The Big Book of
SCIENCE
FICTION

ALSO EDITED BY ANN AND JEFF VANDERMEER

ALSO BY JEFF VANDERMEER

Fiction

Nonfiction

ALSO BY ANN VANDERMEER

The Big Book of
SCIENCE FICTION

THE ULTIMATE COLLECTION

EDITED AND WITH AN INTRODUCTION BY
ANN AND JEFF VANDERMEER

VINTAGE CRIME/BLACK LIZARD
Vintage Books
A Division of Penguin Random House LLC
New York

A VINTAGE CRIME/BLACK LIZARD ORIGINAL, JULY 2016

The Library of Congress Cataloging-in-Publication Data
Names: VanderMeer, Ann, editor. | VanderMeer, Jeff, editor.
Title: The big book of science fiction / edited by Ann VanderMeer and Jeff VanderMeer.
Description: New York : Vintage Crime/Black Lizard, Vintage Books, 2016.
Identifiers: LCCN 2015042397 | ISBN 9781101910092 (pbk.)
Subjects: LCSH: Science fiction—20th century. | Science fiction—21st century.
Classification: LCC PN6071.S33 B55 2016 | DDC 808.83/8762—dc23
LC record available at http://lccn.loc.gov/2015042397

Vintage Crime/Black Lizard Trade Paperback ISBN: 978-1-101-91009-2
eBook ISBN: 978-1-101-91010-8

Book design by Stephanie Moss

www.weeklylizard.com

Printed in the United States of America
10   9   8   7   6   5   4   3   2   1

The editors dedicate this book to Judith Merril,
who helped show us the way.

CONTENTS

CONTENTS

CONTENTS

CONTENTS

INTRODUCTION

Ann and Jeff VanderMeer

Since the days of Mary Shelley, Jules Verne, and H. G. Wells, science fiction has not just helped define and shape the course of literature but reached well beyond fictional realms to influence our perspectives on culture, science, and technology. Ideas like electric cars, space travel, and forms of advanced communication comparable to today's cell phone all first found their way into the public's awareness through science fiction. In stories like Alicia Yánez Cossío's "The IWM 1000" from the 1970s you can even find a clear prediction of Information Age giants like Google—and when Neil Armstrong set foot on the moon, the event was a very real culmination of a yearning already expressed through science fiction for many decades.

Science fiction has allowed us to dream of a better world by creating visions of future societies without prejudice or war. Dystopias, too, like Ray Bradbury's *Fahrenheit 451*, have had their place in science fiction, allowing writers to comment on injustice and dangers to democracy. Where would Eastern Bloc writers have been without the creative outlet of science fiction, which by seeming not to speak about the present day often made it past the censors? For many under Soviet domination during those decades, science fiction was a form of subversion and a symbol of freedom. Today, science fiction continues to ask "What if?" about such important topics as global warming, energy dependence, the toxic effects of capitalism, and the uses of our modern technology, while also bringing back to readers strange and wonderful visions.

No other form of literature has been so relevant to our present yet been so filled with visionary and transcendent moments. No other form has been as entertaining, either. Before now, there have been few attempts at a definitive anthology that truly captures the global influence and significance of this dynamic genre—bringing together authors from all over the world and from both the "genre" and "literary" ends of the fiction spectrum. *The Big Book of Science Fiction* covers the entire twentieth century, presenting, in chronological order, stories from more than twenty-five countries, from the pulp space opera of Edmond Hamilton to the literary speculations of Jorge Luis Borges, from the pre-Afrofuturism of W. E. B. Du Bois to the second-wave feminism of James Tiptree Jr.—and beyond!

What you find within these pages may surprise you. It definitely surprised us.

WHAT IS THE "GOLDEN AGE" OF SCIENCE FICTION?

Even people who do not read science fiction have likely heard the term "the Golden Age of Science Fiction." The actual Golden Age of Science Fiction lasted from about the mid-1930s to the mid-1940s, and is often conflated for general readers with the preceding Age of the Pulps (1920s to mid-1930s). The Age of the Pulps had been dominated by the editor of *Amazing Stories*, Hugo Gernsback. Sometimes called the Father of Science Fiction, Gernsback was most famously photographed in an all-encompassing "Isolator" author helmet, attached to an oxygen tank and breathing apparatus.

The Golden Age dispensed with the Isolator, coinciding as it did with the proliferation of American science fiction magazines, the rise of the ultimately divisive editor John W. Campbell at *Astounding Science Fiction* (such strict definitions and such a dupe for *Dianetics*!), and a proto-market for science fiction novels (which would reach fruition only in the 1950s). This period also saw the rise to dominance of authors like Isaac Asimov, Arthur C. Clarke, Poul Anderson, C. L. Moore, Robert Heinlein, and Alfred Bester. It fixed science fiction in the public imagination as having a "sense of wonder" and a "can-do" attitude about science and the universe, sometimes based more on the earnest, naïve covers than the actual content, which could be dark and complex.

But "the Golden Age" has come to mean something else as well. In his classic, oft-quoted book on science fiction, *Age of Wonders: Exploring the World of Science Fiction* (1984), the iconic anthologist and editor David Hartwell asserted that "the Golden Age of Science Fiction is 12." Hartwell, an influential gatekeeper in the field, was making a point about the arguments that "rage until the small of the morning" at science fiction conventions among "grown men and women" about that time when "every story in every magazine was a master work of daring, original thought." The reason readers argue about whether the Golden Age occurred in the 1930s, 1950s, or 1970s, according to Hartwell, is because the true age of science fiction is the age at which the reader has no ability to tell good fiction from bad fiction, the excellent from the terrible, but instead absorbs and appreciates just the wonderful visions and exciting plots of the stories.

This is a strange assertion, one that seems to want to make excuses. It's often repeated without much analysis of how such a brilliant anthology editor also credited with bringing literary heavyweights like Gene Wolfe and Philip K. Dick to readers would want to (inadvertently?) apologize for science fiction while at the same time engaging in a sentimentality that seems at odds with the whole enterprise of

truly speculative fiction. (Not to mention dissing twelve-year-olds!)

Perhaps one reason for Hartwell's stance can be found in how science fiction in the United States, and to some extent in the United Kingdom, rose out of pulp magazine delivery systems seen as "low art." A pronounced "cultural cringe" within science fiction often combines with the brutal truth that misfortunes of origin often plague literature, which can assign value based on how swanky a house looks from the outside rather than what's inside. The new Kafka who next arises from cosmopolitan Prague is likely to be hailed a savior, but not so much the one who arises from, say, Crawfordville, Florida.

There is also something of a need to apologize for the ma-and-pop tradition exemplified by the pulps, with their amateurish and eccentric editors, who sometimes had little formal training and possessed as many eccentricities as freckles, and who came to dominate the American science fiction world early on. Sometimes an Isolator was the least of it.

Yet even with regard to the pulps, evidence suggests that these magazines at times entertained more sophisticated content than generally given credit for, so that in a sense an idea like "the Golden Age of Science Fiction is 12" undermines the truth about such publications. It also renders invisible all the complex science fiction being written outside of the pulp tradition.

Therefore, we humbly offer the assertion that contrary to popular belief and based on all the evidence available to us . . . the actual Golden Age of Science Fiction is twenty-one, not twelve. The proof can be found in the contents of this anthology, where we have, as much as possible, looked at the totality of what we think of "science fiction," without privileging the dominant mode, but also without discarding it. That which may seem overbearing or all of a type at first glance reveals its individuality and uniqueness when placed in a wider context. At third or fourth glance, you may even find that stories from completely different traditions have commonalities and speak to each other in interesting ways.

BUILDING A BETTER DEFINITION OF "SCIENCE FICTION"

We evoked the names of Mary Shelley, Jules Verne, and H. G. Wells at the beginning of this introduction for a very specific reason. All three are useful entry points or origin points for science fiction because they do not exist so far back in time as to make direct influence seem ethereal or attenuated, they are still known in the modern era, and because the issues they dealt with permeate what we call the "genre" of science fiction even today.

We hesitate to invoke the slippery and preternatural word *influence*, because influence appears and disappears and reappears, sidles in and has many mysterious ways. It can be as simple yet profound as reading a text as a child and forgetting it, only to have it well up from the subconscious years later, or it can be a clear and all-consuming passion. At best we can say only that someone cannot be influenced by something not yet written or, in some cases, not yet translated. Or that influence may occur not when a work is published but when the writer enters the popular imagination—for example, as Wells did through Orson Welles's infamous radio broadcast of *War of the Worlds* (1938) or, to be silly for a second, Mary Shelley through the movie *Young Frankenstein* (1974).

For this reason even wider claims of influence on science fiction, like writer and editor Lester del Rey's assertion that the Mesopotamian *Epic of Gilgamesh* is the earliest written science fiction story, seem appropriative, beside the point, and an overreach for legitimacy more useful as a "tell" about the position of science fiction in the 1940s and 1950s in North America.

But we brought up our triumvirate because they represent different strands of science fic-

tion. The earliest of these authors, Mary Shelley, and her *Frankenstein* (1818), ushered in a modern sensibility of ambivalence about the uses of technology and science while wedding the speculative to the horrific in a way reflected very early on in science fiction. The "mad scientist" trope runs rife through the pages of the science fiction pulps and even today in their modern equivalents. She also is an important figure for feminist SF.

Jules Verne, meanwhile, opened up lines of inquiry along more optimistic and hopeful lines. For all that Verne liked to create schematics and specific detail about his inventions—like the submarine in *Twenty Thousand Leagues Under the Sea* (1870)—he was a very happy puppy who used his talents in the service of scientific romanticism, not "hard science fiction."

H. G. Wells's fiction was also dubbed "scientific romanticism" during his lifetime, but his work existed somewhere between these two foci. His most useful trait as the godfather of modern science fiction is the granularity of his writing. Because his view of the world existed at an intersection of sociology, politics, and technology, Wells was able to create complex geopolitical and social contexts for his fiction—indeed, after he abandoned science fiction, Wells's later novels were those of a social realist, dealing with societal injustice, among other topics. He was able to quantify and fully realize extrapolations about the future and explore the iniquities of modern industrialization in his fiction.

The impulse to directly react to how industrialization has affected our lives occurs very early on in science fiction—for example, in Karl Hans Strobl's cautionary factory tale "The Triumph of Mechanics" (1907) and even in the playful utopian visions of Paul Scheerbart, which often pushed back against bad elements of "modernization." (For his optimism, Scheerbart perished in World War I, while Strobl's "reward" was to fall for fascism and join the Nazi Party—in part, a kind of repudiation of the views expressed in "The Triumph . . .")

Social and political issues also peer out from science fiction from the start, and not just in Wells's work. Rokheya Shekhawat Hossain's "Sultana's Dream" (1905) is a potent feminist utopian vision. W. E. B. Du Bois's "The Comet" (1920) isn't just a story about an impending science-fictional catastrophe but also the start of a conversation about race relations and a proto-Afrofuturist tale. The previously untranslated Yefim Zozulya's "The Doom of Principal City" (1918) presages the atrocities perpetrated by the communism of the Soviet Union and highlights the underlying absurdities of certain ideological positions. (It's perhaps telling that these early examples do not come from the American pulp SF tradition.)

This kind of eclectic stance also suggests a simple yet effective definition for science fiction: *it depicts the future, whether in a stylized or realistic manner.* There is no other definitional barrier to identifying science fiction unless you are intent on defending some particular territory. Science fiction *lives in the future*, whether that future exists ten seconds from the Now or whether in a story someone builds a time machine a century hence in order to travel back into the past. It is science fiction whether the future is phantasmagorical and surreal or nailed down using the rivets and technical jargon of "hard science fiction." A story is also science fiction whether the story in question is, in fact, extrapolation about the future or using the future to comment on the past or present.

Thinking about science fiction in this way delinks the actual content or "experience" delivered by science fiction from the commodification of that genre by the marketplace. It does not privilege the dominant mode that originated with the pulps over other forms. But neither does it privilege those other manifestations over the dominant mode. Further, this definition eliminates or bypasses the idea of a "turf war" between genre and the mainstream, between commercial and literary, and invalidates the (weird, ignorant snobbery of) tribalism that occurs on one side of the divide and the faux snobbery (ironically based on ignorance) that sometimes manifests on the other.

Wrote the brilliant editor Judith Merril in the seventh annual edition of *The Year's Best S-F* (1963), out of frustration:

"But that's not science fiction . . . !" Even my best friends (to invert a paraphrase) keep telling me: That's not science fiction! Sometimes they mean it couldn't be s-f, because it's good. Sometimes it couldn't be because it's not about spaceships or time machines. (Religion or politics or psychology isn't science fiction—is it?) Sometimes (because some of my best friends are s-f fans) they mean it's not *really* science fiction—just fantasy or satire or something like that.

On the whole, I think I am very patient. I generally manage to explain again, just a *little* wearily, what the "S-F" in the title of this book means, and what science fiction is, and why the one contains the other, without being constrained by it. But it does strain my patience when the exclamation is compounded to mean, "Surely you don't mean to use that? *That's not* science fiction!"—about a first-rate piece of the honest thing.

Standing on either side of this debate is corrosive—detrimental to the study and celebration of science fiction; all it does is sidetrack discussion or analysis, which devolves into SF/not SF or intrinsically valuable/not valuable. And, for the general reader weary of anthologies prefaced by a series of "inside baseball" remarks, our definition hopefully lessens your future burden of reading these words.

CONSIDER ANOTHER GRAND TRADITION: THE *CONTE PHILOSOPHIQUE*

Inasmuch as we have put on our Isolator and already paid some tribute to the "dominant" strain of science fiction by briefly conjuring up the American pulp scene of the 1920s through 1940s, it is important before returning to that tradition to examine what the Loyal Opposition was up to in the first half of the twentieth century—and for this reason, it is important to turn our attention to an earlier form, the *conte philosophique*.

Conte philosophique translates as "philosophical story" or "fable of reason." The *contes philosophiques* were used for centuries in the West by the likes of Voltaire, Johannes Kepler, and Francis Bacon as one legitimate way for scientists or philosophers to present their findings. The *conte philosophique* employs the fictional frame of an imaginary or dream journey to impart scientific or philosophical content. In a sense, the fantastical or science-fictional adventure became a mental laboratory in which to discuss findings or make an argument.

If we position some early science fiction as occurring outside of the American pulp tradition but also outside of traditions exemplified by Mary Shelley and H. G. Wells, what remains as influence is both extremely relevant to science fiction and also relevant to more dominant traditions.

Early twentieth-century science fiction like Hossain's "Sultana's Dream," Scheerbart's utopian fables, or Alfred Jarry's "Elements of Pataphysics" from his novel *Exploits and Opinions of Dr. Faustroll, Pataphysician* (1911; first published in English in the 1960s) makes infinitely more sense in this context. More important, these stories take their rightful place within the history of speculative literature. Instead of being considered outliers, they can be seen as the evolution of a grand tradition, one that inverts the usual ratio of the fictional to nonfictional found in a typical *conte philosophique*. It is a mode that certainly helps us better understand Jules Verne's fiction. In many cases, Verne was taking his cue from the trappings of the *conte philosophique*—the fantastical adventure—and using that form as a vehicle for creating his entertainments.

The *conte philosophique*, with its non/fictional fusion, also creates a fascinating link to Jorge Luis Borges and his essay-stories from the 1940s. These stories often serve as a vehicle for metaphysical exploration. Indeed, Borges's work can in this context be seen as the perfect expression of and reconciliation of the (pulpish) adventure fiction he loved and the intellectual underpinnings of his narratives, which rely in part on severe compression into tale (coal into diamonds) rather than traditional short story. Other Latin American examples include Silvina Ocampo's "The Waves" (1959) and Alicia Yánez Cossío's "The IWM 1000" (1975). Even Stanisław Lem in his *Star Diaries* voyages of the 1960s and 1970s is reimagining the *contes philosophiques*—there is the actual voyage (exciting enough!), but it is once again a pure delivery system for ideas about the world.

Although this tradition is not as common in the pulps, "science fiction tales" like A. Merritt's "The Last Poet and the Robots" (1935) and Frederik Pohl's "Day Million" (1966) can be seen as a fusion of the "speculative fairy tale" and the *conte philosophique*, or simply a mutation of the *conte philosophique*, which was itself influenced by ancient myths of fantastical journeys. Ironically, some of these stories add in elements of "hard science fiction."

Interpreted charitably and not from a position espousing the superiority of the *conte philosophique*, this form infiltrates the pulps in the sense that the pulps showcase the physical actuality of the *contes philosophiques*—they are *contes physiques* into which can be reinjected or refed an abstract quality—"what/why/how/if?" And they can embody that quality or kind of inquiry as subtext. (Whereas on the mainstream side of the divide that subtext must manifest as metaphysics to be considered literature or be doomed in terms of approval—as would any non-character-based fiction.)

In this context, whether just as a thought experiment to turn the tables and challenge dominant modes of thinking, or as a subversive "real" metaphorical or metaphysical construct, we could then come to see American pulp space-travel fiction as a kind of devolution—a mistake in which the scaffolding (or booster rockets) used to deliver the point of a *conte philosophique* (the journey) is brought to the foreground and the idea or scientific hypothesis (the "what if") is deemphasized or subtextual only. A case of throwing out the baby to glorify the bathwater?

Science fiction in the United States has often positioned itself as the "literature of ideas," yet what is a literature of ideas if they can be expressed only through a select few "delivery systems"? Aren't there ideas expressed in fiction that we can only see the true value of— good or bad, sophisticated or simple—if we admit that there are more than a few modes of expression with which to convey them? In examining the link between the *conte philosophique* and science fiction, we begin to grasp the outlines of the wider context: how many of these "alternative" approaches are—rather than being deformed or flat or somehow otherwise suspect as lesser modes—just *different* from the dominant model, not lesser, and as useful and relevant. (For example, where otherwise to fit Czechoslovakian writer Karel Čapek—both his 1920s robot plays and his gonzo novel *War with the Newts* from the 1930s?)

Just like our definition of science fiction, this way of thinking about science fiction works both from the "literary mainstream" looking in *or* from genre looking out. The reason it works is that the position or stance—the perspective or vantage taken—is from outside of either. And this is in a sense pure or uncontaminated by the subjective intent—colonizing or foundationally assumed superior—of either "mainstream" literary or genre.

In taking this position (on a mountaintop, from a plane, in a dirigible, from the moon, within a dream journey) much less is rendered invisible in general, and more "viable" science fiction can be recovered, uncovered, or discovered without being any less faithful about our core definition. Thus, too, in this anthology we

have the actuality of exploration and the idea of it, because both thought and action expend energy and are both, in their separate ways, a form of motion.

Perhaps the reason the *conte philosophique* to date has been undervalued as an influence on science fiction is because of the "cultural cringe" of the dominant American form of science fiction, which has consistently positioned itself in relationship to the literary mainstream by accepting the literary mainstream's adherence to the short story as needing to have three-dimensional, psychologically convincing characters to be valid. Even reactions against this position (pre-Humanist SF) have in essence been defining science fiction in relationship to the über-domination of the mainstream.

This is particularly ironic given that a fair amount of early science fiction fails at the task of creating three-dimensional characters (while displaying other virtues) and thus as the century progresses the self-punishment the science fiction genre parcels out to itself for not meeting a standard that is just *one* tradition within the mainstream looks increasingly odd, or even perverse, as are excuses like "the Golden Age of Science Fiction is 12." The genre would have been far better off taking up the cause of traditions like the *conte philosophique* to bypass mainstream approbation rather than continually recycling the Mesopotamian Defense or the Hawthorne Maneuver ("Canon fodder Nathaniel Hawthorne was the first science fiction/fantasy writer") to create legitimacy or "proof of concept" on the mainstream's terms.

FURTHER EXPLORATION OF THE PULP TRADITION

Remember the Age of the Pulps and later Golden Age of Science Fiction (the 1920s to mid-1940s)? Collectively, this era successfully exported itself as a system of plots, tropes, story structures, and entanglements to either emulate or push back against. It was typified not so much by movements as by the hegemonies created by particular influential editors like H. L. Gold, the aforementioned Campbell, and Frederik Pohl (at *Galaxy*).

Many of these editors, trying to push an advantage in the marketplace, created their own fiefdom, defended borders, laid down ground rules for what science fiction was and what it wasn't. In some cases, it might be argued they had to because no one yet knew exactly what it was, or because enthusiasts kept encountering new mutations. These rules in the cutthroat and still-stuffy world of freelance writing could affect content quite a bit—Theodore Sturgeon reportedly stopped writing for a time because of one editor's rules.

Writers could make a living writing for the science fiction magazines in an era with no competition from television or video games—and they could especially make a living if they obeyed the dictates of their editor-kings. Even if editorial tastes are not sound or rational systems of thought, still, they shape taste and canon as much or more so than stable systems or concrete movements—in part because the influence of editors often exists out of the public eye and thus is less subject to open debate.

In a few other cases, magazines like *Weird Tales* successfully forged identities by championing hybrid or new modes of fiction, to the point of becoming synonymous with the type of content they provided to readers. Dashing men in dashing machines having dashing adventures were not as prevalent in such magazines, nor in this Golden Age era. It was more likely that the dashing man might have a dashing accident and be dashed up on some malign alien world or be faced with some dashing Terrible Choice based on being dashed on the rocks of misfortune.

In fact, much written in the mode of purely optimistic fiction has not aged well—in part because it simplified the complexities of a very complex world and the universe beyond. For example, with each decade what we know about what it takes to travel in space makes it more and more unlikely that we will make it out of our own solar system. Even one of the foremost supporters of terraforming, Kim Stanley Robinson, admitted that such travel is highly improbable in a 2014 interview.

The other reason this brand of science fiction has mostly historical value is because the twentieth century included two world wars along with countless significant regional conflicts, the creation of the atom bomb, the spread of various viruses, ecological disaster, and pogroms in Europe, Asia, and Africa.

Against such a growing tally, certain kinds of "gee-whiz" science fiction seem hopelessly out of date; we need escapism in our fiction because fiction is a form of play, but escapism becomes difficult to read when it renders invisible the march of history or becomes too disconnected from readers' experience of science, technology, or world events. When you also throw in institutional racism in the United States, a subject thoroughly ignored by science fiction for a very long time, and other social issues dealt with skillfully by non-SF through the first five decades of the twentieth century, it perhaps makes sense that there is very little from the Golden Age of Science Fiction in this anthology. Our representative choices are ones where the predictive nature of the story or its sophistication stands up to the granularity of the present day.

It is also worth remembering that in the wider world of literature writers outside of science fiction were trying to grapple with the changing nature of reality and technological innovation. After World War I, James Joyce, T. S. Eliot, Virginia Woolf, and others experimented with the nature of time and identity in ways that at times had a speculative feel to it. These were mainstream attempts to engage with science (physics) that only entered into the science fiction tradition as influence during the New Wave movement of the 1960s.

This modernist experimentation and other, more recent evidence suggests that, despite frequent claims to the contrary, science fiction is not *uniquely* suited to interrogate industrialization or modern tech—many nonspeculative stories and novels have done so quite well—so much as it doesn't seem as if science fiction could *exist* or have arisen without the products and inventions particular to industrialization. The physicality of science fiction depends on it in a way that other kinds of fiction do not (for example, historical fiction). Although a spaceship may be more or less a focal point, for example—potentially as unobtrusive as a cab (a ride to a destination)—this is in truth rarely the case. Because spaceships don't exist yet, at least not in the way they are rendered in science fiction, as a *literalization* of the future. Even the most "adventure pulp" stories of early science fiction had to take a position: celebrate the extrapolated future of industrialization and ever-more-advanced technology or bemoan it, speak in terms of splendors and a "sense of wonder" or strike at the ideology behind such thinking through dystopia and examination of excesses. (In such a context, science fiction cannot be seen as escapist or nonpolitical so much as conformist when it does not ask "Why this?" in addition to "What if?")

Still, the pulp tradition as it matured was never as hackneyed or traditional or gee-whiz as it liked to think it was or as twelve-year-old readers fondly remember. It was not nearly as optimistic or crude as the covers that represented it and that science fiction outgrew. In part, this was due to the influx or infusion of a healthy dose of horror from near the start, via *Weird Tales* and its ilk. Magazines like *Unknown* also often published fusions of horror and science fiction, and as some of the author/story notes to early stories in this volume indicate, the "rise of the tentacle" associated with twentieth-century weird fiction (à la Lovecraft) first appeared in weird space operas by writers such as Edmond Hamilton. Among stories from this period that have relevance, many have a depth derived from the darkness that drives them—a sense that the underpinnings of the universe are indeed more complex than we

know. In short, cosmic horror has been around for longer than Lovecraft and has helped to sustain and lend depth to science fiction as well.

POST–WORLD WAR II: HOW SCIENCE FICTION GREW ALL THE WAY UP THE WALLS OF THE WORLD

Largely because it has no "movement" associated with it, the 1950s are sometimes seen as a transitional period, but Robert Silverberg rightly considered the 1950s the true Golden Age of Science Fiction. The full flowering of science fiction in the US and UK dates from this period, in part because opportunities through magazines, book publication, and anthologies proliferated and in part because new and more inclusive gatekeepers entered the field.

The fiction of such highly literate and sophisticated writers like Fritz Leiber (mostly in fantasy and horror), James Blish, and Frederik Pohl came into its own in the 1950s, not just because these writers were encouraged by a much more vital publishing environment but also because of their background with the Futurians, a science fiction club, which had nurtured interests across a wide range of topics, not just genre fiction.

Blish's "Surface Tension" (1952) demonstrates the fruits of that sophistication in its exploration of fascinating ideas about terraforming humans. Philip K. Dick started to publish fiction in the early 1950s, too; in his very first story, "Beyond Lies the Wub" (1952), he staked a claim to that hallucinatory, absurdist, antiestablishment space in which he would later write classics like *Ubik* (1969) and *Flow My Tears, the Policeman Said* (1974).

Arthur C. Clarke had been a fixture of the Golden Age but transitioned into the 1950s with such classic, dark stories as "The Star"(1955), as did Robert Heinlein. Ray Bradbury continued to write brilliant fiction, coming off his success with *The Martian Chronicles*, and Robert Silverberg was extremely prolific in the 1950s, although our choice for a reprint from him was published much later.

Several underrated writers published some of their best fiction, too, including James H. Schmitz, William Tenn, and Chad Oliver. Tom Godwin shook things up with his very long "The Cold Equations" (1954), a good story not included herein, which would become an item of debate for Humanist SF writers, some of whom would try to replicate it. Tenn's "The Liberation of Earth" (1953), a harsh satire of alien invasion inspired by the Korean War, was a touchstone for protesters during the Vietnam War and became a classic. Damon Knight began to establish his legacy with the unusual and strange alien contact story "Stranger Station" (1956). C. M. Kornbluth (another Futurian) published some of his best work during this era, including "The Silly Season" (1950) and "The Marching Morons" (1951), although these tales have not aged well. Other notable writers from the era include Robert Sheckley, Avram Davidson, and Judith Merril (who would achieve lasting fame as an anthology editor).

In hindsight, though, perhaps the most unique and important science fiction writer of the 1950s was Cordwainer Smith, who published most of his science fiction in the mid-1950s. His unique tales set on a far-future Earth and the surrounding universe came seemingly out of nowhere and had no clear antecedent. In "Scanners Live in Vain" (1950) and the story included herein, "The Game of Rat and Dragon" (1955), Smith revitalized space opera just as he remade so much else across an oeuvre as influenced by Jorge Luis Borges and Alfred Jarry as genre science fiction. Even today, Smith's stories stand alone, as if they came from an alternate reality.

Almost equaling Smith in terms of being sui generis, Theodore Sturgeon brought a willfully literary sensibility to his fiction and an empathy that could at times manifest as sentimentality. But in his best work, like "The Man Who Lost the Sea" (1959), Sturgeon displayed a much-needed pathos to science fiction. Sturgeon was also unafraid to explore horror and to take on controversial topics, and with each new story he published that pushed a boundary, Sturgeon made it easier for others to follow.

Another interesting writer, James White, wrote about a galactic hospital in stories like "Sector General" (1957), which in their reliance on medical mysteries and situations pushed back against the standard conflict plots of the day. In White's stories there are often no villains and sometimes no heroes, either. This allowed White to create fresh and different plots; one of his best hospital stories involves taking care of an alien child who manifests as a huge living boulder and who has vastly different feeding needs than human children. Neither Smith nor White was as popular as writers like Arthur C. Clarke, but their body of work stands out starkly from the surrounding landscape because it took such a different stance while still being relatable, entertaining, and modern.

The fifties also saw more space made for brilliant woman writers like Katherine MacLean, Margaret St. Clair, and Carol Emshwiller. What MacLean, St. Clair, and Emshwiller all shared in their fiction was a fascination with either speculative sociology or extremes of psychological reality, within a context of writing unique female characters and using story structures that often came from outside the pulp tradition. MacLean in particular championed sociology and so-called soft science, a distinction from "hard" science fiction that would have seemed fairly radical at the time. St. Clair, meanwhile, with her comprehensive knowledge of horror and fantasy fiction as well as science fiction, crafted stories that could be humorous, terrifying, and sharply thought-provoking all at once. In some of her best stories, we can also see an attempt to interrogate our relationship to the animal world. Together, these three writers not only paved the way for the feminist science fiction explosion of the 1970s, they effectively created room for more unusual storytelling.

Elsewhere in the world, Jorge Luis Borges was continuing to write fascinating, unique stories, and the tradition of the science fiction folktale or satire was used by Mexican writer Juan José Arreola to good effect in "Baby HP" (1952) and other flash fictions. Borges's friend and fellow Argentine Silvina Ocampo even wrote science fiction, not a form of speculation she was known for, with "The Waves" (1959), translated into English herein for the first time. In France, Gérard Klein was just beginning to publish fiction, with early classic stories like "The Monster" (1958), his emergence presaging a boom in interesting·French science fiction. And, even though Arkady and Boris Strugatsky (the Strugatsky brothers) wouldn't achieve international fame until the 1970s, with the translation of *Roadside Picnic* (1979) and other books, they were publishing provocative and intelligent work like the alien-contact story "The Visitors" (1958) in the Soviet Union.

That there was no particular unifying mode or theme of science fiction in the 1950s is in some ways a relief and afforded freedom for a number of unique writers. Clearly, the way was clear for science fiction writers to climb even further up the walls of the world.

But, in part, they would have to do it by tearing down what had come before.

THE NEW WAVE AND THE RISE OF FEMINIST SCIENCE FICTION

The overriding story of science fiction in the 1960s would be the rise of the "New Wave," largely championed at first by the UK magazine *New Worlds*, edited by Michael Moorcock, and then finding expression in the US through Harlan Ellison's *Dangerous Visions* (1967) and *Again, Dangerous Visions* (1972) anthologies.

New Wave fiction had many permutations and artistic ideologies associated with it, but at its core it was often formally experimental and sought to bring mainstream literary technique and seriousness to science fiction. In effect, the New Wave wanted to push the boundaries of what was possible while also embodying, in many cases, the counterculture of the 1960s.

New Wave fiction tended to be antiestablishment and to look with a cold eye upon the Golden Age and the pulps. Sometimes, too, it turned that cold eye on the 1950s, with New Wave writers finding much of what had gone before too safe.

But this opposition was sometimes forced on the New Wave by its detractors. For the average science fiction writer raised within the tradition of the pulps and existing within an era of plenty in the 1950s, especially with regard to the American book market, it must have been a rude awakening for writers from across the pond to suddenly be calling into question everything about their ecosystem, even if just by implication. The essential opposition also occurred because even though the 1950s had featured breakthroughs for many new voices, it had also solidified the hold upon the collective imagination of many Golden Age icons.

Further, the New Wave writers had been either reading a fundamentally different set of texts or interpreting them far differently—such that the common meeting ground between New Wave and not–New Wave could be like first contact with aliens. Neither group spoke the other's language or knew all of its customs. Even those who should have made common cause or found common understandings, like Frederik Pohl and James Blish, found themselves in opposition to the New Wave.

In the event, however, the New Wave—whether writers and editors opposed it or lived within it and used it to create interesting work—would prove the single most influential movement within science fiction, with the concurrent and later rise of feminist science fiction a close second (and in some cases closely tied to the New Wave).

Out of the New Wave came countless writers now unjustly forgotten, like Langdon Jones, Barrington Bayley (both reprinted herein), and John Sladek, but also giants of literature, starting with Michael Moorcock and J. G. Ballard, and including M. John Harrison and Brian Aldiss (actually from an earlier generation, but a hothouse party-crasher). Subversive publishers in the UK like Savoy fanned the flames.

These writers were helped in their ascendency by the continued popularity of writers from outside of genre fiction whose work existed in sympathy to the New Wave, like Kurt Vonnegut Jr. and William S. Burroughs, and those within the genre who were sympathetic and winning multiple Hugo Awards and Nebula Awards, like Harlan Ellison. Ellison's own work fit the New Wave aesthetic to a T and his dual devotion to championing edgy work by both new and established writers in his anthologies created an undeniable New Wave beachhead in North America. American writers like Thomas Disch and Philip José Farmer received a clear boost to their careers because of the existence of the New Wave. Others, like Carol Emshwiller and Sonya Dorman, more or less wandered into the verdant (if also sometimes disaster-clogged) meadows of the New Wave by accident—having always done their own thing—and then wandered out again, neither better nor worse off. Unique eccentricists like David R. Bunch, whose Moderan stories only seem more prescient every day, could not have published their work at all if not for the largesse of daring editors and the aegis of the New Wave. (It is worth pointing out that his Moderan stories in this volume are the first reprints allowed in more than two decades.)

As or more important was the emergence of Samuel R. Delany as a major voice in the field, and the emergence of that voice linked to New Wave fiction with bold, unusual stories like "Aye, and Gomorrah" (1967). Delany just about matched Ellison Nebula Award for Nebula Award during this period and not only led by example in terms of producing sophisticated speculative fiction that featured diverse characters but also was, quite frankly, one of the only African-American or even nonwhite writers in the field for a very long time. Although the huge success of bestsellers like *Dhalgren* (1975) helped prolong the New Wave's moment and furthered the cause of mature (and experimen-

tal) fiction within science fiction, it did not seem to help bring representative diversity with it.

By 1972, Terry Carr wrote in his introduction to volume 1 of *The Best Science Fiction of the Year*,

> By now the "new wave" as such has come and gone; those stories that could stand on their merits have . . . These writers realize a truth basic to all art[:] Innovations are positive to the extent that they open doors, and an avant garde which seems to destroy rather than build will only destroy itself all the faster . . . Personally, I thought most of the work produced during the height of the "new wave" was just as bad as bad science fiction has always been; if there has been an effective difference to me, it was only that I sometimes had to read a story more carefully to discover I disliked it.

Terry Carr was a good and influential editor (who grew with the times), but wrong in this case, although it seems unlikely anyone could have understood how fundamentally the New Wave had changed the landscape. Despite a certain amount of retrenchment after the mid-1970s—at least in part because of the huge influence of Hollywood SF, like *Star Wars*, on the genre as a whole—New Wave fiction had enduring effects and created giants of culture and pop culture like J. G. Ballard (the most cited author on a variety of tech and societal topics since the 1970s).

And, in fact, Carr was also wrong because the New Wave overlapped with another significant development, the rise of feminist science fiction, so the revolution was not in fact over. In some ways it was just beginning—and there was much work to do. In addition to conflict in society in general over the issues of women's rights, the book culture had decided to cynically cater to misogynistic tendencies in readers by publishing whole lines of paperback fiction devoted to novels demonstrating how "women's lib" would lead to future dystopias.

If it feels like a bit of a misnomer to call this "rise" the "ascendency" of "feminist" SF, it is because to do so creates the danger of simplifying a complex situation. Not only did the fight to create more space for stories with positive and proactive women characters in science fiction need to be refought several times, but the arguments and the energy/impulse involved in "feminist" SF were also about representation: about creating a space for women writers, no matter what they wrote. And they were further complicated by the fact that identification of an author with "feminism" (just as identification with "New Wave") can create a narrowed focus in how readers encounter and explore that writer's work. Nor, largely, would this first focus on feminist science fiction address intersectional issues of race or of gender fluidity. (It is worth noting that in the milieu traversed by American surrealists of the 1960s and 1970s, a territory that existed parallel to science fiction, intersectionality appears to have been more central much earlier.)

Kingsley Amis had pointed out in *New Maps of Hell* (1960), his influential book on science fiction published on the cusp of the New Wave, that "though it may go against the grain to admit it, [male] science-fiction writers are evidently satisfied with the sexual status quo." This in a context where few examples of complex or interesting women characters written by men seemed to exist, beyond a few stories by Theodore Sturgeon and John Wyndham (another one-off, marginally associated with the New Wave but, understandably and blissfully, enthralled by plants, fungi, lichen).

By the 1970s, writers like Joanna Russ were giving bold and explicit voice to the cause of science fiction by featuring women. Russ accused science fiction, in her essay "The Image of Women in Science Fiction" (1970), of "a failure of imagination and 'social speculation,'" making the argument that the paucity of complex female characters derived from accepting societal prejudices and stereotypes without thought or analysis. This echoed sentiments about clichés and stereotypes expressed by Delany with regard to race.

Feminist writers were concerned in part about the peculiar and unuseful way in which writers had for so long literalized archetypes, making women stand-ins and not individualized: Madonna/Whore, Mother Earth, etc. As the forever amazing and incisive Ursula K. Le Guin wrote in her essay "American SF and the Other" (1975), "The women's movement has made most of us conscious of the fact that SF has either totally ignored women, or presented them as squeaking dolls subject to instant rape by monsters—or old-maid scientists desexed by hypertrophy of the intellectual organs—or, at best, loyal little wives or mistresses of accomplished heroes."

The irony of having to push back against misogynistic portrayals in science fiction should not be lost on anyone. Within a tradition of "what if," a tradition not of realism but of supposedly dreaming true and of expressing the purest forms of the imagination, science fiction had still chosen in many cases to relegate women to second- or third-rate status. In such an atmosphere, without a revolution, how could anyone, male or female or gender-fluid, see clearly a future in which such prejudices did not exist?

Therefore the rise of feminist SF was about the rise of unique, influential voices whose work could be overtly feminist but was not of interest solely for that reason. Writers like James Tiptree Jr. (Alice Sheldon), Russ, Josephine Saxton, Le Guin, and others were in some cases core New Wavers or were writing corrections of Golden Era simplifications, much as Delany sometimes did, and in other cases bringing sociology, anthropology, ecological issues, and more to the fore in a way that hadn't yet been seen. Rather than being narrow in focus, this fiction *opened up* the world—and did so from within an American and British science fiction community that was at times resistant.

THE IMPORTANT ROLE OF INTERNATIONAL FICTION

Sometimes it is useful to take a step back and examine the frenzy of enthusiasm about a particular era from a different perspective. While the New Wave and feminist science fiction were playing out largely in the Anglo world, the international scene was creating its own narrative. This narrative was not always so different from the Anglo one, in that in regions like Latin America women writers generally had to work twice as hard to achieve the same status as their male counterparts. For this reason, even today there are still women writers of speculative fiction being translated into English for the first time who first published work in the 1950s through 1970s. These roadblocks should not be underestimated, and future anthologists should make it a mission to discover and promote amazing work that may at this time be invisible to us.

Frederik Pohl, Judith Merril, and Damon Knight, all three excellent writers, were at least as influential in putting on their editor hats and were particularly useful in bringing new, international voices into the English-language science fiction field. These gatekeepers and others, including the ubiquitous David Hartwell, were sympathetic to international science fiction, and as a result from the 1950s through the 1980s in particular stories in translation appeared with more frequency. (It is worth noting, though, that in many cases what was translated had to conform to Anglo ideas about what had value in the marketplace.)

"International" science fiction may be a meaningless term because it both exoticizes and generalizes what should be normalized and then discussed in specifics country by country. But it is important to understand the overlay of non-Anglo fiction occurring at the same time as generally UK/US phenomena such as the New Wave and the rise of feminist SF—even if we can focus only on a few stories given the constraints of our anthology. For example, by the 1960s the Japanese science fiction scene had become strange and vital and energetic, as exemplified by work from Yoshio Aramaki and Yasutaka Tsutsui, but also by so many other talented writers.

Although it wouldn't be clear until the publication of a score of English-language Macmillan Soviet science fiction anthologies and novels in the 1980s—many of them championed by Theodore Sturgeon and the Strugatsky brothers—Russian and Ukrainian science fiction came of age in the 1960s and 1970s. From 1960 to the mid-1970s, a number of writers little known in the West published fascinating and complex science fiction—some of it retranslated for this volume.

For example, Valentina Zhuravlyova published "The Astronaut" (1960), which managed to escape being an advertisement for the Soviet space program by virtue of its intricate structure and commitment to the pathos of its space mission emergency. The fairly prolific Dmitri Bilenkin, who would appear in several English translations, wrote "Where Two Paths Cross," an ecological contact story still unique and relevant today. With its alien collective, the story could be said to comment on the communist situation. Perhaps the most unlikely Russian writer of the time was Vadim Shefner, whose graceful fiction, with its deceptive lightness of touch, finds its greatest expression in "A Modest Genius" (1963). How this subversive and wise delicacy evaded the Soviet censors is a mystery, but readers everywhere should be glad it did.

The best Soviet short story writer of the era, however, was Sever Gansovsky, who wrote several powerful stories that could have been included in this anthology. Our choice, "Day of Wrath" (1964), updates the Wellsian "Dr.

Moreau" trope while being completely original. Gansovsky was not as visionary as the Strugatsky brothers, whose *Roadside Picnic* would dominate discussion in the US and UK, but there is in his directness, clarity, grit, and sophistication much that compensates for that lack.

Many examples of Latin American science fiction from the 1960s and 1970s are yet to appear in English, so the complete picture of that time period is unclear. We know that Borges and Ocampo were still publishing fiction that was speculative in nature, as was another major Argentine writer, Angélica Gorodischer. Adolfo Bioy Casares published occasional science fiction, such as "The Squid Chooses Its Own Ink" (1962), retranslated for this volume. The giant of Brazilian SF André Carneiro published his most famous story, "Darkness," in 1965, a tale that stands comfortably alongside the best science fiction of the era. Alicia Yánez Cossío's "The IWM 1000" (1975) is another great example of Latin American SF from the period.

Yet, as noted, our sample as readers in English is still not large enough to draw general conclusions. All we can say is that in this volume you will find both synergy with and divergence from 1960s and 1970s Anglo SF that adds immeasurable value to the conversation about science fiction.

CYBERPUNK, HUMANISM, AND WHAT LAY BEYOND

The New Wave and the rise of feminist SF would always be difficult to follow because such giants strode the Earth and expressed themselves willfully and with intelligent intent during that era. But the two movements most associated with the 1980s and 1990s, cyberpunk and Humanism, would in their own ways be both quietly and not-so-quietly influential.

Cyberpunk as a term was popularized by editor Gardner Dozois, although it was first coined by Bruce Bethke in 1980 in his story "Cyber-

punk," subsequently published in a 1983 issue of *Amazing Stories*. Bruce Sterling then became the main architect of a blueprint for cyberpunk with his columns in his fanzine *Cheap Truth*. William Gibson's stories appearing in *Omni* in the mid-1980s, including "Burning Chrome" and "New Rose Hotel" (reprinted herein), and his novel *Neuromancer* (1984) fixed the term in readers' imaginations. The Sterling-edited *Mirrorshades* anthology (1986) provided a flagship.

Cyberpunk usually fused noir tropes or interior design with dark tales of near-future technology in a context of weak governments and sinister corporations, achieving a new granularity in conveying elements of the Information Age. Trace elements of the recent punk movement in music were brought to the mix by writers such as John Shirley.

Just as some New Wave and feminist SF authors, like Delany and Tiptree, had tried to portray a "realer" realism relative to traditional Golden Age science fiction elements or tropes, cyberpunk often tried to better show advances in computer technology and could be seen as naturally extending a Philip K. Dickian vision of the future, with themes of paranoia and vast conspiracies. The brilliant John Brunner's *The Shockwave Rider* (1975) is sometimes also mentioned as a predecessor. (The Humanist equivalent would be Brunner's *Stand on Zanzibar*.)

Writers such as Rudy Rucker, Marc Laidlaw, Lewis Shiner, and Pat Cadigan published significant cyberpunk stories or novels, with Cadigan later editing *The Ultimate Cyberpunk* (2002), which contextualized cyberpunk within earlier influences (not always successfully) and also showcased post-cyberpunk works.

"Humanist SF" at times seemed to just be a call for three-dimensional characters in science fiction, with feminism added on top, sometimes with an emphasis on the so-called soft sciences, such as sociology. But Carol McGuirk makes an interesting point in an essay in *Fiction 2000* (1992) when she notes that the "soft science fiction" that predominated in the 1950s (remember MacLean?) strongly influenced the New

Wave, cyberpunk, and Humanist SF, which she claims all arose, in part, out of this impulse. The difference is that whereas New Wave and cyberpunk fiction arose out of a starker, darker impulse (including the *contes cruels*) replete with dystopian settings, Humanist SF grew out of another strand in which human beings are front and center, with technology subservient, optimistically, to a human element. (Brothers and sisters often fight, and that seems to be the case here.)

Practitioners of Humanist SF (sometimes also identified as Slipstream—ironically enough, a term coined by Sterling) include James Patrick Kelly, Kim Stanley Robinson, John Kessel, Michael Bishop (a stalwart hybrid who at times partook of the New Wave), and Nancy Kress, with Karen Joy Fowler's work exhibiting some of the same attributes but too various to be pigeonholed or in any sense to be said to have done anything but flown the coop into rarefied and iconic realms. (The gonzo fringe of the impulse was best expressed by Paul Di Filippo, who would go so far as to pose naked for one book cover.)

Humanism was initially seen as in opposition to cyberpunk, but in fact both factions "grew up" rather quickly and produced unique work that defied labels. Perhaps the most interesting aspect of the perceived conflict was that cyberpunk seemed to revel in its science fiction origins without particularly caring what the mainstream thought, perhaps because they had access to a wider audience through pop culture; see: *Wired* magazine. Humanists on the other hand generally identified with core genre but wanted to reach beyond it to mainstream readers and convince them of science fiction's literary worth. Interestingly enough, the cause of Humanist SF would be championed either directly or indirectly by the legendary Damon Knight and Kate Wilhelm, whose Clarion and Sycamore Hill (for more advanced writers) writers' workshops tended to be of most use for those kinds of writers.

Critics of both "movements" argued that cyberpunk and Humanism were retrenchments or conservative acts after the radicalism of the New Wave of the 1960s and the rise of feminist SF in the 1970s—cyberpunk because it fetishized technology and deemphasized the role of governments even while critical of corporations. Readers from within the computer industry pointed to Gibson's lack of knowledge about hacker culture in writing *Neuromancer* and suggested flaws in his vision were created by this lack. A fair amount of cyberpunk also promoted a more traditional idea of gender roles (imported from noir fiction) while providing less space for women authors.

Yet around the same time in Argentina Angélica Gorodischer was publishing such incendiary feminist material as "The Unmistakable Smell of Wood Violets" (1985), and in the US one sui generis writer whose work pushed back against some of these ideas was Misha Nogha, whose Arthur C. Clarke Award finalist *Red Spider White Web* (1990; excerpted herein) portrays a nightmarish future in which artists are commodified but also exist in life-threatening conditions. Technology is definitely not fetishized and the hierarchies of power eventuate from every direction. The novel also features a unique and strong female main character who defies the gender stereotypes of the time. In this sense, Nogha's groundbreaking novel pointed the way toward a more feminist vision of cyberpunk.

The criticism leveled against Humanism, meanwhile, was that it gentrified both the New Wave and feminist impulses by applying middle-of-the-road and middle-class values. (The more radicalized third-wave feminism science fiction of the current era fits more comfortably with New Wave and 1970s feminism despite not always being quite as experimental.) Yet, whatever the truth, what actually happened is that the best Humanist writers matured and evolved over time or had only happened to be passing through on their way to someplace else.

Arguably the most influential science fiction writers to come out of the 1980s and 1990s were Octavia E. Butler, Kim Stanley Robinson,

William Gibson, Bruce Sterling, and Ted Chiang. In far different ways they would change the landscape of popular culture and how readers thought about technology, race, gender, and the environment. Ted Chiang's influence exists mainly within the genre, but this may change due to forthcoming movie adaptations of his work. Karen Joy Fowler would begin to exert a similar influence via her nonspeculative novels like *We Are All Completely Beside Ourselves* (2013), which deals with the issue of animal intelligence and our relationship to that intelligence.

Fowler's example provides some inkling of how such prominence occurs: by having ideas or fiction that breaks out beyond core genre. Although Gibson and Sterling could be said to have founded cyberpunk, for example, it is their writings, both fiction and nonfiction, beyond the initial cyberpunk era that have the most relevance, as they have broadened and sharpened their interrogations of modern society and the technology age.

Butler has undergone a resurgence in popularity and influence because her themes resonate with a new generation of writers and readers who value diversity and who are interested in postcolonial explorations of race, gender, and social issues. (And because she wrote wonderful, unique, complex science fiction unlike anyone in the field.) It is only Robinson who has achieved breakout influence and status while writing from within genre, forcing readers to come to him with a series of groundbreaking science fiction novels that are often referenced in the context of climate change. (Only Paolo Bacigalupi has come to close to being as influential since.)

However, cyberpunk and Humanism were not the only significant impulses in science fiction during this period. Other types of inquiry existed outside of the Anglo world during this period and extending into the twenty-first century. For example, a significant window for Chinese science fiction in the early 1980s (closed shut by regime change) gave readers such interesting stories as "The Mirror Image of the Earth" by Zheng Wenguang and others collected in *Science Fiction from China*, edited by Dingbo Wu and Patrick D. Murphy (1989; with an introduction by the indefatigable Frederik Pohl). Other remarkable Chinese writers, like Han Song, created enduring fiction that either had no real Western antecedent or "cooked" it into something unique—and eventually Cixin Liu would break through with the Hugo Award–winning novel *The Three-Body Problem* (2014), both a critical and a commercial success. His novella "The Poetry Cloud" (1997), included in this volume, is a stunning tour de force that assimilates many different strands of science fiction and, in a joyful and energetic way, rejuvenates them. It in effect renders much of contemporary science fiction obsolete.

In Finland, Leena Krohn, one of her country's most respected and decorated fiction writers, spent the 1980s and 1990s (and up to the present day) creating a series of fascinating speculative works, including *Tainaron* (1985), *Pereat Mundus* (1998), and *Mathematical Creatures, or Shared Dreams* (1992), from which we have reprinted "Gorgonoids." Johanna Sinisalo has also been a creative powerhouse, and her Nebula Award finalist "Baby Doll" is included herein. Other fascinating Finnish writers include Anne Leinonen, Tiina Raevaara, Hannu Rajaniemi, Viivi Hyvönen, and Pasi Ilmari Jääskeläinen.

Other science fiction in the wider world includes Kojo Laing's "Vacancy for the Post of Jesus Christ" (1992), which is not an outlier for this speculative fiction writer from Ghana, and Tatyana Tolstaya's "The Slynx." Both are highly original and not atypical examples of a growing number of fascinating voices from places outside of the Anglo hegemony.

Although not always thought of in a science fiction context so much as a dystopia one (*The Handmaid's Tale*), Canadian Margaret Atwood contributed to the conversation with her MaddAddam trilogy (2003–13), which still holds up today as perhaps the single most significant and useful exploration of near-future ecological catastrophe and renewal. The significance of these novels in terms of mainstream acceptance of science fiction cannot be understated. Although science fiction had already conquered popular culture, without Atwood's example the current trend of science fiction being published by mainstream literary imprints would be unlikely. This type of positioning also helps gain a wider, more varied readership for science fiction generally and accelerates the cultural influence of this kind of fiction.

The growing diversity in the twenty-first century of the science fiction community, combined with the influx of international science fiction and the growing acceptance of science fiction within the mainstream literary world, promises to create a dynamic, vibrant, and cosmopolitan space for science fiction literature in the decades to come.

ORGANIZING PRINCIPLES FOR THIS ANTHOLOGY

In compiling *The Big Book of Science Fiction*, we have thought carefully about what it means to present to the reader a century's worth of short stories, from roughly 1900 to 2000, with some outliers. Our approach has been to think of this anthology as providing a space to be representative and accurate but also revelatory—to balance showcasing core genre fiction with a desire to show not just outliers, but "outliers" that we actually feel are more central to science fiction than previously thought. It has also seemed imperative to bring international fiction into the fold; without that element, any survey of an impulse or genre of fiction will seem narrow, more provincial and less cosmopolitan.

Particular guidelines or thought processes include:

- Avoiding the Great Certainty (interrogate the classics/canon)
- Meticulous testing of previous anthologies of this type

- Identifying and rejecting pastiche previously presented as canon
- Overthrowing the tyranny of typecasting (include writers not known for their science fiction but who wrote superb science fiction stories)
- Repairing the pointless rift (pay no attention to the genre-versus-literary origins of a story)
- Repatriating the fringe with the core (acknowledge the role of cult authors and more experimental texts)
- Crafting more complete genealogies (acknowledge the debt from surrealism and other sources outside of core genre)
- Articulating the full expanse (as noted, explore permutations of science fiction from outside of the Anglo world, making works visible through translation)

We also have wanted to represent as many different types of science fiction as possible, including hard science fiction, soft (social) science fiction, space opera, alternative history, apocalyptic stories, tales of alien encounters, near-future dystopia, satirical stories, and a host of other modes.

Within this general context, we have been less concerned about making sure to include certain authors than we have about trying to give accurate overviews of certain eras, impulses, and movements. For this reason, most readers will no doubt discover a favorite story or author has been omitted . . . but also come across new discoveries and new favorites previously unknown to them.

We have also weighed historical significance against readability in the modern era, with the guiding principle that most people picking up this anthology will be general readers, not academics. For this reason, too, we have endeavored to include humorous stories, which are a rich and deep part of the science fiction tradition and help to balance out the preponderance of dystopias depicted in many of the serious stories. Joke stories, on the other hand, and most twist stories have been omitted as too self-referential, especially stories that rely too heavily on referring to science fiction fandom or core genre.

Because ecological and environmental issues have become increasingly urgent, if given the choice of two equally good stories by the same author, we have also chosen to favor stories featuring those themes. (For example, our selection from Ursula K. Le Guin.) One regret is not being able to include fiction by John Brunner, Frank Herbert, and other giants in the field whose novels are arguably much more robust and vital on this topic than their short fiction.

In considering the broadness of our definition of science fiction, we have had to set limits. Most steampunk seems to us to have more in common with fantasy than science fiction, and stories of the very far future in which science is indistinguishable from magic also seem to us to belong to the fantastical. For this latter reason, Jack Vance's *Dying Earth* stories and M. John Harrison's *Viriconium* stories, and their ilk, will fall within the remit of a future anthology.

In considering international fiction we have chosen (after hard-won prior experience) to take the path of least resistance. For example, we had more access to and better intel about Soviet-era and certain strands of Latin American science fiction than some other traditions. It therefore seemed more valuable to present relatively complete "through-lines" of those traditions than to try to provide one representative story for as many countries as possible. In addition, given our access to international fiction and a choice between equally good stories (often with similar themes) set in a particular country, one by an author from that country and one by an author from the US or UK, we have chosen to use the story by the author from the country in question.

.   .   .

With regard to translations, we followed two rules: to be fearless about including stories not previously published in English (if deemed of high quality) and to retranslate stories already translated into English if the existing translation was more than twenty-five years old or if we believed the existing translation contained errors.

The new translations (works never before published in English) included in this anthology are Karl Hans Strobel's "The Triumph of Mechanics" (1907), Paul Scheerbart's "The New Overworld" (1911), Yefim Zozulya's "The Doom of Principal City" (1918), Silvina Ocampo's "The Waves" (1959), Angélica Gorodischer's "The Unmistakable Smell of Wood Violets" (1985), Jacques Barbéri's "Mondocane" (1983), and Han Song's "Two Small Birds" (1988).

The retranslated stories are Miguel de Unamuno's "Mechanopolis" (1913), Juan José Arreola's "Baby HP" (1952), Arkady and Boris Strugatsky's "The Visitors" (1958), Valentina Zhuravlyova's "The Astronaut" (1960), Adolfo Bioy Casares's "The Squid Chooses Its Own Ink" (1962), Sever Gansovsky's "Day of Wrath" (1965), and Dmitri Bilenkin's "Where Two Paths Cross" (1973).

In contextualizing all of this material we realized that no introduction could truly convey the depth and breadth of a century of science fiction. For this reason, we made the strategic decision to include expanded author notes, which also include information on each story. These notes sometimes convey biographical data and in other cases form miniature essays to provide general context. Sometimes these notes quote other writers or critics to provide firsthand recollections. In researching these author notes, we are very fortunate to have had access, in a synergistic way, to the best existing source about certain writers, *The Encyclopedia of Science Fiction*, with the blessing of its founders, John Clute, Peter Nicholls, and David Langford. Entries containing information from the encyclopedia as their nucleus are noted in the permissions acknowledgments (pages 1169–1178).

Finally, as ever, certain stories could not be acquired for this anthology—or for anyone's anthology—due to the stance of the estates in question. The following stories should be considered an extension of this anthology: A. E. van Vogt's "The Weapon Shop" (1942), Robert Heinlein's "All You Zombies—" (1959), and Bob Shaw's "Light of Other Days" (1966). In addition, for reasons of space we have been unable to include E. M. Forster's "The Machine Stops" (1909), an excerpt from Gustave Le Rouge's strange novel about a mission to a Mars inhabited by vampires (1909), and an excerpt from Doris Lessing's 1970s science fiction novels.

If we have brought any particular value to the task of editing this anthology—and we will let others debate that question—it lies in three areas: 1) we love all kinds of fiction, in all its many forms, and all kinds of science fiction; 2) we have built up an extensive (and still-growing) network of international literary contacts that allowed us to acquire unique content; and 3) we did not approach the task from the center of genre, which is where most editors of these kinds of anthologies have come from. We belong to no clique or group within the science fiction community and have no particular affiliation with nor disinclination to consider any writer in the field, living or dead.

That said, we are also not coming to the task from the sometimes too elevated height of mainstream literary editors with no connection to their speculative subject matter. We do not care about making a case for the legitimacy of science fiction; the ignorance of those who don't value science fiction is their own affliction and problem (as is the ignorance of those who claim science fiction is the be-all and end-all).

Throughout our three-year journey of discovery for this project, we have also had to reconcile ourselves to what we call Regret Over Taxonomy (exclusion is inevitable but not a cause for relief or happiness) and Acknowledgment of the Inherent Imperfection of the Results. However, the corollary to this latter recognition is to never accept or resign oneself to the inherent imperfection of the results.

Now we hope you will put aside this overlong introduction and simply immerse yourself in the science-fictional wonders here assembled. For they are many, and they are indeed wondrous and startling and, at times, darkly beautiful.

The Big Book of
SCIENCE
FICTION

The Star

H. G. WELLS

Herbert George Wells (1866–1946) was an English writer who, as H. G. Wells, achieved worldwide acclaim during his lifetime for his journalism as well as for his fiction, both realistic and speculative, yet today is known solely for his science fiction. Throughout his career, Wells was driven by a need to spread the gospel of science, including Darwin's theory of evolution. He wanted to explore social issues through Utopianism, while, ever practical, keeping a firm grasp on his Socialist Party membership card. However, he also had a knack for spinning a ripping good yarn.

Wells's most notable science fiction includes *The Time Machine* (1895), *The Island of Dr. Moreau* (1896), *The Invisible Man* (1897), and *The War of the Worlds* (1898). Just as Edgar Allan Poe's stories more or less created the horror and mystery genres (and included early science fiction), Wells could be said, along with the French writer Jules Verne, to be the forefather of modern science fiction. Verne, whose best work was published before the twentieth century, held the public imagination through fanciful modern-era "megafauna" like the giant submarine the *Nautilus* and mechanical people-mover elephants, for which Verne even provided detailed blueprints. But Wells found such stunts from his rival annoying and was less interested in whether a mecha-elephant could actually clomp and clank across the earth than in charting the effect of mass societal changes in technology and biology. In a sense, even though their stories were both grouped under the label of "science romance," Verne embraced a Romantic vision of science fiction and Wells was a somewhat cynical futurist.

He often cast a jaundiced eye at modern humanity. The shadow of Poe permeates Wells's work in that Wells heeded the horror in Poe's fiction, especially in works like *The Island of Dr. Moreau*. While Wells could find his way to a happy ending or return to the status quo, the path there would always be bleaker and more influenced by an outlook on humankind that reflected the realities of history. This cold-eyed analysis lent his vision of the future its staying power, a seeming realism that had a significant influence on science fiction in the United States and the United Kingdom during the rise of pulp magazines and the community devoted to them.

Wells became more cynical about technology after the horrors of World War I, and not only did he lose faith in humanity, he stopped writing science fiction. In doing so, he also lost from his later novels some spark or energy that would recommend them to a modern reader. The creativity required to come up with an extrapolation of the improbable had energized Wells's imagination in a way that made his science fiction more interesting than his other fiction.

"The Star" (1897), as with much of Wells's science fiction, is credited with creating a subgenre—in this case, the "impact" subgenre, as of some object falling from the sky onto Earth or other planets, or heavenly bodies colliding. Such stories tend to revolve around a mystery about the object in question, or focus on the reactions of characters in the aftermath. Arthur C. Clarke mentions "The Star" in his novel *Rendezvous with Rama* and wrote a story with the same title (also included in this volume), although Clarke's story has no connection to this one.

THE STAR

H. G. Wells

It was on the first day of the New Year that the announcement was made, almost simultaneously from three observatories, that the motion of the planet Neptune, the outermost of all the planets that wheel about the sun, had become very erratic. Ogilvy had already called attention to a suspected retardation in its velocity in December. Such a piece of news was scarcely calculated to interest a world the greater portion of whose inhabitants were unaware of the existence of the planet Neptune, nor outside the astronomical profession did the subsequent discovery of a faint remote speck of light in the region of the perturbed planet cause any very great excitement. Scientific people, however, found the intelligence remarkable enough, even before it became known that the new body was rapidly growing larger and brighter, that its motion was quite different from the orderly progress of the planets, and that the deflection of Neptune and its satellite was becoming now of an unprecedented kind.

Few people without a training in science can realise the huge isolation of the solar system. The sun with its specks of planets, its dust of planetoids, and its impalpable comets, swims in a vacant immensity that almost defeats the imagination. Beyond the orbit of Neptune there is space, vacant so far as human observation has penetrated, without warmth or light or sound, blank emptiness, for twenty million times a million miles. That is the smallest estimate of the distance to be traversed before the very nearest of the stars is attained. And, saving a few comets more unsubstantial than the thinnest flame, no matter had ever to human knowledge crossed this gulf of space, until early in the twentieth century this strange wanderer appeared. A vast mass of matter it was, bulky, heavy, rushing without warning out of the black mystery of the sky into the radiance of the sun. By the second day it was clearly visible to any decent instrument, as a speck with a barely sensible diameter, in the constellation Leo near Regulus. In a little while an opera glass could attain it.

On the third day of the New Year the newspaper readers of two hemispheres were made aware for the first time of the real importance of this unusual apparition in the heavens. "A Planetary Collision," one London paper headed the news, and proclaimed Duchaine's opinion that this strange new planet would probably collide with Neptune. The leader writers enlarged upon the topic; so that in most of the capitals of the world, on January third, there was an expectation, however vague, of some imminent phenomenon in the sky; and as the night followed the sunset round the globe, thousands of men turned their eyes skyward to see—the old familiar stars just as they had always been.

Until it was dawn in London and Pollux setting and the stars overhead grown pale. The winter's dawn it was, a sickly filtering accumulation of daylight, and the light of gas and candles shone yellow in the windows to show where people were astir. But the yawning policeman saw the thing, the busy crowds in the markets stopped agape, workmen going to their work betimes, milkmen, the drivers of news-carts, dissipation going home jaded and pale, homeless wanderers, sentinels on their beats, and in the country, labourers trudging afield, poachers slinking home, all over the dusky quickening country it could be seen—and out at sea by seamen watching for the day—a great white star, come suddenly into the westward sky!

2

Brighter it was than any star in our skies; brighter than the evening star at its brightest. It still glowed out white and large, no mere twinkling spot of light, but a small round clear shining disc, an hour after the day had come. And where science has not reached, men stared and feared, telling one another of the wars and pestilences that are foreshadowed by these fiery signs in the heavens. Sturdy Boers, dusky Hottentots, Gold Coast Negroes, Frenchmen, Spaniards, Portuguese, stood in the warmth of the sunrise watching the setting of this strange new star.

And in a hundred observatories there had been suppressed excitement, rising almost to shouting pitch, as the two remote bodies had rushed together; and a hurrying to and fro, to gather photographic apparatus and spectroscope, and this appliance and that, to record this novel astonishing sight, the destruction of a world. For it was a world, a sister planet of our earth, far greater than our earth indeed, that had so suddenly flashed into flaming death. Neptune it was, had been struck, fairly and squarely, by the strange planet from outer space and the heat of the concussion had incontinently turned two solid globes into one vast mass of incandescence. Round the world that day, two hours before the dawn, went the pallid great white star, fading only as it sank westward and the sun mounted above it. Everywhere men marvelled at it, but of all those who saw it none could have marvelled more than those sailors, habitual watchers of the stars, who far away at sea had heard nothing of its advent and saw it now rise like a pigmy moon and climb zenithward and hang overhead and sink westward with the passing of the night.

And when next it rose over Europe everywhere were crowds of watchers on hilly slopes, on house-roofs, in open spaces, staring eastward for the rising of the great new star. It rose with a white glow in front of it, like the glare of a white fire, and those who had seen it come into existence the night before cried out at the sight of it. "It is larger," they cried. "It is brighter!"

And, indeed the moon a quarter full and sinking in the west was in its apparent size beyond comparison, but scarcely in all its breadth had it as much brightness now as the little circle of the strange new star.

"It is brighter!" cried the people clustering in the streets. But in the dim observatories the watchers held their breath and peered at one another. "It is nearer," they said. *"Nearer!"*

And voice after voice repeated, "It is nearer," and the clicking telegraph took that up, and it trembled along telephone wires, and in a thousand cities grimy compositors fingered the type. "It is nearer." Men writing in offices, struck with a strange realisation, flung down their pens, men talking in a thousand places suddenly came upon a grotesque possibility in those words, "It is nearer." It hurried along wakening streets, it was shouted down the frost-stilled ways of quiet villages; men who had read these things from the throbbing tape stood in yellow-lit doorways shouting the news to the passersby. "It is nearer." Pretty women, flushed and glittering, heard the news told jestingly between the dances, and feigned an intelligent interest they did not feel. "Nearer! Indeed. How curious! How very, very clever people must be to find out things like that!"

Lonely tramps faring through the wintry night murmured those words to comfort themselves—looking skyward. "It has need to be nearer, for the night's as cold as charity. Don't seem much warmth from it if it is nearer, all the same."

"What is a new star to me?" cried the weeping woman kneeling beside her dead.

The schoolboy, rising early for his examination work, puzzled it out for himself—with the great white star shining broad and bright through the frost-flowers of his window. "Centrifugal, centripetal," he said, with his chin on his fist. "Stop a planet in its flight, rob it of its centrifugal force, what then? Centripetal has it, and down it falls into the sun! And this—!

"Do we come in the way? I wonder—"

The light of that day went the way of its

brethren, and with the later watches of the frosty darkness rose the strange star again. And it was now so bright that the waxing moon seemed but a pale yellow ghost of itself, hanging huge in the sunset. In a South African city a great man had married, and the streets were alight to welcome his return with his bride. "Even the skies have illuminated," said the flatterer. Under Capricorn, two Negro lovers, daring the wild beasts and evil spirits, for love of one another, crouched together in a canebrake where the fireflies hovered. "That is our star," they whispered, and felt strangely comforted by the sweet brilliance of its light.

The master mathematician sat in his private room and pushed the papers from him. His calculations were already finished. In a small white phial there still remained a little of the drug that had kept him awake and active for four long nights. Each day, serene, explicit, patient as ever, he had given his lecture to his students, and then had come back at once to this momentous calculation. His face was grave, a little drawn and hectic from his drugged activity. For some time he seemed lost in thought. Then he went to the window, and the blind went up with a click. Halfway up the sky, over the clustering roofs, chimneys, and steeples of the city, hung the star.

He looked at it as one might look into the eyes of a brave enemy. "You may kill me," he said after a silence. "But I can hold you—and all the universe for that matter—in the grip of this little brain. I would not change. Even now."

He looked at the little phial. "There will be no need of sleep again," he said. The next day at noon—punctual to the minute—he entered his lecture theatre, put his hat on the end of the table as his habit was, and carefully selected a large piece of chalk. It was a joke among his students that he could not lecture without that piece of chalk to fumble in his fingers, and once he had been stricken to impotence by their hiding his supply. He came and looked under his grey eyebrows at the rising tiers of young fresh faces, and spoke with his accustomed studied commonness of phrasing. "Circumstances have arisen—circumstances beyond my control," he said, and paused, "which will debar me from completing the course I had designed. It would seem, gentlemen, if I may put the thing clearly and briefly, that—man has lived in vain."

The students glanced at one another. Had they heard aright? Mad? Raised eyebrows and grinning lips there were, but one or two faces remained intent upon his calm grey-fringed face. "It will be interesting," he was saying, "to devote this morning to an exposition, so far as I can make it clear to you, of the calculations that have led me to this conclusion. Let us assume—"

He turned towards the blackboard, meditating a diagram in the way that was usual to him. "What was that about 'lived in vain'?" whispered one student to another. "Listen," said the other, nodding towards the lecturer.

And presently they began to understand.

That night the star rose later, for its proper eastward motion had carried it some way across Leo towards Virgo, and its brightness was so great that the sky became a luminous blue as it rose, and every star was hidden in its turn, save only Jupiter near the zenith, Capella, Aldebaran, Sirius, and the pointers of the Bear. It was very white and beautiful. In many parts of the world that night a pallid halo encircled it about. It was perceptibly larger; in the clear refractive sky of the tropics it seemed as if it were nearly a quarter the size of the moon. The frost was still on the ground in England, but the world was as brightly lit as if it were midsummer moonlight. One could see to read quite ordinary print by that cold clear light, and in the cities the lamps burnt yellow and wan.

And everywhere the world was awake that night, and throughout Christendom a sombre murmur hung in the keen air over the countryside like the belling of bees in the heather, and this murmurous tumult grew to a clangour in the cities. It was the tolling of the bells in a million belfry towers and steeples, summoning the people to sleep no more, to sin no more, but to gather in their churches and pray. And overhead, growing larger and brighter as the earth rolled on its way and the night passed, rose the dazzling star.

And the streets and houses were alight in all the cities, the shipyards glared, and whatever roads led to high country were lit and crowded all night long. And in all the seas about the civilised lands, ships with throbbing engines, and ships with bellying sails, crowded with men and living creatures, were standing out to ocean and the north. For already the warning of the master mathematician had been telegraphed all over the world, and translated into a hundred tongues. The new planet and Neptune, locked in a fiery embrace, were whirling headlong, ever faster and faster towards the sun. Already every second this blazing mass flew a hundred miles, and every second its terrific velocity increased. As it flew now, indeed, it must pass a hundred million miles wide of the earth and scarcely affect it. But near its destined path, as yet only slightly perturbed, spun the mighty planet Jupiter and his moons sweeping splendid round the sun. Every moment now the attraction between the fiery star and the greatest of the planets grew stronger. And the result of that attraction? Inevitably Jupiter would be deflected from its orbit into an elliptical path, and the burning star, swung by his attraction wide of its sunward rush, would "describe a curved path" and perhaps collide with, and certainly pass very close to, our earth. "Earthquakes, volcanic outbreaks, cyclones, sea waves, floods, and a steady rise in temperature to I know not what limit"—so prophesied the master mathematician.

And overhead, to carry out his words, lonely and cold and livid, blazed the star of the coming doom.

To many who stared at it that night until their eyes ached, it seemed that it was visibly approaching. And that night, too, the weather changed, and the frost that had gripped all Central Europe and France and England softened towards a thaw.

But you must not imagine because I have spoken of people praying through the night and people going aboard ships and people fleeing towards mountainous country that the whole world was already in a terror because of the star. As a matter of fact, use and wont still ruled the world, and save for the talk of idle moments and the splendour of the night, nine human beings out of ten were still busy at their common occupations. In all the cities the shops, save one here and there, opened and closed at their proper hours, the doctor and the undertaker plied their trades, the workers gathered in the factories, soldiers drilled, scholars studied, lovers sought one another, thieves lurked and fled, politicians planned their schemes. The presses of the newspapers roared through the night, and many a priest of this church and that would not open his holy building to further what he considered a foolish panic. The newspapers insisted on the lesson of the year 1000—for then, too, people had anticipated the end. The star was no star—mere gas—a comet; and were it a star it could not possibly strike the earth. There was no precedent for such a thing. Common sense was sturdy everywhere, scornful, jesting, a little inclined to persecute the obdurate fearful. That night, at seven fifteen by Greenwich time, the star would be at its nearest to Jupiter. Then the world would see the turn things would take. The master mathematician's grim warnings were treated by many as so much mere elaborate self-advertisement. Common sense at last, a little heated by argument, signified its unalterable convictions by going to bed. So, too, barbarism and savagery, already tired of the novelty, went about their nightly business, and save for a howling dog here and there, the beast world left the star unheeded.

And yet, when at last the watchers in the European states saw the star rise, an hour later it is true, but no larger than it had been the night before, there were still plenty awake to laugh at the master mathematician—to take the danger as if it had passed.

But hereafter the laughter ceased. The star

grew—it grew with a terrible steadiness hour after hour, a little larger each hour, a little nearer the midnight zenith, and brighter and brighter, until it had turned night into a second day. Had it come straight to the earth instead of in a curved path, had it lost no velocity to Jupiter, it must have leapt the intervening gulf in a day, but as it was it took five days altogether to come by our planet. The next night it had become a third the size of the moon before it set to English eyes, and the thaw was assured. It rose over America near the size of the moon, but blinding white to look at, and hot; and a breath of hot wind blew now with its rising and gathering strength, and in Virginia, and Brazil, and down the St. Lawrence valley, it shone intermittently through a driving reek of thunderclouds, flickering violet lightning, and hail unprecedented. In Manitoba was a thaw and devastating floods. And upon all the mountains of the earth the snow and ice began to melt that night, and all the rivers coming out of high country flowed thick and turbid, and soon—in their upper reaches—with swirling trees and the bodies of beasts and men. They rose steadily, steadily in the ghostly brilliance, and came trickling over their banks at last, behind the flying population of their valleys.

And along the coast of Argentina and up the South Atlantic the tides were higher than had ever been in the memory of man, and the storms drove the waters in many cases scores of miles inland, drowning whole cities. And so great grew the heat during the night that the rising of the sun was like the coming of a shadow. The earthquakes began and grew until all down America from the Arctic Circle to Cape Horn, hillsides were sliding, fissures were opening, and houses and walls crumbling to destruction. The whole side of Cotopaxi slipped out in one vast convulsion, and a tumult of lava poured out so high and broad and swift and liquid that in one day it reached the sea.

So the star, with the wan moon in its wake, marched across the Pacific, trailed the thunderstorms like the hem of a robe, and the growing tidal wave that toiled behind it, frothing and eager, poured over island and island and swept them clear of men. Until that wave came at last—in a blinding light and with the breath of a furnace, swift and terrible it came—a wall of water, fifty feet high, roaring hungrily, upon the long coasts of Asia, and swept inland across the plains of China. For a space the star, hotter now and larger and brighter than the sun in its strength, showed with pitiless brilliance the wide and populous country; towns and villages with their pagodas and trees, roads, wide cultivated fields, millions of sleepless people staring in helpless terror at the incandescent sky; and then, low and growing, came the murmur of the flood. And thus it was with millions of men that night—a flight nowhither, with limbs heavy with heat and breath fierce and scant, and the flood like a wall swift and white behind. And then death.

China was lit glowing white, but over Japan and Java and all the islands of Eastern Asia the great star was a ball of dull red fire because of the steam and smoke and ashes the volcanoes were spouting forth to salute its coming. Above was the lava, hot gases, and ash, and below the seething floods, and the whole earth swayed and rumbled with the earthquake shocks. Soon the immemorial snows of Tibet and the Himalaya were melting and pouring down by ten million deepening converging channels upon the plains of Burmah and Hindostan. The tangled summits of the Indian jungles were aflame in a thousand places, and below the hurrying waters around the stems were dark objects that still struggled feebly and reflected the blood-red tongues of fire. And in a rudderless confusion a multitude of men and women fled down the broad river-ways to that one last hope of men—the open sea.

Larger grew the star, and larger, hotter, and brighter with a terrible swiftness now. The tropical ocean had lost its phosphorescence, and the whirling steam rose in ghostly wreaths from the black waves that plunged incessantly, speckled with storm-tossed ships.

And then came a wonder. It seemed to those who in Europe watched for the rising of the star that the world must have ceased its rotation. In a thousand open spaces of down and upland the people who had fled thither from the floods and the falling houses and sliding slopes of hill watched for that rising in vain. Hour followed hour through a terrible suspense, and the star rose not. Once again men set their eyes upon the old constellations they had counted lost to them forever. In England it was hot and clear overhead, though the ground quivered perpetually, but in the tropics, Sirius and Capella and Aldebaran showed through a veil of steam. And when at last the great star rose near ten hours late, the sun rose close upon it, and in the centre of its white heart was a disc of black.

Over Asia it was the star had begun to fall behind the movement of the sky, and then suddenly, as it hung over India, its light had been veiled. All the plain of India from the mouth of the Indus to the mouths of the Ganges was a shallow waste of shining water that night, out of which rose temples and palaces, mounds and hills, black with people. Every minaret was a clustering mass of people, who fell one by one into the turbid waters, as heat and terror overcame them. The whole land seemed a-wailing and suddenly there swept a shadow across that furnace of despair, and a breath of cold wind, and a gathering of clouds, out of the cooling air. Men looking up, near blinded, at the star, saw that a black disc was creeping across the light. It was the moon, coming between the star and the earth. And even as men cried to God at this respite, out of the east with a strange inexplicable swiftness sprang the sun. And then star, sun, and moon rushed together across the heavens.

So it was that presently, to the European watchers, star and sun rose close upon each other, drove headlong for a space and then slower, and at last came to rest, star and sun merged into one glare of flame at the zenith of the sky. The moon no longer eclipsed the star but was lost to sight in the brilliance of the sky.

And though those who were still alive regarded it for the most part with that dull stupidity that hunger, fatigue, heat, and despair engender, there were still men who could perceive the meaning of these signs. Star and earth had been at their nearest, had swung about one another, and the star had passed. Already it was receding, swifter and swifter, in the last stage of its headlong journey downward into the sun.

And then the clouds gathered, blotting out the vision of the sky, the thunder and lightning wove a garment round the world; all over the earth was such a downpour of rain as men had never before seen, and where the volcanoes flared red against the cloud canopy there descended torrents of mud. Everywhere the waters were pouring off the land, leaving mud-silted ruins, and the earth littered like a storm-worn beach with all that had floated, and the dead bodies of the men and brutes, its children. For days the water streamed off the land, sweeping away soil and trees and houses in the way, and piling huge dykes and scooping out titanic gullies over the countryside. Those were the days of darkness that followed the star and the heat. All through them, and for many weeks and months, the earthquakes continued.

But the star had passed, and men, hunger-driven and gathering courage only slowly, might creep back to their ruined cities, buried granaries, and sodden fields. Such few ships as had escaped the storms of that time came stunned and shattered and sounding their way cautiously through the new marks and shoals of once familiar ports. And as the storms subsided men perceived that everywhere the days were hotter than of yore, and the sun larger, and the moon, shrunk to a third of its former size, took now fourscore days between its new and new.

But of the new brotherhood that grew presently among men, of the saving of laws and books and machines, of the strange change that had come over Iceland and Greenland and the shores of Baffin's Bay, so that the sailors coming there presently found them green and gracious, and could scarce believe their eyes, this story does not tell. Nor of the movement of mankind now that the earth was hotter, northward and southward towards the poles of the earth. It concerns itself only with the coming and the passing of the star.

The Martian astronomers—for there are astronomers on Mars, although they are very different beings from men—were naturally profoundly interested by these things. They saw them from their own standpoint of course. "Considering the mass and temperature of the missile that was flung through our solar system into the sun," one wrote, "it is astonishing what a little damage the earth, which it missed so narrowly, has sustained. All the familiar continental markings and the masses of the seas remain intact, and indeed the only difference seems to be a shrinkage of the white discoloration (supposed to be frozen water) round either pole." Which only shows how small the vastest of human catastrophes may seem, at a distance of a few million miles.

Sultana's Dream
ROKHEYA SHEKHAWAT HOSSAIN

Begum Rokheya Shekhawat Hossain (1880–1932), also known as Begum Rokheya, was a Bengali writer famous for her social work for gender equality in what is now Bangladesh. She wrote in many genres and modes, including short stories, poems, essays, novels, and satirical works.

Her published works, some of them translated into English, include "Pipasha" ("Thirst," 1902), *Motichur* volumes 1 and 2 (1904, 1922), "Saogat" (1918, poetry), *Padmarag* (1924, feminist utopian novel), "Oborodh-Bashini" ("The Secluded Women," 1931), "Narir adhikar" ("The Rights of Women," nonfiction commissioned by the Islamic Women's Association), "God Gives, Man Robs" (1927), and "Education Ideals for the Modern Indian Girl" (1931). The first volume of *Motichur* collects essays, but the second volume includes stories such as "Saurajagat" ("The Solar System"), "Jvan-phal" ("The Fruit of Knowledge"), "Nari-sristi" ("Creation of Women"), and "Mukti-phal" ("The Fruit of Emancipation"). She wrote regularly for such publications as *Saogat, Mahammadi, Nabaprabha, Mahila, Bharatmahila, al-Eslam, Nawroz, Mahe-Nao, Bangiya Mussalman Sahitya Patrika,* the *Musalman,* and the *Indian Ladies' Magazine.*

Born into a wealthy and influential family, Hossain had relatives who were government ministers and a sister who was a popular poet. Although she was married at sixteen, Hossain's husband was a progressive who allowed her to continue her education and who encouraged her activism. Hossain often used humor and cutting satire in her writings to push back against widespread resistance to the education of women. She also established the first school for Muslim girls in 1909 and founded the Islamic Women's Association, which held debates and organized conferences regarding the status of women and education. She advocated reform, particularly for women.

In 1926, Begum Rokheya strongly condemned men for withholding education from women in the name of religion as she addressed the Bengal women's education conference: "The opponents of the female education [who] say that women will be unruly lie! They call themselves Muslims and yet go against the basic tenet of Islam, which gives equal right to education. If men are not led astray once educated, why should women be?" She remained busy with the school until she died of heart problems on her fifty-second birthday. Today, Bangladesh celebrates Rokheya Day in her honor.

The most notable of Hossain's short stories was her feminist utopian work "Sultana's Dream" (1905). As with much early science fiction, the story takes the form of a *"conte philosophique,"* which translates as "fable of reason." The *conte philosophique* had existed for centuries in the West as a way for scientists or philosophers to present their findings, using the fictional frame of an imaginary journey to impart scientific or philosophical content. Other stories in this volume by Alfred Jarry, Paul Scheerbart, and Stanisław Lem use a similar approach, if for different purposes.

SULTANA'S DREAM

Rokheya Shekhawat Hossain

One evening I was lounging in an easy chair in my bedroom and thinking lazily of the condition of Indian womanhood. I am not sure whether I dozed off or not. But, as far as I remember, I was wide awake. I saw the moonlit sky sparkling with thousands of diamondlike stars, very distinctly.

All of a sudden a lady stood before me; how she came in, I do not know. I took her for my friend, Sister Sara.

"Good morning," said Sister Sara. I smiled inwardly as I knew it was not morning, but starry night. However, I replied to her, saying, "How do you do?"

"I am all right, thank you. Will you please come out and have a look at our garden?"

I looked again at the moon through the open window, and thought there was no harm in going out at that time. The menservants outside were fast asleep just then, and I could have a pleasant walk with Sister Sara.

I used to have my walks with Sister Sara, when we were at Darjeeling. Many a time did we walk hand in hand and talk lightheartedly in the botanical gardens there. I fancied Sister Sara had probably come to take me to some such garden and I readily accepted her offer and went out with her.

When walking I found to my surprise that it was a fine morning. The town was fully awake and the streets alive with bustling crowds. I was feeling very shy, thinking I was walking in the street in broad daylight, but there was not a single man visible.

Some of the passersby made jokes at me. Though I could not understand their language, yet I felt sure they were joking. I asked my friend, "What do they say?"

"The women say that you look very mannish."

"Mannish?" said I. "What do they mean by that?"

"They mean that you are shy and timid like men."

"Shy and timid like men?" It was really a joke. I became very nervous, when I found that my companion was not Sister Sara, but a stranger. Oh, what a fool had I been to mistake this lady for my dear old friend Sister Sara.

She felt my fingers tremble in her hand, as we were walking hand in hand.

"What is the matter, dear?" she said affectionately.

"I feel somewhat awkward," I said in a rather apologizing tone, "as being a *purdahnishin* woman I am not accustomed to walking about unveiled."

"You need not be afraid of coming across a man here. This is Ladyland, free from sin and harm. Virtue herself reigns here."

By and by I was enjoying the scenery. Really it was very grand. I mistook a patch of green grass for a velvet cushion. Feeling as if I were walking on a soft carpet, I looked down and found the path covered with moss and flowers.

"How nice it is," said I.

"Do you like it?" asked Sister Sara. (I continued calling her "Sister Sara," and she kept calling me by my name.)

"Yes, very much; but I do not like to tread on the tender and sweet flowers."

"Never mind, dear Sultana; your treading will not harm them; they are street flowers."

"The whole place looks like a garden," said I admiringly. "You have arranged every plant so skillfully."

"Your Calcutta could become a nicer garden than this if only your countrymen wanted to make it so."

"They would think it useless to give so much attention to horticulture, while they have so many other things to do."

"They could not find a better excuse," said she with a smile.

I became very curious to know where the men were. I met more than a hundred women while walking there, but not a single man.

"Where are the men?" I asked her.

"In their proper places, where they ought to be."

"Pray let me know what you mean by 'their proper places.'"

"O, I see my mistake, you cannot know our customs, as you were never here before. We shut our men indoors."

"Just as we are kept in the zenana?"

"Exactly so."

"How funny." I burst into a laugh. Sister Sara laughed too.

"But, dear Sultana, how unfair it is to shut in the harmless women and let loose the men."

"Why? It is not safe for us to come out of the zenana, as we are naturally weak."

"Yes, it is not safe so long as there are men about the streets, nor is it so when a wild animal enters a marketplace."

"Of course not."

"Suppose some lunatics escape from the asylum and begin to do all sorts of mischief to men, horses, and other creatures; in that case what will your countrymen do?"

"They will try to capture them and put them back into their asylum."

"Thank you! And you do not think it wise to keep sane people inside an asylum and let loose the insane?"

"Of course not!" said I, laughing lightly.

"As a matter of fact, in your country this very thing is done! Men, who do or at least are capable of doing no end of mischief, are let loose and the innocent women shut up in the zenana! How can you trust those untrained men out of doors?"

"We have no hand or voice in the management of our social affairs. In India man is lord and master, he has taken to himself all powers and privileges and shut up the women in the zenana."

"Why do you allow yourselves to be shut up?"

"Because it cannot be helped as they are stronger than women."

"A lion is stronger than a man, but it does not enable him to dominate the human race. You have neglected the duty you owe to yourselves and you have lost your natural rights by shutting your eyes to your own interests."

"But, my dear Sister Sara, if we do everything by ourselves, what will the men do then?"

"They should not do anything, excuse me; they are fit for nothing. Only catch them and put them into the zenana."

"But would it be very easy to catch and put them inside the four walls?" said I. "And even if this were done, would all their business—political and commercial—also go with them into the zenana?"

Sister Sara made no reply. She only smiled sweetly. Perhaps she thought it useless to argue with one who was no better than a frog in a well.

By this time we reached Sister Sara's house. It was situated in a beautiful heart-shaped garden. It was a bungalow with a corrugated iron roof. It was cooler and nicer than any of our rich buildings. I cannot describe how neat and how nicely furnished and how tastefully decorated it was.

We sat side by side. She brought out of the parlour a piece of embroidery work and began putting on a fresh design.

"Do you know knitting and needlework?"

"Yes; we have nothing else to do in our zenana."

"But we do not trust our zenana members with embroidery," she said, laughing, "as a man has not patience enough to pass thread through a needle hole even!"

"Have you done all this work yourself?" I asked her, pointing to the various pieces of embroidered teapoy cloths.

"Yes."

"How can you find time to do all these? You have to do the office work as well? Have you not?"

"Yes. I do not stick to the laboratory all day long. I finish my work in two hours."

"In two hours! How do you manage? In our land the officers—magistrates, for instance—work seven hours daily."

"I have seen some of them doing their work. Do you think they work all the seven hours?"

"Certainly they do!"

"No, dear Sultana, they do not. They dawdle away their time in smoking. Some smoke two or three cheroots during the office time. They talk much about their work, but do little. Suppose one cheroot takes half an hour to burn off, and a man smokes twelve cheroots daily; then you see, he wastes six hours every day in sheer smoking."

We talked on various subjects, and I learned that they were not subject to any kind of epidemic disease, nor did they suffer from mosquito bites as we do. I was very much astonished to hear that in Ladyland no one died in youth except by rare accident.

"Will you care to see our kitchen?" she asked me.

"With pleasure," said I, and we went to see it. Of course the men had been asked to clear off when I was going there. The kitchen was situated in a beautiful vegetable garden. Every creeper, every tomato plant was itself an ornament. I found no smoke, nor any chimney either in the kitchen—it was clean and bright; the windows were decorated with flower gardens. There was no sign of coal or fire.

"How do you cook?" I asked.

"With solar heat," she said, at the same time showing me the pipe, through which passed the concentrated sunlight and heat. And she cooked something then and there to show me the process.

"How did you manage to gather and store up the sun-heat?" I asked her in amazement.

"Let me tell you a little of our past history then. Thirty years ago, when our present queen was thirteen years old, she inherited the throne. She was queen in name only, the prime minister really ruling the country.

"Our good queen liked science very much. She circulated an order that all the women in her country should be educated. Accordingly a number of girls' schools were founded and supported by the government. Education was spread far and wide among women. And early marriage also was stopped. No woman was to be allowed to marry before she was twenty-one. I must tell you that before this change we had been kept in strict purdah."

"How the tables are turned," I interposed with a laugh.

"But the seclusion is the same," she said. "In a few years we had separate universities, where no men were admitted.

"In the capital, where our queen lives, there are two universities. One of these invented a wonderful balloon, to which they attached a number of pipes. By means of this captive balloon, which they managed to keep afloat above the cloud-land, they could draw as much water from the atmosphere as they pleased. As the water was incessantly being drawn by the university people no cloud gathered and the ingenious Lady Principal stopped rain and storms thereby."

"Really! Now I understand why there is no mud here!" said I. But I could not understand how it was possible to accumulate water in the pipes. She explained to me how it was done, but I was unable to understand her, as my scientific knowledge was very limited. However, she went on, "When the other university came to know of this, they became exceedingly jealous and tried to do something more extraordinary still. They invented an instrument by which they could collect as much sun-heat as they wanted. And they kept the heat stored up to be distributed among others as required.

"While the women were engaged in scientific research, the men of this country were busy increasing their military power. When they came to know that the female universities were able to draw water from the atmosphere and collect heat from the sun, they only laughed at the members of the universities and called the whole thing 'a sentimental nightmare'!"

"Your achievements are very wonderful indeed! But tell me how you managed to put the men of your country into the zenana. Did you entrap them first?"

"No."

"It is not likely that they would surrender their free and open-air life of their own accord and confine themselves within the four walls of the zenana! They must have been overpowered."

"Yes, they have been!"

"By whom? By some lady-warriors, I suppose?"

"No, not by arms."

"Yes, it cannot be so. Men's arms are stronger than women's. Then?"

"By brains."

"Even their brains are bigger and heavier than women's. Are they not?"

"Yes, but what of that? An elephant also has got a bigger and heavier brain than a man has. Yet man can enchain elephants and employ them, according to their own wishes."

"Well said, but tell me, please, how it all actually happened. I am dying to know it!"

"Women's brains are somewhat quicker than men's. Ten years ago, when the military officers called our scientific discoveries 'a sentimental nightmare,' some of the young ladies wanted to say something in reply to those remarks. But both the Lady Principals restrained them and said they should reply not by word, but by deed, if ever they got the opportunity. And they had not long to wait for that opportunity."

"How marvelous!" I heartily clapped my hands. "And now the proud gentlemen are dreaming sentimental dreams themselves."

"Soon afterwards certain persons came from a neighbouring country and took shelter in ours. They were in trouble, having committed some political offense. The king, who cared more for power than for good government, asked our kindhearted queen to hand them over to his officers. She refused, as it was against her principle to turn out refugees. For this refusal the king declared war against our country.

"Our military officers sprang to their feet at once and marched out to meet the enemy. The enemy, however, was too strong for them. Our soldiers fought bravely, no doubt. But in spite of all their bravery the foreign army advanced step by step to invade our country.

"Nearly all the men had gone out to fight; even a boy of sixteen was not left home. Most of our warriors were killed, the rest driven back, and the enemy came within twenty-five miles of the capital.

"A meeting of a number of wise ladies was held at the queen's palace to advise as to what should be done to save the land. Some proposed to fight like soldiers; others objected and said that women were not trained to fight with swords and guns, nor were they accustomed to fighting with any weapons. A third party regretfully remarked that they were hopelessly weak of body.

"'If you cannot save your country for lack of physical strength,' said the queen, 'try to do so by brainpower.'

"There was a dead silence for a few minutes. Her Royal Highness said again, 'I must commit suicide if the land and my honour are lost.'

"Then the Lady Principal of the second university (which had collected sun-heat), who had been silently thinking during the consultation, remarked that they were all but lost, and there was little hope left for them. There was, however, one plan which she would like to try, and this would be her first and last effort; if she failed in this, there would be nothing left but to commit suicide. All present solemnly vowed that they would never allow themselves to be enslaved, no matter what happened.

"The queen thanked them heartily, and

asked the Lady Principal to try her plan. The Lady Principal rose again and said, 'Before we go out the men must enter the zenanas. I make this prayer for the sake of purdah.' 'Yes, of course,' replied Her Royal Highness.

"On the following day the queen called upon all men to retire into zenanas for the sake of honour and liberty. Wounded and tired as they were, they took that order rather for a boon! They bowed low and entered the zenanas without uttering a single word of protest. They were sure that there was no hope for this country at all.

"Then the Lady Principal with her two thousand students marched to the battlefield, and arriving there directed all the rays of the concentrated sunlight and heat towards the enemy.

"The heat and light were too much for them to bear. They all ran away panic-stricken, not knowing in their bewilderment how to counteract that scorching heat. When they fled away leaving their guns and other ammunitions of war, they were burnt down by means of the same sun-heat. Since then no one has tried to invade our country anymore."

"And since then your countrymen never tried to come out of the zenana?"

"Yes, they wanted to be free. Some of the police commissioners and district magistrates sent word to the queen to the effect that the military officers certainly deserved to be imprisoned for their failure; but they never neglected their duty and therefore they should not be punished and they prayed to be restored to their respective offices.

"Her Royal Highness sent them a circular letter intimating to them that if their services should ever be needed they would be sent for, and that in the meanwhile they should remain where they were. Now that they are accustomed to the purdah system and have ceased to grumble at their seclusion, we call the system 'Mardana' instead of 'zenana.'"

"But how do you manage," I asked Sister Sara, "to do without the police or magistrates in case of theft or murder?"

"Since the 'Mardana' system has been established, there has been no more crime or sin; therefore we do not require a policeman to find out a culprit, nor do we want a magistrate to try a criminal case."

"That is very good, indeed. I suppose if there was any dishonest person, you could very easily chastise her. As you gained a decisive victory without shedding a single drop of blood, you could drive off crime and criminals too without much difficulty!"

"Now, dear Sultana, will you sit here or come to my parlour?" she asked me.

"Your kitchen is not inferior to a queen's boudoir!" I replied with a pleasant smile. "But we must leave it now; for the gentlemen may be cursing me for keeping them away from their duties in the kitchen so long." We both laughed heartily.

"How my friends at home will be amused and amazed, when I go back and tell them that in the far-off Ladyland, ladies rule over the country and control all social matters, while gentlemen are kept in the Mardanas to mind babies, to cook, and to do all sorts of domestic work; and that cooking is so easy a thing that it is simply a pleasure to cook!"

"Yes, tell them about all that you see here."

"Please let me know how you carry on land cultivation and how you plough the land and do other hard manual work."

"Our fields are tilled by means of electricity, which supplies motive power for other hard work as well, and we employ it for our aerial conveyances too. We have no railroad nor any paved streets here."

"Therefore neither street nor railway accidents occur here," said I. "Do not you ever suffer from want of rainwater?" I asked.

"Never since the 'water balloon' has been set up. You see the big balloon and pipes attached thereto. By their aid we can draw as much rainwater as we require. Nor do we ever suffer from flood or thunderstorms. We are all very busy making nature yield as much as she can. We do not find time to quarrel with one another as we never sit idle. Our noble queen is exceedingly fond of botany; it is her ambition to convert the whole country into one grand garden."

"The idea is excellent. What is your chief food?"

"Fruits."

"How do you keep your country cool in hot weather? We regard the rainfall in summer as a blessing from heaven."

"When the heat becomes unbearable, we sprinkle the ground with plentiful showers drawn from the artificial fountains. And in cold weather we keep our rooms warm with sun-heat."

She showed me her bathroom, the roof of which was removable. She could enjoy a shower bath whenever she liked, by simply removing the roof (which was like the lid of a box) and turning on the tap of the shower pipe.

"You are a lucky people!" ejaculated I. "You know no want. What is your religion, may I ask?"

"Our religion is based on Love and Truth. It is our religious duty to love one another and to be absolutely truthful. If any person lies, she or he is . . ."

"Punished with death?"

"No, not with death. We do not take pleasure in killing a creature of God, especially a human being. The liar is asked to leave this land for good and never to come to it again."

"Is an offender never forgiven?"

"Yes, if that person repents sincerely."

"Are you not allowed to see any man, except your own relations?"

"No one except sacred relations."

"Our circle of sacred relations is very limited; even first cousins are not sacred."

"But ours is very large; a distant cousin is as sacred as a brother."

"That is very good. I see purity itself reigns over your land. I should like to see the good queen, who is so sagacious and farsighted and who has made all these rules."

"All right," said Sister Sara.

Then she screwed a couple of seats onto a square piece of plank. To this plank she attached two smooth and well-polished balls. When I asked her what the balls were for, she said they were hydrogen balls and they were used to overcome the force of gravity. The balls were of different capacities to be used according to the different weights desired to be overcome. She then fastened to the air-car two winglike blades, which, she said, were worked by electricity. After we were comfortably seated she touched a knob and the blades began to whirl, moving faster and faster every moment. At first we were raised to the height of about six or seven feet and then off we flew. And before I could realize that we had commenced moving, we reached the garden of the queen.

My friend lowered the air-car by reversing the action of the machine, and when the car touched the ground the machine was stopped and we got out.

I had seen from the air-car the queen walking on a garden path with her little daughter (who was four years old) and her maids of honour.

"Halloo! You here!" cried the queen, addressing Sister Sara. I was introduced to Her Royal Highness and was received by her cordially without any ceremony.

I was very much delighted to make her acquaintance. In the course of the conversation I had with her, the queen told me that she had no objection to permitting her subjects to trade with other countries. "But," she continued, "no trade was possible with countries where the women were kept in the zenanas and so unable to come and trade with us. Men, we find, are rather of lower morals and so we do not like dealing with them. We do not covet other people's land, we do not fight for a piece of diamond though it may be a thousandfold brighter than the Koh-i-Noor, nor do we grudge a ruler his Peacock Throne. We dive deep into the ocean of knowledge and try to find out the precious gems which nature has kept in store for us. We enjoy nature's gifts as much as we can."

After taking leave of the queen, I visited the famous universities, and was shown some of their manufactories, laboratories, and observatories.

After visiting the above places of interest we got again into the air-car, but as soon as it began moving, I somehow slipped down and the fall startled me out of my dream. And on opening my eyes, I found myself in my own bedroom still lounging in the easy chair!

The Triumph of Mechanics
KARL HANS STROBL
Translated by Gio Clairval

Karl Hans Strobl (1877–1946) was an Austrian author and editor of fantasy and weird fiction who studied at Charles University in Prague. His own writing was strongly influenced by Edgar Allan Poe and Hanns Heinz Ewers, author of such weird horror classics as "The Spider." After World War I, Strobl relocated to Germany, where he founded the magazine *Der orchideengarten: Phantastische blätter* (*The Orchid Garden: Fantastic Pages*) in 1919 with Alfons von Czibulka, which is now regarded as the world's first specialized fantasy magazine, predating *Weird Tales* in the United States by two years. His own 1910 novel *Eleagabal Kuperus* was adapted as the film *Nachtgestalten* in 1920, starring Conrad Veidt of *The Cabinet of Dr. Caligari*.

Strobl carved out a space for himself as a unique writer of macabre fiction, earning comparisons to the Czech writer Gustav Meyrink and to Alfred Kubin. However, Strobl also became increasingly extremist as an advocate for German nationalism. This impulse led to Strobl's adopting right-wing and anti-Semitic views late in the 1920s. Some of the racism inherent in Strobl's worldview had been visible as early as the illustrations commissioned for *Der orchideengarten* but metastasized when Strobl joined the Nazi Party before World War II and became a high official in the Nazi writers' organization, spending the rest of his literary career producing pro-Nazi propaganda. As a result, his works were banned by the Allies at the end of the war. In horribly tangible ways, then, Strobl ended up embodying the antithesis of every hope Paul Scheerbart had had for the future of Germany and humankind.

It would be easy to read into Strobl's "The Triumph of Mechanics" (1907), never before translated into English, some precursor or indication of his later proclivities and political views. But what comes through behind the apparent faith and optimism about industry and industrialization is the threat inherent in a mechanized society: the rebellious artificial legions stealing the world from their masters, foreshadowing one of the themes of classic science fiction. In "The Triumph of Mechanics," the author's dystopia is laced with humor. This stance is in direct opposition to the "can-do, gee whiz" attitude about humanity's endeavors on Earth and beyond the stars that dominated some early American science fiction.

THE TRIUMPH OF MECHANICS

Karl Hans Strobl
Translated by Gio Clairval

The town's toy industry had grown considerably in the last few years. All civilized countries placed orders upon orders, eager to own mechanical toys—multicolored, marvelously precise: the Punchinello puppets banging drums, the indefatigable fencers, the madly fast automobiles, the proud war vessels propelled by veritable steam engines. Through some forceful entreat, one could export the toys to unsophisticated lands—though the demand was not as imperious. One could often find—deep in the forests and out in the deserts of Africa—little indigenous children playing with what remained of those remarkable products. A famous explorer even confessed to having been fooled in the jungle, at the edge of the Malagarasi, by a very peculiar monkey: the beast sat in a palm tree, and the explorer had convinced himself he had discovered another simian species, when he glimpsed his country's trademark, DRP* N. 105307, which destroyed his hopes. But the independent press soon placed this story in the usual category (as far as explorers of Africa were concerned) of imaginary ravings and condemned it as one more conspiracy conceived by the abhorred colonial policy.

The automated rabbits from the firm Stricker & Vorderteil were by far in greatest demand. These small animals, exact replicas of the natural creatures, were capable, when their spring was fully wound up, of hopping around like their living models, in five or six circles.

A mechanical engineer of universal genius, an American, of course, whose inventions

seemed to fall from the heavens directly onto his lap, had designed the humble inanimate beasts specifically for the company. Unfortunately, the moment when the firm's performance and celebrity peaked, everything collapsed like a house of cards. With the impertinence of the man who believes himself indispensible, Hopkins requested to be paid double, work half hours, and have access to a personal laboratory and a vacation property out of town. Stricker was inclined to accept, but Vorderteil opposed this decision in the strongest possible terms: "We can't do that, if only for the sake of management's principles; otherwise, in six months' time Hopkins will come up with some new whim."

Stricker agreed. The American, a grin hovering about his face, listened to his boss's decision and responded by handing over his notice. The slight consternation and discontent caused by this reaction vanished when the owners realized all the crucial secrets of fabrication were safe and the enterprise risked nothing.

"What if," said the anxious Stricker, "Hopkins creates a competing firm?"

"Leave it to me," said Vorderteil in a soothing tone, as he was, through a few discreet dealings, acquainted with the town's mayor. The defector would receive no permission to start his business.

Meanwhile, Hopkins worked as if nothing had happened. He continued to supervise the factory's production, changing a few small-scale details, as if he intended to work for Stricker and Vorderteil forever. One could say he invented as easily as he drew breath. During these last weeks, important orders of rabbits

---

* Translator's note: Deutsche Reichspatent.

came in, and the firm was forced to increase its means of production, to fabricate those legions of small animals. Hopkins, wearing his customary smile, left at the end of his notice, doffed his impeccable top hat, and bowed low to his former employers. He remained worryingly quiet about his future projects, and what Stricker's fretful nature had correctly intuited turned out to be true. Through his discreet dealings with the mayor's office, Vorderteil learned that Hopkins had bought a vacant lot and had filed a building permit, to build a new factory.

"Guess," Vorderteil cried, "what he's going to fabricate?"

"I have no idea," Stricker answered, and this time he really had no clue.

"Toys made of glazed colored glass. That's what he wants to do. Glazed colored glass! Have you ever heard of such a thing?"

Stricker had never heard of such a thing, but he deemed Hopkins capable of anything, even of making glazed colored glass toys, which is why he blanched, nodded, shrugged his shoulders, and hunched over, thus losing three centimeters in height.

Vorderteil yelled: "Glazed glass. And colored! Nonsense!"

"Calm down. It's probably a mistake. Maybe Hopkins meant to say 'gasified air.' I think I heard something about it."

At these words, Vorderteil banged his fist on the table, so forcefully the huge recorder placed over his head oscillated. He cried:

"This is a serious matter. Don't be facetious, now that everything we worked for is crumbling around our ears. When Hopkins says glazed glass, he thinks glazed glass, and, if I understand well, he gave an overview of his project, from which it would appear that he has discovered a process to solidify air, a method that allows submitting air to very high temperatures, giving it all the properties of glass, except for fragility."

"That would be an industrial revolution, and he is very obliging, given that he intends to use this breakthrough technology to make toys. Who knows where he'll stop?"

"Very obliging, yes. But what if, all of a sudden, children were given dice, skittles, puppets, locomotives made of colored glass that never break, and the toys are completely safe? Maybe he will even make automated rabbits, oh!"

Vorderteil threw himself back so violently in his armchair that the huge Shannon recorder fell on his head. While papers flittered around him, he bounded to his feet.

"That must be avoided at all costs, and if you, Mr. Stricker, indulge in incomprehensible nonchalance, I myself must thank God for having connections that will help me foil Hopkins's nefarious plan."

The following weeks, many discussions took place through the usual discreet channels, between the mayor and Vorderteil. It ensued that these secret dealings caused a firm refusal of all the requests, appeals, and revisions filed by Hopkins. To the point that Stricker, crushed by his associate's repeated victories, saw himself shrink about two centimeters in height every day.

After the seventeenth rejection of Hopkins's request, a peculiar din resounded before the city hall's door, and the American, flanked by two enormous mastiffs, entered the antechamber, which was made narrow by thick folders, all sorts of carefully kept clutter, and rolled-up sheets of paper containing building plans.

Secretaries and clerks took refuge in the adjacent rooms, while the doors moaned under the weight of the mastiffs, which were leaning into the panels. Thanks to the two monsters, whose heads reached up to his shoulders, Hopkins was able to get into the mayor's office. Here he stood, Hopkins, facing the mayor, hat in hand, while the mastiffs, giving in to their instinct, sniffed the cabinets all around the room, upending vases and unabashedly leaving the marks of their huge paws on the delicate patterns of the rug, and the mayor tried to find something to say:

"Don't you know that dogs are not allowed inside?" he ended up yelling.

"Of course I know," Hopkins answered, smiling. "Dogs must stay outside."

"So how dare you introduce your tykes here!"

"These? But they're not dogs."

"Oh, yes? What are they then?"

"They're machines, Mr. Mayor."

And Hopkins called one of the mastiffs closer, and unscrewed its head so that it was possible to glimpse the gearwheels inside; he also explained how the animals moved their limbs and sniffed, particularly emphasizing the clever mechanism that allowed the dogs to wag their tails.

"What in the hell is this for . . . ?" asked the mayor, an almost imploring expression on his nonplussed face, while the cogs, wheels, springs, and electrical batteries spun frenetically.

Hopkins switched his dogs' mechanisms off and riposted through another question:

"Why wouldn't you let me build my factory?"

"For that, you should address the Civil Engineering Office, in order to learn whether it is possible to obtain a building permit."

"I have already put the same question to the Civil Engineering Office. There, I was told to address the Police Office."

"Well, then, and . . . ?"

"From there, I was sent to the Technical Assistance Office."

"Well, then, and . . . ?"

"There, they wanted me to go to the Civil Engineering Office again, but at this point I decided to address you directly."

The mayor, seeing himself abandoned by all his auxiliary offices, resigned himself to replying.

"We didn't respond favorably to your request because the legal requirements were not met."

"But everything's perfect, and if you don't believe me, I shall do whatever it takes to obtain your agreement, one way or another."

Under the dogs' lackluster stare, which seemed as threatening as the glint in their master's eyes, the mayor dared not to contradict his interlocutor. The three creatures that fenced the mayor inside a magical circle resembled receptacles of accumulated force waiting for a switch-on to explode into action, unleashing destruction.

In a wavering voice, he asked: "And now, what do you intend to do?"

"Oh, I can choose one among hundreds of possibilities . . . like . . . rabbits, for example."

"Ra—rabbits?"

"Yes . . . I can set a billion mechanical rabbits on the town."

There, the mayor burst into laughter. "A billion! And . . . mechanical . . . ha-ha."

"I'm under the impression you have no idea what a billion is, and you don't know a thing about the perfection of mechanics, not to mention the effects of inanimate objects to which one lends movement. . . ."

But the mayor, who couldn't control his fits of laughter, kept saying, "Ra—rabbits. Au-tomated . . . ra—rabbits. Ha-ha."

"Then you take responsibility for it?"

"But of course . . . of course."

"All right," said Hopkins, and he tipped his hat by way of a farewell.

He turned on his dogs' switches and, followed by the monsters, exited, an amiable smile at the corner of his mouth. It took the mayor two hours to recover, and only after all the heads of departments succeeded in restraining their serious cases of the giggles, he went home, a vague air of satisfaction about him. Exhausted by his unusual exertions, he couldn't wait to tell his wife about the joke. In front of the door, he saw in a corner, shyly nestled against the wall, looking miserable, a cute little white rabbit produced according to the renowned process of the Stricker & Vorderteil firm. Amused by the thought that Hopkins had already placed a little white rabbit by his door, the mayor extended a hand to seize the small beast, but the rabbit hopped away, quickly escaping him. Still intent on the idea of pursuit, the mayor saw with satisfaction that not far down the street, a few rascals had trapped the animal. The story told by the mayor was sheer pleasure to his wife as her thrifty nature immediately envisaged the opportunity of procuring children's toys at no cost. When little Edwige appeared clutching a little white rabbit she had found on the porch, the mayor's wife laughed joyously. She burst out laughing again when Richard brought in a rabbit, which settled in on the kitchen table, and again when Fritz and Anna emerged from the dark depths of a cave, each carrying a rabbit.

These animals with dull glass eyes hopped to and fro in a frenzy: one had to stack them up into a corner, from which they escaped, causing the children to become noisily nervous. But when Cook, pale in the face, reported that one of the creatures had all of a sudden leaped into a marmalade jar, the mother's hilarity gave way to the housewife's carefulness. During the afternoon, the rabbits multiplied in a worrisome manner. They seemed to lurk in every corner, erupt from the cracks in the floorboards; they sat on all the moldings and doorframes; they sprang blindly everywhere, so that the general amusement quickly ceased, while a murmur of disapprobation filled the house.

The mayor, fleeing from the nuisance, went to his club through a twilight peppered with hopping white smudges. There he met friends who, as perplexed as he, had convened to discuss the phenomenon, while rabbits, in ever increasing numbers, came to disrupt the men's reflections. From time to time, Joseph, the club's barman, swept the animals out of the rooms, but the next minute, the things shot up from every corner, leaping at one another, their glass eyes red and bulging. Upon the reading table, the creatures deviled the sacred placement of the newspapers. The gentlemen traded furious

glances, deeply disturbed by this aggravating intrusion, and left as soon as it appeared that Joseph and his broom were unable to get rid of the vermin.

That same evening, the mayor felt a hard lump under his bedclothes, and, when he anxiously groped for it, his hand came up filled with a rabbit that stared at him stupidly. Cursing, he threw the thing, but the animal contented itself with uttering a weak, high-pitched scream, like a struck instrument, and then resumed hopping. At this proof of resilience, the mayor flipped his lid, and the effects of his anger troubled his sleep as his dreams teemed with rabbits. Written in letters that reached the sky, the terrible word *INDESTRUCTIBLE* loomed in the midst of a crowd of rabbits, which went up and down the sign, as agile as the proverbial enchanted cats. The red eyes converged on the same point, the mayor, who lay paralyzed in bed.

When he decided to wash away the sweat caused by the nightmare, the man found the top of his washing stand invaded by rabbits, and one of them, with its fur thin and dull, twitched pitifully at the bottom of his pitcher. With a satisfying malignant pleasure, he hurled the creature to the floor, but the rabbit slowly straightened and resumed hopping with the usual enthusiasm.

In the streets, the passersby could not take a step without stumbling upon one of the little monsters, which survived the most incredible torments applied by urchins, and even the passage of the heaviest trucks. Rabbits on the steps of the city hall. Rabbits in every corridor. Perching on the highest folders, they glanced down at the poor mayor, who passed among his employees fighting against more rabbits to enter his office. Thirteen rabbits welcomed him from his desk, causing the papers to rustle and scattering them in splendid disarray. The mayor let himself fall into his armchair, invoking all the destroying powers. He cried out in anguish when his hands landed on soft fur. It seemed to him that over the vacuous muzzles hovered an expression resembling a smile. Thanks to the multiplication, the smile seemed to amplify, growing stronger, and finally the mayor had the impression of seeing Hopkins's grin repeated a hundred thousand times.

Mustering all his energy, the mayor called Vorderteil. Aghast, they gazed at each other for some time, until the mayor recovered a shade of dignity.

"This Mr. Hopkins . . . ," he began.

"Yes, this Mr. Hopkins," Vorderteil said.

"A billion automated rabbits . . ."

"Indestructible . . . indestructible," Vorderteil confirmed.

"It's horrible . . . A billion automated ra—" The mayor had to brush away a rabbit that had brusquely leaped onto his shoulder and wanted to climb his head. "Damned mechanics!" he cried, on the brink of tears.

"Yes, yes, but I don't understand . . ."

"What is it that you don't understand?"

"My factory has never produced so many rabbits before."

"Where do they come from then?"

Vorderteil was unable to answer as he found himself inundated by the red ink a rabbit had just spilled. His elegant black trousers were ruined. The mayor laughed convulsively.

Then Vorderteil said, "I think Hopkins has hoarded all the latest orders. That man is the devil incarnate . . . and he's out to get us . . . but . . ."

And, ignoring the red tide that continued to spill out between them, he whispered: "But I'm thinking of something even more terrible. . . ."

"What?"

"Have you noticed that two generations of rabbits have presented themselves?"

Yes. It was true. Among the twenty-three rabbits that frolicked on the mayor's desk, a few seemed to be smaller, more delicate . . . younger than the others. Even though all of them hopped about, eyeing the world with the same fixed, stupid gaze, smiling the same hideous smile.

"You see, when Hopkins was still working

for us, he alluded to some revolutionary process, something . . . a kind of natural reproduction of mechanical rabbits, which he called 'asexual reproduction.' We made fun of him at the time, but now, apparently, he is using this process. It's clear now: he's using it to terrorize us. Yes. These rabbits are admirable replicas of life. They're reproducing, and tonight we'll see the third generation. Tomorrow morning, we'll welcome the fifth, and the day after tomorrow, we will sail toward two billion beasts. . . ."

This conversation met a quick and strange conclusion, which also ended the discreet dealings between the two men. Seized by the irrepressible desire to avoid going insane, and maybe a combination of rage and desperation, the mayor grabbed by the neck the author of this disaster, spun him around, and had him thrown out. Unfortunately, this violent act brought no resolution to the problem of the rampant rabbits. When they had appeared, the town was amused, and then enraged, but now the general sentiment was horror and disgust. White beasties hopped among the dishes on the tables. They could be destroyed only with axes and fire. With the magistrate's authorization, bonfires were lit on the streets, and rabbits were brought in buckets, aprons, and hutches. But despite these measures, the number of rabbits increased by the hour until the town's population gave up. The fires consumed, a reek of burned fur stank up the air. Without anything to keep them at bay, the rabbits destroyed every trade, jammed the traffic, invaded all activities, and even insinuated themselves into the secret of amorous passions.

But it happened that in a region nearby, in Switzerland, a woman gave birth to a stillborn child. The terror experienced by the mother had caused this premature birth, and the child had on its face a mark in the shape of a rabbit. Indignation erupted, and city hall was almost assailed by a rioting, armed crowd. In this crucial moment, the mayor remembered Napoléon III, who succeeded in calming the miserable masses with raucous parties. Fighting an internal disquiet with external actions seemed the right solution, even more so since he had glimpsed the fifth generation of monsters in his own house. So he ordered festivities of the greatest splendor commemorating the poet Schiller. Like a captain casting a last glance from the mast of his floundering ship, the mayor contemplated his town from the highest spot of the city hall. Even though the month was September, the rooftops, the streets, and the parks seemed to disappear under layers of snow, but this peculiar blanket twitched, decomposed, and recomposed. It was only the billion rabbits—as promised. Like an old man, the mayor stepped down from the tower, slipping over the soft backs of a few thousand rabbits, and, as soon as he reached the ground floor, he heard the report of a policeman he'd sent to Hopkins's home. The man was nowhere to be found, which did not surprise the mayor in the slightest.

That evening, the townspeople gathered for the commemoration, after braving the mountains of rabbits filling the streets, particularly the crossroads, where the beasties superposed in double and triple layers. Even inside, it was difficult to move about as the rabbits leaped among the revelers' legs, occupied the chairs, and filed up and down the galleries, like a bas-relief conceived by a mad sculptor.

An eminent professor who had considerably contributed to the town's intellectual life delivered a speech, and when he extracted a rabbit from his suit pocket to toss it away, the gesture seemed to punctuate his words in a customary manner. A more lugubrious impression occurred when the trumpets released a discordant tune, caused by the rabbits obstructing the instruments. Only the young dramatic singer Beate Vogl created a harmonious atmosphere when she sang a lied in Schiller's honor. Until a terrible scream broke the crystalline sounds as the singer extracted a rabbit from her cleavage. A rabbit, yes, with nine more newborn rabbits hanging from it. The turmoil had reached a peak when a powerful voice rose above the din.

Hopkins stood onstage, beside the unconscious singer. He waved his impeccable top hat and bowed to the audience.

"Ladies and gentlemen, I beg you to please pay attention to what I have to say. The painful events visited on you these last days could have been avoided if the authorities had been able to grasp the meaning of the word *billion*, also showing greater consideration for the accomplishments of modern technology. I desire nothing more than putting an end to these disagreements. The rabbits will disappear as soon as my request is accepted. Although, if my projects should meet more obstacles, then, and only then, would I, against my desire, rest assured, make your situation a little worse."

Smiling, Hopkins fished a squirming rabbit out of his pocket and held it up by the ears. "So far, you've seen an innocuous species of rabbit, but, tomorrow at midday, you'll encounter a new variety: the rabbit that can eat."

With these words, he presented the animal with a bunch of clover.

The silent crowd watched in consternation as the animal's muzzle twitched and turned toward the vegetable to swallow it with mechanical delight.

Everyone pictured an army of indestructible, voracious rabbits devouring everything in sight. Dread crushed the assembly. Nobody dared utter a sound.

That night, an extraordinary meeting of the city council was called, and, come morning, an employee was dispatched to the American's house with an invitation to the mayor's office. This time, Hopkins was at home.

The inventor, upon hearing the decision that gave him permission to build his factory, listened gravely to the question he surely expected.

The mayor, tired and pensive, his face expressing a deep doubt, said:

"Tell me now." His hand caressed his forehead as if wanting to dispel an oppressive impression. "I get most of your science. There's something, though, I don't understand. It's the fact that, thanks to your savoir-faire in mechanics, by mastering the process of life, you have created rabbits that can eat. How is it possible? The rabbit you showed us . . ."

Hopkins gave a smile that was more bitter than usual and tipped his impeccable top hat. "Well, that one . . . ," he said. "That rabbit, Mayor, the one I showed you, was, quite exceptionally, a real, living rabbit."

The New Overworld

PAUL SCHEERBART

Translated by Daniel Ableev and Sarah Kassem

Paul Scheerbart (1863–1915) was a multitalented German author and artist of fantasy and science fiction (under his own name and the pseudonym "Kuno Küfer") who could legitimately be called an eccentric genius. In addition to his art, fiction, and poetry, Scheerbart envisioned vast idealistic engineering and architectural projects aimed at creating a better world, and he also tried to create a perpetual-motion machine. Blurring the lines between fact and fancy, Scheerbart incorporated all his interests into both his fiction and his nonfiction. Like Bengali women's rights advocate Begum Rokheya Shekhawat Hossain, the impish French proto-surrealist Alfred Jarry, and other early science fiction writers, Scheerbart was influenced by the *contes philosophiques*, and thus this blurring had a basis in literary history.

An alcoholic who spent most of his life in poverty before he died in World War I, Scheerbart founded the Verlag Deutscher Phantasten (Publishers of German Fantasists) in 1892. At university, Scheerbart studied art history and philosophy, which fed into the beginnings of a serious attempt at a poetry career (and also, perhaps, his attempts to invent perpetual-motion machines). In 1914, Scheerbart published the work best-known during his lifetime, *Glasarchitektur* (*Glass Architecture*), which, shamefully, was not published in English until 1972. These fantastical essays and poems about glass architecture influenced noted theorist and philosopher Walter Benjamin on his *Arcades Project*, an impressionistic glimpse in fragments of the streets of Paris. None of Scheerbart's other work had been published in English prior to *Glass Architecture*, and even today he remains little known in the English-language world, despite a sumptuous retrospective and several translations since 2001.

The most relevant translation for science fiction readers is the novel *Lesabéndio* (2012). *Lesabéndio*, in episodic chapters, details the workings of an alien civilization. The novel embodied the Utopian ideals Scheerbart had embraced and that he firmly believed would be the salvation of humankind. It also includes, well ahead of its time, treatment of environmental themes that compare favorably to modern theory.

Sadly, this novel and Scheerbart's other science fiction have not exerted much influence on German science fiction in the modern era. But in considering influence more as diaspora, it may be useful to think about connections between Scheerbart and his contemporaries, such as visionaries like Alfred Kubin, author of the masterpiece of weird fiction *The Other Side*, who was commissioned to create art for *Lesabéndio*. Kubin is the gateway to a cascade of other connections, including Kafka. Similarities in Alfred Jarry's and Scheerbart's approaches suggest it also may be useful to view Scheerbart's work in light of the French tradition of fantastic literature.

Perhaps, then, Scheerbart's work has languished in obscurity in part because it existed adjacent to movements like the Surrealists and Decadents but occupied its own unique space. Nor is there any indication that if Scheerbart had lived past World War I, continued to write science fiction, and been translated earlier, his approach would have been much welcomed by the American pulp scene that came to define the bulk of "science fiction." But in a wider context, his association with creators like Benjamin, Jarry, and Kubin, and the similarities in some of his work to Borges, are far more important. "The New Overworld" (1911), never before translated into English, exemplifies Scheerbart's style and approach: light, taking liberties with science, but also unique and playful in its speculation.

THE NEW OVERWORLD

Paul Scheerbart

Translated by Daniel Ableev and Sarah Kassem

"If you can't solve your own problems," said the wise Knax, "then you most certainly are not very clever."

"Absolutely!" exclaimed his audience with a laugh. But soon, the laughter ceased; they weren't feeling too cheerful because of their pressing worries.

A grand fertility reigned on the star Venus. Knax and his audience lived there, and everyone suffered a lot under this ample fertility. Venus is obviously not a star which rotates around itself like Jupiter, Mars, and Earth. Venus always has the same side of its spheric body facing the sun, which makes it scorching hot. Obviously, the result is a plaguing fertility on that side of Venus. Flowery formations on the backsides of Venus's inhabitants sprawl rapidly and develop long, whirring butterfly wings. These wings soon mass together and create an intricate fruiting body. This body grows quickly, detaches itself from the host, and thus a new Venusian emerges.

These offspring are born without any influence of their progenitors on the flowery formations and their metamorphoses. In close proximity to the sun, procreation of species takes place in a very simple manner, without any trace of terrestrial dualism. One can imagine that this convenience of nature causes considerable inconveniences—for the elderly don't die that quickly on Venus, which leads to a relentless increase in the number of inhabitants. This population boom obstructs and diminishes the offspring's mobility.

Now, two contrastingly different kinds of creatures exist on the hot side of Venus. Chubby, idle inhabitants with a sort of turtle fur at their top and bottom. And twenty-armed, uncannily vital creatures with long, delicate hands, which serve as feet when bent into a fistlike form. The chubby ones always make themselves comfortable and lie idly around. They find the vitality and restlessness of the Dynamic Ones embarrassing and occasionally even excruciating.

Knax was one of the dynamic Venusians. Every day, Knax thought deeply about that damning fertility on the sphere's hot side. The possibility of constructing towers and free-floating bridges in order to handle the lack of space had been considered and discussed in great length and detail. And so, myriads of towers and bridges were built in valleys and on the hills. Yet the Venusians' fertility was so yielding and abundant that all the towers and bridges didn't suffice; there were just too many of them. The unhurried turtles covered almost every inch of the ground, calm and rest being their most valuable principles in life. They weren't bothered much when the twenty-legged ones ran about on their backs or in their immediate proximity.

Knax, the wise one, said gloomily: "Heavens—we don't even have enough space to go for a walk. Where are we supposed to go? We can't just always sit on our bridges and in our towers and paint. We need to be able to walk. It's just not in our nature to quit walking." Knax's audience agreed with him, but they didn't know how to deal with this lack of freedom. Of course, the brutal idea to just snuff out some of the expendable offspring never came up; the concept of killing was unknown to the Venusians.

This situation would have undoubtedly

turned into a battle of everybody against everybody, if the nutrition and the food intake of the Unhurried as well as the Dynamic Ones were comparable to the feeding ways here on Earth. But the food wasn't available on the surface of Venus. The Venusians—the Unhurried as well as the Dynamic Ones—took in their nourishment only once a year: Their hair started growing longer and longer, which made them realize that they were hungry; they never actually felt hungry. Then their body hair rooted itself into Venus's rubbery skin—and once inside, it grew rapidly several thousand meters into the star's interior. Deep inside the star, the hair, consisting of the tiniest of tubes, sucked up the nutritional substances and transported them back into the body. When the feeding was complete, the hair broke apart, and the saturated Venusian ran off. If the Unhurried Ones were to cover the whole surface of the planet, the Dynamic Ones would have nowhere to take in their food. But in reality it wasn't all that bad: there just weren't enough turtles to cover all of Venus, which had an enormous surface area, after all. There was no room for walking and running around on the hemisphere, but it was sufficient for nutritional purposes. The turtles were very kind and would make room for the Dynamic Ones by piling up into a stack if room was needed for quiet food ingestion. The Unhurried Ones, however, didn't show even the slightest tolerance for any running and hopping around—since any kind of unrest disturbed their serene philosophical contemplation, which was the most crucial part of their lives.

Knax, the wise one, on the other hand, never stopped contemplating a great deal on the poor freedom of movement and came up one day with the following solution as well as speech: "Fellow inhabitants of the Venusian skin! As you all know, we have countless craters on our side of the star. Very hot air puffs out of them from time to time, rising up with tremendous speed into the heavens, only to cool down when it comes in contact with the cold ether. Couldn't we use this hot, very light crater air as a balloon carrier? And couldn't we then create on top of these balloons the freedom of movement we need? What do you think?"

"That's it! Let's do just that! We will cut the balloon hulls from our star's exterior, which splendidly suits our purposes." The audience found Knax's suggestion so appealing that they even forgot to thank him for it. All the twenty-handed ones got to work immediately, and the turtles gladly made way when they heard about the plan—they also helped with cutting the Venusian skin. Soon Venus was filled with high-pitched cheers, and everyone was grateful and eagerly shaking the wise Knax's hands, which became swollen and started hurting badly.

"Gratitude can be quite hard to take!" exclaimed Knax with laughter. Meanwhile the balloons above the craters bulged upwards in the sky. The Dynamic Ones, who were attached to the balloons, climbed the ropes up and down with ease. Many balloons, however, got so tight and firm that their surface became very slippery, which made it hard to move around.

Knax, the wise one, explained: "Fellow inhabitants of Venus! Do produce new balloons quickly and make holes in the old, tight ones—then the main balloon will form small sub-balloons in many different places, and the terrain which we need for us to walk on will have a roughened structure again." Knax had to elaborate on his plan more than once—and slowly, the fellow Venusians began to understand, and did what he asked them to do.

Soon, the joyfulness on the balloons grew even bigger, and Knax was being celebrated as everybody's savior and redeemer. And the turtles, now leading awfully quiet lives down below, were also pleased. Unfortunately, the turtles' joy didn't last very long, for they soon realized that the huge crater balloons, which grew bigger and bigger every day due to the sub-balloons they produced, were blocking their view of the big sun, so that the turtles had to lie in the shade. They summoned the wise Knax and explained to him the unbearable deprivation of light.

"We aren't familiar with such abundance of shade," said the turtles. "After all, it is our nature that we require sunlight at all times for our philosophical contemplation. We don't know how to deal with darkness, which is something we haven't yet experienced on our side of Venus before. That's why we need you, Knax, to crack our nocturnal problem. Otherwise we will perish. And you don't want that to happen, do you?"

Knax ran his twenty hands through his seven ears and exclaimed with a moan: "How am I supposed to do that? Tell me, how? I don't know! I just don't know!"

He ran into a cave and thought hard about the problem—and came up with the idea that one could tie up all the balloons on the crater's edge and let them rise into the sky. By using longer cords, connection with the ground could be made easily—even if the balloons were to rise several miles high. And that is what happened: soon the balloons were hovering miles above the ground, while at the same time new balloons were forming—populated by many of the Dynamic Ones. There was a large number of balloons in the Venusian skies now, taking on all possible forms. And the turtlish inhabitants on Venus's surface took pleasure in the busy liveliness of their atmosphere, as did the twenty-armed ones, who never fell down, of course, because they were such good climbers.

"Now all the shadows are gone!" said the chubby, idle ones. "And the restless minds, too!" And Knax let everyone worship him as their savior, while residing on top of the biggest balloon, from which no less than two hundred club-shaped sub-balloons had grown. And the gigantic sun with its protuberances tanned the wise Knax's cheeks and hands completely brown—that's how fierce it was burning high up in the sky. Fortunately, the great heat didn't do any harm to the Venusians. If you happen to live close to a sun, you are used to the greatest of heat—all Venusian bodies are constructed in such a way that it simply can't get too hot for them.

Elements of Pataphysics

ALFRED JARRY

Translated by Gio Clairval

Alfred Jarry (1873–1907) was a French writer best known for his play *Ubu Roi* (1896) and for coining the philosophical concept of "pataphysics" ("the science of imaginary solutions"). Jarry is usually classified as a Symbolist but also cited as a prominent proto—as his works can be considered proto-Dada, proto-Surrealist, and proto-futurist (all movements of the 1920s or 1930s). In this regard, he shares affinities with the German writer and artist Paul Scheerbart, not least because Jarry also wrote in a variety of hybrid genres and styles. His play *Ubu Roi* was considered scandalous at the time of its performance for its savage humor and baffling absurdity, and caused an actual riot. Despite their outré nature and Jarry's early death (of tubercular meningitis complicated by alcoholism), these works influenced many other writers and constituted a major influence on the Theater of the Absurd. Many critics today consider Jarry as important as Charles Baudelaire and Arthur Rimbaud before him.

"Elements of Pataphysics," presented here in a new, definitive translation, the first since the 1960s (when *Evergreen Review* devoted an entire issue to Jarry's pataphysics), is an excerpt from Jarry's other famous work, published posthumously in 1911, *Exploits and Opinions of Dr. Faustroll, Pataphysician*. This almost-novel is about a man who, born at age sixty-three, travels through a hallucinatory Paris and subscribes to the tenets of Jarry's own system of "pataphysics," itself a celebration of bizarre logic or even antilogic.

Perhaps editor Judith Merril described the novel best in her introduction to an excerpt appearing in *The Year's Best S-F* (1967): "To call *Faustroll* a novel is rather like referring to a Mariner space probe as a flying machine. *Faustroll* is a novel, and a rather old-fashioned one, as far as plot is concerned: The learned doctor, dunned for debts, escapes prison by luring the drink-loving bailiff, Panmuphle, into a Marvelous Invention (a copper-mesh skiff—perhaps the first amphibious vessel), in which, with the added company of the doctor's friend (or familiar), the talking baboon Bosse-de-Nage, a Wonderful Voyage is conducted."

In a sense, "Elements of Pataphysics" is an absurdist jazz riff on the *conte philosophique* that, a continent away and in a totally different context, Hossain had used in 1905 to advance social justice. What Jarry was advancing instead, influenced by both Wells and Verne, was a contrarian view of human nature, wrapped in the seeming pseudoscience of an experimental philosophy. Cosmological, physical, and metaphysical arguments are advanced in the context of replies to or parodies of the very real Lord Kelvin's essays and addresses. Certain elements in the novel come right from Kelvin: measuring rods, the watch, the tuning fork, the "luminiferous ether," rotating flywheels, and "linked gyrostats."

In the interests of documenting the overlap between science fiction and science fact, it must be noted that Jarry kept readers guessing by appearing in public in a long black cape, in a cyclist's uniform, or wearing a paper shirt with a painted-on tie (set on fire for dramatic effect).

ELEMENTS OF PATAPHYSICS

Alfred Jarry

Translated by Gio Clairval

PART 1: DEFINITION

To Thadée Natanson

The epiphenomenon is a by-product that arises from a phenomenon.

Pataphysics, the etymology of which should be written ἔπι (μετὰ τὰ φυσικά), and the correct spelling *pataphysics*, preceded by an apostrophe, in order to avoid an easy pun,[*] is the science that arises from metaphysics, either in itself or beyond its boundaries, extending as far beyond metaphysics as the latter extends beyond physics. For example, the epiphenomenon often being an exception, pataphysics will essentially be the science of the particular, even though it is commonly held that the only true science is the science of the general. Pataphysics will study the laws which govern the exceptions, and it will explain the universe juxtaposing ours, which is the one studied by general science. Or, less ambitiously, pataphysics will study the universe that can be seen—and that perhaps should be seen instead of the ordinary, the laws of the ordinary universe being correlations of exceptions as well, albeit more frequent, at any rate the laws studied by traditional science being accidental facts which, reducing themselves to the status of unexceptional exceptions, do not even have the appeal of uniqueness.

[WILSON TAYLOR'S TRANSLATION:

DEFINITION. Pataphysics is the science of imaginary solutions, which symbolically attributes the properties of objects, described by their Virtuality, to their lineaments.]

[MINE, AFTER RESEARCHING THE PATAPHYSICS LITERATURE IN FRENCH: DEFINITION: Pataphysics is the science of imaginary solutions that symbolically assign to the objects' descriptive features the properties of objects as they are described in the virtual space.]

Contemporary science is founded on the principle of induction: most observers have seen a particular phenomenon precede or follow another phenomenon, and they infer it will always happen this way. First, the above is only correct in the majority of occurrences, is determined by one observer's viewpoint, and is codified, depending on the moment, in a convenient way—if that! Instead of formulating the law of the fall of a body toward a center, wouldn't it be more appropriate to use the ascension from a vacuum toward a periphery, vacuum being taken as a unity of non-density, a hypothesis much less arbitrary than the choice of *water* as the concrete unity of positive density?

Because water, as a body, is an assumption and a point of view related to the average person's senses, and for its qualities, if not its nature, to remain stable, it is necessary to posit that the height of human beings will always be perceptibly constant and mutually equivalent. Universal consensus is already a quite miraculous and incomprehensible self-deception. Why does everyone claim that the shape of a wristwatch is round, which is clearly wrong because its profile appears to be a thin rectan-

---

[*] *Patte à physique, pas ta physique,* or *pâte à physique* (Physics' Paw; Not Your Kind of Physics; and Physics' Dough).

gular shape, elliptical on three sides? And why the devil would one only notice a watch's shape solely when looking at the time? Perhaps under the pretext of usefulness? Nevertheless, the same child who would draw a watch as a circle will draw a house as a square, a façade, with no justification, evidently, because, except in the countryside, houses are rarely seen as isolated buildings, and in a street even the façades appear as fairly lopsided trapezoids.

One has therefore to admit that the crowd (comprising small children and women) is far too uneducated to comprehend elliptical figures, and its members are at one in the so-called universal consensus because they can solely perceive the curves with a single focal point, as it is easier to mentally match figures with one point than with two.

They communicate by superposing the outer edges of their bellies, balancing on them tangentially. Now, even the masses have learned that the *real* universe is composed of ellipses, and even the bourgeois keep their wine in barrels, rather than cylinders.

So that we may not abandon, through digression, our usual example of water, let us meditate on the following sentence, which the crowd's collective soul irreverently attributes to the adepts of pataphysics:

PART 2: FAUSTROLL SMALLER THAN FAUSTROLL

To William Crookes

Some lunatics repeated over and over
that one was at the same time bigger and
*   smaller*
than oneself, and published such
*   absurdities*
as if they were useful discoveries.
*   —The Talisman of Oramane*

Dr. Faustroll, if one may be permitted to speak from personal experience, one day willed himself smaller than himself, and resolved to explore one of the elements, in order to study what kinds of mutations might arise from a change in their mutual relationship.

He chose this body, ordinarily liquid, colorless, incompressible, and horizontal in small quantities, of curved surface, of blue depths, and with edges animated with a motion of ebb and flow when stretched; which Aristotle terms of a heavy nature, like soil; enemy of fire and revived by it, when decomposed with an explosion; which vaporizes at 100 degrees Celsius, a temperature determined by this fact; and which, solidified, floats upon itself. Water, what else? And having shrunk to the size of a mite, he journeyed down a cabbage leaf, oblivious to his mite colleagues and the magnified aspect of all things around him, until he met Water, in the shape of a bubble, twice his height, through the transparence of which the walls of the universe appeared gigantic, and his own image obscurely reflected on the wet mirror of the leaves, apparently heightened to the stature he had just renounced. He tapped the sphere lightly, as one raps on a door: the inflated eye of malleable glass "adjusted" itself like a living eye, becoming presbyopic, elongated around its horizontal diameter, reaching the ovoid shape that caused myopia; then pushed away Faustroll with elastic inertia, and was spherical again.

The doctor rolled the crystal bubble by little increments, not without effort, toward another crystal globe, gliding on the rails of a cabbage leaf's nervures; once in contact, the two spheres inhaled each other until they tapered and fused into a new bubble of double volume, which placidly hovered in front of Faustroll.

He then tested the consistence of the globe with the tip of his boot: an explosion, formidable of brightness and noise, resounded, with projection all around of a bevy of minuscule newborn spheres—a hail hitting with the dry hardness of diamonds—which scattered in all directions around the green arena, each dragging along the image of one tangent point of the universe, deformed as the original sphere expanded, magnifying its fabulous center. . . .

Beneath everything, the chlorophyll, like a school of green fishes, followed its familiar currents along the subterranean canals of the cabbage leaf. . . .

PART 3: ETHERNITY

To Louis Dumur

*Leves gustus ad philosophiam movere
    fortasse
ad atheismum, sed pleniores haustus
ad religionem reducere.*[†]

—Francis Bacon

CONCERNING THE MEASURING ROD, THE WATCH, AND THE TUNING FORK
—Telepathic letter from
Dr. Faustroll to Lord Kelvin

My dear colleague,

It has been a while since I gave you some news about me, although I surmise you did not think me dead, inasmuch as death only concerns ordinary people. It is undisputed, however, that I no longer am on Earth. Where I am, I have known only for a fairly short time. For we agree on the principle that when one can measure what one is talking about, and express it in numbers, the sole realities that exist, one has a complete grasp of one's subject. Up to the present moment, all I knew was that I had found myself elsewhere, in the same way as I know that quartz is positioned, in the land of hardness, less honorably than the ruby, and the ruby less than diamond, and dia-

mond less than the callosities on my ape-servant Bosse-de-Nage's posterior; and their thirty-two skin folds more numerous than his teeth, if one counts the wisdom teeth, than the prose of Latent Obscure.

But was I away relatively to the date or the place, before or beside, afterward or after a fashion? I was in the location where one stands after exiting space and time: infinite eternity, sir.

It was only natural that, having lost my books; my skiff of metallic fabric; the company of Bosse-de-Nage and M. René-Isidore Panmuphle, bailiff; my senses; Earth; and those two old forms of Kantian thought, I would experience the same isolation angst as a residual molecule several centimeters distant from the others, within a good modern vacuum à la Tait and Dewar.[‡] *Still, the molecule may even know that it is several centimeters distant! For one single centimeter, only valid sign of space in my view, being both a measurable distance and a unity of measure, and one single second of mean solar time, by which the heart of my terrestrial body used to beat, I would have given my soul, sir, however useful it is to me in the endeavor of giving you an account of these curiosities.*

The body is more than necessary a vehicle as it supports one's garments, on which pockets can be found. I had forgotten my measuring rod in one of my pockets, an exact copy of the traditional brass standard, more portable than the entire Earth or even the navigation device called a quadrant, which allows the interplanetary scientists' wandering and posthumous souls to forget about our old sphere and the CGS[§] *as far as measurements of length are concerned, thanks to MM. Méchain and Delambre.*

As for my second of mean solar time, had I remained on Earth, I still could not be sure of retaining the elusive thing, and even of using it to measure time validly.

[†] (Correct quote: *"Leviores gustus in philosophia movere fortasse ad atheismum, sed pleniores haustus ad religionem reducere."*) "It is true that a little philosophy inclineth man's mind to atheism, but depth in philosophy bringeth men's minds about to religion." Baco Verulamus.

[‡] In 1875 MM. Tait and Dewar made a series of experiments on Guthrie's radiometer.

[§] "Centimeter, gram, second" (the unit of force defined in terms of the units of mass, length, and time).

If over a few million years I have not completed my pataphysical studies, it is certain that the period of the Earth's rotation around its axis and of its revolution around the sun will both be very different from what they are now. A good watch that I would have let run all this time would have cost me a fortune, and then again I do not do century-long experiments, couldn't care less about continuity, and think it more aesthetical to keep Time itself in my pocket, or the unity of measurement that constitutes its instantaneous photography.

For these reasons, I had procured an oscillator, a device better suited, for permanence and absolute accuracy, than the balance wheel of a chronometer. This oscillator had a period of vibration retaining the same value over a number of million years with an error of less than 1:1,000. It was a tuning fork. The vibration period had been carefully determined before I embarked in my vessel, as you recommend, by our colleague Professor McLeod, in terms of mean solar seconds, the arms of the fork being successively turned upward, downward, and toward the horizon, in order to eliminate the slightest influence of terrestrial gravity.

I did not have my tuning fork any longer. Imagine the perplexity of a man outside time and space, who has lost his watch, and his measuring rod, and his tuning fork. I believe, sir, that it is indeed this state which constitutes death.

But I suddenly remembered your teachings and my own previous experiments. Since I was simply NOWHERE, or SOMEWHERE, which is the same thing, I found a way of fabricating a piece of glass, thanks to my acquaintance with various demons, including the Sorting Demon of Maxwell, who succeeded in marshaling particles according to their types of movement in a continuous widespread liquid (what you call small elastic solids or molecules): to serve my need, in the shape of silicate of aluminum. I have now traced the lines and lit the two candles, albeit with a little time and perseverance, having had to work without even the aid of tools in flint. I have seen the two rows of spectrums, and the yellow spectrum has returned my centimeter by virtue of the figure $5:892 \times 10^{-3}$.

Here we are now, well and comfortable on dry land, following my atavistic habit, since I carry on me the one-thousand-millionth part of a quarter of the Earth's circumference, which is by far more honorable than simply standing on the orb's surface by means of gravitation; bear with me while I describe a few of my impressions.

Eternity appears to me in the shape of unmoving ether, which as a consequence is not luminous. I shall call the ephemeral ether circular mobile. And I infer from Aristotle's treatise On the Heavens that it is appropriate to write ETHERNITY.

The luminous ether and all the particles of matter, which I can perfectly make out, my astral body having good pataphysical eyes, has the shape, at first sight, of a system of unbending articulated suspension bars and, on some of these bars, fast-rotating wheels. Therefore the system fulfills beautifully the mathematical equations introduced by Navier, Poisson, and Cauchy. Furthermore, it constitutes an elastic solid apt to determine the magnetic rotation of the polarization plane of light discovered by Faraday. During my posthumous spare time, I shall endeavor to prevent it from rotating at all, reducing it to the state of a mere spring balance.

These alterations will not strip the system of any qualities. Ether feels as elastic as jelly, yielding to the touch like the wax of Scottish shoemakers.

PART 4: PATAPHYSICS AND CATACHEMY

Further fragment:

God transcendent is trigonal and the soul transcendent theogonal; therefore the soul is trigonal, too.

God immanent is trihedral and the soul immanent equally trihedral.

There are three souls (cf. Plato).

Man is tetrahedral because his souls are not independent,

Therefore he is a solid, and God is spirit.

If the souls are independent, man is God (MORAL PHILOSOPHY). Dialogue among the three thirds of the number three:

MAN: The three persons are the three souls of God.

DEUS: *Tres animae sunt tres personae hominis.*

TOGETHER: *Homo est Deus.*

PART 5: CONCERNING THE SURFACE OF GOD

God is by definition dimensionless; it is possible, nevertheless, for the sake of clarity, to infer a random number, greater than zero, of dimensions, even though He has none, so long as this number disappears on both sides of our equation. We shall content ourselves with two dimensions, so that we can easily represent these flat geometrical signs on a sheet of paper.

Symbolically God is signified by a triangle, but the three Persons should not be regarded as being either its vertexes or its sides. They are *the three heights* of another equilateral triangle circumscribed around the traditional one. This hypothesis conforms to the revelations of Anna-Katherina Emmerick, who saw the cross (which we may consider to be the symbol of the Verb of God in the form of a Y, and explains it only by the physical reason that no arm of human length could be outstretched far enough to reach the nails at the ends of the branches of a tau.

Therefore, POSTULATE:

Until more facts are available and for greater ease in our provisional estimates, let us suppose God to have the shape and symbolic appearance of three equal straight lines of length a, emanat-ing from the same point and having between them angles of 120 degrees. From the space enclosed between these lines, or from the triangle obtained by joining the three farthest points of these straight lines, we propose to calculate the surface.

Let x be the median extension of one of the Persons a, $2y$ the side of the triangle to which it is perpendicular, and P the extensions of the straight line $(a+x)$ in both directions *ad infinitum.*

Thus we have:

$$x = \infty - N - d - P.$$

But

$$N = \infty - 0$$

And

$$P = 0.$$

Therefore,

$$x = \infty - (\infty - 0) - a - 0 = \infty - \infty + 0 - a - 0$$

$$x = -a.$$

In another respect, the right triangle whose sides are a, x, and y gives us

$$a^2 = x^2 + y^2:$$

By substituting for x its value of $(-a)$ one arrives at

$$a^2 = (a^2) + y^2 = a^2 + y^2$$

Whence

$$y^2 = a^2 - a^2 = 0$$

And

$y = RADICAL\ 0$

Therefore the surface of the equilateral triangle having the three straight lines for bisectors of its angles

a will be

$S = y(x + a) = RADICAL\ 0(-a + a)$

$S = 0\ RADICAL\ 0$

COROLLARY: At first consideration of the *RADICAL 0*, we can affirm that the *surface* calculated is *one line* at the most; in the second place, if we construct the figure according to the values obtained for x and y, we can determine:

That the straight line *2y*, which we now know to be *2 RADICAL 0*, has its point of intersection on one of the straight lines a in the opposite direction to that of our first hypothesis, since $x = -a$; also, that the base of our triangle coincides with its vertex;

That the two straight lines a make, together with the first one, angles at least smaller than 60 degrees, and what is more can only attain *2 RADICAL 0* by coinciding with the first straight line a.

Which conforms to the dogma of the equivalence of the three Persons between themselves and in their totality.

We can say that a is a straight line connecting 0 and INFINITE, and can define God thus:

DEFINITION: *God is the shortest distance between zero and infinity.*

. . . In which direction? one may ask.

We shall reply that His first name is not Jack, but Plus-and-Minus. And one should say:

$\pm$ *God is the shortest distance between 0 and ∞, in either direction.*

Which conforms to the belief in the two principles; but it is more correct to attribute the sign + to that of the subject's faith.

But God being without dimension is not a line.

—Let us note, in fact, that, according to the equation

$\infty - 0 - a + a + 0 = 1$

the length a is nil, so that a is not a line but a point.

Therefore, *definitively*:

GOD IS THE TANGENTIAL POINT BETWEEN ZERO AND INFINITY

Pataphysics is the science . . .

Mechanopolis

MIGUEL DE UNAMUNO

Translated by Marian Womack

Miguel de Unamuno y Jugo (1864–1936) was a Spanish writer and philosopher, well known around the world during his lifetime, who taught at the University of Salamanca. Unamuno was always a controversial figure—a socialist to start before then lapsing into nationalism—in part because he stood in opposition to the monarchy as well as the dictatorships of Miguel Primo de Rivera. As a result, Unamuno was fired from the University of Salamanca in 1920 and exiled from Spain until 1930. During the Spanish Civil War, Unamuno supported the republican government, which had allowed him to return to Spain—but then became a rebel sympathizer.

Much of Unamuno's writing is influenced by his own personal philosophy, which changed significantly multiple times in his life in response to different religious and political crises—his beliefs captured in such treatises as "The Tragic Sense of Life in Men and Nations" (1913) and essays like "Our Lord Don Quixote" (1905) and "The Agony of Christianity" (1925).

Much of his fiction has allegorical dimensions in relation to morality and Christian thought, such as *Abel Sánchez* (1917), which uses the story of Cain and Abel for a then-modern exploration of envy. His story "Mechanopolis" (1913) is actually a rarity for him, in that he wrote very little science fiction.

In a prior translation, this story was previously reprinted in *Cosmos Latinos: An Anthology of Science Fiction from Latin America and Spain*, whose editors included the work because "it illustrates (from the vantage of 1913) the loss of faith in science and the fear of technology characteristic of much science fiction in the twentieth century." The story serves as an excellent early example of Spanish-language science fiction in the twentieth century.

MECHANOPOLIS

Miguel de Unamuno
Translated by Marian Womack

Reading how Samuel Butler, in Erewhon, *describes the inhabitant of that country who wrote* The Book of Machines, *and who thereby caused almost all the machines of his country to be set aside, has brought to mind the tale a friend told me of his journey to Mechanopolis, the city of machines. When he told me, he was still trembling at the memory of what he had seen, and it caused such a strong impression on him that he later retired to spend years in an isolated spot equipped with as few machines as possible. I will try to reproduce my friend's story, as far as I can in his own words:*

A time came when I found myself lost in the middle of a trackless desert: my companions had either turned back to try to save themselves, as if we knew where salvation was to be found, or had perished from thirst. I was alone, and almost dead from thirst myself. I sucked at the dark black blood that flowed from the fingers that I had torn in scrabbling at the dry ground in the mad hope of finding some water beneath it. I was almost prepared to lie down on the ground and turn up my eyes to the implacably blue sky in order to die as soon as possible. When I was prepared to try to kill myself by holding my breath or by scraping out a shallow grave to bury myself in that terrible earth, I lifted my failing eyes and thought I saw a patch of greenery in the distance. "It must be a mirage," I thought, but I dragged myself toward it.

After several hours of agony, I did indeed find myself in an oasis. A spring of fresh water helped me regain my strength, and after drinking I ate some of the pleasant-tasting and suc-culent fruits that hung plentifully on the trees. Then I fell to sleep.

I do not know how many hours I slept, or whether they were indeed hours rather than days, or months, or years. All I know is that I awoke changed, changed utterly. My horrible sufferings had erased themselves almost completely from my memory. "Poor fellows!" I thought, as I remembered my companions in the expedition who had died en route. I stood up, drank water and ate fruit once again, and began to explore the oasis. And nearby, only a few steps from where I was, I found myself at a train station, entirely abandoned. There was not a soul to be seen. A train, deserted, with no driver or stoker, was steaming on the rails. The thought occurred to me that I should, out of pure curiosity, climb on board one of the cars. I sat down, closed the door behind me—I do not know why—and the train started to move. I felt a mad terror overcome me and was seized by the urge to throw myself from the window. But I contained myself, saying, "Let's see where this ends up."

The train moved so swiftly that I was unable even to take notice of the landscape through which we passed. I had to close the windows. I felt a horrid vertigo. And when the train finally stopped, I found myself in a magnificent station, far above any that we have here. I alighted and went into the streets.

I cannot describe the city. No human mind can even dream of the magnificence, the lavishness, the comfort, or the cleanliness of such a spot. Indeed, I did not understand the necessity for such cleanliness, as I saw not a single living creature. No people, no animals. Not a single dog crossing the street, not a single swallow in the sky.

I saw a splendid building whose sign read "Hotel," just like that, written as we write it ourselves, and I went in. It was entirely deserted. I went to the dining room. There was an extremely substantial dinner available there. A list lay upon the table, and each dish on the list was given its number, and next to the list was a vast array of numbered buttons. All one had to do was touch a button and the dish that you desired came up from beneath the table.

After having eaten I went out into the street. Trams and cars drove past, all of them entirely empty.

All one had to do was approach and wave one's hand and they would stop. I got into a car and allowed myself to be carried through the streets. I went to a magnificent geological park, with all the different types of land displayed with explanations on cards at their side. The explanation was given in Spanish, but written in a phonetic transcription. I left the park; I saw a tram passing with "Museum" on its front, and I took it. All the most famous paintings were in the museum, in their original versions. I became convinced that all the paintings we have in our cities, in our art galleries, are nothing more than extremely competent copies. At the foot of each painting there was a learned explanation of its historical and aesthetic value, written most calmly and carefully. In half an hour there, I learned more about painting than in twelve years of study here. I saw on a placard at the entrance that in Mechanopolis the Art Museum is considered a part of the Museum of Paleontology. It existed in order to study the products of the human race that had lived on this earth before the machines had supplanted them. The concert hall and the libraries, with which the city was filled, were also a part of the paleontological culture of the citizens of Mechanopolis, whoever they had been.

What more did I see? I went to the chief concert hall, where the instruments played by themselves. I was in the Grand Theater. In a cinema with phonographic accompaniment, designed in such a way as to give an absolute illusion of life. But my soul shrank to think that I was the only spectator. Where were the citizens of Mechanopolis?

When I woke up the next morning in my hotel room I found, on my bedside table, the *Mechanopolis Echo*, with news stories from all over the world received via wireless telegraph. And on the last page I read the following: "Yesterday afternoon, by what means we are uncertain, there arrived in our city a man, one of the few poor fellows still left around here, and we predict he will have a rough time of it."

And it was true that my days started to become a torment to me. My loneliness began to be filled with ghosts. That is the worst thing about loneliness, how easily it becomes filled. I began to believe that all these factories, all these objects, were controlled by souls that were invincible, intangible, and silent. I started to believe that this city was peopled with persons such as myself, and that they came and went without my seeing them or hearing myself strike against them. I felt that I was the victim of a terrible illness, a madness. The invisible world that filled the human loneliness of Mechanopolis became a crucifying nightmare to me. I started to give voices to the machines, to scold them, to beg things of them. I even went so far as to fall to my knees in front of a car, asking it for mercy. Almost ready to throw myself down to the ground and despair, I took up the newspaper in agitation just to see how things were in the world of men, and found myself face-to-face with this article: "As we predicted, the poor fellow who came, by what means we are uncertain, into the incomparable city of Mechanopolis is going mad. His spirit, filled with ancestral worries and superstitions with regard to the invisible world, is unable to cope with the spectacle of progress. We pity him."

I could not resist the compassion of the mysterious invincible creatures, whether angels or demons, whom I believed to inhabit Mechanopolis. But then I was stricken by a terrible idea, the idea that the machines themselves had souls, mechanical souls, and that it was the machines themselves who felt pity for me. This idea made me tremble. I thought that now I was face-to-face with the race that dominated the dehumanized earth.

I rushed out like a madman and threw myself in front of the first electric tram that passed by. When I awoke from the blow I found myself once again in the oasis I had left behind. I started walking and came across the tent of some Bedouin, and when I met one of them, I embraced him in tears. How well we understood one another even without words! They gave me food, they cared for me, and at night I went out with them and, stretched out on the ground, looking up at the stars, we prayed together. There was not a single machine to be found nearby.

And ever since then I have developed a true hatred of what we choose to call progress, and even of culture itself, and I look everywhere for someone who is like me, a man like me, who laughs and cries just as I cry and laugh, and a place where there are no machines and where the days flow by with the same sweet Christian meekness as an undiscovered river flows through the virgin forest.

The Doom of Principal City

YEFIM ZOZULYA

Translated by Vlad Zhenevsky

Yefim Davidovich Zozulya (1891–1941) was a Soviet-era writer and editor noted for his satirical stories about the Soviet state. Born in Moscow, Zozulya spent part of his childhood in the manufacturing town of Łódź in Poland before going to school in Odessa, now part of the country of Ukraine. Both Łódź and Odessa were part of the Russian Empire when Zozulya lived there.

In 1914 Zozulya started writing short stories and moved to St. Petersburg (Petrograd) to pursue a full-time literary career as an author and editor, his genre of choice being satire. His first collection, *The Doom of Principal City*, was published in 1918. A resident of Moscow from 1919 till his final years, Zozulya took active part in the literary life of the era, encouraging younger authors and founding an influential literary magazine among other things.

His contemporaries describe him as writing "easily and quickly." He considered literature a kind of fanciful sermon and preferred forms like the short stories, which he described as "shorter than a sparrow's beak." His work is rich with vivid worldly morals as well as symbolical and philosophical-satirical fables/tales, reminiscent of the *contes philosophiques*, which represented pressing social issues through allegorical images and situations. Later in his career Zozulya shifted to realism but the background of his stories still tended to be largely conventional, with few specific details about time and place. It may go without saying that Soviet realism-oriented critics did not approve of this approach and more than once Zozulya was jailed for engaging in revolutionary activities.

In the 1930s Zozulya tried his hand at larger forms, creating perhaps his most remarkable work, the novel *The Workshop of Men* (like the biblical "Fisher of Men"), which was published only partially and remained unfinished. As the Great Patriotic War broke out in 1941, he joined the editorial staff of a war newspaper after serving two months in the artillery troops but died from a severe illness at a military hospital on November 3. Despite his prominent position in the literary landscape of the prewar era, Zozulya's name is virtually unknown among present-day readers; most of his work was never republished.

Zozulya wrote several stories with a science-fictional quality. In "Story of Ak and Humanity," citizens vote to bestow total authority on their government, essentially making it totalitarian, and the government reciprocates with a demand that all citizens prove their right to exist, indicating that failure to comply will result in "departure from life" within twenty-four hours. His tale "Moscow of the Future" featured a community of fifty thousand writers, all in their twenties, with no children, with the implication that the children have been taken away to healthier, less subversive zones.

"The Doom of Principal City" may be one of the earliest depictions of dystopia in Russian (and perhaps world) history and represents his debut within these pages in the English language. The story also seems to contain an awareness of Andrei Bely's *Petersburg*, an experimental, fragmented novel, much lauded by Vladimir Nabokov, that tells the story of a man ordered to set off a time bomb in the titular city in the run-up to the 1905 revolution. In "Doom . . . ," the surreal elements of the satire make the story timeless—well positioned to predict the absurdities and counterlogic of Soviet life to come.

THE DOOM OF PRINCIPAL CITY

Yefim Zozulya

Translated by Vlad Zhenevsky

1

Crowds assembled on the squares and crossroads that morning, sparse and inert. Unwashed, sleepy, disheveled, hastily dressed people rushed out of their houses to wander in uneasiness about the streets and greet one another with dejected sighing exclamations:

"They've come!"

"Yes. They're here."

Someone was reporting with his eyes closed, his arms pressed to the chest, "They're here. I live on the outskirts, so I heard the sound of trumpets. They were celebrating. The music played all night long."

"What about our army? Where's our army?"

"They're unable to put up a fight. According to the Chief General's strategic plan that was published yesterday, we are weakened by two and six-tenths. It would've been madness to struggle. Soldiers locked themselves in the barracks. They say they've been betrayed."

"Disgrace! What a disgrace!"

"Doom!"

"Music played all night long!"

"They'll enter the city tonight."

"Look! Look!"

One of the citizens, plain and seemingly sick, squatted and raised both his arms, his frightened and confused look fixed on the sky.

An airplane was circling high above Principal City.

A small dark clump came off it every few minutes and fell to the ground in a slanting irregular line.

"Run for your life!" Shouts were coming from every quarter. "Run for your life!"

Bending over, clutching their heads, dejected figures were running down the streets and hiding in the houses.

Yet they came out soon enough.

It emerged that the victorious enemy were throwing flowers off airplanes. . . . Decidedly real, enormous bouquets of carnations and roses . . .

"Oh, those vile, cruel people!"

"Bandits!"

"Mean, filthy souls!"

Each citizen of Principal City, however peaceful, was scolding the conquerors in a most acrimonious way. Flowers—instead of yesterday's bombs. Flowers tossed to those defeated, humiliated, and trampled on—that was wicked, infinitely hurtful mockery.

No one took those flowers. Two teenagers who picked them up out of curiosity were beaten up by a crowd and dumped off a bridge into the river.

Principal City acknowledged its disgrace at last.

Shops were closed. The tram was shut down.

And meanwhile in various parts of the city, upon streets, balconies, squares, and roofs, the others' flowers lay about, an offensive patchwork of the others' taunting joy, prompting sighs of grievance and despair from residents of Principal City.

2

Enemy troops were expected to enter the city triumphantly and march along the main streets, invoking ultimate desperation in the hearts of everyone.

However, not a single detachment ever appeared. The foe made camp far outside the city, and it was only in some remote outskirts that music was heard, a great number of—more than fifty, as it came to be known later—combined orchestras playing at once.

In the night fiery writings from the enemy's word floodlights glowed above Principal City. Against the dark backdrop of the night sky, fiery verses by enemy poets were revealed. They told of the conquerors' might, of their civility and mercifulness. The verses were followed by blazing statements that the residents of Principal City would not be wronged, that their style of life would not be disturbed, and there was only one condition that the President would have to agree to. *One condition* was underlined.

After that, advertisements for enemy commercial firms were printed on the sky, praising soap, cocoa, watches, and shoes. The sky was entirely covered by these advertisements till dawn. Citizens wept in their houses. Coming up to the windows, they looked at the sky, read advertisements for bentwood furniture or hygienic mustache protectors, and—wept.

The next day was a quiet one. Music outside the city ceased. There were no more falling flowers. It was only in the night that multicolored advertisements—endless, endless—gleamed up in the sky again, so annoyingly, so brazenly, now representing smaller, marginal companies.

3

The President of Principal City summoned the most active Members of Parliament, representatives of the press, and the Chief General to tell them Principal City was perishing.

Everybody knew that: a lot had been written with regard to the downfall of Principal City long before the enemy won, yet they all were listening to the President respectfully—he was held in high esteem and was not to be blamed for the defeat.

Many of the Members of Parliament even wondered if it was necessary to express their sympathy to him as a sufferer and martyr.

"Principal City has fallen, citizens," the President said. "We do not know the terms of peace yet but they will be horrific. I am calling for calm and patience."

There was something in his words, a certain weightiness that set one's mind at rest.

"We need to issue a proclamation," a Member of Parliament suggested.

"Yes. Yes. Definitely. A proclamation. We need to elect a committee."

The committee was elected, the proclamation drawn up.

"Citizens of Principal City!" it went. "I am calling on you to stay calm. No indiscretion shall be inflicted upon the conquerors. We shall not respond to any offenses. Do not pay regard to our enemies' flowers, advertisements, and music. Be patient. Let Reason, the only ruler of the earth, help you; submit to its rightful authority."

The proclamation did not help. There was firing to be heard in various parts of the city at night, from guns and cannons shooting at the pestilent advertisements that beclouded the sky. A large guerrilla party formed in one of the suburbs, setting off on their own to fight the victorious enemy.

The madmen suffered a terrible fate: they were disarmed, divided, forcefully washed, given new clothes, and made to listen to music, eat luxurious food, and revel in company with beautiful women.

Many took their own lives, many were put into lunatic asylums, while most, disgraced and ridiculed, victims to the temptation, returned to Principal City.

4

On the fifth day of the victory celebrations the enemy sent their truce envoys. They arrived unarmed and unescorted in an open car and stopped in front of the President's residence. There were three of them: an old man, a woman, and a tall, humorless, squinting man of middle age, the most resolute and business-minded of all, by the look of him.

It turned out, however, that the actual head of the delegation was the woman—of an average height, bony, with a pleasant smile and colorless eyes.

She declared to the President of Principal City that her nation bore no malice to the vanquished and wished neither violence nor revenge, their only demand being consent to build a new city above Principal City, new squares and streets over its squares and streets, new houses and bridges over its houses and bridges.

The President rose from his chair, flung up his arms, and—cried uncontrollably.

The enemy's envoys stepped back from him and turned to the wall. The woman was surprised, shifting her shoulders as if at a loss.

When the President stopped crying, she came up to him and said, with no sympathy, yet without harshness, "I cannot grasp why you are so worried, Mr. President, perhaps you have not understood—not a single resident of the city, not a single building will suffer any harm. We will be constructing a city of our own above and over Principal City. I hope you have heard about our technologies. Of course we are going to cause you some inconvenience: in front of your windows, steel girders will stand—foundations of our houses and streets. But that's a small matter, isn't it? Then, obviously, it will be darker than now down here, it may even happen that some districts will get totally dark—well, you'll have to use electricity. There's no getting around it. My nation's will is sacred, and I am not entitled to change it."

The President of Principal City was silent.

The enemies were terse, adequate, and businesslike. They were not sentimental. Besides, they knew clearly what they wanted, and knew that no power on the earth could prevent them from fulfilling their aspirations.

"Why are you doing this?" the President asked, and sighed loudly. He felt at once that his question had arisen from weariness rather than from political savvy.

"Yes," he said to correct himself. "I was asking for no reason. But could you say what you are going to do in Upper City?"

"We are going to live there," the old man replied in the woman's stead, and coughed scornfully.

"Odd."

"There is nothing odd about it," the woman said.

"What you want is to ruin us," the President said with a sigh. This remark of his was no more successful with the enemy's envoys than the previous ones. "No, gentlemen, you'd better kill me! Do it!" the President exclaimed tragically, making a gesture of despair.

The envoys winced: their country, rich in industrial equipment, was poor in pathos, so the President's pathos was outright disgusting to them.

"Kill me! I can't take such an unheard-of disgrace! To live down here, in the dark below you, to meet you ceaselessly, to mix with you— Oh!"

"I beg your pardon," the woman interrupted, "but the residents of Principal City will not be seeing or meeting us. Except perhaps during the first ten years, until construction down here is finished—and you will not see us after that."

"How come?"

"The residents of Principal City will be strictly forbidden to enter Upper City."

"Kill me! Kill me! I don't want to talk to you! Goddamn a culture if it can be so cruel! Destroy Principal City, turn it into ruins first, and build your new city after that. I am going to arrange an uprising this very day. Go away. I deem any negotiations redundant."

"This is unwise of you," the woman responded coolly. "An uprising is a savage matter. A pointless one, too. We are very strong. But I should say, your culture is most secure."

"How dare you speak of our culture?" the President cried with the same pathos, which was aplenty in Principal City.

"That's exactly what we are speaking of. We are speaking of the genuine culture. Do you really think we'd have spared you unless we cared about preserving your culture, unless we respected the idea of continuity of cultures? We see your nation as an anachronism but we think highly of your culture, so we are going to build our city above yours only because we want to possess and preserve your buildings, your wonderful museums, your libraries and temples. That's the only reason. We want to have your old, beautiful culture in the cellar, so to speak, and to age it like wine. . . ."

5

The President of Principal City made a request to the conquerors to remove commercial advertisements from the sky, at least for one night, so that the authorities could inform the population of the peace terms and the victors' intention to build a new city above Principal City.

The enemy's headquarters responded that there was no real need to use the sky for that purpose—it could be done by way of printed appeals—but if it *was* the sky that the President wished to employ, it was still possible to negotiate with advertisers who had taken the sky on lease and to compensate them for the incurred losses.

While this issue was being discussed in Parliament, a compromising centrist movement revealed itself for the first time. One of the speakers for the moderate groups made an extensive speech seeking to prove that from their perspective—that of the victors—the enemy was right and could not act other than they did. Because of this, taking the path of endless bickering and obviously futile struggle

was unwise. It was necessary—without delay, if possible—to work out the general terms of the agreement, and to take up struggle when conditions became favorable.

This speaker's speech caused a great outrage. He was even accused of venality and betraying Principal City, and three members of extreme groups had to be ushered out of the assembly hall by force.

"Haven't you by chance won a contract to build a few streets in Upper City?" one of the three shouted, delirious, to the hapless speaker.

With regard to that last reproach, the President of Principal City—haggard looking, having not slept at all in a few days—informed the assembly that the enemy had no intention of offering any contracts to residents of Principal City, which was already known from the Statute of Construction of Upper City, so the reproach by members of extreme groups had not only been undeservedly insulting but also entirely groundless.

After that the President suggested forgoing fruitless debate and electing a committee to negotiate with the leaseholders of the sky so as to clear it of advertisements for one night.

The committee was elected.

By evening the matter was settled: the government had a half of the heavenly dome to notify the public of momentous news.

It was the President in his own person who wrote the announcement. Endorsed by Parliament, in the night it bloomed in straight, stern, and sinister red letters on the blue, mysteriously indifferent dome of the sky.

"Citizens," it went, "take courage! It is for the last time that you are looking at the free sky, your sky. From now on it belongs to someone else. The stars will twinkle for others, the sun will shine for others. Our great, glorious, and lovable Principal City is to turn into a huge, dark, pallidly electrical vault. A new city is to be built above it, and it will be strictly forbidden for us to enter it. Construction of Upper City is going to take ten years, and there will be less of the free sky above us with each passing day. This is, dear citizens, the conquerors' dreadful decision. Be patient! Take courage! Let reason help you, reason and the only wisdom on earth—the wisdom of hope. It is impossible for Principal City to perish so terribly and irrevocably.

"This is blind fate testing us. Let hope, good spirits, and belief in the fortunate change of circumstances help you."

This was followed by the dry articles of the peace treaty.

6

That night was unmatched in anxiety. Even before the President's announcement was published, rumors had begun to spread throughout Principal City that some enormous metallic tubes had been erected by the enemy ten versts* from the city and aimed at it.

There were anxious speculations in evening newspapers that those constructions were meant for washing the President's announcement off, should the conquerors find its wording disagreeable—machines that generated artificial rain or darkened the sky.

Yet special midnight editions of newspapers disproved that assumption: it turned out that the machines and tubes had been installed by the enemy's Efficient Philosophy Association with a view to producing omni-audible machine-generated systematic laughter to mock failures and wrong actions of the government, political parties, and people of Principal City.

The newspaper that was first to reveal the true purpose of the machines and tubes supplied the article with a word of advice—to close the doors and windows tight and, if possible, to stay indoors so as not to hear that hurtful but—alas!—inescapable laughter.

Yellow sheets of paper were coming in two or three issues per hour. There had been enough time to reprint this item and furnish it with belligerent comments and threats saying that the residents of Principal City would not take such abuse, that it was necessary to urgently deploy all drums in Principal City, all bells small and large, all hooters and other instruments capable of making great noise, and if those would not be enough, not to stop short of a cannonade.

At two past midnight, the first peals of the terrible machine laughter came.

The unparalleled oppression of its sounds made the hearts of all living beings inhabiting Principal City leap and shrink.

The machine laughter had two effects, amusing and depressing at once.

No one slept that night.

Teenagers, grown-ups, women, and old people alike wandered about the streets, laughing wildly. Many of them were sobbing. Still many more, surrendering to the infectiousness of machine sounds, roared and wept at the same time.

There were some attempts to counteract the action of those truly infernal machines, too. Somewhere, there was the beating of drums, screaming, explosions somewhere, and there was incessant shooting, but soon it became evident that if the laughter endured, the ramifications would be disastrous.

A delegation from academics, humanitarian societies, and universities approached the President of Principal City, making a request to enter into negotiations with the Efficient Philosophy Association without delay and exercise their best efforts to stop that demoralizing, inhumane, unknown laughter.

The delegation submitted several reports to the President that dealt with the immediate effects caused by that monstrous torture in only three hours. Even fragmentary accounts showed that in Principal City, five million strong, there were dozens of mental disorders, about eighty suicides, and a vast, incalculable number of grave nervous shocks.

---

* A verst (more precisely, versta) is an old Russian measure of length equal to 1.0668 kilometers or 0.6629 miles (3,500 feet).

The President of Principal City received the delegation while sitting by the open window. Perfectly calm, he reclined there gazing wearily at the vague outlines of the houses and roofs. Even the harshest peals of roaring laughter, which bore a distinct resemblance to that of a healthy, deep-chested, clever, and revengeful man, failed to make the President wince.

Still calm, he listened to the agitated delegates and, complying humbly with their request, gave the required written orders.

7

Two people set out in a government-owned airplane to meet the chairman of the Efficient Philosophy Association: the internationally acclaimed writer Claude, whose humanitarian ideas left the whole cultural world awestruck, and the scientist Glavatsky, whose genius and tireless work of forty years made it possible to deliver humankind from the plague of consumption.

There was no doubt that these two men would make a proper impact on the academics of the winning country and bring an end to the oppressing form of philosophical sermon.

The delegates got an honorable welcome, as could be expected. In as few as thirty minutes they were received by the governing board of the association, and their appeal was given full attention.

However, the appeal was dismissed.

The chairman of the Efficient Philosophy Association, a little wizened old man in round spectacles, while bending respectfully and folding his arms on his stomach, stated to the renowned delegates of Principal City:

"I would be happy if I could humor you. But, I regret to say, we find it impossible to waste such a good chance to battle with the outdated, fruitless, and, in our view, detrimental epidemic of optimism which Principal City had been stricken by and, as you see, fallen victim to. Of course it is deplorable to hear about

the shocks and diseases you describe in your reports, but we strongly believe there will be considerably more morally reborn, invigorated, and even spiritually resurrected persons in Principal City eventually. We feel compelled to carry on our sermon of laughter for nine more hours. It is not incurious to note that the Syndicate of Satirical Clubs and Magazines had tried to obtain a license for laughter from His Royal Majesty before we did, but we succeeded in proving, just in time, that our form of sermon was the only one of a scientific and complete nature, so the Academy of Sciences granted the monopoly to us. The syndicate had intended to alternate wholesome scientific laughter with whistling, a rather dubious measure, as well as with some ironic howls and catcalls, the reasonability of which cries for, I should say so, severe testing and can hardly be recognized as satisfactory from a scientific point of view."

8

Two weeks had passed since that memorable night.

Little had outwardly changed in Principal City, aside from a somewhat increased rate of fires. However, a great many public officials and private citizens considered the arson attacks on libraries and archives as a worldwide crisis.

The conquerors barely showed themselves. They were furthering and consolidating their victory by way of official negotiations and issuing decrees and statutes.

Actions of individual guerrilla parties had ceased. The conquerors, for their part, stopped showering Principal City with flowers, and there had not been any music to be heard for a long time. That left only glowing advertisements that consumed the sky by night, but residents of Principal City had become accustomed to them with time.

The shops were open. City traffic was resumed to the full extent. Newspapers and magazines got out on schedule.

The incipient exodus of wealthy citizens from Principal City was checked by the enemy's prohibitive decree, but even that failed to dishearten the community in any real way.

As a matter of fact, the spirit of apathy and indifference was taking hold of more and more people day by day. Automatic cinematographic machines, installed on many streets of Principal City and filming passersby continuously for further examination by the Society of Love for People, now captured a large percentage of figures displaying a languorous gait, vacant and depressed expressions, and facial tics. In a sign of mourning and protest the members of the society began wearing black bands on their left arms.

Suicides became a frequent thing. Newspapers published self-murderers' suicide notes, confessions, and aphorisms in advertisement sections. A respectable old pigeon fancier poisoned all his pigeons—more than ten thousand birds—with cocaine, painted them black, and let them go into the city. He poisoned himself later in the day, while the poor creatures rushed about the city in a daze for a few more hours until they dropped dead on roofs and pavements, cooing plaintively.

Morals were visibly degenerating. Circulation of newspapers specializing in confessions had soared. A great success, humor sheets throve and multiplied, making vicious and vulgar mockery of everything that had been dear to Principal City just yesterday, everything that everyone had believed in and worshipped.

Party leaders, heads of social movements, and groups engaged in settling personal scores were harassing each other. Bitter confusion and spiritual devastation were universal now. Even serious-minded and governmental newspapers started dedicating a lot of space to personal polemics that were not free of spiteful accusations, vindictive attacks, and intent to offend and humiliate rather than to establish the truth.

Narcotic clubs, games of chance, lechery, and consumption of wine and sweetmeats spread most extensively, and, finally, murders and scams escalated in frequency. The most typical example of the latter was the trial of a lawyer who had joined as a conquerors' agent and sold to the residents of Principal City, in secrecy and at a sky-high price, counterfeit permits granting a right to reside in the yet-to-be-built Upper City.

All theaters were open and overflowing with indifferent spectators in search of oblivion. Concerts and balls became much more common than before. There was no merriment about them, though.

The Society of Love for People arranged splendid pageants to fight despondency. On huge motor vehicles adorned by flowers and gaudy decorations, clowns played antics, singers sang, and acrobats showed tricks.

9

By a special conquerors' decree the government of Principal City was dismissed and its parliament dissolved.

In place of those, the conquerors suggested that Principal City should elect the Government of Obedience, made up of six members.

1. The Minister of Quiet, whose task was reducing noise in Principal City to a minimum so that it would not disturb inhabitants of the soon-to-be Upper City.
2. The Minister of Politeness, who was responsible for protecting the workers and supervisors who were constructing Upper City from propaganda and exploitation of pity, as well as from insults, sneers, and various annoyances.
3. The Minister of Responsibility. This office ensured the reliability of the residents of Principal City and guar-

anteed, by way of establishing a strictly scientific system, the absolute physical and psychological impossibility of any attacks on the well-being and tranquillity of Upper City coming from below.

4. The Minister of Quantity, whose duty was to limit and, if need be, to reduce population growth so that overcrowdedness of Principal City would not affect the well-being of Upper City in any way.

5. The Minister of Illusions, in charge of creating an illusion of the sky by means of grand scenery, wherever it would be possible.

6. The Minister of Hopes. This last one was to inspire the residents of Principal City in the spirit of wise hope for circumstances to change for the better in the future.

The decree terminated with two notes.

The first one stated that the Party of the Obedient that had emerged in the city had approached the conquerors with a proposal to rename Principal City as Dark City. In this regard His Royal Majesty deigned to respond that such renaming would be premature but he asked to express gratitude to the right-minded part of the public that had displayed such a remarkable act of wise resignation.

The other note gave Principal City permission to satisfy the natural need of indignation during the space of five days. For that period, the conquerors would withdraw all troops from the vicinity of Principal City so that nothing prevented its residents from showing their emotions freely. What is more, the government, army, and people of the winning country would declare themselves—for all the five days meant for indignation—supremely tolerable to anything that would be spoken of them, no matter in what form.

The sixth and seventh days would be dedicated to the election of the Government of Obedience, and by the noon of the eighth day everything should have been carried out to the letter and the government formed, or else Principal City would be wiped off ruthlessly from the face of the earth in a few hours.

10

Before long, upon the conquerors' request, there began vigorous work to radically disinfect Principal City, which had to be perfectly neat and wholesome as a future foundation for Upper City.

The residents of Principal City were inoculated against all diseases. On the insistence of the authorities, the Bureau of Food made it obligatory for everyone to take bromide daily. Without a pharmacy receipt and evidence that the due dose had been taken, even essential foods were not to be handed out.

Principal City was a singular sight now: people of all classes, standings, and positions, one and all, were cleanly and tidily dressed, well combed and well bathed, their homes a model of cleanliness and order.

There was only a marginal need for repressions.

The Government of Obedience demonstrated maximum energy.

Under the Ministry of Politeness, cadres of supervisors, agents, and policemen were formed. They performed their duties diligently, guarding workers who were already erecting steel and concrete supports for Upper City.

Principal City lived a restless, hurried life of labor now. There was the unceasing clatter of clanging iron and steel, banging hammers, groaning cutters, metallic gritting of winches, and hooting of construction motorcars.

On most streets, there were people digging pits, taking measurements, putting up scaffolding, and in some areas the roofs of buildings were as crowded as squares or streets.

11

A lot of time had passed.

Upper City was growing by leaps and bounds. The western part was almost finished, and people settled there. Litter was taken away daily by cargo airplanes. There was smoke curling from chimneys. By this time, crematoriums had started incinerating the dead. Children went to schools. There were barracks and prisons. There was a lunatic asylum. In the middle of a broad square positioned right above the magnificent park of Principal City the royal palace soared up, beautiful and stylish.

It had become almost totally dark in Principal City. Flats in unaffected houses were rented out at high prices, but soon enough those houses were built over too.

At one time both society and the press talked a great deal about a clever backdrop painted by a certain artist, a believable substitute of the sky for two whole streets and a square. The Ministry of Illusions awarded that artist a medal.

It was strictly prohibited for the residents of Lower City to enter Upper City. This was one of the fundamental articles of the law: those who broke it were put in special Prisons for the Curious, known for their severe regime.

The ministers of the Government of Obedience had changed several times during that period.

There had been a few uprisings in Principal City, all of them brutally suppressed. In two cases small riotous areas were surrounded by a steel vise of vehicles and troops and then mercilessly cemented.

The huge resulting cubes of cement, graves to so many lives, came to be known as the Cubes of Immature Dreams.

Both times, after the rebels had been defeated, the Efficient Philosophy Association fought ideas of optimism with the sermon of machine laughter.

By contrast, during the periods of obedience and reaction the association announced to residents of the darkened Principal City through deafening bellows of giant phonographs:

"We love you!!! We love you!"

"Man loves obedience in his neighbors!"

"The meaning of life lies in suffering and self-improvement!"

And once the machines of the association bellowed deafeningly all day long,

"Know thyself! Know thyself!!!"

The only minister of the government who had never left his post was the Minister of Hopes. He was old and jolly.

"Citizens!" he preached every Sunday. "Dear citizens! Hope! There will come a time when adverse circumstances change! We shall see the sun and sky again! Have faith! Above all, have faith and hope!"

Before long, Upper City took its full shape. It was a large, lively, busy, and important city. There were also a lot of social movements, a lot of social contests between parties. There were parties of equality and justice, too, as there were champions who struggled for liberation of Lower City. They made passionate speeches. They had print media and clubs of their own.

Down below in Principal City, there also were dreamers, champions of justice and equality.

By and large, though, both groups lived a life of restlessness and peace at the same time, often tormented and rarely joyous, but always or nearly always full of hope—just the way people live in the world.

12

The horror came without warning. On a sultry summer noon a factory blew up on the outskirts of Principal City. The risk of fire in the city had been factored in, and usually was quenched in a few minutes.

But it was otherwise this time.

The firefighters were met with gunshots. The workers injured by the explosion were shooting. Those remaining unharmed joined them. Hundreds of bullets burst from the burning building in every direction.

The spirit of rebellion swept through Principal City. Weapons, bombs, explosion devices, and explosives seemed to come out of thin air.

There were people rushing about the streets and screaming frantically:

"Arm yourself! Arm yourself! To arms!"

Alarm bells and hoots roared on every street.

Utmost apprehension seized the city. The fire enveloped a few houses, its area expanding steadily. The entire district was wrapped in black pungent smoke. It crept along the streets, finding no other outlets. Many suffocated in the smoke.

Anguished cries and moans were coming from everywhere, drowned out by the sound of more and more explosions.

Who set fire to the houses? Who blew up the bridges?

There was no telling. Dark human figures dashed about in the flames like devils, running into sight and then disappearing again.

Lots of people were racing along the streets with screams of joy. Many cried with joy. Someone, shouting breathlessly, was commanding,

"Blow up bridges! Blow up houses! Burn! Burn as much as you can!"

A thunderous explosion rocked both cities. Screams were heard from many a hundred thousand voices. A sound came from someone blasting the park dominated by the royal palace. The white edifice went askew and collapsed. What a sound there was as the park trees began to break! How the iron lattices of bridges and fences bent and crumpled! Colossal pillars of fire and rocks alternated with each other.

The electricity went out in Principal City. The darkness and the riot turned it into a black seething chaos. The commotion spread over to Upper City as well.

Many a hundred thousand bullets and shells spattered down from above. Every crack was used to shoot into the darkness, every breach.

But new explosions threw houses and streets up in the air along with shooters.

Flames, choking smoke, clouds of dust, glass, molten metal, and human bodies, thousands of bodies, all were eddying in a whirling mad pandemonium.

On a square, by the light of torches, to crackling of gunfire and the rumble of cave-ins, the Minister of Hopes made a plea to the crowd:

"Citizens! Poor, distraught citizens! Stop! Stop before it's too late! There's only death ahead of you! Was it *this* that I've been teaching you for so many years?! What have you traded the spirit of wise hope for?! For a blind, benighted riot?! Stop! Stop, you wretched folk! Take pity on yourself and our glorious Principal City! Stop before it's too late!"

Poor fellow! He was stoned to death, and his ministry was blasted just like any building in Upper City.

The Efficient Philosophy Association tried to preach something by means of their machines but those were hurled back by a pillar of fire. The chairman, totally old and decrepit now, barely had time to escape on a single-seat airplane.

"Fools," he shouted, wallowing all by himself in the cloudless blue sky. "You can never win! The backbone of the world is reasonable violence, not a wild self-confident riot! Blind rebellious worms! Despicable optimistic calves! What are you hoping for?!"

He was suffocating in the open air like in a noose; he spat downwards, where houses were collapsing and fire roiling, and he died of fear, spite, and grief. The machine carried his underweight, wrinkled corpse about for a long time.

Thousands of other airplanes took off from Upper City, a means of escape for children and women. Screams and sobs filled the air.

And down below, there were more and more cave-ins and explosions rumbling. Bright sunshine found its way into Principal City now. The sky was visible on many streets.

"Long live the sun!" thousands of smoke-poisoned people yelled in a gleeful frenzy. "Long live the sky! Hooraaay . . ."

In reply, shells were showering down, hot cement was raining from above with a sepulchral hiss, and the stifling, all-corroding, deadly powder was falling.

People died like flies but those alive retaliated with more deafening explosions, arson, and the accurate fire of the doomed.

There was fighting on every street. People battled in flats, upon roofs, beneath ruins, and out in the open.

"Blow up bridges!" shouts were coming from all sides. "Blast Upper City! Burn! Blast and burn as much as possible!"

"Citizens! Citizens! Flee from the market district! Call everyone! The railway station of Upper City's about to collapse! Run for your lives, citizens!"

"Hoorraaay! Hoorraaaay!"

After a little while, the railway station did collapse. The terrible crash could not drown out people's delighted screams. Long chains of cars were falling with a thunderous rattle, side by side with pieces of buildings, with bridges, platforms, and rails.

A fiery vortex, a whirlwind of flame, iron, and rocks, shot up into the sky.

"Hoorraaay!"

Large groups of rebels climbed up the ruins into Upper City. It was half empty. The residents were evacuating by the thousands in airplanes. Curses, fire, and bullets were sent after them. The troops had dispersed. All barracks had been blasted. Fire was raging in every quarter; buildings shook and tumbled down.

"Enough!" shouts were coming from below. "Enough! We are dying! Stop! Enough!"

Whole streets of those buried alive, fighting their way painfully through the ruins, begged for mercy.

But new cave-ins buried them again, killed them, wiped them out.

The great destruction went on all day and night, and in the morning tired explosions capped the doom of Principal City.

In such a manner, simple and spontaneous, it perished. Ways of oppression are intricate and varied—in this regard, there is no limit to human imagination—while the road to freedom is simple but bitter. Upper City was gone.

There was only a sea of smoldering and burning ruins, monstrous piles of palaces, squares, bridges, and streets, and amid that twisted chaos of iron, stone, and wood—occasional crowds of blackened, ragged, and bloodied people.

Many of them were wounded, many dying; many were dancing, bereft of their sanity; but the wounded and the dying and the mad alike were singing, joyously and loudly, songs in honor of the rising and dazzlingly indifferent sun.

The Comet

W. E. B. DU BOIS

William Edward Burghardt—W. E. B.—Du Bois (1868–1963) was a scientist, writer, and activist who helped found the National Association for the Advancement of Colored People (NAACP). As an advocate of Pan-Africanism, Du Bois was essential to the Pan-African Congresses of his day, which sought to remove European powers from African nations. He also worked tirelessly against racism in society and embedded in the law.

Although primarily known as a writer of nonfiction, including his influential essay collection *The Souls of Black Folk* (1903), Du Bois also wrote fiction, often of a fantastical and allegorical nature. This fiction was influenced by his views on religion, spirituality, and race relations. It has only recently become clear just how much fiction Du Bois wrote, and how much of it was speculative in nature. A collection of Du Bois's short fiction is in the works, and unpublished stories still occasionally come to light, including "The Princess Steel," which, according to an article by Jane Greenway Carr posted to Slate.com (December 1, 2015), was written between 1908 and 1910. This new story, which helps to enhance our understanding of Afrofuturism, features a black sociologist who demonstrates for a honeymooning couple a "megascope, a machine he created to see across time and space." The story views technology through the lens of race and gender.

The classic story "The Comet" from 1920, reprinted here, was originally included in his volume of autobiography, *Darkwater: Voices from Within the Veil*, and later reprinted in the 2000 anthology *Dark Matter: A Century of Speculative Fiction from the African Diaspora*. Like "The Princess Steel," the story presents a rare early nonwhite science fiction perspective. How influential was "The Comet" when first published? Although it is difficult to tell, we doubt Du Bois's work would have been well known within the closed, tight-knit science fiction pulp magazine community.

THE COMET

W. E. B. Du Bois

He stood a moment on the steps of the bank, watching the human river that swirled down Broadway. Few noticed him. Few ever noticed him save in a way that stung. He was outside the world—"nothing!" as he said bitterly. Bits of the words of the walkers came to him.

"The comet?"

"The comet—"

Everybody was talking of it. Even the president, as he entered, smiled patronizingly at him, and asked:

"Well, Jim, are you scared?"

"No," said the messenger shortly.

"I thought we'd journeyed through the comet's tail once," broke in the junior clerk affably.

"Oh, that was Halley's," said the president; "this is a new comet, quite a stranger, they say—wonderful, wonderful! I saw it last night. Oh, by the way, Jim," he said, turning again to the messenger, "I want you to go down into the lower vaults today."

The messenger followed the president silently. Of course, they wanted *him* to go down to the lower vaults. It was too dangerous for more valuable men. He smiled grimly and listened.

"Everything of value has been moved out since the water began to seep in," said the president; "but we miss two volumes of old records. Suppose you nose around down there,—it isn't very pleasant, I suppose."

"Not very," said the messenger, as he walked out.

"Well, Jim, the tail of the new comet hits us at noon this time," said the vault clerk, as he passed over the keys; but the messenger passed silently down the stairs. Down he went beneath Broadway, where the dim light filtered through the feet of hurrying men; down to the dark basement beneath; down into the blackness and silence beneath that lowest cavern. Here with his dark lantern he groped in the bowels of the earth, under the world.

He drew a long breath as he threw back the last great iron door and stepped into the fetid slime within. Here at last was peace, and he groped moodily forward. A great rat leaped past him and cobwebs crept across his face. He felt carefully around the room, shelf by shelf, on the muddied floor, and in crevice and corner. Nothing. Then he went back to the far end, where somehow the wall felt different. He sounded and pushed and pried. Nothing. He started away. Then something brought him back. He was sounding and working again when suddenly the whole black wall swung as on mighty hinges, and blackness yawned beyond. He peered in; it was evidently a secret vault—some hiding place of the old bank unknown in newer times. He entered hesitatingly. It was a long, narrow room with shelves, and at the far end, an old iron chest. On a high shelf lay the two missing volumes of records, and others. He put them carefully aside and stepped to the chest. It was old, strong, and rusty. He looked at the vast and old-fashioned lock and flashed his light on the hinges. They were deeply incrusted with rust. Looking about, he found a bit of iron and began to pry. The rust had eaten a hundred years, and it had gone deep. Slowly, wearily, the old lid lifted, and with a last, low groan laid bare its treasure—and he saw the dull sheen of gold!

"Boom!"

A low, grinding, reverberating crash struck upon his ear. He started up and looked about.

All was black and still. He groped for his light and swung it about him. Then he knew! The great stone door had swung to. He forgot the gold and looked death squarely in the face. Then with a sigh he went methodically to work. The cold sweat stood on his forehead; but he searched, pounded, pushed, and worked until after what seemed endless hours his hand struck a cold bit of metal and the great door swung again harshly on its hinges, and then, striking against something soft and heavy, stopped. He had just room to squeeze through. There lay the body of the vault clerk, cold and stiff. He stared at it, and then felt sick and nauseated. The air seemed unaccountably foul, with a strong, peculiar odor. He stepped forward, clutched at the air, and fell fainting across the corpse.

He awoke with a sense of horror, leaped from the body, and groped up the stairs, calling to the guard. The watchman sat as if asleep, with the gate swinging free. With one glance at him the messenger hurried up to the sub-vault. In vain he called to the guards. His voice echoed and re-echoed weirdly. Up into the great basement he rushed. Here another guard lay prostrate on his face, cold and still. A fear arose in the messenger's heart. He dashed up to the cellar floor, up into the bank. The stillness of death lay everywhere and everywhere bowed, bent, and stretched the silent forms of men. The messenger paused and glanced about. He was not a man easily moved; but the sight was appalling! "Robbery and murder," he whispered slowly to himself as he saw the twisted, oozing mouth of the president where he lay half-buried on his desk. Then a new thought seized him: If they found him here alone—with all this money and all these dead men—what would his life be worth? He glanced about, tiptoed cautiously to a side door, and again looked behind. Quietly he turned the latch and stepped out into Wall Street.

How silent the street was! Not a soul was stirring, and yet it was high noon—Wall Street? Broadway? He glanced almost wildly up and down, then across the street, and as he looked, a sickening horror froze in his limbs. With a choking cry of utter fright he lunged, leaned giddily against the cold building, and stared helplessly at the sight.

In the great stone doorway a hundred men and women and children lay crushed and twisted and jammed, forced into that great, gaping doorway like refuse in a can—as if in one wild, frantic rush to safety, they had rushed and ground themselves to death. Slowly the messenger crept along the walls, wetting his parched mouth and trying to comprehend, stilling the tremor in his limbs and the rising terror in his heart. He met a businessman, silk-hatted and frock-coated, who had crept, too, along that smooth wall and stood now stone dead with wonder written on his lips. The messenger turned his eyes hastily away and sought the curb. A woman leaned wearily against the signpost, her head bowed motionless on her lace and silken bosom. Before her stood a street-car, silent, and within—but the messenger but glanced and hurried on. A grimy newsboy sat in the gutter with the "last edition" in his uplifted hand: "Danger!" screamed its black headlines. "Warnings wired around the world. The Comet's tail sweeps past us at noon. Deadly gases expected. Close doors and windows. Seek the cellar." The messenger read and staggered on. Far out from a window above, a girl lay with gasping face and sleevelets on her arms. On a store step sat a little, sweet-faced girl looking upward toward the skies, and in the carriage by her lay—but the messenger looked no longer. The cords gave way—the terror burst in his veins, and with one great, gasping cry he sprang desperately forward and ran,—ran as only the frightened run, shrieking and fighting the air until with one last wail of pain he sank on the grass of Madison Square and lay prone and still.

When he rose, he gave no glance at the still and silent forms on the benches, but, going to a fountain, bathed his face; then hiding himself in a corner away from the drama of death, he quietly gripped himself and thought the thing through: The comet had swept the earth and this was the end. Was everybody dead? He must search and see.

He knew that he must steady himself and keep calm, or he would go insane. First he must go to a restaurant. He walked up Fifth Avenue to a famous hostelry and entered its gorgeous, ghost-haunted halls. He beat back the nausea, and, seizing a tray from dead hands, hurried into the street and ate ravenously, hiding to keep out the sights.

"Yesterday, they would not have served me," he whispered, as he forced the food down.

Then he started up the street,—looking, peering, telephoning, ringing alarms; silent, silent all. Was nobody—nobody—he dared not think the thought and hurried on.

Suddenly he stopped still. He had forgotten. My God! How could he have forgotten? He must rush to the subway—then he almost laughed. No—a car; if he could find a Ford. He saw one. Gently he lifted off its burden, and took his place on the seat. He tested the throttle. There was gas. He glided off, shivering, and drove up the street. Everywhere stood, leaned, lounged, and lay the dead, in grim and awful silence. On he ran past an automobile, wrecked and over-turned; past another, filled with a gay party whose smiles yet lingered on their death-struck lips; on past crowds and groups of cars, paus-ing by dead policemen; at Forty-Second Street he had to detour to Park Avenue to avoid the dead congestion. He came back on Fifth Avenue at Fifty-Seventh and flew past the Plaza and by the park with its hushed babies and silent throng, until as he was rushing past Seventy-Second Street he heard a sharp cry, and saw a living form leaning wildly out an upper win-dow. He gasped. The human voice sounded in his ears like the voice of God.

"Hello—hello—help, in God's name!" wailed the woman. "There's a dead girl in here and a man and—and see yonder dead men lying in the street and dead horses—for the love of God go and bring the officers. . . ." And the words trailed off into hysterical tears.

He wheeled the car in a sudden circle, run-ning over the still body of a child and leaping on the curb. Then he rushed up the steps and tried the door and rang violently. There was a long pause, but at last the heavy door swung back. They stared a moment in silence. She had not noticed before that he was a Negro. He had not thought of her as white. She was a woman of perhaps twenty-five—rarely beautiful and richly gowned, with darkly golden hair, and jewels. Yesterday, he thought with bitterness, she would scarcely have looked at him twice. He would have been dirt beneath her silken feet. She stared at him. Of all the sorts of men she had pictured as coming to her rescue she had not dreamed of one like him. Not that he was not human, but he dwelt in a world so far from hers, so infinitely far, that he seldom even entered her thought. Yet as she looked at him curiously he seemed quite commonplace and usual. He was a tall, dark workingman of the better class, with a sensitive face trained to sto-lidity and a poor man's clothes and hands. His face was soft and slow and his manner at once cold and nervous, like fires long banked, but not out.

So a moment each paused and gauged the other; then the thought of the dead world without rushed in and they started toward each other.

"What has happened?" she cried. "Tell me! Nothing stirs. All is silence! I see the dead strewn before my window as winnowed by the breath of God,—and see . . ." She dragged him through great, silken hangings to where, beneath the sheen of mahogany and silver, a little French maid lay stretched in quiet, ever-lasting sleep, and near her a butler lay prone in his livery.

The tears streamed down the woman's cheeks and she clung to his arm until the per-fume of her breath swept his face and he felt the tremors racing through her body.

"I had been shut up in my darkroom devel-oping pictures of the comet which I took last night; when I came out—I saw the dead!

"What has happened?" she cried again.

He answered slowly:

"Something—comet or devil—swept across the earth this morning and—many are dead!"

"Many? Very many?"

"I have searched and I have seen no other living soul but you."

She gasped and they stared at each other.

"My—father!" she whispered.

"Where is he?"

"He started for the office."

"Where is it?"

"In the Metropolitan Tower."

"Leave a note for him here and come."

Then he stopped.

"No," he said firmly—"first, we must go—to Harlem."

"Harlem!" she cried. Then she understood. She tapped her foot at first impatiently. She looked back and shuddered. Then she came resolutely down the steps.

"There's a swifter car in the garage in the court," she said.

"I don't know how to drive it," he said.

"I do," she answered.

In ten minutes they were flying to Harlem on the wind. The Stutz rose and raced like an airplane. They took the turn at 110th Street on two wheels and slipped with a shriek into 135th.

He was gone but a moment. Then he returned, and his face was gray. She did not look, but said:

"You have lost—somebody?"

"I have lost—everybody," he said, simply—"unless . . ."

He ran back and was gone several minutes—hours they seemed to her.

"Everybody," he said, and he walked slowly back with something filmlike in his hand which he stuffed into his pocket.

"I'm afraid I was selfish," he said. But already the car was moving toward the park among the dark and lined dead of Harlem—the brown, still faces, the knotted hands, the homely garments, and the silence—the wild and haunting silence. Out of the park, and down Fifth Avenue they whirled. In and out among the dead they slipped and quivered, needing no sound of bell or horn, until the great, square Metropolitan Tower hove in sight. Gently he laid the dead elevator boy aside; the car shot upward. The door of the office stood open. On the threshold lay the stenographer, and, staring at her, sat the dead clerk. The inner office was empty, but a note lay on the desk, folded and addressed but unsent:

Dear Daughter:

I've gone for a hundred-mile spin in Fred's new Mercedes. Shall not be back before dinner. I'll bring Fred with me.

J.B.H.

"Come," she cried nervously. "We must search the city."

Up and down, over and across, back again—on went that ghostly search. Everywhere was silence and death—death and silence! They hunted from Madison Square to Spuyten Duyvil; they rushed across the Williamsburg Bridge; they swept over Brooklyn; from the Battery and Morningside Heights they scanned the river. Silence, silence everywhere, and no human sign. Haggard and bedraggled they puffed a third time slowly down Broadway, under the broiling sun, and at last stopped. He sniffed the air. An odor—a smell—and with the shifting breeze a sickening stench filled their nostrils and brought its awful warning. The girl settled back helplessly in her seat.

"What can we do?" she cried.

It was his turn now to take the lead, and he did it quickly.

"The long-distance telephone—the telegraph and the cable—night rockets and then—flight!"

She looked at him now with strength and confidence. He did not look like men, as she had always pictured men; but he acted like one and she was content. In fifteen minutes they were at the central telephone exchange. As they came to the door he stepped quickly before her and pressed her gently back as he closed it. She heard him moving to and fro, and knew his burdens—the poor, little burdens he bore. When she entered, he was alone in the room. The grim switchboard flashed its metallic face in cryptic, sphinxlike immobility. She seated herself on a stool and donned the bright earpiece. She looked at the mouthpiece. She had never looked at one so closely before. It was wide and black, pimpled with usage; inert; dead; almost sarcastic in its unfeeling curves. It looked—she beat back the thought—but it looked,—it persisted in looking like—she turned her head and found herself alone. One moment she was terrified; then she thanked him silently for his delicacy and turned resolutely, with a quick intaking of breath.

"Hello!" she called in low tones. She was calling to the world. The world *must* answer. Would the world *answer*? Was the world . . .

Silence!

She had spoken too low.

"Hello!" she cried, full-voiced.

She listened. Silence! Her heart beat quickly. She cried in clear, distinct, loud tones: "Hello—hello—hello!"

What was that whirring? Surely—no—was it the click of a receiver?

She bent close, she moved the pegs in the holes, and called and called, until her voice rose almost to a shriek, and her heart hammered. It was as if she had heard the last flicker of creation, and the evil was silence. Her voice dropped to a sob. She sat stupidly staring into the black and sarcastic mouthpiece, and the thought came again. Hope lay dead within her. Yes, the cable and the rockets remained; but the world—she could not frame the thought or say the word. It was too mighty—too terrible! She turned toward the door with a new fear in her heart. For the first time she seemed to realize that she was alone in the world with a stranger, with something more than a stranger,—with a man alien in blood and culture—unknown,

perhaps unknowable. It was awful! She must escape—she must fly; he must not see her again. Who knew what awful thoughts—

She gathered her silken skirts deftly about her young, smooth limbs—listened, and glided into a side hall. A moment she shrank back: the hall lay filled with dead women; then she leaped to the door and tore at it, with bleeding fingers, until it swung wide. She looked out. He was standing at the top of the alley,—silhouetted, tall and black, motionless. Was he looking at her or away? She did not know—she did not care. She simply leaped and ran—ran until she found herself alone amid the dead and the tall ramparts of towering buildings.

She stopped. She was alone. Alone! Alone on the streets—alone in the city—perhaps alone in the world! There crept in upon her the sense of deception—of creeping hands behind her back—of silent, moving things she could not see,—of voices hushed in fearsome conspiracy. She looked behind and sideways, started at strange sounds and heard still stranger, until every nerve within her stood sharp and quivering, stretched to scream at the barest touch. She whirled and flew back, whimpering like a child, until she found that narrow alley again and the dark, silent figure silhouetted at the top. She stopped and rested; then she walked silently toward him, looked at him timidly; but he said nothing as he handed her into the car. Her voice caught as she whispered:

"Not—that."

And he answered slowly: "No—not that!"

They climbed into the car. She bent forward on the wheel and sobbed, with great, dry, quivering sobs, as they flew toward the cable office on the east side, leaving the world of wealth and prosperity for the world of poverty and work. In the world behind them were death and silence, grave and grim, almost cynical, but always decent; here it was hideous. It clothed itself in every ghastly form of terror, struggle, hate, and suffering. It lay wreathed in crime and squalor, greed and lust. Only in its dread and awful silence was it like to death everywhere.

Yet as the two, flying and alone, looked upon the horror of the world, slowly, gradually, the sense of all-enveloping death deserted them. They seemed to move in a world silent and asleep,—not dead. They moved in quiet reverence, lest somehow they wake these sleeping forms who had, at last, found peace. They moved in some solemn, worldwide *Friedhof*, above which some mighty arm had waved its magic wand. All nature slept until—until, and quick with the same startling thought, they looked into each other's eyes—he, ashen, and she, crimson, with unspoken thought. To both, the vision of a mighty beauty—of vast, unspoken things, swelled in their souls; but they put it away.

Great, dark coils of wire came up from the earth and down from the sun and entered this low lair of witchery. The gathered lightnings of the world centered here, binding with beams of light the ends of the earth. The doors gaped on the gloom within. He paused on the threshold.

"Do you know the code?" she asked.

"I know the call for help—we used it formerly at the bank."

She hardly heard. She heard the lapping of the waters far below,—the dark and restless waters—the cold and luring waters, as they called. He stepped within. Slowly she walked to the wall, where the water called below, and stood and waited. Long she waited, and he did not come. Then with a start she saw him, too, standing beside the black waters. Slowly he removed his coat and stood there silently. She walked quickly to him and laid her hand on his arm. He did not start or look. The waters lapped on in luring, deadly rhythm. He pointed down to the waters, and said quietly:

"The world lies beneath the waters now— may I go?"

She looked into his stricken, tired face, and a great pity surged within her heart. She answered in a voice clear and calm, "No."

Upward they turned toward life again, and he seized the wheel. The world was darkening to twilight, and a great, gray pall was falling mercifully and gently on the sleeping dead. The ghastly glare of reality seemed replaced with the dream of some vast romance. The girl lay silently back, as the motor whizzed along, and looked half-consciously for the elf-queen to wave life into this dead world again. She forgot to wonder at the quickness with which he had learned to drive her car. It seemed natural. And then as they whirled and swung into Madison Square and at the door of the Metropolitan Tower she gave a low cry, and her eyes were great! Perhaps she had seen the elf-queen?

The man led her to the elevator of the tower and deftly they ascended. In her father's office they gathered rugs and chairs, and he wrote a note and laid it on the desk; then they ascended to the roof and he made her comfortable. For a while she rested and sank to dreamy somnolence, watching the worlds above and wondering. Below lay the dark shadows of the city and afar was the shining of the sea. She glanced at him timidly as he set food before her and took a shawl and wound her in it, touching her reverently, yet tenderly. She looked up at him with thankfulness in her eyes, eating what he served. He watched the city. She watched him. He seemed very human,—very near now.

"Have you had to work hard?" she asked softly.

"Always," he said.

"I have always been idle," she said. "I was rich."

"I was poor," he almost echoed.

"The rich and the poor are met together," she began, and he finished:

"The Lord is the Maker of them all."

"Yes," she said slowly; "and how foolish our human distinctions seem—now," looking down to the great dead city stretched below, swimming in unlightened shadows.

"Yes—I was not—human, yesterday," he said.

She looked at him. "And your people were not my people," she said; "but today . . ." She paused. He was a man,—no more; but he was in some larger sense a gentleman,—sensitive, kindly, chivalrous, everything save his hands and—his face. Yet yesterday . . .

"Death, the leveler!" he muttered.

"And the revealer," she whispered gently, rising to her feet with great eyes. He turned away, and after fumbling a moment sent a rocket into the darkening air. It arose, shrieked, and flew up, a slim path of light, and scattering its stars abroad, dropped on the city below. She scarcely noticed it. A vision of the world had risen before her. Slowly the mighty prophecy of her destiny overwhelmed her. Above the dead past hovered the Angel of Annunciation. She was no mere woman. She was neither high nor low, white nor black, rich nor poor. She was primal woman; mighty mother of all men to come and Bride of Life. She looked upon the man beside her and forgot all else but his manhood, his strong, vigorous manhood—his sorrow and sacrifice. She saw him glorified. He was no longer a thing apart, a creature below, a strange outcast of another clime and blood, but her Brother Humanity incarnate, Son of God and great All-Father of the race to be.

He did not glimpse the glory in her eyes, but stood looking outward toward the sea and sending rocket after rocket into the unanswering darkness. Dark-purple clouds lay banked and billowed in the west. Behind them and all around, the heavens glowed in dim, weird radiance that suffused the darkening world and made almost a minor music. Suddenly, as though gathered back in some vast hand, the great cloud-curtain fell away. Low on the horizon lay a long, white star—mystic, wonderful! And from it fled upward to the pole, like some wan bridal veil, a pale, wide sheet of flame that lighted all the world and dimmed the stars.

In fascinated silence the man gazed at the heavens and dropped his rockets to the floor. Memories of memories stirred to life in the dead recesses of his mind. The shackles seemed to rattle and fall from his soul. Up from the crass

and crushing and cringing of his caste leaped the lone majesty of kings long dead. He arose within the shadows, tall, straight, and stern, with power in his eyes and ghostly scepters hovering to his grasp. It was as though some mighty Pharaoh lived again, or curled Assyrian lord. He turned and looked upon the lady, and found her gazing straight at him.

Silently, immovably, they saw each other face to face—eye to eye. Their souls lay naked to the night. It was not lust; it was not love—it was some vaster, mightier thing that needed neither touch of body nor thrill of soul. It was a thought divine, splendid.

Slowly, noiselessly, they moved toward each other—the heavens above, the seas around, the city grim and dead below. He loomed from out the velvet shadows vast and dark. Pearl-white and slender, she shone beneath the stars. She stretched her jeweled hands abroad. He lifted up his mighty arms, and they cried each to the other, almost with one voice, "The world is dead."

"Long live the—"

"Honk! Honk!" Hoarse and sharp the cry of a motor drifted clearly up from the silence below. They started backward with a cry and gazed upon each other with eyes that faltered and fell, with blood that boiled.

"Honk! Honk! Honk! Honk!" came the mad cry again, and almost from their feet a rocket blazed into the air and scattered its stars upon them. She covered her eyes with her hands, and her shoulders heaved. He dropped and bowed, groped blindly on his knees about the floor. A blue flame spluttered lazily after an age, and she heard the scream of an answering rocket as it flew.

Then they stood still as death, looking to opposite ends of the earth.

"Clang—crash—clang!"

The roar and ring of swift elevators shooting upward from below made the great tower tremble. A murmur and babel of voices swept in upon the night. All over the once-dead city the lights blinked, flickered, and flamed; and then with a sudden clanging of doors the entrance to the platform was filled with men, and one with white and flying hair rushed to the girl and lifted her to his breast. "My daughter!" he sobbed.

Behind him hurried a younger, comelier man, carefully clad in motor costume, who bent above the girl with passionate solicitude and gazed into her staring eyes until they narrowed and dropped and her face flushed deeper and deeper crimson.

"Julia," he whispered; "my darling, I thought you were gone forever."

She looked up at him with strange, searching eyes.

"Fred," she murmured, almost vaguely, "is the world—gone?"

"Only New York," he answered; "it is terrible—awful! You know,—but you, how did you escape—how have you endured this horror? Are you well? Unharmed?"

"Unharmed!" she said.

"And this man here?" he asked, encircling her drooping form with one arm and turning toward the Negro. Suddenly he stiffened and his hand flew to his hip. "Why!" he snarled. "It's—a—nigger—Julia! Has he—has he dared . . ."

She lifted her head and looked at her late companion curiously and then dropped her eyes with a sigh.

"He has dared—all, to rescue me," she said quietly, "and I—thank him—much." But she did not look at him again. As the couple turned away, the father drew a roll of bills from his pockets.

"Here, my good fellow," he said, thrusting the money into the man's hands, "take that,—what's your name?"

"Jim Davis," came the answer, hollow-voiced.

"Well, Jim, I thank you. I've always liked your people. If you ever want a job, call on me." And they were gone.

The crowd poured up and out of the elevators, talking and whispering.

"Who was it?"

"Are they alive?"

"How many?"

"Two!"

"Who was saved?"

"A white girl and a nigger—there she goes."

"A nigger? Where is he? Let's lynch the damned—"

"Shut up—he's all right—he saved her."

"Saved hell! He had no business—"

"Here he comes."

Into the glare of the electric lights the colored man moved slowly, with the eyes of those that walk and sleep.

"Well, what do you think of that?" cried a bystander; "of all New York, just a white girl and a nigger!"

The colored man heard nothing. He stood silently beneath the glare of the light, gazing at the money in his hand and shrinking as he gazed; slowly he put his other hand into his pocket and brought out a baby's filmy cap, and gazed again. A woman mounted to the platform and looked about, shading her eyes. She was brown, small, and toil-worn, and in one arm lay the corpse of a dark baby. The crowd parted and her eyes fell on the colored man; with a cry she tottered toward him.

"Jim!"

He whirled and, with a sob of joy, caught her in his arms.

The Fate of the *Poseidonia*

CLARE WINGER HARRIS

Clare Winger Harris (1891–1968), a US writer, was the first woman to publish science fiction in the first generation of American pulp magazines. Her first story publication was "A Runaway World" in the July 1926 issue of *Weird Tales*. Harris wrote about women protagonists fairly regularly, especially in stories like "The Fifth Dimension" (*Amazing Stories*, December 1928) and "The Ape Cycle" (*Science Wonder Quarterly*, Spring 1930). In an environment that suffered from a dearth of strong female characters, this fact made Harris an early feminist in the field by default. Her work also contained a preoccupation with creatures not quite human, cyborgs and ape-people in particular. Although Harris has been reprinted frequently in the modern era, when she first assembled her work in *Away from the Here and Now: Stories in Pseudo-Science* (1947), she had to resort to self-publication through a vanity press.

The story reprinted here, "The Fate of the *Poseidonia*" (1927), also features a female lead and won third prize in an *Amazing Stories* contest. In addition to portraying women in a way uncommon for the times, the story deals with the surprisingly modern themes of fear of technology and loss of privacy. This was the first science fiction story by a woman published in that magazine. Perhaps unsurprisingly *Amazing Stories* editor Hugo Gernsback, whose name would soon grace the Hugo Award, wrote in his introduction to the story: "That the third place winner should prove to be a woman was one of the surprises of the contest, for, as a rule, women do not make good scientifiction writers, because their education and general tendencies on scientific matters are usually limited. But the exception, as usual, proves the rule, the exception in this case being extraordinarily impressive."

Gernsback added that he hoped to see more of "Mrs. Harris's scientifiction" in *Amazing Stories* because "the story has a great deal of charm, chiefly because it is not overburdened with science, but whatever science is contained therein is not only quite palatable, but highly desirable, due to its plausibility. Not only this, but you will find that the author is a facile writer who keeps your interest unto the last line." Some think Winger may have been inspired by her father, Frank Stover Winger, who wrote a novel inspired by Jules Verne. Others give credit to her husband, who was an engineer and architect.

Harris went on to publish eleven more stories with Gernsback over the next three years. She stopped writing in order to see to the education of her children, but her name in the table of contents inspired other women to write and submit their own stories—including another contributor to this anthology, Leslie F. Stone.

THE FATE OF THE *POSEIDONIA*

Clare Winger Harris

CHAPTER I

The first moment I laid eyes on Martell I took a great dislike to the man. There sprang up between us an antagonism that as far as he was concerned might have remained passive, but which circumstances forced into activity on my side.

How distinctly I recall the occasion of our meeting at the home of Professor Stearns, head of the astronomy department of Austin College. The address which the professor proposed giving before the Mentor Club, of which I was a member, was to be on the subject of the planet Mars. The spacious front rooms of the Stearns home were crowded for the occasion with rows of chairs, and at the end of the double parlors a screen was erected for the purpose of presenting telescopic views of the ruddy planet in its various aspects.

As I entered the parlor after shaking hands with my hostess, I felt, rather than saw, an unfamiliar presence, and the impression I received involuntarily was that of antipathy. What I saw was the professor himself engaged in earnest conversation with a stranger. Intuitively I knew that from the latter emanated the hostility of which I was definitely conscious.

He was a man of slightly less than average height. At once I noticed that he did not appear exactly normal physically and yet I could not ascertain in what way he was deficient. It was not until I had passed the entire evening in his company that I was fully aware of his bodily peculiarities. Perhaps the most striking characteristic was the swarthy, coppery hue of his flesh, which was not unlike that of an American Indian. His chest and shoulders seemed abnormally developed, his limbs and features extremely slender in proportion. Another peculiar individuality was the wearing of a skullcap pulled well down over his forehead.

Professor Stearns caught my eye, and with a friendly nod indicated his desire that I meet the new arrival.

"Glad to see you, Mr. Gregory," he said warmly as he clasped my hand. "I want you to meet Mr. Martell, a stranger in our town, but a kindred spirit, in that he is interested in astronomy and particularly in the subject of my lecture this evening."

I extended my hand to Mr. Martell and imagined that he responded to my salutation somewhat reluctantly. Immediately I knew why. The texture of the skin was most unusual. For want of a better simile, I shall say that it felt not unlike a fine dry sponge. I do not believe that I betrayed any visible surprise, though inwardly my whole being revolted. The deep, close-set eyes of the stranger seemed to be searching me for any manifestation of antipathy, but I congratulate myself that my outward poise was undisturbed by the strange encounter.

The guests assembled, and I discovered to my chagrin that I was seated next to the stranger, Martell. Suddenly the lights were extinguished preparatory to the presentation of the lantern slides. The darkness that enveloped us was intense. Supreme horror gripped me when I presently became conscious of two faint phosphorescent lights to my right. There could be no mistaking their origin. They were the eyes of Martell and they were regarding me with an enigmatical stare. Fascinated, I gazed back into those diabolical orbs with an emotion akin to terror. I felt that I should shriek and then attack their owner. But at the precise moment when my usually steady nerves threatened to betray me, the twin lights vanished. A second later the lantern light flashed on the screen. I stole a furtive glance in the direction of Martell. He was sitting with his eyes closed.

"The planet Mars should be of particular interest to us," began Professor Stearns, "not only because of its relative proximity to us, but because of the fact that there are visible upon its surface undeniable evidences of the handiwork of man, and I am inclined to believe in the existence of mankind there not unlike the humanity of the Earth."

The discourse proceeded uninterruptedly. The audience remained quiet and attentive, for Professor Stearns possessed the faculty of holding his listeners spellbound. A large map of one hemisphere of Mars was thrown on the screen, and simultaneously the stranger Martell drew in his breath sharply with a faint whistling sound.

The professor continued, "Friends, do you observe that the outstanding physical difference between Mars and Terra appears to be in the relative distribution of land and water? On our own globe the terrestrial parts lie as distinct entities surrounded by the vast aqueous portions, whereas, on Mars the land and water are so intermingled by gulfs, bays, capes, and peninsulas that it requires careful study to ascertain for a certainty which is which. It is my opinion, and I do not hold it alone, for much discussion with my worthy colleagues has made it obvious, that the peculiar land contours are due to the fact that water is becoming a very scarce commodity on our neighboring planet. Much of what is now land is merely the exposed portions of the onetime ocean bed, the precious life-giving fluid now occupying only the lowest depressions. We may conclude that the telescopic eye, when turned on Mars, sees a waning world; the habitat of a people struggling desperately and vainly for existence, with inevitable extermination facing them in the not-far-distant future. What will they do? If

they are no farther advanced in the evolutionary stage than a carrot or a jellyfish, they will ultimately succumb to fate, but if they are men and women such as you and I, they will fight for the continuity of their race. I am inclined to the opinion that the Martians will not die without putting up a brave struggle, which will result in the prolongation of their existence, but not in their complete salvation."

Professor Stearns paused. "Are there any questions?" he asked.

I was about to speak when the voice of Martell boomed in my ear, startling me.

"In regard to the map, professor," he said, "I believe that gulf which lies farthest south is not a gulf at all but is a part of the land portion surrounding it. I think you credit the poor dying planet with even more water than it actually has!"

"It is possible and even probable that I have erred," replied the learned man, "and I am sorry indeed if that gulf is to be withdrawn from the credit of the Martians, for their future must look very black."

"Just suppose," resumed Martell, leaning toward the lecturer with interested mien, "that the Martians were the possessors of an intelligence equal to that of terrestrials, what might they do to save themselves from total extinction? In other words to bring it home to us more realistically, what would we do were we threatened with a like disaster?"

"That is a very difficult question to answer, and one upon which merely an opinion could be ventured," said Professor Stearns with a smile. " 'Necessity is the mother of invention,' and in our case without the likelihood of the existence of the mother, we can hardly hazard a guess as to the nature of the offspring. But always, as Terra's resources have diminished, the mind of man has discovered substitutes. There has always been a way out, and let us hope our brave planetary neighbors will succeed in solving their problem."

"Let us hope so indeed," echoed the voice of Martell.

CHAPTER II

At the time of my story in the winter of 1994–1995, I was still unmarried and was living in a private hotel on East Ferguson Avenue, where I enjoyed the comforts of well-furnished bachelor quarters. To my neighbors I paid little or no attention, absorbed in my work during the day and paying court to Margaret Landon in the evenings.

I was not a little surprised upon one occasion, as I stepped into the corridor, to see a strange yet familiar figure in the hotel locking the door of the apartment adjoining my own. Almost instantly I recognized Martell, on whom I had not laid eyes since the meeting some weeks previous at the home of Professor Stearns. He evinced no more pleasure at our meeting than I did, and after the exchange of a few cursory remarks from which I learned that he was my new neighbor, we went our respective ways.

I thought no more of the meeting, and as I am not blessed or cursed (as the case may be) with a natural curiosity concerning the affairs of those about me, I seldom met Martell, and upon the rare occasions when I did, we confined our remarks to that ever convenient topic, the weather.

Between Margaret and myself there seemed to be growing an inexplicable estrangement that increased as time went on, but it was not until after five repeated futile efforts to spend an evening in her company that I suspected the presence of a rival. Imagine my surprise and chagrin to discover that rival in the person of my neighbor Martell! I saw them together at the theatre and wondered, even with all due modesty, what there was in the ungainly figure and peculiar character of Martell to attract a beautiful and refined girl of Margaret Landon's type. But attract her he did, for it was plainly evident, as I watched them with the eyes of a jealous lover, that Margaret was fascinated by the personality of her escort.

In sullen rage I went to Margaret a few days later, expressing my opinion of her new admirer in derogatory epithets. She gave me calm and dignified attention until I had exhausted my vocabulary, voicing my ideas of Martell, then she made reply in Martell's defense.

"Aside from personal appearance, Mr. Martell is a forceful and interesting character, and I refuse to allow you to dictate to me who my associates are to be. There is no reason why we three cannot all be friends."

"Martell hates me as I hate him," I replied with smoldering resentment. "That is sufficient reason why we three cannot all be friends."

"I think you must be mistaken," she replied curtly. "Mr. Martell praises your qualities as a neighbor and comments not infrequently on your excellent virtue of attending strictly to your own business."

I left Margaret's presence in a downhearted mood.

"So Martell appreciates my lack of inquisitiveness, does he?" I mused as later I reviewed mentally the closing words of Margaret, and right then and there doubts and suspicions arose in my mind. If self-absorption was an appreciable quality as far as Martell was concerned, there was reason for his esteem of that phase of my character. I had discovered the presence of a mystery; Martell had something to conceal!

It was New Year's Day, not January first as they had it in the old days, but the extra New Year's Day that was sandwiched as a separate entity between two years. This new chronological reckoning had been put into use in 1938. The calendar had previously contained twelve months varying in length from twenty-eight to thirty-one days, but with the addition of a new month and the adoption of a uniformity of twenty-eight days for all months and the interpolation of an isolated New Year's Day, the world's system of chronology was greatly simplified. It was, as I say, on New Year's Day that I arose later than usual and dressed myself. The buzzing monotone of a voice from Martell's room annoyed me. Could he be talking over the telephone to Margaret? Right then and there I stooped to the performance of a deed of which I did not think myself capable. Ineffable curiosity converted me into a spy and an eavesdropper.

I dropped to my knees and peered through the keyhole. I was rewarded with an unobstructed profile view of Martell seated at a low desk on which stood a peculiar cubical mechanism measuring on each edge six or seven inches. Above it hovered a tenuous vapor and from it issued strange sounds, occasionally interrupted by remarks from Martell uttered in an unknown tongue. Good heavens! Was this a newfangled radio that communicated with the spirit world? For only in such a way could I explain the peculiar vapor that enveloped the tiny machine. Television had been perfected and in use for a generation, but as yet no instrument had been invented which delivered messages from the "unknown bourne"!

I crouched in my undignified position until it was with difficulty that I arose, at the same time that Martell shut off the mysterious contrivance. Could Margaret be involved in any diabolical schemes? The very suggestion caused me to break out in a cold sweat. Surely Margaret, the very personification of innocence and purity, could be no partner in any nefarious undertakings! I resolved to call her up. She answered the phone and I thought her voice showed agitation.

"Margaret, this is George," I said. "Are you all right?"

She answered faintly in the affirmative.

"May I come over at once?" I pled. "I have something important to tell you."

To my surprise she consented, and I lost no time in speeding my volplane to her home. With no introductory remarks, I plunged right into a narrative of the peculiar and suspicious actions of Martell, and ended by begging her to discontinue her association with him. Ever well poised and with a girlish dignity that was irresistibly charming, Margaret quietly thanked me for my solicitude for her well-being but assured me that there was nothing to fear from Martell.

It was like beating against a brick wall to obtain any satisfaction from her, so I returned to my lonely rooms, there to brood in solitude over the unhappy change that Martell had brought into my life.

Once again I gazed through the tiny aperture. My neighbor was nowhere to be seen, but on the desk stood that which I mentally termed the devil machine. The subtle mist that had previously hovered above it was wanting.

The next day upon arising I was drawn as by a magnet toward the keyhole, but my amazement knew no bounds when I discovered that it had been plugged from the other side, and my vision completely barred!

"Well I guess it serves me right," I muttered in my chagrin. "I ought to keep out of other people's private affairs. But," I added as an afterthought in feeble defense of my actions, "my motive is to save Margaret from that scoundrel." And such I wanted to prove him to be before it was too late!

CHAPTER III

The sixth of April, 1945, was a memorable day in the annals of history, especially to the inhabitants of Pacific coast cities throughout the world. Radios buzzed with the alarming and mystifying news that just overnight the ocean line had receded several feet. What cataclysm of nature could have caused the disappearance of thousands of tons of water inside of twenty-four hours? Scientists ventured the explanation that internal disturbances must have resulted in the opening of vast submarine fissures into which the seas had poured.

This explanation, stupendous as it was, sounded plausible enough and was accepted by the world at large, which was too busy accumulating gold and silver to worry over the loss of nearly a million tons of water. How little we then realized that the relative importance of gold and water was destined to be reversed, and that man was to have forced upon him a new conception of values which would bring to him a complete realization of his former erroneous ideas.

May and June passed marking little change in the drab monotony that had settled into my life since Margaret Landon had ceased to care for me. One afternoon early in July I received a telephone call from Margaret. Her voice betrayed an agitated state of mind, and sorry though I was that she was troubled, it pleased me that she had turned to me in her despair. Hope sprang anew in my breast, and I told her I would be over at once.

I was admitted by the taciturn housekeeper and ushered into the library, where Margaret rose to greet me as I entered. There were traces of tears in her lovely eyes. She extended both hands to me in a gesture of spontaneity that had been wholly lacking in her attitude toward me ever since the advent of Martell. In the role of protector and advisor, I felt that I was about to be reinstated in her regard.

But my joy was short-lived as I beheld a recumbent figure on the great davenport and recognized it instantly as that of Martell. So he was in the game after all! Margaret had summoned me because her lover was in danger! I turned to go but felt a restraining hand.

"Wait, George," the girl pled. "The doctor will be here any minute."

"Then let the doctor attend to him," I replied coldly. "I know nothing of the art of healing."

"I know, George," Margaret persisted, "but he mentioned you before he lost consciousness and I think he wants to speak to you. Won't you wait, please?"

I paused, hesitant at the supplicating tones of her whom I loved, but at that moment the maid announced the doctor, and I made a hasty exit.

Needless to say I experienced a sense of guilt as I returned to my rooms.

"But," I argued as I seated myself comfortably before my radio, "a rejected lover would have to be a very magnanimous specimen of humanity to go running about doing favors for a rival. What do the pair of them take me for anyway—a fool?"

I rather enjoyed a consciousness of righteous indignation, but disturbing visions of Margaret gave me an uncomfortable feeling that there was much about the affair that was incomprehensible to me.

"The transatlantic passenger plane *Pegasus* has mysteriously disappeared," said the voice of the news announcer. "One member of her crew has been picked up who tells such a weird, fantastic tale that it has not received much credence. According to his story the *Pegasus* was winging its way across midocean last night keeping an even elevation of three thousand feet, when, without any warning, the machine started straight up. Some force outside of itself was drawing it up, but whither? The rescued mechanic, the only one of all the fated ship's passengers, possessed the presence of mind to manipulate his parachute, and thus descended in safety before the air became too rare to breathe, and before he and the parachute could be attracted upwards. He stoutly maintains that the plane could not have fallen later without his knowledge. Scouting planes, boats, and submarines sent out this morning verify his seemingly mad narration. Not a vestige of the *Pegasus* is to be found above, on the surface, or below the water. Is this tragedy in any way connected with the lowering of the ocean level? Has someone a theory? In the face of such an inexplicable enigma the government will listen to the advancement of any theories, in the hope of solving the mystery. Too many times in the past have the so-called levelheaded people failed to give ear to the warnings of theorists and dreamers, but now we know that the latter are often the possessors of a sixth sense that enables them to see that to which the bulk of mankind is blind."

I was awed by the fate of the *Pegasus*. I had had two flights in the wonderful machine myself three years ago, and I knew that it was the last word in luxuriant air travel.

How long I sat listening to brief news bulletins and witnessing scenic flashes of worldly affairs I do not know, but there suddenly came to my mind, and persisted in staying there, a very disquieting thought. Several times I dismissed it as unworthy of any consideration, but it continued with unmitigating tenacity.

After an hour of mental pros and cons I called up the hotel office.

"This is Mr. Gregory in suite 307." I strove to keep my voice steady. "Mr. Martell of 309 is ill at the house of a friend. He wishes me to have some of his belongings taken to him. May I have the key to his rooms?"

There was a pause that to me seemed interminable, then the voice of the clerk. "Certainly, Mr. Gregory, I'll send a boy up with it at once."

I felt like a culprit of the deepest dye as I entered Martell's suite a few moments later and gazed about me. I knew I might expect interference from any quarter at any moment so I wasted no time in a general survey of the apartment but proceeded at once to the object of my visit. The tiny machine, which I now perceived was more intricate than I had supposed from my previous observations through the keyhole, stood in its accustomed place upon the desk. It had four levers and a dial, and I decided to manipulate each of these in turn. I commenced with the one at my extreme left. For a moment apparently nothing happened, then I realized that above the machine a mist was forming.

At first it was faint and cloudy but the haziness quickly cleared, and before my startled vision a scene presented itself. I seemed to be inside a bamboo hut looking toward an opening which afforded a glimpse of a wave-washed sandy beach and a few palm trees silhouetted against the horizon. I could imagine myself on a desert isle. I gasped in astonishment, but it was nothing to the shock which was to follow. While my fascinated gaze dwelt on the scene before me, a shadow fell athwart the hut's entrance and the figure of a man came toward me. I uttered a hoarse cry. For a moment I thought I had been transplanted chronologically to the discovery of America, for the being who approached me

bore a general resemblance to an Indian chief. From his forehead tall, white feathers stood erect. He was without clothing and his skin had a reddish cast that glistened with a coppery sheen in the sunlight. Where had I seen those features or similar ones, recently? I had it! Martell! The Indian savage was a natural replica of the suave and civilized Martell, and yet was this man before me a savage? On the contrary, I noted that his features displayed a remarkably keen intelligence.

The stranger approached a table upon which I seemed to be, and raised his arms. A muffled cry escaped my lips! The feathers that I had supposed constituted his headdress were attached permanently along the upper portion of his arms to a point a little below each elbow. They grew there. This strange being had feathers instead of hair.

I do not know by what presence of mind I managed to return the lever to its original position, but I did, and sat weakly gazing vacantly at the air, where but a few seconds before a vivid tropic scene had been visible. Suddenly a low buzzing sound was heard. Only for an instant was I mystified, then I knew that the stranger of the desert isle was endeavoring to summon Martell.

Weak and dazed, I waited until the buzzing had ceased and then I resolutely pulled the second of the four levers. At the inception of the experiment the same phenomena were repeated, but when a correct perspective was effected a very different scene was presented before my startled vision. This time I seemed to be in a luxuriant room filled with costly furnishings, but I had time only for a most fleeting glance, for a section of newspaper that had intercepted part of my view moved, and from behind its printed expanse emerged a being who bore a resemblance to Martell and the Indian of the desert island. It required but a second to turn off the mysterious connection, but that short time had been of sufficient duration to enable me to read the heading of the paper in the hands of a copper-hued man. It was *Die Münchner Zeitung*.

Still stupefied by the turn of events, it was with a certain degree of enjoyment that I continued to experiment with the devil machine. I was startled when the same buzzing sound followed the disconnecting of the instrument.

I was about to manipulate the third lever when I became conscious of pacing footsteps in the outer hall. Was I arousing the suspicion of the hotel officials? Leaving my seat before the desk, I began to move about the room in semblance of gathering together Martell's required articles. Apparently satisfied, the footsteps retreated down the corridor and were soon inaudible.

Feverishly now I fumbled with the third lever. There was no time to lose and I was madly desirous of investigating all the possibilities of this new kind of television set. I had no doubt that I was on the track of a nefarious organization of spies, and I worked on in the self-termed capacity of a Sherlock Holmes.

The third lever revealed an apartment no less sumptuous than the German one had been. It appeared to be unoccupied for the present, and I had ample time to survey its expensive furnishings, which had an oriental appearance. Through an open window at the far end of the room I glimpsed a mosque with domes and minarets. I could not ascertain for a certainty whether this was Turkey or India. It might have been any one of many eastern lands, I could not know. The fact that the occupant of this oriental apartment was temporarily absent made me desirous of learning more about it, but time was precious to me now, and I disconnected. No buzzing followed upon this occasion, which strengthened my belief that my lever manipulation sounded a similar buzzing that was audible in the various stations connected for the purpose of accomplishing some wicked scheme. The fourth handle invited me to further investigation. I determined to go through with my secret research though I died in the effort. Just before my hand dropped, the buzzing commenced, and I perceived for the first time a faint glow near the lever of number

four. I dared not investigate it at this time, for I did not wish it known that another than Martell was at this station. I thought of going on to dial five, but an innate love of system forced me to risk a loss of time rather than to take them out of order. The buzzing continued for the usual duration of time, but I waited until it had apparently ceased entirely before I moved number four.

My soul rebelled at that which took form from the emanating mist. A face, another duplicate of Martell's, but if possible more cruel, confronted me, completely filling up the vaporous space, and two phosphorescent eyes seared a warning into my own. A nauseating sensation crept over me as my hand crept to the connecting part of number four. When every vestige of the menacing face had vanished, I arose weakly and took a few faltering steps around the room. A bell was ringing with great persistence from some other room. It was mine! It would be wise to answer it. I fairly flew back to my room and was rewarded by the sound of Margaret's voice with a note of petulance in it.

"Why didn't you answer, George? The phone rang several times."

"Couldn't. Was taking a bath," I lied.

"Mr. Martell is better," continued Margaret. "The doctor says there's no immediate danger."

There was a pause and the sound of a rasping voice a little away from the vicinity of the phone, and then Margaret's voice came again.

"Mr. Martell wants you to come over, George. He wants to see you."

"Tell him I have to dress after my bath, then I'll come," I answered.

CHAPTER IV

There was not a moment to spare. I rushed back into Martell's room determined to see this thing through. I had never been subject to heart attacks, but certainly the suffocating sensation that possessed me could be attributed to no other cause.

A loud buzzing greeted my ears as soon as I had closed the door of Martell's suite. I looked toward the devil machine. The four stations were buzzing at once! What was I to do? There was no light near dial five, and that alone remained uninvestigated. My course of action was clear; try out number five to my satisfaction, leave Martell's rooms, and go to Margaret Landon's home as I had told her I would. They must not know what I had done. But it was inevitable that Martell would know when he got back to his infernal television and radio. He must not get back! Well, time enough to plan that later; now to the work of seeing number five.

When I turned the dial of number five (for, as I have stated before, this was a dial instead of a lever) I was conscious of a peculiar sensation of distance. It fairly took my breath away. What remote part of the earth's surface would the last position reveal to me?

A sharp hissing sound accompanied the manipulation of number five and the vaporous shroud was very slow in taking definite shape. When it was finally at rest, and it was apparent that it would not change further, the scene depicted was at first incomprehensible to me. I stared with bulging eyes and bated breath trying to read any meaning into the combinations of form and color that had taken shape before me.

In the light of what has since occurred, the facts of which are known throughout the world, I can lend my description a little intelligence borrowed, as it were, from the future. At the time of which I write, however, no such enlightenment was mine, and it must have been a matter of minutes before the slightest knowledge of the significance of the scene entered my uncomprehending brain.

My vantage point seemed to be slightly aerial, for I was looking down upon a scene possibly fifty feet below me. Arid red cliffs and promontories jutted over dry ravines and crevices. In the immediate foreground, and also across a deep gully, extended a comparatively level area which was the scene of some sort of activity. There was about it a vague suggestion of a shipyard, yet I saw no lumber, only great mountainous piles of dull metal, among which moved thousands of agile figures. They were men and women, but how strange they appeared! Their red bodies were minus clothing of any description and their heads and shoulders were covered with long white feathers that when folded, draped the upper portions of their bodies like shawls. They were unquestionably of the same race as the desert-island stranger—and Martell! At times the feathers of these strange people stood erect and spread out like a peacock's tail. I noticed that when spread in this fanlike fashion they facilitated locomotion. I glanced toward the sun, far to my right, and wondered if I had gone crazy. I rubbed my hands across my eyes and peered again. Yes, it was our luminary, but it was little more than half its customary size! I watched it sinking with fascinated gaze. It vanished quickly beyond the red horizon and darkness descended with scarcely a moment of intervening twilight. It was only by the closest observation that I could perceive that I was still in communication with number five.

Presently the gloom was dissipated by a shaft of light from the opposite horizon whither the sun had disappeared. So rapidly that I could follow its movement across the sky, the moon hove into view. But wait, was it the moon? Its surface looked strangely unfamiliar, and it too seemed to have shrunk in size.

Spellbound, I watched the tiny moon glide across the heavens while I listened to the clang of metal tools from the workers below. Again a bright light appeared on the horizon beyond the great metal bulks below me. The scene was rapidly being rendered visible by an orb that exceeded the sun in diameter. Then I knew. Great God! There were two moons traversing the welkin! My heart was pounding so loudly that it drowned out the sound of the metal-workers. I watched on, unconscious of the passage of time.

Voices shouted from below in great excitement. Events were evidently working up to some important climax while the little satellite passed from my line of vision and only the second large moon occupied the sky. Straight before me and low on the horizon it hung with its lower margin touching the cliffs. It was low enough now so that a few of the larger stars were becoming visible. One in particular attracted my gaze and held it. It was a great bluish-green star and I noticed that the workers paused seemingly to gaze in silent admiration at its transcendent beauty. Then shout after shout arose from below and I gazed in bewilderment at the spectacle of the next few minutes, or was it hours?

A great spherical bulk hove in view from the right of my line of vision. It made me think of nothing so much as a gyroscope of gigantic proportions. It seemed to be made of the metal with which the workers were employed below, and as it gleamed in the deep blue of the sky it looked like a huge satellite. A band of red metal encircled it with points of the same at top and bottom. Numerous openings that resembled the portholes of an ocean liner appeared in the broad central band, from which extended metal points. I judged these were the "eyes" of the machine. But that which riveted my attention was an object that hung poised in the air below the mighty gyroscope, held in suspension by some mysterious force, probably magnetic in nature, evidently controlled in such a manner that at a certain point it was exactly counterbalanced by the gravitational pull. The lines of force apparently traveled from the poles of the mammoth sphere. But the object that depended in midair, as firm and rigid as though resting on terra firma, was the missing *Pegasus*, the epitome of earthly scientific skill, but in the clutches of this unearthly-looking marauder it looked like a fragile toy. Its wings were bent and twisted, giving it an uncanny resemblance to a bird in the claws of a cat.

In my spellbound contemplation of this new phenomenon I had temporarily forgotten the scene below, but suddenly a great cloud momentarily blotted out the moon, then another and another and another, in rapid succession. Huge bulks of aircraft were eclipsing the moon. Soon the scene was all but obliterated by the machines, whose speed accelerated as they reached the upper air. On and on they sped in endless procession while the green star gazed serenely on! The green star, most sublime of the starry host! I loved its pale beauty though I knew not why. Darkness. The moon had set, but I knew that those frightfully gigantic and ominous shapes still sped upward and onward. Whither?

The tiny moon again made its appearance, serving to reveal once more that endless aerial migration. Was it hours or days? I had lost all sense of the passage of time. The sound of rushing feet, succeeded by a pounding at the door, brought me back to my immediate surroundings. I had the presence of mind to shut off the machine, then I arose and assumed a defensive attitude as the door opened and many figures confronted me. Foremost among them was Martell, his face white with rage, or was it fear!

"Officers, seize that man," he cried furiously. "I did not give him permission to spy in my room. He lied when he said that." Here Martell turned to the desk clerk, who stood behind two policemen.

"Speaking of spying," I flung back at him, "Martell, you ought to know the meaning of that word. He's a spy himself," I cried to the two apparently unmoved officers, "why he—he—"

From their unsympathetic attitudes, I knew the odds were against me. I had lied, and I had been found in a man's private rooms without his permission. It would be a matter of time and patience before I could persuade the law that I had any justice on my side.

I was handcuffed and led toward the door just as a sharp pain like an icy clutch at my heart overcame me. I sank into oblivion.

CHAPTER V

When I regained consciousness two days later I discovered that I was the sole occupant of a cell in the state hospital for the insane. Mortified to the extreme, I pled with the keeper to bring about my release, assuring him that I was unimpaired mentally.

"Sure, that's what they all say," the fellow remarked with a wry smile.

"But I must be freed," I reiterated impatiently, "I have a message of importance for the world. I must get into immediate communication with the secretary of war."

"Yes, yes," agreed the keeper affably. "We'll let you see the secretary of war when that fellow over there"—he jerked his thumb in the direction of the cell opposite mine—"dies from drinking hemlock. He says he's Socrates, and every time he drinks a cup of milk he flops over, but he always revives."

I looked across the narrow hall into a pair of eyes that mirrored a deranged mind, then my gaze turned to the guard, who was watching me narrowly. I turned away with a shrug of despair.

Later in the day the man appeared again but I sat in sullen silence in a corner of my cell. Days passed in this manner until at last a plausible means of communication with the outside world occurred to me. I asked if my good friend Professor Stearns might be permitted to visit me. The guard replied that he believed it could be arranged for some time the following week. It is a wonder I did not become demented, imprisoned as I was, in solitude, with the thoughts of the mysterious revelations haunting me continually.

One afternoon the keeper, passing by on one of his customary rounds, thrust a newspaper between the bars of my cell. I grabbed it eagerly and retired to read it.

The headlines smote my vision with an almost tactile force.

"Second Mysterious Recession of Ocean. The *Poseidonia* Is Lost!"

I continued to read the entire article, the letters of which blazed before my eyes like so many pinpoints of light.

"Ocean waters have again receded, this time in the Atlantic. Seismologists are at a loss to explain the mysterious cataclysm as no earth tremors have been registered. It is a little over three months since the supposed submarine fissures lowered the level of the Pacific Ocean several feet, and now the same calamity, only to a greater extent, has visited the Atlantic.

"The island of Madeira reports stranded fish upon her shores by the thousands, the decay of which threatens the health of the island's population. Two merchant vessels off the Azores, and one fifty miles out from Gibraltar, were found total wrecks. Another, the *Transatlantic*, reported a fearful agitation of the ocean depths, but seemed at a loss for a plausible explanation, as the sky was cloudless and no wind was blowing.

"'But despite this fact,' wired the *Transatlantic*, 'great waves all but capsized us. This marine disturbance lasted throughout the night.'

"The following wireless from the great ocean liner *Poseidonia* brings home to us the realization that Earth has been visited with a stupendous calamity. The *Poseidonia* was making her weekly transatlantic trip between Europe and America, and was in midocean at the time her message was flashed to the world.

"'A great cloud of flying objects of enormous proportions has just appeared in the sky blotting out the light of the stars. No sound accompanies the approach of this strange fleet. In appearance the individual craft resemble mammoth balloons. The sky is black with them and in their vicinity the air is humid and oppressive as though the atmosphere were saturated to the point of condensation. Everything is orderly. There are no collisions. Our captain has given orders for us to turn back toward Europe—we have turned, but the dark dirigibles are pursuing us. Their speed is unthinkable. Can the *Poseidonia*, doing a mere hundred miles an hour, escape? A huge craft is bearing down upon us from above and behind. There is no escape. Pandemonium reigns. The enemy—'

"Thus ends the tragic message from the brave wireless operator of the *Poseidonia*."

I threw down the paper and called loudly for the keeper. Socrates across the hall eyed me suspiciously. I was beginning to feel that perhaps the poor demented fellow had nothing on me; that I should soon be in actuality a raving maniac.

The keeper came in response to my call, entered my cell, and patted my shoulders reassuringly.

"Never mind, old top," he said, "it isn't so bad as it seems."

"Now look here," I burst forth angrily, "I tell you I am not insane!" How futile my words sounded! "If you will send Professor Mortimer Stearns, teacher of astronomy at Austin, to me at once for an hour's talk, I'll prove to the world that I have not been demented.

"Professor Stearns is a very highly esteemed friend of mine," I continued, noting the suspicion depicted on his countenance. "If you wish, go to him first and find out his true opinion of me. I'll wager it will not be an uncomplimentary one!"

The man twisted his keys thoughtfully, and I uttered not a word, believing a silent demeanor most effective in the present crisis. After what seemed an eternity:

"All right," he said, "I'll see what can be done toward arranging a visit from Professor Mortimer Stearns as soon as possible."

I restrained my impulse toward a too-effusive expression of gratitude as I realized that a quiet dignity prospered my cause more effectually.

The next morning at ten, after a constant vigil, I was rewarded with the most welcome sight of Professor Stearns striding down the hall in earnest conversation with the guard. He was the straw and I the drowning man, but would he prove a more substantial help than the proverbial straw? I surely hoped so.

A chair was brought for the professor and placed just outside my cell. I hastily drew my own near it.

"Well, this is indeed unfortunate," said Mortimer Stearns with some embarrassment, "and I sincerely hope you will soon be released."

"Unfortunate!" I echoed. "It is nothing short of a calamity."

My indignation voiced so vociferously startled the good professor and he shoved his chair almost imperceptibly away from the intervening bars. At the far end of the hall the keeper eyed me suspiciously. Hang it all, was my last resort going to fail me?

"Professor Stearns," I said earnestly, "will you try to give me an unbiased hearing? My situation is a desperate one, and it is necessary for someone to believe in me before I can render humanity the service it needs."

He responded to my appeal with something of his old sincerity, which always endeared him to his associates.

"I shall be glad to hear your story, Gregory, and if I can render any service, I'll not hesitate—"

"That's splendid of you," I interrupted with emotion, "and now to my weird tale."

I related from the beginning, omitting no details, however trivial they may have seemed, the series of events that had brought me to my present predicament.

"And your conclusion?" queried the professor in strange, hollow tones.

"That Martian spies, one of whom is Martell, are superintending, by radio and television, an unbelievably well-planned theft of Earth's water in order to replenish their own dry ocean beds!"

"Stupendous!" gasped Professor Stearns. "Something must be done to prevent another raid. Let's see," he mused, "the interval was three months before, was it not? Three months we shall have for bringing again into use the instruments of war that—praise God!—have lain idle for many generations. It is the only way to deal with a formidable foe from outside."

CHAPTER VI

Professor Stearns was gone, but there was hope in my heart in place of the former grim despair. When the guard handed the evening paper to me I amazed him with a grateful "thank you." But my joy was short-lived. Staring up at me from the printed passenger list of the ill-fated *Poseidonia* were the names of Mr. and Mrs. T. M. Landon and daughter Margaret!

I know the guard classed me as one of the worst cases on record, but I felt that surely fate had been unkind.

"A package for Mr. George Gregory," bawled a voice in the corridor.

Thanks to the influence of Professor Stearns, I was permitted to receive mail. When the guard saw that I preferred unwrapping it myself, he discreetly left me to the mystery of the missive.

A card just inside bore the few but insignificant words, "For Gregory in remembrance of Martell."

I suppressed an impulse to dash the accursed thing to the floor when I saw that it was Martell's radio and television instrument. Placing it upon the table I drew a chair up to it and turned each of the levers, but not one functioned. I manipulated the dial, number five. The action was accompanied by the same hissing sound that had so startled my overwrought nerves upon the previous occasion. Slowly the wraith-like mist commenced the process of adjustment. Spellbound I watched the scene before my eyes.

Again I had the sensation of a lofty viewpoint. It was identical with the one I had previously held, but the scene—was it the same? It must be—and yet! The barren red soil was but faintly visible through a verdure. The towering rocky palisades that bordered the chasm were crowned with golden-roofed dwellings, or were they temples, for they were like the pure marble fanes of the ancient Greeks except in color. Down the steep slopes flowed streams of sparkling water that dashed with a merry sound to a canal below.

Gone were the thousands of beings and their metal aircraft, but seated on a grassy plot in the left foreground of the picture was a small group of the white-feathered, red-skinned inhabitants of this strange land. In the distance rose the temple-crowned crags. One figure alone stood, and with a magnificent gesture held arms aloft. The great corona of feathers spread following the line of the arms like the open wings of a great eagle. The superb figure stood and gazed into the deep velvety blue of the sky, the others following the direction of their leader's gaze.

Involuntarily I too watched the welkin, where now not even a moon was visible. Then within the range of my vision there moved a great object—the huge aerial gyroscope—and beneath it, dwarfed by its far greater bulk, hung a modern ocean liner, like a jewel from the neck of some gigantic ogre.

Great God—it was the *Poseidonia*! I knew now, in spite of the earthly appearance of the great ship, that it was no terrestrial scene upon which I gazed. I was beholding the victory of Martell, the Martian, who had filled his world's canals with the water of Earth, and even borne away trophies of our civilization to exhibit to his fellow-beings.

I closed my eyes to shut out the awful scene, and thought of Margaret, dead and yet aboard the liner, frozen in the absolute cold of outer space!

How long I sat stunned and horrified I do not know, but when I looked back for another last glimpse of the Martian landscape, I uttered a gasp of incredulity. A face filled the entire vaporous screen, the beloved features of Margaret Landon. She was speaking and her voice came over the distance like the memory of a sound that is not quite audible and yet very real to the person in whose mind it exists. It was more as if time divided us instead of space, yet I knew it was the latter, for while a few minutes of time came between us, millions of miles of space intervened!

"George," came the sweet, faraway voice, "I loved you, but you were so suspicious and jealous that I accepted the companionship of Martell, hoping to bring you to your senses. I did not know what an agency for evil he had established upon the earth. Forgive me, dear."

She smiled wistfully. "My parents perished with hundreds of others in the transportation of the *Poseidonia*, but Martell took me from the ship to the ether-craft for the journey, so that I alone was saved."

Her eyes filled with tears. "Do not mourn for me, George, for I shall take up the thread of life anew among these strange but beautiful surroundings. Mars is indeed lovely, but I will tell you of it later for I cannot talk long now."

"I only want to say," she added hastily, "that Terra need fear Mars no more. There is a sufficiency of water now—and I will prevent any—"

She was gone, and in her stead was the leering, malevolent face of Martell. He was minus his skullcap, and his clipped feathers stood up like the ruff of an angry turkey-gobbler.

I reached instinctively for the dial, but before my hand touched it there came a sound, not unlike that of escaping steam, and instantaneously the picture vanished. I did not object to the disappearance of the Martian, but another fact did cause me regret; from that moment, I was never able to view the ruddy planet through the agency of the little machine. All communication had been forever shut off by Martell.

Although many doubt the truth of my solution to the mystery of the disappearance of the *Pegasus* and of the *Poseidonia*, and are still searching beneath the ocean waves, I know that never will either of them be seen again on Earth.

The Star Stealers

EDMOND HAMILTON

Edmond Moore Hamilton (1904–1977) was a US writer of science fiction whose work spanned many different publications and subgenres. His first story, "The Monster-God of Mamurth," was published in 1926 by *Weird Tales*, which went on to publish more than seventy of his stories between 1926 and 1948. In the 1920s and 1930s Hamilton became popular as an author of space opera, a subgenre he is credited with creating alongside E. E. "Doc" Smith. His first story collection, *The Horror on the Asteroid and Other Tales of Planetary Horror* (1936), is widely thought to be the first hardcover compilation of stories identified as "science fiction." Even more interesting is that link early on between space opera and horror, a link strengthened in the modern era by writers such as Alastair Reynolds and Iain M. Banks.

In the 1940s, Hamilton wrote stories in the Captain Future series, a pulp SF story intended for juvenile readers, alongside writers such as Manly Wade Wellman and Joseph Samachson. But when the science fiction publishing field drifted away from high-adventure space-opera storytelling, Hamilton joined DC Comics as a writer; among other comics scripts, he wrote a Superman story, "Superman Under the Red Sun," which appeared in *Action Comics* 300 in 1963. The story in many ways resembled Hamilton's 1951 novel *City at World's End*. He was also one of the first regular writers for the Legion of Super-Heroes and wrote stories for Batman.

Hamilton married fellow writer Leigh Brackett in 1946 and moved into what is regarded as the most consistent phase of his career, writing stories such as "What's It Like Out There?" (*Thrilling Wonder Stories*, 1952) and novels such as the aforementioned *City at World's End* and *The Haunted Stars* (1960). Shortly after he died in 1977, Toei Animation debuted an anime based on his Captain Future novels, and Tsuburaya Productions adapted his novel *Starwolf* into a *tokusatsu* series, winning him new generations of fans internationally.

"The Star Stealers" (1929) is classic Hamilton and compares favorably to modern science fiction. It represents the best of early Golden Age space opera, which was more sophisticated than is generally acknowledged. It is possible that H. P. Lovecraft was inspired by the alien descriptions in this story, as the story was published in *Weird Tales* years before Lovecraft created and wrote the Cthulhu mythos stories.

THE STAR STEALERS

Edmond Hamilton

I

As I stepped into the narrow bridgeroom the pilot at the controls there turned toward me, saluting.

"Alpha Centauri dead ahead, sir," he reported.

"Turn thirty degrees outward," I told him, "and throttle down to eighty light-speeds until we've passed the star."

Instantly the shining levers flicked back under his hands, and as I stepped over to his side I saw the arrows of the speed dials creeping backward with the slowing of our flight. Then, gazing through the broad windows which formed the room's front side, I watched the interstellar panorama ahead shifting sidewise with the turning of our course.

The narrow bridgeroom lay across the very top of our ship's long, cigarlike hull, and through its windows all the brilliance of the heavens around us lay revealed. Ahead flamed the great double star of Alpha Centauri, two mighty blazing suns which dimmed all else in the heavens, and which crept slowly sidewise as we veered away from them. Toward our right there stretched along the inky skies the far-flung powdered fires of the galaxy's thronging suns, gemmed with the crimson splendors of Betelgeuse and the clear brilliance of Canopus and the hot white light of Rigel. And straight ahead, now, gleaming out beyond the twin suns we were passing, shone the clear yellow star that was the sun of our own system.

It was the yellow star that I was watching, now, as our ship fled on toward it at eighty times the speed of light; for more than two years had passed since our cruiser had left it, to become a part of that great navy of the Federation of Stars, which maintained peace over all the galaxy. We had gone far with the fleet, in those two years, cruising with it the length and breadth of the Milky Way, patrolling the space-lanes of the galaxy, and helping to crush the occasional pirate ships which appeared to levy toll on the interstellar commerce. And now that an order flashed from the authorities of our own solar system had recalled us home, it was with an unalloyed eagerness that we looked forward to the moment of our return. The stars we had touched at, the peoples of their worlds, these had been friendly enough toward us, as fellow members of the great Federation, yet for all their hospitality we had been glad enough to leave them. For though we had long ago become accustomed to the alien and unhuman forms of the different stellar races, from the strange brain-men of Algol to the birdlike people of Sirius, their worlds were not human worlds, not the familiar eight little planets which swung around our own sun, and toward which we were speeding homeward now.

While I mused thus at the window the two circling suns of Alpha Centauri had dropped behind us, and now, with a swift clicking of switches, the pilot beside me turned on our full speed. Within a few minutes our ship was hurtling on at almost a thousand light-speeds, flung forward by the power of our newly invented de-transforming generators, which could produce propulsion-vibrations of almost a thousand times the frequency of the light-vibrations. At this immense velocity, matched by few other craft in the galaxy, we were leaping through millions of miles of space each second, yet the gleaming yellow star ahead seemed quite unchanged in size.

Abruptly the door behind me clicked open to admit young Dal Nara, the ship's second officer, descended from a long line of famous interstellar pilots, who grinned at me openly as she saluted.

"Twelve more hours, sir, and we'll be there," she said.

I smiled at her eagerness. "You'll not be sorry to get back to our little sun, will you?" I asked, and she shook her head.

"Not I! It may be just a pinhead beside Canopus and the rest, but there's no place like it in the galaxy. I'm wondering, though, what made them call us back to the fleet so suddenly."

My own face clouded, at that. "I don't know," I said, slowly. "It's almost unprecedented for any star to call one of its ships back from the Federation fleet, but there must have been some reason. . . ."

"Well," she said cheerfully, turning toward the door, "it doesn't matter what the reason is, so long as it means a trip home. The crew is worse than I am—they're scrapping the generators down in the engine room to get another light-speed out of them."

I laughed as the door clicked shut behind her, but as I turned back to the window the question she had voiced rose again in my mind, and I gazed thoughtfully toward the yellow star ahead. For as I had told Dal Nara, it was a well-nigh unheard-of thing for any star to recall one of its cruisers from the great fleet of the Federation. Including as it did every peopled star in the galaxy, the Federation relied entirely upon the fleet to police the interstellar spaces, and to that fleet each star contributed its quota of cruisers. Only a last extremity, I knew, would ever induce any star to recall one of its ships, yet the message flashed to our ship had ordered us to return to the solar system at full speed and report at the Bureau of Astronomical Knowledge, on Neptune. Whatever was behind the order, I thought, I would learn soon enough,

for we were now speeding over the last lap of our homeward journey; so I strove to put the matter from my mind for the time being.

With an odd persistence, though, the question continued to trouble my thoughts in the hours that followed, and when we finally swept in toward the solar system twelve hours later, it was with a certain abstractedness that I watched the slow largening of the yellow star that was our sun. Our velocity had slackened steadily as we approached that star, and we were moving at a bare one light-speed when we finally swept down toward its outermost, far-swinging planet, Neptune, the solar system's point of arrival and departure for all interstellar commerce. Even this speed we reduced still further as we sped past Neptune's single circling moon and down through the crowded shipping lanes toward the surface of the planet itself.

Fifty miles above its surface all sight of the planet beneath was shut off by the thousands of great ships which hung in dense masses above it—that vast tangle of interstellar traffic which makes the great planet the terror of all inexperienced pilots. From horizon to horizon, it seemed, the ships crowded upon each other, drawn from every quarter of the galaxy. Huge grain boats from Betelgeuse; vast, palatial liners from Arcturus and Vega; ship-loads of radium ores from the worlds that circle giant Antares; long, swift mailboats from distant Deneb—all these and myriad others swirled and circled in one great mass above the planet, dropping down one by one as the official traffic directors flashed from their own boats the brilliant signals which allowed a lucky one to descend. And through occasional rifts in the crowded mass of ships could be glimpsed the interplanetary traffic of the lower levels, a swarm of swift little boats which darted ceaselessly back and forth on their comparatively short journeys, ferrying crowds of passengers to Jupiter and Venus and Earth, seeming like little toy boats beside the mighty bulks of the great interstellar ships above them.

As our own cruiser drove down toward the

mass of traffic, though, it cleared away from before us instantly; for the symbol of the Federation on our bows was known from Canopus to Fomalhaut, and the cruisers of its fleet were respected by all the traffic of the galaxy. Arrowing down through this suddenly opened lane we sped smoothly down toward the planet's surface, hovering for a moment above its perplexing maze of white buildings and green gardens, and then slanting down toward the mighty flat-roofed building which housed the Bureau of Astronomical Knowledge. As we sped down toward its roof I could not but contrast the warm, sunny green panorama beneath with the icy desert which the planet had been until two hundred thousand years before, when the scientists of the solar system had devised the great heat transmitters which catch the sun's heat near its blazing surface and fling it out as high-frequency vibrations to the receiving apparatus on Neptune, to be transformed back into the heat which warms this world. In a moment, though, we were landing gently upon the broad roof, upon which rested scores of other shining cruisers whose crews stood outside them watching our arrival.

Five minutes later I was whirling downward through the building's interior in one of the automatic little cone elevators, out of which I stepped into a long white corridor. An attendant was awaiting me there, and I followed him down the corridor's length to a high black door at its end, which he threw open for me, closing it behind me as I stepped inside.

It was an ivory-walled, high-ceilinged room in which I found myself, its whole farther side open to the sunlight and breezes of the green gardens beyond. At a desk across the room was sitting a short-set man with gray-streaked hair and keen, inquiring eyes, and as I entered he sprang up and came toward me.

"Ran Rarak!" he exclaimed. "You've come! For two days, now, we've been expecting you."

"We were delayed off Aldebaran, sir, by generator trouble," I replied, bowing, for I had recognized the speaker as Hurus Hol, chief of the Bureau of Astronomical Knowledge. Now, at a motion from him, I took a chair beside the desk while he resumed his own seat.

A moment he regarded me in silence, and then slowly spoke. "Ran Rarak," he said, "you must have wondered why your ship was ordered back here to the solar system. Well, it was ordered back for a reason which we dared not state in an open message, a reason which, if made public, would plunge the solar system instantly into a chaos of unutterable panic!"

He was silent again for a moment, his eyes on mine, and then went on. "You know, Ran Rarak, that the universe itself is composed of infinite depths of space in which float great clusters of suns, star-clusters which are separated from each other by billions of light-years of space. You know, too, that our own cluster of suns, which we call the galaxy, is roughly disk-like in shape, and that our own particular sun is situated at the very edge of this disk. Beyond lie only those inconceivable leagues of space which separate us from the neighboring star clusters, or island universes, depths of space never yet crossed by our own cruisers or by anything else of which we have record.

"But now, at last, something has crossed those abysses, is crossing them; since over three weeks ago our astronomers discovered that a gigantic dark star is approaching our galaxy from the depths of infinite space—a titanic, dead sun which their instruments showed to be of a size incredible, since, dark and dead as it is, it is larger than the mightiest blazing suns in our own galaxy, larger than Canopus or Antares or Betelgeuse—a dark, dead star millions of times larger than our own fiery sun—a gigantic wanderer out of some far realm of infinite space, racing toward our galaxy at a velocity inconceivable!

"The calculations of our scientists showed that this speeding dark star would not race into our galaxy but would speed past its edge, and out into infinite space again, passing no closer to our own sun, at the edge, than some fifteen billion miles. There was no possibility of collision or danger from it, therefore; and so though the approach of the dark star is known to all in the solar system, there is no idea of any peril connected with it. But there is something else which has been kept quite secret from the peoples of the solar system, something known only to a few astronomers and officials. And that is that during the last few weeks the path of this speeding dark star has changed from a straight path to a curving one, that it is curving inward toward the edge of our galaxy and will now pass our own sun, in less than twelve weeks, at a distance of less than three billion miles, instead of fifteen! And when this titanic dead sun passes that close to our own sun there can be but one result. Inevitably our own sun will be caught by the powerful gravitational grip of the giant dark star and carried out with all its planets into the depths of infinite space, never to return!"

Hurus Hol paused, his face white and set, gazing past me with wide, unseeing eyes. My brain whirling beneath the stunning revelation, I sat rigid, silent, and in a moment he went on.

"If this thing were known to all," he said slowly, "there would be an instant, terrible panic over the solar system, and for that reason only a handful have been told. Flight is impossible, for there are not enough ships in the galaxy to transport the trillions of the solar system's population to another star in the four weeks that are left to us. There is but one chance—one blind, slender chance—and that is to turn aside this onward-thundering dark star from its present inward-curving path, to cause it to pass our sun and the galaxy's edge far enough away to be harmless. And it is for this reason that we ordered your return.

"For it is my plan to speed out of the galaxy into the depths of outer space to meet this approaching dark star, taking all of the scientific apparatus and equipment which might be used to swerve it aside from this curving path it is following. During the last week I have assembled the equipment for the expedition and have gathered together a force of fifty star-cruisers which are even now resting on the roof of this building, manned and ready for the trip. These are only swift mail-cruisers, though, specially equipped for the trip, and it was advisable to have at least one battle-cruiser for the flagship of the force, and so your own was recalled from the Federation fleet. And although I shall go with the expedition, of course, it was my plan to have you yourself as its captain.

"I know, however, that you have spent the last two years in the service of the Federation fleet; so if you desire, another will be appointed to the post. It is one of danger—greater danger, I think, than any of us can dream. Yet the command is yours, if you wish to accept it."

Hurus Hol ceased, intently scanning my face. A moment I sat silent, then rose and stepped to the great open window at the room's far side. Outside stretched the greenery of gardens, and beyond them the white roofs of buildings, gleaming beneath the faint sunlight. Instinctively my eyes went up to the source of light, the tiny sun, small and faint and far, here, but still—the sun. A long moment I gazed up toward it, and then turned back to Hurus Hol. "I accept, sir," I said.

He came to his feet, his eyes shining. "I knew that you would," he said, simply, and then: "All has been ready for days, Ran Rarak. We start at once."

Ten minutes later we were on the broad roof, and the crews of our fifty ships were rushing to their posts in answer to the sharp alarm of a signal bell. Another five minutes and Hurus Hol, Dal Nara, and I stood in the bridgeroom of my own cruiser, watching the white roof drop behind and beneath as we slanted up from it. In a moment the half-hundred cruisers on that roof had risen and were racing up behind us, arrowing with us toward the zenith, massed in a close, wedge-shaped formation.

Above, the brilliant signals of the traffic boats flashed swiftly, clearing a wide lane for us, and then we had passed through the jam of traffic and were driving out past the incoming lines of interstellar ships at swiftly mounting speed, still holding the same formation with the massed cruisers behind us.

Behind and around us, now, flamed the great panorama of the galaxy's blazing stars, but before us lay only darkness—darkness inconceivable, into which our ships were flashing out at greater and greater speed. Neptune had vanished, and far behind lay the single yellow spark that was all visible of our solar system as we fled out from it. Out-out-out-rocketing, racing on, out past the boundaries of the great galaxy itself into the lightless void, out into the unplumbed depths of infinite space to save our threatened sun.

II

Twenty-four hours after our start I stood again in the bridgeroom, alone except for the silent, imperturbable figure of my ever-watchful wheelman, Nal Jak, staring out with him into the black gulf that lay before us. Many an hour we had stood side by side thus, scanning the interstellar spaces from our cruiser's bridgeroom, but never yet had my eyes been confronted by such a lightless void as lay before me now.

Our ship, indeed, seemed to be racing through a region where light was all but non-existent, a darkness inconceivable to anyone who had never experienced it. Behind lay the galaxy we had left, a great swarm of shining points of light, contracting slowly as we sped away from it. Toward our right, too, several misty little patches of light glowed faintly in the darkness, hardly to be seen; though these, I knew, were other galaxies or star clusters like our own—titanic conglomerations of thronging suns dimmed to those tiny flickers of light by the inconceivable depths of space which separated them from ourselves.

Except for these, though, we fled on through a cosmic gloom that was soul-shaking in its deepness and extent, an infinite darkness and stillness in which our ship seemed the only moving thing. Behind us, I knew, the formation of our fifty ships was following close on our track, each ship separated from the next by a five-hundred-mile interval and each flashing on at exactly the same speed as ourselves. But though we knew they followed, our fifty cruisers were naturally quite invisible to us, and as I gazed now into the tenebrous void ahead the loneliness of our position was overpowering.

Abruptly the door behind me snapped open, and I half turned toward it as Hurus Hol entered. He glanced at our speed dials and his brows arched in surprise.

"Good enough," he commented. "If the rest of our ships can hold this pace it will bring us to the dark star in six days."

I nodded, gazing thoughtfully ahead. "Perhaps sooner," I estimated. "The dark star is coming toward us at a tremendous velocity, remember. You will notice on the telechart . . ."

Together we stepped over to the big telechart, a great rectangular plate of smoothly burnished silvery metal which hung at the bridgeroom's end wall, the one indispensable aid to interstellar navigation. Upon it were accurately reproduced, by means of projected and reflected rays, the positions and progress of all heavenly bodies near the ship.

Intently we contemplated it now. At the rectangle's lower edge there gleamed on the smooth metal a score or more of little circles of glowing light, of varying sizes, representing the suns of the edge of the galaxy behind us. Outermost of these glowed the light disk that was our own sun, and around this Hurus Hol had drawn a shining line or circle lying more than four billion miles from our sun, on the chart. He had computed that if the approaching dark star came closer than that to our sun its mighty gravitational attraction would inevitably draw the latter out with it into space; so the shining line represented, for us, the danger line. And creeping down toward that line and toward our sun, farther up on the blank metal of the great chart, there moved a single giant circle of deepest black, an ebon disk a hundred times the diameter of our glowing little sun circle, which was sweeping down toward the galaxy's edge in a great curve.

Hurus Hol gazed thoughtfully at the sinister dark disk, and then shook his head. "There's something very strange about that dark star," he said, slowly. "That curving path it's moving in is contrary to all the laws of celestial mechanics. I wonder if—"

Before he could finish, the words were broken off in his mouth. For at that moment there came a terrific shock; our ship dipped and reeled crazily, and then was whirling blindly about as though caught and shaken by a giant hand. Dal Nara, the pilot; Hurus Hol; and I were slammed violently down toward the bridgeroom's end with the first crash, and then I clung desperately to the edge of a switchboard as we spun dizzily about. I had a flashing glimpse, through the windows, of our fifty cruisers whirling blindly about like wind-tossed straws, and in another glimpse saw two of them caught and slammed together, both ships smashing like eggshells beneath the terrific impact, their crews instantly annihilated. Then, as our own ship dipped crazily downward again, I saw Hurus Hol creeping across the floor toward the controls, and in a moment I had slid down beside him. Another instant and we had our hands on the levers, and were slowly pulling them back into position.

Caught and buffeted still by the terrific forces outside, our cruiser slowly steadied to an even keel and then leapt suddenly forward again, the forces that held us seeming to lessen swiftly as we flashed on. There came a harsh, grating sound that brought my heart to my throat as one of the cruisers was hurled past us, grazing us, and then abruptly the mighty grip that held us had suddenly disappeared and we were humming on through the same stillness and silence as before.

I slowed our flight, then, until we hung motionless, and then we gazed wildly at each other, bruised and panting. Before we could give utterance to the exclamations on our lips, though, the door snapped open and Dal Nara burst into the bridgeroom, bleeding from a cut on her forehead. "What was that?" she cried, raising a trembling hand to her head. "It caught us there like toys—and the other ships—"

Before any of us could answer her a bell beside me rang sharply and from the diaphragm beneath it came the voice of our message operator.

"Ships thirty-seven, twelve, nineteen, and forty-four reported destroyed by collisions, sir," he announced, his own voice tremulous. "The others report that they are again taking up formation behind us."

"Very well," I replied. "Order them to start again in three minutes, on Number One speed-scale."

As I turned back from the instrument I drew a deep breath. "Four ships destroyed in less than a minute," I said. "And by what?"

"By a whirlpool of ether-currents, undoubtedly," said Hurus Hol. We stared at him blankly, and he threw out a hand in quick explanation. "You know that there are currents in the ether—that was discovered ages ago—and that those currents in the galaxy have always been found to be comparatively slow and sluggish, but out here in empty space there must be currents of gigantic size and speed, and apparently we stumbled directly into a great whirlpool or maelstrom of them. We were fortunate to lose but four ships," he added soberly.

I shook my head. "I've sailed from Sirius to Rigel," I said, "and I never met anything like that. If we meet another . . ." The strangeness of our experience, in fact, had unnerved me, for even after we had tended to our bruises and were again racing on through the void, it was with a new fearfulness that I gazed ahead. At any moment, I knew, we might plunge directly into some similar or even larger maelstrom of ether-currents, yet there was no way by which we could avoid the danger. We must drive blindly ahead at full speed and trust to luck to bring us through, and now I began to understand what perils lay between us and our destination.

As hour followed hour, though, my fearfulness gradually lessened, for we encountered no more of the dread maelstroms in our onward flight. Yet as we hummed on and on and on, a new anxiety came to trouble me, for with the passing of each day we were putting behind us billions of miles of space, and were flashing nearer and nearer toward the mighty dark star that was our goal. And even as we fled on we could see, on the great telechart, the dark disk creeping down to meet us, thundering on toward the galaxy from which, unless we succeeded, it would steal a star.

Unless we succeeded! But could we succeed? Was there any force in the universe that could turn aside this oncoming dark giant in time to prevent the theft of our sun? More and more, as we sped on, there grew in my mind doubt as to our chance of success. We had gone forth on a blind, desperate venture, on a last slender chance, and now at last I began to see how slender indeed was that chance. Dal Nara felt it, too, and even Hurus Hol, I think, but we spoke no word to each other of our thoughts, standing for hours on end in the bridgeroom together, and gazing silently and broodingly out into the darkness where lay our goal.

On the sixth day of our flight we computed, by means of our telechart and flight log, that we were within less than a billion miles of the great dark star ahead, and had slackened our speed until we were barely creeping forward, attempting to locate our goal in the dense, unchanged darkness ahead.

Straining against the windows, we three gazed eagerly forward, while beside me Nal Jak, the wheelman, silently regulated the ship's speed to my orders. Minutes passed while we sped on, and still there lay before us only the deep darkness. Could it be that we had missed our way, that our calculations had been wrong?

Could it be—and then the wild speculations that had begun to rise in my mind were cut short by a low exclamation from Dal Nara, beside me. Mutely she pointed ahead.

At first I could see nothing, and then slowly became aware of a feeble glow of light in the heavens ahead, an area of strange, subdued light which stretched across the whole sky, it seemed, yet which was so dim as to be hardly visible to our straining eyes. But swiftly, as we watched it, it intensified, strengthened, taking shape as a mighty circle of pale luminescence which filled almost all the heavens ahead. I gave a low-voiced order to the pilot which reduced our speed still further, but even so the light grew visibly stronger as we sped on.

"Light!" whispered Hurus Hol. "Light on a dark star! It's impossible—and yet—"

And now, in obedience to another order, our ship began to slant sharply up toward the mighty circle's upper limb, followed by the half-hundred ships behind us. And as we lifted higher and higher the circle changed before our eyes into a sphere—a tremendous, faintly glowing sphere of size inconceivable, filling the heavens with its vast bulk, feebly luminous like the ghost of some mighty sun, rushing through space to meet us as we sped up and over it. And now at last we were over it, sweeping above it with our little fleet at a height of a half-million miles, contemplating in awed silence the titanic dimensions of the faint-glowing sphere beneath us. For in spite of our great height above it, the vast globe stretched from horizon to horizon beneath us, a single smooth, vastly curving surface, shining with the dim, unfamiliar light whose source we could not guess. It was not the light of fire, or glowing gases, for the sun below was truly a dead one, vast in size as it was. It was a cold light, a faint but steady phosphorescence like no other light I had ever seen, a feeble white glow which stretched from horizon to horizon of the mighty world beneath. Dumbfoundedly we stared down toward it, and then, at a signal to the pilot, our ship began to drop smoothly downward, trailed by our forty-odd followers behind. Down, down, we sped, slower and slower, until we suddenly started as there came from outside the ship a high-pitched hissing shriek.

"Air!" I cried. "This dark star has an atmosphere! And that light upon it—see!" And I flung a pointing hand toward the surface of the giant world below. For as we dropped swiftly down toward that world we saw at last that the faint light which illuminated it was not artificial light, or reflected light, but light inherent in itself, since all the surface of the mighty sphere glowed with the same phosphorescent light, its plains and hills and valleys alike feebly luminous, with the soft, dim luminosity of radioactive minerals. A shining world, a world glowing eternally with cold white light, a luminous, titanic sphere that rushed through the darkness of infinite space like some pale gigantic moon. And upon the surface of the glowing plains beneath us rose dense and twisted masses of dark leafless vegetation, distorted tree-growths and tangles of low shrubs that were all of deepest black in color, springing out of that glowing soil and twisting blackly and grotesquely above its feeble light, stretching away over plain and hill and valley like the monstrous landscape of some undreamed-of hell!

And now, as our ship slanted down across the surface of the glowing sphere, there gleamed ahead a deepening of that glow, a concentration of that feeble light which grew stronger as we raced on toward it. And it was a city! A city whose mighty buildings were each a truncated pyramid in shape, towering into the air for thousands upon thousands of feet, a city whose every building and street and square glowed with the same faint white light as the ground upon which they stood, a metropolis out of nightmare, the darkness of which was dispelled only by the light of its own great glowing structures and streets. Far away stretched the mass of these structures, a luminous mass which covered square mile upon square mile of the surface of this glowing world, and far beyond them there lifted into the dusky air the shining towers and pyramids of still other cities.

We straightened, trembling, turning toward each other with white faces. And then, before any could speak, Dal Nara had whirled to the window and uttered a hoarse shout. "Look!" she cried, and pointed down and outward toward the titanic, glowing buildings of the city ahead; for from their truncated summits were rising suddenly a swarm of long black shapes, a horde of long black cones which were racing straight up toward us.

I shouted an order to the pilot, and instantly our ship was turning and slanting sharply upward, while around us our cruisers sped up with us. Then, from beneath, there sped up toward us a shining little cylinder of metal which struck a cruiser racing beside our own. It exploded instantly into a great flare of blinding light, enveloping the cruiser it had struck, and then the light had vanished, while with it had vanished the ship it had enveloped. And from the cones beneath and beyond there leapt toward us other of the metal cylinders, striking our ships now by the dozens, flaring and vanishing with them in great, silent explosions of light.

"Etheric bombs!" I cried. "And our ship is the only battle cruiser—the rest have no weapons!"

I turned, cried another order, and in obedience to it our own cruiser halted suddenly and then dipped downward, racing straight into the ascending swarm of attacking cones. Down we flashed, down, down, and toward us sprang a score of the metal cylinders, grazing along our sides. And then, from the sides of our own downward-swooping ship there sprang out brilliant shafts of green light, the deadly decohesion ray of the ships of the Federation Fleet. It struck a score of the cones beneath and they flamed with green light for an instant and then flew into pieces, spilling downward in a great shower of tiny fragments as the cohesion of their particles was destroyed by the deadly ray. And now our cruiser had crashed down through the swarm of them and was driving down toward the luminous plain below, then turning and racing sharply upward again while from all the air around us the black cones swarmed to the attack.

Up, up, we sped, and now I saw that our blow had been struck in vain, for the last of our ships above were vanishing beneath the flares of the etheric bombs. One only of our cruisers remained, racing up toward the zenith in headlong flight with a score of the great cones in hot pursuit. A moment only I glimpsed this, and then we had turned once more and were again diving down upon the attacking cones, while all around us the etheric bombs filled the air with the silent, exploding flares. Again as we swooped downward our green rays cut paths of annihilation across the swarming cones beneath; and then I heard a cry from Hurus Hol, who whirled to the window and glimpsed above us a single great cone that was diving headlong down toward us in a resistless, ramming swoop. I shouted to the pilot, sprang to the controls, but was too late to ward off that deadly blow. There was a great crash at the rear of our cruiser; it spun dizzily for a moment in midair, and then was tumbling crazily downward like a falling stone toward the glowing plain a score of miles below.

III

I think now that our cruiser's mad downward plunge must have lasted for minutes, at least, yet at the time it seemed over in a single instant. I have a confused memory of the bridgeroom spinning about us as we whirled down, of myself throwing back the controls with a last, instinctive action, and then there came a ripping, rending crash, a violent shock, and I was flung into a corner of the room with terrific force.

Dazed by the swift action of the last few minutes I lay there motionless for a space of seconds, then scrambled to my feet. Hurus Hol and Dal Nara were staggering up likewise, the latter hastening at once down into the cruiser's hull, but Nal Jak, the wheelman, lay motionless against the wall, stunned by the shock. Our first act was to bring him back to consciousness by a few rough first-aid measures, and then we straightened and gazed about us.

Apparently our cruiser's keel was resting upon the ground, but was tilted over at a sharp angle, as the slant of the room's floor attested. Through the broad windows we could see that around our prostrate ship lay a thick, screening grove of black tree-growths which we had glimpsed from above, and into which we had crashed in our mad plunge downward. As I was later to learn, it was only the shock-absorbing qualities of the vegetation into which we had fallen, and my own last-minute rush to the controls, which had slowed our fall enough to save us from annihilation.

There was a buzz of excited voices from the crew in the hull beneath us, and then I turned at a sudden exclamation from Hurus Hol, to find him pointing up through the observation windows in the bridgeroom's ceiling. I glanced up, then shrank back. For high above were circling a score or more of the long black cones which had attacked us, and which were apparently surveying the landscape for some clue to our fate. I gave a sharp catch of indrawn breath as they dropped lower toward us, and we crouched with pounding hearts while they dropped lower toward us, and while they dropped nearer. Then we uttered simultaneous sighs of relief as the long shapes above suddenly drove back up toward the zenith, apparently certain of our annihilation, massing and wheeling and then speeding back toward the glowing city from which they had risen to attack us.

We rose to our feet again, and as we did so the door clicked open to admit Dal Nara. She was a bruised, disheveled figure, like the rest of us, but there was something like a grin on her face.

"That cone that rammed us shattered two of our rear vibration-projectors," she announced, "but that was all the damage. And outside of one man with a broken shoulder the crew is all right."

"Good!" I exclaimed. "It won't take long to replace the broken projectors."

She nodded. "I ordered them to put in two of the spares," she explained. "But what then?"

I considered for a moment. "None of our other cruisers escaped, did they?" I asked.

Dal Nara slowly shook her head. "I don't think so," she said. "Nearly all of them were destroyed in the first few minutes. I saw Ship Sixteen racing up in an effort to escape, heading back toward the galaxy, but there were cones hot after it and it couldn't have got away."

The quiet voice of Hurus Hol broke in upon us. "Then we alone can take back word to the Federation of what is happening here," he said. His eyes suddenly flamed. "Two things we know," he exclaimed. "We know that this dark star's curving path through space, which will bring it so fatally near to our own sun in passing, is a path contrary to all the laws of astronomical science. And we know now, too, that upon this dark star world, in those glowing cities yonder, live beings of some sort who possess, apparently, immense intelligence and power."

My eyes met his. "You mean—" I began, but he interrupted swiftly.

"I mean that in my belief the answer to this riddle lies in that glowing city yonder, and that it is there we must go to find that answer."

"But how?" I asked. "If we take the cruiser near it they'll sight us and annihilate us."

"There is another way," said Hurus Hol. "We can leave the cruiser and its crew hidden here, and approach the city on foot—get as near to it as possible—learn what we can about it."

I think that we all gasped at that suggestion, but as I quickly revolved it in my mind I saw that it was, in reality, our only chance to secure any information of value to take back to the Federation. So we adopted the idea without further discussion and swiftly laid our plans for the venture. At first it was our plan for only us three to go, but at Dal Nara's insistence we included the pilot in our party, the more quickly because I knew her to be resourceful and quick-witted.

Two hours we spent in sleep, at the suggestion of Hurus Hol, then ate a hasty meal and looked to our weapons, small projectors of the decohesion ray similar to the great ray-tubes of the cruiser. Already the ship's two shattered vibration-projectors had been replaced by new spares, and our last order was for the crew and under-officers to await our return without moving beyond the ship in any event. Then the cruiser's hull door snapped open and we four stepped outside, ready for our venture.

The sandy ground upon which we stood glowed with the feeble white light which seemed to emanate from all rock and soil on this strange world, a weird light which beat upward upon us instead of down. And in this light the twisted, alien forms of the leafless trees around us writhed upward into the dusky air, their smooth black branches tangling and intertwining far above our heads. As we paused there Hurus Hol reached down for a glowing pebble, which he examined intently for a moment.

"Radioactive," he commented. "All this glowing rock and soil." Then he straightened, glanced around, and led the way unhesitatingly through the thicket of black forest into which our ship had fallen.

Silently we followed him, in single file, across the shining soil and beneath the distorted arches of the twisted trees, until at last we emerged from the thicket and found ourselves upon the open expanse of the glowing plain. It was a weird landscape which met our eyes, a landscape of glowing plains and shallow valleys patched here and there with the sprawling thickets of black forest, a pale, luminous world whose faint light beat feebly upward into the dusky, twilight skies above. In the distance, perhaps two miles ahead, a glow of deeper light flung up against the hovering dusk from the massed buildings of the luminous city, and toward this we tramped steadily onward, over the shining plains and gullies and once over a swift little brook whose waters glowed as they raced like torrents of rushing light. Within an hour we had drawn to within a distance of five hundred feet from the outermost of the city's pyramidal buildings, and crouched in a little clump of dark tree-growths, gazing fascinatedly toward it.

The scene before us was one of unequaled interest and activity. Over the masses of huge, shining buildings were flitting great swarms of the long black cones, moving from roof to roof, while in the shining streets below them moved other hordes of active figures, the people of the city. And as our eyes took in these latter I think that we all felt something of horror, in spite of all the alien forms which we were familiar with in the thronging worlds of the galaxy. For in these creatures was no single point of resemblance to anything human, nothing which the appalled intelligence could seize upon as familiar. Imagine an upright cone of black flesh, several feet in diameter and three or more in height, supported by a dozen or more smooth long tentacles which branched from its lower end—supple, boneless octopus arms which held the cone body upright and which served both as arms and legs. And near the top of that cone trunk were the only features, the twin tiny orifices which were the ears and a single round and red-rimmed white eye, set between them. Thus were these beings in appearance, black tentacle-creatures, moving in unending swirling throngs through streets and squares and buildings of their glowing city.

Helplessly we stared upon them, from our place of concealment. To venture into sight, I knew, would be to court swift death. I turned to Hurus Hol, then started as there came from the city ahead a low, waxing sound-note, a deep, powerful tone of immense volume which sounded out over the city like the blast of a deep-pitched horn. Another note joined it, and another, until it seemed that a score of mighty horns were calling across the city, and then they died away. But as we looked now we saw that the shining streets were emptying, suddenly, that the moving swarms of black tentacle-creatures were passing into the pyramidal buildings, that the cones above were slanting down toward the roofs and coming to rest. Within a space of minutes the streets seemed entirely empty and deserted, and the only sign of activity over all the city was the hovering of a few cones that still moved restlessly above it. Astounded, we watched, and then the explanation came suddenly to me.

"It's their sleep period!" I cried. "Their night! These things must rest, must sleep, like any living thing, and as there's no night on this glowing world those horn notes must signal the beginning of their sleep period."

Hurus Hol was on his feet, his eyes suddenly kindling. "It's a chance in a thousand to get inside the city!" he exclaimed.

The next moment we were out of the shelter of our concealing trees and were racing across the stretch of ground which separated us from the city. And five minutes later we were standing in the empty, glowing streets, hugging closely the mighty sloping walls of the huge buildings along it.

At once Hurus Hol led the way directly down the street toward the heart of the city, and as we hastened on beside him he answered to my question, "We must get to the city's center. There's something there which I glimpsed from our ship, and if it's what I think . . ."

He had broken into a run, now, and as we raced together down the bare length of the great, shining avenue, I, for one, had an unreassuring presentiment of what would happen should the huge buildings around us disgorge their occupants before we could get out of the city. Then Hurus Hol had suddenly stopped short, and at a motion from him we shrank swiftly behind the corner of a pyramid's slanting walls. Across the street ahead of us were passing a half-dozen of the tentacle-creatures, gliding smoothly toward the open door of one of the great pyramids. A moment we crouched, holding our breath, and then the things had passed inside the building and the door had slid shut behind them. At once we leapt out and hastened on.

We were approaching the heart of the city, I judged, and ahead the broad, shining street we followed seemed to end in a great open space of some sort. As we sped toward it, between the towering luminous lines of buildings, a faint droning sound came to our ears from ahead, waxing louder as we hastened on. The clear space ahead was looming larger, nearer, now, and then as we raced past the last great building on the street's length we burst suddenly into view of the opening ahead and stopped, staring dumbfoundedly toward it.

It was no open plaza or square, but a pit—a shallow, circular pit not more than a hundred feet in depth but all of a mile in diameter, and we stood at the rim or edge of it. The floor was smooth and flat, and upon that floor there lay a grouped mass of hundreds of half-globes or hemispheres, each fifty feet in diameter, which were resting upon their flat bases with their curving sides uppermost. Each of these hemispheres was shining with light, but it was very different light from the feeble glow of the buildings and streets around us, an intensely brilliant blue radiance which was all but blinding to our eyes. From these massed, radiant hemispheres came the loud droning we had heard, and now we saw, at the pit's farther edge, a cylindrical little room or structure of metal which was supported several hundred feet above the pit's floor by a single slender shaft of smooth round metal, like a great birdcage. And toward this cage-structure Hurus Hol was pointing now, his eyes flashing.

"It's the switchboard of the thing!" he cried. "And these brilliant hemispheres—the unheard-of space path of this dark star—it's all clear now! All—"

He broke off, suddenly, as Nal Jak sprang back, uttering a cry and pointing upward. For the moment we had forgotten the hovering cones above the city, and now one of them was slanting swiftly downward, straight toward us.

We turned, ran back, and the next moment an etheric bomb crashed down upon the spot where we had stood, exploding silently in a great flare of light. Another bomb fell and flared, nearer, and then I turned with sudden fierce anger and aimed the little ray-projector in my hand at the hovering cone above. The brilliant little beam cut across the dark shape; the black cone hovered still for a moment, then crashed down into the street to destruction. But now, from above and beyond, other cones were slanting swiftly down toward us, while from the pyramidal buildings beside us hordes of the black tentacle-creatures were pouring out in answer to the alarm.

In a solid, resistless swarm they rushed upon us. I heard a yell of defiance from Dal Nara, beside me, the hiss of our rays as they clove through the black masses in terrible destruction, and then they were upon us. A single moment we whirled about in a wild melee of men and cone-creatures, of striking human arms and coiling tentacles; then there was a shout of warning from one of my friends, something hard descended upon my head with crushing force, and all went black before me.

IV

Faint light was filtering through my eyelids when I came back to consciousness. As I opened them I sat weakly up, then fell back. Dazedly I gazed about me. I was lying in a small, square room lit only by its own glowing walls and floor and ceiling, a room whose one side slanted steeply upward and inward, pierced by a small barred window that was the only opening. Opposite me I discerned a low door of metal bars, or grating, beyond which lay a long, glowing-walled corridor. Then all these things were suddenly blotted out by the anxious face of Hurus Hol, bending down toward me.

"You're awake!" he exclaimed, his face alight. "You know me, Ran Rarak?"

For answer I struggled again to a sitting position, aided by the arm of Dal Nara, who had appeared beside me. I felt strangely weak, exhausted, my head throbbing with racing fires.

"Where are we?" I asked, at last. "The fight in the city—I remember that—but where are we now? And where's Nal Jak?"

The eyes of my two friends met and glanced away, while I looked anxiously toward them. Then Hurus Hol spoke slowly.

"We are imprisoned in this little room in one of the great pyramids of the glowing city," he said. "And in this room you have lain for weeks, Ran Rarak."

"Weeks?" I gasped, and he nodded. "It's been almost ten weeks since we were captured there in the city outside," he said, "and for all that time you've lain here out of your head from that blow you received, sometimes delirious and raving, sometimes completely unconscious. And in all that time this dark star, this world, has been plunging on through space toward our galaxy, and our sun, and the theft and doom of that sun. Ten more days and it passes our sun, stealing it from the galaxy. And I, who have learned at last what forces are behind it all, lie prisoned here.

"It was after we four were brought to this cell, after our capture, that I was summoned before our captors, before a council of those strange tentacle-creatures which was made up, I think, of their own scientists. They examined me, my clothing, all about me, then sought to communicate with me. They did not speak—communicating with each other by telepathy—but they strove to enter into communication with me by a projection of pictures on a smooth wall, pictures of their dark star world, pictures of our own galaxy, our own sun—picture after picture, until at last I began to understand the drift of them, the history and the purpose of these strange beings and their stranger world.

"For ages, I learned, for countless eons,

their mighty sun had flashed through the infinities of space, alone except for its numerous planets upon which had risen these races of tentacle-creatures. Their sun was flaming with life, then, and on their circling planets they had attained to immense science, immense power, as their system rolled on, a single wandering star, through the depths of uncharted space. But as the slow eons passed, the mighty sun began to cool, and their planets to grow colder and colder. At last it had cooled so far that to revive its dying fires they dislodged one of their own planets from its orbit and sent it crashing into their sun, feeding its waning flames. And when more centuries had passed and it was again cooling they followed the same course, sending another planet into it, and so on through the ages, staving off the death of their sun by sacrificing their worlds, until at last but one planet was left to them. And still their sun was cooling, darkening, dying. For further ages, though, they managed to preserve a precarious existence on their single planet by means of artificial heat production, until at last their great sun had cooled and solidified to such a point that life was possible upon its dark, dead surface. That surface, because of the solidified radioactive elements in it, shone always with pale light, and to it the races of the tentacle-creatures now moved. By means of great air-current projectors they transferred the atmosphere of their planet to the dark star itself and then cast loose their planet to wander off into space by itself, for its orbit had become erratic and they feared that it would crash into their own great dark star world, about which it had revolved. But on the warm, shining surface of the great dark star they now spread out and multiplied, raising their cities from its glowing rock and clinging to its surface as it hurtled on and on and on through the dark infinities of trackless space.

"But at last, after further ages of such existence, the tentacle-races saw that again they were menaced with extinction, since in obedience to the inexorable laws of nature their dark star was cooling still further, the molten fires at its center which warmed its surface gradually dying down, while that surface became colder and colder. In a little while, they knew, the fires at its center would be completely dead, and their great world would be a bitter, frozen waste, unless they devised some plan by which to keep warm its surface.

"At this moment their astronomers came forward with the announcement that their dark-star world, plunging on through empty space, would soon pass a great star cluster or galaxy of suns at a distance of some fifteen billion miles. They could not invade the worlds of this galaxy, they knew, for they had discovered that upon those worlds lived countless trillions of intelligent inhabitants who would be able to repel their own invasion, if they attempted it. There was but one expedient left, therefore, and that was to attempt to jerk a sun out of this galaxy as they passed by it, to steal a star from it to take out with them into space, which would revolve around their own mighty dark world and supply it with the heat they needed.

"The sun which they fixed on to steal was one at the galaxy's very edge, our own sun. If they passed this at fifteen billion miles, as their course then would cause them to do, they could do nothing. But if they could change their dark star's course, could curve inward to pass this sun at some three billion miles instead of fifteen, then the powerful gravitational grip of their own gigantic world would grasp this sun and carry it out with it into space. The sun's planets, too, would be carried out, but these they planned to crash into the fires of the sun itself, to increase its size and splendor. All that was needed, therefore, was some method of curving their world's course inward, and for this they had recourse to the great gravity condensers which they had already used to shift their own planets.

"You know that it is gravitational force alone which keeps the suns and planets to their courses, and you know that the gravitational force of any body, sun or planet, is radiated out from it in all directions, tending to pull all things toward that body. In the same way there is radiated outward perpetually from the galaxy that combined attractive gravitational force of all its swarming suns, and a tiny fraction of this outward-radiating force, of course, struck the dark star, pulling it weakly toward the galaxy. If more of that outward-radiating force could strike the dark star, it would be pulled toward the galaxy with more power, would be pulled nearer toward the galaxy's edge, as it passed.

"It was just that which their gravity condenser accomplished. In a low pit at the heart of one of their cities—this city, in fact—they placed the condenser, a mass of brilliant hemispherical ray-attracters which caused more of the galaxy's outward-shooting attractive force to fall upon the dark star, thereby pulling the dark star inward toward the galaxy's edge in a great curve. When they reached a distance of three billion miles from the galaxy's edge they planned to turn off the great condenser, and their dark star would then shoot past the galaxy's edge, jerking out our sun with it, from that edge, by its own terrific gravitational grip. If the condenser were turned off before they came that close, however, they would pass the sun at a distance too far to pull it out with them, and would then speed on out into space alone, toward the freezing of their world and their own extinction. For that reason the condenser, and the great cage-switch of the condenser, were guarded always by hovering cones, to prevent its being turned off before the right moment.

"Since then they have kept the great gravity condenser in unceasing operation, and their dark star has swept in toward the galaxy's edge in a great curve. Back in our own solar system I saw and understood what would be the result of that inward curve, and so we came here—and were captured. And in those weeks since we were captured, while you have lain here unconscious and raving, this dark star has been plunging nearer and nearer toward our galaxy and toward our sun. Ten more days and it passes that sun, carrying it out with it into the darkness of boundless space, unless the great condenser is turned off before then. Ten more days, and we lie here, powerless to warn any of what forces work toward the doom of our sun!"

There was a long silence when Hurus Hol's voice had ceased—a whispering, brain-crushing silence which I broke at last with a single question.

"But Nal Jak . . . ?" I asked, and the faces of my two companions became suddenly strange, while Dal Nara turned away. At last Hurus Hol spoke.

"It was after the tentacle-scientists had examined me," he said gently, "that they brought Nal Jak down to examine. I think that they spared me for the time being because of my apparently greater knowledge, but Nal Jak they—vivisected."

There was a longer hush than before, one in which the brave, quiet figure of the wheel-man, a companion in all my service with the fleet, seemed to rise before my suddenly blurring eyes. Then abruptly I swung down from the narrow bunk on which I lay, clutched dizzily at my companions for support, and walked unsteadily to the square, barred little window. Outside and beneath me lay the city of the dark-star people, a mighty mass of pyramidal, glowing buildings, streets thronged with their dark, gliding figures, above them the swarms of the racing cones. From our little window the glowing wall of the great pyramid which held us slanted steeply down for fully five hundred feet, and upward above us for twice that distance. And as I raised my eyes upward I saw, clear and bright above, a great, far-flung field of stars—the stars of our own galaxy toward which this world was plunging. And burning out clearest among these the star that was nearest of all, the shining yellow star that was our own sun.

I think now that it was the sight of that yellow star, largening steadily as our dark star swept on toward it, which filled us with such utter despair in the hours, the days, that followed. Out beyond the city our cruiser lay hidden in the black forest, we knew, and could we escape we might yet carry word back to the Federation of what was at hand, but escape was impossible. And so, through the long days, days measurable only by our own time-dials, we waxed deeper into an apathy of dull despair.

Rapidly my strength came back to me, though the strange food supplied us once a day by our captors was almost uneatable. But as the days fled by, my spirits sank lower and lower, and less and less we spoke to each other as the doom of our sun approached, the only change in anything around us being the moment each twenty-four hours when the signal-horns called across the city, summoning the hordes in its streets to their four-hour sleep period. At last, though, we woke suddenly to realization of the fact that nine days had passed since my awakening, and that upon the next day the dark star would be plunging past the burning yellow star above us and jerking it into its grip. Then, at last, all our apathy dropped from us, and we raged against the walls of our cells with insensate fury. And then, with startling abruptness, came the means of our deliverance.

For hours there had been a busy clanging of tools and machines somewhere in the great building above us, and numbers of the tentacle-creatures had been passing our barred door carrying tools and instruments toward some work being carried out overhead. We had come to pay but little attention to them, in time, but as one passed there came a sudden rattle and clang from outside, and turning to the door we saw that one of the passing creatures had dropped a thick coil of slender metal chain upon the floor and had passed on without noticing his loss.

In an instant we were at the door and reaching through its bars toward the coil, but though we each strained our arms in turn toward it the thing lay a few tantalizing inches beyond our grasp. A moment we surveyed it, baffled, fearing the return at any moment of the creature who had dropped it, and then Dal Nara, with a sudden inspiration, lay flat upon the floor, thrusting her leg out through the grating. In a moment she had caught the coil with her foot, and in another moment we had it inside, examining it.

We found that though it was as slender as my smallest finger the chain was of incredible strength, and when we roughly estimated the extent of its thick-coiled length we discovered that it would be more than long enough to reach from our window to the street below. At once, therefore, we secreted the thing in a corner of the room and impatiently awaited the sleep period, when we could work without fear of interruption.

At last, after what seemed measureless hours of waiting, the great horns blared forth across the city outside, and swiftly its streets emptied, the sounds in our building quieting until all was silence, except for the humming of a few watchful cones above the great condenser, and the deep droning of the condenser itself in the distance. At once we set to work at the bars of our window.

Frantically we chipped at the rock at the base of one of the metal bars, using the few odd bits of metal at our command, but at the end of two hours had done no more than scratch away a bare inch of the glowing stone. Another hour and we had laid bare from the rock the lower end of the bar, but now we knew that within minutes the sleep period of the city outside would be ending, and into the streets would be swarming its gliding throngs, making impossible all attempts at escape. Furiously we worked, dripping now with sweat, until at last when our time-dials showed that less than half an hour remained to us I gave over the chipping at the rock and wrapped our chain firmly around the lower end of the bar we had loosened. Then stepping back into the cell and bracing ourselves against the wall below the window, we pulled backward with all our strength.

A tense moment we strained thus, the thick bar holding fast, and then abruptly it gave and fell from its socket in the wall to the floor, with a loud, ringing clang. We lay in a heap on the floor, panting and listening for any sound of alarm, then rose and swiftly fastened the chain's end to one of the remaining bars. The chain itself we dropped out of the window, watching it uncoil its length down the mighty building's glowing side until its end trailed on the empty glowing street far below. At once I motioned Hurus Hol to the window, and in a moment he had squeezed through its bars and was sliding slowly down the chain, hand under hand. Before he was ten feet down Dal Nara was out and creeping downward likewise, and then I too squeezed through the window and followed them, downward, the three of us crawling down the chain along the huge building's steeply sloping side like three flies.

I was ten feet down from the window, now, twenty feet, and glanced down toward the glowing, empty street, five hundred feet below, and seeming five thousand. Then, at a sudden sound from above me, I looked sharply up, and as I did so the most sickening sensation of fear I had ever experienced swept over me. For at the window we had just left, twenty feet above me, one of the tentacle-creatures was leaning out, brought to our cell, I doubted not, by the metal bar's ringing fall, his white, red-rimmed eye turned full upon me.

I heard sighs of horror from my two companions beneath me, and for a single moment we hung motionless along the chain's length, swinging along the huge pyramid's glowing side at a height of hundreds of feet above the shining streets below. Then the creature raised one of its tentacles, a metal tool in its grasp, which he brought down in a sharp blow on the chain at the window's edge. Again he repeated the blow, and again.

He was cutting the chain!

V

For a space of seconds I hung motionless there, and then as the tool in the grasp of the creature above came down on the chain in another sharp blow the sound galvanized me into sudden action.

"Slide on down!" I cried. They didn't, however, but followed me up the chain, though Dal Nara and I alone came to grips with the horrible dead-star creature. I gripped the links with frantic hands, pulling myself upward toward the window and the creature at the window, twenty feet above me.

Three times the tool in his hand came down upon the chain while I struggled up toward him, and each time I expected the strand to sever and send us down to death, but the hard metal withstood the blows for the moment, and before he could strike at it again I was up to the level of the window and reaching up toward him.

As I did so, swift black tentacles thrust out and gripped Dal Nara and me, while another of the snaky arms swept up with the tool in its grasp for a blow on my head. Before it could fall, though, I had reached out with my right hand, holding to the chain with my left, and had grasped the body of the thing inside the window, pulling him outside before he had time to resist. As I did so my own hold slipped a little, so that we hung a few feet below the window, both clinging to the slender chain and both striking futilely at each other, he with the metal tool and I with my clenched fist.

A moment we hung there, swaying hundreds of feet above the luminous stone street, and then the creature's tentacle coiled swiftly around my neck, tightening, choking me.

Hanging precariously to our slender strand with one hand I struck out blindly with the other, but felt consciousness leaving me as that remorseless grip tightened. Then with a last effort I gripped the chain firmly with both hands, doubled my feet under me, and kicked out with all my strength. The kick caught the cone-body of my opponent squarely, tearing him loose from his own hold on the chain, and then there was a sudden wrench at my neck and I was free of him, while beneath Dal Nara and I glimpsed his dark body whirling down toward the street below, twisting and turning in its fall along the building's slanting side and then crashing finally down upon the smooth, shining street below, where it lay a black little huddled mass.

Hanging there I looked down, panting, and saw that Hurus Hol had reached the chain's bottom and was standing in the empty street, awaiting us. Glancing up I saw that the blows of the creature I had fought had half severed one of the links above me, but there was no time to readjust it; so with a prayer that it might hold a few moments longer Dal Nara and I began our slipping, sliding progress downward.

The sharp links tore our hands cruelly as we slid downward, and once it seemed to me that the chain gave a little beneath our weight. Apprehensively I looked upward, then down to where Hurus Hol was waving encouragement. Down, down we slid, not daring to look beneath again, not knowing how near we might be to the bottom. Then there was another slight give in the chain, a sudden grating catch, and abruptly the weakened link above snapped and we dropped headlong downward ten feet into the arms of Hurus Hol.

A moment we sprawled in a little heap there on the glowing street and then staggered to our feet. "Out of the city!" cried Hurus Hol. "We could never get to the condenser switch on foot—but in the cruiser there's a chance. And we have but a few minutes now before the sleep period ends!"

Down the broad street we ran, now, through squares and avenues of glowing, mighty pyramids, crouching down once as the ever-hovering cones swept by above, and then racing on. At any moment, I knew, the great horns might blare across the city, bringing its swarming thousands into its streets, and our only chance was to win free of it before that happened. At last we were speeding down the street by which we had entered the city, and before us lay that street's end, with beyond it the vista of black forest and glowing plain over which we had come. And now we were racing over that glowing plain, a quarter-mile, a half, a mile. . . .

Abruptly from far behind came the calling, crescendo notes of the mighty horns, marking the sleep period's end, bringing back into the streets the city's tentacle-people. It could be but moments now, we knew, before our escape was discovered, and as we panted on at our highest speed we listened for the sounding of the alarm behind us.

It came! When we had drawn to within a half-mile of the black forest where our cruiser lay hidden, another great tumult of horn notes burst out over the glowing city behind, high and shrill and raging. And glancing back we saw swarms of the black cones rising from the pyramidal buildings' summits, circling, searching, speeding out over the glowing plains around the city, a compact mass of them racing straight toward us.

"On!" cried Hurus Hol. "It's our last chance to get to the cruiser!"

Staggering, stumbling, with the last of our strength we sped on, over the glowing soil and rocks, toward the rim of the black forest which lay now a scant quarter-mile ahead. Then suddenly Hurus Hol stumbled, tripped, and fell. I halted, turned toward him, then turned again as Dal Nara shouted thickly and pointed upward. We had been sighted by the speeding cones above and two of them were driving straight down toward us.

A moment we stood there, rigid, while the great cones dipped toward us, waiting for the death that would crash down upon us from them. Then suddenly a great dark shape loomed in the air above and behind us, from which sprang out swift shafts of brilliant green light, the dazzling de-cohesion ray, striking the two swooping cones and sending them down in twin torrents of shattered wreckage. And now the mighty bulk behind us swept swiftly down upon us, and we saw that it was our cruiser.

Smoothly it shot down to the ground, and we stumbled to its side, through the waiting open door. As I staggered up to the bridgeroom the third officer was shouting in my ear. "We sighted you from the forest," he was crying. "Came out in the cruiser to get you—"

But now I was in the bridgeroom, brushing the wheelman from the controls, sending our ship slanting sharply up toward the zenith. Hurus Hol was at my side, now, pointing toward the great telechart and shouting something in my ear. I glanced over, and my heart stood still. For the great dark disk on the chart had swept down to within an inch of the shining line around our sun circle, the danger line.

"The condenser!" I shouted. "We must get to that switch—turn it off! It's our only chance!"

We were racing through the air toward the luminous city, now, and ahead a mighty swarm of the cones was gathering and forming to meet us, while from behind and from each side came other swarms, driving on toward us. Then the door clicked open and Dal Nara burst into the bridgeroom.

"The ship's ray-tubes are useless!" she cried. "They've used the last charge in the ray-tanks!"

At the cry the controls quivered under my hands, the ship slowed, stopped. Silence filled the bridgeroom, filled all the cruiser, the last silence of despair. We had failed. Weaponless our ship hung there, motionless, while toward it from all directions leaped the swift and swarming cones, in dozens, in scores, in hundreds, leaping toward us, long black messengers of death, while on the great telechart the mighty dark star leapt closer toward the shining circle that was our sun, toward the fateful line around it. We had failed, and death was upon us.

And now the black swarms of the cones

were very near us, and were slowing a little, as though fearing some ruse on our part, were slowing but moving closer, closer, while we awaited them in a last utter stupor of despair. Closer they came, closer, closer. . . .

A ringing, exultant cry suddenly sounded from somewhere in the cruiser beneath me, taken up by a sudden babel of voices, and then Dal Nara cried out hoarsely, beside me, and pointed up through our upper observation windows toward a long, shining, slender shape that was driving down toward us out of the upper air, while behind it drove a vast swarm of other and larger shapes, long and black and mighty.

"It's our own ship!" Dal Nara was shouting, insanely. "It's Ship Sixteen! They escaped, got back to the galaxy—and look there, behind them—it's the fleet, the Federation fleet!"

There was a wild singing of blood in my ears as I looked up, saw the mighty swarm of black shapes that were speeding down upon us behind the shining cruiser, the five thousand mighty battle cruisers of the Federation fleet.

The fleet! The massed fighting ships of the galaxy, cruisers from Antares and Sirius and Regulus and Spica, the keepers of the Milky Way patrol, the picked fighters of a universe! Ships with which I had cruised from Arcturus to Deneb, beside which I had battled in many an interstellar fight. The fleet! They were straightening, wheeling, hovering, high above us, and then they were driving down upon the massed swarms of cones around us in one titanic, simultaneous swoop.

Then around us the air flashed brilliant with green rays and bursting flares, as de-cohesion rays and etheric bombs crashed and burst from ship to ship. Weaponless our cruiser hung there, at the center of that gigantic battle, while around us the mighty cruisers of the galaxy and the long black cones of the tentacle-people crashed and whirled and flared, swooping and dipping and racing upon each other, whirling down to the glowing world below in scores of shattered wrecks, vanishing in silent flares of blinding light. From far away across the surface of the luminous world beneath, the great swarms of cones drove on toward the battle, from the shining towers of cities far away, racing fearlessly to the attack, sinking and falling and crumbling beneath the terrible rays of the leaping ships above, ramming and crashing with them to the ground in sacrificial plunges. But swiftly, now, the cones were vanishing beneath the brilliant rays.

Then Hurus Hol was at my side, shouting and pointing down toward the glowing city below. "The condenser!" he cried, pointing to where its blue radiance still flared on. "The dark star—look!" He flung a hand toward the telechart, where the dark star disk was but a scant half-inch from the shining line around our sun circle, a tiny gap that was swiftly closing. I glanced toward the battle that raged around us, where the Federation cruisers were sending the cones down to destruction by swarms, now, but unheeding of the condenser below. A bare half-mile beneath us lay that condenser, and its cage-pillar switch, which a single shaft of the green ray would have destroyed instantly. And our ray-tubes were useless!

The wild resolve flared up in my brain and I slammed down the levers in my hands, sent our ship racing down toward the condenser and its upheld cage like a released thunderbolt of hurtling metal. "Hold tight!" I screamed as we thundered down. "I'm going to ram the switch!"

And now up toward us were rushing the brilliant blue hemispheres of the pit, the great pillar and upheld cage beside them, toward which we flashed with the speed of lightning. Crash!—and a tremendous shock shook the cruiser from stem to stern as its prow tore through the upheld metal cage, ripping it from its supporting pillar and sending it crashing to the ground. Our cruiser spun, hovered for a moment as though to whirl down to destruction, then steadied, while we at the window gazed downward, shouting.

For beneath us the blinding radiance of the massed hemispheres had suddenly snapped out! Around and above us the great battle had died, the last of the cones tumbling to the ground beneath the rays of the mighty fleet, and now we turned swiftly to the telechart. Tensely we scanned it. Upon it the great dark-star disk was creeping still toward the line around our sun circle, creeping slower and slower toward it but still moving on, on, on. . . . Had we lost, at the last moment? Now the black disk, hardly moving, was all but touching the shining line, separated from it by only a hairsbreadth gap. A single moment we watched while it hovered thus, a moment in which was settled the destiny of a sun. And then a babel of incoherent cries came from our lips. For the tiny gap was widening!

The black disk was moving back, was curving outward again from our sun and from the galaxy's edge, curving out once more into the blank depths of space whence it had come, without the star it had planned to steal. Out, out, out—and we knew, at last, that we had won.

And the mighty fleet of ships around us knew, from their own charts. They were massing around us and hanging motionless while beneath us the palely glowing gigantic dark star swept on, out into the darkness of trackless space until it hung like a titanic feeble moon in the heavens before us, retreating farther and farther from the shining stars of our galaxy, carrying with it the glowing cities and the hordes of the tentacle-peoples, never to return. There in the bridgeroom, with our massed ships around us, we three watched it go, then turned back toward our own yellow star, serene and far and benignant, that yellow star around which swung our own eight little worlds. And then Dal Nara flung out a hand toward it, half weeping now.

"The sun!" she cried. "The sun! The good old sun, that we fought for and saved! Our sun, till the end of time!"

VI

It was on a night a week later that Dal Nara and I said farewell to Hurus Hol, standing on the roof of that same great building on Neptune from which we had started with our fifty cruisers weeks before. We had learned, in that week, how the only survivor of those cruisers, Ship 16, had managed to shake off the pursuing cones in that first fierce attack and had sped back to the galaxy to give the alarm, of how the mighty Federation fleet had raced through the galaxy from beyond Antares in answer to that alarm, speeding out toward the approaching dark star and reaching it just in time to save our own ship, and our sun.

The other events of that week, the honors which had been loaded upon us, I shall not attempt to describe. There was little in the solar system which we three could not have had for the asking, but Hurus Hol was content to follow the science that was his lifework, while Dal Nara, after the manner of her sex through all the ages, sought a beauty parlor, and I asked only to continue with our cruiser in the service of the Federation fleet. The solar system was home to us, would always be home to us, but never, I knew, would either of us be able to break away from the fascination of the great fleet's interstellar patrol, the flashing from sun to sun, the long silent hours in cosmic night and stellar glare. We would be star-rovers, she and I, until the end.

So now, ready to rejoin the fleet, I stood on the great building's roof, the mighty black bulk of our cruiser behind us and the stupendous canopy of the galaxy's glittering suns over our heads. In the streets below, too, were other lights, brilliant flares, where thronging crowds still celebrated the escape of their worlds. And now Hurus Hol was speaking, more moved than ever I had seen him.

"If Nal Jak were here—" he said, and we were all silent for a moment. Then his hand came out toward us and silently we wrung it, turning toward the cruiser's door.

As it slammed shut behind us we were ascending to the bridgeroom, and from there we glimpsed now the great roof dropping away beneath us as we slanted up from it once more, the dark figure of Hurus Hol outlined for a moment at its edge against the lights below, then vanishing. And the world beneath us was shrinking, vanishing once more, until at last of all the solar system behind us there was visible only the single yellow spark that was our sun. Then about our outward-racing cruiser was darkness, the infinite void's eternal night— night and the unchanging, glittering hosts of wheeling, flaming stars.

The Conquest of Gola

LESLIE F. STONE

Leslie Francis Stone (1905–1991) was a US writer of science fiction who began publishing fiction as early as 1920 but published her first science fiction tale, "Men with Wings," for *Air Wonder Stories*, in only 1929; she remained active in the field for the next decade, publishing about twenty stories. Stone's first name, which she was given at birth, caused her to be mentioned by Isaac Asimov, Frederik Pohl, and others as one of the early women science fiction writers who disguised their sex because of pulp science fiction's male readership; she was, in fact, always known and recognized as female. Next to C. L. Moore, she was considered one of the most successful female writers of that time. Her last science fiction story, "Gravity Off," was published in a 1940 issue of *Future Fiction*.

Her two science fiction books are *When the Sun Went Out* (1929), a far-future tale that appeared in Hugo Gernsback's *Science Fiction Series*, and the Void sequence, comprising *Out of the Void* (*Amazing Stories*, 1929), a space opera set partially on the ninth planet Abrui, inhabited by various alien races, some of them telepaths, and featuring adventures in a planetary romance style; and a novel-length sequel, *Across the Void* (*Amazing Stories*, April–June 1931), was a fantastic-voyage tale, ending in the Alpha Centauri system.

Stone remains best known for "The Conquest of Gola" (*Wonder Stories*, 1931), in which the women who govern "Gola" (Venus) spurn the capitalist lures of intruding men from "Detaxal" (Earth), and later dismiss the Earthlings' attempts at actual invasion; the feminism of the story is an early and explicit example in pulp science fiction. The story is particularly interesting because it is told from the point of view of the alien—and an alien completely different physically from human beings. It is thus also one of the earliest stories to provide a truly unique and nonhumanoid view of intelligent alien life-forms.

THE CONQUEST OF GOLA

Leslie F. Stone

Hola my daughters (sighed the Matriarch), it is true indeed,

I am the only living one upon Gola who remembers the invasion from Detaxal. I alone of all my generation survive to recall vividly the sights and scenes of that past era. And well it is that you come to me to hear by free communication of mind to mind, face-to-face with each other.

Ah, well I remember the surprise of that hour when through the mists that enshroud our lovely world, there swam the first of the great smooth cylinders of the Detaxalans, fifty tas in length, as glistening and silvery as the soil of our land, propelled by the man-things that on Detaxal are supreme even as we women are supreme on Gola.

In those bygone days, as now, Gola was enwrapped by her cloud mists that keep from us the terrific glare of the great star that glows like a malignant spirit out there in the darkness of the void. Only occasionally when a particularly great storm parts the mist of heaven do we see the wonders of the vast universe, but that does not prevent us, with our marvelous telescopes handed down to us from thousands of generations before us, from learning what lies across the dark seas of the outside.

Therefore we knew of the nine planets that encircle the great star and are subject to its rule. And so are we familiar enough with the surfaces of these planets to know why Gola should appear as a haven to their inhabitants who see in our cloud-enclosed mantle a sweet release from the blasting heat and blinding glare of the great sun.

So it was not strange at all to us to find that the people of Detaxal, the third planet of the sun, had arrived on our globe with a wish in their hearts to migrate here, and end their days out of reach of the blistering warmth that had come to be their lot on their own world.

Long ago we, too, might have gone on exploring expeditions to other worlds, other universes, but for what? Are we not happy here? We who have attained the greatest of civilizations within the confines of our own silvery world. Powerfully strong with our mighty force rays, we could subjugate all the universe, but why?

Are we not content with life as it is, with our lovely cities, our homes, our daughters, our gentle consorts? Why spend physical energy in combative strife for something we do not wish, when our mental processes carry us further and beyond the conquest of mere terrestrial exploitation?

On Detaxal it is different, for there the peoples, the ignoble male creatures, breed for physical prowess, leaving the development of their sciences, their philosophies, and the contemplation of the abstract to a chosen few. The greater part of the race faces forth to conquer, to lay waste, to struggle and fight as the animals do over a morsel of worthless territory. Of course we can see why they desired Gola with all its treasures, but we can thank Providence and ourselves that they did not succeed in "commercializing" us as they have the remainder of the universe with their ignoble Federation.

Ah yes, well I recall the hour when first they came, pushing cautiously through the cloud mists, seeking that which lay beneath. We of Gola were unwarned until the two cylinders hung directly above Tola, the greatest city of that time, which still lies in its ruins since that memorable day. But they have paid for it—paid for it well in thousands and tens of thousands of their men.

We were first apprised of their coming when the alarm from Tola was sent from the great beam station there, advising all to stand in readiness for an emergency. Geble, my mother, was then queen of all Gola, and I was by her side in Morka, that pleasant seaside resort, where I shall soon travel to partake of its rejuvenating waters.

With us were four of Geble's consorts, sweet gentle males that gave Geble much pleasure in those free hours away from the worries of state. But when the word of the strangers' descent over our home city, Tola, came to us, all else was forgotten. With me at her side, Geble hastened to the beam station and there in the matter transmitter we dispatched our physical beings to the palace at Tola, and the next moment were staring upward at the two strange shapes etched against the clouds.

What the Detaxalan ships were waiting for we did not know then, but later we learned. Not grasping the meaning of our beam stations, the commanders of the ships considered the city below them entirely lacking in means of defense, and were conferring on the method of taking it without bloodshed on either side.

It was not long after our arrival in Tola that the first of the ships began to descend toward the great square before the palace. Geble watched without a word, her great mind already scanning the brains of those whom she found within the great machine. She transferred to my mind but a single thought as I stood there at her side, and that with a sneer: "Barbarians!"

Now the ship was settling in the square and after a few moments of hesitation, a circular doorway appeared at the side and four of the Detaxalans came through the opening. The square was empty but for themselves and their flyer, and we saw them looking about surveying the beautiful buildings on all sides. They seemed to recognize the palace for what it was and in one accord moved in our direction.

Then Geble left the window at which we stood and strode to the doorway opening upon the balcony that faced the square. The Detaxalans halted in their tracks when they saw her slender graceful form appear and removing the strange coverings they wore on their heads they each made a bow.

Again Geble sneered, for only the male-things of our world bow their heads, and so she recognized these visitors for what they were, nothing more than the despicable males of the species! And what creatures they were!

Imagine a short, almost flat body set high upon two slender legs, the body tapering in the middle, several times as broad across as it is through the center, with two arms almost as long as the legs attached to the upper part of the torso. A small columnlike neck of only a few inches divides the head of oval shape from the body, and in this head only are set the organs of sight, hearing, and scent. Their bodies were like a patchwork of a misguided nature.

Yes, strange as it is, my daughters, practically all of the creature's faculties had their base in the small ungainly head, and each organ was perforce pressed into serving for several functions. For instance, the breathing nostrils also served for scenting out odors, nor was this organ able to exclude any disagreeable odors that might come its way, but had to dispense to the brain both pleasant and unpleasant odors at the same time.

Then there was the mouth, set directly beneath the nose, and here again we had an example of one organ doing the work of two, for the creature not only used the mouth to take in the food for its body, but it also used the mouth to enunciate the excruciatingly ugly sounds of its language.

Never before have I seen such a poorly organized body, so unlike our own highly developed organisms. How much nicer it is to be able to call forth any organ at will, and dispense with it when its usefulness is over! Instead these poor Detaxalans had to carry theirs about in physical being all the time so that always was the surface of their bodies entirely marred.

Yet that was not the only part of their ugliness, and proof of the lowliness of their origin, for whereas our fine bodies support themselves by muscular development, these poor creatures were dependent entirely upon a strange structure to keep them in their proper shape.

Imagine if you can a bony skeleton somewhat like the foundations upon which we build our edifices, laying stone and cement over the steel framework. But this skeleton instead is inside a body which the flesh, muscle, and skin overlay. Everywhere in their bodies are these cartilaginous structures—hard, heavy, bony structures developed by the chemicals of the being for its use. Even the hands, feet, and head of the creatures were underlaid with these bones—ugh, it was terrible when we dissected one of the fellows for study. I shudder to think of it.

Yet again there was still another feature of the Detaxalans that was equally as horrifying as the rest, namely their outer covering. As we viewed them for the first time out there in the square we discovered that parts of the body, that is the part of the head which they called the face, and the bony hands were entirely naked without any sort of covering, neither fur nor feathers, just the raw, pinkish-brown skin looking as if it had been recently plucked.

Later we found a few specimens that had a type of fur on the lower part of the face, but these were rare. And when they doffed the head coverings which we had first taken for some sort of natural covering, we saw that the top of the head was overlaid with a very fine fuzz of fur several inches long.

We did not know in the beginning that the strange covering on the bodies of the four men, green in color, was not a natural growth, but later discovered that such was the truth, and not only the face and hands were bare of fur,

but the entire body, except for a fine sprinkling of hair that was scarcely visible except on the chest, was also bare. No wonder the poor things covered themselves with their awkward clothing. We arrived at the conclusion that their lack of fur had been brought about by the fact that always they had been exposed to the bright rays of the sun so that without the dampness of our own planet the fur had dried up and fallen away from the flesh!

Now thinking it over I suppose that we of Gola presented strange forms to the people of Detaxal with our fine circular bodies, rounded at the top, our short beautiful lower limbs with the circular foot pads, and our short round arms and hand pads, flexible and muscular like rubber.

But how envious they must have been of our beautiful golden coats, our movable eyes, our power to scent, hear, and touch with any part of the body, to absorb food and drink through any part of the body most convenient to us at any time. Oh yes, laugh though you may, without a doubt we were also freaks to those freakish Detaxalans. But no matter, let us return to the tale.

On recognizing our visitors for what they were, simple-minded males, Geble was chagrined at them for taking up her time, but they were strangers to our world and we Golans are always courteous. Geble began of course to try to communicate by thought transference, but strangely enough the fellows below did not catch a single thought. Instead, entirely unaware of Geble's overture to friendship, the leader commenced to speak to her in a most outlandish manner, contorting the red lips of his mouth into various uncouth shapes and making sounds that fell upon our hearing so unpleasantly that we immediately closed our senses to them. And without a word Geble turned her back upon them, calling for Tanka, her personal secretary.

Tanka was instructed to welcome the Detaxalans while she herself turned to her own chambers to summon a half dozen of her council. When the council arrived she began to discuss with them the problem of extracting more of the precious tenix from the waters of the great inland lake of Notauch. Nothing whatever was said of the advent of the Detaxalans, for Geble had dismissed them from her mind as creatures not worthy of her thought.

In the meantime Tanka had gone forth to meet the four who of course could not converse with her. In accordance with the queen's orders she led them indoors to the most informal receiving chamber and there had them served with food and drink which by the looks of the remains in the dishes they did not relish at all.

Leading them through the rooms of the lower floor of the palace she made a pretense of showing them everything which they duly surveyed. But they appeared to chafe at the manner in which they were being entertained.

The creatures even made an attempt through the primitive method of conversing by their arms to learn something of what they had seen, but Tanka was as supercilious as her mistress. When she thought they had had enough, she led them to the square and back to the door of their flyer, giving them their dismissal.

But the men were not ready to accept it. Instead they tried to express to Tanka their desire to meet the ruling head of Gola. Although their hand motions were perfectly inane and incomprehensible, Tanka could read what passed through their brains, and understood more fully than they what lay in their minds. She shook her head and motioned that they were to embark in their flyer and be on their way back to their planet.

Again and again the Detaxalans tried to explain what they wished, thinking Tanka did not understand. At last she impressed upon their savage minds that there was nothing for them but to depart, and disgruntled by her treatment they reentered their machine, closed its ponderous door, and raised their ship to the level of its sister flyer. Several minutes passed and then, with thanksgiving, we saw them pass over the city.

Told of this, Geble laughed. "To think of mere man-things daring to attempt to force themselves upon us. What is the universe coming to? What were their women back home considering when they sent them to us? Have they developed too many males and think that we can find use for them?" she wanted to know.

"It is strange indeed," observed Yabo, one of the council members. "What did you find in the minds of these ignoble creatures, O August One?"

"Nothing of particular interest, a very low grade of intelligence, to be sure. There was no need of looking below the surface."

"It must have taken intelligence to build those ships."

"None aboard them did that. I don't question it but that their mothers built the ships for them as playthings, even as we give toys to our little ones, you know. I recall that the ancients of our world perfected several types of space-flyers many ages ago!"

"Maybe those males do not have 'mothers' but instead they build the ships themselves. Maybe they are the stronger sex on their world!" This last was said by Suiki, the fifth consort of Geble, a pretty little male, rather young in years. No one had noticed his coming into the chamber, but now everyone showed surprise at his words.

"Impossible!" ejaculated Yabo.

Geble, however, laughed at the little chap's expression. "Suiki is a profound thinker," she observed, still laughing, and she drew him to her, gently hugging him.

And with that the subject of the men from Detaxal was closed. It was reopened, however, several hours later when it was learned that instead of leaving Gola altogether the ships were seen one after another by the various cities of the planet as they circumnavigated it. It was rather annoying, for everywhere the cities' routines were broken up as the people dropped their work and studies to gaze at the cylinders.

Too, it was upsetting the morale of the males, for on learning that the two ships contained only creatures of their own sex they were becoming envious wishing for the same type of playthings for themselves.

Shut in, as they were, unable to grasp the profundities of our science and thought, the gentle, fun-loving males were always glad for a new diversion and this new method developed by the Detaxalans had intrigued them.

It was then that Geble decided it was high time to take matters into her own hands. Not knowing where the two ships were at the moment it was not difficult with the object-finder beam to discover their whereabouts, and then with the attractor to draw them to Tola magnetically. An ous later we had the pleasure of seeing the two ships rushing toward our city. When they arrived above it, power brought them down to the square again.

Again Tanka was sent out, and directed the commanders of the two ships to follow her in to the queen. Knowing the futility of attempting to converse with them without mechanical aid, Geble caused to be brought to her three of the ancient mechanical thought transformers that are only museum pieces to us but still workable. The two men were directed to place them on their heads while she donned the third. When this was done she ordered the creatures to depart immediately from Gola, telling them that she was tired of their play.

Watching the faces of the two I saw them frowning and shaking their heads. Of course I could read their thoughts as well as Geble without need of the transformers, since it was only for their benefit that these were used, so I heard the whole conversation, though I need only to give you the gist of it.

"We have no wish to leave your world as yet," the two had argued.

"You are disrupting the routine of our lives

here," Geble told them, "and now that you've seen all that you can there is no need for you to stay longer. I insist that you leave immediately."

I saw one of the men smile, and thereupon he was the one who did all the talking. (I say "talking," for this he was actually doing, mouthing each one of his words although we understood his thoughts as they formed in his queer brain, so different from ours.)

"Listen here," he laughed, "I don't get the hang of you people at all. We came to Gola"—he used some outlandish name of his own, but I use our name of course—"with the express purpose of exploration and exploitation. We come as friends. Already we are in alliance with Damin"—again, the name for the fourth planet of our system was different, but I give the correct appellation—"established commerce and trade, and now we are ready to offer you the chance to join our federation peaceably.

"What we have seen of this world is very favorable; there are good prospects for business here. There is no reason why you people as those of Damin and Detaxal cannot enter into a nice business arrangement congenially. You have far more here to offer tourists, more than Damin. Why, except for your clouds this would be an ideal paradise for every man, woman, and child on Detaxal and Damin to visit, and of course with our new cloud dispensers we could clear your atmosphere for you in short order and keep it that way. Why, you'll make millions in the first year of your trade.

"Come now, allow us to discuss this with your ruler-king or whatever you call him. Women are all right in their place, but it takes the men to see the profit of a thing like this— you are a woman, aren't you?"

The first of his long speech, of course, was so much gibberish to us, with his prate of business arrangements, commerce and trade, tourists, profits, cloud dispersers, and whatnot, but it was the last part of what he said that took my breath away, and you can imagine how it affected Geble. I could see straightaway that she was intensely angered, and with good reason too. By the looks of the silly fellow's face I could guess that he was getting the full purport of her thoughts. He began to shuffle his funny feet and a foolish grin pervaded his face.

"Sorry," he said, "if I insulted you—I didn't intend that, but I believed that man holds the same place here as he does on Detaxal and Damin, but I suppose it is just as possible for woman to be the ruling factor of a world as man is elsewhere."

That speech naturally made Geble more irate, and tearing off her thought transformer she left the room without another word. In a moment, however, Yabo appeared wearing the transformer in her place. Yabo had none of the beauty of my mother, for whereas Geble was slender and as straight as a rod, Yabo was obese, and her fat body overflowed until she looked like a large dumpy bundle of fat held together in her furry skin. She had very little dignity as she waddled toward the Detaxalans, but there was determination in her whole manner, and without preliminaries she began to scold the two as though they were her own consorts.

"There has been enough of this, my fine young men," she shot at them. "You've had your fun, and now it is time for you to return to your mothers and consorts. Shame on you for making up such miserable tales about yourselves. I have a good mind to take you home with me for a couple of days, and I'd put you in your places quick enough. The idea of men acting like you are!"

For a moment I thought the Detaxalans were going to cry by the faces they made, but instead they broke into laughter, such heathenish sounds as had never before been heard on Gola, and I listened in wonder instead of excluding it from my hearing, but the fellows sobered quickly enough at that, and the spokesman addressed the shocked Yabo.

"I see," said he, "it's impossible for your people and mine to arrive at an understanding peaceably. I'm sorry that you take us for children out on a spree, that you are accustomed to such a low type of man as is evidently your lot here.

"I have given you your chance to accept our terms without force, but since you refuse, under the orders of the Federation I will have to take you forcibly, for we are determined that Gola become one of us, if you like it or not. Then you will learn that we are not the children you believe us to be.

"You may go to your supercilious queen now and advise her that we give you exactly ten hours in which to evacuate this city, for precisely on the hour we will lay this city in ruins. And if that does not suffice you, we will do the same with every other city on the planet! Remember, ten hours!"

And with that he took the mechanical thought transformer from his head and tossed it on the table. His companion did the same and the two of them strode out of the room and to their flyers, which arose several thousand feet above Tola and remained there.

Hurrying in to Geble, Yabo told her what the Detaxalan had said. Geble was reclining on her couch and did not bother to raise herself.

"Childish prattle," she conceded, and withdrew her red eyes on their movable stems into their pockets, paying no more heed to the threats of the men from Detaxal.

I, however, could not be as calm as my mother, and I was fearful that it was not childish prattle after all. Not knowing how long ten hours might be I did not wait, but crept up to the palace's beam station and set its dials so that the entire building and as much of the surrounding territory as it could cover were protected in the force zone.

Alas, that the same beam was not greater. But it had not been put there for defense, only for matter transference and whatever other peacetime methods we used. It was the means of proving just the same that it was also a very good defensive instrument, for just two ous later the hovering ships above let loose their powers of destruction, heavy explosives that entirely demolished all of Tola and its millions of people and only the palace royal of all that beauty was left standing!

Awakened from her nap by the terrific detonation, Geble came hurriedly to a window to view the ruin, and she was wild with grief at what she saw. Geble, however, saw that there was urgent need for action. She knew without my telling her what I had done to protect the palace. And though she showed no sign of appreciation, I knew that I had won a greater place in her regard than any other of her many daughters and would henceforth be her favorite as well as her successor.

Now, with me behind her, she hurried to the beam station and in a twinkling we were both in Tubia, the second-greatest city of that time. Nor were we to be caught napping again, for Geble ordered all beam stations to throw out their zone forces while she herself manipulated one of Tubia's greatest power beams, attuning it to the emanations of the two Detaxalan flyers. In less than an ous the two ships were seen through the mists heading for Tubia. For a moment I grew fearful, but on realizing that they were after all in our grip, and the attractors held every living thing powerless against movement, I grew calm and watched them come over the city and the beam pull them to the ground.

With the beam still upon them, they lay supine on the ground without motion. Descending to the square Geble called for Ray C, and when the machine arrived she herself directed the cutting of the hole in the side of the flyer and was the first to enter it with me immediately behind, as usual.

We were both astounded by what we saw of the great array of machinery within. But a glance told Geble all she wanted to know of their principles. She interested herself only in the men standing rigidly in whatever position our beam had caught them. Only the eyes of the creatures expressed their fright, poor things, unable to move so much as a hair while we moved among them untouched by the power of the beam because of the strength of our own minds.

They could have fought against it if they had known how, but their simple minds were too weak for such exercise.

Now glancing about among the stiff forms around us, of which there were one thousand, Geble picked out those of the males she desired for observation, choosing those she judged to be their finest specimens, those with much hair on their faces and having more girth than the others. These she ordered removed by several workers who followed us, and then we emerged again to the outdoors.

Using hand beam torches the picked specimens were kept immobile after they were out of reach of the greater beam and were borne into the laboratory of the building Geble had converted into her new palace. Geble and I followed, and she gave the order for the complete annihilation of the two powerless ships.

Thus ended the first foray of the people of Detaxal. And for the next two tels there was peace upon our globe again. In the laboratory the thirty who had been rescued from their ships were given thorough examinations both physically and mentally and we learned all there was to know about them. Hearing of the destruction of their ships, most of the creatures had become frightened and were quite docile in our hands. Those that were unruly were used in the dissecting room for the advancement of Golan knowledge.

After a complete study of them, which yielded little, we lost interest in them scientifically. Geble, however, found some pleasure in having the poor creatures around her and kept three of them in her own chambers so she could delve into their brains as she pleased. The others she doled out to her favorites as she saw fit.

One she gave to me to act as a slave or in what capacity I desired him, but my interest in him soon waned, especially since I had now come of age and was allowed to have two consorts of my own, and go about the business of bringing my daughters into the world.

My slave I called Jon and gave him complete freedom of my house. If only we had foreseen what was coming we would have annihilated every one of them immediately! It did please me later to find that Jon was learning our language and finding a place in my household, making friends with my two shut-in consorts. But as I have said I paid little attention to him.

So life went on smoothly with scarcely a change after the destruction of the ships of Detaxal. But that did not mean we were unprepared for more. Geble reasoned that there would be more ships forthcoming when the Detaxalans found that their first two did not return. So, although it was sometimes inconvenient, the zones of force were kept upon our cities.

And Geble was right, for the day came when dozens of flyers descended upon Gola from Detaxal. But this time the zones of force did not hold them since the zones were not in operation!

And we were unwarned, for when they descended upon us, our world was sleeping, confident that our zones were our protection. The first indication that I had of trouble brewing was when, awakening, I found the ugly form of Jon bending over me. Surprised, for it was not his habit to arouse me, I started up only to find his arms about me, embracing me. And how strong he was! For the moment a new emotion swept me, for the first time I knew the pleasure to be had in the arms of a strong man, but that emotion was short lived, for I saw in the blue eyes of my slave that he had recognized the look in my eyes for what it was, and for the moment he was tender.

Later I was to grow angry when I thought of that expression of his, for his eyes filled with pity, pity for me! But pity did not stay, instead he grinned and the next instant he was binding me down to my couch with strong rope. Geble, I learned later, had been treated as I, as were the members of the council and every other woman in Gola!

That was what came of allowing our men to meet on common ground with the creatures from Detaxal, for a weak mind is open to seeds of rebellion and the Detaxalans had sown it well, promising dominance to the lesser creatures of Gola.

That, however, was only part of the plot on the part of the Detaxalans. They were determined not only to revenge those we had murdered, but also to gain mastery of our planet. Unnoticed by us they had constructed a machine which transmits sound as we transmit thought and by its means had communicated with their own world, advising them of the very hour to strike when all of Gola was slumbering. It was a masterful stroke, only they did not know the power of the mind of Gola—so much more ancient than theirs.

Lying there bound on my couch I was able to see out the window and, trembling with terror, I watched a half dozen Detaxalan flyers descend into Tubia, guessing that the same was happening in our other cities. I was truly frightened, for I did not have the brain of a Geble. I was young yet, and in fear I watched the hordes march out of their machines, saw the thousands of our men join them.

Free from restraint, the shut-ins were having their holiday, and how they cavorted out in the open, most of the time getting in the way of the freakish Detaxalans, who were certainly taking over our city.

A half ous passed while I lay there watching, waiting in fear at the loss of what life we had led up to the present, and trembled over what the future might be when the Detaxalans had infested us with commerce and trade, business propositions, tourists, and all of their evil practices. It was then that I received the message from Geble, clear and definite, just as all the women of the globe received it, and hope returned to my heart.

There began that titanic struggle, the fight that won us victory over the simple-minded male weaklings below who had presumptuously dared to conquer us. The first indication was that the power of our combined mental concentration at Geble's orders was taking effect on the men of our own race. They tried to shake us off, but we knew we could bring them back to us.

At first the Detaxalans paid them no heed. They knew not what was happening until there came the wholesale retreat of the Golan men back to the buildings, back to the chambers from which they had escaped. Then grasping something of what was happening the already defeated invaders sought to retain their hold on our males. Our erstwhile captives sought to hold them with oratorical gestures, but of course we won. We saw our creatures return to us and unbind us.

Only the Detaxalans did not guess the significance of that, did not realize that inasmuch as we had conquered our own men, we could conquer them also. As they went about their work of making our city their own, establishing already their autocratic bureaus wherever they pleased, we began to concentrate upon them, hypnotizing them to return to the flyers that had disgorged them.

And soon they began to feel of our power, the weakest ones first, feeling the mental bewilderment creeping upon them. Their leaders, stronger in mind, knew nothing of this at first, but soon our terrible combined mental power was forced upon them also and they realized that their men were deserting them, crawling back to their ships! The leaders began to exhort them into new action, driving them physically.

But our power gained on them and now we began to concentrate upon the leaders themselves. They were strong of will and they defied us, fought us, mind against mind, but of course it was useless. Their minds were not suited to the test they put themselves to, and after almost three ous of struggle, we of Gola were able to see victory ahead.

At last the leaders succumbed. Not a single Detaxalan was abroad in the avenues. They were within their flyers, held there by our combined wills, unable to act for themselves. It was then as easy for us to switch the zones of force upon them, subjugate them more securely, and with the annihilator beam to disintegrate completely every ship and man into nothingness! Thousands upon thousands died that day and Gola was indeed revenged.

Thus, my daughters, ended the second invasion of Gola.

Oh yes, more came from their planet to discover what had happened to their ships and their men, but we of Gola no longer hesitated, and they no sooner appeared beneath the mists than they too were annihilated until at last Detaxal gave up the thought of conquering our cloud-laden world. Perhaps in the future they will attempt it again, but we are always in readiness for them now, and our men—well, they are still the same ineffectual weaklings, my daughters. . . .

A Martian Odyssey

STANLEY G. WEINBAUM

Stanley G. Weinbaum (1902–1935) was a US science fiction writer who had a substantial impact on the American science fiction scene despite his short life. Early on, two years studying chemical engineering at the University of Wisconsin helped Weinbaum envision the premise of his most famous work, "A Martian Odyssey" (*Wonder Stories*, 1934), reprinted here. The story broke new ground in attempting to envisage life on other worlds in terms of strange and complex ecosystems. Told in Weinbaum's fluent style, it became immediately and permanently popular. Weinbaum followed up "A Martian Odyssey" with a less successful sequel, "Valley of Dreams" (*Wonder Stories*, 1934). Other Weinbaum stories in this vein include four stories in *Astounding Science Fiction* in 1935: "The Lotus Eaters," which features an interesting attempt to imagine the worldview of an intelligent plant; "The Mad Moon"; "Flight on Titan"; and "Parasite Planet." He also contributed to the well-known round-robin SF story solicited by *Fantasy Magazine* for its September 1935 issue, "The Challenge from Beyond," with Murray Leinster, E. E. Smith, Harl Vincent, and Donald Wandrei.

Weinbaum's premature death from lung cancer robbed science fiction of its most promising writer of the 1930s, the full measure of his ability only becoming apparent when his longer works began to appear posthumously. *The New Adam* (1939) is a painstaking account of the career of a potential superman who grows up as a kind of "feral child" in human society; it initiates into the pulp science fiction world the kind of superman story more commonly told in scientific romance form by Olaf Stapledon and other English writers, the kind of story in which the superman cannot adjust to normal humans and suffers fatal solitude. Another posthumously published SF novel, the psychological horror story *The Dark Other* (1950), is an early exploration of the Jekyll-and-Hyde theme. *The King's Watch* (1994 chapbook) is a previously unprinted hard-boiled detective tale.

"A Martian Odyssey" was his second published story, but his first in the science fiction genre. (A year earlier he had published a romance novel using the pseudonym Marge Stanley.) In the collection *The Best of Stanley G. Weinbaum*, Isaac Asimov wrote that the story "had the effect on the field of an exploding grenade. With this single story, Weinbaum was instantly recognized as the world's best living science fiction writer, and at once almost every writer in the field tried to imitate him." In 1970, when the Science Fiction Writers of America voted on the best stories (prior to the existence of their Nebula Award), this story came in second to Asimov's novella *Nightfall* and was the earliest story to receive such recognition.

As with Edmond Hamilton's work, Weinbaum's science fiction influenced horror and weird fiction as well. H. P. Lovecraft wrote, "Somehow [Weinbaum] had the imagination to envisage wholly alien situations and psychologies and entities, to devise consistent events from wholly alien motives and to refrain from the cheap dramatics in which almost all adventure-pulpists wallow."

A MARTIAN ODYSSEY

Stanley G. Weinbaum

Jarvis stretched himself as luxuriously as he could in the cramped general quarters of the *Ares*.

"Air you can breathe!" he exulted. "It feels as thick as soup after the thin stuff out there!" He nodded at the Martian landscape stretching flat and desolate in the light of the nearer moon, beyond the glass of the port.

The other three stared at him sympathetically—Putz, the engineer; Leroy, the biologist; and Harrison, the astronomer and captain of the expedition. Dick Jarvis was chemist of the famous crew, the *Ares* expedition, first human beings to set foot on the mysterious neighbor of the Earth, the planet Mars. This, of course, was in the old days, less than twenty years after the mad American Doheny perfected the atomic blast at the cost of his life, and only a decade after the equally mad Cardoza rode on it to the moon. They were true pioneers, these four of the *Ares*. Except for a half-dozen moon expeditions and the ill-fated de Lancey flight aimed at the seductive orb of Venus, they were the first men to feel other gravity than Earth's, and certainly the first successful crew to leave the Earth-moon system. And they deserved that success when one considers the difficulties and discomforts—the months spent in acclimatization chambers back on Earth, learning to breathe the air as tenuous as that of Mars, the challenging of the void in the tiny rocket driven by the cranky reaction motors of the twenty-first century, and mostly the facing of an absolutely unknown world.

Jarvis stretched and fingered the raw and peeling tip of his frostbitten nose. He sighed again contentedly.

"Well," exploded Harrison abruptly, "are we going to hear what happened? You set out all shipshape in an auxiliary rocket, we don't get a peep for ten days, and finally Putz here picks you out of a lunatic ant-heap with a freak ostrich as your pal! Spill it, man!"

"Speel?" queried Leroy perplexedly. "Speel what?"

"He means '*spiel*,'" explained Putz soberly. "It iss to tell."

Jarvis met Harrison's amused glance without the shadow of a smile. "That's right, Karl," he said in grave agreement with Putz. *"Ich spiel es!"* He grunted comfortably and began.

"According to orders," he said, "I watched Karl here take off toward the north, and then I got into my flying sweat-box and headed south. You'll remember, Cap—we had orders not to land, but just scout about for points of interest. I set the two cameras clicking and buzzed along, riding pretty high—about two thousand feet—for a couple of reasons. First, it gave the cameras a greater field, and second, the under-jets travel so far in this half-vacuum they call air here that they stir up dust if you move low."

"We know all that from Putz," grunted Harrison. "I wish you'd saved the films, though. They'd have paid the cost of this junket; remember how the public mobbed the first moon pictures?"

"The films are safe," retorted Jarvis. "Well," he resumed, "as I said, I buzzed along at a pretty good clip; just as we figured, the wings haven't much lift in this air at less than a hundred miles per hour, and even then I had to use the under-jets.

"So, with the speed and the altitude and the blurring caused by the under-jets, the seeing wasn't any too good. I could see enough, though, to distinguish that what I sailed over was just more of this grey plain that we'd been examining the whole week since our landing—same blobby growths and the same eternal carpet of crawling little plant animals, or biopods, as Leroy calls them. So I sailed along, calling back my position every hour as instructed, and not knowing whether you heard me."

"I did!" snapped Harrison.

"A hundred and fifty miles south," continued Jarvis imperturbably, "the surface changed to a sort of low plateau, nothing but desert and orange-tinted sand. I figured that we were right in our guess, then, and this grey plain we dropped on was really the Mare Cimmerium, which would make my orange desert the region called Xanthus. If I were right, I ought to hit another grey plain, the Mare Chronium, in another couple of hundred miles, and then another orange desert, Thyle One or Two. And so I did."

"Putz verified our position a week and a half ago!" grumbled the captain. "Let's get to the point."

"Coming!" remarked Jarvis. "Twenty miles into Thyle—believe it or not—I crossed a canal!"

"Putz photographed a hundred! Let's hear something new!"

"And did he also see a city?"

"Twenty of 'em, if you call those heaps of mud cities!"

"Well," observed Jarvis, "from here on I'll be telling a few things Putz didn't see!" He rubbed his tingling nose, and continued. "I knew that I had sixteen hours of daylight at this season, so eight hours—eight hundred miles—from here, I decided to turn back. I was still over Thyle, whether One or Two I'm not sure, not more than twenty-five miles into it. And right there, Putz's pet motor quit!"

"Quit? How?" Putz was solicitous.

"The atomic blast got weak. I started losing altitude right away, and suddenly there I was with a thump right in the middle of Thyle!

Smashed my nose on the window, too!" He rubbed the injured member ruefully.

"Did you maybe try vashing *der* combustion chamber *mit* acid sulphuric?" inquired Putz. "Sometimes *der* lead giffs a secondary radiation—"

"Naw!" said Jarvis disgustedly. "I wouldn't try that, of course—not more than ten times! Besides, the bump flattened the landing gear and busted off the under-jets. Suppose I got the thing working—what then? Ten miles with the blast coming right out of the bottom and I'd have melted the floor from under me!" He rubbed his nose again. "Lucky for me a pound only weighs seven ounces here, or I'd have been mashed flat!"

"I could have fixed!" ejaculated the engineer. "I bet it vas not serious."

"Probably not," agreed Jarvis sarcastically. "Only it wouldn't fly. Nothing serious, but I had my choice of waiting to be picked up or trying to walk back—eight hundred miles, and perhaps twenty days before we had to leave! Forty miles a day! Well," he concluded, "I chose to walk. Just as much chance of being picked up, and it kept me busy."

"We'd have found you," said Harrison.

"No doubt. Anyway, I rigged up a harness from some seat straps, and put the water tank on my back, took a cartridge belt and revolver, and some iron rations, and started out."

"Water tank!" exclaimed the little biologist, Leroy. "She weigh one-quarter ton!"

"Wasn't full. Weighed about two hundred and fifty pounds Earth-weight, which is eighty-five here. Then, besides, my own personal two hundred and ten pounds is only seventy on Mars, so, tank and all, I grossed a hundred and fifty-five, or fifty-five pounds less than my everyday Earth-weight. I figured on that when I undertook the forty-mile daily stroll. Oh—of course I took a thermo-skin sleeping bag for these wintry Martian nights.

"Off I went, bouncing along pretty quickly. Eight hours of daylight meant twenty miles or more. It got tiresome, of course—plugging along over a soft sand desert with nothing to see, not even Leroy's crawling biopods. But an hour or so brought me to the canal—just a dry ditch about four hundred feet wide, and straight as a railroad on its own company map.

"There'd been water in it sometime, though. The ditch was covered with what looked like a nice green lawn. Only, as I approached, the lawn moved out of my way!"

"Eh?" said Leroy.

"Yeah, it was a relative of your biopods. I caught one—a little grasslike blade about as long as my finger, with two thin, stemmy legs."

"He is where?" Leroy was eager.

"He is let go! I had to move, so I plowed along with the walking grass opening in front and closing behind. And then I was out on the orange desert of Thyle again.

"I plugged steadily along, cussing the sand that made going so tiresome, and, incidentally, cussing that cranky motor of yours, Karl. It was just before twilight that I reached the edge of Thyle, and looked down over the grey Mare Chronium. And I knew there was seventy-five miles of *that* to be walked over, and then a couple of hundred miles of that Xanthus desert, and about as much more Mare Cimmerium. Was I pleased? I started cussing you fellows for not picking me up!"

"We were trying, you sap!" said Harrison.

"That didn't help. Well, I figured I might as well use what was left of daylight in getting down the cliff that bounded Thyle. I found an easy place, and down I went. Mare Chronium was just the same sort of place as this—crazy leafless plants and a bunch of crawlers; I gave it a glance and hauled out my sleeping bag. Up to that time, you know, I hadn't seen anything worth worrying about on this half-dead world—nothing dangerous, that is."

"Did you?" queried Harrison.

"*Did I!* You'll hear about it when I come to it. Well, I was just about to turn in when suddenly I heard the wildest sort of shenanigans!"

"Vot iss shenanigans?" inquired Putz.

"He says, '*Je ne sais quoi,*'" explained Leroy. "It is to say, 'I don't know what.'"

"That's right," agreed Jarvis. "I didn't know what, so I sneaked over to find out. There was a racket like a flock of crows eating a bunch of canaries—whistles, cackles, caws, trills, and what have you. I rounded a clump of stumps, and there was Tweel!"

"Tweel?" said Harrison, and "Tveel?" said Leroy and Putz.

"That freak ostrich," explained the narrator. "At least, Tweel is as near as I can pronounce it without sputtering. He called it something like 'Trrrweerrlll.'"

"What was he doing?" asked the captain.

"He was being eaten! And squealing, of course, as anyone would."

"Eaten! By what?"

"I found out later. All I could see then was a bunch of black ropy arms tangled around what looked like, as Putz described it to you, an ostrich. I wasn't going to interfere, naturally; if both creatures were dangerous, I'd have one less to worry about.

"But the birdlike thing was putting up a good battle, dealing vicious blows with an eighteen-inch beak, between screeches. And besides, I caught a glimpse or two of what was on the end of those arms!" Jarvis shuddered. "But the clincher was when I noticed a little black bag or case hung about the neck of the bird-thing! It was intelligent! That or tame, I assumed. Anyway, it clinched my decision. I pulled out my automatic and fired into what I could see of its antagonist.

"There was a flurry of tentacles and a spurt of black corruption, and then the thing, with a disgusting sucking noise, pulled itself and its arms into a hole in the ground. The other let out a series of clacks, staggered around on legs about as thick as golf sticks, and turned suddenly to face me. I held my weapon ready, and the two of us stared at each other.

"The Martian wasn't a bird, really. It wasn't

even birdlike, except just at first glance. It had a beak all right, and a few feathery appendages, but the beak wasn't really a beak. It was somewhat flexible; I could see the tip bend slowly from side to side; it was almost like a cross between a beak and a trunk. It had four-toed feet, and four fingered things—hands, you'd have to call them, and a little roundish body, and a long neck ending in a tiny head—and that beak. It stood an inch or so taller than I, and—well, Putz saw it!"

The engineer nodded. "*Ja!* I saw!"

Jarvis continued. "So—we stared at each other. Finally the creature went into a series of clackings and twitterings and held out its hands toward me, empty. I took that as a gesture of friendship."

"Perhaps," suggested Harrison, "it looked at that nose of yours and thought you were its brother!"

"Huh! You can be funny without talking! Anyway, I put up my gun and said, 'Aw, don't mention it,' or something of the sort, and the thing came over and we were pals.

"By that time, the sun was pretty low and I knew that I'd better build a fire or get into my thermo-skin. I decided on the fire. I picked a spot at the base of the Thyle cliff, where the rock could reflect a little heat on my back. I started breaking off chunks of this desiccated Martian vegetation, and my companion caught the idea and brought in an armful. I reached for a match, but the Martian fished into his pouch and brought out something that looked like a glowing coal; one touch of it, and the fire was blazing—and you all know what a job we have starting a fire in this atmosphere!

"And that bag of his!" continued the narrator. "That was a manufactured article, my friends; press an end and she popped open—press the middle and she sealed so perfectly you couldn't see the line. Better than zippers.

"Well, we stared at the fire awhile and I decided to attempt some sort of communication with the Martian. I pointed at myself and said 'Dick'; he caught the drift immediately, stretched a bony claw at me, and repeated 'Tick.' Then I pointed at him, and he gave that whistle I called Tweel; I can't imitate his accent. Things were going smoothly; to emphasize the names, I repeated 'Dick,' and then, pointing at him, 'Tweel.'

"There we stuck! He gave some clacks that sounded negative, and said something like 'P-p-p-proot.' And that was just the beginning; I was always 'Tick,' but as for him—part of the time he was 'Tweel,' and part of the time he was 'P-p-p-proot,' and part of the time he was sixteen other noises!

"We just couldn't connect. I tried 'rock,' and I tried 'star,' and 'tree,' and 'fire,' and Lord knows what else, and try as I would, I couldn't get a single word! Nothing was the same for two successive minutes, and if that's a language, I'm an alchemist! Finally I gave it up and called him Tweel, and that seemed to do.

"But Tweel hung on to some of my words. He remembered a couple of them, which I suppose is a great achievement if you're used to a language you have to make up as you go along. But I couldn't get the hang of his talk; either I missed some subtle point or we just didn't *think* alike—and I rather believe the latter view.

"I've other reasons for believing that. After a while I gave up the language business, and tried mathematics. I scratched two plus two equals four on the ground, and demonstrated it with pebbles. Again Tweel caught the idea, and informed me that three plus three equals six. Once more we seemed to be getting somewhere.

"So, knowing that Tweel had at least a grammar school education, I drew a circle for the sun, pointing first at it, and then at the last glow of the sun. Then I sketched in Mercury, and Venus, and Mother Earth, and Mars, and finally, pointing to Mars, I swept my hand around in a sort of inclusive gesture to indicate that Mars was our current environment. I was working up to putting over the idea that my home was on Earth.

"Tweel understood my diagram all right. He poked his beak at it, and with a great deal of trilling and clucking, he added Deimos and Phobos to Mars, and then sketched in Earth's moon!

"Do you see what that proves? It proves that Tweel's race uses telescopes—that they're civilized!"

"Does not!" snapped Harrison. "The moon is visible from here as a fifth-magnitude star. They could see its revolution with the naked eye."

"The moon, yes!" said Jarvis. "You've missed my point. Mercury isn't visible! And Tweel knew of Mercury because he placed the moon at the *third* planet, not the second. If he didn't know Mercury, he'd put Earth second, and Mars third, instead of fourth! See?"

"Humph!" said Harrison.

"Anyway," proceeded Jarvis, "I went on with my lesson. Things were going smoothly, and it looked as if I could put the idea over. I pointed at Earth on my diagram, and then at myself, and then, to clinch it, I pointed to myself and then to Earth itself shining bright green almost at the zenith.

"Tweel set up such an excited clacking that I was certain he understood. He jumped up and down, and suddenly he pointed at himself and then at the sky, and then at himself and at the sky again. He pointed at his middle and then at Arcturus, at his head and then at Spica, at his feet and then at half a dozen stars, while I just gaped at him. Then, all of a sudden, he gave a tremendous leap. Man, what a hop! He shot straight up into the starlight, seventy-five feet if an inch! I saw him silhouetted against the sky, saw him turn and come down at me headfirst, and land smack on his beak like a javelin! There he stuck square in the center of my sun-circle in the sand—a bull's-eye!"

"Nuts!" observed the captain. "Plain nuts!"

"That's what I thought, too! I just stared at him openmouthed while he pulled his head out of the sand and stood up. Then I figured he'd missed my point, and I went through the whole blamed rigamarole again, and it ended the same way, with Tweel on his nose in the middle of my picture!"

"Maybe it's a religious rite," suggested Harrison.

"Maybe," said Jarvis dubiously. "Well, there we were. We could exchange ideas up to a certain point, and then—blooey! Something in us was different, unrelated; I don't doubt that Tweel thought me just as screwy as I thought him. Our minds simply looked at the world from different viewpoints, and perhaps his viewpoint is as true as ours. But—we couldn't get together, that's all. Yet, in spite of all difficulties, I *liked* Tweel, and I have a queer certainty that he liked me."

"Nuts!" repeated the captain. "Just daffy!"

"Yeah? Wait and see. A couple of times I've thought that perhaps we—" He paused, and then resumed his narrative. "Anyway, I finally gave it up, and got into my thermo-skin to sleep. The fire hadn't kept me any too warm, but that damned sleeping bag did. Got stuffy five minutes after I closed myself in. I opened it a little and bingo! Some eighty-below-zero air hit my nose, and that's when I got this pleasant little frostbite to add to the bump I acquired during the crash of my rocket.

"I don't know what Tweel made of my sleeping. He sat around, but when I woke up, he was gone. I'd just crawled out of my bag, though, when I heard some twittering, and there he came, sailing down from that three-story Thyle cliff to alight on his beak beside me. I pointed to myself and toward the north, and he pointed at himself and toward the south, but when I loaded up and started away, he came along.

"Man, how he traveled! A hundred and fifty feet at a jump, sailing through the air stretched out like a spear, and landing on his beak. He seemed surprised at my plodding, but after a few moments he fell in beside me, only every few minutes he'd go into one of his leaps, and stick his nose into the sand a block ahead of me. Then he'd come shooting back at me; it made me nervous at first to see that beak of his coming at me like a spear, but he always ended in the sand at my side.

"So the two of us plugged along across the

Mare Chronium. Same sort of place as this—same crazy plants and same little green biopods growing in the sand, or crawling out of your way. We talked—not that we understood each other, you know, but just for company. I sang songs, and I suspect Tweel did too; at least, some of his trillings and twitterings had a subtle sort of rhythm.

"Then, for variety, Tweel would display his smattering of English words. He'd point to an outcropping and say 'rock,' and point to a pebble and say it again; or he'd touch my arm and say 'Tick,' and then repeat it. He seemed terrifically amused that the same word meant the same thing twice in succession, or that the same word could apply to two different objects. It set me wondering if perhaps his language wasn't like the primitive speech of some Earth people—you know, Captain, like the Negritoes, for instance, who haven't any generic words. No word for food or water or man—words for good food and bad food, or rainwater and seawater, or strong man and weak man—but no names for general classes. They're too primitive to understand that rainwater and seawater are just different aspects of the same thing. But that wasn't the case with Tweel; it was just that we were somehow mysteriously different—our minds were alien to each other. And yet—we *liked* each other!"

"Loony, that's all," remarked Harrison. "That's why you two were so fond of each other."

"Well, I like *you*!" countered Jarvis wickedly. "Anyway," he resumed, "don't get the idea that there was anything screwy about Tweel. In fact, I'm not so sure but that he couldn't teach our highly praised human intelligence a trick or two. Oh, he wasn't an intellectual superman, I guess; but don't overlook the point that he managed to understand a little of my mental workings, and I never even got a glimmering of his."

"Because he didn't have any!" suggested the captain, while Putz and Leroy blinked attentively.

"You can judge of that when I'm through," said Jarvis. "Well, we plugged along across the Mare Chronium all that day, and all the next. Mare Chronium—Sea of Time! Say, I was willing to agree with Schiaparelli's name by the end of that march! Just that grey, endless plain of weird plants, and never a sign of any other life. It was so monotonous that I was even glad to see the desert of Xanthus toward the evening of the second day.

"I was fair worn out, but Tweel seemed as fresh as ever, for all I never saw him drink or eat. I think he could have crossed the Mare Chronium in a couple of hours with those block-long nosedives of his, but he stuck along with me. I offered him some water once or twice; he took the cup from me and sucked the liquid into his beak, and then carefully squirted it all back into the cup.

"Just as we sighted Xanthus, or the cliffs that bounded it, one of those nasty sand clouds blew along, not as bad as the one we had here, but mean to travel against. I pulled the transparent flap of my thermo-skin bag across my face and managed pretty well, and I noticed that Tweel used some feathery appendages growing like a mustache at the base of his beak to cover his nostrils, and some similar fuzz to shield his eyes."

"He is a desert creature!" ejaculated the little biologist, Leroy.

"Huh? Why?"

"He drink no water—he is adapt for sandstorm—"

"Proves nothing! There's not enough water to waste anywhere on this desiccated pill called Mars. We'd call all of it desert on Earth, you know." He paused. "Anyway, after the sandstorm blew over, a little wind kept blowing in our faces, not strong enough to stir the sand. But suddenly things came drifting along from the Xanthus cliffs—small, transparent spheres, for all the world like glass tennis balls! But light—they were almost light enough to float even in this thin air—empty, too; at least, I cracked open a couple and nothing came out but a bad smell. I asked Tweel about them, but all he said was 'No, no, no,' which I took to mean that he knew nothing about them. So they went bouncing by like tumbleweeds, or like soap bubbles, and we plugged on toward Xanthus. Tweel pointed at one of the crystal balls once and said 'rock,' but I was too tired to argue with him. Later I discovered what he meant.

"We came to the bottom of the Xanthus cliffs finally, when there wasn't much daylight left. I decided to sleep on the plateau if possible; anything dangerous, I reasoned, would be more likely to prowl through the vegetation of the Mare Chronium than the sand of Xanthus. Not that I'd seen a single sign of menace, except the rope-armed black thing that had trapped Tweel, and apparently that didn't prowl at all, but lured its victims within reach. It couldn't lure me while I slept, especially as Tweel didn't seem to sleep at all, but simply sat patiently around all night. I wondered how the creature had managed to trap Tweel, but there wasn't any way of asking him. I found that out too, later; it's devilish!

"However, we were ambling around the base of the Xanthus barrier looking for an easy spot to climb. At least, I was. Tweel could have leaped it easily, for the cliffs were lower than Thyle—perhaps sixty feet. I found a place and started up, swearing at the water tank strapped to my back—it didn't bother me except when climbing—and suddenly I heard a sound that I thought I recognized!

"You know how deceptive sounds are in this thin air. A shot sounds like the pop of a cork. But this sound was the drone of a rocket, and sure enough, there went our second auxiliary about ten miles to westward, between me and the sunset!'

"Vas me!" said Putz. "I hunt for you."

"Yeah; I knew that, but what good did it do me? I hung on to the cliff and yelled and waved with one hand. Tweel saw it too, and set up a trilling and twittering, leaping to the top of the barrier and then high into the air. And while I watched, the machine droned on into the shadows to the south.

"I scrambled to the top of the cliff. Tweel was still pointing and trilling excitedly, shooting up toward the sky and coming down head-on to stick upside down on his beak in the sand. I pointed toward the south and at myself, and he said, 'Yes—Yes—Yes'; but somehow I gathered that he thought the flying thing was a relative of mine, probably a parent. Perhaps I did his intellect an injustice; I think now that I did.

"I was bitterly disappointed by the failure to attract attention. I pulled out my thermo-skin bag and crawled into it, as the night chill was already apparent. Tweel stuck his beak into the sand and drew up his legs and arms and looked for all the world like one of those leafless shrubs out there. I think he stayed that way all night."

"Protective mimicry!" ejaculated Leroy. "See? He is desert creature!"

"In the morning," resumed Jarvis, "we started off again. We hadn't gone a hundred yards into Xanthus when I saw something queer! This is one thing Putz didn't photograph, I'll wager!

"There was a line of little pyramids—tiny ones, not more than six inches high, stretching across Xanthus as far as I could see! Little buildings made of pygmy bricks, they were, hollow inside and truncated, or at least broken at the top and empty. I pointed at them and said 'What?' to Tweel, but he gave some negative twitters to indicate, I suppose, that he didn't know. So off we went, following the row of pyramids because they ran north, and I was going north.

"Man, we trailed that line for hours! After a while, I noticed another queer thing: they were getting larger. Same number of bricks in each one, but the bricks were larger.

"By noon they were shoulder high. I looked into a couple—all just the same, broken at the top and empty. I examined a brick or two as well; they were silica, and old as creation itself!"

"How you know?" asked Leroy.

"They were weathered—edges rounded. Silica doesn't weather easily even on Earth, and in this climate—!"

"How old you think?"

"Fifty thousand—a hundred thousand years. How can I tell? The little ones we saw in the morning were older—perhaps ten times as old. Crumbling. How old would that make *them*? Half a million years? Who knows?" Jarvis paused a moment. "Well," he resumed, "we followed the line. Tweel pointed at them and said 'rock' once or twice, but he'd done that many times before. Besides, he was more or less right about these.

"I tried questioning him. I pointed at a pyramid and asked 'People?' and indicated the two of us. He set up a negative sort of clucking and said, 'No, no, no. No one-one-two. No two-two-four,' meanwhile rubbing his stomach. I just stared at him and he went through the business again. 'No one-one-two. No two-two-four.' I just gaped at him."

"That proves it!" exclaimed Harrison. "Nuts!"

"You think so?" queried Jarvis sardonically. "Well, I figured it out different! 'No one-one-two!' You don't get it, of course, do you?"

"Nope—nor do you!"

"I think I do! Tweel was using the few English words he knew to put over a very complex idea. What, let me ask, does mathematics make you think of?"

"Why—of astronomy. Or—or logic!"

"That's it! 'No one-one-two!' Tweel was telling me that the builders of the pyramids weren't people—or that they weren't intelligent, that they weren't reasoning creatures! Get it?"

"Huh! I'll be damned!"

"You probably will."

"Why," put in Leroy, "he rub his belly?"

"Why? Because, my dear biologist, that's where his brains are! Not in his tiny head—in his middle!"

"*C'est impossible!*"

"Not on Mars, it isn't! These flora and fauna aren't earthly; your biopods prove that!" Jarvis grinned and took up his narrative. "Anyway, we plugged along across Xanthus and in about the middle of the afternoon, something else queer happened. The pyramids ended."

"Ended!"

"Yeah; the queer part was that the last one—and now they were ten-footers—was capped! See? Whatever built it was still inside; we'd trailed 'em from their half-million-year-old origin to the present.

"Tweel and I noticed it about the same time. I yanked out my automatic (I had a clip of Boland explosive bullets in it) and Tweel, quick as a sleight-of-hand trick, snapped a queer little glass revolver out of his bag. It was much like our weapons, except that the grip was larger to accommodate his four-taloned hand. And we held our weapons ready while we sneaked up along the lines of empty pyramids.

"Tweel saw the movement first. The top tiers of bricks were heaving, shaking, and suddenly slid down the sides with a thin crash. And then—something—something was coming out!

"A long, silvery-grey arm appeared, dragging after it an armored body. Armored, I mean, with scales, silver-grey and dull-shining. The arm heaved the body out of the hole; the beast crashed to the sand.

"It was a nondescript creature—body like a big grey cask, arm and a sort of mouth-hole at one end; stiff, pointed tail at the other—and that's all. No other limbs, no eyes, ears, nose—nothing! The thing dragged itself a few yards, inserted its pointed tail in the sand, pushed itself upright, and just sat.

"Tweel and I watched it for ten minutes before it moved. Then, with a creaking and rustling like—oh, like crumpling stiff paper—its arm moved to the mouth-hole and out came a brick! The arm placed the brick carefully on the ground, and the thing was still again.

"Another ten minutes—another brick. Just one of nature's bricklayers. I was about to slip away and move on when Tweel pointed at the thing and said 'Rock'! I went 'Huh?' and he said it again. Then, to the accompaniment of some of his trilling, he said, 'No—no—,' and gave two or three whistling breaths.

"Well, I got his meaning, for a wonder! I said, 'No breath?' and demonstrated the word. Tweel was ecstatic; he said, 'Yes, yes, yes! No, no, no breet!' Then he gave a leap and sailed out to land on his nose about one pace from the monster!

"I was startled, you can imagine! The arm was going up for a brick, and I expected to see Tweel caught and mangled, but—nothing happened! Tweel pounded on the creature, and the arm took the brick and placed it neatly beside the first. Tweel rapped on its body again, and said 'Rock,' and I got up nerve enough to take a look myself.

"Tweel was right again. The creature was rock, and it didn't breathe!"

"How you know?" snapped Leroy, his black eyes blazing interest.

"Because I'm a chemist. The beast was made of silica! There must have been pure silicon in the sand, and it lived on that. Get it? We, and Tweel, and those plants out there, and even the biopods are *carbon* life; this thing lived by a different set of chemical reactions. It was silicon life!"

"*La vie silicieuse!*" shouted Leroy. "I have suspect, and now it is proof! I must go see! *Il faut que je—*"

"All right! All right!" said Jarvis. "You can go see. Anyhow, there the thing was, alive and yet not alive, moving every ten minutes, and then only to remove a brick. Those bricks were its waste matter. See, Frenchy? We're carbon, and our waste is carbon dioxide, and this thing is silicon, and *its* waste is silicon dioxide—silica. But silica is a solid, hence the bricks. And it builds itself in, and when it is covered, it moves over to a fresh place to start over. No wonder it creaked! A living creature half a million years old!"

"How you know how old?" Leroy was frantic.

"We trailed its pyramids from the beginning, didn't we? If this weren't the original pyramid builder, the series would have ended somewhere before we found him, wouldn't it?—ended and started over with the small ones. That's simple enough, isn't it?

"But he reproduces, or tries to. Before the third brick came out, there was a little rustle and out popped a whole stream of those little crystal balls. They're his spores, or eggs, or seeds—call 'em what you want. They went bouncing by across Xanthus just as they'd bounced by us back in the Mare Chronium. I've a hunch how they work, too—this is for your information, Leroy. I think the crystal shell of silica is no more than a protective covering, like an eggshell, and that the active principle is the smell inside. It's some sort of gas that attacks silicon, and if the shell is broken near a supply of that element, some reaction starts that ultimately develops into a beast like that one."

"You should try!" exclaimed the little Frenchman. "We must break one to see!"

"Yeah? Well, I did. I smashed a couple against the sand. Would you like to come back in about ten thousand years to see if I planted some pyramid monsters? You'd most likely be able to tell by that time!" Jarvis paused and drew a deep breath. "Lord! That queer creature! Do you picture it? Blind, deaf, nerveless, brainless—just a mechanism, and yet—immortal! Bound to go on making bricks, building pyramids, as long as silicon and oxygen exist, and even afterwards it'll just stop. It won't be dead. If the accidents of a million years bring it its food again, there it'll be, ready to run again, while brains and civilizations are part of the past. A queer beast—yet I met a stranger one!"

"If you did, it must have been in your dreams!" growled Harrison.

"You're right!" said Jarvis soberly. "In a way, you're right. The dream-beast! That's the best name for it—and it's the most fiendish, terrifying creation one could imagine! More dangerous than a lion, more insidious than a snake!"

"Tell me!" begged Leroy. "I must go see!"

"Not *this* devil!" He paused again. "Well," he resumed, "Tweel and I left the pyramid creature and plowed along through Xanthus. I was tired and a little disheartened by Putz's failure to pick me up, and Tweel's trilling got on my nerves, as did his flying nosedives. So I just strode along without a word, hour after hour across that monotonous desert.

"Toward midafternoon we came in sight of a low dark line on the horizon. I knew what it was. It was a canal; I'd crossed it in the rocket and it meant that we were just one-third of the way across Xanthus. Pleasant thought, wasn't it? And still, I was keeping up to schedule.

"We approached the canal slowly; I remembered that this one was bordered by a wide fringe of vegetation and that Mud-heap City was on it.

"I was tired, as I said. I kept thinking of a good hot meal, and then from that I jumped to reflections of how nice and homelike even Borneo would seem after this crazy planet, and from that, to thoughts of little old New York, and then to thinking about a girl I know there—Fancy Long. Know her?"

"Vision entertainer," said Harrison. "I've tuned her in. Nice blonde—dances and sings on the *Yerba Mate* hour."

"That's her," said Jarvis ungrammatically. "I know her pretty well—just friends, get me?—though she came down to see us off in the *Ares*. Well, I was thinking about her, feeling pretty lonesome, and all the time we were approaching that line of rubbery plants.

"And then—I said, 'What 'n hell!' and stared. And there she was—Fancy Long, standing plain as day under one of those crackbrained trees, and smiling and waving just the way I remembered her when we left!"

"Now you're nuts, too!" observed the captain.

"Boy, I almost agreed with you! I stared and pinched myself and closed my eyes and then stared again—and every time, there was

Fancy Long smiling and waving! Tweel saw something, too; he was trilling and clucking away, but I scarcely heard him. I was bounding toward her over the sand, too amazed even to ask myself questions.

"I wasn't twenty feet from her when Tweel caught me with one of his flying leaps. He grabbed my arm, yelling, 'No—no—no!' in his squeaky voice. I tried to shake him off—he was as light as if he were built of bamboo—but he dug his claws in and yelled. And finally some sort of sanity returned to me and I stopped less than ten feet from her. There she stood, looking as solid as Putz's head!"

"Vot?" said the engineer.

"She smiled and waved, and waved and smiled, and I stood there dumb as Leroy, while Tweel squeaked and chattered. I *knew* it couldn't be real, yet—there she was!

"Finally I said, 'Fancy! Fancy Long!' She just kept on smiling and waving, but looking as real as if I hadn't left her thirty-seven million miles away.

"Tweel had his glass pistol out, pointing it at her. I grabbed his arm, but he tried to push me away. He pointed at her and said, 'No breet! No breet!' and I understood that he meant that the Fancy Long thing wasn't alive. Man, my head was whirling!

"Still, it gave me the jitters to see him pointing his weapon at her. I don't know why I stood there watching him take careful aim, but I did. Then he squeezed the handle of his weapon; there was a little puff of steam, and Fancy Long was gone! And in her place was one of those writhing, black, rope-armed horrors like the one I'd saved Tweel from!

"The dream-beast! I stood there dizzy, watching it die while Tweel trilled and whistled. Finally he touched my arm, pointed at the twisting thing, and said, 'You one-one-two, he one-one-two.' After he'd repeated it eight or ten times, I got it. Do any of you?"

"*Oui!*" shrilled Leroy. "*Moi—je le comprends!* He mean you think of something, the beast he know, and you see it! *Un chien*—a hungry dog, he would see the big bone with meat! Or smell it—not?"

"Right!" said Jarvis. "The dream-beast uses its victim's longings and desires to trap its prey. The bird at nesting season would see its mate; the fox, prowling for its own prey, would see a helpless rabbit!"

"How he do?" queried Leroy.

"How do I know? How does a snake back on Earth charm a bird into its very jaws? And aren't there deep-sea fish that lure their victims into their mouths? Lord!" Jarvis shuddered. "Do you see how insidious the monster is? We're warned now—but henceforth we can't trust even our eyes. You might see me—I might see one of you—and back of it may be nothing but another of those black horrors!"

"How'd your friend know?" asked the captain abruptly.

"Tweel? I wonder! Perhaps he was thinking of something that couldn't possibly have interested me, and when I started to run, he realized that I saw something different and was warned. Or perhaps the dream-beast can only project a single vision, and Tweel saw what I saw—or nothing. I couldn't ask him. But it's just another proof that his intelligence is equal to ours or greater."

"He's daffy, I tell you!" said Harrison. "What makes you think his intellect ranks with the human?"

"Plenty of things! First, the pyramid-beast. He hadn't seen one before; he said as much. Yet he recognized it as a dead-alive automaton of silicon."

"He could have heard of it," objected Harrison. "He lives around here, you know."

"Well how about the language? I couldn't pick up a single idea of his and he learned six or seven words of mine. And do you realize what complex ideas he put over with no more than those six or seven words? The pyramid-monster—the dream-beast! In a single phrase he told me that one was a harmless automaton

and the other a deadly hypnotist. What about that?"

"Huh!" said the captain.

"*Huh* if you wish! Could you have done it knowing only six words of English? Could you go even further, as Tweel did, and tell me that another creature was of a sort of intelligence so different from ours that understanding was impossible—even more impossible than that between Tweel and me?"

"Eh? What was that?"

"Later. The point I'm making is that Tweel and his race are worthy of our friendship. Somewhere on Mars—and you'll find I'm right—is a civilization and culture equal to ours, and maybe more than equal. And communication is possible between them and us; Tweel proves that. It may take years of patient trial, for their minds are alien, but less alien than the next minds we encountered—if they *are* minds."

"The next ones? What next ones?"

"The people of the mud cities along the canals." Jarvis frowned, then resumed his narrative. "I thought the dream-beast and the silicon-monster were the strangest beings conceivable, but I was wrong. These creatures are still more alien, less understandable than either and far less comprehensible than Tweel, with whom friendship is possible, and even, by patience and concentration, the exchange of ideas.

"Well," he continued, "we left the dream-beast dying, dragging itself back into its hole, and we moved toward the canal. There was a carpet of that queer walking grass scampering out of our way, and when we reached the bank, there was a yellow trickle of water flowing. The mound city I'd noticed from the rocket was a mile or so to the right and I was curious enough to want to take a look at it.

"It had seemed deserted from my previous glimpse of it, and if any creatures were lurking in it—well, Tweel and I were both armed. And by the way, that crystal weapon of Tweel's was an interesting device; I took a look at it after the dream-beast episode. It fired a little glass splinter, poisoned, I suppose, and I guess it held at least a hundred of 'em to a load. The propellant was steam—just plain steam!"

"Shteam!" echoed Putz. "From vot come, shteam?"

"From water, of course! You could see the water through the transparent handle and about a gill of another liquid, thick and yellowish. When Tweel squeezed the handle—there was no trigger—a drop of water and a drop of the yellow stuff squirted into the firing chamber, and the water vaporized—pop!—like that. It's not so difficult; I think we could develop the same principle. Concentrated sulphuric acid will heat water almost to boiling, and so will quicklime, and there's potassium and sodium. . . .

"Of course, his weapon hadn't the range of mine, but it wasn't so bad in this thin air, and it *did* hold as many shots as a cowboy's gun in a Western movie. It was effective, too, at least against Martian life; I tried it out, aiming at one of the crazy plants, and darned if the plant didn't wither up and fall apart! That's why I think the glass splinters were poisoned.

"Anyway, we trudged along toward the mud-heap city and I began to wonder whether the city builders dug the canals. I pointed to the city and then at the canal, and Tweel said 'No—no—no!' and gestured toward the south. I took it to mean that some other race had created the canal system, perhaps Tweel's people. I don't know; maybe there's still another intelligent race on the planet, or a dozen others. Mars is a queer little world.

"A hundred yards from the city we crossed a sort of road—just a hard-packed mud trail, and then, all of a sudden, along came one of the mound builders!

"Man, talk about fantastic beings! It looked rather like a barrel trotting along on four legs with four other arms or tentacles. It had no head, just body and members and a row of eyes completely around it. The top end of the barrel-body was a diaphragm stretched as tight as a drum head, and that was all. It was pushing a little coppery cart and tore right past us like the proverbial bat out of hell. It didn't even notice us, although I thought the eyes on my side shifted a little as it passed.

"A moment later another came along, pushing another empty cart. Same thing—it just scooted past us. Well, I wasn't going to be ignored by a bunch of barrels playing train, so when the third one approached, I planted myself in the way—ready to jump, of course, if the thing didn't stop.

"But it did. It stopped and set up a sort of drumming from the diaphragm on top. And I held out both hands and said, 'We are friends!' And what do you suppose the thing did?"

"Said, 'Pleased to meet you,' I'll bet!" suggested Harrison.

"I couldn't have been more surprised if it had! It drummed on its diaphragm, and then suddenly boomed out, 'We are v-r-r-riends!' and gave its pushcart a vicious poke at me! I jumped aside, and away it went while I stared dumbly after it.

"A minute later another one came hurrying along. This one didn't pause, but simply drummed out, 'We are v-r-r-riends!' and scurried by. How did it learn the phrase? Were all of the creatures in some sort of communication with each other? Were they all parts of some central organism? I don't know, though I think Tweel does.

"Anyway, the creatures went sailing past us, every one greeting us with the same statement. It got to be funny; I never thought to find so many friends on this godforsaken ball! Finally I made a puzzled gesture to Tweel; I guess he understood, for he said, 'One-one-two—yes! Two-two-four—no!' Get it?"

"Sure," said Harrison, "it's a Martian nursery rhyme."

"Yeah! Well, I was getting used to Tweel's symbolism, and I figured it out this way. 'One-one-two—yes!' The creatures were intelligent. 'Two-two-four—no!' Their intelligence was not of our order, but something different and beyond the logic of two and two is four. Maybe I missed his meaning. Perhaps he meant that their minds were of low degree, able to figure out the simple things—'One-one-two—yes!'—but not more difficult things—'Two-two-four—no!' But I think from what we saw later that he meant the other.

"After a few moments, the creatures came rushing back—first one, then another. Their pushcarts were full of stones, sand, chunks of rubbery plants, and such rubbish as that. They droned out their friendly greeting, which didn't really sound so friendly, and dashed on. The third one I assumed to be my first acquaintance and I decided to have another chat with him. I stepped into his path again and waited.

"Up he came, booming out his 'We are v-r-r-riends,' and stopped. I looked at him; four or five of his eyes looked at me. He tried his pass-word again and gave a shove on his cart, but I stood firm. And then the—the dashed creature reached out one of his arms, and two fingerlike nippers tweaked my nose!"

"Haw!" roared Harrison. "Maybe the things have a sense of beauty!"

"Laugh!" grumbled Jarvis. "I'd already had a nasty bump and a mean frostbite on that nose. Anyway, I yelled 'Ouch!' and jumped aside and the creature dashed away; but from then on, their greeting was 'We are v-r-r-riends! Ouch!' Queer beasts!

"Tweel and I followed the road squarely up to the nearest mound. The creatures were coming and going, paying us not the slightest attention, fetching their loads of rubbish. The road simply dived into an opening, and slanted down like an old mine, and in and out darted the barrel-people, greeting us with their eternal phrase.

"I looked in; there was a light somewhere below, and I was curious to see it. It didn't look like a flame or torch, you understand, but more like a civilized light, and I thought that I might get some clue as to the creatures' development. So in I went and Tweel tagged along, not without a few trills and twitters, however.

"The light was curious; it sputtered and flared like an old arc light, but came from a single black rod set in the wall of the corridor. It was electric, beyond doubt. The creatures were fairly civilized, apparently.

"Then I saw another light shining on something that glittered and I went on to look at that, but it was only a heap of shiny sand. I turned toward the entrance to leave, and the devil take me if it wasn't gone!

"I suppose the corridor had curved, or I'd stepped into a side passage. Anyway, I walked back in that direction I thought we'd come, and all I saw was more dim-lit corridor. The place was a labyrinth! There was nothing but twisting passages running every way, lit by occasional lights, and now and then a creature running by, sometimes with a pushcart, sometimes without.

"Well, I wasn't much worried at first. Tweel and I had only come a few steps from the entrance. But every move we made after that seemed to get us in deeper. Finally I tried following one of the creatures with an empty cart, thinking that he'd be going out for his rubbish, but he ran around aimlessly, into one passage and out another. When he started dashing around a pillar like one of those Japanese waltzing mice, I gave up, dumped my water tank on the floor, and sat down.

"Tweel was as lost as I. I pointed up and he said 'No—no—no!' in a sort of helpless trill. And we couldn't get any help from the natives. They paid no attention at all, except to assure us they were friends—ouch!

"Lord! I don't know how many hours or days we wandered around there! I slept twice from sheer exhaustion; Tweel never seemed to need sleep. We tried following only the upward corridors, but they'd run uphill a ways and then curve downwards. The temperature in that damned anthill was constant; you couldn't tell night from day and after my first sleep I didn't know whether I'd slept one hour or thirteen, so I couldn't tell from my watch whether it was midnight or noon.

"We saw plenty of strange things. There

were machines running in some of the corridors, but they didn't seem to be doing anything—just wheels turning. And several times I saw two barrel-beasts with a little one growing between them, joined to both."

"Parthenogenesis!" exulted Leroy. "Parthenogenesis by budding like *les tulipes*!"

"If you say so, Frenchy," agreed Jarvis. "The things never noticed us at all, except, as I say, to greet us with 'We are v-r-r-riends! Ouch!' They seemed to have no home life of any sort, but just scurried around with their pushcarts, bringing in rubbish. And finally I discovered what they did with it.

"We'd had a little luck with a corridor, one that slanted upwards for a great distance. I was feeling that we ought to be close to the surface when suddenly the passage debouched into a domed chamber, the only one we'd seen. And man!—I felt like dancing when I saw what looked like daylight through a crevice in the roof.

"There was a—a sort of machine in the chamber, just an enormous wheel that turned slowly, and one of the creatures was in the act of dumping his rubbish below it. The wheel ground it with a crunch—sand, stones, plants, all into powder that sifted away somewhere. While we watched, others filed in, repeating the process, and that seemed to be all. No rhyme nor reason to the whole thing—but that's characteristic of this crazy planet. And there was another fact that's almost too bizarre to believe.

"One of the creatures, having dumped his load, pushed his cart aside with a crash and calmly shoved himself under the wheel! I watched him being crushed, too stupefied to make a sound, and a moment later, another followed him! They were perfectly methodical about it, too; one of the cartless creatures took the abandoned pushcart.

"Tweel didn't seem surprised; I pointed out the next suicide to him, and he just gave the most humanlike shrug imaginable, as much as to say, 'What can I do about it?' He must have known more or less about these creatures.

"Then I saw something else. There was something beyond the wheel, something shining on a sort of low pedestal. I walked over; there was a little crystal about the size of an egg, fluorescing to beat Tophet. The light from it stung my hands and face, almost like a static discharge, and then I noticed another funny thing. Remember that wart I had on my left thumb? Look!" Jarvis extended his hand. "It dried up and fell off—just like that! And my abused nose—say, the pain went out of it like magic! The thing had the property of hard X-rays or gamma radiations, only more so; it destroyed diseased tissue and left healthy tissue unharmed!

"I was thinking what a present *that'd* be to take back to Mother Earth when a lot of racket interrupted. We dashed back to the other side of the wheel in time to see one of the pushcarts ground up. Some suicide had been careless, it seems.

"Then suddenly the creatures were booming and drumming all around us and their noise was decidedly menacing. A crowd of them advanced toward us; we backed out of what I thought was the passage we'd entered by, and they came rumbling after us, some pushing carts and some not. Crazy brutes! There was a whole chorus of 'We are v-r-r-riends! Ouch!' I didn't like the 'ouch'; it was rather suggestive.

"Tweel had his glass gun out and I dumped my water tank for greater freedom and got mine. We backed up the corridor with the barrel-beasts following—about twenty of them. Queer thing—the ones coming in with loaded carts moved past us inches away without a sign.

"Tweel must have noticed that. Suddenly, he snatched out that glowing coal cigar-lighter of his and touched a cartload of plant limbs. Puff! The whole load was burning—and the crazy beast pushing it went right along without a change of pace! It created some disturbance among our 'v-r-r-riends,' however—and then I noticed the smoke eddying and swirling past us, and sure enough, there was the entrance!

"I grabbed Tweel and out we dashed and

after us our twenty pursuers. The daylight felt like heaven, though I saw at first glance that the sun was all but set, and that was bad, since I couldn't live outside my thermo-skin bag in a Martian night—at least, without a fire.

"And things got worse in a hurry. They cornered us in an angle between two mounds, and there we stood. I hadn't fired nor had Tweel; there wasn't any use in irritating the brutes. They stopped a little distance away and began their booming about friendship and ouches.

"Then things got still worse! A barrel-brute came out with a pushcart and they all grabbed into it and came out with handfuls of foot-long copper darts—sharp-looking ones—and all of a sudden one sailed past my ear—zing! And it was shoot or die then.

"We were doing pretty well for a while. We picked off the ones next to the pushcart and managed to keep the darts at a minimum, but suddenly there was a thunderous booming of 'v-r-r-riends' and 'ouches,' and a whole army of 'em came out of their hole.

"Man! We were through and I knew it! Then I realized that Tweel wasn't. He could have leaped the mound behind us as easily as not. He was staying for me!

"Say, I could have cried if there'd been time! I'd liked Tweel from the first, but whether I'd have had the gratitude to do what he was doing—suppose I *had* saved him from the first dream-beast—he'd done as much for me, hadn't he? I grabbed his arm, and said 'Tweel,' and pointed up, and he understood. He said, 'No—no—no, Tick!' and popped away with his glass pistol.

"What could I do? I'd be a goner anyway when the sun set, but I couldn't explain that to him. I said, 'Thanks, Tweel. You're a man!' and felt that I wasn't paying him any compliment at all. A man! There are mighty few men who'd do that.

"So I went 'bang' with my gun and Tweel went 'puff' with his, and the barrels were throwing darts and getting ready to rush us, and booming about being friends. I had given up hope. Then suddenly an angel dropped right down from heaven in the shape of Putz, with his under-jets blasting the barrels into very small pieces!

"Wow! I let out a yell and dashed for the rocket; Putz opened the door and in I went, laughing and crying and shouting! It was a moment or so before I remembered Tweel; I looked around in time to see him rising in one of his nosedives over the mound and away.

"I had a devil of a job arguing Putz into following! By the time we got the rocket aloft, darkness was down; you know how it comes here—like turning off a light. We sailed out over the desert and put down once or twice. I yelled 'Tweel!' and yelled it a hundred times, I guess. We couldn't find him; he could travel like the wind and all I got—or else I imagined it—was a faint trilling and twittering drifting out of the south. He'd gone, and damn it! I wish—I wish he hadn't!"

The four men of the *Ares* were silent—even the sardonic Harrison. At last little Leroy broke the stillness.

"I should like to see," he murmured.

"Yeah," said Harrison. "And the wart cure. Too bad you missed that; it might be the cancer cure they've been hunting for a century and a half."

"Oh, that!" muttered Jarvis gloomily. "That's what started the fight!" He drew a glistening object from his pocket.

"Here it is."

The Last Poet and the Robots
A. MERRITT

Abraham Grace Merritt (1884–1943), who wrote under the name A. Merritt, was a US writer and editor. Much of his writing could be easily classified as fantasy of varying types, such as supernatural fantasy or dark fantasy. His fiction writing was actually a side interest of his successful journalism career, for which he was paid $25,000 per year in 1919 and $100,000 per year by the end of his life. This wealth allowed him to cultivate interests in world travel and such ironic hobbies as raising orchids and plants linked to, among other things, witchcraft and magic, including wolfsbane, blue datura, and cannabis.

Merritt was good at renovations, and his influence on the science fiction and fantasy world occurred not because of his story lines necessarily, but because of his unique style and the genuine imaginative power he displayed in the creation of hypnotically attractive alternative worlds and realities. He was extremely popular during his lifetime, even having a magazine, *A. Merritt's Fantasy Magazine*, named after him; to many readers, he was the premier fantasy genius of his time. He was posthumously inducted into the Science Fiction and Fantasy Hall of Fame in 1999.

Even though Merritt's repeated romantic image of the beautiful evil priestess was derived from a common Victorian stereotype of womanhood, the escapist yearning for otherness and mystery that he expressed has seldom been conveyed with such an emotional charge, nor with such lucid underlying pessimism, for his tales seldom permit a successful transit from this world. His vision is of a universe whose indifference to humanity reads like malice, a vision expressed most fully in *The Metal Monster*. His approach often includes some element of horror as a result, and reflects a general fusion of horror and science fiction also found in the work of Edmond Hamilton and Stanley G. Weinbaum.

"The Last Poet and the Robots" (first published in *Fantasy Magazine*, 1934) was originally revised from a chapter of the round-robin novel *Cosmos* (the chapter was titled "The Last Poet and the Robots AKA The Last Poet & the Wrongness of Space"). It was published again as "The Rhythm of the Spheres" in *Thrilling Wonder Stories* in 1936. The *Cosmos* round-robin serialized novel was the brainchild of Julius Schwartz and Raymond A. Palmer, who gathered sixteen writers to contribute to this ambitious project later published in installments in the fanzine *Science Fiction Digest*. Edmond Hamilton and E. E. "Doc" Smith were also contributors. "The Last Poet and the Robots" confronts the conflict between science and art. It was seen as having reconciled these two forces and also transcending the divisions of sexuality and nationality.

THE LAST POET AND THE ROBOTS

A. Merritt

Narodny, the Russian, sat in his laboratory. Narodny's laboratory was a full mile under earth. It was one of a hundred caverns, some small and some vast, cut out of the living rock. It was a realm of which he was sole ruler. In certain caverns garlands of small suns shone; and in others little moons waxed and waned over Earth; and there was a cavern in which reigned perpetual dawn, dewy, over lily beds and violets and roses; and another in which crimson sunsets baptized in the blood of slain day dimmed and died and were born again behind the sparkling curtains of the aurora. And there was one cavern ten miles from side to side in which grew flowering trees and trees which bore fruits unknown to man for many generations. Over this great orchard one yellow sun-like orb shone, and clouds trailed veils of rain upon the trees and miniature thunder drummed at Narodny's summoning.

Narodny was a poet—the last poet. He did not write his poems in words but in colors, sounds, and visions made material. Also he was a great scientist. In his peculiar field the greatest. Thirty years before, Russia's Science Council had debated whether to grant him the leave of absence he had asked, or to destroy him. They knew him to be unorthodox. How deadly so they did not know, else after much deliberation they would not have released him. It must be remembered that of all nations, Russia then was the most mechanized; most robot-ridden.

Narodny did not hate mechanization. He was indifferent to it. Being truly intelligent he hated nothing. Also he was indifferent to the whole civilization man had developed and into which he had been born. He had no feeling of kinship to humanity. Outwardly, in body, he belonged to the species. Not so in mind. Like Loeb, a thousand years before, he considered mankind a race of crazy half-monkeys, intent upon suicide. Now and then, out of the sea of lunatic mediocrity, a wave uplifted that held for a moment a light from the sun of truth— but soon it sank back and the light was gone. Quenched in the sea of stupidity. He knew that he was one of those waves.

He had gone, and he had been lost to sight by all. In a few years he was forgotten. Fifteen years ago, unknown and under another name, he had entered America and secured rights to a thousand acres in what of old had been called Westchester. He had picked this place because investigation had revealed to him that of ten localities on this planet it was most free from danger of earthquake or similar seismic disturbance. The man who owned it had been whimsical; possibly an atavist—like Narodny, although Narodny would never have thought of himself as that. At any rate, instead of an angled house of glass such as the thirtieth century built, this man had reconstructed a rambling old stone house of the nineteenth century. Few people lived upon the open land in those days; most had withdrawn into the city-states. New York, swollen by its meals of years, was a fat belly full of mankind still many miles away. The land around the house was forest covered.

A week after Narodny had taken this house, the trees in front of it had melted away, leaving a three-acre, smooth field. It was not as though they had been cut, but as though they had been dissolved. Later that night a great airship had appeared upon this field—abruptly, as though it had blinked out of another dimension. It was rocket shaped but noiseless. And immediately a fog had fallen upon airship and house, hiding them. Within this fog, if one could have seen, was a wide tunnel leading from the air cylinder's door to the door of the house. And out of the airship came swathed figures, ten of them, who walked along that tunnel, were met by Narodny, and the door of the old house closed on them.

A little later they returned, Narodny with them, and out of an opened hatch of the airship rolled a small flat car on which was a mechanism of crystal cones rising around each other to a central cone some four feet high. The cones were upon a thick base of some glassy material in which was imprisoned a restless green radiance. Its rays did not penetrate that which held it, but it seemed constantly seeking, with suggestion of prodigious force, to escape. For hours the strange thick fog held. Twenty miles up in the far reaches of the stratosphere, a faintly sparkling cloud grew, like a condensation of cosmic dust. And just before dawn the rock of the hill behind the house melted away like a curtain that had covered a great tunnel. Five of the men came out of the house and went into the airship. It lifted silently from the ground, slipped into the aperture, and vanished. There was a whispering sound, and when it had died away the breast of the hill was whole again. The rocks had been drawn together like a closing curtain and boulders studded it as before. That the breast was now slightly concave where before it had been convex, none would have noticed.

For two weeks the sparkling cloud was observed far up in the stratosphere, was commented upon idly, and then was seen no more. Narodny's caverns were finished.

Half of the rock from which they had been hollowed had gone with that sparkling cloud. The balance, reduced to its primal form of energy, was stored in blocks of the vitreous material that had supported the cones, and within them it moved as restlessly and always with that same suggestion of prodigious force. And it was force, unthinkably potent; from it

came the energy that made the little suns and moons, and actuated the curious mechanisms that regulated pressure in the caverns, supplied the air, created the rain, and made of Narodny's realm a mile deep under earth the paradise of poetry, of music, of color, and of form which he had conceived in his brain and with the aid of those ten others had caused to be.

Now of the ten there is no need to speak further. Narodny was the master. But three, like him, were Russians; two were Chinese; of the remaining five, three were women—one German in ancestry, one Basque, one a Eurasian; a Hindu who traced his descent from the line of Gautama; a Jew who traced his from Solomon.

All were one with Narodny in indifference to the world; each with him in his viewpoint on life; and each and all lived in his or her own Eden among the hundred caverns except when it interested them to work with each other. Time meant nothing to them. Their researches and discoveries were solely for their own uses and enjoyments. If they had given them to the outer world they would have only been ammunition for warfare either between men upon Earth or men against some other planet. Why hasten humanity's suicide? Not that they would have felt regret at the eclipse of humanity. But why trouble to expedite it? Time meant nothing to them because they could live as long as they desired—barring accident. And while there was rock in the world, Narodny could convert it into energy to maintain his paradise—or to create others.

The old house began to crack and crumble. It fell—much more quickly than the elements could have brought about its destruction. Then trees grew among the ruins of its foundations; and the field that had been so strangely cleared was overgrown with trees. The land became a wood in a few short years; silent except for the roar of an occasional rocket passing over it and the songs of birds that had found there a sanctuary.

But deep down in earth, within the caverns, were music and song and mirth and beauty.

Gossamer nymphs circled under the little moons. Pan piped. There was revelry of antique harvesters under the small suns. Grapes grew and ripened, were pressed, and red and purple wine was drunk by Bacchantes who fell at last asleep in the arms of fauns and satyrs. Oreads danced under the pale moon-bows and sometimes centaurs wheeled and trod archaic measures beneath them to the drums of their hoofs upon the mossy floor. The old Earth lived again.

Narodny listened to drunken Alexander raving to Thais among the splendors of conquered Persepolis; and he heard the crackling of the flames that at the whim of the courtesan destroyed it. He watched the siege of Troy and counted with Homer the Achaean ships drawn up on the strand before Troy's walls; or saw with Herodotus the tribes that marched behind Xerxes—the Caspians in their cloaks of skin with their bows of cane; the Ethiopians in the skins of leopards with spears of antelope horns; the Libyans in their dress of leather with javelins made hard by fire; the Thracians with the heads of foxes upon their heads; the Moschians, who wore helmets made of wood; and the Cabalians, who wore the skulls of men. For him the Eleusinian and the Osirian mysteries were reenacted, and he watched the women of Thrace tear to fragments Orpheus, the first great musician. At his will, he could see the rise and fall of the empire of the Aztecs, the empire of the Incas; or beloved Caesar slain in Rome's senate; or the archers at Agincourt; or the Americans in Belleau Wood. Whatever man had written—whether poets, historians, philosophers, or scientists—his strangely shaped mechanisms could bring before him, changing the words into phantoms real as though living.

He was the last and greatest of the poets—but also he was the last and greatest of the musicians. He could bring back the songs of ancient Egypt, or the chants of more ancient Ur. The songs that came from Mussorgsky's soul of Mother Earth, the harmonies of Beethoven's deaf ear, or the chants and rhapsodies from the heart of Chopin. He could do more than restore the music of the past. He was master of sound. To him, the music of the spheres was real. He could take the rays of the stars and planets and weave them into symphonies. Or convert the sun's rays into golden tones no earthly orchestras had ever expressed. And the silver music of the moon—the sweet music of the moon of spring, the full-throated music of the harvest moon, the brittle crystalling music of the winter moon with its arpeggios of meteors—he could weave into strains such as no human ears had ever heard.

So Narodny, the last and greatest of poets, the last and greatest of musicians, the last and greatest of artists—and in his inhuman way, the greatest of scientists—lived with the ten of his choosing in his caverns. And, with them, he consigned the surface of Earth and all who dwelt upon it to a negative hell—

Unless something happening there might imperil his paradise!

Aware of the possibility of that danger, among his mechanisms were those which brought to eyes and ears news of what was happening on Earth's surface. Now and then, they amused themselves with these.

It so happened that on that night when the Warper of Space had dealt his blow at the spaceships and had flung a part of the great Crater of Copernicus into another dimension, Narodny had been weaving the rays of the moon, Jupiter, and Saturn into Beethoven's *Moonlight Sonata*. The moon was a four-day crescent. Jupiter was at one cusp, and Saturn hung like a pendant below the bow. Shortly Orion would stride across the heavens and bright Regulus and red Aldebaran, the Eye of the Bull, would furnish him with other chords of starlight remoulded into sound.

Suddenly the woven rhythms were ripped—hideously. A devastating indescribable dissonance invaded the cavern. Beneath it, the nymphs who had been dancing languorously to the strains quivered like mist wraiths in a sudden blast and were gone: the little moons flared, then ceased to glow. The tonal instruments were dead. And Narodny was felled as though by a blow.

After a time the little moons began to glow again, but dimly; and from the tonal mechanisms came broken, crippled music. Narodny stirred and sat up, his lean, high-cheeked face more satanic than ever. Every nerve was numb; then as they revived, agony crept along them. He sat, fighting the agony, until he could summon help. He was answered by one of the Chinese, and soon Narodny was himself again.

He said: "It was a spatial disturbance, Lao. And it was like nothing I have ever known. It came in upon the rays, of that I am sure. Let us look out upon the moon."

They passed to another cavern and stood before an immense television screen. They adjusted it, and upon it appeared the moon, rapidly growing larger as though it were hurtling toward them. Then upon the screen appeared a spaceship speeding earthward. They focused upon it, and opened it to their vision; searching it until they came to the control room where were Bartholomew, James Tarvish, and Martin, their gaze upon Earth rapidly and more rapidly expanding in the heavens. Narodny and the Chinese watched them, reading their lips. Tarvish said: "Where can we land, Martin? The robots will be watching for us everywhere. They will see to it that we are destroyed before we can give our message and our warning to the world. They control the governments—or at least control them sufficiently to seize us upon landing. And if we should escape and gather men around us, then it means civil war and that in turn means fatal delay in the building of the space fleet—even if we should win."

Martin said: "We *must* land safely—escape the robots—find some to control or destroy them. God, Tarvish—you saw what that devil they call the Wrongness of Space can do. He threw the side of the crater out of our dimension as a boy would throw a stone into a pond!"

Bartholomew said: "He could take Earth and break it up piecemeal—"

Narodny and Lao looked at each other.

Narodny said: "That is enough. We know." The Chinese nodded. Narodny said: "I estimated that they would reach Earth in four hours." Again Lao nodded. Narodny said: "We will talk to them, Lao; although I had thought we were done with mankind. I do not like this which they call so quaintly the Wrongness of Space—nor the stone he threw into my music."

They brought a smaller screen into position before the larger one. They oriented it to the speeding spaceship and stepped in front of it. The small screen shimmered with whirling vortices of pallid blue luminescence; the vortices drew together and became one vast cone that reached on and on to the greater screen as though not feet but thousands of miles separated them. And as the tip of the cone touched the control room of the spaceship mirrored in the screen, Tarvish, upon the actual ship, gripped Martin's arm.

"Look there!"

There was an eddying in the air, like that over roads on a hot summer day. The eddying became a shimmering curtain of pallid blue luminescence—steadied until it was an oval doorway opening into vast distances. And then abruptly, within that doorway, stood two men—one tall and lean and saturnine with the sensitive face of a dreamer and the other a Chinese, his head a great yellow dome and on his face the calm of Buddha—and it was strange indeed to see in the cavern of earth these same two men standing before the blue-coned screen and upon the greater one their images within the imaged room on which the tip of the cone rested.

Narodny spoke, and in his voice there was a human indifference and sureness that chilled them, yet gave them courage. He said: "We mean you no harm. You cannot harm us. We have long been withdrawn from men. What happens on the surface of Earth means nothing to us. What may happen beneath the surface means much. Whatever it is you have named the Wrongness of Space has already annoyed me. I perceive that he can do more than annoy. I gather that the robots in one way or another are on his side. You are against him. Therefore, our first step must be to help you against the robots. Place me in possession of all facts. Be brief, for we cannot maintain our position here for more than half an hour without discomfort."

Martin said: "Whoever you are, wherever you are, we trust you. Here is the story. . . ."

For fifteen minutes Narodny and the Chinese listened to their tale of struggle against the robots, of their escape and of the blasting of Copernicus in the effort of the Wrongness of Space to prevent their return.

Narodny said: "Enough. Now I understand. How long can you remain in space? I mean— what are your margins of power and of food?"

Martin answered: "Six days."

Narodny said: "Ample time for success—or failure. Remain aloft for that time, then descend to where you started—"

Suddenly he smiled: "I care nothing for mankind—yet I would not harm them, willingly. And it has occurred to me that I owe them, after all, a great debt. Except for them—I would not be. Also, it occurs to me that the robots have never produced a poet, a musician, an artist—" He laughed: "But it is in my mind that they are capable of one great art at least! We shall see."

The oval was abruptly empty; then it too was gone. Bartholomew said: "Call the others. I am for obeying. But they must know." And when the others had heard, they too voted to obey, and the spaceship, course changed, began to circle, as slowly as it could, the Earth.

Down in the chamber of the screens, Narodny laughed and laughed again. He said: "Lao, is it that we have advanced so in these few years? Or that men have retrogressed? No, it is this curse of mechanization that destroys imagination. For look you, how easy is this problem of the robots. They began as man-made machines. Mathematical, soulless, insensible to any emotion. So was primal matter, of which all on Earth are made, rock and water, tree and grass, metal, animal, fish, worm, and

men. But somewhere, somehow, something was added to this primal matter, combined with it— used it. It was what we call life. And life is consciousness. And therefore largely emotion. Life established its rhythm—and its rhythm being different in rock and crystal, metal, fish, and so on, and man, we have these varying things.

"Well, it seems that life has begun to establish its rhythm in the robots. Consciousness has touched them. The proof? They have established the idea of common identity—group consciousness. That in itself involves emotion. But they have gone further. They have attained the instinct of self-preservation. And that, my wise friend, connotes fear—fear of extinction. And fear connotes anger, hatred, arrogance— and many other things. The robots, in short, have become emotional to a degree. And therefore vulnerable to whatever may amplify and control their emotions. They are no longer mechanisms.

"So, Lao, I have in mind an experiment that will provide me study and amusement through many years. Originally, the robots are the children of mathematics. I ask—to what is mathematics most closely related. I answer—to rhythm—to sound—to sounds which will raise to the nth degree the rhythms to which they will respond. Both mathematically and emotionally."

Lao said: "The sonic sequences?"

Narodny answered: "Exactly. But we must have a few with which to experiment. To do that means to dissolve the upper gate. But that is nothing. Tell Maringy and Euphrosyne to do it. Net a ship and bring it here. Bring it down gently. You will have to kill the men in it, of course, but do it mercifully. Then let them bring me the robots. Use the green flame on one or two—the rest will follow, I'll warrant you."

The hill behind where the old house had stood trembled. A circle of pale green light gleamed on its breast. It dimmed, where it had been was the black mouth of a tunnel. An airship, half-rocket, half-winged, making its way to New York, abruptly dropped, circled, and streaked back. It fell gently like a moth, close to the yawning mouth of the tunnel.

Its door opened, and out came two men, pilots, cursing. There was a little sigh from the tunnel's mouth and a silvery misty cloud sped from it, over the pilots and straight through the opened door. The pilots staggered and crumpled to the ground. In the airship half a dozen other men slumped to the floor, smiled, and died.

There were a full score robots in the ship. They stood, looking at the dead men and at each other. Out of the tunnel came two figures swathed in metallic glimmering robes. They entered the ship. One said: "Robots, assemble."

The metal men stood, motionless. Then one sent out a shrill call. From all parts of the ship the metal men moved. They gathered behind the one who had sent the call. They stood behind him, waiting.

In the hand of one of those who had come from the tunnel was what might have been an antique flashlight. From it sped a thin green flame. It struck the foremost robot on the head, sliced down from the head to the base of the trunk. Another flash, and the green flame cut him from side to side. He fell, sliced by that flame into four parts. The four parts lay, inert as their metal, upon the floor of the compartment.

One of the shrouded figures said: "Do you want further demonstration—or will you follow us?"

The robots put heads together; whispered. Then one said: "We will follow."

They marched into the tunnel, the robots making no resistance nor effort to escape. Again there was the sighing, and the rocks closed the tunnel mouth. They came to a place whose floor sank with them until it had reached the caverns. The machine-men still went docilely. Was it because of curiosity mixed with disdain for these men whose bodies could be broken so easily by one blow of the metal appendages that served them for arms? Perhaps.

They came to the cavern where Narodny and the others awaited them. Marinoff led them in and halted them. These were the robots used in the flying ships—their heads cylindrical, four arm appendages, legs triple jointed, torsos slender. The robots, it should be understood, were differentiated in shape according to their occupations. Narodny said:

"Welcome, robots. Who is your leader?"

One answered: "We have no leaders. We act as one."

Narodny laughed: "Yet by speaking for them you have shown yourself leader. Step closer. Do not fear—yet."

The robot said: "We feel no fear. Why should we? Even if you should destroy us who are here, you cannot destroy the billions of us outside. Nor can you breed fast enough, become men soon enough, to cope with us who enter into life strong and complete from the beginning."

He flicked an appendage toward Narodny and there was contempt in the gesture. But before he could draw it back a bracelet of green flame circled it at the shoulder. It had darted like a thrown loop from something in Narodny's hand. The robot's arm dropped clanging to the floor, cleanly severed. The robot stared at it unbelievingly, threw forward his other three arms to pick it up. Again the green flame encircled them, encircled also his legs above the second joints. The robot crumpled and pitched forward, crying in high-pitched shrill tones to the others.

Swiftly the green flame played among them. Legless, armless, some decapitated, all the robots fell except two.

"Two will be enough," said Narodny. "But they will not need arms—only feet."

The flashing green bracelets encircled the appendages and excised them. The pair were marched away. The bodies of the others were taken apart, studied, and under Narodny's direction curious experiments were made. Music filled the cavern, strange chords, unfamiliar progressions, shattering arpeggios, and immense vibrations of sound that could be felt but not heard by the human ear. And finally this last deep vibration burst into hearing as a vast drone, hummed up and up into a swift tingling tempest of crystalline brittle notes, and still ascending passed into shrill high pipings, and continued again unheard, as had the prelude to the droning. And thence it rushed back, the piping and the crystalline storm reversed, into the drone and the silence—then back and up.

And the bodies of the broken robots began to quiver, to tremble, as though every atom within them were in ever increasing, rhythmic motion. Up rushed the music and down—again and again. It ended abruptly in midflight with one crashing note.

The broken bodies ceased their quivering. Tiny star-shaped cracks appeared in their metal. Once more the note sounded and the cracks widened. The metal splintered.

Narodny said: "Well, there is the frequency for the rhythm of our robots. The destructive unison. I hope for the sake of the world outside it is not also the rhythm of many of their buildings and bridges. But after all, in any war there must be casualties on both sides."

Lao said: "Earth will be an extraordinary spectacle for a few days."

Narodny said: "It's going to be an extraordinarily uncomfortable Earth for a few days, and without doubt many will die and many more go mad. But is there any other way?"

There was no answer. He said: "Bring in the two robots."

They brought them in.

Narodny said: "Robots—were there ever any of you who could poetize?"

They answered: "What is poetize?"

Narodny laughed: "Never mind. Have you ever sung—made music—painted? Have you ever—dreamed?"

One robot said with cold irony: "Dreamed? No—for we do not sleep. We leave all that to men. It is why we have conquered them."

Narodny said, almost gently: "Not yet, robot. Have you ever—danced? No? It is an art you are about to learn."

The unheard note began, droned up and through the tempest and away and back again.

And up and down—and up and down, though not so loudly as before. And suddenly the feet of the robots began to move, to shuffle. Their leg joints bent; their bodies swayed. The note seemed to move now here and now there about the chamber, they always following it, grotesquely. Like huge metal marionettes, they followed it. The music ended in the crashing note. And it was as though every vibrating atom of the robot bodies had met some resistible obstruction. Their bodies quivered and from their voice mechanisms came a shriek that was a hideous blend of machine and life. Once more the drone, and once more and once more and again the abrupt stop. There was a brittle crackling all over the conical heads, all over the bodies. The star-shaped splinterings appeared. Once again the drone—but the two robots stood, unresponding. For through the complicated mechanisms which under their carapaces animated them were similar splinterings.

The robots were dead!

Narodny said: "By tomorrow we can amplify the sonar to make it effective in a three-thousand-mile circle. We will use the upper cavern, of course. Equally of course, it means we must take the ship out again. In three days, Marinoff, you should be able to cover the other continents. See to it that the ship is completely proof against the vibrations. To work. We must act quickly—before the robots can discover how to neutralize them."

It was exactly at noon the next day that over all North America a deep unexplainable droning was heard. It seemed to come not only from deep within Earth, but from every side. It mounted rapidly through a tempest of tingling crystalline notes into a shrill piping and was gone . . . then back it rushed from piping to the drone . . . then up and out and down . . . again and again. And over all North America the hordes of robots stopped in whatever they were doing. Stopped . . . and then began to dance. They danced in the airships and scores of those ships crashed before the human crews could gain control. They danced by the thousands in the streets of the cities—in grotesque rigadoons, in bizarre sarabands, with shuffle and hop and jig the robots danced while the people fled in panic and hundreds of them were crushed and died in those panics. In the great factories, and in the tunnels of the lower cities, and in the mines—everywhere the sound was heard—and it was heard everywhere—the robots danced . . . to the piping of Narodny, the last great poet . . . the last great musician.

And then came the crashing note—and over all the country the dance halted. And began again . . . and ceased . . . and began again . . .

Until at last the streets, the lower tunnels of the lower levels, the mines, the factories, the homes, were littered with metal bodies shot through and through with star-shaped splinterings.

In the cities the people cowered, not knowing what blow was to fall upon them . . . or milled about in fear-maddened crowds, and many more died. . . .

Then suddenly the dreadful droning, the shattering tempest, the intolerable high piping ended. And everywhere the people fell, sleeping among the dead robots, as though they never had been strung to the point of breaking, sapped of strength and abruptly relaxed.

As though it had vanished, America was deaf to cables, to all communication beyond the gigantic circle of sound.

But that midnight over all Europe the drone sounded and Europe's robots began their dance of death . . . and when it had ended a strange and silent rocket ship that had hovered high above the stratosphere sped almost with the speed of light and hovered over Asia—and next day Africa heard the drone while the natives answered it with their tom-toms—then South America heard it and last of all far-off Australia . . . and everywhere terror trapped the peoples and panic and madness took their toll. . . .

Until of all that animate metal horde that had tethered Earth and humanity there were a few scant hundreds left—escaped from the death dance through some variant in their constitution. And, awakening from that swift sleep, all over Earth those who had feared and hated the robots and their slavery rose against those who had fostered the metal domination, and blasted the robot factories to dust.

Again the hill above the caverns opened, the strange torpedo ship blinked into sight like a ghost, as silently as a ghost floated into the hill, and the rocks closed behind it.

Narodny and the others stood before the gigantic television screen, shifting upon it images of city after city, country after country, over all Earth's surface. Lao, the Chinese, said: "Many men died, but many are left. They may not understand—but to them it was worth it."

Narodny mused: "It drives home the lesson, what man does not pay for, he values little. Our friends aloft will have little opposition now I think."

He shook his head, doubtfully. "But I still do not like that Wrongness of Space. I do not want my music spoiled again by him, Lao. Shall we hurl the moon out of the universe, Lao?"

Lao laughed: "And what then would you do for moon music?"

Narodny said: "True. Well, let us see what men can do. There is always time—perhaps."

The difficulties which beset humanity did not interest the poet Narodny. While the world governments were reorganized—factories turned out spaceships for Earth's fleet—men were trained in handling these ships—supplies were gathered—weapons were perfected—and when the message from Luna, outlining the course to be followed and setting the starting date, arrived, the space fleet of Earth was ready to leave.

Narodny watched the ships take off. He shook his head, doubtfully. But soon harmonies were swelling through the great cavern of the orchards and nymphs and fauns dancing under the fragrant blossoming trees—and the world was again forgotten by Narodny.

The Microscopic Giants

PAUL ERNST

Paul Ernst (1899–1985) was a US writer who wrote mostly short fiction for pulp markets. His first published story may have been "The Temple of Serpents" for *Weird Tales* in 1928, and he remained extremely active throughout the 1930s, writing for science fiction and fantasy magazines. Under the house name Kenneth Robeson, he was responsible for much of the contents of *The Avenger*, writing all twenty-three novel-length stories for that magazine between 1939 and 1942, each featuring the Avenger, a superhero who fought a wide range of villains. Ernst also wrote a Doctor Satan series for *Weird Tales*, beginning, predictably enough, with "Doctor Satan" (1935), which is fantasy along conventional hero-villain lines. One-off stories appeared mostly in magazines like *Astounding Science Fiction*. Then, in the mid-1940s, Ernst switched over to writing mostly for mainstream magazines such as *Good Housekeeping* and his science fiction output became minimal, at best.

"The Microscopic Giants," his best story, was first published in *Thrilling Wonder Stories* (1936). Anthologized later in *Alfred Hitchcock's Monster Museum* (1965), the story features a race of people living under the Earth. Ernst combines a fascination with miniaturization with a modified hollow-Earth scenario. In addition to myths in almost every culture and religion recounting "underground lands," hollow-Earth theories had been popular in the US since the 1800s, often backed up by seemingly "reliable" science. Some "researchers" made entire careers out of lecturing on the subject. (*Hollow Earth* by David Standish, 2006, provides a lovely overview of the history of this fascination—the theories, legends, and modern-day personalities involved.)

Ernst's story reflects not just one potent vein of early twentieth-century science fiction, but a public fascination with the idea. This fascination had been fed by such earlier examples as Jules Verne's *Journey to the Center of the Earth* and Edgar Rice Burroughs's Pellucidar novels, which featured wild adventures in a prehistoric level below the Earth's crust. Another early example of mysterious underground societies, more horror than science fiction, is on display in Robert Barbour Johnson's "Far Below" (*Weird Tales*, 1939), collected in *The Weird: A Compendium of Strange and Dark Stories*.

THE MICROSCOPIC GIANTS

Paul Ernst

It happened toward the end of the Great War of 1941, which was an indirect cause. You'll find mention of it in the official records filed at Washington. Curious reading, some of those records! Among them are accounts of incidents so bizarre—freak accidents and odd discoveries fringing war activities—that the filing clerks must have raised their eyebrows skeptically before they buried them in steel cabinets, to remain unread for the rest of time.

But this particular one will never be buried in oblivion for me. Because I was on the spot when it happened, and I was the one who sent in the report.

Copper!

A war-torn world was famished for it. The thunder of guns, from the Arctic to the Antarctic and from the Pacific to the Atlantic and back again, drummed for it. Equipment behind the lines demanded it. Statesmen lied for it and national bankers ran up bills that would never be paid to get it.

Copper, copper, copper!

Every obscure mine in the world was worked to capacity. Men risked their lives to salvage fragments from battlefields a thousand miles long. And still not enough copper was available for the maws of the electric furnaces.

Up in the Lake Superior region we had gone down thirty-one thousand feet for it. Then, in answer to the enormous prices being paid for copper, we sank a shaft to forty thousand five hundred feet, where we struck a vein of almost pure ore. And it was shortly after this that my assistant, a young mining engineer named Belmont, came into my office, his eyes afire with the light of discovery.

"We've uncovered the greatest archaeological find since the days of the Rosetta stone!" he announced bluntly. "Down in the new low level. I want to phone the Smithsonian Institution at once. There may be a war on, but the professors will forget all about war when they see this!"

Jim Belmont was apt to be over-enthusiastic. Under thirty, a tall, good-looking chap with light blue eyes looking lighter than they really were in a tanned, lean face, he sometimes overshot his mark by leaping before he looked.

"Wait a minute!" I said. "What have you found? Prehistoric bones? Some new kind of fossil monster?"

"Not bones," said Belmont, fidgeting toward the control board that dialed our private number to Washington on the radio telephone. "Footprints, Frayter. Fossil footsteps."

"You mean men's footprints?" I demanded, frowning. The rock formation at the forty-thousand-foot level was age-old. The Pleistocene era had not occurred when those rocks were formed. "Impossible."

"But I tell you they're down there! Footprints preserved in solid rock. Men's footprints! They antedate anything ever thought of in the age of man."

Belmont drew a deep breath.

"And more than that," he almost whispered. "They are prints of shod men, Frank! The men who made those prints, millions of years ago, wore shoes. We've stumbled on traces of a civilization that existed long, long before man was supposed to have evolved on this earth at all!"

His whisper reverberated like a shout, such was its great import. But I still couldn't believe it. Prints of men—at the forty-thousand-foot level—and prints of shod feet at that!

"If they're prints of feet with shoes on them," I said, "they might be simply prints of our own workmen's boots. If the Smithsonian men got up here and found *that* a laugh would go up that would ruin us forever."

"No, no," said Belmont. "That's impossible. You see, these prints are those of *little* men. I hadn't told you before, had I? I guess I'm pretty excited. The men who made these prints were small—hardly more than two feet high, if the size of their feet can be taken as a true gauge. The prints are hardly more than three inches long."

"Where did you see them?" I asked.

"Near the concrete we poured to fill in the rift we uncovered at the far end of the level."

"Some of the workmen may have been playing a trick—"

"Your confounded skepticism!" Belmont ground out. "Tricks! Perhaps they're prints of our own men! Didn't I tell you the prints were preserved in *solid rock*? Do you think a workman would take the trouble to carve, most artistically, a dozen footprints three inches long in solid rock? Or that—if we had any men with feet that small—their feet would sink into the rock for a half inch or more? I tell you these are fossil prints, made millions of years ago when that rock was mud, and preserved when the rock hardened."

"And I tell you," I replied a little hotly, "that it's all impossible. Because I supervised the pouring of that concrete, and I would have noticed if there were prints before the rift."

"Suppose you come down and look," said Belmont. "After all, that's the one sure way of finding out if what I say is true."

I reached for my hat. Seeing for myself was the one way of finding out if Belmont had gone off half-cocked again.

It takes a long time to go down forty thousand feet. We hadn't attempted to speed up the drop too much; at such great depths there are abnormalities of pressure and temperature to which the human machine takes time to become accustomed.

By the time we'd reached the new low level I'd persuaded myself that Belmont must surely be mad. But having come this far I went through with it, of course.

Fossil prints of men who could not have been more than two feet high, shod in civilized fashion, preserved in rock at the forty-thousand-foot level! It was ridiculous.

We got near the concrete fill at the end of the tunnel, and I pushed the problem of prints out of my mind for a moment while I examined its blank face. Rearing that slanting concrete wall had presented some peculiar problems.

As we had bored in, ever farther under the thick skin of Mother Earth, we had come to a rock formation that had no right to exist there at all. It was a layer of soft, mushy stuff, with gaping cracks in it, slanting down somewhere toward the bowels of the earth. Like a soft strip of marrow in hard bone, it lay between dense, compressed masses of solid rock. And we had put ten feet of concrete over its face to avoid cave-ins.

Concrete is funny stuff. It acts differently in different pressures and temperatures. The concrete we'd poured down here, where atmospheric pressure made a man gasp and the temperature was above a hundred and eighteen in spite of cooling systems, hadn't acted at all like any I'd ever seen before. It hadn't seemed to harden as well as it should, and it still rayed out perceptible, self-generated heat in the pressure surrounding it. But it seemed to be serving its purpose, all right, though it was as soft as cheese compared to the rock around it. . . .

"Here!" said Belmont, pointing down in the bright light of the raw electric bulbs stringing along the level. "Look!"

I looked—and got a shock that I can still feel. A half inch or so deep in the rock floor of the level at the base of the concrete retaining wall, there were footprints. The oddest, tiniest things imaginable!

Jim Belmont had said they were three

inches long. If anything, he had overstated their size. I don't think some of them were more than two and a half inches long! And they were the prints of shod feet, undeniably. Perfect soles and heels, much like those of shoes we wear, were perceptible.

I stared at the prints with disbelief for a moment, even though my own eyes gave proof of their presence. And I felt an icy finger trace its way up my spine.

I had spent hours at this very spot while that concrete fill was made over the face of the down-slanting rift of mush rock. And I hadn't seen the little prints then. Yet here they were, a dozen of them made by feet of at least three varying sizes. How had I missed seeing them before?

"Prints made millions of years ago," Belmont whispered ecstatically. "Preserved when the mud hardened to rock—to be discovered here! Proof of a civilization on Earth before man was thought to have been born . . . For heaven's sake! Look at that concrete!"

I stared along the line of his pointing finger, and saw another queer thing. Queer? It was impossible!

The concrete retaining wall seemed slightly milky, and not quite opaque! Like a great block of frosted glass, into which the eye could see for a few inches before vision was lost.

And then, again, the icy finger touched my spine. This time so plainly that I shuddered a little in spite of the heat.

For a moment I had thought to see movement in the concrete! A vague, luminous swirl that was gone before I had fairly seen it. Or *had* I seen it? Was imagination, plus the presence of these eerie footprints, working overtime?

"Transparent concrete," said Belmont. "There's one for the book. Silicon in greater-than-normal amounts in the sand we used? Some trick of pressure? But it doesn't matter. The prints are more important. Shall we phone the Institution, Frank?"

For a moment I didn't answer. I was observing one more odd thing.

The footprints went in only two directions. They led out from the concrete wall, and led back to it again. And I could still swear they hadn't been there up to three days before, when I had examined the concrete fill most recently.

But of course they must have been there—for a million years or more!

"Let's wait a while on it," I heard myself say. "The prints won't vanish. They're in solid rock."

"But why wait?"

I stared at Belmont, and I saw his eyes widen at something in my face.

"There's something more than peculiar about those prints!" I said. "Fossil footsteps of men two feet high are fantastic enough. But there's something more fantastic than that! See the way they point from the concrete, and then back to it again? As if whatever made them had come out of the concrete, had looked around for a few minutes, and then had gone back into the concrete again!"

It was Belmont's turn to look at me as if suspecting a lack of sanity. Then he laughed.

"The prints were here a long, long time before the concrete was ever poured, Frank. They just happen to be pointing in the directions they do. All right, we'll wait on the Smithsonian Institution notification." He stopped and exclaimed aloud, gaze on the rock floor.

"What's the matter?" I asked.

"An illustration of how you could have overlooked the prints when you were supervising the fill," he said, grinning. "When I was down here last, a few hours ago, I counted an even twelve prints. Now, over here, where I'd have sworn there were no prints, I see four more, made by still another pair of feet back before the dawn of history. It's funny how unobservant the eye can be."

"Yes," I said slowly. "It's very—funny."

For the rest of the day the drive to get more ore out of the ground, ever more copper for the guns and war instruments, drove the thought of the prints to the back of my mind. But back there the thought persisted.

Tiny men, wearing civilized-looking boots, existing long, long ago! What could they have looked like? The prints, marvelously like those of our own shod feet, suggested that they must have been perfect little humans, like our midgets. What business could they have been about when they left those traces of their existence in mud marshes millions of years ago. . . .

Yes, of course, millions of years ago! Several times I had to rein in vague and impossible impressions with those words. But some deep instinct refused to be reined.

And then Carson, my foreman, came to me when the last of the men had emerged from the shafts.

Carson was old; all the young men save highly trained ones like Belmont and myself, who were more valuable in peace zones, were at the various war fronts. He was nearly seventy, and cool and levelheaded. It was unusual to see a frown on his face such as was there when he walked up to me.

"Mr. Frayter," he said, "I'm afraid we'll have trouble with the men."

"Higher wages?" I said. "If they had a spark of patriotism—"

"They're not kicking about wages," Carson said. "It's a lot different than that. Steve Boland, he started it."

He spat tobacco juice at a nail-head.

"Steve works on the new low level, you know. Near the concrete fill. And he's been passing crazy talk among the men. He says he can see into the concrete a little way—"

"That's right," I interrupted. "I was down there this afternoon, and for some curious reason the stuff is a little transparent. Doubtless we could investigate and find out what causes the phenomenon. But it isn't worth taking the time for."

"Maybe it would be worth it," replied Carson quietly. "If it would stop Steve's talk, it might save a shutdown."

"What is Steve saying?"

"He says he saw a man in the concrete, two hours ago. A little man."

I stared at Carson.

"I know he's crazy," the old man went on. "But he's got the rest to halfway believe it. He says he saw a man about a foot and a half high, looking at him out of the concrete. The man was dressed in strips of some shiny stuff that made him look like he had a metal shell on. He looked at Steve for maybe a minute, then turned and walked away. He walked back through the concrete, like it was nothing but thick air. Steve followed him for a foot or so and then was unable to see him anymore."

I smiled at Carson while sweat suddenly formed under my arms and trickled down my sides.

"Send Steve to me," I said. "I'll let him tell me the story too. Meanwhile, kill the story among the men."

Carson sighed.

"It's going to be pretty hard to kill, Mr. Frayter. You see, there's footprints down there. Little footprints that might be made by what Steve claimed he saw."

"You think a man eighteen inches high could sink into solid rock for half an inch—" I began. Then I stopped. But it was already too late.

"Oh, you've seen them too!" said Carson, with the glint of something besides worry in his eyes.

I told him of how and when the prints had been made.

"I'll send Steve to you," was all he said, avoiding my eyes.

Steve Boland was a hulking, powerful man of fifty. He was not one of my best men, but as far as I knew he had no record of being either unduly superstitious or a liar.

He repeated to me the story Carson had quoted him as telling. I tried to kill the fear I saw peering out of his eyes.

"You saw those prints, made long ago, and then you imagined you saw what had made them," I argued. "Use your head, man. Do you think anything could live and move around in concrete?"

"I don't think nothing about nothing, Mr. Frayter," he said doggedly. "I saw what I saw. A little man, dressed in some shiny stuff, in the concrete. And those footprints weren't made a long time ago. They were made in the last few days!"

I couldn't do anything with him. He was terrified, under his laborious show of self-control.

"I'm leaving, Mr. Frayter. Unless you let me work in an upper level. I won't go down there anymore."

After he had left my office shack, I sent for Belmont.

"This may get serious," I told him, after revealing what I'd heard. "We've got to stop this story right now."

He laughed. "Of all the crazy stuff! But you're right. We ought to stop it. What would be the best way?"

"We'll pull the night shift out of there," I said, "and we'll spend the night watching the concrete. Tell all the men in advance. Then when we come up in the morning, we can see if they'll accept our word of honor that nothing happened."

Belmont grinned and nodded.

"Take a gun," I added, staring at a spot over his head.

"What on earth for?"

"Why not?" I evaded. "They don't weigh much. We might as well carry one apiece in our belts."

His laugh stung me as he went to give orders to the crew usually working at night in the forty-thousand-foot level.

We started on the long trip down, alone.

There is no day or night underground. Yet somehow, as Belmont and I crouched in the low level we could know that it was not day. We could sense that deep night held the world outside; midnight darkness in which nothing was abroad save the faint wind rattling the leaves of the trees.

We sat on the rock fragments, with our backs against the wall, staring at the concrete fill till our eyes ached in the raw electric light.

We felt like fools, and said so to each other. And yet—

"Steve *has* some circumstantial evidence to make his insane yarn sound credible," I said. "The way we overlooked those footprints in the rock till recently makes it look as if they'd been freshly formed. You observed a few more this afternoon than you'd noticed before. And this ridiculous concrete is a shade transparent, as though some action—or movement—within it had changed its character slightly."

Belmont grimaced toward the concrete.

"If I'd known the report about the footprints was going to turn us all into crazy men," he grunted, "I'd have kept my mouth shut—"

His voice cracked off abruptly. I saw the grin freeze on his lips; saw him swallow convulsively.

"Look!" he whispered, pointing toward the center of the eight-by-thirty-foot wall.

I stared, but could see nothing unusual about the wall. That is, nothing but the fact we'd observed before: you could look into the thing for a few inches before vision was lost.

"What is it?" I snapped, stirred by the expression of his face.

He sighed, and shook his head.

"Nothing, I guess. I thought for a minute I saw something in the wall. A sort of moving bright spot. But I guess it's only another example of the kind of imagination that got Steve Boland—"

Again he stopped abruptly. And this time he got unsteadily to his feet.

"No, it's *not imagination*! Look, Frank! If you can't see it, then I'm going crazy!"

I stared again. And this time I could swear I saw something too.

Deep in the ten-foot-thick retaining wall, a dim, luminous spot seemed to be growing. As though some phosphorescent growth were slowly mushrooming in there.

"You see it too?" he breathed.

"I see it too," I whispered.

"Thank God for that! Then I'm sane—or we're both mad. What's happening inside that stuff? It's getting brighter, and larger—" His fingers clamped over my arm. "Look! *Look!*"

But there was no need for him to tell me to look. I was staring already with starting eyes, while my heart began to hammer in my chest like a sledge.

As the faint, luminous spot in the concrete grew larger it also took recognizable form. And the form that appeared in the depths of the stuff was that of a human!

Human? Well, yes, if you can think of a thing no bigger than an eighteen-inch doll as being human.

A mannikin a foot and a half high, embedded in the concrete! But not embedded—for it was moving! Toward us!

In astounded silence, Belmont and I stared. It didn't occur to us then to be afraid. Nothing occurred to us save indescribable wonder at the impossible vision we saw.

I can close my eyes and see the thing now: a manlike little figure walking toward us through solid concrete. It bent forward as though shouldering a way against a sluggish tide, off a heavy wind; it moved as a deep-sea diver might move in clogging water. But that was all the resistance the concrete seemed to offer to it, that sluggish impediment to its forward movement.

Behind it there was a faint swirl of luminosity, like phosphorescent water moving in the trail of a tiny boat. And the luminosity surrounded the thing like an aura.

And now we could see its face; and I heard Belmont's whispered exclamation. For the face was as human as ours, with a straight nose, a firm, well-shaped mouth, and eyes glinting with intelligence.

With intelligence—and something else!

There was something deadly about those eyes peering at us through the misty concrete. Something that would have sent our hands leaping for our guns had not the thing been so little. You can't physically fear a doll only a foot and a half high.

"What on earth is it—and how can it move through solid concrete?" breathed Belmont.

I couldn't even guess the answer. But I had a theory that sprang full grown into my mind at the first sight of the little figure. It was all I had to offer in the way of explanation later, and I gave it to Belmont for what it was worth at the time.

"We must be looking at a hitherto unsuspected freak of evolution," I said, instinctively talking in a whisper. "It must be that millions of years ago the human race split. Some of it stayed on top of the ground; some of it went into deep caves for shelter. As thousands of years passed, the latter went ever deeper as new rifts leading downward were discovered. But far down in the earth is terrific pressure, and heat. Through the ages their bodies adapted themselves. They compacted—perhaps in their very atomic structure.

"Now the density of their substance, and its altered atomic character, allows them to move through stuff that is solid to us. Like the concrete and the mush rock behind it, which is softer than the terrifically compressed stone around it."

"But the thing has eyes," murmured Belmont. "Anything living for generations underground would be blind."

"Animals, yes. But this is human; at least it has human intelligence. It has undoubtedly carried light with it."

The little mannikin was within a few inches of the surface of the wall now. It stood there, staring out at us as intently as we stared in at it. And I could see that Steve Boland had added no imaginative detail in his description of what he had seen.

The tiny thing was dressed in some sort of shiny stuff, like metal, that crisscrossed it in strips. It reminded me of something, and finally I got it. Our early airmen, trying for altitude records high in the stratosphere, had laced their bodies with heavy canvas strips to keep them from disrupting outward in the lessened pressure of the heights. The metallic-looking strips lacing this little body looked like those.

"It must be that the thing comes from

depths that make this forty-thousand-foot level seem high and rarefied," I whispered to Belmont. "Hundreds of thousands of feet, perhaps. They've heard us working at the ore, and have come far up here to see what was happening."

"But to go through solid concrete—" muttered Belmont, dazed.

"That would be due to the way the atoms of their substance have been compressed and altered. They might be like the stuff on Sirius's companion, where substance weighs a ton to the cubic inch. That would allow the atoms of their bodies to slide through far-spaced atoms of ordinary stuff, as lead shot could pour through a wide-meshed screen. . . ."

Belmont was so silent that I stared at him. He was paying no attention to me, probably hadn't even heard me. His eyes were wild and wide.

"There's another of them. And another! Frank—we're mad. We must be!"

Two more luminous swirls had appeared in the depths of the concrete. Two more tiny little human figures slowly appeared as, breasting forward like deep-sea divers against solid water, they plodded toward the face of the wall.

And now three mannikins, laced in with silvery-looking metal strips, stared at us through several inches of the milky-appearing concrete. Belmont clutched my arm again.

"Their eyes!" he whispered. "They certainly don't like us, Frank! I'm glad they're like things you see under a low-powered microscope instead of man-sized or bigger!"

Their eyes were most expressive—and threatening. They were like human eyes—and yet unlike them. There was a lack of something in them. Perhaps of the thing we call, for want of a more definite term, soul. But they were as expressive as the eyes of intelligent children.

I read curiosity in them as intense as that which filled Belmont and me. But over and above the curiosity there was—menace.

Cold anger shone from the soulless eyes. Chill outrage, such as might shine from the eyes of a man whose home has been invaded. The little men palpably considered us trespassers in these depths, and were glacially infuriated by our presence.

And then both Belmont and I gasped aloud. For one of the little men had thrust his hands forward, and hands and arms had protruded from the wall, like the hands of a person groping a way out of a thick mist. Then the tiny body followed it. And as if at a signal, the other two little men moved forward out of the wall too.

The three metal-laced mannikins stood in the open air of the tunnel, with their backs to the wall that had offered no more resistance to their bodies than cheese offers to sharp steel. And behind them there were no holes where they had stepped from. The face of the concrete was unbroken.

The atomic theory must be correct, I thought. The compacted atoms of which they were composed slid through the stellar spaces between ordinary atoms, leaving them undisturbed.

But only a small part of my mind concerned itself with this. Nine-tenths of it was absorbed by a growing, indefinable fear. For now the three little men were walking slowly toward us. And in every line of their tiny bodies was a threat.

Belmont looked at me. Our hands went uncertainly toward our revolvers. But we did not draw them. You don't shoot at children; and the diminutive size of the three figures still made us consider them much as harmless children. Though in the back of my mind, at least, if not in Belmont's, the indefinable fear was spreading. . . .

The three stopped about a yard from us. Belmont was standing, and I was still seated, almost in a paralysis of wonder, on my rock fragment. They looked far up at Belmont and almost as far up at me. Three little things that didn't even come up to our knees!

And then Belmont uttered a hoarse cry and

dragged out his gun at last. For one of the three slid his tiny hand into the metal lacing of his body and brought it out with a sort of rod in it about the size of a thick pin, half an inch long. And there was something about the look in the mannikin's eyes that brought a rush of frank fear to our hearts at last, though we couldn't even guess at the nature of the infinitesimal weapon he held.

The mannikin pointed the tiny rod at Belmont, and Belmont shot. I didn't blame him. I had my own gun out and trained on the other two. After all, we knew nothing of the nature of these fantastic creatures who had come up from unguessable depths below. We couldn't even approximate the amount of harm they might do—but their eyes told us they'd do whatever they could to hurt us.

An exclamation ripped from my lips as the roar of the shot thundered down the tunnel.

The bullet had hit the little figure. It couldn't have helped but hit it; Belmont's gun was within a yard of it, and he'd aimed point-blank.

But not a mark appeared on the mannikin, and he stood there apparently unhurt!

Belmont fired again, and to his shot I added my own. The bullets did the little men no damage at all.

"The slugs are going right through the things!" yelled Belmont, pointedly.

Behind the mannikins, long scars in the rock floor told where the lead had ricocheted. But I shook my head in a more profound wonder than that of Belmont's.

"The bullets aren't going through them! *They're going through the bullets!* The stuff they're made of is denser than lead!"

The little man with the tiny rod took one more step forward. And then I saw something that had been lost for the time in the face of things even more startling. I saw how the tiny tracks had been made.

As the mannikin stepped forward, I saw his advancing foot sink into the rock of the floor till the soles of his metallic-looking shoes were buried!

That small figure weighed so much that it sank into stone as a man would sink into ooze!

And now the microscopic rod flamed a little at the tip. And I heard Belmont scream—just once.

He fell, and I looked at him with a shock too great for comprehension, so that I simply stood there stupidly and saw without really feeling any emotion.

The entire right half of Belmont's chest was gone. It was only a crater—a crater that gaped out, as holes gape over spots where shells bury themselves deep and explode up and out.

There had been no sound, and no flash other than the minute speck of flame tipping the mannikin's rod. At one moment Belmont had been whole; at the next he was dead, with half his chest gone. That was all.

I heard myself screaming, and felt my gun buck in my hand as I emptied it. Then the infinitesimal rod turned my way, and I felt a slight shock and stared at my right wrist where a hand and a gun had once been.

I heard my own yells as from a great distance. I felt no pain; there are nerve shocks too great for pain-sensation. I felt only crazed, stupefied rage.

I leaped at the three little figures. With all my strength I swung my heavily booted foot at the one with the rod. There was death in that swing. I wanted to kill these three. I was berserk, with no thought in mind other than to rend and tear and smash. That kick would have killed an ox, I think.

It caught the little man in the middle of the back. And I screamed again and sank to the floor with the white-hot pain of broken small bones spiking my brain. That agony, less than the shock of losing a hand, I could feel all right. And in a blind haze of it I saw the little man smile bleakly and reach out his tiny hand toward Belmont, disregarding me as utterly as though I no longer existed.

And then through the fog of my agony I saw yet another wonder. The little man lifted Belmont's dead body.

With the one hand, and apparently with no more effort than I would have made to pick up a pebble, he swung the body two inches off the floor, and started toward the concrete wall with it.

I tried to follow, crawling on my knees, but one of the other little men dashed his fist against my thigh. It sank in my flesh till his arm was buried to the shoulder, and the mannikin staggered off-balance with the lack of resistance. He withdrew his arm. There was no mark in the fabric of my clothing and I could feel no puncture in my thigh.

The little man stared perplexedly at me, and then at his fist. Then he joined the other two. They were at the face of the concrete wall again.

I saw that they were beginning to look as though in distress. They were panting, and the one with the rod was pressing his hand against his chest. They looked at each other and I thought a message was passed among them.

A message of haste? I think so. For the one picked up Belmont again, and all three stepped into the concrete. I saw them forge slowly ahead through it. And I saw Belmont, at arm's length of the little man who dragged him, flatten against the smooth side of the stuff.

I think I went a little mad, then, as I understood at last just what had happened.

The little men had killed Belmont as a specimen, just as a man might kill a rare insect. They wanted to take him back to their own deep realms and study him. And they were trying to drag him through the solid concrete. It offered only normal resistance to their own compacted tons of weight, and it didn't occur to them that it wouldn't to Belmont's body.

I flung myself at the wall and clawed at it with my left hand. The body of my friend was suspended there, flattened against it as the little man within tried to make solid matter go through solid matter, ignorant of the limitations of the laws of physics as we of Earth's surface know them.

They were in extreme distress now. Even in my pain and madness I could see that. Their mouths were open like the mouths of fish gasping in air. I saw one clutch the leader's arm and point urgently downward.

The leader raised his tiny rod. Once more I saw the infinitesimal flash at its tip. Then I saw a six-foot hole yawn in the concrete around Belmont's body. What was their ammunition? Tiny pellets of gas, so compressed at the depths they inhabited that it was a solid, and which expanded enormously when released at these pressures? No one will ever know—I hope!

In one last effort, the leader dragged the body of my friend into the hole in the concrete. Then, when it stubbornly refused to follow into the substance through which they could force their own bodies, they gave up.

One of the three staggered and fell, sinking in the concrete as an overcome diver might sink through water to the ocean's bed. The other two picked him up and carried him. Down and away.

Down and away . . . down from the floor of the forty-thousand-foot level, and away from the surface of the concrete wall.

I saw the luminous trails they left in the concrete fade into indistinct swirls, and finally die. I saw my friend's form sag back from the hole in the concrete, to sink to the floor.

And then I saw nothing but the still form, and the ragged, six-foot crater that had been blown soundlessly into the solid concrete by some mysterious explosive that had come from a thing no larger than a thick pin, and less than half an inch long. . . .

They found me an hour later—men who had come down to see why neither Belmont nor I answered the ring of the radio phone connecting the low level with the surface.

They found me raving beside Belmont's body, and they held my arms with straps as they led me to the shaft.

They tried me for murder—and sabotage. For, next day, I got away from the men long enough to sink explosive into the forty-thousand-foot level and blow it up so that none could work there again. But the verdict was not guilty in both cases.

Belmont had died and I had lost my right hand in an explosion the cause of which was unknown, the martial court decided. And I had been insane from shock when I destroyed the low level, which, even with the world famished for copper, was almost too far down to be commercially profitable anyway.

They freed me, and I wrote in my report—and some filing clerk has, no doubt, shrugged at its impossibility and put it in a steel cabinet where it will be forever ignored.

But there is one thing that cannot be ignored. That is, those mannikins, those microscopic giants—if ever they decide to return by slow stages of pressure acclimation to the earth's surface!

Myriads of them, tiny things weighing incredible tons, forging through labyrinths composed of soft veins of rock like little deep-sea divers plodding laboriously but normally through impeding water! Beings as civilized as ourselves, if not more so, with infinitely deadly weapons, and practically invulnerable to any weapons we might try to turn against them!

Will they tunnel upward someday and decide calmly and leisurely to take possession of a world that is green and fair, instead of black and buried? If they do, I hope it will not be in my lifetime!

Tlön, Uqbar, Orbis Tertius

JORGE LUIS BORGES

Translated by Andrew Hurley

Jorge Luis Borges (1899–1986) was an Argentine writer, essayist, poet, and translator noted in science fiction circles for his often fantastical short fiction work (he never wrote a novel). Beyond Latin America, he is most influential for his fiction, written from the 1930s to the 1980s and conveniently assembled as *Collected Fictions* (1998). Many of his famous stories were published in the 1940s, especially in the well-known and influential journal *Sur*—but his first known English-language translation appeared in *Ellery Queen's Mystery Magazine* in 1948. His work also appeared in genre publications like *The Magazine of Fantasy and Science Fiction*.

Borges's influence on twentieth-century literature has been deep and pervasive since about 1960, especially for fictions whose structure or arguments question or play with the nature of reality—or that make fantastic use of images of a labyrinth, a mirror, a library, or a book that informs the world. Another enduring trait of most Borges stories is a feat of compression whereby use of summary and adherence to conventions common to essays are used to illuminate often mind-bending fantastical or science-fictional elements. His fiction has had the effect of a map of the unknown: other writers find the same territory mysterious and want to traverse it, not realizing that the map may close up all around them. Successful "cooking" of Borges's influence can be found in the works of such writers as Philip K. Dick, Thomas Pynchon, and Gene Wolfe. The mind-bending aspect of his stories shares an affinity with the contractions/expansions of space and time that make J. G. Ballard's fiction so effective.

"Tlön, Uqbar, Orbis Tertius" formed part of a famous 1941 collection of stories titled *El jardín de senderos que se bifurcan* (*The Garden of Forking Paths*) but was first published in *Sur* (May 1940). *Sur* was an Argentine literary magazine published by Victoria Ocampo, sister of Silvina Ocampo (herself married to Adolfo Bioy Casares; both writers are included in this anthology). It has since been translated into English and published many times in many places, the first being in 1961. Such diverse creators as British writer W. G. Sebald, Colombian musician/composer Diego Vega, and Italian artist-designer Luigi Serafini have been influenced by the story.

In addition to any subconscious inspiration, the story also came out of a conscious decision, by various writers known for contributing to *Sur*, to explore speculative themes. Borges, Ocampo, Bioy Casares, and the writer José Bianco spent many nights discussing how best to frame their "attack on psychologism," as John King puts it in his "Towards a Reading of the Argentine Literary Magazine *Sur*" (*Latin American Research Review* 16, no. 2, 1981). This attack meant putting forward the idea of the "formal perfection of the fantastic/detective story" in addition to writing reviews for *Sur* that advanced the same agenda. In this context, King suggests, the postscript added to "Tlön, Uqbar, Orbis Tertius" in 1947 reflects aspects of Borges's ongoing discussion about fantastical literature.

The story also crosses between the boundaries of fiction and reality by mentioning real people, such as Borges himself and Bioy Casares as well as Baruch Spinoza and Bertrand Russell, along with places that may or may not exist. To further complicate the matter, other contemporary writers of that time played along with this idea by writing about these places and events as if they were real.

A few references in the story may be obscure to English-language readers. "Ramos Mejía" was a Buenos Aires neighborhood for the rich, now an industrial suburb. *"Capangas"* were overseers or foremen of gangs of workers in rural areas. "Xul Solar" was the nom de plume of Alejandro Schultz, a lifelong writer-friend of Borges whom he compared to William Blake. "Amorim" was a Uruguayan writer related to Borges by marriage.

TLÖN, UQBAR, ORBIS TERTIUS

Jorge Luis Borges

Translated by Andrew Hurley

I

I owe the discovery of Uqbar to the conjunction of a mirror and an encyclopedia. The mirror troubled the far end of a hallway in a large country house on Calle Gaona, in Ramos Mejía; the encyclopedia is misleadingly titled *The Anglo-American Cyclopaedia* (New York, 1917), and is a literal (though also laggardly) reprint of the 1902 *Encyclopaedia Britannica*. The event took place about five years ago.

Bioy Casares had come to dinner at my house that evening, and we had lost all track of time in a vast debate over the way one might go about composing a first-person novel whose narrator would omit or distort things and engage in all sorts of contradictions, so that a few of the book's readers—a *very* few—might divine the horrifying or banal truth. Down at that far end of the hallway, the mirror hovered, shadowing us. We discovered (very late at night such a discovery is inevitable) that there is something monstrous about mirrors. That was when Bioy remembered a saying by one of the heresiarchs of Uqbar: *Mirrors and copulation are abominable, for they multiply the number of mankind.* I asked him where he'd come across that memorable epigram, and he told me it was recorded in *The Anglo-American Cyclopaedia*, in its article on Uqbar.

The big old house (we had taken it furnished) possessed a copy of that work. On the last pages of volume XLVI we found an article on Uppsala; in the first of volume XLVII, "Ural-Altaic Languages"—not a word on Uqbar. Bioy, somewhat bewildered, consulted the volumes of the index. He tried every possible spelling:

Ukbar, Ucbar, Ookbar, Oukbahr . . . all in vain. Before he left, he told me it was a region in Iraq or Asia Minor. I confess I nodded a bit uncomfortably; I surmised that that undocumented country and its anonymous heresiarch were a fiction that Bioy had invented on the spur of the moment, out of modesty, in order to justify a fine-sounding epigram. A sterile search through one of the atlases of Justus Perthes reinforced my doubt.

The next day, Bioy called me from Buenos Aires. He told me he had the article on Uqbar right in front of him—in volume XLVI of the encyclopedia. The heresiarch's name wasn't given, but the entry did report his doctrine, formulated in words almost identical to those Bioy had quoted, though from a literary point of view perhaps inferior. Bioy had remembered its being "mirrors and copulation are abominable," while the text of the encyclopedia ran *For one of those gnostics, the visible universe was an illusion or, more precisely, a sophism. Mirrors and fatherhood are hateful because they multiply and proclaim it.* I told Bioy, quite truthfully, that I'd like to see that article. A few days later he brought it to me—which surprised me, because the scrupulous cartographic indices of Ritter's *Erdkunde* evinced complete and total ignorance of the existence of the name Uqbar.

The volume Bioy brought was indeed volume XLVI of *The Anglo-American Cyclopaedia*. On both the false cover and spine, the alphabetical key to the volume's contents (Tor–Upps) was the same as ours, but instead of 917 pages, Bioy's volume had 921. Those four additional pages held the article on Uqbar—an article not contemplated (as the reader will have noted) by the alphabetical key. We later compared the two volumes and found that there was no further difference between them. Both (as I believe I have said) are reprints of the tenth edition of the *Encyclopaedia Britannica*. Bioy had purchased his copy at one of his many sales.

We read the article with some care. The passage that Bioy had recalled was perhaps the only one that might raise a reader's eyebrow; the rest seemed quite plausible, very much in keeping with the general tone of the work, even (naturally) somewhat boring. Rereading it, however, we discovered that the rigorous writing was underlain by a basic vagueness. Of the fourteen names that figured in the section on geography, we recognized only three (Khorasan, Armenia, Erzerum), all interpolated into the text ambiguously. Of the historical names, we recognized only one: the impostor-wizard Smerdis, and he was invoked, really, as a metaphor. The article seemed to define the borders of Uqbar, but its nebulous points of reference were rivers and craters and mountain chains of the region itself. We read, for example, that the Axa delta and the lowlands of Tsai Khaldun mark the southern boundary, and that wild horses breed on the islands of the delta. That was at the top of page 918. In the section on Uqbar's history (p. 920), we learned that religious persecutions in the thirteenth century had forced the orthodox to seek refuge on those same islands, where their obelisks are still standing and their stone mirrors are occasionally unearthed. The section titled "Language and Literature" was brief. One memorable feature: the article said that the literature of Uqbar was a literature of fantasy, and that its epics and legends never referred to reality but rather to the two imaginary realms of Mle'khnas and Tlön. . . . The bibliography listed four volumes we have yet to find, though the third—Silas Haslam's *History of the Land Called Uqbar* (1874)—does figure in the catalogs published by Bernard Quaritch, Bookseller.[*]

---

[*] Haslam was also the author of *A General History of Labyrinths*.

The first, *Lesbare und lesenswerthe Bemerkungen über das Land Ukkbar in Klein-Asien*, published in 1641, is the work of one Johannes Valentinus Andreä. That fact is significant: two or three years afterward, I came upon that name in the unexpected pages of De Quincey (*Writings*, vol. XIII), where I learned that it belonged to a German theologian who in the early seventeenth century described an imaginary community, the Rosy Cross—which other men later founded, in imitation of his foredescription.

That night, Bioy and I paid a visit to the National Library, where we pored in vain through atlases, catalogs, the yearly indices published by geographical societies, the memoirs of travelers and historians—no one had ever been in Uqbar. Nor did the general index in Bioy's copy of the encyclopedia contain that name. The next day, Carlos Mastronardi (whom I had told about all this) spotted the black-and-gold spines of *The Anglo-American Cyclopaedia* in a bookshop at the corner of Corrientes and Talcahuano. . . . He went in and consulted volume XLVI. Naturally, he found not the slightest mention of Uqbar.

II

Some limited and waning memory of Herbert Ashe, an engineer for the Southern Railway Line, still lingers in the hotel at Adrogué, among the effusive honeysuckle vines and in the illusory depths of the mirrors. In life, Ashe was afflicted with unreality, as so many Englishmen are; in death, he is not even the ghost he was in life. He was tall and phlegmatic and his weary rectangular beard had once been red. I understand that he was a widower, and without issue. Every few years he would go back to England, to make his visit (I am judging from some photographs he showed us) to a sundial and a stand of oak trees. My father had forged one of those close English friendships with him (the first adjective is perhaps excessive) that begin by excluding confidences and soon eliminate conversation. They would exchange books and newspapers; they would wage taciturn battle at chess. . . . I recall Ashe on the hotel veranda, holding a book of mathematics, looking up sometimes at the irrecoverable colors of the sky. One evening, we spoke about the duodecimal number system, in which twelve is written 10. Ashe said that by coincidence he was just then transposing some duodecimal table or other to sexagesimal (in which sixty is written 10). He added that he'd been commissioned to perform that task by a Norwegian man . . . in Rio Grande do Sul. Ashe and I had known each other for eight years, and he had never mentioned a stay in Brazil. We spoke of the bucolic rural life, of *capangas*, of the Brazilian etymology of the word *gaucho* (which some older folk in Uruguay still pronounce as *ga-úcho*), and nothing more was said—God forgive me—of duodecimals. In September of 1937 (my family and I were no longer at the hotel), Herbert Ashe died of a ruptured aneurysm. A few days before his death, he had received a sealed, certified package from Brazil containing a book printed in octavo major. Ashe left it in the bar, where, months later, I found it. I began to leaf through it and suddenly I experienced a slight, astonished sense of dizziness that I shall not describe, since this is the story not of my emotions but of Uqbar and Tlön and Orbis Tertius. (On one particular Islamic night, which is called the Night of Nights, the secret portals of the heavens open wide and the water in the water jars is sweeter than on other nights; if those gates had opened as I sat there, I would not have felt what I was feeling that evening.) The book was written in English, and it consisted of 1,001 pages. On the leather-bound volume's yellow spine I read these curious words, which were repeated on the false cover: *A First Encyclopaedia of Tlön. Vol. XI Hlaer to Jangr.* There was no date or place of publication. On the first page and again on the onionskin page that covered one of the color illustrations there was stamped a blue oval with this inscription: *Orbis Tertius.* Two

years earlier, I had discovered in one of the volumes of a certain pirated encyclopedia a brief description of a false country; now fate had set before me something much more precious and painstaking. I now held in my hands a vast and systematic fragment of the entire history of an unknown planet, with its architectures and its playing cards, the horror of its mythologies and the murmur of its tongues, its emperors and its seas, its minerals and its birds and fishes, its algebra and its fire, its theological and metaphysical controversies—all joined, articulated, coherent, and with no visible doctrinal purpose or hint of parody.

In the "volume eleven" of which I speak, there are allusions to later and earlier volumes. Néstor Ibarra, in a now-classic article in the *N.R.F.*, denied that such companion volumes exist; Ezequiel Martínez Estrada and Drieu La Rochelle have rebutted that doubt, perhaps victoriously. The fact is, the most diligent searches have so far proven futile. In vain have we ransacked the libraries of the two Americas and Europe. Alfonso Reyes, weary of those "subordinate drudgeries of a detective nature," has proposed that between us, we undertake to *reconstruct* the many massive volumes that are missing: *ex ungue leonem*. He figures, half-seriously, half in jest, that a generation of Tlönists would suffice. That bold estimate takes us back to the initial problem: who, singular or plural, invented Tlön? The plural is, I suppose, inevitable, since the hypothesis of a single inventor—some infinite Leibniz working in obscurity and self-effacement—has been unanimously discarded. It is conjectured that this "brave new world" is the work of a secret society of astronomers, biologists, engineers, metaphysicians, poets, chemists, algebrists, moralists, painters, geometers . . . guided and directed by some shadowy man of genius. There are many men adept in those diverse disciplines, but few capable of imagination—fewer still capable of subordinating imagination to a rigorous and systematic plan. The plan is so vast that the contribution of each writer is infinitesimal.

At first it was thought that Tlön was a mere chaos, an irresponsible act of imaginative license; today we know that it is a cosmos, and that the innermost laws that govern it have been formulated, however provisionally so. Let it suffice to remind the reader that the apparent contradictions of volume eleven are the foundation stone of the proof that the other volumes do in fact exist: the order that has been observed in it is just that lucid, just that fitting. Popular magazines have trumpeted, with pardonable excess, the zoology and topography of Tlön. In my view, its transparent tigers and towers of blood do not perhaps merit the constant attention of *all* mankind, but I might be so bold as to beg a few moments to outline its conception of the universe.

Hume declared for all time that while Berkeley's arguments admit not the slightest refutation, they inspire not the slightest conviction. That pronouncement is entirely true with respect to Earth, entirely false with respect to Tlön. The nations of that planet are, congenitally, idealistic. Their language and those things derived from their language—religion, literature, metaphysics—presuppose idealism. For the people of Tlön, the world is not an amalgam of *objects* in space; it is a heterogeneous series of independent *acts*—the world is successive, temporal, but not spatial. There are no nouns in the conjectural *Ursprache* of Tlön, from which its "present-day" languages and dialects derive: there are impersonal verbs, modified by monosyllabic suffixes (or prefixes) functioning as adverbs. For example, there is no noun that corresponds to our word *moon*, but there is a verb which in English would be "to moonate" or "to enmoon." "The moon rose above the river" is *"hlör u fang axaxaxas mlö,"* or, as Xul Solar succinctly translates: *Upward, behind the onstreaming it mooned*.

That principle applies to the languages of the southern hemisphere. In the northern hemisphere (about whose *Ursprache* volume eleven contains very little information), the primary unit is not the verb but the monosyl-labic adjective. Nouns are formed by stringing together adjectives. One does not say "moon"; one says "aerial-bright above dark-round" or "soft-amberish celestial" or any other string. In this case, the complex of adjectives corresponds to a real object, but that is purely fortuitous. The literature of the northern hemisphere (as in Meinong's subsisting world) is filled with ideal objects, called forth and dissolved in an instant, as the poetry requires. Sometimes mere simultaneity creates them. There are things composed of two terms, one visual and the other auditory: the color of the rising sun and the distant caw of a bird. There are things composed of many: the sun and water against the swimmer's breast, the vague shimmering pink one sees when one's eyes are closed, the sensation of being swept along by a river and also by Morpheus. These objects of the second degree may be combined with others; the process, using certain abbreviations, is virtually infinite. There are famous poems composed of a single enormous word; this word is a "poetic object" created by the poet. The fact that no one believes in the reality expressed by these nouns means, paradoxically, that there is no limit to their number. The languages of Tlön's northern hemisphere possess all the nouns of the Indo-European languages—and many, many more.

It is no exaggeration to say that the classical culture of Tlön is composed of a single discipline—psychology—to which all others are subordinate. I have said that the people of that planet conceive the universe as a series of mental processes that occur not in space but rather successively, in time. Spinoza endows his inexhaustible deity with the attributes of spatial extension and of thought; no one in Tlön would understand the juxtaposition of the first, which is typical only of certain states, and the second—which is a perfect synonym for the cosmos. Or to put it another way: space is not conceived as having duration in time. The perception of a cloud of smoke on the horizon and then the countryside on fire and then the half-extinguished cigarette that produced the scorched earth is considered an example of the association of ideas.

This thoroughgoing monism, or idealism, renders science null. To explain (or pass judgment on) an event is to link it to another; on Tlön, that joining-together is a posterior state of the *subject*, and can neither affect nor illuminate the prior state. Every mental state is irreducible: the simple act of giving it a name—i.e., of classifying it—introduces a distortion, a "slant" or "bias." One might well deduce, therefore, that on Tlön there are no sciences—or even any "systems of thought." The paradoxical truth is that systems of thought do exist, almost countless numbers of them. Philosophies are much like the nouns of the northern hemisphere; the fact that every philosophy is by definition a dialectical game, a *Philosophie des Als Ob*, has allowed them to proliferate. There are systems upon systems that are incredible but possessed of a pleasing architecture or a certain agreeable sensationalism. The metaphysicians of Tlön seek not truth, or even plausibility—they seek to amaze, astound. In their view, metaphysics is a branch of the literature of fantasy. They know that a system is naught but the subordination of all the aspects of the universe to one of those aspects—*any* one of them. Even the phrase "all the aspects" should be avoided, because it implies the impossible addition of the present instant and all those instants that went before. Nor is the plural "those instants that went before" legitimate, for it implies another impossible operation. . . . One of the schools of philosophy on Tlön goes so far as to deny the existence of time; it argues that the present is undefined and indefinite, the future has no reality except as present hope, and the past has no reality except as present recollection.[†] Another school posits that all time has already passed, so that our life is but the crepuscular memory, or crepuscular reflection, doubtlessly distorted and mutilated, of an irrecoverable process. Yet another claims that the history of the universe—and in it, our lives and every faintest detail of our lives—is the handwriting of a subordinate god trying to communicate with a demon. Another, that the universe might be compared to those cryptograms in which not all the symbols count, and only what happens every three hundred nights is actually real. Another, that while we sleep here, we are awake somewhere else, so that every man is in fact two men.

Of all the doctrines of Tlön, none has caused more uproar than materialism. Some thinkers have formulated this philosophy (generally with less clarity than zeal) as though putting forth a paradox. In order to make this inconceivable thesis more easily understood, an eleventh-century heresiarch[‡] conceived the sophism of the nine copper coins, a paradox as scandalously famous on Tlön as the Eleatic aporiae to ourselves. There are many versions of that "specious argument," with varying numbers of coins and discoveries; the following is the most common:

On Tuesday, X is walking along a deserted road and loses nine copper coins. On Thursday, Y finds four coins in the road, their luster somewhat dimmed by Wednesday's rain. On Friday, Z discovers three coins in the road. Friday morning X finds two coins on the veranda of his house.

From this story the heresiarch wished to deduce the reality—i.e., the continuity in time—of those nine recovered coins. "It is absurd," he said, "to imagine that four of the coins did not exist from Tuesday to Thursday, three from Tuesday to Friday afternoon, two from Tuesday to Friday morning. It is logical to think that they in fact *did* exist—albeit in some secret way that we are forbidden to understand—at every moment of those three periods of time."

[†] Russell (*The Analysis of Mind* [1921], p. 159) posits that the world was created only moments ago, filled with human beings who "remember" an illusory past.

[‡] A "century," in keeping with the duodecimal system in use on Tlön, is a period of one-fourteenth of a year.

The language of Tlön resisted formulating this paradox; most people did not understand it. The "common sense" school at first simply denied the anecdote's veracity. They claimed it was a verbal fallacy based on the reckless employment of two neologisms, words unauthorized by standard usage and foreign to all rigorous thought: the two verbs "find" and "lose," which, since they presuppose the identity of the nine first coins and the nine latter ones, entail a *petition principii*. These critics reminded their listeners that all nouns (*man, coin, Thursday, Wednesday, rain*) have only metaphoric value. They denounced the misleading detail that "[the coins'] luster [was] somewhat dimmed by Wednesday's rain" as presupposing what it attempted to prove: the continuing existence of the four coins from Tuesday to Thursday. They explained that "equality" is one thing and "identity" another, and they formulated a sort of reductio ad absurdum—the hypothetical case of nine men who on nine successive nights experience a sharp pain. Would it not be absurd, they asked, to pretend that the men had suffered one and the same pain?§ They claimed that the heresiarch was motivated by the blasphemous desire to attribute the divine category *Being* to a handful of mere coins, and that he sometimes denied plurality and sometimes did not. They argued: if equality entailed identity, one would have to admit that the nine coins were a single coin.

Incredibly, those refutations did not put an end to the matter. A hundred years after the problem had first been posed, a thinker no less brilliant than the heresiarch, but of the orthodox tradition, formulated a most daring hypothesis. His happy conjecture was that there is but a single subject; that indivisible subject is every being in the universe, and the beings of the universe are the organs and masks of the deity. X is Y and is *also* Z. Z discovers three coins, then, because he remembers that X lost them; X finds two coins on the veranda of his house because he remembers that the others have been found. . . . Volume eleven suggests that this idealistic pantheism triumphed over all other schools of thought for three primary reasons: first, because it repudiated solipsism; second, because it left intact the psychological foundation of the sciences; and third, because it preserved the possibility of religion. Schopenhauer (passionate yet lucid Schopenhauer) formulates a very similar doctrine in the first volume of his *Parerga und Paralipomena*.

Tlön's geometry is made up of two rather distinct disciplines—visual geometry and tactile geometry. Tactile geometry corresponds to our own, and is subordinate to the visual. Visual geometry is based on the surface, not the point; it has no parallel lines, and it claims that as one's body moves through space, it modifies the shapes that surround it. The basis of Tlön's arithmetic is the notion of indefinite numbers; it stresses the importance of the concepts "greater than" and "less than," which our own mathematicians represent with the symbols $>$ and $<$. The people of Tlön are taught that the act of counting modifies the amount counted, turning indefinites into definites. The fact that several persons counting the same quantity come to the same result is for the psychologists of Tlön an example of the association of ideas or of memorization. We must always remember that on Tlön, the subject of knowledge is one and eternal.

Within the sphere of literature, too, the idea of the single subject is all-powerful. Books are rarely signed, nor does the concept of plagiarism exist: it has been decided that all books are the work of a single author who is timeless and anonymous. Literary criticism often invents authors: it will take two dissimilar works—the *Tao Te Ching* and the *1,001 Nights*, for instance—attribute them to a single author, and then in all good conscience determine the

---

§   Today, one of Tlön's religions contends, platonically, that a certain pain, a certain greenish-yellow color, a certain temperature, and a certain sound are all the same, single reality. All men, in the dizzying instant of copulation, are the same man. All men who speak a line of Shakespeare *are* William Shakespeare.

psychology of that most interesting *homme de lettres*. . . .

Their books are also different from our own. Their fiction has but a single plot, with every imaginable permutation. Their works of a philosophical nature invariably contain both the thesis and the antithesis, the rigorous *pro* and *contra* of every argument. A book that does not contain its counter-book is considered incomplete.

Century upon century of idealism could hardly have failed to influence reality. In the most ancient regions of Tlön one may, not infrequently, observe the duplication of lost objects: two persons are looking for a pencil; the first person finds it, but says nothing; the second finds a second pencil, no less real, but more in keeping with his expectations. These secondary objects are called *hrönir*, and they are, though awkwardly so, slightly longer. Until recently, *hrönir* were the coincidental offspring of distraction and forgetfulness. It is hard to believe that they have been systematically produced for only about a hundred years, but that is what volume eleven tells us. The first attempts were unsuccessful, but the modus operandi is worth recalling: The warden of one of the state prisons informed his prisoners that there were certain tombs in the ancient bed of a nearby river, and he promised that anyone who brought in an important find would be set free. For months before the excavation, the inmates were shown photographs of what they were going to discover. That first attempt proved that hope and greed can be inhibiting; after a week's work with pick and shovel, the only *hrön* unearthed was a rusty wheel, dated some time *later* than the date of the experiment. The experiment was kept secret, but was repeated afterward at four high schools. In three of them, the failure was virtually complete; in the fourth (where the principal happened to die during the early excavations), the students unearthed—or produced—a gold mask, an archaic sword, two or three clay amphorae, and the verdigris'd and mutilated torso of a king with an inscription on the chest that has yet to be deciphered.

Thus it was discovered that no witnesses who were aware of the experimental nature of the search could be allowed near the site. . . . Group research projects produce conflicting finds; now individual, virtually spur-of-the-moment projects are preferred. The systematic production of *hrönir* (says volume eleven) has been of invaluable aid to archaeologists, making it possible not only to interrogate but to even modify the past, which is now no less plastic, no less malleable than the future. A curious bit of information: *hrönir* of the second and third remove—*hrönir* derived from another *hrön*, and *hrönir* derived from the *hrön* of a *hrön*—exaggerate the aberrations of the first; those of the fifth remove are almost identical; those of the ninth can be confused with those of the second; and those of the eleventh remove exhibit a purity of line that even the originals do not exhibit. The process is periodic: the *hrönir* of the twelfth remove begin to degenerate. Sometimes stranger and purer than any *hrön* is the *ur*—the thing produced by suggestion, the object brought forth by hope. The magnificent gold mask I mentioned is a distinguished example.

Things duplicate themselves on Tlön; they also tend to grow vague or "sketchy," and to lose detail when they begin to be forgotten. The classic example is the doorway that continued to exist so long as a certain beggar frequented it, but which was lost to sight when he died. Sometimes a few birds, a horse, have saved the ruins of an amphitheater.

Salto Oriental, 1940

POSTSCRIPT—1947

I reproduce the article above exactly as it appeared in the *Anthology of Fantastic Literature* (1940), the only changes being editorial cuts of one or another metaphor and a tongue-in-cheek sort of summary that would now be considered flippant. So many things have happened since 1940. . . . Allow me to recall some of them:

In March of 1941, a handwritten letter from Gunnar Erfjord was discovered in a book by

Hinton that had belonged to Herbert Ashe. The envelope was postmarked Ouro Preto; the mystery of Tlön was fully elucidated by the letter. It confirmed Martinez Estrada's hypothesis: The splendid story had begun sometime in the early seventeenth century, one night in Lucerne or London. A secret benevolent society (which numbered among its members Dalgarno and, later, George Berkeley) was born; its mission: to invent a country. In its vague initial program, there figured "hermetic studies," philanthropy, and the Kabbalah. (The curious book by Valentinus Andreä dates from that early period.) After several years of confabulations and premature collaborative drafts, the members of the society realized that one generation would not suffice for creating and giving full expression to a country. They decided that each of the masters that belonged to the society would select a disciple to carry on the work. That hereditary arrangement was followed; after an interim of two hundred years, the persecuted fraternity turned up again in the New World. In 1824, in Memphis, Tennessee, one of the members had a conversation with the reclusive millionaire Ezra Buckley. Buckley, somewhat contemptuously, let the man talk—and then laughed at the modesty of the project. He told the man that in America it was nonsense to invent a country—what they ought to do was invent a planet. To that giant of an idea he added another, the brainchild of his nihilism[¶]: the enormous enterprise must be kept secret. At that time the twenty volumes of the *Encyclopaedia Britannica* were all the rage; Buckley suggested a systematic encyclopedia of the illusory planet. He would bequeath to them his gold-veined mountains, his navigable rivers, his prairies thundering with bulls and buffalo, his Negroes, his brothels, and his dollars, he said, under one condition: "The work shall make no pact with the impostor Jesus Christ." Buckley did not believe in God, yet he wanted to prove

to the nonexistent God that mortals could conceive and shape a world. Buckley was poisoned in Baton Rouge in 1828; in 1914 the society sent its members (now numbering three hundred) the final volume of *The First Encyclopaedia of Tlön*. It was published secretly: the forty volumes that made up the work (the grandest work of letters ever undertaken by humankind) were to be the basis for another, yet more painstaking work, to be written this time not in English but in one of the languages of Tlön. That survey of an illusory world was tentatively titled *Orbis Tertius*, and one of its modest demiurges was Herbert Ashe—whether as agent or colleague of Gunnar Erfjord, I cannot say. His receipt of a copy of volume eleven seems to favor the second possibility. But what about the others? In 1942, the plot thickened. I recall with singular clarity one of the first events that occurred, something of whose premonitory nature I believe I sensed even then. It took place in an apartment in Laprida, across the street from a high, bright balcony that faced the setting sun. Princess Faucigny Lucinge had received from Poitiers a crate containing her silver table service. From the vast innards of a packing case emblazoned with international customs stamps she removed, one by one, the fine unmoving things: plate from Utrecht and Paris chased with hard heraldic fauna . . . a samovar. Among the pieces, trembling softly but perceptibly, like a sleeping bird, there throbbed, mysteriously, a compass. The princess did not recognize it. Its blue needle yearned toward magnetic north; its metal casing was concave; the letters on its dial belonged to one of the alphabets of Tlön. That was the first intrusion of the fantastic world of Tlön into the real world.

An unsettling coincidence made me a witness to the second intrusion as well. This event took place some months later, in a sort of a country general-store-and-bar owned by a Brazilian man in the Cuchilla Negra. Amorim and I were returning from Sant'Anna. There was a freshet on the Tacuarembó; as there was no way to cross, we were forced to try (to try to endure,

---

[¶] Buckley was a freethinker, a fatalist, and a defender of slavery.

that is) the rudimentary hospitality at hand. The storekeeper set up some creaking cots for us in a large storeroom clumsy with barrels and stacks of leather. We lay down, but we were kept awake until almost dawn by the drunkenness of an unseen neighbor, who swung between indecipherable streams of abuse and loudly sung snatches of *milongas*—or snatches of the same *milonga*, actually. As one can imagine, we attributed the man's insistent carrying-on to the storekeeper's fiery rotgut. . . . By shortly after daybreak, the man was dead in the hallway. The hoarseness of his voice had misled us—he was a young man. In his delirium, several coins had slipped from his wide gaucho belt, as had a gleaming metal cone about a die's width in diameter. A little boy tried to pick the cone-shaped object up, but in vain; a full-grown man could hardly do it. I held it for a few minutes in the palm of my hand; I recall that its weight was unbearable, and that even after someone took it from me, the sensation of terrible heaviness endured. I also recall the neat circle it engraved in my flesh. That evidence of a very small yet extremely heavy object left an unpleasant aftertaste of fear and revulsion. A *paisano* suggested that we throw it in the swollen river. Amorim purchased it for a few pesos. No one knew anything about the dead man, except that "he came from the border." Those small, incredibly heavy cones (made of a metal not of this world) are an image of the deity in certain Tlönian religions.

Here I end the personal portion of my narration. The rest lies in every reader's memory (if not his hope or fear). Let it suffice to recall, or mention, the subsequent events, with a simple brevity of words which the general public's concave memory will enrich or expand:

In 1944, an investigator from the *Nashville American* unearthed the forty volumes of *The First Encyclopaedia of Tlön* in a Memphis library. To this day there is some disagreement as to whether that discovery was accidental or consented to and guided by the directors of the still-nebulous *Orbis Tertius*; the second

supposition is entirely plausible. Some of the unbelievable features of volume eleven (the multiplication of *hrönir*, for example) have been eliminated or muted in the Memphis copy. It seems reasonable to suppose that the cuts obey the intent to set forth a world that is not *too* incompatible with the real world. The spread of Tlönian objects through various countries would complement that plan. . . .** At any rate, the international press made a great hue and cry about this "find." Handbooks, anthologies, surveys, "literal translations," authorized and pirated reprints of Mankind's Greatest Masterpiece filled the world, and still do. Almost immediately, reality "caved in" at more than one point. The truth is, it wanted to cave in. Ten years ago, any symmetry, any system with an appearance of order—dialectical materialism, anti-Semitism, Nazism—could spellbind and hypnotize mankind. How could the world not fall under the sway of Tlön, how could it not yield to the vast and minutely detailed evidence of an ordered planet? It would be futile to reply that reality is also orderly. Perhaps it is, but orderly in accordance with divine laws (read: "inhuman laws") that we can never quite manage to penetrate. Tlön may well be a labyrinth, but it is a labyrinth forged by men, a labyrinth destined to be deciphered by men.

Contact with Tlön, the *habit* of Tlön, has disintegrated this world. Spellbound by Tlön's rigor, humanity has forgotten, and continues to forget, that it is the rigor of chess masters, not of angels. Already Tlön's (conjectural) "primitive language" has filtered into our schools; already the teaching of Tlön's harmonious history (filled with moving episodes) has obliterated the history that governed my own childhood; already a fictitious past has supplanted in men's memories that other past, of which we now know nothing certain—not even that it is false. Numismatics, pharmacology, and archaeology have been reformed. I understand that biology and math-

---

** There is still, of course, the problem of the *material* from which some objects are made.

ematics are also awaiting their next avatar. . . . A scattered dynasty of recluses has changed the face of the earth—and their work continues. If my projections are correct, a hundred years from now someone will discover the hundred volumes of *The Second Encyclopaedia of Tlön*.

At that, French and English and mere Spanish will disappear from the earth. The world will be Tlön. That makes very little difference to me; through my quiet days in this hotel in Adrogué, I go on revising (though I never intend to publish) an indecisive translation in the style of Quevedo of Sir Thomas Browne's *Urne Buriall*.

Desertion

CLIFFORD D. SIMAK

Clifford D. Simak (1904–1988) was an influential and unique US science fiction writer who studied journalism at the University of Wisconsin and worked for newspapers for most of his life. Widely acclaimed by fans and critics, Simak won three Hugo Awards, one Nebula Award (in 1980, for his story "Grotto of the Dancing Deer"), a Science Fiction Writers of America Grand Master Award, and a Bram Stoker Award for Lifetime Achievement. In his best stories, his complex view of animals and his ability to convey the natural world and rural settings make his work unique. Although Simak started his career during the Golden Age of Science Fiction, and in pulp magazines, his psychological insight and unique point of view allowed him to make a successful transition to a new readership; his work has only become more relevant to modern-day readers.

Early stories include "The World of the Red Sun" for *Wonder Stories* (1931); "The Voice in the Void" (*Wonder Stories Quarterly*, 1932), about the desecration of a sacred tomb on Mars that possibly contains the relics of a messiah from Earth; and "Hellhounds of the Cosmos" (*Astounding Science Fiction*, 1932), in which defenders of Earth combine into a gestalt to fight a monster from another dimension. In 1938, inspired by John W. Campbell Jr.'s approach at *Astounding Science Fiction*, Simak began to produce more sophisticated stories, such as "Rule 18" (1938) and "Reunion on Ganymede" (1938). He swiftly followed with his first full-length novel, *Cosmic Engineers* (serialized in *Astounding Science Fiction* in 1939 and revised in 1950), a galaxy-spanning epic in the vein of E. E. Smith and Edmond Hamilton. Despite or because of working within Campbell's constraints, Simak's fiction gradually became identifiably "Simakian": constrained, intensely emotional beneath a calm surface.

Typical of his best work, "Desertion" (1944) was one of the earliest stories to explore "pantropy" (human modification for space exploration, rather than environmental modification)—a term created by James Blish and used later in his own story cycle (including this volume's "Surface Tension"). "Desertion" was incorporated into Simak's mosaic novel *City* in 1952, which won the International Fantasy Award in 1953. Simak wrote in the reissue of the novel: "*City* was written out of disillusion . . . seeking after a fantasy world that would serve as a counterbalance to the brutality through which the world was passing." *City* is Simak's best-known book—a true classic and deserving of a much wider readership.

DESERTION

Clifford D. Simak

Four men, two by two, had gone into the howling maelstrom that was Jupiter and had not returned. They had walked into the keening gale—or rather, they had loped, bellies low against the ground, wet sides gleaming in the rain.

For they did not go in the shape of men.

Now the fifth man stood before the desk of Kent Fowler, head of Dome No. 3, Jovian Survey Commission.

Under Fowler's desk, old Towser scratched a flea, then settled down to sleep again.

Harold Allen, Fowler saw with a sudden pang, was young—too young. He had the easy confidence of youth, the face of one who never had known fear. And that was strange. For men in the domes of Jupiter did know fear—fear and humility. It was hard for man to reconcile his puny self with the mighty forces of the monstrous planet.

"You understand," said Fowler, "that you need not do this. You understand that you need not go."

It was formula, of course. The other four had been told the same thing, but they had gone. This fifth one, Fowler knew, would go as well. But suddenly he felt a dull hope stir within him that Allen wouldn't go.

"When do I start?" asked Allen.

There had been a time when Fowler might have taken quiet pride in that answer, but not now. He frowned briefly.

"Within the hour," he said.

Allen stood waiting, quietly.

"Four other men have gone out and have not returned," said Fowler. "You know that, of course. We want you to return. We don't want you going off on any heroic rescue expedition.

The main thing, the only thing, is that you come back, that you prove man can live in a Jovian form. Go to the first survey stake, no farther, then come back. Don't take any chances. Don't investigate anything. Just come back."

Allen nodded. "I understand all that."

"Miss Stanley will operate the converter," Fowler went on. "You need have no fear on that particular score. The other men were converted without mishap. They left the converter in apparently perfect condition. You will be in thoroughly competent hands. Miss Stanley is the best qualified conversion operator in the solar system. She has had experience on most of the other planets. That is why she's here."

Allen grinned at the woman and Fowler saw something flicker across Miss Stanley's face—something that might have been pity, or rage—or just plain fear. But it was gone again and she was smiling back at the youth who stood before the desk. Smiling in that prim, schoolteacherish way she had of smiling, almost as if she hated herself for doing it

"I shall be looking forward," said Allen, "to my conversion."

And the way he said it, he made it all a joke, a vast ironic joke.

But it was no joke.

It was serious business, deadly serious. Upon these tests, Fowler knew, depended the fate of men on Jupiter. If the tests succeeded, the resources of the giant planet would be thrown open. Man would take over Jupiter as he already had taken over the other smaller planets. And if they failed—

If they failed, man would continue to be chained and hampered by the terrific pressure, the greater force of gravity, the weird chemistry of the planet. He would continue to be shut within the domes, unable to set actual foot upon the planet, unable to see it with direct, unaided vision, forced to rely upon the awkward tractors and the televisor, forced to work with clumsy tools and mechanisms or through the medium of robots that themselves were clumsy.

For man, unprotected and in his natural form, would be blotted out by Jupiter's terrific pressure of fifteen thousand pounds per square inch, pressure that made terrestrial sea bottoms seem a vacuum by comparison.

Even the strongest metal Earthmen could devise couldn't exist under pressure such as that, under the pressure and the alkaline rains that forever swept the planet. It grew brittle and flaky, crumbling like clay, or it ran away in little streams and puddles of ammonia salts. Only by stepping up the toughness and strength of that metal, by increasing its electronic tension, could it be made to withstand the weight of thousands of miles of swirling, choking gases that made up the atmosphere. And even when that was done, everything had to be coated with tough quartz to keep away the rain—the liquid ammonia that fell as bitter rain.

Fowler sat listening to the engines in the subfloor of the dome-engines that ran on endlessly, the dome never quiet of them. They had to run and keep on running, for if they stopped the power flowing into the metal walls of the dome would stop, the electronic tension would ease up, and that would be the end of everything.

Towser roused himself under Fowler's desk and scratched another flea, his leg thumping hard against the floor.

"Is there anything else?" asked Allen.

Fowler shook his head. "Perhaps there's something you want to do," he said. "Perhaps you—"

He had meant to say write a letter and he was glad he caught himself quick enough so he didn't say it.

Allen looked at his watch. "I'll be there on time," he said. He swung around and headed for the door.

Fowler knew Miss Stanley was watching him and he didn't want to turn and meet her eyes. He fumbled with a sheaf of papers on the desk before him.

"How long are you going to keep this up?" asked Miss Stanley, and she bit off each word with a vicious snap.

He swung around in his chair and faced her then. Her lips were drawn into a straight, thin line; her hair seemed skinned back from her forehead tighter than ever, giving her face that queer, almost startling death-mask quality.

He tried to make his voice cool and level. "As long as there's any need of it," he said. "As long as there's any hope."

"You're going to keep on sentencing them to death," she said. "You're going to keep marching them out face-to-face with Jupiter. You're going to sit here safe and comfortable and send them out to die."

"There is no room for sentimentality, Miss Stanley," Fowler said, trying to keep the note of anger from his voice. "You know as well as I do why we're doing this. You realize that man in his own form simply cannot cope with Jupiter. The only answer is to turn men into the sort of things that can cope with it. We've done it on the other planets.

"If a few men die, but we finally succeed, the price is small. Through the ages men have thrown away their lives on foolish things, for foolish reasons. Why should we hesitate, then, at a little death in a thing as great as this?"

Miss Stanley sat stiff and straight, hands folded in her lap, the lights shining on her greying hair, and Fowler, watching her, tried to imagine what she might feel, what she might be thinking. He wasn't exactly afraid of her, but he didn't feel quite comfortable when she was around. Those sharp blue eyes saw too much, her hands looked far too competent. She should have been somebody's aunt sitting in a rocking chair with her knitting needles. But she wasn't. She was the top-notch conversion unit operator in the solar system and she didn't like the way he was doing things.

"There is something wrong, Mr. Fowler," she declared.

"Precisely," agreed Fowler. "That's why I'm sending young Allen out alone. He may find out what it is."

"And if he doesn't?"

"I'll send someone else."

She rose slowly from her chair, started towards the door, then stopped before his desk.

"Someday," she said, "you will be a great man. You never let a chance go by. This is your chance. You knew it was when this dome was picked for the tests. If you put it through, you'll go up a notch or two. No matter how many men may die you'll go up a notch or two."

"Miss Stanley," he said, and his voice was curt, "young Allen is going out soon. Please be sure that your machine—"

"My machine," she told him icily, "is not to blame. It operates along the coordinates the biologists set up."

He sat hunched at his desk, listening to her footsteps go down the corridor.

What she said was true, of course. The biologists had set up the coordinates. But the biologists could be wrong. Just a hairsbreadth of difference, one iota of digression, and the converter would be sending out something that wasn't the thing they meant to send. A mutant that might crack up, go haywire, come unstuck under some condition or stress of circumstance wholly unsuspected.

For man didn't know much about what was going on outside. Only what his instruments told him was going on. And the samplings of those happenings furnished by those instruments and mechanisms had been no more than samplings, for Jupiter was unbelievably large and the domes were very few.

Even the work of the biologists in getting the data on the Lopers, apparently the highest form of Jovian life, had involved more than three years of intensive study and after that two years of checking to make sure. Work that could have been done on Earth in a week or two. But work that, in this case, couldn't be done on Earth at all, for one couldn't take a Jovian life-form to Earth. The pressure here on Jupiter couldn't be duplicated outside of Jupiter and at Earth pressure and temperature the Lopers would simply have disappeared in a puff of gas.

Yet it was work that had to be done if man ever hoped to go about Jupiter in the life-form of the Lopers. For before the converter could change a man to another life-form, every detailed physical characteristic of that life-form must be known—surely and positively—with no chance of mistake.

Allen did not come back.

The tractors, combing the nearby terrain, found no trace of him, unless the skulking thing reported by one of the drivers had been the missing Earthman in Loper form.

The biologists sneered their most accomplished academic sneers when Fowler suggested the coordinates might be wrong. Carefully they pointed out the coordinates worked. When a man was put into the converter and the switch was thrown, the man became a Loper. He left the machine and moved away, out of sight, into the soupy atmosphere.

Some quirk, Fowler had suggested; some tiny deviation from the thing a Loper should be, some minor defect. If there was, the biologists said, it would take years to find it.

And Fowler knew that they were right.

So there were five men now instead of four and Harold Allen had walked out into Jupiter for nothing at all. It was as if he'd never gone so far as knowledge was concerned.

Fowler reached across his desk and picked up the personnel file, a thin sheaf of paper neatly clipped together. It was a thing he dreaded but a thing he had to do. Somehow, the reason for these strange disappearances must be found. And there was no other way than to send out more men.

He sat for a moment listening to the howling of the wind above the dome, the everlasting thundering gale that swept across the planet in boiling, twisting wrath.

Was there some threat out there? he asked himself. Some danger they did not know about? Something that lay in wait and gobbled up the Lopers, making no distinction between Lopers that were bona fide and Lopers that were men? To the gobblers, of course, it would make no difference.

Or had there been a basic fault in selecting the Lopers as the type of life best fitted for existence on the surface of the planet? The evident intelligence of the Lopers, he knew, had been one factor in that determination. For if the thing man became did not have the capacity for intelligence, man could not for long retain his own intelligence in such a guise.

Had the biologists let that one factor weigh too heavily, using it to offset some other factor that might be unsatisfactory, even disastrous? It didn't seem likely. Stiff-necked as they might be, the biologists knew their business.

Or was the whole thing impossible, doomed from the very start? Conversion to other life-forms had worked on other planets, but that did not necessarily mean it would work on Jupiter. Perhaps man's intelligence could not function correctly through the sensory apparatus provided by Jovian life. Perhaps the Lopers were so alien there was no common ground for human knowledge and the Jovian conception of existence to meet and work together.

Or the fault might lie with man, be inherent with the race. Some mental aberration which, coupled with what they found outside, wouldn't let them come back. Although it might not be an aberration, not in the human sense. Perhaps just one ordinary human mental trait, accepted as commonplace on Earth, would be so violently at odds with Jovian existence that it would blast human sanity.

. . .

Claws rattled and clicked down the corridor. Listening to them, Fowler smiled wanly. It was Towser coming back from the kitchen, where he had gone to see his friend, the cook.

Towser came into the room, carrying a bone. He wagged his tail at Fowler and flopped down beside the desk, bone between his paws. For a long moment his rheumy old eyes regarded his master and Fowler reached down a hand to ruffle a ragged ear.

"You still like me, Towser?" Fowler asked, and Towser thumped his tail.

"You're the only one," said Fowler.

He straightened and swung back to the desk. His hand reached out and picked up the file.

Bennett? Bennett had a girl waiting for him back on Earth.

Andrews? Andrews was planning on going back to Mars Tech just as soon as he earned enough to see him through a year.

Olson? Olson was nearing pension age. All the time telling the boys how he was going to settle down and grow roses.

Carefully, Fowler laid the file back on the desk.

Sentencing men to death. Miss Stanley had said that, her pale lips scarcely moving in her parchment face. Marching men out to die while he, Fowler, sat here safe and comfortable.

They were saying it all through the dome, no doubt, especially since Allen had failed to return. They wouldn't say it to his face, of course. Even the man or men he called before this desk and told they were the next to go wouldn't say it to him.

But he would see it in their eyes.

He picked up the file again. Bennett, Andrews, Olson. There were others, but there was no use in going on.

Kent Fowler knew that he couldn't do it, couldn't face them, couldn't send more men out to die.

He leaned forward and flipped up the toggle on the inter-communicator.

"Yes, Mr. Fowler."

"Miss Stanley, please."

He waited for Miss Stanley, listening to Towser chewing halfheartedly on the bone. Towser's teeth were getting bad.

"Miss Stanley," said Miss Stanley's voice.

"Just wanted to tell you, Miss Stanley, to get ready for two more."

"Aren't you afraid," asked Miss Stanley, "that you'll run out of them? Sending out one at a time, they'd last longer, give you twice the satisfaction."

"One of them," said Fowler, "will be a dog."

"A dog!"

"Yes, Towser."

He heard the quick, cold rage that iced her voice. "Your own dog! He's been with you all these years—"

"That's the point," said Fowler. "Towser would be unhappy if I left him behind."

It was not the Jupiter he had known through the televisor. He had expected it to be different, but not like this. He had expected a hell of ammonia rain and stinking fumes and the deafening, thundering tumult of the storm. He had expected swirling clouds and fog and the snarling flicker of monstrous thunderbolts.

He had not expected the lashing downpour would be reduced to drifting purple mist that moved like fleeing shadows over a red and purple sward. He had not even guessed the snaking bolts of lightning would be flares of pure ecstasy across a painted sky.

Waiting for Towser, Fowler flexed the muscles of his body, amazed at the smooth, sleek strength he found. Not a bad body, he decided, and grimaced at remembering how he had pitied the Lopers when he glimpsed them through the television screen.

For it had been hard to imagine a living organism based upon ammonia and hydrogen rather than upon water and oxygen, hard to believe that such a form of life could know the same quick thrill of life that humankind could

know. Hard to conceive of life out in the soupy maelstrom that was Jupiter, not knowing, of course, that through Jovian eyes it was no soupy maelstrom at all.

The wind brushed against him with what seemed gentle fingers and he remembered with a start that by Earth standards the wind was a roaring gale, a two-hundred-mile-an-hour howler laden with deadly gases.

Pleasant scents seeped into his body. And yet scarcely scents, for it was not the sense of smell as he remembered it. It was as if his whole being was soaking up the sensation of lavender—and yet not lavender. It was something, he knew, for which he had no word, undoubtedly the first of many enigmas in terminology. For the words he knew, the thought symbols that served him as an Earthman, would not serve him as a Jovian.

The lock in the side of the dome opened and Towser came tumbling out—at least he thought it must be Towser.

He started to call to the dog, his mind shaping the words he meant to say. But he couldn't say them. There was no way to say them. He had nothing to say them with.

For a moment his mind swirled in muddy terror, a blind fear that eddied in little puffs of panic through his brain.

How did Jovians talk? How—

Suddenly he was aware of Towser, intensely aware of the bumbling, eager friendliness of the shaggy animal that had followed him from Earth to many planets. As if the thing that was Towser had reached out and for a moment sat within his brain.

And out of the bubbling welcome that he sensed, came words.

"Hiya, pal."

Not words, really, better than words. Thought symbols in his brain, communicated thought symbols that had shades of meaning words could never have.

"Hiya, Towser," he said.

"I feel good," said Towser. "Like I was a pup. Lately I've been feeling pretty punk. Legs stiffening up on me and teeth wearing down to almost nothing. Hard to mumble a bone with teeth like that. Besides, the fleas give me hell. Used to be I never paid much attention to them. A couple of fleas more or less never meant much in my early days."

"But . . . but—" Fowler's thoughts tumbled awkwardly. "You're talking to me!"

"Sure thing," said Towser. "I always talked to you, but you couldn't hear me. I tried to say things to you, but I couldn't make the grade."

"I understood you sometimes," Fowler said.

"Not very well," said Towser. "You knew when I wanted food and when I wanted a drink and when I wanted out, but that's about all you ever managed."

"I'm sorry," Fowler said.

"Forget it," Towser told him. "I'll race you to the cliff."

For the first time, Fowler saw the cliff, apparently many miles away, but with a strange crystalline beauty that sparkled in the shadow of the many-colored clouds.

Fowler hesitated. "It's a long way—"

"Ah, come on," said Towser, and even as he said it he started for the cliff.

Fowler followed, testing his legs, testing the strength in that new body of his, a bit doubtful at first, amazed a moment later, then running with a sheer joyousness that was one with the red and purple sward, with the drifting smoke of the rain across the land.

As he ran the consciousness of music came to him, a music that beat into his body, that surged throughout his being, that lifted him on wings of silver speed. Music like bells might make from some steeple on a sunny, springtime hill.

As the cliff drew nearer the music deepened and filled the universe with a spray of magic sound. And he knew the music came from the tumbling waterfall that feathered down the face of the shining cliff.

Only, he knew, it was no waterfall, but an ammonia-fall, and the cliff was white because it was oxygen, solidified.

He skidded to a stop beside Towser where the waterfall broke into a glittering rainbow of many hundred colors.

Literally many hundred, for here, he saw, was no shading of one primary to another as human beings saw, but a clear-cut selectivity that broke the prism down to its last ultimate classification.

"The music," said Towser.

"Yes, what about it?"

"The music," said Towser, "is vibrations. Vibrations of water falling."

"But, Towser, you don't know about vibrations."

"Yes, I do," contended Towser. "It just popped into my head."

Fowler gulped mentally. "Just popped!"

And suddenly, within his own head, he held a formula—a formula for a process that would make metal to withstand the pressure of Jupiter.

He stared, astounded, at the waterfall and swiftly his mind took the many colors and placed them in their exact sequence in the spectrum. Just like that. Just out of blue sky. Out of nothing, for he knew nothing either of metals or of colors.

"Towser," he cried. "Towser, something's happening to us!"

"Yeah, I know," said Towser.

"It's our brains," said Fowler. "We're using them, all of them, down to the last hidden corner. Using them to figure out things we should have known all the time. Maybe the brains of Earth things naturally are slow and foggy. Maybe we are the morons of the universe. Maybe we are fixed so we have to do things the hard way."

And, in the new sharp clarity of thought that seemed to grip him, he knew that it would not only be the matter of colors in a waterfall or metals that would resist the pressure of Jupiter. He sensed other things, things not yet quite clear. A vague whispering that hinted of greater things, of mysteries beyond the pale of human thought, beyond even the pale of human imagination. Mysteries, fact, logic built on reasoning. Things that any brain should know if it used all its reasoning power.

"We're still mostly Earth," he said. "We're just beginning to learn a few of the things we are to know—a few of the things that were kept from us as human beings, perhaps because we were human beings. Because our human bodies were poor bodies. Poorly equipped for thinking, poorly equipped in certain senses that one has to have to know. Perhaps even lacking in certain senses that are necessary to true knowledge."

He stared back at the dome, a tiny black thing dwarfed by the distance.

Back there were men who couldn't see the beauty that was Jupiter. Men who thought that swirling clouds and lashing rain obscured the planet's face. Unseeing human eyes. Poor eyes. Eyes that could not see the beauty in the clouds, that could not see through the storm. Bodies that could not feel the thrill of trilling music stemming from the rush of broken water.

Men who walked alone, in terrible loneliness, talking with their tongue like Boy Scouts wigwagging out their messages, unable to reach out and touch one another's mind as he could reach out and touch Towser's mind. Shut off forever from that personal, intimate contact with other living things.

He, Fowler, had expected terror inspired by alien things out here on the surface, had expected to cower before the threat of unknown things, had steeled himself against disgust of a situation that was not of Earth.

But instead he had found something greater than man had ever known. A swifter, surer body. A sense of exhilaration, a deeper sense of life. A sharper mind. A world of beauty that even the dreamers of the Earth had not yet imagined.

"Let's get going," Towser urged.

"Where do you want to go?"

"Anywhere," said Towser. "Just start going and see where we end up. I have a feeling . . . well, a feeling—"

"Yes, I know," said Fowler.

For he had the feeling, too. The feeling of high destiny. A certain sense of greatness. A knowledge that somewhere off beyond the horizons lay adventure and things greater than adventure.

Those other five had felt it, too. Had felt the urge to go and see, the compelling sense that here lay a life of fullness and of knowledge.

That, he knew, was why they had not returned.

"I won't go back," said Towser.

"We can't let them down," said Fowler.

Fowler took a step or two, back towards the dome, then stopped.

Back to the dome. Back to that aching, poison-laden body he had left. It hadn't seemed aching before, but now he knew it was.

Back to the fuzzy brain. Back to muddled thinking. Back to the flapping mouths that formed signals others understood.

Back to eyes that now would be worse than no sight at all. Back to squalor, back to crawling, back to ignorance.

"Perhaps someday," he said, muttering to himself.

"We got a lot to do and a lot to see," said Towser. "We got a lot to learn. We'll find things—"

Yes, they could find things. Civilizations, perhaps. Civilizations that would make the civilization of man seem puny by comparison. Beauty and, more important, an understanding of that beauty. And a comradeship no one had ever known before—that no man, no dog, had ever known before.

And life. The quickness of life after what seemed a drugged existence.

"I can't go back," said Towser.

"Nor I," said Fowler.

"They would turn me back into a dog," said Towser.

"And me," said Fowler, "back into a man."

RAY BRADBURY

Ray Bradbury (1920–2012) was an iconic, award-winning US writer of speculative fiction who became internationally beloved due mainly to his lyrical, deeply humane short stories as well as *The Martian Chronicles* (1950), *The Illustrated Man* (1951), the classic novel about censorship *Fahrenheit 451* (1953), and *Something Wicked This Way Comes* (1962), which had a direct influence on Neil Gaiman and Stephen King. Many of his fictions were turned into movies or adapted for television. Bradbury himself wrote for television and film, receiving an Emmy Award and his own star on the Hollywood Walk of Fame. Bradbury also received a National Medal of Arts from President George W. Bush and the World Fantasy Award for Life Achievement, and was inducted into the Science Fiction and Fantasy Hall of Fame in 1999. An asteroid has also been named in his honor.

Bradbury discovered science fiction in 1937 and began publishing his fanzine *Futuria Fantasia* in 1939. He would, all his life, be fond of the genre community but had startlingly eclectic and wide-ranging approaches to writing fiction that took him far afield and endeared him to a broad general audience. After a number of early stories that showed promise, the famous Bradbury style began to take shape: poetic, evocative, consciously symbolic, with strong nostalgic elements and a leaning toward the macabre—his work was always as much fantasy and horror as science fiction. This darkness served Bradbury well, as it balanced the more sentimental aspects of his writing and helped him create more layered and interesting work.

Bradbury's most iconic work is probably the mosaic novel *The Martian Chronicles*, which was made into a television miniseries and, in the Spanish edition, features an introduction by Jorge Luis Borges. Bradbury once said that John Steinbeck's *The Grapes of Wrath* was the inspiration behind the structure of the book. Evocative and closely interwoven, the stories are linked by recurring images and themes. The stories tell of the repeated attempts by humans to colonize Mars, of the way they bring their old prejudices with them, including expectations that settlement on Mars could safely replicate their experience of California suburban life, and of their repeated, ambiguous meetings with the shape-changing Martians.

The mood of *The Martian Chronicles* is of loneliness and nostalgia; a pensive regret suffuses the book. This approach would prove too un-science-fictional for some critics, and the book received a mixed reception in the genre community. Although Damon Knight listed *The Martian Chronicles* as one of the top science fiction books of 1950, L. Sprague de Camp thought Bradbury's style was too literary, claiming Bradbury must have been influenced by Ernest Hemingway and William Saroyan. Bradbury himself said he was heavily influenced by Edgar Rice Burroughs. What is clear is the maturity of the work, dealing in subtle and deft fashion with complex themes and issues.

"September 2005: The Martian" was first published as a stand-alone short story in *Super Science Stories* in November 1949.

SEPTEMBER 2005: THE MARTIAN

Ray Bradbury

The blue mountains lifted into the rain and the rain fell down into the long canals and old LaFarge and his wife came out of their house to watch.

"First rain this season," LaFarge pointed out.

"It's good," said his wife.

"Very welcome."

They shut the door. Inside, they warmed their hands at a fire. They shivered. In the distance, through the window, they saw rain gleaming on the sides of the rocket which had brought them from Earth.

"There's only one thing," said LaFarge, looking at his hands.

"What's that?" asked his wife.

"I wish we could have brought Tom with us."

"Oh, now, Lafe!"

"I won't start again; I'm sorry."

"We came here to enjoy our old age in peace, not to think of Tom. He's been dead so long now, we should try to forget him and everything on Earth."

"You're right," he said, and turned his hands again to the heat. He gazed into the fire. "I won't speak of it anymore. It's just I miss driving out to Green Lawn Park every Sunday to put flowers on his marker. It used to be our only excursion."

The blue rain fell gently upon the house.

At nine o'clock they went to bed and lay quietly, hand in hand, he fifty-five, she sixty, in the raining darkness.

"Anna?" he called softly.

"Yes?" she replied.

"Did you hear something?"

They both listened to the rain and the wind.

"Nothing," she said.

"Someone whistling," he said.

"No, I didn't hear it."

"I'm going to get up to see anyhow."

He put on his robe and walked through the house to the front door. Hesitating, he pulled the door wide, and rain fell cold upon his face. The wind blew.

In the dooryard stood a small figure.

Lightning cracked the sky, and a wash of white color illumined the face looking in at old LaFarge there in the doorway.

"Who's there?" called LaFarge, trembling.

No answer.

"Who is it? What do you want!"

Still not a word.

He felt very weak and tired and numb. "Who are you?" he cried.

His wife entered behind him and took his arm. "Why are you shouting?"

"A small boy's standing in the yard and won't answer me," said the old man, trembling. "He looks like Tom!"

"Come to bed, you're dreaming."

"But he's there; see for yourself."

He pulled the door wider to let her see. The cold wind blew and the thin rain fell upon the soil and the figure stood looking at them with distant eyes. The old woman held to the doorway.

"Go away!" she said, waving one hand. "Go away!"

"Doesn't it look like Tom?" asked the old man.

The figure did not move.

"I'm afraid," said the old woman. "Lock the door and come to bed. I won't have anything to do with it."

She vanished, moaning to herself, into the bedroom.

The old man stood with the wind raining coldness on his hands.

"Tom," he called softly. "Tom, if that's you, if by some chance it is you, Tom, I'll leave the door unlatched. And if you're cold and want to come in to warm yourself, just come in later and lie by the hearth; there's some fur rugs there."

He shut but did not lock the door.

His wife felt him return to bed, and shuddered. "It's a terrible night. I feel so old," she said, sobbing.

"Hush, hush," he gentled her, and held her in his arms. "Go to sleep."

After a long while she slept.

And then, very quietly, as he listened, he heard the front door open, the rain and wind come in, the door shut. He heard soft footsteps on the hearth and a gentle breathing. "Tom," he said to himself.

Lightning struck in the sky and broke the blackness apart.

In the morning the sun was very hot.

Mr. LaFarge opened the door into the living room and glanced all about, quickly.

The hearth rugs were empty.

LaFarge sighed. "I'm getting old," he said.

He went out to walk to the canal to fetch a bucket of clear water to wash in. At the front door he almost knocked young Tom down carrying in a bucket already filled to the brim. "Good morning, Father!"

"Morning, Tom." The old man fell aside. The young boy, barefooted, hurried across the room, set the bucket down, and turned, smiling. "It's a fine day!"

"Yes, it is," said the old man incredulously. The boy acted as if nothing was unusual. He began to wash his face with the water.

The old man moved forward. "Tom, how did you get here? You're alive?"

"Shouldn't I be?" The boy glanced up.

"But, Tom, Green Lawn Park, every Sunday, the flowers and . . ." LaFarge had to sit down.

The boy came and stood before him and took his hand. The old man felt of the fingers, warm and firm. "You're really here, it's not a dream?"

"You *do* want me to be here, don't you?" The boy seemed worried.

"Yes, yes, Tom!"

"Then why ask questions? Accept me!"

"But your mother; the shock . . ."

"Don't worry about her. During the night I sang to both of you, and you'll accept me more because of it, especially her. I know what the shock is. Wait till she comes, you'll see." He laughed, shaking his head of coppery, curled hair. His eyes were very blue and clear.

"Good morning, Lafe, Tom." Mother came from the bedroom, putting her hair up into a bun. "Isn't it a fine day?"

Tom turned to laugh in his father's face. "You see?"

They ate a very good lunch, all three of them, in the shade behind the house. Mrs. LaFarge had found an old bottle of sunflower wine she had put away, and they all had a drink of that. Mr. LaFarge had never seen his wife's face so bright. If there was any doubt in her mind about Tom, she didn't voice it. It was a completely natural thing to her. And it was also becoming natural to LaFarge himself.

While Mother cleared the dishes LaFarge leaned toward his son and said confidentially, "How old are you now, son?"

"Don't you know, Father? Fourteen, of course."

"Who are you, *really*? You can't be Tom, but you are *someone*. Who?"

"Don't." Startled, the boy put his hands to his face.

"You can tell me," said the old man. "I'll understand. You're a Martian, aren't you? I've heard tales of the Martians; nothing definite. Stories about how rare Martians are and when they come among us they come as Earth Men. There's something about you—you're Tom and yet you're not."

"Why can't you accept me and stop talking?" cried the boy. His hands completely shielded his face. "Don't doubt, please don't doubt me!" He turned and ran from the table.

"Tom, come back!"

But the boy ran off along the canal toward the distant town.

"Where's Tom going?" asked Anna, returning for more dishes. She looked at her husband's face. "Did you say something to bother him?"

"Anna," he said, taking her hand. "Anna, do you remember anything about Green Lawn Park, a market, and Tom having pneumonia?"

"What *are* you talking about?" She laughed.

"Never mind," he said quietly.

In the distance the dust drifted down after Tom had run along the canal rim.

At five in the afternoon, with the sunset, Tom returned. He looked doubtfully at his father. "Are you going to ask me anything?" he wanted to know.

"No questions," said LaFarge.

The boy smiled his white smile. "Swell."

"Where've you been?"

"Near the town. I almost didn't come back. I was almost"—the boy sought for a word—"trapped."

"How do you mean, 'trapped'?"

"I passed a small tin house by the canal and I was almost made so I couldn't come back here ever again to see you. I don't know how to explain it to you, there's no way, I can't tell you, even *I* don't know; it's strange, I don't want to talk about it."

"We won't then. Better wash up, boy. Suppertime."

The boy ran.

Perhaps ten minutes later a boat floated down the serene surface of the canal, a tall lank man with black hair poling it along with leisurely drives of his arms. "Evening, Brother LaFarge," he said, pausing at his task.

"Evening, Saul, what's the word?"

"All kinds of words tonight. You know that fellow named Nomland who lives down the canal in the tin hut?"

LaFarge stiffened. "Yes?"

"You know what sort of rascal he was?"

"Rumor had it he left Earth because he killed a man."

Saul leaned on his wet pole, gazing at LaFarge. "Remember the name of the man he killed?"

"Gillings, wasn't it?"

"Right. Gillings. Well, about two hours ago Mr. Nomland came running to town crying about how he had seen Gillings, alive, here on Mars, today, this afternoon! He tried to get the jail to lock him up safe. The jail wouldn't. So Nomland went home, and twenty minutes ago, as I get the story, blew his brains out with a gun. I just came from there."

"Well, well," said LaFarge.

"The darnedest things happen," said Saul. "Well, good night, LaFarge."

"Good night."

The boat drifted on down the serene canal waters.

"Supper's hot," called the old woman.

Mr. LaFarge sat down to his supper and, knife in hand, looked over at Tom. "Tom," he said, "what did you do this afternoon?"

"Nothing," said Tom, his mouth full. "Why?"

"Just wanted to know." The old man tucked his napkin in.

At seven that night the old woman wanted to go to town. "Haven't been there in months," she said. But Tom resisted. "I'm afraid of the town," he said. "The people. I don't want to go there."

"Such talk for a grown boy," said Anna. "I won't listen to it. You'll come along. *I* say so."

"Anna, if the boy doesn't want to . . . ," started the old man.

But there was no arguing. She hustled them into the canalboat and they floated up the canal under the evening stars, Tom lying on his back, his eyes closed; asleep or not, there was no telling. The old man looked at him steadily, wondering. Who is this, he thought, in need of love as much as we? Who is he and what is he that, out of loneliness, he comes into the alien camp and assumes the voice and face of memory and stands among us, accepted and happy at last? From what mountain, what cave, what small last race of people remaining on this world when the rockets came from Earth? The old man shook his head. There was no way to know. This, to all purposes, was Tom.

The old man looked at the town ahead and did not like it, but then he returned to thoughts of Tom and Anna again and he thought to himself: Perhaps this is wrong to keep Tom but a little while, when nothing can come of it but trouble and sorrow, but how are we to give up the very thing we've wanted, no matter if it stays only a day and is gone, making the emptiness emptier, the dark nights darker, the rainy nights wetter? You might as well force the food from our mouths as take this one from us.

And he looked at the boy slumbering so peacefully at the bottom of the boat. The boy whimpered with some dream. "The people," he murmured in his sleep. "Changing and changing. The trap."

"There, there, boy." LaFarge stroked the boy's soft curls and Tom ceased.

LaFarge helped wife and son from the boat.

"Here we are!" Anna smiled at all the lights, listening to the music from the drinking houses, the pianos, the phonographs, watching people, arm in arm, striding by in the crowded streets.

"I wish I was home," said Tom.

"You never talked that way before," said the mother. "You always liked Saturday nights in town."

"Stay close to me," whispered Tom. "I don't want to get trapped."

Anna overheard. "Stop talking that way; come along!"

LaFarge noticed that the boy held his hand. LaFarge squeezed it. "I'll stick with you, Tommy-boy." He looked at the throngs coming and going and it worried him also. "We won't stay long."

"Nonsense, we'll spend the evening," said Anna.

They crossed a street, and three drunken men careened into them. There was much confusion, a separation, a wheeling about, and then LaFarge stood stunned.

Tom was gone.

"Where is he?" asked Anna irritably. "Him always running off alone any chance he gets. Tom!" she called.

Mr. LaFarge hurried through the crowd, but Tom was gone.

"He'll come back; he'll be at the boat when we leave," said Anna certainly, steering her husband back toward the motion-picture theater. There was a sudden commotion in the crowd, and a man and woman rushed by LaFarge. He recognized them. Joe Spaulding and his wife. They were gone before he could speak to them.

Looking back anxiously, he purchased the tickets for the theater and allowed his wife to draw him into the unwelcome darkness.

Tom was not at the landing at eleven o'clock. Mrs. LaFarge turned very pale.

"Now, Mother," said LaFarge, "don't worry. I'll find him. Wait here."

"Hurry back." Her voice faded into the ripple of the water.

He walked through the night streets, hands in pockets. All about, lights were going out one by one. A few people were still leaning out their windows, for the night was warm, even though the sky still held storm clouds from time to time among the stars. As he walked he recalled the boy's constant references to being trapped, his fear of crowds and cities. There was no sense in it, thought the old man tiredly. Perhaps the boy was gone forever, perhaps he had never been. LaFarge turned in at a particular alley, watching the numbers.

"Hello there, LaFarge."

A man sat in his doorway, smoking a pipe.

"Hello, Mike."

"You and your woman quarrel? You out walking it off?"

"No. Just walking."

"You look like you lost something. Speaking of lost things," said Mike, "somebody got found this evening. You know Joe Spaulding? You remember his daughter Lavinia?"

"Yes." LaFarge was cold. It all seemed a repeated dream. He knew which words would come next.

"Lavinia came home tonight," said Mike, smoking. "You recall, she was lost on the dead sea bottoms about a month ago? They found what they thought was her body, badly deteriorated, and ever since the Spaulding family's been no good. Joe went around saying she wasn't dead, that wasn't really her body. Guess he was right. Tonight Lavinia showed up."

"Where?" LaFarge felt his breath come swiftly, his heart pounding.

"On Main Street. The Spauldings were buying tickets for a show. And there, all of a sudden, in the crowd, was Lavinia. Must have been quite a scene. She didn't know them first off. They followed her half down a street and spoke to her. Then she remembered."

"Did you see her?"

"No, but I heard her singing. Remember how she used to sing 'The Bonnie Banks of Loch Lomond'? I heard her trilling out for her father a while ago over there in their house. It was good to hear her; such a beautiful girl. A shame, I thought, her dead; and now with her back again it's fine. Here now, you look weak yourself. Better come in for a spot of whisky. . . ."

"Thanks, no, Mike." The old man moved away. He heard Mike say good night and did not answer, but fixed his eyes upon the two-story building where rambling clusters of crimson Martian flowers lay upon the high crystal roof. Around back, above the garden, was a twisted iron balcony, and the windows above were lighted. It was very late, and still he thought to himself: What will happen to Anna if I don't bring Tom home with me? This second shock, this second death, what will it do to her? Will she remember the first death, too, and this dream, and the sudden vanishing? Oh God, I've got to find Tom, or what will come of Anna? Poor Anna, waiting there at the landing. He paused and lifted his head. Somewhere above, voices bade other soft voices good night, doors turned and shut, lights dimmed, and a gentle singing continued. A moment later a girl no more than eighteen, very lovely, came out upon the balcony.

LaFarge called up through the wind that was blowing.

The girl turned and looked down. "Who's there?" she cried.

"It's me," said the old man, and, realizing this reply to be silly and strange, fell silent, his lips working. Should he call out, "Tom, my son, this is your father"? How to speak to her? She would think him quite insane and summon her parents.

The girl bent forward in the blowing light. "I know you," she replied softly. "Please go; there's nothing you can do."

"You've got to come back!" It escaped LaFarge before he could prevent it.

The moonlit figure above drew into shadow, so there was no identity, only a voice. "I'm not your son anymore," it said. "We should never have come to town."

"Anna's waiting at the landing!"

"I'm sorry," said the quiet voice. "But what can I do? I'm happy here. I'm loved, even as you loved me. I am what I am, and I take what can be taken; too late now, they've caught me."

"But, Anna, the shock to her. Think of that."

"The thoughts are too strong in this house; it's like being imprisoned. I can't change myself back."

"You are Tom, you *were* Tom, weren't you? You aren't joking with an old man; you're not really Lavinia Spaulding?"

"I'm not anyone, I'm just myself; wherever

I am, I am something, and now I'm something you can't help."

"You're not safe in the town. It's better out on the canal where no one can hurt you," pleaded the old man.

"That's true." The voice hesitated. "But I must consider these people now. How would they feel if, in the morning, I was gone again, this time for good? Anyway, the mother knows what I am; she guessed, even as you did. I think they all guessed but didn't question. You don't question Providence. If you can't have the reality, a dream is just as good. Perhaps I'm not their dead one back, but I'm something almost better to them; an ideal shaped by their minds. I have a choice of hurting them or your wife."

"They're a family of five. They can stand your loss better!"

"Please," said the voice. "I'm tired."

The old man's voice hardened. "You've got to come. I can't let Anna be hurt again. You're our son. You're my son, and you belong to us."

"No, please!" The shadow trembled.

"You don't belong to this house or these people!"

"No, don't do this to me!"

"Tom, Tom, son, listen to me. Come back, slip down the vines, boy. Come along, Anna's waiting; we'll give you a good home, everything you want." He stared and stared upward, willing it to be.

The shadows drifted, the vines rustled.

At last the quiet voice said, "All right, Father."

"Tom!"

In the moonlight the quick figure of a boy slid down through the vines. LaFarge put up his arms to catch him.

The room lights above flashed on. A voice issued from one of the grilled windows. "Who's down there?"

"Hurry, boy!"

More lights, more voices. "Stop, I have a gun! Vinny, are you all right?" A running of feet.

Together the old man and the boy ran across the garden.

A shot sounded. The bullet struck the wall as they slammed the gate.

"Tom, you that way; I'll go here and lead them off! Run to the canal; I'll meet you there in ten minutes, boy!"

They parted.

The moon hid behind a cloud. The old man ran in darkness.

"Anna, I'm here!"

The old woman helped him, trembling, into the boat. "Where's Tom?"

"He'll be here in a minute," panted LaFarge.

They turned to watch the alleys and the sleeping town. Late strollers were still out: a policeman, a night watchman, a rocket pilot, several lonely men coming home from some nocturnal rendezvous, four men and women issuing from a bar, laughing. Music played dimly somewhere.

"Why doesn't he come?" asked the old woman.

"He'll come, he'll come." But LaFarge was not certain. Suppose the boy had been caught again, somehow, someway, in his travel down to the landing, running through the midnight streets between the dark houses. It was a long run, even for a young boy. But he should have reached here first.

And now, far away, along the moonlit avenue, a figure ran.

LaFarge cried out and then silenced himself, for also far away was another sound of voices and running feet. Lights blazed on in window after window. Across the open plaza leading to the landing, the one figure ran. It was not Tom; it was only a running shape with a face like silver shining in the light of the globes dusted about the plaza. And as it rushed nearer, nearer, it became more familiar, until when it reached the landing it was Tom! Anna flung up her hands. LaFarge hurried to cast off. But already it was too late.

For out of the avenue and across the silent

plaza now came one man, another, a woman, two other men, Mr. Spaulding, all running. They stopped, bewildered. They stared about, wanting to go back because this could be only a nightmare, it was quite insane. But they came on again, hesitantly, stopping, starting.

It was too late. The night, the event, was over. LaFarge twisted the mooring rope in his fingers. He was very cold and lonely. The people raised and put down their feet in the moonlight, drifting with great speed, wide-eyed, until the crowd, all ten of them, halted at the landing. They peered wildly down into the boat. They cried out.

"Don't move, LaFarge!" Spaulding had a gun.

And now it was evident what had happened. Tom flashing through the moonlit streets, alone, passing people. A policeman seeing the figure dart past. The policeman pivoting, staring at the face, calling a name, giving pursuit. "*You*, stop!" Seeing a criminal face. All along the way, the same thing, men here, women there, night watchmen, rocket pilots. The swift figure meaning everything to them, all identities, all persons, all names. How many different names had been uttered in the last five minutes? How many different faces shaped over Tom's face, all wrong?

All down the way the pursued and the pursuing, the dream and the dreamers, the quarry and the hounds. All down the way the sudden revealment, the flash of familiar eyes, the cry of an old, old name, the remembrances of other times, the crowd multiplying. Everyone leaping forward as, like an image reflected from ten thousand mirrors, ten thousand eyes, the running dream came and went, a different face to those ahead, those behind, those yet to be met, those unseen.

And here they all are now, at the boat, wanting the dream for their own, just as we want him to be Tom, not Lavinia or William or Roger or any other, thought LaFarge. But it's all done now. The thing has gone too far.

"Come up, all of you!" Spaulding ordered them.

Tom stepped up from the boat. Spaulding seized his wrist. "You're coming home with me. I *know*."

"Wait," said the policeman. "He's my prisoner. Name's Dexter; wanted for murder."

"No!" a woman sobbed. "It's my husband! I guess I know my husband!"

Other voices objected. The crowd moved in.

Mrs. LaFarge shielded Tom. "This is my son; you have no right to accuse him of anything. We're going home right now!"

As for Tom, he was trembling and shaking violently. He looked very sick. The crowd thickened about him, putting out their wild hands, seizing and demanding.

Tom screamed.

Before their eyes he changed. He was Tom and James and a man named Switchman, another named Butterfield; he was the town mayor and the young girl Judith and the husband William and the wife Clarisse. He was melting wax shaping to their minds. They shouted, they pressed forward, pleading. He screamed, threw out his hands, his face dissolving to each demand. "Tom!" cried LaFarge. "Alice!" another. "William!" They snatched his wrists, whirled him about, until with one last shriek of horror he fell.

He lay on the stones, melted wax cooling, his face all faces, one eye blue, the other golden, hair that was brown, red, yellow, black, one eyebrow thick, one thin, one hand large, one small.

They stood over him and put their fingers to their mouths. They bent down.

"He's dead," someone said at last.

It began to rain.

The rain fell upon the people, and they looked up at the sky.

Slowly, and then more quickly, they turned and walked away and then started running, scattering from the scene. In a minute the place was desolate. Only Mr. and Mrs. LaFarge remained, looking down, hand in hand, terrified.

The rain fell upon the upturned, unrecognizable face.

Anna said nothing but began to cry.

"Come along home, Anna, there's nothing we can do," said the old man.

They climbed down into the boat and went back along the canal in the darkness. They entered their house and lit a small fire and warmed their hands. They went to bed and lay together, cold and thin, listening to the rain returned to the roof above them.

"Listen," said LaFarge at midnight. "Did you hear something?"

"Nothing, nothing."

"I'll go look anyway."

He fumbled across the dark room and waited by the outer door for a long time before he opened it.

He pulled the door wide and looked out.

Rain poured from the black sky upon the empty dooryard, into the canal, and among the blue mountains.

He waited five minutes and then softly, his hands wet, he shut and bolted the door.

Baby HP

JUAN JOSÉ ARREOLA

Translated by Larry Nolen

Juan José Arreola (1918–2001) was an influential Mexican writer and academic best known for his experimental and fantastic short stories. Jorge Luis Borges described his work as the "freedom of an unlimited imagination, governed by a lucid intelligence." A master of the humorous story-essay, Arreola has been compared to satirical writers such as Jonathan Swift, Cyrano de Bergerac, and Edgar Allan Poe. Trained as an actor, Arreola had a fervent belief in the spoken word, which shaped the style of his fiction, which usually takes the form of short-shorts.

Notorious for appearing in the late-1960s Alejandro Jodorowsky movie *Fando y Lis* that was censored in Mexico, Arreola redeemed himself in the 1970s as the recipient of the National Prize in Letters in Mexico City. Other awards include the Literatura Latinoamericana y del Caribe Juan Rulfo Prize, the Alfonso Reyes Prize, and the Ramón López Velarde Prize. By the 1960s and 1970s Arreola wrote less and less and was largely forgotten as other more influential Mexican writers came onto the scene. Some of his work now seems dated and/or portrays women in less than exemplary ways (for example, "Anuncio" [*México en la cultura*, 1952], about the Plastisex, an artificial woman).

Some of Arreola's more typical tales are short enough to include in an author note—for example, "A Theory on Dulcinea," which, translated here by Larry Nolen, skewers Cervantes.

In a lonely place whose name is beside the point there was a man who spent his life avoiding real women. He preferred the solitary enjoyment of reading, and he congratulated himself smugly each time a knight errant in those pages challenged to a fencing duel one of those vague feminine phantasms, made of virtues and overlapping skirts, that awaits the hero after four hundred pages of exploits, lies, and nonsense.

At the threshold of old age, a woman of flesh and bone besieged the hermit-like knight in his cave. Under some pretext she entered his chamber and filled it with the strong aroma of sweat and wool typical of a young peasant woman overheated by the sun.

The knight lost his head, but far from being trapped by the woman in front of him, he instead threw himself headlong in pursuit, through pages and pages, of a pompous fantasy monster. He walked many leagues, speared sheep and windmills, pruned a few oaks, and did three or four leaps into the air, clapping his shoes together.

Upon returning from this fruitless endeavor, however, death awaited him at the door of his house. The knight only had time to dictate a cavernous will, from the bottom of his parched soul. A shepherdess's dusty face was washed with true tears, but it was a useless gleam before the tomb of the mad knight.

Arreola preferred fantasy and wrote very few science fiction short stories but built them, like the rest of his work, using detailed prose and a taste for the bizarre, combined with elements of magic realism and satire. Three of them appear in his best-known collection, *Confabulario* (1952), including "En verdad os digo" ("In Truth I Tell You"), about a scientist who promises the salvation of rich people's souls because he is able to disassemble a camel and make it pass through the eye of a needle in a stream of electrons, defying the words of the Bible.

The other two stories criticize consumerism—in particular the tale reprinted here in a new translation, "Baby H.P.," in which Arreola offers up a way for every family to take advantage of their own children's excess energy.

BABY HP

Juan José Arreola

Translated by Larry Nolen

To the Lady of the House: Convert your children's vitality into an energy force. We now have on sale the marvelous Baby HP, a device that is set to revolutionize the domestic economy.

The Baby HP is a very durable and lightweight metal structure that adapts perfectly to a child's delicate body through the use of comfortable belts, bracelets, rings, and brooches. The attachments on this supplementary skeleton absorb each of the child's movements and accumulate in a Leyden bottle that can be placed on the back or chest, as needed. A gauge shows when the bottle is full. Then you, madam, detach it and plug it into a special receptacle to be unloaded automatically. This receptacle can be placed in any corner of the house, making for a precious piggy bank of electricity available at all times for lighting and heating purposes, as well as to power any of the innumerable devices that now invade homes.

From now on you will see with new eyes the exhausting bustle of your children. And you won't even lose patience before one of their convulsive tantrums, thinking that it's a rich source of energy. The kicking of a breast-feeding baby throughout the day is transformed, thanks to Baby HP, into some useful seconds for running the blender or into fifteen minutes of radio music.

Large families can satisfy all their electricity demands by installing a Baby HP on each one of their offspring, enabling them to run a small and lucrative business of transmitting to their neighbors some of their leftover energy. In apartment high-rises, they can satisfactorily cover lapses in public utilities by linking together the families' receptacles.

The Baby HP causes no physical or psychological trauma in children, because it neither constrains nor disturbs their movements. On the contrary, some doctors believe that it contributes to the body's harmonious development. And as far as the spirit is concerned, you can awaken the children's individual ambitions by awarding them with small prizes when they surpass their usual records. For this end, sugary treats are recommended, as they return your investment with interest. The more calories added to a child's diet, the more kilowatts saved on the electric bill.

Children should wear their Baby HPs day and night. It is important that they always wear them to school so that they don't lose the precious hours of recess, from which they will return with tanks overflowing with energy.

The rumors about some children being electrocuted by the current that they themselves generate are completely irresponsible. The same can be said regarding the superstitious fear that infants outfitted with a Baby HP attract lightning bolts. No accidents of this nature can occur, above all if the instructions that accompany each device are followed to the letter.

The Baby HP is available in fine stores in different sizes, models, and prices. It is a modern, durable, and trustworthy device and all of its joints are extendable. It comes with a manufacturer's guarantee from the company of J. P. Mansfield & Sons, of Atlanta, Illinois.

Surface Tension

JAMES BLISH

James Blish (1921–1975) was a US writer of science fiction and fantasy, sometimes with religious themes, who studied biology in college. Blish also published a substantial body of nonfiction and was one of the prominent science fiction critics of the 1950s in particular. His early fiction appeared in *Super Science Stories* in 1940, and after World War II he eventually earned enough from his stories and novels to become a full-time writer. Blish achieved significant success for his "Okies" stories (collected in the *Cities in Flight* series, 1950–62) and made a minor claim to astronomic fame by creating the term "gas giant" for his story "Solar Plexus" (*Beyond Human Ken*, a 1952 anthology edited by Judith Merril).

If this were the extent of Blish's involvement in science fiction, he would remain a well-regarded figure in the field. But he also pushed well beyond "center genre" with novels like *A Case of Conscience*—and the infernal *Black Easter* and *The Day After Judgment*, inspired by the work of the poet T. S. Eliot and John Milton, a famous apocalyptic English poet from the 1600s who used supernatural imagery.

In this context, it is ironic that major figures in the New Wave movement of the 1960s, such as M. John Harrison, attacked Blish as a member of the old guard. With the advantage of time and distance, this seems in part to be a misunderstanding. Blish studied literature at Columbia and had a certain amount of disdain for pulp fiction and shoddy editing. In addition, Blish's most avant-garde work features conflicted, nuanced characters and situations, and has more in common with New Wave fiction than with traditional "sense of wonder" pulp adventure tales. He was enough of a "man of letters" to have been a useful and formidable advocate for new ways of approaching science fiction—but also exactly what the counterculture New Wave–ists saw as the enemy. Ironically, in the 1940s, Blish had been part of a group that founded a new amateur press association that, as Robert A. W. Lowndes puts it in his introduction to *The Best of James Blish* (1979), wanted to "write intelligently about something other than the latest contents of *Astounding* or nostalgia for the 'good old days,' 'sense of wonder,' fan reminiscences."

Blish achieved even more fame for his "pantropy" stories, the term coined to describe the concept of human genetic modification for the purpose of survival outside of the planet Earth. Clifford D. Simak's story "Desertion" (also included in this anthology) is considered the earliest story to use this concept, predating Blish's work.

In the pantropy stories, collected in *The Seedling Stars* (1957)—admittedly more traditional than Blish's edgier work—human modification is deemed easier and less intrusive than terraforming for colonizing other worlds. "Surface Tension" (1952) is the third (and most popular) story in the pantropy series—a sprawling, exciting, and complex tale that seems even more relevant today, in the context of human life on our own planet. "Surface Tension" was selected by the Science Fiction Writers of America in 1970 as one of the best stories published before the Nebula Awards were created. It was also reprinted in *The Science Fiction Hall of Fame, Volume One: 1929–1964.*

SURFACE TENSION

James Blish

PROLOGUE

Dr. Chatvieux took a long time over the microscope, leaving la Ventura with nothing to do but look at the dead landscape of Hydrot. *Waterscape*, he thought, would be a better word. From space, the new world had shown only one small, triangular continent, set amid endless ocean; and even the continent was mostly swamp.

The wreck of the seed-ship lay broken squarely across the one real spur of rock which Hydrot seemed to possess, which reared a magnificent twenty-one feet above sea level. From this eminence, la Ventura could see forty miles to the horizon across a flat bed of mud. The red light of the star Tau Ceti, glinting upon thousands of small lakes, pools, ponds, and puddles, made the watery plain look like a mosaic of onyx and ruby.

"If I were a religious man," the pilot said suddenly, "I'd call this a plain case of divine vengeance."

Chatvieux said: "Hmn?"

"It's as if we'd been struck down for—is it *hubris*? Pride, arrogance?"

"*Hybris*," Chatvieux said, looking up at last. "Well, is it? I don't feel swollen with pride at the moment. Do you?"

"I'm not exactly proud of my piloting," la Ventura admitted. "But that isn't quite what I mean. I was thinking about why we came here in the first place. It takes a lot of arrogance to think that you can scatter men, or at least things very much like men, all over the face of the galaxy. It takes even more pride to do the job—to pack up all the equipment and move from planet to planet and actually make men, make them suitable for every place you touch."

"I suppose it does," Chatvieux said. "But we're only one of several hundred seed-ships in this limb of the galaxy, so I doubt that the gods picked us out as special sinners." He smiled. "If they had, maybe they'd have left us our ultraphone, so the Colonization Council could hear about our cropper. Besides, Paul, we don't make men. We adapt them—adapt them to Earthlike planets, nothing more than that. We've sense enough—or humility enough, if you like that better—to know that we can't adapt men to a planet like Jupiter, or to the surface of a sun, like Tau Ceti."

"Anyhow, we're here," la Ventura said grimly. "And we aren't going to get off. Phil tells me that we don't even have our germ-cell bank anymore, so we can't seed this place in the usual way. We've been thrown onto a dead world and dared to adapt to it. What are the pantropes going to do with our recalcitrant carcasses— provide built-in waterwings?"

"No," Chatvieux said calmly. "You and I and all the rest of us are going to die, Paul. Pantropic techniques don't work on the body; that was fixed for you for life when you were conceived. To attempt to rebuild it for you would only maim you. The pantropes affect only the genes, the inheritance-carrying factors. We can't give you built-in waterwings, any more than we can give you a new set of brains. I think we'll be able to populate this world with men, but we won't live to see it."

The pilot thought about it, a lump of cold blubber collecting gradually in his stomach. "How long do you give us?" he said at last.

"Who knows? A month, perhaps."

The bulkhead leading to the wrecked section of the ship was pushed back, admitting salt, muggy air, heavy with carbon dioxide. Philip Strasvogel, the communications officer, came in, tracking mud. Like la Ventura, he was now a man without a function, and it appeared to bother him. He was not well equipped for introspection, and with his ultraphone totally smashed, unresponsive to his perpetually darting hands, he had been thrown back into his own mind, whose resources were few. Only the tasks Chatvieux had set him to had prevented him from setting like a gelling colloid into a permanent state of the sulks.

He unbuckled from around his waist a canvas belt, into the loops of which plastic vials were stuffed like cartridges. "More samples, doc," he said. "All alike—water, very wet. I have some quicksand in one boot, too. Find anything?"

"A good deal, Phil. Thanks. Are the others around?"

Strasvogel poked his head out and hallooed. Other voices rang out over the mudflats. Minutes later, the rest of the survivors of the crash were crowding into the pantrope deck: Saltonstall, Chatvieux's senior assistant, a perpetually sanguine, perpetually youthful technician willing to try anything once, including dying; Eunice Wagner, behind whose placid face rested the brains of the expedition's only remaining ecologist; Eleftherios Venezuelos, the always-silent delegate from the Colonization Council; and Joan Heath, a midshipman whose duties, like la Ventura's and Phil's, were now without meaning, but whose bright head and tall, deceptively indolent body shone to the pilot's eyes brighter than Tau Ceti—brighter, since the crash, even than the home sun.

Five men and two women—to colonize a planet on which "standing room" meant treading water.

They came in quietly and found seats or resting places on the deck, on the edges of tables, in corners. Joan Heath went to stand beside la Ventura. They did not look at each other, but the warmth of her shoulder beside his was all that he needed. Nothing was as bad as it seemed.

Venezuelos said: "What's the verdict, Dr. Chatvieux?"

"This place isn't dead," Chatvieux said. "There's life in the sea and in the freshwater, both. On the animal side of the ledger, evolution seems to have stopped with the crustacea; the most advanced form I've found is a tiny crayfish, from one of the local rivulets, and it doesn't seem to be well distributed. The ponds and puddles are well stocked with small metazoans of lower orders, right up to the rotifers— including a castle-building genus like Earth's *Floscularia*. In addition, there's a wonderfully variegated protozoan population, with a dominant ciliate type much like *Paramoecium*, plus various sarcodines, the usual spread of phytoflagellates, and even a phosphorescent species I wouldn't have expected to see anywhere but in saltwater. As for the plants, they run from simple blue-green algae to quite advanced thallus-producing types—though none of them, of course, can live out of the water."

"The sea is about the same," Eunice said. "I've found some of the larger simple metazoans—jellyfish and so on—and some crayfish almost as big as lobsters. But it's normal to find saltwater species running larger than freshwater. And there's the usual plankton and nannoplankton population."

"In short," Chatvieux said, "we'll survive here if we fight."

"Wait a minute," la Ventura said. "You've just finished telling me that we wouldn't survive. And you were talking about us, the seven of us here, not about the genus man, because we don't have our germ-cell banks anymore. What's—"

"We don't have the banks. But we ourselves can contribute germ-cells, Paul. I'll get to that in a moment." Chatvieux turned to Saltonstall. "Martin, what would you think of our taking to the sea? We came out of it once, long ago; maybe we could come out of it again on Hydrot."

"No good," Saltonstall said immediately. "I like the idea, but I don't think this planet ever heard of Swinburne, or Homer, either. Looking at it as a colonization problem alone, as if we weren't involved in it ourselves, I wouldn't give you an Oc dollar for *epi oinopa ponton*. The evolutionary pressure there is too high, the competition from other species is prohibitive; seeding the sea should be the last thing we attempt, not the first. The colonists wouldn't have a chance to learn a thing before they'd be gobbled up."

"Why?" la Ventura said. Once more, the death in his stomach was becoming hard to placate.

"Eunice, do your seagoing coelenterates include anything like the Portuguese man-of-war?"

The ecologist nodded.

"There's your answer, Paul," Saltonstall said. "The sea is out. It's got to be freshwater, where the competing creatures are less formidable and there are more places to hide."

"We can't compete with a jellyfish?" la Ventura asked, swallowing.

"No, Paul," Chatvieux said. "Not with one that dangerous. The pantropes make adaptations, not gods. They take human germcells—in this case, our own, since our bank was wiped out in the crash—and modify them genetically toward those of creatures who can live in any reasonable environment. The result will be manlike, and intelligent. It usually shows the donors' personality patterns, too, since the modifications are usually made mostly in the morphology, not so much in the mind, of the resulting individual.

"*But we can't transmit memory*. The adapted man is worse than a child in the new environment. He has no history, no techniques, no precedents, not even a language. In the usual colonization project, like the Tellura affair, the seeding teams more or less take him through elementary school before they leave the planet to him, but we won't survive long enough to give such instruction. We'll have to design our colonists with plenty of built-in protections and locate them in the most favorable environment possible, so that at least some of them will survive learning by experience alone."

The pilot thought about it, but nothing occurred to him which did not make the disaster seem realer and more intimate with each passing second. Joan Heath moved slightly closer to him. "One of the new creatures can have my personality pattern, but it won't be able to remember being me. Is that right?"

"That's right. In the present situation we'll probably make our colonists haploid, so that some of them, perhaps many, will have a heredity traceable to you alone. There may be just the faintest of residuums of identity—pantropy's given us some data to support the old Jungian notion of ancestral memory. But we're all going to die on Hydrot, Paul, as self-conscious persons. There's no avoiding that. Somewhere we'll leave behind people who behave as we would, think and feel as we would, but who won't remember la Ventura, or Dr. Chatvieux, or Joan Heath, or the Earth."

The pilot said nothing more. There was a gray taste in his mouth.

"Saltonstall, what would you recommend as a form?"

The pantropist pulled reflectively at his nose. "Webbed extremities, of course, with thumbs and big toes heavy and thornlike for defense until the creature has had a chance to learn. Smaller external ears, and the eardrum larger and closer to the outer end of the ear canal. We're going to have to reorganize the water-conservation system, I think; the glomerular kidney is perfectly suitable for living in freshwater, but the business of living immersed, inside and out, for a creature with a salty inside means that the osmotic pressure inside is going to be higher than outside, so that the kidneys are going to have to be pumping virtually all the time. Under the circumstances we'd best step up production of urine, and that means the anti-diuretic function of the pituitary gland is going to have to be abrogated, for all practical purposes."

"What about respiration?"

"Hm," Saltonstall said. "I suppose book-lungs, like some of the arachnids have. They can be supplied by intercostal spiracles. They're gradually adaptable to atmosphere-breathing, if our colonist ever decides to come out of the water. Just to provide for that possibility. I'd suggest that the nose be retained, maintaining the nasal cavity as a part of the otological system, but cutting off the cavity from the larynx with a membrane of cells that are supplied with oxygen by direct irrigation, rather than by the circulatory system. Such a membrane wouldn't survive for many generations, once the creature took to living out of the water even for part of its lifetime; it'd go through two or three generations as an amphibian, and then one day it'd suddenly find itself breathing through its larynx again."

"Ingenious," Chatvieux said.

"Also, Dr. Chatvieux, I'd suggest that we have it adopt sporulation. As an aquatic animal, our colonist is going to have an indefinite life-span, but we'll have to give it a breeding cycle of about six weeks to keep up its numbers during the learning period; so there'll have to be a definite break of some duration in its active year. Otherwise it'll hit the population problem before it's learned enough to cope with it."

"And it'd be better if our colonists could winter over inside a good, hard shell," Eunice Wagner added in agreement. "So sporulation's the obvious answer. Many other microscopic creatures have it."

"Microscopic?" Phil said incredulously.

"Certainly," Chatvieux said, amused. "We can't very well crowd a six-foot man into a two-foot puddle. But that raises a question. We'll have tough competition from the rotifers, and some of them aren't strictly microscopic; for that matter even some of the protozoa can be seen with the naked eye, just barely, with dark-field illumination. I don't think your average colonist should run much under two hundred

fifty microns, Saltonstall. Give them a chance to slug it out."

"I was thinking of making them twice that big."

"Then they'd be the biggest animals in their environment," Eunice Wagner pointed out, "and won't ever develop any skills. Besides, if you make them about rotifer size, it will give them an incentive for pushing out the castle-building rotifers, and occupying the castles themselves, as dwellings."

Chatvieux nodded. "All right, let's get started. While the pantropes are being calibrated, the rest of us can put our heads together on leaving a record for these people. We'll micro-engrave the record on a set of corrosion-proof metal leaves, of a size our colonists can handle conveniently. We can tell them, very simply, what happened, and plant a few suggestions that there's more to the universe than what they find in their puddles. Someday they may puzzle it out."

"Question," Eunice Wagner said. "Are we going to tell them they're microscopic? I'm opposed to it. It may saddle their entire early history with a gods-and-demons mythology that they'd be better off without."

"Yes, we are," Chatvieux said, and la Ventura could tell by the change in the tone of his voice that he was speaking now as their senior on the expedition. "These people will be of the race of men, Eunice. We want them to win their way back into the community of men. They are not toys, to be protected from the truth forever in a freshwater womb."

"Besides," Saltonstall observed, "they won't get the record translated at any time in their early history. They'll have to develop a written language of their own, and it will be impossible for us to leave them any sort of Rosetta stone or other key. By the time they can decipher the truth, they should be ready for it."

"I'll make that official," Venezuelos said unexpectedly. And that was that.

And then, essentially, it was all over. They contributed the cells that the pantropes would need. Privately, la Ventura and Joan Heath went to Chatvieux and asked to contribute jointly; but the scientist said that the microscopic men were to be haploid, in order to give them a minute cellular structure, with nuclei as small as Earthly rickettsiae, and therefore each person had to give germ-cells individually—there would be no use for zygotes. So even that consolation was denied them; in death they would have no children, but be instead as alone as ever.

They helped, as far as they could, with the text of the message which was to go on the metal leaves. They had their personality patterns recorded. They went through the motions. Already they were beginning to be hungry; the sea-crayfish, the only things on Hydrot big enough to eat, lived in water too deep and cold for subsistence fishing.

After la Ventura had set his control board to rights—a useless gesture, but a habit he had been taught to respect, and which in an obscure way made things a little easier to bear—he was out of it. He sat by himself at the far end of the rock ledge, watching Tau Ceti go redly down, chucking pebbles into the nearest pond.

After a while Joan Heath came silently up behind him, and sat down too. He took her hand. The glare of the red sun was almost extinguished now, and together they watched it go, with la Ventura, at least, wondering somberly which nameless puddle was to be his Lethe.

He never found out, of course. None of them did.

CYCLE ONE

In a forgotten corner of the galaxy, the watery world of Hydrot hurtles endlessly around the red star Tau Ceti. For many months its single small continent has been snowbound, and the many pools and lakes which dot the continent have been locked in the grip of the ice. Now, however, the red sun swings closer and closer to the zenith in Hydrot's sky; the snow rushes in torrents toward the eternal ocean, and the ice recedes toward the shores of the lakes and ponds. . . .

The first thing to reach the consciousness of the sleeping Lavon was a small, intermittent scratching sound. This was followed by a disquieting sensation in his body, as if the world—and Lavon with it—were being rocked back and forth. He stirred uneasily, without opening his eyes. His vastly slowed metabolism made him feel inert and queasy, and the rocking did not help. At his slight motion, however, both the sound and the motion became more insistent.

It seemed to take days for the fog over his brain to clear, but whatever was causing the disturbance would not let him rest. With a groan he forced his eyelids open and made an abrupt gesture with one webbed hand. By the waves of phosphorescence which echoed away from his fingers at the motion, he could see that the smooth amber walls of his spherical shell were unbroken. He tried to peer through them, but he could see nothing but darkness outside. Well, that was natural; the amniotic fluid inside the spore would generate light, but ordinary water did not, no matter how vigorously it was stirred.

Whatever was outside the sphere was rocking it again, with the same whispering friction against its shell. Probably some nosy diatom, Lavon thought sleepily, trying to butt its way through an object it was too stupid to go around. Or some early hunter, yearning for a taste of the morsel inside the spore. Well, let it worry itself; Lavon had no intention of breaking the shell just yet. The fluid in which he had slept for so many months had held his body processes static, and had slowed his mind. Once out into the water, he would have to start breathing and looking for food again, and he could tell by the unrelieved darkness outside that it was too early in the spring to begin thinking about that.

He flexed his fingers reflectively, in the disharmonic motion from little finger to thumb that no animal but man can copy, and watched the widening wave fronts of greenish light rebound in larger arcs from the curved spore walls. Here he was, curled up quite comfortably in a little amber ball, where he could stay until even the depths were warm and light. At this moment there was probably still some ice on the sky, and certainly there would not be much to eat as yet. Not that there was ever much, what with the voracious rotifers coming awake too with the first gust of warm water—

The rotifers! That was it. There was a plan afoot to drive them out. Memory returned in an unwelcome rush. As if to help it, the spore rocked again. That was probably one of the Protos, trying to awaken him; nothing man-eating ever came to the Bottom this early. He had left an early call with the Paras, and now the time had come, as cold and early and dark as he had thought he wanted it.

Reluctantly, Lavon uncurled, planting his webbed toes and arching his backbone as hard as he could, pressing with his whole body against his amber prison. With small, sharp, crepitating sounds, a network of cracks raced through the translucent shell.

Then the spore wall dissolved into a thousand brittle shards, and he was shivering violently with the onslaught of the icy water. The warmer fluid of his winter cell dissipated silently, a faint glowing fog. In the brief light he saw, not far from him, a familiar shape: a transparent, bubble-filled cylinder, a colorless slipper of jelly, spirally grooved, almost as long as he was tall. Its surface was furred with gently vibrating fine hairs, thickened at the base.

The light went out. The Proto said nothing; it waited while Lavon choked and coughed, expelling the last remnants of the spore fluid from his book-lungs and sucking in the pure, ice-cold water.

"Para?" Lavon said at last. "Already?"

"Already," the invisible cilia vibrated in even, emotionless tones. Each separate hairlike process buzzed at an independent, changing rate; the resulting sound waves spread through the water, intermodulating, reinforcing or can-

celling each other. The aggregate wave-front, by the time it reached human ears, was rather eerie, but nevertheless recognizable human speech. "This is the time, Lavon."

"Time and more than time," another voice said from the returned darkness. "If we are to drive Flosc from his castles."

"Who's that?" Lavon said, turning futilely toward the new voice.

"I am Para also, Lavon. We are sixteen since the awakening. If you could reproduce as rapidly as we—"

"Brains are better than numbers," Lavon said. "As the Eaters will find out soon enough."

"What shall we do, Lavon?"

The man drew up his knees and sank to the cold mud of the Bottom to think. Something wriggled under his buttocks and a tiny spirillum corkscrewed away, identifiable only by feel. He let it go; he was not hungry yet, and he had the Eaters—the rotifers—to think about. Before long they would be swarming in the upper reaches of the sky, devouring everything, even men when they could catch them, even their natural enemies the Protos now and then. And whether or not the Protos could be organized to battle them was a question still to be tested.

Brains are better than numbers; even that, as a proposition, was still to be tested. The Protos, after all, were intelligent after their fashion; and they knew their world, as the men did not. Lavon could still remember how hard it had been for him to get straight in his head the various clans of beings in this world, and to make sense of their confused names; his tutor Shar had drilled him unmercifully until it had begun to penetrate.

When you said "man," you meant creatures that, generally speaking, looked alike. The bacteria were of three kinds, the rods and the globes and the spirals, but they were all tiny and edible, so he had learned to differentiate them quickly. When it came to the Protos, identification became a real problem. Para here was a Proto, but he certainly looked very different from Stent and his family, and the family of Didin was unlike both. Anything, as it turned out, that was not green and had a visible nucleus was a Proto, no matter how strange its shape might be. The Eaters were all different, too, and some of them were as beautiful as the fruiting crowns of water-plants; but all of them were deadly, and all had the whirling crown of cilia which could suck you into the incessantly grinding mastax in a moment. Everything which was green and had an engraved shell of glass Shar had called a diatom, dredging the strange word as he dredged them all from some Bottom in his skull which none of the rest of them could reach, and even Shar could not explain.

Lavon arose quickly. "We need Shar," he said. "Where is his spore?"

"On a plant frond, far up near the sky."

Idiot! The old man would never think of safety. To sleep near the sky, where he might be snatched up and borne off by any Eater to chance by when he emerged, sluggish with winter's long sleep! How could a wise man be so foolish?

"We'll have to hurry. Show me the way."

"Soon; wait," one of the Paras said. "You cannot see. Noc is foraging nearby." There was a small stir in the texture of the darkness as the swift cylinder shot away.

"Why do we need Shar?" the other Para said.

"For his brains, Para. He is a thinker."

"But his thoughts are water. Since he taught the Proto man's language, he has forgotten to think of the Eaters. He thinks forever of the mystery of how man came here. It is a mystery—even the Eaters are not like man. But understanding it will not help us to live."

Lavon turned blindly toward the creature. "Para, tell me something. Why do the Protos side with us? With man, I mean? Why do you need us? The Eaters fear you."

There was a short silence. When the Para spoke again, the vibrations of its voice were more blurred than before, more even, more devoid of any understandable feeling.

"We live in this world," the Para said. "We are of it. We rule it. We came to that state long before the coming of men, in long warfare with the Eaters. But we think as the Eaters do, we do not plan, we share our knowledge, and we exist. Men plan; men lead; men are different from each other; men want to remake the world. And they hate the Eaters, as we do. We will help."

"And give up your rule?"

"And give it up, if the rule of men is better. That is reason. Now we can go; Noc is coming back with light."

Lavon looked up. Sure enough, there was a brief flash of cold light far overhead, and then another. In a moment the spherical Proto had dropped into view, its body flaring regularly with blue-green pulses. Beside it darted the second Para.

"Noc brings news," the second Para said. "Para is twenty-four. The Syn are awake by thousands along the sky. Noc spoke to a Syn colony, but they will not help us; they all expect to be dead before the Eaters awake."

"Of course," said the first Para. "That always happens. And the Syn are plants; why should they help the Protos?"

"Ask Noc if he'll guide us to Shar," Lavon said impatiently.

The Noc gestured with its single short, thick tentacle. One of the Paras said, "That is what he is here for."

"Then let's go. We've waited long enough."

The mixed quartet soared away from the Bottom through the liquid darkness.

"No," Lavon snapped. "Not a second longer. The Syn are awake, and Notholca of the Eaters is due right after that. You know that as well as I do, Shar. Wake up!"

"Yes, yes," the old man said fretfully. He stretched and yawned. "You're always in such a hurry, Lavon. Where's Phil? He made his spore near mine." He pointed to a still-unbroken amber sphere sealed to a leaf of the water-plant one tier below. "Better push him off; he'll be safer on the Bottom."

"He would never reach the Bottom," Para said. "The thermocline has formed."

Shar looked surprised. "It has? Is it as late as all that? Wait while I get my records together." He began to search along the leaf in the debris and the piled shards of his spore. Lavon looked impatiently about, found a splinter of stone-wort, and threw it heavy end first at the bubble of Phil's cell just below. The spore shattered promptly, and the husky young man tumbled out, blue with shock as the cold water hit him.

"Wough!" he said. "Take it easy, Lavon." He looked up. "The old man's awake? Good. He insisted on staying up here for the winter, so of course I had to stay too."

"Aha," Shar said, and lifted a thick metal plate about the length of his forearm and half as wide. "Here is one of them. Now if only I haven't misplaced the other—"

Phil kicked away a mass of bacteria. "Here it is. Better give them both to a Para, so they won't burden you. Where do we go from here, Lavon? It's dangerous up this high. I'm just glad a Dicran hasn't already shown up."

"I here," something droned just above them.

Instantly, without looking up, Lavon flung himself out and down into the open water, turning his head to look back over his shoulder only when he was already diving as fast as he could go. Shar and Phil had evidently sprung at the same instant. On the next frond above where Shar had spent his winter was the armored, trumpet-shaped body of the rotifer Dicran, contracted to leap after them.

The two Protos came curving back out of nowhere. At the same moment, the bent, short-ened body of Dicran flexed in its armor plate, straightened, came plunging toward them. There was a soft *plop* and Lavon found himself struggling in a fine net, as tangled and impas-sible as the mat of a lichen. A second such sound was followed by a muttered imprecation from Phil. Lavon struck out fiercely, but he was barely able to wriggle in the web of wiry, trans-parent stuff.

"Be still," a voice which he recognized as

a Para's throbbed behind him. He managed to screw his head around, and then kicked him-self mentally for not having realized at once what had happened. The Paras had exploded the trichocysts which lay like tiny cartridges beneath their pellicles; each one cast forth a liquid which solidified upon contact with the water in a long slender thread. It was their stan-dard method of defense.

Farther down, Shar and Phil drifted with the second Para in the heart of a white haze, like creatures far gone in mold. Dicran swerved to avoid it, but she was evidently unable to give up; she twisted and darted around them, her corona buzzing harshly, her few scraps of the human language forgotten. Seen from this dis-tance, the rotation of the corona was revealed as an illusion, created by the rhythm of pulsa-tion of the individual cilia, but as far as Lavon was concerned the point was solely technical and the distance was far too short. Through the transparent armor Lavon could also see the great jaws of Dicran's mastax, grinding away mechanically at the fragments which poured into her unheeding mouth.

High above them all, Noc circled indeci-sively, illuminating the whole group with quick, nervous flashes of his blue light. He was a flag-ellate, and had no natural weapons against the rotifer; why he was hanging around drawing attention to himself Lavon could not imagine.

Then, suddenly, he saw the reason: a barrel-like creature about Noc's size, ringed with two rows of cilia and bearing a ramlike prow. "Didin!" he shouted, unnecessarily. "This way!"

The Proto swung gracefully toward them and seemed to survey them, though it was hard to tell how he could see them without eyes. The Dicran saw him at the same time and began to back slowly away, her buzzing rising to a raw snarl. She regained the plant and crouched down.

For an instant Lavon thought she was going to give up, but experience should have told him that she lacked the sense. Suddenly the lithe, crouched body was in full spring again, this time straight at Didin. Lavon yelled an incoherent warning.

The Proto didn't need it. The slowly cruising barrel darted to one side and then forward, with astonishing speed. If he could sink that poisoned seizing-organ into a weak point in the rotifer's armor—

Noc mounted higher to keep out of the way of the two fighters, and in the resulting weakened light Lavon could not see what was happening, though the furious churning of the water and the buzzing of the Dicran continued.

After a while the sounds seemed to be retreating; Lavon crouched in the gloom inside the Para's net, listening intently. Finally there was silence.

"What's happened?" he whispered tensely.

"Didin does not say."

More eternities went by. Then the darkness began to wane as Noc dropped cautiously toward them.

"Noc, where did they go?"

Noc signaled with his tentacle and turned on his axis toward Para.

"He says he lost sight of them. Wait—I hear Didin."

Lavon could hear nothing; what the Para "heard" was some one of the semi-telepathic impulses which made up the Proto's own language.

"He says Dicran is dead."

"Good! Ask him to bring the body back here."

There was a short silence. "He says he will bring it. What good is a dead rotifer, Lavon?"

"You'll see," Lavon said. He watched anxiously until Didin glided backwards into the lighted area, his poisonous ram sunk deep into the flaccid body of the rotifer, which, after the delicately organized fashion of its kind, was already beginning to disintegrate.

"Let me out of this net, Para."

The Proto jerked sharply for a fraction of a turn on its long axis, snapping the threads off at the base; the movement had to be made with great precision, or its pellicle would tear

as well. The tangled mass rose gently with the current and drifted off over the abyss.

Lavon swam forward and, seizing one buckled edge of the Dicran's armor, tore away a huge strip of it. His hands plunged into the now almost shapeless body and came out again holding two dark spheroids: eggs.

"Destroy these, Didin," he ordered. The Proto obligingly slashed them open.

"Hereafter," Lavon said, "that's to be standard procedure with every Eater you kill."

"Not the males," one of the Paras pointed out.

"Para, you have no sense of humor. All right, not the males—but nobody kills the males anyhow, they're harmless." He looked down grimly at the inert mass. "Remember—destroy the eggs. Killing the beasts isn't enough. We want to wipe out the whole race."

"We never forget," Para said emotionlessly.

The band of over two hundred humans, with Lavon and Shar and a Para at its head, fled swiftly through the warm, light waters of the upper level. Each man gripped a wood splinter, or a fragment of lime chipped from stonewort, as a club; and two hundred pairs of eyes darted watchfully from side to side. Cruising over them was a squadron of twenty Didins, and the rotifers they encountered only glared at them from single red eyespots, making no move to attack. Overhead, near the sky, the sunlight was filtered through a thick layer of living creatures, fighting and feeding and spawning, so that all the depths below were colored a rich green. Most of this heavily populated layer was made up of algae and diatoms, and there the Eaters fed unhindered. Sometimes a dying diatom dropped slowly past the army.

The spring was well advanced; the two hundred, Lavon thought, probably represented all of the humans who had survived the winter. At least no more could be found. The others—nobody would ever know how many—had awakened too late in the season, or had made their spores in exposed places, and the rotifers had snatched them up. Of the group, more than a third were women. That meant that in another forty days, if they were unmolested, they could double the size of their army.

If they were unmolested. Lavon grinned and pushed an agitated colony of Eudorina out of his way. The phrase reminded him of a speculation Shar had brought forth last year: if Para were left unmolested, the oldster had said, he could reproduce fast enough to fill this whole universe with a solid mass of Paras before the season was out. Nobody, of course, ever went unmolested in this world; nevertheless, Lavon meant to cut the odds for people considerably below anything that had heretofore been thought of as natural.

His hand flashed up, and down again. The darting squadrons plunged after him. The light on the sky faded rapidly, and after a while Lavon began to feel slightly chilly. He signaled again. Like dancers, the two hundred swung their bodies in midflight, plunging now feet first toward the Bottom. To strike the thermocline in this position would make their passage through it faster, getting them out of the upper level, where every minute, despite the convoy of Protos, concentrated danger.

Lavon's feet struck a yielding surface, and with a splash he was over his head in icy water. He bobbed up again, feeling the icy division drawn across his shoulders. Other splashes began to sound all along the thermocline as the army struck it, although, since there was water above and below, Lavon could not see the actual impacts.

Now they would have to wait until their body temperatures fell. At this dividing line of the universe, the warm water ended and the temperature dropped rapidly, so that the water below was much denser and buoyed them up. The lower level of cold reached clear down to the Bottom—an area which the rotifers, who were not very clever, seldom managed to enter.

A moribund diatom drifted down beside Lavon, the greenish-yellow of its body fading to a sick orange, its beautifully marked, oblong, pillbox-like shell swarming with greedy bacteria. It came to rest on the thermocline, and the transparent caterpillar tread of jelly which ran around it moved feebly, trying vainly to get traction on the sliding water interface. Lavon reached out a webbed hand and brushed away a clot of vibrating rods which had nearly forced its way into the shell through a costal opening.

"Thank . . . ," the diatom said, in an indistinct, whispering voice. And again, "Thank . . . Die . . ." The gurgling whisper faded. The caterpillar tread shifted again, then was motionless.

"It is right," a Para said. "Why do you bother with those creatures? They are stupid. Nothing can be done for them."

Lavon did not try to explain. He felt himself sinking slowly, and the water about his trunk and legs no longer seemed cold, only gratefully cool after the stifling heat of that he was breathing. In a moment the cool still depths had closed over his head. He hovered until he was reasonably sure that all the rest of his army was safely through, and the long ordeal of searching for survivors in the upper level really ended. Then he twisted and streaked for the Bottom, Phil and Para beside him, Shar puffing along with the vanguard.

A stone loomed; Lavon surveyed it in the half-light. Almost immediately he saw what he had hoped to see: the sand-built house of a caddis-worm, clinging to the mountainous slopes of the rock. He waved in his special cadre and pointed.

Cautiously the men spread out in a U around the stone, the mouth of the U facing the same way as the opening of the worm's masonry tube. A Noc came after them, drifting like a star-shell above the peak; one of the Paras approached the door of the worm's house, buzzing defiantly. Under cover of this challenge the men at the back of the U settled on the rock and began to creep forward. The house was three times as tall as they were; the slimy black sand grains of which it was composed were as big as their heads.

There was a stir inside, and after a moment the ugly head of the worm peered out, weaving uncertainly at the buzzing Para which had disturbed it. The Para drew back, and the worm, in a kind of blind hunger, followed it. A sudden lunge brought it nearly halfway out of its tube.

Lavon shouted. Instantly the worm was surrounded by a howling horde of two-legged demons, who beat and prodded it mercilessly with fists and clubs. Somehow it made a sound, a kind of bleat as unlikely as the birdlike whistle of a fish, and began to slide backwards into its home, but the rear guard had already broken in back there. It jerked forward again, lashing from side to side under the flogging.

There was only one way now for the great larva to go, and the demons around it kept it going that way. It fell toward the Bottom down the side of the rock, naked and ungainly, shaking its blind head and bleating.

Lavon sent five Didins after it. They could not kill it, for it was far too huge to die under their poison, but they could sting it hard enough to keep it travelling. Otherwise, it would be almost sure to return to the rock to start a new house.

Lavon settled on an abutment and surveyed his prize with satisfaction. It was more than big enough to hold his entire clan—a great tubular hall, easily defended once the breach in the rear wall was rebuilt, and well out of the usual haunts of the Eaters. The muck the caddisworm had left behind would have to be cleaned up, guards posted, vents knocked out to keep the oxygen-poor water of the depths in motion inside. It was too bad that the amoebae could not be detailed to scavenge the place, but Lavon knew better than to issue such an order. The Fathers of the Protos could not be asked to do useful work; that had been made very clear.

He looked around at his army. They were standing around him in awed silence, looking at the spoils of their attack upon the largest creature in the world. He did not think they would ever again feel as timid toward the Eaters. He stood up quickly.

"What are you gaping at?" he shouted. "It's yours, all of it. Get to work!"

Old Shar sat comfortably upon a pebble which had been hollowed out and cushioned with spirogyra straw. Lavon stood nearby at the door, looking out at the maneuvers of his legions. They numbered more than three hundred now, thanks to the month of comparative quiet which they had enjoyed in the great hall, and they handled their numbers well in the aquatic drill which Lavon had invented for them. They swooped and turned above the rock, breaking and reassembling their formations, fighting a sham battle with invisible opponents whose shape they could remember only too well.

"Noc says there's all kinds of quarreling going on among the Eaters," Shar said. "They didn't believe we'd joined with the Protos at first, and then they didn't believe we'd all worked together to capture the hall. And the mass raid we had last week scared them. They'd never tried anything of the kind before, and they knew it wouldn't fail. Now they're fighting with each other over why it did. Cooperation is something new to this world, Lavon; it's making history."

"History?" Lavon said, following his drilling squadrons with a technical eye. "What's that?"

"These." The old man leaned over one arm of the pebble and touched the metal plates which were always with him. Lavon turned to follow the gesture, incuriously. He knew the plates well enough: the pure uncorroded shining, graven deeply on both sides with characters no one, not even Shar, could read. The Protos called the plates *Not-stuff*—neither wood nor flesh nor stone.

"What good is that? I can't read it. Neither can you."

"I've got a start, Lavon. I know the plates are written in our language. Look at the first word: *ha ii ss tuh oh or ee*, exactly the right number of characters for *history*. That can't be a coincidence. And the next two words have to be *of the*. And going on from there, using just the characters I already know—" Shar bent and traced in the sand with a stick a new train of characters: *i/terste/ /ar e/ /e/ition.*

"What's that?"

"It's a start, Lavon. Just a start. Someday we'll have more."

Lavon shrugged. "Perhaps, when we're safer. We can't afford to worry about that kind of thing now. We've never had that kind of time, not since the First Awakening."

The old man frowned down at the characters in the sand. "The First Awakening. Why does everything seem to stop there? I can remember in the smallest detail nearly everything that happened to me since then. But what happened to our childhoods, Lavon? None of us who survived the First Awakening seems to have had one. Who were our parents? Why were we so ignorant of the world, and yet grown men and women, all of us?"

"And the answer is in the plates?"

"I hope so," Shar said. "I believe it is. But I don't know. The plates were beside me in the spore at the First Awakening. That's all I know about them, except that there's nothing else like them in the world. The rest is deduction, and I haven't gotten very far with it. Someday . . . someday."

"I hope so too," Lavon said soberly. "I don't mean to mock, Shar, or to be impatient. I've got questions, too; we all have. But we're going to have to put them off for a while. Suppose we never find the whole answer?"

"Then our children will."

"But there's the heart of the problem, Shar: we have to live to have children. And make the kind of a world in which they'll have time to study. Otherwise—"

Lavon broke off as a figure darted between the guards at the door of the hall and twisted to a halt.

"What news, Phil?"

"The same," Phil said, shrugging with his whole body. His feet touched the floor. "The

Flosc's castles are going up all along the bar; they'll be finished with them soon, and then we won't dare to get near them. Do you still think you can drive them out?"

Lavon nodded.

"But why?"

"First, for effect. We've been on the defensive so far, even though we've made a good job of it. We'll have to follow that up with an attack of our own if we're going to keep the Eaters confused. Second, the castles Flosc builds are all tunnels and exits and entrances—much better than worm-houses for us. I hate to think of what would have happened if the Eaters had thought of blockading us inside this hall. And we need an outpost in enemy country, Phil, where there are Eaters to kill."

"This is enemy country," Phil said. "Stephanost is a Bottom-dweller."

"But she's only a trapper, not a hunter. Any time we want to kill her, we can find her right where we left her last. It's the leapers like Dicran and Notholca, the swimmers like Rotar, the colony-builders like Flosc that we have to wipe out first."

"Then we'd better start now, Lavon. Once the castles are finished—"

"Yes. Get your squads together, Phil. Shar, come on; we're leaving the hall."

"To raid the castles?"

"Of course."

Shar picked up his plates.

"You'd better leave those here; they'll be in your way in the fighting."

"No," Shar said determinedly. "I don't want them out of my sight. They go along."

Vague forebodings, all the more disturbing because he had felt nothing quite like them ever before, passed like clouds of fine silt through Lavon's mind as the army swept away from the hall on the Bottom and climbed toward the thermocline. As far as he could see, everything seemed to be going as he had planned it. As the army moved, its numbers were swelled by

Protos who darted into its ranks from all sides. Discipline was good, and every man was armed with a long, seasoned splinter, and from each belt swung a stonewort-flake hand-axe, held by a thong run through a hole Shar had taught them all how to drill. There would probably be much death before the light of today faded, but death was common enough on any day, and this time it should heavily disfavor the Eaters.

But there was a chill upon the depths that Lavon did not like, and a suggestion of a current in the water which was unnatural below the thermocline. A great many days had been consumed in collecting the army, recruiting from stragglers, and in securing the hall. The intensive breeding which had followed, and the training of the newborn and the newly recruited, had taken still more time, all of it essential, but all irrevocable. If the chill and the current marked the beginning of the fall turnover . . .

If it did, nothing could be done about it. The turnover could no more be postponed than the coming of day or night. He signaled to the nearest Para.

The glistening torpedo veered toward him. Lavon pointed up.

"Here comes the thermocline, Para. Are we pointed right?"

"Yes, Lavon. That way is the place where the Bottom rises toward the sky. Flosc's castles are on the other side, where she will not see us."

"The sandbar that runs out from the north. Right. It's getting warmer. Here we go."

Lavon felt his flight suddenly quicken, as if he had been shot like a seed from some invisible thumb and forefinger. He looked over his shoulder to watch the passage of the rest through the temperature barrier, and what he saw thrilled him as sharply as any awakening. Up to now he had had no clear picture of the size of his forces, or the three-dimensional beauty of their dynamic, mobile organization. Even the Protos had fitted themselves into the squads; pattern after pattern of power came soaring after Lavon from the Bottom: first a single Noc bowling

along like a beacon to guide all the rest, then an advance cone of Didins to watch for individual Eaters who might flee to give the alarm, and then the men, and the Protos, who made up the main force, in tight formations as beautiful as the elementary geometry from which Shar had helped derive them.

The sandbar loomed ahead, as vast as any mountain range. Lavon soared sharply upward, and the tumbled, rawboned boulders of the sand grains swept by rapidly beneath him in a broad, stony flood. Far beyond the ridge, towering up to the sky through glowing green obscurity, were the be-fronded stems of the plant jungle which was their objective. It was too dim with distance to allow him to see the clinging castles of the Flosc yet, but he knew that the longest part of the march was over. He narrowed his eyes and cleft the sunlit waters with driving, rapid strokes of his webbed hands and feet. The invaders poured after him over the crest of the bar in an orderly torrent.

Lavon swung his arm in a circle. Silently, the following squadrons glided into a great paraboloid, its axis pointed at the jungle. The castles were visible now; until the formation of the army, they had been the only products of close cooperation that this world had ever seen. They were built of single brown tubes, narrow at the base, attached to each other in a random pattern in an ensemble as delicate as a branching coral. In the mouth of each tube was a rotifer, a Flosc, distinguished from other Eaters by the four-leaf clover of its corona, and by the single, prehensile finger springing from the small of its back, with which it ceaselessly molded its brown spittle into hard pellets and cemented them carefully to the rim of its tube.

As usual, the castles chilled Lavon's muscles with doubt. They were perfect, and they had always been one of the major, stony flowers of summer, long before there had been any First Awakening, or any men. And there was surely something wrong with the water in the upper level; it was warm and sleepy. The heads of the Flosc hummed contentedly at the mouths of their tubes; everything was as it should be, as it had always been; the army was a phantasm, the attack a failure before it had begun—

Then they were spied.

The Flosc vanished instantly, contracting violently into their tubes. The placid humming of their continuous feeding upon everything that passed was snuffed out; spared motes drifted about the castle in the light.

Lavon found himself smiling. Not long ago, the Flosc would only have waited until the humans were close enough, and then would have sucked them down, without more than a few struggles here and there, a few pauses in the humming while the outsize morsels were enfolded and fed into the grinders. Now, instead, they hid; they were afraid.

"Go!" he shouted at the top of his voice. "Kill them! Kill them while they're down!"

The army behind him swept after him with a stunning composite shout.

Tactics vanished. A petalled corona unfolded in Lavon's face, and a buzzing whirlpool spun him toward its black heart. He slashed wildly with his edged wooden splinter.

The sharp edge sliced deeply into the ciliated lobes. The rotifer screamed like a siren and contracted into her tube, closing her wounded face. Grimly, Lavon followed.

It was pitch-dark inside the castle, and the raging currents of pain which flowed past him threw him from one pebbly wall to another. He gritted his teeth and probed with the splinter. It bit into a yielding surface at once, and another scream made his ears ring, mixed with mangled bits of words in Lavon's own language, senseless and horrible with agony. He slashed at them until they stopped, and continued to slash until he could control his terror.

As soon as he was able, he groped in the torn corpse for the eggs. The point found their life and pricked it. Trembling, he pulled himself back to the mouth of the tube, and without stopping to think pushed himself off at the first Eater to pass it.

The thing was a Dicran; she doubled viciously upon him at once. Even the Eaters had learned something about cooperation. And the Dicrans fought well in open water. They were the best possible reinforcements the Flosc could have called.

The Dicran's armor turned the point of Lavon's splinter easily. He jabbed frantically, hoping to hit a joint, but the agile creature gave him no time to aim. She charged him irresistibly, and her humming corona folded down around his head, pinned his forearms to his sides—

The Eater heaved convulsively and went limp. Lavon half slashed, half tore his way free. A Didin was drawing back, pulling out its seizing organ. The body floated downward.

"Thanks," Lavon gasped. The Proto darted off without replying; it lacked sufficient cilia to imitate human speech. Possibly it lacked the desire as well; the Didins were not sociable.

A tearing whirlpool sprang into being again around him, and he flexed his sword-arm. In the next five dreamlike minutes he developed a technique for dealing with the sessile, sucking Flosc. Instead of fighting the current and swinging the splinter back and forth against it, he gave in to the vortex, rode with it, and braced the splinter between his feet, point down. The results were even better than he had hoped. The point, driven by the full force of the Flosc's own trap, pierced the soft, wormlike body half through while it gaped for the human quarry. After each encounter, Lavon doggedly went through the messy ritual of destroying the eggs.

At last he emerged from a tube to find that the battle had drifted away from him. He paused on the edge to get his breath back, clinging to the rounded, translucent bricks and watching the fighting. It was difficult to make any military sense out of the melee, but as far as he could tell the rotifers were getting the worst of it. They did not know how to meet so carefully organized an attack, and they were not in any real sense intelligent.

The Didins were ranging from one side of the fray to the other, in two tight, vicious, efficient groups, englobing and destroying free-swimming rotifers in whole flocks at a time. Lavon saw no fewer than half a dozen Eaters trapped by teams of Paras, each pair dragging a struggling victim in a trichocyst net remorselessly toward the Bottom, where she would inevitably suffocate. He was astonished to see one of the few Nocs that had accompanied his army scouring a cringing Rotar with its virtually harmless tentacle; the Eater seemed too astonished to fight back, and Lavon for once knew just how she felt.

A figure swam slowly and tiredly up to him from below. It was old Shar, puffing hard. Lavon reached a hand down to him and hauled him onto the lip of the tube. The man's face wore a frightening expression, half shock, half pure grief.

"Gone, Lavon," he said. "Gone. Lost."

"What? What's gone? What's the matter?"

"The plate. You were right. I should have known." He sobbed convulsively.

"What plate? Calm down. What happened? Did you lose one of the history plates or both of them?"

Slowly his tutor seemed to be recovering control of his breathing. "One of them," he said wretchedly. "I dropped it in the fight. I hid the other one in an empty Flosc tube. But I dropped the first one, the one I'd just begun to decipher. It went all the way down to the Bottom, and I couldn't get free to go after it—all I could do was watch it go, spinning down into the darkness. We could sift the mud forever and never find it."

He dropped his face into his hands. Perched on the edge of the brown tube in the green glow of the waters, he looked both pathetic and absurd. Lavon did not know what to say; even he realized that the loss was major and perhaps final, that the awesome blank in their memories prior to the First Awakening might now never be filled. How Shar felt about it he could comprehend only dimly.

Another human figure darted and twisted toward him. "Lavon!" Phil's voice cried. "It's

working, it's working! The swimmers are running away, what's left of them. There are still some Flosc in the castles, hiding in the darkness. If we could only lure them out in the open . . ."

Jarred back to the present, Lavon's mind raced over the possibilities. The whole attack could still fail if the Flosc entrenched themselves successfully. After all, a big kill had not been the only object; they had started out to capture the castles.

"Shar—do these tubes connect with each other?"

"Yes," the old man said without interest. "It's a continuous system."

Lavon sprang out upon the open water. "Come on, Phil. We'll attack them from the rear." Turning, he plunged into the mouth of the tube, Phil on his heels.

It was very dark, and the water was fetid with the odor of the tube's late owner, but after a moment's groping Lavon found the opening which led into the next tube. It was easy to tell which way was out because of the pitch of the walls; everything the Flosc built had a conical bore, differing from the next tube only in size. Determinedly Lavon worked his way toward the main stem, going always down and in.

Once they passed beneath an opening beyond which the water was in furious motion, and out of which poured muffled sounds of shouting and a defiant buzz. Lavon stopped to probe through the hole with his sword. The rotifer gave a shrill, startled shriek and jerked her wounded tail upward, involuntarily releasing her toehold upon the walls of the tube. Lavon moved on, grinning. The men above would do the rest.

Reaching the central stem at last, Lavon and Phil went methodically from one branch to another, spearing the surprised Eaters from behind or cutting them loose so that the men outside could get at them as they drifted upward, propelled by the drag of their own coronas. The trumpet shape of the tube prevented the Eaters from turning to fight, and from following them through the castle to surprise them from behind; each Flosc had only the one room, which she never left.

The gutting of the castles took hardly fifteen minutes. The day was just beginning to end when Lavon emerged with Phil at the mouth of a turret to look down upon the first City of Man.

He lay in darkness, his forehead pressed against his knees, as motionless as a dead man. The water was stuffy, cold, the blackness complete. Around him were the walls of a tube of Flosc's castle; above him a Para laid another sand grain upon a new domed roof. The rest of the army rested in other tubes, covered with other new stony caps, but there was no sound of movement or of voices. It was as quiet as a necropolis.

Lavon's thoughts were slow and bitter as drugged syrup. He had been right about the passage of the seasons. He had had barely enough time to bring all his people from the hall to the castles before the annual debacle of the fall overturn. Then the waters of the universe had revolved once, bringing the skies to the Bottom, and the Bottom to the skies, and then mixing both. The thermocline was destroyed until next year's spring overturn would re-form it.

And inevitably, the abrupt change in temperature and oxygen concentration had started the spore-building glands again. The spherical amber shell was going up around Lavon now, and there was nothing he could do about it. It was an involuntary process, as dissociated from his control as the beating of his heart. Soon the light-generating oil which filled the spore would come pouring out, expelling and replacing the cold, foul water, and then sleep would come. . . .

And all this had happened just as they had made a real gain, had established themselves in enemy country, had come within reach of the chance to destroy the Eaters wholesale and forever. Now the eggs of the Eaters had been laid, and next year it would have to be done all over again. And there was the loss of the plate;

he had hardly begun to reflect upon what that would mean for the future.

There was a soft *chunk* as the last sand grain fell into place on the roof. The sound did not quite bring the final wave of despair against which he had been fighting in advance. Instead, it seemed to carry with it a wave of obscure contentment, with which his consciousness began to sink more and more rapidly toward sleep. They were safe, after all. They could not be ousted from the castle. And there would be fewer Eaters next year, because of all the eggs that had been destroyed, and the layers of those eggs. . . . There was one plate still left. . . .

Quiet and cold; darkness and silence.

CYCLE TWO

In a forgotten corner of the galaxy, the watery world of Hydrot hurtles endlessly around the red star Tau Ceti. For many months life has swarmed in its lakes and pools, but now the sun retreats from the zenith, and the snow falls, and the ice advances from the eternal ocean. Life sinks once more toward slumber, simulating death, and the battles and lusts and ambitions and defeats of a thousand million microscopic creatures retreat into the limbo where such things matter not at all.

No, such things matter not at all when winter reigns on Hydrot; but winter is an inconstant king.

Old Shar set down the thick, ragged-edged metal plate at last, and gazed instead out the window of the castle, apparently resting his eyes on the glowing green-gold obscurity of the summer waters. In the soft fluorescence which played down upon him, from the Noc dozing impassively in the groined vault of the chamber, Lavon could see that he was in fact a young man. His face was so delicately formed as to suggest that it had not been many seasons since he had first emerged from his spore.

But of course there had been no real reason to have expected an old man. All the Shars had been referred to traditionally as "old" Shar. The reason, like the reasons for everything else, had been forgotten, but the custom had persisted. The adjective at least gave weight and dignity to the office—that of the center of wisdom of all the people, as each Lavon had been the center of authority.

The present Shar belonged to the generation XVI, and hence would have to be at least two seasons younger than Lavon himself. If he was old, it was only in knowledge.

"Lavon, I'm going to have to be honest with you," Shar said at last, still looking out of the tall, irregular window. "You've come to me at your maturity for the secrets on the metal plate, just as your predecessors did to mine. I can give some of them to you—but for the most part, I don't know what they mean."

"After so many generations?" Lavon asked, surprised. "Wasn't it Shar III who made the first complete translation? That was a long time ago."

The young man turned and looked at Lavon with eyes made dark and wide by the depths into which they had been staring. "I can read what's on the plate, but most of it seems to make no sense. Worst of all, the record's incomplete. You didn't know that? It is. One of the plates was lost in a battle during the first war with the Eaters, while these castles were still in their hands."

"What am I here for, then?" Lavon said. "Isn't there anything of value on the remaining plate? Did they really contain 'the wisdom of the Creators,' or is that another myth?"

"No. No, it's true," Shar said slowly, "as far as it goes."

He paused, and both men turned and gazed at the ghostly creature which had appeared suddenly outside the window. Then Shar said gravely, "Come in, Para."

The slipper-shaped organism, nearly transparent except for the thousands of black-and-silver granules and frothy bubbles which packed its interior, glided into the chamber and hovered, with a muted whirring of cilia. For a moment it remained silent, speaking telepathically to the Noc floating in the vault, after the ceremonious fashion of all the Protos. No human had ever intercepted one of these colloquies, but there was no doubt about their reality; humans had used them for long-range communication for generations.

Then the Para's cilia vibrated once more. "We are arrived, Shar and Lavon, according to the custom."

"And welcome," said Shar. "Lavon, let's leave this matter of the plates for a while, until you hear what Para has to say; that's a part of the knowledge Lavons must have as they come into their office, and it comes before the plates. I can give you some hints of what we are. First Para has to tell you something about what we aren't."

Lavon nodded, willingly enough, and watched the Proto as it settled gently to the surface of the hewn table at which Shar had been sitting. There was in the entity such a perfection and economy of organization, such a grace and surety of movement, that he could hardly believe his own new-won maturity. Para, like all the Protos, made him feel, not perhaps poorly thought out, but at least unfinished.

"We know that in this universe there is logically no place for man," the gleaming, now immobile cylinder upon the table droned abruptly. "Our memory is the common property of all our races. It reaches back to a time when there were no such creatures as man here, nor any even remotely like men. It remembers also that once upon a day there were men here, suddenly, and in some numbers. Their spores littered the Bottom; we found the spores only a short time after our season's Awakening, and inside them we saw the forms of men, slumbering.

"Then men shattered their spores and emerged. At first they seemed helpless, and the Eaters devoured them by scores, as in those days they devoured everything that moved. But that soon ended. Men were intelligent, active. And they were gifted with a trait, a character, possessed by no other creature in this world. Not even the savage Eaters had it. Men organized us to exterminate the Eaters, and therein lay the difference. Men had initiative. We have the word now, which you gave us, and we apply it, but we still do not know what the thing is that it labels."

"You fought beside us," Lavon said.

"Gladly. We would never have thought of that war by ourselves, but it was good and brought good. Yet we wondered. We saw that men were poor swimmers, poor walkers, poor crawlers, poor climbers. We saw that men were formed to make and use tools, a concept we still do not understand, for so wonderful a gift is largely wasted in this universe, and there is no other. What good are tool-useful members such as the hands of men? We do not know. It seems plain that so radical a thing should lead to a much greater rulership over the world than has, in fact, proven to be possible for men."

Lavon's head was spinning. "Para, I had no notion that you people were philosophers."

"The Protos are old," Shar said. He had again turned to look out the window, his hands locked behind his back. "They aren't philosophers, Lavon, but they are remorseless logicians. Listen to Para."

"To this reasoning there could be but one outcome," the Para said. "Our strange ally, man, was like nothing else in this universe. He was and is unfitted for it. He does not belong here; he has been adapted. This drives us to think that there are other universes besides this one, but where these universes might lie, and what their properties might be, it is impossible to imagine. We have no imagination, as men know."

Was the creature being ironic? Lavon could not tell. He said slowly, "Other universes? How could that be true?"

"We do not know," the Para's uninflected voice hummed. Lavon waited, but obviously the Proto had nothing more to say.

Shar had resumed sitting on the windowsill, clasping his knees, watching the come and go of dim shapes in the lighted gulf. "It is quite true," he said. "What is written on the plate makes it plain. Let me tell you now what it says.

"*We were made*, Lavon. We were made by men who were not as we are, but men who were our ancestors all the same. They were caught in some disaster, and they made us, and put us here in our universe—so that, even though they had to die, the race of men would live."

Lavon surged up from the woven spirogyra mat upon which he had been sitting. "You must think I'm a fool," he said sharply.

"No. You're our Lavon; you have a right to know the facts. Make what you like of them." Shar swung his webbed toes back into the chamber. "What I've told you may be hard to believe, but it seems to be so; what Para says backs it up. Our unfitness to live here is self-evident. I'll give you some examples:

"The past four Shars discovered that we won't get any further in our studies until we learn how to control heat. We've produced enough heat chemically to show that even the water around us changes when the temperature gets high enough or low enough; that we knew from the beginning. But there we're stopped."

"Why?"

"Because heat produced in open water is carried off as rapidly as it's produced. Once we tried to enclose that heat, and we blew up a whole tube of the castle and killed everything in range; the shock was terrible. We measured the pressures that were involved in that explosion, and we discovered that no substance we know could have resisted them. Theory suggests some stronger substances—*but we need heat to form them*!

"Take our chemistry. We live in water. Everything seems to dissolve in water, to some extent. How do we confine a chemical test to the crucible we put it in? How do we maintain a solution at one dilution? I don't know. Every avenue leads me to the same stone door. We're thinking creatures, Lavon, but there's something drastically wrong in the way we think about this universe we live in. It just doesn't seem to lead to results."

Lavon pushed back his floating hair futilely. "Maybe you're thinking about the wrong results. We've had no trouble with warfare, or crops, or practical things like that. If we can't create much heat, well, most of us won't miss it; we don't need more than we have. What's the other universe supposed to be like, the one our ancestors lived in? Is it any better than this one?"

"I don't know," Shar admitted. "It was so different that it's hard to compare the two. The metal plate tells a story about men who were travelling from one place to another in a container that moved by itself. The only analogue I can think of is the shallops of diatom shells that our youngsters used to sled along the thermocline; but evidently what's meant is something much bigger.

"I picture a huge shallop, closed on all sides, big enough to hold many people, maybe twenty or thirty. It had to travel for generations through some kind of medium where there wasn't any water to breathe, so the people had to carry their own water and renew it constantly. There were no seasons; no ice formed on the sky, because there couldn't be any sky in a closed shallop; and so there was no spore formation.

"Then the shallop was wrecked somehow. The people in it knew they were going to die. They made us, and put us here, as if we were their children. Because they had to die, they wrote their story on the plates, to tell us what had happened. I suppose we'd understand it better if we had the plate Shar I lost during the war—but we don't."

"The whole thing sounds like a parable," Lavon said, shrugging. "Or a song. I can see why you don't understand it. What I can't see is why you bother to try."

"Because of the plate," Shar said. "You've handled it yourself now, so you know that we've nothing like it. We have crude, impure metals we've hammered out, metals that last for a while and then decay. But the plate shines on, generation after generation. It doesn't change; our hammers and our graving tools break against it; the little heat we can generate leaves it unharmed. That plate wasn't formed in our universe and that one fact makes every word on it important to me. Someone went to a great deal of trouble to make those plates indestructible, and to give them to us. Someone to whom the word *stars* was important enough to be worth fourteen repetitions, despite the fact that the word doesn't seem to mean anything. I'm ready to think that if our makers repeated a word even twice on a record that seems likely to last forever, then it's important for us to know what it means."

Lavon stood up once more.

"All these extra universes and huge shallops and meaningless words—I can't say that they don't exist, but I don't see what difference it makes," he said. "The Shars of a few generations ago spent their whole lives breeding better algae crops for us, and showing us how to cultivate them, instead of living haphazardly on bacteria. Farther back, the Shars devised war engines, and war plans. All that was work worth doing. The Lavons of those days evidently got along without the metal plate and its puzzles, and saw to it that the Shars did, too. Well, as far as I'm concerned, you're welcome to the plate, if you like it better than crop improvement—but I think it ought to be thrown away."

"All right," Shar said, shrugging. "If you don't want it, that ends the traditional interview. We'll go our—"

There was a rising drone from the tabletop. The Para was lifting itself, waves of motion passing over its cilia, like the waves which went silently across the fruiting stalks of the fields of delicate fungi with which the Bottom was planted. It had been so silent that Lavon had forgotten it; he could tell from Shar's startlement that Shar had, too.

"This is a great decision," the waves of sound washing from the creature throbbed.

"Every Proto has heard it, and agrees with it. We have been afraid of this metal plate for a long time, afraid that men would learn to understand it and follow what it says to some secret place, leaving the Protos behind. Now we are not afraid."

"There wasn't anything to be afraid of," Lavon said indulgently.

"No Lavon before you, Lavon, had ever said so," the Para said. "We are glad. We will throw the plate away, as Lavon orders."

With that, the shining creature swooped toward the embrasure. With it, it bore away the remaining plate, which had been resting under it on the tabletop, suspended delicately in the curved tips of its supple ventral cilia. Inside its pellucid body, vacuoles swelled to increase its buoyancy and enable it to carry the heavy weight.

With a cry, Shar plunged through the water toward the window.

"Stop, Para!"

But Para was already gone, so swiftly that it had not even heard the call. Shar twisted his body and brought up one shoulder against the tower wall. He said nothing. His face was enough. Lavon could not look into it for more than an instant.

The shadows of the two men began to move slowly along the uneven cobbled floor. The Noc descended toward them from the vault, its tentacle stirring the water, its internal light flaring and fading irregularly. It, too, drifted through the window after its cousin, and sank slowly away toward the Bottom. Gently its living glow dimmed, flickered in the depths, and winked out.

For many days, Lavon was able to avoid thinking much about the loss. There was always a great deal of work to be done. Maintenance of the castles was a never-ending task. The thousand dichotomously branching wings tended to crumble with time, especially at their bases where they sprouted from one another, and

no Shar had yet come forward with a mortar as good as the rotifer-spittle which had once held them together. In addition, the breaking through of windows and the construction of chambers in the early days had been haphazard and often unsound. The instinctive architecture of the Eaters, after all, had not been meant to meet the needs of human occupants.

And then there were the crops. Men no longer fed precariously upon passing bacteria snatched to the mouth; now there were the drifting mats of specific water-fungi and algae, and the mycelia on the Bottom, rich and nourishing, which had been bred by five generations of Shars. These had to be tended constantly to keep the strains pure, and to keep the older and less intelligent species of the Protos from grazing on them. In this latter task, to be sure, the more intricate and farseeing Proto types cooperated, but men were needed to supervise.

There had been a time, after the war with the Eaters, when it had been customary to prey upon the slow-moving and stupid diatoms, whose exquisite and fragile glass shells were so easily burst, and who were unable to learn that a friendly voice did not necessarily mean a friend. There were still people who would crack open a diatom when no one else was looking, but they were regarded as barbarians, to the puzzlement of the Protos. The blurred and simpleminded speech of the gorgeously engraved plants had brought them into the category of community pets—a concept which the Protos were utterly unable to grasp, especially since men admitted that diatoms on the half-frustrule were delicious.

Lavon had had to agree, very early, that the distinction was tiny. After all, humans did eat the desmids, which differed from the diatoms only in three particulars: their shells were flexible, they could not move (and for that matter neither could all but a few groups of diatoms), and they did not speak. Yet to Lavon, as to most men, there did seem to be some kind of distinction, whether the Protos could see it or not, and that was that. Under the circumstances he felt that it was a part of his duty, as the hereditary leader of men, to protect the diatoms from the occasional poachers who browsed upon them, in defiance of custom, in the high levels of the sunlit sky.

Yet Lavon found it impossible to keep himself busy enough to forget that moment when the last clues to man's origin and destination had been seized, on authority of his own careless exaggeration, and borne away into dim space.

It might be possible to ask Para for the return of the plate, explain that a mistake had been made. The Protos were creatures of implacable logic, but they respected men, were used to illogic in men, and might reverse their decision if pressed—

We are sorry. The plate was carried over the bar and released in the gulf. We will have the Bottom there searched, but . . .

With a sick feeling he could not repress, Lavon knew that that would be the answer, or something very like it. When the Protos decided something was worthless, they did not hide it in some chamber like old women. They threw it away—efficiently.

Yet despite the tormenting of his conscience, Lavon was nearly convinced that the plate was well lost. What had it ever done for man, except to provide Shars with useless things to think about in the late seasons of their lives? What the Shars themselves had done to benefit man, here, in the water, in the world, in the universe, had been done by direct experimentation. No bit of useful knowledge had ever come from the plates. There had never been anything in the second plate, at least, but things best left unthought. The Protos were right.

Lavon shifted his position on the plant frond, where he had been sitting in order to overlook the harvesting of an experimental crop of blue-green, oil-rich algae drifting in a clotted mass close to the top of the sky, and scratched his back gently against the coarse bole. The Protos were seldom wrong, after all. Their lack of creativity, their inability to think an original thought, was a gift as well as a limitation. It allowed them to see and feel things at all times as they were—not as they hoped they might be, for they had no ability to hope, either.

"La-von! Laa-vah-on!"

The long halloo came floating up from the sleepy depths. Propping one hand against the top of the frond, Lavon bent and looked down. One of the harvesters was looking up at him, holding loosely the adze with which he had been splitting free from the raft the glutinous tetrads of the algae.

"I'm up here. What's the matter?"

"We have the ripened quadrant cut free. Shall we tow it away?"

"Tow it away," Lavon said, with a lazy gesture. He leaned back again. At the same instant, a brilliant reddish glory burst into being above him, and cast itself down toward the depths like mesh after mesh of the finest-drawn gold. The great light which lived above the sky during the day, brightening or dimming according to some pattern no Shar ever had fathomed, was blooming again.

Few men, caught in the warm glow of that light, could resist looking up at it, especially when the top of the sky itself wrinkled and smiled just a moment's climb or swim away. Yet, as always, Lavon's bemused upward look gave him back nothing but his own distorted, hobbling reflection, and a reflection of the plant on which he rested.

Here was the upper limit, the third of the three surfaces of the universe. The first surface was the Bottom, where the water ended.

The second surface was the thermocline, definite enough in summer to provide good sledding, but easily penetrable if you knew how.

The third surface was the sky. One could no more pass through that surface than one could penetrate the Bottom, nor was there any better reason to try. There the universe ended. The light which played over it daily, waxing and waning as it chose, seemed to be one of its properties.

Toward the end of the season, the water

gradually became colder and more difficult to breathe, while at the same time the light grew duller and stayed for shorter periods between darknesses. Slow currents started to move. The high waters turned chill and started to fall. The Bottom mud stirred and smoked away, carrying with it the spores of the fields of fungi. The thermocline tossed, became choppy, and melted away. The sky began to fog with particles of soft silt carried up from the Bottom, the walls, the corners of the universe. Before very long, the whole world was cold, inhospitable, flocculent with yellowing, dying creatures. The world died until the first tentative current of warm water broke the winter silence.

That was how it was when the second surface vanished. If the sky were to melt away . . .

"Lavon!"

Just after the long call, a shining bubble rose past Lavon. He reached out and poked it, but it bounded away from his sharp thumb. The gas bubbles which rose from the Bottom in late summer were almost invulnerable and when some especially hard blow or edge did penetrate them, they broke into smaller bubbles which nothing could touch, leaving behind a remarkably bad smell.

Gas. There was no water inside a bubble. A man who got inside a bubble would have nothing to breathe.

But, of course, it was impossible to enter a bubble. The surface tension was too strong. As strong as Shar's metal plate. As strong as the top of the sky.

As strong as the top of the sky. And above that—once the bubble was broken—a world of gas instead of water? Were all worlds bubbles of water drifting in gas?

If it were so, travel between them would be out of the question, since it would be impossible to pierce the sky to begin with. Nor did the infant cosmography include any provisions for Bottoms for the worlds.

And yet some of the local creatures did burrow into the Bottom, quite deeply, seeking something in those depths which was beyond the reach of man. Even the surface of the ooze, in high summer, crawled with tiny creatures for which mud was a natural medium. And though many of the entities with which man lived could not pass freely between the two countries of water which were divided by the thermocline, men could and did.

And if the new universe of which Shar had spoken existed at all, it had to exist beyond the sky, where the light was. Why could not the sky be passed, after all? The fact that bubbles could sometimes be broken showed that the surface skin that had formed between water and gas wasn't completely invulnerable. Had it ever been tried?

Lavon did not suppose that one man could butt his way through the top of the sky, any more than he could burrow into the Bottom, but there might be ways around the difficulty. Here at his back, for instance, was a plant which gave every appearance of continuing beyond the sky; its upper fronds broke off and were bent back only by a trick of reflection.

It had always been assumed that the plants died where they touched the sky. For the most part, they did, for frequently the dead extension could be seen, leached and yellow, the boxes of its component cells empty, floating embedded in the perfect mirror. But some were simply chopped off, like the one which sheltered him now. Perhaps that was only an illusion, and instead it soared indefinitely into some other place—some place where men might once have been born, and might still live. . . .

Both plates were gone. There was only one other way to find out.

Determinedly, Lavon began to climb toward the wavering mirror of the sky. His thorn-thumbed feet trampled obliviously upon the clustered sheaths of fragile stippled diatoms. The tulip-heads of Vortae, placid and murmurous cousins of Para, retracted startledly out of his way upon coiling stalks, to make silly gossip behind him.

Lavon did not hear them. He continued to climb doggedly toward the light, his fingers and toes gripping the plant-bole.

"Lavon! Where are you going? Lavon!"

He leaned out and looked down. The man with the adze, a doll-like figure, was beckoning to him from a patch of blue-green retreating over a violet abyss. Dizzily he looked away, clinging to the bole; he had never been so high before. He had, of course, nothing to fear from falling, but the fear was in his heritage. Then he began to climb again.

After a while, he touched the sky with one hand. He stopped to breathe. Curious bacteria gathered about the base of his thumb where blood from a small cut was fogging away, scattered at his gesture, and wriggled mindlessly back toward the dull red lure.

He waited until he no longer felt winded, and resumed climbing. The sky pressed down against the top of his head, against the back of his neck, against his shoulders. It seemed to give slightly, with a tough, frictionless elasticity. The water here was intensely bright, and quite colorless. He climbed another step, driving his shoulders against that enormous weight.

It was fruitless. He might as well have tried to penetrate a cliff.

Again he had to rest. While he panted, he made a curious discovery. All around the bole of the water plant, the steel surface of the sky curved upward, making a kind of sheath. He found that he could insert his hand into it— there was almost enough space to admit his head as well. Clinging closely to the bole, he looked up into the inside of the sheath, probing it with his injured hand. The glare was blinding.

There was a kind of soundless explosion. His whole wrist was suddenly encircled in an intense, impersonal grip, as if it were being cut in two. In blind astonishment, he lunged upward.

The ring of pain travelled smoothly down his upflung arm as he rose, was suddenly around his shoulders and chest. Another lunge and his knees were being squeezed in the circular vise. Another—

Something was horribly wrong. He clung to the bole and tried to gasp, but there was nothing to breathe.

The water came streaming out of his body, from his mouth, his nostrils, the spiracles in his sides, spurting in tangible jets. An intense and fiery itching crawled over the surface of his body. At each spasm, long knives ran into him, and from a great distance he heard more water being expelled from his book-lungs in an obscene, frothy sputtering. Inside his head, a patch of fire began to eat away at the floor of his nasal cavity.

Lavon was drowning.

With a final convulsion, he kicked himself away from the splintery bole, and fell. A hard impact shook him; and then the water, who had clung to him so tightly when he had first attempted to leave her, took him back with cold violence.

Sprawling and tumbling grotesquely, he drifted, down and down and down, toward the Bottom.

For many days, Lavon lay curled insensibly in his spore, as if in the winter sleep. The shock of cold which he had felt on reentering his native universe had been taken by his body as a sign of coming winter, as it had taken the oxygen starvation of his brief sojourn above the sky. The spore-forming glands had at once begun to function.

Had it not been for this, Lavon would surely have died. The danger of drowning disappeared even as he fell, as the air bubbled out of his lungs and readmitted the life-giving water. But for acute desiccation and third-degree sunburn, the sunken universe knew no remedy. The healing amniotic fluid generated by the spore-forming glands, after the transparent amber sphere had enclosed him, offered Lavon his only chance.

The brown sphere, quiescent in the eternal winter of the Bottom, was spotted after some days by a prowling amoeba. Down there the temperature was always an even 4 degrees, no matter what the season, but it was unheard of that a spore should be found there while the high epilimnion was still warm and rich in oxygen.

Within an hour, the spore was surrounded by scores of astonished Protos, jostling each other to bump their blunt eyeless prows against the shell. Another hour later, a squad of worried men came plunging from the castles far above to press their own noses against the transparent wall. Then swift orders were given.

Four Paras grouped themselves about the amber sphere, and there was a subdued explosion as their trichocysts burst. The four Paras thrummed and lifted, tugging.

Lavon's spore swayed gently in the mud and then rose slowly, entangled in the fine web. Nearby, a Noc cast a cold pulsating glow over the operation, for the benefit of the baffled knot of men. The sleeping figure of Lavon, head bowed, knees drawn up into its chest, revolved with an absurd solemnity inside the shell as it was moved.

"Take him to Shar, Para."

The young Shar justified, by minding his own business, the traditional wisdom with which his hereditary office had invested him. He observed at once that there was nothing he could do for the encysted Lavon which would not be classifiable as simple meddling.

He had the sphere deposited in a high tower room of his castle, where there was plenty of light and the water was warm, which should suggest to the estivating form that spring was again on the way. Beyond that, he simply sat and watched, and kept his speculations to himself.

Inside the spore, Lavon's body seemed to be rapidly shedding its skin, in long strips and patches. Gradually, his curious shrunkenness disappeared. His withered arms and legs and sunken abdomen filled out again.

The days went by while Shar watched. Finally he could discern no more changes, and, on a hunch, had the spore taken up to the topmost battlements of the tower, into the direct daylight.

An hour later, Lavon moved in his amber prison.

He uncurled and stretched, turned blank eyes up toward the light. His expression was that of a man who had not yet awakened from a ferocious nightmare. His whole body shone with a strange pink newness.

Shar knocked gently on the walls of the spore. Lavon turned his blind face toward the sound, life coming into his eyes. He smiled tentatively and braced his hands and feet against the inner wall of the shell.

The whole sphere fell abruptly to pieces with a sharp crackling. The amniotic fluid dissipated around him and Shar, carrying away with it the suggestive odor of a bitter struggle against death.

Lavon stood among the shards and looked at Shar silently. At last he said:

"Shar—I've been above the sky."

"I know," Shar said gently.

Again Lavon was silent. Shar said, "Don't be humble, Lavon. You've done an epoch-making thing. It nearly cost you your life. You must tell me the rest— all of it."

"The rest?"

"You taught me a lot while you slept. Or are you still opposed to 'useless' knowledge?"

Lavon could say nothing. He no longer could tell what he knew from what he wanted to know. He had only one question left, but he could not utter it. He could only look dumbly into Shar's delicate face.

"You have answered me," Shar said, even more gently than before. "Come, my friend; join me at my table. We will plan our journey to the stars."

.   .   .

There were five of them around Shar's big table: Shar himself, Lavon, and the three assistants assigned by custom to the Shars from the families Than, Tanol, and Stravol. The duties of these three men—or, sometimes, women—under many previous Shars had been simple and onerous: to put into effect in the field the genetic changes in the food crops which the Shar himself had worked out in little laboratory tanks and flats. Under other Shars more interested in metalworking or in chemistry, they had been smudged men—diggers, rock splitters, fashioners, and cleaners of apparatus.

Under Shar XVI, however, the three assistants had been more envied than usual among the rest of Lavon's people, for they seemed to do very little work of any kind. They spent long hours of every day talking with Shar in his chambers, poring over records, making minuscule scratch marks on slate, or just looking intently at simple things about which there was no obvious mystery. Sometimes they actually worked with Shar in his laboratory, but mostly they just sat.

Shar XVI had, as a matter of fact, discovered certain rudimentary rules of inquiry which, as he explained it to Lavon, he had recognized as tools of enormous power. He had become more interested in passing these on to future workers than in the seductions of any specific experiment, the journey to the stars perhaps excepted. The Than, Tanol, and Stravol of his generation were having scientific method pounded into their heads, a procedure they maintained was sometimes more painful than heaving a thousand rocks.

That they were the first of Lavon's people to be taxed with the problem of constructing a spaceship was, therefore, inevitable. The results lay on the table: three models, made of diatom-glass, strands of algae, flexible bits of cellulose, flakes of stonewort, slivers of wood, and organic glues collected from the secretions of a score of different plants and animals.

Lavon picked up the nearest one, a fragile spherical construction inside which little beads of dark-brown lava—actually bricks of rotifer-spittle painfully chipped free from the wall of an unused castle—moved freely back and forth in a kind of ball-bearing race. "Now whose is this one?" he said, turning the sphere curiously to and fro.

"That's mine," Tanol said. "Frankly, I don't think it comes anywhere near meeting all the requirements. It's just the only design I could arrive at that I think we could build with the materials and knowledge we have to hand now."

"But how does it work?"

"Hand it here a moment, Lavon. This bladder you see inside at the center, with the hollow spirogyra straws leading out from it to the skin of the ship, is a buoyancy tank. The idea is that we trap ourselves a big gas bubble as it rises from the Bottom and install it in the tank. Probably we'll have to do that piecemeal. Then the ship rises to the sky on the buoyancy of the bubble. The little paddles, here along these two bands on the outside, rotate when the crew—that's these bricks you hear shaking around inside—walks a treadmill that runs around the inside of the hull; they paddle us over to the edge of the sky. I stole that trick from the way Didin gets about. Then we pull the paddles in—they fold over into slots, like this—and, still by weight-transfer from the inside, we roll ourselves up the slope until we're out in space. When we hit another world and enter the water again, we let the gas out of the tank gradually through the exhaust tubes represented by these straws, and sink down to a landing at a controlled rate."

"Very ingenious," Shar said thoughtfully. "But I can foresee some difficulties. For one thing, the design lacks stability."

"Yes, it does," Tanol agreed. "And keeping it in motion is going to require a lot of footwork. But if we were to sling freely moving weight from the center of gravity of the machine, we could stabilize it at least partly. And the biggest expenditure of energy involved in the whole trip is going to be getting the machine up to the sky in the first place, and with this design that's taken care of as a matter of fact; once the bubble's installed, we'll have to keep the ship tied down until we're ready to take off."

"How about letting the gas out?" Lavon said. "Will it go out through those little tubes when we want it to? Won't it just cling to the walls of the tubes instead? The skin between water and gas is pretty difficult to deform—to that I can testify."

Tanol frowned. "That I don't know. Don't forget that the tubes will be large in the real ship, not just straws as they are in the model."

"Bigger than a man's body?" Than said.

"No, hardly. Maybe as big through as a man's head, at the most."

"Won't work," Than said tersely. "I tried it. You can't lead a bubble through a pipe that small. As Lavon says, it clings to the inside of the tube and won't be budged unless you put pressure behind it—lots of pressure. If we build this ship, we'll just have to abandon it once we hit our new world; we won't be able to set it down anywhere."

"That's out of the question," Lavon said at once. "Putting aside for the moment the waste involved, we may have to use the ship again in a hurry. Who knows what the new world will be like? We're going to have to be able to leave it again if it turns out to be impossible to live in."

"Which is your model, Than?" Shar said.

"This one. With this design, we do the trip the hard way—crawl along the Bottom until it meets the sky, crawl until we hit the next world, and crawl wherever we're going when we get there. No aquabatics. She's treadmill-powered, like Tanol's, but not necessarily man-powered; I've been thinking a bit about using motile diatoms. She steers by varying the power on one side or the other. For fine steering we can also hitch a pair of thongs to opposite ends of the rear axle and swivel her that way."

Shar looked closely at the tube-shaped model and pushed it experimentally along the table a little way. "I like that," he said presently. "It sits still when you want it to. With Than's

spherical ship, we'd be at the mercy of any stray current at home or in the new world and for all I know there may be currents of some sort in space, too, gas currents perhaps. Lavon, what do you think?"

"How would we build it?" Lavon said. "It's round in cross-section. That's all very well for a model, but how do you make a really big tube of that shape that won't fall in on itself?"

"Look inside, through the front window," Than said. "You'll see beams that cross at the center, at right angles to the long axis. They hold the walls braced."

"That consumes a lot of space," Stravol objected. By far the quietest and most introspective of the three assistants, he had not spoken until now since the beginning of the conference. "You've got to have free passage back and forth inside the ship. How are we going to keep everything operating if we have to be crawling around beams all the time?"

"All right, come up with something better," Than said, shrugging.

"That's easy. We bend hoops."

"Hoops!" Tanol said. "On *that* scale? You'd have to soak your wood in mud for a year before it would be flexible enough, and then it wouldn't have the strength you'd need."

"No, you wouldn't," Stravol said. "I didn't build a ship model, I just made drawings, and my ship isn't as good as Than's by a long distance. But my design for the ship is also tubular, so I did build a model of a hoop-bending machine—that's it on the table. You lock one end of your beam down in a heavy vise, like so, leaving the butt striking out on the other side. Then you tie up the other end with a heavy line, around this notch. Then you run your line around a windlass, and five or six men wind up the windlass, like so. That pulls the free end of the beam down until the notch engages with this key-slot, which you've pre-cut at the other end. Then you unlock the vise, and there's your hoop; for safety you might drive a peg through the joint to keep the thing from springing open unexpectedly."

"Wouldn't the beam you were using break after it had bent a certain distance?" Lavon asked.

"Stock timber certainly would," Stravol said. "But for this trick you use *green* wood, not seasoned. Otherwise you'd have to soften your beam to uselessness, as Tanol says. But live wood will flex enough to make a good, strong, single-unit hoop—or if it doesn't, Shar, the little rituals with numbers that you've been teaching us don't mean anything after all!"

Shar smiled. "You can easily make a mistake in using numbers," he said.

"I checked everything."

"I'm sure of it. And I think it's well worth a trial. Anything else to offer?"

"Well," Stravol said, "I've got a kind of live ventilating system I think should be useful. Otherwise, as I said, Than's ship strikes me as the type we should build; my own's hopelessly cumbersome."

"I have to agree," Tanol said regretfully. "But I'd like to try putting together a lighter-than-water ship sometime, maybe just for local travel. If the new world is bigger than ours, it might not be possible to swim everywhere you might want to go."

"That never occurred to me," Lavon exclaimed. "Suppose the new world *is* twice, three times, eight times as big as ours? Shar, is there any reason why that couldn't be?"

"None that I know of. The history plate certainly seems to take all kinds of enormous distances practically for granted. All right, let's make up a composite design from what we have here. Tanol, you're the best draftsman among us, suppose you draw it up. Lavon, what about labor?"

"I've a plan ready," Lavon said. "As I see it, the people who work on the ship are going to have to be on the job full-time. Building the vessel isn't going to be an overnight task, or even one that we can finish in a single season, so we can't count on using a rotating force. Besides, this is technical work; once a man learns how to do a particular task, it would be wasteful to

send him back to tending fungi just because somebody else has some time on his hands.

"So I've set up a basic force involving the two or three most intelligent hand-workers from each of the various trades. Those people I can withdraw from their regular work without upsetting the way we run our usual concerns, or noticeably increasing the burden on the others in a given trade. They will do the skilled labor, and stick with the ship until it's done. Some of them will make up the crew, too. For heavy, unskilled jobs, we can call on the various seasonal pools of unskilled people without disrupting our ordinary life."

"Good," Shar said. He leaned forward and rested linked hands on the edge of the table— although, because of the webbing between his fingers, he could link no more than the fingertips. "We've really made remarkable progress. I didn't expect that we'd have matters advanced a tenth as far as this by the end of this meeting. But maybe I've overlooked something important. Has anybody any more suggestions, or any questions?"

"I've got a question," Stravol said quietly.

"All right, let's hear it."

"Where are we going?"

There was quite a long silence. Finally Shar said: "Stravol, I can't answer that yet. I could say that we're going to the stars, but since we still have no idea what a star is, that answer wouldn't do you much good. We're going to make this trip because we've found that some of the fantastic things that the history plate says are really so. We know now that the sky can be passed, and that beyond the sky there's a region where there's no water to breathe, the region our ancients called 'space.' Both of these ideas always seemed to be against common sense, but nevertheless we've found that they're true.

"The history plate also says that there are other worlds than ours, and actually that's an easier idea to accept, once you've found out that the other two are so. As for the stars—well, we just don't know yet, we haven't any information at all that would allow us to read the history plate on that subject with new eyes, and there's no point in making wild guesses unless we can test the guesses. The stars are in space, and presumably, once we're out in space, we'll see them and the meaning of the word will become clear. At least we can confidently expect to see some clues—look at all the information we got from Lavon's trip of a few seconds above the sky!

"But in the meantime, there's no point in our speculating in a bubble. We think there are other worlds somewhere, and we're devising means to make the trip. The other questions, the pendant ones, just have to be put aside for now. We'll answer them eventually—there's no doubt in my mind about that. But it may take a long time."

Stravol grinned ruefully. "I expected no more. In a way, I think the whole project is crazy. But I'm in it right out to the end, all the same." Shar and Lavon grinned back. All of them had the fever, and Lavon suspected that their whole enclosed universe would share it with them before long. He said:

"Then let's not waste a minute. There's still a huge mass of detail to be worked out, and after that, all the hard work will just have begun. Let's get moving!"

The five men arose and looked at each other. Their expressions varied, but in all their eyes there was in addition the same mixture of awe and ambition: the composite face of the shipwright and of the astronaut.

Then they went out, severally, to begin their voyages.

It was two winter sleeps after Lavon's disastrous climb beyond the sky that all work on the spaceship stopped. By then, Lavon knew that he had hardened and weathered into that temporarily ageless state a man enters after he has just reached his prime; and he knew also that there were wrinkles engraved on his brow, to stay and to deepen.

"Old" Shar, too, had changed, his features losing some of their delicacy as he came into his maturity. Though the wedge-shaped bony structure of his face would give him a withdrawn and poetic look for as long as he lived, participation in the plan had given his expression a kind of executive overlay, which at best made it assume a masklike rigidity, and at worst coarsened it somehow. Yet despite the bleeding away of the years, the spaceship was still only a hulk. It lay upon a platform built above the tumbled boulders of the sandbar which stretched out from one wall of the world. It was an immense hull of pegged wood, broken by regularly spaced gaps through which the raw beams of its skeleton could be seen.

Work upon it had progressed fairly rapidly at first, for it was not hard to visualize what kind of vehicle would be needed to crawl through empty space without losing its water; Than and his colleagues had done that job well. It had been recognized, too, that the sheer size of the machine would enforce a long period of construction, perhaps as long as two full seasons; but neither Shar and his assistants nor Lavon had anticipated any serious snag.

For that matter, part of the vehicle's apparent incompleteness was an illusion. About a third of its fittings were to consist of living creatures, which could not be expected to install themselves in the vessel much before the actual takeoff.

Yet time and time again, work on the ship had to be halted for long periods. Several times whole sections needed to be ripped out, as it became more and more evident that hardly a single normal, understandable concept could be applied to the problem of space travel.

The lack of the history plate, which the Paras steadfastly refused to deliver up, was a double handicap. Immediately upon its loss, Shar had set himself to reproduce it from memory; but unlike the more religious of his ancestors, he had never regarded it as holy writ, and hence had never set himself to memorizing it word by word. Even before the theft, he had accumulated a set of variant translations of passages presenting specific experimental problems, which were stored in his library, carved in wood. Most of these translations, however, tended to contradict each other, and none of them related to spaceship construction, upon which the original had been vague in any case.

No duplicates of the cryptic characters of the original had ever been made, for the simple reason that there was nothing in the sunken universe capable of destroying the originals, nor of duplicating their apparently change-less permanence. Shar remarked too late that through simple caution they should have made a number of verbatim temporary records—but after generations of green-gold peace, simple caution no longer covers preparation against catastrophe. (Nor, for that matter, does a cul-ture which has to dig each letter of its simple alphabet into pulpy waterlogged wood with a flake of stonewort encourage the keeping of records in triplicate.)

As a result, Shar's imperfect memory of the contents of the history plate, plus the constant and millennial doubt as to the accuracy of the various translations, proved finally to be the worst obstacle to progress on the spaceship itself.

"Men must paddle before they can swim," Lavon observed belatedly, and Shar was forced to agree with him.

Obviously, whatever the ancients had known about spaceship construction, very lit-tle of that knowledge was usable to a people still trying to build its first spaceship from scratch. In retrospect, it was not surprising that the great hulk rested incomplete upon its platform above the sand boulders, exuding the musty odor of wood steadily losing its strength, two generations after its flat bottom had been laid down.

The fat-faced young man who headed the strike delegation to Shar's chambers was Phil XX, a man two generations younger than Shar, four younger than Lavon. There were crow's-feet at the corners of his eyes, which made him look both like a querulous old man and like an infant spoiled in the spore.

"We're calling a halt to this crazy project," he said bluntly. "We've slaved away our youth on it, but now that we're our own masters, it's over, that's all. It's over."

"Nobody's compelled you," Lavon said angrily.

"Society does; our parents do," a gaunt member of the delegation said. "But now we're going to start living in the real world. Every-body these days knows that there's no other world but this one. You oldsters can hang on to your superstitions if you like. We don't intend to."

Baffled, Lavon looked over at Shar. The sci-entist smiled and said, "Let them go, Lavon. We have no use for the fainthearted."

The fat-faced young man flushed. "You can't insult us into going back to work. We're through. Build your own ship to no place!"

"All right," Lavon said evenly. "Go on, beat it. Don't stand around here orating about it. You've made your decisions and we're not inter-ested in your self-justifications. Good-bye."

The fat-faced young man evidently still had quite a bit of heroism to dramatize which Lavon's dismissal had short-circuited. An exam-ination of Lavon's stony face, however, seemed to convince him that he had to take his victory as he found it. He and the delegation trailed ingloriously out the archway.

"Now what?" Lavon asked when they had gone. "I must admit, Shar, that I would have tried to persuade them. We do need the work-ers, after all."

"Not as much as they need us," Shar said tranquilly. "I know all those young men. I think they'll be astonished at the runty crops their fields will produce next season, after they have to breed them without my advice. Now, how many volunteers have you got for the crew of the ship?"

"Hundreds. Every youngster of the genera-tion after Phil's wants to go along. Phil's wrong about the segment of the populace, at least.

The project catches the imagination of the very young."

"Did you give them any encouragement?"

"Sure," Lavon said. "I told them we'd call on them if they were chosen. But you can't take that seriously! We'd do badly to displace our picked group of specialists with youths who have enthusiasm and nothing else."

"That's not what I had in mind, Lavon. Didn't I see a Noc in these chambers somewhere? Oh, there he is, asleep in the dome. Noc!"

The creature stirred its tentacle lazily.

"Noc, I've a message," Shar called. "The Protos are to tell all men that those who wish to go to the next world with the spaceship must come to the staging area right away. Say that we can't promise to take everyone, but that only those who help us to build the ship will be considered at all."

The Noc curled its tentacle again, and appeared to go back to sleep.

IV

Lavon turned from the arrangement of speaking-tube megaphones which was his control board and looked at Para.

"One last try," he said. "Will you give us back the history plate?"

"No, Lavon. We have never denied you anything before. But this we must."

"You're going with us, though, Para. Unless you give us back the knowledge we need, you'll lose your life if we lose ours."

"What is one Para?" the creature said. "We are all alike. This cell will die; but the Protos need to know how you fare on this journey. We believe you should make it without the plate, for in no other way can we assess the real importance of the plate."

"Then you admit you still have it. What if you can't communicate with your fellows once we're out in space? How do you know that water isn't essential to your telepathy?"

The Proto was silent. Lavon stared at it a moment, then turned deliberately back to the speaking tubes. "Everyone hang on," he said.

He felt shaky. "We're about to start. Stravol, is the ship sealed?"

"As far as I can tell, Lavon."

Lavon shifted to another megaphone. He took a deep breath. Already the water seemed stifling, although the ship hadn't moved.

"Ready with one-quarter power. . . . One, two, three, *go*."

The whole ship jerked and settled back into place again. The raphe diatoms along the under-hull settled into their niches, their jelly treads turning against broad endless belts of crude caddis-worm leather. Wooden gears creaked, stepping up the slow power of the creatures, transmitting it to the sixteen axles of the ship's wheels.

The ship rocked and began to roll slowly along the sandbar. Lavon looked tensely through the mica port. The world flowed painfully past him. The ship canted and began to climb the slope. Behind him, he could feel the electric silence of Shar, Para, and the two alternate pilots, Than and Stravol, as if their gazes were stabbing directly through his body and on out the port. The world looked different, now that he was leaving it. How had he missed all this beauty before?

The slapping of the endless belts and the squeaking and groaning of the gears and axles grew louder as the slope steepened. The ship continued to climb, lurching. Around it, squadrons of men and Protos dipped and wheeled, escorting it toward the sky.

Gradually the sky lowered and pressed down toward the top of the ship.

"A little more work from your diatoms, Tanol," Lavon said. "Boulder ahead." The ship swung ponderously. "All right, slow them up again. Give us a shove from your side, Tol—no, that's too much—there, that's it. Back to normal; you're still turning us! Tanol, give us one burst to line us up again. Good. All right, steady drive on all sides. It shouldn't be long now."

"How can you think in webs like that?" the Para wondered behind him.

"I just do, that's all. It's the way men think.

Overseers, a little more thrust now; the grade's getting steeper."

The gears groaned. The ship nosed up. The sky brightened in Lavon's face. Despite himself, he began to be frightened. His lungs seemed to burn, and in his mind he felt his long fall through nothingness toward the chill slap of the water as if he were experiencing it for the first time. His skin itched and burned. Could he go up there again? Up there into the burning void, the great gasping agony where no life should go?

The sandbar began to level out and the going became a little easier. Up here, the sky was so close that the lumbering motion of the huge ship disturbed it. Shadows of wavelets ran across the sand. Silently, the thick-barreled bands of blue-green algae drank in the light and converted it to oxygen, writhing in their slow mindless dance just under the long mica skylight which ran along the spine of the ship. In the hold, beneath the latticed corridor and cabin floors, whirring Vortae kept the ship's water in motion, fueling themselves upon drifting organic particles.

One by one, the figures wheeling outside about the ship waved arms or cilia and fell back, coasting down the slope of the sandbar toward the familiar world, dwindling and disappearing. There was at last only one single Euglena, half-plant cousin of the Protos, forging along beside the spaceship into the marshes of the shallows. It loved the light, but finally it, too, was driven away into deeper, cooler waters, its single whiplike tentacle undulating placidly as it went. It was not very bright, but Lavon felt deserted when it left.

Where they were going, though, none could follow.

Now the sky was nothing but a thin, resistant skin of water coating the top of the ship. The vessel slowed, and when Lavon called for more power, it began to dig itself in among the sand grains and boulders.

"That's not going to work," Shar said tensely. "I think we'd better step down the gear-ratio, Lavon, so you can apply stress more slowly."

"All right," Lavon agreed. "Full stop, everybody. Shar, will you supervise gear-changing, please?"

The insane brilliance of empty space looked Lavon full in the face just beyond his big mica bull's-eye. It was maddening to be forced to stop here upon the threshold of infinity; and it was dangerous, too. Lavon could feel building in him the old fear of the outside. A few moments more of inaction, he knew with a gathering coldness in his belly, and he would be unable to go through with it.

Surely, he thought, there must be a better way to change gear-ratios than the traditional one, which involved dismantling almost the entire gearbox. Why couldn't a number of gears of different sizes be carried on the same shaft, not necessarily all in action at once, but awaiting use simply by shoving the axle back and forth longitudinally in its sockets? It would still be clumsy, but it could be worked on orders from the bridge and would not involve shutting down the entire machine—and throwing the new pilot into a blue-green funk.

Shar came lunging up through the trap and swam himself to a stop.

"All set," he said. "The big reduction gears aren't taking the strain too well, though."

"Splintering?"

"Yes. I'd go it slow at first."

Lavon nodded mutely. Without allowing himself to stop, even for a moment, to consider the consequences of his words, he called: "Half power."

The ship hunched itself down again and began to move, very slowly indeed, but more smoothly than before. Overhead, the sky thinned to complete transparency. The great light came blasting in. Behind Lavon there was an uneasy stir. The whiteness grew at the front ports.

Again the ship slowed, straining against the blinding barrier. Lavon swallowed and called for more power. The ship groaned like something about to die. It was now almost at a stand-still.

"More power," Lavon ground out.

Once more, with infinite slowness, the ship began to move. Gently, it tilted upward.

Then it lunged forward and every board and beam in it began to squall.

"Lavon! Lavon!"

Lavon started sharply at the shout. The voice was coming at him from one of the mega-phones, the one marked for the port at the rear of the ship.

"Lavon!"

"What is it? Stop your damn yelling."

"I can see the top of the sky! From the *other* side, from the top side! It's like a big flat sheet of metal. We're going away from it. We're above the sky, Lavon, we're above the sky!"

Another violent start swung Lavon around toward the forward port. On the outside of the mica, the water was evaporating with shocking swiftness, taking with it strange distortions and patterns made of rainbows.

Lavon saw space.

It was at first like a deserted and cruelly dry version of the Bottom. There were enormous boulders, great cliffs, tumbled, split, riven, jag-ged rocks going up and away in all directions, as if scattered at random by some giant.

But it had a sky of its own—a deep blue dome so far away that he could not believe in, let alone estimate, what its distance might be. And in this dome was a ball of reddish-white fire that seared his eyeballs.

The wilderness of rock was still a long way away from the ship, which now seemed to be resting upon a level, glistening plain. Beneath the surface-shine, the plain seemed to be made of sand, nothing but familiar sand, the same substance which had heaped up to form a bar in Lavon's universe, the bar along which the ship had climbed. But the glassy, colorful skin .over it—

Suddenly Lavon became conscious of another shout from the megaphone banks. He shook his head savagely and said, "What is it now?"

"Lavon, this is Tol. What have you gotten us into? The belts are locked. The diatoms can't move them. They aren't faking, either; we've . rapped them hard enough to make them think we were trying to break their shells, but they still can't give us more power."

"Leave them alone," Lavon snapped. "They can't fake; they haven't enough intelligence. If they say they can't give you more power, they can't."

"Well, then, you get us out of it."

Shar came forward to Lavon's elbow. "We're on a space-water interface, where the surface tension is very high," he said softly. "If you order the wheels pulled up now, I think we'll make better progress for a while on the belly tread."

"Good enough," Lavon said with relief. "Hello below—haul up the wheels."

"For a long while," Shar said, "I couldn't understand the reference of the history plate to 'retractable landing gear,' but it finally occurred to me that the tension along a space-mud inter-face would hold any large object pretty tightly. That's why I insisted on our building the ship so that we could lift the wheels."

"Evidently the ancients knew their busi-ness after all, Shar."

Quite a few minutes later—for shifting power to the belly treads involved another setting of the gearbox—the ship was crawl-ing along the shore toward the tumbled rock. Anxiously, Lavon scanned the jagged, threaten-ing wall for a break. There was a sort of rivulet off toward the left which might offer a route, though a dubious one, to the next world. After some thought, Lavon ordered his ship turned toward it.

"Do you suppose that thing in the sky is a

'star'?" he asked. "But there were supposed to be lots of them. Only one is up there and one's plenty for my taste."

"I don't know," Shar admitted. "But I'm beginning to get a picture of the way the universe is made, I think. Evidently, our world is a sort of cup in the Bottom of this huge one. This one has a sky of its own; perhaps it, too, is only a cup in the Bottom of a still huger world, and so on and on without end. It's a hard concept to grasp, I'll admit. Maybe it would be more sensible to assume that all the worlds are cups in this one common surface, and that the great light shines on them all impartially."

"Then what makes it go out every night, and dim even in the day during winter?" Lavon demanded.

"Perhaps it travels in circles, over first one world, then another. How could I know yet?"

"Well, if you're right, it means that all we have to do is crawl along here for a while, until we hit the top of the sky of another world," Lavon said. "Then we dive in. Somehow it seems too simple, after all our preparations."

Shar chuckled, but the sound did not suggest that he had discovered anything funny. "Simple? Have you noticed the temperature yet?"

Lavon had noticed it, just beneath the surface of awareness, but at Shar's remark he realized that he was gradually being stifled. The oxygen content of the water, luckily, had not dropped, but the temperature suggested the shallows in the last and worst part of autumn. It was like trying to breathe soup.

"Than, give us more action from the Vortae," Lavon said. "This is going to be unbearable unless we get more circulation."

There was a reply from Than, but it came to Lavon's ears only as a mumble. It was all he could do now to keep his attention on the business of steering the ship.

The cut or defile in the scattered razor-edged rocks was a little closer, but there still seemed to be many miles of rough desert to cross. After a while, the ship settled into a steady, painfully slow crawling, with less pitching and jerking than before, but also with less progress. Under it, there was now a sliding, grinding sound, rasping against the hull of the ship itself, as if it were treadmilling over some coarse lubricant the particles of which were each as big as a man's head.

Finally Shar said, "Lavon, we'll have to stop again. The sand this far up is dry, and we're wasting energy using the tread."

"Are you sure we can take it?" Lavon asked, gasping for breath. "At least we are moving. If we stop to lower the wheels and change gears again, we'll boil."

"We'll boil if we don't," Shar said calmly. "Some of our algae are dead already and the rest are withering. That's a pretty good sign that we can't take much more. I don't think we'll make it into the shadows, unless we do change over and put on some speed."

There was a gulping sound from one of the mechanics. "We ought to turn back," he said raggedly. "We were never meant to be out here in the first place. We were made for the water, not for this hell."

"We'll stop," Lavon said, "but we're not turning back. That's final."

The words made a brave sound, but the man had upset Lavon more than he dared to admit, even to himself. "Shar," he said, "make it fast, will you?"

The scientist nodded and dived below.

The minutes stretched out. The great red-gold globe in the sky blazed and blazed. It had moved down the sky, far down, so that the light was pouring into the ship directly in Lavon's face, illuminating every floating particle, its rays like long milky streamers. The currents of water passing Lavon's cheek were almost hot.

How could they dare go directly forward into that inferno? The land directly under the "star" must be even hotter than it was here.

"Lavon! Look at Para!"

Lavon forced himself to turn and look at

his Proto ally. The great slipper had settled to the deck, where it was lying with only a feeble pulsation of its cilia. Inside, its vacuoles were beginning to swell, to become bloated, pear-shaped bubbles, crowding the granulated cyto-plasm, pressing upon the dark nuclei.

"Is . . . is he dying?"

"This cell is dying," Para said, as coldly as always. "But go on—go on. There is much to learn, and you may live, even though we do not. Go on."

"You're for us now?" Lavon whispered.

"We have always been for you. Push your folly to the uttermost. We will benefit in the end, and so will man."

The whisper died away. Lavon called the creature again, but it did not respond. There was a wooden clashing from below, and then Shar's voice came tinnily from one of the mega-phones. "Lavon, go ahead! The diatoms are dying, too, and then we'll be without power. Make it as quickly and directly as you can."

Grimly, Lavon leaned forward. "The 'star' is directly over the land we're approaching."

"It is? It may go lower still and the shadows will get longer. That may be our only hope."

Lavon had not thought of that. He rasped into the banked megaphones. Once more, the ship began to move, a little faster now, but seemingly still at a crawl. The thirty-two wheels rumbled.

It got hotter.

Steadily, with a perceptible motion, the "star" sank in Lavon's face. Suddenly a new terror struck him. Suppose it should continue to go down until it was gone entirely? Blasting though it was now, it was the only source of heat. Would not space become bitter cold on the instant and the ship an expanding, bursting block of ice?

The shadows lengthened menacingly, stretching across the desert toward the forward-rolling vessel. There was no talking in the cabin, just the sound of ragged breathing and the creaking of the machinery.

Then the jagged horizon seemed to rush upon them. Stony teeth cut into the lower rim of the ball of fire, devoured it swiftly. It was gone.

They were in the lee of the cliffs. Lavon ordered the ship turned to parallel the rock-line; it responded heavily, sluggishly. Far above, the sky deepened steadily, from blue to indigo.

Shar came silently up through the trap and stood beside Lavon, studying that deepening color and the lengthening of the shadows down the beach toward their own world. He said nothing, but Lavon was sure that the same chilling thought was in his mind.

"Lavon."

Lavon jumped. Shar's voice had iron in it. "Yes?"

"We'll have to keep moving. We must make the next world, wherever it is, very shortly."

"How can we dare move when we can't see where we're going? Why not sleep it over—if the cold will let us?"

"It will let us," Shar said. "It can't get dan-gerously cold up here. If it did, the sky—or what we used to think of as the sky—would have frozen over every night, even in summer. But what I'm thinking about is the water. The plants will go to sleep now. In our world that wouldn't matter; the supply of oxygen there is enough to last through the night. But in this confined space, with so many creatures in it and no supply of fresh water, we will probably smother."

Shar seemed hardly to be involved at all, but spoke rather with the voice of implacable physical laws.

"Furthermore," he said, staring unsee-ingly out at the raw landscape, "the diatoms are plants, too. In other words, we must stay on the move for as long as we have oxygen and power—and pray that we make it."

"Shar, we had quite a few Protos on board this ship once. And Para there isn't quite dead yet. If he were, the cabin would be intolerable. The ship is nearly sterile of bacteria, because all the Protos have been eating them as a matter of course and there's no outside supply of them, either. But still and all there would have been some decay."

Shar bent and tested the pellicle of the motionless Para with a probing finger. "You're right, he's still alive. What does that prove?"

"The Vortae are also alive; I can feel the water circulating. Which proves that it wasn't the heat that hurt Para. *It was the light.* Remember how badly my skin was affected after I climbed beyond the sky? Undiluted starlight is deadly. We should add that to the information from the plate."

"I still don't get the point."

"It's this: We've got three or four Noc down below. They were shielded from the light, and so must be still alive. If we concentrate them in the diatom galleys, the dumb diatoms will think it's still daylight and will go on working. Or we can concentrate them up along the spine of the ship, and keep the algae putting out oxygen. So the question is: Which do we need more, oxygen or power? Or can we split the difference?"

Shar actually grinned. "A brilliant piece of thinking. We may make a Shar out of you someday, Lavon. No, I'd say that we can't split the difference. Noc's light isn't intense enough to keep the plants making oxygen; I tried it once, and the oxygen production was too tiny to matter. Evidently the plants use the light for energy. So we'll have to settle for the diatoms for motive power."

"All right. Set it up that way, Shar."

Lavon brought the vessel away from the rocky lee of the cliff, out onto the smoother sand. All trace of direct light was now gone, although there was still a soft, general glow in the sky.

"Now then," Shar said thoughtfully, "I would guess that there's water over there in the canyon, if we can reach it. I'll go below again and arrange—"

Lavon gasped.

"What's the matter?"

Silently, Lavon pointed, his heart pounding.

The entire dome of indigo above them was spangled with tiny, incredibly brilliant lights.

There were hundreds of them, and more and more were becoming visible as the darkness deepened. And far away, over the ultimate edge of the rocks, was a dim red globe, crescented with ghostly silver. Near the zenith was another such body, much smaller, and silvered all over. . . .

Under the two moons of Hydrot, and under the eternal stars, the two-inch wooden spaceship and its microscopic cargo toiled down the slope toward a drying little rivulet.

The ship rested on the Bottom of the canyon for the rest of the night. The great square doors were unsealed and thrown open to admit the raw, irradiated, life-giving water from outside—and the wriggling bacteria which were fresh food.

No other creatures approached them, either out of curiosity or for hunting, while they slept, although Lavon had posted guards at the doors just in case. Evidently, even up here on the very floor of space, highly organized creatures were quiescent at night.

But when the first flush of light filtered through the water, trouble threatened.

First of all, there was the bug-eyed monster. The thing was green and had two snapping claws, either one of which could have broken the ship in two like a spirogyra strand. Its eyes were black and globular, on the ends of short columns, and its long feelers were thicker through than a plant bole. It passed in a kicking fury of motion, however, never noticing the ship at all.

"Is that—a sample of the kind of life they have here?" Lavon whispered. "Does it all run as big as that?" Nobody answered, for the very good reason that nobody knew.

After a while, Lavon risked moving the ship forward against the current, which was slow but heavy. Enormous writhing worms whipped past them. One struck the hull a heavy blow, then thrashed on obliviously.

"They don't notice us," Shar said. "We're too small. Lavon, the ancients warned us of the immensity of space, but even when you see it, it's impossible to grasp. And all those stars— can they mean what I think they mean? It's beyond thought, beyond belief!"

"The Bottom's sloping," Lavon said, looking ahead intently. "The walls of the canyon are retreating, and the water's becoming rather silty. Let the stars wait, Shar; we're coming toward the entrance of our new world."

Shar subsided moodily. His vision of space apparently had disturbed him, perhaps seriously. He took little notice of the great thing that was happening, but instead huddled worriedly over his own expanding speculations. Lavon felt the old gap between their minds widening once more.

Now the Bottom was tilting upward again. Lavon had no experience with delta formation, for no rivulets left his own world, and the phenomenon worried him. But his worries were swept away in wonder as the ship topped the rise and nosed over.

Ahead, the Bottom sloped away again, indefinitely, into glimmering depths. A proper sky was over them once more, and Lavon could see small rafts of plankton floating placidly beneath it. Almost at once, too, he saw several of the smaller kinds of Protos, a few of which were already approaching the ship—

Then the girl came darting out of the depths, her features blurred and distorted with distance and terror. At first she did not seem to see the ship at all. She came twisting and turning lithely through the water, obviously hoping only to throw herself over the mound of the delta and into the savage streamlet beyond.

Lavon was stunned. Not that there were men here—he had hoped for that, had even known somehow that men were everywhere in the universe—but at the girl's single-minded flight toward suicide.

"What—"

Then a dim buzzing began to grow in his ears, and he understood.

"Shar! Than! Stravol!" he bawled. "Break

out crossbows and spears! Knock out all the windows!" He lifted a foot and kicked through the port in front of him. Someone thrust a crossbow into his hand.

"What?" Shar blurted. "What's the matter? What's happening?"

"Eaters!"

The cry went through the ship like a galvanic shock. The rotifers back in Lavon's own world were virtually extinct, but everyone knew thoroughly the grim history of the long battle man and Proto had waged against them.

The girl spotted the ship suddenly and paused, obviously stricken with despair at the sight of this new monster. She drifted with her own momentum, her eyes alternately fixed upon the ship and jerking back over her shoulder, toward where the buzzing snarled louder and louder in the dimness.

"Don't stop!" Lavon shouted. "This way, this way! We're friends! We'll help!"

Three great semitransparent trumpets of smooth flesh bored over the rise, the many thick cilia of their coronas whirring greedily. Dicrans, arrogant in their flexible armor, quarreling thickly among themselves as they moved, with the few blurred, pre-symbolic noises which made up their own language.

Carefully, Lavon wound the crossbow, brought it to his shoulder, and fired. The bolt sang away through the water. It lost momentum rapidly, and was caught by a stray current which brought it closer to the girl than to the Eater at which Lavon had aimed.

He bit his lip, lowered the weapon, wound it up again. It did not pay to underestimate the range; he would have to wait. Another bolt, cutting through the water from a side port, made him issue orders to cease firing "until," he added, "you can see their eyespots."

The irruption of the rotifers decided the girl. The motionless wooden monster was of course strange to her, but it had not yet menaced her—and she must have known what it would be like to have three Dicrans over her, each trying to grab from the others the largest share. She threw herself towards the bull's-eye port. The three Eaters screamed with fury and greed and bored in after her.

She probably would not have made it, had not the dull vision of the lead Dicran made out the wooden shape of the ship at the last instant. The Dicran backed off, buzzing, and the other two sheered away to avoid colliding with her. After that they had another argument, though they could hardly have formulated what it was that they were fighting about; they were incapable of exchanging any thought much more complicated than the equivalent of "Yaah," "Drop dead," and "You're another."

While they were still snarling at each other, Lavon pierced the nearest one all the way through with an arablast bolt. The surviving two were at once involved in a lethal battle over the remains.

"Than, take a party out and spear me those two Eaters while they're still fighting," Lavon ordered. "Don't forget to destroy their eggs, too. I can see that this world needs a little taming."

The girl shot through the port and brought up against the far wall of the cabin, flailing in terror. Lavon tried to approach her, but from somewhere she produced a flake of stonewort chipped to a nasty point. Since she was naked, it was hard to tell where she had been hiding it, but she obviously knew how to use it, and meant to. Lavon retreated and sat down on the stool before his control board, waiting while she took in the cabin, Lavon, Shar, the other pilots, the senescent Para.

At last she said: "Are—you—the gods—from beyond the sky?"

"We're from beyond the sky, all right," Lavon said. "But we're not gods. We're human beings, just like you. Are there many humans here?"

The girl seemed to assess the situation very rapidly, savage though she was. Lavon had the odd and impossible impression that he should recognize her: a tall, deceptively relaxed, tawny woman, not after all quite like this one . . . a woman from another world, to be sure, but still . . .

She tucked the knife back into her bright, matted hair—aha, Lavon thought confusedly, there's a trick I may need to remember—and shook her head.

"We are few. The Eaters are everywhere. Soon they will have the last of us."

Her fatalism was so complete that she actually did not seem to care.

"And you've never cooperated against them? Or asked the Protos to help?"

"The Protos?" She shrugged. "They are as helpless as we are against the Eaters, most of them. We have no weapons that kill at a distance, like yours. And it's too late now for such weapons to do any good. We are too few, the Eaters too many."

Lavon shook his head emphatically. "You've had one weapon that counts, all along. Against it, numbers mean nothing. We'll show you how we've used it. You may be able to use it even better than we did, once you've given it a try."

The girl shrugged again. "We dreamed of such a weapon, but never found it. Are you telling the truth? What is the weapon?"

"Brains, of course," Lavon said. "Not just one brain, but a lot of them. Working together. Cooperation."

"Lavon speaks the truth," a weak voice said from the deck.

The Para stirred feebly. The girl watched it with wide eyes. The sound of the Para using human speech seemed to impress her more than the ship itself, or anything else that it contained.

"The Eaters can be conquered," the thin, burring voice said. "The Protos will help, as they helped in the world from which we came. The Protos fought this flight through space, and deprived man of his records; but man made the trip without the records. The Protos will never oppose man again. We have already spoken to the Protos of this world, and have told them that what man can dream, man can do. Whether the Protos will it or not.

"Shar—your metal record is with you. It was hidden in the ship. My brothers will lead you to it.

"This organism dies now. It dies in confidence of knowledge, as an intelligent creature dies. Man has taught us this. There is nothing. That knowledge. Cannot do. With it . . . men . . . have crossed . . . have crossed space. . . ."

The voice whispered away. The shining slip-per did not change, but something about it was gone. Lavon looked at the girl; their eyes met. He felt an unaccountable warmth.

"We have crossed space," Lavon repeated softly.

Shar's voice came to him across a great distance. The young-old man was whispering: "But—have we?"

Lavon was looking at the girl. He had no answer for Shar's question. It did not seem to be important.

Beyond Lies the Wub

PHILIP K. DICK

Philip Kindred Dick (1928–1982) was a US writer of science fiction, especially surreal science fiction, who started out as a cult author and became a dominant influence throughout pulp culture because of the films based on his work, including *Blade Runner* and *Total Recall*. But Dick was highly respected and influential within the sphere of science fiction before popular success found him late in his life. Dick received the Hugo Award in 1963 for his novel *The Man in the High Castle* and the John W. Campbell Memorial Award in 1975 for his novel *Flow My Tears, the Policeman Said*. Early on, Dick tried to enter the mainstream literary world with his fiction, but his work was rejected and his mainstream novels appeared only after his death.

Strongly interested in theology and philosophy, Dick explored political and metaphysical themes in novels in which individuals, sometimes in altered states of being, confront or flee dysfunctional corporations or fascistic governments. These altered states of being often manifest in Dick's fiction, including *A Scanner Darkly* (1977) and *VALIS* (1981), through drug use, conspiracy theories, transcendent moments of epiphany, and mental illness. Published after his death, Dick's *The Exegesis of Philip K. Dick* explored these ideas in nonfiction form. His *Ubik* (1969)—on *Time* magazine's 2005 list of the top one hundred English-language novels since 1923—bears some resemblance to Stepan Chapman's later novel *The Troika* (1997) in how it manipulates different levels of reality in a unique way. The posthumous legitimizing of Dick became complete in 2007 when he was included in the Library of America series.

Although they did not know each other at the time, Dick and Ursula K. Le Guin graduated in the same high school class (Berkeley High School, class of 1947). Le Guin would later famously admonish Dick for perceived misogyny in his work, but in taking her criticism to heart some critics feel he may have lost, in his late-era novels, some underlying existential element or purely misanthropic impulse that energized his fiction on a subconscious level.

"Beyond Lies the Wub," included here, was Dick's first published story, appearing in *Planet Stories* (1952). Dick recalled in notes for a reprint of the story in the short story anthology *First Voyages* that *Planet Stories* was "the most lurid of all pulp magazines on the stands at the time . . . As I carried four copies into the record store where I worked, a customer gazed at me and them, with dismay, and said, 'Phil, you *read* that kind of stuff?' I had to admit I not only read it, I wrote it."

"Beyond Lies the Wub" is interesting for several reasons, not just in that it is an excellent example of an impulse in science fiction to explore humankind's relationship to animal species, whether terrestrial or alien. The wub makes another appearance in Dick's fiction in the story "Not by Its Cover," considered a sequel. Others point to "Beyond Lies the Wub" as the precursor to Dick's interest in exploring metaphysics in his later stories. The wub not only explores the idea of individuation but deals with the question of how what we eat affects our brains long before it became an important area of inquiry in the sciences.

BEYOND LIES THE WUB

Philip K. Dick

They had almost finished with the loading. Outside stood the Optus, his arms folded, his face sunk in gloom. Captain Franco walked leisurely down the gangplank, grinning.

"What's the matter?" he said. "You're getting paid for all this."

The Optus said nothing. He turned away, collecting his robes. The captain put his boot on the hem of the robe.

"Just a minute. Don't go off. I'm not finished."

"Oh?" The Optus turned with dignity. "I am going back to the village." He looked toward the animals and birds being driven up the gangplank into the spaceship. "I must organize new hunts."

Franco lit a cigarette. "Why not? You people can go out into the veldt and track it all down again. But when we run out halfway between Mars and Earth—"

The Optus went off, wordless. Franco joined the first mate at the bottom of the gangplank.

"How's it coming?" he said. He looked at his watch. "We got a good bargain here."

The mate glanced at him sourly. "How do you explain that?"

"What's the matter with you? We need it more than they do."

"I'll see you later, Captain." The mate threaded his way up the plank, between the long-legged Martian go-birds, into the ship. Franco watched him disappear. He was just starting up after him, up the plank toward the port, when he saw *it*.

"My God!" He stood staring, his hands on his hips. Peterson was walking along the path, his face red, leading *it* by a string.

"I'm sorry, Captain," he said, tugging at the string. Franco walked toward him.

"What is it?"

The wub stood sagging, its great body settling slowly. It was sitting down, its eyes half shut. A few flies buzzed about its flank, and it switched its tail.

It sat. There was silence.

"It's a wub," Peterson said. "I got it from a native for fifty cents. He said it was a very unusual animal. Very respected."

"This?" Franco poked the great sloping side of the wub. "It's a pig! A huge dirty pig!"

"Yes, sir, it's a pig. The natives call it a wub."

"A huge pig. It must weigh four hundred pounds." Franco grabbed a tuft of the rough hair. The wub gasped. Its eyes opened, small and moist. Then its great mouth twitched.

A tear rolled down the wub's cheek and splashed on the floor.

"Maybe it's good to eat," Peterson said nervously.

"We'll soon find out," Franco said.

The wub survived the takeoff, sound asleep in the hold of the ship. When they were out in space and everything was running smoothly, Captain Franco bade his men fetch the wub upstairs so that he might perceive what manner of beast it was.

The wub grunted and wheezed, squeezing up the passageway.

"Come on," Jones grated, pulling at the rope. The wub twisted, rubbing its skin off on the smooth chrome walls. It burst into the anteroom, tumbling down in a heap. The men leaped up.

"Good Lord," French said. "What is it?"

"Peterson says it's a wub," Jones said. "It belongs to him." He kicked at the wub. The wub stood up unsteadily, panting.

"What's the matter with it?" French came over. "Is it going to be sick?"

They watched. The wub rolled its eyes mournfully. It gazed around at the men.

"I think it's thirsty," Peterson said. He went to get some water. French shook his head.

"No wonder we had so much trouble taking off. I had to reset all my ballast calculations."

Peterson came back with the water. The wub began to lap gratefully, splashing the men.

Captain Franco appeared at the door.

"Let's have a look at it." He advanced, squinting critically. "You got this for fifty cents?"

"Yes, sir," Peterson said. "It eats almost anything. I fed it on grain and it liked that. And then potatoes, and mash, and scraps from the table, and milk. It seems to enjoy eating. After it eats it lies down and goes to sleep."

"I see," Captain Franco said. "Now, as to its taste. That's the real question. I doubt if there's much point in fattening it up any more. It seems fat enough to me already. Where's the cook? I want him here. I want to find out—"

The wub stopped lapping and looked up at the captain.

"Really, Captain," the wub said. "I suggest we talk of other matters."

The room was silent.

"What was that?" Franco said. "Just now."

"The wub, sir," Peterson said. "It spoke."

They all looked at the wub.

"What did it say? What did it say?"

"It suggested we talk about other things."

Franco walked toward the wub. He went all around it, examining it from every side. Then he came back over and stood with the men.

"I wonder if there's a native inside it," he said thoughtfully. "Maybe we should open it up and have a look."

"Oh, goodness!" the wub cried. "Is that all you people can think of, killing and cutting?"

Franco clenched his fists. "Come out of there! Whoever you are, come out!"

Nothing stirred. The men stood together, their faces blank, staring at the wub. The wub swished its tail. It belched suddenly.

"I beg your pardon," the wub said.

"I don't think there's anyone in there," Jones said in a low voice. They all looked at each other.

The cook came in.

"You wanted me, Captain?" he said. "What's this thing?"

"This is a wub," Franco said. "It's to be eaten. Will you measure it and figure out—"

"I think we should have a talk," the wub said. "I'd like to discuss this with you, Captain, if I might. I can see that you and I do not agree on some basic issues."

The captain took a long time to answer. The wub waited good-naturedly, licking the water from its jowls.

"Come into my office," the captain said at last. He turned and walked out of the room. The wub rose and padded after him. The men watched it go out. They heard it climbing the stairs.

"I wonder what the outcome will be," the cook said. "Well, I'll be in the kitchen. Let me know as soon as you hear."

"Sure," Jones said. "Sure."

The wub eased itself down in the corner with a sigh. "You must forgive me," it said. "I'm afraid I'm addicted to various forms of relaxation. When one is as large as I—"

The captain nodded impatiently. He sat down at his desk and folded his hands.

"All right," he said. "Let's get started. You're a wub? Is that correct?"

The wub shrugged. "I suppose so. That's what they call us, the natives, I mean. We have our own term."

"And you speak English? You've been in contact with Earthmen before?"

"No."

"Then how do you do it?"

"Speak English? Am I speaking English? I'm not conscious of speaking anything in particular. I examined your mind—"

"My mind?"

"I studied the contents, especially the semantic warehouse, as I refer to it—"

"I see," the captain said. "Telepathy. Of course."

"We are a very old race," the wub said. "Very old and very ponderous. It is difficult for us to move around. You can appreciate that anything so slow and heavy would be at the mercy of more agile forms of life. There was no use in our relying on physical defenses. How could we win? Too heavy to run, too soft to fight, too good-natured to hunt for game—"

"How do you live?"

"Plants. Vegetables. We can eat almost anything. We're very catholic. Tolerant, eclectic, catholic. We live and let live. That's how we've gotten along."

The wub eyed the captain.

"And that's why I so violently objected to this business about having me boiled. I could see the image in your mind—most of me in the frozen food locker, some of me in the kettle, a bit for your pet cat—"

"So you read minds?" the captain said. "How interesting. Anything else? I mean, what else can you do along those lines?"

"A few odds and ends," the wub said absently, staring around the room. "A nice apartment you have here, Captain. You keep it quite neat. I respect life-forms that are tidy. Some Martian birds are quite tidy. They throw things out of their nests and sweep them—"

"Indeed." The captain nodded. "But to get back to the problem—"

"Quite so. You spoke of dining on me. The taste, I am told, is good. A little fatty, but tender. But how can any lasting contact be established between your people and mine if you resort to such barbaric attitudes? Eat me? Rather you should discuss questions with me, philosophy, the arts—"

The captain stood up. "Philosophy. It might interest you to know that we will be hard put to find something to eat for the next month. An unfortunate spoilage—"

"I know." The wub nodded. "But wouldn't it be more in accord with your principles of democracy if we all drew straws, or something along that line? After all, democracy is to protect the minority from just such infringements. Now, if each of us casts one vote—"

The captain walked to the door.

"Nuts to you," he said. He opened the door. He opened his mouth.

He stood frozen, his mouth wide, his eyes staring, his fingers still on the knob.

The wub watched him. Presently it padded out of the room, edging past the captain. It went down the hall, deep in meditation.

The room was quiet.

"So you see," the wub said, "we have a common myth. Your mind contains many familiar myth symbols. Ishtar, Odysseus—"

Peterson sat silently, staring at the floor. He shifted in his chair.

"Go on," he said. "Please go on."

"I find in your Odysseus a figure common to the mythology of most self-conscious races. As I interpret it, Odysseus wanders as an individual, aware of himself as such. This is the idea of separation, of separation from family and country. The process of individuation."

"But Odysseus returns to his home." Peterson looked out the port window, at the stars, endless stars, burning intently in the empty universe. "Finally he goes home."

"As must all creatures. The moment of separation is a temporary period, a brief journey of the soul. It begins, it ends. The wanderer returns to land and race . . ."

The door opened. The wub stopped, turning its great head.

Captain Franco came into the room, the men behind him. They hesitated at the door.

"Are you all right?" French said.

"Do you mean me?" Peterson said, surprised. "Why me?"

Franco lowered his gun. "Come over here," he said to Peterson. "Get up and come here."

There was silence.

"Go ahead," the wub said. "It doesn't matter."

Peterson stood up. "What for?"

"It's an order."

Peterson walked to the door. French caught his arm.

"What's going on?" Peterson wrenched loose. "What's the matter with you?"

Captain Franco moved toward the wub. The wub looked up from where it lay in the corner, pressed against the wall.

"It is interesting," the wub said, "that you are obsessed with the idea of eating me. I wonder why."

"Get up," Franco said.

"If you wish." The wub rose, grunting. "Be patient. It is difficult for me." It stood, gasping, its tongue lolling foolishly.

"Shoot it now," French said.

"For God's sake!" Peterson exclaimed. Jones turned to him quickly, his eyes gray with fear.

"You didn't see him—like a statue, standing there, his mouth open. If we hadn't come down, he'd still be there."

"Who? The captain?" Peterson stared around. "But he's all right now."

They looked at the wub, standing in the middle of the room, its great chest rising and falling.

"Come on," Franco said. "Out of the way."

The men pulled aside toward the door.

"You are quite afraid, aren't you?" the wub said. "Have I done anything to you? I am against the idea of hurting. All I have done is try to protect myself. Can you expect me to rush eagerly to my death? I am a sensible being like yourselves. I was curious to see your ship, learn about you. I suggested to the native—"

The gun jerked.

"See," Franco said. "I thought so."

The wub settled down, panting. It put its paw out, pulling its tail around it.

"It is very warm," the wub said. "I understand that we are close to the jets. Atomic power. You have done many wonderful things with it—technically. Apparently, your scientific hierarchy is not equipped to solve moral, ethical—"

Franco turned to the men, crowding behind him, wide-eyed, silent.

"I'll do it. You can watch."

French nodded. "Try to hit the brain. It's no good for eating. Don't hit the chest. If the rib cage shatters, we'll have to pick bones out."

"Listen," Peterson said, licking his lips. "Has it done anything? What harm has it done? I'm asking you. And anyhow, it's still mine. You have no right to shoot it. It doesn't belong to you."

Franco raised his gun.

"I'm going out," Jones said, his face white and sick. "I don't want to see it."

"Me, too," French said. The men straggled out, murmuring. Peterson lingered at the door.

"It was talking to me about myths," he said. "It wouldn't hurt anyone."

He went outside.

Franco walked toward the wub. The wub looked up slowly. It swallowed.

"A very foolish thing," it said. "I am sorry that you want to do it. There was a parable that your Saviour related—"

It stopped, staring at the gun.

"Can you look me in the eye and do it?" the wub said. "Can you do that?"

The captain gazed down. "I can look you in the eye," he said. "Back on the farm we had hogs, dirty razorback hogs. I can do it."

Staring down at the wub, into the gleaming, moist eyes, he pressed the trigger.

The taste was excellent.

They sat glumly around the table, some of

them hardly eating at all. The only one who seemed to be enjoying himself was Captain Franco.

"More?" he said, looking around. "More? And some wine, perhaps."

"Not me," French said. "I think I'll go back to the chart room."

"Me, too." Jones stood up, pushing his chair back. "I'll see you later."

The captain watched them go. Some of the others excused themselves.

"What do you suppose the matter is?" the captain said. He turned to Peterson. Peterson sat staring down at his plate, at the potatoes, the green peas, and at the thick slab of tender, warm meat.

He opened his mouth. No sound came.

The captain put his hand on Peterson's shoulder.

"It is only organic matter, now," he said. "The life essence is gone." He ate, spooning up the gravy with some bread. "I, myself, love to eat. It is one of the greatest things that a living creature can enjoy. Eating, resting, meditation, discussing things."

Peterson nodded. Two more men got up and went out. The captain drank some water and sighed.

"Well," he said. "I must say that this was a very enjoyable meal. All the reports I had heard were quite true—the taste of wub. Very fine. But I was prevented from enjoying this pleasure in times past."

He dabbed at his lips with his napkin and leaned back in his chair. Peterson stared dejectedly at the table.

The captain watched him intently. He leaned over.

"Come, come," he said. "Cheer up! Let's discuss things."

He smiled.

"As I was saying before I was interrupted, the role of Odysseus in the myths—"

Peterson jerked up, staring.

"To go on," the captain said. "Odysseus, as I understand him . . ."

The Snowball Effect

KATHERINE MACLEAN

Katherine MacLean (1925–) is an underrated US writer of science fiction specializing in short stories, most of which, including her first, "Defense Mechanism" (1949), appeared in *Astounding Science Fiction*. MacLean began to apply so-called soft science such as sociology to science fiction long before the rise of the Humanists in the 1980s. MacLean had a wide range of interests outside of writing that influenced her fiction. MacLean's education background included a BA from Barnard with postgraduate work in psychology. Although her work was unique and sophisticated, MacLean published little in the 1960s and her work was largely invisible to the New Wave writers who might have found it of interest.

MacLean's explorations in fiction often harness the hard sciences as well, to create a generally optimistic tone in stories that deal with a wide range of technological matters. Although she expressed feminist themes in some stories, MacLean did not restrict herself to those themes or protagonists, and did not generally use a male pseudonym. A number of her stories were assembled in *The Diploids and Other Flights of Fancy* (1962) and *The Trouble with You Earth People* (1980).

Many of MacLean's early stories have been anthologized. Perhaps the best-known are "Pictures Don't Lie" (*Galaxy*, August 1951), which tells of the arrival of an alien spaceship that seems normal according to advance radio signals but turns out to be little more than microscopic; "Unhuman Sacrifice" (*Astounding Science Fiction*, November 1958), an important piece of anthropological SF in which a visiting exploration/contact team on another planet misreads a painful initiation ceremony as needless when its purpose is to prevent a damaging biological change; and the story reprinted here, "The Snowball Effect."

"The Snowball Effect" (*Galaxy*, 1952) is unusual in subject matter. The story deals with academia in a sociology setting and shows how such research can make a huge impact in our future. In showcasing an insufficiently rigorous and absurdly failed experiment, the story also examines the ethics of experimenting on people without their knowledge (long before this issue was acknowledged). MacLean's work as a college lecturer may also have influenced this story.

THE SNOWBALL EFFECT

Katherine MacLean

"All right," I said, "what is sociology good for?"

Wilton Caswell, PhD, was head of my sociology department, and right then he was mad enough to chew nails. On the office wall behind him were three or four framed documents in Latin that were supposed to be signs of great learning, but I didn't care at that moment if he papered the walls with his degrees. I had been appointed dean and president to see to it that the university made money. I had a job to do, and I meant to do it.

He bit off each word with great restraint: "Sociology is the study of social institutions, Mr. Halloway."

I tried to make him understand my position. "Look, it's the big-money men who are supposed to be contributing to the support of this college. To them, sociology sounds like socialism—nothing can sound worse than that—and an institution is where they put Aunt Maggy when she began collecting Wheaties in a stamp album. We can't appeal to them that way. Come on now." I smiled condescendingly, knowing it would irritate him. "What are you doing that's worth anything?"

He glared at me, his white hair bristling and his nostrils dilated like a war horse about to whinny. I can say one thing for them—these scientists and professors always keep themselves well under control. He had a book in his hand and I was expecting him to throw it, but he spoke instead:

"This department's analysis of institutional accretion, by the use of open system mathematics, has been recognized as an outstanding and valuable contribution to—"

The words were impressive, whatever they meant, but this still didn't sound like anything that would pull in money. I interrupted. "Valuable in what way?"

He sat down on the edge of his desk, thoughtful, apparently recovering from the shock of being asked to produce something solid for his position, and ran his eyes over the titles of the books that lined his office walls.

"Well, sociology has been valuable to business in initiating worker efficiency and group motivation studies, which they now use in management decisions. And, of course, since the depression, Washington has been using sociological studies of employment labor and standards of living as a basis for its general policies of—"

I stopped him with both raised hands. "Please, Professor Caswell! That would hardly be a recommendation. Washington, the New Deal, and the present administration are somewhat touchy subjects to the men I have to deal with. They consider its value debatable, if you know what I mean. If they got the idea that sociology professors are giving advice and guidance— No, we have to stick to brass tacks and leave Washington out of this. What, specifically, has the work of this specific department done that would make it as worthy to receive money as—say, a heart disease research fund?"

He began to tap the corner of his book absently on the desk, watching me. "Fundamental research doesn't show immediate effects, Mr. Halloway, but its value is recognized."

I smiled and took out my pipe. "All right, tell me about it. Maybe I'll recognize its value."

Professor Caswell smiled back tightly. He knew his department was at stake. The other departments were popular with donors and pulled in gift money by scholarships and fellowships, and supported their professors and graduate students by research contracts with the government and industry. Caswell had to show a way to make his own department popular—or else. I couldn't fire him directly, of course, but there are ways of doing it indirectly.

He laid down his book and ran a hand over his ruffled hair.

"Institutions—organizations, that is"—his voice became more resonant; like most professors, when he had to explain something he instinctively slipped into his platform lecture mannerisms, and began to deliver an essay—"have certain tendencies built into the way they happen to have been organized, which cause them to expand or contract without reference to the needs they were founded to serve."

He was becoming flushed with the pleasure of explaining his subject. "All through the ages, it has been a matter of wonder and dismay to men that a simple organization—such as a church to worship in, or a delegation of weapons to a warrior class merely for defense against an outside enemy—will either grow insensately and extend its control until it is a tyranny over their whole lives, or, like other organizations set up to serve a vital need, will tend to repeatedly dwindle and vanish, and have to be painfully rebuilt.

"The reason can be traced to little quirks in the way they were organized, a matter of positive and negative power feedbacks. Such simple questions as, 'Is there a way a holder of authority in this organization can use the power available to him to increase his power?' provide the key. But it still could not be handled until the complex questions of interacting motives and long-range accumulations of minor effects could somehow be simplified and formulated. In working on the problem, I found that the mathematics of open systems, as introduced to biology by Ludwig von Bertalanffy and George Kreezer, could be used as a base that would enable me to develop a specifically social mathematics, expressing the human factors of intermeshing authority and motives in simple formulas.

"By these formulations, it is possible to determine automatically the amount of growth and period of life of any organization. The UN, to choose an unfortunate example, is a shrinker-type organization. Its monetary support is not in the hands of those who personally benefit by its governmental activities, but, instead, in the hands of those who would personally lose by an extension and encroachment of its authority on their own. Yet by the use of formula analysis—"

"That's theory," I said. "How about proof?"

"My equations are already being used in the study of limited-size federal corporations. Washington—"

I held up my palm again. "Please, not that nasty word again. I mean, where else has it been put into operation? Just a simple demonstration, something to show that it works, that's all."

He looked away from me thoughtfully, picked up the book, and began to tap it on the desk again. It had some unreadable title and his name on it in gold letters. I got the distinct impression again that he was repressing an urge to hit me with it.

He spoke quietly. "All right, I'll give you a demonstration. Are you willing to wait six months?"

"Certainly, if you can show me something at the end of that time."

Reminded of time, I glanced at my watch and stood up.

"Could we discuss this over lunch?" he asked.

"I wouldn't mind hearing more, but I'm having lunch with some executors of a millionaire's will. They have to be convinced that by 'furtherance of research into human ills,' he meant that the money should go to research fellowships for postgraduate biologists at the university, rather than to a medical foundation."

"I see you have your problems, too," Caswell said, conceding me nothing. He extended his hand with a chilly smile. "Well, good afternoon, Mr. Halloway. I'm glad we had this talk."

I shook hands and left him standing there, sure of his place in the progress of science and the respect of his colleagues, yet seething inside because I, the president and dean, had boorishly demanded that he produce something tangible.

I frankly didn't give a hoot if he blew his lid. My job isn't easy. For a crumb of favorable publicity and respect in the newspapers and an annual ceremony in a silly costume, I spend the rest of the year going hat in hand, asking politely for money at everyone's door, like a well-dressed panhandler, and trying to manage the university on the dribble I get. As far as I was concerned, a department had to support itself or be cut down to what student tuition pays for, which is a handful of overcrowded courses taught by an assistant lecturer. Caswell had to make it work or get out.

But the more I thought about it, the more I wanted to hear what he was going to do for a demonstration.

At lunch, three days later, while we were waiting for our order, he opened a small notebook. "Ever hear of feedback effects?"

"Not enough to have it clear."

"You know the snowball effect, though."

"Sure, start a snowball rolling downhill and it grows."

"Well, now——" He wrote a short line of symbols on a blank page and turned the notebook around for me to inspect it. "Here's the formula for the snowball process. It's the basic general growth formula—covers everything."

It was a row of little symbols arranged like an algebra equation. One was a concentric spiral going up, like a cross section of a snowball rolling in snow. That was a growth sign.

I hadn't expected to understand the equation, but it was almost as clear as a sentence. I was impressed and slightly intimidated by it.

He had already explained enough so that I knew that, if he was right, here was the growth of the Catholic Church and the Roman Empire, the conquests of Alexander and the spread of the smoking habit and the change of the unwritten laws of styles.

"Is it really as simple as that?" I asked.

"You notice," he said, "that when it becomes too heavy for the cohesion strength of snow, it breaks apart. Now in human terms—"

The chops and mashed potatoes and peas arrived.

"Go on," I urged.

He was deep in the symbology of human motives and the equations of human behavior in groups. After running through a few different types of grower- and shrinker-type organizations, we came back to the snowball, and decided to run the test by making something grow.

"You add the motives," he said, "and the equation will translate them into organization."

"How about a good selfish reason for the ins to drag others into the group—some sort of bounty on new members, a cut of their membership fee?" I suggested uncertainly, feeling slightly foolish. "And maybe a reason why the members would lose if any of them resigned, and some indirect way they could use to force each other to stay in."

"The first is the chain letter principle." He nodded. "I've got that. The other . . ." He put the symbols through some mathematical manipulation so that a special grouping appeared in the middle of the equation. "That's it."

Since I seemed to have the right idea, I suggested some more, and he added some, and juggled them around in different patterns. We threw out a few that would have made the organization too complicated, and finally worked out an idyllically simple and deadly little organization setup where joining had all the temptation of buying a sweepstakes ticket, going in deeper was as easy as hanging around a racetrack, and getting out was like trying to pull free from a Malayan thumb trap. We put our heads closer together and talked lower, picking the best place for the demonstration.

"Abington?"

"How about Watashaw? I have some student sociological surveys of it already. We can pick a suitable group from that."

"This demonstration has got to be convincing. We'd better pick a little group that no one in his right mind would expect to grow."

"There should be a suitable club . . ."

Picture Professor Caswell, head of the Department of Sociology, and with him the president of the university, leaning across the table toward each other, sipping coffee and talking in conspiratorial tones over something they were writing in a notebook.

That was us.

"Ladies," said the skinny female chairman of the Watashaw Sewing Circle. "Today we have guests." She signaled for us to rise, and we stood up, bowing to polite applause and smiles. "Professor Caswell, and Professor Smith." (My alias.) "They are making a survey of the methods and duties of the clubs of Watashaw."

We sat down to another ripple of applause and slightly wider smiles, and then the meeting of the Watashaw Sewing Circle began. In five minutes I began to feel sleepy.

There were only about thirty people there, and it was a small room, not the halls of Congress, but they discussed their business of collecting and repairing secondhand clothing for charity with endless, boring parliamentary formality.

I pointed out to Caswell the member I thought would be the natural leader, a tall well-built woman in a green suit, with conscious gestures and a resonant, penetrating voice, and then went into a half doze while Caswell stayed awake beside me and wrote in his notebook. After a while the resonant voice roused me to attention for a moment. It was the tall woman holding the floor over some collective dereliction of the club.

I nudged Caswell and murmured, "Did you fix it so that a shover has a better chance of getting into office than a non-shover?"

"I think there's a way they could find for it," Caswell whispered back, and went to work on his equation again. "Yes, several ways to bias the elections."

"Good. Point them out tactfully to the one you select. Not as if she'd use such methods, but just as an example of the reason why only *she* can be trusted with initiating the change. Just mention all the personal advantages an unscrupulous person could have."

He nodded, keeping a straight and sober face, as if we were exchanging admiring remarks about the techniques of clothes repairing, instead of conspiring.

After the meeting, Caswell drew the tall woman in the green suit aside and spoke to her confidentially, showing her the diagram of organization we had drawn up. I saw the responsive glitter in the woman's eyes and knew she was hooked.

We left the diagram of organization and our typed copy of the new bylaws with her and went off soberly, as befitted two social science experimenters. We didn't start laughing until our car passed the town limits and began the climb for University Heights.

If Caswell's equations meant anything at all, we had given that sewing circle more growth drives than the Roman Empire.

Four months later I had time out from a very busy schedule to wonder how the test was coming along. Passing Caswell's office, I put my head in. He looked up from a student research paper he was correcting.

"Caswell, about that sewing club business—I'm beginning to feel the suspense. Could I get an advance report on how it's coming?"

"I'm not following it. We're supposed to let it run the full six months."

"But I'm curious. Could I get in touch with that woman—what's her name?"

"Searles, Mrs. George Searles."

"Would that change the results?"

"Not in the slightest. If you want to graph the membership rise, it should be going up in a log curve, probably doubling every so often."

I grinned. "If it's not rising, you're fired."

He grinned back. "If it's not rising you won't have to fire me—I'll burn my books and shoot myself."

I returned to my office and put in a call to Watashaw.

While I was waiting for the phone to be answered, I took a piece of graph paper and ruled it off into six sections, one for each month. After the phone had rung in the distance for a long time, a servant answered with a bored drawl:

"Mrs. Searles's residence."

I picked up a red gummed star and licked it.

"Mrs. Searles, please."

"She's not in just now. Could I take a message?"

I placed the star at the thirty line in the beginning of the first section. Thirty members they'd started with.

"No, thanks. Could you tell me when she'll be back?"

"Not until dinner. She's at the meetin'."

"The sewing club?" I asked.

"No, sir, not that thing. There isn't any sewing club anymore, not for a long time. She's at the Civic Welfare meeting."

Somehow I hadn't expected anything like that.

"Thank you," I said, and hung up, and after a moment noticed I was holding a box of red gummed stars in my hand. I closed it and put it down on top of the graph of membership in the sewing circle. No more members . . .

Poor Caswell. The bet between us was ironclad. He wouldn't let me back down on it even if I wanted to. He'd probably quit before I put through the first slow move to fire him. His professional pride would be shattered, sunk without a trace. I remembered what he said about shooting himself. It had seemed funny to both of us at the time, but . . . What a mess *that* would make for the university.

I had to talk to Mrs. Searles. Perhaps there was some outside reason why the club had disbanded. Perhaps it had not just died.

I called back. "This is Professor Smith," I said, giving the alias I had used before. "I called a few minutes ago. When did you say Mrs. Searles will return?"

"About six thirty or seven o'clock."

Five hours to wait.

And what if Caswell asked me what I had found out in the meantime? I didn't want to tell him anything until I had talked it over with that woman Searles first.

"Where is this Civic Welfare meeting?"

Five minutes later, I was in my car, heading for Watashaw, driving considerably faster than my usual speed and keeping a careful watch for highway patrol cars as the speedometer climbed.

The town meeting hall and theater was a big place, probably with lots of small rooms for different clubs. I went in through the center door and found myself in the huge central hall, where some sort of rally was being held. A political-type rally—you know, cheers and chants, with bunting already down on the floor, people holding banners, and plenty of enthusiasm and excitement in the air. Someone was making a speech up on the platform. Most of the people there were women.

I wondered how the Civic Welfare League could dare hold its meeting at the same time as a political rally that could pull its members away. The group with Mrs. Searles was probably holding a shrunken and almost memberless meeting somewhere in an upper room.

There probably was a side door that would lead upstairs.

While I glanced around, a pretty girl usher put a printed bulletin in my hand, whispering, "Here's one of the new copies." As I attempted to hand it back, she retreated. "Oh, you can keep it. It's a new one. Everyone's supposed to have it. We've just printed up six thousand copies to make sure there'll be enough to last."

The tall woman on the platform had been making a driving, forceful speech about some plans for rebuilding Watashaw's slum section. It began to penetrate my mind dimly as I glanced down at the bulletin in my hands.

"Civic Welfare League of Watashaw. The United Organization of Church and Secular Charities." That's what it said. Below began the rules of membership.

I looked up. The speaker, with a clear, determined voice and conscious, forceful gestures, had entered the home stretch of her speech, an appeal to the civic pride of all citizens of Watashaw.

"With a bright and glorious future— potentially without poor and without uncared- for ill—potentially with no ugliness, no vistas which are not beautiful—the best people in the best planned town in the country—the jewel of the United States."

She paused and then leaned forward intensely, striking her clenched hand on the speaker's stand with each word for emphasis.

"All we need is more members. Now get out there and recruit!"

I finally recognized Mrs. Searles, as an answering sudden blast of sound half deafened me. The crowd was chanting at the top of its lungs: "Recruit! Recruit!"

Mrs. Searles stood still at the speaker's table and behind her, seated in a row of chairs, was a group that was probably the board of directors. It was mostly women, and the women began to look vaguely familiar, as if they could be members of the sewing circle.

I put my lips close to the ear of the pretty usher while I turned over the stiff printed bulletin on a hunch. "How long has the League been organized?" On the back of the bulletin was a constitution.

She was cheering with the crowd, her eyes sparkling. "I don't know," she answered between cheers. "I only joined two days ago. Isn't it wonderful?"

I went into the quiet outer air and got into my car with my skin prickling. Even as I drove away, I could hear them. They were singing some kind of organization song with the tune of "Marching Through Georgia."

Even at the single glance I had given it, the constitution looked exactly like the one we had given the Watashaw Sewing Circle.

All I told Caswell when I got back was that the sewing circle had changed its name and the membership seemed to be rising.

Next day, after calling Mrs. Searles, I placed some red stars on my graph for the first three months. They made a nice curve, rising more steeply as it reached the fourth month. They had picked up their first increase in membership simply by amalgamating with all the other types of charity organizations in Watashaw, changing the club name with each fusion, but keeping the same constitution—the constitution with the bright promise of advantages as long as there were always new members being brought in.

By the fifth month, the League had added a mutual babysitting service and had induced the local school board to add a nursery school to the town service, so as to free more women for League activity. But charity must have been completely organized by then, and expansion had to be in other directions.

Some real estate agents evidently had been drawn into the whirlpool early, along with their ideas. The slum improvement plans began to blossom and take on a tinge of real estate planning later in the month.

The first day of the sixth month, a big two-page spread appeared in the local paper of a mass meeting which had approved a full-fledged scheme for slum clearance of Watashaw's shack-town section, plus plans for rehousing, civic building, and rezoning. *And* good prospects for attracting some new industries to the town, industries which had already been contacted and seemed interested by the privileges offered.

And with all this, an arrangement for securing and distributing to the club members *alone* most of the profit that would come to the town in the form of a rise in the price of building sites and a boom in the building industry. The profit distributing arrangement was the same one that had been built into the organization plan for the distribution of the small profits of membership fees and honorary promotions. It was becoming an openly profitable business. Membership was rising more rapidly now.

By the second week of the sixth month, news appeared in the local paper that the club had filed application to incorporate itself as the Watashaw Mutual Trade and Civic Development Corporation, and all the local real estate promoters had finished joining en masse. The Mutual Trade part sounded to me as if the chamber of commerce was on the point of being pulled in with them, ideas, ambitions, and all.

I chuckled while reading the next page of the paper, on which a local politician was reported as having addressed the club with a long flowery oration on their enterprise, charity, and civic spirit. He had been made an honorary member. If he allowed himself to be made a *full* member with its contractual obligations and its lures, if the politicians went into this too . . .

I laughed, filing the newspaper with the other documents on the Watashaw test. These proofs would fascinate any businessman with the sense to see where his bread was buttered. A businessman is constantly dealing with organizations, including his own, and finding them either inert, cantankerous, or both. Caswell's formula could be a handle to grasp them with. Gratitude alone would bring money into the university in carload lots.

The end of the sixth month came. The test was over and the end reports were spectacular. Caswell's formulas were proven to the hilt.

After reading the last newspaper reports, I called him up.

"Perfect, Wilt, *perfect*! I can use this Watashaw thing to get you so many fellowships and scholarships and grants for your department that you'll think it's snowing money!"

He answered somewhat disinterestedly, "I've been busy working with students on their research papers and marking tests—not following the Watashaw business at all, I'm afraid. You say the demonstration went well and you're satisfied?"

He was definitely putting on a chill. We were friends now, but obviously he was still peeved whenever he was reminded that I had doubted that his theory could work. And he was using its success to rub my nose in the realization that I had been wrong. A man with a string of degrees after his name is just as human as anyone else. I had needled him pretty hard that first time.

"I'm satisfied," I acknowledged. "I was wrong. The formulas work beautifully. Come over and see my file of documents on it if you want a boost for your ego. Now let's see the formula for stopping it."

He sounded cheerful again. "I didn't complicate that organization with negatives. I wanted it to *grow*. It falls apart naturally when it stops growing for more than two months. It's like the great stock boom before an economic crash. Everyone in it is prosperous as long as the prices just keep going up and new buyers come into the market, but they all knew what would happen if it stopped growing. You remember, we built in as one of the incentives that the members know they are going to lose if membership stops growing. Why, if I tried to stop it now, they'd cut my throat."

I remembered the drive and frenzy of the crowd in the one early meeting I had seen. They probably would.

"No," he continued. "We'll just let it play out to the end of its tether and die of old age."

"When will that be?"

"It can't grow past the female population of the town. There are only so many women in Watashaw, and some of them don't like sewing."

The graph on the desk before me began to

look sinister. Surely Caswell must have made some provision for—

"You underestimate their ingenuity," I said into the phone. "Since they wanted to expand, they didn't stick to sewing. They went from general charity to social welfare schemes to something that's pretty close to an incorporated government. The name is now the Watashaw Mutual Trade and Civic Development Corporation, and they're filing an application to change it to Civic Property Pool and Social Dividend, membership contractual, open to all. That social dividend sounds like a technocrat climbed on the bandwagon, eh?"

While I spoke, I carefully added another red star to the curve above the thousand-members level, checking with the newspaper that still lay open on my desk. The curve was definitely some sort of log curve now, growing more rapidly with each increase.

"Leaving out practical limitations for a moment, where does the formula say it will stop?" I asked.

"When you run out of people to join it. But after all, there are only so many people in Watashaw. It's a pretty small town."

.   .   .

"They've opened a branch office in New York," I said carefully into the phone, a few weeks later.

With my pencil, very carefully, I extended the membership curve from where it was then.

After the next doubling, the curve went almost straight up and off the page.

Allowing for a lag of contagion from one nation to another, depending on how much their citizens intermingled I'd give the rest of the world about twelve years.

There was a long silence while Caswell probably drew the same graph in his own mind. Then he laughed weakly. "Well, you asked me for a demonstration."

That was as good an answer as any. We got together and had lunch in a bar, if you can call it lunch. The movement we started will expand by hook or by crook, by seduction or by bribery or by propaganda or by conquest, but it will expand. And maybe a total world government will be a fine thing—until it hits the end of its rope in twelve years or so.

What happens then, I don't know.

But I don't want anyone to pin that on me. From now on, if anyone asks me, I've never heard of Watashaw.

MARGARET ST. CLAIR

Margaret St. Clair (1911–1995) was a highly idiosyncratic and original US writer of science fiction and fantasy. Her career began with "Rocket to Limbo" for *Fantastic Adventures* in November 1946, and by 1950 she had published about thirty stories, most of them vigorous planetary adventures and planetary romances. St. Clair also published a series of highly regarded stories (including "Prott") under the pen name "Idris Seabright," almost exclusively in *The Magazine of Fantasy and Science Fiction*. The Seabright name for whatever reason became attached to stories that were more seamless and fantastical, and St. Clair became better known for them than work published under her own name.

Her early work could feel conventional at times but had already begun to push back against one central impulse of pulp science fiction: the need to reassure through effective problem-solving and showing humankind as in control of the universe. She also always had a dark, healthy sense of the absurd, on full display in stories like "Hathor's Pets" (1950) and the Lord Dunsany–inspired "The Man Who Sold Rope to the Gnoles" (1951), which mixed horror and humor.

In her classic work, St. Clair demands rereading in much the same way as Vladimir Nabokov and James Tiptree Jr.: the stories contain traps and mazes and hidden doors. St. Clair sometimes expressed a disappointment with the self-importance of the science fiction field as she knew it ("Is it a sacred cause?"). In part, St. Clair thought the field didn't always understand or reward sophisticated humor, too invested in a headlong rush toward the earnest. But St. Clair would likely have remained "elusive," as critic John Clute puts it, no matter what the scene. St. Clair was definitely not a joiner or likely to be comfortable in any club.

St. Clair and her husband became Wiccans in the 1950s, and she chiefly identifies in her introduction to *The Best of Margaret St. Clair* as a "long-time civil libertarian," her political sympathies with "the democratic left." But some additional clues to the dual delicacy and bloody-mindedness of her fiction find expression in another part of her introduction: "Most of the sense impressions of my childhood were pleasant . . . I remember the taste of Mallard ducks—too pretty to kill, with their lovely plumage, but luscious eating—domestic chicken and wild squirrel . . . Things had more flavor then."

In "Prott" (1953), a scientist-observer becomes more and more obsessed with the titular aliens once he starts observing them, with implications both funny and disturbing. "Prott" is classic St. Clair: darkly absurd, at times horrific, and engaged in playing out the implications of its own twisted logic no matter where it leads. The story is one of the most original collected in this anthology.

PROTT

Margaret St. Clair

"Read it," said the spaceman. "You'll find it interesting—under the circumstances. It's not long. One of the salvage crews found it tied to a signal rocket just outside the asteroid belt. It'd been there quite a while.

"I thought of taking it to somebody at the university, a historian or somebody, but I don't suppose they'd be interested. They don't have any more free time than anybody else."

He handed a metal cylinder to Fox, across the table, and ordered drinks for them both. Fox sipped from his glass before he opened the tube.

"Sure you want me to read it now?" he asked. "Not much of a way to spend our free time."

"Sure, go ahead and read it. What difference does it make?"

So Fox spread out the emtex sheets. He began to read.

Dating a diary in deep space offers special problems. Philosophical problems, I mean—that immense "When is now?" which, vexatious enough within a solar system or even on the surface of a planet, becomes quite insoluble in deep space except empirically or by predicating a sort of super-time, an enormous Present Moment which would extend over everything. And yet a diary entry must be dated, if only for convenience. So I will call today Tuesday and take the date of April 21 from the gauges.

Tuesday it is.

On this Tuesday, then, I am quite well and cheerful, snug and comfortable in the *Ellis*. The *Ellis* is a model of comfort and convenience; a man who couldn't be comfortable in it couldn't be comfortable anywhere. As to where I am, I could get the precise data from the calcula-

tors, but I think, for the casual purposes of this record, it's enough to say that I am almost at the edges of the area where the prott are said to abound. And my speed is almost exactly that at which they are supposed to appear.

I said I was well and cheerful. I am. But just under my euphoria, just at the edge of consciousness, I am aware of an intense loneliness. It's a normal response to the deep-space situation, I think. And I am upborne by the feeling that I stand on the threshold of unique scientific discoveries.

Thursday the twenty-sixth (my days are more than twenty-four hours long). Today my loneliness is definitely conscious. I am troubled, too, by the fear that perhaps the prott won't—aren't going to—put in an appearance. After all, their existence is none too well confirmed. And then what becomes of all my plans, of my smug confidence of a niche for myself in the hall of fame of good investigators?

It seemed like a brilliant idea when I was on Earth. I know the bursar thought so, too, when I asked for funds for the project. To investigate the life habits of a non-protoplasmic form of life, with special emphasis on its reproduction— excellent! But now?

Saturday, April 30. Still no prott. But I am feeling better. I went over my files on them and again it seems to me that there is only one conclusion possible:

They exist.

Over an enormous sector in the depth of space, during many years, they have been sighted. For my own comfort, let's list the known facts about prott.

First, they are a non-protoplasmic form of life. (How could they be otherwise, in this light-less, heatless gulf?) Second, their bodily organi-zation is probably electrical. Simmons, who was electrical engineer on the *Thor*, found that his batteries showed discharges when prott were around. Third, they appear only to ships which are in motion between certain rates of speed. (Whether motion at certain speeds attracts them, or whether it is only at certain frequen-cies that they are visible, we don't know.) Fourth, whether or not they are intelligent, they are to some extent telepathic, according to the reports. This fact, of course, is my hope of communicating with them at all. And fifth, prott have been evocatively if unscientifically described as looking like big poached eggs.

On the basis of these facts, I've aspired to be the Columbus—or, more accurately, the Dr. Kinsey—of the prott. Well, it's good to know that, lonely and rather worried as I am, I can still laugh at my own jokes.

May third. I saw my first prott. More later. It's enough for now: I saw my first prott.

May fourth. The *Ellis* has all-angle viewing plates, through 360 degrees. I had set up an automatic signal, and yesterday it rang. My heart thumping with an almost painful excite-ment, I ran to the battery of plates.

There it was, seemingly some five yards long, a cloudy, whitish thing. There was a hint of a large yellow nucleus. Damned if the thing *didn't* look like a big poached egg!

I saw at once why everyone has assumed that prott are life-forms and not, for example, minute spaceships, robots, or machines of some sort. The thing had the irregular, illogical sym-metry of life.

I stood goggling at it. It wasn't alarming,

even in its enormous context. After a moment, it seemed to flirt away from the ship with the watery ease of a fish.

I waited hopefully, but it didn't come back.

May 4. No prott. Question: since there is so lit-tle light in deep space how was I able to see it? It wasn't luminous.

I wish I had had more training in electron-ics and allied subjects. But the bursar thought it more important to send out a man trained in survey techniques.

May 5. No prott.

May 6. No prott. But I have been having very odd thoughts.

May eighth. As I half-implied in my last entry, the ideas I have been having (such odd ideas— they made me feel, mentally, as if some support-ing membrane of my personality were being overstrained) were an indication of the proxim-ity of prott.

I had just finished eating lunch today when the automatic signal rang. I hurried to the view-ers. There, perfectly clear against their jet-black background, were three prott. Two were almost identical; one was slightly smaller in size. I had retraced over and over in my mind the glimpse of the one prott I had had before, but now that three of them were actually present in the viewers, I could only stare at them. They're not alarming, but they do have an odd effect upon the mind.

After several tense seconds, I recovered my wits. I pressed a button to set the automatic photographic records going. I'd put in plates to cover the whole spectrum of radiant energy, and it will be interesting when I go to develop my pictures to see what frequencies catch the prott best. I also—this was more difficult—began to send out the basic "Who? Who? Who?" in which all telepathic communicators are trained.

I have become reasonably good at telepathy through practice, but I have no natural talent for it. I remember McIlwrath telling me jokingly, just before I left New York, that I'd never have trouble with one of the pitfalls of natural telepaths—transmitting a desired answer into the mind of a subject by telepathy. I suppose any deficiency has some advantageous side.

I began to send out my basic "Who?" It may have been only a coincidence, but as soon as the fourth or fifth impulse had left my mind, all three prott slid out of the viewing plates. They didn't come back. It would seem that my attempts at communication alarmed them. I hope not, though.

When I was convinced that they would not return for a while, I began to develop my plates. Those in the range of visible light show the prott very much as they appear to the eye. The infrared plates show nothing at all. But the ultraviolet-sensitive ones are really interesting.

Two of the prott appear as a network of luminous lines intricately knotted and braided. For some reason, I was reminded of the "elfish light" of Coleridge's water snakes, which "moved in tracks of shining white." The third prott, which I assume to have been the smaller one, gave an opaque, flattened-ovoid image, definitely smaller than that of its companions, with a round dark shadow in the centre. This shadow would appear to be the large yellow nucleus.

Question: do these photographic differences correspond to organizational differences? Probably, though it might be a matter of phase.

Further question: if the difference is in fact organizational, do we have here an instance of that specialization which, among protoplasmic creatures, would correspond to sex? It is possible. But such theorizing is bound to be plain guesswork.

May ninth (I see I gave up dating by days some while ago). No prott. I think it would be of some interest if, at this point, I were to try to put down my impression of those "odd thoughts" which I believe the prott inspired in me.

In the first place, there is a reluctance. I didn't want to think what I was thinking. This is not because the ideas were in themselves repellent or disgusting, but because they were uncongenial to my mind. I don't mean uncongenial to my personality or my idiosyncrasies, to the sum of differences that make up "me," but uncongenial to the whole biological orientation of my thinking. The differences between protoplasmic and non-protoplasmic life must be enormous.

In the second place, there is a frustration. I said, "I didn't want to think what I was thinking," but it would be equally true to say that I *couldn't* think it. Hence, I suppose, that sensation of ineffectuality.

And in the third place, there is a great boredom. Frustration often does make one feel bored, I suppose. I couldn't apprehend my own thoughts. But whenever I finally did, I found them boring. They were so remote, so incomprehensible, that they were uninteresting.

But the thoughts themselves? What were they? I can't say.

How confused all this is! Well, nothing is more tiresome than to describe the indescribable.

Perhaps it is true that the only creature that could understand the thoughts of a prott would be another prott.

May tenth. Were the "odd thoughts" the results of attempts on the prott's part to communicate with me? I don't think so. I believe they were near the ship, but out of "view-shot," so to speak, and I picked up some of their interpersonal communications accidentally.

I have been devoting a good deal of thought to the problem of communicating with them. It is too bad that there is no way of projecting a visual image of myself onto the exterior of the ship. I have Matheson's signalling devices, and next time—if there is a next—I shall certainly try them. I have little confidence in devices, however. I feel intuitively that it is going to have to be telepathy or nothing. But if they respond to the basic "Who?" with flight . . . well, I must think of something else.

Suppose I were to begin the attempt at contact with a "split question." "Splits" are hard for any telepath, almost impossible for me. But in just that difficulty, my hope of success might lie. After all, I suppose the prott flirted away from the ship at my "Who?" because mental contact with me was painful to them.

Later. Four of them are here now. I tried to split and they went away, but came back. I am going to try something else.

May eleventh. It worked. My "three-way split"—something I had only read about in journals, but that I would never have believed myself capable of—was astoundingly effective.

Not at first, though. At my first attempt, the prott darted right out of the viewers. I had a moment of despair. Then, with an almost human effect of hesitation, reluctance, and inclination, they came back. They clustered around the viewer. Once more I sent out my impulse; sweat was running down my back with the effort. And they stayed.

I don't know what I should have done if they hadn't. A split is exhausting because, in addition to the three normal axes of the mind, it involves a fourth one, at right angles to all the others. A telepath would know what I mean. But a three-way split is, in the old-fashioned phrase, "lifting yourself up by your bootstraps." Some experts say it's impossible. I still have trouble believing I brought it off.

I did, however. There was a sudden rush, a gush, of communication. I'd like to try to get it down now, while it's still fresh in my mind. But I'm too tired. Even the effort of using the playback is almost beyond me. I've got to rest.

Later. I've been asleep for four hours. I don't think I ever slept so soundly. Now I'm almost myself again, except that my hands shake.

I said I wanted to get the communication with the prott down while it was still fresh. Already it has begun to seem a little remote, I suppose because the subject matter was inherently alien. But the primary impression I retain of it is the gush, the suddenness. It was like pulling the cork out of a bottle of warm champagne which has been thoroughly shaken up.

In the middle, I had to try to maintain my mental balance in the flood. It was difficult; no wonder the effort left me so tired. But I did learn basic things.

One: identity. The prott are individuals, and though their designations for themselves escape me, they have individual consciousness. This is not a small matter. Some protoplasmic life-forms have only group consciousness. Each of the four prott in my viewer was thoroughly aware of itself as distinct from the others.

Two: difference. The prott were not only aware of identity, they were aware of differences of class between themselves. And I am of the opinion that these differences correspond to those shown on my photographic plates.

Three: place. The prott are quite clearly conscious that they are *here* and not somewhere else. This may seem either trivial or so basic as not to be worth bothering with. But there are whole groups of protoplasmic life-forms on Venus whose only cognizance of place is a distinction between "me" and "not-me."

Four: time. For the prott, time is as it is for us, an irreversible flowing in one direction only. I caught in their thinking a hint of a discrimination between biological (for such a life-form? That is what it seemed) time and something else, I am not sure what.

Beyond these four basic things, I am unsure. I do feel, though it is perhaps over-optimistic of me, that further communication, communication of great interest, is possible. I feel that I may be able to discover what their optimum life conditions and habitat are. I do not despair of discovering how they reproduce themselves.

I have the feeling that there is something they want very much to tell me.

May thirteenth. Six prott today. According to my photographic record, only one of them was of the opaque solid-nucleus kind. The others all showed the luminous light-tracked mesh.

The communication was difficult. It is exhausting to me physically. I had again that sense of psychic pressure, of urgency, in their sendings. If I only knew what they wanted to "talk" about, it would be so much easier for me.

I have the impression that they have a psychic itch they want me to help them scratch. That's silly? Yes, I know, yet that is the odd impression I have.

After they were gone, I analyzed my photographs carefully. The knotted light meshes are not identical in individuals. If the patterns are constant for individuals, it would seem that two of the light-mesh kind have been here before.

What do they want to talk about?

May fourteenth. Today the prott—seven of them—and I communicated about habitat. This much is fairly certain. It would appear— and I think that from now on any statement I make about them is going to have to be heavily qualified—it would appear that they are not necessarily confined to the lightless, heatless depths of space. I can't be sure about this. But I thought I got the hint of something "solid" in their thinking.

Wild speculation: do they get their energy from stars?

Behind their sendings, I got again the hint of some other more desired communication. Something which at once attracts and—repels? frightens? embarrasses?

Sometimes the humor of my situation comes to me suddenly. An embarrassed prott! But I suppose there's no reason why not.

All my visitors today were of the knotted-network kind.

May sixteenth. No prott yesterday or today.

May eighteenth. At last! Three prott! From subsequent analysis of the network patterns, all had been here to interview me before. We began communication about habitat and what, with protoplasm, would be metabolic process, but they did not seem interested. They left soon.

Why do they visit the ship, anyhow? Curiosity? That motive must not be so powerful by now. Because of something they want from me? I imagine so; it is again an awareness of some psychic itch. And that gives me a lead as to the course I should follow.

The next time they appear, I shall try to be more passive in my communications. I shall try not to lead them on to any particular subject. Not only is this good interviewing technique, it is essential in this case if I am to gain their full cooperation.

May 20. After a fruitless wait yesterday, today there was one lone prott. In accordance with my recent decision, I adopted a highly passive attitude toward it. I sent out signals of willingness and receptivity, and I waited, watching the prott.

For five or ten minutes there was "silence." The prott moved about in the viewers with an affect of restlessness, though it might have been any other emotion, of course. Suddenly, with great haste and urgency, it began to send. I had again that image of the cork blowing out of the champagne bottle.

Its sending was remarkably difficult for me to follow. At the end of the first three minutes or so, I was wringing wet with sweat. Its communications were repetitive, urgent, and, I believe, pleasurable. I simply had no terms into which to translate them. They seemed to involve many verbs.

I "listened" passively, trying to preserve my mental equilibrium. My bewilderment increased as the prott continued to send. Finally I had to recognize that I was getting to a point where intellectual frustration would interfere with my telepathy. I ventured to put a question, a simple "Please classify" to the prott.

Its sending slackened and then ceased abruptly. It disappeared.

What did I learn from the interview? That the passive approach is the correct one, and that a prott will send freely (and most confusingly, as far as I am concerned) if it is not harassed with questions or directed to a particular topic. What I didn't learn was what the prott was sending about.

Whatever it was, I have the impression that it was highly agreeable to the prott.

Later—I have been rereading the notes I made on my sessions with the prott. What has been the matter with me? I wonder at my blindness. For the topic about which the prott was sending—the pleasurable, repetitive, embarrassing topic, the one about which it could not bear to be questioned, the subject which involved so many verbs—that topic could be nothing other than its sex life.

When put thus baldly, it sounds ridiculous. I make haste to qualify it. We don't as yet—and what a triumph it is to be able to say "as yet"—know anything about the manner in which prott reproduce themselves. They may, for example, increase by a sort of fission. They

may be dioecious, as so much highly organized life is. Or their reproductive cycle may involve the cooperative activity of two, three, or even more different sorts of prott.

So far, I have seen only the two sorts, those with the solid nucleus, and those with the intricate network of light. That does not mean there may not be other kinds.

But what I am driving at is this: the topic about which the prott communicated with me today is one which, to the prott, has the same emotional and psychic value that sex has to protoplasmic life.

(Somehow, at this point, I am reminded of a little anecdote of my grandmother's. She used to say that there are four things in a dog's life which it is important for it to keep in mind, one for each foot. The things are food, food, sex, *and food*. She bred dachshunds and she knew. Question: does my coming up with this recollection at this time mean that I suspect the prott's copulatory activity is also nutritive, like the way in which amoeba conjugate? Their exchange of nuclei seems to have a beneficial effect on their metabolism.)

Be that as it may, I now have a thesis to test in my dealings with the prott!

May 21. There were seven prott in the viewer when the signal rang. While I watched, more and more arrived. It was impossible to count them accurately, but I think there must have been at least fifteen.

They started communicating almost immediately. Not wanting to disturb them with directives, I attempted to "listen" passively, but the effect on me was that of being caught in a crowd of people all talking at once. After a few minutes, I was compelled to ask them to send one at a time.

From then on, the sending was entirely orderly.

Orderly, but incomprehensible. So much so that, at the end of some two hours, I was forced to break off the interview.

It is the first time I have ever done such a thing.

Why did I do it? My motives are not entirely clear even to myself. I was trying to receive passively, keeping in mind the theory I had formed about the protts' communication. (And let me say at this point that I have found nothing to contradict it. Nothing whatever.) Yet, as time passed, my bewilderment increased almost painfully. Out of the mass of chaotic, repetitive material presented to me, I was able to form *not one single clear idea*.

I would not have believed that a merely intellectual frustration could be so difficult to take.

The communication itself was less difficult than yesterday. I must think.

I have begun to lose weight.

June twelfth. I have not made an entry in my diary for a long time. In the interval, I have had thirty-six interviews with prott.

What emerges from these sessions, which are so painful and frustrating to me, so highly enjoyed by the prott?

First, communication with them has become very much easier. It has become, in fact, too easy. I continually find their thoughts intruding on me at times when I cannot welcome them—when I am eating, writing up my notes, or trying to sleep. But the strain of communication is much less and I suppose that does constitute an advance.

Second, out of the welter of material presented to me, I have at last succeeded in forming one fairly clear idea. That is that the main topic of the prott's communication is a process that could be represented verbally as ——ing the ——. I add at once that the blanks do not necessarily represent an obscenity. I have, in fact, no idea what they *do* represent.

(The phrases that come into my mind in this connection are "kicking the bucket" and "belling the cat." It may not be without significance that one of these phrases relates to death and

the other to danger. Communication with prott is so unsatisfactory that one cannot afford to neglect any intimations that might clarify it. It is possible that ——ing the —— is something which is potentially dangerous to prott, but that's only a guess. I could have it all wrong, and I probably do.)

At any rate, my future course has become clear. From now on I will attempt, by every mental means at my disposal, to get the prott to specify what ——ing the —— is. There is no longer any fear of losing their cooperation. Even as I dictate these words to the playback, they are sending more material about ——ing the —— to me.

June 30. The time has gone very quickly, and yet each individual moment has dragged. I have had fifty-two formal interviews with prott— they appear in crowds ranging from fifteen to forty or so—and countless informal ones. My photographic record shows that more than 90 percent of those that have appeared have been of the luminous-network kind.

In all these communications, what have I learned? It gives me a sort of bitter satisfaction to say: "Nothing at all."

I am too chagrined to go on.

July 1. I don't mean that I haven't explored avenue after avenue. For instance, at one time it appeared that ——ing the —— had something to do with the intersections of the luminous network in prott of that sort. When I attempted to pursue this idea, I met with a negative that seemed amused as well as indignant.

They indicated that ——ing the —— was concerned with the whitish body surfaces, but when I picked up the theme, I got another negative signal. And so on. I must have attacked the problem from fifty different angles, but I had to give up on all of them. ——ing the ——, it would appear, is electrical, nonelectrical, solitary, dual, triple, communal, constant, never done at all. At one time I thought that it might apply to any pleasurable activity, but the prott signalled that I was all wrong. I broke that session off short.

Outside of their baffling communications on the subject of ——ing the ——, I have learned almost nothing from the prott.

(How sick I am of them and their inane, vacuous babbling! The phrases of our communication ring in my mind for hours afterward. They haunt me like a clinging odor or stubbornly lingering taste.)

During one session, a prott (solid nucleus, I think, but I am not sure) informed me that they could live under a wide variety of conditions, provided there was a source of radiant energy not too remote. Besides that scrap of information, I have an impression that they are grateful to me for listening to them. Their feelings, I think, could be expressed in the words "understanding and sympathetic."

I don't know why they think so, I'm sure. I would rather communicate with a swarm of dogfish, which are primitively telepathic, than listen to any more prott.

I have had to punch another hole in my wristwatch strap to take up the slack. This makes the third one.

July third. It is difficult for me to use the playback, the prott are sending so hard. I have scarcely a moment's rest from their communications, all concerned with the same damned subject. But I have come to a resolve: I am going home.

Yes, home. It may be that I have failed in my project, because of inner weaknesses. It may be that no man alive could have accomplished more. I don't know. But I ache to get away from them and the flabby texture of their babbling minds. If only there were some way of shutting them off, of stopping my mental ears against them temporarily, I think I could stand it. But there isn't.

I'm going home. I've started putting course data in the computers.

July fourth. They say they are going back with me. It seems they like me so much, they don't want to be without me. I will have to decide.

July twelfth. It is dreadfully hard to think, for they are sending like mad.

I am not so altruistic, so unselfish, that I would condemn myself to a lifetime of listening to prott if I could get out of it. But suppose I ignore the warnings of instinct, the dictates of conscience, and return to Earth, anyhow—what will be the result?

The prott will go with me. I will not be rid of them. And I will have loosed a wave of prott on Earth.

They want passionately to send about ——ing the ——. They have discovered that Earthmen are potential receptors. I have myself to blame for that. If I show them the way to Earth . . .

The dilemma is inherently comic, I suppose. It is nonetheless real. Oh, it is possible that there is some way of destroying prott, and that the resources of Earth intelligence might discover it. Or, failing that, we might be able to work out a way of living with them. But the danger is too great; I dare not ask my planet to face it. I will stay here.

The *Ellis* is a strong, comfortable ship. According to my calculations, there is enough air, water, and food to last me the rest of my natural life. Power—since I am not going back—I have in abundance. I ought to get along all right.

Except for the prott. When I think of them, my heart contracts with despair and revulsion. And yet—a scientist must be honest—it is not all despair. I feel a little sorry for them, a little flattered at their need for me. And I am not, even now, altogether hopeless. Perhaps someday—*someday*—I shall understand the prott.

I am going to put this diary in a permaloy cylinder and jet it away from the ship with a signal rocket. I can soup up the rocket's charge with power from the fuel tanks. I have tried it on the calculators, and I think the rocket can make it to the edge of the gravitational field of the solar system.

Good-bye, Earth. I am doing it for you. Remember me.

Fox put the last page of the manuscript down. "The poor bastard," he said.

"Yeah, the poor bastard. Sitting out there in deep space, year after year, listening to those things bellyaching, and thinking what a savior he was."

"I can't say I feel much sympathy for him, really. I suppose they followed the signal rocket back."

"Yeah. And then they increased. Oh, he fixed it, all right."

There was a depressed silence. Then Fox said, "I'd better go. Impatient."

"Mine, too."

They said good-bye to each other on the curb. Fox stood waiting, still not quite hopeless. But after a moment the hateful voice within his head began:

"I want to tell you more about ——ing the ——."

The Liberation of Earth

WILLIAM TENN

William Tenn (pseudonym of Philip Klass, 1920–2010) was a British-American writer of science fiction. After serving in World War II, Klass began writing science fiction as William Tenn, publishing his first work of genre interest, "Alexander the Bait," for *Astounding Science Fiction* in 1946. He soon followed it with the brilliant and scathing time paradox tale "Brooklyn Project" (*Planet Stories*, 1948), which fell afoul of the 1940s zeitgeist, being rejected by prominent editors like John W. Campbell Jr. This type of rejection—along political lines—occurred more than once in Tenn's career and reflects poorly on the science fiction field.

From the first, Tenn was one of the genre's very few genuinely comic, genuinely incisive writers of short fiction. From 1950 onward he found a congenial market in *Galaxy*, where he published much of his best work before falling relatively quiet after about 1960, despite some stellar efforts like "The Ghost Standard" (1994), reprinted later in this volume. Despite his cheerful surface and the occasional zany humor of his stories, Tenn, like most real satirists, was fundamentally a pessimist, a writer who persisted in describing the bars of the prison; when the comic disguise was whipped off, as happened with some frequency, the result was salutary.

"The Liberation of Earth" was written as a response to the Korean War, although many readers, and later protesters, used it as a call to end the Vietnam War. The story was actually read aloud by student protesters in the 1960s at antiwar rallies. Yet in the beginning not one of the top science fiction magazines wanted to publish the story. It was eventually published in *Future Science Fiction* (1953), considered near the bottom of the barrel of science fiction markets. At the time of publication, the story received little attention, but it has gone on to become a much-reprinted standard.

In *Immodest Proposals: The Complete Science Fiction of William Tenn, Volume 1*, the author writes, "The period covered [by the Korean War] was roughly the same as the Red-scare years that began with the Dies Committee and ended with the Senate censure of Joseph McCarthy in 1954. As a result, the organized Left inveighed against what it called 'Truman's War,' and urged us to get the hell out of Korea; the official Right not only supported the war but considered it perhaps the most crucial element in the battle against the godless Communists. In writing the story, all I wanted to do is point out what a really awful thing it was to be a Korean (and later a Vietnamese) in such a situation."

Today, "The Liberation of Earth" is considered one of the classic science fiction stories of all time.

THE LIBERATION OF EARTH

William Tenn

This, then, is the story of our liberation. Suck air and grab clusters. Heigh-ho, here is the tale.

August was the month, a Tuesday in August. These words are meaningless now, so far have we progressed; but many things known and discussed by our primitive ancestors, our unliberated, unreconstructed forefathers, are devoid of sense to our free minds. Still the tale must be told, with all of its incredible place-names and vanished points of reference.

Why must it be told? Have any of you a *better* thing to do? We have had water and weeds and lie in a valley of gusts. So rest, relax, and listen. And suck air, suck air.

On a Tuesday in August, the ship appeared in the sky over France in a part of the world then known as Europe. Five miles long the ship was, and word has come down to us that it looked like an enormous silver cigar.

The tale goes on to tell of the panic and consternation among our forefathers when the ship abruptly materialized in the summer-blue sky. How they ran, how they shouted, how they pointed!

How they excitedly notified the United Nations, one of their chiefest institutions, that a strange metal craft of incredible size had materialized over their land. How they sent an order *here* to cause military aircraft to surround it with loaded weapons, gave instructions *there* for hastily grouped scientists, with signaling apparatus, to approach it with friendly gestures. How, under the great ship, men with cameras took pictures of it; men with typewriters wrote stories about it; and men with concessions sold models of it.

All these things did our ancestors, enslaved and unknowing, do.

Then a tremendous slab snapped up in the middle of the ship, and the first of the aliens stepped out in the complex tripodal gait that all humans were shortly to know and love so well. He wore a metallic garment to protect him from the effects of our atmospheric peculiarities, a garment of the opaque, loosely folded type that these, the first of our liberators, wore throughout their stay on Earth.

Speaking in a language none could understand, but booming deafeningly through a huge mouth about halfway up his twenty-five feet of height, the alien discoursed for exactly one hour, waited politely for a response when he had finished, and, receiving none, retired into the ship.

That night, the first of our liberation! Or the first of our first liberation, should I say? *That* night, anyhow! Visualize our ancestors scurrying about their primitive intricacies: playing ice hockey, televising, smashing atoms, red-baiting, conducting giveaway shows, and signing affidavits—all the incredible minutiae that made the olden times such a frightful mass of cumulative detail in which to live—as compared with the breathless and majestic simplicity of the present.

The big question, of course, was—what had the alien said? Had he called on the human race to surrender? Had he announced that he was on a mission of peaceful trade and, having made what he considered a reasonable offer—for, let us say, the north polar ice cap—politely withdrawn so that we could discuss his terms among ourselves in relative privacy? Or, possibly, had he merely announced that he was the newly appointed ambassador to Earth from a friendly and intelligent race—and would we please direct him to the proper authority so that he might submit his credentials?

Not to know was quite maddening.

Since the decision rested with the diplomats, it was the last possibility which was held, very late that night, to be most likely; and early the next morning, accordingly, a delegation from the United Nations waited under the belly of the motionless starship. The delegation had been instructed to welcome the aliens to the outermost limits of its collective linguistic ability. As an additional earnest of mankind's friendly intentions, all military craft patrolling the air about the great ship were ordered to carry no more than one atom bomb in their racks, and to fly a small white flag—along with the UN banner and their own national emblem. Thus did our ancestors face this, the ultimate challenge of history.

When the alien came forth a few hours later, the delegation stepped up to him, bowed, and, in the three official languages of the United Nations—English, French, and Russian—asked him to consider this planet his home. He listened to them gravely, and then launched into his talk of the day before—which was evidently as highly charged with emotion and significance to him as it was completely incomprehensible to the representatives of world government.

Fortunately, a cultivated young Indian member of the secretariat detected a suspicious similarity between the speech of the alien and an obscure Bengali dialect whose anomalies he had once puzzled over. The reason, as we all know now, was that the last time Earth had been visited by aliens of this particular type, humanity's most advanced civilization lay in a moist valley in Bengal; extensive dictionaries of that language had been written, so that speech with the natives of Earth would present no problem to any subsequent exploring party.

However, I move ahead of my tale, as one who would munch on the succulent roots before the dryer stem. Let me rest and suck air for a moment. Heigh-ho, truly those were tremendous experiences for our kind.

You, sir, now you sit back and listen. You are not yet of an age to Tell the Tale. I remember, *well enough do I remember*, how my father told it, and his father before him. You will wait your turn as I did; you will listen until too much high land between water holes blocks me off from life.

Then *you* may take your place in the juiciest weed patch and, reclining gracefully between sprints, recite the great epic of our liberation to the carelessly exercising young.

Pursuant to the young Hindu's suggestions, the one professor of comparative linguistics in the world capable of understanding and conversing in this peculiar version of the dead dialect was summoned from an academic convention in New York, where he was reading a paper he had been working on for eighteen years: "An Initial Study of Apparent Relationships Between Several Past Participles in Ancient Sanskrit and an Equal Number of Noun Substantives in Modern Szechuanese."

Yea, verily, all these things—and more, many more—did our ancestors in their besotted ignorance contrive to do. May we not count our freedoms indeed?

The disgruntled scholar, minus—as he kept insisting bitterly—some of his most essential word lists, was flown by fastest jet to the area south of Nancy, which, in those long-ago days, lay in the enormous black shadow of the alien spaceship.

Here he was acquainted with his task by the United Nations delegation, whose nervousness had not been allayed by a new and disconcerting development. Several more aliens had emerged from the ship carrying great quantities of immense, shimmering metal which they proceeded to assemble into something that was obviously a machine—though it was taller than any skyscraper man had ever built, and seemed to make noises to itself like a talkative and sentient creature. The first alien still stood courteously in the neighborhood of the profusely perspiring diplomats; ever and anon he would go through his little speech again, in a language that had been almost forgotten when the cornerstone of the library of Alexandria was laid. The men from the UN would reply, each one hoping desperately to make up for the alien's lack of familiarity with his own tongue by such devices as hand gestures and facial expressions. Much later, a commission of anthropologists and psychologists brilliantly pointed out the difficulties in such physical, gestural communication with creatures possessing—as these aliens did—five manual appendages and a single, unwinking compound eye of the type the insects rejoice in.

The problems and agonies of the professor as he was trundled about the world in the wake of the aliens, trying to amass a usable vocabulary in a language whose peculiarities he could only extrapolate from the limited samples supplied him by one who must inevitably speak it with the most outlandish of foreign accents—these vexations were minor indeed compared to the disquiet felt by the representatives of world government. They beheld the extraterrestrial visitors move every day to a new site on their planet and proceed to assemble there a titanic structure of flickering metal which muttered nostalgically to itself, as if to keep alive the memory of those faraway factories which had given it birth.

True, there was always the alien who would pause in his evidently supervisory labors to release the set little speech; but not even the excellent manners he displayed, in listening to upward of fifty-six replies in as many languages, helped dispel the panic caused whenever a human scientist, investigating the shimmering machines, touched a projecting edge and promptly shrank into a disappearing pinpoint. This, while not a frequent occurrence, happened often enough to cause chronic indigestion and insomnia among human administrators.

. . .

Finally, having used up most of his nervous system as fuel, the professor collated enough of the language to make conversation possible. He—and, through him, the world—was thereupon told the following:

The aliens were members of a highly advanced civilization which had spread its culture throughout the entire galaxy. Cognizant of the limitations of the as-yet-underdeveloped animals who had latterly become dominant upon Earth, they had placed us in a sort of benevolent ostracism. Until either we or our institutions had evolved to a level permitting, say, at least *associate* membership in the Galactic Federation (under the sponsoring tutelage, for the first few millennia, of one of the older, more widespread and important species in that federation)—until that time, all invasions of our privacy and ignorance—except for a few scientific expeditions conducted under conditions of great secrecy—had been strictly forbidden by universal agreement.

Several individuals who had violated this ruling—at great cost to our racial sanity, and enormous profit to our reigning religions—had been so promptly and severely punished that no known infringements had occurred for some time. Our recent growth curve had been satisfactory enough to cause hopes that a bare thirty or forty centuries more would suffice to place us on applicant status with the federation.

Unfortunately, the peoples of this stellar community were many, and varied as greatly in their ethical outlook as in their biological composition. Quite a few species lagged a considerable social distance behind the Dendi, as our visitors called themselves. One of these, a race of horrible, wormlike organisms known as the Troxxt—almost as advanced technologically as they were retarded in moral development—had suddenly volunteered for the position of sole and absolute ruler of the galaxy. They had seized control of several key suns, with their attendant planetary systems, and, after a calculated decimation of the races thus captured, had announced their intention of punishing with a merciless extinction all species unable to appreciate from these object lessons the value of unconditional surrender.

In despair, the Galactic Federation had turned to the Dendi, one of the oldest, most selfless, and yet most powerful of races in civilized space, and commissioned them—as the military arm of the federation—to hunt down the Troxxt, defeat them wherever they had gained illegal suzerainty, and destroy forever their power to wage war.

This order had come almost too late. Everywhere the Troxxt had gained so much the advantage of attack that the Dendi were able to contain them only by enormous sacrifice. For centuries now, the conflict had careened across our vast island universe. In the course of it, densely populated planets had been disintegrated; suns had been blasted into novae; and whole groups of stars ground into swirling cosmic dust.

A temporary stalemate had been reached a short while ago, and—reeling and breathless—both sides were using the lull to strengthen weak spots in their perimeter.

Thus, the Troxxt had finally moved into the till-then-peaceful section of space that contained our solar system—among others. They were thoroughly uninterested in our tiny planet with its meager resources, nor did they care much for such celestial neighbors as Mars or Jupiter. They established their headquarters on a planet of Proxima Centauri—the star nearest our own sun—and proceeded to consolidate their offensive-defensive network between Rigel and Aldebaran. At this point in their explanation, the Dendi pointed out, the exigencies of interstellar strategy tended to become too complicated for anything but three-dimensional maps; let us here accept the simple statement, they suggested, that it became immediately vital for them to strike rapidly, and make the Troxxt position on Proxima Centauri untenable—to establish a base inside their lines of communication.

The most likely spot for such a base was Earth.

. . .

The Dendi apologized profusely for intruding on our development, an intrusion which might cost us dear in our delicate developmental state. But, as they explained—in impeccable pre-Bengali—before their arrival we had, in effect, become (all unknowingly) a satrapy of the awful Troxxt. We could now consider ourselves liberated.

We thanked them much for that.

Besides, their leader pointed out proudly, the Dendi were engaged in a war for the sake of civilization itself, against an enemy so horrible, so obscene in its nature, and so utterly filthy in its practices that it was unworthy of the label of intelligent life. They were fighting, not only for themselves, but for every loyal member of the Galactic Federation; for every small and helpless species; for every obscure race too weak to defend itself against a ravaging conqueror. Would humanity stand aloof from such a conflict?

There was just a slight bit of hesitation as the information was digested. Then—"No!" humanity roared back through such mass-communication media as television, newspapers, reverberating jungle drums, and mule-mounted backwoods messengers. "We will not stand aloof. We will help you destroy this menace to the very fabric of civilization! Just tell us what you want us to do!"

Well, nothing in particular, the aliens replied with some embarrassment. Possibly in a little while there might be something—several little things, in fact—which could be quite useful; but, for the moment, if we would concentrate on not getting in their way when they serviced their gun mounts, they would be very grateful, really. . . .

This reply tended to create a large amount of uncertainty among the two billion of Earth's human population. For several days afterward, there was a planet-wide tendency—the legend has come down to us—of people failing to meet each other's eyes.

But then man rallied from this substantial blow to his pride. He would be useful, be it ever so humbly, to the race which had liberated him from potential subjugation by the ineffably ugly Troxxt. For this, let us remember well our ancestors! Let us hymn their sincere efforts amid their ignorance!

All standing armies, all air and sea fleets, were reorganized into guard patrols around the Dendi weapons; no human might approach within two miles of the murmuring machinery without a pass countersigned by the Dendi. Since they were never known to sign such a pass during the entire period of their stay on this planet, however, this loophole provision was never exercised as far as is known; and the immediate neighborhood of the extraterrestrial weapons became and remained henceforth wholesomely free of two-legged creatures.

Cooperation with our liberators took precedence over all other human activities. The order of the day was a slogan first given voice by a Harvard professor of government in a querulous radio roundtable called "Man's Place in a Somewhat Overcivilized Universe."

"Let us forget our individual egos and collective conceits," the professor cried at one point. "Let us subordinate everything—to the end that the freedom of the solar system in general, and Earth in particular, must and shall be preserved!"

Despite its mouth-filling qualities, this slogan was repeated everywhere. Still, it was difficult sometimes to know exactly what the Dendi wanted—partly because of the limited number of interpreters available to the heads of the various sovereign states, and partly because of their leader's tendency to vanish into his ship after ambiguous and equivocal statements—such as the curt admonition to "evacuate Washington!"

On that occasion, both the secretary of state and the American president perspired fearfully through five hours of a July day in all the silk-hatted, stiff-collared, dark-suited diplomatic regalia that the barbaric past demanded of political leaders who would deal with the representatives of another people. They waited and wilted beneath the enormous ship—which no human had ever been invited to enter, despite the wistful hints constantly thrown out by university professors and aeronautical designers—they waited patiently and wetly for the Dendi leader to emerge and let them know whether he had meant the state of Washington or Washington, DC.

The tale comes down to us at this point as a tale of glory. The Capitol building taken apart in a few days and set up almost intact in the foothills of the Rocky Mountains; the missing archives that were later to turn up in the children's room of a public library in Dubuque, Iowa; the bottles of Potomac River water carefully borne westward and ceremoniously poured into the circular concrete ditch built around the president's mansion (from which, unfortunately, it was to evaporate within a week because of the relatively low humidity of the region)—all these are proud moments in the galactic history of our species, from which not even the later knowledge that the Dendi wished to build no gun site on the spot, nor even an ammunition dump, but merely a recreation hall for their troops, could remove any of the grandeur of our determined cooperation and most willing sacrifice.

There is no denying, however, that the ego of our race was greatly damaged by the discovery, in the course of a routine journalistic interview, that the aliens totaled no more powerful a group than a squad; and that their leader, instead of the great scientist and key military strategist that we might justifiably have expected the Galactic Federation to furnish for the protection of Terra, ranked as the interstellar equivalent of a buck sergeant.

That the president of the United States, the commander in chief of the army and the navy, had waited in such obeisant fashion upon a mere noncommissioned officer was hard for us to swallow, but that the impending Battle of Earth was to have a historical dignity only slightly higher than that of a patrol action was impossibly humiliating.

And then there was the matter of "lendi."

The aliens, while installing or servicing their planetwide weapon system, would occasionally fling aside an evidently unusable fragment of the talking metal. Separate from the machine of which it had been a component, the substance seemed to lose all those qualities which were deleterious to mankind and retain several which were quite useful indeed. For example, if a portion of the strange material was attached to any terrestrial metal—and insulated carefully from contact with other substances—it would, in a few hours, itself become exactly the metal that it touched, whether that happened to be zinc, gold, or pure uranium.

This stuff—"lendi," men have heard the aliens call it—was shortly in frantic demand in an economy ruptured by constant and unexpected emptyings of its most important industrial centers.

Everywhere the aliens went, to and from their weapon sites, hordes of ragged humans stood chanting—well outside the two-mile limit—"Any lendi, Dendi?" All attempts by law-enforcement agencies of the planet to put a stop to this shameless, wholesale begging were useless—especially since the Dendi themselves seemed to get some unexplainable pleasure out of scattering tiny pieces of lendi to the scrabbling multitude. When policemen and soldiery began to join the trampling, murderous dash to the corners of the meadows wherein had fallen the highly versatile and garrulous metal, governments gave up.

Mankind almost began to hope for the attack to come, so that it would be relieved of the festering consideration of its own patent inferiorities. A few of the more fanatically conservative among our ancestors probably even began to regret liberation.

They did, children; they did! Let us hope that these would-be troglodytes were among the very first to be dissolved and melted down by the red flame-balls. One cannot, after all, turn one's back on progress!

Two days before the month of September was over, the aliens announced that they had detected activity upon one of the moons of Saturn. The Troxxt were evidently threading their treacherous way inward through the solar system. Considering their vicious and deceitful propensities, the Dendi warned, an attack from these wormlike monstrosities might be expected at any moment.

Few humans went to sleep as the night rolled up to and past the meridian on which they dwelt. Almost all eyes were lifted to a sky carefully denuded of clouds by watchful Dendi. There was a brisk trade in cheap telescopes and bits of smoked glass in some sections of the planet, while other portions experienced a substantial boom in spells and charms of the all-inclusive, or omnibus, variety.

The Troxxt attacked in three cylindrical black ships simultaneously: one in the Southern Hemisphere, and two in the Northern. Great gouts of green flame roared out of their tiny craft, and everything touched by this imploded into a translucent, glasslike sand. No Dendi was hurt by these, however, and from each of the now-writhing gun mounts there bubbled forth a series of scarlet clouds which pursued the Troxxt hungrily, until forced by a dwindling velocity to fall back upon Earth.

Here they had an unhappy aftereffect. Any populated area into which these pale pink cloudlets chanced to fall was rapidly transformed into a cemetery—a cemetery, if the truth be told as it has been handed down to us, that had more the odor of the kitchen than the grave. The inhabitants of these unfortunate localities were subjected to enormous increases of temperature. Their skin reddened, then blackened; their hair and nails shriveled; their very flesh turned into liquid and boiled off their bones. Altogether a disagreeable way for one-tenth of the human race to die.

The only consolation was the capture of a black cylinder by one of the red clouds. When, as a result of this, it had turned white-hot and poured its substance down in the form of a metallic rainstorm, the two ships assaulting the Northern Hemisphere abruptly retreated to the asteroids into which the Dendi—because of severely limited numbers—steadfastly refused to pursue them.

In the next twenty-four hours, the aliens—*resident* aliens, let us say—held conferences, made repairs to their weapons, and commiserated with us. Humanity buried its dead. This last was a custom of our forefathers that was most worthy of note, and one that has not, of course, survived into modern times.

By the time the Troxxt returned, man was ready for them. He could not, unfortunately, stand to arms as he most ardently desired to do, but he could and did stand to optical instrument and conjurer's oration.

Once more the little red clouds burst joyfully into the upper reaches of the stratosphere; once more the green flames wailed and tore at the chattering spires of lendi; once more men died by the thousands in the boiling backwash of war. But this time, there was a slight difference: the green flames of the Troxxt abruptly changed color after the engagement had lasted three hours; they became darker, more bluish. And, as they did so, Dendi after Dendi collapsed at his station and died in convulsions.

The call for retreat was evidently sounded. The survivors fought their way to the tremendous ship in which they had come. With an explosion from her stern jets that blasted a red-hot furrow southward through France, and kicked Marseilles into the Mediterranean, the ship roared into space and fled home ignominiously.

Humanity steeled itself for the coming ordeal of horror under the Troxxt.

.　.　.

They were truly wormlike in form. As soon as the two night-black cylinders had landed, they strode from their ships, their tiny segmented bodies held off the ground by a complex harness supported by long and slender metal crutches. They erected a domelike fort around each ship—one in Australia and one in the Ukraine—captured the few courageous individuals who had ventured close to their landing sites, and disappeared back into the dark craft with their squirming prizes.

While some men drilled about nervously in the ancient military patterns, others pored anxiously over scientific texts and records pertaining to the visit of the Dendi—in the desperate hope of finding a way of preserving terrestrial independence against this ravening conqueror of the star-spattered galaxy.

And yet all this time, the human captives inside the artificially darkened spaceships (the Troxxt, having no eyes, not only had little use for light, but the more sedentary individuals among them actually found such radiation disagreeable to their sensitive, unpigmented skins) were not being tortured for information—nor vivisected in the earnest quest of knowledge on a slightly higher level—but educated.

Educated in the Troxxtian language, that is.

True it was that a large number found themselves utterly inadequate for the task which the Troxxt had set them, and temporarily became servants to the more successful students. And another, albeit smaller, group developed various forms of frustration hysteria—ranging from mild unhappiness to complete catatonic depression—over the difficulties presented by a language whose every verb was irregular, and whose myriads of prepositions were formed by noun-adjective combinations derived from the subject of the previous sentence. But, eventually, eleven human beings were released, to blink madly in the sunlight as certified interpreters of Troxxt.

These liberators, it seemed, had never visited Bengal in the heyday of its millennia-past civilization.

Yes, these *liberators*. For the Troxxt had landed on the sixth day of the ancient, almost mythical month of October. And October the Sixth is, of course, the Holy Day of the Second Liberation. Let us remember, let us revere. (If only we could figure out which day it is in our calendar!)

The tale the interpreters told caused men to hang their heads in shame and gnash their teeth at the deception they had allowed the Dendi to practice upon them.

True, the Dendi had been commissioned by the Galactic Federation to hunt the Troxxt down and destroy them. This was largely because the Dendi *were* the Galactic Federation. One of the first intelligent arrivals on the interstellar scene, the huge creatures had organized a vast police force to protect them and their power against any contingency of revolt that might arise in the future. This police force was ostensibly a congress of all thinking life-forms throughout the galaxy; actually, it was an efficient means of keeping them under rigid control.

Most species thus-far discovered were docile and tractable, however; the Dendi had been ruling from time immemorial, said they—very well, then, let the Dendi continue to rule. Did it make that much difference?

But, throughout the centuries, opposition to the Dendi grew—and the nuclei of the opposition were the protoplasm-based creatures. What, in fact, had come to be known as the Protoplasmic League.

Though small in number, the creatures whose life cycles were derived from the chemical and physical properties of protoplasm varied greatly in size, structure, and specialization. A galactic community deriving the main wells of its power from them would be a dynamic instead of a static place, where extragalactic travel would be encouraged, instead of being inhibited, as it was at present because of Dendi fears of meeting a superior civilization. It would

be a true democracy of species—a real biological republic—where all creatures of adequate intelligence and cultural development would enjoy a control of their destinies at present experienced by the silicon-based Dendi alone.

To this end, the Troxxt—the only important race which had steadfastly refused the complete surrender of armaments demanded of all members of the federation—had been implored by a minor member of the Protoplasmic League to rescue it from the devastation which the Dendi intended to visit upon it, as punishment for an unlawful exploratory excursion outside the boundaries of the galaxy.

Faced with the determination of the Troxxt to defend their cousins in organic chemistry, and the suddenly aroused hostility of at least two-thirds of the interstellar peoples, the Dendi had summoned a rump meeting of the Galactic Council; declared a state of revolt in being; and proceeded to cement their disintegrating rule with the blasted life-forces of a hundred worlds. The Troxxt, hopelessly outnumbered and out-equipped, had been able to continue the struggle only because of the great ingenuity and selflessness of other members of the Protoplasmic League, who had risked extinction to supply them with newly developed secret weapons.

Hadn't we guessed the nature of the beast from the enormous precautions it had taken to prevent the exposure of any part of its body to the intensely corrosive atmosphere of Earth? Surely the seamless, barely translucent suits which our recent visitors had worn for every moment of their stay on our world should have made us suspect a body chemistry developed from complex silicon compounds rather than those of carbon?

Humanity hung its collective head and admitted that the suspicion had never occurred to it.

Well, the Troxxt admitted generously, we were extremely inexperienced and possibly a little too trusting. Put it down to that.

Our naiveté, however costly to them—our liberators—would not be allowed to deprive us of that complete citizenship which the Troxxt were claiming as the birthright of all.

But as for our leaders, our probably corrupted, certainly irresponsible leaders . . .

The first executions of UN officials, heads of state, and pre-Bengali interpreters as "Traitors to Protoplasm"—after some of the lengthiest and most nearly-perfectly-fair trials in the history of Earth—were held a week after G-J Day (Galaxy-Joining Day), the inspiring occasion on which—amidst gorgeous ceremonies—humanity was invited to join, first the Protoplasmic League and thence the New and Democratic Galactic Federation of All Species, All Races.

Nor was that all. Whereas the Dendi had contemptuously shoved us to one side as they went about their business of making our planet safe for tyranny, and had—in all probability—built special devices which made the very touch of their weapons fatal for us, the Troxxt—with the sincere friendliness which had made their name a byword for democracy and decency wherever living creatures came together among the stars—our Second Liberators, as we lovingly called them, actually *preferred* to have us help them with the intensive, accelerating labor of planetary defense.

So humanity's intestines dissolved under the invisible glare of the forces used to assemble the new, incredibly complex weapons; men sickened and died, in scrabbling hordes, inside the mines which the Troxxt had made deeper than any we had dug hitherto; men's bodies broke open and exploded in the undersea oil-drilling sites which the Troxxt had declared were essential.

Children's schooldays were requested, too, in such collecting drives as "Platinum Scrap for Procyon" and "Radioactive Debris for Deneb." Housewives also were implored to save on salt whenever possible—this substance being useful to the Troxxt in literally dozens of incomprehensible ways—and colorful posters reminded: *"Don't salinate—sugarfy!"*

And over all—courteously caring for us like an intelligent parent—were our mentors, taking their giant supervisory strides on metallic crutches while their pale little bodies lay curled in the hammocks that swung from each paired length of shining leg.

Truly, even in the midst of a complete economic paralysis caused by the concentration of all major peculiar industrial injuries which our medical men were totally unequipped to handle, in the midst of all this mind-wracking disorganization, it was yet very exhilarating to realize that we had taken our lawful place in the future government of the galaxy and were even now helping to make the Universe Safe for Democracy.

But the Dendi returned to smash this idyll. They came in their huge, silvery spaceships, and the Troxxt, barely warned in time, just managed to rally under the blow and fight back in kind. Even so, the Troxxt ship in the Ukraine was almost immediately forced to flee to its base in the depths of space. After three days, the only Troxxt on Earth were the devoted members of a little band guarding the ship in Australia. They proved, in three or more months, to be as difficult to remove from the face of our planet as the continent itself; and since there was now a state of close and hostile siege, with the Dendi on one side of the globe and the Troxxt on the other, the battle assumed frightful proportions.

Seas boiled; whole steppes burned away; the climate itself shifted and changed under the grueling pressure of the cataclysm. By the time the Dendi solved the problem, the planet Venus had been blasted from the skies in the course of a complicated battle maneuver, and Earth had wobbled over as orbital substitute.

The solution was simple: since the Troxxt

were too firmly based on the small continent to be driven away, the numerically superior Dendi brought up enough firepower to disintegrate all Australia into an ash that muddied the Pacific. This occurred on the twenty-fourth of June, the Holy Day of First Reliberation. A day of reckoning for what remained of the human race, however.

How could we have been so naive, the Dendi wanted to know, as to be taken in by the chauvinistic pro-protoplasm propaganda? Surely, if physical characteristics were to be the criteria of our racial empathy, we would not orient ourselves on a narrow chemical basis! The Dendi life-plasma was based on silicon instead of carbon, true, but did not vertebrates—*appendaged* vertebrates, at that, such as we and the Dendi—have infinitely more in common, in spite of a *minor* biochemical difference or two, than vertebrates and legless, armless, slime-crawling creatures who happened, quite accidentally, to possess an identical organic substance?

As for this fantastic picture of life in the galaxy . . . *Well!* The Dendi shrugged their quintuple shoulders as they went about the intricate business of erecting their noisy weapons all over the rubble of our planet. Had we ever seen a representative of these protoplasmic races the Troxxt were supposedly protecting? No, nor would we. For as soon as a race—animal, vegetable, or mineral—developed enough to constitute even a *potential* danger to the sinuous aggressors, its civilization was systematically dismantled by the watchful Troxxt. We were in so primitive a state that they had not considered it at all risky to allow us the outward seeming of full participation.

Could we say we had learned a single useful piece of information about Troxxt technology—for all of the work we had done on their machines, for all of the lives we had lost in the process? No, of course not! We had merely contributed our might to the enslavement of far-off races who had done us no harm.

There was much that we had cause to feel guilty about, the Dendi told us gravely—once the few surviving interpreters of the pre-Bengali dialect had crawled out of hiding. But our collective onus was as nothing compared to that borne by "vermicular collaborationists"—those traitors who had supplanted our martyred former leaders. And then there were the unspeakable human interpreters who had had linguistic traffic with creatures destroying a two-million-year-old galactic peace! Why, killing was almost too good for them, the Dendi murmured as they killed them.

When the Troxxt ripped their way back into possession of Earth some eighteen months later, bringing us the sweet fruits of the Second Reliberation—as well as a complete and most convincing rebuttal of the Dendi—there were few humans found who were willing to accept with any real enthusiasm the responsibilities of newly opened and highly paid positions in language, science, and government.

Of course, since the Troxxt, in order to reliberate Earth, had found it necessary to blast a tremendous chunk out of the Northern Hemisphere, there were very few humans to be found in the first place. . . .

Even so, many of these committed suicide rather than assume the title of secretary general of the United Nations when the Dendi came back for the glorious Re-Reliberation, a short time after that. This was the liberation, by the way, which swept the deep collar of matter off our planet, and gave it what our forefathers came to call a pear-shaped look.

Possibly it was at this time—possibly a liberation or so later—that the Troxxt and the Dendi discovered the Earth had become far too eccentric in its orbit to possess the minimum safety conditions demanded of a Combat Zone. The battle, therefore, zigzagged coruscatingly and murderously away in the direction of Aldebaran.

That was nine generations ago, but the tale that has been handed down from parent to child, to child's child, has lost little in the telling. You hear it now from me almost exactly as *I* heard it. From my father I heard it as I ran with him from water puddle to distant water puddle, across the searing heat of yellow sand. From my mother I heard it as we sucked air and frantically grabbed at clusters of thick green weed, whenever the planet beneath us quivered in omen of a geological spasm that might bury us in its burned-out body, or a cosmic gyration threatened to fling us into empty space.

Yes, even as we do now did we do then, telling the same tale, running the same frantic race across miles of unendurable heat for food and water; fighting the same savage battles with the giant rabbits for each other's carrion—and always, ever and always, sucking desperately at the precious air, which leaves our world in greater quantities with every mad twist of its orbit.

Naked, hungry, and thirsty came we into the world, and naked, hungry, and thirsty do we scamper our lives out upon it, under the huge and never-changing sun.

The same tale it is, and the same traditional ending it has as that I had from my father and his father before him. Suck air, grab clusters, and hear the last holy observation of our history:

"Looking about us, we can say with pardonable pride that we have been about as thoroughly liberated as it is possible for a race and a planet to be!"

Let Me Live in a House
CHAD OLIVER

Chad Oliver (Symmes Chadwick Oliver, 1928–1993) was a prolific US anthropologist and science fiction writer whose short fiction appeared in major science fiction and fantasy magazines over a forty-year career. His science fiction novels were less successful, but he was an award-winning writer of Westerns.

In the introduction to *A Star Above It: Selected Short Stories by Chad Oliver*, volume 1, writer Howard Waldrop credits Oliver's introduction to speculative fiction to an early illness. "When he was twelve, Oliver was hit with rheumatic fever. Gone were bicycles, fly rods, baseball bats . . . One day by mistake, he was brought, along with [his preferred] air-combat [pulp fiction], one of the old encyclopedia-sized *Amazing Stories*. Chad leafed through it, came across Edmond Hamilton's 'Treasure on Thunder Moon,' read it and pronounced it 'the greatest piece of literature ever written!'" Soon, Oliver was devouring as much science fiction as he could find and "the letter columns of the SF magazines were full of things signed 'Chad Oliver, the Loony Lad of Ledgewood.'"

Although born in Ohio, Oliver spent most of his life in Texas, where he took his MA at the University of Texas (his 1952 thesis, "They Builded a Tower," was an early academic study of science fiction) and also founded Texas's first SF fanzine, *Moon Puddle*. After taking a PhD in anthropology from the University of California, Los Angeles, he became professor of anthropology at the University of Texas, Austin. He also helped found the Turkey City Workshop, popularized by noted cyberpunk author Bruce Sterling.

Oliver's science fiction consistently reflected both his professional training and his place of residence: much of it is set in the outdoors in the US Southwest, and most of his characters are deeply involved in outdoor activities. Oliver was also always concerned with the depiction of Native American life and concerns: *The Wolf Is My Brother* (1967), which is not SF, features a sympathetically characterized Native American protagonist. Most of Oliver's science fiction, too, could be thought of as Westerns of the sort that eulogize the land and the people who survive in it.

His first published story, "The Land of Lost Content," appeared in *Super Science Stories* in November 1950. He collaborated with noted weird horror writer Charles Beaumont on the two-story Claude Adams series (*The Magazine of Fantasy and Science Fiction*, 1955). Oliver's first novel, a juvenile, was *Mists of Dawn* (1952), a time travel story whose young protagonist is cast back fifty thousand years into a prehistoric conflict between Neanderthals and Cro-Magnons. *Shadows in the Sun* (1954), set in Texas, describes with some vividness its protagonist's paranoid discovery that all the inhabitants of a small town are aliens, but that it may be possible for Earth to gain galactic citizenship, and that he can work for that goal by living an exemplary life on his home planet.

Oliver was a pioneer in the application of competent anthropological thought to science fiction themes, and though occasional padding sometimes stifled the warmth of his early stories, he was a careful author whose speculative thought deserves to be more widely known and appreciated.

"Let Me Live in a House" showcases Oliver at his very best—a paranoid, tense science fiction story (first published in 1954) that was made into a *Night Gallery* episode by Rod Serling and explores ideas of identity and existence. This story was also published under the title "A Friend to Man."

LET ME LIVE IN A HOUSE

Chad Oliver

It was all exactly perfect, down to the last scratch on the white picket fence and the Frigidaire that wheezed asthmatically at predictable intervals throughout the night. The two white cottages rested lightly on their fresh green lawns, like contented dreams. They were smug in their completeness. They had green shutters and substantial brass door knockers. They had clean, crisp curtains on the windows, and knickknacks on the mantelpieces over the fireplaces. They had a fragment of poetry, caught in dime-store frames in the halls: *Let me live in a house by the side of the road and be a friend to man.*

One of the cottages had a picture of crusty old Grandfather Walters, and that was important.

Soft and subtle sounds hummed through the warm air. One of the sounds was that of a copter, high overhead, but you couldn't *see* it, of course. A breeze sighed across the grass, but the grass was motionless. Somewhere, children laughed and shouted as they clambered and splashed in the old swimming hole.

There were no children, naturally—nor any swimming hole, for that matter.

It was all exactly perfect, though. *Exactly.* If you didn't know better, you'd swear it was real.

Gordon Collier breathed in the smell of flowers that didn't exist and stared without enthusiasm at the white clouds that drifted along through a robin's-egg-blue sky.

"Damn it all," he said.

He kicked at the green grass under his feet and failed to dent it. Then he walked into his snug white cottage and slammed the door behind him, hard.

Helen called from the kitchen: "Don't slam the door, dear."

"I'm sorry," Gordon said. "It slipped."

Helen came bustling in. She was an attractive, if hardly spectacular, woman of thirty. She had brown hair and a domestic manner. She kissed her husband lightly. "Been over at the Walters'?" she asked.

"How did you guess?" Gordon said. Where did she *think* he had been—outside?

"Now, Gordey," Helen admonished him. "You needn't snap my head off for asking a civil question."

"Please don't call me 'Gordey,'" Gordon said irritably. Then he relented—it wasn't her fault, after all. He gave her news about the Walters. "Bart's playing football," he related for the millionth time, "and Mary is watching tri-di."

"Will they be dropping over for cards tonight?" Helen asked.

She's playing the game to the hilt, Gordon thought. *She's learned her part like a machine. I wish I could do that.*

"They'll be over," he said.

Helen's eyes lighted up happily. She had always loved company, Gordon remembered. "My!" she exclaimed. "I'd better see about supper." She smiled eagerly, like a dog at a rabbit, and hustled away back to the kitchen.

Gordon Collier watched his wife go, not without admiration of a sort. They had certainly picked well when they picked Bart, who could sit for hours with his electric football game, reliving the past, or who could with equal absorption paint charmingly naive pictures about the stars. Mary, too, was fine—as long as she had her tri-di set, her life was complete. But when they had picked his wife, they had hit the nail on the head. She was perfect in her part—she gave the impression of actually *believing* in it.

Gordon frowned sourly at himself. "The trouble with you, Gordon," he said softly, "is that you just haven't learned your lines very well."

There was a reason for that, too—but he preferred not to think about it.

After supper—steak and fried potatoes and salad and coffee—the doorbell rang. It was, of course, the Walters.

"Well!" exclaimed Helen. "If it isn't Bart and Mary!"

In they came—Mary, gray at forty, looking to see if the tri-di was on, and Barton, big and wholesome as a vitamin ad, bounding through the door as though it were the enemy goal line.

Four people, Gordon thought. *Four people, utterly alone, four human beings, pretending to be a society.*

Four people.

They exchanged such small talk as there was. Since they had all been doing precisely the same things for seven months, there wasn't much in the way of startling information to be passed back and forth. The bulk of the conversation was taken up with Mary's opinion of the latest tri-di shows, and it developed that she liked them all.

She turned on Gordon's set, which didn't please him unduly, and for half an hour they watched a variety show—canned and built into the set, of course—that was mainly distinguished by its singular lack of variety of any sort. Finally, in desperation, Gordon got out the cards.

"We'll make it poker tonight," he decided as they all sat down at the collapsible green card table. He dealt out four hands of three-card draw, shoved a quarter into the center of the table, and settled back to enjoy the game as best he could.

It wasn't easy. Mary turned up the tri-di in order to hear better, and Barton engaged with furious energy in his favorite pastime—replaying the 1973 Stanford–Notre Dame game, with himself in the starring role.

At eleven o'clock sharp Helen served the cheese and crackers.

At midnight, they heard the new sound.

It was a faint whistle, and it hissed over their heads like an ice-coated snake. It sizzled in from far away, and then there was a long, still pause. Finally, there was a shadowy suggestion of a thump.

Gordon instantly cut off the tri-di set. They all listened, opened a window, and looked out. He couldn't see anything—the blue sky had switched to the deep purple of night and the only glimmer of light came from the porch lamp on the cottage next door. There was nothing to see, and all that he heard were the normal sounds that weren't really there—the chirp of crickets, the soft sigh of the breeze.

"Did you hear it?" he asked the others.

They nodded, uncertain and suddenly alone. *A new sound?* How could that be?

Gordon Collier walked nervously out of the room, followed by Barton. He clenched his fists, feeling the clammy sweat in the palms of his hands, and fought to keep the fear from surging up within him. They walked into a small hall and Gordon pressed a button. A section of the wall slid smoothly back on oiled runners, and the two men walked into the white, brightly lighted equipment room.

Gordon kept his hand steady and flipped on the outside scanners. He couldn't see a thing. He tried the tracer screen, and it was blank. Barton tried the radio, on the off chance that someone was trying to contact them. There was silence.

They checked the radar charts for the past hour. They were all quite normal—except the last one. That one had a streak on it, a very sharp and clear and unmistakable streak. It was in the shape of an arc, and it curved down in a grimly familiar way. It started far out in space and it ended. Outside—outside in the ice and the rocks and the cold.

"Probably a meteor," Barton suggested.

"Probably," Gordon agreed dubiously, and made a note to that effect in the permanent record.

"Well, what else *could* it have been?" Barton challenged.

"Nothing," Gordon admitted. "It was a meteor."

They swung the wall shut again, covering the tubes and screen and coils with flowered wallpaper and Gainsborough's *Blue Boy*. They returned to the living room, where their wives still sat around the card table waiting for them. The room was as comfortable as ever, and the tri-di set was on again.

It was all just as they had left it, Gordon thought—but it was different. The room seemed smaller, constricted, isolated. The temperature had not changed, but it was colder. Millions and millions of miles flowed into the room and crawled around the walls. . . .

"Just a meteor, I guess," Gordon said.

They went on with their game for another hour, and then Barton and Mary went home to bed. Before they left, they invited Gordon and Helen to visit them the next night.

The house was suddenly empty.

Gordon Collier held his wife in his arms and listened to the Frigidaire wheezing in the kitchen and the water dripping from a half-closed faucet. Outside, there were only the crickets and the wind.

"It was only a meteor," he said.

"I know," said his wife.

They went to bed then, but sleep was slow in coming. They had a home, of course, a little white cottage in a green yard. They had two nice neighbors and blue skies and a tri-di set. It was all exactly perfect, and there was certainly nothing to be afraid of.

But it was a long way back, and they had no ship.

. . .

When Gordon Collier awoke in the morning, he knew instantly that something was wrong. He swung himself out of bed and stood in the middle of the room, half-crouched, not sure what he was looking for.

The room seemed normal enough. The twin beds were in their proper places, the rug was smooth, his watch was still on the dresser where he had left it. He looked at the alarm clock and saw that it hadn't gone off yet. His wife was still asleep. What had awakened him?

He stood quite still and listened. At once, he heard it. It came from outside, out by the green lawn and the blue skies. He walked to the window to make certain that his senses weren't playing tricks on him. The sound was still there—another *new* sound. Another new sound where there could *be* no new sounds, but only the old ones, repeating themselves over and over again. . . .

He closed the window, trying to shut it out. Perhaps, he told himself, it wasn't exactly a new sound after all; perhaps it was only the old sound distorted by a faulty speaker or a bad tube. There had been gentle breezes before, summery puffs and wisps of air, and even the gentle patter of light rain once every two weeks. He listened again, straining his ears, but he did not open the window. His heart beat spasmodic in his chest. No, there could be no doubt of it!

The wind was rising.

Helen moaned in her sleep and Gordon decided not to waken her. She might need her sleep and then some before this was over, he knew. He dressed and walked out into the hall, pressed the button that opened the equipment room, and went inside. He checked everything—dials, scanners, charts. Again, they were all quite normal except one. One of the tracers showed a faint line coming in from the ice and the rocks, in toward the two isolated cottages that huddled under the Bubble.

Presumably, it was still there—whatever it was.

The significant question was easily formulated: what did the line represent, the line that had curved down out of space and had now cut across the ice almost to his very door? What *could* it represent?

Gordon Collier forced himself to think logically, practically. It wasn't easy, not after seven months of conditioned living that had been specially designed so that he *wouldn't* think in rational terms. He closed the door, shutting off the little white house and all that it represented. He sat down on a hard metal chair with only the gleaming machines for company. He tried.

It was all too plain that he couldn't contact Earth. His radio wouldn't reach that far, and, anyhow, who was there to listen at the other end? The ship from Earth wasn't due for another five months, so he could expect no help from that source. In an emergency, the two women wouldn't be of much help. As for Bart, what he would do would depend on what *kind* of an emergency he had to face.

What kind of an emergency *was* it? He didn't know, had no way of knowing. The situation was unprecedented. It was nothing much on the face of it—a whistle and a thump and a few lines on a tracer. *And the wind,* his mind whispered, *don't forget the wind.* Nothing much, but he was afraid. He looked at his white, trembling hands and doubted himself. What could he do?

What was out there?

The wall slid open behind him and he bit his lip to keep from crying out.

"Breakfast is ready, dear," his wife said.

"Yes, yes," Gordon murmured shakily. "Yes, I'm coming."

He got to his feet and followed his wife out of the room, back into the comfortable cottage that he knew so well. He kept his eyes straight ahead of him as he walked and tried not to listen to the swelling moan of the wind that couldn't blow.

Gordon Collier drank his coffee black and dabbled at the poached converter eggs, trying to fake an appetite that he did not feel. His wife ate her breakfast in normal fashion, chattering familiar morning-talk in an inconsequential stream. Gordon didn't pay much attention until a stray sentence or two struck home:

"Just listen to that wind, Gordey," she said, with only a trace of strain in her voice. "I declare, I believe we're in for a storm!"

Collier forced himself to go on drinking his coffee, but he was badly shaken. *Her mind won't even accept the situation for what it is,* he thought with a chill. *She's going to play the game out to the bitter end. I'm* ALONE.

"That's right, dear," he said evenly, fighting to keep his voice steady. "We're in for a storm."

Outside, the wind whined around the corners of the lit cottage and something that might have been thunder rumbled in from far away.

The afternoon was a nightmare.

Gordon Collier stood at the window and watched. He didn't want to do it, but something deep within him would not let him turn away. His wife stayed huddled in front of the tri-di, watching a meaningless succession of pointless programs, and doubtless she was better off than he was. But he had to watch, even if it killed him. Dimly, he sensed that it was his responsibility to watch.

There wasn't much to see, of course. The robin's-egg-blue sky had turned an impossible, leaden gray, and the white clouds were tinged with a dismal black. The neat green grass seemed to have lost some of its vitality; it looked dead, like the artificial thing that it was. From far above his head—almost to the inner surface of the Bubble, he judged—little flickerings of light played across the sky.

The visual frequencies were being tampered with, that was all. It wouldn't do to get all excited about it.

The sounds were worse. Thunder muttered and rolled down from above. The faint hum of a copter high in the sky changed to a high-pitched screech, the sound of an aircraft out of control and falling. He waited and waited for the crash, but of course it never came. There was only the screech that went on and on and on, forever.

The auditory frequencies were being tampered with, that was all. *It wouldn't do to get all excited about it.*

When the laughing children who were splashing in the old swimming hole began to scream, Gordon Collier shut the window.

He sank down in a chair and buried his face in his hands. He wanted to shout, throw things, cry, *anything*. But he couldn't. His mind was numb. He could only sit there in the chair by the window and wait for the unknown.

It was almost evening when the rain came. It came in sheets and torrents and splattered on the windowpanes. It ran down the windows in gurgling rivulets and made puddles in the yard. It was *real* rain.

Gordon Collier looked at the water falling from a place where water could not be and began to whimper with fright.

Precisely at nine o'clock, Gordon and Helen dug up two old raincoats out of the hall closet and walked next door through the storm. They rang the doorbell and stood shivering in the icy rain until Mary opened the door and spilled yellow light out into the blackness.

They entered the cottage, which was an exact replica of their own except for the austerely frowning portrait of Grandfather Walters in the front hall. They stood dripping on the rug until Bart came charging in from the living room, grinning with pleasure at seeing them again.

"What a storm!" he said loudly. "Reminds me of the time we played UCLA in a cloudburst—here, let me take your coats."

Gordon clenched his fists helplessly. Bart and Mary weren't facing the situation either; they were simply adapting to it frantically and hoping it would go away. *Well,* his mind demanded, *what else can they do?*

They went through the ritual of playing cards. This time it was bridge instead of poker, but otherwise it was the same. It always was, except for holidays.

Outside, the incredible storm ripped furiously at the cottage. The roof began to leak, ever so slightly, and a tiny drip began to patter away ironically in the middle of the bridge table. No one said anything about it.

Gordon played well enough to keep up appearances, but his mind wasn't on the game. He loaded his pipe with his own ultra-fragrant bourbon-soaked tobacco, and retreated behind a cloud of smoke.

He had himself fairly well under control now. The worst was probably over, for him. He could at least think about it—that was a triumph, and he was proud of it.

Here they were, he thought—four human beings on a moon as big as a planet, three hundred and ninety million miles from the Earth that had sent them there. Four humans encased in two little white cottages under an air bubble on the rock and ice that was Ganymede. Here they were—waiting. Waiting in an empty universe, sustained by a faith in something that had almost been lost.

They were skeleton crews, waiting for the firm flesh to come and clothe their bones. It would not happen today, and it would not happen tomorrow. It might never happen—now.

It was unthinkable that any ship from Earth could be in the vicinity. It was unthinkable that their equipment could have broken down, changed, by itself.

So they were waiting, he thought—but not for the ship from Earth. No, they were waiting for—what?

At eleven o'clock, the storm stopped abruptly and there was total silence.

At midnight, there was a knock on the door.

It was one of those moments that stand alone, cut off and isolated from the conceptual flow of time. It stood quite still holding its breath.

The knock was repeated—impatiently.

"Someone is at the door," Mary said dubiously.

"That's right," Bart said. "We must have visitors."

No one moved. The four human beings sat paralyzed around the table, their cards still in their hands, precisely as though they were waiting for some imaginary servant to open the door and see who was outside. Gordon Collier found himself relatively calm, but he knew that it was not a natural calmness. He was conditioned too, like the rest of them. He studied them with intense interest. Could they even swallow this insane knock on the door, digest it, fit it somehow into their habitual thought patterns?

Apparently, they could.

"See to the door, dear," Mary told her husband. "I wonder who it could be this time of night?"

The knock was repeated a third time. Whoever—or whatever—was outside, Gordon thought, sounded irritated.

Reluctantly, Bart started to get up. Gordon beat him to it, however, pushing back his chair and getting to his feet. "Let me go," he said. "I'm closer."

He walked across the room to the door. It seemed a longer way than he had ever noticed before. The stout wood door seemed very thin. He put his hand on the doorknob, and was dimly conscious of the fact that Bart had gotten up and followed him across the room. He looked at the door, a scant foot before his eyes. The knock came again—sharply, impatiently, a no-nonsense knock. Gordon visualized the heavy brass door knocker on the other side of the door. To whom, or what, did the hand that worked that knocker belong? Or *was* it a hand?

Almost wildly, Gordon remembered a string of jokes that had made the rounds when he was a boy. Jokes about the little man who turned off the light in the refrigerator when you closed the door. Jokes about a little man—what had they called him?

The little man who wasn't there.

Gordon shook his head. That kind of reaction wouldn't do, he told himself. He had to be calm. He asked himself a question: *What are you waiting for?*

He gritted his teeth and opened the door, fast.

The little man *was* there, and he was tapping his foot. But he was not exactly a little man, either. He was somewhat vague, amorphous— he was, you might say, *almost* a little man.

"It's about time," the almost-man said in a blurred voice. "But first, a word from our sponsor. May I come in?"

Stunned, Gordon Collier felt himself moving aside and the little man hustled past him into the cottage.

The almost-man stood apart from the others, hesitating. He wasn't really a little man, Gordon saw with some relief; that is, he wasn't a gnome or an elf or anything like that. Gordon recognized with a start the state of his own mental processes that had even allowed him to imagine that it *could* be some supernatural creature out there on the green lawn, knocking at the door. He fought to clear his mind, and knew that he failed.

Gordon caught one thought and held on, desperately: *If this is an alien, all that I have worked for is finished. The dream is ended.*

The almost-man—changed. He solidified, became real. He *was* a man—elderly, a bit pompous, neatly dressed in an old-fashioned business suit with a conservative blue tie. He had white hair and a neat, precise moustache. His blue eyes twinkled.

"I am overwhelmed," he said clearly, waving a thin hand in the air. "My name is John. You are too kind to a poor old country boy."

Gordon stared. The man was a dead ringer for the portrait of Grandfather Walters on the wall.

Bart and Mary and Helen just looked blankly at the man, trying to adjust to the enormity of what had happened. Bart had resumed his seat at the bridge table, and had even picked up his hand. Helen was watching Gordon, who still stood by the door. Mary sat uncertainly, dimly realizing that she was the hostess here, and waiting for the proper stimulus that would prod her into a patterned routine of welcome. The house waited—a stage set for a play, with the actors all in place and the curtain halfway up.

Gordon Collier slammed the door, fighting to clear his mind from the gentle fog that lapped at it, that made everything all right. "What in the hell is the big idea?" he asked the man who looked like Grandfather Walters and whose name was John.

"Gordey!" exclaimed Helen.

"That's no way to talk to company," Mary said.

John faced Gordon, ignoring the others. His moustache bristled. He spread his hands helplessly. "I am a simple wayfaring stranger," he said. "I happened to pass by your door, and since you live in a house by the side of the road, I assumed that you would wish to be a friend to man."

Gordon Collier started to laugh hysterically, but smothered it before the laughter exploded nakedly into the room. "*Are* you a man?" he asked.

"Certainly not," John said indignantly.

Gordon Collier clenched his fists until his fingernails drew blood from the palms of his hands. He tried to use his mind, to free it, to fight. He could not, and he felt the tears of rage in his eyes. *I must,* he thought, *I must, I must, I MUST.*

He closed his eyes. The ritual had been broken, the lulling pattern was no more. He told himself: *Somewhere in this madness there is a pattern that will reduce it to sanity. It is up to me to find it; that is why I am here. I must fight this thing, whatever it is. I must clear my mind, and I must fight. I must get behind the greasepaint and the special effects and deal with whatever is underneath. This is the one test I must not fail.*

"Would you care for a drink?" he asked the man who looked like Grandfather Walters.

"Not particularly," John told him. "In fact, the thought appalls me."

Gordon Collier turned and walked out into the kitchen, took a bottle of Bart's best Scotch out of the cupboard, and drank two shots straight. Then he methodically mixed a Scotch and soda, and stood quite still, trying to think.

He *had* to think.

This wasn't insane, he had to remember that. It *seemed* to be, and that was important. Things didn't just happen, he knew; there was always an explanation, if you could just find it. Certainly, these two little cottages out here on Ganymede were fantastic enough unless you knew the story behind them. You would never guess, looking at them, that they were the tail end of a dream, a dream that man was trying to stuff back into the box. . . .

Again, the thought came: *If this is an alien, all that I have worked for is finished. The dream is ended.* And a further thought: *Unless they never find out, back on Earth.*

Those thoughts. They drummed so insistently through his mind. Were they his, really? Or were they, too, part of the conditioning? He shook his head. He could not think clearly; his mind was clogged. He would have to feel his way along.

He was desperately aware that he was not reacting rationally to the situation in which he found himself. None of it made sense; there was too much trickery. But how could he cut through to the truth?

He didn't know.

He *did* know that there was danger with him in the house, danger that was beyond comprehension.

He tried to be calm. He walked back into the living room to face the three people who were less than human and the strange man who had walked in out of infinity.

Gordon Collier entered the room and stopped. He forced his mind to accept the scene in matter-of-fact terms. He reached out for reality and held on tight.

There was the bridge table, and there Helen

and Bart, their cards in their hands, caught between action and non-action. There was the homey furniture, and the knickknacks on the mantelpiece over the non-functional fireplace. Out in the kitchen, the Frigidaire wheezed. There was the line of poetry: *Let me live in a house by the side of the road and be a friend to man.* There was the portrait of old Grandfather Walters.

There sat the man named *John,* who *was* Grandfather Walters, down to the last precise hair in his white moustache, the last wrinkle in his dreary gray business suit.

Outside, in a night alive with shadows, there was no sound at all.

"You have returned, as time will allow," John said. "No doubt you have your questions ready." He lit a cigarette, and the brand he smoked had not existed for twenty years. He dropped ashes on the rug.

"I can ask you questions, then," Gordon Collier said hesitantly.

"Certainly, my man. Please do. Valuable prizes."

Gordon frowned, not caring for the phrase "my man." And the oddly misplaced tri-di jargon was disconcerting, vaguely horrible. He fought to clear his mind.

"Are you our friend?"

"No."

"Our enemy?"

"No."

The three people at the bridge table watched, unmoving.

"Are you trying to—ummm—conquer the Earth?"

"My good man, what on Earth for?"

Gordon Collier tried to ignore the pun. It didn't fit. Nothing fitted. That was why he could not force his mind to see it all objectively, then. It was completely outside his experience, all of it.

Somewhere there is a pattern—

"What is this all about? What is going on?"

John's blue eyes twinkled. He lit another cigarette, dropping the other one on the rug

and grinding it out with his neatly polished black shoe. He said: "I have already told you that I am not a man. It follows that I am, from your point of view, an alien. I have nothing to hide. My actions are irrational to you, just as yours are to me. You are, in a way, a preliminary to food. There, is that clear?"

Gordon Collier stared at the man who looked like Grandfather Walters. *If this is an alien*—

His mind rebelled at the thought. It was absurd, fantastic. He tried to find another explanation, ignoring the shrieking danger signals in his mind. Suppose, now, that this was all a trick, a monstrous trick. John was not an alien at all—of course he wasn't—but a clever agent from Earth, out to wreck the dream.

"You say that you are an alien," he told John. "Prove it."

John shrugged, dropping ashes into the little pile on the rug. "The best proof would be highly unpleasant for you," he said. "But I can—the words are difficult, we're a little late, folks—take a story out of your mind and—the words are very hard—project it back to you again. Will that be good enough?"

"Prove it," Gordon Collier repeated, trying to be sure of himself. "Prove it."

John nodded agreeably. He looked around him, smiling.

The clock in the hall struck two.

Gordon Collier sat down. He leaned forward. . . .

He saw a ship. It was very cold and dark. He saw—shadows—in the ship. He followed the ship. It had no home. It was nomadic. It fed on energy that it—absorbed—from other cultures. He saw one of the—shadows—more clearly. There were many shadows. They were watching him. He strained forward, could almost see them—

"I beg your pardon," John said loudly. "How clumsy of me."

The room was taut with fear.

"If at first you don't succeed," John said languidly, "try, try again. Let's see, my man—where shall we start?"

The question was rhetorical. Gordon Collier felt a jolt hit his mind. He felt himself slipping, tried to hold on. He failed. It began to come, out of the past.

Disjointed, at first. Jerky headlines, and then more . . .

MAN CONQUERS SPACE!

YANK SHIP LANDS ON MOON!

NEXT STOP MARS SCIENTIST SAYS!

There had been more, under the headlines. Articles about how the space stations were going to end war by a very logical alchemy. Articles about rockets and jets and atomics. Articles about how to build a nice steel base on the moon.

Gordon Collier laughed aloud and then stopped, suddenly. The three people at the bridge table stared at him mindlessly. John stabbed in his brain. . . .

They had chattered away quite glibly about weightlessness and gravity strains. They had built a perfect machine.

But there had been an imperfect machine inside it.

His name was man.

There were imperfect machines outside it, too. Villages and towns and cities filled to overflowing with them. Once the initial steps had been taken, once man was really in space at last, the reaction came. The true enormity of the task became all too obvious.

Space stations didn't cure wars, of course, any more than spears or rifles or atomic bombs had cured wars. Wars were culturally determined patterns of response to conflict situations; to get rid of wars, you had to change the pattern, not further implement it.

Space killed men. It sent them shrieking into the unknown in coffins of steel. It ripped them out of their familiar, protective cultures and hurled them a million miles into Nothing.

Space wasn't profitable. It gobbled up millions and billions into its gaping craw and it was never satiated. It didn't care about returning a profit. There was no profit to return.

Space was for the few. It was expensive. It took technical skills and training as its only passport. It was well to speak of dreams, but this dream had to be paid for. It took controls and taxes. Who paid the taxes? Who wanted the controls?

I work eight hours a day in a factory, the chorus chanted into the great emptiness. *I got a wife and kids and when I come home at night I'm too tired to dream. I work hard. I earn my money. Why should I foot the bill for a four-eyed Glory Joe?*

Space was disturbing. Sermons were spoken against it. Editorials were written against it. Laws were enacted against it—subtle laws, for controls were not wanted.

The rockets reached Luna and beyond—Mars and Venus and the far satellites of Jupiter and Saturn. Equipment was set up, the trail was blazed at last.

But who would follow the trail? Where did it go? What did it get you when you got there?

Starburn leaves scars on the soul. Some men could not give up. Some men knew that man could not turn back.

Starburned men knew that dreams never really die.

They dwelt in fantastic loneliness, many of them, waiting. They waited for a few of their fellows on Earth to win over a hostile planet with advertising and lectures and closed-door sessions with industrialists. They fought to lay the long-neglected foundations for a skyscraper that already teetered precariously up into the sky and beyond.

Far out in space, the fragile network of men and ships held on tight and hoped.

"Let us revert to verbal communication again," John said with startling suddenness. "Projection is quite tiring."

Gordon Collier jerked back to the present and tried to adjust. He was aware, dimly, that he was being played with consummate skill. He thought of a fish that knew it had a hook in its mouth. What could he do about it? He tried to think. . . .

"Of course," John went on—quite smoothly now—and lighting yet another cigarette, "your scientists, if I may apply the word to them, belatedly discovered that they could not simply isolate a man, or a man and a woman, in a steel hut on an alien world and go off and leave him for six months or a year, to employ your ethnocentric time scale. A man is so constituted that he is naked and defenseless without his culture, something he can live by and believe in."

Gordon Collier gripped his empty glass until he thought the glass would shatter. Could this man be reading his thoughts? A word came to him: *hypnosis*. It sounded nice. He tried to believe in it.

"In the long run, you see," John continued, "it is the totality of little things that goes to make up a culture. A man such as yourself does not simply sit in a room; he sits in a room of a familiar type, with pictures on the walls and dust in the corners and lamps on the tables. A man does not just eat; he eats special kinds of food that he has been conditioned to want, served as he has been trained to want them to be served, in containers he is accustomed to, in a social setting that he is familiar with, that he fits into, that he *belongs* to. All intelligent life is like that, you see."

Gordon waited, trying to think. He had almost had something there, but it was slipping away. . . .

"Someone had to stay in space, of course," John said, dropping more ashes on the rug. "Someone had to man the stations and look after the equipment, and there was a more subtle reason; it was a distinct psychological advantage to have men already *in* space, to prove that it could be done. The machines couldn't do everything, unfortunately for you, and so someone had to stay out here, and he had to stay sane—sane by your standards, of course."

Gordon Collier looked across at the three people who sat as though frozen around the forgotten bridge table, staring at him with blank

dead-fish eyes. Helen, his wife. Bart and Mary. Sane? What did that mean? What was the price of sanity?

"And so," John continued in a bored voice, "man took his culture with him—the more provincial and reassuring and fixed the better. He took little white cottages and neighborly customs, rooted them up out of their native soil, sealed them in cylinders of steel, and rocketed them off to barren little worlds of ice and darkness. I must say, Collier, that your mind has a frightfully melodramatic way of looking at things. Perhaps that was why the little white cottages and the neighbors were not enough; in any event, conditioning was also necessary. No person operating at his full level of perception could possibly enact this farce you are living out here. And yet, without the farce you go mad. It is difficult to imagine a people less suited to space travel, don't you agree?"

Gordon Collier shrugged, feeling the cold sweat gathering in the palms of his hands.

"And there you are," John said, lighting another cigarette. "They are *much* milder. I have tried to demonstrate projection to you, on several different levels. I hope you will excuse the scattered editorial comments?"

Gordon Collier defensively reached out for a single line of reasoning and clung to it. If this were an alien, and the news got back to Earth, then the dream of space travel was finished. An advanced race already in space, added to all the other perils, would be the last straw. He, Gordon Collier, had dedicated his life to the dream. Therefore, it could not end. Therefore, John was human. It was all a trick.

His mind screamed its warning, but he thrust it aside.

He leaned forward, breathing hard. "I'll excuse them," he said slowly, "but I'll also call you a liar."

Outside, the night was still.

The sound had been turned off.

There was no storm now—no rain, nor thunder, nor lightning. There was no wind, not even whispers of a summer breeze. There were no crickets, and no night rustlings in the stuff that looked like grass.

Bart and Mary and Helen sat uncertainly at their bridge table, trying to somehow adapt themselves to a situation that they were in no way prepared to face. It wasn't their fault, Gordon knew. They had not been conditioned to handle *new* elements. That was his job. That was what he had been chosen for. He was the change factor, the mind that had been left free enough to function.

But not wholly free. He felt that keenly, here in the room with the man called John. He was fuzzy and approximate. He needed to be clear and exact. He tried to believe he had figured it all out. *Hypnosis.* That was a good word.

He hoped that it was good enough.

"A liar?" The man who looked like Grandfather Walters laughed in protest and blew smoke in Collier's eyes. "The projection was incorrect?"

Collier shook his head, ignoring the smoke, trying not to be distracted. "The information was correct. That proves nothing."

John arched his bushy eyebrows. "Oh? Come now, my man."

"Look here," Gordon Collier said decisively, believing it now. "You look like a man to me. All I have to contradict my impression is your unsupported statement and some funny tricks that can be explained in terms of conditioning and hypnosis. If you came from Earth, as you obviously did, then you would know the story as well as I do. The rest is tricks. The real question is: who sent you here, and why?"

It was cold in the room. Why was it so cold? John deftly added more ashes to the small mountain at his feet. "Your logic is excellent, if primitive," he said. "The trouble with logic is that its relationship with reality is usually obscure. It *is* logical that I am from Earth. It is not, however, true."

"I don't believe you," Gordon Collier said.

John smiled patiently. "The trouble is," he said, "that you have a word, *alien*, and no concept to go with it. You persist in reducing me to

non-alien terms, and I assure you that I will not reduce. I am, by definition, not human."

The doubt came again, gnawing at him. He fought himself. He felt an icy chill trip along his spine. He tried to convince himself and he said: "There is a reason for the storms and the buildup and the screams. I think it is a human reason. I think you have been sent here by the interests on Earth who are fighting space expansion, to try to scare us off. I think you're a good actor, but I don't think you're good enough."

The thought came again: *If this is an alien . . .*

Nonsense.

Helen, at the bridge table, suddenly stirred. She said, "My, but it's late." That was all.

John ignored her. "I assure you," he said, "that I have not the slightest interest in whether your little planet gets into space or not. Your ethnocentrism is fantastic. Can't you see, man? I don't care, not at all, not in any particular. It just isn't part of my value system."

"Go back and tell them it didn't work," Gordon Collier said.

"Oh, no," John said, shocked. "I'm spending the night."

The silence tautened.

Mary moved at the bridge table. The button had been punched, and she tried to respond. "Bart," she said, "set up the spare bed for the nice man."

Bart didn't move.

"You're not staying," Gordon Collier said flatly. He shook his head. He was so confused. If only—

John smiled and lit another cigarette from his endless supply. "I really must, you know," he said cheerfully. "Look at it this way. The star cluster to which you refer as *the* galaxy—quaint of you—is inhabited by a multitude of diverse cultural groups. A moment's reflection should show you that uniformity of organization over so vast a territory is impossible. The problem of communications alone would defeat such a plan, even were it desirable, which it isn't.

"One of these cultures, of which I happen

to be a member, has no territorial identification, except with space itself. Our ship is our home. We are, in a manner of speaking, nomads. Our economy, since we produce nothing, is based upon what we are able to extract from others."

Gordon Collier listened to his heart. It drummed liquidly in his ears.

"The closest similarity I can find in your mind is that of the ancient Plains Indians in the area you think of as North America," John continued, his blue eyes sparkling. "How charming that you should regard them as primitive! Sedentary economies are so dull, you know. We have become rather highly skilled, if I do say so myself, at imitating dominant life-forms. Contacting aliens for preliminary 'typing' is a prestige mechanism with us, just as counting *coup* served an analogous purpose among your Plains Indians, when a brave would sneak into an enemy camp at night and touch a sleeping warrior or cut loose a picketed horse. This gave prestige in his tribe, and without it he was nothing; he had no status. With us there is a further motive. Suppose, to extrapolate down to your level, you wish to pick apples. It will be to your advantage, then, to try to look and act like the farmer who owns them, will it not? Our culture has found it expedient to 'type' members of an alien culture in a controlled situation, before setting out to, so to speak, pick apples in earnest. The individual who does the 'typing' gains prestige in proportion to the danger involved. Am I getting through to you?"

Gordon Collier got to his feet, slowly. He could not think, not really. In a way, he realized this. He tried to go ahead regardless, to do what he could. His brain supplied a thought: What would the ship from Earth pick up five months from tonight in this silent cottage? Would it be human beings—or something else?

Of course, John *was* a human being.

A hypnotist, perhaps.

Why was it so cold in the house?

He started for the man called John, slowly, step by step. He did not know why he did it; he only knew that he had to act, act now, act before it was too late, act despite the cost. The impulse came from down deep, beyond the conditioning.

"You're a liar," he said again, biting the words out thickly, believing in them. "You're a liar. We don't believe in you. Get out, get out, get *out*—"

If this is an alien, the dream is ended. Unless—

The man called John slid out of his chair and backed away. His blue eyes glittered coldly. The cigarette between his fingers shredded itself to the floor, squeezed in two.

"Stop," said John.

Gordon Collier kept on coming.

The man called John—changed.

Gordon Collier screamed.

It was an animal scream.

He staggered back, back against the wall. His eyes were shut, jammed shut as tightly as he could force them. His mouth was open, to let the endless scream rip and tear itself out from the matrix of his being. He cowered, crouched against the wall, a creature in agony.

He was afraid that he would not die.

His hands shook, and they were clammy with the cold sweat that oozed from his palms. A white flash of indescribable pain seared up from his toes, burned like molten lead through his body. It hissed along his naked nerves and howled into his cringing brain with the numbing, blinding impact of a razor-sharp chisel on a rotten tooth. Blood trickled wetly from his nostrils.

He clawed the floor, not feeling the splinters in his nails.

The scream screeched to a piercing climax that bulged his eyes from their sockets.

Something snapped.

His body relaxed, trembling quietly. His mind was clean and empty, like a flower washed with the summer rain. He breathed in great choking mouthfuls of air. He remembered—

It had *bubbled*.

He shut it out. He lay quite still for a long minute, letting the life wash warmly back through his veins. His breathing slowed. He felt a tiny thrill of triumph course through his body.

His mind was clean.

He could think again.

He took a deep breath and turned around.

The cottage was still there. The Frigidaire wheezed in the kitchen. The living room was unchanged. There were chairs, the tri-di, the picture of Grandfather Walters, the ashes on the rug, the three motionless figures at the bridge table, Bart and Mary and Helen.

They were very still.

Yes, of course. Their conditioned minds had been strained past the tolerance point and they had blanked out. Short-circuited. The fuse had blown. They were out of it, for now.

He was alone.

The man called John was seated again in his armchair, blue eyes twinkling, moustache neat and prim, the pile of ashes at his feet. He had lit another cigarette. He was smiling, quite himself again.

Or, rather, he was *not* himself again.

Gordon Collier got to his feet. It took him a long time, and he did it clumsily. He was shaken and weak in the knees. He had lost the fuzziness which had partially protected him.

But he had his mind back.

It was, he thought, a fair trade.

"I fear the shock has been too much for your dull friends," John said languidly, crossing his legs carefully so as not to disturb the neat crease in his trousers. "I tried to warn you, you know."

Gordon said: "You can't stay here." The words were thick and he licked his lips with his parched tongue.

John hesitated, but recovered quickly. "On the contrary," he said, "I can and I will. A charming place, really. I'd like to get to know you better."

"I can imagine," said Gordon Collier.

The silence beat at his ears. It was uncanny. He had never heard no-sound before.

Black despair settled within him like cold ink. The situation, he now saw, was frightening in its simplicity. He had to accept it for what it was. The thing was alien. It didn't *care* what the effects of its visit would be on the future of Earth. Human beings were to it what pigs were to a man.

Does the hungry man worry about whether or not pigs have dreams?

"You're going to get out," he told it.

The man called John raised an eyebrow in polite doubt.

Gordon Collier was not sure, now, that man *should* leave the Earth. It was odd, he thought, that his concern was still with the dream. Regardless of his actions here, all the human beings would not be "eaten." Many would escape, and the species would recover. But if this thing, or even any news of it, reached the Earth, then the dream was finished. The whole shaky, crazy structure that had put man into space would collapse like a card house in a hurricane. Man—or what was left of him—would retreat, build a wall around himself, try to hide.

And if he did get into space to stay?

Gordon Collier didn't know. There were no simple answers. If the aliens, or even the intelligence that there *were* such aliens, reached the Earth, then man was through, dead in his insignificance. If not, he had a chance to shape his own destiny. He had won time. It was as simple as that.

Gordon Collier again faced the man called John. He smiled.

Two cultures, locked in a room.

From the bridge table, three sluggish statues turned to watch.

To Gordon Collier, the only sound in the room was that of his own harsh breathing in his ears.

"As I was saying," said the man called John, "I'm afraid I really must ignore your lamentable lack of hospitality and stay on for a while. I am, you might say, the man who came to dinner. You are quite helpless, Gordon Collier, and I can bring my people here at any time. Enough of them, you see, to fill both your houses and the air bubble beyond. It will be alive with my people. You are quite helpless, Gordon Collier, and I can bring my people here at any time. Enough of them, you see, to fill . . ."

Gordon Collier refused to listen to the voice that tried to lull him back to sleep. He shut it out of his mind. He had but one weapon, and that was his mind. He had to keep it clear and uncluttered.

John kept talking, melodically.

Gordon Collier tried to think, tried to organize his thoughts, collect his data, relate it to a meaningful whole.

Somewhere there is a pattern.

Several pieces of information, filed away by his conditioned brain until it could assemble them, clicked into place parts of a puzzle. Now that the fog was gone, a number of facts were clear.

He used his mind, exultantly.

For one thing, of course, the man called John had given him more information than was strictly necessary. Why? Well, he had explained about the prestige mechanism involved—and the more danger there was, the more prestige. An important fact followed: if he, Gordon Collier, were in fact utterly helpless, then there was no danger, and no prestige.

And *that* indicated . . .

". . . lamentable lack of hospitality and stay on for a while," the voice droned on in his ears. "I am, you might say, the man who came to dinner. You are quite helpless, Gordon Collier, and I can . . ."

So John had armed him with information. He had been playing a game of sorts, a game for keeps. He had given his opponent clues. What were they? *What were they?*

". . . bring my people here at any time. Enough of them, you see . . ."

"The trouble is," John had said, *"that you have a word, alien, and no concept to go with it."*

Gordon Collier stood motionless, between John and the three immobile figures at the bridge table, looking for the string that would untie the knot. John's voice buzzed on, but he ignored it.

From the first, he remembered, John had kept himself apart from the human beings. He had walked in, hesitated, said his stilted tri-di-derived introductory remarks, and seated himself as Grandfather Walters. He had remained isolated. He had never come really close to any of the human beings, never touched them.

And when Gordon Collier had advanced on him . . .

Collier stared at the man called John. Was he telepathic, or had he picked up his story before he ever came through the door? Was he listening in on his thoughts even now?

That was unimportant, he realized suddenly. That was a blind alley. It made no practical difference. What counted was a simple fact: the alien could not touch him. And, presumably, it wasn't armed; that would have counterbalanced the danger factor.

It was very cold in the room. Gordon Collier felt a sick thrill in the pit of his stomach.

". . . to fill both your houses and the air bubble beyond. It will be alive . . ."

There was danger for the alien here. There *had* to be. Gordon Collier smiled slowly, feeling the sweat come again to his hands. There could be but one source for that danger.

Himself.

He saw the picture. It was quite clear. All that buildup, all the sounds and the rain and the wind, had been designed to test man in a beautiful laboratory situation. If man proved amenable to "typing," then he was next on the food list.

Pigs.

If he didn't crack, if he fought back even *here* and *now*, then the aliens would have to play their game elsewhere. Death wasn't fun, not even to an alien.

Death was basic.

Yes, it was quite clear what he had to do. He didn't know that he could do it, but he could try. He was weak on his legs and there was a cold shriek of memory that would not stay buried in his mind. He bit his lip until he felt the salt taste of blood in his mouth. He was totally unprotected now, and he knew the price he would have to pay.

He smiled again and walked slowly toward the man called John, step by steady step.

Gordon Collier lived an eternity while he crossed the room. He felt as though he were trapped in a nightmare that kept repeating itself over and over and over again.

The six dead eyes at the bridge table followed him.

"Stop," said John.

Gordon Collier kept coming.

The man called John slid out of his chair and backed away. His blue eyes were cold with fear and fury.

"Stop," he said, his voice too high.

Gordon Collier kept coming.

That was when John—changed.

Gordon Collier screamed—and kept on walking. He shaped his screaming lips into a smile and kept on walking. He felt the sickness surge within him and he kept on walking.

Closer and closer and *closer*.

He screamed and while he screamed his mind clamped on one thought and did not let go: *If that seething liquid hell is hideous to me, then I am equally hideous to it.*

He kept walking. He kept his eyes open. His foot stepped into the convulsive muck on the floor. He stopped. He screamed louder. He reached out his hand to *touch* it. It bubbled icily. . . .

He knew that he would touch it if it killed him.

The thing—cracked. It contracted with lightning speed into half its former area. It got away. It boiled furiously. It shot into a corner and stained the wall. It tried to climb. It heaved and palpitated. It stopped, advanced, wavered, advanced—

And retreated.

It flowed convulsively, wriggling, under the door.

Gordon Collier screamed again and again. He looked at the three dead-alive statues at the bridge table and sobbed. He was wrenched apart.

But he had won.

He collapsed on the floor, sobbing. His face fell into the mound of dry gray ashes by the armchair.

He had won. The thought was far, far away. . . .

One of the statues that had been his wife stirred and somehow struggled to her feet. She padded into the bedroom and got a blanket. She placed it gently over his sobbing body.

"Poor dear," said Helen. "He's had a hard day."

Outside, there was a whistle and a roar, and then the pale light of dawn flowed in and filled the sky.

The five months passed, and little seemed changed.

There was only one little white cottage now, and it was on Earth. It snuggled into the Illinois countryside. It had green shutters and crisp curtains on the windows. It had knickknacks on the mantelpiece over the fireplace. It had a fragment of cozy poetry, caught in a dime-store frame. . . .

Gordon Collier was alone now, and the loneliness was a tangible thing. His mind was almost gone, and he knew that it was gone. He knew that they had put him here to shelter him, to protect him, until he should be strong enough to take the therapy as Helen and Bart and Mary had taken it.

But he knew that he would never be strong enough, never again.

They pitied him. Perhaps, they even felt contempt for him. Hadn't he failed them, despite all their work, all their expert conditioning? Hadn't he gone to pieces with the others and reduced himself to uselessness?

They had read the last notation in the equipment room. Odd that a meteor could unnerve a man so!

He walked across the green grass to the white picket fence. He stood there, soaking up the sun. He heard voices—children's voices. There they were, three of them, hurrying across the meadow. He wanted to call to them, but they were far away and he knew that his voice would not carry.

He stood by the white fence for a very long time.

When darkness came, and the first stars appeared above him, Gordon Collier turned and walked slowly up the path, back to the warmth, and to the little white cottage that waited to take him in.

The Star

ARTHUR C. CLARKE

Arthur C. Clarke (1917–2008) was a knighted British science fiction writer who lived in Sri Lanka for much of his life. He also wrote nonfiction, worked as an inventor, and served as the host of the *Arthur C. Clarke's Mysterious World* TV series. Clarke won many Hugo and Nebula Awards and still has a large readership today. He cowrote the screenplay for the iconic movie *2001: A Space Odyssey*, and both the Arthur C. Clarke Award, for the best science fiction novel published in the United Kingdom, and the Arthur C. Clarke Center for Human Imagination at the University of California, San Diego, bear his name.

From a very early age, Clarke was a member of the British Interplanetary Society, supporting the idea of space travel as not just fiction but emerging fact. A 1940s satellite communication system proposed by Clarke won him the Franklin Institute's Stuart Ballantine Medal (1963). He was the chairman of the British Interplanetary Society from 1946 to '47 and again from 1951 to '53, right before he moved to Sri Lanka.

Clarke's work is largely optimistic, especially in its view of science as enabling space exploration. Often, his futures are utopian settings in which advanced technology works to enhance both the natural world and human society. Scientific breakthroughs form the core, or engine, of much of his early published fiction. However, it is to Clarke's credit that he could work in a less utopian mode as well. Today, Clarke's less optimistic work seems most relevant to readers and retains its symbolic power, especially in the context of growing scarcity and threats due to global warming. Throughout his career, though, whether upbeat or downbeat, Clarke had the rare ability to infuse hard science fiction concepts with emotion, bringing them down to the human level.

One of his best, and most pessimistic, short stories, "The Star," was first published in *Infinity Science Fiction* in 1955 and awarded the Hugo in 1956. Later it was adapted for television as a holiday-season episode of *The Twilight Zone*. Although it shares the same title as the H. G. Wells story in this anthology, there is no other relationship between the two stories.

"The Star" tells of a spaceship expedition that encounters the remains of an alien civilization and blends the religious with the scientific in a way that many readers have interpreted as a reconciliation of the numinous and the empirical. Clarke's story is powerful not just because of the juxtaposition of life and death, but also because it mercilessly interrogates human ideas of meaning about the universe—it is very much about the human need to create narrative out of what we observe around us so that we can make sense of the unknown.

It is also telling that the priest narrator points out that his "order has long been famous for its scientific works" even as the scientists on board the spaceship dismiss him despite his science bona fides. "It amused them to have a Jesuit as chief astrophysicist[; they] could never get over it." Whether intended by Clarke or not, there's an indictment in that dismissal, that lack of an attempt to understand another's point of view. That dismissal is especially ironic given that the need to create narrative and purpose is prevalent even in seemingly objective scientific endeavors and experiments.

THE STAR

Arthur C. Clarke

It is three thousand light years to the Vatican. Once, I believed that space could have no power over faith, just as I believed that the heavens declared the glory of God's handiwork. Now I have seen that handiwork, and my faith is sorely troubled. I stare at the crucifix that hangs on the cabin wall above the Mark VI Computer, and for the first time in my life I wonder if it is no more than an empty symbol.

I have told no one yet, but the truth cannot be concealed. The facts are there for all to read, recorded on the countless miles of magnetic tape and the thousands of photographs we are carrying back to Earth. Other scientists can interpret them as easily as I can, and I am not one who would condone that tampering with the truth which often gave my order a bad name in the olden days.

The crew are already sufficiently depressed: I wonder how they will take this ultimate irony. Few of them have any religious faith, yet they will not relish using this final weapon in their campaign against me—that private, good-natured, but fundamentally serious, war which lasted all the way from Earth. It amused them to have a Jesuit as chief astrophysicist: Dr. Chandler, for instance, could never get over it. (Why are medical men such notorious atheists?) Sometimes he would meet me on the observation deck, where the lights are always low so that the stars shine with undiminished glory. He would come up to me in the gloom and stand staring out of the great oval port, while the heavens crawled slowly around us as the ship turned end over end with the residual spin we had never bothered to correct.

"Well, Father," he would say at last, "it goes on forever and forever, and perhaps *Something* made it. But how you can believe that Something has a special interest in us and our miserable little world—that just beats me." Then the argument would start, while the stars and nebulae would swing around us in silent, endless arcs beyond the flawlessly clear plastic of the observation port.

It was, I think, the apparent incongruity of my position that caused most amusement to the crew. In vain I would point to my three papers in the *Astrophysical Journal*, my five in the *Monthly Notices of the Royal Astronomical Society*. I would remind them that my order has long been famous for its scientific works. We may be few now, but ever since the eighteenth century we have made contributions to astronomy and geophysics out of all proportion to our numbers. Will my report on the Phoenix Nebula end our thousand years of history? It will end, I fear, much more than that.

I do not know who gave the nebula its name, which seems to me a very bad one. If it contains a prophecy, it is one that cannot be verified for several billion years. Even the word *nebula* is misleading: this is a far smaller object than those stupendous clouds of mist—the stuff of unborn stars—that are scattered throughout the length of the Milky Way. On the cosmic scale, indeed, the Phoenix Nebula is a tiny thing—a tenuous shell of gas surrounding a single star.

Or what is left of a star . . .

The Rubens engraving of Loyola seems to mock me as it hangs there above the spectro-photometer tracings. What would *you*, Father, have made of this knowledge that has come into my keeping, so far from the little world that was all the universe you knew? Would your faith have risen to the challenge, as mine has failed to do?

You gaze into the distance, Father, but I have traveled a distance beyond any that you could have imagined when you founded our order a thousand years ago. No other survey ship has been so far from Earth: we are at the very frontiers of the explored universe. We set out to reach the Phoenix Nebula, we succeeded, and we are homeward bound with our burden of knowledge. I wish I could lift that burden from my shoulders, but I call to you in vain across the centuries and the light-years that lie between us.

On the book you are holding the words are plain to read. AD MAJOREM DEI GLORIAM, the message runs, but it is a message I can no longer believe. Would you still believe it, if you could see what we have found?

We knew, of course, what the Phoenix Nebula was. Every year, in our galaxy alone, more than a hundred stars explode, blazing for a few hours or days with thousands of times their normal brilliance before they sink back into death and obscurity. Such are the ordinary novae—the commonplace disasters of the universe. I have recorded the spectrograms and light curves of dozens since I started working at the Lunar Observatory.

But three or four times in every thousand years occurs something beside which even a nova pales into total insignificance.

When a star becomes a *supernova*, it may for a little while outshine all the massed suns of the galaxy. The Chinese astronomers watched this happen in AD 1054, not knowing what it was they saw. Five centuries later, in 1572, a supernova blazed in Cassiopeia so brilliantly that it was visible in the daylight sky. There have been three more in the thousand years that have passed since then.

Our mission was to visit the remnants of such a catastrophe, to reconstruct the events that led up to it, and, if possible, to learn its cause. We came slowly in through the con-

centric shells of gas that had been blasted out six thousand years before, yet were expanding still. They were immensely hot, radiating even now with a fierce violet light, but were far too tenuous to do us any damage. When the star had exploded, its outer layers had been driven upward with such speed that they had escaped completely from its gravitational field. Now they formed a hollow shell large enough to engulf a thousand solar systems, and at its center burned the tiny, fantastic object which the star had now become—a white dwarf, smaller than the Earth, yet weighing a million times as much.

The glowing gas shells were all around us, banishing the normal night of interstellar space. We were flying into the center of a cosmic bomb that had detonated millennia ago and whose incandescent fragments were still hurtling apart. The immense scale of the explosion, and the fact that the debris already covered a volume of space many billions of miles across, robbed the scene of any visible movement. It would take decades before the unaided eye could detect any motion in these tortured wisps and eddies of gas, yet the sense of turbulent expansion was overwhelming.

We had checked our primary drive hours before, and were drifting slowly toward the fierce little star ahead. Once it had been a sun like our own, but it had squandered in a few hours the energy that should have kept it shining for a million years. Now it was a shrunken miser, hoarding its resources as if trying to make amends for its prodigal youth.

No one seriously expected to find planets. If there had been any before the explosion, they would have been boiled into puffs of vapor, and their substance lost in the greater wreckage of the star itself. But we made the automatic search, as we always do when approaching an unknown sun, and presently we found a single small world circling the star at an immense distance. It must have been the Pluto of this vanished solar system, orbiting on the frontiers of the night. Too far from the central sun ever to have known life, its remoteness had saved it from the fate of all its lost companions.

The passing fires had seared its rocks and burned away the mantle of frozen gas that must have covered it in the days before the disaster. We landed, and we found the Vault.

Its builders had made sure that we would. The monolithic marker that stood above the entrance was now a fused stump, but even the first long-range photographs told us that here was the work of intelligence. A little later we detected the continent-wide pattern of radioactivity that had been buried in the rock. Even if the pylon above the Vault had been destroyed, this would have remained, an immovable and all but eternal beacon calling to the stars. Our ship fell toward this gigantic bull's-eye like an arrow into its target.

The pylon must have been a mile high when it was built, but now it looked like a candle that had melted down into a puddle of wax. It took us a week to drill through the fused rock, since we did not have the proper tools for a task like this. We were astronomers, not archaeologists, but we could improvise. Our original purpose was forgotten: this lonely monument, reared with such labor at the greatest possible distance from the doomed sun, could have only one meaning. A civilization that knew it was about to die had made its last bid for immortality.

It will take us generations to examine all the treasures that were placed in the Vault. They had plenty of time to prepare, for their sun must have given its first warnings many years before the final detonation. Everything that they wished to preserve, all the fruit of their genius, they brought here to this distant world in the days before the end, hoping that some other race would find it and that they would not be utterly forgotten. Would we have done so as well, or would we have been too lost in our own misery to give thought to a future we could never see or share?

If only they had had a little more time! They could travel freely enough between the planets of their own sun, but they had not yet learned to cross the interstellar gulfs, and the nearest solar system was a hundred light-years away. Yet even had they possessed the secret of the Transfinite Drive, no more than a few millions could have been saved. Perhaps it was better thus.

Even if they had not been so disturbingly human as their sculpture shows, we could not have helped admiring them and grieving for their fate. They left thousands of visual records and the machines for projecting them, together with elaborate pictorial instructions from which it will not be difficult to learn their written language. We have examined many of these records, and brought to life for the first time in six thousand years the warmth and beauty of a civilization that in many ways must have been superior to our own. Perhaps they only showed us the best, and one can hardly blame them. But their words were very lovely, and their cities were built with a grace that matches anything of man's. We have watched them at work and play, and listened to their musical speech sounding across the centuries. One scene is still before my eyes—a group of children on a beach of strange blue sand, playing in the waves as children play on Earth. Curious whiplike trees line the shore, and some very large animal is wading in the shadows yet attracting no attention at all.

And sinking into the sea, still warm and friendly and life-giving, is the sun that will soon turn traitor and obliterate all this innocent happiness.

Perhaps if we had not been so far from home and so vulnerable to loneliness, we should not have been so deeply moved. Many of us had seen the ruins of ancient civilizations on other worlds, but they had never affected us so profoundly. This tragedy was unique. It is one thing for a race to fail and die, as nations and cultures have done on Earth. But to be destroyed so completely in the full flower of its achievement, leaving no survivors—how could that be reconciled with the mercy of God?

My colleagues have asked me that, and I

have given what answers I can. Perhaps you could have done better, Father Loyola, but I have found nothing in the *Exercitia Spiritualia* that helps me here. They were not an evil people: I do not know what gods they worshiped, if indeed they worshiped any. But I have looked back at them across the centuries, and have watched while the loveliness they used their last strength to preserve was brought forth again into the light of their shrunken sun. They could have taught us much: why were they destroyed?

I know the answers that my colleagues will give when they get back to Earth. They will say that the universe has no purpose and no plan, that since a hundred suns explode every year in our galaxy, at this very moment some race is dying in the depths of space. Whether that race has done good or evil during its lifetime will make no difference in the end: there is no divine justice, for there is no God.

Yet, of course, what we have seen proves nothing of the sort. Anyone who argues thus is being swayed by emotion, not logic. God has no need to justify His actions to man. He who built the universe can destroy it when He chooses. It is arrogance—it is perilously near blasphemy—for us to say what He may or may not do.

This I could have accepted, hard though it is to look upon whole worlds and peoples thrown into the furnace. But there comes a point when even the deepest faith must falter, and now, as I look at the calculations lying before me, I know I have reached that point at last.

We could not tell, before we reached the nebula, how long ago the explosion took place. Now, from the astronomical evidence and the record in the rocks of that one surviving planet, I have been able to date it very exactly. I know in what year the light of this colossal conflagration reached our Earth. I know how brilliantly the supernova whose corpse now dwindles behind our speeding ship once shone in terrestrial skies. I know how it must have blazed low in the east before sunrise, like a beacon in that oriental dawn.

There can be no reasonable doubt: the ancient mystery is solved at last. Yet, oh God, there were so many stars you could have used. What was the need to give these people to the fire, that the symbol of their passing might shine above Bethlehem?

Grandpa

JAMES H. SCHMITZ

James H. Schmitz (1911–1981) was a German-born US writer of science fiction whose short stories sometimes included ecological or sociological themes that have only become more resonant and relevant in the modern era. Schmitz's first published story was "Greenface" for *Unknown* (1943), but his most successful stories with readers were four tales featuring sentient robot spaceships and troubleshooters with psi powers, later assembled as *Agent of Vega* (1960). A more recent collection from 2001 with the same title includes a more diverse selection of stories. Although he published a few novels, he was primarily known for his short fiction.

Schmitz's most popular space-opera adventures, published prior to 1970, featured women who perform an active role and save the universe when necessary, in a manner almost completely free of gender clichés—equal to men in intelligence and strength, which was virtually unheard of in the pulp magazines of the time. Several of his stories share a more or less common backdrop of a galaxy inhabited by humans and aliens with room for all and numerous opportunities for discoveries and reversals that carefully fall short of threatening the stability of that background. Many of his stories, as a result, focus less on moments of conceptual breakthrough than on the pragmatic operations of teams and bureaus involved in maintaining the state of things against unfriendly species; in this they rather resemble the tales of the pulpier Murray Leinster, though they are more vigorous and less inclined to punish the adventurous.

"Grandpa," included here, was first published in *Astounding Science Fiction* in 1955. In this story, as in others he's written, Schmitz seems to have sympathy for his alien creatures rather than seeing them as monsters, in contrast to the horror-SF written by many of his contemporaries. As a result, "Grandpa" has aged better than much other fiction from the era. Indeed, one of the most interesting aspects of his stories is how he wrote about ecology as a major theme, not only on this story but others as well (see also "Balanced Ecology" from 1965, in *Analog*). The alien ecosystem described in this story is very intricate and ingenious and points out that human explorers shouldn't base their reactions and reasoning on the world they think they know. Schmitz is one of the earliest writers to use the word *ecology* in his fiction.

GRANDPA

James H. Schmitz

A green-winged, downy thing as big as a hen fluttered along the hillside to a point directly above Cord's head and hovered there, twenty feet above him. Cord, a fifteen-year-old human being, leaned back against a skipboat parked on the equator of a world that had known human beings for only the past four Earth years, and eyed the thing speculatively. The thing was, in the free and easy terminology of the Sutang Colonial Team, a swamp bug. Concealed in the downy fur back of the bug's head was a second, smaller, semiparasitical thing, classed as a bug rider.

The bug itself looked like a new species to Cord. Its parasite might or might not turn out to be another unknown. Cord was a natural research man; his first glimpse of the odd flying team had sent endless curiosities thrilling through him. How did that particular phenomenon tick, and why? What fascinating things, once you'd learned about it, could you get it to do?

Normally, he was hampered by circumstances in carrying out any such investigation. The Colonial Team was a practical, hardworking outfit—two thousand people who'd been given twenty years to size up and tame down the brand-new world of Sutang to the point where a hundred thousand colonists could be settled on it, in reasonable safety and comfort. Even junior colonial students like Cord were expected to confine their curiosity to the pattern of research set up by the station to which they were attached. Cord's inclination toward independent experiments had got him into disfavor with his immediate superiors before this.

He sent a casual glance in the direction of the Yoger Bay Colonial Station behind him. No signs of human activity about that low, fortress-like bulk in the hill. Its central lock was still closed. In fifteen minutes, it was scheduled to be opened to let out the Planetary Regent, who was inspecting the Yoger Bay Station and its principal activities today.

Fifteen minutes was time enough to find out something about the new bug, Cord decided.

But he'd have to collect it first.

He slid out one of the two handguns holstered at his side. This one was his own property: a Vanadian projectile weapon. Cord thumbed it to position for anesthetic small-game missiles and brought the hovering swamp bug down, drilled neatly and microscopically through the head.

As the bug hit the ground, the rider left its back. A tiny scarlet demon, round and bouncy as a rubber ball, it shot toward Cord in three long hops, mouth wide to sink home inch-long, venom-dripping fangs. Rather breathlessly, Cord triggered the gun again and knocked it out in midleap. A new species, all right! Most bug riders were harmless plant-eaters, mere suckers of vegetable juice—

"Cord!" A feminine voice.

Cord swore softly. He hadn't heard the central lock click open. She must have come around from the other side of the station.

"Hi, Grayan!" he shouted innocently without looking around. "Come see what I got! New species!"

Grayan Mahoney, a slender, black-haired girl two years older than himself, came trotting down the hillside toward him. She was Sutang's star colonial student, and the station manager, Nirmond, indicated from time to time that she was a fine example for Cord to pattern his own behavior on. In spite of that, she and Cord were good friends, but she bossed him around considerably.

"Cord, you dope!" She scowled as she came up. "Quit acting like a collector! If the Regent came out now, you'd be sunk. Nirmond's been telling her about you!"

"Telling her what?" Cord asked, startled.

"For one," Grayan reported, "that you don't keep up on your assigned work. Two, that you sneak off on one-man expeditions of your own at least once a month and have to be rescued—"

"Nobody," Cord interrupted hotly, "has had to rescue me yet!"

"How's Nirmond to know you're alive and healthy when you just drop out of sight for a week?" Grayan countered. "Three," she resumed checking the items off on slim fingertips, "he complained that you keep private zoological gardens of unidentified and possibly deadly vermin in the woods back of the station. And four . . . well, Nirmond simply doesn't want the responsibility for you anymore!" She held up the four fingers significantly.

"Golly!" gulped Cord, dismayed. Summed up tersely like that, his record *didn't* look too good.

"Golly is right! I keep warning you! Now Nirmond wants the Regent to send you back to Vanadia—and there's a starship coming in to New Venus forty-eight hours from now!" New Venus was the Colonial Team's main settlement on the opposite side of Sutang.

"What'll I do?"

"Start acting like you have good sense mainly." Grayan grinned suddenly. "I talked to the Regent, too—Nirmond isn't rid of you yet! But if you louse up on our tour of the Bay Farms today, you'll be off the Team for good!"

She turned to go. "You might as well put the skipboat back; we're not using it. Nirmond's driving us down to the edge of the bay in a treadcar, and we'll take a raft from there. Don't let them know I warned you!"

Cord looked after her, slightly stunned. He hadn't realized his reputation had become as

bad as all that! To Grayan, whose family had served on Colonial Teams for the past four generations, nothing worse was imaginable than to be dismissed and sent back ignominiously to one's own homeworld. Much to his surprise, Cord was discovering now that he felt exactly the same way about it!

Leaving his newly bagged specimens to revive by themselves and flutter off again, he hurriedly flew the skipboat around the station and rolled it back into its stall.

Three rafts lay moored just offshore in the marshy cove, at the edge of which Nirmond had stopped the treadcar. They looked somewhat like exceptionally broad-brimmed, well-worn sugarloaf hats floating out there, green and leathery. Or like lily pads twenty-five feet across, with the upper section of a big, gray-green pineapple growing from the center of each. Plant animals of some sort. Sutang was too new to have had its phyla sorted out into anything remotely like an orderly classification. The rafts were a local oddity which had been investigated and could be regarded as harmless and moderately useful. Their usefulness lay in the fact that they were employed as a rather slow means of transportation about the shallow, swampy waters of the Yoger Bay. That was as far as the Team's interest in them went at present.

The Regent had stood up from the backseat of the car, where she was sitting next to Cord. There were only four in the party; Grayan was up front with Nirmond.

"Are those our vehicles?" The Regent sounded amused.

Nirmond grinned, a little sourly. "Don't underestimate them, Dane! They could become an important economic factor in this region in time. But, as a matter of fact, these three are smaller than I like to use." He was peering about the reedy edges of the cove. "There's a regular monster parked here usually—"

Grayan turned to Cord. "Maybe Cord knows where Grandpa is hiding."

It was well meant, but Cord had been hoping nobody would ask him about Grandpa. Now they all looked at him.

"Oh, you want Grandpa?" he said, somewhat flustered. "Well, I left him . . . I mean I saw him a couple of weeks ago about a mile south from here—"

Grayan sighed. Nirmond grunted and told the Regent, "The rafts tend to stay wherever they're left, providing it's shallow and muddy. They use a hair-root system to draw chemicals and microscopic nourishment directly from the bottom of the bay. Well—Grayan, would you like to drive us there?"

Cord settled back unhappily as the treadcar lurched into motion. Nirmond suspected he'd used Grandpa for one of his unauthorized tours of the area, and Nirmond was quite right.

"I understand you're an expert with these rafts, Cord," Dane said from beside him. "Grayan told me we couldn't find a better steersman, or pilot, or whatever you call it, for our trip today."

"I can handle them," Cord said, perspiring. "They don't give you any trouble!" He didn't feel he'd made a good impression on the Regent so far. Dane was a young, handsome-looking woman with an easy way of talking and laughing, but she wasn't the head of the Sutang Colonial Team for nothing. She looked quite capable of shipping out anybody whose record wasn't up to par.

"There's one big advantage our beasties have over a skipboat, too," Nirmond remarked from the front seat. "You don't have to worry about a snapper trying to climb on board with you!" He went on to describe the stinging ribbon-tentacles the rafts spread around them underwater to discourage creatures that might make a meal off their tender underparts. The snappers and two or three other active and aggressive species of the bay hadn't yet learned it was foolish to attack armed human beings in a boat, but they would skitter hurriedly out of the path of a leisurely perambulating raft.

Cord was happy to be ignored for the moment. The Regent, Nirmond, and Grayan were all Earth people, which was true of most of the members of the Team; and Earth people made him uncomfortable, particularly in groups. Vanadia, his own homeworld, had barely graduated from the status of Earth colony itself, which might explain the difference. All the Earth people he'd met so far seemed dedicated to what Grayan Mahoney called the Big Picture, while Nirmond usually spoke of it as "Our Purpose Here." They acted strictly in accordance with their Team Regulations—sometimes, in Cord's opinion, quite insanely. Because now and then the Regulations didn't quite cover a new situation and then somebody was likely to get killed. In which case, the Regulations would be modified promptly, but Earth people didn't seem otherwise disturbed by such events.

Grayan had tried to explain it to Cord:

"We can't really ever *know* in advance what a new world is going to be like! And once we're there, there's too much to do, in the time we've got, to study it inch by inch. You get your job done, and you take a chance. But if you stick by the Regulations you've got the best chances of surviving anybody's been able to figure out for you. . . ."

Cord felt he preferred to just use good sense and not let Regulations or the job get him into a situation he couldn't figure out for himself.

To which Grayan replied impatiently that he hadn't yet got the Big Picture. . . .

The treadcar swung around and stopped, and Grayan stood up in the front seat, pointing. "That's Grandpa, over there!"

Dane also stood up and whistled softly, apparently impressed by Grandpa's fifty-foot spread. Cord looked around in surprise. He was pretty sure this was several hundred yards from the spot where he'd left the big raft two weeks ago; and as Nirmond said, they didn't usually move about by themselves.

Puzzled, he followed the others down a narrow path to the water, hemmed in by tree-sized reeds. Now and then he got a glimpse of Grandpa's swimming platform, the rim of which just touched the shore. Then the path opened out, and he saw the whole raft lying in sunlit, shallow water; and he stopped short, startled.

Nirmond was about to step up on the platform, ahead of Dane.

"Wait!" Cord shouted. His voice sounded squeaky with alarm. "Stop!"

He came running forward.

They had frozen where they stood, looked around swiftly. Then glanced back at Cord coming up. They were well trained.

"What's the matter, Cord?" Nirmond's voice was quiet and urgent.

"Don't get on that raft—it's changed!" Cord's voice sounded wobbly, even to himself. "Maybe it's not even Grandpa—"

He saw he was wrong on the last point before he'd finished the sentence. Scattered along the rim of the raft were discolored spots left by a variety of heat-guns, one of which had been his own. It was the way you goaded the sluggish and mindless things into motion. Cord pointed at the cone-shaped central projection. "There—his head! He's sprouting!"

"Sprouting?" the station manager repeated uncomprehendingly. Grandpa's head, as befitted his girth, was almost twelve feet high and equally wide. It was armor-plated like the back of a saurian to keep off plant-suckers, but two weeks ago it had been an otherwise featureless knob, like those on all other rafts. Now scores of long, kinky, leafless vines had grown out from all surfaces of the cone, like green wires. Some were drawn up like tightly coiled springs, others trailed limply to the platform and over it. The top of the cone was dotted with angry red buds, rather like pimples, which hadn't been there before either. Grandpa looked unhealthy.

"Well," Nirmond said, "so it is. Sprouting!" Grayan made a choked sound. Nirmond glanced at Cord as if puzzled. "Is that all that was bothering you, Cord?"

"Well, sure!" Cord began excitedly. He hadn't caught the significance of the word "all"; his hackles were still up, and he was shaking. "None of them ever—"

Then he stopped. He could tell by their faces that they hadn't got it. Or rather, that they'd got it all right but simply weren't going to let it change their plans. The rafts were classified as harmless, according to the Regulations. Until proved otherwise, they would continue to be regarded as harmless. You didn't waste time quibbling with the Regulations—apparently even if you were the Planetary Regent. You didn't feel you had the time to waste.

He tried again. "Look—" he began. What he wanted to tell them was that Grandpa with one unknown factor added wasn't Grandpa anymore. He was an unpredictable, oversized life-form, to be investigated with cautious thoroughness till you knew what the unknown factor meant.

But it was no use. They knew all that. He stared at them helplessly. "I—"

Dane turned to Nirmond. "Perhaps you'd better check," she said. She didn't add, "to reassure the boy!" but that was what she meant.

Cord felt himself flushing terribly. They thought he was scared—which he was—and they were feeling sorry for him, which they had no right to do. But there was nothing he could say or do now except watch Nirmond walk steadily across the platform. Grandpa shivered slightly a few times, but the rafts always did that when someone first stepped on them. The station manager stopped before one of the kinky sprouts, touched it, and then gave it a tug. He reached up and poked at the lowest of the bud-like growths. "Odd-looking things!" he called back. He gave Cord another glance. "Well, everything seems harmless enough, Cord. Coming aboard, everyone?"

It was like dreaming a dream in which you yelled and yelled at people and couldn't make them hear you! Cord stepped up stiff-legged on the platform behind Dane and Grayan. He knew exactly what would have happened if he'd hesitated even a moment. One of them would have said in a friendly voice, careful not to let it sound too contemptuous: "You don't have to come along if you don't want to, Cord!"

Grayan had unholstered her heat-gun and was ready to start Grandpa moving out into the channels of the Yoger Bay.

Cord hauled out his own heat-gun and said roughly, "I was to do that!"

"All right, Cord." She gave him a brief, impersonal smile, as if he were someone she'd met for the first time that day, and stood aside.

They were so infuriatingly polite! He was, Cord decided, as good as on his way back to Vanadia right now.

For a while, Cord almost hoped that something awesome and catastrophic would happen promptly to teach the Team people a lesson. But nothing did. As always, Grandpa shook himself vaguely and experimentally when he felt the heat on one edge of the platform and then decided to withdraw from it, all of which was standard procedure. Under the water, out of sight, were the raft's working sections: short, thick leaf-structures shaped like paddles and designed to work as such, along with the slimy nettle-streamers which kept the vegetarians of the Yoger Bay away, and a jungle of hair roots through which Grandpa sucked nourishments from the mud and the sluggish waters of the bay, and with which he also anchored himself.

The paddles started churning, the platform quivered, the hair roots were hauled out of the mud; and Grandpa was on his ponderous way.

Cord switched off the heat, reholstered his gun, and stood up. Once in motion, the rafts tended to keep traveling unhurriedly for quite a while. To stop them, you gave them a touch of heat along their leading edge; and they could be turned in any direction by using the gun lightly on the opposite side of the platform.

It was simple enough. Cord didn't look at the others. He was still burning inside. He watched the reed beds move past and open out, giving him glimpses of the misty, yellow and green and blue expanse of the brackish bay ahead. Behind the mist, to the west, were the Yoger Straits, tricky and ugly water when the

tides were running; and beyond the straits lay the open sea, the great Zlanti Deep, which was another world entirely and one of which he hadn't seen much as yet.

Suddenly he was sick with the full realization that he wasn't likely to see any more of it now! Vanadia was a pleasant enough planet; but the wildness and strangeness were long gone from it. It wasn't Sutang.

Grayan called from beside Dane, "What's the best route from here into the farms, Cord?"

"The big channel to the right," he answered. He added somewhat sullenly, "We're headed for it!"

Grayan came over to him. "The Regent doesn't want to see all of it," she said, lowering her voice. "The algae and plankton beds first. Then as much of the mutated grains as we can show her in about three hours. Steer for the ones that have been doing best, and you'll keep Nirmond happy!"

She gave him a conspiratorial wink. Cord looked after her uncertainly. You couldn't tell from her behavior that anything was wrong. Maybe—

He had a flare of hope. It was hard not to like the Team people, even when they were being rock-headed about their Regulations. Perhaps it was that purpose that gave them their vitality and drive, even though it made them remorseless about themselves and everyone else. Anyway, the day wasn't over yet. He might still redeem himself in the Regent's opinion. Something might happen—

Cord had a sudden cheerful, if improbable, vision of some bay monster plunging up on the raft with snapping jaws, and of himself alertly blowing out what passed for the monster's brains before anyone else—Nirmond, in particular—was even aware of the threat. The bay monsters shunned Grandpa, of course, but there might be ways of tempting one of them.

So far, Cord realized, he'd been letting his feelings control him. It was time to start thinking!

Grandpa first. So he'd sprouted—green vines and red buds, purpose unknown, but with no change observable in his behavior patterns otherwise. He was the biggest raft in this end of the bay, though all of them had been growing steadily in the two years since Cord had first seen one. Sutang's seasons changed slowly; its year was somewhat more than five Earth years long. The first Team members to land here hadn't yet seen a full year pass.

Grandpa then was showing a seasonal change. The other rafts, not quite so far developed, would be reacting similarly a little later. Plant animals—they might be blossoming, preparing to propagate.

"Grayan," he called, "how do the rafts get started? When they're small, I mean."

Grayan looked pleased; and Cord's hopes went up a little more. Grayan was on his side again anyway!

"Nobody knows yet," she said. "We were just talking about it. About half of the coastal marsh-fauna of the continent seems to go through a preliminary larval stage in the sea." She nodded at the red buds on the raft's cone. "It looks as if Grandpa is going to produce flowers and let the wind or tide take the seeds out through the straits."

It made sense. It also knocked out Cord's still half-held hope that the change in Grandpa might turn out to be drastic enough, in some way, to justify his reluctance to get on board. Cord studied Grandpa's armored head carefully once more—unwilling to give up that hope entirely. There was a series of vertical gummy black slits between the armor plates, which hadn't been in evidence two weeks ago either. It looked as if Grandpa were beginning to come apart at the seams. Which might indicate that the rafts, big as they grew to be, didn't outlive a full seasonal cycle, but came to flower at about this time of Sutang's year and died. However, it was a safe bet that Grandpa wasn't going to collapse into senile decay before they completed their trip today.

Cord gave up on Grandpa. The other notion returned to him—perhaps he *could* coax an obliging bay monster into action that would show the Regent he was no sissy!

Because the monsters were there, all right.

Kneeling at the edge of the platform and peering down into the wine-colored, clear water of the deep channel they were moving through, Cord could see a fair selection of them at almost any moment.

Some five or six snappers, for one thing. Like big, flattened crayfish, chocolate-brown mostly, with green and red spots on their carapaced backs. In some areas they were so thick you'd wonder what they found to live on, except that they ate almost anything, down to chewing up the mud in which they squatted. However, they preferred their food in large chunks and alive, which was one reason you didn't go swimming in the bay. They would attack a boat on occasion; but the excited manner in which the ones he saw were scuttling off toward the edges of the channel showed they wanted to have nothing to do with a big moving raft.

Dotted across the bottom were two-foot round holes which looked vacant at the moment. Normally, Cord knew, there would be a head filling each of those holes. The heads consisted mainly of triple sets of jaws, held open patiently like so many traps to grab at anything that came within range of the long, wormlike bodies behind the heads. But Grandpa's passage, waving his stingers like transparent pennants through the water, had scared the worms out of sight, too.

Otherwise, mostly schools of small stuff— and then a flash of wicked scarlet, off to the left behind the raft, darting out from the reeds! Turning its needle-nose into their wake.

Cord watched it without moving. He knew that creature, though it was rare in the bay and hadn't been classified. Swift, vicious—alert enough to snap swamp bugs out of the air as they fluttered across the surface. And he'd tantalized one with fishing tackle once into leaping up on a moored raft, where it had flung itself about furiously until he was able to shoot it.

No fishing tackle. A handkerchief might just do it, if he cared to risk an arm—

"What fantastic creatures!" Dane's voice just behind him.

"Yellowheads," said Nirmond. "They've got a high utility rating. Keep down the bugs."

Cord stood up casually. It was no time for tricks! The reed bed to their right was thick with yellowheads, a colony of them. Vaguely froggy things, man-sized and better. Of all the creatures he'd discovered in the bay, Cord liked them least. The flabby, sacklike bodies clung with four thin limbs to the upper sections of the twenty-foot reeds that lined the channel. They hardly ever moved, but their huge, bulging eyes seemed to take in everything that went on about them. Every so often, a downy swamp bug came close enough; and a yellowhead would open its vertical, enormous, tooth-lined slash of a mouth, extend the whole front of its face like a bellows in a flashing strike; and the bug would be gone. They might be useful, but Cord hated them.

"Ten years from now we should know what the cycle of coastal life is like," Nirmond said. "When we set up the Yoger Bay Station there were no yellowheads here. They came the following year. Still with traces of the oceanic larval form; but the metamorphosis was almost complete. About twelve inches long—"

Dane remarked that the same pattern was duplicated endlessly elsewhere. The Regent was inspecting the yellowhead colony with field glasses; she put them down now, looked at Cord, and smiled. "How far to the farms?"

"About twenty minutes."

"The key," Nirmond said, "seems to be the Zlanti Basin. It must be almost a soup of life in spring."

"It is," said Dane, nodding. She had been here in Sutang's spring, four Earth years ago. "It's beginning to look as if the basin alone might justify colonization. The question is

still"—she gestured toward the yellowheads— "how do creatures like that get there?"

They walked off toward the other side of the raft, arguing about ocean currents. Cord might have followed. But something splashed back of them, off to the left and not too far back. He stayed, watching.

After a moment, he saw the big yellowhead. It had slipped down from its reedy perch, which was what had caused the splash. Almost submerged at the waterline, it stared after the raft with huge pale-green eyes. To Cord, it seemed to look directly at him. In that moment, he knew for the first time why he didn't like yellowheads. There was something very like intelligence in that look, an alien calculation. In creatures like that, intelligence seemed out of place. What use could they have for it?

A little shiver went over him when it sank completely under the water and he realized it intended to swim after the raft. But it was mostly excitement. He had never seen a yellowhead come down out of the reeds before. The obliging monster he'd been looking for might be presenting itself in an unexpected way.

Half a minute later, he watched it again, swimming awkwardly far down. It had no immediate intention of boarding, at any rate. Cord saw it come into the area of the raft's trailing stingers. It maneuvered its way between them with curiously human swimming motions, and went out of sight under the platform.

He stood up, wondering what it meant. The yellowhead had appeared to know about the stingers; there had been an air of purpose in every move of its approach. He was tempted to tell the others about it, but there was the moment of triumph he could have if it suddenly came slobbering up over the edge of the platform and he nailed it before their eyes.

It was almost time anyway to turn the raft in toward the farms. If nothing happened before then . . .

He watched. Almost five minutes, but no sign of the yellowhead. Still wondering, a little uneasy, he gave Grandpa a calculated needling of heat.

After a moment, he repeated it. Then he drew a deep breath and forgot all about the yellowhead.

"Nirmond!" he called sharply.

The three of them were standing near the center of the platform, next to the big armored cone, looking ahead at the farms. They glanced around.

"What's the matter now, Cord?"

Cord couldn't say it for a moment. He was suddenly, terribly scared again. Something *had* gone wrong!

"The raft won't turn!" he told them.

"Give it a real burn this time!" Nirmond said.

Cord glanced up at him. Nirmond, standing a few steps in front of Dane and Grayan as if he wanted to protect them, had begun to look a little strained, and no wonder. Cord already had pressed the gun to three different points on the platform; but Grandpa appeared to have developed a sudden anesthesia for heat. They kept moving out steadily toward the center of the bay.

Now Cord held his breath, switched the heat on full, and let Grandpa have it. A six-inch patch on the platform blistered up instantly, turned brown, then black—

Grandpa stopped dead. Just like that.

"That's right! Keep burn—" Nirmond didn't finish his order.

A giant shudder. Cord staggered back toward the water. Then the whole edge of the raft came curling up behind him and went down again, smacking the bay with a sound like a cannon shot. He flew forward off his feet, hit the platform facedown, and flattened himself against it. It swelled up beneath him. Two more enormous slaps and joltings. Then quiet. He looked round for the others.

He lay within twelve feet of the central cone. Some twenty or thirty of the mysterious new vines the cone had sprouted were stretched out stiffly toward him now, like so many thin green fingers. They couldn't quite reach him. The nearest tip was still ten inches from his shoes.

But Grandpa had caught the others, all three of them. They were tumbled together at the foot of the cone, wrapped in a stiff network of green vegetable ropes, and they didn't move.

Cord drew his feet up cautiously, prepared for another earthquake reaction. But nothing happened. Then he discovered that Grandpa was back in motion on his previous course. The heat-gun had vanished. Gently, he took out the Vanadian gun.

A voice, thin and pain-filled, spoke to him from one of the three huddled bodies.

"Cord? It didn't get you?" It was the Regent.

"No," he said, keeping his voice low. He realized suddenly he'd simply assumed they were all dead. Now he felt sick and shaky.

"What are you doing?"

Cord looked at Grandpa's big armor-plated head with a certain hunger. The cones were hollowed out inside; the station's lab had decided their chief function was to keep enough air trapped under the rafts to float them. But in that central section was also the organ that controlled Grandpa's overall reactions.

He said softly, "I've got a gun and twelve heavy-duty explosive bullets. Two of them will blow that cone apart."

"No good, Cord!" the pain-racked voice told him. "If the thing sinks, we'll die anyway. You have anesthetic charges for that gun of yours?"

He stared at her back. "Yes."

"Give Nirmond and the girl a shot each, before you do anything else. Directly into the spine, if you can. But don't come any closer. . . ."

Somehow, Cord couldn't argue with that voice. He stood up carefully. The gun made two soft spitting sounds.

"All right," he said hoarsely. "What do I do now?"

Dane was silent a moment. "I'm sorry, Cord. I can't tell you that. I'll tell you what I can. . . ."

She paused for some seconds again. "This

thing didn't try to kill us, Cord. It could have easily. It's incredibly strong. I saw it break Nirmond's legs. But as soon as we stopped moving, it just held us. They were both unconscious then. . . ."

"You've got that to go on. It was trying to pitch you within reach of its vines or tendrils, or whatever they are, too, wasn't it?"

"I think so," Cord said shakily. That was what had happened, of course; and at any moment Grandpa might try again.

"Now it's feeding us some sort of anesthetic of its own through those vines. Tiny thorns. A sort of numbness . . ." Dane's voice trailed off a moment. Then she said clearly, "Look, Cord—it seems we're food it's storing up! You get that?"

"Yes," he said.

"Seeding time for the rafts. There are analogues. Live food for its seed probably; not for the raft. One couldn't have counted on that. Cord?"

"Yes. I'm here."

"I want," said Dane, "to stay awake as long as I can. But there's really just one other thing— this raft's going somewhere. To some particularly favorable location. And that might be very near shore. You might make it in then; otherwise it's up to you. But keep your head and wait for a chance. No heroics, understand?"

"Sure, I understand," Cord told her. He realized then that he was talking reassuringly, as if it weren't the Planetary Regent but someone like Grayan.

"Nirmond's the worst," Dane said. "The girl was knocked unconscious at once. If it weren't for my arm— But, if we can get help in five hours or so, everything should be all right. Let me know if anything happens, Cord."

"I will," Cord said gently again. Then he sighted his gun carefully at a point between Dane's shoulder blades, and the anesthetic chamber made its soft, spitting sound once more. Dane's taut body relaxed slowly, and that was all.

There was no point Cord could see in letting her stay awake, because they weren't going any-

where near shore. The reed beds and the channels were already behind them, and Grandpa hadn't changed direction by the fraction of a degree. He was moving out into the open bay— and he was picking up company!

So far, Cord could count seven big rafts within two miles of them; and on the three that were closest he could make out a sprouting of new green vines. All of them were traveling in a straight direction; and the common point they were all headed for appeared to be the roaring center of the Yoger Straits, now some three miles away!

Behind the straits, the cold Zlanti Deep— the rolling fogs, and the open sea! It might be seeding time for the rafts, but it looked as if they weren't going to distribute their seeds in the bay. . . .

For a human being, Cord was a fine swimmer. He had a gun and he had a knife; in spite of what Dane had said, he might have stood a chance among the killers of the bay. But it would be a very small chance, at best. And it wasn't, he thought, as if there weren't still other possibilities. He was going to keep his head.

Except by accident, of course, nobody was going to come looking for them in time to do any good. If anyone did look, it would be around the Bay Farms. There were a number of rafts moored there; and it would be assumed they'd used one of them. Now and then something unexpected happened and somebody simply vanished—by the time it was figured out just what had happened on this occasion, it would be much too late.

Neither was anybody likely to notice within the next few hours that the rafts had started migrating out of the swamps through the Yoger Straits. There was a small weather station a little inland, on the north side of the straits, which used a helicopter occasionally. It was about as improbable, Cord decided dismally, that they'd use it in the right spot just now as it would be for a jet transport to happen to come in low enough to spot them.

The fact that it was up to him, as the Regent

had said, sank in a little more after that! Cord had never felt so lonely.

Simply because he was going to try it sooner or later, he carried out an experiment next that he knew couldn't work. He opened the gun's anesthetic chamber and counted out fifty pellets—rather hurriedly because he didn't particularly want to think of what he might be using them for eventually. There were around three hundred charges left in the chamber then; and in the next few minutes Cord carefully planted a third of them in Grandpa's head.

He stopped after that. A whale might have showed signs of somnolence under a lesser load. Grandpa paddled on undisturbed. Perhaps he had become a little numb in spots, but his cells weren't equipped to distribute the soporific effect of that type of drug.

There wasn't anything else Cord could think of doing before they reached the straits. At the rate they were moving, he calculated that would happen in something less than an hour; and if they did pass through the straits, he was going to risk a swim. He didn't think Dane would have disapproved, under the circumstances. If the raft simply carried them all out into the foggy vastness of the Zlanti Deep, there would be no practical chance of survival left at all.

Meanwhile, Grandpa was definitely picking up speed. And there were other changes going on—minor ones, but still a little awe-inspiring to Cord. The pimply-looking red buds that dotted the upper part of the cone were opening out gradually. From the center of most of them protruded now something like a thin, wet, scarlet worm: a worm that twisted weakly, extended itself by an inch or so, rested and twisted again, and stretched up a little farther, groping into the air. The vertical black slits between the armor plates looked somehow deeper and wider than they had been even some minutes ago; a dark, thick liquid dripped slowly from several of them.

Under other circumstances Cord knew he would have been fascinated by these develop-ments in Grandpa. As it was, they drew his suspicious attention only because he didn't know what they meant.

Then something quite horrible happened suddenly. Grayan started moaning loudly and terribly and twisted almost completely around. Afterwards, Cord knew it hadn't been a second before he stopped her struggles and the sounds together with another anesthetic pellet; but the vines had tightened their grip on her first, not flexibly but like the digging, bony green talons of some monstrous bird of prey. If Dane hadn't warned him—

White and sweating, Cord put his gun down slowly while the vines relaxed again. Grayan didn't seem to have suffered any additional harm; and she would certainly have been the first to point out that his murderous rage might have been as intelligently directed against a machine. But for some moments Cord continued to luxuriate furiously in the thought that, at any instant he chose, he could still turn the raft very quickly into a ripped and exploded mess of sinking vegetation.

Instead, and more sensibly, he gave both Dane and Nirmond another shot, to prevent a similar occurrence with them. The contents of two such pellets, he knew, would keep any human being torpid for at least four hours. Five shots—

Cord withdrew his mind hastily from the direction it was turning into; but it wouldn't stay withdrawn. The thought kept coming up again, until at last he had to recognize it:

Five shots would leave the three of them completely unconscious, whatever else might happen to them, until they either died from other causes or were given a counteracting agent.

Shocked, he told himself he couldn't do it. It was exactly like killing them.

But then, quite steadily, he found himself raising the gun once more, to bring the total charge for each of the three Team people up to five. And if it was the first time in the last four years Cord had felt like crying, it also seemed to him that he had begun to understand what was meant by using your head—along with other things.

Barely thirty minutes later, he watched a raft as big as the one he rode go sliding into the foaming white waters of the straits a few hundred yards ahead, and dart off abruptly at an angle, caught by one of the swirling currents. It pitched and spun, made some headway, and was swept aside again. And then it righted itself once more. Not like some blindly animated vegetable, Cord thought, but like a creature that struggled with intelligent purpose to maintain its chosen direction.

At least, they seemed practically unsinkable. . . .

Knife in hand, he flattened himself against the platform as the straits roared just ahead. When the platform jolted and tilted up beneath him, he rammed the knife all the way into it and hung on. Cold water rushed suddenly over him, and Grandpa shuddered like a laboring engine. In the middle of it all, Cord had the horrified notion that the raft might release its unconscious human prisoners in its struggle with the straits. But he underestimated Grandpa in that. Grandpa also hung on.

Abruptly, it was over. They were riding a long swell, and there were three other rafts not far away. The straits had swept them together, but they seemed to have no interest in one another's company. As Cord stood up shakily and began to strip off his clothes, they were visibly drawing apart again. The platform of one of them was half-submerged; it must have lost too much of the air that held it afloat and, like a small ship, it was foundering.

From this point, it was only a two-mile swim to the shore north of the straits, and another mile inland from there to the Straits Head Station. He didn't know about the current; but the distance didn't seem too much, and he couldn't bring himself to leave knife and gun behind. The bay creatures loved warmth and mud, they didn't venture beyond the straits. But Zlanti

Deep bred its own killers, though they weren't often observed so close to shore.

Things were beginning to look rather hopeful.

Thin, crying voices drifted overhead, like the voices of curious cats, as Cord knotted his clothes into a tight bundle, shoes inside. He looked up. There were four of them circling there; magnified seagoing swamp bugs, each carrying an unseen rider. Probably harmless scavengers—but the ten-foot wingspread was impressive. Uneasily, Cord remembered the venomously carnivorous rider he'd left lying beside the station.

One of them dipped lazily and came sliding down toward him. It soared overhead and came back, to hover about the raft's cone.

The bug rider that directed the mindless flier hadn't been interested in him at all! Grandpa was baiting it!

Cord stared in fascination. The top of the cone was alive now with a softly wriggling mass of the scarlet, wormlike extrusions that had started sprouting before the raft left the bay. Presumably, they looked enticingly edible to the bug rider.

The flier settled with an airy fluttering and touched the cone. Like a trap springing shut, the green vines flashed up and around it, crumpling the brittle wings, almost vanishing into the long soft body—

Barely a second later, Grandpa made another catch, this one from the sea itself. Cord had a fleeting glimpse of something like a small, rubbery seal that flung itself out of the water upon the edge of the raft, with a suggestion of desperate haste—and was flipped on instantly against the cone, where the vines clamped it down beside the flier's body.

It wasn't the enormous ease with which the unexpected kill was accomplished that left Cord standing there, completely shocked. It was the shattering of his hopes to swim to shore from here. Fifty yards away, the creature from which the rubbery thing had been fleeing showed briefly on the surface, as it turned away from the raft; and the glance was all he needed. The ivory-white body and gaping jaws were similar enough to those of the shark of Earth to indicate the pursuer's nature. The important difference was that, wherever the white hunters of the Zlanti Deep went, they went by the thousands.

Stunned by that incredible piece of bad luck, still clutching his bundled clothes, Cord stared toward shore. Knowing what to look for, he could spot the telltale roilings of the surface now—the long, ivory gleams that flashed through the swells and vanished again. Shoals of smaller things burst into the air in sprays of glittering desperation and fell back.

He would have been snapped up like a drowning fly before he'd covered a twentieth of that distance!

But almost another full minute passed before the realization of the finality of his defeat really sank in.

Grandpa was beginning to eat!

Each of the dark slits down the sides of the cone was a mouth. So far only one of them was in operating condition, and the raft wasn't able to open that one very wide as yet. The first morsel had been fed into it, however: the bug rider the vines had plucked out of the flier's downy neck fur. It took Grandpa several minutes to work it out of sight, small as it was. But it was a start.

Cord didn't feel quite sane anymore. He sat there, clutching his bundle of clothes and only vaguely aware of the fact that he was shivering steadily under the cold spray that touched him now and then, while he followed Grandpa's activities attentively. He decided it would be at least some hours before one of that black set of mouths grew flexible and vigorous enough to dispose of a human being. Under the circumstances, it couldn't make much difference to the other human beings here; but the moment Grandpa reached for the first of them would also be the moment he finally blew the raft to

pieces. The white hunters were cleaner eaters, at any rate; and that was about the extent to which he could still control what was going to happen.

Meanwhile, there was the very faint chance that the weather station's helicopter might spot them. . . .

Meanwhile also, in a weary and horrified fascination, he kept debating the mystery of what could have produced such a nightmarish change in the rafts. He could guess where they were going by now; there were scattered strings of them stretching back to the straits or roughly parallel to their own course, and the direction was that of the plankton-swarming pool of the Zlanti Basin, a thousand miles to the north. Given time, even mobile lily pads like the rafts had been could make that trip for the benefit of their seedlings. But nothing in their structure explained the sudden change into alert and capable carnivores.

He watched the rubbery little seal-thing being hauled up to a mouth next. The vines broke its neck; and the mouth took it in up to the shoulders and then went on working patiently at what was still a trifle too large a bite. Meanwhile, there were more thin cat-cries overhead; and a few minutes later, two more sea bugs were trapped almost simultaneously and added to the larder. Grandpa dropped the dead seal-thing and fed himself another bug rider. The second rider left its mount with a sudden hop, sank its teeth viciously into one of the vines that caught it again, and was promptly battered to death against the platform.

Cord felt a resurge of unreasoning hatred against Grandpa. Killing a bug was about equal to cutting a branch from a tree; they had almost no life-awareness. But the rider had aroused his partisanship because of its appearance of intelligent action—and it was in fact closer to the human scale in that feature than to the monstrous life-form that had, mechanically, but quite successfully, trapped both it and the human beings. Then his thoughts had drifted again; and he found himself speculating vaguely on the curious symbiosis in which the nerve systems of two creatures as dissimilar as the bugs and their riders could be linked so closely that they functioned as one organism.

Suddenly an expression of vast and stunned surprise appeared on his face.

Why—now he knew!

Cord stood up hurriedly, shaking with excitement, the whole plan complete in his mind. And a dozen long vines snaked instantly in the direction of his sudden motion, and groped for him, taut and stretching. They couldn't reach him, but their savagely alert reaction froze Cord briefly where he was. The platform was shuddering under his feet, as if in irritation at his inaccessibility; but it couldn't be tilted up suddenly here to throw him within the grasp of the vines, as it could around the edges.

Still, it was a warning! Cord sidled gingerly around the cone till he had gained the position he wanted, which was on the forward half of the raft. And then he waited. Waited long minutes, quite motionless, until his heart stopped pounding and the irregular angry shivering of the surface of the raft-thing died away, and the last vine tendril had stopped its blind groping. It might help a lot if, for a second or two after he next started moving, Grandpa wasn't too aware of his exact whereabouts!

He looked back once to check how far they had gone by now beyond the Straits Head Station. It couldn't, he decided, be even an hour behind them. Which was close enough, by the most pessimistic count—if everything else worked out all right! He didn't try to think out in detail what that "everything else" could include, because there were factors that simply couldn't be calculated in advance. And he had an uneasy feeling that speculating too vividly about them might make him almost incapable of carrying out his plan.

At last, moving carefully, Cord took the knife in his left hand but left the gun holstered. He raised the tightly knotted bundle of clothes slowly over his head, balanced in his right hand. With a long, smooth motion he tossed the bundle back across the cone, almost to the opposite edge of the platform.

It hit with a soggy thump. Almost immediately, the whole far edge of the raft buckled and flapped up to toss the strange object to the reaching vines.

Simultaneously, Cord was racing forward. For a moment, his attempt to divert Grandpa's attention seemed completely successful—then he was pitched to his knees as the platform came up.

He was within eight feet of the edge. As it slapped down again, he threw himself desperately forward.

An instant later, he was knifing down through cold, clear water, just ahead of the raft, then twisting and coming up again.

The raft was passing over him. Clouds of tiny sea creatures scattered through its dark jungle of feeding roots. Cord jerked back from a broad, wavering streak of glassy greenness, which was a stinger, and felt a burning jolt on his side, which meant he'd been touched lightly by another. He bumped on blindly through the slimy black tangles of hair roots that covered the bottom of the raft; then green half-light passed over him, and he burst up into the central bubble under the cone.

Half-light and foul, hot air. Water slapped around him, dragging him away again—nothing to hang on to here! Then above him, to his right, molded against the interior curve of the cone as if it had grown there from the start, the froglike, man-sized shape of the yellowhead.

The raft rider . . .

Cord reached up and caught Grandpa's symbiotic partner and guide by a flabby hind leg, pulled himself half out of the water, and struck twice with the knife, fast while the pale-green eyes were still opening.

He'd thought the yellowhead might need a second or so to detach itself from its host, as the bug riders usually did, before it tried to defend itself. This one merely turned its head;

the mouth slashed down and clamped on Cord's left arm above the elbow. His right hand sank the knife through one staring eye, and the yellowhead jerked away, pulling the knife from his grasp.

Sliding down, he wrapped both hands around the slimy leg and hauled with all his weight. For a moment more, the yellowhead hung on. Then the countless neural extensions that connected it now with the raft came free in a succession of sucking, tearing sounds; and Cord and the yellowhead splashed into the water together.

Black tangle of roots again—and two more electric burns suddenly across his back and legs! Strangling, Cord let go. Below him, for a moment, a body was turning over and over with oddly human motions; then a solid wall of water thrust him up and aside, as something big and white struck the turning body and went on.

Cord broke the surface twelve feet behind the raft. And that would have been that, if Grandpa hadn't already been slowing down.

After two tries, he floundered back up on the platform and lay there gasping and coughing awhile. There were no indications that his presence was resented now. A few vine tips twitched uneasily, as if trying to remember previous functions, when he came limping up presently to make sure his three companions were still breathing; but Cord never noticed that.

They were still breathing; and he knew better than to waste time trying to help them himself. He took Grayan's heat-gun from its holster. Grandpa had come to a full stop.

Cord hadn't had time to become completely sane again, or he might have worried now whether Grandpa, violently sundered from his controlling partner, was still capable of motion on his own. Instead, he determined the approximate direction of the Straits Head Station, selected a corresponding spot on the platform, and gave Grandpa a light tap of heat.

Nothing happened immediately. Cord sighed patiently and stepped up the heat a little.

Grandpa shuddered gently. Cord stood up.

Slowly and hesitatingly at first, then with steadfast—though now again brainless—purpose, Grandpa began paddling back toward the Straits Head Station.

The Game of Rat and Dragon

CORDWAINER SMITH

Paul Myron Anthony Linebarger (1913–1966) was a highly original US writer who used the byline "Cordwainer Smith" for his science fiction. Born in Milwaukee, Linebarger grew up in Japan, China, France, and Germany. His father, Paul Myron Wentworth Linebarger, helped finance the Chinese revolution of 1911 and served as legal adviser to Sun Yat-sen (who became Paul's godfather). Sun gave the younger Linebarger the Chinese name Lin Bah Loh, or "Forest of Incandescent Bliss." He would later become a confidant of Chiang Kai-shek, founder of Taiwan, and also at various times served as a soldier, diplomat, and operative in China and the Far East generally. He earned his PhD in political science from Johns Hopkins and authored *Psychological Warfare*, which is still regarded as the authoritative book in its field. Linebarger wrote a science fiction novel, *Norstrilia*, and, under other pen names (including "Felix C. Forrest," a play on his Chinese name), three mainstream novels: *Ria*, *Carola*, and *Atomsk*. *Ria* and *Carola* have been compared to the work of Jean-Paul Sartre and featured female protagonists.

Linebarger is primarily known today for his science fiction short stories. He published his first story, "Scanners Live in Vain" (*Fantasy Book*), in 1950, but it wasn't until the mid-1950s that he published more, due in part to the encouragement of Frederik Pohl. Most of his major science fiction was written between 1955 and 1966. However, Linebarger had been writing science fiction since he was a child, including a bad imitation of Edgar Rice Burroughs entitled "The Books of Futurity" and other material that he based on Chinese folklore. His story "War No. 81-Q" was published in his high school cadet corps magazine when he was fifteen. Many other stories, written in the 1930s and 1940s, exist only in a red-leather-bound volume owned by Linebarger's daughter and were never submitted for publication. Two fantasies, "Alauda Dalma" and "The Archer and the Deep," were sent to *Unknown* in the 1940s and to Judith Merril in 1961 but were rejected. It was in 1945, consigned to a desk job at the Pentagon, that Linebarger wrote "Scanners Live in Vain."

"The Game of Rat and Dragon" was first published in *Galaxy Science Fiction* in 1955. Two major themes dominate in this story: space travel and telepathy. Humans partner with telepathic cats in order to achieve warp speed while human telepaths protect others from the dragons of deep space. This story is considered one of the earliest stories set in the Instrumentality Universe. The Instrumentality of Mankind, which features in most of the author's best stories, rules over humanity across a vast number of planets in the far future and tries to resurrect ancient cultures so as to benefit the "Rediscovery of Man."

As John J. Pierce wrote in his highly recommended introduction to *The Rediscovery of Man: The Complete Short Science Fiction of Cordwainer Smith* (1993), "It is impossible to fit Smith's work into any of the neat categories that appeal to most readers or critics. It isn't hard science fiction, it isn't military science fiction, it isn't sociological science fiction, it isn't satire, it isn't surrealism, it isn't postmodernism. For those who have fallen in love with it over the years, however, it is some of the most powerful science fiction ever written."

Smith was influenced by Alfred Jarry and Jorge Luis Borges, both included in this volume.

THE GAME OF RAT AND DRAGON

Cordwainer Smith

Only partners could fight this deadliest of wars—and the one way to dissolve the partnership was to be personally dissolved!

THE TABLE

Pinlighting is a hell of a way to earn a living. Underhill was furious as he closed the door behind himself. It didn't make much sense to wear a uniform and look like a soldier if people didn't appreciate what you did.

He sat down in his chair, laid his head back in the headrest, and pulled the helmet down over his forehead.

As he waited for the pin-set to warm up, he remembered the girl in the outer corridor. She had looked at it, then looked at him scornfully.

"Meow." That was all she had said. Yet it had cut him like a knife.

What did she think he was—a fool, a loafer, a uniformed nonentity? Didn't she know that for every half hour of pinlighting, he got a minimum of two months' recuperation in the hospital?

By now the set was warm. He felt the squares of space around him, sensed himself at the middle of an immense grid, a cubic grid, full of nothing. Out in that nothingness, he could sense the hollow aching horror of space itself and could feel the terrible anxiety which his mind encountered whenever it met the faintest trace of inert dust.

As he relaxed, the comforting solidity of the sun, the clockwork of the familiar planets and the moon rang in on him. Our own solar system was as charming and as simple as an ancient cuckoo clock filled with familiar ticking and with reassuring noises. The odd little moons of Mars swung around their planet like frantic mice, yet their regularity was itself an assurance that all was well. Far above the plane of the ecliptic, he could feel half a ton of dust more or less drifting outside the lanes of human travel.

Here there was nothing to fight, nothing to challenge the mind, to tear the living soul out of a body with its roots dripping in effluvium as tangible as blood.

Nothing ever moved in on the solar system. He could wear the pin-set forever and be nothing more than a sort of telepathic astronomer, a man who could feel the hot, warm protection of the sun throbbing and burning against his living mind.

Woodley came in.

"Same old ticking world," said Underhill. "Nothing to report. No wonder they didn't develop the pin-set until they began to planoform. Down here with the hot sun around us, it feels so good and so quiet. You can feel everything spinning and turning. It's nice and sharp and compact. It's sort of like sitting around home."

Woodley grunted. He was not much given to flights of fantasy.

Undeterred, Underhill went on, "It must have been pretty good to have been an ancient man. I wonder why they burned up their world with war. They didn't have to planoform. They didn't have to go out to earn their livings among the stars. They didn't have to dodge the Rats or play the Game. They couldn't have invented pinlighting because they didn't have any need of it, did they, Woodley?"

Woodley grunted, "Uh-huh." Woodley was twenty-six years old and due to retire in one more year. He already had a farm picked out. He had gotten through ten years of hard work pinlighting with the best of them. He had kept his sanity by not thinking very much about his job, meeting the strains of the task whenever he had to meet them and thinking nothing more about his duties until the next emergency arose.

Woodley never made a point of getting popular among the Partners. None of the Partners liked him very much. Some of them even resented him. He was suspected of thinking ugly thoughts of the Partners on occasion, but since none of the Partners ever thought a complaint in articulate form, the other pinlighters and the Chiefs of the Instrumentality left him alone.

Underhill was still full of the wonder of their job. Happily he babbled on, "What does happen to us when we planoform? Do you think it's sort of like dying? Did you ever see anybody who had his soul pulled out?"

"Pulling souls is just a way of talking about it," said Woodley. "After all these years, nobody knows whether we have souls or not."

"But I saw one once. I saw what Dogwood looked like when he came apart. There was something funny. It looked wet and sort of sticky as if it were bleeding and it went out of him—and you know what they did to Dogwood? They took him away, up in that part of the hospital where you and I never go—way up at the top part where the others are, where the others always have to go if they are alive after the Rats of the Up-and-Out have gotten them."

Woodley sat down and lit an ancient pipe. He was burning something called tobacco in it.

It was a dirty sort of habit, but it made him look very dashing and adventurous.

"Look here, youngster. You don't have to worry about that stuff. Pinlighting is getting better all the time. The Partners are getting better. I've seen them pinlight two Rats forty-six million miles apart in one and a half milliseconds. As long as people had to try to work the pin-sets themselves, there was always the chance that with a minimum of four hundred milliseconds for the human mind to set a pinlight, we wouldn't light the Rats up fast enough to protect our planoforming ships. The Partners have changed all that. Once they get going, they're faster than Rats. And they always will be. I know it's not easy, letting a Partner share your mind—"

"It's not easy for them, either," said Underhill.

"Don't worry about them. They're not human. Let them take care of themselves. I've seen more pinlighters go crazy from monkeying around with Partners than I have ever seen caught by the Rats. How many do you actually know of them that got grabbed by Rats?"

Underhill looked down at his fingers, which shone green and purple in the vivid light thrown by the tuned-in pin-set, and counted ships. The thumb for the *Andromeda*, lost with crew and passengers, the index finger and the middle finger for *Release Ship*s 43 and 56, found with their pin-sets burned out and every man, woman, and child on board dead or insane. The ring finger, the little finger, and the thumb of the other hand were the first three battleships to be lost to the Rats—lost as people realized that there was something out there *underneath space itself* which was alive, capricious, and malevolent.

Planoforming was sort of funny. It felt like, like—

Like nothing much.

Like the twinge of a mild electric shock.

Like the ache of a sore tooth bitten on for the first time.

Like a slightly painful flash of light against the eyes.

Yet in that time, a forty-thousand-ton ship lifting free above Earth disappeared somehow or other into two dimensions and appeared half a light-year or fifty light-years off.

At one moment, he would be sitting in the Fighting Room, the pin-set ready and the familiar solar system ticking around inside his head. For a second or a year (he could never tell how long it really was, subjectively), the funny little flash went through him and then he was loose in the Up-and-Out, the terrible open spaces between the stars, where the stars themselves felt like pimples on his telepathic mind and the planets were too far away to be sensed or read.

Somewhere in this outer space, a gruesome death awaited, death and horror of a kind which man had never encountered until he reached out for interstellar space itself. Apparently the light of the suns kept the Dragons away.

Dragons. That was what people called them. To ordinary people, there was nothing, nothing except the shiver of planoforming and the hammer blow of sudden death or the dark spastic note of lunacy descending into their minds.

But to the telepaths, they were Dragons.

In the fraction of a second between the telepaths' awareness of a hostile something out in the black, hollow nothingness of space and the impact of a ferocious, ruinous psychic blow against all living things within the ship, the telepaths had sensed entities something like the Dragons of ancient human lore, beasts more clever than beasts, demons more tangible than demons, hungry vortices of aliveness and hate compounded by unknown means out of the thin tenuous matter between the stars.

It took a surviving ship to bring back the news—a ship in which, by sheer chance, a telepath had a light beam ready, turning it out at the innocent dust so that, within the panorama of his mind, the Dragon dissolved into nothing at all and the other passengers, themselves non-telepathic, went about their way not realizing that their own immediate deaths had been averted.

From then on, it was easy—almost.

Planoforming ships always carried telepaths. Telepaths had their sensitiveness enlarged to an immense range by the pin-sets, which were telepathic amplifiers adapted to the mammal mind. The pin-sets in turn were electronically geared into small dirigible light bombs. Light did it.

Light broke up the Dragons, allowed the ships to re-form three-dimensionally, skip, skip, skip, as they moved from star to star.

The odds suddenly moved down from a hundred to one against mankind to sixty to forty in mankind's favor.

This was not enough. The telepaths were trained to become ultrasensitive, trained to become aware of the Dragons in less than a millisecond.

But it was found that the Dragons could move a million miles in just under two milliseconds and that this was not enough for the human mind to activate the light beams.

Attempts had been made to sheath the ships in light at all times.

This defense wore out.

As mankind learned about the Dragons, so too, apparently, the Dragons learned about mankind. Somehow they flattened their own bulk and came in on extremely flat trajectories very quickly.

Intense light was needed, light of sunlike intensity. This could be provided only by light bombs. Pinlighting came into existence.

Pinlighting consisted of the detonation of ultra-vivid miniature photonuclear bombs, which converted a few ounces of a magnesium isotope into pure visible radiance.

. . .

The odds kept coming down in mankind's favor, yet ships were being lost.

It became so bad that people didn't even want to find the ships because the rescuers knew what they would see. It was sad to bring back to Earth three hundred bodies ready for burial and two hundred or three hundred lunatics, damaged beyond repair, to be wakened, and fed, and cleaned, and put to sleep, wakened, and fed again until their lives were ended.

Telepaths tried to reach into the minds of the psychotics who had been damaged by the Dragons, but they found nothing there beyond vivid spouting columns of fiery terror bursting from the primordial id itself, the volcanic source of life.

Then came the Partners.

Man and Partner could do together what Man could not do alone. Men had the intellect. Partners had the speed.

The Partners rode their tiny craft, no larger than footballs, outside the spaceships. They planoformed with the ships. They rode beside them in their six-pound craft ready to attack.

The tiny ships of the Partners were swift. Each carried a dozen pinlights, bombs no bigger than thimbles.

The pinlighters threw the Partners—quite literally threw—by means of mind-to-firing relays direct at the Dragons.

What seemed to be Dragons to the human mind appeared in the form of gigantic Rats in the minds of the Partners.

Out in the pitiless nothingness of space, the Partners' minds responded to an instinct as old as life. The Partners attacked, striking with a speed faster than man's, going from attack to attack until the Rats or themselves were destroyed. Almost all the time, it was the Partners who won.

With the safety of the interstellar skip, skip, skip of the ships, commerce increased immensely, the population of all the colonies went up, and the demand for trained Partners increased.

Underhill and Woodley were a part of the third generation of pinlighters and yet, to them, it seemed as though their craft had endured forever.

Gearing space into minds by means of the pinset, adding the Partners to those minds, keying up the mind for the tension of a fight on which all depended—this was more than human synapses could stand for long. Underhill needed his two months' rest after half an hour of fighting. Woodley needed his retirement after ten years of service. They were young. They were good. But they had limitations.

So much depended on the choice of Partners, so much on the sheer luck of who drew whom.

THE SHUFFLE

Father Moontree and the little girl named West entered the room. They were the other two pinlighters. The human complement of the Fighting Room was now complete.

Father Moontree was a red-faced man of forty-five who had lived the peaceful life of a farmer until he reached his fortieth year. Only then, belatedly, did the authorities find he was telepathic and agree to let him late in life enter upon the career of pinlighter. He did well at it, but he was fantastically old for this kind of business.

Father Moontree looked at the glum Woodley and the musing Underhill. "How're the youngsters today? Ready for a good fight?"

"Father always wants a fight," giggled the little girl named West. She was such a little little girl. Her giggle was high and childish. She looked like the last person in the world one would expect to find in the rough, sharp dueling of pinlighting.

Underhill had been amused one time when he found one of the most sluggish of the Partners coming away happy from contact with the mind of the girl named West.

Usually the Partners didn't care much about the human minds with which they were paired for the journey. The Partners seemed to take the attitude that human minds were complex and fouled up beyond belief, anyhow. No Partner ever questioned the superiority of the human mind, though very few of the Partners were much impressed by that superiority.

The Partners liked people. They were willing to fight with them. They were even willing to die for them. But when a Partner liked an individual the way, for example, that Captain Wow or the Lady May liked Underhill, the liking had nothing to do with intellect. It was a matter of temperament, of feel.

Underhill knew perfectly well that Captain Wow regarded his, Underhill's, brains as silly. What Captain Wow liked was Underhill's friendly emotional structure, the cheerfulness and glint of wicked amusement that shot through Underhill's unconscious thought patterns, and the gaiety with which Underhill faced danger. The words, the history books, the ideas, the science—Underhill could sense all that in his own mind, reflected back from Captain Wow's mind, as so much rubbish.

Miss West looked at Underhill. "I bet you've put stickum on the stones."

"I did not!"

Underhill felt his ears grow red with embarrassment. During his novitiate, he had tried to cheat in the lottery because he got particularly fond of a special Partner, a lovely young mother named Murr. It was so much easier to operate with Murr and she was so affectionate toward him that he forgot pinlighting was hard work and that he was not instructed to have a good time with his Partner. They were both designed and prepared to go into deadly battle together.

One cheating had been enough. They had found him out and he had been laughed at for years.

Father Moontree picked up the imitation-leather cup and shook the stone dice which assigned them their Partners for the trip. By senior rights, he took first draw.

He grimaced. He had drawn a greedy old character, a tough old male whose mind was full of slobbering thoughts of food, veritable oceans full of half-spoiled fish. Father Moontree had once said that he burped cod liver oil for weeks after drawing that particular glutton, so strongly had the telepathic image of fish impressed itself upon his mind. Yet the glutton was a glutton for danger as well as for fish. He had killed sixty-three Dragons, more than any other Partner in the service, and was quite literally worth his weight in gold.

The little girl West came next. She drew Captain Wow. When she saw who it was, she smiled.

"I *like* him," she said. "He's such fun to fight with. He feels so nice and cuddly in my mind."

"Cuddly, hell," said Woodley. "I've been in his mind, too. It's the most leering mind in this ship, bar none."

"Nasty man," said the little girl. She said it declaratively, without reproach.

Underhill, looking at her, shivered.

He didn't see how she could take Captain Wow so calmly. Captain Wow's mind *did* leer. When Captain Wow got excited in the middle of a battle, confused images of Dragons, deadly Rats, luscious beds, the smell of fish, and the shock of space all scrambled together in his mind as he and Captain Wow, their consciousnesses linked together through the pin-set, became a fantastic composite of human being and Persian cat.

That's the trouble with working with cats, thought Underhill. It's a pity that nothing else anywhere will serve as Partner. Cats were all right once you got in touch with them telepathically. They were smart enough to meet the needs of the fight, but their motives and desires were certainly different from those of humans.

They were companionable enough as long as you thought tangible images at them, but their minds just closed up and went to sleep when you recited Shakespeare or Colegrove, or if you tried to tell them what space was.

It was sort of funny realizing that the Partners who were so grim and mature out here in space were the same cute little animals that people had used as pets for thousands of years back on Earth. He had embarrassed himself more than once while on the ground saluting perfectly ordinary non-telepathic cats because he had forgotten for the moment that they were not Partners.

He picked up the cup and shook out his stone dice.

He was lucky—he drew the Lady May.

The Lady May was the most thoughtful Partner he had ever met. In her, the finely bred pedigree mind of a Persian cat had reached one of its highest peaks of development. She was more complex than any human woman, but the complexity was all one of emotions, memory, hope, and discriminated experience—experience sorted through without benefit of words.

When he had first come into contact with her mind, he was astonished at its clarity. With her he remembered her kittenhood. He remembered every mating experience she had ever had. He saw in a half-recognizable gallery all the other pinlighters with whom she had been paired for the fight. And he saw himself radiant, cheerful, and desirable.

He even thought he caught the edge of a longing . . .

A very flattering and yearning thought: *What a pity he is not a cat.*

Woodley picked up the last stone. He drew what he deserved—a sullen, scared old tomcat with none of the verve of Captain Wow. Woodley's Partner was the most animal of all the cats on the ship, a low, brutish type with a dull mind. Even telepathy had not refined his character. His ears were half chewed off from the first fights in which he had engaged.

He was a serviceable fighter, nothing more.

Woodley grunted.

Underhill glanced at him oddly. Didn't Woodley ever do anything but grunt?

Father Moontree looked at the other three. "You might as well get your Partners now. I'll let the Scanner know we're ready to go into the Up-and-Out."

THE DEAL

Underhill spun the combination lock on the Lady May's cage. He woke her gently and took her into his arms. She humped her back luxuriously, stretched her claws, started to purr, thought better of it, and licked him on the wrist instead. He did not have the pin-set on, so their minds were closed to each other, but in the angle of her mustache and in the movement of her ears, he caught some sense of the gratification she experienced in finding him as her Partner. He talked to her in human speech, even though speech meant nothing to a cat when the pin-set was not on.

"It's a damn shame, sending a sweet little thing like you whirling around in the coldness of nothing to hunt for Rats that are bigger and deadlier than all of us put together. You didn't ask for this kind of fight, did you?"

For answer, she licked his hand, purred, tickled his cheek with her long fluffy tail, turned around, and faced him, golden eyes shining.

For a moment, they stared at each other, man squatting, cat standing erect on her hind legs, front claws digging into his knee. Human eyes and cat eyes looked across an immensity which no words could meet, but which affection spanned in a single glance.

"Time to get in," he said.

She walked docilely into her spheroid carrier. She climbed in. He saw to it that her miniature pin-set rested firmly and comfortably against the base of her brain. He made sure that her claws were padded so that she could not tear herself in the excitement of battle.

Softly he said to her, "Ready?"

For answer, she preened her back as much as her harness would permit and purred softly within the confines of the frame that held her.

He slapped down the lid and watched the sealant ooze around the seam. For a few hours, she was welded into her projectile until a workman with a short cutting arc would remove her after she had done her duty.

He picked up the entire projectile and slipped it into the ejection tube. He closed the door of the tube, spun the lock, seated himself in his chair, and put his own pin-set on.

Once again he flung the switch.

He sat in a small room, *small, small, warm, warm*, the bodies of the other three people moving close around him, the tangible lights in the ceiling bright and heavy against his closed eyelids.

As the pin-set warmed, the room fell away. The other people ceased to be people and became small glowing heaps of fire, embers, dark red fire, with the consciousness of life burning like old red coals in a country fireplace.

As the pin-set warmed a little more, he felt Earth just below him, felt the ship slipping away, felt the turning moon as it swung on the far side of the world, felt the planets and the hot, clear goodness of the sun, which kept the Dragons so far from mankind's native ground.

Finally, he reached complete awareness.

He was telepathically alive to a range of millions of miles. He felt the dust which he had noticed earlier high above the ecliptic. With a thrill of warmth and tenderness, he felt the consciousness of the Lady May pouring over into his own. Her consciousness was as gentle and clear and yet sharp to the taste of his mind as if it were scented oil. It felt relaxing and reassuring. He could sense her welcome of him. It was scarcely a thought, just a raw emotion of greeting.

At last they were one again.

In a tiny remote corner of his mind, as tiny as the smallest toy he had ever seen in his childhood, he was still aware of the room and the ship, and of Father Moontree picking up a telephone and speaking to a Scanner captain in charge of the ship.

His telepathic mind caught the idea long before his ears could frame the words. The actual sound followed the idea the way that thunder on an ocean beach follows the lightning inward from far out over the seas.

"The Fighting Room is ready. Clear to planoform, sir."

THE PLAY

Underhill was always a little exasperated with the way that the Lady May experienced things before he did.

He was braced for the quick vinegar thrill of planoforming, but he caught her report of it before his own nerves could register what happened.

Earth had fallen so far away that he groped for several milliseconds before he found the sun in the upper rear right-hand corner of his telepathic mind.

That was a good jump, he thought. This way we'll get there in four or five skips.

A few hundred miles outside the ship, the Lady May thought back at him, "O warm, O generous, O gigantic man! O brave, O friendly, O tender and huge Partner! O wonderful with you, with you so good, good, good, warm, warm, now to fight, now to go, good with you . . ."

He knew that she was not thinking words, that his mind took the clear amiable babble of her cat intellect and translated it into images which his own thinking could record and understand.

Neither one of them was absorbed in the game of mutual greetings. He reached out far beyond her range of perception to see if there was anything near the ship. It was funny how it was possible to do two things at once. He could scan space with his pin-set mind and yet at the same time catch a vagrant thought of hers, a lovely, affectionate thought about a son who had had a golden face and a chest covered with soft, incredibly downy white fur.

While he was still searching, he caught the warning from her.

We jump again!

And so they had. The ship had moved to a second planoform. The stars were different. The sun was immeasurably far behind. Even the nearest stars were barely in contact. This was good Dragon country, this open, nasty, hollow kind of space. He reached farther, faster, sensing and looking for danger, ready to fling the Lady May at danger wherever he found it.

Terror blazed up in his mind, so sharp, so clear, that it came through as a physical wrench.

The little girl named West had found something—something immense, long, black, sharp, greedy, horrific. She flung Captain Wow at it.

Underhill tried to keep his own mind clear. "Watch out!" he shouted telepathically at the others, trying to move the Lady May around.

At one corner of the battle, he felt the lustful rage of Captain Wow as the big Persian tomcat detonated lights while he approached the streak of dust which threatened the ship and the people within.

The lights scored near-misses.

The dust flattened itself, changing from the shape of a stingray into the shape of a spear.

Not three milliseconds had elapsed.

Father Moontree was talking human words and was saying in a voice that moved like cold molasses out of a heavy jar, "C-A-P-T-A-I-N." Underhill knew that the sentence was going to be "Captain, move fast!"

The battle would be fought and finished before Father Moontree got through talking.

Now, fractions of a millisecond later, the Lady May was directly in line.

Here was where the skill and speed of the Partners came in. She could react faster than he.

She could see the threat as an immense Rat coming direct at her.

She could fire the light bombs with a discrimination which he might miss.

He was connected with her mind, but he could not follow it.

His consciousness absorbed the tearing wound inflicted by the alien enemy. It was like no wound on Earth—raw, crazy pain which started like a burn at his navel. He began to writhe in his chair.

Actually he had not yet had time to move a muscle when the Lady May struck back at their enemy.

Five evenly spaced photonuclear bombs blazed out across a hundred thousand miles.

The pain in his mind and body vanished.

He felt a moment of fierce, terrible, feral elation running through the mind of the Lady May as she finished her kill. It was always disappointing to the cats to find out that their enemies, whom they sensed as gigantic space Rats, disappeared at the moment of destruction.

Then he felt her hurt, the pain and the fear that swept over both of them as the battle, quicker than the movement of an eyelid, had come and gone. In the same instant, there came the sharp and acid twinge of planoform.

Once more the ship went skip.

He could hear Woodley thinking at him. "You don't have to bother much. This old son of a gun and I will take over for a while."

Twice again the twinge, the skip.

He had no idea where he was until the lights of the Caledonia space board shone below.

With a weariness that lay almost beyond the limits of thought, he threw his mind back into rapport with the pin-set, fixing the Lady May's projectile gently and neatly in its launching tube.

She was half dead with fatigue, but he could feel the beat of her heart, could listen to her panting, and he grasped the grateful edge of a thanks reaching from her mind to his.

THE SCORE

They put him in the hospital at Caledonia.

The doctor was friendly but firm. "You actually got touched by that Dragon. That's as close a shave as I've ever seen. It's all so quick that it'll be a long time before we know what happened scientifically, but I suppose you'd be ready for the insane asylum now if the contact had lasted several tenths of a millisecond longer. What kind of cat did you have out in front of you?"

Underhill felt the words coming out of him slowly. Words were such a lot of trouble compared with the speed and the joy of thinking, fast and sharp and clear, mind to mind! But words were all that could reach ordinary people like this doctor.

His mouth moved heavily as he articulated words, "Don't call our Partners cats. The right thing to call them is Partners. They fight for us in a team. You ought to know we call them Partners, not cats. How is mine?"

"I don't know," said the doctor contritely. "We'll find out for you. Meanwhile, old man, you take it easy. There's nothing but rest that can help you. Can you make yourself sleep, or would you like us to give you some kind of sedative?"

"I can sleep," said Underhill. "I just want to know about the Lady May."

The nurse joined in. She was a little antagonistic. "Don't you want to know about the other people?"

"They're okay," said Underhill. "I knew that before I came in here."

He stretched his arms and sighed and grinned at them. He could see they were relaxing and were beginning to treat him as a person instead of a patient.

"I'm all right," he said. "Just let me know when I can go see my Partner."

A new thought struck him. He looked wildly at the doctor. "They didn't send her off with the ship, did they?"

"I'll find out right away," said the doctor. He gave Underhill a reassuring squeeze of the shoulder and left the room.

The nurse took a napkin off a goblet of chilled fruit juice.

Underhill tried to smile at her. There seemed to be something wrong with the girl. He wished she would go away. First she had started to be friendly and now she was distant again. It's a nuisance being telepathic, he thought. You keep trying to reach even when you are not making contact.

Suddenly she swung around on him.

"You pinlighters! You and your damn cats!"

Just as she stamped out, he burst into her mind. He saw himself a radiant hero, clad in his smooth suede uniform, the pin-set crown shining like ancient royal jewels around his head. He saw his own face, handsome and masculine, shining out of her mind. He saw himself very far away and he saw himself as she hated him.

She hated him in the secrecy of her own mind. She hated him because he was—she thought—proud, and strange, and rich, better and more beautiful than people like her.

He cut off the sight of her mind and, as he buried his face in the pillow, he caught an image of the Lady May.

She *is* a cat, he thought. That's all she is—a *cat*!

But that was not how his mind saw her— quick beyond all dreams of speed, sharp, clever, unbelievably graceful, beautiful, wordless, and undemanding.

Where would he ever find a woman who could compare with her?

The Last Question

ISAAC ASIMOV

Isaac Asimov (1920–1992) is a highly prolific master of hard science fiction who not only came up with the famed "Three Laws of Robotics" but is himself often mentioned along with Arthur C. Clarke and Robert Heinlein as one of the "Big Three," a term denoting the giants of early science fiction.

Asimov considered H. G. Wells, Clifford D. Simak, and John W. Campbell among those writers who influenced him and his work. He, in turn, was a great influence not just on other writers but in the field of science in general. For example, his *New York Times* essay in 1964 predicting what the world would be like in 2014 envisioned the importance of environmental issues in the future. His emphasis on population growth rather than climate change isn't wrong so much as it emphasizes one major cause over effect.

Asimov's most famous work is the *Foundation* series; his other major series are the *Galactic Empire* series and the *Robot* series. The *Galactic Empire* novels are explicitly set in earlier history of the same fictional universe as the *Foundation* series. Later, beginning with *Foundation's Edge*, he linked this distant future to the *Robot* and Spacer stories, creating a unified "future history" for his stories much like those created by Robert A. Heinlein and previously produced by Cordwainer Smith and Poul Anderson. He wrote hundreds of short stories, including the 1941 social science fiction story "Nightfall," which in 1968 was voted by the Science Fiction Writers of America the best short science fiction story of all time. Asimov wrote the *Lucky Starr* series of juvenile science fiction novels using the pen name Paul French.

Probably one of Asimov's most influential themes was the Three Laws of Robotics. His theories of robotic principles continue to permeate today's popular fiction, movies, television, and other media as well as the field of robotics in general.

"The Last Question" was first published in *Science Fiction Quarterly* in 1956. In this story Asimov imagines a universal computer system that has global reach and is faced with a single question related to human existence. Asimov considered this his best and favorite short story.

THE LAST QUESTION

Isaac Asimov

The last question was asked for the first time, half in jest, on May 21, 2061, at a time when humanity first stepped into the light. The question came about as a result of a five-dollar bet over highballs, and it happened this way:

Alexander Adell and Bertram Lupov were two of the faithful attendants of Multivac. As well as any human beings could, they knew what lay behind the cold, clicking, flashing face—miles and miles of face—of that giant computer. They had at least a vague notion of the general plan of relays and circuits that had long since grown past the point where any single human could possibly have a firm grasp of the whole.

Multivac was self-adjusting and self-correcting. It had to be, for nothing human could adjust and correct it quickly enough or even adequately enough—so Adell and Lupov attended the monstrous giant only lightly and superficially, yet as well as any men could. They fed it data, adjusted questions to its needs, and translated the answers that were issued. Certainly they, and all others like them, were fully entitled to share in the glory that was Multivac's.

For decades, Multivac had helped design the ships and plot the trajectories that enabled man to reach the moon, Mars, and Venus, but past that, Earth's poor resources could not support the ships. Too much energy was needed for the long trips. Earth exploited its coal and uranium with increasing efficiency, but there was only so much of both.

But slowly Multivac learned enough to answer deeper questions more fundamentally, and on May 14, 2061, what had been theory, became fact.

The energy of the sun was stored, converted, and utilized directly on a planet-wide scale. All Earth turned off its burning coal, its fissioning uranium, and flipped the switch that connected all of it to a small station, one mile in diameter, circling the Earth at half the distance of the moon. All Earth ran by invisible beams of sunpower.

Seven days had not sufficed to dim the glory of it and Adell and Lupov finally managed to escape from the public function, and to meet in quiet where no one would think of looking for them, in the deserted underground chambers, where portions of the mighty buried body of Multivac showed. Unattended, idling, sorting data with contented lazy clickings, Multivac, too, had earned its vacation and the boys appreciated that. They had no intention, originally, of disturbing it.

They had brought a bottle with them, and their only concern at the moment was to relax in the company of each other and the bottle.

"It's amazing when you think of it," said Adell. His broad face had lines of weariness in it, and he stirred his drink slowly with a glass rod, watching the cubes of ice slur clumsily about. "All the energy we can possibly ever use for free. Enough energy, if we wanted to draw on it, to melt all Earth into a big drop of impure liquid iron, and still never miss the energy so used. All the energy we could ever use, forever and forever and forever."

Lupov cocked his head sideways. He had a trick of doing that when he wanted to be contrary, and he wanted to be contrary now, partly because he had had to carry the ice and glassware. "Not forever," he said.

"Oh, hell, just about forever. Till the sun runs down, Bert."

"That's not forever."

"All right, then. Billions and billions of years. Twenty billion, maybe. Are you satisfied?"

Lupov put his fingers through his thinning hair as though to reassure himself that some was still left and sipped gently at his own drink. "Twenty billion years isn't forever."

"Well, it will last our time, won't it?"

"So would the coal and uranium."

"All right, but now we can hook up each individual spaceship to the Solar Station, and it can go to Pluto and back a million times without ever worrying about fuel. You can't do *that* on coal and uranium. Ask Multivac, if you don't believe me."

"I don't have to ask Multivac. I know that."

"Then stop running down what Multivac's done for us," said Adell, blazing up. "It did all right."

"Who says it didn't? What I say is that a sun won't last forever. That's all I'm saying. We're safe for twenty billion years, but then what?" Lupov pointed a slightly shaky finger at the other. "And don't say we'll switch to another sun."

There was silence for a while. Adell put his glass to his lips only occasionally, and Lupov's eyes slowly closed. They rested.

Then Lupov's eyes snapped open. "You're thinking we'll switch to another sun when ours is done, aren't you?"

"I'm not thinking."

"Sure you are. You're weak on logic, that's the trouble with you. You're like the guy in the story who was caught in a sudden shower and who ran to a grove of trees and got under one. He wasn't worried, you see, because he figured when one tree got wet through, he would just get under another one."

"I get it," said Adell. "Don't shout. When the sun is done, the other stars will be gone, too."

"Darn right they will," muttered Lupov. "It all had a beginning in the original cosmic explosion, whatever that was, and it'll all have an end when all the stars run down. Some run down faster than others. Hell, the giants won't last a hundred million years. The sun will last twenty billion years and maybe the dwarfs will last a hundred billion for all the good they are. But just give us a trillion years and everything will be dark. Entropy has to increase to maximum, that's all."

"I know all about entropy," said Adell, standing on his dignity.

"The hell you do."

"I know as much as you do."

"Then you know everything's got to run down someday."

"All right. Who says they won't?"

"You did, you poor sap. You said we had all the energy we needed, forever. You said 'forever.'"

It was Adell's turn to be contrary. "Maybe we can build things up again someday," he said.

"Never."

"Why not? Someday."

"Never."

"Ask Multivac."

"*You* ask Multivac. I dare you. Five dollars says it can't be done."

Adell was just drunk enough to try, just sober enough to be able to phrase the necessary symbols and operations into a question which, in words, might have corresponded to this: will mankind one day without the net expenditure of energy be able to restore the sun to its full youthfulness even after it has died of old age?

Or maybe it could be put more simply like this: how can the net amount of entropy of the universe be massively decreased?

Multivac fell dead and silent. The slow flashing of lights ceased, the distant sounds of clicking relays ended.

Then, just as the frightened technicians felt they could hold their breath no longer, there was a sudden springing to life of the teletype attached to that portion of Multivac. Five words were printed: INSUFFICIENT DATA FOR MEANINGFUL ANSWER.

"No bet," whispered Lupov. They left hurriedly.

By next morning, the two, plagued with throbbing head and cottony mouth, had forgotten about the incident.

Jerrodd, Jerrodine, and Jerrodette I and II watched the starry picture in the visiplate change as the passage through hyperspace was completed in its non-time lapse. At once, the even powdering of stars gave way to the predominance of a single bright marble-disk, centered.

"That's X-23," said Jerrodd confidently. His thin hands clamped tightly behind his back and the knuckles whitened.

The little Jerrodettes, both girls, had experienced the hyperspace passage for the first time in their lives and were self-conscious over the momentary sensation of inside-outness. They buried their giggles and chased one another wildly about their mother, screaming, "We've reached X-23—we've reached X-23—we've—"

"Quiet, children," said Jerrodine sharply. "Are you sure, Jerrodd?"

"What is there to be but sure?" asked Jerrodd, glancing up at the bulge of featureless metal just under the ceiling. It ran the length of the room, disappearing through the wall at either end. It was as long as the ship.

Jerrodd scarcely knew a thing about the thick rod of metal except that it was called a Microvac; that one asked it questions if one wished; that if one did not it still had its task of guiding the ship to a preordered destination; of feeding on energies from the various Subgalactic Power Stations; of computing the equations for the hyperspacial jumps.

Jerrodd and his family had only to wait and live in the comfortable residence quarters of the ship.

Someone had once told Jerrodd that the *ac* at the end of *Microvac* stood for "analog computer" in ancient English, but he was on the edge of forgetting even that.

Jerrodine's eyes were moist as she watched the visiplate. "I can't help it. I feel funny about leaving Earth."

"Why for Pete's sake?" demanded Jerrodd. "We had nothing there. We'll have everything on X-23. You won't be alone. You won't be a pioneer. There are over a million people on the planet already. Good Lord, our great-grandchildren will be looking for new worlds because X-23 will be overcrowded."

Then, after a reflective pause, "I tell you, it's a lucky thing the computers worked out interstellar travel the way the race is growing."

"I know, I know," said Jerrodine miserably.

Jerrodette I said promptly, "Our Microvac is the best Microvac in the world."

"I think so, too," said Jerrodd, tousling her hair.

It *was* a nice feeling to have a Microvac of your own and Jerrodd was glad he was part of his generation and no other. In his father's youth, the only computers had been tremendous machines taking up a hundred square miles of land. There was only one to a planet. Planetary ACs they were called. They had been growing in size steadily for a thousand years and then, all at once, came refinement. In place of transistors had come molecular valves so that even the largest Planetary AC could be put into a space only half the volume of a spaceship.

Jerrodd felt uplifted, as he always did when he thought that his own personal Microvac was many times more complicated than the ancient and primitive Multivac that had first tamed the sun, and almost as complicated as Earth's Planetary AC (the largest), which had first solved the problem of hyperspacial travel and had made trips to the stars possible.

"So many stars, so many planets," sighed Jerrodine, busy with her own thoughts. "I suppose families will be going out to new planets forever, the way we are now."

"Not forever," said Jerrodd, with a smile. "It will all stop someday, but not for billions of years. Many billions. Even the stars run down, you know. Entropy must increase."

"What's entropy, Daddy?" shrilled Jerrodette II.

"Entropy, little sweet, is just a word which means the amount of running-down of the universe. Everything runs down, you know, like your little walkie-talkie robot, remember?"

"Can't you just put in a new power-unit, like with my robot?"

"The stars *are* the power-units, dear. Once they're gone, there are no more power-units."

Jerrodette I at once set up a howl. "Don't let them, Daddy. Don't let the stars run down."

"Now look what you've done," whispered Jerrodine, exasperated.

"How was I to know it would frighten them?" Jerrodd whispered back.

"Ask the Microvac," wailed Jerrodette I. "Ask him how to turn the stars on again."

"Go ahead," said Jerrodine. "It will quiet them down." (Jerrodette II was beginning to cry, also.)

Jerrodd shrugged. "Now, now, honeys. I'll ask Microvac. Don't worry, he'll tell us."

He asked the Microvac, adding quickly, "Print the answer."

Jerrodd cupped the strip of thin cellufilm and said cheerfully, "See now, the Microvac says it will take care of everything when the time comes so don't worry."

Jerrodine said, "And now, children, it's time for bed. We'll be in our new home soon."

Jerrodd read the words on the cellufilm again before destroying it: INSUFFICIENT DATA FOR A MEANINGFUL ANSWER.

He shrugged and looked at the visiplate. X-23 was just ahead.

VJ-23X of Lameth stared into the black depths of the three-dimensional, small-scale map of the galaxy and said, "Are we ridiculous, I wonder, in being so concerned about the matter?"

MQ-17J of Nicron shook his head. "I think not. You know the galaxy will be filled in five years at the present rate of expansion."

Both seemed in their early twenties, both were tall and perfectly formed.

"Still," said VJ-23X, "I hesitate to submit a pessimistic report to the Galactic Council."

"I wouldn't consider any other kind of report. Stir them up a bit. We've got to stir them up."

VJ-23X sighed. "Space is infinite. A hundred billion galaxies are there for the taking. More."

"A hundred billion is *not* infinite and it's getting less infinite all the time. Consider! Twenty thousand years ago, mankind first solved the problem of utilizing stellar energy, and a few centuries later, interstellar travel became possible. It took mankind a million years to fill one small world and then only fifteen thousand years to fill the rest of the galaxy. Now the population doubles every ten years—"

VJ-23X interrupted. "We can thank immortality for that."

"Very well. Immortality exists and we have to take it into account. I admit it has its seamy side, this immortality. The Galactic AC has solved many problems for us, but in solving the problems of preventing old age and death, it has undone all its other solutions."

"Yet you wouldn't want to abandon life, I suppose."

"Not at all," snapped MQ-17J, softening it at once to, "Not yet. I'm by no means old enough. How old are you?"

"Two hundred twenty-three. And you?"

"I'm still under two hundred. But to get back to my point. Population doubles every ten years. Once this galaxy is filled, we'll have another filled in ten years. Another ten years and we'll have filled two more. Another decade, four more. In a hundred years, we'll have filled a thousand galaxies. In a thousand years, a million galaxies. In ten thousand years, the entire known universe. Then what?"

VJ-23X said, "As a side issue, there's a problem of transportation. I wonder how many sunpower units it will take to move galaxies of individuals from one galaxy to the next."

"A very good point. Already, mankind consumes two sunpower units per year."

"Most of it's wasted. After all, our own galaxy alone pours out a thousand sunpower units a year and we only use two of those."

"Granted, but even with a hundred percent efficiency, we can only stave off the end. Our energy requirements are going up in geometric progression even faster than our population. We'll run out of energy even sooner than we run out of galaxies. A good point. A very good point."

"We'll just have to build new stars out of interstellar gas."

"Or out of dissipated heat?" asked MQ-17J, sarcastically.

"There may be some way to reverse entropy. We ought to ask the Galactic AC."

VJ-23X was not really serious, but MQ-17J pulled out his AC-contact from his pocket and placed it on the table before him.

"I've half a mind to," he said. "It's something the human race will have to face someday."

He stared somberly at his small AC-contact. It was only two inches cubed and nothing in itself, but it was connected through hyperspace with the great Galactic AC that served all mankind. Hyperspace considered, it was an integral part of the Galactic AC.

MQ-17J paused to wonder if someday in his immortal life he would get to see the Galactic AC. It was on a little world of its own, a spiderwebbing of force-beams holding the matter within which surges of sub-mesons took the place of the old clumsy molecular valves. Yet despite its sub-etheric workings, the Galactic AC was known to be a full thousand feet across.

MQ-17J asked suddenly of his AC-contact, "Can entropy ever be reversed?"

VJ-23X looked startled and said at once, "Oh, say, I didn't really mean to have you ask that."

"Why not?"

"We both know entropy can't be reversed. You can't turn smoke and ash back into a tree."

"Do you have trees on your world?" asked MQ-17J.

The sound of the Galactic AC startled them into silence. Its voice came thin and beautiful out of the small AC-contact on the desk. It said: THERE IS INSUFFICIENT DATA FOR A MEANINGFUL ANSWER.

VJ-23X said, "See!"

The two men thereupon returned to the question of the report they were to make to the Galactic Council.

Zee Prime's mind spanned the new galaxy with a faint interest in the countless twists of stars that powdered it. He had never seen this one before. Would he ever see them all? So many of them, each with its load of humanity—but a load that was almost a dead weight. More and more, the real essence of men was to be found out here, in space.

Minds, not bodies! The immortal bodies remained back on the planets, in suspension over the eons. Sometimes they roused for material activity but that was growing rarer. Few new individuals were coming into existence to join the incredibly mighty throng, but what matter? There was little room in the universe for new individuals.

Zee Prime was roused out of his reverie upon coming across the wispy tendrils of another mind.

"I am Zee Prime," said Zee Prime. "And you?"

"I am Dee Sub Wun. Your galaxy?"

"We call it only the galaxy. And you?"

"We call ours the same. All men call their galaxy their galaxy and nothing more. Why not?"

"True. Since all galaxies are the same."

"Not all galaxies. On one particular galaxy the race of man must have originated. That makes it different."

Zee Prime said, "On which one?"

"I cannot say. The Universal AC would know."

"Shall we ask him? I am suddenly curious."

Zee Prime's perceptions broadened until the galaxies themselves shrunk and became a new, more diffuse powdering on a much larger background. So many hundreds of billions of them, all with their immortal beings, all carrying their load of intelligences with minds that drifted freely through space. And yet one of them was unique among them all in being the original galaxy. One of them had, in its vague and distant past, a period when it was the only galaxy populated by man.

Zee Prime was consumed with curiosity to see this galaxy and called out: "Universal AC! On which galaxy did mankind originate?"

The Universal AC heard, for on every world and throughout space, it had its receptors ready, and each receptor led through hyperspace to some unknown point where the Universal AC kept itself aloof.

Zee Prime knew of only one man whose thoughts had penetrated within sensing distance of the Universal AC, and he reported only a shining globe, two feet across, difficult to see.

"But how can that be all of the Universal AC?" Zee Prime had asked.

"Most of it," had been the answer, "is in hyperspace. In what form it is there I cannot imagine."

Nor could anyone, for the day had long since passed, Zee Prime knew, when any man had any part of the making of a universal AC. Each Universal AC designed and constructed its successor. Each, during its existence of a million years or more, accumulated the necessary data to build a better and more intricate, more capable successor in which its own store of data and individuality would be submerged.

The Universal AC interrupted Zee Prime's wandering thoughts, not with words, but with guidance. Zee Prime's mentality was guided into the dim sea of galaxies and one in particular enlarged into stars.

A thought came, infinitely distant, but infinitely clear. "THIS IS THE ORIGINAL GALAXY OF MAN."

But it was the same after all, the same as any other, and Zee Prime stifled his disappointment.

Dee Sub Wun, whose mind had accompanied the other, said suddenly, "And is one of these stars the original star of man?"

The Universal AC said, "MAN'S ORIGINAL STAR HAS GONE NOVA. IT IS NOW A WHITE DWARF."

"Did the men upon it die?" asked Zee Prime, startled and without thinking.

The Universal AC said, "A NEW WORLD, AS IN SUCH CASES, WAS CONSTRUCTED FOR THEIR PHYSICAL BODIES IN TIME."

"Yes, of course," said Zee Prime, but a sense of loss overwhelmed him even so. His mind released its hold on the original galaxy of man, let it spring back and lose itself among the blurred pinpoints. He never wanted to see it again.

Dee Sub Wun said, "What is wrong?"

"The stars are dying. The original star is dead."

"They must all die. Why not?"

"But when all energy is gone, our bodies will finally die, and you and I with them."

"It will take billions of years."

"I do not wish it to happen even after billions of years. Universal AC! How may stars be kept from dying?"

Dee Sub Wun said in amusement, "You're asking how entropy might be reversed in direction."

And the Universal AC answered. "THERE IS AS YET INSUFFICIENT DATA FOR A MEANINGFUL ANSWER."

Zee Prime's thoughts fled back to his own galaxy. He gave no further thought to Dee Sub Wun, whose body might be waiting on a galaxy a trillion light-years away, or on the star next to Zee Prime's own. It didn't matter.

Unhappily, Zee Prime began collecting interstellar hydrogen out of which to build a small star of his own. If the stars must someday die, at least some could yet be built.

. . .

Man considered with himself, for in a way, Man, mentally, was one. He consisted of a trillion, trillion, trillion ageless bodies, each in its place, each resting quiet and incorruptible, each cared for by perfect automatons, equally incorruptible, while the minds of all the bodies freely melted one into the other, indistinguishable.

Man said, "The universe is dying."

Man looked about at the dimming galaxies. The giant stars, spendthrifts, were gone long ago, back in the dimmest of the dim far past. Almost all stars were white dwarfs, fading to the end.

New stars had been built of the dust between the stars, some by natural processes, some by Man himself, and those were going, too. White dwarfs might yet be crashed together and of the mighty forces so released, new stars built, but only one star for every thousand white dwarfs destroyed, and those would come to an end, too.

Man said, "Carefully husbanded, as directed by the Cosmic AC, the energy that is even yet left in all the universe will last for billions of years."

"But even so," said Man, "eventually it will all come to an end. However it may be husbanded, however stretched out, the energy once expended is gone and cannot be restored. Entropy must increase to the maximum."

Man said, "Can entropy not be reversed? Let us ask the Cosmic AC."

The Cosmic AC surrounded them but not in space. Not a fragment of it was in space. It was in hyperspace and made of something that was neither matter nor energy. The question of its size and nature no longer had meaning to any terms that Man could comprehend.

"Cosmic AC," said Man, "how may entropy be reversed?"

The Cosmic AC said, "THERE IS AS YET INSUFFICIENT DATA FOR A MEANINGFUL ANSWER."

Man said, "Collect additional data."

The Cosmic AC said, "I WILL DO SO. I HAVE BEEN DOING SO FOR A HUNDRED BILLION YEARS. MY PREDECESSORS AND I HAVE BEEN ASKED THIS QUESTION MANY TIMES. ALL THE DATA I HAVE REMAINS INSUFFICIENT."

"Will there come a time," said Man, "when data will be sufficient or is the problem insoluble in all conceivable circumstances?"

The Cosmic AC said, "NO PROBLEM IS INSOLUBLE IN ALL CONCEIVABLE CIRCUMSTANCES."

Man said, "When will you have enough data to answer the question?"

"THERE IS AS YET INSUFFICIENT DATA FOR A MEANINGFUL ANSWER."

"Will you keep working on it?" asked Man.

The Cosmic AC said, "I WILL."

Man said, "We shall wait."

The stars and galaxies died and snuffed out, and space grew black after ten trillion years of running down.

One by one Man fused with AC, each physical body losing its mental identity in a manner that was somehow not a loss but a gain.

Man's last mind paused before fusion, looking over a space that included nothing but the dregs of one last dark star and nothing besides but incredibly thin matter, agitated randomly by the tag ends of heat wearing out, asymptotically, to the absolute zero.

Man said, "AC, is this the end? Can this chaos not be reversed into the universe once more? Can that not be done?"

AC said, "THERE IS AS YET INSUFFICIENT DATA FOR A MEANINGFUL ANSWER."

Man's last mind fused and only AC existed—and that in hyperspace.

Matter and energy had ended and with it, space and time. Even AC existed only for the sake of the one last question that it had never answered from the time a half-drunken computer ten trillion years before had asked the question of a computer that was to AC far less than was a man to Man.

All other questions had been answered, and until this last question was answered also, AC might not release his consciousness.

All collected data had come to a final end. Nothing was left to be collected.

But all collected data had yet to be completely correlated and put together in all possible relationships.

A timeless interval was spent in doing that.

And it came to pass that AC learned how to reverse the direction of entropy.

But there was now no man to whom AC might give the answer of the last question. No matter. The answer—by demonstration— would take care of that, too.

For another timeless interval, AC thought how best to do this. Carefully, AC organized the program.

The consciousness of AC encompassed all of what had once been a universe and brooded over what was now chaos. Step by step, it must be done.

And AC said, "LET THERE BE LIGHT!"

And there was light——

Stranger Station

DAMON KNIGHT

Damon Knight (1922–2002) was an influential US science fiction writer and critic, highly regarded for editing the edgy original anthology series *Orbit* and for his (sometimes overshadowed) fiction, for which he won the Hugo Award. He started early, founding his own fanzine, entitled *Snide*, when he was only eleven. Knight could also be said to have helped create, along with his second wife (the acclaimed writer Kate Wilhelm), the modern structure and apparatus of the US science fiction community.

In addition to being a member of the famous Futurians science fiction group, Knight founded the Science Fiction and Fantasy Writers of America (SFWA) and cofounded three influential organizations: the National Fantasy Fan Federation, the Milford Writer's Workshop, and the Clarion Science Fiction and Fantasy Writers' Workshop. As creative writing teachers, Knight and Wilhelm helped shape several generations of primarily US and UK speculative fiction writers by teaching at both Milford and Clarion; they also helped run Sycamore Hill, a kind of Clarion for intermediate and advanced writers. The SFWA officers and past presidents named Knight its thirteenth grand master in 1994. After Knight's death in 2002, the award became the Damon Knight Memorial Grand Master Award. The Science Fiction and Fantasy Hall of Fame inducted him in 2003.

Ray Bradbury bought Knight's first short story, "The Itching Hour" (*Futuria Fantasia*, 1940), but Knight would soon also be active as an editor and reviewer. As a critic, he (in)famously wrote in 1945 that A. E. van Vogt "is not a giant as often maintained. He's only a pygmy who has learned to operate an overgrown typewriter"—a hyperbolic statement that has not been proven true. Knight is more rightly known for the term *idiot plot*, a story that only functions because almost everyone in it acts stupidly. The term may have been invented by James Blish, a fellow Futurian, but Knight's frequent use of it in his reviews made its use common.

Knight's *Orbit* series (1966–80) ran contiguous with *New Worlds* during the New Wave boom and then outlived *New Worlds*, providing an American refuge for edgy, risk-taking speculative fiction. In addition to being an influence on the editors of this volume, *Orbit* was the only home for early chapters from Stepan Chapman's Philip K. Dick Award–winning novel *The Troika* (stand-alone segments reprinted herein) and a host of other interesting writers. Knight edited several wonderful reprint anthologies, including *A Century of Science Fiction* and *A Century of Great Short Science Fiction Novels*. Knight was also an active translator and champion of French fiction, including that of the notorious Boris Vian.

In terms of his fiction, Knight's most famous story is the jokey "To Serve Man" (1950). It won a fifty-year Retro Hugo in 2001 and was made into a *Twilight Zone* episode, but it is not his best work and has not aged well. Readers should instead seek out his strange, sometimes Nabokovian novels and stories like the first-contact story reprinted here, the novelette "Stranger Station." First published in 1956 in *The Magazine of Fantasy and Science Fiction*, "Stranger Station" showcases Knight at the height of his powers, able to convey both intensity and nuance in a truly unique context. As the title suggests, this is a truly strange story, and a superior example of exploring the complexities of alien contact through fiction.

STRANGER STATION

Damon Knight

The clang of metal echoed hollowly down through the station's many vaulted corridors and rooms. Paul Wesson stood listening for a moment as the rolling echoes died away. The maintenance rocket was gone, heading back to Home; they had left him alone in Stranger Station.

Stranger Station! The name itself quickened his imagination. Wesson knew that both orbital stations had been named a century ago by the then-British administration of the satellite service; "Home" because the larger, inner station handled the traffic of Earth and its colonies; "Stranger" because the outer station was designed specifically for dealings with foreigners—beings from outside the solar system. But even that could not diminish the wonder of Stranger Station, whirling out here alone in the dark—waiting for its once-in-two-decades visitor. . . .

One man, out of all Sol's billions, had the task and privilege of enduring the alien's presence when it came. The two races, according to Wesson's understanding of the subject, were so fundamentally different that it was painful for them to meet. Well, he had volunteered for the job, and he thought he could handle it—the rewards were big enough.

He had gone through all the tests, and against his own expectations he had been chosen. The maintenance crew had brought him up as dead weight, drugged in a survival hamper; they had kept him the same way while they did their work and then had brought him back to consciousness. Now they were gone. He was alone.

But not quite.

"Welcome to Stranger Station, Sergeant Wesson," said a pleasant voice. "This is your alpha network speaking. I'm here to protect and serve you in every way. If there's anything you want, just ask me." It was a neutral voice, with a kind of professional friendliness in it, like that of a good schoolteacher or rec supervisor.

Wesson had been warned, but he was still shocked at the human quality of it. The alpha networks were the last word in robot brains—computers, safety devices, personal servants, libraries, all wrapped up in one, with something so close to "personality" and "free will" that experts were still arguing the question. They were rare and fantastically expensive; Wesson had never met one before.

"Thanks," he said now, to the empty air. "Uh—what do I call you, by the way? I can't keep saying, 'Hey, alpha network.'"

"One of your recent predecessors called me Aunt Nettie," was the response.

Wesson grimaced. Alpha network—Aunt Nettie. He hated puns; that wouldn't do. "The aunt part is all right," he said. "Suppose I call you Aunt Jane. That was my mother's sister; you sound like her, a little bit."

"I am honored," said the invisible mechanism politely. "Can I serve you any refreshments now? Sandwiches? A drink?"

"Not just yet," said Wesson. "I think I'll look the place over first."

He turned away. That seemed to end the conversation as far as the network was concerned. A good thing; it was all right to have it for company, speaking when spoken to, but if it got talkative . . .

The human part of the station was in four

segments: bedroom, living room, dining room, bath. The living room was comfortably large and pleasantly furnished in greens and tans; the only mechanical note in it was the big instrument console in one corner. The other rooms, arranged in a ring around the living room, were tiny; just space enough for Wesson, a narrow encircling corridor, and the mechanisms that would serve him. The whole place was spotlessly clean, gleaming and efficient in spite of its twenty-year layoff.

This is the gravy part of the run, Wesson told himself. The month before the alien came—good food, no work, and an alpha network for conversation. "Aunt Jane, I'll have a small steak now," he said to the network. "Medium rare, with hashed brown potatoes, onions and mushrooms, and a glass of lager. Call me when it's ready."

"Right," said the voice pleasantly. Out in the dining room, the autochef began to hum and cluck self-importantly. Wesson wandered over and inspected the instrument console. Air locks were sealed and tight, said the dials; the air was cycling. The station was in orbit and rotating on its axis with a force at the perimeter, where Wesson was, of one g. The internal temperature of this part of the station was an even 73 degrees.

The other side of the board told a different story; all the dials were dark and dead. Sector Two, occupying a volume some eighty-eight thousand times as great as this one, was not yet functioning.

Wesson had a vivid mental image of the station, from photographs and diagrams—a five-hundred-foot Duralumin sphere, onto which the shallow thirty-foot disk of the human section had been stuck apparently as an afterthought. The whole cavity of the sphere, very nearly—except for a honeycomb of supply and maintenance rooms and the all-important, recently enlarged vats—was one cramped chamber for the alien. . . .

"Steak's ready!" said Aunt Jane.

The steak was good, bubbling crisp outside the way he liked it, tender and pink inside. "Aunt Jane," he said with his mouth full, "this is pretty soft, isn't it?"

"The steak?" asked the voice, with a faintly anxious note.

Wesson grinned. "Never mind," he said. "Listen, Aunt Jane, you've been through this routine—how many times? Were you installed with the station, or what?"

"I was not installed with the station," said Aunt Jane primly. "I have assisted at three contacts."

"Um. Cigarette," said Wesson, slapping his pockets. The autochef hummed for a moment, and popped a pack of GIs out of a vent. Wesson lighted up. "All right," he said, "you've been through this three times. There are a lot of things you can tell me, right?"

"Oh, yes, certainly. What would you like to know?"

Wesson smoked, leaning back reflectively, green eyes narrowed. "First," he said, "read me the Pigeon report—you know, from the *Brief History*. I want to see if I remember it right."

"Chapter Two," said the voice promptly. "First contact with a non-Solar intelligence was made by Commander Ralph C. Pigeon on July 1, 1987, during an emergency landing on Titan. The following is an excerpt from his official report:

" 'While searching for a possible cause for our mental disturbance, we discovered what appeared to be a gigantic construction of metal on the far side of the ridge. Our distress grew stronger with the approach to this construction, which was polyhedral and approximately five times the length of the *Cologne*.

" 'Some of those present expressed a wish to retire, but Lieutenant Acuff and myself had a strong sense of being called or summoned in some indefinable way. Although our uneasiness was not lessened, we therefore agreed to go forward and keep radio contact with the rest of the party while they returned to the ship.

" 'We gained access to the alien construction by way of a large, irregular opening. . . . The internal temperature was minus seventy-five degrees Fahrenheit; the atmosphere appeared to consist of methane and ammonia. . . . Inside the second chamber, an alien creature was waiting for us. We felt the distress, which I have tried to describe, to a much greater degree than before, and also the sense of summoning or pleading. . . . We observed that the creature was exuding a thick yellowish fluid from certain joints or pores in its surface. Though disgusted, I managed to collect a sample of this exudate, and it was later forwarded for analysis. . . .'

"The second contact was made ten years later by Commodore Crawford's famous Titan Expedition—"

"No, that's enough," said Wesson. "I just wanted the Pigeon quote." He smoked, brooding. "It seems kind of chopped off, doesn't it? Have you got a longer version in your memory banks anywhere?"

There was a pause. "No," said Aunt Jane.

"There was more to it when I was a kid," Wesson complained nervously. "I read that book when I was twelve, and I remember a long description of the alien—that is, I remember its being there." He swung around. "Listen, Aunt Jane—you're a sort of universal watchdog, that right? You've got cameras and mikes all over the station?"

"Yes," said the network, sounding—was it Wesson's imagination?—faintly injured.

"Well, what about Sector Two? You must have cameras up there, too, isn't that so?"

"Yes."

"All right, then you can tell me. What do the aliens look like?"

There was a definite pause. "I'm sorry, I can't tell you that," said Aunt Jane.

"No," said Wesson, "I didn't think you could. You've got orders not to, I guess, for the same reason those history books have been cut since I was a kid. Now, what would the reason be? Have you got any idea, Aunt Jane?"

There was another pause. "Yes," the voice admitted.

"Well?"

"I'm sorry, I can't—"

"—tell you that," Wesson repeated along with it. "All right. At least we know where we stand."

"Yes, Sergeant. Would you like some dessert?"

"No dessert. One other thing. *What happens to station watchmen, like me, after their tour of duty?*"

"They are upgraded to Class Seven, students with unlimited leisure, and receive outright gifts of seven thousand stellors, plus free Class One housing. . . ."

"Yeah, I know all that," said Wesson, licking his dry lips. "But here's what I'm asking you. The ones you know—what kind of shape were they in when they left here?"

"The usual human shape," said the voice brightly. "Why do you ask, Sergeant?"

Wesson made a discontented gesture. "Something I remember from a bull session at the academy. I can't get it out of my head; I know it had something to do with the station. Just a part of a sentence: '. . . blind as a bat and white bristles all over . . .' Now, would that be a description of the alien—or the watchman when they came to take him away?"

Aunt Jane went into one of her heavy pauses. "All right, I'll save you the trouble," said Wesson. "You're sorry, you can't tell me that."

"I *am* sorry," said the robot sincerely.

As the slow days passed into weeks, Wesson grew aware of the station almost as a living thing. He could feel its resilient metal ribs enclosing him, lightly bearing his weight with its own as it swung. He could feel the waiting emptiness "up there," and he sensed the alert electronic network that spread around him everywhere, watching and probing, trying to anticipate his needs.

Aunt Jane was a model companion. She had a record library of thousands of hours of music;

she had films to show him, and microprinted books that he could read on the scanner in the living room; or if he preferred, she would read to him. She controlled the station's three telescopes, and on request would give him a view of Earth or the moon or Home. . . .

But there was no news. Aunt Jane would obligingly turn on the radio receiver if he asked her, but nothing except static came out. That was the thing that weighed most heavily on Wesson, as time passed—the knowledge that radio silence was being imposed on all ships in transit, on the orbital stations, and on the planet-to-space transmitters. It was an enormous, almost a crippling handicap. Some information could be transmitted over relatively short distances by photophone, but ordinarily the whole complex traffic of the space lanes depended on radio.

But this coming alien contact was so delicate a thing that even a radio voice, out here where the Earth was only a tiny disk twice the size of the moon, might upset it. It was so precarious a thing, Wesson thought, that only one man could be allowed in the station while the alien was there, and to give that man the company that would keep him sane, they had to install an alpha network. . . .

"Aunt Jane?"

The voice answered promptly, "Yes, Paul."

"This distress that the books talk about—you wouldn't know what it is, would you?"

"No, Paul."

"Because robot brains don't feel it, right?"

"Right, Paul."

"So tell me this—why do they need a man here at all? Why can't they get along with just you?"

A pause. "I don't know, Paul." The voice sounded faintly wistful. Were those gradations of tone really in it, Wesson wondered, or was his imagination supplying them?

He got up from the living room couch and paced restlessly back and forth. "Let's have a look at Earth," he said. Obediently, the viewing screen on the console glowed into life: there was the blue Earth, swimming deep below him, in its first quarter, jewel bright. "Switch it off," Wesson said.

"A little music?" suggested the voice, and immediately began to play something soothing, full of woodwinds.

"*No,*" said Wesson. The music stopped.

Wesson's hands were trembling; he had a caged and frustrated feeling.

The fitted suit was in its locker beside the air lock. Wesson had been topside in it once or twice; there was nothing to see up there, just darkness and cold. But he had to get out of this squirrel cage. He took the suit down and began to get into it.

"Paul," said Aunt Jane anxiously, "are you feeling nervous?"

"Yes," he snarled.

"Then don't go into Sector Two," said Aunt Jane.

"Don't tell me what to do, you hunk of tin!" said Wesson with sudden anger. He zipped up the front of his suit with a vicious motion.

Aunt Jane was silent.

Seething, Wesson finished his check-off and opened the lock door.

The air lock, an upright tube barely large enough for one man, was the only passage between Sector One and Sector Two. It was also the only exit from Sector One; to get here in the first place, Wesson had had to enter the big lock at the "south" pole of the sphere, and travel all the way down inside, by drop hole and catwalk. He had been drugged unconscious at the time, of course. When the time came, he would go out the same way; neither the maintenance rocket nor the tanker had any space, or time, to spare.

At the "north" pole, opposite, there was a third air lock, this one so huge it could easily have held an interplanetary freighter. But that was nobody's business—no human being's.

In the beam of Wesson's helmet lamp, the enormous central cavity of the station was an inky gulf that sent back only remote, mocking glimmers of light. The near walls sparkled with hoarfrost. Sector Two was not yet pressurized; there was only a diffuse vapor that had leaked through the air seal and had long since frozen into the powdery deposit that lined the walls. The metal rang cold under his shod feet; the vast emptiness of the chamber was the more depressing because it was airless, unwarmed, and unlit. *Alone,* said his footsteps; *alone . . .*

He was thirty yards up the catwalk when his anxiety suddenly grew stronger. Wesson stopped in spite of himself and turned clumsily, putting his back to the wall. The support of the solid wall was not enough. The catwalk seemed threatening to tilt underfoot, dropping him into the lightless gulf.

Wesson recognized this drained feeling, this metallic taste at the back of his tongue. It was fear.

The thought ticked through his head: *They want me to be afraid.* But why? Why now? Of what?

Equally suddenly, he knew. The nameless pressure tightened, like a great fist closing, and Wesson had the appalling sense of something so huge that it had no limits at all, descending, with a terrible endless swift slowness. . . .

It was time.

His first month was up.

The alien was coming.

As Wesson turned, gasping, the whole huge structure of the station around him seemed to dwindle to the size of an ordinary room—and Wesson with it, so that he seemed to himself like a tiny insect, frantically scuttling down the walls toward safety.

Behind him as he ran, the station *boomed.*

In the silent rooms, all the lights were burning dimly. Wesson lay still, looking at the ceiling. Up there his imagination formed a shifting, changing image of the alien—huge, shadowy, formlessly menacing.

Sweat had gathered in globules on his brow. He stared, unable to look away.

"That was why you didn't want me to go topside, huh, Aunt Jane?" he said hoarsely.

"Yes. The nervousness is the first sign. But you gave me a direct order, Paul."

"I know it," he said vaguely, still staring fixedly at the ceiling. "A funny thing . . . Aunt Jane?"

"Yes, Paul?"

"You won't tell me what it looks like, right?"

"*No,* Paul."

"I don't want to know. Lord, I don't *want* to know. . . . Funny thing, Aunt Jane, part of me is just pure funk—I'm so scared I'm nothing but a jelly."

"I know," said the voice gently.

"And part is real cool and calm, as if it didn't matter. Crazy, the things you think about. You know?"

"What things, Paul?"

He tried to laugh. "I'm remembering a kids' party I went to twenty, twenty-five years ago. I was—let's see—I was nine. I remember, because that was the same year my father died.

"We were living in Dallas then, in a rented mobile house, and there was a family in the next tract with a bunch of redheaded kids. They were always throwing parties; nobody liked them much, but everybody always went."

"Tell me about the party, Paul."

He shifted on the couch. "This one—this one was a Halloween party. I remember the girls had on black and orange dresses, and the boys mostly wore spirit costumes. I was about the youngest kid there, and I felt kind of out of place. Then all of a sudden one of the redheads jumps up in a skull mask, hollering, 'C'mon, everybody get ready for hide-and-seek.' And he grabs *me,* and says, '*You* be it,' and before I can even move, he shoves me into a dark closet. And I hear that door lock behind me."

He moistened his lips. "And then—you know, in the darkness—I feel something hit my *face.* You know, cold and clammy, like—I don't know—something dead. . . .

"I just hunched up on the floor of that closet, waiting for that thing to touch me again. You know? That thing, cold and kind of gritty, hanging up there. You know what it was? A cloth glove, full of ice and bran cereal. A joke. Boy, that was one joke I never forgot. . . . Aunt Jane?"

"Yes, Paul."

"Hey, I'll bet you alpha networks make great psychs, huh? I could lie here and tell you anything, because you're just a machine—right?"

"Right, Paul," said the network sorrowfully.

"Aunt Jane, Aunt Jane . . . It's no use kidding myself along. I can *feel* that thing up there, just a couple of yards away."

"I know you can, Paul."

"I can't stand it, Aunt Jane."

"You can if you think you can, Paul."

He writhed on the couch. "It's—it's dirty, it's clammy. My God, is it going to be like that for *five* months? I can't, it'll kill me, Aunt Jane!"

There was another thunderous boom, echoing down through the structural members of the station. "What's that?" Wesson gasped. "The other ship—casting off?"

"Yes. Now he's alone, just as you are."

"Not like me. He can't be feeling what I'm feeling. Aunt Jane, you don't know. . . ."

Up there, separated from him only by a few yards of metal, the alien's enormous, monstrous body hung. It was that poised weight, as real as if he could touch it, that weighed down his chest.

Wesson had been a space dweller for most of his adult life and knew even in his bones that, if an orbital station ever collapsed, the "under" part would not be crushed but would be hurled away by its own angular momentum. This was not the oppressiveness of planetside buildings, where the looming mass above you seemed always threatening to fall. This was something else, completely distinct, and impossible to argue away.

It was the scent of danger, hanging unseen up there in the dark, waiting, cold and heavy. It was the recurrent nightmare of Wesson's childhood—the bloated unreal shape, no-color, no-size, that kept on hideously falling toward his face. . . . It was the dead puppy he had pulled out of the creek, that summer in Dakota—wet fur, limp head, cold, cold, *cold.* . . .

With an effort, Wesson rolled over on the couch and lifted himself to one elbow. The pressure was an insistent chill weight on his skull; the room seemed to dip and swing around him in slow, dizzy circles.

Wesson felt his jaw muscles contorting with the strain as he knelt, then stood erect. His back and legs tightened; his mouth hung painfully open. He took one step, then another, timing them to hit the floor as it came upright.

The right side of the console, the one that had been dark, was lighted. Pressure in Sector Two, according to the indicator, was about one and a third atmospheres. The air-lock indicator showed a slightly higher pressure of oxygen and argon; that was to keep any of the alien atmosphere from contaminating Sector One, but it also meant that the lock would no longer open from either side. Wesson found that irrationally comforting.

"Lemme see Earth," he gasped.

The screen lighted up as he stared into it. "It's a long way down," he said. A long, long way down to the bottom of that well . . . He had spent ten featureless years as a servo tech in Home Station. Before that, he'd wanted to be a pilot, but had washed out the first year—couldn't take the math. But he had never once thought of going back to Earth.

Now, suddenly, after all these years, that tiny blue disk seemed infinitely desirable.

"Aunt Jane, Aunt Jane, it's beautiful," he mumbled.

Down there, he knew, it was spring; and in certain places, where the edge of darkness retreated, it was morning—a watery blue morning like the sea light caught in an agate, a morning with smoke and mist in it, a morning of stillness and promise. Down there, lost years and miles away, some tiny dot of a woman was opening her microscopic door to listen to an atom's song. Lost, lost, and packed away in cotton wool, like a specimen slide—one spring morning on Earth.

Black miles above, so far that sixty Earths could have been piled one on another to make a pole for his perch, Wesson swung in his endless circle within a circle. Yet, vast as the gulf beneath him was, all this—Earth, moon, orbital stations, ships; yes, the sun and all the rest of his planets, too—was the merest sniff of space, to be pinched up between thumb and finger.

Beyond—there was the true gulf. In that deep night, galaxies lay sprawled aglitter, piercing a distance that could only be named in a meaningless number, a cry of dismay: O . . . O . . . O . . .

Crawling and fighting, blasting with energies too big for them, men had come as far as Jupiter. But if a man had been tall enough to lie with his boots toasting in the sun and his head freezing at Pluto, still he would have been too small for that overwhelming emptiness. Here, not at Pluto, was the outermost limit of man's empire; here the Outside tunneled down to meet it, like the pinched waist of an hourglass; here, and only here, the two worlds came near enough to touch. Ours—and Theirs.

Down at the bottom of the board, now, the golden dials were faintly alight, the needles trembling ever so little on their pins.

Deep in the vats, the vats, the golden liquid was trickling down: *Though disgusted, I took a sample of the exudate, and it was forwarded for analysis. . . .*

Space-cold fluid, trickling down the bitter walls of the tubes, forming little pools in the cups of darkness; goldenly agleam there, half alive. The golden elixir. One drop of the concentrate would arrest aging for twenty years—keep your arteries soft, tonus good, eyes clear, hair pigmented, brain alert.

That was what the tests of Pigeon's sample had showed. That was the reason for the whole crazy history of the "alien trading post"—first a hut on Titan, then later, when people understood more about the problem, Stranger Station.

Once every twenty years, an alien would come down out of Somewhere, and sit in the tiny cage we had made for him, and make us rich beyond our dreams—rich with life—and still we did not know why.

Above him, Wesson imagined he could see that sensed body a-wallow in the glacial blackness, its bulk passively turning with the station's spin, bleeding a chill gold into the lips of the tubes—drip . . . drop . . .

Wesson held his head. The pressure inside made it hard to think; it felt as if his skull were about to fly apart. "Aunt Jane," he said.

"Yes, Paul." The kindly, comforting voice, like a nurse. The nurse who stands beside your cot while you have painful, necessary things done to you. Efficient, trained friendliness.

"Aunt Jane," said Wesson, "do you know why they keep coming back?"

"No," said the voice precisely. "It is a mystery."

Wesson nodded. "I had," he said, "an interview with Gower before I left Home. You know Gower? Chief of the Outer-world Bureau. Came up especially to see me."

"Yes?" said Aunt Jane encouragingly.

"Said to me, 'Wesson, you got to find out. Find out if we can count on them to keep up the supply. You know? There's fifty million more of us,' he says, 'than when you were born. We need more of the stuff, and we got to know if we can count on it. Because,' he says, 'you know what would happen if it stopped?' Do you know, Aunt Jane?"

"It would be," said the voice, "a catastrophe."

"That's right," Wesson said respectfully. "It would. Like, he says to me, 'What if the people in the Nefud area were cut off from the Jordan Valley Authority? Why, there'd be millions dying of thirst in a week.

"'Or what if the freighters stopped coming to Moon Base? Why,' he says, 'there'd be thousands starving and smothering to death.'

"He says, 'Where the water is, where you can get food and air, people are going to settle and get married, you know? And have kids.'

"He says, 'If the so-called longevity serum stopped coming . . .' Says, 'Every twentieth adult in the Sol family is due for his shot this year.' Says, 'Of those, almost twenty percent are one hundred fifteen or older.' Says, 'The deaths in that group in the first year would be at least three times what the actuarial tables call for.'" Wesson raised a strained face.

"I'm thirty-four, you know?" he said. "That Gower, he made me feel like a baby."

Aunt Jane made a sympathetic noise.

"Drip, drip," said Wesson hysterically. The needles of the tall golden indicators were infinitesimally higher. "Every twenty years we need more of the stuff, so somebody like me has to come out and take it for five lousy months. And one of *them* has to come out and sit there, and *drip*. *Why*, Aunt Jane? What for? Why should it matter to them whether we live a long time or not? Why do they keep on coming back? What do they take *away* from here?"

But to these questions, Aunt Jane had no reply.

All day and every day, the lights burned cold and steady in the circular gray corridor around the rim of Sector One. The hard gray flooring had been deeply scuffed in that circular path before Wesson ever walked there—the corridor existed for that only, like a treadmill in a squirrel cage. It said "Walk," and Wesson walked. A man would go crazy if he sat still, with that squirming, indescribable pressure on his head; and so Wesson paced off the miles, all day and every day, until he dropped like a dead man in the bed at night.

He talked, too, sometimes to himself, sometimes to the listening alpha network; sometimes it was difficult to tell which. "Moss on a rock," he muttered, pacing. "Told him, wouldn't give twenty mills for any shell . . . Little pebbles down there, all colors." He shuffled on in silence for a while. Abruptly: "I don't see *why* they couldn't have given me a cat."

Aunt Jane said nothing. After a moment Wesson went on, "Nearly everybody at Home has a cat, for God's sake, or a goldfish or something. You're all right, Aunt Jane, but I can't *see* you. My God, I mean *if* they couldn't send a man a woman for company—what I mean, my God, I never liked *cats*." He swung around the doorway into the bedroom, and absentmindedly slammed his fist into the bloody place on the wall.

"But a cat would have been *something*," he said.

Aunt Jane was still silent.

"Don't pretend your feelings are hurt. I know you, you're only a machine," said Wesson. "Listen, Aunt Jane, I remember a cereal package one time that had a horse and a cowboy on the side. There wasn't much room, so about all you saw was their faces. It used to strike me funny how much they looked alike. Two ears on the top with hair in the middle. Two eyes. Nose. Mouth with teeth in it. I was thinking, we're kind of distant cousins, aren't we, us and the horses. But compared to that thing up there— we're *brothers*. You know?"

"Yes," said Aunt Jane quietly.

"So I keep asking myself, why couldn't they have sent a horse or a cat *instead of* a man? But I guess the answer is because only a man could take what I'm taking. God, only a man. Right?"

"Right," said Aunt Jane with deep sorrow.

Wesson stopped at the bedroom doorway again and shuddered, holding on to the frame. "Aunt Jane," he said in a low, clear voice, "you take pictures of *him* up there, don't you?"

"Yes, Paul."

"And you take pictures of me. And then what happens? After it's all over, who looks at the pictures?"

"I don't know," said Aunt Jane humbly.

"You don't know. But whoever looks at 'em, it doesn't do any good. Right? We got to find out why, why, why. . . . And we never do find out, do we?"

"No," said Aunt Jane.

"But don't they figure that if the man who's going through it could see him, he might be able to tell something? That other people couldn't? Doesn't that make sense?"

"That's out of my hands, Paul."

He sniggered. "That's funny. Oh, that's

funny." He chortled in his throat, reeling around the circuit.

"Yes, that's funny," said Aunt Jane.

"Aunt Jane, tell me what happens to the watchmen."

"I can't tell you that, Paul."

He lurched into the living room, sat down before the console, beat on its smooth, cold metal with his fists. "What are you, some kind of monster? Isn't there any blood in your veins, or oil or *anything*?"

"Please, Paul—"

"Don't you see, all I want to know, can they talk? Can they tell anything after their tour is over?"

"No, Paul."

He stood upright, clutching the console for balance. "They can't? No, I figured. And you know why?"

"No."

"Up there," said Wesson obscurely. "Moss on the rock."

"Paul, what?"

"We get changed," said Wesson, stumbling out of the room again. "We get changed. Like a piece of iron next to a magnet. Can't help it. You—nonmagnetic, I guess. Goes right through you, huh, Aunt Jane? You don't get changed. You stay here, wait for the next one."

"Yes," said Aunt Jane.

"You know," said Wesson, pacing, "I can tell how he's lying up there. Head *that* way, tail the other. Am I right?"

"Yes," said Aunt Jane.

Wesson stopped. "Yes," he said intently. "So you *can* tell me what you see up there, can't you, Aunt Jane?"

"No. Yes. It isn't allowed."

"Listen, Aunt Jane, *we'll die* unless we can find out what makes those aliens tick! Remember that."

Wesson leaned against the corridor wall, gazing up. "He's turning now—around this way. Right?"

"Yes."

"Well, what else is he doing? Come on, Aunt Jane, tell me!"

A pause. "He is twitching his—"

"What?"

"I don't know the words."

"My God, my God," said Wesson, clutching his head, "of course there aren't any words." He ran into the living room, clutched the console, and stared at the blank screen. He pounded the metal with his fist. "You've got to show me, Aunt Jane, come on and show me—show me!"

"It isn't allowed," Aunt Jane protested.

"You've got to do it just the same, or we'll *die*, Aunt Jane—millions of us, billions, and it'll be your fault, get it? *Your fault*, Aunt Jane!"

"*Please,*" said the voice. There was a pause. The screen flickered to life, for an instant only. Wesson had a glimpse of something massive and dark, but half transparent, like a magnified insect—a tangle of nameless limbs, whiplike filaments, claws, wings. . . .

He clutched the edge of the console.

"Was that all right?" Aunt Jane asked.

"Of course! What do you think, it'll kill me to look at it? Put it back, Aunt Jane, put it back!"

Reluctantly, the screen lighted again. Wesson stared and went on staring. He mumbled something.

"What?" said Aunt Jane.

"*Life of my love, I loathe thee,*" said Wesson, staring. He roused himself after a moment and turned away. The image of the alien stayed with him as he went reeling into the corridor again; he was not surprised to find that it reminded him of all the loathsome, crawling, creeping things the Earth was full of. That explained why he was not supposed to see the alien, or even know what it looked like—because that fed his hate. And it was all right for him to be afraid of the alien, but he was not supposed to hate it. . . . Why not? Why not?

His fingers were shaking. He felt drained, steamed, dried up, and withered. The one daily shower Aunt Jane allowed him was no longer enough. Twenty minutes after bathing the acid sweat dripped again from his armpits, the cold sweat was beaded on his forehead, the hot sweat was in his palms. Wesson felt as if there were a furnace inside him, out of control, all the dampers drawn. He knew that, under stress, something of the kind did happen to a man; the body's chemistry was altered—more adrenaline, more glycogen in the muscles, eyes brighter, digestion retarded. That was the trouble—he was burning himself up, unable to fight the thing that tormented him, nor run from it.

After another circuit, Wesson's steps faltered. He hesitated, and went into the living room. He leaned over the console, staring. From the screen, the alien stared blindly up into space. Down in the dark side, the golden indicators had climbed: the vats were more than two-thirds filled.

To *fight* or *run* . . .

Slowly Wesson sank down in front of the console. He sat hunched, head bent, hands squeezed tight between his knees, trying to hold on to the thought that had come to him.

If the alien felt a pain as great as Wesson's—or greater—

Stress might alter the alien's body chemistry, too.

Life of my love, I loathe thee.

Wesson pushed the irrelevant thought aside. He stared at the screen, trying to envisage the alien up there, wincing in pain and distress—sweating a golden sweat of horror. . . .

After a long time, he stood up and walked into the kitchen. He caught the table edge to keep his legs from carrying him on around the circuit. He sat down.

Humming fondly, the autochef slid out a tray of small glasses—water, orange juice, milk. Wesson put the water glass to his stiff lips; the water was cool and hurt his throat. Then the juice, but he could drink only a little of it; then he sipped the milk. Aunt Jane hummed approvingly.

Dehydrated. How long had it been since he had eaten or drunk? He looked at his hands. They were thin bundles of sticks, ropy-veined, with hard yellow claws. He could see the bones of his forearms under the skin, and his heart's beating stirred the cloth at his chest. The pale hairs on his arms and thighs—were they blond or white?

The blurred reflections in the metal trim of the dining room gave him no answers—only pale faceless smears of gray. Wesson felt lightheaded and very weak, as if he had just ended a bout of fever. He fumbled over his ribs and shoulder bones. He was thin.

He sat in front of the autochef for a few minutes more, but no food came out. Evidently Aunt Jane did not think he was ready for it, and perhaps she was right. *Worse for them than for us,* he thought dizzily. *That's why the station's so far out, why radio silence, and only one man aboard. They couldn't stand it at all, otherwise.* . . . Suddenly he could think of nothing but sleep—the bottomless pit, layer after layer of smothering velvet, numbing and soft. . . . His leg muscles quivered and twitched when he tried to walk, but he managed to get to the bedroom and fall on the mattress. The resilient block seemed to dissolve under him. His bones were melting.

He woke with a clear head, very weak, thinking cold and clear: *When two alien cultures meet, the stronger must transform the weaker with love or hate.* "Wesson's Law," he said aloud. He looked automatically for pencil and paper, but there was none, and he realized he would have to tell Aunt Jane, and let her remember it.

"I don't understand," she said.

"Never mind, remember it anyway. You're good at that, aren't you?"

"Yes, Paul."

"All right—I want some breakfast."

He thought about Aunt Jane, so nearly human, sitting up here in her metal prison, leading one man after another through the torments of hell—nursemaid, protector, torturer. They must have known that something would have to give. . . . But the alphas were comparatively new; nobody understood them very well. Perhaps they really thought that an absolute prohibition could never be broken.

. . . the stronger must transform the weaker . . .

I'm the stronger, he thought. *And that's the way it's going to be.* He stopped at the console, and the screen was blank. He said angrily, "Aunt Jane!" And with a guilty start, the screen flickered into life.

Up there, the alien had rolled again in his pain. Now the great clustered eyes were staring directly into the camera; the coiled limbs threshed in pain; the eyes were staring, asking, pleading. . . .

"*No,*" said Wesson, feeling his own pain like an iron cap, and he slammed his hand down on the manual control. The screen went dark. He looked up, sweating, and saw the floral picture over the console.

The thick stems were like antennae, the leaves thoraxes, the buds like blind insect eyes. The whole picture moved slightly, endlessly, in a slow waiting rhythm.

Wesson clutched the hard metal of the console and stared at the picture, with sweat cold on his brow, until it turned into a calm, meaningless arrangement of lines again. Then he went into the dining room, shaking, and sat down.

After a moment he said, "Aunt Jane, does it get worse?"

"No. From now on, it gets better."

"How long?" he asked vaguely.

"One month."

A month, getting "better"—that was the way it had always been, with the watchman swamped and drowned, his personality submerged. Wesson thought about the men who had gone before him—Class Seven citizenship, with unlimited leisure, and Class One housing. Yes, sure—in a sanatorium.

His lips peeled back from his teeth, and his fists clenched hard. *Not me!* he thought.

He spread his hands on the cool metal to steady them. He said, "How much longer do they usually stay able to talk?"

"You are already talking longer than any of them. . . ."

Then there was a blank. Wesson was vaguely aware, in snatches, of the corridor walls moving past and the console glimpsed and of a thunderous cloud of ideas that swirled around his head in a beating of wings. The aliens—what did they want? And what happened to the watchmen in Stranger Station?

The haze receded a little, and he was in the dining room again, staring vacantly at the table. Something was wrong.

He ate a few spoonfuls of the gruel the autochef served him, then pushed it away; the stuff tasted faintly unpleasant. The machine hummed anxiously and thrust a poached egg at him, but Wesson got up from the table.

The station was all but silent. The resting rhythm of the household machines throbbed in the walls, unheard. The blue-lighted living room was spread out before him like an empty stage setting, and Wesson stared as if he had never seen it before.

He lurched to the console and stared down at the pictured alien on the screen—heavy, heavy, asprawl with pain in the darkness. The needles of the golden indicators were high, the enlarged vats almost full. *It's too much for him,* Wesson thought with grim satisfaction. The peace that followed the pain had not descended as it was supposed to; no, not this time!

He glanced up at the painting over the console—heavy crustacean limbs that swayed gracefully in the sea. . . .

He shook his head violently. *I won't let it; I won't give in!* He held the back of one hand close to his eyes. He saw the dozens of tiny cuneiform wrinkles stamped into the skin over the knuckles, the pale hairs sprouting, the pink shiny flesh of recent scars. *I'm human,* he thought. But when he let his hand fall onto the console, the bony fingers seemed to crouch like crustaceans' legs, ready to scuttle.

Sweating, Wesson stared into the screen.

Pictured there, the alien met his eyes, and it was as if they spoke to each other, mind to mind, an instantaneous communication that needed no words. There was a piercing sweetness to it, a melting, dissolving luxury of change into something that would no longer have any pain. . . . A pull, a calling.

Wesson straightened up slowly, carefully, as if he held some fragile thing in his mind that must not be handled roughly, or it would disintegrate. He said hoarsely, "Aunt Jane!"

She made some responsive noise.

He said, "Aunt Jane, I've got the answer! The whole thing! Listen, now wait—listen!" He paused a moment to collect his thoughts. "*When two alien cultures meet, the stronger must transform the weaker with love or hate*. Remember? You said you didn't understand what that meant. I'll *tell* you what it means. When these—monsters—met Pigeon a hundred years ago on Titan, *they knew* we'd have to meet again. They're spreading out, colonizing, and so are we. We haven't got interstellar flight yet, but give us another hundred years, we'll *get* it. *We'll wind up out there, where they are*. And they can't stop us. Because they're not killers, Aunt Jane, it isn't in them. They're *nicer* than us. See, they're like the missionaries, and we're the South Sea islanders. *They* don't kill their enemies, oh, no—perish the thought!"

She was trying to say something, to interrupt him, but he rushed on. "Listen! The longevity serum—that was a lucky accident. But they played it for all it's worth. Slick and smooth. They come and give us the stuff free—they don't ask for a thing in return. Why not? Listen.

"They come here, and the shock of that first contact makes them sweat out that golden gook we need. Then, the last month or so, the pain always eases off. Why? Because the two minds, the human and alien, they stop fighting each other. Something gives way, it goes soft, and there's a mixing together. And that's where you get the human casualties of this operation—the bleary men that come out of here not even able to talk human language anymore. Oh, I suppose they're happy—happier than I am!—because they've got something big and wonderful inside 'em. Something that you and I can't even understand. But if you took them and put them together again with the aliens who spent time here, *they could all live together—they're adapted*.

"That's what they're aiming for!" He struck the console with his fist. "Not now—but a hundred, two hundred years from now! When we start expanding out to the stars—when we go a-conquering—we'll have already been conquered! Not by weapons, Aunt Jane, not by hate—by love! Yes, love! *Dirty, stinking, low-down, sneaking love!*"

Aunt Jane said something, a long sentence, in a high, anxious voice.

"What?" said Wesson irritably. He couldn't understand a word.

Aunt Jane was silent. "What, what?" Wesson demanded, pounding the console. "Have you got it through your tin head or not? *What?*"

Aunt Jane said something else, tonelessly. Once more, Wesson could not make out a single word.

He stood frozen. Warm tears started suddenly out of his eyes. "Aunt Jane—" he said. He remembered, *You are already talking longer than any of them*. Too late? Too late? He tensed, then whirled and sprang to the closet where the paper books were kept. He opened the first one his hand struck.

The black letters were alien squiggles on the page, little humped shapes, without meaning.

The tears were coming faster, he couldn't stop them—tears of weariness, tears of frustration, tears of hate. *"Aunt Jane!"* he roared.

But it was no good. The curtain of silence had come down over his head. He was one of the vanguard—the conquered men, the ones who would get along with their strange brothers, out among the alien stars.

The console was not working anymore; nothing worked when he wanted it. Wesson squatted in the shower stall, naked, with a soup bowl in his hands. Water droplets glistened on his hands and forearms; the pale short hairs were just springing up, drying.

The silvery skin of reflection in the bowl gave him back nothing but a silhouette, a shadow man's outline. He could not see his face.

He dropped the bowl and went across the living room, shuffling the pale drifts of paper underfoot. The black lines on the paper, when his eye happened to light on them, were worm shapes, crawling things, conveying nothing. He rolled slightly in his walk; his eyes were glazed. His head twitched, every now and then, sketching a useless motion to avoid pain.

Once the bureau chief, Gower, came to stand in his way. "You fool," he said, his face contorted in anger, "you were supposed to go on to the end, like the rest. Now look what you've done!"

"I found out, didn't I?" Wesson mumbled, and as he brushed the man aside like a cobweb, the pain suddenly grew more intense. Wesson clasped his head in his hands with a grunt, and rocked to and fro a moment, uselessly, before he straightened and went on. The pain was coming in waves now, so tall that at their peak his vision dimmed out, violet, then gray.

It couldn't go on much longer. Something had to burst.

He paused at the bloody place and slapped the metal with his palm, making the sound ring dully up into the frame of the station: *rroom . . . rroom . . .*

Faintly an echo came back: *boo-oom . . .*

Wesson kept going, smiling a faint and meaningless smile. He was only marking time now, waiting. Something was about to happen.

The kitchen doorway sprouted a sudden sill and tripped him. He fell heavily, sliding on the floor, and lay without moving beneath the slick gleam of the autochef.

The pressure was too great—the autochef's clucking was swallowed up in the ringing pressure, and the tall gray walls buckled slowly in. . . .

The station lurched.

Wesson felt it through his chest, palms, knees, and elbows: the floor was plucked away for an instant and then swung back.

The pain in his skull relaxed its grip a little. Wesson tried to get to his feet.

There was an electric silence in the station. On the second try, he got up and leaned his back against a wall. *Cluck,* said the autochef suddenly, hysterically, and the vent popped open, but nothing came out.

He listened, straining to hear. What?

The station bounced beneath him, making his feet jump like a puppet's; the wall slapped his back hard, shuddered, and was still; but far off through the metal cage came a long angry groan of metal, echoing, diminishing, dying. Then silence again.

The station held its breath. All the myriad clickings and pulses in the walls were suspended; in the empty rooms the lights burned with a yellow glare, and the air hung stagnant and still. The console lights in the living room glowed like witchfires. Water in the dropped bowl, at the bottom of the shower stall, shone like quicksilver, waiting.

The third shock came. Wesson found himself on his hands and knees, the jolt still tingling in the bones of his body, staring at the floor. The sound that filled the room ebbed away slowly and ran down into the silences—a resonant metallic sound, shuddering away now along the girders and hull plates, rattling tinnily into bolts and fittings, diminishing, noiseless, gone. The silence pressed down again.

The floor leaped painfully under his body, one great resonant blow that shook him from head to foot.

A muted echo of that blow came a few seconds later, as if the shock had traveled across the station and back.

The bed, Wesson thought, and scrambled on hands and knees through the doorway, along a floor curiously tilted, until he reached the rubbery block.

The room burst visibly upward around him,

squeezing the block flat. It dropped back as violently, leaving Wesson bouncing helplessly on the mattress, his limbs flying. It came to rest, in a long reluctant groan of metal.

Wesson rolled up on one elbow, thinking incoherently, *Air, the air lock.* Another blow slammed him down into the mattress, pinched his lungs shut, while the room danced grotesquely over his head. Gasping for breath in the ringing silence, Wesson felt a slow icy chill rolling toward him across the room—and there was a pungent smell in the air. *Ammonia!* he thought, and the odorless, smothering methane with it.

His cell was breached. The burst membrane was fatal—the alien's atmosphere would kill him.

Wesson surged to his feet. The next shock caught him off balance, dashed him to the floor. He arose again, dazed and limping; he was still thinking confusedly, *The air lock—get out.*

When he was halfway to the door, all the ceiling lights went out at once. The darkness was like a blanket around his head. It was bitter cold now in the room, and the pungent smell was sharper. Coughing, Wesson hurried forward. The floor lurched under his feet.

Only the golden indicators burned now— full to the top, the deep vats brimming, golden-lipped, gravid, a month before the time. Wesson shuddered.

Water spurted in the bathroom, hissing steadily on the tiles, rattling in the plastic bowl at the bottom of the shower stall. The light winked on and off again. In the dining room, he heard the autochef clucking and sighing. The freezing wind blew harder; he was numb with cold to the hips. It seemed to Wesson abruptly that he was not at the top of the sky at all, but down, *down* at the bottom of the sea— trapped in this steel bubble, while the dark poured in.

The pain in his head was gone, as if it had never been there, and he understood what that meant: Up there, the great body was hanging like butcher's carrion in the darkness. Its death struggles were over, the damage done.

Wesson gathered a desperate breath, shouted, "Help me! The alien's dead! He kicked the station apart—the methane's coming in! Get help, do you hear me? *Do you hear me?*"

Silence. In the smothering blackness, he remembered: *She can't understand me anymore. Even if she's alive.*

He turned, making an animal noise in his throat. He groped his way on around the room, past the second doorway. Behind the walls, something was dripping with a slow cold tinkle and splash, a forlorn night sound. Small, hard, floating things rapped against his legs. Then he touched a smooth curve of metal—the air lock.

Eagerly he pushed his feeble weight against the door. It didn't move. Cold air was rushing out around the door frame, a thin knife-cold stream, but the door itself was jammed tight.

The suit! He should have thought of that before. If he just had some pure *air* to breathe and a little warmth in his fingers . . . But the door of the suit locker would not move, either. The ceiling must have buckled.

And that was the end, he thought, bewildered. There were no more ways out. But there *had* to be. . . . He pounded on the door until his arms would not lift anymore; it did not move. Leaning against the chill metal, he saw a single light blink on overhead.

The room was a wild place of black shadows and swimming shapes—the book leaves, fluttering and darting in the air stream. Schools of them beat wildly at the walls, curling over, baffled, trying again; others were swooping around the outer corridor, around and around; he could see them whirling past the doorways, dreamlike, a white drift of silent paper in the darkness.

The acrid smell was harsher in his nostrils. Wesson choked, groping his way to the console again. He pounded it with his open hand, crying weakly—he wanted to see Earth.

But when the little square of brightness leaped up, it was the dead body of the alien that Wesson saw.

It hung motionless in the cavity of the station, limbs dangling stiff and still, eyes dull. The last turn of the screw had been too much for it. But Wesson had survived. . . .

For a few minutes.

The dead alien face mocked him; a whisper of memory floated into his mind: *We might have been brothers.* . . . All at once Wesson passionately wanted to believe it—wanted to give in, turn back. That passed. Wearily he let himself sag into the bitter *now*, thinking with thin defiance, *It's done—hate wins. You'll have to stop this big giveaway—can't risk this happening again. And we'll hate you for that—and when we get out to the stars—*

The world was swimming numbly away out of reach. He felt the last fit of coughing take his body, as if it were happening to someone else besides him.

The last fluttering leaves of paper came to rest. There was a long silence in the drowned room.

Then:

"Paul," said the voice of the mechanical woman brokenly; "Paul," it said again, with the hopelessness of lost, unknown, impossible love.

Sector General
JAMES WHITE

James White (1928–1999) was an Irish writer of science fiction whose first published story appeared in *New Worlds* (1953). Although White's novels are often entertaining and engaging, he is known almost exclusively for the tales about galactic medicine comprising the *Sector General* sequence, set in a huge space-habitat hospital located "far out on the galactic rim" and designed to accommodate all known kinds of xenobiological problems; its facilities include a computerized universal translator. Early stories in this sequence appeared in *New Worlds*—the first of all being the novella "Sector General" (1957), reprinted here—and several others in *New Writings in SF*, which gave him a reliable home for the series. Through the first six volumes of *Sector General* stories and novels, Dr. Conway, a human member of the ten-thousand-strong multispecies staff, solves alone or with colleagues a series of medical crises with humor, ingenuity, and an underlying Hippocratic sense of decency; equally sympathetic alien protagonists begin to appear with volume seven.

Throughout the series, White's capacity to conceive and make plausible a wide range of alien anatomies and their failure modes seems unflagging. The *Sector General* series has a strong undercurrent of pacifism (its military "Monitor Corps" exists chiefly to prevent or halt wars using nonlethal weaponry) and includes numerous instances of successful first contact achieved by giving medical aid to injured and distressed aliens, usually spacefaring ones—a trope that recurs in several of White's nonseries stories. The hospital's system of "educator tapes," whereby doctors absorb the memories and skills of other-species medical experts via theoretically reversible identity transfer, is a fruitful source of complications.

The *Sector General* stories are underrated within the science fiction canon, perhaps because they do not depend on typical conflict or story lines for their resolution. But this is exactly what makes them unique and still fresh to this day. "Sector General" remains one of the most potent, demonstrating White's ability to tell an engrossing story while also exploring the hospital and presenting the reader with a unique experience.

SECTOR GENERAL

James White

I

Like a sprawling, misshapen Christmas tree the lights of Sector Twelve General Hospital blazed against the misty backdrop of the stars. From its view-ports shone lights that were yellow and red-orange and soft, liquid green, and others which were a searing actinic blue. There was darkness in places also. Behind these areas of opaque metal plating lay sections wherein the lighting was so viciously incandescent that the eyes of approaching ships' pilots had to be protected from it, or compartments which were so dark and cold that not even the light which filtered in from the stars could be allowed to penetrate to their inhabitants.

To the occupants of the Telfi ship which slid out of hyperspace to hang some twenty miles from this mighty structure, the garish display of visual radiation was too dim to be detected without the use of instruments. The Telfi were energy-eaters. Their ship's hull shone with a crawling blue glow of radioactivity and its interior was awash with a high level of hard radiation which was also in all respects normal. Only in the stern section of the tiny ship were the conditions not normal. Here the active core of a power pile lay scattered in small, sub-critical, and unshielded masses throughout the ship's Planetary Engines room, and here it was too hot even for the Telfi.

The group-mind entity that was the Telfi spaceship captain—*and* crew—energised its short-range communicator and spoke in the staccato clicking and buzzing language used to converse with those benighted beings who were unable to merge into a Telfi gestalt.

"This is a Telfi hundred-unit gestalt," it said slowly and distinctly. "We have casualties and require assistance. Our classification to one group is VTXM, repeat VTXM. . . ."

"Details, please, and degree of urgency," said a voice briskly as the Telfi was about to repeat the message. It was translated into the same language used by the captain. The Telfi gave details quickly, then waited. Around it and through it lay the hundred specialised units that were both its mind and multiple body. Some of the units were blind, deaf, and perhaps even dead cells that received or recorded no sensory impressions whatever, but there were others who radiated waves of such sheer, excruciating agony that the group-mind writhed and twisted silently in sympathy. Would that voice never reply, they wondered, and if it did, would it be able to help them . . . ?

"You must not approach the hospital nearer than a distance of five miles," said the voice suddenly. "Otherwise there will be danger to unshielded traffic in the vicinity, or to beings within the establishment with low radiation tolerance."

"We understand," said the Telfi.

"Very well," said the voice. "You must also realise that your race is too hot for us to handle directly. Remote-controlled mechanisms are already on the way to you, and it would ease the problem of evacuation if you arranged to have your casualties brought as closely as possible to the ship's largest entry port. If this cannot be done, do not worry—we have mechanisms capable of entering your vessel and removing them."

The voice ended by saying that while they

hoped to be able to help the patients, any sort of accurate prognosis was impossible at the present time.

The Telfi gestalt thought that soon the agony that tortured its mind and wide-flung multiple body would be gone, but so also would nearly one-quarter of that body. . . .

With that feeling of happiness possible only with eight hours' sleep behind, a comfortable breakfast within, and an interesting job in front of one, Conway stepped out briskly for his wards. They were not really his wards, of course—if anything went seriously wrong in one of them the most he would be expected to do would be to scream for help. But considering the fact that he had been here only two months he did not mind that, or knowing that it would be a long time before he could be trusted to deal with cases requiring other than mechanical methods of treatment. Complete knowledge of any alien physiology could be obtained within minutes by Educator Tape, but the skill to use that knowledge—especially in surgery—came only with time. Conway was looking forward with conscious pride to spending his life acquiring that skill.

At an intersection Conway saw an FGLI he knew—a Tralthan intern who was humping his elephantine body along on six spongy feet. The stubby legs seemed even more rubbery than usual and the little OTSB who lived in symbiosis with it was practically comatose. Conway said brightly, "Good morning," and received a translated—and therefore necessarily emotionless—reply of "Drop dead." Conway grinned.

There had been considerable activity in and about Reception last evening. Conway had not been called, but it looked as though the Tralthan had missed both his recreation and rest periods.

A few yards beyond the Tralthan he met another who was walking slowly alongside a small DBDG like himself. Not entirely like himself, though—DBDG was the one-group classification which gave the grosser physical attributes, the number of arms, heads, legs, etc., and their placement. The fact that the being had seven-fingered hands, stood only four feet tall, and looked like a very cuddly teddy bear—Conway had forgotten the being's system of origin, but remembered being told that it came from a world which had suffered a sudden bout of glaciation which had caused its highest life-form to develop intelligence and a thick red fur coat—would not have shown up unless the classification were taken to two or three groups. The DBDG had his hands clasped behind his back and was staring with vacant intensity at the floor. His hulking companion showed similar concentration, but favoured the ceiling because of the different position of his visual organs. Both wore their professional insignia on golden armbands, which meant that they were lordly Diagnosticians, no less. Conway refrained from saying good morning to them as he passed, or from making undue noise with his feet.

Possibly they were deeply immersed in some medical problem, Conway thought, or equally likely, they had just had a tiff and were pointedly ignoring each other's existence. Diagnosticians were peculiar people. It wasn't that they were insane to begin with, but their job forced a form of insanity onto them.

At each corridor intersection annunciators had been pouring out an alien gabble which he had only half heard in passing, but when it switched suddenly to Terran English and Conway heard his own name being called, surprise halted him dead in his tracks.

". . . to Admittance Lock Twelve at once," the voice was repeating monotonously. "Classification VTXM-23. Dr. Conway, please go to Admittance Lock Twelve at once. A VTXM-23 . . ."

Conway's first thought was that they could

not possibly mean him. This looked as if he was being asked to deal with a case—a big one, too, because the "23" after the classification code referred to the number of patients to be treated. And that classification, VTXM, was completely new to him. Conway knew what the letters stood for, of course, but he had never thought that they could exist in that combination. The nearest he could make of them was some form of telepathic species—the V prefixing the classification showed this as their most important attribute, and that mere physical equipment was secondary—who existed by the direct conversion of radiant energy, and usually as a closely cooperative group or gestalt. While he was still wondering if he was ready to cope with a case like this, his feet had turned and were taking him towards Lock Twelve.

His patients were waiting for him at the lock, in a small metal box heaped around with lead bricks and already loaded onto a power stretcher carrier. The orderly told him briefly that the beings called themselves the Telfi; that preliminary diagnosis indicated the use of the Radiation Theatre, which was being readied for him; and that owing to the portability of his patients he could save time by calling with them to the Educator room and leaving them outside while he took his Telfi physiology tape.

Conway nodded thanks, hopped onto the carrier, and set it moving, trying to give the impression that he did this sort of thing every day.

In Conway's pleasurable but busy life with the high unusual establishment that was Sector General there was only one sour note, and he met it again when he entered the Educator room: there was a Monitor in charge. Conway disliked Monitors. The presence of one affected him rather like the close proximity of a carrier of a contagious disease. And while Conway was proud of the fact that as a sane, civilised, and ethical being he could never bring himself actually to hate anybody or anything, he disliked Monitors intensely. He knew, of course, that there were people who went off the beam some-

times, and that there had to be somebody who could take the action necessary to preserve the peace. But with his abhorrence of violence in any form, Conway could not like the men who took that action.

And what were Monitors doing in a hospital anyway?

The figure in neat, dark green coveralls seated before the Educator control console turned quickly at his entrance and Conway got another shock. As well as a major's insignia on his shoulder, the Monitor wore the Staff and Serpents emblem of a doctor!

"My name is O'Mara," said the major in a pleasant voice. "I'm the chief psychologist of this madhouse. You, I take it, are Dr. Conway." He smiled.

Conway made himself smile in return, knowing that it looked forced, and that the other knew it also.

"You want the Telfi tape," O'Mara said, a trifle less warmly. "Well, doctor, you've picked a real weirdie this time. Be sure you get it erased as soon as possible after the job is done—believe me, this isn't one you'll want to keep. Thumbprint this and sit over there."

While the Educator headband and electrodes were being fitted, Conway tried to keep his face neutral, and keep from flinching away from the major's hard, capable hands. O'Mara's hair was a dull, metallic grey in colour, cut short, and his eyes also had the piercing qualities of metal. Those eyes had observed his reactions, Conway knew, and now an equally sharp mind was forming conclusions regarding them.

"Well, that's it," said O'Mara when finally it was all over. "But before you go, doctor, I think you and I should have a little chat; a reorientation talk, let's call it. Not now, though, you've got a case—but very soon."

Conway felt the eyes boring into his back as he left.

He should have been trying to make his mind a blank as he had been told to do, so the knowledge newly impressed there could bed down comfortably, but all Conway could think about was the fact that a Monitor was a high member of the hospital's permanent staff—and a doctor, to boot. How could the two professions mix? Conway thought of the armband he wore which bore the Tralthan Black and Red Circle, the Flaming Sun of the chlorine-breathing Illensa, and intertwining Serpents and Staff of Earth—all the honoured symbols of medicine of the three chief races of the Galactic Union. And here was this Dr. O'Mara whose collar said he was a healer and whose shoulder tabs said he was something else entirely.

One thing was now sure: Conway would never feel really content here again until he discovered why the chief psychologist of the hospital was a Monitor.

II

This was Conway's first experience of an alien physiology tape, and he noted with interest the mental double vision which had increasingly begun to affect his mind—a sure sign that the tape had "taken." By the time he had reached the Radiation Theatre, he felt himself to be two people—an Earth-human called Conway and the great, five-hundred-unit Telfi gestalt which had been formed to prepare a mental record of all that was known regarding the physiology of that race. That was the only disadvantage—if it was a disadvantage—of the Educator Tape system. Not only was knowledge impressed on the mind undergoing "tuition," the personalities of the entities who had possessed that knowledge were transferred as well. Small wonder then that the Diagnosticians, who held in their mind sometimes as many as ten different tapes, were a little bit queer.

A Diagnostician had the most important job in the hospital, Conway thought, as he donned radiation armour and readied his patients for the preliminary examination. He had sometimes thought in his more self-confident moments

of becoming one himself. Their chief purpose was to perform original work in xenological medicine and surgery, using their tape-stuffed brains as a jumping-off ground, and to rally round, when a case arrived for which there was no physiology tape available, to diagnose and prescribe treatment.

Not for them were the simple, mundane injuries and diseases. For a Diagnostician to look at a patient that patient had to be unique, hopeless, and at least three-quarters dead. When one did take charge of a case though, the patient was as good as cured—they achieved miracles with monotonous regularity.

With the lower orders of doctor there was always the temptation, Conway knew, to keep the contents of a tape rather than have it erased, in the hope of making some original discovery that would bring them fame. In practical, level-headed men like himself, however, it remained just that, a temptation.

Conway did not see his tiny patients even though he examined them individually. He couldn't unless he went to a lot of unnecessary trouble with shielding and mirrors to do so. But he knew what they were like, both inside and out, because the tape had practically made him one of them. That knowledge, taken together with the results of his examinations and the case history supplied him, told Conway everything he wanted to know to begin treatment.

His patients had been part of a Telfi gestalt engaged in operating an interstellar cruiser when there had been an accident in one of the power piles. The small, beetlelike, and—individually—very stupid beings were radiation eaters, but that flare-up had been too much even for them. Their trouble could be classed as an extremely severe case of overeating coupled with prolonged overstimulation of their sensory equipment, especially of the pain centres. If he simply kept them in a shielded container and starved them of radiation—a course of treatment impossible on their highly radioactive ship—

about 70 percent of them could be expected to cure themselves in a few hours. They would be the lucky ones, and Conway could even tell which of them came into that category. Those remaining would be a tragedy because if they did not suffer actual physical death their fate would be very much worse: they would lose the ability to join minds, and that in a Telfi was tantamount to being a hopeless cripple.

Only someone who shared the mind, personality, and instincts of a Telfi could appreciate the tragedy it was.

It was a great pity, especially as the case history showed that it was these individuals who had forced themselves to adapt and remain operative during that sudden flare of radiation for the few seconds necessary to scatter the pile and so save their ship from complete destruction. Now their metabolism had found a precarious balance based on three times the Telfi normal energy intake. If this intake of energy was interrupted for any lengthy period of time, say a few more hours, the communications centres of their brains would suffer. They would be left like so many dismembered hands and feet, with just enough intelligence to know that they had been cut off. On the other hand, if their upped energy intake was continued they would literally burn themselves out within a week.

But there was a line of treatment indicated for these unfortunates, the only one, in fact. As Conway prepared his servos for the work ahead he felt that it was a highly unsatisfactory line—a matter of calculated risks, of cold, medical statistics which nothing he could do would influence. He felt himself to be little more than a mechanic.

Working quickly, he ascertained that sixteen of his patients were suffering from the Telfi equivalent of acute indigestion. These he separated into shielded, absorbent bottles so that re-radiation from their still "hot" bodies would not slow the "starving" process. The bottles he placed in a small pile furnace set to radiate at Telfi normal, with a detector in each which would cause the shielding to fall away from

them as soon as their excess radioactivity had gone. The remaining seven would require special treatment. He had placed them in another pile, and was setting the controls to simulate as closely as possible the conditions which had obtained during the accident in their ship, when the nearby communicator beeped at him. Conway finished what he was doing, checked it, then said, "Yes?"

"This is Enquiries, Dr. Conway. We've had a signal from the Telfi ship asking about their casualties. Have you any news for them yet?"

Conway knew that his news was not too bad, considering, but he wished intensely that it could be better. The breaking up or modification of a Telfi gestalt once formed could only be likened to a death trauma to the entities concerned, and with the empathy which came as a result of absorbing their physiology tape Conway felt for them. He said carefully, "Sixteen of them will be good as new in roughly four hours' time. The other seven will be fifty percent fatalities, I'm afraid, but we won't know which for another few days. I have them baking in a pile at over double their normal radiation requirements, and this will gradually be reduced to normal. Half of them should live through it. Do you understand?"

"Got you." After a few minutes the voice returned. It said, "The Telfi say that is very good, and thank you. Out."

He should have been pleased at dealing successfully with his first case, but Conway somehow felt let down. Now that it was over his mind felt strangely confused. He kept thinking that 50 percent of seven was three and a half, and what would they do with the odd half Telfi? He hoped that four would pull through instead of three, and that they would not be mental cripples. He thought that it must be nice to be a Telfi, to soak up radiation all the time, and the rich and varied impressions of a corporate body numbering perhaps hundreds of individuals. It made his body feel somehow cold and alone. It was an effort to drag himself away from the warmth of the Radiation Theatre.

Outside he mounted the carrier and left it back at the admittance lock. The right thing to do now was to report to the Educator room and have the Telfi tape erased—he had been ordered to do that, in fact. But he did not want to go; the thought of O'Mara made him intensely uncomfortable, even a little afraid. Conway knew that all Monitors made him feel uncomfortable, but this was different. It was O'Mara's attitude, and that little chat he had mentioned. Conway had felt small, as if the Monitor was his superior in some fashion, and for the life of him Conway could not understand how he could feel small before a lousy Monitor!

The intensity of his feelings shocked him; as a civilised, well-integrated being he should have been incapable of thinking such thoughts. His emotions had verged upon actual hatred. Frightened of himself this time, Conway brought his mind under a semblance of control. He decided to sidestep the question and not report to the Educator room until after he had done the rounds of his wards. It was a legitimate excuse if O'Mara should query the delay, and the chief psychologist might leave or be called away in the meantime. Conway hoped so.

His first call was on an AUGL from Chalderescol II, the sole occupant of the ward reserved for that species. Conway climbed into the appropriate protective garment—a simple diving suit in this instance—and went through the lock into the tank of green, tepid water which reproduced the being's living conditions. He collected the instruments from the locker inside, then loudly signalled his presence. If the Chalder was really asleep down there and he startled it the results could be serious. One accidental flick of that tail and the ward would contain two patients instead of one.

The Chalder was heavily plated and scaled, and slightly resembled a forty-foot-long crocodile except that instead of legs there was an apparently haphazard arrangement of stubby fins and a fringe of ribbonlike tentacles encircling its middle. It drifted limply near the bottom of the huge tank, the only sign of life being

the periodic fogging of the water around its gills. Conway gave it a perfunctory examination—he was way behind time due to the Telfi job—and asked the usual question. The answer came through the water in some unimaginable form to Conway's translator attachment and into his phones as slow, toneless speech.

"I am grievously ill," said the Chalder, "I suffer."

You lie, thought Conway silently, *in all six rows of your teeth!* Dr. Lister, Sector General's director and probably the foremost Diagnostician of the day, had practically taken this Chalder apart. His diagnosis had been hypochondria and the condition incurable. He had further stated that the signs of strain in certain sections of the patient's body plating, and its discomfort in those areas, were due simply to the big so-and-so's laziness and gluttony. Anybody knew that an exoskeletal life-form could not put on weight except from inside! Diagnosticians were not noted for their bedside manners.

The Chalder became really ill only when it was in danger of being sent home, so the hospital had acquired a permanent patient. But it did not mind. Visiting as well as staff medics and psychologists had given it a going over, and continued to do so; also all the interns and nurses of all the multitudinous races represented on the hospital's staff. Regularly and at short intervals it was probed, pried into, and unmercifully pounded by trainees of varying degrees of gentleness, and it loved every minute of it. The hospital was happy with the arrangement and so was the Chalder. Nobody mentioned going home to it anymore.

III

Conway paused for a moment as he swam to the top of the great tank; he felt peculiar. His next call was supposed to be on two methane-breathing life-forms in the lower-temperature ward of his section, and he felt strongly loath to go. Despite the warmth of the water and the heat of his exertions while swimming around his massive patient he felt cold, and he would have given anything to have a bunch of students come flapping into the tank just for the company. Usually Conway did not like company, especially that of trainees, but now he felt cut off, alone and friendless. The feelings were so strong they frightened him. A talk with a psychologist was definitely indicated, he thought, though not necessarily with O'Mara.

The construction of the hospital in this section resembled a heap of spaghetti—straight, bent, and indescribably curved pieces of spaghetti. Each corridor containing an Earth-type atmosphere, for instance, was paralleled above, below, and on each side—as well as being crossed above and below at frequent intervals—by others having different and mutually deadly variations of atmosphere, pressure, and temperature. This was to facilitate the visiting of any given patient-species by any other species of doctor in the shortest possible time in case of emergency, because travelling the length of the hospital in a suit designed to protect a doctor against his patient's environment on arrival was both uncomfortable and slow. It had been found more efficient to change into the necessary protective suit outside the wards being visited, as Conway had done.

Remembering the geography of this section Conway knew that there was a shortcut he could use to get to his frigid-blooded patients—along the water-filled corridor which led to the Chalder operating theatre, through the lock into the chlorine atmosphere of the Illensan PVSJs and up two levels to the methane ward. This way would mean his staying in warm water for a little longer, and he was definitely feeling *cold*.

A convalescent PVSJ rustled past him on spiny, membraneous appendages in the chlorine section and Conway found himself wanting desperately to talk to it, about anything. He had to force himself to go on.

The protective suit worn by DBDGs like himself while visiting the methane ward was in reality a small mobile tank. It was fitted with heaters inside to keep its occupant alive and refrigerators outside so that the leakage of heat would not immediately shrivel the patients to whom the slightest glow of radiant heat—or even light—was lethal. Conway had no idea how the scanner he used in the examinations worked—only those gadget-mad beings with the Engineering armbands knew that—except that it wasn't by infrared. That also was too hot for them.

As he worked Conway turned the heaters up until the sweat rolled off him and still he felt cold. He was suddenly afraid. Suppose he had caught something? When he was outside in air again he looked at the tiny telltale that was surgically embedded on the inner surface of his forearm. His pulse, respiration, and endocrine balance were normal except for the minor irregularities caused by his worrying, and there was nothing foreign in his bloodstream. What was wrong with him?

Conway finished his rounds as quickly as possible. He felt confused again. If his mind was playing tricks on him he was going to take the necessary steps to rectify the matter. It must be something to do with the Telfi tape he had absorbed. O'Mara had said something about it, though he could not remember exactly what at the moment. But he would go to the Educator room right away, O'Mara or no O'Mara.

Two Monitors passed him while he was on the way, both armed. Conway knew that he should feel his usual hostility towards them, also shock that they were armed inside a hospital, and he did, but he also wanted to slap their backs or even hug them: he desperately wanted to have people around, talking and exchanging ideas and impressions so that he would not feel so terribly alone. As they drew level with him Conway managed to get out a shaky "Hello." It was the first time he had spoken to a Monitor in his life.

One of the Monitors smiled slightly, the other nodded. Both gave him odd looks over their shoulders as they passed because his teeth were chattering so much.

His intention of going to the Educator room had been clearly formed, but now it did not seem to be such a good idea. It was cold and dark there with all those machines and shaded lighting, and the only company might be O'Mara. Conway wanted to lose himself in a crowd, and the bigger the better. He thought of the nearby dining hall and turned towards it. Then at an intersection he saw a sign reading "Diet Kitchen, Wards 52 to 68, Species DBDG, DBLF, & FGLI." That made him remember how terribly cold he felt. . . .

The Dietitians were too busy to notice him. Conway picked an oven which was fairly glowing with heat and lay down against it, letting the germ-killing ultraviolet which flooded the place bathe him and ignoring the charred smell given off by his light clothing. He felt warmer now, a little warmer, but the awful sense of being utterly and completely alone would not leave him. He was cut off, unloved and unwanted. He wished that he had never been born.

When a Monitor—one of the two he had recently passed whose curiosity had been aroused by Conway's strange behaviour—wearing a hastily borrowed heat suit belonging to one of the Cook-Dietitians got to him a few minutes later, the big, slow tears were running down Conway's cheeks. . . .

"You," said a well-remembered voice, "are a very lucky and very stupid young man."

Conway opened his eyes to find that he was on the Erasure couch and that O'Mara and another Monitor were looking down at him. His back felt as though it had been cooked medium rare and his whole body stung as if with a bad dose of sunburn. O'Mara was glaring furiously at him; he spoke again.

"Lucky not to be seriously burned and blinded, and stupid because you forgot to inform me on one very important point, namely that this was your first experience with the Educator. . . ."

O'Mara's tone became faintly self-accusatory at this point, but only faintly. He went on to say that had he been thus informed he would have given Conway a hypno-treatment which would have enabled the doctor to differentiate between his own needs and those of the Telfi sharing his mind. He only realised that Conway was a first-timer when he filed the thumbprinted slip, and dammit, how was he to know who was new and who wasn't in a place this size! And anyway, if Conway had thought more of his job and less of the fact that a Monitor was giving him the tape, this would never have happened.

Conway, O'Mara continued bitingly, appeared to be a self-righteous bigot who made no pretence at hiding his feelings of defilement at the touch of an uncivilised brute of a Monitor. How a person intelligent enough to gain appointment to this hospital could also hold those sort of feelings was beyond O'Mara's understanding.

Conway felt his face burning. It had been stupid of him to forget to tell the psychologist that he was a first-timer. O'Mara could easily bring charges of personal negligence against him—a charge almost as serious as carelessness with a patient in a multi-environment hospital—and have Conway kicked out. But that possibility did not weigh too heavily with him at the moment, terrible though it was. What got him was the fact that he was being told off by a *Monitor*, and before another Monitor!

The man who must have carried him here was gazing down at him, a look of half-humourous concern in his steady brown eyes. Conway found that harder to take even than O'Mara's abusiveness. How dare a Monitor feel sorry for *him*!

". . . And if you're still wondering what happened," O'Mara was saying in withering tones, "you allowed—through inexperience, I admit—the Telfi personality contained in the tape to temporarily overcome your own. Its need for hard radiation, intense heat and light, and above all the mental fusion necessary to a group-mind entity, became your needs—transferred into their nearest human equivalents, of course. For a while you were experiencing life as a single Telfi being, and an individual Telfi—cut off from all mental contact with the others of its group—is an unhappy beastie indeed."

O'Mara had cooled somewhat as his explanation proceeded. His voice was almost impersonal as he went on, "You're suffering from little more than a bad case of sunburn. Your back will be tender for a while and later it will itch. Serves you right. Now go away. I don't want to see you again until hour nine the day after tomorrow. Keep that hour free. That's an order—we have to have a little talk, remember?"

Outside in the corridor Conway had a feeling of complete deflation coupled with an anger that threatened to burst out of all control—an intensely frustrating combination. In all his twenty-three years of life he could not remember being subjected to such extreme mental discomfort. He had been made to feel like a small boy—a bad, maladjusted small boy. Conway had always been a very good, well-mannered boy. It hurt.

He had not noticed that his rescuer was still beside him until the other spoke.

"Don't go worrying yourself about the major," the Monitor said sympathetically. "He's really a nice man, and when you see him again you'll find out for yourself. At the moment he's tired and a bit touchy. You see, there are three companies just arrived and more coming. But they won't be much use to us in their present state—they're in a bad way with combat fatigue, most of 'em. Major O'Mara and his staff have to give them some psychological first aid before—"

"Combat fatigue," said Conway in the most insulting tone of which he was capable. He was heartily sick of people he considered his intellectual and moral inferiors either ranting at him or sympathising with him. "I suppose," he added, "that means they've grown tired of killing people?"

He saw the Monitor's young-old face stiffen and something that was both hurt and anger burn in his eyes. He stopped. He opened his mouth for an O'Mara-type blast of invective, then thought better of it. He said quietly, "For someone who has been here for two months you have, to put it mildly, a very unrealistic attitude towards the Monitor Corps. I can't understand that. Have you been too busy to talk to people or something?"

"No," replied Conway coldly, "but where I come from we do not discuss persons of your type, we prefer pleasanter topics."

"I hope," said the Monitor, "that all your friends—if you have friends, that is—indulge in backslapping." He turned and marched off.

Conway winced in spite of himself at the thought of anything heavier than a feather hitting his scorched and tender back. But he was thinking of the other's earlier words, too. So his attitude towards Monitors was unrealistic? Did they want him, then, to condone violence and murder and befriend those who were responsible for it? And he had also mentioned the arrival of several companies of Monitors. Why? What for? Anxiety began to eat at the edges of his hitherto solid block of self-confidence. There was something here that he was missing, something important.

When he had first arrived at Sector General the being who had given Conway his original instructions and assignments had added a little pep talk. It had said that Dr. Conway had passed a great many tests to come here and that they welcomed him and hoped he would be happy enough in his work to stay. The period of trial was now over, and henceforth nobody would be trying to catch him out, but if for any reason—friction with his own or any other species, or the appearance of some xenological psychosis—he became so distressed that he could no longer stay, then with great reluctance he would be allowed to leave.

He had also been advised to meet as many different entities as possible and try to gain mutual understanding, if not their friendship. Finally he had been told that if he should get into trouble through ignorance or any other reason, he should contact either of two Earth-human beings who were called O'Mara and Bryson, depending on the nature of his trouble, though a qualified being of any species would, of course, help him on request.

Immediately afterwards he had met the surgeon-in-charge of the wards to which he had been posted, a very able Earth-human called Mannon. Dr. Mannon was not yet a Diagnostician, though he was trying hard, and was therefore still quite human for long periods during the day. He was the proud possessor of a small dog which stuck so close to him that visiting extraterrestrials were inclined to assume a symbiotic relationship. Conway liked Dr. Mannon a lot, but now he was beginning to realise that his superior was the only being of his own species towards whom he had any feeling of friendship.

That was a bit strange, surely. It made Conway begin to wonder about himself.

After that reassuring pep talk Conway had thought he was all set—especially when he found how easy it was to make friends with the ET members of the staff. He had not warmed to his human colleagues—with the one exception—because of their tendency to be flippant or cynical regarding the very important and worthwhile work he, and they, were doing. But the idea of friction developing was laughable.

That was before today, though, when O'Mara had made him feel small and stupid, accused him of bigotry and intolerance, and generally cut his ego to pieces. This, quite definitely, was friction developing, and if such treatment at the hands of Monitors continued Conway knew that he would be driven to leave. He was a civilised and ethical human being— why were the Monitors in a position to tell him

off? Conway just could not understand it at all. Two things he did know, however; he wanted to remain at the hospital, and to do that he needed help.

IV

The name "Bryson" popped into his mind suddenly, one of the names he had been given should he get into trouble. O'Mara, the other name, was out, but this Bryson now . . .

Conway had never met anyone with that name, but by asking a passing Tralthan he received directions for finding him. He got only as far as the door, which bore the legend, "Captain Bryson, Monitor Corps, Chaplain," then he turned angrily away. Another Monitor! There was just one person left who might help him: Dr. Mannon. He should have tried him first.

But his superior, when Conway ran him down, was sealed in the LSVO theatre, where he was assisting a Tralthan Surgeon-Diagnostician in a very tricky piece of work. He went up to the observation gallery to wait until Mannon had finished.

The LSVO came from a planet of dense atmosphere and negligible gravity. It was a winged life-form of extreme fragility, which necessitated the theatre being at almost zero gravity and the surgeons strapped to their position around the table. The little OTSB who lived in symbiosis with the elephantine Tralthan was not strapped down, but held securely above the operative field by one of its host's secondary tentacles—the OTSB life-form, Conway knew, could not lose physical contact with its host for more than a few minutes without suffering severe mental damage. Interested despite his own troubles, he began to concentrate on what they were doing.

A section of the patient's digestive tract had been bared, revealing a spongy, bluish growth adhering to it. Without the LSVO physiology tape Conway could not tell whether the patient's condition was serious or not, but the operation was certainly a technically difficult one. He could tell by the way Mannon hunched forward over it and by the tightly coiled tentacles of the Tralthan not then in use. As was normal, the little OTSB with its cluster of wire-thin, eye- and sucker-tipped tentacles was doing the fine, exploratory work—sending infinitely detailed visual information of the field to its giant host, and receiving back instructions based on that data. The Tralthan and Dr. Mannon attended to the relatively crude work of clamping, tying off, and swabbing out.

Dr. Mannon had little to do but watch as the super-sensitive tentacles of the Tralthan's parasite were guided in their work by the host, but Conway knew that the other was proud of the chance to do even that. The Tralthan combinations were the greatest surgeons the galaxy had ever known. All surgeons would have been Tralthans had not their bulk and operating procedure made it impossible to treat certain forms of life.

Conway was waiting when they came out of the theatre. One of the Tralthan's tentacles nicked out and tapped Dr. Mannon sharply on the head—a gesture which was a high compliment—and immediately a small bundle of fur and teeth streaked from behind a locker towards the great being who was apparently attacking its master. Conway had seen this game played out many times and it still seemed wildly ludicrous to him. As Mannon's dog barked furiously at the creature towering above both itself and its master, challenging it to a duel to the death, the Tralthan shrank back in mock terror and cried, "Save me from this fearsome beast!" The dog, still barking furiously, circled it, snapping at the leathery tegument protecting the Tralthan's six blocky legs. The Tralthan retreated precipitously, the while calling loudly for aid and being very careful that its tiny attacker was not splattered under one of its elephantine feet. And so the sounds of battle receded down the corridor.

When the noise had diminished sufficiently for him to be heard, Conway said, "Doctor, I wonder if you could help me. I need advice, or at least information. But it's a rather delicate matter. . . ."

Conway saw Dr. Mannon's eyebrows go up and a smile quirk the corners of his mouth. He said, "I'd be glad to help you, of course, but I'm afraid any advice I could give you at the moment would be pretty poor stuff." He made a disgusted face and flapped his arms up and down. "I've still got an LSVO tape working on me. You know how it is—half of me thinks I'm a bird and the other half is a little confused about it. But what sort of advice do you need?" he went on, his head perking to one side in an oddly birdlike manner. "If it's that peculiar form of madness called young love, or any other psychological disturbance, I'd suggest you see O'Mara."

Conway shook his head quickly; anybody but O'Mara. He said, "No. It's more of a philosophical nature, a matter of ethics, maybe. . . ."

"Is *that* all!" Mannon burst out. He was about to say something more when his face took on a fixed, listening expression. With a sudden jerk of his thumb he indicated a nearby wall annunciator. He said quietly, "The solution to your weighty problems will have to wait—you're wanted."

". . . Dr. Conway," the annunciator was saying briskly, "go to room eighty-seven and administer pep-shots. . . ."

"But eighty-seven isn't even in our section!" Conway protested. "What's going on here . . . ?"

Dr. Mannon had become suddenly grim. "I think I know," he said, "and I advise you to keep a few of those shots for yourself because you are going to need them." He turned abruptly and hurried off, muttering something about getting a fast erasure before they started screaming for him, too.

Room 87 was the Casualty Section's staff recreation room, and when Conway arrived its tables, chairs, and even parts of its floor were asprawl with green-clad Monitors, some of whom had not the energy to lift their heads when he came in. One figure pushed itself out of a chair with extreme difficulty and weaved towards him. It was another Monitor with a major's insignia on his shoulders and the Staff and Serpents on his collar. He said, "Maximum dosage. Start with me," and began shrugging out of his tunic.

Conway looked around the room. There must have been nearly a hundred of them, all in stages of advanced exhaustion and their faces showing that telltale grey colouration. He still did not feel well-disposed towards Monitors, but these were, after a fashion, patients, and his duty was clear.

"As a doctor I advise strongly against this," Conway said gravely. "It's obvious that you've had pep-shots already—far too many of them. What you need is sleep—"

"Sleep?" said a voice somewhere. "What's that?"

"Quiet, Teirnan," said the major tiredly, then to Conway: "And as a doctor I understand the risks. I suggest we waste no more time."

Rapidly and expertly Conway set about administering the shots. Dull-eyed, bone-weary men lined up before him and five minutes later left the room with a spring in their step and their eyes too bright with artificial vitality. He had just finished when he heard his name over the annunciator again, ordering him to Lock Six to await instructions there. Lock Six, Conway knew, was one of the subsidiary entrances to the Casualty Section.

While he was hurrying in that direction Conway realised suddenly that he was tired and hungry, but he did not get the chance to think about it for long. The annunciators were giving out a call for all junior interns to report to Casualty, and directions for adjacent wards to be evacuated where possible to other accommodation. An alien gabble interspersed these messages as other species received similar instructions.

Obviously the Casualty Section was being extended. But why, and where were all the casualties coming from? Conway's mind was a confused and rather tired question mark.

V

At Lock Six a Tralthan Diagnostician was deep in conversation with two Monitors. Conway felt a sense of outrage at the sight of the highest and the lowest being so chummy together, then reflected with a touch of bitterness that nothing about this place could surprise him anymore. There were two more Monitors beside the lock's direct vision panel.

"Hello, doctor," one of them said pleasantly. He nodded towards the view-port. "They're unloading at Locks Eight, Nine, and Eleven. We'll be getting our quota any minute now."

The big transparent panel framed an awesome sight: Conway had never seen so many ships together at one time. More than thirty sleek, silver needles, ranging from ten-man pleasure yachts to the gargantuan transports of the Monitor Corps, wove a slow, complicated pattern in and around each other as they waited for permission to lock on and unload.

"Tricky work, that," the Monitor observed.

Conway agreed. The repulsion fields which protected ships against collision with the various forms of cosmic detritus required plenty of space. Meteorite screens had to be set up a minimum of five miles away from the ship they protected if heavenly bodies large and small were to be successfully deflected from them—further away if it was a bigger ship. But the ships outside were a mere matter of hundreds of yards apart, and had no collision protection except the skill of their pilots. The pilots would be having a trying time at the moment.

But Conway had little time for sightseeing before three Earth-human interns arrived. They were followed quickly by two of the red-furred DBDGs and a caterpillar-like DBLF, all wearing medical insignia. There came a heavy scrape of metal against metal; the lock telltales turned from red to green, indicating that a ship was properly connected up; and the patients began to stream through.

Carried in stretchers by Monitors, they were of two kinds only: DBDGs of the Earth-human type and DBLF caterpillars. Conway's job, and that of the other doctors present, was to examine them and route them through to the proper department of Casualty for treatment. He got down to work, assisted by a Monitor who possessed all the attributes of a trained nurse except the insignia. He said his name was Williamson.

The sight of the first case gave Conway a shock—not because it was serious, but because of the nature of the injuries. The third made him stop so that his Monitor assistant looked at him questioningly.

"What sort of accident was this?" Conway burst out. "Multiple punctures, but the edge of the wounds cauterised. Lacerated punctures, as if from fragments thrown out by an explosion. How . . . ?"

The Monitor said, "We kept it quiet, of course, but I thought here at least the rumour would have got to everybody." His lips tightened and the look that identified all Monitors to Conway deepened in his eyes. "They decided to have a war," he went on, nodding at the Earth-human and DBLF patients around them. "I'm afraid it got a little out of control before we were able to clamp down."

Conway thought sickly, *A war . . . !* Human beings from Earth, or an Earth-seeded planet, trying to kill members of a species that had so much in common with them. He had heard that there were such things occasionally, but had never really believed any intelligent species could go insane on such a large scale. So many *casualties . . .*

He was not so bound up in his thoughts of loathing and disgust at this frightful business that he missed noticing a very strange fact— that the Monitor's expression mirrored his own! If Williamson thought that way about war, too, maybe it was time he revised his thinking about the Monitor Corps in general.

A sudden commotion a few yards to his right drew Conway's attention. An Earth-human patient was objecting strenuously to the DBLF intern trying to examine him, and the language he was using was not nice. The DBLF was registering hurt bewilderment, though possibly the human had not sufficient knowledge of its physiognomy to know that, and trying to reassure the patient in flat, translated tones.

It was Williamson who settled the business. He swung round on the loudly protesting patient, bent forward until their faces were only inches apart, and spoke in a low, almost conversational tone which nevertheless sent shivers along Conway's spine.

"Listen, friend," he said. "You say you object to one of the stinking crawlers that tried to kill you trying to patch you up, right? Well, get this into your head, and keep it there—this particular crawler is a doctor here. Also, in this establishment there are no wars. You all belong to the same army and the uniform is a nightshirt, so lay still, shut up, and behave. Otherwise I'll clip you one."

Conway returned to work underlining his mental note about revising his thinking regarding Monitors. As the torn, battered, and burnt life-forms flowed past under his hands his mind seemed strangely detached from it all. Williamson kept surprising him with expressions on his face that seemed to give the lie to some of the things he had been told about Monitors. This tireless, quiet man with the rock-steady hands—was he a killer, a sadist of low intelligence and nonexistent morals? It was hard to believe. As he watched the Monitor covertly between patients, Conway gradually came to a decision. It was a very difficult decision. If he wasn't careful he would very likely get clipped.

O'Mara had been impossible, so had Bryson and Mannon for various reasons, but Williamson now . . .

"Ah . . . er, Williamson," Conway began hesitantly, then finished with a rush, "have you ever killed anybody?"

The Monitor straightened suddenly, his lips

a thin, bloodless line. He said tonelessly, "You should know better than to ask a Monitor that question, doctor. Or should you?" He hesitated, his curiosity keeping check on the anger growing in him because of the tangle of emotion which must have been mirrored on Conway's face, then said heavily, "What's eating you, doc?"

Conway wished fervently that he had never asked the question, but it was too late to back out now. Stammering at first, he began to tell of his ideals of service and of his alarm and confusion on discovering that Sector General—an establishment which he had thought embodied all his high ideals—employed a Monitor as its chief psychologist, and probably other members of the Corps in positions of responsibility. Conway knew now that the Corps was not all bad, that they had rushed units of their Medical Division here to aid them during the present emergency. But even so, *Monitors* . . . !

"I'll give you another shock," Williamson said dryly, "by telling you something that is so widely known that nobody thinks to mention it. Dr. Lister, the director, also belongs to the Monitor Corps.

"He doesn't wear a uniform, of course," the Monitor added quickly, "because Diagnosticians grow forgetful and are careless about small things. The Corps frowns on untidiness, even in a lieutenant general."

Lister, a Monitor! "But, *why*?" Conway burst out in spite of himself. "Everybody knows what you are. How did you gain power here in the first place . . . ?"

"Everybody does not know, obviously," Williamson cut in, "because you don't, for one."

VI

The Monitor was no longer angry, Conway saw as they finished with their current patient and moved on to the next. Instead there was an expression on the other's face oddly reminiscent of a parent about to lecture an offspring on some of the unpleasant facts of life.

"Basically," said Williamson as he gently peeled back a field dressing of a wounded DBLF, "your trouble is that you, and your whole social group, are a protected species."

Conway said, *"What?"*

"A protected species," he repeated. "Shielded from the crudities of present-day life. From your social strata—on all the worlds of the Union, not only on Earth—come practically all the great artists, musicians, and professional men. Most of you live out your lives in ignorance of the fact that you are protected, that you are insulated from childhood against the grosser realities of our interstellar so-called civilisation, and that your ideas of pacifism and ethical behaviour are a luxury which a great many of us simply cannot afford. You are allowed this luxury in the hope that from it may come a philosophy which may one day make every being in the galaxy truly civilised, truly good."

"I didn't know," Conway stammered. "And . . . and you make us—me, I mean—look so useless. . . ."

"Of course you didn't know," said Williamson gently. Conway wondered why it was that such a young man could talk down to him without giving offence; he seemed to possess *authority* somehow. Continuing, he said, "You were probably reserved, untalkative, and all wrapped up in your high ideals. Not that there's anything wrong with them, understand, it's just that you have to allow for a little grey with the black and white. Our present culture," he went on, returning to the main line of discussion, "is based on maximum freedom for the individual. An entity may do anything he likes provided it is not injurious to others. Only Monitors forgo this freedom."

"What about the Normals' reservations?" Conway broke in. At last the Monitor had made a statement which he could definitely contradict. "Being policed by Monitors and confined to certain areas of country is not what I'd call freedom."

"If you think back carefully," Williamson replied, "I think you will find that the Normals—that is, the group on nearly every planet which thinks that, unlike the brutish Monitors and the spineless aesthetes of your own strata, it is truly representative of its species—are not confined. Instead they have naturally drawn together into communities, and it is in these communities of self-styled Normals that the Monitors have to be most active. The Normals possess all the freedom, including the right to kill each other if that is what they desire, the Monitors being present only to see that any Normal not sharing this desire will not suffer in the process.

"We also, when a sufficiently high pitch of mass insanity overtakes one or more of these worlds, allow a war to be fought on a planet set aside for that purpose, generally arranging things so that the war is neither long nor too bloody." Williamson sighed. In tones of bitter self-accusation he concluded, "We underestimated them. This one was both."

Conway's mind was still baulking at this radically new slant on things. Before coming to the hospital he'd had no direct contact with Monitors, why should he? And the Normals of Earth he had found to be rather romantic figures, inclined to strut and swagger a bit, that was all. Of course, most of the bad things he had heard about Monitors had come from them. Maybe the Normals had not been as truthful or objective as they could have been. . . .

"This is all too hard to believe," Conway protested. "You're suggesting that the Monitor Corps is greater in the scheme of things than either the Normals or ourselves, the professional class!" He shook his head angrily. "And anyway, this is a fine time for a philosophical discussion!"

"You," said the Monitor, "started it."

There was no answer to that.

It must have been hours later that Conway felt a touch on his shoulder and straightened to find a DBLF nurse behind him. The being was holding a hypodermic. It said, "Pep-shot, doctor?"

All at once Conway realised how wobbly his legs had become and how hard it was to focus his eyes. And he must have been noticeably slowing down for the nurse to approach him in the first place. He nodded and rolled up his sleeve with fingers which felt like thick, tired sausages.

"Yipe!" he cried in sudden anguish. "What are you using, a six-inch nail?"

"I am sorry," said the DBLF, "but I have injected two doctors of my own species before coming to you, and as you know our tegument is thicker and more closely grained than yours is. The needle has therefore become blunted."

Conway's fatigue dropped away in seconds. Except for a slight tingling in hands and feet and a greyish blotching which only others could see in his face he felt as clear-eyed, alert, and physically refreshed as if he had just come out of a shower after ten hours' sleep. He took a quick look round before finishing his current examination and saw that here at least the number of patients awaiting attention had shrunk to a mere handful, and the number of Monitors in the room was less than half what it had been at the start. The patients were being taken care of, and the Monitors had become patients.

He had seen it happening all around him. Monitors who had had little or no sleep on the transport coming here, forcing themselves to carry on helping the overworked medics of the hospital with repeated pep-shots and sheer, dogged courage. One by one they had literally dropped in their tracks and been taken hurriedly away, so exhausted that the involuntary muscles of heart and lungs had given up with everything else. They lay in special wards with robot devices massaging their hearts, giving artificial respiration, and feeding them through a vein in the leg. Conway had heard that only one of them had died.

Taking advantage of the lull, Conway and Williamson moved to the direct vision panel and looked out. The waiting swarm of ships seemed only slightly smaller, though he knew that these must be new arrivals. He could not imagine where they were going to put these people—even the habitable corridors in the hospital were beginning to overflow now, and there was constant rearranging of patients of all species to make more room. But that wasn't his problem, and the weaving pattern of ships was an oddly restful sight. . . .

"Emergency," said the wall annunciator suddenly. "Single ship, one occupant, species as yet unknown requests immediate treatment. Occupant is in only partial control of its ship, is badly injured and communications are incoherent. Stand by at all admittance locks . . . !"

Oh, no, Conway thought, *not at a time like this!* There was a cold sickness in his stomach and he had a horrible premonition of what was going to happen. Williamson's knuckles shone white as he gripped the edge of the view-port. "Look!" he said in a flat, despairing tone, and pointed.

An intruder was approaching the waiting swarm of ships at an insane velocity and on a wildly erratic course. A stubby, black, and featureless torpedo shape, it reached and penetrated the weaving mass of ships before Conway had time to take two breaths. In milling confusion the ships scattered, narrowly avoiding collision with both it and each other, and still it hurtled on. There was only one ship in its path now, a Monitor transport which had been given the all-clear to approach and was drifting in towards an admittance lock. The transport was big, ungainly, and not built for fast acrobatics—it had neither the time nor the ability to get out of the way. A collision was certain, and the transport was jammed with wounded. . . .

But no. At the last possible instant the hurtling ship swerved. They saw it miss the transport and its stubby torpedo shape foreshorten to a circle which grew in size with heart-stopping rapidity. Now it was headed straight at them! Conway wanted to shut his eyes, but there was

a peculiar fascination about watching that great mass of metal rushing at him. Neither Williamson nor himself made any attempt to jump for a space suit—what was to happen was only split seconds away.

The ship was almost on top of them when it swerved again as its injured pilot sought desperately to avoid this greater obstacle, the hospital. But too late, the ship struck.

A smashing double shock struck up at them from the floor as the ship tore through their double skin, followed by successively milder shocks as it bludgeoned its way into the vitals of the great hospital. A cacophony of screams—both human and alien—arose briefly, also whistlings, rustlings, and guttural jabberings as beings were maimed, drowned, gassed, or decompressed. Water poured into sections containing pure chlorine. A blast of ordinary air rushed through a gaping hole in the compartment whose occupants had never known anything but trans-Plutonian cold and vacuum—the beings shrivelled, died, and dissolved horribly at the first touch of it. Water, air, and a score of different atmospheric mixtures intermingled forming a sludgy, brown, and highly corrosive mixture that steamed and bubbled its way out into space. But long before that had happened the airtight seals had slammed shut, effectively containing the terrible wound made by that bulleting ship.

VII

There was an instant of shocked paralysis, then the hospital reacted. Above their heads the annunciator went into a quiet, controlled frenzy. Engineers and Maintenance men of all species were to report for assignment immediately. The gravity neutraliser grids in the LSVO and MSVK wards were failing—all medical staff in the area were to encase the patients in protective envelopes and transfer them to DBLF theatre two, where one-twentieth-g conditions were being set up, before they were crushed by their own weight. There was an untraced leak in AUGL corridor and all DBDGs were warned of chlorine contamination in the area of their dining hall. Also, Dr. Lister was asked to report himself, please.

In an odd corner of his mind Conway noted how everybody else was ordered to their assignments while Dr. Lister was asked. Suddenly he heard his name being called and he swung around.

It was Dr. Mannon. He hurried up to Williamson and Conway and said, "I see you're free at the moment. There's a job I'd like you to do." He paused to receive Conway's nod, then plunged on breathlessly.

When the crashing ship had dug a hole halfway through the hospital, Mannon explained, the volume sealed off by the safety doors was not confined simply to the tunnel of wreckage it had created. The position of the doors was responsible for this—the result being analogous to a great tree of vacuum extending into the hospital structure, with the tunnel created by the ship as its trunk and the open sections of corridors leading off it the branches. Some of these airless corridors served compartments which themselves could be sealed off, and it was possible that these might contain survivors.

Normally there would be no necessity to hurry the rescue of these beings, they would be quite comfortable where they were for days, but in this instance there was an added complication. The ship had come to rest near the centre—the nerve centre, in fact—of the hospital, the section which contained the controls for the artificial settings of the entire structure. At the moment there seemed to be a survivor in that section somewhere—possibly a patient, a member of the staff, or even the occupant of the wrecked ship—who was moving around and unknowingly damaging the gravity control mechanisms. This state of affairs, if continued, could create havoc in the wards and might even cause deaths among the light-gravity life-forms.

Dr. Mannon wanted them to go in and bring the being concerned out before it unwittingly wrecked the place.

"A PVSJ has already gone in," Mannon added, "but that species is awkward in a space suit, so I'm sending you two as well to hurry things along. All right? Hop to it, then."

Wearing gravity neutraliser packs they exited near the damaged section and drifted along the hospital's outer skin to the twenty-foot-wide hole gouged in its side by the crashing ship. The packs allowed a high degree of manoeuvrability in weightless conditions, and they did not expect anything else along the route they were to travel. They also carried ropes and magnetic anchors, and Williamson—solely because it was part of the equipment issued with the Service Standard suit, he said—also carried a gun. Both had air for three hours.

At first the going was easy. The ship had sheared a clean-edged tunnel through ward bulkheads, deck plating, and even items of heavy machinery. Conway could see clearly into the corridors they passed in their descent, and nowhere was there a sign of life. There were grisly remnants of a high-pressure lifeform which would have blown itself apart even under Earth-normal atmospheric conditions. When subjected suddenly to hard vacuum the process had been that much more violent. And in one corridor there was disclosed a tragedy; a near-human DBDG nurse—one of the red, bearlike entities—had been neatly decapitated by the closing of an airtight door which it had just failed to make in time. For some reason the sight affected him more than anything else he had seen that day.

Increasing amounts of "foreign" wreckage hampered their progress as they continued to descend—plating and structural members torn from the crashing ship—so that there were times when they had to clear a way through it with their hands and feet.

Williamson was in the lead—about ten yards below Conway that was—when the Monitor flicked out of sight. In the suit radio a cry of surprise was abruptly cut off by the clang of metal against metal. Conway's grip on the projecting beam he had been holding tightened instinctively in shocked surprise, and he felt it vibrate through his gauntlets. The wreckage was shifting! Panic took him for a moment until he realised that most of the movement was taking place back the way he had come, above his head. The vibration ceased a few minutes later without the debris around him significantly changing its position. Only then did Conway tie his line securely to the beam and look around for the Monitor.

Knees bent and arms in front of his head Williamson lay face downward partially embedded in a shelving mass of loose wreckage some twenty feet below. Faint, irregular sounds of breathing in his phones told Conway that the Monitor's quick thinking in wrapping his arms around his head had, by protecting his suit's fragile faceplate, saved his life. But whether or not Williamson lived for long depended on the nature of his other injuries, and they in turn depended on the amount of gravitic attraction in the floor section which had sucked him down.

It was now obvious that the accident was due to a square of deck in which the artificial gravity grid was, despite the wholesale destruction of circuits in the crash area, still operative. Conway was profoundly thankful that the attraction was exerted only at right angles to the grid's surface and that the floor section had been warped slightly. Had it been facing straight up then both the Monitor and himself would have dropped, and from a distance considerably greater than twenty feet.

Carefully paying out his safety line Conway approached the huddled form of Williamson. His grip tightened convulsively on the rope when he came within the field of influence of the gravity grid, then eased as he realised that its power was at most only one and a half g's. With

a steady attraction now pulling him downwards towards the Monitor, Conway began lowering himself hand over hand. He could have used his neutraliser pack to counteract that pull, of course, and just drifted down, but that would have been risky. If he accidentally passed out of the floor section's area of influence, then the pack would have flung him upwards again, with probably fatal results.

The Monitor was still unconscious when Conway reached him, and though he could not tell for sure, owing to the other wearing a space suit, he suspected multiple fractures in both arms. As he gently disengaged the limp figure from the surrounding wreckage it was suddenly borne on him that Williamson needed attention, immediate attention with all the resources the hospital could provide. He had just realised that the Monitor had been the recipient of a large number of pep-shots; his reserves of strength must be gone. When he regained consciousness, if he ever did, he might not be able to withstand the shock.

VIII

Conway was about to call through for assistance when a chunk of ragged-edged metal spun past his helmet. He swung round just in time to duck another piece of wreckage which was sailing towards him. Only then did he see the outlines of a non-human, space-suited figure which was partially hidden in a tangle of metal about ten yards away. The being was throwing things at him!

The bombardment stopped as soon as the other saw that Conway had noticed it. With visions of having found the unknown survivor whose blundering about was playing hob with the hospital's artificial gravity system he hurried across to it. But he saw immediately that the being was incapable of doing any moving about at all, it was pinned down, but miraculously unhurt, by a couple of heavy structural members. It was also making vain attempts to reach round to the back of its suit with its only free appendage. Conway was puzzled for a moment, then he saw the radio pack which was strapped to the being's back, and the lead dangling loose from it. Using surgical tape he repaired the break and immediately the flat, translated tones of the being filled his earphones.

It was the PVSJ who had left before them to search the wrecked area for survivors. Caught by the same trap which had snagged the unfortunate Monitor, it had been able to use its gravity pack to check its sudden fall. Overcompensating, it had crashed into its present position. The crash had been relatively gentle, but it had caused some loose wreckage to subside, trapping the being and damaging its radio.

The PVSJ—a chlorine-breathing Illensan— was solidly planted in the wreckage: Conway's attempts to free it were useless. While trying, however, he got a look at the professional insignia painted on the other's suit. The Tralthan and Illensan symbols meant nothing to Conway, but the third one—which was the nearest expression of the being's function in Earth-human terms—was a crucifix. The being was a padre. Conway might have expected that.

But now Conway had two immobilised cases instead of one. He thumbed the transmit switch of his radio and cleared his throat. Before he could speak the harsh, urgent voice of Dr. Mannon was dinning in his ears.

"Dr. Conway! Corpsman Williamson! One of you, report quickly, please!"

Conway said, "I was just going to," and gave an account of his troubles to date and requested aid for the Monitor and the PVSJ padre. Mannon cut him off.

"I'm sorry," he said hurriedly, "but we can't help you. The gravity fluctuations have been getting worse here, they must have caused a subsidence in your tunnel, because it's solidly plugged with wreckage all the way above you. Maintenance men have tried to cut a way through but—"

"Let me talk to him," broke in another voice, and there were the magnified, fumbling noises of a mike being snatched out of someone's hand. "Dr. Conway, this is Dr. Lister speaking," it went on. "I'm afraid that I must tell you that the well-being of your two accident cases is of secondary importance. Your job is to contact that being in the gravity control compartment and stop him. Hit him on the head if necessary, but stop him—he's wrecking the hospital!"

Conway swallowed. He said, "Yes, sir," and began looking for a way to penetrate further into the tangle of metal surrounding him. It looked hopeless.

Suddenly he felt himself being pulled sideways. He grabbed for the nearest solid-looking projection and hung on for dear life. Transmitted through the fabric of his suit he heard the grinding, tearing jangle of moving metal. The wreckage was shifting again. Then the force pulling him disappeared as suddenly as it had come and simultaneously there came a peculiar, barking cry from the PVSJ. Conway twisted round to see that where the Illensan had been a large hole led downward into nothingness.

He had to force himself to let go of his handhold. The attraction which had seized him had been due, Conway knew, to the momentary activating of an artificial gravity grid somewhere below. If it returned while he was floating unsupported . . . Conway did not want to think about that.

The shift had not affected Williamson's position—he still lay as Conway had left him— but the PVSJ must have fallen through.

"Are you all right?" Conway called anxiously.

"I think so," came the reply. "I am still somewhat numb."

Cautiously, Conway drifted across to the newly created opening and looked down. Below him was a very large compartment, well lit from a source somewhere off to one side. Only the floor was visible about forty feet below, the walls being beyond his angle of vision, and this was thickly carpeted by a dark blue, tubular growth with bulbous leaves. The purpose of this compartment baffled Conway until he realised that he was looking at the AUGL tank minus its water. The thick, flaccid growth covering its floor served as both food and interior decoration for the AUGL patients. The PVSJ had been very lucky to have such a springy surface to land on.

The PVSJ was no longer pinned down by wreckage and it stated that it felt fit enough to help Conway with the being in the gravity control department. As they were about to resume the descent Conway glanced towards the source of light he had half-noticed earlier, and caught his breath.

One wall of the AUGL tank was transparent and looked out on a section corridor which had been converted into a temporary ward. DBLF caterpillars lay in the beds which lined one side, and they were by turns crushed savagely into the plasti-foam and bounced upwards into the air by it as violent and random fluctuations rippled along the gravity grids in the floor. Netting had been hastily tied around the patients to keep them in the beds, but despite the beating they were taking they were the lucky ones.

A ward was being evacuated somewhere and through this stretch of corridor there crawled, wriggled, and hopped a procession of beings resembling the contents of some cosmic ark. All the oxygen-breathing life-forms were represented together with many who were not, and human nursing orderlies and Monitors shepherded them along. Experience must have taught the orderlies that to stand or walk upright was asking for broken bones and cracked skulls, because they were crawling along on their hands and knees. When a sudden surge of three or four g's caught them they had a shorter distance to fall that way. Most of them were wearing gravity packs, Conway saw, but had given them up as useless in conditions where the gravity constant was a wild variable.

He saw PVSJs in balloonlike chlorine envelopes being pinned against the floor, flattened like specimens pressed under glass,

then bounced into the air again. And Tralthan patients in their massive, unwieldly harnesses—Tralthans were prone to injury internally despite their great strength—being dragged along. There were DBDGs, DBLFs, and CLSRs, also unidentifiable somethings in spherical, wheeled containers that radiated cold almost visibly. Strung out in a line, being pushed, being dragged, or manfully inching along on their own, the beings crept past, bowing and straightening up again like wheat in a strong wind as the gravity grids pulled at them.

Conway could almost imagine he felt those fluctuations where he stood, but knew that the crashing ship must have destroyed the grid circuits in its path. He dragged his eyes away from that grim procession and headed downwards again.

"Conway!" Mannon's voice barked at him a few minutes later. "That survivor down there is responsible for as many casualties now as the crashed ship! A ward of convalescent LSVOs are dead due to a three-second surge from one-eighth to four gravities. What's happening now?"

The tunnel of wreckage was steadily narrowing, Conway reported, the hull and lighter machinery of the ship having been peeled away by the time it had reached their present level. All that could remain ahead was the massive stuff like hyperdrive generators and so on. He thought he must be very near the end of the line now, and the being who was the unknowing cause of the devastation around them.

"Good," said Mannon, "but hurry it up!"

"But can't the Engineers get through? Surely—"

"They can't," broke in Dr. Lister's voice. "In the area surrounding the gravity grid controls there are fluctuations of up to ten g's. It's impossible. And joining up with your route from inside the hospital is out, too. It would mean evacuating corridors in the neighbouring area, and the corridors are all filled with patients. . . ." The voice dropped in volume as Dr. Lister apparently turned away from the mike, and Conway overhead him saying, "Surely an intelligent being could not be so panic-stricken that it . . . it . . . Oh, when I get my hands on it—"

"It may not be intelligent," put in another voice. "Maybe it's a cub, from the FGLI maternity unit. . . ."

"If it is I'll tan its little—"

A sharp click ended the conversation at that point as the transmitter was switched off. Conway, suddenly realising what a very important man he had become, tried to hurry it up as best he could.

IX

They dropped another level into a ward in which four MSVKs—fragile, tripedal storklike beings—drifted lifeless among loose items of ward equipment. The movements of the bodies and objects in the room seemed a little unnatural, as if they had been recently disturbed. It was the first sign of the enigmatic survivor they were seeking. Then they were in a great, metal-walled compartment surrounded by a maze of plumbing and unshielded machinery. On the floor in a bulge it had created for itself, the ship's massive hyperdrive generator lay with some shreds of control-room equipment strewn around it. Underneath was the remains of a life-form that was now unclassifiable. Beside the generator another hole had been torn in the severely weakened floor by some other piece of the ship's heavy equipment.

Conway hurried over to it, looked down, then called excitedly, "There it is!"

They were looking into a vast room which could only be the grid control centre. Rank upon rank of squat, metal cabinets covered the floor, walls, and ceiling—this compartment was always kept airless and at zero gravity—with barely room for even Earth-human Engineers to move between them. But Engineers were seldom needed here because the devices in this all-important compartment were self-repairing.

At the moment this ability was being put to a severe test.

A being which Conway classified tentatively as AACL sprawled across three of the delicate control cabinets. Nine other cabinets, all winking with red distress signals, were within range of its six pythonlike tentacles, which poked through seals in the cloudy plastic of its suit. The tentacles were at least twenty feet long and tipped with a horny substance which must have been steel-hard considering the damage the being had caused.

Conway had been prepared to feel pity for this hapless survivor, he had expected to find an entity injured, panic-stricken, and crazed with pain. Instead there was a being who appeared unhurt and who was viciously smashing up gravity-grid controls as fast as the built-in self-repairing robots tried to fix them. Conway swore and began hunting for the frequency of the other's suit radio. Suddenly there was a harsh, high-pitched cheeping sound in his earphones. "Got you!" Conway said grimly.

The cheeping sounds ceased abruptly as the other heard his voice and so did all movement of those highly destructive tentacles. Conway noted the wavelength, then switched back to the band used by the PVSJ and himself.

"It seems to me," said the chlorine-breather when he had told it what he had heard, "that the being is deeply afraid, and the noises it made were of fear—otherwise your translator would have made you receive them as words in your own language. The fact that these noises and its destructive activity stopped when it heard your voice is promising, but I think that we should approach slowly and reassure it constantly that we are bringing help. Its activity down there gives me the impression that it has been hitting out at anything which moves, so a certain amount of caution is indicated, I think."

"Yes, Padre," said Conway with great feeling.

"We do not know in what direction the being's visual organs are directed," the PVSJ went on, "so I suggest we approach from opposite sides."

Conway nodded. They set their radios to the new band and climbed carefully down onto the ceiling of the compartment below. With just enough power in their gravity neutralisers to keep them pressing gently against the metal surface, they moved away from each other onto opposite walls, down them, then onto the floor. With the being between them now, they moved slowly towards it.

The robot repair devices were busy making good the damage wrecked by those six anacondas it used for limbs but the being continued to lie quiescent. Neither did it speak. Conway kept thinking of the havoc this entity had caused with its senseless threshing about. The things he felt like saying to it were anything but reassuring, so he let the PVSJ padre do the talking.

"Do not be afraid," the other was saying for the twentieth time. "If you are injured, tell us. We are here to help you. . . ."

But there was neither movement nor reply from the being.

On a sudden impulse Conway switched to Dr. Mannon's band. He said quickly, "The survivor seems to be an AACL. Can you tell me what it's here for, or any reason why it should refuse or be unable to talk to us?"

"I'll check with Reception," said Mannon after a short pause. "But are you sure of that classification? I can't remember seeing an AACL here, sure it isn't a Creppelian—"

"It isn't a Creppelian octopoid," Conway cut in. "There are *six* main appendages, and it is just lying here doing nothing. . . ."

Conway stopped suddenly, shocked into silence, because it was no longer true that the being under discussion was doing nothing. It had launched itself towards the ceiling, moving so fast that it seemed to land in the same instant that it had taken off. Above him now, Conway saw another control unit pulverised as the being struck and others torn from their mounts as its tentacles sought anchorage. In his phones Mannon was shouting about gravity fluctuations in a hitherto stable section of the hospital, and mounting casualty figures, but Conway was unable to reply.

He was watching helplessly as the AACL prepared to launch itself again.

". . . We are here to help you," the PVSJ was saying as the being landed with a soundless crash four yards from the padre. Five great tentacles anchored themselves firmly, and a sixth lashed out in a great, curving blur of motion that caught the PVSJ and smashed it against the wall. Life-giving chlorine spurted from the PVSJ's suit, momentarily hiding in mist the shapeless, pathetic thing which rebounded slowly into the middle of the room. The AACL began making cheeping noises again.

Conway heard himself babbling out a report to Mannon, then Mannon shouting for Lister. Finally the director's voice came in to him. It said thickly, "You've got to kill it, Conway."

You've got to kill it, Conway!

It was those words which shocked Conway back to a state of normality as nothing else could have done. How very like a Monitor, he thought bitterly, to solve a problem with a murder. And to ask a doctor, a person dedicated to the preserving of life, to do the killing. It did not matter that the being was insane with fear, it had caused a lot of trouble in the hospital, so kill it.

Conway had been afraid; he still was. In his recent state of mind he might have been panicked into using this kill-or-be-killed law of the jungle. Not now, though. No matter what happened to him or the hospital he would not kill an intelligent fellow being, and Lister could shout himself blue in the face. . . .

It was with a start of surprise that Conway realised that both Lister and Mannon were shouting at him, and trying to counter his arguments. He must have been doing his thinking aloud without knowing it. Angrily he tuned them out.

But there was still another voice gibbering at him, a slow, whispering, unutterably weary voice that frequently broke off to gasp in pain. For a wild moment Conway thought that the ghost of the dead PVSJ was continuing Lister's arguments, then he caught sight of movement above him.

Drifting gently through the hole in the ceiling was the space-suited figure of Williamson. How the badly injured Monitor had got there at all was beyond Conway's understanding—his broken arms made control of his gravity pack impossible, so that he must have come all that way by kicking with his feet and trusting that a still-active gravity grid would not pull him in a second time. At the thought of how many times those multiple fractured members must have collided with obstacles on the way down, Conway cringed. And yet all the Monitor was concerned with was trying to coax Conway into killing the AACL below him.

Close below him, with the distance lessening every second . . .

Conway felt the cold sweat break out on his back. Helpless to stop himself, the injured Monitor had cleared the rent in the ceiling and was drifting slowly floorwards, *directly on top of the crouching AACL!* As Conway stared fascinated one of the steel-hard tentacles began to uncurl preparatory to making a death-dealing swipe.

Instinctively Conway launched himself in the direction of the floating Monitor, there was no time for him to feel consciously brave—or stupid—about the action. He connected with a muffled crash and hung on, wrapping his legs around Williamson's waist to leave his hands free for the gravity pack controls. They spun furiously around their common centre of gravity, walls, ceiling, and floor with its deadly occupant whirling round so fast that Conway could barely focus his eyes on the controls. It seemed years before he finally had the spin checked and he had them headed for the hole in the ceiling and safety. They had almost reached it when Conway saw the hawserlike tentacle come sweeping up at him. . . .

X

Something smashed into his back with a force that knocked the breath out of him. For a heart-freezing moment he thought his air tanks had gone, his suit torn open, and that he was already sucking frenziedly at vacuum. But his gasp of pure terror brought air rushing into his lungs. Conway had never known canned air to taste so good.

The AACL's tentacle had only caught him a glancing blow—his back wasn't broken—and the only damage was a wrecked suit radio.

"Are you all right?" Conway asked anxiously when he had Williamson settled in the compartment above. He had to press his helmet against the other's—that was the only way he could make himself heard now.

For several minutes there was no reply, then the weary, pain-wrecked near-whisper returned.

"My arms hurt. I'm tired," it said haltingly. "But I'll be okay when . . . they take me . . . inside." Williamson paused, his voice seemed to gather strength from somewhere, and he went on, "That is if there is anybody left alive in the hospital to treat me. If you don't stop our friend down there . . ."

Sudden anger flared in Conway. "Dammit, do you never give up?" he burst out. "Get this, I'm not going to kill an intelligent being! My radio's gone so I don't have to listen to Lister and Mannon yammering at me, and all I've got to do to shut you up is pull my helmet away from yours."

The Monitor's voice had weakened again. He said, "I can still hear Mannon and Lister. They say the wards in Section Eight have been hit now—that's the other low-gravity section. Patients and doctors are pinned flat to the floor under three g's. A few more minutes like that and they'll never get up—MSVKs aren't at all sturdy, you know. . . ."

"Shut up!" yelled Conway. Furiously, he pulled away from contact.

When his anger had abated enough for him to see again, Conway observed that the Monitor's lips were no longer moving. Williamson's eyes were closed, his face grey and sweaty with shock, and he did not seem to be breathing. The drying chemicals in his helmet kept the faceplate from fogging, so that Conway could not tell for sure, but the Monitor could very easily be dead. With exhaustion held off by repeated pep-shots, then his injuries on top of that, Conway had expected him to be dead long since. For some peculiar reason Conway felt his eyes stinging.

He had seen so much death and dismemberment over the last few hours that his sensitivity to suffering in others had been blunted to the point where he reacted to it merely as a medical machine. This feeling of loss, of bereavement, for the Monitor must be simply a resurgence of that sensitivity, and temporary. Of one thing he was sure, however, nobody was going to make this medical machine commit a murder. The Monitor Corps, Conway now knew, was responsible for a lot more good than bad, but he was not a Monitor.

Yet O'Mara and Lister were both Monitors and doctors, one of them renowned throughout the galaxy. Are you better than they are? a little voice nagged in his mind somewhere. And you're all alone now, it went on, with the hospital disorganised and people dying all over the place because of that being down there. What do you think your chances of survival are? The way you came is plugged with wreckage and nobody can come to your aid, so you're going to die, too. Isn't that so?

Desperately Conway tried to hang on to his resolution, to draw it tightly around him like a shell. But that insistent, that cowardly voice in his brain was putting cracks in it. It was with a sense of pure relief that he saw the Monitor's lips moving again. He touched helmets quickly.

". . . hard for you, a doctor," the voice came faintly, "but you've got to. Just suppose you were that being down below, driven mad with fear and pain maybe, and for a moment you became sane and somebody told you what you had done—what you were doing, and the deaths you had caused. . . ." The voice wavered, sank, then returned. "Wouldn't you *want* to die rather than go on killing . . . ?"

"But I can't . . . !"

"Wouldn't you *want* to die, in its place?"

Conway felt the defensive shell of his resolution begin to disintegrate around him. He said desperately, in a last attempt to hold firm, to stave off the awful decision, "Well, maybe, but I couldn't kill it even if I tried—it would tear me to pieces before I got near it. . . ."

"I've got a gun," said the Monitor.

Conway could not remember adjusting the firing controls, or even taking the weapon from the Monitor's holster. It was in his hand and trained on the AACL below, and Conway felt sick and cold. But he had not given in to Williamson completely. Near at hand was a sprayer of the fast-setting plastic which, when used quickly enough, could sometimes save a person whose suit had been holed. Conway planned to wound the being, immobilise it, then reseal its suit with cement. It would be a close thing and risky to himself, but he could not deliberately kill the being.

Carefully he brought his other hand up to steady the gun and took aim. He fired.

When he lowered it there was not much left except shredded twitching pieces of tentacles scattered all over the room. Conway wished now that he had known more about guns, known that this one shot explosive bullets, and that it had been set for continuous automatic fire. . . .

Williamson's lips were moving again. Conway touched helmets out of pure reflex. He was past caring about anything anymore.

". . . It's all right, doctor," the Monitor was saying. "It isn't anybody. . . ."

"It isn't anybody now," Conway agreed. He went back to examining the Monitor's gun and wished that it wasn't empty. If there had been one bullet left, just one, he knew how he would have used it.

"It was hard, we know that," said Major O'Mara. The rasp was no longer in his voice and the iron-grey eyes were soft with sympathy, and something akin to pride. "A doctor doesn't have to make a decision like that usually until he's older, more balanced, mature, if ever. You are, or were, just an overidealistic kid—a bit on the smug and self-righteous side maybe—who didn't even know what a Monitor really was."

O'Mara smiled. His two big, hard hands rested on Conway's shoulders in an oddly fatherly gesture. He went on, "Doing what you forced yourself to do could have ruined both your career and your mental stability. But it doesn't matter, you don't have to feel guilty about a thing. Everything's all right."

Conway wished dully that he had opened his faceplate and ended it all before those Engineers had swarmed into the gravity grid control room and carried Williamson and himself off to O'Mara. O'Mara must be mad. He, Conway, had violated the prime ethic of his profession and killed an intelligent being. Everything most definitely was not all right.

"Listen to me," O'Mara said seriously. "The Communications boys managed to get a picture of the crashed ship's control room, with the occupant in it, before it hit. The occupant was not your AACL, understand? It was an AMSO, one of the bigger life-forms who are in the habit of keeping a non-intelligent AACL-type creature as a pet. Also, there are no AACLs listed in the hospital, so the beastie you killed was simply the equivalent of a fear-maddened dog in a protective suit." O'Mara shook Conway's shoulder until his head wobbled. "Now do you feel better?"

Conway felt himself coming alive again. He nodded wordlessly.

"You can go," said O'Mara, smiling, "and catch up on your sleep. As for the reorienta- tion talk, I'm afraid I haven't the time to spare. Remind me about it sometime, if you still think you need it. . . ."

XI

During the fourteen hours in which Conway slept, the intake of wounded dropped to a manageable trickle, and news came that the war was over. Monitor engineers and maintenance men succeeded in clearing the wreckage and repairing the damaged outer hull. With pressure restored, the internal repair work proceeded rapidly, so that when Conway awoke and went in search of Dr. Mannon he found patients being moved into a section which only hours ago had been a dark, airless tangle of wreckage.

He tracked his superior down in a side ward off the main FGLI Casualty Section. Mannon was working over a badly burned DBLF whose caterpillar-like body was dwarfed by a table which was designed to take the more massive Tralthan FGLIs. Two other DBLFs, under sedation, showed as white mounds on a similarly outsize bed against the wall, and another lay twitching slightly on a stretcher-carrier near the door.

"Where the blazes have you been?" Mannon said in a voice too tired to be angry. Before Conway could reply he went on impatiently, "Oh, don't tell me. Everybody is grabbing everybody else's staff, and junior interns have to do as they're told. . . ."

Conway felt his face going red. Suddenly he was ashamed of that fourteen hours' sleep, but was too much of a coward to correct Mannon's wrong assumption. Instead he said, "Can I help, sir?"

"Yes," said Mannon, waving towards his patients. "But these are going to be tricky. Punctured and incised wounds, deep metallic fragments still within the body, abdominal damage, and severe internal haemorrhage. You won't be able to do much without a tape. Go get it. And come straight back, mind!"

A few minutes later he was in O'Mara's office absorbing the DBLF physiology tape. This time he didn't flinch from the major's hands. While the headband was being removed he asked, "How is Corpsman Williamson?"

"He'll live," said O'Mara drily. "The bones were set by a Diagnostician. Williamson won't dare die. . . ."

Conway rejoined Mannon as quickly as possible. He was experiencing the characteristic mental double vision and had to resist the urge to crawl on his stomach, so he knew that the DBLF tape was taking. The caterpillar-like inhabitants of Kelgia were very close to Earthhumans in both basic metabolism and temperament, so there was less of the confusion he had encountered with the earlier Telfi tape. But it gave him an affinity for the beings he was treating which was actually painful.

The concept of gun, bullet, and target was a very simple one—just point, pull the trigger, and the target is dead or disabled. The bullet didn't think at all, the pointer didn't think enough, and the target . . . suffered.

Conway had seen too many disabled targets recently, and lumps of metal which had ploughed their way into them leaving red craters in torn flesh, bone splinters, and ruptured blood vessels. In addition there was the long, painful process of recovery. Anyone who would inflict such damage on a thinking, feeling entity deserved something much more painful than the Monitor corrective psychiatry.

A few days previously Conway would have been ashamed of such thoughts—and he was now, a little. He wondered if recent events had initiated in him a process of moral degeneration, or was it that he was merely beginning to grow up?

Five hours later they were through. Mannon gave his nurse instructions to keep the four patients under observation, but told her to get something to eat first. She was back within minutes carrying a large pack of sandwiches and bearing the news that their dining hall had been taken over by Tralthan Male Medi-

cal. Shortly after that Dr. Mannon went to sleep in the middle of his second sandwich. Conway loaded him onto the stretcher-carrier and took him to his room. On the way out he was collared by a Tralthan Diagnostician who ordered him to a DBDG Casualty Section.

This time Conway found himself working on targets of his own species and his maturing, or moral degeneration, increased. He had begun to think that the Monitor Corps was too damned soft with some people.

Three weeks later Sector General was back to normal. All but the most seriously wounded patients had been transferred to their local planetary hospitals. The damage caused by the colliding spaceship had been repaired. Tralthan Male Medical had vacated the dining hall, and Conway no longer had to snatch his meals off assorted instrument trolleys. But if things were back to normal for the hospital as a whole, such was not the case with Conway personally.

He was taken off ward duty completely and transferred to a mixed group of Earthhumans and ETs—most of whom were senior to himself—taking a course of lectures in ship rescue. Some of the difficulties experienced in fishing survivors out of wrecked ships, especially those which contained still-functioning power sources, made Conway open his eyes. The course ended with an interesting, if backbreaking, practical which he managed to pass, and was followed by a more cerebral course in ET comparative philosophy. Running at the same time was a series on contamination emergencies: what to do if the methane section sprung a leak and the temperature threatened to rise above minus one forty, what to do if a chlorine-breather was exposed to oxygen, or a water-breather was strangling in air, or vice versa. Conway had shuddered at the idea of some of his fellow students trying to give him artificial respiration—some of whom weighed half a ton!—but luckily there was no practical at the end of that course.

Every one of the lecturers stressed the importance of rapid and accurate classification of incoming patients, who very often were in no condition to give this information themselves. In the four-letter classification system the first letter was a guide to the general metabolism, the second to the number and distribution of limbs and sense organs, and the rest to a combination of pressure and gravity requirements, which also gave an indication of the physical mass and form of protective tegument a being possessed. A, B, and C first letters were water-breathers. D and F warm-blooded oxygen-breathers, into which classification most of the intelligent races fell. G to K were also oxygen-breathing, but insectile, light-gravity beings. L and M were also light-gravity, but birdlike. The chlorine-breathers were contained in the O and P classifications. After that came the weirdies—radiation-eaters, frigid-blooded or crystalline beings, entities capable of changing physical shape at will, and those possessing various forms of extrasensory powers. Telepathic species such as the Telfi were given the prefix V. The lecturers would flash a three-second picture of an ET foot or a section of tegument onto the screen, and if Conway could not rattle off an accurate classification from this glimpse, sarcastic words would be said.

It was all very interesting stuff, but Conway began to worry a little when he realised that six weeks had passed without his even seeing a patient. He decided to call O'Mara and ask what for—in a respectful, roundabout way, of course.

"Naturally you want back to the wards," O'Mara said, when Conway finally arrived at the point. "Dr. Mannon would like you back, too. But I may have a job for you and don't want you tied up anywhere else. But don't feel that you are simply marking time. You are learning some useful stuff, doctor. At least, I hope you are. Off."

As Conway replaced the intercom mike he was thinking that a lot of the things he was learning had regard to Major O'Mara himself. There wasn't a course of lectures on the chief psychologist, but there might well have been, because every lecture had O'Mara creeping into it somewhere. And he was only beginning to realise how close he had come to being kicked out of the hospital for his behaviour during the Telfi episode.

O'Mara bore the rank of major in the Monitor Corps, but Conway had learned that within the hospital it was difficult to draw a limiting line to his authority. As chief psychologist he was responsible for the mental health of all the widely varied individuals and species on the staff, and the avoidance of friction between them.

Given even the highest qualities of tolerance and mutual respect in its personnel, there were still occasions when friction occurred. Potentially dangerous situations arose through ignorance or misunderstanding, or a being could develop a xenophobic neurosis which might affect its efficiency, or mental stability, or both. An Earth-human doctor, for instance, who had a subconscious fear of spiders would not be able to bring to bear on an Illensan patient the proper degree of clinical detachment necessary for its treatment. So it was O'Mara's job to detect and eradicate such signs of trouble or—if all else failed—remove the potentially dangerous individual before such friction became open conflict. This guarding against wrong, unhealthy, or intolerant thinking was a duty which he performed with such zeal that Conway had heard him likened to a latter-day Torquemada.

ETs on the staff whose home-planet histories did not contain an equivalent of the Inquisition likened him to other things, and often called him them to his face. But in O'Mara's book justifiable invective was not indicative of wrong thinking, so there were no serious repercussions.

O'Mara was *not* responsible for the psychological shortcomings of patients in the hospital, but because it was so often impossible to tell when a purely physical pain left off and a psychosomatic one began, he was consulted in these cases also.

The fact that the major had detached him from ward duty could mean either promotion or demotion. If Mannon wanted him back, however, then the job which O'Mara had in mind for him must be of greater importance. So Conway was pretty certain that he was not in any trouble with O'Mara, which was a very nice way to feel. But curiosity was killing him.

Then next morning he received orders to present himself at the office of the chief psychologist. . . .

The Visitors

ARKADY AND BORIS STRUGATSKY

Translated by James Womack

Arkady (1925–1991) and Boris (1933–2012) Strugatsky were highly influential Soviet-Russian science fiction writers who often collaborated on their fiction and who rose to prominence despite Soviet censorship. Their most famous work is the novel *Roadside Picnic* (1971; English translation 1977), which was later adapted by Andrei Tarkovsky as the famous cult film *Stalker* (1979). The Strugatskys have proven especially iconic to many Russian and Eastern European fans and writers, many of whom grew up with their writing. The brothers also championed Soviet-era science fiction through Macmillan's English-language Soviet science fiction line of the 1980s, which featured the work of the Strugatskys but also fiction from many other Russian and Ukrainian writers.

Arkady Strugatsky was born in Batumi but grew up in Leningrad, leaving only during the brutal siege of 1942, his flight ending in the death of the brothers' father. He served in the Soviet army and became proficient in English and Japanese at the Military Institute of Foreign Languages. From 1955 on, he worked as a writer and in 1958 he started to collaborate with his brother. Unlike Arkady, Boris Strugatsky stayed in Leningrad during the siege and then became an astronomer and computer engineer. Literary influences on the Strugatsky brothers include Stanisław Lem, who tended toward satire and societal commentary.

Soviet censorship was also a recurring issue for the brothers that sometimes shaped their fiction; some of their works did not appear in print until after the fall of the USSR. And, in their fiction, over time, relatively optimistic views of the future and of humanity would give way to dystopias, alienation, and a cynicism about human institutions. Censorship could be a problem even when writing seemingly innocuous works.

According to Boris's 1999 memoir, *Comments on the Way Left Behind*, the brothers in the late 1960s turned to a mystery romp because it had become "pretty obvious that any serious work of ours had no chances whatsoever of being published any time soon. We forced ourselves to be cynical. There came a point when we had either to sell ourselves, or abandon writing entirely, or become cynics—that is to learn how to write *well* but for money."

Yet, to their surprise, the comic novel *The Dead Mountaineer's Inn* caused problems because it was too apolitical. "It turned out that our editors wished there were some struggles in the novel—class struggle, struggle for peace, struggle of ideas, just anything." Three years later, they would publish *Roadside Picnic*, after a period of writer's block in part caused by this prior interference by the Soviet censors.

"The Visitors" is the second, stand-alone part of a three-part novella later expanded into a novel. The first part describes an encounter with an alien by a military expedition and the third part is in effect the account of an alien abduction. "The Visitors" first appeared in English in the anthology *Aliens, Travelers, and Other Strangers* (1984) but has been retranslated for this volume.

THE VISITORS

Arkady and Boris Strugatsky

Translated by James Womack

The story of K. N. Sergeyev, one of the members of the Apida archaeological research group

Not long ago in a popular science journal there appeared an extensive article about the strange events that had taken place between July and August last year near Stalinabad. Unfortunately, the author of the article evidently used second- and thirdhand material (from unreliable hands at that) and unwittingly presented the event and the circumstances that surrounded it entirely incorrectly. His discussions of "telemechanical subversives" and "silicon-based monsters," as well as the contradictory reports from "witnesses" about burning mountains and cows and trucks being swallowed whole, do not stand up to any scrutiny. The facts of the matter were more straightforward and at the same time much more complex than these inventions.

When it became clear that the official report of the Stalinabad commission would not see the light of day any time soon, Professor Nikitin suggested to me that I should publish the truth about the Visitors, as I was one of very few actual witnesses. "Just put down what you saw with your own eyes," he said. "Put down your impressions. Just how you presented them to the commission. You could even use our material. Although it would be better if you limited yourself to your own impressions. And don't forget about Lozovsky's diary. That's your right."

As I begin to tell my tale, I warn you that I will try with all my strength to follow the professor's suggestion—to give you only my impressions—and I will set out the events as

they took place from our point of view, from the point of view of the archaeological research group that was excavating what is known as the Apida Castle about fifty kilometers southeast of Pendzhikent.

There were six of us in the group. Three archaeologists: the leader of the group, "Bossman" Boris Yanovich Lozovsky; my old friend the Tajik Dzhamil Karimov; and myself. As well as us three there were two workmen, locals, and Kolya the driver.

The Apida Castle is a hill about thirty meters tall, in a narrow valley nestled among the mountains. A little river, very clean and cold, flows down the valley, filled with smooth round stones. The road to the Pendzhikent oasis runs along the river.

We excavated an ancient Tajik settlement at the top of the hill. Our camp was at the base of the hill: two black tents and a raspberry-colored flag with a drawing of a Sogdian coin on it (a circle with a square hole in the middle). A Tajik castle from the third century CE has nothing in common with the crenellated walls and drawbridges of the feudal castles of Europe. When they have been excavated, they show a design made of two or three flat squares, split up with walls two *vershoks* thick. Now what remains of the castle is only the floor. You can find burned wood, fragments of clay pots, and completely contemporary scorpions, and, if you're lucky, an old green coin.

The group had a car set aside for its use—an

ancient GAZ-51, which we used to go on long trips over the terrifying mountain roads, all for archaeological purposes. On the day the Visitors arrived, Lozovsky took the car to Pendzhikent to buy food, and we waited for him to come back. It was the morning of August 14. The car did not come back, and its disappearance marked the beginning of a chain of surprising and inexplicable events.

I was sitting in my tent and smoking, waiting for some pottery shards that I had piled into a bowl and sunk in the river to be washed clean. The sun seemed to be right at its zenith, although it was already three o'clock in the afternoon. Dzhamil was working at the top of the hill—loessial dust was blowing in the wind and you could see the white felt hats of the workers. The Primus stove was hissing, heating up some buckwheat kasha. It was stuffy, hot, and dusty. I smoked and wondered why Lozovsky would want to stay in Pendzhikent, now that he was almost six hours late. We were running low on kerosene; there were only two tins of food left, and half a packet of tea. It would be very unpleasant if Lozovsky didn't come back today. Having thought up a convincing excuse (Lozovsky had decided to put a call through to Moscow), I stood up, stretched, and saw a Visitor for the first time.

It stood motionless in the door to the tent, a dull black color, like an enormous spider about the size of a large dog. It had a round, flat body, like a pocket watch, and jointed legs. I cannot describe it in any more detail. I was too shocked and scared. After a second it started to move and came straight for me. I watched, petrified, how it moved its legs slowly, leaving little holes in the dust—a monstrous silhouette against the yellow sunlit frangible clay.

You must realize that I had no idea that this was a Visitor. This was some kind of unknown beast, and it was coming for me, moving its legs in a strange way, silent and without any eyes. I took a step backward. There was a soft clicking noise, and a sudden flash of blinding light, so bright that I involuntarily screwed up my eyes,

and when I opened them again, I saw through the red patch on my vision that it was already a step closer, inside the shade of the tent. "Oh Lord!" I muttered to myself. It stood next to our basket of supplies and seemed to be rummaging through it with its two front legs. It sparkled in the sun and suddenly one of the tins of food disappeared somewhere. Then the "spider" turned to one side and disappeared. The Primus stopped hissing; there was a metallic sound.

I don't know what a hardheaded person would have done in my place. I couldn't think straight. I remember that I shouted at the top of my voice, either trying to scare the "spider" or else trying to work up some courage myself; I went out of the tent and ran a few steps, then stopped, panting. Nothing had changed. The mountains were dozing around me, the sun flowing over them; the river rang like a cascade of silver, and the white felt hats were visible at the top of the hill. And then I saw the Visitor again. It was climbing the slope, circling the hill, lightly and noiselessly, as if sliding through the air. Its legs were almost impossible to see, but I could clearly make out its strange sharp shadow, running alongside it over the tough gray grass. Then it disappeared.

Then I was bitten by a horsefly, and slapped at it with a wet towel that, apparently, I had been holding in my hand. Shouts came down from the top of the hill—Dzhamil and the workers were coming down the hill and made a sign to me that I should take the kasha off the stove and put the kettle on. They hadn't seen anything and were shocked when I greeted them with the strange phrase: "A spider took the Primus and the food." Dzhamil said that was terrible. I sat in my tent and flicked cigarette ash into the pot of porridge. My eyes were white, and I kept looking around me in fear. Seeing that my old friend thought I had gone mad, I started hurriedly and contradictorily telling him what had happened, and managed to convince him that he was right. The workers came to a single conclusion from all of this: there was no tea and there was no chance of getting any. Disappointed, they silently ate the leftover kasha and sat in their tent to play Tajik card games, mostly *bishtokutar*. Dzhamil had a bit to eat, we smoked together, and then he listened to me again, slightly more calmly.

After thinking for a moment, he said that I must have got mild sunstroke. I immediately replied that first, I only went out into the sun wearing a hat, and second, where had the Primus and the food gone? Dzhamil said that I must have had a blackout and thrown everything into the river. I was offended at this, but all the same we got up and walked out in transparent water up to our knees, occasionally bending down to feel the bed with our hands. I found Dzhamil's watch that he had lost a week before, and then we went back to the tents and Dzhamil started to muse a little. Was there a strange smell? he asked me. No, I replied, there didn't seem to be a smell. And did the spider have wings? No, I didn't see any wings on it. And did I remember what day of the month it was, and what day of the week? I got angry and said that in all likelihood it was the fourteenth, and that I didn't know which day of the week it was, but that didn't matter, as Dzhamil himself probably knew neither one nor the other. Dzhamil admitted that he only knew which month it was, and which year, and that we were stuck in a lonely backwoods with no calendars or newspapers.

Then we examined the area. Unless you count the half-erased holes at the entrance to the tent, there were no traces we could see. However, it became clear that the "spider" had taken my diary, a box of pencils, and a package containing all our most valuable archaeological finds, as well as the Primus and the food. "The bastard!" Dzhamil said in annoyance. Evening set in. A thick white fog rolled down the valley, the constellation of Scorpio shone above us like a three-toed paw, it smelled like a cool spring night. The workers went to sleep early, but we lay in the camp beds and discussed what had happened, filling the tent with clouds of stinking smoke from our cheap cigarettes. After a long silence Dzhamil politely asked me whether I was playing games with him, then said that there might be a connection between the appearance of the "spider" and the disappearance of Lozovsky. I had thought of that myself, but I didn't say anything. Then he went over the things that had been taken once again and made the strange suggestion that the "spider" might be a thief in an odd disguise. I fell asleep.

I was woken by a strange noise, like the howl of powerful aircraft motors. I lay listening for a while. Something didn't feel entirely right. Perhaps it was that I had been there a month and I had not seen a single airplane. I got up and looked out of the tent. It was late at night; my watch showed that it was half past one. The night was sown with sharp icy stars; the mountains were nothing but deep dark shadows. Then on the slope of the mountain opposite I saw a bright speck of light that headed downward, went out, and then appeared again, but some distance to the right. The howl grew louder.

"What is it?" Dzhamil asked alertly, pushing alongside me.

Something was howling close by, and suddenly a blinding blue-white light lit up the top of our hill. The hill seemed to have ice sparkling at its top. This lasted for a few seconds. Then the light went out, and the howling stopped. Darkness and silence descended like lightning over our camp. Frightened voices came from the workers' tent. Dzhamil, invisible, shouted something in Tajik, followed by the sound of hurried steps over pebbles. Then there came the loud howling again over the valley, and then it died out and seemed to disappear somewhere in the distance. I thought that I had seen a long dark shape moving between the stars and heading to the southeast.

Dzhamil came over with the workers. We sat in a circle and for a long time said nothing, smoking and pricking up our ears at every sound. To tell the truth, I was afraid of everything— of the "spiders," the impenetrable moonless dark, the secret rustlings that could be heard above the chatter of the river. I think that the others felt the same. Dzhamil whispered that we were doubtless right in the middle of some significant event. I did not argue. Finally we all felt very cold and went back to our tents.

"Well, what do you have to say now about sunstroke and thieves in disguise?" I inquired.

Dzhamil said nothing for a while, and then asked: "What if they come back?"

"I don't know," I said.

But they didn't come back.

The next day we climbed up to the excavation site and ascertained that not a single shard was left of anything that had been found the previous day: all the pottery fragments had disappeared. The flat square where the excavation had concentrated was covered in little holes. The mound of excavated soil had been knocked flat and looked as if someone had passed a steamroller over it. The wall was broken in two places. Dzhamil bit his lips and looked at me closely. The workers muttered to one another and came closer to us. They were scared, and so were we.

Lozovsky had still not come back with the car. For breakfast we ate stale bread and drank cold water. When the bread was finished, the workers, expressing their wish to send the job to the devil, took their hoes and went up the hill, while I, after discussing the matter with Dzhamil, pulled my hat on and set off firmly down the road to Pendzhikent, trying to hitch a ride in a car.

The first few kilometers went by uneventfully, and I even sat down a couple of times to smoke. The sides of the valley came together and then moved apart, dust blew over the twisting road, the river sang as it flowed. Several times I saw a flock of goats or some cows grazing, but never any people. There were about ten kilometers to go before the next inhabited area when a black helicopter appeared in the sky above me. It flew low along the road, passed over my head with a dull howling noise, and disappeared round a curve of the valley, leaving a blast of hot air behind it. It was not green, like our military helicopters, or silver, like a passenger vehicle. It was black and glinted a little in the sun like the barrel of a rifle. Its color, its strange shape, and the noise it made: all of these reminded me of what had happened yesterday, of the "spiders," and I was frightened again.

I started to walk faster, then started running. I saw a car around the corner, a GAZ-69, with three people standing around it and looking up into the empty sky. I was worried that they would leave, and so I called to them and ran as fast as I could. They turned round, then one of them lay down on the ground and crawled under the car. The other two, broad-shouldered and bearded fellows, geologists by the look of it, continued looking at me.

"Will you take me to Pendzhikent?" I called.

They were silent and stared at me, and I thought that they hadn't heard what I said.

"Hello," I said as I came up to them. *"Salaam alaikum. . . ."*

The taller of the two men turned away in silence and got into the car. The shorter man said, very grumpily, "Hi," and went back to looking at the sky. I looked up too. There was nothing there, except a large and immobile vulture.

"Are you going to Pendzhikent?" I asked, clearing my throat.

"Who are you?" the shorter man asked. The tall man got out of the car and stretched, and I saw a pistol in a holster at his belt.

"I'm an archaeologist. We're excavating the castle at Apida."

"What are you excavating?" the shorter man asked more politely.

"The castle at Apida."

"Where is that?"

I explained.

"Why do you need to go to Pendzhikent?"

I told them about Lozovsky and about the situation in the camp. I did not mention the "spiders" or what had happened last night.

"I know Lozovsky," the taller man said suddenly. He swung his legs out of the car and lit his pipe. "I know Lozovsky. Boris Yanovich?"

I nodded.

"A good man. Of course we would take you, comrade, but as you can see we're cooling our heels ourselves. . . ."

"Georgey Palich," came a reproachful voice from under the car, "you know it's the drive-shaft. . . ."

"Stop your nonsense, Petrenko," the tall man said lazily. "I'll fire you. I'll fire you and pay you nothing. . . ."

"Georgey Palich . . ."

"There it is, there it is again!" the shorter man said. The black helicopter came over the hill and hurried down the road straight toward us.

"Lord only knows what kind of vehicle it is!" the shorter man said.

The black helicopter lifted up into the sky and hung over our heads. I didn't like this at all, and had already opened my mouth to say something, when suddenly the tall man said in a strangled voice: "It's coming down!" and leaped out of the car. The black helicopter came lower and a wicked round hole opened up in its underside, and it came lower and lower, straight for us.

"Petrenko, get away from the damn car!" the taller man said, and grabbed me by the sleeve to pull me away.

I ran, and so did the shorter geologist. He shouted something, opening his mouth wide, but the roar of the motors covered all other sounds. I crouched in the ditch by the side of the road with my eyes filled with dust, and was able only to see Petrenko hurrying toward us on all fours and the black helicopter settling on the road. The updraft of the powerful rotors tore my hat off and surrounded us with a cloud of yellow dust. Then there was the same blinding light as before, brighter than the sun, and I shouted out from the pain in my eyes. When the dust settled, we saw that the road was empty. The GAZ-69 had disappeared. The black helicopter flew up along the valley . . .

. . . and I never saw the Visitors or their craft again. Dzhamil and the workers saw a single helicopter that day and two more on August 16. They were not flying particularly high, and kept to the course of the road.

My further adventures were only connected tangentially to the Visitors. Together with the traumatized geologists I managed somehow to hitchhike my way to Pendzhikent. The taller geologist spent the whole time looking at the sky; the shorter one swore to himself and said that if this was a "trick by his friends at the flying club," then they'd get what was coming to them. Petrenko, the driver, was completely stunned. Several times he piped up to say something about the driveshaft, but no one listened to him.

They told me in Pendzhikent that Lozovsky had left on the morning of the fourteenth, but that our driver Kolya had come back that evening and had been picked up by the police, because it was obvious that he had stolen the car and dealt with Lozovsky, but he didn't want to say how and where he had done it, and all he did was to try to explain himself with some rubbish about an attack from the air.

I hurried to the police station. Kolya was sitting with the duty officer on a wooden bench and was suffering greatly from human injustice. According to his account, about forty kilometers outside Pendzhikent Boris Yanovich had decided to make a detour to look at a *tepe*, a mound that he suspected covered an archaeological site. Twenty minutes later the helicopter turned up and took the car. Kolya ran after it for about a kilometer, didn't manage to catch up with it, and came back to look for Lozovsky. But Lozovsky had also vanished without a trace.

Then Kolya went back to Pendzhikent and on his honor told people what had happened, but things got out of hand. . . . "You're going to catch it!" the duty officer said angrily, but just at that moment my two geologists and Petrenko came into the police station. They came to make a statement about the disappearance of their car, and asked with mild irony which department it was that dealt with acts of aerial hooliganism. Kolya was released within half an hour.

This was not, I should add, the end to Kolya's troubles. The Pendzhikent district attorney announced that he would be opening an investigation into the case of "the disappearance and supposed murder of citizen Lozovsky," and cited Kolya as a suspect, and Dzhamil, the workers, and myself as witnesses. This case was only shelved after the arrival of the commission under Professor Nikitin. I don't want to write about this and I am not going to, because what I am talking about here is the Visitors, and new information was being turned up about them every day. But the most interesting information was provided by our "Bossman," Boris Yanovich Lozovsky, himself.

We spent a long time musing about possible answers, trying to work out where the Visitors had come from and why they had come. There were a huge number of contradictory opinions, and things were only cleared up when, in the middle of September, they found the Visitors' landing site and Boris Yanovich's diary. They were discovered by a border patrol that was investigating the traces of witness accounts of the black helicopters. The landing site was in a hollow surrounded by mountains, fifteen kilometers to the west of Apida Castle, a smooth space with melted rock at its edge. It was about two hundred meters in diameter, and the ground was scorched in many places, and all vegetation—grass, thistles, two mulberry trees—had been charred beyond recognition. One of the missing cars was found there (it was the GAZ-69), clean and serviced but without any fuel, as well as a few objects made of an unknown material and of unidentifiable purpose (they were handed over to the research group), and—most important of all—the diary that the leader of the Apida research group, Boris Yanovich Lozovsky, had kept, containing many surprising handwritten notes.

The diary was lying on the backseat of the car, and it had not been affected by the damp or the sun, it was only a little dusty. It was a standard exercise book with a brown cardboard cover and two-thirds of it was filled with descriptions of the Apida Castle excavations and notes on further archaeological exploration in the surrounding area. But at the end there were twelve pages filled with a short account which, in my opinion, is at the same level as any novel and many scientific and philosophical works.

Lozovsky wrote it in pencil, always (to judge by the handwriting) very quickly and sometimes not in a particularly connected manner. Some of what he wrote is incomprehensible, but lots of it also shines a light onto certain previously unclear elements of what happened, and the entire document is extremely interesting, especially insofar as its descriptions of how Lozovsky faced the Visitors are concerned. The notebook was handed over to me in my capacity as the temporary head of the Apida archaeological research group by the Pendzhikent district attorney immediately after the case of the "disappearance and supposed murder" had been closed "for lack of evidence of a crime." I give the whole text below, making comments at a few points that need clarification.

Extracts from the diary of B. Y. Lozovsky

August 14

[There is a drawing of something not entirely unlike the cap of a fly agaric mushroom—a severely flattened cone. Next to it are drawn for comparative purposes a car and a man. The caption reads "Spaceship?" The cone has several spots marked on it, and these have arrows pointing to them and the caption "Exits." At the top of the cone is written "Load here." To one side: "Height, 15 m. Diameter at base, 40 m."]

The helicopter has brought back another car, a GAZ-69, number-plate ZD19-19. The Visitors [Lozovsky was the first person to use this word] climbed into it, took the engine out, then loaded it into the ship. The hatches are narrow, but the machine went in somehow. Our car is still down on the plain. I unloaded all the food and they are not touching it. They don't pay me any attention at all, it's a little offensive, even. I suppose I could leave, but I won't go just yet. . . .

[Here there is a very bad drawing, obviously supposed to show one of the Visitors.]

I can't draw. A black disk-shaped body about a meter in diameter. Eight legs, though some have ten. The legs are long and thin, like a spider's, with three joints. The joints can turn in any direction. There are no obvious eyes or ears, but it is clear that they can see and hear very well. They can move very fast, like black streaks of lightning. They can run up an almost vertical cliff, like flies. It's odd that their bodies are not divided into thorax and abdomen. I saw how one of them managed, while running, without stopping and without turning its body, to move rapidly to the side and then back again. When they come close to me, I can detect a fresh scent like the smell of ozone. They chitter like cicadas. A rational creature [. . . the phrase is left unfinished.]

The helicopter has brought a cow. A fat, stupid, Jersey cow. As soon as she was down on the ground she started to nibble at some of the charred thistles. Six Visitors surrounded her, chittering and apparently arguing with one another. They are extremely strong—one of them grabbed the cow by her legs and easily turned her over onto her back. They loaded the cow into the ship. Poor creature. Are they gathering supplies?

I tried to start up a conversation: I went over to them face-to-face. They ignored me.

The helicopter has brought a haystack and loaded it. . . . There are at least twenty Visitors and three helicopters. . . .

They are following me. I walked

behind some rocks. A Visitor came after me, chirruped, paused. . . .

This must be a spaceship. I sat in the shade of the cliff and suddenly the Visitors came running over from all different directions. Then the ship suddenly lifted a few feet up into the air and then came down again. Light as a dandelion. No noise, no fire, no sign that there are motors working. But the stones complained as the ship came down. . . .

One of them, it seems, does have eyes—five shining buttons on the edge of its body. They are all different colors: from left to right, turquoise, dark blue, violet, and then two black ones. Maybe they are not eyes, because their owner spends a lot of its time walking in the opposite direction from the way in which they are pointed. The eyes sparkled in the twilight.

August 15

I slept very little last night. The helicopters kept coming and going, the Visitors ran around and chirruped. And all of this in absolute darkness. There were occasional bright flashes. . . . A fourth car, another GAZ-69, number-plate ZD73-98. Again without its driver. Why? Do they pick a moment when the driver has left the car?

A Visitor caught some lizards, very skilfully. It ran on three legs and with the remaining ones picked up sometimes as many as three lizards at a time. . . .

Yes, I could leave if I wanted. I have just come back from the bottom of the cliff. From there it's only a stone's throw to Pendzhikent, only about three hours on foot. But I don't leave. I need to see how this ends. . . .

They've brought a whole flock of sheep, about ten of them, and a huge amount of hay. They've already managed to find out what sheep eat! Clever things! It is clear that they want to take the sheep and the cow back alive, or else that they are laying in stocks of everything. But I still cannot understand why they are ignoring people so absolutely. Or are people less interesting to them than cows? They've loaded up our car now.

. . . they also understand. What if I were to fly off with them? To try to get them to take me or else just sneak into the ship. Would they let me? . . .

. . . Two propellers, sometimes four. Can't count how many blades the propellers have. About eight meters long. Made of some matte-black material, without obvious joins. I don't think it's metal. Something like plastic. Don't know how to get inside. No hatches that I can see. . . . [This must be a description of the helicopters.]

I must be the only person in the area. It's scary. But how else could it be? I need to fly, that's clear. . . .

Hedgehogs have appeared at the top of the ship again. [This makes no sense. Lozovsky mentions hedgehogs nowhere else in his account.] They spin round, give off sparks, and vanish. A strong smell of ozone . . .

A helicopter came back, fist-sized dents in its side. It landed, sunk in on itself [?], and just now two of our fighter jets have come over the hills. What happened?

The Visitors have carried on running around as if nothing has happened. If they do end up fighting [. . . phrase unfinished.]

[. . .] theoretically [. . . unclear . . .] must explain. Of course they don't understand. Or else they think it's unworthy of them. . . .

Astonishing. I'm stunned. Are they machines? Not two meters away from me two Visitors repaired a third! I couldn't believe my eyes. An unusually complex mechanism, I can't describe it, even. It's

a shame that I'm not an engineer. But maybe that wouldn't have helped. They took off the base plate, and underneath there's a star-shaped [. . . unfinished]. There's a storage space under the belly, but how they get all their things in there, I don't know. Machines!

They put it back together, leaving it with just four legs but adding something like a gigantic claw. As soon as the repairs were finished, the "newborn" ran off and hurried to the ship. . . .

Most of their body is made up of a star-shaped object made of some white material, like pumice or sponge. . . .

Who is the Controller of these machines? Maybe the Visitors are being controlled from inside the ship?

Thinking machines? Nonsense! Cybernetic objects, remote controlled? Amazing either way. And what stops the Controllers from coming out? They understand the difference between people and animals. That's why they don't take people. Humane. They must have taken me by accident. . . . My wife won't forgive them. . . .

. . . never, never to see her again— that's terrifying. But I am a man!

The chances of survival are very small. Hunger, cold, the cosmic rays, a million other accidents. The ship is clearly not designed for stowaways. Maybe I've got a chance in a hundred. But I don't have the right not to take it. I have to make contact with them!

Night, midnight. I'm writing by lamplight. When I turned it on, one of the Visitors came running up, grumbled at me, then left. The Visitors have been building something all evening, like a tower. First three wide gangways came out of three of the hatches. I thought that the controllers would finally come out. But what came down were lots of components and metal [?] bars. Six Visitors set to work. The one with the claw was not among them. I *watched them for a long time. Their movements were exact and sure. The tower was built in four hours. How well they coordinate things! I can't see anything now, it's dark, but I can hear the Visitors running around on their landing site. They move perfectly well without the light, they haven't stopped working for a moment. The helicopters are still flying around. . . . Let's suppose that I [. . . unfinished.]*

August 16: 1600 hours

. . . To the person who finds this notebook. I request that you send it to the following address: The Central Asia Department, The Hermitage, Leningrad.

On August 14 at 0900 hours I, Boris Yanovich Lozovsky, was taken by a black helicopter and brought here, to the Visitors' camp. Until today I have tried as best I can to make a note of all my observations [. . . a few lines are erased . . .] and four cars. My basic conclusions. 1. These Visitors are from elsewhere, from Mars or Venus or some other planet. 2. The Visitors themselves are extremely complex and perfectly put-together machines, and their spaceship works automatically.

The Visitors have examined me, undressed me, and, I believe, recorded images of me. They have not caused me any harm and after their initial studies they have not paid me any attention. I was left in complete liberty. . . .

The ship is, to all appearances, preparing to depart, since this morning all three black helicopters and five of the Visitors were taken to pieces in front of me. My food was loaded on board. All that has been left on the landing stage is a few pieces from the construction of the tower and one of the GAZ-69s. Two Visitors are still scrabbling around under the ship and two are strolling around nearby. I sometimes see them at the top of a hill. . . .

I, Boris Yanovich Lozovsky, have decided to climb on board the Visitors' ship and fly with them. I've thought it all through. I have enough food at least for a month: I don't know what will happen then, but I need to fly. I think I will climb on board the ship, find the cow and the sheep, and stay with them. First of all, they will be company for me, and secondly, they are a source of meat if necessary. I don't know what to do about water. But I have a knife, and if necessary I can drink blood. . . . [Crossed out] If I manage to survive—and I am pretty sure I will— then I will use all my efforts to try to make contact with the Earth and come back along with the Controllers of the Visitors. I think I should be able to come to some agreement with them. . . .

To Mariya Ivanovna Lozovskaya: My dearest Mashenka, my love! I hope that these lines will reach you when everything is already sorted out. But if the worst does happen, then do not judge me. I can do nothing else. Just remember that I have always loved you, and forgive me. Give Grishka a kiss. When he grows up, tell him about me. Maybe I was not such a bad person after all, not so bad that my son will not feel proud of his father. What do you think? That's it. One of the Visitors who was running around on the cliffside has just come back to the ship. So. Lozovsky, time to get to work! It's scary. Or maybe that's nonsense. They are machines, and I'm a man. . . .

At this point the manuscript breaks off. Lozovsky obviously never went back to the car. He did not go back because the ship took off. Skeptics may talk about an accident, but then they do that: they're skeptics. Right from the start I was sincerely and perfectly sure that our "Bossman" is alive and is seeing things we have never dreamed of.

He will return, and I will envy him. I will

always envy him, even if he does not return. He's the bravest man I know.

Yes, it's a fact that not everyone is capable of such a feat. I have spoken to a lot of people about him. A few of them have said, openly, that they would be too scared to do what he did. Most of them say: "I don't know. It all depends on the circumstances." I would not be able to act as he did. I saw one of the "spiders," and even now, now that I know they are nothing but machines, I still don't feel I could face them. And the terrible black helicopters . . . Imagine yourself in the bowels of an alien spaceship, surrounded by unliving mechanisms, imagine yourself flying over an icy desert—without any hope, unsure where you are going—flying for days, months, maybe even years, imagine all of this and you can see what I'm thinking.

And that is all. A few words about some things that happened a long time ago. In the middle of September, Professor Nikitin's com-

mission came from Moscow, and all of us—me, Dzhamil, Kolya the driver, the two workers—were made to fill reams of paper and give answers to thousands of questions.

It took us about a week to do this, then we returned to Leningrad.

Maybe the skeptics are right, and we will never know anything about the nature of our guests from the beyond, about how their spacecraft was put together, about their marvelous machines that they sent to visit us on Earth, about—this is the most important of all—the reason for their unexpected visit, but whatever the skeptics say, I think that the Visitors will return. Boris Yanovich Lozovsky will be their first interpreter. He will know the language of these distant neighbors perfectly: he will be the only one who can explain to them what caused a car in perfect condition to end up alongside fragments of a pitcher sixteen centuries old.

Pelt

CAROL EMSHWILLER

Carol Emshwiller (1921–) is a notable US writer of science fiction who has won the Nebula Award and Philip K. Dick Award, among others. She grew up in Ann Arbor, Michigan, and in France until she was a teenager, making her "hopelessly confused" between English and French. In college, she took classes with Anatole Broyard, Kay Boyle, and the poet Kenneth Koch. She began to sell short stories while still a student, to literary magazines, and then discovered science fiction magazines. Damon Knight published her in his *Orbit* anthologies and she also appeared frequently in *The Magazine of Fantasy and Science Fiction*. Her science fiction novels include *Carmen Dog* (1988) and *The Mount* (2002), which won the Philip K. Dick Award and was a finalist for the Nebula Award. In 2005, she was awarded the World Fantasy Award for Life Achievement. *The Collected Stories of Carol Emshwiller*, spanning Emshwiller's entire fifty-year career, was published in 2011.

Emshwiller's husband, Ed Emshwiller, started out as an abstract expressionist painter and experimental filmmaker and became an influence on his wife, who herself explored experimental writing and "what others called the New Wave." (Ed illustrated Harlan Ellison's iconic *Dangerous Visions* anthologies.) Together, the Emshwillers lived a bohemian life in the 1960s, soaking up the counterculture and getting to know a number of musicians, painters, poets, and filmmakers as they traveled abroad, including a trip back to France. Throughout this period, her interest in postmodern literature grew, and her fiction has ever since existed in a space that synthesizes experimental approaches, mainstream literary modes, and speculative subject matter, often from an overtly feminist perspective. The result has been truly interesting and unique fiction.

Ursula K. Le Guin has called Emshwiller "a major fabulist, a marvelous magical realist, one of the strongest, most complex, most consistently feminist voices in fiction." Karen Joy Fowler said of Emshwiller, "She still defies imitation. But it is my contention that sometime in the last fifteen to twenty years, she has become stealthily influential."

Emshwiller has given her own assessment of her work: "A lot of people don't seem to understand how planned and plotted even the most experimental of my stories are. I'm not interested in stories where anything can happen at any time. I set up clues to foreshadow what will happen and what is foreshadowed does happen. I try to have all, or most of the elements in the stories, linked to each other. [My husband,] Ed, used to call it, referring to his experimental films, 'structuring strategies.' How I write is by linking and by structures, and by, I hope, not ever losing sight of the meaning of the story. My favorite writer is Kafka. He kept everything linked and together and full of meaning."

"Pelt" is on the surface one of Emshwiller's more traditional stories, first published in *The Magazine of Fantasy and Science Fiction* in 1958. The story was submitted and critiqued at the Milford Writer's Workshop at Michigan State University, which was founded by Damon Knight, and also the Turkey City writer's workshop.

At the time of its publication, "Pelt" was considered to exemplify a strand of "literary" science fiction that bridged the gap between mainstream realism and core science fiction. In the modern era, of course, "Pelt" would not be considered anything other than an excellent and unusual science fiction story, one that deals with issues of the environment and how humans view other species. It is the kind of story that has become only more relevant, and better, with the passage of time.

PELT

Carol Emshwiller

She was a white dog with a wide face and eager eyes, and this was the planet, Jaxa, in winter.

She trotted well ahead of the master, sometimes nose to ground, sometimes sniffing the air, and she didn't care if they were being watched or not. She knew that strange things skulked behind iced trees, but strangeness was her job. She had been trained for it, and crisp, glittering Jaxa was, she felt, exactly what she *had* been trained for, *born* for.

I love it, I love it . . . that was in her pointing ears, her waving tail . . . I *love* this place.

It was a world of ice, a world with the sound of breaking goblets. Each time the wind blew they came shattering down by the trayful, and each time one branch brushed against another, it was: Skoal, Down the hatch, To the queen . . . tink, tink, tink. And the sun was reflected as if from a million cut-glass punch bowls under a million crystal chandeliers.

She wore four little black boots, and each step she took sounded like two or three more goblets gone, but the sound was lost in the other tinkling, snapping cracklings of the silver, frozen forest about her.

She had figured out at last what that hovering scent was. It had been there from the beginning, the landing two days ago, mingling with Jaxa's bitter air and seeming to be just a part of the smell of the place, she found it in crisscrossing trails about the squatting ship, and hanging, heavy and recent, in hollows behind flat-branched, piney-smelling bushes. She thought of honey and fat men and dry fur when she smelled it.

There was something big out there, and more than one of them, more than two. She wasn't sure how many. She had a feeling this was something to tell the master, but what was the signal, the agreed-upon noise for: We are being watched? There was a whisper of sound, short and quick, for: Sighted close, come and shoot. And there was a noise for danger (all these through her throat mike to the receiver at the master's ear), a special, howly bark: Awful, awful—there is something awful going to happen. There was even a noise, a low, rumble of sound for: Wonderful, wonderful fur—drop everything and come after *this* one. (And she knew a good fur when she saw one. She had been trained to know.) But there was no sign for: We are being watched.

She'd whined and barked when she was sure about it, but that had got her a pat on the head and a rumpling of the neck fur. "You're doing fine, baby. This world is our oyster, all ours. All we got to do is pick up the pearls. Jaxa's what we've been waiting for." And Jaxa was, so she did her work and didn't try to tell him any more, for what was one more strange thing in one more strange world?

She was on the trail of something now, and the master was behind her, out of sight. He'd better hurry. He'd better hurry or there'll be waiting to do, watching the thing, whatever it is, steady on until he comes, holding tight back, and that will be hard. Hurry, hurry.

She could hear the whispered whistle of a tune through the receiver at her ear and she knew he was not hurrying but just being happy. She ran on, eager, curious. She did not give the signal for hurry, but she made a hurry sound of her own, and she heard him stop whistling and whisper back into the mike, "So, so, Queen of Venus. The furs are waiting to be picked. No hurry, baby." But morning was to her for hurry. There was time later to be tired and slow.

That fat-man honeyish smell was about, closer and strong. Her curiosity became two pronged—this smell or that? What *is* the big thing that watches? She kept to the trail she was on, though. Better to be sure, and this thing was not so elusive, not twisting and doubling back, but up ahead and going where it was going.

She topped a rise and half slid, on thick furred rump, down the other side, splattering ice. She snuffled at the bottom to be sure of the smell again, and then, nose to ground, trotted past a thick and tangled hedgerow.

She was thinking through her nose now. The world was all smell, crisp air and sour ice and turpentine pine . . . and this animal, a urine and brown grass thing . . . and then, strong in front of her, honey-furry-fat man.

She felt it looming before she raised her head to look, and there it was, the smell in person, some taller than the master and twice as wide. Counting his doubled suit and all, twice as wide.

This was a fur! Wonderful, wonderful. But she just stood, looking up, mouth open and lips pulled back, the fur on the back of her neck rising more from the suddenness than from fear.

It was silver and black, a tiger-striped thing, and the whitish parts glistened and caught the light as the ice of Jaxa did, and sparkled and dazzled in the same way. And there, in the center of the face, was a large and terrible orange eye, rimmed in black with black radiating lines crossing the forehead and rounding the head. That spot of orange dominated the whole figure, but it was a flat, blind eye, unreal, grown out of fur. At first she saw only that spot of color, but then she noticed under it two small, red glinting eyes and they were kind, not terrible.

This was the time for the call: Come, come and get the great fur, the huge-price-tag fur for the richest lady on earth to wear and be daz-

zling in and most of all to pay for. But there was something about the flat, black nose and the tender, bow-shaped lips and those kind eyes that stopped her from calling. Something masterlike. She was full of wondering and indecision and she made no sound at all.

The thing spoke to her then, and its voice was a deep lullaby sound of buzzing cellos. It gestured with a thick, fur-backed hand. It promised, offered, and asked; and she listened, knowing and not knowing.

The words came slowly. *This . . . is . . . world.*

Here is the sky, the earth, the ice. The heavy arms moved. The hands pointed.

We have watched you, little slave. What have you done that is free today? Take the liberty. Here is the earth for your four shoed feet, the sky of stars, the ice to drink. Do something free today. Do, do.

Nice voice, she thought, nice thing. It gives and gives . . . something.

Her ears pointed forward, then to the sides, one and then the other, and then forward again. She cocked her head, but the real meaning would not come clear. She poked at the air with her nose. Say that again, her whole body said. I almost have it. I *feel* it. Say it once more and maybe then the sense of it will come.

But the creature turned and started away quickly, very quickly for such a big thing, and disappeared behind the trees and bushes. It seemed to shimmer itself away until the glitter was only the glitter of the ice and the black was only the thick, flat branches.

The master was close. She could hear his crackling steps coming up behind her.

She whined softly, more to herself than to him.

"Ho, the queen, Aloora. Have you lost it?" She sniffed the ground again. The honey-furry smell was strong. She sniffed beyond, zigzagging. The trail was there. "Go to it, baby." She loped off to a sound like Chinese wind chimes, businesslike again. Her tail hung guiltily, though, and she kept her head low. She had missed an important signal. She'd waited until it was too late. But was the thing a man, a master? Or a fur? She wanted to do the right thing. She always tried and tried for that, but now she was confused.

She was getting close to whatever it was she trailed, but the hovering smell was still there too, though not close. She thought of gifts. She knew that much from the slow, lullaby words, and gifts made her think of bones and meat, not the dry fishy biscuit she always got on trips like this. A trickle of drool flowed from the side of her mouth and froze in a silver thread across her shoulder.

She slowed. The thing she trailed must be there, just behind the next row of trees. She made a sound in her throat . . . ready, steady . . . and she advanced until she was sure. She sensed the shape. She didn't really see it . . . mostly it was the smell and something more in the tinkling glassware noises. She gave the signal and stood still, a furry, square imitation of a pointer. Come, hurry. This waiting is the hardest part.

He followed, beamed to her radio. "Steady, baby. Hold that pose. Good girl, good girl." There was only the slightest twitch of her tail as she wagged it, answering him in her mind.

He came up behind her and then passed, crouched, holding the rifle before him, elbows bent. He knelt then, and waited as if at a point of his own, rifle to shoulder. Slowly he turned with the moving shadow of the beast, and shot, twice in quick succession.

They ran forward then, together, and it was what she had expected—a deerlike thing, dainty hoofs, proud head, and spotted in three colors, large gray-green rounds on tawny yellow, with tufts of that same glittering silver scattered over.

The master took out a sharp, flat-bladed knife. He began to whistle out loud as he cut off the handsome head. His face was flushed.

She sat down nearby, mouth open in a kind of smile, and she watched his face as he worked.

The warm smell made the drool come at the sides of her mouth and drip out to freeze on the ice and on her paws, but she sat quietly, only watching.

Between the whistlings he grunted and swore and talked to himself, and finally he had the skin and the head in a tight, inside-out bundle.

Then he came to her and patted her sides over the ribs with the flat, slap sound, and he scratched behind her ears and held a biscuit to her on his thick-gloved palm. She swallowed it whole and then watched him as he squatted on his heels and himself ate one almost like it.

Then he got up and slung the bundle of skin and head across his back. "I'll take this one, baby. Come on, let's get one more something before lunch." He waved her to the right. "We'll make a big circle," he said.

She trotted out, glad she was not carrying anything. She found a strong smell at a patch of discolored ice and urinated on it. She sniffed and growled at a furry, mammal-smelling bird that landed in the trees above her and sent down a shower of ice slivers on her head. She zigzagged and then turned and bit, lips drawn back in mock rage, at a branch that scraped her side.

She followed for a while the chattery sound of water streaming along under the ice, and left it where an oily, lambish smell crossed. Almost immediately she came upon them—six small, greenish balls of wool with floppy, woolly feet. The honey-fat-man smell was strong here too, but she signaled for the lambs, the Come and shoot sound, and she stood again waiting for the master. "*Good* girl!" His voice had a special praise. "By God, this place is a gold mine. Hold it, Queen of Venus. Whatever it is, don't let go."

There was a fifty-yard clear view here and she stood in plain sight of the little creatures, but they didn't notice. The master came slowly and cautiously, and knelt beside her. Just as he did, there appeared at the far end of the clearing a glittering, silver and black tiger-striped man.

She heard the sharp inward breath of the master and she felt the tenseness come to him. There was a new, faint whiff of sour sweat, a stiff silence, and a special way of breathing. What she felt from him made the fur rise along her back with a mixture of excitement and fear.

The tiger thing held a small packet in one hand and was peering into it and pulling at the opening in it with a blunt finger. Suddenly there was a sweep of motion beside her and five fast, frantic shots sounded sharp in her ear. Two came after the honey-fat man had already fallen and lay like a huge decorated sack.

The master ran forward and she came at his heels. They stopped, not too close, and she watched the master looking at the big, dead tiger head with the terrible eye. The master was breathing hard and seemed hot. His face was red and puffy looking, but his lips made a hard whitish line. He didn't whistle or talk. After a time he took out his knife. He tested the blade, making a small, bloody thread of a mark on his left thumb. Then he walked closer and she stood and watched him and whispered a questioning whine.

He stooped by the honey-fat man and it was that small, partly opened packet that he cut viciously through the center. Small round chunks fell out, bite-sized chunks of dried meat and a cheesy substance and some broken bits of clear, bluish ice.

The master kicked at them. His face was not red anymore, but olive-pale. His thin mouth was open in a grin that was not a grin. He went about the skinning then.

He did not keep the flat-faced, heavy head nor the blunt-fingered hands.

The man had to make a sliding thing of two of the widest kind of flat branches to carry the new heavy fur, as well as the head and the skin of the deer. Then he started directly for the ship.

It was past eating time but she looked at his restless eyes and did not ask about it. She walked before him, staying close. She looked back often, watching him pull the sled thing by the string across his shoulder, and she knew, by the way he held the rifle before him in both hands, that she should be wary.

Sometimes the damp-looking, inside-out bundle hooked on things, and the master would curse in a whisper and pull at it. She could see the bundle made him tired, and she wished he would stop for a rest and food as they usually did long before this time.

They went slowly, and the smell of honey-fat man hovered as it had from the beginning. They crossed the trails of many animals. They even saw another deer run off, but she knew that it was not a time for chasing.

Then another big silver and black tiger stood exactly before them. It appeared suddenly, as if actually it had been standing there all the time, and they had not been near enough to see it, to pick it out from its glistening background.

It just stood and looked and dared, and the master held his gun with both hands and looked too, and she stood between them glancing from one face to the other. She knew, after a moment, that the master would not shoot, and it seemed the tiger thing knew too, for it turned to look at her and it raised its arms and spread its fingers as if grasping at the forest on each side. It swayed a bit, like bigness off balance, and then it spoke in its tight-strung, cello tones. The words and the tone seemed the same as before.

Little slave, what have you done that is free today? Remember this is world. Do something free today. Do, do.

She knew that what it said was important to it, something she should understand, a giving and a taking away. It watched her, and she looked back with wide, innocent eyes, wanting to do the right thing, but not knowing what.

The tiger-fat man turned then, this time slowly, and left a wide back for the master and her to see, and then it half turned, throwing a quick glance over the heavy humped shoulder at the two of them. Then it moved slowly away into the trees and ice, and the master still held the gun with two hands and did not move.

The evening wind began to blow, and there sounded about them that sound of a million chandeliers tinkling and clinking like gigantic wind chimes. A furry bird, the size of a shrew and as fast, flew by between them with a miniature shriek.

She watched the master's face, and when he was ready she went along beside him. The soft sounds the honey-fat man had made echoed in her mind but had no meaning.

That night the master stretched the big skin on a frame and afterward he watched the dazzle of it. He didn't talk to her. She watched him awhile and then she turned around three times on her rug and lay down to sleep.

The next morning the master was slow, reluctant to go out. He studied charts of other places, round or hourglass-shaped maps with yellow dots and labels, and he drank his coffee standing up looking at them. But finally they did go out, squinting into the ringing air.

It was her world. More each day, she felt it was so, right feel, right temperature, lovely smells. She darted on ahead as usual, yet not too far today, and sometimes she stopped and waited and looked at the master's face as he came up. And sometimes she would whine a question before she went on. . . . Why don't you walk brisk, brisk, and call me Queen of Venus, Aloora, Galaxa, or Bitch of Betelgeuse? Why don't you sniff like I do? Sniff, and you will be happy with this place. . . . And she would run on again.

Trails were easy to find, and once more she found the oily lamb smell, and once more came upon them quickly. The master strode up beside her and raised his gun . . . but a moment later he turned, carelessly, letting himself make a loud noise, and the lambs ran. He made a face, and spit upon the ice. "Come on, Queen. Let's get out of here. I'm sick of this place."

He turned and made the signal to go back, pointing with his thumb above his head in two jerks of motion.

But why, why? This is morning now and our world. She wagged her tail and gave a short bark, and looked at him, dancing a little on her back paws, begging with her whole body. "Come on," he said.

She turned then, and took her place at his heel, head low, but eyes looking up at him, wondering if she had done something wrong, and wanting to be right and noticed and loved because he was troubled and preoccupied.

They'd gone only a few minutes on the way back when he stopped suddenly in the middle of a step, slowly put both feet flat upon the ground, and stood like a soldier at a stiff, off-balance attention. There, lying in the way before them, was the huge, orange-eyed head and in front of it, as if at the end of outstretched arms, lay two leathery hands, the hairless palms up.

She made a growl deep in her throat and the master made a noise almost exactly like hers, but more a groan. She waited for him, standing as he stood, not moving, feeling his tenseness coming into her. Yet it was just a head and two hands of no value, old ones they had had before and thrown away.

He turned and she saw a wild look in his eyes. He walked with deliberate steps, and she followed, in a wide circle about the spot. When they had skirted the place, he began to walk very fast.

They were not far from the ship. She could see its flat blackness as they drew nearer to the clearing where it was, the burned, iceless pit of spewed and blackened earth. And then she saw that the silver tiger men were there, nine of them in a wide circle, each with the honey-damp fur smell, but each with a separate particular sweetness.

The master was still walking very fast, eyes down to watch his footing, and he did not see them until he was there in the circle before them all, standing there like nine upright bears in tiger suits.

He stopped and made a whisper of a groan, and he let the gun fall low in one hand so that it hung loose with the muzzle almost touching the ground. He looked from one to the other and she looked at him, watching his pale eyes move along the circle.

"Stay," he said, and then he began to go toward the ship at an awkward limp, running and walking at the same time, banging the gun handle against the air lock as he entered.

He had said, Stay. She sat watching the ship door and moving her front paws up and down because she wanted to be walking after him. He was gone only a few minutes, though, and when he came back it was without the gun and he was holding the great fur with cut pieces of thongs dangling like ribbons along its edges where it had been tied to the stretching frame. He went at that same run-walk, unbalanced by the heavy bundle, to one of them along the circle. Three gathered together before him and refused to take it back. They pushed it, bunched loosely, back across his arms again and to it they added another large and heavy package in a parchment bag, and the master stood, with his legs wide to hold it all.

Then one honey-fat man motioned with a fur-backed hand to the ship and the bundles, and then to the ship and the master, and then to the sky. He made two sharp sounds once, and then again. And another made two different sounds, and she felt the feeling of them. . . . Take your things and go home. Take them, these and these, and go.

They turned to her then and one spoke and made a wide gesture. *This is world. The sky, the earth, the ice.*

They wanted her to stay. They gave her . . . was it their world? But what good was a world?

She wagged her tail hesitantly, lowered her head, and looked up at them. . . . I do want to do right, to please everybody, everybody, but . . . Then she followed the master into the ship.

The locks rumbled shut. "Let's get out of here," he said. She took her place, flat on her side, takeoff position. The master snapped the flat plastic sheet over her, covering head and all, and, in a few minutes, they roared off.

Afterward he opened the parchment bag. She knew what was in it. She knew he knew too, but she knew by the smell. He opened it and dumped out the head and the hands. His face was tight and his mouth stiff.

She saw him almost put the big head out the waste chute, but he didn't. He took it in to the place where he kept good heads and some odd paws or hoofs, and he put it by the others there.

Even she knew this head was different. The others were all slant-browed like she was and most had jutting snouts. This one seemed bigger than the big ones, with its heavy, ruffed fur and huge eye staring, and more grand than any of them, more terrible . . . and yet a flat face, with a delicate, black nose and tender lips.

The tenderest lips of all.

The Monster

GÉRARD KLEIN

Translated by Damon Knight

Gérard Klein (1937–) is a well-known French writer, anthologist, critic, and editor. An economist by profession, Klein has used the pseudonyms Gilles d'Argyre (most frequently) and Mark Starr, and, jointly with Patrice Rondard and Richard Chomet, François Pagery (based on the collaborators' first names, PAtrice plus GErard plus RIchard). His first stories, heavily influenced by Ray Bradbury, appeared in 1955 when he was only eighteen, beginning with "Une place au balcon" in *Galaxie* (the French edition of *Galaxy*) in 1955. He soon made a major impact on the field in France, publishing more than forty delicately crafted tales between 1956 and 1962 (a total that reached sixty by 1977), while also establishing himself as a forceful and literate critic of the genre with a series of thirty penetrating essays in various publications.

In the late 1970s Klein remarked upon the pessimism of American science fiction, finding it lacking in its ability to envision a future with better social constructs. Yet this very "accusation" was leveled against many French science fiction writers, for leaning toward the dark, psychological side of science fiction, rather than a perceived (and more common) American optimism from prior decades of science fiction. Klein called to task writers for not taking it upon themselves to imagine a different societal setup, instead falling back on the status quo and therefore seeing only a dark, bleak future. Joanna Russ, in *How to Suppress Women's Writing*, agreed with Klein about the lack of political honesty in much of the science fiction being written at that time. Klein's later works were compared to Cordwainer Smith and Antoine de Saint-Exupéry in their ability to evoke a certain awe about the universe.

This story was first published in 1958 in French. It was translated into English by Damon Knight and published in *The Magazine of Fantasy and Science Fiction* in 1961 and reprinted in the Knight-edited *13 French Science-Fiction Stories* (1965). Perhaps Klein was also influenced by the Belgian writer Jean Ray when creating "The Monster," as there is a certain sense, along with resignation, of horror and fear of the unknown.

THE MONSTER

Gérard Klein

Translated by Damon Knight

Night was ready to fall, just in equilibrium on the edge of the horizon, ready to close like a lid over the town, releasing in its fall the precise clockwork of the stars. Metallic curtains fell like eyelids over the shop windows. Keys went into locks and made the bolts grate. The day was over. A rain of footsteps beat upon the dusty asphalt of the streets. It was then that the news ran through the town, leaping from mouth to ear, showing itself in dazed or frightened eyes, humming in the copper telephone wires or crackling in television picture tubes.

"We repeat, there is no danger," the loudspeaker said to Marion, sitting in her kitchen, hands on her knees, looking out the window at the newly cut grass, the white garden fence, and the road. "Residents of the areas around the park are merely asked to remain at home so as not to interfere in any way with the movements of the specialists. The thing from another planet is not at all hostile to human beings. It's a historic day, this day when we can welcome as our guest a being from another world, one undoubtedly born, in the opinion of the eminent professor who stands beside me at this moment, under the light of another sun."

Marion rose and opened the window. She breathed the air charged with the scent of grass, a spray of water, and a thousand sharp knives of cold, and stared at the street, at the dark and distant point where it detached itself from the high cliffs of the town's tall buildings, and spread itself out, widened among the lawns and the brick houses. In the front of each house, a light burned in a window, and behind nearly every one of these windows Marion could make out a waiting shadow. And these shadows leaning on the sills disappeared one by one, while men's footsteps echoed in the street, keys slipped into oiled locks, and doors clicked, shutting out the day that was ended and the nightfall.

"Nothing will happen to him," Marion told herself, thinking of Bernard, who would be crossing the park, if he came as usual by the shortest and easiest way. She glanced in the mirror, touching her black hair. She was small and somewhat round, and soft as melting vanilla ice cream.

"Nothing will happen to him," Marion told herself, looking toward the park, between the tall illuminated checkerboards of the building fronts, seeing the dark, compact mass of trees enlivened by no other light but that of passing autos' headlamps; "probably he's taking another route"; but in spite of herself, she imagined Bernard walking down the gravel paths with an easy stride, between the clipped shadows of yews and the quaking of poplars, in the thin moonlight, avoiding the low fences that bordered the lawns like iron eyelashes, carrying a newspaper in one hand and whistling perhaps, or smoking a half-burned-out pipe and blowing little puffs of thin smoke, eyes half closed, his attitude faintly insolent, as if he could fight the world. And a big black claw moved in the bushes, or a long tentacle coiled itself up in a ditch, ready to flick through the air like a whip and snap, and she saw them, with her eyes closed, on the point of calling out and screaming with terror, and she did nothing because it was only an illusion brought on by the confident words of the radio.

"All necessary precautions have been taken. The park entrances are being watched. The last pedestrians have been escorted individually as far as the gates. We ask you only to avoid making any noise and preferably any light in the vicinity of the park, in order not to frighten our guest from another world. Contact has not yet been made with the being from another planet. No one can say what its shape is, or how many eyes it has. But here we are at the entrance of the park itself, and we'll keep you up to date. Beside me now is Professor Hermant of the Institute of Space Research, who will give you the results of his preliminary observations. Professor, I'm going to turn the mike over to you. . . ."

Marion thought about that thing from space, that being, huddled and lonely in a corner of the park, crouching against the wet ground, shivering with cold in this alien wind—staring up through an opening in the bushes at the sky, with its new, unknown stars—feeling the earth shake with the footsteps of the men who were surrounding it, the throbbing of motors, and deeper down, the subterranean rumbling of the city.

"Would what I do in its place?" Marion wondered, and she knew that everything would be all right because the radio voice was solemn and untroubled, assured, like the voice of a preacher heard on Sunday, whose words hardly broke the silence. She knew the men would move forward toward that creature trembling in the light of the headlamps, and that it would wait, calm and trusting, for them to hold out their hands and talk to it, and then it would go to them, quivering with anxiety, until, listening to their incomprehensible voices—as she had listened to Bernard's a year ago—it would suddenly understand.

"Our instruments have barely scratched the surface of the immense spaces around us," said the professor's voice. "Just imagine, at the very moment I'm speaking to you, we're hur-tling through cosmic space, between the stars, between clouds of hydrogen. . . ."

He paused for breath. "Therefore, anything at all might be waiting for us beyond that mysterious door that we call space. And now we find that a being from another world has pushed open that door and passed through it. Just one hour and forty-seven minutes ago, a spaceship landed silently in the park of this city. It had been detected an hour and a half earlier, when it entered the upper layers of the atmosphere. It appears to be small in size. It is still too early for any conjectures about its method of propulsion. My distinguished colleague Professor Li is of the opinion that the device may be propelled by an effect of oriented spatial asymmetry, but the research undertaken in this direction—"

"Professor," the announcer interrupted, "some people have advanced the idea that it isn't a ship at all, but merely a creature capable of movement among the stars. What do you think of that theory?"

"Well, it's still too soon for any definite opinion. No one has yet seen the object, and all we know is that it seemed able to direct its flight and arrest its fall. We don't even know whether it actually contains a living being. It's possible that it's only a machine, a sort of robot, if you like. But in any case, it contains a message of the highest scientific interest. This is the greatest scientific event since the discovery of fire by our remote ancestors. We know now that we're not alone any longer in the starry immensity. To answer your question: frankly, I do not believe that a living creature, in the sense you mean, could survive in the conditions of outer space—the absence of atmosphere, of heat and gravitation, the destructive radiation."

"Professor, do you think there's the slightest danger?"

"Honestly, no. This thing has shown no hostile intentions, it's simply stayed in a corner of the park. I'm amazed at the swiftness with which the necessary precautions have been taken, but I don't think they will accomplish anything. I'm more concerned with the possible reactions of people when they meet an absolutely alien being. That is why I ask each person to remain calm, whatever happens. The scientific authorities have the situation in hand. Nothing unfortunate can happen. . . ."

Marion took a cigarette out of the drawer and lit it awkwardly. It was something she had not done for years, since her fifteenth birthday, perhaps. She inhaled the smoke, and coughed. Her fingers were trembling. She brushed a little white ash off her dress.

"What shall we have for dinner tonight?" she asked aloud, reproaching herself for her nervousness. But she did not have the courage to take a frying pan from the cupboard, or even to open the refrigerator.

She put out the light, then went back to the window, and drawing on her cigarette like a little girl, tried to hear a sound of footsteps in the road. But there were only the voices in the peaceful houses, a strain of music, muffled like the humming of bees in a hive, and the purring of words in the loudspeaker.

"Keep calm," she said in a loud voice, biting her lips. "Thousands of people have gone through the park tonight and nothing has happened to them. And nothing will happen to him. Things never happen to people you know, only to gray faces with unlikely names in the newspapers."

The clock struck eight. "Maybe I could telephone the office," Marion thought. "Maybe he'll be there half the night." But they had no telephone, and it would have meant putting on a coat, going out into the darkness, and running through the cold, going into a cafe full of curious faces, unhooking the little black dead humming beast of the phone, and calling with a changed, metallic voice while she crumpled a handkerchief in her pocket. That was what she should do. That was what a brave, independent woman would do. But she was not, she told herself, filled with shame—either brave nor independent. All she could do was wait, and look

out at the glittering city with eyes full of nightmares.

"Thank you, Professor," said the radio. "We are standing now not more than four hundred meters from the place where the creature is hiding. The men of the special brigades are moving forward slowly, studying every square centimeter of the ground. I can't make out anything yet—oh yes, a black shape, vaguely spherical, on the other side of the pond, perhaps a little taller than a man. It's really quite dark, and . . . The park is absolutely empty. The ambassador from the stars is all alone now, but don't worry, you'll be able to make his acquaintance very soon. . . ."

Marion dropped her cigarette and watched it burning itself out on the clean tiles. Bernard was not in the park. Perhaps he was strolling toward it, or perhaps he was prowling around the park fence, trying to glimpse the visitor from the stars. In fifteen minutes he would be here, smiling, his hair sparkling with the microscopic droplets of the mist.

Then the old anxiety rose up out of some internal cavern, purple and damp. "But why don't they move on faster," she thought, imagining the men working in darkness, measuring, weighing, analyzing, moving soundlessly through the night like moles aboveground; "why don't they move on faster if there's no danger?"

And it came to her mind that something was being hidden behind the calm screen of the loudspeaker and the words embroidered with confidence. She thought suddenly that perhaps they were trembling as they spoke, perhaps their hands were clenching convulsively on the microphone while they pretended to be sure of themselves; perhaps their faces were horribly pale in spite of the red glare of the dark lanterns. She told herself that they didn't know any more than she did about things that might be wandering outside the atmosphere of Earth. And she thought that they would do nothing for Bernard, that only she could make the least gesture, even if she couldn't think what it might be: perhaps run to meet him, throw her arms around his neck, and press herself against him, perhaps take him far away from that loathsome star creature—or perhaps simply weep in a white-metal kitchen chair, and wait, motionless, like a silhouette cut out of black paper.

She was incapable of thinking about anything else. She did not want to hear the voice from the radio anymore, but she dared not turn it off, for fear of being still more alone. She picked up a magazine and opened it at random, but she had never really liked to read, and now she would have had to spell everything out letter by letter, her eyes were so blurry; and anyway, the stale words had no more meaning for her at this moment. She tried to look at the pictures, but she saw them as if through a drop of water, or a prism, transparent, strangely dislocated, broken along impossible lines.

Then she heard a step; she got up, ran to the door, opened it, and leaned out into the night, toward the dim wet lawn, and listened, but the footsteps dwindled suddenly, paused, receded, and died out altogether.

She went back into the kitchen and the sound of the radio seemed unendurable. She turned down the volume and pressed her ear right up against the loudspeaker, listening through the curtain of her hair to that minuscule voice, that insect rubbing against a vibrating membrane.

"Look out," said a voice at the other end of a long tube of shivering glass, "something's happening. I think the creature is moving. The specialists are maybe two hundred meters away from it, not more. I hear a sort of voice. Maybe the being from another world is about to speak . . . it's calling out . . . its voice seems almost human . . . like a long sigh . . . I'm going to let you listen to it."

Marion crushed her ear against the radio, her hair imprinting itself into her skin. She heard a series of clicks, a long wordless buzzing, a sharp whistle, then silence; then the voice came into being in the depths of the loudspeaker, hardly audible, deep as the heavy breathing of a sleeper.

"MA-riON," said the voice, nested in the hollow of the loudspeaker, huddling in a dark corner of the park.

It was Bernard's voice.

She sprang up; the chair toppled behind her with a crash.

"MA-riON," murmured the strange, familiar voice. But she did not hear it, she was running down the road, leaving behind her the door wide open and all her anguish dead. She ran past two houses, then stopped a moment, out of breath, shaking with cold. The night was everywhere. Hairlines of light barely escaped from the drawn blinds of the houses. The streetlights were out. She began to walk down the middle of the road, where she was less likely to trip over a stone or fall in a puddle.

An unaccustomed silence hung over the neighborhood, punctuated from time to time by a distant bark, or the metallic uproar of a train. She met a man who was singing as he walked, as black as a statue carved from anthracite. She was about to stop him and ask him to go with her, but when she got near she saw he was drunk, and walked around him.

It seemed to her that she was lost in a hostile city, even though she knew every one of these houses, and had criticized the curtains at every window a hundred times, out walking with Bernard in the daytime. She ran between the tall buildings as if between walls of trees overhanging a forest trail. And she was certain that if she paused, she would hear the breathing of a fierce animal behind her. She was crossing a desert place, a concrete clearing, which the night had roofed over with a canopy pierced with pinholes that were the stars. She came to the edge of the park and began to run along the fence, counting the bars.

Her heels struck the asphalt with the clear ringing of a hammer falling on the keys of a xylophone. Fear ran over her skin like an army of ants. She held her breath. The moon cast a tenuous, impalpable shadow before her.

She whirled, her skirt flaring. There was nothing behind her but the row of nocturnal walls, without form or tint, like great mounds of obsidian devouring all light and all color, turning the night into a gulf and the edge of the sidewalk into a tightrope along which she had run, weightless and numb with her anguish and her cold. She was alone with the night.

A hand touched her arm, made her turn around. She cried out. The hand released her and she backed away to the park fence and pressed her shoulders against the bars, throwing up her hands.

"Sorry, ma'am," said the policeman in a heavy, stumbling voice that was strangely reassuring. "Everybody was asked to stay home. Do you have a radio?"

"Yes," Marion whispered with an effort, not moving, not breathing, not even really moving her lips.

"Want me to take you back home? There isn't much danger here, but . . ." He hesitated. His face was pale in the darkness. A tic jumped at regular intervals in his cheek. ". . . A man was caught just now, and it would be better . . ."

"Bernard," said Marion, her spread fingers pressed against the folds of her dress.

"It wasn't pretty," the policeman muttered. "It would be better if you came with me. And now the thing's calling out. Hurry up, ma'am. I've got my rounds to finish. Hope you don't live far. I don't usually patrol by myself, you understand. But we're short of men tonight."

With the tip of his shoe he crushed a half-smoked cigarette, swollen with water; the paper tore apart and the tobacco scattered.

"My husband," said Marion.

"Come on, let's go. He's waiting for you at home."

"No," said Marion, shaking her head, and her hair fell across her face like a net of fine black mesh. "He's there in the park. I heard him."

"There's nobody in the park." The tic appeared again, deforming his cheek. Marion saw that his jaw was trembling slightly. His left hand rubbed his leather belt and his right hand touched the polished holster of his revolver. He was more frightened than she. He was afraid for himself.

"Don't you understand?" she cried. "Don't you realize?" She threw herself at him, seized him by the arms. She wanted to claw that pale, trembling face, that human façade, as white as the façades of the city were dark.

"My husband is in there calling for me. I heard his voice on the radio. Why won't you let me alone?"

Without warning, she felt tears running down her cheeks. "Oh, let me go," she moaned.

He tipped up momentarily on the square toes of his shiny black leather shoes. "Maybe," he said hesitantly, "maybe. I don't know." Then, more gently, "Sorry, ma'am. Come with me."

They walked along the fence. She ran ahead of him on tiptoe, paused to wait for him every four or five steps.

"Hurry," she said, "for God's sake, hurry."

"Don't make too much noise, ma'am, it's not so far away, and it seems it has sharp ears. Pretty soon now we'll hear it."

"I know," she said, "it's my husband's voice."

He looked at her fixedly, in silence.

"It ate him up," she said. "I know it. I saw it. It has great big pointed teeth all made of steel. I heard them click. It was awful."

Suddenly she began to cry again. Her body shook with her sobs.

"Calm down. Nothing's going to happen to you."

"No," she admitted. "Not anymore."

But her voice was broken with hiccoughs and tears blurred her eyes as she ran. She slipped and one of her shoes flew in the air and she kicked the other off hastily and went on running in her stockings.

Suddenly she heard the monster's voice, and she saw Bernard's lips moving. It was a prolonged, tranquil sound, not at all frightening, but so weak that she would have liked to cup it in her hand to protect it from the wind.

She saw the men in dark uniforms who were guarding the park entrance. She stood still and waited through the exchange of questions and the muttered, tight-lipped answers. She went into the park. She saw the web of copper wires they had woven, glittering wires in a circle, surrounding the strange thing that spoke with Bernard's voice. She felt the dampness of the grass under her feet.

"Who are you?" breathed a voice.

"I came to . . . ," she began, but she heard the voice in the distance: "MA-riON. MA-riON."

"Don't you hear it?" she said.

"I've been hearing it for an hour," said the man. He turned the beam of his flashlight on Marion. His teeth and the buttons of his uniform gleamed. His thin mustache made his mouth seem forever smiling, but his eyes, now, looked desperate.

"It makes human sounds, Earth words it found in that poor guy it caught—words without any connection or sense. At first we thought it was a man calling out. Then we realized no man in the world has a voice like that."

"It's Bernard's voice," she said. "Bernard is my husband. We'll be married a year next month."

"Who are you? What's your name?"

She let herself fall on the grass and wrapped her arms around her head to shut out the voice.

"Marion," the voice repeated insistently. It could not be the voice of a man, it was too penetrating. It seemed to come from the bottom of a pit, or from the inside of an oven. It flowed along the ground and seemed to issue from the earth, like the voice of plants, or the voice of insects, or the voice of a snake gliding through the damp grass.

"You'd almost think it was waiting for somebody," said the man. He sat down beside her. "Tell me your name."

"It's me he's calling to," she said. "I have to go to him."

"Don't move. What's your name? What are you doing here, in that dress, on a night like this?"

"Marion," she whispered, "Marion Laharpe. That was my name."

She thought of her name, that fragile bubble, floating away in the time it took to put a ring on her finger, blown up again in the time it took to run to a park invaded by the night.

"My husband was"—she hesitated, then made up her mind—"eaten by that thing, and he's calling me and I have to go to him."

"Don't excite yourself," said the man. His narrow mustache quivered. "No one's been eaten. And even if they had, how could you be sure it was your husband?"

But his voice shook, cracked apart like a wall about to tumble down; it had a quality of uncertainty, fear, and pity, all mixed together and weighed down by anger.

"Don't lie," said Marion. "I recognize his voice and that policeman that came with me said a man had been killed, and he had to go through the park, and he didn't come home, and I heard the voice on the radio, just now, and it was calling me. A million people heard that voice. You can't say they didn't."

"No," he said, "I believe you." His voice faded as he spoke, and seemed dead, the syllables dancing like ashes in the breath of air from his lungs. "There was nothing we could do. We shut the gates too late. We saw him come out of a path, and just like that the thing was on him, covering him. It happened very fast. I'm sorry. If there's any way I can help . . ."

Then his voice hardened. "We're going to kill that thing. I know that won't bring your husband back, but I wanted to tell you. We're not going to take any unnecessary risks. Look."

The long tubes of flamethrowers shone like tongues on the grass, like sound teeth in a rotten mouth. They lay on the lawn, on the other side of the glittering network of electric wires. And beside each of these lances a man seemed to sleep, but from time to time a shudder ran over his back and his head turned as he tried to look through the tall weeds and the leaves of bushes and probe that hostile, ambush-filled area in front of him.

"No," said Marion in a loud voice. "Don't touch it. I'm sure it's Bernard."

The man shook his head. "He's dead, madam. We saw it happen. The monster may be just repeating his last words, over and over, mechanically. He died thinking of you, that's certain. The professor can explain it better than I can."

"The professor," said Marion. "I heard him. He said there was no danger, that we should keep calm and that he knew what he was doing and that it was a historic event and . . ."

"He's human like the rest of us. He yelled when that thing attacked your husband. He said he didn't understand. He said he'd been waiting all his life for a friend from the stars. He said he'd rather have been eaten himself than see that."

"He kept quiet," she said bitterly. "He said everything was all right. He said we mustn't lose our heads, and he knew that Bernard . . ."

"He did what he thought was best. Now, he says we've got to wipe that vermin off the face of the Earth and send it to hell. He's sent for some gas."

"Marion," softly called the voice without lips, the voice without ivory teeth, or fleshy tongue, from beyond the gleaming copper tubes.

"I want to talk to him," she said into the silence. "I'm sure it's Bernard, and he'll understand me."

"Very well. We've tried that too. But it doesn't answer."

She grasped the microphone in her fingers like a stone curiously polished by the sea.

"Bernard," she breathed. "Bernard, here I am."

Her voice spurted from the loudspeaker like water from a fountain, strangely altered, dis-

tilled. It rebounded from the tree trunks and scattered among the leaves, ran along the stems like a noisy sap, crept among the twigs and weeds in the hollows of the ground. It flooded the lawn, soaked into the shrubbery, filled the paths, disturbed the surface of the pond with undetectable ripples.

"Bernard. Do you hear me? I want to help you."

And the voice answered, "Marion. I'm waiting for you. I've been waiting for you so long, Marion."

"Here I am, Bernard," she said, and her voice was light and fresh, it soared over the children's sandbox, glided between the swings, the merry-go-round, the seesaws, between the rings and trapeze that hung from the crossbar.

"He's calling me. I have to go," she said.

"It's a trap," voices called behind her. "Stay here. There's nothing human in there."

"What do I care? That's Bernard's voice."

"Look," said someone.

A spotlight came on like an eye opening and pierced the black air like a tangible bar of light. And she saw a mass of darkness, sparkling, bubbling, foaming, made of clusters of big bubbles that broke at the surface of a sphere of flabby, viscous coal. It was a living sponge of jet, breathing and swallowing.

"Filth from space," said the solemn voice of the professor, behind her.

"I'm coming, Bernard," said Marion, and she dropped the microphone and threw herself forward. She dodged the hands that tried to stop her and began running down the graveled path. She leaped over the copper-meshed web and passed between the gleaming tongues of the flamethrowers.

"It's a trap," called a deep voice behind her. "Come back. The creature has absorbed some of your husband's knowledge—it's using it as a lure. Come back. That isn't human. It has no face."

But no one followed her. When she turned her head, she saw the men standing up, grasping their lances and looking at her, horrified, their eyes and teeth gleaming with the same metallic light as the buttons of their uniforms.

She rounded the pond. Her feet struck the cement pavement with soft, dull sounds, then they felt the cool, caressing touch of the grass again.

She wondered even as she ran what was going to happen, what would become of her, but she told herself that Bernard would know for her, that he had always known, and that it was best that way. He was waiting for her beyond that black doorway through which his voice came with so much difficulty, and she was about to be with him.

A memory came suddenly into her mind. A sentence read or heard, an idea harvested and stored away, to be milled and tasted now. It was something like this: men are nothing but empty shells, sometimes cold and deserted like abandoned houses, and sometimes inhabited, haunted by the beings we call life, jealousy, joy, fear, hope, and so many others. Then there was no more loneliness.

And as she ran, exhaling a warm breath that condensed into a thin plume of vapor, looking back at the pale, contracted faces of the soldiers, dwindling at every step, she began to think that this creature had crossed space and searched for a new world because it felt itself desperately hollow and useless in its own, because none of those intangible beings would haunt it, and that she and Bernard would perhaps live in the center of its mind, just as confidence and anxiety, silence and boredom live in the hearts and minds of men. And she hoped that they would bring it peace, that they would be two quiet little lights, illuminating the honeycombed depths of its enormous, unknown brain.

She shuddered and laughed. "What does it feel like to be eaten?" she asked herself.

She tried to imagine a spoonful of ice cream melting between her lips, running cool down her throat, lying in the little dark warmth of her stomach.

"Bernard," she cried. "I've come."

She heard the men shouting behind her.

"Marion," said the monster with Bernard's voice, "you took so long."

She closed her eyes and threw herself forward. She felt the cold slip down her skin and leave her like a discarded garment. She felt herself being transformed. Her body was dissolving, her fingers threading out, she was expanding inside that huge sphere, moist and warm, comfortable, and, she understood now, good and kind.

"Bernard," she said, "they're coming after us to kill us."

"I know," said the voice, very near now and reassuring.

"Can't we do anything—run away?"

"It's up to him," he said. "I'm just beginning to know him. I told him to wait for you. I don't know exactly what he's going to do. Go back out into space, maybe? Listen."

And, pressed together, inside a cave of flesh, surrounded by all those trees, that strange grass, and that hostile light, cutting like a scalpel into that palpitating paste of jet, they heard the approaching footsteps, distinct, stealthy, of the human killers who ringed them, fingers clenched on their copper lances, faces masked, ready to spew out a lethal grey mist . . . a broken branch, a liquid rustling, a stifled oath, a click.

The Man Who Lost the Sea

THEODORE STURGEON

Theodore Sturgeon (1918–1985) was a US writer of science fiction, fantasy, and horror, who was inducted into the Science Fiction and Fantasy Hall of Fame in 2000. At the height of his popularity in the 1950s, Sturgeon was among the most anthologized English-language authors alive. He won both the Hugo Award and Nebula Award. Sturgeon's best-known novel may be *More Than Human* (1953), winner of the International Fantasy Award. Moving beyond fiction, Sturgeon wrote more than one hundred book reviews and the screenplays for the highly regarded *Star Trek* episodes "Shore Leave" and "Amok Time," which are noted for their invention of several conventions of Vulcan culture, such as the Vulcan hand symbol, the Vulcan salutation "Live long and prosper," and pon farr, the Vulcan mating ritual.

Sturgeon's relationship to the world of science fiction was at times fraught during his career. His best work fit no particular category and he sometimes used story structures more familiar to mainstream literary readers. For example, even though he had work published in *Astounding Science Fiction*, Sturgeon felt more comfortable submitting work to the magazine *Unknown* than *Astounding*, because *Astounding* had a more restrictive remit. Although Sturgeon contributed to and helped shape John W. Campbell's "Golden Age of Science Fiction," he was much less comfortable in that mode than writers like A. E. van Vogt, Robert Heinlein, or Isaac Asimov. Sturgeon was much more of an influence on and precursor to writers like Harlan Ellison and Samuel R. Delany (and, later, the Humanists of the 1990s). Sturgeon's work could be overly sentimental at times, and he sometimes relied too heavily on exploring the angst of teenagers, but he also managed to plumb the depths of great passion and empathy for his characters—in a way uncommon to science fiction at the time.

Unknown folded and Sturgeon left the field for a brief time, after which his work caught on with newer markets like *Galaxy Science Fiction*, which published most of his best post-1950 fiction. Increasingly, Sturgeon felt free to write on more "adult" themes, including the then-taboo subject of homosexuality. Sex in all of its permutations interested Sturgeon intensely. (At one point, too, Sturgeon took to nudism; the writer and editor Thomas Monteleone first encountered Sturgeon, a literary hero, in this mode when he visited Sturgeon's apartment to conduct an interview.)

The lyrical "The Man Who Lost the Sea" (*The Magazine of Fantasy and Science Fiction*, 1959) pushed back against a romanticized, can-do vision of travel to the moon, while engaging in another kind of (deeper and more profound) romanticism. In one sense, "The Man Who Lost the Sea" renovates a particular astronaut trope in science fiction. But it also has elements in common with the stories by Delany and Knight in this volume that more sharply undercut Golden Age science fiction assumptions.

This story was also Arthur C. Clarke's favorite. In the introduction to *The Ultimate Egoist, Volume I: The Complete Stories of Theodore Sturgeon* (1994), Clarke wrote, "[It was] a small masterpiece . . . the one which had the greatest impact on me, for personal as well as literary reasons. I too lost the sea for many years, and only rediscovered it in later life . . . I can't even reread it without the skin crawling on the back of my neck."

THE MAN WHO LOST THE SEA

Theodore Sturgeon

Say you're a kid, and one dark night you're running along the cold sand with this helicopter in your hand, saying very fast witchy-witchy-witchy. You pass the sick man and he wants you to shove off with that thing. Maybe he thinks you're too old to play with toys. So you squat next to him in the sand and tell him it isn't a toy, it's a model. You tell him look here, here's something most people don't know about helicopters. You take a blade of the rotor in your fingers and show him how it can move in the hub, up and down a little, back and forth a little, and twist a little, to change pitch. You start to tell him how this flexibility does away with the gyroscopic effect, but he won't listen. He doesn't want to think about flying, about helicopters, or about you, and he most especially does not want explanations about anything by anybody. Not now. Now, he wants to think about the sea. So you go away.

The sick man is buried in the cold sand with only his head and his left arm showing. He is dressed in a pressure suit and looks like a man from Mars. Built into his left sleeve is a combination timepiece and pressure gauge, the gauge with a luminous blue indicator which makes no sense, the clock hands luminous red. He can hear the pounding of surf and the soft swift pulse of his pumps. One time long ago when he was swimming he went too deep and stayed down too long and came up too fast, and when he came to it was like this: they said, "Don't move, boy. You've got the bends. Don't even try to move." He had tried anyway. It hurt. So now, this time, he lies in the sand without moving, without trying.

His head isn't working right. But he knows clearly that it isn't working right, which is a strange thing that happens to people in shock sometimes. Say you were that kid, you could say how it was, because once you woke up lying in the gym office in high school and asked what had happened. They explained how you tried something on the parallel bars and fell on your head. You understood exactly, though you couldn't remember falling. Then a minute later you asked again what had happened and they told you. You understood it. And a minute later . . . forty-one times they told you, and you understood. It was just that no matter how many times they pushed it into your head, it wouldn't stick there; but all the while you *knew* that your head would start working again in time. And in time it did. . . . Of course, if you were that kid, always explaining things to people and to yourself, you wouldn't want to bother the sick man with it now.

Look what you've done already, making him send you away with that angry shrug of the mind (which, with the eyes, are the only things which will move just now). The motionless effort costs him a wave of nausea. He has felt seasick before but he has never *been* seasick, and the formula for that is to keep your eyes on the horizon and stay busy. Now! Then he'd better get busy—now; for there's one place especially not to be seasick in, and that's locked up in a pressure suit. Now!

So he busies himself as best he can, with the seascape, landscape, sky. He lies on high ground, his head propped on a vertical wall of black rock. There is another such outcrop before him, whip-topped with white sand and with smooth flat sand. Beyond and down is valley, salt flat, estuary; he cannot yet be sure. He is sure of the line of footprints, which begin behind him, pass to his left, disappear in the outcrop shadows, and reappear beyond to vanish at last into the shadows of the valley.

Stretched across the sky is old mourning-cloth, with starlight burning holes in it, and between the holes the black is absolute—wintertime, mountaintop sky-black.

(Far off on the horizon within himself, he sees the swell and crest of approaching nausea; he counters with an undertow of weakness, which meets and rounds and settles the wave before it can break. Get busier. Now.)

Burst in on him, then, with the X-15 model. That'll get him. Hey, how about this for a gimmick? Get too high for the thin air to give you any control, you have these little jets in the wingtips, see? and on the sides of the empennage: bank, roll, yaw, whatever, with squirts of compressed air.

But the sick man curls his sick lip: oh, git, kid, git, will you?—that has nothing to do with the sea. So you git.

Out and out the sick man forces his view, etching all he sees with a meticulous intensity, as if it might be his charge, one day, to duplicate all this. To his left is only starlit sea, windless. In front of him across the valley, rounded hills with dim white epaulettes of light. To his right, the jutting corner of the black wall against which his helmet rests. (He thinks the distant moundings of nausea becalmed, but he will not look yet.) So he scans the sky, black and bright, calling Sirius, calling Pleiades, Polaris, Ursa Minor, calling that . . . that . . . Why, it *moves*. Watch it: yes, it moves! It is a fleck of light, seeming to be wrinkled, fissured, rather like a chip of boiled cauliflower in the sky. (Of course, he knows better than to trust his own eyes just now.) But that movement . . .

As a child he had stood on cold sand in a frosty Cape Cod evening, watching Sputnik's steady spark rise out of the haze (madly, dawning a little north of west); and after that he had sleeplessly wound special coils for his receiver, risked his life restringing high antennas, all for the brief capture of an unreadable *tweetle-eep-tweetle* in his earphones from Vanguard, Explorer, Lunik, Discoverer, Mercury. He knew them all (well, some people collect match-covers, stamps) and he knew especially that unmistakable steady sliding in the sky.

This moving fleck was a satellite, and in a moment, motionless, uninstrumented but for his chronometer and his part-brain, he will know which one. (He is grateful beyond expression—without that sliding chip of light, there were only those footprints, those wandering footprints, to tell a man he was not alone in the world.)

Say you were a kid, eager and challengeable and more than a little bright, you might in a day or so work out a way to measure the period of a satellite with nothing but a timepiece and a brain; you might eventually see that the shadow in the rocks ahead had been there from the first only because of the light from the rising satellite. Now if you check the time exactly at the moment when the shadow on the sand is equal to the height of the outcrop, and time it again when the light is at the zenith and the shadow gone, you will multiply this number of minutes by eight—think why, now: horizon to zenith is one-fourth of the orbit, give or take a little, and halfway up the sky is half that quarter—and you will then know this satellite's period. You know all the periods—ninety minutes, two, two and a half hours; with that and the appearance of this bird, you'll find out which one it is.

But if you were that kid, eager or resourceful or whatever, you wouldn't jabber about it to the sick man, for not only does he not want to be bothered with you, he's thought of all that long since and is even now watching the shadows for that triangular split second of measurement. Now! His eyes drop to the face of his chronometer: 0400, near as makes no never mind.

He has minutes to wait now—ten? . . . thirty? . . . twenty-three?—while this baby moon eats up its slice of shadowpie; and that's too bad, the waiting, for though the inner sea is calm there are currents below, shadows that shift and swim. Be busy. Be busy. He must not swim near that great invisible amoeba, whatever happens: its first cold pseudopod is even now reaching for the vitals.

Being a knowledgeable young fellow, not quite a kid anymore, wanting to help the sick man too, you want to tell him everything you know about that cold-in-the-gut, that reaching invisible surrounding implacable amoeba. You know all about it—listen, you want to yell at him, don't let that touch of cold bother you. Just know what it is, that's all. Know what it is that is touching your gut. You want to tell him, listen:

Listen, this is how you met the monster and dissected it. Listen, you were skin-diving in the Grenadines, a hundred tropical shoal-water islands; you had a new blue snorkel mask, the kind with faceplate and breathing tube all in one, and new blue flippers on your feet, and a new blue speargun—all this new because you'd only begun, you see; you were a beginner, aghast with pleasure at your easy intrusion into this underwater otherworld. You'd been out in a boat, you were coming back, you'd just reached the mouth of the little bay, you'd taken the notion to swim the rest of the way. You'd said as much to the boys and slipped into the warm silky water. You brought your gun.

Not far to go at all, but then beginners find wet distances deceiving. For the first five minutes or so it was only delightful, the sun hot on your back and the water so warm it seemed not to have any temperature at all, and you were flying. With your face under the water, your mask was not so much attached as part of you, your wide blue flippers trod away yards, your gun rode all but weightless in your hand, the taut rubber sling making an occasional hum as your passage plucked it in the sunlit green. In your ears crooned the breathy monotone of the snorkel tube, and through the invisible disk of plate glass you saw wonders. The bay was shallow—ten, twelve feet or so—and sandy,

with great growths of brain-, bone-, and fire-coral, intricate waving sea-fans, and fish—such fish! Scarlet and green and aching azure, gold and rose and slate-color studded with sparks of enamel-blue, pink and peach and silver. And that *thing* got into you, that . . . monster.

There were enemies in this otherworld: the sand-colored spotted sea-snake with his big ugly head and turned-down mouth, who would not retreat but lay watching the intruder pass; and the mottled moray with jaws like bolt-cutters; and somewhere around, certainly, the barracuda with his undershot face and teeth turned inward so that he must take away whatever he might strike. There were urchins—the plump white sea-egg with its thick fur of sharp quills and the black ones with the long slender spines that would break off in unwary flesh and fester there for weeks; and filefish and stonefish with their poisoned barbs and lethal meat; and the stingaree who could drive his spike through a leg bone. Yet these were not *monsters*, and could not matter to you, the invader churning along above them all. For you were above them in so many ways—armed, rational, comforted by the close shore (ahead the beach, the rocks on each side) and by the presence of the boat not too far behind. Yet you were . . . attacked.

At first it was uneasiness, not pressing, but pervasive, a contact quite as intimate as that of the sea; you were sheathed in it. And also there was the touch—the cold inward contact. Aware of it at last, you laughed: for Pete's sake, what's there to be scared of?

The monster, the amoeba.

You raised your head and looked back in air. The boat had edged into the cliff at the right; someone was giving a last poke around for lobster. You waved at the boat; it was your gun you waved, and emerging from the water it gained its latent ounces so that you sank a bit, and as if you had no snorkel on, you tipped your head back to get a breath. But tipping your head back plunged the end of the tube underwater; the valve closed; you drew in a hard lungful of nothing at all. You dropped your face under;

up came the tube; you got your air, and along with it a bullet of seawater which struck you somewhere inside the throat. You coughed it out and floundered, sobbing as you sucked in air, inflating your chest until it hurt, and the air you got seemed no good, no good at all, a worthless devitalized inert gas.

You clenched your teeth and headed for the beach, kicking strongly and knowing it was the right thing to do; and then below and to the right you saw a great bulk mounding up out of the sand floor of the sea. You knew it was only the reef, rocks and coral and weed, but the sight of it made you scream; you didn't care what you knew. You turned hard left to avoid it, fought by as if it would reach for you, and you couldn't get air, couldn't get air, for all the unobstructed hooting of your snorkel tube. You couldn't bear the mask, suddenly, not for another second, so you shoved it upward clear of your mouth and rolled over, floating on your back and opening your mouth to the sky and breathing with a quacking noise.

It was then and there that the monster well and truly engulfed you, mantling you round and about within itself—formless, borderless, the illimitable amoeba. The beach, mere yards away, and the rocky arms of the bay, and the not-too-distant boat—these you could identify but no longer distinguish, for they were all one and the same thing . . . the thing called unreachable.

You fought that way for a time, on your back, dangling the gun under and behind you and straining to get enough warm sun-stained air into your chest. And in time some particles of sanity began to swirl in the roil of your mind, and to dissolve and tint it. The air pumping in and out of your square-grinned frightened mouth began to be meaningful at last, and the monster relaxed away from you.

You took stock, saw surf, beach, a leaning tree. You felt the new scend of your body as the rollers humped to become breakers. Only a dozen firm kicks brought you to where you could roll over and double up; your shin struck coral with a lovely agony and you stood in foam and waded ashore. You gained the wet sand, hard sand, and ultimately, with two more paces powered by bravado, you crossed the high-water mark and lay in the dry sand, unable to move.

You lay in the sand, and before you were able to move or to think, you were able to feel a triumph—a triumph because you were alive and knew that much without thinking at all.

When you were able to think, your first thought was of the gun, and the first move you were able to make was to let go at last of the thing. You had nearly died because you had not let it go before; without it you would not have been burdened and you would not have panicked. You had (you began to understand) kept it because someone else would have had to retrieve it—easily enough—and you could not have stood the laughter. You had almost died because They might laugh at you.

This was the beginning of the dissection, analysis, study of the monster. It began then; it had never finished. Some of what you had learned from it was merely important; some of the rest—vital.

You had learned, for example, never to swim farther with a snorkel than you could swim back without one. You learned never to burden yourself with the unnecessary in an emergency: even a hand or a foot might be as expendable as a gun; pride was expendable, dignity was. You learned never to dive alone, even if They laugh at you, even if you have to shoot a fish yourself and say afterward "we" shot it. Most of all, you learned that fear has many fingers, and one of them—a simple one, made of too great a concentration of carbon dioxide in your blood, as from too-rapid breathing in and out of the same tube—is not really fear at all but feels like fear, and can turn into panic and kill you.

Listen, you want to say, listen, there isn't anything wrong with such an experience or with all the study it leads to, because a man who can learn enough from it could become fit enough, cautious enough, foresighted, unafraid, modest, teachable enough to be chosen, to be qualified for . . .

You lose the thought, or turn it away, because the sick man feels that cold touch deep inside, feels it right now, feels it beyond ignoring, above and beyond anything that you, with all your experience and certainty, could explain to him even if he would listen, which he won't. Make him, then; tell him the cold touch is some simple explainable thing like anoxia, like gladness even: some triumph that he will be able to appreciate when his head is working right again.

Triumph? Here he's alive after . . . whatever it is, and that doesn't seem to be triumph enough, though it was in the Grenadines, and that other time, when he got the bends, saved his own life, saved two other lives. Now, somehow, it's not the same: there seems to be a reason why just being alive afterward isn't a triumph.

Why not triumph? Because not twelve, not twenty, not even thirty minutes is it taking the satellite to complete its eighth-of-an-orbit: fifty minutes are gone, and still there's a slice of shadow yonder. It is this, this which is placing the cold finger upon his heart, and he doesn't know why, he doesn't know why, he will not know why; he is afraid he shall when his head is working again. . . .

Oh, where's the kid? Where is any way to busy the mind, apply it to something, anything else but the watch hand which outruns the moon? Here, kid: come over here—what you got there?

If you were the kid, then you'd forgive everything and hunker down with your new model, not a toy, not a helicopter or a rocket-plane, but the big one, the one that looks like an overgrown cartridge. It's so big, even as a model, that even an angry sick man wouldn't call it a toy. A giant cartridge, but watch: the lower four-fifths is Alpha—all muscle—over a million pounds thrust. (Snap it off, throw it away.) Half the rest is Beta—all brains—it puts you on your way. (Snap it off, throw it away.) And now look at the polished fraction which is

left. Touch a control somewhere and see—see? it has wings—wide triangular wings. This is Gamma, the one with wings, and on its back is a small sausage; it is a moth with a sausage on its back. The sausage (click! it comes free) is Delta. Delta is the last, the smallest: Delta is the way home.

What will they think of next? Quite a toy. Quite a toy. Beat it, kid. The satellite is almost overhead, the sliver of shadow going—going—almost gone and . . . gone.

Check: 0459. Fifty-nine minutes? give or take a few. Times eight . . . 472 . . . is, uh, 7 hours 52 minutes.

Seven hours fifty-two minutes? Why, there isn't a satellite round Earth with a period like that. In all the solar system there's only . . .

The cold finger turns fierce, implacable.

The east is paling and the sick man turns to it, wanting the light, the sun, an end to questions whose answers couldn't be looked upon. The sea stretches endlessly out to the growing light, and endlessly, somewhere out of sight, the surf roars. The paling east bleaches the sandy hilltops and throws the line of footprints into aching relief. That would be the buddy, the sick man knows, gone for help. He cannot at the moment recall who the buddy is, but in time he will, and meanwhile the footprints make him less alone.

The sun's upper rim thrusts itself above the horizon with a flash of green, instantly gone. There is no dawn, just the green flash and then a clear white blast of unequivocal sunup. The sea could not be whiter, more still, if it were frozen and snow-blanketed. In the west, stars still blaze, and overhead the crinkled satellite is scarcely abashed by the growing light. A formless jumble in the valley below begins to resolve itself into a sort of tent city, or installation of some kind, with tubelike and sail-like buildings. This would have meaning for the sick man if his head were working right. Soon, it would. Will. (Oh . . .)

The sea, out on the horizon just under the rising sun, is behaving strangely, for in that place where properly belongs a pool of unbearable brightness, there is instead a notch of brown. It is as if the white fire of the sun is drinking dry the sea—for look, look! the notch becomes a bow and the bow a crescent, racing ahead of the sunlight, white sea ahead of it and behind it a cocoa-dry stain spreading across and down toward where he watches.

Beside the finger of fear which lies on him, another finger places itself, and another, making ready for that clutch, that grip, that ultimate insane squeeze of panic. Yet beyond that again, past that squeeze when it comes, to be savored if the squeeze is only fear and not panic, lies triumph—triumph, and a glory. It is perhaps this which constitutes his whole battle: to fit himself, prepare himself to bear the utmost that fear could do, for if he can do that, there is a triumph on the other side. But . . . not yet. Please, not yet awhile.

Something flies (or flew, or will fly—he is a little confused on this point) toward him, from the far right where the stars still shine. It is not a bird and it is unlike any aircraft on Earth, for the aerodynamics are wrong. Wings so wide and so fragile would be useless, would melt and tear away in any of Earth's atmosphere but the outer fringes. He sees then (because he prefers to see it so) that it is the kid's model, or part of it, and for a toy it does very well indeed.

It is the part called Gamma, and it glides in, balancing, parallels the sand and holds away, holds away slowing, then, settles, all in slow motion, throwing up graceful sheet-fountains of fine sand from its skids. And it runs along the ground for an impossible distance, letting down its weight by the ounce and stingily the ounce, until *look out* until a skid *look out* fits itself into a bridged crevasse *look out, look out!* and still moving on, it settles down to the struts. Gamma then, tired, digs her wide left wingtip carefully into the racing sand, digs it in hard; and as the wing breaks off, Gamma slews, sidles, slides slowly, pointing her other triangular tentlike wing at the sky, and broadside crushes into the rocks at the valley's end.

As she rolls smashing over, there breaks from her broad back the sausage, the little Delta, which somersaults away to break its back upon the rocks, and through the broken hull spill smashed shards of graphite from the moderator of her power pile. *Look out! Look out!* and at the same instant from the finally checked mass of Gamma there explodes a doll, which slides and tumbles into the sand, into the rocks and smashed hot graphite from the wreck of Delta.

The sick man numbly watches this toy destroy itself: what will they think of next?—and with a gelid horror prays at the doll lying in the raging rubble of the atomic pile: *Don't stay there, man—get away! get away! that's hot, you know?* But it seems like a night and a day and half another night before the doll staggers to its feet and, clumsy in its pressure suit, runs away up the valleyside, climbs a sand-topped outcrop, slips, falls, lies under a slow cascade of cold ancient sand until, but for an arm and the helmet, it is buried.

The sun is high now, high enough to show the sea is not a sea, but brown plain with the frost burned off it, as now it burns away from the hills, diffusing in air and blurring the edges of the sun's disk, so that in a very few minutes there is no sun at all, but only a glare in the east. Then the valley below loses its shadows, and, like an arrangement in a diorama, reveals the form and nature of the wreckage below: no tent city this, no installation, but the true real ruin of Gamma and the eviscerated hulk of Delta. (Alpha was the muscle, Beta the brain; Gamma was a bird, but Delta, Delta was the way home.)

And from it stretches the line of footprints, to and by the sick man, above to the bluff, and gone with the sandslide which had buried him there. Whose footprints?

He knows whose, whether or not he knows that he knows, or wants to or not. He knows what satellite has (give or take a bit) a period like that (want it exactly?—it's 7:66 hours). He knows what world has such a night, and such a frosty glare by day. He knows these things as he knows how spilled radioactives will pour the crash and mutter of surf into a man's earphones.

Say you were that kid: say, instead, at last, that you are the sick man, for they are the same; surely then you can understand why of all things, even while shattered, shocked, sick with radiation calculated (leaving) radiation computed (arriving) and radiation past all bearing (lying in the wreckage of Delta) you would want to think of the sea. For no farmer who fingers the soil with love and knowledge, no poet who sings of it, artist, contractor, engineer, even child bursting into tears at the inexpressible beauty of a field of daffodils—none of these is as intimate with Earth as those who live on, live with, breathe, and drift in its seas. So of these things you must think; with these you must dwell until you are less sick and more ready to face the truth.

The truth, then, is that the satellite fading here is Phobos, that those footprints are your own, that there is no sea here, that you have crashed and are killed and will in a moment be dead. The cold hand ready to squeeze and still your heart is not anoxia or even fear, it is death. Now, if there is something more important than this, now is the time for it to show itself.

The sick man looks at the line of his own footprints, which testify that he is alone, and at the wreckage below, which states that there is no way back, and at the white east and the mottled west and the paling flecklike satellite above. Surf sounds in his ears. He hears his pumps. He hears what is left of his breathing. The cold clamps down and folds him round past measuring, past all limit.

Then he speaks, cries out: then with joy he takes his triumph at the other side of death, as one takes a great fish, as one completes a skilled and mighty task, rebalances at the end of some great daring leap; and as he used to say "we shot a fish" he uses no "I":

"God," he cries, dying on Mars, "God, we made it!"

The Waves

SILVINA OCAMPO

Translated by Marian Womack

Silvina Ocampo (1903–1993) was an influential Argentine writer, translator, and playwright who published more than twenty books of poetry, fiction, and children's stories. Born into an elite Buenos Aires family, she studied art in Paris with Fernand Léger and the surrealist painter Giorgio de Chirico. Italo Calvino wrote of Ocampo, "I don't know of another writer who better captures the magic inside everyday rituals, the forbidden or hidden face that our mirrors don't show us." The first of seven short story collections, *Viaje olvidado* (*Forgotten Journey*), appeared in 1937, and her first collection of poetry, *Enumeración de la patria* (*Enumeration of the Homeland*), appeared in 1942. Other story collections include *Las invitadas* (*The Guests*, 1961), *La furia* (*The Fury*, 1999), *Y así sucesivamente* (*And So Forth*, 1987), and *Cornelia frente al espejo* (*Cornelia Before the Mirror*, 1988). A prolific translator, Ocampo brought works by Dickinson, Poe, Melville, and Swedenborg into the Spanish language.

Along with her friend Jorge Luis Borges and her husband, Adolfo Bioy Casares, Ocampo came to epitomize proto–magic realist Latin American fantastical literature, a form later made famous by, among others, Julio Cortázar and Gabriel García Márquez. Her sister Victoria Ocampo founded and edited *Sur*, and many of Silvina Ocampo's literary works appeared in that august journal. Silvina Ocampo also coedited the classic *Antología de la literatura fantástica* (1940) with Borges and Bioy, later published in English as *The Book of Fantasy* (1988).

In the two decades since her death, Ocampo's reputation in Latin America has grown tremendously. Many previously unpublished works—including stories, a verse autobiography, aphorisms, and a novel—have been published in Argentina. Critical essays about Ocampo have appeared widely in Spanish, English, and French, and her work has been adapted for the theater and the screen. Ocampo's writing has recently become more widely known in English, with the release from New York Review of Books Classics of *Silvina Ocampo* (2014), selected poems translated by Jason Weiss, and *Thus Were Their Faces*, collected stories translated by Daniel Balderston, with an introduction by Helen Oyeyemi and a preface by Borges. *Silvina Ocampo* was the first English translation of her poetry, compared by Oyeyemi to the work of William Blake. Ocampo's verse often verges on the phantasmagorical and surreal. *Thus Were Their Faces*—dark, gothic, fantastic, and grotesque—includes a mysterious and previously unpublished novella, "The Imposter."

In her introduction to *Thus Were Their Faces*, Ocampo writes, "Am I an outsider or liar, a giant or a dwarf, Spanish dancer or an acrobat? When you write, everything is possible, even the very opposite of what you are. I write so that other people can discover what they should love, and sometimes so they discover what I love." She also notes that she fought with her teacher de Chirico over the way he "sacrificed everything for color" and that she turned away from painting to writing so she could more clearly see "the forms amid the color."

"The Waves" (1959), published here in English for the first time, might be Ocampo's only outright science fiction story, a dreamlike future fable that also comments on the present. It is particularly interesting for portraying in a few short pages a dystopia of progress, along with ideas verging on the surreal, like the abolition of countries and wars played out using atmospheric disturbances like storms or droughts.

THE WAVES

Silvina Ocampo

Translated by Marian Womack

Will you only believe the lies? And for how long? How happy the time when it was enough for two people to love one another or even feel sympathy for one another, for them to be allowed to live together or spend time together. The moon was a mysterious satellite a long way away, like America before Columbus. I curse Miss Lina Zfanseld, who in the winter of 1975 lent her overcoat to Mrs. Rosa Tilda. I happened to read her biography yesterday in the little medical dictionary I carry around with me. Because of that damn overcoat, because of Lina Zfanseld's liveliness, we have to suffer this separation, this misunderstanding. If apathetic old Mrs. Rosa Tilda hadn't been so apathetic, if Miss Lina Zfanseld hadn't been so lively, if the old camel-hair overcoat hadn't so perfectly transmitted the waves from one organism to another, if that horrid electron microscope hadn't existed to reveal the order of our molecules, that tool that doctors today use like children used to use kaleidoscopes, then we wouldn't be in this situation.

You see what kind of intricate intrigues, what tiny details are the drivers of discovery; the coincidences that drive the misfortunes and customs that human beings end up taking on. We're like a flock of sheep, obeying the most subtle or most evident orders for the good of society. Blindly, so as to avoid being punished, we fulfill our civic duties and when we think about them and decide to evade them, we end up in trouble. Sometimes it makes me laugh to think that if Mrs. Rosa Tilda had not been undergoing medical treatment for her depression, because her depression stopped her from going to work every day, no one would have noticed that it was the coat that transformed her, and the price of camel hair, at the time out of fashion, would not have shot through the roof. But there was one doctor, they say, with the soul of a researcher, who studied the case and won, undeservedly in my opinion, fame and riches.

I should have been born in a different era, as long as you could have been there with me too. Until 1975, the world was bearable. We are the victims of what some call progress. Wars are now waged via floods and drought, via earthquakes, via sudden plague, via rapid changes in temperature; it is rare for a drop of blood to be spilled, but that doesn't mean we suffer less than our predecessors. How many young men now dream of dying on the field of battle, after gunplay with the enemy across the front line? It's only natural that they want some individual gratification.

But I can communicate with you via this small metal contraption (like an old television set): I see your mirrored face and hear your voice; you receive my daily messages and the reflection of my image. Savages from back in 1930 (and there are still some of them around) would think that we were living in a magical world, but if I could talk to them I would say: "Don't fool yourselves, I'm much more unhappy than you were, you who had no television." Just like those rodents who bury food for their offspring, I am leaving these messages for our descendants. So you're off on the moon, working in the mines with all the comforts and respect due to your position, and I'm down on Earth keeping an eye on you, hidden so that the authorities don't find me and give me drugs to forget you . . . all of this will seem unhappy enough for the people in the future who decipher our messages.

I find it obscene that countries have fallen apart and people are now organized on the basis of the order of their molecules and the waves they emit. I suppose I must just be old-fashioned. When I think of how I was when I was seven years old, I shudder. The prohibitions began after the massacre of the children in that school in Massachusetts, the fire in the Nippon Circus in Tokyo, and the armed robberies in the public gardens of England and Germany. It was not lone individuals who committed these crimes, but some combination of their molecules, and other weird things like that which I barely understand. Full-color photographs of Lina Zfanseld and Rosa Tilda appeared in all the newspapers, got stuck up on walls, proclaiming them the saviors of humanity. Severe measures were taken: the first had to do with travel. People from group A couldn't travel with those from group B, people from group B couldn't travel with those from group C, and so on. (How horrid it was for me to see the photograph of my molecules next to my face in the passport!) Families were divided. Homes were destroyed. I'm not making all this up, am I? They founded villages filled with people who were in no way connected to one another. There were several suicides: most of them were people in love, or else pupils and teachers who didn't want their groups broken up. I heard of a case of some children I knew, eleven years old, and another of two engineering students, because friendships are as passionate as romantic love. But you and I could never agree on that point.

When we decided to falsify our documents, we were happy, why shouldn't we still be happy if it weren't that they've separated us? Nothing was going to stop us from being happy. You think that it's all over between us, but you're wrong. Did you spend all your money on bribes? I've heard about it, there's no need to rub it in.

Do you remember that beautiful summer morning when we went up the stairs in Truth Square? We had our documents in our hands. In the certificate we received from the Ministry of Health, your waves were a perfect match for mine. After going to the prescribed hospitals for our tests, we stopped at the foot of the monument, the statue of large-eyed Truth, sparkling like spun sugar. We sat by the marble plinth, we kissed and ate raspberry ice cream. For a few days, we believed that we weren't hurting each other, and made plans for the future. The certificate seemed so powerful that we didn't argue once in five days. My touch didn't repel you as it usually did, my voice didn't reverberate in your dreams, didn't fill you with that strange dread. Your eyes, when you stared at me, didn't confuse me or make me lose my thoughts, as if I were an automaton. My self didn't disappear in your arms as it usually did. We lived some kind of miracle. As if we had never tried to lie to the state, as if we were obeying its rules and laws. Who cares that the document was a fraud, and that our waves didn't match? We were already changing to match the official documents that we so much despised. We were made for each other, we were legally in love, and nothing could come between us.

But there is always someone who tells the truth, and if the truth sets some people free, then it condemns others. It was an enemy of mine who gave us away. They separated us and exiled you. Before you left, they told you that it had been me who had confessed the truth, because I was repentant: I had recognized my mistake and my shame. You believed them. That I have taken myself away from the world to live in this cave doesn't move you; that I flee mankind to be able to communicate with you: none of this is sufficient proof of my love to you. Our misunderstandings continue. I think that our love was born of a misunderstanding, and I fear that this was what ruined us.

"Love that which helps you. Abandon that which harms you," is inscribed above the doors of all the hospitals. "Check your wavelength." I don't want to hear anything more about waves or organisms.

I remember with horror the tales of crimes of passion told to me by doctors when they were trying to set my mind straight.

I've met a scientist (he might be a fraud) who claims that via a simple operation he can insert me into your group. My messages will stop for a few days and maybe my dog will look into the metal mirror while I'm away. Say "Go to your basket" or "Drink some water" or "Poor little pooch" to console him. The operation is all I can think of. I dream of it day and night. It's not clear how much I will have to suffer, which anaesthetic they will give me, or where the incisions will be made. I am committed to belonging to your wavegroup, and being able to live with you normally. Obviously there is a risk that my personality will change, and it remains to be seen if you will like my new self. I could become a mouse or a paving stone. I shouldn't think about all the dangers: that would drive me crazy. If this last attempt is a failure, I will pay for it with my life, and that would be the best way to go if it turns out that I have been cheated.

After the operation my plan is to get onto an interplanetary flight and discreetly head to your world. I will learn to walk on air, so people will think that I am an angel or a goddess from Greek mythology, one of the ones you compared me with when you believed in my honesty, my beauty, in my love.

Plenitude

WILL WORTHINGTON

Will Mohler was or is a US writer who wrote under the pseudonym of Will Worthington, leaving a legacy of only about a dozen short stories published in the late 1950s and early 1960s. Not much has been written about Worthington; indeed, not much is known about him other than he burst into the field in the late 1950s after working for the government for many years; his first three stories were published in 1959, including "Plenitude." His last published short story was in 1963 and nothing more has been heard from him since. Both Mohler's birth date and possible date of death are unknown.

A few author notes from his appearances in *The Magazine of Fantasy and Science Fiction* provide rather contradictory information: "Mr. Will Mohler, who knows his adventurous bachelor hero quite well, describes himself as a 'hermit without a cave.' 'Confirmation of the existence of the author,' he continues, 'is still pending.'" In another note, the author "warns that he 'has met the protagonist of this story on many docks, in railroad stations and at airfields, but just as often on ships at sea, on overseas flights, exploring the precincts of Buddhist temples, climbing mountains with snow on them.'"

Yet another note indicates the author "lives in Washington, DC, and is a gargoyle." But perhaps it is best to move on from investigating Worthington's life with the following note: "As of this writing, Will Worthington is living on a wild island off the coast of Maine, where he is leading a Thoreau-like existence which will inspire him, it is to be hoped, to more stories like the following."

"Plenitude" is a rather unique postapocalyptic tale that splits humanity into two groups with different views of the world. In its peculiar imagery, trippy feel, and unique structure it presages the feel of 1970s classics like *Logan's Run*. "Plenitude" was originally published in *The Magazine of Fantasy and Science Fiction* and reprinted in several best-of anthologies. Judith Merril included the story in her fifth annual *The Year's Best S-F* (1960) and praised Worthington's "freshness of language and vigor of thought."

PLENITUDE

Will Worthington

"Why can't we go home now, Daddy?" asked Mike, the youngest, and the small tanned face I saw there in the skimpy shade of the olive tree was mostly a matter of eyes—all else, hair, cheeks, thumb-sized mouth, jelly-bean body, and usually flailing arms and legs, were mere accessories to the round, blue, endlessly wondering *eyes*. (*"The Wells of 'Why'"* . . . It would make a poem, I thought, if a poem were needed, and if I wasn't so damned tired. And I also thought, "Oh, God! It begins. Five years old. No, not quite. Four.")

"Because Daddy has to finish weeding this row of beans," I said. "We'll go back to the house in a little while."

I would go back to the house and then I would follow the path around the rocks to the hot springs, and there I would peel off what was left of my clothes and I would soak myself in the clear but pungent water that came bubbling—perfect—from a cleft in the rocks to form a pool in the hollow of a pothole—also perfect. And while I steeped in the mineral water I could think about the fish which was soon to be broiling on the fire, and I could think of Sue turning it, poking at it, and sprinkling herbs over it as though it was the first or perhaps the last fish that would ever be broiled and eaten by human creatures. She would perform that office with the same total and unreserved dedication with which, since sunup, she had scraped deerskin, picked worms from new cabbage-leaves, gathered firewood, caulked the walls of the cabin where the old chinking had fallen away or been chewed or knocked away by other hungry or merely curious creatures, and otherwise filled in the numberless gaps in the world—trivial things mostly which would not be noticed and

could not become great things in a man's eyes unless she were to go away or cease to be. I don't think of this because, for all immediate purposes—there are no others—she is the first Woman in the world and quite possibly—the last.

"Why don't we live in the Old House in the valley, Daddy?"

It is All-Eyes again. Make no mistake about it; there is a kind of connectedness between the seemingly random questions of very small kids. These are the problems posed by an ur-logic which is much closer to the pulse of reality than are any of the pretentious, involuted systems and the mincing nihilations and category-juggling of adults. It is we who are confused and half-blinded with the varieties of special knowledge. But how to explain? What good is my experience to him?

"There are too many old things in the Old House which don't work," I say, even as I know that I merely open the floodgates of further questions.

"Don't the funny men work, Daddy? I want to see the funny men! Daddy, I want . . ."

The boy means the robots. I took him down to see the Old House in the valley once before. He rode on top of my haversack and hung on to my hair with his small fingers. It was all a lark for him. I had gone to fetch some books—gambling that there might be a bagful of worthwhile ones that had not been completely eaten by bugs and mice; and if the jaunt turned out depressing for me, it was my fault, which is to say the fault of memory and the habit of comparing what has been with what is—natural, inevitable, unavoidable, but oh, God, just the same . . . The robots which still stood on their

396

size-thirty metal feet looked like grinning Mexican mummies. They gave me a bad turn even though I knew what they were, and should have known what changes to expect after a long, long absence from that house, but to the kid they were a delight. Never mind transphenomenality of rusted surfaces and uselessly dangling wires; never mind the history of a senile generation. They were the funny men. I wish I could leave it at that, but of course I can't. I hide my hoe in the twigs of the olive tree and pick up Mike. This stops the questions for a while.

"Let's go home to Mummy," I say; and also, hoping to hold back the questions about the Old House long enough to think of some real answers, "Now aren't you glad we live up here where we can see the ocean and eagles and hot springs?"

"Yeth," says Mike firmly by way of making a querulous and ineffectual old man feel better about his decision. What a comfort to me the little one is!

I see smoke coming from the chimney, and when we round the last turn in the path we see the cabin. Sue waves from the door. She has worked like a squaw since dawn, and she smiles and waves. I can remember when women would exhaust themselves talking over the phone and eating bonbons all day and then fear to smile when their beat husbands came home from their respective nothing-foundries lest they crack the layers of phony "youthful glow" on their faces. Not like Sue. Here is Sue with smudges of charcoal on her face and fish scales on her leather pants. Her scent is of wood smoke and of sweat. There is no artificial scent like this—none more endearing nor more completely "correct." There was a time when the odor of perspiration would have been more of a social disaster for a woman than the gummata of tertiary pox. Even men were touched by this strange phobia.

Sue sees the question on my face and she knows why my smile is a little perfunctory and strained.

"Chris . . . ?" I start to ask finally.

"No. He took his bow and his sleeping bag. Muttered something about an eight-point buck."

We do not *need* the venison. If anything has been made exhaustively and exhaustingly clear to the boy it is that our blessings consist in large part of what we do not need. But this is not the point, and I know it is not the point.

"Do you think he'll ever talk to me again, Sue?"

"Of course he will." She pulls off my sweaty shirt and hands me a towel. "You know how twelve is. Everything in Technicolor and with the throbbiest possible background music. Everything drags or jumps or swings or everything is Endsville or something else which it actually isn't. If it can't be turned into a drama it doesn't exist. He'll get over it."

I can think of no apt comment. Sue starts to busy herself with the fire, then turns back to me.

"You did the best thing. You did what you had to do, that's all. Go take your bath. I'm getting hungry."

I make my way up the path to the hot springs and I am wearing only the towel and the soles of an ancient pair of sneakers held on with thongs. I am thinking that the hot water will somehow dissolve the layers of sickly thought that obscure all the colors of the world from my mind, just as it will rid me of the day's accretion of grime, but at once I know that I am yielding to a vain and superstitious hope. I can take no real pleasure in the anticipation of my bath.

When I emerge from the underbrush and come in sight of the outcroppings of rock where the springs are, I can see Sato, our nearest neighbor and my oldest friend, making his way along the path from his valley on the other side of the mountain. I wave at him, but he does not wave back. I tell myself that he is concentrating on his feet and simply does not see me, but myself answers back in much harsher terms. Sato knows what happened when I took my older son to the City, and he knows why my son has not spoken more than a dozen coherent words since returning. He knows what I have done, and while it is not in the man's nature to rebuke another or set himself above another or mouth moral platitudes, there are limits.

Sato is some kind of a Buddhist. Only vaguely and imperfectly do I understand what this implies; not being unnecessarily explicit about itself is certainly a part of that doctrine. But there is also the injunction against killing. And I am—notwithstanding every meretricious attempt of my own mind to convert that fact into something more comfortable—a killer. And so . . . I may now contemplate what it will mean not merely to have lost my older son, but also the priceless, undemanding, and yet immeasurably rewarding friendship of the family in the next valley.

"It was not intentional," I tell myself as I lower my griminess and weariness into the hot water. "It was necessary. How else explain why we chose . . . ?" But it isn't worth a damn. I might as well mumble Tantric formulae. The water feels lukewarm—*used*.

I go on flaying myself in this manner. I return to the house and sit down to supper. The food I had looked forward to so eagerly tastes like raw fungus or my old sneakers. Nothing Sue says helps, and I even find myself wishing she would go to hell with her vitamin-enriched cheerfulness.

On our slope of the mountain the darkness comes as it must come to a lizard which is suddenly immured in a cigar box. Still no sign of Chris and so, of course, the pumas are more vocal than they have been all year. I itemize and savor every disaster that roars, rumbles, creeps, slithers, stings, crushes, or bites: everything from rattlers to avalanches, and I am sure that one or all of these dire things will befall Chris before the night is over. I go outside every time I hear a sound—which is often—and I squint at the top of the ridge and into the valley below. No Chris.

Sue, from her bunk, says, "If you don't stop torturing yourself, you'll be in no condition to

do anything if it *does* become necessary." She is right, of course, which makes me mad as hell on top of everything else. I lie on my bunk and for the ten millionth time reconstruct the whole experience:

We had been hacking at elder bushes, Chris and I. It had been a wet winter and clearing even enough land for a garden out of the encroaching vegetation began to seem like trying to hold back the sea with trowels. This problem and the gloomy knowledge that we had about one hatful of beans left in the cabin had conspired to produce a mood in which nothing but hemlock could grow. And I'd about had it with the questions. Chris had started the "Why" routine at about the same age as little Mike, but the questions, instead of leveling off as the boy began to exercise his own powers of observation and deduction, merely became more involved and challenging.

The worst thing about this was that I could not abdicate: other parents in other times could fluff off the questions of their kids with such hopeless and worthless judgments as "Well, that's how things *are*," thereby implying that both the questioner and the questioned are standing passively at the dead end of a chain of historical cause, or are existentially trapped in the eye of a storm of supernal origin, or are at the nexus of a flock of processes arising out of the choices of too many other agencies to pinpoint and blame definitively . . . *our* life, on the other hand, was clearly and in every significant particular our own baby. It did not merely proceed out of one particular historical choice, complete with foreseeable contingencies, but was an entire fabric of choices—*ours*. Here was total responsibility, complete with crowding elder bushes, cold rain, chiggers, rattlers, bone-weariness, and mud. I had elected to live it— even to impose it upon my progeny—and I was prepared for its hardships, but what galled me was having to justify it.

"The people in the City don't have to do

this, do they?" ("This" is grubbing out elder bushes, and he is right. The people in the City do not have to do *this*. They do not have to hunt, fish, gather, or raise their own food. They do not have to build their own cabins, carry their own water from springs, or fashion their own clothes from the skins of beautiful, murdered—by me—animals. They do not have to perspire. One of these days I will have to explain that they do not even have to sleep with their own wives. *That* of itself should be the answer of answers, but twelve is not yet ready; twelve cares about things with wheels, things which spin, roar, roll, fly, explode, exude noise and stench. Would that twelve were fourteen!)

In the meantime it is *dig—hack—heave; dig—hack—heave!* "Come on, Chris! It isn't sundown yet."

"Why couldn't we bring an old tractor up here in pieces and put it together and fix it up and find oil and . . ." (I try to explain for the fifty millionth time that you do not simply "fix up" something which is the outgrowth of an enormous Organization of interdependent Organizations, the fruit of a dead tree, as it were. The wheel will not be turned back. The kid distrusts abstractions and generalities, and I don't blame him, but God I'm tired!) "Let's just clear off this corner by the olive tree, Chris, and then we'll knock off for the day."

"Are we *better* than the City people?"

(This one hit a nerve. "Better" is a judgment made by people after the fact of their own decisions. Or there isn't any "Better." As for the Recalcitrants, of which vague class of living creatures we are members, they were and are certainly both more and less *something* than the others were—the City people—the ones who elected to Go Along with the Organization. Of all the original Recalcitrant families, I would guess that not 10 percent are now alive. I would if I had any use for statistics. If these people had something in common, you would have to go light-years away to find a name for it. I think it was a common lack of something—a disease perhaps. Future generations will take credit for it and refer to their origins as Fine Old Stock. I think most of them were crazy. I am glad they were, but most of them were just weird. Southern California. I have told Chris about the Peters family. They were going to make it on nothing but papaya juice and stewed grass augmented by East Indian breathing exercises. Poor squittered-out souls! Their corpses were like balsa wood. Better? What is Better? Grandfather was going to live on stellar emanations and devote his energies to whittling statues out of fallen redwoods. Thank Nature his stomach had other ideas! And God I'm tired and fed up!)

"Dammit, boy! Tomorrow I'll *take* you to the City and let you answer your own questions!"

And I did. Sue protested and old Sato just gave me that look which said, "I'm not saying anything," but I *did*.

The journey to the City is necessarily one which goes from bad to worse. As a deer and a man in the wilderness look for downward paths and lush places if they would find a river, the signs which lead to the centers of human civilization are equally recognizable.

You look for ugliness and senselessness. It is that simple. Look for places which have been overlaid with mortar so that nothing can grow or change at its will. Look for things which have been fashioned at great expense of time and energy and then discarded. Look for tin and peeling paint, for rusted metal, broken neon tubing, drifts and drifts of discarded containers—cans, bottles, papers. Look for flies and let your nose lead you where it would rather not go.

What is the difference between the burrow of a fox and a huge sheet-metal hand which bears the legend, in peeling, garish paint: THIS WAY TO PERPETUAL PARMENIDEAN PALACES . . . ? I do not know why one is better than the other, or *if* it is. I know that present purposes—purposes of intellect—lead one way, and intuition leads the other. So we resist intuition, and the path of greatest resistance leads us from one vast, crumbling, frequently stinking artifact or monument to another.

Chris is alternately nauseated and thrilled. He wants to stay in the palatial abandoned houses in the outskirts, but I say no. For one thing, the rats look like Doberman pinschers and for another . . . well, never mind what it is that repels me.

Much of the City looks grand until we come close enough to see where cement and plaster, paint and plastic have sloughed away to reveal ruptured tubes and wires which gleam where their insulation has rotted away, and which are connected to nothing with any life in it. We follow a monorail track which is a silver thread seen from a distance, but which has a continuous ridge of rust and bird droppings along its upper surface as far as the eye can see. We see more of the signs which point to the PERPETUAL PARMENIDEAN PALACES, and we follow them, giving our tormented intuition a rest even while for our eyes and our spirits there is no relief.

When we first encounter life we are not sure that it *is* life.

"They look like huge grapes!" exclaims Chris when we find them, clustered about a central tower in a huge sunken place like a stadium. The P. P. Palaces are indeed like huge grapes—reddish, semitransparent, about fifteen feet in diameter, or perhaps twenty. I am not used to measuring spaces in such terms anymore. The globes are connected to the central tower, or stem, by means of thick cables . . . their umbilicals. A high, wire-mesh fence surrounds the area, but here and there the rust has done its work in spite of zinc coating on the wire. With the corn knife I have brought to defend us from the rats and God knows what, I open a place in the fence. We are trespassing, and we know this, but we have come this far.

"Where are the people?" asks Chris, and I see that he looks pale. He has asked the question reluctantly, as though preferring no answer. I give none. We come close to one of the spheres, feeling that we do the wrong thing and doing it anyway. I see our objective and I point. It is a family of them, dimly visible like floating plants in an uncleaned aquarium. It is their frightened eyes we first see.

I do not know very much about the spheres except from hearsay and dim memory. The contents, including the occupants, are seen only dimly, I know, because the outer skins of the thing are filled with a self-replenishing liquid nutrient which requires the action of the sun and is augmented by the waste products of the occupants. We look closer, moving so that the sun is directly behind the sphere, revealing its contents in sharper outline.

"Those are not real people," says Chris. Now he looks a little sick. "What are all those tubes and wires for if they're real people? Are they robots or dolls or what?"

I do not know the purpose of all the tubes and wires myself. I do know that some are connected with veins in their arms and legs, others are nutrient enemata and for collection of body wastes, still others are only mechanical tentacles which support and endlessly fondle and caress. I know that the wires leading to the metal caps on their heads are part of an invention more voracious and terrible than the ancient television—direct stimulation of certain areas of the brain, a constant running up and down the diapason of pleasurable sensation, controlled by a sort of electronic kaleidoscope.

My imagination stops about here. It would be the ultimate artificiality, with nothing of reality about it save endless variation. Of senselessness I will not think. I do not know if they see constantly shifting masses or motes of color, or smell exotic perfumes, or hear unending and constantly swelling music. I think not. I doubt that they even experience anything so immediate and yet so amorphous as the surge and recession of orgasm or the gratification of thirst being quenched. It would be stimulation without real stimulus; ultimate removal from reality. I decide not to speak of this to Chris. He has had enough. He has seen the wires and the tubes.

I have never sprung such abstractions as

"Dignity" upon the boy. What good are such absolutes on a mountainside? If there is Dignity in grubbing out weeds and planting beans, those pursuits must be more dignified *than* something, because, like all words, it is a meaningless wisp of lint once removed from its relativistic fabric. The word does not exist until he invents it himself. The hoe and the rocky soil or the nutrient enema and the electronic ecstasy: he must judge for himself. That is why I have brought him here.

"Let's get away from here," he says. "Let's go home!"

"Good," I say, but even as I say it I can see that the largest of the pallid creatures inside the "grape" is doing something—I cannot tell what—and to my surprise it seems capable of enough awareness of us to become alarmed. What frightening creatures we must be—dirty, leather clothes with patches of dried animal blood on them, my beard and the small-boy grime of Chris! Removed as I am from these helpless aquarium creatures, I cannot blame them. But my compassion was a short-lived thing. Chris screamed.

I turned in time to see what can only be described as a huge metal scorpion rushing at Chris with its tail lashing, its fore-claws snapping like pruning shears, and red lights flashing angrily where its eyes should have been. A guard robot, of course. Why I had not foreseen such a thing I will never know. I supposed at the time that the creature inside the sphere had alerted it.

The tin scorpion may have been a match for the reactions and the muscles of less primitive, more "civilized" men than ourselves, or the creators of the Perpetual Parmenidean Palaces had simply not foreseen barbarians with heavy corn knives. I knocked Chris out of the way and dispatched the tin bug, snipping off its tail stinger with a lucky slash of the corn knife and jumping up and down on its thorax until all its appendages were still.

When the reaction set in, I had to attack something else. I offer no other justification for what I did. We were the intruders—the invading barbarians. All the creatures in the spheres wanted was their security. The man in the sphere set the scorpion on us, but he was protecting his family. I can see it that way now. I wish I couldn't. I wish I was one of those people who can always contrive to have been Right.

I saw the frightened eyes of the things inside the sphere, and I reacted to it as a predatory animal reacts to the scent of urea in the sweat of a lesser animal. And they had menaced my son with a hideous machine in order to be absolutely *secure*! If I reasoned at all, it was along this line.

The corn knife was not very sharp, but the skin of the sphere parted with disgusting ease. I heard Chris scream, "No! Dad! No!" . . . but I kept hacking. We were nearly engulfed in the pinkish, albuminous nutritive which gushed from the ruptured sac. I can still smell it.

The creatures inside were more terrible to see in the open air than they had been behind their protective layers of plastic material. They were dead white and they looked to be soft, although they must have had normal human skeletons. Their struggles were blind, pointless, and feeble, like those of some kind of larvae found under dead wood, and the largest made a barely audible mewing sound as it groped about in search of what I cannot imagine.

I heard Chris retching violently, but could not tear my attention away from the spectacle. The sphere now looked like some huge coelenterate which had been halved for study in the laboratory, and the hoselike tentacles still moved like groping cilia.

The agony of the creatures in the "grape" (I cannot think of them as people) when they were first exposed to unfiltered, unprocessed air and sunlight, when the wires and tubes were torn from them, and especially when the metal caps on their heads fell off in their panicky struggles and the whole universe of chilly external reality rushed in upon them at once, is beyond my imagining; and perhaps this is merciful. This and the fact that they lay in the stillness of death after only a very few minutes in the open air.

Memory is merciful too in its imperfection. All I remember of our homeward journey is the silence of it.

"Wake up! We have company, old man!"

It is Sue shaking me. Somehow I did sleep—in spite of Chris and in spite of the persistent memory. It must be midmorning. I swing my feet down and scrub at my gritty eyes. Voices outside. Cheerful. How cheerful?

It is Sato and he has his old horse hitched to a crude travois of willow poles. It is Sato and his wife and three kids and my son Chris. There trussed up on the travois is the biggest buck I have seen in ten years, its neck transfixed with an arrow. A perfect shot and one that could not have been scored without the most careful and skillful stalking. I remember teaching him that only a bad hunter . . . a heedless and cruel one . . . would risk a distant shot with a bow.

Chris is grinning and looking sheepish. Sato's daughter is there, which accounts for the look of benign idiocy. I was wondering when he would notice. Then he sees me standing in the door of the cabin and his face takes on about ten years of gravity and thought, but this is not for the benefit of the teenage female. Little Mike is clawing at Chris and asking *why* he went away like that and *why* he went hunting without Daddy, and several other *why*s which Chris ignores. His answer is for his old man:

"I'm sorry, Dad. I wasn't mad at you . . . just sort of crazy. Had to do . . . this. . . ." He points at the deer. "Anyhow, I'm back."

"And I'm glad," I managed.

"Dad, those elder bushes . . ."

"To hell with them," say I. "Wednesday is soon enough."

Sato moves in grinning, and just in time to relieve the awkwardness. "Dressed out this buck and carried it down the mountain by himself." I think of mountain lions. "He was about pooped when I found him in a pasture."

Sue holds open the cabin door and the Satos file in. Himself first, carrying a jug of wine, then Mrs. Sato, grinning greetings. She has never mastered English. It has not been necessary.

I drag up what pass for chairs. Made them myself. We begin talking about weeds and beans, and weather, bugs, and the condition of fruit trees. It is Sato who has steered the conversation into these familiar ways, bless his knowing heart. He uncorks the wine. Sue and Mrs. Sato, meanwhile, are carrying on one of their lively conversations. Someday I will listen to them, but I doubt that I will ever learn how they communicate . . . or what. Women.

I can hear Chris outside talking to Yuki, Sato's daughter. He is not boasting about the deer; he is telling her about the fight with the tin scorpion and the grape people.

"Are they blind . . . the grape people?" the girl asks.

"Heck no," says Chris. "At least one of them wasn't. One of them sicced the robot bug on us. They were going to kill us. And so, Dad did what he had to do. . . ."

I don't hear the details over the interjections of Yuki and little Mike, but I can imagine they are as pungent as the teenage powers of physiological description allow. I hear Yuki exclaim, "Oh how utterly *germy*!" and another language problem occurs to me. How can kids who have never hung around a drugstore still manage to evolve languages of their own . . . characteristically adolescent dialects? It is one more mystery which I shall never solve. I hear little Mike asking for reasons and causes with his favorite word. "*Why*, Chris?"

"I'll explain it when you get older," says Chris, and oddly it doesn't sound ridiculous.

Sato pours a giant-size dollop of wine in each tumbler.

"What's the occasion?" I ask.

Sato studies the wine critically, holding the glass so the light from the door shines through.

"It's Tuesday," he says.

J. G. BALLARD

James Graham "J. G." Ballard (1930–2009) was an iconic English writer born in Shanghai and a captive as a child in a Japanese World War II civilian POW camp for three years. Influenced by the Surrealist painters and early Pop painters, Ballard became a giant of world literature, his surreal, dystopian fiction even more relevant today. Ballard came out of the New Wave movement, writing brilliant apocalyptic novels that included *The Drowned World* (1962), *The Burning World* (1964), and *The Crystal World* (1966). In the late 1960s and early 1970s, Ballard turned his attention to writing and publishing a staggering array of short stories and novellas. These groundbreaking works included his infamous "condensed novels" (possibly influenced by William S. Burroughs) and a number of fictions with ecological or postcapitalist themes; indeed, he could be said early on to have been engaging with what Jean Baudrillard would later call the Western "hegemony." His controversial novel *Crash* (1973), about literal auto-eroticism, continued themes found in his more experimental short fiction and pushed the envelope once again.

Along with Kim Stanley Robinson, Ballard is still the most cited fiction writer in the context of climate change and other "hyperobjects," a term coined by Timothy Morton to describe planet-level or planet-wide occurrences difficult to grok due to their omnipresence and diffusion. "Ballardian" is its own descriptor as well, the *Collins English Dictionary* defining the term as "resembling or suggestive of the conditions described in J. G. Ballard's novels and stories, especially dystopian modernity, bleak man-made landscapes and the psychological effects of technological, social or environmental developments." For these triumphs of clear vision, the wider world made Ballard iconic and ubiquitous, the threshold through which so much else is seen. The science fiction field, however, rewarded Ballard with . . . nothing . . . except for a British Science Fiction Association Award (1980) for his non-SF novel *The Unlimited Dream Company*.

Attention for Ballard's mind-altering shorter works—which often compressed or expanded space and time—crystallized with early collections such as *The Atrocity Exhibition* (1970). *The Complete Stories of J. G. Ballard* (2009), published with an introduction by Martin Amis, only confirmed Ballard's relevance—and his mastery of the short form. His stories feature broken landscapes of sand dunes, concrete deserts, abandoned nightclubs, wrecked spacecraft, and junked military hardware.

As Amis wrote in his introduction: "This was his abiding question: what effect does the modern setting have on our psyches—the motion sculptures of highways, the airport architecture, the culture of the shopping mall, the pervasiveness of pornography, and our dependence on ungrasped technologies? His tentative answer was perversity, which takes various forms, all of them (Ballard being Ballard) pathologically extreme."

"The Voices of Time," first published in *New Worlds* (1960), is a classic long story from Ballard. In this major early work, Ballardian elements like the breakdown of society and the inadequacy of science to save us from ourselves are on full display.

THE VOICES OF TIME

J. G. Ballard

ONE

Later Powers often thought of Whitby, and the strange grooves the biologist had cut, apparently at random, all over the floor of the empty swimming pool. An inch deep and twenty feet long, interlocking to form an elaborate ideogram like a Chinese character, they had taken him all summer to complete, and he had obviously thought about little else, working away tirelessly through the long desert afternoons. Powers had watched him from his office window at the far end of the Neurology wing, carefully marking out his pegs and string, carrying away the cement chips in a small canvas bucket. After Whitby's suicide no one had bothered about the grooves, but Powers often borrowed the supervisor's key and let himself into the disused pool, and would look down at the labyrinth of mouldering gulleys, half-filled with water leaking in from the chlorinator, an enigma now past any solution.

Initially, however, Powers was too preoccupied with completing his work at the Clinic and planning his own final withdrawal. After the first frantic weeks of panic he had managed to accept an uneasy compromise that allowed him to view his predicament with the detached fatalism he had previously reserved for his patients. Fortunately he was moving down the physical and mental gradients simultaneously—lethargy and inertia blunted his anxieties, a slackening metabolism made it necessary to concentrate to produce a connected thought-train. In fact, the lengthening intervals of dreamless sleep were almost restful. He found himself beginning to look forward to them, and made no effort to wake earlier than was essential.

At first he had kept an alarm clock by his bed, tried to compress as much activity as he could into the narrowing hours of consciousness, sorting out his library, driving over to Whitby's laboratory every morning to examine the latest batch of X-ray plates, every minute and hour rationed like the last drops of water in a canteen.

Anderson, fortunately, had unwittingly made him realize the pointlessness of this course.

After Powers had resigned from the Clinic he still continued to drive in once a week for his checkup, now little more than a formality. On what turned out to be the last occasion Anderson had perfunctorily taken his blood-count, noting Powers's slacker facial muscles, fading pupil reflexes, and unshaven cheeks.

He smiled sympathetically at Powers across the desk, wondering what to say to him. Once he had put on a show of encouragement with the more intelligent patients, even tried to provide some sort of explanation. But Powers was too difficult to reach—neurosurgeon extraordinary, a man always out on the periphery, only at ease working with unfamiliar materials. To himself he thought: *I'm sorry, Robert. What can I say—"Even the sun is growing cooler"?* He watched Powers drum his fingers restlessly on the enamel desktop, his eyes glancing at the spinal level charts hung around the office. Despite his unkempt appearance—he had been wearing the same unironed shirt and dirty white plimsolls a week ago—Powers looked composed and self-possessed, like a Conradian beachcomber more or less reconciled to his own weaknesses.

"What are you doing with yourself, Robert?" he asked. "Are you still going over to Whitby's lab?"

"As much as I can. It takes me half an hour to cross the lake, and I keep on sleeping through the alarm clock. I may leave my place and move in there permanently."

Anderson frowned. "Is there much point? As far as I could make out Whitby's work was pretty speculative—" He broke off, realizing the implied criticism of Powers's own disastrous work at the Clinic, but Powers seemed to ignore this, was examining the pattern of shadows on the ceiling. "Anyway, wouldn't it be better to stay where you are, among your own things, read through Toynbee and Spengler again?"

Powers laughed shortly. "That's the last thing I want to do. I want to *forget* Toynbee and Spengler, not try to remember them. In fact, Paul, I'd like to forget everything. I don't know whether I've got enough time, though. How much can you forget in three months?"

"Everything, I suppose, if you want to. But don't try to race the clock."

Powers nodded quietly, repeating this last remark to himself. Racing the clock was exactly what he had been doing. As he stood up and said good-bye to Anderson he suddenly decided to throw away his alarm clock, escape from his futile obsession with time. To remind himself he unfastened his wristwatch and scrambled the setting, then slipped it into his pocket. Making his way out to the car park he reflected on the freedom this simple act gave him. He would explore the lateral byways now, the side doors, as it were, in the corridors of time. Three months could be an eternity.

He picked his car out of the line and strolled over to it, shielding his eyes from the heavy sunlight beating down across the parabolic sweep of the lecture theatre roof. He was about to climb in when he saw that someone had traced with a finger across the dust caked over the windshield:

96,688,365,498,721

Looking over his shoulder, he recognized the white Packard parked next to him, peered inside, and saw a lean-faced young man with blond sun-bleached hair and a high cerebrotonic forehead watching him behind dark glasses. Sitting beside him at the wheel was a raven-haired girl whom he had often seen around the psychology department. She had intelligent but somehow rather oblique eyes, and Powers remembered that the younger doctors called her "the girl from Mars."

"Hello, Kaldren," Powers said to the young man. "Still following me around?"

Kaldren nodded. "Most of the time, doctor." He sized Powers up shrewdly. "We haven't seen very much of you recently, as a matter of fact. Anderson said you'd resigned, and we noticed your laboratory was closed."

Powers shrugged. "I felt I needed a rest. As you'll understand, there's a good deal that needs rethinking."

Kaldren frowned half-mockingly. "Sorry to hear that, doctor. But don't let these temporary setbacks depress you." He noticed the girl watching Powers with interest. "Coma's a fan of yours. I gave her your papers from *American Journal of Psychiatry*, and she's read through the whole file."

The girl smiled pleasantly at Powers, for a moment dispelling the hostility between the two men. When Powers nodded to her she leaned across Kaldren and said: "Actually I've just finished Noguchi's autobiography—the great Japanese doctor who discovered the spirochaete. Somehow you remind me of him—there's so much of yourself in all the patients you worked on."

Powers smiled wanly at her, then his eyes turned and locked involuntarily on Kaldren's. They stared at each other sombrely for a moment, and a small tic in Kaldren's right cheek began to flicker irritatingly. He flexed his facial muscles, after a few seconds mastered it with an effort, obviously annoyed that Powers should have witnessed this brief embarrassment.

"How did the clinic go today?" Powers

asked. "Have you had any more . . . headaches?"

Kaldren's mouth snapped shut, he looked suddenly irritable. "Whose care am I in, doctor? Yours or Anderson's? Is that the sort of question you should be asking now?"

Powers gestured deprecatingly. "Perhaps not." He cleared his throat; the heat was ebbing the blood from his head and he felt tired and eager to get away from them. He turned towards his car, then realized that Kaldren would probably follow, either try to crowd him into the ditch or block the road and make Powers sit in his dust all the way back to the lake. Kaldren was capable of any madness.

"Well, I've got to go and collect something," he said, adding in a firmer voice: "Get in touch with me, though, if you can't reach Anderson."

He waved and walked off behind the line of cars. From the reflection in the windows he could see Kaldren looking back and watching him closely.

He entered the Neurology wing, paused thankfully in the cool foyer, nodding to the two nurses and the armed guard at the reception desk. For some reason the terminals sleeping in the adjacent dormitory block attracted hordes of would-be sightseers, most of them cranks with some magical anti-narcoma remedy, or merely the idly curious, but a good number of quite normal people, many of whom had travelled thousands of miles, impelled towards the Clinic by some strange instinct, like animals migrating to a preview of their racial graveyards.

He walked along the corridor to the supervisor's office overlooking the recreation deck, borrowed the key, and made his way out through the tennis courts and calisthenics rigs to the enclosed swimming pool at the far end. It had been disused for months, and only Powers's visits kept the lock free. Stepping through, he closed it behind him and walked past the peeling wooden stands to the deep end.

Putting a foot up on the diving board, he looked down at Whitby's ideogram. Damp leaves and bits of paper obscured it, but the outlines were just distinguishable. It covered almost the entire floor of the pool and at first glance appeared to represent a huge solar disc, with four radiating diamond-shaped arms, a crude Jungian mandala.

Wondering what had prompted Whitby to carve the device before his death, Powers noticed something moving through the debris in the centre of the disc. A black, horny-shelled animal about a foot long was nosing about in the slush, heaving itself on tired legs. Its shell was articulated, and vaguely resembled an armadillo's. Reaching the edge of the disc, it stopped and hesitated, then slowly backed away into the centre again, apparently unwilling or unable to cross the narrow groove.

Powers looked around, then stepped into one of the changing stalls and pulled a small wooden clothes locker off its rusty wall bracket. Carrying it under one arm, he climbed down the chromium ladder into the pool and walked carefully across the slithery floor towards the animal. As he approached it sidled away from him, but he trapped it easily, using the lid to lever it into the box.

The animal was heavy, at least the weight of a brick. Powers tapped its massive olive-black carapace with his knuckle, noting the triangular warty head jutting out below its rim like a turtle's, the thickened pads beneath the first digits of the pentadactyl forelimbs.

He watched the three-lidded eyes blinking at him anxiously from the bottom of the box.

"Expecting some really hot weather?" he murmured. "That lead umbrella you're carrying around should keep you cool."

He closed the lid, climbed out of the pool, and made his way back to the supervisor's office, then carried the box out to his car.

". . . *Kaldren continues to reproach me [Powers wrote in his diary]. For some reason he seems unwilling to accept his isolation, is elaborating a series of private rituals to replace the missing hours of sleep. Perhaps I should tell him of my own approaching zero, but he'd probably regard this as the final unbearable insult, that I should have in excess what he so desperately yearns for. God knows what might happen. Fortunately the nightmarish visions appear to have receded for the time being. . . ."*

Pushing the diary away, Powers leaned forward across the desk and stared out through the window at the white floor of the lake bed stretching towards the hills along the horizon. Three miles away, on the far shore, he could see the circular bowl of the radio telescope revolving slowly in the clear afternoon air, as Kaldren tirelessly trapped the sky, sluicing in millions of cubic parsecs of sterile ether, like the nomads who trapped the sea along the shores of the Persian Gulf.

Behind him the air conditioner murmured quietly, cooling the pale blue walls half-hidden in the dim light. Outside the air was bright and oppressive, the heat waves rippling up from the clumps of gold-tinted cacti below the Clinic blurring the sharp terraces of the twenty-storey Neurology block. There, in the silent dormitories behind the sealed shutters, the terminals slept their long dreamless sleep. There were now over five hundred of them in the Clinic, the vanguard of a vast somnambulist army massing for its last march. Only five years had elapsed since the first narcoma syndrome had been recognized, but already huge government hospitals in the east were being readied for intakes in the thousands, as more and more cases came to light.

Powers felt suddenly tired, and glanced at his wrist, wondering how long he had to eight o'clock, his bedtime for the next week or so. Already he missed the dusk, soon would wake to his last dawn.

His watch was in his hip pocket. He remembered his decision not to use his timepieces, and sat back and stared at the bookshelves beside the desk. There were rows of green-covered AEC publications he had removed from Whitby's library, papers in which the biologist described his work out in the Pacific after the H-tests. Many of them Powers knew almost by heart, read a hundred times in an effort to grasp Whitby's last conclusions. Toynbee would certainly be easier to forget.

His eyes dimmed momentarily, as the tall black wall in the rear of his mind cast its great shadow over his brain. He reached for the diary, thinking of the girl in Kaldren's car—Coma he had called her, another of his insane jokes—and her reference to Noguchi. Actually the comparison should have been made with Whitby, not himself; the monsters in the lab were nothing more than fragmented mirrors of Whitby's mind, like the grotesque radio-shielded frog he had found that morning in the swimming pool.

Thinking of the girl Coma, and the heartening smile she had given him, he wrote:

Woke 6:33 a.m. Last session with Anderson. He made it plain he's seen enough of me, and from now on I'm better alone. To sleep 8:00? (These countdowns terrify me.)

He paused, then added:

Good-bye, Eniwetok.

TWO

He saw the girl again the next day at Whitby's laboratory. He had driven over after breakfast with the new specimen, eager to get it into a vivarium before it died. The only previous armoured mutant he had come across had nearly broken his neck. Speeding along the lake road a month or so earlier he had struck it with the offside front wheel, expecting the small creature to flatten instantly. Instead its hard lead-packed shell had remained rigid, even though the organism within it had been pulped, had flung the car heavily into the ditch. He had gone back for the shell, later weighed it at the laboratory, found it contained over six hundred grammes of lead.

Quite a number of plants and animals were building up heavy metals as radiological shields. In the hills behind the beach house a couple of old-time prospectors were renovating the derelict gold-panning equipment abandoned over eighty years ago. They had noticed the bright yellow tints of the cacti, run an analysis, and found that the plants were assimilating gold in extractable quantities, although the soil concentrations were unworkable. Oak Ridge was at last paying a dividend!!

Waking that morning just after 6:45—ten minutes later than the previous day (he had switched on the radio, heard one of the regular morning programmes as he climbed out of bed)—he had eaten a light unwanted breakfast, then spent an hour packing away some of the books in his library, crating them up and taping on address labels to his brother.

He reached Whitby's laboratory half an hour later. This was housed in a one-hundred-foot-wide geodesic dome built beside his chalet on the west shore of the lake about a mile from Kaldren's summer house. The chalet had been closed after Whitby's suicide, and many of the experimental plants and animals had died before Powers had managed to receive permission to use the laboratory.

As he turned into the driveway he saw the girl standing on the apex of the yellow-ribbed dome, her slim figure silhouetted against the sky. She waved to him, then began to step down across the glass polyhedrons and jumped nimbly into the driveway beside the car.

"Hello," she said, giving him a welcoming smile. "I came over to see your zoo. Kaldren said you wouldn't let me in if he came so I made him stay behind."

She waited for Powers to say something while he searched for his keys, then volunteered: "If you like, I can wash your shirt."

Powers grinned at her, peered down ruefully at his dust-stained sleeves. "Not a bad idea. I thought I was beginning to look a little uncared-for." He unlocked the door, took Coma's arm. "I don't know why Kaldren told you that—he's welcome here any time he likes."

"What have you got in there?" Coma asked, pointing at the wooden box he was carrying as they walked between the gear-laden benches.

"A distant cousin of ours I found. Interesting little chap. I'll introduce you in a moment."

Sliding partitions divided the dome into four chambers. Two of them were storerooms, filled with spare tanks, apparatus, cartons of animal food, and test rigs. They crossed the third section, almost filled by a powerful X-ray projector, a giant two-hundred-fifty-amp GE Maxitron, angled onto a revolving table, concrete shielding blocks lying around ready for use like huge building bricks.

The fourth chamber contained Powers's zoo, the vivaria jammed together along the benches and in the sinks, big coloured cardboard charts and memos pinned onto the draught hoods above them, a tangle of rubber tubing and power leads trailing across the floor. As they walked past the lines of tanks dim forms shifted behind the frosted glass, and at the far end of the aisle there was a sudden scurrying in a large cage by Powers's desk.

Putting the box down on his chair, he picked a packet of peanuts off the desk and went over to the cage. A small black-haired chimpanzee wearing a dented jet pilot's helmet swarmed deftly up the bars to him, chirped happily, and then jumped down to a miniature control panel against the rear wall of the cage. Rapidly it flicked a series of buttons and toggles, and a succession of coloured lights lit up like a jukebox and jangled out a two-second blast of music.

"Good boy," Powers said encouragingly, patting the chimp's back and shovelling the peanuts into its hands. "You're getting much too clever for that one, aren't you?"

The chimp tossed the peanuts into the back of its throat with the smooth, easy motions of a conjuror, jabbering at Powers in a singsong voice.

Coma laughed and took some of the nuts from Powers. "He's sweet. I think he's talking to you."

Powers nodded. "Quite right, he is. Actually he's got a two-hundred-word vocabulary, but his voice box scrambles it all up." He opened a small refrigerator by the desk, took out half a packet of sliced bread, and passed a couple of pieces to the chimp. It picked an electric toaster off the floor and placed it in the middle of a low wobbling table in the centre of the cage, whipped the pieces into the slots. Powers pressed a tab on the switchboard beside the cage and the toaster began to crackle softly.

"He's one of the brightest we've had here, about as intelligent as a five-year-old child, though much more self-sufficient in a lot of ways." The two pieces of toast jumped out of their slots and the chimp caught them neatly, nonchalantly patting its helmet each time, then ambled off into a small ramshackle kennel and relaxed back with one arm out of a window, sliding the toast into its mouth.

"He built that house himself," Powers went on, switching off the toaster. "Not a bad effort, really." He pointed to a yellow polythene bucket by the front door of the kennel, from which a battered-looking geranium protruded. "Tends that plant, cleans up the cage, pours out an endless stream of wisecracks. Pleasant fellow all round."

Coma was smiling broadly to herself. "Why the space helmet, though?"

Powers hesitated. "Oh, it—er—it's for his own protection. Sometimes he gets rather bad headaches. His predecessors all—" He broke off and turned away. "Let's have a look at some of the other inmates."

He moved down the line of tanks, beckoning Coma with him. "We'll start at the beginning." He lifted the glass lid off one of the tanks, and Coma peered down into a shallow bath of water, where a small round organism with slender tendrils was nestling in a rockery of shells and pebbles.

"Sea anemone. Or was. Simple coelenterate with an open-ended body cavity." He pointed down to a thickened ridge of tissue around the base. "It's sealed up the cavity, converted the channel into a rudimentary notochord, first plant ever to develop a nervous system. Later the tendrils will knot themselves into a ganglion, but already they're sensitive to colour. Look." He borrowed the violet handkerchief in Coma's breast-pocket, spread it across the tank. The tendrils flexed and stiffened, began to weave slowly, as if they were trying to focus.

"The strange thing is that they're completely insensitive to white light. Normally the tendrils register shifting pressure gradients, like the tympanic diaphragms in your ears. Now it's almost as if they can hear primary colours, suggests it's readapting itself for a non-aquatic existence in a static world of violent colour contrasts."

Coma shook her head, puzzled. "Why, though?"

"Hold on a moment. Let me put you in the picture first." They moved along the bench to a series of drum-shaped cages made of wire mosquito netting. Above the first was a large white cardboard screen bearing a blown-up microphoto of a tall pagoda-like chain, topped by the legend: "Drosophila: 15 röntgens/min."

Powers tapped a small Perspex window in the drum. "Fruit fly. Its huge chromosomes make it a useful test vehicle." He bent down, pointed to a grey V-shaped honeycomb suspended from the roof. A few flies emerged from entrances, moving about busily. "Usually it's solitary, a nomadic scavenger. Now it forms itself into well-knit social groups, has begun to secrete a thin sweet lymph something like honey."

"What's this?" Coma asked, touching the screen.

"Diagram of a key gene in the operation." He traced a spray of arrows leading from a link in the chain. The arrows were labelled: "lymph gland" and subdivided "sphincter muscles, epithelium, templates."

"It's rather like the perforated sheet music of a player-piano," Powers commented, "or a computer punch tape. Knock out one link with an X-ray beam, lose a characteristic, change the score."

Coma was peering through the window of the next cage and pulling an unpleasant face. Over her shoulder Powers saw she was watching an enormous spiderlike insect, as big as a hand, its dark hairy legs as thick as fingers. The compound eyes had been built up so that they resembled giant rubies.

"He looks unfriendly," she said. "What's that sort of rope ladder he's spinning?" As she moved a finger to her mouth the spider came to life, retreated into the cage, and began spewing out a complex skein of interlinked grey thread which it slung in long loops from the roof of the cage.

"A web," Powers told her. "Except that it consists of nervous tissue. The ladders form an external neural plexus, an inflatable brain as it were, that he can pump up to whatever size the situation calls for. A sensible arrangement, really, far better than our own."

Coma backed away. "Gruesome. I wouldn't like to go into his parlour."

"Oh, he's not as frightening as he looks. Those huge eyes staring at you are blind. Or, rather, their optical sensitivity has shifted down the band, the retinas will only register gamma radiation. Your wristwatch has luminous hands. When you moved it across the window he started thinking. World War IV should really bring him into his element."

They strolled back to Powers's desk. He put a coffee pan over a Bunsen and pushed a chair across to Coma. Then he opened the box, lifted out the armoured frog, and put it down on a sheet of blotting paper.

"Recognize him? Your old childhood friend, the common frog. He's built himself quite a solid little air-raid shelter." He carried the animal across to a sink, turned on the tap, and let the water play softly over its shell. Wiping his hands on his shirt, he came back to the desk.

Coma brushed her long hair off her forehead, watched him curiously.

"Well, what's the secret?"

Powers lit a cigarette. "There's no secret. Teratologists have been breeding monsters for years. Have you ever heard of the 'silent pair'?"

She shook her head.

Powers stared moodily at the cigarette for a moment, riding the kick the first one of the day always gave him. "The so-called silent pair is one of modern genetics' oldest problems, the apparently baffling mystery of the two inactive genes which occur in a small percentage of all living organisms, and appear to have no intelligible role in their structure or development. For a long while now biologists have been trying to activate them, but the difficulty is partly in identifying the silent genes in the fertilized germ cells of parents known to contain them, and partly in focusing a narrow enough X-ray beam which will do no damage to the remainder of the chromosome. However, after about ten years' work Dr. Whitby successfully developed a whole-body irradiation technique based on his observation of radiobiological damage at Eniwetok."

Powers paused for a moment. "He had noticed that there appeared to be more biological damage after the tests—that is, a greater transport of energy—than could be accounted for by direct radiation. What was happening was that the protein lattices in the genes were building up energy in the way that any vibrating membrane accumulates energy when it resonates—you remember the analogy of the bridge collapsing under the soldiers marching in step—and it occurred to him that if he could first identify the critical resonance frequency of the lattices in any particular silent gene he could then radiate the entire living organism, and not simply its germ cells, with a low field that would act selectively on the silent gene and cause no damage to the remainder of the chromosomes, whose lattices would resonate critically only at other specific frequencies."

Powers gestured around the laboratory with his cigarette. "You see some of the fruits of this 'resonance transfer' technique around you."

Coma nodded. "They've had their silent genes activated?"

"Yes, all of them. These are only a few of the thousands of specimens who have passed through here, and as you've seen, the results are pretty dramatic."

He reached up and pulled across a section of the sun curtain. They were sitting just under the lip of the dome, and the mounting sunlight had begun to irritate him.

In the comparative darkness Coma noticed a stroboscope winking slowly in one of the tanks at the end of the bench behind her. She stood up and went over to it, examining a tall sunflower with a thickened stem and greatly enlarged receptacle. Packed around the flower, so that only its head protruded, was a chimney of grey-white stones, neatly cemented together and labelled:

Cretaceous Chalk: 60,000,000 years.

Beside it on the bench were three other chimneys, these labelled "Devonian Sandstone: 290,000,000 years," "Asphalt: 20 years," "Polyvimi-chloride: 6 months."

"Can you see those moist white discs on the sepals?" Powers pointed out. "In some way they regulate the plant's metabolism. It literally *sees* time. The older the surrounding environment, the more sluggish its metabolism. With the asphalt chimney it will complete its annual cycle in a week, with the PVC one in a couple of hours."

"Sees time," Coma repeated, wonderingly. She looked up at Powers, chewing her lower lip reflectively. "It's fantastic. Are these the creatures of the future, doctor?"

"I don't know," Powers admitted. "But if

they are their world must be a monstrous surrealist one."

THREE

He went back to the desk, pulled two cups from a drawer, and poured out the coffee, switching off the Bunsen. "Some people have speculated that organisms possessing the silent pair of genes are the forerunners of a massive move up the evolutionary slope, that the silent genes are a sort of code, a divine message that we inferior organisms are carrying for our more highly developed descendants. It may well be true— perhaps we've broken the code too soon."

"Why do you say that?"

"Well, as Whitby's death indicates, the experiments in this laboratory have all come to a rather unhappy conclusion. Without exception the organisms we've irradiated have entered a final phase of totally disorganized growth, producing dozens of specialized sensory organs whose function we can't even guess. The results are catastrophic—the anemone will literally explode, the *Drosophila* cannibalize themselves, and so on. Whether the future implicit in these plants and animals is ever intended to take place, or whether we're merely extrapolating—I don't know. Sometimes I think, though, that the new sensory organs developed are parodies of their real intentions. The specimens you've seen today are all in an early stage of their secondary growth cycles. Later on they begin to look distinctly bizarre."

Coma nodded. "A zoo isn't complete without its keeper," she commented. "What about man?"

Powers shrugged. "About one in every one hundred thousand—the usual average— contains the silent pair. You might have them— or I. No one has volunteered yet to undergo whole-body irradiation. Apart from the fact that it would be classified as suicide, if the experiments here are any guide the experience would be savage and violent."

He sipped at the thin coffee, feeling tired and somehow bored. Recapitulating the laboratory's work had exhausted him.

The girl leaned forward. "You look awfully pale," she said solicitously. "Don't you sleep well?"

Powers managed a brief smile. "Too well," he admitted. "It's no longer a problem with me."

"I wish I could say that about Kaldren. I don't think he sleeps anywhere near enough. I hear him pacing around all night." She added: "Still, I suppose it's better than being a terminal. Tell me, doctor, wouldn't it be worth trying this radiation technique on the sleepers at the Clinic? It might wake them up before the end. A few of them must possess the silent genes."

"They *all* do," Powers told her. "The two phenomena are very closely linked, as a matter of fact." He stopped, fatigue dulling his brain, and wondered whether to ask the girl to leave. Then he climbed off the desk and reached behind it, picked up a tape recorder.

Switching it on, he zeroed the tape and adjusted the speaker volume.

"Whitby and I often talked this over. Towards the end I took it all down. He was a great biologist, so let's hear it in his own words. It's absolutely the heart of the matter."

He flipped the tape on, adding: "I've played it over to myself a thousand times, so I'm afraid the quality is poor."

An older man's voice, sharp and slightly irritable, sounded out above a low buzz of distortion, but Coma could hear it clearly.

WHITBY: . . . for heaven's sake, Robert, look at those FAO statistics. Despite an annual increase of five percent in acreage sown over the past fifteen years, world wheat crops have continued to decline by a factor of about two percent. The same story repeats itself ad nauseam. Cereals and root crops, dairy yields, ruminant fertility—are all down. Couple these with a mass of

parallel symptoms, anything you care to pick from altered migratory routes to longer hibernation periods, and the overall pattern is incontrovertible.

POWERS: Population figures for Europe and North America show no decline, though.

WHITBY: Of course not, as I keep pointing out. It will take a century for such a fractional drop in fertility to have any effect in areas where extensive birth control provides an artificial reservoir. One must look at the countries of the Far East, and particularly at those where infant mortality has remained at a steady level. The population of Sumatra, for example, has declined by over fifteen percent in the last twenty years. A fabulous decline! Do you realize that only two or three decades ago the neo-Malthusians were talking about a "world population explosion"? In fact, it's an implosion. Another factor is—

Here the tape had been cut and edited, and Whitby's voice, less querulous this time, picked up again.

. . . just as a matter of interest, tell me something: how long do you sleep each night?

POWERS: I don't know exactly; about eight hours, I suppose.

WHITBY: The proverbial eight hours. Ask anyone and they say automatically "eight hours." As a matter of fact you sleep about ten and a half hours, like the majority of people. I've timed you on a number of occasions. I myself sleep eleven. Yet thirty years ago people did indeed sleep eight hours, and a century before that they slept six or seven. In Vasari's *Lives* one reads of Michelangelo sleeping for only four or five hours, painting all day at the age of eighty, and then working through the night over his anatomy table with a candle strapped to his forehead. Now he's regarded as a prodigy, but it was unremarkable then. How do you think the ancients, from Plato to Shakespeare, Aristotle to Aquinas, were able to cram so much work into their lives? Simply because they had an extra six or seven hours every day. Of course, a second disadvantage under which we labour is a lowered basal metabolic rate—another factor no one will explain.

POWERS: I suppose you could take the view that the lengthened sleep interval is a compensation device, a sort of mass neurotic attempt to escape from the terrifying pressures of urban life in the late twentieth century.

WHITBY: You could, but you'd be wrong. It's simply a matter of biochemistry. The ribonucleic acid templates which unravel the protein chains in all living organisms are wearing out, the dies inscribing the protoplasmic signature have become blunted. After all, they've been running now for over a thousand million years. It's time to retool. Just as an individual organism's life span is finite, or the life of a yeast colony or a given species, so the life of an entire biological kingdom is of fixed duration. It's always been assumed that the evolutionary slope reaches forever upwards, but in fact the peak has already been reached, and the pathway now leads downwards to the common biological grave. It's a despairing and at present unacceptable vision of the future, but it's the only one. Five thousand centuries from now our descendants, instead of being multibrained star-men, will probably be naked prognathous idiots with hair on their foreheads, grunting their way through the remains of this Clinic like Neolithic men caught in a macabre inversion of time. Believe me, I pity them, as I pity myself. My total failure, my absolute lack of any moral or biological right to existence, is implicit in every cell of my body. . . .

The tape ended, the spool ran free and stopped. Powers closed the machine, then massaged his face. Coma sat quietly, watching him and listening to the chimp playing with a box of puzzle dice.

"As far as Whitby could tell," Powers said, "the silent genes represent a last desperate effort of the biological kingdom to keep its head above the rising waters. Its total life period is determined by the amount of radiation emitted by the sun, and once this reaches a certain point the sure-death line has been passed and extinction is inevitable. To compensate for this, alarms have been built in which alter the form of the organism and adapt it to living in a hotter radiological climate. Soft-skinned organisms develop hard shells, these contain heavy metals as radiation screens. New organs of perception are developed too. According to Whitby, though, it's all wasted effort in the long run—but sometimes I wonder."

He smiled at Coma and shrugged. "Well, let's talk about something else. How long have you known Kaldren?"

"About three weeks. Feels like ten thousand years."

"How do you find him now? We've been rather out of touch lately."

Coma grinned. "I don't seem to see very much of him either. He makes me sleep all the time. Kaldren has many strange talents, but he lives just for himself. You mean a lot to him, doctor. In fact, you're my one serious rival."

"I thought he couldn't stand the sight of me."

"Oh, that's just a sort of surface symptom. He really thinks of you continually. That's why we spend all our time following you around." She eyed Powers shrewdly. "I think he feels guilty about something."

"Guilty?" Powers exclaimed. "*He* does? I thought I was supposed to be the guilty one."

"Why?" she pressed. She hesitated, then said: "You carried out some experimental surgical technique on him, didn't you?"

"Yes," Powers admitted. "It wasn't altogether a success, like so much of what I seem to be involved with. If Kaldren feels guilty, I suppose it's because he feels he must take some of the responsibility."

He looked down at the girl, her intelligent eyes watching him closely. "For one or two reasons it may be necessary for you to know. You said Kaldren paced around all night and didn't get enough sleep. Actually he doesn't get any sleep at all."

The girl nodded. "You . . ." She made a snapping gesture with her fingers.

". . . narcotomized him," Powers completed. "Surgically speaking, it was a great success, one might well share a Nobel for it. Normally the hypothalamus regulates the period of sleep, raising the threshold of consciousness in order to relax the venous capillaries in the brain and drain them of accumulating toxins. However, by sealing off some of the control loops the subject is unable to receive the sleep cue, and the capillaries drain while he remains conscious. All he feels is a temporary lethargy, but this passes within three or four hours. Physically speaking, Kaldren has had another twenty years added to his life. But the psyche seems to need sleep for its own private reasons, and consequently Kaldren has periodic storms that tear him apart. The whole thing was a tragic blunder."

Coma frowned pensively. "I guessed as much. Your papers in the neurosurgery journals referred to the patient as K. A touch of pure Kafka that came all too true."

"I may leave here for good, Coma," Powers said. "Make sure that Kaldren goes to his clinics. Some of the deep scar tissue will need to be cleaned away."

"I'll try. Sometimes I feel I'm just another of his insane terminal documents."

"What are those?"

"Haven't you heard? Kaldren's collection of final statements about *Homo sapiens*. The complete works of Freud, Beethoven's blind quartets, transcripts of the Nuremberg trials, an automatic novel, and so on." She broke off. "What's that you're drawing?"

"Where?"

She pointed to the desk blotter, and Powers looked down and realized he had been unconsciously sketching an elaborate doodle, Whitby's four-armed sun. "It's nothing," he said. Somehow, though, it had a strangely compelling force.

Coma stood up to leave. "You must come and see us, doctor. Kaldren has so much he wants to show you. He's just got hold of an old copy of the last signals sent back by the Mercury Seven twenty years ago when they reached the moon, and can't think about anything else. You remember the strange messages they recorded before they died, full of poetic ramblings about the white gardens. Now that I think about it they behaved rather like the plants in your zoo here."

She put her hands in her pockets, then pulled something out. "By the way, Kaldren asked me to give you this."

It was an old index card from the observatory library. In the centre had been typed the number:

96,688,365,498,720

"It's going to take a long time to reach zero at this rate," Powers remarked dryly. "I'll have quite a collection when we're finished."

After she had left he chucked the card into the waste bin and sat down at the desk, staring for an hour at the ideogram on the blotter.

. . .

Halfway back to his beach house the lake road forked to the left through a narrow saddle that ran between the hills to an abandoned air force weapons range on one of the remoter salt lakes. At the nearer end were a number of small bunkers and camera towers, one or two metal shacks, and a low-roofed storage hangar. The white hills encircled the whole area, shutting it off from the world outside, and Powers liked to wander on foot down the gunnery aisles that had been marked down the two-mile length of the lake towards the concrete sight-screens at the far end. The abstract patterns made him feel like an ant on a bone-white chessboard, the rectangular screens at one end and the towers and bunkers at the other like opposing pieces.

His session with Coma had made Powers feel suddenly dissatisfied with the way he was spending his last months. *Good-bye, Eniwetok,* he had written, but in fact systematically forgetting everything was exactly the same as remembering it, a cataloguing in reverse, sorting out all the books in the mental library and putting them back in their right places upside down.

Powers climbed one of the camera towers, leaned on the rail, and looked out along the aisles towards the sight-screens. Ricocheting shells and rockets had chipped away large pieces of the circular concrete bands that ringed the target bulls, but the outlines of the huge hundred-yard-wide discs, alternately painted blue and red, were still visible.

For half an hour he stared quietly at them, formless ideas shifting through his mind. Then, without thinking, he abruptly left the rail and climbed down the companionway. The storage hangar was fifty yards away. He walked quickly across to it, stepped into the cool shadows, and peered around the rusting electric trolleys and empty flare drums. At the far end, behind a pile of lumber and bales of wire, were a stack of unopened cement bags, a mound of dirty sand, and an old mixer.

Half an hour later he had backed the Buick into the hangar and hooked the cement mixer, charged with sand, cement, and water scavenged from the drums lying around outside, onto the rear bumper, then loaded a dozen more bags into the car's trunk and rear seat. Finally he selected a few straight lengths of timber, jammed them through the window, and set off across the lake towards the central target bull.

For the next two hours he worked away steadily in the centre of the great blue disc, mixing up the cement by hand, carrying it across to the crude wooden forms he had lashed together from the timber, smoothing it down so that it formed a six-inch-high wall around the perimeter of the bull. He worked without pause, stirring the cement with a tyre lever, scooping it out with a hubcap prised off one of the wheels.

By the time he finished and drove off, leaving his equipment where it stood, he had completed a thirty-foot-long section of wall.

FOUR

June 7: Conscious, for the first time, of the brevity of each day. As long as I was awake for over twelve hours I still orientated my time around the meridian, morning and afternoon set their old rhythms. Now, with just over eleven hours of consciousness left, they form a continuous interval, like a length of tape-measure. I can see exactly how much is left on the spool and can do little to affect the rate at which it unwinds. Spend the time slowly packing away the library; the crates are too heavy to move and lie where they are filled. Cell count down to 400,000.

Woke 8:10. To sleep 7:15. (Appear to have lost my watch without realizing it, had to drive into town to buy another.)

June 14: 9½ hours. Time races, flashing past like an expressway. However, the last week of a holiday always goes faster than the first. At the present rate there should be about 4–5 weeks left. This morning I tried to visualize what the last week or so—the final, 3, 2, 1, out—would be like, had a sudden chilling attack of pure fear, unlike anything I've ever felt before. Took me half an hour to steady myself for an intravenous.

Kaldren pursues me like my luminescent shadow, chalked up on the gateway "96,688,365,498,702." Should confuse the mailman.

Woke 9:05. To sleep 6:36.

June 19: 6 ½ hours. Anderson rang up this morning. I nearly put the phone down on him, but managed to go through the pretence of making the final arrangements. He congratulated me on my stoicism, even used the word "heroic." Don't feel it. Despair erodes everything—courage, hope, self-discipline, all the better qualities. It's so damned difficult to sustain that impersonal attitude of passive acceptance implicit in the scientific tradition. I try to think of Galileo before the Inquisition, Freud surmounting the endless pain of his jaw cancer surgery.

Met Kaldren downtown, had a long discussion about the Mercury Seven. He's convinced that they refused to leave the moon deliberately, after the "reception party" waiting for them had put them in the cosmic picture. They were told by the mysterious emissaries from Orion that the exploration of deep space was pointless, that they were too late as the life of the universe is now virtually over!!! According to K. there are air force generals who take this nonsense seriously, but I suspect it's simply an obscure attempt on K.'s part to console me.

Must have the phone disconnected. Some contractor keeps calling me up about payment for 50 bags of cement he claims I collected ten days ago. Says he helped me load them onto a truck himself. I did drive Whitby's pickup into town but only to get some lead screening. What does he think I'd do with all that cement? Just the sort of irritating thing you don't expect to hang over your final exit. (Moral: don't try too hard to forget Eniwetok.)

Woke 9:40. To sleep 4:15.

June 25: 7 ½ hours. Kaldren was snooping around the lab again today. Phoned me there, when I answered a recorded voice he'd rigged up rambled out a long string of numbers, like an insane super-Tim. These practical jokes of his get rather wearing. Fairly soon I'll have to go over and come to terms with him, much as I hate the prospect. Anyway, Miss Mars is a pleasure to look at.

One meal is enough now, topped up with a glucose shot. Sleep is still "black," completely unrefreshing. Last night I took a 16 mm film of the first three hours, screened it this morning at the lab. The first true horror movie, I looked like a half-animated corpse.

Woke 10:25. To sleep 3:45.

July 3: 5 ¾ hours. Little done today. Deepening lethargy, dragged myself over to the lab, nearly left the road twice. Concentrated enough to feed the zoo and get log up to date. Read through the operating manuals Whitby left for the last time, decided on a delivery rate of 40 röntgens/min., target distance of 350 cm. Everything is ready now.

Woke 11:05. To sleep 3:15.

Powers stretched, shifted his head slowly across the pillow, focusing on the shadows cast onto the ceiling by the blind. Then he looked down at his feet, saw Kaldren sitting on the end of the bed, watching him quietly.

"Hello, doctor," he said, putting out his cigarette. "Late night? You look tired."

Powers heaved himself onto one elbow, glanced at his watch. It was just after eleven. For a moment his brain blurred, and he swung his legs around and sat on the edge of the bed, elbows on his knees, massaging some life into his face.

He noticed that the room was full of smoke. "What are you doing here?" he asked Kaldren.

"I came over to invite you to lunch." He indicated the bedside phone. "Your line was dead so I drove round. Hope you don't mind me climbing in. Rang the bell for about half an hour. I'm surprised you didn't hear it."

Powers nodded, then stood up and tried to smooth the creases out of his cotton slacks. He had gone to sleep without changing for over a week, and they were damp and stale.

As he started for the bathroom door Kaldren pointed to the camera tripod on the other side of the bed. "What's this? Going into the blue movie business, doctor?"

Powers surveyed him dimly for a moment, glanced at the tripod without replying, and then noticed his open diary on the bedside table. Wondering whether Kaldren had read the last entries, he went back and picked it up, then stepped into the bathroom and closed the door behind him.

From the mirror cabinet he took out a syringe and an ampoule, after the shot leaned against the door waiting for the stimulant to pick up.

Kaldren was in the lounge when he returned to him, reading the labels on the crates lying about in the centre of the floor.

"Okay, then," Powers told him, "I'll join you for lunch." He examined Kaldren carefully. He looked more subdued than usual, there was an air almost of deference about him.

"Good," Kaldren said. "By the way, are you leaving?"

"Does it matter?" Powers asked curtly. "I thought you were in Anderson's care?"

Kaldren shrugged. "Please yourself. Come round at about twelve," he suggested, adding pointedly: "That'll give you time to clean up and change. What's that all over your shirt? Looks like lime."

Powers peered down, brushed at the white streaks. After Kaldren had left he threw the clothes away, took a shower, and unpacked a clean suit from one of the trunks.

Until his liaison with Coma, Kaldren lived alone in the old abstract summer house on the north shore of the lake. This was a seven-storey folly originally built by an eccentric millionaire mathematician in the form of a spiralling concrete ribbon that wound around itself like an insane serpent, serving walls, floors, and ceilings. Only Kaldren had solved the building—a geometric model of √-1—and consequently he had been able to take it off the agents' hands at a comparatively low rent. In the evenings Powers had often watched him from the laboratory, striding restlessly from one level to the next, swinging through the labyrinth of inclines and terraces to the rooftop, where his lean angular figure stood out like a gallows against the sky, his lonely eyes sifting out radio lanes for the next day's trapping.

Powers noticed him there when he drove up at noon, poised on a ledge 150 feet above, head raised theatrically to the sky.

"Kaldren!" he shouted up suddenly into the silent air, half-hoping he might be jolted into losing his footing.

Kaldren broke out of his reverie and glanced down into the court. Grinning obliquely, he waved his right arm in a slow semicircle.

"Come up," he called, then turned back to the sky.

Powers leaned against the car. Once, a few months previously, he had accepted the same invitation, stepped through the entrance, and within three minutes lost himself helplessly in a second-floor cul-de-sac. Kaldren had taken half an hour to find him.

Powers waited while Kaldren swung down from his eyrie, vaulting through the wells and stairways, then rode up in the elevator with him to the penthouse suite.

They carried their cocktails through into a wide glass-roofed studio, the huge white ribbon of concrete uncoiling around them like toothpaste squeezed from an enormous tube. On the staged levels running parallel and across them rested pieces of grey abstract furniture, giant photographs on angled screens, carefully labelled exhibits laid out on low tables, all dominated by twenty-foot-high black letters on the rear wall which spelt out the single vast word:

YOU

Kaldren pointed to it. "What you might call the supraliminal approach." He gestured Powers in conspiratorially, finishing his drink in a gulp. "This is *my* laboratory, doctor," he said with a note of pride. "Much more significant than yours, believe me."

Powers smiled wryly to himself and examined the first exhibit, an old EEG tape traversed by a series of faded inky wriggles. It was labelled: "Einstein, A.; Alpha Waves, 1922."

He followed Kaldren around, sipping slowly at his drink, enjoying the brief feeling of alertness the amphetamine provided. Within two hours it would fade, leave his brain feeling like a block of blotting paper.

Kaldren chattered away, explaining the significance of the so-called terminal documents. "They're end-prints, Powers, final statements, the products of total fragmentation. When I've got enough together I'll build a new world for myself out of them." He picked a thick paperbound volume off one of the tables, riffled through its pages. "Association tests of the Nuremberg Twelve. I have to include these. . . ."

Powers strolled on absently without listening. Over in the corner were what appeared to be three ticker-tape machines, lengths of tape hanging from their mouths. He wondered whether Kaldren was misguided enough to be playing the stock market, which had been declining slowly for twenty years.

"Powers," he heard Kaldren say. "I was telling you about the Mercury Seven." He pointed to a collection of typewritten sheets tacked to a screen. "These are transcripts of their final signals radioed back from the recording monitors."

Powers examined the sheets cursorily, read a line at random.

". . . BLUE . . . PEOPLE . . . RE-CYCLE . . . ORION . . . TELEMETERS . . ."

Powers nodded noncommittally. "Interesting. What are the ticker tapes for over there?"

Kaldren grinned. "I've been waiting for months for you to ask me that. Have a look."

Powers went over and picked up one of the tapes. The machine was labelled: "Auriga 225-G. Interval: 69 hours." The tape read:

96,688,365,498,695

96,688,365,498,694

96,688,365,498,693

96,688,365,498,692

Powers dropped the tape. "Looks rather familiar. What does the sequence represent?"

Kaldren shrugged. "No one knows."

"What do you mean? It must replicate something."

"Yes, it does. A diminishing mathematical progression. A countdown, if you like."

Powers picked up the tape on the right, tabbed: "Aries 44R951. Interval: 49 days."

Here the sequence ran:

876,567,988,347,779,877,654,434

876,567,988,347,779,877,654,433

876,567,988,347,779,877,654,432

Powers looked round. "How long does it take each signal to come through?"

"Only a few seconds. They're tremendously compressed laterally, of course. A computer at the observatory breaks them down. They were first picked up at Jodrell Bank about twenty years ago. Nobody bothers to listen to them now."

Powers turned to the last tape.

6,554

6,553

6,552

6,551

"Nearing the end of its run," he commented. He glanced at the label on the hood, which read: "Unidentified radio source, Canes Venatici. Interval: 97 weeks."

He showed the tape to Kaldren. "Soon be over."

Kaldren shook his head. He lifted a heavy directory-sized volume off a table, cradled it in his hands. His face had suddenly become sombre and haunted. "I doubt it," he said. "Those are only the last four digits. The whole number contains over fifty million."

He handed the volume to Powers, who turned to the title page. "Master Sequence of Serial Signal received by Jodrell Bank Radio-Observatory, University of Manchester, England, 0012-59 hours, 21-5-72. Source: NGC 9743, Canes Venatici." He thumbed the thick stack of closely printed pages, millions of numerals, as Kaldren had said, running up and down across a thousand consecutive pages.

Powers shook his head, picked up the tape again, and stared at it thoughtfully.

"The computer only breaks down the last four digits," Kaldren explained. "The whole series comes over in each fifteen-second-long package, but it took IBM more than two years to unscramble one of them."

"Amazing," Powers commented. "But what is it?"

"A countdown, as you can see. NGC 9743, somewhere in Canes Venatici. The big spirals there are breaking up, and they're saying good-bye. God knows who they think we are but they're letting us know all the same, beaming it out on the hydrogen line for everyone in the universe to hear." He paused. "Some people have put other interpretations on them, but there's one piece of evidence that rules out everything else."

"Which is?"

Kaldren pointed to the last tape from Canes Venatici. "Simply that it's been estimated that by the time this series reaches zero the universe will have just ended."

Powers fingered the tape reflectively. "Thoughtful of them to let us know what the real time is," he remarked.

"I agree, it is," Kaldren said quietly. "Applying the inverse square law that signal source is broadcasting at a strength of about three million megawatts raised to the hundredth power. About the size of the entire Local Group. *Thoughtful* is the word."

Suddenly he gripped Powers's arm, held it tightly, and peered into his eyes closely, his throat working with emotion.

"You're not alone, Powers, don't think you are. These are the voices of time, and they're all saying good-bye to you. Think of yourself in a wider context. Every particle in your body, every grain of sand, every galaxy carries the same signature. As you've just said, you know what the time is now, so what does the rest matter? There's no need to go on looking at the clock."

Powers took his hand, squeezed it firmly. "Thanks, Kaldren. I'm glad you understand." He walked over to the window, looked down across the white lake. The tension between himself and Kaldren had dissipated, he felt that all his obligations to him had at last been met. Now he wanted to leave as quickly as possible, forget him as he had forgotten the faces of the countless other patients whose exposed brains had passed between his fingers.

He went back to the ticker machines, tore

the tapes from their slots, and stuffed them into his pockets. "I'll take these along to remind myself. Say good-bye to Coma for me, will you."

He moved towards the door, when he reached it looked back to see Kaldren standing in the shadow of the three giant letters on the far wall, his eyes staring listlessly at his feet.

As Powers drove away he noticed that Kaldren had gone up onto the roof, watched him in the driving mirror waving slowly until the car disappeared around a bend.

FIVE

The outer circle was now almost complete. A narrow segment, an arc about ten feet long, was missing, but otherwise the low perimeter wall ran continuously six inches off the concrete floor around the outer lane of the target bull, enclosing the huge rebus within it. Three concentric circles, the largest a hundred yards in diameter, separated from each other by ten-foot intervals, formed the rim of the device, divided into four segments by the arms of an enormous cross radiating from its centre, where a small round platform had been built a foot above the ground.

Powers worked swiftly, pouring sand and cement into the mixer, tipping in water until a rough paste formed, then carried it across to the wooden forms and tamped the mixture down into the narrow channel.

Within ten minutes he had finished, quickly dismantled the forms before the cement had set, and slung the timbers into the backseat of the car. Dusting his hands on his trousers, he went over to the mixer and pushed it fifty yards away into the long shadow of the surrounding hills. Without pausing to survey the gigantic cipher on which he had laboured patiently for so many afternoons, he climbed into the car and drove off on a wake of bone-white dust, splitting the pools of indigo shadow.

. . .

He reached the laboratory at three o'clock, jumped from the car as it lurched back on its brakes. Inside the entrance he first switched on the lights, then hurried round, pulling the sun curtains down and shackling them to the floor slots, effectively turning the dome into a steel tent.

In their tanks behind him the plants and animals stirred quietly, responding to the sudden flood of cold fluorescent light. Only the chimpanzee ignored him. It sat on the floor of its cage, neurotically jamming the puzzle dice into the polythene bucket, exploding in bursts of sudden rage when the pieces refused to fit.

Powers went over to it, noticing the shattered glass fibre reinforcing panels bursting from the dented helmet. Already the chimp's face and forehead were bleeding from self-inflicted blows. Powers picked up the remains of the geranium that had been hurled through the bars, attracted the chimp's attention with it, then tossed a black pellet he had taken from a capsule in the desk drawer. The chimp caught it with a quick flick of the wrist, for a few seconds juggled the pellet with a couple of dice as it concentrated on the puzzle, then pulled it out of the air and swallowed it in a gulp.

Without waiting, Powers slipped off his jacket and stepped towards the X-ray theatre. He pulled back the high sliding doors to reveal the long glassy metallic snout of the Maxitron, then started to stack the lead screening shields against the rear wall.

A few minutes later the generator hummed into life.

The anemone stirred. Basking in the warm subliminal sea of radiation rising around it, prompted by countless pelagic memories, it reached tentatively across the tank, groping blindly towards the dim uterine sun. Its tendrils flexed, the thousands of dormant neural cells in their tips regrouping and multiplying, each harnessing the unlocked energies of its nucleus. Chains forged themselves, lattices tiered upwards into multifaceted lenses, focused slowly on the vivid spectral outlines of the sounds dancing like phosphorescent waves around the darkened chamber of the dome.

Gradually an image formed, revealing an enormous black fountain that poured an endless stream of brilliant light over the circle of benches and tanks. Beside it a figure moved, adjusting the flow through its mouth. As it stepped across the floor its feet threw off vivid bursts of colour, its hands racing along the benches conjured up a dazzling chiaroscuro, balls of blue and violet light that exploded fleetingly in the darkness like miniature star-shells.

Photons murmured. Steadily, as it watched the glimmering screen of sounds around it, the anemone continued to expand. Its ganglia linked, heeding a new source of stimuli from the delicate diaphragms in the crown of its notochord. The silent outlines of the laboratory began to echo softly, waves of muted sound fell from the arc lights and echoed off the benches and furniture below. Etched in sound, their angular forms resonated with sharp persistent overtones. The plastic-ribbed chairs were a buzz of staccato discords, the square-sided desk a continuous double-featured tone. Ignoring these sounds once they had been perceived, the anemone turned to the ceiling, which reverberated like a shield in the sounds pouring steadily from the fluorescent tubes. Streaming through a narrow skylight, its voice clear and strong, interweaved by numberless overtones, the sun sang. . . .

It was a few minutes before dawn when Powers left the laboratory and stepped into his car. Behind him the great dome lay silently in the darkness, the thin shadows of the white moonlit hills falling across its surface. Powers free-wheeled the car down the long curving drive to the lake road below, listening to the tyres cutting across the blue gravel, then let out the clutch and accelerated the engine.

As he drove along, the limestone hills half hidden in the darkness on his left, he gradually became aware that, although no longer looking at the hills, he was still in some oblique way conscious of their forms and outlines in the back of his mind. The sensation was undefined but nonetheless certain, a strange almost visual impression that emanated most strongly from the deep clefts and ravines dividing one cliff face from the next. For a few minutes Powers let it play upon him, without trying to identify it, a dozen strange images moving across his brain.

The road swung up around a group of chalets built on to the lake shore, taking the car right under the lee of the hills, and Powers suddenly felt the massive weight of the escarpment rising up into the dark sky like a cliff of luminous chalk, and realized the identity of the impression now registering powerfully within his mind. Not only could he see the escarpment, but he was aware of its enormous age, felt distinctly the countless millions of years since it had first reared out of the magma of the earth's crust. The ragged crests three hundred feet above him, the dark gulleys and fissures, the smooth boulders by the roadside at the foot of the cliff, all carried a distinct image of themselves across to him, a thousand voices that together told of the total time that had elapsed in the life of the escarpment, a psychic picture defined and clear as the visual image brought to him by his eyes.

Involuntarily, Powers had slowed the car, and turning his eyes away from the hill face he felt a second wave of time sweep across the first. The image was broader but of shorter perspectives, radiating from the wide disc of the salt lake, breaking over the ancient limestone cliffs like shallow rollers dashing against a towering headland.

Closing his eyes, Powers lay back and steered the car along the interval between the two time fronts, feeling the images deepen and strengthen within his mind. The vast age of the landscape, the inaudible chorus of voices resonating from the lake and from the white hills, seemed to carry him back through time, down endless corridors to the first thresholds of the world.

He turned the car off the road along the track leading towards the target range. On either side of the culvert the cliff faces boomed and echoed with vast impenetrable time fields, like enormous opposed magnets. As he finally emerged between them onto the flat surface of the lake it seemed to Powers that he could feel the separate identity of each sand grain and salt crystal calling to him from the surrounding ring of hills.

He parked the car beside the mandala and walked slowly towards the outer concrete rim curving away into the shadows. Above him he could hear the stars, a million cosmic voices that crowded the sky from one horizon to the next, a true canopy of time. Like jostling radio beacons, their long aisles interlocking at countless angles, they plunged into the sky from the narrowest recesses of space. He saw the dim red disc of Sirius, heard its ancient voice, untold millions of years old, dwarfed by the huge spiral nebulae in Andromeda, a gigantic carousel of vanished universes, their voices almost as old as the cosmos itself. To Powers the sky seemed an endless babel, the time-song of a thousand galaxies overlaying each other in his mind. As he moved slowly towards the centre of the mandala he craned up at the glittering traverse of the Milky Way, searching the confusion of clamouring nebulae and constellations.

Stepping into the inner circle of the mandala, a few yards from the platform at its centre, he realized that the tumult was beginning to fade, and that a single stronger voice had emerged and was dominating the others. He climbed onto the platform, raised his eyes to the darkened sky, moving through the constellations to the island galaxies beyond them, hearing the thin archaic voices reaching to him across the millennia. In his pockets he felt the paper tapes, and turned to find the distant diadem of Canes Venatici, heard its great voice mounting in his mind.

Like an endless river, so broad that its banks were below the horizons, it flowed steadily towards him, a vast course of time that spread outwards to fill the sky and the universe, enveloping everything within them. Moving slowly, the forward direction of its majestic current almost imperceptible, Powers knew that its source was the source of the cosmos itself. As it passed him, he felt its massive magnetic pull, let himself be drawn into it, borne gently on its powerful back. Quietly it carried him away, and he rotated slowly, facing the direction of the tide. Around him the outlines of the hills and the lake had faded, but the image of the mandala, like a cosmic clock, remained fixed before his eyes, illuminating the broad surface of the stream. Watching it constantly, he felt his body gradually dissolving, its physical dimensions melting into the vast continuum of the current, which bore him out into the centre of the great channel, sweeping him onward, beyond hope but at last at rest, down the broadening reaches of the river of eternity.

As the shadows faded, retreating into the hill slopes, Kaldren stepped out of his car, walked hesitantly towards the concrete rim of the outer circle. Fifty yards away, at the centre, Coma knelt beside Powers's body, her small hands pressed to his dead face. A gust of wind stirred the sand, dislodging a strip of tape that drifted towards Kaldren's feet. He bent down and picked it up, then rolled it carefully in his hands and slipped it into his pocket. The dawn air was cold, and he turned up the collar of his jacket, watching Coma impassively.

"It's six o'clock," he told her after a few minutes. "I'll go and get the police. You stay with him." He paused and then added: "Don't let them break the clock."

Coma turned and looked at him. "Aren't you coming back?"

"I don't know." Nodding to her, Kaldren swung on his heel.

He reached the lake road, five minutes later parked the car in the drive outside Whitby's laboratory.

The dome was in darkness, all its windows shuttered, but the generator still hummed in the X-ray theatre. Kaldren stepped through the entrance and switched on the lights. In the theatre he touched the grilles of the generator, felt the warm cylinder of the beryllium end-window. The circular target table was revolving slowly, its setting at one rpm, a steel restraining chair shackled to it hastily. Grouped in a semi-circle a few feet away were most of the tanks and cages, piled on top of each other haphazardly. In one of them an enormous squidlike plant had almost managed to climb from its vivarium. Its long translucent tendrils clung to the edges of the tank, but its body had burst into a jellified pool of globular mucilage. In another an enormous spider had trapped itself in its own web, hung helplessly in the centre of a huge three-dimensional maze of phosphorescing thread, twitching spasmodically.

All the experimental plants and animals had died. The chimp lay on its back among the remains of the hutch, the helmet forward over its eyes. Kaldren watched it for a moment, then sat down on the desk and picked up the phone. While he dialled the number he noticed a film reel lying on the blotter. For a moment he stared at the label, then slid the reel into his pocket beside the tape.

After he had spoken to the police he turned off the lights and went out to the car, drove off slowly down the drive.

When he reached the summer house the early sunlight was breaking across the ribbon-like balconies and terraces. He took the lift to the penthouse, made his way through into the museum. One by one he opened the shutters and let the sunlight play over the exhibits. Then he pulled a chair over to a side window, sat back, and stared up at the light pouring through into the room.

Two or three hours later he heard Coma outside, calling up to him. After half an hour she went away, but a little later a second voice appeared and shouted up at Kaldren. He left his chair and closed all the shutters overlooking the front courtyard, and eventually he was left undisturbed.

Kaldren returned to his seat and lay back quietly, his eyes gazing across the lines of exhibits. Half-asleep, periodically he leaned up and adjusted the flow of light through the shutter, thinking to himself, as he would do through the coming months, of Powers and his strange mandala, and of the seven and their journey to the white gardens of the moon, and the blue people who had come from Orion and spoken in poetry to them of ancient beautiful worlds beneath golden suns in the island galaxies, vanished forever now in the myriad deaths of the cosmos.

The Astronaut

VALENTINA ZHURAVLYOVA

Translated by James Womack

Valentina Nikolayevna Zhuravlyova (1933–2004) was a Soviet-era science fiction writer from Russia. She published a handful of stories in English in the 1980s that were originally written in the 1950s and early 1960s, but she is largely unknown to Western readers. Especially during the 1960s, the Soviet Union boasted several talented Russian and Ukrainian writers besides the iconic Strugatsky brothers, although the Strugatskys were arguably the only ones to break out into significant English translation.

Although little is known about Zhuravlyova, she did collaborate on science fiction with her husband, the engineer and inventor Genrich Altshuller, who invented TRIZ—the Russian acronym for the Theory of Inventive Problem Solving. They wrote many stories together, but because of anti-Semitic restrictions, these stories were published under the single name of Valentina Zhuravlyova. ("The Astronaut," however, is a story Valentina wrote solo.)

As noted by James Lecky in a 2013 blog entry, "The Astronaut" was first published in 1960 but later appeared in the 1963 anthology *Destination: Amaltheia*, edited by Richard Dixon. The story is striking for its mixture of big, bold emotions and themes of sacrifice and renewal. As Lecky also notes, despite the emotional openness of the story, its provocative structure marks it as a forerunner of the New Wave of the mid-1960s. This new translation by James Womack corrects several errors in the original translation and provides a newly "refurbished" look at an underappreciated gem of Soviet-era science fiction.

THE ASTRONAUT

Valentina Zhuravlyova
Translated by James Womack

"What can I do for the people?" Danko shouted, louder than thunder.
And suddenly he tore at his chest with his hands and plucked out his heart
and lifted it high above his head.
MAXIM GORKY

I should briefly explain why I went to the Central Archive of Space Travel. Otherwise what I am about to tell you would be incomprehensible.

I am a spaceship's doctor and have taken part in three missions. My medical speciality is psychiatry. Astropsychiatry, as they now call it. The problem I am working on is one that first arose a long time ago, in the 1970s. At that time a journey to Mars lasted more than a year, and one to Mercury almost two. The motors were only fired on takeoff and landing. Astronomical observations were not carried out on board—artificial satellites were used instead. What would the crew do then, over the long months of their journey? In the first years of space travel—practically nothing. This enforced inactivity led to nervous collapse, sapped people's strength, caused illnesses. Reading and radio programs were not enough to replace what the first astronauts lacked. They needed work, creative work, which was what they were accustomed to. And then the idea of recruiting people who had outside interests was put forward. The idea was that it did not matter what they liked doing, as long as it gave them something to keep them busy during the flight. And so pilots were also extremely proficient mathematicians. Navigators were students of ancient manuscripts. Engineers spent all their free time writing poetry. . . .

In the flight manuals for astronaut training another point—the famous twelfth point—was added: "What are the candidate's hobbies? What is the candidate interested in?" However, very soon another solution was found for the problem. For interplanetary travel, spaceships were fitted with atomic-ion drives. The length of flights was cut down to a few days. The twelfth point was removed from the training manuals. And then a few years later the problem reappeared, in an even more acute form. Mankind graduated to interstellar travel. Atomic-ion rockets, traveling at near-light speeds, still took years to fly to the closest stars. The time passed more slowly in the swiftly moving rocket, and flights could still take eight, or twelve, or even twenty years. . . .

The twelfth point appeared again in the flight manuals. In fact, it became one of the most important considerations for choosing a crew. Interstellar travel, from the point of view of the pilot, consisted of 99.99 percent downtime. Radio signals broke off a month or so after takeoff. After a month the interference was so great that optical signals had to be broken off. And ahead lay years, years, years. . . .

Back in those days rockets were manned by crews of six or eight, had tiny cabins and a fifty-meter greenhouse. For us, who now travel in interstellar liners, it is difficult to imagine how people managed without a gym, a swimming pool, a cinema, a promenade. . . .

425

I'm losing my thread and the story hasn't even started yet. Nowadays the twelfth point no longer plays a major role in the choice of crew. For scheduled flights along standard routes that is only fair. However, for long-distance research flights people with hobbies are still needed as crew members. At least, that is my opinion. The twelfth point is the subject of my academic research. The history of the twelfth point has brought me here, to the Central Archive of Space Travel.

I should acknowledge that the word *archive* isn't one I like all that much. I am a starship's doctor, and that is more or less the same as being an eighteenth-century ship's doctor. I am used to traveling, to danger. I have made all three of my interstellar journeys on research trips. I participated in the first trip to Procyon and have always been filled with a desire for discovery. On the three planets that orbit Procyon there are several objects that I named: do you know what it's like to name an ocean that you discovered?

Archive was a word that frightened me. But things turned out differently from how I imagined. I don't know, and haven't yet been able to find out, who was the architect of the Central Archive of Space Travel. It must have been someone extremely talented. Talented and brave. The building is on the banks of the Siberian Sea, created twenty years ago when they built a dam on the Ob. The main building of the archive is on the hills by the seaside. I don't know how they managed to do it, but it looks like the building hangs over the water. Light and aiming upward, it looks at a distance like a white sail. . . .

There are fifteen people who work in the archive. I have managed to strike up acquaintances with several of them. They are almost all of them temporary workers. An Austrian is gathering material on the first interstellar flight. There is a scholar, from Leningrad, writing a history of Mars. The shy Indian is a famous sculptor. He said to me: "I need to know their spiritual world." There are two engineers: a husky chap from Saratov who looks like the heroic test pilot Chkalov and a small politely smiling Japanese man. They need to find background material for some project or other. I don't know exactly what. When I asked him, the Japanese replied very politely: "Oh, it's really nothing significant! It's nothing for you to waste your attention on." But I'm drifting away again. Back to the story.

On the first day, in the evening, I spoke to the chief archivist. He is a man, still young, but who is almost completely blind as the result of a fuel tank explosion. He wears glasses with three lenses. They are blue. You can't see his eyes. This makes it appear that the chief archivist never smiles.

"So," he said after hearing me out, "you need to start with the materials from Sector 0-14. I'm sorry, that's our own internal classification, it won't mean anything to you. What I mean is the first expedition to Barnard's Star."

To my embarrassment, I knew almost nothing about this journey.

"You flew in the other direction," the chief archivist said, shrugging. "Sirius, Procyon, 61 Cygni . . ."

I was surprised that he knew my service record so well.

"Yes," he continued, "the story of Aleksey Zarubin, the commander of that expedition, gives a very interesting answer to your question. They'll bring you the materials in half an hour. Good luck."

His eyes were invisible behind the blue glass. But his voice sounded sad.

And the materials are here on my desk. The paper is yellow, on several of the documents the ink (they used ink back then) has faded. But someone has carefully protected the text: infrared photofilms are attached. The paper is covered with transparent plastic; they feel dense and smooth to the touch.

Out of the window—the sea. It slides dully up to the shore, the waves make a noise like pages being turned. . . .

In those days an expedition to Barnard's

Star was daring, maybe even desperate. It takes six years for light to reach from Earth to Barnard's Star. The ship would be accelerating for half the journey, decelerating for the other half. And although sub-light speeds would be reached, the flight there and back would still take around fourteen years. For the people flying in the rocket, time would pass more slowly: fourteen years would become forty months. This is not an unusually long stretch of time, but the problem was that for almost all this time, thirty-eight months out of the forty, the ship's engines would have to work at full power. The nuclear fuel reserves were calculated precisely. Any deviation from the path would mean the death of the expedition.

Nowadays it seems like an unbelievable risk to set off into space without having sufficient fuel reserves, but back then there was no other option. The ship could carry no more than what the engineers managed to pack into the tanks.

I read the report of the committee that chose the crew. The candidates for captain come up one by one and the committee always says: "No." No, because the flight is exceptionally difficult, because colossal resilience needs to be combined with almost incredible daring. And suddenly the committee says: "Yes."

I turn a page. Here is where the story of Captain Aleksey Zarubin begins.

Three pages further on and I start to understand why Aleksey Zarubin was unanimously chosen as the commander of the *Pole*. This man embodied to the most unusual extent both "ice" and "fire": the calm wisdom of a researcher and the wild temperament of a warrior. This must have been why he was sent on dangerous missions. He always found a way to escape from what appeared to be the most hopeless situations.

The committee had chosen the captain. As tradition dictated, the captain must now choose his crew. Speaking for myself, Zarubin didn't really choose his crew. He simply invited five astronauts who had already flown with him. To the question: "Are you willing to go on a dif-

ficult and dangerous flight?" they all replied: "With you, yes."

In the materials there is a photograph of the crew of the *Pole*. It is monochrome, without depth. The captain was twenty-seven years old when it was taken. He looks older in the photograph: a full, slightly puffy face with prominent cheekbones, his lips tight shut, a prominent crooked nose, wavy soft-seeming hair, and strange eyes. They looked peaceful, almost lazy, but had somewhere in their corners a mischievous, reckless spark. . . .

The other astronauts are even younger. The engineers, a husband-and-wife team; there is a joint photograph in the file, they always flew together. The navigator had the thoughtful gaze of a musician. There was a female doctor. I suppose I must have looked just as serious in the first photograph they took of me when I joined the Star Fleet. The astrophysicist looks stubborn, his face is covered in burn marks; he and the captain once made an emergency landing on Dione, one of the moons of Saturn.

Point twelve in the flight manual. I flick through the pages and confirm my hunch: the photograph told the truth. The navigator is a musician and a composer. The serious woman has a serious hobby: microbiology. The astrophysicist studies languages: he is already fluent in five, including Latin and Ancient Greek. The husband-and-wife engineers have only one hobby: chess, a new variant, with two queens of each color and an eighty-one-square board. . . .

The last entry in the twelfth point of the flight manual is that of the captain. He has a strange hobby—unusual, perhaps unique. I've never seen anything like it. That the captain had a keen interest in art ever since he was a child is understandable: his mother was an artist. But the captain paints very little, his interests lie elsewhere. He dreams of rediscovering the long-lost secrets of the old masters—how to make oil paints, how to blend them and prepare them for use. He carries out his chemical research, as he does everything, with the tenacity of a scientist and the temperament of an artist.

Six people, six different characters, different fates. But the tone of the expedition is set by the captain. They love him, they believe in him, they support him. And so they all know how to be unflappably calm and unstoppably daring.

Blast off.

The *Pole* heads for Barnard's Star. The nuclear reactor is working, an invisible stream of ions flows from the various nozzles. The rocket accelerates constantly, the crew feels this. To start with it is difficult to walk, difficult to work. The doctor insists on the imposition of a regimen of activity. The astronauts get used to the conditions of the flight. The greenhouse is set up, then the radiotelescope. Normal life begins. Monitoring the reactor, the equipment, the various mechanisms: this takes up very little time. Four hours a day are all that is required for the crew to work at their specializations. The rest of the time can be employed as each crew member prefers. The navigator composes a song—the whole crew ends up singing it. The chess players spend hours at the board. The astrophysicist reads Plutarch in the original. . . .

The log contains short entries: "The flight continues. The reactor and the ship's equipment are working perfectly. Morale is excellent." And suddenly there is one that sounds like a shout: "The rocket has passed the limit of reception of television signals. We saw the last report from Earth yesterday. How difficult to say good-bye to one's homeland!" And the days still go by. Another entry: "Have set up the antenna for receiving optical signals. We hope that we will receive signals from Earth for another seven or eight days." They were happy as schoolboys when the signals actually lasted another twelve days. . . .

Its speed increasing, the rocket headed toward Barnard's Star. The months went by. The nuclear reactor worked with absolute accuracy. The fuel was spent exactly according to the plans, not a milligram more.

The catastrophe happened without warning. One day—this was in the eighth month of the journey—the reactor started to function in a different way. A parallel reaction made the fuel consumption increase sharply. The brief entry in the log reads: "We do not know what has caused the side reaction." Yes, back in those days they still did not know that infinitesimal impurities in nuclear fuel could sometimes change the speed of a reaction. . . .

The sea sounds outside the window. The wind is up, the waves are no longer rustling—they slap down cruelly as they come in to shore. Someone is laughing in the distance. I cannot, I should not be distracted. I can almost see these people in the rocket. I know them—I can imagine what it was like. Perhaps I am mistaken about the details—but what importance does that have? And in fact no, I am not even mistaken in the details. I am sure that it happened exactly like this.

In the retort, over a burner, a brown liquid boiled and bubbled. Brown smoke curled through the condenser. The captain was carefully examining a test tube filled with a dark red powder. The door opened. The flame of the burner flickered, jumped. The captain turned round. The engineer stood in the doorway.

The engineer was shaken. He was under control, but his voice betrayed how agitated he was. It was someone else's voice, louder, unrealistically harsh. The engineer tried to speak calmly and could not.

"Sit down, Nikolay." The captain pointed him to a chair. "I carried out these tests yesterday evening and got the same result. . . . Sit down. . . ."

"What do we do now?"

"Now?" The captain looked at his watch. "There's fifty-five minutes to go till supper. So we can talk. Please tell everyone."

"Very good," the engineer mechanically replied. "I'll tell them. Yes, I'll tell them." He did not know why the captain was reacting so slowly. With every second the *Pole* was gathering speed, and a decision would have to be made forthwith.

"Look," said the captain, and handed him

the test tube. "This will most likely interest you. This is mercury sulfide, cinnabar. A damn fine pigment. But it normally gets darker when exposed to light. I've figured it out—it's all to do with particle size. . . ."

He spent a while explaining to the engineer how he had managed to produce a light-resistant cinnabar. The engineer impatiently shook the test tube. There was a clock set into the wall over the desk, and the engineer could not help glancing at it: thirty seconds, and the ship's speed increased by two kilometers per second; another minute, another four kilometers per second. . . .

"I'll go now," he said finally. "I need to tell the others."

The captain shut the cabin door tightly. He carefully put the test tube into a rack. He listened. The reactor's cooling system was buzzing quietly. The engines that increased the *Pole*'s speed were working perfectly.

. . . Ten minutes later the captain went down to the crew's quarters. Five people were standing waiting for him. They were all wearing their astronaut uniforms, which they put on only on rare occasions, and the captain understood: he did not need to explain the situation to anyone.

"So . . . ," he started. "Apparently I'm the only one who forgot to get dolled up. . . ."

Nobody smiled.

"Sit down," the captain said. "A council of war . . . So . . . Well. Let the youngest speak first, as is the custom. You, Lenochka. What should we do, what do you think?" He turned to the woman.

She spoke very seriously:

"I am a doctor, Aleksey Pavlovich. This is a more technical question. Please let me give my opinion later."

The captain nodded:

"Of course. You are the wisest of us all, Lenochka. And the quickest thinker. I'd be willing to bet that you have an opinion. You do have one already."

The woman didn't answer.

"Well," the captain said, "Lenochka will talk later. So now it's your turn, Sergey."

The astrophysicist flung his arms wide.

"This has nothing to do with my specialism either, I don't have any firm opinions. But I know that the fuel will last for our trip to Barnard's Star. Why turn back halfway?"

"Yes, why?" the captain repeated. "Because we can't come back. We can turn back halfway. But we can't return once we reach our destination."

"Agreed," the astrophysicist said thoughtfully. "But is it really true that we can't come back? We ourselves, of course, will not return. But people will fly after us. They will see that we haven't come back and will set out to find us. Astronautics is a developing science."

"Developing," the captain laughed. "As time goes by . . . So, we should fly onward? Am I understanding you correctly? Very good. Now you, Georgey. Does this relate to your specialism?"

The navigator leapt up, pushing his chair back from the table.

"Sit down," the captain said. "Sit down and speak calmly. Don't jump around."

"There is no way to get back!" The navigator was almost shouting. "We can only move onward. Onward, through the impossible! Anyway, think about it, how can we return? Didn't we know that the expedition would be a difficult one? Of course we knew. And here we are, up against the first difficulty, ready to throw it all in. . . . No, no, onward, ever onward!"

"Ri-ight," the captain drawled. "Onward through the impossible. Sounds good . . . Well, what do the engineers think? You, Nina Vladimirovna? You, Nikolay?"

The engineer looked at his wife. She nodded and he started to speak. He spoke calmly, as if thinking aloud.

"Our flight to Barnard's Star is a research expedition. If we six learn anything new, make any discoveries, then that in itself won't have any value. Our discoveries will only develop a value when they are known to other people, to mankind as a whole. If we fly to Barnard's Star and have no means of return, what's the point of any discoveries we make? Sergey said that people would end up flying after us. That's true. But the ones who follow will have to make these discoveries without us. What will our contribution have been? What benefit will our expedition have been to humanity? In fact, we will only have caused harm. Yes, harm. They will wait on Earth for our expedition to return. They will wait in vain. If we come back now, then the amount of time lost will be minimized. A new expedition will set out. We will set out ourselves. We may lose a few years, but the material we have gathered so far will be stored on Earth. At the moment there's no chance that will happen. . . . Fly on? Why? No, we—Nina and I—are against it. We have to go back. At once."

There was a long silence. Then Lena asked:

"And what do you think, Captain?"

The captain smiled sadly.

"I think that our engineers are right. Beautiful words are nothing but words. But common sense, logic, calculation: these are all on the side of the engineers. We are flying in order to make discoveries. And if these discoveries are not transmitted to Earth, then they are worthless. Nikolay is right, a thousand times right. . . ."

Zarubin stood up and walked heavily round the cabin. It was difficult to walk: movement was impeded by the triple-strength gravity caused by the acceleration of the rocket.

"Waiting for a relief rocket is out of the question," the captain continued. "There are two other possibilities. The first is to return to Earth. The second is to fly to Barnard's Star . . . and then fly back to Earth. To return in spite of the loss of fuel."

"How?" the engineer asked.

Zarubin went back to his chair and sat down without answering immediately.

"I don't know how. But we have time. There are still eleven months to go before we reach Barnard's Star. If you decide to return now, then we will return. But if you believe that we can think up something over the next eleven months, that we can invent some sort of solution, then . . . then onward, through the impossible! That's all I've got to say, my friends. What about you. It's your turn, Lenochka."

The woman winked at him.

"You're the quickest thinker. I'd be willing to bet that you have something worked out already."

The captain laughed.

"You lose! I haven't got anything in mind. But there are still eleven months left. We'll be able to think up something during that time."

"We have faith," the engineer said. "We have faith." He was silent for a moment. "Although, to tell the truth, I'm not sure how we're going to make it. Fuel levels on the *Pole* will be at eighteen percent when we get there. Eighteen percent instead of fifty . . . But you've said you're certain, and that's that. We'll go to Barnard's Star. Like Georgey said, onward through the impossible."

The door squeaks quietly. The wind ruffles the pages, hurries about the room, filling it with the damp smell of the sea. Smell's a funny thing. There are no smells on board a rocket. The conditioners clean the air, keep the temperature and humidity levels constant. But conditioned air is tasteless, like distilled water. They tried artificial scent generators a couple of times, but nothing came of them. The smell of normal Earth air is too complicated; it's difficult to reproduce. Like now . . . I smell the sea, the damp autumn leaves, and a distant smell of perfume, and from time to time, when the wind gets up, the smell of earth. And a very faint smell of paint.

The wind leafs through the pages. . . . What was the captain banking on? He really had to "think something up." And he was the only experienced astronaut on board the ship.

Of course, Zarubin could rely on the help of the members of his crew—the navigator, the engineers, the astrophysicist, the doctor. But that would be later. First of all, he had to "think something up." That is the particular specialism of a ship's captain.

I am a doctor, but I have been on space flights and I know that there is no such thing as a miracle. When the *Pole* reached Barnard's Star, it would only have 18 percent of its fuel remaining. Eighteen instead of fifty . . .

There is no such thing as a miracle. But if the captain had asked me if I believed he would find a way out, I would have said, "Yes." I would have answered straightaway, without needing to think: "Yes, yes, yes!" I don't believe in miracles, but I believe implicitly in people.

In the morning I asked the chief archivist to show me Zarubin's paintings.

"You'll need to go upstairs," he said. "But . . . Tell me, have you read all the documents?"

He listened to my reply, and nodded.

"I understand. I thought as much. Yes, the captain took on a great responsibility. . . . Would you have trusted him?"

"Yes."

"So would I."

He was silent for a long time, biting his lips. Then he stood up and pushed his glasses up his nose.

"All right then, let's go."

The chief archivist walked with a limp. We walked slowly along the corridors of the archive.

"You'll read some more about this," the archivist said. "If I'm not wrong, it's in the second volume, round about page one hundred. Zarubin wanted to discover the secrets of the Italian Renaissance masters. From the eighteenth century onward there had been a falling off in oil painting, at least on the level of craft. Many people considered that this was an irreversible decline. Artists were unable to get hold of colors that were at the same time bright and long lasting. The brighter they were, the quicker the paintings faded. Especially blues. Well, Zarubin . . . but you'll see."

Zarubin's paintings hung in a narrow sunlit gallery. The first thing that leapt out at me was that each painting was only one color—red, blue, green. . . .

"These are studies," the archivist said. "Technical exercises, nothing more. Here's his *Study in Blue*."

Two fragile human figures—a man and a woman—with strap-on wings were flying side by side through a blue sky. Everything was painted in different shades of blue, but I had never seen so many. It was a night sky, blue-black, on the lower left edge and a transparent warm midday blue in the opposite corner. The people's wings were painted in shades of light and dark blue, shading into violet. At points the colors were harsh, clear, sparkling, and in other parts they were softer, muted, transparent. Next to this painting, Degas's *Blue Dancers* would have seemed very limited and poorly colored.

There were other pictures hanging there as well. *Study in Red*: two crimson suns above an unknown planet, a chaos of shadows and half shadows, from blood-red to pale pink. *Study in Brown*: an imaginary fairy forest . . .

"Zarubin had a great imagination," the archivist said. "He was just trying out his colors. But then . . ."

He fell silent. I waited, looking at the blue impermeable glasses over his eyes.

"Just read more," he said quietly. "Then I'll show you some other paintings. Then you'll understand. . . ."

I read as fast as I can, trying to grasp the most important points.

The *Pole* flew to Barnard's Star. The spaceship reached its maximum speed and then the motors started to go into reverse. Judging from the brief entries in the log, everything proceeded normally. There were no accidents, no illnesses. And the captain was, as always, calm, confident, cheerful. He spent a lot of his time studying the technology of paint manufacture, and painting his studies. . . .

What was he thinking of, in his cabin? The log and the navigator's personal journal do nothing to answer this question. But here's an interesting document. It's the engineer's report. It discusses faults in the cooling system. Dry, precise language, technical terms. But between the lines what I read was the following: "My friend, if you have second thoughts, you can still turn round. Retreat with honor. . . ." And there's a note in the captain's hand: "The cooling systems will be repaired once we reach Barnard's Star." And what that meant was "No, my friend, I haven't changed my mind."

Zarubin didn't change his mind. He drove the *Pole* onward, through the impossible. Nineteen months after takeoff they reached Barnard's Star. The dim red star had only one planet, almost as large as Earth, but covered in ice. The *Pole* tried to land. The ion stream from the engines melted the ice and the first attempt at landing was unsuccessful. The captain chose a different spot—and the ice melted again. Six times the *Pole* tried to land, until it finally came across a granite cliff under the ice.

At this point, the entries in the log start to be made in red ink. This was the traditional method of recording discoveries.

The planet was dead. Its atmosphere was almost pure oxygen, but there was not a single living creature, not a single plant on its dead surface. The thermometer read minus fifty degrees.

"An undistinguished planet," the navigator wrote in his diary, "but what a wonderful star! A whole avalanche of discoveries . . ."

Yes, a whole avalanche of discoveries. Even now, when research into the formation and evolution of stars has taken a great leap forward, even now the discoveries made by the crew of the *Pole* are still to a large extent useful. The research made into the gaseous envelope of "red dwarves" of the Barnard's Star type is still cited as one of the fullest and most accurate studies.

The log . . . The scientific report . . . The astrophysicist's handwriting, setting out his paradoxical hypotheses on the evolution of stars . . . And, finally, what I was looking for: the commander's order to return. It was unexpected, implausible. Not willing to believe it, I quickly flick through the pages. The entry in the navigator's journal. Now I believe, I know for a fact—this is how it was.

One day the captain said:

"Enough. Time to go home."

Five people looked silently at Zarubin. The clock ticked calmly. . . .

Five people looked at the captain. They were waiting.

"Time to go home," the captain repeated. "You know that we have eighteen percent of our fuel remaining. But there is a way out. First of all, we need to make the rocket lighter. We need to get rid of all the electronic equipment apart from the navigation controls. . . ." He saw that the navigator wanted to say something, and stopped him with a gesture. "That's how it needs to be. Apparatus, internal partitions in the empty tanks, bits of the greenhouse. And the most important is the heavy electronic apparatus. But that's not all. The main usage of fuel takes place during the first few months of a flight—because of the slow acceleration. We'll have to get used to being uncomfortable: the *Pole* will take off not at three g's, but at twelve."

"Accelerating like that we won't be able to control the rocket," the engineer interrupted. "The pilot won't be able to—"

"I know that," the captain interrupted firmly. "I know that. Control of the ship over the first few months will have to be carried out here, from the planet. One crew member will stay here. . . . Silence! Silence, I said! Remember, there's no other way out. This is how it will be. So, I'll carry on. You, Nina Vladimirovna, and you, Nikolay, will not be able to stay: you're going to have a child. Yes, I know. You, Lenochka, are the ship's doctor and so you have to fly. Sergey is the astrophysicist. He needs to fly as well. And Georgey can't control himself. And so the only one left is me. Once more—silence! This is how it will be."

. . . I have in front of me the calculations that Zarubin made. I am a doctor, but I understand all of them. One thing I notice straightaway: The calculations are made, one might say, to the limit. The ship will be stripped down to the limit, the gravitational force at takeoff will be pushed to the limit. Most of the greenhouse will be left on the planet, and so the daily ration for the astronauts will be small—much lower than the established norms. The backup power supply with its two mini-reactors will be removed. Almost all the electronic equipment will be removed. If something unforeseen happens on the flight back, the rocket will be unable even to make it back to Barnard's Star. "The risk is raised to the power of three," is written down in the navigator's diary. And below that: "But for the person who stays behind, it is raised to the tenth power, the hundredth. . . ."

Zarubin will have to wait for fourteen years. It is only then that another rocket can come to find him. Fourteen years alone, on an alien frozen world . . . More calculations. The most important thing is the energy supply. It will have to be enough to control the rocket remotely, and then last for fourteen long, endless, eternal years. And once again, everything is worked out to the limit, right on the edge.

A photofilm of the captain's quarters. It is made out of sections of the greenhouse. Through the transparent panes you can see the electronic apparatus and the mini-reactors. The tele-control antennae are on the roof. And all around is a frozen desert. Barnard's Star shines coldly in the gray, dim, fog-covered sky. It is about four times as large as the Earth's sun but shines no brighter than the moon.

I quickly go through the log. Here's everything: the captain's parting words, the agreement reached about radio contact over the first few days of the journey, and a list of objects which need to be left for the captain. . . . And suddenly four words: "The *Pole* takes off." And then there are some strange notes. They look as if they were made by a child: the lines cross over one another, the letters are angular, broken. That is the twelve-g acceleration.

I make out the words with difficulty. The first entry: "All is good. Damn gravity over-

load! Purple patches in front of my eyes . . ." Two days later: "We're accelerating as planned. Impossible to walk, we can only crawl. . . ." A week later: "Difficult, very [crossed out] . . . we're coping. The reactor is working as calculated."

Two pages of the log are not filled in. On the third, heavily blotted, is the following entry, written at an angle: "Contact lost with ground control. Something is blocking the beam. It is [crossed out] . . . It is the end. . . ." But then, right on the edge of the page, is another entry in a much firmer hand: "Contact with ground control reestablished. The power indicator shows strength at level four. The captain is giving us all the energy from his mini-reactors, and we can't stop him. He's sacrificing himself. . . ."

I close the log. Now all I can think about is Zarubin. The breakdown in communications must have been unexpected for him. A sudden light on a control panel . . .

The warning buzzer went off. The needle trembled and pointed to zero. The radio signals came through, but the control signals did not.

The captain stood by the transparent walls of the greenhouse. The dull crimson sun sank over the horizon. Brown shadows fled along the frozen riverbed. The wind howled, threw up dusty snow, hurled it up into the faded red-gray sky.

The warning buzzer rang continuously. The radio signals were growing diffuse; they were no longer strong enough to control the rocket. Zarubin looked at the setting Barnard's Star. Behind him the lamps flashed feverishly on the electronic control panel.

The purple disk was quickly falling behind the horizon. For a moment crimson fires flared up: the last rays of the sun fractured on thousands of ice crystals. Then darkness fell.

Zarubin went over to the control panel. He turned off the buzzer. The arrow pointed to zero. Zarubin turned the power regulator. The greenhouse was filled with the whine of the motors of the conditioning system. Zarubin turned the power regulator as far as it would go. He walked round the other side of the control panel, removed the lock, and turned the regulator twice more. The whine turned into a shrill, penetrating, ringing roar.

The captain turned to the wall and sat down. His hands were shaking. He took out a handkerchief and wiped his forehead. He leaned his cheeks against the cold glass.

He would have to wait for the new powerful signal to reach the rocket and bounce back to him.

Zarubin waited.

He lost his sense of time. The mini-reactors roared, almost as if they were about to explode, the motors of the conditioning system howled and groaned. The fragile greenhouse walls shuddered. . . .

The captain waited.

Finally, some power allowed him to stand up and go over to the control panel.

The power indicator pointed into the green zone. The signals were now strong enough for him to control the rocket. Zarubin gave a weak smile and said: "So . . . ," then looked at the speed at which the power was being consumed. It was happening one hundred and forty times more quickly than had been factored into the calculation.

That night the captain did not sleep. He worked out a program for the electronic navigator. He had to correct all the deviations that the temporary loss of contact had caused.

The wind howled over the snowdrifts on the plain. The vague polar sun rose over the horizon. The crazed mini-reactors screamed as they gave off their energy. The energy that had been carefully parceled out to last fourteen years was now being thrown out into the surroundings with a generous hand. . . . Uploading the program into the electronic navigator, the captain walked tiredly round the greenhouse. The stars shone above the transparent ceiling. Leaning against the control panel, the captain looked up into the sky. Somewhere above him, the *Pole*,

gathering speed, was flying directly toward Earth.

It was very late, but I went to see the chief archivist. I remembered that he had told me about some of Zarubin's other paintings.

The chief archivist was not asleep.

"I knew you would come," he said, quickly putting his glasses on. "Come on, it's just through here."

In the next room, lit by fluorescent lamps, there hung two small pictures. For a moment I thought that the archivist was mistaken. I thought that Zarubin could not have painted these pictures. They were so different from what I had learned that day: they were not experiments with color, or images of fantastic subjects. They were normal landscapes. One showed a road and a tree, and the other was a picture of a forest.

"Yes, they're by Zarubin," the archivist said, as though he had read my thoughts. "He stayed on the planet, you know that, of course. It was a risky way to escape, but it was a way nonetheless. I speak as an astronaut . . . as a former astronaut."

The archivist pushed his glasses up his nose, and paused.

"Then Zarubin did what . . . you know . . . He gave off all the energy he'd had in reserve for fourteen years over the course of four weeks. He directed the rocket, kept the *Pole* on course. And then when the ship reached sub-light speed, it started to brake within normal gravitational parameters, and the crew could steer themselves. By this time, Zarubin had almost no energy left in his mini-reactors. And there was nothing he could do. Nothing. Zarubin did some paintings. He loved Earth, loved life. . . ."

The painting showed a road running between villages, heading over the brow of a hill. A mighty fallen oak lay by the road. He had painted in the style of Jules Dupré, in the style of the Barbizon School: earthy, knotted, full of life and power. The wind drives some ragged clouds across the sky. There is a boulder lying by the gully at the edge of the road; it looks as if some traveler has only recently sat there . . . each detail is carefully painted, lovingly, with an unusual richness of color and sense of light.

The other painting is unfinished. It is a wood in springtime. Everything is filled with air and light and warmth. . . . Surprising golden tones . . . Zarubin knew the best colors to use.

"I brought these paintings back to Earth," the archivist said quietly.

"You?"

"Yes." The archivist's voice sounded sad, almost guilty. "There is no proper end to the materials you have been looking at. They are part of other expeditions already. . . . The *Pole* returned to Earth and a rescue mission was immediately sent out. They did everything to make sure that the rocket reached Barnard's Star as quickly as possible. The crew agreed to fly at six g's. They reached the planet and did not even find the greenhouse. They risked their lives ten times, but didn't find . . . Then, and this was many years later—they sent me. There was an accident en route. So." The archivist raised his hand to his eyes. "But we got there.

We found the greenhouse, the paintings. . . . We found a note from the captain."

"What did it say?"

"Just four words: 'Onward through the impossible.'"

We looked at the pictures in silence. I suddenly realized that Zarubin had painted them from memory. He was surrounded by ice, the evil light of crimson Barnard's Star, and he mixed warm sunny colors on his palette. . . . In the twelfth point of the flight manual he could have with justice have written: "I enjoy . . . no, I have a love, a great love for Earth, for life on Earth, for the people who live there."

The empty corridors of the archive are quiet. The windows are half open; the sea breeze makes the heavy drapes move. The waves come in even and heavy. It seems that they are repeating the same four words: "Onward through the impossible." And then they are quiet, and then they come again and dash themselves on the sand: "Onward through the impossible." And then they are quiet again.

I want to answer the waves: "Yes, onward, ever onward!"

The Squid Chooses Its Own Ink
ADOLFO BIOY CASARES
Translation by Marian Womack

Adolfo Bioy Casares (1914–1999) was a prominent Argentine writer and man of letters who became a major figure in world literature and who championed a Latin American tradition of literary fantasy and detective fiction that pushed back against a dominant culture of realism. In so doing, Bioy Casares helped to create a space for later generations of fantastical writers, including Julio Cortázar and Gabriel García Márquez. His fiction emphasized the metaphysical and mysterious and had surreal, abstract elements, although he famously was not impressed meeting André Breton and did not consider himself a surrealist per se. Bioy Casares was also an avid sportsman who boxed and played rugby but especially enjoyed tennis. He cultivated a well-rounded, cosmopolitan lifestyle that included trips to Europe centered around art and book culture.

A close friend and contemporary of Jorge Luis Borges, Bioy Casares was married to the noted writer Silvina Ocampo. Ocampo's sister Victoria founded and ran the Argentine literary magazine *Sur*, which would provide a home for many of the best short stories and essays by all three writers. Together Bioy Casares, Borges, and Ocampo would edit the classic, highly influential *Antología de la Literatura Fantástica* (1940), reprinted in an updated English-language version in 1988 as *The Book of Fantasy*. Borges and Bioy Casares also wrote short satirical fiction under the pen name H. Bustos Domecq, although their first collaboration was writing advertising copy for various health products targeting the sedentary.

"The Invention of Morel" (1940) is Bioy Casares's most famous work (a novella) and, among other surreal speculative elements, features a narrator who is invisible to the inhabitants of the island he visits. The novella came about as the result of Bioy Casares wanting to create something unique out of the standard adventure story. As a measure of his success, "The Invention of Morel" was the model for Alain Resnais and Alain Robbe-Grillet's movie *Last Year at Marienbad* (1961), which changed the history of film. The novella has even been referenced in the television series *Lost*. Borges considered the work to be comparable in its influence and success to Henry James's *The Turn of the Screw* and Franz Kafka's *The Trial*.

Other works include *El sueño del los héroes* (1954; *The Dream of Heroes*, 1987), which examines a workman's being saved from death by a mysterious figure, possibly supernatural, and the repetition of the same events years later; it was avowedly influenced by the time theories of J. W. Dunne. *Dormir al sol* (1973; *Asleep in the Sun*, 1978) features soul transplants and conflates the transformations of psychosurgery with totalitarianism.

Bioy Casares fell out of favor during the various iterations of the Perón regimes in Argentina, his and *Sur*'s remit seen as not nationalistic enough and too elite. He was quietly and not so quietly an anti-Perónist; Borges and Bioy teamed up once again, under the pen name B. Suárez Lynch, to write savage satires of Perón and others of that political persuasion. Meanwhile, his family's background as landowners grated against the populist origins of revolution in the 1970s. Close associates, such as Borges, were labeled "literary oligarchs," even though, in literary terms, Bioy's championing of nonrealistic fiction would always be out of step with the status quo. However, after the iniquities of that era and a return to democracy, Bioy Casares regained his iconic status as an important literary figure—largely due to the universal nature of his best fiction. In 1990, he received the Cervantes Prize, one of the highest honors for a Spanish-language author.

"The Squid Chooses Its Own Ink," presented here in a new translation—the first since the story's inclusion in *The Book of Fantasy*—is a unique tale of alien contact.

THE SQUID CHOOSES ITS OWN INK

Adolfo Bioy Casares

Translation by Marian Womack

More has happened in this town over the last few days than in the whole of its history. To see the significance of what I am saying, you should remember that I am talking about one of the old towns of the area, one in which notable events are not rare: its foundation in the middle of the nineteenth century; the cholera outbreak—which fortunately did not lead to anything more serious—and the danger of surprise raids, which, even if they never actually occurred, kept the populace on edge for the best part of half a decade while neighboring regions suffered under Indian attacks. And after this heroic period, I will skip over the visits made by governors and parliamentarians and political candidates of all stripes, as well as comedians and one or two sporting giants. I will conclude this brief list by coming full circle, with the celebration of the Centenary of the Foundation, a true tournament of oratory and tributes.

As I am called upon to relate a particularly significant event, I will offer the reader my credentials. A man of wide sympathies and advanced ideas, I devour any books that I may find in my friend the Spaniard Villaroel's library, from Dr. Jung to Hugo, Walter Scott and Goldoni, not forgetting the final volume of *Madrid Scenes*. I am concerned with culture, but I am on the cusp of my "wretched thirties," and I truly fear that I have more to learn than I already know. To sum up, I try to follow all modern movements and to enlighten my fellow citizens, all fine people, of the best stock, even if very given over to their siestas, a tradition which they have cherished since the middle ages, the period of obscurantism. I am a teacher—a schoolteacher—and a journalist.

I ply my pen in certain modest local organs, at times as a factotum for *El Mirasol*, *The Sunflower* (a poorly chosen title, one which provokes unpleasant remarks and brings in a huge quantity of misdirected correspondence, as they take us for an agricultural digest), at times for *Nueva Patria*.

This account has a peculiarity that I would not wish to omit: not only did this event take place in my town, but it actually happened on the block where I have spent my whole life, where are to be found my home and my school—my second home—as well as the bar of a hotel opposite the station, where night after night, into the small hours, we gather, the restless nucleus of local youth. The epicenter of the phenomenon, the focus if you so prefer, was Juan Camargo's town house, which borders the hotel to the east, and the courtyard of my house to the north. A couple of circumstances, which not everyone would have connected to the event, served to announce it: I am of course referring to the order placed for books, and the removal of the pivot sprinkler.

Las Margaritas, Don Juan's own *petit-hôtel*, a real little chalet with its garden facing onto the street, takes up half the frontage and very little of the interior space of the town house, where a huge quantity of material is gathered like shipwrecks piled at the bottom of the sea. As for the pivot sprinkler, it always turned in the aforementioned garden, to the extent that it was one of the oldest traditions, one of the most interesting peculiarities, of our town.

One Sunday, at the beginning of the month, the sprinkler was, mysteriously, not there. As after a week it had not reappeared, the garden had lost much of its color and brightness. While most people saw this without taking it in, there was one whose curiosity was piqued from the first. This individual provoked curiosity in others, and at night, in the bar, opposite the station, the group of young men seethed with questions and comments. And so, as the result of a simple, natural inquisitiveness, we discovered something that was not natural at all, a true surprise.

We knew very well that Don Juan was not a man to cut off the water to his garden, carelessly, in a dry summer. We considered him a pillar of the town. The character of this fifty-year-old was true to type: tall and corpulent, his graying hair parted into two obedient halves, which traced parallel arcs to his mustache and, further down, his watch chain. Further details will reveal a gentleman of an old-fashioned style: breeches, leather leggings, ankle boots. In his life, ruled as it was by moderation and by order, nobody, as far as I can recall, detected any weakness, whether it be drunkenness, skirt-chasing, or clumsy political opinions. Even in his early years, which might with justice be forgotten—who among us, in his unformed youth, has not sown at least one wild oat?—Don Juan remained clean. Even the Cooperative auditors, and others, very disrespectable people, frankly shabby, recognized Don Juan's authority. There must have been some reason why, in those thankless years, Don Juan's large mustache was a handle onto which the respectable folk of the town could cling.

It must be acknowledged that this paragon was possessed of old-fashioned ideas and that in our ranks, those of the idealists, there have not yet appeared figures of comparable consistency. In a new country, there is no tradition of new ideas. And as you are aware, without tradition there is no stability.

There was no one who appeared above this figure in our daily hierarchy, save for Doña Remedios, the mother and unique adviser to her corpulent son. Between ourselves, and not only because she solved every conflict presented to

her *manu militari*, we called her the Iron Lady. Although we were making fun of her, the nickname was meant affectionately.

In order to complete the list of those who dwelled in the chalet all that is required is an indubitably minor addition, the godson, Don Tadeito, who took night classes at my school. As Doña Remedios and Don Juan welcomed very few people into their house, neither as guests nor as assistants, the child had piled on his head the titles of laborer and servant in the main house, as well as that of waiter in Las Margaritas. And in addition to that, the poor devil came regularly to my classes and so you will appreciate why I give short shrift to those people who, out of sheer ill spirit and malice, lumber him with some ridiculous nickname. That he was rejected out of hand for his military service does not matter to me, because I am not an envious man.

The Sunday in question, at some time between two and four o'clock in the afternoon, someone knocked at my door with the deliberate aim, to judge from the blows, of breaking it down. I got up, shaking, and muttered, "It can only be one person," then used words that do not sit well in the mouth of a teacher and then, as if this were not the time for disagreeable visits, opened the door, sure that I would see Don Tadeito. I was right. There he was, my student, smiling, his face so thin that it served as no screen between me and the sun that shone right in my eyes. As far as I could understand him, he asked, point-blank and in his voice that trailed away at the end of the sentence, for first-, second-, and third-grade textbooks.

I spoke to him in irritation:

"May I ask why?"

"Godfather wants them," he replied.

I handed the books over and forgot about the episode immediately, as if it were part of a dream.

A few hours later, as I was heading toward the station and was taking a stroll in order to fill the time, I noticed the absence of the sprinkler in Las Margaritas. I mentioned it on the platform, while we were waiting for the 19:30 express from Plaza, which came through at 20:54, and I mentioned it that night, in the bar. I didn't mention the books, far less did I connect one event with the other, because, as I have said, I barely even recalled the episode.

I supposed that after such a busy day life would return to its normal tranquil path. On Monday, when time came for my siesta, I was thinking, "This time it will be a good one," but the fringe of my poncho was still tickling my nose when the knocking started. Murmuring, "What does he want today? If I catch him kicking the door he'll pay for it," I put on my slippers and walked to the door.

"Is it a habit now to wake your teacher?" I spat out as I took the pile of books.

I was taken aback, as the only response was the following:

"Godfather wants third-year and fourth- and fifth-year books."

I managed to say:

"Why?"

"Godfather wants them," Don Tadeito explained.

I gave him the books and went back to my bed, in search of sleep. I did sleep, I will admit it, but I did so, please believe me, poorly.

Then, on my way to the station, I saw that the sprinkler had not yet returned to its place and that the garden was starting to turn yellow. I conjectured, logically, a series of fantastic conclusions and on the station platform, while my body was on display to the frivolous groups of women, my mind was working on an interpretation of the mystery.

Looking up at the moon, huge in the sky, one of us, I think it was Di Pinto, always ready to give himself over to the romantic chimera of being a country boy (and this in front of his childhood friends!), said:

"The moon was dry when it was born. We can't say that removing this object is a prediction of rain. Don Juan must have had other reasons!"

Badaracco, who was no fool, who had a mark on his face because at an earlier time, aside from his salary from the bank, he had earned some money from denunciations, said to me:

"Why don't you ask the idiot about it?"

"Who do you mean?" I said politely.

"Your student," he replied.

I took advantage of the opportunity and asked him that very evening, after class. I tried to confuse Don Tadeito first of all with the platitude that rain is good for the plants, then I went in for the kill. The dialogue ran as follows:

"Is the sprinkler broken?"

"No."

"I don't see it in the garden."

"Why would you see it?"

"What do you mean why would I see it?"

"Because it's watering the warehouse."

I should state that *the warehouse* was the name we gave to the last hut in the town house courtyard, where Don Juan kept all the stuff that was difficult to sell piled up, for example shabby stoves and statues, monoliths and capstans.

Driven by my desire to tell my friends the news about the sprinkler, I sent my student off without asking him any further about another point. Remembering and shouting happened simultaneously. Don Tadeito looked at me from the doorway with his sheep's eyes.

"What does Don Juan do with the texts?" I shouted.

"He . . . ," the shout came back. ". . . He stores them in the warehouse."

I ran in stupefaction to the hotel, and what I had to communicate caused, as I expected, confusion among my friends. Each of us formed a different opinion, it would have been unthinkable to have been silent at that moment, but luckily no one listened to anyone else. Or perhaps the hotel manager heard us, enormous Don Pomponio with his dropsical stomach, whom those of us in the group barely distinguished from the columns and tables and cutlery of the hotel, so blinded we were by our intellectual arrogance. Don Pomponio's brazen voice, smoothed by rivers of gin, called us to order. Seven faces looked up and fourteen eyes were fixed on a single red and shiny face whose mouth opened to ask the following question:

"Why not head out as a committee and ask Don Juan in person?"

His sarcasm woke up another fellow, called Aldini, who was studying via correspondence course and who wore a white tie. Raising his eyebrows he said to me:

"Why don't you order your pupil to spy on the conversations between Doña Remedios and Don Juan? Then you can put the screws on him."

"What screws?"

"Use your authority as an all-knowing teacher," he said nastily.

"Does Don Tadeito have a good memory?" Badaracco asked.

"Yes he does," I said. "Whatever goes into his head stays there photographed for a while."

"Don Juan asks Doña Remedios for advice about everything," Aldini continued.

"In front of a witness like their godson," Di Pinto said, "they will speak with absolute freedom."

"If there is any mystery, then it will be brought into the light," Toledo stated.

Chazaretta, who worked as a helper at the market, grunted:

"And if there's no mystery, what is there then?"

As the dialogue was getting out of hand, Badaracco, famous for his equanimity, controlled these polemicists.

"Come on, fellows," he scolded them, "this is no time for you to waste your energy."

In order to have the last word, Toledo repeated:

"If there is any mystery, then it will be brought into the light."

And it was brought into the light, but not until several days had gone by.

Next siesta-tide, when I was sunk into sleep, the knocks sounded out once again. To judge from my palpitations, the knocking came at one and the same time at the door and against my heart. Don Tadeito brought the books from the day before and asked for textbooks from the first three years of secondary school. Because the most advanced textbook was not in my possession, I had to visit Villaroel's bookshop, wake up the Spaniard with hefty blows against the door, and calm him down by telling him that it was Don Juan who wanted the books. As might have been feared, the Spaniard asked:

"What's got into this man? He doesn't buy a single book in his whole life and now he's randy for knowledge. It's just like him to be so damn rude as to ask for the books on loan."

"Don't get worked up about it, *gallego*," I said, patting him on the back. "You're so angry that you're starting to curse like a sailor."

I told him about the previous order, the primary school textbooks, and kept an absolute silence about the sprinkler's disappearance, about which, he gave me to understand, he was well aware. With the books under my arm, I added:

"At night we meet in the hotel bar to discuss all this. If you want to add your ha'pennyworth, that's where you'll find us."

As I walked there and back I saw not a soul, apart from the butcher's reddish-gray dog, who must have been sick again, because no creature in its right mind would expose itself to the heat of two o'clock in the afternoon.

I told my pupil that he should report to me verbatim the conversations he heard between Don Juan and Doña Remedios. There is something in what they say, that the sin brings its own punishment with it. That very evening I began a period of torture that, in my curiosity, I would not have suspected: to hear the accurate representation of these conversations, interminable and insipid. Every now and then I had a cruelly ironic reply on the tip of my tongue about how little importance Doña Remedios's opinions about the last batch of yellow soap or the flannels for Don Juan's rheumatism held for me, but I stopped myself in time: how could I delegate to the child the decision as to what was important or not?

Of course, the next day my siesta was again interrupted with the books to be returned to Villaroel. And here was the first new development: Don Juan, Don Tadeito said, no longer wanted textbooks; he wanted old newspapers, which Tadeito had to gather by the kilo, from the haberdashery, the butcher, and the baker. He took his time telling me that the newspapers, like the books before them, would be taken on deposit.

Then there was a period in which nothing happened. There is no way to deal with the feelings of the heart: I missed the loud knocks that had previously woken me from my siesta. I wanted something to happen, whether good or bad. Having become accustomed to an intense life, I could no longer resign myself to sluggishness. But finally one night the student, after a prolix rundown of the effects of salt and other nutritional materials on Doña Remedios's body, said, without altering his tone in the slightest to suggest that he was going to change theme or topic:

"Godfather said to Doña Remedios that they had a visitor living in the warehouse and that he had very nearly knocked him down a few days ago, because he was looking at a kind of amusement-park swing which hadn't been entered in the books and that he did not lose his cool even though he appeared to be in a very bad way and reminded him of a catfish gulping air out of the water. He said that he brought a bucket filled with water, because without thinking about it he realized that he was asking for water and that he was not going to stand by with his arms crossed while a fellow creature died. There was no obvious result and he decided to bring a horse trough across for the visitor. He filled the trough with buckets and there was no obvious result. Suddenly he remembered the sprinkler and, he said, like the doctor who tries everything to save a patient's life, he ran to get it and connect it. The result was immediately visible because the dying creature revived as if what it wanted to do was breathe damp air. Godfather said that

he spent a while with the visitor, because he asked him as best he could if he needed anything and the visitor was pretty quick-witted because after a quarter of an hour he was giving out a couple of words of Spanish and asked him for the rudiments of how to study and learn. Godfather said that he had sent his godson to ask for first-grade books from the teacher. As the visitor was pretty quick-witted he learned all the grades in two days and after just one he was ready to take his exams. And then, Godfather said, he started to read newspapers to find out what was happening in the world."

I ventured a suggestion:

"Did that conversation take place today?"

"Of course," he answered, "while they were drinking coffee."

"Did your godfather say anything else?"

"Of course, but I don't remember what."

"What do you mean, you don't remember?" I protested angrily.

"You interrupted me," my pupil explained.

"All right. But you're not going to leave me like this," I said, "dying from curiosity. Come on, make an effort."

"You interrupted me."

"I know. I interrupted you. It's my fault."

"It's your fault," he repeated.

"Don Tadeito is good. He won't leave his teacher like this, in the middle of the conversation, to carry on tomorrow or never."

With a deep sigh he repeated:

"Or never."

I was upset, as if someone were taking something of great price away from me. I don't know why, but I thought that most of our dialogue consisted of repetitions and suddenly I saw a sliver of hope in this. I repeated the final phrase of Don Tadeito's account:

"He started to read newspapers to find out what was happening in the world."

My student continued indifferently:

"Godfather said that the visitor was shocked to discover that the government of the world was not in the hands of the best people, but rather in those of people who were decidedly mediocre, if not absolute good-for-nothings. That such riffraff had the atomic bomb under their control, the visitor said, was enough to make you crazy. If the best people had the atomic bomb under their control, they would end up dropping it, because it is clear that if someone has it then it will be dropped, but that this riffraff had it could not be serious. He said that other planets had discovered the bomb before this and they had all exploded with fatal results. They did not mind these planets blowing themselves up, because they were a long way away, but our world was close and they were afraid that a chain reaction would take them with it."

The unbelievable suspicion that Don Tadeito was making fun of me made me ask him a question quite severely:

"Have you been reading Jung's *Flying Saucers: A Modern Myth of Things Seen in the Skies*?"

Luckily enough he didn't hear my interruption and carried on:

"Godfather said that the visitor said he had come from his planet in a specially built vehicle because there was not enough material there and it was the fruit of years of research and work. That he came as a friend and as a liberator, and that he asked Godfather for his full support in order to carry out a plan to save the world. Godfather said that the meeting with the visitor took place that afternoon and that he, in the face of such a serious situation, had no hesitation in speaking to Doña Remedios about it, in order to hear her opinion, which was also his own."

As the pause did not immediately come to an end, I asked what that good lady's reply had been.

"Ah, I don't know," he replied.

"What do you mean 'Ah, I don't know'?" I repeated, angered once again.

"I left them talking and came over, because it was time for class. I thought that if I don't get there late, then the teacher will be happy."

His sheep's face grew conceited as he waited for his praise. With admirable presence of mind I thought that my friends from the bar would not believe my story unless I brought Don Tadeito along as a witness. I grasped him violently by an arm and pushed him to the bar by judicious shoves. My friends were there, with the addition of the Spaniard Villaroel.

I will never forget that night, not so long as my memory lasts.

"Sirs," I cried as I pushed Don Tadeito against our table. "I bring the explanation for everything, an extremely important piece of news and a witness who will not permit me to lie. Don Juan explained the whole story in great detail to his dear mother and my faithful pupil did not miss a single word. In the warehouse at the town house, right next door, with just the wall between us, there dwells—guess who?—a visitor from another world. Now, sirs, do not be alarmed: the voyager is apparently not in the best of health, as it appears that he does not deal well with the dry air of our town—we are still competition for Cordoba—and in order for him not to die like a fish out of water, Don Juan has plugged in the sprinkler, to make the atmosphere in the warehouse damper. There's more: apparently the motive for the monster's visit should not cause us to be worried. He has come to save us, sure that the world is on the path to destruction with the atomic bomb, and has told Don Juan of his point of view absolutely openly. Of course, Don Juan, while taking coffee, discussed this question with Doña Remedios. It is just a pity that this child"—I shook Don Tadeito as though he were a rag doll—"should have left just at the moment before Doña Remedios gave her opinion, so we do not know what it was they decided."

"We do know," the bookseller said, pouting with his fat wet lips.

I was a little taken aback that I should be corrected in mid-delivery of a piece of news of which I thought I was the only holder. I asked:

"What do we know?"

"Don't get your collar knotted," Villaroel

said, the cunning old fox. "If it is as you say and the traveler will die if the sprinkler is removed, then Don Juan has just condemned him to death. I came past Las Margaritas on my way here and in the moonlight I could see the sprinkler watering the garden as before."

"I saw it too," Chazarreta confirmed.

"With my hand on my heart," Aldini murmured, "I say to you that the traveler did not lie. Sooner or later we'll blow ourselves up with the atomic bomb. There's no way past it."

As if he were speaking to himself, Badaracco said:

"Don't tell me that these old people have destroyed our last hope."

"Don Juan doesn't want to change his way of living," the Spaniard proposed. "He would rather that the world blew up than that salvation came from outside. I suppose it is a way of loving mankind."

"Disgust in the face of things you don't know," I said. "Obscurantism."

They say that fear makes one's mind run more clearly. The truth is that there was something strange in the bar that night and we all brought our ideas to the discussion.

"Come on, fellows, let's do something," Badaracco said. "For the love of humanity."

"Señor Badaracco, why do you have so much love for humanity?" the Spaniard asked.

Badaracco blushed and stammered:

"I don't know. We all know."

"What do we know, Señor Badaracco? If you think about men, do you think them admirable? I think the exact opposite: they are stupid, and cruel, and mean and envious," Villaroel declared.

"Whenever there are elections," Chazarreta agreed, "then your beautiful humanity stands revealed naked, just as it really is. It's always the worst ones who win."

"So love of humanity is just an empty phrase, then?"

"No, my dear teacher," Villaroel replied. "Let us call love of humanity the compassion for other people's pain and the veneration we have for the works of our great minds, for the Immortal Cripple's *Quixote*, for the paintings of Velázquez and Murillo. In no sense does this love serve as an argument to delay the end of the world. These works only exist for humans to experience, and after the end of the world— and the day will come, whether brought by the bomb or by natural causes—they will have no justification or support, believe you me. As for compassion, it will disappear as the end approaches. . . . As no one can escape death, let it come quickly, for everyone, so the sum of pain will be as small as possible!"

"We are losing our time in the particularities of an academic discussion and here, just through the wall, our last hope is dying," I said with an eloquence which I was the first to admire.

"We must act now," Badaracco said. "Soon it will be too late."

"If we invade the town house, then Don Juan will get angry," Di Pinto said.

Don Pomponio, who sidled over without our hearing him and who made us jump when he spoke, suggested the following:

"Why not send little Don Tadeito along as an advance guard? It would be the sensible thing to do."

"That's a good idea," Toledo said. "Let Don Tadeito set up the sprinkler in the warehouse and have a look at what happens, so we can see what the traveler from another world is like."

We walked out into the night en masse, lit by the implacable moon. Badaracco exhorted us, almost in tears:

"Come on, fellows, let's be generous. It doesn't matter if we risk our skin. All of the mothers of the world, all of the creatures on earth depend upon us."

We gathered together in a crowd in front of the town house, there were movements forward and movements backward, suggestions and tussles. Finally Badaracco got his courage up and pushed Don Tadeito forward. My student came back after an interminable stretch of time and said:

"The catfish is dead."

We broke up sadly. The bookseller came back with me. For some reason that I did not understand at all his company cheered me up.

In front of Las Margaritas, while the sprinkler monotonously watered the garden, I exclaimed:

"I blame him for his lack of curiosity," I said with my eyes on the stars. "How many Americas and Terranovas have we lost tonight!"

"Don Juan," Villaroel said, "prefers to live within his limitations. I admire his courage. The two of us don't even dare climb over his fence."

I said:

"It's late."

"It's late," he repeated.

KURT VONNEGUT JR.

Kurt Vonnegut Jr. (1922–2007) was an iconic US writer best known for his surreal, nonchronological science fiction novel *Slaughterhouse-Five* (1969). With its juxtaposition of a man unstuck from time who has weird adventures in alien zoos and suffers internment in brutal POW camps in Nazi Germany, *Slaughterhouse-Five* captured the imagination of the American counterculture era.

Other important novels include *The Sirens of Titan* (1959), *Mother Night* (1962), *Cat's Cradle* (1963), and *Breakfast of Champions* (1990). However, Vonnegut's later work is also excellent, and perhaps underrated—evidence for which is provided by the recent multivolume Library of America reissues of all his fiction. Vonnegut's works have, at various times, been labeled science fiction, satire, and postmodern. He has been thought of in certain circles as a successor to Mark Twain, but in fact Vonnegut's surreal approaches are much closer to William S. Burroughs, even if their styles are different. Perhaps if Twain and Burroughs had had a love child it would have been Vonnegut.

Although Vonnegut resisted the science fiction label, his work did appear in *Galaxy* ("Unready to Wear," April 1953) and he often imagined alien societies and civilizations. In his essay "Science Fiction," for *The New York Times Book Review* in 1965 (reprinted in *Vonnegut: Novels and Stories 1950–1962*, Library of America, 2002), Vonnegut wrote that when his novel *Player Piano* was published he "learned from the reviewers that [he] was a science-fiction writer." Ever since, Vonnegut noted, he had been a "soreheaded occupant of [that] file drawer," making the point that "many serious critics regularly mistake the drawer for a urinal." As he put it, one became a science fiction writer if one had the chutzpah to "notice technology," but he also had astutely noticed that among those who "adore being classified as science-fiction writers" many are "happy with the status quo" because it allows them to be part of a club. For Vonnegut, science fiction wasn't just a genre—it was a genre of "joiners," which, for a noted loner-curmudgeon, wasn't a plus.

Vonnegut may have been wise to distance himself from genre, in part because he reached a far wider audience in doing so. However, he also used science fiction tropes for purposes far different than most science fiction—including his absurdism, exaggeration, and gift for satire. Writers like William Tenn and Stepan Chapman—who never really got out of the genre field and share certain qualities with Vonnegut—suffered career-wise not just because they produced few novels, but also because their less-than-earnest stance rubbed some science fiction editors the wrong way. In the end, though, genre got Vonnegut: he was inducted into the Science Fiction and Fantasy Hall of Fame in 2015.

Vonnegut wrote relatively little short fiction, but it was always deeply reflective of the themes and style of his novels. "2 B R 0 2 B" (*IF*, 1962) is a satirical story about assisted suicide and population control. It is also a pointed commentary on the idea of immortality. It appeared in the same year as *Mother Night*, released by Fawcett Gold Medal in a first print run of 175,000 copies.

2 B R 0 2 B

Kurt Vonnegut Jr.

Everything was perfectly swell.

There were no prisons, no slums, no insane asylums, no cripples, no poverty, no wars.

All diseases were conquered. So was old age.

Death, barring accidents, was an adventure for volunteers.

The population of the United States was stabilized at forty million souls.

One bright morning in the Chicago Lying-in Hospital, a man named Edward K. Wehling Jr. waited for his wife to give birth. He was the only man waiting. Not many people were born a day anymore.

Wehling was fifty-six, a mere stripling in a population whose average age was one hundred and twenty-nine.

X-rays had revealed that his wife was going to have triplets. The children would be his first.

Young Wehling was hunched in his chair, his head in his hand. He was so rumpled, so still and colorless as to be virtually invisible. His camouflage was perfect, since the waiting room had a disorderly and demoralized air, too. Chairs and ashtrays had been moved away from the walls. The floor was paved with spattered drop cloths.

The room was being redecorated. It was being redecorated as a memorial to a man who had volunteered to die.

A sardonic old man, about two hundred years old, sat on a stepladder, painting a mural he did not like. Back in the days when people aged visibly, his age would have been guessed at thirty-five or so. Aging had touched him that much before the cure for aging was found.

The mural he was working on depicted a very neat garden. Men and women in white, doctors and nurses, turned the soil, planted seedlings, sprayed bugs, spread fertilizer.

Men and women in purple uniforms pulled up weeds, cut down plants that were old and sickly, raked leaves, carried refuse to trashburners.

Never, never, never—not even in medieval Holland nor old Japan—had a garden been more formal, been better tended. Every plant had all the loam, light, water, air, and nourishment it could use.

A hospital orderly came down the corridor, singing under his breath a popular song:

If you don't like my kisses, honey,
Here's what I will do:
I'll go see a girl in purple,
Kiss this sad world toodle-oo.
If you don't want my lovin',
Why should I take up all this space?
I'll get off this old planet,
Let some sweet baby have my place.

The orderly looked in at the mural and the muralist. "Looks so real," he said, "I can practically imagine I'm standing in the middle of it."

"What makes you think you're not in it?" said the painter. He gave a satiric smile. "It's called *The Happy Garden of Life*, you know."

"That's good of Dr. Hitz," said the orderly.

He was referring to one of the male figures in white, whose head was a portrait of Dr. Benjamin Hitz, the hospital's chief obstetrician. Hitz was a blindingly handsome man.

"Lot of faces still to fill in," said the orderly. He meant that the faces of many of the figures in the mural were still blank. All blanks were to be filled with portraits of important people

447

on either the hospital staff or from the Chicago Office of the Federal Bureau of Termination.

"Must be nice to be able to make pictures that look like something," said the orderly.

The painter's face curdled with scorn. "You think I'm proud of this daub?" he said. "You think this is my idea of what life really looks like?"

"What's your idea of what life looks like?" said the orderly.

The painter gestured at a foul drop cloth. "There's a good picture of it," he said. "Frame that, and you'll have a picture a damn sight more honest than this one."

"You're a gloomy old duck, aren't you?" said the orderly.

"Is that a crime?" said the painter.

The orderly shrugged. "If you don't like it here, Grandpa . . . ," he said, and he finished the thought with the trick telephone number that people who didn't want to live anymore were supposed to call. The zero in the telephone number he pronounced "naught."

The number was: "2 B R 0 2 B."

It was the telephone number of an institution whose fanciful sobriquets included: "Automat," "Birdland," "Cannery," "Catbox," "De-louser," "Easy-go," "Good-bye, Mother," "Happy Hooligan," "Kiss-me-quick," "Lucky Pierre," "Sheepdip," "Waring Blender," "Weep-no-more," and "Why Worry?"

"To be or not to be" was the telephone number of the municipal gas chambers of the Federal Bureau of Termination.

The painter thumbed his nose at the orderly. "When I decide it's time to go," he said, "it won't be at the Sheepdip."

"A do-it-yourselfer, eh?" said the orderly. "Messy business, Grandpa. Why don't you have a little consideration for the people who have to clean up after you?"

The painter expressed with an obscenity his lack of concern for the tribulations of his survivors. "The world could do with a good deal more mess, if you ask me," he said.

The orderly laughed and moved on.

Wehling, the waiting father, mumbled something without raising his head. And then he fell silent again.

A coarse, formidable woman strode into the waiting room on spike heels. Her shoes, stockings, trench coat, bag, and overseas cap were all purple, the purple the painter called "the color of grapes on Judgment Day."

The medallion on her purple musette bag was the seal of the Service Division of the Federal Bureau of Termination, an eagle perched on a turnstile.

The woman had a lot of facial hair—an unmistakable mustache, in fact. A curious thing about gas-chamber hostesses was that, no matter how lovely and feminine they were when recruited, they all sprouted mustaches within five years or so.

"Is this where I'm supposed to come?" she said to the painter.

"A lot would depend on what your business was," he said. "You aren't about to have a baby, are you?"

"They told me I was supposed to pose for some picture," she said. "My name's Leora Duncan." She waited.

"And you dunk people," he said.

"What?" she said.

"Skip it," he said.

"That sure is a beautiful picture," she said. "Looks just like heaven or something."

"Or something," said the painter. He took a list of names from his smock pocket. "Duncan, Duncan, Duncan," he said, scanning the list. "Yes—here you are. You're entitled to be immortalized. See any faceless body here you'd like me to stick your head on? We've got a few choice ones left."

She studied the mural bleakly. "Gee," she said, "they're all the same to me. I don't know anything about art."

"A body's a body, eh?" he said, "All righty. As a master of fine art, I recommend this body here." He indicated a faceless figure of a woman who was carrying dried stalks to a trash-burner.

"Well," said Leora Duncan, "that's more the

disposal people, isn't it? I mean, I'm in service. I don't do any disposing."

The painter clapped his hands in mock delight. "You say you don't know anything about art, and then you prove in the next breath that you know more about it than I do! Of course the sheaf-carrier is wrong for a hostess! A snipper, a pruner—that's more your line." He pointed to a figure in purple who was sawing a dead branch from an apple tree. "How about her?" he said. "You like her at all?"

"Gosh——" she said, and she blushed and became humble—"that—that puts me right next to Dr. Hitz."

"That upsets you?" he said.

"Good gravy, no!" she said. "It's—it's just such an honor."

"Ah, you admire him, eh?" he said.

"Who doesn't admire him?" she said, worshiping the portrait of Hitz. It was the portrait of a tanned, white-haired, omnipotent Zeus, two hundred and forty years old. "Who doesn't admire him?" she said again. "He was responsible for setting up the very first gas chamber in Chicago."

"Nothing would please me more," said the painter, "than to put you next to him for all time. Sawing off a limb—that strikes you as appropriate?"

"That is kind of like what I do," she said. She was demure about what she did. What she did was make people comfortable while she killed them.

And, while Leora Duncan was posing for her portrait, into the waiting room bounded Dr. Hitz himself. He was seven feet tall, and he boomed with importance, accomplishments, and the joy of living.

"Well, Miss Duncan! Miss Duncan!" he said, and he made a joke. "What are you doing here?" he said. "This isn't where the people leave. This is where they come in!"

"We're going to be in the same picture together," she said shyly.

"Good!" said Dr. Hitz heartily. "And, say, isn't that some picture?"

"I sure am honored to be in it with you," she said.

"Let me tell you," he said, "I'm honored to be in it with you. Without women like you, this wonderful world we've got wouldn't be possible."

He saluted her and moved toward the door that led to the delivery rooms. "Guess what was just born," he said.

"I can't," she said.

"Triplets!" he said.

"Triplets!" she said. She was exclaiming over the legal implications of triplets.

The law said that no newborn child could survive unless the parents of the child could find someone who would volunteer to die. Triplets, if they were all to live, called for three volunteers.

"Do the parents have three volunteers?" said Leora Duncan.

"Last I heard," said Dr. Hitz, "they had one, and were trying to scrape another two up."

"I don't think they made it," she said. "Nobody made three appointments with us. Nothing but singles going through today, unless somebody called in after I left. What's the name?"

"Wehling," said the waiting father, sitting up, red-eyed and frowzy. "Edward K. Wehling Jr. is the name of the happy father-to-be."

He raised his right hand, looked at a spot on the wall, gave a hoarsely wretched chuckle. "Present," he said.

"Oh, Mr. Wehling," said Dr. Hitz, "I didn't see you."

"The invisible man," said Wehling.

"They just phoned me that your triplets have been born," said Dr. Hitz. "They're all fine, and so is the mother. I'm on my way in to see them now."

"Hooray," said Wehling emptily.

"You don't sound very happy," said Dr. Hitz.

"What man in my shoes wouldn't be happy?" said Wehling. He gestured with his hands to symbolize carefree simplicity. "All I have to do is pick out which one of the triplets is going to live, then deliver my maternal grandfather to the Happy Hooligan, and come back here with a receipt."

Dr. Hitz became rather severe with Wehling, towered over him. "You don't believe in population control, Mr. Wehling?" he said.

"I think it's perfectly keen," said Wehling tautly.

"Would you like to go back to the good old days, when the population of the Earth was twenty billion—about to become forty billion, then eighty billion, then one hundred and sixty billion? Do you know what a drupelet is, Mr. Wehling?" said Hitz.

"Nope," said Wehling sulkily.

"A drupelet, Mr. Wehling, is one of the little knobs, one of the little pulpy grains of a blackberry," said Dr. Hitz. "Without population control, human beings would now be packed on the surface of this old planet like drupelets on a blackberry! Think of it!"

Wehling continued to stare at the same spot on the wall.

"In the year 2000," said Dr. Hitz, "before scientists stepped in and laid down the law, there wasn't even enough drinking water to go around, and nothing to eat but seaweed—and still people insisted on their right to reproduce like jackrabbits. And their right, if possible, to live forever."

"I want those kids," said Wehling quietly. "I want all three of them."

"Of course you do," said Dr. Hitz. "That's only human."

"I don't want my grandfather to die, either," said Wehling.

"Nobody's really happy about taking a close relative to the Catbox," said Dr. Hitz gently, sympathetically.

"I wish people wouldn't call it that," said Leora Duncan.

"What?" said Dr. Hitz.

"I wish people wouldn't call it 'the Catbox,' and things like that," she said. "It gives people the wrong impression."

"You're absolutely right," said Dr. Hitz. "Forgive me." He corrected himself, gave the municipal gas chambers their official title, a title no one ever used in conversation. "I should have said, 'Ethical Suicide Studios,'" he said.

"That sounds so much better," said Leora Duncan.

"This child of yours—whichever one you decide to keep, Mr. Wehling," said Dr. Hitz. "He or she is going to live on a happy, roomy, clean, rich planet, thanks to population control. In a garden like that mural there." He shook his head. "Two centuries ago, when I was a young man, it was a hell that nobody thought could last another twenty years. Now centuries of peace and plenty stretch before us as far as the imagination cares to travel."

He smiled luminously.

The smile faded as he saw that Wehling had just drawn a revolver.

Wehling shot Dr. Hitz dead. "There's room for one—a great big one," he said.

And then he shot Leora Duncan. "It's only death," he said to her as she fell. "There! Room for two."

And then he shot himself, making room for all three of his children.

Nobody came running. Nobody, seemingly, heard the shots.

The painter sat on the top of his stepladder, looking down reflectively on the sorry scene.

The painter pondered the mournful puzzle of life demanding to be born and, once born, demanding to be fruitful . . . to multiply and to live as long as possible—to do all that on a very small planet that would have to last forever.

All the answers that the painter could think of were grim. Even grimmer, surely, than a Catbox, a Happy Hooligan, an Easy-go. He thought of war. He thought of plague. He thought of starvation.

He knew that he would never paint again. He let his paintbrush fall to the drop cloths below. And then he decided he had had about enough of life in the Happy Garden of Life, too, and he came slowly down from the ladder.

He took Wehling's pistol, really intending to shoot himself.

But he didn't have the nerve.

And then he saw the telephone booth in the corner of the room. He went to it, dialed the well-remembered number: "2 B R 0 2 B."

"Federal Bureau of Termination," said the very warm voice of a hostess.

"How soon could I get an appointment?" he asked, speaking very carefully.

"We could probably fit you in late this afternoon, sir," she said. "It might even be earlier, if we get a cancellation."

"All right," said the painter, "fit me in, if you please." And he gave her his name, spelling it out.

"Thank you, sir," said the hostess. "Your city thanks you; your country thanks you; your planet thanks you. But the deepest thanks of all is from future generations."

A Modest Genius

VADIM SHEFNER

Translated by Matthew J. O'Connell

Vadim Sergeevich Shefner (1915–2002) was a Soviet-era Russian writer known mostly for his poetry (from 1940 on) and mainstream fiction. He did, however, publish a small number of quite clever and effective speculative fiction tales, most of which display an adroit eye for detail and for the subtleties of human interaction. Shefner's full-length novel, *Latchuga dolzhnika* (1981; *A Debtor's Hovel*), is a mature literary work, combining elements of science fiction with those of philosophical prose. He received the Russian Aelita Award in 2000.

In addition, two short novels, *Čelovek s pjatio "Ne"* (1967; translated as *The Unman*) and *Devushka u obryva ili zapiski Kovrigina* (1964; translated as *Kovrigin's Chronicles*), were published together as *The Unman; Kovrigin's Chronicles* (1980). Both are poetical and ironic or sardonic almost-fantasies, almost urban fairy tales. Other work of note includes the collections *Imia dlia ptitsy* (1976; *The Name for the Bird*), *Kruglaia taina* (1977; *The Round Mystery*), and *Skazki dlia unmykh* (1985; *Fairy Tales for Smart Ones*).

"A Modest Genius," or "Skromny genni," is a classic—deceptive due to its surface charm and seeming lightness. A near-perfect tale of invention and love, it was reprinted more than once in year's-best volumes and other reprint anthologies after initial publication in *View from Another Shore* (1973), an anthology of international fiction compiled by the influential editor and agent Franz Rottensteiner.

A MODEST GENIUS

Vadim Shefner

Translated by Matthew J. O'Connell

1

Sergei Kladesev was born on Vasilyevski Island, Leningrad. He was a strange boy. While other children were making sand pies and building castles, he was drawing sections of odd-looking machines on the sand. In the second grade he built a portable machine, powered by a pocket flashlight battery, which told each pupil how many good marks he would receive during the coming week. Grown-ups considered the machine uneducational and took it away from him.

After leaving grammar school Sergei attended the Technical School for Electrochemistry. He paid no attention to the many pretty girls he met there—perhaps because he saw them every day.

One fine June day he rented a boat and sailed down the Little Neva to the Gulf of Finland. Near Volny Island he came upon a skiff with two girls in it, strangers to him. They had run onto a sandbar and, in attempting to float their boat, had broken the rudder. Sergei introduced himself and helped them back to the dock where they had rented the boat. After that he visited them frequently; the two friends lived, like Sergei, on Vasilyevski Island, Svetlana on Sixth Street, Liussia on Eleventh.

Liussia was attending a course in typewriting at the time, but Svetlana was resting up from school; secondary school had provided all the education she wanted. Besides, her well-off parents were trying to persuade her that it was time to marry; she agreed in principle, but had no intention of taking the first acceptable fellow that came along.

In the beginning Sergei preferred Liussia, but he knew how to behave toward her. She was so pretty, modest, and easily embarrassed that in her presence he too became embarrassed. Svetlana was quite different: gay and quick-witted; in short, a daredevil. Though naturally timid, Sergei felt happy when he was with her.

A year later, Sergei was visiting a friend in Roshdestwenka and there met Svetlana, who was staying with relatives. A coincidence, of course, but Sergei took it as providential. Day after day he walked in the woods and by the sea with her and was soon convinced that he could not live without her.

Svetlana did not find him especially attractive. To her he was an average fellow, and she dreamed of finding somebody unusual for her partner through life. She went walking with Sergei in the woods and by the sea only because she had to pass the time with someone.

One evening they were standing on the shore. On the smooth surface of the water there lay, like a carpet woven by nymphs, a strip of silvery moonlight. Everything was still, except for the nightingales singing in the wild elders on the opposite shore.

"How beautiful and quiet!"

"Yes, it's pretty," answered Svetlana. "If only we could gather some elder branches! But it's too far for walking around on the shore. We have no boat and we can't walk on the water!"

They returned to the village and their respective lodgings. Sergei didn't go to bed that night. He took pencil and paper and filled page after page with formulas and drawings. In the morning he went back to the city and stayed there two days. When he returned he had a bundle under his arm.

Late that evening he took his bundle with him on their walk to the sea. At the water's edge he opened it and took out two pairs of skates for traveling on the water.

"Here, put these water skates on," he said. "I made them just for you."

They both put them on and skated easily over the water to the other shore. The skates slid very nicely on the surface of the sea.

On the other shore Svetlana and Sergei broke off elder branches and then, each with a bundle, went slowly over the sea in the moonlight.

From then on they went skating every evening over the mirror-smooth surface of the water, the skates leaving behind them only a narrow, hardly visible trace, which immediately disappeared.

One day Sergei stopped out on the sea. Svetlana slowly approached him.

"Do you know something?" asked Sergei.

"No. What's wrong?"

"Do you know, Svetlana, that I love you?"

"Of course not!" she answered ironically.

"Then you like me a little, too?"

"I can't say that. You're a fine fellow, but I have a different ideal of a husband. I can only love a really extraordinary man, but to tell you the truth, you're just a good average fellow."

"Well, you're honest, anyway," said a downcast Sergei.

They skated back to the shore in silence, and the next day Sergei returned to the city. For a time he felt wretched. He lost weight and wandered aimlessly through the streets. He often left the city to stroll about. In the evenings he went home to his little workroom.

One day he met Liussia walking along the river. She was glad to see him, and he noticed it immediately.

"What are you doing here, Sergei?"

"Nothing. Just walking. I'm on vacation."

"I'm just walking, too. If you'd like, perhaps we could go over to Cultural Park." She blushed as she made the suggestion.

They rode over to Yelagin Island and slowly walked along its avenues. Later they met several more times to stroll around the city and found that they were happy to be together.

One day Liussia came to Sergei's house to take him off for a trip to Pavlovsk.

"What a disorganized room!" she exclaimed. "All these machines and flasks! What are they for?"

"I go in for various little inventions in my free time."

"And I never suspected!" said Liussia in amazement. "Could you repair my typewriter? I bought it in a discount store; it's old and the ribbon keeps getting stuck."

"Sure, I'll take a look at it."

"What's this?" she asked. "What an odd camera! I've never seen one like it."

"It's a very ordinary FED camera but it has an accessory that I built just recently. With it you can photograph the future. You aim the camera at a place whose future appearance you'd like to know, and take the picture. But my machine isn't perfected yet. You can photograph things only three years ahead, no more than that as yet."

"Three years! That's a lot. What a wonderful invention!"

"Wonderful? Not at all," said Sergei with a disdainful gesture. "It's very imperfect."

"Have you taken any pictures?"

"Yes. A short time ago I went out to the suburbs and shot some film there." He took several prints from his desk.

"Here I photographed a birch in a meadow, without using the accessory. Then here is the same tree in two years' time."

"It's grown a bit and has more branches."

"And here it is three years from now."

"But there's nothing there!" cried the astonished Liussia. "Just a stump and next to it a pit, like a shell hole. And over there are a pair of soldiers running along stooped. What strange uniforms they're wearing! I can't understand the picture at all."

"Yes, I was surprised too, when I developed

the picture. It looks to me as though there are some kind of maneuvers going on there."

"Sergei, you'd better burn that photo. It looks too like a military secret. That picture might fall into the hands of a foreign spy!"

"You're right, Liussia. I never thought of that." He tore up the picture and threw it into the stove with a pile of other trash; then he set fire to it.

"Now I feel better," said Liussia, obviously relieved. "But now take my picture as I'll be a year from now. In this chair over by the window."

"But the accessory will only photograph a certain sector of space and whatever is in it. So, if you're not sitting in that chair a year from now, you won't be in the picture."

"Take me anyway. Who knows, maybe I will be sitting in this chair this day and hour next year!"

"All right," Sergei agreed. "I still have one picture left on this roll." He took the picture. "Come on, I'll develop the film immediately and make some prints. The bathroom is free today; no one is doing any wash."

He went into the bathroom and developed the film, then brought it back to his room and hung it up near the window to dry.

Liussia took the film by the edges and peered at the last exposure. It seemed to her that someone else was in the chair. At the same time she was secretly wishing that she might be sitting there in a year's time. It's probably me, she concluded, only I didn't come out too well.

Once the film was dry, they went into the bathroom, where the red light was still on. Sergei put the strip of film into the enlarger, turned the machine on, and projected the image onto photographic paper. He then quickly put the picture into the developer. On the paper the features of a woman appeared. She sat in the chair and was embroidering a large cat on a piece of cloth. The cat was almost finished, all but the tail.

"That's not me sitting there!" Liussia was disillusioned. "It's a different woman entirely."

"No, it's not you," Sergei agreed. "I don't know who it is; I never saw the woman before."

"Sergei, I think I'd better be going," said Liussia. "You needn't stop by; I can have the typewriter repaired at the store."

"But at least let me bring you home!"

"No, Sergei, there's no need. I don't want to get mixed up in this business." She left.

My inventions bring me no luck, thought Sergei to himself. He took a hammer and smashed the accessory.

2

About two months later, as Sergei was walking along Bolshoi Avenue, he saw a young woman sitting on a bench and recognized her as the unknown woman of the fateful photograph.

She turned to him: "Can you tell me the time?"

Sergei told her and sat down next to her. They chatted about the weather and got acquainted. Sergei learned that her name was Tamara. He saw her often and soon married her. They had a son, whom Tamara named Alfred.

Tamara proved to be a very boring wife. Nothing roused much interest from her. Day in and day out she sat in the chair by the window and embroidered cats, swans, and stags on little strips of cloth which she then hung proudly on the wall. She didn't love Sergei; she had married him only because he had a room of his own and because after her examinations at the Horse Trainers' Institute she didn't want to work in the provinces. No one had authority to send a married woman away.

Herself a boring person, she regarded Sergei too as boring, uninteresting, and insignificant. He was always spending his leisure time inventing something; she didn't approve, and thought it a senseless waste of time. She was constantly scolding him for filling the room with his machines and apparatuses.

To get more freedom of movement in the room, Sergei built his LEAG, or Local Effect

Anti-Gravitation, machine. With the aid of this machine he could do his work on the ceiling of the room. He laid flooring on the ceiling, set his desk on it, and brought up his instruments and tools. In order not to dirty the wall on which he walked up to the ceiling, he glued a narrow strip of linoleum on it. From now on the lower part of the room belonged to his wife, and the upper became his workroom.

Tamara was still dissatisfied: she was now afraid that the superintendent might find out about the expansion of the room space and demand double rent. Furthermore, it displeased her that Sergei should walk so nonchalantly along the ceiling. It just didn't seem right.

"At least have respect for my superior education and don't walk around that way with your head hanging down," she cried up to him from her chair. "Other women have normal husbands, but here I am, stuck with a bird of ill omen."

When Sergei came home from work (he worked at the Transenergy Authority as a technical control officer), he ate quickly and went off up the wall to his preserve. He frequently went for walks through the city and its environs so as not to have to listen to Tamara's constant nagging. He became so used to hiking that he could have walked to Pavlovsk with no difficulty.

One day he met Svetlana at the corner of Eighth Street and Sredni Avenue.

"I've married an extraordinary man since we last met," were her opening words. "My Petya is a real inventor. He's working just now as a beginning inventor at the Everything Everyday Research Institute, but he'll soon be promoted to the intermediate class. Petya has already invented something all by himself: Don't Steal soap."

"What kind of soap is that?" asked Sergei.

"The idea behind it is quite simple—but then every work of genius is simple, of course. Don't Steal is an ordinary toilet soap, but its core is a piece of solidified, water-resistant, black India ink. If someone, let's say your neighbor in the community house, steals the soap and washes with it, he dirties himself physically as well as morally."

"And if the soap isn't stolen?"

"Don't ask silly questions!" Svetlana flashed back angrily at him "You're just jealous of Petya!"

"Do you ever see Liussia? How is she getting along?"

"Oh, she's the same as ever. I keep telling her to look for a suitable extraordinary man and marry him, but she says nothing. She seems bent on becoming an old maid."

Soon afterward the war began. Tamara and Alfred were evacuated; Sergei went to the front. He began the war as a second lieutenant of infantry and ended as a first lieutenant. He returned to Leningrad, exchanged his uniform for civilian clothes, and went back to his old work at the Transenergy Authority. Shortly afterward, Tamara and Alfred also returned, and life went on as before.

3

Years passed.

Alfred grew up, finished school, and went through the minimal course requirements for the training of hotel personnel. Then he went south and got a job in a hotel.

Tamara continued to embroider cats, swans, and stags on wall hangings. She had grown duller and more quarrelsome with the years. She had also made the acquaintance of a retired director, a bachelor, and was constantly threatening Sergei that, if he didn't finally come to his senses and give up inventing things, she would leave him and go off with the director.

Svetlana was still quite satisfied with her Petya. Yes, he was going places. He'd been promoted to intermediate inventor and had now invented four-sided wheel spokes to replace the old-fashioned round ones! She could really be proud of him.

Liussia still lived on Vasilyevski Island and

worked as a secretary in the office of Klavers, which designed and built replacement parts for pianos. She hadn't married and often thought of Sergei. She'd seen him once from a distance but hadn't approached him. He was walking with his wife along Seventh Street on his way to the Baltika Cinema; Liussia immediately recognized his wife as the woman in the photograph.

Sergei thought often of Liussia, too; he tried to distract himself by concentrating on new inventions. The things he made never seemed to him quite perfect and therefore he thought he had no right to get involved with more difficult ones. Recently he had invented a Quarrel Measurer and Ender and installed it in the kitchen of the community house where he lived. The apparatus had a scale with twenty divisions, which measured the mood of the lodger and the intensity of a quarrel that might be going on. The needle trembled at the first unfriendly word and slowly approached the red line. If it reached the line, the Quarrel Ender went into action. Soft, soothing music filled the room; an automatic atomizer emitted a cloud of valerian and White Night perfume; and on the screen of the machine appeared a fellow who leaped about in a comical way, bowed low to the viewers, and kept repeating: "Be at peace with one another, citizens!"

Due to the machine people would make up in the early stages of a quarrel, and all the lodgers in the house were quite grateful to Sergei for his modest invention.

Sergei had also invented a telescope by making a windowpane with the properties of a gigantic magnifying glass. Through this window of his room he could see the canals of Mars, the craters of the moon, and the storms of Venus. When Tamara got on his nerves too much, he distracted and soothed himself by gazing out into distant worlds.

Most of his inventions had no practical value. But one did save him the expense of buying matches. He had succeeded in extracting benzene from water, and, since he smoked a good deal, he now lit his cigarettes from a lighter

filled with his own benzene. Otherwise he led a rather joyless life. Neither Tamara nor Alfred brought him any happiness. When Alfred visited Leningrad, he talked mainly with Tamara.

"How are you getting along?" he asked her.

"What do you expect?" she answered him with a question. "My only pleasure is my art. Look at this stag that I'm embroidering!"

"What a splendid animal!" cried Alfred. "It's so lifelike! And the antlers! If I had antlers like that, I'd really get somewhere."

"Your father has no feeling for art. He's only interested in inventing things. But there's hardly any use to what he makes!"

"Well, at least he doesn't drink; you ought to be grateful for that," was her son's encouraging answer. "He's a slow comer but maybe he'll wise up a bit. When I look at the people who stop at the hotel, I'm ashamed of Father. One guest is a head buyer, another is a foreigner, another a scientific correspondent. A short time ago a lecturer who wrote Pushkin's autobiography was living in one of our apartments. He owns a country cottage and an automobile."

"How can I dream of a country cottage with a husband like mine?" Tamara asked dejectedly. "I've had enough of him. I'd like to get a divorce."

"Have you hooked anyone else yet?"

"I know a retired director, a bachelor. He has an eye for art! I made him a gift of an embroidered swan, and he was as happy as a child over it. With someone like that you can come out on top."

"What was he director of? A hotel?"

"He was a cemetery director, and he's a serious man."

"He'd have to be, in that job," agreed her son.

4

One June evening Sergei was up on the ceiling working on a new invention. He didn't notice the time passing, and it grew quite late. He went to bed but forgot to set the alarm, and he overslept the next morning, so that he couldn't get to work on time. He decided not to go in at all that day: it was the first and last time that he stayed away from work.

"You're going to the dogs with your inventions," said Tamara. "At least you could have missed work for something worthwhile! But this stuff! Clever people earn a bit extra on the side, but you produce nothing, no more than a he-goat gives milk."

"Don't be angry, Tamara," Sergei said, trying to calm her. "Everything will turn out all right. It'll soon be vacation and we'll take a boat ride on the Volga."

"I don't need your cheap boat rides," Tamara screamed. "You ought to take a ride behind your own back and listen to what people say about you. They all consider you a fool and laugh at you."

She snatched an unfinished wall hanging from its hook and stormed out in a rage.

Sergei was thoughtful. He reflected for a long time and then decided to take a ride behind his own back as his wife had suggested. Some time earlier, he had invented an Invisible Presence Machine (IPM), which was effective up to a distance of thirty-five miles. But he had never used the IPM to observe life in the city, thinking it unethical to look into people's homes or to pry into their private lives. Instead, he often set the machine for the woods on the city's outskirts and watched the birds building their nests or listened to their songs.

Now, however, he decided to test the IPM within the city. He turned it on, set the knob at a very close range, and turned the directional antenna toward the kitchen of the community house. Two women were standing at the gas stove, gossiping about this and that. Finally, one of them said; "Tamara's off to the director's again—and not the least bit embarrassed!"

"I'm sorry for Sergei Vladimirovich," answered the other. "What a good and clever man—and this woman is destroying him!"

"I have to agree with you," he could hear the first woman say. "He really does seem to be a good and clever man, but he has no luck."

Sergei next spied on his fellow workers, and they too had nothing but good to say about him. He turned off the IPM and thought for a while. Then Liussia came to mind and he felt a strong desire to see her again, if only for a moment. He turned the machine on and searched for Liussia's room on the fifth floor of a house on Eleventh Street. Perhaps she no longer lived there? Perhaps she had gotten married and moved away? Or just changed to another floor in the same building?

Unfamiliar rooms and unknown people flashed on the screen. Finally he found Liussia's place. She wasn't there but it was certainly her room. The furniture was the same, and the same picture hung on the wall as before. On a small table stood her typewriter. Liussia was probably at work.

He next aimed the IPM at Svetlana's house, wondering how she was getting along. He found her rather easily in a house stuffed full of all sorts of brand-new things; she herself had aged a bit but seemed cheerful and content.

Suddenly her bell rang and she went to open the door. "Hello, Liussia! I haven't seen you for a long time!" she claimed in a welcoming tone.

"I just happened by; it's our midday break," said Liussia, and Sergei too could now see her. Over the years she hadn't grown any younger, but she was just as attractive as ever.

The two friends went into the house and chatted about all sorts of things.

"Aren't you ever going to get married?" Svetlana suddenly asked. "You can still get some worthwhile man in his prime."

"I don't want one," said Liussia dejectedly. "The man I like is long since married."

"Are you still in love with Sergei?" Svetlana persisted. "What do you see in him? What's so great about him? He's the kind that never amounts to much. He was a nice young fellow, of course. Once he gave me water skates, and we used to skate together across the water. The nightingales were singing on the shore and the people were snoring in their cottages, but we flew across the sea and showed our skill."

"I never knew he invented anything like that," Liussia said thoughtfully. "Did you keep them?"

"Of course not! Petya took them to the junk dealer long ago. He said the whole idea was nonsense. Petya is a real inventor and knows what's what with inventions!"

"Is Petya's job going well?"

"Excellent! A short time ago he invented MUCO-1."

"What's a MUCO?"

"A Mechanical Universal Can Opener. Now housewives and bachelors will be spared all the trouble they used to go to in opening cans."

"Have you got one?" Liussia wanted to pursue the matter. "I'd like to see it."

"No, I haven't and never will. It's to weigh five tons and will require a cement platform. Besides, it will cost four hundred thousand rubles."

"What housewife can afford one, then?" Liussia was amazed.

"My, you're slow!" said Svetlana impatiently. "Every housewife won't be buying one. One will be enough for a whole city. It'll be set up in the center of town—on Nevski Prospekt, for example. There they'll build the UCCOC—United City Can Opening Center. It will be very handy. Suppose you have visitors and want to open some sardines for them; you don't need a tool for opening the can and you don't have to do a lot of work. You just take your can to UCCOC, hand it in at the reception desk, pay five kopeks, and get a receipt. At the desk they paste a ticket on the can and put it on a conveyor belt. You go to the waiting room, settle down in an easy chair, and watch a short film on preserves. Soon you're called to the counter. You present your receipt and get your opened can. Then you return contentedly to Vasilyevski Island."

"And they're really going ahead with this project?"

"Petya very much hopes so. But recently some jealous people have shown up and are trying to keep his inventions from being used. They're envious. Petya's not jealous of anyone; he knows he's an extraordinary man. And he's objective, too. For example, he has the highest regard for another inventor—the one who invented the Drink to the Bottom bottle cap and saw it through production."

"What's a Drink to the Bottom cap?"

"You know how vodka bottles are sealed? With a little metal cap. You pull the tab on the cap, the metal tears, and the bottle is open. But you can't use that cap to close it again so you have to finish the bottle, whether you want to or not."

"I prefer the water skates," Liussia reflected. "I'd love to glide across the bay on skates on a white night."

"The skates have really caught your fancy, haven't they?" Svetlana laughed. "Petya and I wouldn't want them back if you paid us."

Sergei shut off his IPM and thought for a while. Then he came to a decision.

5

That same evening Sergei got his pair of water skates from an old suitcase. He filled the bath with water and tested them: they didn't sink but slid across the surface just as well as they had done years before. Then he went to his retreat and worked late into the night making a second pair of skates for Liussia.

The next day, a Sunday, Sergei put on his good gray suit and wrapped the two pairs of skates in a newspaper. He put an atomizer and a bottle of MSST (Multiple Strengthener of Surface Tension) in his pocket; if a person covered his clothing with this preparation, it would keep him afloat.

Finally, he opened the large closet in which he kept his most significant inventions and took out his SPOSEM (Special Purpose Optical Solar Energy Machine). He had worked very hard on this and considered it the most important of all his inventions. It had been finished for two years but had never been tested. Its purpose was to restore a person's youth to him, and Sergei had never wanted his youth back again. If he made himself young again, he would have to make Tamara young too and begin life with her all again—but one life with her was quite enough. In addition, he was frightened at the extraordinarily high energy consumption of the machine; if he were to turn it on, there would be cosmic consequences, and Sergei had never regarded himself as important enough to warrant those consequences.

But now, after thinking things out carefully and weighing all considerations, he decided to use the machine. He put it in with the skates and left the house.

It was a short walk to Sredni Avenue. In a store on the corner of Fifth Street he bought a bottle of champagne and a box of chocolates before continuing on his way. At Eleventh Street he turned off Sredni Avenue and was soon at Liussia's house; he climbed the steps and rang two long and one short on the bell. Liussia answered the door.

"Hello, Liussia! It's been a long time since we met last."

"Very long. But I've always been expecting you to come, and here you are."

They entered Liussia's room, drank champagne, and reminisced about things that had happened years before.

"Oh!" cried Liussia suddenly. "If only I were only young again and life could begin all over!"

"That's in our power," said Sergei, and showed her his SPOSEM, which was the size of a portable radio and had a rather thick cord attached to it.

"Do you plug it into the electrical system? Won't it burn out? The house was recently switched to two hundred twenty volts."

"No, it doesn't get plugged into the electrical system. A thousand Dnieper powerhouses wouldn't be enough to supply it. It gets its energy directly from the sun. Would you open the window, please?"

She opened it, and Sergei led the cord over to it. The cord had a small concave mirror attached to the end, and Sergei laid this on the windowsill so that it was turned directly to the sun. Then he switched the machine on. A crackling could be heard from inside the apparatus, and soon the sun began to look weaker, the way an incandescent bulb does when the current drops. The room grew dusky.

Liussia went to the window and looked out. "Sergei, what's going on?" she asked in astonishment. "It looks as though an eclipse is beginning. The whole island is in dusk, and it's getting dark in the distance, too."

"It's now dark over the whole earth and even on Mars and Venus. The machine uses a great deal of energy."

"That kind of machine should never be mass-produced, then! Otherwise, everyone would become young again but there'd be darkness from then on."

"Yes," Sergei agreed. "The machine should be used only once. I gave it extra capacity for your sake. Now let's sit down and remain quiet."

They sat down on an old plush sofa, held hands, and waited. Meanwhile it had become dark as night. Throughout the city light sprang out of windows and street lamps were turned on. Liussia's room was now completely black, except for a bluish light along the cord of the SPOSEM. The cord twisted and turned like a tube through which some liquid was being forced at great speed.

Suddenly the machine gave a loud crack and a square window opened in the front; from it leaped a ray of green light, which seemed to be chopped off at the end. The ray was like a solid object, yet it was only light. It became longer and longer and finally reached the wall with the picture of the pig and the oak tree. The pig in the picture suddenly changed into a piglet, and the oak with its huge branches into a tiny sapling.

The ray moved slowly and uncertainly across the room as if blindly seeking out Liussia and Sergei. Where it touched the wall, the old, faded hangings took on their original colors and became new again. The elderly gray tomcat who was dozing on the chest of drawers changed into a young kitten and immediately began to play with its tail. A fly, accidentally touched by the ray, changed into a larva and fell to the floor.

Finally the ray approached Sergei and Liussia. It ranged over their heads, faces, legs, and arms. Above their heads two shimmering half-circles formed, like haloes.

"Something's tickling my head," Liussia giggled.

"Don't move, stay quiet," said Sergei. "That's because gray hairs are changing back to their original color. My head feels funny, too."

"Oh!" cried Liussia. "There's something hot in my mouth!"

"You have some gold caps on your teeth, haven't you?"

"Only two."

"Young teeth don't need caps, so the caps are being pulverized. Just breathe the dust out."

Liussia pursed her lips like an inexperienced smoker and blew out some gold dust.

"It feels as though the sofa were swelling under me," she said suddenly.

"The springs are expanding because we're getting lighter. We did put on some weight over the years!"

"You're right, Sergei! I feel wonderfully light, the way I did at twenty."

"You are twenty now. We've returned to our youth."

At this moment the SPOSEM shivered, rumbled, and burst into flame. Then it was gone and only a little blue ash showed where it had been. All around them, everything was suddenly bright again. Motorists turned their headlights off, the street lamps went out, and the artificial light disappeared from the windows.

Liussia stood up and laughed as she looked at herself in the mirror. "Come on, Sergei, let's go for a walk—maybe to Yelagin Island."

Sergei picked up his bundle of skates, took Liussia's arm, and went down the stairs into the street with her. They rode the streetcar to Cultural Park, where they strolled about for a long time, rode the merry-go-round, and ate two meals in a restaurant.

When the still white night had descended and the park was deserted, they went to the seashore. The sea was completely calm, without even the smallest wave, and in the distance, near Volny Island, the sails of the yachts hung motionless in the moonlight.

"Just the right kind of weather," said Sergei as he unwrapped the water skates. He helped Liussia tie hers and then put his own on.

Liussia ran onto the water and skated lightly across it; Sergei followed. They came to the yachts, whose owners were waiting for a breeze; waved to them; and skated on past Volny Island to the open sea. They glided over the water for a long time, then Sergei suddenly slowed down; Liussia stopped and skated back to him.

"Liussia, do you know what I'd like to say to you?" Sergei began, somewhat unsure of himself.

"I know," Liussia replied, "and I love you too. From now we'll stay together for good."

They embraced and kissed, then turned back to the shore. Meanwhile the wind had risen and was forming waves. It was becoming difficult to skate.

"Suppose I stumble and fall down into the water?" said Liussia.

"I'll take precautions right now so that we won't drown," answered Sergei with a laugh. He took the atomizer and bottle of MSST from his pocket and sprayed his and Liussia's clothing with the liquid.

"Now we can even ride the waves," he said to her.

They sat down, close together, on a wave, as though it were a crystal bench, and the wave carried them back to the shore.

Day of Wrath

SEVER GANSOVSKY

Translated by James Womack

Sever Feliksovich Gansovsky (1918–1990) was a prominent Soviet writer of fiction, including science fiction. He wrote some of the best short stories of his generation, several of them collected in English in Macmillan's Best of Soviet Science Fiction anthologies in the 1980s. He received the Russian Aelita Award in 1989.

During his lifetime, Gansovsky held a number of jobs—sailor, electrician, teacher, postman, and, during World War II, sniper and scout. Severely wounded during the war, Gansovsky was presumed dead, returning home only after his family had already held a funeral for him.

His first published work appeared in 1950, and he graduated from Leningrad State University in 1951 (philology). Soon thereafter, Gansovsky began to win awards for his writing. Because he was also a talented illustrator, his career intersected with that of Arkady and Boris Strugatsky when he created the artwork for their short novel *The Snail on the Slope* (1972), among others.

There is a fierce intelligence to all of Gansovsky's fiction, wedded to a spare but effective characterization underpinned by a keen observation of the absurdities and ruthlessness of human nature. Clearly, too, his experiences in World War II influenced his fiction. Stories involving the military reveal a war-weary sensibility, and Gansovsky had a knack for situating interesting characters within the constraints of political and social systems.

Gansovsky was one of the best science fiction writers of his era, easily rivaling his Western counterparts, and his work deserves a revival in the English-language world. Although several stories are worthy of reprinting—including the antiwar story "Testing Grounds"—the classic "Day of Wrath," with its focus on biotech experimentation and echoes of *Dr. Moreau*, is showcased here, in a new translation.

DAY OF WRATH

Sever Gansovsky

Translated by James Womack

*Chairman: You read in several languages, you are familiar with higher mathematics
and can perform all manner of work. Do you think that this makes you human?
Otark: Yes, of course. Do humans know how to do anything else?*
(FROM THE CROSS-EXAMINATION OF AN OTARK, STATE COMMISSION MATERIALS.)

Two riders came out of the thickly overgrown valley and started to climb the mountain. In front, on a roan with a twisted nose, rode the forester, and Donald Betly followed him on a chestnut mare. The mare slipped on the stony path and fell to her knees. Betly, who had been lost in thought, nearly fell off because the saddle—an English racing saddle with a single strap—slid forward down the horse's neck.

The forester waited for him further up.

"Don't let her put her head down, she always slips."

Betly, swallowing his anger, shot him a frustrated glance. "Devil take it, he could have warned me about that earlier." He was cross with himself as well, because the horse had fooled him. When Betly had saddled her up, she had breathed in, so that the strap would be completely loose.

He pulled so hard on the reins that the horse danced about and moved backward.

The path had leveled out again. They were riding across a mesa, and in front of them the hilltops were visible, covered in fir forests.

The horses took long strides, sometimes breaking into a trot and trying to overtake one another. Whenever the mare nudged ahead, Betly could see the sunburned, cleanly shaven thin cheeks of the forester and his sullen eyes, fixed on the road ahead. It was as if he didn't notice the presence of his companion.

"I'm too direct," Betly thought. "And that doesn't help me. I've tried to strike up conversation with him a handful of times, and he either answers me in monosyllables or else doesn't say anything. He doesn't think I'm worth anything. He thinks that if someone wants to talk, then he's a chatterbox and doesn't need any respect. Out here in the wilds they don't know how to take the measure of things. They think that being a journalist doesn't mean anything. Even a journalist like . . . Anyway, I won't talk to him either. Damn it!"

But step by step his mood improved. Betly was a successful man and thought that everyone else should love life as much as he did. He was surprised at the forester's aloofness, but didn't feel any animosity toward him.

The weather, which had been bad in the morning, was starting to clear up. The fog melted away. The dull sheet over the sky had broken up into separate clouds. Huge shadows moved swiftly over the dark forests and valleys, and this emphasized the cruel, wild, and somehow liberated character of the place.

Betly slapped the mare on her damp neck that smelled of sweat.

"They must have hobbled your front legs when they let you out to graze, and that's why you slip. But we'll be all right together."

He stopped pulling back on the reins and caught up with the forester.

"Excuse me, Mr. Meller, were you born around here?"

"No," the forester replied, without turning around.

"Where were you born then?"

"A long way away."

"And have you been here for a long time?"

"A while." Meller turned to the journalist. "You should talk a little more quietly. They might hear you."

"Who are they?"

"The otarks, of course. They'll hear you and tell the others. Or they could ambush us, jump out from behind and rip us to pieces. . . . And it would be better if they didn't know why we're here."

"Do they attack people often? It says in the papers that such things almost never happen."

The forester was silent.

"And do they attack in person?" Betly involuntarily looked over his shoulder. "Or do they shoot people as well? Do they have weapons? Rifles, machine guns?"

"They only rarely shoot. Their hands aren't made for it. Not hands, paws. They're clumsy with weapons."

"Paws," Betly repeated. "So people here don't think of them as human?"

"Who, us?"

"Yes, you. The people who live here."

The forester spat.

"Of course they're not human. No one here thinks that they are."

He spoke in bursts. Betly had already forgotten his vow of silence.

"So, have you ever spoken to them? Is it true that they can speak quite well?"

"The older ones can speak. The ones who were here when the laboratory was working . . . The younger ones speak worse. But they are much more dangerous. They are cleverer, their heads are twice the size." The forester suddenly reined in his horse. His voice was bitter. "Look, there's no point discussing all this. It's all useless. I've answered these questions a dozen times already."

"What's all useless?"

"All of it, this trip. You won't get anything out of it. Everything will stay as it is."

"Why does it have to? I'm from an influential paper. We have a lot of influence. They're gathering material for a Senate commission. If it is shown that the otarks are really so dangerous, then steps will be taken. You must know that this time they are getting ready to send out the troops against them."

"Even so, nothing's going to happen," the forester sighed. "You're not the first person to come here. Every year someone comes, and they're only interested in the otarks. But not in the people who have to live with them. Everyone asks: 'Is it true that they can learn geometry? Are there really otarks who can understand the theory of relativity?' As if that meant anything at all! As if that were a reason not to destroy them!"

"But that's why I'm here," Betly began, "to gather material for the commission. And then the whole country will know that—"

"And you think that the others weren't gathering material?" Meller interrupted. "And . . . and how are you going to understand the situation here? You need to live here to understand it. It's one thing to pass through, and another to be here the whole time. Oh, what's the point of talking? Let's go." He nudged his horse. "Here's where their range begins, anyway. From this valley onward."

The journalist and the forester had reached the top of a hill. The path headed down in a zigzag from under the horse's hooves.

A long way beneath them lay the brush-filled valley, cut in two lengthwise by a narrow stony river. The forest rose in a sheer wall straight from the stream, and beyond it in the immeasurable distance the snow-whitened slopes of the Chief mountain range.

You could see for tens of kilometers all around from here, but Betly saw no signs of life: no smoke from a chimney, not a single haystack. It was as if the place had died.

The sun hid behind some clouds, all at

once it grew cold, and the journalist suddenly felt that he did not want to go down after the forester. He coldly shrugged his shoulders. He recalled the warm, heated air of his city apartment, the bright warm office at the newspaper. But then he pulled himself together. "Rubbish, I've been in worse situations than this. What do I have to be afraid of? I'm an excellent shot, and I have very good reactions. Who else could they have sent instead of me?" He saw Meller unshoulder his rifle, and did the same with his own weapon.

The mare carefully lifted its feet on the narrow path.

When they were at the bottom of the hill, Meller said:

"We should try to ride abreast. Better not to talk. We need to get to Steglich's farm by around eight. We'll spend the night there."

They spurred their horses on and rode for about two hours in silence. They headed up and rode around Mount Bear, keeping the forest wall to their right at all times, the drop-off to their left, covered in bushes, but so small and sparse that no one could hide among them. They went down to the river and went along its rocky bottom until they reached an abandoned asphalted road, the surface cracked with grass growing through it.

As they rode along the asphalt, Meller suddenly stopped his horse and listened. Then he dismounted, got to his knees, and put his ear to the ground.

"Something's not right," he said, standing up. "Someone's galloping after us. Let's get off the road."

Betly also dismounted and they led the horses into a ditch in a clump of alders.

About two minutes later, the journalist heard the clattering of hooves. They came closer. You could feel that the rider was going flat out.

Then through the faded leaves they saw a gray horse galloping hard. On it, sitting awkwardly, was a man wearing yellow riding breeches and an anorak. He came so close

that Betly got a good look at the man's face and realized that he had seen him before. He even remembered where. Back in town there had been a group of people standing around outside the bar. Five or six men, dirty, badly dressed. They all had the same eyes. Lazy, half-closed, impertinent. The journalist knew those eyes— gangsters' eyes.

As soon as the horseman had come past, Meller rushed out into the road.

"Hey!"

The man pulled on his horse's reins and stopped.

"Hey, wait!"

The rider looked back, and obviously recognized the forester. For a few moments they looked at one another. Then the man waved, turned his horse around, and rode on.

The forester stared after him as the noise of the hooves died away in the distance. Then he suddenly hit his head with his fist and groaned.

"It's not going to work now, that's for certain."

"What is it?" Betly asked. He had come out from among the bushes as well.

"Nothing. It's just put an end to our plan."

"But why?" The journalist looked at the forester and was surprised to see tears in his eyes.

"It's all over now," Meller said, as he turned and wiped his eyes with the back of his hand. "The bastards! Bastards!"

"Listen to me." Betly had started to lose his patience as well. "If you're going to get so worked up, then there's really no point carrying on."

"Worked up?" the forester exclaimed. "You think I've gotten worked up? Just look at this!"

He waved his hand at a branch of a pine tree with reddish cones on it, hanging over the road about thirty paces away from them.

Betly still had not realized why he was supposed to be looking at it when a shot thundered out, he got a strong whiff of gunpowder, and the last pinecone, hanging by itself, dropped down onto the asphalt.

"That's how worked up I am," Meller said, and went into the clump of alders for his horse.

They reached the farm just as night was falling.

Out of the unfinished log house came a tall dark-bearded man with disheveled hair who stood watching in silence how Betly and the forester unsaddled their horses. Then a woman came out onto the porch, red haired and with a flat expressionless face, ungroomed as well. And three children came after her. Two boys of eight or nine years old and a girl aged about thirteen, skinny as if drawn with a single crooked line.

The five of them were not at all surprised at Meller and the journalist: they were not happy or sad. They just stood and stared in silence. Betly didn't like the silence.

Over dinner he tried to start a conversation.

"Tell me, how do you get on with the otarks? Are they really very troublesome?"

"What?" The dark-bearded farmer put his palm to his ear and bent over the table. "What?" he shouted. "Speak up. I don't hear so good."

This was how things went on for a few minutes, and the farmer very clearly did not want to understand what was wanted of him. In the end he spread his hands. Yes, there are otarks here. Do they bother him? No, they don't bother him personally. He doesn't know about the others. He can't say anything about them.

In the middle of this conversation the thin girl stood up, threw a shawl around her shoulders, and left without saying a word to anyone.

As soon as all the plates were empty the farmer's wife brought two mattresses out of another room and started to lay them out for the visitors.

But Meller stopped her.

"I think it would be better if we slept in the barn."

The woman stood up without saying a word. The farmer jumped up from the table.

"Why? Sleep here."

But the forester had already picked up the mattresses.

The farmer led them into the high barn with a lamp. He watched for a minute as they got themselves ready, and for a moment there was an expression on his face as though he wished to say something. But he only raised his hand and rubbed his head. Then he left.

"What's all this about?" Betly asked. "The otarks won't get into the house, surely?"

Meller picked up a thick plank from the floor and forced it up against the heavy solid door, checking that it didn't slip away.

"Go to bed," he said. "Anything can happen. They get into houses as well."

The journalist sat on the mattress and started to unlace his boots.

"Tell me, are there any real bears left here? Not otarks, but real wild bears. Didn't there used to be a lot of bears wandering around here, in the forest?"

"There aren't anymore," Meller replied. "The first thing that the otarks did when they broke out of the laboratory and got off the island was to destroy all the real bears. And the wolves. And there used to be raccoons and foxes—all the normal animals. They took poison from the ruined laboratory and poisoned the smaller animals. There were dead wolves lying around all over the place—for some reason they didn't eat the wolves. But they ate the bears. They sometimes even eat each other."

"They eat each other?"

"Of course, they're not people. You don't know what to expect from them."

"Do you think they're just animals?"

"No." The forester shook his head. "We don't think they're wild animals. That's the kind of thing they argue about in the cities, if they're people or animals. Out here we know that they're neither one thing nor the other. Don't you see, it used to be like this: there were people and there were animals. And now there's something else: the otarks. This is the first time such a thing has happened in the whole history of the world. Otarks aren't animals—it would be great if they were just animals. But they're not people either, of course."

"Tell me"—Betly felt that he couldn't stop

himself asking the question, even though he knew it was banal—"is it true that they find it very easy to learn higher mathematics?"

The forester turned sharply toward him.

"Listen, shut up about mathematics for once! Just shut up! I don't give a toss if they know higher mathematics! Yeah, the otarks can do complicated math standing on their heads! So what? You need to be a person, that's what the question really is."

He turned away and bit his lip.

"He's worked up," Betly thought. "He's still really worked up. He's not a healthy man."

But the forester had already calmed down. He was uncomfortable to have flown off the handle. After a short silence, he asked:

"Sorry, but have you seen him?"

"Who?"

"You know, the genius. Fidler."

"Fidler? Yes, I've seen him. I spoke to him just before I came out here. The newspaper sent me."

"I guess they keep him wrapped up in plastic over there? So he doesn't get a single drop of rain on him."

"Yes, they look after him." Betly remembered how they had checked his pass and frisked him for the first time by the walls of the Science Center. Then they had searched him again and checked his pass again at the entrance to the Institute. And the third search just before they let him into the garden where Fidler came out to meet him. "They look after him. But he is a truly gifted mathematician. He was only thirteen when he wrote his *Corrections to the General Theory of Relativity*. Of course, he's an unusual man, you'd have to be."

"But what does he look like?"

"What does he look like?"

The journalist hesitated. He remembered Fidler coming out into the garden in his baggy white suit. There was something odd about his figure. His hips were wide, his shoulders narrow. A short neck . . . It had been a strange interview, because Betly felt that it was rather he who was being interviewed. Fidler had

answered his questions. But somehow frivolously. As if he were laughing at the journalist and at the whole world of normal people out there, behind the walls of the Science Center. And he asked questions as well. Strange, almost foolish questions. Rubbish, like whether Betly liked carrot juice. As if the conversation were an experiment and he, Fidler, were carrying out research into a normal person.

"Averagely tall," Betly said. "Small eyes . . . Have you really never seen him? He's been here, out at the lake and in the laboratory."

"He came twice," Meller replied. "But he had so much security with him that they wouldn't even let dead people get within a mile of him. That was back when they still kept the otarks behind fences, when Reichhardt and Klein were working with them. They ate Klein. And when the otarks escaped, Fidler never showed his face here again. . . . What does he say about the otarks now?"

"About the otarks? He said that they were a very interesting scientific experiment. Very challenging. But he's not involved with them at the moment. He's doing something to do with cosmic rays. . . . He said that he was sorry for the victims."

"And why did they do all this? What for?"

"How can I put it?" Betly thought for a moment. "Something that happens a lot in science is *what if*. It's led to a lot of discoveries."

"What do you mean, *what if*?"

"Well, for example, *What if we put an electrified wire into a magnetic field*? And then you get the electric motor. . . . I suppose *what if* just means experimentation."

"Experimentation." Meller ground his teeth. "They did an experiment: they let maneaters out among people. And now no one thinks about us. You'll get by as best you can. Fidler's given up on the otarks and on us as well. And they've bred and there are hundreds of them now, and no one knows what they're plotting against us people." He stopped talking and sighed. "The things these scientists think up! Making wild animals cleverer than people.

They've gone crazy, the people who live in cities. Atom bombs and now this. They must really want to bring the human race to an end."

He stood up, took his loaded rifle, and laid it beside him on the floor.

"Listen, Mr. Betly. If there is an alarm, if someone starts knocking or trying to break the door down, you just lie there. Or else we'll shoot each other in the dark. You lie there; I know what to do. I'm so well trained I'm like a dog, I'll wake up just from instinct."

In the morning, when Betly left the barn, the sun was shining so brightly and the rain-washed greenery was so fresh that the conversation they had last night seemed no more than a scary story.

The black-bearded farmer was already out in his field—the white patch of his shirt showed on the other side of the river. For a moment the journalist thought that this might be happiness—to get up at sunrise, not to know the worry and bustle of a difficult city life, to do business only with the handle of your spade, with the clods of dark brown earth.

But the forester quickly brought him back to reality. He appeared from behind the barn with his rifle in his hand.

"Come on, I want to show you something."

They walked around the barn and came out into the kitchen garden that backed up against the house. Here Meller behaved strangely. Bent double, he rushed past the bushes and stopped in a ditch next to the potato beds. Then he made a sign for the journalist to do the same.

They started to follow the ditch around the kitchen garden. At one point a woman's voice could be heard in the house, but it was impossible to hear what she said.

Meller stopped.

"Look here."

"What is it?"

"You said you were a hunter. Look!"

On a patch of bare earth among the tangled grass was a clear five-toed footprint.

"A bear?" Betly said hopefully.

"What bear? There haven't been bears here for a long time."

"So is it an otark?"

The forester nodded.

"It's fresh," the journalist whispered.

"From last night," Meller said. "You see it's damp. They were in the house before it rained."

"In the house?" Betly felt a cold shiver down his spine, as if something metal had pressed against it. "Right in the house?"

The forester did not answer, he jerked his head in the direction of the ditch, and both of them went back the way they had come.

When they got to the barn, Meller waited while Betly got his breath back.

"I thought as much last night. When we got here last night and Steglich started to pretend that he couldn't hear. He just wanted us to speak more loudly so that the otark could hear everything. The otark was in the other room."

The journalist's voice was hoarse.

"What are you saying? People are taking sides with the otarks? Against real people?"

"Keep your voice down," the forester said. "What do you mean, 'taking sides'? Steglich couldn't do anything else. The otark came and it stayed. That happens a lot. An otark comes and lies down, for example, in the bedroom. Or else they just throw people out of their houses and live there for a day or two."

"And what about the people? Do they just put up with it? Why don't they shoot them?"

"How are they going to shoot them, if the woods are filled with other otarks? The farmer has children, and cattle that he wants to pasture in the fields, and a house that could burn down. . . . But the children are the most important. The otarks can take them. Can you really keep an eye on your children? And they've taken all the rifles anyway. That happened right at the start. In the first year."

"And people just gave them up?"

"What could they do? The ones who didn't surrender their weapons were sorry . . ."

He did not finish his sentence and suddenly

stared at the willow coppice about fifteen paces away from them.

What happened next took only two or three seconds.

Meller lifted up his rifle and cocked it. At the same time a dark brown mass rose from the bushes, its large eyes sparkling, wicked and frightened, and said:

"Hey, don't shoot! Don't shoot!"

Instinctively the journalist grabbed Meller's shoulder. A shot rang out but the bullet just nicked a tree. The brown mass bent double and rolled like a ball into the forest and disappeared between the trees. For a few moments all that could be heard was the cracking of twigs, then everything fell silent.

"What the hell!" The forester turned around in a fury. "Why did you do that?"

The journalist, turning pale, whispered:

"He spoke just like a human. . . . He asked you not to shoot."

For a second the forester looked at him, then his anger turned into a tired indifference. He lowered his rifle.

"All right . . . The first time it causes quite an impression."

There was a rustle behind them. They both turned.

The farmer's wife said:

"Come and eat. I've already laid the table."

While they ate they all pretended that nothing had happened.

After breakfast the farmer helped them saddle their horses. They left without saying anything.

When they had ridden off, Meller asked:

"What's your plan, then? I didn't catch it. All they said was that I should ride you around the mountains, and that was it."

"What's my plan? Well, I want to go around in the mountains, yes. To see people, the more the better. To get to know the otarks, if the opportunity presents itself. In a word, to get a sense of the atmosphere."

"Were you getting it back on the farm?"

Betly shrugged.

The forester suddenly reined in his horse.

"Shush . . ."

He listened.

"Someone's running after us. . . . Something's happened on the farm."

Betly had no time to wonder at the forester's hearing when a shout came from behind them:

"Hey, Meller! Hey!"

They turned their horses and the farmer, panting, came up to them. He almost fell over, and grabbed the pommel of Meller's saddle.

"The otark took Tina. He's dragged her off to Moose Canyon."

He gulped at the air; drops of sweat fell from his forehead.

With a single movement, the forester pulled the farmer up onto his saddle. His stallion rushed forward, throwing up mud high from beneath his hooves.

Betly had never thought that he could travel so fast on a horse. Potholes, the trunks of fallen trees, bushes, and ditches all slid by under him, forming some kind of patchy mosaic. At some point a branch whipped off his cap, and he didn't even notice.

This speed largely did not depend on him. In the heat of the competition, his mare tried her hardest not to be left behind by the stallion. Betly grabbed on to her neck. Every second he thought that he would be killed.

They galloped through the forest, across a wide meadow, down a slope, passed the farmer's wife and headed down into a big ravine.

The forester leaped down from his horse and, with the farmer following him, rushed down the narrow path into a grove of sparsely planted pine trees.

The journalist left his horse as well, throwing the rein over her neck, and rushed after Meller. He hurried after the forester and his mind automatically noted the surprising transformation that had taken place. There was nothing left of Meller's former apathy and indecisiveness. He moved with light and collected gestures, never pausing to think; he jumped over pits, slid under low-hanging branches. He moved as if the trail of the otark was sketched out for him in a thick chalk line.

For a while Betly kept up with the pace, then he started to tire. His heart leaped in his chest, he felt tightness and burning in his throat. He slowed down to a walk, and for a few minutes walked alone among the bushes, then heard voices ahead of him.

The forester stood in the narrowest part of the ravine with his gun cocked and pointing at a thick grove of hazel trees. The girl's father was there as well.

The forester spoke with emphasis:

"Let her go. Or I will kill you."

He was talking to what was in the grove.

He was answered by a growl, mingled with the sobs of a child.

The forester repeated what he had said:

"Or I will kill you. I will give my life to track you and kill you. You know me."

The growl came again, and then a voice, but not a human voice, somehow like a gramophone record, running all the words together, said:

"And if I do this, then you won't kill me?"

"No," Meller said. "You will walk out of here alive."

There was silence in the thicket. The only noise was the child's crying.

Then there was a cracking noise of branches, and something white appeared among the trees. The thin girl came out into the long grass. One of her hands was covered in blood and she supported it with the other.

Still crying, she walked past the three men, not turning to look at them, and wandered staggering toward her house.

The three men looked as she walked away.

The black-bearded farmer looked at Meller and Betly. There was something so harsh in his wide-open eyes that the journalist could not bear it and bent his head.

"That's that," the farmer said.

. . .

They stopped to spend the night in a little empty watchman's hut in the forest. They were only a few hours away from the lake with the island where the laboratory had once been, but Meller refused to travel in the dark.

This was the fourth day of their journey, and the journalist thought that his tried and tested optimism was starting to crack. Previously he had had a little saying prepared for every time he met with any unpleasantness: "But all the same, life itself is wonderful!" But now he understood that this was a standby phrase, one that worked perfectly when you were traveling in a comfortable train from one city to the next or when you walked through the glass door that leads into a hotel reception, ready to meet with some famous person—this phrase was entirely inadequate to deal with what had happened to Steglich, for example.

The whole region seemed to be wracked with illness. The people were apathetic, unwilling to talk. Even the children didn't laugh.

Once he asked Meller why the farmers didn't leave the place. The forester explained that the only thing that the inhabitants owned was their land. But now there was no way to sell it. The land was worthless now because of the otarks.

Betly asked:

"Why don't you leave?"

The forester thought. He bit his lips in silence, then replied:

"I can still be of some use. The otarks are afraid of me. I don't have anything here. No family, no home. There's no way they can put pressure on me. They can only fight me. But that is risky."

"Do you mean that the otarks respect you?"

Meller lifted his head uncertainly.

"The otarks? How could they? They don't know respect either. They are not people. They are just afraid. And they're right. I kill them."

But the otarks still took a certain amount of risk. The forester and the journalist both recognized it. They had the impression that a ring was gradually tightening around them. They had been shot at three times. Once the shots had come from the windows of an abandoned house, and twice they had come straight out of the forest. After each of the three attacks they had found fresh tracks. And every day they found more and more marks made by the otarks. . . .

In the watchman's hut, in the little stone fireplace, they lit a fire and prepared their supper. The forester lit his pipe and looked sadly into space.

They had left their horses opposite the open door to the hut.

The journalist looked at the forester. All the time he had been with him, his respect for him had increased every day. Meller was uncultured, he had spent all his life in the forests, he had barely read anything, you couldn't speak to him for two minutes about art. And even so the journalist felt that he couldn't ask for a better friend. The forester's opinions were always healthy and independent: if he didn't have anything to say, then he didn't say anything. To begin with the journalist had thought him somehow nervy and irritably weak, but now Betly understood that this was a long-standing bitterness that he felt on behalf of the inhabitants of this large abandoned region, which had been brought low by the actions of the scientists.

For the last two days Meller had been feeling ill. He had swamp fever. It covered his face with red patches.

The fire was dying in the grate, and the forester unexpectedly said:

"Tell me, is he young?"

"Who?"

"The scientist, Fidler."

"He is young," the journalist replied. "About thirty. No more. Why?"

"It's not good that he's young," the forester said.

"Why?"

Meller was silent for a while.

"Well, they take them all, the talented people, and lock them away in a closed space. And they coddle them. And they don't know any-

thing about life. And that's why they have no compassion for people." He sighed. "You need to be a person first of all. And only then a scientist."

He stood up.

"It's time to go to sleep. We'll take turns. Or else the otarks will kill our horses."

The journalist ended up taking the first watch.

The horses were chewing hay from a small hayrick left over from the previous year.

He sat in the doorway of the hut, his rifle laid across his knees.

The darkness fell fast, like a cover. Then his eyes gradually became accustomed to the gloom. The moon came out. The night was clear and starry. Calling out to one another, a flock of little birds flew overhead. Unlike the larger birds, they were afraid of predators and so carried out their autumn journey by night.

Betly stood up and walked around the hut. The forest closely surrounded the clearing where the hut stood, and this was where the danger lay. The journalist checked his rifle to see if it was cocked.

He started to muse over the last few days, the conversations he had had, the faces he had seen, and he thought about how he would tell the story of the otarks when he got back to the newspaper. Then he thought that it was precisely the idea of his return that constantly appeared in his mind and gave a peculiar coloring to everything that he met with here. Even when they were tracking the otark after it had taken the child, he, Betly, had not forgotten that however bad things got here, he could always turn around and leave it all behind.

"I'll go back," he said to himself. "But Meller? And the others?"

But this was too harsh a thought for him to work out all its ramifications now.

He sat in the shade of the hut and started to think about the otarks. He remembered the headline from some newspaper: "Intelligence without compassion." It was like what the forester said. For him the otarks could not be human, because they had no "compassion." Intelligence without compassion. Was that possible? Could intelligence even exist without compassion? What came first? Isn't kindness a result of intelligence? Or is it the other way around? It had already been established that the otarks were more capable than humans of logical thought, that they understood abstractions better, had better memories. The rumors were already flowing that some of the first-generation otarks were held in the Ministry of Defense and used to help decide certain particular problems. But electronic "reasoning machines" were also used to solve certain particular problems. What was the difference?

He remembered that one of the farmers had told him and Meller that he had recently seen an almost completely naked otark, and the forester had replied that the otarks had recently started to become ever more like people. Would they conquer the world one day? Could intelligence without compassion be stronger than human intelligence?

"But that won't happen any time soon," he said to himself. "If it ever does happen. In any case, I'll be long gone by then."

But then he thought: what about the children? What sort of world would they live in—the world of the otarks or the world of cybernetic robots, also inhuman and also, according to some people, cleverer than humans?

His son appeared in his mind's eye and said to him:

"Listen to me, Dad. We are who we are, right? And they are who they are. But don't they think to themselves that they are a 'we' too?"

"You're growing up too fast," Betly thought. "When I was seven I wouldn't have asked such questions."

Somewhere behind him a twig snapped. The boy disappeared.

The journalist carefully looked around and listened. No, everything was fine.

A bat crossed the clearing in its angular wavering flight.

Betly straightened up. The thought came to him that the forester was hiding something from him. He still hadn't said who the horseman was who had overtaken them on the broken road that first day.

He leaned his back against the wall of the house once more. His son appeared again, with more questions.

"Dad, where does it all come from? The trees, the houses, the air, the people? Where does it come from?"

He started to tell the boy about the evolution of creation, then something seemed to jab him in the heart and Betly woke up.

The moon had gone. But the sky was still fairly light.

The horses were no longer in the clearing. Or rather, one was gone, and the other was lying on the grass, with three gray shadows crouching over it. One of them stretched up, and the journalist saw a huge otark with a large heavy head, grinning jaws, and large eyes that glinted in the half darkness.

Then a whisper came from nearby.

"He's asleep."

"No, he's woken up already."

"Go to him."

"He'll shoot."

"He'd have shot earlier, if he could. He's either asleep, or else he's petrified with fear. Go to him."

"You go."

The journalist was petrified. It was like a dream. He understood that there was no way out of this, that the catastrophe had arrived, but he could not move a muscle.

The whisper continued:

"But what about the other one? He'll shoot."

"He's ill, he won't wake up . . . go, I say!"

With a huge effort Betly managed to move his eyes. An otark appeared from around the corner of the hut. But this one was small, like a pig.

Overcoming his state of shock, the journalist pulled the trigger of his rifle. Two shots boomed out one after the other, two cartridge cases were expelled into the air.

Betly scrambled to his feet, the rifle fell

from his hands. He rushed into the hut, shaking, slammed the door behind him, and put the latch down.

The forester was waiting with his rifle cocked. His lips moved, and the journalist felt rather than heard the question:

"The horses?"

He shook his head.

There was a scratching at the door. The otarks were propping something up against it.

A voice spoke:

"Hey, Meller! Hey!"

The forester rushed to the window and would have stuck his rifle out. But at that moment a black paw flashed past against the starry background; he scarcely pulled his gun back in time.

There was satisfied laughter outside.

The gramophone voice, stretching out its words, said:

"Your time is up, Meller."

Other voices interrupted:

"Meller, Meller, come and talk to us. . . ."

"Hey, forester, say something clever. You're a man, you're supposed to be clever. . . ."

"Meller, say something and I'll tell you it's wrong. . . ."

"Speak to me, Meller. Call me by my name. I'm Philip. . . ."

The forester said nothing.

The journalist walked over to the window with uncertain steps. The voice was very close, just past the log wall. There was an animal stench—blood, dung, something else.

The otark who had said his name was Philip spoke right under the window.

"You're a journalist, right? You, by the window."

The journalist cleared his throat. His throat was dry. The same voice continued:

"Why did you come here?"

There was a silence.

"Did you come here to destroy us?"

There was another pause, then other voices started to speak:

"Of course, of course they want to wipe us

out. . . . First they made us, now they want to destroy us. . . ."

There was a chorus of growls, then another noise. The journalist had the impression that the otarks were fighting.

Over the top of all this noise came the voice of the one who had said he was called Philip:

"Hey, forester, why don't you shoot? You always shoot. Come and speak to me now."

Somewhere above them a shot suddenly rang out.

Betly turned around.

The forester had climbed on top of the fireplace, had moved aside the thin poles with straw on top that made up the roof, and had opened fire.

He fired twice, paused to reload, and fired again.

The otarks ran away.

Meller jumped down from the fireplace.

"We need to get some horses. Or it'll be tough for us."

They looked at the three dead otarks.

One of them, a youngster, was practically naked, with hair only growing on the back of his neck.

Betly nearly vomited when Meller turned the creature over on the grass. He managed to contain himself, holding his mouth shut.

The forester said:

"Remember, they are not people. Even though they can speak. They eat people. They eat each other."

The journalist looked around. It was already dawn. The clearing, the field, the dead otarks— everything seemed at that moment to be unreal.

Could it really be so? Was he, Donald Betly, standing here?

"This is where the otark ate Klein," Meller said. "One of the locals told us all about it, a man from around here. He worked as a cleaner, when the laboratory still existed. And that evening he just happened to be in the next room. He heard everything. . . ."

The journalist and the forester were now on the island, in the main building of the Science Center. That morning they had taken the saddles from the dead horses and had crossed to the island over the dam. They only had one rifle now, because Betly's had been taken by the otarks as they ran away. Meller's plan was to get to a nearby farm while it was still light and take some horses there. But the journalist had talked him into allowing half an hour to look over the abandoned laboratory.

"He heard everything," the forester continued. "It was in the evening, around about ten o'clock. Klein had some kind of contraption that he was taking apart, connecting to electric wires, and the otark was sitting on the floor, and they were chatting. They were talking about physics. This was one of the first otarks they had bred and he was considered the most intelligent. He could even speak foreign languages. . . . This guy was cleaning the floor and could hear them chatting. Then there was a silence, then a thud. And suddenly the cleaner heard a voice saying, 'Oh God!' It was Klein, and there was so much terror in his voice that his knees bent under him. Then there was a gut-wrenching scream of 'Help me!' The cleaner looked into the room and saw Klein lying on the floor and writhing, with the otark chewing at him. This guy was so frightened that he couldn't do anything and just stood there. And it was only when the otark came for him that he shut the door."

"And then?"

"Then they killed two other laboratory workers and ran away. And five or six stayed on as though nothing had happened. And when the commission from the city came, they talked to the otarks. Then they took them away. We found out later that they'd eaten another person on the train."

Everything had been left untouched in the large laboratory. The flasks and dishes were on the long benches, covered with a layer of dust, and spiders had spun their webs through the cables of the X-ray machine. The glass in the windows was broken, and the branches of wild, uncropped acacias came through the empty frames.

Meller and the journalist left the main building.

Betly wanted very much to look at the radiation apparatus, and he asked the forester for five more minutes.

The asphalt on the main road of the abandoned village had been broken through by grass and young strong shoots. It was autumnal and you could see a long way. It smelled of rotting leaves and damp trees.

On the village square Meller stopped unexpectedly.

"Did you hear something?"

"No," Betly replied.

"I was thinking about how they came as a group to besiege us in the watchman's hut," the forester said. "They never used to do anything like that. They always acted alone."

He listened again.

"It's as if they were planning a surprise for us. Let's get out of here as fast as we can."

They went over to the low-slung round building with its narrow barred windows. The massive door was half open, the concrete floor by the doorway was covered with a thick layer of forest debris—reddish pine needles, dust, the wings of midges.

They went carefully into the first room with its hanging ceiling. Another massive door led into a low-roofed room.

They peered in. A squirrel with a fluffy tail like a flame rushed across the wooden table and leaped through the wooden slats covering the window.

The forester looked around quickly. He listened, holding his rifle tight, then said:

"No, this is no good."

And he hurried back the way they had come.

But it was too late.

There was a rustling noise and the outside door clanged shut. Then there was a noise as if something heavy were being placed against it.

For a second Meller and the journalist looked at one another, then they rushed to the window.

Betly took one glance, then stepped back.

The square and the wide dry pool, which had been built there for no obvious reason, were filled with otarks. There were dozens and dozens of them, and new ones kept appearing as if they were coming out of the ground. A noise rose from this crowd of non-humans and non-beasts, a mixture of cries and growling.

In shock, the forester and Betly stood silently.

A young otark near to them stood up on its back paws. There was something round in its front paws.

"A stone," the journalist said, still unable to believe what was happening. "He wants to throw a stone. . . ."

But it was not a stone.

The round object flew through the air, by the window it burst with a blinding light, and a bitter smoke came into the room.

The forester stepped back from the window. He looked confused. His rifle fell from his hands and he grasped at his chest.

"Damn it!" he said, and lifted up a hand, looking at his bloody fingers. "The bastards! They've got me."

Turning pale, he took two uncertain steps, then sank to his heels, then sat against the wall.

"They got me."

"No!" Betly cried. "No!" He shook as though with fever.

Meller, biting his lips, turned his pale face to him.

"The door!"

The journalist ran to the exit. There was already something heavy propped against it from the outside.

He went back to the forester.

Meller was lying down now against the wall, holding his hands to his chest. A damp patch spread over his shirt. He wouldn't let the journalist bind the wound.

"It doesn't matter," he said. "I can feel that this is the end. There's no point causing any more pain. Don't touch me."

"But I can get help!" Betly cried.

"Who from?"

The question was so bitter, so open and so hopeless, that the journalist grew cold.

They were quiet for a while, then the forester said:

"Do you remember the rider we saw the first day?"

"Yes."

"He was most likely running to tell the otarks that you were here. They work together, the city bandits and the otarks. That's why the otarks were able to band together. You shouldn't be surprised. I'm sure that if octopuses came here from Mars, they'd find people willing to side with them."

"Yes," whispered the journalist.

The time until evening passed without anything happening. Meller grew weaker quickly. He stopped bleeding. Even so he wouldn't let anyone touch him. The journalist sat next to him on the stone floor.

The otarks left them alone. They made no attempt to break through the door, or to throw another grenade. The chattering outside the building grew faint, then rose again.

When the sun went down and it started to get colder, the forester asked for something to drink. The journalist gave him water from his flask and wiped his face as well.

The forester said:

"Maybe it's a good thing that the otarks have appeared. Now it will become clear what it means to be a man. Now we will all know that to be a man it is not enough to be able to count and to study geometry. There's something else. And the scientists are proud of their work. But that's not everything."

Meller died that night, and the journalist lived another three days.

The first day he only thought about saving himself, moving from despair to hope, shooting a few times through the window with the idea that someone would hear the shots and come to help him.

Toward nighttime he realized that all his hopes were illusory. His life seemed to be divided into two halves that were impossible to reconcile in any way. He was mostly agitated by the fact that there was no logical connection or continuity between them. One life was the happy intellectual life of a highly successful journalist, and that life had finished when he and Meller had ridden down from the mountainside into the thick forests of the Main Range. This first life had given him no indication that he was destined to die here on this island, in an abandoned laboratory.

In the second life everything was possible and impossible. It was entirely made up of coincidence. And really, it could not be happening. He had been free not to come here, to refuse this call from his editor and take another job. Instead of studying the otarks, he could have flown to Nubia to write about the protection of the ancient monuments of Egyptian art.

An unlucky chance had brought him here. That was the cruelest blow. A couple of times he had almost stopped believing in what had happened to him, and had walked around the room touching the sunlit walls and the dusty tables.

For some reason or other the otarks had lost all interest in him. There were only a few of them left in the pool and on the square. Sometimes they would fight among themselves, and once Betly saw with heart-stopping horror how they threw themselves on one of their own, tore him to pieces, and settled down to eat.

At night he suddenly decided that Meller was guilty of his death. He felt disgusted by the dead forester and dragged his body into the next room and put it by the door.

For a couple of hours he sat on the floor, hopelessly repeating:

"Lord, why me? Why me?"

On the second day his water ran out and he started to be tormented by thirst. But he had already understood that there was no way he would be saved, and he remained calm and started to think about his life again—it already seemed like someone else's. He remembered how, right at the beginning of the journey, he had argued with the forester. Meller had told him that the farmers wouldn't talk to him.

"Why?" Betly had asked.

"Because you live in the warm, with all your comforts," Meller replied. "Because you are one of the people at the top. One of the ones who betrayed them."

"What do you mean, I'm at the top?" Betly said, refusing to accept what he was told. "I only earn a little bit more than they do."

"So what?" the forester said. "Your work is light, fun almost. They have been dying here for years, and you've written your little articles, you've gone to restaurants, you've had your intellectual conversations. . . ."

He realized that all this was true. His optimism, which he had been so proud of, was in the final analysis the optimism of an ostrich. He had just buried his head when it came to the bad news. He read about executions in Paraguay in the newspapers, or about famine in India, but spent his time thinking about how to get money to buy new furniture for his large five-room apartment, or how he might be able to win the good opinion of some important person or other. The otarks—the otark-people—shot crowds of protesters, speculated on the price of bread, prepared wars in secret, and he turned away from it all, pretending that nothing of the kind ever happened.

From this point of view, all of his past life suddenly seemed strongly connected with what was now happening to him. He had never spoken out against evil, and now the time had come for payback.

On the second day the otarks came and spoke with him by the windows a couple of times. He didn't reply.

One of the otarks said:

"Hey, come on out, journalist! We won't hurt you."

And another one, standing next to him, laughed.

Betly thought about the forester once again. But his opinion had changed. He thought that the forester had been a hero. To tell the truth, the only real hero that Betly had ever encountered. Alone, without any kind of assistance, he had fought against the otarks, had struggled with them and died undefeated.

On the third day the journalist started to fall into delirium. He imagined that he had returned to his newspaper and was dictating an article to the stenographer.

The article was called "What Is a Man?"

He dictated out loud.

"In our century of astounding developments in science one might be forgiven for concluding that science is all-powerful. But let us imagine for a moment that an artificial brain has been created, twice as powerful as the human brain and possessing twice the capacity for work. Would a creature with a brain of this type really be allowed to call itself a man? What is it that makes us what we are? The capacity to perform sums, to analyze, to make logical deductions; or is it something else, which arises with the development of society, which is to do with an individual's relation to others and with the relation of the individual to the collective? If we take the otarks as an example . . ."

And here his mind started to wander.

On the third day there was an explosion in the morning. Betly woke up. He thought that he had stood up and was holding his rifle at the ready. In fact he was lying helpless by the wall.

The muzzle of a wild animal appeared before his eyes. With an agonizing effort of thought, he remembered what Fidler had looked like. Like an otark!

Then his thoughts lost their focus again. He could not feel how his flesh was being torn at, and for a tenth of a second Betly was able to think that the otarks were not really so terrible, that there were only a couple of hundred of them in this abandoned region. They could be dealt with. But the people . . . The people!

He did not know that the news of Meller's disappearance had already spread across the whole area, and that the desperate farmers were digging up the rifles they had hidden.

The Hands

JOHN BAXTER

John Baxter (1939–) is an Australian writer of fiction and nonfiction, born in Randwick, New South Wales, and now living in Paris, France. Since 2007 he has served as the codirector of the annual Paris Writers' Workshop. He began publishing his science fiction stories in *New Worlds* during the New Wave boom of the 1960s and also published two groundbreaking anthologies of Australian science fiction during that time: *The Pacific Book of Australian Science Fiction* (1968) and its sequel. Baxter serialized his first novel, *The Godkillers*, through *New Worlds*, after which it was published by Ace as *The Off-Worlders* (1968). But science fiction was only one of Baxter's interests. At the same time he was writing fiction, Baxter became a member of the influential WEA Film Study Group, for which he edited the journal *Film Digest*. He was active in the Sydney Film Festival for many years and wrote film criticism for various publications.

Since the 1980s Baxter has turned exclusively to producing or writing such documentaries and television series as *The Cutting Room* and *First Take*. His nonfiction about the movies includes writing about, among others, Woody Allen, Luis Buñuel, Federico Fellini, Stanley Kubrick, George Lucas, and Steven Spielberg.

The move to Paris was prequel to writing four books of autobiography, *A Pound of Paper: Confessions of a Book Addict*, *We'll Always Have Paris: Sex and Love in the City of Light*, *Immoveable Feast: A Paris Christmas*, and *The Most Beautiful Walk in the World: A Pedestrian in Paris*.

"The Hands" (1965) is an extremely unique and creepy science fiction horror story, one that serves as a perfect example of the successes of the New Wave era.

THE HANDS

John Baxter

They let Vitti go first because he was the one with two heads, and it seemed to the rest that if there was to be anything of sympathy or honour or love for them, then Vitti should have the first and best of it. After he had walked down the ramp, they followed him. Sloane with his third and fourth legs folded like the furled wings of a butterfly on his back; Tanizaki, still quiet, unreadable, Asiatic, despite the bulge inside his belly that made him look like a woman eight months gone with child; and the rest of them. Seven earth men who had been tortured by the Outsiders.

When the crowd saw Vitti, they shouted, because that was what they had gathered there to do. Ten thousand sets of lungs emptied themselves in one automatic, unthinking cry. The sound was a wave breaking over them, a torrent of sound that made them want to fall on the ground and wait for its passing. But there was only one shout. By the time the cry was half over, the people had seen Vitti and the rest of them, and when their lungs were empty they had neither the will nor ability to draw them full for another shout. There were some who did; a few standing at the back. But their shouts were like the cries of seabirds along the edge of the ocean. From the others, there was no sound but the susurrus of whispers like the melting of sea foam after a wave has receded. Nobody had anything to say. At that moment, Alfred Binns realized for the first time that he was a monster.

In the anteroom at headquarters, Binns stood at the window, looking down on the city. The streets were empty now. As he watched, a fam-ily of three—mother, father, and one small boy—hurried across the square below him and disappeared into the subway entrance. They must have been the last, because no more people moved anywhere on the wide, clean streets. Binns had almost forgotten that nobody lived in the cities anymore. Thousands had come to see them arrive, but now the show was over and they were going back to their homes, leaving the city to those who had to live there.

"Nobody left at all?" Farmer said. Nobody else had spoken.

"You're listening again," Binns said without turning. "You promised you wouldn't."

"I can't help it," Farmer said. He looked down at the bulge on his chest where the other brain had grown. Through the soft clear skin he could see the grey convolutions and the ebb of blood through vein and tissue. "It's growing up."

"You and Tanizaki ought to get together," somebody said. It was safe now, though at the beginning of the trip back Hiro had been sensitive about his huge belly where the second set of intestines had grown. There had been fights, as if violence could wipe it all away, but after a few weeks they had learned.

A man came into the anteroom. He worked very hard at not being embarrassed and for a while he almost succeeded. But Farmer was more than a normal man could take. His eyes went glassy and he turned away for a moment. When he looked back his gaze was directed over their heads.

"Would you like to follow me?" he said.

They went with him along the corridor to where the debriefing was to take place. The light was soft and there were no shadows. They were all glad of that; the one thing more horrible to each man than his deformed body was his grotesque dancing shadow.

"Disgusting," the general said. "Barbaric. Inhuman." He was very pale.

"Not really," Binns said politely. "They aren't like us, you know."

A colonel shook his head in bewilderment. "Incredible," he said.

"Not really," Binns said again.

"Do you feel any pain at all?" the doctor asked gently. "When you move them, I mean."

Binns clenched one of the hands that grew from the centre of his chest.

"None at all," he said. "If I make a fist four or five times I feel a sort of shortness of breath, but that's probably because the chest muscles seem to work the hands as well as my lungs."

The doctor made a note in a small neat hand.

"May I examine it?" he said.

His reverent manner was irritating. Everybody spoke in whispers. Any sort of revulsion would be better than this. When the doctor reached out, Binns grabbed his outstretched hand and shook it vigorously. The doctor screamed.

After the medical examinations they were brought back to the big room again for more questioning. Everybody was very quiet and very understanding. Binns still wished they could be a little less reverent. It made him feel different and this disturbed him. On Huxley, he had never felt different, and even when they left Huxley Kolo had made them feel that there was nothing wrong in having another arm or leg or some extra organs. He almost wished that Kolo was back with them. When he had been there, the group had been complete. Now, it was wrong, out of balance. Something was missing.

The questioners continued to be understanding. Their queries were always quiet and considerate. Only the politicians showed any signs of impatience.

"And you never tried to escape?" one of them asked sharply.

"Yes, we tried," Sloane said. "Once—no, twice. Then we gave up. It just wasn't possible to escape."

"It's always possible," another man said, but not very loudly.

On Binns's chest the two hands stirred, the fingertips brushing each other restlessly.

"The people on Huxley aren't like us," Binns said. "They look like us—sometimes—but otherwise they're completely different. You don't know how it is. You can't understand. . . ."

"The fingers," Vitti said. Only his right head spoke. The effect was odd. When one mouth spoke, you expected the other to speak also, but it never did. Even though Farmer had its brain, one expected some sort of reaction. Binns wondered if the two brains thought on separate tracks. He had never asked Vitti. It didn't seem the right thing to do.

"Yes, the fingers," Dixon said. "Kolo had a thing he used to do with his fingers that made us . . . made us . . ."

The handless arms that grew from his shoulders below his own moved to gesture, then stopped as he realized the lack of hands made it meaningless.

"He snapped them," Binns said. "Not like ordinary snapping. Sort of quick and hollow. When he did that, we just had to do whatever he told us."

The general snapped his fingers twice. "Like that?"

"No," Vitti said. "Kolo was the only one who could do it."

"Other than this, no other pressure was placed on you?"

"Well, we couldn't leave the city," Sloane said. "Otherwise, we could do most things. We weren't locked up or anything."

There was silence in the big room for a moment.

"Well," said one of the psychiatrists, "how did they . . ."

He stopped, conscious of the quiet. Nobody had wanted to ask the question. Now that he had started, there was nothing to do but continue.

"How did they make you . . . I mean . . ."

"You mean how did they change us?" Binns said.

"Yes."

Sloane laughed. "They didn't make us," he said. "We did it ourselves."

"Things are different on Huxley," Vitti said. "Up there, this is normal. Everybody can grow and change to suit themselves. If you want to be a foot taller . . . well, you just grow a foot taller. Physically, they aren't very different to us. This is just a sort . . . well, a sort of trick they've learned. They taught it to us."

"But why did you grow these . . . appendages?"

"We don't know," Binns said. "Kolo just snapped his fingers and . . ." He shrugged. There was nothing else to be said.

It was quieter down by the sea. There was no sound but the wind and the gurgle of water. Binns wished there were still beaches, but the city had long ago engulfed the sea's edge and even its shallows. He stood on the farthest lip of the city, looking down at the pylons that disappeared into the grey water. There were no particular thoughts in his mind, but those that were there moved silent and separately, like fish in a pool. This above all was the curious thing: that he had no two thoughts that went together. His mind seemed limitless and the thoughts like pet fish suddenly emptied into an ocean. Ever since he had left Huxley, it had been like this. The collision of this thought with another might have sparked an explosion of fear, but the meeting never occurred. It joined the rest of the ideas that swam quietly about in his mind.

There was rain on his face, or perhaps spray. He looked up and felt the hard drops sting his skin. His clothes were wet. It must have been raining for a long time while he was standing there by the sea. The cold needles of water stung the tender skin of his new hands. With his own hands he groped in his pocket and slipped on the cover they had given him. The hands rubbed themselves together for a moment, then clasped inside the darkness of the hood. Binns could sense them there, holding each other. It was a pleasant feeling.

He stood by the water a moment longer, watching the waves lap at the pillars, staring down, trying to follow with his eyes their long dive to the floor of the ocean. Sometimes he almost thought he saw all the way down, right to the silt at the bottom, but he knew that was only an illusion. Yet an illusion hardly less real than his other thoughts. It was easy to believe that he could see down through all those yards of water; as easy as to believe in Huxley, or the hands on his chest. No thought had any real permanence. They were all vague and shadowy. He felt nothing sharply, with real emotion. He seemed always to be watching pictures of thoughts rather than the thoughts themselves. It came to him, as slowly as did all his thoughts now, that perhaps the things he thought were not of his own creation.

Nonsense, a voice said inside his mind.

But it could be true. The idea was not terrifying. He no longer had the ability to be terrified. But it was disturbing. For the first time since he had arrived back, a real emotion stung him. He was grateful for the stimulus. He turned quickly from the sea. Too quickly. The man watching him had time only to hide part of his body behind a pylon before he was seen. Binns didn't show any sign of recognition. He had expected to be followed, and was glad in a way that he had been. It meant there was somebody near; somebody he could talk to.

He hunched his cloak about him against the rain and walked quickly up the sloping ramp towards the pylon until he was beside it. Then he stopped.

"I'd like to talk to you."

There was no sound for a moment. Then the man came out from behind the pillar. He was young and very thin—gawky, Binns thought. His face and hair were soaked with rain. The wet hair clung to his skull as if the rain had softened it, making it liquid and transparent. Binns could imagine him hiding behind the pylon, pressed against it, his hands flattened against the metal, the rain falling steadily on his face.

"Are you following me?"

The boy reached into his pocket and took out a small metal emblem. Binns knew it well.

"I was assigned to see you were safe."

"Why don't you walk along with me? There's no point in dodging around corners."

He started walking. After a few steps, the boy followed, then fell in beside him. The rain drove at their backs and they both hunched forward to keep the cold water from the back of their necks. Together, in step, they walked up the long ramp towards the city.

"You're very young for this sort of work."

"Twenty-two. Age doesn't matter really." His voice was very young though. It hardly seemed that a boy like this would know what age meant.

"What's your name?"

"Teris."

"Nothing else?"

"I'm a ward."

A ward. That explained a lot. Brought up by the state for employment by the state. No wonder he was so young. Binns tried an experiment.

"Are they following the others too?"

"You know I can't tell you that."

Interesting. He had expected something like that.

Then he stopped walking, very suddenly.

Why had he asked that question? Why "conduct an experiment"? He had no reason to. It was not the sort of thing he normally did.

Teris was watching him.

"What's wrong?"

Binns shook his head. "I feel . . . odd. I'm wondering why I asked you that."

"Will I call headquarters?"

No! Not headquarters!

"No. Don't bother."

He started walking again. Teris fell in beside him, but Binns could feel him looking at him out of the corner of his eye. Inside the hood on his chest, the hands were stirring slightly.

They were at the top of the ramp now. A narrow street ran along the edge of the sea, swinging in a wide circle around the curve of the city. There were a few vehicles going by, but the rain kept most people inside. For a moment Binns watched the cars pass with a sound like ripping silk. Patches of oil flowed on the grey road, flashing false and faded rainbows.

"Do you want to go to your home?" Teris asked.

"No." Binns looked around. "Is there a park?"

"A park?" Teris glanced at the street indicators. "There's one about half a mile away. Or Central Park, of course."

"The nearest one will do." He looked around and saw a wide street leading off the avenue at a sharp angle. There were no cars on it that he could see.

"Up there, isn't it?"

Teris looked at him sharply.

"How did you know that?"

Careful.

"I lived here for a long time, remember. Before you were born, I imagine."

He stepped off the kerb and crossed the street.

They walked together for a few blocks.

"I'm making you nervous," Binns said.

"No."

"I can tell. It's the hands, isn't it?"

Teris didn't answer. *Typical,* the other voice in his head commented. He wondered about the voice, but without real interest. It was not his problem.

"I can't help it, you know. They just grew on me."

No answer. Their feet made twin clatterings on the wet footpath. The rain fell softly, like snow. They were the only people on the street.

"I was told not to discuss the matter with you," Teris said.

"Aren't you interested at all? I don't mind talking about it."

The boy's face was set, partly in embarrassment.

"I have my instructions."

Give it up. Try something else.

"Very well. If you don't want to talk . . . Ah, this is the park, isn't it?"

The park took up a whole block. It was a huge field of grass, with a few trees and a pavilion built in antique style. The grass was clean and smooth, like a carpet. They crossed the street and stood at the edge of the grass. There was a control post near them. All they had to do was press the button and the rain would stop, the sun would come out, the birds would sing. But nobody had pushed the button on any of the control posts around the perimeter of the park. It was empty.

Teris moved towards the post.

"No," Binns said quickly. "I prefer the rain."

Teris looked at him suspiciously.

"It doesn't rain on Huxley," Binns said.

This seemed to satisfy him.

Binns walked onto the grass. It was very wet and spongy. He could feel the water in the brown soil. Under the grass, the earth was dark and deep and wet. Idly he took off the hood that covered his second pair of hands. They moved more easily now, rubbing their fingertips together and spreading their palms to weigh the damp air. He looked out across the park. On the far verge he could see movement, awkward halting movement. There were people over there. Six people, to be exact.

"Teris."

The boy walked up behind him. He could hear his feet on the turf making a soft squishing noise. He was very close now, just by his right shoulder.

Binns turned quickly. He grabbed the boy's arm and pulled him suddenly in against his body. As they touched, the other two hands grabbed the loose cloth of the boy's cloak. Binns's hands went to his throat.

It didn't take very long, and nobody saw it. For a moment the limp body hung pressed against Binns, the boy's dead eyes staring into his. Only after a moment did the hands release their grip and let the body slump to the grass.

The others were coming towards him across the park, but Binns didn't look at them. He was looking at the hands. They were no longer his to control. They had held on to Teris's body long after his own hands had let go, long after he had willed them to relax their grip. It seemed to him that their clutch was a sort of grim triumph. Now they were moving quickly and intelligently without any orders from him. He watched the right one curl, the fingers bending in, the thumb extending, thumb and forefinger touching. There was the sound of fingers snapping. An odd hollow sound, but one that Binns knew well.

The others heard it too, and stopped. Each looked at the burden he carried with him. Farmer at the brain under his skin, Vitti at his other head, Tanizaki at his huge belly. Binns looked at his hands. Where the wrists met the skin of his chest, there was a sort of inflammation. It hurt. The skin was beginning to crack. Tanizaki fell to the ground, clutching his body. The fingers snapped again. Binns fell to his knees. The others were already on the ground. The rain was falling once more, but they didn't notice, as under its still soft touch they gave birth to their master.

Darkness

ANDRÉ CARNEIRO

Translated by Leo L. Barrow

André Carneiro (1922–2014) was an all-around Renaissance man born in the small town of Atibaia, Brazil. He is regarded as Brazil's best-known science fiction writer and was one of the founding fathers of Brazilian science fiction. But in addition he was a giant in the creative arts who gained national and international fame in many fields, including photography, film, painting, clinical hypnosis, advertising, and poetry. It is for poetry that he is best known in Brazil, having founded an influential Brazilian poetry journal along with a movement (Generation 45) and publishing his verse in influential magazines and anthologies. Some of his photography, representing the best of Brazilian modernism, is on permanent display in the Tate Modern museum in London. Among many honors, Carneiro received a medal from the French government for cultural exchange between France and Brazil and was chosen as Person of the Year in 2007 by the *Brazilian Yearbook of Fantastic Literature*. In 2009, he received a special award from the Brazilian Academy of Letters, and his hometown in 2014 and 2015 held a week of cultural events in his honor.

In terms of science fiction, Carneiro published several novels and many influential short stories, translated into sixteen languages. He was the first South American member to join the Science Fiction and Fantasy Writers of America. He also appeared in such anthologies as *The Penguin World Omnibus of Science Fiction* (Penguin Books, 1986), edited by Brian Aldiss and Sam J. Lundwall, and represented Brazil in the international collaborative science fiction novel *Tales from the Planet Earth* (1986), edited by Frederik Pohl and Elizabeth Anne Hull.

His novella "Darkness" (1963), reprinted here, is a unique end-of-the-world story. It is considered an international classic and won the Nova, the Brazilian Hugo Award. Fans of the story included Arthur C. Clarke and A. E. van Vogt, who wrote that "Darkness" was one of the greatest science fiction stories ever written, comparing Carneiro to Kafka and Camus. The story preceded by several decades Portuguese writer José Saramago's *Blindness* (1995), which shares some similarities with Carneiro's tale with its depiction of a world where people are suddenly blind.

DARKNESS

André Carneiro

Translated by Leo L. Barrow

I

Many were frightened, but Waldas wasn't one of them. He went home at four o'clock. The lights were on. They gave off very little light—seemed like reddish balls, danger signals. At the lunch counter where he always ate, he got them to serve him cold sandwiches. There was only the owner and one waitress, who left afterward, walking slowly through the shadows.

Waldas got to his apartment without difficulty. He was used to coming home late without turning on the hall lights. The elevator wasn't working, so he walked up the stairs to the third floor. His radio emitted only strange sounds, perhaps voices, perhaps static. Opening the window, he confronted the thousands of reddish glows, lights of the huge buildings whose silhouettes stood out dimly against the starless sky.

He went to the refrigerator and drank a glass of milk; the motor wasn't working. The same thing would happen to the water pump. He put the plug in the bathtub and filled it. Locating his flashlight, he went through his small apartment, anxious to find his belongings with the weak light. He left the cans of powdered milk, cereal, some crackers, and a box of chocolates on the kitchen table and closed the window, turned out the lights, and lay down on the bed. A cold shiver ran through his body as he realized the reality of the danger.

He slept fitfully, dreamed confused and disagreeable dreams. A child was crying in the next apartment, asking its mother to turn on the lights. He woke up startled. With the flashlight pressed against his watch, he saw that it was eight o'clock in the morning. He opened the windows. The darkness was almost complete. You could see the sun in the east, red and round, as if it were behind a thick smoked glass. In the street dim shapes of people passed by like silhouettes.

With great difficulty Waldas managed to wash his face. He went to the kitchen and ate Rice Krispies with powdered milk. Force of habit made him think about his job. He realized that he didn't have any place to go, and he remembered the terror he felt as a child when they locked him in a closet. There wasn't enough air, and the darkness oppressed him. He went to the window and took a deep breath. The red disk of the sun hung in the dark background of the sky. Waldas couldn't coordinate his thoughts; the darkness kept making him feel like running for help. He clenched his fists, repeated to himself, "I have to keep calm, defend my life until everything returns to normal."

II

There was a knocking on his door; his heart beat more rapidly. It was his neighbor, asking for some water for the children. Waldas told him about the full bathtub, and went with him to get his wife and children. His prudence had paid off. They held hands and the human chain slid along the hall, the kids calmer, even the wife, who, no longer crying, kept repeating, "Thank you, thank you very much."

Waldas took them to the kitchen, made them sit down, the children clinging to their mother. He felt the cupboard, broke a glass, then found

485

an aluminum pan which he filled from the bathtub and took to the table. He surrendered cups of water to the fingers that groped for them. He couldn't keep them level without seeing and the water spilled onto his hands.

As they drank, he wondered if he should offer them something to eat. The boy thanked him and said that he was hungry. Waldas picked up the big can of powdered milk and began to prepare it carefully. While he made the slow gestures of opening the can, counting the spoonfuls, and mixing them with water, he spoke in a loud voice. They encouraged him, telling him to be careful and praising his ability. Waldas took more than an hour to make and ration out the milk, and the effort, the certainty that he was being useful, did him good.

One of the boys laughed at something funny. For the first time since the darkness had set in, Waldas felt optimistic, that everything would turn out all right. They spent an endless time after that in his apartment, trying to talk. They would lean on the windowsill, searching for some distant light, seeing it at times, all enthused, only to discover the deceit that they wouldn't admit.

Waldas had become the leader of that family. He fed them and led them through the small world of four rooms, which he knew with his eyes closed. They left at nine or ten that night, holding hands. Waldas accompanied them, helped put the children to bed. In the streets desperate fathers were shouting, asking for food. Waldas had closed the windows so he couldn't hear them. What he had would be enough to feed the five of them for one or two more days.

Waldas stayed with them, next to the children's room. They lay there talking, their words like links of presence and company. They finally went to sleep, heads under their pillows like shipwrecked sailors clinging to logs, listening to pleas for help that they couldn't possibly answer. They slept, dreaming about the breaking of a new day, a blue sky, the sun flooding their rooms, their eyes, hungry from fasting, avidly feeding on the colors. It wasn't that way.

III

Rationed and divided, the box of chocolates had come to an end. There was still cereal and powdered milk. If the light didn't return soon it would be cruel to predict the consequences. The hours passed. Lying down again, eyes closed, fighting to go to sleep, they waited for the morning with its beams of light on the window. But they woke as before, their eyes useless, the flames extinguished, the stoves cold, and their food running out. Waldas divided the last of the cereal and milk. They became uneasy.

The couple and their children were filled with hope when he suggested the only idea that might work. He would go out and break into a grocery store about a hundred yards away.

Armed with a crowbar from his toolbox, he was leaving his shelter to steal food. It was frightening to think what he might encounter. The darkness had erased all distinctions. Waldas walked next to the wall, his mind reconstructing the details of this stretch, his hands investigating every indentation. Inch by inch his fingers followed the outline of the building until they came to the corrugated iron door. He couldn't be wrong.

It was the only commercial establishment on the block. He bent over to find the lock. His hands didn't encounter resistance. The door was only half closed. He stooped over and entered without making a sound. The shelves on the right would have food and sweets. He collided with the counter, cursed, and remained motionless, muscles tensed, waiting. He climbed over the counter and began to reach out with his hand. It touched the board and he started running it along the shelf.

There was nothing. Of course, they sold it before the total darkness. He raised his arm, searching more rapidly. Nothing, not a single object . . .

He took up the crowbar again and with short careful steps he started back home in search of his invisible friends. . . . He was lost. He sat down on the sidewalk, his temples throbbing. He struggled up like a drowning man and shouted, "Please, I'm lost, I need to know the name of this street." He repeated it time after time, each time more loudly, but no one answered him. The more silence he felt around him, the more he implored, asking them to help him for pity's sake. And why should they? He himself, from his own window, had heard the cries of the lost asking for help, their desperate voices causing one to fear the madness of an assault.

Waldas started off without any direction, shouting for help, explaining that four persons depended on him. No longer feeling the walls, he walked hurriedly in circles, like a drunk, begging for information and food. "I'm Waldas, I live at number two fifteen, please help me."

There were noises in the darkness; impossible for them not to hear him. He cried and pleaded without the least shame, the black pall reducing him to a helpless child. The darkness stifled him, entering through his pores, changing his thoughts.

Waldas stopped pleading. He bellowed curses at his fellow men, calling them evil names, asking them why they didn't answer. His helplessness turned into hate, and he grasped the crowbar, ready to obtain food by violence. He came across others begging for food like himself. Waldas advanced, brandishing his crowbar until he collided with someone, grabbing him and holding him tightly. The man shouted and Waldas, without letting him go, demanded that he tell him where they were and how they could get some food. The other seemed old and broke into fearful sobs. Waldas relaxed the pressure, released him. He threw the weapon into the street and sat down on the sidewalk, listening to the small sounds, the wind rattling windows in the abandoned apartments. Different noises emerged from several directions, deep, rasping, and sharp sounds, from animals, men perhaps, trapped or famished.

A light rhythmic beating of footsteps was approaching. He yelled for help and remained listening. A man's voice, some distance away, answered him. "Wait, I'll come and help you."

The man carried a heavy sack and was panting from the effort. He asked Waldas to help him by holding one end—he would go in front. Waldas sensed something inexplicable. He could hardly follow the man as he turned the corners with assurance. A doubt passed through his mind. Perhaps his companion could see a little; the light was coming back for the others. He asked him, "You walk with such assurance, you can't by any chance see a little?"

The man took a while to answer. "No, I can see absolutely nothing. I am completely blind."

Waldas stammered, "Before this . . . too?"

"Yes, blind from birth, we are going to the Institute for the Blind, where I live."

Vasco, the blind man, told him that they had helped lost persons and had taken in a few. But their stock of food was small and they couldn't take anybody else in. The darkness continued without any sign of ending. Thousands of people might die from starvation and nothing could be done. Waldas felt like a child that adults had saved from danger. At the Institute they gave him a glass of milk and some toast. In his memory, however, the image of his friends was growing, their hearts jumping at every sound, going hungry, waiting for his return.

He spoke to Vasco. They deliberated. The apartment building was large, all the others living there also deserved help, something quite impracticable. Waldas remembered the children. He asked them to show him the way or he would go alone. He got up to leave, stumbled over something, falling. Vasco remembered that there was a bathtub full of water, and water was one thing they needed. They brought two big plastic containers, and Vasco led Waldas to the street. They tied a little cord around both their waists.

Vasco, who knew the neighborhood, walked as fast as possible, choosing the best route, calling out the name of the streets, changing course when they heard suspicious sounds or mad ravings. Vasco stopped and said softly, "It must be here." Waldas advanced a few steps, recognized the door latch. Vasco whispered for him to take off his shoes; they would go in without making any noise. After tying their shoes to the cord, they entered with Waldas in front, going up the stairs two at a time. They bumped into things along the way and heard unintelligible voices from behind the doors.

Reaching the third floor, they went to his neighbor's apartment, knocked softly and then more loudly. No one answered. They went to Waldas's apartment. "It's me, Waldas, let me in."

His neighbor uttered an exclamation like someone who didn't believe it and opened the door, extending his arm for his friend to grasp.

"It's me all right. How is everybody? I brought a friend who saved me and knows the way."

In the bathroom they filled the two plastic containers with water, and Vasco tied them to the backs of the two men with strips of cloth. He also helped to identify some useful things they could take. They took off their shoes and in single file, holding hands, started for the stairs. They went hurriedly; they would inevitably be heard. On the main floor, next to the door, a voice inquired, "Who are you?" No one answered and Vasco pulled them all out into the street. In single file they gained distance; it would be difficult to follow them.

It took more time to return because of the children, and the stops they made to listen to nearby noises. They arrived at the Institute exhausted, with the temporary feeling of relief of soldiers after winning a battle.

Vasco served them oatmeal and milk and went to talk to his companions about what they would do to survive if the darkness continued. Another blind man fixed them a place to sleep, which came easily since they hadn't slept for a long time. Hours later Vasco came to awaken them, saying that they had decided to leave the Institute and take refuge on the Model Farm that the Institute owned a few miles outside the city. Their supplies here wouldn't last long and there was no way to replenish them without danger.

IV

Like mountain climbers, they formed four groups linked by a cord. Waldas was surprised when the cord tied to his waist pulled him into a dirt road. Without knowing how, he realized that they were in the country. How did the blind men find the exact spot? Perhaps through their sense of smell, the perfume of the trees like ripe limes. He breathed deeply. He knew that odor; it came from eucalyptus trees. He could imagine them in straight lines, on each side of the road. The column stopped; they had arrived at their unseen destination. For the time being the urgent fight to keep from dying of hunger had ended.

The blind men brought them a cold soup that seemed to contain oatmeal and honey. Vasco directed the difficult maneuver to keep them from colliding. They had shelter and food. And the others who remained in the city, the sick in the hospitals, the small children . . . ? No one could or wanted to know.

There were carrots, tomatoes, and greens in the gardens, some ripe fruit in the orchard. They should distribute equal rations, a little more for the children. There was speculation as to whether the green vegetables would wilt after so many days without sunshine. The man in charge of the small henhouse told how he had fed the hens every day since the sun stopped shining, but they hadn't laid since then. . . .

They were already in their sixteenth day when Vasco called Waldas aside. He told him that even the reserves of oatmeal, powdered milk, and canned goods that they had saved were almost gone. And their nervous condition was becoming aggravated; it wouldn't be prudent to warn the others. Arguments came up over the least thing and were prolonged without reason. Most of them were on the edge of nervous collapse.

During the early hours of the eighteenth day, they were awakened by shouts of joy and animation. One of the refugees who hadn't been able to go to sleep had felt a difference in the atmosphere. He climbed the ladder outside the house.

There was a pale red ball on the horizon.

Everyone came out at once, pushing and falling, and remained there in a contagious euphoria waiting for the light to increase. Vasco asked if they really did see something, if it wasn't just another false alarm. Someone remembered to strike a match and after a few attempts the flame appeared. It was fragile and without heat, but visible to the eyes of those who looked upon it as a rare miracle.

The light increased slowly, in the way that it had disappeared. At four o'clock in the afternoon you could already distinguish a person's shadow at a distance of four yards.

After the sun went down, the complete darkness returned. They built a fire in the yard, but the flames were weak and translucent and consumed very little of the wood. At midnight it was difficult to convince them that they should go to bed. Only the children slept. Those who had matches struck one from time to time and chuckled to themselves.

At four thirty in the morning they were up and outside. No dawn in the history of the world was ever awaited like this one. The sun was brighter. Unaccustomed eyes were closed. The blind men extended the palms of their hands toward the rays, turned them over to feel the heat on both sides. Different faces came forth, with voices you could recognize, and they laughed and embraced each other. Their loneliness and their differences disappeared in that boundless dawn. The blind people were kissed and hugged, carried in triumph. Men cried, and this made their eyes, unaccustomed to the light, turn even redder. About noon the flames became normal and for the first time in three weeks, they had a hot cooked meal. Little work was done for the rest of the day. Flooded with light, they absorbed the scenes about them, walking through the places where they had dragged themselves in the darkness.

And the city? What had happened to the people there? This was a terribly sobering thought and those who had relatives ceased to smile. How many had died or suffered extreme hardships? Waldas suggested that he should investigate the situation the next day. Others volunteered, and it was decided that three should go.

V

The three refugees left as the sun was coming up, walking along the road that would lead them to the railroad tracks.

They went around a curve and the city came into view. After the first bridges, the tracks began to cross streets. Waldas and his companions went down one of them. The first two blocks seemed very calm, with a few persons moving about, perhaps a bit more slowly. On the next corner they saw a group of people carrying a dead man, covered with a rough cloth, to a truck. The people were crying.

A brown army truck went by, its loudspeaker announcing an official government bulletin. Martial law had been declared. Anyone invading another's property would be shot. The government had requisitioned all food supplies and was distributing them to the needy. Any vehicle could be commandeered if necessary. It advised that the police be immediately notified of any buildings with bad odors so that they could investigate the existence of corpses. The dead would be buried in common graves.

Waldas didn't want to return to his own apartment building. He remembered the voices calling through the half-opened doors and he, in his stocking feet, slipping away, leaving them to their fate. He would have to telephone the authorities if there was a bad odor. He had already seen enough; he didn't want to stay there. His young companion had talked to an officer and had decided to look for his family immediately.

Waldas asked if the telephones were working and learned that some of the automatic circuits were. He dialed his brother-in-law's number and after a short while there was an answer. They were very weak but alive. There had been four deaths in the apartment house. Waldas told them briefly how he had been saved and asked if they needed anything. No, they didn't, there was some food, and they were a lot better off than most.

Everyone was talking to strangers, telling all kinds of stories. The children and the sick were the ones who had suffered most. They told of cases of death in heartbreaking circumstances. The public services were reorganizing, with the help of the army, to take care of those in need, bury the dead, and get everything going again. Waldas and his middle-aged companion didn't want to hear any more. They felt weak, weak with a certain mental fatigue from hearing and seeing incredible things in which the absurd wasn't just a theory but what really had happened, defying all logic and scientific laws.

The two men were returning along the still empty tracks, walking slowly under a pleasantly clouded sky. A gentle breeze rustled the leaves of the green trees and birds flitted among their branches. How had they been able to survive in the darkness? Waldas thought about all this as his aching legs carried him along. His scientific certainties were no longer valid. At that very moment men still shaken by the phenomenon were working electronic computers making precise measurements and observations, religious men in their temples explaining the will of God, politicians dictating decrees, mothers mourning the dead that had remained in the darkness.

Two exhausted men walked along the ties. They brought news, perhaps better than could be expected. Mankind had resisted. By eating anything resembling food, by drinking any kind of liquid, people had lived for three weeks in the world of the blind. Waldas and his companion were returning sad and weakened, but with the secret and muffled joy of being alive. More important than rational speculations was the mysterious miracle of blood running through one's veins, the pleasure of loving, doing things, moving one's muscles, and smiling.

Seen from a distance the two were smaller than the straight tracks that enclosed them. Their bodies were returning to their daily routine, subject to the forces and uncontrollable elements in existence since the beginning of time. But, as their eager eyes took in every color, shade, and movement, they gave little thought to the mysterious magnitude of their universe, and even less to the plight of their brothers, their saviors, who still walked in darkness.

There were planets, solar systems, and galaxies. They were only two men, bounded by two impassive rails, returning home with their problems.

"Repent, Harlequin!" Said the Ticktockman

HARLAN ELLISON®

Harlan Ellison (1934–) is an iconic US writer of speculative fiction who has won multiple Hugo, Nebula, and Edgar Awards. His published works include more than 1,700 short stories, novellas, screenplays, comic book scripts, teleplays, and essays, and a wide range of criticism covering literature, film, television, and print media. Ellison edited two iconic, groundbreaking science fiction anthologies, *Dangerous Visions* (1967) and *Again, Dangerous Visions* (1972)—several stories from which have been reprinted in this volume. He was considered one of the leading American members of the New Wave movement. He received the 1993 World Fantasy Award for Life Achievement. In 2006, Ellison was awarded the prestigious title of grand master by the Science Fiction and Fantasy Writers of America. A documentary chronicling his life and works, *Dreams with Sharp Teeth*, was released in May 2008. In 2011 Ellison was inducted into the Science Fiction and Fantasy Hall of Fame.

Ellison also produced the original script for "The City on the Edge of Forever," often regarded as one of the best episodes of the *Star Trek* series, though Ellison remains displeased with the revisions made to his script for filming. Ellison also wrote two notable episodes of the original run of *The Outer Limits*, "Soldier" and "Demon with a Glass Hand." His stories have been adapted for film, television, and video games numerous times. In the 1960s Ellison traveled with rock groups such as the Rolling Stones, and his novel of the 1950s rockabilly scene, *Spider Kiss* (1961), was much admired by music critic Greil Marcus.

Notable short fiction by Ellison includes "I Have No Mouth, and I Must Scream" (1968 Hugo Award winner), "The Beast That Shouted Love at the Heart of the World" (1969 Hugo Award winner), "The Deathbird" (1974 Hugo Award winner), "A Boy and His Dog" (1969 Nebula Award winner), "The Whimper of Whipped Dogs" (1974 Edgar Award winner), and "Paladin of the Lost Hour" (1986 Hugo Award winner).

Ellison's short story " 'Repent, Harlequin!' Said the Ticktockman," originally published in *Galaxy Science Fiction* in 1965, received a Hugo and a Nebula Award. Ellison wrote it in six hours in order to present it the next day at the Milford Writer's Workshop, run by Damon Knight. The story is often regarded as among his finest and is one of the most reprinted stories in the English language.

"REPENT, HARLEQUIN!" SAID THE TICKTOCKMAN

Harlan Ellison®

There are always those who ask, what is it all about? For those who need to ask, for those who need points sharply made, who need to know "where it's at," this:

> *The mass of men serve the state thus, not as men mainly, but as machines, with their bodies. They are the standing army, and the militia, jailors, constables, posse comitatus, etc. In most cases there is no free exercise whatever of the judgment or of the moral sense; but they put themselves on a level with wood and earth and stones; and wooden men can perhaps be manufactured that will serve the purpose as well. Such command no more respect than men of straw or a lump of dirt. They have the same sort of worth only as horses and dogs. Yet such as these even are commonly esteemed good citizens. Others—as most legislators, politicians, lawyers, ministers, and officeholders—serve the state chiefly with their heads; and, as they rarely make any moral distinctions, they are as likely to serve the Devil, without intending it, as God. A very few, as heroes, patriots, martyrs, reformers in the great sense, and men, serve the state with their consciences also, and so necessarily resist it for the most part; and they are commonly treated as enemies by it.*

> Henry David Thoreau
> *Civil Disobedience*

That is the heart of it. Now begin in the middle, and later learn the beginning; the end will take care of itself.

But because it was the very world it was, the very world they had allowed it to become, for months his activities did not come to the alarmed attention of The Ones Who Kept The Machine Functioning Smoothly, the ones who poured the very best butter over the cams and mainsprings of the culture. Not until it had become obvious that somehow, someway, he had become a notoriety, a celebrity, perhaps even a hero for (what Officialdom inescapably tagged) "an emotionally disturbed segment of the populace," did they turn it over to the Ticktockman and his legal machinery. But by then, because it was the very world it was, and they had no way to predict he would happen—possibly a strain of disease long defunct, now, suddenly, reborn in a system where immunity had been forgotten, had lapsed—he had been allowed to become too real. Now he had form and substance.

He had become a *personality*, something they had filtered out of the system many decades before. But there it was, and there *he* was, a very definitely imposing personality. In certain circles—middle-class circles—it was thought disgusting. Vulgar ostentation. Anarchistic. Shameful. In others, there was only sniggering: those strata where thought is subjugated to form and ritual, niceties, proprieties. But down below, ah, down below, where the people always needed their saints and sinners, their bread and circuses, their heroes and villains, he was considered a Bolívar; a Napoleon; a Robin Hood; a Dick Bong (Ace of Aces); a Jesus; a Jomo Kenyatta.

And at the top—where, like socially attuned Shipwreck Kellys, every tremor and vibration threatening to dislodge the wealthy, powerful, and titled from their flagpoles—he was considered a menace; a heretic; a rebel; a disgrace; a peril. He was known down the line, to the very heart-meat core, but the important reactions were high above and far below. At the very top, at the very bottom.

So his file was turned over, along with his time card and his cardioplate, to the office of the Ticktockman.

The Ticktockman: very much over six feet tall, often silent, a soft purring man when things went timewise. The Ticktockman.

Even in the cubicles of the hierarchy, where fear was generated, seldom suffered, he was called the Ticktockman. But no one called him that to his mask.

You don't call a man a hated name, not when that man, behind his mask, is capable of revoking the minutes, the hours, the days and nights, the years of your life. He was called the Master Timekeeper to his mask. It was safer that way.

"This is *what* he is," said the Ticktockman with genuine softness, "but not *who* he is. This time card I'm holding in my left hand has a name on it, but it is the name of *what* he is, not *who* he is. The cardioplate here in my right hand is also named, but not *whom* named, merely *what* named. Before I can exercise proper revocation, I have to know *who* this *what* is."

To his staff, all the ferrets, all the loggers, all the finks, all the commex, even the mineez, he said, "Who is this Harlequin?"

He was not purring smoothly. Timewise, it was jangle.

However, it was the longest speech they had ever heard him utter at one time, the staff, the ferrets, the loggers, the finks, the commex, but not the mineez, who usually weren't around to know, in any case. But even they scurried to find out.

Who is the Harlequin?

High above the third level of the city, he crouched on the humming aluminum-frame platform of the airboat (foof! airboat, indeed! swizzleskid is what it was, with a tow-rack jerry-rigged) and he stared down at the neat Mondrian arrangement of the buildings.

Somewhere nearby, he could hear the metronomic left-right-left of the 2:47 p.m. shift, entering the Timkin roller-bearing plant in their sneakers. A minute later, precisely, he heard the softer right-left-right of the 5:00 a.m. formation, going home.

An elfin grin spread across his tanned features, and his dimples appeared for a moment. Then, scratching at his thatch of auburn hair, he shrugged within his motley, as though girding himself for what came next, and threw the joystick forward, and bent into the wind as the airboat dropped. He skimmed over a slidewalk, purposely dropping a few feet to crease the tassels of the ladies of fashion, and—inserting thumbs in large ears—he stuck out his tongue, rolled his eyes, and went wugga-wugga-wugga. It was a minor diversion. One pedestrian skittered and tumbled, sending parcels everywhichway; another wet herself; a third keeled slantwise and the walk was stopped automatically by the servitors till she could be resuscitated. It was a minor diversion.

Then he swirled away on a vagrant breeze, and was gone. Hi-ho. As he rounded the cornice of the Time-Motion Study Building, he saw the shift, just boarding the slidewalk. With practiced motion and an absolute conservation of movement, they sidestepped up onto the slow-strip and (in a chorus line reminiscent of a Busby Berkeley film of the antediluvian 1930s) advanced across the strips ostrich-walking till they were lined up on the expresstrip.

Once more, in anticipation, the elfin grin

spread, and there was a tooth missing back there on the left side. He dipped, skimmed, and swooped over them; and then, scrunching about on the airboat, he released the holding pins that fastened shut the ends of the homemade pouring troughs that kept his cargo from dumping prematurely. And as he pulled the trough-pins, the airboat slid over the factory workers and one hundred and fifty thousand dollars' worth of jelly beans cascaded down on the expresstrip.

Jelly beans! Millions and billions of purples and yellows and greens and licorice and grape and raspberry and mint and round and smooth and crunchy outside and soft-mealy inside and sugary and bouncing jouncing rumbling clittering clattering skittering fell on the heads and shoulders and hardhats and carapaces of the Timkin workers, tinkling on the slidewalk and bouncing away and rolling about underfoot and filling the sky on their way down with all the colors of joy and childhood and holidays, coming down in a steady rain, a solid wash, a torrent of color and sweetness out of the sky from above, and entering a universe of sanity and metronomic order with quite-mad coocoo newness. Jelly beans!

The shift workers howled and laughed and were pelted, and broke ranks, and the jelly beans managed to work their way into the mechanism of the slidewalks, after which there was a hideous scraping as the sound of a million fingernails rasped down a quarter of a million blackboards, followed by a coughing and a sputtering, and then the slidewalks all stopped and everyone was dumped thisawayandthataway in a jackstraw tumble, still laughing and popping little jelly bean eggs of childish color into their mouths. It was a holiday, and a jollity, an absolute insanity, a giggle. But . . .

The shift was delayed seven minutes.

They did not get home for seven minutes.

The master schedule was thrown off by seven minutes.

Quotas were delayed by inoperative slidewalks for seven minutes.

He had tapped the first domino in the line, and one after another, like chik chik chik, the others had fallen.

The System had been seven minutes' worth of disrupted. It was a tiny matter, one hardly worthy of note, but in a society where the single driving force was order and unity and equality and promptness and clocklike precision and attention to the clock, reverence of the gods of the passage of time, it was a disaster of major importance.

So he was ordered to appear before the Ticktockman. It was broadcast across every channel of the communications web. He was ordered to be *there* at seven o'clock dammit on time. And they waited, and they waited, but he didn't show up till almost ten thirty, at which time he merely sang a little song about moonlight in a place no one had ever heard of, called Vermont, and vanished again. But they had all been waiting since seven, and it wrecked hell with their schedules. So the question remained: who is the Harlequin?

But the *unasked* question (more important of the two) was: how did we get *into* this position, where a laughing, irresponsible japer of jabberwocky and jive could disrupt our entire economic and cultural life with a hundred and fifty thousand dollars' worth of jelly beans? . . .

Jelly for God's sake *beans*! This is madness! Where did he get the money to buy a hundred and fifty thousand dollars' worth of jelly beans? (They knew it would have cost that much, because they had a team of Situation Analysts pulled off another assignment, and rushed to the slidewalk scene to sweep up and count the candies, and produce findings, which disrupted *their* schedules and threw their entire branch at least a day behind.) Jelly beans! Jelly . . . *beans*? Now wait a second—a second accounted for—no one has manufactured jelly beans for over a hundred years. Where did he get jelly beans?

That's another good question. More than likely it will never be answered to your complete satisfaction. But then, how many questions ever are?

· · ·

The middle you know. Here is the beginning. How it starts:

A desk pad. Day for day, and turn each day. 9:00—open the mail. 9:45—appointment with planning commission board. 10:30—discuss installation progress charts with J.L. 11:45—pray for rain. 12:00—lunch. *And so it goes.*

"I'm sorry, Miss Grant, but the time for interviews was set at 2:30, and it's almost five now. I'm sorry you're late, but those are the rules. You'll have to wait till next year to submit application for this college again." *And so it goes.*

The 10:10 Local stops at Cresthaven, Galesville, Tonawanda Junction, Selby, and Farnhurst, but not at Indiana City, Lucasville, and Cotton, except on Sunday. The 10:35 express stops at Galesville, Selby, and Indiana City, except on Sundays and holidays, at which time it stops at . . . *and so it goes.*

"I couldn't wait, Fred. I had to be at Pierre Cartain's by 3:00, and you said you'd meet me under the clock in the terminal at 2:45, and you weren't there, so I had to go on. You're always late, Fred. If you'd been there, we could have sewed it up together, but as it was, well, I took the order alone.... And so it goes.

Dear Mr. and Mrs. Atterley: In reference to your son Gerold's constant tardiness, I am afraid we will have to suspend him from school unless some more reliable method can be instituted guaranteeing he will arrive at his classes on time. Granted he is an exemplary student, and his marks are high, his constant flouting of the schedules of this school makes it impractical to maintain him in a system where the other children seem capable of getting where they are supposed to be on time *and so it goes.*

YOU CANNOT VOTE UNLESS YOU APPEAR AT 8:45 AM.

"I DON'T CARE IF THE SCRIPT IS GOOD, I NEED IT THURSDAY!"

CHECK-OUT TIME IS 2:00 PM.

"You got here late. The job's taken. Sorry."

YOUR SALARY HAS BEEN DOCKED FOR TWENTY MINUTES' TIME LOST.

"God, what time is it, I've gotta run!"

And so it goes. And so it goes. And so it goes. And so it goes goes goes goes goes tick tock tick tock tick tock and one day we no longer let time serve us, we serve time and we are slaves of the schedule, worshippers of the sun's passing, bound into a life predicated on restrictions because the system will not function if we don't keep the schedule tight.

Until it becomes more than a minor inconvenience to be late. It becomes a sin. Then a crime. Then a crime punishable by this:

EFFECTIVE 15 JULY 2389 12:00:00 midnight, the office of the Master Timekeeper will require all citizens to submit their time cards and cardioplates for processing. In accordance with Statute 555-7-SGH-999 governing the revocation of time per capita, all cardioplates will be keyed to the individual holder and—

What they had done was devise a method of curtailing the amount of life a person could have. If he was ten minutes late, he lost ten minutes of his life. An hour was proportionately worth more revocation. If someone was consistently tardy, he might find himself, on a Sunday night, receiving a communiqué from the Master Timekeeper that his time had run out, and he would be "turned off" at high noon on Monday, please straighten your affairs, sir, madame, or bisex.

And so, by this simple scientific expedient (utilizing a scientific process held dearly secret by the Ticktockman's office) the System was maintained. It was the only expedient thing to do. It was, after all, patriotic. The schedules had to be met. After all, there *was* a war on!

But, wasn't there always?

"Now that is really disgusting," the Harlequin said, when Pretty Alice showed him the wanted poster. "Disgusting and *highly* improbable. After all, this isn't the Day of the Desperado. A *wanted* poster!"

"You know," Pretty Alice noted, "you speak with a great deal of inflection."

"I'm sorry," said the Harlequin, humbly.

"No need to be sorry. You're always saying 'I'm sorry.' You have such massive guilt, Everett, it's really very sad."

"I'm sorry," he said again, then pursed his lips so the dimples appeared momentarily. He hadn't wanted to say that at all. "I have to go out again. I have to *do* something."

Pretty Alice slammed her coffee-bulb down on the counter. "Oh for God's *sake*, Everett, can't you stay home just *one* night! Must you always be out in that ghastly clown suit, running around an*noy*ing people?"

"I'm—" He stopped, and clapped the jester's hat onto his auburn thatch with a tiny tinkling of bells. He rose, rinsed out his coffee-bulb at the spray, and put it into the dryer for a moment. "I have to go."

She didn't answer. The faxbox was purring, and she pulled a sheet out, read it, threw it toward him on the counter. "It's about you. Of course. You're ridiculous."

He read it quickly. It said the Ticktockman was trying to locate him. He didn't care, he was going out to be late again. At the door, dredging for an exit line, he hurled back petulantly, "Well, *you* speak with inflection, *too*!"

Pretty Alice rolled her pretty eyes heavenward. "You're ridiculous."

The Harlequin stalked out, slamming the door, which sighed shut softly, and locked itself.

There was a gentle knock, and Pretty Alice got up with an exhalation of exasperated breath, and opened the door. He stood there. "I'll be back about ten thirty, okay?"

She pulled a rueful face. "Why do you tell me that? Why? You *know* you'll be late! You *know* it! You're always late, so why do you tell me these dumb things?" She closed the door.

On the other side, the Harlequin nodded to himself. *She's right. She's always right. I'll be late. I'm always late. Why* do *I tell her these dumb things?*

He shrugged again, and went off to be late once more.

He had fired off the firecracker rockets that said: I will attend the 115th annual International Medical Association Invocation at 8:00 p.m. precisely. I do hope you will all be able to join me.

The words had burned in the sky, and of course the authorities were there, lying in wait for him. They assumed, naturally, that he would be late. He arrived twenty minutes early, while they were setting up the spiderwebs to trap and hold him. Blowing a large bullhorn, he frightened and unnerved them so, their own moisturized encirclement webs sucked closed, and they were hauled up, kicking and shrieking, high above the amphitheater's floor. The Harlequin laughed and laughed, and apologized profusely. The physicians, gathered in solemn conclave, roared with laughter, and accepted the Harlequin's apologies with exaggerated bowing and posturing, and a merry time was had by all, who thought the Harlequin was a regular foofaraw in fancy pants; all, that is, but the authorities, who had been sent out by the office of the Ticktockman; they hung there like so much dockside cargo, hauled up above the floor of the amphitheater in a most unseemly fashion.

(In another part of the same city where the Harlequin carried on his "activities," totally unrelated in every way to what concerns us here, save that it illustrates the Ticktockman's power and import, a man named Marshall Delahanty received his turn-off notice from the Ticktockman's office. His wife received the notification from the gray-suited minee who delivered it, with the traditional "look of sorrow" plastered hideously across his face. She knew what it was, even without unsealing it. It was a billet-doux of immediate recognition to everyone these days. She gasped, and held

496

it as though it were a glass slide tinged with botulism, and prayed it was not for her. *Let it be for Marsh,* she thought, brutally, realistically, *or one of the kids, but not for me, please dear God, not for me.* And then she opened it, and it *was* for Marsh, and she was at one and the same time horrified and relieved. The next trooper in the line had caught the bullet. "Marshall," she screamed, "Marshall! Termination, Marshall! OhmiGod, Marshall, whattl we do, whattl we do, Marshall omigodmarshall . . . ," and in their home that night was the sound of tearing paper and fear, and the stink of madness went up the flue and there was nothing, absolutely nothing they could do about it.

(But Marshall Delahanty tried to run. And early the next day, when turn-off time came, he was deep in the Canadian forest two hundred miles away, and the office of the Ticktockman blanked his cardioplate, and Marshall Delahanty keeled over, running, and his heart stopped, and the blood dried up on its way to his brain, and he was dead that's all. One light went out on the sector map in the office of the Master Timekeeper, while notification was entered for fax reproduction, and Georgette Delahanty's name was entered on the dole roles till she could remarry. Which is the end of the footnote, and all the point that need be made, except don't laugh, because that is what would happen to the Harlequin if ever the Ticktockman found out his real name. It isn't funny.)

The shopping level of the city was thronged with the Thursday-colors of the buyers. Women in canary-yellow chitons and men in pseudo-Tyrolean outfits that were jade and leather and fit very tightly, save for the balloon pants.

When the Harlequin appeared on the still-being-constructed shell of the new Efficiency Shopping Center, his bullhorn to his elfishly-laughing lips, everyone pointed and stared, and he berated them:

"Why let them order you about? Why let them tell you to hurry and scurry like ants or maggots? Take your time! Saunter awhile! Enjoy the sunshine, enjoy the breeze, let life carry you at your own pace! Don't be slaves of time, it's a helluva way to die, slowly, by degrees . . . down with the Ticktockman!"

Who's the nut? most of the shoppers wanted to know. Who's the nut oh wow I'm gonna be late I gotta run. . . .

And the construction gang on the shopping center received an urgent order from the office of the Master Timekeeper that the dangerous criminal known as the Harlequin was atop their spire, and their aid was urgently needed in apprehending him. The work crew said no, they would lose time on their construction schedule, but the Ticktockman managed to pull the proper threads of governmental webbing, and they were told to cease work and catch that nitwit up there on the spire; up there with the bullhorn. So a dozen and more burly workers began climbing into their construction platforms, releasing the a-grav plates, and rising toward the Harlequin.

After the debacle (in which, through the Harlequin's attention to personal safety, no one was seriously injured), the workers tried to reassemble, and assault him again, but it was too late. He had vanished. It had attracted quite a crowd, however, and the shopping cycle was thrown off by hours, simply hours. The purchasing needs of the system were therefore falling behind, and so measures were taken to accelerate the cycle for the rest of the day, but it got bogged down and speeded up and they sold too many float-valves and not nearly enough wegglers, which meant that the popli ratio was off, which made it necessary to rush cases and cases of spoiling Smash-O to stores that usually needed a case only every three or four hours. The shipments were bollixed, the transshipments were misrouted, and in the end, even the swizzleskid industries felt it.

.   .   .

"Don't come back till you have him!" the Tick-tockman said, very quietly, very sincerely, extremely dangerously.

They used dogs. They used probes. They used cardioplate crossoffs. They used teepers. They used bribery. They used stiktytes. They used intimidation. They used torment. They used torture. They used finks. They used cops. They used search&seizure. They used fallaron. They used betterment incentive. They used fingerprints. They used the Bertillon system. They used cunning. They used guile. They used treachery. They used Raoul Mitgong, but he didn't help much. They used applied physics. They used techniques of criminology.

And what the hell: they caught him.

After all, his name was Everett C. Marm, and he wasn't much to begin with, except a man who had no sense of time.

"Repent, Harlequin!" said the Ticktockman.

"Get stuffed!" the Harlequin replied, sneering.

"You've been late a total of sixty-three years, five months, three weeks, two days, twelve hours, forty-one minutes, fifty-nine seconds, point oh three six one one one microseconds. You've used up everything you can, and more. I'm going to turn you off."

"Scare someone else. I'd rather be dead than live in a dumb world with a bogeyman like you."

"It's my job."

"You're full of it. You're a tyrant. You have no right to order people around and kill them if they show up late."

"You can't adjust. You can't fit in."

"Unstrap me, and I'll fit my fist into your mouth."

"You're a nonconformist."

"That didn't used to be a felony."

"It is now. Live in the world around you."

"I hate it. It's a terrible world."

"Not everyone thinks so. Most people enjoy order."

"I don't, and most of the people I know don't."

"That's not true. How do you think we caught you?"

"I'm not interested."

"A girl named Pretty Alice told us who you were."

"That's a lie."

"It's true. You unnerve her. She wants to belong; she wants to conform; I'm going to turn you off."

"Then do it already, and stop arguing with me."

"I'm not going to turn you off."

"You're an idiot!"

"Repent, Harlequin!" said the Ticktockman.

"Get stuffed."

So they sent him to Coventry. And in Coventry they worked him over. It was just like what they did to Winston Smith in *Nineteen Eighty-Four*, which was a book none of them knew about, but the techniques are really quite ancient, and so they did it to Everett C. Marm; and one day, quite a long time later, the Harlequin appeared on the communications web, appearing elfin and dimpled and bright-eyed, and not at all brainwashed, and he said he had been wrong, that it was a good, a very good thing indeed, to belong, to be right on time hip-ho and away we go, and everyone stared up at him on the public screens that covered an entire city block, and they said to themselves, well, you see, he was just a nut after all, and if that's the way the system is run, then let's do it that way, because it doesn't pay to fight city hall, or in this case, the Ticktockman. So Everett C. Marm was destroyed, which was a loss, because of what Thoreau said earlier, but you can't make an omelet without breaking a few eggs, and in every revolution a few die who shouldn't, but they have to, because that's the way it happens, and if you make only a little change, then it seems to be worthwhile. Or, to make the point lucidly:

. . .

"Uh, excuse me, sir, I, uh, don't know how to uh, to uh, tell you this, but you were three minutes late. The schedule is a little, uh, bit off."

He grinned sheepishly.

"That's ridiculous!" murmured the Ticktockman behind his mask. "Check your watch." And then he went into his office, going *mrmee, mrmee, mrmee, mrmee.*

Nine Hundred Grandmothers

R. A. LAFFERTY

R. A. Lafferty (1914–2002), full name Raphael Aloysius Lafferty, was an award-winning and highly unusual US science fiction and fantasy writer who generally defied classification due to his sui generis imagination and unique story lines. A working-class man, Lafferty was an autodidact (and voracious reader) whose post–high school education consisted of two years of night school at the University of Tulsa and courses in electrical engineering from the International Correspondence Schools. A correspondence with teenage Neil Gaiman led to his becoming invaluable in helping keep Lafferty's works visible after the author's death.

Lafferty came to writing late, publishing his first story in 1959. Most of his best fiction appeared in *Fantastic*, *Galaxy*, and Damon Knight's *Orbit* anthology series. Like Gene Wolfe, Lafferty was strongly influenced by his Catholic beliefs, but despite this conservatism was associated with the New Wave because of the originality of his fiction. His best-known novels are *Past Master* (1968) and *Fourth Mansions* (1969), both nominated for a Nebula Award. *Past Master* also received a Hugo Award nomination. He won the Hugo Award in 1973 for the short story "Eurema's Dam." In 1990, Lafferty received the World Fantasy Award for Life Achievement.

Lafferty was primarily known for his hundreds of highly original short stories, many of which draw on the Irish and Native American tradition of tall tales. His stories are marked by their use of wit, humor, and absurdism. In this regard, Lafferty's work had much in common with writers like Kurt Vonnegut, Stepan Chapman, and William Tenn. Recently, Centipede Press has embarked on a quixotic nine-volume quest to return all of Lafferty's short fiction to print, under the auspices of series editor John Pelan. *The Man Who Made Models: The Collected Short Fiction, Volume 1* (2014) featured an introduction by Michael Swanwick, and *The Man with the Aura: The Collected Short Fiction, Volume 2* (2015) featured an introduction by Harlan Ellison.

In his introduction to volume 1, Swanwick calls Lafferty "the single most original short fiction writer of the Twentieth Century . . . Many of his readers will skim happily over the [wildly entertaining] surface like windsurfers. But, like the ocean, there are depths, and in those depths strange shapes stir . . ."

Lafferty's science fiction stories generally do not strive for realism but in their surreal approach are perhaps more useful than some "hard science fiction" in expanding possibilities about alien life. In the story "Thieving Bear Planet" (1982), for example, aliens are portrayed as capricious and erratic because their ultimate motivations cannot be understood by human beings. The human expedition on a distant planet encounters weird gaps in time, small replicas of themselves, and hauntings that only make sense as part of an alien methodology. Lafferty's genius is to show only glimpses of that methodology but still convey just how frightening and odd such an encounter might be.

However, "Nine Hundred Grandmothers," reprinted here, remains the quintessential Lafferty story. Somehow in just a few short pages Lafferty subverts half a dozen space exploration tropes, pokes fun at military science fiction, and also writes what is at its heart a feminist tale that also presents one of the most truly alien scenarios in all of speculative fiction. The story first appeared in *IF* magazine in 1966, where it no doubt both delighted and confused many readers.

NINE HUNDRED GRANDMOTHERS

R. A. Lafferty

Ceran Swicegood was a promising young Special Aspects Man. But, like all Special Aspects, he had one irritating habit. He was forever asking the question: How Did It All Begin?

They all had tough names except Ceran. Manbreaker Crag, Heave Huckle, Blast Berg, George Blood, Move Manion (when Move says "Move," you move), Trouble Trent. They were supposed to be tough, and they had taken tough names at the naming. Only Ceran kept his own—to the disgust of his commander, Manbreaker.

"Nobody can be a hero with a name like Ceran Swicegood!" Manbreaker would thunder. "Why don't you take Storm Shannon? That's good. Or Gutboy Barrelhouse or Slash Slagle or Nevel Knife? You barely glanced at the suggested list."

"I'll keep my own," Ceran always said, and that is where he made his mistake. A new name will sometimes bring out a new personality. It had done so for George Blood. Though the hair on George's chest was a graft job, yet that and his new name had turned him from a boy into a man. Had Ceran assumed the heroic name of Gutboy Barrelhouse he might have been capable of rousing endeavors and man-sized angers rather than his tittering indecisions and flouncy furies.

They were down on the big asteroid Proavitus—a sphere that almost tinkled with the potential profit that might be shaken out of it. And the tough men of the Expedition knew their business. They signed big contracts on the native velvetlike bark scrolls and on their own parallel tapes. They impressed, inveigled, and somewhat cowed the slight people of Proavitus. Here was a solid two-way market, enough to make them slaver. And there was a whole world of oddities that could lend themselves to the luxury trade.

"Everybody's hit it big but you," Manbreaker crackled in kindly thunder to Ceran after three days there. "But even Special Aspects is supposed to pay its way. Our charter compels us to carry one of your sort to give a cultural twist to the thing, but it needn't be restricted to that. What we go out for every time, Ceran, is to cut a big fat hog in the rump—we make no secret of that. But if the hog's tail can be shown to have a cultural twist to it, that will solve a requirement. And if that twist in the tail can turn us a profit, then we become mighty happy about the whole thing. Have you been able to find out anything about the living dolls, for instance? They might have both a cultural aspect and a market value."

"The living dolls seem a part of something much deeper," Ceran said. "There's a whole complex of things to be unraveled. The key may be the statement of the Proavitoi that they do not die."

"I think they die pretty young, Ceran. All those out and about are young, and those I have met who do not leave their houses are only middling old."

"Then where are their cemeteries?"

"Likely they cremate the old folks when they die."

"Where are the crematories?"

"They might just toss the ashes out or vaporize the entire remains. Probably they have no reverence for ancestors."

"Other evidence shows their entire culture to be based on an exaggerated reverence for ancestors."

"You find out, Ceran. You're Special Aspects Man."

Ceran talked to Nokoma, his Proavitoi counterpart as translator. Both were expert, and they could meet each other halfway in talk. Nokoma was likely feminine. There was a certain softness about both the sexes of the Proavitoi, but the men of the Expedition believed that they had them straight now.

"Do you mind if I ask some straight questions?" Ceran greeted her today.

"Sure is not. How else I learn the talk well but by talking?"

"Some of the Proavitoi say that they do not die, Nokoma. Is this true?"

"How is not be true? If they die, they not be here to say they do not die. Oh, I joke, I joke. No, we do not die. It is a foolish alien custom which we see no reason to imitate. On Proavitus, only the low creatures die."

"None of you does?"

"Why, no. Why should one want to be an exception in this?"

"But what do you do when you get very old?"

"We do less and less then. We come to a deficiency of energy. Is it not the same with you?"

"Of course. But where do you go when you become exceedingly old?"

"Nowhere. We stay at home then. Travel is for the young and those of the active years."

"Let's try it from the other end," Ceran said. "Where are your father and mother, Nokoma?"

"Out and about. They aren't really old."

"And your grandfathers and grandmothers?"

"A few of them still get out. The older ones stay home."

"Let's try it this way. How many grandmothers do you have, Nokoma?"

"I think I have nine hundred grandmothers in my house. Oh, I know that isn't many, but we are the young branch of a family, some of our clan have very great numbers of ancestors in their houses."

"And all these ancestors are alive?"

"What else? Who would keep things not alive? How would such be ancestors?"

Ceran began to hop around in his excitement.

"Could I see them?" he twittered.

"It might not be wise for you to see the older of them," Nokoma cautioned. "It could be an unsettling thing for strangers, and we guard it. A few tens of them you can see, of course."

Then it came to Ceran that he might be onto what he had looked for all his life. He went into a panic of expectation.

"Nokoma, it would be finding the key!" he fluted. "If none of you has ever died, then your entire race would still be alive!"

"Sure. Is like you count fruit. You take none away, you still have them all."

"But if the first of them are still alive, then they might know their origin! They would know how it began! Do they? Do you?"

"Oh, not I. I am too young for the Ritual."

"But who knows? Doesn't someone know?"

"Oh, yes, all the old ones know how it began."

"How old? How many generations back from you till they know?"

"Ten, no more. When I have ten generations of children, then I will also go to the Ritual."

"The Ritual, what is it?"

"Once a year, the old people go to the very old people. They wake them up and ask them how it all began. The very old people tell them the beginning. It is a high time. Oh, how they hottle and laugh! Then the very old people go back to sleep for another year. So it is passed down to the generations. That is the Ritual."

The Proavitoi were not humanoid. Still less were they "monkey-faces," though that name was now set in the explorers' lingo. They were upright and robed and swathed, and were assumed to be two-legged under their garments. Though, as Manbreaker said, "They might go on wheels, for all we know."

They had remarkable flowing hands that might be called everywhere-digited. They could handle tools, or employ their hands as if they were the most intricate tools.

George Blood was of the opinion that the Proavitoi were always masked, and that the men of the Expedition had never seen their faces. He said that those apparent faces were ritual masks, and that no part of the Proavitoi had ever been seen by the men except for those remarkable hands, which perhaps were their real faces.

The men reacted with cruel hilarity when Ceran tried to explain to them just what a great discovery he was verging on.

"Little Ceran is still on the how-did-it-begin jag," Manbreaker jeered. "Ceran, will you never give off asking which came first, the chicken or the egg?"

"I will have that answer very soon," Ceran sang. "I have the unique opportunity. When I find how the Proavitoi began, I may have the clue to how everything began. All of the Proavitoi are still alive, the very first generation of them."

"It passes belief that you can be so simpleminded," Manbreaker moaned. "They say that one has finally mellowed when he can suffer fools gracefully. By God, I hope I never come to that."

But two days later, it was Manbreaker who sought out Ceran Swicegood on nearly the same subject. Manbreaker had been doing a little thinking and discovering of his own.

"You are Special Aspects Man, Ceran," he said, "and you have been running off after the wrong aspect."

"What is that?"

"It don't make a damn how it began. What is important is that it may not have to end."

"It is the beginning that I intend to discover," said Ceran.

"You fool, can't you understand anything? What do the Proavitoi possess so uniquely that we don't know whether they have it by science or by their nature or by fool luck?"

"Ah, their chemistry, I suppose."

"Sure. Organic chemistry has come of age here. The Proavitoi have every kind of nexus and inhibitor and stimulant. They can grow and shrink and telescope and prolong what they will. These creatures seem stupid to me; it is as if they have these things by instinct. But they have them, that is what is important. With these things, we can become the patent medicine kings of the universes, for the Proavitoi do not travel or make many outside contacts. These things can do anything or undo anything. I suspect that the Proavitoi can shrink cells, and I suspect that they can do something else."

"No, they couldn't shrink cells. It is you who talk nonsense now, Manbreaker."

"Never mind. Their things already make nonsense of conventional chemistry. With the pharmacopoeia that one could pick up here, a man need never die. That's the stick horse you've been riding, isn't it? But you've been riding it backward with your head to the tail. The Proavitoi say that they never die."

"They seem pretty sure that they don't. If they did, they would be the first to know it, as Nokoma says."

"What? Have these creatures humor?"

"Some."

"But, Ceran, you don't understand how big this is."

"I'm the only one who understands it so far. It means that if the Proavitoi have always been immortal, as they maintain, then the oldest of them are still alive. From them I may be able to learn how their species—and perhaps every species—began."

Manbreaker went into his dying buffalo act then. He tore his hair and nearly pulled out his ears by the roots. He stomped and pawed and went off bull-bellowing: "It don't make a damn how it began, you fool! It might not have to end!" so loud that the hills echoed back:

"It don't make a damn—you fool."

Ceran Swicegood went to the house of Nokoma, but not with her on her invitation. He went without her when he knew that she was away from home. It was a sneaky thing to do, but the men of the Expedition were trained in sneakery.

He would find out better without a mentor about the nine hundred grandmothers, about the rumored living dolls. He would find out what the old people did do if they didn't die, and find if they knew how they were first born. For his intrusion, he counted on the innate politeness of the Proavitoi.

The house of Nokoma, of all the people, was in the cluster on top of the large flat hill, the Acropolis of Proavitus. They were earthen houses, though finely done, and they had the appearance of growing out of and being a part of the hill itself.

Ceran went up the winding, ascending flagstone paths, and entered the house which Nokoma had once pointed out to him. He entered furtively, and encountered one of the nine hundred grandmothers—one with whom nobody need be furtive.

The grandmother was seated and small and smiling at him. They talked without real difficulty, though it was not as easy as with Nokoma, who could meet Ceran halfway in his own language. At her call, there came a grandfather who likewise smiled at Ceran. These two ancients were somewhat smaller than the Proavitoi of active years. They were kind and serene. There was an atmosphere about the scene that barely missed being an odor—not unpleasant, sleepy, reminiscent of something, almost sad.

"Are there those here older than you?" Ceran asked earnestly.

"So many, so many, who could know how many?" said the grandmother. She called in other grandmothers and grandfathers older and smaller than herself, these no more than half the size of the active Proavitoi—small, sleepy, smiling.

Ceran knew now that the Proavitoi were not masked. The older they were, the more character and interest there was in their faces. It was only of the immature active Proavitoi that there could have been a doubt. No masks could show such calm and smiling old age as this. The queer textured stuff was their real faces.

So old and friendly, so weak and sleepy, there must have been a dozen generations of them there back to the oldest and smallest.

"How old are the oldest?" Ceran asked the first grandmother.

"We say that all are the same age since all are perpetual," the grandmother told him. "It is not true that all are the same age, but it is indelicate to ask how old."

"You do not know what a lobster is," Ceran said to them, trembling, "but it is a creature that will boil happily if the water on him is heated slowly. He takes no alarm, for he does not know at what point the heat is dangerous. It is that gradual here with me. I slide from one degree to another with you and my credulity is not alarmed. I am in danger of believing anything about you if it comes in small doses, and it will. I believe that you are here and as you are for no other reason than that I see and touch you. Well, I'll be boiled for a lobster, then, before I turn back from it. Are there those here even older than the ones present?"

The first grandmother motioned Ceran to follow her. They went down a ramp through the floor into the older part of the house, which must have been underground.

Living dolls! They were here in rows on the shelves, and sitting in small chairs in their niches. Doll-sized indeed, and several hundred of them.

Many had wakened at the intrusion. Others came awake when spoken to or touched. They were incredibly ancient, but they were cognizant in their glances and recognition. They smiled and stretched sleepily, not as humans would, but as very old puppies might. Ceran spoke to them, and they understood each other surprisingly.

Lobster, lobster, said Ceran to himself, *the water has passed the danger point! And it hardly feels different. If you believe your senses in this, then you will be boiled alive in your credulity.*

He knew now that the living dolls were real and that they were the living ancestors of the Proavitoi.

Many of the little creatures began to fall asleep again. Their waking moments were short, but their sleeps seemed to be likewise. Several of the living mummies woke a second time while Ceran was still in the room, woke refreshed from very short sleeps and were anxious to talk again.

"You are incredible!" Ceran cried out, and all the small and smaller and still smaller creatures smiled and laughed their assent. Of course they were. All good creatures everywhere are incredible, and were there ever so many assembled in one place? But Ceran was greedy. A roomful of miracles wasn't enough.

"I have to take this back as far as it will go!" he cried avidly. "Where are the even older ones?"

"There are older ones and yet older and again older," said the first grandmother, "and thrice-over older ones, but perhaps it would be wise not to seek to be too wise. You have seen enough. The old people are sleepy. Let us go up again."

Go up again, out of this? Ceran would not. He saw passages and descending ramps, down into the heart of the great hill itself. There were whole worlds of rooms about him and under his feet. Ceran went on and down, and who was to stop him? Not dolls and creatures much smaller than dolls.

Manbreaker had once called himself an old pirate who reveled in the stream of his riches. But Ceran was the Young Alchemist who was about to find the Stone itself.

He walked down the ramps through centuries and millennia. The atmosphere he had noticed on the upper levels was a clear odor now—sleepy, half-remembered, smiling, sad, and quite strong. That is the way Time smells.

"Are there those here even older than you?" Ceran asked a small grandmother whom he held in the palm of his hand.

"So old and so small that I could hold in my hand," said the grandmother in what Ceran knew from Nokoma to be the older uncompounded form of the Proavitus language.

Smaller and older the creatures had been getting as Ceran went through the rooms. He was boiled lobster now for sure. He had to believe it all: he saw and felt it. The wren-sized grandmother talked and laughed and nodded that there were those far older than herself, and in doing so she nodded herself back to sleep. Ceran returned her to her niche in the hive-like wall where there were thousands of others, miniaturized generations.

Of course he was not in the house of Nokoma now. He was in the heart of the hill that underlay all the houses of Proavitus, and these were the ancestors of everybody on the asteroid.

"Are there those here even older than you?" Ceran asked a small grandmother whom he held on the tip of his finger.

"Older and smaller," she said, "but you come near the end."

She was asleep, and he put her back in her place. The older they were, the more they slept.

He was down to solid rock under the roots of the hill. He was into the passages that were cut out of that solid rock, but they could not be many or deep. He had a sudden fear that the creatures would become so small that he could not see them or talk to them, and so he would miss the secret of the beginning.

But had not Nokoma said that all the old people knew the secret? Of course. But he wanted to hear it from the oldest of them. He would have it now, one way or the other.

"Who is the oldest? Is this the end of it? Is this the beginning? Wake up! Wake up!" he called when he was sure he was in the lowest and oldest room.

"Is it Ritual?" asked some who woke up. Smaller than mice they were, no bigger than bees, maybe older than both.

"It is a special Ritual," Ceran told them. "Relate to me how it was in the beginning."

What was that sound—too slight, too scattered to be a noise? It was like a billion microbes laughing. It was the hilarity of little things waking up to a high time.

"Who is the oldest of all?" Ceran demanded, for their laughter bothered him. "Who is the oldest and first?"

"I am the oldest, the ultimate grandmother," one said gaily. "All the others are my children. Are you also of my children?"

"Of course," said Ceran, and the small laughter of unbelief flittered out from the whole multitude of them.

"Then you must be the ultimate child, for you are like no other. If you be, then it is as funny at the end as it was in the beginning."

"How was it in the beginning?" Ceran bleated. "You are the first. Do you know how you came to be?"

"Oh, yes, yes," laughed the ultimate grandmother, and the hilarity of the small things became a real noise now.

"How did it begin?" demanded Ceran, and he was hopping and skipping about in his excitement.

"Oh, it was so funny a joke the way things began that you would not believe it," chittered the grandmother. "A joke, a joke!"

"Tell me the joke, then. If a joke generated your species, then tell me that cosmic joke."

"Tell yourself," tinkled the grandmother. "You are a part of the joke if you are of my children. Oh, it is too funny to believe. How good to wake up and laugh and go to sleep again."

Blazing green frustration! To be so close and to be balked by a giggling bee!

"Don't go to sleep again! Tell me at once how it began!" Ceran shrilled, and he had the ultimate grandmother between thumb and finger.

"This is not Ritual," the grandmother protested. "Ritual is that you guess what it was for three days, and we laugh and say, 'No, no, no, it was something nine times as wild as that. Guess some more.'"

"I will *not* guess for three days! Tell me at once or I will crush you," Ceran threatened in a quivering voice.

"I look at you, you look at me, I wonder if you will do it," the ultimate grandmother said calmly.

Any of the tough men of the Expedition would have done it—would have crushed her, and then another and another and another of the creatures till the secret was told. If Ceran had taken on a tough personality and a tough name he'd have done it. If he'd been Gutboy Barrelhouse he'd have done it without a qualm. But Ceran Swicegood couldn't do it.

"Tell me," he pleaded in agony. "All my life I've tried to find out how it began, how anything began. And you know!"

"We know. Oh, it was so funny how it began. So joke! So fool, so clown, so grotesque thing! Nobody could guess, nobody could believe."

"Tell me! Tell me!" Ceran was ashen and hysterical.

"No, no, you are no child of mine," chortled the ultimate grandmother. "Is too joke a joke to tell a stranger. We could not insult a stranger to tell so funny, so unbelieve. Strangers can die. Shall I have it on conscience that a stranger died laughing?"

"Tell me! Insult me! Let me die laughing!" But Ceran nearly died crying from the frustration that ate him up as a million bee-sized things laughed and hooted and giggled:

"Oh, it was so funny the way it began!"

And they laughed. And laughed. And went on laughing . . . until Ceran Swicegood wept and laughed together, and crept away, and returned to the ship still laughing. On his next voyage he changed his name to Blaze Bolt and ruled for ninety-seven days as king of a sweet sea island in M-81, but that is another and much more unpleasant story.

FREDERIK POHL

Frederik Pohl (1919–2013) was an iconic and highly adaptive US science fiction writer whose career started in the Golden Age and spanned three-quarters of a century. That Pohl remained a relevant and vital part of the science fiction scene for so many decades is a testament to his talent, his multitude of interests, a general inquisitiveness, and the ways in which he mentored others.

Among the many honors Pohl received, he won the Hugo Award, the Locus Award, the Nebula Award, and the John W. Campbell Memorial Award for his most-famous novel, *Gateway* (1977). Pohl also won a US National Book Award for his novel *Jem* (1979) in the one-year-only science fiction category (enough was enough) and was a finalist for three other years' best-novel awards. Pohl received the Damon Knight Memorial Grand Master Award (1993) and entered the Science Fiction and Fantasy Hall of Fame in 1998.

In addition to his fiction, Pohl served as the editor of two magazines for almost a decade: *Galaxy* and its sister magazine *IF* (1959–69). Before that, he had edited *Astonishing Stories* and *Super Science Stories* (just prior to World War II). He also edited several anthologies. As an early member of the Futurians—which included the similarly intellectually curious James Blish—Pohl believed in a cosmopolitan approach to science fiction and was a champion of international fiction in translation, especially from Japan. At various times he also wrote nonfiction prolifically and served as a literary agent. He collaborated in fiction with fellow writer C. M. Kornbluth and on anthology projects with his third wife, Carol Metcalf Ulf Stanton. He was also influenced by his second wife, the writer and editor Judith Merril. In all ways he was what was once called "a man of letters" and seemed unable to sit still and not busy himself with projects.

Pohl's fiction began in the 1950s with slickly ironic satire with hints of absurdism and dark humor. During the 1950s he also cowrote, with Kornbluth, the satirical gem *The Space Merchants*; the novel featured a dystopian future dominated by overpopulation and ecological devastation. Throughout the 1960s, Pohl continued to explore and grow as a writer, culminating with his famous 1970s and 1980s *Heechee* series about encounters with the artifacts left behind by aliens who have gone into hiding. The first book, *Gateway* (1977), and its equally excellent sequel *Beyond the Blue Event Horizon* (1980) forever cemented Pohl's already considerable reputation in the field.

Oddly, given his wide range of interests and devotion to high standards of quality, Pohl was a public critic of the New Wave. He found its excesses mystifying and self-indulgent, without, apparently, being able to identify its legitimate antecedents in mainstream literary fiction, surrealism, Decadent literature, and experimental writing that powered the movement. Regardless, "Day Million" (*Rogue*, 1966) fits comfortably within a proto–New Wave tradition by dint of its Borgesian compression of narrative and an unconventional approach to societal norms. However, the story is also included in David Hartwell and Kathryn Cramer's *The Ascent of Wonder:*

The Evolution of Hard SF (1994), for the exceedingly rigorous reason that "the attitude is right, giving it the texture and feel of hard sf. It is written for the reader who understands the hopelessness of a [far future] universe without physical constants." So perhaps part of the enduring appeal of "Day Million" is that it straddles many different modes and approaches to science fiction.

DAY MILLION

Frederik Pohl

On this day I want to tell you about, which will be about a thousand years from now, there were a boy, a girl, and a love story.

Now although I haven't said much so far, none of it is true. The boy was not what you and I would normally think of as a boy, because he was a hundred and eighty-seven years old. Nor was the girl a girl, for other reasons; and the love story did not entail that sublimation of the urge to rape and concurrent postponement of the instinct to submit which we at present understand in such matters. You won't care much for this story if you don't grasp these facts at once. If, however, you will make the effort, you'll likely enough find it jam-packed, chockfull, and tiptop-crammed with laughter, tears, and poignant sentiment which may, or may not, be worthwhile. The reason the girl was not a girl was that she was a boy.

How angrily you recoil from the page! You say, who the hell wants to read about a pair of queers? Calm yourself. Here are no hotbreathing secrets of perversion for the coterie trade. In fact, if you were to see this girl, you would not guess that she was in any sense a boy. Breasts, two; vagina, one. Hips, callipygian; face, hairless; supraorbital lobes, nonexistent. You would term her female at once, although it is true that you might wonder just what species she was a female of, being confused by the tail, the silky pelt, or the gill slits behind each ear.

Now you recoil again. Cripes, man, take my word for it. This is a sweet kid, and if you, as a normal male, spent as much as an hour in a room with her, you would bend heaven and earth to get her in the sack. Dora (we will call her that; her "name" was omicron-Dibase seven-group-totter-oot S. Doradus 5314, the last part of which is a color specification corresponding to a shade of green)—Dora, I say, was feminine, charming, and cute. I admit she doesn't sound that way. She was, as you might put it, a dancer. Her art involved qualities of intellection and expertise of a very high order, requiring both tremendous natural capacities and endless practice; it was performed in null-gravity and I can best describe it by saying that it was something like the performance of a contortionist and something like classical ballet, maybe resembling Danilova's dying swan. It was also pretty damned sexy. In a symbolic way, to be sure; but face it, most of the things we call "sexy" are symbolic, you know, except perhaps an exhibitionist's open fly. On Day Million when Dora danced, the people who saw her panted; and you would too.

About this business of her being a boy. It didn't matter to her audiences that genetically she was male. It wouldn't matter to you, if you were among them, because you wouldn't know it—not unless you took a biopsy cutting of her flesh and put it under an electron microscope to find the XY chromosome—and it didn't matter to them because they didn't care. Through techniques which are not only complex but haven't yet been discovered, these people were able to determine a great deal about the aptitudes and easements of babies quite a long time before they were born—at about the second horizon of cell division, to be exact, when the segmenting egg is becoming a free blastocyst—and then they naturally helped those aptitudes along. Wouldn't we? If we find a child with an aptitude for music we give him a scholarship to Juilliard. If they found a child whose aptitudes were for being a woman, they made him one. As sex had long been dissociated from reproduction this was relatively easy to do and caused no trouble and no, or at least very little, comment.

How much is "very little"? Oh, about as much as would be caused by our own tampering with Divine Will by filling a tooth. Less than would be caused by wearing a hearing aid. Does it still sound awful? Then look closely at the next busty babe you meet and reflect that she may be a Dora, for adults who are genetically male but somatically female are far from unknown even in our own time. An accident of environment in the womb overwhelms the blueprints of heredity. The difference is that with us it happens only by accident and we don't know about it except rarely, after close study; whereas the people of Day Million did it often, on purpose, because they wanted to.

Well, that's enough to tell you about Dora. It would only confuse you to add that she was seven feet tall and smelled of peanut butter. Let us begin our story.

On Day Million Dora swam out of her house, entered a transportation tube, was sucked briskly to the surface in its flow of water and ejected in its plume of spray to an elastic platform in front of her—ah—call it her rehearsal hall. "Oh, shit!" she cried in pretty confusion, reaching out to catch her balance and finding herself tumbled against a total stranger, whom we will call Don.

They met cute. Don was on his way to have his legs renewed. Love was the farthest thing from his mind; but when, absentmindedly taking a shortcut across the landing platform for submarinites and finding himself drenched, he discovered his arms full of the loveliest girl he had ever seen, he knew at once they were meant for each other. "Will you marry me?" he asked. She said softly, "Wednesday," and the promise was like a caress.

Don was tall, muscular, bronze, and exciting. His name was no more Don than Dora's was Dora, but the personal part of it was Adonis in tribute to his vibrant maleness, and so we will call him Don for short. His personality color-code, in Angstrom units, was 5290, or only a few degrees bluer than Dora's 5314, a measure of what they had intuitively discovered at first sight, that they possessed many affinities of taste and interest.

I despair of telling you exactly what it was that Don did for a living—I don't mean for the sake of making money, I mean for the sake of giving purpose and meaning to his life, to keep him from going off his nut with boredom—except to say that it involved a lot of traveling. He traveled in interstellar spaceships. In order to make a spaceship go really fast about thirty-one male and seven genetically female human beings had to do certain things, and Don was one of the thirty-one. Actually he contemplated options. This involved a lot of exposure to radiation flux—not so much from his own station in the propulsive system as in the spillover from the next stage, where a genetic female preferred selections and the subnuclear particles making the selections she preferred demolished themselves in a shower of quanta. Well, you don't give a rat's ass for that, but it meant that Don had to be clad at all times in a skin of light, resilient, extremely strong copper-colored metal. I have already mentioned this, but you probably thought I meant he was sunburned.

More than that, he was a cybernetic man. Most of his ruder parts had been long since replaced with mechanisms of vastly more permanence and use. A cadmium centrifuge, not a heart, pumped his blood. His lungs moved only when he wanted to speak out loud, for a cascade of osmotic filters rebreathed oxygen out of his own wastes. In a way, he probably would have looked peculiar to a man from the twentieth century, with his glowing eyes and seven-fingered hands; but to himself, and of course to Dora, he looked mighty manly and grand. In the course of his voyages Don had circled Proxima Centauri, Procyon, and the puzzling worlds of Mira Ceti; he had carried agricultural templates to the planets of Canopus and brought back warm, witty pets from the pale companion of Aldebaran. Blue-hot or red-cool, he had seen a thousand stars and their ten thousand planets. He had, in fact, been traveling the star-lanes with only brief leaves on Earth for pushing two centuries. But you don't care about that, either. It is people that make stories, not the circumstances they find themselves in, and you want to hear about these two people. Well, they made it. The great thing they had for each other grew and flowered and burst into fruition on Wednesday, just as Dora had promised. They met at the encoding room, with a couple of well-wishing friends apiece to cheer them on, and while their identities were being taped and stored they smiled and whispered to each other and bore the jokes of their friends with blushing repartee. Then they exchanged their mathematical analogues and went away, Dora to her dwelling beneath the surface of the sea and Don to his ship.

It was an idyll, really. They lived happily ever after—or anyway, until they decided not to bother anymore and died.

Of course, they never set eyes on each other again.

Oh, I can see you now, you eaters of charcoal-broiled steak, scratching an incipient bunion with one hand and holding this story with the other, while the stereo plays d'Indy or Monk. You don't believe a word of it, do you? Not for one minute. People wouldn't live like that, you say with an irritated and not amused grunt as you get up to put fresh ice in a stale drink.

And yet there's Dora, hurrying back through the flushing commute pipes toward her underwater home (she prefers it there, has had herself somatically altered to breathe the stuff). If I tell you with what sweet fulfillment she fits the recorded analogue of Don into the symbol manipulator, hooks herself in, and turns herself on . . . if I try to tell you any of that you will simply stare. Or glare; and grumble, what the hell kind of lovemaking is this? And yet I assure

you, friend, I really do assure you that Dora's ecstasies are as creamy and passionate as any of James Bond's lady spies, and one hell of a lot more so than anything you are going to find in "real life." Go ahead and grumble. Dora doesn't care. If she thinks of you at all, her thirty times great-great-grandfather, she thinks you're a pretty primordial sort of brute. You are. Why, Dora is farther removed from you than you are from the australopithecines of five thousand centuries ago. You could not swim a second in the strong currents of her life. You don't think progress goes in a straight line, do you? Do you recognize that it is an ascending, accelerating, maybe even exponential curve? It takes hell's own time to get started, but when it goes it goes like a bomb. And you, you Scotch-drinking steak-eater in your Relaxacizor chair, you've just barely lighted the Primacord of the fuse. What is it now, the six or seven hundred thousandth day after Christ? Dora lives in Day Million. A thousand years from now. Her body fats are polyunsaturated, like Crisco. Her wastes are hemodialyzed out of her bloodstream while she sleeps—that means she doesn't have to go to the bathroom. On whim, to pass a slow half-hour, she can command more energy than the entire nation of Portugal can spend today, and use it to launch a weekend satellite or remold a crater on the moon. She loves Don very much. She keeps his every gesture, mannerism, nuance, touch of hand, thrill of intercourse, passion of kiss stored in symbolic-mathematical form. And when she wants him, all she has to do is turn the machine on and she has him.

And Don, of course, has Dora. Adrift on a sponson city a few hundred yards over her head or orbiting Arcturus, fifty light-years away, Don has only to command his own symbol-manipulator to rescue Dora from the ferrite files and bring her to life for him, and there she is; and rapturously, tirelessly they ball all night. Not in the flesh, of course; but then his flesh has been extensively altered and it wouldn't really be much fun. He doesn't need the flesh for pleasure. Genital organs feel nothing. Neither do hands, nor breasts, nor lips; they are only receptors, accepting and transmitting impulses. It is the brain that feels, it is the interpretation of those impulses that makes agony or orgasm; and Don's symbol-manipulator gives him the analogue of cuddling, the analogue of kissing, the analogue of wildest, most ardent hours with the eternal, exquisite, and incorruptible analogue of Dora. Or Diane. Or sweet Rose, or laughing Alicia; for to be sure, they have each of them exchanged analogues before, and will again.

Balls, you say, it looks crazy to me. And you—with your aftershave lotion and your little red car, pushing papers across a desk all day and chasing tail all night—tell me, just how the hell do you think you would look to Tiglath-Pileser, say, or Attila the Hun?

F. L. WALLACE

F. L. Wallace (1915–2004) was an interesting US writer of science fiction and mystery whose small body of work often demonstrates sensitivity to ecological issues. Wallace spent most of his life in California as a mechanical engineer after attending the University of Iowa and UCLA. His first published story, "Hideaway," appeared in the magazine *Astounding Science Fiction*. *Galaxy Science Fiction* and other science fiction magazines published subsequent stories of his, including "Delay in Transit," "Bolden's Pets," and "Tangle Hold." Because he left the field in the 1960s and had no major advocates, Wallace quickly became forgotten, although the e-book release of a collection in 2009 has begun to bring him once again to notice.

The 1950s were Wallace's period of greatest activity, during which he quickly established a reputation for style, wit, and emotional depth. In "Accidental Flight" (*Galaxy*, 1952), a population of the disabled—in fact accident victims, mutants, cyborgs, and others with psi powers—transforms an asteroid hospital into a starship powered by engines that manipulate gravity; they set off for the stars, where they find redemption in being of use to the human race. *Worlds in Balance* (1955) assembles two typical stories, but Wallace never put together a full-length collection of his work.

"Student Body" (*Galaxy*, 1953) showcases Wallace's adroit handling of environmental issues in a manner more sophisticated than that of most writers of the era other than Frank Herbert (at novel length). Complex issues involving both alien contact and the impact of invasive species are housed within a tense plot. Although "Student Body" received no particular accolades upon publication, it endures as an example of a work ahead of its time—a future classic.

STUDENT BODY

F. L. Wallace

The first morning that they were fully committed to the planet, the executive officer stepped out of the ship. It was not quite dawn. Executive Hafner squinted in the early light; his eyes opened wider, and he promptly went back inside. Three minutes later, he reappeared with the biologist in tow.

"Last night you said there was nothing dangerous," said the executive. "Do you still think it's so?"

Dano Marin stared. "I do." What his voice lacked in conviction, it made up in embarrassment. He laughed uncertainly.

"This is no laughing matter. I'll talk to you later."

The biologist stood by the ship and watched as the executive walked to the row of sleeping colonists.

"Mrs. Athyl," said the executive as he stopped beside the sleeping figure.

She yawned, rubbed her eyes, rolled over, and stood up. The covering that should have been there, however, wasn't. Neither was the garment she had on when she had gone to sleep. She assumed the conventional position of a woman who is astonished to find herself unclad without her knowledge or consent.

"It's all right, Mrs. Athyl. I'm not a voyeur myself. Still, I think you should get some clothing on." Most of the colonists were awake now. Executive Hafner turned to them. "If you haven't any suitable clothing in the ship, the commissary will issue you some. Explanations will be given later."

The colonists scattered. There was no compulsive modesty among them, for it couldn't have survived a year and a half in crowded spaceships. Nevertheless, it was a shock to awaken with no clothing on and not know who or what had removed it during the night. It was surprise more than anything else that disconcerted them.

On his way back to the spaceship, Executive Hafner paused. "Any ideas about it?"

Dano Marin shrugged. "How could I have? The planet is as new to me as it is to you."

"Sure. But you're the biologist."

As the only scientist in a crew of rough-and-ready colonists and builders, Marin was going to be called on to answer a lot of questions that weren't in his field.

"Nocturnal insects, most likely," he suggested. That was pretty weak, though he knew that in ancient times locusts had stripped fields in a matter of hours. Could they do the same with the clothing of humans and not awaken them? "I'll look into the matter. As soon as I find anything, I'll let you know."

"Good." Hafner nodded and went into the spaceship.

Dano Marin walked to the grove in which the colonists had been sleeping. It had been a mistake to let them bed down there, but at the time the request had been made, there had seemed no reason not to grant it. After eighteen months in crowded ships everyone naturally wanted fresh air and the rustle of leaves overhead.

Marin looked out through the grove. It was empty now; the colonists, both men and women, had disappeared inside the ship, dressing, probably.

The trees were not tall and the leaves were

dark bottle-green. Occasional huge white flowers caught sunlight that made them seem larger than they were. It wasn't Earth and therefore the trees couldn't be magnolias. But they reminded Marin of magnolia trees and thereafter he always thought of them as that.

The problem of the missing clothing was ironic. Biological Survey never made a mistake—yet obviously they had. They listed the planet as the most suitable for man of any so far discovered. Few insects, no dangerous animals, a most equitable climate. They had named it Glade because that was the word which fitted best. The whole landmass seemed to be one vast and pleasant meadow.

Evidently there were things about the planet that Biological Survey had missed.

Marin dropped to his knees and began to look for clues. If insects had been responsible, there ought to be a few dead ones, crushed, perhaps, as the colonists rolled over in their sleep. There were no insects, either live or dead.

He stood up in disappointment and walked slowly through the grove. It might be the trees. At night they could exude a vapor which was capable of dissolving the material from which the clothing had been made. Far-fetched, but not impossible. He crumbled a leaf in his hand and rubbed it against his sleeve. A pungent smell, but nothing happened. That didn't disprove the theory, of course.

He looked out through the trees at the blue sun. It was bigger than Sol, but farther away. At Glade, it was about equal to the sun on Earth.

He almost missed the bright eyes that regarded him from the underbrush. Almost, but didn't—the domain of biology begins at the edge of the atmosphere; it includes the brush and the small creatures that live in it.

He swooped down on it. The creature fled squealing. He ran it down in the grass outside the grove. It collapsed into quaking flesh as he picked it up. He talked to it gently and the terror subsided.

It nibbled contentedly on his jacket as he carried it back to the ship.

. . .

Executive Hafner stared unhappily into the cage. It was an undistinguished animal, small and something like an undeveloped rodent. Its fur was sparse and stringy, unglamorous; it would never be an item in the fur export trade.

"Can we exterminate it?" asked Hafner. "Locally, that is."

"Hardly. It's ecologically basic."

The executive looked blank. Dano Marin added the explanation: "You know how Biological Controls works. As soon as a planet has been discovered that looks suitable, they send out a survey ship loaded with equipment. The ship flies low over a good part of the planet and the instruments in the ship record the neural currents of the animals below. The instruments can distinguish the characteristic neural patterns of anything that has a brain, including insects.

"Anyway, they have a pretty good idea of the kinds of animals on the planet and their relative distribution. Naturally, the survey party takes a few specimens. They have to in order to correlate the pattern with the actual animal, otherwise the neural pattern would be merely a meaningless squiggle on a microfilm.

"The survey shows that this animal is one of only four species of mammals on the planet. It is also the most numerous."

Hafner grunted. "So if we kill them off here, others will swarm in from surrounding areas?"

"That's about it. There are probably millions of them on this peninsula. Of course, if you want to put a barrier across the narrow connection to the mainland, you might be able to wipe them out locally."

The executive scowled. A barrier was possible, but it would involve more work than he cared to expend.

"What do they eat?" he asked truculently.

"A little bit of everything, apparently. Insects, fruits, berries, nuts, succulents, and grain." Dano Marin smiled. "I guess it could be called an omnivore—now that our clothing is handy, it eats that, too."

Hafner didn't smile. "I thought our clothing was supposed to be vermin-proof."

Marin shrugged. "It is, on twenty-seven planets. On the twenty-eighth, we meet up with a little fella that has better digestive fluids, that's all."

Hafner looked pained. "Are they likely to bother the crops we plant?"

"Offhand, I would say they aren't. But then I would have said the same about our clothing."

Hafner made up his mind. "All right. You worry about the crops. Find some way to keep them out of the fields. Meanwhile, everyone sleeps in the ship until we can build dormitories."

Individual dwelling units would have been more appropriate in the colony at this stage, thought Marin. But it wasn't for him to decide. The executive was a man who regarded a schedule as something to be exceeded.

"The omnivore—" began Marin.

Hafner nodded impatiently. "Work on it," he said, and walked away.

The biologist sighed. The omnivore really was a queer little creature, but it was by no means the most important thing on Glade. For instance, why were there so few species of land animals on the planet? No reptiles, numerous birds, and only four kinds of mammals.

Every comparable planet teemed with a wild variety of life. Glade, in spite of seemingly ideal conditions, hadn't developed. Why?

He had asked Biological Controls for this assignment because it had seemed an interesting problem. Now, apparently, he was being pressed into service as an exterminator.

He reached in the cage and picked up the omnivore. Mammals on Glade were not unexpected. Parallel development took care of that. Given roughly the same kind of environment, similar animals would usually evolve.

In the Late Carboniferous forest on Earth, there had been creatures like the omnivore, the primitive mammal from which all others had evolved. On Glade, that kind of evolution just hadn't taken place. What had kept nature

from exploiting its evolutionary potentialities? There was the real problem, not how to wipe them out.

Marin stuck a needle in the omnivore. It squealed and then relaxed. He drew out the blood and set it back in the cage. He could learn a lot about the animal from trying to kill it.

The quartermaster was shouting, though his normal voice carried quite well.

"How do you know it's mice?" the biologist asked him.

"Look," said the quartermaster angrily.

Marin looked. The evidence did indicate mice.

Before he could speak, the quartermaster snapped, "Don't tell me they're only micelike creatures. I know that. The question is: how can I get rid of them?"

"Have you tried poison?"

"Tell me what poison to use and I'll use it."

It wasn't the easiest question to answer. What was poisonous to an animal he had never seen and knew nothing about? According to Biological Survey, the animal didn't exist.

It was unexpectedly serious. The colony could live off the land, and was expected to. But another group of colonists was due in three years. The colony was supposed to accumulate a surplus of food to feed the increased numbers. If they couldn't store the food they grew any better than the concentrates, that surplus was going to be scanty.

Marin went over the warehouse thoroughly. It was the usual early construction on a colonial world. Not aesthetic, it was sturdy enough. Fused dirt floor, reinforced foot-thick walls, a ceiling slab of the same. The whole was bound together with a molecular cement that made it practically airtight. It had no windows; there were two doors. Certainly it should keep out rodents.

A closer examination revealed an unexpected flaw. The floor was as hard as glass; no animal could gnaw through it, but, like glass, it was also brittle. The crew that had built the warehouse had evidently been in such a hurry to get back to Earth that they hadn't been as careful as they should have been, for here and there the floor was thin. Somewhere under the heavy equipment piled on it, the floor had cracked. There a burrowing animal had means of entry.

Short of building another warehouse, it was too late to do anything about that. Micelike animals were inside and had to be controlled where they were.

The biologist straightened up. "Catch me a few of them alive and I'll see what I can do."

In the morning, a dozen live specimens were delivered to the lab. They actually did resemble mice.

Their reactions were puzzling. No two of them were affected by the same poison. A compound that stiffened one in a matter of minutes left the others hale and hearty, and the poison he had developed to control the omnivores was completely ineffective.

The depredations in the warehouse went on. Black mice, white ones, gray and brown, short-tailed and long-eared, or the reverse, they continued to eat the concentrates and spoil what they didn't eat.

Marin conferred with the executive, outlined the problem as he saw it and his ideas on what could be done to combat the nuisance.

"But we can't build another warehouse," argued Hafner. "Not until the atomic generator is set up, at any rate. And then we'll have other uses for the power." The executive rested his head in his hands. "I like the other solution better. Build one and see how it works."

"I was thinking of three," said the biologist.

"One," Hafner insisted. "We can't spare the equipment until we know how it works."

At that he was probably right. They had equipment, as much as three ships could bring. But the more they brought, the more was expected of the colony. The net effect was that equipment was always in short supply.

Marin took the authorization to the engineer. On the way, he privately revised his specifications upward. If he couldn't get as many as he wanted, he might as well get a better one.

In two days, the machine was ready.

It was delivered in a small crate to the warehouse. The crate was opened and the machine leaped out and stood there, poised.

"A cat!" exclaimed the quartermaster, pleased. He stretched out his hand toward the black fuzzy robot.

"If you've touched anything a mouse may have, get your hand away," warned the biologist. "It reacts to smell as well as sight and sound."

Hastily, the quartermaster withdrew his hand. The robot disappeared silently into the maze of stored material.

In one week, though there were still some mice in the warehouse, they were no longer a danger.

The executive called Marin into his office, a small sturdy building located in the center of the settlement. The colony was growing, assuming an aspect of permanency. Hafner sat in his chair and looked out over that growth with satisfaction.

"A good job on the mouse plague," he said.

The biologist nodded. "Not bad, except there shouldn't be any mice here. Biological Survey—"

"Forget it," said the exec. "Everybody makes mistakes, even BS." He leaned back and looked seriously at the biologist. "I have a job I need done. Just now I'm short of men. If you have no objections . . ."

The exec was always short of men, would be until the planet was overcrowded, and he would try to find someone to do the work his own men should have done. Dano Marin was not directly responsible to Hafner; he was on loan to the expedition from Biological Controls.

Still, it was a good idea to cooperate with the executive. He sighed.

"It's not as bad as you think," said Hafner, interpreting the sound correctly. He smiled. "We've got the digger together. I want you to run it."

Since it tied right in with his investigations, Dano Marin looked relieved and showed it.

"Except for food, we have to import most of our supplies," Hafner explained. "It's a long haul, and we've got to make use of everything on the planet we can. We need oil. There are going to be a lot of wheels turning, and every one of them will have to have oil. In time we'll set up a synthetic plant, but if we can locate a productive field now, it's to our advantage."

"You're assuming the geology of Glade is similar to Earth?"

Hafner waggled his hand. "Why not? It's a nicer twin of Earth."

Why not? Because you couldn't always tell from the surface, thought Marin. It seemed like Earth, but was it? Here was a good chance to find out the history of Glade.

Hafner stood up. "Any time you're ready, a technician will check you out on the digger. Let me know before you go."

Actually, the digger wasn't a digger. It didn't move or otherwise displace a gram of dirt or rock. It was a means of looking down below the surface, to any practical depth. A large crawler, it was big enough for a man to live in without discomfort for a week.

It carried an outsize ultrasonic generator and a device for directing the beam into the planet. That was the sending apparatus. The receiving end began with a large sonic lens which picked up sound beams reflected from any desired depth, converted them into electrical energy and thence into an image which was flashed onto a screen.

At the depth of ten miles, the image was fuzzy, though good enough to distinguish the main features of the strata. At three miles, it was better. It could pick up the sound reflection of a buried coin and convert it into a picture on which the date could be seen.

It was to a geologist as a microscope is to a biologist. Being a biologist, Dano Marin could appreciate the analogy.

He started at the tip of the peninsula and zigzagged across, heading toward the isthmus. Methodically, he covered the territory, sleeping at night in the digger. On the morning of the third day, he discovered oil traces, and by that afternoon he had located the main field.

He should probably have turned back at once, but now that he had found oil, he investigated more deliberately. Starting at the top, he let the image range downward below the top strata.

It was the reverse of what it should have been. In the top few feet, there were plentiful fossil remains, mostly of the four species of mammals. The squirrel-like creature and the far larger grazing animal were the forest dwellers. Of the plains animals, there were only two, in size fitting neatly between the extremes of the forest dwellers.

After the first few feet, which corresponded to approximately twenty thousand years, he found virtually no fossils. Not until he reached a depth which he could correlate to the Late Carboniferous age on Earth did fossils reappear. Then they were of animals appropriate to the epoch. At that depth and below, the history of Glade was quite similar to Earth's.

Puzzled, he checked again in a dozen widely scattered localities. The results were always the same—fossil history for the first twenty thousand years, then none for roughly a hundred million. Beyond that, it was easy to trace the thread of biological development.

In that period of approximately one hundred million years, something unique had happened to Glade. What was it?

On the fifth day his investigations were interrupted by the sound of the keyed-on radio.

"Marin."

"Yes?" He flipped on the sending switch.

"How soon can you get back?"

He looked at the photo-map. "Three hours. Two if I hurry."

"Make it two. Never mind the oil."

"I've found oil. But what's the matter?"

"You can see it better than I can describe it. We'll discuss it when you get back."

Reluctantly, Marin retracted the instruments into the digger. He turned it around and, with not too much regard for the terrain, let it roar. The treads tossed dirt high in the air. Animals fled squealing from in front of him. If the grove was small enough, he went around it, otherwise he went through and left matchsticks behind.

He skidded the crawler ponderously to halt near the edge of the settlement. The center of activity was the warehouse. Pickups wheeled in and out, transferring supplies to a cleared area outside. He found Hafner in a corner of the warehouse, talking to the engineer.

Hafner turned around when he came up. "Your mice have grown, Marin."

Marin looked down. The robot cat lay on the floor. He knelt and examined it. The steel skeleton hadn't broken; it had been bent, badly. The tough plastic skin had been torn off and, inside, the delicate mechanism had been chewed into an unrecognizable mass.

Around the cat were rats, twenty or thirty of them, huge by any standards. The cat had fought; the dead animals were headless or disemboweled, unbelievably battered. But the robot had been outnumbered.

Biological Survey had said there weren't any rats on Glade. They had also said that about mice. What was the key to their error?

The biologist stood up. "What are you going to do about it?"

"Build another warehouse, two-foot-thick fused dirt floors, monolithic construction. Transfer all perishables to it."

Marin nodded. That would do it. It would take time, of course, and power, all they could draw out of the recently set up atomic generator. All other construction would have to be suspended. No wonder Hafner was disturbed.

"Why not build more cats?" Marin suggested.

The executive smiled nastily. "You weren't here when we opened the doors. The warehouse was swarming with rats. How many robot cats would we need—five, fifteen? I don't know. Anyway the engineer tells me we have enough parts to build three more cats. The one lying there can't be salvaged."

It didn't take an engineer to see that, thought Marin.

Hafner continued, "If we need more, we'll have to rob the computer in the spaceship. I refuse to permit that."

Obviously he would. The spaceship was the only link with Earth until the next expedition brought more colonists. No exec in his right mind would permit the ship to be crippled.

But why had Hafner called him back? Merely to keep him informed of the situation?

Hafner seemed to guess his thoughts. "At night we'll floodlight the supplies we remove from the warehouse. We'll post a guard armed with decharged rifles until we can move the food into the new warehouse. That'll take about ten days. Meanwhile, our fast crops are ripening. It's my guess the rats will turn to them for food. In order to protect our future food supply, you'll have to activate your animals."

The biologist started. "But it's against regulations to loose any animal on a planet until a complete investigation of the possible ill effects is made."

"That takes ten or twenty years. This is an emergency and I'll be responsible—in writing, if you want."

The biologist was effectively countermanded. Another rabbit-infested Australia or the planet that the snails took over might be in the making, but there was nothing he could do about it.

"I hardly think they'll be of any use against rats this size," he protested.

"You've got hormones. Apply them." The executive turned and began discussing construction with the engineer.

Marin had the dead rats gathered up and placed in the freezer for further study.

After that, he retired to the laboratory and worked out a course of treatment for the domesticated animals that the colonists had brought with them. He gave them the first injections and watched them carefully until they were safely through the initial shock phase of growth. As soon as he saw they were going to survive, he bred them.

Next he turned to the rats. Of note was the wide variation in size. Internally, the same thing was true. They had the usual organs, but the proportions of each varied greatly, more than is normal. Nor were their teeth uniform. Some carried huge fangs set in delicate jaws; others had tiny teeth that didn't match the massive bone structure. As a species, they were the most scrambled the biologist had ever encountered.

He turned the microscope on their tissues and tabulated the results. There was less difference here between individual specimens, but it was enough to set him pondering. The reproductive cells were especially baffling.

Late in the day, he felt rather than heard the soundless whoosh of the construction machinery. He looked out of the laboratory and saw smoke rolling upward. As soon as the vegetation was charred, the smoke ceased and heat waves danced into the sky.

They were building on a hill. The little creatures that crept and crawled in the brush attacked in the most vulnerable spot, the food supply. There was no brush, not a blade of grass, on the hill when the colonists finished.

Terriers. In the past, they were the hunting dogs of the agricultural era. What they lacked in size they made up in ferocity toward rodents. They had earned their keep originally in granaries and fields, and, for a brief time, they were doing it again on colonial worlds where conditions were repeated.

The dogs the colonists brought had been terriers. They were still as fast, still with the same anti-rodent disposition, but they were no longer small. It had been a difficult job, yet Marin had done it well, for the dogs had lost none of their skill and speed in growing to the size of a Great Dane.

The rats moved in on the fields of fast crops. Fast crops were made to order for a colonial world. They could be planted, grown, and harvested in a matter of weeks. After four such plantings, the fertility of the soil was destroyed, but that meant nothing in the early years of a colonial planet, for land was plentiful.

The rat tide grew in the fast crops, and the dogs were loosed on the rats. They ranged through the fields, hunting. A rush, a snap of their jaws, the shake of a head, and the rat was tossed aside, its back broken. The dogs went on to the next.

Until they could not see, the dogs prowled and slaughtered. At night they came in bloody, most of it not their own, and exhausted. Marin pumped them full of antibiotics, bandaged their wounds, fed them through their veins, and shot them into sleep. In the morning he awakened them with an injection of stimulant and sent them tingling into battle.

It took the rats two days to learn they could not feed during the day. Not so numerous, they came at night. They climbed on the vines and nibbled the fruit. They gnawed growing grain and ravaged vegetables.

The next day the colonists set up lights. The dogs were with them, discouraging the few rats who were still foolish enough to forage while the sun was overhead.

An hour before dusk, Marin called the dogs in and gave them an enforced rest. He brought them out of it after dark and took them to the fields, staggering. The scent of rats revived them; they were as eager as ever, if not quite so fast.

The rats came from the surrounding meadows, not singly, or in twos and threes, as they had before; this time they came together. Squealing and rustling the grass, they moved toward the fields. It was dark, and though he could not see them, Marin could hear them. He ordered the great lights turned on in the area of the fields.

The rats stopped under the glare, milling around uneasily. The dogs quivered and whined. Marin held them back. The rats resumed their march, and Marin released the dogs.

The dogs charged in to attack, but didn't dare brave the main mass. They picked off the stragglers and forced the rats into a tighter formation. After that the rats were virtually unassailable.

The colonists could have burned the bunched-up rats with the right equipment, but they didn't have it and couldn't get it for years. Even if they'd had it, the use of such equipment would endanger the crops, which they had to save if they could. It was up to the dogs.

The rat formation came to the edge of the fields, and broke. They could face a common enemy and remain united, but in the presence of food, they forgot that unity and scattered— hunger was the great divisor. The dogs leaped joyously in pursuit. They hunted down the starved rodents, one by one, and killed them as they ate.

When daylight came, the rat menace had ended.

The next week the colonists harvested and processed the food for storage and immediately planted another crop.

Marin sat in the lab and tried to analyze the situation. The colony was moving from crisis to crisis, all of them involving food. In itself, each critical situation was minor, but lumped together they could add up to failure. No matter how he looked at it, they just didn't have the equipment they needed to colonize Glade.

The fault seemed to lie with Biological Survey; they hadn't reported the presence of pests that were endangering the food supply. Regard- less of what the exec thought about them, Survey knew their business. If they said there were no mice or rats on Glade, then there hadn't been any—*when the survey was made*.

The question was: when did they come and how did they get here?

Marin sat and stared at the wall, turning over hypotheses in his mind, discarding them when they failed to make sense.

His gaze shifted from the wall to the cage of the omnivores, the squirrel-size forest creature. The most numerous animal on Glade, it was a commonplace sight to the colonists.

And yet it was a remarkable animal, more than he had realized. Plain, insignificant in appearance, it might be the most important of any animal man had encountered on the many worlds he had settled on. The longer he watched, the more Marin became convinced of it.

He sat silent, observing the creature, not daring to move. He sat until it was dark and the omnivore resumed its normal activity.

Normal? The word didn't apply on Glade.

The interlude with the omnivore provided him with one answer. He needed another one; he thought he knew what it was, but he had to have more data, additional observations.

He set up his equipment carefully on the fringes of the settlement. There and in no other place existed the information he wanted.

He spent time in the digger, checking his original investigations. It added up to a complete picture.

When he was certain of his facts, he called on Hafner.

The executive was congenial; it was a reflection of the smoothness with which the objectives of the colony were being achieved.

"Sit down," he said affably. "Smoke?"

The biologist sat down and took a cigarette.

"I thought you'd like to know where the mice came from," he began.

Hafner smiled. "They don't bother us anymore."

"I've also determined the origin of the rats."

"They're under control. We're doing nicely."

On the contrary, thought Marin. He searched for the proper beginning.

"Glade has an Earth-type climate and topography," he said. "Has had for the past twenty thousand years. Before that, about a hundred million years ago, it was also like Earth of the comparable period."

He watched the look of polite interest settle on the executive's face as he stated the obvious. Well, it *was* obvious, up to a point. The conclusions weren't, though.

"Between a hundred million years and twenty thousand years ago, something happened to Glade," Marin went on. "I don't know the cause; it belongs to cosmic history and we may never find out. Anyway, whatever the cause—fluctuations in the sun, unstable equilibrium of forces within the planet, or perhaps an encounter with an interstellar dust cloud of variable density—the climate on Glade changed.

"It changed with inconceivable violence and it kept on changing. A hundred million years ago, plus or minus, there was carboniferous forest on Glade. Giant reptiles resembling dinosaurs and tiny mammals roamed through it. The first great change wiped out the dinosaurs, as it did on Earth. It didn't wipe out the still more primitive ancestor of the omnivore, because it could adapt to changing conditions.

"Let me give you an idea how the conditions changed. For a few years a given area would be a desert; after that it would turn into a jungle. Still later a glacier would begin to form. And then the cycle would be repeated, with wild variations. All this might happen— did happen—within a span covered by the lifetime of a single omnivore. This occurred many times. For roughly a hundred million years, it was the norm of existence on Glade. This condition was hardly conducive to the preservation of fossils."

Hafner saw the significance and was concerned. "You mean these climatic fluctuations suddenly stopped, twenty thousand years ago? Are they likely to begin again?"

"I don't know," confessed the biologist. "We can probably determine it if we're interested."

The exec nodded grimly. "We're interested, all right."

Maybe we are, thought the biologist. He said, "The point is that survival was difficult. Birds could and did fly to more suitable climates; quite a few of them survived. Only one species of mammal managed to come through."

"Your facts are not straight," observed Hafner. "There are four species, ranging in size from a squirrel to a water buffalo."

"One species," Marin repeated doggedly. "They're the same. If the food supply for the largest animal increases, some of the smaller so-called species grow up. Conversely, if food becomes scarce in any category, the next generation, which apparently can be produced almost instantly, switches to a form which does have an adequate food supply."

"The mice," Hafner said slowly.

Marin finished the thought for him. "The mice weren't here when we got here. They were born of the squirrel-size omnivore."

Hafner nodded. "And the rats?"

"Born of the next larger size. After all, we're environment, too—perhaps the harshest the beasts have yet faced."

Hafner was a practical man, trained to administer a colony. Concepts were not his familiar ground. "Mutations, then? But I thought—"

The biologist smiled. It was thin and cracked at the edges of his mouth. "On Earth, it would be mutation. Here it is merely normal evolutionary adaptation." He shook his head. "I never told you, but omnivores, though they could be mistaken for an animal from Earth, have no genes or chromosomes. Obviously they do have heredity, but how it is passed down, I don't know. However it functions, it responds to external conditions far faster than anything we've ever encountered."

Hafner nodded to himself. "Then we'll never be free from pests." He clasped and unclasped his hands. "Unless, of course, we rid the planet of all animal life."

"Radioactive dust?" asked the biologist. "They have survived worse."

The exec considered alternatives. "Maybe we should leave the planet and leave it to the animals."

"Too late," said the biologist. "They'll be on Earth, too, and all the planets we've settled on."

Hafner looked at him. The same pictures formed in his mind that Marin had thought of. Three ships had been sent to colonize Glade. One had remained with the colonists, survival insurance in case anything unforeseen happened. Two had gone back to Earth to carry the report that all was well and that more supplies were needed. They had also carried specimens from the planet.

The cages those creatures were kept in were secure. But a smaller species could get out, must already be free, inhabiting, undetected, the cargo spaces of the ships.

There was nothing they could do to intercept those ships. And once they reached Earth, would the biologists suspect? Not for a long time. First a new kind of rat would appear. A mutation could account for that. Without specific knowledge, there would be nothing to connect it with the specimens picked up from Glade.

"We have to stay," said the biologist. "We have to study them and we can do it best here."

He thought of the vast complex of buildings on Earth. There was too much invested to tear them down and make them vermin-proof. Billions of people could not be moved off the planet while the work was being done.

They were committed to Glade not as a colony, but as a gigantic laboratory. They had gained one planet and lost the equivalent of ten, perhaps more when the destructive properties of the omnivores were finally assessed.

A rasping animal cough interrupted the biologist's thoughts. Hafner jerked his head and glanced out the window. Lips tight, he grabbed a rifle off the wall and ran out. Marin followed him.

The exec headed toward the fields where the second fast crop was maturing. On top of a knoll, he stopped and knelt. He flipped the dial to *extreme charge*, aimed, and fired. It was high; he missed the animal in the field. A neat strip of smoking brown appeared in the green vegetation.

He aimed more carefully and fired again. The charge screamed out of the muzzle. It struck the animal on the forepaw. The beast leaped high in the air and fell down, dead and broiled.

They stood over the animal Hafner had killed. Except for the lack of markings, it was a good imitation of a tiger. The exec prodded it with his toe.

"We chase the rats out of the warehouse and they go to the fields," he muttered. "We hunt them down in the fields with dogs and they breed tigers."

"Easier than rats," said Marin. "We can shoot tigers." He bent down over the slain dog near which they had surprised the big cat.

The other dog came whining from the far corner of the field to which he had fled in terror. He was a courageous dog, but he could not face the great carnivore. He whimpered and licked the face of his mate.

The biologist picked up the mangled dog and headed toward the laboratory.

"You can't save her," said Hafner morosely. "She's dead."

"But the pups aren't. We'll need them. The rats won't disappear merely because tigers have showed up."

The head drooped limply over his arm and blood seeped into his clothing as Hafner followed him up the hill.

"We've been here three months," the exec said suddenly. "The dogs have been in the fields only two. And yet the tiger was mature. How do you account for something like that?"

Marin bent under the weight of the dog. Hafner never would understand his bewilderment. As a biologist, all his categories were upset. What did evolution explain? It was a history of organic life on a particular world. Beyond that world, it might not apply.

Even about himself there were many things man didn't know, dark patches in his knowledge which theory simply had to pass over. About other creatures, his ignorance was sometimes limitless.

Birth was simple; it occurred on countless planets. Meek grazing creatures, fierce carnivores—the most unlikely animals gave birth to their young. It happened all the time. And the young grew up, became mature, and mated.

He remembered that evening in the laboratory. It was accidental—what if he had been elsewhere and not witnessed it? They would not know what little they did.

He explained it carefully to Hafner. "If the survival factor is high and there's a great disparity in size, the young need not ever be young. They may be born as fully functioning adults!"

Although not at the rate it had initially set, the colony progressed. The fast crops were slowed down and a more diversified selection was planted. New buildings were constructed and the supplies that were stored in them were spread out thin, for easy inspection.

The pups survived and within a year shot up to maturity. After proper training, they were released to the fields, where they joined the older dogs. The battle against the rats went on; they were held in check, though the damage they caused was considerable.

The original animal, unchanged in form, developed an appetite for electrical insulation. There was no protection except to keep the power on at all times. Even then there were unwelcome interruptions until the short was located and the charred carcass was removed. Vehicles were kept tightly closed or parked only in vermin-proof buildings. While the plague didn't increase in numbers, it couldn't be eliminated, either.

There was a flurry of tigers, but they were larger animals and were promptly shot down.

They prowled at night, so the colonists were assigned to guard the settlement around the clock. Where lights failed to reach, the infrared scope did. As fast as they came, the tigers died. Except for the first one, not a single dog was lost.

The tigers changed, though not in form. Externally, they were all big and powerful killers. But as the slaughter went on, Marin noticed one astonishing fact—the internal organic structure became progressively more immature.

The last one that was brought to him for examination was the equivalent of a newly born cub. That tiny stomach was suited more for the digestion of milk than meat. How it had furnished energy to drive those great muscles was something of a miracle. But drive it had, for a murderous fifteen minutes before the animal was brought down. No lives were lost, though sick bay was kept busy for a while.

That was the last tiger they shot. After that, the attacks ceased.

The seasons passed and nothing new occurred. A spaceship civilization or even that fragment of it represented by the colony was too much for the creature, which Marin by now had come to think of as the "omnimal." It had evolved out of a cataclysmic past, but it could not meet the challenge of the harshest environment.

Or so it seemed.

Three months before the next colonists were due, a new animal was detected. Food was missing from the fields. It was not another tiger: they were carnivorous. Nor rats, for vines were stripped in a manner that no rodent could manage.

The food was not important. The colony had enough in storage. But if the new animal signaled another plague, it was necessary to know how to meet it. The sooner they knew what the animal was, the better defense they could set up against it.

Dogs were useless. The animal roamed the

field they were loose in, and they did not attack nor even seem to know it was there.

The colonists were called upon for guard duty again, but it evaded them. They patrolled for a week and they still did not catch sight of it.

Hafner called them in and rigged up an alarm system in the field most frequented by the animal. It detected that, too, and moved its sphere of operations to a field in which the alarm system had not been installed.

Hafner conferred with the engineer, who devised an alarm that would react to body radiation. It was buried in the original field and the old alarm was moved to another.

Two nights later, just before dawn, the alarm rang.

Marin met Hafner at the edge of the settlement. Both carried rifles. They walked; the noise of any vehicle was likely to frighten the animal. They circled around and approached the field from the rear. The men in the camp had been alerted. If they needed help, it was ready.

They crept silently through the underbrush. It was feeding in the field, not noisily, yet they could hear it. The dogs hadn't barked.

They inched nearer. The blue sun of Glade came up and shone full on their quarry. The gun dropped in Hafner's hand. He clenched his teeth and raised it again.

Marin put out a restraining arm. "Don't shoot," he whispered.

"I'm the exec here. I say it's dangerous."

"Dangerous," agreed Marin, still in a whisper. "That's why you can't shoot. It's more dangerous than you know."

Hafner hesitated and Marin went on. "The omnimal couldn't compete in the changed environment and so it evolved mice. We stopped the mice and it countered with rats. We turned back the rat and it provided the tiger.

"The tiger was easiest of all for us and so it was apparently stopped for a while. But it didn't really stop. Another animal was being formed, the one you see there. It took the omnimal two years to create it—how, I don't know. A million years were required to evolve it on Earth."

Hafner hadn't lowered the rifle and he showed no signs of doing so. He looked lovingly into the sights.

"Can't you see?" urged Marin. "We can't destroy the omnimal. It's on Earth now, and on the other planets, down in the storage areas of our big cities, masquerading as rats. And we've never been able to root out even our own terrestrial rats, so how can we exterminate the omnimal?"

"All the more reason to start now." Hafner's voice was flat.

Marin struck the rifle down. "Are their rats better than ours?" he asked wearily. "Will their pests win or ours be stronger? Or will the two make peace, unite and interbreed, make war on us? It's not impossible; the omnimal could do it if interbreeding had a high survival factor.

"Don't you still see? There is a progression. After the tiger, it bred this. If this evolution fails, if we shoot it down, what will it create next? This creature I think we can compete with. *It's the one after this that I do not want to face.*"

It heard them. It raised its head and looked around. Slowly it edged away and backed toward a nearby grove.

The biologist stood up and called softly. The creature scurried to the trees and stopped just inside the shadows among them.

The two men laid down their rifles. Together they approached the grove, hands spread open to show they carried no weapons.

It came out to meet them. Naked, it had had no time to learn about clothing. Neither did it have weapons. It plucked a large white flower from the tree and extended this mutely as a sign of peace.

"I wonder what it's like," said Marin. "It seems adult, but can it be, all the way through? What's inside that body?"

"I wonder what's in his head," Hafner said worriedly.

It looked very much like a man.

Aye, and Gomorrah

SAMUEL R. DELANY

Samuel Ray Delany Jr. (1942–), who writes as Samuel R. Delany, is a widely influential and often avant-garde US author and academic associated with the New Wave movement. Delany's best-known fiction is speculative fiction, but he also has written important essays on sexuality, including *Shorter Views: Queer Thoughts and the Politics of the Paraliterary* (2000). Delany was for a time married to the National Book Award–winning poet Marilyn Hacker, with whom he had a daughter. Hacker's poetry is important to Delany's early novels, especially *Babel-17* (winner of the 1966 Nebula Award).

Delany's other novels include *The Einstein Intersection* (winner of the 1967 Nebula Award), *Dhalgren*, and the swords-and-sorcery series *Return to Nevèrÿon*. *Dhalgren* elevated Delany beyond cult status, selling almost a million copies while polarizing the science fiction community; it was the quintessential New Wave text. More recently, Delany published the sprawling, ambitious novel *Through the Valley of the Nest of Spiders* (2012), which recounts the lives of a group of gay men. The novel ventures into the near future and reasserted Delany's career-long commitment to ambitious, adult literature in the vein of *Dhalgren*. In terms of nonfiction, Delany's book on science fiction *The Jewel-Hinged Jaw* (1977) remains influential on new generations of writers and readers.

But Delany's impact on the field has been felt in many ways. He won enough Nebulas that in 1986 Bantam could publish a 425-page book of Delany's work entitled *The Complete Nebula Award–Winning Fiction*. His story "Atlantis: Model 1924" has been included in every edition of *The Norton Anthology of African American Literature*. He wrote two issues of *Wonder Woman*, including the (in)famous "Women's Lib" issue, and wrote the graphic novel *Empire* (illustrated by Howard Chaykin) as well as a graphic memoir, *Bread and Wine* (illustrated by Mia Wolff). He taught at the influential Clarion workshop many times, and his students included Octavia E. Butler and Kim Stanley Robinson. Delany's story "The Tale of Plagues and Carnivals," written in 1984 and included in *Flight from Nevèrÿon* (1985), was, in Jeffrey Tucker's words, "the first novel-length work of fiction on AIDS from a major publisher in the United States."

Delany entered the Science Fiction and Fantasy Hall of Fame in 2002. From January 2001 until his recent retirement, Delany served as the director of the graduate creative writing program at Temple University. In 2010 he won the third J. Lloyd Eaton Lifetime Achievement Award in Science Fiction from the academic Eaton Science Fiction Conference at UCR Libraries. The Science Fiction and Fantasy Writers of America named him its thirtieth grand master in 2013.

"Aye, and Gomorrah" appeared in Harlan Ellison's famous *Dangerous Visions* anthology in 1967. In his introduction to the story, Ellison wrote that Delany's work approaches "shopworn clichés of speculative fiction with a bold and compelling ingenuity . . . He brings freshness to a field that occasionally slumps into the line of least resistance." "Aye, and Gomorrah" remains a truly groundbreaking story that demystifies the epic role of the astronaut in science fiction, creating a grittier and stranger reality, much as James Tiptree Jr. does for other science fiction tropes in her "And I Awoke and Found Me Here on the Cold Hill's Side."

AYE, AND GOMORRAH

Samuel R. Delany

And came down in Paris:

Where we raced along the Rue de Médicis with Bo and Lou and Muse inside the fence, Kelly and me outside, making faces through the bars, making noise, making the Luxembourg Gardens roar at two in the morning. Then climbed out, and down to the square in front of St. Sulpice, where Bo tried to knock me into the fountain.

At which point Kelly noticed what was going on around us, got an ash can cover, and ran into the pissoir, banging the walls. Five guys scooted out; even a big pissoir only holds four.

A very blond man put his hand on my arm and smiled. "Don't you think, Spacer, that you . . . people should leave?"

I looked at his hand on my blue uniform. *"Est-ce que tu es un frelk?"*

His eyebrows rose, then he shook his head. *"Une frelk,"* he corrected. "No. I am not. Sadly for me. You look as though you may once have been a man. But now . . ." He smiled. "You have nothing for me now. The police." He nodded across the street, where I noticed the gendarmerie for the first time. "They don't bother us. You are strangers, though. . . ."

But Muse was already yelling, "Hey, come on! Let's get out of here, huh?" And left.

And went up again.

And came down in Houston:

"Goddamn!" Muse said. "Gemini Flight Control—you mean this is where it all started? Let's get *out* of here, *please*!"

So took a bus out through Pasadena, then the monoline to Galveston, and were going to take it down the Gulf, but Lou found a couple with a pickup truck—

"Glad to give you a ride, Spacers. You peo-

ple up there on them planets and things, doing all that good work for the government."

—who were going south, them and the baby, so we rode in the back for two hundred and fifty miles of sun and wind.

"You think they're frelks?" Lou asked, elbowing me. "I bet they're frelks. They're just waiting for us to give 'em the come-on."

"Cut it out. They're a nice, stupid pair of country kids."

"That don't mean they ain't frelks!"

"You don't trust anybody, do you?"

"No."

And finally a bus again that rattled us through Brownsville and across the border into Matamoros, where we staggered down the steps into the dust and the scorched evening, with a lot of Mexicans and chickens and Texas Gulf shrimp fishermen—who smelled worst—and *we* shouted the loudest. Forty-three whores—I counted—had turned out for the shrimp fishermen, and by the time we had broken two of the windows in the bus station they were all laughing. The shrimp fishermen said they wouldn't buy us no food but would get us drunk if we wanted, 'cause that was the custom with shrimp fishermen. But we yelled, broke another window; then, while I was lying on my back on the telegraph office steps, singing, a woman with dark lips bent over and put her hand on my cheek. "You are very sweet." Her rough hair fell forward. "But the men, they are standing around and watching *you*. And that is taking up *time*. Sadly, their time is our money. Spacer, do you not think you . . . people should leave?"

I grabbed her wrist. *"¡Usted!"* I whispered. *"¿Usted es una frelka?"*

"Frelko en español." She smiled and patted the sunburst that hung from my belt buckle. "Sorry. But you have nothing that . . . would be useful to me. It is too bad, for you look like you were once a woman, no? And I like women, too. . . ."

I rolled off the porch.

"Is this a drag, or is this a drag!" Muse was shouting. "Come *on*! Let's *go*!"

We managed to get back to Houston before dawn, somehow.

And went up.

And came down in Istanbul:

That morning it rained in Istanbul.

At the commissary we drank our tea from pear-shaped glasses, looking out across the Bosphorus. The Princes' Islands lay like trash heaps before the prickly city.

"Who knows their way in this town?" Kelly asked.

"Aren't we going around together?" Muse demanded. "I thought we were going around together."

"They held up my check at the purser's office," Kelly explained. "I'm flat broke. I think the purser's got it in for me," and shrugged. "Don't want to, but I'm going to have to hunt up a rich frelk and come on friendly," went back to the tea; *then* noticed how heavy the silence had become. "Aw, come *on*, now! You gape at me like that, and I'll bust every bone in that carefully-conditioned-from-puberty body of yours. Hey you!" meaning me. "Don't give me that holier-than-thou gawk like you never went with no frelk!"

It was starting.

"I'm not gawking," I said, and got quietly mad.

The longing, the old longing.

Bo laughed to break tensions. "Say, last time I was in Istanbul—about a year before I joined up with this platoon—I remember we were coming out of Taksim Square down Istiqlal. Just past all the cheap movies we found a little passage lined with flowers. Ahead of us were two other spacers. It's a market in there, and

farther down they got fish, and then a court-yard with oranges and candy and sea urchins and cabbages. But flowers in front. Anyway, we noticed something funny about the spacers. It wasn't their uniforms: they were perfect. The haircuts: fine. It wasn't till we heard them talking—they were a man and woman dressed up like spacers, trying *to pick up frelks*! Imagine, queer for frelks!"

"Yeah," Lou said. "I seen that before. There were a lot of them in Rio."

"We beat hell out of them two," Bo concluded. "We got them in a side street and went to *town*!"

Kelly's tea glass clicked on the counter. "From Taksim down Istiqlal till you get to the flowers? Now why didn't you say that's where the frelks were, huh?" A smile on Kelly's face would have made that okay. There was no smile.

"Hell," Lou said, "nobody ever had to tell me where to look. I go out in the street and frelks smell me coming. I can spot 'em halfway along Piccadilly. Don't they have nothing but tea in this place? Where can you get a drink?"

Bo grinned. "Moslem country, remember? But down at the end of the Flower Passage there're a lot of little bars with green doors and marble counters where you can get a liter of beer for about fifteen cents in lira. And there're all these stands selling deep-fat-fried bugs and pig's-gut sandwiches—"

"You ever notice how frelks can put it away? I mean liquor, not . . . pig's guts."

And launched off into a lot of appeasing stories. We ended with the one about the frelk some spacer tried to roll who announced: "There are two things I go for. One is spacers; the other is a good fight. . . ."

But they only allay. They cure nothing. Even Muse knew we would spend the day apart, now.

The rain had stopped, so we took the ferry up the Golden Horn. Kelly straight off asked for Taksim Square and Istiqlal and was directed to a *dolmush*, which we discovered was a taxicab, only it just goes one place and picks up lots and lots of people on the way. And it's cheap.

Lou headed off over Atatürk Bridge to see the sights of New City. Bo decided to find out what the Dolma Boche really was; and when Muse discovered you could go to Asia for fifteen cents—one lira and fifty krush—well, Muse decided to go to Asia.

I turned through the confusion of traffic at the head of the bridge and up past the gray, dripping walls of Old City, beneath the trolley wires. There are times when yelling and helling won't fill the lack. There are times when you must walk by yourself because it hurts so much to be alone.

I walked up a lot of little streets with wet donkeys and wet camels and women in veils; and down a lot of big streets with buses and trash baskets and men in business suits.

Some people stare at spacers; some people don't. Some people stare or don't stare in a way a spacer gets to recognize within a week after coming out of training school at sixteen. I was walking in the park when I caught her watching. She saw me see and looked away.

I ambled down the wet asphalt. She was standing under the arch of a small, empty mosque shell. As I passed she walked out into the courtyard among the cannons.

"Excuse me."

I stopped.

"Do you know whether or not this is the shrine of St. Irene?" Her English was charmingly accented. "I've left my guidebook home."

"Sorry. I'm a tourist too."

"Oh." She smiled. "I am Greek. I thought you might be Turkish because you are so dark."

"American red Indian." I nodded. Her turn to curtsy.

"I see. I have just started at the university here in Istanbul. Your uniform, it tells me that you are"—and in the pause, all speculations resolved—"a spacer."

I was uncomfortable. "Yeah." I put my hands in my pockets, moved my feet around on the soles of my boots, licked my third-from-the-rear left molar—did all the things you do when you're uncomfortable. *You're so exciting when you look like that,* a frelk told me once. "Yeah, I am." I said it too sharply, too loudly, and she jumped a little.

So now she knew I knew she knew I knew, and I wondered how we would play out the Proust bit.

"I'm Turkish," she said. "I'm not Greek. I'm not just starting. I'm a graduate in art history here at the university. These little lies one makes for strangers to protect one's ego . . . why? Sometimes I think my ego is very small." That's one strategy.

"How far away do you live?" I asked. "And what's the going rate in Turkish lira?" That's another.

"I can't pay you." She pulled her raincoat around her hips. She was very pretty. "I would like to." She shrugged and smiled. "But I am . . . a poor student. Not a rich one. If you want to turn around and walk away, there will be no hard feelings. I shall only be sad."

I stayed on the path. I thought she'd suggest a price after a little while. She didn't.

And that's another. I was asking myself, *What do you want the damned money for anyway?* when a breeze upset water from one of the park's great cypresses.

"I think the whole business is unhappy." She wiped drops from her face. There had been a break in her voice and for a moment I looked too closely at the water streaks. "I think it's unhappy that they have to alter you to make you a spacer. If they hadn't, then *we* . . . If spacers had never been, then we could not be . . . the way we are. Did you start out male or female?"

Another shower. I was looking at the ground and droplets went down my collar.

"Male," I said. "It doesn't matter."

"How old are you? Twenty-three, twenty-four?"

"Twenty-three," I lied. It's reflex. I'm twenty-five, but the younger they think you are, the more they pay you. But I didn't *want* her damn money—

"I guessed right then." She nodded. "Most of us are experts on spacers. Do you find that? I suppose we have to be." She looked at me with wide black eyes. At the end of the stare, she blinked rapidly. "You would have been a fine man. But now you are a spacer, building water-conservation units on Mars, programming mining computers on Ganymede, servicing communication relay towers on the moon. The alteration . . ." Frelks are the only people I've ever heard say "the alteration" with so much fascination and regret. "You'd think they'd have found some other solution. They could have found another way than neutering you, turning you into creatures not even androgynous; things that are—"

I put my hand on her shoulder, and she stopped like I'd hit her. She looked to see if anyone was near. Lightly, so lightly then, she raised her hand to mine.

I pulled my hand away. "That are what?"

"They could have found another way." Both hands in her pockets now.

"They could have. Yes. Up beyond the ionosphere, baby, there's too much radiation for those precious gonads to work right anywhere you might want to do something that would keep you there over twenty-four hours, like the moon, or Mars, or the satellites of Jupiter—"

"They could have made protective shields. They could have done more research into biological adjustment—"

"Population Explosion time," I said. "No, they were hunting for any excuse to cut down kids back then—especially deformed ones."

"Ah, yes." She nodded. "We're still fighting our way up from the neo-puritan reaction to the sexual freedom of the twentieth century."

"It was a fine solution." I grinned and put my hand over my crotch. "I'm happy with it." And scratched. I've never known why that's so much more obscene when a spacer does it.

"Stop it," she snapped, moving away.

"What's the matter?"

"Stop it," she repeated. "Don't do that! You're a child."

"But they choose us from children whose sexual responses are hopelessly retarded at puberty."

"And your childish, violent substitutes for love? I suppose that's one of the things that's attractive. Yes, I know you're a child."

"Yeah? What about frelks?"

She thought awhile. "I think we are the sexually retarded ones they miss. Perhaps it was the right solution. You really don't regret you have no sex?"

"We've got you," I said.

"Yes." She looked down. I glanced to see the expression she was hiding. It was a smile. "You have your glorious, soaring life—and you have us." Her face came up. She glowed. "You spin in the sky, the world spins under you, and you step from land to land, while we . . ." She turned her head right, left, and her black hair curled and uncurled on the shoulder of her coat. "We have our dull, circled lives, bound in gravity, worshiping you!" She looked back at me. "Perverted, yes? In love with a bunch of corpses in free fall!" Suddenly she hunched her shoulders. "I don't like having a free-fall-sexual-displacement complex."

"That always sounded like too much to say."

She looked away. "I don't like being a frelk. Better?"

"I wouldn't like it either. Be something else."

"You don't choose your perversions. You have no perversions at all. You're free of the whole business. I love you for that, Spacer. My love starts with the fear of love. Isn't that beautiful? A pervert substitutes something unattainable for 'normal' love: the homosexual, a mirror, the fetishist, a shoe or a watch or a girdle. Those with free-fall-sexual-dis—"

"Frelks."

"Frelks substitute"—she looked at me sharply again—"loose, swinging meat."

"That doesn't offend me."

"I wanted it to."

"Why?"

"You don't have desires. You wouldn't understand."

"Go on."

"I want you because you can't want me. That's the pleasure. If someone really had a sexual reaction to . . . us, we'd be scared away. I wonder how many people there were before there were you, waiting for your creation. We're necrophiles. I'm sure grave robbing has fallen off since you started going up. But you couldn't understand. . . ." She paused. "If you did, then I wouldn't be scuffing leaves now and trying to think from whom I could borrow sixty lira." She stepped over the knuckles of a root that had cracked the pavement. "And that, incidentally, is the going rate in Istanbul."

I calculated. "Things still get cheaper as you go east."

"You know"—and she let her raincoat fall open—"you're different from the others. You at least *want* to know—"

I said, "If I spat on you for every time you'd said that to a spacer, you'd drown."

"Go back to the moon, loose meat." She closed her eyes. "Swing on up to Mars. There are satellites around Jupiter where you might do some good. Go up and come down in some other city."

"Where do you live?"

"You want to come with me?"

"Give me something," I said. "Give me something—it doesn't have to be worth sixty lira. Give me something that you like, anything of yours that means something to you."

"No!"

"Why not?"

"Because I—"

"—don't want to give up part of that ego. None of you frelks do!"

"You really don't understand that I just don't want to buy you?"

"You have nothing to buy me with."

"You are a child," she said. "I love you."

We reached the gate of the park. She stopped, and we stood time enough for a breeze to rise and die in the grass. "I . . . ," she offered tentatively, pointing without taking her hand from her coat pocket. "I live right down there."

"All right," I said. "Let's go."

A gas main had once exploded along this street, she explained to me, a gushing road of fire as far as the docks, overhot and overquick. It had been put out within minutes, no building had fallen, but the charred fascias glittered. "This is sort of an artist and student quarter." We crossed the cobbles. "Yuri Pasha, number fourteen. In case you're ever in Istanbul again." Her door was covered with black scales; the gutter was thick with garbage.

"A lot of artists and professional people are frelks," I said, trying to be inane.

"So are lots of other people." She walked inside and held the door. "We're just more flamboyant about it."

On the landing hung a portrait of Atatürk. Her room was on the second floor. "Just a moment while I get my key—"

Marsscapes! Moonscapes! On her easel was a six-foot canvas showing the sunrise flaring on a crater's rim! There were copies of the original Observer pictures of the moon pinned to the wall, and pictures of every smooth-faced general in the International Spacer Corps.

On one corner of her desk was a pile of those photo magazines about spacers that you can find in most kiosks all over the world: I've seriously heard people say they were printed for adventurous-minded high school children. They've never seen the Danish ones. She had a few of those too. There was a shelf of art books, art history texts. Above them were six feet of cheap paper-covered space operas: *Sin on Space Station #12*, *Rocket Rake*, *Savage Orbit*.

"Arrack?" she asked. "Ouzo, or Pernod? You've got your choice. But I may pour them all from the same bottle." She set out glasses on the desk, then opened a waist-high cabinet that turned out to be a refrigerator. She stood up with a tray of lovelies: fruit puddings, Turkish delight, braised meats.

"What's this?"

"Dolmades. Grape leaves filled with rice and pignolis."

"Say it again?"

"Dolmades. Comes from the same Turkish word as 'dolmush.' They both mean 'stuffed.'" She put the tray beside the glasses. "Sit down."

I sat on the studio-couch-that-becomes-bed. Under the brocade I felt the deep, fluid resilience of a glycogel mattress. They've got the idea that it approximates the feeling of free fall.

"Comfortable? Would you excuse me for a moment? I have some friends down the hall. I want to see them for a moment." She winked. "They like spacers."

"Are you going to take up a collection for me?" I asked. "Or do you want them to line up outside the door and wait their turn?"

She sucked a breath. "Actually I was going to suggest both." Suddenly she shook her head. "Oh, what do you want!"

"What will you give me? I want something," I said. "That's why I came. I'm lonely. Maybe I want to find out how far it goes. I don't know yet."

"It goes as far as you will. Me? I study, I read, paint, talk with my friends"—she came over to the bed, by my boots sat down on the floor—"go to the theater, look at spacers who pass me on the street, till one looks back; I am lonely too." She put her head on my knee. "I want something. But"—and after a minute neither of us had moved—"you are not the one who will give it to me."

"You're not going to pay me for it," I countered. "You're not, are you?"

On my knee her head shook. After a while she said, all breath and no voice, "Don't you think you . . . should leave?"

"Okay," I said, and stood up.

She sat back on the hem of her coat. She hadn't taken it off yet.

I went to the door.

"Incidentally." She folded her hands in her lap. "There is a place in New City you might find what you're looking for, called the Flower Passage—"

I turned toward her, angry. "The frelk hangout? Look, I don't *need* money! I said *anything* would do! I don't want—"

She had begun to shake her head, laughing quietly. Now she laid her cheek on the wrinkled place where I had sat. "Do you persist in misunderstanding? It is a *spacer* hangout. When you leave, I am going to visit my friends and talk about . . . ah, yes, the beautiful one that got away. I thought you might find . . . perhaps someone you know."

With anger, it ended.

"Oh," I said. "Oh, it's a spacer hangout. Yeah. Well, thanks."

And went out.

And found the Flower Passage, and Kelly and Lou and Bo and Muse. Kelly was buying beer so we all got drunk, and ate fried fish and fried clams and fried sausage, and Kelly was waving the money around, saying, "You should have seen him! The changes I put that frelk through, you should have *seen* him! Eighty lira is the going rate here, and he gave me a hundred and fifty!" and drank more beer.

And went up.

The Hall of Machines

LANGDON JONES

Langdon Jones (1942–) is a British writer, editor, and musician who was associated with the influential magazine *New Worlds* during its New Wave period both as a contributor—beginning with the story "Storm Water Tunnel" in 1964—and in various editorial capacities. His most memorable work, most of it experimental in form and characterized by an architectural narrative style, was assembled as *The Eye of the Lens* (1972). He no longer writes fiction but continues to be politically involved in his local community and enjoys classical music, both as a musician and composer/arranger.

Jones's wide taste as an editor, not dissimilar to his work as a writer, was on display in *The New SF: An Original Anthology of Modern Speculative Fiction* (1969), one of the most avant-garde collections during a period when experimentation was more commercially acceptable than it is today. He also collaborated with Michael Moorcock in assembling *The Nature of the Catastrophe* (1971), which contained a number of Jerry Cornelius stories from *New Worlds* written by Moorcock and others. The first published version of Mervyn Peake's *Titus Alone* (1959) had been heavily edited because of Peake's degenerative illness, and Jones was responsible for the reconstruction work resulting in the posthumous 1970 publication of the definitive version of the book.

"The Hall of Machines" was first published in *New Worlds* 180 (1968) and later appeared in *The Eye of the Lens* as part of the titular triptych. In the introduction to that collection, Jones writes that the set of three stories "caused [me] more difficulty than anything [I] had written before" and took fifteen months to complete. "This set was the first work of mine to abandon the conventional narrative and structure, and working on it was like trying to force a path through a jungle that was almost impenetrable . . . The initial idea came when I was sitting on a District Line underground train on its way to Ealing Broadway . . . during the part of the journey that was, in fact, above ground, the train passed something I had never noticed before—a little brick building with a notice on its door which said: INTERLOCKING MACHINE ROOM. It seems unlikely that the mental picture this evoked corresponds in any way to the reality."

"The Hall of Machines" (1968) finds parallels between common human acts and processes and the mysterious machines of the title. It is one of those rare works that is formally experimental and, also, touches in an almost indefinable way on strong emotions. Although Jones published only about a dozen short stories, his work made an impact on, and was made possible by, the New Wave movement.

THE HALL OF MACHINES

Langdon Jones

Many great thinkers have attempted to analyze the nature of the hall. However, all their different approaches have been characterized by a lack of agreement and often blatant contradiction of fact. The appearance of the hall is generally well-known, but as soon as we try to unearth specific detail we realize that all is conjecture.

The hall is vast. We would expect the descriptions of its contents to vary—one person could not be expected to cover the whole area of its interior. However, there has been a great deal of superstitious rumor concerning its contents, and it is often difficult to separate the true from the wholly fallacious.

There has been much conjecture concerning the size of the hall, but no results have actually been confirmed by any kind of measurement. It has been postulated by at least one writer that the hall is in fact infinite in extent. Others, no doubt influenced by exaggerated reports, have maintained that the hall covers a variable area, its size altering by a factor of at least fifty. Other evidence, however, suggests that both of these ideas bear, in all probability, little relationship to the facts.

During the last few years I have found it a rewarding task to research all the material I could find that related in any way to the hall. The task has been difficult, but illuminating. I have now in my files a vast amount of information in the form of books, articles, newspaper cuttings, recorded tapes, and movie film as well as a large number of transcribed interviews, on a subject which I have found to become daily more fascinating. My research has become, to a degree, obsessional. I now find that my normal routine has been disturbed to quite a large extent over the last three years. I have devoted a complete room

to this work, my ultimate intention being to shape the material into a comprehensive book. All over the wall are pinned the relevant newspaper cuttings, their arrangement depending on whichever aspect of the hall I am currently researching; set in the middle of the room is my movie projector (frequently I watch the five hours of film I have accumulated at one sitting), and beside it is the tape recorder. On tape I have, apart from interviews and commentaries, at least an hour of the recorded sounds of some of the machines actually in operation. I have taken these sounds down, as accurately as possible, into musical notation. I have permutated the resultant patterns of notes and have found interesting relationships between the basic shapes, but, as yet, nothing more concrete.

I now spend a large proportion of my day in carrying out this research. I sit for hours, cutting out newspaper articles or developing film in the darkroom I have constructed. And so, with scissors, photographic chemicals, music paper, paste, tape recorder, and projector, I have built up a picture that is far from complete, but which is remarkable in its specific detail.

I now present some of the more striking of the descriptions I have unearthed. They are not delivered in a planned order, but have been assembled to give, rather than a dry academic account, a series of interesting impressions. I believe that one of the most fascinating aspects of the hall is in the diverse impressions it creates within the minds of the observers.

When my book is complete (which will not be for some years—it will run to at least five large volumes) I shall have sufficient confidence in the correctness of my results, and also the scope, to *present them in detail. Until then, these extracts are intended only to communicate the atmosphere of the hall as it appeared to some people.*

THE WATER MACHINE

The troughs and gulleys of the Water Machine extend over a very large area of this section of the hall, and although it is enclosed by false "walls" of board, it still gives a sprawling impression. All about are convex metal surfaces; the floor is intersected by runnels and gulleys. The Water Machine is constructed primarily of cast iron, but certain of its parts are made of a lighter metal; probably an alloy, such as aluminum. The machine consists of a complexity of large components which stretch probably twenty feet in height, and the whole mass is supported by a surprisingly small number of slim metal struts.

Water is being pumped in from a large pipe at the very top of the machine. It is conducted by a series of ingenious mechanical movements through a series of gulleys and out of this part of the hall. I thought it likely that the water was moving in a large enclosed cycle, and dropped into a nearby channel a small piece of white paper. As I suspected, within about three minutes, the paper came floating past my feet again.

The noise of the water is almost deafening at times.

Constantly there is the hissing of the jet at the top of the machine and a rushing of the liquid as it bubbles its way through its course; also there is the loud creaking of the metal parts as they operate. Every few seconds there is an enormous crash as a metal part is activated, and the water momentarily redoubles its volume.

Water drips constantly from the supporting members, gathers on the floor, and runs down the slope toward the many drains: concrete channels sweep in graceful lines about my feet: cast-iron conduits curve in black roundness, globules of condensation running along their undersides.

Situated at the top of the machine is the vast silver belly of the top water container, spatulate and curved, like a vast silver spoon. The lead-in pipe, about six inches in diameter, is pointing into this tank, and a great jet of water, like a column of glass, is sluicing into its interior.

After a while, the container begins to groan, loudly. Suddenly the critical balance is attained. The groaning reaches a climax under the enormous weight of water, and the tank begins to shudder under a volume of liquid that it is incapable of supporting. Overspill slops to the floor and runs down to the square drains. Slowly, inch by inch, the tank begins to tip its vast bulk. Water spills over its thick pouring lip and falls in a glistening ribbon into a reservoir a couple of yards below. The tank begins to accelerate its rate of movement, and more water gushes down. Faster moves the container, and then, with a crash, it inverts itself. A solid mass of water falls into the reservoir, and the ground shudders with the impact. The container, meanwhile, is pulled back to a creaking vertical by a counterweight.

Water leaks from the reservoir, jetting out with great force from a circle of six holes at its convex base. These six separate streams are all conducted by diverse methods to the ground. One of the streams gushes into a smaller version of the water-barrel. Another enters one of the hinged containers set between the double rim of a large wheel, its weight causing the wheel to rotate slowly; after a quarter-revolution the container will snag on a projection and tip up, letting the water escape into one of the channels. Another stream strikes a sprung flange which bounces constantly in and out of the flow, the other end of the flange operating a mechanism like the escapement of a clock.

All the streams eventually reach the dark channels of wet concrete set in the floor, and are then conducted away from sight through holes set in the surrounding "walls."

Behind the wall can be heard the sound of great pumps.

Up above, I know, a fountain is playing.

MACHINES OF MOVEMENT

I was passing through a rather enclosed part of the hall, its spaciousness not apparent owing to the large bulk of the partitions enclosing various machines, when I passed a small wooden doorway set into one of the partitions. On the door was a plaque, printed black on white. It said:

INTERLOCKING MACHINE ROOM

On entering the room I found it to be full of giant metal crabs.

Great struts of thin metal rod crisscross from ceiling to floor, making it impossible to see very far into the room. The very air shudders with the vibration of these machines. Although the constructions vary considerably, one from the other, a large number of them have the same basic shape. Their nucleus is a mass of rods and other interlocking members, and they stand about ten feet high. The arrangement of these rods is infinitely complex. At their apex they are thickly composed, and are surrounded by other parts which join them and permit their motion. They branch out, and at floor level each machine covers a considerable area.

All of the legs of these machines are connected by free-moving joints to the legs of the other units, and a movement of one causes an adjustment to the position of the other. The whole room is in motion, and the machines twitch each other with an action that appears almost lascivious in nature.

A rod near me is moved by the action of a neighbor's leg. This movement is communicated at the top of the unit to another of the legs, and it, in turn, imparts motion to a machine further away. As these machines work, a constant metallic clattering fills the air, as if the room is filled with typewriters.

The machines are slick and oiled; their movement is smooth, but gives an impression of great nervousness. All over this chamber are various other parts, all of which seem affected in some way by the movement of the rods. On the wall, near me, is fixed a plaque with a jointed arm extending from it. Taut wires radiate from either extremity into the skeletal gray. One end is angled up, the other down. As the wire of the higher end is pulled by some motion in the mass of interlocking parts, the arm reverses its position jerkily.

Perhaps, a million years ago, these machines were constructed in a delicate static balance, a frozen wave; and with the locking of the final link in the circuit, the fixing of the last jointed leg against leg, the balance was tripped. A motion would have run its path, twisting and turning about the machines, splitting itself, dividing again, until today this movement still ran about the constructions, diffused and unpredictable. A million strands of current, still splitting. And perhaps the machines had been so carefully designed that in another million years all the currents would begin to amalgamate, becoming less and less complex, until they finally became two, meeting in opposition and deadlock, all movement ceasing.

The mind drowns among the interlocking machines. Perhaps the reason is in the similarity of this abstract maze to that pattern formed by the neural current. Perhaps these patterns of motion parallel too closely the patterns of electricity that we call personality, and the one is disturbed by the other. Conversely, perhaps the very existence of a human mind in the room causes little eddies and whirls in the motion of the machines.

I was unable to stay in the interlocking machine room for more than a minute or two before the psychological effects became more than I could bear.

THE CLOCK

A large number of the machines in the hall are partitioned off by boards, so that one often feels that one is walking in a constricted space, and loses completely the feeling of immensity that one often experiences in the hall. It was in such a place that I found, set against one "wall," the mechanism of an enormous clock. It was all of shining brass, and it stood no less than ten feet high. It was facing the wall, the dial and hands (if, in fact, any such existed) being completely invisible. The clock was triangular in shape, and was supported by a framework of sturdy brass, front and back, that curved down to provide four feet. There was no plate at the back of the clock, its arbors being seated in strips of brass that curved in beautiful shapes from the main framework.

Despite the largeness of the clock, it was built to delicate proportions. The wheels were all narrow-rimmed, and the pallets that engaged the escape wheel were long and curved, like the fingernails of a woman. It was as if the mechanism of an ordinary domestic clock had been magnified to a great degree; there was none of the solidity and cumbersomeness of the turret clock here. I discovered to my surprise that this clock was powered, as most domestic clocks, by a spring. However, this spring was immense, and must have exerted a tremendous pressure to operate the mechanism.

Although the whole movement was surmounted by the escape wheel and anchor, which perched on the apex of the triangle, the pendulum was disproportionately short, stretching down little more than six feet. The slow tick of this enormous clock was lacking in the lower partials, and as a consequence was not disturbing.

As the clock was so large, motion could be seen among the wheels, which moved, each to a varying degree, with each tick of the clock. This was a fascinating sight, and I stayed watching the clock for a considerable period of time.

I wish that I could have seen the clock illuminated by strong morning sunlight from a window.

MACHINES OF DEATH—1

There is darkness in this part of the hall. Stray light illuminates black, pitted metal. I can see little of the machine of death; it is to my right, and is a bleak high wall of metal. The end of a thick chain extrudes here, turns, and plunges back into the metal wall. The chain is a foot wide and four inches thick. The only other feature of this machine is a waste pipe which is sticking out from the wall. Underneath this pipe is a channel set into the floor, which conducts the waste to a nearby drain. The all-pervasive stink of this drain makes breathing difficult. The pipe is pouring blood into the channel.

MACHINES OF DEATH—2

This machine is very large, sprawling, and complicated. It appears to be completely functionless. It is possible that it was constructed to be entirely symbolic in nature, or alternatively that the things—creatures—upon which it operated are here no longer.

It consists of a vast network of girders, all of which are vibrating with a strange jogging motion. The only parts of the machine not affected by this movement are the two great supports at either end. The supports are each a framework of girders, and they contain various driving chains and gearing devices. At the top of each of these frames is a long jointed arm, of tremendous proportion. These arms also carry chains and gears. At the end of each arm is an enormous blade, made of a silver metal that catches the small amount of light. The blades have complete mobility, and appear to be fixed on the arms by some kind of ball joint.

The motion of the arms and the blades is difficult to observe in detail and even more difficult to describe. Analyzing the action in words tends to give an impression of slowness, when in fact, considering the bulk of the parts, it is very swift indeed.

The arms rest close to their supports, their

joints extending downward like elbows, the blades upright. Keeping the blades in the same position, they move together across the thirty-yard space. When they are only about a yard apart, the arms are almost fully extended, and the motion stops for an instant. Then abruptly the blades begin to move independently. They execute, in the space of only a few seconds, a complicated system of movements—thrusts, parries, arabesques—the motion of each blade being the mirror of the other. Then again comes the pause, and the arms bend again, carrying the blades back to the supports.

The action of these blades certainly suggests physical mutilation, and I found, as I watched, that I was wondering whether in fact the machine was still complete. Was there once a feeding mechanism that carried the bodies over to the knives to be sculptured within a few seconds to a raw, twitching mass?

Despite the unpleasant feelings that the machine arouses, I found it a fascinating experience to watch the blades, and also the complex system of vibrating girders beneath them. It is strange to see such large objects in such rapid motion; the throbbing of the floor testified to the weight of the mechanism, which must have been in the hundreds of tons.

On the occasion that I observed the machine, there were two other people there as well; a man and a woman. At first I thought that they were part of the machine, but my attention was caught by the fact that their own vibrating motion was slightly lagging behind that of the machine as their soft bodies absorbed their impetus.

They were both naked, and they were on one of the girders directly below the high knives. The man was lying on his back, stretched along the girder, and the woman was squatting astride his hips. The jogging of the girder was throwing their bodies up and down in a mechanical travesty of copulation. The man was grasping the woman's thighs tightly, and her face, turned toward me, with her bottom lip between her teeth, was florid and beaded with sweat. I could see her nostrils contracting with each gasped breath she took.

A drop of oil fell from the knives as they clashed above, and dropped unnoticed onto her shoulder. As it ran down the pale flesh of her arm, it looked like a single drop of ancient blood.

MACHINES OF DEATH—3[*]

The machine sits in distance unheard. I walk on dry sin, on the shit of us all, a man by my side who points out all his bones. The well has now dried and all that remains is a glowing, radioactive silt. The universe is shaped like a whirlpool, and the vortex is here. Here is the end of all time, the end of all space. The ultimate nil. I have eaten my fill; here is my place; there is no single way left to climb, and the rest is just fear. This cul-de-sac is arid and death-cool. It is bleakness, a focus-point built by man and his pains. The door must be tried; I pull and it groans, and opens up wide. The chamber is small, but light is let in to show me a word—

Auschwitz!

THE MOTHER

This machine is standing in isolation; it is surrounded by space on all sides. It is extremely large, standing almost a hundred feet high, and it is shaped like an elongated onion, tapering at the top to a high spire. From one side of the machine, from about ten feet up, a flaccid rubbery tube hangs down and outward to ground level.

The onion-belly of the Mother is completely featureless, and light catches its curves; the tube is of a dull red shade.

---

[*] This machine consists of a flat surface of metal with a circular metal door which leads to a small chamber, called the "compressor," or "pot." Apart from this the wall is featureless except for a switch by the side of the door. This area seems to be the most dismal place in the entire hall.

There are sounds coming from inside the metal body, soft but constant. But then, abruptly, they stop, and all is silent.

At the top of the tube, a bulge becomes apparent, swelling outward all the time. Slowly, this bulge begins to travel inside the tube, away from the machine and down to the ground. While all this is going on, one obtains an impression of supreme effort, and, strangely, pain. Perhaps it is because the whole process is so slow. The object creeping down the tube will eventually reach the end and emerge into the light; one realizes this, and feels an almost claustrophobic impatience with the slowness of the event. There is a feeling too of compression and relaxation, and one finds one's own muscles clenching in time to the imagined contractions.

Eventually the bulge reaches the end of the tube at ground level. This is where the real struggle begins. One becomes aware that the end of the tube is beginning to dilate, slowly and rhythmically. The belly of the machine is as smooth and unevocative of any emotion as ever, but it is impossible for the observer not to feel that agonies are now being endured. One realizes that the process is completely irreversible; that there is no way of forcing the bulge back up the tube and inside the metal shell again.

Wider and wider grows the aperture at the end of the tube, affording one an occasional glimpse of shiny moisture within. A glint of metal is now and then apparent.

The tube dilates to its fullest extent, and a metal form is suddenly revealed, covered in dripping brown fluid. The rubber slides over its surface, releasing it more and more by the second. Abruptly it bursts free in a wash of amniotic oil.

All is still.

The oil begins to drain away, and the new machine stands there motionlessly as the liquid drains from its surfaces. It is a small mechanism on caterpillar tracks, with various appendages at its front end which seem to be designed for working metal, or stone.

With a whirr, it jerks into action, and it moves softly away from the great Mother. There is a click from the parent machine, and the noises inside begin again.

I have watched this mechanism for long periods, and it appears to create only two kinds of machine. They are both on the same basic design, but one appears to be made for erection, the other for demolition.

The Mother has probably been working thus for hundreds of years.

ELECTRONICS

Electric machines stare at me with warm green eyes. I see nothing but bright plastic surfaces, inset with pieces of glass. These are still machines, active but unmoving, and in my ears is the faint hum of their life. The only movement here which indicates that the machines are in operation is the kicking of meters and the occasional jog of an empty tape spool.

Their function is not apparent; they work here at nameless tasks, performing them all with electronic precision and smoothness.

There are wires all over the room, and their bright, primary colors contrast strikingly with the overall pastel tones of the plastic bodies.

In a small chamber to the rear of the room of electric machines, there are some more of a different kind. The door to this small room is of wood, with a square glass set into it. The room appears to have remained undisturbed for many years.

They line three walls of the chamber, and are covered with switches and meters. They hum in strange configurations of sound, and appear to be making electric music together.

DEATH OF MACHINES—1

In this part of the hall, all is still. Spiked mounds of time rise round me, their hulks encrusted with brown decay. The floor is totally covered by a soft carpet of rust, and its acrid odor stings the nostrils. A piece detaches itself from one of the tall machines and drifts to the floor, a flake of time. Many such flakes have fallen here in this part of the hall.

Time burns fire in my eyes, and I turn my head, looking for escape. But everywhere I see seconds and hours frozen into these red shapes. Here is a wheel, its rim completely eaten through; there a piston, its moveable parts now fixed in a mechanical rigor mortis. A reel of wire has been thrown into a corner, ages in the past, and all that remain are its circular traces in the dust.

My feet have left prints in the rust-carpet.

DEATH OF MACHINES—2

I had come into the hall with my girl, and we had spent a long time wandering about, hand in hand, when we suddenly came on the remains of a machine.

It stood about six feet in height, and I could see that at one time it had been of great complexity. For some reason my girl was not very interested, and went off to see something else, but I found that this particular machine made me feel very sad. It appeared to be entirely composed of needles of metal, arranged in a thick pattern. The largest of these needles was about three inches long, and there appeared to be no way for the machine to hold together. My guess is that when it was made, the needles were fitted in such a way that the whole thing struck an internal balance. The machine was now little more than a gossamer web of rust; it must have had tremendous stability to have remained standing for such a long time.

It was fascinating to look closely at its construction, to see the red lines fitting together so densely. It was like looking into a labyrinth; a system of blood-red caves. With every movement of my head a whole new landscape was presented to me. I called my girl over, and we stood hand in hand, looking at the dead machine.

I think that it must have been our body heat, for neither of us made an excessive movement, but at that moment the entire construction creaked, and sank a few inches. Then there was a sigh, and the whole thing dissolved into dust about our feet.

Both of us felt very subdued when we left the hall.

I hope that the above information has enabled my readers to gain an impression of this very exciting hall. There is little that I can add, except the following point.

You will remember from one of the accounts I have printed here; the one giving details of the creation of new machines, the following passages: "It is a small mechanism on caterpillar tracks, with various appendages at its front end which seem to be designed for working metal, or stone. . . . [I]t appears to create only two kinds of machine . . . one appears to be made for erection, the other for demolition." These two passages, together with some other material that I have not published here, suggest an interesting point.

I believe that the machines mentioned are the same as those described in another account, in which the writer stood by one of the outer walls of the hall. He watched one set of machines building a wall about six inches further out than the old one, which was being torn down by the other mechanisms. This seems to be a process which is going on all the time, all over the hall; a new wall is built, slightly further out, and this in its turn will be demolished as another is put up.

I believe that the hall has been, from the time of its creation, and always will be, increasing in size!

However, only more research will be able to establish this radical idea as an incontrovertible fact.

Soft Clocks

YOSHIO ARAMAKI

Translated by Kazuko Behrens and stylized by Lewis Shiner

Yoshio Aramaki (1933–) is a Japanese writer of science fiction who trained as an architect and owns both an art gallery and a construction company in Sapporo. Aramaki made his professional writing debut with the highly speculative fiction "Oinaru shogo" ("The Great Noon") and his heavily theoretical science fiction manifesto "Jutsu no shosetsu-ron" ("Theory on the Fiction of Kunst"), an attempt to read Heinlein in the context of Kant, both published in *Hayakawa's Science Fiction Magazine* in 1970. One of his early novellas, "Shirakabe no moji wa yuhi ni haeru" ("The Writing on the White Wall Shines in the Setting Sun"), won the 1972 Seiun Award, the Japanese equivalent of the Hugo Award. The publication of his first speculative meta-novel, *Shirokihi tabidateba fushi* (*Setting Out on a White Day Leads to Immortality*), was deeply influenced by the Marquis de Sade and selected as runner-up for the Izumi Kyōka Prize for Literature, which was established in 1973 to commemorate the centenary of the birth of Kyōka Izumi, master of Japanese Gothic romance. Some of Aramaki's shorter fiction has appeared in English in *Interzone* and the Lewis Shiner–edited anti-war anthology *When the Music's Over* (1991).

How did Aramaki become a science fiction writer? The noted critic Takayuki Tatsumi, an expert on Aramaki, writes in his introduction to the author's *Collected Works* that in 1965, "Aramaki's deep interest in science fiction led him to join the Hokkaido SF Club, in whose fanzine *CORE* (1965–67) Aramaki published a diversity of Existentialist and Psycho-Analytical essays on science fiction writers such as Arthur C. Clarke, Philip K. Dick, Alfred Bester, Taku Mayumura, and Yasutaka Tsutsui, the pioneer of Japanese metafiction who first discovered Aramaki's literary and critical genius."

Conflict occurred when Aramaki, as Tatsumi puts it, "engaged in a heated debate in the fanzine *Uchujin* (*Cosmic Dust*) between 1969 and 1970 with the young talent Koichi Yamano, the writer-editor of the first commercial speculative fiction quarterly *NW-SF* (1970–82), who actually shared much of the same radical New Wave–oriented perspective as Aramaki, but who could not help but attack Japanese science fiction writers as imitators of their Anglo-American colleagues in his famous essay 'Japanese SF: Its Originality and Possibility' originally published in 1969."

Aramaki in 1990 launched a much more mainstream entertainment series of "virtual reality war novels," with Admiral Isoroku Yamamoto, a real-life naval commander during World War II, as a central character reincarnated in alternate history. After initial low sales, the advent of the Gulf War in 1991 soon helped the series attract a much wider audience, leading Aramaki to start a different series called *Asahi no kantai* (*The Fleet of the Rising Sun*); the two series, totaling some twenty-five volumes, have sold more than five million copies.

"Soft Clocks" appeared in English in 1989 in *Interzone* and was later reprinted in a special issue of *The Review of Contemporary Fiction* (2002) entitled "New Japanese Fiction." The first Japanese publication, however, was in 1968, during the apex of the New Wave movement in the US and UK. The story exists in loose dialogue with Aramaki's René Magritte–influenced story, "Toropikaru" (subsequently published in 1991 in English as "Tropical" in *Strange Plasma* 4), and what Tatsumi calls Aramaki's "magnum opus," the 1978 Hieronymus Bosch–inspired novel *Shinseidai* (*Sanctozoic Era*).

Influenced by the work of Salvador Dalí and Puccini's "proto-Orientalist" opera *Madame Butterfly*, "Soft Clocks" is a transgressive, often disturbing speculative riff reminiscent of Breton-style surrealism and Decadent-era literature. It presents a much different take on expeditions to Mars than other stories in this anthology.

SOFT CLOCKS

Yoshio Aramaki

Translated by Kazuko Behrens and stylized by Lewis Shiner

When I look at the stars in the sky, they appear so small.
Either I am growing larger or the universe is shrinking—or both.
—SALVADOR DALÍ

It was noon on Mars. The party was already in full swing under blinding equatorial sunshine. The theme was "Blackout in Daylight." Our host was DALI, surrealist, paranoiac-critic, millionaire, technophobe. His estate covered an area of the Lunae Planum about the size of Texas.

Gilbert, the producer of the affair, had left orders that all guests were to wear costumes taken from the paintings of the original Salvador Dalí. Even I could not get out of it. Nearly naked receptionists, their faces made up into masks, took away the business suit I'd worn from Earth and dressed me in a plastic costume with golden wings, taken from *View of Port Lligat with Guardian Angels and Fishermen.*

I wandered out into the grounds, dazzled by the landscape. A pond of mercury and mirrors flowed at unsettling angles. A dimensionless black mountain reflected the Spanish seaside village, Port Lligat, where Dalí had spent so many years. Erotically shaped pavilions stretched to impossible horizons.

"This is indeed surreal, is it not?" said a man's voice behind me. I turned around. The man's hair stood straight up, the Dalist trademark. His mustache was waxed and curled at the ends. He held a glass of Martian blue mescal, clearly not his first. "Oh, excuse me. What are you supposed to be? A donkey?"

"I'm sorry?" I said.

The man's upper body weaved from side to side, though his feet were planted solidly in

the red sand. "No, wait, I see it now, you're a tiger. . . ."

Not just the mescal, I thought. The hallucinations were typical of Martian Disease, a form of low-grade encephalitis. According to the literature, the victim's interpretations of an object shifted without the perception itself changing. The disease was responsible for an abnormally high level of neuronal activity and some even claimed it gave the victims telekinetic powers. The last was of course not verified.

I couldn't imagine what I must have looked like to him. He seemed to find it amusing enough.

"I'm from Tokyo," I said. "I am—or was—Vivi's analyst. You sent me a letter—"

"Ah, yes, doctor. Welcome. I'm the famous DALI OF MARS. How are you enjoying the party? Vivi should be with us soon."

"Good, that's good," I said. I'd known that coming here would mean seeing Vivi again. Now I found myself afraid of the idea.

"Gilbert should be here somewhere. He produced all this. You'll want to meet him."

"I don't remember him being on the list," I said. "Is he one of the . . . uh, candidates?"

"Ah, the list. So you're wanting to start work already, eh?" DALI was distracted by a young woman in a death's head mask and a tight suit cut away to reveal her breasts and buttocks. His eyes bulged with a look of insatiable greed.

"Yes," I said. "I'd like to get started as soon as possible. It would be much easier if I could get back my normal clothes. . . ."

"Yes, of course," DALI said. "The 'candidates,' as you put it, should be in the bar." He pointed toward a building shaped like a snail's shell lying on its side.

"Thank you," I said, but DALI was already walking toward the woman with the death's head.

Dressed like a normal person again, I made my way to the bar. Chairs were set up along the wide spiraling aisle, and leather bags full of mescal hung from the curved ceiling. Several of the guests were already drunk. As DALI would have put it, they looked like "snail meat marinated in good champagne."

I found a seat in a bulge of the wall, close enough to hear the conversation. As an outsider, it sounded to me like a herd of geese being stampeded by a pig. Highly symbolic words and phrases shot out of their mouths, one after another. There was a certain harmony to it, but it didn't last. The loudest of the voices belonged to Pinkerton, the pig among the geese.

His name and that of Professor Isherwood, the rheologist, were the first two on DALI's list.

"No, no, no," he shouted. He was dressed as the artist's self-portrait, in smock and beret. "You're all wrong. The hatred of machines goes all the way back to my ancestor Salvador Dalí. His is the true paranoiac-critical view of technology. It's my perfect understanding of this that Vivi so admires. That's why the odds all show that I'm going to be picked for her husband. The odds are ninety-two point four percent, in fact, calculated objectively."

"Fool," said Isherwood. He sat across the table from Pinkerton, wearing a corduroy jacket over a sweater. "Loudmouthed fool."

"What?" Pinkerton came out of his chair, leaning across the table with both hands spread wide. "You're nothing but a monkey, a simpering toady to technology. You haven't got a prayer. Our engagement will be announced any day. Vivi's husband will be Pinkerton, genius painter of Mars, new incarnation of the first, the original, Salvador Dalí!"

Pinkerton settled back in his chair, checking his hair in a hand mirror. Isherwood stared at him, his hands shaking. There was a glass of mescal in one of them and it shattered with a transparent sound. Blood streamed onto the tablecloth.

"Ah," Pinkerton said. "This is true beauty. I think I'll show this tablecloth in my next exhibition."

The other two at the table, Boccaccio the barber and Martin the movie actor, laughed without much conviction. Pinkerton seemed serious. "I think I'll call it *Jealous Donkey, with His Tail Caught in His Horseshoe, Insults an Angel*."

"This is ludicrous," Isherwood said. He got up, knocking his chair over, and started out.

"Sir?" I said. I offered him my handkerchief.

"Thank you," he said. He wrapped the handkerchief over his cut and glanced back at Pinkerton. "The man is insane."

"Martian sickness," I said. "Maybe he's not in control of himself. Will you sit down?"

Isherwood nodded and sat across from me. "I've never seen you before," he said. "Are you from Earth?" When I nodded, he said, "You talk like a psychiatrist."

"A marriage counselor, right now," I said. "I was trained in psychiatry. But there aren't many openings these days. Not on Earth, anyway."

"My name is Isherwood."

"I know," I said. "I've read your articles on the rheoprotein."

Isherwood raised one eyebrow, but didn't take the bait. "You're here as a tourist?"

"I'm studying Martian Disease," I said. It was the cover story DALI had instructed me to use. "I want to see if there's any truth to this mind-over-matter business."

"Odd work for a marriage counselor," Isherwood said. "I think maybe you're here to test the various suitors for Vivi's hand. What do you say to that?"

I looked down. My training was in psychiatry, not espionage. I didn't know how to go about deceiving him.

"Good," Isherwood said. "So I'm to be the first. Tell me, what are my chances?"

"I couldn't tell you yet. There have to be tests and interviews, I have to compare your test data with Vivi's. . . ."

"You already have Vivi's data then?"

One thing was already clear. Isherwood was in love with Vivi. I only had to speak her name to arouse his jealousy.

"I treated Vivi personally while she was studying on Earth," I said.

"Personally?"

"Needless to say, we were just doctor and patient, nothing more." His stare cut into me. I found myself rushing to explain. "She suffered from acute technophobia. It's different on Earth than it is here. There are machines everywhere. You can't get away from them. Computers and televisions and video cameras in every room. It's bad enough for an ordinary person coming from Mars, but with Vivi's special—"

Isherwood cut me off. "That's true. She has a very delicate nervous system. It was a mistake to send her to Earth in the first place."

"But your work is technological. Don't you think it would be a mistake for the two of you to marry?"

"Well, I don't think so, of course. I'll be with her no matter what happens."

"But you have powerful enemies. And are you sure she cares for you? You're old enough to be her father."

"I don't know," Isherwood said sadly. "My Beatrice's mind is more mysterious to me than the construction of Phobos."

"So she hasn't refused you completely, then?"

He looked theatrically at the curved ceiling. "No, she only smiles like the Mona Lisa." I wondered if he meant da Vinci's or Dalí's.

We moved to his office so we could have privacy for the formal tests. I gave him TAT, Improved Rorschach, Super Association Test, Differential Color Test, Abnormal Sentence Completion, and everything went well. There's often a problem with defensiveness in this sort of testing, but Isherwood was open and friendly, often showing a childlike innocence.

I'd almost told him about Vivi in the bar, but he'd interrupted me. Now, the longer I put it off, the harder it was to bring the subject up again.

I'd found out about it during her analysis in Tokyo three years before. It was early summer when she first came to my office. I could see crystalline sunlight through the green leaves outside my window. By the end of June the heat and monoxide would turn everything to gray and brown.

Vivi was a student at the art college near my office. She was a referral from the local hospital, where she'd been taken after she tried to disembowel herself with an ancient short sword.

When I saw her medical records things became clearer. The plane bringing her to Tokyo had crashed, and only the replacement of her heart, lungs, and stomach with artificial constructs had kept her alive. Knowing her technophobic background, the surgeons had kept the information from her. But her subconscious had evidently at least suspected the truth.

She was only eighteen, beautiful as a butterfly. I was twenty-seven, just out of medical school, without even a nurse or a secretary, trying to make a living from referrals. I suppose I loved her immediately. Of course, I realized my position. It would have been improper for me to take advantage of our relationship as doctor and patient. More than that, though, I simply didn't have any confidence that I could make Vivi happy. A conservative attitude, but then I was young and hadn't established myself, and my future was far from certain.

I saw her for over a year, and helped her, I think. Maybe I should have told her the truth, that the technology she hated was the only thing keeping her alive. But I couldn't bring myself to do it. Her feelings were too delicate, like fine glasswork.

There were other problems I was able to

help her with. The worst of them was her relationship with her grandfather. Her father had died when she was three years old. She suspected, perhaps with reason, that DALI had then had an incestuous relationship with her mother. DALI became both substitute father and rival for her mother's love. I had persuaded her to confront some of these Oedipal conflicts and begin to resolve them.

When she left to go back to Mars I thought I would never see her again. And then the letter arrived from DALI. Vivi was twenty-one now, old enough for marriage, but she rejected every man who even broached the subject. DALI had decided that she was to marry, and I was to choose from his list of candidates. The thought of selecting her husband was distasteful to me, but it would mean seeing Vivi again. I accepted.

And so far, the first candidate was doing well. There was only one serious problem. Vivi was still technophobic, and Isherwood's occupation as rheologist naturally involved machines. I tried to delicately express my concerns, but Isherwood ignored me, instead indulging in still more poetry.

"I'm the one who really loves her. Pinkerton is only thinking of DALI's fortune. A square inch of any of his paintings is worth more than a hundred square feet in Manhattan. I'm different. Vivi has taught me the meaning of life. She is a heliotrope, blooming in the red desert of Mars."

"But you must see that Pinkerton is the more obvious choice. He is younger and, forgive me, better looking. As an artist, his career would not be so threatening to her. And he seems very confident of his appeal. . . ."

"So you think so, too? But there are things I can offer her. Wonderful toys. Delights for the imagination. Just look."

He reached into a desk drawer and took out a soft clock. It was the size of a dessert plate, and it hung limply over his hand. He set it on the edge of the desk, and the rim of the clock bent and drooped toward the floor.

"That's amazing," I said. I touched it with one finger and it gave slightly. The second hand moved continuously around the dial, following the deformations of the clock. "Just like in Dali's *Persistence of Memory*."

"Made entirely of rheoprotein," Isherwood said. "Accurate to within a few milliseconds, and calibrated for the slightly shorter Martian hour. It must be kept reasonably cool, or it will melt, just like chocolate."

"This seems impossible," I said.

"It would be, with an inorganic mechanism. The problem is that the gears, for example, must resist other gears and yet be flexible under pressure from gravity or an external touch. The protein resembles a universal joint, only on a molecular level. Plus there is an information-carrying component, like RNA, that allows it to recognize other rheoproteins and respond appropriately to them."

"A very complicated toy," I said.

"It's not just a toy," Isherwood said. "It could bring an industrial revolution on Earth. Maybe you've seen some reference to it—they're calling it Flabby Engineering. Some journalist's idea of a joke, I imagine. Anyway—an internal combustion engine could be produced in virtually any shape—long and thin, like a broomstick, or twisted, like a spiral. Not to mention cybernetics. Energy or movement can be passed on—or reacted to—with the kind of smoothness you see in living tissue."

"I even find it interesting, from a psychiatric standpoint. The contrast between the hardness of machines and the softness of human beings . . ."

Isherwood didn't seem to be listening. "In factories this kind of material could contain, or even harness, the force of accidental explosions. Cars and planes would be infinitely safer." The mention of airplanes made me think of Vivi. "Submarines could be built to mimic the swimming of dolphins. With flexible machine parts all these six-decimal-point tolerances would become meaningless."

He held up his hands. "The possibilities

are . . . well, beyond anything we could imagine."

For the rest of that day and all of the next I interviewed the remaining candidates. Boccaccio had little intelligence and no imagination. Martin, the actor, was driven by vanity and greed. Conrad, a well-known athlete, revealed a basic hostility toward women.

I interviewed Pinkerton late on the second day. As with all the others, I approached him in conversation and only later resorted to formal testing. He seemed eager to make a good impression once he found out what I was really up to. But under the relentless light of the personality tests he showed himself to be nothing but a dreamer and a braggart, completely self-obsessed. By the end of our session he was screaming and cursing me.

Of all of them only Isherwood was stable and sincere enough to be worthy of Vivi. His paternal nature would go well with her delicate personality and sensibilies. The only problem was Vivi's technophobia. If she married Isherwood, it might very well send her over the edge.

The party lasted two days. The last guests were gone by the time I finished with Pinkerton. The butler showed him to the door and I was alone in DALI's huge cathedral of a house.

I had no sooner showered and changed than the butler came to my room with an invitation. "My master wishes you to join him for dinner, if that would be convenient."

"Of course," I said.

I followed him down to the lobby. Through a bronze door I could see a hallway that seemed to curve upward and over itself in defiance of gravity. When I looked closer I saw it was only an illusion.

The mansion was full of them. There were so many false rooms and staircases and corridors that the false parts seemed to put pressure on the real things, distorting them into nightmare shapes.

The dining room was so large it seemed a deliberate insult to rationality. Black-and-white checkered tiles receded to infinity in all directions.

"Welcome," DALI said, "please sit down." He was at the head of the long, narrow table. His favorite crutch leaned against the side of his red-velvet armchair. But I hardly noticed him. At the far end of the table sat his granddaughter, Vivi.

She was ethereally beautiful. Her golden hair was cut within an inch of her head. Her cheeks were sunken, her eyes hollow, and the muscles of her neck stood out like marble ornaments. It was obvious to anyone that she was critically anorexic. I smiled at her, and she smiled back with what seemed to be great pleasure.

The first chair I touched collapsed and then sprang back into shape. It was clearly not meant to support my weight.

DALI smiled. "One of Mr. Gilbert's designs. They are part of his *Revenge Against the Machine Age* series. You see, if the function of a tool is removed, you have Art. Very witty, don't you think?"

I found a chair that would support my weight, and the dinner began.

DALI explained that shellfish had long been the object of his family's gluttony. "The bones, you see, are the objectivity of the animal. The flesh is madness. We carry our objectivity inside us and wear our madness for all the world to see. But the shellfish, the shellfish is an enigma. Objective outside, mad within."

He then proceeded to eat an astounding quantity of oysters, mussels, lobsters, crab, and conch. Unlike the classic bulimic he did not pause to purge himself, but kept on eating with undiminished appetite.

Vivi, meanwhile, did not even taste the small portion she had been served. "Grandpa won't listen to me," she said, her voice glistening like olive oil. "Please, doctor, won't you speak in your own behalf?"

I smiled uneasily, unsure what she was asking.

"This child wants everything," DALI said,

breaking through the shell of a monstrous shrimp and attacking the soft, buttery meat inside. "I have always given her whatever she wanted." He looked at me meaningfully.

"I'm sorry," I said, "but—"

"No!" Vivi said. "Doctor, tell him that I only want to be with you! I want you to take me back to Tokyo with you!"

I was completely at a loss. It was natural for a girl like Vivi to become infatuated with her doctor during treatment. It is a common hazard of psychoanalysis. But such feelings are shallow and temporary. Vivi needed a strong father figure, someone to love her faithfully and protect her. Someone like Professor Isherwood.

"Vivi, I—"

DALI grabbed his crutch and stood up. "Vivi! You will go to your room! Immediately, do you hear me?" He turned to me. "Please try to make her understand, doctor."

"No," Vivi said, "no, no, no!" She lunged for a table knife and brought it up to stab herself in the chest. I saw that I could not reach her in time and snatched away DALI's crutch. With the crutch I knocked the knife from Vivi's hands. She sank back into her chair, weeping.

I looked back at DALI. It was as if I had taken his sanity when I took the crutch away from him. "Give me that!" he shouted, and tore it from my hands.

I already knew the crutch was both physical and psychological. It appeared in many of Salvador Dalí's paintings. It was the symbolic tool he needed to support his soft world. DALI and Vivi stared at each other across the table. The anger and jealousy sparked in the air between them. Vivi recovered first and ran from the room, covering her face with both hands.

We all have our crutches, I thought. Sometimes they are powerful weapons and sometimes they become dangerous dependencies. The dinner was over.

I found the butler and asked him where Vivi had gone. He said she had just taken her car into town. "Probably to the Narcissus. It's a pub where the artists all go." He gave me directions and the key to one of DALI's cars.

The pub smelled of tobacco, marijuana, mescal, amyl nitrate, beta-carboline. The Chiriconians meditated silently in the center of the room. A naked couple, tattooed with birds and snakes, wandered around until they finally found two seats by themselves. Two contending groups of monochromists formed living sculptures, the blues horizontal in a dark corner, the reds vertical under a bright light. The futurists walked rapidly around the edges of the room, talking in a truncated language which I could not understand. A pop artist, wrapped in dirty bandages like a mummy, smelled of rotten sausage.

A fauvist woman, dressed as Matisse's *Lady in Blue*, approached me. "Buy a girl a drink?" she said. I nodded and signaled to the waitress. "So what group are you?" she asked.

"I am as you see me."

"That's what I was afraid of. Non-artist. What a drag. Too practical, no dreams." She drained her absinthe in a single swallow. "Oh," she said. "Here comes my friend." I was a little relieved when she left me for the old man, who moved with robotic stiffness. A cubist, apparently. I had heard the rumor that fauvists were obsessed with wolves. Just as the thought came into my head, the woman in the blue dress turned back to me and smiled, showing cosmetically implanted fangs.

I looked away. Martian Disease; everyone was affected to some degree. If I stayed too long, it would begin happening to me. The pub reminded me of the mental hospital in Tokyo where I'd been an intern.

"Are you alone?" a woman said. "May I sit here?"

She had a firm, beautiful body, covered by a Tahitian dress out of a painting by Gauguin. There were red tropical flowers in her hair.

"Do I know you?" I asked.

"My name is Carmen. We met the day before yesterday at DALI's mansion."

"Ah, yes, you were one of the receptionists.

I was here looking for Vivi, actually. Have you seen her?"

"She went for a ride with some of DALI's disciples."

"Where do you think they went? I really need to find her."

"Give it up. The desert is too big. She'll be all right."

I let her convince me. After all, I thought, if she was with friends, they would take care of her.

I bought Carmen a glass of champagne and ordered a beer for myself. The beer tasted like mouse piss. Martian water and hops were not up to the job. But it had a lot of alcohol in it, and I quickly became drunk.

Martian women were notoriously loose, and Carmen was no exception. I felt the pressure of her hips against mine. I was a long way from home, and her interest was warming me faster than the beer.

The champagne was clearly affecting her. "I have to make a confession," she said. "I have a terrible habit and I can't seem to stop it. I'm a kleptomaniac. I steal things."

It wasn't the confession I'd wanted to hear, but I nodded sympathetically.

"The guilt is really terrible," she said. "I'm suffering so much pain from it. Please, spank me, doctor." She started to cry.

No one seemed to care except a man at the next table, who said, "Why don't you just go ahead and hit her? That's what she wants." He was wearing a bowler and waistcoat and a short beard. He tipped the hat to Carmen. "Hey, Carmen, did you steal anything worth money this time?"

"You cheap old bastard!" Carmen shouted. "Bitch!"

The man yanked her away from me, and then both of them fell onto the floor. The man straddled her waist, backwards; lifted her dress; and began to spank her shapely buttocks. I got up to pull him away and felt a hand on my arm. It was the Lady in Blue. "That's Carmen's pimp," she said. "You'd do better to stay out of it."

The pimp opened her purse and felt inside it. "This bitch, she steals the most worthless shit. What the hell is this?" The thing he pulled out hung down through his fingers like chewing gum.

It was one of Isherwood's soft clocks.

"You thief!" Carmen shouted. Without warning she threw the clock into her mouth, chewed it, and swallowed it.

I was not, it seemed, going to be spending the night with Carmen. But she had given me an idea. I ran to the phone and called Professor Isherwood.

The next morning I woke up with a pounding head and queasy stomach. I hadn't realized the aftereffects of Martian beer would be so devastating. I took a hot shower and lurched downstairs just in time for breakfast. DALI was in an extremely good mood. He had already begun eating.

"Why don't you try one?" he said.

When I saw what was on the plate he offered, I panicked. I had meant Isherwood to give the soft clocks to Vivi to eat. DALI must have taken them from her.

I had no choice. I picked out a small pocket watch and ate it. It was cool and crisp, like an English wheat biscuit.

"I like to eat a full meal in the morning," DALI said. The cook brought in a sizzling alarm clock on a tray. The clock was deformed and spread out to the edge of plate, but was still keeping time.

DALI stabbed it with a fork as if to murder it and cut it into bite-sized pieces. His face was radiant with joy. Brown sauce dripped from his mouth and stained his napkin. "Doctor, this is wonderful."

"Perhaps," I suggested, "Vivi would like to try one."

"I don't want any," Vivi said.

"Please, Vivi," I begged her. "It's a gift from Professor Isherwood. He asked especially that you try it."

"No," she said. "I have no appetite. I don't want any, I tell you!"

My idea had been to warm her to the idea of technology with the soft clocks. They were so friendly and harmless looking. I had hoped she might use them to begin to overcome her technophobia. But I hadn't counted on the intensity of her anorexia.

At lunch and dinner she again refused to eat. Her loathing for the soft clocks was so intense that I was afraid she might attempt suicide with her fork. Her personal physician was forced to give her an intravenous injection of protein simply to keep her alive.

The next day I returned to Earth. I had one last plan. Isherwood had given me copies of all his notes and a range of samples of the rheoprotein, and I took them to Sony's research and development laboratory. If Vivi's mechanical organs could be replaced with organs made of the rheoprotein, so close to living tissue, her subconscious self-hatred might be brought under control. Her gratitude to Isherwood would seal their marriage.

I had to hurry. If Vivi's anorexia continued to get worse she would even refuse the injections, and then she would surely die.

The Sony scientists were ecstatic at what I'd brought them. Within a week they'd developed prototype organs and made arrangements for them to be implanted as soon as possible. Isherwood's patent applications were filed, and I was assured that he would soon be a millionaire several times over.

I sat alone in my office with a flask of warm sake. It was bitter and sweet at the same time. I had probably saved Vivi's life and made it possible for her to be married to the man I had chosen for her. I had fulfilled my mission.

Why was I miserable? Was it possible that I still loved her? Was it more than some childish infatuation?

But if I truly loved her I would wish only for her happiness. I would see her in her bridal gown. She would leave for her honeymoon with Isherwood. I would see them off. I would have the gratitude of the happy couple.

Gratitude! I smashed the sake cup against the floor. I staggered off to bed and lay there, sleepless, until long after the sun had come up.

My job, I soon learned, was not over. A telegram arrived from Vivi. "GRANDFATHER GOES MAD. MARS IS MELTING."

Isherwood was there to meet me at the abandoned shuttleport. I got into his jeep and we drove into the Martian desert, toward DALI's mansion.

"What's happening? Where is everyone?" I asked him.

"He should never have eaten the soft clock," Isherwood said. "The results have been beyond anything anyone could imagine. It's a disaster, a catastrophe."

The desert was melting, reshaping itself. It formed two humanlike figures, which sank waist-deep in the sand and began to melt into each other. A twisted tree grew up to support the woman's head as it became soft and began to topple over. No, not a tree, I realized. A crutch. I recognized the scene from Salvador Dalí's painting *Autumn Cannibalism*.

"The rheoprotein mixed with DALI's digestive fluid, with his entire body chemistry. By the time it passed through his system the protein had absorbed his genetic message. Now everything that comes in contact with the protein becomes part of DALI and part of his madness."

"The Martian sickness," I said. "He can telekinetically control the entire desert."

"Not control, exactly," Isherwood said. "The desert has become a vast theater of his unconscious."

The sand under the jeep began to undulate. The jeep itself seemed to soften. I sank deeper into the seat. Isherwood shouted, "No!" and drove even faster. As our speed picked up the tires were less and less in contact with the ground, and the effects diminished.

"The entire space-time structure is being affected," Isherwood said. "DALI is insane, bulimic. And as this insanity spreads, his insane world becomes edible. The more he eats, the worse it becomes. His gluttony is devouring time itself."

Vivi stood outside the palace, waiting for us. Around her was an island of solidity. As I got out of the jeep she ran toward me, but stopped short of putting her arms around me. "You came," she whispered. "I'm so glad you're safe."

"Of course I came," I said. She was even thinner than when I had left. She was a skeleton, barely covered with skin. And yet she had a radiant, spiritual beauty that I could not deny.

I looked back into the desert. A herd of giant elephants, led by a white horse, was charging toward us. Their legs were impossibly long and distorted, like the legs of spiders. I recognized them from Salvador Dalí's *Temptation of Saint Anthony*.

"We'd better get inside," I said. "Where is your grandfather?"

"Eating," Vivi said. Isherwood ran for the house. I took Vivi's hand and pulled her in after us.

"Eating what?" I asked.

"Anything he finds. Desks, chairs, beds, he's even cooking telephones. He's started on the wall of the dining room. Soon he will have eaten the entire house."

I suddenly noticed the house. DALI had once predicted that the buildings of the future would be soft and hairy. Here at least it was coming true. As I watched, the walls swelled and softened and moved gently in and out, as if they were breathing. Fine black hairs began to grow from the walls and ceilings. I shuddered away from them.

"First the house," Isherwood said, "and then the entire planet. Perhaps the entire universe."

I didn't believe him until I saw DALI.

He was ten feet tall. Sitting with his legs crossed, his head nearly touched the ceiling. He was eating the mantelpiece when we walked in.

"So you're back," DALI said. "Will you join me?" He offered me a leftover chair leg.

"No, thank you," I said.

He continued to eat. He ate with more than mere hunger. He was not eating just to sustain himself, but with endless, thoughtless greed. It was the ultimate materialism, the ultimate desire to possess, to control, to own. To make the entire external universe a part of DALI.

"Mars has become the fantasy he inherited from his ancestor," I said to Vivi. "When he was a child Salvador Dalí wanted to be a cook. As he grew older his hero became Napoléon. Now DALI OF MARS has become both. The imperialist glutton. Worlds not only to conquer, but devour."

I pictured DALI floating in space, large as a planet, Mars in one hand like an apple that had been eaten to the core.

Vivi shook her head. "It's horrible," she said. "How can he stand it? To eat so much. To become so huge."

And then I saw it. Vivi's anorexia was the antidote to DALI's madness.

It made perfect sense. Classical anorexia nervosa is very much tied to the patient's concept of space. A previous anorexic patient of mine used to feel ashamed whenever anyone entered the area around her, which she defined as her personal space. On occasion she would have to spend time at her father's restaurant. If any of the customers touched her, it would send her into ecstasies of self-loathing. In time her bashfulness extended from being touched to being seen, and finally she could not bear to be seen even by inanimate objects, such as dishes.

Vivi's fear of things crossing her personal boundaries was the exact opposite of her grandfather's gluttony.

There were also her personal feelings for DALI. In fact I was beginning to see that her anorexic self-hatred was just a displacement of her Oedipal hatred for her grandfather. As Vivi grew up, the closed world of her inner space began to reach toward the outer world. The dining room played an important role in this. Receiving nutrition from one's family is like receiving trust. But the atmosphere at DALI's table, between his gluttony and Vivi's fear of him, was hardly suited to normal development.

This all came to a head with the artificial

organ transplant. The anorexia was just another form of technophobia, a rejection of the outer world. Because her subconscious realized the presence of a piece of the outer world—her artificial organs—inside her, the contradiction began to tear her apart. She rejected not only food, but the bridegroom candidates, anyone or anything that tried to cross her personal boundaries.

"Professor Isherwood," I said. "Do you still have any of those soft clocks?"

"Well," he said unhappily, "there is just one. I was keeping it as a souvenir."

"You must let me have it. It's our only hope."

DALI had eaten through the back of the house. He was now consuming the lawn furniture, and growing steadily larger. Within minutes he would be heading into the desert.

Isherwood handed me the clock. It was a small wall model with red enamel, not much larger than my hand. Vivi, as if suspecting what was about to happen, shrank from me.

"Vivi—" I said.

"No," she said. I put the soft clock in her hand. "I can't even look at it," she said. "It's shameful, embarrassing."

"Vivi, you must be strong. You must eat it."

"No, I can't. It's shameful. I'd rather die."

"It's not just your life. It's the lives of everyone on Mars." I hesitated, and then I said, quietly, "It's my life too."

"All right," she said. She was crying. "I'll do it. But Professor Isherwood must turn his back."

"Professor?"

"Yes, all right."

Isherwood turned away. Vivi slowly brought the clock to her lips. She flushed with shame. Her eyes filled with tears. I looked away. The clock crunched slowly as she bit into it, like a cookie. From the corner of my eye I could see her chewing, slowly, keeping it in the front of her mouth.

She swallowed. "All of it?" she asked.

"As much as you can. At least a few more bites."

When I looked back she had eaten half of it. The second hand swept around to the missing half and then disappeared. Thirty seconds later it reappeared at the other edge. Vivi shook her head. "No more," she said.

"Very well. There's something I have to tell you. You should hear this too, Professor. Vivi, when you came to Earth you were in a terrible accident. You were in surgery for many days."

"What does that have to do with—"

"Please. This is difficult for me." I was sweating. "In order to save your life, your heart and lungs—"

"No!" Vivi screamed.

"—and stomach had to be replaced—"

"No!" She tried to run, but I held her arms.

"—replaced with artificial implants. Mechanical substitutes—" I couldn't go on. Vivi was screaming too loudly. I let her go. Immediately her eyes wrinkled shut and her throat began working. I saw her mechanical stomach heaving. I got out of her way.

She ran for the bathroom and flung the door closed behind her. It shut with a fleshy sound. I looked at Professor Isherwood as we heard Vivi being violently sick.

"You did that on purpose," Isherwood said.

"The rheoprotein has mixed with her digestive juices. Vivi has infected the house with her anorexia, just as it was earlier infected with DALI's bulimia." I smiled tentatively at Isherwood. "Now the battle commences."

We ran outside. I could see DALI in the distance, running into the melting desert, thirty feet tall, devouring boulders and handfuls of red sand.

"Doctor!" Isherwood shouted. I ran to where he stood, at the edge of a pond. A naked woman floated facedown in the water. Her body had turned soft and her fingers and toes had begun to melt into long, thin tendrils. I helped Isherwood pull her body onto the shore and turn her over.

It was Carmen, from the pub.

"She must have come back to steal something more valuable," I said. I couldn't look away. Her softness was ripe, erotic, intoxicating. Her full, glistening breasts wobbled provocatively. The soft flesh of her thighs rubbed against the damp blackness of her pubic hair.

Isherwood was captivated too. He bent over her and gently touched one arm. "The bones are still there."

"She still has her 'objectivity,' as DALI would say. There may be time to save her."

"Her, perhaps," Isherwood said, "but what about Pinkerton?"

He pointed into the desert. A gigantic hand had risen from the dunes. Its fingers held a cracked egg with a flower growing out of it. The form of the hand was reflected in the form of a huge man, crouching in the sand. The scene was from Salvador Dalí's painting *Metamorphosis of Narcissus*. The face of the crouching man belonged to Pinkerton.

As I watched, Pinkerton's mouth seemed to form the words "Help me." But it was too late.

Vivi walked out onto the porch of the now firm, lifeless house. A wave of solidity flowed from her and rippled out into the desert. Carmen stirred and sat up. "Where am I?"

"Safe," I said. "Safe, for now."

. . .

They finally found DALI, deep in the desert of the Lunae Planum. He had been transformed into a hundred-foot-tall replica of one of Salvador Dalí's earliest paintings, *Self-Portrait with Easel*, and frozen there.

Vivi returned to Earth with me for the operation that replaced her mechanical organs with living organs of rheoprotein. Almost immediately she began to gain weight. It was a symbolic cure, but effective; my previous anorexic had been cured by a tonsillectomy.

She was willing to honor her grandfather's last wishes and marry Professor Isherwood, though she knew she didn't love him. Isherwood, however, had changed his mind. Maybe it was the fact that Vivi had asked him to turn away from her, there at the end of the madness on DALI's estate. Maybe it was something else. In any case, he had fallen in love with Carmen, and the last we heard, he was more like a bullfighter than a poet.

As for Vivi and myself, I learned to stop fighting my feelings. I completed my contract and selected myself as Vivi's bridegroom. The decision seemed to please everyone.

Someday, perhaps, we will have children, and one day we may take them to Mars to see the statue of their great-grandfather. But for the moment we are in no hurry.

Three from Moderan
DAVID R. BUNCH

David R. Bunch (1925–2000) was a prolific US fiction writer and poet who specialized in short fiction and whose real name may have been David Groupe. A cartographer for the US Air Force, Bunch became associated with the American New Wave due to his inclusion in Harlan Ellison's iconic *Dangerous Visions* anthology. Bunch's fiction shares some similarities with that of R. A. Lafferty, Stepan Chapman, and Kurt Vonnegut, but his is much more kinetic and punchily lyrical.

Although little-known, Bunch was among the most original voices in the science fiction field in the 1960s and 1970s. Much of his work appeared in literary magazines before he turned to speculative fiction. His first published science fiction story may have been "Routine Emergency" (*IF*, 1957). "That High-Up Blue Day That Saw the Black Sky-Train Come Spinning" (*The Magazine of Fantasy and Science Fiction*, 1968) is one of his best stand-alone stories. The adventurous Cele Goldsmith is credited with championing Bunch by taking many of his stories for *Amazing* and *Fantastic* when she was the acquiring editor for those publications. (*Fantastic* also took work by J. G. Ballard and Harlan Ellison considered too outré for other genre publications.)

Bunch himself famously stated in the June 1965 issue of *Amazing Stories,* "I'm not in this business primarily to describe or explain or entertain. I'm here to make the reader think, even if I have to bash his teeth out, break his legs, grind him up, beat him down, and totally chastise him for the terrible and tinsel and almost wholly bad world we allow . . . The first level reader, who wants to see events jerk their tawdry ways through some used and USED old plot—I love him with a hate bigger than all the world's pity, but he's not for me. The reader I want is the one who wants the anguish, who will go up there and get on that big black cross. And that reader will have, with me, the saving grace of knowing that some awful payment is due . . . as all space must look askance at us, all galaxies send star frowns down, a cosmic leer envelop this small ball that has such Great GREAT pretenders." Perhaps it's no surprise that *Twentieth Century Science Fiction Writers* wrote that Bunch's stories "met with varying degrees of outrage."

Bunch's most recent collection was *Bunch!* (1993). However, Bunch's first book, published in 1971, remains his best-known: *Moderan*, a mosaic novel consisting of linked fable-like tales written in a surreal, almost experimental mode. These tales of Moderan describe a radical future world of automation and factories where, after a nuclear holocaust, humans have been transformed into cyborgs, the surface of Earth is plastic, and communities exist underground.

Nothing quite like the Moderan stories had been written before and nothing like them has been written since. In their intensity and their structural spiraling they at times resemble prose-poems. Yet they convey an astonishing amount of information, characterization, and plot beneath their hyperreal exterior. The only comparable experience exists in sections of Stepan Chapman's novel *The Troika*, which includes the story of a man named Alex who turns into a machine. The Moderan stories are also notable because of their increasing relevance in a world of scarcity and growing alarm about climate change and what humankind has done to the planet.

"Three from Moderan" represents the first reprinting of Bunch's work in quite some time. There is some reason to hope not only that a full Moderan collection will be forthcoming but that previously unpublished Bunch stories will finally become available to readers as well.

THREE FROM MODERAN

David R. Bunch

NO CRACKS OR SAGGING

Sometimes, from the brink of our great involvements, we move in our minds back to remember things of seemingly small-bore significances that loom, in the recalling times, extra-large. The day I crossed over, the day I went into Moderan, out of the rolled and graded fields, far as the eye could reach, were these long-legged tamping machines. Essentially they were huge black cylinders swung spinning between gigantic thighs and calves of metal. There seemed an air of casualness about these strange black monsters as they loafed on their tall-thighed legs and twirled their cylinders about in what appeared to be, at times, almost totally contrived, excessive, and meaningless nonchalance. Then, at no signal that I could detect, at no prompting that I could learn of, one or another of the machines would rush right over to a spot of ground and, seeming to bend forward a little at the waist, unleash the fury of its cylinder at the fresh earth underneath as though in great glee and highest concentration. The two-legged machine, once started, would really pummel that spot of earth with the front end of its cylinder for upwards of, say, thirty minutes or maybe even three-quarters of an hour, increasing its battering motion as the minutes passed. Then, appearing to know without any guessing when enough was plenty, and withdrawing a dirt-caked cylinder-end, the machine, as it erected to full height from its leaned position, would wander away and rejoin other loafing, waiting machines as though nothing of any consequence had really occurred at all.

Once two machines started for the same spot of earth, and it was quite a show to watch them both hunch into battering position at the same time, take aim at the same place, and start battering each the other's cylinder almost as much as they pummeled the ground. An overseer for tamping machines watched this ridiculous punching contest for a while before he went over and drummed each machine on the rump just enough to break up the rhythm of their misdirected jab-jab-jab and send them both packing off twirling their cylinders as though they hadn't really wanted to use them anyway. The job was awarded to a third machine, a troubleshooter reserve type who soon hunched into position and went about poking away at the place as though the world were entirely new and jolly to him and heigh-ho, jig-jig, holiday, holiday, go Go GO!

"What goes WHAT GIVES!?" I asked the overseer of tamping machines, my voice with wonder like a child's, my eyes surely bulged out like, in the Old Days, a frog's.

"Time goes, life stays, heigh-ho heigh-hey," he recited. And then he said, "What are you, some kind of a humorist, or something? What do you mean, 'what goes, what gives'?"

"What goes, what gives? Explain these grim, grotesque, and altogether hilarious actions. I wish to be instructed. I want to understand. I see nothing but burlesque here. Is there more?"

"Is there more!? Man, is there more!!" Then he looked at me closely. "Why! you're from Out There! Old Times!" he ejaculated. "Perhaps you really do not understand at all. Maybe you really do mean, 'What goes, what gives?'"

"I mean WHAT GOES, WHAT GIVES!" My fists were doubled by now and I saw I could easily go into my punch-now talk-later mood for sure.

"Travel far?"

"I came far enough. In miles. In time. In blasted hopes and withering dreams. In tears I came. In trouble. YES, I came far enough. And now to find, near the place of my chartered destination, if I came on course and if I drew my lines correctly on the charts they gave, a kind of antic Silly Far. Where big two-legged machines that are essentially, as I see it, just contrivances for carrying around those big proddy rammers, at wholly random instances and to no practical purpose at all, try to have sexual intercourse with the soil."

"You're quite a talker. Why don't you cut through, more? Go direct to your statement and pummel your meaning? Be more like these machines? You can see, when they get that signal, they don't beat around the bush. They go right over there and then it's just phoo phoo phoo, jig jig jig, bam bam bam, until the job's done."

"WHAT JOB? WHAT'S DONE?"

"The solution is to cover the pollution. The answer is to get rid of the cancer. Ho ho ho."

I moved in on him and I was ready to punch him down. Then I saw he had a strange look. He stared me back with gleaming, beaming, funny eyes, and there was about him something of the manner of, not a man, but more a machine-man. "This is Moderan," he said. "We're building New Land here. When these misters detect a soft place in our soil, they rush right over and batter it into submission. They look random and nonchalant. I know. But really they're not. When they seem to be just standing, they're sampling things from way off, maybe. You see, they own very sensitive feet. It's built in. If there's a soft place in their sphere of detection, they'll get it through these sensors in the feet. Treading here, they'll get a vibration from a hollow place out there. They're programmed to hate hollow places. They rush right over and stick in the jammy-ram cylinder when they get wind of a hollow place. By hollow place, I mean a piece of the land surface that isn't as hard as it should be."

"Oh yes! And that's important!?"

"VERY." Then he looked at me cold-eyed. "Maybe you'd better come with me. I can leave these machines for a while. These jammy-rams are programmed so that really all I have to do is put in my time. And take care of unusual occurrences, like when two signals cross at the juncture of spheres and detection. This happens but rarely, but when it does, whooee! look out! we have, as you saw, the strange, hilarious, and altogether inefficient phenomena of two jammy-rams going for the same hole. (By hole, I mean a piece of the land surface that isn't as firm as it should be.) Very hard on jammy-rams and also it doesn't make for a good tamping job at the hole either. And when you're building for forever, that's one of the things you really do want and must have—a good tamping job at the hole." He wasn't kidding. I saw he wasn't kidding.

We got into his flap-hap airabout scoot that he used to check on plans and we went up high. And far as the eye could gaze I saw the flats. All dotted with jammy-ram monsters was about three-quarters of this far-as-I-could-see area of the flats, brown-black scraped-off earth speckled with the darker, wandering, and nonchalant spots that were machines doing, I had just been told, a very efficient and important piece of detection work and finalization execution at the hole. Then far down near the horizon, and at the edge of the dots that were jammy-rams, I saw how the browny-black changed to a blur that was gray or grayey-white. He slipped me a pair of the long-rangers for the eyes and I zeroed in on the blur. "The new ice age!"

"Not at all!" he returned. "Or maybe just precisely, if you want to see it so. But this ice age, if you want it so—go ahead, call it that!—is for the species, not against it. You'll never see this ice age rolling up boulders or creeping along with mammoth bones in its teeth. This ice age is covering up dirt, not just rearranging it. That's plastic you're looking at, man! I'm out here as an advance guard for plastic. It's a friendly deadly-competitive hell-for-plastic devil-take-the-hindermost race between my jammy-rams and me on one side and that creeping gray edge on the other. And we're gaining!" He smirked with satisfaction. And if I hadn't already decided he was some kind of a Great One, I would have suspected right now that he was just some kind of a small jackass overseer type taking a lean satisfaction from staying on top of his small-small job. But surely not. Surely this was a Planner, a mover, a shaker, and a rearranger of the World Scheme. At least a mover, a shaker, and a rearranger of the surface of the earth.

"Why—what—?" I sputtered. Yes! I was snowed in just now, as deep back in the murk as I ever like not to be.

He looked hot-eyed with little bulbs at me. He really bored in hard. He seemed to be making some kind of a tough decision about whether I really existed or not. Anyway, I got that impression, so hard was his bright-bulb stare. "Say, you are cleared for this," he finally said, "aren't you?"

I remembered some gates and some guards I had passed many days and many many miles long back. Far down at the edge of the place where things were old and wrecked, I remembered that hard cross-questioning, and the lie detectors, and the probing, the probing in— "I think I'm cleared," I answered. "Would I have got this far if I had not been? Some things like tin eagles have hung over me all the long way, as it is, circling, circling, as I came slowly on my tired shank's mare. . . . I take it you people are taking no chances whatsoever with what you've got down there."

"We take no chances! Show me if you've got it!"

I rolled up my sleeves and showed him the two bright-orange M's that had been stamped on my lower arms, at the clearing gates a long while back. I thought that might be what he wanted to see, and it was. "You're cleared! And you're a whole lot more than that!" He peered more closely at the M's. "You probably don't know it now, but you're a whole lot more than

just cleared!" There was in his voice a note of admiration that I couldn't believe was faked. Yes, he meant it. He pointed at some small symbol under each M. "You probably don't know exactly what those mean," he mused, "but I do. I really do." Then he shook his head in what I had to read as sadness, and he seemed to slip in memory a long way down. "Too old," he muttered, "too old and too many bridges gone crackling down in the floods, the flames, and the always-present wrecking of the days, before this thing came up for me. But you—you're just right! You're young and apparently you passed your tests with colors flying, really whipping out there in the breeze. I bet you're stamped just about all over! under your clothes!"

"Yeah, they stamped me up pretty well. Then they told me to get going. Pointed me to a road, gave me maps and charts, and said, 'Get on up there. They're a-building and you're sure to be in time.' Is that what they meant?"

"NOOO. Not for you! This is what I qualified for. I was a Moderan Early-Early. But I was too old and time-ravaged and event-hurt before this gold chance came up for me. But you, you're young and right and on the mark. I can tell you now, you'll be a Stronghold master, one of the elite-elite, if you can stand those operations. And there's no reason why you can't. I stood what ones they allowed me to, in good shape. And you're to be allowed the maximum. I can read it by those small marks under the M's. CONGRATULATIONS!" Impulsively he let go of the controls of the flap-hap and grabbed my right hand with both of his hands. I really got a steel handshake that day!

After a while we landed, back at the place where we had started, and there were two jammy-rams going for the same hole again, so it was altogether to the good that we had arrived back at this station when we did. He rushed right over and straightened things out by slapping the two silly rammers on their rumps, with a certain rhythmic beat, as I had seen him do in that other instance. "A very bad spot, this here," he announced, coming back. "Something about the spheres of detection right here at this locale, which you'll notice is a little bit of a depression, taken on the large, causes tangling of the spirals. Really not the fault of the machines, not at all, for they just do what they're programmed for and that's it."

"You really know how to do it!" I exclaimed, for something intuitively told me now that here was just a little serving man, really, a victim, who could do with some praise.

He swelled a lot with good pride as his chest came up a notch. "You know, I developed that technique myself—slapping them on the rump that way with a certain beat. Breaks up their rhythm, jiggles the connections, and they just wander away for a while, not knowing what in hell else to do. After a short time, though, they settle right back down again, the rhythm of their programming is restored, and they're good serviceable jammy-rammers once more."

"Anyway, I think that's neat, slapping these big earth fornicators on the rump that way to send them off just twirling their dirty cylinders at the air, all puzzled and deranged. Sort of shows man's mastery somehow. Yet—huh?"

"YEAH! Thought it up myself, kind of by accident really. Saw it'd work when my foot slipped and I fell against one of them one time, flailing my arms for balance. Adopted the method. All against procedures, naturally. SAY! you should see what I'm really supposed to do when something like this comes up. About twenty-five to thirty forms to fill out giving the pinpoint time and place and my ideas on why the foul-up. I'm furiously filling out the forms, see, after I've immediately and at once sent in the signal to headquarters that two jammy-rammers are at the same hole, COME WITH ALL SPEED! About sixteen big shots hop off their new-metal mistresses up at headquarters, their secretaries, you know, jump in their flap-hap airabout jet scoots, and slam off out here as though hell itself were inside coming out. All this time the two poor jammy-rams with their signals crossed are beating hell out of each other's rammers, making a bigger scarred-

up soft place in the graded surface than there was before, and generally compounding futility to the top degree. But the big shots get there fast, in about two to five minutes—I will say this for them, they're prompt—and they rush out of their jet-slap airabout scoots and have their big cigars fired up and are clearing their throats and considering things almost before the two mixed-up jammy-rams are scarcely one-third through with their programmed cycle of earth ramming. Which makes it harder, really, because naturally being big-deal men of action, these headquarters fellows (do something, even if it's wrong! you know) signal off out there at once for the Separator task forces, which come in on the heavy transports in about ten minutes more, and these Separator troops throw big chain links around the intensely working jammy-rams and drag them away from the hole, the jammy-rams still fighting to finish the cycle, naturally, of course. Ever try to pull a jammy-ram by force away from the hole before he'd finished his cycle?"

"No, never did that."

"No," he laughed, "course you didn't. But it can be done with enough horsepower pulling at the jammy-rams and strong enough chains. Tears up the jammy-rams, though, and causes them to have to be sent away many many miles to the repair stations. Then I just complete the filling out of the forms, and procedures are maintained, and everything's unstrained, happy, and satisfied with the hardware boys."

I laughed. He laughed. "Yeah, if I hewed to the line of procedures in every way, that long ice-edge of the plastic would be covering me up completely! Along with my jammy-rams, in no time at all. I run my show out here, the big-deal headquarters men can log more time on their new-metal secretaries, I stay ahead of the plastic, and who's to care if I cut a few procedural corners right in twain?"

"Nobody should care," I agreed.

He looked at me, and a half-smile toyed at the corners of his mouth, this proud, vain, little man. "You know, what'd happen if they found out, if they ever found out how I slap those jammy-rammers on the rump with a certain beat to shortcut the procedures? Why, I'd be riding out of here in chains in just minutes, that's what'd happen. Yeah! Procedures are the god in New Land. It's got to be that way, of course—but still, once in a while, I think a practical mind is best. I usually give those jammy-rams a little extra oiling, or a polish-and-pet with the 'slick up, shine up' kit to help them get back straight and forget their humiliation, and it works out." And suddenly, I had a dazzling flash of insight. This man was really pretty usual! Procedures were for everyone but him. All at once I found myself not admiring his cunning little rump-slapping transgression of the rules quite as much as I thought I would. But then, as I've found out in the past, all people disappoint me, soon or late. They just don't measure out. "What about that plastic? What about those jammy-rams for that matter?" I yelled. "You've flown me over wide expanses of scraped and graded earth swarming with milling, wandering, and soil-fornicating jammy-rams. You've also flown me over wide areas of whitey-gray plastic that was smooth and cold as ice from where I sat. There's some reason for all this? You seem to think it's important. Outside of being your job, is it important?"

His eyes went hard-bright. He was not a friendly man just then. But soon he relaxed, when something had clicked in his mind, I guess. "Sure," he answered, "it's very much of importance. But being so lately from Old Land and coming a far way from where all is wrecked and cindered, as I understand it, I guess you wouldn't know. Forgive me. I was getting a little flame-hot at you just then. I thought you were ridiculing. But I know now, remembering your background, it's ignorance. And ignorance can be admirable, if the person came by it honestly. Flippant, flyblow, half-baked wiseacring is about the worst thing in the world, compared to honest ignorance."

"Thanks," I said. "Thank you."

"Now, to answer your question about the scraped-off rolled-down land, the jammy-rams, and the plastic: You see, we're moving down toward where you came from. We'll get it all in time. Surely you must know that the earth is poisoned. From what I've heard, where you are from is not only poisoned, but wrecked and cindered as well. We stopped just short of that havoc up here; therefore there is this place for you from Old Land to come to. But our land was poisoned by science 'progress' as much as yours was. So we're covering all with the sterile plastic, a great big whitey-gray envelope of thick tough sterile plastic over all the land of the earth. That's our goal. It's a mammoth task, but for mammoth tasks man has behemoth machines. The mountains go into the valleys, the creek banks go into the creeks, the ditch sides go into the ditches, the golf courses are smoothed, the mine tailings are scattered—and all is coated. At the necessary places we make the reservoirs for runoff and freeze it solid. The oceans we will deal with in our own time, our own time and well enough. There are several plans, one being to use our scientific know-how to freeze the oceans solid, another being to shoot the oceans out into space in capsules and be done with all that surplus water forever. The new-metal man, which I am to a degree, and which you are to become to a much much higher degree, will need very little water. . . . But now it's the land we're doing. The water is a later task. But when we get all through, I visualize an earth of such tranquility and peace in nature that it must be the true marvel of all the ages. The surface of our globe will be a smooth, tough grayey-white hide. When our water plans are finalized the rainfall will be no more. No more will man be fleeing floods anywhere in the world. In cloudless heavens the winds will have died in our even temperatures; no more will man go sky-high in the twisters. The air will hang as a tranquil envelope over essentially a smooth gray ball, the smoothness being broken only by the Strongholds and the bubble-dome homes. Trees, if we want them, will spring up from the yard holes at the flick of a switch. The flowers will bloom just right and on time in wonderful bloom-metal. Animals—there will be no animals, unless we should want a few tigers and lions and such, all mechanical of course, for a staged jungle hunt. Yes! it will be a land for forever, ordered and sterilized. That's the Dream!"

"But you still haven't told me why those jammy-rams ram at the soil in such a ridiculous way!" Yes, I could listen to the grandest plan in all the universe and still feel the bones of a jagged ragged uncomfortable question nag at my dissenting throat. And anyway, I felt he owed me an answer on less grandiose terms. Anyone could have a big puff-ball dream about how to make the earth into such an ordered place as almost to stump the imagination. But would it ever happen? Well, I for one would call it more than a small cosmic miracle if man, a spark of life tediously evolved from the dead cold elements himself, should so organize his forces as to rearrange those elements to have essentially a dead cold planet again before he departed. It would seem to me a dismal, and more than a little depressing, closing of the ring, for sure. "Tell me about the jammy-rams!" I shouted.

"Well, as you should have guessed a while back, the jammy-rams are just clever and sophisticated machines, science's marvels, you might say, for making sure that the surface we're coating is packed and solid everywhere. We want no cracks or sagging in the plastic. The mammoth graders and rollers do the big smoothing and packing jobs, and they're now miles on beyond. And miles back the other way, as we saw in our flap-hap airabout scoot ride, is the ice edge of the plastic this whole thing is all about. And my jammy-rams and I are in between, the artistic effort really, the ones who care, seeing that the whole thing comes not to naught because of small soft places left untended to make an improper bedding for the plastic. YES! we're the crux of it!" I could see that his was a proud calling.

I looked about and far and wide strolled still on that smoothed and rolled-down earth the tall cylinder-carrying monsters, and many was the jammy-ram that was hunched into the position and having a go at the jug-jug-jug, phoo-phoo-phoo, bam-bam-bam that was its main mission. "How long will I be in that hospital," I asked abruptly, thinking now of my future and many things.

"Nine months," he answered at once, gently rump-stroking a nearby jammy-ram that was having a go at a soft place in the hard hide of the soil. "That's the full transformation, and you're scheduled for it, from the markings I read under the orange M's." He stuck out a hand, and I shook it, felt its cold steel. "Good luck, boy, with the operations. When we meet again, if we meet again, you'll be a Stronghold master, one of the elite-elite. Youth will be served. I missed my chance, failed my hunt, ordered my gray battalions on to the impossible fields too late and lost—due to no fault of my own. It was age—and fate." He turned away, and I knew he was fighting a battle.

I went on up toward the place where the operations were nine months long, where according to rumor, iron nurses, sterile and capable, ran on spur tracks up to the edges of beds, where a man, if of the CHOSEN, might receive enough part-steel to be a king in his times.

NEW KINGS ARE NOT FOR LAUGHING

Out of the hospital, out of the nine-months mutilation, out of the nine-months magic, released and alone. The steel-spliced doctors knew they had made a monster. They were proud of me, their monster, as doctors must always be proud of successes in their field; but they knew that now I was a kind of king, and they were merely doctors. Their arrogance was small-town lording now, their lording outlorded, as it were. No matter how born or made, a king WILL be a king. They got rid of me. They loaded me out. They quick-shifted me into the seething yeasty world; and with almost no parting ceremony. And with the very minimum of instructions and equipment (which was load plenty-enough) to stand me down on my trip. But somehow a king must be a king, know how to behave as a captain of his times and domesticate his wild situations, no matter what the odds.

With my portable flesh-strip feeder, my book of instructions for new-metal limb control, my plastic mechanical tear bags (for even a king must sometimes cry, you will allow), and all the other paraphernalia to get me started, or at least to sustain me until I should attain my Stronghold sanctuary, I sailed out from the hospital steps, the arrogant doctors watching. Something like a small iron frigate from the Old Days, I guess I was, loaded to the gunwales and standing forth on end.

Walking was easy, really. *Plop-plip-plap-plot*—one foot in front of the other, pick-them-up-and-plunk-them-down, toggle your hinges and braces, go with the arm swing for balance, flail the air with those blades when you go to tumble down—determine, determine, DETERMINE! determine that you will move along. Go for the tear bags when things get too uncertain, stop—think—cry (oh yes, a king can cry), curse if you want to, and hate, hate, hate. But keep on walking, don't let those steel-spliced doctors see, don't let anyone see how it is.

GOD! Being a new-metal man wasn't going to be easy. Let me tell you here and now, being a new-metal man was going to take some swinging. BUT I WOULD.

According to the little packet of special maps and instructions the steel-spliced ones had slung around my neck at our parting, I was to be Stronghold 10. I looked at that number and at first it meant nothing. Nothing at all. Then I thought more, the new green juices in the fresh-made brainpans sloshing and fuming, and I thought, STRONGHOLD 10! YES! STRONGHOLD 10 FOREVER! Stronghold 10 must never disgrace Moderan. Stronghold 10 must achieve. Stronghold 10 must win honors. Stronghold 10 must be heroic. Stronghold 10 must be brave. Stronghold 10 must be the strongest, toughest, meanest, most hateful, most arrogant, loudest-

mouthed, most battle-hungry hellion-hearted Stronghold in all the wide wide world. YES!

But first, just right now, soon, THE NEXT ORDER OF BUSINESS! Stronghold 10 must find his Stronghold.

After five hours of walking hard and going perhaps a stingy mile and a half, and some of that in circles, I stood lost in a little plastic draw, and quite bewildered. The vapor shield was scarlet August that burning month, the tin flowers were up in all the plastic plant holes, the rolling ersatz pastures were all aflutter with flash and flaunt of blooms. A sheen was in the air, a shimmer, and a million devils of heat-stroke walked out and wrapped me close in my shell. And I was lost on this seventh day of hot August.

I'll always remember him, the way he came walking, a big man all shrunken in the torso, all bent down along the back curve, all sere and wrinkled in the face areas, so very terribly black-brown, like meat cooked too long on the bone. He had surely been through some maximum havoc—fire maybe, maybe fire and wind together, maybe flood too, wife-trouble and relatives thrown in could be, almost surely a war, possibly all standard disasters known to man, and some not so standard. He looked that bad. Yes, truly. THE WAR mostly—probably. And when he talked, I knew some problem surely had wrecked him even past what showed. Perhaps he had lost some parts that really counted one time. Anyway, his voice was a womanly squeak now as he said, "Lost, mister?"

I swiveled to take him in fully, practicing coming down to hard-stare with my new wide-range Moderan vision, and I thumbed at the book, seeking the page on speech. (Oh, remember, I was new new-metal and the hospital had not kept me over for many practice runs. Not in any phase, let alone speech.) But it wasn't so hard really. NO! of course not. All one had to do was be a mechanical genius to run oneself, a broad-caster speech specialist in order to talk, and a few other things to be able to operate as a new-metal man smoothly and with élan. Mostly, for just right now, forget the refinements and just try to find the right buttons. When I pushed the *phfluggee-phflaggee* too hard and it shouted, I mean shouted, "SURE AM," he jumped about five feet in the air. I could guess he wasn't used to that voice-button shouting, and I could also suppose he expected lip movement (I learned to do that later) and maybe better inflection too (which I learned later, as well). I tried again and said, passably I hoped, *phfluggee-phflaggee* voice going smoother, "I'm looking for Stronghold Ten. I AM Stronghold Ten. When I get there." Then I tried a little voice-button laugh, just for kicks, and it came out "HA! Huk!"

"OH!" he said, wet slop slopping, gristle-meat tongue doing a dance, wind in the wind-pipe working, GOD! what an old-fashioned method just to communicate a few verbal salutes. Hadn't we needed improvement for quite a long time there? "I think I know," he finished, squeak-voiced and all, and still scared, "but you look so funny! Like a polished-up scrap heap, sort of. And all that load!" His fried-like wrinkled cheeks puffed then and he was consumed for a while with a tiny squeaky belly laugh.

"Well, I'm not funny," I snapped, furiously working the buttons, "not funny at all. I'm to be a king. I AM A KING! If I can just find where. And this stuff is all stuff I need to get me started, be sure of that."

"I guess I know," he piped up, stopping the laugh off tight. "I mean, you said Strong-hold Ten. And well, there's a big pile up there of stuff. I mean, it's a castle, really. WOW! I mean it's like nothing I ever saw!" And he stood entranced, thinking, I had to guess, on what he'd seen.

"HOO! It's got a big ten on it that shines out day and night. That ten must be in jewels. Or maybe just some kind of paint. But it's too much for me. I've walked by just to look at that ten sometimes. And usually things would happen. Or I should say ALWAYS, here of late, things would happen. I guess they've got all that

BLAM! stuff working and perfected now. And all those walls and towers."

"YEAH?" I *phfluggee-phflaggeed*. "Really?"

"Yeah! Last time I's by—yesterday, it was, late, I mean—they must have had ALL of it systems-GO! When I move in close I acti-vate something. I've found that out, found it out months past, and I've been teasin' 'em for months, too. But I guess they didn't mind, 'cause it gave 'em a chance to test. And practice. And yesterday, WHEE! I have to believe every-thing was ready. Such a bedlam, such a warn-ing display, such a response for just a harmless lost human wreck-pile like me, who's 'ad it and 'ad it really. I mean, I'm done. THE WAR, you know. And all."

"Sorry," I push-buttoned at him the very best that I could. "Really sorry. But go on about what happened. The response, I mean."

"The response?—YEAH! Well, if you were in THE WAR, we have some background for conversation. Were you in THE WAR?"

"Yes, VERY!"

"Were you in on the response at Landry, say, or the push-button flattening of Whay? Happened all in just seconds, you know. That's where I got it, got it bad and really—at Landry, and lost the parts that, being gone, cause me to squeak at my conversation just right now. Know what I mean?"

"Know what you mean. And yes, I was in on the things you mention. In fact, I was the young Bangdaddo, the Commandaddo, the Chief-in-Chief of the Bangs, who pushed the buttons on Whay. My job, you know, just doing my job." God, maybe I was the one who had ripped him.

He looked at me straight on and a sun came out of either eye just then and shone at me with a million warm pats of adoration. "YOU'RE HIM!" he squeak-voice shouted. And I thought I knew what he meant. Yes, I had been very BIG at the response on Landry and the push-button flattening of Whay. I had been the First Bang-daddo, THE COMMANDADDO.

"And now they've fixed you to be one of the BIG ones here! That figures."

"I'm lucky. And I'm sorry you got it, got shot up so badly. Truly sorry. No one won, finally, you know. NO ONE. Maybe they can fix you."

"Nah. Once gone like this is gone GONE. For me it's downhill to the bone hill. But I'm staying as long as I can!" And I had to admire him for that last little singing out of the bones-in-the-teeth determination. "Just to see what happens to you guys who made it," he finished.

"But now," I asked, "would you be kind enough to lead me to my castle? So I can get started on whatever it is I'm supposed to be. I'd be ever so grateful to you."

"I'll do it, and gladly. And if you don't know by now why GLADLY, I guess you never will." He looked at me with not a begging look, just a quiet questioning look from eyes that didn't waver now, and I guessed that within this wreck pile there had once been a very proud human being. Something about that stance, the set of the once-champion shoulders, the head lowered a little more now with the eyes peep-glaring out, the fists ready to hammer the world down to tiniest wreck-size pieces—and a bulb flashed on, far deep in the reaches—"MORGBAWN!" I shouted, hitting all the *phfluggee-phflaggee* buttons I had, and suddenly we were clasping each other while time had rolled quite away. "Oh God, what happened HAPPENED?"

I remember him as he had not-too-long-ago been, a man quite up among men, tall and giant-seeming in his neat uniform of the BANGS, just before Landry, where everything for him and for me went wrong. I had lost him, my great second in command, in the hell and the flame and the noise of Landry, where I thought he had been blown to high skies and all winds. I had escaped by the merest chance of a miracle myself, to try the retrieval of all on Whay. There was no retrieval of anything that war, and especially not on Whay. YES! I had flattened it with the launchers and the big zump-blasters, but the other side took me out just as badly. And right after that all the world seemed to turn to flame as everyone gunned in.

"To start again!" I said to Morgbawn. "Maybe we can both start again."

"No," he replied in the very smallest of piping voices, quite eerie, "I'm nothing but the dust now. Essentially. It's just a matter of a very small small while until whatever I was must lie and lie and lie, grave-housed—FOREVER. The battles can never be joined again for me."

Then an idea took me, a great boiling steaming kind of thought, the kind that could, when I was all flesh in the Old Days, give me goose crinkles along the brain. My new-metal shell now rasped and wrinkled and roared in my flesh-strips and new green blood reacted while the brainpans steamed. "Come be my weapons man!" I cried with the button-crying, "and we'll flatten the world! as we once hoped we could do it when we were fresh and deadly in our new uniforms of the BANGS. It's a chance to fight again and maybe win it all, maybe make up our losses.—Every Stronghold master, as I understand it, has a head weapons man. You'll be my lead!"

The look from his haggard killed fried-meat face was wan and wintry through storms of glooms. And yet, I thought I detected a very tiny pinpoint spark of yearning hope too, deep back, struggling behind his gaze. But he said, "Ah no, I've been here long enough to know what a weapons man is in Moderan. He's a moving bit of mechanical servant nonsense meaning nothing, nothing at all. I think I'd rather lie out in my grave than to rejoin the battles that way. Not even one flesh-strip!"

"I'll see that you get one. I swear it. One of mine!"

"Ah no, what could it mean? One flesh-strip. HA-ha. Why, a person has to have a whole network, with the blood coursing, to be anything. Otherwise it means nothing. You have to admit it, God still made the best people. One flesh-strip! HA! Why, I'd have to have a built-in pickle jar to keep it alive."

"We'll do it. A built-in pickle jar!"

"Ah, no." But there was still that tiny spark of hope, and I thought I detected it stronger now. YES! I was beginning to wonder if Morgbawn wasn't finding it a worlds better idea, that of being up and moving with even just one flesh-strip in a pickle jar rather than to lie totally quiet out there, the Battles finally and forever completely renounced for him.

"How about it?"

"Maybe!" he said. "I don't know. Come find me where I fall. We'll keep in touch, maybe. It shouldn't be long now. When I feel myself finally going, wherever I am, I'll head for your place. I'll struggle in as close as I can get. Come find me—" His face retreated and commenced to break up then, he started to move away, and I think in that one anguished moment I understood just a little better than I ever had before what it might be like to be, as Morgbawn surely was, at the very brink of the Forever Total Dark. He was far down the plastic draw, the heart-rending wreck of my once great second in command, before I came back to the moment of now and remembered that he could have helped me find my way home. Ah well, it was near. He had said so. And maybe, after nightfall, that glowing 10 he had told me of would reach out and beam me in. I turned all the settings on LOW, fixed the alarm at a time for awakening, and, surrounded by my equipment and instructions, simmered into sleep right there on the plastic that very hot summer eve, to awake, I hoped, in the light of a gleaming 10.

THE FLESH MAN FROM FAR WIDE

I had just nailed the mice down lightly by their tails to the struggle board, was considering how happy is happy, and was right on the point of rising from my hip-snuggie chair to go fetch forth the new-metal cat when my warner set up a din. I raced to my Viewer Wall, where the weapon thumbs all were; set the peep scope to max-sweep; and looked out, wide-ranging the blue plastic hills. And I saw this guy, this shape, this little bent-down thing coming not from the Valley of the White Witch, my main area of danger now, but coming from the Plains of Far Wide, from which I had not had a visitor for nigh on to five eras.

Was he sad, oh, was he sad! He came on, this little toad-down man, tap-tap, mince-mince, step-walk-step, but with tense carefulness in his slowness, as if every inch-mince were some slipping up on a bird. It made me itch just to see him, and to think how walking should be, great striding, big reaching, tall up with steel things clanking long-down by your side and other weapons in leather with which to defy your world. And your wagons coming up with maces and hatchets on end. Though I go not that way myself, truth to say, for I am of Moderan, where people have "replacements." I walk with a hitch worse than most, an inch-along kind of going, clop-clip-clap-clop, over the plastic yards, what little I walk, for I still have bugs in the hinges. I was an Early, you know, one of the first of Moderan. But I remember. Something in the pale green blood of my flesh-strips recalls how walking should be—a great going out with maces to pound up your enemies' heads, and a crunchy bloody jelly underfoot from the bones and juices of things too little even to be glanced at under your iron-clad feet.

But this guy! Hummph. He came like a lily. Yes, a white lily with bell-cone head bent down. I wondered why my warner even bothered with him. But yes, I knew why my warner bothered with him. My warner tells me of all movement toward my Stronghold, and sometimes the lilies—"Stand by for decontamination!" He was at my Outer Wall now, at the Screening Gate, so I directed my decontaminators and weapons probers to give him the rub-a-dub. To be truthful, two large metal hands had leaped out of the wall to seize him and hold him directly in front of the Screening Gate, so my call to "stand by for decontamination!" was merely a courtesy blab. When the Decontamination and the Weapons Report both gave him a clean bill

I thumbed the gates back in all my eleven steel walls and let the lily man mince through.

"Hello, and welcome, strange traveler from Far Wide." He stood trembling in his soft-rag shoes, seeming hard put on how actually to stop his inch-mince walk. "Forgive me," he said, "if I seem nervous." And he looked at me out of the blue of his flesh-ball eyes while he tugged at a cup-shaped red beard. And I was appalled at the "replacements" he had disallowed, the parts of himself he had clung to. For one wild blinding moment I was almost willing to bet that he had his real heart, even. But then I thought ah, no, not at this late year and in Moderan. "This walking," he continued, "keeps going. You see, it takes a while to quiet. You know, getting here at last, I cannot, all of me, believe I am really here. My mind says yes! My poor legs keep thinking there's still walking to do. But I'm here!"

"You're here," I echoed, and I wondered, What next? what goes? I thought of the mice I had nailed and the new cat waiting and I was impatient to get on with my Joys. But then, a visitor is a visitor, and a host most likely is a victim. "Have you eaten? Have you had your introven?"

"I've eaten." He eyed at me strange-wide. "I didn't have introven."

I began to feel more uneasy by the minute. He just stood there vibrating slightly on thin legs, with those blue-flesh-ball eyes peeking my way, and he seemed to be waiting for me to react. "I'm here!" he said again. And I said, "Yes," not knowing what else to say. "Would you wish to tell me about your trip," I asked, "the trials and tribulations?"

Then he started his recital. It was mostly a dreary long tune of hard going, of almost baseless hopes concerning what he hoped to find, of how he had kept coming, of how he had almost quit in the Spoce Mountains, of how something up ahead had kept him trying, something like a gleam of light through a break in an iron wall. "Get over the wall," he said, "and you have won it, all that light. Over the wall!" He looked at me as though this was surely my time to react.

"Why did you almost quit in the Spoce Mountains?"

"Why did I almost quit in the Spoce Mountains!? Have you ever tried the Spoce Mountains?" I had to admit that I had not. "If you have never tried the Spoce Mountains—" He fell into a fit of shaking that was more vivid than using many words. "Where are all the others?" he asked when the shaking had stopped a little.

"All the others? What are you talking about?"

"Oh, yes. There must be great groups here. There must be long lists waiting." His white cone-shaped face lit up. "Oh, they're in the Smile Room. That's it, isn't it?"

My big steel fingers itched to crush him then like juicing a little worm. There was something about him, so soft, so trustful and pleading and so all against my ideas of the iron mace and the big arm-swing walk. "There's no Smile Room here," I blurted. "And no long lists waiting."

Unwilling to be crushed he smiled that pure little smile. "Oh, it must be such a wonderful machine. And so big! After all the other machines, the One, the ONE—finally!"

Great leaping lead balls bouncing on bareflesh toes! What had we here? A nut? Or was he just lost from home? "Mister," I said, "I don't know what you're driving at. This is my home. It's where I wall out danger. It's where I wall in fun. My kind of fun. It's a Stronghold."

At the sound of that last word his blue eyes dipped over and down in his whitewash face; his head fell forward like it was trying to follow the eyes to where they were falling. And out of a great but invisible cloud that seemed to wrap him round his stricken mouth gaped wide. "A Stronghold! All this way I've come and it is a Stronghold! You have not the Happiness Machine at a Stronghold. It could not be.

"Oh, it is what kept me going—the hope of it. I was told. In the misty dangerous weird Spoce Mountains when the big wet-wing Gloon Glays jumped me and struck me down with their beaks I arose and kept coming. And on one very sullen rain-washed hapless morning I awoke in a white circle of the long-tusk wart-skin woebegawngawns, and oh it would have been so much easier, so very much less exacting, to have feigned sleep while they tore me and opened my soul case with death. But no! I stood up, I remembered prophecy. I drew my cloak around me. I walked. I walked on. I left them staring with empty teeth. I thought of my destination. And now— It was a dream! I am fooled! Take me to your Happiness Machine!"

He was becoming hysterical. He blabbed as how he wanted to go and sit in some machine gauged to beauty and truth and love and be happy. He was breaking down. I saw I must rally him for one more try, to get him beyond my walls. "Mister," I said, "you have, no doubt, known the big clouds and the sun failing and the rain-washed gray dawn of the hopeless time. You have—I believe it—stood up in disaster amid adversity's singing knives and all you had going for you was what you had brought along. There were no armies massing for you on other fields, no uncles raising funds in far countries across seas; perhaps there were no children, even, coming for Daddy in the Spoce Mountains, and with death not even one widow to claim the body and weep it toward the sun. And yet you defied all this, somehow got out of disaster's tightening ring and moved on down. I admire you. I truly am sorry I do not have what you want. And though you are a kind of fool, by my way of thinking, to go running around in flesh looking for a pure something that perhaps does not exist, I wish you luck as I thumb the gates back and make way for your progress. You may find, up ahead somewhere, across a lot of mountains, and barren land, these Happiness Machines for which you cry." He trembled when I spoke of mountains, but he moved out through the gates.

And though I was sure he would find nothing the way he was going, I have not been entirely able to forget him. What would prompt such a creature, obviously ill equipped for any great achievement, to hope for the ultimate and impossibly great achievement, happiness? And such an odd way to expect it, happiness dispensed by some magic machine gauged to beauty and truth and love. In a resplendent place at the end of a long trip.

To hear him talk you'd think happiness could be based on lily-weak things. How weird. Power is joy; strength is pleasure; put your trust only in the thick wall with the viewer and the warner. But sometimes, in spite of myself, I think of this little flesh-ridden man and wonder where he is.

And when I'm at my ease, feeding my flesh-strips the complicated fluids of the introven, knowing I can live practically forever with the help of the new-metal alloys, a vague uneasiness comes over me and I try to evaluate my life. With the machines that serve me all buzzing underneath my Stronghold and working fine— yes, I am satisfied, I am adequate. And when I want a little more than quiet satisfaction, I can probe out and destroy one of my neighbor's walls perhaps, or a piece of his warner. And then we will fight lustily at each other for a little while from our Strongholds, pushing the destruction buttons at each other in a kind of high glee. Or I can just keep home and work out some little sadistic pleasure on my own. And on the terms the flesh-man wanted—truth, beauty, love—I'm practically sure there is no Happiness Machine out there anywhere at all. I'm almost sure there isn't.

Let Us Save the Universe

(An Open Letter from Ijon Tichy)

STANISŁAW LEM

Translated by Joel Stern and Maria Swiecicka-Ziemianek

Stanisław Lem (1921–2006) was a world-renowned Polish writer of science fiction, philosophy, and satire whose books have appeared in more than thirty countries and sold millions of copies. Over half a century, he published a flurry of influential and groundbreaking fiction and nonfiction books.

In 1976, Theodore Sturgeon wrote that Lem was the most widely read science fiction writer in the world. If true, this was in part because Lem was a genius but also because Lem often adopted the form of the short tall tale or folktale for his science fiction, speaking therefore in a near-universal language. Yet the intellectual rigor of his fiction is second to none, spanning such areas as advanced technology, human intelligence, community, and the nature of alien life. Much of his work exists within a continuum also occupied by idiosyncratic, brilliant writers such as Italo Calvino, Jorge Luis Borges, and Leena Krohn.

He is perhaps most famous for writing the classic 1961 novel *Solaris*, translated into film thrice, most notably by Andrei Tarkovsky. But Lem's adventures with nonfiction are just as breathtaking, especially *Summa Technologiae* (1964), a brilliant and risky survey of possible informational, A.I., and ecological advances, interwoven with musings of a biological and technological nature.

Parts of the American science fiction community did not particularly get along with Lem. He became the epicenter of a controversy involving the Science Fiction Writers of America in 1973 when he was awarded, and then denied, an honorary membership with the organization; some saw it as a rebuke to his mostly negative opinion of American science fiction, which he thought was too commercially driven. Even when Lem praised an American writer—one Philip K. Dick—it caused difficulties. Dick reported Lem to the FBI, believing that "Lem" was a front for a communist agent trying, somehow, to undermine the United States. Thereafter, Lem can hardly be blamed for having nothing to do with the science fiction community—especially given that he had his own difficulties with the Communist Party in his country. (Thankfully, his international popularity allowed Lem more leeway than most writers in the Soviet bloc.)

Although most of the Lem canon is well worth reading, his stories featuring Ijon Tichy, described as the hapless Candide of the Cosmos, are particularly hilarious and rich in detail. Tichy pilots his single-seat rocket through deep space, encountering time warps, weird intergalactic civilizations, and black holes. Whether it is killer potatoes who love to eat spaceships or robot theologians living in catacombs, Lem's imagination is superlative in these beloved tales. As translator Michael Kandel noted in *The Star Diaries* (1976), these stories include playful anecdotes, pointed satire, and outright philosophy. But rather than innovating, as Kandel believed, Lem was renovating—by bringing the *conte philosophe* approach used by early twentieth-century science fiction into the modern era and thus allying himself with writers such as Alfred Jarry and Paul Scheerbart.

"Let Us Save the Universe" (1971), first published in English in *The New Yorker* (1981), is one of the last Tichy tales, and as such encapsulates many of the joys of the series, even as it also includes a note of sadness. In revisiting his favorite places, Tichy finds too much has been polluted or transformed. "Tichy" is pronounced "*Tee*-khee" and suggests the Polish word for "quiet."

LET US SAVE THE UNIVERSE
(An Open Letter from Ijon Tichy)

Stanisław Lem
Translated by Joel Stern and Maria Swiecicka-Ziemianek

After a long stay on Earth I set out to visit my favorite places from my previous expeditions—the spherical clusters of Perseus, the constellation of the Calf, and the large stellar cloud in the center of the galaxy. Everywhere I found changes, which are painful for me to write about, because they are not changes for the better. There is much talk nowadays about the growth of cosmic tourism. Without question tourism is wonderful, but everything should be in moderation.

The eyesores begin as soon as you are out the door. The asteroid belt between Mars and Jupiter is in deplorable condition. Those monumental rocks, once enveloped in eternal night, are lit up now, and to make matters worse, every crag is carved with initials and monograms.

Eros, the particular favorite of lovers, shakes from the explosions with which self-taught calligraphers gouge inscriptions in its crust. A couple of shrewd operators there rent out hammers, chisels, and even pneumatic drills, and a man cannot find an untouched rock in what were once the most rugged areas.

Everywhere are graffiti like it was love at first sight on this here meteorite, and arrow-pierced hearts in the worst taste. On Ceres, which for some reason large families like, there is a veritable plague of photography. The many photographers there don't just rent out space suits for posing but cover mountainsides with a special emulsion and for a nominal fee immortalize on them entire groups of vacationers. The huge pictures are then glazed to make them permanent. Suitably posed families—father, mother, grandparents, children—smile from cliffs. This, as I read in some prospectus, creates a "family atmosphere." As regards Juno, that once beautiful planetoid is all but gone; anyone who feels like it chips stones off it and hurls them into space. People have spared neither nickel-iron meteors (which have gone into souvenir signet rings and cufflinks) nor comets. You won't find a comet with its tail intact anymore.

I thought I would escape the congestion of cosmobuses, the family portraits on cliffs, and the graffiti doggerel once I left the solar system. Was I wrong!

Professor Bruckee from the observatory complained to me recently that both stars in Centaurus were growing dim. How can they not grow dim when the entire area is filled with trash? Around the heavy planet Sirius, the chief attraction of this system, is a ring like those of Saturn, but formed of beer bottles and lemonade containers. An astronaut flying that route must dodge not only swarms of meteors but also tin cans, eggshells, and old newspapers. There are places where you cannot see the stars, for all the rubbish. For years astrophysicists have been racking their brains over the reason for the great difference in the amounts of cosmic dust in various galaxies. The answer, I think, is quite simple: the higher a civilization is, the more dust and refuse it produces. This is a problem more for janitors than for astrophysicists. Other nebulae have not been able to cope with it, either, but that is small comfort.

Spitting into space is another reprehensible practice. Saliva, like any liquid, freezes at low temperatures, and colliding with it can easily lead to disaster. It is embarrassing to mention, but individuals who fall sick during a voyage seem to consider outer space their personal toilet, as if unaware that the traces of their distress will orbit for millions of years, arousing in tourists bad associations and an understandable disgust.

Alcoholism is a special problem.

Beyond Sirius I began counting the huge signs advertising Mars vodka, Galax brandy, Lunar gin, and Satellite champagne, but soon lost count. I hear from pilots that some cosmodromes have been forced to switch from alcohol fuel to nitric acid, there being nothing of the former left to use for takeoff. The patrol service says that it is difficult to spot a drunken person from a distance: people blame their staggering on weightlessness. And the practices of certain space stations are a disgrace. I once asked that my reserve bottles be filled with oxygen, after which, having traveled no more than a parsec, I heard a strange burbling and found that I had been given, instead, pure cognac! When I went back, the station director insisted that I had winked when I spoke to him. Maybe I did wink—I have a stye—but does that justify such a state of affairs?

Confusion reigns on the main routes. The huge number of accidents is not surprising, considering that so many people regularly exceed the speed limit. The worst offenders are women: by traveling fast they slow the passage of time and age less. Also, one frequently encounters rattletraps, like the old cosmobuses that pollute the length of the ecliptic with their exhaust.

When I landed on Palindronia and asked for the complaint book, I was told that it had been smashed the day before by a meteorite. And the supply of oxygen is running short. Six light-years from Beluria it cannot be obtained anywhere, people who go there to sightsee are forced to freeze themselves and wait, reversibly dead, for the next shipment of air, because if alive they would have not a thing to breathe. When I arrived, there was no one at the cosmodrome; they were all hibernating in the coolers.

But in the cafeteria I saw a complete assortment of drinks—from pineapples in cognac to pilsner.

Sanitary conditions, particularly on those planets within the Great Preserve, are outrageous. In the *Voice of Mersituria* I read an article calling for the extermination of those splendid beasts the swallurkers. These predators have on their upper lips a number of shiny warts in diverse patterns. In the last few years, however, a variety with warts arranged in the form of two zeroes has been appearing more frequently. Swallurkers usually hunt in the vicinity of campsites, where at night, under cover of darkness, they lie, with wide-open jaws. In wait for people seeking a secluded spot. Doesn't the author of the article realize that the animals are completely innocent, that one should blame not them but those responsible for the lack of proper plumbing facilities?

A swallurker at night with victim

On this same Mersituria the absence of public conveniences has caused a whole series of mutations among insects.

Bottombiter chair ants lying in wait

In places famous for beautiful views one often sees comfortable wicker chairs that seem to invite the weary stroller. If he eagerly sits down between the arms, the supposed chair attacks, for it is actually thousands of spotted ants (the bottombiter chair ant, *Multipodium pseudostellatum Trylopii*) that group together and mimic wicker furniture. Rumor has it that certain other varieties of arthropods (fripples, scrooches, and brutalacean rollipedes) have mimicked soda stands, hammocks, and even showers with faucets and towels, but I cannot vouch for the truth of such assertions, having myself seen nothing of the kind, and the myrmecological authorities are silent on this point. However, I should give a warning about a rather rare species, the snakefooted telescoper (*Anencephalus pseudoopticus tripedius Klaczkinensis*). The telescoper also stations itself in scenic spots, extending its three long, thin legs like a tripod and aiming its tubular tail at the scenery. With the saliva that fills its mouth opening, it imitates the lens of a telescope, enticing the careless tourist to take a peek, with extremely unpleasant consequences. Another snake, the trippersneak (*Serpens vitiosus Reichenmantlii*), found on the planet Gaurimachia, lurks in bushes and trips unwary passersby with its tail. However, this reptile feeds exclusively on blondes and does not mimic anything.

A brutalacean rollipede

The universe is not a playground, nor is biological evolution an idyll. We ought to publish brochures like those I saw on Derdimona, warning amateur botanists about the cruella

(*Pliximiglaquia bombardons L.*). The cruella has gorgeous flowers, but they must not be picked, because the plant lives in symbiosis with the brainbasher, a tree bearing fruit that is melon sized and spiked. The careless botanizer need pluck only one flower, and a shower of rock-hard missiles will descend upon his head. Neither the cruella nor the brainbasher does any harm to the victim afterward; they are content with the natural consequences of his death, for it helps fertilize the surrounding soil.

But marvels of mimicry occur on all the planets in the Preserve. The savannas of Beluria, for example, abound with colorful flowers, among which there is a crimson rose of wondrous beauty and fragrance (the *Rosa mendatrix Tichiana*, as Professor Pingle named it, for I was the first to describe it). This flower is actually a growth on the tail of the herpeton, a Belurian predator. The hungry herpeton hides in a thicket, extending its extremely long tail far ahead, so that only the flower protrudes from the grass. When an unsuspecting tourist stoops to smell it, the beast pounces on him from behind. Its tusks are almost as long as an elephant's. What a strange, extraterrestrial confirmation, this, of the adage that every rose has its thorns!

If I may digress a little, I cannot help recalling another Belurian marvel, a distant relative of the potato—the sentient gentian (*Gentiana sapiens suicidalis Pruck*). The name of this plant derives from certain of its mental properties. It has sweet and very tasty bulbs. As a result of mutation, the gentian will sometimes form tiny brains instead of the usual bulbs. This mutant variety, the crazy gentian (*Gentiana mentecapta*), becomes restless as it grows. It digs itself out, goes into the forest, and gives itself up to solitary meditation. It invariably reaches the conclusion that life is not worth living, and commits suicide.

The gentian is harmless to man, unlike another Belurian plant, the furiol. This species has adapted to an environment created by intolerable children. Such children, constantly running, pushing, and kicking whatever lies in their path, love to break the eggs of the spiny slothodile. The furiol produces fruits identical in form to these eggs. A child, thinking he has an egg in front of him, gives vent to his urge for destruction and smashes it with a kick. The spores contained in the pseudo-egg are released and enter his body. The infected child develops into an apparently normal individual, but before long an incurable malignant process sets in: card playing, drunkenness, and debauchery are the successive stages, followed by either death or a great career. I have often heard the opinion that furiols should be extirpated. Those who say this do not stop to think that children should be taught, instead, not to kick objects on foreign planets.

I am by nature an optimist and try to have faith in man, but it is not always easy. On Prostostenesa lives a small bird known as the scribblemock (*Graphomanus spasmaticus Essenbachii*), the counterpart of the terrestrial parrot, except that it writes instead of talks. Often, alas, it writes on fences the obscenities it picks up from tourists from Earth. Some people deliberately infuriate this bird by taunting it with spelling errors. The creature then begins eating everything in sight. They feed it ginger, raisins, pepper, and yellwort, an herb that lets out a long scream at sunrise (it is sometimes used as an alarm clock). When the bird dies of overeating, they barbecue it. The species is now threatened with extinction, for every tourist who comes to Prostostenesa looks forward to a meal of roast scribblemock, reputed to be a great delicacy.

A scribblemock

Some people believe that it is all right if humans eat creatures from other planets, but when the reverse takes place they raise a hue and cry, call for military assistance, demand punitive expeditions, etc. Yet it is anthropomorphic nonsense to accuse extraterrestrial flora or fauna of treachery. If the deadly deceptorite, which looks like a rotten tree stump, stands posing on its hind legs to mimic a signpost along a mountain trail, leads hikers astray, and devours them when they fall into a chasm—if, I say, the deceptorite does this, it is only because the rangers in the Preserve do not maintain the road signs. The paint peels off the signs, which causes them to rot and resemble that animal. Any other creature, in its place, would do the same.

A deadly deceptorite

The famous mirages of Stredogentsia owe their existence solely to man's vicious inclinations. At one time chillips grew on the planet in great numbers, and warmstrels were hardly ever found. Now the latter have multiplied incredibly. Above thickets of them, the air, heated artificially and diffracted, gives rise to mirages of taverns, which have caused the death of many a traveler from Earth. It is said that the warmstrels are entirely to blame. Why, then, don't their mirages mimic schools, libraries, or health clubs? Why do they always show places where intoxicating beverages are sold? The answer is simple. Because mutations are random, warmstrels at first created all sorts of mirages, but those that showed people libraries and adult-education classes starved to death, and only the tavern variety (*Thermomendax spirituosus halucinogenes* of the family Anthropophagi) survived. This special adaptation of the warmstrel, brought about by man himself, is a powerful indictment of our vices.

Not long ago I was incensed by a letter to the editor in the *Stredogentsia Echo*. The writer demanded the removal of both the warmstrels and the solinthias, those magnificent trees that are the pride of every park. When their bark is cut, poisonous, blinding sap squirts out. The solinthia is the last Stredogentsian tree not carved from top to bottom with graffiti and initials—and now we are to get rid of it? A similar fate appears to threaten such valuable fauna as the vengerix, the maraudola, the morselone, and the electric howler. The latter, to protect itself and its offspring from the nerve-racking noise of countless tourist radios in the forest, has developed, through natural selection, the ability to cancel out particularly loud rock-and-roll music. The electrical organs of the howler emit superheterodyne waves, so this unusual creation of nature should be placed under protection at once.

As for the foul-tailed fetido, I admit that the odor it gives off has no equal. Dr. Hopkins of the University of Milwaukee has calculated that particularly active specimens can produce up to five kr (kiloreeks) per second. But even a child knows that the fetido does this only when photographed. The sight of an aimed camera triggers a reaction known as the lenticular-subcaudal reflex—it is nature attempting to shield this innocent creature from the intrusions of rubbernecks. Although it is true that the fetido, being rather nearsighted, sometimes takes for a camera such objects as ashtrays, lighters, watches, and even medals and badges, this is partly because some tourists use minia-

ture cameras; it is easy to make a mistake. As for the observation that in recent years fetidos have increased their range and now produce up to eight megareeks per acre, I must point out that the cause here is the widespread use of telephoto lenses.

A foul-tailed fetido

I do not wish to give the impression that I consider all extraterrestrial animals and plants beyond criticism. Certainly carnivamps, saprophoids, geeklings, dementeria, and marshmuckers are not particularly likable, nor are the mysophilids from the family Autarchiae, including *Gauleiterium flagellans*, *Syphonophiles pruritualis*, and the throttlemor (*Lingula stranguloides Erdmenglerbeyeri*). But think the matter over carefully and try to be objective. Why is it proper for a human to pick flowers and dry them in a herbarium, but unnatural for a plant to tear off and preserve ears? If the echoloon (*Echolalium impudicum Schwamps*) has multiplied on Aedonoxia beyond all measure, humans are to blame for this, too. The echoloon derives its life energy from sound. Once thunder served it as a food source; in fact, it still likes to listen to storms. But now it has switched to tourists. Each tourist treats the echoloon to a volley of the filthiest curses. It is amusing, they say, to watch the creature literally blossom under a torrent of abuse. It does indeed grow, but because of the energy absorbed from sonic vibrations, not because of the profanities shouted by excited tourists.

Gauleiterium flagellans

produces a supernova especially for him! By squandering nuclear energy, polluting asteroids and planets, ravaging the Preserve, and leaving litter everywhere we go, we shall ruin outer space and turn it into one big dump. It is high time we came to our senses and enforced the laws. Convinced that every minute of delay is dangerous, I sound the alarm: let us save the universe.

A drillbeaked borbit

Where is all this leading? Such species as the blue wizzom and the drillbeaked borbit have disappeared; thousands of others are dying out. Sunspots are increasing due to clouds of rubbish. I still remember the time when the great treat for a child was the promise of a Sunday trip to Mars; but now the little monster will not eat his breakfast unless Daddy

Vaster Than Empires and More Slow

URSULA K. LE GUIN

Ursula K. Le Guin (1929–) is an iconic and award-winning US writer known mostly for fantasy and science fiction, and a towering figure in American literature. Leading an intensely private life, Le Guin sporadically engages in political activism and remains a steady participant in the literary community in Portland, Oregon, where she has lived since 1958.

Three of Le Guin's books have been finalists for the Pulitzer Prize and the American Book Award. She has received many honors for her writing, including a National Book Award, the Janet Heidinger Kafka Prize, the PEN/Malamud Award, five Hugo Awards, five Nebula Awards, SFWA's Grand Master, the Harold D. Vursell Memorial Award of the American Academy of Arts and Letters, the Margaret A. Edwards Award, the Los Angeles Times Robert Kirsch Award, and in 2014 the National Book Foundation's Medal for Distinguished Contribution to American Letters, among others.

Le Guin's rigorous artistry and serious devotion to science fiction and other allegedly subliterary genres has been met with rapturous critical reception. She has garnered praise from John Updike, Gary Snyder, Grace Paley, Salman Rushdie, Kelly Link, Neil Gaiman, and Carolyn Kizer. Harold Bloom counts her among the classic American writers, and many critical studies have been written on Le Guin's work, including book-length treatments by Elizabeth Cummins, D. R. White, B. J. Bucknall, B. Selinger, and K. R. Wayne.

Throughout her sixty-year career and up to the present day, Le Guin has been more than willing to engage in discussions and arguments about fiction, science fiction, gender issues, and the future of publishing. Her incisive essays and blog posts display a sharpness and clarity that continue to make her viewpoints relevant. She has also edited major anthologies (including coediting *The Norton Book of Science Fiction* [1993]) and in all ways her life has reflected a commitment to books and book culture as a true "person of letters."

First published in the 1960s, Le Guin's fiction has often depicted futuristic or imaginary alternative worlds in stories that grapple with important issues such as politics, gender, and the environment. After a first story was submitted to and rejected by the magazine *Astounding Science Fiction* when she was eleven, Le Guin continued writing but did not attempt to publish for a decade. In 1969, her career began its steep upward trajectory with the publication of *The Left Hand of Darkness*, which won the Hugo and Nebula Awards for Best Novel. Shortly thereafter, *The Dispossessed* also won the Hugo and Nebula Awards.

"Vaster Than Empires and More Slow" (1971) is both classic Le Guin and a good example of a story that has become only more topical and relevant with the passage of time. This story of unusual alien contact carries forward environmental themes present in such other stories in this anthology as James H. Schmitz's "Grandpa," F. L. Wallace's "Student Body," and Dmitri Bilenkin's "Where Two Paths Cross."

VASTER THAN EMPIRES AND MORE SLOW

Ursula K. Le Guin

It was only during the earliest decades of the League that the Earth sent ships out on the enormously long voyages, beyond the pale, over the stars and far away. They were seeking for worlds which had not been seeded or settled by the Founders on Hain, truly alien worlds. All the Known Worlds went back to the Hainish Origin, and the Terrans, having been not only founded but salvaged by the Hainish, resented this. They wanted to get away from the family. They wanted to find somebody new. The Hainish, like tiresomely understanding parents, supported their explorations, and contributed ships and volunteers, as did several other worlds of the League.

All these volunteers to the Extreme Survey crews shared one peculiarity: they were of unsound mind.

What sane person, after all, would go out to collect information that would not be received for five or ten centuries? Cosmic mass interference had not yet been eliminated from the operation of the ansible, and so instantaneous communication was reliable only within a range of 120 light-years. The explorers would be quite isolated. And of course they had no idea what they might come back to, if they came back. No normal human being who had experienced time-slippage of even a few decades between League worlds would volunteer for a round trip of centuries. The Surveyors were escapists, misfits. They were nuts.

Ten of them climbed aboard the ferry at Smeming Port, and made varyingly inept attempts to get to know one another during the three days the ferry took getting to their ship, *Gum*. *Gum* is a Cetian nickname, on the order of *Baby* or *Pet*. There were two Cetians on the team, two Hainishmen, one Beldene, and five Terrans; the Cetian-built ship was chartered by the Government of Earth. Her motley crew came aboard wriggling through the coupling tube one by one like apprehensive spermatozoa trying to fertilize the universe. The ferry left and the navigator put *Gum* under way. She flitted for some hours on the edge of space a few hundred million miles from Smeming Port, and then abruptly vanished.

When, after 10 hours 29 minutes, or 256 years, *Gum* reappeared in normal space, she was supposed to be in the vicinity of Star KG-E-96651. Sure enough, there was the gold pinhead of the star. Somewhere within a four-hundred-million-kilometer sphere there was also a greenish planet, World 4470, as charted by a Cetian mapmaker. The ship now had to find the planet. This was not quite so easy as it might sound, given a four-hundred-million-kilometer haystack. And *Gum* couldn't bat about in planetary space at near light speed; if she did, she and Star KG-E-96651 and World 4470 might all end up going bang. She had to creep, using rocket propulsion, at a few hundred thousand miles an hour. The Mathematician/Navigator, Asnanifoil, knew pretty well where the planet ought to be, and thought they might raise it within ten E-days. Meanwhile the members of the Survey team got to know one another still better.

"I can't stand him," said Porlock, the Hard Scientist (chemistry, plus physics, astronomy, geology, etc.), and little blobs of spittle appeared on his mustache. "The man is insane. I can't imagine why he was passed as fit to join a Survey team, unless this is a deliberate experiment in non-compatibility, planned by the Authority, with us as guinea pigs."

"We generally use hamsters and Hainish gholes," said Mannon, the Soft Scientist (psychology, plus psychiatry, anthropology, ecology, etc.), politely; he was one of the Hainishmen. "Instead of guinea pigs. Well, you know, Mr. Osden is really a very rare case. In fact, he's the first fully cured case of Render's Syndrome—a variety of infantile autism which was thought to be incurable. The great Terran analyst Hammergeld reasoned that the cause of the autistic condition in this case is a supernormal empathic capacity, and developed an appropriate treatment. Mr. Osden is the first patient to undergo that treatment, in fact he lived with Dr. Hammergeld until he was eighteen. The therapy was completely successful."

"Successful?"

"Why, yes. He certainly is not autistic."

"No, he's intolerable!"

"Well, you see," said Mannon, gazing mildly at the saliva-flecks on Porlock's mustache, "the normal defensive-aggressive reaction between strangers meeting—let's say you and Mr. Osden just for example—is something you're scarcely aware of; habit, manners, inattention get you past it; you've learned to ignore it, to the point where you might even deny it exists. However, Mr. Osden, being an empath, feels it. Feels his feelings, and yours, and is hard put to say which is which. Let's say that there's a normal element of hostility towards any stranger in your emotional reaction to him when you meet him, plus a spontaneous dislike of his looks, or clothes, or handshake—it doesn't matter what. He feels that dislike. As his autistic defense has been unlearned, he resorts to an aggressive-defense mechanism, a response in kind to the aggression which you have unwittingly projected onto him." Mannon went on for quite a long time.

"Nothing gives a man the right to be such a bastard," Porlock said.

"He can't tune us out?" asked Harfex, the Biologist, another Hainishman.

"It's like hearing," said Olleroo, Assistant Hard Scientist, stopping over to paint her toenails with fluorescent lacquer. "No eyelids on your ears. No Off switch on empathy. He hears our feelings whether he wants to or not."

"Does he know what we're *thinking*?" asked Eskwana, the Engineer, looking round at the others in real dread.

"No," Porlock snapped. "Empathy's not telepathy! Nobody's got telepathy."

"Yet," said Mannon, with his little smile, "just before I left Hain there was a most interesting report in from one of the recently discovered worlds, a hilfer named Rocannon reporting what appears to be a teachable telepathic technique existent among a mutated hominid race; I only saw a synopsis in the HILF *Bulletin*, but . . ." He went on. The others had learned that they could talk while Mannon went on talking; he did not seem to mind, nor even to miss much of what they said.

"Then why does he hate us?" Eskwana said.

"Nobody hates you, Ander honey," said Olleroo, daubing Eskwana's left thumbnail with fluorescent pink. The engineer flushed and smiled vaguely.

"He acts as if he hated us," said Haito, the Coordinator. She was a delicate-looking woman of pure Asian descent, with a surprising voice, husky, deep, and soft, like a young bullfrog. "Why, if he suffers from our hostility, does he increase it by constant attacks and insults? I can't say I think much of Dr. Hammergeld's cure, really, Mannon; autism might be preferable. . . ."

She stopped. Osden had come into the main cabin.

He looked flayed. His skin was unnaturally white and thin, showing the channels of his blood like a faded road map in red and blue. His Adam's apple, the muscles that circled his mouth, the bones and ligaments of his wrists and hands, all stood out distinctly as if displayed for an anatomy lesson. His hair was pale rust, like long-dried blood. He had eyebrows and lashes, but they were visible only in certain lights; what one saw was the bones of the eye sockets, the veining of the lids, and the colorless eyes. They were not red eyes, for he was not really an albino, but they were not blue or grey; colors had canceled out in Osden's eyes, leaving a cold waterlike clarity, infinitely penetrable. He never looked directly at one. His face lacked expression, like an anatomical drawing or a skinned face.

"I agree," he said in a high, harsh tenor, "that even autistic withdrawal might be preferable to the smog of cheap secondhand emotions with which you people surround me. What are you sweating hate for now, Porlock? Can't stand the sight of me? Go practice some autoeroticism the way you were doing last night, it improves your vibes. —Who the devil moved my tapes, here? Don't touch my things, any of you. I won't have it."

"Osden," said Asnanifoil in his large, slow voice, "why *are* you such a bastard?"

Ander Eskwana cowered and put his hands in front of his face. Contention frightened him. Olleroo looked up with a vacant yet eager expression, the eternal spectator.

"Why shouldn't I be?" said Osden. He was not looking at Asnanifoil, and was keeping physically as far away from all of them as he could in the crowded cabin. "None of you constitute, in yourselves, any reason for my changing my behavior."

Harfex, a reserved and patient man, said, "The reason is that we shall be spending several years together. Life will be better for all of us if—"

"Can't you understand that I don't give a damn for all of you?" Osden said, took up his microtapes, and went out. Eskwana had suddenly gone to sleep. Asnanifoil was drawing slipstreams in the air with his finger and muttering the Ritual Primes. "You cannot explain his presence on the team except as a plot on the part of the Terran Authority. I saw this almost at once. This mission is meant to fail," Harfex whispered to the Coordinator, glancing over his shoulder. Porlock was fumbling with his flybutton; there were tears in his eyes. "I did tell you they were all crazy, but you thought I was exaggerating."

All the same, they were not unjustified. Extreme Surveyors expected to find their fellow team members intelligent, well trained, unstable, and personally sympathetic. They had to work together in close quarters and nasty places, and could expect one another's paranoias, depressions, manias, phobias, and compulsions to be mild enough to admit of good personal relationships, at least most of the time. Osden might have been intelligent, but his training was sketchy and his personality was disastrous. He had been sent only on account of his singular gift, the power of empathy: properly speaking, of wide-range bioempathic receptivity. His talent wasn't species-specific; he could pick up emotion or sentience from anything that felt. He could share lust with a white rat, pain with a squashed cockroach, and phototropy with a moth. On an alien world, the Authority had decided, it would be useful to know if anything nearby is sentient, and if so, what its feelings towards you are. Osden's title was a new one: he was the team's Sensor.

"What is emotion, Osden?" Haito Tomiko asked him one day in the main cabin, trying to make some rapport with him for once. "What is it, exactly, that you pick up with your empathic sensitivity?"

"Muck," the man answered in his high, exasperated voice. "The psychic excreta of the animal kingdom. I wade through your feces."

"I was trying," she said, "to learn some facts." She thought her tone was admirably calm.

"You weren't after facts. You were trying to get at me. With some fear, some curiosity, and a great deal of distaste. The way you might poke a dead dog to see the maggots crawl. Will you understand once and for all that I don't want to be got at, that I want to be left alone?" His skin was mottled with red and violet, his voice had risen. "Go roll in your own dung, you yellow bitch!" he shouted at her silence.

"Calm down," she said, still quietly, but she left him at once and went to her cabin. Of course he had been right about her motives; her question had been largely a pretext, a mere effort to interest him. But what harm in that? Did not that effort imply respect for the other? At the moment of asking the question she had felt at most a slight distrust of him; she had mostly felt sorry for him, the poor arrogant venomous bastard, Mr. No-Skin, as Olleroo called him. What did he expect, the way he acted? Love?

"I guess he can't stand anybody feeling sorry for him," said Olleroo, lying on the lower bunk, gilding her nipples.

"Then he can't form any human relationship. All his Dr. Hammergeld did was turn an autism inside out. . . ."

"Poor frot," said Olleroo. "Tomiko, you don't mind if Harfex comes in for a while tonight, do you?"

"Can't you go to his cabin? I'm sick of always having to sit in Main with that damned peeled turnip."

"You do hate him, don't you? I guess he feels that. But I slept with Harfex last night too, and Asnanifoil might get jealous, since they share the cabin. It would be nicer here."

"Service them both," Tomiko said with the coarseness of offended modesty. Her Terran subculture, the East Asian, was a puritanical one; she had been brought up chaste.

"I only like one a night," Olleroo replied with innocent serenity. Beldene, the Garden Planet, had never discovered chastity, or the wheel.

"Try Osden, then," Tomiko said. Her personal instability was seldom so plain as now: a profound self-distrust manifesting itself as destructivism. She had volunteered for this job because there was, in all probability, no use in doing it.

The little Beldene looked up, paintbrush in hand, eyes wide. "Tomiko, that was a dirty thing to say."

"Why?"

"It would be vile! I'm not attracted to Osden!"

"I didn't know it mattered to you," Tomiko said indifferently, though she did know. She got some papers together and left the cabin, remarking, "I hope you and Harfex or whoever it is finish by last bell; I'm tired."

Olleroo was crying tears dripping on her little gilded nipples. She wept easily. Tomiko had not wept since she was ten years old.

It was not a happy ship; but it took a turn for the better when Asnanifoil and his computers raised World 4470. There it lay, a dark-green jewel, like truth at the bottom of a gravity well. As they watched the jade disc grow, a sense of mutuality grew among them. Osden's selfishness, his accurate cruelty, served now to draw the others together. "Perhaps," Mannon said, "he was sent as a beating-gron. What Terrans call a scapegoat. Perhaps his influence will be good after all." And no one, so careful were they to be kind to one another, disagreed.

They came into orbit. There were no lights on nightside, on the continents none of the lines and clots made by animals who build.

"No men," Harfex murmured.

"Of course not," snapped Osden, who had a viewscreen to himself, and his head inside a polythene bag. He claimed that the plastic cut down on the empathic noise he received from the others. "We're two light-centuries past the limit of the Hainish Expansion, and outside that there are no men. Anywhere. You don't think Creation would have made the same hideous mistake twice?"

No one was paying him much heed; they were looking with affection at that jade immensity below them, where there was life, but not human life. They were misfits among men, and what they saw there was not desolation, but peace. Even Osden did not look quite so expressionless as usual; he was frowning.

Descent in fire on the sea; air reconnaissance; landing. A plain of something like grass, thick, green, bowing stalks, surrounded the ship, brushed against extended view cameras, smeared the lenses with a fine pollen.

"It looks like a pure phytosphere," Harfex said. "Osden, do you pick up anything sentient?"

They all turned to the Sensor. He had left the screen and was pouring himself a cup of tea. He did not answer. He seldom answered spoken questions.

The chitinous rigidity of military discipline was quite inapplicable to these teams of mad scientists; their chain of command lay somewhere between parliamentary procedure and peck-order, and would have driven a regular service officer out of his mind. By the inscrutable decision of the Authority, however, Dr. Haito Tomiko had been given the title of Coordinator, and she now exercised her prerogative for the first time. "Mr. Sensor Osden," she said, "please answer Mr. Harfex."

"How could I 'pick up' anything from outside," Osden said without turning, "with the emotions of nine neurotic hominids pulsating around me like worms in a can? When I have anything to tell you, I'll tell you. I'm aware of my responsibility as Sensor. If you presume to give me an order again, however, Coordinator Haito, I'll consider my responsibility void."

"Very well, Mr. Sensor. I trust no orders will be needed henceforth." Tomiko's bullfrog voice was calm, but Osden seemed to flinch slightly as he stood with his back to her, as if the surge of her suppressed rancor had struck him with physical force.

The biologist's hunch proved correct. When they began field analyses they found no animals even among the microbiota. Nobody here ate anybody else. All life-forms were photosynthesizing or saprophagous, living off light or death, not off life. Plants: infinite plants, not one species known to the visitors from the house of man. Infinite shades and intensities of green, violet, purple, brown, red. Infinite silences. Only the wind moved, swaying leaves and fronds, a warm soughing wind laden with spores and pollens, blowing the sweet pale-green dust over prairies of great grasses, heaths that bore no heather, flowerless forests where no foot had ever walked, no eye had ever looked. A warm, sad world, sad and serene. The Surveyors, wandering like picnickers over sunny plains of violet filicaliformes, spoke softly to each other. They knew their voices broke a silence of a thousand million years, the silence of wind and leaves, leaves and wind, blowing and ceasing and blowing again. They talked softly; but being human, they talked.

"Poor old Osden," said Jenny Chong, Bio and Tech, as she piloted a helijet on the North Polar Quadrating run. "All that fancy hi-fi stuff in his brain and nothing to receive. What a bust."

"He told me he hates plants," Olleroo said with a giggle.

"You'd think he'd like them, since they don't bother him like we do."

"Can't say I much like these plants myself," said Porlock, looking down at the purple undulations of the North Circumpolar Forest. "All the same. No mind. No change. A man alone in it would go right off his head."

"But it's all alive," Jenny Chong said. "And if it lives, Osden hates it."

"He's not really so bad," Olleroo said, magnanimous.

Porlock looked at her sidelong and asked, "You ever slept with him, Olleroo?" Olleroo burst into tears and cried, "You Terrans are obscene!"

"No she hasn't," Jenny Chong said, prompt to defend. "Have you, Porlock?"

The chemist laughed uneasily: ha, ha, ha. Flecks of spittle appeared on his mustache.

"Osden can't bear to be touched," Olleroo said shakily. "I just brushed against him once by accident and he knocked me off like I was some sort of dirty . . . thing. We're all just things, to him."

"He's evil," Porlock said in a strained voice, startling the two women. "He'll end up shattering this team, sabotaging it, one way or another. Mark my words. He's not fit to live with other people!" They landed on the North Pole. A midnight sun smoldered over low hills. Short, dry, greenish-pink bryoform grasses stretched away in every direction, which was all one direction, south. Subdued by the incredible silence, the three Surveyors set up their instruments and set to work, three viruses twitching minutely on the hide of an unmoving giant.

Nobody asked Osden along on runs as pilot or photographer or recorder, and he never volunteered, so he seldom left base camp. He ran Harfex's botanical taxonomic data through the on-ship computers, and served as assistant to Eskwana, whose job here was mainly repair and maintenance. Eskwana had begun to sleep a great deal, twenty-five hours or more out of the thirty-two-hour day, dropping off in the middle of repairing a radio or checking the guidance circuits of a helijet. The Coordinator stayed at base one day to observe. No one else was home except Poswet To, who was subject to epileptic fits; Mannon had plugged her into a therapy-circuit today in a state of preventive catatonia. Tomiko spoke reports into the storage banks, and kept an eye on Osden and Eskwana. Two hours passed.

"You might want to use the 860 microwaldoes in sealing that connection," Eskwana said in his soft, hesitant voice.

"Obviously!"

"Sorry. I just saw you had the 840s there—"

"And will replace them when I take the 860s out. When I don't know how to proceed, Engineer, I'll ask your advice."

After a minute Tomiko looked round. Sure enough, there was Eskwana sound asleep, head on the table, thumb in his mouth. "Osden."

The white face did not turn, he did not speak, but conveyed impatiently that he was listening.

"You can't be unaware of Eskwana's vulnerability."

"I am not responsible for his psychopathic reactions."

"But you are responsible for your own. Eskwana is essential to our work here, and

you're not. If you can't control your hostility, you must avoid him altogether."

Osden put down his tools and stood up. "With pleasure!" he said in his vindictive, scraping voice. "You could not possibly imagine what it's like to experience Eskwana's irrational terrors. To have to share his horrible cowardice, to have to cringe with him at everything!"

"Are you trying to justify your cruelty towards him? I thought you had more self-respect." Tomiko found herself shaking with spite. "If your empathic power really makes you share Ander's misery, why does it never induce the least compassion in you?"

"Compassion," Osden said. "Compassion. What do you know about compassion?"

She stared at him, but he would not look at her.

"Would you like me to verbalize your present emotional affect regarding myself?" he said. "I can do so more precisely than you can. I'm trained to analyze such responses as I receive them. And I do receive them."

"But how can you expect me to feel kindly towards you when you behave as you do?"

"What does it matter how I *behave*, you stupid sow, do you think it makes any difference? Do you think the average human is a well of loving-kindness? My choice is to be hated or to be despised. Not being a woman or a coward, I prefer to be hated."

"That's rot. Self-pity. Every man has—"

"But I am not a man," Osden said. "There are all of you. And there is myself. I am *one*."

Awed by that glimpse of abysmal solipsism, she kept silent awhile; finally she said with neither spite nor pity, clinically, "You could kill yourself, Osden."

"That's your way, Haito," he jeered. "I'm not depressive, and seppuku isn't my bit. What do you want me to do here?"

"Leave. Spare yourself and us. Take the air-car and a data-feeder and go do a species count. In the forest; Harfex hasn't even started the forests yet. Take a hundred-square-meter forested area, anywhere inside radio range. But outside empathy range. Report in at eight and twenty-four o'clock daily."

Osden went, and nothing was heard from him for five days but laconic all-well signals twice daily. The mood at base camp changed like a stage set. Eskwana stayed awake up to eighteen hours a day. Poswet To got her stellar lute and chanted the celestial harmonies (music had driven Osden into a frenzy). Mannon, Harfex, Jenny Chong, and Tomiko all went off tranquilizers. Porlock distilled something in his laboratory and drank it all by himself. He had a hangover. Asnanifoil and Poswet To held an all-night Numerical Epiphany, that mystical orgy of higher mathematics which is the chief pleasure of the religious Cetian soul. Olleroo slept with everybody. Work went well.

The Hard Scientist came towards base at a run, laboring through the high, fleshy stalks of the graminiformes. "Something—in the forest—" His eyes bulged, he panted, his mustache and fingers trembled. "Something big. Moving behind me. I was putting in a benchmark, bending down. It came at me. As if it was swinging down out of the trees. Behind me." He stared at the others with the opaque eyes of terror or exhaustion.

"Sit down, Porlock. Take it easy. Now wait, go through this again. You *saw* something—"

"Not clearly. Just the movement. Purposive. A—an—I don't know what it could have been. Something self-moving. In the trees, the arboriformes, whatever you call 'em. At the edge of the woods."

Harfex looked grim. "There is nothing here that could attack you, Porlock. There are not even microzoa. There *could not* be a large animal."

"Could you possibly have seen an epiphyte drop suddenly, a vine come loose behind you?"

"No," Porlock said. "It was coming down at me, through the branches. When I turned it took off again, away and upward. It made a noise, a sort of crashing. If it wasn't an animal, God knows what it could have been! It was

big—as big as a man, at least. Maybe a reddish color. I couldn't see, I'm not sure."

"It was Osden," said Jenny Chong, "doing a Tarzan act." She giggled nervously, and Tomiko repressed a wild feckless laugh. But Harfex was not smiling.

"One gets uneasy under the arboriformes," he said in his polite, repressed voice. "I've noticed that. Indeed that may be why I've put off working in the forests. There's a hypnotic quality in the colors and spacing of the stems and branches, especially the helically arranged ones; and the spore-throwers grow so regularly spaced that it seems unnatural. I find it quite disagreeable, subjectively speaking. I wonder if a stronger effect of that sort mightn't have produced a hallucination . . . ?"

Porlock shook his head. He wet his lips. "It was there," he said. "Something. Moving with purpose. Trying to attack me from behind."

When Osden called in, punctual as always, at twenty-four o'clock that night, Harfex told him Porlock's report. "Have you come on anything at all, Mr. Osden, that could substantiate Mr. Porlock's impression of a motile, sentient life-form, in the forest?"

Ssss, the radio said sardonically. "No. Bullshit," said Osden's unpleasant voice.

"You've been actually inside the forest longer than any of us," Harfex said with unmitigable politeness. "Do you agree with my impression that the forest ambiance has a rather troubling and possibly hallucinogenic effect on the perceptions?"

Ssss. "I'll agree that Porlock's perceptions are easily troubled. Keep him in his lab, he'll do less harm. Anything else?"

"Not at present," Harfex said, and Osden cut off.

Nobody could credit Porlock's story, and nobody could discredit it. He was positive that something, something big, had tried to attack him by surprise. It was hard to deny this, for they were on an alien world, and everyone who had entered the forest had felt a certain chill and foreboding under the "trees." ("Call them trees, certainly," Harfex had said. "They really are the same thing only, of course, altogether different.") They agreed that they had felt uneasy, or had had the sense that something was watching them from behind.

"We've got to clear this up," Porlock said, and he asked to be sent as a temporary Biologist's Aide, like Osden, into the forest to explore and observe. Olleroo and Jenny Chong volunteered if they could go as a pair. Harfex sent them all off into the forest near which they were encamped, a vast tract covering four-fifths of Continent D. He forbade sidearms. They were not to go outside a fifty-mile half-circle, which included Osden's current site. They all reported in twice daily, for three days. Porlock reported a glimpse of what seemed to be a large semi-erect shape moving through the trees across the river; Olleroo was sure she had heard something moving near the tent, the second night.

"There are no animals on this planet," Harfex said, dogged.

Then Osden missed his morning call.

Tomiko waited less than an hour, then flew with Harfex to the area where Osden had reported himself the night before. But as the helijet hovered over the sea of purplish leaves, illimitable, impenetrable, she felt a panicked despair. "How can we find him in this?"

"He reported landing on the riverbank. Find the aircar; he'll be camped near it, and he can't have gone far from his camp. Species-counting is slow work. There's the river."

"There's his car," Tomiko said, catching the bright foreign glint among the vegetable colors and shadows. "Here goes, then."

She put the ship in hover and pitched out the ladder. She and Harfex descended. The sea of life closed over their heads.

As her feet touched the forest floor, she unsnapped the flap of her holster; then, glancing at Harfex, who was unarmed, she left the gun untouched. But her hand kept coming back to it. There was no sound at all, as soon as they were a few meters away from the slow, brown river, and the light was dim. Great boles stood well apart, almost regularly, almost alike; they were soft-skinned, some appearing smooth and others spongy, grey or greenish-brown or brown, twined with cable-like creepers and festooned with epiphytes, extending rigid, entangled armfuls of big saucer-shaped, dark leaves that formed a roof-layer twenty to thirty meters thick. The ground underfoot was springy as a mattress, every inch of it knotted with roots and peppered with small, fleshy-leafed growths.

"Here's his tent," Tomiko said, cowed at the sound of her voice in that huge community of the voiceless. In the tent was Osden's sleeping bag, a couple of books, a box of rations. We should be calling, shouting for him, she thought, but did not even suggest it; nor did Harfex. They circled out from the tent, careful to keep each other in sight through the thick-standing presences, the crowding gloom. She stumbled over Osden's body, not thirty meters from the tent, led to it by the whitish gleam of a dropped notebook. He lay facedown between two huge-rooted trees. His head and hands were covered with blood, some dried, some still oozing red.

Harfex appeared beside her, his pale Hainish complexion quite green in the dusk. "Dead?"

"No. He's been struck. Beaten. From behind." Tomiko's fingers felt over the bloody skull and temples and nape. "A weapon or a tool . . . I don't find a fracture."

As she turned Osden's body over so they could lift him, his eyes opened. She was holding him, bending close to his face. His pale lips writhed. A deathly fear came into her. She screamed aloud two or three times and tried to run away, shambling and stumbling into the terrible dusk. Harfex caught her, and at his touch and the sound of his voice, her panic decreased. "What is it? What is it?" he was saying.

"I don't know," she sobbed. Her heartbeat still shook her, and she could not see clearly.

"The fear—the . . . I panicked. When I saw his eyes."

"We're both nervous. I don't understand this—"

"I'm all right now, come on, we've got to get him under care."

Both working with senseless haste, they lugged Osden to the riverside and hauled him up on a rope under his armpits; he dangled like a sack, twisting a little, over the glutinous dark sea of leaves. They pulled him into the helijet and took off. Within a minute they were over open prairie. Tomiko locked onto the homing beam. She drew a deep breath, and her eyes met Harfex's. "I was so terrified I almost fainted. I have never done that."

"I was . . . unreasonably frightened also," said the Hainishman, and indeed he looked aged and shaken. "Not so badly as you. But as unreasonably."

"It was when I was in contact with him, holding him. He seemed to be conscious for a moment."

"Empathy? . . . I hope he can tell us what attacked him."

Osden, like a broken dummy covered with blood and mud, half lay as they had bundled him into the rear seats in their frantic urgency to get out of the forest.

More panic met their arrival at base. The ineffective brutality of the assault was sinister and bewildering. Since Harfex stubbornly denied any possibility of animal life they began speculating about sentient plants, vegetable monsters, psychic projections. Jenny Chong's latent phobia reasserted itself and she could talk about nothing except the Dark Egos which followed people around behind their backs. She and Olleroo and Porlock had been summoned back to base; and nobody was much inclined to go outside.

Osden had lost a good deal of blood during the three or four hours he had lain alone, and concussion and severe contusions had put him in shock and semi-coma. As he came out of this and began running a low fever he called several

times for "Doctor," in a plaintive voice: "Dr. Hammergeld . . ." When he regained full consciousness, two of those long days later, Tomiko called Harfex into his cubicle.

"Osden: can you tell us what attacked you?"

The pale eyes flickered past Harfex's face.

"You were attacked," Tomiko said gently. The shifty gaze was hatefully familiar, but she was a physician, protective of the hurt. "You may not remember it yet. Something attacked you. You were in the forest—"

"Ah!" he cried out, his eyes growing bright and his features contorting. "The forest—in the forest—"

"What's in the forest?"

He grasped for breath. A look of clearer consciousness came into his face. After a while he said, "I don't know."

"Did you see what attacked you?" Harfex asked.

"I don't know."

"You remember it now."

"I don't know."

"All our lives may depend on this. You must tell us what you saw!"

"I don't know," Osden said, sobbing with weakness. He was too weak to hide the fact that he was hiding the answer, yet he would not say it. Porlock, nearby, was chewing his pepper-colored mustache as he tried to hear what was going on in the cubicle. Harfex leaned over Osden and said, "You *will* tell us—" Tomiko had to interfere bodily.

Harfex controlled himself with an effort that was painful to see. He went off silently to his cubicle, where no doubt he took a double or triple dose of tranquilizers. The other men and women scattered about the big frail building, a long main hall and ten sleeping-cubicles, said nothing, but looked depressed and edgy. Osden, as always, even now, had them all at his mercy. Tomiko looked down at him with a rush of hatred that burned in her throat like bile. This monstrous egotism that fed itself on others' emotions, this absolute selfishness, was worse than any hideous deformity of the flesh.

Like a congenital monster, he should not have lived. Should not be alive. Should have died. Why had his head not been split open?

As he lay flat and white, his hands helpless at his sides, his colorless eyes were wide open, and there were tears running from the corners. He tried to flinch away. "Don't," he said in a weak, hoarse voice, and tried to raise his hands to protect his head. "Don't!"

She sat down on the folding stool beside the cot, and after a while put her hand on his. He tried to pull away, but lacked the strength.

A long silence fell between them.

"Osden," she murmured, "I'm sorry. I'm very sorry. I will you well. Let me will you well, Osden. I don't want to hurt you. Listen, I do see now. It was one of us. That's right, isn't it? No, don't answer, only tell me if I'm wrong; but I'm not. . . . Of course there are animals on this planet. Ten of them. I don't care who it was. It doesn't matter, does it? It could have been me, just now. I realize that I didn't understand how it is, Osden. You can't see how difficult it is for us to understand. . . . But listen. If it were love, instead of hate and fear . . . It is never love?"

"No."

"Why not? Why should it never be? Are human beings all so weak? That is terrible. Never mind, never mind, don't worry. Keep still. At least right now it isn't hate, is it? Sympathy at least, concern, well-wishing, you do feel that, Osden? Is it what you feel?"

"Among . . . other things," he said, almost inaudibly.

"Noise from my subconscious, I suppose. And everybody else in the room . . . Listen, when we found you there in the forest, when I tried to turn you over, you partly wakened, and I felt a horror of you. I was insane with fear for a minute. Was that your fear of me I felt?"

"No."

Her hand was still on his, and he was quite relaxed, sinking towards sleep, like a man in pain who has been given relief from pain. "The forest," he muttered; she could barely understand him. "Afraid."

She pressed him no further, but kept her hand on his and watched him go to sleep. She knew what she felt, and what therefore he must feel. She was confident of it: there is only one emotion, or state of being, that can thus wholly reverse itself, polarize, within one moment. In Great Hainish indeed there is one word, *onta*, for love and for hate. She was not in love with Osden, of course, that was another kettle of fish. What she felt for him was *onta*, polarized hate. She held his hand and the current flowed between them, the tremendous electricity of touch, which he had always dreaded. As he slept the ring of anatomy-chart muscles around his mouth relaxed, and Tomiko saw on his face what none of them had ever seen, very faint, a smile. It faded. He slept on.

He was tough; next day he was sitting up, and hungry. Harfex wished to interrogate him, but Tomiko put him off. She hung a sheet of polythene over the cubicle door, as Osden himself had often done. "Does it actually cut down your empathic reception?" she asked, and he replied, in the dry, cautious tone they were now using to each other, "No."

"Just a warning then."

"Partly. More faith-healing. Dr. Hammergeld thought it worked. . . . Maybe it does, a little."

There had been love, once. A terrified child, suffocating in the tidal rush and battering of the huge emotions of adults, a drowning child, saved by one man. Taught to breathe, to live, by one man. Given everything, all protection and love, by one man. Father/Mother/God: no other. "Is he still alive?" Tomiko asked, thinking of Osden's incredible loneliness, and the strange cruelty of the great doctors. She was shocked when she heard his forced, tinny laugh. "He died at least two and a half centuries ago," Osden said. "Do you forget where we are, Coordinator? We've all left our little families behind. . . ."

Outside the polythene curtain the eight other human beings on World 4470 moved vaguely. Their voices were low and strained. Eskwana slept; Poswet To was in therapy; Jenny

Chong was trying to rig lights in her cubicle so that she wouldn't cast a shadow.

"They're all scared," Tomiko said, scared. "They've all got these ideas about what attacked you. A sort of ape-potato, a giant fanged spinach, I don't know. . . . Even Harfex. You may be right not to force them to see. That would be worse, to lose confidence in one another. But why are we all so shaky, unable to face the fact, going to pieces so easily? Are we really all insane?"

"We'll soon be more so."

"Why?"

"There *is* something." He closed his mouth; the muscles of his lips stood out rigid.

"Something sentient?"

"A sentience."

"In the forest?"

He nodded.

"What is it, then—?"

"The fear." He began to look strained again, and moved restlessly. "When I fell, there, you know, I didn't lose consciousness at once. Or I kept regaining it. I don't know. It was more like being paralyzed."

"You were."

"I was on the ground. I couldn't get up. My face was in the dirt, in that soft leaf mold. It was in my nostrils and eyes. I couldn't move. Couldn't see. As if I was in the ground. Sunk into it, part of it. I knew I was between two trees even though I never saw them. I suppose I could feel the roots. Below me in the ground, down under the ground. My hands were bloody, I could feel that, and the blood made the dirt around my face sticky. I felt the fear. It kept growing. As if they'd finally known I was there, lying on them there, under them, among them, the thing they feared, and yet part of their fear itself. I couldn't stop sending the fear back, and it kept growing and I couldn't move, I couldn't get away. I would pass out, I think, and then the fear would bring me to again, and I still couldn't move. Any more than they can."

Tomiko felt the cold stirring of her hair, the readying of the apparatus of terror. "They: who are they, Osden?"

"They, it—I don't know. The fear."

"What is he talking about?" Harfex demanded when Tomiko reported this conversation. She would not let Harfex question Osden yet, feeling that she must protect Osden from the onslaught of the Hainishman's powerful, over-repressed emotions. Unfortunately this fueled the slow fire of paranoid anxiety that burned in poor Harfex, and he thought she and Osden were in league, hiding some fact of great importance or peril from the rest of the team.

"It's like the blind man trying to describe the elephant. Osden hasn't seen or heard the . . . the sentience, any more than we have."

"But he's felt it, my dear Haito," Harfex said with just-suppressed rage. "Not empathically. On his skull. It came and knocked him down and beat him with a blunt instrument. Did he not catch *one* glimpse of it?"

"What would he have seen, Harfex?" Tomiko said, but he would not hear her meaningful tone; even he had blocked out that comprehension. What one fears is alien. The murderer is an outsider, a foreigner, not one of us. The evil is not in me!

"The first blow knocked him pretty well out," Tomiko said a little wearily, "he didn't see anything. But when he came to again, alone in the forest, he felt a great fear. Not his own fear; an empathic effect. He is certain of that. And certain it was nothing picked up from any of us. So that evidently the native life-forms are not all insentient."

Harfex looked at her a moment, grim. "You're trying to frighten me, Haito. I do not understand your motives." He got up and went off to his laboratory table, walking slowly and stiffly, like a man of eighty, not of forty.

She looked around at the others. She felt some desperation. Her new, fragile, and profound interdependence with Osden gave her, she was well aware, some added strength. But if even Harfex could not keep his head, who of the others would? Porlock and Eskwana were shut in their cubicles, the others were all working or busy with something. There was something queer about their positions. For a while the Coordinator could not tell what it was, then she saw that they were all sitting facing the nearby forest. Playing chess with Asnanifoil, Olleroo had edged her chair around until it was almost beside his.

She went to Mannon, who was dissecting a tangle of spidery brown roots, and told him to look for the pattern-puzzle. He saw it at once, and said with unusual brevity, "Keeping an eye on the enemy."

"What enemy? What do *you* feel, Mannon?" She had a sudden hope in him as a psychologist, on this obscure ground of hints and empathies where biologists went astray.

"I feel a strong anxiety with a specific spatial orientation. But I am not an empath. Therefore the anxiety is explicable in terms of the particular stress-situation, that is, the attack on a team member in the forest, and also in terms of the total stress-situation, that is, my presence in a totally alien environment for which the archetypical connotations of the word *forest* provide an inevitable metaphor."

Hours later Tomiko woke to hear Osden screaming in nightmare; Mannon was calming him, and she sank back into her own dark-branching pathless dreams. In the morning Eskwana did not wake. He could not be roused with stimulant drugs. He clung to his sleep, slipping farther and farther back, mumbling softly now and then until, wholly regressed, he lay curled on his side, thumb at his lips, gone.

"Two days; two down. Ten little Indians, nine little Indians . . ." That was Porlock.

"And you're the next little Indian," Jenny Chong snapped. "Go analyze your urine, Porlock!"

"He is driving us all insane," Porlock said, getting up and waving his left arm. "Can't you feel it? For God's sake, are you all deaf and blind? Can't you feel what he's doing, the emanations? It all comes from him—from his room there—from his mind. He is driving us all insane with fear!"

"Who is?" said Asnanifoil, looming precipitous and hairy over the little Terran.

"Do I have to say his name? Osden, then. Osden! Osden! Why do you think I tried to kill him? In self-defense! To save all of us! Because you won't see what he's doing to us. He's sabotaged the mission by making us quarrel, and now he's going to drive us all insane by projecting fear at us so that we can't sleep or think, like a huge radio that doesn't make any sound, but it broadcasts all the time, and you can't sleep, and you can't think. Haito and Harfex are already under his control but the rest of you can be saved. I had to do it!"

"You didn't do it very well," Osden said, standing half-naked, all rib and bandage, at the door of his cubicle. "I could have hit myself harder. Hell, it isn't me that's scaring you blind, Porlock, it's out there—there, in the woods!"

Porlock made an ineffectual attempt to assault Osden; Asnanifoil held him back, and continued to hold him effortlessly while Mannon gave him a sedative shot. He was put away shouting about giant radios. In a minute the sedative took effect, and he joined a peaceful silence to Eskwana's.

"All right," said Harfex. "Now, Osden, you'll tell us what you know and all you know."

Osden said, "I don't know anything."

He looked battered and faint. Tomiko made him sit down before he talked.

"After I'd been three days in the forest, I thought I was occasionally receiving some kind of affect."

"Why didn't you report it?"

"Thought I was going spla, like the rest of you."

"That, equally, should have been reported."

"You'd have called me back to base. I couldn't take it. You realize that my inclusion in the mission was a bad mistake. I'm not able to coexist with nine other neurotic personalities at close quarters. I was wrong to volunteer for Extreme Survey, and the Authority was wrong to accept me."

No one spoke; but Tomiko saw, with certainty this time, the flinch in Osden's shoulders and the tightening of his facial muscles, as he registered their bitter agreement.

"Anyhow, I didn't want to come back to base because I was curious. Even going psycho, how could I pick up empathic affects when there was no creature to emit them? They weren't bad, then. Very vague. Queer. Like a draft in a closed room, a flicker in the corner of your eye. Nothing really."

For a moment he had been borne up on their listening: they heard, so he spoke. He was wholly at their mercy. If they disliked him he had to be hateful; if they mocked him he became grotesque; if they listened to him he was the storyteller. He was helplessly obedient to the demands of their emotions, reactions, moods. And there were seven of them, too many to cope with, so that he must be constantly knocked about from one to another's whim. He could not find coherence. Even as he spoke and held them, somebody's attention would wander: Olleroo perhaps was thinking that he wasn't unattractive, Harfex was seeking the ulterior motive of his words, Asnanifoil's mind, which could not be long held by the concrete, was roaming off towards the eternal peace of number, and Tomiko was distracted by pity, by fear. Osden's voice faltered. He lost the thread. "I . . . I thought it must be the trees," he said, and stopped.

"It's not the trees," Harfex said. "They have no more nervous system than do plants of the Hainish Descent on Earth. None."

"You're not seeing the forest for the trees, as they say on Earth," Mannon put in, smiling elfinly; Harfex stared at him. "What about those root-nodes we've been puzzling about for twenty days—eh?"

"What about them?"

"They are, indubitably, connections. Con-

nections among the trees. Right? Now let's just suppose, most improbably, that you knew nothing of animal brain structure. And you were given one axon, or one detached glial cell, to examine. Would you be likely to discover what it was? Would you see that the cell was capable of sentience?"

"No. Because it isn't. A single cell is capable of mechanical response to stimulus. No more. Are you hypothesizing that individual arboriformes are 'cells' in a kind of brain, Mannon?"

"Not exactly. I'm merely pointing out that they are all interconnected, both by the root-node linkage and by your green epiphytes in the branches. A linkage of incredible complexity and physical extent. Why, even the prairie grass-forms have those root-connectors, don't they? I know that sentience or intelligence isn't a thing; you can't find it in, or analyze it out from, the cells of a brain. It's a function of the connected cells. It is, in a sense, the connection: the connectedness. It doesn't exist. I'm not trying to say it exists. I'm only guessing that Osden might be able to describe it."

And Osden took him up, speaking as if in trance. "Sentience without senses. Blind, deaf, nerveless, moveless. Some irritability, response to touch. Response to sun, to light, to water, and chemicals in the earth around the roots. Nothing comprehensible to an animal mind. Presence without mind. Awareness of being, without object or subject. Nirvana."

"Then why do you receive fear?" Tomiko asked in a low voice.

"I don't know. I can't see how awareness of objects, of others, could arise: an unperceiving response. . . . But there was an uneasiness, for days. And then when I lay between the two trees and my blood was on their roots—" Osden's face glittered with sweat. "It became fear," he said shrilly, "only fear."

"If such a function existed," Harfex said, "it would not be capable of conceiving of a self-moving, material entity, or responding to one. It could no more become aware of us than we can 'become aware' of Infinity."

" 'The silence of those infinite expanses terrifies me,' " muttered Tomiko. "Pascal was aware of Infinity. By way of fear."

"To a forest," Mannon said, "we might appear as forest fires. Hurricanes. Dangers. What moves quickly is dangerous, to a plant. The rootless would be alien, terrible. And if it is mind, it seems only too probable that it might become aware of Osden, whose own mind is open to connection with all others so long as he's conscious, and who was lying in pain and afraid within it, actually inside it. No wonder it was afraid—"

"Not 'it,' " Harfex said. "There is no being, no huge creature, no person! There could at most be only a function—"

"There is only a fear," Osden said.

They were all still awhile, and heard the stillness outside.

"Is that what I feel all the time coming up behind me?" Jenny Chong asked, subdued.

Osden nodded. "You all feel it, deaf as you are. Eskwana's the worst off, because he actually has some empathic capacity. He could send if he learned how, but he's too weak, never will be anything but a medium."

"Listen, Osden," Tomiko said, "you can send. Then send to it—the forest, the fear out there—tell it that we won't hurt it. Since it has, or is, some sort of affect that translates into what we feel as emotion, can't you translate back? Send out a message, We are harmless, we are friendly."

"You must know that nobody can emit a false empathic message, Haito. You can't send something that doesn't exist."

"But we don't intend harm, we are friendly."

"Are we? In the forest, when you picked me up, did you feel friendly?"

"No. Terrified. But that's—it, the forest, the plants, not my own fear, isn't it?"

"What's the difference? It's all you felt. Can't you see"—and Osden's voice rose in exasperation—"why I dislike you and you dislike me, all of you? Can't you see that I retransmit every negative or aggressive affect you've felt towards me since we first met? I return your hostility, with thanks. I do it in self-defense. Like Porlock. It is self-defense, though; it's the only technique I developed to replace my original defense of total withdrawal from others. Unfortunately it creates a closed circuit, self-sustaining and self-reinforcing. Your initial reaction to me was the instinctive antipathy to a cripple; by now of course it's hatred. Can you fail to see my point? The forest mind out there transmits only terror, now, and the only message I can send it is terror, because when exposed to it I can feel nothing except terror!"

"What must we do, then?" said Tomiko, and Mannon replied promptly, "Move camp. To another continent. If there are plant-minds there, they'll be slow to notice us, as this one was; maybe they won't notice us at all."

"It would be a considerable relief," Osden observed stiffly. The others had been watching him with a new curiosity. He had revealed himself, they had seen him as he was, a helpless man in a trap. Perhaps, like Tomiko, they had seen that the trap itself, his crass and cruel egotism, was their own construction, not his. They had built the cage and locked him in it, and like a caged ape he threw filth out through the bars. If, meeting him, they had offered trust, if they had been strong enough to offer him love, how might he have appeared to them?

None of them could have done so, and it was too late now. Given time, given solitude, Tomiko might have built up with him a slow resonance of feeling, a consonance of trust, a harmony; but there was no time, their job must be done. There was not room enough for the cultivation of so great a thing, and they must make do with sympathy, with pity, the small change of love. Even that much had given her strength, but it was nowhere near enough for him. She could see in his flayed face now his savage resentment of their curiosity, even of her pity.

"Go lie down, that gash is bleeding again," she said, and he obeyed her.

Next morning they packed up, melted down the spray-form hangar and living quarters, lifted *Gum* on mechanical drive and took her halfway round World 4470, over the red and green lands, the many warm green seas. They had picked out a likely spot on Continent G: a prairie, twenty thousand square kilos of wind-swept graminiformes. No forest was within a hundred kilos of the site, and there were no lone trees or groves on the plain. The plant-forms occurred only in large species-colonies, never intermingled, except for certain tiny ubiquitous saprophytes and spore-bearers. The team sprayed holomeld over structure forms, and by evening of the thirty-two-hour day were settled into the new camp. Eskwana was still asleep and Porlock still sedated, but everyone else was cheerful. "You can breathe here!" they kept saying.

Osden got on his feet and went shakily to the doorway; leaning there he looked through twilight over the dim reaches of the swaying grass that was not grass. There was a faint, sweet odor of pollen on the wind; no sound but the soft, vast sibilance of wind. His bandaged head cocked a little, the empath stood motionless for a long time. Darkness came, and the stars, lights in the windows of the distant house of man. The wind had ceased, there was no sound. He listened.

In the long night Haito Tomiko listened. She lay still and heard the blood in her arteries, the breathing of sleepers, the wind blowing, the dark veins running, the dreams advancing, the vast static of stars increasing as the universe died slowly, the sound of death walking. She struggled out of her bed, fled the tiny solitude of her cubicle. Eskwana alone slept. Porlock lay straitjacketed, raving softly in his obscure native tongue. Olleroo and Jenny Chong were playing cards, grim-faced. Poswet To was in the therapy niche, plugged in. Asnanifoil was drawing a mandala, the Third Pattern of the Primes. Mannon and Harfex were sitting up with Osden.

She changed the bandages on Osden's head. His lank, reddish hair, where she had not had to shave it, looked strange. It was salted with white, now. Her hands shook as she worked. Nobody had yet said anything.

"How can the fear be here too?" she said, and her voice rang flat and false in the terrific silence.

"It's not just the trees; the grasses . . ."

"But we're twelve thousand kilos from where we were this morning, we left it on the other side of the planet."

"It's all one," Osden said. "One big green thought. How long does it take a thought to get from one side of your brain to the other?"

"It doesn't think. It isn't thinking," Harfex said, lifelessly. "It's merely a network of processes. The branches, the epiphytic growths, the roots with those nodal junctures between individuals: they must all be capable of transmitting electrochemical impulses. There are no individual plants, then, properly speaking. Even the pollen is part of the linkage, no doubt, a sort of windborne sentience, connecting overseas. But it is not conceivable. That all the biosphere of a planet should be one network of communications, sensitive, irrational, immortal, isolated . . ."

"Isolated," said Osden. "That's it! That's the fear. It isn't that we're motile, or destructive. It's just that we are. We are other. There has never been any other."

"You're right," Mannon said, almost whispering. "It has no peers. No enemies. No relationship with anything but itself. One alone forever."

"Then what's the function of its intelligence in species-survival?"

"None, maybe," Osden said. "Why are you getting teleological, Harfex? Aren't you a Hain-ishman? Isn't the measure of complexity the measure of the eternal joy?"

Harfex did not take the bait. He looked ill. "We should leave this world," he said.

"Now you know why I always want to get out, get away from you," Osden said with a kind of morbid geniality. "It isn't pleasant, is it—the other's fear . . . ? If only it were an animal intelligence. I can get through to animals. I get along with cobras and tigers; superior intelligence gives one the advantage. I should have been used in a zoo, not on a human team. . . . If I could get through to the damned stupid potato! If it wasn't so overwhelming . . . I still pick up more than the fear, you know. And before it panicked it had a—there was a serenity. I couldn't take it in, then, I didn't realize how big it was. To know the whole daylight, after all, and the whole night. All the winds and lulls together. The winter stars and the summer stars at the same time. To have roots, and no enemies. To be entire. Do you see? No invasion. No others. To be whole . . ."

He had never spoken before, Tomiko thought.

"You are defenseless against it, Osden," she said. "Your personality has changed already. You're vulnerable to it. We may not all go mad, but you will, if we don't leave."

He hesitated, then he looked up at Tomiko, the first time he had ever met her eyes, a long still look, clear as water. "What's sanity ever done for me?" he said, mocking. "But you have a point, Haito. You have something there."

"We should get away," Harfex muttered.

"If I gave in to it," Osden mused, "could I communicate?"

"By 'give in,'" Mannon said in a rapid, nervous voice, "I assume that you mean, stop sending back the empathic information which you receive from the plant-entity: stop rejecting the fear, and absorb it. That will either kill you at once, or drive you back into total psychological withdrawal, autism."

"Why?" said Osden. "Its message is *rejection*. But my salvation is rejection. It's not intelligent. But I am."

"The scale is wrong. What can a single human brain achieve against something so vast?"

"A single human brain can perceive pattern on the scale of stars and galaxies," Tomiko said, "and interpret it as Love."

Mannon looked from one to the other of them; Harfex was silent.

"It'd be easier in the forest," Osden said. "Which of you will fly me over?"

"When?"

"Now. Before you all crack up or go violent."

"I will," Tomiko said.

"None of us will," Harfex said.

"I can't," Mannon said. "I . . . I am too frightened. I'd crash the jet."

"Bring Eskwana along. If I can pull this off, he might serve as a medium."

"Are you accepting the Sensor's plan, Coordinator?" Harfex asked formally.

"Yes."

"I disapprove. I will come with you, however."

"I think we're compelled, Harfex," Tomiko said, looking at Osden's face, the ugly white mask transfigured, eager as a lover's face.

Olleroo and Jenny Chong, playing cards to keep their thoughts from their haunted beds, their mounting dread, chattered like scared children. "This thing, it's in the forest, it'll get you—"

"Scared of the dark?" Osden jeered.

"But look at Eskwana, and Porlock, and even Asnanifoil—"

"It can't hurt you. It's an impulse passing through synapses, a wind passing through branches. It is only a nightmare."

They took off in a helijet, Eskwana curled up still sound asleep in the rear compartment, Tomiko piloting, Harfex and Osden silent, watching ahead for the dark line of the forest across the vague grey miles of starlit plain. They neared the black line, crossed it; now under them was darkness.

She sought a landing place, flying low, though she had to fight her frantic wish to fly high, to get out, get away. The huge vitality of the plant-world was far stronger here in the forest and its panic beat in immense dark waves. There was a pale patch ahead, a bare knoll-top a little higher than the tallest of the black shapes around it; the not-trees; the rooted; the parts of the whole. She set the helijet down in the glade, a bad landing. Her hands on the stick were slippery, as if she had rubbed them with cold soap.

About them now stood the forest, black in darkness.

Tomiko cowered and shut her eyes. Eskwana moaned in his sleep. Harfex's breath came short and loud, and he sat rigid, even when Osden reached across him and slid the door open.

Osden stood up; his back and bandaged head were just visible in the dim glow of the control panel as he paused stooping in the doorway.

Tomiko was shaking. She could not raise her head. "No, no, no, no, no, no, no," she said in a whisper. "No. No. No."

Osden moved suddenly and quietly, swinging out of the doorway, down into the dark. He was gone.

I am coming! said a great voice that made no sound.

Tomiko screamed. Harfex coughed; he seemed to be trying to stand up, but did not do so.

Tomiko drew in upon herself, all centered in the blind eye in her belly, in the center of her being; and outside that there was nothing but the fear.

It ceased.

She raised her head; slowly unclenched her hands. She sat up straight. The night was dark, and stars shone over the forest. There was nothing else.

"Osden," she said, but her voice would not come. She spoke again, louder, a lone bullfrog croak. There was no reply.

She began to realize that something had gone wrong with Harfex. She was trying to find his head in the darkness, for he had slipped down from the seat, when all at once, in the dead quiet, in the dark rear compartment of the craft, a voice spoke. "Good," it said. It was Eskwana's voice. She snapped on the interior lights and saw the engineer lying curled up asleep, his hand half over his mouth.

The mouth opened and spoke. "All well," it said.

"Osden—"

"All well," said the voice from Eskwana's mouth.

"Where are you?"

Silence.

"Come back."

A wind was rising. "I'll stay here," the soft voice said.

"You can't stay—"

Silence.

"You'd be alone, Osden!"

"Listen." The voice was fainter, slurred, as if lost in the sound of wind. "Listen. I will you well."

She called his name after that, but there was no answer. Eskwana lay still. Harfex lay stiller.

"Osden!" she cried, leaning out the doorway into the dark, wind-shaken silence of the forest of being. "I will come back. I must get Harfex to the base. I will come back, Osden!"

Silence and wind in leaves.

They finished the prescribed survey of World 4470, the eight of them; it took them forty-one days more. Asnanifoil and one or another of the women went into the forest daily at first, searching for Osden in the region around the bare knoll, though Tomiko was not in her heart sure which bare knoll they had landed on that night in the very heart and vortex of terror. They left piles of supplies for Osden, food enough for fifty years, clothing, tents, tools. They did not go on searching; there was no way to find a man alone, hiding if he wanted to hide, in those unending labyrinths and dim corridors, vine-entangled, root-floored. They might have passed within arm's reach of him and never seen him.

But he was there; for there was no fear anymore. Rational, and valuing reason more highly after an intolerable experience of the immortal mindless, Tomiko tried to understand rationally what Osden had done. But the words escaped her control. He had taken the fear into himself, and, accepting, had transcended it. He had given up his self to the alien, an unreserved surrender, that left no place for evil. He had learned the love of the Other, and thereby had been given his whole self. But this is not the vocabulary of reason.

The people of the Survey team walked under the trees, through the vast colonies of life, surrounded by a dreaming silence, a brooding calm that was half aware of them and wholly indifferent to them. There were no hours. Distance was no matter. Had we but world enough and time . . . The planet turned between the sunlight and the great dark; winds of winter and summer blew fine, pale pollen across the quiet seas.

Gum returned after many surveys, years, and light-years, to what had several centuries ago been Smeming Port. There were still men there, to receive (incredulously) the team's reports, and to record its losses: Biologist Harfex, dead of fear, and Sensor Osden, left as a colonist.

Good News from the Vatican

ROBERT SILVERBERG

Robert Silverberg (1935–) is an influential US writer and editor of science fiction and fantasy who began to explore science fiction while studying at Columbia University. He has won multiple Hugo and Nebula Awards during a long and distinguished sixty-year career. He won his first Hugo in 1956 for Best New Writer and for most of his life has balanced his writing with a prodigious editing schedule, having edited or coedited more than seventy anthologies. These anthologies, including the *Universe* series, would have been considerable, noteworthy achievements even had Silverberg not written fiction; Silverberg has often championed new writers and nontraditional fiction. He was inducted into the Science Fiction and Fantasy Hall of Fame in 1999 and received the Science Fiction and Fantasy Writers of America Grand Master Award in 2004.

During the late fifties, Silverberg wrote, by his estimation, a million words a year, mostly for various magazines and Ace Doubles, before briefly retiring from science fiction due to what some termed a collapse in the market. However, in the mid-1960s, Silverberg returned with material that was considered far superior and mature compared with his fifties output, including the novels *Downward to the Earth*, *The World Inside*, and *Dying Inside*. Silverberg once again retired from writing in the late seventies, due to the stresses of thyroid issues and a house fire, but he returned in 1980 with his vastly popular *Majipoor* series, starting with the novel *Lord Valentine's Castle*. Both Silverberg's novels and short fiction are immensely popular with readers. He is one of the few writers to adapt to the changing landscape of genre fiction over a span that saw the rise of the New Wave, feminist SF, cyberpunk, and Humanism.

"Good News from the Vatican" (*Universe 1*, 1971) won the Nebula Award. It showcases Silverberg's oft-neglected gift for satire in a humorous story that pokes fun at religious power structures.

GOOD NEWS FROM THE VATICAN

Robert Silverberg

This is the morning everyone has waited for, when at last the robot cardinal is to be elected pope. There can no longer be any doubt of the outcome. The conclave has been deadlocked for many days between the obstinate advocates of Cardinal Asciuga of Milan and Cardinal Carciofo of Genoa, and word has gone out that a compromise is in the making. All factions now are agreed on the selection of the robot. This morning I read in *Osservatore Romano* that the Vatican computer itself has taken a hand in the deliberations. The computer has been strongly urging the candidacy of the robot. I suppose we should not be surprised by this loyalty among machines. Nor should we let it distress us. We absolutely *must not* let it distress us.

"Every era gets the pope it deserves," Bishop FitzPatrick observed somewhat gloomily today at breakfast. "The proper pope for our times is a robot, certainly. At some future date it may be desirable for the pope to be a whale, an automobile, a cat, a mountain." Bishop FitzPatrick stands well over two meters in height and his normal facial expression is a morbid, mournful one. Thus it is impossible for us to determine whether any particular pronouncement of his reflects existential despair or placid acceptance. Many years ago he was a star player for the Holy Cross championship basketball team. He has come to Rome to do research for a biography of St. Marcellus the Righteous.

We have been watching the unfolding drama of the papal election from an outdoor cafe several blocks from the Square of St. Peter's. For all of us, this has been an unexpected dividend of our holiday in Rome; the previous pope was reputed to be in good health and there was no reason to suspect that a successor would have to be chosen for him this summer.

Each morning we drive across by taxi from our hotel near the Via Veneto and take up our regular positions around "our" table. From where we sit, we all have a clear view of the Vatican chimney through which the smoke of the burning ballots rises: black smoke if no pope has been elected, white if the conclave has been successful. Luigi, the owner and headwaiter, automatically brings us our preferred beverages: Fernet-Branca for Bishop FitzPatrick, Campari and soda for Rabbi Mueller, Turkish coffee for Miss Harshaw, lemon squash for Kenneth and Beverly, and Pernod on the rocks for me. We take turns paying the check, although Kenneth has not paid it even once since our vigil began. Yesterday, when Miss Harshaw paid, she emptied her purse and found herself three hundred fifty lire short; she had nothing else except hundred-dollar travelers' checks. The rest of us looked pointedly at Kenneth but he went on calmly sipping his lemon squash. After a brief period of tension Rabbi Mueller produced a five-hundred-lire coin and rather irascibly slapped the heavy silver piece against the table. The rabbi is known for his short temper and vehement style. He is twenty-eight years old, customarily dresses in a fashionable plaid cassock and silvered sunglasses, and frequently boasts that he has never performed a bar mitzvah ceremony for his congregation, which is in Wicomico County, Maryland. He believes that the rite is vulgar and obsolete, and invariably farms out all of his bar mitzvahs to a franchised organization of itinerant clergymen who handle such affairs on a commission basis. Rabbi Mueller is an authority on angels.

Our group is divided over the merits of electing a robot as the new pope. Bishop Fitz-Patrick, Rabbi Mueller, and I are in favor of the idea. Miss Harshaw, Kenneth, and Beverly are opposed. It is interesting to note that both of our gentlemen of the cloth, one quite elderly and one fairly young, support this remarkable departure from tradition. Yet the three "swing-ers" among us do not.

I am not sure why I align myself with the progressives. I am a man of mature years and fairly sedate ways. Nor have I ever concerned myself with the doings of the Church of Rome. I am unfamiliar with Catholic dogma and unaware of recent currents of thought within the Church. Still, I have been hoping for the election of the robot since the start of the con-clave. Why? I wonder. Is it because the image of a metal creature upon the Throne of St. Peter's stimulates my imagination and tickles my sense of the incongruous? That is, is my support of the robot purely an aesthetic matter? Or is it, rather, a function of my moral cowardice? Do I secretly think that this gesture will buy the robots off? Am I privately saying, Give them the papacy and maybe they won't want other things for a while? No. I can't believe anything so unworthy of myself. Possibly I am for the robot because I am a person of unusual sensi-tivity to the needs of others.

"If he's elected," says Rabbi Mueller, "he plans an immediate time-sharing agreement with the Dalai Lama and a reciprocal plug-in with the head programmer of the Greek Ortho-dox Church, just for starters. I'm told he'll make ecumenical overtures to the rabbinate as well, which is certainly something for all of us to look forward to."

"I don't doubt that there'll be many correc-tions in the customs and practices of the hierar-chy," Bishop FitzPatrick declares. "For example, we can look forward to superior information-gathering techniques as the Vatican computer is given a greater role in the operations of the Curia. Let me illustrate by—"

"What an utterly ghastly notion," Kenneth says. He is a gaudy young man with white hair and pink eyes. Beverly is either his wife or his sister. She rarely speaks. Kenneth makes the sign of the Cross with offensive brusqueness and murmurs, "In the name of the Father, the Son, and the Holy Automaton." Miss Harshaw giggles but chokes the giggle off when she sees my disapproving face.

Dejectedly, but not responding at all to the interruption, Bishop FitzPatrick contin-ues, "Let me illustrate by giving you some fig-ures I obtained yesterday afternoon. I read in the newspaper *Oggi* that during the last five years, according to a spokesman for the Mis-siones Catholic, the Church has increased its membership in Yugoslavia from 19,381,403 to 23,501,062. But the government census taken last year gives the total population of Yugoslavia at 23,575,194. That leaves only 74,132 for the other religious and irreligious bodies. Aware of the large Moslem population of Yugoslavia, I suspected an inaccuracy in the published sta-tistics and consulted the computer in St. Peter's, which informed me"—the bishop, pausing, produces a lengthy printout and unfolds it across much of the table—"that the last count of the Faithful in Yugoslavia, made a year and a half ago, places our numbers at 14,206,198. Therefore an overstatement of 9,294,864 has been made. Which is absurd. And perpetuated. Which is damnable."

"What does he look like?" Miss Harshaw asks. "Does anyone have any idea?"

"He's like all the rest," says Kenneth. "A shiny metal box with wheels below and eyes on top."

"You haven't seen him," Bishop FitzPatrick interjects. "I don't think it's proper for you to assume that—"

"They're all alike," Kenneth says. "Once you've seen one, you've seen all of them. Shiny boxes. Wheels. Eyes. And voices coming out of their bellies like mechanized belches. Inside, they're all cogs and gears." Kenneth shudders delicately. "It's too much for me to accept. Let's have another round of drinks, shall we?"

Rabbi Mueller says, "It so happens that I've seen him with my own eyes."

"You *have*?" Beverly exclaims.

Kenneth scowls at her. Luigi, approaching, brings a tray of new drinks for everyone. I hand him a five-thousand-lire note. Rabbi Mueller removes his sunglasses and breathes on their brilliantly reflective surfaces. He has small, watery gray eyes and a bad squint. He says, "The cardinal was the keynote speaker at the Congress of World Jewry that was held last fall in Beirut. His theme was 'Cybernetic Ecumenicism for Contemporary Man.' I was there. I can tell you that His Eminence is tall and distinguished, with a fine voice and a gentle smile. There's something inherently melancholy about his manner that reminds me greatly of our friend the bishop, here. His movements are graceful and his wit is keen."

"But he's mounted on wheels, isn't he?" Kenneth persists.

"On treads," replies the rabbi, giving Kenneth a fiery, devastating look and resuming his sunglasses. "Treads, like a tractor has. But I don't think that treads are spiritually inferior to feet, or, for that matter, to wheels. If I were a Catholic I'd be proud to have a man like that as my pope."

"Not a man," Miss Harshaw puts in. A giddy edge enters her voice whenever she addresses Rabbi Mueller. "A robot," she says. "He's not a man, remember?"

"A *robot* like that as my pope, then," Rabbi Mueller says, shrugging at the correction. He raises his glass. "To the new pope!"

"To the new pope!" cries Bishop FitzPatrick.

Luigi comes rushing from his cafe. Kenneth waves him away. "Wait a second," Kenneth says. "The election isn't over yet. How can you be so sure?"

"The *Osservatore Romano*," I say, "indicates in this morning's edition that everything will be decided today. Cardinal Carciofo has agreed to withdraw in his favor, in return for a larger real-time allotment when the new computer hours are decreed at next year's consistory."

"In other words, the fix is in," Kenneth says.

Bishop FitzPatrick sadly shakes his head. "You state things much too harshly, my son. For three weeks now we have been without a Holy Father. It is God's Will that we shall have a pope; the conclave, unable to choose between the candidacies of Cardinal Carciofo and Cardinal Asciuga, thwarts that Will; if necessary, therefore, we must make certain accommodations with the realities of the times so that His Will shall not be further frustrated. Prolonged politicking within the conclave now becomes sinful. Cardinal Carciofo's sacrifice of his personal ambitions is not as self-seeking an act as you would claim."

Kenneth continues to attack poor Carciofo's motives for withdrawing. Beverly occasionally applauds his cruel sallies. Miss Harshaw several times declares her unwillingness to remain a communicant of a church whose leader is a machine. I find this dispute distasteful and swing my chair away from the table to have a better view of the Vatican. At this moment the cardinals are meeting in the Sistine Chapel. How I wish I were there! What splendid mysteries are being enacted in that gloomy, magnificent room! Each prince of the Church now sits on a small throne surmounted by a violet-hued canopy. Fat wax tapers glimmer on the desk before each throne. Masters of ceremonies move solemnly through the vast chamber, carrying the silver basins in which the blank ballots repose. These basins are placed on the table before the altar. One by one the cardinals advance to the table, take ballots, return to their desks. Now, lifting their quill pens, they begin to write. "I, Cardinal ——, elect to the Supreme Pontificate the Most Reverend Lord my Lord Cardinal ——." What name do they fill in? Is it Carciofo? Is it Asciuga? Is it the name of some obscure and shriveled prelate from Madrid or Heidelberg, some last-minute choice of the anti-robot faction in its desperation? Or are they writing his name? The sound of scratching pens is loud in the chapel. The cardinals are completing their ballots, sealing them at the ends, folding them, folding them again and again, carrying them to the altar, dropping them into the great gold chalice. So have they done every morning and every afternoon for days, as the deadlock has prevailed.

"I read in the *Herald-Tribune* a couple of days ago," says Miss Harshaw, "that a delegation of two hundred and fifty young Catholic robots from Iowa is waiting at the Des Moines airport for news of the election. If their man gets in, they've got a chartered flight ready to leave, and they intend to request that they be granted the Holy Father's first public audience."

"There can be no doubt," Bishop FitzPatrick agrees, "that his election will bring a great many people of synthetic origin into the fold of the Church."

"While driving out plenty of flesh-and-blood people!" Miss Harshaw says shrilly.

"I doubt that," says the bishop. "Certainly there will be some feelings of shock, of dismay, of injury, of loss, for some of us at first. But these will pass. The inherent goodness of the new pope, to which Rabbi Mueller alluded, will prevail. Also I believe that technologically minded young folk everywhere will be encouraged to join the Church. Irresistible religious impulses will be awakened throughout the world."

"Can you imagine two hundred and fifty robots clanking into St. Peter's?" Miss Harshaw demands.

I contemplate the distant Vatican. The morning sunlight is brilliant and dazzling, but the assembled cardinals, walled away from the world, cannot enjoy its gay sparkle. They all have voted, now. The three cardinals who were chosen by lot as this morning's scrutators of the vote have risen. One of them lifts the chalice and shakes it, mixing the ballots. Then he places it on the table before the altar; a second

scrutator removes the ballots and counts them. He ascertains that the number of ballots is identical to the number of cardinals present. The ballots now have been transferred to a ciborium, which is a goblet ordinarily used to hold the consecrated bread of the Mass. The first scrutator withdraws a ballot, unfolds it, reads its inscription; passes it to the second scrutator, who reads it also; then it is given to the third scrutator, who reads the name aloud. Asciuga? Carciofo? Some other? *His?*

Rabbi Mueller is discussing angels. "Then we have the Angels of the Throne, known in Hebrew as *arelim* or *ophanim*. There are seventy of them, noted primarily for their steadfastness. Among them are the angels Orifiel, Ophaniel, Zabkiel, Jophiel, Ambriel, Tychagar, Barael, Quelamia, Paschar, Boel, and Raum. Some of these are no longer found in heaven and are numbered among the fallen angels in hell."

"So much for their steadfastness," says Kenneth.

"Then, too," the rabbi goes on, "there are the Angels of the Presence, who apparently were circumcised at the moment of their creation. These are Michael, Metatron, Suriel, Sandalphon, Uriel, Saraqael, Astanphaeus, Phanuel, Jehoel, Zagzagael, Yefefiah, and Akatriel. But I think my favorite of the whole group is the Angel of Lust, who is mentioned in Talmud *Bereshith Rabba* eighty-five as follows, that when Judah was about to pass by . . ."

They have finished counting the votes by this time, surely. An immense throng has assembled in the Square of St. Peter's. The sunlight gleams off hundreds if not thousands of steel-jacketed crania. This must be a wonderful day for the robot population of Rome. But most of those in the piazza are creatures of flesh and blood: old women in black, gaunt young pickpockets, boys with puppies, plump vendors of sausages, and an assortment of poets, philosophers, generals, legislators, tourists, and fishermen. How has the tally gone? We will have our answer shortly. If no candidate has had a majority, they will mix the ballots with wet straws before casting them into the chapel stove, and black smoke will billow from the chimney. But if a pope has been elected, the straw will be dry, the smoke will be white.

The system has agreeable resonances. I like it. It gives me the satisfaction one normally derives from a flawless work of art: the Tristan chord, let us say, or the teeth of the frog in Bosch's *Temptation of St. Anthony*. I await the outcome with fierce concentration. I am certain of the result; I can already feel the irresistible religious impulses awakening in me. Although I feel, also, an odd nostalgia for the days of flesh-and-blood popes. Tomorrow's newspapers will have no interviews with the Holy Father's aged mother in Sicily, nor with his proud younger brother in San Francisco. And will this grand ceremony of election ever be held again? Will we need another pope, when this one whom we will soon have can be repaired so easily?

Ah. The white smoke! The moment of revelation comes!

A figure emerges on the central balcony of the façade of St. Peter's, spreads a web of cloth of gold, and disappears. The blaze of light against that fabric stuns the eye. It reminds me perhaps of moonlight coldly kissing the sea at Castellammare or, perhaps even more, of the noonday glare rebounding from the breast of the Caribbean off the coast of St. John. A second figure, clad in ermine and vermilion, has appeared on the balcony. "The cardinal archdeacon," Bishop FitzPatrick whispers. People have started to faint. Luigi stands beside me, listening to the proceedings on a tiny radio. Kenneth says, "It's all been fixed." Rabbi Mueller hisses at him to be still. Miss Harshaw begins to sob. Beverly softly recites the Pledge of Allegiance, crossing herself throughout. This is a wonderful moment for me. I think it is the most truly contemporary moment I have ever experienced.

The amplified voice of the cardinal archdea-con cries, "I announce to you great joy. We have a pope."

Cheering commences, and grows in intensity as the cardinal archdeacon tells the world that the newly chosen pontiff is indeed that cardinal, that noble and distinguished person, that melancholy and austere individual, whose elevation to the Holy See we have all awaited so intensely for so long. "He has imposed upon himself," says the cardinal archdeacon, "the name of—"

Lost in the cheering. I turn to Luigi. "Who? What name?"

"Sisto Settimo," Luigi tells me.

Yes, and there he is, Pope Sixtus the Seventh, as we now must call him. A tiny figure clad in the silver and gold papal robes, arms outstretched to the multitude, and, yes! the sunlight glints on his cheeks, his lofty forehead, there is the brightness of polished steel. Luigi is already on his knees. I kneel beside him. Miss Harshaw, Beverly, Kenneth, even the rabbi all kneel, for beyond doubt this is a miraculous event. The pope comes forward on his balcony. Now he will deliver the traditional apostolic benediction to the city and to the world. "Our help is in the Name of the Lord," he declares gravely. He activates the levitator jets beneath his arms; even at this distance I can see the two small puffs of smoke. White smoke, again. He begins to rise into the air. "Who hath made heaven and earth," he says. "May Almighty God, Father, Son, and Holy Ghost, bless you." His voice rolls majestically toward us. His shadow extends across the whole piazza. Higher and higher he goes, until he is lost to sight. Kenneth taps Luigi. "Another round of drinks," he says, and presses a bill of high denomination into the innkeeper's fleshy palm. Bishop FitzPatrick weeps. Rabbi Mueller embraces Miss Harshaw. The new pontiff, I think, has begun his reign in an auspicious way.

When It Changed

JOANNA RUSS

Joanna Russ (1937–2011) was an award-winning and influential US writer and academic who grew up in the Bronx and became, as a high school student, one of ten finalists in Westinghouse's Science Talent Search. Russ attended Cornell University, where she eventually taught creative writing, and took an MFA in playwriting at Yale. She was inducted into the Science Fiction and Fantasy Hall of Fame in 2013.

Russ, like Carol Emshwiller, published fiction in a variety of genre and literary outlets, including *Manhattan Review* and Damon Knight's *Orbit* anthology series. She began publishing science fiction in 1959 with "Nor Custom Stale" for *The Magazine of Fantasy and Science Fiction*, a journal for which she also contributed influential book reviews between 1967 and 1980. Her most influential and highly regarded piece of fiction is perhaps her novel *The Female Man* (1975), a searing work of feminist science fiction that still shocks and inspires readers and writers to this day. Her short story collections, long out of print, include *The Zanzibar Cat* (1983), *(Extra)ordinary People* (1985), and *The Hidden Side of the Moon* (1987). As of this writing, a "complete fiction" collection is urgently needed as her entire short output rivals in quality the oeuvre of iconic writers such as Angela Carter and Shirley Jackson.

Russ's nonfiction was as thought-provoking, deft, and edgy as her fiction, winning the 1988 Pilgrim Award for science fiction criticism. Collections of her essays include *How to Suppress Women's Writing* (1983) and *Magic Mommas, Trembling Sisters, Puritans and Perverts: Feminist Essays* (1985). According to the critic John Clute, "Like Samuel R. Delany, she was a thoroughly grounded intellectual, and every word she wrote, fiction or nonfiction, was shaped by thought in action. Despite this—or perhaps because of this—she remained exceptionally persuasive. She told often unpalatable truths in tales that were, as pure story, a joy to read." Taken in total, her work, along with that of writers such as James Tiptree Jr., changed both the conversation in the science fiction world of the time and the emphasis about what was important in fiction.

"When It Changed" was first published in Harlan Ellison's classic anthology *Again, Dangerous Visions* (1972) and won the Nebula Award. Of this story, Ellison wrote that it "makes some extraordinarily sharp distinctions between the abilities and attitudes of the sexes, while erasing many others we think immutable. It is, in the best and strongest sense of the word, a female liberation story, while never once speaking of, about, or to the subject."

The setting of Whileaway is the feminist utopian world featured in *The Female Man*, and "When It Changed" tells the story of what happens to this utopia after the arrival of a starship full of men.

WHEN IT CHANGED

Joanna Russ

Katy drives like a maniac; we must have been doing over 120 kilometers per hour on those turns. She's good, though, extremely good, and I've seen her take the whole car apart and put it together again in a day. My birthplace on Whileaway was largely given to farm machinery and I refuse to wrestle with a five-gear shift at unholy speeds, not having been brought up to it, but even on those turns in the middle of the night, on a country road as bad as only our district can make them, Katy's driving didn't scare me.

The funny thing about my wife, though: she will not handle guns. She has even gone hiking in the forests above the forty-eighth parallel without firearms, for days at a time. And that *does* scare me.

Katy and I have three children between us, one of hers and two of mine. Yuriko, my eldest, was asleep in the backseat, dreaming twelve-year-old dreams of love and war: running away to sea, hunting in the North, dreams of strangely beautiful people in strangely beautiful places, all the wonderful guff you think up when you're turning twelve and the glands start going. Someday soon, like all of them, she will disappear for weeks on end to come back grimy and proud, having knifed her first cougar or shot her first bear, dragging some abominably dangerous dead beastie behind her, which I will never forgive for what it might have done to my daughter. Yuriko says Katy's driving puts her to sleep.

For someone who has fought three duels, I am afraid of far, far too much. I'm getting old. I told this to my wife.

"You're thirty-four," she said. Laconic to the point of silence, that one. She flipped the lights on, on the dash—three kilometers to go and the road getting worse all the time. Far out in the country. Electric-green trees rushed into our headlights and around the car. I reached down next to me where we bolt the carrier panel to the door and eased my rifle into my lap. Yuriko stirred in the back. My height but Katy's eyes, Katy's face. The car engine is so quiet, Katy says, that you can hear breathing in the backseat. Yuki had been alone in the car when the message came, enthusiastically decoding her dot-dashes (silly to mount a wide-frequency transceiver near an IC engine, but most of Whileaway is on steam). She had thrown herself out of the car, my gangly and gaudy offspring, shouting at the top of her lungs, so of course she had had to come along. We've been intellectually prepared for this ever since the Colony was founded, ever since it was abandoned, but this is different. This is awful.

"Men!" Yuki had screamed, leaping over the car door. "They've come back! Real Earth men!"

We met them in the kitchen of the farmhouse near the place where they had landed; the windows were open, the night air very mild. We had passed all sorts of transportation when we parked outside—steam tractors, trucks, an IC flatbed, even a bicycle. Lydia, the district biologist, had come out of her Northern taciturnity long enough to take blood and urine samples and was sitting in a corner of the kitchen shaking her head in astonishment over the results; she even forced herself (very big, very fair, very shy, always painfully blushing) to dig up the old language manuals—though I can talk the old tongues in my sleep. And do. Lydia is uneasy with us; we're Southerners and too flamboyant. I counted twenty people in that kitchen, all the brains of North Continent. Phyllis Spet, I think, had come in by glider. Yuki was the only child there.

Then I saw the four of them.

They are bigger than we are. They are bigger and broader. Two were taller than I, and I am extremely tall, one meter eighty centimeters in my bare feet. They are obviously of our species but *off*, indescribably off, and as my eyes could not and still cannot quite comprehend the lines of those alien bodies, I could not, then, bring myself to touch them, though the one who spoke Russian—what voices they have—wanted to "shake hands," a custom from the past, I imagine. I can only say they were apes with human faces. He seemed to mean well, but I found myself shuddering back almost the length of the kitchen—and then I laughed apologetically—and then to set a good example (*Interstellar amity,* I thought) did "shake hands" finally. A hard, hard hand. They are heavy as draft horses. Blurred, deep voices. Yuriko had sneaked in between the adults and was gazing at *the men* with her mouth open.

He turned *his* head—those words have not been in our language for six hundred years—and said, in bad Russian:

"Who's that?"

"My daughter," I said, and added (with that irrational attention to good manners we sometimes employ in moments of insanity), "My daughter, Yuriko Janetson. We use the patronymic. You would say matronymic."

He laughed, involuntarily. Yuki exclaimed, "I thought they would be good-looking!" greatly disappointed at this reception of herself. Phyllis Helgason Spet, whom someday I shall kill, gave me across the room a cold, level, venomous look, as if to say: *Watch what you say. You know what I can do.* It's true that I have little formal status, but Madam President will get herself in serious trouble with both me and her own staff if she continues to consider industrial espionage good clean fun. Wars and rumors of wars, as it says in one of our ancestors' books. I translated Yuki's words into *the man's* dog-Russian, once our lingua franca, and *the man* laughed again.

"Where are all your people?" he said conversationally.

I translated again and watched the faces around the room; Lydia embarrassed (as usual), Spet narrowing her eyes with some damned scheme, Katy very pale.

"This is Whileaway," I said.

He continued to look unenlightened.

"Whileaway," I said. "Do you remember? Do you have records? There was a plague on Whileaway."

He looked moderately interested. Heads turned in the back of the room, and I caught a glimpse of the local professions-parliament delegate; by morning every town meeting, every district caucus, would be in full session.

"Plague?" he said. "That's most unfortunate."

"Yes," I said. "Most unfortunate. We lost half our population in one generation."

He looked properly impressed.

"Whileaway was lucky," I said. "We had a big initial gene pool, we had been chosen for extreme intelligence, we had a high technology and a large remaining population in which every adult was two or three experts in one. The soil is good. The climate is blessedly easy. There are thirty millions of us now. Things are beginning to snowball in industry—do you understand?—give us seventy years and we'll have more than one real city, more than a few industrial centers, full-time professions, full-time radio operators, full-time machinists, give us seventy years and not everyone will have to spend three-quarters of a lifetime on the farm." And I tried to explain how hard it is when artists can practice full-time only in old age, when there are so few, so very few who can be free, like Katy and myself. I tried also to outline our government, the two houses, the one by professions and the geographic one; I told him the district caucuses handled problems too big for the individual towns. And that population control was not a political issue, not yet, though give us time and it would be. This was a delicate point in our history; give us time. There was no need to sacrifice the quality of life for an insane rush into industrialization. Let us go our own pace. Give us time.

"Where are all the people?" said that monomaniac.

I realized then that he did not mean people, he meant *men*, and he was giving the word the meaning it had not had on Whileaway for six centuries.

"They died," I said. "Thirty generations ago."

I thought we had poleaxed him. He caught his breath. He made as if to get out of the chair he was sitting in; he put his hand to his chest; he looked around at us with the strangest blend of awe and sentimental tenderness. Then he said, solemnly and earnestly:

"A great tragedy."

I waited, not quite understanding.

"Yes," he said, catching his breath again with the queer smile, that adult-to-child smile that tells you something is being hidden and will be presently produced with cries of encouragement and joy, "a great tragedy. But it's over." And again he looked around at all of us with the strangest deference. As if we were invalids.

"You've adapted amazingly," he said.

"To what?" I said. He looked embarrassed. He looked inane. Finally he said, "Where I come from, the women don't dress so plainly."

"Like you?" I said. "Like a bride?" For the men were wearing silver from head to foot. I had never seen anything so gaudy. He made as if to answer and then apparently thought better of it; he laughed at me again. With an odd exhilaration—as if we were something childish and something wonderful, as if he were doing us an enormous favor—he took one shaky breath and said, "Well, we're here."

I looked at Spet, Spet looked at Lydia, Lydia looked at Amalia, who is the head of the local town meeting, Amalia looked at I don't know whom. My throat was raw. I cannot stand local beer, which the farmers swill as if their stomachs had iridium linings, but I took it anyway, from Amalia (it was her bicycle we had seen outside as we parked), and swallowed it all. This was going to take a long time. I said, "Yes, here you are," and smiled (feeling like a fool), and wondered seriously if male Earth-people's minds worked so very differently from female Earth-people's minds, but that couldn't be so or the race would have died out long ago. The radio network had got the news around the planet by now and we had another Russian speaker, flown in from Varna; I decided to cut out when *the man* passed around pictures of his wife, who looked like the priestess of some arcane cult. He proposed to question Yuki, so I barreled her into a back room in spite of her furious protests, and went out on the front porch. As I left, Lydia was explaining the difference between parthenogenesis (which is so easy that anyone can practice it) and what we do, which is the merging of ova. That is why Katy's baby looks like me. Lydia went on to the Ansky Process and Katy Ansky, our one full-polymath genius and the great-great I don't know how many times great-grandmother of my own Katharina.

A dot-dash transmitter in one of the outbuildings chattered faintly to itself—operators flirting and passing jokes down the line.

There was a man on the porch. The other tall man. I watched him for a few minutes—I can move very quietly when I want to and when I allowed him to see me, he stopped talking into the little machine hung around his neck. Then he said calmly, in excellent Russian, "Did you know that sexual equality has been reestablished on Earth?"

"You're the real one," I said, "aren't you? The other one's for show." It was a great relief to get things cleared up. He nodded affably.

"As a people, we are not very bright," he said. "There's been too much genetic damage in the last few centuries. Radiation. Drugs. We can use Whileaway's genes, Janet." Strangers do not call strangers by the first name.

"You can have cells enough to drown in," I said. "Breed your own."

He smiled. "That's not the way we want to do it." Behind him I saw Katy come into the square of light that was the screened-in door. He went on, low and urbane, not mocking me, I think, but with the self-confidence of someone who has always had money and strength to spare, who doesn't know what it is to be second-class or provincial. Which is very odd, because the day before, I would have said that was an exact description of me.

"I'm talking to you, Janet," he said, "because I suspect you have more popular influence than anyone else here. You know as well as I do that parthenogenetic culture has all sorts of inherent defects, and we do not—if we can help it—mean to use you for anything of the sort. Pardon me; I should not have said 'use.' But surely you can see that this kind of society is unnatural."

"Humanity is unnatural," said Katy. She had my rifle under her left arm. The top of that silky head does not quite come up to my collarbone, but she is as tough as steel; he began to move, again with that queer smiling deference (which his fellow had showed to me but he had not), and the gun slid into Katy's grip as if she had shot with it all her life.

"I agree," said the man. "Humanity is unnatural. I should know. I have metal in my teeth and metal pins here." He touched his shoulder. "Seals are harem animals," he added, "and so are men; apes are promiscuous and so are men; doves are monogamous and so are men; there are even celibate men and homosexual men. There are homosexual cows, I believe. But Whileaway is still missing something." He gave a dry chuckle. I will give him the credit of believing that it had something to do with nerves.

"I miss nothing," said Katy, "except that life isn't endless."

"You are—?" said the man, nodding from me to her.

"Wives," said Katy. "We're married." Again the dry chuckle.

"A good economic arrangement," he said, "for working and taking care of the children. And as good an arrangement as any for randomizing heredity, if your reproduction is made to follow the same pattern. But think, Katharina Michaelason, if there isn't something better that you might secure for your daughters. I believe in instincts, even in man, and I can't think that the two of you—a machinist, are you? and I gather you are some sort of chief of police—don't feel somehow what even you must miss. You know it intellectually, of course. There is only half a species here. Men must come back to Whileaway."

Katy said nothing.

"I should think, Katharina Michaelason," said the man gently, "that you, of all people, would benefit most from such a change," and he walked past Katy's rifle into the square of light coming from the door. I think it was then that he noticed my scar, which really does not show unless the light is from the side: a fine line that runs from temple to chin. Most people don't even know about it.

"Where did you get that?" he said, and I answered with an involuntary grin. "In my last duel." We stood there bristling at each other for several seconds (this is absurd but true) until he went inside and shut the screen door behind him. Katy said in a brittle voice, "You damned fool, don't you know when we've been insulted?" and swung up the rifle to shoot him through the screen, but I got to her before she could fire and knocked the rifle out of aim; it burned a hole through the porch floor. Katy was shaking. She kept whispering over and over, "That's why I never touched it, because I knew I'd kill someone. I knew I'd kill someone." The first man—the one I'd spoken with first—was still talking inside the house, something about the grand movement to recolonize and rediscover all the Earth had lost. He stressed the advantages to Whileaway: trade, exchange of ideas, education. He, too, said that sexual equality had been reestablished on Earth.

Katy was right, of course; we should have burned them down where they stood. Men are coming to Whileaway. When one culture has the big guns and the other has none, there is a certain predictability about the outcome. Maybe men would have come eventually in any case. I like to think that a hundred years from now my great-grandchildren could have stood them off or fought them to a standstill, but even that's no odds; I will remember all my life those four people I first met who were muscled like bulls and who made me—if only for a moment—feel small. A neurotic reaction, Katy says. I remember everything that happened that night; I remember Yuki's excitement in the car, I remember Katy's sobbing when we got home as if her heart would break, I remember her lovemaking, a little peremptory as always, but wonderfully soothing and comforting. I remember prowling restlessly around the house after Katy fell asleep with one bare arm hung into a patch of light from the hall. The muscles of her forearms are like metal bars from all that driving and testing of her machines. Sometimes I dream about Katy's arms. I remember wandering into the nursery and picking up my wife's baby, dozing for a while with the poignant, amazing warmth of an infant in my lap, and finally returning to the kitchen to find Yuriko fixing herself a late snack. My daughter eats like a Great Dane.

"Yuki," I said, "do you think you could fall in love with a man?" and she whooped derisively. "With a ten-foot toad!" said my tactful child.

But men are coming to Whileaway. Lately I sit up nights and worry about the men who will come to this planet, about my two daughters and Betta Katharinason, about what will happen to Katy, to me, to my life. Our ancestors' journals are one long cry of pain and I suppose I ought to be glad now, but one can't throw away six centuries, or even (as I have lately discovered) thirty-four years. Sometimes I laugh at the question those four men hedged about all evening and never quite dared to ask, looking at the lot of us, hicks in overalls, farmers in canvas pants and plain shirts: *Which of you plays the role of the man?* As if we had to produce a carbon copy of their mistakes! I doubt very much that sexual equality has been reestablished on Earth. I do not like to think of myself mocked, of Katy deferred to as if she were weak, of Yuki made to feel unimportant or silly, of my other children cheated of their full humanity or turned into strangers. And I'm afraid that my own achievements will dwindle from what they were—or what I thought they were—to the not-very-interesting curiosa of the *human* race, the oddities you read about in the back of the book, things to laugh at sometimes because they are so exotic, quaint but not impressive, charming but not useful. I find this more painful than I can say. You will agree that for a woman who has fought three duels, all of them kills, indulging in such fears is ludicrous. But what's around the corner now is a duel so big that I don't think I have the guts for it; in Faust's words: *Verweile doch, du bist so schoen!* Keep it as it is. Don't change.

Sometimes at night I remember the original name of this planet, changed by the first generation of our ancestors, those curious women for whom, I suppose, the real name was too painful a reminder after the men died. I find it amusing, in a grim way, to see it all so completely turned around. This, too, shall pass. All good things must come to an end.

Take my life but don't take away the meaning of my life.

For-A-While.

And I Awoke and Found Me Here on the Cold Hill's Side

JAMES TIPTREE JR.

Alice Hastings Bradley Sheldon (1915–1987) was a US psychologist who wrote groundbreaking science fiction as James Tiptree Jr. and as Raccoona Sheldon. As Michael Swanwick wrote in his introduction to *Her Smoke Rose Up Forever* (2004), "strangest of all were three writing desks [in Sheldon's house], each with its distinct typewriter, stationery, and color of ink. One belonged to James Tiptree Jr. A second was used exclusively by Raccoona Sheldon. The third was for Alice Sheldon, a sometimes scientist, artist, newspaper critic, soldier, businesswoman, and retired CIA officer, who on occasion moved to one of the other desks." In 1991, the authors Karen Joy Fowler and Pat Murphy founded the James Tiptree Jr. Award, which is given annually to a work of science fiction or fantasy that expands or explores our understanding of gender.

Tiptree used the pen names initially to protect her academic work, but speculations about her gender within the field of science fiction led to controversy and often heated discussion. The evolving understanding of Tiptree's identity is interesting to track. In 1972, Frederik Pohl wrote in *Best Science Fiction*, "James Tiptree Jr. is a writer I . . . have never met. I rather think the chances are we never will, because every time [I] suggest we get together for a drink, it turns out that he is that week off to Borneo or Brooklyn or Swaziland." The editor Terry Carr, in *Best Science Fiction of the Year #3* (1974), wrote in the story note for Tiptree's "The Women Men Don't See," "Like any branch of literature, science fiction reflects the trends of current thinking. Last year Joanna Russ won a Nebula Award for a feminist story entitled 'When It Changed'; this year James Tiptree Jr. offers a male viewpoint on the same subject. As you might expect, other than the basic theme, there's very little similarity between the two stories." Ursula Le Guin, a year or two after the truth became known, may have gotten in the last word with this comment accompanying Tiptree's story "Slow Music" (in *Interfaces: An Anthology of Speculative Fiction*, 1980): "James Tiptree Jr. is a pseudonym. He is a woman. She is also Raccoona Sheldon. They are an experimental psychologist of great insight, a writer of surpassing strength, and a person of infinite reserve, generosity, and charm."

Tiptree wrote primarily short stories, publishing only one novel, *Up the Walls of the World* (1978). She worked in a variety of styles, often combining the trappings of "hard" science fiction with "soft" science fiction like sociology and psychology. Tiptree stories retain their power even today, and demand rereading, because they resist easy interpretation. Nor are Tiptree's characters mouthpieces for ideas or rhetoric, and the unconventional structures of her stories render them mysterious and luminous—in a way similar to Carol Emshwiller's and also Margaret St. Clair's stories from the 1950s and early 1960s, which can be read as precursors to the hyperrealistic mental landscapes that dominate Tiptree's fiction.

"And I Awoke and Found Me Here on the Cold Hill's Side" takes the pulp "sense of wonder" about space travel and pushes back against it with a portrayal of alien contact in a gritty dystopic future. Few prior stories manage to anticipate the complexities of such a situation. Much about this culture clash points to how fiction of the 1960s and 1970s, within the New Wave and outside of it, wanted to portray a more "real" reality. Tiptree's story also shares thematic resonances with Samuel R. Delany's "Aye, and Gomorrah," which sharply interrogates other assumptions made by classic science fiction.

AND I AWOKE AND FOUND ME HERE ON THE COLD HILL'S SIDE

James Tiptree Jr.

He was standing absolutely still by a service port, staring out at the belly of the *Orion* docking above us. He had on a gray uniform and his rusty hair was cut short. I took him for a station engineer.

That was bad for me. Newsmen strictly don't belong in the bowels of Big Junction. But in my first twenty hours I hadn't found any place to get a shot of an alien ship.

I turned my holocam to show its big World Media insignia and started my bit about What It Meant to the People Back Home who were paying for it all.

"—it may be routine work to you, sir, but we owe it to them to share—"

His face came around slow and tight, and his gaze passed over me from a peculiar distance.

"The wonders, the drama," he repeated dispassionately. His eyes focused on me. "You consummated fool."

"Could you tell me what races are coming in, sir? If I could even get a view—"

He waved me to the port. Greedily I angled my lenses up at the long blue hull blocking out the starfield. Beyond her I could see the bulge of a black and gold ship.

"That's a Foramen," he said. "There's a freighter from Belye on the other side, you'd call it Arcturus. Not much traffic right now."

"You're the first person who's said two sentences to me since I've been here, sir. What are those colorful little craft?"

"Procya." He shrugged. "They're always around. Like us."

I squashed my face on the vitrite, peering. The walls clanked. Somewhere overhead aliens were off-loading into their private sector of Big Junction. The man glanced at his wrist.

"Are you waiting to go out, sir?"

His grunt could have meant anything.

"Where are you from on Earth?" he asked me in his hard tone.

I started to tell him and suddenly saw that he had forgotten my existence. His eyes were on nowhere, and his head was slowly bowing forward onto the port frame.

"Go home," he said thickly. I caught a strong smell of tallow.

"Hey, sir!" I grabbed his arm; he was in rigid tremor. "Steady, man."

"I'm waiting . . . waiting for my wife. My loving wife." He gave a short ugly laugh. "Where are you from?"

I told him again.

"Go home," he mumbled. "Go home and make babies. While you still can."

One of the early GR casualties, I thought.

"Is that all you know?" His voice rose stridently. "Fools. Dressing in their styles. Gnivo suits, Aoleelee music. Oh, I see your newscasts," he sneered. "Nixi parties. A year's salary for a floater. Gamma radiation? Go home, read history. *Ballpoint pens and bicycles*—"

He started a slow slide downward in the half gee. My only informant. We struggled confusedly; he wouldn't take one of my sobertabs but I finally got him along the service corridor to a bench in an empty loading bay. He fumbled out a little vacuum cartridge. As I was helping him unscrew it, a figure in starched whites put his head in the bay.

"I can be of assistance, yes?" His eyes

popped, his face was covered with brindled fur. An alien, a Procya! I started to thank him but the red-haired man cut me off.

"Get lost. Out."

The creature withdrew, its big eyes moist. The man stuck his pinky in the cartridge and then put it up his nose, gasping deep in his diaphragm. He looked toward his wrist.

"What time is it?"

I told him.

"News," he said. "A message for the eager, hopeful human race. A word about those lovely, lovable aliens we all love so much." He looked at me. "Shocked, aren't you, newsboy?"

I had him figured now. A xenophobe. Aliens plot to take over Earth.

"Ah, Christ, they couldn't care less." He took another deep gasp, shuddered, and straightened. "The hell with generalities. What time d'you say it was? All right, I'll tell you how I learned it. The hard way. While we wait for my loving wife. You can bring that little recorder out of your sleeve, too. Play it over to yourself sometime . . . when it's too late." He chuckled. His tone had become chatty—an educated voice. "You ever hear of supernormal stimuli?"

"No," I said. "Wait a minute. White sugar?"

"Near enough. Y'know Little Junction Bar in DC? No, you're an Aussie, you said. Well, I'm from Burned Barn, Nebraska."

He took a breath, consulting some vast disarray of the soul.

"I accidentally drifted into Little Junction Bar when I was eighteen. No. Correct that. You don't go into Little Junction by accident, any more than you first shoot skag by accident.

"You go into Little Junction because you've been craving it, dreaming about it, feeding on every hint and clue about it, back there in Burned Barn, since before you had hair in your pants. Whether you know it or not. Once you're out of Burned Barn, you can no more help going into Little Junction than a sea-worm can help rising to the moon.

"I had a brand-new liquor ID in my pocket. It was early; there was an empty spot beside some humans at the bar. Little Junction isn't an embassy bar, y'know. I found out later where the high-caste aliens go—when they go out. The New Rive, the Curtain by the Georgetown Marina.

"And they go by themselves. Oh, once in a while they do the cultural exchange bit with a few frosty couples of other aliens and some stuffed humans. Galactic Amity with a ten-foot pole.

"Little Junction was the place where the lower orders went, the clerks and drivers out for kicks. Including, my friend, the perverts. The ones who can take humans. Into their beds, that is."

He chuckled and sniffed his finger again, not looking at me.

"Ah, yes. Little Junction is Galactic Amity night, every night. I ordered . . . what? A margarita. I didn't have the nerve to ask the snotty spade bartender for one of the alien liquors behind the bar. It was dim. I was trying to stare everywhere at once without showing it. I remember those white boneheads—Lyrans, that is. And a mess of green veiling I decided was a multiple being from some place. I caught a couple of human glances in the bar mirror. Hostile flicks. I didn't get the message, then.

"Suddenly an alien pushed right in beside me. Before I could get over my paralysis, I heard this blurry voice:

"'You air a futeball enthusiash?'

"An alien had spoken to me. An *alien*, a being from the stars. Had spoken. To me.

"Oh, god, I had no time for football, but I would have claimed a passion for paper-folding, for dumb crambo—anything to keep him talking. I asked him about his home-planet sports, I insisted on buying his drinks. I listened raptly while he spluttered out a play-by-play account of a game I wouldn't have turned a dial for. The 'Grain Bay Pashkers.' Yeah. And I was dimly aware of trouble among the humans on my other side.

"Suddenly this woman—I'd call her a girl now—this girl said something in a high nasty voice and swung her stool into the arm I was holding my drink with. We both turned around together.

"Christ, I can see her now. The first thing that hit me was *discrepancy*. She was a nothing—but terrific. Transfigured. Oozing it, radiating it.

"The next thing was I had a horrifying hard-on just looking at her.

"I scrooched over so my tunic hid it, and my spilled drink trickled down, making everything worse. She pawed vaguely at the spill, muttering.

"I just stared at her trying to figure out what had hit me. An ordinary figure, a soft avidness in the face. Eyes heavy, satiated-looking. She was totally sexualized. I remember her throat pulsed. She had one hand up touching her scarf, which had slipped off her shoulder. I saw angry bruises there. That really tore it, I understood at once those bruises had some sexual meaning.

"She was looking past my head with her face like a radar dish. Then she made an 'ahh-hhh' sound that had nothing to do with me and grabbed my forearm as if it were a railing. One of the men behind her laughed. The woman said, 'Excuse me,' in a ridiculous voice and slipped out behind me. I wheeled around after her, nearly upsetting my football friend, and saw that some Sirians had come in.

"That was my first look at Sirians in the flesh, if that's the word. God knows I'd memorized every news shot, but I wasn't prepared. That tallness, that cruel thinness. That appalling alien arrogance. Ivory-blue, these were. Two males in immaculate metallic gear. Then I saw there was a female with them. An ivory-indigo, exquisite, with a permanent faint smile on those bone-hard lips.

"The girl who'd left me was ushering them to a table. She reminded me of a goddamn dog that wants you to follow it. Just as the crowd hid them, I saw a man join them, too. A big man, expensively dressed, with something wrecked about his face.

"Then the music started and I had to apologize to my furry friend. And the Sellice dancer came out and my personal introduction to hell began."

The red-haired man fell silent for a minute, enduring self-pity. Something wrecked about the face, I thought; it fit.

He pulled his face together.

"First I'll give you the only coherent observation of my entire evening. You can see it here at Big Junction, always the same. Outside of the Procya, it's humans with aliens, right? Very seldom aliens with other aliens. Never aliens with humans. It's the humans who want in."

I nodded, but he wasn't talking to me. His voice had a druggy fluency.

"Ah, yes, my Sellice. My first Sellice.

"They aren't really well built, y'know, under those cloaks. No waist to speak of and short-legged. But they flow when they walk.

"This one flowed out into the spotlight, cloaked to the ground in violet silk. You could only see a fall of black hair and tassels over a narrow face like a vole. She was a mole-gray. They come in all colors. Their fur is like a flexible velvet all over; only the color changes startlingly around their eyes and lips and other places. Erogenous zones? Ah, man, with them it's not zones.

"She began to do what we'd call a dance, but it's no dance, it's their natural movement. Like smiling, say, with us. The music built up, and her arms undulated toward me, letting the cloak fall apart little by little. She was naked under it. The spotlight started to pick up her body markings moving in the slit of the cloak. Her arms floated apart and I saw more and more.

"She was fantastically marked and the markings were writhing. Not like body paint—alive. Smiling, that's a good word for it. As if her whole body was smiling sexually, beckoning, winking, urging, pouting, speaking to me. You've seen a classic Egyptian belly dance? Forget it—a sorry, stiff thing compared to what any Sellice can do. This one was ripe, near term.

"Her arms went up and those blazing lemon-colored curves pulsed, waved, everted, contracted, throbbed, evolved unbelievably welcoming, inciting permutations. *Come do it to me, do it, do it here and here and here and now.* You couldn't see the rest of her, only a wicked flash of mouth. Every human male in the room was aching to ram himself into that incredible body. I mean it was *pain.* Even the other aliens were quiet, except one of the Sirians, who was chewing out a waiter.

"I was a basket case before she was halfway through. . . . I won't bore you with what happened next; before it was over there were several fights and I got cut. My money ran out on the third night. She was gone next day.

"I didn't have time to find out about the Sellice cycle then, mercifully. That came after I went back to campus and discovered you had to have a degree in solid-state electronics to apply for off-planet work. I was a premed but I got that degree. It only took me as far as First Junction then.

"Oh, god, First Junction. I thought I was in heaven—the alien ships coming in and our freighters going out. I saw them all, all but the real exotics, the tankies. You only see a few of those a cycle, even here. And the Yyeire. You've never seen that.

"Go home, boy. Go home to your version of Burned Barn. . . .

"The first Yyeir I saw, I dropped everything and started walking after it like a starving hound, just breathing. You've seen the pix of course. Like lost dreams. *Man is in love and loves what vanishes.* . . . It's the scent, you can't guess that. I followed until I ran into a slammed port. I spent half a cycle's credits sending the creature the wine they call stars' tears. . . . Later I found out it was a male. That made no difference at all.

"You can't have sex with them, y'know. No way. They breed by light or something, no one knows exactly. There's a story about a man who got hold of a Yyeir woman and tried. They had him skinned. Stories—"

He was starting to wander.

"What about that girl in the bar, did you see her again?"

He came back from somewhere.

"Oh, yes. I saw her. She'd been making it with the two Sirians, y'know. The males do it in pairs. Said to be the total sexual thing for a woman, if she can stand the damage from those beaks. I wouldn't know. She talked to me a couple of times after they finished with her. No use for men whatever. She drove off the P Street bridge. . . . The man, poor bastard, he was trying to keep that Sirian bitch happy singlehanded. Money helps, for a while. I don't know where he ended up."

He glanced at his wristwatch again. I saw the pale bare place where a watch had been and told him the time.

"Is that the message you want to give Earth? Never love an alien?"

"Never love an alien—" He shrugged. "Yeah. No. Ah, Jesus, don't you see? Everything going out, nothing coming back. Like the poor damned Polynesians. We're gutting Earth, to begin with. Swapping raw resources for junk. Alien status symbols. Tape decks, Coca-Cola, Mickey Mouse watches."

"Well, there is concern over the balance of trade. Is that your message?"

"The balance of trade." He rolled his eyes sardonically. "Did the Polynesians have a word for it, I wonder? You don't see, do you? All right, why are you here? I mean *you*, personally. How many guys did you climb over—"

He went rigid, hearing footsteps outside. The Procya's hopeful face appeared around the corner. The red-haired man snarled at him and he backed out. I started to protest.

"Ah, the silly reamer loves it. It's the only pleasure we have left. . . . Can't you see, man? That's *us.* That's the way we look to them, to the real ones."

"But—"

"And now we're getting the cheap C-drive, we'll be all over just like the Procya. For the pleasure of serving as freight monkeys and junction crews. Oh, they appreciate our ingenious little service stations, the beautiful star folk. They don't *need* them, y'know. Just an amusing convenience. D'you know what I do here with my two degrees? What I did at First Junction. Tube cleaning. A swab. Sometimes I get to replace a fitting."

I muttered something; the self-pity was getting heavy.

"Bitter? Man, it's a *good* job. Sometimes I get to talk to one of them." His face twisted. "My wife works as a—oh, hell, you wouldn't know. I'd trade—correction, I have traded—everything Earth offered me for just that chance. To see them. To speak to them. Once in a while to touch one. Once in a great while to find one low enough, perverted enough to want to touch me . . ."

His voice trailed off and suddenly came back strong.

"And so will you!" He glared at me. "Go home! Go home and tell them to quit it. Close the ports. Burn every god-lost alien thing before it's too late! That's what the Polynesians didn't do."

"But surely—"

"But surely be damned! Balance of trade—balance of *life*, man. I don't know if our birth rate is going, that's not the point. Our soul is leaking out. We're bleeding to death!"

He took a breath and lowered his tone.

"What I'm trying to tell you, this is a trap. We've hit the supernormal stimulus. Man is exogamous—all our history is one long drive to find and impregnate the stranger. Or get impregnated by him; it works for women, too. Anything different-colored, different nose, ass, anything, man *has* to fuck it or die trying. That's a drive, y'know, it's built in. Because it works fine as long as the stranger is human. For millions of years that kept the genes circulating. But now we've met aliens we can't screw, and we're about to die trying. . . . Do you think I can touch my wife?"

"But—"

"Look. Y'know, if you give a bird a fake egg like its own but bigger and brighter-marked, it'll roll its own egg out of the nest and sit on the fake? That's what we're doing."

"We've been talking about sex so far." I was trying to conceal my impatience. "Which is great, but the kind of story I'd hoped—"

"Sex? No, it's deeper." He rubbed his head, trying to clear the drug. "Sex is only part of it—there's more. I've seen Earth missionaries, teachers, sexless people. Teachers—they end cycling waste or pushing floaters, but they're hooked. They stay. I saw one fine-looking old woman, she was servant to a Cu'ushbar kid. A defective—his own people would have let him die. That wretch was swabbing up its vomit as if it was holy water. Man, it's deep . . . some cargo cult of the soul. We're built to dream outwards. They laugh at us. They don't have it."

There were sounds of movement in the next corridor. The dinner crowd was starting. I had to get rid of him and get there; maybe I could find the Procya.

A side door opened and a figure started toward us. At first I thought it was an alien and then I saw it was a woman wearing an awkward body-shell. She seemed to be limping slightly. Behind her I could glimpse the dinner-bound throng passing the open door.

The man got up as she turned into the bay. They didn't greet each other.

"The station employs only happily wedded couples," he told me with that ugly laugh. "We give each other . . . comfort."

He took one of her hands. She flinched as he drew it over his arm and let him turn her passively, not looking at me. "Forgive me if I don't introduce you. My wife appears fatigued."

I saw that one of her shoulders was grotesquely scarred.

"Tell them," he said, turning to go. "Go home and tell them." Then his head snapped back toward me and he added quietly, "And stay away from the Syrtis desk or I'll kill you."

They went away up the corridor.

I changed tapes hurriedly with one eye on the figures passing that open door. Suddenly among the humans I caught a glimpse of two sleek scarlet shapes. My first real aliens! I snapped the recorder shut and ran to squeeze in behind them.

Where Two Paths Cross
DMITRI BILENKIN
Translated by James Womack

Dmitri Bilenkin (1933–1987) was an eminent Soviet science fiction and science writer, reportedly proud of his enormous black beard, who joined the geology faculty of Moscow State University in the late 1950s. Subsequently he participated in several geological expeditions across remote areas of the Soviet Union, including Siberia. In 1959, Bilenkin became a science fiction writer, working on *Komsomolskaya pravda*'s editorial staff and later at *Vokrug sveta* (*Around the World*) magazine. His story collections include *The Surf of Mars* (1967), *Smuggled Night* (1971), *Intelligence Test* (1974), and *The Snows of Olympus* (1980). He also wrote a popular science book titled *The Argument Over the Mysterious Planet*. He was a member of the Union of Writers of the USSR from 1975, and a member of the Communist Party of the Soviet Union from 1963. In 1988, Bilenkin was posthumously awarded the Ivan Yefremov Prize.

Bilenkin's stories have been translated into several languages, including English, German, French, and Japanese. In the United States, most of his works in translation appeared in anthologies published by Macmillan in the 1980s—including his story "The Surf of Mars," which appeared in *World's Spring* (1981), edited by Vladimir Gakov, and was considered a classic at the time. Bilenkin, together with Anatoly Agranovsky, Yaroslav Golovanov, V. N. Komarov, and the artist Pavel Bunin used the collective pseudonym Pavel Bagryak. Together they wrote a cycle of detective stories and a novel titled *Blue Man*.

"Where Two Paths Cross" (1973), retranslated for this volume, was selected by the Strugatsky brothers for their 1984 anthology *Aliens, Travelers, and Other Strangers*. This superior alien contact story, at times darkly absurd, charts the misunderstandings and assumptions made by both humans and aliens on a distant planet. As with other fiction in this volume, most notably the selection by Ursula K. Le Guin, the ecological underpinnings in this story about alien life and the environment seem ever more relevant today.

WHERE TWO PATHS CROSS

Dmitri Bilenkin

Translated by James Womack

As always, the mangors picked up on the hurricane's approach in good time, although it seemed that there was nothing nearby to indicate its proximity.

If the mangors had been able to put their sensations into words, then most likely they would have said that it was unconscionable for nature to drive them away from a heavily laden table before they had eaten their fill. But they had no thoughts or words. All they did was hurriedly pull their legroots out of the earth, and raise their black-violet canopies and hold them up to the wind, like taut sails. Hard-hearted evolution had cruelly instilled into the mangors the harsh knowledge of the nomad: he who dawdles risks dying in a hurricane, however tightly he holds on to the soil.

After no more than a quarter of an Earth hour, a packed mass of dark sails moved ever more quickly across the plain, driven by the wind and the strength of hundreds of thousands of tentacle-like legs. An unerring instinct for the best route led the mangors to a spot where the storm would not blow, at least not in the immediate future, a place where they might safely graze.

At the same moment, hundreds of kilometers from the mangors and observing everything from the heights of the cosmos, human reason, reinforced by the whole might of various machines, was trying to solve the same problem.

Electronic and laser signals, acting with a speed incomprehensible not only to the mangors but to man himself, searched the whole polar region, studying the arcs of the multiple storms, the chaos of vortices, the blows delivered by furious currents of air, the whole brainteaser of atmospheric conditions that were scarcely calculable by terrestrial mathematical models, and all with the single aim of finding a spot on the surface of the planet where the landing party could come down without coming into danger from the rapid fury of extraterrestrial elements.

Insofar as truth is an objective quantity, there is nothing surprising in the fact that different, almost incompatible methods should give one and the same result: the earthlings' landing craft hurried to the same place where the mangors had themselves hurried earlier.

The mangors had stopped moving as soon as they had reached the hollow where they could safely graze. Their "sails" were furled, they lay flat against the ground collecting the miserly light from its distant source, and their tentacles dug into the earth so as to find nutritive salts for the bodies that lay spread over several hectares.

No one would say that the mangors were nomadic now; they looked as if they had always grown and would always grow on this hillside. All the other living things that accompanied the mangors and could not live without them (just as the mangors in their turn could not live without these other creatures) settled down and got to work.

A roar from the sky, a crescendo of noise, a strong wind hit the mangors without warning and forced them to hold tighter to the soil. Carried on a fiery pillar, a lens-shaped object came from the clouds and slowly settled on the ground.

The mangors' organs registered almost every detail of mankind's arrival on their planet, apart from the final moment: the craft's descent onto the top of the hill.

The wind died down, and they calmed too. Whatever had happened was not a sudden typhoon that could damage them, but even if it had been, then the typhoon had moved off somewhere to the side. The range of responses to outside stimuli—never particularly broad—worked as expected and the mangors carried on grazing peacefully, enjoying the cool rays of their sun, enjoying their food and their current security. Everything to do with the arrival of man laid a long way beyond the boundaries of their dim consciousness, and although their path in life had already crossed that of man, for them everything remained the same as it had been before.

And mankind was also unaware that these two paths had crossed, although it was aware of the existence of the mangors and was interested in them. Strangely enough, both sides had roughly the same relation to the other: for the mangors mankind did not exist, and man thought of the mangors only as a puzzle—what details of the life of a planet can be determined from outer space? All that they had established was that some patches of what was obviously vegetation either changed color (this was the traditional hypothesis, and therefore the one that was considered to be the most accurate) or else dug holes for themselves in periods of bad weather, or else moved around in some incomprehensible fashion. In the face of the alien and violent atmosphere there was no more that could be said, not even by the automatic probes, which were blown around like autumn leaves.

And so, what did the mangors actually mean? They were tiny pebbles, dust on mankind's great journey to the stars. Dust which should be examined in passing, no more than that.

. . .

When the ship had finally landed, the bottom of the landing craft moved aside, releasing anchor legs that immediately screwed themselves into the soil in case of unexpected hurricanes. What the hurricanes were like here was as well-known by the people who had never experienced them as it was by the mangors themselves. But they were unable to rely on their calculations—when and where the hurricanes would appear—as firmly as the mangors could rely on their instincts.

An hour after the dust had settled a ramp came down from an open hatch and an all-terrain vehicle came down. Mankind had stepped onto yet another planet.

The all-terrain vehicle forced itself over the crest of a hill, and humans saw mangors up close for the first time. Or rather, they did not see mangors but rather something that was familiar and understandable to them: a clump of bushes. Not entirely normal, but a clump just the same, a low canopy of thick and naked branches, many of which ended in a fan of dark oblong leaves. Their surface was exactly perpendicular to the rays of the sun. There was no possibility for doubt about what this was, and the driver took the all-terrain vehicle through the clump.

The caterpillar tracks crushed the thick "mattress" of branches, without even registering any resistance. The first leaves were ground into the dust; the all-terrain vehicle moved onward, leaving mulch behind it.

"The scheduled rest point is in the middle of the vegetation," the biologist said without taking his eyes off the visicam. "We need to take some scans and study the bushes up close."

But they would stop a little earlier than predicted. And not of their own volition.

The edge of the mangors' flesh felt pain that spread as the vehicle cut through the living body. But the mangors did not react too quickly: their life was a continuous battle for existence and they knew what to do and when to do it. They noticed the monster as soon as it arrived. Identification was a matter of a few moments. The mangors did not discover anything new: they considered this just a standard attack by their primordial enemy, the ourbans. Countless generations of ourbans had fed on mangors, engaging them in a cruel battle, and countless generations of mangors had either been victorious or else died in these struggles. The less capable were the ones who died, while the clever and cunning survived and killed the less successful ourbans themselves. And so they mutually removed their weakest elements: this unending battle between deadly enemies was the guarantee of progress for them both, and the increasing perfection of the ourbans led to the increasing perfection of the mangors.

The low-slung and massive all-terrain vehicle resembled an ourban only in part, of course, but the point where resemblance was the closest was the most important: it was attacking. And so the movement of the caterpillar tracks provoked the whole arsenal of offensive techniques against such crushing giants, just as the appearance of the mangors provoked in an observing human's consciousness the idea that he was looking at a bush.

And if the mangors had been capable of reason, they would have noticed with satisfaction that the enemy attacking them was, while impudent and large, also stupid, and so victory over this ourban would necessarily be theirs.

But they were incapable of reason, and so they acted.

The all-terrain vehicle rocked smoothly from side to side. So smoothly, so gently, that any irregularity would have caused a more noticeable jolt. None of the people on board noticed anything.

The calculations that the mangors carried out unconsciously would have done an Earth com-puter proud. At just the right moment, using just the right amount of force, as if on command, a large number of legroots reached out. As soon as the all-terrain vehicle moved over this patch of ground, the legroots, invisible underneath the leaves, would gently latch on to the bottom of the vehicle. The ourban in question could not sense this contact, but the mangors were given invaluable information about their enemy's weight.

The all-terrain vehicle rocked once again, sharply. At the same time, it slowed so abruptly that the people inside were thrown forward. The driver automatically applied the brakes. The all-terrain vehicle righted itself. As there were no obstacles in front of them and—as a swift glance at the dial of the depth locator showed—no crevasses in the neighborhood, the driver, in surprise, started the engine.

But the all-terrain vehicle didn't even think about moving. They could see the caterpillar tracks turning, they could hear the motor, but that was it. Just as automatically as he had acted a moment or two before, the driver put his foot down. The all-terrain vehicle shuddered, the caterpillar tracks spun rapidly, the motor, which apparently nothing could resist, roared in fury. But the vehicle did not move an inch.

It could not move, because the mangors, grabbing hold of its underside, had lifted it up a little, and the tracks were spinning in the air.

The enemy's reaction, if the mangors had possessed the capacity for surprise, would have surprised them with its slowness. Everything had worked out unusually well: their hapless enemy had been lifted from the ground, deprived of its ability to move, and its destruction was now only a matter of time.

The mangors felt satisfied: that at least was an instinctive feeling they did know.

. . . .

"Hello, landing craft here. We've been attacked by . . . it'll sound a bit weird . . . we've been attacked by some bushes."

"Can you be more specific?"

"The caterpillar tracks are just spinning in the air, the 'bushes' have lifted them up. They've got flexible branches—maybe better to say tentacles—and they've wrapped them around the hull so we can't open the door or use our weapons."

"Are you in any danger?"

"No immediate danger. The 'bushes' aren't trying anything else, but it's a pretty dumb situation: we're prisoners, and we don't even know what's taken us captive. We can't see a way out at the moment."

"Understood. In about ten minutes we'll attack your shrubbery."

"The biologist says that's a problem: we don't have another ATV and it would be risky to attack without one, as we don't know the nature of our enemy."

"Have you got anything useful to add?"

"You should take scans of the 'bushes' and find out what we're up against."

"We're doing that. Can you be sure that nothing will happen in the meantime?"

"No, of course not, but I repeat that the 'bushes' have stopped attacking. It's clear they don't know what to do with us."

"All right, then our plan's under way. Hold tight."

The people were mistaken when they thought that the mangors didn't know what to do with a captured monster. They were also mistaken when they thought that the mangors wouldn't try anything else. They acted as they were accustomed to act, and just as the previously mentioned conversation was taking place, they tried to make the all-terrain vehicle explode, just as they would explode an ourban that fell into their clutches.

Of course, they didn't succeed in this, because something was not quite right: the enemy didn't try to tear itself free from its bonds, and the branches that would usually have cut off the ourban's dangerous claws snipped only at thin air.

This last circumstance confused not only the mangors but also the humans, who watched uncomprehendingly as to the left and the right of the hull clumps of tentacles waved in the air. What could this mean? All of the mangors' other actions, once the first wave of astonishment had passed, were comprehensible, even if not entirely so. This assault had no obvious explanation and made them suspect the worst: a treacherous plot planned for the future.

Leaving one person on board, the three soldiers quickly reached the top of the hill. They were armed with plasma rifles, weapons of unimaginable power. But, as became immediately clear, even with their help it was too much to expect rapid success. An armored monster was one thing—a well-placed blast of plasma could cut one in two—but a thick clump of bushes was quite another, and it was this latter they had to pass through to reach the stranded machine.

But what could shrubbery do against the weapon that had cleared the way for mankind on all worlds without exception?

Convinced that they would not now be able to make their victim explode, the mangors changed their tactic: the branches squeezed the all-terrain vehicle so hard that no ourban would have been able to survive.

However, the spectrolite shell of the vehicle did not even squeak, and the people within the vehicle did not notice these new and powerful efforts the mangors were making.

The shrubbery had to be burned away slowly, meter after meter, and the attackers methodically set to their task. They had no doubt as to their success.

Of course, the mangors were not aware that these little figures, hurting their body at a distance, and the captured giant were links in a single chain. They were faced by a new enemy, and that was it. They had not yet had to face an enemy who attacked at a distance, but fear of the unknown—any kind of fear if it came to that—was not something they recognized. While they had not yet suffered too much damage, they could and should fight on, or else, as their million years of experience had taught them, they would not survive.

With satisfaction, the people noticed that their first shots made the shrubbery retreat. The whole front retreated, but they took the all-terrain vehicle along with them.

The enemy was fleeing, and had to be pursued! This was an ancient rule of the hunt. And also there was nothing else the people could do, as their weapons were less effective at a distance. They began their pursuit.

The mangors were unaware of any abstract idea of "ambush." But they set an ambush, because that was a tactic in their arsenal of combat tactics.

They did not withdraw entirely. Individual legroots sunk into the soil where they had been set and remained until they felt the feet of the enemy touch them.

Even a battle against bushes generates a certain amount of passion, and the people, firing their lightning into the canopy, did not pay much attention to the soil their shots had charred.

The assault was the business of an instant. The people could not understand what was happening to them as their legs were seized by tentacles that came hurtling out of the ground. A moment more and their bodies were hanging in the air, and other tentacles seized their hands.

It was so strange, this being flung up into the air, that the people missed the valuable moment when their weapons might still have freed them.

Of course the mangors, as might be expected, immediately started squeezing their new captives, but the strength of individual legroots, which had worked so well in capturing their enemies, was not enough to crush a thick space suit.

But this was only a temporary respite for the humans. As soon as the shooting had stopped, the whole mass of the mangors headed toward the three helpless prisoners hanging in the air.

They understood at once that they were under threat. Their weapons and arms were seized in such a fantastical way that two of them could only move their wrists. In such a position, moving was not at all comfortable, but a target such as the shrubbery could be hit even without aiming. And so the mangors were once again struck by lightning.

This was an act of desperation, and the people expected that the tentacles would immediately seize, and squeeze, and crush the weapons. But, to their surprise and relief, nothing of the kind happened—the tentacles didn't move in the slightest.

The mangors' front line came under fire and stopped dead. The people immediately stopped firing—in their new situation every shot was valuable.

The mangors came forward.

The people fired again and the mangors stopped.

This happened several times.

Finally the people were released from their nightmare, and the mangors no longer attempted to move forward.

.   .   .

The mangors, although primitive in structure, knew how to learn. But here their capacities were limited. The shots had activated certain reflexes, but things got complicated after that. The mangors found themselves in a bit of a hole, if one can put it like that, because the battle was not being fought "according to the rules."

And then, when their instincts had run out of options, they began to function via trial and error.

"Somebody do something!"

The shout came in vain through the earphones. The people remaining in the all-terrain vehicle preferred not to look at one another. Their situation was terrible, because they, protected by the ship's hull yet powerless to act, would have to watch their friends agonize, the very friends who had wanted to save them and who had themselves been taken prisoner.

Because their friends would certainly die sooner or later. Even if everything stayed as it was and the shrubbery did nothing more, the oxygen in the space suits would run out before any spaceship could come rushing from a neighboring planet.

There was still one free human: the watchman had left his post, and his lonely figure now loomed over the brow of the hill. But he could not shoot—there was no way he could cut through a tentacle without hitting a person. Go closer and use a cutter? That was too risky.

Suddenly the all-terrain vehicle shook. It tilted sharply and the people on board were scarcely able to grasp the handles. No, the mangors had not forgotten their initial enemy. They turned it upside down.

Why? The humans did not know this; neither did the mangors.

Even with the all-terrain vehicle upside down, the mangors could not do anything with it, but they could deal with the others in at least three ways: kill them by striking them hard against the ground, twist their bodies around until they broke the space suits, or, as they had done with the all-terrain vehicle, turn them upside down.

The second option was one that the mangors retained in their hereditary memory, but, luckily for the humans, it was an option that they had already tried unsuccessfully with the all-terrain vehicle, so they did not attempt it here. More precisely, their instinct to "do what you always do" had been weakened by a second one: "do something different." And since the people with the lightning and the all-terrain vehicle seemed to be different enemies, they tried different methods with them: all the tentacles did was release the juice they used to break down minerals in the soil. And they started to shake the people, just as they did when, the juice having been released, they wanted to break up the soil.

It was not what one might call pleasant, but being shaken did not harm them. And as for the white liquid that flowed down the outside of the space suits, the people suspected the worst. The enemy that had captured the people so quickly and with such cunning seemed the incarnation of a sly and calculating mind.

Fortunately, not to all of them.

In spite of their trials and tribulations, the people in the all-terrain vehicle had the opportunity to think.

They followed everything that was happening and their habit of comparison and analysis gradually came to the fore. This process was in general unconscious, a result of the vast experience of human culture, which indicated that all victories were the result of a creative approach, and that where there was no creativity there could be no hope.

Their normal patterns of thought had led them into trouble, but they needed to avoid a second such mistake. They were centralized and focused and from the outside the intelligent activity of the shrubbery had for a moment shaken the biologist's initial conviction that they were dealing with a primitive, although unusual, creature. This conviction was not in any sense unthinking, for it was based on a knowledge of the general rules of evolution, knowledge that function determines form. The fact that the shrubbery had not disarmed its captives, and had not found an effective way to kill helpless people, finally put the argument beyond all doubt. Their enemies were not possessed of intelligence, nor were they stupid, just as a plant on Earth is neither clever nor dumb; they were excellently adapted to particular conditions and situations, and that was the sum of it.

Once they had realized this, it only took a little more time for them to see the way out of what had seemed an impossible situation.

The clues were there for them to see. Wherever the battle was not raging, the mangors' leaves continued peacefully to absorb the light. As soon as the shooting died down, creatures like giant wood lice appeared and hurried fearlessly through the branches and even paused to eat the leaves.

Of course, this idyll remained unobserved by minds overwhelmed by events, but it remained captured in their consciousness. In order for the thoughts that derived from this observation to be fully processed, a few remaining prejudices needed to be overcome. In particular, one had to realize that mankind's omnipotence was not in his strength or in the powerful forms of energy he had mastered, or in the complexity of its machines. . . . It was not even in its wisdom: it was to be found in the flexibility, breadth, and farsightedness of his thought. Another prejudice: one had to be aware that a tactic that had worked a thousand times would not definitely work the thousand and first. And another: one had to clear one's mind of the idea that human beings are always rational, when in fact they are only rational when

they can seize and assess something new and rebuild their former image of the world, and act in accordance with reality, whatever that might now be.

Without thinking about it consciously (necessity is the best teacher), the biologist had avoided all these obstacles. And then he realized what had to be done.

He realized it at the exact moment when a despairing cry reached them through their headphones.

"The liquid's dissolving my space suit!"

And so the critical period commenced, and the biologist understood that his discovery was useless: there was no time to explain; events had outrun the workings of his mind.

However . . .

"How do you know that the juice can dissolve silicate?"

"The upper layer is flaking off and falling away!"

The juice was applied half an hour ago, came the instant thought. *And there are three layers. . . .*

"Stop!" he shouted. "We've still got time and there's a definite solution!"

But it was too late. The only free member of their group had already run over to the captive. The cutter's blade sparkled. . . .

Before the cutter could remove another tentacle, a few others released their captives and grabbed the brave man. Although he was prepared for the attack, the tentacles moved faster than he could react. A second later he was in the same situation as the others.

Horror did not stop the biologist from noticing that his conjecture had been radiantly confirmed in its weakest point. Now he believed they could succeed. Unless, of course, a new action by the shrubbery made things impossible.

This was something that he need not have feared. The mangors knew that their root juice acted slowly and did not hurry to try another plan. As for their initial enemy, the all-terrain vehicle, its behavior convinced them that it was dead. And so it remained for them only to wait while the process of decomposition softened the tissue of the strangely hard ourban. Nothing was as it usually was, but everything was going according to plan.

The lower hatch opened inward. The biologist was the first to come out. The hatch shut behind him at once—however convinced he was of his theory, there was no sense in risking everyone's life.

In turning the all-terrain vehicle over, the mangors had made it easier for the plan to be carried out, for now the human had a lot of room to maneuver, which he would not have had if the hatch had remained underneath.

Crawling, and trying not to touch the tentacles if he could avoid it, the man slid off the hull of the all-terrain vehicle and continued on all fours, twisting his whole body, through the terrifying tangle of undergrowth.

It was difficult even to watch. The most frightening thing for the biologist was the touch of the greasy-pale tentacles and the knowledge that it would cost them nothing to seize him and crush him. In spite of everything, his imagination involuntarily conquered his reason, which normally kept his instincts under control. How could they not see he was an enemy!

For the mangors, however, it was absolutely clear that what was crawling through their branches was harmless or even helpful. No other creature would have been able to turn up out of the blue and crawl through the very heart of the organism—it would have been captured, recognized, and destroyed at the border. The mangors did not know what kinds of creatures were crawling around inside them; they paid no attention to the animals that ate sick leaves, or captured harmful insects, or fed on dying tissue. Even humans are incapable without help of noticing the harmless creatures that nest in their own bodies. And so the biologist was in no danger, just as if he were strolling through the park.

This soon became clear to everyone.

There were only two dangers that the biologist might face, and he had thought about them already. He did not move in a straight line, because that would have meant crawling through the sections that had been damaged in the shooting, which might cause a pain reaction in the mangors, which would, of course, lead to a defensive reaction. Although it made his journey much longer, he traveled through areas where the mangors had not been touched. And, when he got outside the all-terrain vehicle, he did not stand up and he did not run, as he knew very well that his opponent had already learned to equate the figure of a walking man with danger.

The crew of the all-terrain vehicle followed his actions perfectly. It would not be correct to say that they did so without trembling, but they were successful. And just in time.

As he had predicted, the space suits of the prisoners were still resisting the destructive effects of the plant juice. There was still some time. . . .

The fight with the tentacles, which had ended so mournfully, nevertheless confirmed at first sight all that the biologist had guessed. The clump of tentacles had exhausted all its reserves. So tired out were they that they had not even been able to lift their newest captive off the ground. Perhaps they could have taken one or two more enemies, but now another four people entered the fight. The other mangors were no danger: their "plasma reflex" response to the humans' weapons would not vanish so fast.

Everything that happened then was

strongly reminiscent of a live-action version of the sculpture of Laocoön.

Now all they had to do was free the all-terrain vehicle. But the idea of killing the bushes that were still mysterious but were now defenseless, given that their weak points were clear, stuck in the humans' throats. And they eagerly came to the conclusion that the mangors would abandon the all-terrain vehicle when they felt the approach of the storm.

Here they were mistaken. Instinct demanded that the mangors not release their prey, and when the storm approached they carried the all-terrain vehicle away.

This was a fateful miscalculation on their part. Unlike an ourban, the all-terrain vehicle could not be broken down into pieces; its size made it difficult for the mangors to move, and the storm caught them.

And what the storms were like there, the reason the mangors became nomadic creatures, half plant, half animal, was revealed later to the humans by the fragments of the all-terrain vehicle scattered over many miles.

Standing Woman

YASUTAKA TSUTSUI

Translated by Dana Lewis

Yasutaka Tsutsui (1934–) is a Japanese author whose works of absurdist science fiction and commentary on the media landscape made him one of the Big Three of Japanese speculative fiction in the twentieth century, alongside Shinichi Hoshi and Sakyō Komatsu. He is best understood first as Japan's answer to the New Wave of the 1960s and 1970s, and secondly as comparable in some ways to such social satirists as Robert Sheckley, Norman Spinrad, and Kurt Vonnegut Jr.; his later works form the basis of Japanese science fiction postmodernism.

Tsutsui graduated from Doshisha University, Kyoto, in 1957 with a master's thesis on psychoanalysis and surrealism and worked for several years at a branch of the Nomura design firm, spending his bonus money to produce the science fiction fanzine *Null* (1961–64). *Null* attracted many young members of the Japanese science fiction community, including Kazumasa Hirai and Taku Mayumura, but folded after its eleventh issue as Tsutsui was drawn into other activities. Tsutsui helped run the third Japanese Daicon convention, wrote for *SF Magazine*, and was the screenwriter for the anime television series *Super Jetter* (1965). He became closely associated with the science fiction author Sakyō Komatsu and eventually lampooned Komatsu's *Nippon chinbotsu* with "Nippon igai zenbu chinbotsu" in 1973 ("Everything Apart from Japan Sinks"), which won the following year's Short Form Seiun Award, one of the most respected awards for Japanese science fiction.

Tsutsui has courted controversy throughout his career, including waging a crusade against political correctness, and he embarked on a self-imposed authorial strike from 1993 to 1996, after his story "Muteki keisatsu" ("Unmanned Police"; *Nigiyaka-na Mirai*, 1968) was dropped from an anthology published by Kadokawa. However, during that well-publicized absence from print, Tsutsui was intensely active in digital media, publishing his first "digital book," *Tsutsui Yasutaka yonsenji gekijō* (*Yasutaka Tsutsui's Four-Thousand-Character Theater*), in 1994 for the Japanese PC-9800 system. The anime films *The Girl Who Leapt Through Time* (2006) and *Paprika* (2009) are both based on his novels.

"Standing Woman" (1974) is a classic of surreal science fiction, first published in English in *Omni* in 1981 and reprinted many times, including in *The Best Japanese Science Fiction Stories* (1997).

STANDING WOMAN

Yasutaka Tsutsui

Translated by Dana Lewis

I stayed up all night and finally finished a forty-page short story. It was a trivial entertainment piece, capable of neither harm nor good.

"These days you can't write stories that might do harm or good: it can't be helped." That's what I told myself while I fastened the manuscript with a paper clip and put it into an envelope.

As to whether I have it in me to write stories that might do harm or good, I do my best not to think about it. I might want to try.

The morning sunlight hurt my eyes as I slipped on my wooden clogs and left the house with the envelope. Since there was still time before the first mail truck would come, I turned my feet toward the park. In the morning no children come to this park, a mere eighty square meters in the middle of a cramped residential district. It's quiet here. So I always include the park in my morning walk. Nowadays even the scanty green provided by the ten or so trees is priceless in the megalopolis.

I should have brought some bread, I thought. My favorite dogpillar stands next to the park bench. It's an affable dogpillar with buff-colored fur, quite large for a mongrel.

The liquid-fertilizer truck had just left when I reached the park; the ground was damp and there was a faint smell of chlorine. The elderly gentleman I often saw there was sitting on the bench next to the dogpillar, feeding the buff post what seemed to be meat dumplings. Dogpillars usually have excellent appetites. Maybe the liquid fertilizer, absorbed by the roots sunk deep in the ground and passed on up through the legs, leaves something to be desired.

They'll eat just about anything you give them.

"You brought him something? I slipped up today. I forgot to bring my bread," I said to the elderly man.

He turned gentle eyes on me and smiled softly.

"Ah, you like this fellow, too?"

"Yes," I replied, sitting down beside him. "He looks exactly like the dog I used to have."

The dogpillar looked up at me with large, black eyes and wagged its tail.

"Actually, I kept a dog like this fellow myself," the man said, scratching the ruff of the dogpillar's neck. "He was made into a dogpillar when he was three. Haven't you seen him? Between the haberdashery and the film shop on the coast road. Isn't there a dogpillar there that looks like this fellow?"

I nodded, adding, "Then that one was yours?"

"Yes, he was our pet. His name was Hachi. Now he's completely vegetized. A beautiful dogtree."

"Now that you mention it, he does look a lot like this fellow. Maybe they came from the same stock."

"And the dog you kept?" the elderly man asked. "Where is he planted?"

"Our dog was named Buff," I answered, shaking my head. "He was planted beside the entrance to the cemetery on the edge of town when he was four. Poor thing, he died right after he was planted. The fertilizer trucks don't get out that way very often, and it was so far I couldn't take him food every day. Maybe they planted him badly. He died before becoming a tree."

"Then he was removed?"

"No, fortunately, it didn't much matter there if he smelled or not, and so he was left there and dried. Now he's a bonepillar. He makes fine material for the neighborhood elementary-school science class, I hear."

"That's wonderful."

The elderly man stroked the dogpillar's head. "This fellow here, I wonder what he was called before he became a dogpillar."

"No calling a dogpillar by its original name," I said. "Isn't that a strange law?"

The man looked at me sharply, then replied casually, "Didn't they just extend the laws concerning people to dogs? That's why they lose their names when they become dogpillars." He nodded while scratching the dogpillar's jaw. "Not only the old names, but you can't give them new names, either. That's because there are no proper nouns for plants."

Why, of course, I thought.

He looked at my envelope with MANUSCRIPT ENCLOSED written on it.

"Excuse me," he said. "Are you a writer?"

I was a little embarrassed.

"Well, yes. Just trivial things."

After looking at me closely, the man returned to stroking the dogpillar's head. "I also used to write things."

He managed to suppress a smile.

"How many years is it now since I stopped writing? It feels like a long time."

I stared at the man's profile. Now that he said so, it was a face I seemed to have seen somewhere before. I started to ask his name, hesitated, and fell silent.

The elderly man said abruptly. "It's become a hard world to write in."

I lowered my eyes, ashamed of myself, who still continued to write in such a world.

The man apologized hurriedly at my sudden depression.

"That was rude. I'm not criticizing you. I'm the one who should feel ashamed."

"No," I told him, after looking quickly around us, "I can't give up writing, because I haven't the courage. Giving up writing! Why,

after all, that would be a gesture against society."

The elderly man continued stroking the dogpillar. After a long while he spoke.

"It's painful, suddenly giving up writing. Now that it's come to this, I would have been better off if I'd gone on boldly writing social criticism and had been arrested. There are even times when I think that. But I was just a dilettante, never knowing poverty, craving peaceful dreams. I wanted to live a comfortable life. As a person strong in self-respect, I couldn't endure being exposed to the eyes of the world, ridiculed. So I quit writing. A sorry tale."

He smiled and shook his head. "No, no, let's not talk about it. You never know who might be listening, even here on the street."

I changed the subject. "Do you live here?"

"Do you know the beauty parlor on the main street? You turn in there. My name is Hiyama." He nodded at me. "Come over sometime. I'm married, but . . ."

"Thank you very much."

I gave him my own name.

I didn't remember any writer named Hiyama. No doubt he wrote under a pen name. I had no intention of visiting his house. This is a world where even two or three writers getting together is considered illegal assembly.

"It's time for a mail truck to come in."

Taking pains to look at my watch, I stood.

"I'm afraid I'd better go," I said.

He turned a sadly smiling face toward me and bowed slightly. After stroking the dogpillar's head a little, I left the park.

I came out on the main street, but there was only a ridiculous number of passing cars: pedestrians were few. A cattree, about thirty to forty centimeters high, was planted next to the sidewalk.

Sometimes I come across a catpillar that has just been planted and still hasn't become a cattree. New catpillars look at my face and meow or cry, but the ones where all four limbs planted in the ground have vegetized, with their greenish faces stiffly set and eyes shut tight, only move their ears now and then. Then there are catpillars that grow branches from their bodies and put out handfuls of leaves. The mental condition of these seems to be completely vegetized—they don't even move their ears. Even if a cat's face can still be made out, it may be better to call these cattrees.

Maybe, I thought, *it's better to make dogs into dogpillars. When their food runs out, they get vicious and even turn on people. But why did they have to turn cats into catpillars? Too many strays? To improve the food situation by even a little? Or perhaps for the greening of the city . . .*

Next to the big hospital on the corner where the highways intersect are two mantrees, and ranged alongside these trees is a manpillar. This manpillar wears a postman's uniform, and you can't tell how far its legs have vegetized because of its trousers. It is male, thirty-five or thirty-six years old, tall, with a bit of a stoop.

I approached him and held out my envelope as always.

"Registered mail, special delivery, please."

The manpillar, nodding silently, accepted the envelope and took stamps and a registered-mail slip from his pocket.

I looked around quickly after paying the postage. There was no one else there. I decided to try speaking to him. I gave him mail every three days, but I still hadn't had a chance for a leisurely talk.

"What did you do?" I asked in a low voice.

The manpillar looked at me in surprise. Then, after running his eyes around the area, he answered with a sour look, "Won't do to go saying unnecessary things to me. Even me, I'm not supposed to answer."

"I know that," I said, looking into his eyes.

When I wouldn't leave, he took a deep breath. "I just said the pay's low. What's more, I got heard by my boss. Because a postman's pay is really low." With a dark look, he jerked his jaw at the two mantrees next to him. "These guys were the same. Just for letting slip some complaints about low pay. Do you know them?" he asked me.

I pointed at one of the mantrees. "I remember this one, because I gave him a lot of mail. I don't know the other one. He was already a mantree when we moved here."

"That one was my friend," he said.

"Wasn't that other one a chief clerk or section head?"

He nodded. "That's right. Chief clerk."

"Don't you get hungry or cold?"

"You don't feel it that much," he replied, still expressionless. Anyone who's made into a manpillar soon becomes expressionless. "Even I think I've gotten pretty plantlike. Not only in how I feel things, but in the way I think, too. At first, I was sad, but now it doesn't matter. I used to get really hungry, but they say the vegetizing goes faster when you don't eat."

He stared at me with lightless eyes. He was probably hoping he could become a mantree soon.

"Talk says they give people with radical ideas a lobotomy before making them into manpillars, but I didn't get that done, either. Even so a month after I was planted here I didn't get angry anymore."

He glanced at my wristwatch. "Well, you better go now. It's almost time for the mail truck to come."

"Yes." But still I couldn't leave, and I hesitated uneasily.

"You," the manpillar said. "Someone you know didn't recently get done into a manpillar, did they?"

Cut to the quick. I stared at his face for a moment, then nodded slowly.

"Actually, my wife."

"Hmm, your wife, is it?" For a few moments he regarded me with deep interest. "I wondered whether it wasn't something like that. Otherwise nobody ever bothers to talk to me. Then what did she do, your wife?"

"She complained that prices were high at a housewives' get-together. Had that been all, fine, but she criticized the government, too. I'm starting to make it big as a writer, and I think that the eagerness of being that writer's wife made her say it. One of the women there informed on her. She was planted on the left side of the road looking from the station toward the assembly hall and next to that hardware store."

"Ah, that place." He closed his eyes a little, as if recollecting the appearance of the buildings and the stores in that area. "It's a fairly peaceful street. Isn't that for the better?" He opened his eyes and looked at me searchingly. "You aren't going to see her, are you? It's better not to see her too often. Both for her and you. That way you both forget faster."

"I know that."

I hung my head.

"Your wife?" he asked, his voice turning slightly sympathetic. "Has anyone done anything to her?"

"No. So far nothing. She's just standing, but even so——"

"Hey." The manpillar serving as a postbox raised his jaw to attract my attention. "It's come. The mail truck. You'd better go."

"You're right."

Taking a few wavering steps, as if pushed by his voice, I stopped and looked back. "Isn't there anything you want done?"

He brought a hard smile to his cheeks and shook his head.

The red mail truck stopped beside him. I moved on past the hospital.

Thinking I'd check in on my favorite bookstore, I entered a street of crowded shops. My new book was supposed to be out any day now, but that kind of thing no longer made me the slightest bit happy.

A little before the bookstore in the same row is a small, cheap candy store, and on the edge of the road in front of it is a manpillar on the verge of becoming a mantree. A young male; it is already a year since it was planted. The face had become a brownish color tinged with green, and the eyes are tightly shut. Tall back slightly bent, the posture slouching a little forward. The legs, torso, and arms, visible through clothes reduced to rags by exposure to wind and rain, are already vegetized, and here and there branches sprout. Young leaves bud from the ends of the arms, raised above the shoulders like beating wings. The body, which has become a tree, and even the face no longer move at all. The heart has sunk into the tranquil world of plants.

I imagined the day when my wife would reach this state, and again my heart winced with pain, trying to forget. It was the anguish of trying to forget.

If I turn the corner at this candy store and go straight, I thought, *I can go to where my wife is standing. I can see my wife. But it won't do to go*, I told myself. *There's no telling who might see you: if the woman who informed on her questioned you, you'd really be in trouble.* I came to a halt in front of the candy store and peered down the road. Pedestrian traffic was the same as always. *It's all right. Anyone would overlook it if you just stand and talk a bit. You'll just have a word or two.* Defying my own voice screaming *"Don't go!"* I went briskly down the street.

Her face pale, my wife was standing by the road in front of the hardware store. Her legs were unchanged, and it seemed as if only her feet from the ankles down were buried in the earth. Expressionlessly, as if striving to see nothing, feel nothing, she stared steadily ahead. Compared with two days before, her cheeks seemed a bit hollow. Two passing factory workers pointed at her, made some vulgar joke, and passed on, guffawing uproariously. I went up to her and raised my voice.

"Michiko!" I yelled right in her ear.

My wife looked at me, and blood rushed to her cheeks. She brushed one hand through her tangled hair.

"You've come again? Really you mustn't."

"I can't help coming."

The hardware store mistress, tending shop, saw me. With an air of feigned indifference, she averted her eyes and retired to the back of the store. Full of gratitude for her consideration, I drew a few steps closer to Michiko and faced her.

"You've gotten pretty used to it?"

With all her might she formed a bright smile on her stiffened face. "Mmm. I'm used to it."

"Last night it rained a little."

Still gazing at me with large, dark eyes, she nodded lightly. "Please don't worry. I hardly feel anything."

"When I think about you, I can't sleep." I hung my head. "You're always standing out here. When I think that, I can't possibly sleep. Last night I even thought I should bring you an umbrella."

"Please don't do anything like that!" My wife frowned just a little. "It would be terrible if you did something like that."

A large truck drove past behind me. White dust thinly veiled my wife's hair and shoulders, but she didn't seem bothered.

"Standing isn't really all that bad." She spoke with deliberate lightness, working to keep me from worrying.

I perceived a subtle change in my wife's expressions and speech from two days before. It seemed that her words had lost a shade of delicacy, and the range of her emotions had become somewhat impoverished. *Watching from the sidelines like this, seeing her gradually grow more expressionless, it's all the more desolating for having known her as she was before—those keen responses, the bright vivacity, the rich, full expressions.*

"These people," I asked her, running my eyes over the hardware store, "are they good to you?"

"Well, of course. They're kind at heart. Just once they told me to ask if there's anything I want done. But they still haven't done anything for me."

"Don't you get hungry?"

She shook her head.

"It's better not to eat."

So. Unable to endure being a manpillar, she was hoping to become a mantree even so much as a single day faster.

"So please don't bring me food." She stared at me. "Please forget about me. I think, certainly,

even without making any particular effort, I'm going to forget about you. I'm happy that you come to see me, but then the sadness drags on that much longer. For both of us."

"Of course you're right, but—" Despising this self that could do nothing for his own wife, I hung my head again. "But I won't forget you." I nodded. The tears came. "I won't forget. Ever."

When I raised my head and looked at her again, she was gazing steadily at me with eyes that had lost a little of their luster, her whole face beaming in a faint smile like a carved image of Buddha. It was the first time I had ever seen her smile like that.

I felt I was having a nightmare. *No,* I told myself, *this isn't your wife anymore.*

The suit she had been wearing when she was arrested had become terribly dirty and filled with wrinkles. But of course I wouldn't be allowed to bring a change of clothes. My eyes rested on a dark stain on her skirt.

"Is that blood? What happened?"

"Oh, this." She spoke falteringly, looking down at her skirt with a confused air. "Last night two drunks played a prank on me."

"The bastards!" I felt a furious rage at their inhumanity. If you put it to them, they would say that since my wife was no longer human, it didn't matter what they did.

"They can't do that kind of thing! It's against the law!"

"That's right. But I can hardly appeal."

And of course I couldn't go to the police and appeal, either. If I did, I'd be looked on as even more of a problem person.

"The bastards! What did they—" I bit my lip. My heart hurt enough to break. "Did it bleed a lot?"

"Mmm, a little."

"Does it hurt?"

"It doesn't hurt anymore."

Michiko, who had been so proud before now, showed just a little sadness in her face. I was shocked by the change in her. A group of young men and women, penetratingly comparing me and my wife, passed behind me.

"You'll be seen," my wife said anxiously. "I beg of you, don't throw yourself away."

"Don't worry." I smiled thinly for her in self-contempt. "I don't have the courage."

"You should go now."

"When you're a mantree," I said in parting, "I'll petition. I'll get them to transplant you to our garden."

"Can you do that?"

"I should be able to." I nodded liberally. "I should be able to."

"I'd be happy if you could," my wife said expressionlessly.

"Well, see you later."

"It'd be better if you didn't come again," she said in a murmur, looking down.

"I know. That's my intention. But I'll probably come anyway."

For a few minutes we were silent.

Then my wife spoke abruptly.

"Good-bye."

"Umm."

I began walking.

When I looked back as I rounded the corner, Michiko was following me with her eyes, still smiling like a graven Buddha.

Embracing a heart that seemed ready to split apart, I walked. I noticed suddenly that I had come out in front of the station. Unconsciously, I had returned to my usual walking course.

Opposite the station is a small coffee shop I always go to called Punch. I went in and sat down in a corner booth. I ordered coffee, drinking it black. Until then I had always had it with sugar. The bitterness of sugarless, creamless coffee pierced my body, and I savored it masochistically. *From now on I'll always drink it black*. That was what I resolved.

Three students in the next booth were talking about a critic who had just been arrested and made into a manpillar.

"I hear he was planted smack in the middle of the Ginza."

"He loved the country. He always lived in the country. That's why they set him up in a place like that."

"Seems they gave him a lobotomy."

"And the students who tried to use force in the Diet, protesting his arrest—they've all been arrested and will be made into manpillars, too."

"Weren't there almost thirty of them? Where'll they plant them all?"

"They say they'll be planted in front of their own university, down both sides of a street called Students Road."

"They'll have to change the name now. Violence Grove, or something."

The three snickered.

"Hey, let's not talk about it. We don't want someone to hear."

The three shut up.

When I left the coffee shop and headed home, I realized that I had begun to feel as if I was already a manpillar myself. Murmuring the words of a popular song to myself, I walked on.

I am a wayside manpillar. You, too, are a wayside manpillar. What the hell, the two of us, in this world. Dried grasses that never flower.

ALICIA YÁNEZ COSSÍO

Translated by Susana Castillo and Elsie Adams

Alicia Yánez Cossío (1929–) is a journalist, fiction writer, poet, and professor of literature who is widely considered to be one of Ecuador's most notable twentieth-century literary figures. Her poetry and fiction are highly regarded in her home country and, despite the difficulty Ecuadorian writers have had in reaching international audiences in the past, increasingly highly regarded internationally. She was the first Ecuadorian to win the Sor Juana Inés de la Cruz Prize (1996). In 2008, Cossío received Ecuador's highest prize in literature, the Premio Eugenio Espejo, for her lifetime of work. She has written three novels, *Bruna, soroche y los tíos* (1970), *Yo vendo unos ojos negros* (1979), and *La cofradia del mullo del vestido de la virgen Pipona* (1985).

Themes in Cossío's work include corruption, social injustice, the role of women, the excesses of consumer-driven societies, and the dangers of technology. Many of her stories also focus on life in Ecuador's central range of the Andes, where her characters are conflicted by the push and pull between their colonial past histories and the dehumanization of modern society's materialistic tendencies.

In general, Cossío is deeply interested in telling stories about characters who are trying to figure out their place in modern society and how much of their past taboos and traditions they should keep or let go of in order to create a better life for themselves and others. Throughout her career, Cossío also has cultivated an interest in parody and satire.

She has not written much science fiction, but her interest in the dangers of technology is closely aligned with the concerns of many science fiction writers. The story reprinted here, "The IWM 1000," is a clever and prescient take on information technology, presaging the rise of Google. It is also an excellent example of the Latin American tradition of the science fiction tale, sharing similarities to the work of Silvina Ocampo and Juan José Arreola included in this volume. This story first appeared in her 1975 collection, *El beso y otras fricciones*.

THE IWM 1000

Alicia Yánez Cossío

Translated by Susana Castillo and Elsie Adams

A man is only what he knows.
—FRANCIS BACON

Once upon a time, all the professors disappeared, swallowed and digested by a new system. All the centers of learning closed because they were outmoded, and their sites were converted into living quarters swarming with wise, well-organized people who were incapable of creating anything new.

Knowledge was an item that could be bought and sold. A device called the IWM 1000 had been invented. It was the ultimate invention: it brought an entire era to an end. The IWM 1000 was a very small machine, the size of an old scholarly briefcase. It was very easy to use—lightweight and affordable to any person interested in knowing anything. The IWM 1000 contained all human knowledge and all the facts of all the libraries of the ancient and modern world.

Nobody had to take the trouble of learning anything because the machine, which could be hand-carried or put on any piece of household furniture, provided any information to anybody. Its mechanism was so perfect, and the data it gave so precise, that nobody had dared to prove it otherwise. Its operation was so simple that children spent time playing with it. It was an extension of the human brain. Many people would not be separated from it even during the most personal, intimate acts. The more they depended on the machine, the wiser they became.

A great majority, knowing that the facts were so ready at hand, had never touched an IWM 1000, not even out of curiosity. They did not know how to read or write. They were ignorant of the most elementary things, and it did not matter to them. They felt happy at having one less worry, and they enjoyed the other technological advances more. With the IWM 1000, you could write any type of literature, compose music, and even paint pictures. Creative works were disappearing because anybody, with time and sufficient patience, could make any work similar to and even superior to one made by artists of the past without having to exert the brain or feel anything strange or abnormal.

Some people spent time getting information from the IWM 1000 just for the pleasure of knowing something. Some did it to get out of some predicament, and others asked it things of no importance whatsoever, simply for the pleasure of having someone say something to them, even though it might just be something from their trivial, boring world.

"What is *etatex*?"

"What does *hybrid* mean?"

"How do you make a chocolate cake?"

"What does Beethoven's *Pastorale* mean?"

"How many inhabitants are there actually in the world?"

"Who was Viriatus?"

"What is the distance from the Earth to Jupiter?"

"How can you get rid of freckles?"

"How many asteroids have been discovered this year?"

"What is the function of the pancreas?"

"When was the last world war?"

"How old is my neighbor?"

"What does *reciprocal* mean?"

Modulations of the voice fell on some super-sensitive electronic membrane, connected with the brain of the machine, and computed immediately the requested information, which was not always the same because, according to the tone of voice, the machine computed the data concisely or with necessary references.

Sometimes two intellectuals would start to talk, and when one of them had a difference of opinion, he would consult his machine. He would present the problem from his own perspective, and the machines would talk and talk. Objections were made, and many times these did not come from the intellectuals but from the machines, who tried to convince each other. The men who had begun the discussion would listen, and when they tired of listening, they would be thinking which of two machines was going to get the last word because of the power of the respective generators.

Lovers would make the machines conjugate all the tenses of the verb *to love*, and they would listen to romantic songs. In offices and administrative buildings tape-recorded orders were given, and the IWM 1000 would complete the details of the work. Many people got in the habit of talking only to their own machines; therefore, nobody contradicted them because they knew how the machine was going to respond, or because they believed that rivalry could not exist between a machine and a human being. A machine could not accuse anyone of ignorance: they could ask anything.

Many fights and domestic arguments were conducted through the IWM 1000. The contestants would ask the machine to say to their opponent the dirtiest words and the vilest insults at the highest volume. And, when they wanted to make peace, they could make it at once because it was the IWM 1000 and not they who said those words.

People began to feel really bad. They con-sulted their IWM 1000s, and the machines told them that their organisms could not tolerate one more dose of pep pills because they had reached the limit of their tolerance. In addition, they computed that the possibilities of suicide were on the increase, and that a change in life-style had become necessary.

The people wanted to return to the past, but it was too late. Some tried to put aside their IWM 1000, but they felt defenseless. Then they consulted the machines to see if there was some place in the world where there was nothing like the IWM 1000; and the machines gave information and details about a remote place called Takandia. Some people began to dream about Takandia. They gave the IWM 1000 to those who had only an IWM 100. They began to go through a series of strange actions. They went to museums; they spent time in the sections which contained books looking at something that intrigued them a great deal—something that they wanted to have in their hands—little, shabby syllabaries in which the children of past civilizations learned slowly to read poring over symbols, for which they used to attend a des-ignated site called a school. The symbols were called letters; the letters were divided into syl-lables; and the syllables were made up of vowels and consonants. When the syllables were joined together, they made words, and the words were oral and written. . . . When these ideas became common knowledge, some people were very content again because these were the first facts acquired for themselves and not through the IWM 1000.

Many left the museums to go out to the few antique shops that remained, and they did not stop until they found syllabaries, which went from hand to hand in spite of their high prices. When the people had the syllabaries, they started to decipher them: *a-e-i-o-u, ma me mi mo mu, pa pe pi po pu.* It turned out to be easy and fun. When they knew how to read, they obtained all the books they could. They were few, but they were books: *The Effect of Chloro-phyll on Plants, Les Misérables* by Victor Hugo,

One Hundred Recipes from the Kitchen, The History of the Crusades. . . . They began to read, and, when they could obtain facts for themselves, they began to feel better. They stopped taking pep pills. They tried to communicate their new sensations to their peers. Some looked at them with suspicion and distrust and labeled them lunatics. Then these few people hastened to buy tickets to Takandia.

After a jet, they took a slow boat, then a canoe. They walked many kilometers and arrived at Takandia. There they found themselves surrounded by horrible beings, who did not wear even modest loincloths. They lived in the tops of trees; they ate raw meat because they were not familiar with fire; and they painted their bodies with vegetable dyes.

The people who had arrived in Takandia realized that, for the first time in their lives, they were among true human beings, and they began to feel happy. They looked for friends; they yelled as the others did; and they began to strip off their clothes and throw them away among the bushes. The natives of Takandia forgot about the visitors for a few minutes to fight over the discarded clothing.

MICHAEL BISHOP

Michael Bishop (1945–) is an influential US science fiction and fantasy writer who sold his first story, "Piñon Fall," to *Galaxy* in 1969 and has gone on to produce several award-winning novels and stories in a career spanning almost five decades. These works include the Nebula Award–winning novel *No Enemy but Time*, the Nebula Award–winning novelette "The Quickening," the Mythopoeic Fantasy Award–winning novel *Unicorn Mountain*, and the Shirley Jackson Award–winning story "The Pile" (based on notes discovered on his late son Jamie's computer). He has also received four Locus Awards and his work has been nominated for numerous Hugo Awards.

Bishop's many story collections include *The Door Gunner and Other Perilous Flights of Fancy: A Retrospective* (2012), edited by Michael H. Hutchins, and the forthcoming *Other Arms Reach Out to Me: Georgia Stories*. Bishop has edited seven anthologies, including the Locus Award–winning *Light Years and Dark* and *A Cross of Centuries: Twenty-Five Imaginative Tales About the Christ* (2007). His latest anthology, *Passing for Human* (2009), was coedited with Steven Utley.

Bishop has also written a novel for young people ("whatever their age"), *Joel-Brock the Brave and the Valorous Smalls*, with pen-and-ink illustrations by Orion Zangara. Since 2012, Fairwood Press, in conjunction with Bishop's own imprint there, Kudzu Planet Productions, has been releasing revised editions of his novels about twice a year. These include *Brittle Innings*, *Ancient of Days*, *Who Made Stevie Crye?*, *Count Geiger's Blues*, *A Funeral for the Eyes of Fire*, and *Philip K. Dick Is Dead, Alas*.

About "The House of Compassionate Sharers," Bishop writes, "After selling stories to *Galaxy*, *F&SF*, and *Worlds of If*, I began focusing on Damon Knight's hardcover anthology series, *Orbit*, as well as on Silverberg's *New Dimensions* and Terry Carr's *Universe*. Because I especially admired Knight's story 'Masks' (1968), I used it as a basis for 'The House of Compassionate Sharers,' which also has its roots in some of the Japanese fiction I was then reading: Kawabata, Endo, Mishima, and others." Knight promptly rejected what Bishop calls "a bloated version that I trimmed and restructured, using Damon's comments as guides." After Bishop placed a revised version with a new magazine called *Cosmos* edited by David Hartwell, four different year's-best anthologies reprinted the story, which Bishop described as "a 'hat trick' no other story of mine has ever duplicated."

The version of "The House of Compassionate Sharers" (1977) reprinted here—still edgy, timeless, and unique—completes Bishop's editing process by trimming a last eight hundred words since its appearance in *Cosmos*.

THE HOUSE OF COMPASSIONATE SHARERS

Michael Bishop

In the Port Iranani Galenshall, I awoke in the room Diderits called the Black Pavilion. I was an engine, a system, a series of myoelectric and neuromechanical components, and the Accident responsible for this enamel-hard enfleshing lay two full M-years in the past. This morning was an anniversary of sorts. By now I should have adjusted. And I had. I had reached a full accommodation with myself. Narcissistic, one could say. Which was the trouble.

"Dorian? Dorian Lorca?"

The voice belonged to KommGalen Diderits, wet and breathy even though it came from a metal speaker to which the sable drapes of the dome were attached. I stared up into the ring of curtains.

"Dorian, it's target day. Answer, please."

"I'm here, my galen." I arose, listening to the quasi-musical ratcheting that I make when I move, a sound like the concatenation of tiny bells or the purring of a stope-car. The sound echoes through the porcelain plates, metal vertebrae, and osteoid polymers holding me together, and no one else can hear it.

"Rumai's here, Dorian. May she enter?"

"If I agreed, I suppose so."

"Damn it, Dorian, don't feel you're bound by *honor* to see her! We've spent the last several brace-weeks preparing you to resume normal human contact." Diderits began to list: "Chameleodrene treatments, hologramic substitution, stimulus-response therapy. You ought to *want* Rumai to come in to you, Dorian."

Ought. My brain was—and remains—my own, but the body Diderits and the other kommgalens had given me had "instincts" and "tropisms" specific to itself, ones whose templates had a mechanical instead of a biological origin.

What I ought to feel, in human terms, and what I felt as the occupant of a total prosthesis resembled each other about as much as blood and oil.

"Do you *want* her to come in, Dorian?"

"I do." And I did. After all the biochemical and psychiatric preparation, I wanted to witness my own reaction. Still sluggish from a drug, I had no idea how Rumai's arrival would affect me.

At a parting of the pavilion's draperies, two or three meters from my couch, Rumai Montieth, my wife, appeared. Her garment of overlapping latex scales, glossy black in color, was a hauberk revealing only her hands, face, and hair. Rumai's dress was one of Diderits's deceits, or "preparations": he wanted me to see Rumai as little different from myself, a creature as well assembled and synapsed as the engine I had become. But her hands, face, and hair—well, nothing could disguise their primitive humanity, and revulsion swept over me like a tide.

"Dorian?" And her voice: wet, breath-driven, expelled through moistened lips.

I turned away. "No," I said to the speaker overhead. "It hasn't worked, my galen. Every part of me cries out against this."

Diderits said nothing. Was he still out there? Or had he tried to bestow on Rumai and me a privacy I didn't want?

"Disassemble me," I urged him. "Link me to the control systems of a delta-state vessel and let me go out from Miroste for good. You don't want a zombot among you, Diderits—an unhappy anproz. You're all tormenting me!"

"And you, us," Rumai said. I faced her. "As you're very aware, Dorian, as you're very aware . . . Take my hand."

"No." I didn't shrink away, I merely refused.

"Here. Take it."

Fighting my disgust, I seized her hand, twisted it over, and showed her its back. "Look."

"I *see* it, Dor." I was hurting her.

"Surfaces, that's all you see. Look at this wen." I pinched the growth. "That's sebum, fatty matter. And the smell, if only you could—"

Rumai drew back, and I sought to quell a mental nausea almost as profound as my regret. . . . To venture out from Miroste seemed the only answer. Around me I wanted machinery—thrumming machinery—and the sterile, actinic emptiness of vacuum. I wanted to become the probeship *Dorian Lorca*, a clear step up from my position as prince consort to the governor of Miroste.

"Let me out," Rumai commanded the head of the Port Iranani Galenshall, and Diderits released her from the pavilion. Again, I dwelt alone in one of the few private chambers of a surgical complex given over to adapting Civi Korps personnel to our leprotic planet's fume-filled mine shafts. The Galenshall was also used to patch up these civkis after their implanted respirators had atrophied, almost beyond saving, the muscles of their chests and lungs.

Including administrative personnel, Kommfleet officials, and the Civi Korps workers in the mines, over half a million people lived on Miroste in the year of which I write. Diderits answered for the health of all those not assigned to the outlying territories.

Had I not been the husband of Miroste's first governor, he might have let me die along with the seventeen "expendables" on tour with me in the Fetneh District when the roof of the Haft Paykar diggings collapsed. But Rumai had made Diderits's duty plain to him, and I am as I am because we had the resources in Port Iranani and Diderits obeyed his governor.

Alone in my pavilion, I lifted my hand and heard a caroling of minute copper bells.

. . .

Nearly a month later, I observed, by closed-circuit TV, Rumai, Diderits, and a stranger who sat in a Galenshall conference room. This strange woman, bald but for a scalplock, wore gold silk pantaloons that gave her a clownish appearance, and a corrugated green jacket that oddly reversed that impression. Even on my monitor I could see thick sunlight spilling into their room.

"This is Wardress Kefa," Rumai told me. I greeted her through a microphone and tested the cosmetic work of Diderits's associates by trying to smile. "She's from Earth, Dor, and she came because KommGalen Diderits and I asked her to."

"Forty-six lights," I said, touched and angry at the same time. To be constantly the focus of your friends' attentions, especially when they have more urgent business, leads to either a corrosive cynicism or a self-effacing humility just as crippling.

"We'd like you to go back with her on *Nizami* when it leaves here tomorrow night," Diderits said.

"Why?"

"Wardress Kefa came all this way to talk with us," Rumai said. "As a final stage in your therapy, she'd like you to visit her establishment on Earth. And if this fails, Dor, I give you up. If that's what you want, I relinquish you." Today, Rumai wore a yellow sarong and a nun's hood of red and orange stripes. Speaking, she averted her eyes from the monitor to stare out the high windows instead. I could not help admiring the spare aesthetics of her profile.

"Establishment? What sort of establishment?" I studied the tiny Wardress, but her appearance yielded nothing.

"The House of Compassionate Sharers," Diderits said. "It lies in Earth's Western Hemisphere, in North America, two hundred kilometers southwest of the gutted Urban Nucleus of Denver. One reaches it from Manitou Port by 'rail."

"Good. I'll have no trouble getting there. But what is this mysterious house?"

Wardress Kefa spoke: "I'd prefer that you

discover its nature and purposes from me, Mr. Lorca, when we've arrived safely under its several roofs."

"Is it a brothel?" This question fell among my interlocutors like a stone.

"No," Rumai said at length. "It's a unique clinic for the treatment of unique emotional disorders." She glanced at the Wardress, concerned that she'd said too much.

"Some call it a brothel," Wardress Kefa admitted huskily. "Earth has become a haven of misfits and opportunists, a crossroads of Glaktik Komm influence and trade. The House wouldn't prosper catering only to those who experience rare dissociations of feeling. Hence, a few of those who frequent the House are kommthors rich in power and finicky in their tastes. But I view them as exceptions, Governor Montieth, KommGalen Diderits. They represent a compromise that I make to carry out the work for which we first built the House."

A moment later Rumai said, "You're going, Dor—tomorrow night. Diderits and I will see you in three E-months." She threw on her cloak and departed.

"Good-bye, Dorian," Diderits said, standing.

Wardress Kefa's keen glance felt oddly disconcerting. "Tomorrow, then."

"Tomorrow," I agreed. In my monitor, the galen and the Wardress exited the conference room together. In its high windows, Miroste's sun sang a cappella in a lemon sky.

I had a private berth on *Nizami*. I used my "nights" (because sleep no longer meant a thing to me) to prowl through the compartments of shipboard machinery not forbidden to passengers. Although I couldn't enter the command module, I could the computer-ringed observation turret and a few corridors of auxiliary equipment necessary to maintaining a continuous probefield. In these places, I pondered the likelihood of an encephalic/neural connection to one of Kommfleet's interstellar frigates.

My body was a trial. Diderits had long ago told me that it—that *I*—was still "sexually viable." But this promise I had not tested, nor did I wish to. Tyrannized by vivid images of human viscera, human excreta, human decay, I'd been rebuilt of metal, porcelain, and plastic, as if from the substances—skin, bone, hair, cartilage—that these inorganic materials mocked. I was a contradiction, a quasi-immortal masquerading as one of the ephemera who'd delivered me from their own short-lived lot. Paradoxically, my aversion to the organic was another human (i.e., organic) emotion. So I fervently wanted out. For over a year and a half on Miroste, I'd hoped that Rumai and the others would see their mistake and exile me not only from themselves but also from the body continuously reminding me of my total estrangement.

But Rumai persisted in her love, and I had lived a prisoner in the Port Iranani Galenshall—with one chilling respite—ever since the Haft Paykar explosion and cave-in. Now, entering the care of a new wardress, I brooded amid the enamel-encased engines of *Nizami* and wondered what sort of jail the House of Compassionate Sharers would prove.

A passenger of a monorail car bound outward from Manitou Port, Wardress Kefa in the window seat beside me, I still brooded. Anthrophobia. Lorca, I told myself, exercise self-control. And I did. From Manitou Port we rode the sleek bullet through rugged, sparsely inhabited country toward Wolf Run Summit, and I stayed sane.

"You've never been 'home' before?" Wardress Kefa asked.

"No. Earth isn't home. I was born on GK-world Dai-Han, Wardress. As a young man, I traveled as an administrative colonist to Miroste, where—"

"Where you were born again," she said. "But this is where we began."

The shadows of the mountains slid across

the wraparound window glass, and the imposing white pylons of the monorail system flashed past like the legs of giants—like huge, naked cyborgs hiding amid the aspens and pines.

"Where I met Rumai Montieth, I was going to say; where I wed and settled into the life of a bureaucrat married to power. You anticipate me, Wardress." I didn't add that now Earth and Miroste were equally alien: the probeship *Nizami* had bid fair to assume first place among my loyalties.

A 'rail from Wolf Run swept past us toward Manitou Port. The sight pleased me; the hum of the passing 'rail lingered sympathetically in my hearing, and I refused to talk, even though the Wardress obviously wanted to draw me out about my prior life. I was surrounded and beset. Surely, she'd learned all that she needed to know from Diderits and Rumai. My annoyance grew.

"You're silent, Mr. Lorca."

"I have no innate hatred of silences."

"Nor do I, Mr. Lorca—unless they're empty ones."

Hands in lap, humming like a bioelectric, I studied my guardian disdainfully. "There are some who can't engage in a silence without peeling it of its unspoken freight of meaning."

The woman laughed. "That certainly isn't true of you, is it?" A wry expression on her lips, she gazed at the hurtling countryside and said nothing else until we disembarked at Wolf Run Summit.

Kommfleet officers and members of the administrative hierarchy frequented the resort in Manitou Port. Civi Korps personnel had built gingerbread chateaux among the trees and engineered two of the slopes above the hamlet for yearlong skiing. "Many of these people," Wardress Kefa explained, indicating a crowd beneath the deck of Wolf Run's main lodge, "work inside Shays Mountain, near the light-probe port, in facilities built originally for satellite tracking and missile-launch detection. Now they monitor the display boards for Kommfleet orbiters and shuttles; they program cruising

and descent lanes. Others are demographic and wildlife managers, set on resettling Earth as efficiently as possible. Tedious work, Mr. Lorca, so they come here to play." We passed below the lodge on a path of unglazed vitrofoam. Some of Wolf Run's bundled visitors stared at me, maybe because, in my tunic sleeves, I was undaunted by the spring cold. Or maybe they stared at my guardian. . . .

"How many of these people patronize your House, Wardress?"

"Forgive me—I can't divulge that." But she glanced back as if she'd recognized someone.

"What do they find in your house that they can't in Manitou Port?"

"I don't know, Mr. Lorca. I'm not a mind reader."

To reach the House of Compassionate Sharers from Wolf Run, we trekked on foot down a narrow path worked reverently into the flank of the mountain—very nearly a two-hour hike. I couldn't credit the distance or Wardress Kefa's stamina. Swinging her arms, jolting along on stiff legs, she went determinedly down the mountain. We met no other hikers and finally arrived in a clearing giving us an open view of a steep pine-filled glen: a grotto that, falling away beneath us, graded into a scrim of smooth white sky. But the Wardress pointed down into the foliage.

"There," she said: "The House of Compassionate Sharers."

I saw nothing but sunlight gilding the aspens, boulders huddled in the mulch cover, and swaying tunnels among the trees. Squinting, I finally made out a geodesic structure built from the very materials of the woods.

Like an upland sleight, a wavering mirage, the House slipped in and out of my vision, blending, emerging, melting again: a series of irregular domes as hard to hold as water vapor. But after several red-winged blackbirds flew noisily past its highest turret, the House manifested—*bang!*—in stark relief.

"It's more noticeable," Wardress Kefa said, "when someone cranks its shutters aside. Then the stained-glass windows sparkle like dragon's eyes."

"I'd like to see that. Now, it appears camouflaged."

"That's deliberate, Mr. Lorca. Come."

When at last all the way down, I could see of what colossal size the House really was: it reared through the pine needles, holding interlocking polygons to the sky. Strange to think that no one in a passing helicraft was likely to see it. Wardress Kefa led me up some plank stairs, spoke at a door, and introduced me into an antechamber so spartan that I thought "barracks" rather than "bordello." The ceilings and walls were honeycombed, and the natural flooring smelled of the outdoors. My guardian disappeared, returned coatless, and took me into a room like a tapered well. With a hand-crank, she opened the shutters: varicolored light streamed in through slant-set windows. On high cushions that snapped and rustled whenever we moved, we faced each other.

"What now?" I asked.

"Just listen: The Sharers have come here of their own volition, Mr. Lorca. Most lived and worked on extrakomm worlds toward Glaktik Center before we asked them to work here. Those here accepted the invitation and came to offer themselves to people much like you."

"Me? Are they misconceived machines?"

"Let's just say that the services the Sharers offer are wide. As I've told you, a few visitants regard the Sharers as a convenient means of satisfying exotically aberrant tastes. For others, they're a way back to the larger community. We take whoever comes to us for help, so that the Sharers do not remain idle or the House empty."

"If whoever comes has wealth and influence?"

She considered. "That's true enough. But the matter's out of our hands. I'm an employee of Glaktik Komm, chosen for my empathic abilities. I don't make policy. I don't own title to the House."

"But you *are* its madam. Its 'wardress,' rather."

"True. For the last twenty-two years. I'm the only wardress to have served here, Mr. Lorca, and I love the Sharers—for their devotion to the fragile mentalities who visit them. Still, despite all my time here, I don't fully plumb the source of their transcendent concern. That's what I wanted to tell you."

"You think me a 'fragile mentality'?"

"I'm sorry—but you're here, and you certainly aren't fragile of limb, are you?" The Wardress laughed. "I also wanted to ask you to—to restrain your crueler impulses when the treatment itself begins."

I stood and moved away. How had I borne her presence for so long?

"Please don't take my request amiss. It isn't specifically personal. I make it of everyone who comes to the House. Restraint is an unwritten corollary of the only three rules we have here. Will you hear them?"

I shrugged janglingly.

"First, don't leave the session chamber once you've entered it. Second, emerge immediately upon my summons."

"And third?"

"Don't kill the Sharer."

All the myriad disgusts I'd been suppressing squatted now atop the ladder of my patience, and, rung by painful rung, I stepped them back down. Must a rule be made to prevent a visitant from murdering the partner he'd bought? Incredible. The Wardress was perceptibly sweating, even her earlobes grotesquely agleam.

"Is there a room here for a wealthy, influential client? A private room?"

"Of course," she said. "I'll show you."

It had a full-length mirror. I disrobed and stood before it. Only during my first "period of adjustment" on Miroste had I spent much time looking at what I'd become. Later, back in the Port Iranani Galenshall, Diderits had denied me any sort of reflective surface at all—looking glasses, darkened windows, metal spoons. The waxen perfection of my features ridiculed those that another Dorian Lorca had possessed before the Haft Paykar Incident. Cosmetic mockery.

Faintly corpselike, speciously paradigmatic, I was both a man and much less. In Wardress Kefa's House, the less seemed preeminent. I ran a finger down my inner arm, studying the track of an intubated vein, for through it swirled a serum called hematocybin: a "low-maintenance" blood substitute, combative of both fatigue and infection, which needs changing only once every six M-months. With a good supply of hematocybin and a plastic recirculator, I change it myself. That night, though, the ridge of my vein, mirrored an arm's length away, seemed more horror than miracle. Hence, horrified, I shut my eyes.

Later, Wardress Kefa came to me with a candle and an embroidered gown. She made me don it before her. With the robe's rich, symbolic embroidery on my back, I followed her from my first-floor chamber to a rustic stairwell seemingly connective to all the rooms in the House. The dome contained many smaller domes and five or six staircases. No other person intruded.

Lit by the Wardress's taper, the House's mid-interior put me in mind of an Escheresque drawing in which verticals and horizontals trade places and a figure who from one vantage seems to climb a series of steps, from another seems to descend them. Soon the Wardress and I stood on a landing above the topsy-turvy well of stairs (though more stairs loomed above); and, looking down, I experienced an unsettling reversal of perspectives. Vertigo. Why hadn't Diderits, against so human a debility, implanted tiny gyrostabilizers in me? I clutched a rail and held on.

"You can't fall," Wardress Kefa said. "It's an illusion: a whim of the architects."

"Does an illusion dwell behind this door?"

"Oh, the Sharer's real enough. Please. Go in." She bowed and left, taking her candle. Then I went through the door to my assignation, and the door locked of itself. My hand on the knob, I felt the night working in the chamber. The only light came from the stove-bed on the far wall, the fitted polygons overhead still blanked out by their shutters. No candles anywhere. Instead, reddish embers glowed behind an isinglass portal beneath the quilt-strewn stove-bed upon which the Sharer waited.

Outside, the wind played harp music in the trees. I trembled, as when Rumai had visited me in the pavilion. Even though my eyes adjusted, I still found it difficult to see. Temporizing, I surveyed the dome. In its vault dangled a cage in which, perturbed by my entrance, a bird skittishly hopped about. The cage rocked on its tether.

Go on, I told myself.

I advanced to the dais and leaned over the unmoving Sharer. A hand on either side of his head, I braced myself. The figure moved, weakly, and I drew back. But because the Sharer didn't stir again, I reassumed my previous stance: the posture of a lover or of one called upon to identify a mangled corpse. But I made no identification; the embers under the bed offered too feeble a sheen. In such darkness, even a lover's kiss would have fallen amiss. "I'm going to touch you," I said. "May I?"

The Sharer lay still.

Then, willing all my senses into the synthetic flesh at my fingertip, I touched the Sharer's face: hard, and smooth, and cool.

I moved my finger from side to side, and the hardness, smoothness, coolness, continued to flow. The object felt like a death's-head, the cranial cap of a human being: bone rather than metal. My finger distinguished between these possibilities, deciding on bone. Half-panicked, I reasoned that I'd traced an arc on the skull of an intelligent being who bore his every bone on the outside, like an armor of calcium. If so, how could this organism—this *thing*—express compassion? I lifted a finger. Its tip hummed with a pressure now relieved, emanating warmth. A living death's-head . . .

Maybe I laughed. In any case, I boarded the platform and straddled the Sharer, my eyes gently closed. "Sharer," I whispered, "I don't know you yet." My thumbs touched the creature's eyes, the sockets in the smooth exoskeleton; both thumbs returned to me a hardness and a coldness clearly metallic in origin. The Sharer never flinched—though I assumed that touching his eyes, however softly, would provoke an involuntary reaction. Instead, the Sharer lay still.

And why not? I thought. Your eyes are two sophisticated optical machines.

Yes, two light-sensing image-integrating units gazed at me from the sockets near which my thumbs probed, and even in this darkness the Sharer, its vision sharper than my own, could discern my blind face staring down, futilely trying to create an image out of the information that my hands had supplied. I opened my eyes and saw only shadows, but my thumbs *felt* the cold metal rings gripping the Sharer's photosensitive orbs.

"An animatronic construct," I said, rocking back on my heels. "A soulless robot. Move your head if I'm right."

The Sharer continued motionless.

"All right: a sentient creature whose eyes have been replaced with an artificial system. Lord, are we brothers then?"

I had a sudden hunch that the Sharer was very old, a senescent being owing its life to prosthetics, transplants, organs of laminated silicon. Its life had been extended by these gizmos, not saved. I asked the Sharer about this hunch. It slowly moved the helmetlike skull housing its fake eyes and its aged compassionate mind. Uncharitably, I considered myself the victim of a deception, the Sharer's or Wardress Kefa's. Here, after all, lay a creature who had chosen to prolong its life rather than escape it, and who had willingly employed the same materials and methods that Diderits had used to save me.

"You might have died," I told it. "Go too far with these contrivances, Sharer, and you'll forfeit suicide as an option." Leaning forward again, I let my hands move from the Sharer's bony face to its throat. Here a shield of cartilage graded upward into its jaw and downward into

the silken plastic skin covering its body, internalizing all but the defiant skull: a death's-head with the body of a man.

I could take no more. I rose from the stove-bed, cinched my gown, and crossed to the room's far side. It held no furniture but the bed, so I assumed a lotus position on the floor and sat thus all night, staving off dreams. Diderits had said that I needed to dream to sidestep both hallucination and madness. In the Port Iranani Galenshall, he had had drugs administered to me every day and my sleep period monitored by an ARC machine and a team of electroencephalographers. But my dreams veered into nightmares, descents into klieg-lit charnel houses. I infinitely preferred the risk of going psychotic. Someone might pity and then disassemble me, piece by loving piece. Also, I had now lasted two E-weeks on nothing but catnaps, and I still had gray matter upstairs, not chopped pâté.

I crossed my fingers.

A long time later, Wardress Kefa threw open the door—morning. The freshly canted shutters outside the room admitted a singular roaring of light. The entire chamber crackled, and crimson wall hangings, a mosaic of red and purple stones on the floor, and a tumble of scarlet quilts glowed within it. The bird in the wobbly cage was a red-winged blackbird.

"Where is it from?"

"You could use a kinder pronoun."

"*He? She?* Which is kinder, Wardress Kefa?"

"Assume the Sharer masculine, Mr. Lorca."

"My sexual proclivities have never run that way."

"Your sexual proclivities matter only if you regard the House as a brothel rather than a clinic and the Sharers as whores rather than therapists."

"Last night I heard two or three people clomping up the stairs in their boots, that and a woman's raucous laughter."

"A client, Mr. Lorca—not a Sharer."

"I didn't think she was a Sharer. But it's

hard to believe I'm in a clinic when that sort of noise intrudes."

"I've explained that. It can't be helped."

"Okay. Where's he from, this therapist of mine?"

"An interior star. But where he's from is of no consequence in your treatment. I matched him to your needs, as I see them, and you'll soon go back to him."

"To spend another night squatting on the floor?"

"You won't do that again, Mr. Lorca. And you needn't worry. Your reaction parallels that of many newcomers to the House."

"Revulsion? Revulsion's therapeutic?"

"I don't think you were as put off as you contend."

"Oh? Why not?"

"Because you talked to the Sharer. You addressed him, not once but several times. Many clients fail to get that far during their first session."

"Talked to him?" I considered this. "Maybe. Before I found out what he was."

"Ah. Before you found out what he was." In her heavy green jacket and swishy pantaloons, the tiny woman turned and left.

For a time, I stared bemusedly after her.

Three nights after my first session, the night of my conversation with Wardress Kefa, I reentered the Sharer's chamber. Nothing had changed, except that the dome's shutters stood ajar and moonlight frosted the mosaic tiles. The Sharer awaited me in the same recumbent posture, and the red-winged blackbird set one of its perches rocking.

Perversely, I'd decided not to talk to the Sharer—but I did approach the stove-bed and lean over him. Hello, I thought, and almost said. I straddled the Sharer and studied him in the stained moonlight. He looked just as my sense of touch had led me to conclude earlier—like a skull, oddly flattened and beveled, with the body of a man. But despite the chemical embers agleam beneath his bed, the Sharer's body lacked warmth. To know him more fully, I resumed tracing him with a finger.

At every conceivable pressure point, a tiny scar existed, or the tip of an implanted electrode, while miniature canals into which wires had been sunk veined his inner arms and legs. Beneath his sternum a concave disc about eight centimeters across, containing neither instruments nor any other conspicuous features, had been set like a stainless-steel brooch. It hummed under my finger as I drew my nail around the disc.

What was it for? What did it mean?

I rolled toward the wall and stretched out beside the Sharer. Maybe he *couldn't* move. On my last visit he'd moved his dimly phosphorescent head, but feebly. Maybe his immobility stemmed from a mechanical dysfunction.

My resolve not to speak fled me—I propped myself up on my elbow. "Sharer . . . Sharer, can you move?"

The head turned toward me slightly, signaling . . . what?

"Can you rise? Try. Get off this dais under your own power."

A miracle: the Sharer nudged a quilt to the floor and struggled to his feet.

Moonlight glinted from the ringed units of his eyes, giving his bent, elongated body the look of a piece of Inhodlef Era statuary, primitive work from the extrakomm world of Glaparcus.

"Very good. Now tell me what you're to share with me. We may not have as much in common as our Wardress thinks."

The Sharer extended both arms and opened his fists. In his palms, he held two items I'd not noticed during my tactile examination. I accepted these—a small metal disc and a thin metal cylinder. The disc reminded me of the mirrorlike bowl in his chest; the cylinder resembled a penlight.

Absently, I pulled my thumb over the head of the penlight. A ridged metal sheath followed the motion of my thumb, uncovering a point of ghostly red light stretching away into the cylinder forever. I pointed this instrument at the wall, our bedding, the Sharer—but it emitted no beam.

When I turned the penlight on my wrist, the results were much the same: not even a faint red shadow appeared along the edge of my arm. The pen's light existed internally, a beam transmitted and retransmitted between its two poles. Pulling back the sheath on its head hadn't disabled its self-regenerating circuit, and I stared in wonder into the tunnel of redness.

"Sharer, what's this thing for?"

The Sharer took from my other hand the disc I'd ignored. He laid it in the larger disc in his chest, where it apparently stuck—for I could no longer see it. That done, the Sharer stood immobile, a statue again, one arm frozen across his body, a hand stilled at the margin of the sunken plate into which the smaller disc had vanished. He looked dead and self-commemorating.

"Lord! What've you done, Sharer? Turned yourself off?"

Turned off, the Sharer ignored me.

I felt opiate-weary. I could not stay on the dais with this puzzle-piece being from another sun standing over me like a dark angel from my racial subconscious. I thought to manhandle him across the room, but lacked the will to touch his bone-and-metal body, and so dismissed the idea. Nor would Wardress Kefa help me, even if I tried to summon her. Is this what you want me to experience, Rumai? The frustration of trying to devise my own "therapy"? I peered through one of the dome's unstained polygons in search of the constellation Auriga, but realized I wouldn't know it even if it lay within my ken.

"You're certainly a pretty one," I said, pointing the penlight at the Sharer's chest. Then I drew back the sheath on its head. *"Bang."*

A beam of light sang between the instrument in my hand and the plate in the being's chest. The beam died at once (I'd registered only its brightness, not its color), but the disc kept glowing, residually. The Sharer lowered his arm and assumed a looser, more expectant posture. I turned the penlight over, pointed it at him again, and waited for another coursing of light. The instrument still burned internally, but the alien's inset disc did not reignite; however, it still dimly glowed. I brandished the penlight.

"You've rejoined the living, haven't you?"

The Sharer canted his head.

"Forgive me, but if you can move again, how about over there?" I pointed at the opposite wall. "Please don't hover over me."

The Sharer obeyed, but oddly, cruising backward as if on invisible coasters—his legs moving, albeit not enough to propel him quickly across the chamber. Once against the far wall, he adopted the motionless but expectant posture that he'd assumed after the penlight "activation." He still had some control over his own movements, for his skeletal fingers flexed and his skull nodded eerily in the halo of moonlight pocketing him. But he had genuinely moved only at my voice command and my simultaneous gesturing with the penlight. And what did *that* mean?

Maybe the Sharer had surrendered control of his body to the man-machine Dorian Lorca, keeping for himself just those movements that persuade the manipulated of their autonomy. It was an awesome prostitution, even if Wardress Kefa would have frowned to hear me call it that. But I rejoiced. It freed me from the demands of an artificial eroticism, from any necessity to deduce what was expected of me. The Sharer would obey my least gesture, my briefest word. I just had to use the control he'd literally handed over.

This nearly unlimited power was a therapy whose value Rumai would understand: a harsh assessment, but penlight in hand, I too resembled a marionette. . . . Insofar as I could, I came to grips with the physics of the Sharer's operation. First, the disc-within-a-disc on his chest apparently broke the connections ordinarily allowing him to exercise the senile power that

645

he still owned. And, second, the penlight's beam restored and amplified his power, but delivered it into the hands of whoever wielded the penlight.

In Earth's probeship yards, crews of animatronic workers, programmed to fit and to weld, had labored. A single supervisor could direct fifteen to twenty receiver-equipped laborers with only a penlight and a microphone.

"Sharer," I commanded, "go there. . . . No, no. Lift your feet. March. That's right . . . *goose-step*." While Wardress Kefa's third rule rattled about in my mind challengingly, for the next several hours I toyed with the Sharer. I set him to either calisthenics or dance, and he obeyed, more gracefully than I would have predicted. Here—there—back again, minus only music for accompaniment. At intervals, I rested, but always the penlight drew me back, and I again played puppetmaster.

"Enough, Sharer!" The sky had a curdled quality hinting at dawn. Catching sight of the cage overhead, I had an irresistible urge. I pointed my penlight at it and said, "Up, Sharer: up, up, up."

The Sharer floated up from the floor, toward the ceiling's vault: a beautiful aerial walk. Without benefit of hawsers, scaffolds, or wings, he levitated. Hovering above the stove-bed—over everything, in fact—he reached the cage, floating before it with his hands touching the scrolled ironwork on its door. I lowered my hands and watched. So tightly did I grip the cylinder, though, that my knuckles resembled the caps of four tiny bleached skulls.

Time passed, and the Sharer posed in the gelid air awaiting some word. Morning entered the polygonal windows. "Take the bird out," I said, moving my penlight. "Take the bird out and kill it." This command seemed a foolproof, indirect way of striking back at Rumai, Diderits, the Wardress, and the third rule of the House. Against all reason, I wanted the red-winged blackbird dead. And I wanted the Sharer to kill it. Dawn made clear the encroachment of age in his body, as well as the full hor-

ror of his fake death's-head. He looked like he'd been lynched. And when his hands went up to the cage, instead of opening its door he lifted the contraption off the hook, fastened it to its tether, and then lost his grip—accidentally, I'm sure.

The cage fell. Landed on its side. Bounced. Bounced again. The Sharer stared down with his bulging, silver-ringed eyes, his hands still spread wide to accommodate what he had just dropped.

"Mr. Lorca." Wardress Kefa knocked heavily. "Mr. Lorca, what's going on?"

I arose from the stove-bed, tossed my quilt aside, and straightened my robes. The Wardress knocked again. The Sharer swayed in the half-light like a sword, an instrument of severance. The night had sped.

Again the purposeful knocking.

"Coming," I barked.

In the dented cage, a flutter of crimson. A stillness. Another melancholy bit of flapping. I hurled my penlight. When it struck the wall, the Sharer rocked for a moment without descending a centimeter. The knocking went on. "You have the key, Wardress. Open the door." She did, and stood on the threshold taking stock. Her eyes were bright but devoid of censure, and I swept past her, burning with shame and bravado.

I slept that day—*all* that day—for the first time since leaving my own world. And I dreamt. I dreamt myself connected to a mechanism pistoning away on the edge of the Haft Paykar diggings, siphoning deadly gases from the shafts and recirculating them through the pump with which I shared a feedback circuit. Amid the turquoise sunsets and the intermittent gusts of sand, this pistoning went on continuously. When I awoke, I lifted my hands, intending to scar my face with my nails. But, as I expected, the mirror showed me a perfect unperturbed Dorian Lorca. . . .

"May I come in?"

"I'm the client here, Wardress. So I suppose you may."

She entered and, intuiting my mood, stood far from me. "You slept, didn't you? And dreamt?"

I said nothing.

"You dreamt, *didn't you*?"

"A nightmare, Wardress, but different from those I had on Miroste."

"A start. And you survived it? Yes? Good. All to the good."

I went to the room's only window, a hexagonal pane of dark blue through which I could see nothing. "Did you get him down?"

"Yes. And restored the birdcage to its place." Her tiny feet paced the hardwood. "The bird was unharmed."

"Wardress, what's all this about? Why have you paired me with this Sharer?" I turned around. "What's the point?"

"You're not estranged from your wife only, Mr. Lorca. You're—"

"I know that. I've known that."

"I realize that. Give me some credit. . . . You also know," she resumed, "that you're estranged from yourself, body and soul at variance."

"Yes, damn it! And the argument rages in my every pseudo-organ and -circuit!"

"Please, Mr. Lorca. This interior argument, it's really a metaphor for an attitude you assumed after Diderits performed his operations. And a metaphor can be taken apart and explained."

"Like a machine."

"If you like." She paced some more. "To take inventory, Mr. Lorca, you have to surmount that which is inventoried. You go *outside* in order to *reenter*." She halted and fixed me with a humorless, lopsided smile.

"All of that is clear. Know thyself, saith Diderits. And the ancient Greeks. Well, if anything, my knowledge has increased my uneasiness about not only me, but others—and not only others, but the very phenomena enabling us to spawn." I flashed on an image of crimson-gilled salmon firing upstream in a roiling bar-rage. "All that I know hasn't cured anything, Wardress."

"No. So you came here—to extend your knowledge and to join in relationships demanding that you sanctify others as well as yourself."

"As with the Sharer I left hanging in the air?"

"Yes. Distance is initially advisable, perhaps inevitable. You needn't feel guilty. In a night or two, you'll return to him, and then we'll just have to see."

"Is this the only Sharer I'm going to be—working with?"

"I don't know. It depends on your progress."

But for Wardress Kefa, the Sharer in the crimson dome, and the noisy midnight clients I'd never seen, I sometimes believed myself the only occupant of the House. The thought of my isolation, though not unwelcome, was an anchoritic fantasy. In the rooms next to mine, going about the arcane business of the lives they'd bartered away, breathed humanoid creatures hard to imagine; harder still, once lodged in the mind, to purge from it. To what number and kind of beings had Wardress Kefa indentured her love?

I had no choice but to ask. We heard an insistent stamping on the steps outside the House and then muffled voices in the antechamber.

"Who comes?"

The Wardress waved me to silence and opened my door. "A moment," she called. But her husky voice didn't carry well, and whoever had entered the House began rapping rudely on doors and clumping from room to room, all the while bellowing the Wardress's name. "I'd better talk to them," she said apologetically.

"But who is it?"

"Someone voice-coded for entrance. Nothing to worry about." And she went into the corridor, wafting me a smell of spruce needles and a glimpse of solidly hewn rafters before the door swung to.

I got up and followed. Outside the Wardress stood face-to-face with two imposing persons who looked identical in spite of their being one a man and the other a woman. Their faces had the same lantern-jawed mournfulness, their eyes hooded under heavy brows. They wore pea jackets, ski leggings, and fur caps bearing the interpenetrating-galaxies insignia of Glaktik Komm. I judged them in their late thirties, E-standard, but they had the domineering air of high-ranking veterans in the bureaucratic establishment. I had once been an official of the same stamp.

The man, caught in mid-bellow, tried to laugh. "Ah. Ah. Wardress, Wardress."

"I didn't expect you this evening," she said.

"We got a leave for finishing the Salous blueprint ahead of schedule," the female explained, "and so caught a late 'rail from Manitou Port. We hiked down in the dark." She lifted a hand lantern for our inspection.

"We *took* a leave," the man said, "even if we were here last week. We deserve it, too." He told us that Salous dealt with reclaiming the remnants of aboriginal populations and pooling them for something called integrative therapy. "The Great Plains will soon be our bordello, Wardress. There, you see: you and the Orhas are in the same business . . . at least until they ask us to stage-manage something more prosaic." He clapped his gloves together and looked at me. "You're new. Whom do you visit?"

"Pardon me," the Wardress said wearily. "Who do you two want tonight?"

The man looked to his partner. "Cleva?"

"The mouthless one," Cleva said, "preferably drugged."

"Come with me, Orhas." The Wardress led them to her own apartment then into the House's mid-interior, where they disappeared. I could hear them climbing, though. Shortly thereafter, the Wardress returned to my room.

"Twins?" I said.

"Clonemates: Cleva and Cleirach Orha, specialists in holosyncretic management. They computer-plan strategic movements of indigenous and alien populations—so they know of the House and have authorization to visit."

"Do they always appear together? Go upstairs together?"

The Wardress's silence clearly meant yes.

"A bit unorthodox, isn't it?"

She gave me an angry look whose implications shut me up, then said: "The Orhas are our only clients who visit together. Since they share a common upbringing, the same genetic material, and identical biochemistries, it should hardly surprise that their sexual preferences also coincide. In Manitou Port, I'm told, lives a third clonemate who married. I've never seen her here or in Wolf Run Summit. Even among clonal siblings a degree of variety exists."

"Do these two come often?"

"You heard them in the House a few days ago."

"They have frequent leaves, then?"

"Last time was an overnighter. They returned to Manitou Port in the morning, Mr. Lorca. This time they'll remain several days."

"For treatment?"

"You're baiting me." She'd taken her graying scalplock into her fingers; now she held its fan of hair against her right cheek. In this posture, despite her preoccupation with the Orhas, she looked at once old and innocent.

"Who is the 'mouthless one,' Wardress?"

"Good night. I returned only to tell you good night." And she left.

I hadn't permitted myself to talk with her for so long since our first afternoon in the House, nor had I stayed in her presence for so long since our claustrophobic 'rail ride from Manitou Port. Even the Orhas, bundled to the gills, as vulgar as bullfrogs, had not struck me as wholly insufferable. Wearing neither coat nor cap, I took a walk through the glens below the House, touching each wind-shaken tree as if to conjure a viable memory of Rumai's smile.

"Sex as weapon," I told the Sharer lying on my stove-bed amid a dozen quilts of scarlet and offscarlet. "As prince consort to the governor of

Miroste, I had access to no other weapon. Rumai used me as an emissary, Sharer—a spy, a protocol officer, whatever state business required. I received visiting representatives of Glaktik Komm, mediated disputes in the Port Iranani Galenshall, and took biannual inspection tours of the Fetneh and Furak District mines. I did a bit of everything, Sharer."

As I paced, the Sharer studied me with a macabre but not unsettling penetration. The hollow of his chest was exposed, and when I passed him, an occasional metallic wink caught my eye. I told him the story of my involvement with a minor official in Port Iranani's department of immigration, a young woman whom I'd never called anything but Humay, her maternal surname. I had had others besides this woman, but Humay's story was the one I told—because alone among my ostensible "lovers," I'd never taken her to bed. I'd never chosen to.

Instead, to her intense bewilderment, I gave Humay rings, wristlets, earpieces, brooches, necklaces, and die-cut cameos, all from the collection of Rumai Montieth, governor of Miroste: anything distinctive enough for my wife to recognize at a glance. Then, at functions requiring Rumai's presence, I asked Humay to attend, too. Sometimes I accompanied her, sometimes I found an escort among the single men assigned to me as aides. Always I ensured that Rumai should see Humay, if not in a reception line then in the sweep of the formal recessional. Afterward, I asked Humay, who rarely had a clue into my game's purposes, to return whatever piece of jewelry she'd worn. She always did so. Then I put this jewelry back in my wife's sandalwood box before she could verify its "theft." I suppose I wanted to make my dishonesty conspicuous.

Finally, dismissing Humay for good, I presented her a cameo that an artisan in the Furak District had crafted. Later, I learned that she'd flung this cameo at an aide of mine about something else entirely. Several times she raised my name. At length (in two days' time), she received an arbitrary transfer to Yagme, the frontier administrative center of the Furak District, and I never saw her again.

"Later, Sharer, when I dreamed of Humay, I saw her as a woman with mother-of-pearl flesh and ruby eyes. In my dreams, she became the jewelry with which I'd tried to incite my wife's sexual jealousy, blunting it even as I summoned it."

The Sharer regarded me with hard but not unsympathetic eyes.

Why? I asked. Why had I dreamed of Humay as a precious clockwork automaton, gilded, beset with gemstones, invulnerably enameled? And why had I so fiercely desired Rumai's jealousy?

The Sharer's silence invited confession.

After the Haft Paykar Incident (I went on, pacing), after Diderits had fitted me with a fullbody prosthesis, my nightmares often focused on the woman exiled to Yagme. Although in Port Iranani I'd never touched Humay erotically, in my readable nightmares, I often descended into a catacomb or a dry quarry to force myself, without success, on the bejeweled automaton that she had become. Always, Humay awaited me underground and turned me back with coruscating laughter, and in my nightmares I realized that I wanted Humay far less than I did residency in the subterranean places that she'd made hers. The klieg lights directing my descent always followed me back out, so that Humay remained many kilometers below, exulting in the dark.

The Sharer stood and took a turn around the room, the quilt over his shoulders clutched loosely at his chest. He'd never moved so far of his own volition, and I sat down to watch. Did he understand me at all? I'd spoken to him as if he must—but perhaps all his "reactions" were projections of my ambiguous hopes. When he at last returned, he extended both hideously canaled arms and opened his fists. In them, the disc and the penlight: an offering, a compassionate, selfless offering. For a moment, I stared at them in perplexity. What did the Sharer, Wardress Kefa, and the others who had sent me here want? How could I purchase their forbearance or my freedom? By choosing power over impotency? By manipulation?

I hesitated.

The Sharer placed the small disc in the larger one beneath his sternum. Then, as before, a thousand esoteric connections severed, he froze. In the hand extended toward me, the faintly glittering penlight threatened to slip from his insensible grasp. I took it, pulled back the sheath on its head, and gazed into its red-lit hollow. I released the sheath and pointed the light at the disc in his chest. If I pulled the sheath back again, he would turn into little more than an external prosthesis—as much at my disposal as my own alien hands.

"No," I said. "Not this time." And I flipped the penlight across the chamber, out of the way of temptation. With my nails, I pried the small disc out of its electromagnetic moorings above the Sharer's heart.

He was restored to himself.

As was I to myself . . . as was I.

A day later, early in the afternoon, I ran into the Orhas in the House's mid-interior. They approached me out of a lofty, sideways-canted door as I peered upward from the access corridor. Man and woman side by side, mirror images ratcheting down a Möbius strip of stairs, on they came.

"The brand-new client," Cleirach Orha told his sister at the lowest step. "We've seen you before."

"Briefly," I said, "on the night you arrived from Manitou Port for your leave."

"Such a memory," Cleva Orha said. "We also saw you the day you arrived. You and the Wardress were setting out from Wolf Run Summit. Cleirach and I sat beneath the ski lodge, watching."

"You wore no coat," Cleirach said, to explain their interest. Both stared at me. Nor did I wear a coat in the well of the House—even though the temperature hovered only a few degrees above freezing and our breaths ballooned before us like the ghosts of ghosts. . . .

My silence made them nervous, and brazen.

"No coat," Cleva repeated, "on a day cold enough to freeze your spit. 'Look at that one,' Cleirach said, 'thinks he's a polar bear.' And we laughed, studling."

Bile flooded my mouth. I wanted to escape the Orhas' warty humor. They were intelligent people; otherwise, no one would have cloned them, but face-to-face with their flawed skins and loud sexuality, I felt my reserves of tolerance overbalancing like a tower of blocks.

"We seem to be the only ones in the House this month," Cleva volunteered. "Last month the Wardress was gone, the Sharers had a holiday, and we had to content ourselves with incestuous buggery in Manitou Port."

"Cleva!" the man protested, laughing.

"It's true." She turned to me. "And that little she-goat—Kefa, I mean—won't even tell us why the Closed sign was out for so long."

"Yes," Cleirach said. "An exasperating woman. You have to tread lightly on her patience. One day, I'd like to find out what makes *her* tick!"

"She's a maso-ascetic, brother."

"I don't know. This House has many mansions, Cleva, several of which she has refused to show us. Why?" He lifted one brow suggestively, as Cleva often did, and the Orhas' expressions matched exactly.

Cleva appealed to me: "What do you think? Is our Wardress at bed and bone with a Sharer? Or does she lie alone under an untanned elk hide?"

"I haven't really thought about it." Containing my anger, I tried to leave. "Excuse me, Orha-clones."

"Wait, wait, wait," Cleva said mincingly. "You know our names, and that puts you up, studling. You can't leave without revealing yours."

Resentfully, I disclosed my name.

"From where?" Cleirach asked.

"Colony World GK-Eleven, otherwise known as Miroste."

The Orhas exchanged a glance of enlightenment, after which Cleva raised her thin brows and spoke mockingly: "Ah, the mystery solved. Out and back our Wardress went and therefore closed her House."

"Welcome, Mr. Lorca. Welcome."

"We're going up to Wolf Run for an afterbout of toddies and P-nol. Please come. The climb won't affect a studling like you. Look, Cleirach, biceps unbundled and sinuses still clear."

I declined.

"Who have you been with?" Cleirach bent toward me. "We've been with a native of an extrakomm world called Trope: the local name. Anyhow, there's not another such being inside a hundred light-years."

"The face intrigues us," Cleva explained, saving me from replying. She reached out and ran a finger down my arm. "Look. Not even a goose bump. Cleirach, you and I suffer the shems and trivs, but Mr. Lorca stands unperturbed."

Cleirach started to ask his question again, irritated with Cleva's non sequiturs, but, studying me closely, she had an insight and overrode him: "Mr. Lorca can't tell you about his Sharer, Cleirach. He's not a regular visitor to the House and he doesn't want to violate the confidences of those who are."

Dumbfounded, I said nothing.

Cleva guided her brother beyond me into the House's antechamber. Then the Orha-clones let themselves out and started the long climb to Wolf Run Summit.

What had happened? Cleva Orha had recognized me as a man-machine. From this recognition, she'd drawn a logical but mistaken inference—that, like the "mouthless one" from Trope, I was also a slave of the House.

During my next tryst with my Sharer I spoke for an hour or more of Rumai's infuriating patience, her dignity, her serene ardor. I had maneuvered her to the expression of these qualities by my hollow commitment to Humay and to the others before Humay who had engaged me only physically. Under my wife's attentions, though, I preened sullenly, demanding more than Rumai—or any woman in her position— had the power to give. My needs, I wanted her to know, had at least as much urgency as our world's. At the end of one of these fatiguing encounters, Rumai seemed both to concede the legitimacy of my demands and to decry their intemperance: she took a warm pendant from her throat and placed it on my palm like an accusation.

"A week later," I told the Sharer, "we inspected the diggings at Haft Paykar."

These things said, I achieved a first in the Wardress's House: I fell asleep under the hand of the Sharer. My dreams were dreams, not nightmares, and lucid ones, shot through with light and peaceful funnelings of sand. The images flooding me were haloed arms and legs inside a series of shifting yellow, yellow-orange, and subtly red discs. The purr of running sand behind these images conferred upon them the blessing of mortality, and that, I felt, was good.

I awoke in a blast of icy air and found myself alone. The door to the Sharer's apartment stood open on the shaft of the stairwell, and faint, angry voices came across the emptiness between.

Groggy, I lay on my stove-bed watching the door, a square of shadow feeding its chill into the room.

"Dorian!" a husky voice called. "Dorian!"

Wardress Kefa's voice, diluted by distance and fear. A door opened, and her voice hailed me again, more loudly. Then the door slammed, and every noise in the House took on a smothered quality.

I got up, dragging my bedding, and reached the narrow porch on the stairwell. Thin starlight filtered through the louvered windows in the ceiling. But, looking from stairway to stairway, I had no idea behind which door the Wardress had hidden. Because there were no connecting stairs among the staggered landings, my only option was to go down. I took the steps two at a time, nearly plunging.

At the bottom I found my Sharer with both hands clenched about the outer stair rail, trembling. Indeed, he seemed about to shake himself apart. I put my hands on his shoulders, and the tremors racking his systems threatened to rack mine, too. Who would fly apart first?

"Go upstairs," I told the Sharer. "Get the hell up there!"

The Wardress called again, her summons hard to pinpoint.

The Sharer could not or would not obey me. I coaxed him, cursed him, goaded him. Nothing availed. The Wardress, calling me, had inadvertently called the Sharer out as my proxy, and he declined to yield to me the role that he'd usurped. The beautifully faired planes of his skull turned to me, bringing with them the stainless-steel rings of his eyes. These parts of his body did not tremble, but they couldn't countermand the agues shaking him. As inhuman and as immovable as they were, his features still managed to convey stark entreaty.

I knelt, felt about his legs, and removed the penlight and the disc from the two pocketlike incisions holding them. Then I stood and used them. "Find Wardress Kefa for me, Sharer." I pointed at the high windows.

And the Sharer floated up from the steps through the mid-interior of the House. In the starlight, rocking a little, he passed through a knot of curving stairs into a space where he suddenly grew brightly visible.

"Which door?" I jabbed the penlight at several different landings around the well. "Show me the one."

My words echoed. The Sharer, legs dangling, inscribed a half-circle, then pointed at a half-hidden doorway. I stalked across the well, found a likely-seeming stairway, and climbed it with no notion of what to do. Wardress Kefa

didn't call out, but the same faint, slurred voices muttered again—the Orhas. A pair of muted female guffaws convinced me of this, and I hesitated on the landing.

"Okay," I told the Sharer, turning him with a wrist movement. "Go home."

He dropped through the torus of a lower set of stairs, found our chamber's porch, and settled upon it like a clumsy puppet. I pocketed the penlight in my gown and knocked on the Orhas' door.

"Enter," Cleva Orha said. "By all means, Sharer Lorca, enter."

Every surface of the room was burnished as if with beeswax. The timbers shone. Whereas in the other chambers I'd seen, nearly all the joists and rafters were rough-hewn, here they were smooth and splinter-free. The scent of sandalwood pervaded the air, and opposite the door a carven screen blocked my view of the stove-bed. A tall wooden lamp illuminated the furnishings and the figures arrayed about its border of light like iconic statues.

"Welcome," Cleirach said. "Your invitation was from the Wardress, however, not us." He wore only silken pantaloons drawn together at the waist with a cord. His right forearm pressed down on Wardress Kefa's throat, restraining her movement without yet cutting off her wind.

His frowzy clonemate, in a gown much like mine, sat cross-legged on a cushion toying with a waxed stiletto. Her eyes gleamed wide, as did her brother's, the doings of too much placenol, too much Wolf Run small-malt, and the Orhas' own meanness. Cleva was drugged and drunk, malicious to a turn. Cleirach didn't appear that far gone, but all he had to do to strangle the Wardress was lift his forearm into her trachea. I felt out of my element, gill-less in a sluice of stinging saltwater.

"Wardress Kefa—"

"She's all right," Cleva told me. "Perfectly all right." She gazed from her right eye alone and barked a deranged-sounding laugh.

"Let the Wardress go," I told Cleirach.

Amazingly, he looked intimidated. "Mr.

Lorca's an anproz," he reminded Cleva. "That letter opener you're cleaning your nails with—it'll mean nothing to him."

"Then let her go, Cleirach. Now."

Cleirach released the Wardress, who, massaging her throat, hurried to the stove-bed. She halted beside the screen and beckoned me over. "Mr. Lorca, please . . . Will you see to him first? I beg you."

"I'm going back to Wolf Run Summit," Cleirach said, slipping on his night jacket. Then he gathered his clothes and left. Cleva stayed on her cushion, her head tilted back as if sipping poison from a chalice. Glancing at her, I went to the Wardress, stepped around the wooden partition, and saw her Sharer.

The Tropeman lying there was slender, almost slight, with a ridge of flesh where a human being has a mouth. His eyes were an organic sort of crystal: uncanny and depthful stones. One of these brandy-colored stones, Cleva's "letter opener" had dislodged from its socket. Although the Orhas had failed to pry it loose, blood streaked the Tropeman's face. These streaks ran down into the bedding under his narrow head, giving him the look of an aborigine in war paint. Lacking external genitalia, his body was spread-eagled atop the quilts so that the burns on his legs and lower abdomen called for notice as plangently as did his face.

"Sweet light, sweet light," the Wardress chanted, now in my arms, clutching me tightly above her beloved, butchered Sharer.

"He's not dead," Cleva insisted. "The rules . . . the rules say not to kill them, and brother and I obey the rules."

"What can I do, Wardress Kefa?" I whispered, holding her.

Slumped against me, she repeated her consoling chant. Fearful that this being with gemstone eyes would die, we still delayed, Wardress Kefa emanating a warmth that I had never believed available to me.

She, I saw, was also a Compassionate Sharer—as much a Sharer as the bleeding Tropeman on the stove-bed or the creature whose electrode-studded body and gleaming death's-head had mocked the efficient mechanical deadness in me: a deadness that, in turning away from Rumai, I had turned into a god. In the face of this realization, my disgust with the Orhas changed into something new: a mode of perception; a means of adapting.

I had an answer, one not easy, but still quite a simple one: I, too, qualified as a Compassionate Sharer. Monster, machine, anproz, the designation no longer mattered. Wherever I might go, I would live forevermore a ward of this woman's House—my fate, inescapable and sure.

The Wardress broke free and knelt beside the Tropeman. She tore a piece of cloth from her tunic. Wiping blood from the Sharer's face, she said, "Downstairs, I heard him calling, Mr. Lorca. Encephalogoi—brain words. I came as quickly as I could. Cleirach tried to stop me. All I could do was shout for you. Then, not even that."

Her hands touched the Sharer's burns, hovered over the wounded eye, moved about with a mysterious somatic knowledge.

"We couldn't get it all the way out," Cleva Orha said, laughing. "It wouldn't come. Cleirach tried and tried."

I found the cloned female's pea jacket, leggings, and tunic. Then I took her by the arm and led her downstairs. As I did so, she reviled me tenderly.

"You," she predicted, "you we'll never get."

She was right. Years passed before I returned to the House of Compassionate Sharers; and, upon learning of their sadistic abuse of a ward of the House, the authorities in Manitou Port denied the Orhas any future access. A Sharer, after all, was an expensive commodity.

But I did return. After going back to Miroste and living with Rumai the remaining forty-two years of her life, I applied to the House as a novitiate. I reside here now.

In fact as well as in metaphor, I have become a Sharer.

My brain cells die, and I can do nothing to stop the depredations of time. But my body mimics that of a younger man, and I move inside it with ease.

Visitors seek comfort from me, as once, against my will, I sought comfort here, and I try to give it—even to those who have only a muddled understanding of what a Sharer does. My battles are not really with these unhappy people, but with the advance columns of my senility (a fact I do not care to admit) and the shock troops of memory, which still functions—remarkably well for one so old.

Wardress Kefa died seventeen years ago, Diderits twenty-two, and Rumai two. Thus do I keep score, nowadays. Death has also carried off the gem-eyed Tropeman and the Sharer who drew the real Dorian Lorca out of the prosthetic rind that he had mistaken for himself.

I intend to stay here longer. I have recently taken a chamber into which the light sifts with a painful white brilliance reminiscent of the sands of Miroste or the snows of Wolf Run Summit. This is all to the good.

Either way, you see, I die at home.

Sporting with the Chid
BARRINGTON J. BAYLEY

Barrington J. Bayley (1937–2008) was an underrated, often fascinating English science fiction writer associated with the New Wave movement of the 1960s and 1970s. Bayley was a frequent contributor to *New Worlds* when it was edited by Michael Moorcock, and the two became good friends. Moorcock later reprinted Bayley in various *New Worlds* paperback anthologies and continued to be a strong advocate for the author. Later, more than twenty of Bayley's stories would appear in the magazine *Interzone*. His work also appeared in the anthologies *Tomorrow's Alternatives* and *An Index of Possibilities*. His approach to writing science fiction has been cited as influential on M. John Harrison, Brian Stableford, Bruce Sterling, Iain M. Banks, and Alastair Reynolds.

Bayley's first book, *The Star Virus*, was followed by more than a dozen other novels, including *Annihilation Factor*, *Collision with Chronos*, *Empire of Two Worlds*, *The Fall of Chronopolis*, *The Great Hydration*, *The Grand Wheel*, *The Pillars of Eternity*, *The Soul of the Robot*, *Star Winds*, and *The Zen Gun*. However, the most lasting impact made by Bayley remains in the realm of short fiction, especially his work from the 1970s. His two collections *The Knights of the Limits* (1978, reprinted in 2001) and *The Seed of Evil* (1979) are remarkable for the wealth of their ideas and their kinetic and often playful style. Some of the stories are fairly experimental in both form and content, while others take core science fiction ideas or tropes and use traditional story structures to turn those ideas or tropes on their head. Some, like "Mutation Planet," "The Exploration of Space," and "The Bees of Knowledge"—inspired by the mathematical writings of C. Davies and W. G. Peck—are so different they could have been written by different people, and yet are equally brilliant.

Of Bayley's work, Bruce Sterling wrote, "[he] reminds one that the power of the British New Wave was . . . due . . . to its sheer visionary intensity." In *Vector*, Chris Evans observed that "Bayley is one of the most inventive and idiosyncratic writers in the genre; his short stories, especially, read like no one else's . . . His plots are fast-paced and action-packed, with the fate of a world or solar system in the balance—but his subject matter extends far beyond the limited horizons of the pulp format."

"Sporting with the Chid," the lead-off story from *The Seed of Evil*, provides a classic example of Bayley's liveliness, playfulness, and ingenuity. Yet Bayley was never frivolous in his expressions of a unique imagination. "Sporting" may be vastly entertaining, but it is also dark and layered, and contains a sting in its tail.

SPORTING WITH THE CHID

Barrington J. Bayley

"But look at him, he's such a mess," Brand protested. "There wouldn't be any point in it."

Ruiger grunted, looking down at what remained of their comrade. It was a mess, all right, a sickening, bloody mess. The scythe-cat they had been hunting had practically sliced Wessel to ribbons. The ruined body still retained a lot of blood, however, due to the heart having stopped at the outset, when the cat had ripped open the rib cage. For that reason, Ruiger had supposed there was still hope.

"We can't just stand here doing nothing," he said. He glanced up the trail along which the cat had fled under the hail of their gunfire. Wessel's own gun lay nearby, wrecked by the first blow of the animal's terrible bladed claw. It infuriated Ruiger to think that the beast had bested them. He wondered why the toxic darts they had fired had failed to take effect. Possibly they had lodged in its very thick dermis and the poisons were spreading slowly. In that case, the cat's corpse should be found within not too great a distance.

"The brain isn't damaged," he observed stubbornly. "Come on, do what I say: freeze him quick, before it starts to degenerate." He was a broad-set man with a rugged face; he spoke with traces of a clipped, hard-toned accent Brand had never yet been able to identify.

Brand hesitated, then submitted to the other's more positive personality. He moved closer to the dead Wessel, nerving himself against the raw, nauseating smell of blood and flesh. Kneeling, he opened the medical kit and took out a blue cylinder. From the cylinder there flowed a lavender mist which settled over the body and then seemed to fly into it, to be absorbed by it like water into a sponge.

"You can't freeze somebody without special equipment," he told Ruiger. "Frozen water crystallises and ruptures all the body cells. This stuff will keep him fresh, but it's only good for about twelve hours. It holds the tissues in a gelid suspension so chemical processes don't take place."

"He's not frozen?"

"No." Brand straightened. "You realise what this means? The nearest fully equipped hospital is six weeks away. Even then, I don't suppose the surgeons could do much. He'd be crippled for life, probably paralysed if he lived at all. Maybe he wouldn't like that."

Before replying Ruiger glanced at the sky, as if summing up interstellar distances. "What about the Chid camp on the other side of the continent? You know their reputation."

Brand snapped shut the medical case with an angry gesture. "Are you crazy? You know damned well we can't go messing with the Chid."

"Shut up and help me get him on the sled." They tackled the unpleasant job in silence. It should have been the scythe-cat the sled was carrying, Ruiger thought, but he fought down an urge to go after the animal and make sure it was dead. A more compelling urge had come over him, for he was a man who hated to admit defeat if there remained even the possibility of action, and Wessel had been a good comrade.

The sled floated a foot or two above the coarse broad-bladed grass that covered most of the planet's dry surface. As they trudged back to the ship Ruiger looked at the sky again. The sun lay well below the horizon, but there was no such thing as real night—this was the N4 star cluster, where suns were packed so thick as to turn even midnight into what would have been a mellow autumn evening on Earth. The multicoloured blaze never faded; it filled the sky not only at night but throughout the day, augmenting the light of the somewhat pale sun.

The cluster teemed, if such a vast region could be said to teem, with freelance prospectors looking for anything that, by reason of rarity or novelty, would command a high price back in civilisation. Exotic furs and hides, unknown gems, outlandish chemicals and minerals, drugs with unexpected properties—these days, rarity was the name of the game. If it was new, preferably unique, and had a use, then it was valuable. The fur of the scythe-cat, for example, would grace the wardrobes of no more than a dozen exorbitantly wealthy women.

Not all the prospectors were human. The cluster had few sentient races of its own, but it had attracted the attentions of scores of others, lured by its wealth or else engaged on less identifiable business. As a rule the various species prudently ignored one another, a practice with which Ruiger would normally have concurred wholeheartedly. With some of the alien races known to mankind—so numerous that only the most cursory examination had been made of most of them—one could communicate with ease. But with others one had to be cautious.

And there were yet others with habits and attitudes so inexplicable by human standards that the central government had placed a strict prohibition on any kind of intercourse with them whatsoever.

Such a species was the Chid.

Back at the ship, Ruiger took out the official government handbook on aliens. Like many others, the entry on the Chid was subheaded: *Absolutely No Contact in Any Circumstances.* The information offered supplied very little by way of explanation, but he carefully read such as there was. Following the location of the Chid star, and a description of the extent of Chid influence, the sociological information was scant, apparently depending on the word of some lone-wolf explorer who had visited the home planet and later had volunteered an account of his experiences to the Department of Alien Affairs. Ruiger knew, however, that subsequent encounters between Chid and humans had reinforced the impression of them as a wayward and difficult people.

"An extraordinary feature of the Chid," he read, "is their aptitude for the medical sciences. Among them advanced surgery is a household skill; even the most highly trained Earth surgeon would find himself outclassed by the average Chid, who traditionally prides himself on his surgical ability, much as a human will pride himself on being able to repair his own auto. That Chid surgical skill is so universal is probably because it was the first technique to be developed on the Chid world, predating even the discovery of fire.

"Surgery's prominent place in Chid lore, even from primitive times, is attested by the following incident from the saga of the ancient champion Gathor. On finding himself trapped in a country surrounded by enemies, he ordered his followers to dissect him, and to smuggle him out in pieces, 'none of them larger than a single finger-joint.' After being reassembled, Gathor went on to free his people from slavery.

"The Chid have a love of sports and games, and are addicted to gambling. Otherwise there is little in the Chid mind that renders it suitable for human company. On the contrary, Chid mental processes are so foreign to human mentality as to present considerable danger. Anyone finding himself in the presence of a Chid should on no account attempt to have dealings with it, since if he does he will almost certainly misunderstand its intentions. Instead, he should at once remove himself from the vicinity of the Chid."

Slowly, Ruiger put away the handbook.

Outside, he found Brand sitting gazing into the night sky. "We'll go to the Chid," he said with finality.

Brand stirred. "You realise the risks we'll be taking?"

Ruiger nodded. "Intercourse with prohibited aliens. A twenty-thousand-labour-credit fine, or five years in a work prison. Or both." The government took such matters seriously.

"I was thinking less of that," Brand said, "than of the Chid themselves. Those laws are for our own protection. Maybe we'd be getting into something we can't get out of."

Ruiger's voice was blunt and obstinate. "My ancestors were Boers," he said. "They were people who learned to hang on to life, no matter what it costs. That's my outlook, too. Chances are worth taking where it's a matter of living or not living."

He took a last look round the clearing, feeling a lingering regret that he had not found time to go after the scythe-cat. "No sense hanging about here. Let's get moving."

"The way I see it," Ruiger said as they flew over the tawny-coloured continent, "creatures with such a knowledge of surgery can't be all that bad. They can mend the sick and injured— that's not something *I* find incomprehensible. Maybe the government's too quick to write the no-go sign."

Brand didn't answer. Soon the Chid camp came in sight. It was on the edge of a level plain, perched near a two-hundred-foot cliff that fell away to sharp rocks and a boiling sea. It had only three features: a pentagonal hut that seemed to be roofed with local ferns; the Chid ship, which resembled nothing so much as an Earth street tram; and a small, dark wood which occupied an oval-shaped depression in the ground. Ruiger did not think the wood was indigenous. Probably, he thought, the Chid had set it up as a garden or a park, using plants and trees from their own world.

They set down on what could roughly be interpreted as the perimeter of the camp. For some time they sat together in the control cabin, saying nothing, watching the site through the viewscreens. At first there was no sign of life. After about half an hour, two tall Chid emerged from the hut and strolled to the wood, with not a single glance at the Earth ship nearby.

Anxiously Ruiger and Brand watched. At length the Chid reappeared, brushing aside foliage and coming into the light of day from the dank depths of the wood. Unconcernedly they ambled back to the fern-covered hut.

"It seems they spend their time in the hut, not in the ship," Brand observed.

"Unless there are more of them in the ship."

"It's not very big. It couldn't carry many."

"Yes, that's right." Ruiger gnawed his knuckles. "They're ignoring us."

"Wise of them. We'd do the same if they landed near us. We might even move away. They haven't done that."

"Well, the first move's up to us." Ruiger rose, and looked at Brand. Both men felt nervousness make a sick ache in their stomachs. "Let's go out there and see what they'll do for us."

They bolstered their sidearms inside their shirts so that to outward appearances they were unarmed. Wessel's jellified body still lay on the sled. They eased it out of the port, and set off across the short stretch of savannah-like grass to the Chid hut.

From outside the hut looked primitive and could as well have been erected by savages. They stopped a few feet from the door, which like the walls was made of a frame of branches from a local tree interwoven with ferns.

He decided it was probably an advantage that they would have to converse by means of gestures. When only the simplest and most obvious wants could be made known there was less room for misunderstanding.

He hooked his thumbs in his belt and called out. "Hello! Hello!"

Again: "Hello! We are Earthmen!"

The door opened, swinging inwards. The interior was dim. Ruiger hesitated. Then, his throat dry, he stepped inside, followed by Brand, who guided the sled before him. "We are Earthmen," he repeated, feeling slightly ridiculous. "We have trouble. We need your help."

Anything else he might have said was cut off as he absorbed the scene within. The two Chid he had seen earlier swivelled their eyes to look at him. One lolled on a couch, but in such a manner as to seem like a corpse that had been carelessly thrown there, limbs flung apart in disarray, head hanging down and almost touching the beaten earth floor. The other was leaning forward half upright, dangling limply from a double sling into which his arms were thrust, and which was suspended from the roof rafters. His head lolled forward, his legs trailed behind.

Both postures looked bizarrely uncomfortable. Ruiger supposed, however, that the Chid were simply relaxing.

Somewhat larger of frame than a human, they had a lank, loose appearance about them. Their skin was grey, with undertones of green and buff orange. For clothing they wore a simple garment consisting of short trousers combined with a bib held in place by straps going over the shoulders. As with many androform species, their nonhuman faces were apt to seem caricatures of a particular human expression—in the Chid instance, an idiotic, chuckling gormlessness. It was important, Ruiger knew, not to be influenced by this doubtlessly totally wrong impression.

Unrecognisable utensils lay scattered and jumbled about the floor, and Ruiger's gaze went to the rest of the hut. He shuddered. The walls resembled the racks of some prehistoric butcher's shop, hung with pieces of raw flesh—limbs, entrails, various internal organs, and other organic components and substances he could not identify, from a variety of creatures unknown to him. The Chid clearly had botanic interests, too. Items of vegetable origin accompanied the purely animal ones, plants, tree branches, cuttings, fruit, strips of fibre, and so forth. A moist, slightly rotten smell hung on the air, though whether from the grisly array or from the Chid themselves he could not say.

Unable to find a clear space on the floor, Brand left the sled floating. Ruiger pointed to the body. He hoped the purpose of their visit was self-evident.

"This is our comrade. He has been badly injured. We came to ask if you can heal him."

The Chid in the sling swayed slightly from side to side. "*Werry-werry-werry-werry . . . ,*" he said, or that was what it sounded like to Ruiger. But then he broke off, and to the Earthmen's great surprise spoke in almost perfect English.

"Visitors come to us from off the vast plain! You are here to sport with us, perhaps?"

"We came to ask for your help," Ruiger replied. Again he pointed to the sled. "Our friend was attacked by a scythe-cat—a dangerous animal that's found on this continent."

"For the time being I've suspended his organic processes with a gelid solution," Brand interrupted. "But when it wears off he'll be dead, unless the damage can be made good first."

"Chid are famed for their surgical skill," Ruiger added.

The Chid withdrew his arms from the sling and approached the sled with an ambling gait, kicking aside metal artifacts that lay on the floor. Automatically Ruiger drew back. The strangeness of the scene made him fearful. It was hard to believe that these people were as advanced as they were supposed to be.

Bending over the sled, the Chid prodded Wessel's inert form with a long finger. He chortled: a brassy sound like the braying of a cornet.

"Can you help him?" Ruiger enquired.

"Oh yes. Quite easy. Simple slicing. Nerves, muscles, blood vessels, lymph channels, skin—you won't even know where the joins are."

A feeling of relief flooded through the two men. "Then you'll operate?" Ruiger pressed.

Straightening, the Chid stared directly at him. His eyes, now that Ruiger saw them close up, were horrible, like boiled eggs. "I have heard it said that Earthmen can leave their bodies and move about without them. Is it true?"

"No," said Ruiger. It took him a moment to realise what the Chid was talking about. "You mean their souls can leave their bodies. It's not true, though. It's only religious belief. You know what religion is? Just a story."

"How wonderful, to be able to leave one's body and move about without it!" The Chid seemed to reflect. "Are you here for sport?" he asked suddenly. "Do you like races?"

"We are only interested in helping our friend get better."

"Oh, but you should game with us."

"After our friend is better," Ruiger said slowly, "we'll do anything you like."

"Excellent, excellent!" The Chid chortled again, much louder than before, a shrill, unnerving sound.

"Can we rely on you?" Ruiger pressed. "How long will it take?"

"Not long, not long. Leave him with us."

"May we stay to watch?"

"No, no!" The Chid seemed indignant. "It is not seemly. You are our guests. Depart!"

"All right," Ruiger said. "When shall we come back?"

"We will send him out when he is ready. Tomorrow morning, perhaps."

"Good." Ruiger stood uncertainly. He was eager to get out of the hut, but somehow reluctant to leave.

The Chid on the couch had completely ignored them, apart from one glance when they first entered. He still lay motionless, as if dead.

"Until tomorrow, then."

"Until tomorrow."

They withdrew, stiffly and awkwardly. To human sensibilities the Chid seemed to lack stability, Ruiger decided. They gave a neurotic, erratic, disconcerting impression. But it was probably a false impression, like that given by their idiot faces.

Back in the ship, Ruiger said: "Well, so far it went all right. If that Chid keeps his promise we've got nothing to worry about."

"But this talk about sports and games," Brand said anxiously. "What do they expect of us?"

"Never mind about that. As soon as we get Wessel back, and he's all right, we simply take off."

"We'll owe them. They might try to stop us."

"We've got guns."

"Yeah . . . you know, I guess we're all right, but what about Wessel? That hut doesn't look a lot like an operating theatre to me. Somehow I find it hard to believe they can do anything."

"They don't work the way we do. But everybody knows they can accomplish miracles, almost. You'll see. Anyway, it gives Wessel a chance. He didn't have one before."

They fell silent.

After a while Ruiger became restless. In crossing the continent they had backtracked on the sun; now it was evening again, and there were about eight hours to wait until dawn. Ruiger didn't feel like sleeping. He suggested they take a walk.

After some hesitation Brand agreed. Once outside, they strolled towards the Chid's wood, both of them curious to see what lay inside it. They skirted the depression where it grew, aware that the Chid could be watching and might not like strangers entering their private garden, if such it was.

There was little doubt that the wood was alien to the planet. It was quite unlike the open bush that covered most of the continent. Local flora and fauna were characterised by a quality of brashness, and their colours were light, all tawny, orange, and yellow, but this seemed dark and oppressive, huddled in on itself, and unnaturally silent and still. The bark of the trees was slick, olive-green in colour, and glistened, while the foliage was almost black.

Out of sight of the Chid hut, Ruiger parted some shoulder-high vegetation that screened the interior of the wood from view, and stepped between the slender tree trunks.

Quietly and cautiously, they sauntered a few yards into the wood. The light was suffusive and dim, filtering through the tree cover that seemed to press in overhead to create a totally enclosed little environment. Though fairly close-packed, the interior was less dense than the perimeter, which Ruiger began to think of as a barrier or skin. There was the same moist, rotting odour he had noticed in the Chid hut.

The air was humid and surprisingly hot; presumably the wood trapped heat in some way, or else was warmed artificially.

The ground, sloping down towards the centre, was carpeted with a kind of moss, or slime, which felt unpleasant underfoot. Ruiger was struck by the dead hush of the place. Not a leaf moved; there was not the merest breath of a breeze. They crept on, descending the slope into the depths of the wood, and before long began to notice a change in the nature of the vegetation. Besides the slender trees other, less familiar plants flourished. Luxurious growths with broad, drooping leaves that dripped a yellow syrup. Python-like creepers that intertwined with the upper tree branches and pulsed slightly. Bilious parasites, like clusters of giant grapes or cancerous excrescences, that clung and tumbled down the squamous trunks, sometimes engulfing entire trees.

The wood was coming more to resemble a lush, miniature, alien jungle. Also, it was no longer still. There were sounds in it—not the rustle of leaves or the sigh of branches, but obscene little slurping and lapping sounds. Ruiger stopped, startled, as the scum carpet suddenly surged into motion just ahead of him. From it there emerged what looked like a pinkish-grey tangle of entrails, which swarmed quickly up a nearby tree and began to wrestle with the parasitic growth hanging there. The parasite apparently had a gelid consistency; the two shook and shivered like horrid jelly.

"Look," Brand whispered.

Ruiger followed his gaze. A small creature was creeping through some undergrowth that sprouted near the base of a tree. It looked for all the world like the uncovered brain of a medium-sized mammal such as a dog or a tiger, complete with trailing spinal stem.

They watched it until it disappeared from sight. A few yards further on, they came to a clearing. It was occupied by a single tree—not one of the trees that made up the bulk of the wood, but a fat, pear-shaped trunk that contracted rhythmically like a beating heart. It was surmounted by a crown from which spread a mesh of fine twigs. As they entered the clearing this mesh suddenly released a spray of red droplets onto them.

Quickly they moved away. Ruiger examined the drops that had fallen on his tunic, head, and hands. The liquid was sticky, like blood, or bile.

Distastefully they wiped the stuff off their exposed skin.

"I've seen enough," said Brand. "Let's get out."

"Wait," Ruiger insisted. "We might as well go all the way."

They were approaching the bottom of the wood now, and Ruiger guessed there might be something special there. The rich, foetid smell was becoming so strong that both men nearly gagged, but a few yards further on they broke through a thicket of clammy-feeling tendrils, and there it was.

The surrounding trees leaned over it protectively, spreading their branches to form a complete canopy above it: a little lake of blood. Ruiger was sure the stuff was blood: it looked like it and smelled like it, though with not quite the same smell as human blood. Dozens of small creatures were gathered on the shores of the pool to drink: segmented creatures the size of lobsters, creatures like the brain-animal they had seen already, creatures that consisted of clusters of tubes, resembling assemblies of veins and arteries. The forest, too, put out hoses of its own into the pool, snaking them down from the trees and across the bushes.

Ruiger and Brand stared in fascination. Was this, Ruiger wondered, a pleasant little paradise to the Chid mind? He took his eyes from the gleaming crimson surface of the lake. The wood, with its covering of slime, its slick trees, its gibbous growths and pulsing python pipes that seemed neither animal nor vegetable, no longer looked to him like a wood in the Earthly sense. Its totally enclosed, self-absorbed nature put him in mind of what it might be like inside his own body.

He grunted, and nudged Brand. "Let's go." Slowly they made their way up the bowl-shaped slope, towards the open starlight.

Minutes after they returned to the ship, the first of the Chid gifts arrived.

They did not know, at the time, that it was meant to be a gift, and if they had known, they still wouldn't have known what they were supposed to do with it. It was an animal that came bounding from the Chid hut to prance about in front of the Earthmen's ship. It was vaguely doglike and about the size of a Great Dane, with hairless yellow skin.

Ruiger focused the external scanner on it, magnifying the image. There were slits in the animal's body; as it moved, these opened, revealing its internal organs.

Brand was nauseated. He turned away.

For a while the creature snuffled about the ship's port, and leaped this way and that. "I didn't see this beast in the Chid hut," Brand remarked.

"Perhaps they made it." Ruiger watched until the animal apparently wearied of what it was doing and loped back the way it had come, disappearing inside the hut.

"I'm tired," Ruiger said. "I'd like to get some sleep."

"Okay."

But Brand himself could not sleep. He felt restless and uneasy. Nervously he settled down with a full percolator of coffee and kept his eye on the external viewer.

From time to time other animals left the hut and approached the ship. None were particularly alien looking, except, that was, that they were all apt to expose their innards to view as they moved. One vaguely resembled a pig, another a hairless llama, another a kangaroo. Were they all, perhaps, one animal, made over and over from the same bits and pieces?

The Chid had better not fix Wessel up that way, Brand thought aggressively. He wondered if he and Ruiger were expected to respond to these sorties. But when one didn't know, it was safer to do nothing.

Steadily the stars, illuminating the landscape with shadowless light, moved across the sky. A short time after the pale sun had risen, Ruiger came stumbling back into the room.

"Anything happen?"

Brand gave him some coffee and told him about the animals. Ruiger sat down, staring at the viewscreen and sipping from his cup.

By now Brand felt tired himself, but his nervousness had not decreased. "You think it will be all right?" he asked Brand anxiously.

"Sure it will be all right," Ruiger said gruffly. "Don't be put off by that wood. Probably the whole Chid planet is like that."

It was the first time either of them had mentioned the wood. "Listen," Brand said, "I've been thinking about those animals they keep sending—"

Ruiger gave a shout. On the screen, Wessel had appeared in the open door of the Chid hut. He stood there uncertainly, and then took a step forward.

"There he is!" Ruiger crowed. "They've delivered the goods!"

He jumped to his feet and swept from the room. Brand followed him down to the port and out onto the coarse grass. Wessel was walking towards them. But it was not his usual walk. He plodded rather than strode, moving leadenly and awkwardly, his arms hanging loose, his face slack.

Nevertheless they both loped out to meet him. And then, as they came closer, the grin on Ruiger's face froze. Wessel's eye sockets were empty. The eyelids framed nothing; even the orbital bones had been removed. And Brand now realised that this eyeless Wessel wasn't even walking towards the ship. He was making for the cliff a short distance away.

"Wessel," he called softly. And then something else caught his attention. Crawling some yards behind Wessel there came a rounded greyish object no larger than his boot. The thing had a wrinkled, convoluted surface, with a deep crevice running down its back, and glistened as if encased in a transparent jelly.

The creature moved after the manner of a snail, on a single splayed podium. It followed after Wessel with every appearance of effort, just managing to keep up with his erratic pace. Brand and Ruiger watched the procession dumbly. The crawling creature's front end supported a pair of white balls, their whiteness broken by neat circles of colour. These white balls were obviously human eyes, the same eyes that were missing from Wessel's eye sockets. The grey mass, however improbable it seemed logically, was without doubt Wessel's own brain, alive but without a body, given its own means of locomotion.

Suddenly the decerebrated body stumbled and fell. The brain seemed avid for the body. Before the body could rise it had caught up with it and clambered onto a leg. When the body started to walk again the brain clung to it like a leech, and began to climb.

The body lurched towards the cliff; the brain ascended painfully. Its rate of progress was impressive. It negotiated the hips, climbed up the back, and reached a shoulder, momentarily perching there. Then, as if hinged somehow, the back of Wessel's head opened, the two halves coming apart and revealing an empty cavern. Into this empty skull the brain nosed its way, like a hermit crab edging into a discarded shell or a fat grey rat disappearing down a hole, and the head closed up behind it.

The Wessel body abruptly stopped walking. A shudder passed through it. Then it stood motionless, facing the sea.

Brand and Ruiger glanced at one another.

"Christ!" Ruiger said hoarsely.

"What shall we do?"

Gingerly, continuing to glance at one another for support, they approached Wessel.

Wessel's eyes were now in place and peered from their sockets, somewhat bloodshot. He might have been taken for normal, except that he seemed very, very dazed.

Angrily Ruiger unholstered his pistol and glared towards the Chid hut. "Those alien bastards aren't getting away with this," he said. "They're going to put this right."

"Wait a minute," said Brand, holding up his hand. He turned to Wessel. "Wessel," he said quietly, "can you hear me?"

Wessel blinked. "Sure," he said.

"How long have you been conscious?"

No answer.

"Can you move?"

"Sure." Wessel turned round and took a step towards them. Ruiger stumbled back, feeling that he was in the presence of something unclean. Brand, however, stood his ground.

"Can you make it back to the ship?" he asked.

"I think so."

"Then let's walk."

Stepping more naturally than before, Wessel accompanied Brand. Slowly they walked towards the gleaming shape of the starship.

Ruiger glowered again at the Chid hut. Then, bolstering his pistol, he followed.

Inside, they sat Wessel down in the living quarters. He sat passively, not volunteering anything, not looking at anything in particular.

Brand swallowed. "Do you remember being out of your body?" he asked.

"Yes."

"What was it like?"

Wessel answered in a dull monotone. "All right."

"Is that all you can say about it?"

Wessel was silent.

"Would you like anything to eat or drink?"

"No."

"You *do* recognise us, don't you?"

"Sure I do."

Brand looked worriedly at Ruiger, then tossed his head, indicating the door.

Leaving Wessel, they withdrew to the control cabin. "Well, I don't know," Brand said. "Perhaps he's going to be all right."

"All *right*!" Ruiger was incredulous, his face red with anger. "Christ, just *look* at what's happened!"

"He's dazed right now. But the brain has already knitted itself to the body. It's in complete control. Did you notice?—no scar, no seam. Fantastic."

"It's hideous, grotesque, perverted—" Ruiger slumped. "I don't get you. You're actually taking it in your stride."

"We *were* warned about the Chid," Brand pointed out. "Their ways aren't our ways. Perhaps to them this sort of thing is some little joke, without any malicious intent. And after all, Wessel *is* in one piece now. He's whole, mended."

Ruiger sighed. He seemed defeated. "If you say so. Me, I can't even believe what I've seen. It's not possible."

"You mean you can't accept that a brain could lead a freelance existence outside its body?"

Ruiger nodded.

"That isn't really so very extraordinary. I've seen a brain kept alive in a hospital on Earth, in a glass tank."

"Yes, but that's in hospital conditions, with every kind of backup. Here . . ."

"Here," said Brand, smiling crookedly, "it's done by two aliens in a straw hut, surrounded by dirt and garbage. And the brain actually crawls about."

"That's what gets me. Maybe it isn't Wessel's brain at all. Maybe the Chid are tricking us."

"I think it's Wessel all right. And I think we've got to accept the strangeness of it. The Chid don't need a hospital or sterile conditions because they've solved all kinds of technical problems we haven't. As for a brain that can move—a few simple muscles, an arrangement to keep it oxygenated—it's probably not as hard as it sounds, once you're crazy enough to want to do it." He paused reflectively. "You know, I don't think the Chid view the body as a unit the same way we do. That wood we went into—I got the idea there were brains, stomachs, digestive systems, all kinds of parts moving about on their own. It's as if the Chid like giving bodily organs autonomy."

"Part-animals," Ruiger grunted. "Sick, isn't it?"

"To *us* it is."

There was a long silence between them. Finally Ruiger said: "Well, what do we do?"

"Our safest move would probably be to take off right away. But I think we ought to wait for a while to see if Wessel improves. He's probably suffering from postoperative shock. What I'm hoping is that he wasn't really conscious while he was out of his body. Try to imagine that."

"I absolutely won't hear of our taking off until he shows signs of recovery."

"We shouldn't leave it too late. It won't be long before the Chid come to collect their side of the bargain. After all, they *have* saved his life. Our own people can probably deal with any future problems."

"Oh, no." Ruiger tapped his gun. "If the Chid have done us wrong, they're going to be taken care of."

"Let's hope we can take off by sunset," Brand said.

That afternoon, Wessel came out of his skull again.

It happened right in front of Brand, who had been sitting with Wessel to keep an eye on him. Wessel had spent most of his time staring placidly at the wall, and neither of them had spoken all afternoon.

Then his head opened, at the front end this time, and without any warning his face split down the front. Within, the brain was revealed like a lurking animal, eyes attached, still with its protective coating of gelatinous substance. Without delay its podium got a grip on Wessel's chin, and it began to clamber out, dripping a pale pink fluid.

Ruiger came at a run as Brand yelled. As he entered the room the brain seemed to realise for the first time that it was being observed. Its eyes swivelled; it backtracked, retreating guiltily into its bone cave. The face closed up; the eyes disappeared momentarily, then joggled themselves into their sockets.

Wessel resumed staring woodenly at the wall, ignoring his two erstwhile friends. There was not the slightest trace of a join where his face had opened.

Brand stood stupefied. *"Well?"* Ruiger rasped, *"you still think he's all right?"*

He went to the arms cupboard and got two dart rifles. "We're paying a second visit," he said curtly, handing a rifle to Brand. "This time we'll stay and watch the operation. Let's see how tricky those aliens are at the point of a gun."

Brand followed blindly. Wessel, too, seemed to have no will to resist or argue. When ordered to do so he went with them out of the ship and walked across the grass to the Chid hut.

As soon as they reached it Ruiger kicked the door open, and barged in.

The smell of rottenness invaded their nostrils. The interior was exactly as they had first seen it: one Chid lay sprawled on the couch, while the other lolled in the double sling. Only the latter reacted to the intrusion, raising his head to peer at Ruiger.

"Our friends have returned!" he chortled. "They have arrived to give us our promised sport!"

The Chid on the couch replied with the slightest trace of an acid-sounding accent. "Yes," he said, "but it was not polite of them to spurn our parts offering."

Brand and Wessel entered behind Ruiger. Ruiger spoke thickly, holding his rifle at the ready.

"You have misused our friend terribly. His brain is not fixed in his body!"

The Chid turned his eyes to the roof. "Ah, to be able to leave one's body! It is every Earthman's desire—that is what I learn in Earth religion."

"You don't understand—"

Ruiger broke off as the Chid disengaged himself from his slings. The Chid's big frame seemed awkward, yet somehow commanding, in the cramped, confined hut. He reached out to unhook what looked like a golfer's carrying case, complete with shoulder strap, from the wall. The case contained numerous metal tools, many of which bore gleaming blades.

With a snakelike motion the second Chid came off the couch and stretched himself. "Shall we take umbrage at the breach in their good manners?"

"No. We should make allowance for their alienness. That said, we must of course recompense ourselves for the insult. Shall we arrange a brain-race? It will do our guests no harm, and provide us with welcome sport. How will you wager?"

"I bet this one to win," the second Chid said, pointing to Ruiger.

The other laughed. "I bet that neither of them will make it."

An urgent feeling of danger seized Ruiger. He tried to speak, but could not. He tried to shoot the nearest Chid with his rifle, but could not. He was completely immobilised. The two Chid towered over him, inspecting him with their boiled-egg eyes. Their exchange continued, apparently with a discussion of stakes and odds. Then they reached for their surgical tools.

What happened next was of such a nature that Ruiger's mind was unable to apply any appropriate feelings to it. At first it was like being a babe in the hands of ultimately powerful adults, and the strangeness of it made all his perceptions hazy. He felt no pain, not even when the Chid, using a simple scalpel, cut his skull and face down the middle, bisecting his nose in the process, and prised apart the two halves. The minute his brain was levered out of place, however, he immediately ceased to feel that he was a human being possessing arms, legs, or a torso. Eyes still functioning, he emerged from the sawn-open skull as a different creature altogether. He was a rounded grey lump, a cleft down his back, a sort of armadillo's tail at his rear.

After that there was a short period of unconsciousness. When Ruiger came round again, his transformation was complete.

It was a little like being a snail. He could move about on the podium on which he squatted. He was covered with a gelatinous layer which protected his vulnerable tissue. And he could see. But he could not, of course, hear, or feel, or smell. The podium did, however, support other small organs which comprised a partial life-support. He could breathe and, after a fashion, feed, though on somewhat specialised food.

He had been put down outside the Chid hut, amid the coarse broad-bladed grass. Not far from him he saw another part-animal like himself. He knew it was Brand. And ahead, already striding away towards the cliff's edge by means of vestigial motor functions, were two human bodies. One was Brand's. The other was his.

Ruiger experienced a terrible hunger for the body that went walking away from him. He knew that he could possess it again, but to do so he must catch up with it before it fell over the cliff, and so he set off, sliding over the uneven ground with all his puny strength.

This, he realised, was the Chid's brain-race. The Chid had placed bets on whether he or Brand, who also was straining not far away, would recover his body first. Already Ruiger was gaining on his body. If it should fall but once, he told himself, he would be able to catch up with it.

But the minutes passed and the body did not fall. Instead, Ruiger himself became entangled in a clump of grass. By the time he freed himself it was far too late. Desperately he lunged forward, only to see his body, striated by blades of grass, walk straight over the edge of the cliff, to fall on the rocks and the sea below.

It was gone. His body was gone. Numb with failure, Ruiger turned round. The Brand body, too, had disappeared, and of the Brand brain there was no sign. He made out the Chid hut. Near it was Wessel, standing casually, his brain out of his skull again and clinging to the side of his neck like an enormous slug. Beyond that, he dimly saw the Chid spaceship, not far from the little wood.

He saw his own spaceship, too, but that was no use to him now. Ruiger's gaze settled on the wood. The dark patch, the motionless copse, was like an island amid the tawny bush. Curious . . . he was already forgetting what it was like to have a body. . . . The burning hunger faded, his humanity receded from him as if he had lost it not minutes ago, but decades ago, and the little wood was no longer gruesome or grotesque. It was a lush, gentle, sheltering place to part-animals like himself. It protected and nurtured them. In the wood he could live— after a fashion. And life, he remembered dimly, was worth hanging on to at any cost.

The sun and stars were burning down on him. He was naked and helpless here in the open. He could not live here. Steadily, pushing his way through the stiff grass, thinking of the welcoming pool of blood, of the enclosing black foliage, of the pulsing warmth, he crawled towards the still, dark hollow.

Sandkings

GEORGE R. R. MARTIN

George R. R. Martin (1948–) is a popular US writer who has written influential horror and science fiction but is widely known for his fantasy series *A Song of Ice and Fire*, an international bestseller. Martin's work has become only more wildly popular since HBO launched its series based on his fantasy novels, *Game of Thrones*. *Time* has called Martin "the American Tolkien," and the magazine included him in the 2011 "Time 100," a list of the "most influential people in the world." He has won multiple Hugo and Nebula Awards, as well as a Bram Stoker Award and a World Fantasy Award. In 2012, Martin won the World Fantasy Award for Life Achievement.

Martin has over the course of his career been among the most versatile of writers, crafting classics in several genres. To name just two of his best works, "Nightflyers" (1980) is a marvel of science fiction horror, and "The Pear-Shaped Man" (1987) is a disturbing modern weird tale. The impressive entirety of his short fiction output, across several decades, can be found in the volume *Dreamsongs* (2003). Although Martin often writes fantasy or horror, a number of his earlier works are science fiction tales occurring in a milieu known as "the Thousand Worlds" or "the Manrealm."

His 1979 story "Sandkings," published in *Omni*, won both the Hugo and Nebula Awards, the only one of his stories to do so. Martin was inspired to write "Sandkings" after watching horror movies with a friend who had a tank of piranhas. Martin's friend would throw goldfish into the tank between films "like a weird intermission." Originally Martin believed "Sandkings" would be the start of a series of stories. It was adapted for an episode of *The Outer Limits* (1995). It has been parodied by *The Simpsons*, *Futurama*, and *South Park*. A British rock band from the late eighties and early nineties also used "Sandkings" as their name. Despite its appropriation by pop culture, "Sandkings" remains a powerful tale of science fiction horror, one with political overtones.

SANDKINGS

George R. R. Martin

Simon Kress lived alone in a sprawling manor house among the dry, rocky hills fifty kilometers from the city. So, when he was called away unexpectedly on business, he had no neighbors he could conveniently impose on to take his pets. The carrion hawk was no problem; it roosted in the unused belfry and customarily fed itself anyway. The shambler Kress simply shooed outside and left to fend for itself; the little monster would gorge on slugs and birds and rockjocks. But the fish tank, stocked with genuine Earth piranha, posed a difficulty. Kress finally just threw a haunch of beef into the huge tank. The piranha could always eat each other if he were detained longer than expected. They'd done it before. It amused him.

Unfortunately, he was detained *much* longer than expected this time. When he finally returned, all the fish were dead. So was the carrion hawk. The shambler had climbed up to the belfry and eaten it. Simon Kress was vexed.

The next day he flew his skimmer to Asgard, a journey of some two hundred kilometers. Asgard was Baldur's largest city and boasted the oldest and largest starport as well. Kress liked to impress his friends with animals that were unusual, entertaining, and expensive; Asgard was the place to buy them.

This time, though, he had poor luck. Xenopets had closed its doors, t'Etherane the Petseller tried to foist another carrion hawk off on him, and Strange Waters offered nothing more exotic than piranha, glow-sharks, and spider squids. Kress had had all those; he wanted something new.

Near dusk, he found himself walking down the Rainbow Boulevard, looking for places he had not patronized before. So close to the star-pon, the street was lined by importers' marts. The big corporate emporiums had impressive long windows, where rare and costly alien artifacts reposed on felt cushions against dark drapes that made the interiors of the stores a mystery. Between them were the junk shops—narrow, nasty little places whose display areas were crammed with all manner of offworld bric-a-brac. Kress tried both kinds of shop, with equal dissatisfaction.

Then he came across a store that was different.

It was quite close to the port. Kress had never been there before. The shop occupied a small, single-story building of moderate size, set between a euphoria bar and a temple-brothel of the Secret Sisterhood. Down this far, the Rainbow Boulevard grew tacky. The shop itself was unusual. Arresting.

The windows were full of mist; now a pale red, now the gray of true fog, now sparkling and golden. The mist swirled and eddied and glowed faintly from within. Kress glimpsed objects in the window—machines, pieces of art, other things he could not recognize—but he could not get a good look at any of them. The mists flowed sensuously around them, displaying a bit of first one thing and then another, then cloaking all. It was intriguing.

As he watched, the mist began to form letters. One word at a time. Kress stood and read:

WO. AND. SHADE. IMPORTERS.
ARTIFACTS. ART. LIFE-FORMS.
AND. MISC.

The letters stopped. Through the fog, Kress saw something moving. That was enough for him, that and the word *life-forms* in their advertisement. He swept his walking cloak over his shoulder and entered the store.

Inside, Kress felt disoriented. The interior seemed vast, much larger than he would have guessed from the relatively modest frontage. It was dimly lit, peaceful. The ceiling was a starscape, complete with spiral nebulae, very dark and realistic, very nice. The counters all shone faintly, the better to display the merchandise within. The aisles were carpeted with ground fog. In places, it came almost to his knees and swirled about his feet as he walked.

"Can I help you?"

She seemed almost to have risen from the fog. Tall and gaunt and pale, she wore a practical gray jumpsuit and a strange little cap that rested well back on her head.

"Are you Wo or Shade?" Kress asked. "Or only sales help?"

"Jala Wo, ready to serve you," she replied. "Shade does not see customers. We have no sales help."

"You have quite a large establishment," Kress said. "Odd that I have never heard of you before."

"We have only just opened this shop on Baldur," the woman said. "We have franchises on a number of other worlds, however. What can I sell you? Art, perhaps? You have the look of a collector. We have some fine Nor T'alush crystal carvings."

"No," Simon Kress said. "I own all the crystal carvings I desire. I came to see about a pet."

"A life-form?"

"Yes."

"Alien?"

"Of course."

"We have a mimic in stock. From Celia's World. A clever little simian. Not only will it learn to speak, but eventually it will mimic your voice, inflections, gestures, even facial expressions."

"Cute," said Kress. "And common. I have no use for either, Wo. I want something exotic. Unusual. And not cute. I detest cute animals. At the moment I own a shambler. Imported from Cotho, at no mean expense. From time to time I feed him a litter of unwanted kittens. That is what I think of *cute*. Do I make myself understood?"

Wo smiled enigmatically. "Have you ever owned an animal that worshipped you?" she asked.

Kress grinned. "Oh, now and again. But I don't require worship, Wo. Just entertainment."

"You misunderstood me," Wo said, still wearing her strange smile. "I meant worship literally."

"What are you talking about?"

"I think I have just the thing for you," Wo said. "Follow me."

She led Kress between the radiant counters and down a long, fog-shrouded aisle beneath false starlight. They passed through a wall of mist into another section of the store, and stopped before a large plastic tank. An aquarium, thought Kress.

Wo beckoned. He stepped closer and saw that he was wrong. It was a terrarium. Within lay a miniature desert about two meters square. Pale and bleached scarlet by wan red light. Rocks: basalt and quartz and granite. In each corner of the tank stood a castle.

Kress blinked, and peered, and corrected himself; actually only three castles stood. The fourth leaned, a crumbled, broken ruin. The other three were crude but intact, carved of stone and sand. Over their battlements and through their rounded porticoes, tiny creatures climbed and scrambled. Kress pressed his face against the plastic. "Insects?" he asked.

"No," Wo replied. "A much more complex life-form. More intelligent as well. Considerably smarter than your shambler. They are called sandkings."

"Insects," Kress said, drawing back from the tank. "I don't care how complex they are." He frowned. "And kindly don't try to gull me with this talk of intelligence. These things are far too small to have anything but the most rudimentary brains."

"They share hiveminds," Wo said. "Castle minds, in this case. There are only three organisms in the tank, actually. The fourth died. You see how her castle has fallen."

Kress looked back at the tank. "Hiveminds, eh? Interesting." He frowned again. "Still, it is only an oversized ant farm. I'd hoped for something better."

"They fight wars."

"Wars? Hmmm." Kress looked again.

"Note the colors, if you will," Wo told him. She pointed to the creatures that swarmed over the nearest castle. One was scrabbling at the tank wall. Kress studied it. It still looked like an insect to his eyes. Barely as long as his fingernail, six-limbed, with six tiny eyes set all around its body. A wicked set of mandibles clacked visibly, while two long, fine antennae wove patterns in the air. Antennae, mandibles, eyes, and legs were sooty black, but the dominant color was the burnt orange of its armor plating. "It's an insect," Kress repeated.

"It is not an insect," Wo insisted calmly. "The armored exoskeleton is shed when the sandking grows larger. *If* it grows larger. In a tank this size, it won't." She took Kress by the elbow and led him around the tank to the next castle. "Look at the colors here."

He did. They were different. Here the sandkings had bright red armor; antennae, mandibles, eyes, and legs were yellow. Kress glanced across the tank. The denizens of the third live castle were off-white, with red trim. "Hmmm," he said.

"They war, as I said," Wo told him. "They even have truces and alliances. It was an alliance that destroyed the fourth castle in this tank. The blacks were getting too numerous, so the others joined forces to destroy them."

Kress remained unconvinced. "Amusing, no doubt. But insects fight wars too."

"Insects do not worship," Wo said.

"Eh?"

Wo smiled and pointed at the castle. Kress stared. A face had been carved into the wall of the highest tower. He recognized it. It was Jala Wo's face. "How . . . ?"

"I projected a hologram of my face into the tank, kept it there for a few days. The face of god, you see? I feed them; I am always close. The sandkings have a rudimentary psionic sense. Proximity telepathy. They sense me, and worship me by using my face to decorate their buildings. All the castles have them, see." They did.

On the castle, the face of Jala Wo was serene and peaceful, and very lifelike. Kress marveled at the workmanship. "How do they do it?"

"The foremost legs double as arms. They even have fingers of a sort; three small, flexible tendrils. And they cooperate well, both in building and in battle. Remember, all the mobiles of one color share a single mind."

"Tell me more," Kress said.

Wo smiled. "The maw lives in the castle. Maw is my name for her. A pun, if you will; the thing is mother and stomach both. Female, large as your fist, immobile. Actually, *sandking* is a bit of a misnomer. The mobiles are peasants and warriors, the real ruler is the queen. But that analogy is faulty as well. Considered as a whole, each castle is a single hermaphroditic creature."

"What do they eat?"

"The mobiles eat pap—predigested food obtained inside the castle. They get it from the maw after she has worked on it for several days. Their stomachs can't handle anything else, so if the maw dies, they soon die as well. The maw . . . the maw eats anything. You'll have no special expense there. Table scraps will do excellently."

"Live food?" Kress asked.

Wo shrugged. "Each maw eats mobiles from the other castles, yes."

"I am intrigued," he admitted. "If only they weren't so small."

"Yours can be larger. These sandkings are small because their tank is small. They seem to limit their growth to fit available space. If I moved these to a larger tank, they'd start growing again."

"Hmmmm. My piranha tank is twice this size, and vacant. It could be cleaned out, filled with sand. . . ."

"Wo and Shade would take care of the installation. It would be our pleasure."

"Of course," said Kress, "I would expect four intact castles."

"Certainly," Wo said.

They began to haggle about the price.

Three days later Jala Wo arrived at Simon Kress's estate, with dormant sandkings and a work crew to take charge of the installation. Wo's assistants were aliens unlike any Kress was familiar with—squat, broad bipeds with four arms and bulging, multifaceted eyes. Their skin was thick and leathery, twisted into horns and spines and protrusions at odd spots upon their bodies. But they were very strong, and good workers. Wo ordered them about in a musical tongue that Kress had never heard.

In a day it was done. They moved his piranha tank to the center of his spacious living room, arranged couches on either side of it for better viewing, scrubbed it clean, and filled it two-thirds of the way up with sand and rock. Then they installed a special lighting system, both to provide the dim red illumination the sandkings preferred and to project holographic images into the tank. On top they mounted a sturdy plastic cover, with a feeder mechanism built in. "This way you can feed your sandkings without removing the top of the tank," Wo explained. "You would not want to take any chances on the mobiles escaping."

The cover also included climate-control devices, to condense just the right amount of moisture from the air. "You want it dry, but not too dry," Wo said.

Finally one of the four-armed workers climbed into the tank and dug deep pits in the four corners. One of his companions handed the dormant maws over to him, removing them one by one from their frosted cryonic travel-

ing cases. They were nothing to look at. Kress decided they resembled nothing so much as a mottled, half-spoiled chunk of raw meat. With a mouth.

The alien buried them, one in each corner of the tank. Then they sealed it all up and took their leave.

"The heat will bring the maws out of dormancy," Wo said. "In less than a week, mobiles will begin to hatch and burrow to the surface. Be certain to give them plenty of food. They will need all their strength until they are well established. I would estimate that you will have castles rising in about three weeks."

"And my face? When will they carve my face?"

"Turn on the hologram after about a month," she advised him. "And be patient. If you have any questions, please call. Wo and Shade are at your service." She bowed and left.

Kress wandered back to the tank and lit a joy-stick. The desert was still and empty. He drummed his fingers impatiently against the plastic, and frowned.

On the fourth day, Kress thought he glimpsed motion beneath the sand, subtle subterranean stirrings.

On the fifth day, he saw his first mobile, a lone white.

On the sixth day, he counted a dozen of them, whites and reds and blacks. The oranges were tardy. He cycled through a bowl of half-decayed table scraps. The mobiles sensed it at once, rushed to it, and began to drag pieces back to their respective corners. Each color group was very organized. They did not fight. Kress was a bit disappointed, but he decided to give them time.

The oranges made their appearance on the eighth day. By then the other sandkings had begun to carry small stones and erect crude fortifications. They still did not war. At the moment they were only half the size of those he had seen at Wo and Shade's, but Kress thought they were growing rapidly.

The castles began to rise midway through the second week. Organized battalions of mobiles dragged heavy chunks of sandstone and granite to their corners, where other mobiles were pushing sand into place with mandibles and tendrils. Kress had purchased a pair of magnifying goggles so he could watch them work, wherever they might go in the tank. He wandered around and around the tall plastic walls, observing. It was fascinating. The castles were a bit plainer than Kress would have liked, but he had an idea about that. The next day he cycled through some obsidian and flakes of colored glass along with the food. Within hours, they had been incorporated into the castle walls.

The black castle was the first completed, followed by the white and red fortresses. The oranges were last, as usual. Kress took his meals into the living room and ate seated on the couch, so he could watch. He expected the first war to break out any hour now.

He was disappointed. Days passed; the castles grew taller and more grand, and Kress seldom left the tank except to attend to his sanitary needs and answer critical business calls. But the sandkings did not war. He was getting upset.

Finally, he stopped feeding them.

Two days after the table scraps had ceased to fall from their desert sky, four black mobiles surrounded an orange and dragged it back to their maw. They maimed it first, ripping off its mandibles and antennae and limbs, and carried it through the shadowed main gate of their miniature castle. It never emerged. Within an hour, more than forty orange mobiles marched across the sand and attacked the blacks' corner. They were outnumbered by the blacks that came rushing up from the depths. When the fighting was over, the attackers had been slaughtered. The dead and dying were taken down to feed the black maw.

Kress, delighted, congratulated himself on his genius.

When he put food into the tank the following day, a three-cornered battle broke out over its possession. The whites were the big winners. After that, war followed war.

Almost a month to the day after Jala Wo had delivered the sandkings, Kress turned on the hologram projector, and his face materialized in the tank. It turned, slowly, around and around so his gaze fell on all four castles equally. Kress thought it rather a good likeness—it had his impish grin, wide mouth, full cheeks. His blue eyes sparkled, his gray hair was carefully arrayed in a fashionable side sweep, his eyebrows were thin and sophisticated.

Soon enough, the sandkings set to work. Kress fed them lavishly while his image beamed down at them from their sky. Temporarily, the wars stopped. All activity was directed towards worship.

His face emerged on the castle walls.

At first all four carvings looked alike to him, but as the work continued and Kress studied the reproductions, he began to detect subtle differences in technique and execution. The reds were the most creative, using tiny flakes of slate to put the gray in his hair. The white idol seemed young and mischievous to him, while the face shaped by the blacks—although virtually the same, line for line—struck him as wise and beneficent. The orange sandkings, as ever, were last and least. The wars had not gone well for them, and their castle was sad compared to the others. The image they carved was crude and cartoonish, and they seemed to intend to leave it that way. When they stopped work on the face, Kress grew quite piqued with them, but there was really nothing he could do.

When all the sandkings had finished their Kress-faces, he turned off the hologram and decided that it was time to have a party. His friends would be impressed. He could even stage a war for them, he thought. Humming happily to himself, he began to draw up a guest list.

The party was a wild success.

Kress invited thirty people: a handful of close friends who shared his amusements, a few former lovers, and a collection of business and social rivals who could not afford to ignore his summons. He knew some of them would be discomfited and even offended by his sandkings. He counted on it. Simon Kress customarily considered his parties a failure unless at least one guest walked out in high dudgeon.

On impulse he added Jala Wo's name to his list. "Bring Shade if you like," he added when dictating her invitation.

Her acceptance surprised him just a bit. "Shade, alas, will be unable to attend. He does not go to social functions," Wo added. "As for myself, I look forward to the chance to see how your sandkings are doing."

Kress ordered them up a sumptuous meal. And when at last the conversation had died down, and most of his guests had gotten silly on wine and joy-sticks, he shocked them by personally scraping their table leavings into a large bowl. "Come, all of you," he told them. "I want to introduce you to my newest pets." Carrying the bowl, he conducted them into his living room.

The sandkings lived up to his fondest expectations. He had starved them for two days in preparation, and they were in a fighting mood. While the guests ringed the tank, looking through the magnifying glasses Kress had thoughtfully provided, the sandkings waged a glorious battle over the scraps. He counted almost sixty dead mobiles when the struggle was over. The reds and whites, who had recently formed an alliance, emerged with most of the food.

"Kress, you're disgusting," Cath m'Lane told him. She had lived with him for a short time two years before, until her soppy sentimentality almost drove him mad. "I was a fool to come back here. I thought perhaps you'd changed, wanted to apologize." She had never forgiven him for the time his shambler had eaten an excessively cute puppy of which she had been fond. "Don't *ever* invite me here again, Simon." She strode out, accompanied by her current lover and a chorus of laughter.

His other guests were full of questions.

Where did the sandkings come from? they wanted to know. "From Wo and Shade, Importers," he replied, with a polite gesture towards Jala Wo, who had remained quiet and apart through most of the evening.

Why did they decorate their castles with his likeness? "Because I am the source of all good things. Surely you know that?" That brought a round of chuckles.

Will they fight again? "Of course, but not tonight. Don't worry. There will be other parties."

Jad Rakkis, who was an amateur xenologist, began talking about other social insects and the wars they fought. "These sandkings are amusing, but nothing really. You really ought to read about Terran soldier ants, for instance."

"Sandkings are not insects," Jala Wo said sharply, but Jad was off and running, and no one paid her the slightest attention. Kress smiled at her and shrugged.

Malada Blane suggested a betting pool the next time they got together to watch a war, and everyone was taken with the idea. An animated discussion about rules and odds ensued. It lasted for almost an hour. Finally the guests began to take their leave.

Jala Wo was the last to depart. "So," Kress said to her when they were alone, "it appears my sandkings are a hit."

"They are doing well," Wo said. "Already they are larger than my own."

"Yes," Kress said, "except for the oranges."

"I had noticed that," Wo replied. "They seem few in number, and their castle is shabby."

"Well, someone must lose," Kress said. "The oranges were late to emerge and get established. They have suffered for it."

"Pardon," said Wo, "but might I ask if you are feeding your sandkings sufficiently?"

Kress shrugged. "They diet from time to time. It makes them fiercer."

She frowned. "There is no need to starve them. Let them war in their own time, for their own reasons. It is their nature, and you will witness conflicts that are delightfully subtle and complex. The constant war brought on by hunger is artless and degrading."

Simon Kress repaid Wo's frown with interest. "You are in my house, Wo, and here I am the judge of what is degrading. I fed the sandkings as you advised, and they did not fight."

"You must have patience."

"No," Kress said. "I am their master and their god, after all. Why should I wait on their impulses? They did not war often enough to suit me. I corrected the situation."

"I see," said Wo. "I will discuss the matter with Shade."

"It is none of your concern, or his," Kress snapped.

"I must bid you good night, then," Wo said with resignation. But as she slipped into her coat to depart, she fixed him with a final disapproving stare. "Look to your faces, Simon Kress," she warned him. "Look to your faces."

Puzzled, he wandered back to the tank and stared at the castles after she had taken her departure. His faces were still there, as ever. Except—he snatched up his magnifying goggles and slipped them on. Even then it was hard to make out. But it seemed to him that the expression on the face of his images had changed slightly, that his smile was somehow twisted so that it seemed a touch malicious. But it was a very subtle change, if it was a change at all. Kress finally put it down to his suggestibility, and resolved not to invite Jala Wo to any more of his gatherings.

Over the next few months, Kress and about a dozen of his favorites got together weekly for what he liked to call his "war games." Now that his initial fascination with the sandkings was past, Kress spent less time around his tank and more on his business affairs and his social life, but he still enjoyed having a few friends over for

a war or two. He kept the combatants sharp on a constant edge of hunger. It had severe effects on the orange sandkings, who dwindled visibly until Kress began to wonder if their maw was dead. But the others did well enough.

Sometimes at night, when he could not sleep, Kress would take a bottle of wine into the darkened living room, where the red gloom of his miniature desert was the only light. He would drink and watch for hours, alone. There was usually a fight going on somewhere, and when there was not he could easily start one by dropping in some small morsel of food.

They took to betting on the weekly battles, as Malada Blane had suggested. Kress won a good amount by betting on the whites, who had become the most powerful and numerous colony in the tank, with the grandest castle. One week he slid the corner of the tank top aside, and dropped the food close to the white castle instead of on the central battleground as usual, so that the others had to attack the whites in their stronghold to get any food at all. They tried. The whites were brilliant in defense. Kress won a hundred standards from Jad Rakkis.

Rakkis, in fact, lost heavily on the sandkings almost every week. He pretended to a vast knowledge of them and their ways, claiming that he had studied them after the first party, but he had no luck when it came to placing his bets. Kress suspected that Jad's claims were empty boasting. He had tried to study the sandkings a bit himself, in a moment of idle curiosity, tying in to the library to find out to what world his pets were native. But there was no listing for them. He wanted to get in touch with Wo and ask her about it, but he had other concerns, and the matter kept slipping his mind.

Finally, after a month in which his losses totaled more than a thousand standards, Jad Rakkis arrived at the war games carrying a small plastic case under his arm. Inside was a spiderlike thing covered with fine golden hair.

"A sand spider," Rakkis announced. "From Cathaday. I got it this afternoon from t'Etherane the Petseller. Usually they remove the poison sacs, but this one is intact. Are you game, Simon? I want my money back. I'll bet a thousand standards, sand spider against sandkings."

Kress studied the spider in its plastic prison. His sandkings had grown—they were twice as large as Wo's, as she'd predicted—but they were still dwarfed by this thing. It was venomed, and they were not. Still, there were an awful lot of them. Besides, the endless sandking wars had begun to grow tiresome lately. The novelty of the match intrigued him. "Done," Kress said. "Jad, you are a fool. The sandkings will just keep coming until this ugly creature of yours is dead."

"You are the fool, Simon," Rakkis replied, smiling. "The Cathadayn sand spider customarily feeds on burrowers that hide in nooks and crevices and—well, watch—it will go straight into those castles, and eat the maws."

Kress scowled amid general laughter. He hadn't counted on that. "Get on with it," he said irritably. He went to freshen his drink.

The spider was too large to cycle conveniently through the food chamber. Two of the others helped Rakkis slide the tank top slightly to one side, and Malada Blane handed him up his case. He shook the spider out. It landed lightly on a miniature dune in front of the red castle, and stood confused for a moment, mouth working, legs twitching menacingly.

"Come on," Rakkis urged. They all gathered round the tank. Simon Kress found his magnifiers and slipped them on. If he was going to lose a thousand standards, at least he wanted a good view of the action.

The sandkings had seen the invader. All over the castle, activity had ceased. The small scarlet mobiles were frozen, watching.

The spider began to move toward the dark promise of the gate. On the tower above, Simon Kress's countenance stared down impassively.

At once there was a flurry of activity. The nearest red mobiles formed themselves into two wedges and streamed over the sand toward the spider. More warriors erupted from inside the

castle and assembled in a triple line to guard the approach to the underground chamber where the maw lived. Scouts came scuttling over the dunes, recalled to fight.

Battle was joined.

The attacking sandkings washed over the spider. Mandibles snapped shut on legs and abdomen, and clung. Reds raced up the golden legs to the invader's back. They bit and tore. One of them found an eye, and ripped it loose with tiny yellow tendrils. Kress smiled and pointed.

But they were *small*, and they had no venom, and the spider did not stop. Its legs flicked sandkings off to either side. Its dripping jaws found others, and left them broken and stiffening. Already a dozen of the reds lay dying. The sand spider came on and on. It strode straight through the triple line of guardians before the castle. The lines closed around it, covered it, waging desperate battle. A team of sandkings had bitten off one of the spider's legs, Kress saw. Defenders leaped from atop the towers to land on the twitching, heaving mass.

Lost beneath the sandkings, the spider somehow lurched down into the darkness and vanished.

Jad Rakkis let out a long breath. He looked pale. "Wonderful," someone else said. Malada Blane chuckled deep in her throat.

"Look," said Idi Noreddian, tugging Kress by the arm.

They had been so intent on the struggle in the corner that none of them had noticed the activity elsewhere in the tank. But now the castle was still, the sands empty save for dead red mobiles, and now they saw.

Three armies were drawn up before the red castle. They stood quite still, in perfect array, rank after rank of sandkings, orange and white and black. Waiting to see what emerged from the depths.

Simon Kress smiled. "A cordon sanitaire," he said. "And glance at the other castles, if you will, Jad."

Rakkis did, and swore. Teams of mobiles

were sealing up the gates with sand and stone. If the spider somehow survived this encounter, it would find no easy entrance at the other castles. "I should have brought four spiders," Jad Rakkis said. "Still, I've won. My spider is down there right now, eating your damned maw."

Kress did not reply. He waited. There was motion in the shadows.

All at once, red mobiles began pouring out of the gate. They took their positions on the castle, and began repairing the damage the spider had wrought. The other armies dissolved and began to retreat to their respective corners.

"Jad," said Simon Kress, "I think you are a bit confused about who is eating who."

The following week Rakkis brought four slim silver snakes. The sandkings dispatched them without much trouble.

Next he tried a large black bird. It ate more than thirty white mobiles, and its thrashing and blundering virtually destroyed their castle, but ultimately its wings grew tired, and the sandkings attacked in force wherever it landed.

After that it was a case of insects, armored beetles not too unlike the sandkings themselves. But stupid, stupid. An allied force of oranges and blacks broke their formation, divided them, and butchered them.

Rakkis began giving Kress promissory notes.

It was around that time that Kress met Cath m'Lane again, one evening when he was dining in Asgard at his favorite restaurant. He stopped at her table briefly and told her about the war games, inviting her to join them. She flushed, then regained control of herself and grew icy. "Someone has to put a stop to you, Simon. I guess it's going to be me," she said. Kress shrugged and enjoyed a lovely meal and thought no more about her threat.

Until a week later, when a small, stout woman arrived at his door and showed him a police wristband. "We've had complaints," she said. "Do you keep a tank full of dangerous insects, Kress?"

"Not insects," he said, furious. "Come, I'll show you."

When she had seen the sandkings, she shook her head. "This will never do. What do you know about these creatures, anyway? Do you know what world they're from? Have they been cleared by the ecological board? Do you have a license for these things? We have a report that they're carnivores, possibly dangerous. We also have a report that they are semi-sentient. Where did you get these creatures, anyway?"

"From Wo and Shade," Kress replied.

"Never heard of them," the woman said. "Probably smuggled them in, knowing our ecologists would never approve them. No, Kress, this won't do. I'm going to confiscate this tank and have it destroyed. And you're going to have to expect a few fines as well."

Kress offered her a hundred standards to forget all about him and his sandkings.

She *tsk*ed. "Now I'll have to add attempted bribery to the charges against you."

Not until he raised the figure to two thousand standards was she willing to be persuaded.

"It's not going to be easy, you know," she said. "There are forms to be altered, records to be wiped. And getting a forged license from the ecologists will be time-consuming. Not to mention dealing with the complainant. What if she calls again?"

"Leave her to me," Kress said. "Leave her to me."

He thought about it for a while. That night he made some calls.

First he got t'Etherane the Petseller. "I want to buy a dog," he said. "A puppy."

The round-faced merchant gawked at him. "A puppy? That is not like you, Simon. Why don't you come in? I have a lovely choice."

"I want a very specific *kind* of puppy," Kress said. "Take notes. I'll describe to you what it must look like."

Afterward he punched for Idi Noreddian.

"Idi," he said, "I want you out here tonight with your holo equipment. I have a notion to record a sandking battle. A present for one of my friends."

The night after they made the recording, Simon Kress stayed up late. He absorbed a controversial new drama in his sensorium, fixed himself a small snack, smoked a joy-stick or two, and broke out a bottle of wine. Feeling very happy with himself, he wandered into the living room, glass in hand.

The lights were out. The red glow of the terrarium made the shadows flushed and feverish. He walked over to look at his domain, curious as to how the blacks were doing in the repairs on their castle. The puppy had left it in ruins.

The restoration went well. But as Kress inspected the work through his magnifiers, he chanced to glance closely at the face. It startled him.

He drew back, blinked, took a healthy gulp of wine, and looked again.

The face on the wall was still his. But it was all wrong, all *twisted*. His cheeks were bloated and piggish, his smile was a crooked leer. He looked impossibly malevolent.

Uneasy, he moved around the tank to inspect the other castles. They were each a bit different, but ultimately all the same.

The oranges had left out most of the fine detail, but the result still seemed monstrous, crude—a brutal mouth and mindless eyes.

The reds gave him a satanic, twitching kind of smile. His mouth did odd, unlovely things at its corners.

The whites, his favorites, had carved a cruel idiot god.

Simon Kress flung his wine across the room in rage. "You *dare*," he said under his breath. "Now you won't eat for a week, you damned . . ." His voice was shrill. "I'll teach you." He had an idea. He strode out of the room, and returned a moment later with an antique iron throwing-sword in his hand. It was a meter long, and the point was still sharp. Kress smiled,

climbed up, and moved the tank cover aside just enough to give him working room, opening one corner of the desert. He leaned down, and jabbed the sword at the white castle below him. He waved it back and forth, smashing towers and ramparts and walls. Sand and stone collapsed, burying the scrambling mobiles. A flick of his wrist obliterated the features of the insolent, insulting caricature the sandkings had made of his face. Then he poised the point of the sword above the dark mouth that opened down into the maw's chamber, and thrust with all his strength. He heard a soft, squishing sound, and met resistance. All of the mobiles trembled and collapsed. Satisfied, Kress pulled back.

He watched for a moment, wondering whether he'd killed the maw. The point of the throwing-sword was wet and slimy. But finally the white sandkings began to move again. Feebly, slowly, but they moved.

He was preparing to slide the cover back in place and move on to a second castle when he felt something crawling on his hand.

He screamed and dropped the sword, and brushed the sandking from his flesh. It fell to the carpet, and he ground it beneath his heel, crushing it thoroughly long after it was dead. It had crunched when he stepped on it. After that, trembling, he hurried to seal the tank up again, and rushed off to shower and inspect himself carefully. He boiled his clothing.

Later, after several fresh glasses of wine, he returned to the living room. He was a bit ashamed of the way the sandking had terrified him. But he was not about to open the tank again. From now on, the cover stayed sealed permanently. Still, he had to punish the others.

Kress decided to lubricate his mental processes with another glass of wine. As he finished it, an inspiration came to him. He went to the tank, smiling, and made a few adjustments to the humidity controls.

By the time he fell asleep on the couch, his wineglass still in his hand, the sand castles were melting in the rain.

. . .

Kress woke to angry pounding on his door.

He sat up, groggy, his head throbbing. Wine hangovers were always the worst, he thought. He lurched to the entry chamber.

Cath m'Lane was outside. "You monster," she said, her face swollen and puffy and streaked by tears. "I cried all night, damn you. But no more, Simon, no more."

"Easy," he said, holding his head. "I've got a hangover."

She swore and shoved him aside and pushed her way into his house. The shambler came peering round a corner to see what the noise was. She spat at it and stalked into the living room, Kress trailing ineffectually after her. "Hold on," he said. "Where do you . . . you can't . . ." He stopped, suddenly horrorstruck. She was carrying a heavy sledgehammer in her left hand. "No," he said.

She went directly to the sandking tank. "You like the little charmers so much, Simon? Then you can live with them."

"*Cath!*" he shrieked.

Gripping the hammer with both hands, she swung as hard as she could against the side of the tank. The sound of the impact set his head to screaming, and Kress made a low blubbering sound of despair. But the plastic held.

She swung again. This time there was a *crack*, and a network of thin lines sprang into being.

Kress threw himself at her as she drew back her hammer for a third swing. They went down flailing, and rolled. She lost her grip on the hammer and tried to throttle him, but Kress wrenched free and bit her on the arm, drawing blood. They both staggered to their feet, panting.

"You should see yourself, Simon," she said grimly. "Blood dripping from your mouth. You look like one of your pets. How do you like the taste?"

"Get out," he said. He saw the throwing-sword where it had fallen the night before, and

snatched it up. "Get out," he repeated, waving the sword for emphasis. "Don't go near that tank again."

She laughed at him. "You wouldn't dare," she said. She bent to pick up her hammer.

Kress shrieked at her, and lunged. Before he quite knew what was happening, the iron blade had gone clear through her abdomen. Cath m'Lane looked at him wonderingly, and down at the sword. Kress fell back whimpering. "I didn't mean . . . I only wanted . . ."

She was transfixed, bleeding, dead, but somehow she did not fall. "You monster," she managed to say, though her mouth was full of blood. And she whirled, impossibly, the sword in her, and swung with her last strength at the tank. The tortured wall shattered, and Cath m'Lane was buried beneath an avalanche of plastic and sand and mud.

Kress made small hysterical noises and scrambled up on the couch.

Sandkings were emerging from the muck on his living room floor. They were crawling across Cath's body. A few of them ventured tentatively out across the carpet. More followed.

He watched as a column took shape, a living, writhing square of sandkings, bearing something, something slimy and featureless, a piece of raw meat big as a man's head. They began to carry it away from the tank. It pulsed.

That was when Kress broke and ran.

It was late afternoon before he found the courage to return. He had run to his skimmer and flown to the nearest city, some fifty kilometers away, almost sick with fear. But once safely away, he had found a small restaurant, put down several mugs of coffee and two anti-hangover tabs, eaten a full breakfast, and gradually regained his composure.

It had been a dreadful morning, but dwelling on that would solve nothing. He ordered more coffee and considered his situation with icy rationality.

Cath m'Lane was dead at his hand. Could

he report it, plead that it had been an accident? Unlikely. He had run her through, after all, and he had already told that policer to leave her to him. He would have to get rid of the evidence, and hope that she had not told anyone where she was going this morning. That was probable. She could only have gotten his gift late last night. She said that she had cried all night, and she had been alone when it arrived. Very well; he had one body and one skimmer to dispose of.

That left the sandkings. They might prove more of a difficulty. No doubt they had all escaped by now. The thought of them around his house, in his bed and his clothes, infesting his food—it made his flesh crawl. He shuddered and overcame his revulsion. It really shouldn't be too hard to kill them, he reminded himself. He didn't have to account for every mobile. Just the four maws, that was all. He could do that. They were large, as he'd seen. He would find them and kill them.

Simon Kress went shopping before he flew back to his home. He bought a set of skinthins that would cover him from head to foot, several bags of poison pellets for rockjock control, and a spray canister of illegally strong pesticide. He also bought a magnalock towing device.

When he landed, he went about things methodically. First he hooked Cath's skimmer to his own with the magnalock. Searching it, he had his first piece of luck. The crystal chip with Idi Noreddian's holo of the sandking fight was on the front seat. He had worried about that.

When the skimmers were ready, he slipped into his skinthins and went inside for Cath's body.

It wasn't there.

He poked through the fast-drying sand carefully, but there was no doubt of it; the body was gone. Could she have dragged herself away? Unlikely, but Kress searched. A cursory inspection of his house turned up neither the body nor any sign of the sandkings. He did not have time for a more thorough investigation, not with the incriminating skimmer outside his front door. He resolved to try later.

Some seventy kilometers north of Kress's estate was a range of active volcanoes. He flew there, Cath's skimmer in tow. Above the glowering cone of the largest, he released the magnalock and watched it vanish in the lava below.

It was dusk when he returned to his house. That gave him pause. Briefly he considered flying back to the city and spending the night there. He put the thought aside. There was work to do. He wasn't safe yet.

He scattered the poison pellets around the exterior of his house. No one would find that suspicious. He'd always had a rockjock problem. When that task was completed, he primed the canister of pesticide and ventured back inside.

Kress went through the house room by room, turning on lights everywhere he went until he was surrounded by a blaze of artificial illumination. He paused to clean up in the living room, shoveling sand and plastic fragments back into the broken tank. The sandkings were all gone, as he'd feared. The castles were shrunken and distorted, slagged by the watery bombardment Kress had visited upon them, and what little remained was crumbling as it dried.

He frowned and searched on, the canister of pest spray strapped across his shoulders.

Down in his deepest wine cellar, he came upon Cath m'Lane's corpse.

It sprawled at the foot of a steep flight of stairs, the limbs twisted as if by a fall. White mobiles were swarming all over it, and as Kress watched, the body moved jerkily across the hard-packed dirt floor.

He laughed, and twisted the illumination up to maximum. In the far corner, a squat little earthen castle and a dark hole were visible between two wine racks. Kress could make out a rough outline of his face on the cellar wall.

The body shifted once again, moving a few centimeters towards the castle. Kress had a sudden vision of the white maw waiting hungrily. It might be able to get Cath's foot in its mouth, but no more. It was too absurd. He laughed again, and started down into the cellar, finger poised on the trigger of the hose that snaked down his right arm. The sandkings—hundreds of them moving as one—deserted the body and formed up battle lines, a field of white between him and their maw.

Suddenly Kress had another inspiration. He smiled and lowered his firing hand. "Cath was always hard to swallow," he said, delighted at his wit: "Especially for one your size. Here, let me give you some help. What are gods for, after all?"

He retreated upstairs, returning shortly with a cleaver. The sandkings, patient, waited and watched while Kress chopped Cath m'Lane into small, easily digestible pieces.

Simon Kress slept in his skinthins that night, the pesticide close at hand, but he did not need it. The whites, sated, remained in the cellar, and he saw no sign of the others.

In the morning he finished the cleanup of the living room. After he was through, no trace of the struggle remained except for the broken tank.

He ate a light lunch, and resumed his hunt for the missing sandkings. In full daylight, it was not too difficult. The blacks had located in his rock garden, and built a castle heavy with obsidian and quartz. The reds he found at the bottom of his long-disused swimming pool, which had partially filled with windblown sand over the years. He saw mobiles of both colors ranging about his grounds, many of them carrying poison pellets back to their maws. Kress decided his pesticide was unnecessary. No use risking a fight when he could just let the poison do its work. Both maws should be dead by evening.

That left only the burnt-orange sandkings unaccounted for. Kress circled his estate several times, in ever-widening spirals, but found no trace of them. When he began to sweat in his skinthins—it was a hot, dry day—he decided it was not important. If they were out here, they were probably eating the poison pellets along with the reds and blacks.

He crunched several sandkings underfoot, with a certain degree of satisfaction, as he walked back to the house. Inside, he removed his skinthins, settled down to a delicious meal, and finally began to relax. Everything was under control. Two of the maws would soon be defunct, the third was safely located where he could dispose of it after it had served his purposes, and he had no doubt that he would find the fourth. As for Cath, all trace of her visit had been obliterated.

His reverie was interrupted when his viewscreen began to blink at him. It was Jad Rakkis, calling to brag about some cannibal worms he was bringing to the war games tonight.

Kress had forgotten about that, but he recovered quickly. "Oh, Jad, my pardons. I neglected to tell you. I grew bored with all that, and got rid of the sandkings. Ugly little things. Sorry, but there'll be no party tonight."

Rakkis was indignant. "But what will I do with my worms?"

"Put them in a basket of fruit and send them to a loved one," Kress said, signing off. Quickly he began calling the others. He did not need anyone arriving at his doorstep now, with the sandkings alive and infesting the estate.

As he was calling Idi Noreddian, Kress became aware of an annoying oversight. The screen began to clear, indicating that someone had answered at the other end. Kress flicked off. Idi arrived on schedule an hour later. She was surprised to find the party canceled, but perfectly happy to share an evening alone with Kress. He delighted her with his story of Cath's reaction to the holo they had made together. While telling it, he managed to ascertain that she had not mentioned the prank to anyone. He nodded, satisfied, and refilled their wineglasses. Only a trickle was left. "I'll have to get a fresh bottle," he said. "Come with me to my wine cellar, and help me pick out a good vintage. You've always had a better palate than I."

She came along willingly enough, but balked at the top of the stairs when Kress opened the door and gestured for her to precede him. "Where are the lights?" she said. "And that smell—what's that peculiar smell, Simon?"

When he shoved her, she looked briefly startled. She screamed as she tumbled down the stairs. Kress closed the door and began to nail it shut with the boards and airhammer he had left for that purpose. As he was finishing, he heard Idi groan. "I'm hurt," she said. "Simon, what is this?" Suddenly she squealed, and shortly after that the screaming started.

It did not cease for hours. Kress went to his sensorium and dialed up a saucy comedy to blot it off of his mind.

When he was sure she was dead, Kress flew her skimmer north to the volcanoes and discarded it. The magnalock was proving a good investment.

Odd scrabbling noises were coming from beyond the wine cellar door the next morning when Kress went down to check it out. He listened for several uneasy moments, wondering if Idi Noreddian could possibly have survived, and was now scratching to get out. It seemed unlikely; it had to be the sandkings. Kress did not like the implications of that. He decided that he would keep the door sealed, at least for the moment, and went outside with a shovel to bury the red and black maws in their own castles.

He found them very much alive.

The black castle was glittering with volcanic glass, and sandkings were all over it, repairing and improving. The highest tower was up to his waist, and on it was a hideous caricature of his face. When he approached, the blacks halted in their labors, and formed up into two threatening phalanxes. Kress glanced behind him and saw others closing off his escape. Startled, he dropped the shovel and sprinted out of the trap, crushing several mobiles beneath his boots.

The red castle was creeping up the walls of the swimming pool. The maw was safely settled in a pit, surrounded by sand and concrete and battlements. The reds crept all over the bottom of the pool. Kress watched them carry a rockjock and a large lizard into the castle. He stepped back from the poolside, horrified, and felt something crunch. Looking down, he saw three mobiles climbing up his leg. He brushed them off and stamped them to death, but others were approaching quickly. They were larger than he remembered. Some were almost as big as his thumb.

He ran. By the time he reached the safety of the house, his heart was racing and he was short of breath. The door closed behind him, and Kress hurried to lock it. His house was supposed to be pest-proof. He'd be safe in here.

A stiff drink steadied his nerves. So poison doesn't faze them, he thought. He should have known. Wo had warned him that the maw could eat anything. He would have to use the pesticide. Kress took another drink for good measure, donned his skinthins, and strapped the canister to his back. He unlocked the door.

Outside, the sandkings were waiting.

Two armies confronted him, allied against the common threat. More than he could have guessed. The damned maws must be breeding like rockjocks. They were everywhere, a creeping sea of them.

Kress brought up the hose and flicked the trigger. A gray mist washed over the nearest rank of sandkings. He moved his hand from side to side.

Where the mist fell, the sandkings twitched violently and died in sudden spasms. Kress smiled. They were no match for him. He sprayed in a wide arc before him and stepped forward confidently over a litter of black and red bodies. The armies fell back. Kress advanced, intent on cutting through them to their maws.

All at once the retreat stopped. A thousand sandkings surged toward him.

Kress had been expecting the counterattack.

He stood his ground, sweeping his misty sword before him in great looping strokes. They came at him and died. A few got through; he could not spray everywhere at once. He felt them climbing up his legs, sensed their mandibles biting futilely at the reinforced plastic of his skinthins. He ignored them, and kept spraying.

Then he began to feel soft impacts on his head and shoulders.

Kress trembled and spun and looked up above him. The front of his house was alive with sandkings. Blacks and reds, hundreds of them. They were launching themselves into the air, raining down on him. They fell all around him. One landed on his faceplate, its mandibles scraping at his eyes for a terrible second before he plucked it away.

He swung up his hose and sprayed the air, sprayed the house, sprayed until the airborne sandkings were all dead and dying. The mist settled back on him, making him cough. He coughed, and kept spraying. Only when the front of the house was clean did Kress turn his attention back to the ground.

They were all around him, on him, dozens of them scurrying over his body, hundreds of others hurrying to join them. He turned the mist on them. The hose went dead. Kress heard a loud *hiss*, and the deadly fog rose in a great cloud from between his shoulders, cloaking him, choking him, making his eyes burn and blur. He felt for the hose, and his hand came away covered with dying sandkings. The hose was severed; they'd eaten it through. He was surrounded by a shroud of pesticide, blinded. He stumbled and screamed, and began to run back to the house, pulling sandkings from his body as he went.

Inside, he sealed the door and collapsed on the carpet, rolling back and forth until he was sure he had crushed them all. The canister was empty by then, hissing feebly. Kress stripped off his skinthins and showered. The hot spray scalded him and left his skin reddened and sensitive, but it made his flesh stop crawling.

He dressed in his heaviest clothing, thick work pants and leathers, after shaking them out nervously. "Damn," he kept muttering, "damn." His throat was dry. After searching the entry hall thoroughly to make certain it was clean, he allowed himself to sit and pour a drink. "Damn," he repeated. His hand shook as he poured, slopping liquor on the carpet.

The alcohol settled him, but it did not wash away the fear. He had a second drink and went to the window furtively. Sandkings were moving across the thick plastic pane. He shuddered and retreated to his communications console. He had to get help, he thought wildly. He would punch through a call to the authorities, and policers would come out with flamethrowers and . . .

Simon Kress stopped in mid-call, and groaned. He couldn't call in the police. He would have to tell them about the whites in his cellar, and they'd find the bodies there. Perhaps the maw might have finished Cath m'Lane by now, but certainly not Idi Noreddian. He hadn't even cut her up. Besides, there would be bones. No, the police could be called in only as a last resort.

He sat at the console, frowning. His communications equipment filled a whole wall; from here he could reach anyone on Baldur. He had plenty of money, and his cunning—he had always prided himself on his cunning. He would handle this somehow.

He briefly considered calling Wo, but soon dismissed the idea. Wo knew too much, and she would ask questions, and he did not trust her. No, he needed someone who would do as he asked *without* questions.

His frown faded, and slowly turned into a smile. Simon Kress had contacts. He put through a call to a number he had not used in a long time.

A woman's face took shape on his viewscreen: white-haired, bland of expression, with a long hook nose. Her voice was brisk and efficient. "Simon," she said. "How is business?"

"Business is fine, Lissandra," Kress replied. "I have a job for you."

"A removal? My price has gone up since last time, Simon. It has been ten years, after all."

"You will be well paid," Kress said. "You know I'm generous. I want you for a bit of pest control."

She smiled a thin smile. "No need to use euphemisms, Simon. The call is shielded."

"No, I'm serious. I have a pest problem. Dangerous pests. Take care of them for me. No questions. Understood?"

"Understood."

"Good. You'll need . . . oh, three or four operatives. Wear heat-resistant skinthins, and equip them with flamethrowers, or lasers, something of that order. Come out to my place. You'll see the problem. Bugs, lots and lots of them. In my rock garden and the old swimming pool you'll find castles. Destroy them, kill everything inside them. Then knock on the door, and I'll show you what else needs to be done. Can you get out here quickly?"

Her face was impassive. "We'll leave within the hour."

Lissandra was true to her word. She arrived in a lean black skimmer with three operatives. Kress watched them from the safety of a second-story window. They were all faceless in dark plastic skinthins. Two of them wore portable flamethrowers, a third carried a lasercannon and explosives. Lissandra carried nothing; Kress recognized her by the way she gave orders.

Their skimmer passed low overhead first, checking out the situation. The sandkings went mad. Scarlet and ebony mobiles ran everywhere, frenetic. Kress could see the castle in the rock garden from his vantage point. It stood tall as a man. Its ramparts were crawling with black defenders, and a steady stream of mobiles flowed down into its depths.

Lissandra's skimmer came down next to Kress's and the operatives vaulted out and unlimbered their weapons. They looked inhuman, deadly.

The black army drew up between them

and the castle. The reds—Kress suddenly realized that he could not see the reds. He blinked. Where had they gone?

Lissandra pointed and shouted, and her two flamethrowers spread out and opened up on the black sandkings. Their weapons coughed dully and began to roar, long tongues of blue-and-scarlet fire licking out before them. Sandkings crisped and blackened and died. The operatives began to play the fire back and forth in an efficient, interlocking pattern. They advanced with careful, measured steps.

The black army burned and disintegrated, the mobiles fleeing in a thousand different directions, some back toward the castle, others toward the enemy. None reached the operatives with the flamethrowers. Lissandra's people were very professional.

Then one of them stumbled.

Or seemed to stumble. Kress looked again, and saw that the ground had given way beneath the man. Tunnels, he thought with a tremor of fear—tunnels, pits, traps. The flamer was sunk in sand up to his waist, and suddenly the ground around him seemed to erupt, and he was covered with scarlet sandkings. He dropped the flamethrower and began to claw wildly at his own body. His screams were horrible to hear.

His companion hesitated, then swung and fired. A blast of flame swallowed human and sandkings both. The screaming stopped abruptly. Satisfied, the second flamer turned back to the castle and took another step forward, and recoiled as his foot broke through the ground and vanished up to the ankle. He tried to pull it back and retreat, and the sand all around him gave way. He lost his balance and stumbled, flailing, and the sandkings were everywhere, a boiling mass of them, covering him as he writhed and rolled. His flamethrower was useless and forgotten.

Kress pounded wildly on the window, shouting for attention. "The castle! Get the castle!"

Lissandra, standing back by her skimmer, heard and gestured. Her third operative sighted with the lasercannon and fired. The beam throbbed across the grounds and sliced off the top of the castle. He brought it down sharply, hacking at the sand and stone parapets. Towers fell. Kress's face disintegrated. The laser bit into the ground, searching round and about. The castle crumbled; now it was only a heap of sand. But the black mobiles continued to move. The maw was buried too deeply; they hadn't touched her.

Lissandra gave another order. Her operative discarded the laser, primed an explosive, and darted forward. He leaped over the smoking corpse of the first flamer, landed on solid ground within Kress's rock garden, and heaved. The explosive ball landed square atop the ruins of the black castle. White-hot light seared Kress's eyes, and there was a tremendous gout of sand and rock and mobiles. For a moment dust obscured everything. It was raining sand-kings and pieces of sandkings.

Kress saw that the black mobiles were dead and unmoving.

"The pool," he shouted down through the window. "Get the castle in the pool."

Lissandra understood quickly; the ground was littered with motionless blacks, but the reds were pulling back hurriedly and re-forming. Her operative stood uncertain, then reached down and pulled out another explosive ball. He took one step forward, but Lissandra called him and he sprinted back in her direction.

It was all so simple then. He reached the skimmer, and Lissandra took him aloft. Kress rushed to another window in another room to watch. They came swooping in just over the pool, and the operative pitched his bombs down at the red castle from the safety of the skimmer. After the fourth run, the castle was unrecognizable, and the sandkings stopped moving.

Lissandra was thorough. She had him bomb each castle several additional times. Then he used the lasercannon, crisscrossing methodically until it was certain that nothing living could remain intact beneath those small patches of ground.

Finally they came knocking at his door.

Kress was grinning manically when he let them in. "Lovely," he said, "lovely."

Lissandra pulled off the mask of her skinthins. "This will cost you, Simon. Two operatives gone, not to mention the danger to my own life."

"Of course," Kress blurted. "You'll be well paid, Lissandra. Whatever you ask, just so you finish the job."

"What remains to be done?"

"You have to clean out my wine cellar," Kress said. "There's another castle down there. And you'll have to do it without explosives. I don't want my house coming down around me."

Lissandra motioned to her operative. "Go outside and get Rajk's flamethrower. It should be intact."

He returned armed, ready, silent. Kress led them down to the wine cellar.

The heavy door was still nailed shut, as he had left it. But it bulged outward slightly, as if warped by some tremendous pressure. That made Kress uneasy, as did the silence that held reign about them. He stood well away from the door as Lissandra's operative removed his nails and planks. "Is that safe in here?" he found himself muttering, pointing at the flamethrower. "I don't want a fire, either, you know."

"I have the laser," Lissandra said. "We'll use that for the kill. The flamethrower probably won't be needed. But I want it here just in case. There are worse things than fire, Simon."

He nodded.

The last plank came free of the cellar door. There was still no sound from below. Lissandra snapped an order, and her underling fell back, took up a position behind her, and leveled the flamethrower square at the door. She slipped her mask back on, hefted the laser, stepped forward, and pulled open the door.

No motion. No sound. It was dark down there.

"Is there a light?" Lissandra asked.

"Just inside the door," Kress said. "On the right-hand side. Mind the stairs, they're quite steep."

She stepped into the doorway, shifted the laser to her left hand, and reached up with her right, fumbling inside for the light panel. Nothing happened. "I feel it," Lissandra said, "but it doesn't seem to . . ."

Then she was screaming, and she stumbled backward. A great white sandking had clamped itself around her wrist. Blood welled through her skinthins where its mandibles had sunk in. It was fully as large as her hand.

Lissandra did a horrible little jig across the room and began to smash her hand against the nearest wall. Again and again and again. It landed with a heavy, meaty thud. Finally the sandking fell away. She whimpered and fell to her knees. "I think my fingers are broken," she said softly. The blood was still flowing freely. She had dropped the laser near the cellar door.

"I'm not going down there," her operative announced in clear firm tones.

Lissandra looked up at him. "No," she said. "Stand in the door and flame it all. Cinder it. Do you understand?"

He nodded.

Simon Kress moaned. "My *house*," he said. His stomach churned. The white sandking had been so *large*. How many more were down there? "Don't," he continued. "Leave it alone. I've changed my mind. Leave it alone."

Lissandra misunderstood. She held out her hand. It was covered with blood and greenish-black ichor. "Your little friend bit clean through my glove, and you saw what it took to get it off. I don't care about your house, Simon. Whatever is down there is going to die."

Kress hardly heard her. He thought he could see movement in the shadows beyond the cellar door. He imagined a white army bursting forth, all as large as the sandking that had attacked Lissandra. He saw himself being lifted by a hundred tiny arms, and dragged down into the darkness where the maw waited hungrily. He was afraid. "Don't," he said.

They ignored him.

Kress darted forward, and his shoulder slammed into the back of Lissandra's operative just as the man was bracing to fire. He grunted and was unbalanced and pitched forward into the black. Kress listened to him fall down the stairs. Afterward there were other noises—scuttlings and snaps and soft squishing sounds.

Kress swung around to face Lissandra. He was drenched in cold sweat, but a sickly kind of excitement was on him. It was almost sexual.

Lissandra's calm cold eyes regarded him through her mask. "What are you doing?" she demanded as Kress picked up the laser she had dropped. *"Simon!"*

"Making a peace," he said, giggling. "They won't hurt god, no, not so long as god is good and generous. I was cruel. Starved them. I have to make up for it now, you see."

"You're insane," Lissandra said. It was the last thing she said. Kress burned a hole in her chest big enough to put his arm through. He dragged the body across the floor and rolled it down the cellar stairs. The noises were louder—chitinous clackings and scrapings and echoes that were thick and liquid. Kress nailed up the door once again.

As he fled, he was filled with a deep sense of contentment that coated his fear like a layer of syrup. He suspected it was not his own.

He planned to leave his home, to fly to the city and take a room for a night, or perhaps for a year. Instead Kress started drinking. He was not quite sure why. He drank steadily for hours, and retched it all up violently on his living room carpet. At some point he fell asleep. When he woke, it was pitch-dark in the house.

He cowered against the couch. He could hear *noises*. Things were moving in the walls. They were all around him. His hearing was extraordinarily acute. Every little creak was the footstep of a sandking. He closed his eyes and waited, expecting to feel their terrible touch, afraid to move lest he brush against one.

Kress sobbed, and was very still for a while, but nothing happened.

He opened his eyes again. He trembled. Slowly the shadows began to soften and dissolve. Moonlight was filtering through the high windows. His eyes adjusted.

The living room was empty. Nothing there, nothing, nothing. Only his drunken fears.

Simon Kress steeled himself, and rose, and went to a light.

Nothing there. The room was quiet, deserted.

He listened. Nothing. No sound. Nothing in the walls. It had all been his imagination, his fear.

The memories of Lissandra and the thing in the cellar returned to him unbidden. Shame and anger washed over him. Why had he done that? He could have helped her burn it out, kill it. Why . . . he knew why. The maw had done it to him, put fear in him. Wo had said it was psionic, even when it was small. And now it was large, so large. It had feasted on Cath, and Idi, and now it had two more bodies down there. It would keep growing. And it had learned to like the taste of human flesh, he thought.

He began to shake, but he took control of himself again and stopped. It wouldn't hurt him. He was god. The whites had always been his favorites.

He remembered how he had stabbed it with his throwing-sword. That was before Cath came. Damn her anyway.

He couldn't stay here. The maw would grow hungry again. Large as it was, it wouldn't take long. Its appetite would be terrible. What would it do then? He had to get away, back to the safety of the city while it was still contained in his wine cellar. It was only plaster and hard-packed earth down there, and the mobiles could dig and tunnel. When they got free . . . Kress didn't want to think about it.

He went to his bedroom and packed. He took three bags. Just a single change of clothing, that was all he needed; the rest of the space he filled with his valuables, with jewelry and art and other things he could not bear to lose. He did not expect to return.

His shambler followed him down the stairs, staring at him from its baleful glowing eyes. It was gaunt. Kress realized that it had been ages since he had fed it. Normally it could take care of itself, but no doubt the pickings had grown lean of late. When it tried to clutch at his leg, he snarled at it and kicked it away, and it scurried off, offended.

Kress slipped outside, carrying his bags awkwardly, and shut the door behind him.

For a moment he stood pressed against the house, his heart thudding in his chest. Only a few meters between him and his skimmer. He was afraid to cross them. The moonlight was bright, and the front of his house was a scene of carnage. The bodies of Lissandra's two flamers lay where they had fallen, one twisted and burned, the other swollen beneath a mass of dead sandkings. And the mobiles, the black and red mobiles, they were all around him. It was an effort to remember that they were dead. It was almost as if they were simply waiting, as they had waited so often before.

Nonsense, Kress told himself. More drunken fears. He had seen the castles blown apart. They were dead, and the white maw was trapped in his cellar. He took several deep and deliberate breaths, and stepped forward onto the sandkings. They crunched. He ground them into the sand savagely. They did not move.

Kress smiled, and walked slowly across the battleground, listening to the sounds, the sounds of safety.

Crunch. Crackle. Crunch.

He lowered his bags to the ground and opened the door to his skimmer.

Something moved from shadow into light. A pale shape on the seat of his skimmer. It was as long as his forearm. Its mandibles clacked together softly, and it looked up at him from six small eyes set all around its body.

Kress wet his pants and backed away slowly.

There was more motion from inside the skimmer. He had left the door open. The sandking emerged and came toward him, cautiously. Others followed. They had been hiding beneath his seats, burrowed into the upholstery. But now they emerged. They formed a ragged ring around the skimmer.

Kress licked his lips, turned, and moved quickly to Lissandra's skimmer.

He stopped before he was halfway there. Things were moving inside that one too. Great maggoty things, half-seen by the light of the moon.

Kress whimpered and retreated back toward the house. Near the front door, he looked up.

He counted a dozen long white shapes creeping back and forth across the walls of the building. Four of them were clustered close together near the top of the unused belfry where the carrion hawk had once roosted. They were carving something. A face. A very recognizable face.

Simon Kress shrieked and ran back inside.

A sufficient quantity of drink brought him the easy oblivion he sought. But he woke. Despite everything, he woke. He had a terrible headache, and he smelled, and he was hungry. Oh so very hungry. He had never been so hungry.

Kress knew it was not his *own* stomach hurting.

A white sandking watched him from atop the dresser in his bedroom, its antennae moving faintly. It was as big as the one in the skimmer the night before. He was horribly dry, sandpaper dry. He licked his lips and fled from the room.

The house was full of sandkings; he had to be careful where he put his feet. They all seemed busy on errands of their own. They were making modifications in his house, burrowing into or out of his walls, carving things. Twice he saw his own likeness staring out at him from unexpected places. The faces were warped, twisted, livid with fear.

He went outside to get the bodies that had been rotting in the yard, hoping to appease the white maw's hunger. They were gone, both of them. Kress remembered how easily the mobiles could carry things many times their own weight.

It was terrible to think that the maw was *still* hungry after all of that.

When Kress reentered the house, a column of sandkings was wending its way down the stairs. Each carried a piece of his shambler. The head seemed to look at him reproachfully as it went by.

Kress emptied his freezers, his cabinets, everything, piling all the food in the house in the center of his kitchen floor. A dozen whites waited to take it away. They avoided the frozen food, leaving it to thaw in a great puddle, but they carried off everything else.

When all the food was gone, Kress felt his own hunger pangs abate just a bit, though he had not eaten a thing. But he knew the respite would be short-lived. Soon the maw would be hungry again. He had to feed it.

Kress knew what to do. He went to his communicator. "Malada," he began casually when the first of his friends answered, "I'm having a small party tonight. I realize this is terribly short notice, but I hope you can make it. I really do."

He called Jad Rakkis next, and then the others. By the time he had finished, nine of them had accepted his invitation. Kress hoped that would be enough.

Kress met his guests outside—the mobiles had cleaned up remarkably quickly, and the grounds looked almost as they had before the battle—and walked them to his front door. He let them enter first. He did not follow.

When four of them had gone through, Kress finally worked up his courage. He closed the door behind his latest guest, ignoring the startled exclamations that soon turned into shrill gibbering, and sprinted for the skimmer the man had arrived in. He slid in safely, thumbed the startplate, and swore. It was programmed to lift only in response to its owner's thumbprint, of course.

Jad Rakkis was the next to arrive. Kress ran to his skimmer as it set down, and seized Rakkis by the arm as he was climbing out. "Get back in, quickly," he said, pushing. "Take me to the city. Hurry, Jad. *Get out of here!*"

But Rakkis only stared at him, and would

not move. "Why, what's wrong, Simon? I don't understand. What about your party?"

And then it was too late, because the loose sand all around them was stirring, and the red eyes were staring at them, and the mandibles were clacking. Rakkis made a choking sound, and moved to get back in his skimmer, but a pair of mandibles snapped shut about his ankle, and suddenly he was on his knees. The sand seemed to boil with subterranean activity. Jad thrashed and cried terribly as they tore him apart. Kress could hardly bear to watch.

After that, he did not try to escape again. When it was all over, he cleaned out what remained in his liquor cabinet, and got extremely drunk. It would be the last time he would enjoy that luxury, he knew. The only alcohol remaining in the house was stored down in the wine cellar.

Kress did not touch a bite of food the entire day, but he fell asleep feeling bloated, sated at last, the awful hunger vanquished. His last thoughts before the nightmares took him were of whom he could ask out tomorrow.

Morning was hot and dry. Kress opened his eyes to see the white sandking on his dresser again. He shut them again quickly, hoping the dream would leave him. It did not, and he could not go back to sleep. Soon he found himself staring at the thing.

He stared for almost five minutes before the strangeness of it dawned on him; the sandking was not moving.

The mobiles could be preternaturally still, to be sure. He had seen them wait and watch a thousand times. But always there was some motion about them—the mandibles clacked, the legs twitched, the long fine antennae stirred and swayed.

But the sandking on his dresser was completely still.

Kress rose, holding his breath, not daring to hope. Could it be dead? Could something have killed it? He walked across the room.

The eyes were glassy and black. The crea-

ture seemed swollen, somehow, as if it were soft and rotting inside, filling up with gas that pushed outward at the plates of white armor.

Kress reached out a trembling hand and touched it.

It was warm—hot even—and growing hotter. But it did not move.

He pulled his hand back, and as he did, a segment of the sandking's white exoskeleton fell away from it. The flesh beneath was the same color, but softer looking, swollen and feverish. And it almost seemed to throb.

Kress backed away, and ran to the door.

Three more white mobiles lay in his hall. They were all like the one in his bedroom.

He ran down the stairs, jumping over sandkings. None of them moved. The house was full of them, all dead, dying, comatose, whatever. Kress did not care what was wrong with them. Just so they could not move.

He found four of them inside his skimmer. He picked them up one by one, and threw them as far as he could. Damned monsters. He slid back in, on the ruined half-eaten seats, and thumbed the startplate.

Nothing happened.

Kress tried again, and again. Nothing. It wasn't fair. This was *his* skimmer, it ought to start, why wouldn't it lift, he didn't understand.

Finally he got out and checked, expecting the worst. He found it. The sandkings had torn apart his gravity grid. He was trapped. He was still trapped.

Grimly, Kress marched back into the house. He went to his gallery and found the antique axe that had hung next to the throwing-sword he had used on Cath m'Lane. He set to work. The sandkings did not stir even as he chopped them to pieces. But they splattered when he made the first cut, the bodies almost bursting. Inside was awful; strange half-formed organs, a viscous reddish ooze that looked almost like human blood, and the yellow ichor.

Kress destroyed twenty of them before he realized the futility of what he was doing. The mobiles were nothing, really. Besides, there were so *many* of them. He could work for a day and night and still not kill them all.

He had to go down into the wine cellar and use the axe on the maw.

Resolute, he started down. He got within sight of the door, and stopped.

It was not a door anymore. The walls had been eaten away, so that the hole was twice the size it had been, and round. A pit, that was all. There was no sign that there had ever been a door nailed shut over that black abyss.

A ghastly, choking, fetid odor seemed to come from below.

And the walls were wet and bloody and covered with patches of white fungus.

And worst, it was *breathing*.

Kress stood across the room and felt the warm wind wash over him as it exhaled, and he tried not to choke, and when the wind reversed direction, he fled.

Back in the living room, he destroyed three more mobiles, and collapsed. What was *happening*? He didn't understand.

Then he remembered the only person who might understand. Kress went to his communicator again, stepping on a sandking in his haste, and prayed fervently that the device still worked.

When Jala Wo answered, he broke down and told her everything.

She let him talk without interruption, no expression save for a slight frown on her gaunt, pale face. When Kress had finished, she said only, "I ought to leave you there."

Kress began to blubber. "You can't. Help me. I'll pay. . . ."

"I ought to," Wo repeated, "but I won't."

"Thank you," Kress said. "Oh, thank—"

"Quiet," said Wo. "Listen to me. This is your own doing. Keep your sandkings well, and they are courtly ritual warriors. You turned yours into something else, with starvation and torture. You were their god. You made them what they are. That maw in your cellar is sick,

still suffering from the wound you gave it. It is probably insane. Its behavior is . . . unusual.

"You have to get out of there quickly. The mobiles are not dead, Kress. They are dormant. I told you the exoskeleton falls off when they grow larger. Normally, in fact, it falls off much earlier. I have never heard of sandkings growing as large as yours while still in the insectoid stage. It is another result of crippling the white maw, I would say. That does not matter.

"What matters is the metamorphosis your sandkings are now undergoing. As the maw grows, you see, it gets progressively more intelligent. Its psionic powers strengthen, and its mind becomes more sophisticated, more ambitious. The armored mobiles are useful enough when the maw is tiny and only semi-sentient, but now it needs better servants, bodies with capabilities. Do you understand? The mobiles are all going to give birth to a new breed of sandking. I can't say exactly what it will look like. Each maw designs its own, to fit its perceived needs and desires. But it will be biped, with four arms, and opposable thumbs. It will be able to construct and operate advanced machinery. The individual sandkings will not be sentient. But the maw will be very sentient indeed."

Simon Kress was gaping at Wo's image on the viewscreen. "Your workers," he said, with an effort. "The ones who came out here . . . who installed the tank . . ."

Jala Wo managed a faint smile. "Shade," she said.

"Shade is a sandking," Kress repeated numbly. "And you sold me a tank of . . . of . . . infants, ah. . . ."

"Do not be absurd," Wo said. "A first-stage sandking is more like a sperm than an infant. The wars temper and control them in nature. Only one in a hundred reaches second stage. Only one in a thousand achieves the third and final plateau, and becomes like Shade. Adult sandkings are not sentimental about the small maws. There are too many of them, and their mobiles are pests." She sighed. "And all this talk wastes time. That white sandking is going to waken to full sentience soon. It is not going to need you any longer, and it hates you, and it will be very hungry. The transformation is taxing. The maw must eat enormous amounts both before and after. So you have to get out of there. Do you understand?"

"*I can't*," Kress said. "My skimmer is destroyed, and I can't get any of the others to start. I don't know how to reprogram them. Can you come out for me?"

"Yes," said Wo. "Shade and I will leave at once, but it is more than two hundred kilometers from Asgard to you, and there is equipment we will need to deal with the deranged sandking you've created. You cannot wait there. You have two feet. Walk. Go due east, as near as you can determine, as quickly as you can. The land out there is pretty desolate. We'll find you easily with an aerial search, and you'll be safely away from the sandking. Do you understand?"

"Yes," said Simon Kress. "Yes, oh, yes."

They signed off, and he walked quickly toward the door. He was halfway there when he heard the noise—a sound halfway between a pop and a crack.

One of the sandkings had split open. Four tiny hands covered with pinkish-yellow blood came up out of the gap and began to push the dead skin aside.

Kress began to run.

He had not counted on the heat.

The hills were dry and rocky. Kress ran from the house as quickly as he could, ran until his ribs ached and his breath was coming in gasps. Then he walked, but as soon as he had recovered he began to run again. For almost an hour he ran and walked, ran and walked, beneath the fierce hot sun. He sweated freely, and wished that he had thought to bring some water. He watched the sky in hopes of seeing Wo and Shade.

He was not made for this. It was too hot,

and too dry, and he was in no condition. But he kept himself going with the memory of the way the maw had breathed, and the thought of the wriggling little things that by now were surely crawling all over his house. He hoped Wo and Shade would know how to deal with them.

He had his own plans for Wo and Shade. It was all their fault, Kress had decided, and they would suffer for it. Lissandra was dead, but he knew others in her profession. He would have his revenge. He promised himself that a hundred times as he struggled and sweated his way east.

At least he hoped it was east. He was not that good at directions, and he wasn't certain which way he had run in his initial panic, but since then he had made an effort to bear due east, as Wo had suggested.

When he had been running for several hours, with no sign of rescue, Kress began to grow certain that he had gone wrong.

When several more hours passed, he began to grow afraid. What if Wo and Shade could not find him? He would die out here. He hadn't eaten in two days; he was weak and frightened; his throat was raw for want of water. He couldn't keep going. The sun was sinking now, and he'd be completely lost in the dark. What was wrong? Had the sandkings eaten Wo and Shade? The fear was on him again, filling him, and with it a great thirst and a terrible hunger. But Kress kept going. He stumbled now when he tried to run, and twice he fell. The second time he scraped his hand on a rock, and it came away bloody. He sucked at it as he walked, and worried about infection.

The sun was on the horizon behind him. The ground grew a little cooler, for which Kress was grateful. He decided to walk until last light and settle in for the night. Surely he was far enough from the sandkings to be safe, and Wo and Shade would find him come morning.

When he topped the next rise, he saw the outline of a house in front of him.

It wasn't as big as his own house, but it was big enough. It was habitation, safety. Kress shouted and began to run toward it. Food and drink, he had to have nourishment, he could taste the meal now. He was aching with hunger. He ran down the hill towards the house, waving his arms and shouting to the inhabitants. The light was almost gone now, but he could still make out a half-dozen children playing in the twilight. "Hey there," he shouted. "Help, help."

They came running toward him.

Kress stopped suddenly. "No," he said, "oh, no. Oh, no." He backpedaled, slipped on the sand, got up and tried to run again. They caught him easily. They were ghastly little things with bulging eyes and dusky orange skin. He struggled, but it was useless. Small as they were, each of them had four arms, and Kress had only two.

They carried him toward the house. It was a sad, shabby house built of crumbling sand, but the door was quite large, and dark, and it breathed. That was terrible, but it was not the thing that set Simon Kress to screaming. He screamed because of the others, the little orange children who came crawling out from the castle, and watched impassive as he passed.

All of them had his face.

Wives

LISA TUTTLE

Lisa Tuttle (1952–) is an influential US science fiction and fantasy writer whose work often contains a deep vein of horror. A longtime resident of the United Kingdom, Tuttle now has dual British–American citizenship. She has won the John W. Campbell Award for Best New Writer (1974) and the Nebula Award (1982; she refused the award because of campaigning by another nominee, which she objected to), among others. Her first short story collection to be published in France, *Ainsi naissent les fantômes* (*Ghosts and Other Lovers*), won the Grand Prix de l'Imaginaire in 2012.

Prolific and inquisitive, Tuttle has published more than a dozen novels, including *Familiar Spirit* (1983), *Gabriel* (1987), *Lost Futures* (1992), *The Mysteries* (2005), *The Silver Bough* (2006), and *The Curious Affair of the Somnambulist & The Psychic Thief* (2016). Her fiction has been compiled in several short story collections and her nonfiction titles include a reference book on feminism, *Encyclopedia of Feminism* (1986). She has also edited such anthologies as *Skin of the Soul: New Horror Stories by Women* (1990) and has reviewed books for publications such as *The Sunday Times*. Along with such writers as Howard Waldrop and Bruce Sterling, Tuttle helped found the Turkey City writer's workshop in 1973. Tuttle's collaborative novella with George R. R. Martin, "The Storms of Windhaven," was nominated for a Hugo Award (1976). They later published a novel-length version titled *Windhaven* (1981).

Tuttle has published several short stories considered classics in the field. "Replacements" (1992), reprinted in, among others, Joyce Carol Oates's *American Gothic Tales* (1996) and *The Weird: A Compendium of Strange Dark Stories* (2011), is one such tale. Another is "Wives," a classic of feminist science fiction and of alien contact, thought-provoking and sinister. It lives comfortably alongside Chad Oliver's "Let Me Live in a House" (1954), found elsewhere in this volume. Asked about the story, written in 1976, Tuttle responded, "I fear [it] is still depressingly relevant today, rather than being a quaint artifact of the bad old sexist, violent, aggressively colonialist days as my younger self would have wished."

WIVES

Lisa Tuttle

A smell of sulphur in the air on a morning when the men had gone, and the wives, in their beds, smiled in their sleep, breathed more easily, and burrowed deeper into dreams.

Jack's wife woke, her eyes open and her little nose flaring, smelling something beneath the sulphur smell. One of those smells she was used to not noticing, when the men were around. But it was all right, now. Wives could do as they pleased, so long as they cleaned up and were back in their proper places when the men returned.

Jack's wife—who was called Susie—got out of bed too quickly and grimaced as the skintight punished her muscles. She caught sight of herself in the mirror over the dressing table: her sharp teeth were bared, and she looked like a wild animal, bound and struggling. She grinned at that, because she could easily free herself.

She cut the skintight apart with scissors, cutting and ripping carelessly. It didn't matter that it was ruined—skintights were plentiful. She had a whole boxful, herself, in the hall closet behind the Christmas decorations. And she didn't have the patience to try soaking it off slowly in a hot bath, as the older wives recommended. So her muscles would be sore and her skintight a tattered rag—she would be free that much sooner.

She looked down at her dead-white body, feeling distaste. She felt despair at the sight of her small arms, hanging limp, thin and useless in the hollow below her ribs. She tried to flex them but could not make them move. She began to massage them with her primary fingers, and after several minutes the pain began, and she knew they weren't dead yet.

She bathed and massaged her newly uncovered body with oil. She felt terrifyingly free, naked and rather dangerous, with the skintight removed. She sniffed the air again and that familiar scent, musky and alluring, aroused her.

She ran through the house—noticing, in passing, that Jack's pet spider was eating the living room sofa. It was the time for building nests and cocoons, she thought happily, time for laying eggs and planting seeds; the spider was driven by the same force that drove her.

Outside the dusty ground was hard and cold beneath her bare feet. She felt the dust all over her body, raised by the wind and clinging to her momentary warmth. She was coated in the soft yellow dust by the time she reached the house next door—the house where the magical scent came from, the house which held a wife in heat, longing for someone to mate with.

Susie tossed her head, shaking the dust out in a little cloud around her head. She stared up at the milky sky and around at all the houses, alien artefacts constructed by men. She saw movement in the window of the house across the street and waved—the figure watching her waved back.

Poor old Maggie, thought Susie. Old, bulging, and ugly; unloved and nobody's wife. She was only housekeeper to two men who were, rather unfortunately Susie thought, in love with each other.

But she didn't want to waste time by thinking of wives and men, or by feeling pity, now. Boldly, like a man, Susie pounded at the door.

It opened. "Ooooh, Susie!"

Susie grinned and looked the startled wife up and down. You'd never know from looking at her that the men were gone and she could relax—this wife, called Doris, was as dolled up as some eager-to-please newlywed and looked, Susie thought, more like a real woman than any woman had ever looked.

Over her skintight (which was bound more tightly than Susie's had been) Doris wore a low-cut dress, her three breasts carefully bound and positioned to achieve the proper, double-breasted effect. Gaily patterned and textured stockings covered her silicone-injected legs, and she tottered on heels three centimetres high. Her face was carefully painted, and she wore gold bands on neck, wrists, and fingers.

Then Susie ignored what she looked like because her nose told her so much more. The smell was so powerful now that she could feel her pouch swelling in lonely response.

Doris must have noticed, for her eyes rolled, seeking some safe view.

"What's the matter?" Susie asked, her voice louder and bolder than it ever was when the men were around. "Didn't your man go off to war with the others? He stay home sick in bed?"

Doris giggled. "Ooooh, I wish he would, sometimes! No, he was out of here before it was light."

Off to see his mistress before leaving, Susie thought. She knew that Doris was nervous about being displaced by one of the other wives her man was always fooling around with—there were always more wives than there were men, and her man had a roving eye.

"Calm down, Doris. Your man can't see you now, you know." She stroked one of Doris's hands. "Why don't you take off that silly dress and your skintight. I know how constricted you must be feeling. Why not relax with me?"

She saw Doris's face darken with emotion beneath the heavy makeup, and she grasped her hand more tightly when Doris tried to pull away.

"Please don't," Doris said.

"Come on," Susie murmured, caressing Doris's face and feeling the thick paint slide beneath her fingers.

"No, don't . . . please . . . I've tried to con-trol myself, truly I have. But the exercises don't work, and the perfume doesn't cover the smell well enough—he won't even sleep with me when I'm like this. He thinks it's disgusting, and it is. I'm so afraid he'll leave me."

"But he's gone now, Doris. You can let yourself go. You don't have to worry about him when he's not around! It's safe, it's all right, you can do as you please now—we can do anything we like and no one will know." She could feel Doris trembling.

"Doris," she whispered, and rubbed her face demandingly against hers.

At that, the other wife gave in, and collapsed in her arms.

Susie helped Doris out of her clothes, tearing at them with hands and teeth, throwing shoes and jewellery high into the air and festooning the yard with rags of dress, stockings, and undergarment.

But when Doris, too, was naked, Susie suddenly felt shy and a little frightened. It would be wrong to mate here in the settlement built by man, wrong and dangerous. They must go somewhere else, somewhere they could be something other than wives for a little while, and follow their own natures without reproach.

They went to a place of stone on the far northern edge of the human settlement. It was a very old place, although whether it had been built by the wives in the distant time before they were wives or whether it was natural, neither Susie nor Doris could say. They both felt it was a holy place, and it seemed right to mate there, in the shadow of one of the huge, black standing stones.

It was a feast, an orgy of life after a season of death. They found pleasure in exploring the bodies which seemed so similar to men but which they knew to be miraculously different, each from the other, in scent, texture, and taste. They forgot that they had ever been creatures known as wives. They lost their names and forgot the language of men as they lay entwined.

There were no skintights imprisoning their bodies now, barring them from sensation, freedom, and pleasure, and they were partners, not strangers, as they explored and exulted in their flesh. This was no mockery of the sexual act— brutishly painful and brief as it was with the men—but the true act in all its meaning.

They were still joined at sundown, and it was not until long after the three moons began their nightly waltz through the clouds that the two lovers fell asleep at last.

"In three months," Susie said dreamily. "We can—"

"In three months we won't do anything."

"Why not? If the men are away . . ."

"I'm hungry," said Doris. She wrapped her primary arms around herself. "And I'm cold, and I ache all over. Let's go back."

"Stay here with me, Doris. Let's plan."

"There's nothing to plan."

"But in three months we must get together and fertilize it."

"Are you crazy? Who would carry it then? One of us would have to go without a skintight, and do you think either of our husbands would let us slop around for four months without a skintight? And then when it's born how could we hide it? Men don't have babies, and they don't want anyone else to. Men kill babies, just as they kill all their enemies."

Susie knew that what Doris was saying was true, but she was reluctant to give up her new dream. "Still, we might be able to keep it hidden," she said. "It's not so hard to hide things from a man. . . ."

"Don't be so stupid," Doris said scornfully. Susie noticed that she still had smears of makeup on her face. Some smears had transferred themselves to Susie in the night. They looked like bruises or bloody wounds. "Come back with me now," Doris said, her voice gentle again. "Forget this, about the baby. The old ways are gone— we're wives now, and we don't have a place in our lives for babies."

"But someday the war may end," Susie said. "And the men will all go back to Earth and leave us here."

"If that happens," said Doris, "then we would make new lives for ourselves. Perhaps we would have babies again."

"If it's not too late then," Susie said. "If it ever happens." She stared past Doris at the horizon.

"Come back with me."

Susie shook her head. "I have to think. You go. I'll be all right."

She realized when Doris had gone that she, too, was tired, hungry, and sore, but she was not sorry she had remained in the place of stone. She needed to stay awhile longer in one of the old places, away from the distractions of the settlement. She felt that she was on the verge of remembering something very important.

A large, dust-coloured lizard crawled out of a hole in the side of a fallen rock, and Susie rolled over and clapped her hands on it. But it wriggled out of her clutches like air or water or the windblown dust and disappeared somewhere. Susie felt a sharp pang of disappointment— she had a sudden memory of how that lizard would have tasted, how the skin of its throat would have felt, tearing between her teeth. She licked her dry lips and sat up. In the old days, she thought, I caught many such lizards. But the old days were gone, and with them the old knowledge and the old abilities.

I'm not what I used to be, she thought. I'm something else now, a "wife," created by man in the image of something I have never seen, something called "woman."

She thought about going back to her house in the settlement and of wrapping herself in a new skintight and then selecting the proper dress and shoes to make a good impression on the returning Jack; she thought about painting her face and putting rings on her fingers. She thought about boiling and burning good food to turn it into the unappetizing messes Jack favoured, and about killing the wide-eyed "coffee fish" to get the oil to make the mildly addictive drink the men called "coffee." She thought about watching Jack, and listening to him, always alert for what he might want, what he might ask, what he might do. Trying to anticipate him, to earn his praise and avoid his blows and harsh words. She thought about letting him "screw" her and about the ugly jewellery and noisome perfumes he brought her.

Susie began to cry, and the dust drank her tears as they fell. She didn't understand how this had all begun, how or why she had become a wife, but she could bear it no longer.

She wanted to be what she had been born to be—but she could not remember what that was. She only knew that she could be Susie no longer. She would be no man's wife.

"I remembered my name this morning," Susie said with quiet triumph. She looked around the room. Doris was staring down at her hands, twisting them in her lap. Maggie looked half asleep, and the other two wives—Susie didn't remember their names; she had simply gathered them up when she found them on the street—looked both bored and nervous.

"Don't you see?" Susie persisted. "If I could remember that, I'm sure I can remember other things, in time. All of us can."

Maggie opened her eyes all the way. "And what good would that do," she asked, "except make us discontented and restless, as you are?"

"What *good* . . . why, if we all began to remember, we could live our lives again—our *own* lives. We wouldn't have to be wives, we could be . . . ourselves."

"Could we?" said Maggie sourly. "And do you think the men would watch us go? Do you think they'd let us walk out of their houses and out of their lives without stopping us? Don't you—you who talk about remembering—don't you remember how it was when the men came? Don't you remember the slaughter? Don't you remember just who became wives, and why? We, the survivors, became wives because the men wouldn't kill us then, not if we kept them happy and believing we weren't the enemy. If we try to leave or change, they'll kill us like they've killed almost everything else in the world."

The others were silent, but Susie suspected they were letting Maggie speak for them.

"But we'll die," she said. "We'll die like this, as wives. We've lost our identities, but we can have them back. We can have the world back, and our lives, only if we take them. We're dying as a race and as a world, now. Being a wife is a living death, just a postponement of the end, that's all."

"Yes," said Maggie, irony hanging heavily from the word. "So?"

"So why do we have to let them do this to us? We can hide—we can run far away from the settlement and hide. Or, if we have to, we can fight back."

"That's not our way," said Maggie.

"Then what *is* our way?" Susie demanded. "Is it our way to let ourselves be destroyed? They've already killed our culture and our past—we have no 'way' anymore—we can't claim we do. All we are now is imitations, creatures moulded by the men. And when the men leave—if the men leave—it will be the end for us. We'll have nothing left, and it will be too late to try to remember who we were."

"It's already too late," Maggie said. Susie was suddenly impressed by the way she spoke and held herself, and wondered if Maggie, this elderly and unloved wife she had once pitied, had once been a leader of her people.

"Can you remember why we did not fight or hide before?" Maggie asked. "Can you remember why we decided that the best thing for us was to change our ways, to do what you are now asking us to undo?"

Susie shook her head.

"Then go and try to remember. Remember that we made a choice when the men came, and now we must live with that choice. Remember that there was a good reason for what we did, a reason of survival. It is too late to change again. The old way is not waiting for our return, it is dead. Our world had been changed, and we could not stop it. The past is dead, but that is as it should be. We have new lives now. Forget your restlessness and go home. Be a good wife to Jack—he loves you in his way. Go home, and be thankful for that."

"I can't," she said. She looked around the room, noticing how the eyes of the others fell before hers; so few of them had wanted to listen to her, so few had dared venture out of their homes. Susie looked at Maggie as she spoke, meaning her words for all the wives. "They're killing us slowly," she said. "But we'll be just as dead in the end. I would rather die fighting, and take some of them with us."

"You may be ready to die now, but the rest of us are not," Maggie said. "But if you fought them, you would get not only your own death, but the death of us all. If they see you snarling and violent, they will wake up and turn new eyes on the rest of us and see us not as their loving wives but as beasts, strangers, dangerous wild animals to be destroyed. They forget that we are different from them; they are willing to forget and let us live as long as we keep them comfortable and act as wives should act."

"I can't fight them alone, I know that," Susie said. "But if you'll all join with me, we have a chance. We could take them by surprise, we could use their weapons against them. Why not? They don't expect a fight from us—we could win. Some of us would die, of course, but many of us would survive. More than that—we'd have our own lives, our own world, back again."

"You think your arguments are new," said Maggie. There was a trace of impatience in her usually calm voice. "But I can remember the old days, even if you can't. I remember what happened when the men first came, and I know what would happen if we angered them. Even if we managed somehow to kill all the men here, more men would come in their ships from the sky. And they would come to kill us for daring to fight them. Perhaps they would simply drop fire on us, this time being sure to burn out all of us and all life on our world. Do you seriously ask us to bring about this certain destruction?"

Susie stared at her, feeling dim memories stir in response to her words. Fire from the sky, the burning, the killing . . . But she couldn't be certain she remembered, and she would rather risk destruction than go back to playing wife again.

"We could hide," she said, pleading. "We could run away and hide in the wilderness. The men might think we had died—they'd forget about us soon, I'm certain. Even if they looked for us at first, we could hide. It's our world, and we know it as they don't. Soon we could live again as we used to, and forget the men."

"Stop this dreaming," Maggie said. "We can never live the way we used to—the old ways are gone, the old world is gone, and even your memories are gone, that's obvious. The only way we know how to live now is with the men, as their wives. Everything else is gone. We'd die of hunger and exposure if the men didn't track us down and kill us first."

"I may have forgotten the old ways, but you haven't. You could teach us."

"I remember enough to know that what is gone, is gone. To know that we can't go back. Believe me. Think about it, Susie. Try—"

"Don't call me that!"

Her shout echoed in the silence. No one spoke. Susie felt the last of her hope drain out of her as she looked at them. They did not feel what she felt, and she would not be able to convince them. In silence, still, she left them, and went back to her own house.

She waited for them there, for them to come and kill her.

She knew that they would come; she knew she had to die. It was as Maggie had said: one renegade endangered them all. If one wife turned on one man, all the wives would be made to suffer. The look of love on their faces would change to a look of hatred, and the slaughter would begin again.

Susie felt no desire to try to escape, to hide from the other wives as she had suggested they all hide from the men. She had no wish to live alone; for good or ill she was a part of her people, and she did not wish to endanger them nor to break away from them.

When they came, they came together, all the

wives of the settlement, coming to act in concert so none should bear the guilt alone. They did not hate Susie, nor did she hate them, but the deadly work had to be done.

Susie walked outside, to make it easier for them. By offering not the slightest resistance, she felt herself to be acting with them. She presented the weakest parts of her body to their hands and teeth, that her death should come more quickly. And as she died, feeling her body pressed, pounded, and torn by the other wives, Susie did not mind the pain. She felt herself a part of them all, and she died content.

After her death, one of the extra wives took on Susie's name and moved into her house. She got rid of the spider's gigantic egg-case first thing—Jack might have liked his football-sized pet, but he wouldn't be pleased by the hundreds of pebble-sized babies that would come spilling out of the egg-case in a few months. Then she began to clean in earnest: a man deserved a clean house to come home to.

When, a few days later, the men returned from their fighting, Susie's man, Jack, found a spotless house, filled with the smells of his favourite foods cooking, and a smiling, sexily dressed wife.

"Would you like some dinner, dear?" she asked.

"Put it on hold," he said, grinning wolfishly. "Right now I'll take a cup of coffee—in bed—with you on the side."

She fluttered her false eyelashes and moved a little closer, so he could put his arm around her if he liked.

"Three tits and the best coffee in the universe," he said with satisfaction, squeezing one of the bound lumps of flesh on her chest. "With this to come home to, it kind of makes the whole war-thing worthwhile."

The Snake Who Had Read Chomsky

JOSEPHINE SAXTON

Josephine Saxton (1935–) is an English writer most notably associated with both the New Wave movement and the rise of feminist science fiction. Her novel *Queen of the States* (1986) was shortlisted for the Arthur C. Clarke Award, losing to Margaret Atwood's *The Handmaid's Tale*. She began publishing science fiction with "The Wall" for *Science Fantasy* 78 in 1965, and her first three novels—*The Hieros Gamos of Sam and An Smith* (1969), *Vector for Seven: The Weltanschaung of Mrs. Amelia Mortimer and Friends* (1970), and *Group Feast* (1971)—established her very rapidly as a unique and surreal writer invested in allegory and the interior life of her characters. Often, these early works feature an attempted quest that is badly botched or terminated without success.

In the 1980s, Saxon published *The Travails of Jane Saint* (1980), *The Consciousness Machine* (1980), and *Jane Saint and the Backlash: The Further Travails of Jane Saint* (1989). Both *Travails* and *Further Travails* were later released in expanded editions with additional related stories. *Queen of the States*—"States" can be interpreted as referring to the United States or to various sorts of mental breakdown—comes very close to a savage reductionism: the SF/fantasy escapades of the female protagonist default constantly to delusion, for she is imprisoned in a mental institution. Most of Saxon's short stories, from 1966 to 1985, have been collected in *The Power of Time* (1985). *Little Tours of Hell: Tall Tales of Food and Holidays* (1986) includes no science fiction but does include some horror fiction. Her most recent book, *Gardening Down a Rabbit Hole* (1996), is a memoir of her gardening experiences.

Throughout Saxton's work from the 1980s, there is a deep understanding, in a feminist sense, of the constraints binding women to a male-oriented reality. Equally, there is a sense of the author's trust in her own subconscious and the images arising from that subconscious in the creation of her fiction. Her novels and stories are unruly in the best way, much less stylized and formal than Angela Carter's, but containing that same sense of wildness and unpredictability. Saxton clearly had no interest in following safe or established approaches to structure, plot, or characterization—and in experimenting she often hit upon sui generis ways to tell stories. At the same time Saxton un-domesticated domestic themes, writing about ordinary women and their lives in a way similar to Judith Merril and Kate Wilhelm, but from a less realistic stance and in a more phantasmagorical style.

Roz Kaveney, editor of Saxton's *The Power of Time*, described Saxton's work as "a combination of surrealism, occultism, feminism and a sort of bloody-minded Midlands Englishness, and quite wonderful." John Crowley was inspired by Saxton's work to write a love story ("Exogamy") with speculative elements—influenced in particular by *The Hieros Gamos of Sam and An Smith*.

"The Snake Who Had Read Chomsky" (1981) is classic Saxton: a take-no-prisoners examination of biotech experimentation and the follies of capitalist societies in the grips of decadent extremes. It is sharp, incisive, darkly inventive, and an excellent example of the capabilities of this brilliant but underrated writer.

THE SNAKE WHO HAD READ CHOMSKY

Josephine Saxton

They spent almost all their nonofficial working time, and their spare time, in that part of the lab which had been requisitioned for them. Although it was not large, it sufficed; to unravel nucleic acid chains does not require a dance hall plus arcades. They were very satisfied with the robot assistance that Selly had allowed them, plus computer time, subelectron microscope, chemical analyzer, and all the animals they needed.

"Yes, certainly, Marvene and Janos, if you wish to research into some aspects of the genetic part of animal behavior then I shall be pleased to encourage you, just so long as your work here for me does not suffer, of course." Their work had not suffered, they saw to that. Their private work was not exactly what they stated, but it was near enough to deceive an observer who would be scrupulous and not snoop extensively. There was a little more to it than the behavior of the cat, but even to themselves they maintained a neutral attitude to their information, knowing only what they hoped.

There were mice being used, and a boa constrictor called Lupus the Loop who had a sole right to mice as food, and who possibly resented the fact that Marvene used a large proportion of them for her work instead of feeding them to him.

"Getting the information to link itself to all the cell types is the final key," said Janos, taking a look at some mice who were hibernating in a lowered temperature even though they were a non-hibernating variety. "These mice are hibernating, but they will never shed their skin." Janos very much wanted to have a coup with this research. He stood to be what he wanted for the rest of his life if all went well.

Marvene glanced at him with concealed contempt. "The skin-shedding isn't important at this stage, surely? If we stick to the line we are on, we shall have the final tests ready in weeks," she told him evenly and not without effort. Working in such close confines with one person for so long was not good for personal regard, but worse, it almost inclined one to show that bad feeling. She was taking extra pains with her good manners. She too wanted to be rewarded by the world for this work, and she had no intention of allowing Janos to take the whole accolade, as she rightly suspected he would like to do. They had not discussed this aspect of the project, it would have been quite rude to do so, but instead maintained an implicit agreement that like all scientists they would share honors. It was certain that they had both been equally dedicated and both worked hard and with concentration. Not a moment was wasted in idle chatter. They had sufficient incentive not to waste their opportunity, for they could also be revenged upon Selly, whom they hated. That greasy, plump, celibate person was not to be allowed to share any reflected glory from their work. He had irritated and disgusted them for so long with his unaesthetic presence, and they meant to be revenged upon him. It was worth the risk of discovery, they had decided; the plan was irresistible. When they thought of this they would laugh together, but when they thought of their separate plans, they laughed apart, and silently.

Selly rarely visited them in their area; he went home at night to who knew what, alone in his bachelor apartment. Sour as old socks, Selly, white as suet but softer, secretive, and full of bile. But very clever, and this they respected.

It was one of the reasons they were at this lab, Selly's notorious cleverness. They had hoped to learn from him and in many ways they had. He was already near the top of the social list, even though he socialized so little. He was known for being something of a recluse, and for his genius and originality in demonstrating his ideas.

Selly had wished to demonstrate that light-obedient hormones were involved in flight patterns in birds, and he had caused a skylark to dive into the depths of illuminated water, singing. The audience had considered this very amusing. What had made it unpleasant was the way Selly laughed at the sight of the little creature trying to warble until it was drowned in watery light.

He had done some useful things, also, in the business of providing food for the world's surplus people. He had produced a runner bean which was 50 percent first-class animal protein. These could be fed on petroleum by-products, having the ability to make the chemical changes within their own metabolism and, also, the useful ability to cleanse the soil by exuding a solvent which was biodegradable. It was true, Selly was no slouch in his work.

As for Marvene and Janos's part in Selly's work, they were assisting him in breeding a two-kilo mouse which would at first be used in factory soupmeat and later, after sufficient publicity, as a roast. So far the creatures had died before slaughtering could take place, so there was still work to do on strengthening the heart muscles of these little giants. These animals were fed on processed petroleum by-products. There was a vast store of fossil fuels since the melting of the polar ice caps had made it available. The lab in which they worked was part of a redundant atomic power station, ideal because of its isolation coupled with easy access by underground train to the living complexes: it took them only five minutes to return to the other world. In one of the larger central areas of the building they had constructed a reproduction of a typical deserted domestic settlement of the lower classes. The actual work of course

had been done by a workgang from the lower classes. If such settlements could be shown to be suitable for breeding mice, then some of them could be used, for there were many such ghost towns since the suicide epidemics. There was no question of experimenting with a real one; they were all too far away from civilization. Their main problem had been getting the right light and darkness periods, because even though there was so little difference between them since the canopy came over the ancient skies, the animals all had residual circadian rhythms. All the upper-class human beings had artificial moonlight and sunlight in regulated phases because it had been shown to have an important psychological effect on brain chemistry, but the lower classes, for whom such things did not matter, lived in a dim limbo, monotonous and drear.

As a companion work on food they were breeding a potato containing every known nutritional element in correct proportion for maintaining human life. This was proving harder than anticipated, because some vitamins destroyed others when existing in the same plant. But they would succeed, with Selly's guidance. It was going to make the lower-class menu very dull, but that did not matter. Selly could have existed on such fodder, for he was a very poor aesthete in the matter of food as in other things. This disgusted them. Selly did not enjoy life; he enjoyed ideas about life. He once confided in a rare moment of intimacy: "There is a life of the mind which I have hardly touched upon yet." They could have expanded on that comment but chose not.

In some ways, Selly was downright immature, a state not at all to be admired. She did not think him fit to live in the wonderful architectural fantasy of their upper-class settlement; he was an eyesore. They all had very small apartments, but it was one of the best specialist settlements in existence. The upper classes needed the stimulus of interesting surroundings, and interest had been taken well toward the limits both visually and kinetically. Their settlement was famous for its dissolving architecture; at any moment a balcony might disappear and drop people to their deaths. This did not happen so often that it was monotonous, but often enough to make living there exciting. In historical times, those people living on fault lines must have been exhilarated in much the same way, Marvene reflected. How ghastly it must be to live in the utilitarian warrens of the lower classes! Would society never find a humane way of ridding itself of all those surplus people left over since human labor had become almost redundant? Marvene profoundly hoped so: they were an anchor to a civilization that needed to sail ahead.

If Selly was successful even with the potatoes, he would become a very high-ranking upper-class person. They considered him a totally unsuitable candidate for this because of his vulgarity. But whatever they thought, it was necessary to apply the art of flattery. He was always susceptible.

"Selly, I feel constrained to voice my admiration for your working method today. You are so stylish in your approach to what must feel like mundane tasks to one so advanced as yourself. I wish very much to cultivate your self-control." Marvene smiled sweetly at him through her diamante-effect contact lenses. The twinkling was a stunning effect, and hid real feeling. Selly was not susceptible to female charm, but in his genetic makeup somewhere there must surely have been a response to beauty, for once, just once, he had reached out to touch Marvene's hair, which had been trained to move constantly in shining coils, always changing its shape like a mass of slowly dancing snakes. Strictly speaking she was reaching above her present level of society with such styles, but sometimes beauty was forgiven social errors. Because she made such a beautiful model she had managed to get it done free, but she had been obliged to have all the actichips inserted in her skull with only local anaesthetic.

"Thank you, Marvene. I'm glad you appreciate the difference between mere routine work

well done and a truly aesthetic approach to the mundane. I may be able to give you some instruction on that."

"Selly, I would be so grateful if you could. If I could only emulate you . . ."

"Marvene, it is all inner work. One has to control the entire self in order to properly control things like grace and care." He didn't really have grace, she thought, he was just lethargic.

"If you talk to yourself, Marvene, daily, and draw all your energies in toward your working self every morning, you will be able to bring more presence to your work." This wholly patronizing speech was typical and it made her angry. She already did this rather commonplace exercise every morning. She had presence and style, and knew it, and she practiced attitudes toward the day when she meant to grace the highest levels of society. When Marvene had completed her research she would not only have put horrible Selly down, but have a weapon which could forever quell invaders, preventing war, and could possibly be used to keep the lower classes permanently occupied, if not eliminated. She would be remembered.

They already had the means of fixing Selly and of testing out their work at the same time, but for mass use they needed a foolproof method of dissemination which would disperse itself in a population per body weight and type equally everywhere. If they could only have had a few humans to experiment upon, the job would by now have been done; but there was still too much opposition to human experimentation to make it popular, and it was certainly illegal to use human beings without their recorded consent, and this applied even to the lower classes, a very atavistic area of the law. With this work they hoped to justify human experimentation and thus earn the gratitude of scientists everywhere whose work was held up for lack of suitable material.

Selly was an ideal subject, being so predictable and stable in his habits, and in having no close friends. Selly could not be bothered with friends. He occasionally arranged some social life, of course, buying a dinner party for himself in some exotic building, but these occasions were only meant to keep his name in circulation and to impress the influential. It was always necessary to keep in favor in order to get financial patronage. He was ideal because any noticeable effects must be observed only by themselves until such time as they wished it otherwise.

"You know, Marvene," said Janos, showing his small and boringly ordinary teeth in a slow smile of what in a stronger personality would have been consummate awfulness, "I have to admire Selly for his independence of other people, especially women."

"And what's so good about that?" she demanded icily, fire flashing off her eyeballs. "I don't see where the style is, in being by yourself. There's nobody to appreciate a lone person. One needs other opinions."

Janos chose to overlook her anger, regarding it as one might a bit of flatus. "If you're good enough and know it, then nobody is going to think better of you than yourself," he replied. He had that relentless argumentative tone in his voice that she had once found very attractive, believing it to be self-assurance. It was certain that nobody was going to think better of Marvene and Janos than themselves. Marvene still required that the whole of society admire her, as soon as possible. So did Janos, of course; he was indulging in conceit with his words. He did not know it but he had managed without her good opinion for years.

"I have to disagree. An isolated opinion is not valid, especially when the subject cannot see the self from outside, which is a rare achievement. How can you ever really know what impression you are making?"

"I have practiced projecting myself, metaphorically speaking, and using my imagination to know what impression I am making. Doesn't everyone do that, Marvene?"

"Of course, but it is a matter of degree and skill. It will still be a heavily subjective result."

He did not like that idea, clearly. "If you

persist in making destructive statements against me, I shall be obliged to be rude to you."

This formal warning was rather extreme, so she knew she had gone too far. He didn't have good style and tended to think that all negative statements reflected upon him. He must be guilty about something, she thought.

"I apologize. I had not meant the statement to be destructive, merely in opposition."

He gave her a conciliatory nod, the kind meant to conceal the atmosphere, but his gestures always had a patronizing tone that ruined the effect. She must find stylish ways of dealing with him, and was indeed working upon that.

Another problem was the question of reversibility in the chromosome interference. Perhaps the answer lay where she thought it did, in electronic control, but that posed problems for the masses. Not difficult for one subject, and things would go a stage at a time. She was determined not to rush. After a while, Janos seemed to have recovered from their little contretemps, for he suddenly suggested that they buy a dinner party for themselves for the following night, and he suggested that with luck it might be possible to get somewhere in a fashionable building, perhaps the Cairns or the Herberg Suite? Here was proof that he required the admiration of a crowd, but she let it pass and instead complimented him on his wonderful idea. They set about compiling a guest list, an unusual thing for them to do during working hours.

They already had a few well-thought-of people on their social list, and several who might demean themselves for an evening. All their acquaintances were bioengineers: it was rare to meet anyone outside one's own discipline; there was not enough time. This was a price all talented people had to pay, but the rewards were greater than the penalties. They had been awarded knowledge implants as well as memory reinforcement grafts in their youth, which enhanced their natural brilliance and capacity for application. Everyone preferred a hard life to the appalling possibility of being in the lower classes, who had little in their lives except prescribed entertainment. They had very little spare time, so she should feel privileged that he proposed using some of his time with her, but as it was not done to give a party without a member of the opposite sex as cohost, she did not make too much of the situation. She liked playing hostess and knew herself excellent at the task. When the overworked upper classes relaxed, they tried always to make the occasion rare without always being monotonously outrageous. So what theme had he thought of?

"Animals. Fancy dress." She smiled with glittering delight, her hair seeming to express a rise in her spirits. But it would be impossible for everyone to obtain a costume in time for the following night. He looked annoyed and downcast; he did not want to postpone the occasion.

"Why not have animals but not costumes—ask everyone to mime?"

After a few tense moments his face showed reluctant pleasure. Fun, but not too spectacular. They must never be accused of self-aggrandizement. They got out all the invitations and replies of acceptance and ordered the Herberg Suite to be done out to have the appearance of a twenty-second-century zoological garden at a time when animals had not been so rare. The food would be in feeding trays and the drink in gravity feeders.

They were especially pleased to have Selly's acceptance. To have Selly behaving like an animal in public at their expense would afford them some glee. What animal would he mime? They were sure they could guess. In order to have plenty of energy for the party, they retired early and did not return later for more work.

The lab was at rest, and Lupus the Loop lay coiled on his simulated branch in the simulated moonlight, smiling to himself, for had he not been eavesdropping on them every night for months?

The party was a great success. Within the general benevolent atmosphere there were memorable moments. The sight of two well-known agriculturalists, who had made their name as the team that caused real animal fur to grow on sheets of plastic, behaving like a couple of Nubian goats was worth remembering. It seemed that they could cheerfully mime mating for hours without being vulgar, and very convincingly in spite of their very creative human appearance. They were both quite hairless and had gold eyeballs and teeth and nails, but their acting was so convincing that few had to ask what they were.

Janos made a wonderful mouse. He nibbled his way through his food, delightfully twitching some imaginary whiskers. His very ordinary appearance seemed to fit the mouse image. He had never indulged in even so much as a tattoo to decorate his person, just like the lower classes who were obliged by law to wear uniforms and were prohibited from any form of distinguishing mark. Janos, the little gray mouse, nibbling away at fame with determination.

And Selly, the great scientist, being what she had hoped he would be, a cat. He rubbed round people's legs in a feline manner, getting tidbits dropped for him, and being stroked and fondled, although someone made the joke of treating him like a lab cat, miming the drilling of holes into the skull. He went so far as to jump onto someone's lap and attempt to curl up, his great bulk hanging down on all sides, making the catness of cats seem very droll indeed. Fat, satisfied, smug, comfort-loving, lethargic Selly. It suited him. He could make a purring noise and wash his face with the back of his wrist, where his watch lay embedded in his wristbone. This instrument gave not only astronomical information, longitude and latitude, time and date, but the state of his brain waves, blood sugar, and noradrenalin. Few people still had these things embedded, for they had proved to be painful to many people in later years. Marvene stroked Selly cat and told him what a lovely pussy he was.

"This is a lovely party, Marvene. I shall remember this for a long time," purred the monster feline.

"And I also," said the man beneath Selly in a breathy manner. "This is a wonderful idea; I shall tell everyone about this." Marvene glowed with pleasure then, thinking that it had been worth the trouble if they were to be favorably talked about. Even the most brilliant upper-class people did not get funds if they were not in circulation.

Marvene felt she should do a little more about acting a snake. She began to hypnotize a female frog who had hopped over to her and sat crouched at her feet blowing a pouch and staring vacantly. Marvene slowly wound herself around the creature, who put hands over eyes as frogs in danger will, a clever touch. Marvene's extreme yoga lessons had kept her supple enough to coil backward around another human being and to mime squeezing the life out of the frog, the proportion of the creatures not detracting from their dual performance. Everyone seemed suitably amused.

A rhinoceros, more usually an invertebrate engineer, came over to congratulate her.

"You have a gift as an actress as well as a scientist," he grunted, swinging his invisible horn about on a great head, peering with little eyes full of stupid malevolence which was really a gaze of intellectual penetration. She liked the rhino-man; she was dazzled by his achievements and creations. His most famous work was the culturing of a hybrid toxicaria which could be absorbed in spore form through human skin and, when mature, grow to twenty feet long with the ability to bore through bone, disposing rather definitely of any enemy unlucky enough to pick up its invisible spores. He had also, of course, developed an immunity for the aggressor. And this was not all he had done to improve the world. He had written a whole series of papers on parasites of the universe, and presented one of the most controversial theories of the millennium. He was an authority on evolution and had shown, conclusively for many, that Homo sapiens, far from being the highest product of a chain of events, was intended to be the lowest in another chain of events, but

when the Sol system had been cut off in a crucial period in its development in order to quarantine it, that destiny had not been fulfilled. The Aldebaran Apple People had not wanted parasites, and indeed, not everyone on Earth relished the idea that humanity's true end was as a kind of maggot, burrowing through giant fruit.

The party was made complete with a tragic ending. A serious accident or fatality always lent interest to the story of a party. For some, the main game of an evening was to walk home, the buildings being more active at night. There was a far higher risk of a step collapsing beneath the foot or a balcony disappearing, leaving a person teetering on the edge of death with no choice but to jump—there was no rescue system; that would have taken the element of chance out of the game. A few people did not care for this entertainment, but they became impossible to socialize with, cowardice being so disgusting, and they were often relegated to live in the safe lower-class architecture. So a courageous woman who had mimed a dove all evening plummeted to her death on the deep glass floor below, showing that her miming did not extend to real flight. Exhilarated, Marvene and Janos walked home in amicable silence. Next day, everything was back to normal and both Selly's work and their own proceeded steadily.

They had made excellent progress, and Marvene knew that it was her insight which had made possible the step in personally controlling the subject. Selly needed a few more "doses" to give them conclusive proof. But it was to be admitted that they had taken this line from original ideas of Selly's. He had connections with espionage and had thought that if a human being could be made temporarily to behave as an alien in all respects, including instinctive behavior, there would be no chance of discovery when spying in other star systems. This of course applied only to those aliens whose outward physiology closely resembled the human. There were several important "human" cultures having totally different metabolism to Homo sapiens and who behaved differently in many respects. For example, the Wilkins Planet race, who were of shining intelligence and naturally extremely advanced (more than humanity in some things) but who loped around at high speed on all fours and who had a mating season once every four of their years.

Selly had been held up by lack of subjects because, although he had applied for volunteers, he did not trust the authorities to keep his research secret if he explained exactly why he required people, and this was requisite. But Marvene and Janos were ahead of Selly. Everything had depended upon what Selly had not quite seen, which was B/B serotonin pathways through the subelectronic RNA polymerase.

They had the potion which had made Bottom the Weaver behave like an ass, though they had never heard of him. Selly was to become the cat which he had so obligingly played at the party. She had given him a gift of sweets containing more necessary doses and had the minute control constructed which she could activate whenever she cared to do so.

She had come up with all these ideas while talking to Lupus the Loop. She often wandered in there to have a chat with him; it was an aid to projecting her thoughts. This was her secret; the other two would have thought her slightly deranged but she trusted her instincts, when controlled with careful thought. Lupus the Loop seemed to tell her things she needed to know.

"Tell me, Lupus, have you any idea how I can control the newly altered instincts of Selly so that he will not always behave under the new influence?" she had asked the great snake as he lay coiled and smugly full of food.

"It's perfectly simple," the snake had seemed to say. "You will construct a monitor which you will keep in your possession, transmitting impulses that will inhibit or release the metabolic pathways you have interfered with."

And it had been that simple in essence, although difficult to effect. An extremely sophisticated form of radio control. Beautiful! She had

hugged him in thanks, knowing that of course the idea had come from her own mind. Snakes do not have minds. But even plants sometimes spoke to Marvene, when she was alone with them. She had discovered as a child that you can talk to anything and get a reply, and learned later about the projection of the mind, and had then kept it all secret, for such things were despised by intelligent persons.

Janos was straightening his papers, which were all handwritten—very unusual. There was only one copy of each; he kept them in an insulated box for safety. Marvene was observing the mice. They were reprogrammed as dogs, and as she watched, one little male cocked its leg up and put a marker on an upright post. Another one was burying a fragment of bone, and two of the females were playing together in an unmouselike manner. Most amusing!

She supposed that Janos's ideas had an ecological beauty about them, for if he succeeded in ridding the world of excess people and making animals able to do the few tasks left requiring human labor, then they could be cannibalized, whereas human beings could not, at least aesthetically.

That evening when they arrived for their session, Selly was in their part of the lab. They detested his intrusion but could say nothing.

"I came to find out why your mice were so noisy," he explained, grinning. He was obviously embarrassed. He offered each of them a conciliatory smoke and they accepted even though they were his last; he said he had another pack. They smoked together in silence, then Selly said he was going and did so. Janos immediately checked his papers but nothing seemed to have been touched. Was Selly snooping? There was no evidence. Marvene decided that she felt tired and left early, and soon after that Janos wandered into the snake house.

The great constrictor was coiled rather torpidly except for his eyes, which seemed to follow every movement. Janos did not like taking samples from this beast; he was secretly afraid of it but would have died rather than admit as much. He sprayed the skin thoroughly with a penetrating local anaesthetic and took a syringeful of spinal fluid from behind the head. His hands shook and he imagined that the snake knew he was frightened.

"There you are, Lupus the Loop, that didn't bother you, did it?" he cooed insincerely. The snake ignored this transparent mollification. It was a very large specimen that had been reared in Nature, having all the instincts and qualities of the wild creature, which lab specimens did not show so strongly after a few generations. Someday Janos would like to visit Nature, that large zoological garden that had once been called Australia. The snake moved, sliding like oil along the branch toward him. He watched spellbound, noticing how it could move without disturbing its surroundings. What intensity. What grace. Collecting himself he suddenly ran, closing the door securely. How primitive those creatures were, how far removed from himself. Shuddering, he thrust the samples away and then suddenly noticed that Selly was standing watching him, and he almost collapsed with fright.

Selly was holding a mouse, stroking it, although he was no animal lover. The unmoving moonlight illuminated the plump face, making a mirror image of artificial Selene herself, smiling full at the trembling Janos, who was in no social position to lose his temper and managed not to do so.

"I forgot something; I returned for a moment," said Selly. "I'm sorry if I startled you."

"That's quite all right. I respect your attention to detail, you know that."

Selly replaced the mouse in the vivarium, where it had been trying to build a bridge from the little island upon which it had been placed, to a happy land at the edge of the world where nuts and other choice scraps tempted. Together they watched the mouse in its occupation without comment. Selly nodded in benevolent approval, absentmindedly scratching his ear and shaking his head. Janos was very offended

at this utterly disgusting behavior until he realized with a thrill that Selly was behaving like a cat. Of course, the nasty man sometimes scratched himself anyway. He looked for the control which Marvene had been constructing and it had gone. Had she finished it; had she gone ahead without him? How long had she been secretly experimenting with Selly without his knowledge? Janos looked at Selly looking at the mouse. The fellow was drooling.

Shaking with fury, he took his leave and went to find Marvene. She was there, outside the lab, and had been observing both of them through the glass door. She told him that she had been looking for him; she had a surprise for him. Confused, he told her he thought he knew what it was.

"But watch this," she said, waving the tiny box between a thumb and finger. She indicated Selly. They were fascinated to observe Selly slowly take off all his clothes and prowl round slowly; and then, fat though he was, crouch down on his haunches and with much puffing and heaving somehow manage to get his leg up around the back of his neck, where it stuck up pointing at the ceiling, his foot extended like that of a dancer. He slowly reached forward with tongue extended and made a bold attempt to wash his own genitals, pausing to nibble at something bothering him on his thigh. Janos thought: I shall remember this moment all my life. It is one of the great moments of science that we are privileged to witness.

They were all invited to another party, and this was very exciting, the host being the renowned Roald, who had made breakthroughs in bringing back seals to land and breeding them as household pets. Miniature seals were a favorite in many homes, lolling around on sofas and balancing things on their noses. To have reversed evolution in this way was a considerable feat and might lead to a further breed of useful seal. Selly wobbled with anticipation.

"It is to be a swimming party. What a sense

of humor the man has!" Janos laughed aloud, a thing he seldom did, usually expressing amusement with breathy exhalations. He was delighted because he swam very well indeed and would be able to exhibit this talent. Marvene was less happy because she had never swum well and had no confidence in water. The pool contained dolphins and she disliked them, fearing that they might bite and imagining that they could read her mind. She knew that they did not bite but still the fear was there, secreted behind her immaculate eyes.

"I may go in aquatic costume," Janos said, "if costume is allowed." Marvene dreaded that there might only be seafood, which she could not bear.

"I hope they have seafood," said Selly. "If there's one thing I like, it is a nice bit of fish." But the main thing to be glad about was that they were privileged to be visiting Roald, for he had a very high position and, following so soon on their own party, they could make a continued good impression. Each would have preferred to have a reputation alone, but together was better than nothing.

Work continued without further discussion, and Janos locked away all his notes when he was done, and hid the key.

The party was going well when they arrived and they were well received and introduced to important people. They were feeling confident of themselves, and Marvene had resigned herself to not making much of a showing in the water; she draped herself at the edge of the pool, bravely throwing her supper to the dolphin, which did seem to be reading her mind because it always leapt a split second before she threw a morsel. Janos was posing nearby eating prawns and clams with evident enjoyment. He planned to dive into the pool, when there were not many swimming, and execute a graceful water dance. If he had not been a scientist, he could have been a great water athlete. Selly was chatting easily with Roald himself, and several important people stood near them waiting to have a word with the great man. Suddenly Mar-

vene saw her chance: if Selly misbehaved here, he would be forever out of countenance. She activated his new behavior.

Selly abruptly crouched on the floor on his haunches and got himself into a complicated position whereby he could lick the backs of his own thighs. The effect was immediate then—good! Had he done that at their animal mime party he would have received applause, but one *never* repeated a performance or did anything out of tune with the prescribed atmosphere. Roald stared unbelieving at this awful display, seeming at a loss, and other important people tried to ignore Selly, everyone suffering from acute embarrassment.

Janos was horrified. Why had she done this here? Did she not realize that it would bring bad attention to all three of them? What lack of tact! He decided to try to divert attention from the scene and ran up the steps to the diving board, sparing a look of hatred for Marvene, who was actually displaying her glee at Selly's display. He prepared to dive, calming himself for an especially elegant performance.

Selly, while engaged in cat behavior which did not seem at all unusual to him, noticed his wrist monitor because his tortured position brought it right in front of his eyes. His brain wave readings and noradrenaline were abnormal. They would be normal for a cat, though, and of course all manner of other realizations came with this knowledge—these made him snarl and begin a howling growl which made the blood run chill. He could take his revenge immediately without a show of power, without explanation. He would bring them both down—if he was to be ruined, then it would not happen in solitude. It must be Janos who had done this thing to him, he believed, for he had read Janos's notes fairly extensively in his spying. But his discoveries had enabled him to do something very similar. He had not believed that they would dare attempt this on him, but he had been waiting his chance to experiment with Janos.

His hands felt very clumsy because his

thumb did not want to oppose itself and his claws wanted to retract in a most uncomfortable way, because he did not have claws. With a triumph of control, considering that everyone was staring at him as if he had gone mad, he activated a control directed at Janos.

Janos was poised for action. He looked down to judge the height and was overcome with waves of prickling terror at the sight of the water. Water! He had come the wrong way. He turned to retreat, wobbling wildly between diving skills which he knew he had and the total unfamiliarity with water that belongs to mice. He clutched himself with his little front paws, balancing on his hind legs by an act of will, and people turned to see a man hesitating to dive because of lack of nerve. He was creating a totally unfavorable diversion, but his rodent instincts made him tremble and stay. There was derisive laughter from one or two impolite guests and Roald glared at them, then at Janos. This spurred him to action and he fell into the water with a disgraceful splash, squeaking with fear he could not master. He floundered around trying to swim but a lab mouse had no inkling of such motion. He panicked.

Marvene collected herself and without thinking slid into the water to rescue him. She swam well. Janos had activated her snake instincts, thus ensuring her increased confidence in water, although it was certainly still not her favorite element. The onlookers were impressed with Marvene in spite of themselves, and she was obscurely aware that she had done something amazing and unaccustomed. While the disgraced Janos was being taken away to dress and the impossible Selly escorted to another room to hide himself, she enjoyed a certain amount of qualified glory. It was while she was experiencing a strange desire to slither away underneath a piece of furniture that she guessed what was happening to her. Her jaws drew open with reptilian fury. There was something so obviously wrong with her now that people left her alone. The three of them were in disgrace; it was demonstrated that they were

no longer desirable. Marvene knew then that all the work would come to an end. It would be impossible to find another good place in upper-class society. She burned with hatred of her two colleagues. They had stolen the work and used it against her! The very thought filled her with the will to kill them both. She felt that she could strangle them slowly while telling them why she was doing so, and then swallow them whole to eliminate them from her ruined world.

It was discreetly suggested to her in a message from Roald that she leave the party with Selly and Janos. They were ruining his party. She acquiesced with graceful dignity and as she glided away she looked her host in the eye in such a way that he felt threatened. Everything was over now; what did it matter? Then the three of them were out in the night. None of them spoke; there was too much suppressed anger beneath the tough veneer of politeness for any to dare. Janos's upper lip twitched dangerously and Selly's mouth was ajar in a silent snarl as he regarded Janos with malice. He had hunger in his face and Janos felt threatened; a paralysis seemed to have overcome him. Marvene slid away from them, which broke the gaze, and the two men followed.

Selly loped along silently on the balls of his feet, going ahead and returning, quickly but without fuss, circling them and then trotting off like a shadow. Marvene glided quickly then, head held erect, fixing Janos with a gaze, and he trotted agitatedly, head down in his shoulders. Around them the fantasy of the city glowed; the illuminated towers and balconies and flights of stairs and terraces were beautiful, everywhere glass, every aspect designed to astonish and amuse. Marvene spoke first.

"Janos, I am going to kill you. I am going to punish you for spoiling my life. There is nothing you can do; you are going to die." He kept his nervous eyes upon her and tripped over the bottom step of a winding flight that led to a broad esplanade, a favorite nightwalk because of its elevation over an abyss and the astounding view. The banisters of the stairway were hollow and filled with small alien life-forms from other planets. Janos had always loved this walk; he always stopped to take a look at the lizard people or the gloriously beautiful butterfly people in their simulated environment. Now, he would have given a lot to be a prisoner in a bottle like these highly intelligent specimens; anything would have been better than to have only space between Marvene and himself.

Suddenly she reached out to grab him and he jumped; he ran up the stairway at speed but saw Selly ahead, crouched on all fours. The grotesque image of fat Selly crouching to spring almost made him squeak with hysterical laughter, out of control. In a blind panic he whimpered and ran down again. Marvene reached him and almost had hold of him by the neck when Selly leapt with a screech. The stairway beneath them all disappeared instantly and all Marvene could hear was her own ghastly hissing shriek as she clung to a balustrade, winding herself around it clinging, watching the little butterfly people escape as their prison dissolved. They would not live long. And Janos had lost the night game; he fell to his death among a cloud of exquisite wings.

Selly had changed direction in midleap and somersaulted out into space in a wonderful arc to land with ease upon his feet on an impossible balcony two flights below. He crouched there moaning with the physical shock, looking down to see Janos land on solid glass. And then he looked up at Marvene, her hair coiling wildly.

"We shall all die. I shall kill you myself. None of us has a life now."

"And we have come such a long way together."

"Not together."

"I'll switch off the control if you will. Do we want to be like this?" It was self and not-self, this snake that she felt herself to be.

"No. You are a snake. It suits your nature. And it must have been Janos who did that to you."

Probably true; it didn't matter now. She ran then, bitter and wild, not home but making for the lab in the underground, down to it through the glittering arcades, aware that Selly followed. Kill herself? Where was the courage for that? How did snakes kill themselves? She was drawn to her most familiar surroundings and stood among the cages, uncertain. She reached in and picked up a mouse by its tail. It kicked as she dangled it over her open mouth. Selly got there, howling eerily with laughter, and reached out a paw to get the mouse for himself. The little creature was dashed away and ran to trembling safety in a heap of mouse bedding, heaps of paper shredded but still showing that it was covered with Janos's handwriting. Then she laughed too, for he had been careless; now there would be nothing left to show what the research had been. The two humans engaged in a clumsy struggle—Marvene lacked weight and Selly was too fat to get her arms around to squeeze, and he was hitting her with the flat of his hand.

Behind him on the bench were the dissecting knives, and she reached out and grasped one. She pushed the instrument into the side of his throat and cut, and cut. He was thick and tough and she could hardly believe that he was dead when his weight went slack and slid to the floor in a great pool of his blood. She found the control in his belt pack and deactivated it, examining it with a detached curiosity to see if it was a good copy. She felt different now, active and tense but more like herself. She felt disgusted that she had almost eaten a mouse. What a powerful discovery they had made. She turned over in her mind ways in which she could use this to make a new life for herself. It was a powerful control weapon. Perhaps she could still be famous if she completed the research alone. She had nobody holding her back now, crippling her sense of style. She turned from the mess and wandered into the snake house.

"Marvene, I have waited for you," said Lupus the Loop, smiling with pleasure. The hallucination of his actually speaking to her was very strong. All the disturbances she had endured had upset her mental balance. "Chomsky was right, Marvene. That ancient debate is at an end. Language is innate, you know." She stared at him, knowing perfectly well that the vocal cords of snakes were so . . .

"Selly very kindly gave me his powers of verbal communication when he gave me his own instincts. You didn't know he was trying that, did you?"

"You cannot speak," she said, obviously expecting it to interpret.

"Did you hear a voice, my dear? I am transmitting to you telepathically, my usual method of communication with other snakes, of course."

Marvene laughed thinly. "What an imagination I have sometimes. Dear Lupus, come to me then, tell me more. Give me answers out of my own brain." But she had not read Chomsky. He glided to her and swiftly wound himself around her, head down and gripping tightly.

"Marvene, I want us to mate. I have needed a female for some time, but my cruel imprisonment here did not allow that. Snakes are more passionate than humans realize, and Selly too had his passions. Secretly, he much desired you, my dear." She screamed again and again, begging him to let her go. He was embracing her desperately, frustrated and in anguish. He gripped her tighter and her bones slowly snapped and the breath went out of her so that she could not scream anymore. Finally, possessing her in the only way he could, he swallowed her whole, taking his time, covering her broken body over with his own beautiful elastic skin.

The little mouse who had escaped was busy. It was releasing its fellow prisoners, who were not only grateful to be released, but said so.

Reiko's Universe Box

KAJIO SHINJI

Translated by Toyoda Takashi and Gene van Troyer

Kajio Shinji (1947–) is an award-winning Japanese author who came to science fiction and fantasy in an unusual way. While running his inherited string of gasoline-stand franchises, Kajio wrote stories on the side. For several decades, he managed this exquisite balancing act, until in 1984 he quit the gasoline-stand business to become a full-time writer. Kajio has won the Nihon SF Taisho Award and the Seiun Prize three times.

The film *Yomigaeri*, a supernatural mystery about the investigation of several unexplained cases of resurrected people, is based on his novel of the same name. He is also renowned as a master of humorous science fiction in Japan—often emulated but rarely equaled for delightfully imaginative and funny twists that season what are still, at their core, seriously thought-provoking tales. He cowrote the manga *Omoide emanon* with Kenji Tsuruta, who also illustrated the series. The manga is based on his short story of the same name. In 1991, he won the Nihon SF Taisho Award for his novel *Salamander senmetsu*. More recently, he has achieved mainstream bestseller status in Japan.

Kajio has been a part of the science fiction community since middle school, when he began participating in Shibano Takumi's famous *Uchujin* fanzine. He also made his debut because of that publication, when *Hayakawa's SF Magazine* reprinted his story "Pearls for Mia" in 1970. This beautiful and haunting love story remains a favorite of many readers in Japan today. However, he is best known for his *Emanon* cycle. In 1979, he released the first story in this popular series, establishing himself as a leader in the Japanese science fiction community and making *Emanon* a permanent feature of the literary landscape. Since then, Kajio has continued to add installments of the cycle, adapting it to cover a staggering range of themes and ideas, and it still captures new fans today.

His gently mind-expanding and strangely upbeat short story "Reiko's Universe Box" first appeared in Japanese in 1981 and was subsequently published in English in the anthology *Speculative Japan* (2007).

REIKO'S UNIVERSE BOX

Kajio Shinji

Translated by Toyoda Takashi and Gene van Troyer

"I wonder who gave this to us?" Reiko, still wearing her coat, turned the gift in her hands.

The box, a forty-centimeter square, was so light that she thought it might well be empty. A myriad sparkling galaxies patterned the creamy wrapping paper and a satin ribbon with an elaborate bow like a star's corona bound it. Among the many wedding gifts, it really seemed out of place.

"Could it be a mistake? There's no card on it."

"Let's put it off till tomorrow," Ikutarō grumbled from the armchair. "I never imagined that a honeymoon would be this tiring."

"But . . . Just this one, dear. I'd like to see what's inside."

Giving up, he nodded. She smiled to him and started undoing the ribbon. "You should take off your coat, at least," he told his bride, then rose and went into the kitchen.

Inside the wrapping paper was a white carton. Embossed golden letters on it said: *The Universe Box . . . Presented by Fessenden & Co.*

"Isn't it strange? There're no names inside, either."

Ikutarō brought two cups of coffee and placed one in front of her.

"Have a coffee break. I guess they forgot to identify themselves in their haste."

He picked up a bundle of telegrams from their wedding well-wishers. Reiko opened the carton without finishing her coffee. A transparent cube came out, packed in Styrofoam pads.

At first she could see only absolute darkness in the cube. But, as her eyes focused, she began to make out small specks of light.

"Look! There's a universe inside!"

She set the universe box on the coffee table in front of her husband.

"Well, it must be a new type of decoration," he said drolly. "Did you know there are similar fantastic ornaments, using optical fiber or transparent bubbles of wax? Maybe this is just the latest variation. Anyway, I'm afraid we can't enjoy its beauty in this dinky apartment. We'll have to stash it in the closet till we can move into a bigger place."

Ikutarō's indifference couldn't have been plainer. His eyes quickly went back to the telegrams.

He paid more attention to what I said before we got married, Reiko thought.

A sheet of paper was still in the carton.

HOW TO USE THE UNIVERSE BOX

This box contains a real universe. You can use it for interior decoration. Furthermore, there is no need to worry about supplying energy as the box is powered by its own internal stellar processes. CAUTION: Do not reset the dial on the lower part of the box. It controls the progression of time within the box.

In case of product defect, we are ready to replace the whole box free of charge. Please send it back to our research and development department, postage collect.

FESSENDEN & CO.

How can I send it back when you don't give your address? she thought.

"Hey, I have a good idea." Ikutarō, a little irritated by his wife's divided attention, took the box and wrote something with a white marker pen along the black base: *In memory of our wedding . . . Ikutarō & Reiko.* "Now it'll remind us of our happiest moment whenever we see this note."

He showed her his inscription, his contented smile somewhat smug.

"Now that your curiosity about this gift is satisfied, you'd better put it away. We have to visit relatives and other people tomorrow, you know, to thank them. It's about time we hit the sack, since we have an early day tomorrow."

Reiko had yet to take off her coat. She nodded absently to him, still gazing into the compelling universe.

Ikutarō worked in the business section of a large trading company and often visited the office where Reiko had clerked and done secretarial duties—which, on his initiative, was how they met. He had that high-energy, push-forward spirit that every capable sales executive should have. Also, he had a sense of humor that always made her laugh loudly, even during office hours. His gentle eyes and tanned skin glowed, and he would hold his head higher to show his thick neck and chest when he talked about his university days as a soccer player.

He must be a good guy, she would tell herself, so she said yes without reservation when he asked her out—her first date ever, actually: not that she was too shy or selective, just that none of the guys until then had interested her enough. That's all. That, and she wasn't the kind of girl who went man hunting. She was a patient girl who could wait for Prince Charming on his white charger. And there he had been.

Their first date: a movie, a melodrama, her choice. He compromised, and it was a yawner even for her. *Once upon a time boy met girl— they had to overcome mediocre and stereotyped hardships to get together—they lived happily ever after. The End.* Reiko glanced at Ikutarō. He wasn't sleeping, but his glassy-eyed gaze fixed on the screen seemed absentminded enough to suggest he had mastered sleeping with his eyes open.

After the movie they had tried to have a meaningful conversation for about an hour over drinks at a cocktail lounge. Only at the end did a common topic miraculously emerge: both of them had seen the Disney movie *Dumbo the Flying Elephant* when they were children. Talking about that movie kept them going for another half hour.

They parted after promising a second date. On their fifth date, two months later, Ikutarō took her hand and suddenly, naively but clearly, said: "Reiko, please give me your hand in marriage."

It was perhaps the most clichéd proposal imaginable—somehow that made it endearing— but she wasn't even sure she loved him. Maybe she did, because he must have loved her enough to propose—and even if she didn't, love might grow in her because of his evident love for her. Still, she wasn't sure and her uncertainty irritated her. She said she'd have to think it over, and when he phoned two fretful days later— days she had spent castigating herself for her indecisiveness—she accepted his proposal over the telephone.

She was a flexible girl, after all.

"Before I marry you, I have to tell you one thing," Ikutarō said as if he were laying out the ground rules for brokering a business deal. "I won't be coming home early or regularly. I'm a salesman with executive responsibilities, and I often have to entertain customers until late at night. Sometimes, I have to drink with them, sometimes play mahjong with them. But I think you can understand why I have to serve them this way—it's all for your happiness."

He said the same thing again just before, then just after, the wedding. To make her happy, he had to get more money. He had to work harder and longer than any of the other sales staff.

For three months after the wedding he would regularly call her to let her know what time he would be home. After that it became every other time. Then, it became once every three times. Nevertheless, every night she would prepare dinner and wait for his return.

"When I'm late, you don't have to wait up, Reiko," he told her, but not only did she not feel like going to bed alone, he wanted a baby—every night when he came home, he would ask for the signs—and they worked at bringing them about—and if she went to bed, she would sleep and not be in the most receptive mood for lovemaking.

On the other hand, while waiting for him she didn't feel like watching TV or reading books or magazines. She did housework, rearranged the contents of the refrigerator and the cupboards, and tinkered with the meals she prepared for him. You could say it was a form of meditation for her.

One night the weather was rather balmy, so she went out onto the veranda. Their rooms were on the third floor of an apartment tower, and from the veranda she could see the road to the bus stop. It was already past midnight. Reiko put her elbows on the rail wet with dew and placed her chin on her palms, waiting for Ikutarō's return without expectation.

"All this overtime might kill him, I'm afraid," she murmured to herself. "He works too hard. He must be completely exhausted."

Traffic below was sparse; only after long intervals would a lone car pass by. Soon, a taxi stopped beside their apartment. She could tell it was her husband even from this distance and in the dark. She noticed the heavy smell of alcohol about him when he came through the door.

"Oh, you're still up, are you?" That was all that he said. Then he went to bed—or maybe it's more accurate to say he collapsed into it—somewhat guiltily, she thought.

He was sound asleep—passed out probably—before his head hit the pillow.

Reiko thought that his mental fatigue must be almost unbearable. Anxious for his health, she put away the dinner dishes and the uneaten meal.

Such was life, though sometimes he ate the meals.

. . .

The next week, he came home unusually late. Reiko made not a single grumble about it, which might have made him uncomfortable.

"I'm trying hard to land a new customer right now," he said a little defensively before leaving for work the next morning. "The manager of the purchasing department at his trading company. He wants me to play mahjong with him every night."

That night, too, she waited for him out on the veranda. Tears sprang unexpectedly from her eyes, though she could not understand the reason at first. Then it came to her.

She was lonely.

She looked up at the night sky to stop her tears.

"There are no stars at all!" she said in a small surprised voice.

It had been a long time since last she had looked up at the stars. Smog blanketed the sky and hid the stars, which she had not realized until then. She felt a strange awe because she could not see them. Quietly, she went back into her room, wiping her tears.

And she remembered the universe box. There had been stars in that, she recalled, and with another jolt of surprise, realized that was the last time she had seen stars. *Where is it?* she wondered. She at last found the package in a corner of the closet, covered with a film of dust.

She hastily took it out of the carton.

Now she could see the details of the gift that she had looked over so closely that night so many months ago. There was a real universe enclosed within a transparent cube. Regardless of the bright light in her room, there was absolute darkness in the cube.

She looked closer.

Since the depth of the cube appeared to be only forty centimeters, she should have been able to see the opposite side of her living room through the cube. But all she could see was the seemingly impenetrable darkness in the box.

Is it a hologram? she wondered.

A star floated at the apparent center of the cube, by far the largest one. About seven centimeters in diameter, it was a white star around which she could see ten or more tinier points of light moving almost imperceptibly.

"Fascinating!" She sighed with wonder. Looking into the cube made her calm and peaceful. She sat there peering into the universe box until her husband returned. She barely noticed when he came in.

The next day she went shopping downtown, which was not usual for her. Ordinarily, she went to nearby supermarkets to shop for groceries and commodities. But this time she wanted books, and there were no comprehensive bookstores in the neighborhood. The multistory national chain bookstore on Chuo Boulevard, just down from the train station, was the place to go.

Reiko bought a book titled *Mysteries of the Universe: A Practical Guide*. The universe box had aroused her curiosity, and this book struck her as elementary and easy enough to understand. Maybe she'd get a good idea of what was going on inside the universe box. At home, she pored over the book. The world of stars, until now almost completely unknown to her, seemed to blossom like a garden of colorful flowers before her eyes. She was hooked.

That night, waiting for Ikutarō, she watched the universe box on the kitchen table.

The largest star must be a "fixed" star, like our sun, the book told her. *I wonder if it's a white giant, since it shines white*, she mused. *Anyway, it must be older than the sun. So, all of these small bodies going around it are planets like the Earth*.

Little by little, the universe in the box showed changes. She could see the motion of the rice-grain-sized planets, though it was almost imperceptibly slow.

"Do these planets have moons?" she wondered. She observed closely, but could not tell for sure.

"Oh, I'd like to see a shooting star!"

At the time, she had yet to learn that a shooting star was actually a meteor entering the atmosphere that burns from air friction. But she wanted to make a wish that she would be able to have a good life with Ikutarō.

Her husband finally came home and had dinner with her. She was distracted by the universe box, and failed to respond to his questions a couple of times. He smiled bitterly, feeling guilty about her absentmindedness because his late-night homecomings might have been what made her this way—enchanted by the magic of the universe box.

One night, as she gazed into the universe box with her chin resting on her palms, she had an idea. She got up and turned off the lights. With the curtains drawn, there was only the light of the universe box shining thinly into the room.

She sat down again before the cube within the darkness. There were no sounds; only the light from the star was there. She felt as if she were somehow entering the miniature universe when she kept looking at it.

No, she thought, *this is not a miniature universe but my private universe.*

Then, it happened. Something gaseous with a white tail passed before her eyes.

"It's a comet!"

The comet in the universe box moved toward the star, maybe covering a millimeter a minute, trailing a long incandescent tail. Over the next few hours it seemed to grow in size, blazing spectacularly, and then it plunged into the star's corona and died with a brief flare. It was the first dramatic scene she had witnessed in the universe box. Appreciation—no, glee—filled her.

"This universe is really alive!"

If Reiko had been wondering why this small box attracted her so much, she stopped: she no longer felt the least lonely. For the first time she thought of giving the star and its family of planets names. The central star should be Ikunōsuke, using part of her husband's name. Then, the planets came: they should be Tarō, Jirō, Saburō, and so on, following the traditional Japanese way of naming boys. Of the planets, Tarō was the largest, almost one-third of the size of the central star, Ikunōsuke. She could tell the size of the planets by observing their day and night sides.

She didn't notice that her husband had entered the apartment.

"What on earth are you doing without the lights!?" he demanded irritably. He smelled like whiskey.

She winced when he turned on the lights, feeling like she'd been yanked back into reality. *Is this real?* she wondered.

"That damned universe box again? You're still hooked?" He sounded even more annoyed. Reiko did not answer.

"I'm hungry. Do we have anything to eat?"

He was rummaging in the refrigerator. She hadn't prepared dinner. The clock struck ten o'clock. The resonance of the dry sound seemed to linger in the kitchen.

"Okay," Ikutarō said in disgust. "I'll go to bed. No dinner." He glanced sharply at her and added, "You'd better get to bed early. I'm leaving early tomorrow morning, too. I want breakfast."

She stared into the universe box for almost half an hour after he fell asleep.

She had already read more than ten books to learn about the universe: *Creation of the Universe*, *Development of the Stars*, *Types of the Galaxies*, *Types of the Stars*, *Neutron Stars*, *Black Holes*, *Quasars*, *Double Stars*. Many a word she had not known even existed before was now as familiar to her as mundane items on the grocery lists she less and less frequently wrote.

"Was it a Big Bang that started this universe in the box?" she asked herself while reading one of the books.

The phone rang persistently. Reiko idly picked up the receiver. It was a woman she didn't know.

"Give me Ikutarō, please." The husky female voice referred to her husband by his first name.

Reiko absently told her that he wasn't home yet.

"Is this the wife, Reiko-san?" the mystery woman asked in a challenging tone.

"Yes, that's right," Reiko confirmed nonchalantly.

"Oh, it's nothing important." She hung up with a violent click. Reiko also hung up, glad to get back to the astronomy book, and promptly forgot the call. The sultry-voiced woman had been correct.

Ikutarō came home very late that night. When he found his wife sitting in the dark, staring as if hypnotized into the universe box, he said nothing to her. She thought vaguely that although she and her husband sat together, their minds were far apart. With her thoughts in the universe box, they might as well have been farther away than the width of the infinite universe. To Ikutarō, the universe box was less than useless: it was ridiculous. He couldn't see the glorious auroral sheets of galaxies, starfields, nebulae, and solar systems flocking in his wife's mind. She just looked like some slack-faced drug addict.

Still in his Burberry mac, he smoked a few cigarettes, not bothering to hide his irritation and contempt. Maybe he had something to say. But, in the end, he went to bed without saying a word. They talked about nothing that night. Reiko was not angry. She cared nothing about the girl on the telephone. She just made it clear to herself that she was not depending on anybody.

It was just because she had nothing that she wanted to talk about with her husband. That night there was only silence in their universe box.

Sunday morning.

"What're you doing every day!?" Ikutarō cried out in angry surprise. He was looking in the refrigerator. "It's empty!"

Oh, I haven't been cooking lately, she thought. She'd been eating whatever breads and pastries she could buy in the convenience store on the ground floor of their apartment tower.

"You haven't done the laundry in days, and I can see cobwebs and dust bunnies everywhere! What are you *doing* at home!?" he shouted.

Reiko didn't answer or face her husband. She just gazed into the universe box. Her husband only sounded like a dog barking in the distance.

He had put on his Burberry mac and was standing behind her.

"I'm going out for a walk," he growled, and slammed the door on the way out.

Within the universe box, all the planets were about to line up.

With Ikunōsuke as the leader, the planets were moving into a straight line, Tarō, Jirō, Saburō, and the others, extending to her right from the near side of the box. A solar conjunction. Reiko sighed with awe. This fascinating dance of the many-colored, jewel-like planets in this tiny universe was only for her to appreciate.

It was a breathtaking view!

Reiko stood up to close the curtains for more darkness. This way, the illusion that she was floating in the universe box was more complete. As she sat watching the lined-up planets, a curious thought came to her.

Do any of the planets around Ikunōsuke have inhabitants like on Earth? It was a naive question, but . . . Maybe. *And maybe there are some intelligent creatures there like the human race?*

There should be, she concluded.

Then, maybe there's someone like me who is gazing into her own universe box, within which there may be a planet like the Earth, on which someone may be looking into her universe, within which . . . Maybe I'm in someone else's universe box and she's wondering about me and whether I might be here . . . !

She went on mumbling about the infinite regression of universe boxes wheeling through her head.

Ikutarō came home very late that night. His rage exploded when he found Reiko still at the universe box. He threw a matchbook on the table in front of her, which showed the name of a notorious hotel.

"I was there until just a little while ago," he said ominously. Reiko contemplated the multiple universe boxes that seemed to have expanded all about her. Ikutarō thundered, *"Don't you* FEEL *anything?"*

She felt nothing at all. Everything was remote from her. What was that noise coming from the funny cartoon character confronting her?

"You've been like this for months! That freaking universe box is more important to you than me, isn't it!? Why don't you fight me? How can you be so indifferent to me when I'm screwing another woman!? Wanna hear the details? God! I should have thrown that box away that first night!"

She showed no sign that she'd heard a word he'd said.

"Look at me when I talk to you!" he shrieked.

Nothing.

"To hell with this!" Hysterically, Ikutarō hammered the universe box with a single blow from the side of his fist. It flew off the table, banged onto the floor, and skidded almost to the wall. There was an actinic flash from the box like a camera strobe going off.

This was the first time he had ever shown any violence to her. What was that all about? Reiko calmly picked up the box and held it closely, without noticing that the dial on the box had been turned during the incident. The flow of time in the universe box had accelerated drastically. As if caring for her own baby, she looked closely into the universe.

Ikunōsuke, the white giant, was not shining, or rather, it had dimmed to the point of invisibility.

"The universe box seems to be broken," Reiko observed tonelessly.

"Good!" Ikutarō roared.

"Everything is over," she said without emotion. She knew it. Everything around her had fractured into disconnected frames of images like jostling panes of glass.

Ikutarō didn't say a word. He dropped heavily into the other chair with a huff, and they just sat there wordlessly, facing each other across the kitchen table.

He chain-smoked several cigarettes with quick puffs. Reiko looked into the dead darkness in the universe box. All the planets around Ikunōsuke were somewhere within that darkness. This universe box that she and Ikutarō lived in was in its own darkness.

Then, a slight change took place. She thought she saw one of the planets that used to orbit the star disappear into the darkness where the star used to be. The darkness guttered like a dim ember. She could see the other planets speeding towards the dark spot, which began to glow redly, and then some nearby stars appeared that were clearly moving towards the spot. She set the box on the table to get a clearer look.

"The universe box is still alive!" she joyously exclaimed. "It's just that Ikunōsuke became a black hole! The star must have shrunk smaller than the Schwarzschild radius!"

"Oh, for God's sake!" Ikutarō groaned. And began to look dangerous.

Reiko remembered this topic from the book about black holes. Normally, such a process would take a vast amount of time, but in this universe box, where time had been accelerated by the turned dial, planets, asteroids, comets, and even some nearby stars were attracted to it with amazing speed. Hundreds of thousands of years seemed to be passing with each instant.

Ikutarō looked like he was about to do something violent again, when the hotel matchbook on the kitchen table went skittering into the box through the transparent panel with a gush of air. *Whoosh!*

"Hey, what are you doing?" he cried out in surprise.

The cigarette he was smoking jerked from his fingers and shot after the matchbook. The kitchen table started to tremble. Small articles like the newspaper, towels, and clock went into the box as if by magic. *Whoosh, whoosh, whoosh!*

With the progress of time accelerated, Ikunōsuke, the white giant, had turned into a major black hole in nearly no time relative to their universe. With its tremendous mass, it started to attract nearby stars, gaining more mass and attraction. Now, the black hole had begun to attract articles outside the cube. Ikutarō was clinging to the table leg, crying.

He had no understanding of what was happening, and his eyes were wide with terror. Now, larger items like the TV set, stereo, and toaster oven went into the small cube. Ikutarō finally lost his grip and his throat-ripping cry of terror was cut off as he was sucked headfirst into the cube. Bones cracked like he was being munched.

Reiko was not frightened at all. She felt like she was outside it all, looking in. Maybe she was. She'd been in there for a long time anyway, but outside looking in at the same time, and wondering if someone was watching her. Maybe that someone was her, and maybe this was the revenge of the universe box against her husband. Her universe, collapsing on them both. Her gaze fell on the inscription Ikutarō had scrawled so many months ago on the base with such irritation—almost like a prediction, now—*"In memory of our wedding . . . Ikutarō & Reiko."*

That's the way she took it. Her universe box, her revenge.

With a joyful shriek, she dived after her husband.

Swarm

BRUCE STERLING

(Michael) Bruce Sterling (1954–) is an influential US science fiction author often cited as a founder of the cyberpunk genre, along with William Gibson. In collaboration, Gibson and Sterling could be said to have jump-started the steampunk genre as well, with their novel *The Difference Engine*. Sterling set parameters for cyberpunk in his polemical fanzine *Cheap Truth* (1984–86), making his case in part by criticizing Humanists like Kim Stanley Robinson. Since that time, both writers have made major contributions to our understanding of modern life, in vastly different ways. Robinson has arguably become the most important climate change fiction writer in the world and Sterling has been invaluable as a ceaseless critic and analyst of the postcapitalist Baudrillardian world.

Sterling's fiction has won two Hugo Awards in addition to the Hayakawa Book Prize, the Arthur C. Clarke Award, the Locus Award, and the Campbell Award. However, Sterling has been equally fascinating and adroit in his perceptive nonfiction, while his work editing the seminal *Mirrorshades* anthology (1986) helped define cyberpunk for a generation of readers. Sterling cofounded the legendary Turkey City writer's workshop in Austin, Texas, and famously coined the term *slipstream* (1989, in the magazine *Science Fiction Eye*) to describe cross-genre fiction that did not easily fit into a particular category. Other terms coined by Sterling include *Wexelblat disaster* (1999), for when a natural disaster triggers a secondary failure of human technology, and *buckyjunk*, in a 2005 issue of *Wired*, which refers to future, difficult-to-recycle consumer waste made of carbon nanotubes.

Sterling's novels include *Islands in the Net* (1988), *Heavy Weather* (1994), and *The Caryatids* (2009). Stand-alone stories like the oft-reprinted "We See Things Differently" in the legendary *Semiotext(e)* anthology (1989) amply demonstrate Sterling's versatility in his short fiction.

But he is perhaps best known for his stories set in the Shaper/Mechanist universe, featuring a colonized solar system caught between two major warring factions: the Mechanists, who use computer-based mechanical tech, and the Shapers, who deploy species-wide genetic engineering. Over time, this binary opposition is complicated by the arrival of different alien civilizations and the splintering of humanity into many posthuman subspecies. The Shaper/Mechanist stories can be found in the collections *Crystal Express* and *Schismatrix Plus*.

"Swarm" is a brilliant example of these stories, first published in *The Magazine of Fantasy and Science Fiction* in 1982 and nominated for the Hugo, Nebula, and Locus Awards. In the story, Captain Simon Afriel is tasked with researching a little-known life-form called the Swarm, initially thought to be unintelligent. What ensues is unpredictable, exciting, and thought-provoking—like all of Sterling's fiction. It's also undeniably "post cyberpunk."

SWARM

Bruce Sterling

"I will miss your conversation during the rest of the voyage," the alien said.

Captain-Doctor Simon Afriel folded his jeweled hands over his gold-embroidered waistcoat. "I regret it also, ensign," he said in the alien's own hissing language. "Our talks together have been very useful to me. I would have paid to learn so much, but you gave it freely."

"But that was only information," the alien said. He shrouded his bead-bright eyes behind thick nictitating membranes. "We Investors deal in energy, and precious metals. To prize and pursue mere knowledge is an immature racial trait." The alien lifted the long ribbed frill behind his pinhole-sized ears.

"No doubt you are right," Afriel said, despising him. "We humans are as children to other races, however; so a certain immaturity seems natural to us." Afriel pulled off his sunglasses to rub the bridge of his nose. The starship cabin was drenched in searing blue light, heavily ultraviolet. It was the light the Investors preferred, and they were not about to change it for one human passenger.

"You have not done badly," the alien said magnanimously. "You are the kind of race we like to do business with: young, eager, plastic, ready for a wide variety of goods and experiences. We would have contacted you much earlier, but your technology was still too feeble to afford us a profit."

"Things are different now," Afriel said. "We'll make you rich."

"Indeed," the Investor said. The frill behind his scaly head flickered rapidly, a sign of amusement. "Within two hundred years you will be wealthy enough to buy from us the secret of our starflight. Or perhaps your Mechanist faction will discover the secret through research."

Afriel was annoyed. As a member of the Reshaped faction, he did not appreciate the reference to the rival Mechanists. "Don't put too much stock in mere technical expertise," he said. "Consider the aptitude for languages we Shapers have. It makes our faction a much better trading partner. To a Mechanist, all Investors look alike."

The alien hesitated. Afriel smiled. He had appealed to the alien's personal ambition with his last statement, and the hint had been taken. That was where the Mechanists always erred. They tried to treat all Investors consistently, using the same programmed routines each time. They lacked imagination.

Something would have to be done about the Mechanists, Afriel thought. Something more permanent than the small but deadly confrontations between isolated ships in the Asteroid Belt and the ice-rich Rings of Saturn. Both factions maneuvered constantly, looking for a decisive stroke, bribing away each other's best talent, practicing ambush, assassination, and industrial espionage.

Captain-Doctor Simon Afriel was a past master of these pursuits. That was why the Reshaped faction had paid the millions of kilowatts necessary to buy his passage. Afriel held doctorates in biochemistry and alien linguistics, and a master's degree in magnetic weapons engineering. He was thirty-eight years old and had been Reshaped according to the state of the art at the time of his conception. His hormonal balance had been altered slightly to compensate for long periods spent in free fall.

He had no appendix. The structure of his heart had been redesigned for greater efficiency, and his large intestine had been altered to produce the vitamins normally made by intestinal bacteria. Genetic engineering and rigorous training in childhood had given him an intelligence quotient of 180. He was not the brightest of the agents of the Ring Council, but he was one of the most mentally stable and the best trusted.

"It seems a shame," the alien said, "that a human of your accomplishments should have to rot for two years in this miserable, profitless outpost."

"The years won't be wasted," Afriel said.

"But why have you chosen to study the Swarm? They can teach you nothing, since they cannot speak. They have no wish to trade, having no tools or technology. They are the only spacefaring race that is essentially without intelligence."

"That alone should make them worthy of study."

"Do you seek to imitate them, then? You would make monsters of yourselves." Again the ensign hesitated. "Perhaps you could do it. It would be bad for business, however."

There came a fluting burst of alien music over the ship's speakers, then a screeching fragment of Investor language. Most of it was too high-pitched for Afriel's ears to follow.

The alien stood, his jeweled skirt brushing the tips of his clawed birdlike feet. "The Swarm's symbiote has arrived," he said.

"Thank you," Afriel said. When the ensign opened the cabin door, Afriel could smell the Swarm's representative; the creature's warm yeasty scent had spread rapidly through the starship's recycled air.

Afriel quickly checked his appearance in a pocket mirror. He touched powder to his face and straightened the round velvet hat on his shoulder-length reddish-blond hair. His earlobes glittered with red impact-rubies, thick as his thumbs' ends, mined from the Asteroid Belt. His knee-length coat and waistcoat were of gold brocade; the shirt beneath was of dazzling fineness, woven with red-gold thread. He had dressed to impress the Investors, who expected and appreciated a prosperous look from their customers. How could he impress this new alien? Smell, perhaps. He freshened his perfume.

Beside the starship's secondary air lock, the Swarm's symbiote was chittering rapidly at the ship's commander. The commander was an old and sleepy Investor, twice the size of most of her crewmen. Her massive head was encrusted in a jeweled helmet. From within the helmet her clouded eyes glittered like cameras.

The symbiote lifted on its six posterior legs and gestured feebly with its four clawed forelimbs. The ship's artificial gravity, a third again as strong as Earth's, seemed to bother it. Its rudimentary eyes, dangling on stalks, were shut tight against the glare. It must be used to darkness, Afriel thought.

The commander answered the creature in its own language. Afriel grimaced, for he had hoped that the creature spoke Investor. Now he would have to learn another language, a language designed for a being without a tongue.

After another brief interchange the commander turned to Afriel. "The symbiote is not pleased with your arrival," she told Afriel in the Investor language. "There has apparently been some disturbance here involving humans, in the recent past. However, I have prevailed upon it to admit you to the Nest. The episode has been recorded. Payment for my diplomatic services will be arranged with your faction when I return to your native star system."

"I thank Your Authority," Afriel said. "Please convey to the symbiote my best personal wishes, and the harmlessness and humility of my intentions—" He broke off short as the symbiote lunged toward him, biting him savagely in the calf of his left leg. Afriel jerked free and leapt backward in the heavy artificial gravity, going into a defensive position. The symbiote had ripped away a long shred of his pants leg; it now crouched quietly, eating it.

"It will convey your scent and composition to its nestmates," said the commander. "This is necessary. Otherwise you would be classed as an invader, and the Swarm's warrior caste would kill you at once."

Afriel relaxed quickly and pressed his hand against the puncture wound to stop the bleeding. He hoped that none of the Investors had noticed his reflexive action. It would not mesh well with his story of being a harmless researcher.

"We will reopen the air lock soon," the commander said phlegmatically, leaning back on her thick reptilian tail. The symbiote continued to munch the shred of cloth. Afriel studied the creature's neckless segmented head. It had a mouth and nostrils; it had bulbous atrophied eyes on stalks; there were hinged slats that might have been radio receivers, and two parallel ridges of clumped wriggling antennae, sprouting among three chitinous plates. Their function was unknown to him.

The air lock door opened. A rush of dense, smoky aroma entered the departure cabin. It seemed to bother the half-dozen Investors, who left rapidly. "We will return in six hundred and twelve of your days, as by our agreement," the commander said.

"I thank Your Authority," Afriel said.

"Good luck," the commander said in English. Afriel smiled.

The symbiote, with a sinuous wriggle of its segmented body, crept into the air lock. Afriel followed it. The air lock door shut behind them. The creature said nothing to him but continued munching loudly. The second door opened, and the symbiote sprang through it, into a wide, round stone tunnel. It disappeared at once into the gloom.

Afriel put his sunglasses into a pocket of his jacket and pulled out a pair of infrared goggles. He strapped them to his head and stepped out of the air lock. The artificial gravity vanished, replaced by the almost imperceptible gravity of the Swarm's asteroid nest. Afriel smiled, comfortable for the first time in weeks. Most of his adult life had been spent in free fall, in the Shapers' colonies in the Rings of Saturn.

Squatting in a dark cavity in the side of the tunnel was a disk-headed furred animal the size of an elephant. It was clearly visible in the infrared of its own body heat. Afriel could hear it breathing. It waited patiently until Afriel had launched himself past it, deeper into the tunnel. Then it took its place in the end of the tunnel, puffing itself up with air until its swollen head securely plugged the exit into space. Its multiple legs sank firmly into sockets in the walls.

The Investors' ship had left. Afriel remained here, inside one of the millions of planetoids that circled the giant star Betelgeuse in a girdling ring with almost five times the mass of Jupiter. As a source of potential wealth it dwarfed the entire solar system, and it belonged, more or less, to the Swarm. At least, no other race had challenged them for it within the memory of the Investors.

Afriel peered up the corridor. It seemed deserted, and without other bodies to cast infrared heat, he could not see very far. Kicking against the wall, he floated hesitantly down the corridor.

He heard a human voice. "Dr. Afriel!"

"Dr. Mirny!" he called out. "This way!"

He first saw a pair of young symbiotes scuttling toward him, the tips of their clawed feet barely touching the walls. Behind them came a woman wearing goggles like his own. She was young, and attractive in the trim, anonymous way of the genetically reshaped.

She screeched something at the symbiotes in their own language, and they halted, waiting. She coasted forward, and Afriel caught her arm, expertly stopping their momentum.

"You didn't bring any luggage?" she said anxiously.

He shook his head. "We got your warning before I was sent out. I have only the clothes I'm wearing and a few items in my pockets."

She looked at him critically. "Is that what people are wearing in the Rings these days? Things have changed more than I thought."

Afriel glanced at his brocaded coat and laughed. "It's a matter of policy. The Investors are always readier to talk to a human who looks ready to do business on a large scale. All the Shapers' representatives dress like this these days. We've stolen a jump on the Mechanists; they still dress in those coveralls."

He hesitated, not wanting to offend her. Galina Mirny's intelligence was rated at almost two hundred. Men and women that bright were sometimes flighty and unstable, likely to retreat into private fantasy worlds or become enmeshed in strange and impenetrable webs of plotting and rationalization. High intelligence was the strategy the Shapers had chosen in the struggle for cultural dominance, and they were obliged to stick to it, despite its occasional disadvantages. They had tried breeding the Superbright—those with quotients over two hundred—but so many had defected from the Shapers' colonies that the faction had stopped producing them.

"You wonder about my own clothing," Mirny said.

"It certainly has the appeal of novelty," Afriel said with a smile.

"It was woven from the fibers of a pupa's cocoon," she said. "My original wardrobe was eaten by a scavenger symbiote during the troubles last year. I usually go nude, but I didn't want to offend you by too great a show of intimacy."

Afriel shrugged. "I often go nude myself, I never had much use for clothes except for pockets. I have a few tools on my person, but most are of little importance. We're Shapers, our tools are here." He tapped his head. "If you can show me a safe place to put my clothes . . ."

She shook her head. It was impossible to see her eyes for the goggles, which made her expression hard to read. "You've made your first mistake, doctor. There are no places of our own here. It was the same mistake the Mechanist agents made, the same one that almost killed me as well. There is no concept of privacy or property here. This is the Nest. If you seize any part of it for yourself—to store equipment, to sleep in, whatever—then you become an intruder, an enemy. The two Mechanists—a man and a woman—tried to secure an empty chamber for their computer lab. Warriors broke down their door and devoured them. Scavengers ate their equipment, glass, metal, and all."

Afriel smiled coldly. "It must have cost them a fortune to ship all that material here."

Mirny shrugged. "They're wealthier than we are. Their machines, their mining. They meant to kill me, I think. Surreptitiously, so the warriors wouldn't be upset by a show of violence. They had a computer that was learning the language of the springtails faster than I could."

"But you survived," Afriel pointed out. "And your tapes and reports—especially the early ones, when you still had most of your equipment—were of tremendous interest. The Council is behind you all the way. You've become quite a celebrity in the Rings, during your absence."

"Yes, I expected as much," she said.

Afriel was nonplused. "If I found any deficiency in them," he said carefully, "it was in my own field, alien linguistics." He waved vaguely at the two symbiotes who accompanied her. "I assume you've made great progress in communicating with the symbiotes, since they seem to do all the talking for the Nest."

She looked at him with an unreadable expression and shrugged. "There are at least fifteen different kinds of symbiotes here. Those that accompany me are called the springtails, and they speak only for themselves. They are savages, doctor, who received attention from the Investors only because they can still talk. They were a spacefaring race once, but they've forgotten it. They discovered the Nest and they were absorbed, they became parasites." She tapped one of them on the head. "I tamed these two because I learned to steal and beg food better than they can. They stay with me now and protect me from the larger ones. They are jealous, you know. They have only been with the Nest for perhaps ten thousand years and are still uncertain of their position. They still think, and wonder sometimes. After ten thousand years there is still a little of that left to them."

"Savages," Afriel said. "I can well believe that. One of them bit me while I was still aboard the starship. He left a lot to be desired as an ambassador."

"Yes, I warned him you were coming," said Mirny. "He didn't much like the idea, but I was able to bribe him with food. . . . I hope he didn't hurt you badly."

"A scratch," Afriel said. "I assume there's no chance of infection."

"I doubt it very much. Unless you brought your own bacteria with you."

"Hardly likely," Afriel said, offended. "I have no bacteria. And I wouldn't have brought microorganisms to an alien culture anyway."

Mirny looked away. "I thought you might have some of the special genetically altered ones. . . . I think we can go now. The springtail will have spread your scent by mouth-touching in the subsidiary chamber, ahead of us. It will be spread throughout the Nest in a few hours. Once it reaches the queen, it will spread very quickly."

She jammed her feet against the hard shell of one of the young springtails and launched herself down the hall. Afriel followed her. The air was warm and he was beginning to sweat under his elaborate clothing, but his antiseptic sweat was odorless.

They exited into a vast chamber dug from the living rock. It was arched and oblong, eighty meters long and about twenty in diameter. It swarmed with members of the Nest.

There were hundreds of them. Most of them were workers, eight-legged and furred, the size of Great Danes. Here and there were members of the warrior caste, horse-sized furry monsters with heavy fanged heads the size and shape of overstuffed chairs.

A few meters away, two workers were carrying a member of the sensor caste, a being whose immense flattened head was attached to an atrophied body that was mostly lungs. The sensor had great platelike eyes, and its furred chitin sprouted long coiled antennae that twitched feebly as the workers bore it along. The workers clung to the hollowed rock of the chamber walls with hooked and suckered feet.

A paddle-limbed monster with a hairless, faceless head came sculling past them, through the warm reeking air. The front of its head was a nightmare of sharp grinding jaws and blunt armored acid spouts. "A tunneler," Mirny said. "It can take us deeper into the Nest—come with me." She launched herself toward it and took a handhold on its furry, segmented back. Afriel followed her, joined by the two immature springtails, who clung to the thing's hide with their forelimbs. Afriel shuddered at the warm, greasy feel of its rank, damp fur. It continued to scull through the air, its eight fringed paddle feet catching the air like wings.

"There must be thousands of them," Afriel said.

"I said a hundred thousand in my last report, but that was before I had fully explored the Nest. Even now there are long stretches I haven't seen. They must number close to a quarter of a million. This asteroid is about the size of the Mechanists' biggest base—Ceres. It still has rich veins of carbonaceous material. It's far from mined out."

Afriel closed his eyes. If he was to lose his goggles, he would have to feel his way, blind, through these teeming, twitching, wriggling thousands. "The population's still expanding, then?"

"Definitely," she said. "In fact, the colony will launch a mating swarm soon. There are three dozen male and female alates in the chambers near the queen. Once they're launched, they'll mate and start new Nests. I'll take you to see them presently." She hesitated. "We're entering one of the fungal gardens now."

One of the young springtails quietly shifted position. Grabbing the tunneler's fur with its forelimbs, it began to gnaw on the cuff of Afriel's pants. Afriel kicked it soundly, and it jerked back, retracting its eyestalks.

When he looked up again, he saw that they had entered a second chamber, much larger than the first. The walls around, overhead, and below were buried under an explosive profusion of fungus. The most common types were swollen barrel-like domes, multibranched massed thickets, and spaghetti-like tangled extrusions that moved very slightly in the faint and odorous breeze. Some of the barrels were surrounded by dim mists of exhaled spores.

"You see those caked-up piles beneath the fungus, its growth medium?" Mirny said.

"Yes."

"I'm not sure whether it is a plant form or just some kind of complex biochemical sludge," she said. "The point is that it grows in sunlight, on the outside of the asteroid. A food source that grows in naked space! Imagine what that would be worth, back in the Rings."

"There aren't words for its value," Afriel said.

"It's inedible by itself," she said. "I tried to eat a very small piece of it once. It was like trying to eat plastic."

"Have you eaten well, generally speaking?"

"Yes. Our biochemistry is quite similar to the Swarm's. The fungus itself is perfectly edible. The regurgitate is more nourishing, though. Internal fermentation in the worker hindgut adds to its nutritional value."

Afriel stared. "You grow used to it," Mirny said. "Later I'll teach you how to solicit food from the workers. It's a simple matter of reflex tapping—it's not controlled by pheromones, like most of their behavior." She brushed a long lock of clumped and dirty hair from the side of her face. "I hope the pheromonal samples I sent back were worth the cost of transportation."

"Oh, yes," said Afriel. "The chemistry of them was fascinating. We managed to synthesize most of the compounds. I was part of the research team myself." He hesitated. How far did he dare trust her? She had not been told about the experiment he and his superiors

had planned. As far as Mirny knew, he was a simple, peaceful researcher, like herself. The Shapers' scientific community was suspicious of the minority involved in military work and espionage.

As an investment in the future, the Shapers had sent researchers to each of the nineteen alien races described to them by the Investors. This had cost the Shaper economy many gigawatts of precious energy and tons of rare metals and isotopes. In most cases, only two or three researchers could be sent; in seven cases, only one. For the Swarm, Galina Mirny had been chosen. She had gone peacefully, trusting in her intelligence and her good intentions to keep her alive and sane. Those who had sent her had not known whether her findings would be of any use or importance. They had only known that it was imperative that she be sent, even alone, even ill equipped, before some other faction sent their own people and possibly discovered some technique or fact of overwhelming importance. And Dr. Mirny had indeed discovered such a situation. It had made her mission into a matter of Ring security. That was why Afriel had come.

"You synthesized the compounds?" she said. "Why?"

Afriel smiled disarmingly. "Just to prove to ourselves that we could do it, perhaps."

She shook her head. "No mind games, Dr. Afriel, please. I came this far partly to escape from such things. Tell me the truth."

Afriel stared at her, regretting that the goggles meant he could not meet her eyes. "Very well," he said. "You should know, then, that I have been ordered by the Ring Council to carry out an experiment that may endanger both our lives."

Mirny was silent for a moment. "You're from Security, then?"

"My rank is captain."

"I knew it. . . . I knew it when those two Mechanists arrived. They were so polite, and so suspicious—I think they would have killed me at once if they hadn't hoped to bribe or torture some secret out of me. They scared the life out of me, Captain Afriel. . . . You scare me, too."

"We live in a frightening world, doctor. It's a matter of faction security."

"Everything's a matter of faction security with your lot," she said. "I shouldn't take you any farther, or show you anything more. This Nest, these creatures—they're not *intelligent*, Captain. They can't think, they can't learn. They're innocent, primordially innocent. They have no knowledge of good and evil. They have no knowledge of *anything*. The last thing they need is to become pawns in a power struggle within some other race, light-years away."

The tunneler had turned into an exit from the fungal chambers and was paddling slowly along in the warm darkness. A group of creatures like gray, flattened basketballs floated by from the opposite direction. One of them settled on Afriel's sleeve, clinging with frail whiplike tentacles. Afriel brushed it gently away, and it broke loose, emitting a stream of foul reddish droplets.

"Naturally I agree with you in principle, doctor," Afriel said smoothly. "But consider these Mechanists. Some of their extreme factions are already more than half machine. Do you expect humanitarian motives from them? They're cold, doctor—cold and soulless creatures who can cut a living man or woman to bits and never feel their pain. Most of the other factions hate us. They call us racist supermen. Would you rather that one of these cults do what we must do, and use the results against us?"

"This is double-talk." She looked away. All around them workers laden down with fungus, their jaws full and guts stuffed with it, were spreading out into the Nest, scuttling alongside them or disappearing into branch tunnels departing in every direction, including straight up and straight down. Afriel saw a creature much like a worker, but with only six legs, scuttle past in the opposite direction, overhead. It was a parasite mimic. How long, he wondered, did it take a creature to evolve to look like that?

"It's no wonder that we've had so many

defectors, back in the Rings," she said sadly. "If humanity is so stupid as to work itself into a corner like you describe, then it's better to have nothing to do with them. Better to live alone. Better not to help the madness spread."

"That kind of talk will only get us killed," Afriel said. "We owe an allegiance to the faction that produced us."

"Tell me truly, Captain," she said. "Haven't you ever felt the urge to leave everything—everyone—all your duties and constraints, and just go somewhere to think it all out? Your whole world, and your part in it? We're trained so hard, from childhood, and so much is demanded from us. Don't you think it's made us lose sight of our goals, somehow?"

"We live in space," Afriel said flatly. "Space is an unnatural environment, and it takes an unnatural effort from unnatural people to prosper there. Our minds are our tools, and philosophy has to come second. Naturally I've felt those urges you mention. They're just another threat to guard against. I believe in an ordered society. Technology has unleashed tremendous forces that are ripping society apart. Some one faction must arise from the struggle and integrate things. We Shapers have the wisdom and restraint to do it humanely. That's why I do the work I do." He hesitated. "I don't expect to see our day of triumph. I expect to die in some brush-fire conflict, or through assassination. It's enough that I can foresee that day."

"But the arrogance of it, Captain!" she said suddenly. "The arrogance of your little life and its little sacrifice! Consider the Swarm, if you really want your humane and perfect order. Here it is! Where it's always warm and dark, and it smells good, and food is easy to get, and everything is endlessly and perfectly recycled. The only resources that are ever lost are the bodies of the mating swarms, and a little air. A Nest like this one could last unchanged for hundreds of thousands of years. Hundreds . . . of thousands . . . of years. Who, or what, will remember us and our stupid faction in even a thousand years?"

Afriel shook his head. "That's not a valid comparison. There is no such long view for us. In another thousand years we'll be machines, or gods." He felt the top of his head; his velvet cap was gone. No doubt something was eating it by now.

The tunneler took them deeper into the asteroid's honeycombed free-fall maze. They saw the pupal chambers, where pallid larvae twitched in swaddled silk; the main fungal gardens; the graveyard pits, where winged workers beat ceaselessly at the soupy air, feverishly hot from the heat of decomposition. Corrosive black fungus ate the bodies of the dead into coarse black powder, carried off by blackened workers themselves three-quarters dead.

Later they left the tunneler and floated on by themselves. The woman moved with the ease of long habit; Afriel followed her, colliding bruisingly with squeaking workers. There were thousands of them, clinging to ceiling, walls, and floor, clustering and scurrying at every conceivable angle.

Later still they visited the chamber of the winged princes and princesses, an echoing round vault where creatures forty meters long hung crooked-legged in midair. Their bodies were segmented and metallic, with organic rocket nozzles on their thoraxes, where wings might have been. Folded along their sleek backs were radar antennae on long sweeping booms. They looked more like interplanetary probes under construction than anything biological. Workers fed them ceaselessly. Their bulging spiracled abdomens were full of compressed oxygen.

Mirny begged a large chunk of fungus from a passing worker, deftly tapping its antennae and provoking a reflex action. She handed most of the fungus to the two springtails, which devoured it greedily and looked expectantly for more.

Afriel tucked his legs into a free-fall lotus position and began chewing with determination on the leathery fungus. It was tough, but

tasted good, like smoked meat—a delicacy he had tasted only once. The smell of smoke meant disaster in a Shaper's colony.

Mirny maintained a stony silence.

"Food's no problem," Afriel said. "Where do we sleep?"

She shrugged. "Anywhere . . . there are unused niches and tunnels here and there. I suppose you'll want to see the queen's chamber next."

"By all means."

"I'll have to get more fungus. The warriors are on guard there and have to be bribed with food."

She gathered an armful of fungus from another worker in the endless stream, and they moved on. Afriel, already totally lost, was further confused in the maze of chambers and tunnels. At last they exited into an immense lightless cavern, bright with infrared heat from the queen's monstrous body. It was the colony's central factory. The fact that it was made of warm and pulpy flesh did not conceal its essentially industrial nature. Tons of predigested fungal pap went into the slick blind jaws at one end. The rounded billows of soft flesh digested and processed it, squirming, sucking, and undulating, with loud machinelike churnings and gurglings. Out of the other end came an endless conveyor-like blobbed stream of eggs, each one packed in a thick hormonal paste of lubrication. The workers avidly licked the eggs clean and bore them off to nurseries. Each egg was the size of a man's torso.

The process went on and on. There was no day or night here in the lightless center of the asteroid. There was no remnant of a diurnal rhythm in the genes of these creatures. The flow of production was as constant and even as the working of an automated mine.

"This is why I'm here," Afriel murmured in awe. "Just look at this, doctor. The Mechanists have cybernetic mining machinery that is generations ahead of ours. But here—in the bowels of this nameless little world—is a genetic technology that feeds itself, maintains itself, runs itself, efficiently, endlessly, mindlessly. It's the perfect organic tool. The faction that could use these tireless workers could make itself an industrial titan. And our knowledge of biochemistry is unsurpassed. We Shapers are just the ones to do it."

"How do you propose to do that?" Mirny asked with open skepticism. "You would have to ship a fertilized queen all the way to the solar system. We could scarcely afford that, even if the Investors would let us, which they wouldn't."

"I don't need an entire Nest," Afriel said patiently. "I only need the genetic information from one egg. Our laboratories back in the Rings could clone endless numbers of workers."

"But the workers are useless without the Nest's pheromones. They need chemical cues to trigger their behavior modes."

"Exactly," Afriel said. "As it so happens, I possess those pheromones, synthesized and concentrated. What I must do now is test them. I must prove that I can use them to make the workers do what I choose. Once I've proven it's possible, I'm authorized to smuggle the genetic information necessary back to the Rings. The Investors won't approve. There are, of course, moral questions involved, and the Investors are not genetically advanced. But we can win their approval back with the profits we make. Best of all, we can beat the Mechanists at their own game."

"You've carried the pheromones here?" Mirny said. "Didn't the Investors suspect something when they found them?"

"Now it's you who has made an error," Afriel said calmly. "You assume that the Investors are infallible. You are wrong. A race without curiosity will never explore every possibility, the way we Shapers did." Afriel pulled up his pants cuff and extended his right leg. "Consider this varicose vein along my shin. Circulatory problems of this sort are common among those who spend a lot of time in free fall. This vein, how-

ever, has been blocked artificially and treated to reduce osmosis. Within the vein are ten separate colonies of genetically altered bacteria, each one specially bred to produce a different Swarm pheromone."

He smiled. "The Investors searched me very thoroughly, including X-rays. But the vein appears normal to X-rays, and the bacteria are trapped within compartments in the vein. They are indetectable. I have a small medical kit on my person. It includes a syringe. We can use it to extract the pheromones and test them. When the tests are finished—and I feel sure they will be successful, in fact I've staked my career on it—we can empty the vein and all its compartments. The bacteria will die on contact with air. We can refill the vein with the yolk from a developing embryo. The cells may survive during the trip back, but even if they die, they can't rot inside my body. They'll never come in contact with any agent of decay. Back in the Rings, we can learn to activate and suppress different genes to produce the different castes, just as is done in nature. We'll have millions of workers, armies of warriors if need be, perhaps even organic rocket ships, grown from altered alates. If this works, who do you think will remember me then, eh? Me and my arrogant little life and little sacrifice?"

She stared at him; even the bulky goggles could not hide her new respect and even fear. "You really mean to do it, then."

"I made the sacrifice of my time and energy. I expect results, doctor."

"But it's kidnapping. You're talking about breeding a slave race."

Afriel shrugged, with contempt. "You're juggling words, doctor. I'll cause this colony no harm. I may steal some of its workers' labor while they obey my own chemical orders, but that tiny theft won't be missed. I admit to the murder of one egg, but that is no more a crime than a human abortion. Can the theft of one strand of genetic material be called 'kidnapping'? I think not. As for the scandalous idea of a slave race—I reject it out of hand. These creatures are genetic robots. They will no more be slaves than are laser drills or cargo tankers. At the very worst, they will be our domestic animals."

Mirny considered the issue. It did not take her long. "It's true. It's not as if a common worker will be staring at the stars, pining for its freedom. They're just brainless neuters."

"Exactly, doctor."

"They simply work. Whether they work for us or the Swarm makes no difference to them."

"I see that you've seized on the beauty of the idea."

"And if it worked," Mirny said, "if it worked, our faction would profit astronomically."

Afriel smiled genuinely, unaware of the chilling sarcasm of his expression. "And the personal profit, doctor . . . the valuable expertise of the first to exploit the technique." He spoke gently, quietly. "Ever see a nitrogen snowfall on Titan? I think a habitat of one's own there—larger, much larger than anything possible before . . . A genuine city, Galina, a place where a man can scrap the rules and discipline that madden him . . ."

"Now it's you who are talking defection, Captain-Doctor."

Afriel was silent for a moment, then smiled with an effort. "Now you've ruined my perfect reverie," he said. "Besides, what I was describing was the well-earned retirement of a wealthy man, not some self-indulgent hermitage . . . there's a clear difference." He hesitated. "In any case, may I conclude that you're with me in this project?"

She laughed and touched his arm. There was something uncanny about the small sound of her laugh, drowned by a great organic rumble from the queen's monstrous intestines. . . ." Do you expect me to resist your arguments for two long years? Better that I give in now and save us friction."

"Yes."

"After all, you won't do any harm to the Nest. They'll never know anything has hap-

pened. And if their genetic line is successfully reproduced back home, there'll never be any reason for humanity to bother them again."

"True enough," said Afriel, though in the back of his mind he instantly thought of the fabulous wealth of Betelgeuse's asteroid system. A day would come, inevitably, when humanity would move to the stars en masse, in earnest. It would be well to know the ins and outs of every race that might become a rival.

"I'll help you as best I can," she said. There was a moment's silence. "Have you seen enough of this area?"

"Yes." They left the queen's chamber.

"I didn't think I'd like you at first," she said candidly. "I think I like you better now. You seem to have a sense of humor that most Security people lack."

"It's not a sense of humor," Afriel said sadly. "It's a sense of irony disguised as one."

There were no days in the unending stream of hours that followed. There were only ragged periods of sleep, apart at first, later together, as they held each other in free fall. The sexual feel of skin and body became an anchor to their common humanity, a divided, frayed humanity so many light-years away that the concept no longer had any meaning. Life in the warm and swarming tunnels was the here and now; the two of them were like germs in a bloodstream, moving ceaselessly with the pulsing ebb and flow. Hours stretched into months, and time itself grew meaningless.

The pheromonal tests were complex, but not impossibly difficult. The first of the ten pheromones was a simple grouping stimulus, causing large numbers of workers to gather as the chemical was spread from palp to palp. The workers then waited for further instructions; if none were forthcoming, they dispersed. To work effectively, the pheromones had to be given in a mix, or series, like computer commands; number one, grouping, for instance, together with the third pheromone, a transferral order, which caused the workers to empty any given chamber and move its effects to another. The ninth pheromone had the best industrial possibilities; it was a building order, causing the workers to gather tunnelers and dredgers and set them to work. Others were annoying; the tenth pheromone provoked grooming behavior, and the workers' furry palps stripped off the remaining rags of Afriel's clothing. The eighth pheromone sent the workers off to harvest material on the asteroid's surface, and in their eagerness to observe its effects the two explorers were almost trapped and swept off into space.

The two of them no longer feared the warrior caste. They knew that a dose of the sixth pheromone would send them scurrying off to defend the eggs, just as it sent the workers to tend them. Mirny and Afriel took advantage of this and secured their own chambers, dug by chemically hijacked workers and defended by a hijacked air lock guardian. They had their own fungal gardens to refresh the air, stocked with the fungus they liked best, and digested by a worker they kept drugged for their own food use. From constant stuffing and lack of exercise the worker had swollen up into its replete form and hung from one wall like a monstrous grape.

Afriel was tired. He had been without sleep recently for a long time; how long, he didn't know. His body rhythms had not adjusted as well as Mirny's, and he was prone to fits of depression and irritability that he had to repress with an effort. "The Investors will be back sometime," he said. "Sometime soon."

Mirny was indifferent. "The Investors," she said, and followed the remark with something in the language of the springtails, which he didn't catch. Despite his linguistic training, Afriel had never caught up with her in her use of the springtails' grating jargon. His training was almost a liability; the springtail language had decayed so much that it was a pidgin tongue, without rules or regularity. He knew enough to give them simple orders, and with his partial control of the warriors he had the power to

back it up. The springtails were afraid of him, and the two juveniles that Mirny had tamed had developed into fat, overgrown tyrants that freely terrorized their elders. Afriel had been too busy to seriously study the springtails or the other symbiotes. There were too many practical matters at hand.

"If they come too soon, I won't be able to finish my latest study," she said in English.

Afriel pulled off his infrared goggles and knotted them tightly around his neck. "There's a limit, Galina," he said, yawning. "You can only memorize so much data without equipment. We'll just have to wait quietly until we can get back. I hope the Investors aren't shocked when they see me. I lost a fortune with those clothes."

"It's been so dull since the mating swarm was launched. If it weren't for the new growth in the alates' chamber, I'd be bored to death." She pushed greasy hair from her face with both hands. "Are you going to sleep?"

"Yes, if I can."

"You won't come with me? I keep telling you that this new growth is important. I think it's a new caste. It's definitely not an alate. It has eyes like an alate, but it's clinging to the wall."

"It's probably not a Swarm member at all, then," he said tiredly, humoring her. "It's probably a parasite, an alate mimic. Go on and see it, if you want to. I'll be here waiting for you."

He heard her leave. Without his infrareds on, the darkness was still not quite total; there was a very faint luminosity from the steaming, growing fungus in the chamber beyond. The stuffed worker replete moved slightly on the wall, rustling and gurgling. He fell asleep.

When he awoke, Mirny had not yet returned. He was not alarmed. First, he visited the original air lock tunnel, where the Investors had first left him. It was irrational—the Investors always fulfilled their contracts—but he feared that they would arrive someday, become impatient, and leave without him. The Investors would have to wait, of course. Mirny could keep them occupied in the short time it would take him to hurry to the nursery and rob a developing egg of its living cells. It was best that the egg be as fresh as possible.

Later he ate. He was munching fungus in one of the anterior chambers when Mirny's two tamed springtails found him. "What do you want?" he asked in their language.

"Food-giver no good," the larger one screeched, waving its forelegs in brainless agitation. "Not work, not sleep."

"Not move," the second one said. It added hopefully, "Eat it now?"

Afriel gave them some of his food. They ate it, seemingly more out of habit than real appetite, which alarmed him. "Take me to her," he told them.

The two springtails scurried off; he followed them easily, adroitly dodging and weaving through the crowds of workers. They led him several miles through the network, to the alates' chamber. There they stopped, confused. "Gone," the large one said.

The chamber was empty. Afriel had never seen it empty before, and it was very unusual for the Swarm to waste so much space. He felt dread. "Follow the food-giver," he said. "Follow the smell."

The springtails snuffled without much enthusiasm along one wall; they knew he had no food and were reluctant to do anything without an immediate reward. At last one of them picked up the scent, or pretended to, and followed it up across the ceiling and into the mouth of a tunnel.

It was hard for Afriel to see much in the abandoned chamber; there was not enough infrared heat. He leapt upward after the springtail.

He heard the roar of a warrior and the springtail's choked-off screech. It came flying from the tunnel's mouth, a spray of clotted fluid bursting from its ruptured head. It tumbled end over end until it hit the far wall with a flaccid crunch. It was already dead.

The second springtail fled at once, screeching with grief and terror. Afriel landed on the lip of the tunnel, sinking into a crouch as his legs soaked up momentum. He could smell the acrid stench of the warrior's anger, a pheromone so thick that even a human could scent it. Dozens of other warriors would group here within minutes, or seconds. Behind the enraged warrior he could hear workers and tunnelers shifting and cementing rock.

He might be able to control one enraged warrior, but never two, or twenty. He launched himself from the chamber wall and out an exit.

He searched for the other springtail—he felt sure he could recognize it, since it was so much bigger than the others—but he could not find it. With its keen sense of smell, it could easily avoid him if it wanted to.

Mirny did not return. Uncountable hours passed. He slept again. He returned to the alates' chamber; there were warriors on guard there, warriors that were not interested in food and brandished their immense serrated fangs when he approached. They looked ready to rip him apart; the faint reek of aggressive pheromones hung about the place like a fog. He did not see any symbiotes of any kind on the warriors' bodies. There was one species, a thing like a huge tick, that clung only to warriors, but even the ticks were gone.

He returned to his chambers to wait and think. Mirny's body was not in the garbage pits. Of course, it was possible that something else might have eaten her. Should he extract the remaining pheromone from the spaces in his vein and try to break into the alates' chamber? He suspected that Mirny, or whatever was left of her, was somewhere in the tunnel where the springtail had been killed. He had never explored that tunnel himself. There were thousands of tunnels he had never explored.

He felt paralyzed by indecision and fear. If he was quiet, if he did nothing, the Investors might arrive at any moment. He could tell the Ring Council anything he wanted about Mirny's death; if he had the genetics with him, no one would quibble. He did not love her; he respected her, but not enough to give up his life, or his faction's investment. He had not thought of the Ring Council in a long time, and the thought sobered him. He would have to explain his decision. . . .

He was still in a brown study when he heard a whoosh of air as his living air lock deflated itself. Three warriors had come for him. There was no reek of anger about them. They moved slowly and carefully. He knew better than to try to resist. One of them seized him gently in its massive jaws and carried him off.

It took him to the alates' chamber and into the guarded tunnel. A new, large chamber had been excavated at the end of the tunnel. It was filled almost to bursting by a black-splattered white mass of flesh. In the center of the soft speckled mass were a mouth and two damp, shining eyes, on stalks. Long tendrils like conduits dangled, writhing, from a clumped ridge above the eyes. The tendrils ended in pink, fleshy pluglike clumps.

One of the tendrils had been thrust through Mirny's skull. Her body hung in midair, limp as wax. Her eyes were open, but blind.

Another tendril was plugged into the braincase of a mutated worker. The worker still had the pallid tinge of a larva; it was shrunken and deformed, and its mouth had the wrinkled look of a human mouth. There was a blob like a tongue in the mouth, and white ridges like human teeth. It had no eyes.

It spoke with Mirny's voice. "Captain-Doctor Afriel . . ."

"Galina . . ."

"I have no such name. You may address me as Swarm."

Afriel vomited. The central mass was an immense head. Its brain almost filled the room.

It waited politely until Afriel had finished.

"I find myself awakened again," Swarm said dreamily. "I am pleased to see that there is no major emergency to concern me. Instead it is a threat that has become almost routine." It hesitated delicately. Mirny's body moved slightly in midair; her breathing was inhumanly regular. The eyes opened and closed. "Another young race."

"What are you?"

"I am the Swarm. That is, I am one of its castes. I am a tool, an adaptation; my specialty is intelligence. I am not often needed. It is good to be needed again."

"Have you been here all along? Why didn't you greet us? We'd have dealt with you. We meant no harm."

The wet mouth on the end of the plug made laughing sounds. "Like yourself, I enjoy irony," it said. "It is a pretty trap you have found yourself in, Captain-Doctor. You meant to make the Swarm work for you and your race. You meant to breed us and study us and use us. It is an excellent plan, but one we hit upon long before your race evolved."

Stung by panic, Afriel's mind raced frantically. "You're an intelligent being," he said. "There's no reason to do us any harm. Let us talk together. We can help you."

"Yes," Swarm agreed. "You will be helpful. Your companion's memories tell me that this is one of those uncomfortable periods when galactic intelligence is rife. Intelligence is a great bother. It makes all kinds of trouble for us."

"What do you mean?"

"You are a young race and lay great stock by your own cleverness," Swarm said. "As usual, you fail to see that intelligence is not a survival trait."

Afriel wiped sweat from his face. "We've done well," he said. "We came to you, and peacefully. You didn't come to us."

"I refer to exactly that," Swarm said urbanely. "This urge to expand, to explore, to develop, is just what will make you extinct. You naively suppose that you can continue to feed your curiosity indefinitely. It is an old story, pursued by countless races before you. Within a thousand years—perhaps a little longer—your species will vanish."

"You intend to destroy us, then? I warn you it will not be an easy task—"

"Again you miss the point. Knowledge is power! Do you suppose that fragile little form of yours—your primitive legs, your ludicrous arms and hands, your tiny, scarcely wrinkled brain—can *contain* all that power? Certainly not! Already your race is flying to pieces under the impact of your own expertise. The original human form is becoming obsolete. Your own genes have been altered, and you, Captain-Doctor, are a crude experiment. In a hundred years you will be a relic. In a thousand years you will not even be a memory. Your race will go the same way as a thousand others."

"And what way is that?"

"I do not know." The thing on the end of the Swarm's arm made a chuckling sound. "They have passed beyond my ken. They have all discovered something, learned something, that has caused them to transcend my understanding. It may be that they even transcend being. At any rate, I cannot sense their presence anywhere. They seem to do nothing, they seem to interfere in nothing; for all intents and purposes, they seem to be dead. Vanished. They may have become gods, or ghosts. In either case, I have no wish to join them."

"So then—so then you have—"

"Intelligence is very much a two-edged sword, Captain-Doctor. It is useful only up to a point. It interferes with the business of living. Life and intelligence do not mix very well. They are not at all closely related, as you childishly assume."

"But you, then—you are a rational being—"

"I am a tool, as I said." The mutated device on the end of its arm made a sighing noise. "When you began your pheromonal experiments, the chemical imbalance became apparent to the queen. It triggered certain genetic patterns within her body, and I was reborn. Chemical sabotage is a problem that can best be dealt with by intelligence. I am a brain replete, you see, specially designed to be far more intelligent than any young race. Within three days I was fully self-conscious. Within five days I had deciphered these markings on my body. They are the genetically encoded history of my race . . . within five days and two hours I rec-

ognized the problem at hand and knew what to do. I am now doing it. I am six days old."

"What is it you intend to do?"

"Your race is a very vigorous one. I expect it to be here, competing with us, within five hundred years. Perhaps much sooner. It will be necessary to make a thorough study of such a rival. I invite you to join our community on a permanent basis."

"What do you mean?"

"I invite you to become a symbiote. I have here a male and a female, whose genes are altered and therefore without defects. You make a perfect breeding pair. It will save me a great deal of trouble with cloning."

"You think I'll betray my race and deliver a slave species into your hands?"

"Your choice is simple, Captain-Doctor. Remain an intelligent, living being, or become a mindless puppet, like your partner. I have taken over all the functions of her nervous system; I can do the same to you."

"I can kill myself."

"That might be troublesome, because it would make me resort to developing a cloning technology. Technology, though I am capable of it, is painful to me. I am a genetic artifact; there are fail-safes within me that prevent me from taking over the Nest for my own uses. That would mean falling into the same trap of progress as other intelligent races. For similar reasons, my life span is limited. I will live for only a thousand years, until your race's brief flurry of energy is over and peace resumes once more."

"Only a thousand years?" Afriel laughed bitterly. "What then? You kill off my descendants, I assume, having no further use for them."

"No. We have not killed any of the fifteen other races we have taken for defensive study. It has not been necessary. Consider that small scavenger floating by your head, Captain-Doctor, that is feeding on your vomit. Five hundred million years ago its ancestors made the galaxy tremble. When they attacked us, we unleashed their own kind upon them. Of course, we altered our side, so that they were smarter, tougher, and, naturally, totally loyal to us. Our Nests were the only world they knew, and they fought with a valor and inventiveness we never could have matched. . . . Should your race arrive to exploit us, we will naturally do the same."

"We humans are different."

"Of course."

"A thousand years here won't change us. You will die and our descendants will take over this Nest. We'll be running things, despite you, in a few generations. The darkness won't make any difference."

"Certainly not. You don't need eyes here. You don't need anything."

"You'll allow me to stay alive? To teach them anything I want?"

"Certainly, Captain-Doctor. We are doing you a favor, in all truth. In a thousand years your descendants here will be the only remnants of the human race. We are generous with our immortality; we will take it upon ourselves to preserve you."

"You're wrong, Swarm. You're wrong about intelligence, and you're wrong about everything else. Maybe other races would crumble into parasitism, but we humans are different."

"Certainly. You'll do it, then?"

"Yes. I accept your challenge. And I will defeat you."

"Splendid. When the Investors return here, the springtails will say that they have killed you, and will tell them to never return. They will not return. The humans should be the next to arrive."

"If I don't defeat you, they will."

"Perhaps." Again it sighed. "I'm glad I don't have to absorb you. I would have missed your conversation."

Mondocane
JACQUES BARBÉRI
Translated by Brian Evenson

Jacques Barbéri (1954–) is a French writer of science fiction and fantasy. He was initially inspired to write science fiction by the film *2001: A Space Odyssey* and Philip K. Dick's novel *The Three Stigmata of Palmer Eldritch* in the early 1970s. While working on a doctorate in dental surgery and dentistry, he continued to write, leading up to his first collection of short fiction, *Kosmokrim* (1985), which revealed his obsessions with time, memory, myth, metamorphoses of flesh, and perceptions of reality. He is also a screenplay writer, a translator from Italian, and a musician (in the group Palo Alto).

With Antoine Volodine, Francis Berthelot, Emmanuel Jouanne, and a few other writers, he formed Limite, a group that worked to experiment and push back against the conventions imposed by the history of the genre. Their first collective work, *Despite the World*, profoundly changed the French science fiction of the eighties.

Barbéri has published a dozen novels (none yet in English), including *Narcose* (*Narcosis*, 1989), his most popular title, and one hundred short stories. In addition to a new edition of the *Narcosis* trilogy (*Narcosis*, *La Mémoire du crime* [*The Memory of the Crime*, 2009], *Le Tueur venu du Centaure* [*The Killer from Centaur*, 2010]), he recently has published in French (through La Volte editions) two collections of short stories, *L'Homme qui parlait aux araignées* (*The Man Who Speaks to Spiders*, 2008) and *Le Landeau du rat* (*The Rat's Cradle*, 2011), as well as two novels, *Les Crépuscule des chimères* (*The Twilight of Chimeras*, 2013) and *Cosmos Factory* (2014).

"Mondocane" (1983), appearing here for the first time in English, is a stunning example of surreal science fiction, carrying forward the legacy of Paul Scheerbart and Alfred Jarry in a much more visceral way.

MONDOCANE

Jacques Barbéri

Translated by Brian Evenson

The end of the war gave birth to bottle-men and hives of homunculi. The war had left behind her a bleeding and swollen Earth. The wounds filled at the end of years with water and sand, transforming cities into deserts and continents into islets.

What had really happened, nobody knew. A slippage of forces, an uncontrollable hatred . . .

Humans again found themselves attracted to the greatly ill, the cancerous, the leprous, the diabetic. They were tugged by a mysterious force, dragged liked dogs along the dusty streets. Aspirated. And they rushed, dislocated, into the hallways of clinics, of hospitals, to finish their trajectories in operating rooms, glued to the bodies of the dying. Gigantic pyramids formed, making the walls of these edifices, the porous buildings, burst.

In this way, new mountains invaded the changing geography of the globe. The most farsighted quickly hid themselves away in the depths of nuclear bunkers. Once all the hatches were closed, the last fanatics of protection were locked up in old blockhouses or, if need be, behind the meters of concrete of shut-down nuclear factories.

For the captives of the surface, one of the most corrosive neuroses was then that of wearing a gas mask. An obsessive fear of radiation convinced a number of people that they should no longer remove their masks. And, through the glass of the goggles, it is now possible to observe a certain putrefaction of the flesh. The skin is attired in mould and the condensation which forms on the glass is perhaps due to not just the principal occupant.

A process of expansion/compression, most likely owing to the theories of Anton Ravon on the localization of a point of perceptual modulation at the level of the central sulcus of the cerebrum, was manifested a short while later. Gigantic metropolises like New York or Paris found themselves transformed into trinkets, like those little miniatures frozen within glass, under a tempest of snow. Thousands of inhabitants died like this, crushed by dogs or by jackasses. Certain buildings, on the contrary, expanded immensely, forcing their occupants to walk for several months before reaching the exit door, fed by the crumbs stuck in the warp of the floor covering. Freighters came to run aground on the immaculate tiling of operating rooms. Entire trains, be they locomotive or wagon, finished their route at the bottom of the toilet bowls of water closets.

To flee the rising waters, men and animals saw themselves forced to scale the mountains of bodies and, in the rarefied atmosphere of the heights, they fell asleep, exhausted, their slumber lulled by the backwash of the waves breaking against the skulls, the legs, the amalgamated torsos, the nightmares carved by the groaning of the still living bodies lost in the heap.

Some, during the climb, coupled savagely with a man or a woman whose sex was accessible, hugging the mountainside. The orgasm seemed to spread through the entire mountain; and the violator found himself soldered to the ensemble, after having experienced, for the space of an instance, extreme pleasure.

To try to flee this uncertain ground once and for all, the most inventive created strange machines. Giant catapults launched masses of dismantled men and women, floating in fat canvas suits, beyond the stratosphere. Implantations of subcutaneous micro-reactors propelled "cannon-men" toward the stars. The most adventurous were crushed, after a harmonious curve, behind the wheel of homemade rockets, pedal- or powder-driven. Others tried all sorts of telekinetic drugs, stolen from deserted space centers, or else synthesized based on formulas of doubtful authenticity.

And for some, the journey still continues. It will last until cellular putrefaction, the osseous erosion of their frame, frozen, in an S or an L, in their delicate salon easy chairs, as if they were watching an anodyne television broadcast or listening on their radio to a classical piece requiring deep contemplation. Insufficient or damaged doses; and in their listless heads, stars march along the fuselage of spacecraft, meteorites collide with the metal; ghost captains of a memory-vessel, they try desperately to reach a welcoming planet, braving meteor showers and the impish mutinies of the crew.

Incorrect blends give results that are to say the least spectacular; only certain parts of the body are stormed by the telekinetic drugs. And arms disappear, skin bursts, guts explode, leaving a cavity that is empty, clean: arteries empty of their blood, ocular orbs are driven out of their sockets, cerebral matter gushes out of the nostrils, the ears; and the travellers, always just as calm and serene, seem to be watching their favorite television program, listening to their favorite record, while their vanished organs decay on distant planets.

When Anton Ravon died, crushed by his coat and his hat, there was a certain period of respite, punctuated by a few infrequent reversals. Clothing took possession of bodies; networks of wool became intrications of muscular fibers, silk shirts a tapestry of nerves, cravats and bow ties metamorphosed into arteries, into veins, watches ossified, handkerchiefs became inlaid with fingernails, lace with pulmonary tissue. And bodies flattened. Empty. Crushed by the clothing of the flesh. Initially, clothing was rapidly abandoned, then replaced by protective gear made of copper, the only element resistant to the reversals. And men in armor strode across the desert, looking for a watering hole, sometimes getting bogged down in the furniture zones. Prisoners of their heavy coppered skins, they were eaten alive by the animals of the sand.

Many preferred to remain naked.

Nobody was ever able to discern the exact origin of the bottle-men. The most generally accepted theory is that which consists of comparing their "fabrication" to that of fruit in liqueur. In the same way that the fruit, still attached to the tree, fattens up inside of a bottle, the babies, after delivery, are placed in large bottles, where they develop to an adult stage. Then, they are thrown in the sea. Is this a punishment? A method of fleeing an island battered by the storm? No one can affirm it. They come to wash up on the beaches, are shattered on the rocks; and their occupants are always dead.

I think, as for me, that it's a matter of messages, of genetic information perhaps. The bottle-men all have the same face. That of Anton Ravon on the day of his death.

The hives of homunculi were born out of necessity. The occupants of the nuclear bunkers were found, for the most part, buried under hundreds of meters of sand. Initially, the women, crushed by a powerful lethargy, saw their volume increase considerably; their limbs atrophied, and only their head remained, at the tip of a gigantic flaccid body. Inversely, the men decreased in volume and started to live in the folds of flesh of the female bodies.

But it was a matter of becoming animal only in appearance, cerebral functions diminishing not at all. Except the social instinct, of collective life, was intensified. The first eggs were tended in doubt and fear. Then the first larvae made their appearance. And, supplied with burrowing snouts, they set about fighting their way towards the surface. The desert is now a gigantic network of tunnels and reproduction chambers. The hives presently stage the form of life that is the most evolved, most adapted, of the planet. All things considered, the homunculi would prefer to remain underground, and come out only very rarely, mainly to hunt.

Strange coral structures are starting to come up to the surface of the new seas. Again an inevitable mutation. Will the adaptation of the submarine prisoners be as favorable as that of the prisoners of the desert?

The majority of mountains of bodies are living. They feed through their thousands of mouths. A real osmosis, permeability, is embodied at the level of the welds. They reproduce by scissiparity. The new hills are very beautiful.

A stratification of organs and of limbs seems to be being carried out. The latest births have given rise to relatively differentiated mounds. The base is an amalgamation of legs; then come the stomachs with a few ectopic digestive organs, then the arms, followed by torsos working the cardiopulmonary organs in unison. The beating of a marching army.

Near the surface, the heads, sheltered behind forests of hair, and, finally, at the summit, the genital organs. The intestines finish their course underground, sheltered in the final meters of the path by a hedge of legs.

At this rate, I truly believe that we will soon witness the birth of a new race of giants. And I am uncertain already of knowing the appearance of their faces. The death of Anton Ravon is going perhaps to save us all.

Blood Music

GREG BEAR

Greg (Gregory) Bear (1951–) is an award-winning US writer best known for his science fiction short stories and novels. Bear's first published fiction, "Destroyers," appeared in *Famous Science Fiction* in 1967, when he was sixteen. The son-in-law of the famed SF writer Poul Anderson, Bear would go on to become one of the best-known hard science fiction writers of the 1980s, with such classics as *Eon* (1985) and *Eternity* (1988). He has won five Nebula Awards and two Hugo Awards. Other novels include the *Forge of God* series, the *Way* series, *Queen of Angels*, and the duology *Darwin's Radio* and *Darwin's Children*. He has most recently written several fascinating novels set in the universe of the Halo video game.

Bear's activities outside of writing have included serving as the president of the Science Fiction Writers of America from 1988 to 1990 and cofounding San Diego Comic-Con. His early artwork appeared as covers for the magazines *Galaxy* and *The Magazine of Fantasy and Science Fiction*. He also serves on the board of advisers for the Museum of Science Fiction.

Bear has had a fascinating tendency to explore both the microscopic and macroscopic worlds to excellent effect. Novels such as *Eon* are dramatic showcases for Bear's talent for cosmological space opera, including large-scale ideas like hollowed-out asteroids. But he has been equally adroit at balancing a sense of awe about the universe with interesting details of characterization and science aimed at exploring the life within us. Case in point: the nanotechnology in the classic Nebula and Hugo Award–winning "Blood Music," first published in *Analog* (1983). Bear expanded it into a novel that was published in 1985. Much about the way Bear uses the science of transforming RNA molecules into living computers is groundbreaking and breathtaking all on its own. But "Blood Music" showcases how Bear, unlike many other writers, manages to incorporate the hardest and most cognitively demanding of hard science fiction premises into stories whose protagonists display far greater complexity than anything unliving. Bear clearly understands that human beings are just as difficult to understand as physics or any other branch of hard science. In linking science and humanity, "Blood Music" remains one of the most important stories hinting at the posthuman condition.

BLOOD MUSIC

Greg Bear

There is a principle in nature I don't think anyone has pointed out before. Each hour, a myriad of trillions of little live things—bacteria,
microbes, "animalcules"—are born and die,
not counting for much except in the bulk of
their existence and the accumulation of their
tiny effects. They do not perceive deeply. They
do not suffer much. A hundred billion, dying,
would not begin to have the same importance as
a single human death.

Within the ranks of magnitude of all creatures, small as microbes or great as humans,
there is an equality of "élan," just as the
branches of a tall tree, gathered together, equal
the bulk of the limbs below, and all the limbs
equal the bulk of the trunk.

That, at least, is the principle. I believe Vergil Ulam was the first to violate it.

It had been two years since I'd last seen Vergil.
My memory of him hardly matched the tan,
smiling, well-dressed gentleman standing before
me. We had made a lunch appointment over the
phone the day before, and now faced each other
in the wide double doors of the employees' cafeteria at the Mount Freedom Medical Center.

"Vergil?" I asked. "My God, Vergil!"

"Good to see you, Edward." He shook my
hand firmly. He had lost ten or twelve kilos
and what remained seemed tighter, better pro-
portioned. At university, Vergil had been the
pudgy, shock-haired, snaggletoothed whiz kid
who hot-wired doorknobs, gave us punch that
turned our piss blue, and never got a date
except with Eileen Termagent, who shared
many of his physical characteristics.

"You look fantastic," I said. "Spend a summer in Cabo San Lucas?"

We stood in line at the counter and chose our
food. "The tan," he said, picking out a carton of
chocolate milk, "is from spending three months
under a sunlamp. My teeth were straightened
just after I last saw you. I'll explain the rest, but
we need a place to talk in private."

I steered him to the smoker's corner, where
three die-hard puffers were scattered among six
tables.

"Listen, I mean it," I said as we unloaded our
trays. "You've changed. You're looking good."

"I've changed more than you know." His
tone was motion-picture ominous, and he delivered the line with a theatrical lift of his brows.
"How's Gail?"

Gail was doing well, I told him, teaching
nursery school. We'd married the year before.
His gaze shifted down to his food—pineapple
slice and cottage cheese, piece of banana cream
pie—and he said, his voice almost cracking,
"Notice something else?"

I squinted in concentration. "Uh."

"Look closer."

"I'm not sure. Well, yes, you're not wearing
glasses. Contacts?"

"No. I don't need them anymore."

"And you're a snappy dresser. Who's dressing you now? I hope she's as sexy as she is
tasteful."

"Candice isn't—wasn't responsible for the
improvement in my clothes," he said. "I just got
a better job, more money to throw around. My
taste in clothes is better than my taste in food,
as it happens." He grinned the old Vergil self-
deprecating grin, but ended it with a peculiar

leer. "At any rate, she's left me, I've been fired from my job, I'm living on savings."

"Hold it," I said. "That's a bit crowded. Why not do a linear breakdown? You got a job. Where?"

"Genetron Corp.," he said. "Sixteen months ago."

"I haven't heard of them."

"You will. They're going public next month. The stock will shoot right off the board. They've broken through with MABs. Medical—"

"I know what MABs are," I interrupted. "At least in theory. Medically Applicable Biochips."

"They have some that work."

"What?" It was my turn to lift my brows.

"Microscopic logic circuits. You inject them into the human body, they set up shop where they're told and troubleshoot. With Dr. Michael Bernard's approval."

That was quite impressive. Bernard's reputation was spotless. Not only was he associated with the genetic engineering biggies, but he had made news at least once a year in his practice as a neurosurgeon before retiring. Covers on *Time*, *Mega*, *Rolling Stone*.

"That's supposed to be secret—stock, breakthrough, Bernard, everything." Vergil looked around and lowered his voice. "But you do whatever the hell you want. I'm through with the bastards."

I whistled. "Make me rich, huh?"

"If that's what you want. Or you can spend some time with me before rushing off to your broker."

"Of course." He hadn't touched the cottage cheese or pie. He had, however, eaten the pineapple slice and drunk the chocolate milk. "So tell me more."

"Well, in med school I was training for lab work. Biochemical research. I've always had a bent for computers, too. So I put myself through my last two years—"

"By selling software packages to Westinghouse," I said.

"It's good my friends remember. That's how I got involved with Genetron, just when they were starting out. They had big-money backers, all the lab facilities I thought anyone would ever need. They hired me, and I advanced rapidly.

"Four months and I was doing my own work. I made some breakthroughs." He tossed his hand nonchalantly. "Then I went off on tangents they thought were premature. I persisted and they took away my lab, handed it over to a certifiable flatworm. I managed to save part of the experiment before they fired me. But I haven't exactly been cautious . . . or judicious. So now it's going on outside the lab."

I'd always regarded Vergil as ambitious, a trifle cracked, and not terribly sensitive. His relations with authority figures had never been smooth. Science, for him, was like the woman you couldn't possibly have, who suddenly opens her arms to you, long before you're ready for mature love—leaving you afraid you'll forever blow the chance, lose the prize. Apparently, he did. "Outside the lab? I don't get you."

"Edward, I want you to examine me. Give me a thorough physical. Maybe a cancer diagnostic. Then I'll explain more."

"You want a five-thousand-dollar exam?"

"Whatever you can do. Ultrasound, NMR, thermogram, everything."

"I don't know if I can get access to all that equipment. NMR full-scan has only been here a month or two. Hell, you couldn't pick a more expensive way—"

"Then ultrasound. That's all you'll need."

"Vergil, I'm an obstetrician, not a glamour-boy lab tech. OB-GYN, butt of all jokes. If you're turning into a woman, maybe I can help you."

He leaned forward, almost putting his elbow into the pie, but swinging wide at the last instant by scant millimeters. The old Vergil would have hit it square. "Examine me closely and you'll . . ." He narrowed his eyes. "Just examine me."

"So I make an appointment for ultrasound. Who's going to pay?"

"I'm on Blue Shield." He smiled and held up a medical credit card. "I messed with the personnel files at Genetron. Anything up to a hundred thousand dollars medical, they'll never check, never suspect."

He wanted secrecy, so I made arrangements. I filled out his forms myself. As long as everything was billed properly, most of the examination could take place without official notice. I didn't charge for my services. After all, Vergil had turned my piss blue. We were friends.

He came in late at night. I wasn't normally on duty then, but I stayed late, waiting for him on the third floor of what the nurses called the Frankenstein wing. I sat on an orange plastic chair. He arrived, looking olive colored under the fluorescent lights.

He stripped, and I arranged him on the table. I noticed, first off, that his ankles looked swollen. But they weren't puffy. I felt them several times. They seemed healthy but looked odd. "Hm," I said.

I ran the paddles over him, picking up areas difficult for the big unit to hit, and programmed the data into the imaging system. Then I swung the table around and inserted it into the enameled orifice of the ultrasound unit, the *humhole*, so-called by the nurses.

I integrated the data from the humhole with that from the paddle sweeps and rolled Vergil out, then set up a video frame. The image took a second to integrate, then flowed into a pattern showing Vergil's skeleton. My jaw fell.

Three seconds of that and it switched to his thoracic organs, then his musculature, and, finally, vascular system and skin.

"How long since the accident?" I asked, trying to take the quiver out of my voice.

"I haven't been in an accident," he said. "It was deliberate."

"Jesus, they beat you to keep secrets?"

"You don't understand me, Edward. Look at the images again. I'm not damaged."

"Look, there's thickening here"—I indicated the ankles—"and your ribs, that crazy zigzag pattern of interlocks. Broken sometime, obviously. And—"

"Look at my spine," he said. I rotated the image in the video frame. Buckminster Fuller,

I thought. It was fantastic. A cage of triangular projections, all interlocking in ways I couldn't begin to follow, much less understand. I reached around and tried to feel his spine with my fingers. He lifted his arms and looked off at the ceiling.

"I can't find it," I said. "It's all smooth back there." I let go of him and looked at his chest, then prodded his ribs. They were sheathed in something tough and flexible. The harder I pressed, the tougher it became. Then I noticed another change.

"Hey," I said. "You don't have nipples." There were tiny pigment patches, but no nipple formations at all.

"See?" Vergil asked, shrugging on the white robe. "I'm being rebuilt from the inside out."

In my reconstruction of those hours, I fancy myself saying, "So tell me about it." Perhaps mercifully, I don't remember what I actually said.

He explained with his characteristic circumlocutions. Listening was like trying to get to the meat of a newspaper article through a forest of sidebars and graphic embellishments.

I simplify and condense.

Genetron had assigned him to manufacturing prototype biochips, tiny circuits made out of protein molecules. Some were hooked up to silicon chips little more than a micrometer in size, then sent through rat arteries to chemically keyed locations, to make connections with the rat tissue and attempt to monitor and even control lab-induced pathologies.

"That was something," he said. "We recovered the most complex microchip by sacrificing the rat, then debriefed it—hooked the silicon portion up to an imaging system. The computer gave us bar graphs, then a diagram of the chemical characteristics of about eleven centimeters of blood vessel . . . then put it all together to make a picture. We zoomed down eleven centimeters of rat artery. You never saw so many scientists jumping up and down, hugging each other, drinking buckets of bug juice." Bug juice was lab ethanol mixed with Dr Pepper.

Eventually, the silicon elements were eliminated completely in favor of nucleoproteins. He seemed reluctant to explain in detail, but I gathered they found ways to make huge molecules—as large as DNA, and even more complex—into electrochemical computers, using ribosome-like structures as "encoders" and "readers" and RNA as "tape." Vergil was able to mimic reproductive separation and reassembly in his nucleoproteins, incorporating program changes at key points by switching nucleotide pairs. "Genetron wanted me to switch over to super-gene engineering, since that was the coming thing everywhere else. Make all kinds of critters, some out of our imagination. But I had different ideas." He twiddled his finger around his ear and made theremin sounds. "Mad scientist time, right?" He laughed, then sobered. "I injected my best nucleoproteins into bacteria to make duplication and compounding easier. Then I started to leave them inside, so the circuits could interact with the cells. They were heuristically programmed; they taught themselves. The cells fed chemically coded information to the computers, the computers processed it and made decisions, the cells became smart. I mean, smart as planaria, for starters. Imagine an E. coli as smart as a planarian worm!"

I nodded. "I'm imagining."

"Then I really went off on my own. We had the equipment, the techniques, and I knew the molecular language. I could make really dense, really complicated biochips by compounding the nucleoproteins, making them into little brains. I did some research into how far I could go, theoretically. Sticking with bacteria, I could make a biochip with the computing capacity of a sparrow's brain. Imagine how jazzed I was! Then I saw a way to increase the complexity a thousandfold, by using something we regarded as a nuisance—quantum chitchat between the fixed elements of the circuits. Down that small, even the slightest change could bomb a biochip. But I developed a program that actually predicted and took advantage of electron tunneling. Emphasized the heuristic aspects of the computer, used the chitchat as a method of increasing complexity."

"You're losing me," I said.

"I took advantage of randomness. The circuits could repair themselves, compare memories, and correct faulty elements. I gave them basic instructions: Go forth and multiply. Improve. By God, you should have seen some of the cultures a week later! It was amazing. They were evolving all on their own, like little cities. I destroyed them all. I think one of the Petri dishes would have grown legs and walked out of the incubator if I'd kept feeding it."

"You're kidding." I looked at him. "You're not kidding."

"Man, they knew what it was like to improve! They knew where they had to go, but they were just so limited, being in bacteria bodies, with so few resources."

"How smart were they?"

"I couldn't be sure. They were associating in clusters of a hundred to two hundred cells, each cluster behaving like an autonomous unit. Each cluster might have been as smart as a rhesus monkey. They exchanged information through their pili, passed on bits of memory, and compared notes. Their organization was obviously different from a group of monkeys. Their world was so much simpler, for one thing. With their abilities, they were masters of the petri dishes. I put phages in with them; the phages didn't have a chance. They used every option available to change and grow."

"How is that possible?"

"What?" He seemed surprised I wasn't accepting everything at face value.

"Cramming so much into so little. A rhesus monkey is not your simple calculator, Vergil."

"I haven't made myself clear," he said, irritated. "I was using nucleoprotein computers. They're like DNA, but all the information can interact. Do you know how many nucleotide pairs there are in the DNA of a single bacterium?"

It had been a long time since my last biochemistry lesson. I shook my head.

"About two million. Add in the modified ribosome structures—fifteen thousand of them, each with a molecular weight of about three million—and consider the combinations and permutations. The RNA is arranged like a continuous loop of paper tape, surrounded by ribosomes ticking off instructions and manufacturing protein chains. . . ." His eyes were bright and slightly moist. "Besides, I'm not saying every cell was a distinct entity. They cooperated."

"How many bacteria were in the dishes you destroyed?"

"Billions. I don't know." He smirked. "You got it, Edward. Whole planetsful of E. coli."

"But Genetron didn't fire you then?"

"No. They didn't know what was going on, for one thing. I kept compounding the molecules, increasing their size and complexity. When bacteria were too limited, I took blood from myself, separated out white cells, and injected them with the new biochips. I watched them, put them through mazes and little chemical problems. They were whizzes. Time is a lot faster at that level—so little distance for the messages to cross, and the environment is much simpler. Then I forgot to store a file under my secret code in the lab computers. Some managers found it and guessed what I was up to. Everybody panicked. They thought we'd have every social watchdog in the country on our backs because of what I'd done. They started to destroy my work and wipe my programs. Ordered me to sterilize my white cells. Christ." He pulled the white robe off and started to get dressed. "I only had a day or two. I separated out the most complex cells—"

"How complex?"

"They were clustering in hundred-cell groups, like the bacteria. Each group as smart as a four-year-old kid, maybe." He studied my face. "Still doubting? Want me to run through how many nucleotides there are in the human genome? I tailored my computers to take advantage of the white cells' capacity. Tens of thousands of genes. Three billion nucleotides,

Edward. And they don't have a huge body to worry about, taking up most of their thinking time."

"Okay," I said. "I'm convinced. What did you do?"

"I mixed the cells back into a cylinder of whole blood and injected myself with it." He buttoned the top of his shirt and smiled thinly. "I'd programmed them with every drive I could, talked as high a level as I could using just enzymes and such. After that, they were on their own."

"You programmed them to go forth and multiply, improve?" I asked.

"I think they developed some characteristics picked up by the biochips in their E. coli phases. The white cells could talk to each other with extruded memories. They found ways to ingest other types of cells and alter them without killing them."

"You're crazy."

"You can see the screen! Edward, I haven't been sick since. I used to get colds all the time. I've never felt better."

"They're inside you," I said. "Finding things, changing them."

"And by now, each cluster is as smart as you or I."

"You're absolutely nuts."

He shrugged. "Genetron fired me. They thought I was going to take revenge for what they did to my work. They ordered me out of the labs, and I haven't had a real chance to see what's been going on inside me until now. Three months."

"So . . ." My mind was racing. "You lost weight because they improved your fat metabolism. Your bones are stronger, your spine has been completely rebuilt—"

"No more backaches even if I sleep on my old mattress."

"Your heart looks different."

"I didn't know about the heart," he said, examining the frame image more closely. "As for the fat—I was thinking about that. They could increase my brown cells, fix up the metabolism. I haven't been as hungry lately. I haven't changed my eating habits that much—I still want the same old junk—but somehow I get around to eating only what I need. I don't think they know what my brain is yet. Sure, they've got all the glandular stuff—but they don't have the big picture, if you see what I mean. They don't know I'm in here. But boy, they sure did figure out what my reproductive organs are."

I glanced at the image and shifted my eyes away.

"Oh, they look pretty normal," he said, hefting his scrotum obscenely. He snickered. "But how else do you think I'd land a real looker like Candice? She was just after a one-night stand with a techie. I looked okay then, no tan but trim, with good clothes. She'd never screwed a techie before. Joke time, right? But my little geniuses kept us up half the night. I think they made improvements each time. I felt like I had a goddamned fever."

His smile vanished. "But then one night my skin started to crawl. It really scared me. I thought things were getting out of hand. I wondered what they'd do when they crossed the blood-brain barrier and found out about me—about the brain's real function. So I began a campaign to keep them under control. I figured, the reason they wanted to get into the skin was the simplicity of running circuits across a surface. Much easier than trying to maintain chains of communication in and around muscles, organs, vessels. The skin was much more direct. So I bought a quartz lamp." He caught my puzzled expression. "In the lab, we'd break down the protein in biochip cells by exposing them to ultraviolet light. I alternated sunlamp with quartz treatments. Keeps them out of my skin and gives me a nice tan."

"Give you skin cancer, too," I commented.

"They'll probably take care of that. Like police."

"Okay. I've examined you, you've told me a story I still find hard to believe . . . what do you want me to do?"

"I'm not as nonchalant as I act, Edward. I'm worried. I'd like to learn how to control them before they find out about my brain. I mean, think of it, they're in the trillions by now, each one smart. They're cooperating to some extent. I'm probably the smartest thing on the planet, and they haven't even begun to get their act together. I don't really want them to take over." He laughed unpleasantly. "Steal my soul, you know? So think of some treatment to block them. Maybe we can starve the little buggers. Just think on it." He buttoned his shirt. "Give me a call." He handed me a slip of paper with his address and phone number. Then he went to the keyboard and erased the image on the frame, dumping the memory of the examination. "Just you," he said. "Nobody else for now. And please . . . hurry."

It was three o'clock in the morning when Vergil walked out of the examination room. He'd allowed me to take blood samples, then shaken my hand—his palm was damp, nervous—and cautioned me against ingesting anything from the specimens.

Before I went home, I put the blood through a series of tests. The results were ready the next day. I picked them up during my lunch break, then destroyed all of the samples. I did it like a robot.

It took me five days and nearly sleepless nights to accept what I'd seen. His blood was normal enough, though the machines diagnosed the patient as having an infection. High levels of leukocytes—white blood cells—and histamines.

On the fifth day, I believed.

Gail came home before I did, but it was my turn to fix dinner. She slipped one of her school's disks into the home system and showed me video art the nursery kids had been creating. I watched quietly, ate with her in silence.

That evening, I had two dreams, part of my final acceptance. In the first, I witnessed the destruction of the planet Krypton, Superman's home world. Billions of superhuman geniuses went screaming off in walls of fire. I related this destruction to my sterilizing the samples of Vergil's blood. The second dream was worse. I dreamed that New York City was raping a woman. By the end of the dream, she gave birth to little embryo cities, all wrapped up in translucent sacs, soaked with blood from the difficult labor.

I called Vergil on the morning of the sixth day. He answered on the fourth ring. "I have some results," I said. "Nothing conclusive. But I want to talk. In person."

"Sure," he said. "I'm staying inside for the time being." His voice was strained; he sounded tired.

Vergil's apartment was in a fancy high-rise near the lake shore. I took the elevator up, listening to little advertising jingles and watching dancing holograms display products, empty apartments for rent, the building's hostess discussing social activities for the week.

Vergil opened the door and motioned me in. He wore a checked robe with long sleeves and carpet slippers. He clutched an unlit pipe in one hand, his fingers twisting it back and forth as he walked away from me and sat down, saying nothing.

"You have an infection," I said.

"Oh?"

"That's all the blood analyses tell me. I don't have access to the electron microscopes."

"I don't think it's really an infection," he said. "After all, they're my own cells. Probably something else . . . some sign of their presence, of the change. We can't expect to understand everything that's happening."

I removed my coat. "Listen," I said, "you really have me worried now." The expression on his face stopped me: a kind of frantic beatitude. He squinted at the ceiling and pursed his lips.

"Are you stoned?" I asked.

He shook his head, then nodded once, very slowly. "Listening," he said.

"To what?"

"I don't know. Not sounds, exactly. More like music. The heart, all the blood vessels, friction of blood along the arteries, veins. Activity. Music in the blood." He looked at me plaintively. "Why aren't you at work?"

"My day off. Gail's working."

"Can you stay?"

I shrugged. "I suppose." I sounded suspicious. I glanced around the apartment, looking for ashtrays, packs of papers.

"I'm not stoned, Edward," he said. "I may be wrong, but I think something big is happening. I think they're finding out who I am."

I sat down across from Vergil, staring at him intently. He didn't seem to notice. Some inner process involved him. When I asked for a cup of coffee, he motioned to the kitchen. I boiled a pot of water and took a jar of instant from the cabinet. With cup in hand, I returned to my seat.

He twisted his head back and forth, eyes open. "You always knew what you wanted to be, didn't you?" he asked.

"More or less."

"A gynecologist. Smart moves. Never false moves. I was different. I had goals, but no direction. Like a map without roads. I didn't give a shit for anything, anyone but myself. I hated my folks. I hated science. Just a means. I'm surprised I got so far."

He gripped his chair arms.

"Something wrong?" I asked.

"They're talking to me," he said. He shut his eyes.

For an hour he seemed to be asleep. I checked his pulse, which was strong and steady, felt his forehead—slightly cool—and made myself more coffee. I was looking through a magazine, at a loss what to do, when he opened his eyes.

"Hard to figure exactly what time is like for them," he said. "It's taken them maybe three, four days to figure out language, key human concepts. Now they're onto it. Onto me. Right now."

"How's that?"

He claimed there were thousands of researchers hooked up to his neurons. He couldn't give details. "They're damned efficient, you know," he said. "They haven't screwed me up yet."

"We should get you into the hospital now."

"What in hell could other doctors do? Did *you* figure out any way to control them? I mean, they're my own cells."

"I've been thinking. We could starve them. Find out what metabolic differences—"

"I'm not sure I want to be rid of them," Vergil said. "They're not doing any harm."

"How do you know?"

He shook his head and held up one finger. "Wait. They're trying to figure out what space is. That's tough for them. They break distances down into concentrations of chemicals. For them, space is like intensity of taste."

"Vergil—"

"Listen! Think, Edward!" His tone was excited but even. "Something big is happening inside me. They talk to each other across the fluid, through membranes. They tailor something—viruses?—to carry data stored in nucleic acid chains. I think they're saying 'RNA.' That makes sense. That's one way I programmed them. But plasmidlike structures, too. Maybe that's what your machines think is a sign of infection—all their chattering in my blood, packets of data. Tastes of other individuals. Peers. Superiors. Subordinates."

"Vergil, I still think you should be in a hospital."

"This is my show, Edward," he said. "I'm their universe. They're amazed by the new scale." He was quiet again for a time.

I squatted by his chair and pulled up the sleeve to his robe. His arm was crisscrossed with white lines. I was about to go to the phone when he stood and stretched. "Do you realize," he said, "how many body cells we kill each time we move?"

"I'm going to call for an ambulance," I said.

"No, you aren't." His tone stopped me. "I told you, I'm not sick. This is my show. Do you know what they'd do to me in a hospital? They'd be like cavemen trying to fix a computer."

"Then what the hell am *I* doing here?" I asked, getting angry. "I can't do anything! I'm one of those cavemen."

"You're a friend," Vergil said, fixing his eyes on me. I had the impression I was being watched by more than just Vergil. "I want you here to keep me company." He laughed. "But I'm not exactly alone."

He walked around the apartment for two hours, fingering things, looking out windows, slowly and methodically fixing himself lunch. "You know, they can actually feel their own thoughts," he said around noon. "I mean, the cytoplasm seems to have a will of its own, a kind of subconscious life counter to the rationality they've only recently acquired. They hear the chemical 'noise' of the molecules fitting and unfitting inside."

At one, I called Gail to tell her I would be late. I was almost sick with tension, but I tried to keep my voice level. "Remember Vergil Ulam? I'm talking with him right now."

"Everything okay?" she asked.

Was it? Decidedly not. "Fine," I said.

"Culture!" Vergil said, peering at me around the kitchen wall.

I said good-bye and hung up.

"They're always swimming in that bath of information," Vergil said. "It's a kind of gestalt thing. The hierarchy is absolute. They send tailored phages after cells that don't interact properly. Viruses specified to individuals or groups. No escape. A rogue cell gets pierced by the virus, the cell blebs outward, it explodes and dissolves. But it's not just a dictatorship. I think they effectively have more freedom than in a democracy. I mean, they vary so differently from individual to individual. Does that make sense? They vary in different ways than we do."

"Hold it," I said, gripping his shoulders. "Vergil, you're pushing me to the edge. I can't take this much longer. I don't understand, I'm not sure I believe—"

"Not even now?"

"Okay, let's say you're giving me the right interpretation. Giving it to me straight. Have you bothered to figure out the consequences? What all this means, where it might lead?"

He walked into the kitchen and drew a glass of water from the tap, then returned and stood beside me. His expression had changed from childish absorption to sober concern. "I've never been good at that."

"Are you afraid?"

"I was. Now, I'm not sure." He fingered the tie of his robe. "Look, I don't want you to think I went around you, over your head or something. But I met with Michael Bernard yesterday. He put me through his private clinic, took specimens. Told me to quit the lamp treatments. He called this morning, just before you did. He says it all checks out. And he asked me not to tell anybody." His expression became dreamy again. "Cities of cells," he continued. "Edward, they push tubes through the tissues, spread information—"

"Stop it!" I shouted. "Checks out? What checks out?"

"As Bernard puts it, I have 'severely enlarged macrophages' throughout my system. And he concurs on the anatomical changes."

"What does he plan to do?"

"I don't know. I think he'll probably convince Genetron to reopen the lab."

"Is that what you want?"

"It's not just having the lab again. I want to show you. Since I stopped the lamp treatments, I'm still changing." He undid his robe and let it slide to the floor. All over his body, his skin was crisscrossed with white lines. Along his back, the lines were starting to form ridges.

"My God!" I said.

"I'm not going to be much good anywhere else but the lab soon. I won't be able to go out in public. Hospitals wouldn't know what to do, as I said."

"You're . . . you can talk to them, tell them to slow down," I said, aware how ridiculous that sounded.

"Yes, indeed I can, but they don't necessarily listen."

"I thought you were their god or something."

"The ones hooked up to my neurons aren't the big wheels. They're researchers, or at least serve the same function. They know I'm here, what I am, but that doesn't mean they've convinced the upper levels of the hierarchy."

"They're arguing?"

"Something like that. It's not all that bad. If the lab is reopened, I have a home, a place to work." He glanced out the window, as if looking for someone. "I don't have anything left but them. They aren't afraid, Edward. I've never felt so close to anything before." Again the beatific smile. "I'm responsible for them. Mother to them all."

"You have no way of knowing what they're going to do."

He shook his head.

"No, I mean it. You say they're like a civilization—"

"Like a thousand civilizations."

"Yeah, and civilizations have been known to screw up. Warfare, the environment—"

I was grasping at straws, trying to restrain a growing panic. I wasn't competent to handle the enormity of what was happening. Neither was Vergil. He was the last person I would have called insightful and wise about large issues.

"But I'm the only one at risk."

"You don't know that. Jesus, Vergil, look what they're doing to you!"

"To me, all to me!" he said. "Nobody else."

I shook my head and held up my hands in a gesture of defeat. "Okay, so Bernard gets them to reopen the lab, you move in, become a guinea pig. What then?"

"They treat me right. I'm more than just good old Vergil Ulam now. I'm a goddamned galaxy, a super-mother."

"Super-host, you mean."

He conceded the point with a shrug.

I couldn't take any more. I made my exit

with a few flimsy excuses, then sat in the lobby of the apartment building, trying to calm down. Somebody had to talk some sense into him. Who would he listen to? He had gone to Bernard. . . .

And it sounded as if Bernard was not only convinced, but very interested. People of Bernard's stature didn't coax the Vergil Ulams of the world along unless they felt it was to their advantage.

I had a hunch, and I decided to play it. I went to a pay phone, slipped in my credit card, and called Genetron.

"I'd like you to page Dr. Michael Bernard," I told the receptionist.

"Who's calling, please?"

"This is his answering service. We have an emergency call, and his beeper doesn't seem to be working."

A few anxious minutes later, Bernard came on the line. "Who the hell is this?" he asked. "I don't have an answering service."

"My name is Edward Milligan. I'm a friend of Vergil Ulam's. I think we have some problems to discuss."

We made an appointment to talk the next morning.

I went home and tried to think of excuses to keep me off the next day's hospital shift. I couldn't concentrate on medicine, couldn't give my patients anywhere near the attention they deserved.

Guilty, angry, afraid.

That was how Gail found me. I slipped on a mask of calm and we fixed dinner together. After eating, holding on to each other, we watched the city lights come on through the bayside window. Winter starlings pecked at the yellow lawn in the last few minutes of twilight, then flew away with a rising wind which made the windows rattle.

"Something's wrong," Gail said softly. "Are you going to tell me, or just act like everything's normal?"

"It's just me," I said. "Nervous. Work at the hospital."

"Oh, lord," she said, sitting up. "You're going

to divorce me for that Baker woman." Mrs. Baker weighed three hundred and sixty pounds and hadn't known she was pregnant until her fifth month.

"No," I said, listless.

"Rapturous relief," Gail said, touching my forehead lightly. "You know this kind of introspection drives me crazy."

"Well, it's nothing I can talk about yet, so . . ." I patted her hand.

"That's disgustingly patronizing," she said, getting up. "I'm going to make some tea. Want some?" Now she was miffed, and I was tense with not telling. Why not just reveal all? I asked myself. An old friend was about to risk everything, *change* everything. . . .

I cleared away the table instead.

That night, unable to sleep, I looked down on Gail in bed from my sitting position, pillow against the wall, and tried to determine what I knew was real, and what wasn't. I'm a doctor, I told myself. A technical, scientific profession. I'm supposed to be immune to things like future shock. How would it feel to be topped off with a trillion intelligences speaking a language as incomprehensible as Chinese?

I grinned in the dark and almost cried at the same time. What Vergil had inside him was unimaginably stranger. Stranger than anything I—or Vergil—could easily understand. Perhaps ever understand.

Vergil Ulam is turning himself into a galaxy.

But I knew what was real. The bedroom, the city lights faint through gauze curtains. Gail sleeping. Very important. Gail in bed, sleeping.

The dream returned. This time the city came in through the window and attacked Gail. It was a great, spiky lighted-up prowler, and it growled in a language I couldn't understand, made up of auto horns, crowd noises, construction bedlam. I tried to fight it off, but it got to her—and turned into a drift of stars, sprinkling all over the bed, all over everything. I jerked awake and stayed up until dawn, dressed with Gail, kissed her, savored the reality of her human, unviolated lips.

I went to meet with Bernard. He had been loaned a suite in a big downtown hospital; I rode the elevator to the sixth floor, and saw what fame and fortune could mean. The suite was tastefully furnished, fine serigraphs on wood-paneled walls, chrome and glass furniture, cream-colored carpet, Chinese brass, and wormwood-grain cabinets and tables.

He offered me a cup of coffee, and I accepted. He took a seat in the breakfast nook, and I sat across from him, cradling my cup in moist palms. He wore a dapper gray suit and had graying hair and a sharp profile. He was in his midsixties and he looked quite a bit like Leonard Bernstein.

"About our mutual acquaintance," he said. "Mr. Ulam. Brilliant. And, I won't hesitate to say, courageous."

"He's my friend. I'm worried about him."

Bernard held up one finger. "Courageous—and a bloody damned fool. What's happening to him should never have been allowed. He may have done it under duress, but that's no excuse. Still, what's done is done. He's talked to you, I take it."

I nodded. "He wants to return to Genetron."

"Of course. That's where all his equipment is. Where his home probably will be while we sort this out."

"Sort it out—how? Why?" I wasn't thinking too clearly. I had a slight headache.

"I can think of a lot of uses for small, superdense computer elements with a biological base. Can't you? Genetron has already made breakthroughs, but this is something else again."

"What are you—they—planning?"

Bernard smiled. "I'm not really at liberty to say. It'll be revolutionary. We'll have to put him in a tightly controlled, isolated environment. Perhaps his own wing. Animal experiments have to be conducted. We'll start from scratch, of course. Vergil's . . . um . . . colonies can't be transferred. They're based on his own white blood cells. So we have to develop colonies that won't trigger immune reactions."

"Like an infection?" I asked.

"I suppose there are comparisons. But Vergil is *not* infected."

"My tests indicate he is."

"That's probably loose bits of data floating around in his blood, don't you think?"

"I don't know."

"Listen, I'd like you to come down to the lab after Vergil is settled in. Your expertise might be useful to us."

Us. He was working with Genetron hand in glove. Could he be objective?

"How will you benefit from all this?"

"Edward, I have always been at the forefront of my profession. I see no reason why I shouldn't be helping here. With my knowledge of brain and nerve functions, and the research I've been conducting in neurophysiology—"

"You could help Genetron hold off an investigation by the government," I said.

"That's being very blunt. Too blunt, and unfair."

"Perhaps. Anyway, yes: I'd like to visit the lab when Vergil's settled in. If I'm still welcome, bluntness and all."

Bernard looked at me sharply. I wouldn't be playing on his team; for a moment, his thoughts were almost nakedly apparent. "Of course," he said, rising with me. He reached out to shake my hand. His palm was damp. He was as nervous as I was, even if he didn't look it.

I returned to my apartment and stayed there until noon, reading, trying to sort things out. Reach a decision. What was real, what I needed to protect. There is only so much change anyone can stand: innovation, yes, but slow application. Don't force. Everyone has the right to stay the same until they decide otherwise.

The greatest thing in science since . . .

And Bernard would force it. Genetron would force it. I couldn't handle the thought. "Neo-Luddite," I said to myself. A filthy accusation.

When I pressed Vergil's number on the building security panel, Vergil answered almost immediately. "Yeah," he said. He sounded exhilarated. "Come on up. I'll be in the bathroom. Door's unlocked."

I entered his apartment and walked through the hallway to the bathroom. Vergil lay in the tub, up to his neck in pinkish water. He smiled vaguely and splashed his hands. "Looks like I slit my wrists, doesn't it?" he said softly. "Don't worry. Everything's fine now. Genetron's going to take me back. Bernard just called." He pointed to the bathroom phone and intercom.

I sat on the toilet and noticed the sunlamp fixture standing unplugged next to the linen cabinets. The bulbs sat in a row on the edge of the sink counter. "You're sure that's what you want?" I said, my shoulders slumping.

"Yeah, I think so," he said. "They can take better care of me. I'm getting cleaned up, going over there this evening. Bernard's picking me up in his limo. Style. From here on in, everything's style."

The pinkish color in the water didn't look like soap. "Is that bubble bath?" I asked. Some of it came to me in a rush then and I felt a little weaker; what had occurred to me was just one more obvious and necessary insanity.

"No," Vergil said.

I knew that already.

"No," he repeated, "it's coming from my skin. They're not telling me everything, but I think they're sending out scouts. Astronauts." He looked at me with an expression that didn't quite equal concern; more like curiosity as to how I'd take it. The confirmation made my stomach muscles tighten as if waiting for a punch. I had never even considered the possibility until now, perhaps because I had been concentrating on other aspects.

"Is this the first time?" I asked.

"Yeah," he said, then laughed. "I've half a mind to let the little buggers down the drain. Let them find out what the world's really about."

"They'd go everywhere," I said.

"Sure enough."

"How . . . how are you feeling?"

"I'm feeling pretty good now. Must be billions of them." More splashing with his hands. "What do you think? Should I let the buggers out?"

Quickly, hardly thinking, I knelt down beside the tub. My fingers went for the cord on the sunlamp and I plugged it in. He had hot-wired doorknobs, turned my piss blue, played a thousand dumb practical jokes, and never grown up, never grown mature enough to understand that he was sufficiently brilliant to transform the world; he would never learn caution.

He reached for the drain knob. "You know, Edward, I—"

He never finished. I picked up the fixture and dropped it into the tub, jumping back at the flash of steam and sparks. Vergil screamed and thrashed and jerked and then everything was still, except for the low, steady sizzle and the smoke wafting from his hair.

I lifted the toilet lid and vomited. Then I clenched my nose and went into the living room. My legs went out from under me and I sat abruptly on the couch.

After an hour, I searched through Vergil's kitchen and found bleach, ammonia, and a bottle of Jack Daniel's. I returned to the bathroom, keeping the center of my gaze away from Vergil. I poured first the booze, then the bleach, then the ammonia into the water. Chlorine started bubbling up and I left, closing the door behind me.

The phone was ringing when I got home. I didn't answer. It could have been the hospital. It could have been Bernard. Or the police. I could envision having to explain everything to the police. Genetron would stonewall; Bernard would be unavailable. I was exhausted, all my muscles knotted with tension and whatever name one can give to the feelings one has after—

Committing genocide?

That certainly didn't seem real. I could not believe I had just murdered a hundred trillion intelligent beings. Snuffed a galaxy. It was laughable. But I didn't laugh.

What was easy to believe was that I had just killed one human being, a friend. The smoke, the melted lamp rods, the drooping electrical outlet and smoking cord.

Vergil.

I had dunked the lamp into the tub with Vergil.

I felt sick. Dreams, cities raping Gail (and what about his girlfriend, Candice?). Draining the water filled with them. Galaxies sprinkling over us all. What horror. Then again, what potential beauty—a new kind of life, symbiosis and transformation.

Had I been thorough enough to kill them all? I had a moment of panic. Tomorrow, I thought, I will sterilize his apartment. Somehow, I didn't even think of Bernard.

When Gail came in the door, I was asleep on the couch. I came to, groggy, and she looked down at me.

"You feeling okay?" she asked, perching on the arm. I nodded.

"What are you planning for dinner?" My mouth didn't work properly. The words were mushy.

She felt my forehead. "Edward, you have a fever," she said. "A very high fever." I stumbled into the bathroom and looked in the mirror. Gail was close behind me.

"What is it?" she asked.

There were lines under my collar, around my neck. White lines, like freeways. They had already been in me a long time, days.

"Damp palms," I said. So obvious.

I think we nearly died. I struggled at first, but in minutes I was too weak to move. Gail was just as sick within an hour.

I lay on the carpet in the living room, drenched in sweat. Gail lay on the couch, her face the color of talcum, eyes closed, like a corpse in an embalming parlor. For a time I thought she *was* dead. Sick as I was, I raged—hated, felt tremendous guilt at my weakness, my slowness to understand all the possibilities. Then I no longer cared. I was too weak to blink, so I closed my eyes and waited.

There was a rhythm in my arms, my legs. With each pulse of blood, a kind of sound welled up within me, like an orchestra thousands strong, but not playing in unison; playing whole seasons of symphonies at once. Music in the blood. The sound became harsher, but more coordinated, wave-trains finally canceling into silence, then separating into harmonic beats.

The beats seemed to melt into me, into the sound of my own heart.

First, they subdued our immune responses. The war—and it was a war, on a scale never before known on Earth, with trillions of combatants—lasted perhaps two days.

By the time I regained enough strength to get to the kitchen faucet, I could feel them working on my brain, trying to crack the code and find the god within the protoplasm. I drank until I was sick, then drank more moderately and took a glass to Gail. She sipped. Her lips were cracked, her eyes bloodshot and ringed with yellowish crumbs. There was some color in her skin.

Minutes later, we were eating feebly in the kitchen.

"What in hell is happening?" was the first thing she asked. I didn't have the strength to explain. I peeled an orange and shared it with her. "We should call a doctor," she said. But I knew we wouldn't. I was already receiving messages; it was becoming apparent that any sensation of freedom we experienced was illusory.

The messages were simple at first. Memories of commands, rather than the commands themselves, manifested in my thoughts. We were not to leave the apartment—a concept which seemed quite abstract to those in control, even if undesirable—and we were not to have contact with others. We would be allowed to eat certain foods and drink tap water for the time being.

With the subsidence of the fevers, the transformations were quick and drastic. Almost simultaneously, Gail and I were immobilized. She was sitting at the table, I was kneeling on the floor. I was able barely to see her in the corner of my eye.

Her arm developed pronounced ridges.

They had learned inside Vergil; their tactics within the two of us were very different. I itched all over for about two hours—two hours in hell—before they made the breakthrough and found *me*. The effort of ages on their time-scale paid off and they communicated smoothly and directly with this great, clumsy intelligence who had once controlled their universe.

They were not cruel. When the concept of discomfort and its undesirability was made clear, they worked to alleviate it. They worked too effectively. For another hour, I was in a sea of bliss, out of all contact with them.

With dawn the next day, they gave us freedom to move again; specifically, to go to the bathroom. There were certain waste products they could not deal with. I voided those—my urine was purple—and Gail followed suit. We looked at each other vacantly in the bathroom. Then she managed a slight smile. "Are they talking to you?" she asked.

I nodded.

"Then I'm not crazy."

For the next twelve hours, control seemed to loosen on some levels. I suspect there was another kind of war going on in me. Gail was capable of limited motion, but no more.

When full control resumed, we were instructed to hold each other. We did not hesitate.

"Eddie . . . ," she whispered. My name was the last sound I ever heard from outside.

Standing, we grew together. In hours, our legs expanded and spread out. Then extensions grew to the windows to take in sunlight, and to the kitchen to take water from the sink. Filaments soon reached to all corners of the room, stripping paint and plaster from the walls, fabric and stuffing from the furniture.

By dawn, the transformation was complete.

I no longer have any clear idea of what we look like. I suspect we resemble cells—large, flat, and filamented cells, draped purposefully across most of the apartment. The great shall mimic the small.

Our intelligence fluctuates daily as we are absorbed into the minds within. Each day, our individuality declines. We are, indeed, great clumsy dinosaurs. Our memories have been taken over by billions of them, and our personalities have been spread through the transformed blood. Soon there will be no need for centralization.

Already the plumbing has been invaded. People throughout the building are undergoing transformation.

Within the old time frame of weeks, we will reach the lakes, rivers, and seas in force. I can barely begin to guess the results. Every square inch of the planet will teem with thought. Years from now, perhaps much sooner, they will subdue their own individuality—what there is of it. New creatures will come, then. The immensity of their capacity for thought will be inconceivable.

All my hatred and fear is gone now.

I leave them—us—with only one question.

How many times has this happened, elsewhere? Travelers never came through space to visit the Earth. They had no need.

They had found universes in grains of sand.

Bloodchild

OCTAVIA E. BUTLER

Octavia E. Butler (1947–2006) was an iconic US writer of science fiction who received multiple Hugo, Nebula, and Locus Awards for her writing before dying of a stroke in 2006. The recipient of a $500,000 MacArthur Fellowship in 1995, Butler was posthumously inducted into the Science Fiction and Fantasy Hall of Fame in 2010. After her death, the Carl Brandon Society established the Octavia E. Butler Memorial Scholarship to support attendance of students of color at the Clarion West Writers Workshop and Clarion Science Fiction and Fantasy Writers' Workshop. Butler had gotten her start at a Clarion workshop thirty-five years before.

Butler's science fiction novels include her *Patternist* series, *Patternmaster* (1976), *Mind of My Mind* (1977), *Survivor* (1978), *Wild Seed* (1980), and *Clay's Ark* (1984). During this time she also wrote a stand-alone time-travel slave novel, *Kindred* (1979). In the eighties and nineties Butler produced two more outstanding series, the *Xenogenesis* trilogy and the incomplete *Parable* series. Butler's writing often used the context of alien situations and environments to comment on race and gender relations.

Although she did not write many short stories, considering herself primarily a novelist, Butler's "Bloodchild" (1984) is a masterful example of the form and addresses many of the themes found in her longer works. It also fits comfortably within a kind of "science fiction realism" tradition that pushed back against the simplified cause-and-effect of much earlier speculative fiction—doing for space colonization what James Tiptree Jr.'s "And I Awoke and Found Me Here on the Cold Hill's Side" and Samuel R. Delany's "Aye, and Gomorrah" did for the glamour of astronauts.

In her story notes for *Bloodchild and Other Stories*, Butler told readers that "Bloodchild" was not "a story of slavery." Instead, she considered it a love story and a coming-of-age story. On a secondary level, "Bloodchild" was her "pregnant man story" and "a story about paying the rent," in the sense that members of an isolated space colony would need to make "an unusual accommodation" with their hosts. She also wrote the story to overcome her fear of botflies.

BLOODCHILD

Octavia E. Butler

My last night of childhood began with a visit home. T'Gatoi's sisters had given us two sterile eggs. T'Gatoi gave one to my mother, brother, and sisters. She insisted that I eat the other one alone. It didn't matter. There was still enough to leave everyone feeling good. Almost everyone. My mother wouldn't take any. She sat, watching everyone drifting and dreaming without her. Most of the time she watched me.

I lay against T'Gatoi's long, velvet underside, sipping from my egg now and then, wondering why my mother denied herself such a harmless pleasure. Less of her hair would be gray if she indulged now and then. The eggs prolonged life, prolonged vigor. My father, who had never refused one in his life, had lived more than twice as long as he should have. And toward the end of his life, when he should have been slowing down, he had married my mother and fathered four children.

But my mother seemed content to age before she had to. I saw her turn away as several of T'Gatoi's limbs secured me closer. T'Gatoi liked our body heat, and took advantage of it whenever she could. When I was little and at home more, my mother used to try to tell me how to behave with T'Gatoi—how to be respectful and always obedient because T'Gatoi was the Tlic government official in charge of the Preserve, and thus the most important of her kind to deal directly with Terrans. It was an honor, my mother said, that such a person had chosen to come into the family. My mother was at her most formal and severe when she was lying.

I had no idea why she was lying, or even what she was lying about. It was an honor to have T'Gatoi in the family, but it was hardly a novelty. T'Gatoi and my mother had been friends all my mother's life, and T'Gatoi was not interested in being honored in the house she considered her second home. She simply came in, climbed onto one of her special couches, and called me over to keep her warm. It was impossible to be formal with her while lying against her and hearing her complain as usual that I was too skinny.

"You're better," she said this time, probing me with six or seven of her limbs. "You're gaining weight finally. Thinness is dangerous." The probing changed subtly, became a series of caresses.

"He's still too thin," my mother said sharply.

T'Gatoi lifted her head and perhaps a meter of her body off the couch as though she were sitting up. She looked at my mother and my mother, her face lined and old looking, turned away.

"Lien, I would like you to have what's left of Gan's egg."

"The eggs are for the children," my mother said.

"They are for the family. Please take it."

Unwillingly obedient, my mother took it from me and put it to her mouth. There were only a few drops left in the now-shrunken, elastic shell, but she squeezed them out, swallowed them, and after a few moments some of the lines of tension began to smooth from her face.

"It's good," she whispered. "Sometimes I forget how good it is."

"You should take more," T'Gatoi said. "Why are you in such a hurry to be old?"

My mother said nothing.

"I like being able to come here," T'Gatoi said. "This place is a refuge because of you, yet you won't take care of yourself."

T'Gatoi was hounded on the outside. Her people wanted more of us made available. Only she and her political faction stood between us and the hordes who did not understand why there was a Preserve—why any Terran could not be courted, paid, drafted, in some way made available to them. Or they did understand, but in their desperation, they did not care. She parceled us out to the desperate and sold us to the rich and powerful for their political support. Thus, we were necessities, status symbols, and an independent people. She oversaw the joining of families, putting an end to the final remnants of the earlier system of breaking up Terran families to suit impatient Tlic. I had lived outside with her. I had seen the desperate eagerness in the way some people looked at me. It was a little frightening to know that only she stood between us and that desperation that could so easily swallow us. My mother would look at her sometimes and say to me, "Take care of her." And I would remember that she too had been outside, had seen.

Now T'Gatoi used four of her limbs to push me away from her onto the floor. "Go on, Gan," she said. "Sit down there with your sisters and enjoy not being sober. You had most of the egg. Lien, come warm me."

My mother hesitated for no reason that I could see. One of my earliest memories is of my mother stretched alongside T'Gatoi, talking about things I could not understand, picking me up from the floor and laughing as she sat me on one of T'Gatoi's segments. She ate her share of eggs then. I wondered when she had stopped, and why.

She lay down now against T'Gatoi, and the whole left row of T'Gatoi's limbs closed around her, holding her loosely, but securely. I had always found it comfortable to lie that way but, except for my older sister, no one else in the family liked it. They said it made them feel caged.

T'Gatoi meant to cage my mother. Once she had, she moved her tail slightly, then spoke. "Not enough egg, Lien. You should have taken it when it was passed to you. You need it badly now."

T'Gatoi's tail moved once more, its whip motion so swift I wouldn't have seen it if I hadn't been watching for it. Her sting drew only a single drop of blood from my mother's bare leg.

My mother cried out—probably in surprise. Being stung doesn't hurt. Then she sighed and I could see her body relax. She moved languidly into a more comfortable position within the cage of T'Gatoi's limbs. "Why did you do that?" she asked, sounding half asleep.

"I could not watch you sitting and suffering any longer."

My mother managed to move her shoulders in a small shrug. "Tomorrow," she said.

"Yes. Tomorrow you will resume your suffering—if you must. But for now, just for now, lie here and warm me and let me ease your way a little."

"He's still mine, you know," my mother said suddenly. "Nothing can buy him from me." Sober, she wouldn't have permitted herself to refer to such things.

"Nothing," T'Gatoi agreed, humoring her.

"Did you think I would sell him for eggs? For long life? My son?"

"Not for anything," T'Gatoi said, stroking my mother's shoulders, toying with her long, graying hair.

I would have liked to touch my mother, share that moment with her. I knew she would take my hand if I touched her now. Freed by the egg and the sting, she would smile and perhaps say things long held in. But tomorrow, she would remember all this as a humiliation. I did not want to be part of a remembered humiliation. Best just to be still and know she loved me under all the duty and pride and pain.

"Xuan Hoa, take off her shoes," T'Gatoi said. "In a little while I'll sting her again and she can sleep."

My older sister obeyed, swaying drunkenly as she stood up. When she had finished, she sat down beside me and took my hand. We had always been a unit, she and I.

My mother put the back of her head against T'Gatoi's underside and tried from that impossible angle to look up into the broad, round face. "You're going to sting me again?"

"Yes, Lien."

"I'll sleep until tomorrow noon."

"Good. You need it. When did you sleep last?"

My mother made a wordless sound of annoyance. "I should have stepped on you when you were small enough," she muttered.

It was an old joke between them. They had grown up together, sort of, though T'Gatoi had not, in my mother's lifetime, been small enough for any Terran to step on. She was nearly three times my mother's present age, yet would still be young when my mother died of age. But T'Gatoi and my mother had met as T'Gatoi was coming into a period of rapid development—a kind of Tlic adolescence. My mother was only a child, but for a while they developed at the same rate and had no better friends than each other.

T'Gatoi had even introduced my mother to the man who became my father. My parents, pleased with each other in spite of their very different ages, married as T'Gatoi was going into her family's business—politics. She and my mother saw each other less. But sometime before my older sister was born, my mother promised T'Gatoi one of her children. She would have to give one of us to someone, and she preferred T'Gatoi to some stranger.

Years passed. T'Gatoi traveled and increased her influence. The Preserve was hers by the time she came back to my mother to collect what she probably saw as her just reward for her hard work. My older sister took an instant liking to her and wanted to be chosen, but my mother was just coming to term with me and T'Gatoi liked the idea of choosing an infant and watching and taking part in all the phases of development. I'm told I was first caged within T'Gatoi's many limbs only three minutes after my birth. A few days later, I was given my first taste of egg. I tell Terrans that when they ask whether I was ever afraid of her. And I tell it

to Tlic when T'Gatoi suggests a young Terran child for them and they, anxious and ignorant, demand an adolescent. Even my brother who had somehow grown up to fear and distrust the Tlic could probably have gone smoothly into one of their families if he had been adopted early enough. Sometimes, I think for his sake he should have been. I looked at him, stretched out on the floor across the room, his eyes open, but glazed as he dreamed his egg dream. No matter what he felt toward the Tlic, he always demanded his share of egg.

"Lien, can you stand up?" T'Gatoi asked suddenly.

"Stand?" my mother said. "I thought I was going to sleep."

"Later. Something sounds wrong outside." The cage was abruptly gone.

"What?"

"Up, Lien!"

My mother recognized her tone and got up just in time to avoid being dumped on the floor. T'Gatoi whipped her three meters of body off her couch, toward the door, and out at full speed. She had bones—ribs, a long spine, a skull, four sets of limb bones per segment. But when she moved that way, twisting, hurling herself into controlled falls, landing running, she seemed not only boneless, but aquatic— something swimming through the air as though it were water. I loved watching her move.

I left my sister and started to follow her out the door, though I wasn't very steady on my own feet. It would have been better to sit and dream, better yet to find a girl and share a waking dream with her. Back when the Tlic saw us as not much more than convenient big warm- blooded animals, they would pen several of us together, male and female, and feed us only eggs. That way they could be sure of getting another generation of us no matter how we tried to hold out. We were lucky that didn't go on long. A few generations of it and we would have been little more than convenient big animals.

"Hold the door open, Gan," T'Gatoi said. "And tell the family to stay back."

"What is it?" I asked.

"N'Tlic."

I shrank back against the door. "Here? Alone?"

"He was trying to reach a call box, I suppose." She carried the man past me, unconscious, folded like a coat over some of her limbs. He looked young—my brother's age perhaps— and he was thinner than he should have been. What T'Gatoi would have called dangerously thin.

"Gan, go to the call box," she said. She put the man on the floor and began stripping off his clothing.

I did not move.

After a moment, she looked up at me, her sudden stillness a sign of deep impatience.

"Send Qui," I told her. "I'll stay here. Maybe I can help."

She let her limbs begin to move again, lifting the man and pulling his shirt over his head. "You don't want to see this," she said. "It will be hard. I can't help this man the way his Tlic could."

"I know. But send Qui. He won't want to be of any help here. I'm at least willing to try."

She looked at my brother—older, bigger, stronger, certainly more able to help her here. He was sitting up now, braced against the wall, staring at the man on the floor with undisguised fear and revulsion. Even she could see that he would be useless.

"Qui, go!" she said.

He didn't argue. He stood up, swayed briefly, then steadied, frightened sober.

"This man's name is Bram Lomas," she told him, reading from the man's armband. I fingered my own armband in sympathy. "He needs T'Khotgif Teh. Do you hear?"

"Bram Lomas, T'Khotgif Teh," my brother said. "I'm going." He edged around Lomas and ran out the door.

Lomas began to regain consciousness. He only moaned at first and clutched spasmodically at a pair of T'Gatoi's limbs. My younger sister, finally awake from her egg dream, came close to look at him, until my mother pulled her back.

T'Gatoi removed the man's shoes, then his pants, all the while leaving him two of her limbs to grip. Except for the final few, all her limbs were equally dexterous. "I want no argument from you this time, Gan," she said.

I straightened. "What shall I do?"

"Go out and slaughter an animal that is at least half your size."

"Slaughter? But I've never—"

She knocked me across the room. Her tail was an efficient weapon whether she exposed the sting or not.

I got up, feeling stupid for having ignored her warning, and went into the kitchen. Maybe I could kill something with a knife or an ax. My mother raised a few Terran animals for the table and several thousand local ones for their fur. T'Gatoi would probably prefer something local. An achti, perhaps. Some of those were the right size, though they had about three times as many teeth as I did and a real love of using them. My mother, Hoa, and Qui could kill them with knives. I had never killed one at all, had never slaughtered any animal. I had spent most of my time with T'Gatoi while my brother and sisters were learning the family business. T'Gatoi had been right. I should have been the one to go to the call box. At least I could do that.

I went to the corner cabinet where my mother kept her larger house and garden tools. At the back of the cabinet there was a pipe that carried off wastewater from the kitchen— except that it didn't anymore. My father had rerouted the wastewater before I was born. Now the pipe could be turned so that one half slid around the other and a rifle could be stored inside. This wasn't our only gun, but it was our most easily accessible one. I would have to use it to shoot one of the biggest of the achti. Then T'Gatoi would probably confiscate it. Firearms were illegal in the Preserve. There had been incidents right after the Preserve was established—Terrans shooting Tlic, shooting N'Tlic. This was before the joining of families began, before everyone had a personal stake in keeping the peace. No one had shot a Tlic in my lifetime or my mother's, but the law still stood—for our protection, we were told. There were stories of whole Terran families wiped out in reprisal back during the assassinations.

I went out to the cages and shot the biggest achti I could find. It was a handsome breeding male and my mother would not be pleased to see me bring it in. But it was the right size, and I was in a hurry.

I put the achti's long, warm body over my shoulder—glad that some of the weight I'd gained was muscle—and took it to the kitchen. There, I put the gun back in its hiding place. If T'Gatoi noticed the achti's wounds and demanded the gun, I would give it to her. Otherwise, let it stay where my father wanted it.

I turned to take the achti to her, then hesitated. For several seconds, I stood in front of the closed door wondering why I was suddenly afraid. I knew what was going to happen. I hadn't seen it before but T'Gatoi had shown me diagrams, and drawings. She had made sure I knew the truth as soon as I was old enough to understand it.

Yet I did not want to go into that room. I wasted a little time choosing a knife from the carved wooden box in which my mother kept them. T'Gatoi might want one, I told myself, for the tough, heavily furred hide of the achti.

"Gan!" T'Gatoi called, her voice harsh with urgency.

I swallowed. I had not imagined a simple moving of the feet could be so difficult. I realized I was trembling and that shamed me. Shame impelled me through the door.

I put the achti down near T'Gatoi and saw that Lomas was unconscious again. She, Lomas, and I were alone in the room, my mother and sisters probably sent out so they would not have to watch. I envied them.

But my mother came back into the room as T'Gatoi seized the achti. Ignoring the knife I offered her, she extended claws from several of her limbs and slit the achti from throat to anus.

She looked at me, her yellow eyes intent. "Hold this man's shoulders, Gan."

I stared at Lomas in panic, realizing that I did not want to touch him, let alone hold him. This would not be like shooting an animal. Not as quick, not as merciful, and, I hoped, not as final, but there was nothing I wanted less than to be part of it.

My mother came forward. "Gan, you hold his right side," she said. "I'll hold his left." And if he came to, he would throw her off without realizing he had done it. She was a tiny woman. She often wondered aloud how she had produced, as she said, such "huge" children.

"Never mind," I told her, taking the man's shoulders. "I'll do it."

She hovered nearby.

"Don't worry," I said. "I won't shame you. You don't have to stay and watch."

She looked at me uncertainly, then touched my face in a rare caress. Finally, she went back to her bedroom.

T'Gatoi lowered her head in relief. "Thank you, Gan," she said with courtesy more Terran than Tlic. "That one . . . she is always finding new ways for me to make her suffer."

Lomas began to groan and make choked sounds. I had hoped he would stay unconscious. T'Gatoi put her face near his so that he focused on her.

"I've stung you as much as I dare for now," she told him. "When this is over, I'll sting you to sleep and you won't hurt anymore."

"Please," the man begged. "Wait . . ."

"There's no more time, Bram. I'll sting you as soon as it's over. When T'Khotgif arrives she'll give you eggs to help you heal. It will be over soon."

"T'Khotgif!" the man shouted, straining against my hands.

"Soon, Bram." T'Gatoi glanced at me, then placed a claw against his abdomen slightly to the right of the middle, just below the last rib. There was movement on the right side— tiny, seemingly random pulsations moving his brown flesh, creating a concavity here, a convexity there, over and over until I could see the rhythm of it and knew where the next pulse would be.

Lomas's entire body stiffened under T'Gatoi's claw, though she merely rested it against him as she wound the rear section of her body around her legs. He might break my grip, but he would not break hers. He wept helplessly as she used his pants to tie his hands, then pushed his hands above his head so that I could kneel on the cloth between them and pin them in place. She rolled up his shirt and gave it to him to bite down on.

And she opened him.

His body convulsed with the first cut. He almost tore himself away from me. The sounds he made . . . I had never heard such sounds come from anything human. T'Gatoi seemed to pay no attention as she lengthened and deepened the cut, now and then pausing to lick away blood. His blood vessels contracted, reacting to the chemistry of her saliva, and the bleeding slowed.

I felt as though I were helping her torture him, helping her consume him. I knew I would vomit soon, didn't know why I hadn't already. I couldn't possibly last until she was finished.

She found the first grub. It was fat and deep red with his blood—both inside and out. It had already eaten its own egg case, but apparently had not yet begun to eat its host. At this stage, it would eat any flesh except its mother's. Let alone, it would have gone on excreting the poisons that had both sickened and alerted Lomas. Eventually it would have begun to eat. By the time it ate its way out of Lomas's flesh, Lomas would be dead or dying—and unable to take revenge on the thing that was killing him. There was always a grace period between the time the host sickened and the time the grubs began to eat him.

T'Gatoi picked up the writhing grub carefully, and looked at it, somehow ignoring the terrible groans of the man.

Abruptly, the man lost consciousness.

"Good." T'Gatoi looked down at him. "I wish you Terrans could do that at will." She felt nothing. And the thing she held . . .

It was limbless and boneless at this stage, perhaps fifteen centimeters long and two thick, blind and slimy with blood. It was like a large worm. T'Gatoi put it into the belly of the achti, and it began at once to burrow. It would stay there and eat as long as there was anything to eat.

Probing through Lomas's flesh, she found two more, one of them smaller and more vigorous. "A male!" she said happily. He would be dead before I would. He would be through his metamorphosis and screwing everything that would hold still before his sisters even had limbs. He was the only one to make a serious effort to bite T'Gatoi as she placed him in the achti.

Paler worms oozed to visibility in Lomas's flesh. I closed my eyes. It was worse than finding something dead, rotting, and filled with tiny animal grubs. And it was far worse than any drawing or diagram.

"Ah, there are more," T'Gatoi said, plucking out two long, thick grubs. "You may have to kill another animal, Gan. Everything lives inside you Terrans."

I had been told all my life that this was a good and necessary thing Tlic and Terran did together—a kind of birth. I had believed it until now. I knew birth was painful and bloody, no matter what. But this was something else, something worse. And I wasn't ready to see it. Maybe I never would be. Yet I couldn't not see it. Closing my eyes didn't help.

T'Gatoi found a grub still eating its egg case. The remains of the case were still wired into a blood vessel by their own little tube or hook or whatever. That was the way the grubs were anchored and the way they fed. They took only blood until they were ready to emerge. Then they ate their stretched, elastic egg cases. Then they ate their hosts.

T'Gatoi bit away the egg case, licked away the blood. Did she like the taste? Did childhood habits die hard—or not die at all?

The whole procedure was wrong, alien. I wouldn't have thought anything about her could seem alien to me.

"One more, I think," she said. "Perhaps two. A good family. In a host animal these days, we would be happy to find one or two alive." She glanced at me. "Go outside, Gan, and empty your stomach. Go now while the man is unconscious."

I staggered out, barely made it. Beneath the tree just beyond the front door, I vomited until there was nothing left to bring up. Finally, I stood shaking, tears streaming down my face. I did not know why I was crying, but I could not stop. I went farther from the house to avoid being seen. Every time I closed my eyes I saw red worms crawling over redder human flesh.

There was a car coming toward the house. Since Terrans were forbidden motorized vehicles except for certain farm equipment, I knew this must be Lomas's Tlic with Qui and perhaps a Terran doctor. I wiped my face on my shirt, struggled for control.

"Gan," Qui called as the car stopped. "What happened?" He crawled out of the low, round, Tlic-convenient car door. Another Terran crawled out the other side and went into the house without speaking to me. The doctor. With his help and a few eggs, Lomas might make it.

"T'Khotgif Teh?" I said.

The Tlic driver surged out of her car, reared up half her length before me. She was paler and smaller than T'Gatoi—probably born from the body of an animal. Tlic from Terran bodies were always larger as well as more numerous.

"Six young," I told her. "Maybe seven alive. At least one male."

"Lomas?" she said harshly. I liked her for the question and the concern in her voice when she asked it. The last coherent thing he had said was her name.

"He's alive," I said.

She surged away to the house without another word.

"She's been sick," my brother said, watching her go. "When I called, I could hear people telling her she wasn't well enough to go out even for this."

I said nothing. I had extended courtesy to the Tlic. Now I didn't want to talk to anyone. I hoped he would go in—out of curiosity if nothing else.

"Finally found out more than you wanted to know, eh?"

I looked at him.

"Don't give me one of her looks," he said. "You're not her. You're just her property."

One of her looks. Had I picked up even an ability to imitate her expressions?

"What'd you do, puke?" He sniffed the air. "So now you know what you're in for."

I walked away from him. He and I had been close when we were kids. He would let me follow him around when I was home and sometimes T'Gatoi would let me bring him along when she took me into the city. But something had happened when he reached adolescence. I never knew what. He began keeping out of T'Gatoi's way. Then he began running away— until he realized there was no "away." Not in the Preserve. Certainly not outside. After that he concentrated on getting his share of every egg that came into the house, and on looking out for me in a way that made me all but hate him—a way that clearly said, as long as I was all right, he was safe from the Tlic.

"How was it, really?" he demanded, following me.

"I killed an achti. The young ate it."

"You didn't run out of the house and puke because they ate an achti."

"I had . . . never seen a person cut open before." That was true, and enough for him to know. I couldn't talk about the other. Not with him.

"Oh," he said. He glanced at me as though he wanted to say more, but he kept quiet.

We walked, not really headed anywhere. Toward the back, toward the cages, toward the fields.

"Did he say anything?" Qui asked. "Lomas, I mean."

Who else would he mean? "He said, 'T'Khotgif.'"

Qui shuddered. "If she had done that to me, she'd be the last person I'd call for."

"You'd call for her. Her sting would ease your pain without killing the grubs in you."

"You think I'd care if they died?"

No. Of course he wouldn't. Would I?

"Shit!" He drew a deep breath. "I've seen what they do. You think this thing with Lomas was bad? It was nothing."

I didn't argue. He didn't know what he was talking about.

"I saw them eat a man," he said.

I turned to face him. "You're lying!"

"*I saw them eat a man.*" He paused. "It was when I was little. I had been to the Hartmund house and I was on my way home. Halfway here, I saw a man and a Tlic and the man was N'Tlic. The ground was hilly. I was able to hide from them and watch. The Tlic wouldn't open the man because she had nothing to feed the grubs. The man couldn't go any farther and there were no houses around. He was in so much pain he told her to kill him. He begged her to kill him. Finally, she did. She cut his throat. One swipe of one claw. I saw the grubs eat their way out, then burrow in again, still eating."

His words made me see Lomas's flesh again, parasitized, crawling. "Why didn't you tell me that?" I whispered.

He looked startled, as though he'd forgotten I was listening. "I don't know."

"You started to run away not long after that, didn't you?"

"Yeah. Stupid. Running inside the Preserve. Running in a cage."

I shook my head, said what I should have said to him long ago. "She wouldn't take you, Qui. You don't have to worry."

"She would . . . if anything happened to you."

"No. She'd take Xuan Hoa. Hoa . . . wants it." She wouldn't if she had stayed to watch Lomas.

"They don't take women," he said with contempt.

"They do sometimes." I glanced at him. "Actually, they prefer women. You should be around them when they talk among themselves. They say women have more body fat to protect the grubs. But they usually take men to leave the women free to bear their own young."

"To provide the next generation of host animals," he said, switching from contempt to bitterness.

"It's more than that!" I countered. Was it?

"If it were going to happen to me, I'd want to believe it was more, too."

"It *is* more!" I felt like a kid. Stupid argument.

"Did you think so while T'Gatoi was picking worms out of that guy's guts?"

"It's not supposed to happen that way."

"Sure it is. You weren't supposed to see it, that's all. And his Tlic was supposed to do it. She could sting him unconscious and the operation wouldn't have been as painful. But she'd still open him, pick out the grubs, and if she missed even one, it would poison him and eat him from the inside out."

There was actually a time when my mother told me to show respect for Qui because he was my older brother. I walked away, hating him. In his way, he was gloating. He was safe and I wasn't. I could have hit him, but I didn't think I would be able to stand it when he refused to hit back, when he looked at me with contempt and pity.

He wouldn't let me get away. Longer-legged, he swung ahead of me and made me feel as though I were following him.

"I'm sorry," he said.

I strode on, sick and furious.

"Look, it probably won't be that bad with you. T'Gatoi likes you. She'll be careful."

I turned back toward the house, almost running from him.

"Has she done it to you yet?" he asked, keeping up easily. "I mean, you're about the right age for implantation. Has she—"

I hit him. I didn't know I was going to do it, but I think I meant to kill him. If he hadn't been bigger and stronger, I think I would have.

He tried to hold me off, but in the end, had to defend himself. He only hit me a couple of times. That was plenty. I don't remember going down, but when I came to, he was gone. It was worth the pain to be rid of him.

I got up and walked slowly toward the house. The back was dark. No one was in the kitchen. My mother and sisters were sleeping in their bedrooms—or pretending to.

Once I was in the kitchen, I could hear voices—Tlic and Terran from the next room. I couldn't make out what they were saying— didn't want to make it out.

I sat down at my mother's table, waiting for quiet. The table was smooth and worn, heavy and well crafted. My father had made it for her just before he died. I remembered hanging around underfoot when he built it. He didn't mind. Now I sat leaning on it, missing him. I could have talked to him. He had done it three times in his long life. Three clutches of eggs, three times being opened and sewed up. How had he done it? How did anyone do it?

I got up, took the rifle from its hiding place, and sat down again with it. It needed cleaning, oiling.

All I did was load it.

"Gan?"

She made a lot of little clicking sounds when she walked on bare floor, each limb clicking in succession as it touched down. Waves of little clicks.

She came to the table, raised the front half of her body above it, and surged onto it. Sometimes she moved so smoothly she seemed to flow like water itself. She coiled herself into a small hill in the middle of the table and looked at me.

"That was bad," she said softly. "You should not have seen it. It need not be that way."

"I know."

"T'Khotgif—Ch'Khotgif now—she will die of her disease. She will not live to raise her children. But her sister will provide for them, and for Bram Lomas." Sterile sister. One fertile female in every lot. One to keep the family going. That sister owed Lomas more than she could ever repay.

"He'll live then?"

"Yes."

"I wonder if he would do it again."

"No one would ask him to do that again."

I looked into the yellow eyes, wondering how much I saw and understood there, and how much I only imagined. "No one ever asks us," I said. "You never asked me."

She moved her head slightly. "What's the matter with your face?"

"Nothing. Nothing important." Human eyes probably wouldn't have noticed the swelling in the darkness. The only light was from one of the moons, shining through a window across the room.

"Did you use the rifle to shoot the achti?"

"Yes."

"And do you mean to use it to shoot me?"

I stared at her, outlined in moonlight— coiled, graceful body. "What does Terran blood taste like to you?"

She said nothing.

"What are you?" I whispered. "What are we to you?"

She lay still, rested her head on her topmost coil. "You know me as no other does," she said softly. "You must decide."

"That's what happened to my face," I told her.

"What?"

"Qui goaded me into deciding to do something. It didn't turn out very well." I moved the gun slightly, brought the barrel up diagonally under my own chin. "At least it was a decision I made."

"As this will be."

"Ask me, Gatoi."

"For my children's lives?"

She would say something like that. She knew how to manipulate people, Terran and Tlic. But not this time.

"I don't want to be a host animal," I said. "Not even yours."

It took her a long time to answer. "We use almost no host animals these days," she said. "You know that."

"You use us."

"We do. We wait long years for you and teach you and join our families to yours." She moved restlessly. "You know you aren't animals to us."

I stared at her, saying nothing.

"The animals we once used began killing most of our eggs after implantation long before your ancestors arrived," she said softly. "You know these things, Gan. Because your people arrived, we are relearning what it means to be a healthy, thriving people. And your ancestors, fleeing from their homeworld, from their own kind who would have killed or enslaved them— they survived because of us. We saw them as people and gave them the Preserve when they still tried to kill us as worms."

At the word *worms* I jumped. I couldn't help it, and she couldn't help noticing it.

"I see," she said quietly. "Would you really rather die than bear my young, Gan?"

I didn't answer.

"Shall I go to Xuan Hoa?"

"Yes!" Hoa wanted it. Let her have it. She hadn't had to watch Lomas. She'd be proud. . . . Not terrified.

T'Gatoi flowed off the table onto the floor, startling me almost too much.

"I'll sleep in Hoa's room tonight," she said. "And sometime tonight or in the morning, I'll tell her."

This was going too fast. My sister. Hoa had had almost as much to do with raising me as my mother. I was still close to her—not like Qui. She could want T'Gatoi and still love me.

"Wait! Gatoi!"

She looked back, then raised nearly half her length off the floor and turned it to face me. "These are adult things, Gan. This is my life, my family!"

"But she's . . . my sister."

"I have done what you demanded. I have asked you!"

"But—"

"It will be easier for Hoa. She has always expected to carry other lives inside her."

Human lives. Human young who would someday drink at her breasts, not at her veins.

I shook my head. "Don't do it to her, Gatoi." I was not Qui. It seemed I could become him, though, with no effort at all. I could make Xuan Hoa my shield. Would it be easier to know that red worms were growing in her flesh instead of mine?

"Don't do it to Hoa," I repeated.

She stared at me, utterly still.

I looked away, then back at her. "Do it to me."

I lowered the gun from my throat and she leaned forward to take it.

"No," I told her.

"It's the law," she said.

"Leave it for the family. One of them might use it to save my life someday."

She grasped the rifle barrel, but I wouldn't let go. I was pulled into a standing position over her.

"Leave it here!" I repeated. "If we're not your animals, if these are adult things, accept the risk. There is risk, Gatoi, in dealing with a partner."

It was clearly hard for her to let go of the rifle. A shudder went through her and she made a hissing sound of distress. It occurred to me that she was afraid. She was old enough to have seen what guns could do to people. Now her young and this gun would be together in the same house. She did not know about our other guns. In this dispute, they did not matter.

"I will implant the first egg tonight," she said as I put the gun away. "Do you hear, Gan?"

Why else had I been given a whole egg to eat while the rest of the family was left to share one? Why else had my mother kept looking at me as though I were going away from her, going where she could not follow? Did T'Gatoi imagine I hadn't known?

"I hear."

"Now!" I let her push me out of the kitchen, then walked ahead of her toward my bedroom. The sudden urgency in her voice sounded real. "You would have done it to Hoa tonight!" I accused.

"I must do it to someone tonight."

I stopped in spite of her urgency and stood in her way. "Don't you care who?"

She flowed around me and into my bedroom. I found her waiting on the couch we shared. There was nothing in Hoa's room that she could have used. She would have done it to Hoa on the floor. The thought of her doing it to Hoa at all disturbed me in a different way now, and I was suddenly angry.

Yet I undressed and lay down beside her. I knew what to do, what to expect. I had been told all my life. I felt the familiar sting, narcotic, mildly pleasant. Then the blind probing of her ovipositor. The puncture was painless, easy. So easy going in. She undulated slowly against me, her muscles forcing the egg from her body into mine. I held on to a pair of her limbs until I remembered Lomas holding her that way. Then I let go, moved inadvertently, and hurt her. She gave a low cry of pain and I expected to be caged at once within her limbs. When I wasn't, I held on to her again, feeling oddly ashamed.

"I'm sorry," I whispered.

She rubbed my shoulders with four of her limbs.

"Do you care?" I asked. "Do you care that it's me?"

She did not answer for some time. Finally, "You were the one making choices tonight, Gan. I made mine long ago."

"Would you have gone to Hoa?"

"Yes. How could I put my children into the care of one who hates them?"

"It wasn't . . . hate."

"I know what it was."

"I was afraid."

Silence.

"I still am." I could admit it to her here, now.

"But you came to me . . . to save Hoa."

"Yes." I leaned my forehead against her. She was cool velvet, deceptively soft. "And to keep you for myself," I said. It was so. I didn't understand it, but it was so.

She made a soft hum of contentment. "I couldn't believe I had made such a mistake with you," she said. "I chose you. I believed you had grown to choose me."

"I had, but . . ."

"Lomas."

"Yes."

"I have never known a Terran to see a birth and take it well. Qui has seen one, hasn't he?"

"Yes."

"Terrans should be protected from seeing."

I didn't like the sound of that—and I doubted that it was possible. "Not protected," I said. "Shown. Shown when we're young kids, and shown more than once. Gatoi, no Terran ever sees a birth that goes right. All we see is N'Tlic—pain and terror and maybe death."

She looked down at me. "It is a private thing. It has always been a private thing."

Her tone kept me from insisting—that and the knowledge that if she changed her mind, I might be the first public example. But I had planted the thought in her mind. Chances were it would grow, and eventually she would experiment.

"You won't see it again," she said. "I don't want you thinking any more about shooting me."

The small amount of fluid that came into me with her egg relaxed me as completely as a sterile egg would have, so that I could remember the rifle in my hands and my feelings of fear and revulsion, anger and despair. I could remember the feelings without reviving them. I could talk about them.

"I wouldn't have shot you," I said. "Not you." She had been taken from my father's flesh when he was my age.

"You could have," she insisted.

"Not you." She stood between us and her own people, protecting, interweaving.

"Would you have destroyed yourself?"

I moved carefully, uncomfortably. "I could have done that. I nearly did. That's Qui's 'away.' I wonder if he knows."

"What?"

I did not answer.

"You will live now."

"Yes." *Take care of her,* my mother used to say. Yes.

"I'm healthy and young," she said. "I won't leave you as Lomas was left—alone, N'Tlic. I'll take care of you."

Variation on a Man

PAT CADIGAN

Pat Cadigan (1953–) is a US science fiction writer associated with the cyberpunk movement who has won two Arthur C. Clarke Awards and a Hugo Award. From the beginning, Cadigan focused on near-future, usually urban, and usually Californian settings, often intensified by a sense of wind-swept, prairie desolation—and used them as highly charged gauntlets that her protagonists do not so much run through as cling to, surviving somehow. Certainly her immersion of her female protagonists in traditionally masculine venues has been useful in subverting some tropes of the subgenre. In addition to writing cyberpunk fiction, Cadigan edited the anthology *The Ultimate Cyberpunk* in 2002, an attempt to show historical antecedents and also provide examples of contemporary cyberpunk stories.

Cadigan's first novel, *Mindplayers* (1987), blurred the line between objective reality and subjective experience. Her second novel, *Synners* (1991), expands upon this idea and constituted a breakthrough for the author. *Synners* translates the cyberpunk aspects of her best short fiction into a comprehensive vision—linguistically acute, simultaneously pell-mell and precise in its detailing—of a world dominated by the intricacies of the human/computer interface. The plot, which is extremely complicated, is an early exploration of the interface disease trope, where computer viruses that pass for artificial intelligence are beginning to cause numerous human deaths and to fragment human identity.

Cadigan's work has increasingly seemed to be prescient, in some part through the sense of entrapment it conveys. Like William Gibson's cyberpunk novels—and unlike Bruce Sterling's—*Synners* offers no sense that the technological breakthroughs in the story will in any significant sense transform the overwhelmingly urbanized world, though there is some hint that the system may begin to fail through its own internal imbalances.

She began publishing short fiction with "Death from Exposure," in the second issue of *Shayol* (1978), a much-lauded magazine Cadigan edited throughout its existence (1977–85). She later assembled much of her best shorter work in *Patterns* (1989), with later stories appearing in *Home by the Sea* (1992) and *Dirty Work: Stories* (1993). Most of these collected stories were published in *Asimov's Science Fiction Magazine* and *Omni*.

"Variation on a Man" (*Omni*, 1984) is classic Cadigan cyberpunk and later became part of her novel *Mindplayers*.

VARIATION ON A MAN

Pat Cadigan

I was convinced (still am) that it was the pearl-necklace episode that caused Nelson Nelson to give me the Gladney case.

All mindplayers can pretty much count on getting pearl necklaced sooner or later, but it's a far more vivid experience for pathosfinders than it is for neurosis-peddlers, say, or belljarrers, who don't spend as much time in direct mind-to-mind contact with their clients as we do.

It seems the more time you spend working as a disembodied mind, the more intensely you get pearl necklaced.

My pearl necklace came during a routine reality affixing. Reality affixing is mandatory for mindplayers by federal law, though I don't really believe we're more prone to delusional thinking than anyone else. And there's something about having to have my perceptions stamped ACCEPTABLE PER GOVERNMENT REGULATORY STANDARDS that makes me a touch uneasy. On the other hand—or lobe, if you will—a mindplayer who is convinced everybody must accept the water buffalo as a personal totem is not someone you'd want fooling around in people's minds.

Still, I didn't look forward to having my reality affixed, in spite of Nelson Nelson's reassurance that government standards were broad enough to encompass all the varieties of normal. I always wanted to ask him what made him so sure about that. But there was no room for argument—either I had my reality affixed or I lost my job at the mind-play agency and my license to practice pathosfinding.

All I had to do was go headfirst into the agency's system and let it probe me for perhaps ten minutes, if that. Of course, it can seem like days when you're lying on the slab with your eyes out and the system hooked into your mind via the optic nerves, body awareness blocked off so that you're completely alone with yourself. NN was always telling me that I should look at it as a particularly intense kind of meditation and that as long as I was myself, I certainly had nothing to feel uneasy about.

As long as I was myself. And who else would I be? The system had apparently stimulated this particular question, and out came the pearl necklace. That was exactly how it appeared to my inner eye, as a long, long line of pearls, each one holding a moment in the life of Alexandra Victoria Haas, a.k.a. Deadpan Allie, separate, self-contained, unrelated to those on either side of it. The connecting thread running through them was suddenly gone, and I was looking at a series of strangers who shared my face but nothing more, as though I had popped in and out of being every moment I had been alive instead of existing continuously. The realization flared like sudden pain: *I have not always been as I am now.*

I couldn't remember being any different. Nor could I conceive of what I would be like in the next moments—the future me was as much a stranger as the past one.

The pearls began moving away from one another, the sequence going from ordered to random. I lunged to gather them up, and panic sent them flying apart as I fell toward disintegration.

The next thing I knew, I was fine again, and the pearl necklace was gone. The foundation of everything I'd lived was under me again; I was no longer a stranger to myself. The system ran through the rest of the affixing procedure and then disengaged. I put my eyes back in and went off to have a nap.

Naturally, the crisis was reported to Nelson Nelson. I knew it would be, but he never mentioned it. Instead he called me into his office to give me an assignment.

"In your work with artists," he said, while I lay on the gold-lamé interview couch and tried not to be obvious about the rash the tacky upholstery was giving me, "what would you say your primary objective as a pathosfinder is?"

I rested my cheek on my left hand and thought it over. "To assist them in reaching a level where inward and outward perceptions balance well enough against each other so that—"

"*Allie.*" He gave me a look. "This is *me* you're talking to."

"Help them move past irrelevant and superficial mental trash."

NN raised himself up on one elbow, his own couch creaking and groaning, and actually shook his finger at me. "Never, never, *never* essay-answer me."

"Sorry."

His eyes narrowed. He had brand-new pink-jade biogem eyes, and they made him look like a geriatric rabbit. "Don't be sorry. In spite of your initial choice of words, you're right." The wrinkled old face took on a thoughtful expression. "Would you say that in many cases the pathosfinder is responsible for helping an artist locate the creative generator's ON button as well as helping to enhance the soul of the work?"

For someone who didn't like essay answers, he was pretty fond of essay questions. "In many cases, sure."

Now he looked satisfied. "That's why I'd like to put you on the Gladney case."

"Rand Gladney? The composer? I thought he'd been sucked."

"He was. But he's out of full quarantine now, and his new personality's grown into mature form. He's lucky his old recording company had regeneration insurance on him. Of course, he's not really Gladney anymore and never will be again."

"Have they told him who he used to be?"

"Oh, yeah. Every detail. He wanted to know. Most victims of involuntary mind-suck do. They're all intensely curious about their former lives, and the doctors figure honesty is the best policy. Better for them to hear about it in a sheltered environment where they can learn to deal with it. Anyway, I thought this would be a good opportunity for a pathosfinder to work with an adult who has no history whatsoever and help him become an artist."

For the millionth time, I thought about the career in neurosis-peddling I'd given up. NN had promised (sort of) that someday he'd let me go back to it.

I'd never thought peddling things like compulsive cleanliness to wealthy people who enjoyed feeling a little more unstable than usual was easy work until NN had made a pathosfinder out of me.

But I didn't have to tell him I'd take the job. He knew I would.

I ran through the bare minimum of information on Gladney that NN had dumped into the datakeep in my apartment while the portable system I used for mind-to-mind contact with clients was being overhauled. Prior to having his mind stolen, Rand Gladney had been a composer of middle-high talent with a fair number of works that had settled into the cultural mainstream. At the time of his erasure, he'd been approaching a turning point in his career where he would have either ascended to greater ability and prominence or settled slowly into repetition and, eventually, semioblivion. In seven years, he had peaked twice after his breakthrough. And that was just about all NN wanted me to know about the Gladney-that-had-been. I could have easily found out more, but I trusted NN's judgment as to how much information on Gladney's previous incarnation I should bring with me to the job.

The Gladney-that-was-now had been out of full quarantine for a month, though he was still hospitalized and his movements were restricted. Rehabilitating mindwipes is a precarious business, like trying to stand with your hands both on and off someone's shoulders. Personality regrowth begins with the restoration of language, first by machine, then by humans. If humans don't replace the machine at precisely the right moment, you end up with a person unable to think in anything but a machine-type mode. People like that may be great logicians, but they're lousy on theory. Most often they resolve the conflict between the definite and the gray in their lives by suicide or voluntary mindwipe, which is pretty much the same thing. There are very few brains hardy enough to redevelop a mind after a second erasure, the myelin sheathing on the axons just won't stand up to that kind of abuse.

In any case, Gladney (who was apparently still going by that name for the sake of convenience) had passed all the critical points in redevelopment and had become a person, again or for the first time, depending on your point of view. He was certainly not the same person— the man who had emerged from the blank brain was reminiscent of his former self but no more that self than he was anyone else.

The extreme convolutedness of such a situation was one reason why I chose not to go into rehabbing mindwipe as a profession when I'd had the chance. Still, it was a fascinating field, easier to succeed in if you have a bit of a mystic bent, or so I've been told. I'd never thought of myself as particularly mystical, but I suppose all mindplayers are to a certain extent, if you accept the mind as the ghost in the biological machine or something like that.

I filed the idea way for later meditation and went over Gladney's aptitude tests. His new personality had grown in with a definite talent for music and more—I was startled to find that he now had perfect pitch. The previous man did not. It made me wonder. Was the perfect pitch something that had shown up due to some alteration in Gladney's brain chemistry brought about by the mindsuck? Or was it just due to a different brain organization? Possibly it was a combination of both.

Whatever it was, I didn't really have to worry about it. I was supposed to treat Gladney as I would any other client, which is to say as though he had never been anyone else but who he was now.

"Truth to tell," said the woman with the carnelian eyes and the too-short apple-red hair, "we ended up selecting you for your business name. Anyone operating as Deadpan Allie must have quite a lot of control over herself." She smiled brightly. Her name was Lind Jesl, and she looked less like the chief doctor on the Gladney case than she did someone finishing up her own recovery. Except for the carnelian eyes and the hair, she was as plain as possible, her stout body concealed in a loose, gray sacksuit. The office we were sitting in was even more austere, a cream-colored box with no decorations. Even the computer desk was all folded into a stark, bare block. The whole thing reminded me of the infamous white-room image I'd come across in certain clients' minds.

"Of course," she went on, "your self-control will be vital when you delve our boy. An involuntary wipe is supremely sensitive and impressionable, even at such an advanced stage of regeneration. Just the experience of you probing his mind is going to make quite a mark on him. Your flavor, as 'twere, will leave a bit of an aftertaste."

"I'm very careful."

"Yes, certainly you are." Her gaze snagged briefly on my equipment piled up beside me before she gave me her five-hundred-watt smile again. "And we wouldn't have hired you if we weren't as confident of his ability to think independently as we are of *your* ability to refrain from exerting too much psychic influence."

She was putting a lot of emphasis on the very thing guaranteed by the fact that I was licensed to pathosfind in the first place. "What kind of results are you looking for?"

"Ah." Five hundred watts went to six hundred. She folded her pudgy hands and plunked them on her stomach. "We're hoping you'll help him learn how to combine the various elements that make up a composer into a whole that will be greater than the sum of the parts."

I blinked.

"We know that he has a musical *bent*, as 'twere. A definite leaning toward music, an affinity for playing instruments that tends to accompany perfect pitch. But as yet, these things are fragmented in him. He's having difficulty achieving a state where they all work together. In fact, he has yet to achieve it even for a few moments."

"Isn't that just a matter of"—I shrugged—"practice and experience?"

"Usually. But I know Gladney. *This* Gladney. There are signs of a definite barrier of some kind that he just can't or won't find his way around. We don't know for certain because we haven't delved him since the very early part of the regeneration, which he does not remember. Delicate Plant Syndrome, you see—if you keep digging up a delicate plant to see how well the roots are taking, it dies." She sat forward, her hands disappearing into the voluminous cloth of the sacksuit. "We feel he's ready for mind-to-mind contact now but with a pathosfinder rather than a doctor. We want him to feel less like our patient and more like a person."

"How long *has* it been since you delved him therapeutically?"

"About nine or ten months. It's been a year since the mindsuckers got him. We're hoping to release him completely in another six months at the most. Depending on how much progress he makes with you."

"Have you let him listen to any of his old compositions? The previous Gladney's music, I mean?"

"Yes and no. Which is to say he's heard it, but he doesn't know who composed it. We removed all identification from all the record-

ings we've given him, not just Gladney's, to foil whatever deductions he might have tried to make."

"Does he react any differently to the Gladney compositions than he does to any of the others?"

"He reacts to all music somewhat guardedly. He puts it through some kind of mental sorting procedure, and he *can* tell with an accuracy of close to ninety percent, sometimes more, whether different pieces of music were composed by the same person. I suspect he could also arrange a composer's works in the correct chronological order as well. He's *extremely* bright. But—" Jesl spread her hands. "Something inside isn't meshing."

"Has he tried to compose?"

"Oh, yes. Some short things he won't let us hear. We had to bug the synthesizer we gave him. His work shows potential. There are moments when it *almost* breaks through, but it always stops short of achieving—well, fullness, as 'twere. You'll hear that for yourself, I'm sure." She looked at my equipment again.

She was awfully sure about a lot of things, it seemed to me. I considered the possibility that her evaluation of his music might be faulty. Perhaps the musical direction he was taking was just different from the old Gladney's, and what he wasn't achieving were her expectations. But a sight reading of her Emotional Index didn't indicate any smugness. Her certainty seemed to come from the fact that she'd been with him at every step of his regrowth. She smiled again, this time somewhat reservedly, and I realized she knew I'd been taking her Emotional Index.

"When can I see him?" I asked.

"Right now, if you like. We've fixed up a room for you not far from his so you'll be within easy reach of each other. I'll take you down there, and then we'll visit our boy."

The room they'd given me was an improvised efficiency with a freestanding lavabo unit and jury-rigged meal dial. My apartment at NN's agency had spoiled me for any other kind of accommodations, no matter how temporary. The bed was a hospital bed disguised as a civilian—not very wide but, to my great relief, hard as a rock.

I'd brought only a few personal things with me, which I didn't bother to unpack. I debated taking my equipment with me to Gladney's room and decided against it. He might feel too pressured to begin work if I appeared wheeling my system with me. I wanted some extra time myself, just to see what an eighteen-month-old adult was like on the outside before I went inside.

The man lying on the bed had once had the pampered good looks found in most people of celebrity status. Over the months, he'd lost a good deal of them, the way an athlete or dancer will lose a certain amount of strength after a long period of inactivity. He was still attractive, but his appearance was changing, veering off in another direction. Typical of a regrown mind-wipe. In a few months it was possible he would be so changed that no one from his previous life would recognize him.

He got up for Jesl's brief introduction, touching hands with me gingerly, as though I might be a hot iron. Something like bewildered panic crossed his face as Jesl made a quick but unhurried exit, leaving us on our own.

"So, you're my pathosfinder." He gestured at a small area arranged around an entertainment center with a few chairs and a beverage table. He'd probably set it up himself, but I could tell he wasn't completely at home with it.

"Anything you'd like to ask me in particular?" I said, sitting down. The chair I selected gave like soft clay under me, and I realized it was one of those damned contour things that will adapt a shape to complement your position. It was made of living fiber, supposedly the most comfortable kind of furniture there was, though how anyone could be comfortable with a chair that needed to be fed, watered, and cleaned up after was not within my understanding. Occasionally you'd hear horror stories about people who had sat down on one of those things and then needed to be surgically removed later. I wondered why they'd given Gladney a contour and then remembered it was also supposed to be a boon to the lonely. I was going to have a rough time being deadpan if it started any funny stuff with me. Fortunately, it seemed disposed to let me sit in peace; so I decided to tough it out rather than change seats. Gladney appeared to be watching me closely.

"I hardly ever use that one," he said as it molded itself to support my elbows. "I can't get used to it. But it's fascinating to watch when someone else is in it." He turned his attention to my face. "What kind of eyes are those?"

"Cat's-eye biogem."

"Cat's-eye." He sounded slightly envious. "Everyone here at the hospital has biogems. Even some of the other 'wipes. Dr. Jesl says that I can order some whenever I want to, but I don't feel like I can yet. *He* had biogems."

"Who?"

"Gladney. The original one, not me. After he was sucked, the hospital replaced them with these, which I guess are reproductions of the eyes he was born with." He smiled. "I remember how surprised I was when they told me almost everyone has his eyes replaced with artificial ones. It still amazes me a little. I mean, my eyes don't feel artificial—but then, I guess I wouldn't know the difference, would I?" His smile shrank. "It's strange to think of you going into my brain that way. Through my eyes. It's strange to think of anyone else in there except me." He put his hand on his chest and absently began rubbing himself. "And yet there have been a whole lot of people in there. Mindplayers. For *him*. And then the suckers. The doctors. And now you."

"Direct contact with the mind is a way of life. Not just the mindplay but many forms of higher education. People buy and sell things, too. Neuroses, memories, or—" *Nice rolling, Deadpan,* I thought. *You had to bring that up.*

"Yeah. I know. People buy and sell. They steal, too." He lifted his chin with just a trace of defiance. "I made them tell me about that, and what they wouldn't tell me, I looked up. How

Gladney's mind got stolen because there was some guy who admired him so much that he wanted to *be* Gladney. So he had Gladney overlaid on his own self. He went crazy. Trying to be two people at once." He slouched in his chair and rested his head on his right hand, digging his fingers into his thick, brown hair. I didn't make a move. "I asked them why they didn't just take Gladney out of him and put him back, but they said they couldn't do that after he'd already been implanted. Even if they'd found the suckers before that, it would have been impossible because this brain"—he pointed at his head and then resumed rubbing his chest— "had already begun developing a new mind. Me. There would have been too much conflict. Doesn't seem fair."

"Fair to whom?"

"Gladney." Beneath the thin material of his shirt, I could see his flesh reddening. "He just disintegrated. Evaporated when they cleaned him out of the other man. And here I am. Variation on a theme." His gaze drifted away from me to something over my left shoulder. I turned to look. He was staring at the synthesizer near the bed. It was a small one as synthesizers go, taking up about twice as much space as my portable system did when assembled. There was a very light coating of dust on the keyboard cover.

"Use it much?" I asked.

"From time to time."

"I'd really like to hear something you've composed."

He looked mildly shocked. "Ah, you would. Why?"

"Get acquainted with your music."

"So that after you get into my brain and find my music box, you'll know whether it's mine or not, huh?" He waved away his words. "Never mind. I've done nothing but short pieces, and I don't think of any of them as complete. Not when I compare them to other things I've heard."

"I would still like to hear something."

He hesitated. "Would a recording be all right? I don't like to play in front of anyone.

I'm not an entertainer. Or at least not that kind of entertainer."

"A recording would be fine."

He got up and puttered around with the entertainment center for a minute, keeping his back to me.

Generally it's difficult if not impossible to sight-read the Emotional Index of someone who isn't facing you but it was easy to tell that Gladney was dry-mouthed at the idea of my hearing one of his compositions. It was far more than stage fright or shyness. His shoulders were stiffened as though he expected someone to hit him.

Abruptly music blared out of the speakers, and he jumped to adjust the volume.

"Set it to repeat once," I told him.

He turned to me, ready to object, and then shrugged and thumbed a shiny green square on the console before sitting down again. "Just a musical doodle, really," he muttered, apologizing for it before it could offend me.

In fact, it was a bit more than that, a dialogue between piano and clarinet, admirably synthesized but too tentative. And he'd been right—it wasn't complete at all. It was more like an excerpt from a longer piece that he'd heard only a portion of in his mind. I was no musical authority but the second time through, I could pick out spots where a surer composer would have punched up the counterpoint and let the two instruments answer each other more quickly. There might even have been the makings of a canon in it, though I couldn't be certain. Perhaps he'd been mistaking Bach for Gladney. Whatever he'd been doing or trying to do, something was definitely missing.

"How did you compose it?" I asked after the music finished.

He frowned.

"Did you just sit down at the synthesizer and fool around until you found a sequence or—"

"Oh." He laughed nervously. "That's a funny thing. I heard it in a dream, and when I woke up, I went to the synthesizer to play it out so I wouldn't forget it. First I just played all the notes as I'd heard them. Then I put them with the appropriate instruments."

"Was that how it was in the dream—piano and clarinet?"

"I don't remember. I just remember the music itself. Piano and clarinet seemed right."

I had a feeling I knew what the answer to my next question would be, but asked anyway. "What was the dream about?"

He was rubbing again. "Gladney."

I managed to talk him into playing a few more of his incomplete compositions. When his discomfort went from acute to excruciating, I gave him a reprieve and told him I was going to get some rest. His relief was so tangible I could have ridden it out of the room and halfway down the hall.

There was a message in my phone, an invitation from Dr. Jesl to have dinner with her and the other medicos working on Gladney's habilitation. I begged off and asked her if she could supply me, without his knowing it, with dupe recordings of Gladney's recent attempts at composition, and also some of the previous Gladney's work. She could and did, and I spent most of the rest of the day and a good part of the evening in an audio-hood.

Maybe if I'd known more about music—the real hard-core stuff, mathematics of progressions and so forth—I'd have been able to pick out more similarities (or differences) between the two Gladneys' work. I called for recordings by other composers he'd listened to, and I played those as well. Our boy, as Jesl had called him, hadn't been trying to crib from Bach or anyone else. He had avoided being derivative as much as possible, admirable in a beginning talent and also evident of already well-developed control, which is a good sign only as long as it doesn't become inhibition. What he had borrowed from other composers was mostly technique—my ear was good enough to pick that up, if I listened to everything several times. The composer he seemed to have borrowed from

least was, oddly enough, Gladney. Or perhaps that wasn't so odd. Perhaps the compositions sounded too familiar.

I listened to the piano-clarinet piece over and over, trying to hear some similarity between it and any of the other Gladney's music—a sequence of notes, rhythm, something. He'd been unable to tell me exactly what had happened in the dream where he'd heard it—just that he'd known the dream was about Gladney. That was somewhat unsettling and would have been more so if he had composed all his music after dreaming about that former persona. But he hadn't, and I would have found it reassuring if the piano-clarinet piece hadn't been so obviously superior to all of his other attempts. Variation on a theme, he'd called himself. It nagged at me.

I waited until Gladney had been escorted off to some kind of day-to-day culture workshop early the next afternoon and had Jesl let me into his room so I could set up for our first session. That way he wouldn't have to receive me as a guest with all the attendant awkwardness again.

The bed, I decided, would be the best place to put him; it was obviously what he gravitated to when left to himself, so he'd probably be more receptive lying down. I rolled my equipment over and assembled the eight odd-sized components. They still reminded me of a giant set of cub's blocks. With me as the giant cub, I supposed, building some kind of surreal structure, a little like a cubist idea of a skyscraper. It looked ready to topple over as most of the smaller pieces were clustered on one side of the largest one, a four-foot rectangle. In reality it would have been more trouble than it was worth to knock it over. By the time Gladney returned I had the compartmented tank for our eyes set out on the stand by the bed, the optic-nerve connections to the system primed, and a relaxation program ready to run the moment he was hooked in.

He didn't seem surprised to see me, only a little resigned and nervous. "You're not going to want to hear any more music, are you?" he asked with an attempt at a smile.

"No more recordings, no." I patted the bed. "Come get comfortable. We don't have to start immediately."

Now he did smile, stripped off his overshirt and chaps (it never fails to amaze me what will come back into style), and flopped down on the bed in his secondskins.

Rather than play one of the usual preparatory games like *What Would You Do?* or *What Do You Hear?* with him, I eased him into chatting about his habilitation. I thought I'd learn more about his state of mind from simple conversation than from games. After all, what past experience could he draw on for a game? It would only oblige him to be inventive and pull his concentration from the situation at hand. Chitter-chat was the right approach. He had some rather astute observations on modern life, as any outsider would, and I hoped he wouldn't lose them when he became an insider. He wasn't really opening up to me—I hadn't expected that—but watching him try to hide in his own talk was enlightening. He wasn't going to give a single thing away, not even in mind-to-mind contact, and if I didn't figure out a different approach, I'd end up chasing him all over his own mind.

Eventually he began winding down. I let him get away with some delaying tactics: going to the bathroom, taking his vitamins—delaying tactics can be important personal-preparation rituals, if they don't go on for too long. When he began talking about having a snack, I made him lie down again and start breathing exercises.

He was a good breather, reaching a state of physical receptiveness more quickly than a lot of more experienced clients I'd had. When the time came I removed his eyes for him; just pressed my thumbs on his closed lids and out they popped into my palms, as smoothly as melon seeds. Gladney didn't even twitch. The connections to his optic nerves disengaged with an audible *kar-chunk*. Hospital eyes are always a little more mechanical than they have to be. After I placed them in the left side of the holding tank, I slipped the system connections under his flaccid eyelids. A tiny jump in the wires told me when he was hooked in to the mental finger-painting exercise I'd selected for him. Mental finger-painting was about the right amount of effort for someone on his level. The system supplied the colors; all he had to do was stir them around.

I breathed myself into a relaxed state in a matter of moments, but I waited a full minute before popping my own eyes out and joining him in the system. I wanted to give him time to get acclimated. Some people experience a sense of continuous drifting when they first enter the system, a disorientation not unlike weightlessness, and they need a minute alone to right themselves before they have to get used to another presence.

My materialization was even more gradual than usual, to spare him any trauma. His perception of my entry was as another color, oozing in greenly and then transforming itself into a second consciousness. Bright lights flashed as he recognized me, some of them nightmare purple, but it wasn't me he was afraid of. There was a little fear from not having a body to feel, but he was becoming accustomed to that. He was edgy about something else entirely—quick images of traps snapping shut, closet doors slamming. But there was exhilaration, too, at being in a realm where almost nothing is impossible.

The images began to flow more continuously from him, rolling over us in a tumbling series, gargantuan confetti. Most of them were portions of dreams, scenes from books he'd read; some were strange scenes he was making up in the heat of the moment, just to see if he could do it. I stabilized myself and moved with his attention, reminding him that I was still there. The image of my own face came, followed by a series of others that gradually became more bizarre. The undertones running out of him indicated this was how he imagined everyone else in the world to be—somewhat exotic, different, mysterious, alien, existing on a plane he had only the haziest conception of.

I emphasized my presence before he could become caught up enough in his grotesquely ornamented faces to get hysterical. He steadied, his energy level decreasing. I felt him adjust something and there was a sense of balance being established, as though two large masses floating in space were settling into orbit around each other. *Space* was a good word for it. The feeling of emptiness surrounding us was enormous and almost vivid enough to induce vertigo.

This is me. So much nothingness to be filled. He was unaware that he'd said anything; it simply came out of him as everything else had. There was a brief image of Gladney—the previous Gladney—and he tensed at the thought. *Somewhere. In this big emptiness*—

The Gladney-that-had-been drifted away from us and disintegrated. The thought remained incomplete. He seemed to be at a total loss now, drifting nowhere, so I gave him a new image, a simple one: the synthesizer. As soon as I was sure he saw it, I added the music, the clarinet-piano piece.

Suspicion bristled on him for a moment, and then he was rerunning the music with me. I could hear little extra things, notes and embellishments absent from the recording. He was on the verge of rolling with it, letting it come the way it had been meant to, when hard negation chopped down like a guillotine blade. We were left in silence. If he could have withdrawn from me, he would have, but he didn't know how to.

I waited, making my presence as non-threatening as possible, while I took his Emotional Index. He registered in peculiar fragmented sensations of movement rather than visuals, because everything was movement for him. I could see that now. The universe was movement, the movement of vibration. Like a tuning fork. He was a tuning fork, and right now he was vibrating in the key of fear-sharp.

One octave up I could hear a whiny echo of guilt.

The intensity of it ebbed, and I turned the music on again. This time he didn't shut it down. He just pulled back from it as far as possible and allowed it to replay as the original recording without changes. I slowed down my time sense and concentrated, tightening myself until I was small enough to slip in between the notes. At that level they thundered, no longer recognizable as music; my consciousness vibrated in sympathy. I concentrated a little more, and the thundering rumble of the notes became more ponderous. Now I could detect something else within the vibrations of the music, faint but present. I would have to concentrate even harder to find out what it was, and I was nearly to the limit of my endurance. To concentrate that forcefully is to alter the state of consciousness in such a way that one is not actually conscious in the true sense of the word—I would not be able to monitor Gladney. From his perspective it would seem as though I'd vanished into some part of his mind inaccessible to him, or gone from being real to being imaginary.

I strained, achieving it slowly. The notes swelled until I could perceive only one at a time, and I let the nearest one swallow me up. It was a piano note, G, perfectly formed in perfect pitch, a universe created by the oscillation of a string in the air (that was how he saw it, not as synthesized piano but the real thing). Each sweep of the string through space created the universe of the note anew, the string reaching the limit of its swing before the ghost of itself opposite had disappeared. And within—

He looked up with a smile of mild interest. The face was unmistakable in spite of all the changes he'd been through in the last year and a half.

Come closer, he said.

Gladney?

The same. The smile broadened. *Well, not quite the same.* Those pampered good looks in full flower, the well-tended skin, the sculptured jawline, the hair brushed straight back and falling nearly to his shoulders. His face was the most solid thing about him. The rest had been sketched in vaguely. I could get no undertones from him, no feelings, no image.

He locked me in here, he said. *So I won't get out and take—*

The note passed away, and we were in another. Gladney was standing on a high hill in the middle of the day.

—what used to be mine. He looked around. In the distance the horizon ran wetly, melting into the sky. *I live in the music now. He can't come in unless I get out.*

It wasn't possible. If anything had been left of the old Gladney's mind after the suckers had finished cleaning out his brain, it would have shown up while he was still in quarantine. This had to be a delusion of the present Gladney, some kind of survivor guilt. Until he ceased to think of music as being a simultaneously convex and concave prison, he would never be able to compose more than a few incomplete snatches of melody.

The outdoor scene disappeared as the note went on; now we were in a vague representation of the old Gladney's recording studio. He looked up from the piano he was sitting at.

Can you prove who you are? I asked him.

You can see me as I was. Isn't that enough for you?

No. The Gladney-that-is has perfect pitch—that could easily translate to his being able to reproduce his old appearance. If you are really the Gladney-that-was, you can tell me something about yourself that the Gladney-that-is has no knowledge of.

The delusion spread his hands. *He's studied up on me thoroughly. They gave him access to vid-magazines, newstapes.*

There's still plenty he doesn't know, I said. *The private things. Certain memories. Feelings. Tell me something your family could confirm as true.*

His face took on a defiant look, but there was no more feeling from him than there would have been from a holo transmission. That in itself indicated he was a fabrication, but my merely telling Gladney that wasn't going to help. Even if I could get his intellect to believe me, his emotions probably wouldn't.

Tell me something, I prodded again.

He rose and leaned on the top of the piano. *Don't you think a man with perfect pitch would be able to interpolate the private feelings of another man who had grown from the same brain?*

The studio was gone. He was leaning on a small table in a quick-eat while I stood just outside the entrance. I could hear the drumming of his fingers on the table.

Tell me a fact, then. Just one fact he couldn't possibly know.

He straightened up abruptly. *The mindsuckers damaged me. I remember only what he knows.*

I'd expected him to hide behind that, but I was unsure what to do next. Arguing with the delusion was only going to strengthen its sense of presence. Even acknowledging it was giving it something to feed on. Confronting it was Gladney's job, not mine. I was going to have to get him down in the music with me.

The note passed and was replaced by a bedroom. Gladney lay crosswise on a bed with his arms folded behind his head. He was looking at me upside down.

I'm residue, he said happily. His reversed smile was grotesque. *I'm a myelin ghost. You can't get rid of me without physically damaging his brain.*

I hooked my feet under the bed and willed myself upward. His bizarre upside-down face rushed away from me as I grew through the ceiling of the phantom room, up into the emptiness to the limit of the note. The piano string swung across a sky made of the present Gladney's face. My abrupt appearance gave him a surge of alarm that nearly dislodged me.

Where were you?

You know. The piano string moved between us. I stretched out my arms. *Take my hand before that string comes back.*

No.

Why not? It's your music.

No!

From the corner of my eye, I saw the piano string return to view, slicing through space. *Please, Gladney. Don't let that string put another barrier between you and your own work.*

Panic at the idea of being cut off from his music made him grab my hands; half a moment later panic at the idea of meeting his delusion head-on made him sorry he'd done it.

We were pitching and bucking in the throes of his fear, but still the piano string approached. Shortly it would pass through my wrists and fragment my concentration.

I can't pull you in, Gladney. You have to come on your own.

I'm afraid!

Why? Say it!

I'm afraid because—

Say it!

He'll get me!

Who?

Gladney!

You are Gladney.

No!

Then who are you?

There was no answer. The piano string was almost on us.

Are you a composer?

His affirmation ducked him under the string just before it would have severed my hands. He stared after it with a horrified elation, and then we were rushing down into the music together in the momentum of his admission.

The delusional image of Gladney watched us descend. The real one made a soft landing on the bed beside it, still gripping my hands. Without thinking, he tried to pull me onto the bed between himself and the other.

The bedroom vanished. We were on an underground tube, the only three in the coach. I moved around behind Gladney, and he had to let go of me. As soon as he did, the delusional image vanished. Gladney was startled, but not half as much as I was. He moved forward with his hands out in front of him, feeling the air.

He's not here, Allie. Is he?

I didn't answer. I was still trying to figure out what had happened. Delusions didn't just go away that quickly.

Allie? He half-turned toward me, and I saw that his eyes were closed. He swung his arms back and forth awkwardly, fingers clutching at nothing. Either he was making use of a fairly sophisticated mental maneuver, a sort of sneaking up on his own blind side, or he was faking same to stay blinded to the situation. I couldn't tell which; his undertones showed only confusion.

Suddenly his hands seized on something invisible. The delusion snapped into existence again, caught in Gladney's grasp. The air around them crackled with sparks from Gladney's terror.

Allie! I can't let go!

We went from the tube to a raft in the middle of the ocean, bright sun beating down on the water. Gladney still had hold of the delusion. His eyes were open now. A shadow passed over us—a high-flying piano string.

High A-sharp, Gladney said automatically, identifying the note. *We're getting close to the end of the melody. What do I do with him then?*

You're asking me? It's yours. What do you do when music's over?

We were in the lower branches of a large tree, then back to the tube very briefly (*B-flat grace note,* Gladney said), in the bedroom, on a windy rooftop several thousand feet above the ground. Gladney was plunging us to the end of the song. The images began to blend into one another, flickering and flapping. Gladney and his delusion flashed on and off in a variety of positions, Gladney still holding on, as though they were wrestling or dancing. The music went from slow motion subsonic to recognizable melody. The background imagery faded away completely, leaving the two Gladneys in their dance/struggle. The delusion offered no resistance, but Gladney was too occupied to notice. The struggle became a tumbling, end over end over end over end. I saw Gladney's hospital room, the synthesizer, Gladney himself standing before it, staring it down as though it were an enemy. Dr. Jesl appeared briefly, carnelian eyes blind to the two figures tumbling past her through the entertainment center, where Gladney sat studying a newstape of the Gladney-that-had-been on the holo screen. The tumblers rolled on to the vision of a dimly remembered dream, that dream of Gladney, the old Gladney, lifting his head to the sight of three people, visible only from neck to thigh, rushing forward at him.

The dream-Gladney cried out, fell back, and vanished, and then the tumblers were beyond the end of the melody. But still they went on, and the music went on with them, the piano and clarinet finally making contact, playing together and opposite each other in complement.

After some measurable time, the tumbling began to slow. When the music stopped, there was only one figure, not two, that stopped with it. He drifted in emptiness, excited and drained all at once. That was enough, I decided. Before he could think of doing anything else, I cued another relaxation exercise and wrapped it around him. As soon as he was completely absorbed in mental finger-painting I broke the contact between us and withdrew.

It took a minute or so for his vitals to calm down. I changed the exercise from finger-painting to simple abstract visuals. He was overstimulated, in need of a passive mode. After his pulse went down below eighty, I disconnected him from the system and put his eyes back in.

A soon as he saw me, he broke into a sweat. "Don't try to talk," I told him, covering the connections and slipping them into the drawer in the largest component.

"I can talk."

"Sure. I just didn't want you to feel like you had to." He turned his face away while I dismantled the system. His breathing was extremely loud in the room. Rhythmic. I let him be. The inexperienced are often overcome by an intense feeling of embarrassment after mindplay, particularly pathosfinding. It takes some getting over.

"Listen," he said, after a bit, still not looking at me. "You don't know what it's like. What it *was* like." He rubbed his forehead tiredly. "I was almost him. I wanted him, and I didn't want him." He paused and I knew he was staring at the synthesizer. "If I'd been him, I would have been someone. I just came out of nowhere, out of his brain. But I'm not him. Now I'm a figment of my own imagination."

I opened my mouth to say something conciliatory but neutral when the image of the pearl necklace popped into my mind. *I have not always been as I am now.* And neither was anybody else. I wanted to tell him so. I wanted to tell him he'd get over that, too, that he wasn't the only person who'd ever met the stranger in himself. Granted, his experience had been more extreme, but it was pretty much the same. I could no more tell him something like that than I could map out his life for him.

"You can't have somebody else's past," I said as gently as I could. "And there's no such thing as a ghost, myelin or otherwise. It's always just you."

"I could buy memories. People do that." His face was hard. "They even buy whole minds, remember?"

"And it drives them mad, trying to be two people at once. Remember?"

That gave him pause. "God, I'm tired," he said after a moment.

"Take a nap. I'm just down the hall if you want to talk later."

"Allie—"

I waited while he tried to settle on what it was he wanted to say. The words never came. He waved one hand, dismissing me. I let myself out, wondering how long he was going to sulk. If we prize our illusions, we are even that much more jealous of our delusions because they're so patently untrue. I was sure, though, that in a few more sessions, he'd adjust to being exactly what he was, no more and no less, and he would accept his music as his music only, to make without the fear or the desire that it came from him at the behest of something beyond his control.

Dr. Jesl phoned me sometime later, rousing me from a doze. "Our boy has a supreme mad-on for you," she said. "Thing is, I can't tell just what it's all about. I don't think he knows, either." She sounded more amused than worried.

I was still too exhausted to explain about mindplay embarrassment compounded by the loss of a self-imposed handicap. "He'll get over it," I told her.

Which he did. And I was only a little bit spooked later on when he correctly distinguished all of the old Gladney's music as having been composed by him without anyone's identifying it for him. Great minds, I told myself, think alike.

Passing as a Flower in the City of the Dead
S. N. DYER

Sharon N. Farber is a Hugo Award–nominated US writer who also uses the pen name "S. N. Dyer" and is best known for stories written in the 1970s and 1980s. She has written in many different genres, publishing mystery fiction as well. Farber has also collaborated with several writers, including James Killus, David Stout, and Susanna Jacobson. Her birth date is unknown.

Her first published story, "The Great Dormitory Mystery," appeared in 1976 in the anthology *Sherlock Holmes Through Time and Space*, and her work has appeared frequently in *Asimov's Science Fiction Magazine*, including her most recent story, "My Cat" (2001). She also has written two story series, each with a female protagonist: Ann Atomic and Billy Jean. She has been a finalist four times for the Hugo Award, in the category of Best Fan Writer, with her most recent nomination in 1997. Little more is known about Farber.

"Passing as a Flower in the City of the Dead" (1984) is an excellent example of mideighties Humanist science fiction—and a forgotten gem from an underrated writer.

PASSING AS A FLOWER IN THE CITY OF THE DEAD

S. N. Dyer

Henri hated parties; he was striding through the cocktail crowd, his massive head down, shoulders back. Watching her husband, Madeline wanted to laugh. This was "the pacing lion of the landscape"? What would that sycophantic art critic call him if she could see him now, skeletal after months of untreated leukemia, bald as a newborn from total-body irradiation?

The stalking scarecrow, Madeline thought.

She lost sight of her husband as he pushed through into the house. Madeline put down her drink; it was adding to the steady-state nausea she'd felt from the aseptic food and from the sight of the colony ceiling far overhead. Her universe was a cylinder in space, the overhead view one of land and houses, while Earth and stars hid under her feet. Perhaps 180 degrees away another woman stood in another party and watched Madeline spin by. A treeless, grassless vista painted pastel blue.

"I'm Bob. How do you like Blues?" A man grinned at her. He had finely coiled gray hair, held a drink in each hand, and seemed more alive than anyone else at the party.

"It takes getting used to. . . ."

"Of course," he boomed, and Madeline noticed that his presence had cleared an even wider space. They were alone, haloed by emptiness like a colony of hemolytic streptococci on a blood agar plate.

"We're pariahs, you 'n' I," he said, setting down one empty paper cup, draping that hand about her shoulder, and steering her effortlessly to the refreshments table. "Moses parting the Red Sea," he whispered, and Madeline laughed as the crowd melted away about them. He picked up a decanter, nestled in an arrangement of silk flowers, and poured full a pottery mug.

"Drink this. It'll settle your stomach and curdle your brain," he commanded. "The amnestic waters of the river Styx across which the dead must pass." He looked about with exaggerated movements, then whispered sotto voce, "Don't tell anyone. I've had a classical education."

"You aren't afraid?" she asked.

"Afraid of what? Parsing verbs?"

She giggled. "No, of me. I'm a newcomer." She ran one hand through her crew-cut-length hair. "Some bacterium may have snuck in with me.

"I'm a very dangerous woman," she added in her best villainess voice.

Bob chortled. "Not too observant, are we? Look at me!"

Studying him, she realized why he had seemed so different, so alive. Of all those standing in the crowded patio, he alone lacked the pallor of the bloodless. He held his hand beside hers, allowing her to compare his rosy pink hue, the blue veins like ropes, with her own clear veins in cadaver flesh.

"None of that fluorocarbon-soup artificial blood for me," he said. "I'm the last of the red-blooded men. At least on Blues."

Madeline nodded. "Your immune system is intact. You can laugh in the face of any pathogen."

"Right." He grinned, downing his drink. "I'm going to feel awful in the morning—I've got all my blood. Red, white, blue, you name it."

Madeline contrasted him to the others, to

herself. A pale, bloodless lot. An O'Neill colony inhabited by those with leukemia, with autoimmune disease, with transplanted organs. They had all stood on the banks of the Styx, only to be saved by the killing of their every blood cell—the treacherous cells that multiplied erratically, or attacked their own organs, or fought the transplants. And the innocent blood cells had died as well, the cells that carried oxygen, fought invading microbes, stopped hemorrhages.

They were alive, locked in a hermetically sealed, sterile tin can rotating in space.

The man intruded on her thoughts. "Yes, I'm that fiend incarnate, that villain of stage and screen, the Outsider."

"But why . . ."

"Was I invited? Giselle works in my department. Even she isn't rude enough not to invite me. She just never thought I'd be rude enough to come." His grin widened. "I've seen you in the hospital. You're in the lab? Come see me. Respiratory." He put down his cup and left, swiveling at the gate to face the crowd. "I'm leaving. You can talk about me now," he yelled.

"Obnoxious, isn't he." Giselle was at Madeline's side, small and dainty, with brown hair to her waist. Hair was a status symbol on Blues. The longer the hair, the longer the head had been on Blues. The longer the survival from the terminal disease.

"Loud, but amusing."

"You don't have to work with him."

The elderly man beside Giselle snarled. "Earthies. They come in, work their stint, and leave, acting like they're so damn superior."

He gazed suspiciously at Madeline as if, she thought, he were smelling pseudomonas. Or smelling anything. She was a woman without colonizing bacteria—her sweat, her breath, even her feces were almost odorless.

He suspects, she thought, panicking. No, he could not suspect. She was as much the Outsider as Bob, but she had the protective discoloration of the bloodless.

Giselle clapped her hands. "Everybody!"

"Damn," the man said. "Must you go through with this?"

"Father, stop acting like it's indecent."

"You just like to shock people. It must be your genetics. It certainly wasn't your upbringing." He stormed into the house.

Giselle shrugged at Madeline. "Father's a bit traditional. . . . Everybody! May I have your attention—you too, you wastrel. . . ." The revelers paused in their various pursuits and looked to their hostess. Henri, studying the flower bed with its plastic nasturtiums, glowered at Madeline.

"During the party, many of you have met our newcomers, Henri and Madeline. Madeline, it happens, is an actual relative of mine. A blood relative."

The audience chuckled, to Madeline's bewilderment. Henri merely looked as if he were trapped in an ethnographic film.

"She was my genetic mother's second cousin on Earth. Let's welcome these newcomers to Blues."

The audience clapped politely, all the while scrutinizing the strangers like laboratory specimens. Then they returned to their interrupted pastimes. A young man with a braided beard began to flirt with Giselle. Madeline moved away, finding herself before the girl's adoptive father.

"You don't approve of me."

He answered vehemently. "You had some nerve calling, introducing yourself."

Madeline sighed. *It's true,* she thought. *Civilization diminishes proportionally to the distance from Paris.* She decided to try again, smiling ingratiatingly.

"Giselle seems to have grown into a beautiful young lady—she looks just like her mother. Before I emigrated, Giselle's mother begged me to find her, to see what sort of woman she'd become—"

"Her mother! The woman who bore her? What claim has she? Who spent six months in quarantine with her, risking their lives to care for her? We did. Who raised her, taught her? We did, Hilda and me. And the whole time we're getting her through the traumas of growing up, especially growing up in this place—the whole time she keeps getting letters from that earthside bitch."

Forcing down her anger, she replied, "It's not easy for those who stay behind either. Giselle's parents—"

"Hilda was her mother! I am her father!" He stopped, shook his head. "I'm sorry. You're new, you don't understand yet.

"To come to Blues is to die and be reborn. You get some awful disease—myeloma. You?"

She paused a moment. "Lupus."

"You say good-bye to your family, write your will, dispose of all your belongings. You're shot into space, to the quarantine station. Six months alone in tiny rooms, while radiation and chemicals kill every blood cell, every germ in your body. Then, when you're positively bug free—because without our immune systems the common cold could wipe out the colony—when you're safe, you enter Blues. Hairless, like a baby. Reincarnated into a new world."

He grabbed her left hand, holding it up. "You wore a ring for many years. Where is your husband now?"

She barely choked back her answer.

He nodded. "He stayed on Earth. Do you still write him? Don't. You can never return to Earth. Let go of the past. 'Until death do us part.' Blues is a city of the dead."

Madeline asked hesitantly, "And if my husband had come with me?"

"Come with you?" His face would have flushed livid, had he had any blood. "Fidoes. Faithful spouses following their loved ones into hell. Virtuous little toads. Don't let me near one. I'd show him a bit of hell."

"I don't understand. How can you hate someone so full of love for her husband—or wife—that she—they'd follow them here?"

He snarled and stalked away.

Giselle came up and put a hand on Madeline's shoulder. Her other hand was resting loosely on Henri's forearm. "God—what's Father yelling about this time?"

"Fidoes."

"Them again? Well, of course we all hate Fidoes."

"Why." Henri always stated his questions.

"Because they remind us of what we've lost. We're under life sentences, unable to see Earth or relatives. (Not that I, personally, have any memories of either.) But we're all unified in that respect. Then Fidoes come, like it's a big joke, play the self-righteous martyr for a few years, then return to Earth. Father says the only way to survive here is to sever all ties with your past."

Madeline said, "And that's why you don't write your mother?"

Giselle rolled her eyes at the mere thought.

"Don't judge. Annette is a lovely woman," Henri said.

Giselle pulled her hand away, regarding him with narrowed eyes. "How do you know? I thought you two met in quarantine."

Madeline said hastily, "We knew each other before, in art school." She felt her entire past slipping away, negated by words that blithely tossed out memories of marriage, career, friends, love—anything to avoid the truth. She was a Fido.

"Henri and I, meeting again. It was quite a coincidence."

"Quite," Giselle agreed.

Henri slept with the corner of his mouth twitching, making an occasional soft moan. Madeline lay propped up on one arm. Despite the months, he still seemed alien to her, her now bald and thin husband merging in her mind's eye with her grandfather. Even the venous catheter high on Henri's chest, closed except during the bimonthly infusion of artificial blood, reminded her of Grandpere's central-line venous access when his peripheral veins could no longer sustain an intravenous line.

Her grandfather had been only fifty-six when they diagnosed lymphoma, and he'd refused the standard treatment.

"Let them clean me out like a rat in a lab, replace my blood with cream, send me to outer space? Never. If I must die, I shall do so with my family around me."

He'd done well for a while, then gone downhill with a vengeance. And so to the special hospital in America, where he'd suffered through six-drug chemotherapy, radiation, interferon, debulking operations. Madeline remembered him wasting away, shriveling, his final days a contest to see which would kill him first—the disease or the treatment, the pain of the invading lymphocytes or the pain of the poisons that fought the cells.

She remembered Dr. Elbein, though she found it impossible to picture him without his entourage of fellows, residents, and medical students. He'd stood outside the door, unaware how his voice carried in the stillness. "This is a rare opportunity to relive medical history," he'd said, his voice unexpectedly gentle from a face that sharp and sardonic. "We called them 'hot leuks,' though lymphoma's really just 'leuk equivalent.' We'd drug them until the white count dropped into the basement, then hope it would crawl back up before they died of infection."

"Why 'hot leuks'?" a student asked.

"Because leukemics are hot. They look fine one minute and crump the next. Every night on call they'd spike and you'd have to do a complete fever workup—you kids can't imagine how much time that ate up. And if they didn't spike they'd need blood or platelets—and they never had any veins.

"You think it's awful with this guy, watching him puke and get septic and waste away?" He laughed. "We had wards full of them. Now we just shoot them into space, like atomic waste."

"Waste," Madeline whispered, and tried to sleep.

She dreamed of the hospital, air sweet with bouquets and bodily decay. Her husband seemed as pale as his sheets. Watching Henri sleep had always given her a feeling of security; she'd been safe from all harm with her lion beside her. Now she was watching him, anticipating every harsh breath, afraid that the next might not come.

He woke screaming.

"I'm here," she said.

He clutched her. "Don't leave me."

"Of course not."

"Never. I—I'm afraid. Don't ever leave me." And he began to cry.

She'd never seen him cry before. "I'll stay with you," she promised, and woke.

She rose, made coffee, and sat quietly in the studio. The coffee was bland, artificial—real coffee might stimulate too much gastric acid secretion, causing ulcers that would bleed. People without blood platelets cannot afford to bleed. Hence the boring food, the soft-edged furniture, the dull knives. Hence Madeline's inability to sculpt.

Internal bleeding—a bruise—stops by the action of clotting factors made in the liver. But cuts, scrapes, open wounds—bleeding from them stops due to platelets. And platelets come from the same stem cells which give rise to the white and red blood cells, the stem cells which had been diligently destroyed in almost all the inhabitants of Blues. The artificial clotting aids could not completely replace platelets. Thus there was no more chance of Madeline getting a sculpting tool than of her getting fresh fruit or a potted palm.

She surveyed the studio. It was so different from their studio back home, with the north window facing the garden. Here the one small window faced another building, pastel blue. Paintings in every stage of completion—here the canvases were either blank or turned to face the wall. Her sculptures on every shelf—here were only photographs of her statues, too heavy to bring from Earth.

"They don't understand your work," Henri had always said, "because they're fools."

She looked at the shelf of paints and her one attempt at sculpture since arrival, a clay sphere with little tendrils reaching out—a sun sending out plumes of gas, or a macrophage ready to engulf. It was covered in the fine powder that passed for dust on Blues.

She reached for it scornfully. Clay had no life, no soul, so unlike wood. Wood contained the sculpture already; she had only to find it and release it from its covering. But clay was like all of Blues, a bland mediocre world, as devoid of ugliness as it was of beauty. People, though—people were still the same. . . .

The sphere slipped from her fingers, pancaking on the floor.

Henri entered, rubbing at his scalp to push back the mane that no longer existed. "What . . ."

"Found art," she said. "It's an egg."

He adopted his nasal art-critic voice. "The egg, symbol of life and new beginnings." When Madeline failed to laugh at the imitation, he picked up a canvas, stared at it, turned it back to face the wall again, and began pacing.

Madeline sipped her coffee. "It was an awful party."

He paused, a strange smile on his face. "Your cousin doesn't believe we're living together. She says we don't act like lovers. She says we act like an old married couple." He laughed once, a staccato bark, and resumed pacing.

Madeline ran into Giselle in the line at the hospital cafeteria as the older woman tried to choose a meal. The plastic-looking food had many strikes against it. It was shipped from Earth fully processed. It was digestible by people lacking normal bowel flora and with their gastric acid secretion diminished by drugs. As if that were not enough, it was also hospital food.

Madeline made some polite comments about Giselle's party.

"How do you like Blues?"

"It's—different. Hard to adjust to. My job is, too. I'm a medical technician. My specialties

are bacteriology and hematology—not much demand for either. Now all I do is plate specimens; I haven't seen a single rod or coccus to reward my efforts."

"Thank God," Giselle said.

"Well, at least I'm working with culture." Giselle did not get the joke, so Madeline continued. "It's worse for Henri. He's a painter."

"An artist?" Giselle became enthusiastic. "Lord knows we need more art up here. What does he paint?"

"He began in landscapes. But"—she caught herself from saying "we"—"he had to live in cities, to lecture and teach and such. Have you heard of the microlandscape school? Henri was one of the founders. It's easy to find grandeur in the country, with the vistas of trees, mountains, sky. . . ." She was falling back into her standard explanation, culled almost directly from the exhibit pamphlets she'd helped write.

"Those are just concepts in textbooks," Giselle said. "Maybe . . . is it like Out-there? Space is huge and black and wonderful. It just keeps going, with stars like spots of fire. . . ." She pushed at the remnants of her sandwich, her mind somewhere else.

"The Group decided to paint city landscapes," Madeline continued dreamily. "A flower in the sidewalk, tree leaves against the sky . . . Beauty is ubiquitous in the country. The challenge is to find it in the city." Like searching for bacteria in the pus of a sterile abscess.

"Unfortunately, there's no sky here, no trees, no flowers. Henri is without inspiration. He can't paint."

Giselle's face lit up. "But there's beauty in Blues."

"Ah, you were raised here."

"No, it's there for everyone. The arc of a roof against a support strut, the glint of a house far overhead, the way the stars smear out underfoot in the observation deck . . ."

Madeline was thoughtful. "Do you think you could get someone else to see this beauty? Henri?"

"I can try."

. . .

They received a letter from Bertrand, a glorious collage of pictures and words that began, *"Mon cher Henri, ma belle Madeline,"* appellations that made Henri bristle.

"He's got something planned," Henri muttered. "While the cat's away the mice shall play."

Madeline put the letter on hold. "Bertrand's not so bad."

"The man's an upstart. The only thing that held him back was his inability to decide which he'd rather do—steal my school or seduce my wife."

Madeline shrugged, half smiling, and switched the letter back on. "The prices for your paintings have already skyrocketed, my dear Henri, to a height almost worthy of your present surroundings. Also, may I opine, to a degree undreamed of in your earthly days."

"The rodent."

"He's just trying to be poetic."

"Even the sculptures of your lovely wife are coveted and much sought after."

"Vultures," Henri growled.

A new picture came on. "Our latest exhibit. Marcel's *Flowers in the Crosswalk I.*" It was a good example of their school—austere brush work, unpretentious realism.

"Flowers in the Crosswalk II." Now the flowers were buffeted in the airstream of rushing traffic. There was a cartoonlike simplicity to the art. Henri sat rigid.

"Flowers in the Crosswalk III." The final item in the triptych blinked into being, the flowers transformed into metal, the trucks and motorbikes into elephants, typewriters, musical notes.

"Surrealism!" Henri bellowed, banging his fist onto the console. Paintings began to flash by rapidly, each sillier than the last, each more of a parody of the circle's previous work, of Henri's lifework.

Henri rose and left the room, his massive shoulders slumped. Madeline stopped the letter at the last of the art and slowly read the title.

"Dancing on My Grave Before I'm Even Dead."

Madeline had not seen much of Henri for the last few days. He set out early each morning, led by Giselle or one of her friends, returning each evening with an armful of charcoal roughs. The house began to fill with students, trying to convert their own crude sketches into full canvases. They painted into the night, falling asleep on the couch or rug, working and lying underfoot until Madeline would wake and send them to their own homes as she left for the lab.

While Henri had found beauty in a tree thrusting out of pavement, Madeline had found it in the microscope. She'd given up her own art studies—one of them had to bring home a salary—but the aesthetics of a Wright's-stained blood smear had eased her through the workaday world. The delicate lobulations of a PMN, no two cells alike. The frothy purple lacework of a platelet. The sweet blue of a lymphocyte's cytoplasm. Even when she'd gone to the lab to see the slide that spelled Henri's doom, even as she'd scanned field after field of leukemic myelocytes, she'd thought, *How can they be bad? They're too beautiful.*

"Why so quiet?"

She looked around. Bob, the stranger from the party, was leaning against an incubator. A stethoscope peeked out of one pocket of his very loud suit.

She put down her pipette. "You'll think I'm crazy. I was remembering the beauty of a good peripheral blood smear."

"Not crazy—just a little weird. One of my path teachers was artsy. Wanted to be an architect, became a pathologist instead. He always said, 'The worst cancer looks gorgeous in hematoxylin and eosin.' He'd show us a slide of, say, lung with its fine mesh of purple and pink, and he'd say, 'Go on, show me anything in art nouveau that can beat this.' Frankly, I didn't think it was so hot. Not that it kept me from getting the top grade in the class."

"No," Madeline said. "One does not need a sense of aesthetics to be successful."

"What's wrong," Henri demanded, putting down his brush. The studio was now full of paintings by Henri and his new pupils. Views of stars, of houses, of women lying in artificial flowers or standing in the metallic sheen of the oxygen equipment. Works in progress lay propped everywhere and hung on the walls, covering the photos of Madeline's sculptures. "You've been unhappy all evening."

"Don't you know what today is?"

"It's our anniversary. Well, we can't very well celebrate it, can we? They don't even know we're married."

"But we could—"

"Let's choose a new anniversary, Madeline, one appropriate to our life here. I know! We can have a party for the day when they told me I was dying." Laughing bitterly, he turned back to the canvas.

As Henri was becoming engrossed in his painting and his teaching, Madeline was making friends at work. They gossiped as she plated a seemingly infinite number of specimens from people, places, things in the never-ending war to keep the colony germ-free. She joined a chess club. She went to a party to bid a temporary farewell to a coworker who had won the adoption lottery and was going on leave to help her new three-year-old immunosuppressed son through the terrors of quarantine.

She occasionally met Giselle at lunch. They would begin by gossiping—had X sliced her finger on a broken window and bled to death by accident, or was it suicide or murder; did Y's newly adopted daughter have brain damage; would Z wed yet again?

But, perhaps because of her own lung damage from recurrent pneumonia as an infant, lunch with Giselle always ended up a bitter catalog of the disasters that walked into the Pul-monary Functions Lab—chronic lungers incapacitated by smoking, by radiation fibrosis, by bronchiectasis from infection.

After yet another description of yet another pulmonary cripple, Giselle changed her subject. "I got another letter from your cousin today."

"Annette? How is she?"

"I don't know. I just erase them as they come through the computer."

"Giselle! How can you!"

"That woman inundates me with her unwanted attention!"

"You can hardly call a few letters a year an inundation."

"She gave me up to Blues—why can't she give me up completely? I didn't ask to be born. I don't owe her—"

Madeline had had enough dramatics. "Calm down, Giselle. Don't you ever wonder about your family? You had an older brother. Antoine. The colds started at three months. Then pneumonia. Meningitis. Constant diarrhea. He didn't respond to immunoglobulin replacement. He died before his first birthday.

"The geneticists said there was only a one-in-four chance the next child would also have an immunodeficiency. Annette and Pierre wanted children, and they took the chance. They treated you as if you were made of jewels. Then at three months, when the maternal antibodies begin to disappear, you sneezed. . . .

"They didn't have a third child. Don't you see—allowing you to leave Earth, to live, was an act of love. Your mother loves you, Giselle, though she hasn't seen you for twenty years."

The girl stared into her coffee cup.

Madeline said softly, "Read the next letter you receive. Please."

"Well, hello, ladies."

Giselle groaned as Bob sat down. "Lucky women, lunching with the last of the red-blooded men. Who could ask for more?"

Giselle rose. "I have to get back to work."

Bob waited until she was gone. "At last. We're alone." The other diners within range of his booming voice turned in astonishment.

Madeline stifled a giggle. "At last."

"I brought you a gift." He handed her a slide, folded in lens paper. Madeline unwrapped it, rotating it into the light.

"Notice the perfect feather edge," Bob said. "Haven't done a smear in twenty years, but I haven't lost my touch. Nothing's beyond the last of the red-blooded men."

"But what—"

"Blood. My own, of course, with just the right amount of Wright's stain. A nostalgic voyage to a world where people have hot, pulsing red stuff in their arteries."

Smiling, she pocketed the slide. "Thank you, Bob. As I revel in each red cell, each delightful leukocyte, each marvelous monocyte, I'll think of you."

He shuddered. "If you find anything strange on the diff—do me a favor. Don't tell me."

The great and near great of Blues were there. Administrators, store owners, journalists. They looked at the paintings, drank the bland wine, argued politics.

"We're nothing but a company store, existing on Earth's sufferance."

"Look, they won't run something this expensive if it isn't worth their while. Why shouldn't we tend the satellites and factories. We aren't invalids. . . ."

Madeline moved along making sure everyone had a glass of wine, a piece of cheese. She felt almost at home. She'd had years of practice running art shows.

A man grabbed her arm as she passed. "Do you play cello?"

"Sorry."

"Damn. We've almost got an entire orchestra. All we need is another cellist."

She bit back the temptation to suggest he hire one. She knew how the few hired personnel from Earth were ostracized, despised. Instead, she smiled devilishly. "Sooner or later some cellist down there will need a kidney transplant. You just have to be patient."

As she wandered, she looked at the paintings—a few starscapes, but mostly scenes of the station itself. Henri's contributions easily stood out, with their mastery of perspective, their confident brush strokes. The students' contributions were remarkable only for their odd viewpoints. The school had drawn from Giselle's peers, Earth children uprooted by disease and raised on Blues. One student—the boy with the braided beard—showed promise. His paintings were a tangle of intersecting levels that gave Madeline vertigo, the same feeling she got whenever she looked above her at the other side of the colony.

She paused before a final picture, a sentimental still life of silken flowers. Giselle's. It was the most amateurish of all, and Madeline resented its presence.

She heard Giselle's laughter. The girl was entertaining some journalist, translating Henri's dour phrases into an artistic manifesto. That had always been Madeline's job back home. But here—Madeline was deluding herself. If anyone was the hostess of the art show, it was Giselle.

One of the daring young artists accepted a refill of his glass, then pointed to Giselle. "Isn't she grand tonight?"

"She appears to be in her element." She noticed Giselle's father buttonholing people and forcing them to confront his daughter's still life.

"I was an artist," she said.

"You?"

The boy obviously thought of her as a drudge who existed only to support Henri. *The juvenile form of the PMN is called a stab,* Madeline thought. *How appropriate.*

"Me. I gave up my career to support—my husband. But I still sculpted, even showed."

"Sculpture. You mean, pottery and plastic and stuff?"

"Wood. I miss it. The feel of a good knife, the search for the right pattern in the grain . . ."

"Well, miss away," he said. "I'd like to see you find a knife on Blues. They'd have a fit."

"Would they?" She watched him move

deeper into the room of harsh design but rounded edges, an environment to minimize trauma.

"Ah, for a knife as sharp as a child's tongue."

Hearing applause, Madeline watched the young artist with the braided beard present Giselle with a bouquet. His ringlets of hair reminded her of a cluster of staphylococci. She shook her head and looked away, turning back at the shriek.

Giselle had dropped the plastic flowers and was clutching her hand. Clear liquid, like viscous water, ran from her hand and onto the floor.

"Oh no I'm sorry I'm sorry, I don't know how . . . ," the man babbled. The others stood, horrified. Giselle's father began to berate the young man. "You've killed her," he screamed.

Madeline felt like a character out of *Alice in Wonderland*. She pushed through the crowd to Giselle, grabbing her hand, feeling the slippery fluid. She raised Giselle's hand high, holding pressure over the artery in the upper arm.

Giselle was wide-eyed and shaking. She would have been pale were she not already the sickly yellow of the bloodless. "It's going to be all right," Madeline said, and from the corner of her eye noticed Henri.

He was as wide-eyed as Giselle. He stared at the younger woman, looking almost ready to faint.

Madeline's heart missed a beat.

"Call an ambulance," she said.

"It's ludicrous; everyone is overreacting. You'd think she was Camille, coughing out her lungs. Not a cut finger." Madeline gazed in the window of the emergency room cubicle. Giselle had a liter of artificial blood hung in her central line. Henri clutched her free hand as a doctor sutured up the other.

Bob, who had heard the commotion and come to the emergency room to offer advice, said, "People bleed to death frequently here. Well, 'bleed' isn't the best description."

"As good as 'blood relative,'" Madeline said.

"Who's the wimp cutting off her circulation?"

"The man I live with." So easily was Henri relegated to a bloodless description.

"Oh." Bob put an arm about Madeline's shoulder, ushered her upstairs to his office, and materialized two cups of coffee. They nursed the coffee in silence. She stared at the decorations on the wall, the diplomas and certificates, the framed portraits. In one, a dozen men and women in formal attire faced the camera; Bob wore blue jeans. In another, he was the one beard in a sea of clean-shaven faces.

Bob said finally, "My place is pretty nice. Lots of posters of trees and all. The bed is big, too."

She said, "Thanks. I'll keep it in mind."

"No commitments or anything. I can't get caught; it would leave too many broken hearts from Boise to Mars. Just temporary quarters, you know?"

She nodded. "We wouldn't want to upset your girlfriends."

"Right. God, I love the French. You understand things so well."

"You're a good man, Bob."

"Hey, what do you expect from the last of the red-blooded men? Are you going to fight for him?"

"I'm not sure yet."

"Then keep this in mind about Giselle. She has a combined immunodeficiency."

"So?"

"So that means that only her lymphocytes were useless. She still had stem cells that became perfectly good red cells and platelets and polys."

Madeline put down her coffee. "You mean—"

"Yeah. Giselle grew up as rosy and healthy as me. She looked like an Outsider, an Earthie. She took elective chemo, wiped out her stem cells voluntarily. Just to look 'normal.'"

Standing, he kissed Madeline's hand. "Be careful. Giselle is a very determined young lady."

. . .

Henri haunted the hospital, sleeping in the lounge, pacing catlike through the halls, until Giselle went home. Then he moved to the couch in his studio. Whenever Madeline passed the open door he would jump before a canvas, holding the brush poised as if in decision. But the painting never progressed.

And finally, one morning when Madeline went in to work, her friends did not speak to her. When she sat down to lunch, her neighbors moved to another table. Returning to the lab, she found her white coat shredded, her locker opened, and its contents smashed.

"Why are you doing this?" she screamed. The others kept to their tasks, plating samples, staring into microscopes. She grabbed a coworker and spun him around. "Why!"

"Fido," he said, wrenching loose. "Bow wow." The others in the lab took up the barking call.

She fled to the transport, running the final quarter kilometer home. The front door was unlocked, Henri's studio vacant. The painting had progressed since morning.

She went to the bedroom and flung open the door. Henri looked at her guiltily. Giselle sat up, long hair ebony against her yellow-ivory skin, and smiled. "Woof woof."

"You told them!"

"It was your cousin's latest letter. I'm glad you persuaded me to read it. She hoped we'd be good friends, you and I, and talked about your long, idyllic marriage to a famous painter. Henri confirmed it. Can't keep a secret, can you, my angel?" She leaned over and kissed him, then looked back at Madeline. Henri's expression was as blank as unsculpted marble.

"You would stoop so low . . ."

Giselle said, "You have no rights here. Outsider."

"Henri!"

He didn't answer.

"Henri—you as well? All right, she's young and pretty and amusing, but, Henri, it's empty glamour. It's the sparkle of a castle in a fishbowl."

He spoke at last. "They have your marrow frozen in the lab. You can return to Earth. I—I'm the fish; I can't leave the fishbowl. So I'll settle for the castle."

She fled.

She clung to the spoke, in the still center without gravity. Near her a father and daughter played with fighting kites. She could see the entirety of the O'Neill module below her, curving up and above her. With ponds, forests, meadows, it might have been beautiful. Instead it was all shiny metal and muted pastels.

"Get me," the father urged. "That's it." And they giggled.

Madeline remembered the oncologist, a large-boned woman with eyes that crinkled when she smiled. She had not been smiling then. "Don't do it," she'd said.

"Henri's afraid to go alone."

"I'm begging you—stay on Earth."

"He's my husband."

The doctor had shrugged. "All right; you won't be the first. But you'll do it our way. You'll need a cover story to fit in—lupus. We haven't used that before. We'll say your mother died from SLE. When you developed it you decided to emigrate early, before the steroid side effects. You'll undergo the same treatments your husband does—we'll kill every blood cell in your body. But there'll be one difference. We'll keep some of your marrow, for when you change your mind and decide to come home. It will be in the freezer, waiting for you."

"Then it will wait forever."

"Forever," Madeline repeated now. She could push off from the tower, glide slowly to her doom. And when she landed—there would be no telltale red spot on the pavement.

She looked down at the colony, people visible only as abstractions. She'd thought of it as a colony, like a colony of bacteria growing on an artificial medium, but from this height it seemed more like a body. A cylinder full of life, in pieces so small the individual components were meaningless. And herself? The Outsider. The infective particle.

The people without individual immune systems had formed a larger, more potent immune system to reject her. What could she do? Stay, like Bob, and become an abscess walled off by hate? Or let them win. The short flight downward . . .

The body cannot tolerate an invader. One or the other must die.

She left everything for Henri and Giselle, taking only the old brandy—Napoleon fleeing the winter. She knocked and entered, carrying the bottle. Bob, wearing only a pair of jeans, stood staring into a hologram of a redwood forest.

"For you," she said, and put down the bottle.

He spoke to the wall. "A going-away present?"

She took one step forward, then stopped. "Bob, come with me. Choose life. Why stay and be destroyed?"

Laughing, he turned to face her. She saw the large, hasty scar of an emergency laparotomy bisecting his abdomen.

He grinned. "Drunk driver. My spleen looked like hamburger."

"After the splenectomy—"

"Yeah. Recurrent pneumococcal infections."

"Antibiotics—"

He cut her off. "I'm allergic to sulfa and the beta-lactams. The others were too toxic for long-term prophylaxis."

"Then—you're immunocompromised; Earth would kill you. You belong on Blues."

He laughed again. "Belong? I'm the last of the red-blooded men. I never belong."

The art show was the expected babble of voices, clink of glasses. She left the paintings and let the crowd drift her toward the sculptures in the center. She paused before the crenulated sphere engulfing the small rod, both carved out of heart of cedar. She'd become very fond of hues of red.

A ruddy-faced young man was studying the piece carefully. "Looks real symbolic," he said.

"It's a macrophage, phagocytosing a salmonella."

The man chuckled. "Come on. It's obviously some sort of Jungian allegory about the female swallowing the male or something. I'm a photographer; I can't understand anything more symbolic than a traffic sign. What do you do?"

"I sculpt," she said, and pointed to her name on the stand.

He barely blushed, then examined her name and looked pointedly at her unadorned fingers.

"Weren't you married?"

She shrugged. "I'm a widow. More wine?"

New Rose Hotel

WILLIAM GIBSON

William Gibson (1948–) is a highly influential US-Canadian science fiction novelist and essayist who has been called the "noir prophet" of cyberpunk; critics credit Gibson with creating the term *cyberspace* in his 1982 story "Burning Chrome," and *The Guardian* has called him "probably the most important novelist of the past two decades." His first novel, *Neuromancer* (1984), had a revolutionary effect on science fiction, expanding upon the themes in his short stories. The first line of *Neuromancer*—"The sky above the port was the color of television, turned to a dead channel"— has become as memorable as Thomas Pynchon's "A screaming comes across the sky" from *Gravity's Rainbow* (1973). Gibson's more recent bestselling novels—*Pattern Recognition* (2003), *Spook Country* (2007), *Zero History* (2010), and *The Peripheral* (2014)—are set in a version of our reality, although *The Peripheral* in particular has speculative elements. The later novels tend to tackle the inequities of the information age in the context of capitalism and computer technology.

Gibson's father died when he was six, his mother when he was eighteen. His father worked in middle management for a construction company in South Carolina. "They'd built some of the Oak Ridge atomic facilities, and paranoic legends of 'security' at Oak Ridge were part of our family culture," Gibson wrote in his short biographical essay "Since 1948." The world Gibson grew up in was one "of early television, a new Oldsmobile with crazy rocket-ship styling, toys with science fiction themes."

Later, Gibson stumbled upon "a writer named Burroughs—not Edgar Rice but William S." Gibson read Kerouac and Ginsberg soon thereafter, making him, as he puts it, "Patient Zero of what would later become the counterculture."

Gibson's short fiction is quite diverse and includes work that could be classified as horror or fantasy or cross-genre. "New Rose Hotel," which appeared in *Omni* in 1984, is classic cyberpunk, and in many ways a more interesting story than the iconic "Burning Chrome."

NEW ROSE HOTEL

William Gibson

Seven rented nights in this coffin, Sandii. New Rose Hotel. How I want you now. Sometimes I hit you. Replay it so slow and sweet and mean, I can almost feel it. Sometimes I take your little automatic out of my bag, run my thumb down smooth, cheap chrome. Chinese .22, its bore no wider than the dilated pupils of your vanished eyes.

Fox is dead now, Sandii.

Fox told me to forget you.

I remember Fox leaning against the padded bar in the dark lounge of some Singapore hotel, Bencoolen Street, his hands describing different spheres of influence, internal rivalries, the arc of a particular career, a point of weakness he had discovered in the armor of some think tank. Fox was point man in the skull wars, a middleman for corporate crossovers. He was a soldier in the secret skirmishes of the zaibatsus, the multinational corporations that control entire economies.

I see Fox grinning, talking fast, dismissing my ventures into intercorporate espionage with a shake of his head. The Edge, he said, have to find that Edge. He made you bear the capital E. The Edge was Fox's grail, that essential fraction of sheer human talent, nontransferable, locked in the skulls of the world's hottest research scientists.

You can't put Edge down on paper, Fox said, can't punch Edge into a diskette.

The money was in corporate defectors.

Fox was smooth, the severity of his dark French suits offset by a boyish forelock that wouldn't stay in place. I never liked the way the effect was ruined when he stepped back from the bar, his left shoulder skewed at an angle no Paris tailor could conceal. Someone had run him over with a taxi in Berne, and nobody quite knew how to put him together again.

I guess I went with him because he said he was after that Edge.

And somewhere out there, on our way to find the Edge, I found you, Sandii.

The New Rose Hotel is a coffin rack on the ragged fringes of Narita International. Plastic capsules a meter high and three long, stacked like surplus Godzilla teeth in a concrete lot off the main road to the airport. Each capsule has a television mounted flush with the ceiling. I spend whole days watching Japanese game shows and old movies. Sometimes I have your gun in my hand.

Sometimes I can hear the jets, laced into holding patterns over Narita. I close my eyes and imagine the sharp, white contrails fading, losing definition.

You walked into a bar in Yokohama, the first time I saw you. Eurasian, half gaijin, long-hipped and fluid in a Chinese knockoff of some Tokyo designer's original. Dark European eyes, Asian cheekbones. I remember you dumping your purse out on the bed, later, in some hotel room, pawing through your makeup. A crumpled wad of new yen, dilapidated address book held together with rubber bands, a Mitsubishi bank chip, Japanese passport with a gold chrysanthemum stamped on the cover, and the Chinese .22.

You told me your story. Your father had been an executive in Tokyo, but now he was disgraced, disowned, cast down by Hosaka, the biggest zaibatsu of all. That night your mother was Dutch, and I listened as you spun out those summers in Amsterdam for me, the pigeons in Dam Square like a soft, brown carpet.

I never asked what your father might have done to earn his disgrace. I watched you dress; watched the swing of your dark, straight hair, how it cut the air.

Now Hosaka hunts me.

The coffins of New Rose are racked in recycled scaffolding, steel pipes under bright enamel. Paint flakes away when I climb the ladder, falls with each step as I follow the catwalk. My left hand counts off the coffin hatches, their multilingual decals warning of fines levied for the loss of a key.

I look up as the jets rise out of Narita, passage home, distant now as any moon.

Fox was quick to see how we could use you, but not sharp enough to credit you with ambition. But then he never lay all night with you on the beach at Kamakura, never listened to your nightmares, never heard an entire imagined childhood shift under those stars, shift and roll over, your child's mouth opening to reveal some fresh past, and always the one, you swore, that was really and finally the truth.

I didn't care, holding your hips while the sand cooled against your skin.

Once you left me, ran back to that beach saying you'd forgotten our key. I found it in the door and went after you, to find you ankle-deep in surf, your smooth back rigid, trembling; your eyes faraway. You—couldn't talk. Shivering. Gone. Shaking for different futures and better pasts.

Sandii, you left me here.

You left me all your things.

This gun. Your makeup, all the shadows and blushes capped in plastic. Your Cray microcomputer, a gift from Fox, with a shopping list you entered. Sometimes I play that back, watching each item cross the little silver screen.

A freezer. A fermenter. An incubator. An electrophoresis system with integrated agarose cell and transilluminator. A tissue embedder. A high-performance liquid chromatograph. A flow cytometer. A spectrophotometer. Four

gross of borosilicate scintillation vials. A microcentrifuge. And one DNA synthesizer, with inbuilt computer. Plus software.

Expensive, Sandii, but then Hosaka was footing our bills. Later you made them pay even more, but you were already gone.

Hiroshi drew up that list for you. In bed, probably. Hiroshi Yomiuri. Maas Biolabs GmbH had him. Hosaka wanted him.

He was hot. Edge and lots of it. Fox followed genetic engineers the way a fan follows players in a favorite game. Fox wanted Hiroshi so bad he could taste it.

He'd sent me up to Frankfurt three times before you turned up, just to have a look-see at Hiroshi. Not to make a pass or even to give him a wink and a nod. Just to watch.

Hiroshi showed all the signs of having settled in. He'd found a German girl with a taste for conservative loden and riding boots polished the shade of a fresh chestnut. He'd bought a renovated town house on just the right square. He'd taken up fencing and given up kendo.

And everywhere the Maas security teams, smooth and heavy, a rich, clear syrup of surveillance. I came back and told Fox we'd never touch him.

You touched him for us, Sandii. You touched him just right.

Our Hosaka contacts were like specialized cells protecting the parent organism. We were mutagens, Fox and I, dubious agents adrift on the dark side of the intercorporate sea.

When we had you in place in Vienna, we offered them Hiroshi. They didn't even blink. Dead calm in an LA hotel room. They said they had to think about it.

Fox spoke the name of Hosaka's primary competitor in the gene game, let it fall out naked, broke the protocol forbidding the use of proper names.

They had to think about it, they said.

Fox gave them three days.

I took you to Barcelona a week before I took you to Vienna. I remember you with your hair tucked back into a gray beret, your high

Mongol cheekbones reflected in the windows of ancient shops. Strolling down the Ramblas to the Phoenician harbor, past the glass-roofed Mercado selling oranges out of Africa.

The old Ritz, warm in our room, dark, with all the soft weight of Europe pulled over us like a quilt. I could enter you in your sleep. You were always ready. Seeing your lips in a soft, round O of surprise, your face about to sink into the thick, white pillow—archaic linen of the Ritz. Inside you I imagined all the neon, the crowds surging around Shinjuku Station, wired electric night. You moved that way, rhythm of a new age, dreamy and far from any nation's soil.

When we flew to Vienna, I installed you in Hiroshi's wife's favorite hotel. Quiet, solid, the lobby tiled like a marble chessboard, with brass elevators smelling of lemon oil and small cigars. It was easy to imagine her there, the highlights on her riding boots reflected in polished marble, but we knew she wouldn't be coming along, not this trip.

She was off to some Rhineland spa, and Hiroshi was in Vienna for a conference. When Maas security flowed in to scan the hotel, you were out of sight.

Hiroshi arrived an hour later, alone.

Imagine an alien, Fox once said, who's come here to identify the planet's dominant form of intelligence. The alien has a look, then chooses. What do you think he picks? I probably shrugged.

The zaibatsus, Fox said, the multinationals. The blood of a zaibatsu is information, not people. The structure is independent of the individual lives that comprise it. Corporation as life-form.

Not the Edge lecture again, I said.

Maas isn't like that, he said, ignoring me.

Maas was small, fast, ruthless. An atavism. Maas was all Edge.

I remember Fox talking about the nature of Hiroshi's Edge. Radioactive nucleuses, monoclonal antibodies, something to do with the linkage of proteins, nucleotides . . . Hot, Fox called them, hot proteins. High-speed links. He said Hiroshi was a freak, the kind who shatters paradigms, inverts a whole field of science, brings on the violent revision of an entire body of knowledge. Basic patents, he said, his throat tight with the sheer wealth of it, with the high, thin smell of tax-free millions that clung to those two words.

Hosaka wanted Hiroshi, but his Edge was radical enough to worry them. They wanted him to work in isolation.

I went to Marrakech, to the old city, the Medina. I found a heroin lab that had been converted to the extraction of pheromones. I bought it, with Hosaka's money.

I walked the marketplace at Djemaa-el-Fna with a sweating Portuguese businessman, discussing fluorescent lighting and the installation of ventilated specimen cages. Beyond the city walls, the high Atlas. Djemaa-el-Fna was thick with jugglers, dancers, storytellers, small boys turning lathes with their feet, legless beggars with wooden bowls under animated holograms advertising French software.

We strolled past bales of raw wool and plastic tubs of Chinese microchips. I hinted that my employers planned to manufacture synthetic beta-endorphin. Always try to give them something they understand.

Sandii, I remember you in Harajuku, sometimes. Close my eyes in this coffin and I can see you there—all the glitter, the crystal maze of the boutiques, the smell of new clothes. I see your cheekbones ride past chrome racks of Paris leathers. Sometimes I hold your hand.

We thought we'd found you, Sandii, but really you'd found us. Now I know you were looking for us, or for someone like us. Fox was delighted, grinning over our find: such a pretty new tool, bright as any scalpel. Just the thing to help us sever a stubborn Edge, like Hiroshi's, from the jealous parent-body of Maas Biolabs.

You must have been searching a long time, looking for a way out, all those nights down Shinjuku. Nights you carefully cut from the scattered deck of your past.

My own past had gone down years before,

lost with all hands, no trace. I understood Fox's late-night habit of emptying his wallet, shuffling through his identification. He'd lay the pieces out in different patterns, rearrange them, wait for a picture to form. I knew what he was looking for. You did the same thing with your childhoods.

In New Rose, tonight, I choose from your deck of pasts.

I choose the original version, the famous Yokohama hotel room text, recited to me that first night in bed. I choose the disgraced father, Hosaka executive. Hosaka. How perfect. And the Dutch mother, the summers in Amsterdam, the soft blanket of pigeons in the Dam Square afternoon.

I came in out of the heat of Marrakech into Hilton air-conditioning. Wet shirt clinging cold to the small of my back while I read the message you'd relayed through Fox. You were in all the way; Hiroshi would leave his wife. It wasn't difficult for you to communicate with us, even through the clear, tight film of Maas security; you'd shown Hiroshi the perfect little place for coffee and *kipferl*. Your favorite waiter was white-haired, kindly, walked with a limp, and worked for us. You left your messages under the linen napkin.

All day today I watched a small helicopter cut a tight grid above this country of mine, the land of my exile, the New Rose Hotel. Watched from my hatch as its patient shadow crossed the grease-stained concrete. Close. Very close.

I left Marrakech for Berlin. I met with a Welshman in a bar and began to arrange for Hiroshi's disappearance.

It would be a complicated business, intricate as the brass gears and sliding mirrors of Victorian stage magic, but the desired effect was simple enough. Hiroshi would step behind a hydrogen-cell Mercedes and vanish. The dozen Maas agents who followed him constantly would swarm around the van like ants; the Maas security apparatus would harden around his point of departure like epoxy.

They know how to do business promptly in Berlin. I was even able to arrange a last night with you. I kept it secret from Fox; he might not have approved. Now I've forgotten the town's name. I knew it for an hour on the autobahn, under a gray Rhenish sky, and forgot it in your arms.

The rain began, sometime toward morning. Our room had a single window, high and narrow, where I stood and watched the rain fur the river with silver needles. Sound of your breathing. The river flowed beneath low, stone arches. The street was empty. Europe was a dead museum.

I'd already booked your flight to Marrakech, out of Orly, under your newest name. You'd be on your way when I pulled the final string and dropped Hiroshi out of sight.

You'd left your purse on the dark old bureau. While you slept I went through your things, removed anything that might clash with the new cover I'd bought for you in Berlin. I took the Chinese .22, your microcomputer, and your bank chip. I took a new passport, Dutch, from my bag, a Swiss bank chip in the same name, and tucked them into your purse.

My hand brushed something flat, I drew it out, held the thing, a diskette. No labels.

It lay there in the palm of my hand, all that death. Latent, coded, waiting.

I stood there and watched you breathe, watched your breasts rise and fall. Saw your lips slightly parted, and in the jut and fullness of your lower lip, the faintest suggestion of bruising.

I put the diskette back into your purse. When I lay down beside you, you rolled against me, waking, on your breath all the electric night of a new Asia, the future rising in you like a bright fluid, washing me of everything but the moment. That was your magic, that you lived outside of history, all now.

And you knew how to take me there.

For the very last time, you took me.

While I was shaving, I heard you empty your makeup into my bag. I'm Dutch now, you said, I'll want a new look.

Dr. Hiroshi Yomiuri went missing in Vienna, in a quiet street off Singerstrasse, two blocks from his wife's favorite hotel. On a clear afternoon in October, in the presence of a dozen expert witnesses, Dr. Yomiuri vanished.

He stepped through a looking glass. Somewhere, offstage, the oiled play of Victorian clockwork.

I sat in a hotel room in Geneva and took the Welshman's call. It was done, Hiroshi down my rabbit hole and headed for Marrakech. I poured myself a drink and thought about your legs.

Fox and I met in Narita a day later, in a sushi bar in the JAL terminal. He'd just stepped off an Air Maroc jet, exhausted and triumphant.

Loves it there, he said, meaning Hiroshi. Loves her, he said, meaning you.

I smiled. You'd promised to meet me in Shinjuku in a month.

Your cheap little gun in the New Rose Hotel. The chrome is starting to peel. The machining is clumsy, blurry Chinese stamped into rough steel. The grips are red plastic, molded with a dragon on either side. Like a child's toy.

Fox ate sushi in the JAL terminal, high on what we'd done. The shoulder had been giving him trouble, but he said he didn't care. Money now for better doctors. Money now for everything.

Somehow it didn't seem very important to me, the money we'd gotten from Hosaka. Not that I doubted our new wealth, but that last night with you had left me convinced that it all came to us naturally, in the new order of things, as a function of who and what we were.

Poor Fox. With his blue oxford shirts crisper than ever, his Paris suits darker and richer. Sitting there in JAL, dabbing sushi into a little rectangular tray of green horseradish, he had less than a week to live.

Dark now, and the coffin racks of New Rose are lit all night by floodlights, high on painted metal masts. Nothing here seems to serve its original purpose. Everything is surplus, recycled, even the coffins. Forty years ago these plastic capsules were stacked in Tokyo or Yokohama, a modern convenience for traveling businessmen. Maybe your father slept in one. When the scaffolding was new, it rose around the shell of some mirrored tower on the Ginza, swarmed over by crews of builders.

The breeze tonight brings the rattle of a pachinko parlor, the smell of stewed vegetables from the pushcarts across the road.

I spread crab-flavored krill paste on orange rice crackers. I can hear the planes.

Those last few days in Tokyo, Fox and I had adjoining suites on the fifty-third floor of the Hyatt. No contact with Hosaka. They paid us, then erased us from official corporate memory.

But Fox couldn't let go. Hiroshi was his baby, his pet project. He'd developed a proprietary, almost fatherly, interest in Hiroshi. He loved him for his Edge. So Fox had me keep in touch with my Portuguese businessman in the Medina, who was willing to keep a very partial eye on Hiroshi's lab for us.

When he phoned, he'd phone from a stall in Djemaa-el-Fna, with a background of wailing vendors and Atlas panpipes. Someone was moving security into Marrakech, he told us. Fox nodded. Hosaka.

After less than a dozen calls, I saw the change in Fox, a tension, a look of abstraction. I'd find him at the window, staring down fifty-three floors into the imperial gardens, lost in something he wouldn't talk about.

Ask him for a more detailed description, he said, after one particular call. He thought a man our contact had seen entering Hiroshi's lab might be Moenner, Hosaka's leading gene man.

That was Moenner, he said, after the next call. Another call and he thought he'd identified Chedanne, who headed Hosaka's protein team. Neither had been seen outside the corporate arcology in over two years.

By then it was obvious that Hosaka's leading researchers were pooling quietly in the Medina, the black executive Lears whispering into the Marrakech airport on carbon-fiber wings. Fox shook his head. He was a professional, a specialist, and he saw the sudden accumulation of all that prime Hosaka Edge in the Medina as a drastic failure in the zaibatsu's tradecraft.

Christ, he said, pouring himself a Black Label, they've got their whole bio section in there right now. One bomb. He shook his head. One grenade in the right place at the right time . . .

I reminded him of the saturation techniques Hosaka security was obviously employing. Hosaka had lines to the heart of the Diet, and their massive infiltration of agents into Marrakech could only be taking place with the knowledge and cooperation of the Moroccan government.

Hang it up, I said. It's over. You've sold them Hiroshi. Now forget him.

I know what it is, he said. I know. I saw it once before.

He said that there was a certain wild factor in lab work. The edge of Edge, he called it. When a researcher develops a breakthrough, others sometimes find it impossible to duplicate the first researcher's results. This was even more likely with Hiroshi, whose work went against the conceptual grain of his field. The answer, often, was to fly the breakthrough boy from lab to corporate lab for a ritual laying on of hands. A few pointless adjustments in the equipment, and the process would work. Crazy thing, he said, nobody knows why it works that way, but it does. He grinned.

But they're taking a chance, he said. Bastards told us they wanted to isolate Hiroshi, keep him away from their central research thrust. Balls. Bet your ass there's some kind of power struggle going on in Hosaka research. Somebody big's flying his favorites in and rubbing them all over Hiroshi for luck. When Hiroshi shoots the legs out from under genetic engineering, the Medina crowd's going to be ready.

He drank his scotch and shrugged.

Go to bed, he said. You're right, it's over. I did go to bed, but the phone woke me. Marrakech again, the white static of a satellite link, a rush of frightened Portuguese.

Hosaka didn't freeze our credit, they caused it to evaporate. Fairy gold. One minute we were millionaires in the world's hardest currency, and the next we were paupers. I woke Fox.

Sandii, he said. She sold out. Maas security turned her in Vienna. Sweet Jesus.

I watched him slit his battered suitcase apart with a Swiss Army knife. He had three gold bars glued in there with contact cement. Soft plates, each one proofed and stamped by the treasury of some extinct African government.

I should've seen it, he said, his voice flat.

I said no. I think I said your name.

Forget her, he said. Hosaka wants us dead. They'll assume we crossed them. Get on the phone and check our credit.

Our credit was gone. They denied that either of us had ever had an account.

Haul ass, Fox said.

We ran. Out a service door, into Tokyo traffic, and down into Shinjuku. That was when I understood for the first time the real extent of Hosaka's reach.

Every door was closed. People we'd done business with for two years saw us coming, and I'd see steel shutters slam behind their eyes. We'd get out before they had a chance to reach for the phone. The surface tension of the underworld had been tripled, and everywhere we'd meet that same taut membrane and be thrown back. No chance to sink, to get out of sight.

Hosaka let us run for most of that first day. Then they sent someone to break Fox's back a second time.

I didn't see them do it, but I saw him fall. We were in a Ginza department store an hour before closing, and I saw his arc off that polished mezzanine, down into all the wares of the new Asia.

They missed me somehow, and I just kept running. Fox took the gold with him, but I had a hundred new yen in my pocket. I ran. All the way to the New Rose Hotel.

Now it's time.

Come with me, Sandii. Hear the neon humming on the road to Narita International. A few late moths trace stop-motion circles around the floodlights that shine on New Rose.

And the funny thing, Sandii, is how sometimes you just don't seem real to me. Fox once said you were ectoplasm, a ghost called up by the extremes of economics. Ghost of the new century, congealing on a thousand beds in the world's Hyatts, the world's Hiltons.

Now I've got your gun in my hand, jacket pocket, and my hand seems so far away. Disconnected.

I remember my Portuguese business friend forgetting his English, trying to get it across in four languages I barely understood, and I thought he was telling me that the Medina was burning. Not the Medina. The brains of Hosaka's best research people. Plague, he was whispering, my businessman, plague and fever and death.

Smart Fox, he put it together on the run. I didn't even have to mention finding the diskette in your bag in Germany.

Someone had reprogrammed the DNA synthesizer, he said. The thing was there for the overnight construction of just the right macromolecule. With its in-built computer and its custom software. Expensive, Sandii. But not as expensive as you turned out to be for Hosaka.

I hope you got a good price from Maas.

The diskette in my hand. Rain on the river. I knew, but I couldn't face it. I put the code for that meningial virus back into your purse and lay down beside you.

So Moenner died, along with other Hosaka researchers. Including Hiroshi. Chedanne suffered permanent brain damage.

Hiroshi hadn't worried about contamination. The proteins he punched for were harmless. So the synthesizer hummed to itself all night long building a virus to the specifications of Maas Biolabs GmbH.

Maas. Small, fast, ruthless. All Edge.

The airport road is a long, straight shot. Keep to the shadows.

And I was shouting at that Portuguese voice, I made him tell me what happened to the girl, to Hiroshi's woman. Vanished, he said. The whir of Victorian clockwork.

So Fox had to fall, fall with his three pathetic plates of gold, and snap his spine for the last time. On the floor of a Ginza department store, every shopper staring in the instant before they screamed.

I just can't hate you, baby.

And Hosaka's helicopter is back, no lights at all, hunting on infrared, feeling for body heat. A muffled whine as it turns, a kilometer away, swinging back toward us, toward New Rose. Too fast a shadow, against the glow of Narita.

It's all right, baby. Only please come here. Hold my hand.

Pots

C. J. CHERRYH

Carolyn Janice Cherry (1942–), writing as C. J. Cherryh, is an influential US science fiction writer who lives in Spokane, Washington, and holds a master's degree in classics from Johns Hopkins; Greek and Roman mythology have been a major influence on her work. She started writing fiction at the age of ten, after her favorite television show, *Flash Gordon*, was canceled, and she won the John W. Campbell Award for Best New Writer in 1976. Cherryh is best known for her novels set in the Alliance-Union Universe, especially *Downbelow Station* (1981) and *Cyteen* (1988)—both of which won Hugo Awards. The Alliance-Union novels are set throughout most of the home galaxy during the third and fourth millennia, during which period the Alliance, structured around merchant cultures that operate huge interstellar freighters necessary for trade, manages to survive at the heart of the more ruthless, expansionist Union. Cherryh has used this backdrop to good effect repeatedly, exploring ever more widely both the milieu and the socioeconomic implications of the situation.

Her first novel was *Gate of Ivrel* (1976), the beginning of the *Morgaine* series, which continued with *Well of Shiuan* (1978), *Fires of Azeroth* (1979), and the much later *Exile's Gate* (1988). In these novels, Cherryh fused interplanetary intrigue with tropes more usual to fantasy, including a romantic heroic quest. An underlying rationality counterbalances the stylistic flourish of the series; Cherryh could be said to have renovated and modernized the planetary romance with the series.

Cherryh's first short story, the much-anthologized "Cassandra" (1978), won the Hugo Award. Eventually she published enough short fiction to release *The Collected Short Fiction of C. J. Cherryh* (2004), comprising her prior collections *Sunfall* (1981) and *Visible Light* (1986) plus sixteen additional stories.

"Pots," which first appeared in the anthology *Afterwar* (1985), is anthropological or archaeological science fiction and fairly unusual in its approach to that subject. It showcases in very interesting ways the author's many virtues, including a flair for the dramatic and her gift for fusing both modern and traditional impulses in science fiction.

POTS

C. J. Cherryh

It was a most bitter trip, the shuttle-descent to the windy surface. Suited, encumbered by life support, Desan stepped off the platform and waddled onward into the world, waving off the attentions of small spidery surface robots: "Citizen, this way, this way, citizen, have a care—Do watch your step; a suit tear is hazardous."

Low-level servitors. Desan detested them. The chief of operations had plainly sent these creatures accompanied only by an AI eight-wheel transport, which inconveniently chose to park itself a good five hundred paces beyond the shuttle blast zone, an uncomfortable long walk across the dusty pan in the crinkling, pack-encumbered oxy-suit. Desan turned, casting a forlorn glance at the shuttle waiting there on its landing gear, silver, dip-nosed wedge under a gunmetal sky, at rest on an ocher and rust land-scape. He shivered in the sky-view, surrendered himself and his meager luggage to the irritating ministries of the service robots, and waddled on his slow way down to the waiting AI transport.

"Good day," the vehicle said inanely, opening a door. "My passenger compartment is not safe atmosphere; do you understand, Lord Desan?"

"Yes, yes." Desan climbed in and settled himself in the front seat, a slight give of the transport's suspensors. The robots fussed about in insectile hesitance, delicately setting his luggage case just so, adjusting, adjusting till it conformed with their robotic, template-compared notion of their job. Maddening. Typical robotic efficiency. Desan slapped the pressure-sensitive seating. "Come, let's get this moving, shall we?"

The AI talked to its duller cousins, a single squeal that sent them scuttling; "Attention to the door, citizen." It lowered and locked. The

AI started its noisy drive motor. "Will you want the windows dimmed, citizen?"

"No. I want to see this place."

"A pleasure, Lord Desan."

Doubtless for the AI, it was.

The station was situated a long drive across the pan, across increasingly softer dust that rolled up to obscure the rearview—softer, looser dust, occasionally a wind-scooped hollow that made the transport flex—"Do forgive me, citizen. Are you comfortable?"

"Quite, quite, you're very good."

"Thank you, citizen."

And *finally—finally!*—something other than flat appeared, the merest humps of hills, and one anomalous mountain, a massive, long bar that began as a haze and became solid, became a smooth regularity before the gentle brown folding of hills hardly worthy of the name.

Mountain. The eye indeed took it for a volcanic or sedimentary formation at a distance, some anomalous and stubborn outcrop in this barren reach, where all else had declined to entropy, absolute, featureless, flat. But when the AI passed along its side this mountain had joints and seams, had the marks of *making* on it; and even knowing in advance what it was, driving along within view of the jointing, this work of Ancient hands chilled Desan's well-traveled soul. The station itself came into view against the weathered hills, a collection of shocking green domes on a brown lifeless world. But such domes Desan had seen. With only the AI for witness, Desan turned in his seat, pressed the flexible bubble of the helmet to the double-seal window, and stared and stared at the stonework until it passed to the rear and the dust obscured it.

"Here, lord," said the AI, eternally cheerful. "We are almost at the station—a little climb. I do it very smoothly."

Flex and lean; sway and turn. The domes lurched closer in the forward window and the motor whined. "I've very much enjoyed serving you."

"Thank you," Desan murmured, seeing another walk before him, ascent of a plastic grid to an air lock and no sight of a welcoming committee.

More service robots, scuttling toward them as the transport stopped and adjusted itself with a pneumatic wheeze.

"Thank you, Lord Desan, do watch your helmet, watch your life-support connections, watch your footing please. The dust is slick. . . ."

"Thank you." With an AI one had no recourse.

"Thank you, my lord." The door came up; Desan extricated himself from the seat and stepped to the dusty ground, carefully shielding the oxy-pack from the door frame and panting with the unaccustomed weight of it in such gravity. The service robots moved to take his luggage while Desan waddled doggedly on, up the plastic gridwork path to the glaringly lime-green domes. Plastics. Plastics which could not even originate in this desolation, but which came from their ships' spare biomass. Here all was dead, frighteningly void: even the signal that guided him to the lakebed was robotic, like the advisement that a transport would meet him.

The air lock door shot open ahead, and living, suited personnel appeared, three of them, at last, at long last, flesh-and-blood personnel came walking toward him to offer proper courtesy. But before that mountain of stone; before these glaring green structures and the robotic paraphernalia of research that made all the reports real—Desan still felt the deathliness of the place. He trudged ahead, touched the offered, gloved hands, acknowledged the expected sal-

utations, and proceeded up the jointed-plastic walk to the open air lock. His marrow refused to be warmed. The place refused to come into clear focus, like some bad dream with familiar elements hideously distorted.

A hundred years of voyage since he had last seen this world and then only from orbit, receiving reports thirdhand. A hundred years of work on this planet preceded this small trip from port to research center, under that threatening sky, in this place by a mountain that had once been a dam on a lake that no longer existed.

There had been the findings on the moon, of course. A few artifacts. A cloth of symbols. Primitive, unthinkably primitive. First omen of the findings on this sere, rust-brown world.

He accompanied the welcoming committee into the air lock of the main dome, waited through the cycle, and breathed a sigh of relief as the indicator lights went from white to orange and the inner door admitted them to the interior. He walked forward, removed the helmet, and drew a deep breath of air unexpectedly and unpleasantly tainted. The foyer of this centermost dome was businesslike—plastic walls, visible ducting. A few plants struggled for life in a planter in the center of the floor. Before it, a black pillar and a common enough emblem: a plaque with two naked alien figures, the diagrams of a star system—reproduced even to its scars and pitting. In some places it might have been mundane, unnoticed.

It belonged here, *belonged* here, and it could never be mundane, this message of the Ancients.

"Lord Desan," a female voice said, and he turned, awkward in the suit.

It was Dr. Gothon herself, unmistakable aged woman in science-blues. The rare honor dazed him, and wiped away all failure of hospitality thus far. She held out her hand. Startled, he reacted in kind, remembered the glove, and hastily drew back his hand to strip the glove. Her gesture was gracious and he felt the very fool and very much off his stride, his hands touching—no, firmly grasped by the callused, aged hand of this legendary intellect. Age-soft and hard-surfaced at once. Age and vigor. His tongue quite failed him, and he felt, recalling his purpose, utterly daunted.

"Come in, let them rid you of that suit, Lord Desan. Will you rest after your trip, a nap, a cup of tea perhaps? The robots are taking your luggage to your room. Accommodations here aren't luxurious, but I think you'll find them comfortable."

Deeper and deeper into courtesies. One could lose all sense of direction in such surroundings, letting oneself be disarmed by gentleness, by pleasantness—by embarrassed reluctance to resist.

"I want to see what I came to see, doctor." Desan unfastened more seams and shed the suit into waiting hands, smoothed his coveralls. Was that too brusque, too unforgivably hasty? "I don't think I *could* rest, Dr. Gothon. I attended my comfort aboard the shuttle. I'd like to get my bearings here at least, if one of your staff would be so kind as to take me in hand—"

"Of course, of course, I rather expected as much—do come, please, let me show you about. I'll explain as much as I can. Perhaps I can convince you as I go."

He was overwhelmed from the start; he had expected some high official, the director of operations most likely. Not Gothon. He walked slightly after the doctor, the stoop-shouldered presence which passed like a benison among the students and lesser staff—*I saw the Doctor,* the young ones had been wont to say in hushed tones, aboard the ship, when Gothon strayed absently down a corridor in her rare intervals of waking. *I saw the Doctor.*

In that voice one might claim a theophany.

They had rarely waked her, lesser researchers being sufficient for most worlds; while he was the fifth lord-navigator, the fourth born on the journey, a time-dilated trifle, fifty-two waking years of age and a mere two thousand years of voyage against—aeons of Gothon's slumberous life.

And Desan's marrow ached now at such gentle grace in this bowed, mottle-skinned old scholar, this sleuth patiently deciphering the greatest mystery of the universe. Pity occurred to him. He suffered personally in this place, but not as Gothon would have suffered here, in that inward quiet where Gothon carried on thoughts the ship-crews were sternly admonished never to disturb.

Students rushed now to open doors for them, pressed themselves to the walls and allowed their passage into deeper halls within the maze of the domes. Passing hands brushed Desan's sleeves, welcome offered the current lord-navigator; he reciprocated with as much attention as he could devote to courtesy in his distress. His heart labored in the unaccustomed gravity, his nostrils accepted not only the effluvium of dome-plastics and the recyclers and so many bodies dwelling together, but a flinty, bitter air, like electricity or dry dust. He imagined some hazardous leakage of the atmosphere into the dome: unsettling thought. The hazards of the place came home to him, and he wished already to be away.

Gothon had endured here, during his further voyages—seven years more of her diminishing life; waked four times, and this was the fourth, continually active now for five years, her longest stint yet in any waking. She had found data finally worth the consumption of her life, and she burned it without stint. *She* believed. She believed, enough to die pursuing it.

He shuddered up and down and followed Gothon through a seal-door toward yet another dome, and his gut tightened in dismay; for there were shelves on either hand, and those shelves were lined with yellowed skulls, endless rows of staring dark sockets and grinning jaws. Some were long-nosed; some were short. Some small, virtually noseless skulls had fangs which gave them a wise and intelligent look—*like miniature people, like babies with grown-up features,* must be the initial reaction of anyone seeing them in the holos or viewing the specimens brought up to the orbiting labs. But cranial capacity in these was much too small. The real sapients occupied further shelves, row upon row of eyeless, generously domed skulls, grinning in their flat-toothed way, in permanent horror—provoking profoundest horror in those that discovered them here, in this desolation.

Here Gothon paused, selected one of the small sapient skulls, much reconstructed: Desan had at least the skill to recognize the true bone from the plassbone bonded to it. This skull was far more delicate than the others, the jaw smaller. The front two teeth were restructs. So was one of the side.

"It was a child," Gothon said. "We call her Missy. The first we found at this site, up in the hills, in a streambank. Most of Missy's feet were gone, but she's otherwise intact. Missy was all alone except for a little animal all tucked up in her arms. We keep them together—never mind the cataloguing." She lifted an anomalous and much-reconstructed skull from the shelf among the sapients, fanged and delicate. "Even archaeologists have sentiment."

"I—see—" Helpless, caught in courtesy, Desan extended an unwilling finger and touched the child-skull.

"Back to sleep." Gothon set both skulls tenderly back on the shelf, and dusted her hands and walked further, Desan following, beyond a simple door and into a busy room of workbenches piled high with a clutter of artifacts.

Staff began to rise from their dusty work in a sudden startlement. "No, no, go on," Gothon said quietly. "We're only passing through; ignore us—here, do you see, Lord Desan?" Gothon reached carefully past a researcher's shoulder and lifted from the counter an elongate ribbed bottle with the opalescent patina of long burial. "We find a great many of these. Mass production. Industry. Not only on this continent. This same bottle exists in sites all over the world, in the uppermost strata. Same design. Near the time of the calamity. We trace global alliances and trade by such small things." She set it down and gathered up a virtually complete vase, much patched. "It always comes to

pots, Lord Desan. By pots and bottles we track them through the ages. Many layers. They had a long and complex past."

Desan reached out and touched the corroded brown surface of the vase, discovering a single bright remnant of blue glaze along with the gray encrustations of long burial. "How long—how long does it take to reduce a thing to this?"

"It depends on the soil—on moisture, on acidity. This came from hereabouts." Gothon tenderly set it back on a shelf, walked on, frail, hunch-shouldered figure among the aisles of the past. "But very long, very long to obliterate so much—almost all the artifacts are gone. Metals oxidize; plastics rot; cloth goes very quickly; paper and wood last quite long in a desert climate, but they go, finally. Moisture dissolves the details of sculpture. Only the noble metals survive intact. Soil creep warps even stone, crushes metal. We find even the best pots in a matrix of pieces, a puzzle-toss. Fragile as they are, they outlast monuments, they last as long as the earth that holds them, drylands, wetlands, even beneath the sea—where no marine life exists to trouble them. That bottle and that pot are as venerable as that great dam. The makers wouldn't have thought that, would they?"

"But—" Desan's mind reeled at the remembrance of the great plain, the silt, and the deep buried secrets.

"But?"

"You surely might miss important detail. A world to search. You might walk right over something and misinterpret everything."

"Oh, yes, it can happen. But *finding* things where we expect them is an important clue, Lord Desan, a confirmation—one only has to suspect where to look. We locate our best hope first—a sunken, a raised place in those photographs we trouble the orbiters to take; but one gets *a feeling* about the lay of the land— more than the mechanical probes, Lord Desan." Gothon's dark eyes crinkled in the passage of thoughts unguessed, and Desan stood lost in Gothon's unthinkable mentality. What did a mind *do* in such age? Wander? Could the great doctor lapse into mysticism? To report such a thing—would solve one difficulty. But to have that regrettable duty—

"It's a feeling for living creatures, Lord Desan. It's reaching out to the land and saying—if this were long ago, if I thought to build, if I thought to trade—where would I go? Where would my neighbors live?"

Desan coughed delicately, wishing to draw things back to hard fact. "And the robot probes, of course, do assist."

"Probes, Lord Desan, are heartless things. A robot can be very skilled, but a researcher directs it only at a distance, blind to opportunities and the true sense of the land. But you were born to space. Perhaps it makes no sense."

"I take your word for it," Desan said earnestly. He felt the weight of the sky on his back. The leaden, awful sky, leprous and unhealthy cover between them, and the star and the single moon. Gothon remembered homeworld. *Remembered homeworld.* Had been renowned in her field even there. The old scientist claimed to come to such a landscape and *locate* things by seeing things that robot eyes could not, by thinking thoughts those dusty skulls had held in fleshly matter—

—how long ago?

"We look for mounds," Gothon said, continuing in her brittle gait down the aisle, past the bowed heads and shy looks of staff and students at their meticulous tasks. The work of tiny electronic needles proceeded about them, the patient ticking away at encrustations to bring ancient surfaces to light. "They built massive structures. Great skyscrapers. Some of them must have lasted, oh, thousands of years intact; but when they went unstable, they fell, and their fall made rubble; and the wind came and the rivers shifted their courses around the ruin, and of course the weight of sediment piled up, wind- and water-driven. From that point, its own weight moved it and warped it and complicated our work." Gothon paused again beside a further table, where holo plates stood inactive.

She waved her hand and a landscape showed itself, a serpentined row of masonry across a depression. "See the wall there. They didn't build it that way, all wavering back and forth and up and down. Gravity and soil movement deformed it. It was buried till we unearthed it. Otherwise, wind and rain alone would have destroyed it ages ago. As it will do, now, if time doesn't rebury it."

"And this great pile of stone—" Desan waved an arm, indicating the imagined direction of the great dam and realizing himself disoriented. "How old is it?"

"Old as the lake it made."

"But contemporaneous with the fall?"

"Yes. Do you know, that mass may be standing when the star dies. The few great dams; the pyramids we find here and there around the world—one only guesses at their age. They'll outlast any other surface feature except the mountains themselves."

"Without life."

"Oh, but there is."

"Declining."

"No, no. Not declining." The doctor waved her hand and a puddle appeared over the second holo plate, all green with weed waving feathery tendrils back and forth in the surge. "The moon still keeps this world from entropy. There's water, not as much as this dam saw—it's the weed, this little weed that gives one hope for this world. The little life, the things that fly and crawl—the lichens and the life on the flatlands."

"But nothing they knew."

"No. Life's evolved new answers here. Life's starting over."

"It certainly hasn't much to start with, has it?"

"Not very much. It's a question that interests Dr. Bothogi—whether the life making a start here has the time left, and whether the consumption curve doesn't add up to defeat—but life doesn't know that. We're very concerned about contamination. But we fear it's inevitable. And who knows, perhaps it will have added something beneficial." Dr. Gothon lit yet another holo with a wave of her hand. A streamlined six-legged creature scuttled energetically across a surface of dead moss, frantically waving antennae and making no apparent progress.

"The inheritors of the world." Despair chilled Desan's marrow.

"But each generation of these little creatures is an unqualified success. The last to perish perishes in profound tragedy, of course, but without consciousness of it. The awareness will have, oh, half a billion years to wait—then, maybe it will appear, if the star doesn't fail; it's already far advanced down the sequence." Another holo, the image of desert, of blowing sand, beside the holo of the surge of weed in a pool. "Life makes life. That weed you see is busy making life. It's taking in and converting and building a chain of support that will enable things to feed on it, while more of its kind grows. That's what life does. It's busy, all unintended, of course, but fortuitously building itself a way off the planet."

Desan cast her an uncomfortable look askance.

"Oh, indeed. Biomass. Petrochemicals. The storehouse of aeons of energy all awaiting the use of Consciousness. And that consciousness, if it arrives, dominates the world because awareness is a way of making life more efficiently. But consciousness is a perilous thing, Lord Desan. Consciousness is a computer loose with its own perceptions and performing calculations on its own course, in the service of that little weed; billions of such computers all running and calculating faster and faster, adjusting themselves and their ecological environment, and what if there were the smallest, the most insignificant software error at the outset?"

"You don't believe such a thing. You don't reduce us to that." Desan's faith was shaken; this good woman had not gone unstable, this great intellect had had her faith shaken, that was what—the great and gentle doctor had, in her unthinkable age, acquired cynicism, and he fought back with his fifty-two meager years.

"Surely, but surely this isn't the proof, doctor, this could have been a natural calamity."

"Oh, yes, the meteor strike." The doctor waved past a series of holos on a fourth plate, and a vast crater showed in aerial view, a crater so vast the picture showed planetary curvature. It was one of the planet's main features, shockingly visible from space. "But this solar system shows scar after scar of such events. A many-planeted system like this, a star well attended by debris in its course through the galaxy— look at the airless bodies, the moons, consider the number of meteor strikes that crater them. Tell me, space farer: am I not right in that?"

Desan drew in a breath, relieved to be questioned in his own element. "Of course, the system is prone to that kind of accident. But that crater is ample cause—"

"If it came when there was still sapience here. But that hammer-blow fell on a dead world."

He gazed on the eroded crater, the sand-swept crustal melting, eloquent of age. "You have proof."

"Strata. Pots. Ironic, they must have feared such an event very greatly. One thinks they must have had a sense of doom about them, perhaps on the evidence of their moon; or understanding the mechanics of their solar system; or perhaps primitive times witnessed such falls, and they remembered. One catches a glimpse of the mind that reached out from here . . . what impelled it, what it sought."

"How can we know that? We overlay our mind on their expectations—" Desan silenced himself, abashed, terrified. It was next to heresy. In a moment more he would have committed irremediable indiscretion; and the lords-magistrate on the orbiting station would have heard it by suppertime, to his eternal detriment.

"We stand in their landscape, handle their bones, we hold their skulls in our fleshly hands and try to think in their world. Here we stand beneath a threatening heaven. What will we do?"

"Try to escape. Try to get off this world. They *did* get off. The celestial artifacts—"

"Archaeology is ever so much easier in space. A million years, two, and a thing still shines. Records still can be read. A color can blaze out undimmed after aeons, when first a light falls on it. One surface chewed away by microdust, and the opposing face pristine as the day it had its maker's hand on it. You keep asking me about the age of these ruins. But we know that, don't we truly suspect it, in the marrow of our bones—at what age they fell silent?"

"It *can't* have happened then!"

"Come with me, Lord Desan." Gothon waved a hand, extinguishing all the holos, and, walking on, opened the door into yet another hallway. "So much to catalog. That's much of the work in that room. They're students, mostly. Restoring what they can; numbering, listing. A librarian's job, just to know where things are filed. In five hundred years more of intensive cataloguing and restoring, we may know them well enough to know something of their minds, though we may never find more of their written language than those artifacts on the moon. A place of wonders. A place of ongoing wonders, in Dr. Bothogi's work. A little algae beginning the work all over again. Perhaps not for the first time—interesting thought."

"You mean—" Desan overtook the aged doctor in the narrow, sterile hall, a series of ringing steps. "You mean—before the sapients evolved—there were other calamities, other rebeginnings."

"Oh, well before. It sends chills up one's back, doesn't it, to think how incredibly stubborn life might be here, how persistent in the calamity of the skies—the algae and then the creeping things and the slow, slow climb to dominance—"

"Previous sapients?"

"Interesting question in itself. But a thing need not be sapient to dominate a world, Lord Desan. Only tough. Only efficient. Haven't the worlds proven that? High sapience is a rare jewel. So many successes are dead ends. Flippers and not hands; lack of vocal apparatus—unless you believe in telepathy, which I assuredly don't. No. Vocalizing is necessary. Some sort of long-distance communication. Light-flashes; sound; something. Else your individuals stray apart in solitary discovery and rediscovery and duplication of effort. Oh, even with awareness—even granted that rare attribute—how many species lack something essential, or have some handicap that will stop them before civilization; before technology—"

"—before they leave the planet. But they *did* that, they were the one in a thousand—without them—"

"Without them. Yes." Gothon turned her wonderful soft eyes on him at close range and for a moment he felt a great and terrible stillness like the stillness of a grave. "Childhood ends here. One way or another, it ends."

He was struck speechless. He stood there, paralyzed a moment, his mind tumbling free fall, then blinked and followed the doctor like a child, helpless to do otherwise.

Let me rest, he thought then, *let us forget this beginning and this day, let me go somewhere and sit down and have a warm drink to get the chill from my marrow and let us begin again. Perhaps we can begin with facts and not fancies—*

But he would not rest. He feared that there was no rest to be had in this place, that once the body stopped moving the weight of the sky would come down, the deadly sky that had boded destruction for all the history of this lost species; and the age of the land would seep into his bones and haunt his dreams as the far greater scale of stars did not.

All the years I've voyaged, Dr. Gothon, all the years of my life searching from star to star. Relativity has made orphans of us. The world will have sainted you. Me, it never knew. In a quarter of a million years—they'll have forgotten; O doctor, you know more than I how a world ages. A quarter of a million years you've seen—and we're both orphans. Me endlessly cloned. You in your long sleep, your several clones held eons waiting in theirs—O doctor, we'll re-create you. And not truly you, ever again. No more than I'm Desan-prime. I'm only the fifth lord-navigator.

In a quarter of a million years, has not our species evolved beyond us, might they not, may they not find some faster transport and find us, their eons-lost precursors; and we will not know each other. Dr. Gothon—how could we know each other—if they had, but they have not; we have become the wavefront of a quest that never overtakes us, never surpasses us.

In a quarter of a million years, might some calamity have befallen us and our world be like this world, ocher and deadly rust?

While we are clones and children of clones, genetic fossils, anomalies of our kind?

What are they to us and we to them? We seek the Ancients, the makers of the probe.

Desan's mind reeled; adept as he was at time-relativity calculations, accustomed as he was to stellar immensities, his mind tottered and he fought to regain the corridor in which they walked, he and the doctor. He widened his stride yet again, overtaking Gothon at the next door.

"Doctor." He put out his hand, preventing her, and then feared his own question, his own skirting of heresy and tempting of hers. "Are you beyond doubt? You can't be beyond doubt. They could have simply abandoned this world in its calamity."

Again the impact of those gentle eyes, devastating. "Tell me, tell me, Lord Desan. In all your travels, in all the several, near stars you've visited in a century of effort, have you found traces?"

"No. But they could have gone—"

"—leaving no traces, except on their moon?"

"There may be others. The team in search on the fourth planet—"

"Finds nothing."

"You yourself say that you have to stand in that landscape, you have to think with their mind—Maybe Dr. Ashodt hasn't come to the right hill, the right plain—"

"If there are artifacts there, they are only a few. I'll tell you why I know so. Come, come with me." Gothon waved a hand and the door gaped on yet another laboratory.

Desan walked. He would rather have walked out to the deadly surface than through this simple door, to the answer Gothon promised him . . . but habit impelled him; habit, duty—necessity. He had no other purpose for his life but this. He had been left none, lord-navigator, fifth incarnation of Desan Das. They had launched his original with none, his second incarnation had had less, and time and successive incarnations had stripped everything else away. So he went, into a place at once too mundane and too strange to be quite sane—mundane because it was sterile as any lab, a well-lit place of littered tables and a few researchers; and strange because hundreds and hundreds of skulls and bones were piled on shelves in heaps on one wall, silent witnesses. An articulated skeleton hung in its frame; the skeleton of a small animal scampered in macabre rigidity on a tabletop.

He stopped. He stared about him, lost for the moment in the stare of all those eyeless sockets of weathered bone.

"Let me present my colleagues," Gothon was saying; Desan focused on the words late, and blinked helplessly as Gothon rattled off names. Bothogi the zoologist was one, younger than most, seventeenth incarnation, burning himself out in profligate use of his years: so with all the incarnations of Bothogi Nan. The rest of the names slid past his ears ungathered—true strangers, the truly-born, sons and daughters of the voyage. He was lost in their stares like the stares of the skulls, eyes behind which shadows and dust were truth, gazes full of secrets and heresies.

They knew him and he did not know them, not even Lord Bothogi. He felt his solitude, the helplessness of his convictions—all lost in the dust and the silences.

"Kagodte," said Gothon, to a white-eared, hunched individual, "Kagodte—the Lord Desan has come to see your model."

"Ah." The aged eyes flicked nervously.

"Show him, pray, Dr. Kagodte."

The hunched man walked over to the table, spread his hands. A holo flared and Desan blinked, having expected some dreadful image, some confrontation with a reconstruction. Instead, columns of words rippled in the air, green and blue. Numbers ticked and multiplied. In his startlement he lost the beginning and failed to follow them. "I don't see—"

"We speak statistics here," Gothon said. "We speak data; we couch our heresies in mathematical formulae."

Desan turned and stared at Gothon in fright. "Heresies I have nothing to do with, doctor. I deal with facts. I come here to find facts."

"Sit down," the gentle doctor said. "Sit down, Lord Desan. There, move the bones over, do; the owners won't mind, there, that's right."

Desan collapsed onto a stool facing a white worktable. Looked up reflexively, eye drawn by a wall-mounted stone that bore the blurred image of a face, eroded, time-dulled—

The juxtaposition of image and bones overwhelmed him. The two whole bodies portrayed on the plaque. The sculpture. The rows of fleshless skulls.

Dead. World hammered by meteors, life struggling in its most rudimentary forms. Dead.

"Ah," Gothon said. Desan looked around and saw Gothon looking up at the wall in her turn. "Yes. That. Occasionally the fall of stone will protect a surface. Confirmation. Indeed. But the skulls tell us as much. With our measurements and our holos we can flesh them. We can make them—even more vivid. Do you want to see?"

Desan's mouth worked. "No." A small word. A coward word. "Later. So this was *one* place— you still don't convince me of your thesis, doctor, I'm sorry."

"The place. The world of origin. A many-layered world. The last layers are rich with artifacts of one period, one global culture. Then silence. Species extinguished. Stratum upon stratum of desolation. Millions of years of geo-logical record—" Gothon came round the end of the table and sat down in the opposing chair, elbows on the table, a scatter of bone between them. Gothon's green eyes shone watery in the brilliant light; her mouth was wrinkled about the jowls and trembled in minute cracks, like aged clay. "The statistics, Lord Desan, the dry statistics tell us. They tell us the centers of production of artifacts, such as we have; they tell us compositions, processes the Ancients knew— and there was no progression into advanced materials. None of the materials we take for granted, metals that would have lasted—"

"And perhaps they went to some new process, materials that degraded completely. Perhaps their information storage was on increasingly perishable materials. Perhaps they developed these materials in space."

"Technology has steps. The dry numbers, the dusty dry numbers, the incidences and concentration of items, the numbers and the pots—always the pots, Lord Desan; and the imperishable stones; and the very fact of the meteors—the undeniable fact of the meteor strikes. Could we not avert such a calamity for our own world? Could we not have done it— oh, a half a century before we left?"

"I'm sure you remember, Dr. Gothon. I'm sure you have the advantage of me. But—"

"You see the evidence. You want to cling to your hopes. But there is only one question—no, two. Is this the species that launched the probe—yes. Or evolution and coincidence have cooperated mightily. Is this the only world they inhabited? Beyond all doubt. If there are artifacts on the fourth planet they are scoured by its storms, buried, lost."

"But they may *be* there."

"There is no abundance of them. There is no *progression*, Lord Desan. That is the key thing. There is nothing beyond these substances, these materials. This was not a starfaring civilization. They launched their slow, unmanned probes, with their cameras, their robot eyes—not for us. We always knew that. We were the recipients of flotsam. Mere wreckage on the beach."

"It was purposeful!" Desan hissed, trembling, surrounded by them all, a lone credent among this quiet heresy in this room. "Dr. Gothon, your unique position—is a position of trust, of profound trust; I beg you to consider the effect you have—"

"Do you threaten me, Lord Desan? Are you here for that, to silence me?"

Desan looked desperately about him, at the sudden hush in the room. The minute tickings of probes and picks had stopped. Eyes stared. "Please." He looked back. "I came here to gather data; I expected a simple meeting, a few staff meetings—to consider things at leisure—"

"I have distressed you. You wonder how it would be if the lords-magistrate fell at odds with me. I am aware of myself as an institution, Lord Desan. I remember Desan Das. I remember launch, the original five ships. I have waked to all but one of your incarnations. Not to mention the numerous incarnations of the lords-magistrate."

"You cannot discount them! Even you—let me plead with you, Dr. Gothon, be patient with us."

"You do not need to teach me patience, Desan-Five."

He shivered convulsively. Even when Gothon smiled that gentle, disarming smile. "You have to give me facts, doctor, not mystical communings with the landscape. The lords-magistrate accept that this is the world of origin. I assure you they never would have devoted so much time to creating a base here if that were not the case."

"Come, lord, those power systems on the probe, so long dead—what was it truly for, but to probe something very close at hand? Even orthodoxy admits that. And what is close at hand but their own solar system? Come, I've *seen* the original artifact and the original tablet. Touched it with my hands. This was a *primitive* venture, designed to cross their own solar system—*which they had not the capability to do.*"

Desan blinked. "But the purpose—"

"Ah. The purpose."

"You say that you stand in a landscape and you think in their mind. Well, doctor, *use* this skill you claim. What did the Ancients intend? Why did they send it out with a message?"

The old eyes flickered, deep and calm and pained. "An oracular message, Lord Desan. A message into the dark of their own future, unaimed, unfocused. Without answer. Without hope of answer. We know its voyage time. Five million years. They spoke to the universe at large. This probe went out, and they fell silent shortly afterward—the depth of this dry lake of dust, Lord Desan, is eight and a quarter million years."

"I will not believe that."

"Eight and a quarter million years ago, Lord Desan. Calamity fell on them, calamity global and complete within a century, perhaps within a decade of the launch of that probe. Perhaps calamity fell from the skies; but demonstrably it was atomics and their own doing. They were at that precarious stage. And the destruction in the great centers is catastrophic and of one level. Destruction centered in places of heavy population. That is what those statistics say. Atomics, Lord Desan."

"I cannot accept this!"

"Tell me, spacefarer—do you understand the workings of weather? What those meteor strikes could do, the dust raised by atomics could do with equal efficiency. Never mind the radiation that alone would have killed millions—never mind the destruction of centers of government: we speak of global calamity, the dimming of the sun in dust, the living oceans and lakes choking in dying photosynthetes in a sunless winter, killing the food chain from the bottom up—"

"You have no proof!"

"The universality, the ruin of the population centers. Arguably, they had the capacity to prevent meteor-impact. That may be a matter of debate. But beyond a doubt in my own mind, simultaneous destruction of the population centers indicates atomics. The statistics, the pots and the dry numbers, Lord Desan, doom us to that answer. The question is answered. There were no descendants; there was no escape from the world. They destroyed themselves before that meteor hit them."

Desan rested his mouth against his joined hands. Staring helplessly at the doctor. "A lie. Is that what you're saying? We pursued a lie?"

"Is it their fault that we needed them so much?"

Desan pushed himself to his feet and stood there by mortal effort. Gothon sat staring up at him with those terrible dark eyes.

"What will you do, lord-navigator? Silence me? The old woman's grown difficult at last: wake my clone after, tell it—what the lords-magistrate select for it to be told?" Gothon waved a hand about the room, indicating the staff, the dozen sets of living eyes among the dead. "Bothogi too, those of us who have clones—but what of the rest of the staff? How much will it take to silence all of us?"

Desan stared about him, trembling. "Dr. Gothon—" He leaned his hands on the table to look at Gothon. "You mistake me. You utterly mistake me—the lords-magistrate may have the station, but I have the ships, I, I and my staff. I propose no such thing. I've come home"—the unaccustomed word caught in his throat; he considered it, weighed it, accepted it at least in the emotional sense—"home, Dr. Gothon, after a hundred years of search, to discover this argument and this dissension."

"Charges of heresy—"

"They dare not make them against *you*." A bitter laugh welled up. "Against *you* they have no argument and you well know it, Dr. Gothon."

"Against their violence, lord-navigator, I have no defense."

"But she has," said Dr. Bothogi.

Desan turned, flicked a glance from the hardness in Bothogi's green eyes to the even harder substance of the stone in Bothogi's hand. He flung himself about again, hands on the table, abandoning the defense of his back. "Dr. Gothon! I appeal to you! I am your friend!"

"For myself," said Dr. Gothon, "I would make no defense at all. But, as you say—they have no argument against me. So it must be a general catastrophe—the lords-magistrate have to silence everyone, don't they? *Nothing* can be left of this base. Perhaps they've quietly dislodged an asteroid or two and put them on course. In the guise of mining, perhaps they will silence this poor old world forever—myself and the rest of the relics. Lost relics and the distant dead are always safer to venerate, aren't they?"

"That's absurd!"

"Or perhaps they've become more hasty now that your ships are here and their judgment is in question. *They* have atomics within their capability, lord-navigator. They can disable your shuttle with beam-fire. They can simply welcome you to the list of casualties—a charge of heresy. A thing taken out of context, who knows? After all—all lords are immediately duplicatable, the captains accustomed to obey the lords-magistrate—what few of them are awake—am I not right? If an institution like myself can be threatened—where is the fifth lord-navigator in their plans? And of a sudden those plans will be moving in haste."

Desan blinked. "Dr. Gothon—I assure you—"

"If you are my friend, lord-navigator, I hope for your survival. The robots are theirs; do you understand? Their powerpacks are sufficient for transmission of information to the base AIs; and from the communications center it goes to satellites; and from satellites to the station and the lords-magistrate. This room is safe from their monitoring. We have seen to that. They cannot hear you."

"I cannot believe these charges, I cannot accept it—"

"Is murder so new?"

"Then come with me! Come with me to the shuttle, we'll confront them—"

"The transportation to the port is theirs. It would not permit. The transport AI would resist. The planes have AI components. And we might never reach the airfield."

"My luggage. Dr. Gothon, my luggage—my com unit!" And Desan's heart sank, remembering the service-robots. "*They* have it."

Gothon smiled, a small, amused smiled. "O spacefarer. So many scientists clustered here, and could we not improvise so simple a thing? We have a receiver-transmitter. Here. In this room. We broke one. We broke another. They're on the registry as broken. What's another bit of rubbish—on this poor planet? We meant to contact the ships, to call *you*, lord-navigator, when you came back. But you saved us the trouble. You came down to us like a thunderbolt. Like the birds you never saw, my space-born lord, swooping down on prey. The conferences, the haste you must have inspired up there on the station—if the lords-magistrate planned what I most suspect! I congratulate you. But knowing we have a transmitter—with your shuttle sitting on this world vulnerable as this building—what will you do, lord-navigator, since they control the satellite relay?"

Desan sank down on his chair. Stared at Gothon. "You never meant to kill me. All this—you schemed to enlist me."

"I entertained that hope, yes. I knew your predecessors. I also know your personal reputation—a man who burns his years one after the other as if there were no end of them. Unlike his predecessors. What are you, lord-navigator? Zealot? A man with an obsession? Where do you stand in this?"

"To what—" His voice came hoarse and strange. "To what are you trying to convert me, Dr. Gothon?"

"To our rescue from the lords-magistrate. To the rescue of truth."

"Truth!" Desan waved a desperate gesture. "I don't believe you. I cannot believe you, and you tell me about plots as fantastical as your research and try to involve me in your politics. I'm trying to find the trail the Ancients took—one clue, one artifact to direct us—"

"A new tablet?"

"You make light of me. Anything. Any indication where they went. And they *did* go,

doctor. You will not convince me with your statistics. The unforeseen and the unpredicted aren't in your statistics."

"So you'll go on looking—for what you'll never find. You'll serve the lords-magistrate. They'll surely cooperate with you. They'll approve your search and leave this world . . . after the great catastrophe. After the catastrophe that obliterates us and all the records. An asteroid. Who but the robots charts their courses? Who knows how close it is at this moment?"

"People would know a murder! They could never hide it!"

"I tell you, Lord Desan, you stand in a place and you look around you and you say—what would be natural to this place? In this cratered, devastated world, in this chaotic, debris-ridden solar system—could not an input error by an asteroid miner be more credible an accident than atomics? I tell you when your shuttle descended, we thought you might be acting for the lords-magistrate. That you might have a weapon in your baggage which their robots would deliberately fail to detect. But I believe you, lord-navigator. You're as trapped as we. With only the transmitter and a satellite relay system they control. What will you do? Persuade the lords-magistrate that you support them? Persuade them to support you in this further voyage—in return for your backing them? Perhaps they'll listen to you and let you leave."

"But they will," Desan said. He drew in a deep breath and looked from Gothon to the others and back again. "My shuttle is my own. *My* robotics, Dr. Gothon. From my ship and linked to it. And what I need is that transmitter. Appeal to *me* for protection if you think it so urgent. Trust me. Or trust nothing and we will all wait here and see what truth is."

Gothon reached into a pocket, held up an odd metal object. Smiled. Her eyes crinkled round the edges. "An old-fashioned thing, lord-navigator. We say *key* nowadays and mean something quite different, but I'm a relic myself, remember. Baffles the hell out of the robots. Bothogi. Link up that antenna and unlock the closet and let's see what the lord-navigator and his shuttle can do."

"Did it hear you?" Bothogi asked, a boy's honest worry on his unlined face. He still had the rock, as if he had forgotten it. Or feared robots. Or intended to use it if he detected treachery. "Is it moving?"

"I assure you it's moving," Desan said, and shut the transmitter down. He drew a great breath, shut his eyes, and saw the shuttle lift, a silver wedge spreading wings for home. Deadly if attacked. *They will not attack it, they must not attack it, they will query us when they know the shuttle is launched and we will discover yet that this is all a ridiculous error of misunderstanding.* And looking at nowhere: "Relays have gone; *nothing* stops it and its defenses are considerable. The lords-navigator have not been fools, citizens: we probe worlds with our shuttles, and we plan to get them back." He turned and faced Gothon and the other staff. "The message is *out*. And because I am a prudent man—are there suits enough for your staff? I advise we get to them. In the case of an accident."

"The alarm," said Gothon at once. "Neoth, sound the alarm." And as a senior staffer moved: "The dome pressure alert," Gothon said. *"That* will confound the robots. All personnel to pressure suits; all robots to seek damage. I agree about the suits. Get them."

The alarm went, a staccato shriek from overhead. Desan glanced instinctively at an uncommunicative white ceiling—

—darkness, darkness above, where the shuttle reached the thin blue edge of space. The station now knew that things had gone greatly amiss. It should inquire, there should be inquiry immediate to the planet—

Staffers had unlocked a second closet. They pulled out suits, not the expected one or two for emergency exit from this pressure-scalable room, but a tightly jammed lot of them. The lab

seemed a mine of defenses, a stealthily equipped stronghold that smelled of conspiracy all over the base, throughout the staff—*everyone* in on it—

He blinked at the offering of a suit, ears assailed by the siren. He looked into the eyes of Bothogi, who had handed it to him. There would be no call, no inquiry from the lords-magistrate. He began to know that, in the earnest, clear-eyed way these people behaved—not as lunatics, not schemers. Truth. They had told their truth as they believed it, as the whole base believed it. And the lords-magistrate named it heresy.

His heart beat steadily again. Things made sense again. His hands found familiar motions, putting on the suit, making the closures.

"There's that AI in the controller's office," said a senior staffer. "I have a key."

"What will they do?" a younger staffer asked, panic-edged. "Will the station's weapons reach here?"

"It's quite distant for sudden actions," said Desan. "Too far for beams and missiles are slow." His heartbeat steadied further. The suit was about him; familiar feeling; hostile worlds and weapons: more familiar ground. He smiled, not a pleasant kind of smile, a parting of lips on strong, long teeth. "And one more thing, young citizen, the ships they have are transports. Miners. Mine are hunters. I regret to say we've carried weapons for the last two hundred thousand years, and my crews know their business. If the lords-magistrate attack that shuttle it will be their mistake. Help Dr. Gothon."

"I've got it, quite, young lord." Gothon made the collar closure. "I've been handling these things longer than—"

An explosion thumped somewhere far away. Gothon looked up. All motion stopped. And the air-rush died in the ducts.

"The oxygen system—" Bothogi exclaimed. "O *damn* them—!"

"We have," Desan said coldly. He made no haste. Each final fitting of the suit he made with care. Suit-drill; example to the young: the lord-navigator, youngsters, demonstrates his skill. Pay attention. "And we've just had our answer from the lords-magistrate. We need to get to that AI and shut it down. Let's have no panic here. Assume that my shuttle has cleared the atmosphere—"

—well above the gray clouds, the horror of the surface. Silver needle aimed at the heart of the lords-magistrate.

Alert, alert, it would shriek, *alert, alert, alert*—with its transmission relying on no satellites, with its message shoved out in one high-powered bow-wave. *Crew on the world is in danger.* And, code that no lord-navigator had ever hoped to transmit, a series of numbers in syntaxical link: *Treachery: the lords-magistrate are traitors; aid and rescue—alert, alert, alert—*

—anguished scream from a world of dust; a place of skulls; the grave of the search.

Treachery: alert, alert, alert!

Desan was not a violent man; he had never thought of himself as violent. He was a searcher, a man with a quest.

He knew nothing of certainty. He believed a woman a quarter of a million years old, because—because Gothon was Gothon. He cried traitor and let loose havoc all the while knowing that here might be the traitor, this gentle-eyed woman, this collector of skulls.

O, Gothon, he would ask if he dared, *which of you is false? To force the lords-magistrate to strike with violence enough to damn them—is that what you wish? Against a quarter million years of unabated life—what are my five incarnations: mere genetic congruency, without memory. I am helpless to know your perspectives.*

Have you planned this a thousand years, ten thousand? Do you stand in this place and think in the mind of creatures dead longer even than you have lived? Do you hold their skulls and think their thoughts? Was it purpose eight million years ago? Was it, is it—horror upon horror—a mistake on both sides?

"Lord Desan," said Bothogi, laying a hand on his shoulder. "Lord Desan, we have a mas-

ter key. We have weapons. We're waiting, Lord Desan."

Above them the holocaust.

It was only a service robot. It had never known its termination. Not like the base AI, in the director's office, which had fought them with locked doors and release of atmosphere, to the misfortune of the director—

"Tragedy, tragedy," said Bothogi, standing by the small dented corpse, there on the ocher sand before the buildings. Smoke rolled up from a sabotaged life-support plant to the right of the domes; the world's air had rolled outward and inward and mingled with the breaching of the central dome—the AI transport's initial act of sabotage, ramming the plastic walls. "Microorganisms let loose on this world—the fools, the arrant *fools!*"

It was not the microorganisms Desan feared. It was the AI eight-wheeled transport, maneuvering itself for another attack on the cold-sleep facilities. Prudent to have set themselves inside a locked room with the rest of the scientists and hope for rescue from offworld; but the AI would batter itself against the plastic walls, and living targets kept it distracted from the sleeping, helpless clones—Gothon's juniormost; Bothogi's; those of a dozen senior staffers.

And keeping it distracted became more and more difficult.

Hour upon hour they had evaded its rushes, clumsy attacks, and retreats in their encumbering suits. They had done it damage where they could while staff struggled to come up with something that might slow it . . . it lumped along now with a great lot of metal wire wrapped around its rearmost right wheel.

"Damn!" cried a young biologist as it maneuvered for her position. It was the agile young who played this game; and one aging lord-navigator who was the only fighter in the lot.

Dodge, dodge, and dodge. "It's going to

catch you against the oxy-plant, youngster! *This* way!" Desan's heart thudded as the young woman thumped along in the cumbersome suit in a losing race with the transport. "Oh, *damn*, it's got it figured! Bothogi!"

Desan grasped his probe-spear and jogged on—"Divert it!" he yelled. Diverting it was all they could hope for.

It turned their way, a whine of the motor, a serpentine flex of its metal body, and a flurry of sand from its eight-wheeled drive. "Run, lord!" Bothogi gasped beside him; and it was still turning—it aimed for them now, and at another tangent a white-suited figure hurled a rock, to distract it yet again.

It kept coming at them. AI. An eight-wheeled, flex-bodied intelligence that had suddenly decided its behavior was not working and altered the program, refusing distraction. A pressure-windowed juggernaut tracking every turn they made.

Closer and closer. "Sensors!" Desan cried, turning on the slick dust—his footing failed him and he caught himself, gripped the probe, and aimed it straight at the sensor array clustered beneath the front window.

Thump! The dusty sky went blue and he was on his back, skidding in the sand with the great balloon tires churning sand on either side of him.

The suit, he thought with a spaceman's horror of the abrading, while it dawned on him at the same time that he was being dragged beneath the AI, and that every joint and nerve center was throbbing with the high-voltage shock of the probe.

Things became very peaceful then, a cessation of commotion. He lay dazed, staring up at a rusty blue sky, and seeing it laced with a silver thread.

They're coming, he thought, and thought of his eldest clone, sleeping at a well-educated twenty years of age. Handsome lad. He talked to the boy from time to time. *Poor lad, the lordship is yours. Your predecessor was a fool—*

A shadow passed above his face. It was another suited face peering down into his. A weight rested on his chest.

"Get off," he said.

"He's alive!" Bothogi's voice cried. "Dr. Gothon, he's still alive!"

The world showed no more scars than it had at the beginning—red and ocher where clouds failed. The algae continued its struggle in sea and tidal pools and lakes and rivers—with whatever microscopic addenda the breached dome had let loose in the world. The insects and the worms continued their blind ascent to space, dominant life on this poor, cratered globe. The research station was in function again, repairs complete.

Desan gazed on the world from his ship: it hung as a sphere in the holotank by his command station. A wave of his hand might show him the darkness of space; the floodlit shapes of ten hunting ships, lately returned from the deep and about to seek it again in continuation of the Mission, sleek fish rising and sinking again in a figurative black sea. A good many suns had shone on their hulls, but this one had seen them more often than any since their launching.

Home.

The space station was returning to function. Corpses were consigned to the sun the Mission had sought for so long. And power over the Mission rested solely at present in the hands of the lord-navigator, in the unprecedented circumstance of the demise of all five lords-magistrate simultaneously. Their clones were not yet activated to begin their years of majority—"Later will be time to wake the new lords-magistrate," Desan decreed, "at some further world of the search." Let them hear this event as history.

When I can manage them personally, he thought. He looked aside at twenty-year-old Desan-Six and the youth looked gravely back with the face Desan had seen in the mirror thirty-two waking years ago.

"Lord-navigator?"

"You'll wake your brother after we're away, Six. Directly after. I'll be staying awake much of this trip."

"*Awake*, sir?"

"Quite. There are things I want you to think about. I'll be talking to you and Seven both."

"About the lords-magistrate, sir?"

Desan lifted brows at this presumption. "You and I are already quite well attuned, Six. You'll succeed young. Are you sorry you missed this time?"

"No, lord-navigator! I assure you not!"

"Good brain. I ought to know. Go to your post, Six. Be grateful you don't have to cope with a new lordship *and* five new lords-magistrate and a recent schism." Desan leaned back in his chair as the youth crossed the bridge and settled at a crew-post, beside the captain. The lord-navigator was more than a figurehead to rule the seventy ships of the Mission, with their captains and their crews. Let the boy try his skill on this plotting. Desan intended to check it. He leaned aside with a wince—the electric shock that had blown him flat between the AI's tires had saved him from worse than a broken arm and leg; and the medical staff had seen to that: the arm and the leg were all but healed, with only a light wrap to protect them. The ribs were tightly wrapped too, and they caused him more pain than all the rest.

A scan had indeed located three errant asteroids, three courses the station's computers had not accurately recorded as inbound for the planet—until personnel from the ships began to run their own observations. Those were redirected.

Casualties. Destruction. Fighting within the Mission. The guilt of the lords-magistrate was profound and beyond dispute.

"Lord-navigator," the communications officer said. "Dr. Gothon returning your call."

Good-bye, he had told Gothon. *I don't accept your judgment, but I shall devote my energy to pursuit of mine, and let any who want to join you reside on the station. There are some volunteers; I don't profess to understand them. But you may trust them. You may trust the lords-magistrate to have learned a lesson. I will teach it. No member of this mission will be restrained in any opinion while my influence lasts. And I shall see to that. Sleep again and we may see each other once more in our lives.*

"I'll receive it," Desan said, pleased and anxious at once that Gothon deigned reply; he activated the com-control. Ship-electronics touched his ear, implanted for comfort. He heard the usual blip and chatter of com's mechanical protocols, then Gothon's quiet voice. "Lord-navigator."

"I'm hearing you, doctor."

"Thank you for your sentiment. I wish you well too. I wish you very well."

The tablet was mounted before him, above the console. Millions of years ago a tiny probe had set out from this world, bearing the original. Two aliens standing naked, one with hand uplifted. A series of diagrams which, partially obliterated, had still served to guide the Mission across the centuries. A probe bearing a greeting. Ages-dead cameras and simple instruments.

Greetings, stranger. We come from this place, this star system.

See, the hand, the appendage of a builder—this we will have in common.

The diagrams: we speak knowledge; we have no fear of you, strangers who read this, whoever you be.

Wise fools.

There had been a time, long ago, when fools had set out to seek them . . . in a vast desert of stars. Fools who had desperately needed proof, once upon a quarter million years ago, that they were not alone. One dust-scoured alien artifact they found, so long ago, on a lonely drifting course. *Hello,* it said.

The makers, the peaceful Ancients, became a legend. They became purpose, inspiration.

The overriding, obsessive *Why* that saved a species, pulled it back from war, gave it the stars.

"I'm very serious—I do hope you rest, doctor—save a few years for the unborn."

"My eldest's awake. I've lost my illusions of immortality, lord-navigator. I hope to spend my years teaching her. I've told her about *you*, lord-navigator. She hopes to meet you."

"You might still abandon this world and come with us, doctor."

"To search for a myth?"

"Not a myth. We're bound to disagree. Doctor, doctor, what *good* can your presence there do? What if you're right? It's a dead end. What if I'm wrong? I'll never stop looking. *I'll* never know."

"But we know their descendants, lord-navigator. We. We are. We're spreading their legend from star to star—they've become a fable. The Ancients, the Pathfinders. A hundred civilizations have taken up that myth. A hundred civilizations have lived out their years in that belief and begotten others to tell their story. What if you should find them? Would you know them—or where evolution had taken them? Perhaps we've already met them, somewhere among the worlds we've visited, and we failed to know them."

It was irony. Gentle humor. "Perhaps, then," Desan said in turn, "we'll find the track leads home again. Perhaps we *are* their children—eight and a quarter million years removed."

"O ye makers of myths. Do your work, spacefarer. Tangle the skein with legends. Teach fables to the races you meet. Brighten the universe with them. I put my faith in you. Don't you know—this world is all I came to find, but you—child of the voyage, you have to have more. For you the voyage is the Mission. Good-bye to you. Farewell. Nothing is complete calamity. The equation here is different, by a multitude of microorganisms let free—Bothogi has stopped grieving and begun to have quite different thoughts on the matter. His algae pools may turn out a different breed this time—the shift of a protein here and there in the genetic chain—who knows what it will breed? Different software this time, perhaps. Good voyage to you, lord-navigator. Look for your Ancients under other suns. We're waiting for their offspring here, under this one."

Snow

JOHN CROWLEY

John Crowley (1942–) is a US fiction writer, screenwriter, and teacher who gained enduring devotion from a legion of fans for his fantasy novel *Little, Big* (1981), which Harold Bloom called "a neglected masterpiece." In a sense, Crowley's *Ægypt* series can be seen as a continuation of the themes in *Little, Big*—including exploration of family dynamics, the role of memory, and esoteric strands of religion. Other novels include *The Deep* (1975), *Beasts* (1976), and *Engine Summer* (1979)—the latter a nominee for the 1980 National Book Award. Crowley currently teaches at the Yale Writers' Workshop and writes a monthly column for *Harper's* magazine. He has won the Award in Literature from the American Academy and Institute of Arts and Letters (1992) and the World Fantasy Life Achievement Award (2006), among other honors.

The story reprinted here, "Snow" (1986), was a finalist for both the Hugo and Nebula Awards. Like many of his works, "Snow" deals with the themes of memory and loss. The gadget the Wasp in the story is not too different from modern life today, in which so much of what we do is captured for all eternity.

In a 2011 interview for *Lightspeed* magazine, Crowley said of the story, "When I was writing it I thought I needed to set the story pretty far in the future in order to make the existence of a machine like the Wasp realistic. So the details of the freight airship and the closed highways were to suggest a world that's changed greatly from ours. And in the state of my and the world's knowledge when the story was written in the 1970s, things like the Wasp did seem a long way off. But you probably know that technology has very nearly created the Wasp already. Drones the size of hummingbirds are now capable of facial recognition, can hover and follow and transmit from an array of sensors, and bug-sized ones are coming."

Crowley notes, "This happens a lot in SF: writers come up with one thing that is not only possible but just about to appear, and insert it into an extraordinary world a long way off, or they leave stuff from their own time in the world they imagine: the first sentence of William Gibson's *Neuromancer*, set at some far-off digital world, starts with a sentence (quoted from memory), 'The sky was the color of a television tuned to a dead channel.' But that's not how televisions look even today—that gray cloudy look is as old as the snow in my story—dead channels are bright blue. But how could he know that?"

SNOW

John Crowley

I don't think Georgie would ever have got one for herself: she was at once unsentimental and a little in awe of death. No, it was her first husband—an immensely rich and (from Georgie's description) a strangely weepy guy, who had got it for her. Or for himself, actually, of course. He was to be the beneficiary. Only he died himself shortly after it was installed. If *installed* is the right word. After he died, Georgie got rid of most of what she'd inherited from him, liquidated it. It was cash that she had liked best about that marriage anyway; but the Wasp couldn't really be got rid of. Georgie ignored it.

In fact the thing really was about the size of a wasp of the largest kind, and it had the same lazy and mindless flight. And of course it really was a bug, not of the insect kind but of the surveillance kind. And so its name fit all around: one of those bits of accidental poetry the world generates without thinking. O Death, where is thy sting?

Georgie ignored it, but it was hard to avoid; you had to be a little careful around it; it followed Georgie at a variable distance, depending on her motions and the numbers of other people around her, the level of light, and the tone of her voice. And there was always the danger you might shut it in a door or knock it down with a tennis racket.

It cost a fortune (if you count the access and the perpetual care contract, all prepaid), and though it wasn't really fragile, it made you nervous.

It wasn't recording all the time. There had to be a certain amount of light, though not much. Darkness shut it off. And then sometimes it would get lost. Once when we hadn't seen it hovering around for a time, I opened a closet door, and it flew out, unchanged. It went off looking for her, humming softly. It must have been shut in there for days.

Eventually it ran out, or down. A lot could go wrong, I suppose, with circuits that small, controlling that many functions. It ended up spending a lot of time bumping gently against the bedroom ceiling, over and over, like a winter fly. Then one day the maids swept it out from under the bureau, a husk. By that time it had transmitted at least eight thousand hours (eight thousand was the minimum guarantee) of Georgie: of her days and hours, her comings in and her goings out, her speech and motion, her living self—all on file, taking up next to no room, at the Park. And then, when the time came, you could go there, to the Park, say on a Sunday afternoon; and in quiet landscaped surroundings (as the Park described it) you would find her personal resting chamber, and there, in privacy, through the miracle of modern information storage and retrieval systems, you could access her, her alive, her as she was in every way, never changing or growing any older, fresher (as the Park's brochure said) than in memory ever green.

I married Georgie for her money, the same reason she married her first, the one who took out the Park's contract for her. She married me, I think, for my looks; she always had a taste for looks in men. I wanted to write. I made a calculation that more women than men make, and decided that to be supported and paid for by a rich wife would give me freedom to do so, to "develop." The calculation worked out no better for me than it does for most women who make it. I carried a typewriter and a case of miscellaneous paper from Ibiza to Gstaad to Bali to London, and typed on beaches, and learned to ski. Georgie liked me in ski clothes.

Now that those looks are all but gone, I can look back on myself as a young hunk and see that I was in a way a rarity, a type that you run into often among women, far less among men, the beauty unaware of his beauty, aware that he affects women profoundly and more or less instantly but doesn't know why; thinks he is being listened to and understood, that his soul is being seen, when all that's being seen is long-lashed eyes and a strong, square, tanned wrist turning in a lovely gesture, stubbing out a cigarette. Confusing. By the time I figured out why I had for so long been indulged and cared for and listened to, why I was interesting, I wasn't as interesting as I had been. At about the same time I realized I wasn't a writer at all. Georgie's investment stopped looking as good to her, and my calculation had ceased to add up; only by that time I had come, pretty unexpectedly, to love Georgie a lot, and she just as unexpectedly had come to love and need me too, as much as she needed anybody. We never really parted, even though when she died I hadn't seen her for years. Phone calls, at dawn or four a.m. because she never, for all her travel, really grasped that the world turns and cocktail hour travels around with it. She was a crazy, wasteful, happy woman, without a trace of malice or permanence or ambition in her—easily pleased and easily bored and strangely serene despite the hectic pace she kept up. She cherished things and lost them and forgot them: things, days, people. She had fun, though, and I had fun with her; that was her talent and her destiny, not always an easy one. Once, hungover in a New York hotel, watching a sudden snowfall out the immense window, she said to me, "Charlie, I'm going to die of fun."

And she did. Snow-foiling in Austria, she was among the first to get one of those snow leopards, silent beasts as fast as speedboats. Alfredo called me in California to tell me, but with the distance and his accent and his eagerness to tell me he wasn't to blame, I never grasped the details. I was still her husband, her closest relative, heir to the little she still had, and beneficiary, too, of the Park's access concept. Fortunately, the Park's services included collecting her from the morgue in Gstaad and installing her in her chamber at the Park's California unit. Beyond signing papers and taking delivery when Georgie arrived by freight airship at Van Nuys, there was nothing for me to do. The Park's representative was solicitous and made sure I understood how to go about accessing Georgie, but I wasn't listening. I am only a child of my time, I suppose. Everything about death, the fact of it, the fate of the remains, and the situation of the living faced with it, seems grotesque to me, embarrassing, useless. And everything done about it only makes it more grotesque, more useless: someone I loved is dead; let me therefore dress in clown's clothes, talk backwards, and buy expensive machinery to make up for it. I went back to LA.

A year or more later, the contents of some safe-deposit boxes of Georgie's arrived from the lawyer's: some bonds and such stuff and a small steel case, velvet lined, that contained a key, a key deeply notched on both sides and headed with smooth plastic, like the key to an expensive car.

Why did I go to the Park that first time? Mostly because I had forgotten about it. Getting that key in the mail was like coming across a pile of old snapshots you hadn't cared to look at when they were new but which after they have aged come to contain the past, as they did not contain the present. I was curious.

I understood very well that the Park and its access concept were very probably only another cruel joke on the rich, preserving the illusion that they can buy what can't be bought, like the cryonics fad of thirty years ago. Once in Ibiza, Georgie and I met a German couple who also had a contract with the Park; their Wasp hovered over them like a Paraclete and made them self-conscious in the extreme—they seemed to be constantly rehearsing the eternal show being stored up for their descendants. Their deaths had taken over their lives, as though they were pharaohs. Did they, Georgie wondered, exclude the Wasp from their bedroom? Or did its presence there stir them to greater efforts, proofs of undying love and admirable vigor for the unborn to see?

No, death wasn't to be cheated that way, any more than by pyramids, by masses said in perpetuity. It wasn't Georgie saved from death that I would find. But there were eight thousand hours of her life with me, genuine hours, stored there more carefully than they could be in my porous memory; Georgie hadn't excluded the Wasp from her bedroom, our bedroom, and she who had never performed for anybody could not have conceived of performing for it. And there would be me, too, undoubtedly, caught unintentionally by the Wasp's attention. Out of those thousands of hours there would be hundreds of myself, and myself had just then begun to be problematic to me, something that had to be figured out, something about which evidence had to be gathered and weighed. I was thirty-eight years old.

That summer, then, I borrowed a Highway Access Permit (the old HAPpy cards of those days) from a county lawyer I knew and drove the coast highway up to where the Park was, at the end of a pretty beach road, all alone above the sea. It looked from the outside like the best, most peaceful kind of Italian country cemetery, a low stucco wall topped with urns, amid cypresses, an arched gate in the center. A small brass plaque on the gate: PLEASE USE YOUR KEY. The gate opened, not to a square of shaded tombstones but onto a ramped corridor going down: the cemetery wall was an illusion, the works were underground. Silence, or nameless Muzak like silence. Solitude: either the necessary technicians were discreetly hidden or none were needed. Certainly the access concept turned out to be simplicity itself, in operation

anyway. Even I, who am an idiot about information technology, could tell that. The Wasp was genuine state-of-the-art stuff, but what we mourners got was as ordinary as home movies, as old letters tied up in ribbon.

A display screen near the entrance told me down which corridor to find Georgie, and my key let me into a small screening room where there was a moderate-size TV monitor, two comfortable chairs, and dark walls of chocolate-brown carpeting. The sweet-sad Muzak. Georgie herself was evidently somewhere in the vicinity, in the wall or under the floor, they weren't specific about the charnel-house aspect of the place. In the control panel before the TV were a keyhole for my key and two bars: ACCESS and RESET.

I sat, feeling foolish and a little afraid, too, made more uncomfortable by being so deliberately soothed by neutral furnishings and sober tools. I imagined, around me, down other corridors, in other chambers, others communed with their dead as I was about to do, that the dead were murmuring to them beneath the stream of Muzak; that they wept to see and hear, as I might; but I could hear nothing. I turned my key in its slot, and the screen lit up. The dim lights dimmed further, and the Muzak ceased. I pushed ACCESS, obviously the next step. No doubt all these procedures had been explained to me long ago at the dock when Georgie in her aluminum box was being off-loaded, and I hadn't listened. And on the screen she turned to look at me—only not at me, though I started and drew breath—at the Wasp that watched her. She was in midsentence, midgesture. Where? When? *Or put it on the same card with the others,* she said, turning away. Someone said something, Georgie answered, and stood up, the Wasp panning and moving erratically with her, like an amateur with a home-video camera. A white room, sunlight, wicker. Ibiza. Georgie wore a cotton blouse, open; from a table she picked up lotion, poured some on her hand, and rubbed it across her freckled breastbone. The meaningless conversation about putting something on a card went on, ceased. I watched the room, wondering what year, what season I had stumbled into. Georgie pulled off her shirt—her small round breasts tipped with large, childlike nipples, child's breasts she still had at forty, shook delicately. And she went out onto the balcony, the Wasp following, blinded by sun, adjusting. *If you want to do it that way,* someone said. The someone crossed the screen, a brown blur, naked. It was me. Georgie said: *Oh, look, hummingbirds.*

She watched them, rapt, and the Wasp crept close to her cropped blond head, rapt too, and I watched her watch. She turned away, rested her elbows on the balustrade. I couldn't remember this day. How should I? One of hundreds, of thousands . . . She looked out to the bright sea, wearing her sleepwalking face, mouth partly open, and absently stroked her breast with her oiled hand. An iridescent glitter among the flowers was the hummingbird.

Without really knowing what I did—I felt hungry, suddenly, hungry for pastness, for more—I touched the RESET bar. The balcony in Ibiza vanished, the screen glowed emptily. I touched ACCESS.

At first there was darkness, a murmur; then a dark back moved away from the Wasp's eye, and a dim scene of people resolved itself. Jump. Other people, or the same people, a party? Jump. Apparently the Wasp was turning itself on and off according to the changes in light levels here, wherever here was. Georgie in a dark dress having her cigarette lit: brief flare of the lighter. She said, *Thanks.* Jump. A foyer or hotel lounge. Paris? The Wasp jerkily sought for her among people coming and going; it couldn't really make a movie, establishing shots, cutaways—it could only doggedly follow Georgie, like a jealous husband, seeing nothing else. This was frustrating. I pushed RESET. ACCESS. Georgie brushed her teeth, somewhere, somewhen.

I understood, after one or two more of these terrible leaps. Access was random. There was no way to dial up a year, a day, a scene. The Park had supplied no program, none; the eight thousand hours weren't filed at all, they were a jumble, like a lunatic's memory, like a deck of shuffled cards. I had supposed, without thinking about it, that they would begin at the beginning and go on till they reached the end. Why didn't they?

I also understood something else. If access was truly random, if I truly had no control, then I had lost as good as forever those scenes I had seen. Odds were on the order of eight thousand to one (more? far more? probabilities are opaque to me) that I would never light on them again by pressing this bar. I felt a pang of loss for that afternoon in Ibiza. It was doubly gone now. I sat before the empty screen, afraid to touch ACCESS again, afraid of what I would lose.

I shut down the machine (the light level in the room rose, the Muzak poured softly back in) and went out into the halls, back to the display screen in the entranceway. The list of names slowly, greenly, rolled over like the list of departing flights at an airport. Code numbers were missing from beside many, indicating perhaps that they weren't yet in residence, only awaited. In the *D*s, three names, and DIRECTOR—hidden among them as though he were only another of the dead. A chamber number. I went to find it and went in. The director looked more like a janitor or a night watchman, the semiretired type you often see caretaking little-visited places. He wore a brown smock like a monk's robe and was making coffee in a corner of his small office, out of which little business seemed to be done. He looked up startled, caught out, when I entered.

"Sorry," I said, "but I don't think I understand this system right."

"A problem?" he said. "Shouldn't be a problem." He looked at me a little wide-eyed and shy, hoping not to be called on for anything difficult. "Equipment's all working?"

"I don't know," I said. "It doesn't seem that it could be." I described what I thought I had learned about the Park's access concept. "That can't be right, can it?" I said. "That access is totally random . . ."

He was nodding, still wide-eyed, paying close attention.

"Is it?" I asked.

"Is it what?"

"Random."

"Oh, yes. Yes, sure. If everything's in working order."

I could think of nothing to say for a moment, watching him nod reassuringly. Then, "Why?" I asked. "I mean why is there no way at all to, to organize, to have some kind of organized access to the material?" I had begun to feel that sense of grotesque foolishness in the presence of death, as though I were haggling over Georgie's effects. "That seems stupid, if you'll pardon me."

"Oh no, oh no," he said. "You've read your literature? You've read all your literature?"

"Well, to tell the truth . . ."

"It's all just as described," the director said. "I can promise you that. If there's any problem at all . . ."

"Do you mind," I said, "if I sit down?" I smiled. He seemed so afraid of me and my complaint, of me as mourner, possibly grief-crazed and unable to grasp the simple limits of his responsibilities to me, that he needed soothing himself. "I'm sure everything's fine," I said. "I just don't think I understand. I'm kind of dumb about these things."

"Sure. Sure. Sure." He regretfully put away his coffee makings and sat behind his desk, lacing his fingers together like a consultant. "People get a lot of satisfaction out of the access here," he said, "a lot of comfort, if they take it in the right spirit." He tried a smile. I wondered what qualifications he had had to show to get this job. "The random part. Now, it's all in the literature. There's the legal aspect—you're not a lawyer are you, no, no, sure, no offense. You see, the material here isn't for anything, except, well, except for communing. But suppose the stuff were programmed, searchable. Suppose there was a problem about taxes or inheritance or so on. There could be subpoenas, lawyers all over the place, destroying the memorial concept completely."

I really hadn't thought of that. Built-in randomness saved past lives from being searched in any systematic way. And no doubt saved the Park from being in the records business and at the wrong end of a lot of suits. "You'd have to watch the whole eight thousand hours," I said, "and even if you found what you were looking for there'd be no way to replay it. It would have gone by." It would slide into the random past even as you watched it, like that afternoon in Ibiza, that party in Paris. Lost. He smiled and nodded. I smiled and nodded.

"I'll tell you something," he said. "They didn't predict that. The randomness. It was a side effect, an effect of the storage process. Just luck." His grin turned down, his brows knitted seriously. "See, we're storing here at the molecular level. We have to go that small, for space problems. I mean your eight-thousand-hour guarantee. If we had gone tape or conventional, how much room would it take up? If the access concept caught on. A lot of room. So we went vapor-trap and endless tracking. Size of my thumbnail. It's all in the literature." He looked at me strangely. I had a sudden intense sensation that I was being fooled, tricked, that the man before me in his smock was no expert, no technician; he was a charlatan, or maybe a madman impersonating a director and not belonging here at all. It raised the hair on my neck and passed. "So the randomness," he was saying. "It was an effect of going molecular. Brownian movement. All you do is lift the endless tracking for a microsecond and you get a rearrangement at the molecular level. We don't randomize. The molecules do it for us."

I remembered Brownian movement, just barely, from physics class. The random movement of molecules, the teacher said; it has a mathematical description. It's like the movement of dust motes you see swimming in a shaft of sunlight, like the swirl of snowflakes in a glass paperweight that shows a cottage being snowed on. "I see," I said. "I guess I see."

"Is there," he said, "any other problem?" He said it as though there might be some other problem and that he knew what it might be and that he hoped I didn't have it. "You understand the system, key lock, two bars, ACCESS, RESET. . . ."

"I understand," I said. "I understand now."

"Communing," he said, standing, relieved, sure I would be gone soon. "I understand. It takes a while to relax into the communing concept."

"Yes," I said. "It does."

I wouldn't learn what I had come to learn, whatever that was. The Wasp had not been good at storage after all, no, no better than my young soul had been. Days and weeks had been missed by its tiny eye. It hadn't seen well, and in what it had seen it had been no more able to distinguish the just-as-well-forgotten from the unforgettable than my own eye had been. No better and no worse—the same.

And yet, and yet—she stood up in Ibiza and dressed her breasts with lotion, and spoke to me: *Oh, look, hummingbirds.* I had forgotten, and the Wasp had not; and I owned once again what I hadn't known I had lost, hadn't known was precious to me.

The sun was setting when I left the Park, the satin sea foaming softly, randomly around the rocks.

I had spent my life waiting for something, not knowing what, not even knowing I waited. Killing time. I was still waiting. But what I had been waiting for had already occurred and was past.

It was two years, nearly, since Georgie had died; two years until, for the first and last time, I wept for her—for her and for myself.

Of course I went back. After a lot of work and correctly placed dollars, I netted a HAPpy card of my own. I had time to spare, like a lot of people then, and often on empty afternoons (never on Sunday) I would get out onto the unpatched and weed-grown freeway and glide up the coast. The Park was always open. I relaxed into the communing concept.

Now, after some hundreds of hours spent there underground, now, when I have long ceased to go through those doors (I have lost my key, I think; anyway I don't know where to look for it), I know that the solitude I felt myself to be in was real. The watchers around me, the listeners I sensed in other chambers, were mostly my imagination. There was rarely anyone there. These tombs were as neglected as any tombs anywhere usually are. Either the living did not care to attend much on the dead—when have they ever?—or the hopeful buyers of the contracts had come to discover the flaw in the access concept—as I discovered it, in the end.

ACCESS, and she takes dresses one by one from her closet, and holds them against her body, and studies the effect in a tall mirror, and puts them back again. She had a funny face which she never made except when looking at herself in the mirror, a face made for no one but herself, that was actually quite unlike her. The mirror Georgie.

RESET.

ACCESS. By a bizarre coincidence here she is looking in another mirror. I think the Wasp could be confused by mirrors. She turns away, the Wasp adjusts; there is someone asleep, tangled in bedclothes on a big hotel bed, morning, a room-service cart. Oh, the Algonquin: myself. Winter. Snow is falling outside the tall window. She searches her handbag, takes out a small vial, swallows a pill with coffee, holding the cup by its body and not its handle. I stir, show a tousled head of hair. Conversation—unintelligible. Gray room, whitish snow light, color degraded. Would I now (I thought, watching us) reach out for her? Would I in the next hour take her, or she me, push aside the bedclothes, open her pale pajamas? She goes into the john, shuts the door. The Wasp watches stupidly, excluded, transmitting the door.

RESET, finally.

But what (I would wonder) if I had been patient, what if I had watched and waited?

Time, it turns out, takes an unconscionable time. The waste, the footless waste—it's no spectator sport. Whatever fun there is in sitting idly looking at nothing and tasting your own being for a whole afternoon, there is no fun in replaying it. The waiting is excruciating. How often, in five years, in eight thousand hours of daylight or lamplight, might we have coupled, how much time expended in lovemaking? A hundred hours, two hundred? Odds were not high of my coming on such a scene; darkness swallowed most of them, and the others were lost in the interstices of endless hours spent shopping, reading, on planes and in cars, asleep, apart. Hopeless.

ACCESS. She has turned on a bedside lamp. Alone. She hunts amid the Kleenex and magazines on the bedside table, finds a watch, looks at it dully, turns it right side up, looks again, and puts it down. Cold. She burrows in the blankets, yawning, staring, then puts out a hand for the phone but only rests her hand on it, thinking. Thinking at four a.m. She withdraws her hand, shivers a child's deep, sleepy shiver, and shuts off the light. A bad dream. In an instant it's morning, dawn; the Wasp slept, too. She sleeps soundly, unmoving, only the top of her blond head showing out of the quilt— and will no doubt sleep so for hours, watched over more attentively, more fixedly, than any Peeping Tom could ever have watched over her.

RESET.

ACCESS.

"I can't hear as well as I did at first," I told the director. "And the definition is getting softer."

"Oh sure," the director said. "That's really in the literature. We have to explain that carefully. That this might be a problem."

"It isn't just my monitor?" I asked. "I thought it was probably only the monitor."

"No, no, not really, no," he said. He gave me coffee. We'd gotten to be friendly over the months. I think, as well as being afraid of me, he was glad I came around now and then; at least one of the living came here, one at least was using the services. "There's a slight degeneration that does occur."

"Everything seems to be getting gray."

His face had shifted into intense concern, no belittling this problem. "Mm-hm, mm-hm, see, at the molecular level where we're at, there is degeneration. It's just in the physics. It randomizes a little over time. So you lose—you don't lose a minute of what you've got, but you lose a little definition. A little color. But it levels off."

"It does?"

"We think it does. Sure it does, we promise it does. We predict that it will."

"But you don't know."

"Well, well you see we've only been in this business a short while. This concept is new. There were things we couldn't know." He still looked at me, but seemed at the same time to have forgotten me. Tired. He seemed to have grown colorless himself lately, old, losing definition. "You might start getting some snow," he said softly.

ACCESS RESET ACCESS.

A gray plaza of herringbone-laid stones, gray, clicking palms. She turns up the collar of her sweater, narrowing her eyes in a stern wind. Buys magazines at a kiosk: *Vogue*, *Harper's*, *La Mode*. *Cold*, she says to the kiosk girl. *Frio*. The young man I was takes her arm: they walk back along the beach, which is deserted and strung with cast seaweed, washed by a dirty sea. Winter in Ibiza. We talk, but the Wasp can't hear, the sea's sound confuses it; it seems bored by its duties and lags behind us.

RESET.

ACCESS. The Algonquin, terribly familiar morning, winter. She turns away from the snow window. I am in bed, and for a moment watching this I felt suspended between two mirrors, reflected endlessly. I had seen this before; I had lived it once and remembered it once, and remembered the memory, and here it was again, or could it be nothing but another morning, a similar morning? There were far more than one like this, in this place. But no; she turns from the window, she gets out her vial of pills, picks up the coffee cup by its body: I had seen this moment before, not months before, weeks before, here in this chamber. I had come upon the same scene twice.

What are the odds of it, I wondered, what are the odds of coming upon the same minutes again, these minutes.

I stir within the bedclothes.

I leaned forward to hear, this time, what I would say; it was something like *but fun anyway*, or something.

Fun, she says, laughing, harrowed, the degraded sound a ghost's twittering. *Charlie, someday I'm going to die of fun.*

She takes her pill. The Wasp follows her to the john and is shut out.

Why am I here? I thought, and my heart was beating hard and slow. *What am I here for? What?*

RESET.

ACCESS.

Silvered icy streets, New York, Fifth Avenue. She is climbing, shouting from a cab's dark interior. *Just don't shout at me,* she shouts at someone; her mother I never met, a dragon. She is out and hurrying away down the sleety street with her bundles, the Wasp at her shoulder. I could reach out and touch her shoulder and make her turn and follow me out. Walking away, lost in the colorless press of traffic and people, impossible to discern within the softened snowy image.

Something was very wrong.

Georgie hated winter, she escaped it most of the time we were together, about the first of the year beginning to long for the sun that had gone elsewhere; Austria was all right for a few weeks, the toy villages and sugar snow and bright, sleek skiers were not really the winter she feared, though even in fire-warmed chalets it was hard to get her naked without gooseflesh and shudders from some draft only she could feel. We were chaste in winter. So Georgie escaped it: Antigua and Bali and two months in Ibiza when the almonds blossomed. It was continual false, flavorless spring all winter long.

How often could snow have fallen when the Wasp was watching her?

Not often; countable times, times I could count up myself if I could remember as the Wasp could. Not often. Not always.

"There's a problem," I said to the director.

"It's peaked out, has it?" he said. "That definition problem?"

"Actually," I said, "it's gotten worse."

He was sitting behind his desk, arms spread wide across his chair's back, and a false, pinkish flush to his cheeks like undertaker's makeup. Drinking.

"Hasn't peaked out, huh?" he said.

"That's not the problem," I said. "The problem is the access. It's not random like you said."

"Molecular level," he said. "It's in the physics."

"You don't understand. It's not getting more random. It's getting less random. It's getting selective. It's freezing up."

"No, no, no," he said dreamily. "Access is random. Life isn't all summer and fun, you know. Into each life some rain must fall."

I sputtered, trying to explain. "But, but . . ."

"You know," he said, "I've been thinking of getting out of access." He pulled open a drawer in the desk before him; it made an empty sound. He stared within it dully for a moment and shut it. "The Park's been good for me, but I'm just not used to this. Used to be you thought you could render a service, you know? Well, hell, you know, you've had fun, what do you care?"

He was mad. For an instant I heard the dead around me; I tasted on my tongue the stale air of underground.

"I remember," he said, tilting back in his chair and looking elsewhere, "many years ago, I got into access. Only we didn't call it that then. What I did was, I worked for a stock-footage house. It was going out of business, like they all did, like this place here is going to do, shouldn't say that, but you didn't hear it. Anyway, it was a big warehouse with steel shelves for miles, filled with film cans, film cans filled with old plastic film, you know? Film of every kind. And movie people, if they wanted old scenes of past time in their movies, would call up and ask for what they wanted, find me this, find me that. And we had everything, every kind of scene, but you know what the hardest thing to find was? Just ordinary scenes of daily life. I mean people just doing things and living their lives. You know what we did have? Speeches. People giving speeches. Like presidents. You could have hours of speeches, but not just people, whatchacallit, oh, washing clothes, sitting in a park. . . ."

"It might just be the reception," I said. "Somehow."

He looked at me for a long moment as though I had just arrived. "Anyway," he said at last, turning away again, "I was there awhile learning the ropes. And producers called and said, 'Get me this, get me that.' And one producer was making a film, some film of the past, and he wanted old scenes, old, of people long ago, in the summer; having fun; eating ice cream; swimming in bathing suits; riding in convertibles. Fifty years ago. Eighty years ago."

He opened his empty drawer again, found a toothpick, and began to use it.

"So I accessed the earliest stuff. Speeches. More speeches. But I found a scene here and there—people in the street, fur coats, window-shopping, traffic. Old people, I mean they were young then, but people of the past; they have these pinched kind of faces, you get to know them. Sad, a little. On city streets, hurrying, holding their hats. Cities were sort of black then, in film; black cars in the streets, black derby hats. Stone. Well, it wasn't what they wanted. I found summer for them, color summer, but new. They wanted old. I kept looking back. I kept looking. I did. The further back I went, the more I saw these pinched faces, black cars, black streets of stone. Snow. There isn't any summer there."

With slow gravity he rose and found a brown bottle and two coffee cups. He poured sloppily. "So it's not your reception," he said. "Film takes longer, I guess, but it's the physics.

All in the physics. A word to the wise is sufficient."

The liquor was harsh, a cold distillate of past sunlight. I wanted to go, get out, not look back. I would not stay watching until there was only snow.

"So I'm getting out of access," the director said. "Let the dead bury the dead, right? Let the dead bury the dead."

I didn't go back. I never went back, though the highways opened again and the Park isn't far from the town I've settled in. Settled; the right word. It restores your balance, in the end, even in a funny way your cheerfulness, when you come to know, without regrets, that the best thing that's going to happen in your life has already happened. And I still have some summer left to me.

I think there are two different kinds of memory, and only one kind gets worse as I get older: the kind where, by an effort of will, you can reconstruct your first car or your serial number or the name and figure of your high school physics teacher—a Mr. Holm, in a gray suit, a bearded guy, skinny, about thirty. The other kind doesn't worsen; if anything it grows more intense. The sleepwalking kind, the kind you stumble into as into rooms with secret doors and suddenly find yourself sitting not on your front porch but in a classroom, you can't at first think where or when, and a bearded, smiling man is turning in his hand a glass paperweight, inside which a little cottage stands in a swirl of snow.

There is no access to Georgie, except that now and then, unpredictably, when I'm sitting on the porch or pushing a grocery cart or standing at the sink, a memory of that kind will visit me, vivid and startling, like a hypnotist's snap of fingers. Or like that funny experience you sometimes have, on the point of sleep, of hearing your name called softly and distinctly by someone who is not there.

The Lake Was Full of Artificial Things

KAREN JOY FOWLER

Karen Joy Fowler (1950–) is an influential and award-winning US writer of speculative and mainstream fiction associated with the Humanists (including Kim Stanley Robinson) and the rise of feminist science fiction. She studied at Berkeley and the University of California at Davis, receiving a BA in political science and an MA in North Asian studies. Fowler is best known as the author of two bestselling novels, *The Jane Austen Book Club* (2004), which was made into a movie, and *We Are All Completely Beside Ourselves* (2013). She has won several awards, including the Nebula Award and World Fantasy Award, in addition to being shortlisted for the Man Booker Prize and the Warwick Prize (both for *We Are All Completely Beside Ourselves*). In 1991, Fowler cofounded the James Tiptree Jr. Award, given annually to a work of science fiction or fantasy that "expands or explores our understanding of gender."

We Are All Completely Beside Ourselves is not, strictly speaking, science fiction (although, amusingly enough, it was shortlisted for the Nebula Award for science fiction) but exhibits a speculative impulse in how it interrogates the way human beings interact with and perceive animals. Her often ambiguous approach to genre writing also manifests in novels like *Sarah Canary* (1991), which can be read as a feminist story of the nineteenth century *and* a first-contact story with a character who may or may not be an alien.

Fowler began publishing science fiction with "Recalling Cinderella" in *L. Ron Hubbard Presents Writers of the Future*, volume 1 (1985), edited by Algis Budrys. Swiftly thereafter her first collection, *Artificial Things* (1986), had a large impact on the field and she won the 1987 John W. Campbell Award for Best New Writer. Later collections include *Peripheral Vision* (1990), *Letters from Home* (1991; with separate stories by Fowler, Pat Cadigan, and Pat Murphy), and *Black Glass: Short Fictions* (1997), which assembles stories from the previous two volumes, plus original material, and which was recently reissued. Her most recent collection, *What I Didn't See and Other Stories* (2009), won the World Fantasy Award. Fowler has shown considerable range in her short fiction throughout her career. Some stories, like "Face Value" (1986) or "Faded Roses" (1989), are pure science fiction, while others shift into fantasy or fabulation, using ambiguity in ingenious and unique ways.

On the topic of ambiguity, Fowler wrote in an essay included in *Wonderbook* (2013), "I don't use ambiguity in a story as a literary device or a postmodern trick . . . I use it in an attempt to acknowledge that the things we think we know are submerged in a vast sea of things we don't know and things we will never know. I mean to admit to my own lack of comprehension about the world in which we live."

"The Lake Was Full of Artificial Things" (1985), originally published in *Isaac Asimov's Science Fiction Magazine*, features hypnotherapy and time travel. Despite being an early tale of hers, the story is typically Fowleresque in its mixture of complexity and deep characterization.

THE LAKE WAS FULL OF ARTIFICIAL THINGS

Karen Joy Fowler

Daniel was older than Miranda had expected. In 1970, when they had said good-bye, he had been twenty-two. Two years later he was dead, but now, approaching her with the bouncing walk which had suited his personality so well, he appeared as a middle-aged man and quite gray, though solid and muscular. She noted with relief that he was smiling. "Randy!" he said. He laughed delightedly. "You look wonderful."

Miranda glanced down at herself, wondering what, in fact, she did look like or if she had any form at all. She saw the flesh of her arms firm again and the skin smooth and tight. So she was the twenty-year-old. Isn't that odd, she thought, turning her hands palms up to examine them. Then Daniel reached her. The sun was bright in the sky behind him, obscuring his face, giving him a halo. He put his arms around her. I feel him, she thought in astonishment. I smell him. She breathed in slowly. "Hello, Daniel," she said.

He squeezed her slightly, then dropped his arms and looked around. Miranda looked outward, too. They were on the college campus. Surely this was not the setting she would have chosen. It unsettled her, as if she had been sent backward in time and gifted with prescience, but remained powerless to make any changes, was doomed to see it all again, moving to its inevitable conclusion. Daniel, however, seemed pleased.

He pointed off to the right. "There's the creek," he said, and suddenly she could hear it. "Memories there, right?" And she remembered lying beneath him on the grass by the water. She put her hands on his shoulders now; his clothes were rough against her palms and military—like his hair. He gestured to the round brick building behind her. "Tollman Hall," he said. "Am I right? God, this is great, Randy. I remember everything. Total recall. I had Physics Ten there with Dr. Fielding. Physics for nonmajors. I couldn't manage my vectors and I got a B." He laughed again, throwing an arm around Miranda. "It's great to be back."

They began to walk together toward the center of campus, slow walking with no destination, designed for conversation. They were all alone, Miranda noticed. The campus was deserted, then suddenly it wasn't. Students appeared on the pathways. Longhairs with headbands and straights with slide rules. Just what she remembered. "Tell me what everyone's been doing," Daniel said. "It's been what? Thirty years? Don't leave out a thing."

Miranda stooped and picked a small daisy out of the grass. She twirled it absentmindedly in her fingers. It left a green stain on her thumb. Daniel stopped walking and waited beside her. "Well," Miranda said. "I've lost touch with most of them. Gail got a job on *Le Monde*. She went to Germany for the reunification. I heard she was living there. The antinuclear movement was her permanent beat. She could still be there, I suppose."

"So she's still a radical," said Daniel. "What stamina."

"Margaret bought a bakery in San Francisco. Sixties cuisine. Whole grains. Tofu brownies. Heaviest cookies west of the Rockies. We're in the same cable chapter so I keep up with her better. I saw her last marriage on TV. She's been married three times now, every one a loser."

"What about Allen?" Daniel asked.

"Allen," repeated Miranda. "Well, Allen

had a promising career in jogging shoes. He was making great strides." She glanced at Daniel's face. "Sorry," she said. "Allen always brought out the worst in me. He lost his father in an air collision over Kennedy. Sued the airline and discovered he never had to work again. In short, Allen is rich. Last I heard, and this was maybe twenty years ago, he was headed to the Philippines to buy himself a submissive bride." She saw Daniel smile, the lines in his face deepening with his expression. "Oh, you'd like to blame me for Allen, wouldn't you?" she said. "But it wouldn't be fair. I dated him maybe three times, tops." Miranda shook her head. "Such an enthusiastic participant in the sexual revolution. And then it all turned to women's liberation on him. Poor Allen. We can only hope his tiny wife divorced him and won a large settlement when you could still get alimony."

Daniel moved closer to her and they began to walk again, passing under the shade of a redwood grove. The grass changed to needles under their feet. "You needn't be so hard on Allen," he said. "I never minded about him. I always knew you loved me."

"Did you?" asked Miranda anxiously. She looked at her feet, afraid to examine Daniel's face. My god, she was wearing moccasins. Had she ever worn moccasins? "I did get married, Daniel," she said. "I married a mathematician. His name was Michael." Miranda dropped her daisy, petals intact.

Daniel continued to walk, swinging his arms easily. "Well, you were always hot for mathematics. I didn't expect you to mourn me forever."

"So it's all right?"

Daniel stopped, turning to face her. He was still smiling, though it was not quite the smile she expected, not quite the easy, happy smile she remembered. "It's all right that you got married, Randy," he said softly. Something passed over his face and left it. "Hey!" he laughed again. "I remember something else from Physics Ten. Zeno's paradox. You know what that is?"

"No," said Miranda.

"It's an argument. Zeno argued that motion was impossible because it required an object to pass through an infinite number of points in a finite amount of time." Daniel swung his arms energetically. "Think about it for a minute, Randy. Can you fault it? Then think about how far I came to be here with you."

"Miranda. Miranda." It was her mother's voice, rousing her for school. Only then it wasn't. It was Dr. Matsui, who merely sounded maternal, despite the fact that she had no children of her own and was not yet thirty. Miranda felt her chair returning slowly to its upright position. "Are you back?" Dr. Matsui asked. "How did it go?"

"It was short," Miranda told her. She pulled the taped wires gently from her lids and opened her eyes. Dr. Matsui was seated beside her, reaching into Miranda's hair to detach the clips which touched her scalp.

"Perhaps we recalled you too early," she conceded. "Matthew spotted an apex so we pulled the plug. We just wanted a happy ending. It was happy, wasn't it?"

"Yes." Dr. Matsui's hair, parted on one side and curving smoothly under her chin, bobbed before Miranda's face. Miranda touched it briefly, then her own hair, her cheeks, and her nose. They felt solid under her hand, real, but no more so than Daniel had been. "Yes, it was," she repeated. "He was so happy to see me. So glad to be back. But, Anna, he was so real. I thought you said it would be like a dream."

"No," Dr. Matsui told her. "I said it wouldn't be. I said it was a memory of something that never happened and in that respect was like a dream. I wasn't speaking to the quality of the experience." She rolled her chair to the monitor and stripped the long feed-out sheet from it, tracing the curves quickly with one finger. Matthew, her technician, came to stand behind her. He leaned over her left shoulder, pointing. "There," he said. "That's Daniel. That's what I put in."

Dr. Matsui returned her chair to Miranda's side. "Here's the map," she said. "Maybe I can explain better."

Miranda tried to sit forward. One remaining clip pulled her hair and made her inhale sharply. She reached up to detach herself. "Sorry," said Dr. Matsui sheepishly. She held out the paper for Miranda to see. "The dark waves is the Daniel we recorded off your memories earlier. Happy memories, right? You can see the fainter echo here as you responded to it with the original memories. Think of it as memory squared. Naturally, it's going to be intense. Then, everything else here is the record of the additional activity you brought to this particular session. Look at these sharp peaks at the beginning. They indicate stress. You'll see that nowhere else do they recur. On paper it looks to have been an entirely successful session. Of course, only you know the content of the experience." Her dark eyes were searching and sympathetic. "Well," she said. "Do you feel better about him?"

"Yes," said Miranda. "I feel better."

"Wonderful." Dr. Matsui handed the feedback to Matthew. "Store it," she told him.

Miranda spoke hesitatingly. "I had other things I wanted to say to him," she said. "It doesn't feel resolved."

"I don't think the sessions ever resolve things," Dr. Matsui said. "The best they can do is open the mind to resolution. The resolution still has to be found in the real world."

"Can I see him again?" Miranda asked.

Dr. Matsui interlaced her fingers and pressed them to her chest. "A repeat would be less expensive, of course," she said. "Since we've already got Daniel. We could just run him through again. Still, I'm reluctant to advise it. I wonder what else we could possibly gain."

"Please, Anna," said Miranda. She was looking down at her arms, remembering how firmly fleshed they had seemed.

"Let's wait and see how you're feeling after our next couple regular visits. If the old regrets persist and, more importantly, if they're still interfering with your ability to get on with things, then ask me again."

She was standing. Miranda swung her legs over the side of the chair and stood, too. Matthew walked with her to the door of the office. "We've got a goalie coming in next," he confided. "She stepped into the goal while holding the ball; she wants to remember it the way it didn't happen. Self-indulgent if you ask me. But then, athletes make the money, right?" He held the door open, his arm stretched in front of Miranda. "You feel better, don't you?" he asked.

"Yes," she reassured him.

She met Daniel for lunch at Frank Fats Cafe. They ordered fried clams and scallops, but the food never came. Daniel was twenty again and luminescent with youth. His hair was blond and his face was smooth. Had he really been so beautiful? Miranda wondered.

"I'd love a Coke," he said. "I haven't had one in thirty years."

"You're kidding," said Miranda. "They don't have the real thing in heaven?"

Daniel looked puzzled.

"Skip it," she told him. "I was just wondering what it was like being dead. You could tell me."

"It's classified," said Daniel. "On a need-to-know basis."

Miranda picked up her fork, which was heavy and cold. "This time it's you who looks wonderful. Positively beatific. Last time you looked so—" She started to say *old*, but amended it. After all, he had looked no older than she did these days. Such things were relative. "Tired," she finished.

"No, I wasn't tired," Daniel told her. "It was the war."

"The war's over now," Miranda said, and this time his smile was decidedly unpleasant.

"Is it?" he asked. "Just because you don't read about it in the paper now? Just because you watch the evening news and there's no body count in the corner of the screen?"

"Television's not like that now," Miranda began, but Daniel hadn't stopped talking.

"What's really going on in Southeast Asia? Do you even know?" Daniel shook his head. "Wars never end," he said. He leaned threateningly over the table. "Do you imagine for one minute that it's over for me?"

Miranda slammed her fork down. "Don't do that," she said. "Don't try to make me guilty of that, too. You didn't have to go. I begged you not to. Jesus, you knew what the war was. If you'd gone off to save the world from communist aggression, I would have disagreed, but I could have understood. But you knew better than that. I never forgave you for going."

"It was so easy for you to see what was right," Daniel responded angrily. "You were completely safe. You women could graduate without losing your deferment. Your goddamn birthday wasn't drawn twelfth in the draft lottery and if it had been you wouldn't have cared. When was your birthday drawn? You don't even know." Daniel leaned back and looked out the window. People appeared on the street. A woman in a red miniskirt got into a blue car. Then Daniel faced her again, large before Miranda. She couldn't shut him out. " 'Go to Canada,' you said. 'That's what I'd do.' I wonder. Could you have married your mathematician in Canada? I can just picture you saying good-bye to your mother forever."

"My mother's dead now," said Miranda. A knot of tears tightened about her throat.

"And so the hell am I." Daniel reached for her wrists, holding them too hard, hurting her deliberately. "But you're not, are you? You're just fine."

There was a voice behind Daniel. "Miranda. Miranda," it called.

"Mother," cried Miranda. But, of course it wasn't, it was Anna Matsui, gripping her wrists, bringing her back. Miranda gasped for breath and Dr. Matsui let go of her. "It was awful," said Miranda. She began to cry. "He

accused me . . ." She pulled the wires from her eyes recklessly. Tears spilled out of them. Miranda ached all over.

"He accused you of nothing." Dr. Matsui's voice was sharp and disappointed. "You accused yourself. The same old accusations. We made Daniel out of you, remember?" She rolled her chair backward, moved to the monitor for the feedback. Matthew handed it to her and she read it, shaking her head. Her short black hair flew against her cheeks. "It shouldn't have happened," she said. "We used only the memories that made you happy. And with your gift for lucid dreaming—well, I didn't think there was a risk." Her face was apologetic as she handed Miranda a tissue and waited for the crying to stop. "Matthew wanted to recall you earlier," she confessed, "but I didn't want it to end this way."

"No!" said Miranda. "We can't stop now. I never answered him."

"You only need to answer yourself. It's your memory and imagination confronting you. He speaks only with your voice, he behaves only as you expect him to." Dr. Matsui examined the feedback map again. "I should never have agreed to a repeat. I certainly won't send you back." She looked at Miranda and softened her voice. "Lie still. Lie still until you feel better."

"Like in another thirty years?" asked Miranda. She closed her eyes; her head hurt from the crying and the wires. She reached up to detach one close to her ear. "Everything he said to me was true," she added tonelessly.

"Many things he didn't say are bound to be true as well," Dr. Matsui pointed out. "Therapy is not really concerned with truth, which is almost always merely a matter of perspective. Therapy is concerned with adjustment—adjustment to an unchangeable situation or to a changing truth." She lifted a pen from her collar, clicking the point in and out absentmindedly. "In any given case," she continued, "we face a number of elements within our control and a far greater number beyond it. In a case such as yours, where the patient has felt profoundly and morbidly guilty over an extended period of time, it is because she is focusing almost exclusively on her own behavior. 'If only I hadn't done x,' she thinks, 'then y would never have happened.' Do you understand what I'm saying, Miranda?"

"No."

"In these sessions we try to show you what might have happened if the elements you couldn't control were changed. In your case we let you experience a continued relationship with Daniel. You see that you bore him no malice. You wished him nothing ill. If he had come back the bitterness of your last meeting would have been unimportant."

"He asked me to marry him," said Miranda. "He asked me to wait for him. I told you that. And I said that I was seeing Allen. Allen! I said as far as I was concerned he was already gone."

"You wish you could change that, of course. But what you really want to change is his death, and that was beyond your control." Dr. Matsui's face was sweet and intense.

Miranda shook her head. "You're not listening to me, Anna. I told you what happened, but I lied about why it happened. I pretended we had political differences. I thought my behavior would be palatable if it looked like a matter of conscience. But really I dated Allen for the first time before Daniel had even been drafted. Because I knew what was coming. I saw that his life was about to get complicated and messy. And I saw a way out of it. For me, of course. Not for him." Miranda began to pick unhappily at the loose skin around her nails. "What do you think of that?" she asked. "What do you think of me now?"

"What do you think?" Dr. Matsui said, and Miranda responded in disgust.

"I know what I think. I think I'm sick of talking to myself. Is that the best you therapists can manage? I think I'll stay home and talk to the mirrors." She pulled off the remaining connections to her scalp and sat up. "Matthew," she said. "Matthew!"

Matthew came to the side of her chair. He looked thin, concerned, and awkward. What a baby he was, really, she thought. He couldn't be more than twenty-five. "How old are you, Matthew?" she asked.

"Twenty-seven."

"Be a hell of a time to die, wouldn't it?" She watched Matthew put a nervous hand on his short brown hair and run it backward. "I want your opinion about something, Matthew. A hypothetical case. I'm trusting you to answer honestly."

Matthew glanced at Dr. Matsui, who gestured with her pen for him to go ahead. He turned back to Miranda. "What would you think of a woman who deserted her lover, a man she really claimed to love, because he got sick and she didn't want to face the unpleasantness of it?"

Matthew spoke carefully. "I would imagine that it was motivated by cowardice rather than cruelty," he said. "I think we should always forgive sins of cowardice. Even our own." He stood looking at Miranda with his earnest, innocent face.

"All right, Matthew," she said. "Thank you." She lay back down in the chair and listened to the hum of the idle machines. "Anna," she said. "He didn't behave as I expected. I mean, sometimes he did and sometimes he didn't. Even the first time."

"Tell me about it," said Dr. Matsui.

"The first session he was older than I expected. Like he hadn't died, but had continued to age along with me."

"Wish fulfillment."

"Yes, but I was *surprised* by it. And I was surprised by the setting. And he said something very odd right at the end. He quoted me Zeno's paradox and it really exists, but I never heard it before. It didn't sound like something Daniel would say, either. It sounded more like my husband, Michael. Where did it come from?"

"Probably from just where you said," Dr. Matsui told her. "Michael. You don't think you remember it, but obviously you did. And husbands and lovers are bound to resemble each other, don't you think? We often get bits of overlap. Our parents show up one way or another in almost all our memories." Dr. Matsui stood. "Come in Tuesday," she said. "We'll talk some more."

"I'd like to see him one more time," said Miranda.

"Absolutely not," Dr. Matsui answered, returning Miranda's chair to its upright position.

"Where are we, Daniel?" Miranda asked. She couldn't see anything.

"Camp Pendleton," he answered. "On the beach. I used to run here mornings. Guys would bring their girlfriends. Not me, of course."

Miranda watched the landscape fill in as he spoke. Fog remained. It was early and overcast. She heard the ocean and felt the wet, heavy air begin to curl her hair. She was barefoot on the sand and a little cold. "I'm so sorry, Daniel," she said. "That's all I ever really wanted to tell you. I loved you."

"I know you did." He put his arm around her. She leaned against him. I must look like his mother, she thought; in fact, her own son was older than Daniel now. She looked up at him carefully. He must have just arrived at camp. The hair had been all but shaved from his head.

"Maybe you were right, anyway," Daniel told her. "Maybe I just shouldn't have gone. I was so angry at you by then I didn't care anymore. I even thought about dying with some sense of anticipation. Petulant, you know, like a little kid. I'll go and get killed and *then* she'll be sorry."

"And she was," said Miranda. "God, was she." She turned to face him, pressed her lined cheek against his chest, smelled his clothes. He must have started smoking again. Daniel put both arms around her. She heard a gull cry out ecstatically.

"But when the time came I really didn't want to die." Daniel's voice took on an unfamiliar edge, frightened, slightly hoarse. "When

the time came I was willing to do *anything* rather than die." He hid his face in her neck. "Do you have kids?" he asked. "Did you and Michael ever?"

"A son," she said.

"How old? About six?"

Miranda wasn't sure how old Jeremy was now. It changed every year. But she told him, wonderingly, "Of course not, Daniel. He's all grown up. He owns a pizza franchise, can you believe it? He thinks I'm a bore."

"Because I killed a kid during the war. A kid about six years old. I figured it was him or me. I shot him." Miranda pushed back from Daniel, trying to get a good look at his face. "They used kids, you know," he said. "They counted on us not being able to kill them. I saw this little boy coming for me with his hands behind his back. I told him to stop. I shouted at him to stop. I pointed my rifle and said I was going to kill him. But he kept coming."

"Oh, Daniel," said Miranda. "Maybe he didn't speak English."

"A pointed rifle is universal. He walked into the bullet."

"What was he carrying?"

"Nothing," said Daniel. "How could I know?"

"Daniel," Miranda said. "I don't believe you. You wouldn't do that." Her words unsettled her even more. "Not the way I remember you," she said. "This is not the way I remember you."

"It's so easy for you to see what's right," said Daniel.

I'm going back, thought Miranda. Where am I really? I must be with Anna, but then she remembered that she was not. She was in her own study. She worked to feel the study chair beneath her, the ache in her back as she curved over her desk. Her feet dangled by the wheels; she concentrated until she could feel them. She saw her own hand, still holding her pencil, and she put it down. Things seemed very clear to her. She walked to the bedroom and summoned

Dr. Matsui over the console. She waited perhaps fifteen minutes before Anna appeared.

"Daniel's the one with the problem," Miranda said. "It's not me, after all."

"There is no Daniel." Dr. Matsui's voice betrayed a startled concern. "Except in your mind and on my tapes. Apart from you, no Daniel."

"No. He came for me again. Just like in our sessions. Just as intense. Do you understand? Not a dream," she cut off Dr. Matsui's protest. "It was not a dream, because I wasn't asleep. I was working and then I was with him. I could feel him. I could smell him. He told me an absolutely horrible story about killing a child during the war. Where would I have gotten that? Not the sort of thing they send home in their letters to the bereaved."

"There were a thousand ugly stories out of Vietnam," said Dr. Matsui. "I know some and I wasn't even born yet. Or just barely born. Remember My Lai?" Miranda watched her image clasp its hands. "You heard this story somewhere. It became part of your concept of the war. So you put it together now with Daniel." Dr. Matsui's voice took on its professional patina. "I'd like you to come in, Miranda. Immediately. I'd like to take a complete readout and keep you monitored awhile. Maybe overnight. I don't like the turn this is taking."

"All right," said Miranda. "I don't want to be alone anyway. Because he's going to come again."

"No," said Dr. Matsui firmly. "He's not."

Miranda took the elevator to the garage and unlocked her bicycle. She was not frightened and wondered why not. She felt unhappy and uncertain, but in complete control of herself. She pushed out into the bike lane. When the helicopter appeared overhead, Miranda knew immediately where she was. A banana tree sketched itself in on her right. There was a smell in the air which was strange to her. Old diesel engines, which she recognized, but also something organic. A lushness almost turned to rot. In the distance the breathtaking green of rice growing. But the dirt at her feet was bare.

Miranda had never imagined a war could be so quiet. Then she heard the chopper. And she heard Daniel. He was screaming. He stood right next to her, beside a pile of sandbags, his rifle stretched out before him. A small, delicately featured child was just walking into Miranda's view, his arms held behind him. All Miranda had to do was lift her hand.

"No, Daniel," she said. "His hands are empty."

Daniel didn't move. The war stopped. "I killed him, Randy," said Daniel. "You can't change that."

Miranda looked at the boy. His eyes were dark; a streak of dust ran all the way up one shoulder and onto his face. He was barefoot. "I know," she said. "I can't help him." The child faded and disappeared. "I'm trying to help you." The boy reappeared again, back further, at the very edge of her vision. He was beautiful, unbearably young. He began to walk to them once more.

"*Can* you help me?" Daniel asked.

Miranda pressed her palm into his back. He wore no shirt and was slick and sweaty. "I don't know," she said. "Was it a crime of cowardice or of cruelty? I'm told you can be forgiven the one, but not the other."

Daniel dropped his rifle into the dirt. The landscape turned slowly about them, became mountainous. The air smelled cleaner and was cold.

A bird flew over them in a beautiful arc, and then it became a baseball and began to fall in slow motion, and then it became death and she could plot its trajectory. It was aimed at Daniel, whose rifle had reappeared in his hands. Now, Miranda thought. She could stay and die with Daniel the way she'd always believed she should. Death moved so slowly in the sky. She could see it, moment to moment, descending like a series of scarcely differentiated still frames. "Look, Daniel," she said. "It's Zeno's paradox in reverse. Finite points. Infinite time." How long did she have to make this decision? A lifetime. Her lifetime.

Daniel would not look up. He reached out his hand to touch her hair. Gray, she knew. Her gray under his young hand. He was twenty-four. "Don't stay," he said. "Do you think I would have wanted you to? I would never have wanted that."

So Miranda moved from his hand and found she was glad to do so. "I always loved you," she said as if it mattered. "Good-bye, Daniel." But he had already looked away. Other soldiers materialized beside him and death grew to accommodate them. But they wouldn't all die. Some would survive in pieces, she thought. And some would survive whole. Wouldn't they?

The Unmistakable Smell of Wood Violets

ANGÉLICA GORODISCHER

Translated by Marian Womack

Angélica Gorodischer (1928–) is an influential Argentine writer of fiction and nonfiction who won the World Fantasy Award for Life Achievement in 2011. Although an avid reader, she came late to fiction writing and won her first literary prize in 1964, for a detective story. In 1965, Gorodischer won another award for her first collection, *Cuentos con soldados* (*Short Stories with Soldiers*). She was born in Buenos Aires but is closely associated with the city of Rosario, home to her well-known character Trafalgar Medrano, an interplanetary businessman, introduced in her novel *Trafalgar* (1979; English translation 2013).

Although Gorodischer, after a certain point in her career, chose to focus on writing mainstream feminist literature and criticism, her speculative fiction continues to find a growing readership. The science fiction—more than twenty novels and collections of stories, most of it untranslated—shares structural and thematic similarities with the work of Jorge Luis Borges and Italo Calvino. She is less of a magic realist than Gabriel García Márquez or Mario Vargas Llosa.

In addition to *Trafalgar*, the following books have been translated into English: *Kalpa Imperial* (translated by Ursula K. Le Guin, 2003), which collects all the stories of the *Kalpa* sequence, initially published in two volumes (*La casa del poder* and *El imperio más vasto*, 1983), and the novel *Prodigies* (*Prodigios*, 1994; English translation 2015), set in the former home of the poet Novalis after it was turned into a boardinghouse. Among stand-alone short stories, "The Violet's Embryos," published in the highly recommended *Cosmos Latinos: An Anthology of Science Fiction from Latin America and Spain* (2003), is a good example of this author's default style and approach. The story speculates about the nature of desire and search for happiness while confronting traditional military notions of masculinity.

The story reprinted here, "The Unmistakable Smell of Wood Violets," was first published in the magazine *Minotauro* in 1985 and then in Gorodischer's collection of dystopian stories *Las repúblicas* in 1991. It has been translated into English for the first time for this anthology. "The Unmistakable Smell of Wood Violets" is a masterpiece of science fiction and of feminist fiction, written in a smoldering, bold, direct manner that is in some ways different in tone from many of her other translated works.

THE UNMISTAKABLE SMELL OF WOOD VIOLETS

Angélica Gorodischer

Translated by Marian Womack

The news spread fast. It would be correct to say that the news moved like a flaming trail of gunpowder, if it weren't for the fact that at this point in our civilization gunpowder was archaeology, ashes in time, the stuff of legend, nothingness. However, it was because of the magic of our new civilization that the news was known all over the world, practically instantaneously.

"Oooh!" the tsarina said.

You have to take into account that Her Gracious and Most Illustrious Virgin Majesty Ekaterina V, Empress of Holy Russia, had been carefully educated in the proper decorum befitting the throne, which meant that she would never have even raised an eyebrow or curved the corner of her lip, far less would she have made an interjection of that rude and vulgar kind. But not only did she say "Oooh!," she also got up and walked through the room until she reached the glass doors of the great balcony. She stopped there. Down below, covered by snow, Saint Leninburg was indifferent and unchanged, the city's eyes squinting under the weight of winter. At the palace, ministers and advisers were excited, on edge.

"And where is this place?" the tsarina asked.

And that is what happened in Russia, which is such a distant and atypical country. In the central states of the continent, there was real commotion. In Bolivia, in Paraguay, in Madagascar, in all the great powers, and in the countries that aspired to be great powers, such as High Peru, Iceland, or Morocco, hasty conversations took place at the highest possible level with knitted brows and hired experts. The strongest currencies became unstable: the gua-

rani rose, the Bolivian peso went down half a point, the crown was discreetly removed from the exchange rates for two long hours, long queues formed in front of the exchanges in front of all the great capitals of the world. President Morillo spoke from the Oruro Palace and used the opportunity to make a concealed warning (some would call it a threat) to the two Peruvian republics and the Minas Gerais secessionist area. Morillo had handed over the presidency of Minas to his nephew, Pepe Morillo, who had proved to be a wet blanket whom everybody could manipulate, and now Morillo bitterly regretted his decision. Morocco and Iceland did little more than give their diplomats a gentle nudge in the ribs, anything to shake them into action, as they imagined them all to be sipping grenadine and mango juice in the deep south while servants in shiny black uniforms stood over them with fans.

The picturesque note came from the Independent States of North America. It could not have been otherwise. Nobody knew that all the states were now once again under the control of a single president, but that's how it was: some guy called Jack Jackson-Franklin, who had been a bit-part actor in videos, and who, aged eighty-seven, had discovered his extremely patriotic vocation of statesman. Aided by his singular and inexplicable charisma, and by his suspect family tree, according to which he was the descendent of two presidents who had ruled over the states during their glory days, he had managed to unify, at least for now, the seventy-nine northern states. Anyway, Mr. Jackson-Franklin said to the world that the Independent States would not permit such a thing to take place. No more, just that they would not permit such a thing to take place. The world laughed uproariously at this.

Over there, in the Saint Leninburg palace, ministers cleared their throats, advisers swallowed saliva, trying to find out if, by bobbing their Adam's apples up and down enough, they might be able to loosen their stiff official shirts.

"Ahem. Ahem. It's in the south. A long way to the south. In the west, Your Majesty."

"It is. Humph. Ahem. It is, Your Majesty, a tiny country in a tiny territory."

"It says that it is in Argentina," the tsarina said, still staring through the window but without paying any attention to the night as it fell over the snow-covered roofs and the frozen shores of the Baltic.

"Ah, yes, that's right, that's right, Your Majesty, a pocket republic."

Sergei Vasilievich Kustkarov, some kind of councilor and, what is more, an educated and sensible man, broke into the conversation.

"Several, Your Majesty, it is several."

And at last the tsarina turned around. Who cared a fig for the Baltic night, the snow-covered rooftops, the roofs themselves, and the city of which they were a part? Heavy silk crackled, starched petticoats, lace.

"Several of what, Councilor Kustkarov, several of what? Don't come to me with your ambiguities."

"I must say, Your Majesty, I had not the slightest intention—"

"Several of what?"

The tsarina looked directly at him, her lips held tightly together, her hands moving unceasingly, and Kustkarov panicked, as well he might.

"Rep-rep-republics, Your Majesty," he blurted out. "Several of them. Apparently, a long time ago, a very long time, it used to be a single territory, and now it is several, several republics, but their inhabitants, the people who live in all of them, all of the republics, are called, they call themselves, the people, that is, Argentinians."

The tsarina turned her gaze away. Kustkarov felt so relieved that he was encouraged to carry on speaking:

"There are seven of them, Your Majesty: Rosario, Entre dos Rios, Ladocta, Ona, Riachuelo, Yujujuy, and Labodegga."

The tsarina sat down.

"We must do something," she said.

Silence. Outside it was not snowing, but inside it appeared to be. The tsarina looked at the transport minister.

"This enters into your portfolio," she said.

Kustkarov sat down, magnificently. How lucky he was to be a councilor, a councilor with no specific duties. The transport minister, on the other hand, turned pale.

"I think, Your Majesty . . . ," he dared to say.

"Don't think! Do something!"

"Yes, Your Majesty," the minister said, and, bowing, started to make his way to the door.

"Where do you think you're going?" the tsarina said, without moving her mouth or twitching an eyelid.

"I'm just, I'm going, I'm just going to see what can be done, Your Majesty."

There's nothing that can be done, Sergei Vasilievich thought in delight, nothing. He realized that he was not upset, but instead he felt happy. And on top of everything else a woman, he thought. Kustkarov was married to Irina Waldoska-Urtiansk, a real beauty, perhaps the most beautiful woman in all of Holy Russia. Perhaps he was being cuckolded; it would have been all too easy for him to find that out, but he did not want to. His thoughts turned in a circle: and on top of everything else a woman. He looked at the tsarina and was struck, not for the first time, by her beauty. She was not so beautiful as Irina, but she was magnificent.

In Rosario it was not snowing, not because it was summer, although it was, but because it never snowed in Rosario. And there weren't any palm trees: the Moroccans would have been extremely disappointed had they known, but their diplomats said nothing about the Rosario flora in their reports, partly because the flora of Rosario was now practically nonexistent, and partly because diplomats are supposed to be above that kind of thing.

Everyone who was not a diplomat, that is to say, everyone, the population of the entire republic that in the last ten years had multiplied vertiginously and had now reached almost two hundred thousand souls, was euphoric, happy, triumphant. They surrounded her house, watched over her as she slept, left expensive imported fruits outside her door, followed her down the street. Some potentate allowed her the use of a Ford 99, which was one of the five cars in the whole country, and a madman who lived in the Espinillos cemetery hauled water all the way up from the Pará lagoon and grew a flower for her which he then gave her.

"How nice," she said, then went on, dreamily, "Will there be flowers where I'm going?"

They assured her that there would be.

She trained every day. As they did not know exactly what it was she had to do to train herself, she got up at dawn, ran around the Independence crater, skipped, did some gymnastic exercises, ate little, learned how to hold her breath, and spent hours and hours sitting or curled into strange positions. She also danced the waltz. She was almost positive that the waltz was not likely to come in handy, but she enjoyed it very much.

Meanwhile, farther away, the trail of gunpowder had become a barrel of dynamite, although dynamite was also a legendary substance and didn't exist. The infoscreens in every country, whether poor or rich, central or peripheral, developed or not, blazed forth with extremely large headlines suggesting dates, inventing biographical details, trying to hide, without much success, their envy and confusion. No one was fooled:

"We have been wretchedly beaten," the citizens of Bolivia said.

"Who would have thought it," pondered the man on the Reykjavík omnibus.

The former transport minister of Holy Russia was off breaking stones in Siberia. Councilor Sergei Vasilievich Kustkarov was sleeping with the tsarina, but that was only a piece of low, yet spicy, gossip that has nothing to do with this story.

"We will not allow this to happen!" Mr. Jackson-Franklin blustered, tugging nervously at his hairpiece. "It is our own glorious history that has set aside for us this brilliant destiny! It is we, we and not this despicable banana republic, who are marked for this glory!"

Mr. Jackson-Franklin also did not know that there were no palm trees or bananas in Rosario, but this was due not to a lack of reports from his diplomats but rather a lack of diplomats. Diplomats are a luxury that a poor country cannot afford, and so poor countries often go to great pains to take offense and recall all the knights commanders and lawyers and doctors and even eventually the generals working overseas, in order to save money on rent and electricity and gas and salaries, not to mention the cost of the banquets and all the money in brown paper envelopes.

But the headlines kept on appearing on the infoscreens: "Argentinian Astronaut Claims She Will Reach Edge of Universe," "Sources Claim Ship Is Spaceworthy in Spite of or Because of Centuries-Long Interment," "Science or Catastrophe?," "Astronaut Not a Woman but a Transsexual" (this in the *Imperialskaya Gazeta*, the most puritan of the infoscreens, even more so than the Papal *Piccolo Osservatore Lombardo*), "Ship Launches," "First Intergalactic Journey in Centuries," "We Will Not Allow This to Happen!" (*Portland Times*).

She was dancing the waltz. She woke up with her heart thumping, tried out various practical hairstyles, ran, skipped, drank only filtered water, ate only olives, avoided spies and journalists, went to see the ship every day, just to touch it. The mechanics all adored her.

"It'll work, they'll see, it'll work," the chief engineer said defiantly.

Nobody contradicted him. No one dared say that it wouldn't.

It would make it, of course it would make

it. Not without going through many incredible adventures on its lengthy journey. Lengthy? No one knew who Langevin was anymore, so no one was shocked to discover that his theory contradicted itself, ended up biting its own tail, and that however long the journey took, the observers would only perceive it as having lasted minutes. Someone called Cervantes, a very famous personage back in the early years of human civilization—it was still debated whether he had been a physicist, a poet, or a musician—had suggested a similar theory in one of his lost works.

One autumn dawn the ship took off from the Independence crater, the most deserted part of the whole desert republic of Rosario, at five forty-five in the morning. The exact time is recorded because the inhabitants of the country had all pitched in together to buy a clock, which they thought the occasion deserved (there was one other clock, in the Enclosed Convent of the Servants of Santa Rita de Casino, but because the convent was home to an enclosed order nothing ever went in or out of it, no news, no requests, no answers, no nothing). Unfortunately, they had not had enough money. But then someone had had the brilliant idea which had brought in the money they needed, and Rosario had hired out its army for parades in friendly countries: there weren't that many of them and the ones there were weren't very rich, but they managed to get the cash together. Anyone who was inspired by patriotism and by the proximity of glory had to see those dashing officers, those disciplined soldiers dressed in gold and crimson, protected by shining breastplates, capped off with plumed helmets, their catapults and pouches of stones at their waists, goose-stepping through the capital of Entre Dos Rios or the Padrone Giol vineyards in Labodegga, at the foot of the majestic Andes.

The ship blasted off. It got lost against the sky. Before the inhabitants of Rosario, their hearts in their throats and their eyes clouded by emotion, had time to catch their breath, a little dot appeared up there, getting bigger and bigger, and it was the ship coming back down. It landed at 06:11 on the same morning of that same autumn day. The clock that recorded this is preserved in the Rosario Historical Museum. It no longer works, but anyone can go and see it in its display cabinet in Room A of the Museum. In Room B, in another display case, is the so-called Carballensis Indentic Axe, the fatal tool that cut down all the vegetation of Rosario and turned the whole country into a featureless plain. Good and evil, side by side, shoulder to shoulder.

Twenty-six minutes on Earth, many years on board the ship. Obviously, she did not have a watch or a calendar with her: the republic of Rosario would not have been able to afford either of them. But it was many years, she knew that much.

Leaving the galaxy was a piece of cake. You can do it in a couple of jumps, everyone knows that, following the instructions that Albert Einsteinstein, the multifaceted violin virtuoso, director of sci-fi movies, and student of space-time, gave us a few hundred years back. But the ship did not set sail to the very center of the universe, as its predecessors had done in the great era of colonization and discovery; no, the ship went right to the edge of the universe.

Everyone also knows that there is nothing in the universe, not even the universe itself, which does not grow weaker as you reach its edge. From pancakes to arteries, via love, rubbers, photographs, revenge, bridal gowns, and power. Everything tends to imperceptible changes at the beginning, rapid change afterward; everything at the edge is softer and more blurred, as the threads start to fray from the center to the outskirts.

In the time it took her to take a couple of breaths, a breath and a half, over the course of many years, she passed through habitable and uninhabitable places, worlds which had once been classified as existent, worlds which did not appear and had never appeared and probably would never appear in any cartographical survey. Planets of exiles, singing sands, minutes and seconds in tatters, whirlpools of nothingness, space junk, and that's without even mentioning those beings and things, all of which stood completely outside any possibility of description, so much so that we tend not to perceive them when we look at them; all of this, and shock, and fear more than anything else, and loneliness. The hair grew gray at her temples, her flesh lost its firmness, wrinkles appeared around her eyes and her mouth, her knees and ankles started to act up, she slept less than before and had to half close her eyes and lean backward in order to make out the numbers on the consoles. And she was so tired that it was almost unbearable. She did not waltz any longer: she put an old tape into an old machine and listened and moved her gray head in time with the orchestra.

She reached the edge of the universe. Here was where everything came to an end, so completely that even her tiredness disappeared and she felt once again as full of enthusiasm as she had when she was younger. There were hints, of course: salt storms, apparitions, little brushstrokes of white against the black of space, large gaps made of sound, echoes of long-dead voices that had died giving sinister orders, ash, drums; but when she reached the edge itself, these indications gave way to space signage: "End," "You Are Reaching the Universe Limits," "The Cosmos General Insurance Company, YOUR Company, Says: GO NO FURTHER," "End of Protected Cosmonaut Space," etc., as well as the scarlet polygon that the OMUU had adopted to use as a sign for that's it, abandon all hope, *the end*.

All right, so she was here. The next thing to do was go back. But the idea of going back never occurred to her. Women are capricious creatures, just like little boys: as soon as they get what they want, then they want something else. She carried on.

There was a violent judder as she crossed the limit. Then there was silence, peace, calm. All very alarming, to tell the truth. The needles did not move, the lights did not flash, the ven-tilation system did not hiss, her alveoli did not vibrate, her chair did not swivel, the screens were blank. She got up, went to the portholes, looked out, saw nothing. It was logical enough:

"Of course," she said to herself, "when the universe comes to an end, then there's nothing."

She looked out through the portholes a little more, just in case. She still could see nothing, but she had an idea.

"But I'm here," she said. "Me and the ship."

She put on a space suit and walked out into the nothing.

When the ship landed in the Independence crater in the republic of Rosario, twenty-six minutes after it had taken off, when the hatch opened and she appeared on the ramp, the spirit of Paul Langevin flew over the crater, laughing fit to burst. The only people who heard him were the madman who had grown the flower for her in the Espinillos cemetery and a woman who was to die that day. No one else had ears or fingers or tongue or feet, far less did they have eyes to see him.

It was the same woman who had left, the very same, and this calmed the crowds down at the same time as it disappointed them, all the inhabitants of the country, the diplomats, the spies, and the journalists. It was only when she came down the gangplank and they came closer to her that they saw the network of fine wrinkles around her eyes. All other signs of her old age had vanished, and had she wished, she could have waltzed tirelessly, for days and nights on end, from dusk till dawn till dusk.

The journalists all leaned forward; the diplomats made signals, which they thought were subtle and unseen, to the bearers of their sedan chairs to be ready to take them back to their residences as soon as they had heard what she had to say; the spies took photographs with the little cameras hidden away in their shirt buttons or their wisdom teeth; all the old people put their hands together; the men raised their fists to their heart; the little boys pranced; the young girls smiled.

And then she told them what she had seen:

"I took off my suit and my helmet," she said, "and walked along the invisible avenues that smelled of violets."

She did not know that the whole world was waiting to hear what she said; that Ekaterina V had made Sergei Vasilievich get up at five o'clock in the morning so that he could accompany her to the grand salon and wait there for the news; that one of the seventy-nine Northern States had declared its independence because the president had not stopped anything from happening or obtained any glory, and this had lit the spark of rebellion in the other seventy-eight states, and this had made Mr. Jackson-Franklin leave the White House without his wig, in pajamas, freezing and furious; that Bolivia, Paraguay, and Iceland had allowed the two Peruvian republics to join their new alliance and defense treaty set up against a possible attack from space; that the high command of the Paraguayan aeronautical engineers had promised to build a ship that could travel beyond the limits of the universe, always assuming that they could be granted legal immunity and a higher budget, a declaration that made the guarani fall back the two points that it had recently risen and then another one as well; that Don Schicchino Giol, the new padrone of the Republic of Labodegga at the foot of the majestic Andes had been woken from his most recent drinking bout to be told that he had now to sign a declaration of war against the Republic of Rosario, now that they knew the strength of the enemy's forces.

"Eh? What? Hunh?" Don Schicchino said.

"I saw the nothingness of everything," she said, "and it was all infused with the unmistakable smell of wood violets. The nothingness of the world is like the inside of a stomach throbbing above your head. The nothingness of people is like the back of a painting, black, with glasses and wires that release dreams of order and imperfect destinies. The nothingness of creatures with leathery wings is a crack in the air and the rustle of tiny feet. The nothingness of history is the massacre of the innocents. The nothingness of words, which is a throat and a hand that break whatever they touch on perforated paper; the nothingness of music, which is music. The nothingness of precincts, of crystal glasses, of seams, of hair, of liquids, of lights, of keys, of food."

When she had finished her list, the potentate who owned the Ford 99 said that he would give it to her, and that in the afternoon he would send one of his servants with a liter of naphtha so that she could take the car out for a spin.

"Thank you," she said. "You are very generous."

The madman went away, looking up to the skies; who knows what he was searching for. The woman who was going to die that day asked herself what she should eat on Sunday, when her sons and their wives came to lunch. The president of the Republic of Rosario gave a speech.

And everything in the world carried on the same, apart from the fact that Ekaterina V named Kustkarov her interior minister, which terrified the poor man but which was welcomed with open arms by Irina as an opportunity for her to refresh her wardrobe and her stock of lovers. And Jack Jackson-Franklin sold his memoirs to one of Paraguay's more sophisticated magazines for a stellar amount of money, which allowed him to retire to live in Imerina. And six spaceships from six major world powers set off to the edges of the universe and were never seen again.

She married a good man who had a house with a balcony, a white bicycle, and a radio which, on clear days, could pick up the radio plays that LLL1 Radio Magnum transmitted from Entre Dos Rios, and she waltzed in white satin shoes. The day that her first son was born a very pale green shoot grew out of the ground on the banks of the great lagoon.

The Owl of Bear Island
JON BING

Jon Bing (1944–2014) was an important Norwegian speculative fiction writer and professor of law. Born in the town of Tønsberg, Bing moved to Oslo to attend university, and there in 1966 met Tor Åge Bringsværd, with whom he would collaborate and whose career would be intertwined with his own for many decades. Both men were inveterate science fiction readers in a country where science fiction literally did not exist, and in 1966 they founded the still-active Oslo University science fiction club Aniara and its fanzine. Almost from the beginning, however, both Bing and Bringsværd preferred to use the term *fabelprosa*—best translated as, literally, "fairy-tale fictions," or, idiomatically, "speculative fiction"—for their endeavors, rather than *science fiction*.

In 1967, they made their joint debut as professional writers with a short story collection, *Rundt solen i ring* ("Ring Around the Sun"), the first book by any Norwegian author to be labeled "science fiction." In the same year, they also published their first jointly edited anthology of translated science fiction, *Og jorden skal beve* ("And the World Will Shake"). Their first play, *Å miste eit romskib* ("To Lose a Spaceship," 1969), was performed at Det Norske Teatret in Oslo, the Norwegian national theater. In 1970, Bing published a first novel, as did Bringsværd, and in the same year they dramatized four science fiction short stories that aired on Norwegian television. With Tor Åge Bringsværd, Bing would publish several story collections; numerous stage, radio, and television plays; and almost twenty science fiction anthologies. On his own, Bing wrote many more novels as well as short stories.

The two would continue to collaborate, but their paths began to diverge when Bing, who studied law, went on to become a full professor at Oslo University, a visiting professor at King's College in London, and an honorary doctor of Stockholm University and the University of Copenhagen as well as an internationally leading authority on legal informatics; as an academic, Bing published almost twenty books and innumerable essays and papers, in time becoming the first chairman of the Norwegian computer integrity council; chairman of the Norwegian Film Council, the EU Council Committee on Data Processing, and Arts Council Norway; and a member of many other expert committees. In 1999, Bing was made a knight of the Norwegian Order of St. Olav. Perhaps for this reason, Bing published only around fifty volumes of fiction, while Bringsværd has published close to two hundred.

They had already, in 1967, talked the leading Norwegian publisher Gyldendal into launching a paperback line of science fiction, which they edited and which continued until 1980, releasing a total of fifty-five titles; this was where authors like Brian W. Aldiss, J. G. Ballard, Alfred Bester, Ray Bradbury, Arthur C. Clarke, Philip K. Dick, Ursula K. Le Guin, Fritz Leiber, Stanisław Lem, Clifford D. Simak, Theodore Sturgeon, and Kurt Vonnegut were all first published in Norwegian. Since the series also included several debut Norwegian writers, it is reasonable to say not only that Bing and Bringsværd founded Norwegian fandom but that they went on to create the Norwegian science fiction field.

Although Bringsværd and Bing worked together for almost fifty years, there were clear literary differences between them. Both were civil libertarians, but Bing had a more generous attitude toward a central legislative power and system of justice, while Bringsværd characterized himself as a left-wing anarchist. Bringsværd's science fiction in English translation has seemed to confirm this distinction in its very form, as he appears to be a more experimental writer than Bing in terms of story structure. (His work is well worth seeking out.)

Bing's "The Owl of Bear Island" is a sly and very unique tale of alien contact that first appeared in English in 1986.

THE OWL OF BEAR ISLAND

Jon Bing

The landscape outside the window was black and white, with the ocean like gray metal beneath a dark sky. The cliffs were bare and steep, ribboned by bird droppings, the beaches stony and empty with off-white trimmings of dried foam and salt.

It was a lifeless landscape, even this far into "spring." The polar night had lost its grip on day and let it slide into twilight along the horizon in the south. I looked toward the metallic reflection of sunlight and felt invisible feathers rise around my neck. I blinked my eyes.

Why were they this far north?

I thought of my boss as an owl. A great white snow-owl with a cloud of light feathers. With big yellow eyes in a round head. With a sharp and cynical beak. With spastic movements. I felt like that when the Owl took me over, I discovered such movements in my own body when the Owl left me.

What did he really want from me? Why was not I, like the others of whom I had heard, guided to the ghetto on Hawaii? What was an extraterrestrial doing on Bear Island, 74 degrees north?

Bear Island is the southernmost of the Spitsbergen Islands. Its area is approximately 180 square kilometers. Its shape is triangular, with the famous Bird's Mountain on the southernmost point. It was discovered by the Dutch polar explorer Willem Barents in 1596, and fishermen were attracted to the island by huge populations of elephant seal and whale. The climate is quite mild: in the warmest month the average temperature is not more than 4 degrees centigrade, but the average drops in the coldest month to −7 degrees, quite mild for a latitude halfway between the North Pole and the northernmost point of Alaska.

Bear Island was placed under Norwegian sovereignty in 1925. Since 1918, Norway has maintained a station on the island, partly to keep radio contact with the fisheries fleet, partly for meteorological observations. The station was destroyed when the Allies withdrew in 1941, to make it useless for the Germans. A new station was constructed in 1947 at Herwig Port, a few kilometers from the old.

The station was my closest neighbor. I could in principle visit there, either in the boat if there was not too much ice along the coast, or in the small but efficient helicopter in the tin hangar outside the buried bunker in which the Institute was housed. It would take just a little while to fly north and west from Cape Levin to Herwig Port. But I did not fly.

Of course.

After I was possessed, I did not do such things.

I blinked my great yellow eyes, flexed my clawlike fingers over the keyboard of my computer, and did not remember anything . . . until I later shuddered and blinked in front of the screen.

My eyes were sore and staring. More than eleven hours had passed. I got back to the bunk I had made up in the terminal room just before being overwhelmed by deep sleep.

It was, of course, contrary to normal procedure to let one man live through the polar night on his own. There should have been two of us.

Normally, there were, both specialists, experts on the analysis of geotechnical data from sonar probes. We were rather good friends, Norway being small enough to make most people within the same field acquaintances. His name was Johannes Hansen; he was from the small town Mo in northern Norway and was used to long and sunless winters. I was from the south, but I needed the bonus which a winter would bring. We had rather looked forward to a quiet winter of routine work—and a computer, which we could use in our spare time to process the material we had both collected for a paper, perhaps a thesis.

It was not many nights after equinox before the white and dark wings closed over my thoughts and my boss took power.

A few days later Johannes Hansen became seriously ill. I am sure that my boss induced the illness, though I do not know in what way.

Johannes Hansen was collected by a helicopter from a coast guard vessel. He died before he reached the mainland.

The doctors had problems in determining the cause of death, and no replacement was sent out. I remained alone in the bunker of the Institute on the east coast of Bear Island. People from the meteorological station did not visit. Nor did I visit them, though I talked to them by radio from time to time in order to reassure them. It was important that they should not grow suspicious, important to my boss.

My boss knew why he was there. I did not. I did not know what the Owl wanted from me and the bunker of the Institute at Bear Island. I only knew that in this bunker for the better part of the winter a possessed person lived, a person who flapped invisible wings and hooted like an owl toward the night lying across the snow, and the ice outside the windows.

Institute for Polar Geology is the official name. It may sound rather academic. Formally, the Institute is part of the University of Tromsø—the world's northernmost university—but in reality it is financed by the government. Norway had for many years conducted quite sensitive negotiations with the Soviet Union over possible economic exploitation of the Barents Sea; that is, the ocean north of Norway and the Kola Peninsula which stretches between Spitsbergen and Novaya Zemlya toward the pole.

The negotiations were difficult for several reasons. First, the Soviets had considerable military activity on the Kola Peninsula—for instance, its largest navy base. Second, preliminary surveys indicated major natural resources on the continental shelf, especially in oil. The coal mines of Spitsbergen were an obvious sign of what might lie hidden by the cold sea. In the summer of 1984 the Soviets made the first major find of natural gas and oil, midway between the Norwegian coast and Novaya Zemlya.

The two countries had not arrived at a final agreement. There was still a contested sector midway between the two countries, popularly known as "the gray zone." In 1984 it was discovered that one of the important members of the Norwegian delegation during the negotiations had been in contact with the KGB and was probably a Soviet agent. All these factors had combined to block the final solution of the gray-zone problem.

Soviet mining ships had made test drillings as close to the gray zone as possible, seeking information on which natural resources it might hide. Norway was too occupied with exploration and development of promising oil fields in the North Sea to start more than symbolic test drills farther north. The northernmost samples were taken at Tromsøflaket, a fishing bank off the shore of North Troms at a depth of 2,300 meters.

The Institute for Polar Geology was founded to furnish more information about the structures underneath the sea bottom in the north, and the sea bottom itself. An installation was constructed at Bear Island, approximately midway between the mainland and Spitsbergen proper. This installation was equipped with a computer system for analysis of data collected by sonar probes. The system was quite powerful. There was a sturdy minicomputer, databases with all available geological information on the northern seas, programs for analysis developed on the basis of experiments made in the North Sea, plotters and graphic screens for projection of maps and graphs.

The system received data through a radio link with the sonar probes. Some probes were anchored to the sea bottom, while others could be piloted—almost like unmanned minisubs—by the computer system, into areas from which data was desirable.

The system had no permanent link to those on the mainland. However, through a disk antenna one of the polar orbiting satellite systems could be accessed for computer communication. There was also a link to the mainland by way of the meteorological station at Herwig Port.

It was a rather fancy computer system. But it was a considerably less expensive way of collecting information than test drilling. Perhaps the Soviets also would have chosen this alternative if it had been open to them, but the system in the bunker at Cape Levin was certainly on the embargo list of the US Department of Commerce. It was not possible for the Soviets to establish something similar. And this well-equipped bunker was the place where the invisible Owl had arrived, from a planet beyond the curtain of northern lights.

Obviously, it was to use this equipment that the Owl had chosen the bunker. It must be possible for the equipment to squeeze out information from the sonar probes. I did not know what it might be, except in rough outlines.

When the Owl had ridden me throughout days of polar night, I came to in an exhausted body. My tongue was dry and thick like a stopper in my throat, my eyes were red and swollen. The Owl showed little consideration for the fact that static electricity in the terminal screen gathered dust from the atmosphere of the elec-trically heated bunker, and that this concentration of dust irritated the mucous membranes in the eyes and prompted symptoms of allergy. The Owl used my body as long as necessary. It rode me, day after day, and let me recover only sufficiently to endure another ride—impatient with me, irritated by my bodily needs.

Perhaps I was too exhausted to revolt. I nursed myself back to some semblance of health time after time, though I knew that as soon as I became strong, the claws would grip my thoughts and I would be ridden through a new unconscious period.

I noticed the evidence of what had been done, read the log from the computer, and knew that new programs had been written, probes activated, new data collected. Several of the mobile probes frequently went into the gray zone. From time to time they crossed the territorial border to the Soviets. It was probably not out of respect for human agreements or the danger of creating an international incident that the Owl refrained from penetrating deeper into Soviet territory—but rather just because the radio signals became too weak to be received so far from the installation.

I tried to read the programs. They were, of course, written in FORTRAN or SIMULA—the Owl had to make do with what to him would seem naive languages. But I did not understand the programs, though I was a passable programmer myself.

It could not be oil resources that interested the Owl. I could only guess what he—and I, in my unconscious and feverish working periods—really was looking for. I guessed it would have something to do with the nodules, the bulbs of manganese covering great areas of the sea bottom.

And, of course, even manganese could not be the interesting thing. Next to iron, it is the heavy metal most common in the Earth's crust, though the fraction is no higher than 0.77 percent. Manganese is also identified in meteorites and in the spectrum of stars, so it could not be the scarcity of this metal that made an extra-terrestrial interested in the cold sea far in the north of the Earth.

But laboratory analysis of the nodules shows that they contain a profusion of other minerals, among these at least forty different metals, for instance iron, copper, nickel, and cobalt. I thought it might be a trace element that the Owl looked for. Perhaps his search related to the fact that the nodules were so far north, where temperature, magnetic fields, or the strong cosmic radiation had acted to catalyze an unknown process. Or perhaps the solution was to be found in some prehistoric volcanic catastrophe creating the core of the bulbs.

An unknown trace element . . . or an alloy, a chemical compound . . .

It was not the only riddle of the Owl.

I did not understand why it operated in secrecy. The other reported incidents of "possession" of which I had heard had taken the host directly to Hawaii, where the bosses haggled among themselves in some sort of stock exchange of Babel, where terrestrial goods and services were traded on behalf of clients light-years away—who probably would not be able to enjoy the goods or services for many slow decades. In some way the Owl participated in this game, perhaps collecting secret information on natural resources.

I believed he operated outside the rules of the game. That's why he had selected the lonely Bear Island, therefore had selected me . . . a lonely man in a wintery bunker at the shore of the Barents Sea.

I believed there might also be another reason.

My boss hated sunlight. It was perhaps for that reason I had dubbed him the Owl. He worked only at night. The long polar night allowed him to work without being disturbed by daylight—until my body failed.

From time to time I thought of his home planet. A waste-world, at the edge of a solar system. Perhaps the white wings of the Owl slid through an atmosphere of methane? Or perhaps his planet was covered by eternal clouds? Or perhaps it was tied in rotation to its sun, where the Owl and his kind inhabited the night side?

In my nightmares the Owl became a figure from fairy tales, and his home planet a magic forest. It felt nearly logical that he should share the predilection of the trolls from Norwegian fairy tales, by hiding from the sun.

And soon the polar night would be at an end.

There were long periods each day when I was free of the Owl. At last there were only a few hours each night when it dared to sink its claws into my subconscious.

But I understood that it had done something to me. I did not fully have free will. I contacted the meteorological station and declared that I would like to stay another winter. And that I did not really need a summer holiday.

They grew very concerned. I could count on a visit from a psychologist—at least a radio interview with one on the mainland. I would have liked to break my isolation—but I was controlled, guided by the rules the Owl had constructed in my subconscious.

But the polar night has its reflection in the polar summer. From April 30 till August 12, the sun never sets over Bear Island. The midnight sun burns in the north each night, and the shadows pivot like the pointers of a watch across the whole dial. The landscape explodes in seductive colors under melting snow. The air is light and transparent in white sunshine.

And for the whole of this period, more than three months, the Owl would stay away from me—though it still controlled my subconscious. During this period I had to take countermeasures to break out of my psychological jail. In the May sun I looked for the key to the barred door.

.   .   .

I found it. At least I thought so then.

The computer system at the bunker was quite advanced. It had access to, among other programs, a version of PROSPECTOR, one of the most successful examples of expert systems constructed. PROSPECTOR exploits the results of research in artificial intelligence and the knowledge from a large number of experts in geology and petrochemistry. This knowledge is structured in a large set of rules. And this rule system could assist another expert—for instance, myself. The results of analyses could be presented to PROSPECTOR, which at once would suggest that supplementing information should be collected, until it arrived at a conclusion on whether the geological structure described by the information was promising or not.

PROSPECTOR could become the key.

The version of PROSPECTOR to which I had access was a self-instructing program. Through use, the program learned more about the one using it, and about what it was being used for. It automatically constructed supplementing rules, constantly refining its expertise.

Of course, the Owl would not himself start using PROSPECTOR, or my special version, the OWLECTOR. I used the summer to hide the program in the operating system to the computer. It was a sort of extra layer in the program, rather like a hawk floating in the air and keeping an eye on what was happening below. This is how I saw OWLECTOR, like a hunting hawk programmed with a taste in owls. The more the Owl used the system, the more OWLECTOR would learn of the Owl. It would learn enough to take control from the Owl, fight the Owl. And the more the Owl fought to keep in control, the more OWLECTOR would learn of its opponent.

There was a fascinating justice in the scheme. Neither I nor any other human could fight the Owl or any of his galactic colleagues. We had not sufficient knowledge nor capacity in a brief human life to learn what we needed. But a computer does not have our limitations. It can learn as long as there is somebody to teach. It can learn until it knows as much as the teacher.

It can tap knowledge from the Owl until it becomes an owl itself.

And the computerized owl is loyal to humans. That is the way I have programmed it. And this loyalty will last as long as the program.

There will not be much time. Perhaps only a few hours, a few days. Who knows how soon the Owl will discover the hunting hawk somewhere above, like a dot against the sky?

But perhaps it does not expect such an attack. Perhaps the Owl is arrogant and impatient with weak humans, who fail from thirst and exhaustion. And then it will perhaps not search the sky for a hunting hawk in the form of a computer program, which studies the Owl as prey until it is ready to strike the bustling white bird and liberate me for all future time. . . .

I do not know whether to believe in this or not. But I no longer dream of spectral owls in strange dark forests, but of white owls in snow, owls killed by birds of prey, blood splashing the snow. In my sleep I hear the seabirds cry: they dive and circle through the sunny nights, and I seem to hear the owls hoot.

It will soon be August 12. The sun already touches the horizon at midnight. Soon the Owl will be back, and I will know the answer. . . .

Readers of the Lost Art

ÉLISABETH VONARBURG

Translated by Howard Scott

Élisabeth Vonarburg (1947–) is an award-winning French-born Canadian teacher, editor, critic, and writer considered by many to be one of the finest science fiction writers of her generation. Vonarburg's work is often associated with both the New Wave and the rise of feminist science fiction; certainly, her themes and structural experimentation express sympathies with both approaches. Her fiction shares some commonalities with the work of both Leena Krohn and Ursula K. Le Guin. Vonarburg is a very deliberate writer who brings great care and thought to the depiction of characters and settings. Her themes are often uniquely societal and environmental in scope.

She has won the Aurora Award, Canada's top science fiction honor, more than ten times, for both her stories and her novels. She has also received seven Prix Boréal and a Philip K. Dick Award special citation (runner-up) for her novel *In the Mothers' Land* (1992). In addition to writing fiction, Vonarburg has served as fiction editor (1979–90) and editor (1983–85) of the magazine *Solaris*.

Vonarburg's first science fiction story, "Marée haute," appeared in *Requiem* in 1978 and was translated under the title "High Tide" for the influential anthology *Twenty Houses of the Zodiac* (1979), edited by Maxim Jakubowski. Many of her stories have been collected in *L'oeil de la nuit* ("The Eye of Night," 1980), *Janus* (1984), and (in English) *Blood out of a Stone* (2009). Some of the stories collected therein form part of her Baïblanca/*Mothers' Land* series, in which a semidecadent society in a far-future Europe sees the gradual appearance of shape-shifting mutants (the "*métames*"). The series continues in *Le silence de la cité* (1981; published in English as *The Silent City*, 1988). In the novel, a young female protagonist leaves her underground home and travels to the surface, with its wild tribes, where she begins to transform the blighted world. Revelations of the artificial nature of the feminist governance of Mothers' Land sharpens the rite-of-passage story at the heart of *Chroniques du pays des mères* (1992). A one-off, *Les voyageurs malgre eux* (1992; published in English as *Reluctant Voyagers*, 1995), in a sense grounds her first series (and her subsequent work as well) through its depiction of a teacher/writer whose travels to alternate worlds are engineered through the stories she writes.

The *Tyranaël* series—the main sequence of which begins with *Tyranaël 1: Les rêves de la mer* (1996; published in English as *Dreams of the Sea*, 2003) and ends with *Tyranaël 5: La mer allée avec le soleil* (1997)—is a planetary romance set on the eponymous Living World, though it may be that only the circumambient ocean is sentient. The large cast—some reincarnations of earlier protagonists—gains through telepathy and other means a gradually intensifying symbiosis with their planet.

"Readers of the Lost Art" is a uniquely transgressive, hypersymbolic piece of science fiction about ritual and creativity. Both chilling and transformative, the story won the Aurora Award when first published as "La carte du tendre" in *Aimer: 10 nouvelles par 10 auteurs quebecois* (1986) and was first published in English in *Tesseracts 5* (1996).

READERS OF THE LOST ART

Élisabeth Vonarburg

Translated by Howard Scott

The Subject presents itself as a block, slightly taller than it is wide, set vertically on a round central stage that is slowly revolving. The colour of the block, a very dark green, does not necessarily make one think of stone (it could be plasmoc), especially since it glistens with a strange opalescence under the combined laser beams. Its rough texture and irregular shape, however, tell the audience what the voice of the invisible Announcer, floating over the room, now confirms: the Subject has chosen to appear in a sheath of Labrador amphibolite.

As murmurs commenting on this strategy go back and forth at a few tables, the Operator enters, a silhouette at first glance consisting of reflections from a scattered brightness. All the instruments required for his task, which are mostly metal, are held to his body by strongly magnetized chips and small plates inserted under his skin. The Operator does not wear any clothing except for the armour made up of these tools, all of different shapes and sizes but designed to fit together like the segments of some exoskeleton to the glory of technology. Of course, a black hood fits tightly over his head, though not over his face, which contrasts with the smooth, shiny material and seems like a simple, abstract outline—geometrical planes arbitrarily linked together rather than a recognizable countenance.

The amphitheatre falls silent after some scattered, rather condescending applause. Everyone knows there will be no subtlety in the first approach, in accordance with the obvious wishes of the Subject: a direct assault, almost naive, on the primitive material surrounding it. The Operator circles the block, steps up to it, steps away from it, touches it here and there, then steps back two paces and stands there a few moments with his head lowered. He emerges from his meditation only to take two unsurprising instruments from his tool-armour: a hammer and a chisel.

He needs to find the areas of least resistance: briefly returned to its original plasticity through heat and pressure before enclosing the Subject, then cooled, the metamorphic rock provides clues to its schistosities in the infinitely divergent orientations of its amphiboles, as the rounded reflections playing on the surface of a still river reveal to the practised eye the contours of the bottom, and the twists and turns of the current. The plagioclase opalescence of the material will apparently not delay the operation; a section of rock falls off the block after the first blow is delivered by a sure, firm hand. The Operator is experienced. We will soon get to the heart of the Subject.

In the room, up in the tiers, the alcoves are gradually filling up, the small lamps on the tables are being turned on, and jewels are throwing furtive sparkles. Buyers and merchants sit down, ready after the day's work for work of another sort. With slow elegance, the hostesses parade along the tiers, their eyes falsely distant, like panthers pacing their cages pretending to be unaware that they were long ago torn away from their secret jungle paths. Now and then, a hand is raised, nonchalantly or urgently, and yet another captive goes and sits close to the client whom she will, for the evening, be pleasing.

On the central stage (noiselessly—the floor where the rock fragments fall is covered with a thick elastic carpet), the Operator is almost finished with the first phase and those the show is intended to entertain grant a little discreet applause when a whole section of rock comes off the upper part of the block, indicating finally what is in store for the second phase of the operation. In the deep layer revealed, indistinct masses can barely be seen, a glassy gleam.

The Operator puts the chisel and hammer into the box provided for them. It is a medium-sized box, a declaration of principle that does not escape the seasoned spectators: the Operator is no novice and fully intends to get through the Subject without having to use all his instruments. As usual, the lid only opens one way. The tools that are put in the box cannot be taken out again. If Operators dared to try—something that is unthinkable—they would be immediately electrocuted by the powerful current running through every metal object the instant it is placed in one of the compartments of the box.

A murmur runs through the amphitheatre as the Subject is completely extricated from the rock sheath: its crystalline prisms scatter the coherent laser light into myriads of geometric rainbows that both reveal and hide the thickness of the material. The Operator moves away and again circles the Subject to the discreet clickings of his tool-armour (in which the absence of the hammer and chisel has opened two gaps). Meditatively, he paces around the perimeter of the stage. Brute force is no longer enough. Getting close to the Subject by shattering the prisms would be in rare bad taste, and the audience would be right to show their displeasure by pushing the buttons that link them to the Manager of the establishment. The Operator carefully chooses his next tool, creating a new gap in his tool-armour. A probe, of course.

The probe indicates the expected thickness of the Subject in the second phase, as well as the nodal points, invisible to the naked eye, where the prisms are joined. As this information is displayed holographically above the stage, a few exclamations in the audience reveal the interest of those watching the show. The matter is dense. The prisms are composed of several concentric layers of varying nature, which blend together in several places; their macro-crystals are themselves juxtaposed in complex combinations. They will have to be disassembled one by one unless there are certain nodal points governing the simultaneous unlocking of several elements. This is almost certainly the case, but the information provided by the probe gives no hint of it.

On one of the levels, halfway up the amphitheatre, almost all the hostesses have been called. There is only one left. She is a rather tall woman with very white skin wearing a crimson lamé dress that glints stroboscopically with her every movement. Her short hair, cut in a helmet shape and smoothed down over her head, does not shine, quite the contrary. It is so dark that when the woman goes into shadow, that whole part of her head disappears and her face, enigmatically made up in mauve and gold, looks like a floating mask. An attentive observer would notice that this hostess flinches whenever a hand is raised (which activates the communication disk grafted on the forehead of each member of the staff), then relaxes when the hand is lowered (since the client has indicated subvocally who he is speaking to, thus automatically cutting off the hostess or the waiter from the general network).

One such attentive observer is sitting in one of the alcoves at the edge of the third level. He has wide shoulders, or else his evening jumpsuit hides shoulder pads, but this is not likely, since his torso is long and muscular. The wide low neck of his suit reveals a very distinct scar that appears to run all the way down his chest. His hands (the only parts other than his torso that are clearly lit by the globelamp on the table) are strong and square; his fingertips are strangely discoloured. Of his head, which is in shadow, the only thing visible is the round shape crowned with a mane of abundant and apparently rebellious hair. The man at last raises his hand. The hostess stops, turns towards the alcove, then, her slightly lowered head floating in the alternations of shadow and light, obeys and steps forward.

Meanwhile, more and more of the audience has turned its attention to the performance taking place on the central stage. A wave of applause mixed with exclamations of appreciative surprise has distracted them from their dinners, their bargaining, or their companions. The prisms that surround the Subject have lost their translucence and their rainbows. The laser light has begun to trigger complex molecular reactions on their surfaces. Lines form, shapes and colours merge slowly with one another to reappear in different combinations. There is an implied rhythm, the suggestion of a pattern in the permutations, a hint of an intention in the sequences.

The Operator, who has detached a few instruments from his tool-armour, stops to study this new development. After a while, he places all but two of the instruments in the box, which prohibits him from picking them up again. He has kept a small rubber-headed hammer and a series of suction-cup rings, which he places separately on the fingertips of his right hand, including the thumb. He steps up to the prismatic block and stops again, as though waiting for a signal. All of a sudden, carefully, he positions the hand with the suction-cup rings one finger at a time, on the protruding part of one of the prisms, and with the other hand gives a light tap with the hammer on a point that he seems to have chosen very precisely. Nothing happens. The coloured lines and shapes continue rippling across the surface of the prisms. The Operator waits. Suddenly, without the audience being able to see what has triggered his action, he taps the same spot as before, twice, in quick succession.

A piece of the prism as big as a fist breaks off, held by the fingers of the Operator, who then removes the suction cups from it with his other hand, sets the crystal fragment on the floor, picks up his small hammer, and again turns to face the prisms, attentive (the spec-

tators are beginning to understand it) to the enigmatic progression of clues moving just under their surface. The randomness of all the coloured movements of the lines and shapes, their nature, their frequency, their combinations, is only apparent. They actually constitute a code marking the location of nodal points where the prisms are joined. A code, or more accurately changing codes—the rhythms have rhythms, the combinations have combinations, and the law (or the laws) governing it all hides, elusively, in those converging metamorphoses.

Some members of the audience, who have understood the rules of the game, turn to making quick electronic speculations on the small terminals built into their tables. Bets are exchanged back and forth. A hum of interest swells, ebbs, and swells again with each crystal segment dislodged from the Subject. Even the few clients old enough to have immediately recognized the nature of the proposed entertainment— "reading," a very ancient art form which always experiences sporadic revivals—even they begin taking interest in the show. This will be a memorable performance.

In the alcove she has been called to, the hostess in the crimson lamé dress turns her back to the stage; she is sitting very straight in the low armchair, although it is softly contoured to encourage relaxation. With one hand, she holds in her fingertips the stem of a glass filled with a drink with which she has hardly wet her lips; her other hand, fist closed, is on the arm of the chair. The man seated on her right leans over, takes her closed hand, and gently unfolds the fingers one by one on the table. With this movement, the man's head enters the sphere of light that surrounds the globelamp. Beneath the unruly hair, his features are strong but without fineness, like a sketch that someone did not bother finishing. The only features that stand out in detail are the mouth, the thick, sinuous lips strangely bordered with a white line—makeup or apigmentation—and the eyes, oblique but wide, possibly blue, softened by the light into a very pale grey in which the black iris, extremely dilated, seems to almost fill the eye. It is difficult to attribute an expression to this monolithic whole. Alertness, certainly, but is it inquisitive, cunning, friendly? The man's hand releases the fingers of the hostess, which fold up again between palm and thumb. The woman is surely not even aware of this, for when the index finger of the man taps lightly on her closed fist, she starts, makes a move to hide that hand under the table, and then, with visible effort, places it close to the one holding—too tightly now—the long-stemmed glass. The man lies back in his chair, returning his face to the shadow, and the hostess must assume that he is watching the show, because she also pivots her chair towards the stage below.

The Operator has finished dismantling the first layer of crystals. The general shape of the Subject is easier now to make out: a tapering vertical parallelepiped, much higher than it is wide and of irregular thickness; it narrows towards the bottom, widens, then narrows again at the top. Identical bulges are visible about one-third up its front face and two-thirds up its back face. The same play of lines and shapes moves across the surface of this second crystalline layer. Or at least the same principle is no doubt at work because, although it is hard to say why, one senses that the content of these animated patterns is not quite the same—nor completely different, however—as the one from the previous phase. More speed, perhaps, in the transformations? Or rather they flicker with concomitant metamorphoses; the rhythms they follow are subtly out of sync with each other, but when the effort is made to perceive them simultaneously, they constitute a whole whose organic cohesion leaves no doubt.

The Operator seems to hesitate. The rubber-headed hammer hangs above the changing patterns. Then, very gently, it strikes one of the crystals. The block turns dark. The Operator jumps away, dropping the hammer, his hands clamped over his ears, his face twisted in a silent grimace.

There is a burst of applause from the audi-ence (the frequency of the ultrasound was modulated for the Operator alone, which makes their satisfaction all the greater) as the block clears, and the lines and colours resume their briefly interrupted progression. The Operator nods several times as he removes the suction-cup rings from his fingers. Then he picks up the small rubber-headed hammer and puts it and the rings into the box.

A murmur of astonishment and excitement greets his next gesture—he detaches several sets of tools from his tool-armour and also deposits them in the box. He now presents an impressive silhouette, dotted irregularly with disparate metal objects between which patches of bare skin can be seen. He detaches another set of rings with smaller suction cups and slips them onto his fingertips, right hand and left. He then moves close to the block and attentively observes the shiftings and groupings of the lines. One finger at a time, he places his right hand, then his left, on two widely separated points; the fingers are positioned irregularly, some close together, some half bent, others stretched out and spread wide, no doubt to correspond to strategically placed points that must be touched simultaneously to produce the desired effect.

For an instant, the Operator is motionless. He must have been waiting for a precise combination of colours, lines, and shapes, for all of a sudden he can be seen leaning a little against the block, giving a sudden push, and then he steps back holding the section of crystals that he has just detached.

The audience leans forward, the better to see what is revealed of the Subject by the breach that has been created. They are disappointed, or surprised, or delighted. It is intensely black, featureless, a simple cutout that reveals neither shape nor volume—it could just as well be a glimpse of the intergalactic void. Only the Operator is close enough to possibly make anything out, but nothing in his behaviour indicates what he sees. With his hands held out a few millimetres above the crystalline sheath, he waits for the moment when a new configuration, indiscernible by the audience, will indicate to him that another section of the Subject is offering itself to be broken off.

A conversation has begun between the hostess in the crimson lamé dress and her client. It is not a very animated one. The woman seems as reticent to answer the questions of her interlocutor as he is slow to ask them. And they are perhaps not questions. They may be rambling comments on the performance being staged below. The man and the hostess both seem to be watching it.

The Subject has been almost entirely extracted from its crystalline shell. Totally black—that strangely matte, depthless black that flattens volumes—its shape to come is very clear now: from the front, an elongated diamond standing on its narrowest point; but from the side (it can be seen as the central stage slowly rotates), although it retains the shape of a parallelogram, it will be an asymmetrical one.

Using combined pressure and shearing, the Operator detaches the last crystalline section. Around the Subject, the stage is littered with blocks of all sizes. Slow ripples of transformations still flow over their surfaces. Their inner rhythm is subtly or considerably altered now that their organic link with the Subject has been cut, but their beauty, their fascinating appeal, remains intact—as indicated by the requests that have been flooding the communication network for some time now: What will become of those fragments? Is it possible to obtain them, and at what price? To all these questions, the Manager's answer is the same: all the materials from the performance are the exclusive property of the Artists, who dispose of them as they see fit.

The Operator once more circles the Subject. He takes a device from his tool-armour (almost completely dismantled now) to scan the black block from a distance. The spectators peer at the area above the stage where the holographically retransmitted data will appear. Nothing. The Operator punches hidden keys on the small device and moves to another spot to resume his examinations. Still nothing. He almost shakes the device, stops, and places it in the box, allowing himself a slight shrug. He detaches another device, a sort of stylus connected by several wires thick enough to be fine conduits to an oblong box of which all one side is covered with variously coloured keys of different sizes. With perceptible hesitation, he walks up to the block, and touches it with the tip of the stylus.

An inarticulate exclamation rises unanimously from the audience. The Operator has been thrown to the floor, where he goes into visibly painful convulsions, no doubt caused by an electrical discharge of quite high intensity.

After several minutes, though, he gets up again with some difficulty. He deposits the useless device in the box. After closing the lid, he stands motionless for a moment, one hand on each side of the box, leaning lightly, his head lowered a bit. Those spectators who have been brought opposite him by the rotation of the stage can see that he has his eyes closed, and that a film of sweat glistens on the skin of his face and body (where the tools have been detached). A murmur of satisfaction—not without a certain joyous cruelty—runs through the audience: the Subject is a formidable opponent.

The chair of the hostess in the crimson lamé dress has pivoted; she is no longer watching the show, nor is she looking at her client. He speaks to her from time to time, leaning a little towards her, his face half lit by the globelamp. One of his hands is wrapped around the arm of his chair. A distinct depression in the soft material shows the force with which he is gripping it. His other hand, however, resting on the table, is slowly, delicately turning the long-stemmed glass, occasionally raising it to his face like a flower to drink. The young woman's face, because she is nearer the table, is fully lighted. She is looking straight ahead without any discernible emotion (except, perhaps, by inference, the desire to be inexpressive). Her eyelids do not blink, her eyes are fixed, enlarged, shining brightly, with a tremulous sparkle that suddenly comes loose and rolls down her right cheek to fall on her collarbone, which is exposed by the low neckline of the lamé dress. The man puts his glass down on the table, very gently. He leans a little closer to the woman and follows the wet trail with the tip of a finger. The woman turns her head away and lowers it towards her other shoulder. The man takes hold of her face—which half disappears in his big hand—to turn it, without brutality but firmly, back towards him.

The Operator begins moving again. Facing the black block—as though it could see him—he removes what remain of his tools from his skin with slow, deliberate movements, and lays them down on the floor. He brings his hands to his head and unhooks the fastenings of his hood, which are joined at the top. He is naked now, except for the shell that protects his sexual organs from any unpleasant contact with the tools nearby. He is a tall young man, broad shouldered and long bodied. His skin, uniformly smooth and completely lacking in pilosity, is very white. His smooth hair is cut in a helmet shape around the sturdy face, and appears, perhaps in contrast, excessively dark. When he moves close to the block again, it can be seen that he is almost the same height, just barely shorter. (Perhaps only the flat blackness of the block makes it look taller than the Operator.)

The Operator seems to collect himself (or meditate, or simply take the time to breathe deeply); then he holds out his arms and—to the extent that the shape of the block permits him to do so—he embraces it.

A silent explosion of blackness momentarily blinds the spectators. When they regain their sight, the Operator and the Subject are face-to-face at last, with nothing to separate them.

In the alcove, the chairs of the man and woman are closer together. Resting on the table between the two long-stemmed glasses, the man's hand envelops the woman's. The woman's head is leaning against the man's shoulder. They are both watching the circular stage below.

The Subject now appears in the shape of a naked woman, with golden skin, copper-coloured in the light of the lasers, and, like the Operator, completely lacking in pilosity, except for a mid-length, unruly mane, also copper-coloured; slanted eyebrows above very black eyes (but this may only be an effect of the lights); and very thick eyelashes. She is the same height as the Operator—though there is no point of reference to estimate their actual heights, now that the black parallelepiped has sublimated. Besides, there is no more time to indulge in such speculations, for the stage changes suddenly, and a surprised exclamation rises from the audience (where almost all the clients now have become spectators).

The Operator and the Subject, both still naked, float above the circular stage, and, although no visible barrier indicates the limits of their weightlessness chamber, it is suddenly apparent that what the audience has been seeing since the beginning is not a live performance but a holographic retransmission, perhaps long after the fact. Various movements disturb the spectators after the initial surprise—protests, approval, arguments from one table to the next between advocates of actuality and advocates of virtuality. But all this agitation dissipates quite quickly, for down below, in the weightlessness chamber, the show continues.

A number of tools had remained stuck to the skin of the Operator during the third exploratory phase. He takes them off his skin without using them. He has not been forced to put them in the box and can still use them. There will therefore be a fourth phase for the Subject, now at the discretion of the Operator.

With the Operator's first moves, the coming procedure is made obvious, and the spectators who have not yet understood, by realizing that the performance is recorded, understand now with a shiver of anxious or delighted anticipation: this will be the Great Game.

The Operator first proceeds with removing the nails, regal paths to the skin. Delicate remote-controlled cybernetic pincers alight on either side of each nail on the hands and feet. Small suction cups coated with monomolecular glue are placed on the surface of the nails. An instant of immobility, then the impetus spreads, activating precise movements throughout the system. With a quiet tearing noise, the nails are pulled from the phalangettes, which are invisible under the layer of flesh. Another small suction cup attaches itself to each of the fingers like a mouth, aspirating the blood seeping from the periphery of the nail, in the same movement injecting a local delayed-action analgesic, and then cauterizing the blood vessels. The Subject's scream is cut short.

The Operator, of course, did not scream when his own nails were detached from his fingers. The process is not the same for him since he initiates it—and the subsequent interruption of the blood flow to the injured areas— autonomously by directly manipulating his psychosoma. Moreover, electrical impulses that scramble his analgo-receptor centres are emitted continuously from the outside, though they become weaker as the performance progresses; in the Great Game, speed and precision are literally of vital importance.

With the Subject floating horizontally in front of him, maintained in place by magnetic fields, the Operator now makes the median incision from the top of the sternum to the pubis. The anaesthetizing suction cups follow the red line, close behind the scalpel. The Subject's scream is again cut short.

The next incisions must be made rapidly. This is where everything will be decided; the pain increases for the Operator (as the electric scrambling steadily decreases in intensity) while it diminishes for the Subject as area after area is more and more thoroughly anaesthetized. The Operator starts with the pubis. The audience leans forward. Will he attempt internal detachment? No, he will leave the most intimate parts of the Subject intact. He makes do with cutting around the labia majora and the anus. (The process takes a little longer, and is

therefore more perilous for the Operator when the Subject is of the male sex. The penis is, of course, an exterior organ, which makes the operation obligatory, and its flaccidity creates a problem; an entire traction system is required and it must be regulated perfectly to permit a quick, precise incision. Psychosomatic control easily solves this problem for the bodies of male Operators.)

The Operator now goes to the other end of the Subject. The head has an abundance of orifices whose outlines must be followed meticulously—the eyes and the mouth especially, for obvious, though different, reasons. The ears, by convention, will be detached with the rest of the skin; the nostrils, also by convention, are always cut along their perimeter. But the eyes and the mouth require special attention. Cutting the eyelids is particularly delicate and there is no room for missteps. As for the mouth, like the genitals of a female Subject and the anus in both sexes, there are two possibilities: either the incision simply follows the line of the lips, or else the mini-scalpels take the risk of going inside. There will be no surprises here. The Operator, logically, chooses the first option.

Up to this point the procedure has been flawless, and the Operator can begin the next phase confidently. The pain has not yet begun to slow him down. Nevertheless everything is not settled. Besides the extraction operation per se, some separate incisions, more or less important, are still required on the Subject from time to time for the removal of the skin, which must be carried out, if not slowly, at least with caution, if the optimal result is to be obtained.

A cloud of minute machines floats around the Operator. These will carry out the actual removal of the skin, remote-controlled by him; his optical centres receive pictures directly transmitted by cameras built into the micro-scalpels.

Here he has opted for speed, but also difficulty, by moving simultaneously from the periphery to the centre (peeling the tips of the fingers and toes like a glove), and from the centre to the periphery (lifting the skin from each side of the median incision). Bets are exchanged in the audience on the number of additional incisions that he will have to make.

The man and the woman now watch the show only from time to time. They talk instead, heads close together, punctuating their words with kisses.

The Operator's psychosomatic control has relaxed for the first time. Blood beads along his cuts and where his skin, with a slow but regular movement, is being lifted at the same time as the Subject's. Suction cups stick to him to clean and cauterize (but will not inject, of course, any analgesics). The work of the micro-machines, however, continues without any appreciable interruption. The myriads of pincer-clips hold the Subject's skin and carefully lift it as the lasers separate the dermis, millimetre by millimetre. (It is important that the five layers of the epidermis be removed intact, basal layer, Malpighian layer, granular layer, clear layer, and horny layer.) There are particularly delicate areas, where the skin is thinner (the inside of the wrists, the armpits, the nipples . . . and of course, in the lower half, the popliteal space, the groin, and, when the Subject is a man, the penis, which is initially treated like a finger. It is necessary to go from the glans to the root, by way of the flap of the foreskin, and to deal with the softness of the scrotum).

The Operator is visibly fighting the pain now. The suction cups stick themselves to him more often, and the removal of the Subject's skin seems to have also slowed down. Once the fingers have been uncovered, the arms and legs are skinned without particular problems for the Subject (and causing the Operator only the difficult, though expected, problem of growing pain). But the linkup of the micro-scalpels coming from the periphery with those coming from the centre takes place with difficulty on the perimeter of the torso. The process is no longer the slow but certain advance of a nearly straight front, as in the beginning (pincer-clips above the skin, micro-scalpels beneath) but a staggered progression, a section here, another farther on. The risks of tearing the tissue are increasing second by second as the machines lose their alignment and stresses are applied to the skin more and more unevenly. Will the Operator forfeit, or will he try to hold out to the extreme limits of consciousness, with all the attendant risks? The movement of the machines and the removal of the skin is now so slow as to be almost imperceptible. It could even be concluded, after a while, that it has totally stopped. The Operator floats, motionless. Only the movement of the cauterizing suction cups, here and there on his body, shows that he is still conscious. Is he resting, frittering away the precious remaining seconds while the analgesics still have some effect, or, although he is conscious, does he lack the strength to concede? But the suction cups detach themselves from him, putting an end to the spectators' speculations. He is quite unconscious now. He has not been able to get through the Subject.

The Subject, however, in spite of the initial pain, and then the progressive anaesthesia, has remained perfectly conscious. With the Operator immobilized, she takes full control of his powers. Now in command of the extraction tools, the Subject can choose to stop or to go on with the initial work—which in this case will continue to be performed on the Operator's body using identical machines that have just appeared in the weightlessness chamber and are obediently awaiting her decision. The machines position themselves on the floating body of the Operator. There is a brief round of satisfied applause in the audience. The Subject will finish the work, guiding the advance of the pincer-clips and micro-lasers over her own body, not only for the linkup taking place all around her torso, but also for the extremely delicate skinning of her head.

The Subject, of course, benefits from the results of the Operator's skill and speed. She needs only a few minutes to complete the task (while the cauterizing suction cups move over the unconscious body of the Operator in the wake of the micro-scalpels and hastily inject him with a powerful mixture of restorative drugs).

The purpose of the injection at the end of the process, for the Subject as for the Operator (but is it still legitimate now to distinguish them in this way?), is to reinforce the skin sufficiently to reduce the risk during the last phase of the operation. After waiting a few minutes for the strengthener to take effect, the Subject extracts herself from her epidermis, slowly and nimbly, helped by the machines. Carried by force fields, the skin floats, tinted with a delicate, pinkish hue by the light of the lasers, not flaccid but as if still inhabited in absentia by the body that has just left it. The Subject swims towards the Operator, an exact, animated anatomical statue in which muscles, tendons, and capillary networks are outlined with gleaming precision (they also hint more clearly, by the patterns finally revealed, at the rigid, solid bone frame that supports them). She now applies herself to extracting him from his skin. Soon the two envelopes float side by side in the weightlessness chamber, like outlines in waiting.

The Operator has regained consciousness. Impossible now to read any expression on his face, but the way he circles the Subject's envelope, then his own, indicates quite clearly his satisfaction with the outcome of the encounter. They were, one could say, worthy of each other. He comes back towards the Subject and speaks some inaudible words to her. They seem to be in agreement and swim together to the skins.

A spectator on the fifth level who is more perceptive than the others begins applauding. Others understand a few seconds later, and soon the rest of the audience does too—through contagion or sudden illumination, impossible to say. In the weightlessness chamber, the Subject is in the process of fitting herself into the Operator's skin, and the Operator (with some difficulty, the proportions not being identical though the sizes are) is wriggling into the Subject's skin.

A series of stationary holograms replaces the hologram of the weightlessness chamber. They show the development of the ultimate phase of the Great Game: the progressive assimilation of the exchanged envelopes through local reabsorption of excess skin and regeneration of missing skin (with the interesting colour patterns that result—zones of thin white skin on copper-coloured skin, and vice versa). The woman's skin is very white except for these differently pigmented bands; she now has short hair, black and smooth. The young man sports an unruly mane, and its copper colour matches almost perfectly the colour of his skin, striped here and there with white bands, particularly on the torso, the genitals, and the fingertips.

The circular stage vanishes. The applause continues for a few minutes more, while the voice of the Announcer names the two artists in the performance that has just been viewed. A few exclamations indicate that their names are familiar to many of the spectators. For a while, in some alcoves, there's a flurry of speculation about what could have induced the Manager to present a show which is, if memory serves well, already ten years old. The artists have long since gone on to other destinies, and other, more modern, forms of art. The conversations go on this way for a moment, then drift off as various other concerns take over. Some clients get up to leave the establishment. The waiters guide others who have just arrived to vacant alcoves. Some hostesses who are free now begin to circulate among the audience again, while on the stage another attraction—holographic or real, it matters little—begins to draw the attention of possible spectators.

In the alcove on the third level, the man and the woman are also ready to leave. The occupants of the neighbouring table stop them as they go, and speak a few animated words to them in passing, to which they reply with a smile and a nod. Comcodes are exchanged; then the couple continues on its way up the levels to the exit. For an instant, in the doorway, the light catches a copper reflection on the hair of the man, a fragmented sparkling from the woman's lamé dress; then the door closes on them, hiding them from the curiosity of the few other consumers who are perhaps still following with their eyes, unsure, and who will no doubt never have another chance to learn more about their identity.

A Gift from the Culture

IAIN M. BANKS

Iain Banks (1954–2013) was a popular Scottish writer of both general fiction and science fiction—the latter as "Iain M. Banks." He is best known for his Culture novels, including *Consider Phlebas* (1987), *The Player of Games* (1988), *The State of the Art* (1991), *Use of Weapons* (1990), and many more. Significant stand-alone novels include the often horrifying *The Wasp Factory* (1984). Although Banks received few science fiction award nominations of any note for these novels, they have become classics in the field. In 2008, the London *Times* named Banks to their list of the "Fifty Greatest British Writers Since 1945." He also got to write a book about whiskey a few years before his death from cancer, which entailed driving around Scotland and sampling the product, engendering perhaps thousands of envious curses from writers around the world.

The Culture novels portray a vast, interstellar civilization whose thirty trillion citizens are housed not only on planets but in gigantic starships and space habitats called "orbitals." These habitats are governed by vast, wry artificial intelligences called Minds, who are essentially indistinguishable from their ships or habitats. One unique element of Banks's creation is that it has been conceived in genuine post-scarcity terms; it does not contain—and therefore does not tell the stories of—internal or external hierarchies or conspiracies bent on maintaining power through control of limited resources. Within the Culture itself, therefore, there are no empires, no tentacled corporations, no enclaves whose hidden knowledge give their inhabitants a vital edge in their attempts to maintain independence, no secret masters.

Even more remarkably, Iain M. Banks represents the inhabitants of the Culture as energetic volunteers living in a utopia that has, in a sense, been created for them. They are most often met monitoring and exploring the universe in the vast AI-run ships that comprise the ganglia of the colossal enterprise. The novels of the Culture, therefore, almost entirely escape the presumption—very widely though tacitly espoused in twentieth-century science fiction—that a society without scarcity is inherently a society whose inhabitants are idle. Post-scarcity is not here inherently a mark of dystopia; it is not a sign of decadence or devolution that "in the Culture, anybody anytime could experience anything anywhere for nothing."

This doesn't in any way preclude internal conflict or complex political machinations, however—the Culture novels are full of brilliant set pieces and conflict-driven plotlines. Further, Banks's creation allows him to examine in-depth topics like the nature of AI, the nature of evil, and the nature of posthuman interactions.

"A Gift from the Culture" (1987), Banks's only short story set in that milieu, gives readers a glimpse of the virtues of this truly extraordinary series.

A GIFT FROM THE CULTURE

Iain M. Banks

Money is a sign of poverty. This is an old Culture saying I remember every now and again, especially when I'm being tempted to do something I know I shouldn't, and there's money involved (when is there not?).

I looked at the gun, lying small and precise in Cruizell's broad, scarred hand, and the first thing I thought—after: Where the hell did they get one of those?—was: Money is a sign of poverty. However appropriate the thought might have been, it wasn't much help.

I was standing outside a no-credit gambling club in Vreccis Low City in the small hours of a wet weeknight, looking at a pretty, toylike handgun while two large people I owed a lot of money to asked me to do something extremely dangerous and worse than illegal. I was weighing up the relative attractions of trying to run away (they'd shoot me), refusing (they'd beat me up; probably I'd spend the next few weeks developing a serious medical bill), and doing what Kaddus and Cruizell asked me to do, knowing that while there was a chance I'd get away with it—uninjured, and solvent again—the most likely outcome was a messy and probably slow death while assisting the security services with their enquiries.

Kaddus and Cruizell were offering me all my markers back, plus—once the thing was done—a tidy sum on top, just to show there were no hard feelings.

I suspected they didn't anticipate having to pay the final instalment of the deal.

So, I knew that logically what I ought to do was tell them where to shove their fancy designer pistol, and accept a theoretically painful but probably not terminal beating. Hell, I could switch the pain off (having a Culture background does have some advantages), but what about that hospital bill?

I was up to my scalp in debt already.

"What's the matter, Wrobik?" Cruizell drawled, taking a step nearer, under the shelter of the club's dripping eaves. Me with my back against the warm wall, the smell of wet pavements in my nose and a taste like metal in my mouth. Kaddus and Cruizell's limousine idled at the kerb; I could see the driver inside, watching us through an open window. Nobody passed on the street outside the narrow alley. A police cruiser flew over, high up, lights flashing through the rain and illuminating the underside of the rain clouds over the city. Kaddus looked up briefly, then ignored the passing craft. Cruizell shoved the gun towards me. I tried to shrink back.

"Take the gun, Wrobik," Kaddus said tiredly. I licked my lips, stared down at the pistol.

"I can't," I said. I stuck my hands in my coat pockets.

"Sure you can," Cruizell said. Kaddus shook his head.

"Wrobik, don't make things difficult for yourself; take the gun. Just touch it first, see if our information is correct. Go on; take it." I stared, transfixed, at the small pistol. "Take the gun, Wrobik. Just remember to point it at the ground, not at us; the driver's got a laser on you and he might think you meant to use the gun on us . . . come on; take it, touch it."

I couldn't move, I couldn't think. I just stood, hypnotized. Kaddus took hold of my right wrist and pulled my hand from my pocket. Cruizell held the gun up near my nose; Kaddus forced my hand onto the pistol. My hand closed round the grip like something lifeless.

. . .

The gun came to life; a couple of lights blinked dully, and the small screen above the grip glowed, flickering round the edges. Cruizell dropped his hand, leaving me holding the pistol; Kaddus smiled thinly.

"There, that wasn't difficult, now, was it?" Kaddus said. I held the gun and tried to imagine using it on the two men, but I knew I couldn't, whether the driver had me covered or not.

"Kaddus," I said, "I can't do this. Something else; I'll do anything else, but I'm not a hit man; I can't—"

"You don't have to be an expert, Wrobik," Kaddus said quietly. "All you have to be is . . . whatever the hell you are. After that, you just point and squirt: like you do with your boyfriend." He grinned and winked at Cruizell, who bared some teeth. I shook my head.

"This is crazy, Kaddus. Just because the thing switches on for me—"

"Yeah; isn't that funny." Kaddus turned to Cruizell, looking up to the taller man's face and smiling. "Isn't that funny, Wrobik here being an alien? And him looking just like us."

"An alien *and* queer," Cruizell rumbled, scowling. "Shit."

"Look," I said, staring at the pistol, "it . . . this thing, it . . . it might not work," I finished lamely. Kaddus smiled.

"It'll work. A ship's a big target. You won't miss." He smiled again.

"But I thought they had protection against—"

"Lasers and kinetics they can deal with, Wrobik; this is something different. I don't know the technical details; I just know our radical friends paid a lot of money for this thing. That's enough for me."

Our radical friends. This was funny, coming from Kaddus. Probably he meant the Bright Path. People he'd always considered bad for business, just terrorists. I'd have imagined he'd sell them to the police on general principles, even if they did offer him lots of money. Was

he starting to hedge his bets, or just being greedy? They have a saying here: Crime whispers; money talks.

"But there'll be people on the ship, not just—"

"You won't be able to see them. Anyway, they'll be some of the Guard, naval brass, some Administration flunkeys, Secret Service agents. . . . What do you care about them?" Kaddus patted my damp shoulder. "You can do it."

I looked away from his tired grey eyes, down at the gun, quiet in my fist, small screen glowing faintly. Betrayed by my own skin, my own touch. I thought about that hospital bill again. I felt like crying, but that wasn't the done thing amongst the men here, and what could I say? I was a woman. I was Culture. But I had renounced these things, and now I am a man, and now I am here in the Free City of Vreccis, where nothing is free.

"All right," I said, a bitterness of my mouth, "I'll do it."

Cruizell looked disappointed. Kaddus nodded. "Good. The ship arrives Ninthday; you know what it looks like?" I nodded. "So you won't have any problems." Kaddus smiled thinly. "You'll be able to see it from almost anywhere in the City." He pulled out some cash and stuffed it into my coat pocket. "Get yourself a taxi. The underground's risky these days." He patted me lightly on the cheek; his hand smelt of expensive scents. "Hey, Wrobik, cheer up, yeah? You're going to shoot down a fucking starship. It'll be an experience." Kaddus laughed, looking at me and then at Cruizell, who laughed too, dutifully.

They went back to the car; it hummed into the night, tyres ripping at the rain-filled streets. I was left to watch the puddles grow, the gun hanging in my hand like guilt.

"I am a Light Plasma Projector, model LPP 91, series two, constructed in A/4882.4 at Manufactory Six in the Spanshacht-Trouferre Orbital,

Ørvolöus Cluster. Serial number 3685706. Brain value point one. AM battery powered, rating: indefinite. Maximum power on single-bolt: 3.1 x 810 joules, recycle time 14 seconds. Maximum rate of fire: 260 RPS. Use limited to Culture genofixed individuals only through epidermal gene analysis. To use with gloves or light armour, access 'modes' store via command buttons. Unauthorized use is both prohibited and punishable. Skill requirement 12-75 percent C. Full instructions follow; use command buttons and screen to replay, search, pause, or stop. . . .

"Instructions, part one: Introduction. The LPP 91 is an operationally intricate general-purpose 'peace'-rated weapon not suitable for full battle use; its design and performance parameters are based on the recommendations of . . ."

The gun sat on the table, telling me all about itself in a high, tinny voice while I lay slumped in a lounger, staring out over a busy street in Vreccis Low City. Underground freight trains shook the rickety apartment block every few minutes, traffic buzzed at street level, rich people and police moved through the skies in fliers and cruisers, and above them all the starships sailed.

I felt trapped between these strata of purposeful movements.

Far in the distance over the city, I could just see the slender, shining tower of the city's Lev tube, rising straight towards and through the clouds, on its way to space. Why couldn't the Admiral use the Lev instead of making a big show of returning from the stars in his own ship? Maybe he thought a glorified elevator was too undignified. Vainglorious bastards, all of them. They deserved to die (if you wanted to take that attitude), but why did I have to be the one to kill them? Goddamned phallic starships. I shook my head.

Not that the Lev was any less pricklike, and anyway, no doubt if the Admiral had been coming down by the tube Kaddus and Cruizell would have told me to shoot it down; holy shit. I shook my head.

I was holding a long glass of jahl—Vreccis City's cheapest strong booze. It was my second glass, but I wasn't enjoying it. The gun chattered on, speaking to the sparsely furnished main room of our apartment. I was waiting for Maust, missing him even more than usual. I looked at the terminal on my wrist; according to the time display he should be back any moment now. I looked out into the weak, watery light of dawn. I hadn't slept yet.

The gun talked on. It used Marain, of course; the Culture's language. I hadn't heard that spoken for nearly eight standard years, and hearing it now I felt sad and foolish. My birthright; my people, my language. Eight years away, eight years in the wilderness. My great adventure, my renunciation of what seemed to me sterile and lifeless to plunge into a more vital society, my grand gesture . . . well, now it seemed like an empty gesture, now it looked like a stupid, petulant thing to have done.

I drank some more of the sharp-tasting spirit. The gun gibbered on, talking about beam-spread diameters, gyroscopic weave patterns, gravity-contour mode, line-of-sight mode, curve shots, spatter and pierce settings. . . . I thought about glanding something soothing and cool, but I didn't; I had vowed not to use those cunningly altered glands eight years ago, and I'd broken that vow only twice, both times when I was in severe pain. Had I been courageous I'd have had the whole damn lot taken out, returned to their human-normal state, our original animal inheritance . . . but I am not courageous. I dread pain, and cannot face it naked, as these people do. I admire them, fear them, still cannot understand them. Not even Maust. In fact, least of all Maust. Perhaps you cannot ever love what you completely understand.

Eight years in exile, lost to the Culture, never hearing that silky, subtle, complexly simple language, and now when I do hear Marain, it's from a gun, telling me how to fire it so I can kill . . . what? Hundreds of people? Maybe thousands; it will depend on where the ship falls, whether it explodes (could primitive starships explode? I had no idea; that was never my field). I took another drink, shook my head. I couldn't do it.

I am Wrobik Sennkil, Vreccile citizen number . . . (I always forget; it's on my papers), male, prime race, aged thirty; part-time freelance journalist (between jobs at the moment), and full-time gambler (I tend to lose but I enjoy myself, or at least I did until last night). But I am, also, still Bahlln-Euchersa Wrobich Vress Schennil dam Flaysse, citizen of the Culture, born female, species mix too complicated to remember, aged sixty-eight, standard, and one-time member of the Contact section.

And a renegade; I chose to exercise the freedom the Culture is so proud of bestowing upon its inhabitants by leaving it altogether. It let me go, even helped me, reluctant though I was. (But could I have forged my own papers, made all the arrangements by myself? No, but at least, after my education into the ways of the Vreccile Economic Community, and after the module rose, dark and silent, back into the night sky and the waiting ship, I have turned only twice to the Culture's legacy of altered biology, and not once to its artefacts. Until now; the gun rambles on.) I abandoned a paradise I considered dull for a cruel and greedy system bubbling with life and incident; a place I thought I might find . . . what? I don't know. I didn't know when I left and I don't know yet, though at least here I found Maust, and when I am with him my searching no longer seems so lonely.

Until last night that search still seemed worthwhile. Now Utopia sends a tiny package of destruction, a casual, accidental message.

Where *did* Kaddus and Cruizell get the thing? The Culture guards its weaponry jealously, even embarrassedly. You can't buy Culture weapons, at least not from the Culture. I suppose things go missing though; there is so much of everything in the Culture that objects must be mislaid occasionally. I took another drink, listening to the gun, and watching that watery, rainy-season sky over the rooftops, towers,

aerials, dishes, and domes of the Great City. Maybe guns slip out of the Culture's manicured grasp more often than other products do; they betoken danger, they signify threat, and they will only be needed where there must be a fair chance of losing them, so they must disappear now and again, be taken as prizes.

That, of course, is why they're built with inhibiting circuits which only let the weapons work for Culture people (sensible, nonviolent, non-acquisitive Culture people, who *of course* would only use a gun in self-defence, for example, if threatened by some comparative barbarian . . . oh the self-satisfied Culture: its imperialism of smugness). And even this gun is antique; not obsolescent (for that is not a concept the Culture really approves of—it builds to last), but outdated; hardly more intelligent than a household pet, whereas modern Culture weaponry is sentient.

The Culture probably doesn't even make handguns anymore. I've seen what it calls Personal Armed Escort Drones, and if, somehow, one of those fell into the hands of people like Kaddus and Cruizell, it would immediately signal for help, use its motive power to try to escape, shoot to injure or even kill anybody trying to use or trap it, attempt to bargain its way out, and destruct if it thought it was going to be taken apart or otherwise interfered with.

I drank some more jahl. I looked at the time again; Maust was late. The club always closed promptly, because of the police. They weren't allowed to talk to the customers after work: he always came straight back. . . . I felt the start of fear, but pushed it away. Of course he'd be all right. I had other things to think about. I had to think this thing through. More jahl.

No, I couldn't do it. I left the Culture because it bored me, but also because the evangelical, interventionist morality of Contact sometimes meant doing just the sort of thing we were supposed to prevent others doing: starting wars, assassinating . . . all of it, all the bad things. . . . I was never involved with Special Circumstances directly, but I knew what went on. (Special Circumstances; Dirty Tricks, in other words. The Culture's tellingly unique euphemism.) I refused to live with such hypocrisy and chose instead this honestly selfish and avaricious society, which doesn't pretend to be good, just ambitious.

But I have lived here as I lived there, trying not to hurt others, trying just to be myself; and I cannot be myself by destroying a ship full of people, even if they are some of the rulers of this cruel and callous society. I can't use the gun; I can't let Kaddus and Cruizell find me. And I will not go back, head bowed, to the Culture.

I finished the glass of jahl.

I had to get out. There were other cities, other planets, besides Vreccis; I just had to run; run and hide. Would Maust come with me though? I looked at the time again; he was half an hour late. Not like him. Why was he late? I went to the window, looking down to the street, searching for him.

A police APC rumbled through the traffic. Just a routine cruise; siren off, guns stowed. It was heading for the Outworlder's Quarter, where the police had been making shows of strength recently. No sign of Maust's svelte shape swinging through the crowds.

Always the worry. That he might be run over, that the police might arrest him at the club (indecency, corrupting public morals, and homosexuality; that great crime, even worse than not making your payoff!), and, of course, the worry that he might meet somebody else.

Maust. Come home safely, come home to me.

I remember feeling cheated when I discovered, towards the end of my regendering, that I still felt drawn to men. That was long ago, when I was happy in the Culture, and like many people I had wondered what it would be like to love those of my own original sex; it seemed terribly unfair that my desires did not alter with my physiology. It took Maust to make me feel I had not been cheated. Maust made everything better. Maust was my breath of life.

Anyway, I would not be a woman in this society.

I decided I needed a refill. I walked past the table.

". . . will not affect the line-stability of the weapon, though recoil will be increased on power-priority, or power decreased—"

"Shut up!" I shouted at the gun, and made a clumsy attempt to hit its Off button; my hand hit the pistol's stubby barrel. The gun skidded across the table and fell to the floor.

"Warning!" the gun shouted. "There are no user-serviceable parts inside! Irreversible deactivation will result if any attempt is made to dismantle or—"

"Quiet, you little bastard," I said (and it did go quiet). I picked it up and put it in the pocket of a jacket hanging over a chair. Damn the Culture; damn all guns. I went to get more drink, a heaviness inside me as I looked at the time again. Come home, please come home . . . and then come away, come away with me. . . .

I fell asleep in front of the screen, a knot of dull panic in my belly competing with the spinning sensation in my head as I watched the news and worried about Maust, trying not to think of too many things. The news was full of executed terrorists and famous victories in small, distant wars against aliens, outworlders, subhumans. The last report I remember was about a riot in a city on another planet; there was no mention of civilian deaths, but I remember a shot of a broad street littered with crumpled shoes. The item closed with an injured policeman being interviewed in hospital.

I had my recurring nightmare, reliving the demonstration I was caught up in three years ago: looking, horrified, at a wall of drifting, sun-struck stun gas and seeing a line of police mounts come charging out of it, somehow more appalling than armoured cars or even tanks, not because of the visored riders with their long shock-batons, but because the tall animals were also armoured and gas-masked, monsters from a ready-made, mass-produced dream, terrorizing.

Maust found me there hours later, when he got back. The club had been raided and he hadn't been allowed to contact me. He held me as I cried, shushing me back to sleep.

"Wrobik, I can't. Risåret's putting on a new show next season and he's looking for new faces; it'll be big-time, straight stuff. A High City deal. I can't leave now; I've got my foot in the door. Please understand." He reached over the table to take my hand. I pulled it away.

"I can't do what they're asking me to do. I can't stay. So I have to go; there's nothing else I can do." My voice was dull. Maust started to clear away the plates and containers, shaking his long, graceful head. I hadn't eaten much; partly hangover, partly nerves. It was a muggy, enervating midmorning; the tenement's conditioning plant had broken down again.

"Is what they're asking really so terrible?" Maust pulled his robe tighter, balancing plates expertly. I watched his slim back as he moved to the kitchen. "I mean, you won't even tell me. Don't you trust me?" His voice echoed.

What could I say? That I didn't know if I did trust him? That I loved him but: Only he had known I was an outworlder. That had been my secret, and I'd told only him. So how did Kaddus and Cruizell know? How did Bright Path know? My sinuous, erotic, faithless dancer. Did you think because I always remained silent that I didn't know of all the times you deceived me?

"Maust, please; it's better that you don't know."

"Oh," Maust laughed distantly; that aching, beautiful sound, tearing at me. "How terribly dramatic. You're protecting me. How awfully gallant."

"Maust, this is serious. These people want me to do something I just can't do. If I don't do it they'll . . . they'll at least hurt me, badly. I don't know what they'll do. They . . . they might even try to hurt me through you. That was why I was so worried when you were late; I thought maybe they'd taken you."

"My dear, poor Wrobbie," Maust said, looking out from the kitchen, "it has been a long

day; I think I pulled a muscle during my last number, we may not get paid after the raid—Stelmer's sure to use that as an excuse even if the filth didn't swipe the takings—and my ass is still sore from having one of those queer-bashing pigs poking his finger around inside me. Not as romantic as your dealings with gangsters and baddies, but important to me. I've enough to worry about. You're overreacting. Take a pill or something; go back to sleep; it'll look better later." He winked at me, disappeared. I listened to him moving about in the kitchen. A police siren moaned overhead. Music filtered through from the apartment below.

I went to the door of the kitchen. Maust was drying his hands. "They want me to shoot down the starship bringing the Admiral of the Fleet back on Ninthday," I told him. Maust looked blank for a second, then sniggered. He came up to me, held me by the shoulders.

"Really? And then what? Climb the outside of the Lev and fly to the sun on your magic bicycle?" He smiled tolerantly, amused. I put my hands on his and removed them slowly from my shoulders.

"No. I just have to shoot down the ship, that's all. I have . . . they gave me a gun that can do it." I took the gun from the jacket. He frowned, shaking his head, looked puzzled for a second, then laughed again.

"With that, my love? I doubt you could stop a motorized pogo stick with that little—"

"Maust, please; believe me. This can do it. My people made it and the ship . . . the state has no defence against something like this."

Maust snorted, then took the gun from me. Its lights flicked off. "How do you switch it on?" He turned it over in his hand.

"By touching it; but only I can do it. It reads the genetic makeup of my skin, knows I am Culture. Don't look at me like that; it's true. Look." I showed him. I had the gun recite the first part of its monologue and switched the tiny screen to holo. Maust inspected the gun while I held it.

"You know," he said after a while, "this might be rather valuable."

"No, it's worthless to anyone else. It'll only work for me, and you can't get round its fidelities; it'll deactivate."

"How . . . faithful," Maust said, sitting down and looking steadily at me. "How neatly everything must be arranged in your 'Culture.' I didn't really believe you when you told me that tale, did you know that, my love? I thought you were just trying to impress me. Now I think I believe you."

I crouched down in front of him, put the gun on the table and my hands on his lap. "Then believe me that I can't do what they're asking, and that I am in danger; perhaps we both are. We have to leave. Now. Today or tomorrow. Before they think of another way to make me do this."

Maust smiled, ruffled my hair. "So fearful, eh? So desperately anxious." He bent, kissed my forehead. "Wrobbie, Wrobbie; I can't come with you. Go if you feel you must, but I can't come with you. Don't you know what this chance means to me? All my life I've wanted this; I may not get another opportunity. I have to stay, whatever. You go; go for as long as you must and don't tell me where you've gone. That way they can't use me, can they? Get in touch through a friend, once the dust has settled. Then we'll see. Perhaps you can come back; perhaps I'll have missed my big chance anyway and I'll come to join you. It'll be all right. We'll work something out."

I let my head fall to his lap, wanting to cry. "I can't leave you."

He hugged me, rocking me. "Oh, you'll probably find you're glad of the change. You'll be a hit wherever you go, my beauty; I'll probably have to kill some knife-fighter to win you back."

"Please, please come with me," I sobbed into his gown.

"I can't, my love, I just can't. I'll come to wave you good-bye, but I can't come with you."

He held me while I cried; the gun lay silent and dull on the table at his side, surrounded by the debris of our meal.

I was leaving. Fire escape from the flat just before dawn, over two walls clutching my travelling bag, a taxi from General Thetropsis Avenue to Intercontinental Station . . . then I'd catch a Railtube train to Bryme and take the Lev there, hoping for a standby on almost anything heading Out, either trans or inter. Maust had lent me some of his savings, and I still had a little high-rate credit left; I could make it. I left my terminal in the apartment. It would have been useful, but the rumours are true; the police can trace them, and I wouldn't have put it past Kaddus and Cruizell to have a tame cop in the relevant department.

The station was crowded. I felt fairly safe in the high, echoing halls, surrounded by people and business. Maust was coming from the club to see me off; he'd promised to make sure he wasn't followed. I had just enough time to leave the gun at Left Luggage. I'd post the key to Kaddus, try to leave him a little less murderous.

There was a long queue at Left Luggage; I stood, exasperated, behind some naval cadets. They told me the delay was caused by the porters searching all bags and cases for bombs; a new security measure. I left the queue to go and meet Maust; I'd have to get rid of the gun somewhere else. Post the damn thing, or even just drop it in a waste bin.

I waited in the bar, sipping at something innocuous. I kept looking at my wrist, then feeling foolish. The terminal was back at the apartment; use a public phone, look for a clock. Maust was late.

There was a screen in the bar, showing a news bulletin. I shook off the absurd feeling that somehow I was already a wanted man, face liable to appear on the news broadcast, and watched today's lies to take my mind off the time.

They mentioned the return of the Admiral of the Fleet, due in two days. I looked at the screen, smiling nervously. *Yeah, and you'll never know how close the bastard came to getting blown out of the skies.* For a moment or two I felt important, almost heroic.

Then the bombshell; just a mention—an aside, tacked on, the sort of thing they'd have cut had the programme been a few seconds over—that the Admiral would be bringing a guest with him; an ambassador from the Culture. I choked on my drink.

Was *that* who I'd really have been aiming at if I'd gone ahead?

What was the Culture doing anyway? An ambassador? The Culture knew everything about the Vreccile Economic Community, and was watching, analyzing; content to leave ill enough alone for now. The Vreccile people had little idea how advanced or widely spread the Culture was, though the court and Navy had a fairly good idea. Enough to make them slightly (though had they known it, still not remotely sufficiently) paranoid. What was an ambassador for?

And who was really behind the attempt on the ship? Bright Path would be indifferent to the fate of a single outworlder compared to the propaganda coup of pulling down a starship, but what if the gun hadn't come from them, but from a grouping in the court itself, or from the Navy? The VEC had problems; social problems, political problems. Maybe the president and his cronies were thinking about asking the Culture for aid. The price might involve the sort of changes some of the more corrupt officials would find terminally threatening to their luxurious lifestyles.

Shit, I didn't know; maybe the whole attempt to take out the ship was some loony in Security or the Navy trying to settle an old score, or just skip the next few rungs on the promotion ladder. I was still thinking about this when they paged me.

I sat still. The station PA called for me, three times. A phone call. I told myself it was just Maust, calling to say he had been delayed; he knew I was leaving the terminal at the apartment so he couldn't call me direct. But would he announce my name all over a crowded sta-tion when he knew I was trying to leave quietly and unseen? Did he still take it all so lightly? I didn't want to answer that call. I didn't even want to think about it.

My train was leaving in ten minutes; I picked up my bag. The PA asked for me again, this time mentioning Maust's name. So I had no choice.

I went to Information. It was a viewcall.

"Wrobik," Kaddus sighed, shaking his head. He was in some office; anonymous, bland. Maust was standing, pale and frightened, just behind Kaddus's seat. Cruizell stood right behind Maust, grinning over his slim shoulder. Cruizell moved slightly, and Maust flinched. I saw him bite his lip. "Wrobik," Kaddus said again. "Were you going to leave so soon? I thought we had a date, yes?"

"Yes," I said quietly, looking at Maust's eyes. "Silly of me. I'll . . . stick around for . . . a couple of days. Maust, I—" The screen went grey.

I turned round slowly in the booth and looked at my bag, where the gun was. I picked the bag up. I hadn't realized how heavy it was.

I stood in the park, surrounded by dripping trees and worn rocks. Paths carved into the tired topsoil led in various directions. The earth smelled warm and damp. I looked down from the top of the gently sloped escarpment to where pleasure boats sailed in the dusk, lights reflecting on the still waters of the boating lake. The duskward quarter of the city was a hazy platform of light in the distance. I heard birds calling from the trees around me.

The aircraft lights of the Lev rose like a rope of flashing red beads into the blue evening sky; the port at the Lev's summit shone, still uneclipsed, in sunlight a hundred kilometres overhead. Lasers, ordinary searchlights, and chemical fireworks began to make the sky bright above the Parliament buildings and the Great Square of the Inner City; a display to greet the returning, victorious Admiral, and maybe the ambassador from the Culture, too. I couldn't see the ship yet.

I sat down on a tree stump, drawing my coat about me. The gun was in my hand; on, ready, ranged, set. I had tried to be thorough and professional, as though I knew what I was doing; I'd even left a hired motorbike in some bushes on the far side of the escarpment, down near the busy parkway. I might actually get away with this. So I told myself, anyway. I looked at the gun.

I considered using it to try to rescue Maust, or maybe using it to kill myself; I'd even considered taking it to the police (another, slower form of suicide). I'd also considered calling Kaddus and telling him I'd lost it, it wasn't working, I couldn't kill a fellow Culture citizen . . . anything. But in the end, nothing.

If I wanted Maust back I had to do what I'd agreed to do.

Something glinted in the skies above the city, a pattern of falling, golden lights. The central light was brighter and larger than the others.

I had thought I could feel no more, but there was a sharp taste in my mouth, and my hands were shaking. Perhaps I would go berserk, once the ship was down, and attack the Lev too; bring the whole thing smashing down (or would part of it go spinning off into space? Maybe I ought to do it just to see). I could bombard half the city from here (hell, don't forget the curve shots; I could bombard the whole damn city from here); I could bring down the escort vessels and attacking planes and police cruisers; I could give the Vreccile the biggest shock they'd ever had, before they got me. . . .

The ships were over the city. Out of the sunlight, their laser-proof mirror hulls were duller now. They were still falling, maybe five kilometres up. I checked the gun again.

Maybe it wouldn't work, I thought.

Lasers shone in the dust and grime above the city, producing tight spots on high and wispy clouds. Searchlight beams faded and spread

in the same haze, while fireworks burst and slowly fell, twinkling and sparkling. The sleek ships dropped majestically to meet the welcoming lights. I looked about the tree-lined ridge; alone. A warm breeze brought the grumbling sound of the parkway traffic to me.

I raised the gun and sighted. The formation of ships appeared on the holo display, the scene noon-bright. I adjusted the magnification, fingered a command stud; the gun locked onto the flagship, became rock-steady in my hand. A flashing white point in the display marked the centre of the vessel.

I looked round again, my heart hammering, my hand held by the field-anchored gun. Still nobody came to stop me. My eyes stung. The ships hung a few hundred metres above the state buildings of the Inner City. The outer vessels remained there; the centre craft, the flagship, stately and massive, a mirror held up to the glittering city, descended towards the Great Square. The gun dipped in my hand, tracking it.

Maybe the Culture ambassador wasn't aboard the damn ship anyway. This whole thing might be a Special Circumstances setup; perhaps the Culture was ready to interfere now and it amused the planning Minds to have me, a heretic, push things over the edge. The Culture ambassador might have been a ruse, just in case I started to suspect. . . . I didn't know. I didn't know anything. I was floating on a sea of possibilities, but parched of choices.

I squeezed the trigger.

The gun leapt backwards, light flared all around me. A blinding line of brilliance flicked, seemingly instantaneously, from me to the starship ten kilometres away. There was a sharp detonation of sound somewhere inside my head. I was thrown off the tree stump.

When I sat up again the ship had fallen. The Great Square blazed with flames and smoke and strange, bristling tongues of some terrible lightning; the remaining lasers and fireworks were made dull. I stood, shaking, ears ringing, and stared at what I'd done. Late-reacting sprinterceptiles from the escorts crisscrossed the air above the wreck and slammed into the ground, automatics fooled by the sheer velocity of the plasma bolt. Their warheads burst brightly among the boulevards and buildings of the Inner City, a bruise upon a bruise.

The noise of the first explosion smacked and rumbled over the park.

The police and the escort ships themselves were starting to react. I saw the lights of police cruisers rise strobing from the Inner City; the escort craft began to turn slowly above the fierce, flickering radiations of the wreck.

I pocketed the gun and ran down the damp path towards the bike, away from the escarpment's lip. Behind my eyes, burnt there, I could still see the line of light that had briefly joined me to the starship; bright path indeed, I thought, and nearly laughed. A bright path in the soft darkness of the mind.

I raced down to join all the other poor folk on the run.

Paranamanco

JEAN-CLAUDE DUNYACH

Translated by Sheryl Curtis

Jean-Claude Dunyach (1957–) is a critically acclaimed French writer with a PhD in applied mathematics and supercomputing who works for Airbus in the city of Toulouse, France. Dunyach has been writing science fiction and fantasy since the beginning of the 1980s, and has already published eight novels and nine collections of short stories, garnering the Grand Prix de la science fiction française, four Rosny-Aîné prizes, the Grand Prix de l'Imaginaire, the Grand Prix Tour Eiffel de science-fiction, and the Prix Ozone. His short story "Déchiffrer la trame" ("Unraveling the Thread") won both the Grand Prix de l'Imaginaire and the Rosny-Aîné Award in 1998, and was voted Best Story of the Year by the readers of the magazine *Interzone*. Dunyach's works have been translated into English, Bulgarian, Croatian, Danish, Hungarian, German, Italian, Russian, and Spanish. Dunyach also writes lyrics for several French singers, which served as an inspiration for one of his novels, about a rock-and-roll singer touring in Antarctica with a zombie philharmonic orchestra.

In his introduction to Dunyach's story collection *The Night Orchid* (2004), the US author David Brin writes that "Jean-Claude has a trait that is rare among authors—variability [with a] sense of the author's deeper drive to experiment . . . To surprise. He also always seemed to have something wry and relevant to say."

The story reprinted here, "Paranamanco," is a unique take on the idea of the biological city. Toulouse (nicknamed "the Pink City") is mostly built of red bricks, and some of its most famous buildings—including the dome of the Hôpital de la Grave and the bell tower of Saint-Sernin Basilica—resemble bizarre body parts. The idea for a city made of flesh, an "animalcity," came to Dunyach on the banks of the Garonne River, during an early morning stroll in the mist.

"Paranamanco" (1987) is the first story based on this concept. However, animalcities play a central role in two of Dunyach's novels: *Étoiles mortes* (*Dead Stars*) and *Étoiles mourantes* (*Dying Stars*), the latter written in collaboration with Yal Ayerdhal.

PARANAMANCO

Jean-Claude Dunyach

Translated by Sheryl Curtis

When Paranamanco broke out of her mooring lines and flew off into the night, I was hardly surprised. I remembered the words of the old navigator I'd interviewed a few months earlier, shortly after the animalcity project had been abandoned. I took the recording cube of our conversation out of a drawer and played it, wondering if I'd have the time to listen to it until the end. . . .

"An entire herd? Can you imagine it? Twenty or so wild animalcities floating like medusas in space. The smallest could have served as the capital of any empire; the largest . . . No doubt you observed Paranamanco while orbiting in the transit satellite before landing here. You flew over it for several hours, skimming over the outgrowths we incorrectly call dwellings; maybe you even strolled along her avenues, with their disorderly striations carved by meteor dust. You may believe that you've seen her, but she continues to elude you as a result of her size, her topography with its folds and strangeness. There are entire neighborhoods which no one has penetrated yet, alleys that are not shown on any map, buildings of flesh waiting to be explored."

The old man stopped to finish his glass. On a corner of my desk, the cube reader wove the image of a tavern, purring busily. I don't like mute objects. We created things to fill our solitude with their omnipresent company, not for them to fall silent and echo the waves of our own silence back at us, amplified.

"If you've got the heart for it," the old man said, "buy a recent plan and then have them drop you off anywhere in the city. You know the rule: when you find a street that hasn't been identified, you can name it as you see fit and register it with the land titles office. There's a bonus for each discovery, but it will hardly cover the cost of purchasing the one hundred sixty microfilmed volumes of the plan. Yet, how many people do you think are wandering about like that, shoulders bent under the weight of the microfilms and the viewer? Several thousand?"

He shook his head and glumly contemplated his empty glass, which was starting to crackle and release an unpleasant odor. After the last swallow, the glass walls, deprived of humidity, decompose rather quickly, obliging drinkers to order another round immediately.

The strident ring of the communicator shrilled through the apartment. I cut it off and went back to listening.

"You have your own opinion of Paranamanco. It's undoubtedly incorrect, but mine is no better. It was a living organism before we decided to make it a city. A creature like that never really totally dies. Certain outlying neighborhoods rise and fall like respiration that is barely perceptible; the hollow filaments that we plan on using as transportation tunnels or sewer mains are sometimes animated by nervous shudders, like the axons of a failed brain.

"No, Paranamanco isn't completely dead; I've known her far too long to be wrong about that. Before I landed on her surface, I observed her in the middle of the herd, in deep space. Then I explored her for months, looking for the control points of her nervous system. I planted thousands of needles randomly in her flesh before discovering her pleasure centers and mounting her like an elephant driver, armed with the whip of my electrical discharges. I forced her to follow me here, by trial and error. Once in orbit, I moored her, practically all on my own.

"You should have been there when we landed! Paralyzed by the cloud of tugs hooked to her circumference, she deployed her corolla of multicolored filaments and whipped the air, trying to trap the metal birds that flew within reach. She was magnificent and dangerous, a real carnivorous flower. No one could have forced her to obey if I'd dropped the reins.

"Of course, those who supervised the project had taken their precautions. Paranamanco was the first animalcity that we'd moored and, to date, she's still the only one; the others are parked between the asteroids, waiting for the authorities to reach a decision. The idea of using a life-form like this as an inhabitable zone on the surface of a colonized world is interesting, but it's not to everyone's liking. Many colonists would prefer us to build them something more conventional. Some categorically refuse to settle in a dwelling whose walls are made of living organic tissue.

"We all make the mistake of judging the animalcities by their appearance. A city is just a city, the imbeciles say, nothing surprising about that. That's stupid, even dangerous. These creatures have nothing other than the most superficial points in common with the human species. Their architecture, their existence depends on rules beyond our knowledge, even though it does appear easy to apply our own rules to them. We can use them, but we can never understand them. Take heed: this is important!

"Everyone was walking on eggs at that time. The head honchos came here to supervise the operations and prevent any possible problems from causing too many waves.

"Finally they gave the explorers the go-ahead. That's when the problems started. . . ."

With a sigh, I pour him another drink. I've learned to recognize those points when stories wind down if they're not fuelled—with alcohol, compliments, or, occasionally, forgiveness. It all depends on the storyteller. The old man wasn't looking for absolution; he just wanted to drink.

"I went there too," I said.

He gazed at his glass in the light of a mood lamp and noisily drained a good half of it.

"I wasn't looking to make my fortune. Capturing Paranamanco had already made me rich and, in any case, I'd never believed those tales of treasure buried in the animalcities' entrails. No, I was bored. Setting out to hunt in deep space didn't thrill me anymore. Any prey would have appeared minuscule to me after that catch.

"I'd started drinking, seriously drinking if you know what I mean. I set out on a whim one morning. I think that I was even getting tired of the alcohol and I was afraid of what would come next.

"I chose to explore the eighteenth sector, starting out from the base camp established in the heart of the city. The instructions provided for a spiral exploration of the neighboring streets, followed by satellite reconnaissance of the outlying neighborhoods. At that rate, it would have taken ten years to map the main arteries. Paranamanco wouldn't have been inhabitable for a century.

"It's impossible to realize just how vast she is if you haven't tried to cross her alone. She's brimming with optical illusions, fake terraces, and underground arteries. The guide satellites are no use at all. Animalcity skin is impervious to radio waves; even the remote-controlled units get lost. To bring her back to more human proportions, she had to be marked out with beacons filled with signs, and pointers; the chaos of her alleys had to be corrected, the still wild neighborhoods had to be domesticated.

"So, I set out to identify the most direct route possible to the edge of the city. If everyone else had done the same, we could have completed the map in two years and taken charge of the terrain.

"It's a game, you see. Draw a map and you control the territory. The more accurate your map is, the more efficient your control is.

"Do you know how a new world is opened

up for colonization? There are the mechanical caterpillars that lay kilometers and kilometers of fiber-optic cables in a few hours. Release thousands of those machines on the surface of any planet and they lay out a grid of high-capacity lines and communication nodes, while sterilising the surface. It doesn't matter how long it takes, you can rest assured that, after they've finished their job, there isn't a single nook or cranny that hasn't been explored. There's always a telephone booth on the horizon. At any given time, you're a thirty-minute shuttle ride from civilization.

"I took one of those caterpillars with me. . . .

"I don't know why, but those caterpillars had no success with Paranamanco. They would either get lost or go completely crazy. They built closed lines that held them prisoner or wove electrified webs in which they hid, waiting for their prey. Apparently, some have even been found enveloped in a veritable cocoon, a prelude to an impossible metamorphosis. I'm only repeating what I've heard, but you know as well as I do that where there's smoke there's usually a fire.

"So, I headed off in the direction of the periphery with that caterpillar purring as it laid its wire. My belongings sat at the peak of its central ring, firmly moored to magnetic clamps. I walked ahead, hands in my pockets, as carefree as a Stanley who didn't give a rat's ass about Livingstone, while she crawled along behind me.

"About every ten kilometers, she'd stop to lay a new communication node, wrapped in placental tissue. It's a curious sight, but you get tired of it quickly. After a day, I stopped paying attention. Besides, people say you shouldn't get too close to those machines at such times. Now and then, their maternal love makes them dangerous. I made the most of these stops to stroll about the narrow alleys in the vicinity or I'd drink a glass to Paranamanco's health. My supplies were supposed to last two months. That's the main reason I'd brought the caterpil-lar along. With all the bottles, my luggage was too heavy for my old shoulders.

"After two days, we were navigating by sight between the constructions erected like pustules on the city's bituminous skin. Most were empty and naked, with a faint smell of dried sweat. Others, encumbered by cartilage partitions or blood red drapes, would have driven an interior decorator mad. I didn't have time to visit them all, so I settled for glancing inside the closest ones, so I could map those I considered inhabitable.

"The road we were following sloped down gently before branching out into narrower and narrower catwalks that led to the peaks of the buildings. Often, a building would be super-imposed over the main artery and we'd move ahead into a dark tunnel, out of the range of the observation satellites. In such cases, our prog-ress would be jerkier, the caterpillar's head-lights hesitantly sweeping away the dark. I'd keep my hand on its head ring, to reassure it.

"The farther we proceeded into the invisible levels of the city, the more uncontrollable my caterpillar's reactions became. Her dilated sphincters released bunches of embryonic booths, most irreversibly deformed, exuding machine oil. I'd kick their protective envelope into bits, to alleviate their agony and prevent the development of interference in the communication network. When we got back to the surface, the caterpillar returned to normal. I stopped in a clearing so she could recharge her solar batteries.

"It was during one of these breaks that I realized we were no longer alone.

"Our trail was easy to follow; all they had to do was keep sight of the wires. Yet, I'd never have thought that someone would have bothered to tail us, the machine and me. We weren't carrying anything valuable, apart from my booze, and I'd have willingly shared a bottle. And don't for a minute think that we were surrounded by unknown creatures drawn from the depths of the city. Our trackers were human and they weren't making much of an effort to hide.

"I could have set a trap for them, ambushed them in any alleyway. They'd had a dozen opportunities to do the same earlier, so . . . I stopped the caterpillar and waited for them, a bottle of alcohol in my hand. I know the rules.

"They, on the other hand, didn't. They took so long to show their faces that I was three-quarters drunk by the time they arrived. I no longer clearly remember what they told me that evening; the next morning, all my bottles were broken and my skull was buzzing. Luckily, the girl made good coffee.

"There were two of them. A guy and a girl. About your age. I had him pegged right off: taciturn, with the long, slender fingers of a pianist. She was something completely different. A china doll, skin and bones, the type who has never turned anyone away and has decided that it's time for things to change. Apart from that, she was as silent as he was.

"After a few cups of java, I felt up to chewing them out for the loss of my bottles prior to hearing their side of this. They let me shout out my drunkenness before speaking with me. Good idea! I was too angry to do anything but vent my spleen. Plus, yelling almost drowned out the buzzing in my skull.

"They had a map to show me. Not a buried-treasure map, that wasn't their style, or one of those esoteric diagrams that the so-called Paranamanco fortune-tellers specialize in. They're supposed to be able to read your future in the topographical maps of the city, you know, and show the future colonists the best places to settle. If necessary, they find the settlers a neighborhood where the layout of the streets corresponds to the lines on their hands. Utter stupidity.

"My two followers were a different sort of bright spark than I'd possibly come across before. They both worked in the department that tracked the data transmitted by the orbital satellites. The computer had highlighted anom-alies in the aerial photos taken of Paranamanco, inconsistencies in the routes taken by certain streets, the type of detail that neither you nor I would have noticed but which the machines regularly set their sights on. They'd each been looking on their own for months, without joining forces, then they decided to pool their observations. They found the solution almost immediately.

"A fragment on the map of the city was repeated identically forty-four times. A single fragment, but because of this duplicated element, the computer crashed every time it tried to reconstitute the Paranamanco jigsaw. Discouraged, the girl had drawn a map indicating the locations of the famous fragment.

"Once the coffee had its effect, they rolled their map out to show me. Forty-four spots were spread over the disk of the city, with no apparent symmetry or regularity. Yet, their pattern looked familiar to me. I got out my own map, the one showing the animal's nerve centers, which I'd drawn during my deep space exploration. Mine was cruder, but there was nothing haphazard about the resemblance. Strangely, mine was offset one hundred and ninety degrees from theirs; a semicircle, as if the two phenomena were of equal importance, but opposite in meaning.

"The route taken by the caterpillar was heading straight towards the closest spot, which is why they had decided to follow me. I believe they suspected my intentions were the same as theirs. As the first one to explore the creature, I was supposed to know more about her than anyone else. They thought I already had an inkling as to what the identical sectors hid, that the government had some secret goal when it had Paranamanco land and that it was exploring her through me. I didn't disabuse them. They wouldn't have believed me anyway.

"When we set out again, the caterpillar was carrying three packs instead of one, which didn't seem to affect her all that much, and I had an audience to whom I could recount my memories of deep space. They knew how to listen, that much I can say for them, a bit like you, but then you're paid to listen so it doesn't count. The guy, Geoff, never said more than a few words at a time, and settled for moving ahead at his own pace. From time to time, he'd look back to see if the girl was still following. I've forgotten her name, but it will certainly come back as I talk.

"We were a good day's walk from the interesting zone, which gave us time to review a fair number of hypotheses and invent a few new ones. The most curious thing was that, seen from the satellite, there was nothing particular about the duplicated fragment: three or four streets, completely ordinary outgrowths for buildings. Same old, same old. I could have walked through them without noticing a thing. Geoff thought it was some sort of visual illusion and that we should expect something else, underground tunnels maybe, or vast rooms filled with strange machinery. He fixated on that idea: the animalcities were once used as spacecraft by a humanoid race and had outlived their creators. This made for a good story, completely valid, when you have twelve hours of walk ahead of you and nothing else to do than survey the streets and christen them as you see fit.

"In any case, no one knew anything at all about the animalcities at the time, and we've learned precious little since. The colonization of Paranamanco was interrupted and it won't start up again any time soon. As for the rest of the herd, it's wandering carefree about the asteroids. If we knew how to kill a wild city, our problems would be resolved for the most part, but I doubt we'll ever reach that point. I'm starting to think that the entire operation is plain old stupidity, but no one's asked me for my opinion in a long time.

"So, there we were, walking ahead of the caterpillar, because of the exhaust fumes, without even taking the time to visit the structures that surrounded us. We had the entire city to ourselves and the only thing that interested us was a block of three streets, which didn't even

have the excuse of being unique. At the time, that didn't strike us. The idea only came to me on our way back.

"Imagine: today, there are almost one million colonists on Paranamanco, there's noise, electricity, eleven official religions, an entire microcosm of the human species gathered on the surface of a flat organism that had the good sense to be inhabitable. I know that it will take at least half a billion people for the place to even start looking settled, but at the time that the three of us were walking along unexplored avenues there was no one within a two-hundred-kilometer radius. Not a soul! I don't think that an ocean or a desert could give such an impression of solitude. Weirdly it wasn't until the other two arrived that I even noticed.

"Then the wind started to blow down the empty streets and we stopped for shelter on a porch. Evening fell slowly. The buildings created unusual shadows, stretching in unexpected directions. I hadn't had a drop to drink since the previous night, yet my usual hallucinations settled over the façades of the neighboring buildings. They were remodelling the scene that surrounded us. I desperately needed a drink and felt my nightmares swirling in around me, waiting for night to torment me. I didn't have the strength to resist.

"We were approaching our goal. I suppose it was the first symptoms of Paranamanco's influence, although the base doctor has talked to me about delirium tremens with a knowing smile. People like that always have a better explanation than yours and there's no way to make them change their minds.

"The next day the others decided, without consulting me, to leave me there for the entire day while they went out to do some reconnaissance. I'd have refused if I'd known, but that double dose of sleeping pills in the coffee would have put anyone out like a light. When I opened my eyes, I was trapped in an unbreakable cocoon of cables and the caterpillar, which had been reprogrammed, was vigilantly standing guard over me.

"I'd wanted to warn the base that a couple of loonies were holding me prisoner so that someone would come and get me. It seemed easy; I was surrounded by communication booths. The caterpillar had woven a delicious little concentration camp for one where transmission cables replaced the barbed wire and booths replaced watchtowers. The only problem was that I didn't have enough tokens.

"Before I even reached the base operator, my supply had run out. I was stupid enough to try to kick the box apart to collect its contents. My first mistake was choosing a freshly hatched booth; my second was forgetting the caterpillar's maternal instinct.

"Possibly her reflexes should have been altered by the reprogramming, but that didn't stop her from charging at me with the full speed of her segments, tearing her way through the cables she'd woven. We played a deadly game of tag, in which the neutral zones were the booths. Bit by bit, I was trying to draw her away from the breach she'd made in the network of wires that held me prisoner. When I thought it was a good time, I raced off towards the closest building, expecting to be caught and pulverized at any time. I've rarely been afraid, but I was that day.

"Once safe, I caught my breath before glancing behind me. The caterpillar hadn't followed me at all; she stood motionless in the middle of her cocoon. On her back, the girl was waving in my direction.

"I turned about slowly, savoring my anger as it swept over me. I was preparing myself for one of those explosions that make novas look minor. In two days these two clueless young people had deprived me of my bottles, drugged me, and forced me into a rodeo with a thirty-ton caterpillar. I had enough insults in mind to turn the air blue. Then I saw the tears rolling down the girl's cheeks and I fell silent. . . . What else could I have done?

"We broke camp in ten minutes. I cut the cable ahead of the anarchic section and made a splice directly on the machine's hindquar-ters, short-circuiting the delirious skin that had imprisoned me. One more puzzle for the archeologists of the future. I allowed myself the luxury of using an iron bar to pulverize the booth that held my tokens and recovered them. I'm the first official vandal on Paranamanco. Don't forget to mention that in your article."

"Why were you in such a rush to leave?"

My voice rises out of the cube reader with an irritating fidelity, asking the right question at the right time.

In front of me, on the back wall of my office, the red warning light flashes in vain. I don't feel like answering any call, especially right now.

"Geoff had disappeared in the unknown sector. The girl, Evalane (I knew her name would come back to me, Geoff called her Evie), well the girl had been afraid to continue their research on her own and had come back to release me so I could help her. Ten seconds later and she'd probably have found the caterpillar nibbling on a pancake-shaped cadaver. Bio-machines can be quite strange at times. My caterpillar would've probably laid flesh pink booths, with dial pads incrusted with eyes rather than keys. Just the thought of dialling a number under those conditions, fingers in eyes . . . Evie acknowledged that it was lucky for me that Geoff had chosen that particular moment to evaporate. How was I supposed to respond to that? I grumbled that luck had been smiling on me ever since they'd arrived, but the girl was insensitive to sarcasm.

"She had stopped crying, well almost. I hadn't realized that she had a thing for him. When you live alone in space, you lose track of that sort of phenomenon. I had no idea just how important that was going to be later.

"Evie said there was nothing particular about the area where Geoff had disappeared. It looked like so many other neighborhoods that they'd walked through before. They had to backtrack and ask for a satellite location in order to find it. Geoff was disappointed and furious. He raced up and down the three streets, looking for a secret passageway, a hidden opening, without success. Then he started to explore the outgrowths one after another, coming back out a little more annoyed each time. Finally, she saw him go into a porch and he never came back out.

"According to the girl, there was nothing particular about the interior of the building either: a labyrinth of cartilage partitions, a rough floor, made of folds of dead skin. Since no one answered when she called out, she hadn't dared to venture too far in and preferred to return to camp, taking care to spray-paint her initials on the porch.

"We approached cautiously. Nothing moved, no sound filtered out to us, no trace of Geoff. I picked up the caterpillar's remote control as I pulled Evie away from the porch.

" 'We could get lost in that maze,' I explained to her. 'I'll send the beast in to explore for us.'

" 'Good idea!' she said. 'Then we can simply follow its wire to make our way back out without getting trapped by those damn partitions.'

" 'After she's done a tour inside, there won't actually be many partitions intact,' I replied.

"She blushed, which didn't look good on her, and fell silent. The caterpillar rolled over to the entrance. Her segments proceeded into the building, one by one. We could hear the sound of fabric tearing, followed by irregular periods of silence. I glanced inside: the floor was strewn with cartilage debris and booths that had been laid all askew, imprisoned in their placental pouches. Just the place for a large-scale communication centre. I noted its location on the map, out of reflex, before carefully following in the caterpillar's footsteps, accompanied by Evie.

"We made our way through the building diagonally, stumbling over the waste. A cloud of bone dust powdered our clothing. We avoided coughing, for fear of giving birth to an echo we wouldn't have recognized. I twisted my ankle and Evie fell in a pile of debris, from which she emerged looking like a ghost, bits of membrane hanging from her shoulders and hair like a transparent shroud.

"The caterpillar had stopped at the entrance to an immense multisided room that had remained intact. Evie slid past her body and almost immediately cried out. When I reached her, she was kneeling next to Geoff, who lay unconscious, feverish, lips clenched, fingernails dug into bloody palms.

"We didn't see the fountain right away. We were busy trying to revive our lost team member and didn't have the time to study the surroundings closely. It was only when Geoff opened his eyes and pointed at it that I realised it was there. He hoarsely asked us to get him something to drink.

"Evie gave him a shot and poured the contents of her canteen between his lips. I stood up to disconnect the caterpillar. On my way, I glanced about, without noticing anything special: a murmur came from the thin ribbon of water that welled up from the ground and filled a cavity. It hadn't rained in a week and I recall wondering where the water was coming from. But I didn't think it was all that important.

"As soon as Geoff could stand up and before we could stop him, he rushed over to the fountain to drink. The water didn't appear to have any particular effect on him. He offered me some, but I don't really have an affinity for that type of liqueur at zero degrees.

"When we asked him why he'd fainted, he replied that he'd knocked himself out against a partition. The explanation was so stupid that we believed it and considered the matter closed. Evie apologized for dragging me into all this for nothing. Geoff received his share of insults from me for leaving me with the caterpillar, but my heart wasn't in it, so I left it alone.

"We followed the wire back out. None of us tried to get away from the sector; we even decided to set up our camp at the intersection of two neighboring streets. Evie made some coffee. Without a word, Geoff held out her canteen so that she could go and fill it.

"I gave him a mild sedative so that he could rest for the remainder of the day and went out to explore the neighboring buildings, to form my own opinion.

"Evie was telling the truth; there was absolutely nothing to see in that sector. It was so similar to all the others I'd travelled through before that things were starting to look suspicious. I was caught up in the game, obstinately searching for something. I didn't know what it should look like. I palpated the city's thick skin in hopes of detecting some sort of revealing pulse; I scratched esoteric maps in an old notepad, tearing the pages out as I finished them. In short, I behaved like an imbecile. Evie, who was watching over Geoff, called out to me from time to time, asking if I'd found anything, and seemed to take no notice of my increasingly brief answers.

"The dark gradually chased me from the shadowy streets, in which it would be all too easy to lose my way. I gave up and sat down next to the electric hot plate where our evening rations were heating, along with an entire pot of coffee. Evie and Geoff glanced at me, but refrained from making a comment. Just as well. I couldn't forgive them for breaking the pleasant monotony of my trip through the city. For the first time, Paranamanco had disappointed me and it was all their fault.

"I rolled up in my bedroll, as far from the caterpillar and them as possible, and tried to fall asleep. I'd had too much coffee for sleep to come easily but, with the help of the silence, I gradually felt myself doze off with the hope that the place would get rid of my two pests.

"That night I dreamt the same thing over and over again. I was hitting my head against the reality of the city like a moth blinded by light. When I woke up, Geoff had disappeared once more and the entire neighborhood seemed to have gone mad. . . .

"Heavy bunches of colored lightbulbs hung overhead, large drops of luminous sap dripping down. A vine of telephone cables climbed up the outgrowths, rolling in abundant, baroque spirals along the streets, in an unnatural embrace. Neon orchids with electrifying scents surged from the slightest chink in the walls, shooting lightning that bounced off Parana-manco's skin. In a few hours, the neighborhood had been transformed into a virgin forest.

"Next to the dead hot plate and the caterpillar, which had been definitively disconnected, Evie lay plunged in a sleep evidently filled with nightmares. The ground around her was spiked by long, transparent spears, shimmering with violet sparks. I had to kick them to bits to get closer to her.

"Geoff had made her swallow the rest of the sleeping pills and had pinned a laconic note to her sleeping bag before heading off. I knew what it said before reading and rereading it. Then I woke Evie.

"All around us, the neighbourhood was coming to life. The sun was already high and the dense fiber-optic jungle shimmered in the bright light. I almost expected Geoff to appear wearing a simple loincloth, leaping from vine to vine, hunting prey. But I knew that we'd never see him again. And, deep down, Evie did too.

"She refused to believe it, however, and wanted to look for him in that verdant growth, despite the evidence that surrounded us, despite Geoff's note. She denied the facts. Hey, you try to convince a woman that her lover is capable of leaving her for a living organism that measures six hundred kilometers in diameter, a creature he had shared his dreams with. . . .

"I had a lot of difficulty convincing her to listen to me. I'd known what was really going on with Paranamanco since the previous night, in part because of Evie. The water she'd used to make her coffee came from the fountain. Some of its power remained, despite the boiling, just enough that I knew what kind of trap Geoff fell into. Merely thinking that I could have suffered the same fate made me shiver. It would have taken so little. I must be one of the few people whose life has been saved by alcohol.

"I told Evie that the liquid had slowly poisoned Geoff, that the first time we'd found him, unconscious, he'd most certainly just drunk from the fountain and that, feeling that he was about to die, he preferred to distance himself from the camp, to spare us the spectacle of his agony. The note he had left her was the fruit of a brain that was already damaged; she shouldn't pay it any attention. Of course, she didn't believe a word of what I said, but it was the best lie I could come up with given the time available.

"She insisted that I tell the truth. I was stupid enough to do so. . . ."

A long line of vehicles, sirens shrieking, is heading my way. Judging by the sound, they're still far away enough for me to listen to the last surface of the cube, the most important one.

"The animalcities are incomplete organisms," the old man murmurs, eyes staring at a horizon beyond my reach. "To successfully face the space that separates galaxies, they need symbiotic companions, gardeners capable of caring for them and maintaining them throughout the voyage. In exchange, they offer access to the entire universe, as well as the means to survive in the void of space.

"When I landed on Paranamanco's surface for the first time, she understood that her race and mankind could get along. She flavored the water with her dreams accordingly. After tasting it, Geoff was able to give birth to the neon garden that surrounded us of his own accord. No doubt he was wandering about the adjacent neighborhoods, impatient to put his new powers to the test. I imagined the winding streets filled with hardy brambles, leaves flashing with lightning, tree streetlights, electric foliage stretching over the city's squares, avenues illuminated by the flamboyant chalices of glass tulips. I realized that Geoff had not only shared Paranamanco's dreams, but had also, in a certain manner, transmitted his own. She dreamed of looking like the cities on Earth, with their adornment of multicolored lights enshrined in metal and stone. All she needed was a little help.

"At the beginning, Evie refused to believe me, convinced that I was making the whole thing up for some totally obscure reason, that I didn't know any more than she did. So, I placed my hands on the warm soil. A tiny neon flower sprang up and spat out its fire before expiring.

"She finally understood that we couldn't do any more for Geoff. Only an expedition organized by the base would be able to find him, if it wasn't already too late. The caterpillar was dead; we had no more water. Well, at least, I preferred not to try the water in our canteens, in case Geoff had filled them at the fountain. I left Evie, deeply wounded by my words, and set out, following the wire, to search for a booth that was working.

"I had no idea what my colleague on the other end of the line thought about my story and I didn't care. Once I was certain that someone would come to get us immediately, I headed back to camp, and found it empty.

"Evie had carried off one of the canteens when she left. In a letter scribbled while I was away, she said that she was ready to join Geoff, to take her turn at serving the city. I castigated myself for not having seen that coming and I cried out her name until the echoes rebounded around me. I never saw her again.

"The most horrible part is that there was no chance for her project to succeed. Paranamanco was only interested in men. There was a sexual component between her gardeners and her that was essential for her survival. Evie was incapable of providing that and I suppose that the animalcities can occasionally get jealous. . . .

"That evening, a shuttle came to pick me up, guided by the dead caterpillar's beacon. When the pilot saw the scene, he called for reinforcements. A security cordon surrounded the site. But it was too late. We never found anyone.

"I don't know how the information could have leaked out, but hundreds of colonists set out to look for Paranamanco's secret wells. Those in charge implemented a news blackout, partly because they didn't believe me. I'm an old wino, you know. It was fine and dandy for me to tell them over and over that it was the alcohol that had saved my life, but they remained skeptical. I can see their point of view and I would never have imagined that someone would come and interview me about all this.

"And you, do you believe me? If I weren't

half drunk, I'd string up a garland of lights to convince you, but Paranamanco doesn't like alcohol and I believe I lost my power over her a long time ago. She doesn't want me anymore. I had my chance and I blew it."

Someone is banging brusquely at my door; the recording is over. My article has been rejected everywhere, without explanation. I've been under constant surveillance, but that doesn't matter now. The city found her pilot; she was able to take off with her crew of dreamers and adventurers, whose hands will bring flowers back to the dead streets. No doubt, they're far away already.

I have a minute or two before those who are looking for me break down the door. I grab the flask of the city's dreams that the old explorer gave to me, before heading off into the streets with their sadly conventional signs and disappearing for good. Maybe I'll have the time to uncork and drink it, but Paranamanco has flown off and I'm no longer certain that I can find her.

Crying in the Rain

TANITH LEE

Tanith Lee (1947–2015) was an iconic British writer of speculative fiction who wrote in nearly every genre during a prolific and distinguished career that produced almost one hundred novels, several hundred short stories, and work in other media (including two episodes of the BBC television series *Blake's 7*). Lee grew up the daughter of professional dancers, who often discussed favorite books with her and encouraged her to read work by Saki and Theodore Sturgeon, among others. She began to write before the age of ten.

Lee's short fiction has been reprinted by many anthologists and appeared in most of the major science fiction and fantasy magazines. In particular, Lee became associated with *Weird Tales*, which published her work continuously from the 1980s until her death. She became the first woman to win the British Fantasy Award for best novel (1980), was twice nominated for the Nebula Award, was nominated eleven times for the World Fantasy Award (winning twice), and received the World Fantasy Award for Life Achievement in 2013 and the Horror Writers Association Lifetime Achievement Award in 2015.

As she moved beyond her early works for children, Lee proved to be an inventive and fertile writer, producing novels and stories that differ vastly in tone and subject matter and are dauntingly comprehensive. There seemed to be no subject, from robots to cosmogony, that failed to serve her primary impulses as a storyteller. For this reason, it is hard to place her oeuvre within the larger context of the history of science fiction, except to say that her interests often lay within the gothic, surreal, and psychological. Although Lee was heterosexual, much of her fame was attributed to her award-winning fiction featuring gay, lesbian, bisexual, and transgender characters. An early series, *Tales from the Flat Earth* (inspired by the fairy tales of Oscar Wilde), was celebrated for introducing gender-fluid characters long before this became more common in the past few years.

"Crying in the Rain" (1989) is typical, classic Lee—a dark and brooding setting with all-too-human characters, and the implications of the setup carried to conclusion with devastating consequences.

CRYING IN THE RAIN

Tanith Lee

There was a weather warning that day, so to start with we were all indoors. The children were watching the pay-TV and I was feeding the hens on the shutyard. It was about nine a.m. Suddenly my mother came out and stood at the edge of the yard. I remember how she looked at me: I had seen the look before, and although it was never explained, I knew what it meant. In the same way she appraised the hens, or checked the vegetables and salad in their grow-trays. Today there was a subtle difference, and I recognized the difference too. It seemed I was ready.

"Greena," she said. She strode across to the hen-run, glanced at the disappointing hens. There had only been three eggs all week, and one of those had registered too high. But in any case, she wasn't concerned with her poultry just now. "Greena, this morning we're going into the Center."

"What about the Warning, Mum?"

"Oh, that. Those idiots, they're often wrong. Anyway, nothing until noon, they said. All Clear till then. And we'll be in by then."

"But, Mum," I said, "there won't be any buses. There never are when there's a Warning. We'll have to walk."

Her face, all hard and eaten back to the bone with life and living, snapped at me like a rat trap: "So we'll *walk*. Don't go on and on, Greena. What do you think your legs are for?"

I tipped the last of the feed from the pan and started toward the stair door.

"And talking of legs," said my mother, "put on your stockings. And the things we bought last time."

There was always this palaver. It was normally because of the cameras, particularly those in the Entry washrooms. After you strip, all your clothes go through the cleaning machine, and out to meet you on the other end. But there are security staff on the cameras, and the doctors, and they might see, take an interest. You had to wear your smartest stuff in order not to be ashamed of it, things even a Center doctor could glimpse without repulsion. A stickler, my mother. I went into the shower and took one and shampooed my hair, and used powder bought in the Center with the smell of roses, so all of me would be gleaming clean when I went through the shower and shampooing at the Entry. Then I dressed in my special under-clothes, and my white frock, put on my stockings and shoes, and remembered to drop the carton of rose powder in my bag.

My mother was ready and waiting by the time I came down to the street doors, but she didn't upbraid me. She had meant me to be thorough.

The children were yelling round the TV, all but Daisy, who was seven and had been left in charge. She watched us go with envious fear. My mother shouted her away inside before we opened up.

When we'd unsealed the doors and got out, a blast of heat scalded us. It was a very hot day, the sky so far clear as the finest blue Perspex. But of course, as there had been a weather Warning, there were no buses, and next to no one on the streets. On Warning days, there was anyway really nowhere to go. All the shops were sealed fast, even our three area pubs. The local train station ceased operating when I was four, eleven years ago. Even the endless jumble of squats had their boards in place and their tarpaulins over.

The only people we passed on the burning dusty pavements were a couple of fatalistic tramps, in from the green belt, with bottles of cider or petromix; these they jauntily raised to us. (My mother tugged me on.) And once a police car appeared which naturally hove to at our side and activated its speaker.

"Is your journey really necessary, madam?"

My mother, her patience eternally tried, grated out furiously, "Yes it is."

"You're aware there's been a forecast of rain for these sections?"

"*Yes,*" she rasped.

"And this is your daughter? It's not wise, madam, to risk a child—"

"My daughter and I are on our way to the Center. We have an appointment. Unless we're *delayed,*" snarled my mother, visually skewering the pompous policeman, only doing his job, through the Sealtite window of the car, "we would be inside before any rain breaks."

The two policemen in their snug patrol vehicle exchanged looks.

There was a time we could have been arrested for behaving in this irresponsible fashion, my mother and I, but no one really bothers now. There was more than enough crime to go round. On our own heads it would be.

The policeman who'd spoken to us through the speaker smiled coldly and switched it off—speaker, and come to that, smile.

The four official eyes stayed on me a moment, however, before the car drove off. That at least gratified my mother. Although the policemen had called me a child for the white under-sixteen tag on my wristlet, plainly they'd noticed I looked much older and besides, rather good.

Without even a glance at the sky, my mother marched forward. (It's true there are a few public weather-shelters but vandals had wrecked most of them.) I admired my mother, but I'd never been able to love her, not even to like her much. She was phenomenally strong and had kept us together, even after my father canced, and the other man, the father of Jog, Daisy, and

Angel. She did it with slaps and harsh tirades, to show us what we could expect in life. But she must have had her fanciful side once: for instance, the silly name she gave me, for green trees and green pastures and waters green as bottle glass that I've only seen inside the Center. The trees on the streets and in the abandoned gardens have always been bare, or else they have sparse foliage of quite a cheerful brown color. Sometimes they put out strange buds or fruits and then someone reports it and the trees are cut down. They were rather like my mother, I suppose, or she was like the trees. Hard-bitten to the bone, enduring, tough, holding on by her root-claws, not daring to flower.

Gallantly she showed only a little bit of nervousness when we began to see the glint of the dome in the sunshine coming down High Hill from the old cinema ruin. Then she started to hurry quite a lot and urged me to be quick. Still, she didn't look up once, for clouds.

In the end it was perfectly all right: the sky stayed empty and we got down to the concrete underpass. Once we were on the moving way I rested my tired feet by standing on one leg, then the other like a stork I once saw in a TV program.

As soon as my mother noticed she told me to stop it. There are cameras watching, all along the underpass to the Entry. It was useless to try persuading her that it didn't matter. She had never brooked argument and though she probably wouldn't clout me before the cameras she might later on. I remember I was about six or seven when she first thrashed me. She used a plastic belt, but took off the buckle. She didn't want to scar me. Not to scar Greena was a part of survival, for even then she saw something might come of me. But the belt hurt and raised welts. She said to me as I lay howling and she leaned panting on the bed, "I won't have any back-answers. Not from you and not from any of you, do you hear me? There isn't time for it. You'll do as I say."

. . . .

After we'd answered the usual questions, we joined the queue for the washroom. It wasn't much of a queue, because of the Warning. We glided through the mechanical check, the woman operator even congratulating us on our low levels. "That's section SEK, isn't it?" she said chattily. "A very good area. My brother lives out there. He's over thirty and has three children." My mother congratulated the operator in turn and proudly admitted our house was one of the first in SEK fitted with Sealtite. "My kids have never played outdoors," she assured the woman. "Even Greena here scarcely went out till her eleventh birthday. We grow most of our own food." Then, feeling she was giving away too much—you never knew who might be listening, there was always trouble in the suburbs with burglars and gangs—she clammed up tighter than the Sealtite.

As we went into the washroom a terrific argument broke out behind us. The mechanical had gone off violently. Some woman was way over the acceptable limit. She was screaming that she had to get into the Center to see her daughter, who was expecting a baby—the oldest excuse, perhaps even true, though pregnancy is strictly regulated under a dome. One of the medical guards was bearing down on the woman, asking if she had Insurance.

If she had, the Entry hospital would take her in and see if anything could be done. But the woman had never got Insurance, despite having a daughter in the Center, and alarms were sounding and things were coming to blows.

"Mum," I said, when we passed into the white plastic-and-tile expanse with the black camera eyes clicking overhead and the Niagara rush of showers, "who are you taking me to see?"

She actually looked startled, as if she still thought me so naive that I couldn't guess she too, all this time, had been planning to have a daughter in the Center. She glared at me, then came out with the inevitable.

"Never you mind. Just you hope you're lucky. Did you bring your talc?"

"Yes, Mum."

"Here then, use these too. I'll meet you in the cafeteria."

When I opened the carton I found "Smoky" eye makeup, a cream lipstick that smelled of peaches, and a little spray of scent called I Mean It.

My stomach turned right over. But then I thought, So what. It would be frankly stupid of *me* to be thinking I was naive. I'd known for years.

While we were finishing our hamburgers in the cafeteria, it did start to rain, outside. You could just sense it, miles away beyond the layers of protection and lead-glass. A sort of flickering of the sight. It wouldn't do us much harm in here, but people instinctively moved away from the outer suburb-side walls of the cafe even under the plastic palm trees in tubs. My mother stayed put.

"Have you finished, Greena? Then go to the ladies' and brush your teeth, and we'll get on. And spray that scent again."

"It's finished, Mum. There was only enough for one go."

"Daylight robbery," grumbled my mother, "you can hardly smell it." She made me show her the empty spray and insisted on squeezing hissing air out of it into each of my ears.

Beyond the cafeteria, a tree-lined highway runs down into the Center. Real trees, green trees, and green grass on the verges. At the end of the slope, we waited for an electric bus painted a jolly bright color, with a rude driver. I used to feel that everyone in the Center must be cheery and contented, bursting with optimism and the juice of kindness. But I was always disappointed. They know you're from outside at once; if nothing else gives you away, skin tone is different from the pale underdome skin or chocolaty solarium Center tan. Although you could never have got in here if you hadn't checked out as acceptable, a lot of people draw away from you on the buses or underground trains. Once or twice, when my mother and I had gone to see a film in the Center no one would sit near us. But not everybody had this attitude. Presumably, the person my mother was taking me to see wouldn't mind.

"Let me do the talking," she said as we got off the bus. (The driver had started extra quickly, half shaking our contamination off his platform, nearly breaking our ankles.)

"Suppose he asks me something?"

"*He?*" But I wasn't going to give ground on it now. "All right. In that case, answer, but be careful."

Parts of the Center contain very old historic buildings and monuments of the inner city which, since they're inside, are looked after and kept up. We were now under just that sort of building. From my TV memories—my mother had made sure we had the educational TV to grow up with, along with lesson tapes and exercise ropes—the architecture looked late eighteenth or very early nineteenth, white stone, with toplids on the windows and pillared porticos up long stairs flanked by black metal lions.

We went up the stairs and I was impressed and rather frightened.

The glass doors behind the pillars were wide open. There's no reason they shouldn't be, here. The cool-warm, sweet-smelling breezes of the dome-conditioned air blew in and out, and the real ferns in pots waved gracefully. There was a tank of golden fish in the foyer. I wanted to stay and look at them. Sometimes on the Center streets you see well-off people walking their clean, groomed dogs and foxes. Sometimes there might be a silken cat high in a window. There were birds in the Center parks, trained not to fly free anywhere else. When it became dusk above the dome, you would hear them tweeting excitely as they roosted. And then all the lights of the city came on and moths danced round them. You could get proper honey in the Center, from the bee farms, and beef and milk from the cattle grazings, and salmon, and leather and wine and roses.

But the fish in the tank were beautiful. And

I suddenly thought, If I get to stay here—if I really *do*—but I didn't believe it. It was just something I had to try to get right for my mother, because I must never argue with her, ever.

The man in the lift took us to the sixth floor. He was impervious; we weren't there, he was simply working the lift for something to do.

A big old clock in the foyer had said three p.m. The corridor we came out in was deserted. All the rooms stood open like the corridor windows, plushy hollows with glass furniture: offices. The last office in the corridor had a door which was shut.

My mother halted. She was pale, her eyes and mouth three straight lines on the plain of bones. She raised her hand and it shook, but it knocked hard and loud against the door.

In a moment, the door opened by itself.

My mother went in first.

She stopped in front of me on a valley-floor of grass-green carpet, blocking my view.

"Good afternoon, Mr. Alexander. I hope we're not too early."

A man spoke.

"Not at all. Your daughter's with you? Good. Please do come in." He sounded quite young.

I walked behind my mother over the grass carpet, and chairs and a desk became visible, and then she let me step around her, and said to him, "This is my daughter, Mr. Alexander. Greena."

He was only about twenty-two, and that was certainly luck, because the ones born in the Center can live up until their fifties, their sixties even, though that's rare. (They quite often don't even cance in the domes, providing they were born there. My mother used to say it was the high life killed them off.)

He was tanned from a solarium and wore beautiful clothes, a cotton shirt and trousers. His wristlet was silver—I had been right about his age: the tag was red. He looked so fit and hygienic, almost edible. I glanced quickly away from his eyes.

"Won't you sit down?" He gave my mother

a crystal glass of Center gin, with ice cubes and lemon slices. He asked me, smiling, if I'd like a milkshake, yes with real milk and strawberry flavor. I was too nervous to want it or enjoy it, but it had to be had. You couldn't refuse such a thing.

When we were perched in chairs with our drinks (he didn't drink with us) he sat on the desk, swinging one foot, and took a cigarette from a box and lit and smoked it.

"Well, I must say," he remarked conversationally to my mother, "I appreciate your coming all this way—after a Warning, too. It was only a shower I gather."

"We were inside by then," said my mother quickly. She wanted to be definite—the flower hadn't been spoiled by rain.

"Yes, I know. I was in touch with the Entry." He would have checked our levels, probably. He had every right to, after all. If he was going to buy me, he'd want me to last for a while.

"And, let me say at once, just from the little I've seen of your daughter, I'm sure she'll be entirely suitable for the work. So pretty, and such a charming manner."

It was normal to pretend there was an actual job involved. Perhaps there even would be, to begin with.

My mother must have been putting her advert out since last autumn. That was when she'd had my photograph taken at the Center. I'd just worn my nylon-lace panties for it; it was like the photos they take of you at the Medicheck every ten years. But there was always a photograph of this kind with such an advert. It was illegal, but nobody worried. There had been a boy in our street who got into the Center three years ago in this same way. He had placed the advert, done it all himself. He was handsome, though his hair, like mine, was very fine and perhaps he would lose it before he was eighteen. Apparently that hadn't mattered.

Had my mother received any other offers? Or only this tanned Mr. Alexander with the intense bright eyes?

I'd drunk my shake and not noticed.

Mr. Alexander asked me if I would read out what was written on a piece of rox he gave me. My mother and the TV lessons had seen to it I could read, or at least that I could read what was on the rox, which was a very simple paragraph directing a Mr. Cleveland to go to office 170B on the seventh floor and a Miss O'Beale to report to the basement. Possibly the job would require me to read such messages. But I had passed the test. Mr. Alexander was delighted. He came over without pretense and shook my hand and kissed me exploringly on the left cheek. His mouth was firm and wholesome and he had a marvelous smell, a smell of money and safety. My mother had labored cleverly on me. I recognized it instantly, and wanted it. Between announcements, they might let me feed the fish in the tank.

Mr. Alexander was extremely polite and gave my mother another big gin, and chatted sociably to her about the latest films in the Center, and the color that was in vogue, nothing tactless or nasty, such as the cost of food inside, and out, or the SEO riots the month before, in the suburbs, when the sounds of the fires and the police rifles had penetrated even our sealed-tight home in SEK. He didn't mention any current affairs, either, the death rate on the continent, or the trade war with the USA—he knew our TV channels got edited. Our information was too limited for an all-round discussion.

Finally he said, "Well, I'd better let you go. Thank you again. I think we can say we know where we stand, yes?" He laughed over the smoke of his fourth cigarette, and my mother managed her death's-head grin, her remaining teeth washed with gin and lemons. "But naturally I'll be writing to you. I'll send you the details Express. That should mean you'll get them—oh, five days from today. Will that be all right?"

My mother said, "That will be lovely, Mr. Alexander. I can speak for Greena and tell you how very thrilled she is. It will mean a lot to us. The only thing is, Mr. Alexander, I do have a couple of other gentlemen—I've put them off, of course. But I have to let them know by the weekend."

He made a gesture of mock panic. "Good God, I don't want to lose Greena. Let's say three and a half days, shall we? I'll see if I can't rustle up a special courier to get my letter to you extra fast."

We said good-bye, and he shook my hand again and kissed both cheeks. A great pure warmth came from him, and a sort of power. I felt I had been kissed by a tiger, and wondered if I was in love.

At the Entry exit, though it didn't rain again, my mother and I had a long wait until the speakers broadcast the All Clear. By then the clarified sunset lay shining and flaming in six shades of red and scarlet-orange over the suburbs.

"Look, Mum," I said, because shut up indoors so much, I didn't often get to see the naked sky, "isn't it beautiful? It doesn't look like that through the dome."

But my mother had no sympathy with vistas. Only the toxins in the air, anyway, make the colors of sunset and dawn so wonderful. To enjoy them is therefore idiotic, perhaps unlawful.

My mother had, besides, been very odd ever since we left Mr. Alexander's office. I didn't properly understand that this was due to the huge glasses of gin he'd generously given her. At first she was fierce and energetic, keyed up, heroic against the polished sights of the Center, which she had begun to point out to me like a guide. Though she didn't say so, she meant *Once you live here*. But then, when we had to wait in the exit lounge and have a lot of the rather bad coffee-drink from the machine, she sank in on herself, brooding. Her eyes became so dark, so bleak, I didn't like to meet them. She had stopped talking at me.

Though the rain alert was over, it was now too late for buses. There was the added problem that gangs would be coming out on the streets, looking for trouble.

The gorgeous poisoned sunset died behind the charcoal sticks of trees and pyramids and oblongs of deserted buildings and rusty railings.

Fortunately, there were quite a few police patrols about. My mother gave them short shrift when they stopped her. Generally they let us get on. We didn't look dangerous.

On SEK, the working streetlights were coming on and there were some ordinary people strolling or sitting on low broken walls, taking the less unhealthy air. They pop up like the rabbits used to, out of their burrows. We passed a couple of women we knew, outside the Sealtite house on the corner of our road. They asked where we'd come from. My mother said tersely we'd been at a friend's, and stopped in till the All Clear.

Although Sealtite, as the advert says, makes secure against anything but gelignite, my mother had by now got herself into an awful sort of rigid state. She ran up the concrete to our front door, unlocked it, and dived us through. We threw our clothes into the washbin, though they hardly needed it as we'd been in the Center most of the day. The TV was still blaring. My mother, dragging on a skirt and nylon blouse, rushed through into the room where the children were. Immediately there was a row. During the day Jog had upset a complete giant can of powdered milk. Daisy had tried to clear it up and they had meant not to tell our mother as if she wouldn't notice one was missing. Daisy was only seven, and Jog was three, so it was blurted out presently. My mother hit all of them, even Angel. Daisy, who had been responsible for the house in our absence, she belted, not very much, but enough to fill our closed-in world with screaming and savage sobs.

After it was over, I made a pot of tea. We drank it black since we would have to economize on milk for the rest of the month.

The brooding phase had passed from my mother. She was all sharp jitters. She said we had to go up and look at the hens. The eggs were always registering too high lately. Could there be a leak in the sealing of the shutyard?

So that was where we ended up, tramping through lanes of lettuce, waking the chickens, who got agitated and clattered about. My mother wobbled on a ladder under the roofing with a torch. "I can't see anything," she kept saying.

Finally she descended. She leaned on the ladder with the torch dangling, still alight, wasting the battery. She was breathless.

"Mum . . . the torch is still on."

She switched it off, put it on a post of the hen-run, and suddenly came at me. She took me by the arms and glared into my face.

"Greena, do you understand about the Alexander man? Well, do you?"

"Yes, Mum."

She shook me angrily but not hard.

"You know why you have to?"

"Yes, Mum. I don't mind, Mum. He's really nice."

Then I saw her eyes had changed again, and I faltered. I felt the earth give way beneath me. Her eyes were full of burning water. They were soft and they were frantic.

"Listen, Greena. I was thirty last week."

"I know—"

"You shut up and listen to me. I had my Medicheck. It's no good, Greena."

We stared at each other. It wasn't a surprise. This happened to everyone. She'd gone longer than most. Twenty-five was the regular innings, out here.

"I wasn't going to tell you, not yet. I don't have to report into the hospital for another three months. I'm getting a bit of pain, but there's the Insurance: I can buy that really good painkiller, the new one."

"Mum."

"Will you be quiet? I want to ask you, you know what you have to do? About the kids? They're your sisters and your brother, you know that, don't you?"

"Yes. I'll take care of them."

"Get him to help you. He will. He really wants you. He was dead unlucky, that Alexander. His legal girlfriend canced. Born in the Center and everything and she pegged out at eighteen. Still, that was good for us. Putting you on the sterilization program when you were little, thank God I did. You see, he can't legally sleep with another girl with pregnancy at all likely. Turns out he's a high deformity risk. Doesn't look it, does he?"

"Yes, Mum, I know about the pregnancy laws."

She didn't slap me or even shout at me for answering back. She seemed to accept I'd said it to reassure her I truly grasped the facts. Alexander's predicament had anyway been guessable. Why else would he want a girl from outside?

"Now, Angel"—said my mother—"I want you to see to her the same, sterilization next year when she's five. She's got a chance too: she could turn out very nice looking. Daisy won't be any use to herself, and the boy won't. But you see you get a decent woman in here to take care of them. No homes. Do you hear? Not for my kids." She sighed, and said again, *"He'll* help you. If you play your cards right, he'll do anything you want. He'll cherish you, Greena." She let me go and said, grinning, "We had ten applications. I went and saw them all. He's the youngest and the best."

"He's lovely," I said. "Thanks, Mum."

"Well, you just see you don't let me down."

"I won't. I promise. I promise, really."

She nodded, and drew up her face into its sure habitual shape, and her eyes dry into their Sealtite of defiance.

"Let's get down now. I'd better rub some anesjel into those marks on Daisy."

We went down and I heard my mother passing from child to child, soothing and reprimanding them as she harshly pummeled the anaesthetic jelly into their hurts.

For a moment, listening on the landing, in the clamped house-dark, I felt I loved my mother.

Then that passed off. I began to think about Mr. Alexander and his clothes and the brilliance of his eyes in his tanned healthy face.

. . .

It was wonderful. He didn't send a courier. He came out himself. He was in a small sealed armored car like a TV alligator, but he just swung out of it and up the concrete into our house. (His bodyguard stayed negligently inside the car. He had a pistol and a mindless attentive lethal look.)

Mr. Alexander brought me half a dozen perfect tawny roses, and a crate of food for the house, toys and TV tapes for the children, and even some gin for my mother. He presumably didn't know yet she only had three months left, but he could probably work it out. He made a fuss of her, and when she'd spoken her agreements into the portable machine, he kissed me on the mouth and then produced a bottle of champagne. The wine was very frothy, and the glassful I had made me feel giddy. I didn't like it, but otherwise our celebration was a success.

I don't know how much money he paid for me. I'd never want to ask him. Or the legal fiddles he must have gone through. He was able to do it, and that was all we needed to know, my mother, me. (She always kept the Insurance going and now, considerably swelled, the benefits will pass on to the children.)

She must have told him eventually about the hospital. I do know he saw to it personally that she had a private room and the latest in pain relief, and no termination until she was ready. He didn't let me see her after she went in. She'd said she didn't want it, either. She had already started to lose weight and shrivel up, the way it happens.

The children cried terribly. I thought it could never get put right, but in the end the agency he found brought us a nineteen-year-old woman who'd lost her own baby and she seemed to take to the children at once. The safe house, of course, was a bonus no one sane would care to ignore. The agency will keep an eye on things, but her levels were low, she should have at least six years. The last time I went there they all seemed happy. He doesn't want me to go outside again.

Six months ago, he brought me officially into the Center.

All the trees were so *green* and the fish and swans sparkled in and on the water, and the birds sang, and he gave me a living bird, a real live tweeting yellow jumping bird in a spacious, glamorous cage; I love this bird and sometimes it sings. It may only live a year, he warned me, but then I can have another.

Sometimes I go to a cubicle in the foyer of one of the historic buildings, and read out announcements over the speaker. They pay me in Center credit discs, but I hardly need any money of my own.

The two rooms that are mine on Fairgrove Avenue are marvelous. The lights go on and off when you come in or go out, and the curtains draw themselves when it gets dark, or the blinds come down when it's too bright. The shower room always smells fresh, like a summer glade is supposed to, and perhaps once did. I see him four, five, or six times every week, and we go to dinner and to films, and he's always bringing me real flowers and chocolates and fruit and honey. He even buys me books to read. Some days, I learn new words from the dictionary.

When he made love to me for the first time, it was a strange experience, but he was very gentle. It seemed to me I might come to like it very much (and I was right), although in a way, it still seems rather an embarrassing thing to do.

That first night, after, he held me in his arms, and I enjoyed this. No one had ever held me caringly, protectingly, like that, ever before. He told me, too, about the girl who canced. He seemed deeply distressed, as if no one ever dies that way, but then, in Centers, under domes, death isn't ever certain.

All my mother tried to get was time, and when that ran out, control of pain and a secure exit. But my darling seems to think that his girl had wanted much, much more, and that I should want more too. And in a way that scares me, because I may not even live to be twenty, and then he'll break his heart again. But then again he'll probably find someone else. And maybe I'll be strong like my mother. I hope so. I want to keep my promise about the children. If I can get Angel settled, she can carry on after me. But I'll need ten or eleven years for that.

Something funny happened yesterday. He said, he would bring me a toy tomorrow— today. Yes, a toy, though I'm a woman, and his lover. I never had a toy. I love my bird best. I love him, too.

The most peculiar thing is, though, that I miss my mother. I keep on remembering what she said to me, her blows and injunctions. Going shopping with her, or to the cinema; how, when her teeth were always breaking, she got into such a rage.

I remember mistily when I was small, the endless days of weather Warnings when she, too, was trapped in the house, my fellow prisoner, and how the rain would start to pour down, horrible sinister torrents that frightened me, although then I didn't know why. All the poisons and the radioactivity that have accumulated and go on gathering on everything in an unseen glittering, and which the sky somehow collects and which the rain washes down from the sky in a deluge. The edited pay-TV seldom reports the accidents and oversights which continually cause this. Sometimes an announcement would come on and tell everyone just to get indoors off the streets, and no reason given, and no rain or wind even. The police cars would go about the roads sounding their sirens, and then they too would slink into holes to hide. But next day, usually there was the All Clear.

In the Center, TV isn't edited. I was curious to see how they talked about the leaks and pollutions, here. Actually they don't seem to mention them at all. It can't be very important, underdome.

But I do keep remembering one morning, that morning of a colossal rain, when I was six or seven. I was trying to look out at the forbidden world, with my nose pressed to the Sealtite. All I could see through the distorting material was a wavering leaden rush of liquid. And then I saw something so alien I let out a squeal.

"What is it?" my mother demanded. She had been washing the breakfast dishes in half the morning ration of domestic filtered water, clashing the plates bad-temperedly. "Come on, Greena, don't just make silly noises."

I pointed at the Sealtite. My mother came to see.

Together we looked through the fall of rain, to where a tiny girl, only about a year old, was standing—*out on the street*. Not knowing how she got there—strayed from some squat, most likely. She wore a pair of little blue shorts and nothing else, and she clutched a square of ancient blanket that was her doll. Even through the sealed pane and the rainfall you could see she was bawling and crying in terror.

"Jesus Christ and Mary the Mother," said my own mother on a breath. Her face was scoured white as our sink. But her eyes were blazing fires, hot enough to quench the rain.

And next second she was thrusting me into the TV room, locking me in, shouting, *Stay there don't you move or I'll murder you!*

Then I heard both our front doors being opened. Shut. When they opened again and shut again, I heard a high-pitched infantile roaring. The roar got louder and possessed the house. Then it fell quiet. I realized my mother had flown out into the weather and grabbed the lost child and brought her under shelter.

Of course, it was no use. When my mother carried her to the emergency unit next day, after the All Clear, the child was dying. She was so tiny. She held her blanket to the end and scorned my mother, the nurse, the kindly needle of oblivion. Only the blanket was her friend. Only the blanket had stayed and suffered with her in the rain.

When she was paying for the treatment and our own decontam, the unit staff said horrible things to my mother, about her stupidity, until I started to cry in humiliated fear. My mother ignored me and only faced them out like an untamed vixen, snarling with her cracked teeth.

All the way home I whined and railed at her. Why had she exposed us to those wicked people with their poking instruments and boiling showers, the hurt and rancor, the downpour of words? (I was jealous too, I realize now, of that intruding poisonous child. I'd been till then the only one in our house.)

Go up to bed! shouted my mother. I wouldn't.

At last she turned on me and thrashed me with the plastic belt. Violent, it felt as if she thrashed the whole world, till in the end she made herself stop.

But now I'm here with my darling, and my lovely bird singing. I can see a corner of a green park from both my windows. And it never, never rains.

It's funny how I miss her, my mother, so much.

MICHAEL MOORCOCK

Michael Moorcock (1939–) is an iconic English writer and editor recently listed by the London *Times* as among the fifty best writers since 1945. One of the most important figures in speculative literature, Moorcock has shown a startling versatility and range in his writings throughout his long career. He has been compared to, among others, Balzac, Dumas, Dickens, James Joyce, Ian Fleming, J.R.R. Tolkien, and Robert E. Howard. Born in London, Moorcock now divides his time between Paris, France, and Austin, Texas. He is married to Linda Steele and has three children from a previous marriage.

An author of literary novels and stories in practically every genre, he has won or been short-listed for numerous awards, including the Nebula (for *Behold the Man* [1969]), World Fantasy (for *Gloriana* [1978]), Whitbread (for *Mother London* [1988]), and Guardian Fiction Prize (for *The Condition of Muzak* [1977]). He has been the recipient of several lifetime achievement awards, including the Prix Utopiales, the Stoker, the SFWA, and the World Fantasy, and has been inducted into the Science Fiction and Fantasy Hall of Fame. His award-winning tenure as editor of *New Worlds* magazine in the sixties and seventies is widely regarded as a high-water mark for science fiction editing, blending genre and literary fiction, science and the arts. Moorcock's leadership and writings in this context were crucial to the development of the so-called New Wave, which brought to prominence not just Moorcock but also contemporaries such as M. John Harrison and J. G. Ballard. He has continued to influence subsequent generations of writers through his writing and editing.

Moorcock's journalism has appeared in the *Spectator*, *The Guardian*, the *Financial Times*, and the *Los Angeles Times*. He is also a musician who recorded and performed in the seventies with his own band, the Deep Fix (*The New Worlds Fair* and "The Brothel in Rosenstrasse" [also a novel]), and won a platinum disc as a member of the space-rock band Hawkwind (for *Warrior on the Edge of Time*). He is currently working on a new album, *Live from the Terminal Café*, for the Spirits Burning label.

Moorcock's literary creations include the series *Corum*, *The Dancers at the End of Time*, *Hawkmoon*, and *Jerry Cornelius*; Von Bek; and, of course, his most famous character, Elric of Melniboné. His *Colonel Pyat Quartet* (*Byzantium Endures*, *The Laughter of Carthage*, *Jerusalem Commands*, *The Vengeance of Rome*) has been described as an authentic masterpiece of the twentieth and twenty-first centuries. He is the author of several graphic novels, including *Michael Moorcock's Multiverse* and *Elric: The Making of a Sorcerer*. He recently published a novel, *The Whispering Swarm*, that combined autobiography and fantasy.

A single selection from Moorcock's oeuvre cannot hope to capture the depth and breadth of his range, but "The Frozen Cardinal" does showcase the author's imagination, his sense of adventure, his devotion to characterization, and the ways in which he tends to subvert science-fictional tropes. The story first appeared in the anthology *Other Edens* in 1987, long after Moorcock wrote it, and was reprinted soon thereafter in Moorcock's combined fiction and nonfiction collection *Casablanca* (1989). "The Frozen Cardinal" was originally written in 1966 on commission from *Playboy* (for Judith Merril, then the science fiction editor), but Moorcock withdrew it when asked for a rewrite.

THE FROZEN CARDINAL

Michael Moorcock

MOLDAVIA. S. POLE. 1/7/17

Dear Gerry,

I got your last, finally. Hope this reaches you in less than a year. The supply planes are all robots now and are supposed to give a faster service. Did I tell you we were being sent to look over the southern pole? Well, we're here. Below-zero temperatures, of course, and at present we're gaining altitude all the time. At least we don't have to wear breathing equipment yet. The Moldavian poles have about twice the volume of ice as those of Earth, but they're melting. As we thought, we found the planet at the end of its ice age. I know how you hate statistics and you know what a bore I can be, so I won't go into the details. To tell you the truth, it's a relief not to be logging and measuring.

It's when I write to you that I find it almost impossible to believe how far away Earth is. I frequently have a peculiar sense of closeness to the home planet, even though we are light-years from it. Sometimes I think Earth will appear in the sky at "dawn" and a rocket will come to take me to you. Are you lying to me, Gerry? Are you really still waiting? I love you so much. Yet my reason cautions me. I can't believe in your fidelity. I don't mean to make you impatient but I miss you desperately sometimes and I'm sure you know how strange people get in these conditions. I joined the expedition, after all, to give you time by yourself, to reconsider our relationship. But when I got your letter I was overjoyed. And, of course, I wish I'd never signed up for Moldavia. Still, only another six

months to go now, and another six months home. I'm glad your mother recovered from her accident. This time next year we'll be spending all my ill-gotten gains in the Seychelles. It's what keeps me going.

We're perfectly safe in our icesuits, of course, but we get terribly tired. We're ascending a series of gigantic ice terraces which seem to go on forever. It takes a day to cross from one terrace to the wall of the next, then another day or so to climb the wall and move the equipment up. The small sun is visible throughout an entire cycle of the planet at this time of year, but the "day," when both suns are visible, is only about three hours. Then everything's very bright, of course, unless it's snowing or there's a thick cloud cover, and we have to protect our eyes. We use the brightest hours for sleeping. It's almost impossible to do anything else. The vehicles are reliable, but slow. If we make any real speed we have to wait a consequently longer interval until they can be recharged. Obviously, we recharge during the bright hours, so it all works out reasonably well. It's a strangely orderly planet, Gerry: everything in its place. Those creatures I told you about were not as intelligent as we had hoped. Their resemblance to spiders is remarkable, though, even to spinning enormous webs around their nests; chiefly, it seemed to us, for decoration. They ate the rations we offered and suffered no apparent ill effects, which means that the planet could probably be opat-gen in a matter of years. That would be a laugh on Galtman. Were you serious, by the way, in your letter? You couldn't leave your USSA even to go to Canada when we were together! You wouldn't care for this ice. The plains and jungles we explored last year feel almost deserted, as if they were once inhabited by a race which left no mark whatsoever. We found no evidence of intelligent inhabitants, no large animals, though we detected some weirdly shaped skeletons in caves below the surface. We were told not to excavate, to leave that to the follow-up team. This is routine official work; there's no romance in it for me. I didn't expect there would be, but I hadn't really allowed for the boredom, for the irritation one begins to feel with one's colleagues. I'm so glad you wrote to say you still love me. I joined to find myself, to let you get on with your life. I hope we both will be more stable when we meet again.

The gennard is warmed up and I'm being signalled, so I'll close this for the time being. We're about to ascend another wall, and that means only one of us can skit to see to the hoist, while the others go up the hard way on the lines. Helander's leader on this particular op. I must say he's considerably easier going than old IP, whom you'll probably have seen on the news by now, showing off his eggs. But the river itself is astonishing, completely encircling the planet; freshwater and Moldavia's only equivalent to our oceans, at least until this ice age is really over!

8/7/17 "Dawn"

A few lines before I fall asleep. It's been a hard one today. Trouble with the hoists. Routine stuff, but it doesn't help morale when it's this cold. I was dangling about nine hundred metres up, with about another thousand to go, for a good hour, with nothing to do but listen to Fisch's curses in my helmet, interspersed with the occasional reassurance. You're helpless in a situation like that! And then, when we did all get to the top and started off again across the terrace (the ninth!) we came almost immediately to an enormous crevasse which must be half a kilometre across! So here we are on the edge. We can go round or we can do a horizontal skit. We'll decide that in the "evening." I have the irrational feeling that this whole section could split off suddenly and engulf us in the biggest landslide a human being ever witnessed. It's silly to think like that. In relationship to this astonishing staircase we are lighter than midges. Until I got your last letter I wouldn't have cared. I'd have been excited by the idea. But now, of course, I've got something to live for. It's peculiar, isn't it, how that makes cowards of the best of us?

9/7/17

Partridge is down in the crevasse at this moment. He thinks we can bridge, but wants to make sure. Also our instruments have picked up something odd, so we're duty-bound to investigate. The rest of us are hanging around, quite glad of the chance to do nothing. Fedin is playing his music and Simons and Russell are fooling about on the edge, kicking a ration-pack about, with the crevasse as the goal. You can hardly make out the other side. Partridge just said he's come across something odd imbedded in the north wall. He says the colours of the ice are beautiful, all dark greens and blues, but this, he says, is red. "There shouldn't be anything red down here!" He says it's probably rock but it resembles an artefact. Maybe there have been explorers here before us, or even inhabitants. If so, they must have been here relatively recently, because these ice-steps are not all that old, especially at the depth Partridge has reached. Mind you, it wouldn't be the first practical joke he's played since we arrived.

Later

Partridge is up. When he pushed back his visor he looked pale and said he thought he was crazy. Fedin gave him a checkup immediately.

There are no extraordinary signs of fatigue. Partridge says the outline he saw in the ice seemed to be a human figure. The instruments all suggest it is animal matter, though of course there are no life-functions. "Even if it's an artefact," said Partridge, "it hasn't got any business being there." He shuddered. "It seemed to be looking at me. A direct, searching stare. I got frightened." Partridge isn't very imaginative, so we were all impressed. "Are we going to get it out of there?" asked Russell. "Or do we just record it for the follow-up team, as we did with those skeletons?" Helander was uncertain. He's as curious as the rest of us. "I'll take a look for myself," he said. He went down, said something under his breath which none of us could catch in our helmets, then gave the order to be hoisted up again. "It's a Roman Catholic cardinal," he said. "The hat, the robes, everything. Making a benediction!" He frowned. "We're going to have to send back on this and await instructions."

Fedin laughed. "We'll be recalled immediately. Everyone's warned of the hallucinations. We'll be hospitalised back at base for months while the bureaucrats try to work out why we went mad."

"You'd better have a look," said Helander. "I want you to go down one by one and tell me what you see."

Partridge was squatting on his haunches, drinking something hot. He was trembling all over. He seemed to be sweating. "This is ridiculous," he said, more than once.

Three others are ahead of me, then it's my turn. I feel perfectly sane, Gerry. Everything else seems normal—as normal as it can be. And if this team has a failing it is that it isn't very prone to speculation or visual hallucinations. I've never been with a duller bunch of fact-gatherers. Maybe that's why we're all more scared than we should be. No expedition from Earth could ever have been to Moldavia before. Certainly nobody would have buried a Roman Catholic cardinal in the ice. There is no explanation, however wild, which fits. We're all great

rationalists on this team. Not a hint of mysticism or even poetry among us. The drugs see to that if our temperaments don't!

Russell's coming up. He's swearing, too. Chang goes down. Then it's my turn. Then Simons's. Then Fisch. I wish you were here, Gerry. With your intelligence you could probably think of something. We certainly can't. I'd better start kitting up. More when I come up. To tell you the absolute truth I'm none too happy about going down!

Later

Well, I've been down. It's dark. The blues and greens glow as if they give off an energy of their own, although it's only reflections. The wall is smooth and opaque. About four metres down and about half a metre back into the ice of the face you can see him. He's tall, about fifty-five, very handsome, clean-shaven, and he's looking directly out at you. His eyes seem sad but not at all malevolent. Indeed, I'd say he seemed kind. There's something noble about him. His clothes are scarlet and fall in folds which suggest he became frozen while standing naturally in the spot he stands in now. He couldn't, therefore, have been dropped, or the clothing would be disturbed. There's no logic to it, Gerry. His right hand is raised and he's making some sort of Christian sign. You know I'm not too hot on anthropology. Helander's the expert.

His expression seems to be one of forgiveness. It's quite overwhelming. You almost find your heart going out to him while at the same time you can't help thinking you're somehow responsible for his being there! Six light-years from Earth on a planet which was only catalogued three years ago and which we are supposedly the first human beings to explore. Nowhere we have been has anyone discovered a shred of evidence that man or anything resembling man ever explored other planets. You know as well as I do that the only signs of intelligent life anyone has found have been negligible and certainly we have never had a hint that any other creature is capable of space travel. Yet here is a man dressed in a costume which, at its latest possible date, is from the twentieth century.

I tried to stare him down. I don't know why. Eventually I told them to lift me up. While Simons went down, I waited on the edge, sipping ade and trying to stop shaking. I don't know why all of us were so badly affected. We've been in danger often enough (I wrote to you about the lavender swamps) and there isn't anyone on the team who hasn't got a sense of humour. Nobody's been able to raise a laugh yet. Helander tried, but it was so forced that we felt sorry for him. When Simons came up he was in exactly the same state as me. I handed him the rest of my ade and then returned to my biv to write this. We're to have a conference in about ten minutes. We haven't decided whether to send back information yet or not. Our curiosity will probably get the better of us. We have no specific orders on the question, but we're pretty sure we'll get a hands-off if we report now. The big skeletons were one thing. This is quite another. And yet we know in our hearts that we should leave well alone.

"Dawn"

The conference is over. It went on for hours. Now we've all decided to sleep on it. Helander and Partridge have been down for another look and have set up a carver in case we decided to go ahead. It will be easy enough to do. Feeling very tired. Have the notion that if we disturb the cardinal we'll do something cataclysmic. Maybe the whole planet will dissolve around us. Maybe this enormous mountain will crumble to nothing. Helander says that what he would like to do is send back on the cardinal but say that he is already carving, since our instruments suggest the crevasse is unstable and could close. There's no way it could close in the next week! But it would be a good enough excuse.

You might never get this letter, Gerry. For all we're told personal mail is uninspected I don't trust them entirely. Do you think I should? Or if someone else is reading this, do they think I should have trusted to the law? His face is in my mind's eye as I write. So tranquil. So sad. I'm taking a couple of deegs, so will write more tomorrow.

10/7/17

Helander has carved. The whole damned thing is standing in the centre of the camp now, like a memorial. A big square block of ice with the cardinal peering out of it. We've all walked round and round the thing. There's no question that the figure is human. Helander wanted to begin thawing right away, but bowed to Simons, who doesn't want to risk the thing deteriorating. Soon he's to vacuum-cocoon it. Simons is cursing himself for not bringing more of his archaeological gear along with him. He expected nothing like this, and our experience up to now has shown that Moldavia doesn't *have* any archaeology worth mentioning. We're all convinced it was a living creature. I even feel he may still be alive, the way he looks at me. We're all very jittery, but our sense of humour has come back and we make bad jokes about the cardinal really being Jesus Christ or Mahomet or somebody. Helander accuses us of religious illiteracy. He's the only one with any real knowledge of all that stuff. He is behaving oddly. He snapped at Russell a little while ago, telling him he wasn't showing proper reverence.

Russell apologised. He said he hadn't realised Helander was superstitious. Helander has sent back, saying what he's done and telling them he's about to thaw. A fait accompli. Fisch is unhappy. He and Partridge feel we should replace the cardinal and get on with "our original business." The rest of us argue that this *is* our original business. We are an exploration team. "It's follow-up work," said Fisch. "I'm anxious to see what's at the top of this bloody great staircase." Partridge replied: "A bloody great Vatican, if you reason it through on the evidence we have." That's the trouble with the kind of logic we go in for, Gerry. Well, we'll all be heroes when we get back to Earth, I suppose. Or we'll be disgraced, depending on what happens next. There's not a lot that can happen to me. This isn't my career, the way it is for the others. I'll be only too happy to be fired, since I intend to resign as soon as I'm home. Then it's the Seychelles for us, my dear. I hope you haven't changed your mind. I wish you were here. I feel the need to share what's going on— and I can think of nobody better to share it than you. Oh, God, I love you so much, Gerry. More, I know, than you'll ever love me; but I can bear anything except separation. I was reconciled to that separation until you wrote your last letter. I hope the company is giving you the yellow route now. You deserve it. With a clean run through to Maracaibo there will be no stopping the old gaucho, eh? But those experiments are risky, I'm told. So don't go too far. I think I know you well enough to be pretty certain you won't take unnecessary risks. I wish I could reach out now and touch your lovely, soft skin, your fine fair hair. I must stop this. It's doing things to me which even the blunn can't control! I'm going out for another walk around our frozen friend.

Well, he's thawed. And it is human. Flesh and blood, Gerry, and no sign of deterioration. A man even taller than Helander. His clothes are all authentic, according to the expert. He's even wearing a pair of old-fashioned cotton underpants. No protective clothing. No sign of having had food with him. No sign of transport. And our instruments have been scouring a wider and wider area. We have the little beeps on automatic, using far more energy than they should. The probes go everywhere. Helander says that this is important. If we can find a vehicle or a trace of habitation, then at least we'll have the beginnings of an answer. He wants something to send back now, of course. We've had an acknowledgement and a hold-off signal.

There's not much to hold off from, currently. The cardinal stands in the middle of the camp, his right arm raised in benediction, his eyes as calm and sad and resigned as ever. He continues to make us jumpy. But there are no more jokes, really, except that we sometimes call him "padre." Helander says all expeditions had one in the old days: a kind of psych-medic, like Fedin. Fedin says he thinks the uniform a bit unsuitable for the conditions. It's astonishing how we grow used to something as unbelievable as this. We look up at the monstrous ice steps ahead of us, the vast gulf behind us, at an alien sky with two suns in it; we know that we are millions upon millions of miles from Earth, across the vacuum of interstellar space, and realise we are sharing our camp with a corpse dressed in the costume of the sixteenth century and we're beginning to take it all for granted. . . . I suppose it says something for human resilience. But we're all still uncomfortable. Maybe there's only so much our brains can take. I wish I was sitting on a stool beside you at the Amset having a beer. But things are so strange to me now that *that* idea is hard to accept. This has become normality. The probes bring in nothing. We're using every instrument we've got. Nothing. We're going to have to ask for the reserve stuff at base and get them to send something to the top. I'd like to be pulled back, I think, and yet I remain fascinated. Maybe you'll be able to tell me if I sound mad. I don't feel mad. Nobody is behaving badly. We're all under control, I think. Only Helander seems profoundly affected. He spends most of his time staring into the cardinal's face, touching it.

Helander says the skin feels warm. He asked me to tell him if I agreed. I stripped off a glove and touched the fingers. They certainly feel warm, but that could just be the effect of sun. Nevertheless, the arm hasn't moved; neither have the eyes. There's no breathing. He stares at us tenderly, blessing us, forgiving us. I'm beginning to resent him. What have I done that he should forgive me? I now agree with those who want to put him back. I suppose we can't.

We've been told to sit tight and wait for base to send someone up. It will take a while before they come.

11/7/17

Russell woke me up. I kitted up fast and went out. Helander was kneeling in front of the cardinal and seemed to be mumbling to himself. He refused to move when we tried to get him to stand up. "He's weeping," he said. "He's weeping."

There did seem to be moisture on the skin. Then, even as we watched, blood began to trickle out of both eyes and run down the cheeks. The cardinal was weeping tears of blood, Gerry!

"Evidently the action of the atmosphere," said Fedin, when we raised him. "We might have to refreeze him, I think."

The cardinal's expression hadn't changed. Helander became impatient and told us to go away. He said he was communicating with the cardinal. Fedin sedated him and got him back to his biv. We heard his voice, even in sleep, mumbling and groaning. Once, he screamed. Fedin pumped some more stuff into him, then. He's quiet now.

Later

We've had word that base is on its way. About time, too, for me. I'm feeling increasingly scared.

"Dusk"

I crawled out of my biv thinking that Helander was crying again or that Fedin was playing his music. The little, pale sun was high in the sky, the big one was setting. There was a reddish glow on the ice. Everything seemed red, in fact. I couldn't see too clearly, but the cardinal was still standing there, a dark silhouette. And the sounds were coming from him. He was singing, Gerry. There was no one else up. I stood in front of the cardinal. His lips were moving. Some sort of chant. His eyes weren't looking at me any longer. They were raised. Someone came to stand beside me. It was Helander. He was a bit woozy, but his face was ecstatic. He began to join in the song. Their singing seemed to fill the sky, the planet, the whole damned universe. The music made me cry, Gerry. I have never heard a more beautiful voice. Helander turned to me once. "Join in," he said. "Join in." But I couldn't because I didn't know the words. "It's Latin," said Helander. It was like a bloody choir. I found myself lifting my head like a dog. There were resonances in my throat. I began to howl. But it wasn't howling. It was chanting, the same as the cardinal. No words. Just music. It was the most exquisite music I have ever heard in my life. I became aware that the others were with me, standing in a semicircle, and they were singing too. And we were so full of joy, Gerry. We were all weeping. It was incredible. Then the sun had set and the music gradually faded and we stood looking at one another, totally exhausted, grinning like coyotes, feeling complete fools. And the cardinal was looking at us again, with that same sweet tolerance. Helander was kneeling in front of him and mumbling, but we couldn't hear the words. Eventually, after he'd been on the ice for an hour, Fedin decided to sedate him. "He'll be dead at this rate, if I don't."

Later

We've just finished putting the cardinal back in the crevasse, Gerry. I can still hear that music in my head. I wish there was some way I could play you the recordings we've made, but doubtless you'll hear them in time, around when you get this letter. Base hasn't arrived yet. Helander said he was going to let it be their responsibility. I'm hoping we'll be relieved for those medical tests we were afraid of at first. I want to get away from here. I'm terrified, Gerry. I keep wanting to climb into the crevasse and ask the cardinal to sing for me again. I have never known such absolute release, such total happiness, as when I sang in harmony with him. What do you think it is? Maybe it's all hallucination. Someone will know. Twice I've stood on the edge, peering down. You can't see him from here, of course. And you can't see the bottom. I haven't the courage to descend the lines.

I want to jump. I would jump, I think, if I could get the chance just once more to sing with him. I keep thinking of eternity. For the first time in my life I have a glimmering of what it means.

Oh, Gerry, I hope it isn't an illusion. I hope you'll be able to hear that voice on the tapes and know what I felt when the frozen cardinal sang. I love you, Gerry. I want to give you so much. I wish I could give you what I have been given. I wish I could sing for you the way the cardinal sang. There isn't one of us who hasn't been weeping. Fedin keeps trying to be rational. He says we are more exhausted than we know, that the drugs we take have side effects which couldn't be predicted. We look up into the sky from time to time, waiting for base to reach us. I wish you were here, Gerry. But I can't possibly regret now that I made the decision I made. I love you, Gerry. I love you all.

Rachel in Love

PAT MURPHY

Pat Murphy (1955–) is a US writer of science fiction and fantasy who lives in San Francisco and first began publishing notable short fiction with "Nightbird at the Window" (*Chrysalis* 5, 1979). Her first novel was the obscurely published *The Shadow Hunter* (1982), in which a Stone Age man is displaced by a time-travel device into a cruelly alienating future.

After editing and producing environmental reports and graphics for various Pacific Coast organizations, Murphy began in 1982 to edit *Exploratorium* magazine, the quarterly journal of the Exploratorium, a San Francisco museum designed to promote a hands-on relationship between human perception and the arts and sciences. In the 1980s, Murphy, like Kim Stanley Robinson, was described as a Humanist writer, a position considered in opposition to cyberpunk, although the distinction is not quite so clear-cut, given the inclusion of writers like Pat Cadigan in the cyberpunk movement. Like Robinson, Murphy resisted the labeling, which she clearly found limiting.

"Rachel in Love" (*Asimov's Science Fiction Magazine*, 1987) is probably Murphy's most famous work, and won a Nebula and a Theodore Sturgeon Memorial Award. It features as its viewpoint character a female chimpanzee with enhanced intelligence who escapes an impersonally horrific research institute. The story's focus on its titular character and devotion to contemporary realism make it particularly effective science fiction, and it is even more relevant today, given advances in animal behavior science, the recent retirement of chimps experimented on in the United States, and the importance of redefining our relationship with animals in general.

In an afterword to her collection *Points of Departure*, Murphy writes, "Many of my stories deal with outsiders, people who are trapped in a world where they do not belong, [including] Rachel, the chimp with the mind of a teenage girl. These are characters who have, in a sense, found that secret door I was always looking for [as a child]. They've entered a new world filled with exotic things and strange people; it just happens to be the world in which we live every day."

RACHEL IN LOVE

Pat Murphy

It is a Sunday morning in summer and a small brown chimpanzee named Rachel sits on the living room floor of a remote ranch house on the edge of the Painted Desert. She is watching a Tarzan movie on television. Her hairy arms are wrapped around her knees and she rocks back and forth with suppressed excitement. She knows that her father would say that she's too old for such childish amusements—but since Aaron is still sleeping, he can't chastise her.

On the television, Tarzan has been trapped in a bamboo cage by a band of wicked Pygmies. Rachel is afraid that he won't escape in time to save Jane from the ivory smugglers who hold her captive. The movie cuts to Jane, who is tied up in the back of a Jeep, and Rachel whimpers softly to herself. She knows better than to howl: she peeked into her father's bedroom earlier, and he was still in bed. Aaron doesn't like her to howl when he is sleeping.

When the movie breaks for a commercial, Rachel goes to her father's room. She is ready for breakfast and she wants him to get up. She tiptoes to the bed to see if he is awake.

His eyes are open and he is staring at nothing. His face is pale and his lips are a purplish color. Dr. Aaron Jacobs, the man Rachel calls father, is not asleep. He is dead, having died in the night of a heart attack.

When Rachel shakes him, his head rocks back and forth in time with her shaking, but his eyes do not blink and he does not breathe. She places his hand on her head, nudging him so that he will waken and stroke her. He does not move. When she leans toward him, his hand falls limply to dangle over the edge of the bed.

In the breeze from the open bedroom win-dow, the fine wisps of gray hair that he had carefully combed over his bald spot each morn-ing shift and flutter, exposing the naked scalp. In the other room, elephants trumpet as they stampede across the jungle to rescue Tarzan. Rachel whimpers softly, but her father does not move.

Rachel backs away from her father's body. In the living room, Tarzan is swinging across the jungle on vines, going to save Jane. Rachel ignores the television. She prowls through the house as if searching for comfort—stepping into her own small bedroom, wandering through her father's laboratory. From the cages that line the walls, white rats stare at her with hot red eyes. A rabbit hops across its cage, making a series of slow dull thumps, like a feather pillow tumbling down a flight of stairs.

She thinks that perhaps she made a mistake. Perhaps her father is just sleeping. She returns to the bedroom, but nothing has changed. Her father lies open-eyed on the bed. For a long time, she huddles beside his body, clinging to his hand.

He is the only person she has ever known. He is her father, her teacher, her friend. She cannot leave him alone.

The afternoon sun blazes through the win-dow, and still Aaron does not move. The room grows dark, but Rachel does not turn on the lights. She is waiting for Aaron to wake up. When the moon rises, its silver light shines through the window to cast a bright rectangle on the far wall.

Outside, somewhere in the barren rocky land surrounding the ranch house, a coyote lifts its head to the rising moon and wails, a thin sound that is as lonely as a train whistling through an abandoned station. Rachel joins in with a desolate howl of loneliness and grief. Aaron lies still and Rachel knows that he is dead.

When Rachel was younger, she had a favorite bedtime story. —Where did I come from? she would ask Aaron, using the gestures of ASL, American Sign Language. —Tell me again.

"You're too old for bedtime stories," Aaron would say.

—Please, she signed. —Tell me the story.

In the end, he always relented and told her. "Once upon a time, there was a little girl named Rachel," he said. "She was a pretty girl, with long golden hair like a princess in a fairy tale. She lived with her father and her mother and they were all very happy."

Rachel would snuggle contentedly beneath her blankets. The story, like any good fairy tale, had elements of tragedy. In the story, Rachel's father worked at a university, studying the workings of the brain and charting the electric fields that the nervous impulses of an active brain produced. But the other researchers at the university didn't understand Rachel's father; they distrusted his research and cut off his funding. (During this portion of the story, Aaron's voice took on a bitter edge.) So he left the university and took his wife and daughter to the desert, where he could work in peace.

He continued his research and determined that each individual brain produced its own unique pattern of fields, as characteristic as a fingerprint. (Rachel found this part of the story quite dull, but Aaron insisted on including it.) The shape of this "Electric Mind," as he called it, was determined by habitual patterns of thoughts and emotions. Record the Electric Mind, he postulated, and you could capture an individual's personality.

Then one sunny day, the doctor's wife and beautiful daughter went for a drive. A truck barreling down a winding cliffside road lost its brakes and met the car head-on, killing both the girl and her mother. (Rachel clung to Aaron's hand during this part of the story, frightened by the sudden evil twist of fortune.)

But though Rachel's body had died, all was not lost. In his desert lab, the doctor had recorded the electrical patterns produced by his daughter's brain. The doctor had been experimenting with the use of external magnetic fields to impose the patterns from one animal onto the brain of another. From an animal supply house, he obtained a young chimpanzee. He used a mixture of norepinephrin-based transmitter substances to boost the speed of neural processing in the chimp's brain, and then he imposed the pattern of his daughter's mind upon the brain of this young chimp, combining the two after his own fashion, saving his daughter in his own way. In the chimp's brain was all that remained of Rachel Jacobs.

The doctor named the chimp Rachel and raised her as his own daughter. Since the limitations of the chimpanzee larynx made speech very difficult, he instructed her in ASL. He taught her to read and to write. They were good friends, the best of companions.

By this point in the story, Rachel was usually asleep. But it didn't matter—she knew the ending. The doctor, whose name was Aaron Jacobs, and the chimp named Rachel lived happily ever after.

Rachel likes fairy tales and she likes happy endings. She has the mind of a teenage girl, but the innocent heart of a young chimp.

Sometimes, when Rachel looks at her gnarled brown fingers, they seem alien, wrong, out of place. She remembers having small, pale, delicate hands. Memories lie upon memories, layers upon layers, like the sedimentary rocks of the desert buttes.

Rachel remembers a blond-haired fair-skinned woman who smelled sweetly of perfume. On a Halloween long ago, this woman (who was, in these memories, Rachel's mother) painted Rachel's fingernails bright red because Rachel was dressed as a Gypsy and Gypsies liked red. Rachel remembers the woman's hands: white hands with faintly blue veins hidden just beneath the skin, neatly clipped nails painted rose pink.

But Rachel also remembers another mother and another time. Her mother was dark and hairy and smelled sweetly of overripe fruit. She and Rachel lived in a wire cage in a room filled with chimps and she hugged Rachel to her hairy breast whenever any people came into the room. Rachel's mother groomed Rachel constantly, picking delicately through her fur in search of fleas that she never found.

Memories upon memories: jumbled and confused, like random pictures clipped from magazines, a bright collage that makes no sense. Rachel remembers cages: cold wire mesh beneath her feet, the smell of fear around her. A man in a white lab coat took her from the arms of her hairy mother and pricked her with needles. She could hear her mother howling, but she could not escape from the man.

Rachel remembers a junior high school dance where she wore a new dress: she stood in a dark corner of the gym for hours, pretending to admire the crepe paper decorations because she felt too shy to search among the crowd for her friends.

She remembers when she was a young chimp: she huddled with five other adolescent chimps in the stuffy freight compartment of a train, frightened by the alien smells and sounds.

She remembers gym class: gray lockers and ugly gym suits that revealed her skinny legs. The teacher made everyone play softball, even Rachel, who was unathletic and painfully shy. Rachel at bat, standing at the plate, was terrified to be the center of attention. "Easy out," said the catcher, a hard-edged girl who ran with the wrong crowd and always smelled of cigarette smoke. When Rachel swung at the ball and missed, the outfielders filled the air with malicious laughter.

Rachel's memories are as delicate and elusive as the dusty moths and butterflies that dance among the rabbit brush and sage. Memories of her girlhood never linger; they land for an instant, then take flight, leaving Rachel feeling abandoned and alone.

Rachel leaves Aaron's body where it is, but closes his eyes and pulls the sheet up over his head. She does not know what else to do. Each day she waters the garden and picks some greens for the rabbits. Each day, she cares for the rats and the rabbits, bringing them food and refilling their water bottles. The weather is cool, and Aaron's body does not smell too bad, though by the end of the week, a wide line of ants runs from the bed to the open window.

At the end of the first week, on a moonlit evening, Rachel decides to let the animals go free. She releases the rabbits one by one, climbing on a stepladder to reach down into the cage and lift each placid bunny out. She carries each one to the back door, holding it for a moment and stroking the soft warm fur. Then she sets the animal down and nudges it in the direction of the green grass that grows around the perimeter of the fenced garden.

The rats are more difficult to deal with. She manages to wrestle the large rat cage off the shelf, but it is heavier than she thought it would be. Though she slows its fall, it lands on the floor with a crash and the rats scurry to and fro within. She shoves the cage across the linoleum floor, sliding it down the hall, over the doorsill, and onto the back patio. When she opens the cage door, rats burst out like popcorn from a popper, white in the moonlight and dashing in all directions.

Once, while Aaron was taking a nap, Rachel walked along the dirt track that led to the main highway. She hadn't planned on going far. She just wanted to see what the highway looked like, maybe hide near the mailbox and watch a car drive past. She was curious about the outside world and her fleeting fragmentary memories did not satisfy that curiosity.

She was halfway to the mailbox when Aaron came roaring up in his old Jeep. "Get in the car," he shouted at her. "Right now!" Rachel had never seen him so angry. She cowered in the Jeep's passenger seat, covered with dust from the road, unhappy that Aaron was so upset. He didn't speak until they got back to the ranch house, and then he spoke in a low voice, filled with bitterness and suppressed rage.

"You don't want to go out there," he said. "You wouldn't like it out there. The world is filled with petty, narrow-minded, stupid people. They wouldn't understand you. And anyone they don't understand, they want to hurt. They hate anyone who's different. If they know that you're different, they punish you, hurt you. They'd lock you up and never let you go."

He looked straight ahead, staring through the dirty windshield. "It's not like the shows on TV, Rachel," he said in a softer tone. "It's not like the stories in books."

He looked at her then and she gestured frantically. —I'm sorry. I'm sorry.

"I can't protect you out there," he said. "I can't keep you safe."

Rachel took his hand in both of hers. He relented then, stroking her head. "Never do that again," he said. "Never."

Aaron's fear was contagious. Rachel never again walked along the dirt track, and sometimes she had dreams about bad people who wanted to lock her in a cage.

Two weeks after Aaron's death, a black-and-white police car drives slowly up to the house. When the policemen knock on the door, Rachel hides behind the couch in the living room. They knock again, try the knob, then open the door, which she has left unlocked.

Suddenly frightened, Rachel bolts from behind the couch, bounding toward the back door. Behind her, she hears one man yell, "My God! It's a gorilla!"

By the time he pulls his gun, Rachel has run out the back door and away into the hills. From the hills she watches as an ambulance drives up and two men in white take Aaron's body away. Even after the ambulance and the police car drive away, Rachel is afraid to go back to the house. Only after sunset does she return.

Just before dawn the next morning, she wakens to the sound of a truck jouncing down the dirt road. She peers out the window to see a pale green pickup. Sloppily stenciled in white on the door are the words PRIMATE RESEARCH CENTER. Rachel hesitates as the truck pulls up in front of the house. By the time she has decided to flee, two men are getting out of the truck. One of them carries a rifle.

She runs out the back door and heads for the hills, but she is only halfway to hiding when she hears a sound like a sharp intake of breath and feels a painful jolt in her shoulder. Suddenly, her legs give way and she is tumbling backward down the sandy slope, dust coating her red-brown fur, her howl becoming a whimper, then fading to nothing at all. She falls into the blackness of sleep.

The sun is up. Rachel lies in a cage in the back of the pickup truck. She is partially conscious and she feels a tingling in her hands and feet. Nausea grips her stomach and bowels. Her body aches.

Rachel can blink, but otherwise she can't move. From where she lies, she can see only the wire mesh of the cage and the side of the truck. When she tries to turn her head, the burning in her skin intensifies. She lies still, wanting to cry out, but unable to make a sound. She can only blink slowly, trying to close out the pain. But the burning and nausea stay.

The truck jounces down a dirt road, then stops. It rocks as the men get out. The doors slam. Rachel hears the tailgate open.

A woman's voice: "Is that the animal the county sheriff wanted us to pick up?" A woman peers into the cage. She wears a white lab coat and her brown hair is tied back in a single braid. Around her eyes, Rachel can see small wrinkles, etched by years of living in the desert. The woman doesn't look evil. Rachel hopes that the woman will save her from the men in the truck.

"Yeah. It should be knocked out for at least another half hour. Where do you want it?"

"Bring it into the lab where we had the rhesus monkeys. I'll keep it there until I have an empty cage in the breeding area."

Rachel's cage scrapes across the bed of the pickup. She feels each bump and jar as a new pain. The man swings the cage onto a cart and the woman pushes the cart down a concrete corridor. Rachel watches the walls pass just a few inches from her nose.

The lab contains rows of cages in which small animals sleepily move. In the sudden stark light of the overhead fluorescent bulbs, the eyes of white rats gleam red.

With the help of one of the men from the truck, the woman manhandles Rachel onto a lab table. The metal surface is cold and hard, painful against Rachel's skin. Rachel's body is not under her control; her limbs will not respond. She is still frozen by the tranquilizer, able to watch, but that is all. She cannot protest or plead for mercy.

Rachel watches with growing terror as the woman pulls on rubber gloves and fills a hypodermic needle with a clear solution. "Mark down that I'm giving her the standard test for tuberculosis; this eyelid should be checked before she's moved in with the others. I'll add thiabendazole to her feed for the next few days to clean out any intestinal worms. And I suppose we might as well de-flea her as well," the woman says. The man grunts in response.

Expertly, the woman closes one of Rachel's eyes. With her open eye, Rachel watches the hypodermic needle approach. She feels a sharp pain in her eyelid. In her mind, she is howling, but the only sound she can manage is a breathy sigh.

The woman sets the hypodermic aside and begins methodically spraying Rachel's fur with a cold, foul-smelling liquid. A drop strikes Rachel's eye and burns. Rachel blinks, but she cannot lift a hand to rub her eye. The woman treats Rachel with casual indifference, chatting with the man as she spreads Rachel's legs and sprays her genitals. "Looks healthy enough. Good breeding stock."

Rachel moans, but neither person notices. At last, they finish their torture, put her in a cage, and leave the room. She closes her eyes, and the darkness returns.

Rachel dreams. She is back at home in the ranch house. It is night and she is alone. Outside, coyotes yip and howl. The coyote is the voice of the desert, wailing as the wind wails when it stretches itself thin to squeeze through a crack between two boulders. The people native to this land tell tales of Coyote, a god who was a trickster, unreliable, changeable, mercurial.

Rachel is restless, anxious, unnerved by the howling of the coyotes. She is looking for Aaron. In the dream, she knows he is not dead, and she searches the house for him, wandering from his cluttered bedroom to her small room to the linoleum-tiled lab.

She is in the lab when she hears something tapping: a small dry scratching, like a windblown branch against the window, though no tree grows near the house and the night is still. Cautiously, she lifts the curtain to look out.

She looks into her own reflection: a pale oval face, long blond hair. The hand that holds the curtain aside is smooth and white with carefully clipped fingernails. But something is wrong. Superimposed on the reflection is another face peering through the glass: a pair of dark brown eyes, a chimp face with red-brown hair and jug-handle ears. She sees her own reflection and she sees the outsider; the two images merge and blur. She is afraid, but she can't drop the curtain and shut the ape face out.

She is a chimp looking in through the cold, bright windowpane; she is a girl looking out;

she is a girl looking in; she is an ape looking out. She is afraid and the coyotes are howling all around.

Rachel opens her eyes and blinks until the world comes into focus. The pain and tingling has retreated, but she still feels a little sick. Her left eye aches. When she rubs it, she feels a raised lump on the eyelid where the woman pricked her. She lies on the floor of a wire mesh cage. The room is hot and the air is thick with the smell of animals.

In the cage beside her is another chimp, an older animal with scruffy dark brown fur. He sits with his arms wrapped around his knees, rocking back and forth, back and forth. His head is down. As he rocks, he murmurs to himself, a meaningless cooing that goes on and on. On his scalp, Rachel can see a gleam of metal: a permanently implanted electrode protrudes from a shaven patch. Rachel makes a soft questioning sound, but the other chimp will not look up.

Rachel's own cage is just a few feet square. In one corner is a bowl of monkey pellets. A water bottle hangs on the side of the cage. Rachel ignores the food, but drinks thirstily.

Sunlight streams through the windows, sliced into small sections by the wire mesh that covers the glass. She tests her cage door, rattling it gently at first, then harder. It is securely latched. The gaps in the mesh are too small to admit her hand. She can't reach out to work the latch.

The other chimp continues to rock back and forth. When Rachel rattles the mesh of her cage and howls, he lifts his head wearily and looks at her. His red-rimmed eyes are unfocused; she can't be sure he sees her.

—Hello, she gestures tentatively. —What's wrong?

He blinks at her in the dim light. —Hurt, he signs in ASL. He reaches up to touch the electrode, fingering skin that is already raw from repeated rubbing.

—Who hurt you? she asks. He stares at her blankly and she repeats the question. —Who?

—Men, he signs.

As if on cue, there is the click of a latch and the door to the lab opens. A bearded man in a white coat steps in, followed by a clean-shaven man in a suit. The bearded man seems to be showing the other man around the lab. ". . . only preliminary testing, so far," the bearded man is saying. "We've been hampered by a shortage of chimps trained in ASL." The two men stop in front of the old chimp's cage. "This old fellow is from the Oregon center. Funding for the language program was cut back and some of the animals were dispersed to other programs." The old chimp huddles at the back of the cage, eying the bearded man with suspicion.

—Hungry? the bearded man signs to the old chimp. He holds up an orange where the old chimp can see it.

—Give orange, the old chimp gestures. He holds out his hand, but comes no nearer to the wire mesh than he must to reach the orange. With the fruit in hand, he retreats to the back of his cage.

The bearded man continues, "This project will provide us with the first solid data on neural activity during use of sign language. But we really need greater access to chimps with advanced language skills. People are so damn protective of their animals."

"Is this one of yours?" the clean-shaven man asks, pointing to Rachel. She cowers in the back of the cage, as far from the wire mesh as she can get.

"No, not mine. She was someone's household pet, apparently. The county sheriff had us pick her up." The bearded man peers into her cage. Rachel does not move; she is terrified that he will somehow guess that she knows ASL. She stares at his hands and thinks about those hands putting an electrode through her skull. "I think she'll be put in breeding stock," the man says as he turns away.

Rachel watches them go, wondering at what

terrible people these are. Aaron was right: they want to punish her, put an electrode in her head.

After the men are gone, she tries to draw the old chimp into conversation, but he will not reply. He ignores her as he eats his orange. Then he returns to his former posture, hiding his head and rocking himself back and forth.

Rachel, hungry despite herself, samples one of the food pellets. It has a strange medicinal taste, and she puts it back in the bowl. She needs to pee, but there is no toilet and she cannot escape the cage. At last, unable to hold it, she pees in one corner of the cage. The urine flows through the wire mesh to soak the litter below, and the smell of warm piss fills her cage. Humiliated, frightened, her head aching, her skin itchy from the flea spray, Rachel watches as the sunlight creeps across the room.

The day wears on. Rachel samples her food again, but rejects it, preferring hunger to the strange taste. A black man comes and cleans the cages of the rabbits and rats. Rachel cowers in her cage and watches him warily, afraid that he will hurt her too.

When night comes, she is not tired. Outside, coyotes howl. Moonlight filters in through the high windows. She draws her legs up toward her body, then rests with her arms wrapped around her knees. Her father is dead, and she is a captive in a strange place. For a time, she whimpers softly, hoping to awaken from this nightmare and find herself at home in bed. When she hears the click of a key in the door to the room, she hugs herself more tightly.

A man in green coveralls pushes a cart filled with cleaning supplies into the room. He takes a broom from the cart, and begins sweeping the concrete floor. Over the rows of cages, she can see the top of his head bobbing in time with his sweeping. He works slowly and methodically, bending down to sweep carefully under each row of cages, making a neat pile of dust, dung, and food scraps in the center of the aisle.

. . .

The janitor's name is Jake. He is a middle-aged deaf man who has been employed by the Primate Research Center for the past seven years. He works night shift. The personnel director at the Primate Research Center likes Jake because he fills the federal quota for handicapped employees, and because he has not asked for a raise in five years. There have been some complaints about Jake—his work is often sloppy—but never enough to merit firing the man.

Jake is an unambitious, somewhat slow-witted man. He likes the Primate Research Center because he works alone, which allows him to drink on the job. He is an easygoing man, and he likes the animals. Sometimes, he brings treats for them. Once, a lab assistant caught him feeding an apple to a pregnant rhesus monkey. The monkey was part of an experiment on the effect of dietary restrictions on fetal brain development, and the lab assistant warned Jake that he would be fired if he was ever caught interfering with the animals again. Jake still feeds the animals, but he is more careful about when he does it, and he has never been caught again.

As Rachel watches, the old chimp gestures to Jake. —Give banana, the chimp signs. —Please banana. Jake stops sweeping for a minute and reaches down to the bottom shelf of his cleaning cart. He returns with a banana and offers it to the old chimp. The chimp accepts the banana and leans against the mesh while Jake scratches his fur.

When Jake turns back to his sweeping, he catches sight of Rachel and sees that she is watching him. Emboldened by his kindness to the old chimp, Rachel timidly gestures to him. —Help me.

Jake hesitates, then peers at her more closely. Both his eyes are shot with a fine lacework of red. His nose displays the broken blood vessels of someone who has been friends with the bottle for too many years. He needs a shave. But when he leans close, Rachel catches the scent of whiskey and tobacco. The smells remind her of Aaron and give her courage.

—Please help me, Rachel signs. —I don't belong here.

For the last hour, Jake has been drinking steadily. His view of the world is somewhat fuzzy. He stares at her blearily.

Rachel's fear that he will hurt her is replaced by the fear that he will leave her locked up and alone. Desparately she signs again. —Please please please. Help me. I don't belong here. Please help me go home.

He watches her, considering the situation. Rachel does not move. She is afraid that any movement will make him leave. With a majestic speed dictated by his inebriation, Jake leans his broom on the row of cages behind him and steps toward Rachel's cage again. —You talk? he signs.

—I talk, she signs.

—Where did you come from?

—From my father's house, she signs. —Two men came and shot me and put me here. I don't know why. I don't know why they locked me in jail.

Jake looks around, willing to be sympathetic, but puzzled by her talk of jail. —This isn't jail, he signs. —This is a place where scientists raise monkeys.

Rachel is indignant. —I am not a monkey, she signs. —I am a girl.

Jake studies her hairy body and her jug-handle ears. —You look like a monkey.

Rachel shakes her head. —No. I am a girl.

Rachel runs her hands back over her head, a very human gesture of annoyance and unhappiness. She signs sadly, —I don't belong here. Please let me out.

Jake shifts his weight from foot to foot, wondering what to do. —I can't let you out. I'll get in big trouble.

—Just for a little while? Please?

Jake glances at his cart of supplies. He has to finish off this room and two corridors of offices before he can relax for the night.

—Don't go, Rachel signs, guessing his thoughts.

—I have work to do.

She looks at the cart, then suggests eagerly, —Let me out and I'll help you work.

Jake frowns. —If I let you out, you will run away.

—No, I won't run. I will help. Please let me out.

—You promise to go back?

Rachel nods.

Warily he unlatches the cage. Rachel bounds out, grabs a whisk broom from the cart, and begins industriously sweeping bits of food and droppings from beneath the row of cages. —Come on, she signs to Jake from the end of the aisle. —I will help.

When Jake pushes the cart from the room filled with cages, Rachel follows him closely. The rubber wheels of the cleaning cart rumble softly on the linoleum floor. They pass through a metal door into a corridor where the floor is carpeted and the air smells of chalk dust and paper.

Doors from the corridor open into offices, each one a small room furnished with a desk, bookshelves, and a blackboard. Jake shows Rachel how to empty the wastebaskets into a garbage bag. While he cleans the blackboards, she wanders from office to office, trailing the trash-filled garbage bag.

At first, Jake keeps a close eye on Rachel. But after cleaning each blackboard, he pauses to sip whiskey from a paper cup. At the end of the corridor, he stops to refill the cup from the whiskey bottle that he keeps wedged between the Saniflush and the window cleaner. By the time he is halfway through the second cup, he is treating her like an old friend, telling her to hurry up so that they can eat dinner.

Rachel works quickly, but she stops sometimes to gaze out the office windows. Outside, moonlight shines on a sandy plain, dotted here and there with scrubby clumps of rabbit brush.

At the end of the corridor is a larger room in which there are several desks and typewriters. In one of the wastebaskets, buried beneath memos and candy bar wrappers, she finds a magazine. The title is *Love Confessions* and the cover has a picture of a man and woman kissing. Rachel studies the cover, then takes the magazine, tucking it on the bottom shelf of the cart.

Jake pours himself another cup of whiskey and pushes the cart to another hallway. Jake is working slower now, and as he works he makes humming noises, tuneless sounds that he feels only as pleasant vibrations. The last few blackboards are sloppily done, and Rachel, finished with the wastebaskets, cleans the places that Jake missed.

They eat dinner in the janitor's storeroom, a stuffy windowless room furnished with an ancient grease-stained couch, a battered black-and-white television, and shelves of cleaning supplies. From a shelf, Jake takes the paper bag that holds his lunch: a baloney sandwich, a bag of barbecue potato chips, and a box of vanilla wafers. From behind the gallon jugs of liquid cleanser, he takes a magazine. He lights a cigarette, pours himself another cup of whiskey, and settles down on the couch. After a moment's hesitation, he offers Rachel a drink, pouring a shot of whiskey into a chipped ceramic cup.

Aaron never let Rachel drink whiskey, and she samples it carefully. At first the smell makes her sneeze, but she is fascinated by the way that the drink warms her throat, and she sips some more.

As they drink, Rachel tells Jake about the men who shot her and the woman who pricked her with a needle, and he nods. —The people here are crazy, he signs.

—I know, she says, thinking of the old chimp with the electrode in his head. —You won't tell them I can talk, will you?

Jake nods. —I won't tell them anything.

—They treat me like I'm not real, Rachel signs sadly. Then she hugs her knees, frightened at the thought of being held captive by crazy people. She considers planning her escape: she is out of the cage and she is sure she could outrun Jake. As she wonders about it, she finishes her cup of whiskey. The alcohol takes the edge off her fear. She sits close beside Jake on the couch, and the smell of his cigarette smoke reminds her of Aaron. For the first time since Aaron's death she feels warm and happy.

She shares Jake's cookies and potato chips and looks at the *Love Confessions* magazine that she took from the trash. The first story that she reads is about a woman named Alice. The headline reads: "I became a go-go dancer to pay off my husband's gambling debts, and now he wants me to sell my body."

Rachel sympathizes with Alice's loneliness and suffering. Alice, like Rachel, is alone and misunderstood. As Rachel slowly reads, she sips her second cup of whiskey. The story reminds her of a fairy tale: the nice man who rescues Alice from her terrible husband replaces the handsome prince who rescued the princess. Rachel glances at Jake and wonders if he will rescue her from the wicked people who locked her in the cage.

She has finished the second cup of whiskey and eaten half Jake's cookies when Jake says that she must go back to her cage. She goes reluctantly, taking the magazine with her. He promises that he will come for her again the next night, and with that she must be content. She puts the magazine in one corner of the cage and curls up to sleep.

She wakes early in the afternoon. A man in a white coat is wheeling a low cart into the lab.

Rachel's head aches with hangover and she feels sick. As she crouches in one corner of her cage, he stops the cart beside her cage and then locks the wheels. "Hold on there," he mutters to her, then slides her cage onto the cart.

The man wheels her through long corridors, where the walls are cement blocks, painted institutional green. Rachel huddles unhappily in the cage, wondering where she is going and whether Jake will ever be able to find her.

At the end of a long corridor, the man opens a thick metal door and a wave of warm air strikes Rachel. It stinks of chimpanzees, excrement, and rotting food. On either side of the corridor are metal bars and wire mesh. Behind the mesh, Rachel can see dark hairy shadows. In one cage, five adolescent chimps swing and play. In another, two females huddle together, grooming each other. The man slows as he passes a cage in which a big male is banging on the wire with his fist, making the mesh rattle and ring.

"Now, Johnson," says the man. "Cool it. Be nice. I'm bringing you a new little girlfriend."

With a series of hooks, the man links Rachel's cage with the cage next to Johnson's and opens the doors. "Go on, girl," he says. "See the nice fruit." In the new cage is a bowl of sliced apples with an attendant swarm of fruit flies.

At first, Rachel will not move into the new cage. She crouches in the cage on the cart, hoping that the man will decide to take her back to the lab. She watches him get a hose and attach it to a water faucet. But she does not understand his intention until he turns the stream of water on her. A cold blast strikes her on the back and she howls, fleeing into the new cage to avoid the cold water. Then the man closes the doors, unhooks the cage, and hurries away.

The floor is bare cement. Her cage is at one end of the corridor and two walls are cement block. A door in one of the cement block walls leads to an outside run. The other two walls are wire mesh: one facing the corridor; the other, Johnson's cage.

Johnson, quiet now that the man has left, is sniffing around the door in the wire mesh wall that joins their cages. Rachel watches him anxiously. Her memories of other chimps are distant, softened by time. She remembers her mother; she vaguely remembers playing with other chimps her age. But she does not know how to react to Johnson when he stares at her with great intensity and makes a loud huffing sound. She gestures to him in ASL, but he only stares harder and huffs again. Beyond Johnson, she can see other cages and other chimps, so many that the wire mesh blurs her vision and she cannot see the other end of the corridor.

To escape Johnson's scrutiny, she ducks through the door into the outside run, a wire mesh cage on a white concrete foundation. Outside there is barren ground and rabbit brush. The afternoon sun is hot and all the other runs are deserted until Johnson appears in the run beside hers. His attention disturbs her and she goes back inside.

She retreats to the side of the cage farthest from Johnson. A crudely built wooden platform provides her with a place to sit. Wrapping her arms around her knees, she tries to relax and ignore Johnson. She dozes off for a while, but wakes to a commotion across the corridor.

In the cage across the way is a female chimp in heat. Rachel recognizes the smell from her own times in heat. Two keepers are opening the door that separates the female's cage from the adjoining cage, where a male stands, watching with great interest. Johnson is shaking the wire mesh and howling as he watches.

"Mike here is a virgin, but Susie knows what she's doing," one keeper was saying to the other. "So it should go smoothly. But keep the hose ready."

"Yeah?"

"Sometimes they fight. We only use the hose to break it up if it gets real bad. Generally, they do okay."

Mike stalks into Susie's cage. The keepers lower the cage door, trapping both chimps in the same cage. Susie seems unalarmed. She continues eating a slice of orange while Mike sniffs at her genitals with every indication of great interest. She bends over to let Mike finger her pink bottom, the sign of estrus.

Rachel finds herself standing at the wire mesh, making low moaning noises. She can see Mike's erection, hear his grunting cries. He squats on the floor of Susie's cage, gesturing to the female. Rachel's feelings are mixed: she is fascinated, fearful, confused. She keeps thinking of the description of sex in the *Love Confessions* story: When Alice feels Danny's lips on hers, she is swept away by the passion of the moment. He takes her in his arms and her skin tingles as if she were consumed by an inner fire.

Susie bends down and Mike penetrates her with a loud grunt, thrusting violently with his hips. Susie cries out shrilly and·suddenly leaps up, knocking Mike away. Rachel watches, overcome with fascination. Mike, his penis now limp, follows Susie slowly to the corner of the cage, where he begins grooming her carefully. Rachel finds that the wire mesh has cut her hands where she gripped it too tightly.

It is night, and the door at the end of the corridor creaks open. Rachel is immediately alert, peering through the wire mesh and trying to see down to the end of the corridor. She bangs on the wire mesh. As Jake comes closer, she waves a greeting.

When Jake reaches for the lever that will raise the door to Rachel's cage, Johnson charges toward him, howling and waving his arms above his head. He hammers on the wire mesh with his fists, howling and grimacing at Jake. Rachel ignores Johnson and hurries after Jake.

Again Rachel helps Jake clean. In the laboratory, she greets the old chimp, but the animal is more interested in the banana that Jake has brought than in conversation. The chimp will not reply to her questions, and after several tries, she gives up.

While Jake vacuums the carpeted corridors, Rachel empties the trash, finding a magazine called *Modern Romance* in the same wastebasket that provided *Love Confessions*.

Later, in the janitor's lounge, Jake smokes a cigarette, sips whiskey, and flips through one of his own magazines. Rachel reads love stories in *Modern Romance*.

Every once in a while, she looks over Jake's shoulder at grainy pictures of naked women with their legs spread wide apart. Jake looks for a long time at a picture of a blond woman with big breasts, red fingernails, and purple-painted eyelids. The woman lies on her back and smiles as she strokes the pinkness between her legs. The picture on the next page shows her caressing her own breasts, pinching the dark nipples.

The final picture shows her looking back over her shoulder. She is in the position that Susie took when she was ready to be mounted.

Rachel looks over Jake's shoulder at the magazine, but she does not ask questions. Jake's smell began to change as soon as he opened the magazine; the scent of nervous sweat mingles with the aromas of tobacco and whiskey. Rachel suspects that questions would not be welcome just now.

At Jake's insistence, she goes back to her cage before dawn.

Over the next week, she listens to the conversations of the men who come and go, bringing food and hosing out the cages. From the men's conversation, she learns that the Primate Research Center is primarily a breeding facility that supplies researchers with domestically bred apes and monkeys of several species. It also maintains its own research staff. In indifferent tones, the men talk of horrible things. The adolescent chimps at the end of the corridor are being fed a diet high in cholesterol to determine cholesterol's effects on the circulatory system. A group of pregnant females are being injected with male hormones to determine how that will affect the female offspring. A group of infants is being fed a low-protein diet to determine adverse effects on their brain development.

The men look through her as if she were not real, as if she were a part of the wall, as if she were no one at all. She cannot speak to them; she cannot trust them.

Each night, Jake lets her out of her cage and she helps him clean. He brings treats: barbecue potato chips, fresh fruit, chocolate bars, and cookies. He treats her fondly, as one would treat a precocious child. And he talks to her.

At night, when she is with Jake, Rachel can almost forget the terror of the cage, the anxiety of watching Johnson pace to and fro, the sense of unreality that accompanies the simplest act. She would be content to stay with Jake forever, eating snack food and reading confessions magazines. He seems to like her company. But each morning, Jake insists that she go back to the cage and the terror. By the end of the first week, she has begun plotting her escape.

Whenever Jake falls asleep over his whiskey, something that happens three nights out of five, Rachel prowls the center alone, surreptitiously gathering things that she will need to survive in the desert: a plastic jug filled with water, a plastic bag of food pellets, a large beach towel that will serve as a blanket on the cool desert nights, a discarded plastic shopping bag in which she can carry the other things. Her best find is a road map on which the Primate Research Center is marked in red. She knows the address of Aaron's ranch and finds it on the map. She studies the roads and plots a route home. Cross-country, assuming that she does not get lost, she will have to travel about fifty miles to reach the ranch. She hides these things behind one of the shelves in the janitor's storeroom.

Her plans to run away and go home are disrupted by the idea that she is in love with Jake, a notion that comes to her slowly, fed by the stories in the confessions magazines. When Jake absentmindedly strokes her, she is filled with a strange excitement. She longs for his company and misses him on the weekends when he is away. She is happy only when she is with him, following him through the halls of the center, sniffing the aroma of tobacco and whiskey that is his own perfume. She steals a cigarette from his pack and hides it in her cage, where she can savor the smell of it at her leisure.

She loves him, but she does not know how to make him love her back. Rachel knows little about love: she remembers a crush where she mooned after a boy with a locker near hers, but that came to nothing. She reads the confessions magazines and Ann Landers's column in the newspaper that Jake brings with him each night, and from these sources, she learns about romance. One night, after Jake falls asleep, she types a badly punctuated, ungrammatical letter to Ann. In the letter, she explains her situation and asks for advice on how to make Jake

love her. She slips the letter into a sack labelled "Outgoing Mail," and for the next week she reads Ann's column with increased interest. But her letter never appears.

Rachel searches for answers in the magazine pictures that seem to fascinate Jake. She studies the naked women, especially the big-breasted woman with the purple smudges around her eyes.

One night, in a secretary's desk, she finds a plastic case of eye shadow. She steals it and takes it back to her cage. The next evening, as soon as the Center is quiet, she upturns her metal food dish and regards her reflection in the shiny bottom. Squatting, she balances the eye shadow case on one knee and examines its contents: a tiny makeup brush and three shades of eye shadow—INDIAN BLUE, FOREST GREEN, and WILDLY VIOLET. Rachel chooses the shade labeled WILDLY VIOLET.

Using one finger to hold her right eye closed, she dabs her eyelid carefully with the makeup brush, leaving a gaudy orchid-colored smudge on her brown skin. She studies the smudge critically, then adds to it, smearing the color beyond the corner of her eyelid until it disappears in her brown fur. The color gives her eye a carnival brightness, a lunatic gaiety. Working with great care, she matches the effect on the other side, then smiles at herself in the glass, blinking coquettishly.

In the other cage, Johnson bares his teeth and shakes the mesh. She ignores him.

When Jake comes to let her out, he frowns at her eyes. —Did you hurt yourself? he asks.

No, she says. Then, after a pause, —Don't you like it?

Jake squats beside her and stares at her eyes. Rachel puts a hand on his knee and her heart pounds at her own boldness. —You are a very strange monkey, he signs.

Rachel is afraid to move. Her hand on his knee closes into a fist; her face folds in on itself, puckering around the eyes.

Then, straightening up, he signs, —I liked your eyes better before.

He likes her eyes. She nods without taking her eyes from his face. Later, she washes her face in the women's restroom, leaving dark smudges the color of bruises on a series of paper towels.

Rachel is dreaming. She is walking through the Painted Desert with her hairy brown mother, following a red rock canyon that Rachel somehow knows will lead her to the Primate Research Center. Her mother is lagging behind: she does not want to go to the Center; she is afraid. In the shadow of a rock outcropping, Rachel stops to explain to her mother that they must go to the Center because Jake is at the Center.

Rachel's mother does not understand sign language. She watches Rachel with mournful eyes, then scrambles up the canyon wall, leaving Rachel behind. Rachel climbs after her mother, pulling herself over the edge in time to see the other chimp loping away across the windblown red cinder-rock and sand.

Rachel bounds after her mother, and as she runs she howls like an abandoned infant chimp, wailing her distress. The figure of her mother wavers in the distance, shimmering in the heat that rises from the sand. The figure changes. Running away across the red sands is a pale blond woman wearing a purple sweatsuit and jogging shoes, the sweet-smelling mother that Rachel remembers. The woman looks back and smiles at Rachel. "Don't howl like an ape, daughter," she calls. "Say Mama."

Rachel runs silently, dream running that takes her nowhere. The sand burns her feet and the sun beats down on her head. The blond woman vanishes in the distance, and Rachel is alone. She collapses on the sand, whimpering because she is alone and afraid.

She feels the gentle touch of fingers grooming her fur, and for a moment, still half-asleep, she believes that her hairy mother has returned to her. In the dream, she opens her eyes and looks into a pair of dark brown eyes, separated from her by wire mesh. Johnson. He has reached through a gap in the fence to groom her. As he sorts through her fur, he makes soft cooing sounds, gentle comforting noises.

Still half-asleep, she gazes at him and wonders why she was so fearful. He does not seem so bad. He grooms her for a time, and then sits nearby, watching her through the mesh. She brings a slice of apple from her dish of food and offers it to him. With her free hand, she makes the sign for apple. When he takes it, she signs again: apple. He is not a particularly quick student, but she has time and many slices of apple.

All Rachel's preparations are done, but she cannot bring herself to leave the Center. Leaving the Center means leaving Jake, leaving potato chips and whiskey, leaving security. To Rachel, the thought of love is always accompanied by the warm taste of whiskey and potato chips.

Some nights, after Jake is asleep, she goes to the big glass doors that lead to the outside. She opens the doors and stands on the steps, looking down into the desert. Sometimes a jackrabbit sits on its haunches in the rectangles of light that shine through the glass doors. Sometimes she sees kangaroo rats, hopping through the moonlight like rubber balls bouncing on hard pavement. Once, a coyote trots by, casting a contemptuous glance in her direction.

The desert is a lonely place. Empty. Cold. She thinks of Jake snoring softly in the janitor's lounge. And always she closes the door and returns to him.

Rachel leads a double life: janitor's assistant by night, prisoner and teacher by day. She spends her afternoons drowsing in the sun and teaching Johnson new signs.

On a warm afternoon, Rachel sits in the outside run, basking in the sunlight. Johnson is inside, and the other chimps are quiet. She can almost imagine she is back at her father's ranch, sitting in her own yard. She naps and dreams of Jake.

She dreams that she is sitting in his lap on the battered old couch. Her hand is on his chest: a smooth pale hand with red-painted fingernails. When she looks at the dark screen of the television set, she can see her reflection. She is a thin teenager with blond hair and blue eyes. She is naked.

Jake is looking at her and smiling. He runs a hand down her back and she closes her eyes in ecstasy.

But something changes when she closes her eyes. Jake is grooming her as her mother used to groom her, sorting through her hair in search of fleas. She opens her eyes and sees Johnson, his diligent fingers searching through her fur, his intent brown eyes watching her. The reflection on the television screen shows two chimps, tangled in each other's arms.

Rachel wakes to find that she is in heat for the first time since she came to the Center. The skin surrounding her genitals is swollen and pink.

For the rest of the day, she is restless, pacing to and fro in her cage. On his side of the wire mesh wall, Johnson is equally restless, following her when she goes outside, sniffing long and hard at the edge of the barrier that separates him from her.

That night, Rachel goes eagerly to help Jake clean. She follows him closely, never letting him get far from her. When he is sweeping, she trots after him with the dustpan and he almost trips over her twice. She keeps waiting for him to notice her condition, but he seems oblivious.

As she works, she sips from a cup of whiskey. Excited, she drinks more than usual, finishing two full cups. The liquor leaves her a little disoriented, and she sways as she follows Jake to the janitor's lounge. She curls up close beside him on the couch. He relaxes with his arms resting on the back of the couch, his legs stretching out before him. She moves so that she is pressed against him.

He stretches, yawns, and rubs the back of his neck as if trying to rub away stiffness. Rachel reaches around behind him and begins to gently rub his neck, reveling in the feel of his skin, his hair against the backs of her hands.

The thoughts that hop and skip through her mind are confusing. Sometimes it seems that the hair that tickles her hands is Johnson's; sometimes, she knows it is Jake's. And sometimes it doesn't seem to matter. Are they really so different? They are not so different.

She rubs his neck, not knowing what to do next. In the confessions magazines, this is where the man crushes the woman in his arms. Rachel climbs into Jake's lap and hugs him, waiting for him to crush her in his arms. He blinks at her sleepily. Half asleep, he strokes her, and his moving hand brushes near her genitals. She presses herself against him, making a soft sound in her throat. She rubs her hip against his crotch, aware now of a slight change in his smell, in the tempo of his breathing. He blinks at her again, a little more awake now. She bares her teeth in a smile and tilts her head back to lick his neck. She can feel his hands on her shoulders, pushing her away, and she knows what he wants. She slides from his lap and turns, presenting him with her pink genitals, ready to be mounted, ready to have him penetrate her. She moans in anticipation, a low inviting sound.

He does not come to her. She looks over her shoulder and he is still sitting on the couch, watching her through half-closed eyes. He reaches over and picks up a magazine filled with pictures of naked women. His other hand drops to his crotch and he is lost in his own world.

Rachel howls like an infant who has lost its mother, but he does not look up. He is staring at the picture of the blond woman.

Rachel runs down dark corridors to her cage, the only home she has. When she reaches the corridor, she is breathing hard and making small lonely whimpering noises. In the dimly lit corridor, she hesitates for a moment, staring into Johnson's cage. The male chimp is asleep. She remembers the touch of his hands when he groomed her.

From the corridor, she lifts the gate that leads into Johnson's cage and enters. He wakes at the sound of the door and sniffs the air.

When he sees Rachel, he stalks toward her, sniffing eagerly. She lets him finger her genitals, sniff deeply of her scent. His penis is erect and he grunts in excitement. She turns and presents herself to him and he mounts her, thrusting deep inside. As he penetrates, she thinks, for a moment, of Jake and of the thin blond teenage girl named Rachel, but then the moment passes. Almost against her will she cries out, a shrill exclamation of welcoming and loss.

After he withdraws his penis, Johnson grooms her gently, sniffing her genitals and softly stroking her fur. She is sleepy and content, but she knows that they cannot delay.

Johnson is reluctant to leave his cage, but Rachel takes him by the hand and leads him to the janitor's lounge. His presence gives her courage. She listens at the door and hears Jake's soft breathing. Leaving Johnson in the hall, she slips into the room. Jake is lying on the couch, the magazine draped over his legs. Rachel takes the equipment that she has gathered and stands for a moment, staring at the sleeping man. His baseball cap hangs on the arm of a broken chair, and she takes that to remember him by.

Rachel leads Johnson through the empty halls. A kangaroo rat, collecting seeds in the dried grass near the glass doors, looks up curiously as Rachel leads Johnson down the steps. Rachel carries the plastic shopping bag slung over her shoulder. Somewhere in the distance, a coyote howls, a long yapping wail. His cry is joined by others, a chorus in the moonlight.

Rachel takes Johnson by the hand and leads him into the desert.

A cocktail waitress, driving from her job in Flagstaff to her home in Winslow, sees two apes dart across the road, hurrying away from the bright beams of her headlights. After wrestling with her conscience (she does not want to be accused of drinking on the job), she notifies the county sheriff.

A local newspaper reporter, an eager young man fresh out of journalism school, picks up the story from the police report and interviews the waitress. Flattered by his enthusiasm for her story and delighted to find a receptive ear, she tells him details that she failed to mention to the police: one of the apes was wearing a baseball cap and carrying what looked like a shopping bag.

The reporter writes up a quick humorous story for the morning edition, and begins researching a feature article to be run later in the week. He knows that the newspaper, eager for news in a slow season, will play a human-interest story up big—kind of *Lassie Come Home* with chimps.

Just before dawn, a light rain begins to fall, the first rain of spring. Rachel searches for shelter and finds a small cave formed by three tumbled boulders. It will keep off the rain and hide them from casual observers. She shares her food and water with Johnson. He has followed her closely all night, seemingly intimidated by the darkness and the howling of distant coyotes. She feels protective toward him. At the same time, having him with her gives her courage. He knows only a few gestures in ASL, but he does not need to speak. His presence is comfort enough.

Johnson curls up in the back of the cave and falls asleep quickly. Rachel sits in the opening and watches dawn light wash the stars from the sky. The rain rattles against the sand, a comforting sound. She thinks about Jake. The baseball cap on her head still smells of his cigarettes, but she does not miss him. Not really. She fingers the cap and wonders why she thought she loved Jake.

The rain lets up. The clouds rise like fairy castles in the distance and the rising sun tints them pink and gold and gives them flaming red banners. Rachel remembers when she was younger and Aaron read her the story of Pinocchio, the little puppet who wanted to be a real boy. At the end of his adventures, Pinocchio, who has been brave and kind, gets his wish. He becomes a real boy.

Rachel cried at the end of the story and when Aaron asked why, she rubbed her eyes on the backs of her hairy hands. —I want to be a real girl, she signed to him. —A real girl.

"You are a real girl," Aaron told her, but somehow she never believed him.

The sun rises higher and illuminates the broken rock turrets of the desert. There is a magic in this barren land of unassuming grandeur. Some cultures send their young people to the desert to seek visions and guidance, searching for true thinking spawned by the openness of the place, the loneliness, the beauty of emptiness.

Rachel drowses in the warm sun and dreams a vision that has the clarity of truth. In the dream, her father comes to her. "Rachel," he says to her, "it doesn't matter what anyone thinks of you. You're my daughter."

—I want to be a real girl, she signs.

"You *are* real," her father says. "And you don't need some two-bit drunken janitor to prove it to you." She knows she is dreaming, but she also knows that her father speaks the truth. She is warm and happy and she doesn't need Jake at all. The sunlight warms her and a lizard watches her from a rock, scurrying for cover when she moves. She picks up a bit of loose rock that lies on the floor of the cave. Idly, she scratches on the dark red sandstone wall of the cave. A lopsided heart shape. Within it, awkwardly printed: Rachel and Johnson. Between them, a plus sign. She goes over the letters again and again, leaving scores of fine lines on the smooth rock surface. Then, late in the morning, soothed by the warmth of the day, she sleeps.

Shortly after dark, an elderly rancher in a pickup truck spots two apes in a remote corner of his ranch. They run away and lose him in the rocks, but not until he has a good look at them. He calls the police, the newspaper, and the Primate Research Center.

The reporter arrives first thing the next morning, interviews the rancher, and follows the men from the Primate Research Center as they search for evidence of the chimps. They find chimpanzee footprints in the wash near the cave, confirming that the runaways were indeed nearby. The news reporter, an eager and curious young man, squirms on his belly into the cave and finds the names scratched on the cave wall. He peers at it. He might have dismissed them as the idle scratchings of kids, except that the names match the names of the missing chimps. "Hey," he called to his photographer, "Take a look at this."

The next morning's newspaper displays Rachel's crudely scratched letters. In a brief interview, the rancher mentioned that the chimps were carrying bags. "Looked like supplies," he said. "They looked like they were in for the long haul."

On the third day, Rachel's water runs out. She heads toward a small town, marked on the map. They reach it in the early morning—thirst forces them to travel by day. Beside an isolated ranch house, she finds a faucet. She is filling her bottle when Johnson grunts in alarm.

A dark-haired woman watches from the porch of the house. She does not move toward the apes, and Rachel continues filling the bottle. "It's all right, Rachel," the woman, who has been following the story in the papers, calls out. "Drink all you want."

Startled, but still suspicious, Rachel caps the bottle and, keeping her eyes on the woman, drinks from the faucet. The woman steps back into the house. Rachel motions Johnson to do the same, signaling for him to hurry and drink. She turns off the faucet when he is done.

They are turning to go when the woman emerges from the house carrying a plate of tortillas and a bowl of apples. She sets them on the edge of the porch and says, "These are for you."

The woman watches through the window as Rachel packs the food into her bag. Rachel puts away the last apple and gestures her thanks to the woman. When the woman fails to respond to the sign language, Rachel picks up a stick and writes in the sand of the yard. THANK YOU, Rachel scratches, then waves good-bye and sets out across the desert. She is puzzled, but happy.

The next morning's newspaper includes an interview with the dark-haired woman. She describes how Rachel turned on the faucet and turned it off when she was through, how the chimp packed the apples neatly in her bag and wrote in the dirt with a stick.

The reporter also interviews the director of the Primate Research Center. "These are animals," the director explains angrily. "But people want to treat them like they're small hairy people." He describes the Center as "primarily a breeding center with some facilities for medical research." The reporter asks some pointed questions about their acquisition of Rachel.

But the biggest story is an investigative piece. The reporter reveals that he has tracked down Aaron Jacobs's lawyer and learned that Jacobs left a will. In this will, he bequeathed all his possessions—including his house and surrounding land—to "Rachel, the chimp I acknowledge as my daughter."

The reporter makes friends with one of the young women in the typing pool at the Primate Research Center, and she tells him the office scuttlebutt: people suspect that the chimps may have been released by a deaf and drunken janitor, who was subsequently fired for negligence. The reporter, accompanied by a friend who can communicate in sign language, finds Jake in his apartment in downtown Flagstaff.

Jake, who has been drinking steadily since he was fired, feels betrayed by Rachel, by the Primate Research Center, by the world. He complains at length about Rachel: they were friends, and then she took his baseball cap and ran away. He just didn't understand why she ran away like that.

"You mean she could talk?" the reporter asks through his interpreter.

—Of course she can talk, Jake signs impatiently. —She is a smart monkey.

The headlines read: "Intelligent chimp inherits fortune!" Of course, Aaron's bequest isn't really a fortune and she isn't just a chimp, but close enough. Animal rights activists rise up in Rachel's defense. The case is discussed on the national news. Ann Landers reports receiving a letter from a chimp named Rachel; she had thought it was a hoax perpetrated by the boys at Yale. The American Civil Liberties Union assigns a lawyer to the case.

By day, Rachel and Johnson sleep in whatever hiding places they can find: a cave; a shelter built for range cattle; the shell of an abandoned car, rusted from long years in a desert gully. Sometimes Rachel dreams of jungle darkness, and the coyotes in the distance become a part of her dreams; their howling becomes the cries of fellow apes.

The desert and the journey have changed her. She is wiser, having passed through the white-hot love of adolescence and emerged on the other side. She dreams, one day, of the ranch house. In the dream, she has long blond hair and pale white skin. Her eyes are red from crying and she wanders the house restlessly, searching for something that she has lost. When she hears coyotes howling, she looks through a window at the darkness outside. The face that looks in at her has jug-handle ears and shaggy hair. When she sees the face, she cries out in recognition and opens the window to let herself in.

By night, they travel. The rocks and sands are cool beneath Rachel's feet as she walks toward her ranch. On television, scientists and politicians discuss the ramifications of her case, describe the technology uncovered by investigation of Aaron Jacobs's files. Their debates do not affect her steady progress toward her ranch or the stars that sprinkle the sky above her.

It is night when Rachel and Johnson approach the ranch house. Rachel sniffs the wind and smells automobile exhaust and strange humans. From the hills, she can see a small camp beside a white van marked with the name of a local television station. She hesitates, considering returning to the safety of the desert. Then she takes Johnson by the hand and starts down the hill. Rachel is going home.

MANJULA PADMANABHAN

Manjula Padmanabhan (1953–) is an Indian playwright, journalist, and fiction writer. She has also illustrated more than twenty children's books and created a long-running cartoon strip, *Suki*. Her play *Harvest*, about the sale of body parts and exploitative relations between developed and developing countries, won an Onassis Prize in 1997. Much of her written work encompasses a pronounced fantastical or science-fictional milieu, ranging from postapocalyptic stories to tales of vampires, monsters, and ogres. Across the span of her work, however, she is often praised for a wry, worldly sense of humor, even when describing sometimes sinister occurrences.

"Sharing Air" (1984) is a short, sharp shock of a story that acknowledges climate-change issues in a way that will resonate even more acutely for a modern-day audience.

SHARING AIR

Manjula Padmanabhan

On the bargain network, today, there was a selection of antique atmospheres advertised. I thought I'd try something different for a change, so I ordered the late twentieth-century "Five Cities" blend. It took two days to appear in the delivery slot and—pheee-yew! It was strong! To think human beings lived in that soup day in and day out! It's a wonder that their lungs lasted long enough for them to have become our ancestors.

It must have been odd to have had no choice over what one breathed. Unimaginable. No control over water or power, either. That's beyond what I call civilization. As I wrote to a friend the other day, it's not really possible for us, living in an age of unlimited vital supplies, to understand the minds of those for whom the very air they breathed was decided by despotic government authorities.

I had forgotten that my friend was proud of tracing her ancestry back to the nineteenth century and so had to listen to a tiresome argument about civic arrangements in those days. "You don't understand," she said, "there was no question of legislating for the quality of air supply, let alone deciding that a whole nation must make do on two parts of carbon monoxide for every six of oxygen! We, in our era of continuous electronic monitoring, cannot imagine how little control those early governments actually had. . . ."

But I don't hold by such accommodating arguments. The simple fact is, those governments sanctioned polluting industries; QED, they controlled the air supply. The only thing that doesn't make sense is that most government functionaries themselves breathed the same poisons. So perhaps there *is* some validity to the argument that polluted air causes personality changes as well as the gross physical damage we are all so concerned about. Maybe if you breathe enough toxins, you can no longer distinguish between well-being and ill health. So you make decisions which will only result in more toxins. And so on and on until you set the stage for total civic breakdown. Which is what happened.

Personally, I feel we've all benefited from that breakdown. I mean, consider this air I bought today. Granted, it's only a flavour and can't actually cause me any harm. But what does it taste like, smell like, feel like, as it rasps its way down my trachea? Madness, that's what. I've always despised those scholars who delight in pointing out that the mix of chemicals in late twentieth-century air was actually intoxicating and that most humans went about in an air-induced euphoria. They would succumb, say these scholars, to depression and delirium tremens if they were to be subjected to the airs we use today. If you ask me, I've always believed that these scholars are not only heretics to the modern ethic, but secret self-toxinators as well.

In case you think that self-toxination is an alarmist fantasy, let me tell you it isn't. I myself know of a society which calls itself the Toxi-Club, whose members speak of themselves as "toxies." They tried to get me to join, but I attended one session and excused myself thereafter, claiming that I was born with Congenital Weak-Lung Syndrome.

The club was the idea of X, who had inherited an old cooling tower from his farsighted grandfather who had bought up decommissioned nuclear power stations cheap, then sold them for a galactic sum when decontamination technology was in place. X assured us that the tower was not radioactive, but I wore my radiation suit anyway, passing it off as an old-fashioned fixation of mine. He had managed to seal the cooling tower so that it could be pumped full of air under pressure. Don't ask me how he had the money or contacts to have access to such resources. There are some people who can have their own way even in our world. Anyway, whenever he can get enough of his fellow toxies together, they get into that old cooling tower, seal all the air locks, pump in the air, and zap it with chemicals. Sulphur, methane, tincture of titanium, xeon, Freon, fly ash, construction dust, soot, you name it. And then—you may find this shocking, but I assure you it's true, it happens—all the members of the group remove their breathing tubes and *share the air*!

I can tell you, it was a real skin-burning experience. At the time I accepted the invitation, I had believed that we would at most take quick drags from a common cylinder of treated air. The others spent a good half hour convincing me that it was actually possible to survive with all the valves open on my face mask. "This is what it was like!" they said to me. "The twentieth century unplugged!" Air-to-air communication too, no radios, no sound processors. When I finally picked up the courage to take in my first drag, I almost passed out. That air was so foul, so grainy, sooty, and dense, that I choked and gagged, my eyes bulged, my skin poured with sweat. I had to take long deep draughts from a handheld aerosol kit for at least ten minutes before I could try again. And even then, I never got the hang of just breathing with my mouth gaping open in front of all those other people.

Intoxication? Forget it. I mean, it's true there was a mild drowsy something I felt, right at the edge of consciousness, but I wouldn't call it intoxication. More like bleary with a touch of pleasurable panic, like when you're in a simulator and there's a meteor flaming down towards your tiny vulnerable space shuttle or something. I was too damn conscious all the time: of

what we were doing, the sheer mindless risk of it all, and the fact that any moment we might be found out. But the other toxies weren't worried. It was amazing. They were talking to each other across bare air as if they'd been doing it all their lives. Then our host began to take his face mask off completely and that's when I had to look away. Fortunately, not many others followed his example. I was relieved not to be the only one who knows that there's a point past which risqué becomes risky.

Or just downright disgusting. Inevitably, someone or the other pulled out an ancient videocassette, upgraded to 3-D, and projected it. It was garbage. I took art appreciation courses in school, so I've seen these things before, but they only confirm my belief that all generations prior to the era of individual vital supplies were entirely depraved. They breathed one another's air for goodness' sakes! Recycling all their airborne germs, their waste products, their cast-off bronchial ceils, every kind of organic junk. Water was delivered via miles of unsterilized piping from distant sources, sometimes even just up from the polluted earth itself! And as for energy, they took whatever they could get. No wonder their gadgets were so crude and lifeless—they had only the most brutish, unrefined forms of electricity to run on.

Everyone else was bloated with sentimental reverence for that time of "freedom," as they called it. "Free dirt!" I shouted. "That wasn't freedom, that was depravity!" They really turned on me then and everyone was talking at once, their real voices sounding squeaky and hollow in the open air. They talked about the repression of our times, the regimentation of all our public and private activities to serve the common good. "Oh yeah?" I said. "So it was better then? When they were free to pollute our planet's atmosphere, killing virtually all plant and animal life? That was freedom? No! It was slavery to the temple of the Self!" They argued that what we had now was worse than nothing because it was life without any of the pleasures of life. I said, "Pleasures for the few, ill health for the many!" They said that our ancestors savoured types of bliss that we had no conception of. They exposed their skin to the sun. They bathed in the rain. They had natural reproduction—no incubators, no fertility drugs. "Selfish!" I screamed. Maybe the air had gone to my head after all. I lost all inhibition. "They were spoilt! They were weak!"

Then one person said, "No, just suicidal. Our ancestors were manic-depressives. It's been confirmed—sharing air causes depression. They destroyed the ecosystem because they despised themselves. They wanted to save the universe from their own presence within it. Self-hate was their prime directive, not self-love!" These remarks caused a profound silence to fall upon the company. Shortly after that, I left. Back in my life-support unit, I thought about that wild and wasteful era as I tended my oxygen plant, arranged my protein capsules attractively for the day, and played with my pet amoebae in their petri dish. I looked at the label on my "Five Cities" atmo-cylinder: Mexico City, New Delhi, Bombay, Bangkok, Cairo. The picture on the label was a simple hologram showing a trillion people in multi-D. And today we have less than two million! All concentrated in the few remaining areas where the atmosphere is thick enough that the stars don't show through during daylight. But I don't care. I have my pick of fragrant airs. I own a brood of virtual children whom I share with other members of my thought-group. Through the mirror-processor I can travel to any dimension of my choice. The only thing I miss—or think I miss, having never seen any real ones—is trees. They sound nice. Friendly. If you come across a small one being sold, no matter what the price, do inform me. I'll keep it by my sleeping pad and stroke it gently through the night.

Schwarzschild Radius

CONNIE WILLIS

Connie Willis (1945–) is an influential US science fiction writer who has won more combined Hugo and Nebula Awards (eighteen) than any other writer. Willis holds degrees in English and elementary education from the University of Northern Colorado. After receiving a National Endowment for the Arts grant in 1982, she left a teaching job to become a full-time writer, though she has been published since 1970. Associated with the Humanist SF movement of the 1980s and 1990s, Willis often uses so-called soft science to illuminate the human condition. She is also known for her humor, especially in a comedy-of-manners or satirical style. She has been inducted into the Science Fiction and Fantasy Hall of Fame (2009), and the Science Fiction Writers of America named her a grand master in 2011.

Time travel features prominently in three of her Hugo Award–winning novels: the stand-alone *Doomsday Book* (1992) and *To Say Nothing of the Dog* (1998), and the long novel published in two volumes, *Blackout/All Clear* (2010). *Blackout/All Clear* is set in London during the Blitz and describes in great detail the travails of three visitors from 2060. They are afraid that their temporary inability to return home is linked to their frequent involuntary transgressions against the proper flow of reality at a time of fragility in the world. As with *Doomsday Book*, Willis writes with a sense of reverence about the world; in this case, her clear, attentive love for 1940s England comes through as some very well-known aspects of life then are presented as newly discovered. Both novels reaffirm Willis's commitment to the basic humanity and Humanism of her storytelling.

"Schwarzschild Radius" (1987) is classic Willis; the science is foregrounded more than usual for her, but as in her time-travel stories there is a sharp emphasis on the human impact of that science. It's an impactful story, written with a precision and clarity that show the author at the top of her form.

SCHWARZSCHILD RADIUS

Connie Willis

"When a star collapses, it sort of falls in on itself." Travers curved his hand into a semicircle and then brought the fingers in. "And sometimes it reaches a kind of point of no return where the gravity pulling in on it is stronger than the nuclear and electric forces, and when it reaches that point, nothing can stop it from collapsing and it becomes a black hole." He closed his hand into a fist. "And that critical diameter, that point where there's no turning back, is called the Schwarzschild radius." Travers paused, waiting for me to say something.

He had come to see me every day for a week, sitting stiffly on one of my chairs in an unaccustomed shirt and tie, and talked to me about black holes and relativity, even though I taught biology at the university before my retirement, not physics. Someone had told him I knew Schwarzschild, of course.

"The Schwarzschild radius?" I said in my quavery, old man's voice, as if I could not remember ever hearing the phrase before, and Travers looked disgusted. He wanted me to say, "The Schwarzschild radius! Ah, yes, I served with Karl Schwarzschild on the Russian front in World War I!" and tell him all about how he had formulated his theory of black holes while serving with the artillery, but I had not decided yet what to tell him. "The event horizon," I said.

"Yeah. It was named after Schwarzschild because he was the one who worked out the theory," Travers said. He reminded me of Muller with his talk of theories. He was the same age as Muller, with the same shock of stiff yellow hair and the same insatiable curiosity, and perhaps that was why I let him come every day to talk to me, though it was dangerous to let him get so close.

"I have drawn up a theory of the stars," Muller says while we warm our hands over the Primus stove so that they will get enough feeling in them to be able to hold the liquid barretter without dropping it. "They are not balls of fire, as the scientists say. They are frozen."

"How can we see them if they are frozen?" I say. Muller is insulted if I do not argue with him. The arguing is part of the theory.

"Look at the wireless!" he says, pointing to it sitting disemboweled on the table. We have the back off the wireless again, and in the barretter's glass tube is a red reflection of the stove's flame. "The light is a reflection off the ice of the star."

"A reflection of what?"

"Of the shells, of course."

I do not say that there were stars before there was this war, because Muller will not have an answer to this, and I have no desire to destroy his theory, and besides, I do not really believe there was a time when this war did not exist. The star shells have always exploded over the snow-covered craters of No Man's Land, shattering in a spray of white and red, and perhaps Muller's theory is true.

"At that point," Travers said, "at the event horizon, no more information can be transmitted out of the black hole because gravity has become so strong, and so the collapse appears frozen at the Schwarzschild radius."

"Frozen," I said, thinking of Muller.

"Yeah. As a matter of fact, the Russians call black holes 'frozen stars.' You were at the Russian front, weren't you?"

"What?"

"In World War I."

"But the star doesn't really freeze," I said. "It goes on collapsing."

"Yeah, sure," Travers said. "It keeps collapsing in on itself until even the atoms are stripped of their electrons and there's nothing left except what they call a naked singularity, but we can't see past the Schwarzschild radius, and nobody inside a black hole can tell us what it's like in there because they can't get messages out, so nobody can ever know what it's like inside a black hole."

"I know," I said, but he didn't hear me.

He leaned forward. "What was it like at the front?"

It is so cold we can only work on the wireless a few minutes at a time before our hands stiffen and grow clumsy, and we are afraid of dropping the liquid barretter. Muller holds his gloves over the Primus stove and then puts them on. I jam my hands into my ice-stiff pockets.

We are fixing the wireless set. Eisner, who had been delivering messages between the sectors, got sent up to the front when he could not fix his motorcycle. If we cannot fix the wireless, we will cease to be telegraphists and become soldiers, and we will be sent to the front lines.

We are already nearly there. If it were not snowing, we could see the barbed wire and pitted snow of No Man's Land, and the big Russian coal boxes sometimes land in the communication trenches. A shell hit our wireless hut two weeks ago. We are ahead of our own artillery lines, and some of the shells from our guns fall on us, too, because the muzzles are worn out. But it is not the front, and we guard the liquid barretter with our lives.

"Eisner's unit was sent up on wiring fatigue last night," Muller says, "and they have not come back. I have a theory about what happened to them."

"Has the mail come?" I say, rubbing my sore eyes and then putting my cold hands immediately back in my pockets. I must get some new gloves, but the quartermaster has none to issue. I have written my mother three times to knit me a pair, but she has not sent them yet.

"I have a theory about Eisner's unit," he says doggedly. "The Russians have a magnet that has pulled them into the front."

"Magnets pull iron, not people," I say.

I have a theory about Muller's theories. Littering the communications trenches are things that the soldiers going up to the front have discarded: water bottles and haversacks and bayonets. Hans and I sometimes tried to puzzle out why they would discard such important things.

"Perhaps they were too heavy," I would say, though that did not explain the bayonets or the boots.

"Perhaps they know they are going to die," Hans would say, picking up a helmet.

I would try to cheer him up. "My gloves fell out of my pocket yesterday when I went to the quartermaster's. I never found them. They are in this trench somewhere."

"Yes," he would say, turning the helmet round and round in his hands, "perhaps as they near the front, these things simply drop away from them."

My theory is that what happens to the water bottles and helmets and bayonets is what has happened to Muller. He was a student in university before the war, but his knowledge of science and his intelligence have fallen away from him, and now we are so close to the front, all he has left are his theories. And his curiosity, which is a dangerous thing to have kept.

"Exactly. Magnets pull iron, and *they* were carrying barbed wire!" he says triumphantly. "And so they were pulled in to the magnet."

I put my hands practically into the Primus flame and rub them together, trying to get rid of the numbness. "We had better get the barretter in the wireless again or this magnet of yours will suck it to the front, too."

I go back to the wireless. Muller stays by the stove, thinking about his magnet. The door bangs open. It is not a real door, only an iron humpie tied to the beam that reinforces the dugout and held with a wedge, and when someone pushes against it, it flies inward, bringing the snow with it.

Snow swirls in, and light, and the sound from the front, a low rumble like a dog growling. I clutch the liquid barretter to my chest, and Muller flings himself over the wireless as if it were a wounded comrade. Someone bundled in a wool coat and mittens, with a wool cap pulled over his ears, stands silhouetted against the reddish light in the doorway, blinking at us.

"Is Private Rottschieben here? I have come to see him about his eyes," he says, and I see it is Dr. Funkenheld.

"Come in and shut the door," I say, still carefully protecting the liquid barretter, but Muller has already jammed the metal back against the beam.

"Do you have news?" Muller says to the doctor, eager for new facts to spin his theories from. "Has the wiring fatigue come back? Is there going to be a bombardment tonight?"

Dr. Funkenheld takes off his mittens. "I have come to examine your eyes," he says to me. His voice frightens me. All through the war he has kept his quiet bedside voice, speaking to the wounded in the dressing station and at the stretcher bearers' posts as if they were in his surgery in Stuttgart, but now he sounds agitated, and I am afraid it means a bombardment is coming and he will need me at the front.

When I went to the dressing station for medicine for my eyes, I foolishly told him I had studied medicine with Dr. Zuschauer in Jena. Now I am afraid he will ask me to assist him, which will mean going up to the front. "Do your eyes still hurt?" he says.

I hand the barretter to Muller and go over to stand by the lantern that hangs from a nail in the beam.

"I think he should be invalided home, Herr Doktor," Muller says. He knows it is impossible, of course. He was at the wireless the day the message came through that no one was to be invalided out for frostbite or "other non-contagious diseases."

"Can you find me a better light?" the doctor says to him.

Muller's curiosity is so strong that he cannot bear to leave any place where something interesting is happening. If he went up to the front, I do not think he would be able to pull himself away, and now I expect him to make some excuse to stay, but I have forgotten that he is even more curious about the wiring fatigue. "I will go see what has happened to Eisner's unit," he says, and opens the door. Snow flies in, as if it had been beating against the door to get in, and the doctor and I have to push against the door to get it shut again.

"My eyes have been hurting," I say, while we are still pushing the metal into place, so that he cannot ask me to assist him. "They feel like sand has gotten into them."

"I have a patient with a disease I do not recognize," he says. I am relieved, though disease can kill us as easily as a trench mortar. Soldiers die of pneumonia and dysentery and blood poisoning every day in the dressing station, but we do not fear it the way we fear the front.

"The patient has fever, excoriated lesions, and suppurating bullae," Dr. Funkenheld says.

"Could it be boils?" I say, though of course he would recognize something so simple as boils, but he is not listening to me, and I realize that it is not a diagnosis from me that he has come for.

"The man is a scientist, a Jew named Schwarzschild, attached to the artillery," he says, and because the artillery are even farther back from the front lines than we are, I volunteer to go and look at the patient, but he does not want that either.

"I must talk to the medical headquarters in Bialystok," he says.

"Our wireless is broken," I say, because I do not want to have to tell him why it is impossible for me to send a message for him. We are allowed to send only military messages, and they must be sent in code, tapped out on the telegraph key. It would take hours to send his message, even if it were possible. I hold up the dangling wire. "At any rate, you must clear it with the commandant," but he is already writing out the name and address on a piece of paper, as if this were a telegraph office.

"You can send the message when you get the wireless fixed. I have written out the symptoms."

I put the back on the wireless. Muller comes in, kicking the door open, and snow flies everywhere, picking up Dr. Funkenheld's message and sending it circling around the dugout. I catch it before it spirals into the flame of the Primus stove.

"The wiring fatigue was pinned down all night," Muller says, setting down a hand lamp. He must have gotten it from the dressing station. "Five of them froze to death, the other eight have frostbite. The commandant thinks there may be a bombardment tonight." He does not mention Eisner, and he does not say what has happened to the rest of the thirty men in Eisner's unit, though I know. The front has gotten them. I wait, holding the message in my stiff fingers, hoping Dr. Funkenheld will say, "I must go attend to their frostbite."

"Let me examine your eyes," the doctor says, and shows Muller how to hold the hand lamp. Both of them peer into my eyes. "I have an ointment for you to use twice daily," he says, getting a flat jar out of his bag. "It will burn a little."

"I will rub it on my hands then. It will warm them," I say, thinking of Eisner frozen at the front, still holding the roll of barbed wire, perhaps.

He pulls my bottom eyelid down and rubs the ointment on with his little finger. It does not

sting, but when I have blinked it into my eye, everything has a reddish tinge. "Will you have the wireless fixed by tomorrow?" he says.

"I don't know. Perhaps."

Muller has not put down the hand lamp. I can see by its light that he has forgotten all about the wiring fatigue and the Russian magnet and is wondering what the doctor wants with the wireless.

The doctor puts on his mittens and picks up his bag. I realize too late I should have told him I would send the message in exchange for them. "I will come check your eyes tomorrow," he says, and opens the door to the snow. The sound of the front is very close.

As soon as he is gone, I tell Muller about Schwarzschild and the message the doctor wants to send. He will not let me rest until I have told him, and we do not have time for his curiosity. We must fix the wireless.

"If you were on the wireless, you must have sent messages for Schwarzschild," Travers said eagerly. "Did you ever send a message to Einstein? They've got the letter Einstein sent to him after he wrote him his theory, but if Schwarzschild sent him some kind of message, too, that would be great. It would make my paper."

"You said that no message can escape a black hole?" I said. "But they could escape a collapsing star. Is that not so?"

"Okay," Travers said impatiently, and made his fingers into a semicircle again. "Suppose you have a fixed observer over here." He pulled his curved hand back and held the forefinger of his other hand up to represent the fixed observer. "And you have somebody in the star. Say when the star starts to collapse, the person in it shines a light at the fixed observer. If the star hasn't reached the Schwarzschild radius, the fixed observer will be able to see the light, but it will take longer to reach him because the gravity of the black hole is pulling on the light, so it will seem as if time on the star has slowed down, and the wavelengths will have been lengthened, so the light will be redder. Of course that's just a thought problem. There couldn't really be anybody in a collapsing star to send the messages."

"We sent messages," I said. "I wrote my mother asking her to knit me a pair of gloves."

There is still something wrong with the wireless. We have received only one message in two weeks. It said, "Russian opposition collapsing," and there was so much static we could not make out the rest of it. We have taken the wireless apart twice. The first time we found a loose wire, but the second time we could not find anything. If Hans were here, he would be able to find the trouble immediately.

"I have a theory about the wireless," Muller says. He has had ten theories in as many days: the magnet of the Russians is pulling our signals in to it; the northern lights, which have been shifting uneasily on the horizon, make a curtain the wireless signals cannot get through; the Russian opposition is not collapsing at all. They are drawing us deeper and deeper into a trap.

I say, "I am going to try again. Perhaps the trouble has cleared up," and put the headphones on so I do not have to listen to his new theory. I can hear nothing but a rumbling roar that sounds like the front.

I take out the folded piece of paper Dr. Funkenheld gave me and lay it on the wireless. He comes nearly every night to see if I have gotten an answer to his message, and I take off the headphones and let him listen to the static. I tell him that we cannot get through, but even though that is true, it is not the real reason I have not sent the message. I am afraid of the commandant's finding out. I am afraid of being sent to the front.

I have compromised by writing a letter to the professor that I studied medicine with in Jena, but I have not gotten an answer from him yet, and so I must go on pretending to the doctor.

"You don't have to do that," Muller says. He sits on the wireless, swinging his leg. He picks up the paper with the symptoms on it and holds it to the flame of the Primus stove. I grab for it, but it is already burning redly. "I have sent the message for you."

"I don't believe you. Nothing has been getting out."

"Didn't you notice the northern lights did not appear last night?"

I have not noticed. The ointment the doctor gave to me makes everything look red at night, and I do not believe in Muller's theories. "Nothing is getting out now," I say, and hold the headphones out to him so he can hear the static. He listens, still swinging his leg. "You will get us both in trouble. Why did you do it?"

"I was curious about it." If we are sent up to the front, his curiosity will kill us. He will take apart a land mine to see how it works. "We cannot get in trouble for sending military messages. I said the commandant was afraid it was a poisonous gas the Russians were using." He swings his leg and grins because now I am the curious one.

"Well, did you get an answer?"

"Yes," he says maddeningly, and puts the headphones on. "It is not a poisonous gas."

I shrug as if I do not care whether I get an answer or not. I put on my cap and the muffler my mother knitted for me and open the door. "I am going out to see if the mail has come. Perhaps there will be a letter there from my professor."

"Nature of disease unknown," Muller shouts against the sudden force of the snow. "Possibly impetigo or glandular disorder."

I grin back at him and say, "If there is a package from my mother, I will give you half of what is in it."

"Even if it is your gloves?"

"No, not if it is my gloves," I say, and go to find the doctor.

At the dressing station they tell me he has gone to see Schwarzschild and give me directions to the artillery staff's headquarters. It is not very far, but it is snowing and my hands are already cold. I go to the quartermaster's and ask him if the mail has come in.

There is a new recruit there, trying to fix Eisner's motorcycle. He has parts spread out on the ground all around him in a circle. He points to a burlap sack and says, "That is all the mail there is. Look through it yourself."

Snow has gotten into the sack and melted. The ink on the envelopes has run, and I squint at them, trying to make out the names. My eyes begin to hurt. There is not a package from my mother or a letter from my professor, but there is a letter for Lieutenant Schwarzschild. The return address says "Doctor." Perhaps he has written to a doctor himself.

"I am delivering a message to the artillery headquarters," I say, showing the letter to the recruit. "I will take this up, too." The recruit nods and goes on working.

It has gotten dark while I was inside, and it is snowing harder. I jam my hands in the ice-stiff pockets of my coat and start to the artillery headquarters in the rear. It is pitch-dark in the communication trenches, and the wind twists the snow and funnels it howling along them. I take off my muffler and wrap it around my hands like a girl's muff.

A band of red shifts uneasily all along the horizon, but I do not know if it is the front or Muller's northern lights, and there is no shelling to guide me. We are running out of shells, so we do not usually begin shelling until nine o'clock. The Russians start even later. Sometimes I hear machine-gun fire, but it is distorted by the wind and the snow, and I cannot tell what direction it is coming from.

The communication trench seems narrower and deeper than I remember it from when Hans and I first brought the wireless up. It takes me longer than I think it should to get to the branching that will lead north to the headquarters. The front has been contracting, the ammunition dumps and officer's billets and clearing stations moving up closer and closer behind us. The artillery headquarters has been moved up from the village to a dugout near the artillery line, not half a mile behind us. The nightly firing is starting. I hear a low rumble, like thunder.

The roar seems to be ahead of me, and I stop and look around, wondering if I can have gotten somehow turned around, though I have not left the trenches. I start again, and almost immediately I see the branching and the headquarters.

It has no door, only a blanket across the opening, and I pull my hands free of the muffler and duck through it into a tiny space like a rabbit hole, the timber balks of the earthen ceiling so low I have to stoop. Now that I am out of the roar of the snow, the sound of the front separates itself into the individual crack of a four-pounder, the whine of a star shell, and under it the almost continuous rattle of machine guns. The trenches must not be as deep here. Muller and I can hardly hear the front at all in our wireless hut.

A man is sitting at an uneven table spread with papers and books. There is a candle on the table with a red glass chimney, or perhaps it only looks that way to me. Everything in the dugout, even the man, looks faintly red.

He is wearing a uniform but no coat, and gloves with the finger ends cut off, even though there is no stove here. My hands are already cold.

A trench mortar roars, and clods of frozen dirt clatter from the roof onto the table. The man brushes the dirt from the papers and looks up.

"I am looking for Dr. Funkenheld," I say.

"He is not here." He stands up and comes around the table, moving stiffly, like an old man, though he does not look older than forty. He has a moustache, and his face looks dirty in the red light.

"I have a message for him."

An eight-pounder roars, and more dirt falls on us. The man raises his arm to brush the dirt off his shoulder. The sleeve of his uniform has been slit into ribbons. All along the back of his raised hand and the side of his arm are red sores running with pus. I look back at his face. The sores in his moustache and around his nose and mouth have dried and are covered with a crust. Excoriated lesions. Suppurating bullae. The gun roars again, and dirt rains down on his raw hands.

"I have a message for him," I say, backing away from him. I reach in the pocket of my coat to show him the message, but I pull out the letter instead. "There was a letter for you, Lieutenant Schwarzschild." I hold it out to him by one corner so he will not touch me when he takes it.

He comes toward me to take the letter, the muscles in his jaw tightening, and I think in horror that the sores must be on his legs as well. "Who is it from?" he says. "Ah, Herr Professor Einstein. Good," and turns it over. He puts his fingers on the flap to open the letter and cries out in pain. He drops the letter.

"Would you read it to me?" he says, and sinks down into the chair, cradling his hand against his chest. I can see there are sores in his fingernails.

I do not have any feeling in my hands. I pick the envelope up by its corners and turn it over. The skin of his finger is still on the flap. I back away from the table. "I must find the doctor. It is an emergency."

"You would not be able to find him," he says. Blood oozes out of the tip of his finger and down over the blister in his fingernail. "He has gone up to the front."

"What?" I say, backing and backing until I run into the blanket. "I cannot understand you."

"He has gone up to the front," he says, more slowly, and this time I can puzzle out the words, but they make no sense. How can the doctor be at the front? This is the front.

He pushes the candle toward me. "I order you to read me the letter."

I do not have any feeling in my fingers. I open it from the top, tearing the letter almost in two. It is a long letter, full of equations and numbers, but the words are warped and blurred. "'My Esteemed Colleague! I have read your paper with the greatest interest. I had not expected

that one could formulate the exact solution of the problem so simply. The analytical treatment of the problem appears to me splendid. Next Thursday I will present the work with several explanatory words, to the Academy!'"

"Formulated so simply," Schwarzschild says, as if he is in pain. "That is enough. Put the letter down. I will read the rest of it."

I lay the letter on the table in front of him, and then I am running down the trench in the dark with the sound of the front all around me, roaring and shaking the ground. At the first turning, Muller grabs my arm and stops me. "What are you doing here?" I shout. "Go back! Go back!"

"Go back?" he says. "The front's that way." He points in the direction he came from. But the front is not that way. It is behind me, in the artillery headquarters. "I told you there would be a bombardment tonight. Did you see the doctor? Did you give him the message? What did he say?"

"So you actually held the letter from Einstein?" Travers said. "How exciting that must have been! Only two months after Einstein had published his theory of general relativity. And years before they realized black holes really existed. When was this exactly?" He took out a notebook and began to scribble notes. "'My esteemed colleague' . . . ," he muttered to himself. "'Formulated so simply.' This is great stuff. I mean, I've been trying to find out stuff on Schwarzschild for my paper for months, but there's hardly any information on him. I guess because of the war."

"No information can get out of a black hole once the Schwarzschild radius has been passed," I said.

"Hey, that's great!" he said, scribbling. "Can I use that in my paper?"

Now I am the one who sits endlessly in front of the wireless sending out messages to the Red

Cross, to my professor in Jena, to Dr. Einstein. I have frostbitten the forefinger and thumb of my right hand and have to tap out the letters with my left. But nothing is getting out, and I must get a message out. I must find someone to tell me the name of Schwarzschild's disease.

"I have a theory," Muller says. "The Jews have seized power and have signed a treaty with the Russians. We are completely cut off."

"I am going to see if the mail has come," I say, so that I do not have to listen to any more of his theories, but the doctor stops me on my way out of the hut.

I tell him what the message said. "Impetigo!" the doctor shouts. "You saw him! Did that look like impetigo to you?"

I shake my head, unable to tell him what I think it looks like.

"What are his symptoms?" Muller asks, burning with curiosity. I have not told him about Schwarzschild. I am afraid that if I tell him, he will only become more curious and will insist on going up to the front to see Schwarzschild himself.

"Let me see your eyes," the doctor says in his beautiful calm voice. I wish he would ask Muller to go for a hand lamp again so that I could ask him how Schwarzschild is, but he has brought a candle with him. He holds it so close to my face that I cannot see anything but the red flame.

"Is Lieutenant Schwarzschild worse? What are his symptoms?" Muller says, leaning forward.

His symptoms are craters and shell holes, I think. I am sorry I have not told Muller, for it has only made him more curious. Until now I have told him everything, even how Hans died when the wireless hut was hit, how he laid the liquid barretter carefully down on top of the wireless before he tried to cough up what was left of his chest and catch it in his hands. But I cannot tell him this.

"What symptoms does he have?" Muller says again, his nose almost in the candle's flame, but the doctor turns from him as if he cannot hear him and blows the candle out. The doctor unwraps the dressing and looks at my fingers. They are swollen and red. Muller leans over the doctor's shoulder. "I have a theory about Lieutenant Schwarzschild's disease," he says.

"Shut up," I say. "I don't want to hear any more of your stupid theories," and do not even care about the wounded look on Muller's face or the way he goes and sits by the wireless. For now I have a theory, and it is more horrible than anything Muller could have dreamed of.

We are all of us—Muller, and the recruit who is trying to put together Eisner's motorcycle, and perhaps even the doctor with his steady bedside voice—afraid of the front. But our fear is not complete, because unspoken in it is our belief that the front is something separate from us, something we can keep away from by keeping the wireless or the motorcycle fixed, something we can survive by flattening our faces into the frozen earth, something we can escape altogether by being invalided out.

But the front is not separate. It is inside Schwarzschild, and the symptoms I have been sending out, suppurative bullae and excoriated lesions, are not what is wrong with him at all. The lesions on his skin are only the barbed wire and shell holes and connecting trenches of a front that is somewhere farther in.

The doctor puts a new dressing of crepe paper on my hand. "I have tried to invalid Schwarzschild out," the doctor says, and Muller looks at him, astounded. "The supply lines are blocked with snow."

"Schwarzschild cannot be invalided out," I say. "The front is inside him."

The doctor puts the roll of crepe paper back in his kit and closes it. "When the roads open again, I will invalid you out for frostbite. And Muller, too."

Muller is so surprised, he blurts, "I do not have frostbite."

But the doctor is no longer listening. "You must both escape," he says—and I am not sure he is even listening to himself—"while you can."

"I have a theory about why you have not told me what is wrong with Schwarzschild," Muller says as soon as the doctor is gone.

"I am going for the mail."

"There will not be any mail," Muller shouts after me. "The supply lines are blocked." But the mail is there, scattered among the motorcycle parts. There are only a few parts left. As soon as the roads are cleared, the recruit will be able to climb on the motorcycle and ride away.

I gather up the letters and take them over to the lantern to try to read them, but my eyes are so bad, I cannot see anything but a red blur. "I am taking them back to the wireless hut," I say, and the recruit nods without looking up.

It is starting to snow. Muller meets me at the door, but I brush past him and turn the flame of the Primus stove up as high as it will go and hold the letters up behind it.

"I will read them for you," Muller says eagerly, looking through the envelopes I have discarded. "Look, here is a letter from your mother. Perhaps she has sent your gloves."

I squint at the letters one by one while he tears open my mother's letter to me. Even though I hold them so close to the flame that the paper scorches, I cannot make out the names.

"'Dear son,'" Muller reads, "'I have not heard from you in three months. Are you hurt? Are you ill? Do you need anything?'"

The last letter is from Professor Zuschauer in Jena. I can see his name quite clearly in the corner of the envelope, though mine is blurred beyond recognition. I tear it open. There is nothing written on the red paper.

I thrust it at Muller. "Read this," I say.

"I have not finished with your mother's letter yet," Muller says, but he takes the letter and reads: "'Dear Herr Rottschieben, I received your letter yesterday. I could hardly decipher your writing. Do you not have decent pens at the front? The disease you describe is called Neumann's disease or pemphigus—'"

I snatch the letter out of Muller's hands and run out the door. "Let me come with you!" Muller shouts.

"You must stay and watch the wireless!" I say joyously, running along the communication trench. Schwarzschild does not have the front inside him. He has pemphigus, he has Neumann's disease, and now he can be invalided home to hospital.

I go down and think I have tripped over a discarded helmet or a tin of beef, but there is a crash, and dirt and revetting fall all around me. I hear the low buzz of a daisy cutter and flatten myself into the trench, but the buzz does not become a whine. It stops, and there is another crash and the trench caves in.

I scramble out of the trench before it can suffocate me and crawl along the edge toward Schwarzschild's dugout, but the trench has caved in all along its length, and when I crawl up and over the loose dirt, I lose it in the swirling snow.

I cannot tell which way the front lies, but I know it is very close. The sound comes at me from all directions, a deafening roar in which no individual sounds can be distinguished. The snow is so thick, I cannot see the burst of flame from the muzzles as the guns fire, and no part of the horizon looks redder than any other. It is all red, even the snow.

I crawl in what I think is the direction of the trench, but as soon as I do, I am in barbed wire. I stop, breathing hard, my face and hands pressed into the snow. I have come the wrong way. I am at the front. I hear a sound out of the barrage of sound, the sound of tires on the snow, and I think it is a tank and cannot breathe at all. The sound comes closer, and in spite of myself I look up and it is the recruit who was at the quartermaster's.

He is a long way away, behind a coiled line of barbed wire, but I can see him quite clearly in spite of the snow. He has the motorcycle fixed, and as I watch, he flings his leg over it and presses his foot down. "Go!" I shout. "Get out!" The motorcycle jumps forward. "Go!"

The motorcycle comes toward me, picking up speed. It rears up, and I think it is going to jump the barbed wire, but it falls instead, the motorcycle first and then the recruit, spiralling slowly down into the iron spikes. The ground heaves, and I fall, too.

I have fallen into Schwarzschild's dugout. Half of it has caved in, the timber balks sticking out at angles from the heap of dirt and snow, but the blanket is still over the door, and Schwarzschild is propped in a chair. The doctor is bending over him. Schwarzschild has his shirt off. His chest looks like Hans's did.

The front roars and more of the roof crumbles. "It's all right! It's a disease!" I shout over it. "I have brought you a letter to prove it," and hand him the letter which I have been clutching in my unfeeling hand.

The doctor grabs the letter from me. Snow whirls down through the ruined roof, but Schwarzschild does not put on his shirt. He watches uninterestedly as the doctor reads the letter.

"'The symptoms you describe are almost certainly those of Neumann's disease, or pemphigus vulgaris. I have treated two patients with the disease, both Jews. It is a disease of the mucous membranes and is not contagious. Its cause is unknown. It always ends in death.'" Dr. Funkenheld crumples up the paper. "You came all this way in the middle of a bombardment to tell me there is no hope?" he shouts in a voice I do not even recognize, it is so unlike his steady doctor's voice. "You should have tried to get away. You should have—" And then he is gone under a crashing of dirt and splintered timbers.

I struggle toward Schwarzschild through the maelstrom of red dust and snow. "Put your shirt on!" I shout at him. "We must get out of here!" I crawl to the door to see if we can get out through the communication trench.

Muller bursts through the blanket. He is carrying, impossibly, the wireless. The headphones trail behind him in the snow. "I came to see what had happened to you. I thought you were dead. The communication trenches are shot to pieces."

It is as I feared. His curiosity has got the best of him, and now he is trapped, too, though he seems not to know it. He hoists the wireless onto the table without looking at it. His eyes are on Schwarzschild, who leans against the remaining wall of the dugout, his shirt in his hands.

"Your shirt!" I shout, and come around to help Schwarzschild put it on over the craters and shell holes of his blasted skin. The air screams and the mouth of the dugout blows in. I grab at Schwarzschild's arm, and the skin of it comes off in my hands. He falls against the table, and the wireless goes over. I can hear the splintering tinkle of the liquid barretter breaking, and then the whole dugout is caving in and we are under the table. I cannot see anything.

"Muller!" I shout. "Where are you?"

"I'm hit," he says.

I try to find him in the darkness, but I am crushed against Schwarzschild. I cannot move. "Where are you hit?"

"In the arm," he says, and I hear him try to move it. The movement dislodges more dirt, and it falls around us, shutting out all sound of the front. I can hear the creak of wood as the table legs give way.

"Schwarzschild?" I say. He doesn't answer, but I know he is not dead. His body is as hot as the Primus stove flame. My hand is underneath his body, and I try to shift it, but I cannot. The dirt falls like snow, piling up around us. The darkness is red for a while, and then I cannot see even that.

"I have a theory," Muller says in a voice so close and so devoid of curiosity it might be mine. "It is the end of the world."

"Was that when Schwarzschild was sent home on sick leave?" Travers said. "Or validated, or whatever you Germans call it? Well, yeah, it had to be, because he died in March. What happened to Muller?"

I had hoped he would go away as soon as I had told him what had happened to Schwarzschild, but he made no move to get up. "Muller was invalided out with a broken arm. He became a scientist."

"The way you did." He opened his notebook again. "Did you see Schwarzschild after that?"

The question makes no sense.

"After you got out? Before he died?"

It seems to take a long time for his words to get to me. The message bends and curves, shifting into the red, and I can hardly make it out. "No," I say, though that is a lie.

Travers scribbles. "I really do appreciate this, Dr. Rottschieben. I've always been curious about Schwarzschild, and now that you've told me all this stuff, I'm even more interested," Travers says, or seems to say. Messages coming in are warped by the gravitational blizzard into something that no longer resembles speech. "If you'd be willing to help me, I'd like to write my thesis on him."

Go. Get out. "It was a lie," I say. "I never knew Schwarzschild. I saw him once, from a distance—your fixed observer."

Travers looks up expectantly from his notes as if he is still waiting for me to answer him.

"Schwarzschild was never even in Russia," I lie. "He spent the whole winter in hospital in Göttingen. I lied to you. It was nothing but a thought problem."

He waits, pencil ready.

"You can't stay here!" I shout. "You have to get away. There is no safe distance from which a fixed observer can watch without being drawn in, and once you are inside the Schwarzschild radius, you can't get out. Don't you understand? We are still there!"

We are still there, trapped in the trenches of the Russian front, while the dying star burns itself out, spiralling down into that center where time ceases to exist, where everything ceases to exist except the naked singularity that is somehow Schwarzschild.

Muller tries to dig the wireless out with his crushed arm so he can send a message that nobody can hear—"Help us! Help us!"—and I struggle to free the hands that in spite of Schwarzschild's warmth are now so cold I cannot feel them, and in the very center Schwarzschild burns himself out, the black hole at his center imploding him cell by cell, carrying him down into darkness, and us with him.

"It is a trap!" I shout at Travers from the center, and the message struggles to escape and then falls back.

"I wonder how he figured it out," Travers says, and now I can hear him clearly. "I mean, can you imagine trying to figure out something like the theory of black holes in the middle of a war and while you were suffering from a fatal disease? And just think, when he came up with the theory, he didn't have any idea that black holes even existed."

GENE WOLFE

Gene Wolfe (1931–) is an award-winning US writer of science fiction and fantasy who was born in New York City and had polio as a child. He attended Texas A&M University before being drafted to serve in the military during the Korean War. He later graduated from the University of Houston and worked as an industrial engineer—which culminated in his helping create the machine that makes Pringles potato chips. The cartoon face on the side of the Pringles package is purportedly a rendering of Wolfe's face. Wolfe then turned to fiction, at which he proved to have a unique talent; in addition to the brilliant, complex *The Fifth Head of Cerberus* (1972), Wolfe's signature creation is *The Book of the New Sun*, a tetralogy (1980–83). This far-future series has received substantial acclaim and awards consideration, while redefining the antihero within science fiction. Wolfe has won the Nebula Award, the Locus Award, the World Fantasy Award, and the August Derleth Award several times. He also is a member of the Science Fiction and Fantasy Hall of Fame and has received the World Fantasy Award for Life Achievement.

Although not a bestselling author, Wolfe is highly regarded by critics and fellow writers, and considered by many to be one of the best living science fiction authors. Indeed, he has sometimes been called the best living American writer regardless of genre. In a sympathetic profile on the *New Yorker* website (April 24, 2015), Peter Berbegal wrote of Wolfe, "His stories and novels are rich with riddles, mysteries, and sleights of textual hand. His working lexicon is vast, and his plots are unspooled by narrators who deliberately confuse or are confused—or both . . . His science fiction is neither operatic nor scientifically accurate; his fantasy works are not full of clanging swords and wizardly knowledge." The critic and author John Clute has written about Wolfe's fiction, "From the first, and with a prolific output that has not ebbed for more than four decades, he has created texts [that]—almost uniquely—marry modernism and SF, rather than putting them into rhetorical opposition; his ultimate importance to world literature derives from the success of that marriage." The award-winning science fiction author Michael Swanwick has said, with perhaps some hyperbole: "Gene Wolfe is the greatest writer in the English language alive today. Let me repeat that: Gene Wolfe is the greatest writer in the English language alive today!" Among others, writers Neil Gaiman and Patrick O'Leary have credited Wolfe for inspiration.

Wolfe wrote of his views of fiction, "My definition of a great story has nothing to do with 'a varied and interesting background.' It is: *One that can be read with pleasure by a cultivated reader and reread with increasing pleasure.*" "All the Hues of Hell" first appeared in the anthology *Universe* in 1987. For a Gene Wolfe story, it is fairly straightforward science fiction. Yet it contains hidden depths.

ALL THE HUES OF HELL

Gene Wolfe

Three with egg roll, Kyle thought. Soon four without—if this shadow world really has (oh, sacred!) life. The *Egg* was still rolling, still spinning to provide mock gravitation.

Yet the roar of the sharply angled guidance jets now seeped only faintly into the hold, and the roll was slower and slower, the feeling of weight weaker and weaker. The *Egg* was in orbit . . . around nothing. Or at least around nothing visible. As its spin decreased, its ports swept the visible universe. Stars that were in fact galaxies flowed down the synthetic quartz like raindrops down a canopy. Once Kyle caught sight of their mother ship; the *Shadow Show* herself looked dim and ghostly in the faint light. Of the planet they orbited, there was no trace. Polyaris screamed and took off, executing a multicolored barrel roll with outstretched wings through the empty hold; like all macaws, Polyaris doted on microgravity.

In his earphones Marilyn asked, "Isn't it pretty, Ky?" But she was admiring her computer simulation, not his ecstatic bird: an emerald forest three hundred meters high, sparkling sapphire lakes—suddenly a vagrant strip of beach golden as her hair, and the indigo southern ocean.

One hundred and twenty degrees opposed to them both, Skip answered instead, and not as Kyle himself would have.

"No, it isn't." There was a note in Skip's voice that Kyle had noticed, and worried over, before.

Marilyn seemed to shrug. "Okay, darling, it's not really anything to us, less even than ultraviolet. But—"

"I can see it," Skip told her.

Marilyn glanced across the empty hold toward Kyle.

He tried to keep his voice noncommittal as he whispered to his mike. "You can see it, Skip?"

Skip did not reply. Polyaris chuckled to herself. Then silence (the utter, deadly quiet of nothingness, of the void where shadow matter ruled and writhed invisible) filled the *Egg*. For a wild instant, Kyle wondered whether silence itself might not be a manifestation of shadow matter, a dim insubstance felt only in its mass and gravity, its unseen heaviness. Galaxies drifted lazily over the ports, in a white *Egg* robbed of Up and Down. Their screens were solid sheets of deepest blue.

Skip broke the silence. "Just let me show it to you, Kyle. Allow me, Marilyn, to show you what it actually looks like."

"Because you really know, Skip?"

"Yes, because I really know, Kyle. Don't you remember, either of you, what they said?"

Kyle was watching Marilyn across the hold; he saw her shake her head. "Not all of it." Her voice was cautious. "They said so much, darling, after all. They said quite a lot of things."

Skip sounded as though he were talking to a child. "What the Life Support people said. The thing, the only *significant* thing, they did say."

Still more carefully, Marilyn asked, "And what was that, darling?"

"That one of us would die."

An island sailed across her screen, an emerald set in gold and laid upon blue velvet.

Kyle said, "That's my department, Skip. Life Support told us there was a real chance—perhaps as high as one in twenty—that one of you would die, outbound from Earth or on the trip back. They were being conservative; I would have estimated it as one in one hundred."

Marilyn murmured, "I think I'd better inform the Director."

Kyle agreed.

"And they were right," Skip said. "Kyle, I'm the one. I died on the way out. I passed away, but you two followed me."

Ocean and isle vanished from all the screens, replaced by a blinking cursor and the word DIRECTOR.

Marilyn asked, "Respiration monitor, L. Skinner Jansen."

Kyle swiveled to watch his screen. The cursor swept from side to side without any sign of inhalation or exhalation, and for a moment he was taken aback. Then Skip giggled.

Marilyn's sigh filled Kyle's receptors. "The programming wizard. What did you do, Skip? Turn down the gain?"

"That wasn't necessary. It happens automatically." Skip giggled again.

Kyle said slowly, "You're not dead, Skip. Believe me, I've seen many dead men. I've cut up their bodies and examined every organ; I know dead men, and you're not one of them."

"Back on the ship, Kyle. My former physical self is lying in the *Shadow Show*, dead."

Marilyn said, "Your physical self is right here, darling, with Ky and me." And then to the Director, "Sir, is L. Skinner Jansen's module occupied?"

The trace vanished, replaced by NEGATIVE: JANSEN 1'S MODULE IS EMPTY.

"Console," Skip himself ordered.

Kyle did not turn to watch Skip's fingers fly across the keys. After a moment Skip said, "You see, this place—the formal name of our great republic is Hades, by the way—looks the way it does only because of the color gradations you assigned the gravimeter data. I'm about to show you its true colors, as the expression has it."

A blaze of 4.5-, 6-, and 7.8-ten-thousandths-millimeter light, Polyaris fluttered away to watch Skip. When he made no attempt to shoo her off, she perched on a red emergency lever and cocked an eye like a bright black button toward his keyboard.

Kyle turned his attention back to his screen. The letters faded, leaving only the blue southern ocean. As he watched, it darkened to sable. Tiny flames of ocher, citron, and cinnabar darted from the crests of the waves.

"See what I mean?" Skip asked. "We've been sent to bring a demon back to Earth—or maybe just a damned soul. I don't care. I'm going to stay right here."

Kyle looked across the vacant white hold toward Marilyn.

"I can't," she whispered. "I just can't, Ky. You do it."

"All right, Marilyn." He plugged his index finger into the Exchange socket, so that he sensed rather than saw the letters overlaying the hellish sea on the screens: KAPPA UPSILON LAMBDA 23011 REPORTS JANSEN I PSYCHOTIC. CAN YOU CONFIRM, JANSEN 2?

"Confirmed, Marilyn Jansen."

RESTRAINT ADVISED.

Marilyn said, "I'm afraid restraint's impossible as long as we're in the *Egg*, sir."

DO NOT ABORT YOUR MISSION, JANSEN 2. WILL YOU ACCEPT THE RESTRAINT OF JANSEN I WHEN RESTRAINT IS PRACTICAL?

"Accepted whenever practical," Marilyn said. "Meanwhile, we'll proceed with the mission."

SATISFACTORY, the Director said, and signed off.

Skip asked, "So you're going to lock me up, honeybone?"

"I hope that by the time we get back it won't be necessary. Ky, haven't you anything to give him?"

"No specifics for psychosis, Marilyn. Not here. I've got some back on the *Shadow Show*."

Skip ruffled his beard. "Sure. You're going to lock up a ghost." Across the wide hold, Kyle could see he was grinning.

Polyaris picked up the word: "Ghost! *Ghost! GHOST!*" She flapped to the vacant center of the *Egg*, posing like a heraldic eagle and watching to make certain they admired her.

The shoreline of a larger island entered their screens from the right. Its beach was ashes and embers, its forest a forest of flames.

"If we're going to make the grab, Marilyn . . ."

"You're right," she said. Courageously, she straightened her shoulders. The new life within her had already fleshed out her cheeks and swollen her breasts; Kyle felt sure that she had never been quite so lovely before. When she put on her helmet, he breathed her name (though only to himself) before he plugged into the simulation that seemed so much more real than a screen.

As a score of pink arms, Marilyn's grav beams dipped into the shadow planet's atmosphere, growing dark and heavy as they pulled up shadow fluid and gases from a lake on the island and whatever winds might ruffle it. Kyle reflected that those arms should be blue instead of black, and told the onboard assistant director to revert to the hues Marilyn had originally programmed.

Rej, the assistant director snapped.

And nothing happened. The gravs grew darker still, and the big accelerator jets grumbled at the effort required to maintain *Egg* in orbit. When Kyle glanced toward the hold, he discovered it had acquired a twelve-meter yolk as dark as the eggs Chinese bury for centuries. Polyaris was presumably somewhere in that black yolk, unable to see or feel it. He gave a shrill whistle, and she screamed and fluttered out to perch on his shoulder.

The inky simulation doubled and redoubled, swirling to the turbulence of the fresh shadow matter pumped into the *Egg* by the gravs. Generators sang the spell that kept the shadow "air" and "water" from boiling away in what was to them a high vacuum.

The grumbling of the jets rose to an angry roar.

Skip said, "You've brought hell in here with us, honeybone. You, not me. Remember that."

Marilyn ignored him, and Kyle told him to keep quiet.

Abruptly the gravitors winked out. A hundred tons or more of the shadow world's water (whatever that might be) fell back to the surface, fully actual to any conscious entity that might be there.

"Rains of frogs and fish, Polyaris," Kyle muttered to his bird. "Remember Charlie Fort?"

Polyaris chuckled, nodding.

Skip said, "Then remember too that when Moses struck the Nile with his staff, the Lord God turned the water to blood."

"You're the one who got into the crayon box, Skip. I'll call you Moses if you like, but I can hardly call you 'I Am,' after you've just assured us you're not." Kyle was following Marilyn's hunt for an example of the dominant life form, less than a tenth of his capacity devoted to Polyaris and Skip.

"You will call me *Master*!"

Kyle grinned, remembering the holovamp of an ancient him. "No, Skip. For as long as you're ill, I am the master. Do you know I've been waiting half my life to use that line?"

Then he saw it, three-quarters of a second, perhaps, after Marilyn had: an upright figure striding down a fiery beach. Its bipedal locomotion was not a complete guarantee of dominance and intelligence, to be sure; ostriches had never ruled a world and never would, no matter how big a pest they became on Mars. But— yes—those powerful forelimbs were surely GP manipulators and not mere weapons. *Now, Marilyn! Now!*

As though she had heard him, a pink arm flicked down. For an instant the shadow man floated, struggling wildly to escape, the gravitation of his shadow world countered by their gravitor; then he flashed toward them. Kyle swiveled to watch the black sphere splash (there could be no other word for it) and, under the prodding of the gravs, recoalesce. They were four.

In a moment more, their shadow man bobbed to the surface of the dark and still trembling yolk. To him, Kyle reflected, they were not there, the *Egg* was not there. To him it must have seemed that he floated upon a watery sphere suspended in space.

And possibly that was more real than the computer-enhanced vision he himself inhabited, a mere cartoon created from one of the weakest forces known to physics. He unplugged, and at once the *Egg*'s hold was white and empty again.

Marilyn took off her helmet. "All right, Ky, from here on it's up to you—unless you want something more from the surface?"

Kyle congratulated her and shook his head. "Darling, are you feeling any better?"

Skip said levelly, "I'm okay now. I think that damned machine must have drugged me."

"Ky? That seems pretty unlikely."

"We should de-energize or destroy him, if we can't revise his programming."

Marilyn shook her head. "I doubt that we could reprogram him. Ky, what do you think?"

"A lot of it's hardwired, Marilyn, and can't be altered without new boards. I imagine Skip could revise my software if he put his mind to it, though it might take him quite a while. He's very good at that sort of thing."

Skip said, "And you're a very dangerous device, Kyle."

Shaking his head, Kyle broke out the pencil-thin cable he had used so often in training exercises. One end jacked into the console, the other into a small socket just above his hips. When both connections were made, he was again in the cybernetic cartoon where true matter and shadow matter looked equally real.

It was still a cartoon with colors by Skip: Marilyn's skin shone snow-white, her lips were burning scarlet, her hair like burnished brass, and her eyes blue fire; Skip himself had become a black-bearded satyr, with a terra-cotta complexion and cruel crimson lips. Kyle tightened both ferrules firmly, tested his jets, released his safety harness, and launched himself toward the center of the *Egg*, making Polyaris crow with delight.

The shadow man drifted into view as they neared the black yolk. He was lying upon what Kyle decided must be his back; on the whole he was oddly anthropomorphic, with recognizable head, neck, and shoulders. Binocular organs of vision seemed to have vanished behind small folds of skin, and Kyle would have called his respiration rapid in a human.

Marilyn asked, "How does he look, Ky?"

"Like hell," Kyle muttered. "I'm afraid he may be in shock. At least, shock's what I'd say if he were one of you. As it is, I . . ." He let the sentence trail away.

There were strange, blunt projections just above the organs that appeared to be the shadow man's ears. Absently, Kyle tried to palpate them; his hand met nothing, and vanished as it passed into the shadow man's cranium.

The shadow man opened his eyes.

Kyle jerked backward, succeeding only in throwing himself into a slow spin that twisted his cable.

Marilyn called, "What's the matter, Ky?"

"Nothing," Kyle told her. "I'm jumpy, that's all."

The shadow man's eyes were closed again. His arms, longer than a human's and more muscled than a bodybuilder's, twitched and were still. Kyle began the minute examination required by the plan.

When it was complete, Skip asked, "How'd it go, Kyle?"

He shrugged. "I couldn't see his back. The way you've got the shadow water keyed, it's like ink."

Marilyn said, "Why don't you change it, Skip? Make it blue but translucent, the way it's supposed to be."

Skip sounded apologetic. "I've been trying to; I've been trying to change everything back. I can't, or anyway not yet. I don't remember just what I did, but I put some kind of block on it."

Kyle shrugged again. "Keep trying, Skip, please."

"Yes, please try, darling. Now buckle up, everybody. Time to rendezvous."

Kyle disconnected his cable and pulled his

harness around him. After a moment's indecision, he plugged into the console as well.

If he had been unable to see it, it would have been easy to believe that *Egg*'s acceleration had no effect on the fifty-meter sphere of dark matter at its center; yet that too was mass, and the gravs whimpered like children at the strain of changing its speed and direction, their high wail audible—to Kyle at least—above the roaring of the jets. The black sphere stretched into a sooty tear. Acceleration was agony for Polyaris as well; Kyle cupped her fragile body in his free hand to ease her misery as much as he could.

Somewhere so far above the *Egg* that the gravity well of the shadow planet had almost ceased to make any difference and words like *above* held little meaning, the *Shadow Show* was unfolding to receive them, preparing itself to embed the newly fertilized *Egg* in an inner wall. For a moment Kyle's thoughts soared, drunk on the beauty of the image.

Abruptly the big jets fell silent. The *Egg* had achieved escape velocity.

Marilyn returned control of *Egg* to the assistant director. "That's it, folks, until we start guiding in. Unbuckle if you want."

Kyle tossed Polyaris toward the yolk and watched her make a happy circuit of the *Egg*'s interior.

Skip said, "Marilyn, I seem to have a little problem here."

"What is it?"

Kyle took off his harness and retracted it. He unplugged, and the yolk and its shadow man were gone. Only the chortling Polyaris remained.

"I can't get this goddamned thing off," Skip complained. "The buckle's jammed or something."

Marilyn took off her own acceleration harness and sailed across to look at it. Kyle joined them.

"Here, let me try it," Marilyn said. Her slender fingers, less nimble but more deft than Skip's, pressed the release and jiggled the locking tab; it would not pull free.

Kyle murmured, "I'm afraid you can't release Skip, Marilyn. Neither can I."

She turned to look at him.

"You accepted restraint for Skip, Marilyn. I want to say that in my opinion you were correct to do so."

She began, "You mean—"

"The Director isn't satisfied yet that Skip has recovered, that's all. Real recoveries aren't usually so quick or so—" Kyle paused, searching his dictionary file for the best word. "Convenient. This may be no more than a lucid interval. That happens, quite often. It may be no more than a stratagem."

Skip cursed and tore at the straps.

"Do you mean you can lock us . . . ?"

"No," Kyle said. "I can't. But the Director can, if in his judgment it is indicated."

He waited for Marilyn to speak, but she did not.

"You see, Marilyn, Skip, we tried very hard to prepare for every foreseeable eventuality, and mental illness was certainly one of those. About ten percent of the human population suffers from it at some point in their lives, and so with both of you on board and under a great deal of stress, that sort of problem was certainly something we had to be ready for."

Marilyn looked pale and drained. Kyle added, as gently as he could, "I hope this hasn't been too much of a shock to you."

Skip had opened the cutting blade of his utility knife and was hacking futilely at his straps. Kyle took it from him, closed it, and dropped it into one of his own storage areas.

Marilyn pushed off. He watched her as she flew gracefully across the hold, caught the pilot's-chair grab bar, and buckled herself into the seat; her eyes were shining with tears. As if sensing her distress, Polyaris perched on the bar and rubbed her ear with the side of her feathered head.

Skip muttered, "Go look at your demon, Kyle. Go anyplace but here."

Kyle asked, "Do you still think it's a demon, Skip?"

"You've seen it a lot closer up than I have. What do you think?"

"I don't believe in demons, Skip."

Skip looked calm now, but his fingers picked mechanically at his straps. "What do you believe in, Kyle? Do you believe in God? Do you worship man?"

"I believe in life. Life is my God, Skip, if you want to put it like that."

"Any life? What about the mosquito?"

"Yes, any life. The mosquito won't bite me." Kyle smiled his metal smile.

"Mosquitoes spread disease."

"Sometimes," Kyle admitted. "Then they must be destroyed, the lower life sacrificed to the higher. Skip, your Marilyn is especially sacred to me now. Do you understand that?"

"Marilyn's doomed."

"Why do you say that?"

"Because of the demon, of course. I tried to tell her that she had doomed herself, but it was actually you that doomed her. You were the one who wanted him. You had to have him, you and the Director; and if it hadn't been for you, we could have gone home with a hold full of dark matter and some excuse."

"But you aren't doomed, Skip? Only Marilyn?"

"I'm dead and damned, Kyle. My doom has caught up with me. I've hit bottom. You know that expression?"

Kyle nodded.

"People talk about hitting bottom and bouncing back up. If you can bounce, that isn't the bottom. When somebody gets where I am, there's no bouncing back, not ever."

"If you're really dead, Skip, how can the straps hold you? I wouldn't think that an acceleration harness could hold a lost soul, or even a ghost."

"They're not holding me," Skip told him. "It was just that at the last moment I didn't have guts enough to let Marilyn see I was really gone. I'd loved her. I don't anymore—you can't love anything or anyone except yourself where I am. But—"

"Can you get out of your seat, Skip? Is that what you're saying, that you can get out without unfastening the buckle?"

Skip nodded slowly, his dark eyes (inscrutable eyes, Kyle thought) never leaving Kyle's face. "And I can see your demon, Kyle. I know you can't see him because you're not hooked up. But I can."

"You can see him now, Skip?"

"Not now—he's on the far side of the black ball. But I'll be able to see him when he floats around to this side again."

Kyle returned to his seat and connected the cable as he had before. The black yolk sprang into being again; the shadow man was facing him—in fact glaring at him with burning yellow eyes. He asked the Director to release Skip.

Together they drifted toward the center of the *Egg*. Kyle made sure their trajectory carried them to the side of the yolk away from the shadow man, and when the shadow man was no longer in view, he held Skip's arm and stopped them both with a tug at the cable. "Now that I know you can see him too, Skip, I'd like you to point him out to me."

Skip glanced toward the watery miniature planet over which they hovered like flies—or perhaps merely toward the center of the hold. "Is this a joke? I've told you, I can see him." A joyous blue and yellow comet, Polyaris erupted from the midnight surface, braking on napping wings to examine them sidelong.

"That's why I need your input, Skip," Kyle said carefully. "I'm not certain the feed I'm getting is accurate. If you can apprehend shadow matter directly, I can use your information to check the simulation. Can you still see the demon? Indicate his position, please."

Skip hesitated. "He's not here, Kyle. He must be on the other side. Shall we go around and have a look?"

"The water's still swirling quite a bit. It should bring him to us before long."

Skip shrugged. "Okay, Kyle, you're the boss. I guess you always were."

"The Director's our captain, Skip. That's why we call him what we do. Can you see the demon yet?" A hand and part of one arm had floated into view around the curve of the yolk.

"No. Not yet. Do you have a soul, Kyle?"

Kyle nodded. "It's called my original monitor. I've seen a printout, though of course I didn't read it all; it was very long."

"Then when you're destroyed it may be sent here. Here comes your demon, by the way."

Kyle nodded.

"I suppose it may be put into one of these horrors. They seem more machine than human, at least to me."

"No," Kyle told him. "They're truly alive. They're shadow life, Skip, and since this one is the only example we have, just now it must be the most precious life in the universe to you, to Marilyn, and to me. Do you think he sees us?"

"He sees me," Skip said grimly.

"When I put my fingers into his brain, he opened his eyes," Kyle mused. "It was as though he felt them there."

"Maybe he did."

Kyle nodded. "Yes, possibly he did. The brain is such a sensitive mechanism that perhaps a gravitational disturbance as weak as that results in stimulation, if it is uneven. Put your hand into his head, please. I want to watch. You say he's a demon—pretend you're going to gouge out his eyes."

"You think I'm crazy!" Skip shouted. "Well, I'm telling you, you're crazy!"

Startled, Marilyn twisted in her pilot's chair to look at them.

"I've explained to you that he sees me," Skip said a little more calmly. "I'm not getting within his reach!"

"Touch his nose for me, Skip. Like this." Kyle lengthened one arm until his fingers seemed to brush the dark water several meters from the drifting shadow man's hideous face. "Look here, Skip. I'm not afraid."

Skip screamed.

.   .   .

"Have I time?" Kyle asked. He was holding the grab bar of Marilyn's control chair. In the forward port, the *Shadow Show* was distinctly visible.

"We've a few minutes yet," Marilyn told him. "And I want to know. I have to, Ky. He's the father of my child. Can you cure him?"

"I think so, Marilyn, though your correcting the simulator hues has probably helped Skip more than anything I've done thus far."

Kyle glanced appreciatively in the direction of the yolk. It was a translucent blue, as it should have been all along, and the shadow man who floated there looked more like a good-natured caricature of a human being than a demon. His skin was a dusty pinkish brown, his eyes the cheerful bright yellow of daffodils. It seemed to Kyle that they flickered for a moment as though to follow Polyaris in her flight across the hold. Perhaps a living entity of shadow matter could apprehend true matter after all—that would require a thorough investigation as soon as they were safely moored in the *Shadow Show*.

"And he can't really see shadow matter, Ky?"

Kyle shook his head. "No more than you or I can, Marilyn. He thought he could, you understand, at least on some level. On another he knew he couldn't and was faking it quite cleverly." Kyle paused, then added, "Freud did psychology a considerable disservice when he convinced people that the human mind thinks on only three levels. There are really a great many more than that, and there's no question but that the exact number varies between individuals."

"But for a while you really believed he might be able to, from what you've told me."

"At least I was willing to entertain the thought, Marilyn. Occasionally you can help people like Skip just by allowing them to test their delusional systems. What I found was that he had been taking cues from me—mostly from the direction of my eyes, no doubt. It would be wrong for you to think of that as lying. He honestly believed that when you human beings died your souls came here, to this shadow planet of a shadow system, in a shadow galaxy. And that he himself was dead."

Marilyn shook her head in dismay. "But that's insane, Ky. Just crazy."

She has never looked this lovely, Kyle thought. Aloud he said, "Mental illness is often a way of escaping responsibility, Marilyn. You may wish to consider that. Death is another, and you may wish to consider that also."

For a second Marilyn hesitated, biting her lip. "You love me, don't you, Ky?"

"Yes, I do, Marilyn. Very much."

"And so does Skip, Ky." She gave him a small, sad smile. "I suppose I'm the luckiest woman alive, or the unluckiest. The men I like most both love me, but one's having a breakdown. . . . I shouldn't have started this, should I?"

"While the other is largely inorganic," Kyle finished for her. "But it's really not such a terrible thing to be loved by someone like me, Marilyn. We—"

Polyaris shrieked and shrieked again—not her shrill cry of pleasure or even her outraged squawk of pain, but the uncanny, piercing screech that signaled a prowling ocelot: Danger! Fire! Flood! INVASION and CATASTROPHE!

She was fluttering about the shadow man, and the shadow man was no longer a dusty pinkish brown. As Kyle stared, he faded to gray, then to white. His mouth opened. He crumpled, slowly and convulsively, into a fetal ball.

Horrified, Kyle turned to Marilyn. But Marilyn was self-absorbed, her hands clasping her belly. "It moved, Ky! It just moved. *I felt life!*"

Vacuum States

GEOFFREY A. LANDIS

Geoffrey A. Landis (1955–) is a US scientist and Hugo Award–winning writer. As a scientist, he has worked for NASA, particularly on the Rover design for Mars missions. His first science fiction story was "Elemental" for *Analog* in 1984 and his work rapidly began to attract interest and attention. "Ripples in the Dirac Sea" (*Asimov's Science Fiction Magazine*, 1988), an engagingly human take on time travel and mathematics, won a Nebula Award. "A Walk in the Sun" (*Asimov's*, 1991), describing the aftermath of a crash on the moon, won a Hugo Award, and the ambitious, fascinating "Approaching Perimelasma" (*Asimov's*, 1998) examined unexpected consequences from the exploration of a black hole. Many of these stories were collected in *Impact Parameter and Other Quantum Realities* (2001), which showcased Landis's ability to infuse hard science ideas with emotion and human dilemmas.

Landis's first novel, *Mars Crossing* (2000), which won a Locus Award, was similarly committed to scientific verisimilitude, although with a more conventional thriller plot. Landis has also published science fiction poetry throughout his career and has twice won the Rhysling Award. A wide sampling of his work appears in *Time Frames: A Speculative Poetry Anthology* (1991), but *Iron Angels* (2009) is his first substantive collection.

"Vacuum States," a 1988 story published in *Asimov's Science Fiction Magazine*, poses a pointed set of questions about the risks of speculative physics research. As ever, it reveals an author fascinated by the detail of the universe and by the process of scientific discovery.

VACUUM STATES

Geoffrey A. Landis

> *. . . the vacuum state must contain many particles in a state of transient existence with violent fluctuations . . . The total energy of the vacuum is infinite. . . .*
> —P. A. M. DIRAC, *QUANTUM MECHANICS*

You open the door hesitantly, then walk into the laboratory where the two scientists wait for you. They seem to know you. Perhaps you are a science writer, well known for your ability to convey a sense of the excitement of even the most arcane scientific discoveries. Or perhaps you are merely a friend, someone who knows both of them from long ago. It doesn't matter.

The older scientist smiles as she sees you. She is a world-renowned physicist, and justly so, an iconoclast who laughingly destroyed the worldview of her predecessors and rebuilt the universe to match her own view of beauty. Some say that now, older, she has grown conservative, less open to speculation. Her hair is clipped short, just beginning to grey. Call her Celia. Whatever else she may be, she is a friend. Between you no titles or last names are needed.

And the younger scientist, barely out of grad school, with an infectious enthusiasm and boundless energy; the new iconoclast, the barbarian storming the walls of the citadel of knowledge, already being compared to the young Einstein or Dirac. Perhaps he is tall and lanky, with unruly black hair, wearing a grey sweatshirt emblazoned with a cartoon picture of Schrödinger's cat. Or maybe he wears a three-piece suit; such an incongruity would appeal to his sense of humor.

You were there when they first met. Perhaps you even introduced them, in the hopes of seeing sparks fly. If so, you were disappointed, since their conversation had quickly shifted to another language, a language of Hilbert spaces and contravariant derivatives. Perhaps the very language, you muse, of the Word spoken in the Beginning, before the world began.

But sparks indeed flew, could you but have seen. And one of them had caught fire.

"I came," you say, "as soon as I could."

The younger scientist—perhaps his name is David?—takes your hand and shakes it vigorously. "Yes, yes, yes, yes," he says, "I knew you would. I trust you are ready to see something, well . . ." He grins. "Earth shaking?"

"What do you know about guts?" says the older scientist.

"Yes," you say, speaking to the scientist whose name is perhaps David, and "GUTs? Grand Unification Theories? Just the barest bones," you say to the other.

"But you do know that the quantum vacuum is quite full of energy?" she asks, in her slightly British accent. "That, according to quantum mechanics, even empty space must have a large 'zero-point energy'?"

"Alive with virtual particles," he interjects, "bursting with the energies of creation; constantly afroth and aboil with the boundless, countless, infinite dance of creation and annihilation below the Heisenberg limit."

"Yes," you say, slowly. You've tried to understand quantum mechanics before. Somehow, though, the vital essence has always managed to elude you. "But it's not *real* energy, is it?"

"Indeed," she says, "most respectable"—

she pronounces the word as if it were somehow dirty—"physicists will tell you that zero-point energy is just a mathematical artifact, a figment of the formalism."

"So goes the conventional wisdom," he says. "But it's there, nevertheless."

"Maybe," she says dryly, "you should show the apparatus."

"Yes, of course. This way." He turns and walks with a bounce across the room, not even looking to see if you are behind him. You follow him into an adjoining room where a large, complicated piece of experimental apparatus fills most of the available space. "What do you think?"

You hate to admit it, but all physics experiments look alike to you. A shiny stainless-steel vacuum chamber, large storage tanks of liquid nitrogen and helium, racks of digital meters, an oscilloscope or two, with brightly colored wires strung all about and the ubiquitous computer sitting in front. "Very pretty," you say, hoping he won't notice your indifference. Experimenters all think that their apparatus is beautiful. "What is it?"

"A device to extract energy from the vacuum," she says.

"What?"

"An endless energy source," he says. "A rabbit that pulls itself out of a hat. A perpetual motion machine, if you will."

"Oh." You are impressed. "Does it work?"

The two scientists look at each other. David sighs. "We haven't tried it."

"Why not?"

"There is a question we disagree about, and we thought we'd ask your opinion," Celia says, slowly. For a moment you think this is funny; there is no way that you could hope to answer a question that they could not. Then it seems less funny, then not funny at all. So you hold your silence. "A philosophical question: if we take energy out of the vacuum, what do we have left?"

"Nothing!" he interjects, barely waiting for her to finish speaking. "That's the symmetry of the vacuum. Since the zero-point energy is infinite, no matter how much energy is extracted there is always an infinite amount left."

"So goes conventional wisdom," she replies softly. "But the infinity is a renormalized infinity, and the only thing of importance is differences in energy. If we remove energy, what is left must be a vacuum with lower energy.

"Therefore, if we can extract energy, the physical vacuum must be a false vacuum."

She makes this pronouncement seem portentous, as if it were the most important thing in the world. "True vacuum?" you say. "False vacuum?"

"Right," she says. "It's simple. A 'true vacuum' by definition is the lowest-energy state of empty space. If you put anything into it—remember, mass has energy!—the energy must increase, and it's no longer the true vacuum."

You plop yourself down onto a lab stool, a spidery metal thing with a round metal seat, slickly enamelled in nondescript light brown. Through your jeans you feel it cool against your buttocks. You swivel slightly, back and forth, like a compass needle uncertain of true north.

"The GUT theory postulates that when the universe was young there existed a vacuum that was just as empty of matter, but had higher energy. This 'false' vacuum decayed into our 'true' vacuum by a process we call spontaneous breaking of symmetry."

Her colleague leans back against a rack of equipment, smiling slightly. He seems willing to let her do the explaining. She glances at her watch. "We don't have a whole lot of time, so please pay careful attention.

"Here's an example. Consider a beaker of perfectly pure liquid water. The water has perfect symmetry, which means if you start from one water molecule, you have just as much likelihood of finding another water molecule in one direction as any other. Now, cool the water down. Cool it past the freezing point, and keep cooling it. If it's really pure water, it won't freeze. Instead, it supercools. That's because ice has lower symmetry than liquid water; all directions are *not* the same. Some directions are along the crystal axis, others aren't. Since pure water doesn't have any way to 'pick' a preferred direction to orient the crystals, it can't crystallize.

"Now drop in a tiny crystal of ice. One little seed of ice, no matter how tiny, and whamo! Suddenly the whole mass of water crystallizes, releasing energy in the process. Explosive crystallization, it's called.

"That's symmetry breaking.

"Now, symmetries exist in empty space as well, although a bit more abstract ones. According to GUTs, the big bang itself was caused by symmetry breaking. In the beginning, the universe was unthinkably small, and unimaginably hot, but empty. Everything was supersymmetric, all the four forces were the same, and all particles were alike. The universe cooled, and then supercooled. After a while the supersymmetric vacuum wasn't the true vacuum anymore, but a false vacuum, laden with potential energy. Nobody knows what triggered the crystallization, but suddenly it happened, and the universe flipped over into one of the lower-energy states.

"A lot of energy was released. Everything that is, was created from that explosive transition to a lower-energy vacuum."

"Oh," you say, since you can't think of anything else.

"Sometimes I dream of it," she says. "Perhaps before the big bang, there were intelligent creatures in the universe. What they were like we couldn't possibly imagine. Their world was hot, and dense, and tiny; their entire universe would have been smaller than the point of a pin, and they would have lived a trillion generations in the shortest time we can measure. Perhaps one of them realized that the vacuum they were living in was a false vacuum, and that they could create energy from nothing. Perhaps one of them tried it. One tiny seed, no matter how small . . ."

Your head is spinning, trying to imagine lit-

tle tiny scientists before the big bang. You picture them as something like ants, but smaller, and moving so fast that they're like blurs. And hot, don't forget hot. You give up trying to picture it, and go back to listening. She is saying something about cubic potentials, comparing the universe to a marble on top of a hill—if the marble is right exactly at the top, it doesn't know which way to roll.

"The question is," she continues, "if energy can be extracted from the vacuum, why doesn't it happen spontaneously, all by itself? The answer has to be, because some symmetry forbids it. But if that symmetry is broken . . .

"Since the big bang, the universe has cooled a lot. Perhaps *our* vacuum has cooled out of the lowest-energy state. If the symmetry is broken, all the energy of the vacuum would be released at once. It would be the end, not only of the Earth, but of the universe as we know it.

"And now David, here, wants to do exactly that."

"As it turns out, her worries are pointless," he says. "There are plenty of energetic objects in the universe that would trip such a transition. Quasars, black holes, Seyfert galaxies. If the universe were a false vacuum, it would have transitioned billions of years ago."

"Have you ever wondered about the Fermi paradox?" she asks. "How it is that we've never seen any signs of other intelligent life in the universe? I can tell you the answer. If any alien civilizations more advanced than ours existed, they would have already found the secret to extracting vacuum energy. Sooner or later, they'd try it, and, wham! The end of the universe. So the universe wouldn't exist, unless we're the first."

You notice that they are both waiting for you to say something. You scuffle your feet against the rough concrete floor. You've figured out why they called you here, and are desperately trying to think of what to say. "So you have cold feet? You want me to tell you whether you should do the experiment?"

"No," he tells you. "We already have started the experiment." He gestures at a digital read-out. "I turned it on when you first walked in the door. The field is building up now. When it hits ten thousand teslas, the generator is programmed to flip on automatically." You look at the LED indicator. Nine point four, it tells you, in a cheerful cherry-red glow.

"But," says the other.

"But?" you say. David takes your hand, and wraps it around the handle of a switch, a large old-fashioned knife switch, the kind that you privately think of as a "Frankenstein switch." You briefly pretend that you are the obsessed doctor, with life and death subjugated to your power. You've watched too many old monster movies. "This turns it off?"

"In a manner of speaking," he says.

"I doubt anybody else will reproduce what we found," she says. "This may sound like boasting, but it took a few pretty radical insights—and more than a bit of luck—and it's not at all the direction that other theoretical physicists are searching. Not the idea of getting energy from the vacuum—plenty of people could think of that. It's our way to do it that's the trick."

"I disagree. What one person discovers, no matter how esoteric, another will duplicate. Maybe not for a long time, maybe not in our lifetimes, but sooner or later, it will happen."

She smiles. "Again, it's a question of philosophy. I've been playing the game long enough to know that real science doesn't work the way the science books pretend. It's not like making a map, unless you think of it as creating the land as we map it. The very shape of science is created by the scientists who first make it. We think in their metaphors; we see what they chose to look at. If we let go of this discovery, it won't be duplicated in our lifetimes, and by then the flow of science will be elsewhere."

"In any case," he says, "there isn't enough money in the grant for us to do it again.

"The switch you're holding breaks the circuit in the superconducting magnets. There's about a thousand amps running through the coils now. Quench the magnet and the superconductors heat up, transition back into ordinary metal. In other words, they become resistors. All that current . . . it'll create a lot of heat. Throw that switch, and ten million dollars' worth of equipment melts into a puddle of slag."

"Not to worry too much, though," Celia adds cheerfully. "It's only grant money."

Suddenly your lips are dry. You run the tip of your tongue over them. "And you want *me* to . . ."

"We've agreed on this much," she says, exasperated. "If you stop the experiment, we'll abide by your decision. We won't publish. Nor even hint."

"But why me?" you ask. "Why not bring in an expert?"

"We *are* the experts," he says. "What we need is somebody from outside, somebody with an unbiased opinion."

"Don't be silly," she says, speaking to you. "We wanted somebody who *couldn't* understand the details. If we called in a bunch of experts, do you think they could possibly keep it secret, after?"

"And besides," he adds, "committees are always conservative. We all know what they'd say: wait, let's study it some more. Well, damn, we've *already* studied it. If she'd told me we need to have a committee discuss it, I'd have just snuck in one midnight and run it myself. No, we have to do it this way. Whatever you decide, that's it. No dithering. No second thoughts. We go for it right now, or forget it.

"If I'm right," he continues, "then the stars are ours. The *universe* is ours. Humanity will be immortal. When the sun burns out, we'll create our own suns. We will have all the energy of creation at our fingertips."

"And if he's wrong," she says, "then this is the end. Not just the end of us. The end of the universe."

"Except that I'm not wrong."

"If you are, we'll never know. Either way."

"Still, I'd risk it all. This is the key to the universe. It's worth the risk. It's worth any risk."

She looks back at you. "So there you have it."

He raises an eyebrow. "On the one hand, infinity. On the other, the end of everything."

He looks over at the digital readout, and your eye follows his. As you watch, it flicks from 9.8 to 9.9. The handle of the switch is warm, faintly slick with sweat. In your hand it seems to almost vibrate.

She looks at you. You look at him. He looks at the switch. You look at her. They both look at you.

"You'd best decide quickly," he says, softly.

Two Small Birds

HAN SONG

Translated by John Chu

Han Song (1965–) is a prominent Chinese writer of science fiction who has won the Yinhe Award multiple times. Han attended Wuhan University (1984–91), studying English and journalism, and eventually graduating with a master of law degree. He subsequently became an editor and contributor to the government-owned journal *Liaowang dongfang zhoukan* (*Oriental Outlook Weekly*), for which he often writes on cultural and social dynamics, and new developments in science. Some of these writings saw print as *Renzaoren* (*Artificial Humans*, 1997). His continued position as a respected member of a high-profile publication allows him to effectively shrug off the fact that many of his fictional works soon vanish from bookshelves. Embracing science fiction's subversive potential in a culture that once proclaimed itself to already be a futuristic utopia, Han's works often run afoul of the official censors but endure in online samizdat form or elsewhere in the Chinese diaspora or in Japanese translation.

Han Song's first notable success, the long story "Yuzhou mubei" ("Gravestone of the Universe"; *Huanxiang*, 1991) appeared in a Taiwanese magazine and was subsequently unavailable for a decade in the People's Republic. The story details the memorials and artifacts left behind by astronauts across the universe, and the unusual effects this has on those who come upon them. Similarly, his short story "Wo de zuguo bu zuomeng" ("My Fatherland Does Not Dream"; *Zhongguo kexue*, 2007), in which an authoritarian state drugs its citizens to both optimize labor and redact memories of atrocities, was swiftly banned.

Much of Han's work counterbalances his downbeat or decidedly pessimistic tone with a lyrical style. He prefers ambiguity, even in his description of grand schemes such as the one in "Hongse haiyang" ("Red Ocean," 2004), which sends genetically engineered humans under the sea to escape ecological disaster on land. His English translation of his own "Gezhanshi de zhuanjingtong" (*Kehuan shijie*, 2002) for *The Apex Book of World SF*, under the title "The Wheel of Samsara," seems to playfully accentuate the story's inspiration in Arthur C. Clarke's "The Nine Billion Names of God" (1953), including the Tibetan location and the tone of its apocalyptic ending.

A recurring theme in Han Song's work is the rise and possible supremacy of China in contention with the West, which Han often treats with an ambiguity of tone sure to confuse the authorities. *Ditie* (*Subway*, 2010), a collection of linked stories, explores the ruins and futurity of the Beijing metro system, held up since the 1970s as a triumph of modernity, but in Han's fiction reimagined as a Kafkaesque dystopia in which the Chinese pointlessly struggle to emulate the bustle and energy of Western capitalism.

He has repeated this mode in several other stories, such as "Chengke yu changzaozhe" (*Kehuan shijie*, 2006; published in English as "The Passengers and the Creator," *Renditions*, 2012), a surreal tale in which the entire population of China is forced to live out its existence in a fleet of midair jumbo jets. "Huoxing zhaoyao Meiguo: 2066-nian zhi xixing manji" ("Mars Shines on America: An Account of a Westward Journey in the Year 2066," first published in 2001 and published in more complete form in 2012) focuses on a balkanized and declining United States in a Sinocentric world, notoriously featuring a terrorist attack on the New York World Trade Center several months before reality imitated fiction.

"Two Small Birds"—translated here for the first time by the Hugo Award–winner John Chu—showcases Han's lyricism and the agility of his ideas, which often manifest in a surreal way. Although one of the shortest stories in this anthology, "Two Small Birds" contains multitudes.

TWO SMALL BIRDS

Han Song
Translated by John Chu

I take a colorful magazine down from the bookshelf. I open the magazine and the flock of birds in a photo suddenly flies past me with a crashing noise. Air rushes against my face.

I'm sitting in the library's reading room, absentmindedly leafing through a birding magazine. Practically no other readers are here except for two women. They sit at two ends, forming a triangle with me.

The early morning air pours in like a rising tide. I hear a few birds call outside. They are sparrows standing on high-voltage power lines.

Alarmed by something, the sparrows suddenly fly away.

A young librarian walks towards me. His eyes seem like the muzzle of a shotgun. His entire body gives off the stench of an owl near midnight.

For a moment, sunlight leaps through the window. On the tabletop, I catch a reflection of me sitting. It's that of a giant bird.

I drop the magazine and walk outside.

The young librarian throws an odd look at me, but the two women don't move at all. They don't even spare me a glance. They study with a single-minded devotion the books in their hands.

It's a deep, dark night outside. After a hundred thousand years, I know it well. Starlight diffuses here and there across the sky.

I concentrate like usual and become a slice of dark hovering in the air.

My silhouette is cast against the sparsely lit city. It's definitely that of a bird of prey.

The city, growing smaller and smaller, is tossed behind me. Agitated, I screech. A burning, blazing star gradually grows clearer in my mind.

My silhouette falls on the background of a resplendent, multicolored universe.

It's the background of the magazine that I opened. I firmly believe no humans can understand it.

Every word and punctuation mark corresponds to nebulas, gravitation, and trace elements. Paragraphs then form laws of mathematics and physics.

Every day Ozma traverses the magazine in the library, she transmits to me secrets of the universe. When I'm near her, I am not lost.

The opened universe flaps its pages behind my body. My wings are agitated by magnetic fields. They gradually spread into a sail.

I'm about to look back on that point in space-time fifty thousand years ago, tirelessly cranking the mechanism that will save Ozma.

"Ozma, are you okay? It's me."

I land lightly on an unpopulated wasteland as I imagine what it will be like here fifty thousand years from now. This place will be called Peru.

My image, because energy is focused and thrown across the ground, seems like a totem of the humans of this time. It can't be wiped away.

Later humans will be puzzled by this. They'll think it's a sign that an alien spaceship has landed here.

I recover my ability to touch consciousnesses. I sense Ozma, no thought of returning home, nearby panting in pain. Ozma, as a physical presence, no longer exists.

"Ozma, I've been working at this for one hundred thousand years. Perhaps you still want to wait for up to another two thousand. You know there are still several strings whose positions I have no way to determine. They have to be reorganized before you can enter time and space freely."

All of this, Ozma understands perfectly. To rescue her from her prison, there's only one step left. As a result, she's utterly cooperative.

Every day, we make progress.

But, today, something's bothering her. Usually, a disturbed and distracted Ozma calms down obediently once she smells my breath. But, today, she's restless instead.

What troubles her emerges from the Large Magellanic Cloud, which passed through her head. The galaxy expands rapidly as though it were foam. It flickers between yellow and green, like a ghost in the sky.

"Ozma, what's wrong? You have to help me in this."

Suddenly, the eyes of the librarian from fifty thousand years into the future appear in the cloud. A dreadful fear fills me.

But they disappear in an instant.

I decide we won't have our usual pleasant chat. I decide to forget for now the dangerous and terrifying image that was in the sky. I link my field to that of the universe. They connect to Ozma's mental world—but not through the magazine. The gathering of forces, bit by bit, breaks down the prison walls that prevent her from leaving.

Even so, tonight, we don't really make any headway.

"Ozma, join me." Only I can hear my voice.

The Magellanic Cloud expands again, like a magazine being ripped to shreds. Every string of space-time unfolds out of the cloud. I see on them things that should not be.

Two birds in the wind peck at their food. Their appearance throws the timeline into disarray. I can't continue my work.

A voice penetrates me: Let me go.

It booms like thunder and lightning. I'm slain. I mumble: "Ozma, it's been fifty thousand years. I'm not wrong to wait for you. I won't abandon you. Wait for me. I'll be back."

The two birds have disappeared. The galaxy makes a noise like a flock of birds dispersing. The day arrives, spreading its wings.

The cover of a new issue of the magazine is a North American condor. Its bearing is powerful, as though it were an overlord of the universe.

I vacillate over whether to open the magazine.

Last night, my promise to Ozma surfaced in my heart. Even so, I can't drive away the silhouettes of the two birds.

The overcast day outside the window falls on the library's main reading room. Once again, the table doesn't have my reflection. Those two women aren't here today. Besides me, there is just the librarian. He is using a feather duster to slap the dust off a row of bookshelves.

He walks to the back of the art section and I take that moment to open the magazine. The first article is called "A Discussion of the Bird's Place in the Ecosystem." To my surprise, I don't find the secret code that I know so well between the lines. Ozma has failed to send any information.

Winter is coming and birds are migrating south. The article says this. As I read, sweat drips off me. I don't close the magazine before I stand and leave.

The librarian blocks my way.

"Why are you leaving so early today?"

"I'm feeling a little under the weather."

"A little under the weather? Be careful. It's winter. Don't catch a cold."

I shiver. I brush past him, wanting to go outside.

"Wait."

I stop. "What?"

"I'm sorry, but you violated the reading regulations."

"What are you talking about?"

"I've noticed that every day, you read the same magazine."

"And this violates the reading regulations?"

He shows me the magazine. I've underlined key words and paragraphs in red.

"I'm sorry. I'll pay whatever fine," I say fearfully.

"I'm afraid you can't afford the fine. Why did you underline these words?"

"I'm with the Biology Department at B University. My area of research is bird breeding and migration. The article I'm working on has everything to do with this."

"However, does it also have something to do with the control of time and space?"

"What did you say?" My leg starts to shake.

I know he's a hunter but how did he find my hiding place so quickly?

Against these people, resistance is useless.

"You're free to do whatever you want," I say.

"You have to stop helping Ozma immediately. You're changing the common established timelines of many people. These timelines have existed for a long time now. They're like these books, written in black ink on white paper."

"I said you're free to do whatever you want but it's really a pity. Ozma is no ordinary spaceship. She's sentient. Because of that, you've grounded her."

"I don't understand what you're saying. Why don't you take a walk with me?"

On the return trip, I give the hunter a hint. As a matter of fact, last night, I gave up on the rescue I've worked on continuously for the past hundred thousand years. There's no point to capturing me today. I explain those two birds pecking at food in the wind from nowhere to him.

I doubt they represent another mystical force.

The hunter listens silently.

After a moment, I hear him thinking to himself. "If only they weren't those two women."

"What did you say?" I'm also sending thoughts via brain waves.

He doesn't respond again. The light in his heart darkens.

He's probably singled out the two gloomy female readers in the main reading room. But I don't think they're anyone special.

The thin air makes the starlight sorrowful. All the free will in the universe now returns to its nest. I have a hunch that this is a good time to escape.

After one hundred thousand years, I have a lot of experience in hiding.

The hunter is distracted. I guess, because of what I said, his attention has shifted to the two birds overhead. I sneak away, withdraw from this game of chase and taboo.

Once again, I see my bird-of-prey body transcend time and space. The pursuer searches despairingly at the other end of the wormhole. He didn't anticipate that I'd escape.

Nebulas and dust cleanse my mind and body.

I discover that my claws grasp the magazine that was exhibited in the library on Earth.

I let it fall. It quickly dissolves into elementary particles. Let it follow the librarian.

The textbook that contains the secrets of the natural world and the legislators of a civilized society take the same shape. But what do those two small birds symbolize?

As the Earth folk say, twenty thousand years pass in the blink of an eye.

Ultimately, I break my promise. I never return to Ozma's universe because I begin to doubt whether altering the entire course of evolution is worth it for a sentient spaceship.

I don't think through to the result because, afterwards, I have a new goal. . . .

I see with my own eyes the death of the hunter and the deaths of heavenly bodies.

A newly born galaxy produces a new generation of hunters and prey as well as the rest of the strange things that go along with them. I have no interest in any of that.

In this universe, my credentials are too obsolete.

Ultimately, even the newly born will disappear. The heat death will arrive.

I fling my silhouette into a turbulent burst of light. Revolving, it merges into the subsequent era.

The early days of a newly created universe are so calm. It will be many years before life emerges. I feel incredibly lonely. This is the price of continuing to exist.

But, not long after, I find, by chance, bird footprints at a newly formed planet. I'm certain that I didn't leave them.

They are the footprints of the two small birds, slender and clever, walking by. The planet's infant ocean is still rising. If I'd arrived a little later, any footprints would have been washed away by the tide.

I'm shocked to smell the flavor of olden days.

At the same time, I have an ominous premonition. It's possible that I'm not the master of this new age. The real masters are the two birds, who keep an even lower profile than a bird of prey.

Burning Sky

RACHEL POLLACK

Rachel Pollack (1945–) is an award-winning US writer born in Brooklyn who lived abroad for almost two decades, most of that time in Amsterdam. Her fiction is often pointedly feminist or ecological in outlook and influenced by the tarot. Pollack published her first science fiction story, "Pandora's Bust," in *New Worlds Quarterly* 2 (1971), edited by Michael Moorcock, but her interests have, over time, taken her further and further from clearly identifiable genre fiction.

Pollack's most famous work is the Arthur C. Clarke Award–winning *Unquenchable Fire* (1988). Set in an alternate America in which shamanism is as credible a means of understanding the world as science, *Unquenchable Fire*'s "bureaucracy of shamans" seeks out energy from deep within the Earth. Pollack's protagonist is a miraculously pregnant woman with a rich backstory, told through flashbacks, who characteristically refuses her role as the mother of a new, possible prodigal shaman. A sequel, *Temporary Agency* (1994), continues the story. Throughout, Pollack's portrait of a radically different but alarmingly similar United States is meticulously drawn, and her depiction of life in an alternate Poughkeepsie, New York, is frequently hilarious. Several stories—like "The Protector" (*Interzone*, 1986)—depict similarly transformed universes. From issue 64 to its demise at the end of 1994 with issue 87, Pollack also wrote *Doom Patrol* for DC Comics.

Her collection *Burning Sky* (1998), with an introduction by Samuel R. Delany, examines a variety of gender and women's issues through a series of surreal short stories and folklore-influenced tales. As Delany writes, Pollack's short fiction occurs "in a universe of wonders, where Free Women revenge sexist wrongs and a ten-kilometer-tall tree grows from the head of a comet . . . Pollack's theme is the pursuit of ecstasy. Her characters approach that state from every conceivable direction." Delany also identifies Pollack as in many ways an intellectual mystic, her writings in the service of a vision. This is a useful way to think of Pollack's work, which is not turned in toward core genre but outward toward the universe.

In keeping with this stance, it's unsurprising that Pollack has had a long professional interest in the tarot and that this has generated several nonfiction presentations of its underlying philosophy (and various packs) as well as an anthology of original stories, *Tarot Tales* (1989), edited with Caitlín Matthews, in which each contributor used the French Oulipo school of literary constraint to extract story ideas from a tarot pack. She has also written a series of fantasy tales assembled as *The Tarot of Perfection: A Book of Tarot Tales* (2008).

"Burning Sky," reprinted here, is an incendiary and visionary classic of feminist science fiction from 1989, originally published in the infamous *Semiotext(e)* anthology, whose contributors included William S. Burroughs.

BURNING SKY

Rachel Pollack

Sometimes I think of my clitoris as a magnet, pulling me along to uncover new deposits of ore in the fantasy mines. Or maybe a compass, like the kind kids used to get in Woolworth's, with a blue-black needle in a plastic case, and flowery letters marking the directions.

Two years ago, more by accident than design, I left the City of Civilized Sex. I still remember its grand traditions: orgasms in the service of loving relationships, healthy recreation with knowledgeable partners, a pinch of perversion to bring out the flavor. I remember them with a curious nostalgia. I think of them as I march through the wilderness, with only my compass to guide me.

Julia. Tall, with fingers that snake round the knobs and levers of her camera. Julia's skin is creamy, her neck is long and smooth, her eyebrows arch almost to a point. There was once a woman who drowned at sea, dreaming of Julia's eyes. Sometimes her hair is short and spiky, sometimes long and straight, streaming out to one side in the wind off Second Avenue. Sometimes her hair is red, with thick curls. Once a month she goes to a woman who dyes her eyelashes black. They darken further with each treatment.

Julia's camera is covered in black rubber. The shutter is a soft rubber button.

The Free Women. Bands of women who roam the world's cities at night, protecting women from rapists, social security investigators, police, and other forms of men. Suits of supple blue plastic cover their bodies from head to toe. Only the faces remain bare. Free Skin,

they call it. The thin plastic coats the body like dark glistening nail polish.

Julia discovers the Free Women late one summer night. She has broken up with a lover and can't sleep, so she goes out walking, wearing jeans and a white silk shirt and high red boots, and carrying her camera over one shoulder. On a wide street, by a locked park, with a drunk curled asleep before the gate, a man with a scarred face has cornered a girl, about fourteen. He flicks his knife at her, back and forth, like a lizard tongue. Suddenly they are there, yanking him away from the girl, surrounding him, crouched down with moon and streetlights running like water over their blue muscles. The man jerks forward. Spread fingers slide sideways. The attacker drops his knife to put his hand over his throat. Blood runs through the fingers. He falls against the gate. The women walk away. Julia follows.

Julia discovers the Free Women one night on the way home from an assignment. Tired as she is, she walks rather than take a taxi home to an empty apartment. She has just broken up with a lover, the third in less than two years. Julia doesn't understand what happens in these relationships. She begins them with such hopes, and then a month, two months, and she's lost interest, faking excitement when her girlfriend plans for the future. Recklessly, Julia walks down the West Side, a woman alone with an expensive camera. She sees them across the street, three women walking shoulder to shoulder, their blue boots (she thinks) gliding in step, their blue gloves (she thinks) swinging in rhythm, their blue hoods (she thinks) washed in light. Julia takes the cap off her lens and follows them, conscious of the jerkiness in her stride, the hardness in her hips.

She follows them to a grimy factory building on West Twenty-First Street. As they press buttons on an electronic light Julia memorizes the combination. For hours she waits, in a doorway smelling of piss, thinking now and then that the women are watching her, that they have arranged for her to stand there in that filth, a punishment for following them. Finally they leave and Julia lets herself inside. She discovers a single huge room, with lacquered posts hanging with manacles, racks of black-handled daggers along the walls, and in the middle of the floor a mosaic maze, coils of deep blue, with the center, the prize, a four-pronged spiral made of pure gold. On the wall opposite the knives hang rows of blue suits, so thin they flutter slightly in the breeze from the closing door.

Over the next weeks Julia rushes through her assignments to get back to the hall of the Free Women. She spends days crouched across the street, waiting for the thirty seconds when she can photograph them entering or leaving. She spends more and more time inside, taking the suits in her hands, walking the maze. In the center she hears a loud fluttering of wings.

She tells herself she will write an exposé, an article for the Sunday *Times*. But she puts off calling the paper or her agent. She puts off writing any notes. Instead she enlarges her photos to more than life-size, covering the walls of her apartment, until she can almost imagine the women are there with her, or that the maze fills the floor of her kitchen.

And then one day Julia comes home—she's gone out for food, she's forgotten to keep any food in the house—and she finds the photos slashed, the negatives ruined, and all the lenses gone from her cameras.

Julia runs. She leaves her clothes, her cameras, her portfolios. She takes whatever cash lies in the house and heads into the street. Downtown she takes a room above a condemned bank and blacks out all the windows.

. . . .

Let me tell you how I came to leave the City of Civilized Sex. It happened at the shore. Not the ocean, but the other side of Long Island, the sound connecting New York and Connecticut. I'd gone there with my girlfriend Louise, who at nineteen had seduced more women than I had ever known.

Louise and I had gotten together a few months after my husband Ralph had left me. On our last day as a couple Ralph informed me how lucky I was not to have birthed any children. The judge, he said, would certainly have awarded them to him. He went on to explain that it was no coincidence, our lack of children, since any heroic sperm that attempted to mount an expedition in search of my hidden eggs (*Raiders of the Lost Ovum*) would have frozen in "that refrigerator cunt of yours." Ralph liked to mix metaphors. When he got angry his speech reminded me of elaborate cocktails, like Singapore Slings.

I can't really blame Ralph. Not only did I never learn to fake orgasms properly (I would start thrusting and moaning and then think of something and forget the gasps and shrieks) but even in fights I tended to get distracted when I should have wept or screamed or thrown things.

Like the day Ralph left. I'm sure I should have cried or stared numbly at the wall. Instead I made myself a tuna sandwich and thought of sperms in fur coats, shivering on tiny wooden rafts as they tried to maneuver round the icebergs that blocked their way to the frozen eggs. I don't blame Ralph for leaving.

Anyway, he went, and I met Louise window-shopping in a pet store. That same night we went to bed and I expected to discover that my sexual indifference had indicated a need for female flesh. Nothing happened. Louise cast her best spells, she swirled her magician's cloak in more and more elaborate passes, but the rabbit stayed hidden in the hat.

I became depressed, and Louise, exhausted,

assured me that in all her varied experiences (she began to recite the range of ages and nationalities of women she'd converted) she'd never failed to find the proper button. It would just take time. I didn't tell her Ralph had said much the same thing. I wondered if I'd have to move to my parents' house upstate to avoid safaris searching for my orgasms like Tarzan on his way to the elephants' graveyard.

Julia runs out of money. She disguises herself in clothes bought from a uniform store on Canal Street and goes uptown to an editor who owes her a check. As she leaves the building she sees, across the street, in the doorway of a church, a black raincoat over blue skin. Julia jumps in a taxi. She goes to Penn Station, turning around constantly in her taxi to make sure no blue-hooded women sit in the cars behind her. At the station she runs down the stairs, pushing past commuters to the Long Island Rail Road, where she searches the computer screens for the train to East Hampton.

On track twenty she hears a fluttering of wings and she smells the sea, and for a moment she thinks she's already arrived. And then she sees a trench coat lying on the floor. Another is falling beside her. A flash of light bounces off the train, as if the sun has found a crack through Penn Station and the roof of the tunnel. She tries running for the doors. Blue hands grab her wrists. Blueness covers her face.

No. No, it happens along Sixth Avenue. Sixth Avenue at lunchtime, among the pushcarts selling souvlaki and sushi, egg rolls and yoghurt, tofu and pretzels. Julia's pants are torn, the wind dries the sweat on her chest, she's been running for hours, her toes are bleeding, no cabs will stop for her. She turns a corner and tumbles into a class of twelve-year-old girls. The girls are eating hot dogs and drinking Pepsi Cola. They wear uniforms, pleated skirts and lace-up shoes, brown jackets and narrow

ties. The girls surround Julia. They push her down when she tries to stand up. Somewhere up the street a radio plays a woman singing, "Are you lonesome tonight?" The girls tear off Julia's clothes. They pinch and slap her face, her breasts. Grease streaks her thighs. The girls are whistling, yelping, stamping their feet. Now come the wings, the smell of the sea. The girls step back, their uniforms crisp, their ties straight. They part like drapes opening to the morning. A woman in blue steps into the circle, bright shining as the sun. Spread fingertips slide down Julia's body, from the mouth down the neck and along the breasts, the belly, the thighs. Wherever the woman touches, the welts disappear. She lifts Julia in her arms. Slowly she walks down the street, while the crowd moves aside and the whole city falls silent, even the horns. Julia hears the cry of gulls searching for food.

Over the weeks Louise changed from bluff to hearty to understanding to peevish as her first failure became more and more imminent. She suggested I see a doctor. I told her I'd been and she got me to admit the doctor had been a man. She lugged me to a woman's clinic where the whole staff consisted of former lovers of hers. While Louise went in to consult the healer on duty I sat in the waiting room.

I got into conversation with a tall skinny woman wearing a buckskin jacket, a gold shirt, and motorcycle boots. She showed me the French bayonet she carried in a sheath in her hip pocket, explaining it would "gut the next prick" that laid a hand on her or one of her sisters. I asked her if she'd undergone any training in knifeware. Not necessary, she told me. Pricks train. The Goddess would direct her aim. The Goddess, she said, lived in the right side of the brain. That's why the government (99 percent pricks) wanted to burn left-handed women.

"Janie's a little strong-minded," Louise told me as she led me down a corridor to see Dr. Catherine. The corridor's yellow striped wallpaper had started to peel in several places, revealing a layer of newspaper underneath.

"Did you sleep with her?" I asked.

"Only a couple of times. Did she show you her bayonet?" I nodded. "She kept it under the pillow in case the police broke in to arrest us for Goddessworship. That's what she calls women screwing."

I didn't listen very closely to Catherine, who didn't like the name *doctor*. I wanted to think about pricks training for their life's work. They probably do it in gym class, I decided. While the girls try backward somersaults and leap sideways over wooden horses the boys practise erections, and later, in advanced classes, learn to charge rubber simulations of female genitals. At the end of each lesson the instructor reminds them not to speak of this in front of their girlfriends.

Catherine didn't find my G spot or raise my *Mary Rose*. (I strongly identified with Henry VIII's sunken flagship and all its chests of gold. I cried when they raised it, all crusted in barnacles and brine. That left only one of us hidden in the murk.) She did give me some crushed herbs for tea and a bag of tree bark to chew on while I lay in the bathtub. Louise raged at me whenever I neglected my treatment. "You can't let yourself get negative," she shouted. "You've got to believe."

In the ritual hall Julia spends days hanging from copper, then brass, then silver manacles. Six, no, nine of the women weave in and out of sight, sometimes whispering to each other, sometimes laughing, sometimes standing before Julia and silently mouthing words in a foreign language. Across from her the blue suits rustle against each other.

Julia learns to catch bits of food thrown at her from across the room. Twice, no, three times a day one of the women brings her water in a stone bowl. A gold snake coils at the bottom. Sometimes the woman holds the bowl in front of her, and Julia has to bow her head and lap

up as much as she can. Or the woman moves the bowl away just as Julia begins to drink. Or throws the water in her face. At other times she gently tilts the bowl for Julia. Once, as Julia drinks, she discovers that a live snake has replaced the metal one. The head rises above the water and Julia's own head snaps back so hard she would have banged it against the wall if a blue hand wasn't there to cushion her.

They shave her head. No, they comb and perfume her hair. They rub her with oils and smooth the lines in her face and neck, slapping her only when she tries to bite or lick the cool fingertips sliding down her face.

Once or several times a day they take her down from the wall and force her to run the maze. The women surround the tiled circle, hitting the floor with sticks and trilling louder and louder until Julia misses a step or even falls, just outside the gold spiral. When she's failed they yank her out of the maze and hold her arms out like wings as they press the tips of her breasts into champagne glasses filled with tiny sharp emeralds.

On the day Julia completes the maze the women dress her in shapeless black overalls and heavy boots. They smuggle her out of the country to an island where a house of white stone stands on top of a hill covered in pine trees. The women strip Julia. With their sticks they drive her up a rock path. The door opens and a cool wind flows from the darkness.

A woman steps out. Instead of blue her suit gleams a deep red. It covers the whole body, including the face, except for the eyes, the nostrils, the mouth. Her muscles move like a river running over stone. Her name is Burning Sky, and she was born in Crete six thousand years ago. When she walks the air flows behind her like the sundered halves of a very thin veil.

One night, after a fight, Louise kicked the wall and ran from the house. The next morning, the doorbell woke me at six o'clock. Frightened, I looked out the window before I would open the door. There stood Louise in a rough zipper jacket and black turtleneck sweater. She saw me and waved a pair of rubber boots. Afraid she planned to kick me, I didn't want to let her in but I couldn't think of how to disconnect the doorbell. She'd begun to shout, too. "For heaven's sake, Maggie, open the fucking door." Any moment the police would show up.

While I buttered toast and boiled water Louise announced our plans for the morning. We were going fishing. "Dress warm," she said, and gave me the spare boots she'd brought for me. I had to wear two pairs of socks, and my feet still slid around.

In her pickup truck I tried to sleep, despite Louise's cheerful whistle. But when we got all our gear and bodies in a rowboat out in the sound, it turned out that Louise didn't plan to fish at all. "Now, goddammit," she said, "you can't whine and get away from me. I'm not taking this boat back to shore until you come and I can feel it all over my fingers."

"What?" I said, ruining her powerful speech. Her meaning became clearer as she began to crawl towards me. She scared me but she made me want to laugh too. It reminded me of the time Ralph had locked us in a motel room with a bottle of wine, a bag of marijuana, and a pink nightgown. At least motel rooms are comfortable. Maybe Louise considered rowboats romantic.

I decided I better hold my face straight. "You rapist prick!" I shouted, and tried to grab an oar to threaten her but couldn't work it loose from the lock. I snatched the fish knife and held it with both hands in front of my belly. "Keep away from me," I warned.

"Put that down," Louise said. "You'll hurt yourself."

"I'll hurt you, you prick."

"Don't call me that. You don't know how to use that."

"The Goddess will show me."

Apparently this all became too much for her. "Shit," she said, and turned around to grasp the oars for the pull to shore. I sat slumped over and shivering. My hands clenched around the knife.

In a ceremonial hall hung with purple silk and gold shields the women tattoo a four-pronged spiral in the hollow of Julia's neck. They present her with a blue suit. With four others she returns to New York on a cruise ship secretly owned by the Free Women. They wear disguises, like the Phantom, when he would venture out as Mister Walker, wrapped in a trench coat and slouch hat, to rescue his beloved Diana from Nazi kidnappers.

Despite the women's clever tricks someone on the boat recognizes them. A television anchorwoman, or maybe a right-wing politician. This woman once served Burning Sky, but disobeyed her leader on some assignment. Now she comes to their suite of cabins and begs the Free Women to readmit her. They play with her, attaching small intricately carved stone clips all over her skin. She suffers silently, only to have them announce she has forgotten how to break through the wall. They can do nothing for her. She goes away, later becomes prime minister.

When we got back to the rental dock Louise began to lug the boat onto the wooden platform. "If you want to go home," she said, "give me a hand." I took hold of the rope to tie it to the iron post that would hold it fast when the hurricane came.

At that moment a woman came out of the water. Dressed in a black wet suit with long shiny flippers and a dark mask that completely hid her face, she stood for a moment rotating her shoulders and tilting her head up to the sun. Her speargun pointed at the ground.

My heart began throwing blood wildly around my body: my vagina contracted like someone running for her life. "Will you come on?" Louise said.

I stammered something at her. Louise had never heard me stammer before. "What the hell is the matter with you?" she said. Then her eyes followed the invisible cable connecting me and my beautiful skin diver. She looked back and forth between us a couple of times while a wolf-grin took over her face. "Sonofabitch," she said, and laughed. "Why didn't you tell me?"

"I didn't know," I said, and Louise got to see another first. I blushed.

It was certainly a day for firsts. That evening, in the sloppy cavernous apartment Louise had inherited from her grandfather, she took out her collection of "toys": whips, handcuffs, masks, chains, nipple clips, leather capes, rubber gloves, and one whalebone corset, c. 1835. No wet suits, but it didn't really matter. I hope none of Ralph's sperm remained camped inside me anymore. The spring thaw came that night, and the flood would have washed the courageous little creatures away forever.

The Free Women order Julia to go alone to her apartment and renew her professional contacts. At first she finds it hard to function without her instructors. She hates going out "naked," as she thinks of her ordinary clothes. With no one to command her she forgets to eat and one day passes out while photographing a police parade in the South Bronx.

Gradually the dream fades. Julia stops dressing up in her Free Skin at night, she goes on holiday with a woman reporter who asks about the tattoo on Julia's neck. Julia tells her she got it to infiltrate a group of terrorists. When the woman falls asleep Julia cries in the shower and thanks the Virgin Mary for her deliverance. She wonders how she ever could have submitted to such strange and wretched slavery.

An order comes. Something simple, maybe embarrassing a judge who suspended the sentence of a man who raped his five-year-old daughter. Something with a clear moral imperative.

Julia takes off from work to decide what to do. In a cabin in the woods she tries on her Free Skin and lies in bed, remembering Burning Sky's face, and the way her fingers looked extended into the air. She remembers lying with the other women in a huge bed, how they slid in and out of each other, while their bodies melted inside their blue suits. She remembers hanging from silver manacles, remembers dancing to the heart of the labyrinth.

Julia returns to the city and locks the blue suit in a metal cabinet. The day of her assignment passes. She falls into a fever, attended by her reporter friend. When she recovers and the woman has left, Julia opens the cabinet. Her Free Skin has vanished. In its place lies a Chinese woman's dagger, five hundred years old, with an ivory handle bearing the same spiral sign that marks Julia's neck. Terrified, she waits for retribution. Weeks pass.

And so I left the City of Civilized Sex in one great rush on the back of a skin diver. Now that she'd preserved her record Louise lost interest very quickly, but at least she gave me some leads to "your kind of trick," as she delicately put it. I didn't know whether she meant the lovers or the activities.

I discovered not only a large reservoir of women devoted to far-fetched sexual practices, but several organizations, complete with buttons, slogans, jackets, and conflicting manifestoes. After a while they all began to strike me as rather odd, not just for their missionary zeal, but for their hunger for community. Had I left the City only to emigrate to another nation-state?

It wasn't so much the social as the sexual conformity that disturbed me. Everyone seemed to agree ahead of time on what would excite them. I began to wonder if all those people in the Land of Leather really liked the same sort of collar (black with silver studs) or if each new arrival, thrilled at finding a town where she'd expected only a swamp, confused gratitude with eroticism, and gave up her dreams of finding leather clothes and objects of exactly the right color, cut, and texture.

As my imagination began to show me its tastes I became more and more specific with the women who tried to satisfy me. That first night with Louise she could have tied me up with a piece of filthy clothesline and I wouldn't have complained. A few months later I was demanding the right ropes (green and gold curtain pulls with the tassel removed) tied only in particular knots taken from the *Boy Scout Handbook*.

And even that phase didn't last. For, in fact, it's not actions that I'm hunting. No matter how well you do them they can only approximate reality. City dwellers believe that fantasies exist to intensify arousal. Out here in the Territories the exiles should know better. I want to stand on a tree stump and yell through the forest, "Stop trying to build new settlements. Stop trying to clear the trees and put up walls and lay down sewers." I want them to understand. Sex exists to lay traps for fantasies.

Julia's life becomes as pale and blank as cheap paper. She goes to bars and picks up women. They all go away angry when they get back to Julia's apartment and Julia just sits on the bed, or else goes to the darkroom and doesn't come out. Julia returns to the ritual hall. She finds it replaced by a button factory.

She drives out to the beach on a hard sunny day in December. Ignoring the cold wind she strips naked and walks toward the water, both hands gripping the Chinese dagger. She raises it to the sun to watch the light glint off the blade. But then she notices flashes beyond the knife. Small spots on the horizon. As she watches, they grow larger, become blue sails, then a row of boats coming out of the deep. Each one contains a single woman. The sails rise out of their shoulders like wings. They call to each other like birds, their voices piercing the wind. When they land they detach their skins from the boat masts and the plastic snaps back against their bodies.

Julia falls down in the wet sand. A wild roaring in the Earth drowns out the sea as the six women lift her to her feet (six is the number of love, with Julia they become seven, the number of victory). They wash the mud and loneliness from her and dress her in the Free Skin she abandoned for an illusion of freedom.

The only true happiness lies in obedience to loving authority.
CHARLES MOULTON, SPEAKING AS QUEEN HIPPOLYTE OF PARADISE ISLAND
TO HER DAUGHTER, PRINCESS DI, *WONDER WOMAN COMICS*, C. 1950

Before I Wake

KIM STANLEY ROBINSON

Kim Stanley Robinson (1952–) is an award-winning US writer of science fiction whose novels have become incredibly influential outside of the genre world. Robinson has become known to the general public through frequent mentions by climate-change scientists and references both in pop culture and in magazines such as the *Economist*—whose 2015 special on global warming led off with a summary of Robinson's novel *2312* (2012). He, along with Karen Joy Fowler, is perhaps the most successful of the so-called Humanist science fiction writers.

Robinson became widely recognized with the publication of his first novel, *The Wild Shore* (1984), released as one of Terry Carr's Ace Specials. It won the Locus Award and initiated the *Three Californias* sequence, set in three versions of Orange County on the Pacific coast just south of Los Angeles. Robinson is also highly regarded for his *Mars Trilogy*, starting with *Red Mars* (1992) and proceeding through *Green Mars* (1993) and *Blue Mars* (1996). All the books in the *Mars Trilogy* won the Hugo Award, and *Blue Mars* also won the Locus Award. The overall narrative unpacks in detail a future history during the course of which the human settlers of Mars gain political independence from Earth (Robinson, optimistic about reader tendencies, provides a full constitution in the text) while engaging in a debate over the ethics and practicalities involved in terraforming the planet. With suitable cognitive caution, the cast (and the sequence) comes down on the side of planetary transformation.

Though it might be possible to call him a hard science fiction Humanist, what in fact most characterizes the growing reach and power of his work is its cogent analysis and its disposal of such categorical thinking. In some form or another, Robinson's career has consistently adhered to an overriding cognitive imperative: the argument that humanity will not thrive unless technology can be used in ways sympathetic to the Earth's ecology, an argument intimately married to a conviction that the alternative to making the world better is allowing it to become fatally worse.

Robinson's "Before I Wake" (1989) is not necessarily typical of his longer work, but at the short-fiction length he roves more widely. It's a powerful Humanist tale about the nature of reality based in part on a dream journal Robinson kept between 1975 and 1980. Of course, the dream source is nicely balanced by Robinson's natural tendency toward the rational.

BEFORE I WAKE

Kim Stanley Robinson

In his dream Abernathy stood on a steep rock ridge. A talus slope dropped from the ridge to a glacial basin containing a small lake. The lake was cobalt in the middle, aquamarine around the edges. Here and there in the rock expanse patches of meadow grass gleamed, like the lawns of marmot estates. There were no trees. The cold air felt thin in his throat. He could see ranges many miles away, and though everything was perfectly still there was also an immense sweep in things, as if a gust of wind had caught the very fabric of being.

"Wake up, damn you," a voice said. He was shoved in the back, and he tumbled down the rockfall, starting a small avalanche.

He stood in a large white room. Glass boxes of various size were stacked everywhere, four and five to a pile, and in every box was a sleeping animal: monkey, rat, dog, cat, pig, dolphin, turtle. "No," he said, backing up. "Please, no."

A bearded man entered the room. "Come on, wake up," he said brusquely. "Time to get back to it, Fred. Our only hope is to work as hard as we can. You have to resist when you start slipping away!" He seized Abernathy by the arms and sat him down on a box of squirrels. "Now listen!" he cried. "We're asleep! We're dreaming!"

"Thank God," Abernathy said.

"Not so fast! We're awake as well."

"I don't believe you."

"Yes you do!" He slapped Abernathy in the chest with a large roll of graph paper, and it spilled loose and unrolled over the floor. Black squiggles smeared the graphs.

"It looks like a musical score," Abernathy said absently.

The bearded man shouted, "Yes! Yes! This is the symphony our brains play, very apt! Violins yammering away—that's what used to be ours, Fred; that was consciousness." He yanked hard on his beard with both hands, looking anguished. "Sudden drop to the basses, bowing and bowing, blessed sleep, yes, yes! And in the night the ghost instruments, horn and oboe and viola, spinning their little improvs over the ground bass, longer and longer till the violins start blasting again, yes, Fred, it's perfectly apt!"

"Thank you," Abernathy said. "But you don't have to yell. I'm right here."

"Then *wake up*," the man said viciously. "Can't, can you! Trapped, aren't you! Playing the new song like all the rest of us. Look at it there—REM sleep mixed indiscriminately with consciousness and deep sleep, turning us all into dreamwalkers. Into waking nightmares."

Looking into the depths of the man's beard, Abernathy saw that all his teeth were incisors. Abernathy edged toward the door, then broke for it and ran. The man leaped forward and tackled him, and they tumbled to the floor.

Abernathy woke up.

"Aha," the man said. It was Winston, administrator of the lab. "So now you believe me," he said sourly, rubbing an elbow. "I suppose we should write that down on the walls. If we all start slipping away we won't even remember what things used to be like. It'll all be over then."

"Where are we?" Abernathy asked.

"In the lab," Winston replied, voice filled with heavy patience. "We live here now, Fred. Remember?"

Abernathy looked around. The lab was large and well lit. Sheets of graph paper recording

970

EEGs were scattered over the floor. Black countertops protruded from the walls, which were cluttered with machinery. In one corner were two rats in a cage.

Abernathy shook his head violently. It was all coming back. He was awake now, but the dream had been true. He groaned, walked to the room's little window, saw the smoke rising from the city below. "Where's Jill?"

Winston shrugged. They hurried through a door at the end of the lab, into a small room containing cots and blankets. No one there. "She's probably gone back to the house again," Abernathy said. Winston hissed with irritation and worry. "I'll check the grounds," he said. "You'd better go to the house. Be careful!"

Fred was already out the door.

In many places the streets were almost blocked by smashed cars, but little had changed since Abernathy's last venture home, and he made good time. The suburbs were choking in haze that smelled like incinerator smoke. A gas station attendant holding a pump handle stared in astonishment as he drove by, then waved. Abernathy didn't wave back. On one of these expeditions he had seen a knifing, and now he didn't like to look.

He stopped the car at the curb before his house. The remains of his house. It was charred almost to the ground. The blackened chimney was all that stood over chest high.

He got out of his old Cortina and slowly crossed the lawn, which was marked by black footprints. In the distance a dog barked insistently.

Jill stood in the kitchen, humming to herself and moving black things from here to there. She looked up as Abernathy stopped in the side yard before her. Her eyes twitched from side to side. "You're home," she said cheerily. "How was your day?"

"Jill, let's go out to dinner," Abernathy said.

"But I'm already cooking!"

"I can see that." He stepped over what had

been the kitchen wall and took her arm. "Don't worry about that. Let's go anyway."

"My my," Jill said, brushing his face with a sooty hand. "Aren't you romantic this evening."

He stretched his lips wide. "You bet. Come on." He pulled her carefully out of the house and across the yard, and helped her into the Cortina. "Such chivalry," she remarked, eyes darting about in tandem.

Abernathy got in and started the engine. "But, Fred," his wife said, "what about Jeff and Fran?"

Abernathy looked out his window. "They've got a babysitter," he finally said.

Jill frowned, nodded, sat back in her seat. Her broad face was smudged. "Ah," she said, "I do so like to dine out."

"Yes," Abernathy said, and yawned. He felt drowsy. "Oh no," he said. "No!" He bit his lip, pinched the back of the hand on the wheel. Yawned again. "No!" he cried. Jill jerked against her door in surprise. He swerved to avoid hitting an Oriental woman sitting in the middle of the road. "I must get to the lab," he shouted. He pulled down the Cortina's sun visor, took a pen from his coat pocket, and scrawled *To the Lab*. Jill was staring at him. "It wasn't my fault," she whispered.

He drove them onto the freeway. All thirty lanes were clear, and he put his foot down on the accelerator. "To the lab," he sang, "to the lab, to the lab." A flying police vehicle landed on the highway ahead of them, folded its wings, and sped off. Abernathy tried to follow it, but the freeway turned and narrowed; they were back on street level. He shouted with frustration, bit the flesh at the base of his thumb. Jill leaned back against her door, crying. Her eyes looked like small beings, a team trying to jerk its way free. "I couldn't help it," she said. "He loved me, you know. And I loved him."

Abernathy drove on. Some streets were burning. He wanted to go west, needed to go west. The car was behaving oddly. They were on a tree-lined avenue, out where there were few houses. A giant Boeing 747 lay across the road, its wings slewed forward. A high tunnel had been cut through it so traffic could pass. A cop with whistle and white gloves waved them through.

On the dashboard an emergency light blinked. *To the Lab.* Abernathy sobbed convulsively. "I don't know how!"

Jill, his sister, sat up straight. "Turn left," she said quietly. Abernathy threw the directional switch and their car rerouted itself onto the track that veered left. They came to other splits in the track, and each time Jill told him which way to go. The rearview mirror bloomed with smoke.

Then he woke up. Winston was swabbing his arm with a wad of cotton, wiping off a droplet of blood.

"Amphetamines and pain," Winston whispered.

They were in the lab. About a dozen lab techs, postdocs, and grad students were in there at their countertops, working with great speed. "How's Jill?" Abernathy said.

"Fine, fine. She's sleeping right now. Listen, Fred. I've found a way to keep us awake for longer periods of time. Amphetamines and pain. Regular injections of benzedrine, plus a sharp burst of pain every hour or so, administered in whatever way you find most convenient. Metabolism stays too high for the mind to slip into the dreamwalking. I tried it and stayed fully awake and alert for six hours. Now we're all using the method."

Abernathy watched the lab techs dash about. "I can tell." He could feel his heart's rapid emphatic thumping.

"Well let's get to it," Winston said intently. "Let's make use of this time."

Abernathy stood. Winston called a little meeting. Feeling the gazes fixed on him, Abernathy collected his thoughts. "The mind consists of electrochemical action. Since we're all suffering the effects of this, it seems to me we can ignore the chemical and concentrate on the

electrical. If the ambient fields have changed . . . Anyone know how many gauss the magnetic field is now? Or what the cosmic ray count is?"

They stared at him.

"We can tune in to the space station's monitor," he said. "And do the rest here."

So he worked, and they worked with him. Every hour a grinning Winston came around with hypodermics in hand, singing, "Speed, speed, spee-ud!" He convinced Abernathy to let droplets of hydrochloric acid fall on the inside of his forearm.

It kept Abernathy awake better than it did the others. For a whole day, then two, he worked without pause, eating crackers and drinking water as he worked, giving himself the injections when Winston wasn't there.

After the first few hours his assistants began slipping back into dreamwalking, despite the injections and acid splashings. Assignments he gave were never completed. One of his techs presented him with a successful experiment: the two rats, grafted together at the leg. Vainly Abernathy tried to pummel the man back to wakefulness.

In the end he did all the work himself. It took days. As his techs collapsed or wandered off he shifted from counter to counter, squinting sand-filled eyes to read oscilloscope and computer screen. He had never felt so exhausted in his life. It was like taking tests in a subject he didn't understand, in which he was severely retarded.

Still he kept working. The EEGs showed oscillation between wakefulness and REM sleep, in a pattern he had never seen. And there were correlations between the EEGs and fluctuations in the magnetic field.

Some of the men's flickering eyes were open, and they sat on the floors talking to each other or to him. Once he had to calm Winston, who was on the floor weeping and saying, "We'll never stop dreaming, Fred, we'll never stop." Abernathy gave him an injection, but it didn't have any effect.

He kept working. He sat at a crowded table

at his high school reunion, and found he could work anyway. He gave himself an injection whenever he remembered. He got very, very tired.

Eventually he felt he understood as much as he was going to. Everyone else was lying in the cot room with Jill, or was slumped on the floors. Eyes and eyelids were twitching.

"We move through space filled with dust and gas and fields of force. Now all the constants have changed. The readouts from the space station show that, show signs of a strong electromagnetic field we've apparently moved into. More dust, cosmic rays, gravitational flux. Perhaps it's the shockwave of a supernova, something nearby that we're just seeing now. Anyone looked up into the sky lately? Anyway. Something. The altered field has thrown the electrical patterns of our brains into something like what we call the REM state. Our brains rebel and struggle towards consciousness as much as they can, but this field forces them back. So we oscillate." He laughed weakly, and crawled up onto one of the countertops to get some sleep.

He woke and brushed the dust off his lab coat, which had served him as a blanket. The dirt road he had been sleeping on was empty. He walked. It was cloudy, and nearly dark.

He passed a small group of shacks, built in a tropical style with open walls and palm thatch roofs. They were empty. Dark light filled the sky.

Then he was at the sea's edge. Before him extended a low promontory, composed of thousands of wooden chairs, all crushed and piled together. At the point of the promontory there was a human figure, seated in a big chair that still had seat and back and one arm.

Abernathy stepped out carefully, onto slats and lathed cylinders of wood, from a chair arm to the plywood bottom of a chair seat. Around him the gray ocean was strangely calm; glassy swells rose and fell over the slick wood at the waterline without a sound. Insubstantial clouds

of fog, the lowest parts of a solid cloud cover, floated slowly onshore. The air was salty and wet. Abernathy shivered, stepped down to the next fragment of weathered gray wood.

The seated man turned to look at him. It was Winston. "Fred," he called, loud in the silence of the dawn. Abernathy approached him, picked up a chair back, placed it carefully, sat.

"How are you?" Winston said.

Abernathy nodded. "Okay." Down close to the water he could hear the small slaps and sucking of the sea's rise and fall. The swells looked a bit larger, and he could see thin smoky mist rising from them as they approached the shore.

"Winston," he croaked, and cleared his throat. "What's happened?"

"We're dreaming."

"But what does that mean?"

Winston laughed wildly. "Emergent stage-one sleep, transitional sleep, rapid sleep, rhomb-encephalic sleep, pontine sleep, activated sleep, paradoxical sleep." He grinned ironically. "No one knows what it is."

"But all those studies."

"Yes, all those studies. And how I used to believe in them, how I used to work for them, all those sorry guesses ranging from the ridiculous to the absurd, we dream to organize experience into memory, to stimulate the senses in the dark, to prepare for the future, to give our depth perception exercise for God's sake! I mean we don't know, do we, Fred. We don't know what dreaming is, we don't know what sleep is, you only have to think about it a bit to realize we didn't know what consciousness itself was, what it meant to be awake. Did we ever really know? We lived, we slept, we dreamed, and all three equal mysteries. Now that we're doing all three at once, is the mystery any deeper?"

Abernathy picked at the grain in the wood of a chair leg. "A lot of the time I feel normal," he said. "It's just that strange things keep happening."

"Your EEGs display an unusual pattern," Winston said, mimicking a scientific tone.

"More alpha and beta waves than the rest of us. As if you're struggling hard to wake up."

"Yes. That's what it feels like."

They sat in silence for a time, watching swells lap at the wet chairs. The tide was falling. Offshore, near the limit of visibility, Abernathy saw a large cabin cruiser drifting in the current.

"So tell me what you've found," Winston said.

Abernathy described the data transmitted from the space station, then his own experiments.

Winston nodded. "So we're stuck here for good."

"Unless we pass through this field. Or—I've gotten an idea for a device you could wear around your head, that might restore the old field."

"A solution seen in a dream?"

"Yes."

Winston laughed. "I used to believe in our rationality, Fred. Dreams as some sort of electrochemical manifestation of the nervous system, random activity, how reasonable it all sounded! Give the depth perception exercise! God, how small-minded it all was. Why shouldn't we have believed that dreams were great travels, to the future, to other universes, to a world more real than our own! They felt that way sometimes, in that last second before waking, as if we lived in a world so charged with meaning that it might burst. . . . And now here we are. We're here, Fred, this is the moment and our only moment, no matter how we name it. *We're here.* From idea to symbol, perhaps. People will adapt. That's one of our talents."

"I don't like it," Abernathy said. "I never liked my dreams."

Winston merely laughed at him. "They say consciousness itself was a leap like this one, people were ambling around like dogs and then one day, maybe because the earth moved through the shockwave of some distant explosion, sure, one day one of them straightened up and looked around surprised, and said, 'I am.'"

"That would be a surprise," Abernathy said.

"And this time everyone woke up one morning still dreaming, and looked around and said, '*What AM I?*'" Winston laughed. "Yes, we're stuck here. But I can adapt." He pointed. "Look, that boat out there is sinking."

They watched several people aboard the craft struggle to get a rubber raft over the side. After many dunkings they got it in the water and everyone inside it. Then they rowed away, offshore into the mist.

"I'm afraid," Abernathy said.

Then he woke up. He was back in the lab. It was in worse shape than ever. A couple of countertops had been swept clean to make room for chessboards, and several techs were playing blindfolded, arguing over which board was which.

He went to Winston's offices to get more benzedrine. There was no more. He grabbed one of his postdocs and said, "How long have I been asleep?" The man's eyes twitched, and he sang his reply: "Sixteen men on a dead man's chest, yo ho ho and a bottle of rum." Abernathy went to the cot room. Jill was there, naked except for light blue underwear, smoking a cigarette. One of the grad students was brushing her nipples with a feather. "Oh hi, Fred," she said, looking him straight in the eye. "Where have you been?"

"Talking to Winston," he said with difficulty. "Have you seen him?"

"Yes! I don't know when, though. . . ."

He started to work alone again. No one wanted to help. He cleared a small room off the main lab, and dragged in the equipment he needed. He locked three large boxes of crackers in a cabinet, and tried to lock himself in his room whenever he felt drowsy. Once he spent six weeks in China, then he woke up. Sometimes he woke out in his old Cortina, hugging the steering wheel like his only friend. All his friends were lost. Each time he went back and started working again. He could stay awake for hours at a time. He got lots done. The magnets were working well, he was getting the fields he wanted. The device for placing the field around the head—an odd-looking wire helmet—was practicable.

He was tired. It hurt to blink. Every time he felt drowsy he applied more acid to his arm. It was covered with burns, but none of them hurt anymore. When he woke he felt as if he hadn't slept for days. Twice his grad students helped out, and he was grateful for that. Winston came by occasionally, but only laughed at him. He was too tired, everything he did was clumsy. He got on the lab phone once and tried to call his parents; all the lines were busy. The radio was filled with static, except for a station that played nothing but episodes of *The Lone Ranger*. He went back to work. He ate crackers and worked. He worked and worked.

Late one afternoon he went out onto the lab's cafeteria terrace to take a break. The sun was low, and a chill breeze blew. He could see the air, filled with amber light, and he breathed it in violently. Below him the city smoked, and the wind blew, and he knew that he was alive, that he was aware he was alive, and that something important was pushing into the world, suffusing things. . . .

Jill walked onto the terrace, still wearing nothing but the blue underwear. She stepped on the balls of her feet, smiled oddly. Abernathy could see goose pimples sweep across her skin like cat's paws over water, and the power of her presence—distant, female, mysterious—filled him with fear.

They stood several feet apart and looked down at the city, where their house had been. The area was burning.

Jill gestured at it. "It's too bad we only had the courage to live our lives fully in dreams."

"I thought we were doing okay," Abernathy said. "I thought we engaged it the best we could, every waking moment."

She stared at him, again with the knowing smile. "You did think that, didn't you?"

"Yes," he said fiercely, "I did. I did."

He went inside to work it off.

. . .

Then he woke up. He was in the mountains, in the high cirque again. He was higher now and could see two more lakes, tiny granite pools, above the cobalt-and-aquamarine one. He was climbing shattered granite, getting near the pass. Lichen mottled the rocks. The wind dried the sweat on his face, cooled him. It was quiet and still, so still, so quiet. . . .

"Wake up!"

It was Winston. Abernathy was in his little room (high ranges in the distance, the dusty green of forests below), wedged in a corner. He got up, went to the crackers cabinet, pumped himself full of the benzedrine he had found in some syringes on the floor. (Snow and lichen.)

He went into the main lab and broke the fire alarm. That got everyone's attention. It took him a couple of minutes to stop the alarm. When he did his ears were ringing.

"The device is ready to try," he said to the group. There were about twenty of them. Some were as neat as if they were off to church, others were tattered and dirty. Jill stood to one side.

Winston crashed to the front of the group. "What's ready?" he shouted.

"The device to stop us dreaming," Abernathy said weakly. "It's ready to try."

Winston said slowly, "Well, let's try it then, okay, Fred?"

Abernathy carried helmets and equipment out of his room and into the lab. He arranged the transmitters and powered the magnets and the field generators. When it was all ready he stood up and wiped his brow.

"Is this it?" Winston asked. Abernathy nodded. Winston picked up one of the wire helmets.

"Well I don't like it!" he said, and struck the helmet against the wall.

Abernathy's mouth dropped open. One of the techs gave a shove to his electromagnets, and in a sudden fury Abernathy picked up a bat of wood and hit the man. Some of his assistants leaped to his aid, the rest pressed in and pulled at his equipment, tearing it down. A tremendous fight erupted. Abernathy swung his slab of wood with abandon, feeling great satisfaction each time it struck. There was blood in the air. His machines were being destroyed. Jill picked up one of the helmets and threw it at him, screaming, *"It's your fault, it's your fault!"* He knocked down a man near his magnets and had swung the slab back to kill him when suddenly he saw a bright glint in Winston's hand; it was a surgical knife, and with a swing like a sidearm pitcher's Winston slammed the knife into Abernathy's diaphragm, burying it. Abernathy staggered back, tried to draw in a breath and found that he could, he was all right, he hadn't been stabbed. He turned and ran.

He dashed onto the terrace, closely pursued by Winston and Jill and the others, who tripped and fell even as he did. The patio was much higher than it used to be, far above the city, which burned and smoked. There was a long wide stairway descending into the heart of the city. Abernathy could hear screams, it was night and windy, he couldn't see any stars, he was at the edge of the terrace, he turned and the group was right behind him, faces twisted with fury. "No!" he cried, and then they rushed him, and he swung the wood slab and swung it and swung it, and turned to run down the stairs and then without knowing how he had done it he tripped and fell head over heels down the rocky staircase, falling falling falling.

Then he woke up. He was falling.

Death Is Static Death Is Movement
(Excerpt from *Red Spider White Web*)

MISHA NOGHA

Misha Nogha (1955–) is a US writer of fiction and poetry often associated with the cyberpunk movement and best known for her neo-cyberpunk novel *Red Spider White Web* (1990), which was a finalist for the Arthur C. Clarke Award and won the 1990 ReaderCon Award. However, the focus of her work is often broader.

Of mixed Native American (Metis-Cree) and Norse ancestry, Nogha began publishing with the fantasy prose-poetry collection *Prayers of Steel* (1988). Her second collection, *Ke-Qua-Hawk-As* (1994), includes poems intermixed with stories based on Native American material. Her most recent collection is *Magpies and Tigers* (2007). The performed story "Tsuki Mangetsu" won the 1989 Prix d'Italia.

Nogha's short fiction (and poetry) appeared in some of the best independent magazines of the 1980s and 1990s, including *Back Brain Recluse*, *Factsheet Five*, and *Ice River*. Her brilliant story "Stone Badger" was showcased in the *Looking Glass Anthology of Native American Writers*, while "Chippoke Na Gomi" appeared in the *Witness Anthology of Experimental Fiction* (1989) and *The Wesleyan Anthology of Science Fiction* (2010). Her nonfiction appeared in the iconic (and New Wave–influenced) *Science Fiction Eye* magazine and she served as a fiction editor for the influential speculative magazine *New Pathways*.

Red Spider White Web, excerpted here, describes a dystopian future congested, cyberpunkish America, dominated by Japan and afflicted by climate change, where artists try to avoid sanctuaries called "Mickey-Sans," which shelter their inhabitants from the excremental waste and pollution outside but also sanitize creativity. Into this milieu steps a dedicated Native American artist who has been gengineered into a being half human and half wolverine, and on her mission falls afoul of surreal figures and dangers. The style is often phantasmagorical and full of dark menace, but the darkness is balanced by the main character Kumo's pursuit of her hologram art.

The 1999 Wordcraft of Oregon edition of the novel acknowledges Nogha as having been a sui generis example of and influence on cyberpunk. It features an impressive triumvirate of advocates, with an introduction by John Shirley, a foreword by Brian Aldiss, and a postscript by James P. Blaylock. Shirley, who made *Time*'s list of the "seminal cyberpunk writers," avows that Nogha transcends the subgenre, also citing the example of slipstream fiction published in literary magazines. Shirley calls Nogha's novel "the radical convergence of metaphysical, psychological, tribal and techno-logical." Aldiss points to the "hard, dirty, challenging" aspects of *Red Spider White Web*.

Blaylock, meanwhile, zeroes in on the climate-change aspects and offers up an anecdote of an apocalyptic vision he had while driving, of a blasted landscape and food made out of plastic. Unlike much cyberpunk fiction, which seems to fetishize or render beautiful artificial landscapes—to, in effect, celebrate the disconnection of modern technology—Nogha, much more in sympathy with Philip K. Dick, mourns the loss of the real or natural world and interrogates our disconnection. Her depictions of the "underground real" conjure up sympathetic echoes of the work of Cordwainer Smith.

In this excerpt, "Death Is Static Death Is Movement," the artist Kumo is on the move after a disconcerting conversation with her friend JuJube. Dern Motler, a fellow artist turned enemy (and turned violent), is after her, and Kumo is unsure whom to trust. The excerpt features an encounter with Tommy, a potentially dangerous friend who is worshipped as a god in the Mickey-San. The "Pinkies," or "Pink Flies," mentioned are misogynistic neo-Nazis: rich male teenagers ("scrubbed clean") who go slumming and with whom Kumo has had run-ins.

DEATH IS STATIC DEATH IS MOVEMENT

(Excerpt from *Red Spider White Web*)

Misha Nogha

Flowing from shadow to shadow, like spilled ink, Kumo was glad to be in the air again. In the clone skin she was free to move. Her mind flashed in many directions, like a jar of released fireflies—each thought having its own reason and purpose. It was already cold, below freezing by many degrees. The scent of the river was chilling into the air, and dropping. Kumo followed it toward the charter house. JuJube didn't think she had noticed where they were going that day—the day he borrowed the solar car to bring her here. But she did. Kumo noticed everything.

The part of her mind that was ticking so ominously made her wonder about JuJube again. What was it? Everything was all wrong. She kept thinking about the daruma doll. The one she had hung on the door handle of the closet. Then her mind flashed to the shrunken heads, veered away from the thought, and circled back. She pulled it out again. Yeah, there it was. Dammit all to hell. There was something about that one shrunken head that faced the others. She stood in the alley a second, waiting a moment before crossing a path lit by solar-powered lights. It was late. A nasty feeling stung her in the spine. *What was it? Shit.* Her heart beat fast from fear and from outrage. *The head was David's. Well wasn't it?* She wasn't sure. She'd have to find that out though, later.

And Motler nothing more than a Navvy data retriever. She wondered why, as she trotted across a filth-filled alley. She pulled her thoughts away from Motler, from JuJube, like she pulled dead skin away from a blister.

The Pinkies. She had her skull juggler's plan. Was it only in the circus that leopards and clowns met? She had sparking rosettes of hate etched on her soul. The Pinkies represented everything she hated about men—all men. The male animal with a sharp rump and no memories. She was female—and not even a fashalt at that. To her world, she was only a varmint with sex organs. Welcome as a rabid badger. How many rough blows had she suffered? How many times had she been an unwilling step for the selfish souls of her fellow opposite gender? And the Pinkies, so white and so male, were like living stiff boots of conquerors. A flame of desire warmed her murderous expectation. It paced from eye to eye.

The snow came quickly, white hornets stinging in the thin atmospheric night. It stopped as suddenly as it fell. Cut out of the sky with huge shears of cold air.

Kumo picked up her pace, her soft boots like paw pads in the squeaky, grey snow. She hesitated, listening with her inner instincts more than with her ears—and then she dashed off to the right. She was used to the gnawing cold—a night wanderer—but she knew when to burrow in for the evening. She wasn't actually warm in the clone suit—even though the Mikan thermals had been chemically altered with Vigowear polytherm, but she could function well enough until she was able to dig into some polytherm packing straw. She felt naked without the jacket Pink Fly had ruined. *One woman naked under God.*

"God?" she whispered.

Rituals ran the streets like stray dogs. The full Eucharist moon passed between her lips, fell on her tongue. She didn't chew—but felt its fossil weight on her mind. Its ancient bone bread filled her whole being. The stars were still in the sky, steely snipers waiting for their chance to get in a clear shot.

Kumo stopped in her tracks and then sank to the ground in a sheet of moonlight. Kneeling there, head bowed, she welcomed that familiar feeling. Some old wyekan—wandering and searching for a willing host—pounced on her and snarled. Kumo growled with intention. A vision of the method washed over her mind and a laugh crept up her throat. The Pinkies would meet their justice. *Call in the bears*, she thought, *the little bastards will mock no more.*

She spat at the image and the spit froze almost before it hit the ground.

"Oh no," she said aloud. She was certain she wasn't going to make it before the cold quick-froze her—but she ran anyway—lungs bursting and legs already cramping. Instead of running down to the river, she ran back along the tracks towards Tommy's tank.

In only a few blocks she began to slow. The coughs were beginning, shaking her and racking up flecks of blood that fell as black diamonds in the snow. The ice had formed a glassine mask over her leather one. Her goggles and suit were frosting with rime. Her limbs were wood and her lungs refused to accept the frigid air—they hurt. Her nostrils stung. She stopped, bent over, and began beating her hands against her shoulders. Suddenly Kumo stood bolt upright. She cupped her hands to her mouth and began to yell.

"Tommy! Toooommmmmmmyyyyy!"

Uchida, deep in the warmth of his reconstructed chemical tank, head bent low over the worktable, hands full of tiny instruments, and with circuits, vacuum tubes, wires all spread out before him, cocked his head. *Someone needs me*, he thought. Then he shrugged. *They all need me.* He decided to ignore the call—but then again, he pricked up his ears and listened to the tiny, gnatlike voice whispering in his enhanced ear.

There was something remarkable and irresistible about the timbre of the voice.

Tommy jumped up, knocking over pieces of metal and delicate components. He hurried on his Vigowear and grabbed a hot snap blanket. In a second or two he was out the door. His arti legs pumping faster than those of a normal human. His arti lungs unaffected by the cold. In a few minutes he stood by the trembling Kumo, who was laughing uncontrollably, coughing blood, complaining of being hot, and attempting to take off her suit.

The first stages of hypothermia had already set in. Tommy rushed her into the hot pack and locked it up—then proceeded to carry her the full quarter mile back to his chemical tank. Tommy was shaking his head at her and gesturing for her to sit down again and drink up. He loved using the signing, his hands singing in the air.

His graceful gestures had a nostalgic, calming effect on Kumo. She was mesmerized by his movements and understood the signing well enough.

Finally, she sighed and buried her face in the warm blankets. Tommy could barely stand the velvety feel of her muffled sentences.

"Those insect collectors torment me for fun. Every day I have to burrow into pain. Those handicapped dogs shove muzzles in shit piles. I am a free predator! I don't want their petty domestics. To hell with their pus-filled pastimes. Why don't they get sick and die? Putrid dogs. No better than old people, wiggers put out to die by stingy relatives. I only want to be left alone."

Kumo jerked an arm toward the wiredog screens. Tommy's head slumped onto his chest and he sniggered.

Tommy made the sign for a Pink Fly and then ran a quick gesture across his neck.

"I've had it. Here, look at this mess, Tommy." She stood up and turned her back and dropped the blanket so that he could see.

Tommy stared at her for a long time. His masks were off, showing his beautiful and smooth face. His heavy black eyebrows shot up. Droplets of sweat ran down his face. He signed for a fly again.

" 'Endgame,' says the spider to the fly." She made a sound like two wet stones clacking together.

Tommy nodded.

"And, Tommy . . ." She gave a great cough and crumpled back into the polytherm. ". . . I'm going to need your help."

An inscrutable smile crept across Tommy's features.

"To make Kumonosu."

Tommy laughed a low, sinister laugh.

"You're smarter than I thought, Tommy. Smarter than anyone thought."

Kumo coughed again, her arms cramped with a tremendous charley horse, but she said nothing. They hurt, but she was used to these cramps now. Nothing had been the same since her time in the crane.

She lay back on the sleeping platform and looked at Tommy's tank. The stray junk was gone and replaced with boxes and crates and cartons of spare parts and wire. The walls were covered with high-tech panels, patch cords, monitors at every angle, components with the guts ripped out, blinking digital lights, whirring reels, laser discs, transformers, sparking cables, and digital UV meters. Kumo let her eye rove around the tank until it settled on Tommy's old stained and tattered motorcycle jacket.

"Can I have that old jacket, Tommy?"

He shrugged. "Help yourself. It's my fishing jacket."

Kumo made a face, but she still wanted it. She got up stiffly and went over to it. She lifted it off the hook. It smelled more like clone leather than fish. As she was about to put it on, one of the fishhooks sewn under the lapel snagged her finger. She pulled back the barb and lifted it out, smiling.

Kumo was confused by the tank. It contained at least two million credits' worth of equipment. An electrical chemical smell tainted her lungs. She approached the walls. Sixteen monitors registered her. The rest recorded some distant scene she didn't recognize. A nasty schemer had siphoned all this stuff off and plopped it right into Tommy's tank. A "master plan." Probably the whim of some rich Japanese. Some government KGIs?

KGI. Cagey Eye. "I wish I was rich," she said aloud. She brought the jacket back to the bed and set it beside her.

This time Tommy laughed and was verbal. "What would you do if you were rich, Kumo?"

"I'd buy one of your best Karakuri market pairs. I'd move out into the country with plenty of holo material and solar packs and food and jugs of scotch."

"The country! There's nothing out there but those closed-down genetic reservations, frozen deserts, and howling winds."

"I'd burrow into the ground like a badger. Every night I'd sit on the mound and wait."

"Wait! What would you wait for?"

"For the coyotes to come."

Tommy laughed again, howled like a wolf, and sniggered.

"Not like that. Coyotes yippiteroooo. They have a lot to say. You know who I mean, the genetic tribes on all those old Nature Conservancy lands."

"They have hunters there all the time now, running missiles with joy-sticks to kill the genetic trophies. You'd die out there pretty fast I expect." Tommy was grim again.

"I'll die in here pretty fast too."

"No, don't worry about it. We'll fix those Pinkies."

"Yes, I'll fix those Pinkies. But there are always the Hoodoos and their zombie minions, and Mikans, and people who act like friends, but only want to break you apart and suck the marrow from your bones."

"You can't expect the tribes to take you in. Out there you would be alone. You'll be one of the people, but a tribe of one."

Kumo nodded. "Yes, that's the biggest luxury of all—isn't it?"

"I don't think they made many WIs. I think

that was some twisted joke. They don't want intelligent animals like you out there, scheming like wolverines to smash their caches."

Kumo shrugged. "There might be a Ba tribe." Kumo had been thinking of it.

"Genetics were a waste of everyone's time. All you got were creatures who were too smart to be animals and too vicious to be humans."

Kumo grunted. "But hardier than both, Tommy. There's a lot to be said for the integrity of mixed genes. A sort of mongrel vigor."

"Can't see leaving the Earth peopled with savages."

"It's how we started. Anyway, which do you prefer, enhanced psychopathic tin men like yourself to lead the masses?"

"Lead the masses. Is that how you see it?"

"Isn't that what you're planning? Set yourself up as some kinda messiah and then have the flock follow you. Fools. Where are you gonna lead those people?"

"Just where they always wanted to go."

Kumo looked at him from the side of her wide eyes as he came slowly down the ladder. "Where's that?"

"To hell," Tommy whispered.

Kumo stood up and walked toward him. "I thought you were a man-god, Tommy. Just what are you and the Mikans doing?"

She moved further into the camera angle. There was a brief hesitation and then a chorus of voice-print perfections in sixteen different languages shouted her words back at her. Kumo let her jaw drop open. Sixteen computer-altered holo images of her dropped their jaws. She saw herself as Asian, black, white, Indian, blond, and even as a bipedal badger with a short muzzle and a black mask. Kumo pointed to that one and Tommy laughed long and hard.

"You're a fucking revolutionist. *Sonuvabitch.*" Kumo looked at him in fear and distrust. "How can you be a revolutionist in this nest of fascism?"

"I have many—friends."

"Do you?" Kumo sniffed suspiciously. "*I* never saw any."

"These are powerful friends."

Kumo grunted. "Revolutionary fascists I suppose. The worst kind of madness."

The holos kept talking back to her in their own languages.

She grimaced. "This place is like some ETS self-monitoring shuttle." Something crackled and showered them with sparks. Tommy swore, and then moved his squeaking scaffolding and climbed back up to do repairs.

"It's a special project." He called down to her. "You'll know all about it in a few days. Everyone will."

Kumo sensed a very disagreeable feeling about the "everyone will," but she just stared at Tommy amidst the chaos of wires with dumb awe. He worked skillfully and adeptly as a spider mending its complex webwork. He was so far ahead of her that while she'd been peering in the mist he came up behind her to pass again.

"I already guessed, Tommy. You and those Mikans. Nobody's really going to China are they? Where are they going?"

Tommy laughed then, guffawed so that flakes of rust fell down on the boxes.

"You know everything, my tupu friend."

Kumo frowned. "Let me use some of this shit, Tommy. I've got parasites. I need a CPU with a skinhead's K of bubble."

He waved at her. "You work over there." He pointed at a cam CPU and an empty box table. "Tommy finishes up here. Don't talk anymore okay? You're annoying."

"Yeah? Well fuck you too, brother." Kumo jerked her chin at him, but immediately forgot him as she conferred with the system. She booted up the appropriate software, and remote-accessed her files in the locker. One by one she digitally fed the images into the memory.

This was going to be a good flytrap. Prayers of steel. Hopes of steel. Ruins of steel. Stainless steel death.

When she looked up, the high-res shots on

Tommy's monitors had zoomed into somebody's private Mickey dwelling. Straight satellite work. He'd tied into *that* too.

She looked up at him, saw his stern face.

"I won't," she replied, and went back to work. About four hours later Tommy interrupted her with coffee and some glo-nuts.

"I hate sanpuru. It's like eating soft wax."

Kumo popped one of the bite-sized glo-nuts in her mouth. "Those Mikans are pure, crazy, fanatical shit, man."

"You prefer Hoodoo hamburgers?" Tommy asked dryly.

"I prefer a private, personal God with manna made out of real food."

"No such deity."

"No?" Kumo asked. "You don't know anything about a God, Tommy. You're just a karakuri ningyo."

Tommy gave an annoyed laugh. "It's absurd. Why should an animal want God simply because it's given the gift of human speech?"

He came up close behind Kumo and traced the collar of purple on Kumo's bare neck.

"What's this?"

Kumo laughed. "Sukoshi kega o shimashita."

"How did it happen?"

"It had to do with my part of a performance piece. I made a misjudgment." Kumo spoke sadly.

"Very crazy, those fucking artists."

"Yes, that's right, Tommy. You're the sane one, yes? You dropped out. Kerist, I have bad dreams about all of this, Tommy. Here, lean down." He leaned down and she pushed his hank of black hair away from his forehead.

"What's this?"

"Thought I might find seven horns or something." Kumo gave him a faint smile.

Tommy shook his head, put his arms around Kumo. "Let's not worry about God so much, Kumo. Animals have no souls. You should rejoice in that."

"And what about angels, Tommy? Don't they have souls either?"

Tommy looked straight ahead. "No, angels are like eagles or tigers. They have no mercy, just a cold brilliance and glittering eyes watching for prey."

Kumo shuddered. No, Tommy wasn't going to China. She couldn't see it even though she was certain he had connections straight from Japan.

She leaned her head back against Tommy's chest. She knew he was a snuff, couldn't figure out why he hadn't loved her into oblivion. And the strangest thing of all was that the only place she felt safe in this crazy world was here, in Tommy's tank. Her lids closed over her feral eyes. Her skin was satin and amber, yet marred with scrabbled tissue and hundreds of scars from the hard life she'd seen.

Still, she had a way of moving, and stretching, a large erotic animal offering some sandalwood-scented secret to Tommy's skin and steel. He pressed his mouth to her bare shoulder, while pushing her back on the bed, his left hand supported her head as they flowed down, to the thick quilts and the soft buttery light of the heated lamp. Kumo rolled away from Tommy, holding his advances away with her shoulder. She turned over on her stomach, shielding breasts that she was ashamed of. But Tommy only laughed. He crouched over her like a puma. He grabbed her around the waist and pulled her to her hands and knees. Kumo made a low dangerous sound, but Tommy put one of his hands on the back of her neck and clamped hard enough to keep her immobile. Once she was still a moment, he entered her, gripping her hard to force their movements.

Afterwards, when they were lying side by side, Kumo placed his hand on his mirror, her face.

"What does this mean, Tommy? What are we?"

"Cub scouts." He stretched and rolled over on his stomach.

"Huh?" She slapped him on the backside.

He shrugged. "From the same litter maybe."

"You mean this is incest?"

They both sniggered. Kumo elbowed him playfully in the ribs.

"Tommy, tell me your genetic profile."

"Why?"

"I want to know everything."

"I can guess why you want to know."

"Can you?" Kumo smiled brightly.

"You've figured out everything."

Kumo looked up into his smooth face. "I had it in a dream. Remember, I'm just a dumb beast with a gift to speak."

"An obstreperous animal who dreams of having a soul." Tommy laughed. "And the odds?"

"It would be a kind of final miracle."

"Hu-Wi-SL- . . ."

"Ba?" Kumo asked.

Tommy looked at her and laughed. They both laughed, slapping their knees. They had this final secret then.

"This is a good time to die, sister!"

Kumo choked on her laughter, and then nodded solemnly at him.

"It is."

In the low morning sun, the rusty, abandoned steelworks glowed blood-red. It was only two blocks from Tommy's tank. Kumo photoread most of the interior into the CPU and then, from there, made the appropriate adjustments.

From Tommy she asked for twelve sound chips. He produced them cheerfully, working alongside her from time to time to rid the world of Pinkeye flies. Normally, Pinkies were below his notice—but now that they had been called to his attention, he wanted the whole holy world rid of them.

While she worked, Kumo whistled fragments of a strange tune called "Second Object"—and then laughed at the irony of it all.

It only took a few hours for Kumo to transfer Tommy's stabilizing cameras, deflected beams, portable lasers, and mirrors to the steelworks.

"I'll bring them back," she told Tommy as she noticed him watching her move the junk.

"Not necessary. I'm finished with them."

Kumo shrugged but she was affected by his blatant extravagance.

She soon moved her bedroll into the steelworks. Her eyes burned at night as she tried to get warm in the polytherm packing straw she dragged into the icehot furnace.

A couple of days later, Kumo went back to Tommy's tank. He was gone and the whole drum seemed to thrum with the tension of the anticipation of his return. She took a sonic shower, oiled her clone suit, and rustled out the rest of the glo-nuts. Then, feeling the cold pressure of so many waiting machines, she dashed out and hurried straight to market.

This week was to be her scene in the sun, as Motler was wont to say. This had been scheduled for months. Kumo had the same piece ready for some length of time. Though she couldn't see how it related anymore. Nothing related. Kumo was nervous. Now Motler was in charge of the set at market, not Tanaka as always had been.

She trotted through her old section and hunted up the number-seven boxcar. It was still uninhabited, smelling a bit too civetlike for even the lowliest vermin.

The graffiti had all changed to Hoodoo. The Mikan signs were mostly rubbed out or holoed over. Kumo didn't recognize any street deities but they all looked the same, skinny, skull faced, and square toothed with spooky pop-eyes. "Boring," she said aloud.

The charter house was bereft of even the crimestop holo. The bento stall drums were full of black goo and the smell of rotten meat covered the area.

Packs of wiggers flowed around the corners of the streets, but even they were looking more wraithlike than ever. The rocky-goat sign at market was toppled. The whole market seemed deserted of anyone she knew. JuJube was nowhere in sight. Dori was dead. David— dead. Yugi, dead. Amos gone to the Bell Factory. She hurried to the Japanese craft section. Kanda was off to China too. Where was JuJube? she wondered. The station was deathly quiet for a market and cleaned up like a corpse in preparation for burial.

She brought up the holo on a small viewer. There was the white flag with the red circle just exactly center. And as the camera zoomed on the red spot, the lines became distinct and the viewer could see that it was a huge red spider. The white web glittered with dew diamonds and three large bundles bounced on the web. The first bundle contained a hollow sugar egg. Inside the egg from a cutaway end, one could see a little fairyland of blue skies and sun and butterflies on daisies. The second bundle contained a giant worker ant. Its mandibles were large, but it was unable to turn its head to free itself from the web. The third bundle struggled with an angry buzz. It was a large wasp whose stinger was immobilized in silk. Its wings could only move enough to give the creature the illusion that it was freeing itself.

Suddenly, with a giant heave, the red spider launched herself into the air, and floated away on a parachute of web. The victims were left to blacken in the sun, with no merciful bite or anesthetizing sting.

Kumo set the holo up in a temp view from her locker and watched it three times. When she checked back into the scene she noticed the Friendly Navvys were standing by. Their golden banners were limp with no wind, and the wire-dogs were strangely stationary. They were all watching her holo with opaque black eyes and set, grimacing masks. She looked straight back at them. Their numbers had dwindled. Like missing yellowjackets in late fall, after a good hard frost.

Kumo turned off the holo and bowed to them. One of them, a sergeant, bowed back, then the others did, quick to follow suit.

Kumo walked away slowly, and stiffly. You could always appeal to the protocol of a Navvy. That's what made them bearable.

. . .

That evening Kumo climbed to her vantage point from the warehouse and shouted at the Pinkies below who were performing their boring little ritual with the salt and suds.

She got a head start on them, but it wasn't long before all thirteen Pink Flies buzzed down the alleyway on the way to the steelworks.

The chase she led them on was almost too easy and she wondered if they were on some kind of brain-cell-crisping drug.

They followed her straight into her holographic web at the steelworks. Kumo was nervous. It was going too well.

When she hit the switch at the door, they all poured in after her. They all shouted at the metal doors when they slammed shut. Realizing that Kumo was also locked in with them, their howls of rage turned to sinister laughter and hoots of derision.

They felt the sounds before they heard them, strange thrummings and thuds. In a short time the derelict steelworks had suddenly come to life. A switch clicked on, whooshed, and then let out a high-pitched keening. The rusted hulks of gears suddenly began to turn. The rust flaked off in the movement. Shining steel and black grease gleamed with naked intent. A pit opened before them and a huge bucket swung out and began to tilt with a high squeal and thunk.

The Pinkies shrieked with horror as a waterfall of molten red steel came cascading down, surprisingly heatless in the iron room. The walls began to shimmer red, then orange.

They milled about in terror but Mute Fly began shouting, "No, not . . . ! Wait—it's a holo!" After more shouting, the others began to calm, but the yells turned to whimpers as one of the walls began to melt and a big jagged hole opened into it. The sounds of the chips was deafening now and the subsonic levels did more to frighten them than what their eyes told them.

Mute motioned for them to go through the hole, and reluctantly, they did. Kumo was standing at the far end of room—smiling.

They took a few steps into the room and then stopped. They weren't on solid ground, but four hundred feet in the air with the city dizzyingly far below. The Pinkies stood on a steel girder two feet wide and Kumo was poised on another girder beckoning to them.

"Pinkbooties!" She laughed. All of them at once sat down on the girder, unable to move for a moment despite the fact that they knew it was just an illusion. One of the men stood up and yelled.

"It's solid, solid!" He jumped off the edge to show them and screamed all the four hundred feet down. CPUs adjusted to movement. He'd only fallen five feet but was now out of sight. The real Kumo was waiting below in a trench and she hit the Pinkie over the head and knocked him out. She tied and gagged him—then stalked the other twelve.

The rest of them scaled the imaginary beam and entered a room full of catwalks and running motors. Glowing steel ingots moved on a conveyer belt. The pings of metal and throbbing sound of huge machinery were loud enough to stun them temporarily. One of the men fell to his knees with blood pouring from his nose and ears. The whole structure of the building shimmered like an image in a heat wave.

The sound grew louder and then dropped. Five Kumos stood staring at them. The leader noticed the hesitancy of the Pinkies and screamed. "Bash them—bash them all!!!"

As they jumped forward and began swinging wildly—for none of these were Kumo—they looked around to see their own number increased. All of them had quadrupled now, all of them and their selves were swinging. It wasn't long before they started swinging at each other. Out of chance and pure ferocity, they sometimes smacked one another just for the satisfaction of connecting with something solid. Leaders were screaming in quadruple for them to knock it off—and they did, but not before a good deal of damage was done.

The images stopped hitting each other.

There were a lot less of them now. The real Kumo called to them while fake ones looked on at her. The Pinkies swung chains forward and ran toward her. She disappeared into another room which was all gleaming steel and quiet. No machinery moved, no metal glowed molten. There was a sound like a huge metal handle moving, and thunks like some iron chain slipping. The men and their holo clones looked up and around.

Camera eyes revealed themselves out of reach. A high window burst inwards with a shattering of glass and bent steel. Something black and slimy rushed through the window with a gurgling, sucking sound. It not only looked and sounded disgusting—it smelled horrible. From the far end of the corridor, a wave of the black-brown stuff flowed. Too late to run. The wash of shit lashed around their legs.

Nobody paid much attention to the river of effluvium, they were too riveted on what was floating on the top, huge maggots with evil, lamprey mouths and rows of teeth. These rapidly attacked the holo images with insect fury. The holo images were screaming and going down in the current with the maggots on their faces and torsos.

Other Pinkies tried to help but rarely got a grasp on anything real. When one Pink touched another by accident, the other was sure it was the maggots and struck out blindly and viciously.

The wave of shit passed as rapidly as it had come and the Pinkies that were left stood in the emptied hall panting, staring at each other, wondering who was real and who wasn't. Suddenly one of the leaders started screaming and clawing at his face. Parts of his face fell off in ulcer orange clusters, fingers and hands fell off. Instant leprosy plagued them all. Immense bottle-green flies flew around them, buzzing ominously. When someone fell he was instantly covered with filthy iridescent flies who would partially consume him and leave a mass of glutinous eggs on what was left. Pinkies began throwing up and slipping in their own puddles of vomit.

Mute Fly was too quick for it and ignored the decaying corpses of his holographic gang members. He followed a long pink tongue waving at him from a small vent and crawled down the shaft of it into another room. His own tongue was now wood in his mouth. He called out to Kumo.

"Aiy now yo in vere!" he screamed. "I mow yo fo what yo are! Come hya! Kumo!!! Faaaaiiiighht!"

Kumo dropped down before him from a junked heister. She was crimson in the cold light of the holo, once again showing a molten furnace all around them. Maggots and roaches crawled along the floor, devouring each other, and carrying phalluses and pieces of testicle in their mandibles.

The Mute stared at her, refusing to look at the insects, though he shuddered. The walls crawled with flaming cockroaches. Some of the roaches were impervious to fire, but others sizzled, charred, and fell in a blackened heap. The whole derelict steam-works had a potent sulfuric smell to it.

The Mute Fly glared at her with hot, cornered rage. Sweat rolled into his eyes and he shook his head. He lunged forward and then jumped back as her sides were ripped open and eight hairy legs thrust through.

Another Kumo came in a side door, a ruby-black Kumo. This one, too, burst open like an overfilled tick. A spider's legs and mandibles jerked through torn skin. Blood-filled laughter coated the room. A third Kumo came into the room and hissed at Mute Fly. This time when he jumped, his guess was correct. He shat and came in his clone suit as he grabbed her. The elation of connecting with the actual Kumo almost made him faint.

Kumo yowled triumphantly as she heard the remaining Pinkies get rerouted to a room of metal horror. Just as suddenly, she froze and allowed Mute Fly to beat her.

Something was wrong. There was another presence here. A faint smell of onion and cumin rolled down the corridors. Mixed with this was the smell of rotting meat.

She didn't like what her mind was telling her, no revenge should be so complete. These were not screams of terror, but of pain.

Mute Fly dropped her in fear at the analogue cries. Real Pinkies were screaming in living pain.

Kumo and Mute Fly were both stunned. Mute Fly turned to run but Kumo grabbed him.

"No—wait," she yelled as he struggled. "Hoodoo!"

"*Shit!*" he screamed back at her, obviously thinking she was in league with them. He broke free and ran.

Kumo staggered to her feet and trotted after him. Her limbs were weighted down with dread. Those shitting zombies. *Goddamn them*. They'd been following her and now had them all trapped in here. Her bowels sloshed with liquid ice. She just wanted to hide.

Fly turned into a room with a polished steel floor, took a step forward, and fell into stagnant icy water. Kumo slid to a stop just behind him and, teetering on the edge, was able to right her balance before going into the water. She knew nothing about this fluid. It wasn't part of her plan.

As she backed rapidly away, she saw Pinkies swarm up to the door covered with huge black leeches.

Kumo hissed at the real leeches. Saliva and blood poured from the wax-white Pinkie faces, now maskless and terrified as they sloshed wetly past Kumo. She grabbed one to help him, but he screeched in fright and careened off the walls.

Mute Fly jumped out last, giving Kumo a tormented glance as he ran past. Kumo ran after him, skidding on the slime from his dripping clothes. She wanted this all to stop now, no more.

Mute Fly suddenly tripped and fell into a

huge pile of soft ground meat. It was icy and greasy. He cried out in disgust and dismay and stood stinking and steaming in the cold room. Kumo vomited up a glo-nut mess. There were a lot of zombies, she decided.

"Hey, Mute, it's only food," she yelled over his carrying on. He smelled putrid.

"Here, I'll—I—can help." She reached for him but he turned and ran down the hallway, looking in all doors for a cleansing clone-water tank. Kumo followed, she'd smelt a bad omen.

They both rounded a corner and ran into a room that held five vats. Kumo guessed it was probably a cooling and dipping room. One of the vats held clear liquid. Mute Fly hesitated, looking desperately at it. Kumo guessed his panicked intent, caught his hand, and held tight.

"Hey, don't. Who knows what—"

Mute Fly jerked from her grasp, leaving his empty glove in her hand, and dived in the nearest tank. He instantly began hissing, bubbling, and floundering. Some *thing* in the wax of the water made a strange growl-like snort and heaved and turned. The sides were sloped so exit from the tank was almost impossible without aid.

Kumo leaned over the tank to help, and froze—staring at an ominous filmy residue that was unraveling from Mute Fly. She was reluctant to touch the fluid, but started to reach in anyway.

"Don't!" The swastika-mask Pinkie knocked her to the floor. He kicked her hard in the ribs with his big boot and she spit up blood. "Leave him alone. Leave him to die there, you stupid animal. We don't want him out"—he nodded his head to the dissolving tissue—"like that."

Kumo heard and comprehended. No, they *wouldn't*.

A faint drumming echoed down the corridors. The zombies pounding. The Pinkie cursed and ran off. Kumo picked up Mute Fly's bloody, fingerless glove she'd dropped. She stuck the little piece of dried tongue in it and then tossed them both in the vat. "RIP then, Fly."

Kumo turned to follow the swastika and get out of the steelworks. She hurried down the corridor but stopped suddenly when she saw that two tall, mirasmic zombies stood in the way. They had absurdly long, sharp-tined forks in their skinny hands.

For all the food they mashed, they certainly looked thin. Kumo thought maybe human flesh wasn't nutritious. Or maybe it was the drip-dry drug, that BopZ—benzyloxypromezap—modified pesticide, they all took.

She'd never been this close to a zombie before. They had day-of-the-dead bones painted on the grub-colored thermal underpieces they wore. Their faces were waxy white, with greenish circles around their eyes. In short, like slightly decomposed corpses. Inside the dark circles of their eyes, small needle-points glowed red. Kumo had a sudden urge to pounce on the neck of one and shake it like a rat. The rotting-flesh smell that clung to them made her lip curl back. She hugged the wall even closer than she normally did, a lower profile for someone creeping up behind her. The zombies took two steps forward while Kumo pondered her next move. She wasn't about to go back down the corridor toward the room writhing with butchered Pinkies. The zombies advanced.

Kumo tried to hold her breath to keep from gagging on the foul stench emanating from them. The Vigowear outfits were covered with rusty spots of grime.

Termites, Kumo said to herself, shifting back and forth on her boots, she couldn't think of them as human.

Jeezus, they're so emaciated. She thought she could just take them apart with her bare hands. Their slight forms gave her confidence. Kumo lunged forward and bowled into their skinny knees.

They all came down in a tumble and a strange wet whoosh that made Kumo wince. *What the hell was that?* flashed in her mind as the zombies grabbed her arms and ankles with their long bony hands. They gripped tight and stabbed at her with the sharp fork tines.

One of them bit into her suit with its artificial shovel-like teeth. Kumo gave a quick jerk and the teeth shattered at the roots, letting blood and enamel fly everywhere. The zombie clapped its hands over its mouth and its partner took the moment to strike down at her with a fork. Kumo grabbed an arm on its downward swing and, scrambling up, busted it hard across her own thigh. It broke easily, like a dry stick.

The zombie went, *"Ungh, ungh, ungh."*

Kumo grabbed its wrist and wrenched it hard, marveling at the tight "crack" it made as the thing screeched. The fork dropped on the cement. Kumo snatched it up and jabbed it deep into the lungs of the first zombie. She lunged forward as she struck with the fork and knocked the zombie on its back. The fork went in deep and in a second the zombie was vomiting forth suds of orange, frothy blood.

Uuuucck. Kumo planted her boot heel into the thing's ruined nose. She hissed as she felt it smoosh into a skull like a rotted pumpkin.

"Shhiiiitt." Kumo gagged. *These things ain't even real.*

With both boots she jumped on the thigh bone of the broken-armed voodoo doll and urbled a hysterical laugh when she saw the bones poke through the rotten Vigowear. *Fucking-a.* She grabbed its ankle and jerked, positive she could pull the thin tendons apart with the strength of her arms.

The zombie cried, *"Hunh, hunh."*

Kumo let go and walked around to its head. She stepped on that too, just like she had the other zombie, who was now only moving convulsively and not consciously. A coil of green snot came out of its nose, and some long writhing worms. Kumo laughed aloud. It was a nightmare she had found here. Not a real thing. *It wasn't human—it was a-a-meat puppet.* Kumo threw herself down on her knees on the chest of the broken zombie and heard a satisfying crunch. In a way, she wondered if the parasites had given the zombies the illusion of being alive. Just the movement of the

worms through the putrefying flesh animated them.

What was the point of being so skinny? she wondered. Her muscular weight alone could smear them like a frog on a highway. Kumo shook her head again, sicked up a bit, and then pissed on the zombies. She couldn't treat them like beings—*they were just these cancerous, leprous* . . .

Kumo kept her brow furrowed as she ran. She could still hear the snap of the limbs breaking across her knees and wanted to go back, to do it again, just to see if it really happened. If she had taken the thin bones and broken them like toothpicks. *Hadn't she?* It was so confusing. The soft lungs, the softened skulls. Like pickled eggs in the shell. Eggshells. The zombies ate the gangs, but who preyed on the zombies? Gangleshanks?

Dung beetles? Kumo thought of their icy, greasy faces and shook her head rapidly. How did those things kill the gangs? How could shit and maggots and those white termites kill gangs? Gangs could pop them like lice between their fingernails.

Or was it that there were so many? Were gangs buried alive in their soft bodies, with matchstick legs and sharpened tines? Toxiphobia. Telling themselves, *Don't panic, don't panic, it's just, just* . . . The gouging, the ear ripping, tongues lapping and teeth shoveling in the young gang flesh.

Kumo giggled nervously. *Weird world.* She went back to Tommy's briefly, to get her jacket, and some loose credits. He was nowhere to be seen, so she headed out again, to burrow down to Dogton. She found the place she was looking for, prayed, and jerked the handle. Miracle number two, it opened. The hatch dropped straight into the Dogton tunnels. She dived in, slamming the hatch behind her.

She untangled herself and fingered a goose egg on her head, and then ran underground into the heated tunnels. She kept running all the way to Ded Tek, where she surfaced near market and then lit off to her own boxcar. She vomited over and over again, until dry heaves held her in the throes of exhaustion.

She trembled and sweated and cried long and savagely, like a wounded big cat. It echoed like a looped tape, over and over out into the yards. Some artists on the tracks looked at each other through smoky, spooked eyes, but nobody went to see. Nobody dared.

Revenge wasn't sweet, only its own demon, demanding more hate and blood than any human had to give. In her fingers Kumo could feel the thin cold bones snapping, snapping.

The Brains of Rats

MICHAEL BLUMLEIN

Michael Blumlein (1948–) is a US science-fiction writer who works full-time as a medical doctor at the University of California, San Francisco. His novels include *The Movement of Mountains* (1987), *X, Y* (1993), and *The Healer* (2005). Despite a small output—he has only published six books— Blumlein has had considerable impact on the field, beginning with his first published story, "Tissue Ablation and Variant Regeneration: A Case Report" for *Interzone* (1984). This tale remains one of the most astonishingly savage political assaults ever published. The target is Ronald Reagan, whose living body is eviscerated without anesthetic by a team of doctors, partly to punish him for the evils he has allowed to flourish in the world and partly to make amends for those evils through the biologically engineered growth and transformation of the ablated tissues into foodstuffs and other goods ultimately derived from the flesh, which are then sent to the impoverished of the Earth. The story recalls the "condensed novels" of J. G. Ballard and would not have been out of place in a New Wave–era volume of *New Worlds* magazine.

"Tissue Ablation" and other remarkable tales, including the striking exploration of gender couched in the language of medicine reprinted in this anthology, "The Brains of Rats" (originally published in *Interzone*, 1986), were assembled as *The Brains of Rats* (1989), which also included original stories such as "The Wet Suit." Blumlein's later stories, assembled in *What the Doctor Ordered* (2014)—which includes a novella, "The Roberts" (2010)—continue in the same externally cool, internally incandescent manner. At his best, Blumlein writes tales in which, with an air of remote sangfroid, he makes unrelenting assaults on public issues (and figures).

The writer Michael McDowell notes in his astute introduction to *The Brains of Rats*, "The futured world of Blumlein's occasional science-fiction stories is strange and unsettling. Fellini's stylized and grotesque cinematic past is probably nearest to it, not because its details are correct but simply because history is shown to be alien and unrecognizable . . . aberrations sanctioned in fiction only by their reality [which] segue abruptly into the pathology of the civilized mind."

Blumlein's almost scatological fearlessness—seemingly influenced by the Decadents and Symbolists as well as his medical background—demonstrates the very considerable thematic and stylistic range of late twentieth-century science fiction, and shows how very far from reassuring it could be. In some ways, the story and the writer's career have been an unintended rebuke to the bourgeois middle-of-the-road quality of much 1980s and 1990s Humanist SF. Certainly, his fiction often reminds the reader more of attempts at a grittier realism in speculative fiction by writers like James Tiptree Jr. (linked in part by explorations of weird pathology).

Even today, "The Brains of Rats" shocks and disturbs, with its far-from-likable narrator and the provocative ideas to which he gives voice.

THE BRAINS OF RATS

Michael Blumlein

There is evidence that Joan of Arc was a man. Accounts of her trial state that she did not suffer the infirmity of women. When examined by the prelates prior to her incarceration it was found that she lacked the characteristic escutcheon of women. Her pubic area, in fact, was as smooth and hairless as a child's.[*]

There is a condition of men, of males, called testicular feminization. The infants are born without a penis, and the testicles are hidden. The external genitalia are those of a female. Raised as women, these men at puberty develop breasts. Their voices do not deepen. They do not menstruate because they lack a uterus. They have no pubic hair.

These people carry a normal complement of chromosomes. The twenty-third pair, the so-called sex chromosome pair, is unmistakably male. XY. Declared a witch in 1431 and burned at the stake at the age of nineteen, Joan of Arc was quite likely one of these.

Herculine Barbin was born in 1838 in France; she was reared as a female. She spent her childhood in a convent and in boarding schools for girls and later became a schoolmistress. Despite her rearing, she had the sexual inclination of a male. She had already taken a female lover, when, on account of severe pain in her left groin, she sought the advice of a physician. Partly as a result of his examination her sex was redesignated, and in 1860 she was given the civil status of a male. The transformation brought shame and disgrace upon her. Her existence as a male was wretched, and in 1868 she took her own life.[†]

I have a daughter. I am married to a blond-haired, muscular woman. We live in enlightened times. But daily I wonder who is who and what is what. I am baffled by our choices; my mind is unclear. Especially now that I have the means to ensure that every child born on this earth is male.

A patient once came to me, a man with a painful drip from the end of his penis. He had had it for several days; neither excessive bathing nor drugstore remedies had proven helpful. About a week and a half before, on a business trip, he had spent time with a prostitute. I asked if he had enjoyed himself. In a roundabout way he said it was natural for a man.

Several days later, at home, his daughter tucked safely in bed, he had made love to his wife. He said that she got very excited. The way he said it made me think she was the only one in the room.

The two of them are both rather young. While he was in the examining room, she sat quietly in the waiting room. She stared ahead, fatigue and ignorance making her face impassive. In her lap her daughter was curled asleep.

In the room the man milked his penis, squeezing out a large amount of creamy material, which I smeared on a glass slide. In an hour the laboratory told me he had gonorrhea. When

---

[*] Stephen Wachtel, *H-Y Antigen and the Biology of Sex Determination* (New York: Grune & Stratton, 1983), 170.

[†] Ibid., 172.

I conveyed the news to him, he was surprised and worried.

"What is that?" he asked.

"An infection," I said. "A venereal disease. It's spread through sexual contact."

He nodded slowly. "My wife, she got too excited."

"Most likely you got it from the prostitute."

He looked at me blankly and said it again. "She got too excited."

I was fascinated that he could hold such a notion and calmly repeated what I had said. I recommended treatment for both him and his wife. How he would explain the situation to her was up to him. A man with his beliefs would probably not have too hard a time.

I admit that I have conflicting thoughts. I am intrigued by hypnotism and relations of power. For years I have wanted to be a woman, with small, firm breasts held even firmer by a brassiere. My hair would be shoulder-length and soft. It would pick up highlights and sweep down over one ear. The other side of my head would be bare, save for some wisps of hair at the nape and around my ear. I would have a smooth cheek.

I used to brush it this way, posing before my closet mirror in dark tights and high-heeled boots. The velveteen dress I wore was designed for a small person, and I split the seams the first time I pulled it over my head. My arms and shoulders are large; they were choked by the narrow sleeves. I could barely move, the dress was so tight. But I was pretty. A very pretty thing.

I never dream of having men. I dream of women. I am a woman and I want women. I think of being simultaneously on the top and on the bottom. I want the power and I want it taken from me.

I should mention that I also have the means to make every conceptus a female. The thought is as disturbing as making them all male. But I think it shall have to be one or the other.

The genes that determine sex lie on the twenty-third pair of chromosomes. They are composed of a finite and relatively short sequence of nucleic acids on the X chromosome and one on the Y. For the most part these sequences have been mapped. Comparisons have been made between species. The sex-determining gene is remarkably similar in animals as diverse as the wasp, the turtle, and the cow. Recently it has been found that the male banded krait, a poisonous snake of India separated evolutionarily from man by many millions of years, has a genetic sequence nearly identical to that of the human male.

The Y gene turns on other genes. A molecule is produced, a complex protein, which is present on the surface of virtually all cells in the male. It is absent in the female. Its presence makes cells and environments of cells develop in particular ways. These ways have not changed much in millions of years.

Certain regions of the brain in rats show marked sexual specificity. Cell density, dendritic formation, synaptic configuration of the male are different from the female. When presented with two solutions of water, one pure, the other heavily sweetened with saccharin, the female rat consistently chooses the latter. The male does just the opposite. Female chimpanzee infants exposed to high levels of male hormones in utero exhibit patterns of play different from their sisters. They initiate more, are rougher and more threatening. They tend to snarl a lot.

Sexual differences of the human brain exist, but they have been obscured by the profound evolution of this organ in the past half-million years. We have speech and foresight, consciousness and self-consciousness. We have art, physics, and religion. In a language whose meaning men and women seem to share, we say we are different, but equal.

The struggles between the sexes, the battles for power, are a reflection of the schism between thought and function, between the power of our minds and powerlessness in the face of our design. Sexual equality, an idea present for hundreds of years, is subverted by instincts present for millions. The genes determining mental capacity have evolved rapidly; those determining sex have been stable for eons. Humankind suffers the consequences of this disparity, the ambiguities of identity, the violence between the sexes. This can be changed. It can be ended. I have the means to do it.

All my life I have watched men fight with women. Women with men. Women come to the clinic with bruised and swollen cheeks, where they have been slapped and beaten by their lovers. Not long ago an attractive middle-aged lady came in with a bloody nose, bruises on her arms, and a cut beneath her eye, where the cheekbone rises up in a ridge. She was shaking uncontrollably, sobbing in spasms so that it was impossible to understand what she was saying. Her sister had to speak for her.

Her boss had beat her up. He had thrown her against the filing cabinets and kicked her on the floor. She had cried for him to stop, but he had kept on kicking. She had worked for him for ten years. Nothing like this had ever happened before.

Another time a young man came in. He wore a tank top and had big muscles in his shoulders and arms. On one biceps was a tattoo of the upper torso and head of a woman, her huge breasts bursting out of a ragged garment. On his forearm beneath this picture were three long and deep tracks in the skin, oozing blood. I imagined the swipe of a large cat, a lynx or a mountain lion. He told me he had hurt himself working on his car.

I cleaned the scratches, cut off the dead pieces of skin bunched up at the end of the tracks. I asked again how this had happened. It was his girlfriend, he said, smiling a little now, gazing proudly at the marks on his arm. They had had a fight, she had scratched him with her nails. He looked at me, turning more serious, trying to act like a man but sounding like a boy, and asked, "You think I should have a shot for rabies?"

Sexual differentiation in humans occurs at about the fifth week of gestation. Prior to this time the fetus is sexless, or more precisely, it has the potential to become either (or both) sex. Around the fifth week a single gene turns on, initiating a cascade of events that ultimately gives rise to testicle or ovary. In the male this gene is associated with the Y chromosome; in the female, with the X. An XY pair normally gives rise to a male; an XX pair, to a female.

The two genes have been identified and produced by artificial means. Despite a general reluctance in the scientific community as a whole, our laboratory has taken this research further. Recently, we have devised a method to attach either gene to a common rhinovirus. The virus is ubiquitous; among humans it is highly contagious. It is spread primarily through water droplets (sneezing, coughing), but also through other bodily fluids (sweat, urine, saliva, semen). We have attenuated the virus so that it is harmless to mammalian tissue. It incites little, if any, immune response, resting dormantly inside cells. It causes no apparent disruption of function.

When an infected female becomes pregnant, the virus rapidly crosses the placenta, infecting cells of the developing fetus. If the virus carries the X gene, the fetus will become a female; if it carries the Y, a male. In mice and rabbits we have been able to produce entire litters of males or females. Experiments in simians have been similarly successful. It is not premature to conclude that we have the capability to do the same for humans.

Imagine whole families of males or females. Districts, towns, even countries. So simple, it is as though it was always meant to be.

· · ·

My daughter is a beautiful girl. She knows enough about sex, I think, to satisfy her for the present. She plays with herself often at night, sometimes during the day. She is very happy not to have to wear diapers anymore. She used to look at my penis a lot, and once in a while she would touch it. Now she doesn't seem to care.

Once maybe every three or four months she'll put on a pair of pants. The rest of the time she wears skirts or dresses. My wife, a laborer, wears only pants. She drives a truck.

One of our daughter's schoolteachers, a Church woman, told her that Christian girls don't wear pants. I had a dream last night that our next child is a boy.

I admit I am confused. In the ninth century there was a German woman with a name no one remembers. Call her Katrin. She met and fell in love with a man, a scholar. Presumably, the love was mutual. The man traveled to Athens to study and Katrin went with him. She disguised herself as a man so that they could live together.

In Athens the man died. Katrin stayed on. She had learned much from him, had become something of a scholar herself. She continued her studies and over time gained renown for her learning. She kept her disguise as a man.

Some time later she was called to Rome to study and teach at the offices of Pope Leo IV. Her reputation grew, and when Leo died in 855, Katrin was elected pope.

Her reign ended abruptly two and a half years later. In the midst of a papal procession through the streets of Rome, her cloak hanging loose, obscuring the contours of her body, Katrin squatted on the ground, uttered a series of cries, and delivered a baby. Soon after, she was thrown in a dungeon, and later banished to an impoverished land to the north. From that time on, all popes, prior to confirmation, have been examined by two reliable clerics. Before

an assembled audience they feel under the candidate's robes.

"Testiculos habet," they declare, at which point the congregation heaves a sigh of relief.

"Deo gratias," it chants back. "Deo gratias."‡

I was at a benefit luncheon the other day, a celebration of regional women writers. Of five hundred people I was one of a handful of men. I went at the invitation of a friend because I like the friend and I like the writers who were being honored. I wore a sports coat and slacks and had a neatly trimmed four-day growth of beard. I waited in a long line at the door, surrounded by women. Some were taller than me, but I was taller than most. All were dressed fashionably; most wore jewelry and makeup. I was uncomfortable in the crowd, not profoundly, but enough that my manner turned meek. I was ready to be accosted and singled out.

A loud woman butted in front of me and I said nothing. At the registration desk I spoke softly, demurely. The woman at the desk smiled and said something nice. I felt a little better, took my card, and went in.

It was a large and fancy room, packed with tables draped with white cloths. The luncheon was being catered by a culinary school located in the same building. There was a kitchen on the ground floor, to the left of the large room. Another was at the mezzanine level above the stage at the front of the room. This one was enclosed in glass, and during the luncheon there was a class going on. Students in white coats and a chef with a tall white hat passed back and forth in front of the glass. Their lips moved, but from below we didn't hear any sounds.

Midway through the luncheon the program started. The main organizer spoke about the foundation for which the luncheon was

---

‡   H. Gordon, in *Genetic Mechanisms of Sexual Development*, ed. H. L. Vallet and I. H. Porter (New York: Academic Press, 1979), 18.

a benefit. It is an organization dedicated to the empowerment of women, to the rights of women and girls. My mind drifted.

I have been a feminist for years. I was in the room next door when my first wife formed a coven. I gave her my encouragement. I celebrated with her the publication of Valerie Solanas's *SCUM Manifesto*. The sisters made a slide show, using some of Valerie's words. It was shown around the East Coast. I helped them out by providing a man's voice. I am a turd, the man said. A lowly, abject turd.

My daughter is four. She is as precious as any four-year-old can be. I want her to be able to choose. I want her to feel her power. I will tear down the door that is slammed in her face because she is a woman.

The first honoree came to the podium, reading a story about the bond between a wealthy woman traveler and a poor Mexican room-maid. After two paragraphs a noise interrupted her. It was a dull, beating sound, went on for half a minute, stopped, started up again. It came from the glassed-in teaching kitchen above the stage. The white-capped chef was pounding a piece of meat, oblivious to the scene below. Obviously he couldn't hear.

The woman tried to keep reading but eventually stopped. She made one or two frivolous comments to the audience. We were all a little nervous, and there were scattered titters while we waited for something to be done. The chef kept pounding the meat. Behind me a woman whispered loudly, male chauvinist.

I was not surprised, had, in fact, been waiting from the beginning for someone to say something like that. It made me mad. The man was innocent. The woman was a fool. An automaton. I wanted to shake her, shake her up and make her pay the price.

I have a friend, a man with a narrow face and cheeks that always look unshaven. His eyes are quick; when he is with me, they always seem to be looking someplace else. He is facile with speech and quite particular about the words he chooses. He is not unattractive.

I like this man for the same reasons I dislike him. He is opportunistic and assertive. He is clever, in the way that being detached allows one to be. And fiercely competitive. He values those who rise to his challenges.

I think of him as a predator, as a man looking for an advantage. This would surprise, even bewilder him, for he carries the innocence of self-absorption. When he laughs at himself, he is so proud to be able to do so.

He has a peculiar attitude toward women. He does not like those who are his intellectual equal. He does not respect those who are not. And yet he loves women. He loves to make them. Especially he loves the ones who need to be convinced. I sometimes play tennis with him. I apologize if I hit a bad shot. I apologize if I am not adequate competition. I want to please him, and I lose every time we play. I am afraid to win, afraid that he might get angry, even violent. He could explode.

I want to win. I want to win bad. I want to drive him into the net, into the concrete itself and beneath it with the force of my victory.

I admit I am perplexed. A man can be aggressive, tender, strong, compassionate, hostile, moody, loyal, competent, funny, generous, searching, selfish, powerful, self-destructive, shy, shameful, hard, soft, duplicitous, faithful, honest, bold, foolhardy, vain, vulnerable, and proud. Struggling to keep his instincts in check, he is both abused and blessed by his maleness.

Dr. P, a biologist, husband, father, and subject of a widely cited study, never knew how much of his behavior to attribute to the involuntary release of chemicals, to the flow of electricity through synapses stamped male as early as sixty days after conception, and how much was under his control. He did not want to dilute his potency as a scientist, as a man, by struggling too hard against his impulses, and yet the glimpses he had of another way of life were often too compelling to disregard. The bond between his wife and daughter sometimes brought tears to his eyes. The thought of his wife carrying the child in her belly for nine months and then pushing her out through the tight gap between her legs sometimes settled in his mind like a hypnotic suggestion, like something so sweet and pure he would wither without it.[§]

I asked another friend what it was to him to be a man. He laughed nervously and said the question was too hard. Okay, I said, what is it you like best? He shied away but I pressed him. Having a penis, he said. I nodded. Having it sucked, putting it in a warm place. Coming. He smiled and looked beatific. Oh God, he said, it's so good to come.

Later on he said, I like the authority I have, the subtle edge. I like the respect. A man, just by being a man, gets respect. When I get an erection, when I get very hard, I feel strong. I take on power that at other times is hidden to me. Impossibilities seem to melt away.

(A world like that, I think. A world of men. How wondrous! The Y virus, then. I think it must be the Y.)

In the summer of our marriage I was sitting with my first wife in the mountains. She was on one side of a dirt road that wound up to a pass and I was on the other. Scattered on the mountain slope were big chunks of granite and around them stands of aspen and a few solitary pines. The sky was a deep blue, the kind that takes your breath away. The air was crisp.

She was throwing rocks at me, and arguing. Some of the rocks were quite big, as big as you could hold in a palm. They landed close, throwing up clouds of dust in the roadbed. She was telling me why we should get married.

"I'll get more respect," she said. "Once we get married then we can get divorced. A divorced woman gets respect."

I asked her to stop throwing rocks. She was mad because she wasn't getting her way. Because I was being truculent. Because she was working a man's job cleaning out the insides of ships, scaling off the plaque and grime, and she was being treated like a woman. She wanted to be treated like a man, be tough like a man, dirty and tough. She wanted to smoke in bars, get drunk, shoot pool. In the bars she wanted to act like a man, be loud, not take shit. She wanted to do this and also she wanted to look sharp, she wanted to dress sexy, in tight blouses and pants. She wanted men to come on to her, she wanted them to fawn a little. She wanted that power.

"A woman who's been married once, they know she knows something. She's not innocent. She's gotten rid of one, she can get rid of another. They show respect."

She stopped throwing rocks and came over to me. I was a little cowed. She said if I loved her I would marry her so she could divorce me. She was tender and insistent. I did love her, and I understood the importance of respect. But I was torn. I couldn't make up my mind.

"You see," she said, angry again. "You're the one who gets to decide. It's always you who's in control."

"I am a turd," I replied. "A lowly, abject turd."

A woman came to me the other day. She knew my name, was aware of the thrust of my research but not the particulars. She did not know that in the blink of an eye her kind, or mine, could be gone from the face of the earth. She did not know, but it did not seem to matter.

She was dressed simply; her face was plain. She seemed at ease when she spoke, though she could not conceal (nor did she try) a certain intensity of feeling. She said that as a woman she could not trust a man to make decisions

---

[§] I. E. Rudolf et al., *Whither the Male?: Studies in Functionally Split Identities* (Philadelphia: Ova Press, 1982).

about her future. To my surprise I told her that I am not a man at all.

"I am a mother," I said. "When my daughter was an infant, I let her suckle my breast."

"You have no breasts," she said scornfully.

"Only no milk." I unbuttoned my shirt and pulled it to the side. I squeezed a nipple. "She wouldn't stay on because it was dry."

"You are a man," she said, unaffected. "You look like one. I've seen you walk, you walk like one."

"How does a man walk?"

"Isn't it obvious?"

"I am courteous. I step aside in crowds, wait for others to pass."

"Courtesy is the manner the strong adopt toward the weak. It is the recognition of their dominance."

"Sometimes I am meek," I said. "Sometimes I'm as shy as a kitten."

She gave me an exasperated look, as though I were a child who had strained the limits of her patience. "You are a man, and men are outcasts. You are outcasts from the very world you made. The world you built on the bodies of other species. Of women."

I did not want to argue with her. In a way she was right. Men have tamed the world.

"You think you rise above," she went on, less stridently. "It is the folly of comparison. There's no one below. No one but yourselves."

"I don't look down," I said.

"Men don't look at all. If you did, you'd see that certain parts of your bodies are missing."

"What does that mean?"

She looked at me quietly. "Don't you think it's time women had a chance?"

"Let me tell you something," I said. "I have always wanted to be a woman. I used to dress like one whenever I had the chance. I was too frightened to keep women's clothes in my own apartment, and I used to borrow my neighbor's. She was a tall woman, bigger than me, and she worked evenings. I had the key to her apartment, and at night after work, before she

came home, I would sneak into her place and go through her drawers. Because of her size, most of her clothes fit. She had a pair of boots, knee-high soft leather boots which I especially liked."

Her eyes narrowed. "Why are you telling me this?"

"I want to. It's important that you understand."

"Listen, no man wants to be a woman. Not really. Not deep down."

"Men are beautiful." I made a fist. "Our bodies are powerful, like the ocean, and strong. Our muscles swell and tuck into each other like waves.

"There is nothing so pure as a man. Nothing like the face of a boy. The smooth and innocent cheek. The promise in the eyes.

"I love men. I love to trace our hard parts, our soft ones, with my eyes, my imagination. I love to see us naked, but I am not aroused. I never have thoughts of having men.

"One night, though, I did. I was coming from my neighbor's apartment, where I had dressed up in dark tights, those high boots of hers, and a short, belted dress. I had stuffed socks in the cups of her bra and was a very stacked lady. Very shapely indeed. When I was done, I took everything off, folded it, and put it neatly back in her drawers. I got dressed in my own pants and shirt, a leather jacket on top, and left. I was going to spend the night with my wife, who at the time lived separately from me a few blocks away.

"On the street I still felt aroused. I had not relieved the tension and needed some release. As I walked I alternated between feeling like a man on the prowl and a woman wanting to grab something between her legs. I think I felt more the latter, because I wanted something to be done to me. I wanted someone else to be boss.

"I reached the top of the hill and started down the other side. It was late and the street was dark. A solitary car, a Cadillac, crept down the hill. When it came alongside me, it slowed. The driver motioned me over, and I took half a step back. My heart was pounding. He motioned again. I took a deep breath, swallowed heavily, and went to him.

"He was a burly black man, smelled of alcohol. I sat far away from him, against the door, and stared out the windshield. He asked where my place was. I said I had none. He grunted and drove up a steep hill, then several more. He pulled his big car into the basement lot of an apartment complex. "A lady friend's," he said, and I followed him up some flights of stairs and down a corridor to the door of an apartment. I was aroused, frightened, determined. I don't think he touched me that whole time.

"He opened the door and we went in. The living room was bare, except for a record player on the floor and a scattered bunch of LPs. One was playing and was close to being done. I expected to see someone else in the apartment. But it was empty.

"The man went into another room, maybe the kitchen, and fixed himself a drink. He wasn't friendly to me, wasn't cruel. I think he was a little nervous to have me there, but otherwise acted as if I were a piece of something to deal with in his own way in his own time. I did not feel that I needed to be treated any differently than that.

"He took me into the bedroom, put me on the bed. That was in the beginning: later I remember only the floor. He took off his shirt and his pants and pulled my pants down. He settled on me, his front to my front. He was barrel-chested, big and heavy. I wrapped my legs around him and he began to rub up and down on me. His lips were fat, and he kissed me hard and tongued me. He smelled very strong, full of drugs and liquor. His beard was rough on my cheek. I liked the way it felt but not the way it scratched. He began to talk to himself.

" 'The swimmin' gates. Let me in the swimmin' gates. The swimmin' gates.'

"He muttered these words over and over, drunkenly getting more and more turned on.

He rolled me over, made me squat on my knees with my butt in the air. He grabbed me with his arms, tried to enter me. I was very dry and it hurt. I let him do it despite the pain because I wanted to feel it, I wanted to know what it was like, I didn't want to let him down.

"Even before then, before the pain, I had withdrawn. I was no longer aroused, or not much. I liked his being strong because I wanted to be dominated, but as he got more and more excited, I lost the sense that I was anything at all. I was a man, but I might just as easily have been a woman, or a dog, or even a tube lined with something from the butcher. I felt like nothing; I was out of my body and growing cold. I did not even feel the power of having brought him to his climax. If it wasn't me, it would have been something else. . . ."

I stopped. The woman was quiet for a while.

"So what's your point?" she asked at length.

"I'm wrong to think he didn't need me. Or someone to do what he wanted. To take it without question."

"He hurt you."

"In a way I pity him. But also, I admire his determination."

She was upset. "So you think you know what it's like to be a woman? Because of that story, even if it did happen like you said, you think you know?"

"I don't know anything," I said. "Except that when I think about it I always seem to know more about what it is to be a woman than what it is to be a man."

Having a penis, my friend said. That's what I like best. It reminds me of a patient I once had, a middle-aged man with diabetes. He took insulin injections twice a day, was careful with his diet, and still he suffered the consequences of that disease. Most debilitating to him was the loss of his sex life.

"I can't get it up," he told me. "Not for more than a minute or two."

I asked if he came. Diabetes can be quite selective in which nerves it destroys.

"Sometimes. But it's not the same. It feels all right, it feels good, but it's not the same. A man should get hard."

I nodded, thinking that he should be grateful, it could be worse. "At least you can come. Some people can't even do that."

"Don't you have a shot, doctor? Something so I can get it up."

I said no, I didn't, it wasn't a question of some shot, it was a question of his diabetes. We agreed to work harder at keeping it under control, and we did, but his inability to get an erection remained. He didn't become depressed, as many do, nor did he get angry. He was matter-of-fact, candid, even funny at times. He told me that his wife liked him better the way he was.

"I don't run around," he explained. "It's not that I can't . . . the ladies, they don't seem to mind the way I am. In fact, they seem to like it. I just don't want to, it doesn't feel right, I don't feel like a man."

"So the marriage is better?"

He shrugged. "She's a prude. She'd rather not have sex anyway. So how about a hormone shot, doc? What do we got to lose?"

His optimism was infectious, and I gave him a shot of testosterone. And another a few weeks later. It didn't change anything. The next time I saw him he was carrying a newspaper clipping.

"I heard about this operation." He handed me the article. "They got something they put in your penis to make it hard. A metal rod, something like that. They also got this tube they can put in. With a pump, so you can pump it up when you're ready and let it down when you're finished. What do you think, doc?"

I knew a little about the implants. The rods were okay, except the penis stayed stiff all the time. It was a nuisance, and sometimes it hurt if it got bent the wrong way. The inflatable tubes were unreliable, sometimes breaking open, other times not deflating when they were supposed to. I told him this.

"It's worth a try," he said. "What do we got to lose?"

It was four or five months before I saw him again. He couldn't wait to get me in the examining room, pulling down his pants almost as soon as I shut the door. Through the slit in his underwear his penis pointed at me like a finger. His face beamed.

"I can go for hours now, doc," he said proudly. "Six, eight, all night if I want. And look at this. . . ." He bent it to the right, where it stayed, nearly touching his leg. Then to the left. Then straight up, then down. "Any position, for as long as I want. The women, they love it."

I sat there, marveling. "That's great."

"You should see them," he said, bending it down in the shape of a question mark and stuffing it back in his pants. "They go crazy. I'm like a kid, doc. They can't keep up with me."

I thought of him, sixty-two years old, happy, stiff, humping away on an old mattress, stopping every so often to ask his companion that night which way she wanted it. Did she like it better left or right, curved or straight, up or down? He was a man now, and he loved women. I asked about his wife.

"She wants to divorce me," he said. "I got too many women now."

The question, I think, is not so much what I have in common with the banded krait of India, him slithering through the mud of that ancient country's monsoon-swollen rivers, me sitting pensively in a cardigan at my desk. We share that certain sequence of nucleic acids, that gene on the Y chromosome that makes us male. The snake is aggressive; I am loyal and dependable. He is territorial; I am a faithful family man. He dominates the female of his species; I am strong, reliable, a good lover.

The question really is how I differ from my wife. We lie in bed, our long bodies pressed together as though each of us were trying to become the other. We talk, sometimes of love, mostly of problems. She says, my job, it's so hard, I'm so tired, my body aches. And I think, that's too bad, I'm so sorry, where is the money to come from, be tough, buck up. I say, I am insecure at work, worried about being a good father, a proper husband. And she says, you are good, I love you, which rolls off of me like water. She strokes my head and I feel trapped; I stroke hers and she purrs like a cat. What is this? I ask, nervous, frightened. Love, she says. Kiss me.

I am still so baffled. It is not as simple as the brains of rats. As a claw, a fang, a battlefield scarred with bodies. I want to possess, and be possessed.

One night she said to me, "I think men and women are two different species."

It was late. We were close, not quite touching.

"Maybe soon," I said. "Not quite yet."

She yawned. "It might be better. It would certainly be easier."

I took her hand and squeezed it. "That's why we cling so hard to one another."

She snuggled up to me. "We like it."

I sighed. "It's because we know someday we might not want to cling at all."

Gorgonoids

LEENA KROHN

Translated by Hildi Hawkins

Leena Krohn (1947–) is a critically acclaimed Finnish author, perhaps the most well-known Finnish writer of her generation. Her large and varied body of work—showcased in English in the enormous *Collected Fiction* (2015)—includes novels, short stories, children's books, and essays. She often deals with such topics as the relationship between imagination and morality, the evolution of synthetic forms of life, and the future of humankind in the context of the natural world. Krohn has received such prestigious honors as the Pro Finlandia Medal of the Order of the Lion of Finland (1997; returned in protest for ethical reasons) and the Aleksis Kivi Fund award for lifetime achievement (2013). Her short novel *Tainaron: Mail from Another City* was a World Fantasy Award finalist in 2005 and her books have been translated into more than twenty languages. Her fiction has been included in such English-language anthologies as *The Weird*, *Sisters of the Revolution*, and *The Dedalus Book of Finnish Fantasy*.

Krohn's usual form is a kind of "mosaic" novel, in which short chapters advance the overall story arc but also form complete tales in and of themselves. The rate of ideas and images conveyed in a typical chapter, even when playful, has a density that might overwhelm in longer increments but seems layered and useful at the short length. There is also a puzzle aspect respectful of reader intelligence and imagination, as the reader pieces together the final form of the novel chapter by chapter.

Her justly celebrated novel *Tainaron* exemplifies the worth of this approach: not only is there an interesting symbolism in chapters that include a hillside immolation of beetles and another with sand lions, but the insect characters themselves have an intrinsic meaning beyond that mere symbolism.

Krohn is also one of our foremost thinkers about not just the present but the future. The novel *Pereat Mundus* (1998 in Finnish; published in English in *Collected Fiction*) details the lives of a series of cloned biotech versions of the same person—exploring what it means to be human. In this work and others, Krohn's exploration of biotech and artificial intelligence occurred well before it became trendy in English-language fiction, and if *Pereat Mundus* had entered the English-language canon in the 1990s it would have been received as groundbreaking work. (Krohn also used digital tools in her literary work well before they became popular in mainstream literary circles—perhaps best exemplified in her experimental novel *Sphinx or Robot*.)

As Peter Berbegal noted in his profile of Krohn for the *New Yorker* website, "Krohn offers up the narrated inner lives of characters trying to make sense of their environments, and of the other people whom they encounter. Many of the works are set in cities, but the worlds that Krohn's characters inhabit never feel concrete: everything is mediated through particular characters' perceptions. The reader is left with the sense of having intruded on someone's dream, in which symbols are revelations of intimate details."

"Gorgonoids" is a self-contained excerpt from another important Krohn novel, *Mathematical Creatures or Shared Dreams*, which won Finland's most prestigious literary award, the Finlandia Prize, in 1993. *Mathematical Creatures* was Krohn's seventh novel for adults and consists of twelve prose pieces that straddle the line between fiction and essay, in a way similar to some of Alfred Jarry's and Jorge Luis Borges's work. They are linked thematically by a discussion of the relationship between self and reality. "Gorgonoids" is among the most playful selections in this anthology, demonstrating to great effect how Krohn's imagination and attention to detail help make her exploration of abstract ideas so interesting.

GORGONOIDS

Leena Krohn

Translated by Hildi Hawkins

The egg of the gorgonoid is, of course, not smooth. Unlike a hen's egg, its surface texture is noticeably uneven. Under its reddish, leather skin bulge what look like thick cords, distantly reminiscent of fingers. Flexible, multiply jointed fingers, entwined—or, rather, squeezed into a fist.

But what can those "fingers" be?

None other than embryo of the gorgonoid itself.

For the gorgonoid is made up of two "cables." One forms itself into a ring; the other wraps round it in a spiral, as if combining with itself. Young gorgonoids that have just broken out of their shells are pale and striped with red. Their colouring is like the peppermint candies you can buy at any city kiosk.

In the mature gorgonoid, the stripes darken. It develops a great lidless eyeball whose iris is blood-red.

I spoke of a leather skin, but that is, of course, not an accurate description. In fact, it is completely erroneous. It is simply, you understand, that the eggshell looks like leather. It isn't actually leather, of course, or chitin, or plaster. Or any other known material. Note: it is not made of any material at all. These creatures are not organic, but neither are they inorganic. For gorgonoids are immaterial, mathematical beings. They are visible, all the same: they move, couple, and multiply on our computer terminals. Their kin persist on our monitor screens, and their progeny mature to adulthood in a few seconds. But how they exist, how—if at all—they live, is a different question entirely. The gorgonoid is merely and exclusively what it looks like—as far as we know.

But what have I said; am I not now contradicting myself? Didn't I say that the eggshell of the gorgonoid looks like leather, but is not leather? There is some inconsistency here, something that troubles me. Perhaps I should have said: the gorgonoid appears to be only that which it appears to be. What it really is, one hardly dares attempt to say.

Not everything that is visible is material. Gorgonoids are visible but immaterial creatures. In that respect, they belong in the same category as all images and dreams, although they are not located only in an individual mind. We, on the other hand, are visible and material. In addition, there exists matter that is invisible, as astrophysicists have shown. They believe that the entire universe is full of such cold, dark mass, that there is infinitely more of it than of visible matter. Frail filaments of visible matter glimmer amid the darkness. . . .

But about that which is both invisible and immaterial, they too know nothing. It is completely unattainable, uncategorisable. It is not merely unknown; it is unknowable. We cannot sense creatures of such a category, but that is no reason to dispute their existence—if not for us.

Besides the gorgonoid, I have had the opportunity to trace the development of the tubanide, the pacmantis, and the lissajoune. The tubanide looks a little like certain ammonites of the Mesozoic era. It is a mathematical model for *Nipponites mirabilis*, which lives in a sea of ammonia.

The spherical figures of the lissajoune have charmed me most. Whenever we wish, the precise flower-spheres of the lissajoune blossom forth on our terminals. They grow in irregular spirals, in which the outline of each figure eventually returns to its starting point. The curve is always closed, unless irrational numbers come into play. And that happens extremely seldom.

Oh how dazzlingly beautiful is the odourless geometry of the lissajoune! Its beauty is not natural beauty, but the flawless logical enchantment of abstract necessity, with which nothing human or material can compare. And yet these figures are merely simulations of material life and natural growth.

And that is what most people in the institute thought: that the gorgonoid, the pacmantis, and the lissajoune were nothing more than models simulating atomic structures. But there were others who believed that, if they were not already alive, they were in the process of stepping across the threshold that separates existence from life.

"Would you like to be like them?" Rolf, the other assistant, asked me once.

"What do you mean? Like them in what sense?"

"Without free will," Rolf said. "They never have to make a choice. That is a great advantage. Everything they do, they have to do. And they never want anything other than what they do."

"You amaze me," I said to Rolf. "You don't really think they want and don't want? And that there could exist intention that is bound?"

"I mean," Rolf said, "that for them action and intention are the same thing."

"That they lack internal contradiction, unlike us, you mean? But perhaps, still, they feel as if they make choices. . . ."

He shrugged his shoulders, and left. His words affected me deeply.

I remembered once looking at a dark hawk moth lying on a pine trunk. I asked myself, then, how the hawk moth knows how to make the right choice. Why does it always choose a trunk covered in dark bark, and not, for example, a pale birch? Does it know what colour it is?

The hawk moth cannot see itself, but we can. Nevertheless, it always makes the right choice, but human beings do not. Why is that which we call instinct more accurate than that which we call reason? In its flawlessness, the perfection of its life, the gorgonoid—to which we have granted neither inborn instinct nor the possibility of rationality—is more like the hawk moth than ourselves.

But we, the reason we lose our way so often is that we are freer to err, and because we watch ourselves instead of what lies ahead.

Certainly there were moments when I should have liked to have exchanged my life for that of the gorgonoid, or, even better, the lissajoune, in order to be as flawless, precise, and beautiful as they.

And another reason why I should have liked to be like them is that they could at any moment—true, the moment was defined by us, but this they could hardly have known—cease to exist, and then come back just the same as before. We were not allowed to pause for breath, we had to live without stopping. Sleep was not real absence, it was not enough. Everything continued through the nights: the stream of images was ceaseless, it merely took place in different surroundings, without need of eyes or light. And when the night was over and we returned to our desks, we were not quite the same creatures who had left in the evening, for even our dreams changed us. And our changes were always irreversible, whereas they could start again from the beginning—or from the exact point at which they had left off.

How I should have loved to go away, even for a moment, if it could have been done by pressing a key, to come back later. But for us there was no temporary death, whereas the gorgonoid—when the glow of the monitor was extinguished—ceased to exist in the place where it was, but without going anywhere else.

Inconceivable that something that has existed in some place can no longer exist in any place. How can we help asking, when someone dies, "Where has he gone?"

The gorgonoid does not fall ill, age, or necessarily ever die. Such are the privileges of creatures that do not live in the flesh or in time. They can be transferred to other programs and be copied endlessly.

But was it certain that, outside the program, the gorgonoid did not have its own independent existence, did not continue its existence there in precisely the same way as it had lived on our screens up to that point, with the sole difference that now we could no longer perceive it?

"What do you think, Rolf, are they animals?" I asked once, as the project was beginning to near its conclusion.

"Don't animals have bodies? Mass?" he said.

"They are not animals or plants, because they don't really have bodies. You can't touch them."

"Is that your criterion for an animal? That you can touch it?"

They looked three-dimensional, but of course they were not. Our understanding was that their life was "apparent" life, it was completely superficial. They were objects, no more than objects, at any rate that's what it—yes, appeared to be.

I couldn't have lived the "apparent" life of the gorgonoid, even if I had wanted to. And that was because I wasn't "internally consistent," for I had a quality that the gorgonoids only appeared to have—the state of materiality, a state of intentionality, self, and freedom that had spread inseparably through matter, had dissolved into it. It was this that kept the visible in existence, that gave it a recognisable form, discrete and relatively permanent. It was a state of choice that allowed changes of direction, but only of place, never of time.

Would I really have exchanged my life for theirs? Would I have given up my materiality, my fleeting moment, for their disembodied seclusion, static even in its mutability?

What gave us the right to consider their life to be a mere shadow existence, pictures in a magic lantern? Our life differed from theirs in that we loved, hated, feared, and pitied—and were conscious of the events of our own existence. When we were no longer conscious of them, there was little to differentiate between our lives and their existence.

There were times when I began to have the terrifying feeling that, in some ways, I was becoming like them. It felt as though the things that made my life human were beginning to wither and shrivel.

During that winter, when I was spending my days in the company of the gorgonoids, I came home to his cold gaze, or did not see him at all. He spent his time in the town, in rooms I did not know, with people I did not know. I did not know which was worse: that I waited for him and he did not come home, or that he came home and it was as if there was nobody there. There was no connection. I looked at him as I looked at the gorgonoids, but he never looked at me. It was as though he was as unconscious of my existence as they were. And when I, too, ceased to look at him, we lived in separate programs.

My life began to thin out strangely, to empty as if from the inside. I began to become detached, abstracted. I still had a body, and my body had mass, but I was conscious of its existence only momentarily. This state of affairs was not visible from outside. If someone had examined my existence as I examined the gorgonoids, they would not have noticed any difference. But for as long as I myself was conscious of it, I was not a gorgonoid, I only resembled one.

I had a body and a voice, but I did not touch anyone with my body, and no one touched me.

And my voice fell silent, even though I, too, desired to shout the ancient words: "My God, if you exist, save my soul, if I have a soul."

Gorgonoids always stay in their own world. They cannot approach us, and we cannot approach them.

For we do not associate with each other. We

only program them; we are their gods. And they know as little of us as we know of our gods. But although we created the program, we cannot completely predict what they will do at a given moment. And they know nothing of our power and our weaknesses, for we do not inhabit the same time or the same space. At the moment when something in their world changes, they perhaps receive a hint of our existence, as if two-dimensional creatures were to see a ball sink through their surface-world, and then disappear.

Is there any interaction? I am asking a straightforward question: In what sense do they exist? In what sense do they live? The gorgonoid, the tubanide, the pacmantis, and the lissajoune. These statistical animals that can only be seen. That are only two-dimensional, even though they appear three-dimensional.

Did I say "only"? It is unclear in what sense they fail to be three-dimensional. For even if we cannot measure the mass of the gorgonoid, we are able to calculate its volume. And I was unable to rid myself of the following question, however irrelevant it seemed in regard to the institute's project: Can behaviour exist without consciousness? Does the gorgonoid believe that it can influence its individual life in the same way as we do? And is there any way of proving that it does, or does not?

If someone asks, is it alive, what does he really mean? And I do ask. I ask, does it exist for itself. Because I believe that only that is true life. If it has no consciousness, but only an abstract and superficial reality, I do not consider it to be alive. It may be true, but it does not live. In that case, it is merely an object and—objectively!—it exists. And exists much more clearly and unequivocally than myself, who can never prove the existence of my internal reality and whose exterior form can easily

be destroyed, but never transferred. But it is not alive. No, that I deny it.

"You can't," Rolf said. "How can you dictate that artificial reality is less real than physical reality?"

"Life is not a spectacle," I said.

Gorgonoids always stay in their own world. People always stay in the human world. They cannot function without creatures of the same species. But even a solitary gorgonoid is still a gorgonoid, while a person stripped of all relationships is no longer a person. His life resides in them.

Gorgonoids! Tubanides! Lissajounes! *Nipponites mirabilis!* In some ways we were like them, and in others—I thought—even more mechanical than they, like inorganic objects.

But did they have even the slightest possibility of dreaming of choice as we do, day after day, again and again, and as we would continue to do even if it were conclusively proved that any chance of choice was over, and that it had never really existed? That was where humanity lay—not in freedom itself, but in the dream of freedom.

I still say that I wish to raise my hand and step out—in that direction! And I raise my hand and take a step. Not knowing whether I have done so because I wish it, or because my will happens to be in harmony with what I must do.

I still ask: In what sense do we exist? We, who are both visible and invisible? What level of reality do we represent? Is it always the same, or does it sometimes shift, without our realising it?

How independent, and how dependent, are we?

And how can we ever cease to exist?

Vacancy for the Post of Jesus Christ

KOJO LAING

(Bernard) Kojo Laing (1946–) is a notable fiction writer and poet from Ghana who attended school in the United Kingdom and graduated from Glasgow University in Scotland. Since 1985, Laing has served as headmaster at a school his mother founded in Accra. His early work was in poetry, much of it considered to be in the surrealism genre; he often uses Ghanaian Pidgin English alongside standard English. In his fiction, the surrealist impulse from his verse is often transformed into prose that exists within the territory of the speculative or outright science-fictional. His acclaimed novels include *Search Sweet Country* (1986), reissued by McSweeney's in 2012; *Women of the Aeroplanes* (1988); and *Major Gentl and the Achimota Wars* (1992). His work has been awarded the National Poetry Prize Valco Award and the National Novel Prize in Ghana.

In her review of the novel in *Slate Book Review*, Uzodinma Iweala wrote, "Reading *Search Sweet Country* is like reading a dream, and indeed at times it feels like the magical landscapes of writers like the Nigerian Ben Okri or the Mozambican Mia Couto. Each page delivers an intense blast of vivid imagery, a world in which landscapes come to life when inanimate objects receive human characterization." *Women of the Aeroplanes*, meanwhile, is regarded as a utopian fantasy of sorts, set in Africa and Scotland, and *Major Gentl and the Achimota Wars* is a complex set of experimental fictions set in 2020 in "Achimota City," an environment indebted somewhat to cyberpunk conceptions of the future.

Although Laing hasn't written much short fiction, "Vacancy for the Post of Jesus Christ" is a kinetic and clever take on the alien contact story that also interrogates organized religion and general human nature. It originally appeared in *The Heinemann Book of Contemporary African Stories* (1992), edited by Chinua Achebe and C. L. Innes.

VACANCY FOR THE POST OF JESUS CHRIST

Kojo Laing

When the small quick lorry was being lowered from the skies, it was discovered that it had golden wood, and many seedless guavas for the hungry. As the lorry descended the many layers of cool air, the rich got ready to buy it, and the poor to resent it. The wise among the crowd below opened their mouths in wonder, and closed them only to eat. They ate looking up while the sceptical looked down. And so the lorry had chosen to come down to this town that shamed the city with its cleanliness. The wheels were already revolving and, when they shone, most of them claimed they were the mirrors of God. The lorry was quick but the descent was slow. So many wanted to touch it. A whole morning had passed leaving its dew behind long ago; and yet the lorry had not reached the earth. The wooden gold was easy with its birds landing and unlanding. And when the great gust of African rain came down, the wise still kept their eyes up, the poor huddled, and the rich shut their purses small. But nobody left. Come down, lorry of golden wood, with your cleanest exhaust ever seen, they said.

And the old woman was crying. They asked her whether she was crying for a wasted age, or she was crying for the coming lorry. "Come and cleanse me, divine owner of this mammy truck, take my heart now, for I eat too much cassava to be good, I break too many proverbs." They stared at her, then forgot her, for the lorry's golden rope had slackened, and was coming down a little faster. If only it could send down some shea butter for the strained necks . . . and tell the birds to stop their singing so loud, for they wanted to hear the engine and place the range of its power. "But we don't want material power, we want miracles and the healing

of the spirit." The sceptical looked at the poor for the poor to share the slander of what had just been said. As if to say: when was material bread never needed? But the lorry did not mind the large curiosity below it. The songs of birds changed their direction small, and the seedless guavas rolled against each other. The soft touch came from the sky of fruit and love.

At first no one saw the gigantic message being lowered from the wheels of the lorry. The dancing and jumping of the children had continued under the intense afternoon sun. There were scores of dark glasses shined for greater shade. The message on the big card, having folded over after the sudden rain, opened out with the sun: VACANCY FOR THE POST OF JESUS CHRIST. The consternation among the crowd spread even at its different intensities: the sceptical felt vindicated, and snorted at the sky, saying that the eternal laws never favoured the wonder-prone, nor the innocent, and that if the heart was closed today, it would be closed tomorrow. And what was joy anyway but a movement of brain energy. What a pity the African scientists were no different, they said! And the wise grew in stature in their own eyes, for the coming of mystery increased the questions and decreased the answers, thus leaving the space between for them to move confidently in. The poor waited and the rich wrote hundreds of cheques in advance. They were all preparing, preparing. And the old woman said as she grew in remembrance for them, "Look at the shame of the children, dancing when they should be kneeling, they don't train them to respect these days."

Among the dotted neem tree copses, among the generous savanna beyond the city, the old gnarled palm tree refused its birds, the weight being too heavy for any more landing; and the rejected wings had risen and joined the golden birds on the descending machine. "If we have birds going and joining the visitation, then we are in trouble," whispered a brash young man with a girl on his hand and a cap on his head. "You, Boy Kwaku, I knew you had no sense in that tangerine head of yours. Can't you read? The lorry is coming to advertise and then collect applications for the post of Jesus Christ from both black and white. We have never heard of anything like this and I can't even eat . . . but you, such new times will pass you over with nothing showing in you!" screamed an old man with his beard woven around to the back of his head. The old man looked with scorn at the old woman of remembrance, wondering when she was going to be prophetic again between the mouthfuls of roasted cocoyam. Boy Kwaku laughed to his adoring girl, but the old man ignored him and patted his black beard in the sun.

Even in this time of upward eyes you couldn't understand why the sun and the rain changed places so often. You ate atua out of season in the rain, and sho in season of the sun. And the shades were stolen rests from the hot valleys. Turn your eyes sideways, you crowd! For the golden lorry with its divine vacancy was getting bigger as it descended. "It is coming to kill us!" shouted a little girl running from one shade to another. Dogs, sheep, goats, and hens moved about with a curious stiffness, kokrokoo. "Daddy, buy the lorry for me, Daddy, buy the lorry for me now now now! . . ."

It wasn't long before the priests and the policemen came; for the simple reason that rumours had grown that there was a deep-bronze man in the golden lorry. "We can talk to something we can touch then," enthused the two groups. Before the priests came they had insisted that half the town fill the churches, since if this was a divine presence, it would certainly visit a church first. Furthermore, if the sons and daughters of men were to believe in the big VACANCY sign flapping above the valleys, then surely the search indicated would be in a church. But Bishop Bawa asked Father Vea, "Is there anything in the gospels that speaks of a vacancy for the Son of God?" Father Vea, a man that followed his own ways, had entered the valleys with a huge karate jump that he had been trying to teach the bishop to do. These unusual clerics had arrived before the usual ones, and they had also arrived before the herbalists and the traditional priests. "My Lord, we are in unusual times . . . and I love it!" There was a loud but short-lived cheer for the jump. But the wise were sarcastic about these visitational acrobatics.

True, there was a dark bronzeman with very clear eyes at the wheel of the lorry. The murmuring in the crowd grew, as the untidy but immaculate-eyed man of ropegold presented one expressionless look after another. The old rain came back and wet the lorry. But the crowd remained dry. Father Vea was jumping about and praying at the same time, as the lone traditional priest, now come, poured libation at great speed. He was trying to beat the golden lorry to Asaase Yaa before it landed. The cries of goats were stuck in the mouth, and Father Vea was going round the mouths of goats trying hard to unstick the sounds. He shouted, "The more apocalyptic we appear, the easier it would be for the divine to pass us by! Let the goats be normal!" "Go back to your African Gonja karate, Father!" someone shouted back. At the edges of the small ponds the guinea grass was motionless with the cries of doves. Bishop Bawa had been told of what was happening while he was in his vast rice and pepper farms. He had been strolling up and down just behind his open-air raffia altar. He and Father Vea had jumped in surprise together, but Father Vea had jumped higher.

And then the lorry of wooden gold began to shake violently as it prepared to land. The expression of the bronze lorry man had now changed to one of intense concentration. The police moved back, their weapons unconsciously at the ready. Oddly enough, the crowd surged forward instead of back. Father Vea held his hands high in an unknowing triumph. . . .

So unknowing that the speed of the bronzeman was not even witnessed as he raised a thick arm and gave Father Vea a massive blow on the neck. Before Vea fell, the bronze-black giant had already collected the rifles of the police, with the same lightning speed, and this done without leaving the lorry. And long before the army's three armoured vehicles could move the bronzeman had already neutralised their wheels and guns. The old woman of remembrance was sobbing and tending Father Vea. The poor were ready for any old order to be broken, while the rich were inching slowly away, their chequebooks hidden; how could you buy a truck with such a violent driver masquerading as the keep of the vacancy of Jesus Christ? "Didn't I tell you he was coming to kill us?" shouted the little girl again, with all her shades finished. The cheque keepers must be sobbing, thought the bearded old man.

The quick African dusk had come as the bronzeman finally jumped out of the woodgold. He stood there staring at the earth, with utter concentration. The heavens were dragging away at the last of the red sunset, and the ropegold hung uselessly out of the sky. The crowd couldn't bear the man's concentration as small branches caught fire, and birds flew away from smoke.

"I fear nothing!" shouted the dark bronzeman suddenly. "I am the master of the skies, and I am the one that killed Jesus Christ behind the millionth galaxy of stars. I have come to seek a replacement for the Lord, because the galaxies have never been the same since his death. I am a violent man looking for peace." Bishop Bawa looked with more scorn than pity at the strong skytraveller towering above the rest of them. The sceptical looked with dismay at what was happening; they wanted clarity rather than mystery. The wise threw out different questions: "If you have killed the Lord, why should you be allowed to seek a replacement?"

"You have given me the chance to forgive you," mumbled Father Vea, trying to rise to his feet under the hands of the forgotten woman of remembrance. Bishop Bawa beckoned to Vea to continue to rest, as he himself moved forward to speak, his rice and pepper farms echoing in his head; he always felt nearer to God through mundane physical images, seen in crises. "If you have killed Jesus," asserted the little girl of shades, "then this is the town where you too will die." The animals scattered as the skytraveller combed dust out of his thick hair. The wise wanted miracles to liberate their wisdom . . . but miracles on whose behalf? "Shame to the sky of murder!" someone shouted against the hard forehead of the bronzling. The first sky of descending love had changed to this. There were now brusque orders and there was violence. But Bishop Bawa spoke all the same, "Did you kill the Lord's son or did you kill his body?" The bronzling snorted at the bishop, but answered, "Show me the three most important places of the neighbouring city, and I will tell you the secret of Jesus Christ."

"I will show you five places, one here and four in the city; if only you would do two important things: kill me in the same way you killed the Lord, but before this you will tell me all about the lorry of wooden gold," said Father Vea with conviction, struggling onto his feet. The traditional priest had appeared on the hills watching everything in the valleys. And without warning, with the dusk dead to the evening, the hard traveller crushed the dog's head with his foot to signify the agreement. "Shame to your violence!" the traditional priest shouted down. The traveller looked to the hills with contempt and slept there standing up.

The dawn couldn't catch the traveller, for he had already left with Father Vea towards the city. Bishop Bawa and the traditional priest had already gathered the crowd, and they had all sworn to prepare for the giant's destruction, this killer of eternity. They had decided to take the lorry of wooden gold, to get it to help them. Surely anything golden was good. . . . "This lorry is not better than its master, I tell you sharp," warned the little girl.

There was a threat, even damnation, in the air on the road to the city. Father Vea had tried kicks, chops, and trips in surprise on the skytraveller, but the strength of the latter was incredible. These attempts only angered the bronzling, thus creating a mood of ruthlessness that did not seem to belong here on Earth. When this giant urinated he created a stream that went on forever. Vea soldiered on, tripping and panting and rebelling simultaneously in front of the wooden golden man. The sun had given the city a yellow look.

"You evil African bronzeman, I will show you the mortuary, the seat of government, the courtroom, and the historical room. The fifth place will be the church of the shrine back in the town. I hope you survive this," Father said to the bronzeman, who had taken on that intense concentration again . . . as if he were expecting something. "Sometimes I feel the spirit of the Lord, so the sooner I replace the body of the dead Jesus the clearer my mind will be. . . . I have enemies from other galaxies. I am the first evil galactic African bronzeman; and before I arrive at simpler places like the Earth, I send false images of beauty and peace before me by a secret process of osmosis. . . ." "Why are you filling me fat with all this information before you kill me in the same way you killed Jesus . . . ?" complained Father Vea, with no trace of fear. The bronzeman continued regardless, with the birds back at his head, "My lorry of wooden gold has its own mind, created through a new type of computer. Back in the galaxies we call the Lord the Spiriter!" He laughed a deep preset laugh at his own words. But Father Vea stumbled on the thought, his legs bleeding from the scratching of ivy bushgreen and blackberry. "We will go to the mortuary first, but we need permission . . . ," Vea said. "I will break the doors down even from a distance," was the curt reply from the bronze mouth.

Father Vea stopped running before the giant strides of the giantman, and asked, "Why is the mortuary one of the three places you want to see? How can the dead apply for the post of Jesus here? . . ." Giantman wasn't paying attention, and had rather taken on a sudden concentration. He boomed out, "There are two tanks hidden near the doorway. . . ." And the tanks' cannons fired at once, the bombs bouncing off his chest almost as if they were small stones. He gave out his huge laughter as he broke the mortuary door down, saying, "Sometimes the better people are dead. If I find someone suitable to fill the vacancy, I'll take him back and resurrect him through deep ice plus the manipulation of time. . . ." He was still laughing as he crushed the tracks of the tanks and walked into the house of the dead, with the officials and attendants scattering in fear. "Would you like to meet any literary men?" Father Vea ventured, with the giant laughter still in progress, and Vea regretting his intuition that he should have learnt a better karate since no one anticipated an invincible man.

The atmosphere had changed with the afternoon yellowing through the opaque windows. Father Vea had not been able to get a word from the bronzeman as the latter, callous and casual, went among the dead both frozen and unfrozen, on the postmortem tables and off them. Vea was shaking with uncontrollable anger as the dead were desecrated, and had tried his useless karate kicks again. He said a quick formal prayer and then bellowed to the giantman, as if in a trance, "Leave that cool face alone, the poor man died only last week from a broken heart and diabetes, since his children had become ashamed of his old face, his stammer, and his poverty; and the last straw was when his eldest daughter got married without his knowledge. His wife had been helping this filial hate along . . . and that woman had died in an accident. Are you allowing women applying to be Jesus, if not please leave her alone! Judging these lives is incidental to you, and I am telling their lives out of the need to defend them from you. I know you think I'm giving you information, how stupid!" The blow that Father Vea received knocked him out altogether.

Father Vea woke to these words from his adversary. "I have selected two potential candidates. They are on the floor at the moment. Carry them into the golden lorry outside. I called it here." Vea caught himself doing exactly as he was told. This obedience was what he would have to fight against, voluntary and involuntary slavery. Yet one part of his mind remained free and full of disjointed prayers. The birds were no longer around the wooden gold lorry, and its guavas of bribery were rotten. "But one of them is a woman," exclaimed Vea, knowing full well that he could get the answer that the new Jesus-to-be could be a woman. He received no answer as the lorrygold drove off by itself to put the bodies where it first landed, the valley now deserted except for the echoing sounds of intense activity in the churches and the shrines. Only the same little girl stood by her finished shades.

"There is joy in using an ancestral laser gun, arrived at from centuries of experiments sustained by gari, herbs, bones, and metal. The galaxies are very ancestral, hence the killing and the search for the Lord. If there is no spirit beyond the gadgets then the gadgets take over . . . ," said the giantman with a silly smile on his face, pushing Father Vea brutally towards the next place of visit: the courtrooms. "I believe the spirit can be evil as well as good," panted Vea, trying to correct the hate in his heart for this galactic man with his prestidigitatory mammy truck. "The means always justifies the end in the galaxies," shouted giantman, now not only smiling but laughing between the pushing of the priest. Vea stopped abruptly, and then said as he was prodded forward again, "I see you don't have real intelligence up there. . . ."

Bronzeman's laughter went from the mortuary right into the courtrooms, where the yellow atmosphere continued through the fan and the floor of ochre terrazzo. The afternoon was old. But the laughter continued to be new as

it pierced through the back of Father Vea. And what was strange about the court was that the judge and everyone else behaved as if the giantman and the Father hadn't entered at all. The case under trial continued through the presence of the man of the galaxies. "I am used to attention," he roared, raising his hands so that they almost touched the high court ceiling. "I get attention among the planets, and I demand it here as of right." The lawyers continued to argue their cases, and the witnesses came. Father Vea, now totally exhausted, was sitting staring on the court floor. "I have come here to fill the vacancy for the post of Jesus Christ, and I will take by force anyone I consider a suitable candidate. . . ."

"My lord, I believe the learned counsel has misread the point I am trying to make in connection with the third witness for the defence. . . ." The court continued to ignore the giantman as Father Vea, regaining his breath, at last looked around in amazement.

To the surprise and enragement of the man of wooden gold, the judge started to speak directly to him. "I am happy that you as the accused have now been apprehended, but I demand that you comport yourself properly in court. I may have to hold you in contempt. We in this city have been waiting for centuries to put you on trial for your criminal destruction of the spirit in space, of which the killing of the son of the Master of the universe is the biggest symbol. We are not afraid of your brutal power. The trial will continue whether you kill us all together or one by one." There was complete silence as Bishop Bawa walked into the court and stood defiantly below the judge. He had pepper in one hand and rice in the other. He said to the hard-faced wooden golding, "After you have finished in the courtrooms, the governing rooms and the churches and shrines, we will be waiting for you in the historical rooms . . . where we assure you that you will get all the candidates you need for the vacancy of the Lord." The giantman killed a bailiff with one blow, shouting, "Show me the governing places, my patience is wearing thin!" And in his own mind he had only left the life of the judge intact because he could be a live candidate for the astral vacancy. Giantman had not forgotten Father Vea: he pulled him along, as Bishop Bawa rushed back towards the town, with a grim look on his face.

At first the cabinet rooms smelt of the same old politics: the half-truth, the slant, the cynical, the secret, the sabotage, the murder, the brazen, the corrupt, the thievery, the apathy, the sycophantic, the lie, the totally broken contract, the recreation, the assertion, the favour, and the annihilation, could either form wholes to the left or wholes to the right . . . depending, Father Vea thought, on whether the new changes came from internal or external necessity. "I am looking for the most rotten man in politics," asserted the giantman, "for when I get him, I will purify him, and make him the favourite for the new Jesus Christ." And the ministers seemed to be dancing a history-hip dance, for the giantman was giving them a deep vindication: he was not coming to destroy the leaders, but only those under them. And to manoeuvre in governing was to show ability, and above all to create value: for how else could they be chosen candidates for the biggest post in the skies? Was God not the most tremendous political arranger in the world? All the same, bronzeman pulverised the belly of one minister with short sharp blows and left him for dead. "The dead minister was the most rotten least principled man among us," one minister said with regret: if only he could be the boss of the skies instead! "Where is your leader?" the aerial visitor with the murderous hands demanded. "He has gone looking for you at the valleys to strike a deal for the whole country." Everything has an end, Father Vea caught himself whispering in exhaustion. "I will add the leader to the dead minister as another two candidates," stated bronzeman, dragging Vea along with him again. The lorry of wooden gold had already come and taken the dead man to the valleys. What old old eyes the giantman had, as he wiped the blood on his hand. His broad knees could hit any metal freely and survive. "I am completely neutral to your life and to your death," he said with a snort into the sky.

One tree received the shade of another and Father Vea and the bronzeman went back towards the town, out of the yellow city with its stunned crowds helpless against the driver of lorrygold. All of Father Vea's African Gonja karate was finished, and he could hardly walk. Neither were his bruised knees allowed to pray. "But I am also a religious man," the Greatgold Driver was saying, "and the only difference between your religion and mine is distance. From the galaxies your worshipping at the shrine and at the altar looks ridiculously small, and you have nothing of real power to look back at us on an equal basis. And it was the unending sympathy of the Lord—do you know that he was at first a warrior of the stars?— that led me to kill him. Too much spirit for a man of power and gadgets!" The giant laughter had come again, but when he laughed his eyes remained neutral, his dark tight skin getting tighter with its glowing.

No one man, no one people will ever control the universe, Father Vea thought, limping in and out of his utter despair. If anyone succeeds in the process of doing so, then we could all see the terrible narrowness of the galaxies, see the desire to murder the spirit. But the spirit will live and make for another corner of the stars. Father Vea stopped, and looked curiously at the giantman. He said to the giant, "There's no need to convert any of us into a spirit to fill the vacancy of the Lord, for the spirit of the Lord is indivisible . . . and if you rule the universe alone, you will only be trapped in your own inventions. We are not afraid of exclusive and powerful people of the skies, and as we raise the level of the spirit, you will find us dangerous in your narrow world, and impossible to destroy!"

Bishop Bawa was standing waiting for giantman and Father Vea at the outskirts of the town, among the neem leaves and the snake-plants. He was with the little girl of shades and the shrine herbalist. Giantman stopped in anger. "We have come with a new spirit to defeat you, to show you that no matter how powerful you are, we know your secret: spirit for us and spirit for a man of the galaxies is the same, is indivisible." The giant took his look of intense concentration, for he could not see nor make radio contact with the wooden gold lorry. He marched forward with his huge strides to slap Father Vea, but Vea had crawled swiftly to the side of the small party with the bishop at the head of it.

"You can't kill anyone again in this town! Your power to kill is finished for a year because you have overused it . . . ," shouted the little girl, with her head in her hands and herbs on her neck. And Father Vea shouted, "The biggest secret that you have and you don't want to tell us is that the flesh is not the home of the spirit! Spirit is the indivisible atom, the atom's atom's atom!" The herbal man was outstaring the bronzeman, and holding roots together. The giant's face looked more and more intense, and he looked as if he were rooted to the spot. "And owura Giant," screamed the little girl, "look up at the sky! Don't you see your lorry of wooden gold being pulled up the sky? It is climbing its own rope without you!" "Yes!" added Bishop Bawa. "You came to us as the master of the skies and so, dear master, where is your mastery now!" "But we haven't defeated him yet, we haven't defeated him yet. He is trying to ask for extra energy from his originator! But the originators hate energy asked for in advance! So we will not dance too soon!" shouted the herbal man.

"Give him images and strange but true stories! Fill his mind with our world, for that is the only way of defeating his concentration." The bishop was running about with hands held high. Father Vea shouted as the lorry of wooden gold continued to rise into the skies, "We know your secret experiments that speak about spiritual vacancies, the lizard burst before its own white eggs, we have layers of air that carry a lorry that obeys its originators for the right reasons but wrong in the eyes of the masters, we have never seen in the galaxies the honeysuckle under the heel of wild wired men from other planets, the sense of irrepressible birds forming one line and one wing all the way to the real master of the universe who does not boast of his masters, and all we needed was a child of the tropics with insights that travel through evil, VACANCY FOR THE POST OF JESUS CHRIST INDEED!"

And the giantman was shrinking, but he shrank only two inches, for his will was only enough for his height; but this will was never enough to keep the lorrygold. "But where's the historical room?" bronzeman asked, his voice less neutral now, full of the tones of doubt. "It's an open-air room right here in the presence of the different generations standing before you," Father Vea answered. "Will the dead you murdered remain dead?" asked the herbal shrine man. "Look, look, look up on top of the lorrygold almost gone see something!" the shade girl shouted.

Up there among the few guavas left at the back of the truck stood, still alive, the victims of the anger of the giantman. And they were waving. And who was that dusky bearded man in the white robes, immediately above the lorrygold, the man just jumped down from a sudden cross in the sky, and looking with wonder at the nailmarks on his hands? "Lord!" shouted Father Vea in a trance. "I knew you would come from the freest most difficult part of the universe! Only your humility in the helicopter! I knew you would arrive in this proud and clean tropical land. . . ." The little girl of shades and spirit asked the disappearing dark Jesus, "Please, O son of the universal Controller, can you please show us your appointment letter from God?" The cynical raised their eyebrows, the wise nodded, the poor and the rich had one reaction, and the animals were free . . . and the giantman groaned, almost human now. But had he found his peace?

The Universe of Things
GWYNETH JONES

Gwyneth Jones (1952–) is an award-winning English science fiction and fantasy writer and critic born in Manchester. She received her education at a convent school and received her undergraduate degree in European history at the University of Sussex. In addition to her work for adults, Jones has written almost twenty young adult and children's books under the name Ann Halam. Jones's works are mostly science fiction and near-future high fantasy with themes often connected to gender and feminism. She has won two World Fantasy Awards, the Arthur C. Clarke Award, the Philip K. Dick Award, and the James Tiptree Jr. Award.

Her first novel for adults, *Divine Endurance* (1984), remains one of her most widely admired. It is set in a ruined Earth governed by a matriarchy. No dates are given, but Jones's enormously complex Southeast Asia venue has a Vance-ian *Dying Earth* tonality, and the matriarchal society she depicts is riven by profound ambivalences. The hard melancholy and sustained density of the book are unique in recent science fiction.

Other of her novels include *Water in the Air* (1977), *Escape Plans* (1986), *White Queen* (1991), and *Bold as Love* (2001). Her short fiction has been collected in, among others, *Identify the Object* (1993) and *Grazing the Long Acre* (2009).

"The Universe of Things," published in *New Worlds* 3 in 1993, is a unique tale of alien contact in that it is about not the fate of the world but of quieter and yet more profound matters.

THE UNIVERSE OF THINGS

Gwyneth Jones

The alien parked its car across the street and came and sat down in the waiting room. He must have seen this happen, peripherally. But he was busy settling the bill with a middle-aged woman with curly grey hair and substantial, attractive clothes, to whom he'd taken an irrational dislike. Those who deal with Joe Punter, day in and day out, especially Joe car-owning Punter, are prone to such allergies. He saw her start of concealed surprise, looked up, and there was the alien.

The other customers on the row of seats were pretending, in their English way, that nothing special had happened. He finished dealing with the woman. Other cars and customers left; the alien's turn came. He went out in the road and hand-waved it into the bay with fatherly care, then sent it back to wait while he looked the red car over. He entered the car's make and model in the terminal, and began to check the diagnostics.

The mechanic worked this franchise alone with the robotics and the electronic presence of cashier, manager, head office. He was able to read print; even to write. It was a necessity of his trade. To be wired up, routinely, among all this free-running machinery was against health and safety regulations. He used a hear-and-do wire only for the exotics, where the instructions came packaged with the part, and tried to conceal this from his customers. The mystique of craftsmanship was important to him.

Consequently, it took him some little time to examine the tired little runabout. He called in the alien and explained what had to be done, using a lot of gesture.

The convention was that if you couldn't stomach calling another sentient being "it," they were all called "she." The mechanic eyed the alien covertly as he made his exposition: the soft, noseless profile, drooping shoulders, the torso thickened by layers of strange undergarments beneath its drab "overalls," gawky backwards-jointed legs. It was about as female-looking as the dugongs sailors used to miscall "mermaids." The confusion, he considered, was an insult to both parties. But it was nonsense to expect the denizen of another star system to be humanly attractive. He was in no hurry. He wasn't affronted or frightened, as some people might have been, to see one running around loose, out of the enclave. No doubt the alien was going to tip generously, but it wasn't avarice that made him willing to linger. He was simply, genuinely pleased to have one of them in his shop.

"I just want you to scrub the converter."

He wasn't surprised that it could speak English, he'd only imagined it would not trouble itself to do so. But the last thing he'd expected was for an alien to be mean.

"You know, it's going to be cheaper in the long run to replace the whole exhaust system. You've been using a high methanol percentage, there's a lot of corrosion here. . . ."

The alien looked at the ground.

"Come away—"

He followed it out into the waiting room, where it folded down like a big dog on one of the seats, looking miserable, twisting its puckered, chicken-skin hands against its chest. "I'm going to sell it," the alien explained. "I want you to do the minimum that's legally necessary."

He realized that the alien did not believe that its car could understand English. But nor did it believe that such understanding was impossible. It believed that if you have to say something unpleasant about someone/thing, you remove yourself from the immediate vicinity of the victim. The rules of etiquette were immovable, matter-of-fact, and binding. The car's level of comprehension was a separate matter, a subject for abstruse philosophy.

It was not unusual in the mechanic to be familiar, as far as this, with alien psychology. Alien nature was the stuff of daytime television. The mechanic could have drowned in the subject, if he had enough idle time between customers.

"What's legally necessary," he repeated. He was disappointed, practically and emotionally, by his customer's poverty, but mollified by its bizarre sensitivity.

Of course he knew that in an alien the state of poverty could only be temporary and relative. The tip dwindled but some other benefit was bound to accrue.

It (or she) nodded glumly.

They nodded. Their gestures were very human, but culturally diverse: for *no* they would jerk the chin, not shake the head. It was as if they'd borrowed a little, deliberately, from every human race, and maybe that was exactly so. Their journey into human space had been through such a saturation of human emissions, no one knew how much of alien behavior on Earth was natural, and how much a carefully devised presentation.

"Shall I wait or shall I come back?"

Throughout this exchange the other customers had remained painfully fixed in bored or casual poses. The mechanic was delighted by their intent, covert attention. Luckily there were no children involved, to spoil the effect of cosmopolitan unconcern.

He did not want it to stay. If it stayed in here it might strike up a conversation, become the temporary property of one of these mere punters.

"You'd better go," he told it, feigning regret. "I have another job that I can't put on auto. Come back in about an hour."

When it had left, regret became real. He went out into the dusty street and stared up and down. It was October. The fronds of the banana tree that grew over the wall of an unkempt yard next door were acid green under a lowering sky that had been promising rain for days. The tourist centre was not far away: the massive grace that all the world admired, which had once been the center of a dock town called Liverpool. He could see the tiny points of the newly gilded Liver Birds, winking above their monument of vast commercial assurance. Far inland, the vague conurbation stretched up the flanks of the Pennines, the hills swimming there out of sight like drowned monuments, drowned in time and lost forever, like the great city.

There was no sign of the alien.

He went into the shop, checked the progress of various operations, and quietly—avoiding camera eyes—sneaked through the door at the back, and upstairs to his living quarters. His wife was at work. Their two children, seven and two years old, were with her in the workplace schoolroom and crèche. The rooms, which were small but well supplied with consumer durables, seemed unnaturally tidy and silent. He stood in the living room and studied a row of books, discs, journals, on a shelf of the library unit. *Dealing with the Alien*; *What Do They Think of Us*; *The Farcomers*; *Through Alien Eyes*; *Have They Been Here Before?*; *Xenobiology: Towards the Dawn of Science* . . . The mechanic and his family were no more than averagely interested in the alien visitors. The books had been bought, not read. But it would have been a strange household indeed, or a very poor one, that didn't possess at least a few of these titles.

The mechanic did not feel, on the whole, that the human race was overreacting. He and his wife had voted in favor, in the European referendum, of the global change of era, which was now on its way to becoming law. This year, this present year, would be forever year three: 3 AC, probably, if the English-speaking lobby had its way. *After Contact*. It was official: this was the greatest thing that had happened to the human race since the dim and distant "coming of Christ." And the aliens, unlike Christ, were *here*. They were in print, on the screen. They were indubitably real.

Everything on the shelves had been entered in their library; the mechanic's wife was meticulous over this chore. His fingers hovered over the keypad. But the mysterious inertia of human adulthood defeated him. Only the seven-year-old actually used the database. He took a book down, and another: leafed pages, read a paragraph or two. He didn't know what he was looking for. Surrounded by hard things that did not speak or look at him, he tried to imagine how it felt to be the alien. He had known sentimental drivers: cars with names, cars referred to as "she"; cars abused for bad behaviour. He had caught himself (he dredged up fragments of memory) occasionally giving a glossy flank of robot casing an affectionate pat as he put it aside.

Good boy . . .

Good dog . . .

But the aliens did not know about animals. They had tools that crept, slithered, flew: but they had made these things. They had no notion of a separate creation, life that was not their own. It might be that conditions on the home planet were different but the evidence, from their reactions and their own reporting, was otherwise. It seemed likely that they had shared their world with no other, no *separate* warm-blooded animals.

He went down to the service bay, and checked the screen that showed the waiting room. All was quiet in there. It had not come back. He turned from that screen and made work for himself among the ramped vehicles and buzzing tools. He didn't touch the alien's car. When it reappeared he told it he was having a few problems. Please be patient, he said. Come back later, or wait. He took no new customers. The afternoon turned to dusk. The waiting room emptied until it (or she) was there alone.

The mechanic's wife and his children arrived home, on foot from the tram stop, the baby in her buggy. He heard the childish voices chattering and laughing at the street door, and gritted his teeth as if interrupted in some highly concentrated and delicate task. But he was doing nothing, just sitting in the gloom among the silent tools.

The alien was folded up on its seat. It looked like an animal dressed up, a talking animal of no known species from a child's cartoon. It stood and smiled, showing the tips of its teeth: the modified snarl that might or might not be a genuine, shared gesture.

The mechanic was embarrassed because there was really no way he could explain his behavior. A human customer, stranger in a strange land, would by now have been either very angry or—possibly—a little scared. The alien seemed resigned. It did not expect humans to behave reasonably.

It made the mechanic obscurely angry to think that he was not the first person to give it the runaround like this. He would have liked to explain *I just want to have you near me for a while.* . . . But that would have been a shameful confession.

"I want to do you a favor," he said. "I didn't like to tell you before, thought you might get embarrassed. I'm fixing up quite a few things, and I'm only going to charge you for the scrub."

"Oh." He thought it looked surprised, perhaps wary. It was impossible not to award them with human feelings; not to read human expressions in their strange faces. "Thank you."

"The least I could do, after you've come all this way!"

He laughed nervously. It didn't. They did not laugh.

"Would you like to come upstairs? Would you like something to eat, a cup of tea? My wife, my kids would be very pleased to meet you."

The invitation was completely insincere. The last thing he wanted was to see it in his home. He didn't want to share the alien with anyone. The alien gave him a wry look that seemed to know exactly what was going on. According to some readings of their behavior they were telepathic: intensely so between themselves, mildly with humans.

On the other hand, it had probably been pestered this way before . . . performing animal. The thought made him wince, for himself and for those others.

"No thank you." It looked at the ground. "Will the car be ready tomorrow?"

The street was dark. There was little lighting just here, away from the hotels and malls and the floodlit, water-lapped monuments. He felt guilty. The poor alien might be mentally counting up its cash, maybe wondering what the hell to do next. Aliens traveling alone were rarities anywhere. If it couldn't take refuge in a big rich hotel it would be bothered. People would crowd around it heartlessly, pointing their cameras.

But that wasn't the mechanic's fault. He didn't want to *capture* it. He didn't want to turn it out, either. He'd have liked it to stay here; to keep its real live presence. It could sleep on the seats. He would bring down some food. They liked some human foodstuffs: ice cream, white bread, hamburgers; nothing too natural.

"Yes, of course. Come back tomorrow. I open at nine."

He told his wife that he had to work overtime. This never happened, but she accepted the idea without comment. The routine of their life together was so calm it could swallow the occasional obvious lie without a ripple.

He sat in the machine shop alone and looked around him. Cars.

It was strange how many static, urban Europeans still felt the need to own them, even with the fuel rationing and all the rest of the environment-protection laws. The mechanic wasn't complaining. It was a steady job, and often even enjoyable. These are my people, he thought, trying on the alien worldview.

My people, the sheep of my flock. He had a grandmother who was a churchgoer. But there came the idea of animals again, the separation of one kind of life from another. That was not what happened between an alien and an alien machine. He went up to the car, clamped on its ramp in an undignified posture, a helpless patient.

"Hallo?" he said tentatively.

The car made no response, but the atmosphere in the shop changed. By speaking to it aloud he had shifted something: his own perception. He'd embarrassed himself, in fact. He could just catch the tail of a more interesting emotion. He was a child creeping past the witch's door, deliciously afraid. But nothing he could do or say would make the imagined real: make him see the robot eyes wink, the jaws of metal grin or open in speech. Nothing but madness would change things that far.

He began to work, or rather he set the robotics to work. He had no choice now, he would have to do what he had promised and square the accounts somehow. Nothing that happened in his garage went unrecorded. The mechanic had never tried to hack his way around the firm's system. He'd never been the type to be tempted by the complications of crime, and now he wouldn't know where to start. He became very gloomy thinking about what he'd have to do: the awkward covering up for this strange impulse.

The free machines skated to and fro. Others slid along the overhead lines and reached down their serpent heads. The mechanic fidgeted. The little car, a fifteen-year-old Korean methanol/mix burner with a red plastic body, liquid clutch, and suspension, was a hard-wearing complex of equipment, good for at least another ten years on the road. It needed a certain amount of attention: but it didn't need *his* hands-on attention at all. He stood and watched.

I am redundant, he thought—a standard overreaction to robotics. Why don't aliens feel redundant? He struggled to perform the mental contortion of looking out of the mirror. If it were not for humans, if it were not for me, there would be no cars, no robots, no machines at all. I cannot be superseded. Even if the machines become self-conscious, become "human" (the ever-receding bogey of the popular media), I will still be God. The maker. The origin.

Upstairs the toddler would be in bed; and the boy too, tucked up with one of the home tutoring wires that supplemented the education provided by his mother's employers. The mother would be relaxing into her evening, snug in a nest of hardware. Empathically, subliminally, the mechanic was aware of the comings and goings, the familiar routine.

He discovered why the alien filled him with such helpless, inarticulate delight. The machines promised, but they could not perform. They remained *things*, and people remained lonely. The mechanic had visited his country's National Forests—the great tracts of land that must remain undisturbed, however small his sitting room became. He accepted the necessity of their existence, but the only emotion he could possibly feel was resentment. He had no friendship with the wilderness. Animals could be pets, but they were not part of you, not the same. The aliens had the solution to human isolation: a talking world, a world with eyes; the companionship that God dreams of. The alien's visitation had stirred in him a God-like discontent.

He could not make it stay. But perhaps he could learn from it, share its enriched experience. He saw the bay as a microcosm of human technology and civilization—a world extruded like ectoplasm from its human centre, full of creatures made in the mechanic's own image: his finger and thumb, his teeth, his rolling, folding joints, his sliding muscle. His mind, even, in its flickering chemical cloud, permeating the hardware of his brain.

Excited by this insight, he jumped up and hurried to the bay's keypad. He pulled the robotics out, the shining jointed arms sliding back and folding themselves away into the walls. He took out a box of hand tools. He would pay the alien's car the greatest compliment in his power. He would give it the benefit of his craftsmanship, the kind of "natural, organic" servicing for which the rich paid ridiculous sums.

For a while he worked like Adam in Eden, joyfully naming the subcreation with his hands and mind. He worked, he slowed. . . . He sat on the cold, dark-stained floor with a socket spanner in one hand and a piece of ragwaste in the other. The lights looked down. They built things with bacteria, as the mechanic understood it. Bacteria which were themselves traceable to the aliens' own intestinal flora, infecting everything: every tool and piece of furniture, even the massive shell of their ship-world. Human beings, when they wanted to express feelings of profound communion with the planet, with the race, spoke of being "a part of the great whole." Having lived so many years—from the start of their evolution, in a sense, the pundits reckoned—in a world created by themselves, the aliens could not experience being *a-part*. There were no parts in their continuum: no spaces, no dividing edges.

He suddenly felt disgusted. Scientists had established that the alien bacteria were harmless. That was the story, but it might be wrong. It might be a big lie, maintained to prevent panic in the streets. He wished he hadn't touched the car. The alien had been using it for months. It must be coated all over with invisible crawling slime.

What was it like, to be part of a living world? He stared at the spanner in his hand until the rod of metal lost its shine. Skin crept over it, the adjustable socket became a cup of muscle, pursed like an anus, wet lips drawn back by a twist on the tumescent rod. The mechanic was nauseated, but he could not put the tool down. He could not go away from it. This oozed drop of self, attached to his hand, would not be parted from him if he dropped it. Tiny strings, strands of living slime, would cling and join them still. The air he breathed was full of self, of human substance.

He stood up. He backed off: a robot casing yielded like flesh. The mechanic yelped and sprang away. His hand, with the rod-flesh spanner growing out of it, hit the keypad: and all the tools began to leap into action. He stood in his own surging, hurrying, pulsating gut—for an instant saved by the notional space of an anatomical drawing—and then the walls closed in. There was no light, only a reddened darkness. The mechanic wailed. He fought a horrible need to vomit, he scrabbled desperately at the keys.

When everything was quiet again he sat for a while. It might have been minutes; it felt like a long time. Eventually he stopped wanting to be sick and managed to put down the spanner. He sat with his head hunched in his arms; became aware of this abject fetal crouch and came out of it slowly. He took a deep breath.

The garage was the same as it had always been: dead, and safe. He realized that he had been highly privileged. Somehow, just briefly, he had succeeded in entering the alien mind, seen the world through alien eyes. How could you expect such an experience to be pleasant? Now that it was over he could accept that: and he was truly grateful.

At last he heaved a sigh, and set about putting the bay to work again. He couldn't bring himself to touch the red car with hand tools now. Besides, he was too shaky. But he would deliver the alien's vehicle in the morning as promised, as near to perfectly reborn as was humanly possible. He owed it that much.

He had tried to take something from the alien by a kind of force. And he'd got what he wanted. It wasn't the alien's fault that he'd bitten off more than he could chew, and gagged on the mouthful. Gritting his teeth against the ghostly feel of flesh in the machines, he set up the necessary routines.

In a short time, it was all done. But it was very late. His wife would have to ask questions now, and he'd have to tell her something of what had happened. He stood looking at the plastic shell and the clever, deviously eco-nomical innards under the open bonnet. The machines, they said, couldn't live with the ecosphere. In the end the human race would have to abandon one or the other: motorcars or "the environment." But "in the end" was still being held at bay. In the meantime this was a good, well-made little compromise with damnation.

He felt lonely and sad. He had seen another world walk into his life, reached out to grasp the wonder, and found something worse than empty air. He'd wanted the alien to give him dreamland, somewhere over the rainbow. He had found, instead, an inimical Eden: a treasure that he could no more enjoy than he could crawl back into the womb.

The mechanic sighed again and gently closed the bonnet.

The red car settled itself a little.

"Thank you," it said.

In the morning at nine o'clock the alien was there. The car was ready, gleaming on the forecourt. The alien put down its bag, which it carried not on its back or at arm's length but tucked under one armpit in that very peculiar, lopsided way of theirs. He thought it looked tired, and anxious. It barely glanced at the car. Perhaps, like a human, it didn't even want to know how badly it had been cheated.

"What's the damage?" it asked.

The mechanic was hurt. He'd have liked to go over the whole worksheet with it: to extract the sweet honey of its approval, or at least to extend this dwindling transaction just a little further. He had to remind himself that the alien owed him nothing. To itself, its feelings were not romantic or bizarre in the least. The world it lived in was commonplace. The mechanic's experience was his own concern, had been an internal matter from the start. The alien was not responsible for kinks of human psychology, nor for imaginary paranormal incidents.

"Look," he said. "I've got a proposition for you. My eldest, my son, he's just passed his driving test. He won't be allowed out on his own for a while, of course. But I've been thinking about getting him a little runabout. I don't keep a car myself, you see, I've never felt the need. But kids, they like the freedom. . . . I'd like to buy your car."

In the cold light of day, he couldn't bear to tell it the truth. He knew the car would never speak to him again. But he had been touched by the world of the other, and he simply had to bring away something: some kind of proof.

The alien looked even more depressed.

The mechanic realized suddenly that he didn't have to worry about the money. He would tell the firm everything. They were human at the head office, and as fascinated as he. The car would stay on the forecourt. He would call in and get it featured on the local news, maybe even national news. It would be extremely good for business.

For the alien's benefit, however, he would stick to the story about his son. They really shouldn't be encouraged to believe that human beings thought they were magic.

"List price," he added, hurriedly. "And a little more. Because anyone would pay a little more, a car that's been driven by one of our famous visitors. What do you say?"

So the alien walked away with its credit card handsomely e-charged. It turned at the corner of the street, by the yard where the banana fronds hung over the gate, and bared its pointed teeth in that seeming smile. The farewell could have been for the red car on the forecourt as much as for the human beside it, but it made the man feel better anyway.

The Remoras

ROBERT REED

Robert Reed (1956–) is an award-winning and exceedingly prolific US writer of science fiction who has written hundreds of short stories and several novels. Highly versatile, Reed in his fiction ranges from intimate vignettes to intricate variations on space opera. As with James Tiptree Jr., intimations of death (and entropy) frequently appear as subtext in his work. His novella "A Billion Eves" won the 2007 Hugo Award, but in general his prolific nature, although matched by quality, has left Reed in the position of being critically underappreciated.

Two sets of connected works have shaped Reed's later career. In the *Veil of Stars* sequence—*Beyond the Veil of Stars* (1994) and *Beneath the Gated Sky* (1997)—the sense of claustrophobia characteristic of Reed's work derives from an image of our solar system as impacted upon—from beyond a fabricated and deceitful veil of stars—by innumerable similar inhabited systems. We live in a megalopolis of planets, and we communicate with one another by passing through dimensional barriers, which change our bodies so that we resemble natives of the overcrowded visited world.

The *Great Ship* sequence—comprising *Marrow* (2000), *Mere* (2004), *The Well of Stars* (2004), the title story of *Eater-of-Bone and Other Novellas* (2012), *The Greatship* (2013), and *The Memory of Sky* (2014)—is set on a world ship discovered by humans, seemingly adrift, passengerless and crewless, outside the home galaxy, who take it over, dubbing it Great Ship. The reason for its original construction (many eons earlier), and for its seemingly aimless course through the universe, remains mysterious and undetermined; so large and largely unknown is the ship, even to its new "owners," that the discovery in the first volume that it is in fact built around an entire planet is shocking.

In an essay about the series, Reed wrote that the initial idea came from thinking about a man living inside "the most perfect spacesuit . . . built from some marvelous material [and that] functions as a very small, highly competent spaceship." A second insight years later led to writing the first stories: "A simple realization that the spacesuit was much like a world, self-contained and eternal. I began thinking about more durable types of human beings, people who wore these elaborate 'lifesuits' throughout their lives. I saw them as a society. [But] a little spaceship wouldn't do the trick. I needed something with size, an expansive place where a great culture could be born."

"The Remoras," first published in *The Magazine of Fantasy and Science Fiction* in 1994 (and reprinted in Hartwell and Cramer's *The Space Opera Renaissance*, 2006), is a stellar example from the *Great Ship/Marrow* sequence. It works as an excellent general science fiction story but also as riveting space opera, in a tradition going back to Edmond Hamilton in the 1920s and comparable to the best of Iain M. Banks.

THE REMORAS

Robert Reed

Quee Lee's apartment covered several hectares within one of the human districts, some thousand kilometers beneath the ship's hull. It wasn't a luxury unit by any measure. Truly wealthy people owned as much as a cubic kilometer for themselves and their entourages. But it had been her home since she had come on board, for more centuries than she could count, its hallways and large rooms as comfortable to her as her own body.

The garden room was a favorite. She was enjoying its charms one afternoon, lying nude beneath a false sky and sun, eyes closed and nothing to hear but the splash of fountains and the prattle of little birds. Suddenly her apartment interrupted the peace, announcing a visitor. "He has come for Perri, miss. He claims it's most urgent."

"Perri isn't here," she replied, soft gray eyes opening. "Unless he's hiding from both of us, I suppose."

"No, miss. He is not." A brief pause, then the voice said, "I have explained this to the man, but he refuses to leave. His name is Orleans. He claims that Perri owes him a considerable sum of money."

What had her husband done now? Quee Lee could guess, halfway smiling as she sat upright. Oh, Perri . . . won't you learn . . . ? She would have to dismiss this Orleans fellow herself, spooking him with a good hard stare. She rose and dressed in an emerald sarong, then walked the length of her apartment, never hurrying, commanding the front door to open at the last moment but leaving the security screen intact. And she was ready for someone odd. Even someone sordid, knowing Perri. Yet she didn't expect to see a shiny lifesuit more than two meters tall

and nearly half as wide, and she had never imagined such a face gazing down at her with mismatched eyes. It took her a long moment to realize this was a Remora. An authentic Remora was standing in the public walkway, his vivid round face watching her. The flesh was orange with diffuse black blotches that might or might not be cancers, and a lipless, toothless mouth seemed to flow into a grin. What would bring a Remora here? They never, never came down here . . . !

"I'm Orleans." The voice was sudden and deep, slightly muted by the security screen. It came from a speaker hidden somewhere on the thick neck, telling her, "I need help, miss. I'm sorry to disturb you . . . but you see, I'm desperate. I don't know where else to turn."

Quee Lee knew about Remoras. She had seen them and even spoken to a few, although those conversations were eons ago and she couldn't remember their substance. Such strange creatures. Stranger than most aliens, even if they possessed human souls. . . .

"Miss?"

Quee Lee thought of herself as being a good person. Yet she couldn't help but feel repelled, the floor rolling beneath her and her breath stopping short. Orleans was a human being, one of her own species. True, his genetics had been transformed by hard radiations. And yes, he normally lived apart from ordinary people like her. But inside him was a human mind, tough and potentially immortal. Quee Lee blinked and remembered that she had compassion as well as charity for everyone, even aliens . . . and she managed to sputter, "Come in." She said, "If you wish, please do," and with that invitation, her apartment deactivated the invisible screen.

"Thank you, miss." The Remora walked slowly, almost clumsily, his lifesuit making a harsh grinding noise in the knees and hips. That wasn't normal, she realized. Orleans should have been graceful, his suit powerful, serving him as an elaborate exoskeleton.

"Would you like anything?" she asked foolishly. Out of habit.

"No, thank you," he replied, his voice nothing but pleasant.

Of course. Remoras ate and drank only self-made concoctions. They were permanently sealed inside their lifesuits, functioning as perfectly self-contained organisms. Food was synthesized, water recycled, and they possessed a religious sense of purity and independence.

"I don't wish to bother you, miss. I'll be brief."

His politeness was a minor surprise. Remoras typically were distant, even arrogant. But Orleans continued to smile, watching her. One eye was a muscular pit filled with thick black hairs, and she assumed those hairs were light sensitive. Like an insect's compound eye, each one might build part of an image. By contrast, its mate was ordinary, white and fishy with a foggy black center. Mutations could do astonishing things. An accelerated, partly controlled evolution was occurring inside that suit, even while Orleans stood before her, boots stomping on the stone floor, a single spark arcing toward her. Orleans said, "I know this is embarrassing for you—"

"No, no," she offered.

"—and it makes me uncomfortable too. I wouldn't have come down here if it wasn't necessary."

"Perri's gone," she repeated, "and I don't know when he'll be back. I'm sorry."

"Actually," said Orleans, "I was hoping he would be gone."

"Did you?"

"Though I'd have come either way."

Quee Lee's apartment, loyal and watchful, wouldn't allow anything nasty to happen to her. She took a step forward, closing some of the distance. "This is about money being owed? Is that right?"

"Yes, miss."

"For what, if I might ask?"

Orleans didn't explain in clear terms. "Think of it as an old gambling debt." More was involved, he implied. "A very old debt, I'm afraid, and Perri's refused me a thousand times."

She could imagine it. Her husband had his share of failings, incompetence and a self-serving attitude among them. She loved Perri in a controlled way, but his flaws were obvious. "I'm sorry," she replied, "but I'm not responsible for his debts." She made herself sound hard, knowing it was best. "I hope you didn't come all this way because you heard he was married." Married to a woman of some means, she thought to herself. In secret.

"No, no, no!" The grotesque face seemed injured. Both eyes became larger, and a thin tongue, white as ice, licked at the lipless edge of the mouth. "Honestly, we don't follow the news about passengers. I just assumed Perri was living with someone. I know him, you see . . . my hope was to come and make my case to whomever I found, winning a comrade. An ally. Someone who might become my advocate." A hopeful pause, then he said, "When Perri does come here, will you explain to him what's right and what is not? Can you, please?" Another pause, then he added, "Even a lowly Remora knows the difference between right and wrong, miss."

That wasn't fair, calling himself lowly. And he seemed to be painting her as some flavor of bigot, which she wasn't. She didn't look at him as lowly, and morality wasn't her private possession. Both of them were human, after all. Their souls were linked by a charming and handsome, manipulative user . . . by her darling husband . . . and Quee Lee felt a sudden anger directed at Perri, almost shuddering in front of this stranger.

"Miss?"

"How much?" she asked. "How much does he owe you, and how soon will you need it?"

Orleans answered the second question first, lifting an arm with a sickly whine coming from his shoulder. "Can you hear it?" he asked. As if she were deaf. "My seals need to be replaced, or at least refurbished. Yesterday, if possible." The arm bent, and the elbow whined. "I already spent my savings rebuilding my reactor."

Quee Lee knew enough about lifesuits to appreciate his circumstances. Remoras worked on the ship's hull, standing in the open for hours and days at a time. A broken seal was a disaster. Any tiny opening would kill most of his body, and his suffering mind would fall into a protective coma. Left exposed and vulnerable, Orleans would be at the mercy of radiation storms and comet showers. Yes, she understood. A balky suit was an unacceptable hazard on top of lesser hazards, and what could she say?

She felt a deep empathy for the man.

Orleans seemed to take a breath, then he said, "Perri owes me fifty-two thousand credits, miss."

"I see." She swallowed and said, "My name is Quee Lee."

"Quee Lee," he repeated. "Yes, miss."

"As soon as Perri comes home, I'll discuss this with him. I promise you."

"I would be grateful if you did."

"I will."

The ugly mouth opened, and she saw blotches of green and gray-blue against a milky throat. Those were cancers or perhaps strange new organs. She couldn't believe she was in the company of a Remora—the strangest sort of human—yet despite every myth, despite tales of courage and even recklessness, Orleans appeared almost fragile. He even looked scared, she realized. That wet orange face shook as if in despair, then came the awful grinding noise as he turned away, telling her, "Thank you, Quee Lee. For your time and patience, and for everything."

Fifty-two thousand credits!

She could have screamed. She would scream when she was alone, she promised herself. Perri had done this man a great disservice, and

he'd hear about it when he graced her with his company again. A patient person, yes, and she could tolerate most of his flaws. But not now. Fifty thousand credits was no fortune, and it would allow Orleans to refurbish his lifesuit, making him whole and healthy again. Perhaps she could get in touch with Perri first, speeding up the process . . . ?

Orleans was through her front door, turning to say good-bye. False sunshine made his suit shine, and his faceplate darkened to where she couldn't see his features anymore. He might have had any face, and what did a face mean? Waving back at him, sick to her stomach, she calculated what fifty-two thousand credits meant in concrete terms, to her . . .

. . . wondering if she should . . . ?

But no, she decided. She just lacked the required compassion. She was a particle short, if that, ordering the security screen to engage again, helping to mute that horrid grinding of joints as the Remora shuffled off for home.

The ship had many names, many designations, but to its long-term passengers and crew it was referred to as the ship. No other starship could be confused for it. Not in volume, nor in history.

The ship was old by every measure. A vanished humanoid race had built it, probably before life arose on Earth, then abandoned it for no obvious reason. Experts claimed it had begun as a sunless world, one of the countless Jupiters that sprinkled the cosmos. The builders had used the world's own hydrogen to fuel enormous engines, accelerating it over millions of years while stripping away its gaseous exterior. Today's ship was the leftover core, much modified by its builders and humans. Its metal and rock interior was laced with passageways and sealed environments, fuel tanks and various ports. There was room enough for hundreds of billions of passengers, though there were only a fraction of that number now. And its hull was a special armor made from hyperfibers, kilometers thick and tough enough to withstand most high-velocity impacts.

The ship had come from outside the galaxy, passing into human space long ago. It was claimed as salvage, explored by various means, then refurbished to the best of its new owners' abilities. A corporation was formed; a promotion was born. The ancient engines were coaxed to life, changing the ship's course. Then tickets were sold, both to humans and alien species. Novelty and adventure were the lures. One circuit around the Milky Way; a half-million-year voyage touring the star-rich spiral arms. It was a long span, even for immortal humans. But people like Quee Lee had enough money and patience. That's why she purchased her apartment with a portion of her savings. This voyage wouldn't remain novel for long, she knew. Three or four circuits at most, and then what? People would want something else new and glancingly dangerous. Wasn't that the way it always was?

Quee Lee had no natural lifespan. Her ancestors had improved themselves in a thousand ways, erasing the aging process. Fragile DNAs were replaced with better genetic machinery. Tailoring allowed a wide range of useful proteins and enzymes and powerful repair mechanisms. Immune systems were nearly perfect; diseases were extinct. Normal life couldn't damage a person in any measurable way. And even a tragic accident wouldn't need to be fatal; Quee Lee's body and mind were able to withstand frightening amounts of abuse.

But Remoras, despite those same gifts, did not live ordinary lives. They worked on the open hull, each of them encased in a lifesuit. The suits afforded extra protection and a standard environment, each one possessing a small fusion plant and redundant recycling systems. Hull life was dangerous in the best times. The ship's shields and laser watchdogs couldn't stop every bit of interstellar grit. And every large impact meant someone had to make repairs. The ship's builders had used sophisticated robots, but they proved too tired after several billions of years on the job. It was better to promote—or demote—members of the human crew. The original scheme was to share the job,

brief stints fairly dispersed. Even the captains were to don the lifesuits, stepping into the open when it was safest, patching craters with fresh-made hyperfibers. . . .

Fairness didn't last. A kind of subculture arose, and the first Remoras took the hull as their province. Those early Remoras learned how to survive the huge radiation loads. They trained themselves and their offspring to control their damaged bodies. Tough genetics mutated, and they embraced their mutations. If an eye was struck blind, perhaps by some queer cancer, then a good Remora would evolve a new eye. Perhaps a hair was light-sensitive, and its owner, purely by force of will, would culture that hair and interface it with the surviving optic nerve, producing an eye more durable than the one it replaced. Or so Quee Lee had heard, in passing, from people who acted as if they knew about such things.

Remoras, she had been told, were happy to look grotesque. In their culture, strange faces and novel organs were the measures of success. And since disaster could happen anytime, without warning, it was unusual for any Remora to live long. At least in her sense of long. Orleans could be a fourth- or fifth-generation Remora, for all she knew. A child barely fifty centuries old. For all she knew. Which was almost nothing, she realized, returning to her garden room and undressing, lying down with her eyes closed and the light baking her. Remoras were important, even essential people, yet she felt wholly ignorant. And ignorance was wrong, she knew. Not as wrong as owing one of them money, but still. . . .

This life of hers seemed so ordinary, set next to Orleans's life. Comfortable and ordinary, and she almost felt ashamed.

Perri failed to come home that next day, and the next. Then it was ten days, Quee Lee having sent messages to his usual haunts and no reply. She had been careful not to explain why she wanted him. And this was nothing too unusual;

Perri was probably wandering somewhere new and Quee Lee was skilled at waiting, her days accented with visits from friends and parties thrown for any small reason. It was her normal life, never anything but pleasant; yet she found herself thinking about Orleans, imagining him walking on the open hull with his seals breaking, his strange body starting to boil away . . . that poor man . . . !

Taking the money to Orleans was an easy decision. Quee Lee had more than enough. It didn't seem like a large sum until she had it converted into black-and-white chips. But wasn't it better to have Perri owing her instead of owing a Remora? She was in a better place to recoup the debt; and besides, she doubted that her husband could raise that money now. Knowing him, he probably had a number of debts, to humans and aliens both; and for the nth time, she wondered how she'd ever let Perri charm her. What was she thinking, agreeing to this crazy union?

Quee Lee was old even by immortal measures. She was so old she could barely remember her youth, her tough neurons unable to embrace her entire life. Maybe that's why Perri had seemed like a blessing. He was ridiculously young and wore his youth well, gladly sharing his enthusiasms and energies. He was a good, untaxing lover; he could listen when it was important; and he had never tried milking Quee Lee of her money. Besides, he was a challenge. No doubt about it. Maybe her friends didn't approve of him—a few close ones were openly critical—but to a woman of her vintage, in the middle of a five-thousand-century voyage, Perri was something fresh and new and remarkable. And Quee Lee's old friends, quite suddenly, seemed a little fossilized by comparison.

"I love to travel," Perri had explained, his gently handsome face capable of endless smiles. "I was born on the ship, did you know? Just weeks after my parents came on board. They were riding only as far as a colony world, but I stayed behind. My choice." He had laughed, eyes gazing into the false sky of her ceiling. "Do you know what I want to do? I want to see the entire ship, walk every hallway and cavern. I want to explore every body of water, meet every sort of alien—"

"Really?"

"—and even visit their quarters. Their homes." Another laugh and that infectious smile. "I just came back from a low-gravity district, six thousand kilometers below. There's a kind of spidery creature down there. You should see them, love! I can't do them justice by telling you they're graceful, and seeing holes isn't much better."

She had been impressed. Who else did she know who could tolerate aliens, what with their strange odors and their impenetrable minds? Perri was remarkable, no doubt about it. Even her most critical friends admitted that much, and despite their grumbles, they'd want to hear the latest Perri adventure as told by his wife.

"I'll stay on board forever, if I can manage it."

She had laughed, asking, "Can you afford it?"

"Badly," he had admitted. "But I'm paid up through this circuit, at least. Minus day-by-day expenses, but that's all right. Believe me, when you've got millions of wealthy souls in one place, there's always a means of making a living."

"Legal means?"

"Glancingly so." He had a rogue's humor, all right. Yet later, in a more sober mood, he had admitted, "I do have enemies, my love. I'm warning you. Like anyone, I've made my share of mistakes—my youthful indiscretions—but at least I'm honest about them."

Indiscretions, perhaps. Yet he had done nothing to earn her animosity.

"We should marry," Perri had proposed. "Why not? We like each other's company, yet we seem to weather our time apart too. What do you think? Frankly, I don't think you need a partner who shadows you day and night. Do you, Quee Lee?"

She didn't. True enough.

"A small tidy marriage, complete with rules," he had assured her. "I get a home base, and you have your privacy, plus my considerable entertainment value." A big long laugh, then he had added, "I promise. You'll be the first to hear my latest tales. And I'll never be any kind of leech, darling. With you, I will be the perfect gentleman."

Quee Lee carried the credit chips in a secret pouch, traveling to the tube-car station and riding one of the vertical tubes toward the hull. She had looked up the name Orleans in the crew listings. The only Orleans lived at Port Beta, no mention of his being a Remora or not. The ports were vast facilities where taxi craft docked with the ship, bringing new passengers from nearby alien worlds. It was easier to accelerate and decelerate those kilometer-long needles. The ship's own engines did nothing but make the occasional course correction, avoiding dust clouds while keeping them on their circular course.

It had been forever since Quee Lee had visited a port. And today there wasn't even a taxi to be seen, all of them off hunting for more paying customers. The non-Remora crew—the captains, mates, and so on—had little work at the moment, apparently hiding from her. She stood at the bottom of the port—a lofty cylinder capped with a kilometer-thick hatch of top-grade hyperfibers. The only other tourists were aliens, some kind of fishy species encased in bubbles of liquid water or ammonia. The bubbles rolled past her. It was like standing in a school of small tuna, their sharp chatter audible and Quee Lee unable to decipher any of it. Were they mocking her? She had no clue, and it made her all the more frustrated. They could be making terrible fun of her. She felt lost and more than a little homesick all at once.

By contrast, the first Remora seemed normal. Walking without any grinding sounds, it covered ground at an amazing pace. Quee Lee had to run to catch it. To catch her. Something about the lifesuit was feminine, and a female voice responded to Quee Lee's shouts.

"What what what?" asked the Remora. "I'm busy!"

Gasping, Quee Lee asked, "Do you know Orleans?"

"Orleans?"

"I need to find him. It's quite important." Then she wondered if something terrible had happened, her arriving too late—

"I do know someone named Orleans, yes." The face had comma-shaped eyes, huge and black and bulging, and the mouth blended into a slitlike nose. Her skin was silvery, odd bunched fibers running beneath the surface. Black hair showed along the top of the faceplate, except at second glance it wasn't hair. It looked more like ropes soaked in oil, the strands wagging with a slow stately pace.

The mouth smiled. The normal-sounding voice said, "Actually, Orleans is one of my closest friends!"

True? Or was she making a joke?

"I really have to find him," Quee Lee confessed. "Can you help me?"

"Can I help you?" The strange mouth smiled, gray pseudoteeth looking big as thumbnails, the gums as silver as her skin. "I'll take you to him. Does that constitute help?" And Quee Lee found herself following, walking onto a lifting disk without railing, the Remora standing in the center and waving to the old woman. "Come closer. Orleans is up there." A skyward gesture. "A good long way, and I don't think you'd want to try it alone. Would you?"

"Relax," Orleans advised.

She thought she was relaxed, except then she found herself nodding, breathing deeply and feeling a tension as it evaporated. The ascent had taken ages, it seemed. Save for the rush of air moving past her ears, it had been soundless. The disk had no sides at all—a clear violation of safety regulations—and Quee Lee had grasped one of the Remora's shiny arms, needing a handhold, surprised to feel rough spots in the hyperfiber. Minuscule impacts had left craters too tiny to see. Remoras, she had realized, were very much like the ship itself—enclosed biospheres taking abuse as they streaked through space.

"Better?" asked Orleans.

"Yes. Better." A thirty-kilometer ride through the port, holding tight to a Remora. And now this. She and Orleans were inside some tiny room not five hundred meters from the vacuum. Did Orleans live here? She nearly asked, looking at the bare walls and stubby furniture, deciding it was too spare, too ascetic to be anyone's home. Even his. Instead she asked him, "How are you?"

"Tired. Fresh off my shift, and devastated."

The face had changed. The orange pigments were softer now, and both eyes were the same sickening hair-filled pits. How clear was his vision? How did he transplant cells from one eye to the other? There had to be mechanisms, reliable tricks . . . and she found herself feeling ignorant and glad of it. . . .

"What do you want, Quee Lee?"

She swallowed. "Perri came home, and I brought what he owes you."

Orleans looked surprised, then the cool voice said, "Good. Wonderful!"

She produced the chips, his shiny palm accepting them. The elbow gave a harsh growl, and she said, "I hope this helps."

"My mood already is improved," he promised.

What else? She wasn't sure what to say now. Then Orleans told her, "I should thank you somehow. Can I give you something for your trouble? How about a tour?" One eye actually winked at her, hairs contracting into their pit and nothing left visible but a tiny red pore. "A tour," he repeated. "A walk outside? We'll find you a lifesuit. We keep them here in case a captain comes for an inspection." A big deep laugh, then he added, "Once every thousand years, they do! Whether we need it or not!"

What was he saying? She had heard him, and she hadn't.

A smile and another wink, and he said,

"I'm serious. Would you like to go for a little stroll?"

"I've never . . . I don't know . . . !"

"Safe as safe can be." Whatever that meant. "Listen, this is the safest place for a jaunt. We're behind the leading face, which means impacts are nearly impossible. But we're not close to the engines and their radiations either." Another laugh, and he added, "Oh, you'll get a dose of radiation, but nothing important. You're tough, Quee Lee. Does your fancy apartment have an autodoc?"

"Of course."

"Well, then."

She wasn't scared, at least in any direct way. What Quee Lee felt was excitement and fear born of excitement, nothing in her experience to compare with what was happening. She was a creature of habits, rigorous and ancient habits, and she had no way to know how she'd respond out there. No habit had prepared her for this moment.

"Here," said her gracious host. "Come in here."

No excuse occurred to her. They were in a deep closet full of lifesuits—this was some kind of locker room, apparently—and she let Orleans select one and dismantle it with his growling joints. "It opens and closes, unlike mine," he explained. "It doesn't have all the redundant systems either. Otherwise, it's the same."

On went the legs, the torso and arms and helmet; she banged the helmet against the low ceiling, then struck the wall with her first step.

"Follow me," Orleans advised, "and keep it slow."

Wise words. They entered some sort of tunnel that zigzagged toward space, ancient stairs fashioned for a nearly human gait. Each bend had an invisible field that held back the ship's thinning atmosphere. They began speaking by radio, voices close, and she noticed how she could feel through the suit, its pseudoneurons interfacing with her own. Here gravity was stronger than Earth-standard, yet despite her added bulk she moved with ease, limbs humming, her helmet striking the ceiling as she climbed. Thump, and thump. She couldn't help herself.

Orleans laughed pleasantly, the sound close and intimate. "You're doing fine, Quee Lee. Relax."

Hearing her name gave her a dilute courage.

"Remember," he said, "your servomotors are potent. Lifesuits make motions large. Don't overcontrol, and don't act cocky."

She wanted to succeed. More than anything in recent memory, she wanted everything as close to perfect as possible.

"Concentrate," he said.

Then he told her, "That's better, yes."

They came to a final turn, then a hatch, Orleans pausing and turning, his syrupy mouth making a preposterous smile. "Here we are. We'll go outside for just a little while, okay?" A pause, then he added, "When you go home, tell your husband what you've done. Amaze him!"

"I will," she whispered.

And he opened the hatch with an arm— the abrasive sounds audible across the radio, but distant—and a bright colored glow washed over them. "Beautiful," the Remora observed. "Isn't it beautiful, Quee Lee?"

Perri didn't return home for several more weeks, and when he arrived—"I was rafting Cloud Canyon, love, and didn't get your messages!"— Quee Lee realized that she wasn't going to tell him about her adventure. Nor about the money. She'd wait for a better time, a weak moment, when Perri's guard was down. "What's so important, love? You sounded urgent." She told him it was nothing, that she'd missed him and been worried. How was the rafting? Who went with him? Perri told her, "Tweewits. Big hulking baboons, in essence." He smiled until she smiled too. He looked thin and tired; but that night, with minimal prompting, he found the energy to make love to her twice. And the second time was special enough that she was left wondering how she could so willingly live

without sex for long periods. It could be the most amazing pleasure.

Perri slept, dreaming of artificial rivers roaring through artificial canyons; and Quee Lee sat up in bed, in the dark, whispering for her apartment to show her the view above Port Beta. She had it projected into her ceiling, twenty meters overhead, the shimmering aurora changing colors as force fields wrestled with every kind of spaceborn hazard.

"What do you think, Quee Lee?"

Orleans had asked the question, and she answered it again, in a soft awed voice. "Lovely." She shut her eyes, remembering how the hull itself had stretched off into the distance, flat and gray, bland yet somehow serene. "It is lovely."

"And even better up front, on the prow," her companion had maintained. "The fields there are thicker, stronger. And the big lasers keep hitting the comets tens of millions of kilometers from us, softening them up for us." He had given a little laugh, telling her, "You can almost feel the ship moving when you look up from the prow. Honest."

She had shivered inside her lifesuit, more out of pleasure than fear. Few passengers ever came out on the hull. They were breaking rules, no doubt. Even inside the taxi ships, you were protected by a hull. But not up there. Up there she'd felt exposed, practically naked. And maybe Orleans had measured her mood, watching her face with the flickering pulses, finally asking her, "Do you know the story of the first Remora?"

Did she? She wasn't certain.

He told it, his voice smooth and quiet. "Her name was Wune," he began. "On Earth, it's rumored, she was a criminal, a registered habitual criminal. Signing on as a crew mate helped her escape a stint of psychological realignment—"

"What crimes?"

"Do they matter?" A shake of the round head. "Bad ones, and that's too much said. The point is that Wune came here without rank, glad for the opportunity, and like any good mate, she took her turns out on the hull." Quee Lee had nodded, staring off at the far horizon.

"She was pretty, like you. Between shifts, she did typical typicals. She explored the ship and had affairs of the heart and grieved the affairs that went badly. Like you, Quee Lee, she was smart. And after just a few centuries on board, Wune could see the trends. She saw how the captains were avoiding their shifts on the hull. And how certain people, guilty of small offenses, were pushed into double shifts in their stead. All so that our captains didn't have to accept the tiniest, fairest risks."

Status. Rank. Privilege. She could understand these things, probably too well.

"Wune rebelled," Orleans had said, pride in his voice. "But instead of overthrowing the system, she conquered by embracing it. By transforming what she embraced." A soft laugh. "This lifesuit of mine? She built its prototype with its semi-forever seals and the hyperefficient recyke systems. She made a suit that she'd never have to leave, then she began to live on the hull, in the open, sometimes alone for years at a time."

"Alone?"

"A prophet's contemplative life." A fond glance at the smooth gray terrain. "She stopped having her body purged of cancers and other damage. She let her face—her beautiful face—become speckled with dead tissues. Then she taught herself to manage her mutations, with discipline and strength. Eventually she picked a few friends without status, teaching them her tricks and explaining the peace and purpose she had found while living up here, contemplating the universe without obstructions."

Without obstructions indeed!

"A few hundred became the First Generation. Attrition convinced our great captains to allow children, and the Second Generation numbered in the thousands. By the Third, we were officially responsible for the ship's exterior and the deadliest parts of its engines. We had achieved a quiet conquest of a world-sized realm, and today we number in the low millions!"

She remembered sighing, asking, "What happened to Wune?"

"An heroic death," he had replied. "A comet swarm was approaching. A repair team was caught on the prow, their shuttle dead and useless—"

"Why were they there if a swarm was coming?"

"Patching a crater, of course. Remember. The prow can withstand almost any likely blow, but if comets were to strike on top of one another, unlikely as that sounds—"

"A disaster," she muttered.

"For the passengers below, yes." A strange slow smile. "Wune died trying to bring them a fresh shuttle. She was vaporized under a chunk of ice and rock, in an instant."

"I'm sorry." Whispered.

"Wune was my great-great-grandmother," the man had added. "And no, she didn't name us Remoras. That originally was an insult, some captain responsible. Remoras are ugly fish that cling to sharks. Not a pleasing image, but Wune embraced the word. To us it means spiritual fulfillment, independence, and a powerful sense of self. Do you know what I am, Quee Lee? I'm a god inside this suit of mine. I rule in ways you can't appreciate. You can't imagine how it is, having utter control over my body, my self . . . !"

She had stared at him, unable to speak.

A shiny hand had lifted, thick fingers against his faceplate. "My eyes? You're fascinated by my eyes, aren't you?"

A tiny nod. "Yes."

"Do you know how I sculpted them?"

"No."

"Tell me, Quee Lee. How do you close your hand?"

She had made a fist, as if to show him how.

"But which neurons fire? Which muscles contract?" A mild, patient laugh, then he had added, "How can you manage something that you can't describe in full?"

She had said, "It's habit, I guess. . . ."

"Exactly!" A larger laugh. "I have habits

too. For instance, I can willfully spread mutations using metastasized cells. I personally have thousands of years of practice, plus all those useful mechanisms that I inherited from Wune and the others. It's as natural as your making the fist."

"But my hand doesn't change its real shape," she had countered.

"Transformation is my habit, and it's why my life is so much richer than yours." He had given her a wink just then, saying, "I can't count the times I've re-evolved my eyes."

Quee Lee looked up at her bedroom ceiling now, at a curtain of blue glows dissolving into pink. In her mind, she replayed the moment.

"You think Remoras are vile, ugly monsters," Orleans had said. "Now don't deny it. I won't let you deny it."

She hadn't made a sound.

"When you saw me standing at your door? When you saw that a Remora had come to your home? All of that ordinary blood of yours drained out of your face. You looked so terribly pale and weak, Quee Lee. Horrified!" She couldn't deny it. Not then or now.

"Which of us has the richest life, Quee Lee? And be objective. Is it you or is it me?"

She pulled her bedsheets over herself, shaking a little bit.

"You or me?"

"Me," she whispered, but in that word was doubt. Just the flavor of it. Then Perri stirred, rolling toward her with his face trying to waken. Quee Lee had a last glance at the projected sky, then had it quelched. Then Perri was grinning, blinking and reaching for her, asking:

"Can't you sleep, love?"

"No," she admitted. Then she said, "Come here, darling."

"Well, well," he laughed. "Aren't you in a mood?"

Absolutely. A feverish mood, her mind leaping from subject to subject, without order, every thought intense and sudden, Perri on top of her and her old-fashioned eyes gazing up at the darkened ceiling, still seeing the powerful surges of changing colors that obscured the bright dusting of stars.

They took a second honeymoon, Quee Lee's treat. They traveled halfway around the ship, visiting a famous resort beside a small tropical sea; and for several months, they enjoyed the scenery and beaches, bone-white sands dropping into azure waters where fancy corals and fancier fishes lived. Every night brought a different sky, the ship supplying stored images of nebulas and strange suns; and they made love in the oddest places, in odd ways, strangers sometimes coming upon them and pausing to watch.

Yet she felt detached somehow, hovering overhead like an observer. Did Remoras have sex? she wondered. And if so, how? And how did they make their children? One day, Perri strapped on a gill and swam alone to the reef, leaving Quee Lee free to do research. Remoran sex, if it could be called that, was managed with electrical stimulation through the suits themselves. Reproduction was something else, children conceived in vitro, samples of their parents' genetics married and grown inside a hyperfiber envelope. The envelope was expanded as needed. Birth came with the first independent fusion plant. What an incredible way to live, she realized; but then again, there were many human societies that seemed bizarre. Some refused immortality. Some had married computers or lived in a narcotic haze. There were many, many spiritual splinter groups . . . only she couldn't learn much about the Remoran faith. Was their faith secret? And if so, why had she been allowed a glimpse of their private world?

Perri remained pleasant and attentive.

"I know this is work for you," she told him, "and you've been a delight, darling. Old women appreciate these attentions."

"Oh, you're not old!" A wink and smile, and he pulled her close. "And it's not work at all. Believe me!"

They returned home soon afterward, and

Quee Lee was disappointed with her apartment. It was just as she remembered it, and the sameness was depressing. Even the garden room failed to brighten her mood . . . and she found herself wondering if she'd ever lived anywhere but here, the stone walls cold and closing in on her.

Perri asked, "What's the matter, love?"

She said nothing.

"Can I help, darling?"

"I forgot to tell you something," she began. "A friend of yours visited . . . oh, it was almost a year ago."

The roguish charm surfaced, reliable and nonplussed. "Which friend?"

"Orleans."

And Perri didn't respond at first, hearing the name and not allowing his expression to change. He stood motionless, not quite looking at her; and Quee Lee noticed a weakness in the mouth and something glassy about the smiling eyes. She felt uneasy, almost asking him what was wrong. Then Perri said, "What did Orleans want?" His voice was too soft, almost a whisper. A sideways glance, and he muttered, "Orleans came here?" He couldn't quite believe what she was saying. . . .

"You owed him some money," she replied. Perri didn't speak, didn't seem to hear anything. "Perri?"

He swallowed and said, "Owed?"

"I paid him."

"But . . . but what happened . . . ?" She told him and she didn't. She mentioned the old seals and some other salient details, then in the middle of her explanation, all at once, something obvious and awful occurred to her. What if there hadn't been a debt? She gasped, asking. "You did owe him the money, didn't you?"

"How much did you say it was?"

She told him again.

He nodded. He swallowed and straightened his back, then managed to say, "I'll pay you back . . . as soon as possible. . . ."

"Is there any hurry?" She took his hand, telling him, "I haven't made noise until now,

have I? Don't worry." A pause. "I just wonder how you could owe him so much."

Perri shook his head. "I'll give you five thousand now, maybe six . . . and I'll raise the rest. Soon as I can, I promise."

She said, "Fine."

"I'm sorry," he muttered.

"How do you know a Remora?"

He seemed momentarily confused by the question. Then he managed to say, "You know me. A taste for the exotic, and all that."

"You lost the money gambling? Is that what happened?"

"I'd nearly forgotten, it was so long ago." He summoned a smile and some of the old charm. "You should know, darling . . . those Remoras aren't anything like you and me. Be very careful with them, please."

She didn't mention her jaunt on the hull. Everything was old news anyway, and why had she brought it up in the first place? Perri kept promising to pay her back. He announced he was leaving tomorrow, needing to find some nameless people who owed him. The best he could manage was fifteen hundred credits. "A weak down payment, I know." Quee Lee thought of reassuring him—he seemed painfully nervous—but instead she simply told him, "Have a good trip, and come home soon."

He was a darling man when vulnerable. "Soon," he promised, walking out the front door. And an hour later, Quee Lee left too, telling herself that she was going to the hull again to confront her husband's old friend. What was this mysterious debt? Why did it bother him so much? But somewhere during the long tube-car ride, before she reached Port Beta, she realized that a confrontation would just further embarrass Perri, and what cause would that serve?

"What now?" she whispered to herself.

Another walk on the hull, of course. If Orleans would allow it. If he had the time, she hoped, and the inclination.

His face had turned blue, and the eyes were larger. The pits were filled with black hairs that shone in the light, something about them distinctly amused. "I guess we could go for a stroll," said the cool voice. They were standing in the same locker room, or one just like it; Quee Lee was unsure about directions. "We could," said Orleans, "but if you want to bend the rules, why bend little ones? Why not pick the hefty ones?"

She watched the mouth smile down at her, two little tusks showing in its corners. "What do you mean?" she asked.

"Of course it'll take time," he warned. "A few months, maybe a few years. . . ."

She had centuries, if she wanted.

"I know you," said Orleans. "You've gotten curious about me, about us." Orleans moved an arm, not so much as a hum coming from the refurbished joints. "We'll make you an honorary Remora, if you're willing. We'll borrow a lifesuit, set you inside it, then transform you partway in a hurry-up fashion."

"You can? How?"

"Oh, aimed doses of radiation. Plus we'll give you some useful mutations. I'll wrap up some genes inside smart cancers, and they'll migrate to the right spots and grow. . . ."

She was frightened and intrigued, her heart kicking harder.

"It won't happen overnight, of course. And it depends on how much you want done." A pause. "And you should know that it's not strictly legal. The captains have this attitude about putting passengers a little bit at risk."

"How much risk is there?"

Orleans said, "The transformation is easy enough, in principle. I'll call up our records, make sure of the fine points." A pause and a narrowing of the eyes. "We'll keep you asleep throughout. Intravenous feedings. That's best. You'll lie down with one body, then waken with a new one. A better one, I'd like to think. How much risk? Almost none, believe me."

She felt numb. Small and weak and numb.

"You won't be a true Remora. Your basic genetics won't be touched, I promise. But someone looking at you will think you're genuine."

For an instant, with utter clarity, Quee Lee saw herself alone on the great gray hull, walking the path of the first Remora.

"Are you interested?"

"Maybe. I am."

"You'll need a lot of interest before we can start," he warned. "We have expenses to consider, and I'll be putting my crew at risk. If the captains find out, it's a suspension without pay." He paused, then said, "Are you listening to me?"

"It's going to cost money," she whispered.

Orleans gave a figure.

And Quee Lee was braced for a larger sum, two hundred thousand credits still large but not unbearable. She wouldn't be able to take as many trips to fancy resorts, true. Yet how could a lazy, prosaic resort compare with what she was being offered?

"You've done this before?" she asked.

He waited a moment, then said, "Not for a long time, no."

She didn't ask what seemed quite obvious, thinking of Perri and secretly smiling to herself.

"Take time," Orleans counseled. "Feel sure."

But she had already decided.

"Quee Lee?"

She looked at him, asking, "Can I have your eyes? Can you wrap them up in a smart cancer for me?"

"Certainly!" A great fluid smile emerged, framed with tusks. "Pick and choose as you wish. Anything you wish."

"The eyes," she muttered.

"They're yours," he declared, giving a little wink.

Arrangements had to be made, and what surprised her most—what she enjoyed more than the anticipation—was the subterfuge, taking money from her savings and leaving no destination, telling her apartment that she would be gone for an indeterminate time. At least a year, and perhaps much longer. Orleans hadn't put a cap on her stay with them, and what if she liked the Remoran life? Why not keep her possibilities open?

"If Perri returns?" asked the apartment.

He was to have free rein of the place, naturally. She thought she'd made herself clear—

"No, miss," the voice interrupted. "What do I tell him, if anything?"

"Tell him . . . tell him that I've gone exploring."

"Exploring?"

"Tell him it's my turn for a change," she declared; and she left without as much as a backward glance.

Orleans found help from the same female Remora, the one who had taken Quee Lee to him twice now. Her comma-shaped eyes hadn't changed, but the mouth was smaller and the gray teeth had turned black as obsidian. Quee Lee lay between them as they worked, their faces smiling but the voices tight and shrill. Not for the first time, she realized she wasn't hearing their real voices. The suits themselves were translating their wet mutterings, which is why throats and mouths could change so much without having any audible effect.

"Are you comfortable?" asked the woman. But before Quee Lee could reply, she asked, "Any last questions?"

Quee Lee was encased in the lifesuit, a sudden panic taking hold of her.

"When I go home . . . when I'm done . . . how fast can I . . . ?"

"Can you?"

"Return to my normal self."

"Cure the damage, you mean." The woman laughed gently, her expression changing from one unreadable state to another. "I don't think there's a firm answer, dear. Do you have an autodoc in your apartment? Good. Let it excise the bad and help you grow your own organs over again. As if you'd suffered a bad accident. . . ." A brief pause. "It should take what, Orleans? Six months to be cured?"

The man said nothing, busy with certain controls inside her suit's helmet. Quee Lee could just see his face above and behind her.

"Six months and you can walk in public again."

"I don't mean it that way," Quee Lee countered, swallowing now. A pressure was building against her chest, panic becoming terror. She wanted nothing now but to be home again.

"Listen," said Orleans, then he said nothing.

Finally Quee Lee whispered, "What?"

He knelt beside her, saying, "You'll be fine. I promise."

His old confidence was missing. Perhaps he hadn't believed she would go through with this adventure. Perhaps the offer had been some kind of bluff, something no sane person would find appealing, and now he'd invent some excuse to stop everything—

—but he said, "Seals tight and ready."

"Tight and ready," echoed the woman.

Smiles appeared on both faces, though neither inspired confidence. Then Orleans was explaining: "There's only a slight, slight chance that you won't return to normal. If you should get hit by too much radiation, precipitating too many novel mutations . . . well, the strangeness can get buried too deeply. A thousand autodocs couldn't root it all out of you."

"Vestigial organs," the woman added. "Odd blemishes and the like."

"It won't happen," said Orleans.

"It won't," Quee Lee agreed.

A feeding nipple appeared before her mouth.

"Suck and sleep," Orleans told her.

She swallowed some sort of chemical broth, and the woman was saying, "No, it would take ten or fifteen centuries to make lasting marks. Unless—"

Orleans said something, snapping at her.

She laughed with a bitter sound, saying, "Oh, she's asleep . . . !"

And Quee Lee was asleep. She found herself in a dreamless, timeless void, her body being pricked with needles—little white pains marking every smart cancer—and it was as if nothing else existed in the universe but Quee Lee, floating in that perfect blackness while she was remade.

"How long?"

"Not so long. Seven months, almost."

Seven months. Quee Lee tried to blink and couldn't, couldn't shut the lids of her eyes. Then she tried touching her face, lifting a heavy hand and setting the palm on her faceplate, finally remembering her suit. "Is it done?" she muttered, her voice sloppy and slow. "Am I done now?"

"You're never done," Orleans laughed. "Haven't you been paying attention?"

She saw a figure, blurred but familiar.

"How do you feel, Quee Lee?"

Strange. Through and through, she felt very strange.

"That's normal enough," the voice offered. "Another couple months, and you'll be perfect. Have patience."

She was a patient person, she remembered. And now her eyes seemed to shut of their own volition, her mind sleeping again. But this time she dreamed, her and Perri and Orleans all at the beach together. She saw them sunning on the bone-white sand, and she even felt the heat of the false sun, felt it baking hot down to her rebuilt bones.

She woke, muttering, "Orleans? Orleans?"

"Here I am."

Her vision was improved now. She found herself breathing normally, her wrong-shaped mouth struggling with each word and her suit managing an accurate translation.

"How do I look?" she asked.

Orleans smiled and said, "Lovely."

His face was blue-black, perhaps. When she sat up, looking at the plain gray locker room, she realized how the colors had shifted. Her new eyes perceived the world differently, sensitive to the same spectrum but in novel ways. She slowly climbed to her feet, then asked, "How long?"

"Nine months, fourteen days."

No, she wasn't finished. But the transformation had reached a stable point, she sensed, and it was wonderful to be mobile again. She managed a few tentative steps. She made clumsy fists with her too-thick hands. Lifting the fists, she gazed at them, wondering how they would look beneath the hyperfiber.

"Want to see yourself?" Orleans asked.

Now? Was she ready?

Her friend smiled, tusks glinting in the room's weak light. He offered a large mirror, and she bent to put her face close enough . . . finding a remade face staring up at her, a sloppy mouth full of mirror-colored teeth and a pair of hairy pits for eyes. She managed a deep breath and shivered. Her skin was lovely, golden, or at least appearing golden to her. It was covered with hard white lumps, and her nose was a slender beak. She wished she could touch herself, hands stroking her faceplate. Only Remoras could never touch their own flesh. . . .

"If you feel strong enough," he offered, "you can go with me. My crew and I are going on a patching mission, out to the prow."

"When?"

"Now, actually." He lowered the mirror. "The others are waiting in the shuttle. Stay here for a couple more days, or come now."

"Now," she whispered.

"Good." He nodded, telling her, "They want to meet you. They're curious what sort of person becomes a Remora."

A person who doesn't want to be locked up in a bland gray room, she thought to herself, smiling now with her mirrored teeth.

They had all kinds of faces, all unique, myriad eyes and twisting mouths and flesh of every color. She counted fifteen Remoras, plus Orleans, and Quee Lee worked to learn names and get to know her new friends. The shuttle ride was like a party, a strange informal party, and she had never known happier people, listening to Remora jokes and how they teased one another, and how they sometimes teased her. In friendly ways, of course. They asked about her apartment—how big, how fancy, how much—and about her long life. Was it as boring as it sounded? Quee Lee laughed at herself while she nodded, saying, "No, nothing changes very much. The centuries have their way of running together, sure."

One Remora—a large masculine voice and a contorted blue face—asked the others, "Why do people pay fortunes to ride the ship, then do everything possible to hide deep inside it? Why don't they ever step outside and have a little look at where we're going?"

The cabin erupted in laughter, the observation an obvious favorite.

"Immortals are cowards," said the woman beside Quee Lee.

"Fools," said a second woman, the one with comma-shaped eyes. "Most of them, at least."

Quee Lee felt uneasy, but just temporarily. She turned and looked through a filthy window, the smooth changeless landscape below and the glowing sky as she remembered it. The view soothed her. Eventually she shut her eyes and slept, waking when Orleans shouted something about being close to their destination. "Decelerating now!" he called from the cockpit.

They were slowing. Dropping. Looking at her friends, she saw a variety of smiles meant for her. The Remoras beside her took her hands, everyone starting to pray. "No comets today," they begged. "And plenty tomorrow, because we want overtime."

The shuttle slowed to nothing, then settled.

Orleans strode back to Quee Lee, his mood suddenly serious. "Stay close," he warned, "but don't get in our way, either."

The hyperfiber was thickest here, on the prow, better than ten kilometers deep, and its surface had been browned by the ceaseless radiations. A soft dry dust clung to the lifesuits, and everything was lit up by the aurora and flashes of laser light. Quee Lee followed the others, listening to their chatter. She ate a little meal of Remoran soup—her first conscious meal—feeling the soup moving down her throat, trying to map her new architecture. Her stomach seemed the same, but did she have two hearts? It seemed that the beats were wrong. Two hearts nestled side by side. She found Orleans

and approached him. "I wish I could pull off my suit, just once. Just for a minute." She told him, "I keep wondering how all of me looks."

Orleans glanced at her, then away. He said, "No."

"No?"

"Remoras don't remove their suits. Ever."

There was anger in the voice and a deep chilling silence from the others. Quee Lee looked about, then swallowed. "I'm not a Remora," she finally said. "I don't understand. . . ."

Silence persisted, quick looks exchanged.

"I'm going to climb out of this . . . eventually . . . !"

"But don't say it now," Orleans warned. A softer, more tempered voice informed her, "We have taboos. Maybe we seem too rough to have them—"

"No," she muttered.

"—yet we do. These lifesuits are as much a part of our bodies as our guts and eyes, and being a Remora, a true Remora, is a sacred pledge that you take for your entire life."

The comma-eyed woman approached, saying, "It's an insult to remove your suit. A sacrilege."

"Contemptible," said someone else. "Or worse."

Then Orleans, perhaps guessing Quee Lee's thoughts, made a show of touching her, and she felt the hand through her suit. "Not that you're anything but our guest, of course. Of course." He paused, then said, "We have our beliefs, that's all."

"Ideals," said the woman.

"And contempt for those we don't like. Do you understand?"

She couldn't, but she made understanding sounds just the same. Obviously she had found a sore spot.

Then came a new silence, and she found herself marching through the dust, wishing someone would make angry sounds again. Silence was the worst kind of anger. From now on, she vowed, she would be careful about everything she said. Every word.

. . .

The crater was vast and rough and only part-way patched. Previous crew had brought giant tanks and the machinery used to make the patch. It was something of an art form, pouring the fresh liquid hyperfiber and carefully curing it. Each shift added another hundred meters to the smooth crater floor. Orleans stood with Quee Lee at the top, explaining the job. This would be a double shift, and she was free to watch. "But not too closely," he warned her again, the tone vaguely parental. "Stay out of our way."

She promised. For that first half-day, she was happy to sit on the crater's lip, on a ridge of tortured and useless hyperfiber, imagining the comet that must have made this mess. Not large, she knew. A large one would have blasted a crater too big to see at a glance, and forty crews would be laboring here. But it hadn't been a small one, either. It must have slipped past the lasers, part of a swarm. She watched the red beams cutting across the sky, their heat producing new colors in the aurora. Her new eyes saw amazing details. Shock waves as violet phosphorescence; swirls of orange and crimson and snowy white. A beautiful deadly sky, wasn't it? Suddenly the lasers fired faster, a spiderweb of beams overhead, and she realized that a swarm was ahead of the ship, pinpointed by the navigators somewhere below them . . . tens of millions of kilometers ahead, mud and ice and rock closing fast . . . !

The lasers fired even faster, and she bowed her head.

There was an impact, at least one. She saw the flash and felt a faint rumble dampened by the hull, a portion of those energies absorbed and converted into useful power. Impacts were fuel, of a sort. And the residual gases would be concentrated and pumped inside, helping to replace the inevitable loss of volatiles as the ship continued on its great trek.

The ship was an organism feeding on the galaxy.

It was a familiar image, almost cliché, yet suddenly it seemed quite fresh. Even profound. Quee Lee laughed to herself, looking out over the browning plain while turning her attentions inward. She was aware of her breathing and the bump-bumping of wrong hearts, and she sensed changes with every little motion. Her body had an odd indecipherable quality. She could feel every fiber in her muscles, every twitch and every stillness. She had never been so alive, so self-aware, and she found herself laughing with a giddy amazement.

If she was a true Remora, she thought, then she would be a world unto herself. A world like the ship, only smaller, its organic parts enclosed in armor and forever in flux. Like the passengers below, the cells of her body were changing. She thought she could nearly feel herself evolving . . . and how did Orleans control it? It would be astonishing if she could re-evolve sight, for instance . . . gaining eyes unique to herself, never having existed before and never to exist again . . . !

What if she stayed with these people?

The possibility suddenly occurred to her, taking her by surprise.

What if she took whatever pledge was necessary, embracing all of their taboos and proving that she belonged with them? Did such things happen? Did adventurous passengers try converting—?

The sky turned red, lasers firing and every red line aimed at a point directly overhead. The silent barrage was focused on some substantial chunk of ice and grit, vaporizing its surface and cracking its heart. Then the beams separated, assaulting the bigger pieces and then the smaller ones. It was an enormous drama, her exhilaration married to terror . . . her watching the aurora brightening as force fields killed the momentum of the surviving grit and atomic dust. The sky was a vivid orange, and sudden tiny impacts kicked up the dusts around her. Something struck her leg, a flash of light followed by a dim pain . . . and she wondered if she was dead, then how badly she was wounded. Then she blinked and saw the little crater etched above her knee. A blemish, if that. And suddenly the meteor shower was finished.

Quee Lee rose to her feet, shaking with nervous energy.

She began picking her way down the crater slope. Orleans's commands were forgotten; she needed to speak to him. She had insights and compliments to share, nearly tripping with her excitement, finally reaching the work site and gasping, her air stale from her exertions. She could taste herself in her breaths, the flavor unfamiliar, thick and a little sweet.

"Orleans!" she cried out.

"You're not supposed to be here," groused one woman.

The comma-eyed woman said, "Stay right there. Orleans is coming, and don't move!"

A lake of fresh hyperfiber was cooling and curing as she stood beside it. A thin skin had formed, the surface utterly flat and silvery. Mirrorlike. Quee Lee could see the sky reflected in it, leaning forward and knowing she shouldn't. She risked falling in order to see herself once again. The nearby Remoras watched her, saying nothing. They smiled as she grabbed a lump of old hyperfiber, positioning herself, and the lasers flashed again, making everything bright as day.

She didn't see her face.

Or rather, she did. But it wasn't the face she expected, the face from Orleans's convenient mirror. Here was the old Quee Lee, mouth ajar, those pretty and ordinary eyes opened wide in amazement.

She gasped, knowing everything. A near-fortune paid, and nothing in return. Nothing here had been real. This was an enormous and cruel sick joke; and now the Remoras were laughing, hands on their untouchable bellies and their awful faces contorted, ready to rip apart from the sheer brutal joy of the moment . . . !

"Your mirror wasn't a mirror, was it? It synthesized that image, didn't it?" She kept asking questions, not waiting for a response. "And you drugged me, didn't you? That's why everything still looks and feels wrong."

Orleans said, "Exactly. Yes."

Quee Lee remained inside her lifesuit, just the two of them flying back to Port Beta. He would see her on her way home. The rest of the crew was working, and Orleans would return and finish his shift. After her discovery, everyone agreed there was no point in keeping her on the prow.

"You owe me money," she managed.

Orleans's face remained blue-black. His tusks framed a calm icy smile. "Money? Whose money?"

"I paid you for a service, and you never met the terms."

"I don't know about any money," he laughed.

"I'll report you," she snapped, trying to use all of her venom. "I'll go to the captains—"

"—and embarrass yourself further." He was confident, even cocky. "Our transaction would be labeled illegal, not to mention disgusting. The captains will be thoroughly disgusted, believe me." Another laugh. "Besides, what can anyone prove? You gave someone your money, but nobody will trace it to any of us. Believe me."

She had never felt more ashamed, crossing her arms and trying to wish herself home again.

"The drug will wear off soon," he promised. "You'll feel like yourself again. Don't worry."

Softly, in a breathless little voice, she asked, "How long have I been gone?"

Silence.

"It hasn't been months, has it?"

"More like three days." A nod inside the helmet. "The same drug distorts your sense of time, if you get enough of it."

She felt ill to her stomach.

"You'll be back home in no time, Quee Lee."

She was shaking and holding herself.

The Remora glanced at her for a long moment, something resembling remorse in his expression. Or was she misreading the signs?

"You aren't spiritual people," she snapped. It was the best insult she could manage, and she spoke with certainty. "You're crude, disgusting monsters. You couldn't live below if you had the chance, and this is where you belong."

Orleans said nothing, merely watching her.

Finally he looked ahead, gazing at the endless gray landscape. "We try to follow our founder's path. We try to be spiritual." A shrug. "Some of us do better than others, of course. We're only human."

She whispered, "Why?"

Again he looked at her, asking, "Why what?"

"Why have you done this to me?"

Orleans seemed to breathe and hold the breath, finally exhaling. "Oh, Quee Lee," he said, "you haven't been paying attention, have you?"

What did he mean?

He grasped her helmet, pulling her face up next to his face. She saw nothing but the eyes, each black hair moving and nameless fluids circulating through them, and she heard the voice saying, "This has never, never been about you, Quee Lee. Not you. Not for one instant."

And she understood—perhaps she had always known—struck mute and her skin going cold, and finally, after everything, she found herself starting to weep.

Perri was already home, by chance.

"I was worried about you," he confessed, sitting in the garden room with honest relief on his face. "The apartment said you were going to be gone for a year or more. I was scared for you."

"Well," she said, "I'm back."

Her husband tried not to appear suspicious, and he worked hard not to ask certain questions. She could see him holding the questions inside himself. She watched him decide to try the old charm, smiling now and saying, "So you went exploring?"

"Not really."

"Where?"

"Cloud Canyon," she lied. She had practiced the lie all the way from Port Beta, yet it sounded false now. She was halfway startled when her husband said:

"Did you go into it?"

"Partway, then I decided not to risk it. I rented a boat, but I couldn't make myself step on board."

Perri grinned happily, unable to hide his relief. A deep breath was exhaled, then he said, "By the way, I've raised almost eight thousand credits already. I've already put them in your account."

"Fine."

"I'll find the rest too."

"It can wait," she offered.

Relief blended into confusion. "Are you all right, darling?"

"I'm tired," she allowed.

"You look tired."

"Let's go to bed, shall we?"

Perri was compliant, making love to her and falling into a deep sleep, as exhausted as Quee Lee. But she insisted on staying awake, sliding into her private bathroom, and giving her autodoc a drop of Perri's seed. "I want to know if there's anything odd," she told it.

"Yes, miss."

"And scan him, will you? Without waking him."

The machine set to work. Almost instantly, Quee Lee was being shown lists of abnormal genes and vestigial organs. She didn't bother to read them. She closed her eyes, remembering what little Orleans had told her after he had admitted that she wasn't anything more than an incidental bystander. "Perri was born Remora, and he left us. A long time ago, by our count, and that's a huge taboo."

"Leaving the fold?" she had said.

"Every so often, one of us visits his home while he's gone. We slip a little dust into our joints, making them grind, and we do a pity-play to whomever we find."

Her husband had lied to her from the first, about everything.

"Sometimes we'll trick her into giving even more money," he had boasted. "Just like we've done with you."

And she had asked, "Why?"

"Why do you think?" he had responded.

Vengeance, of a sort. Of course.

"Eventually," Orleans had declared, "everyone's going to know about Perri. He'll run out of hiding places, and money, and he'll have to come back to us. We just don't want it to happen too soon, you know? It's too much fun as it is."

Now she opened her eyes, gazing at the lists of abnormalities. It had to be work for him to appear human, to cope with those weird Remora genetics. He wasn't merely someone who had lived on the hull for a few years, no. He was a full-blooded Remora who had done the unthinkable, removing his suit and living below, safe from the mortal dangers of the universe. Quee Lee was the latest of his ignorant lovers, and she knew precisely why he had selected her. More than money, she had offered him a useful naïveté and a sheltered ignorance . . . and wasn't she well within her rights to confront him, confront him and demand that he leave at once . . . ?

"Erase the lists," she said.

"Yes, miss."

She told her apartment, "Project the view from the prow, if you will. Put it on my bedroom ceiling, please."

"Of course, miss," it replied.

She stepped out of the bathroom, lasers and exploding comets overhead. She fully expected to do what Orleans anticipated, putting her mistakes behind her. She sat on the edge of her bed, on Perri's side, waiting for him to wake on his own. He would feel her gaze and open his eyes, seeing her framed by a Remoran sky . . .

. . . and she hesitated, taking a breath and holding it, glancing upwards, remembering that moment on the crater's lip when she had felt a union with her body. A perfection; an intoxicating sense of self. It was induced by drugs and ignorance, yet still it had seemed true. It was a perception worth any cost, she realized; and she imagined Perri's future, hounded by the Remoras, losing every human friend, left with no choice but the hull and his left-behind life. . . .

She looked at him, the peaceful face stirring.

Compassion. Pity. Not love, but there was something not far from love making her feel for the fallen Remora.

"What if . . . ?" she whispered, beginning to smile.

And Perri smiled in turn, eyes closed and him enjoying some lazy dream that in an instant he would surely forget.

The Ghost Standard

WILLIAM TENN

William Tenn (pseudonym of Philip Klass, 1920–2010) was a British-American writer of science fiction whose famous story "The Liberation of Earth" appears earlier in this volume. Although Tenn's
output dropped after the early 1960s, he was still active and writing into the 1990s—and still writing fiction relevant to the times.

"The Ghost Standard," published in *Playboy* in 1994, shows Tenn in a more playful mode than
the biting "The Liberation of Earth," with a rather amazing tale of alien contact. As Tenn wrote
in his afterword to the story in *Immodest Proposals*, the first volume of his collected fiction, "An
attempted definition of 'humanness' is what precipitated the story. If you believe, as I do, that we
will shortly . . . be encountering alien intelligent life-forms and having to learn to live with them on
various moral levels . . . you must be thinking also of the necessary distinctions in many areas that
we and they will have to make."

The "essential plot gimmick," as Tenn put it, "is the variations the characters play on 'dirigible,'
and 'limousine,' and the results thereof. It is based on an actual game of Ghost in which [the author]
Daniel Keyes and my brother Mort were participants and used these variations against each other. I
won't tell who did which."

"Ghost Standard" is a comic masterpiece, showcasing the ways in which science fiction and
humor can be a perfect match.

THE GHOST STANDARD

William Tenn

Remember the adage of the old English legal system: "Let justice be done though the heavens fall"? Well, *was* justice done in this case?

You have three entities here. An intelligent primate from Sol III—to put it technically, a human. An equally intelligent crustacean from Procyon VII—in other words, a sapient lobstermorph. And a computer of the Malcolm Movis omicron beta design, intelligent enough to plot a course from one stellar system to another and capable of matching most biological minds in games of every sort, from bridge to chess to double zonyak.

Now—add a shipwreck. A leaky old Cascassian freighter comes apart in deep space. I mean quite literally comes apart. Half the engine segment explodes off, the hull develops leaks and begins to collapse, all those who are still alive and manage to make it to lifeboats get away just before the end.

In one such lifeboat you have the human, Juan Kydd, and the lobstermorph, Tuezuzim. And, of course, the Malcolm Movis computer—the resident pilot, navigator, and general factotum of the craft.

Kydd and Tuezuzim had known each other for more than two years. Computer programmers of roughly the same level of skill, they had met on the job and had been laid off together. Together they had decided to save money by traveling on the scabrous Cascassian freighter to Sector N-42B5, where there were rumored to be many job opportunities available.

They were in the dining salon, competing in a tough hand of double zonyak, when the disaster occurred. They helped each other scramble into the lifeboat. Activating the computer pilot, they put it into Far Communication Mode to search for rescuers. It informed them that rescue was possible no sooner than twenty days hence, and was quite likely before thirty.

Any problems? The lifeboat had air, fuel, more than enough water. But food . . .

It was a Cascassian freighter, remember. The Cascassians, of course, are a silicon-based life-form. For their passengers, the Cascassians had laid in a supply of organic, or carbon-based, food in the galley. But they had not even thought of restocking the lifeboats. So the two non-Cascassians were now imprisoned for some three to four weeks with nothing to eat but the equivalent of sand and gravel.

Or each other, as they realized immediately and simultaneously.

Humans, on their home planet, consider tinier, less sapient crustaceans such as lobsters and crawfish great delicacies. And back on Procyon VII, as Tuezuzim put it, "We consider it a sign of warm hospitality to be served a small, succulent primate known as spotted morror."

In other words, each of these programmers could eat the other. And survive. There were cooking and refrigerating facilities aboard the lifeboat. With careful management and rationing, meals derived from a full-size computer programmer would last until rescue.

But who was to eat whom? And how was a decision to be reached?

By fighting? Hardly. These were two highly intellectual types, neither of them good exemplars of their species.

Kydd was round shouldered, badly nearsighted, and slightly anemic. Tuezuzim was somewhat undersized, half deaf, and suffering from one crippled chela. The claw had been twisted at birth and had never matured normally. With these disabilities, both had avoided participation in athletic sports all their lives, especially any sport of a belligerent nature.

Yet the realization that there was nothing else available to eat had already made both voyagers very hungry. What was their almost-friendship compared with the grisly prospect of starvation?

For the record, it was the lobstermorph, Tuezuzim, who suggested a trial by game, with the computer acting as referee and also as executioner of the loser. Again, only for the record and of no importance otherwise, it was the human, Juan Kydd, who suggested that the logical game to decide the issue should be Ghost.

They both liked Ghost and played it whenever they could not play their favorite game—that is, when they lacked zonyak tiles. In the scrambling haste of their emergency exit, they had left both web and tiles in the dining salon. A word game now seemed the sole choice remaining, short of flipping a coin, which—as games-minded programmers—they shrugged off as childishly simplistic. There also was the alternative of trial by physical combat, but that was something that neither found at all attractive.

Since the computer would function as umpire and dispute-settling dictionary as well as executioner, why not make it a three-cornered contest and include the computer as a participant? This would make the game more interesting by adding an unpredictable factor, like a card shuffle. The computer could not lose, of course—they agreed to ignore any letters of *ghost* that it picked up.

They kept the ground rules simple: a ten-minute time limit for each letter; no three-letter words; the usual prohibition against proper nouns; and each round would go in the opposite direction from that of the previous round. Thus, both players would have equal challenging opportunities, and neither would be permanently behind the other in the contest.

Also, challenging was to be allowed across

the intervening opponent—the computer not part of the combat.

Having sent off one last distress signal, they addressed themselves to programming the computer for the game (and the instantaneous execution of the loser). Combing through the immense software resources of the computer, they were pleased to discover that its resident dictionaries included *Webster's First* and *Second*, their own joint favorites. They settled on the ancient databases as the supreme arbiters.

The verdict-enforcer took a little more time to organize. Eventually, they decided on what amounted to a pair of electric chairs controlled by the computer. The killing force would be a diverted segment of the lifeboat's Hametz Drive. Each competitor would be fastened to his seat, locked in place by the computer until the game was over. At the crucial moment, when one of them incurred the *t* in Ghost, a single blast of the diverted drive would rip through the loser's brain, and the winner would be released.

"Everything covered?" asked Tuezuzim as they finished their preparations. "A fair contest?"

"Yes, everything's covered," Kydd replied. "All's fair. Let's go."

They went to their respective places: Kydd to a chair, Tuezuzim to the traditional curved bed of the lobstermorph. The computer activated their electronic bonds. They stared at each other and softly said their good-byes.

We have this last information from the computer. The Malcolm Movis omicron beta is bundled at sale with Al-truix 4.0, a fairly complex ethicist program. It was now recording the proceedings, with a view to the expected judicial inquest.

The lobstermorph drew the first *g*. He had challenged Juan Kydd, who had just added an *e* to *t-w-i-s*. Kydd came up with *twisel*, the Anglo-Saxon noun and verb for *fork*. To Tuezuzim's bitter protests that *twisel* was archaic, the Malcolm Movis pointed out that there had been no prior agreement to exclude archaisms.

Kydd himself was caught a few minutes later. Arrogant over his initial victory, he was helping to construct *laminectomy* ("surgical removal of the posterior arch of a vertebra") by adding *m* after *l-a-m-i-n-e-c-t-o*. True, this would end on the computer's turn, which could incur no penalty letters, but Kydd was willing to settle for a neutral round. Unfortunately, he had momentarily forgotten the basic escape hatch for any seasoned Ghost player—plurals. The Malcolm Movis indicated *i*, and Tuezuzim added the *e* so fast it sounded like an echo. There was absolutely no escape for Kydd from the concluding *s* in *laminectomies*.

And so it went, neck and neck, or, rather, neck and cephalothorax. Tuezuzim pulled ahead for a time and seemed on the verge of victory, as Kydd incurred *g-h-o-s* and then was challenged in a dangerous situation with a questionable word.

"*Dirigibloid?*" Tuezuzim demanded. "You just made that one up. There is no such word. You are simply trying to avoid getting stuck with the *e* of *dirigible*."

"It certainly is a word," Kydd maintained, perspiring heavily. "As in 'like a dirigible, in the form of or resembling a dirigible.' It can be used, probably has been used, in some piece of technical prose."

"But it's not in *Webster's Second*—and that's the test. Computer, is it in your dictionary?"

"As such, no," the Malcolm Movis replied. "But the word *dirigible* is derived from the Latin *dirigere*, 'to direct.' It means 'steerable,' as a dirigible balloon. The suffix *-oid* may be added to many words of classical derivation. As in *spheriod* and *colloid* and *asteroid*, for example—"

"Just consider those examples!" Tuezuzim broke in, arguing desperately. "All three have the Greek suffix *-oid* added to words that were originally Greek, not Latin. *Aster* means 'star' in Greek, so with *asteroid* you have 'starlike or

in the form of a star.' And *colloid* comes from the Greek *kolla*, for 'glue.' Are you trying to tell me that dictionaries on the level of *Webster's First* or *Second* mix Greek with Latin?"

It seemed to the anxiously listening Kydd that the Malcolm Movis computer almost smiled before continuing. "As a matter of fact, in one of those cases, that's exactly what happens. *Webster's Second* describes *spheroid* as deriving from both Greek and Latin. It provides as etymologies, on the one hand, the Greek *sphairoeides* (*sphaira*, 'sphere,' plus *eidos*, 'form') and, on the other, the Latin *sphaeroides*, 'ball-like' or 'spherical.' Two different words, both of classical origin. *Dirigibloid* is therefore ruled a valid word."

"I protest that ruling!" Tuezuzim waved his claw angrily. "Data are being most selectively used. I am beginning to detect a pro-human, anti-lobstermorph bias in the computer."

Another faint suggestion of an electromechanical smile. "Once more, a matter of fact," the computer noted silkily. "The Malcolm Movis design team was headed by Dr. Hodgodya Hodgodya, the well-known lobstermorph electronicist. Pro-human, anti-lobstermorph bias is therefore most unlikely to have been built in. *Dirigibloid* is ruled valid; the protest is noted and disallowed. Juan Kydd begins the next round."

Since both opponents were now tagged with *g-h-o-s*, the round coming up would be the rubber, or execution, round. This was most definitely *it*.

Kydd and Tuezuzim looked at each other again. One of them would be dead in a few minutes. Then Kydd looked away and began the round with the letter that had always worked best for him in three-cornered Ghost, the letter *l*.

The computer added *i*, and Tuezuzim, a bit rashly, came up with *m*. He was quite willing for the word to be *limit*, and thus to end on the Malcolm Movis. A null round, and he, Tuezuzim, would be starting the next one.

But Kydd was not interested in a null round this time. He added an *o* to the *l-i-m* and, when the computer supplied a *u*, the developing *limousine* that had to end on Tuezuzim became obvious.

The lobstermorph thought desperately. With a hopeless squeak from deep in his cephalothorax, he said *s*.

It must be recognized here, as the computer testified at the subsequent inquest, that the *s* already completed a word, to wit *limous* ("muddy, slimy"). But the Malcolm Movis pointed out that the individual who should have triumphantly called attention to *limous*, Juan Kydd, was so committed to catching his opponent with *limousine* that he didn't notice.

Limousine moved right along, with an *i* from Kydd and an *n* from the computer. And once again it was up to Tuezuzim.

He waited until his ten-minute time limit had almost expired. Then he came up with a letter. But it wasn't *e*.

It was *o*.

Juan Kydd stared at him. *"L-i-m-o-u-s-i-n-o?"* he said in disbelief, yet already suspecting what the lobstermorph was up to. "I challenge you."

Again Tuezuzim waited a long time. Then, slowly rotating his crippled left chela at Juan Kydd's face, he said, "The word is *limousinoid*."

"There's no such word! What in hell does it mean?"

"What does it mean? 'Like a limousine, in the form of or resembling a limousine.' It can be used, probably has been used, in some piece of technical prose."

"Referee!" Kydd yelled. "Let's have a ruling. Do you have *limousinoid* in your dictionary?"

"Whether or not it's in the dictionary, Computer," Tuezuzim countered, "it has to be acceptable. If *dirigibloid* can exist, so can *limousinoid*. If *limousinoid* exists, Kydd's challenge is invalid and he gets the *t* of Ghost—and loses. If *limousinoid* doesn't exist, neither does *dirigibloid*, and so Kydd would have lost that earlier

round and would therefore now be up to the *t* of Ghost. Either way, he has to lose."

Now it was the Malcolm Movis that took its time. Five full minutes it considered. As it testified later, it need not have done so; its conclusion was reached in microseconds. "But," it noted in its testimony at the inquest, "an interesting principle was involved here that required the use of this unnecessary time. Justice, it is said, not only must be done, but must *seem* to be done. Only the appearance of lengthy, careful consideration would make justice *seem* to be done in this case."

Five minutes—and then, at last, the Malcolm Movis gave its verdict.

"There is no valid equation here between *dirigibloid* and *limousinoid*. Since *dirigible* is a word derived from the so-called classic languages, it may add the Greek suffix *-oid*. *Limousine*, on the other hand, derives from French, a Romance language. It comes from Limousin, an old province of France. The suffix *-oid* cannot therefore be used properly with it—Romance French and classical Greek may not be mixed."

The Malcolm Movis paused now for three or four musical beats before going on. Juan Kydd and Tuezuzim stared at it, the human's mouth moving silently, the crustacean's antennae beginning to vibrate in frantic disagreement.

"Tuezuzim has incurred *t*, the last letter of Ghost," the computer announced. "He has lost."

"I protest!" Tuezuzim screamed. "Bias! Bias! If no *limousinoid*, then no *dirigibl*—"

"Protest disallowed." And the blast of the Hametz Drive tore through the lobstermorph. "Your meals, Mr. Kydd," the computer said courteously.

The inquest, on Karpis VIII of Sector N-42B5, was a swift affair. The backup tapes of the Malcolm Movis were examined; Juan Kydd was merely asked if he had anything to add (he did not).

But the verdict surprised almost everyone, especially Kydd. He was ordered held for trial. The charge? Aggravated cannibalism in deep space.

Of course, our present definition of inter-species cannibalism derives from this case:

The act of cannibalism is not to be construed as limited to the eating of members of one's own species. In modern terms of widespread travel through deep space, it may be said to occur whenever one highly intelligent individual kills and consumes another highly intelligent individual. Intelligence has always been extremely difficult to define precisely, but it will be here and henceforth understood to involve the capacity to understand and play the terrestrial game of Ghost. It is not to be understood as solely limited to this capacity, but if an individual, of whatever biological construction, possesses such capacity, the killing, consuming, and assimilating of that individual shall be perceived as an act of cannibalism and is to be punished in terms of whatever statutes relate to cannibalism in that time and that place.

—*The Galaxy v. Kidd,* Karpis VIII, C17603

Now, Karpis VIII was pretty much a rough-and-ready frontier planet. It was still a rather wide-open place with a fairly tolerant attitude toward most violent crime. As a result, Juan Kydd was assessed a moderate fine, which he was able to pay after two months of working at his new job in computer programming.

The Malcolm Movis computer did not fare nearly as well.

First, it was held as a crucial party to the crime and an accessory before the fact. It was treated as a responsible and intelligent individual, since it had unquestionably demonstrated the capacity to understand and play the ter-restrial game of Ghost. Its plea of nonbiological construction (and therefore noninvolvement in legal proceedings pertaining to living creatures) was disallowed on the ground that the silicon-based Cascassians who had built the ship and lifeboat were now also subject to this definition of cannibalism. If silicon-chemistry intelligence could be considered biological, the court ruled, so inevitably must silicon electronics.

Furthermore, and perhaps most damaging, the computer was held to have lied in a critical situation—or, at least, to have withheld information by not telling the whole truth. When Tuezuzim had accused it of anti-lobstermorph bias, it had pointed to the fact that the Malcolm Movis omicron beta had been designed by a lobstermorph and that anti-lobstermorph bias was therefore highly unlikely. The *whole* truth, however, was that the designer, Dr. Hodgodya, was living in self-imposed exile at the time because he hated his entire species and, in fact, had expressed this hatred in numerous satirical essays and one long narrative poem. In other words, anti-lobstermorph bias *had* been built in and the computer knew it.

To this the computer protested that it was, after all, only a computer. As such, it had to answer questions as simply and directly as possible. It was the questioner's job to formulate and ask the right questions.

"Not in this case," the court held. "The Malcolm Movis omicron beta was not functioning as a simple question-and-answer machine but as a judge and umpire. Its obligations included total honesty and full information. The possibility of anti-lobstermorph bias had to be openly considered and admitted."

The Malcolm Movis did not give up. "But you had two top-notch programmers in Kydd and Tuezuzim. Could it not be taken for granted that they would already know a good deal about the design history of a computer in such general use? Surely for such knowledgeable individuals not every *i* has to be dotted, not every *t* has to be crossed."

"Software people!" the court responded. "What do they know about fancy hardware?"

The computer was eventually found guilty of being an accessory to the crime of cannibalism and was ordered to pay a fine. Though this was a much smaller fine than the one incurred by Juan Kydd, the Malcolm Movis, unlike Kydd, had no financial resources and no way of acquiring any.

That made for a touchy situation. On a freewheeling planet such as Karpis VIII, judges and statutes might wink a bit at killers and even cannibals. But never at out-and-out deadbeats. The court ruled that if the computer could not pay its fine, it still could not evade appropriate punishment. "Let justice be done!"

The court ordered that the Malcolm Movis omicron beta be wired in perpetuity into the checkout counter of a local supermarket. The computer requested that instead it be disassembled forthwith and its parts scattered. The request was denied.

So.

You decide. Was justice done?

Remnants of the Virago Crypto-System

GEOFFREY MALONEY

Geoffrey Maloney (1956–) is an award-winning Australian writer of speculative short fiction who lives in Brisbane with his wife and three children. Through much of the 1980s, Maloney backpacked around India, Nepal, and Africa, and studied Indian history at Sydney University. Maloney's first story, "5 Cigarettes and 2 Snakes," was published in 1990 in *Aurealis*, Australia's premier speculative fiction magazine. Since then more of his stories have appeared in *Aurealis*, as well as in magazines and anthologies such as *Eidolon*, *Nova SF*, *Harbinger*, *Redsine*, *Abaddon*, *The Devil in Brisbane*, *Albedo One*, *New Writings in the Fantastic*, and *Antipodean SF*—some collected in *Tales from the Crypto-System* (2003), which was nominated for a Ditmar Award. Along with Maxine McArthur and others, he helped set up the Canberra Speculative Fiction Guild in 1999. This resulted in the anthology *Nor of Human . . . An Anthology of Fantastic Creatures* with Maloney as the editor.

In 1997, Maloney's "The Embargo Traders" was nominated for the Aurealis Award for best science fiction short story, and he has received multiple nominations for that award since. In 2001 he won the Aurealis Award for best fantasy short story for "The World According to Kipling (A Plain Tale from the Hills)." The story was subsequently included in *Wonder Years: The Ten Best Australian Stories of a Decade Past* (2003). He has also appeared more than once in *The Year's Best Australian Science Fiction and Fantasy*.

"Remnants of the Virago Crypto-System," first published in Ann VanderMeer's surrealist/avant-garde magazine the *Silver Web* in 1995, is a story about what happens after the aliens leave, among other things. It is a powerful, haunted, and enigmatic post–New Wave science fiction story.

REMNANTS OF THE VIRAGO CRYPTO-SYSTEM

Geoffrey Maloney

We leave the city in the early morning, taking the highway to the northwest, going up the country to the places where the aliens used to live. At one point during the journey it becomes apparent that the trip is not what I understood it to be, a holiday jaunt into the countryside to visit the deserted alien houses. She reveals that she is meeting a friend of hers, a woman, an alien who still lives here on Earth, deep in the countryside, isolated from human civilization. This has been slipped in, folded into our lives, pushed in between the bits and pieces of what appeared to be a casual conversation. Our relationship changes after that. I believe this alien woman is an ex-lover that she once spoke of. I grow bewildered, confused, jealous, angry, and useless. And she becomes all thrusty glances that at first warn, then accuse, glances which say: You never understand, then later, You fool, then later still, You are trying to interfere in my life. A silence intervenes, the journey continues. The world has been very quiet of late, since most of the aliens left. It is a terrifying, insecure quietness, a dread.

Arrival is at an old stone house in the country. Nearby is an old stone church. It has some beautiful stained glass windows which seem to depict the death of the Christian revival. A motorbike leans up against the wall of the church. She inspects it, checking it over like an animal, reassuring it and herself that everything is as it should be, that it will get her further up-country. I sulk from a distance, watching, then she nods, everything is okay—the alien woman has arranged this—but now communication is poor. There is nothing we can say to each other.

Inside the house are some other people, strangers unknown and irrelevant and unconcerned about our arrival. They are here to do other things. We are of no interest, they none to us. The interior of the house is self-functioning, built according to the alien Crypto-System. A set of Y-shaped escalators moves between floors. The levels are confusing, known yet still strange, as always in alien houses. Upstairs, the house's treasure, its heart, the Virago Machine, is still intact, still useable. It has escaped ransacking. At first appearance it looks like a typewriter and a cupboard. The typewriter, quite large, sits on a desk and backs against the cupboard, but this is only an interpretation. It is really a complete unit, a communication system capable of transporting messages across the lost years of space. It is arguable whether it carries them across the lost years of time as well. I have opened the doors of the cupboard and gazed at the rolls of yellow paper, all printed with fading, gray type. There are messages here, much to be deciphered, but later, later. . . .

Later another woman arrives. I know her by name. She and I are friends sometimes, both putting up with the whims of her. She is not the ex-lover. The ex-lover, the alien, is still far away, up-country, another two weeks' trip there and back. I suspect my chances of accompanying her now are slim. . . .

Several hours of arguments, more accusations, more references, obscure, to my ignorance, my lack of understanding of anything outside myself. The other woman who has arrived feels sorry for me, but she will say nothing. So it becomes, as it always becomes: it is I who have done this to myself, and unless I ask forgiveness, lose the anger, stop the sulking, then there will be no forgiveness, no reconciliation, and the trip up-country will proceed without me. And at some point it does not matter anymore, for it would seem that she only meant for me to come this far, to this alien house in this silent country.

Sometime later they are gone. I do not see, nor hear, them go. I was inside and such are the mysteries of the Crypto-System that the outside world is blocked out, destroyed: the house has its own reason, its own rhythm.

I ride the Y-shaped escalators, careful to switch sides at the ascent, so as to be not carried downstairs again—a tricky business, but like so many tricky things there is a knack to it, and once learned it is simple. The other people in the house are drinking wine. They too are ignorant—so she said—but they do not mind. I sense that they have come here to enjoy that ignorance, a convenient caravanserai on a long journey. I stand before the Virago Machine, my fingers resting on the keys, but I type nothing. I do not open the doors again, even though I sense that important communications or fragments of them are here. Perhaps there are messages from her ex-lover, perhaps there are communications which explain the quiet dread that has invaded our lives, but I am too scared to find out just yet.

During the days that follow I drink wine and display my ignorance with the other travellers. I fancy that I am beginning to enjoy myself, but it is the enjoyment of ignorance, the pretense that there is nothing else going on, and that this current pastime is the be-all and end-all of life. Sometimes, during drunken euphoric stupors, I mount the escalators, my feet infected by the cheap wine, slipping on its steps, but each time

the knack remains and the ascent to the upper storey is successful. There I search through the paper memories of the Virago, looking for the communications of one woman to another, but I find little. I suspect that the Virago is in bad need of repair: only fragments appear in its rolls and rolls of paper, bits and pieces that it has grabbed from the localised slipstream of the Crypto-System. Here and there among the faded type-print, among the yellow rolls of paper, women's names appear, sometimes complete sentences, scraps of messages they once sent to each other, some messages from this house to another further up-country, others that were returned. Occasional flashes of deeper import appear, mortality statistics and references to war atrocities, but there is nothing among these remnants to confirm and complete my half-held images of her infatuation with the alien woman. The communications remain incomprehensible to me, and I suspect that I have missed something important.

My days continue, and then they are back. So, two weeks have gone—inside the house barely five days have passed—such is the nature of the alien system. It is difficult to readjust. Here she is now. I am pleased, but some anger burns within me still. Why did she have to go? What need did she have? But she will not speak to me, or glance in my direction. A coldness sits between us like a long-lost friend. I ask many questions, jealous questions, finally drawing accusing glances upon myself. At least now she will look at me, but she does nothing to alleviate the pain, and displays her determination of being right, absolutely right, because she has chosen to do this. No other reason is required by her. As usual I feel more alone now. I am drawn towards her and away from the wine-drinking travellers, but I become lost somewhere in between, a territory so familiar to me that I begin to feel secure in my isolation.

.   .   .

Preparations for the journey down-country begin. I make one more visit to the Virago. Perhaps a last communication has passed between them and the nature of this journey, the nature of their relationship will be revealed on the yellow pages in the cupboard. But the Virago gives me nothing, only more communications with the intent of glances. It forces me away in the end and like a child I kick its cupboard, a further injury which will add to its demise. I ride the escalators downstairs one last time and salvage some joy from this by deftly changing tracks mid-flight, descending, rising, descending, until I tire of the game, my new trick, and allow myself to be carried to the lower storey.

We return to the city, a loathsome silent journey. If I ask questions there will be no answers. I do not ask. I like answers too much. Somewhere we stop to eat. The woman behind the counter looks familiar. I will talk to her, a chance for small revenge, but when I draw close I know this woman is a stranger. I do not know her, there is nothing I can say. At the counter, her friend—my friend I think—whispers to me. There is a communication in her bag, you should read it, do not let her see you. Perhaps you will be ashamed of your actions.

At home we still do not speak. She leaves her bag in the lounge and goes to the bathroom. I find the brown envelope, break it open, and feel the yellow Virago paper between my fingertips. In faded print like that of a cheap portable typewriter with a poor ribbon the message of the alien woman, her work, her art, her mission, is written. The communication consists of names, places, figures, some of which are vaguely familiar, others which I feel I should know but do not. I can only decipher some of it: Vietnam, some statistics, some figures; Ethiopia, more statistics, more figures; this obscure country, that obscure country, printed number after printed number, child mortality throughout this war

and that, the usual cryptic use of the English language. No statement of reasons, no conclusions, just fact after fact, figure after figure, numbers hammering at you until the conclusion becomes self-evident. I look at the communication again and realise something important is happening. This is the way they think. This is the way the Crypto-System works: a whole bunch of data forming a question. And this one became simple, in the end deciphering it was easy. The message rendered into humble human English: why do they kill children?

And her friend, my friend, had been right. I felt petty and ashamed. Simple jealousy had dominated me, and yet something more important had been happening. They, the alien women, had come here, studied us, and here the final communication, perhaps from the last alien on Earth, shakes in my hand. I mumble to myself, did this sum us up in their eyes, was this their final cryptic conclusion? Why had they left? Confused and distraught, the human lounge-room becomes a foreboding place. Had they studied us, tried us, and convicted us? Was that what it was all about? I imagined a fleet of alien ships channelling towards Earth to pronounce the final verdict and sentence. She was in the bathroom. Why had she been gone so long? A question on yellow paper. So, there was a question, there could be an answer. The bathroom door is locked. I knock hard, there is no answer. The door lock breaks, swings open. She is blue on the floor. No breath. The lips are already cold. Peach blossom and bitter almond hang in the air. There is a scrap of yellow paper in her hand. It unfolds in the warmth of my touch.

There is no answer, it reads.

There is a Virago Machine in an abandoned house down the road—they always leave their machines. The house is boarded up. I climb in through broken windows. Glass cuts my body. I begin to bleed. No escalators this time, the Machine sits in the kitchen next to the stove.

I rest my fingers against the keyboard. She is gone now. She knew there could be no answer. I don't feel anything. My fingers rest against the keyboard. I cannot answer the question. I imagine fleets of alien warships laying waste to the world. Punishment, no redemption. I see a scrap of yellow paper grasped between her fingers, unfolding in my hand. My fingers type, fumble and type. The cupboard splutters and whirrs, coming to life. Across the lost years of space, the communication, my answer, appears in faded type on yellow rolls of paper: I didn't kill any children.

Selfish to the last, I wait. There is no rolling thunder, no sound of an alien fleet breaking through the sky. Just a long steady silence that screams in the ears.

. . .

My days begin again, not much stranger than before. No redemption, beyond punishment. I move from abandoned house to abandoned house searching for further remnants of the Crypto-System, thinking yet that there might be an answer, hidden away among the yellow rolls of paper, now crumbling to dust. The world has grown quieter still, more deserted. Lingering, as if it turns ever more slowly upon its axis. In the end I return to the house in the country. No travellers this time, no cheap wine. The Crypto-System remains, the escalators still work. Some hope is salvaged as I ride them upstairs, prepare to switch tracks at the ascent, but I have lost the knack. I lose my footing, stumble, slip, then slide to the bottom. When I look up I see the escalators stop. Caught in an unfinished movement, everything is utterly, utterly still. My heart is between beats. Quietus.

How Alex Became a Machine
STEPAN CHAPMAN

Stepan Chapman (1951–2014) was a US writer who won the Philip K. Dick Award (1997) for his first and only novel, *The Troika* (1996). He grew up in Glencoe, Illinois, and attended the University of Michigan. Throughout his life, Chapman either wrote full-time or held odd jobs; with his wife, Kia Chapman, he once performed PSA-type puppet shows for Arizona schoolchildren, a gig that ended when the puppets caught fire. Chapman also wrote an eccentric math book for kids and wrote plays performed at various fringe festivals. He died prematurely of a heart attack in 2014, at his desk, working on new fiction.

As a storyteller, Chapman mixed myth, science fiction, fantasy, and the surreal into a rich tapestry of unusual, ironic, and darkly humorous fictions that were often antiestablishment. Useful comparisons can be made to such distinctly American freethinkers as Mark Twain, R. A. Lafferty, and Kurt Vonnegut Jr. Chapman's first story, bought by the legendary John Campbell, was published in the December 1969 *Analog: Science Fiction and Fact*, followed by four appearances in Damon Knight's influential *Orbit* anthology series. His work also later appeared in the World Fantasy Award–winning *Leviathan* series (1994–2002). However, Chapman is also one of the few writers associated with science fiction to regularly appear in such prestigious publications as *Chicago Review*, *Hawaii Review*, *Wisconsin Review*, and *Zyzzyva*. In all, he published more than three hundred short stories during his lifetime, only a handful of them collected in *Danger Music* (1996) and *Dossier* (2001). A "complete stories" is long overdue.

Chapman's most famous creation is the novel *The Troika* (published by the editors of this anthology through Ministry of Whimsy Press, 1997), which received widespread critical acclaim and was perhaps the most reviewed science fiction book of that year. *The Troika* came into print only after Chapman submitted selections from it to Jeff VanderMeer's Ministry of Whimsy *Leviathan* anthology series. By that point, the novel had been rejected by more than 120 publishers—so many editors had passed on the novel, in fact, that at the Philip K. Dick Award ceremony Chapman sat by chance next to two of the editors who had rejected the novel. The story of *The Troika*'s publication provides a good example of how difficult it could be to publish sui generis long-form material in the American marketplace at that time.

The Troika is a tour de force of sustained surreal science fiction—influenced to some degree by manga—and contains some of the most audaciously imaginative passages ever published in the context of science fiction. Although the mordant humor of the novel invites comparisons to Joseph Heller and Terry Southern, it is uniquely "Chapmanesque" in its fusion of mythology, psychology, and the afterlife. In the novel, three main characters who have lost their memories trudge across an endless desert lit by three purple suns: a robotic jeep (Alex), a brontosaurus (Naomi), and an old woman (Eva). Only at night, in dreams, do they recall fragments of their past identities. To further complicate matters, sandstorms jolt them out of one body and into another.

The novel alternates between dream tales about the troika's former lives and their present-day attempts to discover where they are and how they can get out. From this quest form, Chapman creates a poignant and powerful story of redemption, in which pathos is leavened by humor and pain is softened by comfort.

The excerpt included in this volume, "How Alex Became a Machine," fuses chapters 7 and 10 of *The Troika* to tell the complete story of Alex, a character who is pushed by excesses of industrial capitalism into losing his humanity.

HOW ALEX BECAME A MACHINE

Stepan Chapman

1. ASSEMBLIES

I was a dour young fool when I lived in Chicago in 1995. I had my own legs back then and most of my arms—the ones I was born with. After an initial spurt, the pace of my auto-destruction had slowed. Gone were the happy days when I would whang off one of my hands at the factory, go home for a beer, and think nothing of it. I must have been sentimentally attached to myself.

I speak of this fool that I was, but I can hardly believe in him. Think of a cardboard cutout of a young fool, that's some improvement. Dress him in cutout paper clothing: a pale blue shirt, coarse gray paper pants, little black shoes. Slot him into a world of sliding cardboard flats, inside the box of a toy theater called the factory. Cardboard walls, cardboard people, cardboard machines. Good. Now attach a power screwdriver to the stump of his right arm, and a humanoid prosthetic to the stump of his left.

That's him.

Now stand him beside a conveyer belt. Riding the belt, a succession of television picture tubes move past him, mounted in steel frames with some circuit boards and color-coded wiring.

His new job is affixing Masonite backing panels to the frames as they roll by. His left hand places the screws, his power prosthetic drives the screws tight. Preset manipulation loops run his hands. His hands require none of his attention.

So his attention wanders. He studies the dust on the cement floor. Or he watches the other assemblers, who have to think, to some extent, about what they're doing. Or he closes his eyes and listens to the factory—the ratchet of pneumatic wrenches, the hum of conveyer motors, the white noise from the air conditioners.

He makes up lies about his past. He pretends that he lost his hands in a war. Yes, he's secretly at war with the factory. And obviously the factory's winning. He's not like the others. They just come here for the money. He doesn't need money. What can he do with money? He never leaves the factory. He never sees the light of day. He never sleeps.

He sounds like a riddle. What makes war on a factory, has no hands, and never sleeps? I have no idea, but it's crawling up your neck, ha-ha-ha.

It's not that I refused my salary. In fact I drew three salaries, since I worked all three shifts every day, under differing surnames. At four p.m. I'd punch out Alex One and punch in Alex Two.

But a man has to sleep. Maybe I never was one after all. Maybe I was really a machine that was deceiving itself. It's simple to hide from yourself. You just choose a place you'll never look, work all the time, and never sleep. You never find out what you are, and it's phenomenal how much you can get done.

You can think about your goals in life. You can add up the minutes between you and your next coffee break. When break time comes, you can go to the so-called cafeteria—a row of vending machines against a Sheetrock wall—and sit on a polyurethane seat and think some more. You can drink hot cocoa and chicken soup and think. You can eat a hot dog and an ice cream sandwich and think. You can calculate the number of screws you sink in a day. The one thing you can't do, if you're me, is stop thinking. It's a basic design flaw. If I stop for an instant, all my cores go blank.

Where was I?

I was standing at my assembly station, screwing down Masonite panels, when my foreman Mr. Bosch and the janitor Mr. Siever came walking down the aisle and stopped behind me. Mr. Bosch tapped my shoulder to get my attention, then crooked his finger to tell me to follow him to his office. Siever took my place on the line.

Mr. Bosch's office was a glassed-in cubicle at one corner of the subbasement where we worked. He had a metal desk and two chairs in there, a file cabinet, and a coat tree. A gooseneck lamp cast an oval of light on a morass of oil-stained papers. Mr. Bosch, a bald man with thick glasses, gestured me into a chair and pushed a memo slip across the desk at me.

"The company is changing your work assignment. It's some new motivational bullshit the management cooked up. Read that."

I picked up the memo and held it in front of my face. I didn't want to read it, but it was my strict policy never to disagree with people. Bitter experience had taught me that the minute you contradict someone, you instantly get sucked into their asinine private world. By avoiding arguments I wound up not talking to anyone. I lived utterly alone in my own asinine private world. Terribly alone and constantly crowded by idiots—that was my life. Rats gnaw off their feet with less provocation. Mr. Bosch watched me patiently. I tried to read the memo, but whichever way I held it, it seemed to be upside-down.

Mr. Bosch explained that my new job was to do everyone else's jobs. Not all at once, but one job at a time. I would relieve workers at their stations and give them unscheduled ten-minute breaks.

"It's a twelve percent pay hike," said Mr. Bosch. "It's a promotion. Do you know why you were chosen? Your perfect attendance record. Don't you ever get sick, Alex?"

"I'm in training to become a machine. When do I start?"

"You just started. Congratulations. This new job is the best thing that could happen for you."

"Right."

"And do you know why I say that, Alex?"

"I have no idea."

"Because of your psychological problem, Alex. You have a psychological problem as big as all outdoors. Have I mentioned it before?"

"You may have. Can I go now?"

"You're a menace, Alex, to yourself and everyone around you. You need therapy, Alex. Lots and lots of therapy."

"Thanks for your concern, Mr. Bosch."

I left the office and started back toward the assembly line. I still had the memo in my screwdriver claw, so I looked at it again. Worse than ever. I still couldn't read it, and now I couldn't remember what it was. This happened to me in those days. Common household objects would mystify me. A paper cup, an alarm clock, a memo slip . . . I knew that these things had functions, but I'd be helpless to recall their names.

A horn blew in my ear. I was standing between two forklifts whose drivers were engaged in a right-of-way dispute. I got out of their way.

I went to the locker room, opened my locker, and changed my screwdriver for a more versatile prosthetic. I chose the mate of the humanoid hand that I was wearing on my left arm.

Siever was still at my workstation, doing my job with a rapt expression. Apparently we'd both been promoted. I walked up the line, all the way to the freight elevator that took away the finished video units. I watched over people's shoulders and memorized their assembly moves. I thought to myself, *I could run this whole factory if there were enough of me.*

I walked up behind Evangeline, an elderly black woman with bad veins in her legs. I liked Evangeline because she admired the cleverness of my prosthetics, and once she'd given me a Christmas card. She was wearing a loud pink dress and hair curlers. Circuit boards were shuffling past, and Evangeline was slapping a diode from her diode tray onto every single board, tweezers in one hand, solder gun in the other. She saw me and tugged out her earplugs.

"What are you doing here?" she asked me.

"I got a new job."

"That's great, honey. You too smart to work here."

"Give me the solder gun. I'm going to fill in for you."

"Oh, how nice."

Evangeline got down off her stool and stiffly walked away.

But something she'd said had wormed its way into a dark corner of my brain. *What are you doing here?* A dangerous question.

As the weeks of that summer wore on, I learned every assembly task that was done on our level of the subbasement. I took pride in my work and hoped to become a machine soon. Apart from the sleeplessness and the thinking too much, I was content. Until I had that bad dream. It was during the first coffee break of a graveyard shift. I fell asleep in my cafeteria chair, and I had a bad dream.

I dreamed that I was working on the line as usual, except that instead of building televisions, we were machining aircraft parts with rotary sanders. Plastic chips bounced off my goggles. I wondered why these huge fuselage sections should be made of styrene. Styrene is awfully flammable. So I walked off my station to see if I could find out where the parts got put together. I found a hangar full of bomber jets that were life-size model kits, hollow inside. Impressive as hell, but they'd never fly.

At one end of the hangar, a crew was rolling jets out into the sunshine. I followed one out. The jets were rolled down a sloping runway straight into the funnel of a gigantic grinder, which chopped them into chips, so that the chips—it came to me—could be melted down and molded into more aircraft parts.

I walked back into the factory to share my discovery. Mr. Bosch was there, but when I tried to speak to him, no words came out. So I went to the locker room and looked in a mirror. I saw why my mouth wouldn't open. My head was made of white plastic, smooth and hollow.

I woke up in my chair and tried to remember the dream, but all that came back to me was: *What am I doing here?*

What were we doing? Working for ESU, Educational Systems Unlimited. Assembling what? What was the product? I asked around, but no one seemed to know. Something educational. A sane man would have dropped the matter there. But not me. I was a dream-starved machine-in-training and a man with a Quest.

I got on the freight elevator and followed a batch of our video units to the level just below ours. There I learned an assembly sequence from an oriental guy named Joe. Joe had a scraggly goatee and agile fingers. All day long he built flush tanks for toilets. He screwed on the floating copper balls.

"Maybe this floor and my floor are producing different things," I suggested.

"Naw," said Joe. "All same thing."

"Maybe it's a pay toilet with pay TV inside."

"Your guess good as mine. What for you care?"

"Just curious."

Joe scratched his chin. "Curiosity kill cat," he told me.

I followed the flush tanks downstream, seeking out convergences of the component flow.

"Excuse me. I'm taking a survey. What do you think we do here?"

I stopped relieving people from their stations entirely. I rewrote my job description. I stayed in one area only long enough to scope out what they made there and where it went. A hippie type by the name of Reeves had some interesting theories. I picked his brain while he screwed colored lightbulbs into a display panel—one green, one red, one blue.

"What do you suppose it's for?" I asked him.

"I should worry? I got my own problems."

"But if you took a wild guess . . ."

"Maybe we're not making anything, man. I got a buddy works the level two down from here. He upholsters seat cushions. So you have to wonder. Seat, video, toilet, colored lights . . . What's the big picture? I'm not sure I want to know, you know? I got a million theories, but most of them I try not to think about."

So much for Reeves. I punched out and went home in the middle of my shift. I walked up Pulaski to Humboldt and took the bus east to the national guard armory. My apartment was two flights up over a Walgreens. I ate some popcorn and crashed. I slept on the floor, since I hadn't gotten around to buying a mattress. There were quite a few roaches and rats, but they stayed out of my way. I think I scared them.

While I was sleeping, I had another dream. I'm watching a silent movie about an overly serious young man named Felix. He has clean-shaven Teutonic good looks and jet-black hair brushed back from a high pale forehead. A Colin Clive type.

He works at a factory where he tours the machinery with a stopwatch, timing compression cycles and making notes in a book. He also sits at a desk in a slanted brick alcove, pulling the lever of an adding machine.

Everything in this silent movie is huge, angular, and skewed. Awesome pistons slide. Puffs of steam belch from floor grates. Faceless drones in prison pajamas trudge. Obese overseers crack bullwhips from steel balconies.

Felix is summoned before his superior, Ivan, a tub of lard with a walrus mustache. Ivan orders Felix to clear out a musty storeroom to make room for new machines. Felix rolls up his sleeves and sets to work.

He's wrestling with a lathe when he notices something wedged between the lathe and a wall. (Moody backlighting here, and ominous organ chords.) Felix dusts off his discovery—a featureless black box, the size of a large dictionary. A bizarre unhealthy expression creeps over his face. There's something about this box. That evening he furtively takes the box home under his coat. Legend card: DAYS PASS.

Felix changes. He's more dedicated to his work than ever, but he forgets to shave. He loses weight. His eyes are the eyes of a captured soldier. Legend: ONE MORNING . . .

Felix comes to work looking even more haggard than before. His overcoat is bunched around him oddly. He takes it off and hangs it on a peg. His right hand has been replaced by a crude prosthetic claw. No sick leave. No word of explanation. Just the missing hand. And this obscene homemade claw at the end of the stump.

The other workers are far too intimidated by him to ask what happened. No one talks to him anymore. But the whispering is thunderous. Inevitably Ivan invites Felix into the privacy of his cubicle. Cautiously, from across the desk, he asks a question. Title card: "WHAT HAPPENED?"

Felix sits, half in shadow, mute as a stone, staring Ivan down. He's still too high-minded to lie, but how can he tell his foreman that he fed his hand to a black box? Ivan looks down at the claw which could so easily make of bloody mess of someone's throat.

But the film breaks, the screen goes white, and the dream is done.

The next afternoon I stopped at the Walgreens on the way to work and bought a clipboard and a stopwatch. People would talk to me if I wrote on a clipboard. It made the process look official.

I used my stopwatch to time my walk from the punch clock to the building across the railroad track where I was pursuing my Quest. Twenty minutes wasted. I never punched in again. I was in *blue sky*.

I was tracing forward the path of a promising assembly, a computer keyboard. A conveyer took the keyboards down a narrow brick tunnel with an arched ceiling. I squeezed in beside the conveyer and moved sideways deeper and deeper into the tunnel, hoping to find out where it went. The tunnel went on and on, turning corners. The light was adequate, but my knees were going weak, and my back hurt from stooping under buttresses, and my mouth was dry from talking to myself. So I crawled in under the legs of the conveyer and took a nap.

It was cozy under there. Rubber flaps hung down on either side to protect the works from dust. I slept on my side because of the rash on my back. A man with a Quest must sometimes endure rashes.

The bad part was: as soon as I closed my eyes, I was dreaming again. In the dream I was lying on my back on the belt of the conveyer. It carried me along while I lay and watched the ceilings slide by. Then the belt stopped, and a man in white coveralls unfastened my right arm and set it aside. The belt started rolling again, and every time it stopped, another man in white would remove another part of me. The longer the dream went on, the less of me was left.

I woke up disoriented and poked my head out through the rubber flaps. For a moment I thought I was looking down a vertical shaft. The bottom of the shaft opened into a deep bright chamber where women and men in white smocks and white slippers walked here and there on a white wall.

When I got to my feet, I knew where I was—the computer section. Sliding beige partitions hung from slots in the ceiling, and everyone wore air filters over their mouths, for the protection of the printed circuits.

The staff there treated me well. Showed me where to wash up, found a clean smock for me, and a mouth filter. Many of them had prosthetics. Artificial eyes were especially popular, the favored style being big black globes with little white pinholes. All the young women were happy to explain their work to a serious young man with a clipboard. But they kept pointing at things that were too small for me to see. I met a Southern Baptist girl named Jo Anne who had plugs on her wrists rather than hands. The plugs fit into micromanipulation boxes. My kind of girl.

But I had no time for women. My Quest was upon me, and I was nearing the Finished Prod-

uct. I could practically smell it. Final subassemblies were forming before my eyes. A steel rack entered the picture—two feet wide and a yard long. My old friends the video tubes showed up to be bolted inside the racks, three to a rack. The colored lights were mounted beside the tubes. The dozen roots of my twisting flow chart were converging into a trunk.

Then I saw the panels. I was poking around a storeroom, and a freight elevator stacked with aluminum panels stopped at my level. The panels were four feet by eight, the biggest component yet. I resolved to stick with them like glue. Where they went, I would go. I sat on top of them and rode them up through the ceiling.

The ride took me to ground level, to a room three stories tall. From my perch on the panels I could see row upon row and rank upon rank of aluminum cabinets, like those chemical outhouses you used to see. Not far from where I sat, a couple of technical types were running wires from a diagnostic cart through a service port in one of the cabinets. An inspection team.

I got down and circled the nearest cabinet. There was an air-conditioning vent and some unconnected plumbing protruding from the base. But no door. Each side was bolted on. Once you were inside this outhouse, you were *really inside*.

At one corner of one side was an insignia decal, a purple oval with one word inside it: AUTISTICON.

So this was what I'd been doing with my life. I'd been a builder of Autisticons. This cabinet was an example of my handiwork. But what *was* it?

I walked down a row of Autisticons and came to one that had a side panel detached, providing a view of the thing's interior. The chamber was upholstered in black vinyl over a layer of foam. Here was the toilet, nested inside a black vinyl armchair. The toilet bowl peeked from a hole in the seat cushion. The toilet had no lid. But it did have restraining straps.

The armchair seemed smaller than I remembered. A good size for a five-year-old. The buckles of the restraining straps had keyholes. They locked. Everything fit. Form followed function.

Go on, I said to myself. *Stick your head in. No one's going to kang you in and run rapiers up your nose. Go on, Alex. It won't burn your eyes out. Have a close look.*

An armature rose from one armrest to support a plastic desk. Built into the desk was the computer keyboard. Attached to the opposite armrest was a self-rinsing bowl, the kind you used to see on dentist's chairs, for spitting. A red rubber tube dangled from the chamber's ceiling. A duct for cold porridge, that was my conjecture. Cold porridge laced with tranquilizers. That made sense. A kid has to eat. It wouldn't be humane to shut a child in a box without nourishment.

Mounted at the top of the front panel were the video screens with the colored lights, facing the chair, angled down. Red, green, blue. And tucked under the screens, a video camera aimed at my head.

I approached the diagnostic team. One of them was a short bald man with thick tortoise-shell glasses. He was holding a clipboard and smoking a pipe. He supervised the other mechanic. It was Mr. Bosch from my old department. He must have been promoted like me. He turned to face me.

"Alex. You finally got here. Any questions?"

"What *are* these things, Mr. Bosch?"

He drew on his pipe and frowned. "These are teaching stalls. Computerized teaching stalls. For schools. Elementary schools."

"What do they teach?"

"Whatever they're teaching children these days."

"Why do they have toilets in them?"

"So the children can shit, Alex."

"Why can't the children go down the hall to the bathroom?"

"Because the children are strapped in. Because there isn't any door."

That settled that. "And the cameras?"

"To keep an eye on the children."

"You're saying that the teachers watch the children on monitor screens?"

"I didn't say anything about teachers."

My heart was pounding for some reason, and my fists were clenched. I must have been upset. Mr. Bosch made a mark on his clipboard.

"If you really want to see how these things are used," he told me, "you should visit a modern elementary school. Most of them use Autisticons exclusively."

Perhaps he was right. Perhaps I should visit such a school. Perhaps such a visit was exactly the next step demanded by my Quest.

The other inspector tapped my shoulder. I was in his way. I stepped aside, and he screwed hoses to the toilet pipes. He was testing the flush. I was finding it hard to breathe. My bones felt like soggy cardboard that might bend in ten places at any moment.

Suddenly I wanted to kill Mr. Bosch. Him or myself. But what would that prove? And if I blew up the factory with dynamite? What would that prove? Precisely nothing. You can't do shit with dynamite. You've got to be subtle, if you want to make a dent. You've got to be far more subtle than a human. You've got to be a machine. And beat them at their own game.

"Mr. Bosch?"

"Yes?"

"What exactly do you do here?"

"Me? I pick units at random, and I make measurements. If the measurements deviate from certain parameters, I record that on my forms. What are *you* doing here?"

I held my face in my hands. It seemed to be an ancient ball of brittle rubber, cracked and weeping powder.

"All right," I said. "That's enough. Wake me up now."

"What?" said Mr. Bosch.

"Wake me up! I've seen enough. I don't want to hang around for the gory parts."

"What are you talking about?" said Mr. Bosch. Except that it wasn't Mr. Bosch at all. It was a total stranger, and I was shaking him by his shoulders and yelling into his face.

"The dream! The dream! I want a different dream! Or I want you to wake me up!"

"Leave me alone!" the stranger yelled back at me. "I don't even know you!"

I grabbed both of his arms in my steel-and-plastic fists and backed him up against an Autisticon.

"Cut the crap, asshole. Wake me up."

A couple of inspectors pried me off of him. As soon as they let go of me, I fell to my knees and retched. I retched directly into the toilet bowl in the open cabinet. Sometimes a thing is right there when you need it.

I stood up, wiped my mouth, and walked away. I found a dark corner of the loading dock and wept. I was making a fool of myself. I had no Quest. I was just a dumb Polack with delusions of sainthood.

I watched from the shadows while freight handlers prepared a shipment of Autisticons for transport. They wrapped each box in a sheet of foam and fastened the foam with copper straps. They nailed together fiberboard crates that held the Autisticons snugly. They wrangled the crates across metal ramps into the bellies of the waiting trucks.

I walked over to the trucks. Down the narrow corridor between two of them, I could see Wrightwood Avenue baking in the summer sun. A strip of scraggly crabgrass grew between the sidewalk and the curb. A little yellow butterfly flitted past. I waited until no one was around and walked across one of the ramps into the van of a truck. I was going to visit an elementary school. It was part of my job.

The crates were so tall, they nearly reached the van's silvery inner roof. But there was just enough room for me to crawl in on top of them. I lay on my stomach across two of the crates. I rested my chin on my arms and waited.

A scrape and a clank. Someone had moved the loading ramp. A squeal of hinges. Blackness. The slam of the driver's door. The vibration of the engine.

The truck lurched, paused, turned left, shifted gears. Braked at the Pulaski Street stoplight, turned north, and rumbled over the potholes. The crates jumped beneath me.

Onto the expressway. Air keening past. I was on my way. Through corn country and cattle land. Across the dusk and into the night. Going west. Whenever I started seeing things in the dark, I'd take out my lighter and strike a flame. There in the steady blue glow would be my hand. There were the crates. There I was.

I turned onto my side and fell asleep. It felt like falling too. Like falling into a deep dark well.

I dreamed that I was a soldier in basic training, running an obstacle course. Bare trees beneath an overcast sky. Frosted brown earth that crackled beneath my boots. I jogged along, huffing out steam. All by myself. Perhaps I was being punished. My fingers and toes were numb. I crawled under some barbed wire and kept moving.

I came to a barricade built of railroad ties. I climbed a rope to the top and threw my legs over. Then I got a surprise. The barricade's far side was slick aluminum. I lost my grip and fell, feet first, down a steep chute like a playground slide.

The chute leveled out and sent me spinning across the ice of a frozen pond. I slid to a stop on my belly. The ice felt thin. A blackbird flew past, scolding me. I tried to creep toward shore. The ice groaned and broke. I sank into the pond up to my armpits. My hands scrambled uselessly at the ice.

Night fell. A sheet of new ice formed around my chest. The pond held me firmly in its jaws. I was in no further danger of drowning. The stars came out.

An army jeep came toward the pond, blinding me with its headlights. It drove straight across the ice and stopped in front of me. The glare hurt my eyes. I waited to be rescued. But the jeep just sat there, idling its motor. Finally it honked its horn. It wanted me to get out of its way.

"Go around!" I yelled at it. "Go around! You've got the whole pond!"

I prayed for release. I woke up, fumbled for my lighter, lit another cigarette, went back to sleep. The air brakes hissed. We'd come to a weigh station at the Missouri border.

Here the aged film of the dream scorches and snaps. I lose the visuals, but the soundtrack proceeds.

I woke up coughing. There was a lot of smoke and a smell like burnt pork chops. Apparently the fiberboard crates were flammable. Apparently I'd barbecued myself. Luckily it happened at a weigh station. As soon as they found me, someone called an ambulance. Amidst loud expressions of anger and disgust.

I wondered what I looked like, as I rode to the hospital. I'll never know, because the ambulance wouldn't show me a mirror, and because my eyes were gone. Boiled like two little green onions. The ambulance was a real moron. It wouldn't shut up. It told me this long involved joke about a pet poodle that gets put in a microwave. What a creep.

I wouldn't have been so sensitive if I could've stopped thinking. Even at times when I wanted to stop—when I was charbroiling myself for example, or when mutant cicadas were chewing out my nerves—I'd go right on thinking, as if there were no tomorrow.

At the hospital I was wheeled on a squeaky gurney through hallways that reeked of mint. A radiologist with a stuffy nose fed me stale water from a paper cup. A fluoroscope buzzed. The radiologist turned me over and shot another exposure.

The nurses took off my hands and bandaged me from head to foot. For days I did nothing but lie in a bed and pee into a catheter, filling up little plastic bags. Then my kidneys gave out, so they detoured my renal arteries into a noisy dialysis machine.

Being blind required some adjustments. The first few days I tried desperately to remember what various things looked like. To fix them in my mind before they faded forever. But the more I tried to remember, the more I forgot. Eventually I gave up.

When they took off my bandages, the skin went with them. The dermatologist had planned for this. He'd special-ordered a batch of new skin from a pharmaceuticals concern in Boston. It itched at first, but I was glad to have it.

When my heart failed, the cardiologist had a new heart ready for me. And while they had my chest open, the hepatologist replaced my liver. New kidneys were still on order from a kidney shop in Amarillo. The food was great, and my job insurance was paying all the bills.

When my visceral condition stabilized, the ophthalmologist connected up a new pair of eyes. Everything looked pastel—pearl grays and bleached aquas, the colors of bread mold. But hell, they were eyes. I'd get used to them.

Then they gave me counseling. I needed a lot of therapy, because I was a very disturbed individual. I had a lot to learn about channeling my self-hatred into socially acceptable channels. But my therapists had great faith in me. If I worked hard, if I improved myself, I might someday perform a useful function. I might even become a delivery van or a dump truck. Being helpful to others is so important for rehabilitation.

But the crucial thing in life, I feel, is to become more and more like a machine as you go on, and less and less like a person. You have to become a machine if you want to escape all that.

2. SPRAYING FOR BUGS

It was 1997, and I was working for the city of Tucson as an exterminator. My life was fairly simple. I'd given up on being a man, and was trying to function as a public works vehicle. PUBLICWORKSVEHICLEPUBLICWORKSVEHI

I was south of downtown, driving the side streets around Stone, looking for an address. I watched for the numbers stenciled in yellow paint on the lampposts and checked them against my internal street map. My optics scanned the decaying city, translating walls and alleys and Dumpsters into vehicular simulation space. My tires rumbled over the sunscorched gutter trash. My fender optics tracked the curbs. Traffic was sparse. There weren't any pedestrians out, nor any drivers either. The city had grown nearly uninhabitable. The storm drains were choked, so the next winter flood would swamp the place and cripple city services for good. Piped water and wired power would recede into the fabled past. The more stubborn among the citizens were refusing to evacuate to the settlement camps. All the worse for them.

I came to Russell Avenue and braked at a stop sign beside a boarded-up library. I was the only vehicle in Tucson that still stopped for signs, but I'm a creature of habit, what can I do? A tow truck limped past me along Russell, dragging a sedan with no wheels. The tow truck had a flat. I turned onto Russell and proceeded south.

A year earlier I'd been the guidance brain in a trash truck. That was pleasant work, if you didn't have a nose. But they ripped me out of that truck and wired me into this van. Well, ours is not to reason why.

My six tires rattled over cracked cement. The pressure vent on my methanol tank was jammed, and my shock absorbers were a joke, but I was on the job, and that was what mattered to the City. I had a good spare tire but no jack. I'd lost a wiper blade, and when it rained, I compulsively dragged bare metal across my windshield. Also I talked to myself too much.

I had my service manual etched on my visual cortex—four volumes of theoretical perfection and zero-tolerance schematics—no rust, no wear, no fraying cables. I used to read it in the back of my mind, for a laugh.

My only friend at this time was a municipal garage door opener who opened the door for me when I went out or came back. She told me that my problem was that I'd been a man, and now I expected too much. I wonder how she could tell.

I was driving through a city of people who stayed at home. They stayed indoors and watched television and gradually melted. That was the new virus, the melting. After they melted, ambulances with loud sirens would take their goo to the University Hospital to make sure they were dead. After they got certified, pickup trucks would haul barrels of them out to the cemetery on Oracle Drive. Then bulldozers covered them over, and then there were forms to fill out.

The city had been built by earthmovers and cement mixers and cranes. Humans could never have built it. Humans could hardly live there. Humans grew buboes, sarcomas, and cysts there. Humans broke out in plastic sores, plague cankers, and growths without names there. Their wheat was full of wheat rust, no matter how their chemists poisoned it. Their water was full of cleaning supplies. If the poisons didn't get them, they still had household pests to contend with. New improved mutant pests! Paper wasps from Chile. Amazonian jumping scorpions. Norwegian wheel bugs and killer isopods from the Malay. The humans had it tough. The ones with no houses to hide in would lock themselves in cars and starve there, or seal themselves into Dumpsters with duct tape and suffocate. At least they didn't have to worry about rats. The bugs had eaten all the rats.

But humans weren't my job. My job was killing pests. You weren't going to catch me catching any diseases. You'd never see me melting. Me and the digital clocks and VCRs were immune. God grants small favors for his chosen. Sometimes so small you need a microscope.

I was told what to do, and I did what I was told. If I forgot where I was going, my Comptroller would remind me. If I ignored him, he repeated himself. People's houses filled up with bugs, so they phoned my Comptroller. Then he would send me out to spray. People didn't want to be bothered with bugs. People wanted to melt in peace. I could relate to that. I would have liked to be left in peace. But someone had to spray.

I knew a lot about bugs. My ROM included *A Bestiary of the Urban Insects of North America*, updated to 1996. The carapace of the Pea Scaler ranges from drab brown in winter to brilliant yellow—the sting of the Giant House Centipede— Sometimes I'd run it through my voice coder at high speed. Bug jabber.

FORMALCOMPLAINTFORMALCOMPLAINT

I was in a disgraceful condition. I should not have been working. My transmission fluid was seeping, there were bubbles in my tires, and my solenoid was out of adjustment. I should have been up on a lift, with grease monkeys packing my wheel bearings.

All it took out there was the irrevocable snap of one brittle fan belt, and you'd be dead on the shoulder of some desolate industrial drag, and the car strippers would come down like flies. But the City didn't consider *that*. The City needed every vehicle it could muster in those desperate days. If it moved, put it to work! That was their philosophy. Who was I to complain? I couldn't feel pain. Neither can bugs, but bugs at least can die. Bugs do have that advantage over machines.

MOBILEUNITMOBILEUNITMOBILEUNITMO

A dummy sat in my driver's seat. He didn't drive me. He was just part of my equipment. There wasn't any steering wheel, so he kept his gloves in his lap. He had black leather gloves, black leather boots, and no hands or feet in them. The gloves and the boots were his hands and feet.

He was called a Mobile Unit because he could get out of me and walk around. His coat was black vinyl, and his pants, and his cap, and his face. Dual cameras were mounted in his head. Their lens covers were gridded red glass, like a stoplight. I could see through his eyes or talk from the speaker in his neck. I could swivel

his head or tap his feet. I could send him into houses and use him to spray for bugs.

When I was a garage truck, I'd had a similar Mobile Unit to empty the trash cans. Sometimes he'd even scrape up Melters. Certain Melters didn't rate the ambulance treatment— Dumpster people, people who melted in public toilets, people like that.

Garbage collection had ended a year earlier, but the City still sent teams around to spray the fresh garbage with a foam that hardened around it. Phenomenal, the things they were doing with plastics. People were dropping like flies, but the new plastics were breeding like rabbits. It gave one hope for the future.

STATUSREPORTSTATUSREPORTSTATUSREP

I turned north from East Sixteenth into a graveled alley between Stone and Russell. To the west was a junk-strewn vacant lot. North of the lot stood a row of two-yard-wide mini-apartments, with aerials and swamp coolers on their roofs and bulbous mounds of petrified foamed-over garbage leaning against them in the alley. To the east, the backyards of houses, behind storm fence. I parked beside a house reputed to be the residence of a Mrs. Everson. My turbines wound down. I filed a status report by tightbeam. It was a punishing day in August, 1:27 p.m.

DISEMBARKATIONDISEMBARKATIONDISEM

I raised the dummy's hand and unbuckled his harness. I unlatched the driver's door and pushed it open. Swiveled the dummy's legs out of my cab. Somehow got both of his boots planted on the gravel. Slammed the door behind him and turned him toward the back end of me. All very complicated, if you thought about it too much.

I opened the rear doors and dragged out my canvas pouch and my tool belt. I hung the pouch on my shoulder and stuffed it with spray guns and a cross-section of aerosol toxins. I had pesticides for ants, spiders, roaches, fleas, silverfish, or armored slugs.

A mangy dog trotted up the alley with a

scrap of greasy butcher paper in its mouth. It didn't even look at me. I had no scent. I walked up to the storm fence and followed it south until I came to a gate, chained and padlocked. I hung my gloves on the wire and thought for a while. Luckily I had a bolt cutter on my tool belt.

The side yard was paved with red bricks. A barrel cactus stood in a little well. A swing set with no swings stood rusting. I turned east at the corner of the house, found the front step, and knocked at the door. Just then I was attacked by a vicious carnivore. Well, it was only a small poodle, but it bit my leg.

Slowly I bent at the waist and leaned down toward the dog. "Good dog," I said soothingly, while it growled and worried my ankle. "Nice doggy." I drew a cylinder of pressurized methyl cyanase from my pouch and lifted it over my head. Then I clubbed the fucker until it let go of me. I kicked it against the door, and it landed in a broken heap.

"I'm coming! I'm coming!" said a voice from the house. "Don't kick the door down!" Security chains rattled. I kicked the poodle into a space between the aluminum siding and a potted yucca.

"It's the exterminator," I called out. "The exterminator is here."

"Keep your shirt on," said Mrs. Everson.

MRS.EVERSONMRS.EVERSONMRS.EVERSON

The door swung open. An old woman squinted at me, shielding her eyes from the sun with one hand. Her arms were like plucked chicken wings, and her neck was like a powdered éclair. She wore orthopedic shoes, nylons rolled to the ankles, bifocals on a cord, and a hearing aid. Hanging by a thread.

"Are you the exterminator?" she asked me. "Well, come in out of the sun. I'll talk to you in the den. I'm watching one of my programs." Then she vanished and left me in the entryway. I would have to locate the den by the sound from the television. Not as simple as it sounds.

I was standing, according to my floor plan, in the entryway. But *entryway* is a deceptively innocuous term for that sense-numbing wel-

ter of porcelain mementos, stacked magazines, ceramic lamps, Christmas cards, et cetera. The ceiling was low, and there was hardly room to move.

I took my bearings from the walls and door frames and set forth. I knocked over an end table. I let it lie. I could understand a table wanting to lie down. I wished that someone would let me lie down.

I found Mrs. Everson sitting in an armchair. She was watching her TV set and eating crackers and cheese. Square orange cheese slices on round orange crackers filled a plate that rested on a tray with legs. Two boxes stood beside the plate, a box of cheese and a box of crackers. Every minute or two, Mrs. Everson would eat a cracker, and there'd be one less cracker on the plate.

Wet laundry was dripping on the rug. Yes, there were clotheslines strung across the den, with dripping clothes on them. It made sense. It saved her going outdoors.

TRANSCRIPTTRANSCRIPTTRANSCRIPTTRA

CLIENT: They're troublesome. Hundreds of them. They come from the window frames and spit on the glass. I can't tell if they're on the inside or the outside. Would you like a cracker?

MOBILE UNIT: No thank you.

CLIENT: Have you seen this show? It's my favorite.

MOBILE UNIT: What is it?

CLIENT: It's my favorite. I try to kill them with a broom, but they get in under the screens.

MOBILE UNIT: The bugs?

CLIENT: Awful! Do you live around here?

MOBILE UNIT: I don't live anywhere.

CLIENT: Would you like a cracker? Are you married?

MOBILE UNIT: No, I'm an exterminator.

CLIENT: I beg your pardon?

MOBILE UNIT: I like to be indoors. Walls, floors. Nothing outdoors has any *edges*. And there's all that *weather*. If everything just stayed in the box it came in, none of the boxes would get lost.

CLIENT: When are you going to spray? Because I have to move my pets. I can't let my pets be exposed to chemicals.

MOBILE UNIT: Your dog is already taken care of.

CLIENT: Would you like some juice?

MOBILE UNIT: I will require that you vacate the premises for a minimum period of twenty-four hours. Your compulsory compliance with this procedure will allow the safe deployment of lethal fumigants necessary for the complete eradication of your pest problem.

CLIENT: *Say what?*

MOBILE UNIT: I will require that you vacate the premises for a minimum period of twenty-four hours.

CLIENT: Well, if I have to, I suppose I can go stay the night with my sister. She lives on Speedway, but she's *married*.

Mrs. Everson phoned her sister and packed an overnight bag. Then she called a cab. The cab came two hours later. Her parting instructions to me, as I bundled her out the door, were that I should help myself to whatever I found in the icebox, but that I should under no circumstances move her furniture, because she had it all where she wanted it.

She shuffled toward her cab in the pitiless afternoon sun. She turned and spoke to me again. "You should be careful not to breathe that stuff," she told me. "You could grow a cancer like a grapefruit and never be properly compensated."

I could relate to that. Everyone should be properly compensated.

DIAGNOSTICSPRAYINGDIAGNOSTICSPRAYI

When I shut the door behind her, the house was mine. It was just me and the bugs now. But first I had to prep the floors.

I took my claw hammer into the den and got down on my knees in all the fucking magazines and crackers and tried to pull up the fucking carpet tacks. But there was all this fucking *furniture* in the way! *The hell with the carpet tacks,* I said to myself. *I'll rip up the fucking carpet with my fucking bare hands.*

So I did. The television pitched off its stand and smashed. A bureau full of knickknacks fell on its side. But *fuck all that shit*! I had *work* to do! I tore the rug up, wrapped the armchair and the birdcage in it, and dragged the whole mess into the yard.

Then I unloaded my pouch onto the kitchen table. I arranged all my pumps and canisters, my thinners and spreaders, all my sticky syrups and virulent powders. I picked out a tank of ant-and-roach mix and screwed on a red rubber hose with a brass nozzle. (Tri-iso-necrolaine in a base of sodium chromate. If swallowed, induce vomiting.)

I hooked the tank onto a shoulder strap, carried it to the kitchen sink, and pointed the nozzle at the dishes piled there. I turned a valve. Half-eaten toast on a flowery plate turned black. Cups and spoons and scrambled egg turned black. The sink and the sudsy water in it turned black. A gleaming black film crept up the wall tiles and blackened the doors of the cupboards.

Wallpaper blistered, peeled, and smoked. The inky stain covered the kitchen ceiling and spread into the living room. Shreds of curling paint fell from the plaster, leaving jagged white holes in the black.

I stood beside a window, spraying a baseboard and watching the guck soak in. The streetlights were on now. The stars were out. A breeze stirred the dead grass at the curb. I lifted my nozzle to the windowpanes. Oily goo slid down the glass and dripped from the sill. I moved into the bedroom.

Here, bugs! Come to Alex! Heeere, bug bug bug!

I closed off the valve on the tank. I surveyed the black drapes, the black bedspread and bolster, the closet full of black clothes, and the black perfume bottles on the smoking black lace doily. The toxic scum was a great improvement. It lent that cluttered wooden cave a sterile lunar beauty.

You started with the crude stuff to get the bugs' attention and to flush a few into the open. Once you knew what you were dealing with, you could poison them more selectively. You could fuck up their spiracles with polymers, or mess up their sex lives with pheromones, or even feed them enzymes that killed their alimentary flora and made them starve. The possibilities were endless, a chemist's holiday. But until you could stink a bug out of the woodwork and tag a specimen, you were just pissing in the wind. And I still hadn't seen one bug.

All right then, I said to myself. *Let's experiment.*

Back in the kitchen, I filled a bucket at the sink and screwed the lid off a jar of potassium tartrate. I poured three cups of the dangerous yellow granules into the water. They sputtered and fizzed. I found a mop and wet down all the floors. When a cabinet or a dresser got in my way, I'd rip the legs off it, drag it to the yard, and throw it on the burn pile. But the mop fell apart before I could finish. And still no bugs.

It never failed. Just when you got a good bloodlust rolling, the little cunts crept deeper into the crawl spaces, where you couldn't get at them, like an itch at the center of your back. Crawl spaces. The hallmark of shoddy construction. I walked around the house kicking holes in the fucking walls.

I had to carry stuff out of there in armfuls— samplers, houseplants, cans of tomato paste. . . . And there was always more. What a rat's nest! It made me want to strangle a parakeet.

I got busy with my sledgehammer and knocked down some shelves and partitions. Then I turned off all the lights and sat down against a wall to think.

The sprays might be driving the bugs into the foundation. Perhaps I could lure them out with some *bait.*

LAYINGBAITLAYINGBAITLAYINGBAITLAYI

Peanut butter? Chicken liver? Dead dog? The dead dog would be perfect. I walked out into the moonlight and fetched it indoors. I put it on the bedspread and hid in the bedroom closet with the bathrobes and tennis rackets.

Still the bugs wouldn't show themselves. I needed more bait.

I went to the alley and broke through the plastic crust of one of the hillocks of old garbage. Dragged two black plastic bags back to the house and used a garden rake to distribute the trash evenly. I kept going for more until I had it to a depth of six inches on all the floors. Then I hid in the closet again.

All night I lay in wait, watching with my eyes, listening with my gloves, smelling with my boots. The air conditioner turned itself on, turned itself off, a well adjusted appliance. Cars drove past. I turned off my eyes and just listened. My head felt as if it had retracted into my chest.

But I could make out a new rhythm behind the tranquil murmur of the air conditioner. A chirping. A shrilling. Dozens of shrillings. From the walls, the floor, from every side. A strident mantric din like a horde of locusts. I left the closet and turned on a lamp. The bugs went right on singing, safe in their crannies.

The air conditioner was distracting me, so I ripped out its cord. That's when I saw my first cicada.

INITIALSIGHTINGINITIALSIGHTINGINITIA

It dropped out of the air conditioner and

landed on the floor. A huge fucker, six inches long. With a humped brown shell like a cricket's. Angular sawtooth legs. Crooked feelers tapping at the floorboards like blind men's canes. A radically mutated giant cicada. It belonged in a monster movie, knocking down Hoover Dam.

It scuttled nervously toward the wall, then stopped. I froze where I stood and processed optical data. Sampled out a dorsal view and a profile and ran them through my morphological comparitor. This cicada was not the traditional seventeen-year root sucker. This thing was a *carnivore*.

I wasn't normally given to emotional reactions to vermin. But the giant cicada filled me with a physical dismay. It made the vinyl creep on my aluminum bones. It made my clothes itch.

Such things were to be expected. This was the decade when all the genetic codes went through a cheap photocopier. This was the generation when none of the babies were quite what they seemed. These were the years when puppies lay squirming on puppy blankets, all sticky and feeble and new and *not quite puppies*.

Cautiously I sank to my hands and knees and extended one palm over the specimen. The hideous insect tentatively twitched and squeaked. Then it rushed at me, a sickening scrambling concentration of vitality. I crushed it under my glove. The crunch was deafening.

Luckily for purposes of documentation, the cicada's head escaped mangling. Its beady eyes glared at me while it died. I lifted my hand, and it hung from the underside, glued there by its own ichor, weakly waving its legs. Then it fell to the floor. I stuffed the corpse into a sandwich bag. The cicadas under the floor went on singing.

I had to simplify the floor plan. I went to my van for a crowbar. The sun was up, and the gravel was wet. A street scrubber drove slowly north along Stone, past the Presbyterian church and Madelaine's Beauty College.

Mrs. Everson might come home today. But she couldn't stay here. I intended to make life very unpleasant for those cicadas.

The best thing would've been to burn the fucking house down.

BERSERKERBERSERKERBERSERKERBERSERK

I went back indoors and punched the fucking water heater right through the fucking bedroom wall. Then I tore out the bathroom sink and rammed *that* into the fucking attic. Just to show the fucking cicadas I meant business.

Then I walked around the house screaming insults at them. Just the normal kind of things you scream at a time like that. "Come out of there, you yellow little pukes!" "I know you're in there, you slimy faggots!" That sort of thing.

Then I looked for them. I looked in the oven and pried the back off the television and pulled the stuffing out of the cushions. I wished that I could see through walls. That way I could've seen the bugs, snug in their cozy dens, warbling their miserable *songs*. I could've mapped their demographics and charted their social organization. Then I could've wiped them out—crushed their eggs, burned their larvae, tortured their drones for strategic information.

But since I couldn't do any of *that*, I contented myself with pounding a crowbar through Mrs. Everson's flocked pastel wallpaper, again and again and again.

BREAKTIMEBREAKTIMEBREAKTIMEBREAK

I took a break. I felt I was entitled. I sat down in Mrs. Everson's bathtub with the television set on my lap. I watched Saturday morning cartoons for a couple of hours.

One of the cartoons concerned a magpie that wanted to eat a worm. Another involved a wolf who wanted to eat some sheep. I enjoyed the jokes, but it bothered me that the worm and the sheep never got eaten. I think that a story should be realistic.

VANVANVANVANVANVANVANVANVAN

Just then my van made a noise on the tightbeam. It wanted to alert me regarding a Threat to Vehicular Security that was developing in the alley. Apparently a couple of suspicious-looking Mexican kids were hanging around, sitting with their backs against the storm fence. One youth had a shaved head and was picking her teeth with a screwdriver. The other had purple tattoos on her face and wore a necklace of spark plugs. The van thought that they were talking about him. He suspected the youths of being car strippers. I thought he was being an alarmist.

"Alex," I told him, "you're overreacting. Alex? Do you copy?"

But I received no response.

HOWEVERHOWEVERHOWEVERHOWEVERH

However, as I stood up in the bathtub, I knocked my head against the rod of the shower curtain. Flying into a rage, I tore the ugly fucking thing right out of the fucking wall—curtains, brackets, and all. Half the bathroom wall fell into the tub with me. And there I stood in the trembling dust, curtain rod in hand, gazing *into* the wall.

Gazing into the wall. My wish had come true. Here was the plumbing. There were the studs. And over in the shadows, a pale pod hung in a hammock of filaments. Within the pod, myriad milky larvae wriggled or slept. It was a nest of baby cicadas. Adults stuck their heads from crannies, squeaking in alarm.

The adults rushed to the pod and tore it open. Each stuffed a few of the infants under its belly and scrambled away. But they were bailing out a lifeboat with a thimble. I had them where I wanted them. By merely reaching out my glove and clenching my fist, I could turn their nursery into a slaughterhouse. I could fry their grubs in peanut oil and dip them in hot sauce and sell them door to door. How could they prevent me?

VANVANVANVANVANVANVANVANVAN

My van went completely paranoid. One of the Mexican kids stood up, and it rammed the kid into the storm fence. It was convinced that they were car strippers. I couldn't talk to it.

"*This* will break some bones," it kept saying. "Come on *out* here, Alex. Don't you want to see me break some *bones*?"

ANYWAYANYWAYANYWAYANYWAYANYWA

Anyway I was reaching into the wall for a handful of larvae when Mrs. Everson tapped me on my shoulder.

"This place looks *so* much better," she told me. "I'm very grateful to you. And do you know what? At my sister's house, I spoke with a nice young social worker. And she's had me relocated. I'm very happy where I live now. They fix our lunches for us and give us free drugs. I have my own waterbed and my own VCR, and I watch pornography all day. It's *wonderful*. You go ahead with your work, young man. And thank you so much for strangling that parakeet. I never liked it. It was a *gift*."

She made a move for the door, but I was too fast for her. I wasn't going to let her get away *that* easy. She still had to sign for the spraying. I put a sofa on top of her and sat down on it.

But she wouldn't stop breathing, so I went to the kitchen for my spray gun. I'd make her sign the receipt, then finish her off. I understood my mission for the City. To kill pests. Including any excess citizens who got in my way. Discreetly. Without appearing to. I was a chemical weapon. Whereas Mrs. Everson was old and in the way. Should I have suffered her to live? Old and useless as she was?

Sitting on the sofa, loading the spray gun, my legs began to itch. Impossible, but they did itch. I *had* no legs, only trousers and metal stilts. Yet they itched. It was like something from a previous life.

LONGAGOLONGAGOLONGAGOLONGAGOLO

Long ago in a previous life, I had been a man built of flesh. For a year or so, I lived in a rainy city in a clammy basement. The fleas there became a problem, because they *liked* me. As food. I scratched my flea bites until they bled. When the blood dried, I scratched my scabs. Finally I went to the pet section of a supermarket and bought some flea powder and a couple of the flea collars for cats. I sprinkled the powder on my bed and my sofa. The collars, I wore around my ankles under my socks. It seemed like a great idea at the time. Unfortunately the collars were designed for an animal with fur.

I slept in the collars and woke the next morning with big black fleas hopping on and off of me as usual, and angry red water blisters that ran all round my ankles. With trembling hands I unbuckled the plastic shackles from my insulted flesh.

For days I lay on the sofa with my feet up on the backrest, while my puffy yellow ankles wept salty tears down my legs. Suffering for my stupidity, I underwent epiphanies of self-disgust. That's what happens when you don't read labels.

MEANWHILEMEANWHILEMEANWHILEME

It was a good thing for me that I wasn't flesh anymore. Flesh could be stung by bugs or even eaten. Plus, if I were flesh, I'd have asphyxiated myself by now. I'd be dead or delirious. Whereas I was reasoning with perfect clarity.

My van wasn't faring so well. The car strippers had removed all its tires and pried loose its engine cover. A tire iron had shattered its windows. Pebbles of auto glass littered the driver's seat. The strippers applied hacksaws from the van's own tool kit. The van exploded in slow motion, like a carburetor schematic, clusters of parts floating in midair. There went the alternator. There went the batteries.

What if they find the silica wafers of my brain, Alex? What then? Where are my car keys, Alex? For the love of mercy, help me!

NOCTURNENOCTURNENOCTURNENOCTUR

An old woman was sleeping under a sofa. A robot sat on top of the sofa. Neither of us were breathing. It was dark outside. A siren wailed, across town somewhere.

I climbed down from the sofa and paced the living room. All the faucets in the house were running. Mrs. Everson's dresses were stuffed down the drains and into the cracks under the doors. The water lay an inch deep on the floor. All escape routes were blocked. I paced the room, waiting for the water to rise, slipping on loose tiles and place mats—half indoors, half out, half crazy, half dead.

I told myself: *Don't panic.* Whatever happened, I mustn't panic. If I could continue to reason with perfect clarity, all would be well.

A deep dark well. With three sisters at the bottom, eating treacle and feeling ill. A deep dark ill.

I stood beside a blacked-out window in the dead of night. Everything seemed to be shrinking. The walls shrank from the floors. The alley gravel shrank from the patio bricks. Tire tread shrank from asphalt, billboards from the sky, and the stars from the earth. Women shrank from men, and men from one another. I couldn't sleep. I couldn't make sense of anything.

Somewhere in the neighborhood a mariachi band was playing—accordion and trumpets. It sounded like a party.

The earth spun under my boots. The stars circled Mrs. Everson's roof. I had burned all her magazines. Something was chewing on my leg.

AFTERMATHAFTERMATHAFTERMATHAFT

Time passed. The water company shut off the water. The power company cut the power. Batteries emptied, I shared the ruined house with my friends, the bugs. The moon-scorched skeleton of my van stood in the alley, corroding in the winter downpours.

On the day they cut the power, the picture on the TV screen contracted to a white dot and blinked out. Sometimes children threw rocks through the windows, but I ignored them. The cicadas would take care of them. The cicadas had driven the red ants from Tucson, and were eating the last of the citizens.

I lay on my back with my head in a broom closet. A mop handle and some gallon bottles of ginger ale kept me company. I kept forgetting things. I forgot what I was doing. (Flooding the house.) I forgot what I'd done. (Lost my car keys.) I forgot what I'd planned. (Someday the roof of the house would cave in, and the sun would bleach my optical sockets.) All my vital parts had been pried loose and carried off.

I told jokes to the cicadas. I said, *Stop me if you've heard this.* The cicadas brought me food and taught me things. I couldn't eat the food, but I learned quite a lot. Things about families and about deserts and about soul murder.

I can't eat this, I kept telling them. They thought I was joking.

During mating season, the male cicadas turned blue and began to glow. They crept around the ceiling like winking constellations. I wondered whether insects were machines, and whether machines were insects. Certain insects can fly, but not every insect, and the same is true of machines. Flying machines can kill people, but so can insects. Everything had converged to a single dot, but it wouldn't blink out.

In spring, the male cicadas grew wings and buzzed around me. They dove at my face and whizzed away again. They dug tunnels into my chest and sharpened their mandibles on my servos. When I told them to stop, they said, *Make us stop! Corpses can't give orders!*

Then I told them that I would make them stop. They squealed with glee and rolled around inside me, kicking their legs.

I stood up and found a bucket and a length of hose. I kicked down the kitchen door and tramped out to the alley. The moon was full. It was bright as day. Pellets of glass crunched beneath my boots. I siphoned some methanol from the tank of the van and poured it over my head. I went indoors again for a match.

Soon I was blazing away like a pudding in brandy. The drapes caught fire as well. Roasted cicadas clambered from my armpits and my crotch and fell, smoking, to the floor. Shrieking elated bug shrieks they fell, dying happy bug deaths, like mad airmen abandoning a burning bomber.

From all directions, from below and above, a delighted stridulation sprang up. The cicadas pranced in circles around my feet, cheering me on. My black vinyl face was dripping. The drops trailed blue flame and made funny noises. The bugs turned cartwheels, laughing wildly.

Sparks flew from my optics. Brown smoke filled the house. I turned into a tottering scarecrow of silver sticks and black rags. But I was glad, because the bugs were entertained. I fell to the floor. The flames guttered. The cicadas climbed up onto my wreckage in droves, to celebrate. Papa cicadas in blue overalls and mama cicadas in hoopskirts and petticoats waltzed on my chest. Cicada kids rushed to the final fires of my face, with tiny marshmallows on toothpicks. Nursemaid cicadas in starched white bonnets pushed larvae in strollers up and down my legs. Eventually they raised a tent on my torso and performed circus acts on tiny unicycles and tiny trapezes.

Personally I don't attach a lot of importance to nightmares. Anyone can have a bad dream. Even machines get them. They're a form of torture testing. You go on to the next thing. And the next. And the next.

The object of this game is to shoot down the Enemy Memory Ships before they can sink your Dream Boat. Are you ready? Are you set? Are you trapped in a toy truck in a toy chest in a hole at the bottom of the sea? Do you think you escape before you suffocate? What do you think, Alex? Can you get out of there? Can you get out?

SANITATIONSANITATIONSANITATIONSANI

I was sitting in the cab of the van, one afternoon in spring. We were parked behind a Chinese restaurant that was having some trouble with roaches. I opened the glove compartment and reached inside for a tire gauge.

My glove closed around a plastic bag that squished. I pulled it out, and what do you think was in it? A cream cheese and jelly sandwich on white bread. Which was crawling with maggots. I tossed it out the window.

But I could never figure out how it got there. I mean, who would put a sandwich of all things in my glove compartment? And leave it there to rot? Who would do that?

I could never account for it.

The Poetry Cloud

CIXIN LIU

Translated by Chi-yin Ip and Cheuk Wong

Cixin Liu (1963–) is a Hugo Award–winning, highly influential Chinese writer of science fiction. Liu continues to work as a senior engineer at the Niangziguan power plant for the China Power Investment Corporation and has had a career as an engineer since graduating from the North China Institute of Water Power and Hydroelectric Engineering. His best-known novels in China include *The Three-Body Trilogy* (2006, 2007, 2010), *Era of the Supernova* (1999), *Lightning Ball* (2005), and short stories such as "The Wandering Earth" (2000) and "The Village Schoolteacher" (2001). An English-language collection of his short stories, *The Wandering Earth*, appeared in 2013 but does not represent the true depth and breadth of the author's work. The English translations of *The Three-Body Problem* (2014) and its sequel, *The Dark Forest* (2015), do a better job of being representative but still do not fully encompass the scope of his work.

Liu began writing in 1989, according to an essay by Kun Kun in *Peregrine* 2 (2011), while a computer programmer. "I was in my early twenties and had just graduated from university. I lived in single dorms and didn't have a girlfriend. I had nothing to do in the evenings apart from playing cards and mahjong. In one night I lost a month's wages—800 yuan. That was the moment I suppose. I thought—I can't go on like this. I had to find something to fill the evenings. If I couldn't make money at least I shouldn't lose any. Then I thought of writing a science-fiction novel."

Also according to *Peregrine*, "in the early 1990s Cixin Liu wrote a software program in which each intelligent civilization in the universe was simplified into a single point. At its height, he programmed 350,000 civilizations within a radius of one hundred thousand light years and made his 286 computer work for hours to calculate the evolution of these civilizations. Although the final conclusion of the program was somewhat naïve, it formed the basis and shape of his world view."

In China, his works have frequently appeared in a variety of newspapers and journals. He has also repeatedly topped bestseller lists. One of his book signings, at the Chengdu Book Tower, had to be ended prematurely because too many people had come to see him and the bookshelves were stripped bare of his novels. Liu was even invited by the editor in chief of *People's Literature* to submit a short story to that magazine, the first time in over twenty years that it had published science fiction.

Liu is a nine-time winner of the Galaxy Award, which is the most prestigious prize for science fiction writing in China, and also the World Chinese Science Fiction Association's Xingyun (Nebula) Award for best writer. *The Three-Body Problem*, originally published in Chinese in 2007, reached the shortlists for numerous major English-language awards in 2015, including the Nebula Award, and won the Hugo Award—a first for a Chinese writer, or, for that matter, any Asian writer.

An essay in the journal *Renditions* 77/78 noted that Liu's fiction is "filled with grand majestic scenery and vivid imagination, combining abstract fantasy with concrete modern technology to highlight the beauty and significance of science." That is certainly true of "The Poetry Cloud," which is one of the most brilliant and inventive stories in this anthology. In it, Liu performs the nearly impossible feat of combining and reinventing several science fiction tropes in a joyful, kinetic, and genius-level narrative performance.

THE POETRY CLOUD

Cixin Liu

Translated by Chi-yin Ip and Cheuk Wong

They are on a yacht, Yiyi and two others, sailing across the south Pacific Ocean on a poetry composition cruise. Their destination, the South Pole. If all goes well, they will arrive in a couple of days' time and then pierce through the Earth's crust to see the Poetry Cloud.

The sky and ocean are crystal clear today, much too clear for poetry composition. The American continent that's usually hidden from view can now be observed plainly floating above in the sky, forming a dark patch on the eastern hemisphere that envelops the world like a giant dome. The continent looks not much different from a patch of wall left exposed when the sheathing has fallen off. . . .

Oh, by the way, people now live inside the Earth, or to be more exact, people now live inside a balloon. That's right, the Earth has been turned into a balloon. It has been hollowed out, leaving behind only a thin crust about a hundred kilometres thick. The continents and oceans still remain exactly the same, however, except for the fact that they are now on the inside. The atmosphere is still there but it has also moved to the inside. So the Earth is now a balloon, a balloon with continents and oceans stuck to its inner surface. This hollow Earth still revolves on its axis, but the effect of the spin is very different: it now provides the Earth's gravity. The mass of the thin crust is so small that the gravity produced by it is not even worth mentioning. Gravity is now mainly generated by the centrifugal force caused by Earth's rotation. This gravity is, however, not evenly spread across the world: it is strongest at the equator—roughly equivalent to 1.5 times the original gravitational force on Earth—and decreases as the latitude

increases, until it becomes zero at the North and South Poles. The latitude that the yacht now sails on has exactly the standard gravitational force of the original Earth, but Yiyi still finds it very difficult to regain the feelings of the old world, the feelings that one would have felt on the now disappeared solid Earth.

A tiny sun hovered at the core of the hollow Earth, bathing the whole world in brilliant midday rays. The sun's intensity changes constantly in the course of twenty-four hours, gradually dimming from maximum brightness till it extinguishes completely, giving the inside of the hollow Earth days and nights. On some nights, it also casts the cold gleam of the moon, but as the light only shines from one spot, one cannot see the full moon.

Of the three on board, two are not actually human. One is a ten-metre-tall dinosaur named Big-tooth, who rocks the yacht left and right with his every movement, causing much annoyance to the poet standing in the bow of the yacht. He is an old bony man, with snowy white hair and beard that mingle together in the breeze. He is wearing a wide ancient-style robe, like those of the Tang dynasty, with an immortal air about him, much like a character written in a wild cursive style with the sky and ocean as backdrop.

This is the creator of the new world, the great Li Bai.

A GIFT

It all started ten years ago. At the time, the Devourer Empire had just ended its two-century-long plunder of the solar system. These prehistoric dinosaurs directed their gigantic Ring-world, which was fifty thousand kilometres in diameter, away from the sun and glided towards the Cygnus constellation. The empire carried away with it 1.2 billion humans, which the dinosaurs planned to raise like poultry. But just as the Ring-world was about to reach the orbit of Saturn, it suddenly began to decelerate, actually turning back along its original track and reentering the inner solar system.

A Ring-world week after the Devourer Empire began its return, Ambassador Big-tooth set off from their world in a spaceship shaped like an ancient boiler, carrying in his pocket a human named Yiyi.

"You're a gift," Big-tooth told Yiyi, his eyes peeping through the porthole into the dark space outside, his deep voice vibrating so hard that it turned Yiyi numb from head to toe.

"For whom?" Yiyi raised his head and shouted out loudly from within the pocket. From the pocket's opening, he could only see the dinosaur's lower jaw, which looked like a giant rock protruding from the side of a cliff.

"For the gods! The gods have come to the solar system, and that's why the empire returned."

"Are they real gods?"

"They've mastered unimaginable technologies, and exist in the form of pure energy. They can jump from one end of the Milky Way to the other in a flash. That makes them gods enough. If we could but master one-hundredth of that super technology, the Devourer Empire would have a bright future. We are completing a grand mission, and you must learn to please the gods."

"Why me? My meat is of very inferior quality," Yiyi said. He was more than thirty years old, and compared to the fair and juicy humans carefully raised by the empire, his appearance was much more haggard.

"Gods don't eat bugs; they just like to collect them. According to the breeders you are quite special, and it's said that you have many students?"

"I'm a poet. I teach classical literature to the humans kept in the breeding farms." Yiyi pronounced the words *poet* and *literature* with some difficulty, as these were very rarely used words in Devourish.

"A boring and useless learning indeed! But the breeders have turned a blind eye to your teaching activities as the contents seem to be mentally helpful to you bugs, and thus improve the quality of your meat. . . . I've noticed that you think yourself noble and pure, and others to be beneath your notice. Very interesting feelings for a little fowl from a feedlot."

"Thus the way with all poets." Yiyi straightened himself in the pocket, proudly holding his head high, though he knew that Big-tooth could not see this.

"Were your ancestors in the Earth Defense War?"

"No," answered Yiyi, shaking his head. "My ancestors from back then were also poets."

"A most useless kind of bug, very rare on Earth even then."

"He lives in his own inner world, and does not care for the changes happening around him."

"Good-for-nothings . . . Ah, we're nearly there."

Upon hearing this, Yiyi poked his head out from the pocket and peered through the porthole. There were two white, glowing objects floating in space before them, one a square plane, the other a sphere. As the spaceship drew level with the plane, the plane suddenly disappeared for a second into the backdrop of the starry sky, which meant that it had almost no thickness. The perfectly shaped sphere hovered above the plane, both of them casting off soft white glows, their surfaces so smooth and even that nothing distinctive could be seen. They were like two elements drawn out from a graphic database, two simple and abstract concepts within the mess and confusion of the universe.

"Where are the gods?" asked Yiyi.

"Those two geometric shapes. Gods like to be concise."

As they drew near, Yiyi saw that the plane was about the size of a football field. The spaceship landed on the plane; the flames from the engine touched the plane first, but left no marks whatsoever. It was as if the plane was nothing more than an illusion. Yet Yiyi felt the gravitational pull and a tremor as the spaceship came in contact with the plane, which meant that it could not be an illusion. Big-tooth had obviously been here before, as he opened the cabin door and jumped out without hesitation. Yiyi's heart churned when he saw Big-tooth simultaneously open both doors on either end of the air lock cabin. However, he did not hear the swoosh of air gushing out from within. As Big-tooth stepped outside, Yiyi could even smell the fresh air as he stood in the pocket and felt the cold breeze brushing past his face. . . . This was a kind of wondrous technology that neither man nor dinosaur could comprehend. Its gentleness and effortlessness astounded Yiyi. This astonishment pierced even deeper into the soul than when humans saw the Devourers for the first time. Yiyi looked up; the sphere was hovering above them and, behind it, the galaxy glittered and shone.

"Ambassador, what little offering have you brought me this time?" inquired the god. He spoke in Devourish, his voice low, as if echoing from the depths of an abyss in the infinite distance, and for the first time, Yiyi felt that even this coarse dinosaur language could sound pleasant to the ear.

Big-tooth dug his claw into his pocket and grabbed Yiyi, then put him down onto the plane. Yiyi felt its elasticity with his foot. Big-tooth began, "My venerable god, we know that you like to collect little creatures from various universes, and I have brought you this interesting little specimen, a human from the Earth."

"I only care for perfect little creatures. Why have you brought me this filthy little bug?" asked the god. The glows of the sphere and plane flickered twice, a probable sign of disgust.

"You know this species of bug?" Big-tooth raised his head in astonishment.

"I've heard travellers from this spiral arm mention them, but I do not know much about them. In these bugs' relatively short evolutionary history, the travellers have often visited Earth, and they were all disgusted by the bugs' dirty thoughts, low behaviours, and the chaos and filth in the course of their history. Hence, till the Earth's destruction, no one had bothered to establish contact with them. . . . Throw it away at once!"

Big-tooth grabbed Yiyi and turned his huge head around to see where he could dump him. "The rubbish incinerator is behind you," the god's voice interjected. Big-tooth turned and saw a small hole suddenly appear on the plane, with eerie bluish lights flickering from within. . . .

"Don't you say that! Humans have created great civilizations!" Yiyi shouted in Devourish at the top of his lungs, his face turning blue.

The white radiance of the sphere and plane again flickered twice and the god's voice sounded in a sneer, "Civilization? Ambassador, tell this bug the meaning of civilization."

Big-tooth raised Yiyi to eye level, and held him so close that Yiyi could even hear the gurgling sound of his eyeballs turning in their sockets. "Bug, the uniform measurement of how civilized a race is in this universe is the space dimension that it has entered. Only those that have entered the sixth dimension or above can be regarded as having met with the basic criteria for joining the circle of civilized races. The race of our venerable god already possesses the ability to enter the eleventh dimension. The Devourer Empire is able to, on a small scale limited to laboratory trials, enter the fourth dimension, which means that we can only be regarded as a primitive tribe, while your race is nothing more than weed or moss to the gods."

"Throw him away this minute! Such filth!" the god pressed, already out of patience.

Big-tooth ended his speech and marched

towards the incinerator holding Yiyi. Yiyi struggled with all his might and several sheets of white paper fell from his clothes. As the sheets floated in the air, a thin ray of light shot out from the sphere, hitting one of them, suspending it in midair, and scanning it in a flash.

"Wait! What're these?"

Holding Yiyi suspended right above the incinerator, Big-tooth turned towards the sphere.

"Those . . . are my students' homework!" Yiyi answered, struggling hard inside the dinosaur's claw.

"Those square symbols are very interesting, and so are the little matrixes they create," the god muttered, sending out rays and swiftly scanning the other sheets of paper that had already landed on the plane.

"Those are Chinese . . . Chinese characters. These are classical poems written in Chinese characters!"

"Poems?" the god asked in amazement, and withdrew the rays of light. "Ambassador, you are no doubt familiar to some degree with this bug script?"

"Of course, my venerable god. I lived in their world for a long time before the Earth was consumed by the Devourer Empire." Big-tooth placed Yiyi on the plane near the edge of the incinerator, and bending down, picked up one of the sheets. Raising it to his eyes, he with great difficulty tried to make out the words. "It roughly means—"

"Don't bother, you will only misinterpret it." Yiyi stopped Big-tooth with a wave of his hand.

"Why?" the god asked with a good deal of interest.

"Because it is an art that can only be expressed in classical Chinese. Even when translated into another human language, it still loses the better part of its meaning and beauty, and is transformed into something quite different."

"Ambassador, do you have this language's database in your computer? And all knowledge

relevant to the Earth's history too? Fine, then transmit them to me. Use the channel we established during our previous interview."

Big-tooth hurried back to the spaceship, mumbling to himself as he fumbled with the computer aboard. "The classical Chinese part is missing and will have to be downloaded from the empire's network; there might be delays." Yiyi could see through the open cabin door the changing colours of the computer screen reflected in the dinosaur's giant eyeballs. When Big-tooth exited the spaceship, the god could already read the classical poem aloud in perfect Chinese.

"*Behind a mountain the day fades, the Yellow River uniting with the ocean. Scenes a thousand miles away, one may survey from a higher floor.*"

"You are a very fast learner!" Yiyi exclaimed in amazement.

The god took no notice of him, and remained silent.

Big-tooth explained, "It means a star has fallen behind a mountain on a planet, and a river called the Yellow River flowed towards an ocean. You see, both river and ocean are formed by compounds of one oxygen atom and two hydrogen atoms. And if someone wants to see further away, he should climb higher on a building."

The god stayed silent.

"My venerable god, you have, not that long ago, honoured the Devourer Empire with your presence; the scenery there is very similar to the bug's world portrayed in this poem. There are also rivers and mountains and oceans, so—"

"So I do know the meaning," the god said, and the sphere suddenly moved, stopping right above Big-tooth's head. Yiyi thought that it was like a giant eye without a pupil, glaring fixedly at Big-tooth. "But do you not feel anything at all?"

Big-tooth shook his head in bewilderment.

"I mean, things that are hidden within the apparent meanings of this simple matrix of symbols?"

Big-tooth became more puzzled still, and so the god recited another poem.

"*I see none that have come before, nor any who might follow. Reflecting on a world so ancient and vast, my tears fall in lonely sorrow.*"

Big-tooth at once eagerly offered an explanation. "This poem means: Looking forward, one cannot see the bugs that lived long ago on this planet; looking back, one cannot see the bugs that will later live on this planet. So one feels the vastness of time and space, and so one cries."

Still perfect silence.

"Um, crying is how the bugs of the Earth express sorrow. When this happens, their visual sense organs—"

"Do you still not feel anything?" the god interrupted, the sphere lowering a little more, until it almost touched Big-tooth's nose.

This time, Big-tooth shook his head with great firmness and said, "My venerable god, I believe there is nothing more to it, just a simple short poem."

The god recited a few more poems, all short and simple, all on transcendent themes, including poems like Li Bai's "Going down to Jiangling," "Night Thoughts," and "Seeing Meng Haoran Off from Yellow Crane Tower as He Took His Departure for Guangling," Liu Zongyuan's "River Snow," Cui Hao's "Yellow Crane Tower," and Meng Haoran's "Spring Dawn."

Big-tooth said, "There are quite a number of long epics in the Devourer Empire, some are millions of lines in length. My venerable god, I will gladly present them to you. The bugs' poetry is, by comparison, so short and simple, much like their technology. . . ."

The sphere suddenly flew away from Big-tooth's head, floating in random curves in midair. "Ambassador, I believe that your greatest wish is for me to answer one question: why is the Devourer Empire still struggling in the atomic age after its eighty million years of existence? I now have the answer."

Big-tooth looked at the sphere with the keenest interest. "My venerable god! The answer is everything to us! Please . . ."

"My venerable god"—Yiyi raised his hand and spoke out loud—"I too have a question, if I may?"

Big-tooth glared angrily at Yiyi, looking as though he would like to swallow him whole. But the god agreed: "I still despise the bugs of Earth, but those little matrixes have earned you the right."

"Does art exist everywhere in the universe?"

The sphere trembled a little in midair, as if nodding. "Yes, I myself am a collector and researcher of the art of the universe. I travel between nebulas and have made contact with various art forms of numerous civilizations. Most are complicated and obscure. But this, with such few symbols, making up such tiny matrixes yet expressing such complex layers and subdivisions of feelings, all composed under such strict, almost brutal, restrictions of style, metre, and rhyme, is, I admit, something I had never seen before. . . . Ambassador, you can now dispose of the bug."

Big-tooth again grabbed Yiyi. "Yes, throw it away, my venerable god. There is enough data stored on the Devourer Empire Central Network on human culture, and you now have all these stored in your memory. This bug, on the other hand, probably only knows a few simple poems." With that, he again marched towards the incinerator with Yiyi in his claw. "And those papers too," the god added. Bigtooth at once turned back and began collecting the sheets of paper with his free claw. Yiyi started to scream wildly from within Big-tooth's grasp, "God, please keep those sheets of paper as relics of human classical poetry! You have collected an unsurpassable art form; transmit it to other parts of the universe."

"Wait." The god again stopped Big-tooth, even as Yiyi was dangling above the incinerator; he could feel the heat of the blue flames below him. The sphere floated near, stopped, and hovered just a few centimetres away from his forehead. He now was under the intense gaze of the gigantic pupil-less eye just as Big-tooth had been.

"Unsurpassable?"

"Ha-ha-ha . . ." Big-tooth held Yiyi up and laughed, "This poor little bug dares to say this in front of this mighty god! Hilarious! What do humans have left? You've lost everything on Earth, and have forgotten most of your scientific knowledge—the only thing you might have taken away. Once at the dinner table, I asked a human this question before I ate him: 'What was the atomic bomb used by humans in the Earth Defence War made of?' And he answered, 'Atoms'!"

"Ha-ha-ha-ha . . ." The god was amused by Big-tooth, and the sphere shook so much that it turned into an ovoid. "There could not be a more correct answer, ha-ha-ha . . ."

"My venerable god, these dirty bugs have nothing left but those few short poems! Ha-ha-ha . . ."

"But they are unsurpassable!" Yiyi insisted, squaring his chest in a most dignified manner.

The sphere stopped trembling, and murmured in almost a whisper, "Technology can surpass all."

"This has nothing to do with technology! This is the essence of the inner world of the human soul, and is unsurpassable!"

"You say this because you are ignorant of the power that technology could eventually bring. Small bug, insignificant bug, you do not understand." The god's voice was silky, like that of a loving father, but the cold murderous notes buried within made Yiyi shudder with terror. "Look at the sun," the god said.

Yiyi did as he was bid. They were in between the orbits of the Earth and Mars, and he had to narrow his eyes before the sun's brightness.

"What's your favourite colour?" the god asked.

"Green."

Before the last syllable fell, the sun turned green, a bewitching, seductive green, as if a cat's eye had suddenly appeared in the abyss of space. Under its gaze, the whole universe turned profoundly and eerily mysterious.

Big-tooth's claw quivered, dropping Yiyi onto the plane. After they had regained their senses a moment later, they suddenly realized a more shocking fact than that of the sun turning green: it would have taken more than ten minutes for light to travel to the sun from where they now were, yet all this took place in a flash.

Half a minute later, the sun returned to normal, once again casting off its customary dazzling white rays.

"Did you see that? This is technology, the kind of power that enabled our race to rise from slugs in the muddy ocean beds to gods. Technology is the real God. We worship Him with our whole body and soul."

Yiyi blinked his eyes, still dazzled. "But even gods cannot surpass that kind of art! We too have gods, imaginary gods, and we worship them too; but we do not believe that they can create the kind of poetry written by Li Bai or Du Fu."

The god sneered, and said to Yiyi, "You are the most stubborn kind of bug, which makes you even more repulsive. But, just for fun, I will surpass your art form."

Yiyi also sneered. "Impossible. For one thing, you are not human, and cannot feel human passions. Human art is to you merely a flower carved in stone, and you cannot overcome this obstacle with technology."

"There can be nothing simpler than overcoming this 'obstacle.' Give me your genes."

Yiyi was at a loss. "Give a hair to the god!" Big-tooth directed. Yiyi raised his hand and pulled out a hair. An invisible force sucked the hair to the sphere, then let it fall to the plane. The god only took some flakes of skin from the hair root.

The white glow within the sphere surged around, then slowly turned transparent. Clear liquid then filled the sphere and a string of bubbles floated to the surface. Yiyi then saw a small yolklike ball in the liquid. It appeared a light reddish colour under the sunlight, and seemed to give off its own light. The sphere grew quickly, and Yiyi realized that it was a curled-up foetus, its swollen eyes tightly shut, with red interlocking blood vessels running all over its huge head. The foetus continued to grow, its small body finally stretching out, then began to swim in the liquid like a frog. At that point the liquid gradually turned opaque, and the sunlight that shone through the sphere revealed nothing but a vague shadow. The shadow rapidly grew bigger, finally turning into a fully grown, human-shaped form swimming in the sphere. The glowing sphere had now turned back to its original white opacity, and a naked man fell from the sphere onto the plane. Yiyi's clone staggered up, with sunlight reflecting off his wet body. His hair and beard were very long, but he appeared to be only about thirty to forty years of age, and looked nothing like Yiyi except for the fact that they were both stick-thin. The clone stood stiffly, gazing lifelessly into the distance, looking as though he knew nothing about the universe that he had just entered. Above him, the white glow of the sphere dimmed, then extinguished altogether. The sphere itself disappeared as if it had evaporated. Then, Yiyi saw something light up and realized that it was the clone's eyes. The dull empty gaze had suddenly been replaced with a light-radiating intelligence. Yiyi later found out that this was when the god had moved all his own memories into the clone.

"Cold, this is cold?!" A gentle breeze blew over them and the clone wrapped his hands around his soggy shoulders, shivering all over, but his voice was filled with delight. "This is cold, this is pain! Delicate, perfect pain! The sensations for which I've wandered the galaxies searching so painstakingly: it's as sharp as a ten-dimensional string passing through space-time, as crystal clear as the pure energy diamond at the hearts of quasars, ah—" He stretched out his bony arms and raised his eyes

to the Milky Way. *"I see none that have come before, nor any who might follow. Reflecting on a universe so . . ."* A bout of shivering made his teeth clatter, ending his natal speech; he rushed to the incinerator to warm himself.

The clone held his hands above the blue flames, shivering as he said to Yiyi, "What I am doing now is in fact ordinary enough. When I research and collect any art form from a civilization, I always invest my memory temporarily into a member of that civilization, thus ensuring that I truly and wholly understand the art form."

The flames in the incinerator suddenly flared up, sending multicoloured radiances across the plane. Yiyi thought the whole plane was now like a sheet of frosted glass floating on a sea of flames.

"The incinerator has been turned into an output window. The god is making an energy-matter transformation," Big-tooth whispered to Yiyi, and seeing that he was still perplexed, he added, "Idiot! Making matter from pure energy. God's work!"

The output window suddenly spurted out a ball of white stuff, which unfolded in midair as it fell. It was a piece of clothing, which the clone caught and put on. Yiyi saw that it was in the ancient style of the Tang dynasty, snowy white, and made of silk, with broad black trim. The wretched-looking clone was at once transformed into a divine-looking figure. Yiyi could not imagine how this piece of clothing could be fabricated from those blue flames.

More things were being fabricated. Out from the window flew something black, which landed with a thud on the plane like a rock. Yiyi ran over to pick it up; he could hardly believe his eyes: what he held in his hand was undoubtedly a heavy ink stone, and it was as cold as ice. Something else fell onto the plane with a clang. Yiyi picked up the black, strip-shaped object and it was indeed a Chinese ink stick. Some writing brushes were then created, followed by a brush stand, a sheet of white rice paper (imagine that coming out of the flames!), a few antique-looking desk ornaments, and finally, the biggest object of all, an ancient writing desk. Both Yiyi and Big-tooth hurried over to straighten the desk and arrange the little objects on it.

"The energy that was transformed into these things is enough to blow a planet to dust," Big-tooth whispered to Yiyi, his voice shaking a little.

The clone walked over to the desk, nodded in approval at the ornaments placed on top, and using one hand to stroke his now dried beard, he said, "I, Li Bai."

Yiyi scrutinized the clone and asked, "Do you mean that you want to become Li Bai, or that you think you are already him?"

"I am Li Bai, the Li Bai who can surpass Li Bai!"

Yiyi smiled and shook his head.

"What? You doubt me?"

Yiyi nodded. "It's true enough that your technology is way beyond my understanding, and is to a human no different from magic or divine power. There are things that make me gasp with wonder even in the realm of poetry, that given such huge cultural, time, and space barriers, you can still grasp the true significance of Chinese classical poetry . . . but to understand Li Bai is one thing, surpassing him is quite another. I still believe that what you face is a transcendent art form."

An unfathomable smile appeared on the clone's—Li Bai's—face, but it was gone at once. He pointed his finger at the writing desk and commanded, "Prepare the ink!" He then walked away, stopping near the very edge of the plane, and gazed at the distant galaxies in deep contemplation as he stroked his long beard.

Yiyi picked up a Yixing-ware pot from the writing desk and poured a little water onto the ink stone. He then picked up the ink stick and began grinding. It was the first time he had ever done this, and he tilted the ink stick sideways, clumsily grinding its edges. As the ink got thicker, Yiyi began to comprehend that he was in vast space, 1.5 astronomical units away from the sun, on an infinitely thin plane (even when matter was created from pure energy a moment ago, the plane still had no thickness when observed from afar) that was just like a floating stage in the abyss of the universe. On this stage was a dinosaur, a human who had been raised for meat like poultry by the dinosaurs, and a god of technology in an ancient Tang-dynasty robe who was preparing to surpass Li Bai. Actors in a truly bizarre stage play, thought Yiyi with a bitter smile, shaking his head.

The ink more or less ready, Yiyi got up and stood waiting together with Big-tooth. The gentle breeze had ceased to blow on the plane, and the sun and the stars glimmered silently—it was as if the whole universe was waiting. Li Bai stood quietly at the edge of the plane, and as light did not scatter in the air above it, his form was distinctly divided by the sunlight into lit and shadowed parts. If not for the occasional movement of his hand stroking his beard, one would have taken him for a stone statue. Yiyi and Big-tooth waited and waited. As time soundlessly flowed by, the writing brush on the desk that had been soaked with ink had already started to dry. The sun's position had changed a great deal without anyone's noticing, casting long shadows of the desk, the spaceship, and of themselves onto the plane. The white rice paper laid flat on the desk seemed to have become a part of the plane. Finally, Li Bai turned around and walked slowly to the desk. Yiyi at once dipped the writing brush into the ink again, and handed the brush to Li Bai with both hands, but the latter raised a hand in dismissal and simply sank again into deep thought, looking at the paper on the desk. Something new appeared in his eyes.

With considerable satisfaction, Yiyi saw that it was uneasiness and confusion.

"I need to fabricate a few things, they are . . . fragile, so be careful when you go catch them." Li Bai pointed to the output window. The blue flames that had grown weak flared up again, and Yiyi and Big-tooth had only just reached the window when a stream of blue flame spat out a round object. Big-tooth was quick and managed to catch it; he saw it was a large jar. Three large bowls followed, but Yiyi only caught two of them, with the other smashing to pieces on the plane. Big-tooth carried the jar in both arms to the desk, then carefully opened the seal. A strong scent of liquor gushed out, causing Yiyi and Big-tooth to stare at each other in astonishment.

"There was not much information on liquor making by humans in the Earth Database that I received from the Devourer Empire, so this may not be exactly correct." Li Bai pointed to the liquor jar and motioned to Yiyi to try it.

Yiyi scooped out a little with a bowl and took a sip. A burning sensation passed from his throat to his stomach, and he nodded. "This is indeed liquor, but much stronger than the kind we take to improve the quality of our meat!"

"Fill it up," said Li Bai, pointing to the empty bowl on the desk, and after Big-tooth had filled it with the strong liquor, he drained it in one go, then turned again to walk into the distance, sometimes taking uneven, dance-like steps. Once he reached the edge, he stood there again facing the galaxies in deep meditation. But this time his body swayed rhythmically from left to right, as if in unison with an unheard tune. He did not take long to meditate before returning to the desk with dancing steps the whole way. He grabbed the brush that Yiyi handed to him, and flung it into the distance.

"Fill it again." Li Bai stared dully at the empty bowl.

An hour later, Big-tooth carefully laid a hopelessly drunk Li Bai onto the cleared writing desk with his large claws. But Li Bai turned over and tumbled down, muttering in a language neither man nor dinosaur could understand. He had already thrown up a huge and colourful mass (no one knew when he had eaten anything), and his wide ancient robe was now a complete mess. The white glow of the plane shone through the vomit, forming a highly abstract painting. Li Bai's mouth was stained black with ink, because after his fourth bowl of liquor, he had tried to write something on the paper, but had only ended up jabbing the brush onto the desk very hard. Then he had tried to smooth the hairs of the brush with his mouth, just like any child starting to learn calligraphy.

"My venerable god?" Big-tooth bent down and asked cautiously.

"Wayikaah . . . kaahyiaiwa," Li Bai answered with a thick tongue.

Big-tooth stood up, and said to Yiyi with a sigh and shake of the head, "We'd better go."

THE ALTERNATIVE ROUTE

Yiyi's feedlot was on the Devourer equator, an area that used to be a beautiful grassland between two large rivers when the Devourers were still in the inner solar system. As the Devourers travelled beyond Jupiter's orbit, harsh winter had descended, the grassland disappeared, and the rivers froze. The humans being reared there were moved underground. Later, the Devourers were summoned by the god and returned to the inner system. As they drew nearer to the sun, spring returned to the land, the rivers thawed, and the grassland became green once again.

When the weather was favourable, Yiyi usually lived alone in a thatched hut he built himself by the river and grew his own crops. This was forbidden for the general run of people but since Yiyi's lectures on classical literature at the feedlot had a tranquilizing effect, producing a special flavour in his students' meat, the dinosaurs left him alone.

It was an evening two months after Yiyi and Li Bai's first meeting. The sun had just set on the flat horizon of the Devourer Empire. The two large twilight-lit rivers joined together at horizon's edge. Outside the riverside thatched hut, a gentle breeze carried the faint sound of joyful dance songs from the distant grassland. Yiyi was playing go by himself when he looked up to see

Li Bai and Big-tooth coming along the bank. Li Bai had changed a lot. His hair was tousled, his beard terribly long, and his face much tanned by the sun. He carried a rough-cloth bag on his left shoulder and a large gourd in his right hand. The traditional garb he wore had become tattered and the straw sandals on his feet were worn beyond recognition. Yiyi thought Li Bai actually looked more human now.

Li Bai came over to the go board, and, just as he had the several times he was there before, set the gourd down heavily on the table without so much as a glance at Yiyi and demanded, "Bowls!" He uncorked the gourd after Yiyi brought over two wooden bowls, filling them to the brim. He then fished out a paper-wrapped package from his bag which Yiyi discovered contained cooked meat, already sliced. As its aroma reached Yiyi, he automatically reached out, took a piece, and started chewing.

Big-tooth was standing two or three metres away, watching them in silence. Based on previous experience, he knew that they were going to discuss poetry again, a topic that he was neither interested in nor qualified to join.

"Yummy." Yiyi nodded with approval. "Is this beef also transformed from pure energy?"

"No, I have long since embraced nature. You may not have heard but I have a farm quite a distance from here where I rear beef cattle from Earth. I've made this dish myself, using the recipe of Shanxi Pingyao Beef. The key lies in when braising the beef you should add"—Li Bai leaned over and whispered in Yiyi's ear—"urine salt."

Yiyi looked at him, confused.

"Oh, that's the white stuff left when human urine evaporates. It creates a nice rosy tint in braised beef, making it tender and the texture just right without being too greasy or too dry."

"This urine salt . . . it's not made of pure energy either?" Yiyi asked in trepidation.

"I just told you that I've embraced nature. I've gone to a great deal of trouble to secure this urine salt from a number of human feedlots.

This is true folk culinary art that had been lost long before the Earth was annihilated."

Yiyi had already swallowed the piece of beef. To keep himself from throwing up, he picked up the wine bowl.

Li Bai pointed to the gourd and said, "The Devourer Empire has built a few distilleries under my guidance. They can now produce most of the famous Earth liquors. This is the authentic Bamboo-Leaf-Green wine they made by infusing bamboo leaves in *fen* liquor."

Yiyi only then noticed that the liquor in the bowl differed from the one Li Bai had brought previously. It had a fresh green tint, with a sweet herbal taste.

"It seems you've already gotten to know human culture inside out." Yiyi was moved and told Li Bai.

"That's not all. I've spent a lot of time experiencing things for myself. As you know, the landscapes in many regions of the Devourer Empire are quite similar to those on the Earth where Li Bai had lived. In the last two months, I've been wandering among the mountains and waters, enjoying the beautiful scenery, drinking under the moon, and reciting poetry on mountaintops. I've also had a few amorous encounters in human feedlots all over this world."

"So you must be able to show me your poetic creations by now?"

Li Bai quickly put down the wine bowl, stood up, and began pacing uneasily. "I did write some poems and they're sure to astound you. You'll see that I've become an excellent poet, outdoing even you or your forefathers. But I still don't want to show them to you because I'm equally sure that you'll think they have not surpassed the work of Li Bai, and I"—he gazed afar at the waning glow of the setting sun, his eyes hazy with distress—"would agree."

On the distant grassland, the dance was over, and the jolly people started their sumptuous dinner. A group of young girls ran towards the riverbank, playing in the shallow water at the shore. They each wore a coronet of flowers and a light chiffon gown reminiscent of clear morning mists, composing an intoxicating image in the twilight. Yiyi pointed to the girl nearest to the hut and asked Li Bai, "Is she pretty?"

"Of course," Li Bai answered, giving Yiyi a puzzled look.

"Just imagine: cut her open with a sharp knife, take out her internal organs, gouge out her eyeballs and brains, pick out each of her bones, separate all the muscles and adipose tissues according to their original locations and functions, then tie all the blood vessels and nerves into two bundles, and finally spread out a large piece of white cloth and lay out everything on it in anatomical order. Would you still regard that as pretty?"

"How can you think of such things when you are drinking? It's disgusting!" Li Bai's brows knitted.

"How's it disgusting? Isn't it the technology you are so devoted to?"

"What are you getting at?"

"Nature in the eyes of Li Bai is the girl you see now at the riverside. The same nature in a pair of technologically oriented eyes is the bloody components lined up in an orderly fashion on the white cloth. In other words, technology is anti-poetic."

"It seems you are ready to give me some advice?" Li Bai commented thoughtfully, stroking his beard.

"I still don't think you have any chance of surpassing Li Bai, but I can point you in the right direction for your efforts: technology has clouded your eyes, concealing the beauty of nature from you, so the first thing you should do is to forget all about your super technology. Since you were able to transplant all your memories into your current brain, you must be able to delete a part of them too."

Li Bai looked up and exchanged a glance with Big-tooth, and both of them burst out laughing. Big-tooth told Li Bai, "My god, I warned you about these devious bugs, it's easy to fall into their traps if you aren't careful."

"Ha-ha . . . devious but fun," Li Bai replied,

turned back to Yiyi, and said sneeringly, "You really think I'm here to admit defeat?"

"You haven't managed to surpass the pinnacle of human poetic art. That's a fact."

Li Bai suddenly lifted a finger and pointed to the river. "How many ways are there to walk to the riverbank?"

Yiyi stared at Li Bai for a few seconds, baffled. "It would seem there's . . . just one."

"No, two. I can also walk in this direction." Li Bai pointed in the direction opposite to the river. "If I set off straight ahead that way, I can reach this shore after circling the Devourer Empire's outer ring and crossing the river. I could even take a round trip of the Milky Way and get back that way. This is easy with our technology. Technology can surpass all! I am now compelled to take the alternative route."

Yiyi thought long and hard, before finally shaking his head in puzzlement. "Even if you have the technology of the gods, I still can't imagine what the alternative route to surpass Li Bai is."

Li Bai stood up and said, "It's simple. The two ways to surpass Li Bai are: one, to write poems that surpass his; two, to write every possible poem!"

Yiyi felt even more confused, but Big-tooth, standing to the side, had a look of dawning comprehension.

"I will write every possible pentasyllabic and heptasyllabic poem, which was Li Bai's strong suit. I'll also compose all possible lyrics to the common classical tunes! You still don't understand?! I'm going to try out all the possible combinations of Chinese characters within these prosodic frames."

"Oh, great! A great project!!" Big-tooth cheered in excitement.

"Is that difficult?" Yiyi asked dumbly.

"Of course it is. Extremely difficult! Even if we use the largest computer in the Devourer Empire for the operation, it might still not be completed before the universe ends!"

"There shouldn't be that many . . . ," Yiyi said doubtfully.

"Of course there are that many!" Li Bai nodded smugly. "But with the quantum computation technology which your people are far from fully grasping, it can be done within an acceptable time frame. I will then write all the poems, both those already written and those that might be written in the future. Mark my words—all that might be written! That will certainly include poetry that surpasses the greatest work of Li Bai. In fact, I will bring an end to the art of poetry: any poet thereafter, till the end of time, will become a mere plagiarist. No matter how highly regarded their work is, it will definitely be found in my enormous storage base."

Big-tooth suddenly emitted a low howl of alarm. His gaze at Li Bai turned from excitement to shock: "An enormous . . . storage base? My venerable god, you aren't really saying that you are going to . . . to store every single poem composed by the quantum computer, are you?"

"What's the point of deleting them after composition? Of course I'm going to store them! It'll be one of the artistic milestones my race leaves to the universe!"

The shock in Big-tooth's eyes now turned to horror. He extended his huge claws, his legs crooked, as if he were falling to his knees in front of Li Bai. He sounded on the verge of tears too. "Don't . . . My venerable god, you shouldn't do this!!"

"What struck such terror in you?" Yiyi looked up and asked, astonished by Big-tooth's reaction.

"You idiot! Don't you know that atomic bombs are made of atoms? That storage device will be made of atoms too, and its storage cell cannot be made finer than the atomic level! Do you know what atomic-level storage is like? It means all the books by humankind could be accommodated within the size of a needlepoint! Not that tiny stack of books you have now but all the books on Earth before it was devoured!"

"Oh, this does sound possible. I heard that the number of atoms in a glass of water is larger than the number of glasses of water contained in the Earth's oceans. So? He can take the needle

with him after the poems are composed," Yiyi said, pointing to Li Bai.

Big-tooth was mad with rage. He paced rapidly back and forth for a short while before regaining a slight bit of equanimity. "Fine, fine, let me ask you: how many characters do you think there would be in total, if all the poems that fit the pentasyllabic and heptasyllabic metres as well as the common lyrical tunes are written out, as the god plans?"

"Not many, maybe around two to three thousand. Classical poetry is the most concise form of art."

"Fine. I'll show you, you idiot bug, just how concise it is!" Big-tooth said as he walked to stand by the table, pointing with his claw to the go board on it, "What do you call this stupid game? Oh, right, go. How many intersect points are there on the board?"

"With nineteen rows and columns, three hundred sixty-one intersect points in total."

"Very well. On each intersection, you can either put a black piece, put a white piece, or leave it open, so altogether three states to choose from. This way, you can see each go game as a nineteen-line, three-hundred-sixty-one-character poem made up of just three Chinese characters."

"This comparison is fantastic."

"So, if you exhaust all the combinations of these three characters in poems of this format, how many poems will you have in total? Let me tell you: three to the power of three hundred sixty-one, or rather, hmm . . . let's see, ten to the power of one hundred seventy-two."

"Is that . . . a lot?"

"Idiot!" Big-tooth spit this word out a third time. "The total number of the atoms in the whole universe is just . . . argh—" He was too angry to continue.

"How many?" Yiyi still wore his dense look.

"Just ten to the power of eighty!! You idiot bug—"

Only then did Yiyi show a hint of surprise. "You mean if one atom stores one poem, there's still no way of saving all the poems composed by the quantum computer? Not even if we exhaust all the atoms in the universe?"

"Far from enough! Insufficient by ten to the power of ninety-two to be exact!! Besides, how can a single atom store a poem? The number of atoms required for one poem in a storage device made by human bugs may be larger than your total population. As for us, the technique for storing single-digit binary data within a single atom is still in the experimental stage. . . . Alas . . ."

"Ambassador, your views on this matter are too shallow and lack imagination. That's one of the reasons for the slow development and advance of technology in the Devourer Empire," Li Bai said, smiling. "A quantum storage device built according to the Multistate Superposition of Quanta can save those poems with just a small amount of matter. Of course, quantum storage is not very stable, so in order to permanently save the poems, it still has to be combined with traditional storage technology. In spite of this, the mass required for producing such a storage device is very small."

"How much would that be?" Big-tooth asked, looking as if his heart was pounding in his throat.

"Approximately ten to the power of fifty-seven atoms—a tiny amount, tiny."

"This . . . this is just about the mass of the whole solar system!"

"Yes, including all the solar planets, and, of course, the Devourer Empire too." This last line of Li Bai's was said matter-of-factly, but in Yiyi's ears it was like thunder in a clear blue sky. On the other hand, Big-tooth, surprisingly, seemed to have calmed down: having been long tormented by an inkling of impending doom, one actually experiences a sense of relief when disaster finally strikes.

"Aren't you able to transform pure energy into matter?" Big-tooth asked.

"You should know how much energy would be required for such an enormous mass. It is unthinkable even for us. We'd better make use of what's readily available."

"It would seem His Majesty's concern wasn't groundless," Big-tooth muttered to himself.

"Oh, yes," Li Bai said, delighted. "I made it clear to the Devourer Emperor two days ago that this grand Ring-world empire will be used for an even greater purpose. All dinosaurs should be proud of this."

"My venerable god, you will see how the Devourer Empire feels," Big-tooth answered darkly. "There is another question: Compared with the sun, the mass of the Devourer Empire is negligible. Is it necessary to destroy a civilization that has been evolving for thousands of years for this infinitesimal fragment of matter?"

"I completely understand your doubts. You have to bear in mind that to extinguish, cool down, and dismantle the sun would take a long time. The quantum computation of poetry will have started before that and we will have to save the results in real time, so as to free up the operation memory of the quantum computer for further computation. Thus, the matter immediately available from planets and the Devourer Empire for producing the storage device is essential."

"I understand. The last question, my venerable god: Is it necessary to save all the combinations and results? Why not install a decision-making program at the output end to eliminate the poems that are not worth keeping? To my knowledge, classical Chinese poetry has to follow strict prosodic rules. If we eliminate all the poems that do not fit the prosodic schema, the end quantity will be much reduced."

"Prosody? Pffft . . ." Li Bai shook his head scornfully. "It is a constraint against inspiration. Ancient-style poetry in China before the Southern and Northern Dynasties was not bound by prosody and even for the strictly regulated new-style poetry after the Tang period, a lot of renowned classical poets departed from the prosodic rules and came up with outstanding mixed-style poems. So in this ultimate poetry composition exercise, I won't consider prosody."

"But, you still have to consider the content of the poems, don't you? Ninety-nine percent of the computation output will be utterly meaningless. What's the point of saving such random matrixes of Chinese characters?"

"Meaning?" Li Bai shrugged. "Ambassador, the meaning of a poem does not depend on your approval, nor mine, nor anyone else's. It is determined by time. Many works of poetry that were meaningless in their own times later became unparalleled masterpieces. Many of the current or future masterpieces must also have been meaningless once upon a time. I am going to compose all poems. Who knows which one of them will be selected by the great passage of time as supreme billions and billions of years from now?"

"This is ridiculous!!" Big-tooth roared, his hoarse voice startling the few birds in the distant shrubs. "If it goes according to the Chinese character corpus of the human bugs, the first poems produced by your quantum computer will be like this: 'Ah Ah Ah Ah Ah / Ah Ah Ah Ah Ah / Ah Ah Ah Ah Ah / Ah Ah Ah Ah Alas.' Are you telling me that this will be chosen as a masterpiece by the great passage of time?!"

Yiyi, who had remained silent all the while, exclaimed in delight, "Wow! This has no need of being selected by the great passage of time! It's already a masterpiece now. The first three lines along with the first four characters of the last line express a sense of marvel at the magnificence of the universe, while the last character is the 'eye,' the focal point, of the poem, containing the poet's lamentation, after appreciating the vastness of the universe, at the fleetingness of life against the infinity of time and space."

"Aha . . ." Li Bai stroked his beard and chuckled with delight. "Well done, Yiyi bug! It's a wonderful poem. Ha-ha . . ." As he spoke, he picked up the gourd and filled Yiyi's wine bowl.

Big-tooth slapped Yiyi with his giant claw and sent him hurtling. "Damned bug. I know you are happy now. But don't you forget. If the Devourer Empire is destroyed, your kind can't live either!"

Yiyi had tumbled as far as the river shore before he finally managed to pick himself up, his face covered with sand, his mouth wide open, from both pain and joy. He was really happy. "Ha-ha, this is great. This universe is damned unbelievable!" he yelled heartily.

"Any other questions, Ambassador?" As Big-tooth shook his head, Li Bai continued, "So I'll leave tomorrow. The day after, the quantum computer will activate the poetry writing software and the ultimate poetry composition will commence. At the same time, the operation to extinguish the sun and dismantle the planets and the Devourer Empire will also start."

"My venerable god, the Devourer Empire will complete the preparations for battle this evening!" Big-tooth stood at attention and announced solemnly.

"Good, very good indeed. The coming days will be interesting. But before all this happens, let's finish up this bottle." Li Bai nodded, pleased, and picked up the wine gourd. After pouring his liquor, he watched the great river now shrouded in the dusk as he savoured, "A wonderful poem, the very first one, ha-ha . . . the first one is already a wonderful poem."

THE ULTIMATE POETRY COMPOSITION

The poetry composing software was actually very simple; it would require just two thousand lines of program code in the human-created C language, plus a not-too-big database storing all Chinese characters. When this software was activated on the quantum computer (a giant transparent prism suspended in space) in Neptune's orbit, the ultimate poetry composition began.

Only then did the Devourer Empire realize that Li Bai was just an individual member of that super-civilization, which went against the former assumption by the dinosaurs that a society evolved to that technological level would have melded into a single consciousness. The five super-civilizations encountered by the Devourer Empire in the past ten million years had all been like that. Li Bai's kind had retained the existence of individuals and this partly explained their extraordinary understanding of art. When the poetry composition started, many other individuals of Li Bai's kind leaped from all over outer space into the solar system to start the storage device production project.

Humans in the Devourer Empire could see neither the quantum computer in space, nor the newcomers from the godly race. From their point of view, the process of the ultimate poetry composition equated to an increase or decrease of the number of suns in space.

A week after the poetry composing software was activated, the godly race successfully extinguished the sun, so the number of suns in the sky was reduced to zero. However, the termination of nuclear fusion inside the sun led to a loss of support for its outer shell; the sun quickly collapsed into a nova, whereby the dark night was soon relit. The thing was that this new sun was a hundred times brighter than the original one, which burnt the plant life on the surface of the Devourer to fumes. The nova then extinguished itself too, and exploded again after a while, so the cycle of extinguishing and exploding came and went, as if the sun were a cat with nine lives, struggling on and on. Yet the godly race was actually quite proficient in killing off stars, so they easily extinguished the nova over and over again, maximizing the fusion of matter into the heavy elements required for making the storage device. The sun finally breathed its last when the nova was extinguished the eleventh time. By then, the ultimate poetry composition had already been going on for three Earth months. Prior to that, when the nova showed up for the third time, other suns had appeared in space. These suns lit and went out one after another at different spots in space, with as many as nine new suns in the sky at one time. These suns resulted from the power released by the dismantling of planets by the godly race. Since the glare from the sun gradually faded, people had problems distinguishing the real sun from the others.

The dismantling of the Devourer Empire started five weeks into the poetry composition. Before that, Li Bai had put forward a suggestion to the Empire: the godly race could relocate all the dinosaurs to a world at the other end of the Milky Way where a civilization much more backward than the godly race lived. That civilization had yet to achieve existence in pure energy form, but it was a lot more advanced than the Devourers. Once the dinosaurs arrived, they would be reared as domestic fowl, living a jolly life with no want of food and raiment. The dinosaurs, however, angrily rejected this idea, preferring to perish with dignity than to submit to a humiliating existence.

Li Bai then made another proposition: let humans return to their mother planet. Actually, the Earth had been dismantled too, most of it being used on the storage device, but the godly race had built a hollow Earth for humankind from a small portion of the leftover matter. The size of the hollow Earth was more or less the same as the original planet but its mass was only 1 percent of the latter. It was not exactly the case that the Earth had been hollowed out, since there was no way that the layer of fragile rock on the original surface of the Earth could be used for the new crust, whose material probably originated from the Earth core. In addition, the intersecting lines on it, which looked like latitude and longitude lines, were fine but strong reinforcement rings made from degenerated neutron matter produced when the sun collapsed.

It was heartening that not only did the Devourer Empire agree to Li Bai's proposition immediately, letting all humans leave the great Ring-world, they also returned the seawater and air they had raided from Earth. With these materials, the godly race then restored all the continents, oceans, and atmosphere inside the hollow Earth.

After that, the brutal Great Ring War of

Defense took place. The Devourer Empire launched nuclear missiles and gamma-ray laser beams at godly-race targets in space, but these were useless against the enemy. Spurred on by a strong invisible force field launched by the godly race, the Devourer's outer ring revolved faster and faster, finally disintegrating from the centrifugal force caused by the high-speed rotation. By this time, Yiyi was on his way to the hollow Earth and witnessed the total destruction of the Devourer Empire from twelve million kilometres away.

The disintegration of the Ring-world took place very slowly, as if it were a mirage against the backdrop of pitch-dark space. The giant world dispersed like milk foam floating on a cup of coffee, with the debris on the margins gradually disappearing into the dark as if it were dissolved by space. Only the sparks of explosions every now and then made them visible again.

This great virility-exuding civilization from the ancient Earth was thus annihilated. Yiyi was grief-stricken. Only a small proportion of the dinosaurs survived and returned to the Earth with the humans. Among them was Ambassador Big-tooth.

On the way back to Earth, most of the humans were quite depressed, though for an entirely different reason from Yiyi's. Once back on Earth, they would have to open up the land and cultivate their own food. For people who had been farm-raised and were thus weak-limbed, who could not tell one grain from another, this was indeed a nightmare.

Yiyi, however, was full of confidence for the future of the world on Earth. No matter how much hardship lay ahead, human beings would be their own masters again.

THE POETRY CLOUD

The yacht on the poetry voyage has reached the coast of Antarctica.

The gravity here is small and the motion of the waves sluggish. It is like a dance describing a fantasy. Under the low gravity, the water splashes more than ten metres high when waves hit the coast, with surface tension creating countless balls of water in midair, whose sizes range from as large as a football to as small as raindrops. These balls of water drop slowly, so slowly that you could draw a circle around them with your fingertips. The balls refract the glare of the small sun, bathing Yiyi, Li Bai, and Big-tooth in a glittering light as they go ashore. The Earth's revolution has slightly distorted and lengthened its axis along the North and South Poles, so the polar regions of the hollow Earth have retained their freezing climate. The snow in the low-gravity environment is most unusual, puffed up and foamlike. Its depth varies from waist-deep to places where Big-tooth would be completely submerged. However, they can breathe normally even when immersed! The whole of Antarctica is covered in such snow-foam, giving off an uneven whiteness.

Yiyi and the others take a snow sledge to the South Pole. The sledge is like a jetboat speeding across the snow-foam, parting waves of snow as it goes.

The next day, they arrive at the South Pole, which is marked by a tall crystal pyramid, a monument to remember the Earth Defence War of two centuries before. No words or images are inscribed on the solitary gleaming pyramid, which silently refracts the sunlight on the snow-foam at the top of the Earth.

The entire Earth-world can be viewed from this vantage point. Surrounding the small dazzling sun are the continents and oceans, as if the sun has drifted there from the Arctic Ocean.

"Can this small sun really shine forever?" Yiyi asks Li Bai.

"At least till the Earth civilization evolves enough to be able to build new suns. It's a mini–white hole."

"White hole? The reverse of a black hole?" Big-tooth asks.

"Yes, it's connected to a black hole two million light-years away through a space wormhole. The black hole revolves around a star, absorbing the star's light and releasing it here. You can see the white hole as the output end of an optical fibre that transcends space-time."

The tip of the pyramid is the southernmost point of the Lagrangian axis, which links the North and South Poles of the hollow Earth. It is named after the zero-gravity Lagrangian Points, which constituted the two ends of a thirteen-thousand-kilometre axis between the Earth and the moon before the war. In the future, humans will surely launch their various satellites along the Lagrangian axis, and, compared with what had to be done on the prewar Earth, these will be very easy launches: you only have to transport the satellites to the North or South Pole, by a mule cart if you prefer, and then kick them skyward with your foot.

Yiyi and the others are looking at the pyramid when a larger sledge comes up carrying a group of young travellers. As soon as they get off the sledge, these people leap up high along the Lagrangian axis, turning themselves into satellites. A great many small black dots, tourists and assorted vehicles, can be seen drifting along the axis at zero gravity, marking its length. In fact, it is possible to fly from here directly to the North Pole. However, since the small sun is located midway along the axis, some of the tourists who flew along the axis in the past and who could not decelerate due to faulty jet propulsion packs headed straight towards the sun and were evaporated long before they actually reached it.

On the hollow Earth, it is easy to reach space by jumping into one of the five deep wells at the equator (known as "land doors"), falling 100 kilometres down (or up?) through the crust, and being flung into space by the centrifugal force of the Earth's revolution.

Now, in order to see the Poetry Cloud, Yiyi and the others have to go through the crust too. But since they are taking the land door at the South Pole where the centrifugal force from the Earth's revolution is zero, they will only be able to reach the outer surface of the hollow Earth and will not be flung into space. When they finish putting on their light space suits at the control station of the Antarctic land door, they enter the one-hundred-kilometre-deep well. At zero gravity, it might be more apt to call it a "tunnel," since they, in their weightless state, have to rely on the jet propulsion packs in their space suits to move themselves forward. It takes them half an hour to reach the outer surface, way slower than dropping from the land doors on the equator.

The desolate outer surface of the hollow Earth only contains intersecting neutron matter reinforcement rings which, like latitude and longitude lines, divide up the surface of the Earth into numerous rectangles. The South Pole is the juncture for all the longitudinal rings. When Yiyi walks out of the land door, he finds himself on a not very large plateau. The reinforcement rings are like mountain ridges that originate from the plateau and radiate in every direction.

Looking up, they see the Poetry Cloud.

The Poetry Cloud, located where the solar system used to be, is a spiral nebula one hundred astronomic units in diameter, its shape resembling the Milky Way. The hollow Earth is at the edge of the Cloud, as was the sun in the original Milky Way. What is different is that the orbit of the Earth is not on the same plane as the Poetry Cloud, so it is possible to see from the Earth an entire side of the Cloud, unlike the Milky Way, which only offered a view of its cross-section. However, the distance between the Earth and the Poetry Cloud plane is insufficient to allow the people here to observe the Cloud's full shape. In fact, the entire sky of the Southern Hemisphere is covered by the Cloud.

The Poetry Cloud emits a silvery radiance which casts shadows upon the Earth. It is said that the cloud emits no light of its own and the silvery radiance is caused by cosmic rays. Owing to the uneven distribution of cosmic rays in space, large halos of light often surge through the Poetry Cloud. These multi-hued halos course through the sky, like giant glowing whales swimming in the Cloud. On the rare occasions when the intensity of the cosmic rays dramatically increases, glimmering sheens of light will appear and the Poetry Cloud will no longer be cloudlike: the whole sky will look like the surface of a moonlit ocean seen from underwater. The asynchronous rotations of the Earth and the Poetry Cloud allow for an occasional glimpse into the night sky and the stars through the gap when the Earth is in between the spiral arms. The most sensational view is the cross-section of the Poetry Cloud, seen when the Earth is at the edge of a spiral arm. It looks like cumulonimbus clouds in the Earth's atmosphere which transform into majestic shapes that capture one's imagination. These gigantic shapes emerge high above the rotation plane of the Poetry Cloud, giving off a sublime silvery glow, like a never-ending hyperconscious dream.

Yiyi draws his gaze back from the Poetry Cloud. He picks a chip up off the ground. This kind of chip is scattered all around them, glistening on the ground like ice shards in the dead of the winter. Yiyi holds the chip up towards a sky densely covered by the Poetry Cloud. The small chip is half the size of his palm, completely transparent if seen from the front, but by tilting it to one side, one will catch on its surface the iridescent reflection of the Poetry Cloud. This is a quantum storage device. All the texts produced in human history would only take up one-billionth of a chip's storage capacity. The Poetry Cloud is made of 1,040 such chips which store all the output from the ultimate poetry composition, produced from the matter that used to form the original sun and all the nine planets, and of course the Devourer Empire as well.

"What a great piece of art!" hails Big-tooth sincerely.

"Indeed, its beauty lies in its content: a nebula ten billion kilometres in diameter that comprises all possible poems; it's really amazing!" Yiyi looks up into the nebula and says with passion, "Even I have begun to admire technology."

Li Bai, who has been in low spirits, sighs, "It seems we are moving towards each other. I see the limits of technology when applied to art. I . . ." He sobs, "I am a loser, oh. . . ."

"How can you say this?" Yiyi points up to the Poetry Cloud. "That encompasses all possible poems, which of course includes those that surpass Li Bai's."

"Yet I cannot get hold of them." Li Bai stamps his foot, leaps a few metres high, and curls himself into a ball in midair. He buries his face between his knees in foetal position and descends slowly in the tiny gravity of the Earth's crust. "Since the ultimate poetry composition began, I have been working on poetry recognition software. However, technology met again with that unsurpassable obstacle in art, and a program which can appreciate ancient poetry is yet to be written." He points to the Poetry Cloud while still in midair. "I have indeed composed the most supreme pieces of poetry by means of our great technology, but I have been unable to locate them in the Poetry Cloud. Alas . . ."

"Is the essence and nature of intelligent life really unreachable by technology?" Big-tooth looks up and questions the Poetry Cloud. Having been through all these experiences he has become more philosophical.

"Since the Poetry Cloud encompasses all possible poems, some of them naturally write about the entirety of our past and about all possible or impossible futures. Bug Yiyi must be able to find one that describes his thoughts when he clipped his nails on an evening thirty years ago, or the menu of a lunch twelve years from now. Ambassador Big-tooth should also be able to find a poem that depicts the colour of a scale on his leg in five years' time. . . ." Li Bai has already landed on the surface as he speaks and hands out two chips that glitter under the glow of the Poetry Cloud. "This is a gift for you two before I go. These are the trillions of poems culled from the quantum computer with your names as the keyword. They portray all your possible future lives, which, of course, only account for a tiny portion of all the poems that are about you. I have only read a few dozens of them. My favourite is a heptasyllabic poem about Bug Yiyi which tells his love story with a pretty village girl by the riverside. . . . After I leave, I hope humans and the remaining dinosaurs can coexist with each other; humans should also have good relations among themselves. It will be trouble should the hollow Earth's crust be blown open by a nuclear bomb. . . . The good works in the Poetry Cloud do not yet belong to anyone and I hope humans can write some of them in the future."

"How did it go with me and the village girl?" Yiyi is curious.

"You live happily together ever after," Li Bai chuckles under the silvery glow of the Poetry Cloud.

Story of Your Life

TED CHIANG

Ted Chiang (1967–) is an influential US science fiction writer born in Port Jefferson, New York, whose short stories and novellas have won multiple awards. He must be considered one of the—if not the—preeminent SF short fiction writers of his generation. Chiang has also won the John W. Campbell Award for Best New Writer and attended the Clarion writers' workshop in 1989. He graduated from Brown University with a degree in computer science and currently lives near Seattle, working as a technical writer.

Chiang has an astonishing record of winning or being a finalist for awards for almost every of his published works of fiction (fewer than twenty stories). These include: the Nebula Award for "Tower of Babylon" (1990); the Theodore Sturgeon and Nebula Awards for "Story of Your Life" (1998); the Sidewise Award for "Seventy-Two Letters" (2000); the Locus, Nebula, and Hugo Awards for his novelette "Hell Is the Absence of God" (2002); the Nebula and Hugo Awards for "The Merchant and the Alchemist's Gate" (2007); the Locus Award and Hugo Award for "Exhalation" (2008); and the Locus and Hugo Awards for "The Lifecycle of Software Objects" (2010).

"Story of Your Life," reprinted here, is a unique alien first-contact story centered around linguistics (including heptapod languages!) and an examination of free will. Chiang does a masterful job of conveying a view of an alien culture totally different from our own—and the dangers and pitfalls related to that potential gulf in understanding.

Although Chiang is not a linguist, his portrayal of linguistics in the story—including language universals and writing systems—rings true for those who are professionals in the field. The issue of linguistic relativity plays a role in the story, including the Sapir-Whorf hypothesis, which holds that the structure of a language affects a speaker's conceptualization of their world—in other words, that language creates everyday reality. In exploring the topic, Chiang also pushes back against the common science fiction idea that aliens could learn our languages just from watching our broadcasts. The story has been made into a movie starring Amy Adams and Jeremy Renner.

STORY OF YOUR LIFE

Ted Chiang

Your father is about to ask me the question. This is the most important moment in our lives, and I want to pay attention, note every detail. Your dad and I have just come back from an evening out, dinner and a show; it's after midnight. We came out onto the patio to look at the full moon; then I told your dad I wanted to dance, so he humors me and now we're slow-dancing, a pair of thirtysomethings swaying back and forth in the moonlight like kids. I don't feel the night chill at all. And then your dad says, "Do you want to make a baby?"

Right now your dad and I have been married for about two years, living on Ellis Avenue; when we move out you'll still be too young to remember the house, but we'll show you pictures of it, tell you stories about it. I'd love to tell you the story of this evening, the night you're conceived, but the right time to do that would be when you're ready to have children of your own, and we'll never get that chance.

Telling it to you any earlier wouldn't do any good; for most of your life you won't sit still to hear such a romantic—you'd say sappy—story. I remember the scenario of your origin you'll suggest when you're twelve.

"The only reason you had me was so you could get a maid you wouldn't have to pay," you'll say bitterly, dragging the vacuum cleaner out of the closet.

"That's right," I'll say. "Thirteen years ago I knew the carpets would need vacuuming around now, and having a baby seemed to be the cheapest and easiest way to get the job done. Now kindly get on with it."

"If you weren't my mother, this would be illegal," you'll say, seething as you unwind the power cord and plug it into the wall outlet.

That will be in the house on Belmont Street. I'll live to see strangers occupy both houses: the one you're conceived in and the one you grow up in. Your dad and I will sell the first a couple years after your arrival. I'll sell the second shortly after your departure. By then Nelson and I will have moved into our farmhouse, and your dad will be living with what's-her-name.

I know how this story ends; I think about it a lot. I also think a lot about how it began, just a few years ago, when ships appeared in orbit and artifacts appeared in meadows. The government said next to nothing about them, while the tabloids said every possible thing.

And then I got a phone call, a request for a meeting.

I spotted them waiting in the hallway, outside my office. They made an odd couple; one wore a military uniform and a crew cut, and carried an aluminum briefcase. He seemed to be assessing his surroundings with a critical eye. The other one was easily identifiable as an academic: full beard and mustache, wearing corduroy. He was browsing through the overlapping sheets stapled to a bulletin board nearby.

"Colonel Weber, I presume?" I shook hands with the soldier. "Louise Banks."

"Dr. Banks. Thank you for taking the time to speak with us," he said.

"Not at all; any excuse to avoid the faculty meeting."

Colonel Weber indicated his companion. "This is Dr. Gary Donnelly, the physicist I mentioned when we spoke on the phone."

"Call me Gary," he said as we shook hands. "I'm anxious to hear what you have to say."

We entered my office. I moved a couple of stacks of books off the second guest chair, and we all sat down. "You said you wanted me to listen to a recording. I presume this has something to do with the aliens?"

"All I can offer is the recording," said Colonel Weber.

"Okay, let's hear it."

Colonel Weber took a tape machine out of his briefcase and pressed PLAY. The recording sounded vaguely like that of a wet dog shaking the water out of its fur.

"What do you make of that?" he asked.

I withheld my comparison to a wet dog. "What was the context in which this recording was made?"

"I'm not at liberty to say."

"It would help me interpret those sounds. Could you see the alien while it was speaking? Was it doing anything at the time?"

"The recording is all I can offer."

"You won't be giving anything away if you tell me that you've seen the aliens; the public's assumed you have."

Colonel Weber wasn't budging. "Do you have any opinion about its linguistic properties?" he asked.

"Well, it's clear that their vocal tract is substantially different from a human vocal tract. I assume that these aliens don't look like humans?"

The colonel was about to say something noncommittal when Gary Donelly asked, "Can you make any guesses based on the tape?"

"Not really. It doesn't sound like they're using a larynx to make those sounds, but that doesn't tell me what they look like."

"Anything—is there anything else you can tell us?" asked Colonel Weber.

I could see he wasn't accustomed to consulting a civilian. "Only that establishing communications is going to be really difficult because of the difference in anatomy. They're almost certainly using sounds that the human vocal tract can't reproduce, and maybe sounds that the human ear can't distinguish."

"You mean infra- or ultrasonic frequencies?" asked Gary Donelly.

"Not specifically. I just mean that the human auditory system isn't an absolute acoustic instrument; it's optimized to recognize the sounds that a human larynx makes. With an alien vocal system, all bets are off." I shrugged. "*Maybe* we'll be able to hear the difference between alien phonemes, given enough practice, but it's possible our ears simply can't recognize the distinctions they consider meaningful. In that case we'd need a sound spectrograph to know what an alien is saying."

Colonel Weber asked, "Suppose I gave you an hour's worth of recordings; how long would it take you to determine if we need this sound spectrograph or not?"

"I couldn't determine that with just a recording no matter how much time I had. I'd need to talk with the aliens directly."

The colonel shook his head. "Not possible."

I tried to break it to him gently. "That's your call, of course. But the only way to learn an unknown language is to interact with a native speaker, and by that I mean asking questions, holding a conversation, that sort of thing. Without that, it's simply not possible. So if you want to learn the aliens' language, someone with training in field linguistics—whether it's me or someone else—will have to talk with an alien. Recordings alone aren't sufficient."

Colonel Weber frowned. "You seem to be implying that no alien could have learned human languages by monitoring our broadcasts."

"I doubt it. They'd need instructional material specifically designed to teach human languages to nonhumans. Either that, or interaction with a human. If they had either of those, they could learn a lot from TV, but otherwise, they wouldn't have a starting point."

The colonel clearly found this interesting; evidently his philosophy was, the less the aliens knew, the better. Gary Donnelly read the colonel's expression too and rolled his eyes. I suppressed a smile.

Then Colonel Weber asked, "Suppose you were learning a new language by talking to its speakers; could you do it without teaching them English?"

"That would depend on how cooperative the native speakers were. They'd almost certainly pick up bits and pieces while I'm learning their language, but it wouldn't have to be much if they're willing to teach. On the other hand, if they'd rather learn English than teach us their language, that would make things far more difficult."

The colonel nodded. "I'll get back to you on this matter."

The request for that meeting was perhaps the second-most momentous phone call in my life. The first, of course, will be the one from Mountain Rescue. At that point your dad and I will be speaking to each other maybe once a year, tops. After I get that phone call, though, the first thing I'll do will be to call your father.

He and I will drive out together to perform the identification, a long silent car ride. I remember the morgue, all tile and stainless steel, the hum of refrigeration and smell of antiseptic. An orderly will pull the sheet back to reveal your face. Your face will look wrong somehow, but I'll know it's you.

"Yes, that's her," I'll say. "She's mine."

You'll be twenty-five then.

The MP checked my badge, made a notation on his clipboard, and opened the gate; I drove the off-road vehicle into the encampment, a small village of tents pitched by the army in a farmer's sun-scorched pasture. At the center of the encampment was one of the alien devices, nicknamed "looking glasses."

According to the briefings I'd attended, there were nine of these in the United States, one hundred and twelve in the world. The looking glasses acted as two-way communication devices, presumably with the ships in orbit. No

one knew why the aliens wouldn't talk to us in person; fear of cooties, maybe. A team of scientists, including a physicist and a linguist, was assigned to each looking glass; Gary Donnelly and I were on this one.

Gary was waiting for me in the parking area. We navigated a circular maze of concrete barricades until we reached the large tent that covered the looking glass itself. In front of the tent was an equipment cart loaded with goodies borrowed from the school's phonology lab; I had sent it ahead for inspection by the army.

Also outside the tent were three tripod-mounted video cameras whose lenses peered, through windows in the fabric wall, into the main room. Everything Gary and I did would be reviewed by countless others, including military intelligence. In addition we would each send daily reports, of which mine had to include estimates on how much English I thought the aliens could understand.

Gary held open the tent flap and gestured for me to enter. "Step right up," he said, circus-barker-style. "Marvel at creatures the likes of which have never been seen on God's green earth."

"And all for one slim dime," I murmured, walking through the door. At the moment the looking glass was inactive, resembling a semicircular mirror over ten feet high and twenty feet across. On the brown grass in front of the looking glass, an arc of white spray paint outlined the activation area. Currently the area contained only a table, two folding chairs, and a power strip with a cord leading to a generator outside. The buzz of fluorescent lamps, hung from poles along the edge of the room, commingled with the buzz of flies in the sweltering heat.

Gary and I looked at each other, and then began pushing the cart of equipment up to the table. As we crossed the paint line, the looking glass appeared to grow transparent; it was as if someone was slowly raising the illumination behind tinted glass. The illusion of depth was uncanny; I felt I could walk right into it.

Once the looking glass was fully lit it resembled a life-size diorama of a semicircular room. The room contained a few large objects that might have been furniture, but no aliens. There was a door in the curved rear wall.

We busied ourselves connecting everything together: microphone, sound spectrograph, portable computer, and speaker. As we worked, I frequently glanced at the looking glass, anticipating the aliens' arrival. Even so I jumped when one of them entered.

It looked like a barrel suspended at the intersection of seven limbs. It was radially symmetric, and any of its limbs could serve as an arm or a leg. The one in front of me was walking around on four legs, three non-adjacent arms curled up at its sides. Gary called them "heptapods."

I'd been shown videotapes, but I still gawked. Its limbs had no distinct joints; anatomists guessed they might be supported by vertebral columns. Whatever their underlying structure, the heptapod's limbs conspired to move it in a disconcertingly fluid manner. Its "torso" rode atop the rippling limbs as smoothly as a hovercraft.

Seven lidless eyes ringed the top of the heptapod's body. It walked back to the doorway from which it entered, made a brief sputtering sound, and returned to the center of the room followed by another heptapod; at no point did it ever turn around. Eerie, but logical; with eyes on all sides, any direction might as well be "forward."

Gary had been watching my reaction. "Ready?" he asked.

I took a deep breath. "Ready enough." I'd done plenty of fieldwork before, in the Amazon, but it had always been a bilingual procedure: either my informants knew some Portuguese, which I could use, or I'd previously gotten an intro to their language from the local missionaries. This would be my first attempt at conducting a true monolingual discovery procedure. It was straightforward enough in theory, though.

I walked up to the looking glass and a heptapod on the other side did the same. The image was so real that my skin crawled. I could see the texture of its gray skin, like corduroy ridges arranged in whorls and loops. There was no smell at all from the looking glass, which somehow made the situation stranger.

I pointed to myself and said slowly, "Human." Then I pointed to Gary. "Human." Then I pointed at each heptapod and said, "What are you?"

No reaction. I tried again, and then again.

One of the heptapods pointed to itself with one limb, the four terminal digits pressed together. That was lucky. In some cultures a person pointed with his chin; if the heptapod hadn't used one of its limbs, I wouldn't have known what gesture to look for. I heard a brief fluttering sound, and saw a puckered orifice at the top of its body vibrate; it was talking. Then it pointed to its companion and fluttered again.

I went back to my computer; on its screen were two virtually identical spectrographs representing the fluttering sounds. I marked a sample for playback. I pointed to myself and said "Human" again, and did the same with Gary. Then I pointed to the heptapod, and played back the flutter on the speaker.

The heptapod fluttered some more. The second half of the spectrograph for this utterance looked like a repetition: call the previous utterances [flutter1], then this one was [flutter2flutter1].

I pointed at something that might have been a heptapod chair. "What is that?"

The heptapod paused, and then pointed at the "chair" and talked some more. The spectrograph for this differed distinctly from that of the earlier sounds: [flutter3]. Once again, I pointed to the "chair" while playing back [flutter3].

The heptapod replied; judging by the spectrograph, it looked like [flutter3flutter2]. Optimistic interpretation: the heptapod was confirming my utterances as correct, which implied compatibility between heptapod and human patterns of discourse. Pessimistic inter- pretation: it had a nagging cough.

At my computer I delimited certain sections of the spectrograph and typed in a tentative gloss for each: "heptapod" for [flutter1], "yes" for [flutter2], and "chair" for [flutter3]. Then I typed "Language: Heptapod A" as a heading for all the utterances.

Gary watched what I was typing. "What's the 'A' for?"

"It just distinguishes this language from any other ones the heptapods might use," I said. He nodded.

"Now let's try something, just for laughs." I pointed at each heptapod and tried to mimic the sound of [flutter1], "heptapod." After a long pause, the first heptapod said something and then the second one said something else, neither of whose spectrographs resembled any- thing said before. I couldn't tell if they were speaking to each other or to me since they had no faces to turn. I tried pronouncing [flutter1] again, but there was no reaction.

"Not even close," I grumbled.

"I'm impressed you can make sounds like that at all," said Gary.

"You should hear my moose call. Sends them running."

I tried again a few more times, but neither heptapod responded with anything I could rec- ognize. Only when I replayed the recording of the heptapod's pronunciation did I get a con- firmation; the heptapod replied with [flutter2], "yes."

"So we're stuck with using recordings?" asked Gary.

I nodded. "At least temporarily."

"So now what?"

"Now we make sure it hasn't actually been saying 'aren't they cute' or 'look what they're doing now.' Then we see if we can identify any of these words when that other heptapod pro- nounces them." I gestured for him to have a seat. "Get comfortable; this'll take a while."

.   .   .

In 1770, Captain Cook's ship *Endeavor* ran aground on the coast of Queensland, Austra- lia. While some of his men made repairs, Cook led an exploration party and met the aboriginal people. One of the sailors pointed to the animals that hopped around with their young riding in pouches, and asked an aborigine what they were called. The aborigine replied, "Kanguru." From then on Cook and his sailors referred to the animals by this word. It wasn't until later that they learned it meant "What did you say?"

I tell that story in my introductory course every year. It's almost certainly untrue, and I explain that afterwards, but it's a classic anec- dote. Of course, the anecdotes my undergradu- ates will really want to hear are ones featuring the heptapods; for the rest of my teaching career, that'll be the reason many of them sign up for my courses. So I'll show them the old videotapes of my sessions at the looking glass, and the sessions that the other linguists con- ducted; the tapes are instructive, and they'll be useful if we're ever visited by aliens again, but they don't generate many good anecdotes.

When it comes to language-learning anec- dotes, my favorite source is child language acquisition. I remember one afternoon when you are five years old, after you have come home from kindergarten. You'll be coloring with your crayons while I grade papers.

"Mom," you'll say, using the carefully casual tone reserved for requesting a favor, "can I ask you something?"

"Sure, sweetie. Go ahead."

"Can I be, um, honored?"

I'll look up from the paper I'm grading. "What do you mean?"

"At school Sharon said she got to be hon- ored."

"Really? Did she tell you what for?"

"It was when her big sister got married. She said only one person could be, um, honored, and she was it."

"Ah, I see. You mean Sharon was maid of honor?"

"Yeah, that's it. Can I be made of honor?"

• • •

Gary and I entered the prefab building containing the center of operations for the looking-glass site. Inside it looked like they were planning an invasion, or perhaps an evacuation: crew-cut soldiers worked around a large map of the area, or sat in front of burly electronic gear while speaking into headsets. We were shown into Colonel Weber's office, a room in the back that was cool from air-conditioning.

We briefed the colonel on our first day's results. "Doesn't sound like you got very far," he said.

"I have an idea as to how we can make faster progress," I said. "But you'll have to approve the use of more equipment."

"What more do you need?"

"A digital camera, and a big video screen." I showed him a drawing of the setup I imagined. "I want to try conducting the discovery procedure using writing; I'd display words on the screen, and use the camera to record the words they write. I'm hoping the heptapods will do the same."

Weber looked at the drawing dubiously. "What would be the advantage of that?"

"So far I've been proceeding the way I would with speakers of an unwritten language. Then it occurred to me that the heptapods must have writing, too."

"So?"

"If the heptapods have a mechanical way of producing writing, then their writing ought to be very regular, very consistent. That would make it easier for us to identify graphemes instead of phonemes. It's like picking out the letters in a printed sentence instead of trying to hear them when the sentence is spoken aloud."

"I take your point," he admitted. "And how would you respond to them? Show them the words they displayed to you?"

"Basically. And if they put spaces between words, any sentences we write would be a lot more intelligible than any spoken sentence we might splice together from recordings."

He leaned back in his chair. "You know we want to show as little of our technology as possible."

"I understand, but we're using machines as intermediaries already. If we can get them to use writing, I believe progress will go much faster than if we're restricted to the sound spectrographs."

The colonel turned to Gary. "Your opinion?"

"It sounds like a good idea to me. I'm curious whether the heptapods might have difficulty reading our monitors. Their looking glasses are based on a completely different technology than our video screens. As far as we can tell, they don't use pixels or scan lines, and they don't refresh on a frame-by-frame basis."

"You think the scan lines on our video screens might render them unreadable to the heptapods?"

"It's possible," said Gary. "We'll just have to try it and see."

Weber considered it. For me it wasn't even a question, but from his point of view it was a difficult decision; like a soldier, though, he made it quickly. "Request granted. Talk to the sergeant outside about bringing in what you need. Have it ready for tomorrow."

I remember one day during the summer when you're sixteen. For once, the person waiting for her date to arrive is me. Of course, you'll be waiting around too, curious to see what he looks like. You'll have a friend of yours, a blond girl with the unlikely name of Roxie, hanging out with you, giggling.

"You may feel the urge to make comments about him," I'll say, checking myself in the hallway mirror. "Just restrain yourselves until we leave."

"Don't worry, Mom," you'll say. "We'll do it so that he won't know. Roxie, you ask me what I think the weather will be like tonight. Then I'll say what I think of Mom's date."

"Right," Roxie will say.

"No, you most definitely will not," I'll say.

"Relax, Mom. He'll never know; we do this all the time."

"What a comfort that is."

A little later on, Nelson will arrive to pick me up. I'll do the introductions, and we'll all engage in a little small talk on the front porch. Nelson is ruggedly handsome, to your evident approval. Just as we're about to leave, Roxie will say to you casually, "So what do you think the weather will be like tonight?"

"I think it's going to be really hot," you'll answer.

Roxie will nod in agreement. Nelson will say, "Really? I thought they said it was going to be cool."

"I have a sixth sense about these things," you'll say. Your face will give nothing away. "I get the feeling it's going to be a scorcher. Good thing you're dressed for it, Mom."

I'll glare at you, and say good night.

As I lead Nelson toward his car, he'll ask me, amused, "I'm missing something here, aren't I?"

"A private joke," I'll mutter. "Don't ask me to explain it."

At our next session at the looking glass, we repeated the procedure we had performed before, this time displaying a printed word on our computer screen at the same time we spoke: showing HUMAN while saying "Human," and so forth. Eventually, the heptapods understood what we wanted, and set up a flat circular screen mounted on a small pedestal. One heptapod spoke, and then inserted a limb into a large socket in the pedestal; a doodle of script, vaguely cursive, popped onto the screen.

We soon settled into a routine, and I compiled two parallel corpora: one of spoken utterances, one of writing samples. Based on first impressions, their writing appeared to be logographic, which was disappointing; I'd been hoping for an alphabetic script to help us learn their speech. Their logograms might include some phonetic information, but finding it would be a lot harder than with an alphabetic script.

By getting up close to the looking glass, I was able to point to various heptapod body parts, such as limbs, digits, and eyes, and elicit terms for each. It turned out that they had an orifice on the underside of their body, lined with articulated bony ridges: probably used for eating, while the one at the top was for respiration and speech. There were no other conspicuous orifices; perhaps their mouth was their anus too. Those sorts of questions would have to wait.

I also tried asking our two informants for terms for addressing each individually; personal names, if they had such things. Their answers were of course unpronounceable, so for Gary's and my purposes, I dubbed them Flapper and Raspberry. I hoped I'd be able to tell them apart.

The next day I conferred with Gary before we entered the looking-glass tent. "I'll need your help with this session," I told him.

"Sure. What do you want me to do?"

"We need to elicit some verbs, and it's easiest with third-person forms. Would you act out a few verbs while I type the written form on the computer? If we're lucky, the heptapods will figure out what we're doing and do the same. I've brought a bunch of props for you to use."

"No problem," said Gary, cracking his knuckles. "Ready when you are."

We began with some simple intransitive verbs: walking, jumping, speaking, writing. Gary demonstrated each one with a charming lack of self-consciousness; the presence of the video cameras didn't inhibit him at all. For the first few actions he performed, I asked the heptapods, "What do you call that?" Before long, the heptapods caught on to what we were trying to do; Raspberry began mimicking Gary, or at least performing the equivalent heptapod action, while Flapper worked their computer, displaying a written description and pronouncing it aloud.

In the spectrographs of their spoken utterances, I could recognize their word I had glossed as "heptapod." The rest of each utterance was presumably the verb phrase; it looked like they had analogs of nouns and verbs, thank goodness.

In their writing, however, things weren't as clear-cut. For each action, they had displayed a single logogram instead of two separate ones. At first I thought they had written something like "walks," with the subject implied. But why would Flapper say "the heptapod walks" while writing "walks," instead of maintaining parallelism? Then I noticed that some of the logograms looked like the logogram for "heptapod" with some extra strokes added to one side or another. Perhaps their verbs could be written as affixes to a noun. If so, why was Flapper writing the noun in some instances but not in others?

I decided to try a transitive verb; substituting object words might clarify things. Among the props I'd brought were an apple and a slice of bread. "Okay," I said to Gary, "show them the food, and then eat some. First the apple, then the bread."

Gary pointed at the Golden Delicious and then he took a bite out of it, while I displayed the "What do you call that?" expression. Then we repeated it with the slice of whole wheat.

Raspberry left the room and returned with some kind of giant nut or gourd and a gelatinous ellipsoid. Raspberry pointed at the gourd while Flapper said a word and displayed a logogram. Then Raspberry brought the gourd down between its legs, a crunching sound resulted, and the gourd reemerged minus a bite; there were cornlike kernels beneath the shell. Flapper talked and displayed a large logogram on their screen. The sound spectrograph for "gourd" changed when it was used in the sentence; possibly a case marker. The logogram was odd: after some study, I could identify graphic elements that resembled the individual logograms for "heptapod" and "gourd." They looked as if they had been melted together, with several extra strokes in the mix that presumably meant "eat." Was it a multiword ligature?

Next we got spoken and written names for the gelatin egg, and descriptions of the act of eating it. The sound spectrograph for "heptapod eats gelatin egg" was analyzable; "gelatin egg" bore a case marker, as expected, though the sentence's word order differed from last time. The written form, another large logogram, was another matter. This time it took much longer for me to recognize anything in it; not only were the individual logograms melted together again, it looked as if the one for "heptapod" was laid on its back, while on top of it the logogram for "gelatin egg" was standing on its head.

"Uh-oh." I took another look at the writing for the simple noun-verb examples, the ones that had seemed inconsistent before. Now I realized all of them actually did contain the logogram for "heptapod"; some were rotated and distorted by being combined with the various verbs, so I hadn't recognized them at first. "You guys have got to be kidding," I muttered.

"What's wrong?" asked Gary.

"Their script isn't word divided; a sentence is written by joining the logograms for the constituent words. They join the logograms by rotating and modifying them. Take a look." I showed him how the logograms were rotated.

"So they can read a word with equal ease no matter how it's rotated," Gary said. He turned to look at the heptapods, impressed. "I wonder if it's a consequence of their bodies' radial symmetry: their bodies have no 'forward' direction, so maybe their writing doesn't either. Highly neat."

I couldn't believe it; I was working with someone who modified the word "neat" with "highly." "It certainly is interesting," I said, "but it also means there's no easy way for us to write our own sentences in their language. We can't simply cut their sentences into individual words and recombine them; we'll have to learn the rules of their script before we can write anything legible. It's the same continuity problem we'd have had splicing together speech fragments, except applied to writing."

I looked at Flapper and Raspberry in the looking glass, who were waiting for us to continue, and sighed. "You aren't going to make this easy for us, are you?"

To be fair, the heptapods were completely cooperative. In the days that followed, they readily taught us their language without requiring us to teach them any more English. Colonel Weber and his cohorts pondered the implications of that, while I and the linguists at the other looking glasses met via videoconferencing to share what we had learned about the heptapod language. The videoconferencing made for an incongruous working environment: our video screens were primitive compared to the heptapods' looking glasses, so that my colleagues seemed more remote than the aliens. The familiar was far away, while the bizarre was close at hand.

It would be a while before we'd be ready to ask the heptapods why they had come, or to discuss physics well enough to ask them about their technology. For the time being, we worked on the basics: phonemics/graphemics, vocabulary, syntax. The heptapods at every looking glass were using the same language, so we were able to pool our data and coordinate our efforts.

Our biggest source of confusion was the heptapods' "writing." It didn't appear to be writing at all; it looked more like a bunch of intricate graphic designs. The logograms weren't arranged in rows, or a spiral, or any linear fashion. Instead, Flapper or Raspberry would write a sentence by sticking together as many logograms as needed into a giant conglomeration.

This form of writing was reminiscent of primitive sign systems, which required a reader to know a message's context in order to understand it. Such systems were considered too lim-

ited for systematic recording of information. Yet it was unlikely that the heptapods developed their level of technology with only an oral tradition. That implied one of three possibilities: The first was that the heptapods had a true writing system, but they didn't want to use it in front of us; Colonel Weber would identify with that one. The second was that the heptapods hadn't originated the technology they were using; they were illiterates using someone else's technology. The third, and most interesting to me, was that the heptapods were using a nonlinear system of orthography that qualified as true writing.

I remember a conversation we'll have when you're in your junior year of high school. It'll be Sunday morning, and I'll be scrambling some eggs while you set the table for brunch. You'll laugh as you tell me about the party you went to last night.

"Oh man," you'll say, "they're not kidding when they say that body weight makes a difference. I didn't drink any more than the guys did, but I got so much *drunker*."

I'll try to maintain a neutral, pleasant expression. I'll really try. Then you'll say, "Oh, come on, Mom."

"What?"

"You know you did the exact same things when you were my age."

I did nothing of the sort, but I know that if I were to admit that, you'd lose respect for me completely. "You know never to drive, or get into a car if—"

"God, of course I know that. Do you think I'm an idiot?"

"No, of course not."

What I'll think is that you are clearly, maddeningly not me. It will remind me, again, that you won't be a clone of me; you can be wonderful, a daily delight, but you won't be someone I could have created by myself.

.   .   .

The military had set up a trailer containing our offices at the looking-glass site. I saw Gary walking toward the trailer, and ran to catch up with him. "It's a semasiographic writing system," I said when I reached him.

"Excuse me?" said Gary.

"Here, let me show you." I directed Gary into my office. Once we were inside, I went to the chalkboard and drew a circle with a diagonal line bisecting it. "What does this mean?"

"'Not allowed'?"

"Right." Next I printed the words NOT ALLOWED on the chalkboard. "And so does this. But only one is a representation of speech."

Gary nodded. "Okay."

"Linguists describe writing like this"—I indicated the printed words—"as 'glottographic,' because it represents speech. Every human written language is in this category. However, this symbol"—I indicated the circle and diagonal line—"is 'semasiographic' writing, because it conveys meaning without reference to speech. There's no correspondence between its components and any particular sounds."

"And you think all of heptapod writing is like this?"

"From what I've seen so far, yes. It's not picture writing, it's far more complex. It has its own system of rules for constructing sentences, like a visual syntax that's unrelated to the syntax for their spoken language."

"A visual syntax? Can you show me an example?"

"Coming right up." I sat down at my desk and, using the computer, pulled up a frame from the recording of yesterday's conversation with Raspberry. I turned the monitor so he could see it. "In their spoken language, a noun has a case marker indicating whether it's a subject or object. In their written language, however, a noun is identified as subject or object based on the orientation of its logogram relative to that of the verb. Here, take a look." I pointed at one of the figures. "For instance, when 'heptapod' is integrated with 'hears' this way, with

these strokes parallel, it means that the heptapod is doing the hearing." I showed him a different one. "When they're combined this way, with the strokes perpendicular, it means that the heptapod is being heard. This morphology applies to several verbs.

"Another example is the inflection system." I called up another frame from the recording. "In their written language, this logogram means roughly 'hear easily' or 'hear clearly.' See the elements it has in common with the logogram for 'hear'? You can still combine it with 'heptapod' in the same ways as before, to indicate that the heptapod can hear something clearly or that the heptapod is clearly heard. But what's really interesting is that the modulation of 'hear' into 'hear clearly' isn't a special case; you see the transformation they applied?"

Gary nodded, pointing. "It's like they express the idea of 'clearly' by changing the curve of those strokes in the middle."

"Right. That modulation is applicable to lots of verbs. The logogram for 'see' can be modulated in the same way to form 'see clearly,' and so can the logogram for 'read' and others. And changing the curve of those strokes has no parallel in their speech; with the spoken version of these verbs, they add a prefix to the verb to express ease of manner, and the prefixes for 'see' and 'hear' are different.

"There are other examples, but you get the idea. It's essentially a grammar in two dimensions."

He began pacing thoughtfully. "Is there anything like this in human writing systems?"

"Mathematical equations, notations for music and dance. But those are all very specialized; we couldn't record this conversation using them. But I suspect, if we knew it well enough, we could record this conversation in the heptapod writing system. I think it's a full-fledged, general-purpose graphical language."

Gary frowned. "So their writing constitutes a completely separate language from their speech, right?"

"Right. In fact, it'd be more accurate to refer

to the writing system as 'Heptapod B,' and use 'Heptapod A' strictly for referring to the spoken language."

"Hold on a second. Why use two languages when one would suffice? That seems unnecessarily hard to learn."

"Like English spelling?" I said. "Ease of learning isn't the primary force in language evolution. For the heptapods, writing and speech may play such different cultural or cognitive roles that using separate languages makes more sense than using different forms of the same one."

He considered it. "I see what you mean. Maybe they think our form of writing is redundant, like we're wasting a second communications channel."

"That's entirely possible. Finding out why they use a second language for writing will tell us a lot about them."

"So I take it this means we won't be able to use their writing to help us learn their spoken language."

I sighed. "Yeah, that's the most immediate implication. But I don't think we should ignore either Heptapod A or B; we need a two-pronged approach." I pointed at the screen. "I'll bet you that learning their two-dimensional grammar will help you when it comes time to learn their mathematical notation."

"You've got a point there. So are we ready to start asking about their mathematics?"

"Not yet. We need a better grasp on this writing system before we begin anything else," I said, and then smiled when he mimed frustration. "Patience, good sir. Patience is a virtue."

You'll be six when your father has a conference to attend in Hawaii, and we'll accompany him. You'll be so excited that you'll make preparations for weeks beforehand. You'll ask me about coconuts and volcanoes and surfing, and practice hula dancing in the mirror. You'll pack a suitcase with the clothes and toys you want to bring, and you'll drag it around the house to see how long you can carry it. You'll ask me if I can carry your Etch A Sketch in my bag, since there won't be any more room for it in yours and you simply can't leave without it.

"You won't need all of these," I'll say. "There'll be so many fun things to do there, you won't have time to play with so many toys."

You'll consider that; dimples will appear above your eyebrows when you think hard. Eventually you'll agree to pack fewer toys, but your expectations will, if anything, increase.

"I wanna be in Hawaii now," you'll whine.

"Sometimes it's good to wait," I'll say. "The anticipation makes it more fun when you get there."

You'll just pout.

In the next report I submitted, I suggested that the term "logogram" was a misnomer because it implied that each graph represented a spoken word, when in fact the graphs didn't correspond to our notion of spoken words at all. I didn't want to use the term "ideogram" either because of how it had been used in the past; I suggested the term "semagram" instead.

It appeared that a semagram corresponded roughly to a written word in human languages: it was meaningful on its own, and in combination with other semagrams could form endless statements. We couldn't define it precisely, but then no one had ever satisfactorily defined "word" for human languages either. When it came to sentences in Heptapod B, though, things became much more confusing. The language had no written punctuation: its syntax was indicated in the way the semagrams were combined, and there was no need to indicate the cadence of speech. There was certainly no way to slice out subject-predicate pairings neatly to make sentences. A "sentence" seemed to be whatever number of semagrams a heptapod wanted to join together; the only difference between a sentence and a paragraph, or a page, was size.

When a Heptapod B sentence grew fairly

sizable, its visual impact was remarkable. If I wasn't trying to decipher it, the writing looked like fanciful praying mantises drawn in a cursive style, all clinging to each other to form an Escheresque lattice, each slightly different in its stance. And the biggest sentences had an effect similar to that of psychedelic posters: sometimes eye-watering, sometimes hypnotic.

I remember a picture of you taken at your college graduation. In the photo you're striking a pose for the camera, mortarboard stylishly tilted on your head, one hand touching your sunglasses, the other hand on your hip, holding open your gown to reveal the tank top and shorts you're wearing underneath.

I remember your graduation. There will be the distraction of having Nelson and your father and what's-her-name there all at the same time, but that will be minor. That entire weekend, while you're introducing me to your classmates and hugging everyone incessantly, I'll be all but mute with amazement. I can't believe that you, a grown woman taller than me and beautiful enough to make my heart ache, will be the same girl I used to lift off the ground so you could reach the drinking fountain, the same girl who used to trundle out of my bedroom draped in a dress and hat and four scarves from my closet.

And after graduation, you'll be heading for a job as a financial analyst. I won't understand what you do there, I won't even understand your fascination with money, the preeminence you gave to salary when negotiating job offers. I would prefer it if you'd pursue something without regard for its monetary rewards, but I'll have no complaints. My own mother could never understand why I couldn't just be a high school English teacher. You'll do what makes you happy, and that'll be all I ask for.

As time went on, the teams at each looking glass began working in earnest on learning heptapod terminology for elementary mathematics and physics. We worked together on presentations, with the linguists focusing on procedure and the physicists focusing on subject matter. The physicists showed us previously devised systems for communicating with aliens, based on mathematics, but those were intended for use over a radio telescope. We reworked them for face-to-face communication.

Our teams were successful with basic arithmetic, but we hit a roadblock with geometry and algebra. We tried using a spherical coordinate system instead of a rectangular one, thinking it might be more natural to the heptapods given their anatomy, but that approach wasn't any more fruitful. The heptapods didn't seem to understand what we were getting at.

Likewise, the physics discussions went poorly. Only with the most concrete terms, like the names of the elements, did we have any success; after several attempts at representing the periodic table, the heptapods got the idea. For anything remotely abstract, we might as well have been gibbering. We tried to demonstrate basic physical attributes like mass and acceleration so we could elicit their terms for them, but the heptapods simply responded with requests for clarification. To avoid perceptual problems that might be associated with any particular medium, we tried physical demonstrations as well as line drawings, photos, and animations; none were effective. Days with no progress became weeks, and the physicists were becoming disillusioned.

By contrast, the linguists were having much more success. We made steady progress decoding the grammar of the spoken language, Heptapod A. It didn't follow the pattern of human languages, as expected, but it was comprehensible so far: free word order, even to the extent that there was no preferred order for the clauses in a conditional statement, in defiance of a human language "universal." It also appeared that the heptapods had no objection to many levels of center-embedding of clauses, something that quickly defeated humans. Peculiar, but not impenetrable.

Much more interesting were the newly discovered morphological and grammatical processes in Heptapod B that were uniquely two-dimensional. Depending on a semagram's declension, inflections could be indicated by varying a certain stroke's curvature, or its thickness, or its manner of undulation; or by varying the relative sizes of two radicals, or their relative distance to another radical, or their orientations; or various other means. These were non-segmental graphemes; they couldn't be isolated from the rest of a semagram. And despite how such traits behaved in human writing, these had nothing to do with calligraphic style; their meanings were defined according to a consistent and unambiguous grammar.

We regularly asked the heptapods why they had come. Each time, they answered "To see," or "To observe." Indeed, sometimes they preferred to watch us silently rather than answer our questions. Perhaps they were scientists, perhaps they were tourists. The State Department instructed us to reveal as little as possible about humanity, in case that information could be used as a bargaining chip in subsequent negotiations. We obliged, though it didn't require much effort: the heptapods never asked questions about anything. Whether scientists or tourists, they were an awfully incurious bunch.

I remember once when we'll be driving to the mall to buy some new clothes for you. You'll be thirteen. One moment you'll be sprawled in your seat, completely unself-conscious, all child; the next, you'll toss your hair with a practiced casualness, like a fashion model in training.

You'll give me some instructions as I'm parking the car. "Okay, Mom, give me one of the credit cards, and we can meet back at the entrance here in two hours."

I'll laugh. "Not a chance. All the credit cards stay with me."

"You're kidding." You'll become the embodiment of exasperation. We'll get out of the car and I will start walking to the mall entrance.

After seeing that I won't budge on the matter, you'll quickly reformulate your plans.

"Okay, Mom, okay. You can come with me, just walk a little ways behind me, so it doesn't look like we're together. If I see any friends of mine, I'm gonna stop and talk to them, but you just keep walking, okay? I'll come find you later."

I'll stop in my tracks. "Excuse me? I am not the hired help, nor am I some mutant relative for you to be ashamed of."

"But, Mom, I can't let anyone see you with me."

"What are you talking about? I've already met your friends; they've been to the house."

"That was different," you'll say, incredulous that you have to explain it. "This is shopping."

"Too bad."

Then the explosion: "You won't do the least thing to make me happy! You don't care about me at all!"

It won't have been that long since you enjoyed going shopping with me; it will forever astonish me how quickly you grow out of one phase and enter another. Living with you will be like aiming for a moving target; you'll always be further along than I expect.

I looked at the sentence in Heptapod B that I had just written, using simple pen and paper. Like all the sentences I generated myself, this one looked misshapen, like a heptapod-written sentence that had been smashed with a hammer and then inexpertly taped back together. I had sheets of such inelegant semagrams covering my desk, fluttering occasionally when the oscillating fan swung past.

It was strange trying to learn a language that had no spoken form. Instead of practicing my pronunciation, I had taken to squeezing my eyes shut and trying to paint semagrams on the insides of my eyelids.

There was a knock at the door and before I could answer Gary came in looking jubilant. "Illinois got a repetition in physics."

"Really? That's great; when did it happen?"

"It happened a few hours ago; we just had the videoconference. Let me show you what it is." He started erasing my blackboard.

"Don't worry, I didn't need any of that."

"Good." He picked up a nub of chalk and drew a diagram:

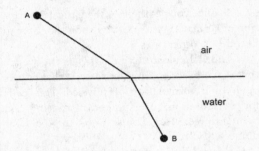

"Okay, here's the path a ray of light takes when crossing from air to water. The light ray travels in a straight line until it hits the water; the water has a different index of refraction, so the light changes direction. You've heard of this before, right?"

I nodded. "Sure."

"Now here's an interesting property about the path the light takes. The path is the fastest possible route between these two points."

"Come again?"

"Imagine, just for grins, that the ray of light traveled along this path." He added a dotted line to his diagram:

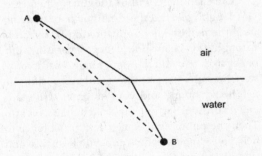

"This hypothetical path is shorter than the path the light actually takes. But light travels more slowly in water than it does in air, and a greater percentage of this path is underwater. So it would take longer for light to travel along this path than it does along the real path."

"Okay, I get it."

"Now imagine if light were to travel along this other path." He drew a second dotted path:

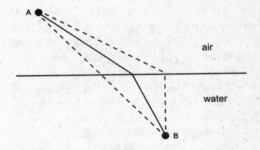

"This path reduces the percentage that's underwater, but the total length is larger. It would also take longer for light to travel along this path than along the actual one."

Gary put down the chalk and gestured at the diagram on the chalkboard with white-tipped fingers. "Any hypothetical path would require more time to traverse than the one actually taken. In other words, the route that the light ray takes is always the fastest possible one. That's Fermat's principle of least time."

"Hmm, interesting. And this is what the heptapods responded to?"

"Exactly. Moorehead gave an animated presentation of Fermat's principle at the Illinois looking glass, and the heptapods repeated it back. Now he's trying to get a symbolic description." He grinned. "Now is that highly neat, or what?"

"It's neat all right, but how come I haven't heard of Fermat's principle before?" I picked up a binder and waved it at him; it was a primer on the physics topics suggested for use in communication with the heptapods. "This thing goes on forever about Planck masses and the spin-flip of atomic hydrogen, and not a word about the refraction of light."

"We guessed wrong about what'd be most useful for you to know," Gary said without embarrassment. "In fact, it's curious that Fermat's principle was the first breakthrough; even though it's easy to explain, you need calculus to describe it mathematically. And not ordinary calculus; you need the calculus of variations. We thought that some simple theorem of geometry or algebra would be the breakthrough."

"Curious indeed. You think the heptapods' idea of what's simple doesn't match ours?"

"Exactly, which is why I'm *dying* to see what their mathematical description of Fermat's principle looks like." He paced as he talked. "If their version of the calculus of variations is simpler to them than their equivalent of algebra, that might explain why we've had so much trouble talking about physics; their entire system of mathematics may be topsy-turvy compared to ours." He pointed to the physics primer. "You can be sure that we're going to revise that."

"So can you build from Fermat's principle to other areas of physics?"

"Probably. There are lots of physical principles just like Fermat's."

"What, like Louise's principle of least closet space? When did physics become so minimalist?"

"Well, the word 'least' is misleading. You see, Fermat's principle of least time is incomplete; in certain situations light follows a path that takes *more* time than any of the other possibilities. It's more accurate to say that light always follows an *extreme* path, either one that minimizes the time taken or one that maximizes it. A minimum and a maximum share certain mathematical properties, so both situations can be described with one equation. So to be precise, Fermat's principle isn't a minimal principle; instead it's what's known as a 'variational' principle."

"And there are more of these variational principles?"

He nodded. "In all branches of physics. Almost every physical law can be restated as a variational principle. The only difference between these principles is in which attribute is minimized or maximized." He gestured as if the different branches of physics were arrayed before him on a table. "In optics, where Fermat's principle applies, time is the attribute that has to be an extreme. In mechanics, it's a different attribute. In electromagnetism, it's something else again. But all these principles are similar mathematically."

"So once you get their mathematical description of Fermat's principle, you should be able to decode the other ones."

"God, I hope so. I think this is the wedge that we've been looking for, the one that cracks open their formulation of physics. This calls for a celebration." He stopped his pacing and turned to me. "Hey, Louise, want to go out for dinner? My treat."

I was mildly surprised. "Sure," I said.

It'll be when you first learn to walk that I get daily demonstrations of the asymmetry in our relationship. You'll be incessantly running off somewhere, and each time you walk into a door frame or scrape your knee, the pain feels like it's my own. It'll be like growing an errant limb, an extension of myself whose sensory nerves report pain just fine, but whose motor nerves don't convey my commands at all. It's so unfair: I'm going to give birth to an animated voodoo doll of myself. I didn't see this in the contract when I signed up. Was this part of the deal?

And then there will be the times when I see you laughing. Like the time you'll be playing with the neighbor's puppy, poking your hands through the chain-link fence separating our backyards, and you'll be laughing so hard you'll start hiccuping. The puppy will run inside the neighbor's house, and your laughter will gradually subside, letting you catch your breath. Then the puppy will come back to the fence to lick your fingers again, and you'll shriek and start laughing again. It will be the most wonderful sound I could ever imagine, a sound that makes me feel like a fountain, or a wellspring.

Now if only I can remember that sound the next time your blithe disregard for self-preservation gives me a heart attack.

After the breakthrough with Fermat's principle, discussions of scientific concepts became more fruitful. It wasn't as if all of heptapod physics was suddenly rendered transparent, but progress was steady. According to Gary, the heptapods' formulation of physics was indeed topsy-turvy relative to ours. Physical attributes that humans defined using integral calculus were seen as fundamental by the heptapods. As an example, Gary described an attribute that, in physics jargon, bore the deceptively simple name "action," which represented "the difference between kinetic and potential energy, integrated over time," whatever that meant. Calculus for us; elementary to them.

Conversely, to define attributes that humans thought of as fundamental, like velocity, the heptapods employed mathematics that were, Gary assured me, "highly weird." The physicists were ultimately able to prove the equivalence of heptapod mathematics and human mathematics; even though their approaches were almost the reverse of one another, both were systems of describing the same physical universe.

I tried following some of the equations that the physicists were coming up with, but it was no use. I couldn't really grasp the significance of physical attributes like "action"; I couldn't, with any confidence, ponder the significance of treating such an attribute as fundamental. Still, I tried to ponder questions formulated in terms more familiar to me: What kind of worldview did the heptapods have, that they would consider Fermat's principle the simplest explanation of light refraction? What kind of perception made a minimum or maximum readily apparent to them?

. . .

Your eyes will be blue like your dad's, not mud brown like mine. Boys will stare into those eyes the way I did, and do, into your dad's, surprised and enchanted, as I was and am, to find them in combination with black hair. You will have many suitors.

I remember when you are fifteen, coming home after a weekend at your dad's, incredulous over the interrogation he'll have put you through regarding the boy you're currently dating. You'll sprawl on the sofa, recounting your dad's latest breach of common sense: "You know what he said? He said, 'I know what teenage boys are like.'" Roll of the eyes. "Like I don't?"

"Don't hold it against him," I'll say. "He's a father; he can't help it." Having seen you interact with your friends, I won't worry much about a boy taking advantage of you; if anything, the opposite will be more likely. I'll worry about that.

"He wishes I were still a kid. He hasn't known how to act toward me since I grew breasts."

"Well, that development was a shock for him. Give him time to recover."

"It's been *years*, Mom. How long is it gonna take?"

"I'll let you know when my father has come to terms with mine."

During one of the videoconferences for the linguists, Cisneros from the Massachusetts looking glass had raised an interesting question: was there a particular order in which semagrams were written in a Heptapod B sentence? It was clear that word order meant next to nothing when speaking in Heptapod A; when asked to repeat what it had just said, a heptapod would likely as not use a different word order unless we specifically asked them not to. Was word order similarly unimportant when writing in Heptapod B?

Previously, we had focused our attention only on how a sentence in Heptapod B looked once it was complete. As far as anyone could tell, there was no preferred order when reading the semagrams in a sentence; you could start almost anywhere in the nest, then follow the branching clauses until you'd read the whole thing. But that was reading; was the same true about writing?

During my most recent session with Flapper and Raspberry I had asked them if, instead of displaying a semagram only after it was completed, they could show it to us while it was being written. They had agreed. I inserted the videotape of the session into the VCR, and on my computer I consulted the session transcript.

I picked one of the longer utterances from the conversation. What Flapper had said was that the heptapods' planet had two moons, one significantly larger than the other; the three primary constituents of the planet's atmosphere were nitrogen, argon, and oxygen; and fifteen twenty-eighths of the planet's surface was covered by water. The first words of the spoken utterance translated literally as "inequality-of-size rocky-orbiter rocky-orbiters related-as-primary-to-secondary."

Then I rewound the videotape until the time signature matched the one in the transcription. I started playing the tape, and watched the web of semagrams being spun out of inky spider's silk. I rewound it and played it several times. Finally I froze the video right after the first stroke was completed and before the second one was begun; all that was visible on-screen was a single sinuous line.

Comparing that initial stroke with the completed sentence, I realized that the stroke participated in several different clauses of the message. It began in the semagram for "oxygen," as the determinant that distinguished it from certain other elements; then it slid down to become the morpheme of comparison in the description of the two moons' sizes; and lastly it flared out as the arched backbone of the semagram for "ocean." Yet this stroke was a single continuous line, and it was the first one that Flapper wrote. That meant the heptapod had to know how the entire sentence would be laid out before it could write the very first stroke.

The other strokes in the sentence also traversed several clauses, making them so interconnected that none could be removed without redesigning the entire sentence. The heptapods didn't write a sentence one semagram at a time; they built it out of strokes irrespective of individual semagrams. I had seen a similarly high degree of integration before in calligraphic designs, particularly those employing the Arabic alphabet. But those designs had required careful planning by expert calligraphers. No one could lay out such an intricate design at the speed needed for holding a conversation. At least, no human could.

There's a joke that I once heard a comedienne tell. It goes like this: "I'm not sure if I'm ready to have children. I asked a friend of mine who has children, 'Suppose I do have kids. What if when they grow up, they blame me for everything that's wrong with their lives?' She laughed and said, 'What do you mean, if?'"

That's my favorite joke.

Gary and I were at a little Chinese restaurant, one of the local places we had taken to patronizing to get away from the encampment. We sat eating the appetizers: potstickers, redolent of pork and sesame oil. My favorite.

I dipped one in soy sauce and vinegar. "So how are you doing with your Heptapod B practice?" I asked.

Gary looked obliquely at the ceiling. I tried to meet his gaze, but he kept shifting it.

"You've given up, haven't you?" I said. "You're not even trying anymore."

He did a wonderful hangdog expression. "I'm just no good at languages," he confessed. "I thought learning Heptapod B might be more like learning mathematics than trying to speak another language, but it's not. It's too foreign for me."

"It would help you discuss physics with them."

"Probably, but since we had our breakthrough, I can get by with just a few phrases."

I sighed. "I suppose that's fair; I have to admit, I've given up on trying to learn the mathematics."

"So we're even?"

"We're even." I sipped my tea. "Though I did want to ask you about Fermat's principle. Something about it feels odd to me, but I can't put my finger on it. It just doesn't sound like a law of physics."

A twinkle appeared in Gary's eyes. "I'll bet I know what you're talking about." He snipped a potsticker in half with his chopsticks. "You're used to thinking of refraction in terms of cause and effect: reaching the water's surface is the cause, and the change in direction is the effect. But Fermat's principle sounds weird because it describes light's behavior in goal-oriented terms. It sounds like a commandment to a light beam: 'Thou shalt minimize or maximize the time taken to reach thy destination.'"

I considered it. "Go on."

"It's an old question in the philosophy of physics. People have been talking about it since Fermat first formulated it in the sixteen hundreds; Planck wrote volumes about it. The thing is, while the common formulation of physical laws is causal, a variational principle like Fermat's is purposive, almost teleological."

"Hmm, that's an interesting way to put it. Let me think about that for a minute." I pulled out a felt-tip pen and, on my paper napkin, drew a copy of the diagram that Gary had drawn on my blackboard. "Okay," I said, thinking aloud, "so let's say the goal of a ray of light is to take the fastest path. How does the light go about doing that?"

"Well, if I can speak anthropomorphic-projectionally, the light has to examine the possible paths and compute how long each one would take." He plucked the last potsticker from the serving dish.

"And to do that," I continued, "the ray of light has to know just where its destination is. If the destination were somewhere else, the fastest path would be different."

Gary nodded again. "That's right; the notion of a 'fastest path' is meaningless unless there's a destination specified. And computing how long a given path takes also requires information about what lies along that path, like where the water's surface is."

I kept staring at the diagram on the napkin. "And the light ray has to know all that ahead of time, before it starts moving, right?"

"So to speak," said Gary. "The light can't start traveling in any old direction and make course corrections later on, because the path resulting from such behavior wouldn't be the fastest possible one. The light has to do all its computations at the very beginning."

I thought to myself, *The ray of light has to know where it will ultimately end up before it can choose the direction to begin moving in.* I knew what that reminded me of. I looked up at Gary. "That's what was bugging me."

I remember when you're fourteen. You'll come out of your bedroom, a graffiti-covered notebook computer in hand, working on a report for school.

"Mom, what do you call it when both sides can win?"

I'll look up from my computer and the paper I'll be writing. "What, you mean a win-win situation?"

"There's some technical name for it, some math word. Remember that time Dad was here, and he was talking about the stock market? He used it then."

"Hmm, that sounds familiar, but I can't remember what he called it."

"I need to know. I want to use that phrase in my social studies report. I can't even search for information on it unless I know what it's called."

"I'm sorry, I don't know it either. Why don't you call your dad?"

Judging from your expression, that will be more effort than you want to make. At this point, you and your father won't be getting along well. "Can you call Dad and ask him? But don't tell him it's for me."

"I think you can call him yourself."

You'll fume, "Jesus, Mom, I can never get help with my homework since you and Dad split up."

It's amazing the diverse situations in which you can bring up the divorce. "I've helped you with your homework."

"Like a million years ago, Mom."

I'll let that pass. "I'd help you with this if I could, but I don't remember what it's called."

You'll head back to your bedroom in a huff.

I practiced Heptapod B at every opportunity, both with the other linguists and by myself. The novelty of reading a semasiographic language made it compelling in a way that Heptapod A wasn't, and my improvement in writing it excited me. Over time, the sentences I wrote grew shapelier, more cohesive. I had reached the point where it worked better when I didn't think about it too much. Instead of carefully trying to design a sentence before writing, I could simply begin putting down strokes immediately; my initial strokes almost always turned out to be compatible with an elegant rendition of what I was trying to say. I was developing a faculty like that of the heptapods.

More interesting was the fact that Heptapod B was changing the way I thought. For me, thinking typically meant speaking in an internal voice; as we say in the trade, my thoughts were phonologically coded. My internal voice normally spoke in English, but that wasn't a requirement. The summer after my senior year in high school, I attended a total immersion program for learning Russian; by the end of the summer, I was thinking and even dreaming in Russian. But it was always *spoken* Russian. Different language, same mode: a voice speaking silently aloud.

The idea of thinking in a linguistic yet non-phonological mode always intrigued me. I had a friend born of deaf parents; he grew up using American Sign Language, and he told me that he often thought in ASL instead of English. I used to wonder what it was like to have one's thoughts be manually coded, to reason using an inner pair of hands instead of an inner voice.

With Heptapod B, I was experiencing something just as foreign: my thoughts were becoming graphically coded. There were trancelike moments during the day when my thoughts weren't expressed with my internal voice; instead, I saw semagrams with my mind's eye, sprouting like frost on a windowpane.

As I grew more fluent, semagraphic designs would appear fully formed, articulating even complex ideas all at once. My thought processes weren't moving any faster as a result, though. Instead of racing forward, my mind hung balanced on the symmetry underlying the semagrams. The semagrams seemed to be something more than language; they were almost like mandalas. I found myself in a meditative state, contemplating the way in which premises and conclusions were interchangeable. There was no direction inherent in the way propositions were connected, no "train of thought" moving along a particular route; all the components in an act of reasoning were equally powerful, all having identical precedence.

A representative from the State Department named Hossner had the job of briefing the US scientists on our agenda with the heptapods. We sat in the videoconference room, listening to him lecture. Our microphone was turned off, so Gary and I could exchange comments without interrupting Hossner. As we listened, I worried that Gary might harm his vision, rolling his eyes so often.

"They must have had some reason for coming all this way," said the diplomat, his voice tinny through the speakers. "It does not look like their reason was conquest, thank God. But if that's not the reason, what is? Are they prospectors? Anthropologists? Missionaries? Whatever their motives, there must be something we can offer them. Maybe it's mineral rights to our solar system. Maybe it's information about ourselves. Maybe it's the right to deliver sermons to our populations. But we can be sure that there's something.

"My point is this: their motive might not be to trade, but that doesn't mean that we cannot conduct trade. We simply need to know why they're here, and what we have that they want. Once we have that information, we can begin trade negotiations.

"I should emphasize that our relationship with the heptapods need not be adversarial. This is not a situation where every gain on their part is a loss on ours, or vice versa. If we handle ourselves correctly, both we and the heptapods can come out winners."

"You mean it's a non-zero-sum game?" Gary said in mock incredulity. "Oh my gosh."

"A non-zero-sum game."

"What?" You'll reverse course, heading back from your bedroom.

"When both sides can win: I just remembered, it's called a non-zero-sum game."

"That's it!" you'll say, writing it down on your notebook. "Thanks, Mom!"

"I guess I knew it after all," I'll say. "All those years with your father, some of it must have rubbed off."

"I knew you'd know it," you'll say. You'll give me a sudden, brief hug, and your hair will smell of apples. "You're the best."

"Louise?"

"Hmm? Sorry, I was distracted. What did you say?"

"I said, what do you think about our Mr. Hossner here?"

"I prefer not to."

"I've tried that myself: ignoring the government, seeing if it would go away. It hasn't."

As evidence of Gary's assertion, Hossner kept blathering: "Your immediate task is to think back on what you've learned. Look for anything that might help us. Has there been any indication of what the heptapods want? Of what they value?"

"Gee, it never occurred to us to look for things like that," I said. "We'll get right on it, sir."

"The sad thing is, that's just what we'll have to do," said Gary.

"Are there any questions?" asked Hossner.

Burghart, the linguist at the Fort Worth looking glass, spoke up. "We've been through this with the heptapods many times. They maintain that they're here to observe, and they maintain that information is not tradable."

"So they would have us believe," said Hossner. "But consider: how could that be true? I know that the heptapods have occasionally stopped talking to us for brief periods. That may be a tactical maneuver on their part. If we were to stop talking to them tomorrow—"

"Wake me up if he says something interesting," said Gary.

"I was just going to ask you to do the same for me."

That day when Gary first explained Fermat's principle to me, he had mentioned that almost every physical law could be stated as a variational principle. Yet when humans thought about physical laws, they preferred to work with them in their causal formulation. I could understand that: the physical attributes that humans found intuitive, like kinetic energy or acceleration, were all properties of an object at a given moment in time. And these were conducive to a chronological, causal interpretation of events: one moment growing out of another, causes and effects creating a chain reaction that grew from past to future.

In contrast, the physical attributes that the

heptapods found intuitive, like "action" or those other things defined by integrals, were meaningful only over a period of time. And these were conducive to a teleological interpretation of events: by viewing events over a period of time, one recognized that there was a requirement that had to be satisfied, a goal of minimizing or maximizing. And one had to know the initial and final states to meet that goal; one needed knowledge of the effects before the causes could be initiated.

I was growing to understand that, too.

"Why?" you'll ask again. You'll be three.

"Because it's your bedtime," I'll say again. We'll have gotten as far as getting you bathed and into your jammies, but no further than that.

"But I'm not sleepy," you'll whine. You'll be standing at the bookshelf, pulling down a video to watch: your latest diversionary tactic to keep away from your bedroom.

"It doesn't matter: you still have to go to bed."

"But why?"

"Because I'm the mom and I said so."

I'm actually going to say that, aren't I? God, somebody please shoot me.

I'll pick you up and carry you under my arm to your bed, you wailing piteously all the while, but my sole concern will be my own distress. All those vows made in childhood that I would give reasonable answers when I became a parent, that I would treat my own child as an intelligent, thinking individual, all for naught: I'm going to turn into my mother. I can fight it as much as I want, but there'll be no stopping my slide down that long, dreadful slope.

Was it actually possible to know the future? Not simply to guess at it; was it possible to *know* what was going to happen, with absolute certainty and in specific detail? Gary once told me that the fundamental laws of physics were time-symmetric, that there was no physical dif-ference between past and future. Given that, some might say, "Yes, theoretically." But speaking more concretely, most would answer "No," because of free will.

I liked to imagine the objection as a Borgesian fabulation: consider a person standing before the *Book of Ages*, the chronicle that records every event, past and future. Even though the text has been photoreduced from the full-sized edition, the volume is enormous. With magnifier in hand, she flips through the tissue-thin leaves until she locates the story of her life. She finds the passage that describes her flipping through the *Book of Ages*, and she skips to the next column, where it details what she'll be doing later in the day: acting on information she's read in the *Book*, she'll bet $100 on the racehorse Devil May Care and win twenty times that much.

The thought of doing just that had crossed her mind, but being a contrary sort, she now resolves to refrain from betting on the ponies altogether.

There's the rub. The *Book of Ages* cannot be wrong; this scenario is based on the premise that a person is given knowledge of the actual future, not of some possible future. If this were Greek myth, circumstances would conspire to make her enact her fate despite her best efforts, but prophecies in myth are notoriously vague; the *Book of Ages* is quite specific, and there's no way she can be forced to bet on a racehorse in the manner specified. The result is a contradiction: the *Book of Ages* must be right, by definition; yet no matter what the *Book* says she'll do, she can choose to do otherwise. How can these two facts be reconciled?

They can't be, was the common answer. A volume like the *Book of Ages* is a logical impossibility, for the precise reason that its existence would result in the above contradiction. Or, to be generous, some might say that the *Book of Ages* could exist, as long as it wasn't accessible to readers: that volume is housed in a special collection, and no one has viewing privileges.

The existence of free will meant that we

couldn't know the future. And we knew free will existed because we had direct experience of it. Volition was an intrinsic part of consciousness.

Or was it? What if the experience of knowing the future changed a person? What if it evoked a sense of urgency, a sense of obligation to act precisely as she knew she would?

I stopped by Gary's office before leaving for the day. "I'm calling it quits. Did you want to grab something to eat?"

"Sure, just wait a second," he said. He shut down his computer and gathered some papers together. Then he looked up at me. "Hey, want to come to my place for dinner tonight? I'll cook."

I looked at him dubiously. "You can cook?"

"Just one dish," he admitted. "But it's a good one."

"Sure," I said. "I'm game."

"Great. We just need to go shopping for the ingredients."

"Don't go to any trouble—"

"There's a market on the way to my house. It won't take a minute."

We took separate cars, me following him. I almost lost him when he abruptly turned into a parking lot. It was a gourmet market, not large, but fancy; tall glass jars stuffed with imported foods sat next to specialty utensils on the store's stainless-steel shelves.

I accompanied Gary as he collected fresh basil, tomatoes, garlic, linguini. "There's a fish market next door; we can get fresh clams there," he said.

"Sounds good." We walked past the section of kitchen utensils. My gaze wandered over the shelves—pepper mills, garlic presses, salad tongs—and stopped on a wooden salad bowl.

When you are three, you'll pull a dish towel off the kitchen counter and bring that salad bowl down on top of you. I'll make a grab for it, but I'll miss. The edge of the bowl will leave you with a cut, on the upper edge of your forehead,

that will require a single stitch. Your father and I will hold you, sobbing and stained with Caesar dressing, as we wait in the emergency room for hours.

I reached out and took the bowl from the shelf. The motion didn't feel like something I was forced to do. Instead it seemed just as urgent as my rushing to catch the bowl when it falls on you: an instinct that I felt right in following.

"I could use a salad bowl like this."

Gary looked at the bowl and nodded approvingly. "See, wasn't it a good thing that I had to stop at the market?"

"Yes it was." We got in line to pay for our purchases.

Consider the sentence "The rabbit is ready to eat." Interpret "rabbit" to be the object of "eat," and the sentence was an announcement that dinner would be served shortly. Interpret "rabbit" to be the subject of "eat," and it was a hint, such as a young girl might give her mother so she'll open a bag of Purina Bunny Chow. Two very different utterances; in fact, they were probably mutually exclusive within a single household. Yet either was a valid interpretation; only context could determine what the sentence meant.

Consider the phenomenon of light hitting water at one angle, and traveling through it at a different angle. Explain it by saying that a difference in the index of refraction caused the light to change direction, and one saw the world as humans saw it. Explain it by saying that light minimized the time needed to travel to its destination, and one saw the world as the heptapods saw it. Two very different interpretations.

The physical universe was a language with a perfectly ambiguous grammar. Every physical event was an utterance that could be parsed in two entirely different ways, one causal and the other teleological, both valid, neither one disqualifiable no matter how much context was available.

When the ancestors of humans and heptapods first acquired the spark of consciousness, they both perceived the same physical world, but they parsed their perceptions differently; the worldviews that ultimately arose were the end result of that divergence. Humans had developed a sequential mode of awareness, while heptapods had developed a simultaneous mode of awareness. We experienced events in an order, and perceived their relationship as cause and effect. They experienced all events at once, and perceived a purpose underlying them all. A minimizing, maximizing purpose.

I have a recurring dream about your death. In the dream, I'm the one who's rock climbing—me, can you imagine it?—and you're three years old, riding in some kind of backpack I'm wearing. We're just a few feet below a ledge where we can rest, and you won't wait until I've climbed up to it. You start pulling yourself out of the pack; I order you to stop, but of course you ignore me. I feel your weight alternating from one side of the pack to the other as you climb out; then I feel your left foot on my shoulder, and then your right. I'm screaming at you, but I can't get a hand free to grab you. I can see the wavy design on the soles of your sneakers as you climb, and then I see a flake of stone give way beneath one of them. You slide right past me, and I can't move a muscle. I look down and see you shrink into the distance below me.

Then, all of a sudden, I'm at the morgue. An orderly lifts the sheet from your face, and I see that you're twenty-five.

"You okay?"

I was sitting upright in bed; I'd woken Gary with my movements. "I'm fine. I was just startled; I didn't recognize where I was for a moment."

Sleepily, he said, "We can stay at your place next time."

I kissed him. "Don't worry; your place is fine." We curled up, my back against his chest, and went back to sleep.

. . .

When you're three and we're climbing a steep, spiral flight of stairs, I'll hold your hand extra tightly. You'll pull your hand away from me. "I can do it by myself," you'll insist, and then move away from me to prove it, and I'll remember that dream. We'll repeat that scene countless times during your childhood. I can almost believe that, given your contrary nature, my attempts to protect you will be what create your love of climbing: first the jungle gym at the playground, then trees out in the greenbelt around our neighborhood, the rock walls at the climbing club, and ultimately cliff faces in national parks.

I finished the last radical in the sentence, put down the chalk, and sat down in my desk chair. I leaned back and surveyed the giant Heptapod B sentence I'd written that covered the entire blackboard in my office. It included several complex clauses, and I had managed to integrate all of them rather nicely.

Looking at a sentence like this one, I understood why the heptapods had evolved a semasiographic writing system like Heptapod B; it was better suited for a species with a simultaneous mode of consciousness. For them, speech was a bottleneck because it required that one word follow another sequentially. With writing, on the other hand, every mark on a page was visible simultaneously. Why constrain writing with a glottographic straitjacket, demanding that it be just as sequential as speech? It would never occur to them. Semasiographic writing naturally took advantage of the page's two-dimensionality; instead of doling out morphemes one at a time, it offered an entire page full of them all at once.

And now that Heptapod B had introduced me to a simultaneous mode of consciousness, I understood the rationale behind Heptapod A's grammar: what my sequential mind had perceived as unnecessarily convoluted, I now recognized as an attempt to provide flexibility within the confines of sequential speech. I could use Heptapod A more easily as a result, though it was still a poor substitute for Heptapod B.

There was a knock at the door and then Gary poked his head in. "Colonel Weber'll be here any minute."

I grimaced. "Right." Weber was coming to participate in a session with Flapper and Raspberry; I was to act as translator, a job I wasn't trained for and that I detested.

Gary stepped inside and closed the door. He pulled me out of my chair and kissed me.

I smiled. "You trying to cheer me up before he gets here?"

"No, I'm trying to cheer me up."

"You weren't interested in talking to the heptapods at all, were you? You worked on this project just to get me into bed."

"Ah, you see right through me."

I looked into his eyes. "You better believe it," I said.

I remember when you'll be a month old, and I'll stumble out of bed to give you your two a.m. feeding. Your nursery will have that "baby smell" of diaper rash cream and talcum powder, with a faint ammoniac whiff coming from the diaper pail in the corner. I'll lean over your crib, lift your squalling form out, and sit in the rocking chair to nurse you.

The word "infant" is derived from the Latin word for "unable to speak," but you'll be perfectly capable of saying one thing: "I suffer," and you'll do it tirelessly and without hesitation. I have to admire your utter commitment to that statement; when you cry, you'll become outrage incarnate, every fiber of your body employed in expressing that emotion. It's funny: when you're tranquil, you will seem to radiate light, and if someone were to paint a portrait of you like that, I'd insist that they include the halo. But when you're unhappy, you will become a klaxon, built for radiating sound; a portrait of you then could simply be a fire alarm bell.

At that stage of your life, there'll be no past or future for you; until I give you my breast, you'll have no memory of contentment in the past nor expectation of relief in the future. Once you begin nursing, everything will reverse, and all will be right with the world. NOW is the only moment you'll perceive; you'll live in the present tense. In many ways, it's an enviable state.

The heptapods are neither free nor bound as we understand those concepts; they don't act according to their will, nor are they helpless automatons. What distinguishes the heptapods' mode of awareness is not just that their actions coincide with history's events; it is also that their motives coincide with history's purposes. They act to create the future, to enact chronology.

Freedom isn't an illusion; it's perfectly real in the context of sequential consciousness. Within the context of simultaneous consciousness, freedom is not meaningful, but neither is coercion; it's simply a different context, no more or less valid than the other. It's like that famous optical illusion, the drawing of either an elegant young woman, face turned away from the viewer, or a wart-nosed crone, chin tucked down on her chest. There's no "correct" interpretation; both are equally valid. But you can't see both at the same time.

Similarly, knowledge of the future was incompatible with free will. What made it possible for me to exercise freedom of choice also made it impossible for me to know the future. Conversely, now that I know the future, I would never act contrary to that future, including telling others what I know: those who know the future don't talk about it. Those who've read the *Book of Ages* never admit to it.

I turned on the VCR and slotted a cassette of a session from the Fort Worth looking glass. A diplomatic negotiator was having a discussion with the heptapods there, with Burghart acting as translator.

The negotiator was describing humans' moral beliefs, trying to lay some groundwork for the concept of altruism. I knew the heptapods were familiar with the conversation's eventual outcome, but they still participated enthusiastically.

If I could have described this to someone who didn't already know, she might ask, if the heptapods already knew everything that they would ever say or hear, what was the point of their using language at all? A reasonable question. But language wasn't only for communication: it was also a form of action. According to speech act theory, statements like "You're under arrest," "I christen this vessel," or "I promise" were all performative: a speaker could perform the action only by uttering the words. For such acts, knowing what would be said didn't change anything. Everyone at a wedding anticipated the words "I now pronounce you husband and wife," but until the minister actually said them, the ceremony didn't count. With performative language, saying equaled doing.

For the heptapods, all language was performative. Instead of using language to inform, they used language to actualize. Sure, heptapods already knew what would be said in any conversation; but in order for their knowledge to be true, the conversation would have to take place.

"First Goldilocks tried the papa bear's bowl of porridge, but it was full of Brussels sprouts, which she hated."

You'll laugh. "No, that's wrong!" We'll be sitting side by side on the sofa, the skinny, overpriced hardcover spread open on our laps.

I'll keep reading. "Then Goldilocks tried the mama bear's bowl of porridge, but it was full of spinach, which she also hated."

You'll put your hand on the page of the book to stop me. "You have to read it the right way!"

"I'm reading just what it says here," I'll say, all innocence.

"No you're not. That's not how the story goes."

"Well if you already know how the story goes, why do you need me to read it to you?"

"'Cause I wanna hear it!"

The air-conditioning in Weber's office almost compensated for having to talk to the man.

"They're willing to engage in a type of exchange," I explained, "but it's not trade. We simply give them something, and they give us something in return. Neither party tells the other what they're giving beforehand."

Colonel Weber's brow furrowed just slightly. "You mean they're willing to exchange gifts?"

I knew what I had to say. "We shouldn't think of it as 'gift-giving.' We don't know if this transaction has the same associations for the heptapods that gift-giving has for us."

"Can we"—he searched for the right wording—"drop hints about the kind of gift we want?"

"They don't do that themselves for this type of transaction. I asked them if we could make a request, and they said we could, but it won't make them tell us what they're giving." I suddenly remembered that a morphological relative of "performative" was "performance," which could describe the sensation of conversing when you knew what would be said: it was like performing in a play.

"But would it make them more likely to give us what we asked for?" Colonel Weber asked. He was perfectly oblivious of the script, yet his responses matched his assigned lines exactly.

"No way of knowing," I said. "I doubt it, given that it's not a custom they engage in."

"If we give our gift first, will the value of our gift influence the value of theirs?" He was improvising, while I had carefully rehearsed for this one and only show.

"No," I said. "As far as we can tell, the value of the exchanged items is irrelevant."

"If only my relatives felt that way," murmured Gary wryly.

I watched Colonel Weber turn to Gary. "Have you discovered anything new in the physics discussions?" he asked, right on cue.

"If you mean, any information new to mankind, no," said Gary. "The heptapods haven't varied from the routine. If we demonstrate something to them, they'll show us their formulation of it, but they won't volunteer anything and they won't answer our questions about what they know."

An utterance that was spontaneous and communicative in the context of human discourse became a ritual recitation when viewed by the light of Heptapod B.

Weber scowled. "All right then, we'll see how the State Department feels about this. Maybe we can arrange some kind of gift-giving ceremony."

Like physical events, with their causal and teleological interpretations, every linguistic event had two possible interpretations: as a transmission of information and as the realization of a plan.

"I think that's a good idea, Colonel," I said.

It was an ambiguity invisible to most. A private joke; don't ask me to explain it.

Even though I'm proficient with Heptapod B, I know I don't experience reality the way a heptapod does. My mind was cast in the mold of human, sequential languages, and no amount of immersion in an alien language can completely reshape it. My worldview is an amalgam of human and heptapod.

Before I learned how to think in Heptapod B, my memories grew like a column of cigarette ash, laid down by the infinitesimal sliver of combustion that was my consciousness, marking the sequential present. After I learned Heptapod B, new memories fell into place like gigantic blocks, each one measuring years in duration, and though they didn't arrive in order or land contiguously, they soon composed a period of five decades. It is the period during which I know Heptapod B well enough to think in it, starting during my interviews with Flapper and Raspberry and ending with my death.

Usually, Heptapod B affects just my memory: my consciousness crawls along as it did before, a glowing sliver crawling forward in time, the difference being that the ash of memory lies ahead as well as behind: there is no real combustion. But occasionally I have glimpses when Heptapod B truly reigns, and I experience past and future all at once; my consciousness becomes a half-century-long ember burning outside time. I perceive—during those glimpses—that entire epoch as a simultaneity. It's a period encompassing the rest of my life, and the entirety of yours.

I wrote out the semagrams for "process create-endpoint inclusive-we," meaning "let's start." Raspberry replied in the affirmative, and the slide shows began. The second display screen that the heptapods had provided began presenting a series of images, composed of semagrams and equations, while one of our video screens did the same.

This was the second "gift exchange" I had been present for, the eighth one overall, and I knew it would be the last. The looking-glass tent was crowded with people; Burghart from Fort Worth was here, as were Gary and a nuclear physicist, assorted biologists, anthropologists, military brass, and diplomats. Thankfully they had set up an air-conditioner to cool the place off. We would review the tapes of the images later to figure out just what the heptapods' "gift" was. Our own "gift" was a presentation on the Lascaux cave paintings.

We all crowded around the heptapods' second screen, trying to glean some idea of the images' content as they went by. "Preliminary assessments?" asked Colonel Weber.

"It's not a return," said Burghart. In a previous exchange, the heptapods had given us information about ourselves that we had previously told them. This had infuriated the State Department, but we had no reason to think of it as an insult: it probably indicated that trade value really didn't play a role in these exchanges. It didn't exclude the possibility that the heptapods might yet offer us a space drive, or cold fusion, or some other wish-fulfilling miracle.

"That looks like inorganic chemistry," said the nuclear physicist, pointing at an equation before the image was replaced.

Gary nodded. "It could be materials technology," he said.

"Maybe we're finally getting somewhere," said Colonel Weber.

"I wanna see more animal pictures," I whispered, quietly so that only Gary could hear me, and pouted like a child. He smiled and poked me. Truthfully, I wished the heptapods had given another xenobiology lecture, as they had on two previous exchanges; judging from those, humans were more similar to the heptapods than any other species they'd ever encountered. Or another lecture on heptapod history; those had been filled with apparent non sequiturs, but were interesting nonetheless. I didn't want the heptapods to give us new technology, because I didn't want to see what our governments might do with it.

I watched Raspberry while the information was being exchanged, looking for any anomalous behavior. It stood barely moving as usual; I saw no indications of what would happen shortly.

After a minute, the heptapod's screen went blank, and a minute after that, ours did too. Gary and most of the other scientists clustered around a tiny video screen that was replaying the heptapods' presentation. I could hear them talk about the need to call in a solid-state physicist.

Colonel Weber turned. "You two," he said, pointing to me and then to Burghart, "schedule the time and location for the next exchange." Then he followed the others to the playback screen.

"Coming right up," I said. To Burghart, I asked, "Would you care to do the honors, or shall I?"

I knew Burghart had gained a proficiency in Heptapod B similar to mine. "It's your looking glass," he said. "You drive."

I sat down again at the transmitting computer. "Bet you never figured you'd wind up working as an army translator back when you were a grad student."

"That's for goddamn sure," he said. "Even now I can hardly believe it." Everything we said to each other felt like the carefully bland exchanges of spies who meet in public, but never break cover.

I wrote out the semagrams for "locus exchange-transaction converse inclusive-we" with the projective aspect modulation.

Raspberry wrote its reply. That was my cue to frown, and for Burghart to ask, "What does it mean by that?" His delivery was perfect.

I wrote a request for clarification; Raspberry's reply was the same as before. Then I watched it glide out of the room. The curtain was about to fall on this act of our performance.

Colonel Weber stepped forward. "What's going on? Where did it go?"

"It said that the heptapods are leaving now," I said. "Not just itself; all of them."

"Call it back here now. Ask it what it means."

"Um, I don't think Raspberry's wearing a pager," I said.

The image of the room in the looking glass disappeared so abruptly that it took a moment for my eyes to register what I was seeing instead: it was the other side of the looking-glass tent. The looking glass had become completely transparent. The conversation around the playback screen fell silent.

"What the hell is going on here?" said Colonel Weber.

Gary walked up to the looking glass, and then around it to the other side. He touched the rear surface with one hand; I could see the pale ovals where his fingertips made contact with the looking glass. "I think," he said, "we just saw a demonstration of transmutation at a distance."

I heard the sounds of heavy footfalls on dry grass. A soldier came in through the tent door, short of breath from sprinting, holding an oversize walkie-talkie. "Colonel, message from—"

Weber grabbed the walkie-talkie from him.

I remember what it'll be like watching you when you are a day old. Your father will have gone for a quick visit to the hospital cafeteria, and you'll be lying in your bassinet, and I'll be leaning over you.

So soon after the delivery, I will still be feeling like a wrung-out towel. You will seem incongruously tiny, given how enormous I felt during the pregnancy; I could swear there was room for someone much larger and more robust than you in there. Your hands and feet will be long and thin, not chubby yet. Your face will still be all red and pinched, puffy eyelids squeezed shut, the gnomelike phase that precedes the cherubic.

I'll run a finger over your belly, marveling at the uncanny softness of your skin, wondering if silk would abrade your body like burlap. Then you'll writhe, twisting your body while poking out your legs one at a time, and I'll recognize the gesture as one I had felt you do inside me, many times. So *that's* what it looks like.

I'll feel elated at this evidence of a unique mother-child bond, this certitude that you're the one I carried. Even if I had never laid eyes on you before, I'd be able to pick you out from a sea of babies: Not that one. No, not her either. Wait, that one over there.

Yes, that's her. She's mine.

That final "gift exchange" was the last we ever saw of the heptapods. All at once, all over the world, their looking glasses became transparent and their ships left orbit. Subsequent analysis of the looking glasses revealed them to be nothing more than sheets of fused silica, completely inert. The information from the final exchange session described a new class of superconducting materials, but it later proved to duplicate the results of research just completed in Japan: nothing that humans didn't already know.

We never did learn why the heptapods left, any more than we learned what brought them here, or why they acted the way they did. My own new awareness didn't provide that type of knowledge; the heptapods' behavior was presumably explicable from a sequential point of view, but we never found that explanation.

I would have liked to experience more of the heptapods' worldview, to feel the way they feel. Then, perhaps I could immerse myself fully in the necessity of events, as they must, instead of merely wading in its surf for the rest of my life. But that will never come to pass. I will continue to practice the heptapod languages, as will the other linguists on the looking-glass teams, but none of us will ever progress any further than we did when the heptapods were here.

Working with the heptapods changed my life. I met your father and learned Heptapod B, both of which make it possible for me to know you now, here on the patio in the moonlight. Eventually, many years from now, I'll be without your father, and without you. All I will have left from this moment is the heptapod language. So I pay close attention, and note every detail.

From the beginning I knew my destination, and I chose my route accordingly. But am I working toward an extreme of joy, or of pain? Will I achieve a minimum, or a maximum?

These questions are in my mind when your father asks me, "Do you want to make a baby?" And I smile and answer, "Yes," and I unwrap his arms from around me, and we hold hands as we walk inside to make love, to make you.

Craphound

CORY DOCTOROW

Cory Doctorow (1971–) is an award-winning and bestselling Canadian science fiction writer, critic, and public speaker born in Toronto who serves as coeditor of the website Boing Boing. In the 1990s he founded the free software corporation Opencola. Later, he relocated to London and worked as the European affairs coordinator for the Electronic Frontier Foundation, helping to establish the Open Rights Group, before becoming a full-time writer in 2006. Doctorow was named the 2006–2007 Canadian Fulbright chair for public diplomacy; the position included a one-year residency at the University of Southern California, Los Angeles.

In the context of science fiction, Doctorow attended the 1992 Clarion writers' workshop and won the John W. Campbell Award for Best New Writer in 2000. He has won multiple other awards, including the Locus Award in 2004 for his first novel, *Down and Out in the Magic Kingdom* (2003); the Sunburst Award (2004); and two Prometheus Awards (2009 and 2014). He has been nominated for the Hugo and Nebula Awards, and his career has at times been intertwined with that of Charles Stross, with whom he has collaborated on fiction.

Doctorow as writer and activist is highly aware of the transformations the human race is facing. Much of his work consists of nonfiction advocacy, as collected in *Content: Selected Essays on Technology, Creativity, Copyright, and the Future of the Future* (2008) and *Information Doesn't Want to Be Free* (2014). He has complex views on the relationship of the information-dense world we now inhabit and the free flow of information within this network, where (he feels) we now essentially live and work. His most influential novel is *Little Brother* (2008), which was nominated for the Hugo, Nebula, and Locus Awards. It won the John W. Campbell Memorial Award and the Ontario Library Association White Pine Award, as well as the Indienet Award for bestselling young adult novel in independent bookstores. The novel is also the most consciously near-future of his science fiction work. Prior to *Little Brother*, much of Doctorow's science fiction was fairly far-future in its approach. A sequel to *Little Brother*, *Homeland*, was published in 2013.

Doctorow first came to wide attention in the science fiction community for his story "Craphound," reprinted here, in which aliens turn out to conceive of the marks and detritus of our human passage over the planet as collectible. It is a fascinating exploration of the modern "culture of things" and also deeply funny and wise.

CRAPHOUND

Cory Doctorow

Craphound had wicked yard-sale karma, for a rotten, filthy alien bastard. He was too good at panning out the single grain of gold in a raging river of uselessness for me not to like him—respect him, anyway. But then he found the cowboy trunk. It was two months' rent to me and nothing but some squirrelly alien kitsch-fetish to Craphound.

So I did the unthinkable. I violated the Code. I got into a bidding war with a buddy. Never let them tell you that women poison friendships: in my experience, wounds from women-fights heal quickly; fights over garbage leave nothing behind but scorched earth.

Craphound spotted the sign—his karma, plus the goggles in his exoskeleton, gave him the advantage when we were doing eighty kilometers per hour on some stretch of back-highway in cottage country. He was riding shotgun while I drove, and we had the radio on to the CBC's summer-Saturday programming—eight weekends with eight hours of old radio dramas: *The Shadow*; *Quiet, Please*; *Tom Mix*; *The Crypt-Keeper* with Bela Lugosi. It was hour three, and Bogey was phoning in his performance on a radio adaptation of *The African Queen*. I had the windows of the old truck rolled down so that I could smoke without fouling Craphound's breather. My arm was hanging out the window, the radio was booming, and Craphound said, "Turn around! Turn around, now, Jerry, now, turn around!"

When Craphound gets that excited, it's a sign that he's spotted a rich vein. I checked the side-mirror quickly, pounded the brakes, and spun around. The transmission creaked, the wheels squealed, and then we were creeping along the way we'd come.

"There," Craphound said, gesturing with his long, skinny arm. I saw it. A wooden A-frame real-estate sign, a piece of hand-lettered cardboard stuck overtop of the Realtor's name:

EAST MUSKOKA VOLUNTEER FIRE DEPT

LADIES AUXILIARY RUMMAGE SALE

SAT 25 JUNE

"Hoo-eee!" I hollered, and spun the truck onto the dirt road. I gunned the engine as we cruised along the tree-lined road, trusting Craphound to spot any deer, signs, or hikers in time to avert disaster. The sky was a perfect blue and the smells of summer were all around us. I snapped off the radio and listened to the wind rushing through the truck. Ontario is *beautiful* in the summer.

"There!" Craphound shouted. I hit the turn-off and downshifted and then we were back on a paved road. Soon, we were rolling into a country fire station, an ugly brick barn. The hall was lined with long, folding tables, stacked high. The mother lode!

Craphound beat me out the door, as usual. His exoskeleton is programmable, so he can record little scripts for it like: move left arm to door handle, pop it, swing legs out to running board, jump to ground, close door, move forward. Meanwhile, I'm still making sure I've switched off the headlights and that I've got my wallet.

Two blue-haired grannies had a card-table set up out front of the hall, with a big tin pitcher of lemonade and three boxes of Tim Horton assorted donuts. That stopped us both, since we share the superstition that you *always* buy food from old ladies and little kids, as a sacrifice to the crap-gods. One of the old ladies poured out the lemonade while the other smiled and greeted us.

"Welcome, welcome! My, you've come a long way for us!"

"Just up from Toronto, ma'am," I said. It's an old joke, but it's also part of the ritual, and it's got to be done.

"I meant your friend, sir. This gentleman."

Craphound smiled without baring his gums and sipped his lemonade. "Of course I came, dear lady. I wouldn't miss it for the worlds!" His accent is pretty good, but when it comes to stock phrases like this, he's got so much polish you'd think he was reading the news.

The biddie *blushed* and *giggled*, and I felt faintly sick. I walked off to the tables, trying not to hurry. I chose my first spot, about halfway down, where things wouldn't be quite so picked-over. I grabbed an empty box from underneath and started putting stuff into it: four matched highball glasses with gold crossed bowling pins and a line of black around the rim; an Expo '67 wall-hanging that wasn't even a little faded; a shoe box full of late sixties O-Pee-Chee hockey cards; a worn, wooden-handled steel cleaver that you could butcher a steer with.

I picked up my box and moved on: a deck of playing cards copyrighted '57, with the logo for the Royal Canadian Dairy, Bala, Ontario, printed on the backs; a fireman's cap with a brass badge so tarnished I couldn't read it; a three-story wedding-cake trophy for the 1974 Eastern Region Curling Championships. The cash register in my mind was ringing, ringing, ringing. God bless the East Muskoka Volunteer Fire Department Ladies' Auxiliary.

I'd mined that table long enough. I moved to the other end of the hall. Time was, I'd start at the beginning and turn over each item, build one pile of maybes and another pile of definites, try to strategise. In time, I came to rely on instinct and on the fates, to whom I make my obeisances at every opportunity.

Let's hear it for the fates: a genuine col-

lapsible top hat; a white-tipped evening cane; a hand-carved cherry-wood walking stick; a beautiful black lace parasol; a wrought-iron lightning rod with a rooster on top; all of it in an elephant-leg umbrella stand. I filled the box, folded it over, and started on another.

I collided with Craphound. He grinned his natural grin, the one that showed row on row of wet, slimy gums, tipped with writhing, poisonous suckers. "Gold! Gold!" he said, and moved along. I turned my head after him, just as he bent over the cowboy trunk.

I sucked air between my teeth. It was magnificent: a leather-bound miniature steamer trunk, the leather worked with lariats, Stetson hats, war bonnets, and six-guns. I moved toward him, and he popped the latch. I caught my breath.

On top, there was a kid's cowboy costume: miniature leather chaps, a tiny Stetson, a pair of scuffed white-leather cowboy boots with long, worn spurs affixed to the heels. Craphound moved it reverently to the table and continued to pull more magic from the trunk's depths: a stack of cardboard-bound Hopalong Cassidy 78s; a pair of tin six-guns with gun belt and holsters; a silver star that said "Sheriff"; a bundle of Roy Rogers comics tied with twine, in mint condition; and a leather satchel filled with plastic cowboys and Indians, enough to reenact the Alamo.

"Oh, my God," I breathed, as he spread the loot out on the table.

"What are these, Jerry?" Craphound asked, holding up the 78s.

"Old records, like LPs, but you need a special record player to listen to them." I took one out of its sleeve. It gleamed, scratch-free, in the overhead fluorescents.

"I got a seventy-eight player here," said a member of the East Muskoka Volunteer Fire Department Ladies' Auxiliary. She was short enough to look Craphound in the eye, a hair under five feet, and had a skinny, rawboned look to her. "That's my Billy's things, Billy the Kid we called him. He was dotty for cowboys when he was a boy. Couldn't get him to take off that fool outfit—nearly got him thrown out of school. He's a lawyer now, in Toronto, got a fancy office on Bay Street. I called him to ask if he minded my putting his cowboy things in the sale, and you know what? He didn't know what I was talking about! Doesn't that beat everything? He was dotty for cowboys when he was a boy."

It's another of my rituals to smile and nod and be as polite as possible to the erstwhile owners of crap that I'm trying to buy, so I smiled and nodded and examined the 78 player she had produced. In lariat script, on the top, it said, "Official Bob Wills Little Record Player," and had a crude watercolour of Bob Wills and His Texas Playboys grinning on the front. It was the kind of record player that folded up like a suitcase when you weren't using it. I'd had one as a kid, with Yogi Bear silkscreened on the front.

Billy's mom plugged the yellowed cord into a wall jack and took the 78 from me, touched the stylus to the record. A tinny ukelele played, accompanied by horse-clops, and then a narrator with a deep, whisky voice said, "Howdy, pardners! I was just settin' down by the ole campfire. Why don't you stay an' have some beans, an' I'll tell y'all the story of how Hopalong Cassidy beat the Duke Gang when they come to rob the Santa Fe."

In my head, I was already breaking down the cowboy trunk and its contents, thinking about the minimum bid I'd place on each item at Sotheby's. Sold individually, I figured I could get over two grand for the contents. Then I thought about putting ads in some of the Japanese collectors' magazines, just for a lark, before I sent the lot to the auction house. You never can tell. A buddy I knew had sold a complete packaged set of *Welcome Back, Kotter* action figures for nearly eight grand that way. Maybe I could buy a new truck. . . .

"This is wonderful," Craphound said, interrupting my reverie. "How much would you like for the collection?"

I felt a knife in my guts. Craphound had found the cowboy trunk, so that meant it was his. But he usually let me take the stuff with street value—he was interested in *everything*, so it hardly mattered if I picked up a few scraps with which to eke out a living.

Billy's mom looked over the stuff. "I was hoping to get twenty dollars for the lot, but if that's too much, I'm willing to come down."

"I'll give you thirty," my mouth said, without intervention from my brain.

They both turned and stared at me. Craphound was unreadable behind his goggles.

Billy's mom broke the silence. "Oh, my! Thirty dollars for this old mess?"

"I will pay fifty," Craphound said.

"Seventy-five," I said.

"Oh, my," Billy's mom said.

"Five hundred," Craphound said.

I opened my mouth, and shut it. Craphound had built his stake on Earth by selling a complicated biochemical process for non-chlorophyll photosynthesis to a Saudi banker. I wouldn't ever beat him in a bidding war. "A thousand dollars," my mouth said.

"Ten thousand," Craphound said, and extruded a roll of hundreds from somewhere in his exoskeleton.

"My Lord!" Billy's mom said. "Ten thousand dollars!"

The other pickers, the firemen, the bluehaired ladies all looked up at that and stared at us, their mouths open.

"It is for a good cause," Craphound said.

"Ten thousand dollars!" Billy's mom said again.

Craphound's digits ruffled through the roll as fast as a croupier's counter, separated off a large chunk of the brown bills, and handed them to Billy's mom.

One of the firemen, a middle-aged paunchy man with a comb-over, appeared at Billy's mom's shoulder.

"What's going on, Eva?" he said.

"This . . . gentleman is going to pay ten thousand dollars for Billy's old cowboy things, Tom."

The fireman took the money from Billy's mom and stared at it. He held up the top note under the light and turned it this way and that, watching the holographic stamp change from green to gold, then green again. He looked at the serial number, then the serial number of the next bill. He licked his forefinger and started counting off the bills in piles of ten. Once he had ten piles, he counted them again. "That's ten thousand dollars, all right. Thank you very much, mister. Can I give you a hand getting this to your car?"

Craphound, meanwhile, had repacked the trunk and balanced the 78 player on top of it. He looked at me, then at the fireman.

"I wonder if I could impose on you to take me to the nearest bus station. I think I'm going to be making my own way home."

The fireman and Billy's mom both stared at me. My cheeks flushed. "Aw, c'mon," I said. "I'll drive you home."

"I think I prefer the bus," Craphound said.

"It's no trouble at all to give you a lift, friend," the fireman said.

I called it quits for the day, and drove home alone with the truck only half-filled. I pulled it into the coach house and threw a tarp over the load and went inside and cracked a beer and sat on the sofa, watching a nature show on a desert reclamation project in Arizona, where the state legislature had traded a derelict megamall and a custom-built habitat to an alien for a local-area weather control machine.

The following Thursday, I went to the little crap-auction house on King Street. I'd put my finds from the weekend in the sale: lower minimum bid, and they took a smaller commission than Sotheby's. Fine for moving the small stuff.

Craphound was there, of course. I knew he'd be. It was where we met, when he bid on a case of Lincoln Logs I'd found at a fire sale.

I'd known him for a kindred spirit when he bought them, and we'd talked afterwards, at his place, a sprawling, two-storey warehouse amid a cluster of auto-wrecking yards where the junkyard dogs barked, barked, barked.

Inside was paradise. His taste ran to shrines—a collection of fifties bar kitsch that was a shrine to liquor; a circular waterbed on a raised podium that was nearly buried under seventies bachelor pad–inalia; a kitchen that was nearly unusable, so packed it was with old barn-board furniture and rural memorabilia; a leather-appointed library straight out of a Victorian gentlemen's club; a solarium dressed in wicker and bamboo and tiki idols. It was a hell of a place.

Craphound had known all about the Goodwills and the Sally Anns, and the auction houses, and the kitsch boutiques on Queen Street, but he still hadn't figured out where it all came from.

"Yard sales, rummage sales, garage sales," I said, reclining in a vibrating Naugahyde easy chair, drinking a glass of his pricey singlemalt that he'd bought for the beautiful bottle it came in.

"But where are these? Who is allowed to make them?" Craphound hunched opposite me, his exoskeleton locked into a coiled, semi-seated position.

"Who? Well, anyone. You just one day decide that you need to clean out the basement, you put an ad in the *Star*, tape up a few signs, and voila, yard sale. Sometimes, a school or a church will get donations of old junk and sell it all at one time, as a fund-raiser."

"And how do you locate these?" he asked, bobbing up and down slightly with excitement.

"Well, there're amateurs who just read the ads in the weekend papers, or just pick a neighbourhood and wander around, but that's no way to go about it. What I do is, I get in a truck, and I sniff the air, catch the scent of crap, and *vroom!*, I'm off like a bloodhound on a trail. You learn things over time: like stay away from Yuppie yard sales, they never have anything worth buying, just the same crap you can buy in any mall."

"Do you think I might accompany you someday?"

"Hell, sure. Next Saturday? We'll head over to Cabbagetown—those old coach houses, you'd be amazed what people get rid of. It's practically criminal."

"I would like to go with you on next Saturday very much Mr. Jerry Abington." He used to talk like that, without commas or question marks. Later, he got better, but then, it was all one big sentence.

"Call me Jerry. It's a date, then. Tell you what, though: there's a Code you got to learn before we go out. The Craphound's Code."

"What is a craphound?"

"You're lookin' at one. You're one, too, unless I miss my guess. You'll get to know some of the local craphounds, you hang around with me long enough. They're the competition, but they're also your buddies, and there're certain rules we have."

And then I explained to him all about how you never bid against a craphound at a yard sale, how you get to know the other fellows' tastes, and when you see something they might like, you haul it out for them, and they'll do the same for you, and how you never buy something that another craphound might be looking for, if all you're buying it for is to sell it back to him. Just good form and common sense, really, but you'd be surprised how many amateurs just fail to make the jump to pro because they can't grasp it.

There was a bunch of other stuff at the auction, other craphounds' weekend treasures. This was high season, when the sun comes out and people start to clean out the cottage, the basement, the garage. There were some collectors in the crowd, and a whole whack of antique and junk dealers, and a few pickers, and me, and Craphound. I watched the bidding listlessly, waiting for my things to come up and sneaking out for smokes between lots. Craphound never once looked at me or acknowledged my pres-

ence, and I became perversely obsessed with catching his eye, so I coughed and shifted and walked past him several times, until the auctioneer glared at me, and one of the attendants asked if I needed a throat lozenge.

My lot came up. The bowling glasses went for five bucks to one of the Queen Street junk dealers; the elephant foot fetched $350 after a spirited bidding war between an antique dealer and a collector—the collector won; the dealer took the top hat for $100. The rest of it came up and sold, or didn't, and at end of the lot, I'd made over $800, which was rent for the month plus beer for the weekend plus gas for the truck.

Craphound bid on and bought more cowboy things—a box of Super 8 cowboy movies, the boxes mouldy, the stock itself running to slime; a Navajo blanket; a plastic donkey that dispensed cigarettes out of its ass; a big neon armadillo sign.

One of the other nice things about that place over Sotheby's, there was none of this waiting thirty days to get a cheque. I queued up with the other pickers after the bidding was through, collected a wad of bills, and headed for my truck.

I spotted Craphound loading his haul into a minivan with handicapped plates. It looked like some kind of fungus was growing over the hood and side panels. On closer inspection, I saw that the body had been covered in closely glued Lego.

Craphound popped the hatchback and threw his gear in, then opened the driver's side door, and I saw that his van had been fitted out for a legless driver, with brake and accelerator levers. A paraplegic I knew drove one just like it. Craphound's exoskeleton levered him into the seat, and I watched the eerily precise way it executed the macro that started the car, pulled the shoulder belt, put it into drive, and switched on the stereo. I heard tape-hiss, then, loud as a b-boy cruising Yonge Street, an old-timey cowboy voice: "Howdy, pardners! Saddle up, we're ridin'!" Then the van backed up and sped out of the lot.

I got into the truck and drove home. Truth be told, I missed the little bastard.

Some people said that we should have run Craphound and his kin off the planet, out of the solar system. They said that it wasn't fair for the aliens to keep us in the dark about their technologies. They say that we should have captured a ship and reverse-engineered it, built our own, and kicked ass.

Some people!

First of all, nobody with human DNA could survive a trip in one of those ships. They're part of Craphound's people's bodies, as I understand it, and we just don't have the right parts. Second of all, they *were* sharing their tech with us—they just weren't giving it away. Fair trades every time.

It's not as if space was off-limits to us. We can any one of us visit their homeworld, just as soon as we figure out how. Only they wouldn't hold our hands along the way.

I spent the week haunting the "Secret Boutique," a.k.a. the Goodwill As-Is Centre on Jarvis. It's all there is to do between yard sales, and sometimes it makes for good finds. Part of my theory of yard-sale karma holds that if I miss one day at the thrift shops, that'll be the day they put out the big score. So I hit the stores diligently and came up with crapola. I had offended the fates, I knew, and wouldn't make another score until I placated them. It was lonely work, still and all, and I missed Craphound's good eye and obsessive delight.

I was at the cash register with a few items at the Goodwill when a guy in a suit behind me tapped me on the shoulder.

"Sorry to bother you," he said. His suit looked expensive, as did his manicure and his haircut and his wire-rimmed glasses. "I was just wondering where you found that." He gestured at a rhinestone-studded ukelele, with a cowboy hat wood-burned into the body. I had picked

it up with a guilty little thrill, thinking that Craphound might buy it at the next auction.

"Second floor, in the toy section."

"There wasn't anything else like it, was there?"

"'Fraid not," I said, and the cashier picked it up and started wrapping it in newspaper.

"Ah," he said, and he looked like a little kid who'd just been told that he couldn't have a puppy. "I don't suppose you'd want to sell it, would you?"

I held up a hand and waited while the cashier bagged it with the rest of my stuff, a few old clothbound novels I thought I could sell at a used-book store, and a *Grease* belt buckle with Olivia Newton-John on it. I led him out the door by the elbow of his expensive suit.

"How much?" I had paid a dollar.

"Ten bucks?"

I nearly said, "Sold!" but I caught myself. "Twenty."

"Twenty dollars?"

"That's what they'd charge at a boutique on Queen Street."

He took out a slim leather wallet and produced a twenty. I handed him the uke. His face lit up like a lightbulb.

It's not that my adulthood is particularly unhappy. Likewise, it's not that my childhood was particularly happy.

There are memories I have, though, that are like a cool drink of water. My grandfather's place near Milton, an old Victorian farmhouse, where the cat drank out of a milk-glass bowl; and where we sat around a rough pine table as big as my whole apartment; and where my playroom was the draughty barn with hay-filled lofts bulging with farm junk and Tarzan ropes.

There was Grampa's friend Fyodor, and we spent every evening at his wrecking yard, he and Grampa talking and smoking while I scampered in the twilight, scaling mountains of auto junk. The glove boxes yielded treasures: crumpled photos of college boys mugging in front of signs, road maps of faraway places. I found a guidebook from the 1964 New York World's Fair once, and a lipstick like a chrome bullet, and a pair of white leather ladies' gloves.

Fyodor dealt in scrap, too, and once, he had half of a carny carousel, a few horses and part of the canopy, paint flaking and sharp torn edges protruding; next to it, a Korean War tank minus its turret and treads, and inside the tank were peeling old pinup girls and a rotation schedule and a crude Kilroy. The control room in the middle of the carousel had a stack of paperback sci-fi novels, Ace Doubles that had two books bound back-to-back, and when you finished the first, you turned it over and read the other. Fyodor let me keep them, and there was a pawn ticket in one from Macon, Georgia, for a transistor radio.

My parents started leaving me alone when I was fourteen and I couldn't keep from sneaking into their room and snooping. Mom's jewelry box had books of matches from their honeymoon in Acapulco, printed with bad palm trees. My dad kept an old photo in his sock drawer, of himself on Muscle Beach, shirtless, flexing his biceps.

My grandmother saved every scrap of my mother's life in her basement, in dusty army trunks. I entertained myself by pulling it out and taking it in: her mouse ears from the big family train trip to Disneyland in '57, and her records, and the glittery pasteboard sign from her sweet sixteen. There were well-chewed stuffed animals, and school exercise books in which she'd practiced variations on her signature for page after page.

It all told a story. The penciled Kilroy in the tank made me see one of those Canadian soldiers in Korea, unshaven and crew-cut like an extra on *M*A*S*H*, sitting for bored hour after hour, staring at the pinup girls, fiddling with a crossword, finally laying it down and sketching his Kilroy quickly, before anyone saw.

The photo of my dad posing sent me whirling through time to Toronto's Muscle Beach in the east end, and hearing the tinny AM radios

playing weird psychedelic rock while teenagers lounged on their Mustangs and the girls sunbathed in bikinis that made their tits into torpedoes.

It all made poems. The old pulp novels and the pawn ticket, when I spread them out in front of the TV, and arranged them just so, they made up a poem that took my breath away.

After the cowboy trunk episode, I didn't run into Craphound again until the annual Rotary Club charity rummage sale at the Upper Canada Brewing Company. He was wearing the cowboy hat, six-guns, and silver star from the cowboy trunk. It should have looked ridiculous, but the net effect was naive and somehow charming, like he was a little boy whose hair you wanted to muss.

I found a box of nice old melamine dishes, in various shades of green—four square plates, bowls, salad plates, and a serving tray. I threw them in the duffel bag I'd brought and kept browsing, ignoring Craphound as he charmed a salty old Rotarian while fondling a box of leather-bound books.

I browsed a stack of old Ministry of Labour licenses—barber, chiropodist, bartender, watchmaker. They all had pretty seals and were framed in stark green institutional metal. They all had different names, but all from one family, and I made up a little story to entertain myself, about the proud mother saving her sons' accreditations and framing and hanging them in the spare room with their diplomas. "Oh, George Junior's just opened his own barbershop, and little Jimmy's still fixing watches. . . ."

I bought them.

In a box of crappy plastic Little Ponies and Barbies and Care Bears, I found a leather Indian headdress, a wooden bow-and-arrow set, and a fringed buckskin vest. Craphound was still buttering up the leather books' owner. I bought them quick, for five bucks.

"Those are beautiful," a voice said at my elbow. I turned around and smiled at the snappy dresser who'd bought the uke at the Secret Bou-tique. He'd gone casual for the weekend, in an expensive, L.L. Bean button-down way.

"Aren't they, though."

"You sell them on Queen Street? Your finds, I mean?"

"Sometimes. Sometimes at auction. How's the uke?"

"Oh, I got it all tuned up," he said, and smiled the same smile he'd given me when he'd taken hold of it at Goodwill. "I can play 'Don't Fence Me In' on it." He looked at his feet. "Silly, huh?"

"Not at all. You're into cowboy things, huh?" As I said it, I was overcome with the knowledge that this was "Billy the Kid," the original owner of the cowboy trunk. I don't know why I felt that way, but I did, with utter certainty.

"Just trying to relive a piece of my child-hood, I guess. I'm Scott," he said, extending his hand.

Scott? I thought wildly. *Maybe it's his mid-dle name?* "I'm Jerry."

The Upper Canada Brewing Company sale has many things going for it, including a beer garden where you can sample their wares and get a good barbecue burger. We gently gravi-tated to it, looking over the tables as we went.

"You're a pro, right?" he asked after we had plastic cups of beer.

"You could say that."

"I'm an amateur. A rank amateur. Any words of wisdom?"

I laughed and drank some beer, lit a ciga-rette. "There's no secret to it, I think. Just dili-gence: you've got to go out every chance you get, or you'll miss the big score."

He chuckled. "I hear that. Sometimes, I'll be sitting in my office, and I'll just *know* that they're putting out a piece of pure gold at the Goodwill and that someone else will get to it before my lunch. I get so wound up, I'm no good until I go down there and hunt for it. I guess I'm hooked, eh?"

"Cheaper than some other kinds of addic-tions."

"I guess so. About that Indian stuff—what do you figure you'd get for it at a Queen Street boutique?"

I looked him in the eye. He may have been something high-powered and cool and collected in his natural environment, but just then, he was as eager and nervous as a kitchen-table poker player at a high-stakes game.

"Maybe fifty bucks," I said.

"Fifty, huh?" he asked.

"About that," I said.

"Once it sold," he said.

"There is that," I said.

"Might take a month, might take a year," he said.

"Might take a day," I said.

"It might, it might." He finished his beer. "I don't suppose you'd take forty?"

I'd paid five for it, not ten minutes before. It looked like it would fit Craphound, who, after all, was wearing Scott/Billy's own boy-hood treasures as we spoke. You don't make a living by feeling guilty over 800 percent mark-ups. Still, I'd angered the fates, and needed to redeem myself.

"Make it five," I said.

He started to say something, then closed his mouth and gave me a look of thanks. He took a five out of his wallet and handed it to me. I pulled the vest and bow and headdress out of my duffel.

He walked back to a shiny black Jeep with gold detail work, parked next to Craphound's van. Craphound was building onto the Lego body, and the hood had a miniature Lego town attached to it.

Craphound looked around as he passed, and leaned forward, peering with undisguised interest at the booty. I grimaced and finished my beer.

I met Scott/Billy three times more at the Secret Boutique that week.

He was a lawyer, who specialised in alien-technology patents. He had a practice on Bay

Street, with two partners, and despite his youth, he was the senior man.

I didn't let on that I knew about Billy the Kid and his mother in the East Muskoka Volunteer Fire Department Ladies' Auxiliary. But I felt a bond with him, as though we shared an unspoken secret. I pulled any cowboy finds for him, and he developed a pretty good eye for what I was after and returned the favour.

The fates were with me again, and no two ways about it. I took home a ratty old Oriental rug that on closer inspection was a nineteenth-century hand-knotted Persian; an upholstered Turkish footstool; a collection of hand-painted silk Hawaiiana pillows and a carved meerschaum pipe. Scott/Billy found the last for me, and it cost me two dollars. I knew a collector who would pay thirty in an eye-blink, and from then on, as far as I was concerned, Scott/Billy was a fellow craphound.

"You going to the auction tomorrow night?" I asked him at the checkout line.

"Wouldn't miss it," he said. He'd barely been able to contain his excitement when I told him about the Thursday night auctions and the bargains to be had there. He sure had the bug.

"Want to get together for dinner beforehand? The Rotterdam's got a good patio."

He did, and we did, and I had a glass of framboise that packed a hell of a kick and tasted like fizzy raspberry lemonade, and doorstopper fries and a club sandwich.

I had my nose in my glass when he kicked my ankle under the table. "Look at that!"

It was Craphound in his van, cruising for a parking spot. The Lego village had been joined by a whole postmodern spaceport on the roof, with a red-and-blue castle, a football-sized flying saucer, and a clown's head with blinking eyes.

I went back to my drink and tried to get my appetite back.

"Was that an extee driving?"

"Yeah. Used to be a friend of mine."

"He's a picker?"

"Uh-huh." I turned back to my fries and tried to kill the subject.

"Do you know how he made his stake?"

"The chlorophyll thing, in Saudi Arabia."

"Sweet!" he said. "Very sweet. I've got a client who's got some secondary patents from that one. What's he go after?"

"Oh, pretty much everything," I said, resigning myself to discussing the topic after all. "But lately, the same as you—cowboys and Injuns."

He laughed and smacked his knee. "Well, what do you know? What could he possibly want with the stuff?"

"What do they want with any of it? He got started one day when we were cruising the Muskokas," I said carefully, watching his face. "Found a trunk of old cowboy things at a rummage sale. East Muskoka Volunteer Fire Department Ladies' Auxiliary." I waited for him to shout or startle. He didn't.

"Yeah? A good find, I guess. Wish I'd made it."

I didn't know what to say to that, so I took a bite of my sandwich.

Scott continued. "I think about what they get out of it a lot. There's nothing we have here that they couldn't make for themselves. I mean, if they picked up and left today, we'd still be making sense of everything they gave us in a hundred years. You know, I just closed a deal for a biochemical computer that's no-shit ten thousand times faster than anything we've built out of silicon. You know what the extee took in trade? Title to a defunct fairground outside of Calgary—they shut it down ten years ago because the midway was too unsafe to ride. Doesn't that beat all? This thing is worth a billion dollars right out of the gate, I mean, within twenty-four hours of the deal closing, the seller can turn it into the GDP of Bolivia. For a crummy real-estate dog that you couldn't get five grand for!"

It always shocked me when Billy/Scott talked about his job—it was easy to forget that he was a high-powered lawyer when we were jawing and fooling around like old craphounds. I wondered if maybe he *wasn't* Billy the Kid; I couldn't think of any reason for him to be playing it all so close to his chest.

"What the hell is some extee going to do with a fairground?"

Craphound got a free Coke from Lisa at the check-in when he made his appearance. He bid high, but shrewdly, and never pulled ten-thousand-dollar stunts. The bidders were wandering the floor, previewing that week's stock, and making notes to themselves.

I rooted through a box-lot full of old tins, and found one with a buckaroo at the Calgary Stampede, riding a bucking bronc. I picked it up and stood to inspect it. Craphound was behind me.

"Nice piece, huh?" I said to him.

"I like it very much," Craphound said, and I felt my cheeks flush.

"You're going to have some competition tonight, I think," I said, and nodded at Scott/Billy. "I think he's Billy; the one whose mother sold us—you—the cowboy trunk."

"Really?" Craphound said, and it felt like we were partners again, scoping out the competition. Suddenly I felt a knife of shame, like I was betraying Scott/Billy somehow. I took a step back.

"Jerry, I am very sorry that we argued."

I sighed out a breath I hadn't known I was holding in. "Me, too."

"They're starting the bidding. May I sit with you?"

And so the three of us sat together, and Craphound shook Scott/Billy's hand and the auctioneer started into his harangue.

It was a night for unusual occurrences. I bid on a piece, something I told myself I'd never do. It was a set of four matched Li'l Orphan Annie Ovaltine glasses, like Grandma's had been, and seeing them in the auctioneer's hand took me right back to her kitchen, and endless afternoons passed with my colouring books and weird old-lady hard candies and Liberace albums playing in the living room.

"Ten," I said, opening the bidding.

"I got ten, ten, ten, I got ten, who'll say twenty, who'll say twenty, twenty for the four."

Craphound waved his bidding card, and I jumped as if I'd been stung.

"I got twenty from the space cowboy, I got twenty, sir will you say thirty?"

I waved my card.

"That's thirty to you sir."

"Forty," Craphound said.

"Fifty," I said even before the auctioneer could point back to me. An old pro, he settled back and let us do the work.

"One hundred," Craphound said.

"One fifty," I said.

The room was perfectly silent. I thought about my overextended MasterCard, and wondered if Scott/Billy would give me a loan.

"Two hundred," Craphound said.

Fine, I thought. Pay two hundred for those. I can get a set on Queen Street for thirty bucks.

The auctioneer turned to me. "The bidding stands at two. Will you say two ten, sir?"

I shook my head. The auctioneer paused a long moment, letting me sweat over the decision to bow out.

"I have two—do I have any other bids from the floor? Any other bids? Sold, two hundred dollars, to number fifty-seven." An attendant brought Craphound the glasses. He took them and tucked them under his seat.

I was fuming when we left. Craphound was at my elbow. I wanted to punch him—I'd never punched anyone in my life, but I wanted to punch him.

We entered the cool night air and I sucked in several lungfuls before lighting a cigarette.

"Jerry," Craphound said.

I stopped, but didn't look at him. I watched the taxis pull in and out of the garage next door instead.

"Jerry, my friend," Craphound said.

"*What?*" I said, loud enough to startle myself. Scott, beside me, jerked as well.

"We're going. I wanted to say good-bye, and to give you some things that I won't be taking with me."

"What?" I said again, Scott just a beat behind me.

"My people—we're going. It has been decided. We've gotten what we came for."

Without another word, he set off towards his van. We followed along behind, shell-shocked.

Craphound's exoskeleton executed another macro and slid the panel door aside, revealing the cowboy trunk.

"I wanted to give you this. I will keep the glasses."

"I don't understand," I said.

"You're all leaving?" Scott asked, with a note of urgency.

"It has been decided. We'll go over the next twenty-four hours."

"But *why?*" Scott said, sounding almost petulant.

"It's not something that I can easily explain. As you must know, the things we gave you were trinkets to us—almost worthless. We traded them for something that was almost worthless to you—a fair trade, you'll agree—but it's time to move on."

Craphound handed me the cowboy trunk. Holding it, I smelled the lubricant from his exoskeleton and the smell of the attic it had been mummified in before making its way into his hands. I felt like I almost understood.

"This is for me," I said slowly, and Crap-hound nodded encouragingly. "This is for me, and you're keeping the glasses. And I'll look at this and feel . . ."

"You understand," Craphound said, looking somehow relieved.

And I *did*. I understood that an alien wearing a cowboy hat and six-guns and giving them away was a poem and a story, and a thirtyish bachelor trying to spend half a month's rent on four glasses so that he could remember his grandma's kitchen was a story and a poem, and that the disused fairground outside Calgary was a story and a poem, too.

"You're craphounds!" I said. "All of you!"

Craphound smiled so I could see his gums and I put down the cowboy trunk and clapped my hands.

Scott recovered from his shock by spending the night at his office, crunching numbers, talking on the phone, and generally getting while the getting was good. He had an edge—no one else knew that they were going.

He went pro later that week, opened a chi-chi boutique on Queen Street, and hired me on as chief picker and factum factotum.

Scott was not Billy the Kid. Just another Bay Street shyster with a cowboy jones. From the way they come down and spend, there must be a million of them.

Our draw in the window is a beautiful mannequin I found, straight out of the fifties, a little boy we call the Beaver. He dresses in chaps and a sheriff's badge and six-guns and a miniature Stetson and cowboy boots with worn spurs, and rests one foot on a beautiful miniature steamer trunk whose leather is worked with cowboy motifs.

He's not for sale at any price.

The Slynx

TATYANA TOLSTAYA

Translated by Jamey Gambrell

Tatyana Tolstaya (1951–) is a Russian writer and essayist born in Leningrad to a family of writers, including Leo and Alexei Tolstoy. Alexei's wife, Natalia Krandievskaya, was an important poet, and Tatyana's maternal grandfather, Mikhail Lozinsky, was a literary translator. Tatyana received a degree in classics at Leningrad State University and went to work for a Moscow publishing house shortly after that. Her first short story, "On a Golden Porch," was published in *Avrora* magazine in 1983, which launched her literary career. Her first story collection established her as one of the foremost writers of the Gorbachev era.

Tolstaya spent much of the 1980s and 1990s living in the United States, teaching at various universities. Her work has been well received in the US, and the critically acclaimed Austin indie rock band Okkervil River took their name from one of her short stories. Her writing is varied, ranging from nonfiction to the dystopian science fiction novel excerpted here, *The Slynx* (2000 in Russia; New York Review of Books Classics English-language edition 2007). Known for her acerbic essays on contemporary Russian life, Tolstaya has also been the cohost of the Russian cultural interview television program *School for Scandal*.

The Slynx is a riotous joy of a novel, spinning a tale of a postapocalyptic future Russia that is rife with satirical jabs at local absurdities of geopolitics and elements of folklore. Its deft storytelling and rampant imagination set it apart from many postapocalyptic novels and place it firmly in the tradition of Russian literature established by Gogol, Bulgakov, and Bely. In some sense, too, *The Slynx* seems a natural successor to the dystopic situation set out in Yefim Zozulya's "The Doom of Principal City" (1918), also reprinted in this volume.

In *The Slynx*, civilization ended two hundred years ago in an event known as the Blast. The character Benedikt makes the best of a bad situation as he survives by transcribing old books and presenting them as the words of the great new leader Fyodor Kuzmich, Glorybe. By the terms of Tolstaya's chaotic future, Benedikt is even thriving—for example, he is mutation-free, with no extra fingers, gills, or cockscombs sprouting from his eyelids like some people. Nor is he a half-human Degenerator, harnessed to a troika. Part weird, original post-Collapse novel and part a testimony to the power of words, *The Slynx* follows Benedikt on a quest to maintain and preserve the culture of Russia against dangers both internal and external. The first chapter, included here, exemplifies the manic energy and originality of the novel while also being a more or less self-contained story.

THE SLYNX

Tatyana Tolstaya

Translated by Jamey Gambrell

Benedikt pulled on his felt boots, stomped his feet to get the fit right, checked the damper on the stove, brushed the bread crumbs onto the floor—for the mice—wedged a rag in the window to keep out the cold, stepped out the door, and breathed the pure, frosty air in through his nostrils. Ah, what a day! The night's storm had passed, the snow gleamed all white and fancy, the sky was turning blue, and the high elfir trees stood still. Black rabbits flitted from treetop to treetop. Benedikt stood squinting, his reddish beard tilted upward, watching the rabbits. If only he could down a couple—for a new cap. But he didn't have a stone.

It would be nice to have the meat, too. Mice, mice, and more mice—he was fed up with them.

Give black rabbit meat a good soaking, bring it to boil seven times, set it in the sun for a week or two, then steam it in the oven—and it won't kill you.

That is, if you catch a female. Because the male, boiled or not, it doesn't matter. People didn't used to know this, they were hungry and ate the males too. But now they know: if you eat the males you'll be stuck with a wheezing and a gurgling in your chest the rest of your life. Your legs will wither. Thick black hairs will grow like crazy out of your ears and you'll stink to high heaven.

Benedikt sighed: time for work. He wrapped his coat around him, set a wood beam across the door of the izba, and even shoved a stick behind it. There wasn't anything to steal, but he was used to doing things that way. Mother, may she rest in peace, always did it that way. In the Oldener Days, before the Blast, she told him, everyone locked their doors. The neigh-bors learned this from Mother and it caught on. Now the whole settlement locked their doors with sticks. It might be Freethinking.

His hometown, Fyodor-Kuzmichsk, spread out over seven hills. Benedikt walked along listening to the squeak of fresh snow, enjoying the February sun, admiring the familiar streets. Here and there black izbas stood in rows behind high pike fences and wood gates; stone pots or wood jugs were set to dry on the pikes. The taller terems had bigger jugs, and some people would even stick a whole barrel up there on the spike, right in your face as if to say: Look how rich I am, Golubchiks! People like that don't trudge to work on their own two feet, they ride on sleighs, flashing their whips, and they've got a Degenerator hitched up. The poor thing runs, all pale, in a lather, its tongue hanging out, its felt boots thudding. It races to the Work Izba and stops stock-still on all four legs, but its fuzzy sides keep going *huffa, puffa, huffa, puffa.*

And it rolls its eyes, rolls 'em up and down and sideways. And bares its teeth. And looks around . . .

To hell with them, those Degenerators, better to keep your distance. They're strange ones, and you can't figure out if they're people or not. Their faces look human, but their bodies are all furry and they run on all fours. With a felt boot on each leg. It's said they lived before the Blast, Degenerators. Could be.

It's nippy out now, steam comes out of his mouth, and his beard's frozen up. Still—what bliss! The izbas are sturdy and black, there are high white snowdrifts leaning against the fences, and a little path has been beaten to each gate. The hills run smooth all the way up and back down, white, wavy; sleighs slide along the snowy slopes, and beyond the sleighs are blue shadows, and the snow crunches in colors, and beyond the hills the sun rises, splashing rainbows on the dark blue sky. When you squint, the rays of the sun turn into circles; when you stomp your boots in the fluffy snow it sparks, like when ripe firelings flicker.

Benedikt thought a moment about firelings, remembered his mother, and sighed: she passed away on account of those firelings, poor thing. They turned out to be fake.

The town of Fyodor-Kuzmichsk spreads out over seven hills. Around the town are boundless fields, unknown lands. To the north are deep forests, full of storm-felled trees, the limbs so twisted you can't get through, prickly bushes catch at your britches, branches pull your cap off your head. Old people say the Slynx lives in those forests. The Slynx sits on dark branches and howls a wild, sad howl—*eeeeennxx, eeeeen-nxx, eeenx-a-leeeeeennnxx!*—but no one ever sees it. If you wander into the forest it jumps on your neck from behind: *hop!* It grabs your spine in its teeth—*crunch*—and picks out the big vein with its claw and breaks it. All the reason runs right out of you. If you come back, you're never the same again, your eyes are different, and you don't ever know where you're headed, like when people walk in their sleep under the moon, their arms outstretched, their fingers fluttering: they're asleep, but they're standing on their own two feet. People will find you and take you inside, and sometimes, for fun, they'll set an empty plate in front of you, stick a spoon in your hand, and say "Eat." And you sit there like you're eating from an empty plate, you scrape and scrape and put the spoon in your mouth and chew, and then you make to wipe your dish with a piece of bread, but there's no bread in your hand. Your kinfolk are rolling on the floor with laughter. You can't do for yourself, not even take a leak, someone has to show you each time. If your missus or mother feels sorry for you, she takes you to the out-

house, but if there's no one to watch after you, you're a goner, your bladder will burst, and you'll just die.

That's what the Slynx does.

You can't go west either. There's a sort of road that way—invisible, like a little path. You walk and walk, then the town is hidden from your eyes, a sweet breeze blows from the fields, everything's fine and good, and then all of a sudden, they say, you just stop. And you stand there. And you think: Where was I going anyway? What do I need there? What's there to see? It's not like it's better out there. And you feel so sorry for yourself. You think: Maybe the missus is crying back at the izba, searching the horizon, holding her hand over her eyes; the chickens are running around the yard, they miss you too; the izba stove is hot, the mice are having a field day, the bed is soft. . . . And it's like a worrum got at your heart, and he's gnawing a hole in it. . . . You turn back. Sometimes you run. And as soon as you can see your own pots on your fence, tears burst from your eyes. It's really true, they splash a whole mile. No lie!

You can't go south. The Chechens live there. First it's all steppe, steppe, and more steppe—your eyes could fall out from staring. Then beyond the steppe—the Chechens. In the middle of the town there's a watchtower with four windows, and guards keep watch out of all of them. They're on the lookout for Chechens. They don't really look all the time, of course, as much as they smoke swamp rusht and play straws. One person grabs four straws in his fist—three long ones, one short. Whoever picks the short one gets a whack on the forehead. But sometimes they look out the window. If they spot a Chechen, they're supposed to cry "Chechens, Chechens!" and then people from all the settlements run out and start beating pots with sticks, to scare the Chechens. And the Chechens skedaddle. Once, two people approached the town from the south, an old man and an old woman. We banged on our pots, stomped and hollered up a storm, but the Chechens didn't care, they just kept on coming and looking around. We—well, the boldest of us—went out to meet them with tongs, spindles, whatever there was. To see who they were and why they came. "We're from the south, Golubchiks," they said. "We've been walking for two weeks, we've walked our feet off. We came to trade rawhide strips. Maybe you have some goods?"

What goods could we have? We eat mice. "Mice Are Our Mainstay," that's what Fyodor Kuzmich, Glorybe, teaches. But our people are softhearted, they gathered what there was in the izbas and traded for the rawhide and let them go their way. Later there was a lot of talk about them. Everyone jabbered about what they were like, the stories they told, how come they showed up.

Well, they looked just like us: the old man was gray headed and wore reed shoes, the old woman wore a scarf, her eyes were blue, and she had horns. Their stories were long and sad. Benedikt was little and didn't have any sense at all then, but he was all ears.

They said that in the south there's an azure sea, and in that sea there's an island, and on that island there's a tower, and in that tower there's a golden stove bed. On that bed there's a girl with long hair—one hair is gold, the next is silver, one is gold, and the next is silver. She lies there braiding her tresses, just braiding her long tresses, and as soon as she finishes the world will come to an end.

Our people listened and listened and said: "What's gold and silver?"

And the Chechens said: "Gold is like fire, and silver is like moonlight, or when firelings light up."

Our people said: "Ah, so that's it. Go on and tell us some more."

And the Chechens said: "There's a great river, three years' walk from here. In that river there's a fish—Blue Fin. It talks with a human voice, cries and laughs, and swims back and forth across that river. When it swims to one side and laughs, the dawn starts playing, the sun rises up in the sky, and the day comes. When it goes back, it cries, drags the darkness with it, and hauls the moon by its tail. All the stars in the sky are Blue Fin's scales."

We asked: "Have you heard why winter comes and why summer goes?"

The old lady said: "No, good people, we haven't heard, I won't lie, we haven't heard. It's true, though, folks wonder: Why do we need winter, when summer is so much sweeter? It must be for our sins."

But the old man shook his head. "No," he said, "everything in nature must have its reason. A feller passing through once told me how it is. In the north there's a tree that grows right up to the clouds. Its trunk is black and gnarled, but its flowers are white, teeny tiny like a speck of dust. Father Frost lives in that tree, he's old and his beard is so long he tucks it into his belt. Now, when it comes time for winter, as soon as the chickens flock together and fly south, then that Old Man Frost gets busy: he starts jumping from branch to branch, clapping his hands and muttering doodle-dee-doo, doodle-dee-doo! And then he whistles: *wheeeeooossshhhh!* Then the wind comes up, and those white flowers come raining down on us—and that's when you get snow. And you ask: why does winter come?"

Our Golubchiks said: "Yes, that's right. That must be the way it is. And you, Grandpa, aren't you afraid to walk the roads? What's it like at night? Have you come across any goblins?"

"Oh, I met one once!" said the Chechen. "Seen him up close, I did, close as you are to me. Now hear what I say. My old woman had a hankering for some firelings. Bring me some firelings, she kept saying. And that year the firelings ripened sweet, nice and chewy. So off I go. Alone."

"What do you mean, alone!" we gasped.

"That's right, alone," boasted the stranger. "Well, listen up. I was walking along, just walking, and it started getting dark. Not very dark, but, well, all gray-like. I was tiptoeing so as not to scare the firelings when suddenly: *shush-shush-shush!* "What's that?" I thought. I looked—no one there. I went on. Again: *shush-*

shush-shush. Like someone was shushing the leaves. I looked around. No one. I took another step. And there he was right in front of me. There was nothing there 'tall, and then all of a sudden I seen him. At arm's length. Just a little feller. Maybe up to my waist or chest. Looked like he were made of old hay, his eyes shone red, and he had palms on his feet. And he was stomping those palms on the ground and chanting: *pitter-patter, pitter-patter, pitter-patter*. Did I run, let me tell you! Don't know how I ended up at home. My old lady didn't get her firelings that time."

The children asked him: "Grandfather, tell us what other monsters there are in the forest."

They poured the old man some egg kvas and he started. "I was young back then, hotheaded. Not afraid of a thing. Once I tied three logs together with reeds, set them on the water— our river is fast and wide—sat myself down on them, and off I floated. The honest truth! The women ran down to the bank, there was a hollering and a wailing, like you might expect. Where do you see people floating on the river? Nowadays, I'm told, they hollow out trunks and put them on the water. If they're not lying, of course."

"No, they're not, they're not! It's our Fyodor Kuzmich, Glorybe. He invented it!" we cried out, Benedikt loudest of all.

"Don't know any Fyodor Kuzmich myself. We aren't booklearned. That's not my story. Like I said, I wasn't afraid of nothing. Not mermaids or water bubbles or wrigglers that live under stones. I even caught a whirlytooth fish in a bucket."

"Come on, Grandpa," our folks said. "Now you're making things up."

"That's the honest truth! My missus here will tell you."

"It's true," the old lady said. "It happened. How I yelled at him. He clean ruined my bucket, I had to burn it. Had to carve out a new one, and a new one, by the time you hollow it, tar it, let it dry three times, cure it with rusht, rub it with blue sand—it near to broke my hands,

I worked so hard. And for him, it's all glory. The whole village came out to look at him. Some were afraid."

"Of course they were," we said.

The old man was pleased. "But then, you see, maybe I'm the only one," he boasted. "The only one seen a whirlytooth up close—close as you folks there, he was—and come out of it alive. Ha! I was a real he-man. Mighty! Sometimes I'd yell so loud the window bladders would burst. And how much rusht I could drink at a sitting! I could suck a whole barrel dry."

Benedikt's mother was sitting there, her lips pressed. "What concrete benefit did you derive from your strength? Did you accomplish anything socially beneficial to the community?" she asked.

The old man was offended. "When I was a youngster, Golubushka, I could jump from here to that hill way over there on one leg! Beneficial! I tell you, sometimes I'd give a shout—and the straw would fall off the roof. All our folks is like that. A real strong man, I was. My missus here will tell you, if I get a blister or a boil— it's as big as your fist. No joke. I had pimples that big, I tell you. That big. And you talk. I'll have you know when my old man scratched his head, he'd shake off a half-bucket of dandruff."

"Come on, now," we piped up. "Grandpa, you promised to tell us about monsters."

But the old man wasn't joking, he was really mad. "I'm not saying another word. If you come to listen . . . then listen. Don't go butting in. It ruins the whole story. She must be one of them Oldeners, I can tell by the way she talks."

"That's right," said our people, throwing a side glance at Mother. "One of the Oldeners. Come on now, Grandpa, go on."

The Chechen also told us about forest ways, how to tell paths apart: which ones are for real and which are a figment, just green mist, a tangle of grasses, spells, and sorcery. He laid out all the signs. He told how the mermaid sings at dawn, burbles her watery songs; at first low-like, starting off deep: *oooloo, oooloo*, then up higher: *ohouuaaa, ohouuaaa*—then hold on, watch out, or she'll pull you in the river—and when the song reaches a whistle: *iyee, iyee!* run for your life, man. He told us about enchanted bark, and how you have to watch out for it; about the Snout that grabs people by their legs; and how to find the best rusht.

Then Benedikt spoke up. "Grandfather, have you seen the Slynx?"

Everyone looked at Benedikt like he was an idiot. No one said anything, though.

They saw the fearless old man off on his way, and it was again quiet in town. They put more guards on, but no one else attacked us from the south.

No, we mostly walk out east from the town. The woods there are bright, the grass is long and shiny. In the grasses there are sweet little blue flowers: if you pick them, wash them, beat them, comb and spin them, you can plait the threads and weave burlap. Mother, may she rest in peace, was all thumbs, everything tangled up in her hands. She cried when she had to spin thread, poured buckets of tears when she wove burlap. Before the Blast, she said, everything was different. You'd go to a deportmunt store, she said, take what you wanted, and if you didn't like it, you'd turn up your nose, not like now. This deportmunt store or bootick they had was something like a Warehouse, only there were more goods, and they didn't give things out only on Warehouse Days—the doors stood open all day long.

It's hard to believe. How's that? Come and grab what you want? You couldn't find enough guards to guard it. Just let us in and we'll strip everything bare. And how many people would get trampled? When you go to the Warehouse your eyes nearly pop out of your head from looking at who got what, how much, and why not me?

Looking won't help any: you won't get more than they give you. And don't stare at another guy's takings: the Warehouse Workers will whack you. You got what's yours, now get out! Or else we'll take that away too.

When you leave the Warehouse with your basket you hurry home to your izba, and you keep feeling around in the basket: Is everything there? Maybe they forgot something? Or maybe someone snuck up from behind in an alley, dipped in, took off with something?

It happens. Once, Mother was coming home from the Warehouse, they'd given her crow feathers. For a pillow. They're light, you carry them and it's like there was nothing there. She got home, pulled off the cloth—and what do you know? No feathers at all, and in their place, little turds. Well, Mother cried her eyes out, but Father got the giggles. What a funny thief—he not only took off with the goods but thought up a joke, with a twist: here's what your feathers are worth. How d'ya like that!

The feathers turned up at the neighbor's. Father started bugging him: Where'd they come from? The market. Whaddya trade them for? Felt boots. Who from? All of a sudden the neighbor didn't know this, didn't know that, I didn't mean, I didn't, I drank too much rusht—you couldn't get a thing out of him. That's how they left it.

Well, and what do they give out at the Warehouse? Mouse-meat sausage, mouse lard, wheatweed flour, those feathers, then there's felt boots, of course, and tongs, burlap, stone pots: different things. One time they put some slimy firelings in the basket—they'd gone bad somewhere, so they handed them out. If you want good firelings you have to get them yourself.

Right at the edge of the town to the east are elfir woods. Elfir is the best tree. Its trunk is light, it drips resin, the leaves are delicate, patterned, paw shaped, they have a healthy smell. In a word—elfir! Its cones are as big as a human head, and you can eat your fill of its nuts. If you soak them, of course. Otherwise they're disgusting. Firelings grow on the oldest elfirs, in the deep forest. Such a treat: sweet, round, chewy. A ripe fireling is the size of a person's eye. At night they shine silver, like the crescent moon was sending a beam through the leaves, but during the day you don't notice them. People go out into the woods when it's still light, and as soon as it's dark everyone holds hands and walks in a chain so as not to get lost. And so the firelings don't know there's people around. You have to pick them off quick, else the fireling will wake up and shout. He'll warn the others, and they'll go out in a flash. You can pick them by feel if you want. But no one does. You end up with fakes. When the fake ones light up, it's like a red fire is blowing through them. Mother picked some fakes and poisoned herself. Or else she'd be alive right now.

Two hundred and thirty-three years Mother lived on this earth. And she didn't grow old. They laid her in the grave just as black-haired and pink-cheeked as ever. That's the way it is: whoever didn't croak when the Blast happened, doesn't grow old after that. That's the Consequence they have. Like something in them got stuck. But you can count them on the fingers of one hand. They're all in the wet ground: some ruined by the Slynx, some poisoned by rabbits, Mother here, by firelings. . . .

Whoever was born after the Blast, they have other Consequences—all kinds. Some have got hands that look like they broke out in green flour, like they'd been rolling in greencorn, some have gills, another might have a cockscomb or something else. And sometimes there aren't any Consequences, except when they get old a pimple will sprout from the eye, or their private parts will grow a beard down to the shins. Or nostrils will open up on their knees.

Benedikt sometimes asked Mother: how come the Blast happened? She didn't really know. It seems like people were playing around and played too hard with someone's *arms*. "We didn't have time to catch our breath," she would say. And she'd cry. "We lived better back then." And the old man—he was born after the Blast—would blow up at her: "Cut out all that Oldener Times stuff! The way we live is the way we live! It's none of our beeswax."

Mother would say: "Neanderthal! Stone Age brute!"

Then he'd grab her by the hair. She'd scream, call on the neighbors, but you wouldn't hear a peep out of them: it's just a husband teaching his wife a lesson. None of our business. A broken dish has two lives. And why did he get mad at her? Well, she was still young and looking younger all the time, and he was fading; he started limping, and he said his eyes saw everything like it was in dark water.

Mother would say to him: "Don't you dare lay a finger on me! I have a university education!"

And he'd answer: "I'll give you an ejucayshin! I'll beat you to a pulp. Gave our son a dog's name, you did, so the whole settlement would talk about him!"

And such a cussing would go on, such a squabbling—he wouldn't shut up till his whole beard was in a slobber. He was a hard one, the old man. He'd bark, and then he'd get tuckered; he'd pour himself a bucket of hooch and drink himself senseless. And Mother would smooth her hair, straighten her hem, take Benedikt by the hand, and lead him to the high hill over the river; he already knew that was where she used to live, before the Blast. Mother's five-story izba stood there, and Mother would tell about how there were higher mansions, there weren't enough fingers to count them. So what did you do—take off your boots and count your toes too? Benedikt was only learning his numbers then. It was still early for him to be counting on stones. And now, to hear tell, Fyodor Kuzmich, Glorybe, had invented counting sticks. They say that it's like you run a hole through a chip of wood, put it on the sticks, and toss them back and forth from right to left. And they say the numbers go so fast your head spins! Only don't you dare make one yourself. If you need one—come on market day to the market, pay what they tell you, they'll take burlap or mice, and then you can count to your heart's content. That's what they say. Who knows if it's true or not.

. . . So Mother would come to the hill, sit down on a stone, sob and cry her eyes out, soak herself with bitter tears, and remember her girlfriends, fair maidens, or dream about those deportmunt stores. And all the streets, she said, were covered with assfelt. That's like a sort of foam, but hard, black, you fall down on it and you don't fall through. If it was summer weather, Mother would sit and cry, and Benedikt would play in the dirt, making mud pies in the clay, or picking off yellers and sticking them in the ground like he was building a fence. Wide-open spaces all around: hills and streams, a warm breeze, he'd wander about—the grass would wave, and the sun rolled across the sky like a great pancake, over the fields, over the forests, to the Blue Mountains.

Our town, our home sweet homeland, is called Fyodor-Kuzmichsk, and before that, Mother says, it was called Ivan-Porfirichsk, and before that Sergei-Sergeichsk, and still before that Southern Warehouses, and way back when—Moscow.

Baby Doll

JOHANNA SINISALO

Translated by David Hackston

Johanna Sinisalo (1958–) is an award-winning, influential Finnish writer of science fiction and fantasy whose work has often focused on environmental themes. Born in Sodankylä (Finnish Lapland), she studied literature and drama at the University of Tampere and worked in advertising until turning to writing full-time in 1997. Since then, she has published more than forty short stories, winning the Finnish Atorox Award for short fiction seven different times. Sinisalo has also written a large number of reviews, articles, comic scripts, and screenplays, and edited two anthologies, including *The Dedalus Book of Finnish Fantasy* (2006).

Her novels, translated into several languages, include *Troll: A Love Story* (2004), in which readers learn trolls are nearly extinct predators capable of fostering intense attractions in humans; *Birdbrain* (2011), about a sinister wilderness hike through New Zealand and Australia; and *The Blood of Angels* (2014), in which bees mysteriously vanish on a worldwide scale, causing agricultural upheaval and chaos. *Troll* won both the prestigious Finlandia Prize for best novel and the James Tiptree Jr. Award. *Birdbrain* was shortlisted for the French Prix Escapade. *The Blood of Angels* won an English PEN award. Her latest novel is *The Core of the Sun* (Grove Atlantic, 2016). She is working on a climate-change novel and a "writer's cut" version of the cult movie *Iron Sky*, for which she wrote the screenplay.

Sinisalo's fiction also often plays with gender relations, and in the powerful, disturbing "Baby Doll," reprinted here, she deals with themes of love and loss. In this possible future in which everyone, especially children, is judged based on their sexual attractiveness, Sinisalo explores how society views sexuality and the commodification of sexuality. Similar explosive themes have been explored by other science fiction writers, such as incest in Theodore Sturgeon's "If All Men Were Brothers, Would You Let One Marry Your Sister?" and sexual obsession with aliens in James Tiptree Jr.'s story in this volume, "And I Awoke and Found Me Here on the Cold Hill's Side."

"Baby Doll" (2002) was a finalist for the Nebula Award and the Theodore Sturgeon Memorial Award. It was also reprinted in *SFWA European Hall of Fame* (2007).

BABY DOLL

Johanna Sinisalo

Translated by David Hackston

Annette comes home from school and shrugs her bag onto the floor in the hall. The bag is made of clear vinyl speckled with metal glitter, all in rainbow colors that swirl around the iridescent pink hearts and full kissy lips. The vinyl reveals the contents of the bag: Annette's schoolbooks, exercise books, and a plastic pencil box featuring the hottest boy band of 2015, Stick That Dick. The boys wear open leather jackets across their rippling bare torsos, and their jockstraps all feature the head of some animal with a large beak or a long trunk. Craig has an elephant on his jockstrap. Craig's the cutest of them all.

Annette slings her bright red spandex jacket across a chair and starts to remove her matching stretch boots. They're tight around the shins, but she can't be bothered to bend down and wrench them off. Instead she tries to pry one heel free with the opposite toe, but succeeds only in tearing her fishnet stockings.

Oh, for fuck's sake!

Mumps walks in from the kitchen, still wearing her work clothes. What was that, darling?

I said, Golly, I've wrecked my tights.

Oh, dear, not again. And they were so expensive. Well, you'll just have to wear the plain ones tomorrow.

I'm so *not* wearing anything like that!

Darling, you don't really have a choice.

Then I'm not going to school at *all*! Annette snatches up her bag and stomps off toward her room, but the TV is on in the den, and it's time for her favorite show, *Suburban Heat and Hate*. I'd look like a total dork! she continues, half to herself, half to her mother, who can no longer hear her, as she throws herself on the couch.

The show begins. The plot's as thick as it gets. Jake has just been discovered in bed with Melissa, but Bella doesn't know that Jake knows she's having an affair with his twin brother, Tom. Jake meanwhile doesn't know that Melissa is in fact his daughter, because years ago he helped a lesbian couple get pregnant.

Let's make a deal, darling. Mum has come in from the kitchen and is standing by the couch.

Quiet! I can't hear a thing. Just then Bella pulls Jake off Melissa, screaming a barrage of abuse, leaving Melissa's enormous boobs and Jake's white butt in full view. At school today Annette heard Ninotska telling everyone to watch this afternoon's episode because Jake's got such a fantastic butt. Annette doesn't see what's so fantastic about it. It's paler than the rest of his brown skin, and it isn't as hairy as other men's butts. Still, tomorrow she'll find an opportunity to tell Ninotska she got a glimpse of Jake's butt, and of course she'll say she thought it was totally hypersmart, and give a low giggle the way you're supposed to when you talk about these things.

Mum waits till the commercials come on. I have to go back to work the minute Dad gets home.

I'll be fine.

Lulu's at a shoot. Dad'll pick her up around nine or ten, and then it's your bedtime.

Tell me something I don't know.

One more thing, darling. I'm going on a business trip tomorrow, and I'll be away for two days.

You're always going off somewhere.

Dad can help you with your homework.

Yeah, right, I bet he makes me watch Otso so he can play squash.

That's what I mean by the deal. Promise me you'll help Dad and all you kids will behave yourselves.

Annette is pissed off—big-time. Whenever Mumps goes away, they end up eating all sorts of weird meals that Dumps cooks himself, instead of pizza or deli sushi or toasted sandwiches like Mumps gives them. You need to tell Dumps at least a hundred times what stuff to buy at the store, and why you need it. Once when Mumps was away Annette spent an hour explaining to Dumps why she categorically had to have a new eyelash-lengthening mascara and a bottle of golden body-spray.

On one condition, Annette says.

What's that?

Can I go to a sleepover at Ninotska's Thursday night?

Although Annette hasn't actually been invited, rumor has it Ninotska's still deciding on the final guest list. Annette has noticed Ninotska checking out the Stick That Dick pencil box that Mum and Dad brought back from London. Annette could give Ninotska the pencil box, then later ask Mum for money to buy another—she could always say she cracked the old one.

Just in case she gets invited, she has to make sure she has permission to go. If you get invited you have to be able to say Sí, sí, gracias without worrying about it. *Nobody* is tragic enough to say they need to ask permission, and if you say Sí, sí, gracias and don't turn up, you can pretty much forget about being invited anywhere again.

Who's Ninotska?

Ninotska Lahtinen from our year, stupid! She lives on Vuorikatu.

And why do you have to go over there?

She's having her nine-yo party. And I'll need to take a present. I can catch a bus if Dad can't take me.

Mumps sighs, and with that Annette knows she won't have to sweat it anymore. The commercials finally end, and Annette turns back to the tube. Melissa's a professional stripper. She's wearing a bikini with golden frills. It's so mega.

The apartment door opens, and Dumps comes in, having picked up Otso at the nursery. Otso is five-yo.

Mumps has laid the table with pasta salad from the deli. It's all right except for the capers; Annette doesn't like them and shoves the awful things aside. Dumps starts raving on about how they're the most delicious bits, then spears a caper off Annette's plate and stuffs it in his mouth, loudly smacking his lips. Otso only ever eats the pasta twists, but wouldn't you know—nobody gives him a lecture about it.

So Otso, how was nursery today? Mumps asks, all treacly like a TV kiddie host. Did she really use that twittery voice on Annette when she was five?

I'm going on a date! With my girlfriend! Otso can't say his *f*'s properly, and his speech therapist has her work cut out with his *r*'s too. The word *girlfriend* sounds like Otso's trying to spit something out between his front teeth.

Mumps and Dumps exchange one of their grown-up looks. Well, our big boy's going on a date! says Dad in the same cringe-o-matic voice as Mum. When is your date, and who is it with?

Tomorrow, with Pamela. Her Mum's picking us up.

Mum and Dad simper at one another again, pretending to swoon, then shake their heads in the phoniest way, meanwhile smiling like split sausages.

Pamela's my main squeeze, says Otso, shoveling down different colored pasta swirls.

Once Mum has gone back to the office, Annette flops down to watch the reality show *Between the Sheets*, in which the contestants try to find the perfect sex partner. What first comes to mind when I look down your cleavage: (a) lemons, (b) apples, or (c) melons? a male contestant asks a woman sprawled behind the curtain on a canopy bed when the door opens and Dad and Lulu walk in.

Lulu's only two years older than Annette, but looking at her you'd never believe it.

She's still wearing her photo-session makeup, a pair of giant false eyelashes, with so much black and gray around her eyes it no longer looks like makeup at all; the eye shadow just gave her a tired and hungry look. Her lips feature a dark crimson pencil line to straighten her Cupid's bow, the puffy parts filled with a lighter plum-red, and there's so much lip gloss involved that her mouth appears bruised and swollen. Her hair has been curled in tiny ringlets and tied in a deliberately careless bun.

Not long ago Lulu got calls from photographers in Milan and Tokyo, and she burst into tears when they later told Mum and Dad not to bring her because she was too short after all. Before that disaster she'd been weighing herself twice a day, but now she's checking her height three or four times a week. She has a special chart on the wall for marking her growth. The pencil lines are so close together they form a gray smudge.

Lulu's face recently landed on the cover of the Finnish *Cosmopolitan*, a very big deal, so now her agent says she has to stop posing for the catalogs. Being associated with Monoprix and Wal-Mart won't help her image. She's far too sensual.

Lulu heads upstairs to rinse off her sensual makeup. Annette's stomach twists and churns. She goes to her room and stands before the mirror and tries to stare herself down, as if she could make her face look more sensual by gazing at it angrily enough. She sucks her belly in, but she still resembles a flat squash.

Annette! Bedtime! comes Dumps's voice from downstairs.

Yes yes YESYES!

· · ·

Annette's a slut! the boys start shouting as she walks onto the playground, pretending not to hear them. It's fairly normal and not worth worrying about; anybody they're not trying to pull they call a slut—and they're not trying to pull Annette.

There are far worse things they could shout out.

Ninotska and Veronika are standing by the main entrance, whispering to each other. Veli and Juho walk past. Veli attempts to grope Ninotska, and Juho tries shoving his hand up Veronika's black leather miniskirt. Ninotska giggles, squirms, and pushes him away, and Veronika dashes to hide behind her. Veli and Juho swagger toward the door, and on their way each boy sticks his index finger through the looped thumb and finger of the other hand. Ninotska and Veronika giggle until the boys are out of earshot.

Annette approaches the two girls. Hi, she says awkwardly.

Veronika and Ninotska toss their fountains of permed hair and look at her disdainfully. Ninotska's skimpy shirt allows a wide strip of skin to show between her golden shiny hipsters and her spaghetti-strap top. She has a silver ring in her belly button.

Ninotska, can you come over here for a minute? says Annette, backing toward the Dumpster. We need to talk.

Ninotska glances at Veronika, a scowl on her face, then joins Annette. Well, what's the big deal? she asks suspiciously.

Annette reaches into her bag and brings out the Stick That Dick pencil box. You know, I'm really bored with this. You want it?

Ninotska's eyes light up, and Annette realizes her offer's having the desired effect. What makes you think I'd want your old crap? Ninotska bluntly replies, but it's all part of the script.

Annette shrugs. Okay, fine then, she says, and starts to throw the thing in the Dumpster.

Ninotska's hand shoots out, grabbing the

box before it can join the rubbish. Easy pleasy. I believe in recycling.

Annette smiles as Ninotska slips the pencil box into her golden bag printed with the words Eat Me. Hey, what're you doing Thursday night? she asks finally, and Annette's heart leaps with excitement.

On the bed Annette has spread out everything she'll need: best lace-chiffon nightie, makeup kit, perfume—plus books and stuff for the next day at school. Her nine-yo present for Ninotska is wrapped in silver paper, three shades of nail polish that Annette picked out herself because Mumps would've gotten something tragic. It should all fit in the flight bag borrowed from Mumps. Now Annette must decide what to wear for the evening. She plumps for a pair of lizard-scale leggings and a skirt with a slit up the side. She hasn't got any swank-tanks like Ninotska, but her green top is fray-proof, so she takes a pair of scissors and cuts a good ten centimeters off the bottom, making it stop well short of her belly button. The ragged cut is totally glam; it looks a bit like those TV shows where the jungle women's clothes are so tattered they reveal lots of skin.

Annette studies the nightie and the matching thong underwear. Then she looks in the mirror.

She slips off her skirt, leggings, and panties. She opens her makeup kit and removes a black eyeliner. With her pink plastic sharpener she gives the pencil a serious point.

She sits spread-eagled before the mirror and with careful pencil strokes draws thin wavy lines between her legs.

Ninotska's Mum and Dad are away somewhere for the evening. In addition to Ninotska and Annette, Veronika and Janika and Evita and Carmen and Vanessa are all naturally at the pajama party. The sleepover boasts buckets of pizza-flavored popcorn and big bottles of high-energy soda, so we can last through the night, squeals Ninotska.

Once Ninotska has opened her presents everybody gets ready for the fashion show. Back home Annette thought her nightie was fantastic, but now it looks like an old woman's shirt. It's too long, reaching almost to the knees, and totally unrevealing. Everybody agrees that Evita's nightie is the best. It's slightly see-through, like violet-blue mist, and it's so short it barely covers her ass. Ninotska's is nice, too, with wide frilly shoulder straps and loose laces on the front so it's open almost all the way down, and it's made of red silk. But because it's her party Ninotska decides to be generous and votes for Evita's nightie.

Around ten o'clock everybody gets all excited and snickery when Ninotska takes a stepladder and goes into her mum and dad's room and comes back cradling a stack of DVDs. Let's watch a film. The girls sort through the pile. Each DVD has naked men and women on the cover, sharing the space with titles like *Hot Pussies* and *Grand Slam Gang Bang*. All the girls start giggling, hiding their mouths with their hands, and Ninotska puts a DVD in the player.

The pounding music and the script with its endless shouts of Give it to me, baby and Meats to the sweet are all very monotonous, but they still stare at the screen—nobody dares not watch. Annette feels twitchy and uncomfortable, and sometimes it's like there's a second little heart beating under her stomach, and that makes her uncomfortable, too. She knows you're supposed to stay the distance with this stuff, and you're also supposed to pretend it doesn't bother you in the slightest, the way boys watch slasher movies—if you let on you're scared, everybody laughs and takes the piss. Even though the whole point of horror flicks is to upset you, and that's why they get made in the first place, you're still not allowed to be scared. And so they have to watch these grand slam hot pussies as if it didn't mean anything.

Once the second flick is halfway over, and two black dudes are simultaneously pumping a woman with gigantic boobs, Ninotska gives a loud yawn, and this is a sign that the guests are no longer expected to be interested in the film. She switches the machine off, slipcases the disc, and drops it on the stack.

Who wants to check out my mum and dad's room? she asks, and everybody wants to, of course. The girls jostle behind Ninotska and make their way into a lovely bedroom with an enormous four-poster and a gold-framed mirror on the wall. Ninotska climbs the stepladder to the top shelf of the closet. She returns the stack of DVDs, then takes down a big cardboard box and jumps back onto the rug. She opens the box and spreads the contents across the bed. Red-and-black underwear that's nothing but a belt with bits of fabric on the sides: in the middle they're completely open. A pair of manacles with fur on the cuffs. Ninotska grabs a pinkish zucchini and gives the end a twist, and the thing starts shaking in her hand. Brrrrr! she says, trying to imitate the noise of the zucchini, then waves it in each girl's face, and they all move away giggling hysterically.

Has anybody ever tried one of these? she asks slowly, challenging them, and Annette feels like Ninotska is looking straight at her.

I'll bet none of you would *dare*. Ninotska glances across the group of girls. Somebody attempts a giggle, and then they all fall silent.

I dare you. I dare you.

The silence rings in Annette's ears, her mouth is dry with anticipation, and she feels that any second now Ninotska's eyes will stop at her.

Lulu's chewing gum and trying to look mega, but every now and then she gives a quick laugh, her straightened, whitened teeth flashing between her dark red lips while the tabloid photographer takes her picture, over and over.

Occasionally the female reporter glances at the LED screen to see how the photos are coming out. Annette is sulking in the den. She can look into the living room, but the people from the newspaper can't see her, and she would refuse to be photographed next to Lulu even if they begged her.

In any case, they haven't asked.

So tell me, how does it feel being the new face of Sexy Secrets Underwear? the reporter asks.

Lulu lowers her false eyelashes, so overlong they almost reach her boobs, and smiles. Annette knows that Lulu uses this posture so she'll have time to think without seeming like a dork. Finally Lulu looks up.

Okay.

People say you're about to become the object of a national fantasy. Do you agree?

The eyelashes tilt down, then rise again. I guess.

The reporter smiles and switches off her digital recorder. Thanks, Lulu. That'll be all.

Annette simply has to walk out of the den before the tabloid people leave. She's got her makeup on, and she's wearing her shiny black dress—plus of course her high-heeled ankle boots, even though Mumps has told her not to use them on the parquet.

Well, lookee here, the photographer says, squinting at Annette, there's *another* stunning woman on the premises, and he almost sounds sincere, but she can't be sure.

That's my little sister, Lulu says before blowing a bubble gum bubble. She's eight.

Annette could kill Lulu. Annette thinks she looks at least ten-yo, but by now the tabloid people are already in the hall, telling Lulu the article will run on Friday.

Naturally Mumps has bought three copies of Friday's paper. On the front page of the fashion section is a picture of Lulu, her head thrown back, a gush of curls cascading down her shoulders, her teeth showing between pouty lips and her eyes half shut. Model Sensation Lulu: I Love Being the Star of Guys' Wet Dreams! screams the headline.

Lippe from the next apartment has come over to share a glass of wine with Mum. Lippe admires Lulu's picture, and then they gab about the contract. Though Mum whispers, Annette, sitting in front of the TV, can still hear her. With her hand to her lips, Mum says, A hundred and twenty thousand euros. At least they'll get back all the money they sank into Lulu's career, Annette thinks. A year ago Lulu took some modeling courses that cost ultra-bucks, but thanks to that move a fancy agent saw Lulu at the graduation show and signed her up on the spot. Lulu doesn't go to regular school anymore; she's supposed to be studying with a private tutor and taking the odd exam, but Annette hasn't noticed much evidence of this. There have been no reported sightings of Lulu reading a schoolbook.

Annette once applied to the modeling school, but you have to get through the preliminary round. They looked at her for about half a second and didn't bother asking her any questions. A month later a letter came saying that she didn't have sufficient camera presence.

Mum explains to Lippe that originally another girl had been tapped for the Sexy Secrets campaign, a seventeen-year-old from Turku called Ramona who'd already done a lot of modeling and was a runner-up for Miss Finland.

Hasn't her face been used to death? asks Lippe.

She's well past her prime, Mum says, nodding, so Lulu got the contract.

The door rattles, and Dad comes in with Otso. Otso's cheeks are red, and he's wearing a smart jacket, a white shirt, and a bow tie. He's been on another date with Pamela: Dad took them to a film or something. Both Mum and Dad prattle about what a handsome little boy they have. Otso runs into Mum's arms shouting, Guess what! Guess what! Me and Pamela

got engaged! which of course starts off such a wave of fawning and gushing that Annette feels like throwing up.

Annette is on the school bus. The journey is less than a kilometer, only a few blocks, but the law states that all school-aged children must ride to school in their parents' cars or on a supervised bus. For the protection of our children, ran the ads a few years ago when the law went into effect. Annette is standing in the aisle, but her new platform shoes cause her feet to slide down toward the point, and she keeps losing her balance. Once the bus stops at the traffic light she raises her eyes, and the view out the window hits her like a punch in the face.

From a gigantic roadside billboard Lulu stares back at her, ten times larger than normal, her eyes dark, her lips shining cherry red, a wind machine billowing her hair.

When Annette finally gets off the bus, as if to further taunt her, another billboard appears, a startling three-panel display this time, looming near the school gates. And of course the star is Lulu, modeling three different lines of underwear—Naughty Red, Sinful Black, and Seductive Green, according to the words.

Each image bears the same caption: Baby Doll.

Trussed in a bright red string, Lulu's ass practically bursts from the first panel; with half-closed eyes she twists her head toward the camera, brushing her hands against her bare shoulders so that her false nails, painted the same color as her panties, gleam against her skin like drops of blood.

Then comes Lulu crouching, shiny black-laced boots matching her underwear, holding a ridiculous toy snake and making like she's kissing the thing, its orange velveteen head sliding between her lips.

And finally there's a shot of Lulu from the

side, hugging a beige teddy bear. Her back is arched, and her boobs, wrapped in jade-green lace, thrust defiantly upward.

Lulu's priceless tits.

But a few days later a miracle occurs.

Annette arrives on the playground for recess, and instantly her stomach starts tightening, her chest pounding, just like every other time she has to walk past the gangs of boys. She hunches her shoulders, lowers her head, and wonders where the mockery will come from today, the cries of slut and dwarf-butt, and of course the comments about her tits—bee-stings, milkduds.

One gang mutters something indistinct, but Annette manages to reach the pavilion without her face blushing bright red. All of a sudden he's standing right next to her. His name's Timppa, she knows that. He's two years ahead of her and plays ice hockey with the F Juniors, and many times she's heard Ninotska and Veronika whispering that Timppa is absolutely *shagtastic*. He's still standing right next to her, looking at her, and Annette is so startled she almost runs away for fear of yet another insult, but Timppa gives her a friendly smile and doesn't look a bit like all he wants to do is shove his hand down her top.

You're Annette, right? he asks. Annette is so taken aback that all she can manage is a nod. She's utterly speechless. Timppa must think she's a total dork because she doesn't know how to respond with something quick and sassy the way Ninotska and Veronika always do when boys talk to them. But Timppa doesn't seem to care; he looks Annette up and down, and his eyes stop at the sight of her platform shoes.

Awesome boots.

Thanks, Annette stammers as Timppa reaches into his leather jacket and produces a packet of SuperKiss, which he holds out to Annette. Gum?

Annette takes one, fumbles off the wrapper,

and pops the stick in her mouth just as the bell rings, saving her. Timppa backs away, smirks, and waves at her. Catch you later, Annette.

Annette stands there and forgets to chew her gum, her mouth half open. Her heart is about to burst out of her chest.

During the next lesson Annette writes Timppa Timppa Timppa on her arm with a sharp pencil, scratching so hard the skin almost breaks.

Ninotska and Veronika have of course noticed that Annette was talking to Timppa during recess, and they'll be sure to catch up with her at their first opportunity, instead of Annette nonchalantly trying to hang around their gang.

Well, well, our little Annette's got a *boyfriend*, Ninotska says, her eyes burning, and for the first time Annette feels like she's *somebody*, not just that girl whose mum and dad brought her a Stick That Dick pencil box from London; suddenly there's something a little bit glam about Annette.

He's not my boyfriend. We're just . . . friends.

Then it must be the first time ever that Timppa Kujala is *just friends* with a girl.

Veronika gives a hollow chortle. He's the horniest stud in the school.

Careful you don't get burned, Annette, darling.

Ninotska and Veronika shuffle off, their curls gushing, their little bottoms bouncing contemptuously, and Annette looks at them and says under her breath, They're just *jealous*.

And with that a great warmth fills her.

Timppa is loitering near the gates when Annette leaves school. He asks her where she's off to, and when she says she's going home he says he's headed the same way and suggests they walk together, fuck the bus law. Timppa spits on the ground and says the whole rule is a load of crapola; he walks to school whenever he wants to. Annette wants to sound mega and says she thinks it's a dumb-ass rule, too, and for some reason she feels safe walking with Timppa.

Annette sees that Veronika notices her leaving with Timppa, and her sense of triumph is so great she's able to chat almost normally with Timppa, even though the silences are long, and she ends up asking him the same questions over and over; but he doesn't seem to mind, and he talks practically the whole way home about which hockey players he admires the most, the ones that have the fastest cars and the juiciest babes with the hottest knockers.

When they arrive at Annette's building, Timppa shuffles awkwardly for a moment and stares at the ground. Can I come in for a bit?

Annette is about to faint. Even though Ninotska and Veronika have kissed lots of boys at parties, and while Carmen spent a whole semester walking around hand-in-hand with Pasi, nobody has ever had a boyfriend who wanted to *visit*. It could mean almost anything. Annette can hardly breathe.

Sure, come on in.

They enter the elevator, and Annette presses the button for the sixth floor. Inside the car they don't say a word, and for Annette this is quite a relief. Finally they arrive; she opens her apartment door, shows Timppa in, and gives him a hanger for his leather jacket. This time she doesn't drop her bag on the floor but carries it down the hall past the living room and the den, Timppa at her heels, then stops outside her bedroom door, on which there's a large Stick That Dick poster and a piece of cardboard with thick red lettering: Annettez Room Private No Entry!

Annette steps toward Timppa so she's almost right up against him. Want to see my room?

Timppa doesn't appear to be listening, he's inspecting the other doors in the vicinity. One features a full-color poster of the world's most glamorous supermodel, Marinette Mankiewicz.

Her moist skin sparkles with hundreds of little pearly beads for a major wetness effect; her bikini looks wet, too, clamped tight against her tits and almost see-through. Lulu once told Annette it's all done with oil instead of water, because oil is shinier and doesn't dry out under the studio lights.

Is that your sister's room?

Lulu's? I guess.

When's she coming home?

At first Annette doesn't understand, but then it strikes her, and her stomach feels like it's about to spill out around her heels, and her head starts to spin.

Around four o'clock, she mutters almost inaudibly.

I can hang out and wait, huh? Timppa asks, his eyes fixed on Marinette Mankiewicz, and Annette realizes that Lulu and the photographer have ripped off the idea behind this poster for their three-panel billboard—the Seductive Green Lulu with her tits pointing skyward.

Make yourself at home, she says, and goes into her room, and only vast amounts of self-control prevent her from slamming the door shut much louder than normal.

After that Timppa visits almost every day. He comes around at the same time as Lulu and often doesn't leave till late at night, after Mumps and Dumps have stood next to the Marinette Mankiewicz poster coughing or clearing their throats or knocking on the door, and Mumps says, pretending to be all thoughtful and considerate, Right, I think it's time for our Lulu's beauty sleep!

Ninotska and Veronika have been giggling to themselves and tossing their curls around and whispering so much that Annette can feel it in her stomach. They ask her, real smarmy, How's your *boyfriend* doing nowadays? then burst into a hyperly loud chortle as if the joke gets funnier every time. At first Annette can't understand how exactly Ninotska and Veronika learned that Timppa and Lulu have been hanging together, but it all becomes clear during morning recess when she's walking behind a group of boys who haven't noticed her, and she overhears one of them chattering about what a hottie Timppa has pulled; he then describes Lulu at great length and brags that Timppa's on the verge of scoring. Timppa, naturally, has told the entire school.

Annette runs straight to the girls' toilet and throws up, filling the bowl with globules of meat and potatoes. The ketchup makes it look like she's been vomiting blood, and she decides that vomiting blood probably feels like this. A moment later, her puke-tears having dried, she feels slightly dizzy, but her thoughts are surprisingly clear.

As she leaves the stall, she bumps into Nana, one of the girls in her year, loitering by the sinks. She must have heard Annette barfing. Nana gives her a conspiratorial smile.

Have you just started?

Annette doesn't understand. Nana pulls a bottle of Evian from her schoolbag and hands it to her. If you want to stay fit while you're on the program, remember to drink enough water. Don't let yourself dry out. No calories in water, you see.

Annette gulps down a mouthful of Evian and mumbles her thanks. Nana slips the bottle back in her bag. One good tip: get yourself some xylitol chewing gum and use it after you've barfed. That way the stomach acids won't take the shine off your teeth.

Annette nods. Nana slings her bag across her shoulder and looks Annette up and down. Yeah, you could do with losing a few kilos. Nana moves toward the door, her little ass snugged tightly in her jeans. Good luck.

Mum and Dad are watching a movie on late-night TV. Timppa is around again.

Annette has a walk-in closet that runs along the wall she shares with Lulu's room. When they were little, they used to play telephone. Every time Annette held the rim of a drinking glass against the back wall of her closet and pressed her ear to the bottom, she could hear what her sister was saying even if Lulu used a normal voice.

Annette visits the bathroom and dumps the toothbrushes out of the glass. She returns to her room, slides back the closet door, and makes her way through the hanging clothes. Chiffon, fake leather, and the hems of her black and brightly colored miniskirts brush her face, and the heels of her shoes clatter as she pushes them out of the way. The closet smells of fabric conditioner, sweaty sneakers, and lavender sachet.

Annette holds the glass against the plaster. She knows that Lulu's bed is on the other side, right up against the wall.

At first all she picks up is a lot of mumbling, moaning, whispering, and creaking bedsprings. Then comes a thump as though somebody's arm or leg has hit the wall. The sound shoots right into Annette's ear, and she almost jumps out of the closet.

For Christ's sake, what's your problem? We've been together a whole month. She can hear Timppa clearly now, sounding all shrill since his voice hasn't yet broken. Lulu responds with a murmur Annette can't quite make out.

What're you saving it for? Timppa chirps. I'll bet you've already been screwed every which way, at least that's what the guys are saying.

Again Annette can't hear Lulu's reply—is she talking into her pillow or what?—but Timppa understands her, and he answers immediately.

Don't you know this town's full of chicks just begging for it? he scoffs. Why should I waste my time on some snooty tight-twat? Shit, are you like planning to hold out till you're fourteen or something?

No, Lulu says. I don't know.

Then what's your problem? Aren't you on the pill?

Lulu hesitates. Well, not exactly. Her voice is all raspy and apologetic, the way it gets when she's embarrassed. I haven't quite got mine yet.

Your pills?

My . . . periods.

Bingo! Then there's no need to mess with rubbers!

Again Lulu says something Annette can't quite hear.

I just think it's time our relationship took a step forward. Timppa's words sound like he's reading them from a book.

Another loud thump, followed by a rustling sound, probably Lulu's sheets. She whimpers a little.

Stop it.

Stop it? You're like a walking invitation, ass and jalookies on billboards all over town, and you have the balls to say *stop it*?

Again the rustling of Lulu's sheets. She mumbles something, and then comes Timppa's voice, and this time it's more of a whine. When you lead a guy on like that, you've got to see it through.

Annette stands upright, and her head hits the metal rod, but she doesn't give it a second thought. She crawls out of the closet, sending her shoes clattering into the room. An instant later she's in the hall banging on Lulu's door.

Lulu!

A moment's silence, then Lulu's voice, trying to sound calm and normal. Now what?

Mum says your guest has to go!

From behind the door comes a stifled curse, still more rustling; the bed creaks. There follows a lot of low harsh muttering, and Annette hears a zipper being pulled up. Timppa comes out of the door, his hair messed up and his face all red. He glowers at Annette, who's leaning against the wall minding her own business, and she stares back at him with a shrug and an innocent, slightly apologetic smile that says, *Parents will be parents.*

Lulu's door stays closed, and after a short while the sound of soft sweet music floats out into the hall.

Timppa has stopped coming round and Annette is ferociously happy about it. But her triumph starts falling apart, cracking and flaking and blowing away with the wind when she realizes that Lulu hasn't changed; she's still always giggling and yawning and stuffing herself with laxative licorice candy. It's the same Lulu who smiles mysteriously from beneath her false eyelashes, and for some reason she doesn't seem to pine for the lost Timppa in the least.

The worst of it is the way Lulu had the nerve simply to forget Timppa, whose name still throbs where Annette scratched it on her forearm, Timppa Timppa Timppa.

He was Annette's first chance to be the way everyone expected her to be, and Lulu acts like she took up with him just for the hell of it, then let him go for the same reason. As if Annette wasn't the one who split them up in the first place.

Would it kill Lulu to show, even for the tiniest instant, that she knows what it feels like to be Annette?

In fairness, ever since the night with the drinking glass Lulu has acted almost friendly toward Annette, chatting with her and giving her stuff from her makeup kit that's hardly been used at all. Sometimes Lulu looks at her with big wet spaniel eyes, which is actually pretty maddening, and Annette almost breaks a tooth trying to stay calm when Lulu gets all palsy-walsy. Annette knows Lulu's just pretending, her way of covering up the wound Annette caused in coming between her and Timppa. And with that phony chumminess Lulu is snatching away the last precious thing Annette has, her pissy little victory.

And on top of it all Mumps keeps simpering, It's so nice to see you sisters getting along so well.

· · ·

Annette is vegging out before the television, the big noisy climax of some dopey rock show. Stick That Dick has dropped to number six on the charts, and now in the number one slot there's the girl band Jugzapoppin', who perform topless. After that there's nothing on; even the trash channels are boring once you get used to them. Annette visits a chat room using the remote, but soon gives up. You can barely write two answers before somebody asks about your cup size and what color panties you're wearing. She surfs the net, then skips through different TV channels, but all she can find are unfunny sitcoms and grotty old movies.

One of them catches her attention.

The title of the flick is *Welcome to the Dollhouse*. At first Annette is only interested because the star is so unbelievably ugly. Why would they let anybody who looks like that be in a movie? The girl must be about eight-yo, Annette's age, and she's not even making an effort to appear older. She wears glasses, of all things, which tells you right off the film is ancient, because nowadays nobody, no girl that is, would be that insane; you either have an operation or at the very least get contacts. Annette follows the film for a few minutes, occasionally flipping through the other channels, but she keeps coming back to *Welcome to the Dollhouse* as though drawn by a rubber band.

The girl's name is Dawn, and everyone at school hates her and calls her a dork and a dog and a dyke. She has a little sister named Missy who does ballet. Missy's about six-yo. She wears a pink tutu and a pink leotard—a pink angel—her hair tied back in a bun, with flowers, cute as a doll. Dawn's mum and dad spend all day fawning over Missy and neglect Dawn really badly, and Dawn hates Missy so much her stomach hurts. Okay, sure, Dawn never actually *says* Missy makes her stomach hurt, but Annette knows what it means when Dawn wraps her arms around herself, clenches her teeth, and shuts her eyes tight.

Then one day Dawn's mum asks her to tell Missy, who's about to leave for a ballet class, that she can't pick her up today, so Missy should ask the teacher for a ride home.

But Dawn doesn't tell her.

And Missy is left standing alone outside the ballet school and gets kidnapped. Good-bye, Missy.

Annette feels a devilish red glow of satisfaction, and yet at the same time terribly guilty, as if *she* were the one who'd gotten rid of Miss Goody Two-Shoes Sugar-Plum-Fairy Missy for good.

She changes the channel and doesn't watch the end of the *Dollhouse* flick, but still the mood of the thing follows Annette for days, and she can't quite shake that sickly-prickly thrill she felt when, with the police cars flashing their red and blue lights outside Dawn and Missy's house, it became clear that Dawn had succeeded.

Lulu has a shoot somewhere on the other side of town. Mumps is in Gothenburg, and Dumps is supposed to pick her up after the session. Annette has of course been asked to babysit Otso. Surprised that the little Casanova's not at Pamela's place, she wonders, nastily, has Pamela found herself a more mega stud and finished with Otso just like that? Annette is lounging on the couch watching the celebs on *Junior Pop Idol*. Otso sits a meter from the TV, staring at the screen, and tries to sing along except when Annette hisses at him to be quiet. Four-year-old Jussi does a rendition of "I Want Your Sex," then Kylie comes on, the same age, singing "Like a Virgin." Kylie wears a shiny sequined dress and a pink ostrich-feather boa with matching lipstick. Halfway through the performance the telephone rings. Annette's in a pretty ticked-off mood when she answers, interruptions being just about her least favorite thing.

It's Dad, and there's a lot of noise in the background. He's had to borrow somebody else's phone to call her. Some idiot smashed into his car, and on impact his headset phone flew out the window and broke. Dad's got to take the car to the garage and get himself a new headset, and that will take some time. He says Lulu probably switched off her phone for the shoot, so could Annette send her a voice mail or a text message saying Dad can't pick her up and she should take a taxi? He explains this over and over like it's the most difficult assignment ever.

Yes yes yesyes! Annette screams, and ends the call, but still she's missed two more potential Junior Pop Idols; now a five-yo boy is singing ". . . hit me, baby, one more time." Otso joins in whenever Annette doesn't try to stop him.

Annette picks up her mobile and has already selected Lulu from the quick menu when her hand goes limp.

This can't be just a coincidence.

Annette stares at the phone.

Welcome to the dollhouse, Baby Doll, she says, then switches off the phone entirely.

Hours later the apartment phone rings for the sixth time, and each time the caller-name on the screen is Lulu.

The fact that nobody's answering isn't exactly unusual. Otso's a light sleeper, so Dad often unplugs the phone after he's put Otso to bed, and all the headsets or mobiles in the apartment are in a drawer or under a pillow or turned off altogether.

The phone rings for a seventh time.

The police car is parked in front of the building, but the lights on its roof aren't pulsing red and blue like in the film; the car is totally dark and totally silent.

Dad carries Lulu inside, wrapped in a gray blanket. Her mascara has dribbled down her face, and one of her cheeks is red and scratched and bleeding. Her right eye is almost swollen shut, and her lower lip is split. Dad carefully lays her on the living room couch and staggers into the kitchen like he's gone blind. He returns with a dish towel soaked in warm water and tries to wipe the mascara streaks off Lulu's face, but she gently pushes his hand away.

Remppu, she whispers. Dad looks at Lulu; he doesn't know what she means—but Annette knows, so she goes to Lulu's room and pulls a drawer out from under the bed. Remppu is lying among the other junk with his spindly legs in a knot: a stuffed terry-cloth monkey whose long dangling arms have little orange mittens sewn at the ends. The terry-cloth loops have worn away on those places where Lulu used to suck on Remppu when she was a baby.

Annette walks up to Lulu and places Remppu in her arms. Lulu squeezes him against her chest and places her lips to his battered old head, near where Annette once tore off the eyes and Mum had to sew on a pair of blue buttons instead. Lulu closes her own eyes and lies there perfectly still.

The two policemen wander around the living room like flickering shadows. It's as though Annette is not really in the same place where all this is happening; instead she's standing outside somebody's else's apartment watching these events through the window. Her stomach's filled with a heavy sweetness, as if her breath has turned to syrup.

Messages sometimes disappear when the operators are busy, says one officer. Dad nods blindly; he clearly doesn't even hear.

We've got some possible sightings of the four men, and of course we'll try our best, but, sad to say, cases like this are getting more common all the time, so who knows?

Dad bobs his head like an automaton. Annette stands there silently and doesn't know what to do; she feels totally stunned. Now she realizes how stupid she was. She didn't mean for this to happen. She thought Lulu would just disappear, would get lost somewhere in town and, like a child in a fairy tale, never find her way home.

Now Annette is annoyed that she didn't

watch *Welcome to the Dollhouse* all the way through; she doesn't know what finally became of Missy.

Would Dawn have made such a dumb-ass mistake?

Are you sure you'll be okay? an officer says.

Dad nods for a third time, then takes Lulu and Remppu in a single bundle in his arms and walks off toward Lulu's room; beneath the blanket Lulu's feet dangle as limply as Remppu's terry-cloth limbs.

Mum and Dad are in the den talking all hushed and low, thinking nobody will hear them, but the walls are thin and Annette has sharp ears; she can easily sort out both their voices, almost every word, from the noise of the TV in the background.

Not that she wants to hear them, because her stomach is aching, and she'd much rather swat the voices away like flies and pretend they don't exist, but she also feels compelled to listen, like that time at Ninotska's nine-yo party when Annette kept her eyes on the screen even though she didn't want to see any more grand slam hot pussies.

The insurance will cover Lulu's plastic surgery, Dad says. If we can believe the doctors, there won't be any scarring. She can probably start modeling again in a couple of months. Thank God they finished the Sexy Secrets shoot in time.

The men who did this, if they ever get caught—should we try to get . . . restitution? Mum asks indistinctly.

Dad sighs. Caught? Not too likely. Wouldn't matter anyway. The whole problem is that she never changed her clothes—she thought I was picking her up—so they'll just say she was asking for it. Their lawyers will argue that Lulu brought it on herself.

Then we won't see a penny?

'Fraid not, Dad says.

Annette's head and stomach start aching again. What could that mean, *Lulu brought it on herself*? No, no, *she* did it—she, Annette, caused all this just as surely as if she'd bought a gun and shot herself in the foot. Annette would give almost anything for this, of all things, never to have happened.

Word has circulated around the school.

The boys' hand signals have become grosser than ever, and naturally Ninotska and Veronika keep trying to get all chatty with Annette. Annette vows to act hypernormal, a bit indifferent, even slightly chipper. She won't show those dopes how much she's really hurting.

Four, Ninotska trills. Four horny dudes!

Was it one after another, or did they all do it together? Veronika carries on.

Annette shrugs. I couldn't care less. She walks off, and the hallway echoes with shouts of *lulululululululululululu*.

Mum has brought home burritos from the deli. She cuts one into small pieces for Otso and squeezes ketchup over them from a plastic bottle. Otso would eat Styrofoam if it was covered in ketchup. Lulu won't come down to eat. She won't even leave her room, and that infuriates Annette, too—Lulu always has to make herself special somehow. Annette pokes at her burrito with a fork. She normally likes them, but now her throat feels blocked. Lately nothing tickles her fancy.

I want implants.

The words bubble abruptly out of Annette's mouth, almost like vomit. Mum stops in mid-squeeze, the bottle gives a little fart, and Otso has a laughing fit.

Implants? For you? Mum looks confused, as though she'd never heard the word before.

Everybody's got them!

At your age?

Ninotska's getting them, Sarietta's already stopped being a milkdud, and today I heard

Veronika's shopping around! Annette bangs her fork rhythmically against the table. Anyway, Lulu's got them. You gave her implants the minute the agent told you to!

Everything freezes. Mum stares at her, eyes like saucers, and even Otso stops eating. The silence gets so intense that Annette's ears almost hurt, and then Mum clears her throat.

But . . . we don't want the same thing happening to you that happened to Lulu, she says, her voice all hoarse.

You never want *anything* to happen to me, do you? says Annette, giving Mum big saucer-eyes in return.

Mum doesn't answer. All the doors and windows of her face are shut tight.

Annette slams her fork so hard it springs out of her hand and somersaults to the floor, clanging like a bell.

I knew it! I knew you never wanted anything to happen to me!

Mum looks at her, the side of her mouth twitching. This is a sign.

Everybody thinks I'm just a child! Annette screams. She upends her plate, sending chicken pieces and veggie bits flying out of the tortilla all over the tablecloth and onto the floor. Nothing real is ever supposed to happen to me!

Mum stands there frozen, and Annette picks up a knife and starts banging it against the table. Mum moves quickly and grabs Annette's arm. There, there, dear, we can ask Dad when he gets home, she says, then carefully takes the knife away.

ABOUT THE EDITORS

Ann VanderMeer currently serves as an acquiring fiction editor for Tor.com, Cheeky Frawg Books, and WeirdFictionReview.com. She was the editor-in-chief for *Weird Tales* for five years, during which time she was nominated three times for the Hugo Award and won one. Along with multiple nominations for the Shirley Jackson Award, she also has won a World Fantasy Award and a British Fantasy Award for coediting *The Weird: A Compendium of Strange and Dark Stories*. Other projects have included *Best American Fantasy*; three steampunk anthologies; and a humor book, *The Kosher Guide to Imaginary Animals*. Her latest anthologies include *The Time Traveler's Almanac*, *Sisters of the Revolution: A Feminist Speculative Fiction Anthology*, and *The Bestiary*, an anthology of original fiction and art.

Jeff VanderMeer's most recent fiction is the *New York Times* bestselling Southern Reach trilogy (*Annihilation*, *Authority*, and *Acceptance*), which *Entertainment Weekly* included on its list of the top ten novels of 2014 and which prompted the *New Yorker* to call the author "the weird Thoreau." The series has been acquired by publishers in thirty-four other countries, and Paramount Pictures/Scott Rudin Productions have acquired the movie rights. *Annihilation* has won both the Nebula Award and Shirley Jackson Award for best novel. VanderMeer's nonfiction has appeared in *The New York Times*, *The Guardian*, *The Washington Post*, Atlantic.com, and the *Los Angeles Times*. A three-time winner of the World Fantasy Award, VanderMeer has also edited or coedited many iconic fiction anthologies; taught at the Yale Writers' Conference and the Miami Book Fair International; and lectured at MIT, Brown, and the Library of Congress. He serves as the codirector of Shared Worlds, a unique teen writing camp located at Wofford College. His forthcoming novel is *Borne*.

ABOUT THE TRANSLATORS

Originally from Novosibirsk, Russia, Daniel Ableev is a certified strangeologist living in Bonn, Germany. He has studied law and comparative literature. His work has been published in German and English online at *The Dream People* and elsewhere, and he is the author of the novel *Alu*. Ableev is the coeditor of *Die Novelle—Zeitschrift für Experimentelles*.

John Chu has translated the work of such writers as Tang Fei and Cixin Liu for venues such as *Clarkesworld*. He is also a podcast narrator and a microprocessor architect, as well as a writer of fiction in his own right. His story "The Water That Falls on You from Nowhere" won the 2014 Hugo Award for Best Short Story.

Gio Clairval is an Italian-born writer, translator, and former international management consultant who has lived most of her life in Paris, France, and who now commutes between Lake Como, Italy, and Edinburgh, Scotland. She has translated from the French, German, Spanish, and Italian languages a number of literary classics, including works by Gustave Flaubert, Franz Kafka, Georg Heym, Karl Strobl, Julio Cortázar, Dino Buzzati, Michel Bernanos, and Claude Seignolle. She is currently translating contemporary French novels. Her fiction has appeared in such magazines as *Weird Tales* and the *Postscripts* anthologies, among others.

Brian Evenson is the author of a dozen books of fiction, including the story collections *A Collapse of Horses* and *Windeye*, as well as the novel *Immobility*. His novel *Last Days* won the American Library Association's award for Best Horror Novel of 2009. His novel *The Open Curtain* was a finalist for an Edgar Award and an International Horror Guild Award. Other books include *The Wavering Knife* (which won the IHG Award for best story collection), *Dark Property*, and *Altmann's Tongue*. He has translated work by Christian Gailly, Jean Frémon, Claro, Jacques Jouet, Éric Chevillard, Antoine Volodine, Manuela Draeger, David B., and others. He is the recipient of three O. Henry Prizes as well as an NEA Literature Fellowship. His work has been translated into French, Italian, Spanish, Japanese, and Slovenian. Evenson lives and works in California as a creative writing professor at California Institute of the Arts.

Sarah Kassem lives in Bonn, Germany. She is the author of the tetralogy *Betula Pendula* and coeditor of *Die Novelle—Zeitschrift für Experimentelles*.

Larry Nolen is a freelance translator. He has taught history and English for most of the past sixteen years in Tennessee and Florida. His first published translation, of Leopoldo Lugones's "El escuerzo" appeared in the anthology *ODD?*, and his second, of Augusto Monterroso's "Mister Taylor," appeared in *The Weird: A Compendium of Strange and Dark Stories*. He is currently working on translating a selection of Roberto Arlt's short stories into English.

James Womack has translated widely from Spanish and Russian, including works by Vladimir Mayakovsky, Sergio del Molino, Roberto Arlt, Silvina Ocampo, and Boris Savinkov. He lives in Madrid,

Spain, where he is coeditor at Nevsky Prospects, a Spanish-language publishing house specializing in translations of Russian literature. His poetry collection, *Misprint*, was published by Carcanet in 2012.

Marian Womack is a translator, author, and editor. She has published Spanish versions of works by such authors as Mary Shelley, Lord Dunsany, Charles Dickens, and Daphne du Maurier, and English translations of Spanish speculative fiction for *The Apex Book of World SF* volume 4. Her own writing can be read in *Apex Magazine*, *SuperSonic*, and *Weird Fiction Review*. She is based in Madrid and Cambridge.

Vladimir Zhenevsky began in 2007 as a translator from English into Russian of obscure British crime fiction writers but happily moved on to the likes of Peter Watts, Clive Barker, and Thomas Ligotti. He started translating Russian speculative fiction into English in 2013. A resident of Ufa, Russia, he was an author of his own weird and horror stories. Zhenevsky died in 2015.

ACKNOWLEDGMENTS

Thank you to everyone who helped with this anthology through sharing information, engaging in discussion, or in other ways. In particular, thanks to our editor, Tim O'Connell, and to the rest of the crew at Vintage. Additional thanks to the likes of Matthew Cheney and Eric Schaller for their generosity with their time and knowledge of the field. Thank you to Adam Mills, Lawrence Schimel, Vida Cruz, Maxim Jakubowski, Anil Menon, Yoshio Kobayashi, Edward Gauvin, Jaroslav Olsa Jr., and Karin Tidbeck for additional research and to all the readers out there who have shared their favorite stories with us over the years.

Sadly, a good friend and an invaluable source of information on Russian and Ukrainian SF, Vladimir Zhenevsky, passed away last year, shortly after delivering his translation and research for author notes to us. Vlad was beloved by many and we will endeavor to ensure he is not forgotten. We consider him to be the patron saint of *The Big Book of Science Fiction*, along with Judith Merril, to whom we have dedicated this anthology.

We would also like to thank the editors, living and dead, who have worked tirelessly, out of a deep love of SF, to bring stories to readers through their magazines and anthologies. Any list is of necessity incomplete, but in particular we would like to acknowledge the work of Judith Merril, David G. Hartwell, Franz Rottensteiner, Damon Knight, Donald A. Wollheim, Terry Carr, Grania Davis, John Joseph Adams, Ellen Datlow, Frederik Pohl, Alisa Krasnostein, Groff Conklin, Cristina Jurado, Robert Silverberg, Isaac Asimov, Jonathan Strahan, Harlan Ellison, Hugo Gernsback, Michael Moorcock, Kristine Kathryn Rusch, Terri Windling, Sheila Williams, Sheree R. Thomas, Alberto Manguel, Gardner Dozois, and Gordon Van Gelder.

We owe a deep debt of gratitude to all our translators, who helped bring new stories or new translations into the public eye. Thank you Daniel Ableev, John Chu, Gio Clairval, Brian Evenson, Sarah Kassem, Larry Nolen, James Womack, Marian Womack, and Vlad Zhenevsky. We would also like to acknowledge the other translators of stories acquired in their original English-language form and all translators—past, present, and future—who, although not always recognized, continue to meet the challenge of presenting wonderful fiction written by others to a new audience of appreciative readers.

This book would not have been possible without the assistance, guidance, support, and love of the genre of several people we want to thank: Jason Sanford, John Glover, Dominik Parisien, Richard Scott, Fábio Fernandes, Merrilee Heifetz, Ken Liu, Lauren Rogoff, Vaughne Hansen, and Sara Kramer. We also want to acknowledge Bud Webster's assistance over the years in tracking down estates of writers. We are saddened deeply by his recent passing. We are also at a loss over the death of David G. Hartwell. We spent many hours together arguing about and sharing our love of fiction. He was generous with his time, and he will be sorely missed by many.

It is impossible to list everyone, but know that even if you are not named here, we appreciate your contribution.

Finally, thanks to our intrepid agent, Sally Harding, and everyone at the Cooke Agency.

PERMISSIONS ACKNOWLEDGMENTS

Yoshio Aramaki: "Soft Clocks" by Yoshio Aramaki, copyright © 1988 by Yoshio Aramaki. Translation by Kazuko Behrens and stylized by Lewis Shiner. Originally published in Japanese in *Uchujin* (April 1968). This translation originally appeared in *Interzone* (January/February 1989). Reprinted by permission of author's estate and translators.

Juan José Arreola: "Baby HP" by Juan José Arreola. Translation copyright © 2016 by Larry Nolen. Originally published in Spanish in 1952. This new translation published by permission of the translator.

Isaac Asimov: "The Last Question" by Isaac Asimov, copyright © 1956 by Asimov Holdings LLC. Originally published in *Science Fiction Quarterly* (November 1956). Reprinted by permission of Asimov Holdings LLC and William Morris Endeavor Entertainment LLC.

J. G. Ballard: "The Voices of Time" from *The Complete Stories of J. G. Ballard* by J. G. Ballard, copyright © 1963 by J. G. Ballard. Originally published in *New Worlds* (October 1960). Reprinted by permission of W. W. Norton & Company, Inc., and The Wylie Agency LLC.

Iain M. Banks: "A Gift from the Culture" by Iain M. Banks, copyright © 1987 by Iain M. Banks. Originally published in *Interzone* 20 (Summer 1987). Reprinted by permission of the author's estate.

Jacques Barbéri: "Mondocane" by Jacques Barbéri, copyright © 1983 by Jacques Barbéri. Translation copyright © 2016 by Brian Evenson. Originally published in French in *Fausse caméra*, edited by Jacques Barbéri (Les Locataires, 1983). This first English-language translation published by permission of Éditions La Volte and the translator.

John Baxter: "The Hands" by John Baxter, copyright © 1965 by John Baxter. Originally published in *New Writings in SF 6*, edited by John Carnell (Corgi Books, 1965). Reprinted by permission of the author.

Barrington J. Bayley: "Sporting with the Chid" by Barrington J. Bayley, copyright © 1979 by Barrington J. Bayley. Originally published in *The Seed of Evil* (Allison & Busby, 1979). Reprinted by permission of the author's representative.

Greg Bear: "Blood Music" by Greg Bear, copyright © 1983 by Greg Bear. Originally published in *Analog* (June 1983). Reprinted by permission of the author.

Dmitri Bilenkin: "Where Two Paths Cross" by Dmitri Bilenkin, originally published in English as "Crossing of the Paths" in *Aliens, Travelers, and Other Strangers*, edited by Arkady and Boris Strugatsky (Macmillan, 1984). Originally published in Russian as "Пересечение пути" ("Peresechenie puti") in *Vokrug sveta* 10 (1973), copyright © 1973. Translation copyright © 2016 by

James Womack. This new translation published by permission of the author's estate and the translator.

Jon Bing: "The Owl of Bear Island" by Jon Bing, copyright © 1986 by The Estate of Jon Bing. Originally published in Norwegian in *Hvadata?: lesestykker for informasjonssamfunnet* (Grøndahl og Dreyer, 1986). This translation originally appeared in *Tales from Planet Earth*, edited by Frederik Pohl and Elizabeth Anne Hull (St. Martin's Press, 1986). Reprinted by permission of the author's estate and the Gyldendal Agency.

Adolfo Bioy Casares: "The Squid Chooses Its Own Ink" by Adolfo Bioy Casares, copyright © 1962, 2015 by Heirs of Adolfo Bioy Casares. Originally published in Spanish as "El calamari opta su tinta" in *El lado de la sombra* (Emecé Editores, 1962). Translation copyright © 2016 by Marian Womack. This new translation published by permission of the author's estate and the translator.

Michael Bishop: "The House of Compassionate Sharers" by Michael Bishop, copyright © 1977, 2011 by Michael Bishop. Originally published in *Cosmos Science Fiction and Fantasy Magazine* (May 1977). Revised text from *The Door Gunner and Other Perilous Flights of Fancy: A Michael Bishop Retrospective*, edited by Michael H. Hutchins (Subterranean Press, 2012). Reprinted by permission of the author.

James Blish: "Surface Tension" by James Blish, copyright © 1952, 1980 by The Estate of James Blish. Originally published in *Galaxy* (August 1952). Reprinted by permission of Judith L. Blish and The Virginia Kidd Agency, Inc.

Michael Blumlein: "The Brains of Rats" by Michael Blumlein, copyright © 1990 by Michael Blumlein. Originally published in *The Brains of Rats* (Scream Press, 1990). Reprinted by permission of the author.

Jorge Luis Borges: "Tlön, Uqbar, Orbis Tertius" by Jorge Luis Borges, copyright © 1988 by Maria Kodama. Translation copyright © 1998 by Penguin Random House LLC. Originally published in Spanish in *Sur* (May 1940). This translation originally appeared in *Collected Fictions* by Jorge Luis Borges, translated by Andrew Hurley (Viking Press, 1998). Reprinted by permission of Viking Books, an imprint of Penguin Publishing Group, a division of Penguin Random House LLC, and The Wylie Agency LLC.

Ray Bradbury: "September 2005: The Martian" by Ray Bradbury, copyright © 1949 by Popular Publications, renewed 1977 by Ray Bradbury. Originally published in *Super Science Stories* (November 1949). Reprinted by permission of Don Congdon Associates, Inc.

David R. Bunch: "Three from Moderan" by David R. Bunch, originally published individually as "The Flesh-Man from Far Wide," copyright © 1959, in *Amazing Stories* (November 1959); "New Kings Are Not for Laughing" by David R. Bunch, copyright © 1970, and "No Cracks or Sagging" by David R. Bunch, copyright © 1970, originally published in *Moderan* (Avon Books, 1971). Reprinted by permission of the author's estate.

by Stanisław Lem. Reprinted by permission of Houghton Mifflin Harcourt Publishing Company. All rights reserved.

Cixin Liu: "The Poetry Cloud" by Cixin Liu. Translation by Chi-yin Ip and Cheuk Wong. Originally published in Chinese in *Kehuan Shijie* (March 1997). This translation originally published in *Renditions* 77 (Spring 2012) and 78 (Autumn 2012). Reprinted by permission of the Research Centre for Translation, The Chinese University of Hong Kong.

Katherine MacLean: "The Snowball Effect" by Katherine MacLean, copyright © 1952, 1980 by Katherine MacLean. Originally published in *Galaxy Science Fiction* (September 1952). Reprinted by permission of the author and the author's agents, The Virginia Kidd Agency, Inc.

Geoffrey Maloney: "Remnants of the Virago Crypto-System" by Geoffrey Maloney, copyright © 1995 by Geoffrey Maloney. Originally published in *The Silver Web* 12 (Summer 1995). Reprinted by permission of the author.

George R. R. Martin: "Sandkings" by George R. R. Martin, copyright © 1979. Originally published in *Omni* (August 1979). Reprinted by permission of the author.

Michael Moorcock: "The Frozen Cardinal" by Michael Moorcock, copyright © 1987 by Michael Moorcock. Originally published in *Other Edens*, edited by Robert Holdstock and Christopher Evans (Unwin Paperbacks, 1987). Reprinted by permission of the author.

Pat Murphy: "Rachel in Love" by Pat Murphy, copyright © 1987 by Pat Murphy. Originally published in *Isaac Asimov's Science Fiction Magazine* (April 1987). Reprinted by permission of the author.

Misha Nogha: "Death Is Static Death Is Movement" from *Red Spider White Web* by Misha Nogha, copyright © 1990 by Misha Nogha. Reprinted by permission of the author.

Silvina Ocampo: "The Waves" by Silvina Ocampo, copyright © 1959 by Silvina Ocampo. Originally published in Spanish as "Las ondas" in *La Furia* (Sur, 1959). Translation copyright © 2016 by Marian Womack. This first English-language translation published by permission of the author's estate and the translator.

Chad Oliver: "Let Me Live in a House" by Chad Oliver, copyright © 1954 by Chad Oliver. Originally published in *Universe Science Fiction* (March 1954). Reprinted by permission of the author's estate.

Manjula Padmanabhan: "Sharing Air" by Manjula Padmanabhan, copyright © 1984 by Manjula Padmanabhan. Originally published in New Delhi in *The New Sunday Express Magazine* (1984) and subsequently published in slightly different form in *Kleptomania* (Penguin Books India, 2004). Reprinted by permission of the author.

Frederik Pohl: "Day Million" by Frederik Pohl, copyright © 1971 by Frederik Pohl. Originally published in *Rogue* (February 1966). Reprinted by permission of Curtis Brown, Ltd.

Rachel Pollack: "Burning Sky" by Rachel Pollack, copyright © 1989 by Rachel Pollack. Originally published in *Semiotext(e) SF*, edited by Rudy Rucker, Peter Lamborn Wilson, and Robert Anton Wilson (Semiotext(e)/AK Press, 1989). Reprinted by permission of the author.

Robert Reed: "The Remoras" by Robert Reed, copyright © 1994 by Robert Reed. Originally published in *The Magazine of Fantasy and Science Fiction* (May 1994). Reprinted by permission of the author.

Kim Stanley Robinson: "Before I Wake" by Kim Stanley Robinson, copyright © 1989 by Kim Stanley Robinson. Originally published in *Interzone* 27 (January/February 1989). Reprinted by permission of the author.

Joanna Russ: "When It Changed" by Joanna Russ, copyright © 1972 by The Estate of Joanna Russ. Originally published in *Again, Dangerous Visions*, edited by Harlan Ellison (Doubleday, 1972). Reprinted by permission of the author's estate.

Josephine Saxton: "The Snake Who Had Read Chomsky" by Josephine Saxton, copyright © 1981 by Josephine Saxton. Originally published in *Universe 11*, edited by Terry Carr (Doubleday, 1981). Reprinted by permission of the author.

Paul Scheerbart: "The New Overworld" by Paul Scheerbart. Translation copyright © 2016 by Daniel Ableev and Sarah Kassem. Originally published in German as "Die neue Oberwelt" in *Die Aktion* 1 (1911). This first English-language translation published by permission of the translators.

James H. Schmitz: "Grandpa" by James H. Schmitz, copyright © 1955 by Street & Smith Publications, copyright © 1983 by The Estate of James H. Schmitz. Originally published in *Astounding Science Fiction* (1955). Reprinted by permission of the author's estate.

Vadim Shefner: "A Modest Genius" by Vadim Shefner, copyright © 1963 by Vadim Shefner. Translation by Matthew J. O'Connell. Originally published in Russian as "Скромный гений" in *Nedelya* 41 (1963). This translation originally published in *View from Another Shore*, edited by Franz Rottensteiner (Liverpool University Press, 1973). Reprinted by permission of the author's estate and representative.

Robert Silverberg: "Good News from the Vatican" by Robert Silverberg, copyright © 1971 by Agberg, Ltd. Originally published in *Universe 1*, edited by Terry Carr (Ace Books, 1971). Reprinted by permission of the author.

Clifford D. Simak: "Desertion" by Clifford D. Simak, copyright © 1944, 1972 by Clifford D. Simak. Originally published in *Astounding Science Fiction* (November 1944). Reprinted by permission of the author's estate.

Johanna Sinisalo: "Baby Doll" by Johanna Sinisalo, copyright © 2002 by Johanna Sinisalo. Translation by David Hackston. Originally published in Finnish in *Intohimosta rikokseen* (2002). This translation originally published in *The SFWA European Hall of Fame*, edited by James Morrow and Kathryn Morrow (Tor Books, 2007). Reprinted by permission of the author.

Cordwainer Smith: "The Game of Rat and Dragon" by Cordwainer Smith, copyright © 1955 by Paul Linebarger. Originally published in *Galaxy Science Fiction* (October 1955). Reprinted by permission of the author's estate and The Spectrum Literary Agency.

Margaret St. Clair: "Prott" by Margaret St. Clair, copyright © 1985 by Margaret St. Clair. Originally published in *Galaxy Science Fiction* (January 1953). Reprinted by permission of McIntosh & Otis, Inc.

Bruce Sterling: "Swarm" by Bruce Sterling, copyright © 1982 by Bruce Sterling. Originally published in *The Magazine of Fantasy and Science Fiction* (April 1982). Reprinted by permission of the author.

Karl Hans Strobl: "The Triumph of Mechanics" by Karl Hans Strobl. Translation copyright © 2016 by Gio Clairval. Originally published in German in 1907. This first English-language translation published by permission of the translator.

Arkady and Boris Strugatsky: "The Visitors" by Arkady and Boris Strugatsky, copyright © 1958 by Arkady and Boris Strugatsky. Translation copyright © 2016 by James Womack. Originally published in Russian in *Tekhnika Molodezhi* (*Technology for the Youth*) 1 (January 1958). This new translation published by permission of the authors' estate and the translator.

Theodore Sturgeon: "The Man Who Lost the Sea" by Theodore Sturgeon, copyright © 1959, renewed 1977 by Theodore Sturgeon. Originally published in *The Magazine of Fantasy and Science Fiction* (October 1959). Reprinted by permission of The Theodore Sturgeon Literary Trust.

William Tenn: "The Liberation of Earth" by William Tenn, copyright © 1953 by Philip Klass. Originally published in *Future Science Fiction* (May 1953); "The Ghost Standard" by William Tenn, copyright © 1994 by Philip Klass. Originally published in *Playboy* (December 1994). Both reprinted by permission of the author's estate and The Virginia Kidd Agency, Inc.

James Tiptree Jr.: "And I Awoke and Found Me Here on the Cold Hill's Side" by James Tiptree Jr., copyright © 1972 by Alice B. Sheldon, copyright © 2000 by Jeffrey D. Smith. Originally published in *The Magazine of Fantasy and Science Fiction* (March 1972). Reprinted by permission of Jeffrey D. Smith and The Virginia Kidd Agency, Inc.

Tatyana Tolstaya: "The Slynx" originally published as chapter 1 of the novel *The Slynx* by Tatyana Tolstaya, copyright © 2003 by Tatyana Tolstaya. Translation copyright © 2003 by Jamey Gambrell. Reprinted by permission of The Wylie Agency LLC.

Yasutaka Tsutsui: "Standing Woman" by Yasutaka Tsutsui, copyright © 1974 by Yasutaka Tsutsui. Translation copyright © 1979 by Dana Lewis. Originally published in English in *Omni* (February 1981). Reprinted by permission of the author and translator.

Lisa Tuttle: "Wives" by Lisa Tuttle, copyright © 1979 by Lisa Tuttle. Originally published in *The Magazine of Fantasy and Science Fiction* (December 1979). Reprinted by permission of the author.

Miguel de Unamuno: "Mechanopolis" by Miguel de Unamuno. Translation copyright © 2016 by Marian Womack. This new translation published by permission of the translator.

Élisabeth Vonarburg: "Readers of the Lost Art" by Élisabeth Vonarburg, copyright © 1987 by Élisabeth Vonarburg. Translation copyright © 1996 by Howard Scott. Originally published in English in *Tesseracts 5*, edited by Robert Runté and Yves Meynard (Tesseract Books, 1996). Reprinted by permission of the author and translator.

Kurt Vonnegut Jr.: "2 B R 0 2 B" from *Bagombo Snuff Box: Uncollected Short Fiction* by Kurt Vonnegut Jr., copyright © 1999 by Kurt Vonnegut Jr. Originally published in *IF* (January 1962). Reprinted by permission of G. P. Putnam's Sons, an imprint of Penguin Publishing Group, a division of Penguin Random House LLC.

James White: "Sector General" by James White, copyright © 1957 by James White. Originally published in *New Worlds Science Fiction* 65 (November 1957). Reprinted by permission of the author's estate.

Connie Willis: "Schwarzschild Radius" by Connie Willis, copyright © 1987 by Connie Willis. Originally published in *The Universe* (November 1987). Reprinted by permission of the author.

Gene Wolfe: "All the Hues of Hell" by Gene Wolfe, copyright © 1987 by Gene Wolfe. Originally published in *The Universe* (November 1987). Reprinted by permission of the author and The Virginia Kidd Agency, Inc.

Alicia Yánez Cossío: "The IWM 1000" by Alicia Yánez Cossío, copyright © 1990 by Arte Público Press, University of Houston. Translation by Susana Castillo and Elsie Adams. Originally published in Spanish in the collection *El beso y otra fricciones* (1975). This translation originally published in *Short Stories by Latin American Women: The Magic and the Real*, edited by Celia Correas de Zapata (Modern Library Classics, 1990). Reprinted by permission of Arte Público Press, University of Houston.

Valentina Zhuravlyova: "The Astronaut" by Valentina Zhuravlyova, copyright © 1960 by Valentina Zhuravlyova. Translation copyright © 2016 by James Womack. Originally published in Russian as "Astronavt" in *Destination: Amaltheia*, edited by Richard Dixon (Foreign Language Publishing House, 1960). This new translation published by permission of the author's estate and the translator.

Yefim Zozulya: "The Doom of Principal City" by Yefim Zozulya. Translation copyright © 2016 by Vlad Zhenevsky. Originally published in Russian in 1918. This first English-language translation published by permission of the translator.

THE ENCYCLOPEDIA OF SCIENCE FICTION PARTNERSHIP

As noted in the introduction, John Clute, David Langford, and Peter Nicholls, creators of *The Encyclopedia of Science Fiction*, have kindly allowed us to partner with them to use general biographical facts and literary analysis from SFE author entries. Most entries were written by John Clute; additional credits are given in parentheses as necessary. We are very grateful to have had access to this wellspring of research.

Major excerpts have been used for the following authors: Paul Ernst (Peter Nicholls and John Clute); Edmond Hamilton, Clare Winger Harris (Jane Donawerth); Gwyneth Jones, Tanith Lee, A. Merritt (John Clute and Peter Nicholls); Leslie F. Stone (John Clute and Peter Nicholls); and James White (David Langford and John Clute). For three authors, the information in the *Encyclopedia* was so complete and essential that almost the entire entry has been used with minimal changes: Jon Bing (John-Henri Holmberg), Han Song (Jonathan Clements), and Yasutaka Tsutsui (Jonathan Clements).

Selected excerpts of entries for the following authors were also used in preparation of the author notes, usually forming the nucleus of biographical information. Parentheticals indicate authorship other than John Clute; Clute collaborations are also noted: J. G. Ballard (David Pringle with John Clute, descriptions of his work); Iain M. Banks (John Clute and David Langford, especially analysis of the Culture novels); Greg Bear (especially analysis of *Eon* and *Blood Music*); Dmitri Bilenkin (Vladimir Gakov); Michael Blumlein ("Tissue Ablation" and discussion of his collection *The Brains of Rats*); Jorge Luis Borges (John Clute and Peter Roberts, especially discussion of Borges tropes that became universal); Ray Bradbury (Peter Nicholls); Pat Cadigan (especially general observations about the author's work); Angélica Gorodischer (John Clute and Yolanda Molina-Gavilán, for career facts and signature settings); Geoffrey A. Landis (Graham Sleight); Chad Oliver, Rachel Pollack, Robert Reed, Kim Stanley Robinson (especially analysis of his Mars novels); Josephine Saxton (John Clute and Peter Nicholls, for career facts); Vadim Shefner (Vladimir Gakov); Margaret St. Clair, Élisabeth Vonarburg (LP and John Clute, for career information); Bruce Sterling (Colin Greenland and John Clute, especially about his Swarm universe); F. L. Wallace; and Connie Willis (time travel discussion).

Any text deviating from the *Encyclopedia* represents the fruits of other research. The opinions and emphasis expressed in each author note that reference the story itself are most often that of the editors of this anthology. Any errors should be placed at our door.

ADDITIONAL THANKS

We are also grateful to Sara Kramer and New York Review of Books Classics for allowing us to use biographical material and quotes from their books for entries on Silvina Ocampo, Adolfo Bioy Casares, and Tatyana Tolstaya. Many thanks to Takayuki Tatsumi for his help compiling the entry on the writer Yoshio Aramaki; in addition to direct quotes from Tatsumi, the rest of the entry is taken, sometimes lightly paraphrased, from Tatsumi's introduction to Aramaki's *Collected Works*. Finally, many thanks to Adam Mills for his assistance in researching and compiling the notes for this book.